THE BLACK HIGHWAYMAN

THE FOLLOWING

SPLENDID PICTURES GRATIS

WITH

THE NEW RE-ISSUE

OF

BLUESKIN,

By the Author of BLACK BESS.

With Nos. 1 and 2, in Illuminated Wrapper,

GRATIS } EDGWORTH BESS BEING RESCUED FROM THE MOHAWKS BY COLONEL THORNE.

GRATIS WITH No. 3. } BLUESKIN AND JACK SHEPPARD ESCAPE FROM JONATHAN WILD.

GRATIS WITH No. 4 } JONATHAN WILD KILLS COLONEL THORNE AND CAPTURES EDGWORTH BESS.

GRATIS WITH No. 5. } JACK SHEPPARD'S ESCAPE FROM NEWGATE

GRATIS WITH No. 6. } BLUESKIN LEAPS FROM THE PARAPET OF LONDON BRIDGE TO EVADE JONATHAN WILD

GRATIS WITH No. 7. } THE BURNING OF NEWGATE DURING THE TIME OF THE LORD GEORGE GORDON RIOTS

GRATIS WITH No. 8. } PORTRAIT OF JACK SHEPPARD.

GRATIS WITH No. 9. } BLUESKIN, JACK SHEPPARD, AND EDGWORTH BESS ARE RESCUED FROM THE POWER OF JONATHAN WILD.

GRATIS WITH No. 10. } THE BURGLARY.

THE FOLLOWING

SPLENDID PICTURES GRATIS

WITH

THE NEW RE-ISSUE

OF

THE BLACK HIGHWAYMAN,

By the Author of BLACK BESS.

With Nos. 1 and 2, in Illuminated Wrapper,

GRATIS } THE BLACK HIGHWAYMAN AND CAPTAIN HAWK RESCUING THE COUNTESS OF BLACK LAKE.

GRATIS WITH No. 3, } CAPTAIN HAWK AND THE BOW STREET RUNNER.

GRATIS WITH No. 4, } LORD HARCLIFFE DENOUNCED AS THE BLACK HIGHWAYMAN.

GRATIS WITH No. 5, } PHANTOM CLEARS TYBURN TOLL-GATE

GRATIS WITH No. 6, } CAPTAIN HAWK TAKEN PRISONER, AND TREATED MAZEPPA FASHION.

GRATIS WITH No. 7, } CAPTAIN HAWK LEAPS SATAN OVER THE STAGE COACH.

GRATIS WITH No. 8. } THE ATTACK UPON THE WAGGON.

GRATIS WITH No. 9. } THE BLACK HIGHWAYMAN LEVIES A CONTRIBUTION ON THE PRINCE OF WALES.

GRATIS WITH No. 10 } "AN AWFUL SHRIEK THRILLED FROM THE LIPS OF THE POLICE OFFICER AS HE FELT THE FLOORING OF THE HUT SUDDENLY GIVE WAY BENEATH HIS FEET."

THE BLACK HIGHWAYMAN AND CAPTAIN HAWK RESCUING THE COUNTESS OF BLACKLAKE.

GRATIS With Nos. 1 & 2 (in a Coloured Wrapper, One Penny) of the BLACK HIGHWAYMAN, being the Second Series of BLACK BESS; OR THE KNIGHT OF THE ROAD, by the same Author.

OBSERVE!—Nos. 1 & 2 AND THE COLOURED PICTURE, ONE PENNY.

☞ GRATIS with Numbers 3 to 6, FOUR COLOURED PLATES.

THE

BLACK HIGHWAYMAN.

BEING THE SECOND SERIES OF

BLACK BESS; OR, THE KNIGHT OF THE ROAD.

BY THE SAME AUTHOR.

[THE DISCOVERY OF THE RIFLED GRAVE.]

CHAPTER I.

THE STORM.—THE GUESTS AT THE OLD CHEQUERS.—THE STRANGER AND WILD WILL.—THE CHURCHYARD BY NIGHT.

"How the wind howls! It shakes the chimneys and the gable-tops of the Old Chequers, but the place has weathered many a fiercer storm than this. Pile on more wood—stir the fire till the blaze mounts up to the gaypole! We can then defy the storm and bid it do its worst."

A tremendous gust of wind that made every window rattle furiously followed the words the landlord had just spoken.

The strangely-assorted company that thronged the old inn kitchen paused involuntarily to listen.

It was when the fury of the blast was at its greatest

Nos. 1 and 2.

that the front door was dashed open with the utmost violence.

A rush of cold air and a cloud of frozen snow came whirling into the room, reducing the temperature instantly to that which prevailed without.

"Shut the door," bawled the landlord, as he caught sight of a muffled figure on the threshold—"shut the door! Was there ever such a night?"

So loud was the howling of the wind that it seemed almost doubtful whether the landlord's injunction had been heard.

But it would seem so, for the door was closed, though not without difficulty, for the wind opposed it with all its strength, as though unwilling to be excluded from such comfortable quarters.

The new-comer then rapidly divested himself of the huge cloak he had muffled closely round him.

"It be nation cold and windy, my masters, bain't it?" he exclaimed. "I can't remember such a night. The snow cuts you like bits of powdered glass."

"Come up close to the fire," cried the landlord, heartily. "You are doubly welcome on such a night as this."

The new-comer did not hesitate to accept this invitation, and as he crossed the sanded floor he exchanged nods of recognition with several of those present, which showed he was no stranger.

"Thanks—thanks!" he cried, as several moved their chairs to enable him to approach. "Don't disturb yourselves. I shall get warm again in time, no doubt. I suppose Dick Turpin lies warm enough in his grave. I thought of him as I came through the churchyard just now."

At this mention of the name of the celebrated highwayman one of the assembled guests started and looked up.

But he lowered his eyes almost immediately, for he saw that his action was noticed by many present.

His elbow was on the corner of the table, and leaning his head upon it in a way by which the greater part of his countenance was concealed, he resumed the attitude he had preserved all the evening, listening to all that was said, but saying nothing.

"Poor Dick's past feeling the weather now," said a smooth-shaven man near the hearth. "As Shakspere says, 'He made a good end.'"

"Who was it that claimed his body and had it buried in the churchyard?" said another. "There's a mystery in that. The doctors made sure of having him for a subject."

A general movement of the whole assembly, indicative of uneasiness and abhorrence, was instantly perceptible.

"And I won't say they don't have him after all," remarked the new-comer, who had by this time seated himself and was engaged in toasting his toes.

"Why—why? How do you make that out?" asked several.

"There are body-snatchers in York, as I have good reason for believing," was the reply; "and what is more, I know one or two doctors who would not mind giving a twenty-pound note for such a celebrated subject as Dick Turpin."

These assertions caused general uneasiness, for at that time the popular feeling against dissection was a thousand times more violent than it is to-day.

"I should not care about their work on such a night as this, at all events," replied the landlord. "Here comes the wind again!"

An immediate silence followed these words.

Then, with a force and fury that seemed to threaten to level the Old Chequers to the ground, the storm came again.

So terrific was it, and so long-enduring, that the ones which had preceded it seemed mere puffs in comparison.

Then came a sudden and startling crash.

All looked towards the window, one-half of which had been dashed against the wall, shivering the diamonded panes to atoms.

Was this the wind's work?

All thought so until they perceived a weird, uncouth-looking figure clinging to the iron-work of the shattered casement.

Dimly seen, he looked more like some wild elfish sprite than an inhabitant of the earth.

His shock of hair, shaggy as a lion's mane, more than half concealed his swarthy physiognomy, and his eyes gleamed as though they contained some latent light of their own.

"Why, bless my life," ejaculated the landlord, "that's Wild Will!"

"Yes, it's Wild Will, sure enough," replied the singular figure at the casement, speaking in unnatural, shrill tones—"it's Wild Will, and there's wild doings in the old churchyard to-night—ha, ha!—wild doings—rare doings among the worms, and coffins, and dead men's bones! But he's sound and whole enough yet, and they'll have him out. Ha, ha! rare doings!"

Then suddenly losing all his excitement, he exclaimed, in tones strikingly at variance with those he had just employed:

"Haven't you got anything for poor Will? Don't be frightened—poor Will is cold."

His teeth chattered as he spoke.

But the stranger who had sat so silent, and who had kept his face so sedulously concealed, had sprung to his feet at the first words, and now, with ill-suppressed excitement, cried:

"What's that you say about the churchyard? Is there some one there?"

"No doubt of it," answered the last-arrived guest, "but he will tell you no more. He has seen the body-snatchers at their work, that's all. I told you how it would be. If you weren't a stranger in these parts you would know that that is a poor idiot who never understands one-half of what is said to him."

"I'll know the truth of it, at all events," said the cloaked stranger, hastening to the door. "It is not far from here to the churchyard."

The next moment he was out in the snow, hastening on as fast as the violent wind would permit.

Those he had left behind him remained for something like a moment in a state of indecision—each one glancing at his neighbour.

Then, all at once, as though animated by the self-same intention, they sprang to their feet, and, leaving their glasses untouched, hastened to the doorway.

So simultaneous was the rush, and so anxious were all to get out, that their intention was defeated.

One by one, however, they emerged, and, with wild cries and frantic shouts, hastened tumultuously towards the churchyard.

The foremost were just in time to catch sight of the cloaked stranger scaling the low boundary wall, and without pausing to consider, they made their way to the same point and imitated his action.

The others followed pell-mell.

The dark cloak of the stranger formed a very conspicuous object when viewed against the snow.

The feathery flakes had ceased to fall, and there was a light-coloured patch in the sky, which seemed to indicate that the moon would ere long break forth.

The stranger made his way towards one corner of the churchyard and then paused.

He saw before him tolerably evident signs that the idiot had told the truth.

The snow had been disturbed, and there were half-filled-up footprints here and there visible in the soft mass.

The next moment, to his surprise, he found himself surrounded by a yelling, agitated crowd of persons.

"They have been at their accursed work," said one, speaking with savage bitterness. "See there—and there! Behold the footprints! They stole my only little one after she had been laid here, as I thought, in safety and in peace. Shall we suffer this? No, no! Down with the body-snatchers!—death to them!"

"Hold!" said the cloaked stranger, springing on the top of an adjoining tomb—"hold a moment—do not be rash! Listen to me a moment!"

There was something so commanding in the stranger's voice that the assembled crowd instinctively and with one accord obeyed him.

Perhaps one cause of this was that he was a stranger, and a strong curiosity arose to know who he was—a question which had been asked in vain more than once that evening.

"Don't let us be too hasty!" he exclaimed, holding up his hand, "the boy may have not told us true. Let us find out. If the body-snatchers have been here we will have such a retribution as shall be a warning for all after time.

He who lies buried here was my dear friend, and if any indignity has been offered his remains, rest assured I will be revenged!"

The last word, sonorously pronounced, struck upon the hearts of all like a key-note.

"Yes—yes!" they cried, in chorus—"revenge upon the resurrectionists!"

The stranger again held up his hand.

It was strange to see what effect that simple gesture had upon the angry, frenzied multitude—for such it now was—the alarm having spread, and a crowd of people having assembled with that celerity which has so often been remarked.

There was a total silence.

The stranger spoke again, and all could tell that he was struggling hard with his emotions.

"You saw him buried here to-day," he said, pointing to the grave at his feet—"you know it was not a deep one; the earth was just scooped out, but no more. It will be easy to tell whether the coffin is under the loose earth. If it is not, then, I say again, we will be revenged!"

"Yes, yes—revenged!" was the universal cry.

The stranger released his hold upon his cloak, and the wind instantly blew it back in such a way as to display his figure fully.

He was tall, and stood with an erectness that was alike indicative of a fearless heart, and that he differed from the ordinary run of mortals.

His tight-fitting, picturesque costume so well displayed his symmetrical yet muscular figure, that it seemed as though it must have been designed for that sole purpose.

He was attired in black, and this sombre hue made his pale, regular-featured face show to all the more advantage.

His eyes were black and piercing, and now excitement had imparted to them a double brightness.

It was not to show off his form, however, that he had allowed his cloak to fall back, but to draw his sword.

As no one till that moment had suspected that he carried such a weapon, all shrank back, for it glittered like a flash of light when, with a sudden movement, he drew it from its scabbard.

Then the way in which he brandished it aloft had so hostile a look that those in front stepped back still further.

"We shall soon know," cried the stranger, leaping from the tomb—"he does not lie so deep as to be out of the reach of my sword's point—I am sure I can touch the coffin-lid."

Leaning forward, he, with a sudden thrust, plunged the weapon into the soft earth.

It descended almost to the hilt, and then it encountered some obstacle.

He struck repeated blows with the sword's point.

A faint muffled sound was returned.

"He has not been moved," said the stranger. "Hark! the coffin is here."

"But it may be empty!" cried the voice which before had spoken with so much bitterness. "The coffin is there, but how do you know whether the body remains in it?"

Evidently the stranger had not thought of this, for he remained as though suddenly deprived of motion, with his sword buried in the ground.

Now that this doubt was started, however, there would be no pausing until it was satisfied.

"A spade—a spade!" continued the man who had last spoken, and whose excitement had risen to a point little short of madness. "They had my child—my only one! But vengeance will yet be mine! A spade—a spade!"

Recovering from the state of stupor in which they had been thrown by the horrible and unexpected nature of these events, some half-dozen rushed off in the direction of the sexton's tool-house behind the vestry.

The distance was but short, and, as they dashed the frail door open by main force, they were not long in reappearing with the implements they wanted.

A shout of approval greeted them, and caused them to quicken their speed.

Eager hands were stretched forth, and no d[illegible] a struggle would have taken place had not the young stranger, who had now recovered himself, interposed his authority.

The excited father seized one of the spades, and, with a rapidity that was wonderful to look on, threw up the mould.

But little labour was involved, for the soil was soft, as it always is when newly dug.

But his very fury exhausted him the sooner, and in a few moments he was compelled to desist.

The perspiration streamed from every pore.

Yet, short as was the time he had been at work, he had managed to clear out at least one-half of the earth that had been thrown upon the coffin.

But there were many strong arms and willing hearts in waiting, and scarcely had he relinquished his strengthless grasp upon the spade than another was in the grave working with scarcely less desperation.

A strange, unnatural calm now feel on all.

They knew that in another half-dozen seconds the coffin would be reached.

They were straining their ears to catch the dull sound that the spade would make in striking against the lid.

"Empty!" ejaculated the worker as the coffin returned a hollow sound to the stroke of the spade. "Empty, for a thousand pounds!"

The intense excitement was now at its highest.

Their impatience would not let them wait until the remainder of the earth was thrown out.

Many strong hands seized upon the handles of the coffin, and so tore it from its resting-place.

But when the last receptacle of sad humanity was placed upon the mound of upturned soil, another death-like silence reigned.

All looked towards the young stranger, as though they expected their further orders should come from him.

But, from some cause or other, he did not speak.

He made a gesture, though, which was interpreted—rightly, no doubt—as a command to break off the lid.

Two blows dealt by a sinewy arm sufficed.

A kind of gasping sound—half sob, half sigh—coming from many breasts, followed each blow.

Then the lid flew off, and all saw that the coffin was, as they expected—empty!

CHAPTER II.

THE RECOVERY OF DICK TURPIN'S BODY.—BACK TO THE GRAVEYARD.—THE RECOGNITION OF THE STRANGER IN THE CLOAK.

Upon finding that their worst anticipations were confirmed, the angry crowd broke forth into howls of rage and frightful threats against those who had committed this outrage on the dead.

The young stranger was deeply affected, for the dread was about his heart that it might be already too late to save his friend's remains from the desecration of the surgeon's scalpel.

But the riotous behaviour manifested by the tumultuous throng around him brought him back to a consideration of time present.

"Death to the doctors! Death to the body-snatchers! Down with them all!" were the threatening cries that arose on every side.

"Get what weapons you can," shrieked the man who had declared himself to be so great a sufferer by these outragers of the dead—"billhooks, scythes, anything will do! Death to them all! We shall have no trouble to find them out—the footprints in the snow will guide us."

The stranger once more raised his hand.

He called aloud, and strove to recover that command over the people which he had possessed such a short time before.

In vain, however.

Their angry passions now were too much roused for them to listen to anything save incitements to further violence.

With the infuriated father at their head, they dashed across the graveyard, treading in the half-filled-up footprints of those who had been engaged in this odious deed.

The young stranger, before he was aware of it, found himself hurried on along with the frenzied mass, and powerless alike to stop or to extricate himself.

He was like some waif carried along by a swift tide.

The churchyard wall was crossed; the streets of old York city were gained.

So little had the peaceful inhabitants been abroad that the track in the snow was as easily and surely followed in the streets as it had been across the level waste of the graveyard.

At every step, however, their ranks were swelled, and the new arrivals for the most part carried something which would serve as an attacking weapon.

Then many, who could, deserted the throng as they found themselves near their habitations; but it was only to provide themselves with some sort of weapon.

The stranger saw clearly that all his power was lost.

He could no more control the infuriated multitude than he could have stayed the course of a swift-rushing torrent.

But, at least, he should be able to witness all that was done, and perhaps he might be able to take advantage of some critical moment, and so reassert his authority.

But his lips compressed as he mentally resolved that he would fight to the last gasp rather than allow the mob to work their pleasure upon Dick Turpin's body—that was, supposing they found it, and this seemed more than likely.

The loud uproar in the usually quiet streets struck a panic into the hearts of all those who happened to catch sight of the procession.

Windows were thrown open—lights gleamed everywhere—shrieks of women and children could be heard—altogether serving to make up a scene which no description can do justice to.

The number of those persons who had sallied forth from the Old Chequers was now increased thirty-fold, and it promised to grow to double its present strength.

At last, however, with a subdued and angry roar—like that sometimes made by the wind immediately before a tempest—the disorderly assemblage stopped before one of the largest and finest residences in the whole city.

Its inhabitants seemed all to be resting peacefully, for not the faintest gleam of light issued from one of the many windows.

But it was to this place, as the footprints indisputably proved, that the body had been brought.

"It is here—it is here!" shouted the frantic father. "Here lives the vampire we have suffered in our midst! Down with the grave-robber—down with him! Death—death to him and his!"

These ominous words found a ready and responsive echo upon many lips.

The furious man who had uttered these inflammatory words had, by some means or other, possessed himself of a pickaxe.

It was a terrible weapon to see in the hands of one so fearfully excited as he was.

Swinging it once round his head, he brought its broadest head down with terrific force on the front door of the surgeon's house.

He struck at the lock, and the accuracy of his aim showed that he was no stranger to the use of the implement he carried.

A crash of broken wood followed the blow.

Another and another stroke followed until the door flew back upon its hinges.

But now arose other sounds which caused a momentary diversion of attention.

Alarmed by the tumult, and perhaps guessing the cause, the surgeon had shown himself at one of the upper windows.

He wished to say something, but the infuriated populace would not listen.

His appearance was the signal for the hurling of a thousand missiles.

Considering how thickly the snow lay, it seemed truly wonderful that so many stones and other objects should be found.

The surgeon was compelled to beat a retreat unheard, and the next moment there was not a whole pane of glass left in any of the windows.

Fain would the young stranger have checked this violence.

But knowing this to be impossible, he did the very wisest thing in his power.

This was, to avail himself of the time while the unruly mob were thus engaged—to gain the front door of the house and slip into the passage.

The man who had wrought the work of demolition had paused when the fresh uproar from without had come upon his ears.

"Come on!" he cried. "Never mind the windows! Follow me! I tell you, we will be revenged!"

Turning round, he found himself most unexpectedly confronted by the stranger in the cloak, who stood just within the doorway, holding his sword in a way that promised little mercy to those who might have the temerity to advance.

"Stand aside!" bawled the man with the pickaxe, who, while he spoke, again raised his fearful weapon.

But the young stranger was undismayed.

"Hold!" he cried, in a voice which sounded in the ears of those who heard it like a sudden blast upon a trumpet.

He accompanied the word by taking a step forward.

The fearlessness of his demeanour caused a murmur of applause.

"Let me ask you all—what would you have? Do not be carried too far! Do not, in your just resentment, mingle the innocent with the guilty—let only the guilty perish! Your first care should be to get possession of Dick Turpin's body. You knew him—all of you knew him well enough when in life. He was ever the friend of the poor and the foe of the rich. Three cheers for Dick Turpin! We will find his body, and when we have it we will carry it in triumph once more to the grave. We will consign him to his last resting-place, and when that is accomplished—I say again, we will be revenged!"

This brief and stirring address produced a greater impression than the young man had dared to hope for.

Dick Turpin's name told well, and the three cheers were given with a lustiness that made the old streets ring again.

But scarcely had the last one died away when a voice cried, in stentorian tones:

"Three groans for the vampire doctors!"

Never were groans more heartily given.

"Follow me!" cried the young stranger, flashing his sword around him—"follow me! We will find Dick Turpin's body, and carry it back again to the grave."

The words were caught up and echoed.

The stranger, turning round, hastened along the passage.

He had an anxious duty before him, but he had high hopes of success.

A moment's reflection convinced him that the body, if on the premises at all, would be in the surgery.

Could he only find his way to this place, all would be well.

But, alas! he was an entire stranger in that dwelling, and it was as a last hope that he cried out:

"The surgery—the surgery! Where is the surgery?"

"Straight on," said a voice—"straight on. Open the door in front of you."

This was enough.

The stranger continued to advance, keeping back with the utmost difficulty the mob which thronged at his heels.

But the door was opened, and, somewhat to his surprise, he found himself in the garden in the rear of the surgeon's abode.

But seeing a small building at a little distance, he guessed that must be the surgery, and made his way towards it.

He was right.

The door, however, was fastened, though this was but a temporary obstacle.

Two blows with the ponderous pickaxe beat down the obstruction.

There was a dim light burning in the surgery, and this, in conjunction with the moon, which was shining brightly through the windows, enabled the young stranger to take a good view of the objects it contained.

But his gaze was riveted instantly upon a long table in the centre.

This was covered over with a white sheet, but it could be seen that it served to cover something else.

"At all hazards, Dick, I will stand by you now," he cried, "even as I would have stood by you in life!"

With remarkable agility he sprang upon the table, and turning his face towards the door, he projected his sword in front of him in a manner that would have made any-one hesitate before venturing to come too close.

"My friends," he cried, addressing the huge throng "we have found him—he is here. Listen to me! Those who think well enough of Dick Turpin to wish to preserve his body from the doctor's knife will place themselves under my direction, and act in accordance with my orders."

"Hurrah!"

The cry of approval issued simultaneously from many throats.

"All that is necessary," continued the young stranger, "will be to carry him back to the churchyard, and once more inter him in his grave."

"We will—we will!" was the universal cry; "and after that we will come back for our revenge upon the vampire!"

This was enough.

In a moment the stranger descended from the table.

"Hold!" he cried. "We must have something that will serve the purpose of a bier."

"The front-door," said a voice.

"A good thought," exclaimed the stranger, quickly—"nothing could be better for our purpose. The front-door!"

There was a hasty rush in the direction of the street.

The front-door of the surgeon's abode had not been knocked down altogether, though it hung in a very frail manner upon its hinges.

The united strength of a dozen hands tore it down in a moment.

With all speed possible they returned to the surgery with their prize.

Tenderly and reverently the last remains of the world-celebrated highwayman were lifted up and placed upon the stout oak door.

Even the most callous and hard of heart are affected by the presence of the dead.

A strange, deep silence fell upon the throng which a short time before had been so turbulent.

"Are you all ready?" asked the stranger, his voice unconsciously becoming deeply solemn in its tone.

"Quite," was the response.

No sooner was the word pronounced than the young man unclasped his ample cloak.

Spreading it open wide, he carefully covered with it the body of the bold highwayman as it laid extended on the door.

In default of anything better, it served well enough for the purpose of a pall.

"Now," said the stranger, "I want a few of you to assist in bearing him back to the graveyard. Remember what your burden will be. Do not forget that it is the inanimate form of one who, when living, would always have extended a helping hand to you."

A faint cheer was given.

About a dozen of the foremost in the throng stood forward.

To raise the extemporised bier was easy enough when so many hands were near.

"Forward!" cried the stranger.

As he spoke, the people of their own accord formed themselves into a kind of procession, and with slow and measured steps they quitted the surgery and made their way—not through the house again, but out at a small gate communicating with the back part of the premises.

The reason for this was that they might avoid the huge crowd which had assembled without, and, in comparison with whom those who had followed the stranger to the surgery were but a handful.

The excited populace had proceeded from one act of violence to another.

Never had there been before such a display of execration on the part of the peaceful inhabitants of the old city.

"Roast him—roast him alive!" called out one of the ringleaders. "Burn down his nest! Don't leave a stick standing! Down with the vampire!—down with the grave-robber!—down with him!"

These violent words were received with a roar of approval.

They suited exactly the state of mind which nearly all present were in.

Lights sprang up as if by magic.

The surgeon's abode was fired in twenty places; and as the light had in every case been applied to some combustible material, the whole of the dwelling was in an incredibly short space of time ablaze.

It was just at this juncture that the little procession, now headed by the sable stranger, came in sight.

For a moment they gazed in silence.

Those who carried the bier had raised it up upon their shoulders—at that time more commonly the mode of carrying the dead than it is now—and, with the same solemn tread, advanced in perfect silence.

The dense mob, however, did not long remain quiescent.

Ere long a general movement in the direction of the line of procession was observable.

Those who carried torches pressed forward eagerly, and in a few moments the funeral throng found themselves surrounded by a tumultuous crowd—the individual members of which were, for the most part, armed with aggressive weapons.

In this manner the churchyard was reached—not in a direct line, however, but by passing down the principal streets.

The determination to adopt this triumphal kind of progress was so strong that the young stranger found it quite in vain to attempt to oppose it.

He would be content so long as his intention was carried into effect—namely, to restore the remains of his friend, for so he had called him, to his violated grave.

By this time it may be said the whole of the population was aroused.

The authorities turned out in the hope of restoring order; but they found themselves in such a ridiculous minority that they could do nothing save remain spectators of this extraordinary and unparalleled scene.

It was noticeable, however, as the churchyard was neared, the violence of the multitude became less and less.

The loud cries and shouts, which had sounded so appallingly to the frightened inmates of the houses, grew fainter until they ceased altogether.

At the churchyard gates a slight delay took place, which threatened to re-arouse the angry passions of the people.

The cause of this was that the strong iron gates were found to be securely locked.

But the stranger, who seemed gifted with the power of discerning every advantage, pointed out that it would be possible to lift the gates off at the hinges, and this was done accordingly.

With the observance of more decorum than might have been expected, the bearers made their way towards the still open grave.

"Rare sport!" cried a shrill voice. "When was ever such doings known in the old churchyard! Ha, ha! A rare funeral! Wild Will is here!"

The idiot boy scrambled up on to the top of the tomb on which the stranger had previously stood; and then, clapping his hands together, manifested in every way the most extravagant delight.

The stranger hastened to place himself beside the upturned coffin; and having succeeded, he made a sign to the foremost bearers to set down their burden.

At the moment when this was done every sound was hushed.

Even Wild Will, the idiot boy, ceased his noisy manifestations; but he looked on the proceedings with an expectant grin that caused all who beheld it to shudder involuntarily.

As for the people, they stood around in a dense circle, all their faculties absorbed in gazing upon the strangest of all scenes.

The young stranger issued his instructions rapidly and clearly.

With reverent care, the lifeless mass was lifted from the bier and placed within the rudely-made coffin from which the body-snatchers had removed it such a short time before.

This done, the lid was replaced.

It could not be fastened, because violence had been used in opening it.

To this, however, they seemed to attach but slight importance, for the coffin was now lowered into the grave that was ready to receive it.

The stranger was the first to begin filling-in the earth.

The first sod, as it fell upon the coffin-lid, raised a strange sound that found an echo in his heart.

His emotions would suffer him to do no more.

He surrendered his spade to the first of the eager, outstretched hands that were waiting to receive it.

Then, gazing down, he murmured:

"Farewell, my old friend! I tried my best to save you, and no one can blame me because I failed. No mortal can perform impossibilities; but I have rendered you what service lies in my power. Farewell, old friend—farewell!"

These words were spoken to himself rather than uttered, yet there were many that stood near who caught their purport.

At the conclusion, he buried his face in his hands, and became entirely unconscious of all that was taking place around him.

Meanwhile, the business of filling-in the grave went on with great rapidity, for there were many hands at work.

So carried away was the stranger by his genuine grief, and so intent were all the spectators in watching the close of the proceedings, that the approach of a considerable body of mounted men was unnoticed.

They even made their way through the gateway and walked their horses over the graves without exciting the least attention.

These men were all well armed, and their faces were expressive of stern, unflinching resolution.

The first intimation of their presence was given by the leader, who, in clear and startling tones, cried out:

"Five hundred pounds!"

Had those three words been some all-potent spell, the people could not have looked up more quickly.

Certainly, the mention of such a sum of money in so strange a way, and on so extraordinary an occasion, was well calculated to excite a more than common interest.

The leader of the troop drew his sword, and pointed with it towards Dick Turpin's grave.

"There is a reward of five hundred pounds for that man! Take him who can!"

Beyond all doubt, the person he indicated was the young and interesting stranger, who had taken such a prominent part in the proceedings of the night.

But the people seemed so amazed and stunned that after this declaration not one moved a limb.

"Five hundred pounds!" said the leader of the troop. "That is the reward to be paid to whoever makes him prisoner!"

The stranger had looked up as soon as the tones of the loud voice struck upon his ear.

He was accustomed to surprises of various kinds, and was rarely disconcerted; but the sight of this large body of armed and mounted men, of whose approach he had not had the least intimation, for a moment or so fairly staggered him.

He glanced about him eagerly.

Flight was his only chance of escape.

But how impossible this seemed, hemmed in by a crowd so dense as that which had assembled.

Yet he did not despair.

He gave one last and yearning glance at Dick Turpin's grave, and then he said, addressing those who stood around him:

"You will not aid in my capture, after doing what I have to-night. Give me a fair chance with my foes, that is all I ask; I have injured none of you!"

"Captain Hawk," cried the leader of the troop, unable to approach closer in consequence of the denseness of the people—"Captain Hawk, I call upon you in the name of his gracious Majesty the King, to surrender yourself into my hands! Escape is impossible, so you may as well yield quietly, and save yourself from further injury!"

This was a revelation to the crowd.

At that time there was no one more popular with the people at large than this said Captain Hawk—all admired him for his bravery and dauntlessness—those qualities which years before had endeared their ancestors to Robin Hood and his companions. Captain Hawk was their champion, the idol of the hour.

The highwayman showed himself in no way moved by the demand just made.

It was indeed in the coolest and calmest tone of voice that he answered:

"Do your own work, and don't ask me to save you trouble. If you want me you must come and take me."

"Three cheers for the brave highwayman, Captain Hawk!" cried the man with the pickaxe, as he once more raised aloft that terrible weapon. "We will stand by him to the last!"

Those words were all that the people wanted to decide them to declare in favour of the highwayman.

"This way—this way!" said several voices, and immediately a narrow lane was opened, along which the captain could make his way speedily enough.

As fast as he went, this living lane was closed up after him, his protectors turning their faces towards his would-be captors.

Seeing this, the officers were furious.

"Down with the rioters," cried their leader—"down with them! Cut them down without mercy! Quick—quick, or he will escape!"

The police officers drew their cutlasses, and charged upon the mob.

Riotous thoughts had, however, been uppermost in the minds of every one of them that night, and now the prospect of a row was far from disagreeable.

But it was not likely that they would be able to make a lengthened stand against so large a body of well-armed, mounted, resolute men.

In spite of their cries, and their determination to stand by the captain to the last, they gave way and fled in all directions, like so much chaff before a sudden gust of wind.

"There he goes!" cried the chief officer, excitedly. "Look, there he is! Now he is down! Quick—quick! No, he is up again! He gains the wall; he is over! Curses on the fellow, he will elude us after all!"

CHAPTER III.

THE PURSUIT AND CAPTURE OF CAPTAIN HAWK.—THE MAD HORSE.—OFF AND AWAY.

Captain Hawk made the best use he could of his powers, and the way in which he bounded over the churchyard was something wonderful.

He stumbled once, and fell.

But, in some mysterious way, he seemed to roll up on to his feet again.

His headlong course was continued until he finally disappeared over the boundary wall.

His pursuers, however, pressed him hard. Being mounted, they naturally had the advantage over him, for they rode their horses among the tombstones in the most reckless manner conceivable.

Captain Hawk's course was directed towards the Old Chequers Inn.

His sole chance lay in the possibility of being able to reach the stables long enough before the officers to enable him to gain the back of his incomparable steed.

Once mounted, he felt he should be in a position to bid defiance to all danger.

With great resolution, however, his pursuers compelled their horses to leap over the boundary wall; and after that they seemed to stand a double chance of success.

Captain Hawk did not look back, but he heard the muffled sound produced by their progress become louder and louder.

He redoubled his efforts.

A narrow street, or rather alley, not more than twenty yards in length, was all that lay between him and the point he so much wished to reach.

This alone was enough to make him strain every nerve.

But just at the moment when he was beginning to felicitate himself upon his success—when the extremity of the alley was all but reached—another party of police officers came in sight.

Captain Hawk involuntarily gave utterance to a loud cry of vexation and despair.

He stopped at once.

To have run further would only have been to precipitate his capture.

The approaching officers numbered some thirteen or fourteen, and were all on foot.

They consisted in part of some of Skellum's men—the remainder were the regular guardians of the city.

Their destination was the churchyard; but when they caught sight of a man flying at the top of his speed and hotly pursued by mounted men, they with great readiness drew themselves up so as to form a perfect barrier across the narrow thoroughfare.

The officers in the rear were not slow to perceive this, to them, fortunate occurrence, and they increased their shouts.

"Stop him!" bawled the leader of the troop, in tones so stentorian that the street fairly echoed—"stop him! That's Captain Hawk! Whoever stops him has the reward!"

As a matter of course, these words produced an immediate effect.

The whole of the party on foot rushed on the captain in a mass.

Thus hemmed in by two forces of his foes, what chance had the hunted highwayman of escape?

There was not a moment for him to consider what to do.

He was trapped.

Both outlets of the narrow street were blocked up by his foes.

On each side of him were houses, the windows and doors of which were securely locked and barred.

He could not escape, that was quite clear.

Captain Hawk saw that at a glance.

But he could resist his capture to the last, and this he prepared to do by drawing a couple of pistols from his belt.

He gasped so for breath, however, and his heart beat so violently, that he could not steady the muscles of his hands.

Placing his back against the wall, he held out his weapons before him, while he half articulately cried:

"Death—death to the man that touches me! Stand off, I say!"

He was not allowed to utter more.

The officers rushed at him in a body.

The pistols were discharged in quick succession.

But the captain's hands shook so that it was impossible for him to take aim; and, moreover, the assault upon him was more rapid and vigorous than he had expected.

Distressed as he was by the immense exertion he had been compelled to make, what chance had he when so many strong hands were laid upon him?

Absolutely none.

He was overpowered, as one may say, instantly, though his struggles, brief as they were, seemed almost superhuman.

"Hold him tight—keep him down!" cried the leader of the mounted troop. "Do not let him escape! You have well earned your reward!"

His own men now hastened to the assistance of the rest.

By their united efforts, Captain Hawk was kept pinned to the ground, while his limbs were strongly bound.

When the last knot was tied, he was about as helpless as a man well could be.

But by this time the people who had made so weak and ineffectual an attempt to protect the captain in the graveyard arrived upon the scene.

Their demeanour now had lost something of its fierceness, though whether this would continue when they found Captain Hawk a prisoner was rather doubtful.

But the manner in which the police had in the first instance laid about them with their cutlasses had inspired them with a great deal of awe.

Crowding closely together and increasing in numbers every moment, they stood looking on, being scarcely able to realise what had taken place.

The bonds being now all perfectly secure, however, the police officers disentangled themselves a little, and raised the prisoner to his feet.

He was quite incapable of raising himself.

Yet, for all that, the first glance which he gave around him fully showed that he had lost none of his dauntlessness—his look and manner, pinioned as he was, were both as proud as ever.

But he saw little that was calculated to give birth to the hope that he might yet extricate himself from the peril which impended over him.

One chance there was—and one only.

It was a frail one—none knew how frail better than the captain did himself.

"I am taken," he cried, addressing the fast-increasing crowd. "You all know what I have done to-night. It was the determination to be faithful to a friend that has brought me to this. Will you suffer it?"

The words were spoken rapidly—so rapidly, that the officers were powerless to stifle his voice.

But they were responded to by an ominous murmur coming from the crowd.

The usually peaceful people, their passions stirred up by the strange things which had happened, pressed forward more closely still and in a threatening manner.

From their aspect it was clear they needed but little to commence an attack.

The chief officer saw this.

"Form round your prisoner!" he cried. "Present your pistols, and if anyone advances upon you, don't wait to receive the word from me, but fire!"

This order was carried out with astonishing promptitude.

When the assembled people found themselves confronted by so many pistols—the muzzles of every one of which were steadily pointed at them—their resolution wavered.

It was just at this juncture that the excitement was heightened by the appearance of a man on horseback.

Where he had come from no one knew, the soft snow gave forth scarcely any sound, and everybody had been too busily engaged in watching what was occurring close to them to look around.

But the behaviour of this horse was what attracted everybody's notice.

He pranced and reared, and then plunging down, flung his hind feet in the air in a manner which created no little consternation, for he dashed right into the thickest of the crowd.

How the man on his back retained his seat was, perhaps, the greatest mystery.

That it was no easy matter could be perceived at a glance, for he clung most desperately to the horse's mane, and seemed every second as though he must fall off.

"Why, blow me," said a voice, in tones indicative of great astonishment—"if that isn't Sam the ostler from the Old Chequers!"

This little incident attracted, as a matter of course, much of the attention of the officers, though they did not relax their vigilance with respect to their prisoner.

Those who had horses had no slight difficulty in retaining their command over them, for they were influenced by the actions of the other.

"It's a mad horse—a mad horse!" cried the chief officer.

Just at this moment Captain Hawk by a sudden jerk freed his mouth from the hand of one of his captors, which had been laid so heavily upon it as to serve well for a gag.

"Hi!" cried the highwayman. "Satan—Satan! Hi, boy—h——"

The hand was once more dashed violently over his mouth, and further speech prevented.

But no sooner did the horse catch the first tones of that well-known voice than he gave so tremendous a leap and plunge that the ostler—good rider as he was—was hurled out of the saddle, turning a complete somersault over Satan's head.

Luckily, he alighted on the snow, and therefore sustained but little injury.

There is something truly terrible in the idea of a mad horse, and certainly the manner in which the highwayman's steed now dashed among the police officers went far towards realising it.

"The horse is mad!" roared the chief officer. "Shoot at it—shoot at it, or we shall all be killed or lamed!"

The scene of confusion at this moment cannot be described.

But the officers prepared to carry out the order they had received, though it was almost too painful to think of wounding such a magnificent creature.

When Captain Hawk saw the danger with which his favourite steed was threatened he was almost maddened.

Desperation gave him double strength.

Again freeing his mouth, he cried:

"Away, away—off and away, old boy—away—away!"

Beyond all dispute, the splendid creature understood the words which had just been addressed to him, for, with a sudden snort, he wheeled round and set off at a gallop.

The people cleared away right and left to allow him free passage. Quick as he was, though, the police officer had time to pull the trigger.

No words can possibly do justice to the captain's feelings when he saw his foe's finger encircling the trigger, and beheld the barrel steadily levelled at the object which he valued above all other earthly things, while he could not so much as raise his hand to save him.

But, urged by desperation, he in some strange way slipped himself from the grasp of his foes, and, all bound and helpless as he was, flung himself forward with all his might.

In falling, his shoulder struck violently against the back of the chief officer, who, totally unprepared to sustain the captain's weight, found himself flung face foremost to the earth.

It was while falling that his pistol was discharged—aimlessly, of course.

Captain Hawk's end was gained—Satan was uninjured.

He had not escaped receiving some serious bruises; but he would not have heeded them had they been ten times as severe.

The police officer was assisted to rise.

His anger was something awful to think of, and no doubt, influenced by it, he would have committed some act of desperation had not a loud roaring cry coming from the mob at this moment warned him that his trouble was by no means over yet.

"Don't flinch if they attempt a rescue," he said, in a low tone, to his men. "I fancy, by the way of them, they mean mischief. Be prepared."

A low murmur was the response.

Captain Hawk saw and heard all.

He read the feelings of the people easily; and he felt assured that could he only manage to renew his appeal to them, they would rush in a body upon his foes—for they outnumbered them ten to one—and set him at liberty.

The captain looked round for the man who had carried the pickaxe, and who had taken so prominent a part in the night's doings. But he was nowhere to be seen.

The cries of the people increased, until at last they assumed a definite shape.

"Give up your prisoner!" was the universal shout.

"Never!" answered the officer in command. "Keep a bold front," he added, to his men. "We shall have assistance soon; and to let the prisoner be wrested from us would be to cover ourselves with disgrace."

The mob slowly advanced.

"Keep the prisoner close to the wall," said the chief officer, in a low tone. "He will be safest there, and hardest to be got at."

Scarcely had he spoken the words before the foremost of the throng pressed forward with menacing gestures.

"Give up the prisoner," they said, resolutely, "and save further disturbance!"

"Never while we live! My lads," cried the chief officer, "if they come any closer, don't hesitate—fire upon them!"

At the word, one of the officers discharged his pistol.

The act was an accidental one, no doubt, but it was taken by the mob as an unprovoked attack.

They rushed on pell-mell.

Those officers who had been told to keep their prisoner closely pressed against the wall had obeyed the order, except that instead of keeping him against the wall it was against the front-door of one of the houses.

Just at the moment the conflict commenced this door suddenly and unexpectedly flew back upon its hinges.

The officers who were pressing Captain Hawk against it, being totally unprepared for such an event, went staggering forwards into the passage.

They found themselves confronted by many men.

Captain Hawk was snatched from their grasp and the front-door closed again before they had time to recover from the first shock of their surprise, and almost before the rest of their comrades comprehended the mystery of their sudden disappearance.

A tremendous uproar from without soon testified that the police officers were aware of what had occurred.

This was immediately followed by heavy blows upon the door.

Probably no one was more surprised at the suddenness and unexpectedness of the turn events had taken than the captain himself.

He felt himself dragged along by some one, and then a rough voice bade him keep still. The next moment he understood the meaning of this injunction.

One of his unknown friends was busily engaged in cutting the cords which bound him, with a knife.

A dim glimmer of light coming from some distant source was now discernible.

By the aid of it, the captain saw that one of those to whom he stood indebted for this great service was the man with the pickaxe.

Judging by the sounds which reached their ears from without, the conflict between the populace and the police had ceased.

The officers, however, were making the most strenuous efforts to effect an entrance.

Although quite unprovided with the weapons requisite for this purpose, yet it seemed tolerably certain that a very few seconds more would elapse before they had achieved their object.

But the last stroke had been given to the captain's cords. He was once more a free man—that is, he was able to make use of his limbs.

"Now, captain," said a familiar voice, "we have done all we can for you—you must trust to yourself for the rest. Cut and run with all your might. You may be able to get off. Keep straight on, and you will get out at the back of the house."

It was Sam the ostler who spoke.

It was probably to him that the captain was indebted for this successful plan of setting him at liberty.

But there was no time to ask questions, or even give expression to his gratitude.

A tremendous crash announced the fact that the police officers had broken down the door.

At the time when this was done the captain was not half a dozen paces off.

Consequently his position now was one of very great danger; though compared with what it had been, it seemed to him to be almost like freedom.

Fixing his eyes upon the faint glimmer of light we have mentioned, he dashed forward with all the speed he was capable of making.

Three steps brought him to the foot of a flight of stairs.

Whether escape lay in this direction, or whether he ought to look for it in some other, he knew not.

There was not the thousandth part of a moment allowed him to decide in.

Indeed, as one may say, without making any pause at all, he dashed up the staircase as though it had been his intention to do so from the first.

A broad red glare of light now illumined the place.

It came from several torches, and as he turned the angle of the stairs Captain Hawk had a good view of his enemies.

Whether he was seen by them or not he could not tell—he fancied so.

At any rate, they were so close upon his heels as to make his chances of ultimate escape more than doubtful.

The speed he made was something amazing; nor did he pause until he reached the top of the flight.

The darkness here was intense. Panting for breath, he strove to make out his surroundings.

But he had no other means of doing this than by the sense of touch.

Groping about, the first thing his hand encountered was the handle of a door.

Just then the foremost officers were at the angle of the staircase. Another second, and he would be seen.

The only means by which he could prevent immediate discovery was by turning the handle and passing through the doorway.

He did this, closing the door again with the utmost silence and rapidity.

He felt down the edge, hoping to come in contac with either bolt or lock, but there was no means whatever of securing the door on the inner side.

And now his difficulties and perplexities were added to by the discovery that this room was tenanted.

[THE BLACK HIGHWAYMAN AND THE BISHOP OF OXFORD.]

He was made aware of the fact by hearing a low gasping cry—such as anyone might be supposed to give vent to when in the last stage of terror and only one remove from unconsciousness.

A rather dim light was burning in the room; but to Captain Hawk, who had been so long in the dark, it seemed absolutely brilliant.

He saw that the apartment was a bed-chamber, and if he might judge upon the many articles of apparel hanging about, it belonged to a member of the female sex.

His swift glance next rested upon the bed, which was hung round with curtains, and which was shaking in a most mysterious manner.

Captain Hawk comprehended all this at one fleeting glance.

He made at once for the window.

But, to his dismay, he found it so well protected by iron bars placed close together as to put an end to all hope or possibility of escape in that direction.

"This way," said a voice outside—"this way! Come on! Mind, there is a good look-out kept upon all the windows and on the roof! Fire at him the moment you see him!"

These words were quite enough to make Captain Hawk shrink with despair.

For one fleeting moment he did seem as though he would give way.

No feeling, however, could have been more transient.

Ever ready of invention and fertile expedients, an idea now entered his mind, and without delay he proceeded to act upon it.

Had he given it any consideration, he would probably have come to the conclusion that it was too monstrous and absurd to be attempted.

But we repeat he had no time for reflection.

He could only act upon impulse.

Quick as thought, he went towards the bed, in which lay the trembling form of a female, who looked almost old enough to be the captain's grandmother.

She was half dead with fright.

Her terror was so great as to make her past giving utterance to any vocal sound.

Her eyes rolled fearfully, and altogether she presented as complete a personification of absolute terror as can be conceived.

Had she possessed the least control over her voice, Captain Hawk's next actions would have brought a loud cry from her lips.

In the twinkling of an eye he turned down the clothes, and placed himself in bed by her side.

Whipping off his hat, he thrust it out of sight, and had just time to snatch off the poor woman's nightcap—which, by-the-by, was furnished with an alarming border—when the latch of the door was lifted.

"Say I am your sister," whispered Captain Hawk, menacingly. "Deny that anyone has entered the room to-night. Betray me, and you die; conceal me, and you shall have whatever you like for your reward."

He had no time to utter more.

The door was opened, and a police officer, carrying a lantern, came in.

CHAPTER IV.

THE WATCH FOR THE BLACK HIGHWAYMAN ON EALING COMMON.—THE BISHOP'S COACH.—A MYSTERIOUS DISAPPEARANCE.—PETERSON GAINS SOME INFORMATION.

"MR. PETERSON—Mr. Peterson! What is that? Look yonder! Can you see it?"

"I can see nothing," answered the officer addressed, straining his eyes the while in a vain endeavour to pierce the darkness.

"Nor I now, sir; but I saw him—I am certain I saw him."

"Saw who?"

"Why, the man we are looking for, to be sure."

"The Black Highwayman?"

"Yes."

"Pooh, pooh, Hopkins!—you must have fallen asleep and dreamt it. I will take my oath there has been nothing stirring about here but the leaves for half an hour at least."

"And, Mr. Peterson, I will take my oath, if you like, that I saw him. I cannot be mistaken. He passed close by. If you will follow me we shall quickly overtake him."

"You saw him, you say?"

"Yes, sir."

"But did you hear him?"

"Well, no, I can't say that I did; but I saw him, and that ought to be enough."

"It must have been a ghost."

"You may laugh at me, Mr. Peterson, and disbelieve me, if you like; but I tell you over again, I saw him just when I spoke—quite as plainly as I can see you now."

"Then I say again, it must have been his ghost, or I should have heard him."

"Very well, sir—have your own opinion. I shouldn't like to say I didn't believe in ghosts—that is, the ghosts of human beings; but when it comes to a horse—excuse me. No, no—I couldn't believe in the ghost of a horse; that would be coming it a little too strong, I rather think."

"But it's preposterous!" said Peterson, vainly endeavouring to conceal his uneasiness. "You must think me a fool to try and make me believe that a mounted man has ridden by without the least sound reaching my ears. It's impossible!"

"Very well, sir, you know best, of course; but, for all that, unaccountable as it seems, I stick to what I said."

"I know you do," answered the other, peevishly, "and I know you will do so; and the fact will become garnished with so many particulars that it will be looked upon as another wonder."

"Will you ride a little way down the road, s—, and see?"

"What's the good? It is through such as you that this Black Highwayman, as he is called, has got to be so much dreaded. I understand now how it is that he is described as dropping suddenly from the clouds and afterwards disappearing without leaving a trace behind. But it's imagination—all imagination. Thank goodness, I never had any."

"Hark!" exclaimed his companion. "Can you hear anything now? Is that imagination?"

"No, I should say not. It sounds remarkably like some one galloping towards us. This is far more likely to be the man we want. Are your weapons ready?"

"Yes."

"Then follow me. Let it be who it may, he does not pass without giving good account of himself."

The clear and rapid strokes of a horse's hoofs upon the hard roadway which bisects Ealing Common could now be heard with unmistakable plainness.

The two police officers, who had been watching beneath the shadow of a dense clump of trees, now emerged, and took up their positions opposite one another on each side of the way.

"You understand, Hopkins," said Peterson, "if he disregards us or offers any resistance, fire upon him. But fetch him down alive if possible; I don't want him killed."

"All right, sir. He's coming at a tremendous pace."

"He is."

"But I don't think it is the Black Highwayman."

"Why not?"

"He would take care not to give us such notice of his approach."

"Pooh—pooh! You would make me believe him to be something more than a man. Hopkins, I'm ashamed of you!"

"We shall soon know, sir."

This was true enough, for the approaching horseman came on with unabated speed.

"Hold!" cried Peterson, at the top of his voice, a moment afterwards. "Pull up, if you value your life! If you refuse, you will have a bullet through you!"

The horseman heard these words, and evidently was disinclined to regard them lightly, for he made the most strenuous efforts to check his flying steed.

But this proved anything but an easy matter, and it is doubtful whether he would have succeeded had not the two officers assisted.

"This isn't him," said Hopkins; "I thought it wasn't."

"Get the light, stupid!" said the superior officer, far from pleased at finding himself at fault.

Thus commanded, Hopkins drew forth a dark lantern from his pocket, and, removing the slide, allowed the broad beam of light to fall full upon the horseman.

At the very first glance it seemed manifest that this could not be the person of whom they were in search, for his appearance corresponded in no way with the description given of the mysterious highwayman.

"Who are you?" said Peterson, savagely. "And what the devil do you want here at this time of night?"

"I decline to answer both your questions," answered the stranger, somewhat haughtily. "Stand aside and let me ride on. I took you at first for police officers."

"And that's what we are, make no mistake. My name's Peterson. Heard of me, no doubt?"

The officer drew out of his pocket a little ebony staff, tipped with a silver crown, which was his badge of office; at the same time, his coat flying back, disclosed the well-known glaring red waistcoat.

"I see you are now," said the horseman, "and I am heartily glad of it."

"Why so—why so?"

"Perhaps you know my lord, the Bishop of Oxford, is on the road to-night. He is carrying with him a large sum of money."

"Then he is in danger of losing it."

"So he thought; and, in case any highwaymen should attempt to stop him, he hit on a scheme to make the attempt fruitless."

"Indeed!" said Peterson, deeply interested.

"He has handed me the valise containing the money. It is here; and my instructions are to gallop with all speed possible to London with it."

"And who may you be, pray?" asked Peterson, edging still closer to the horseman.

"I am my Lord Bishop's private secretary."

"And he has sent you on in advance with the gold, you say?"

"Yes, here it is."

The horseman tapped the little valise as he spoke.

"And whereabouts is the Bishop?" inquired Peterson.

"About a mile off down the road. And if I might give you a word of advice——"

"What is it?"

"I should recommend you to ride on and meet his lordship, and escort him over the heath. He has a great horror of highwaymen, and you would find that it would be nothing out of your pocket to render him this service."

Peterson hesitated.

He was one of those over-cunning men who fancy there is something suspicious in the simplest objects.

For instance, without any adequate cause, he doubted whether this horseman was what he declared himself—the Bishop's secretary.

What this suspicion might have developed itself into it is hard to say, but just at this moment they were all three startled by the report of firearms.

"That's the Black Highwayman, by Jove!" ejaculated the horseman. "His lordship's fears were well grounded, after all. One comfort, the rascal will have nothing for his trouble, provided he does not in his rage ill-use the Bishop."

The sound came from a considerable distance, for it was very faint; and scarcely had the Bishop's secretary ceased speaking when another followed.

"That sounds like business, doesn't it?" ejaculated Hopkins.

"Ride to his lordship's assistance," said the secretary, imploringly. "Quick—quick! I will continue on my way, and so save all this wealth. The loss of it would be almost ruin to my master."

Peterson evidently did not know what to do, and while he was hesitating precious moments were lost.

"Fly—fly!" said the secretary, imploringly; "or, at least, allow me to depart! I ought by this time to be clear of the common, and should have been but for your interruption. Let me entreat you again to make haste! Why on earth do you hesitate?"

"Because, my spark," said Peterson, with an air of profound wisdom, "I have my suspicions of you—that's why; and your anxiety to part company confirms them. But I would have you know you have no fool to deal with."

The horseman laughed.

"Preposterous," he said—"preposterous in the extreme! Bring your lantern and look here. I will soon convince you that I am his lordship's confidential servant."

These words, and the easy way in which he had received the accusation, disconcerted Peterson not a little.

From his breast-pocket the horseman now produced a packet of papers, which he handed to the police officer for inspection.

One glance was sufficient to convince even the sceptical Peterson that he had made a terrible mistake, and had suffered time to elapse which he could not recover.

"I beg your pardon, sir," he said, with great confusion. "Good night! Come on, Hopkins! What the devil are you lingering behind for, d—n you?"

Hopkins grinned, and rode after his commander.

Their speed was something terrific.

In the course of a few moments they caught sight of a couple of twinkling lights in advance.

Doubtless they were the lamps of the Bishop's carriage.

A few minutes more convinced them of the fact.

The first thing they heard was a dismal groaning, as if somebody was enduring more than an ordinary amount of bodily pain.

"Who's that?" said Peterson, suddenly checking his horse.

"Me, poor devil—me!" said a doleful voice. "Oh, we are all robbed and murdered! I knew how it would be—I dreamt it all, I did!"

"Now, stupid, show a light," said Peterson to his subordinate, "and get down off your horse!"

He alighted as he spoke, and Hopkins obeyed both commands as quickly as he could.

The bright beams of the police officer's dark lantern first of all disclosed a human being lying in a strange, huddled-up position in the middle of the road.

This was the individual who had given utterance to the doleful cries.

Peterson saw at a glance that this was the postilion.

The first thing he did consequent upon this discovery was to salute the poor fellow with a couple of hearty kicks in his ribs, and then said:

"Get up, you fool, can't you? What do you want to lie there howling like that for?"

Without waiting to see whether his words were attended to, he came still closer to the carriage, the door of which was swinging open.

At first sight, Peterson took the vehicle to be empty.

But Hopkins pointed to something which could be seen sticking out from under the seat.

Peterson seized it in a moment.

A sudden movement and a dismal cry followed.

Peterson put out his strength, and presently pulled forth the form of a thin, effeminate-looking young man, whose age, perhaps, might have been one-and-twenty.

His face was the picture of consternation, and he trembled all over with the most ludicrous fright.

"Oh, mercy! Spare my life! Good Mr. Robber, do spare my life, and take the old man's money! Spare my life! Oh, mercy—mercy!"

Peterson set this valorous individual up on his legs.

"You have nothing to fear now," said the police officer. "Where is the Bishop?"

"Eh? Ain't you a robber? Oh dear me! I don't know!"

"Never mind him," said Hopkins—"he is half out of his senses. I think I can hear the Bishop over here."

A low gurgling, gasping sound was now audible.

Peterson proceeded at once in the direction of it.

They paused on the brink of a ditch of dangerous depth and unusual width.

Looking down, they perceived the right reverend father, &c., beplastered with slime from head to foot, and making vain efforts to free himself from the thick tenacious mud, into which his violent efforts only seemed to make him sink the more.

By the united efforts of the two police officers and the postilion—for that individual was not hurt in the least, although he made so much uproar—the Bishop of Oxford was dragged from the ditch.

On gaining dry land, the first thing he did was to thrust his hand into the breast of his coat, from which he produced a good-sized bottle, the glass sides of which were well protected with wicker-work.

Placing this to his lips, he allowed a considerable quantity of its contents to trickle down his throat at an alarming rate.

Pausing at length from sheer want of breath, the Bishop gazed upon the forms of his rescuers.

"You have been attacked, my lord," said Peterson, with a low bow. "I am sorry I arrived too late to prevent the perpetration of this atrocious outrage; but your lordship can at least give me the particulars of it. They will be most useful."

"The Black Highwayman!" ejaculated the Bishop, once more applying himself to his pocket-flask.

"I thought as much," said Peterson.

"He fired at the postilion twice—stopped the carriage—opened the door—demanded my money—told him I had none—leaned forward on his horse—took hold of me by the collar—dragged me out—searched me—and flung me in there!"

The Bishop gave a shuddering glance at the ditch

"But he robbed you of nothing?"

"No; but he searched the carriage, though."

"And which way did he go?"

The Bishop pointed along the high-road towards London. He could not speak, for he was just then, for the third time, paying his respects to the wicker bottle.

"Your lordship must be mistaken," answered Peterson. "I have only just come in that direction, and I saw no one whatever."

"He went that way—I am certain of it," answered the Bishop, doggedly.

Peterson did not attempt to argue the point; but went on by saying:

"Did you see him plainly, my lord?"

"Oh yes, quite plainly."

"Then if you would describe him you wo... be rendering me a great service."

"His horse was black, so were his saddle and bridle. His cloak was black, and when it blew back I saw that his whole dress was jet black, faced here and there with very narrow silver lace."

"Did you catch a glimpse of his face, my lord?"

"No, he wore a half-mask, and—— Oh, have mercy upon me, miserable sinner—he's coming!"

The clatter of iron-bound hoofs was distinctly heard by all present, and it was this which had caused his lordship to break off so suddenly in his description, for he jumped at once to the conclusion that it was the Black Highwayman returning.

The two police officers placed themselves in readiness for an attack.

The postilion flung himself down again, and howled with the most abject fright, while the Bishop's valorous son, whose courage had been reviving, felt it collapse altogether, and he again betook himself to the shelter afforded by the small recess beneath the carriage seat.

During the time these events had been taking place, a considerable change was observed in the weather.

The dense black clouds which had before caused the night to be one of unusual darkness had gradually drifted away, and now from out of a clear broad space the moon shone beautifully.

The irregular furze-dotted surface of the common—at that time five times the extent that it is now—looked pisturesque in the extreme.

But the little group around the carriage were in no humour to admire the beauty of the surrounding scene.

All their faculties, indeed, were fixed upon the advancing horseman, whose form could now dimly be distinguished.

He was riding at full speed from the direction of London.

As he increased his speed rather than diminished it, it follows that he reached the carriage in a very short space of time, when he pulled up so suddenly and with so much strength that his horse fairly rose on his haunches and pawed the air with his fore-feet.

"Oh, my lord—my lord!" said the new-comer, in a voice expressive of the deepest despair. "Alas—alas! I grieve to tell you—but we are all ruined and undone!"

The Bishop recognised the voice which spoke in these wobegone accents.

His secretary, whom he hoped had by this time got safely to London, stood before him.

With a dismal groan the Bishop plumped down in the road, and so close to the edge of the ditch that he was within an ace of falling into it again.

"Speak—speak again!" he said. "Villain, do you mean to tell me you have lost the money I confided to your charge? Speak—speak, I say!"

"It was no fault of mine."

"The money is gone, then?"

"It is."

"I am a ruined man, then—a ruined man!"

The Bishop showed more concern for the loss of the worldly vanity, vulgarly called money, than was consistent with his preaching, which invariably tended towards a depreciation of the current coin of the realm.

Money he despised.

That was his constant cry, and people believed him, though few knew how it was.

But the fact was, the Bishop had so great a store of the base dross that he could afford to despise it.

His practice on the present occasion formed a deeply-interesting contrast to his preaching.

"Three thousand pounds," he groaned—"three thousand pounds—and all gone! Villain—villain! You have undone me!"

"Three thousand pounds!" ejaculated Peterson, pricking up his ears. "Does your lordship mean to say that the valise contained so much as that?"

Up to this moment the secretary had not recognised the police officer, but now he knew him again in a moment.

"That is the man who is to blame for what has occurred! That is the fellow who is in fault!"

"You had better mind what you say!" cried Peterson, hotly. "I am more than half inclined to take you into custody on suspicion of having appropriated the money yourself. It is impossible for the Black Highwayman to have taken it."

"Possible or impossible, he has taken it!" answered the secretary, with equal warmth. "A tall, well-made fellow. I saw him distinctly. He was mounted on a black horse, furnished with black trappings, and had a black half-mask on his face."

"And you say he robbed you?"

"He did."

"And from which direction did he approach?"

"That I don't know."

"You don't know? Surely you must have seen him coming towards you?"

"I did not, nor did I hear him eith[er]. I was not aware of his presence until I found him riding by my side."

"Riding by your side?"

"Yes."

"And you could not hear him?"

"I could not."

Hopkins plucked Peterson by the coat sleeve.

"What do you think of that?" he whispered. "Didn't I tell you I caught a sight of him, though I could not hear a sound?"

CHAPTER V.

MR. PETERSON DISCOVERS HIS ERROR.—THE SUDDEN APPEARANCE OF THE BLACK HIGHWAYMAN.—THE PURSUIT OVER THE COMMON.—THE LONE HUT IN THE WOOD.—A MYSTERY.

"SHUT up!" said Peterson, savagely. "If you say another word, d—n me if I don't get you discharged!"

Hopkins muttered something in a semi-audible voice, which Peterson pretended not to hear.

The Bishop still sat in his undignified position on the edge of the ditch, bewailing the loss of what, had it belonged to somebody else and not to himself, he would have stigmatised as evil dross, not worthy of receiving a moment's regret.

Peterson confined his attention to the secretary, against whom his former suspicions were re-awakened with tenfold force.

"And when you saw him, what did he do?" he continued.

"Well, to tell you the truth, I was a good deal flustered at finding some one riding along by the side of me like a ghost or a shadow when I believed myself to be quite alone upon the road—and I did not know how long he had been by the side of me either."

"Well?"

"I don't think it well at all. I tell you I was quite flustered when I first saw him; and before I could recover myself from the shock, he stretched out his arm—which seemed twice as long as mine—snatched away the valise, and then galloped off with it."

"And what did you do then?"

"Drew a pistol, and fired it after him."

"Did you hit him?"

"I think not, for away he went across the common like a whirlwind."

"Now—a—Mr. Secretary," said Peterson, coming closer still, and assuming a confidential air, "I want to know whether you take me for a *hass?*"

"Well, I—a——" said the secretary, hesitatingly.

"You must do so," continued Peterson, oracularly, "or else you would not think of trying to fob me off with such a monstrous story as that."

"As what?"

"As that you have just told me."

"I will take my oath this moment," said the secretary, earnestly, "that all I have told you is the truth, and nothing but the truth!"

"And I would not believe it," said Peterson, deliberately pausing between each word—"not if you were to stand there and say it until every hair on your head grew gray!"

"Then, on my part, I must say that I do think you an ass—since that is the way you put the question to me

—because, if you had one single grain of common sense, you would not stop here talking to me like you have, but would have set spur to your horse, and galloped after the robber."

"Oh, I dessay!" said Peterson, putting one finger against the side of his nose, and wagging his head backwards and forwards in what he intended to be a very sagacious manner indeed. "But it happens that no galloping is wanted, because the thief is within arm's-length."

"Oh, monstrous!" ejaculated the secretary. Fortunately, I can laugh at your accusal, because my Lord Bishop knows me too well to dream for a moment that I should be guilty of such an act. You are on the wrong scent entirely."

But Peterson only clung to his opinion with all the more firmness.

"My lord," said the secretary, addressing himself to the Bishop, who by this time began to evince some signs of having recovered from his panic, "would you believe that this dunder-headed blundering fool has been the main cause of the loss which you have sustained? He stopped me and detained me on the road, when every moment was of the extremest importance, and now he keeps me here, cross-questioning me like a barrister, when he ought to be at work looking for the mysterious robber who, after all, cannot have got very far off."

The Bishop was never a man with brain enough to enable him to grasp two subjects at once, and now his mind was too much engrossed by his loss for him to attend to anything else.

"My lord," continued the secretary, "you will at least give this thick-skulled blockhead the assurance that you think it quite out of the question that I have taken this money?"

"Oh, of course!" said the Bishop, with an air as though he was greatly surprised. "That is quite out of the question—quite."

After this assertion Peterson looked very blank, and his muddy intellect begun to suggest to him that he had made a stupid mistake.

"Hullo!" said Hopkins—"hullo! Look there, everybody, all at once, and let me know whether I am a victim to that unfortunate imagination of mine again! Tell me—can you all see anything yonder?"

He pointed across the common excitedly while he spoke.

The moon's light was now ten times more brilliant than before.

By the aid of the illumination she afforded they were enabled to see distinctly to a considerable distance.

Turning their eyes simultaneously in the direction to which Hopkins pointed, all beheld a figure which requires at our hands a few lines of special description.

Trotting swiftly along, at a distance of about two hundred yards, was a horseman.

His horse was black—jet black—of unusual size, and possessed of wonderful symmetry of limb and splendid action.

His rider sat in the saddle with an easy grace that must have been the result of long and careful practice.

He, too, was black.

His cloak, secured only by a clasp at the throat, fluttered behind him in sable folds, and displaying his body incased with a tight-fitting costume of the same pall-like hue.

The moonbeams shone upon him with so much distinctness and brilliancy that the gazers were able to make out almost every detail.

Hopkins was full of excitement.

He was the first to speak.

By doing so he broke the spell which seemed to have laid hold on all, and which, perhaps, would have continued to have exercised its influence until the disappearance of the mysterious horseman.

"Is it imagination?" gasped Hopkins. "If it is, I'll never trust my eyes again as long as I live! If it isn't, that's the counterpart of the rider I saw glide by while we were watching under the trees, Mr. Peterson."

"That's the man who robbed me!" said the Bishop, who, with preternaturally wide-open eyes, gazed intently upon the swiftly-moving figure.

"That is the robber who snatched the valise from me!" said the secretary. "And he rode as noiselessly by the side of me as he is riding now."

"Murder! The Black Highwayman! Here he comes again! Murder—murder!" bawled the Bishop's son, who, impelled by curiosity, had peeped out to see what was the matter.

No sooner did he catch a glimpse, however, of the flitting, shadowy-looking horseman than, with a frantic rush, he hastened to avail himself of his former place of concealment.

"Forward—forward!" cried the secretary. "Why stand here like sticks and stones? Forward—forward! If we do not overtake him, we may, perhaps, keep on his track until we obtain more assistance."

As for Peterson, he said never a word, but remained like a man suddenly struck dumb with intense amazement.

The last words, however, roused him.

Cursing his companion for his delay, he hastened to regain the saddle.

Hopkins was not a second after him.

"On—on!" cried Peterson—"come on! I see him now. And as I have set eyes on him at last, I will keep on until I hunt him down!"

"Push ahead, then!" said the secretary.

As he spoke he spurred his horse so violently that he started off at a tearing gallop.

The two others followed in an irregular line.

"Murder—murder!" cried the Bishop's son, poking his head out of the carriage window. "Come back—come back! If you leave us we shall all be murdered—I am sure we shall!"

But his cries were totally disregarded.

The Bishop himself did not much relish being thus deserted; and he made a start to follow them on foot; but the folly of this proceeding soon obtruded itself upon him, and he came to a standstill.

For some time he was enabled to be a spectator of the scene.

The Black Highwayman—for by common consent the sable rider was no other—was apparently quite unaware of the fact that he was pursued.

He never once turned his head, but made his way in a direct line across the broken, uneven surface of the common towards a wood of considerable extent, all vestiges of which have long since disappeared under the ruthless hands of improvement.

The secretary kept the lead bravely.

He was the first to make out the highwayman's destination.

"On—on! Faster—faster yet, or all our trouble will be in vain! If he once gets under the shadow of that wood it would be as vain to search for him as to look for a needle in a bottle of hay."

The officers were quite alive to this, and made all the efforts in their power.

But it was manifest that the object of their pursuit was going two yards to their one, yet they were galloping at full speed, while he seemed going at an easy trot.

In spite of the discouraging prospect, they continued the chase until, like a shadow, the black horse and rider seemed to vanish among the trees.

"It's all over," said the secretary.

"Never mind!" bawled Peterson. "Don't stop! On—on!"

Now that they had not the form of the highwayman in view, the distance between them and the wood seemed interminable.

But eventually it was traversed.

All three had kept their eyes upon the exact spot where the rider had seemed to be swallowed up by the still darker shadows of the trees.

On reaching it not a single moving thing was to be seen, nor could any sound be detected save the melancholy rustling of the wind among the tree tops.

"It's all over," said the secretary, breaking the silence. "We may just as well ride back as attempt to follow him in here."

Peterson gave him what he intended should be a glance of withering scorn.

"I daresay you are frightened now. Turn back—turn back, by all means. Thank goodness, I know my duty! Come on, Hopkins. Good night, sir," he added, with mock politeness.

So saying, he rode into the wood, following what bore some resemblance to a bridle-path among the trees.

Hopkins followed at his heels.

The Bishop's secretary remained where he was, watching them until the intervening tree trunks hid them from his view.

"Well, well," he ejaculated, as he turned his head with the intention of making his way back to the carriage, "I am not surprised that highwaymen should have the roads all to themselves, if what I have seen to-night can be taken as a fair specimen of the abilities of those who are set to catch them."

And as he uttered the last words he touched his horse upon the flank, and hastened to leave the wood behind him.

In the meanwhile Peterson followed the half-formed path that we have mentioned.

He was in anything but an amiable frame of mind, and nothing would have afforded him more pleasure than the opportunity to vent his rage upon some one.

On his way he continued to mutter the most horrible curses against the secretary.

Hopkins prudently kept silent.

As a matter of course, the further they penetrated into the wood the slower became their progress, owing to the increase in the density of the vegetation.

All vestiges of the pathway vanished.

At length it became impossible to proceed further on horseback.

Two courses were left open to them.

One was to turn back.

The other to dismount and proceed on foot.

Peterson paused, and looked about him doubtfully.

The silence seemed doubly intense.

Not the faintest trace was there of what they wished to find.

Suddenly Hopkins uttered an exclamation.

"Look there! Do you see that light?—over yonder between the trees."

Peterson turned, and was just able to catch a glimpse of a bright light; but it vanished almost instantly.

"Did you see it?" said Hopkins.

"Yes."

"What is it?"

"How should I know better than you, stupid?"

"It's gone now."

"Yes, there is no doubt of that; and I am going after it. Try to keep your eye upon the spot."

"And the horses, sir?"

"We will lead them by the bridle."

As he spoke he set his follower the example.

It was to a certain extent reasonable enough for Peterson to determine to try and find out what was the cause of the light and of its sudden disappearance.

Under the existing state of things he was quite justified in looking at everything with a suspicious eye.

Having gone a little way, the police officers were agreeably surprised to find that the character of the wood became more open.

Peterson did not mount, but walked forward with increased rapidity and ease.

Still no signs of the light presented themselves.

In a few moments afterwards, however, they emerged into quite a clear space.

For some time past the moon had been hidden by clouds, but now she broke forth again.

Her first rays enabled the two officers to discern a wooden shed, or rather hut, for the building was furnished with both door and windows.

The latter, however, were carefully covered with shutters.

"That is where the light came from," said Peterson; "and it follows that there must have been some one here to show it. That some one we must find, and try to get some information from."

While speaking, he made his way swiftly across the clearing, at the further extremity of which the hut was situated.

Coming nearer, they found that it presented no signs of inhabitation.

"Knock," said Peterson.

Hopkins drew forth a pistol, and hammered away furiously with the butt-end of it.

"Who's there?" said a rough voice within.

"His Majesty's officers of police. Open the door at once, and let us enter!"

"Not if I know it," was the rejoinder. "You may be officers of police or you may not."

"Open the door!" said Peterson, with rising ire.

"Oh, it's all right, I see!" said the rough voice again.

Looking up, Peterson caught sight of a face at a kind of upper window.

But it disappeared almost instantly, and in another moment the sound made by the removal of bolts and bars was heard.

Then the door opened, and the cheerful blaze of a large wood fire was seen.

The ruddy light showed them a burly-looking form clad in coarse clothes, and bearing the appearance of a man who got his living in the woods.

"Walk in," he said, with a little abatement of his roughness. "What do you want?"

"I want to know who you may be."

"A poor wood-cutter, living all alone by himself," was the reply.

The two officers crossed the threshold, leaving their horses without.

The apartment, if so we may call it, was a very rude one, and destitute of almost every article of comfort.

"A wood-cutter, eh?" said Peterson, glancing sharply about him. "Do you happen to have seen anything of a man mounted on a black horse?"

"When?"

"To-night."

"In the wood, here?"

"Yes."

"No—I haven't. I have been sitting here for the last hour, may be two. All I have seen is the fire, and all I have heard is the wind."

Suspicious of everything and everybody as Peterson was—and he believed that a readiness to suspect was the greatest of all virtues in a police officer—yet he could make nothing out of what he saw.

Still, to satisfy himself, he made an examination of the premises.

There was one other rude chamber, and that was all the hut contained.

Nothing was found to recompense him for the trouble of searching, and so he departed to renew his quest elsewhere, with the comforting reflection that he had lost much valuable time.

All hope of getting again upon the track of the Black Highwayman seemed at end.

During the time which had elapsed since his disappearance he had had abundant opportunity either to conceal himself or to get many miles away.

"I am afraid we can do nothing but make our way back again," said Peterson, and addressing his subordinate as though all the blame attached to him; "but we will take our way back through the wood. We may be fortunate enough to get a clue."

The wood-cutter carefully barred his door after his visitors had retired.

Considering, however that a search had been made over the premises, it seemed somewhat strange that, as soon as the police officers had fairly turned their backs, a dusky, shadow-like figure should glide away from the habitation, and immediately vanish among the trees.

Yet such was certainly the case, though both Peterson and Hopkins failed to see it.

The moon could still be seen shining among the tree tops, and by it the officers directed their course.

On the way, however, they disturbed nothing save a few birds, which, with strange cries, flew heavily away.

Suddenly and somewhat unexpectedly they found themselves upon the side of a broad road.

"Here we are," said Peterson. "Come along."

The wood was divided from the roadway by a fence; but it was such a low one that the two police officers leaped their horses over it without difficulty.

"I wonder if he came this way?" ejaculated Hopkins, glancing up the road.

"Hold your row!" was the rejoinder of his companion. "I thought I heard something."

"A horse!" cried Hopkins, after listening a moment. "It's a horse! I can hear his hoofs plainly enough."

About this there could be no mistake.

"Yes, it's a horse," assented Peterson. "Draw to one side of the road. I will stop whoever may be coming, upon the chance of learning something."

Perhaps there may have been an idea in Peterson's mind that the approaching traveller might turn out to be the famous Black Highwayman himself; at any rate, he drew forth a pistol.

A few more minutes convinced him, however, that it was a vehicle which was approaching, for now the rattling of the wheels could be heard mingled with the clatter of the horse's feet.

Peterson put up his pistol.

Directly afterwards the vehicle made its appearance at a slight bend in the road.

The moon was shining clearly.

"Bowling along a bit, sir," said Hopkins. "I don't like a white horse myself; but that is a capital bit of horseflesh in spite of its colour."

"Hold your row!"

So saying, Peterson placed himself a little nearer to the middle of the road.

"Halt!" he said. "Pull up in the name of his Majesty the King!"

The vehicle was a light gig, with particularly large wheels, and was occupied apparently by a gentleman and his servant.

At this command, the gentleman, who was driving, tightened the rein, and brought his fast-trotting horse somewhat abruptly to a standstill.

"Pharoah," he cried to the servant seated beside him, "take care of the valise."

"Yes, my lord,"

Hearing mention made of a valise, Peterson gave a great start, and bumped himself severely on the tree of the saddle in consequence.

"Now, fellows," cried his lordship, haughtily, "what do you want? If you mean robbery you will find you have no chickens to deal with!"

He cocked a long, double-barreled pistol as he spoke.

"I beg pardon, my lord," stammered Peterson, who on the spur of the moment hardly knew how to speak or how to act, "we are no robbers, but his Majesty's officers of police, in search of the Black Highwayman."

And in support of this assertion, Peterson pulled out his staff.

"Is he on this road?" asked his lordship, evincing some little trepidation, despite the bold assertion he had just made.

"He may be—I am not sure. But he has stopped and robbed the Bishop of Oxford on Ealing Common to-night. I was within a hair's-breadth of having him."

"But you lost him?"

"Yes," admitted Peterson, reluctantly.

"But why do you stop me?"

"Upon the chance that you might have seen something of him on the road."

"I haven't, and hope I sha'n't. Good night!"

"Stop—stop!"

"What do you want now?"

"Wh—wh—why, your lordship——" stammered Peterson.

"What is the matter with the fellow? Why don't you speak out?"

"You mentioned a valise, my lord."

"Well?"

"Would your lordship allow me one peep at it?"

This request made the nobleman stare very hard at the police officer.

"Why, I——"

Peterson stopped, because, somehow, he felt conscious in his own mind on this occasion that his suspicions were absurd.

Perhaps his previous failures had made him doubtful.

"It is a strange request," said his lordship, at length; "and certainly I shall not accede to it unless you give me some very strong reasons for doing so. Which do you take me for," he added, noting the officer's embarrassment, "a fool or a robber—which?"

"My lord, I——"

"Do you want anything else?"

Peterson was silent.

"Drive on, Pharoah!" said the nobleman. "We are quite late enough. Good night!"

The police officer offered no opposition to his departure.

The reins were slackened, and away went the white horse and the light gig at a wonderful rate.

"A valise!" muttered Peterson. "How much I should have liked to see that valise! But, then, it's ridiculous to suppose that—yes, yes, ridiculous, I must admit. He is a nobleman, no doubt."

Could it be that Peterson carried his principle of suspiciousness so far as to fancy that his lordship had some share in the robbery?

His muttered words would give colour to such a supposition.

He gazed after the swift-travelling vehicle with a vague yearning sensation which he could neither understand nor account for.

Puzzled and bewildered, he pulled off his hat, and wiped the drops from his steaming forehead.

"A valise!" he muttered again. "What did he mean by crying out, 'Take care of the valise?' It's suspicious—I'm certain it's suspicious! Who is he, I wonder? He called his servant Pharoah! What an odd name! Perhaps that will help me to find out who he is."

CHAPTER VI.

CAPTAIN HAWK FINDS DANGER THICKENS AROUND HIM.

Leaving the pair of highly-astute officers in their perplexity and to fathom the mysteries connected with that most mysterious of all beings the Black Highwayman, we will return to Captain Hawk, whose position cannot but be considered as a most critical one.

But the reader must be careful not to fall into any mistake with respect to the length of time occupied by the events which followed the captain's entrance into the room.

Certainly the period was not over sixty seconds.

The police officer who carried the lantern no sooner crossed the threshold than he cried out:

"Keep the door—be sure you keep the door! If he is here he will make a desperate rush to escape!"

The throng which crowded round the doorway was a dense one—much too dense for anyone to hope to succeed in forcing a way through it.

The officer flashed his lantern around him swiftly, but everything was perfectly quiet, with the exception of the captain's bedfellow, who began to groan dolefully.

Without pausing, the officer hastened to the window.

"He cannot have gone this way, that is certain!" he exclaimed, as soon as he caught sight of the iron bars, "nor I don't think he's in here either!"

But resolved not to quit the room until he had satisfied himself upon the point, he hastily ransacked everywhere—he came at last to the bed.

Dashing aside the curtains roughly, he said:

"Hullo! Excuse me, ma'am, I wouldn't have intruded if I could have helped it, but have you seen a man in this room? We are in pursuit of a notorious highwayman!"

The old lady opened her eyes.

The first thing her glance fell upon was the officer's drawn cutlass, upon which the lantern shone with a very alarming effect.

"Murder!" she shrieked, as she made a frantic effort to get under the bedclothes. "Oh! Murder—murder! Help—help!"

"Don't be alarmed, ma'am—pray don't be alarmed! But just tell us whether you have seen the man we want!"

"A man—in here? Oh, gracious!"

"All right," said the officer, with a grin. "He's in the house somewhere, and we are sure to have him! Don't you be frightened, old lady—no one will hurt you. But you must not object to my placing a man at the door—it will be a protection to you," he added.

With these words, he turned away, and Captain Hawk for the first time permitted himself breathe.

"Jones," he said, addressing one of his men, "stand at this door, and keep a good watch. Wing him if you see him; it will save trouble."

So saying, the officer hastily retreated to carry on his investigations elsewhere.

But as these cannot possibly be successful, there will be little interest in the description of them

The house was searched from top to bottom; but not a trace of the captain could be found.

The officer hailed those outside.

"Have you not seen him?" he bawled. "He is not here."

"He must be!" replied a dozen voices. "He could not have left without being seen by us!"

The officer was baffled.

Rapid as his search had been, yet he was certain that it had been a thorough one.

"He must be in the house somewhere," he muttered.

Then aloud he cried:

"Keep a doubly sharp look out! I don't care how good his hiding-place may be, I will unkennel him!"

These words were distinctly heard by Captain Hawk, and, as the reader may be sure, with anything but a feeling of satisfaction.

But time enough had elapsed to enable him to recover his calmness, and he now asked himself very seriously what should be his next step.

There was no slight risk in attempting to speak even a single word to his companion—the police officer on guard was so close at hand that he could not help hearing every syllable.

The captain, however, while in this state of indecision, was not unoccupied, for he slipped his hand into his pocket and drew forth a well-filled purse.

This he held before the eyes of his strange bedfellow, who was not so terrified as to be unable to tell what it was.

"Be silent," said Captain Hawk, in the faintest of whispers—"that is all I require of you."

He dropped the purse quietly as he spoke.

It was hidden at once, and he took that as a sign that his wishes would be carried out.

But what should he do next?

He was conscious that this second search would be a much more rigorous one than the first.

Detection was almost certain.

But, as we have before remarked, the captain was ready at expedients; and now a fresh thought occurred to him, and, as usual, he set about carrying it into execution without bestowing any attention upon the details.

With perfect noiselessness he slipped out of bed—the voluminous bed-hangings concealing him effectually from the gaze of the police officer at the door.

He peeped through a crevice unobserved, and saw that Jones was just in a position favourable to the carrying out of the wild idea which had darted into his mind—that is to say, he had his back turned to the room, from which he apprehended no danger, his whole attention being turned to what might occur upon the staircase.

"It's simple," said the captain, mentally—"it's very simple."

As he spoke, he stole out of his place of concealment with a degree of stealth that might have made a cat envious.

At the same time he listened and made good use of his eyes.

A good deal of uproar was going on up above, indicating that the search was proceeding rather actively in that quarter, but, save the sentinel officer, no one was in sight.

The captain crept within a few paces of him.

Then seeing how alone he was, the desire to make a rush past came strongly over him, but he recollected the watchers outside and the other men placed at the various doors of exit, and abandoned the notion, for it was plain enough to be seen that it could only eventuate in his own capture.

Nearer and nearer still he crept, until he was close enough to carry out his original intention.

With truly *hawk*-like swiftness, he pounced upon the unsuspecting officer.

The grasp was taken on the throat, and the grip so firm as to stop the windpipe completely.

There was not a sound—at least, not one which could be distinguished among the general confusion.

Putting out all his strength, the captain dragged the officer into the room.

The man himself was too much confounded at the suddenness and unexpectedness of the attack to be able to make much resistance; and before he could recover himself in any degree, he found himself pinned against the wall, and Captain Hawk's face within six inches of his own.

At this his eyes expanded to an extraordinary width; but he was incapable of manifesting his amazement in any other way.

Captain Hawk did not throw away a second, for he did not know how soon some other person might appear upon the scene.

"Look here! Tell me how much you expected to get by making me your prisoner?"

The officer made an ineffectual attempt to speak.

"Raise your voice above a whisper," ejaculated the captain, slightly relaxing his hold, "and I will blow your brains out in a moment!"

He showed a pistol.

"You are wholly at my mercy," continued the captain, for the officer had not breathed enough as yet to speak. "I may be taken; but, mark me, if I am, it will not be until I have lodged a bullet in you, so you must see it is to your personal advantage to aid me to escape."

"I—I——" he gasped.

"You cannot hope to have the whole reward, even if I am taken and you escaped my pistol; but if you will serve me you shall have five hundred pounds and save your life as well. Do you consent?"

The officer's cupidity was aroused by this speech.

"I'll take his money," he thought—"I shall have just as good a chance of nailing him afterwards. I cannot be a loser."

"Do you consent?"

"What must I do?"

"Change hat and coat with me," continued Hawk, speaking with great rapidity—"I want no more of you. And if you consent, if you call to-morrow at the Old Chequers and ask for a parcel marked 'H,' you will find in it five hundred pounds."

"But how do I know whether to trust you?"

"Please yourself."

"If I refuse?"

"I shall be compelled in self-defence to commit a deed which I would gladly shrink from if I could. You understand me?"

"Yes. I consent."

"That's enough—I will trust you; but if I see you attempt to call out, that very moment is your last!"

There was no mistake about the tone of deep determination in which Captain Hawk spoke.

He released his grasp.

Certainly the risk he ran in doing so was very great, for of course there was no dependence whatever to be placed on such a man as this police officer, and no one knew it better than Captain Hawk.

"Off with your coat and hat! Come—quick!"

"All right, captain," said the officer, in a suppressed voice. "I am with you now, so don't be afraid. My business is to get money, and your terms are so high that I cannot hesitate about taking them."

"Very good," said the captain, probably putting down this speech for what it was worth.

By the rapid, noiseless way in which the officer slipped off his coat, however, it would seem that he was really acting in good faith.

Captain Hawk had his off and the change effected in a twinkling.

The alteration was remarkable. By the dim light of the chamber the change was absolutely startling.

"Now," said Hawk, "you must pretend to be me. Lay yourself down on the floor face downwards. There—that will do."

Hawk placed himself upon the prostrate form, as though in the act of holding him down.

"Now for my plan," he said. "You must call out for help and assistance—your companions will rush in, and in this duskness will take you for me. You must struggle, and I will make a great show of holding you down; I will gag you; they will hasten to secure you, and before they are able to find out their mistake I shall slip off."

"But how am I to clear myself?"

"Say that I compelled you by main force, and threatened to take your life if you did not obey me."

"Which would be just the truth."

"Of course. Now call out for help, just as you would if you had really caught me. After that don't speak, but struggle as much as you like."

"Are you ready now?"

"Yes, quite."

CAPTAIN HAWK AND THE BOW STREET RUNNER.

Presented Gratis with No. 3 of the New Re-Issue of The Black Highwayman, by the Author of Black Bess.

GRATIS with Nos. 3 to 6, FOUR COLOURED PICTURES,
GRATIS with Nos 7 to 10, FOUR UNCOLOURED PICTURES.

[CAPTAIN HAWK STOPS AN ECCENTRIC TRAVELLER.]

The police officer raised his head a little way from the oor.

"Help!" he bawled. "Murder—murder! Help—help ere; I have got him!"

"That will do," said the captain.

To all appearance now a furious struggle commenced.

The noise of it and the outcry which had been raised erved to alarm the whole of the house at once.

An uproar of voices and the tread of many feet was eard, and then the officers rushed in.

"Help me—help me, quick!" said Captain Hawk. "I've ot him down, and I think I've gagged him. Help—elp!"

He spoke so exactly like Jones as to startle that indi-idual himself.

As the highwayman had calculated, the police officers, eing a red-coated man on the floor struggling furiously, d a man dressed like a police officer holding him down,

jumped at once to the conclusion that Captain Hawk was captured.

The dim light in the apartment assisted the delusion.

The news flew from mouth to mouth like magic.

"Mind, I caught him myself," said Captain Hawk, but speaking so exactly like Jones that the others were completely deceived; "and I claim all the reward."

But, as we have said before, he had great talent in disguises.

He had heard the officer speak the few words which we have recorded, and that was enough for him.

Jones himself, half bewildered by the rapid and unexpected turn events had taken, felt half disposed to doubt his own identity.

Of course, under ordinary circumstances, we don't pretend to say the captain's *ruse* would have succeeded, but it must not be forgotten that on the present occasion everyone was excited in the highest degree.

NO. 3.

GRATIS with this Number, The COLOURED PICTURE of CAPTAIN HAWK AND THE BOW STREET RUNNER.

One thought filled all their minds.

It was with the utmost precipitation that they all threw themselves upon the prostrate form.

Hawk had taken care to twist a pocket-handkerchief and place it bit-wise in Jones's mouth.

The two ends he tied very firmly at the back of his head, thereby gagging him so effectually as to make it out of the question for him to utter a single syllable of explanation.

He pretended to be very unwilling to make the least movement, lest the safety of his prize should be endangered.

But the others were just as anxious to pull him out of the way, in order that the prisoner might be securely bound.

"Don't be a fool, Jones!" cried the commanding officer. "How the devil are we to do anything with him while you act like that? Get up, can't you!"

The seeming police officer rose with great apparent reluctance.

He pretended to be exhausted by his exertions.

The others pushed him violently on one side.

Truly it might be said that all those present, without any exception whatever, had eyes for nothing but one object—their fancied prisoner.

Everybody was anxious to get closer.

Therefore it was the easiest matter in the world for the captain to slip away unobserved.

When once he gained the staircase, he descended with reckless rapidity, and rushed to the front door.

Seeing him come so fast, the officer placed there on guard held out his arms and stopped him.

But the captain was not taken aback.

Not forgetting to speak as much like Jones as he could, he cried:

"Quick—quick! They have got him! Make haste upstairs! I am going now for further assistance! Just hark! I should not wonder if he slipped through their fingers now!"

A terrific uproar taking place above now well-nigh drowned the captain's words.

But if the mind of the officer at the door had been dimmed with the faintest breath of suspicion, the unmistakable sounds of a contention taking place upstairs would have removed it.

Without pausing a moment, he rushed upstairs as though for his life.

The cause of the disturbance must be guessed.

The officers had discovered their mistake.

In raising Jones to his feet, his hat (or rather, Captain Hawk's hat) was knocked off.

It also happened that what little light there was in the room fell full upon his features.

"Why—why, d—n me, it's—— No—no, it can't be—yes it is—it's Jones!"

The officer who spoke these words relaxed his hold and staggered back aghast.

The others stood as though suddenly changed to stone.

Jones was too well gagged to speak, and too well bound to move any of his limbs.

But he nodded his head with great violence and rapidity, as though anxious to assert his identity by the only means in his power.

The chief officer recovered himself with creditable quickness from the first shock of his surprise.

"A light—a light!" he cried. "That d—d rushlight is worse than darkness! If it had not been for that we should never have made this horrible mistake."

A light was produced, and, of course, the result was to confirm the astounding discovery.

It was Jones beyond all manner of doubt.

Still, they were half incredulous, for such a transformation seemed to them nothing short of being magical.

One had presence of mind enough to cut the pocket-handkerchief, and so restore Jones the use of his speech, by which means alone they could hope to comprehend the mystery.

The first use Jones made of his voice was to cry out:

"After him—after him! Don't lose a moment—he cannot have gone far! He seized on me—he has the strength of ten men—changed coat and hat with me, and now he's gone!"

This was enough, and more than enough, to let the officers into the light of what had occurred.

They looked hastily for the being they had been so eager to thrust aside.

He was nowhere to be seen.

If anything could have aggravated the officers more than another it was the knowledge that several of them had actually had their hands on the man they so much wished to catch.

Bitterly cursing their own stupidity, they did what they could to repair their blunder.

Some rushed headlong down the staircase.

Others made their way frantically to the windows at the front and back of the house.

"Stop him—stop him—seize him! He has escaped—escaped disguised as a police officer! Seize him!"

The intelligence came upon the people outside like a thunder-clap, for they had made quite sure the noted highwayman was a prisoner and firmly bound by this time.

"Which way has he gone?—how did he escape?" they asked.

No one had seen him.

Mortified and crestfallen to a degree which we cannot describe, the police officer in command strode back to the staircase.

"Where's Jones?" he asked.

"Here I am, sir," answered that individual, with all the effrontery imaginable.

"Consider yourself under arrest," was the unexpected rejoinder of his superior. "Your conduct is suspicious—at the best, you have been remiss in your duty."

Jones was taken into custody accordingly, and the chief officer felt a little relieved now that he had made a prisoner of somebody.

CHAPTER VII.

CONTINUES TO RELATE THE UNPARALLELED ADVENTURES OF CAPTAIN HAWK.

Once through the doorway of the house which had been so full of perils, Captain Hawk made the best use of his time.

He was well aware that he had not a minute to waste, being conscious that the deception would not remain long undiscovered.

In fact, when the officer opened the window and called out, he was within hearing.

Making his way forwards as best he could, he glanced around him anxiously in search of his horse.

What had become of it and whither it had gone during the tumult, he had no idea.

He hesitated to give utterance to the whistle which he was certain would bring his horse to him if he happened to be within hearing, because he feared, justly enough, that it would have the effect of directing general attention towards him.

"Captain!" said a familiar voice—"is that you? Ah! I see it is. Hurrah! I got alarmed about you once, but yet I thought you would be all right."

The highwayman gave a sigh of relief.

It was Sam the ostler from the Old Chequers who had addressed him.

"Where's Satan?" he asked.

"Safe and sound, captain, and waiting for you."

"At the old place?"

"Not scarcely twenty paces off. Follow me quickly. You are not out of danger yet."

The truth of this was obvious, and the captain kept close enough to his faithful ally.

"I am puzzled to know how Satan got at liberty," he said. "How was it?"

"Ah! captain, I would rather not say."

"Why not?"

"Because——"

"Speak on. I shall not trust you for the future if you do not."

"Ah! that's just it."

"What do you mean? Speak out, I say."

The ostler evidently had something on his mind which he dreaded to communicate.

The way in which the highwayman spoke the last words, however, convinced him he would have quite as much cause for dread if he remained silent.

"I will make a clean breast, captain."

"You will find it best to do so."

"And rely upon your——"

"Go on—be quick!"

"Well, captain," he began, deprecatingly, "you must not be too hard upon me for once; but do you know many's the time and oft that I have felt I would rather have a ride on Satan's back than be given a hundred pounds in gold."

"Ah!"

"Now, don't be angry, captain—please don't, because, you see, after all, you have not so much to complain of. It happened lucky, I rather think. While you were all so busy at the churchyard the thought struck me the time had come to try what a ride on Satan's back was like. The temptation was too strong to be resisted."

"And that accounts for him being saddled and bridled in the street. But what ailed him?"

"Ah! captain, you know best—he must have been aware that his proper rider was not on his back. Confound him! he behaved like a brute! I thought till to-night that I was capable of riding anything in the shape of a bit of horseflesh. I stuck on his back pretty well, but he threw me at last. There he is, captain, as safe as a church, tied to a hedge. You wouldn't think it of him now. How quiet he does look!"

Captain Hawk was considerably annoyed at what he heard, but the fact of finding his horse all right and ready for the road at the moment when he most needed him went far towards mollifying his anger.

"This way," said the ostler, to a boy who was engaged in holding the highwayman's horse.

Bang! went a pistol at this moment, and Captain Hawk's hat—or rather the one he had taken from Jones—went rolling over the snow.

For a moment the captain was not sure whether or not his head was in it.

He was only convinced by hearing some one cry:

"That's him, I am certain! And he's winged, I fancy! Help, here—help!"

Captain Hawk turned round.

His face was flushed with passion.

"That was a treacherous shot," he said, "and as such it shall be punished!"

He drew a pistol as he spoke, for he caught sight of a dark figure a few paces off.

Aware of his danger, the man who had fired the cowardly shot flung himself down at full length, and rolled over and over in the snow.

The captain fired, and, judging by a dismal howl which mingled with the discharge of the firearm, he hit his mark.

But the whole troop of police officers had now got into view, the reports of the two pistols having probably directed their steps to this particular spot.

Captain Hawk no sooner fired than he hastened to his steed.

With one bound he was fixed in the saddle.

"You will hear from me again, Sam! Good-bye!"

"Halt!" cried the commanding officer, as soon as ever he saw the captain fairly mounted. "If he refuses to surrender when I call upon him, fire!"

The officers hastily pulled out their pistols.

"Good-bye!" cried Captain Hawk, pushing back his hair, which the wind had blown over his face. "I am going to ride, not from London to York, but from York to London; and in spite of all the officers in the kingdom I will take my own time about it. Twelve days will be nearer the mark than twelve hours; so if you are in no hurry we will travel in company. For the present, good night!"

This cool speech angered the commanding officer to such a degree that he found himself deprived of all power of speech.

He opened his mouth, flung his arms about, and stamped his feet, but not a syllable could he squeeze out.

The captain's audacity was dumbfoundering.

It was not until Satan bounded off that the police officer managed to articulate the one word—

"Fire!"

A straggling dropping volley followed, which, so far as could be seen, was productive of no result.

This is not to be wondered at, considering the flurried state every man was in. To imagine them capable of taking a steady aim was absurd.

Captain Hawk had only to give Satan the rein, and the splendid animal bounded off at a truly wonderful rate. A moment of time seemed to suffice, not only to leave the officers far behind, but also to carry them into the open country.

It happened, however, that the horses belonging to the police officers were not very far off, so they mounted and renewed the pursuit with as little loss of time as possible.

After the hairbreadth escapes he had had upon this memorable night, the captain felt himself impressed with a sensation of absolute security when he found he was really seated on the back of his matchless steed.

His rapid motion, too, was peculiarly grateful to him; and so, resigning all command over the reins, he allowed himself to be carried at what speed his horse thought proper.

Every moment increased the exhilaration of his spirits, and in the fulness of heart which he experienced at gaining so complete a victory ever his foes, he gave utterance to loud shouts, which had the effect of causing Satan to redouble his rate of speed.

Trees, hedges, and occasionally a few cottages would flit past like swift-gliding shadows. On—on—still on along the snow-covered highway, until a faint streak of grayish light in the far-off horizon proclaimed the coming of another day.

The eventful night was all but over.

A keen wind had sprung up, and the captain felt it whistle most unpleasantly about his ears, without guessing the reason, till he put up his hand and found his hat was gone.

He tightened the rein.

Satan seemed quite willing to moderate his speed, for of course the speed at which he had been going was one which even he could not perform without feeling the effects somewhat severely.

In a few minutes he was only going at a quiet walk.

"Confound the fellow!" was Captain Hawk's ejaculation. "No wonder I felt the cold so. But fortunately I have the means of making good my loss."

So saying, he stopped his horse completely and then dismounted.

"You have come harder than I thought, old fellow," he said, patting his steed fondly. "But I was too much carried away to note either pace or distance. It won't hurt you, though, and there is some comfort in knowing that we can afford to take it easy now. We are out of reach of our late foes."

Satan pawed the ground while his master spoke, and seemed to be full of impatience to start off afresh.

"Gently now—gently, can't you? Don't I tell you there is no need of hurry? Why don't you take it easy? Gently, I say—gently!"

As he spoke, the captain lifted up the flap of the saddle, which was made to contain a kind of pocket that was very useful for carrying various things.

From this pocket the captain produced a felt hat of the kind then usually worn.

It was pressed very flat, but in the captain's fingers soon assumed its proper shape.

It was trimmed with a narrow band of gold lace, which imparted to it a very stylish look, and was also provided by a kind of half-mask, formed by a strip of thick crape secured to the rim.

At first he felt inclined to remove this, but upon taking a second thought seemed to alter his mind.

"There is this confounded coat, too. I'll have that off without any further delay. It's a capital plan to travel with a few spare things about you.'

Suiting the action to the word, he pulled off the coat and rolled it up.

"I was going to throw it over the hedge," he remarked; "but I won't. It may turn out useful—who knows?"

Going then to the other side of his horse, he lifted up the saddle and disclosed another pocket.

In this there was a coat, but so carefully and cleverly folded that one would have doubted whether such a garment could have been contained in so small a space.

Having shook the coat well to free it from creases, he put it on, and then had more unmistakably the appearance of a highwayman than before.

The officer's coat was carefully placed in the saddle pocket.

"That will do nicely," remarked the captain, again

patting his steed. "You have recovered your wind, old fellow; so we will take another start."

Vaulting into the saddle, he again urged his horse forward.

His speed was rapid, though by no means like it had been.

The morning came on rapidly, and now a cold gray light was shed upon all things.

"Let me see," ejaculated the captain. "If I push on a little further I may reckon upon being free from pursuit for some time to come. I will take a rest then at the first convenient place which offers."

After speaking these words, the captain seemed to have entirely settled the affair in his mind; and this determination looked as though he was quite in earnest about taking his time in journeying to London.

But the sun rose clear and bright to a considerable altitude before the highwayman encountered what looked to him a suitable place to look for shelter.

Presently, however, he saw before him, on the left-hand side of the high-road, a rather tall white post, from the cross-arm of which hung a sign-board.

But what was very strange was, that no signs of a habitation could be discerned.

"That's odd," ejaculated Hawk. "I never saw anything look more like the sign of a roadside inn in my life. But surely it can't be that, unless the house in some mysterious way has been swallowed up."

The nearer he came the more singular did this appear, for there could be no mistake about the character of the post; and, moreover, the square bit of wood dependent from it was swinging backwards and forwards in the chill morning wind, and creaking in a most dismal fashion all the while, as though complaining in peevish tones.

"It's an inn sign," said the captain. "Ah! and now I can make it out. 'This way to the Bleeding Wolf.' And a fine grass-grown way it is, to be sure. I should fancy there is but a poor trade done at the Bleeding Wolf."

As Captain Hawk muttered these words, he brought his horse to a standstill, and by his manner it seemed pretty clear he was doubtful as to whether he should or should not make a trial of the accommodation at the lonely inn.

The sign-post stood just at a point where another road seemed to branch off from the main one—we say seemed, because, although broad and level, the ground was covered with firm turf.

The captain's hesitation did not last very long.

"I will try it," he said. "At any rate, I will have a look at the place, and if it don't please me I can but ride on. As it is, I may go for an hour or two without meeting with what I want."

Accordingly, he turned Satan aside, and before he had gone far, discovered that he was in reality upon a road, though assuredly it was a little-used one.

On and on he went, expecting every moment to catch sight of the inn, but it was not until he had gone at least three-quarters of a mile that he beheld a thin wreath of blue smoke curling upwards in the distance.

Seeing this, he quickened his horse's pace, and having passed a sharp bend in the road, presently caught sight of the wished-for place.

"The very thing!" he ejaculated, as soon as his eyes fell upon the dwelling. "It is as solitary and retired as I could wish. On, boy—on!"

The last words were addressed to Satan, who seemed to know that he was making his way towards a resting-place.

The inn, upon a close approach, proved to have a very old and picturesque appearance—probably a couple of centuries had elapsed since its erection, and it looked as though good for another two to come.

Captain Hawk pulled off his hat, and folded the piece of square crape in such a way that it was invisible when he put his hat on again.

He fully expected that his coming would be either heard or seen, and that in consequence some of the inhabitants of the inn would show themselves outside; but in this expectation he was disappointed.

He rode quite up to the moss-grown, dilapidated horse-trough without any notice being taken of his approach.

And now for the first time he was struck with the notion that the whole place had a forlorn, melancholy air.

"Hallo!" he cried—"hallo, there! House—house! Is no one within?"

His shouts brought to the threshold of the inn a man of middle age, who carried in his countenance unmistakable signs that life had by no means been a pleasant, thornless path to him.

With dejection in every movement, he walked slowly to the horse-trough, his eyes half turned upon the traveller and half seeking the ground.

"Good morning, sir," he said, in a low, melancholy voice. "What are your commands?"

Captain Hawk returned the salutation civilly, and as he did so, looked with an air of deep interest and curiosity at the landlord of the inn.

"I want a few hours' rest for myself and steed, if I can have them," he returned.

"You shall be served as well as my means will admit," answered the man, in the same mournful tones. "Let me hold the stirrup for you. There! Things are not as they used to be," he added, with a weary sigh. "I will see to your horse myself, sir. Trade is so very bad that I am obliged to be ostler, waiter, groom, and everything."

"Then if you have no objection I will go with you to the stables."

"Just as you please, sir," he said, in the same sad way. "I am quite at your commands."

Contrary to his expectations, the captain found the stables were comfortable ones, though there was rather a limited stock of provender.

Entering the house, he requested to be accommodated with a private room.

"They are all private enough," said the landlord, with a smile that made him look more melancholy than ever. "You need not fear being disturbed. What would you like to take?"

The captain ordered a substantial breakfast.

The landlord, with another sigh, left the room.

Captain Hawk went to the window and looked out.

Not a single habitation could be discerned; and the landscape, covered here and there with half-thawed snow, had anything but a pleasant appearance.

The sound made by the opening of the door caused him to turn round.

He then caught sight of a young girl, who possessed one of the sweetest faces he had looked on for many a day.

She carried in her hand a breakfast cloth and some other matters.

"Lovely!" said the captain, mentally, who was very susceptible to female beauty. "A perfect charmer!"

He was about to follow with the utterance of some compliment, but he checked himself suddenly, for he now saw that her eyes were red with weeping, and that dew-like drops of tears rested on her long, dark eyelashes.

CHAPTER VIII.

A DISSOLUTE PARTY.—LORD HARCLIFFE AND HIS ATTENDANT.—THE WAGER, AND ITS RESULT.—NEWS OF THE BLACK HIGHWAYMAN.

"WINE—wine! We will have more wine! Pharoah, you rascal, do you hear me? More champagne, I say! Can't you see the table waits? Pharoah, I say!"

"Coming, my lord."

"Come at once, then—my patience will hold out no longer!"

The young man who uttered these impatient, imperious words occupied a seat in a large, richly-carved arm-chair, which was placed at one end of a long table that took up the greater part of a spacious, luxuriously-furnished apartment.

The seats placed on either side of this long table were occupied by young men, all apparently about the age of the one in the arm-chair, and who was the giver of the entertainment.

A more noisy, riotous, excited assembly could scarcely have been found, and yet each one, both by bearing and apparel, was evidently of high position.

The costume of the occupant of the arm-chair was a marvel of richness—every portion of it which admitted of such adornment being studded with jewels.

Diamond rings of such lustre were upon the fingers of both hands that the least movement caused an absolute glitter of light.

Particularly brilliant did they look upon the present occasion, for the magnificent saloon was lit up with myriads of wax candles, and the sparkling gems seemed to derive a scintillation from each one.

His face, although now much flushed with wine and excitement, was one which could not have been pronounced otherwise than a most handsome one. The features were delicate and regularly formed; his eyes dark and yet so bright that they vied with the many lustrous gems about his person; his teeth, faultlessly even, seemed of the purest white when viewed in contrast with the vivid red of his full lips—lips so full and so suggestive of self-indulgence, as to mar his countenance to some extent.

Such was the young Lord Harcliffe, the only son of the rich Earl of Bartton, and at that time enjoying the reputation of being the wildest and most prodigal young nobleman in London.

Those who sat at the well-spread board before him were all kindred spirits—for the most part sons of peers, who, dazzled by the lavish prodigality of the young lord, had but one ambition, and that was to outshine him.

But as yet all such attempts had failed. Many wondered where all this boundless wealth came from, and shook their heads when speculating upon its probable duration.

The room in which the young men were assembled was situated in one of the finest mansions in the then fashionable part of London—a mansion where reckless pleasure and excitement were ever dominant.

"Pharoah," cried the young nobleman again, knitting his brows threateningly, "am I to be kept all night? Will the wine never come?"

"It is here, my lord."

A door at one end of the spacious saloon was opened, and through it came quite a procession of servants.

Each one carried a small kind of tub, which contained several bottles of wine of the choicest and rarest vintages, all plunged neck downwards into ice water.

One of these tubs of iced wine was set down beside the chair of every guest.

Then, at a wave of the young spendthrift's hand, all retired—all save the one pale, sombre-looking attendant who answered to the strange name of Pharoah.

"Now, gentlemen," he said, "help yourselves, and let the bright wine flow again. This is to be a night's diversion, bear in mind, and as yet we have scarcely made a commencement. No shirking. Let me see a bottle before each one."

He himself set the example by stooping down and taking a bottle of champagne.

"A wager!" he cried, as he set the bottle on the table. "I will lay anyone a hundred that I crack the ceiling with my champagne cork! Who will take the bet?"

"I," said a voice.

"Enough."

The wire was removed, and the strings cut with a rapidity which could only have been acquired by long practice.

To explain what was meant by this strange speech, we must observe that the ceiling of this magnificent apartment was composed of looking-glass, giving to it when lighted up, as on the present occasion, a doubly brilliant aspect.

Richly-carved and gilded ribs of wood crossed and recrossed the ceiling, forming an elaborate design, and it was in the many compartments thus formed that the mirrors were placed.

With a sharp and clear report the cork left the bottle's neck, flying upwards with amazing force.

A sharp cracking sound instantly followed.

The wager was won.

One of the largest of the sheets of looking-glass was cracked and starred in a dozen places.

The successful accomplishment of this piece of wanton mischief was greeted with a loud outbreak of approval.

"Well done, my lord, you have won fairly—there can be no doubt about that; and here is the hundred pounds!"

The speaker drew forth a bank-note from his pocket-book, and handed it to his entertainer, who, crumpling it in his hand like a piece of waste paper, thrust it carelessly into the pocket of his coat.

"Wetherby, my boy," he said, "here's to your health, and better luck! I will give you a chance of winning back your note."

"How so?"

"I will bet you a couple of hundred that you can't do it."

"Not crack another square of looking-glass?"

"I will lay you two hundred pounds you cannot—your own note and mine as well."

He flung two crushed pieces of paper on the table as he spoke.

"Done!"

By common consent, all remained still and silent to see which way the wager would be decided.

Wetherby stooped down and produced his bottle.

His face was slightly flushed, and his hand shook a little as he broke the wire.

Then, with the same sharp report as before, the cork flew upwards.

Its course, however, was erratic.

The ceiling was struck, but the cork came partially in contact with one of the cross-beams we have mentioned.

The glass was unbroken.

"You are an unfortunate devil, Wetherby!" said Lord Harcliffe, carelessly sipping his wine. "Will you try again?"

"No," was the answer, given in a slightly tremulous voice.

"Wetherby don't like it," whispered one who sat near the loser. "But it serves him right! He has no business to be here if such a trifling matter as a few hundreds troubles him!"

"Certainly not."

"Sir!" cried Wetherby, starting up, his face now perfectly scarlet. "Do you presume to make those remarks concerning me?"

"And what if I do?"

"I shall not allow them to pass unresented."

"Peace!" cried Lord Harcliffe. "Remember, I allow no quarrelling at this table!"

"Yes, but surely——"

"Hold, Wetherby! You are an unlucky devil, as I said before. But still, if you want satisfaction, make him lay you another wager about the ceiling."

This proposition was so warmly applauded by everybody that there was no such thing as dissenting from it.

The result was awaited with redoubled interest.

But the young man who had been called Wetherby seemed truly to merit the appellation Lord Harcliffe had given him, for he lost again.

With an angry oath he flung down the money, rising so suddenly as to overturn his chair.

"You shall hear more of this," he said, with great agitation, his face having changed its former florid hue to an ashy paleness—"I will not pocket the affront!"

Turning round rapidly, he hurried to the door.

In a moment all present burst out into a roar of laughter.

The ebullition seemed to drive the young man almost frantic, but with a great effort he controlled himself.

"Don't be a fool, Wetherby!" cried Lord Harcliffe, in such stentorian tones as to be heard distinctly above the laughter of the rest. "It's all right! Come back! Don't be a fool, I say!"

But the young man did not pause.

He crossed the threshold, and closed the door after him with so much violence that everything in the apartment shook again.

A momentary silence fell upon the party after this unexpected departure of one of their number, but it was only momentary.

"He's gone now, and forget him!" cried Lord Harcliffe. "Let the wine flow—the fun flags to-night."

Our readers will doubtless agree that the remark was a just one, for they, like us, must have failed to see any fun at present.

"A—a—really," cried one, with an affected stammering drawl—"really—a—poor Wetherby seems as badly hit by the champagne corks—a—yes—as if they were pistol bullets."

"That's very good for you, Favers—very good," lisped a military-looking young man. "And talking of pistols and bullets must remind you all of the Black Highwayman."

"The Black Highwayman?" echoed several.

"Yes. You must all have heard of him, though you may not be acquainted with his last exploit."

"No, no—what is it?" asked several. "Has he stopped the King?"

"Well, no—not exactly."

"Who, then?"

"The Bishop of Oxford."

The mention of the prelate's name was the signal for a loud burst of laughter.

"And he robbed him?"

"Oh, yes—of something like six or seven thousand pounds, I believe."

Lord Harcliffe gave a peculiar smile.

"Then, if rumour has told the truth on this occasion," he said, "I suppose we shall hear no more of this highly mysterious individual. Such a fortune would enable him to retire from his profession."

There was a general laugh at this, and one of the young men, whose deeply-bronzed countenance spoke plainly enough of a long residence in a foreign land, said:

"What is all this I hear about the Black Highwayman, as you all call him? Hang me if I can make it out at all!"

"Ah, Tracy!" said one who sat near him. "Anyone could tell by that remark that you have been absent a long while from England, and have only just returned."

"Well, satisfy my curiosity—the fellow's name is on everybody's lips."

"It is."

"I have heard him mentioned—but mentioned only. I want to know something definite about him."

"Which just means that you want to be wiser than any of the rest of us."

"How so? What do you mean?"

"Simply that nothing definite is known about him by anyone."

"Nothing definite? You surprise me! I should have thought robbing the Bishop of Oxford of seven thousand pounds was definite with a vengeance; and I'll be bound the Bishop thinks so too."

A hearty round of laughter followed this sally.

"Why, yes, in a manner of speaking it is; but you must understand that the lack of definite knowledge does not concern the actions of the highwayman, but his own proper person."

"Oh, I see!"

"We have had highwaymen before to-day," continued the speaker—"gallant enough fellows in their way, but this Black Highwayman, as he is called, eclipses them all in every particular."

"You interest me deeply."

"I am not surprised at that when every scanty detail that is known about him forms the subject of discussion on almost every tongue. He is a perfect living mystery—that is, if he does live; and there are some who have not scrupled to deny all belief in his existence."

"Who has seen him?"

"I may say no one."

"How does he commit his depredations, then?"

"I will tell you. Just suppose yourself travelling—say on horseback—along any of the roads leading from the metropolis."

"Well?"

"If you had anything about you at all worth the taking, you would all at once become aware that something like a shadow would be riding by your side—so dark, so swift, so noiseless, that you would be in doubt as to whether your fancy was playing you a trick or whether what you saw was reality."

Tracy leaned forward a little more, showing how strongly what he heard had hold of his imagination.

"Well, and what next?" he said.

"Then all at once a long arm would be stretched out, and before you would have time to recover yourself from the first shock of your surprise, you would be despoiled of all the valuables and cash you had about you."

"And the mysterious highwayman?"

"Would vanish as suddenly and as noiselessly as he had appeared—he would seem to fade away into the night air."

"And is this believed?"

"By some—especially those who have been robbed. Some exaggeration there doubtless is about all the recitals, but it is somewhat strange that every account corresponds in its main details—the unanimity is wonderful."

"It is very strange."

"That, I think, is the least you can say of it."

"And his horse," said another, joining in the conversation—"all agree about that, and I confess that is what puzzles me most."

"How do you mean?"

"Why, all, without exception, declare that the horse is as noiseless in his movements as a ghost. He is caught sight of all at once, not the faintest sound having indicated his approach, and he retires as silently."

"And," said Lord Harcliffe, who, during the last few moments had been apparently busily intent upon watching the ebullient globules in his wine, "they say, do they not, that he has never been known to speak—that no one has heard his voice?"

"All are agreed upon that point. Silence is preserved in all things—no spirit could be more noiseless. Last night, it seems, he was seen by several persons at the same moment, so that there can no longer be a doubt entertained as to whether such a personage really exists. The moon was shining at the time, and he was seen distinctly."

"Did his appearance agree with the descriptions formerly given?"

"Perfectly. His horse, an animal of unusual size but of wondrous symmetry of limb, was jet black; the saddle and the rest of the trappings of the same hue; the rider himself clad in the deepest black from head to foot, and wearing a black half-mask over the upper portion of his face."

"And do these people declare they did not hear the horse's hoofs?"

"They most solemnly aver that the movements of no spectre could have been more silent."

"This is strange indeed," said Tracy, after a brief pause. "And do you know that, in spite of what you have told me, I am a disbeliever?"

The narrator shrugged his shoulders.

"I can't help that, my boy. You had better take a ride some night and satisfy yourself."

"I have serious thoughts of doing so," was the response, which, though given with real earnestness, was nevertheless received with a loud laugh.

"Nay, nay—I fully intend it," answered the young man, with a quietness and calmness that spoke volumes as to the genuine quality of the courage he possessed. "You shall all have your doubts set at rest upon the point—to-morrow night I will ride forth to meet him, and something seems to tell me that after I have done so this strange mystery will be at an end."

CHAPTER IX.

LORD HARCLIFFE MAKES ANOTHER BET.—THE LIEUTENANT'S FATE.—MR. PETERSON SENDS IN HIS CARD.

"Tracy, my boy," said Lord Harcliffe, breaking the silence which followed this declaration, "I have a great regard for you—I have indeed, and so I hope you will take a friendly word of advice."

"May I ask what it is?"

"Certainly. It is that you do not trouble yourself about the Black Highwayman until he troubles you."

The young naval officer's lips curled with a disdainful smile.

"What do you mean by saying that, Harcliffe?" he asked. "Do you think me a coward?"

"Certainly not—I know you too well."

"Then why your advice?"

"Because I think you would be running your head unnecessarily into very great danger."

Tracy snapped his fingers with a contemptuous air.

"And, moreover," continued Lord Harcliffe, speaking in a way which made it very doubtful whether he was half in jest or half in earnest, "I prophesy that at the best you will meet with nothing but disappointment."

"I will take my luck about that."

"Very well. Only I happen to have been much interested in this mysterious fellow, and not very long ago took the trouble to make some inquiries concerning him."

"Indeed! And what did you hear?"

"More than you will care to listen to, I am certain. I may mention, though, that, according to my information, the Black Highwayman never shows himself to those who are anxiously on the look-out for him, or who particularly want to see him."

"I thought so," said Tracy, again curling his lip.

"Well, well," cried Lord Harcliffe, with a laugh, "we all know the old proverb of a wilful man having his own way, and I suppose you mean to exemplify it. Don't let me dissuade you, only it seems clear that in this enterprise danger is certain, and the least benefit very doubtful."

"I don't care for that," was the dogged answer. "Whether or not, I'll do my best to make this mystery a thing of the past. I am only surprised it has not been done already."

"I'll tell you what it is, Tracy," broke in another, "you may be a very good hand about a ship, and understand nautical matters very well, but, for all that, you are quite out of your latitude in this matter. The most active members of the police have been ceaselessly occupied for a long time past in trying to do what you seem to think the simplest thing in the world."

"That may be; but my determination is unchanged, and we shall soon see who is right and who is wrong. You must all know there is jugglery and deceit somewhere, and I will find out where."

"Then," said Lord Harcliffe, "as I have been rather lucky with my bets to-night, I don't mind laying you another wager."

"What is it?"

"Or two, rather."

"Name them."

"The first is a level five hundred that you don't meet with the Black Highwayman."

"Well?"

"And another that if you do you will be no nearer the solution of the mystery than you are at the present moment."

"Done!"

"I shall win," said Lord Harcliffe, quietly. "After all, I am in doubt whether it is fair to lay the wagers at all."

"Why?"

"Because they may be the means of causing you to persist in your design, when otherwise you would abandon it."

"Pho—pho! Abandon it? You don't know me, or you would never have made that remark."

"Very good. Then let some one hold the stakes. But do you remember young Lieutenant Leslie?"

"Perfectly well."

"He is dead!"

"Dead? How?—when?"

"It is a sad business," answered Lord Harcliffe—"very sad. About six weeks ago he was found lying quite dead on the high-road, near the east end of Ealing Common."

"Yes, it's quite true," said another of the young guests. "It was a terrible shock to all of us when we heard it. Poor fellow! he was the life and soul of a party."

Without knowing why, Tracy felt a strange sensation creep over him.

But shaking it off, he said:

"And the cause of his death?"

"A bullet through his heart."

"Fired by whom?"

"That is a mystery. Surely, if anyone could have been supposed absolutely without an enemy in the world, he was. Yet, as I have told you, he was found one morning quite dead—and, of course, the general opinion was that he had been murdered."

"And, of course, the Black Highwayman was brought into the affair?" said Tracy, endeavouring to preserve the tone of disdain in which he had all along spoken.

"He was," replied Lord Harcliffe, "and not so unreasonably as you seem to suppose. Would you like to learn the particulars?"

"I should indeed."

"Well, then, I must tell you that after his funeral it was recollected by a few that he had more than once spoken about the Black Highwayman, and, as you have done to-night, he many a time declared that he would solve the mystery."

Tracy felt more uneasy still, though he was ashamed to admit it even to himself.

"Like all the rest," continued his lordship, "I was much concerned about his unhappy fate; and when the Black Highwayman was mentioned as having been the cause of it, I resolved to make further inquiries."

"And with what result?"

"I may say none—certainly with nothing satisfactory. But a police officer who had been investigating the matter gave me his own opinion of it, and I am bound to confess that his suppositions had a very truthlike air indeed."

"I never heard anything of this, Harcliffe," interrupted another.

"Very likely. Would you like to know the police officer's opinion?"

"What a question!"

"His view was simply this: that Leslie, in accordance with his expressed design, had gone out for the purpose of meeting with the Black Highwayman and tearing away the veil with which his actions were surrounded—that he had met with him, and *possibly recognised him.*"

The last words were spoken with a peculiar emphasis.

"It is universally admitted," he continued, speaking amid a breathless silence, "that this Black Highwayman never accompanies his depredations with acts of violence—he appears, effects his purpose, and disappears in a moment, but without harming anyone. That is in accordance with general report, is it not?"

"Quite so."

"From the precautions of secrecy taken, the officer concluded that the identity of the mysterious being would be fatal to him if discovered. Young Leslie, then, he assumed, had recognised him, and the Black Highwayman had, in self-defence, shot him through the heart."

"And I suppose," said Tracy, recovering himself, "that you wish to lead me to think that if I make the discovery this will be my fate? You make a great mistake though if you think that any such recital will frighten me."

"Nay—nay—not——"

"Or dissuade me from my purpose."

Lord Harcliffe bowed.

"And here are the thousand pounds. Suppose, Grantley, that you hold the stakes?"

"I have no objection."

"I am open to make yet another bet," cried Lord Harcliffe, as he passed bank-notes for the same amount. "Not that I could crack another square of glass, because I know I could do that."

He broke the wire of another bottle, and the cork flying upwards, struck one of the largest pieces of looking-glass with so much force as to star it in all directions.

"Somebody asked whether the Black Highwayman had stopped the Prince of Wales, but it turned out to be only the Bishop of Oxford. However, here is another hundred-pound note—no, two—and I will wager them that he does stop the Prince of Wales the next time his Royal Highness goes abroad."

"If he does that," said Tracy, "he will be a bold and daring character indeed."

"I will take you, Harcliffe," said another. "He may be a wonderful fellow, but he won't stop the Prince of Wales. No, you may make up your mind that you will never see that two hundred again, my boy."

Lord Harcliffe laughed.

"Let us change the subject," he said; "and yet, before we do, I must ask Tracy to be careful. If he still persists in his design, I confess frankly that I will aid him how I can—in consideration of plans and so forth."

"I shall not forget your promise, but my purpose is unshaken."

This last sentence was pronounced in so decided a tone as to put an end to any further discussion.

One of those sudden pauses which everyone must have remarked as often succeeding one subject of conversation before another is started now took place.

The silence on the present occasion was all the more remarkable, because of the contrast it afforded to the previous uproar.

Even Lord Harcliffe seemed for the moment at a loss

what to say—indeed, his general aspect was that of one who has experienced some considerable annoyance.

But freeing himself from every manifestation of such a feeling, he glanced around, and opened his lips as if about to address all those assembled, when a sharp unexpected sound rang through the vast saloon.

It had the effect of checking his lordship in what he was about to say.

His lips remained open, but his purpose was at an end—like the rest, he was listening intently.

Bang!

This time there could have been no mistake about the nature of the sound.

Some one desirous of admittance to the mansion had raised the ponderous knocker on the front-door and brought it down with terrific force.

Lord Harcliffe started.

"I am growing nervous, I think," he said, with a laugh, perceiving that the movement had been noticed. "What the devil is it?"

Bang! came the pertinacious knock again, as though the person who gave it was in no hurry, but, nevertheless, determined to effect an entrance.

"I—I—should say—a—that it's—a—somebody at the front-door. A—a—dun, Harcliffe, eh? I—I—I've got a d—d tailor, and he always knocks like that, confound him! It's enough to make a fellow's heart jump into his mouth! It is—a—a—monstrous!"

While the military-attired individual was making this brilliant speech, Lord Harcliffe made a slight, almost imperceptible, signal to Pharoah.

But that discreet attendant both saw and understood it, and like a ghost he glided to the door just as the thundering single knock again raised the echoes of the building.

"Pass the wine, gentlemen," cried Lord Harcliffe. "Confound the Black Highwayman, I say! He has stopped our evening's amusement altogether. Come, come—more wine!"

Some few helped themselves to fresh bottles of wine, but it was plain to see that the mysterious knocking had produced an effect upon them all, and that they were waiting to see what would happen next.

A very few moments elapsed before Pharoah returned.

He brought with him in his hands an elegant silver salver, on the centre of which was a crumpled and dirty piece of cardboard.

"What is it?" asked his lordship, with ill-disguised anxiety.

Pharoah replied by handing the salver.

Lord Harcliffe took up the cardboard between his finger and thumb.

On it was printed as follows:—

"*M. Peterson,*
"*P. O.*"

With a knitted brow his lordship turned the card over and over.

"I am engaged," he said.

"But he insists upon seeing you," whispered his attendant. "He is in the dining-room."

Pharoah accompanied his words with a singular glance.

"Who is it?" asked his master—"what does he want? What does 'P. O.' mean?"

Pharoah sunk his voice to a still lower whisper.

"*P. O. means police officer. The man's name is Peterson. He is one of the head runners at Bow Street, and he insists upon seeing you!*"

CHAPTER X.

CAPTAIN HAWK PERFORMS A KINDLY ACTION.—HURRAH FOR THE ROAD!—THE ECCENTRIC TRAVELLER.—THE STAGE-COACH AND A NEW DANGER.—SATAN TAKES A TERRIFIC LEAP.

CAPTAIN HAWK was a little embarrassed when he suddenly discovered the grief-stricken aspect which the countenance of the young girl had upon it, for he had gone so far in his intention of speaking that the first word was half pronounced.

But the young girl, apparently, was so absorbed that she did not notice, for she went on quietly with her work, and kept her head bent down as much as possible.

Captain Hawk turned to the window, and looked out again.

"I have fallen into the company of a cheerful set of people," he said, mentally. "Whatever can be the cloud that hangs over this household?"

Turning round once more, as though it was his intention to put some question to the girl, he found that she had quitted the room as silently as she had entered it.

Why he should feel the strongest interest in the affairs of these people he hardly knew, nor did he trouble himself to inquire—he only made up his mind, with his usual impulsiveness, to discover the secret cause of this too evident sorrow.

He was speculating upon it, and wondering how he could achieve his purpose, when the chief subject of his thoughts re-entered.

Captain Hawk was particularly impressionable if a young and pretty girl was concerned, and this is the readiest and likeliest explanation we can give for his sudden accession of interest.

In a mechanical kind of way, that was far more expressive of deep grief than the noisiest demonstrations would have been, she placed the various articles in readiness upon the table.

"Will there be anything more, sir?" she asked, with a strong and painful attempt to keep her voice steady.

"Yes, one thing," said the captain, advancing closer to her. "You are in deep sorrow—I can see that affliction of some sort hangs over this house. What is it? Don't hesitate to confide in me," he added, "for I am one most willing to aid you if it lies in my power."

"Don't speak to me, sir," she wailed—"pray don't speak to me! I——"

She paused there, for her sorrow refused any longer to remain in subjection.

It was evidently only by a very great effort that she had controlled herself so far as she had.

Before the captain could recover from his surprise or attempt to stop her she had left the room.

"Well," he said, as he drew a chair close to the table, "that does not look like achieving my purpose. I must try some other plan. What splendid eyes she has—even now they are dulled with tears."

Captain Hawk had a keen appetite, which was not interfered with either by the remembrance of past events or the deep sorrow of the young girl.

"I must find it out, though," he muttered. "That there is a secret is evident—I wonder whether it is a guilty one?"

He rang the bell as he spoke, and when he did so it was with the hope that the young girl in whom he felt so deeply interested would respond to the summons.

He was not disappointed.

"My dear girl," he said, in gentle accents, and placing his hands lightly upon hers, "I cannot rest satisfied and content while I see you thus plunged in grief. Forgive me for my boldness! Do not look upon me as intrusive, but in all sincerity confide in me. I have more power than you may be aware of; and as my will to aid you is strong indeed, I feel a presentiment that I shall be able to remove the cause of your great sorrow!"

The young girl was so much taken by surprise, and so carried away by what Captain Hawk had said, that she neither withdrew her hand nor attempted to interrupt him.

Once she raised her tear-filled eyes to his, but the expression she saw in them caused her in some confusion to turn her eyes again towards the floor.

"I—I—that is you—you are very kind, sir!" she said, with increased embarrassment, and having the greatest difficulty in suppressing her sighs and tears, "but——"

"Nay, do not hesitate," urged the captain, in those low persuasive tones which no one could employ to better advantage than himself.

"My father——" she said.

"What of him?"

"He would be angry."

"Why?"

"If I disclosed——"

"I think not," returned the captain. "At least you can tell me why this house is so overhung with grief."

LORD HARCLIFFE DENOUNCED AS THE BLACK HIGHWAYMAN.

Presented Gratis with No. 4 of the New Re-Issue of the Black Highwayman, by the Author of Black Bess.

GRATIS with Nos. 3 to 6, FOUR COLOURED PICTURES,
GRATIS with Nos. 7 to 10, FOUR UNCOLOURED PICTURES,

[CAPTAIN HAWK DISCOVERS THE SECRET [illegible]]

"[illegible] because, sir," she said, struggling heroically to [illegible] emotion—"because my father has been so un[illegible]. Oh! I am sure he will never forgive me for [illegible] all this to a stranger; he is one——"

But Captain Hawk exerted himself to the utmost to [illegible] her scruples; and the young girl resolved to tell [illegible] because of the hope she had that the young tra[veller] [illegible] show them a way out of their troubles.

"[illegible] must know, sir, that not many years ago this [illegible] one of the most prosperous inns upon the London [Road.]"

"The London Road?" ejaculated Captain Hawk. "This [illegible] of the London Road!"

"The old road, sir. You must have been surprised at [illegible] an inn here, so far removed from what is the [road] now."

"[illegible] I was."

"[illegible] that, sir."

"How? I do not understand."

"I ought to have told you, sir, that this house and a little bit of ground all round it, belongs to my father. It has been the possession of the family for more than two hundred years. You may think we prize it, sir. My father was born here, like his father and grandfather, and he hoped to die here."

"But I suppose the alteration of the road has deprived you of a livelihood?"

"Not exactly [illegible] our wants are few, and I think we could manage to satisfy them and be content. But you must [illegible] piece of land stands quite in the [illegible] greatest squire about these parts [illegible] he has bought all the land [illegible] wanted to buy this [illegible] part with the place [illegible] mortal enemy of the squire."

[illegible] BLACK BESS.

"And an enemy to be dreaded."

"As we have since found, sir, to our cost. When he found my father was firm and fixed in his determination, he set to work to ruin us. His first step was to divert the road. You see it did bend hereabouts, sir, and by cutting the new road, not only a hill was avoided, but half a mile in distance saved. That took us quite away from the high-road, for though we put the sign-board up—which you doubtless saw—very few people trouble themselves to turn out of their way."

"I suppose so."

"And not only that, sir, the squire put up another inn on the new road; but finding my father held out in spite of this, he set to work and bought up all our debts."

"Monstrous!"

Captain Hawk's heart burned to hear this story of oppression on the part of the rich—an oppression which is, alas! too often exercised.

"It has preyed dreadfully on father's mind, and has changed him into an old man. Most people advise him to yield at once—and I daresay you will, sir—and though he knows he is the weaker of the two, he is determined to hold out to the very last."

"And so would I," said the captain; "and I warmly applaud him for it."

The young girl opened her eyes in intense astonishment.

"Are you serious, sir?"

"Why should you doubt it?"

"Because you are the very first who has spoken like that."

"Perhaps those others have been more or less dependent on the squire—or tyrant he ought to be called."

"He ought, sir, for now he has got full power over us, he does not scruple to use it. He has bought father's debts, which are more than they would have been but for the difficulties of carrying on his trade; and more than that, he now suspects that credit was only given him to further the squire's ends. Sir," she added, in a whisper, "my father would die with shame to acknowledge it, but we have now the bailiffs in the house in possession; and unless we can find the whole of the money by noon to-morrow, everything we have will be taken from us, and we shall be turned out of doors, homeless, destitute, penniless."

Her highly-wrought feelings enabled her to speak with excitement; but no sooner was the last word pronounced than, with a low, wailing cry, she flung her apron over her face and gave free rein to her sorrow.

The violence of her emotions greatly alarmed the captain, and he set himself assiduously to work to calm them.

For some time he was totally unsuccessful.

"My dear girl," he said, "look up and listen. Do you not understand me when I say that your troubles are at an end, and that the cloud which has for so long overshadowed you will pass away? I don't say this by way of false comfort, but because such is really the case."

"But how can it be, sir? Oh no, it is impossible!"

"On the contrary, it is simple. Come, dry your tears, and listen to me calmly."

The girl made an effort to obey.

A strong curiosity to know who this stranger could be sprang up in her mind, and it was this powerful feeling which, no doubt, assisted her to stifle her emotions.

"You tell me that this squire is your father's sole creditor—that is, that he has bought up all the debts?"

"Yes, sir, that is right."

"And he has put in a bailiff?"

"He has. He is now in the house."

"But would leave if you paid off what he claims?"

"I suppose so. But there is no fear we shall be able to do that."

"What is the amount?"

"Three hundred pounds!"

The captain gave a long whistle.

"A serious amount," he said.

"Yes," she cried, relapsing into her violent distress—"much greater than we can possibly obtain."

"And I, unfortunately, have not a quarter of the sum about me," murmured the captain.

"What did you say, sir?"

"Nothing—nothing—at least, nothing of importance. But dry your eyes, and take this assurance to heart. The squire shall be baffled in his designs, and you shall retain your home here, and be as happy as you once were."

"Oh, sir, I feel I ought to thank you, but I cannot! I know not what words to say."

"And a good thing too, for they would only embarrass me. But I must see your father."

"Oh! when he knows I have divulged this secret he will never forgive me!"

"Tut—tut! I know better than that! Call him in."

The captain consoled himself with a hastily-snatched kiss.

It was taken before the young girl had any idea of his purpose; but her eyes blazed suddenly, as though she would resent the freedom; but the captain remained so calm as to fill her with embarrassment.

She left the room hastily, merely telling her father that the stranger wished to speak to him.

The landlord entered the parlour, looking gloomy and wretched enough.

"I have been questioning your daughter," said the captain, abruptly, "and from her I have learnt the condition of affairs in this house. Strange as it may seem for one utterly unknown to you to say so, I am both able and willing to get you out of your troubles and set the squire at complete defiance."

The landlord looked the picture of incredulity.

But Captain Hawk soon convinced him that he had heard aright.

"But how—how can you accomplish this?"

"In the easiest manner in the world. If you could pay the bailiff three hundred pounds at noon to-morrow you would be all right."

"Yes, but——"

"Then I will find you three hundred pounds to enable you to do so."

"You will?"

"I certainly will."

"And what is your motive?"

"None further than that I hate oppression and petty tyranny such as you have been subjected to more than anything else on earth, and nothing gratifies me so much as when I find myself in a position to thwart it."

"Is this possible?"

"You will find it so."

"And you are willing to lend me this amount, sir, I suppose?"

"Oh, yes!" answered the captain, with a smile.

"And on what security?"

"The word of an honest and independent man, such as I am sure you must be, or you would have truckled to this squire long ere this, as your neighbours have done."

The landlord's eyes brightened when he heard his guest thus speak, and he murmured out his gratitude as best he could.

"I would rather do something for you," he said, "to convince you of my obligation, than utter a lot of words. It may seem ridiculous for me to think of rendering a service to you——"

"Not at all," said the captain—"not at all."

"Well, sir, if ever you have need of my help, call upon me."

"I will, never fear. Three hundred pounds, you say, will cover the claim made against you?"

"Oh yes!"

"And the money will do if paid by noon to-morrow?"

"Yes, but no later. You may depend, sir, the squire will not wait a moment after the power to act is placed in his hands. He will take everything, and turn me out."

"No, he will not—make your mind quite easy about that. Long before the hour comes you shall be provided with the money; and when the squire finds you can pay he will feel you have had your revenge upon him."

"But, sir," said the landlord, hesitatingly, "I have heard of good, kind-hearted people before to-day, but never was fortunate enough to meet with one, and now I can scarcely believe in my good fortune. If you lend me this money, sir, when shall you expect me to pay you back again?"

"Whenever you are able to do so. Let that be the last thing to trouble your mind."

The landlord's amazement increased.

But the advent of another customer called him away; and the captain having satisfied himself that this new-comer in no way concerned him, bolted the door and flung himself down upon the couch, in order to snatch a deep repose.

The reader will be at no loss to understand that he was badly in need of rest.

Indeed, so thoroughly worn out was he, that as soon as he stretched himself at full length and closed his eyes he fell off into a calm sleep.

On that day the old inn was unusually quiet; and as nothing occurred to disturb him, it will occasion no surprise when we state that Captain Hawk did not awake until the day was fast drawing to a close.

He then felt quite like himself, and ready for anything that might happen.

This was as it should be, for he projected making an adventurous night of it.

Another substantial meal added still more to his comfort, and no small amount of the zest which he enjoyed was owing to the fact that his attendant was the landlord's pretty daughter.

The gaze which she from time to time bent upon the handsome face and form of the bold highwayman eloquently expressed her gratitude and the kindly feelings of her heart.

The captain, on his part, did his best to make himself agreeable; and when all things are taken into consideration, can it be wondered at that he succeeded?

Indeed, he had already made a much deeper impression upon the young girl's heart than he was aware of—or she either.

The temptation to remain was great; but the captain, when he found that the apartment was beginning to grow dim in the fading twilight, shook off the fascination and arose.

"Good night, Lottie," he said, taking her hand. "As I told you, I have not with me the amount I mentioned, nor would it be safe to travel with so much about one while the notorious Captain Hawk holds possession of the road."

The landlord's daughter gave a faint cry of dismay when she heard the name.

Her companion warmly pressed her hand to reassure her.

"I start now," he said, "because I have far to ride. But if I live, you will find me here again some time before noon to-morrow. Have no apprehension that I shall fail to come."

Again he drew her closer to him and pressed his lips to hers.

Her face flushed scarlet, and with a sudden snatch she freed her hand from his detaining grasp.

Whether to be angry or feel pleased she knew not, and it was with a strange conflict of emotions that she turned away.

Captain Hawk looked after her with a faint smile, and again murmuring the words "Good night," he left the room.

He had before told the landlord to have his horse ready saddled at sunset, so he made his way direct to the stables.

Here he found the landlord waiting.

"Your horse is quite ready, sir—and a splendid animal he is! He has been well fed and attended to, though I say it; but his looks will proclaim the fact without a word from anyone being necessary. He is a beauty—a real beauty. I have seen a good few specimens of first-class horseflesh in my time, sir—and believe me I don't say it to flatter you—but to my mind I never before saw his equal."

"I believe he is matchless—incomparable. Woa, Satan, boy—woa—woa! Quiet now—keep your tricksiness till I am on your back!"

Captain Hawk's eyes glowed with enthusiasm and delight.

To his mind his noble steed deserved a much warmer eulogium than had been bestowed upon it.

But the landlord was certainly right when he spoke of the great improvement which had taken place in his appearance since his arrival.

His jet-black hide shone like the richest satin, and his waving mane drooped gracefully over his broad, arching neck, while the brilliancy of his dark eyes, now bent upon his master, and the impatient attitude in which he stood, showed that he was in perfect readiness for the road.

"Brave fellow!" said the captain, fondly, patting him upon the neck—a caress which the splendid creature instantly showed himself appreciative of. "You have a long ride before you, but it will be as nothing."

"You are right," said the landlord. "I am good enough judge to be aware that his performance is equal to his appearance. He looks truly magnificent now—such a study as a painter or a sculptor would be glad of."

There was a proud feeling of satisfaction and delight in the captain's heart when these words fell upon his ear.

But mindful of his purpose, he, with a light and airy movement which greatly excited the landlord's astonishment, placed himself in the saddle.

"Good night," he cried. "To-morrow I shall be here."

He rode out of the inn-yard while he spoke, and the landlord, looking after him, muttered:

"A fit rider for such a steed!"

On reaching the road the captain found that Lottie was standing at the front-door, evidently watching to behold his departure.

He kissed his hand gracefully to her as he rode by, and again repeated his farewell.

Lottie averted her head.

It was only for a moment, though, nor did she remove her gaze from the horseman's retreating form until the fast-increasing darkness completely hid him from her view.

CHAPTER XI.

THE DEPARTURE. — HURRAH FOR THE ROAD! — THE TRAVELLER.—A STRANGE REQUEST.—THE DICE-BOX.—CAPTAIN HAWK IS UNFORTUNATE.—A FRESH MYSTERY.

"I WONDER what sort of luck I am destined to meet with?" muttered Captain Hawk, as soon as he found himself fairly on the high-road. "Those blundering officers seem inclined to let me alone. I wonder what can have become of them?"

He stopped and listened.

His practised ear assured him that there was no one upon the road either way for a mile at least, for the night was a remarkably calm one, when distant sounds would have been heard with twice their ordinary distinctness.

"They have either ridden by," he continued, "or else have abandoned the chase. Both things seem unlikely; but it is quite clear they must have done either one or the other."

It was indeed very strange that Captain Hawk had been allowed to remain for so long a time at the lonely inn without any molestation being offered him.

The highwayman, having gained the high-road, did not hesitate a moment about the direction he should take.

He at once turned his back to York.

"A good gallop now will be the thing," he cried—"just as much as will set our blood in circulation, Satan, my boy! It is a splendid night. My heart is light and free, and you, my gallant steed, seem as fresh as a daisy in the sunlight on a dewy morning! Surely, then, I ought to cry, Hurrah for the road!"

He spoke the last words in a loud voice of enthusiasm.

The ringing sounds rang in his horse's ears, and the magnificent animal neighed loudly, as though he would have cried with his young master, "Hurrah for the road!"

"Well done, Satan, old boy—well done!" cried the captain, in the same bell-like tones. "Now, then, off and awa[illegible], old boy—away—away!"

No further incitement to rapid motion was needed than these few spirit-stirring words.

In a second he broke into a [illegible]ound, swift gallop—not s[illegible]ch a o[illegible] as would convey the least impression of exe[illegible]tion, but a light, spirited motion, as though

> "His hoofs disdained to tread
> The bearing earth."

His rider, with that easy grace for which he was so famous, retained his position in the saddle, doing no more than keeping a firm grasp upon the reins.

Slight as the restraint was, the horse chafed under it. He seemed full of impatience to tear off at full gallop.

Light-hearted as he was before, the highwayman felt his spirits rise higher still under the subtle influence wrought by the pleasant motion. His eyes grew brighter and brighter yet, and his warm blood seemed to dance and tingle in every vein.

Trees, hedgerows, and now and then a human habitation flitted by like swift-gliding shadows as the highwayman's spirits became more and more elate the less he thought of ending his wild ride.

It was not until he had left the Bleeding Wolf Inn many, very many miles behind him, that he began to look around him.

"So far?" he ejaculated, at once drawing in the rein. "What can I have been thinking of? Lottie's sweet, gentle-looking eyes, I suppose. Heigho! she is just the one to set a sensible fellow's heart aching. Hullo! what's that?"

Satan's speed was reduced to a walk now, and, though speaking half aloud, the captain's ears had caught a faint and far-off sound.

He bent all his faculties to listening.

"A single horseman!" he ejaculated. "That seems to promise something. I was beginning to feel afraid that the road was deserted to-night. He seems to be in a great hurry," he added, after a momentary pause, "but he will find that I shall put an end to his gallop!"

As he spoke, he brought Satan to a complete standstill, and, drawing forth his weapons, examined them carefully, in order to see that they were in good order.

With that formidable pistol he called "Death" he was particularly careful.

In the days when percussion caps were undreamt of, and when so many things were necessary to ensure the explosion of a firearm, this examination was a most important thing, especially to one like Captain Hawk.

A very short time sufficed, however, to put everything in perfect readiness, yet it enabled the approaching traveller to get very close at hand indeed.

The spot where the captain had halted was much overshadowed by trees—so much so that the darkness was twice as great there as on either side of it.

A place better adapted for his purpose could not be wished, and so he waited patiently until the approaching horseman made his appearance.

This soon happened.

Captain Hawk took a ready means not only of attracting the attention of the stranger, but also of bringing him to a standstill.

This was by firing a pistol across the road just when the horseman appeared in sight, of course keeping the barrel at such an elevation as would preclude the possibility of the infliction of any injury.

The report was a loud one, and, in the intense silence, very startling.

Nothing could have been more unexpected by the traveller, so it is not to be wondered at that he should, upon the impulse of the moment, rein-in his steed very suddenly.

It is just what nine people out of ten would have done in such a case.

The loud report and the bright flash alarmed the horse, and he rose upon his haunches, pawing the air with his fore-feet.

In a second Captain Hawk was breast to breast with the traveller.

"Hold!" he said. "Upon peril of your life go a step further! Hold, I say!"

"Murder!"

"It may be if you disobey me."

"Woa—woa!"

"I want your purse," continued Captain Hawk, with as much indifference as though he had been making a remark about the weather. "Hand it over, and then you may continue your journey."

"Well, I'll be d—d!"

"I hope not!" said the captain, with mock gravity.

"You take it coolly," responded the traveller.

"Yes, I always do, if I find my demands are complied with; but if not——"

"Well?"

"Why, then it is a bad thing for those who provoke me."

"Oh!"

"Very so, I assure you, for I have a most troublesome and fatiguing habit."

"Indeed, sir!—you surprise me!"

"Very likely."

"And what may be this habit you allude to, sir?"

"Why, I draw my pistol, and blow out the brains of whoever may be foolish enough to resist my demands. But I have an objection to doing it, although in a general way it is very conclusive."

"Oh!" said the traveller; and by the way in which he pronounced the word it might with safety be assumed that he was not a little bewildered by the captain's extraordinary behaviour.

"Yes. I don't suppose you can form any idea how very disagreeable it is after shooting a man to have to dismount and grope about his body in the dark till you find what you want—it makes you feel angry that you have been needlessly put to so much trouble."

The way in which Captain Hawk pronounced these last words horrified the traveller to such a degree that he was incapable of speech entirely.

"But you, sir," continued the highwayman, "judging by your voice and your appearance, as well as this darkness will allow me to distinguish it, have much more discretion than to sacrifice your life for the preservation of a few guineas—of which you will not be able to retain possession after all."

"You are right," gasped the stranger—"quite right."

"I am glad to hear you say so; and as my time is valuable, be good enough to put an end to our agreeable meeting without more delay."

There was something so very outrageous in this last speech—not merely in the words of which it was composed, but in the manner in which it was pronounced—that the traveller could not refrain from bursting into a hearty laugh.

Captain Hawk joined in, but, checking his merriment, he said:

"Come, sir, let us go back to business. Your purse! That is all I want. I won't trouble you for what other valuables you may chance to have about you."

"You are a singular fellow."

"I am single, if that is the same thing."

"Not at all. But as you seem inclined to make a disagreeable business as pleasant as possible, I have a little proposition to make to you."

"I have no objection to hearing it, provided too much time is not taken up."

"It will be over in a moment."

"I am all attention, then."

"Very well. What I have to propose is that we refer this matter to the dice-box."

"Dice-box? How? I do not understand."

"I will throw you, and the one who has most points in three casts shall take the purse of the other. If I throw highest, you must give up your pelf—if lowest, you shall have all the cash I carry about me."

"Agreed!" cried the captain, in a moment. "There would be something amusing in the circumstance of a highwayman having to surrender a purse upon the high-road instead of taking one."

"Very amusing, and decidedly agreeable to me, I can assure you," said the traveller. "Let us come out of the shadow of the trees, and then I make no doubt we shall be able to make out the spots upon the dice, for the moon is shining nicely now."

Captain Hawk was pleased with the humour of the stranger—he admired him, too, for the captain considered bravery the highest of all personal qualifications, and none but a brave man would have taken matters so easily as the traveller did.

He put up his pistols, and followed this whimsical being to an open part of the roadway.

"There!" cried the stranger, "this will suit us admirably—nothing could be better! I will be confidential so far as to tell you that gambling is my passion—my bane, some people would call it; but still, the feeling has so much influence over me, that if luck is on your side I shall surrender my purse without the least regret."

"Very good. But what are we to do for the articles?"

"Trust me, I never travel about without them. Hold your hand a moment—here is a box, and here a couple of dice. Now, you see, my hat flattened will make an admirable substitute for a table. I will hold it while you throw."

"Then you give me the first chance?"

"Just so—it is immaterial."

"You are an extraordinary character?" ejaculated the highwayman. "This is an adventure I shall never forget."

"Ha, ha! Dame Fortune is no friend of mine in a general way, but for once I do hope the fickle jade will stand on my side."

While speaking, the stranger hastily took off his black felt hat, and, after flattening it as much as possible, placed it upon the pommel of his saddle, and held it there as firmly as he could.

Captain Hawk slipped the ivory cubes into the box, and shook them up with quite an artistic flourish.

Then, having thrown, he strained his eyes to make out the number of points.

"Six and five!" he cried. "Not bad for a start."

"On the contrary," cried the stranger, "I call it very good. I shall have my old luck—I know I shall, confound it!"

Captain Hawk threw twice more, gaining three points and seven—in all twenty-one.

"I think I can beat that," the stranger cried, gaily. "Oblige me."

And he handed the captain his flattened hat.

The moon was now shining with great clearness, and as the stranger's head was uncovered, the highwayman had a capital view of his features.

The captain noticed that the moment his hand grasped the dice-box his eyes lighted up with a peculiar lustre, which proclaimed the inveterate gamester.

"Now!" he cried.

Having pronounced the word, he threw thrice with great rapidity, gaining at the first twelve, at the second six, at the third four.

"Hurrah!" he cried. "Twenty-two. Mr. Highwayman, I beat you by one. This is what I call deucedly agreeable, Mr. Highwayman! I must trouble you for your purse. Ha, ha!"

The traveller was so tickled by the termination of the affair that he dropped one of his dice, and then very nearly rolled out of the saddle himself.

"I shall never forget this!" he exclaimed, with the tears in his eyes. "It is rich! The idea of being a gainer by such a transaction as this is amusing—most amusing! Thank you, sir! I see you are a gentleman, though you ride on the highway by night."

These words were elicited by the promptitude with which the captain handed over his money.

But the amount so amazed the stranger that he became suddenly grave.

"Good Heavens!" he ejaculated, in a greatly altered tone of voice. "However much is there here?"

"About a hundred and fifty pounds, I think," returned the highwayman, rather grimly, for just then his thoughts reverted to the landlord's daughter and the solemn assurance he had given.

"Then it isn't fair," said the stranger. "I protest it is not fair."

"How so?"

"Why, I ought to be ashamed to confess it, but I have not so much as five pounds about me. If I had, I should not have been so ready with the dice-box."

"But what is your objection?"

"Simply that I have treated you unfairly. You would have expected to find more about me."

"That is a risk I always have to run. Nothing could be fairer or more straightforward. I have lost, and am content. Good night."

"Nay—nay! Stop a moment. At least let me have a couple more words with you."

"I must request you to be brief."

"I will. Your behaviour, though, has so much struck me with amazement that I can hardly collect myself. I am conscious that I don't feel satisfied with taking this money."

"Suppose you hand it back, then?"

"That is just what I should do without the least hesitation whatever: but the fact is, I have been so confoundedly unlucky of late and have got so low in funds that I have been obliged to make various shifts."

"Very good. That is quite sufficient."

"Nay, one word more—I want you to accept of this ring. Its value is not great, yet it will serve as a remembrance of to-night. Do not hesitate about accepting it; and tell me if you know Leicester House?"

"In London?"

"Yes."

"The residence of the Prince of Wales?"

"The same."

"I know it well."

"Then if ever you are in any great difficulty or danger, send this ring there and you will be aided. I can say no more."

"Many thanks!" said the captain, as he slipped the ring on to his finger. "Don't think me ungracious for saying, however, that when I am in danger I generally trust to myself."

"You despise my gift, then?"

"Not at all—I shall always prize it very highly as a souvenir."

The stranger deliberately put Captain Hawk's hundred and fifty pounds in his pocket.

"Of all the strange beings I have ever met with in the whole course of my life—and there have been no few of them—you are certainly the strangest."

"It may be so. Once more, good night."

"Will you not tell me your name?" asked the stranger, raising his voice, for the highwayman had already got several paces off. "I will give you my word that I will never make use of the knowledge to your injury."

"I have no objection," was the response. "You have often heard of me, no doubt. I am known on the high-road as Captain Hawk."

And without waiting to observe the effect produced by this announcement, the highwayman gave his horse the rein, and in an instant was flying along the road at an amazing gallop.

CHAPTER XII.

THE OLD TOLL-GATE.—NEWS OF THE POLICE OFFICERS.—THE ALARM.—THE HOLLOW.—CAPTAIN HAWK BRINGS THE LONDON MAIL TO A STANDSTILL.

If Captain Hawk had ever permitted himself to be put out of the way by the occurrence of any cross incident, the loss of his money at this particular juncture, when he so much needed it, would certainly have had that effect.

We should be afraid to say that his temper was altogether unruffled; but if so, the hard gallop he took restored him to his usual composure.

"I wouldn't care a rap," he muttered, as he slackened his pace, "if it was not for the fact of my having promised that three hundred pounds to-morrow. I must get it somehow or other, that is certain. No one shall ever say that Captain Hawk broke his word. Time is short, though," he added; "and to-night, of all nights in the year, travellers seem scarcer than ever I have known them to be."

He pulled up as he uttered the last word.

But though he listened well, not a sound of horses' hoofs or carriage wheels could be distinguished.

And what was the worst was that the time was fast approaching when travellers would be scarcer and scarcer, for he well knew how few were to be met with between midnight and sunrise.

He was speculating upon the amount of success he was likely to meet with, and wondering what he should do if he found it impossible to obtain the three hundred pounds, when he all at once caught sight of a dim glimmering light in advance.

His first idea was that it belonged to some vehicle, and his spirits revived accordingly, but a closer approach made him aware that the uncertain illumination proceeded from a lamp over a toll-gate.

He rode forwards towards it at a leisurely rate.

"If I have quite cleared my pockets," he said, "it will be awkward. No, here is a crown-piece—that will recompense the old curmudgeon for being woke out of his slumbers."

"Hilloa!" he cried, in a loud voice, a moment afterwards. "Hi—hi! Gate—gate!"

He had to repeat the summons more than once before a

small latticed window was dashed open and a night-capped head thrust forth.

"What the devil do you want at this time of night?"

"To go through the gate, to be sure!" rejoined the captain, with a laugh. "If you are quick there will be a crown-piece for your trouble—if not, you will have nothing. You understand!"

"Lor! captain! You're a rum 'un, you is, and no mistake! Understand you? I should rather think I did! You mean you would just jump the gate like you did the last time. My eyes! I shall never forget it!"

"Be quick, will you? Do you think I mean waiting here all night?"

"One moment, captain—only one moment!"

The toll-keeper—who, judging by what he had said, knew perfectly well who the late traveller was—made good haste, and appeared at the door after the lapse of not much more time than he had mentioned.

"The road is quiet to-night."

"It is, captain, uncommon—and I am glad of it.

"No doubt. Here is the crown-piece I promised you; and if I should happen to find the gate open when I come galloping back you will find a guinea on your doorstep, most likely."

"All right, captain. A nod and a wink, you know. If you go that way," he continued, pointing in the direction Captain Hawk was taking, and which we need scarcely remind the reader was towards London—"if you go that way you are most likely to want to come back in a hurry."

"Why so?"

"Because a good party of police officers have gone through here in pursuit of you. They called and asked me whether I had seen you, and I said no, but they did not believe me seemingly, for on they went."

"And they have not returned?"

The toll-keeper shook his head.

"Well, if officers are to be on the road with me," said the captain, quietly, "I would much rather have them in front than behind me."

"Oh, that's good—I like that—I do! Ha, ha!"

"Hold your row! What time does the London coach come through here?"

"Five in the morning."

"It is light then?"

"Oh yes—you can see about you pretty well at four!"

"That will do! Good night!"

"Good night!" was the response.

Then, in an undertone, he said to himself:

"The London mail will be a little behind time when it gets to York in the morning, I rather think."

And with this remark on his lips he turned in again.

Meantime, Captain Hawk again pushed his horse forward.

The toll-keeper was right in his surmise—the bold highwayman had determined to stop the stage-coach running between London and York.

This was no inconsiderable feat; but the captain was resolved upon it, because he knew that he should be able thereby to make sure of a good booty.

The danger was proportionably great, of course, but then Captain Hawk always laughed at danger—he would absolutely court it for the excitement which it afforded.

Still, he was aware that he should have a much better chance of success if he stopped the mail-coach before daylight, and as success was in this case of unusual importance, he resolved to push on.

But morning was much closer at hand than he was aware of.

Having placed a considerable interval between him and the toll-gate, he reduced Satan's pace to a walk.

He had now given up all hopes of meeting with another traveller, and therefore determined to jog on quietly until the mail-coach came in sight.

He had been going for some time at this pace, and had reached a very dark part of the road, with tall trees growing on each side, when all at once the loud, clattering sound produced by the approach of a considerable body of horsemen reached his ears.

His first act was to pull up.

Another second convinced him that he had not been mistaken, and he immediately made up his mind what he should do.

"Those are police officers," he said, with a decisive air; "no doubt the ones the toll-man spoke of, and I suppose by this time have satisfied themselves that I am not on the road before them, and so have turned back. How fortunate—just the very thing I wanted! I will get out of the way and allow them to ride by."

The captain pronounced the words as though convinced he was really showing the officers a great favour.

The dense belt of trees on the side of the road offered every facility for concealment that could be wished, and in less than a moment he was securely hidden.

Of course, if anything in the shape of a search was instituted, his discovery would have been inevitable, but this consideration gave him no concern, because he remembered that there was nothing to give the police officers the least idea of his whereabouts.

Quite complacently, then, he awaited their arrival.

Some time elapsed, for on a still night the sound made by a body of horsemen can be heard at a great distance.

The highwayman's patience was well-nigh worn out when they arrived.

They were all coming at a hard gallop, and as there were eight or ten of them, the din made by so many iron-bound hoofs striking the frozen roadway was rather terrific.

But to Captain Hawk's intense surprise—for it seemed as though the officers knew exactly where he was—they all pulled up very suddenly in the road not a dozen paces from him.

This event was so sudden and so unexpected, that had not the captain habitually kept his nerves under great command, he would, ten to one, have betrayed his presence by some slight sound or movement.

Luckily, he had the presence of mind to remain profoundly still.

"D—n me," said a voice, "if I like this—I won't go any further, that's flat!"

"What is the matter, Mr. Trattles?" said another voice, in tones of great respect.

"Matter? Why, this is all an infamous though ingenious device on Gogg's part to do us out of a fair chance of getting our share of the reward! What a confounded dolt I must have been not to see through it at the first!"

Hereupon Mr. Trattles, who seemed of a very irascible temperament, gave himself several hard blows upon the side of his head with his clenched fists.

This operation seemed to soothe his feelings wonderfully.

"Then, do you think of turning back again?" asked another of the party.

"Certainly I do. It's as plain as a pikestaff now! He didn't want us with him—we made too many for the reward to be shared amongst, so he started the foolish notion that we must have passed him on the road somewhere, and I was fool enough to think it a likely idea, because we could hear nothing of the fellow! Oh dear, how that Gogg is grinning at my want of sense, I know!"

This happened to be a most aggravating reflection indeed.

"I think we had better ride on a little further, now we have come back this far, sir!"

"Oh, do you—and may I presume to ask why?"

"Because, sir, there is a toll-gate not such a very long way from here, and if we only ride as far as that we shall be able to make sure whether we passed him."

The strong sense of this suggestion impressed itself even on the mind of Mr. Trattles, and after a little pretended hesitation he agreed that this proposition should be carried into effect.

"If he should really be hereabouts," cried Mr. Trattles, with a chuckle, "and I nabbed him, wouldn't that make old Gogg grin on the wrong side of his mouth! Oh, rather!"

This was a very pleasant thing to have in prospective, so away they all went, highly delighted.

Captain Hawk was not a little amused by this scene, but he did not venture to emerge from his hiding-place for some time, because he thought nothing more likely than that the officers might alter their minds again before they got half way to the toll-gate, which was in reality much farther off than they appeared to imagine.

But the silence having lasted for a long time, Captain Hawk came forth and once more turned his face in the direction of London.

He moved on gently, for he had a long, steep hill before him.

Upon gaining the summit he was enabled to perceive

unmistakable signs that dawn was at hand, and therefore he prepared himself to see the stage-coach.

Satisfied that all his weapons were in perfect order, he descended the hill.

At the foot he found himself in a kind of hollow, for the ground a few yards further on again had an upward tendency.

Just at the bottom of the valley, for such indeed it was, a rather wide stream flowed across the roadway. Horses and vehicles had to splash their way through it as best they could, but for the convenience of passengers there was a rude foot-bridge, composed of a few planks and posts roughly nailed together, and placed at one side of the road.

The trees grew rather densely in the vicinity, and even in the daytime a dim twilight hung around the spot.

On the present occasion a dense white mist rested upon the surface of the little brawling stream, and the more the dawn advanced the more palpable the vapour became.

"I rather think," muttered the captain, as he allowed his horse to drink sparingly of the water—"I rather think this is just the place I want. If it had been contrived on purpose it could not have suited me any better."

Backing as close as he could under the trees, he waited as silently as a statue.

He bent forward in the saddle once or twice, as though he had heard the coach approaching, but each time it would seem that he had been misled by some accidental sound.

Suddenly the dreary silence was broken in upon by the long, winding notes of a horn.

Captain Hawk gave himself a good shake—for the mist had a depressing effect—and prepared for action.

The horn sounded again.

"What the deuce is that for?" he ejaculated. "There is no stopping-place hereabouts. Ah! I have it: it is to warn anyone who might chance to be ascending to draw aside and let the coach roll by."

No doubt this was the correct solution of the affair.

The horn sounded again.

Then the rumbling of wheels could be detected, and a few moments afterwards the highwayman, despite the mist, was enabled to descry the heavy, lumbering vehicle rolling down the hill.

Its speed was now much diminished, for the hill they were descending was almost the worst bit of roadway between London and York.

Not only was it very steep, but it wound about in a very devious manner, and from top to bottom the surface of the road was strewn with loose, round stones, which seemed formed for the express purpose of throwing a horse down.

On the present occasion, the white, fleecy mist rolling up the hill-side increased the difficulty of the descent, and the driver came down much slower than was usual.

No one can fail to see how highly favourable all these circumstances were to Captain Hawk.

The mist made the brook appear much wider than it really was, and the driver accordingly approached with due caution.

It was just as the fore horses splashed their feet in the water that Captain Hawk rode forth from his place of concealment.

The driver of the mail was apparently known to him, for he cried:

"Bill Waddle, pull up! Drive your horses another step, and your life shall pay the penalty! What would your wife and children think if they saw you brought home with a brace of slugs in your skull, and knew that nothing brought them there but your own stupid, pig-headed obstinacy?"

"Murder! Oh dear!—it's all up with us! Here's the captain!"

"And what if there is?" said the man who sat on the box beside him. "Captain or no captain, you don't think for a moment we shall sit here and submit to one man plundering us, and perhaps murdering us afterwards?"

"No, no," said the driver. "Captain Hawk never does that; and if you have got half the amount of common sense I give you credit for, you will keep quiet. If you do, the captain won't hurt you."

In the meanwhile, the highwayman had hastened to place himself at the door of the coach.

He arrived just at the moment when some one inside let down the window, probably with the intention of inquiring the cause of the stoppage.

"Thank you!" said Captain Hawk.

The man drew back with great suddenness, being not a little startled to find a horseman so close to the side of the coach.

"The devil!" he ejaculated.

"Oh dear no!" said the highwayman, in the most musical of accents. "Only Captain Hawk--entirely at your service, ladies and gentlemen."

At the mention of this much-dreaded, well-known name, there was a general cry of dismay.

"D—n it, madam!" said some one, roughly, "don't fall on anybody like that! It's enough to absquatulate a fellow, ma'am. Recollect, you are not a sylph, but more like a great feather-bed. Don't faint away in my arms, don't—don't!"

While this speech was made Captain Hawk was very busily engaged in removing the lamp that was fixed on that side of the coach.

It took him but a moment to lift it from its setting.

Then, holding it before him, he was enabled to take a tolerably good look into the coach, while at the same time, as he kept the dark part of the lamp towards him, he prevented his own face from being at all distinctly seen.

"Ladies and gentlemen," he said—for the coach was quite full, and contained representatives of both sexes—"it will be entirely your own faults, I assure you, if this stoppage is a very long one, or is very disagreeable in its results. Nothing like robbery is intended. I beg you will take that assurance to heart, ladies and gentlemen. Robbery!—I abhor both the name and the deed!"

"Then what the devil did you stop the coach for?" said a growling voice in the far corner.

"That," said Captain Hawk, with a low bow, "I will, with your permission, ladies and gentlemen, at once proceed to explain."

"Oh, d—n his politeness!" said the growling voice again. "We shall all have to pay dearly enough for it, I'll warrant"

CHAPTER XIII.

THE SQUIRE'S STEWARD.—THE HIGHWAYMAN'S STRANGE ALLY.—THE WARNING.—OFF AND AWAY!—THE COACH MEETS WITH A MISHAP, AND CAPTAIN HAWK COMES VERY UNEXPECTEDLY UPON HIS FOES.

THERE was something so ludicrous in the way in which these last words were uttered that the passengers, despite their disagreeable position, could not forbear from laughing.

As for Captain Hawk, he joined in the merriment with right good will.

But, checking himself, he drew from his belt his long-barreled pistol with the peculiar handle, and rested the weapon in a negligent manner upon the sill of the coach window.

The sight of the glittering barrel—for the light of the lamp shone upon it with great effect—caused the laughter to subside with remarkable suddenness.

Most shrank back as far as they could, in the hope that they should by this means escape all danger from the bullets with which it was loaded.

"Ladies and gentlemen," said the highwayman, lightly, and yet somehow in such a way as to make it clear that he was very much in earnest, "I assure you you do me a very great injury to associate the word robbery with my name. As I said before, nothing of the kind is intended. I shall merely call upon you all to make a small contribution, which doubtless you can well afford. If you cannot, that is your misfortune, and not my fault—a contribution I must have."

"Ah!" ejaculated the growling voice, "I thought that was it!"

"Very likely," continued the captain, admirably preserving the same amount of calmness. "I must inform you, however, that the contribution thus raised is not for my own benefit—it is, take my word, for a very praiseworthy purpose, and the knowledge of this fact will doubtless induce you to behave more liberally than you would do otherwise."

"Praiseworthy!" broke in the growling voice, again—"let there be no more of this masquerading! Execute your orders, and let us continue on our journey. I have no pistols with me, or you would find I should act in a very different manner."

"Perhaps so!" returned Captain Hawk. "As you are so obliging I will begin with you. Be kind enough to place your contribution in my hat."

As he spoke, he handed in the article named; but as he held the pistol very carelessly between his fingers the while a great deal of consternation was the result.

"Come—come," he added, "if you are anxious to make haste I assure you I am; and I ought to tell you that the amount I require is three hundred pounds."

"Three hundred devils!"

"No, sir," answered the highwayman, gravely, addressing himself to the man who had given vent to this last ejaculation—"I doubt whether you have the power to supply me with so many, and if you had they would not be of the least use to me, I give you my word."

"Pooh—pooh!"

"But three hundred pounds—and in cash, too—I am determined to have, or the coach goes no further. You understand that perfectly. And rest persuaded I should infallibly be as good as my word in the matter. If you choose to take a reasonable and common-sense view of your position you will at once let me have the amount I mention, in which case not the least further molestation will be offered you. Your journey can be resumed without delay."

"I'll be d—d if ever I heard of such cool impudence!" cried another. "Three hundred pounds! Why, the fellow speaks of this sum as though it was nothing, when instead of that it's a fortune—a fortune!"

The last words were followed by two groans.

"Why, Mr. Goslings," ejaculated the large female, "however can you speak in such a way? What is three hundred pounds to you, I wonder? Why, a mite—a mere mite! Instead of speaking like that, you ought to give the whole amount yourself, and so save anything from being taken from us poor bodies, who can so ill afford it."

"Stop her tongue!" cried Mr. Goslings, frantically. "Can no one stop her infernal tongue? What does the woman mean? Don't pay any attention to her, Mr. Highwayman—she is as rich as a Jew, and has a large purse in her pocket!"

"Oh, you base villain," retaliated the huge female—"you monster, to speak in that way of the mite of a poor widow like myself! You know you have had your eye upon it for a long time; but you won't have it—oh dear no!"

This scene mightily amused Captain Hawk.

Not only did he obtain diversion, however, but the passengers by thus wrangling among themselves were letting him know the amount of booty he might expect to obtain from them.

"Confound you, be quiet!"

"I sha'n't be quiet, Mr. Goslings! What did you want to insult an unprotected female for, you brute? Didn't you call me a feather-bed? But I'll have my revenge upon you!"

"Quite right too," said Captain Hawk, approvingly. "The man who is brute enough to say an insulting or disparaging word to lovely woman deserves to suffer—indeed he does."

"And I know how to do it," continued the lady, triumphantly. "Mr. Highwayman," she added, pointing to the unfortunate Goslings, "that is Squire Pemberton's steward, one of the richest men in these parts—some say richer than the old squire himself; and I should be ready to believe it, for he does just as he likes with his master; and it is entirely through him the poor folks about here have such hard times of it. He exacts what he likes, and pays over what he chooses; and if it wasn't for him the squire would be the best landlord in the world, I am certain."

"Ha!" cried Captain Hawk, with an air of great satisfaction, for this statement threw fresh light upon the tale told him by Lottie. "I am much obliged to you, madam. Your suggestion shall be acted upon, rely on it."

"As it happens, it will be quite in vain on the present occasion," said the steward, falteringly, and trying hard to smile. "I have no money about me now. So you are cheated in your revenge, you old harridan!"

The last opprobrious epithet so inflamed the ire of the huge female, that, with a sudden sound—half a snort, half a scream—she precipitated herself upon the steward.

"Take that!" she cried—"and that!"

"Murder—oh, murder! Ten thousand devils! Free me from this tiger in petticoats, somebody! Murder! Oh, death—and the devil!"

Of course, no one attempted to interfere.

The steward was not liked well enough for anyone to be ready to take up arms in his defence.

"Take that!" repeated his tormentor.

Another yell followed.

"And you, Mr. Highwayman, take that!"

As she spoke she flung a heavy purse at the captain, who caught and slipped it into his pocket with a dexterity and rapidity really wonderful.

"And here's another!" she cried. "And now, you cross-eyed old vampire, I'll let you know better than call a respectable lone female a feather-bed, I will, you wretch!"

In the hands of this Amazonian specimen of the feminine sex the unlucky steward was almost as helpless as a child.

As for his resistance, it did him more harm than good, for it only had the effect of bringing down more ill-usage upon him.

"I'll make you smart for this!" he howled. "I've got my remedy against you at law, that's one comfort—and what's more, I'll have it! Ha, ha! Mrs. Grumpus, you shall smart for this!"

"Then I'll smart for this at the same time!" she cried, pulling out a whole handful of hair. "And do you talk of the law? Bah! Try it! You would find yourself in the wrong box! You know what I know about a certain matter, Mr. Goslings, and I'll out with it—yes, I would if I knew I was going to swing for it!"

As she spoke, Mrs. Grumpus, with a terrible tug, pulled out another heavy bag of money, much larger than the preceding ones.

"There," she cried, "now be off! You have more than you want in those three bags, for I know what he has been receiving to-day! Take it, and be off!"

"I will," said Captain Hawk, who felt sure that he had much more than the sum he had named. "You are all free to continue your journey."

"My money!" shrieked the steward, turning round with a wild air of appeal towards the highwayman. "Give me—oh, give me back my money, or I am a lost, ruined, undone man!"

"And a good thing too!" answered the captain.

"Take care," cried Mrs. Grumpus—"he is going to fire!"

The warning came almost too late.

The captain had just time to make a sudden movement, and that was all.

There was a flash and a loud report.

There was a crash of broken glass, too, and the interior of the coach was instantly plunged into utter darkness.

The bullet from the steward's pistol had struck the coach lamp, and shivered the glass.

"Good night!" cried the highwayman. "Drive on, Bill—off and away!"

He turned Satan's head towards London, and in an instant was off like the wind.

It was fortunate he was so speedy, for the steward, leaning out of the window, fired another pistol.

But it produced no result.

Captain Hawk, when he heard the report, checked Satan's speed very slightly, for the suggestion crossed his mind that it was anything but right to leave a lady exposed to the fury of such a wretch.

But in another second he recollected that the lady in question had shown herself quite capable of taking her own part—so capable that any assistance on his part would be purely superfluous.

The driver of the coach did not need telling twice that he could drive on.

He immediately whipped his horses, and away they splashed through the brook in an amazing style.

The quarrel inside went on most desperately, much to the detriment of the other passengers.

Suddenly, however, all became conscious of a frightful jerk.

A terrible swaying movement followed.

The combatants paused.

PHANTOM CLEARS TYBURN TOLL-GATE.

Presented Gratis with No. 5 of the New Re-Issue of The Black Highwayman, by the Author of Black Bess.

GRATIS with Nos. 3 to 6, FOUR COLOURED PICTURES.
GRATIS with Nos. 7 to 10, FOUR UNCOLOURED PICTURES.

[LORD HARCLIFFE INCREASES PETERSON'S SUSPICIONS.]

Then, with the most awful crash, the stage-coach fell on one side on the roadway.

The coachman at once was flung from his seat, while the horses got most inextricably entangled in the harness.

The guard performed a most astounding somersault, and fell down, along with his blunderbuss, into a hole which had been partially filled up with snow, that was by this time in a half-melted, half-frozen condition.

The shrieks coming from the interior of the vehicle, the oaths, and the sounds of furious, desperate struggling must be imagined—they cannot be described.

The passengers, without exception, all fought like so many wild animals, who, suddenly finding themselves in a cage, were trying their utmost to get out, and wholly disregarding what injuries they inflicted upon others so long as they succeeded.

Captain Hawk in the meanwhile had not continued far along the high-road in the direction of London.

From the first he had not intended to go to any distance, but to make his way by a circuitous route back again to the lonely inn.

All at once, however, on turning a sharp corner of the road, he came upon a troop of mounted men.

In the dim gray light which was shed over all things there was no difficulty in distinguishing them.

They were police officers.

Why they had drawn up in that place, of course, was more than the highwayman knew or had time to ask himself.

For an inappreciable space of time he was deprived of his self-command.

Evidently, too, the officers were not a whit less taken by surprise than himself, for the snow, which in that place covered the roadway rather deeply, prevented them from hearing his approach until he was close upon them.

No. 5.

GRATIS with this Number, The SPLENDID COLOURED PICTURE: PHANTOM CLEARS TYBURN TOLLGATE.

Neither was long in recovering self-possession, but Captain Hawk was first.

"Excuse me, gentlemen," he said, with his usual coolness, "I had no idea you were so close by, or I would not have interrupted you, depend upon it. Allow me the honour and pleasure of wishing you a very good morning!"

As he spoke he made Satan wheel round.

In another instant he was going at full speed.

Such a proceeding as this might well stagger the officers.

For the moment they were speechless and motionless.

Then one cried:

"That is our man for a thousand pounds! After him —after him! Don't spare your horses, we can get a fresh supply a little further on."

With these words the officer set the others the example by sticking his spurs deeply into his horse's flanks.

The whole of them were speedily in motion, and on getting round the bend in the highway which we have mentioned, they had a full view of Captain Hawk galloping along in a wonderful manner.

The highwayman, however, glanced continually from side to side, for he was anxious to descry some spot where the hedgerow was low enough to render a leap practicable.

But no such spot presented itself, for, in order to reduce the ascent of the hill as much as possible, the road had been cut deeply, leaving a steep embankment on both sides of such a character as to make it quite impossible for a horse to gain the meadows.

For a wonder there was a slight shade of uneasiness visible in the highwayman's countenance.

"Confound it!" he cried. "The further I go the more impossible it will be for me to get across the country, and if I go much further at this rate I shall come up with the coach; and although the passengers might not be able to stop me from getting past, yet they could delay me so much as to bring those fellows behind much nearer than I should consider at all agreeable."

Little did Captain Hawk guess what an accident had befallen the mail-coach, and that at that very moment it lay in a confused mass in the high-road, blocking up the way entirely.

He was made acquainted with the circumstance very suddenly.

It was no more than natural that his first impulse should be to pull up.

So suddenly did he draw the rein, that Satan rose upright on his haunches and pawed the air with his forefeet.

A loud, confused shout from the rear made the highwayman aware that his pursuers were conscious of the aspect of affairs as well as himself.

They looked upon the matter as settled—no one who heard their cry of exultation could have had any doubt about it.

Captain Hawk bit his lip and glanced around again.

"We have but one chance, old boy!" he said, addressing his steed. "Away—away! On, boy—on—on! Over —over!"

His voice had a spirit-stirring sound, and produced an immediate and visible effect upon his horse.

Off he went like the wind.

"Curse me," cried one of the officers, "he means going over the coach!"

Just as he spoke, Satan rose in the air in truly beautiful style.

The highwayman uttered another inspiriting cry.

It was followed by a loud yell of alarm, which came from such of the occupants of the coach as had managed partly to extricate themselves.

Mrs. Grumpus and Goslings, the steward, had had a desperate fight, and both were trying to force their way through the window at the same moment.

But when they saw a rider coming with the velocity of a whirlwind, and when they saw his steed rise up in the air, no one can be surprised to learn that they were half frantic with terror.

Nor was their danger inconsiderable, for the hind hoofs of the highwayman's horse escaped the steward's head by the space of about half an inch only.

"Murder," he cried—"murder!"

But before the word was pronounced a loud report shook the air, and made everybody feel as though he had been annihilated.

This was caused by the stupidity of the guard, who had been floundering about for some time, and now thought he would put a period to Captain Hawk's existence by firing his blunderbuss at him.

But he came much nearer to lodging the greater part of the miscellaneous missiles it contained into the skull of Mr. Goslings.

As for the highwayman and his steed, they escaped unhurt, and alighted in safety on the high-road.

"Come on!" cried the captain, looking back over his shoulder at the police officers. "Come on! The reward for my apprehension is so good that you ought not to mind a little extra trouble in earning it!"

A volley of curses was his sole reply as the officers reined-up on the other side of the fallen coach.

Of course, it was not likely that they would hazard such a desperate leap.

It was such a one as Captain Hawk himself would have hesitated to attempt under circumstances of less emergency.

Owing to the exceedingly awkward manner in which the coach had fallen, they had no slight amount of difficulty in making their way past it.

It follows, therefore, that Captain Hawk in the meanwhile got a long way ahead, for he did not allow Satan to relax his speed in the least degree.

But the officers by no means gave way to despair.

"Never mind," said their leader. "We have the certain knowledge that he is before us. It is getting lighter, and as the day advances it is impossible for him to go for any distance unobserved. We shall hear of him at frequent intervals, and, by getting a change of horses, may make sure of running him to earth before sunset."

There seemed a strong degree of probability about this—the officers looked upon the result as certain, and prepared to commence the pursuit with all imaginable ardour.

It was rather a damp on their spirits, however, when, on gaining the summit of the next hill, from which an unusually extensive prospect could be obtained, they were unable to detect the faintest and most distant trace of their prey.

Captain Hawk had indeed made the best use of his time

He knew very well that in the present case his best chance lay in pushing on at the utmost speed of his horse for such a length of time as would carry him completely out of sight of his foes.

We need hardly say that he succeeded.

Yet the officers with a dogged perseverance rode on until they were able to change their horses, and although their inquiries met with no success they pushed on with undiminished hopes.

CHAPTER XIV.

CAPTAIN HAWK ELUDES HIS FOES.—THE STEWARD RECEIVES THE MONEY.—THE SUDDEN APPEARANCE OF THE OFFICERS.—THE HIGHWAYMAN'S RESOLVE.

So soon as ever Captain Hawk felt assured that he was out of sight of his pursuers he suffered his horse gradually to reduce his speed until it became a trot.

By this time, however, the morning was well advanced, and every now and then he would catch sight of some early husbandman making his way towards the scene of his daily labour.

"Things have turned out much better than I could have hoped for or expected," he muttered to himself. "I have the means now beyond all doubt of relieving the landlord from his embarrassment, and one bright smile from Lottie will be to me an ample reward. I will make my way there at once, for it seems I have managed to give those fellows the slip nicely."

He turned his horse round as he spoke, and raised himself in the stirrups.

A careful look around satisfied him that the police officers were not in sight.

"I will go easy," he said; "I have more reasons than one for it I am in no hurry, and if those fellows come within view I can easily get away from them. It will be something to know they are not after me."

To one in Captain Hawk's position this was an important matter indeed.

In the most leisurely manner possible, then, he rode along, his thoughts partly occupied with Lottie and partly fixing themselves upon his adventure with the stage-coach.

"And so that was the squire's steward! I am thankful for that bit of knowledge, because I had such a good look at him that I should be able to tell him again from a thousand—and what is more satisfactory, he did not, I am convinced, catch a glimpse of my features; future recognition by him is impossible."

He was quite sure on this point, because he had taken care to hold the coach lamp in such a way that its dark metal side was turned towards him and the glazed part towards the interior of the vehicle.

"I would wager anything," he continued, "that he is the oppressor of these poor people far more than the squire himself. We shall see, for there is a strong presentiment upon my mind that we shall see each other again before long."

He journeyed on; but no signs of his pursuers appearing, his impatience to see the landlord's daughter overcame his resolution, and Satan was soon flying over the ground at a hard gallop.

On reaching the lonely inn, he felt a pang of disappointment at not seeing Lottie at any of the windows; but shaking off the feeling and laughing lightly to himself at the idea of being so impressed, he went round to the stables.

Here he met the landlord.

"Look up," he said—"better times are in store! You shall have the money you want at the appointed time."

"I wish I could thank you, sir!"

"Never mind about that, but tell me whether the steward will attend at the time when the money should be paid?"

"He will, sir; he would not omit such an opportunity of trampling over me for worlds! He has been a bitter foe to me!"

"Then I think he will be rather late."

"Rather late, sir? What do you mean?"

"Nothing. It was my opinion—nothing more."

He walked towards the house as he spoke.

The landlord followed, wondering what he meant by so odd a remark.

But the captain said not another word on the point to enlighten him.

"I will have breakfast," he said, "and a rest, for I have travelled many miles. When they come to you for the money, let me know."

Much to the landlord's astonishment, twelve o'clock came, but no steward.

An hour elapsed.

His amazement was unbounded, for he had anticipated that he would be there to the moment.

"There is something in all this which I can't make out," said the landlord. "I wonder how my unknown benefactor could have found out that Mr. Goslings would be delayed?"

To ponder over this was quite useless.

In the meantime, afternoon having arrived, the captain looked up the money.

He was well aware of the great necessity there was for absolute caution, because in paying the cash back to the man from whom it had been taken there was the risk that he might recognise some of it.

Much to the highwayman's satisfaction, however, he discovered that the amount was in gold and silver.

He inspected many of the coins with the utmost care, but failed to discover any marks which might lead to their identification.

The three hundred pounds he left counted out upon the table; the remainder—and there was nearly another hundred—he slipped into his pocket, and then rang the bell for the landlord.

"Has not the steward come yet?"

"Not yet, sir."

"That is strange! I scarcely thought he would be so late as this. However, there is the money—take it now, and you will be in readiness to pay. If he is much longer I shall leave without seeing him, and yet I should much like to be a witness."

"Of course, sir!" answered the landlord, upon whom the sight of the money seemed to have produced a stupifying effect.

Then recovering a little, he asked:

"And when shall you want me to repay this?"

"Whenever you can spare the money; I am in no hurry I will call from time to time to see you."

What more the landlord would have said is uncertain, for just then both were startled by the rumbling of carriage wheels.

"At last!" ejaculated the captain.

The landlord looked out from the window, and saw that it was indeed the steward who had just arrived.

"Say that the money has been lent you by a friend," whispered the highwayman; "and refuse to furnish any further information until I give you leave."

"Hullo!—hullo, there!" cried Mr. Goslings, in disagreeable tones. "Where are you? Take possession, Roberts, and bundle them out neck and crop! I am late, but this little job won't take long, thank goodness! Oh dear!"

"What is the matter, sir?" asked another voice.

It belonged to the man who had been left in charge of the place.

"Matter—everything's the matter! I have been stopped and robbed! I am a ruined man! Oh dear!—oh dear! But seize the things and turn these obstinate wretches out! I shall be easier in my mind then."

The way in which the steward spoke affected Captain Hawk to such a degree that he could scarcely control the strong impulse he had to spring out and inflict summary chastisement upon him.

"Go on," he whispered, through his clenched teeth—"go and stop him. Give him the money, but take care to have a proper receipt."

The landlord nodded and obeyed.

Before he appeared, however, the steward called for him at the top of his voice, and poured out a torrent of the grossest abuse.

"Don't distress yourself, Mr. Goslings," said the landlord, quietly. "A friend has found me the money. Take it. Let me have the receipt, and then the sooner you carry your carcass over my threshold the better I shall be pleased."

Absolute amazement prevented the steward from saying a single word.

Nothing could have caused him a greater shock of surprise than thus finding the landlord prepared to satisfy the demands made upon him.

"Write out the receipt," continued the landlord, who intensely enjoyed the discomfiture of his enemy, "and count over the money. Don't stand there like one half-crazed!"

"And who lent you this money, may I ask?" said the steward, with great difficulty recovering the use of his voice.

"You may not ask—I shall not tell you. Once more I say, write out the receipt and then depart."

"But—but——"

"You did not anticipate this, did you? You made sure that I had not a friend in the world. You see, you are mistaken, and all your plans fall to the ground."

Great as was the steward's discomfiture, and much as he wished to have his revenge upon the landlord, he could do nothing else than take the money.

Quivering with mortification, he took a pen and wrote out the receipt.

The landlord pocketed it in a moment, for he knew that while he held it he was safe.

"I have the very great pleasure of wishing you good day," he said. "And good day to you, Roberts, and I heartily hope that neither of you will ever cross my threshold again!"

Up to this moment, Captain Hawk had kept inside his room, where, as the door was a little way open, he had managed to hear every word.

Now he suddenly stepped forth

The steward gazed at him intently, but the captain, without pausing, made his way towards the back part of the house

"Who's that?" asked the steward.

"I don't know," said the landlord—"I never saw him till yesterday. Once more, good day."

Gnashing his teeth, Mr. Goslings walked to the front-door, but before he could emerge a troop of horsemen, with a sudden rush, reined-up in front of the inn.

They were police officers.

"Have you caught him?" asked the steward.

"Caught who?"

"Why, Captain Hawk, of course, blockhead!"

"Blockhead yourself!" answered the officer, hotly, who was by no means good-tempered under his failure. "What's it to do with you?"

"Do with me!" screamed the steward. "Why, if you hulking vagabonds had been doing your duty I should not have been robbed last night!"

"Robbed? What—by Captain Hawk?"

"Yes, of nearly five hundred pounds. I will give two hundred myself to the man that makes him prisoner, and the squire will give another two—so it will pay you all well."

"Curse the fellow!" said the officer. "We have ridden after him until we can scarcely sit in our saddles, or our horses put one foot before another! We have heard of him in fifty places, but downright fatigue prevents us from going any further till we have had a rest."

"Then don't stop here," cried the steward, rejoiced at being able to do the landlord this petty injury. "There is no accommodation here; but if you will go just about half a mile further you will come to the Pemberton Arms on the New Road, where you will find everything you can wish."

"No," said the officer, "I go no further. This will do for me very well."

The steward looked as though about to say something unusually vicious, when he was stopped by a loud shout coming from one of the officers.

"Look—look!" he screamed—"look there!"

With lightning-like swiftness every eye was turned in the direction towards which he pointed.

"May I be d—d!" ejaculated the principal officer. "There he is!"

"After him!" yelled the steward, executing under the influence of his strong excitement a kind of weird, fantastic dance—"after him! I will give another hundred if you will catch him now! That will be five hundred pounds extra to the reward!"

The promise of such a sum as this was well calculated to make the police officers strain every nerve, but under the present state of circumstances it produced no result.

Both horses and men were fairly dead beat.

Yet, in spite of this, they commenced a pursuit

The reader no doubt guesses what had happened.

Captain Hawk, while listening to what was taking place between the landlord and the steward, had chanced to look out at the window.

Fortunate indeed was it for him that he did so, for he caught sight of the troop of police officers approaching.

His mind was made up in a moment.

Emerging from the room in the way we have mentioned, he hastened to the stable, where, with great rapidity, he saddled and bridled his horse.

Having done this, he left the premises at the rear, and proceeded for some distance under cover of the buildings.

But one of the officers caught sight of him riding swiftly away, and recognised him.

Such a pursuit, however, as the present promised to be the highwayman felt he could laugh at, and so literally he turned round and did so.

This manifest mark of contempt annoyed the officers to such a degree that they forgot all about their fatigue.

Unmercifully belabouring and spurring their horses, they endeavoured to come up with him.

The steward flung himself into the carriage, and, with a volley of oaths, bade the coachman drive after the officers.

As for the landlord, he stood like one might be supposed to do who had by some magical process been converted into stone.

His lips, however, moved faintly.

"That Captain Hawk!" he whispered. "My benefactor a highwayman! Surely I dream, or else there is some strange mistake!"

"Oh, father," cried a tearful, trembling voice at his side, "can this be true? No, no—I will never believe it! And yet, look—look! See how he turns round and taunts them, and seems to dare them to follow! Alas—alas!"

It was as Lottie had said—the highwayman's actions could not be misunderstood.

The hour of sunset had by this time almost come.

There was a dim, fast-thickening mist hanging over distant objects, and the night promised to be such a one as would afford every facility for an escape.

But Captain Hawk seemed disinclined to try to get away.

As soon as he found some trees were intervening between himself and his pursuers, making it impossible for them to observe his actions, he drew rein.

"Gently," he said—"gently! I have not done with you yet, Mr. Goslings, as you will find; and I do not intend to allow myself to be scared away so easily! I want to get that three hundred pounds back again—I don't intend to allow the steward to retain it. My friend the landlord has a receipt in full of all demands, so he is all right, and I shall be no loser by the transaction."

By the perfectly cool manner in which Captain Hawk muttered these words to himself, it seemed pretty evident that he had never from the first contemplated allowing the steward to retain the money after it had been paid him by the landlord.

To persevere in this intention when so many police officers were in chase, with Mr. Goslings among them, was, however, almost more than might have been expected of the captain, despite the extreme audacity which characterised all his proceedings.

"This thickening gloom is in my favour," he continued, "and doubtless will enable me to conceal myself somewhere close at hand. But where?—that is the question."

He glanced around while these words were on his lips.

No place holding out the slightest prospect of affording him the shelter he desired could be beheld.

A ringing shout made him aware that the police officers had again got him in sight.

For the last time he waved his hand in defiance; and just touching Satan with the spur, flew off at such an amazing rate that the officers were discouraged from making any attempt to overtake him.

They would have abandoned the chase for the present had it not been for the steward, who, by a mixture of threats and promises of a rich reward, induced them to continue.

Captain Hawk had not to go far at that tremendous gallop before he was quite swallowed up by the evening mist.

Finding himself out of sight again, he once more stopped.

"If I could only see a hiding-place hereabouts," he exclaimed, "all would be well; I would remain in it until I found myself able to carry out my purpose with the steward."

Just at this moment he faintly descried among some tree-tops close at hand the chimneys and gables of a red-brick dwelling, which, from its position and general character, was doubtless an abode of some pretension.

"What place is that?" he said. "The old squire's mansion, perhaps. Yes, yes, that must be it; and I will just make an experiment to-night to see to what pass sheer audacity will carry me."

CHAPTER XV.

CAPTAIN HAWK GAINS THE INTERIOR OF THE SQUIRE'S ABODE, AND LEARNS SOME DEEPLY-INTERESTING PARTICULARS CONCERNING A FAMILY MYSTERY.

It will very soon be seen what Captain Hawk meant by his experiment.

Suddenly changing the direction in which he had been going, he walked his horse in a direct line towards some large wooden gates, which to all appearances communicated with the grounds surrounding the mansion.

Quite unfalteringly, he rode up to them, and with the butt-end of a pistol knocked loudly for admittance.

After a little delay, one half of the ponderous door was opened, and an old woman, bent almost double with age, made her appearance.

"Ha!" she cried—"at last—at last! Have you come from London, sir, with news of the squire's son? If so, you will indeed be welcome! My poor master is almost at death's door; but if he could only see Master George before his death I do believe all will be well."

This greeting took the captain greatly by surprise, as well it might—so much so that he was unable to remember the pretext which he had decided upon giving to procure his admittance.

But he retained his presence of mind sufficiently to pass through the gateway; and the old woman, with an exertion of strength which no one would believe her capable of making, closed the half of the door again.

By the time the clang caused by this operation had died away the highwayman had made up his mind.

It was to keep up, if possible, the delusion into which the old woman had fallen.

"Yes," he said, "I bring important news."

"Then ride on to the Hall," she cried, imploringly. "You will be most welcome. Lose not a moment."

In spite of this adjuration, the highwayman went no faster than at a walk along the fine old avenue.

"And that, then, is Pemberton Hall," he cried, as he came close to the front of the building, "and the old squire lies at the point of death! Strange—very strange! Here, however, of all the places in the world, that rascally steward will never think of looking for me. Yet it is where I am most likely to recover the three hundred pounds—if not, to discover some further tokens of his villany. After all, I think that is the most likely."

Having reached this point in his ruminations, he found himself in front of the main entrance to the Hall.

A man came forward and took his horse.

He resigned Satan with a slight sensation of uneasiness; but to have attempted to go to the stables would have been such an unusual proceeding that suspicion would infallibly be aroused.

All that he could do was to watch the direction taken, though that afforded him but little content.

He was ushered into the building by an obsequious domestic.

The moment he crossed the threshold Captain Hawk was conscious of the existence of that strange stillness which is ever found in a house where either death or sickness reigns.

The servant spoke to him in a funereal whisper.

"What is your pleasure?"

"To see the squire."

"Impossible, sir! I fear he is much worse this evening. If you will step into this room I will call the doctor."

Captain Hawk had no alternative before him than that of entering the reception-room, the door of which the servant noiselessly opened.

He closed it, and the highwayman was alone. He had only time enough to glance around at the various objects in the apartment before the doctor entered.

He stared hard at the captain, who in return saluted him with so courtly a bow as at once convinced the medical man that a gentleman stood before him.

"You wish to see the squire, I believe?"

Hawk bowed.

"Coming at this time, the request is a strange one; but doubtless the business is of urgency, and of an entirely private nature?"

The captain thought he could not make a better reply than by bowing again, and accordingly did so.

"And of an agitating nature, so far as my patient is concerned," continued the doctor; "therefore, despite its urgency, I must ask you to reserve it until the morning, when I trust he will be better able to listen to any communication you may have to make."

The captain professed to be seriously concerned at the delay, when, as we need scarcely say, he was heartily rejoiced, his object being merely to remain for a few hours beneath the shelter of that roof.

"If it must be so," he said, "of course I submit, though I would fain——"

"Believe me, sir, it is imperative. The squire is in a most critical condition. As you must know, his son's misdeeds prey heavily upon him, and anything on that subject would be attended with the worst consequences."

"But in the morning——"

"In the morning, I think, if no change for the worse takes place, you may have your interview."

"Many thanks!"

"In the meantime, you are welcome to the best accommodation the Hall affords. I will have a bed-chamber prepared for your reception."

With these words, the doctor withdrew.

No sooner had the door closed than Captain Hawk, drawing a long breath, muttered:

"Now, I would not mind giving any sum within reason if I could only learn who the deuce they take me to be. However, my object is achieved—I am safely harboured here for awhile. By the morning I shall be miles and miles away."

To speak the truth, when the highwayman decided upon this bold and novel plan of getting out of the way of his pursuers, he little expected that Fortune would favour his audacity in so remarkable a manner.

It was not until some time had elapsed that he called to mind what he had heard about the power exercised by the steward.

That worthy had not yet arrived; but upon his doing so, was there not every probability that he would walk in for the purpose of ascertaining the guest's business.

A very little reflection convinced the captain that there was very great danger indeed of this.

"Confound it!" he cried. "How came I to forget that? Why, it would spoil all! No matter; I see my way out of the difficulty. I will plead fatigue, and make that an excuse for retiring at once to my room, although the hour is such an early one."

When Captain Hawk arrived at a decision he never lost any time in carrying it out, and so, without a moment's pause, he rung the bell.

His request was complied with readily, and in a few minutes he found himself alone, with the door closed, in one of the best-appointed bed-chambers in the Hall.

His first act was to cross the room to the window.

Looking forth, he saw that the scene without was bathed in moonlight.

At any other time he must have been struck with the extreme beauty of the prospect, but now his whole attention was absorbed by some dark, moving figures, upon which his eyes immediately had rested.

They were coming towards the Hall, and as they advanced the highwayman was enabled to recognise them.

Foremost walked the steward, and behind him came the officers.

Captain Hawk shrunk back with a heart beating a little faster than usual.

Had they learned from the old woman at the gate that he had entered?

If so, what was to be done?

The officers were talking, but the distance was too great for him to overhear what they said.

As though deprived of all further motion, the captain stood until the whole party passed round an angle of the building and disappeared.

"Have they tracked me?" he asked, as he drew forth his pistols and examined them. "That I shall soon know, for they will be in no doubt as to my precise position. I fancy they are only coming here because they have found their search to be a successless one."

Nevertheless, he waited for some time in anxious expectation.

All remained still.

"I am right," he added; "but I shall be better satisfied when I see them leave the premises, as I shall do if the steward has only brought them here for the purpose of giving them some refreshment."

He waited long, but had the satisfaction of finding his conjectures verified.

The officers, little dreaming they had been so near their prey, departed, and the captain with a chuckle turned back into the room.

"When all is still within the house," he said, "I will take steps to have my settlement with the steward; till then, I will snatch a little rest."

He flung himself, dressed as he was, upon the bed.

A profound silence prevailed, but he could not believe the hour to be late enough to allow him to put his design into execution.

As he thus lay waiting, a drowsy feeling came over him, from which, however, he was aroused by a sharp snapping sound.

Not only was he awake in a moment, but he also had the presence of mind to remain quite still.

A creaking noise followed, like that which is often given forth when one attempts to open a door stealthily.

Raising his head slightly and stretching open his eyes to their fullest extent, the highwayman tried to make out what was going forward.

The moon was shining in at the window, rendering most of the objects in the room tolerably distinct

The creaking noise continued, and the captain, turning his eyes in the direction whence the sound came, saw the centre door of a massive oak wardrobe slowly opening.

Directly afterwards, something in human shape stepped forth.

The captain held his breath.

With a very slow, gliding movement, and without the least sound of a footfall, this figure made its way across the chamber, passing close to the foot of the bed on which the highwayman lay.

On, steadily on, it went, until the opposite wall was gained.

Here the shadows were thicker and deeper than elsewhere, and Captain Hawk had no little difficulty in making out what was going forward.

But another snap struck very plainly upon his ears, and he fancied he caught sight of an opening door.

About this he was not certain until he heard it closed.

For a moment or two after this he did not venture to move.

Then rising slowly, he slipped off the bed, and with a silentness of tread only equalled by the mysterious being who had crossed the room before him, he made his way to where it had disappeared.

He paused in front of a large wardrobe of carved oak, very similar in its appearance to the one on the other side.

It had a centre door, which was now closed.

"I must fathom this," said the captain, mentally. "When there is so much care taken to be silent the secret is sure to be worth finding out. Now, this intruder is either at this moment within the wardrobe, or else has passed through into another chamber."

Of the two suppositions the latter was by far the most likely to be the true one.

Very carefully the captain now set to work to try to open the door.

This promised to be no easy matter, for, as far as he could ascertain, it was fast locked.

But Captain Hawk was generally prepared to cope with such difficulties as these, and his next act was to take from one of his pockets something which looked like a small steel hook.

This he inserted into the keyhole, and after a few turns succeeded in forcing back the bolt into the wards of the lock.

The snap which this made sounded in his ears very alarmingly, and caused him to suspend his operations.

The door, as though inviting him to pursue his investigations, slowly creaked open.

Finding all was still, he peeped into the wardrobe.

The darkness was too great for him to see anything.

"Dare I show a light?" he asked himself—"that is the question. I am afraid I shall be obliged to run the risk."

The intense silence which prevailed emboldened him to run the risk.

He lighted only a "thieves' match," which gave forth a very faint amount of illumination.

No sooner, however, did its rays enable him to catch a glimpse of the interior of the wardrobe than he gave a sudden start, and scarcely was able to suppress the exclamation which rose to his lips.

"How lucky I did not try to enter!" he ejaculated, in a whisper. "If so, discovery or death would have been certain."

He came a little closer, and held the almost burned-out match close to the flooring—or, rather, what should have been the flooring inside the wardrobe, for none was visible.

Instead, there was a black, yawning space, about the depth of which he was unable to form the least idea before his light went out.

The sudden darkness made the chasm appear doubly terrible.

"I have a lamp," the captain said. "All seems still—very still It will be the safer plan to light it, if I am to continue my investigations—and to discover who it was that crossed this room I am determined!"

Accordingly, he drew forth a very small dark lantern, and, having lighted it, he was enabled to examine anything before him without diffusing much light around.

He found that the wardrobe had a floor or bottom which lifted up like the lid of a box.

This was now fixed up by means of a small iron hook, from which circumstance the captain inferred that the mysterious being intended to choose this way for his return.

It was not until he stooped down and directed the condensed beams of the lamp into the abyss that he discovered some steep steps leading abruptly downwards.

They were blackened by age, and thickly overlaid with dust and cobwebs.

"Not a very inviting place," he said; "but I will find out where it leads to, at all events."

Without any more delay he commenced the descent of the precipitous steps, concealing the light of his lamp as much as possible by keeping it under the skirt of his coat.

"Twelve!" he murmured, as he reached the foot of the staircase. "I ought now to be on the ground floor."

A narrow passage extended itself in front of him.

Along this he made his way with increased caution.

A few steps brought him to what was apparently its termination.

The low and seemingly far-off murmur of voices came now upon his ears.

He turned the dark slide over the lens of his lantern and listened.

Much to his vexation, however, he found himself unable to distinguish one word that was said, though he was tolerably certain that the speakers were only just on the other side of the wooden partition which formed the end of the passage.

After the lapse of a moment or two Captain Hawk ventured to show a little light.

His sole attention was turned to the partition, by the appearance of which he quickly concluded that it formed a secret door of some kind.

On the other side, beyond all doubt, every care had been taken to conceal the existence of such a thing, but on this, where there could be no particular motive for concealment, the long spring which held it in its place was distinctly visible.

After looking at it attentively, the captain fancied that with due care he should be able to draw back the principal portion of the spring in such a way as to release the fastening noiselessly.

Should this turn out to be right, he would most likely be able, by leaving the secret door a very little ajar, to hear what was taking place in the adjoining room.

Perhaps be an eye witness, too.

He tried, and found he had not been mistaken.

The secret door opened noiselessly to the extent of about a quarter of an inch, but in releasing the spring again a slight sound was made.

"What's that?" said a voice, suddenly.

CHAPTER XVI.

CAPTAIN HAWK OVERHEARS A DIABOLICAL PLOT.—THE NARROW ESCAPE.—THE YOUNG MAN'S TERRORS.—CAPTAIN HAWK STEPS THROUGH THE SECRET PANEL.

The tones were plainly expressive of surprise and alarm.

Captain Hawk pressed himself against the wall, covered his lantern, and became profoundly still, fearing even to draw breath.

"What is the matter?" said another voice, which made the captain start slightly, for he knew by the sound who it was that spoke.

"Did you hear nothing?"

"Nothing whatever. It was some chance sound of no importance. You are nervous. If you let such trifles as these affect you, all will be lost. Let me pour you out a drop more brandy."

There was a silence, which was broken only by the gurgle of the spirit as it flowed from the neck of the decanter.

"So, Mr. Steward," said Captain Hawk, mentally, "you

are mixed up in this matter. I am not surprised at that. Was it you that crept through my room, I wonder?"

He did not pursue his speculations further, but bent all his faculties to listening as the conversation recommenced.

"I am nervous," said the first speaker. "I shudder now from head to foot. What horrid brandy that is! I feel as though I had drunk ice-cold water."

"Hush—hush! I tell you this will undo us both. Why not be calm and collected, as I am?" said the steward.

"Because I am not quite so great a villain as you are, I suppose."

"You are merry, Master George. But take care that your pleasantry is not ill-timed. You do not seem to understand what important consequences hinge upon to-night's doings."

"I do—I do."

"All depends, then, on yourself. It rests with you, and you alone, whether you remain for ever an outcast—a beggar in purse and reputation—or whether you assume your true position as head over this household and master of the revenues of this vast estate."

"And the choice is in my hands, you say?"

"It is."

"How so? My father, I am convinced, will never—never forgive me."

The steward uttered an impatient ejaculation.

"Forgive!" he cried—"who talks of forgiveness? You must be a fool, Master George, to think of such a thing. I tell you the will is made!"

"Made?"

"Yes, and it is out of his power to make another!"

"And you are acquainted with the terms of it?" said the other, in a voice which showed how deeply he was agitated.

"I am."

"What are they? Name them—name them at once!"

"I will tell you your share of your father's wealth. He bequeaths you just—one shilling."

An angry oath followed.

"Hush—hush! You will be heard; and if your presence in this house to-night was only guessed at, all hope of adjusting things better will be at an end."

"And the remainder?" asked the other, as though with difficulty repressing an ebullition of anger. "To whom is the rest left?"

"To your cousin."

"Mark Appleton?"

"The same."

"Curse him!"

"So say I! But you need not alarm the house! Drink some more brandy! It is of the best quality, as you would find could you subdue your excitement."

Another pause followed, and Captain Hawk took advantage of it to change his position slightly.

He was now able to have a good look at the speakers.

The room in which they sat was of an antique character, yet the massive furniture, the large portraits, and the panelled wainscoting gave it an air of magnificence, which was heightened by the ruddy glow the bright-burning wood fire dispersed around.

The villanous steward was sitting in an old-fashioned arm-chair with his back towards the secret door, but yet his position was such an enabled the unsuspected listener to observe him well.

Nearly opposite to him sat a young man, whose appearance gave unmistakable evidence that his life was passed in the midst of the haunts of dissipation.

Although well and fashionably dressed, there was an air of general recklessness and carelessness about him.

His countenance now was distorted by the angry feelings which were struggling in his bosom, and the manner in which he clutched the carved arms of the chair in which he sat manifested his extreme agitation.

The steward watched him closely, and all the while he kept a half-pitying smile upon his lips.

"What is to be done?" the young man said, at length. "Why on earth don't you speak out? I can tell by the look of that cur[illegible]ngly face of yours that you have something to propose!"

"Don't lose your temper, Master George," rejoined the other, calmly—"if you do, the consequences will be fatal to us. The evil is great, but——"

"But what?"

"It is not past remedy."

It is impossible to convey an idea of the peculiar significance with which these last few words were uttered.

"What do you propose?"

"You are too much excited for me to speak now. Drink some more brandy."

"Curse the brandy!"

"Hush—hush!"

"Will you speak?"

"I will. But don't be violent, or you will be ruined, and so shall I as well."

"Ay, there it is."

"Of course it is."

"I am calm then, and I will promise to be, no matter what you may say."

The steward gave a half-apprehensive glance about him, and drew his chair a little closer.

"Master George," he said, in a subdued voice, though Captain Hawk heard every word—"Master George, if you will only control yourself a little and be guided by me you may have your revenge upon Mark Appleton, and be the sole and undisputed possessor of your father's property, which by every right belongs to you—no one ought to be able to deprive you of it."

"I—I will be calm."

"Will you listen to my advice?"

"Yes—yes! Go on!"

"Your father has made a will. You know his peculiar ways well enough to feel certain that he would not have done this had he not felt his end was near."

"Then he was compelled to have a lawyer?"

"No—no," answered the steward. "You know his foolish prejudice against every member of the legal profession—he always swore he would die without making a will, and would have done so but for his firmly-fixed purpose of disinheriting you."

The young man ground his teeth.

"How, then, did he make a will?"

"He has written it with his own hand. I and my son—who can be relied on—are the sole witnesses to it."

"And this will?"

"You want to know where it is?"

"I do."

"Ha, ha! Master George, you were not prepared for this; but all the while you must know you have had some one at work whose determination from the first has been to serve your interests, because——"

"Because what?"

"Because I like you," responded the steward, with a hideous smile; "and because I know you are not the one to forget to reward an important service."

"And you will suppress this will for me?"

"I don't say that, Master George. I like to be careful in what I am about—and yet I will aid you."

"Why don't you speak out?"

"Your father is at the point of death. He will not live to witness the setting of another sun, although the doctor professes to hold out hopes of his recovery. Should he die, and the will be found, you are a beggar."

"But should he mention it?"

"Impossible. He is speechless, and has been for many hours."

"In a word," said the young man, impatiently, "what will you do?"

The rascally steward sunk his voice still lower.

"The will is written on a small piece of paper, which lies under your father's pillow. He will not suffer it to be further away from him, so fearful is he that his intentions may be balked."

"Well—well?"

"I will take you to the room; I will open the door. In all probability he is sleeping; if so, all you have to do is to cross the room swiftly, slip your hand beneath the pillow and withdraw the will. When you have that safely in your hand all will be well—the inheritance is yours."

These words produced so great an effect upon the young man to whom they were addressed that he trembled most violently from head to foot, nor had his life depended upon it could he have subdued it.

"Drink again, Master George," continued the tempter "Your nerves are in a sad state indeed; but there is nothing in the world like brandy to steady them. Pour out again."

But the young man's hand shook to such a degree that

he could not grasp the neck of the decanter, so the steward had to pour out the spirit and hold the glass to his dupe's lips.

He drank it eagerly, and, as could be seen, no more effect was produced by it than by so much water.

The glass was drained.

"There," he said, "you will be better directly, and then you must come with me. The house is quite quiet now, and all you have to do is to follow me silently up the grand staircase."

The young man could not, however, yet compose himself enough to speak.

A silence of some moments' duration ensued, which might have lasted much longer had it not been broken by the steward.

"Come," he said, "precious moments are passing now. Give me the word—say one way or the other. Either make up your mind to forego all this which you have ever thought your own and live a life of future misery and embarrassment, or come with me and by one simple act secure yourself from all future ills. Silent still? Will you not tell me your decision?"

The young man had to make several efforts before he could force to his lips the words:

"I—I will do it!"

"Of course you will! You would have been a madman to refuse—you must see that very clearly! And all is so simple, too! There is no danger to be incurred and no risk run worth thinking of for a single moment. All you have to do is to take the paper."

"W-will not you do it for me?" gasped the squire's evil-minded son. "If so, you shall be well rewarded. My nervousness might spoil all. I will stay here until you return with the paper."

"Never!" was the reply, pronounced with unexpected firmness.

"Never? Why not?"

"Because, as you will be the gainer in every way, you must perform the act yourself. I will not."

"Remember, I will be liberal!"

"No matter. The will must be taken by you or not at all."

"Do you think he sleeps?"

"I will ascertain whether he does so before you enter."

"And is there no nurse?"

"Yes."

"And what of her?"

"She will not trouble you. I supplied her with a bottle of comfort, extra strong—she is fast asleep enough by this time, I'll warrant."

"I will do it," said the squire's son, springing to his feet, and speaking with sudden resolution—"I must do it! I cannot help myself! Without this property my life would be a worthless burden to me!"

"Come on! Excuse me, Master George, but the man in your position who would hesitate about doing what I suggest when the means are so very simple and dangerless, would be both a coward and a fool!"

The steward rose while he spoke these words with great vehemence, and pouring out a glassful of brandy, drank it off himself.

His companion, whose courage was of a very inferior quality indeed, showed every sign of trepidation. He glanced around him as though he expected every moment his eye would light upon some spectre.

"Drink this!" cried the steward, once more refilling the glass. "Surely your blood will be warmer then! Ha!"

"Mercy—mercy! Oh! what is it?" cried the young man, in an agony of fright, and letting fall the glass which he had half raised to his lips.

"Nothing. Don't be so scared. I see, when you entered you forgot to close the secret panel properly. It stands a little way open."

"But—but I did close it."

"You could not have done so, unless it has come open itself. The spring is old and worn—that may be it."

The steward, while giving utterance to these words, rapidly crossed the room.

He flung open the secret door.

The young man, shaking like an aspen leaf, remained near the table, by grasping which he strove to steady himself.

Captain Hawk was somewhat to blame for this discovery, for, rendered over bold, he had pushed the door still further open, in order that there should be no impediment to his seeing well into the room.

But at the first warning words from the steward he hastily drew back, and flattened himself as closely as he could against the wall of the passage.

He had no time to take any other precaution against being seen before the steward appeared on the threshold.

There was no light save that which came from the fire, but this was bright enough, though it failed to illuminate the gloomy recesses of the secret passage.

"There's—there's no one there, is there?"

"No one, of course! Who should be?" answered the steward, straining his eyes to pierce the darkness. "Your nervousness will be the ruin of us yet. Hark!"

For a moment he listened most intently.

But all was still.

Satisfied that the cause lay in his companion's negligence, he closed the door with a sharp sound.

Captain Hawk now heard nothing more save an indistinct murmuring sound.

But presently that ceased.

He waited a moment or two.

Then cautiously approached the secret panel.

Pulling back the spring, he opened the door in the same noiseless manner as before.

The room was empty.

Silence was all around.

"A nice pair, truly!" he said, as he pushed the door open to its full extent and stepped into the room. "And what a narrow escape I had of being found! That would have been a slight surprise for the steward, I rather think!"

CHAPTER XVII.

THE SQUIRE'S ROOM.—THE MURDER.—THE STOLEN WILL.—THE FALSE ACCUSATION, AND THE DISCOVERY OF THE HIGHWAYMAN.

Captain Hawk carefully closed the secret panel.

"I will take the steward's word this is a drop of good brandy, and that passage is confoundedly dusty. Ah!"

He took a deep draught of the spirit, and then, with a rapid step, made his way to the door of the room.

It was rather a perilous thing to open it, but he judged that by this time the steward and his companion had got some distance away.

He opened the door accordingly.

Before him, he saw the foot of the principal staircase, which was dimly illuminated by a light at some distance above.

As silently as a ghost, the captain strode across the small space which intervened between the door of the room and the staircase, and began to ascend.

The soft, luxurious carpeting, which suffered his feet to sink in at every step, did away with all fear that his approach would be heard.

He found the light proceeded from a lamp placed upon a bracket at the entrance to a long corridor, from which the doors of the various rooms opened.

It was now necessary for him to be doubly careful, as this lamp would reveal him to anyone who might be on the watch.

"How am I to find out the squire's chamber?" he asked himself. "If I had but an idea of its position I should not care."

Just at this moment the faint sound of whispering voices came upon his ears.

He listened intently.

He was not long in deciding whence the sound proceeded.

This discovered, he ascended another stair, which brought his head a little above the top of the staircase.

Very dimly, at the extremity of the corridor, he could distinguish two shadowy forms.

By the gestures used he concluded that the young man was making a vain attempt to persuade his companion to enter the sick chamber and purloin the will.

But the steward was by far too wily to do anything of the kind.

Then came silence, and after that a door close to them was opened.

[LIEUTENANT TRACY IN PURSUIT OF THE BLACK HIGHWAYMAN.]

A faint light streamed forth, which, falling on the two shadowy forms, made their identity past question.

In obedience to a furious gesture, the young man, after several shrinking efforts, crossed the threshold.

The steward stood without, his features bearing an expression which was by far more fiend-like than human.

Captain Hawk had come thus far without having troubled himself to ask what steps he should take.

His determination, however, was taken—it was to foil the steward and his accomplice in their nefarious plan.

Suddenly a loud cry broke the intense silence.

It was followed by the sound of struggling.

Captain Hawk saw the steward stand irresolute a moment, and then dash suddenly into the room.

After this, to ascend the remaining stairs and hurry along the corridor took the highwayman but a few seconds.

On gaining the door through which the steward had darted so swiftly, he saw before him a long narrow room, at the further end of which was another door standing open a little way.

It was through this inner doorway that the gleam of light came which shone feebly out into the passage.

At full speed Captain Hawk traversed this apartment, and then found before him an antique-looking bedchamber.

There was no struggle now.

The steward, his face the very picture of atrocity, was holding a large pillow over the face of the person occupying the bed—who was, he had no doubt, the squire.

Master George, as he had been called, held in his trembling fingers a folded sheet of bluish-coloured paper.

He had seen Captain Hawk suddenly appear upon the threshold, and, having done so, his terror was so great that he was deprived of all motion save a convulsive twitching of his features.

No. 6.

GRATIS with this Number, The COLOURED PICTURE of CAPTAIN HAWK TAKEN PRISONER, AND TREATED MAZEPPA FASHION.

The steward turned and saw him too.

He, for the moment, was horror-struck at finding himself caught in the diabolical act of murdering his master.

But he was a bold and hardened villain, as his next action proved.

Leaping from the bed, and before the highwayman could imagine what he was about, he rang a bell with all his might.

"Help—help!" he cried. "Robbers and murder! Help—help!"

Then lowering his voice and addressing the young man, he said, with great rapidity of utterance:

"Courage—courage! You have the will. Fly—fly! Make all speed, and leave the rest to me!"

This speech seemed to have the effect of rousing the young man from his stupefaction, and he rushed hastily towards another door.

But Captain Hawk pounced upon him, and in an instant snatched the folded paper from Master George's trembling fingers.

"Foiled!" he exclaimed, as he thrust the precious document into his breast. "Your scheme is foiled!"

Furious at what he saw, the steward, with ungovernable fury, flung himself upon the highwayman.

A terrific struggle ensued, for the captain's strength was scarcely able to cope with the vigour which desperation had lent the steward.

Long ere it was over, the squire's unworthy son had dashed through the doorway and disappeared.

The steward's efforts were all directed towards obtaining possession of the paper which had been snatched from the grasp of his accomplice, but this the captain was able to prevent.

The loud cries of many voices, the trampling of many feet, and all those sounds which accompany the arousal of a household in the middle of the night, could now be heard.

The steward renewed his vociferations.

"Help—help!" he cried. "Quick—quick! There has been murder done! Help me to secure the murderer! Help—help, I say!"

As he pronounced the last words, a tumultuous throng of terrified, bewildered people arrived upon the scene.

Most carried lights, and all had hurried on their clothing with all haste; but on gaining the threshold of the squire's room, they stood motionless and horror-struck.

"Seize him!" cried the steward, again—"seize the murderer of your master! I was in time to witness the perpetration of the deed, yet not to prevent it. Are you all stocks and stones? Help, I say! I can hold him no longer! It is Captain Hawk—Captain Hawk, the highwayman! A thousand pounds reward!"

Sheer amazement made the domestics incapable of speedy interference.

Something like the same feeling also made Captain Hawk cease his furious struggles.

Certainly a more audacious act than that of the steward's could hardly be conceived.

But with that quickness of mind which had enabled him all his life to play the rogue with so much success, he saw that he should not have much difficulty in fixing the odium of his crime upon the highwayman.

"You infernal rascal!" Captain Hawk cried, and renewing his struggles at the same moment. "Let go, I say!"

The captain put forth all his strength.

The steward, exhausted by his former efforts, could not stand against it, and in another second he was hurled heavily to the ground.

But by this time the assembled crowd had recovered themselves from the first shock of their surprise, and with one impulse they rushed forward with the intention of laying violent hands upon the highwayman.

Captain Hawk, however, sprang to the window.

He did not stop to try to undo any of the fastenings, but with one crash forced his way completely through it.

"After him!" yelled the steward, rising partially from the floor. "Don't let him escape! Quick—quick!"

But the space through which Captain Hawk had flung himself was so small and so surrounded with jagged pieces of glass that not one thought of following him.

The act of removing the fastenings of course caused a slight delay—more than was usual, in consequence of the excited state everyone was in.

When the captain made his way so suddenly through the window he was quite prepared for a fall to a considerable distance.

But it happened that there was a balcony on the outside, and on this he alighted without sustaining the least injury.

Gathering himself up, he ran hastily along in what he conceived was the direction of the stables.

The extremity of the balcony was quickly reached, but not before the whole of the aroused household had poured through the window.

Captain Hawk swung himself over the iron boundary railing, and, letting himself down to the full length of his arms, dropped into the garden.

As he alighted upon a well-cultivated flower-bed, the shock of the descent was not worth heeding.

"I must escape," he said. "Flight is my only chance. Some other time I will take care to deliver this will to the rightful owner. Would that I could form an idea of the whereabouts of the stables!"

Stooping down in the hope of being able to avoid observation, he ran swiftly along in a strange, crouching attitude, which, as he kept close to the building, diminished the chances of his being seen.

By this time so general was the alarm, and so widespread, that lights were gleaming from every window; and, as if to spread the catastrophe far and wide, a bell in one of the turrets of the mansion sent forth a tremendous clang.

Yet Captain Hawk ran on until all at once he came upon a party of men-servants carrying stable lanterns, and armed with pitchforks and other formidable weapons.

He stopped and changed his course before the men were aware of what had occurred.

But the cries of the others and the rush of the highwayman's feet quickly enlightened them.

Forced thus to quit the contiguity of the mansion, Captain Hawk despaired of regaining his horse.

There was just the chance that if he gave his signal Satan might hear it, and contrive to gain his side.

It was, however, with no sanguine hopes that he tried the experiment.

He waited breathlessly for a moment, during which his pursuers gained upon him fearfully.

No sound came to his eager ears, however, that indicated his steed's approach.

"I must abandon him for the present," he said, clenching his teeth. "I must seek on foot some secure hiding-place, or I shall be overwhelmed with numbers."

The retinue of servants which the old squire kept was a large one, and every one had eagerly turned out, in the hope of capturing him who they had so artfully been told was the murderer.

Cursing the steward with all his heart, Captain Hawk, with all the speed he was capable of making, rushed across the park, among the trees of which he hoped ere long to elude his pursuers.

But the excited servants were so close behind him as to be able to see the route he took, and, instigated by the cries of the steward, strained every nerve to overtake the fugitive.

It was, therefore, with a sensation of extreme relief that he found himself fairly under cover of the huge trees.

Then gathering himself up for a final effort, he bounded over the ground with so much fleetness that his pursuers were soon left many yards behind.

Breathlessness at length compelled him to come to a standstill, but even then he had not got so far away but that he could see the lights the servants carried flashing through the trees.

"Where shall I hide?" he said, mentally. "If I continue thus, I shall ere long reach the boundary of the park, and then in the open country I shall have no chance. Will a tree serve me?" he added, glancing up at a huge chesnut under whose far-spreading boughs he had chanced to halt. "It may be so. The night is dark, and if they should only pass beneath it, what would be easier than to descend and start off for the stables? Ten to one if anybody is left there now."

There seemed so much feasibility about this proceeding that, without further consideration, he prepared to mount.

This happened to be easy, for there was about eight feet from the ground a stout horizontal bough, which, by springing up, he managed to grasp with both hands, and in less than a moment afterwards he was snugly ensconced amid the dense foliage.

Scarcely, however, had he settled himself than his pursuers arrived beneath the tree.

"Stop," said some one, in a gasping voice—"stop! I can't hear him now. Depend upon it he has hidden himself somewhere! Listen, all of you!"

Captain Hawk held his breath.

The little party was not in very good condition for listening, in consequence of the breathless state of each member of it.

"I can't hear him," said the voice which had before spoken. "This is what I feared. If he has hidden himself in one of these trees, how are we to find out which?"

This was an unanswerable question.

"Hilloa, there!" said another voice, coming from some distance off. "What are you stopping for? Have you lost him?"

This was the steward.

"We fancy he has hidden himself, sir."

"Very likely. Get to the park palings, and form a guard round as well as you can, so as to see he does not leave. By that time the police officers will be here, and they will unkennel him, I'll be bound!"

"Then you have sent for them, sir?"

"Of course I have! But off with you at once!"

In obedience to this command, the servants dispersed themselves in order to gain the park palings at different points, the steward accompanying them.

"Now is my time," murmured the highwayman, lowering himself from the tree as soon as his foes had got to a little distance. "If I can only manage to reach the stables, all will be well."

There was no little peril in making this attempt, but all ordinary danger was despised by Captain Hawk.

He made his way with great swiftness from tree to tree.

But just as he was about to emerge from the park into the open ground which intervened between it and the mansion, he caught sight of flashing lanterns.

He paused, of course, and then his ears were assailed by the sound of voices and the trampling of heavy footsteps.

"Let the park be surrounded," cried a loud voice, "and take care to keep good watch. We will drive him out before long. Remember, there will be something handsome for the man who seizes him."

With great swiftness the men formed themselves into a line across the open piece of garden ground; and such was their proximity that Captain Hawk felt it would be quite impossible to pass them unseen.

In the meanwhile, a small, well-armed party marched into the park.

"What is to be done?" said the highwayman, dashing the heavy drops of perspiration from his brow. "I cannot gain the stables that way, and if I linger here long I shall certainly be discovered."

How to contrive to leave the park he knew not, for by this time, doubtless, the boundary was well watched at every point.

"Luck must befriend me!" he cried, striking off in an opposite direction. "Oh, Mr. Steward, I only wish I was within arm's-length of you!"

He paused abruptly, for a crackling sound among the bushes close by came with unpleasant plainness upon his ears.

CHAPTER XVIII.

THE INTERVIEW BETWEEN LORD HARCLIFFE AND PETERSON, THE OFFICER.—A RIDE ON THE WESTERN ROAD.—THE RETURNING VEHICLE.—THE MYSTERIOUS STRANGER.

We return now to Lord Harcliffe.

A dark shade passed over his features while his attendant spoke, but it was of so transient a character as to make it hard to say whether it had appeared at all.

"Excuse me, friends," he said, rising from his chair; "I have a little business of importance to transact. But do not let my absence interfere with the circulation of the bottle. I will be back again with you in a few moments."

He quitted the room.

As soon as ever he crossed the threshold a deep frown settled upon his countenance, while he murmured some words that were inaudible.

An obsequious servant opened the door of the dining-room, and Lord Harcliffe, with a deeper frown than ever, stalked in.

Peterson, the police officer, was standing in the centre of the spacious apartment, which was only dimly illuminated by a couple of wax candles that were burning on a side-table.

"Well!" said Lord Harcliffe, sternly and angrily. "To what cause may I attribute your visit? Speak quickly, for I have no time to spare!"

Peterson bowed—then tried to speak; but the words dying away upon his lips, he bowed again.

The fact was, just as his lordship entered, he had been struck with the consciousness that he had come upon a very foolish errand, and that, though his suspicions were strong, he ought to have waited until something more happened to confirm them.

Lord Harcliffe flung himself into a chair, and drew forth a watch.

"I have just five minutes that I can devote to you, and no longer," he said; "so be speedy in making your communication, which I assume to be of some importance, or you would not intrude upon me at this unseasonable hour!"

"It—it is of importance, my lord," stammered Peterson; "and I trust your lordship will excuse me——"

"Well, well!"

"You may not recollect me again," Peterson continued; "but I stopped your lordship——"

"Yes, yes—I remember!"

"I told you the Black Highwayman was abroad, and I wish to know whether you reached home unmolested."

"Yes, certainly I did! Why do you ask?"

"Because, my lord, if you will remember, your lordship, on pulling up in your gig, said something about a valise."

"Well; and what of that?"

"Why, simply, your lordship, that as I was riding back to London my man happened to meet with an accident. His horse shied, and flung him into a ditch—fortunately a dry one. Scrambling up, he put his hand on something which excited his curiosity. He called to me, and upon examination, it proved to be a small leather travelling portmanteau or valise."

"Indeed!"

"Yes. Upon further examination still, we found it had been rudely cut open with a knife, and the contents, whatever they might have been, extracted. Evidently, it pointed to the committal of a robbery; and as your lordship had mentioned such an article, I thought I would call to see whether you had been unfortunate enough to have lost it, because——"

Peterson checked himself.

"Because what?"

"I was going to say, my lord, in the event of such a thing, I have a clue to the robber."

"Thanks for the trouble you have taken," said Lord Harcliffe, rising. "Luckily, I reached home safely. The valise you found must have belonged to some other unfortunate—not to me."

"Very good, my lord," said Peterson, rising. "I trust your lordship will forgive my intrusion."

"Oh yes—oh yes! Here, take this guinea, and drink my health with it. Good-bye!"

He rang the bell, and the door was opened.

Bowing again, Peterson took his leave, and Lord Harcliffe returned to the saloon, where his friends were impatiently awaiting him.

"Now, I am inclined to think," muttered Peterson, as soon as he gained the street, "that I managed that little stroke of business rather cleverly. I have had a good look at his lordship, and that, too, without giving him the least occasion to think that I had any particular motive in doing so. That much is accomplished. I should know him again, no matter where it might be."

He walked on briskly until he came to a dark gateway, and here he halted.

He was joined immediately by another person, who proved to be his fellow-officer, Hopkins.

"Have you seen him, Mr. Peterson?"

"Yes."

"And what do you think now?"

"I don't know what to think, Hopkins."

"Has he any suspicions of you?"

"None at all," answered Peterson, with a satisfied chuckle. "I made up a tale about a valise, which I pretended we had found."

"Oh!"

"And I have learned two most important things by doing so."

"What are they, Mr. Peterson?"

"Why, I have had such a long look at his face that I feel sure that I shall never forget it, but be able to tell it again, no matter where I may see it."

"And the other?"

"I have heard him speak, and should always know his voice again—yes, even if I only heard one word."

"But, Mr. Peterson!"

"Well?"

"Do you really think that there is any connection between this young nobleman and the mysterious highway robber?"

"That's what I want to find out, Hopkins; and I am going to keep a watch upon his movements until my doubts are ended one way or the other."

"But it seems too improbable—too outrageous!"

"What is?"

"Why, to suspect that the Black Highwayman and Lord Harcliffe can have anything in common with each other."

"It does—it does," said Peterson, again struck with the monstrous nature of his suspicion. "And mark you, I don't say they have; but I mean to watch, for all that."

"Very good."

"There are many strange things about this young nobleman," continued Peterson, half aloud, and more as though communing with his thoughts than addressing himself to his companion. "In the first place, he spends ten times as much as any young blood in London. His father is rich, granted; but, then, he is disgusted with his son's career, and utterly renounces him. The money to keep up all this lavish expenditure does not come from that quarter, I am certain. It may come from the money-lenders—yes, yes, it may."

"Or it may come from the high-road," interjected Hopkins.

"It may; and if so, he would not be the first of high birth who has taken this means of replenishing an empty purse. But we must wait and watch, Hopkins, and the next time he leaves home follow him wherever he may go."

Peterson and Hopkins agreed to keep watch by turns.

The quiet of the street was unbroken till towards dawn, at which hour the carriages began to call for Lord Harcliffe's dissolute guests, who had spent the night in furious dissipation.

The watch was kept up during the day, but with no result—the simple fact being that his lordship was sleeping off the effects of the previous night's debauch.

Evening came on, and the officer on watch redoubled his vigilance.

Soon after dark had fairly set in, Hopkins aroused his comrade.

"Be quick, Mr. Peterson!" he said. "The white horse is at the front door—his lordship is going out!"

"Then see that our horses are in perfect readiness, for, let him go where he will, I shall follow him."

Peeping out at the gateway, Peterson caught sight of the large-wheeled vehicle and the white horse on the other side of the road.

A dark-looking figure that he took to be Pharoah occupied it.

In a few moments afterwards the front-door of the mansion was opened, and Lord Harcliffe came forth.

Mounting into the vehicle with some difficulty, for the high-mettled creature would not stand still, he seized the reins, and spun off before Peterson was prepared for it.

He was round the next corner like lightning.

"Hopkins, you villain!" he cried. "Where are the horses?"

"Here they are, sir—all ready."

"Mount, then, and follow me!"

Scrambling into the saddle with all haste, Peterson, followed by his coadjutor, rode down the street.

On turning the corner, he found that his lordship was already out of sight.

"Never mind," he said. "If my suspicions have any foundation, we shall meet with him somewhere on the Western Road. Come on!"

Taking as straight a direction as he could to the place he had mentioned, Peterson urged his horse to his full speed, nor did he draw the rein until the glimmering lights at Tyburn Gate met his view.

"Now we shall soon know," he said. "The toll-man will tell us whether a white horse in a large-wheeled gig has passed through recently. Hilloa!" he bawled. "Gate—gate!"

After a slight delay the toll-keeper made his appearance.

"Harkye, my friend," cried Peterson. "One would think, by the way of you, that no one had passed through this gate for an hour—but I know better."

"And what of that?"

"Do you see this?"

He exhibited his staff of office as he spoke.

"Yes, I see it."

"Very well, then. Just tell me whether two men in a large-wheeled gig have gone through the pike lately?"

"A white horse?"

"Yes, a white horse."

"They went through about a quarter of an hour ago."

"That will do! Good night!"

Peterson rode through the gate, followed by Hopkins, who began to be inclined to think that his superior's suspicions were not so very wide of the mark, after all.

At a hard gallop the officers made their way along the high-road.

Just before reaching Ealing Common they turned off to the right, entering upon the broad, cross-country road where Peterson had seen Lord Harcliffe on the previous evening.

The precise spot was gained at length, and here they paused and listened.

The low moaning of the wind was, however, the only sound that was borne to their ears.

"What is to be done next, Mr. Peterson?"

"We will ride on for a mile or two," was the response, "and decide then."

Accordingly this was done.

"What's that yonder?" Peterson cried, stopping abruptly. "Can you see anything by the side of the road?"

"Yes," returned Hopkins, straining his eyes—"something dark."

"It looks to me like the thing we want. We will ride on quietly and see."

But the dark-looking object came towards them—slowly at first, but afterwards more rapidly.

"It's the white horse!" ejaculated Hopkins. "I'll swear to the white horse!"

On came the approaching vehicle at a tremendous rate, passing by with a sudden rush, and then fast disappearing down the road.

Peterson's first impulse was to join in pursuit.

But two considerations induced him to change his intention.

The first was his firmly-grounded conviction that it would be quite impossible for them to overtake it.

The second was that the gig now only contained one person, and that one he felt sure was Pharoah.

"We are on the right scent, Hopkins," cried Peterson, exultingly. "We have only to follow it up quietly and steadily, and we shall be triumphant! I prophesy the mystery of the Black Highwayman's identity will not be a mystery much longer."

"You think now that Lord Harcliffe has been put down somewhere, and is now about to play the highwayman's part?"

"I do."

"It seems strange, I confess; and yet he may have been taken only to some quiet out-of-town box. You know what I mean—you have heard of such things before to-day."

"I have; and if this Lord Harcliffe was not such absolute master of his actions as he is, I should think there might be something in the suggestion. But them, he has no motive for concealment—none whatever."

"But where are we to look for him now?"

"We must trust to our luck! Come on!"

"Hark! I hear some one coming!"

"So do I. Not our man, though, I'll be bound! He comes along too quietly."

"At any rate, we will see."

"Oh yes! Stop where you are."

A single horseman approached them at a very leisurely pace.

As he came nearer it could be seen that he wore a long riding cloak.

"Halt!" cried Peterson—"halt a moment!"

The horseman pulled up his horse—taking plenty of time over the action.

Then looking up at the two police officers, he said, in the calmest way in the world:

"Well?"

Peterson saw at a glance this was not the object of his pursuit.

"Excuse me for stopping you," he said. "We are officers of police. Have you seen anything of a mounted man on this road within the last ten minutes or so?"

The stranger gazed several seconds at his interlocutors before he ventured to reply, and when he did speak it was in his former cool, leisurely manner.

"You say you are officers?"

"Yes, of course I do! Do you doubt it?"

"Oh dear no! But you will please turn your horses' heads the other way and ride back to London."

"Eh!" ejaculated Peterson, who could not believe that he had heard aright.

"You know perfectly well what I said," was the response, "and therefore I shall not take the trouble to repeat it."

"But—but," gasped Peterson, "who are you?"

"I am here," said the calm stranger, "upon secret service, and I cannot allow such fellows as you are to interrupt me. Ride off at once!"

"Well, I rather think things have come to something at last, when his Majesty's officers of police are ordered off the road by nobody knows who! We sha'n't go, that's flat!"

But if Peterson thought his denial would have the effect of ruffling the stranger's self-possession in the slightest degree he was mistaken.

Just as calmly as ever, he said:

"Light your lantern."

"It is lighted," cried Hopkins, at once unmasking it.

"Then oblige me by looking at this paper."

Filled with curiosity, Peterson eagerly obeyed.

The document had a very official look.

Peterson read as follows:—

"By command of the Secretary of State, all persons, upon pain of severe punishment, are ordered to assist the bearer hereof in the execution of the secret service in which he is engaged, and to obey all his directions as though coming from his Majesty the King. Especially all police officers and constables are enjoined to lend their assistance.—MALMESBURY."

Peterson stared at this paper for some time.

"Have you read it?" said the stranger.

"Y-yes."

"Then give it back."

Peterson mechanically complied.

CHAPTER XIX.

THE SECRET SERVICE MESSENGER.—PETERSON'S BEWILDERMENT.—THE BLACK HIGHWAYMAN AND HIS PURSUER.—THE MYSTERY THICKENS.

THE mysterious stranger, with that extreme amount of deliberation which characterised all he said and all he did, folded up the paper and replaced it in his breast pocket.

"Are you satisfied?" he said.

"Well, I—a—a——"

"Let me advise you not to run your head into trouble."

"But that paper——"

"Well, what of it?"

"It tells you to call upon police officers for assistance?"

"Just so. And I call upon you."

"We are here."

"Your assistance will be easily rendered. It is to ride away from this spot and not return to the vicinity—you will only be obstacles in my way by remaining."

"But you must allow me to explain that the duty which brings us to this spot to-night is a most important one."

"Possibly. But the Secretary of State will be responsible."

"But we are on the track of the Black Highwayman," exclaimed Peterson, irritated beyond measure by the extraordinary coolness maintained by the stranger, "and I have every confidence in saying that, if allowed to proceed, he will be a prisoner in the morning."

"You think so?"

"I feel sure of it."

"Then," answered the stranger, "let me advise you to make up your mind to be disappointed."

"Disappointed—the devil, sir! I have discovered his identity."

"Ah!"

"Confound your 'Ah!' sir!"

"Very good. But, my hot-headed friend, I will just take the trouble to inform you that the secret service I am engaged upon is the capture of this very Black Highwayman you speak of."

"What?"

"I spoke distinctly. I am sure you heard what I said," rejoined the stranger, as imperturbably as ever.

"But——"

"Let me have no more words. Too much time has been wasted here already. I tell you once for all that your presence on this road to-night will interfere with the accomplishment of my purpose. The Secretary of State, you see, has confidence enough in me to place the matter absolutely in my hands. He is determined that this Black Highwayman shall be apprehended forthwith, and, pardon me, he is fully sensible that the whole London police force is incompetent to do it."

"But I never heard of such a proceeding in my life."

"Quite likely. No one is more fully aware of its exceptional character than myself. I shall say no more. Ride on. If you refuse obedience it will be at your peril. It would be rather awkward for you if I charged you with being the cause of my failing to capture the highwayman to-night, which seems more than likely."

"Come away," said Hopkins, in a whisper—"come away, and don't make a blessed fool of yourself!"

Quite bewildered and boiling over with wrath as he was, it is a wonder Peterson did not turn round upon his companion; but he happened to be fully sensible that he would get himself into no ordinary difficulty if he persisted in thwarting one who was armed with such indisputable power.

"I shall inquire into this," he said, as he wheeled round. "If the regular police force is to be impeded and set at nought in this manner, the sooner it ceases to be the better."

"Just so. Good night!"

Gnashing his teeth and muttering some diabolical curses, Peterson struck his spurs savagely into his horse's flanks and rode off, followed closely, of course, by Hopkins.

The latter turned his head more than once, but each time he saw the stranger in the middle of the road just as they had left him.

At length the broad, level Western Road was gained, and as soon as this was the case Peterson discharged another volley of imprecations and reined up.

"Curse me," he said, "if I stand this! Secretary of State or not, I don't intend to leave him the field all to himself! No! If I do, I——"

"Take care, sir!" said Hopkins. "It strikes me it will be a difficult and dangerous matter to interfere."

"I don't care!"

"But you will not ride back to him?"

"No—I will ride to Ealing Common. Perhaps we shall be allowed to do what we like there without being interfered with. And what is more, we may stand a better chance of meeting with the Black Highwayman if he is out upon the road."

"There can be no harm in trying, can there?"

"None at all; and if I do see him, it will go hard with me if I do not make a capture! My own life I would risk a thousand times over upon the chance of spoiling that confounded fellow's sport!"

Peterson spoke with such an air of savage determination that there could be no doubt he was thoroughly in earnest.

"Come on!" he cried. "No more waiting! Come on!"

"There is some one coming, sir."

"Yes, so there is; and from the direction of the Common, too! Wait a moment—we will see who it is."

A mounted man was coming towards them at a sharp canter.

"Hold!" cried Peterson, a moment or so afterwards. "Pull up, in the King's name!"

"Mercy—mercy!" cried the new-comer, in tones of terror. Then, changing his note, he cried: "But it's no use—ha, ha!—it's no use! I'm robbed—I've lost all! You can kill me if you like! What's the good of living now?—I might just as well be dead as without my money! Oh—oh!"

"Stop!" bawled Peterson—"stop! What the devil are you gabbling at?"

"Take my life!" continued the traveller, with increasing excitement. "The other fellow had my money, and now you had better take my life—I shall be out of my misery then, I shall! Oh dear!"

"You must be either a madman or a fool," cried Peterson, "or you would see that we are his Majesty's officers of police."

"Police! Are you police?" screamed the traveller, wildly "Then I may yet have some hopes! Help! I have been robbed! I have lost all—all that is worth living for! Alas—alas!"

The traveller seemed quite distracted by the loss which he appeared to have sustained.

"Calm yourself and attend to me," said Peterson, filled with the hope that he might encounter the Black Highwayman after all. "Just answer two or three questions."

"Oh yes—oh dear!—yes, I will answer! I am a miserable wretch!"

"You have just been robbed?"

"Yes, I have—of three hundred and seventy pounds, and all in gold. What shall I do—oh, what shall I do?"

"Why, attend to me, of course, because then you may have a chance of getting it back again."

"Back again?—did you say back again? Oh dear, I fear not! They told me how it would be when I left West Drayton—they said I should be stopped by the Black Highwayman if I attempted to cross the Common; but I was a fool, and laughed at it."

"Hush—hush! I want to know where you were attacked?"

"Why, on the Common."

"And by whom?"

"Why, the Black Highwayman, to be sure! Who else would do it? I saw something by me that I took at first for a shadow, but something very substantial tore open my coat, and before I could recover from my surprise had taken my bag of gold with three hundred and seventy pounds in it, and disappeared."

"Is that how it occurred?"

"Yes. Oh dear!"

The traveller sighed heavily.

"And what did the shadow look like?"

"A man dressed in black, with a black mask on, mounted on a black horse."

"And which way did he go?"

"That I can't tell you."

"Why not?"

"Because I don't know. He was at my side without my seeing or hearing where he came from, and he vanished in the same way."

"That's just what I told you, sir," interrupted Hopkins. "There is some deep mystery at the bottom of it."

"It will go hard with me if I do not find it out to-night!" cried Peterson, resolutely. "But," he added, addressing himself to the traveller, "have you not exaggerated this affair? Confess, now. If you have it will be best for you to do so—that is, if you wish to get your money back."

"Exaggerate?—I exaggerate? Oh dear no!"

"Then how do you account for a horse's tread being noiseless?"

"I can't account for it; but it is a fact, for all that."

"Well, we will do our best. I know there are those who would gladly declare there was something supernatural in the matter, but I am not one of them. Come, Hopkins—we cannot afford to wait any longer."

"And shall I come with you, gentlemen? I may be of some help. And if you get my money back, you may depend upon my being liberal."

"No, no," said Peterson—"I fear you may prove an impediment rather than otherwise. Ride on till you come to the next inn, and stop there until I call. Come on, Hopkins!"

At a hard gallop the two police officers rode towards the Common, from which they were not far distant.

Upon reaching its border they paused.

In the darkness the open space seemed to be at least double its real extent.

The wind came rushing over it with a dismal howl, and both the officers, though well accustomed to all weathers, shrunk back before its fury.

"We will keep to the road," said Peterson, "and trot from here to the other side of the Common. After that, we can decide upon our further proceedings."

To this, Hopkins made no objection.

The night was such a one as would tempt few persons from home, and this accounted for the two officers crossing the Common without meeting with a soul.

"No luck here!" growled Peterson. "Curse that secret service fellow for spoiling our night's sport, as I feel convinced he has done!"

"Where to next, sir?"

"We will draw to one side there, under cover of those trees; they will screen us from this piercing east wind, and then we will consider further."

Scarcely, however, had they taken up this position when the unmistakable sound of some one else being on the road came to their ears.

"Who is this, I wonder?" ejaculated Hopkins.

"Keep quiet—we shall soon see. Whoever it may be must be in a desperate hurry."

"Shall we stop him?"

"By all means. We can scarcely fail to learn something of importance."

"We must be quick, then, or he will be upon us."

The two officers immediately sallied forth, and placed themselves in the middle of the road.

They were evidently observed by the fast-approaching horseman, for he slackened speed as he came towards them.

"Avast there!" he sung out, in loud tones, as soon as he got a little nearer—"avast there! Out of the way!"

"In the King's name," bawled Peterson, "I call upon you to halt!"

"Ay—ay!"

The horseman brought his steed to a standstill, and then looking closely at the two officers, he cried:

"What do you want? Out with it quickly, for I have important business on hand!"

"Show a light, Hopkins!"

The dark lantern was produced, and at the same time Peterson drew forth his staff.

One glance was quite enough to satisfy even the incredulous Peterson that the individual before him was not the man he sought.

Nevertheless, he did not omit to make a display of his power.

"Look here!" he exclaimed, showing his gilt-crowned staff. "I call upon you to state your name and your business on the road to-night!"

"I am no privateer," was the answer; "so you are welcome to overhaul my papers. My name is Tracy—Lieutenant Tracy; and I am out to-night to try if I can get in the wake of that piratical craft, the Black Highwayman."

"The devil!"

"What do you mean?"

"Why, everybody to-night seems on the same errand. But no matter. What authority have you for acting the part of a police officer?"

"None at all."

"And what's your motive?"

"A wager I have made—to rather a considerable amount, too—that I would clear up the mystery about this

Black Highwayman; and, as sure as I am a sailor, I'll do it!"

"Oh!"

"And," continued Lieutenant Tracy, "as I am anxious to get the matter over, I'll stand fifty guineas out of my own pocket if you will render me your assistance."

"And with whom lies your wager?"

"With Lord Harcliffe."

Hopkins uttered a loud exclamation, while Peterson contented himself with giving vent to a low, prolonged whistle.

"And he bet that you would not discover the mystery, I suppose?"

"He did. But what is the meaning of your strange behaviour?"

"No matter. If we have the chance to aid you we will —I can say no more. An officer may have his suspicions, but he is not obliged to utter them. Oh dear no—not by any manner of means! Pass on. Good night!"

"What the deuce does the fellow mean?" muttered Tracy, as he continued his journey. "Can he mean to insinuate—— No—no! That would be too absurd!"

He looked back once or twice, and saw the two officers still planted in the middle of the roadway.

"I do not seem in a very fair way for success to-night," he said. "But I will not despair. Those who know me best will give me credit for persevering in any design that I may have formed. I will ride back again across the Common, and if I fail to see anything then, I suppose I shall have to give it up for to-night."

The dense, heavy clouds which the furious east wind was driving across the sky now lightened a little, enabling the young lieutenant to see better about him.

His eyes were keen, and, during the long night watches on board ship, had grown accustomed to discerning objects in the darkness.

But all he could see were the bushes on the Common and the dark patches here and there which noted the whereabouts of some deep declivity.

Presently, however, as the amount of light increased, he fancied he could descry in the far distance something that was moving swiftly.

He pressed his horse onward and strained his eyes.

The result was a conviction that he had not been mistaken.

Regardless of all perils, he continued to dash on at a rate that would by most people have been considered dangerous to a degree.

"By Heaven!" he ejaculated, burying the spurs in the flanks of his already over-goaded beast. "It is a horse and rider! Yes—yes, and both are black! How his cloak streams out behind him in the wind! It is—it must be the Black Highwayman!"

The young lieutenant's excitement upon making this discovery was greater than he had ever experienced before.

"I am gaining on him," he said—"I am gaining on him. What makes me sure of it is, that I can see him so much plainer now. And what a step! One would almost think no mortal horse could trot like that!"

It was now impossible to entertain a doubt about the character of what the young sailor saw.

It was indeed a horse and rider—a horse and rider that in every point and every way corresponded with the description always given of the Black Highwayman and his wondrous steed.

But what amazed Tracy was, that though he was going at such a headlong gallop, the highwayman's horse was merely trotting, but yet with such extraordinary swiftness as to make it very doubtful whether he would be overtaken.

CHAPTER XX.

TRACY'S PURSUIT OF THE BLACK HIGHWAYMAN, AND ITS TERMINATION.—A STARTLING SUGGESTION.—HOPKINS PROPOSES TO PLAY THE SPY.

What seemed more surprising still was the fact that apparently neither horse nor rider was aware of the pursuit.

The lieutenant dashed away the drops of perspiration which obscured his vision.

On, steadily on, in one unvarying course, and apparently towards some fixed point of destination, went the noble horse.

"Wonderful!" ejaculated Tracy. "I can understand now that people should have exaggerated their description a little. I can hear nothing of his progress—it seems as silent as a shadow But then he is some distance from me, and he may be making his way over soft ground. Get on with you!"

The last words were addressed to his steed, but without effect, as the animal was already going at the utmost speed it was capable of making.

For the first time Tracy now became aware that the Black Highwayman—if it were indeed that mysterious personage—was making his way across the track which he (Tracy) was pursuing.

Every moment the Black Highwayman got further and further to the left.

"Stop now," said Tracey, to himself—"let me think. If he holds that course and I turn off at once to the left I shall meet him somewhere close to those trees yonder, the shelter of which it appears to me he is endeavouring to gain. Yes, yes, I am convinced that is his object. It will be a bit of rough riding, I daresay, but I never felt less inclined to stick at trifles than I do to-night."

As he spoke he pulled the left rein, and the horse, in obedience to the impulse, left the high-road and entered upon the broken surface of the Common.

"On—on! Forward, boy—forward!" his rider cried, in inspiriting tones. "Steady now—steady!"

At a wonderful rate, especially when the nature of the ground underfoot is taken into consideration, Tracy's horse galloped over the Common.

But the young lieutenant was ignorant of the many perils which lay in his path, or he would never have attempted such a course.

Instead, too, of keeping any look-out as to the condition of the ground in front of him, his gaze was fixed upon the object of his pursuit, who still held on his way as though wholly unconscious that anyone else was making in a straight line for his apparent destination, and seemingly in such a way that with little doubt he would arrive at the same moment.

Seeing this, a wild feeling of exultation sprang up in the sailor's breast, which rapidly increasing, rendered him altogether regardless of the least caution; and in his excitement he spurred and urged his horse onward much as he would have done had a good level turnpike-road been before him.

Fortune or chance favoured his recklessness wonderfully.

The ground was extremely rugged, and how it was he escaped a hundred falls is an unaccountable mystery.

Nearer—nearer still he came.

The Black Highwayman could now be distinguished plainly—the black trappings on his steed, his own sombre silver-faced apparel, the crape mask covering the greater part of his face—all were visible.

Still in his progress he made no sound—that is, none reached the ears of the young lieutenant.

All at once, however, the mysterious rider became aware that he was menaced by danger—or rather his magnificent steed apprised him of it, for he snorted loudly, and immediately broke out into a gallop.

Maddened at the thought that his prey would, after all, elude him, Tracy spurred his horse vigorously.

The noble creature, which deserved better treatment, gave a loud scream of pain, and bounded forward madly.

But that good fortune which had before attended its movements now ceased.

A treacherous hollow lay right before its feet—a place abruptly sinking into the earth, and fringed with gorse and brake in such a manner as to conceal the edge of the abyss.

Down into the hollow, then, went Tracy's steed headlong.

The young lieutenant was just conscious of the occurrence of this catastrophe, and of whirling suddenly through the air, but nothing more.

He fell heavily to the ground some distance over the horse's head, where he lay motionless, either insensible or dead.

It was a wonder that the horse did not fall upon him or injure him in the frantic but ineffectual attempts it made to regain a footing.

The Black Highwayman had disappeared.

In the meantime the two police officers, Peterson and Hopkins, had been exerting themselves but to little purpose.

Soon after the young lieutenant had left them, however, Hopkins broke a long period of silence by crying:

"Mr. Peterson, it's my belief now that it was a dead do—a regular out-and-out swindle!"

"What do you mean?"

"Why, that secret service gentleman."

"How so? What of him?"

"Why, I believe we have been thrown off the scent by a bold-faced, outrageous trick!"

"Is—is that your opinion—your honest opinion, Hopkins?"

"It is, Mr. Peterson," was the deeply-emphatic reply—"it is indeed!"

"I confess that I can hardly reconcile myself to the thought that the Secretary of State should adopt such a course, or grant any such authority."

"You may depend he never did," said Hopkins. "I feel surer and surer the more I think about it."

"And—and that paper?"

"Must be nothing but a downright impudent forgery."

Peterson was silent for some moments, and then he said:

"Well, there is some satisfaction in knowing that we can ascertain the point before midday to-morrow."

"Slight satisfaction that," said Hopkins.

"But," interrupted Peterson, "I never heard that this Black Highwayman had any accomplice."

"Nor I."

"Who was it we met, then?"

"No accomplice, you may be sure. Depend upon it, it was the Black Highwayman himself."

"Never," cried Peterson—"never! I am sure you are wrong there!"

"Why?"

"I have two reasons."

"What are they?"

"In the first place, no one would ever have the consummate impudence and boldness to play such a part; and, more than all, to carry it out with such an extraordinary amount of coolness."

"Very good!"

"And, in the second place, the voice was not the same."

"How the same?"

"As Lord Harcliffe's!"

"Then you still believe him to be the Black Highwayman?"

"I do."

"But you may be mistaken. I would sooner say that cool, calm, secret service gentleman is the true Black Highwayman."

"If he is," said Peterson, slowly, "my suspicions about Lord Harcliffe fall to the ground, because I paid so much attention to his lordship's voice that I am certain I could recognise it again anywhere."

"But he could disguise it."

"He might; but not to such an extent as that. Nothing could be more different."

"Wait till the morning, sir," said Hopkins. "The more I think about it, the more certain do I feel that when you come to make inquiries, you will learn that the document you saw was an impudent forgery, and the whole affair a fabrication to get us out of the way."

"If so, Hopkins, it is certain that this Black Highwayman is at the same time the boldest and most audacious fellow that ever took to the highway; and my suspicions against Lord Harcliffe, however, are so strong that I cannot share your opinion altogether. I think it possible it was an accomplice."

"No, no! You admit the boldness and courage required. Rest assured no accomplice could have performed such a part. It is either genuine or else the Black Highwayman himself."

"I should be of your opinion, Hopkins, did I not feel so perfectly assured in my own mind that Lord Harcliffe and the Black Highwayman are one and the same, and that the secret service gentleman is not Lord Harcliffe. The last does not admit of the slightest doubt."

"Make your inquiries carefully, Mr. Peterson. It would never do to let the world know we had been so egregiously deceived."

"Trust me for that."

"And, Mr. Peterson!"

"Well?"

"I have something else to propose."

"What is it?"

"Simply this. You are prepared to admit that, let this Black Highwayman be whom he may, this Common is the chief scene of his exploits?"

"It seems so. But what is your proposition?"

"I am coming to it. It is that you ride towards London, to find out whether the Secretary of State has really taken the apprehension of this highwayman into his own hands, leaving me here."

"Here?"

"Yes. I will set to work to see what I can discover by a little spying and watching. No doubt, when you come again to-morrow night, I shall have something to tell you worth listening to."

"It is possible," said Peterson, reflectively.

"Very possible, I think; and besides, you can manage as well without me as with me. It stands to reason that I must be more useful here than elsewhere."

"You will be careful?"

"Oh yes. Such a little affair as this is quite in my line. I will find out all I am able; but will do nothing unless under sheer necessity."

"And where shall we meet?"

"To-morrow night an hour after sunset, at the spot where we met with the traveller who had been robbed."

"Agreed!"

"And you consent to this arrangement?"

"Yes, I can think of nothing better?"

This resolution having been come to, and feeling that there were little hopes of finding the Black Highwayman on the road now it was so late, Peterson, though with a heavy and unwilling heart, turned his horse's head towards London.

Hopkins accompanied him to the extremity of the Common.

"Here we will meet, Mr. Peterson," he said. "You will not miss the place?"

"No."

"All right, sir. Good night!"

"Good night, Hopkins!"

In anything but a pleasant state of mind, the police officer rode towards London, his brain in a whirl and a ferment about the mysterious nature of all the events which had occurred.

Hopkins sat in the saddle watching the receding form of his chief until the darkness swallowed it up from his view.

He remained gazing for some few moments after this took place, and then with a look of deep thought upon his features, slowly turned his horse's head towards the Common.

"Let me think," he said, "I fancy I could make my way to the very spot where we entered the wood when the Bishop's secretary was with us—I feel pretty sure I can do so." At any rate, I will try. Then I will tie my horse to one of the young trees thereabouts, and make my way straight across the wood to those palings which divide it from the cross-road. If that secret service gentleman is anywhere about there I shall see him, no doubt. That shall be my first plan."

Accordingly, he made his way towards the point to which he had alluded.

To reach it he was compelled to make his way across the open Common, but in his progress he adopted every precaution, and as he went only at a walking pace he escaped the fate which had befallen unfortunate Lieutenant Tracy.

On gaining the confines of the wood he had more trouble than he anticipated in finding the place where they had formerly entered.

"I think this must be it," he said, at length. "At all events, it is sufficiently near to answer my purpose. And let me think, there was a hut, too, in this wood. We failed to make anything of it or of its inmates. Yet it may repay a second examination."

Hopkins only rode into the wood a little way and then dismounted.

Looking about him, he saw hard by a dense thicket.

"If I can only force a way into that," he said, "it will be a capital place for my horse. He will be quite secure against any chance discovery."

CAPTAIN HAWK LEAPS SATAN OVER THE STAGE COACH.

Presented Gratis with No. 7 of the New Re-Issue of The Black Highwayman, by the Author of Black Bess.

GRATIS with Nos. 7 to 10, FOUR UNCOLOURED PICTURES,
GRATIS with Nos. 3 to 6. FOUR COLOURED PICTURES.

[CAPTAIN HAWK AWAITS THE ARRIVAL OF THE OLD WAGGON.]

After some trouble, he found a place where his steed could pass between the dense mass of vegetation; and having tethered him securely by the rein, he left him to his own devices.

It was now fast growing towards morning, and Hopkins therefore had but little time before him to pursue his investigations.

Hastening to leave the thicket, he directed his steps as well as he was able to judge towards the cross-road.

A strange sensation came over him as he fairly plunged into the wood.

What it meant he could not tell, but a strange depression of spirits weighed him down.

"Pooh—pooh!" he said. "Am I growing nervous? It is being in this place alone, I suppose; and yet I have been in worse places by far many a time by myself. It is having Peterson at my side so much, perhaps. And then, this is such a mysterious affair altogether."

He shuddered as he spoke, and yet it would have puzzled him to tell why.

Was it that the subtle essence which we call by the vague names of mind, soul, spirit, was conscious of some forthcoming danger? The sensation is one well known, and, in default of a better word, is termed a presentiment.

It did indeed seem that this police officer's spirit was overshadowed by a presentiment of terrible coming danger to himself, or, in the words of the poet, as though

"Coming events had cast their dark shadow before."

Upon a more sensitive organisation than Hopkins possessed a widely different effect would most probably have been produced.

But he resolved to shake off this weakness—for so he called it—and, having swallowed a quantity of brandy from a pocket-flask, to some extent succeeded in doing it

No. 7.

GRATIS with this Number, The ENGRAVING of CAPTAIN HAWK LEAPS SATAN OVER THE STAGE COACH.

"Better now," he said, though at the moment he spoke he could not repress a shiver—"very much better, and quite ready for what may turn out. Nervousness would ruin all. I must be calm—quite calm."

But in spite of his expressed resolution, his limbs would persist in trembling.

It was, however, with a tolerably firm step that he forced his way among the trees, pausing every now and then to listen, fancying some slight sound had reached his ears.

All at once he saw start up out of the darkness a tiny star-like light.

It jumped into existence instantaneously, and then remained fixed and immovable.

"What's that?" asked Hopkins, in a whisper, and stopping the instant he observed the phenomenon.

All around the stillness of the tomb prevailed.

"I don't feel at all comfortable," he murmured. "I will try a little drop of brandy. Ah! that's better! A wonderful thing brandy is! What can that light mean?—does it come from the woodman's hut? I think not. It does not seem in the right direction. But let it come from where it may, I ought to find out something else concerning it—oh yes, of course I ought—I will not shirk it!"

Yet it was with a most singular inward feeling of reluctance that the police officer cautiously crept through the brushwood with his eyes fixed upon the tiny glimmering light.

CHAPTER XXI.

CAPTAIN HAWK MEETS WITH A STRANGE COMPANION, AND FINDS A STILL STRANGER PLACE OF REFUGE. —THE DISCOVERY.—THE OLD WATERCOURSE.—THE FLIGHT.

THE crackling sound which had startled Captain Hawk was just such as would be produced by some one stealthily endeavouring to force a passage among the underwood and dry dead twigs which, to a depth of a couple of feet or more, covered the ground between the trunks of the trees in the park.

Barely had the highwayman time to draw back as far as possible into the shadow cast by a large tree before a man with an air of extreme caution emerged from a small thicket close by.

He did not at first venture to quit this place of concealment entirely, but, leaning forward, put one hand to his ear and listened attentively.

"Confound it all!" he exclaimed, in a low tone. "What could be more unlucky? The chances are ten to one these fellows will light upon me before I can reach the old den; and if they do my neck will be as good as in the noose at once. Ha! they come!"

He stole swiftly and noiselessly across the small open space before him, and disappeared.

Captain Hawk had only heard this man's muttered words in a very imperfect manner, but yet sufficiently to be able to know that for some reason or other he dreaded the approach of the officers, and—what was of the highest importance—that he had a good place of shelter, provided he could only manage to reach it unseen.

"I'll follow him," he muttered. "If he speaks truth I need have no fear that he will betray me."

The task which the captain had set himself was not in one respect a very difficult one, for, despite all the care exercised by the man, it was impossible for him to proceed without making sound enough to enable him to be tracked readily enough.

The chief fear was that he would prematurely become acquainted with the fact that he was followed by some one, and, in the alarm caused by making the discovery, utter a cry that would bring about the discovery and destruction of both.

Guided entirely by his sense of hearing, the highwayman followed in the footsteps of his unconscious guide.

Suddenly, however, the man stopped.

Captain Hawk hurried forward.

"Hold!" he said. "A single cry, and you are a dead man! Assist me to find a hiding-place, and I will reward you well."

The man was so astounded at hearing these words, that the ejaculation which had risen to his lips died away in a low whisper.

In another second Captain Hawk had taken a firm grasp upon his arm.

"Now," he whispered, "there is no time for discussion. Do you consent?"

"I do."

"Very good—I will trust you."

"I should think you will, when I am going to show you a place which—but you shall see. We will not waste time in talking."

The darkness was too great for Captain Hawk to judge well of minor objects, but, so far as he could make out, the man was attired half like a gamekeeper, half like an ordinary farm labourer.

The highwayman was not long, however, in finding that his new companion's actions were by far more interesting than his personal appearance.

He had stopped at a spot where a huge tree had formerly stood. Whether it had been blown down by the winds, or struck by lightning, or whether it had fallen before the woodman's axe, was hard to say; but, at any rate, a portion of the stump was left, which was about a foot or fourteen inches in height.

Stooping down, the man raised it much as he would have lifted an unusually thick and heavy lid of a circular box.

The precise nature of the contrivance could not be ascertained, for the man said, in suppressed tones:

"Be quick! There is not a moment to be lost. Descend!"

"Are there steps?"

"Yes; rough ones. Be careful!"

The highwayman unhesitatingly complied, placing more trust in this new ally than was prudent, and more than he would have done had he been allowed more time for reflection.

It was not until he had descended several steps, so that his head was actually below the level of the ground, that the alarming thought occurred to him, that if the man chose to play a treacherous part, nothing would be easier for him than to close the secret entrance, which, in all probability, he had some means of securely fastening.

But this fear was proved to be perfectly groundless, for with an impatient exclamation he urged the highwayman to greater speed, and immediately afterwards began to descend the steps.

He pulled the lid of the secret entrance down upon him, after which the darkness was intense.

"Stop as soon as you find yourself at the bottom of the steps," he said, abruptly. "I will get a light then."

"I am at the bottom already."

"Very good. So am I," answered the man, whose familiarity with the place enabled him to make much better speed than our friend.

Without losing much time, he took from his pocket what proved to be a flint and tinder-box, by the aid of which he with no little trouble lighted a small piece of candle.

As soon as the wick was fairly alight he availed himself of the opportunity to have a good look at the highwayman, who on his part gazed with no slight amount of curiosity into the countenance of his strange companion.

"Humph!" ejaculated the latter. "Then I suppose it is you who have been the cause of bringing all these fellows in the park? Who and what are you? Surely I have a right to know that?"

"Perhaps so," answered the captain, coolly. "But I want to be satisfied about the security of this place."

"Oh, be under no apprehension on that score! You are as safe as you would be if a hundred miles away—perhaps safer."

"What is that, then?"

Hush—hush!"

A strange, lumbering noise could be heard overhead.

"Those are the officers," whispered the man. "They are going to beat the park from end to end, feeling sure that they shall discover you by doing so, and that you cannot get away unseen, because the boundary of the park is watched at every point."

From the heavy way in which the officers seemed to tread, Captain Hawk fancied that the roof of his subterranean hiding-place was not of any great thickness.

Both paused to listen.

"Are you sure," whispered Captain Hawk, a moment afterwards, "that the entrance is well enough contrived to elude the vigilance of these men?"

"Oh yes! Why, I——"

What more he would have said cannot be told, for he was interrupted by a crash so terrific as to deprive him not only of speech but of motion.

"Good Heavens!" ejaculated Captain Hawk. "What is that?"

"Hurrah!" cried a voice. "Steps! Come on! We have him now, sure enough!"

The hurried trampling of feet followed.

"The entrance!" cried the captain, shaking his companion, who appeared like one completely stupified—"surely they have discovered it?"

About this there could be no doubt, for the foot of the staircase was close to where they stood, and men could be heard descending it.

In another second lights appeared.

"This way!" exclaimed the man, extinguishing his candle. "Grasp my hand! So! Now run forward with me, and fear nothing. I know all the ins and outs of this place so well that the darkness will make no difference!"

He ran forward hastily while speaking.

Captain Hawk did as he was told, but felt far from comfortable regarding the probable issue of the adventure.

How it was the officers had managed to find out their hiding-place he had no means of knowing.

He could only surmise that the man must have omitted to secure it properly, or it may be that the lighted candle betrayed them.

But about this the highwayman felt it was useless to speculate—it was sufficient for him to be certain that the entrance to the subterranean hiding-place had been found.

As the ground was hard and level beneath the feet, his companion made such good speed that he had no little trouble in keeping pace with it.

Their pursuers, however, were very hard indeed upon their footsteps.

As to the form and nature of the underground region he was in, Captain Hawk was not in a position to give anything like a clear idea.

He remembered that the candle, during the brief period it had given out illumination, had shown that he was standing in a rudely-formed passage hollowed out of the solid earth.

"Where would you lead me?" he asked. "Have you any hope of ultimate escape?"

"Yes—yes! Follow me. All will be well."

But the highwayman, after what had happened, did not feel disposed to place any implicit reliance upon what his new friend should say. Under the circumstances, however, it was clear that he could do nothing better than submit to his guidance.

From some cause a slight amount of delay seemed to take place on the part of the officers, but from what the fugitives did not attempt to ascertain.

"Stop," said the man, suddenly. "Stand there a moment, and I will interpose a barrier that will be a considerable check to their further progress."

The highwayman had to depend entirely upon his ears for cognisance of what took place, the darkness being extreme.

First, then, he heard a sound as though a door of no trifling weight had been slammed shut, and this sound was immediately followed by the creaking of rusty bolts as they were forced into their sockets.

"There," he said. "Now we may venture to take things easier."

"But they will break that door down," said the captain—"for a door I suppose it is?"

"Yes. But it will take them some time to do it, for it is made of hard old oak. In the meanwhile we will gain the open air again."

"Then you have the means of doing so?" the captain said, with an air of great relief.

"Oh yes! In a moment or so you will feel the wind blowing upon your face."

This proved to be the case, and the captain was no sooner sensible of it than he increased his speed.

"Hold—hold, sir! Not so fast. We must have a little care before we emerge."

"Are we still within the precincts of the park?"

"At present we are."

"Then we shall be exposed to the gaze of those who are watching the boundary?"

"I hope not."

The man paused as he spoke, and then went on at a cautious pace, which enabled him to converse without difficulty.

"You see," he said, "we shall come presently upon an old watercourse. The brick channel through which it flows is narrow and confined. We shall have to creep out; but as I believe no one knows that it has any connection with the cavern, and as the night is dark, I hope we shall steal away unseen."

"It is our only chance, I suppose?"

"Yes."

"Then we must make the best of it."

"Here we are, then. Can you hear the water?"

"Yes. Lead on."

"Follow me."

The man advanced.

In advance a very dim sort of twilight could be discerned—so feeble, however, that it could never have been seen unless contrasted with the pitchy blackness of the subterranean region.

It, however, enabled the captain to make out the form of the man in front of him.

"The water is deeper than I expected. But fear nothing. You must not mind wetting your skin a little."

"Go on—say no more."

The man, stooping almost on his hands and knees, crept under a low archway.

Captain Hawk followed.

The water was nearly three feet in depth, but, luckily, the bottom was firm.

"It will be better not to speak again," said the man, in a low whisper—"our voices may get carried to the ears of those above; and be careful not to splash with the water."

"Right! Go on!"

Not another word was said.

Much to Captain Hawk's satisfaction, it grew lighter at every step.

In the distance before him he could see the circular-shaped opening of the watercourse.

It was reached in much less time than he had anticipated.

The man paused on reaching the termination, and stealthily reconnoitred.

The coast seemed clear.

Sounds now came from behind them, however, which showed that their pursuers had triumphed over the strength of the oak door.

Placing his mouth close to the captain's ear, and subduing his voice to the faintest possible murmur, the man said:

"Never mind those behind. We shall be far away before they enter upon the watercourse. We are now just on the outside of the park palings; and if we are cautious I think we may contrive to creep away unnoticed, for of course those on the look-out will have their attention turned to the inner part of the park, not to the boundary."

This seemed probable enough.

"Here," said Captain Hawk, placing a purse in his hand, "is the reward I promised you. We had better separate—it will double the chances of our escape."

"Agreed!"

"We will both steal forth at once. Are you ready?"

"Quite."

According to this arrangement, both crept out from the low archway, each one going in opposite directions—Captain Hawk taking care to choose that route which would lead him towards the Hall.

Scarcely had he gone a dozen yards, however, when the prevailing silence was broken by the loud explosion of a pistol.

So suddenly did the sound come upon the ears of the highwayman that for a moment he fancied he was shot.

The impulse to look back was irresistible, and he saw about half a dozen dusky-looking figures rushing swiftly in the direction taken by his companion.

"They have seen him," he muttered, as he increased

his speed. "That is his misfortune. He must shift as best he can, for it is out of my power to help him.

"It is lucky for me, however," he added, after the lapse of a few moments, "for the pursuit seems diverted from me entirely. I only hope he will have the good fortune to elude them. If not, I may soon expect them on my track again."

One would have thought that Captain Hawk would best have secured his own safety by making all speed to quit the vicinity of a spot that had been to him so deeply fraught with danger, and unquestionably he would have done so but for the fact that his horse Satan was still an inmate of the stables.

Without his gallant steed the highwayman felt he should be nought; and besides, he was well aware that, despite the apparent danger, he should never have a better opportunity of regaining possession of him than the present.

"No, no," he said; "if I can only get to the stables speedily I have little doubt that all will end as I could wish. Ten to one if, in their confusion and excitement, they have given a moment's thought about my horse; but in time, if I elude them, they must remember it, and consequently take such precautions as will make my re-obtainment of him almost impossible. By Jove, they have caught him!"

As he uttered this last hasty exclamation he looked back and saw that his unknown companion had fallen into the hands of his pursuers. In an instant he was densely surrounded.

"I must make the best use of my time," said the highwayman, mentally. "They will not be long in finding out they have captured the wrong person."

A loud outcry in the rear arose at this moment, testifying to the truth of this remark.

Captain Hawk had less difficulty in getting back to the Hall than one might at the first glance imagine.

To use the officer's phrase upon the occasion, no sooner had the game been fairly started than those who had been guarding the boundary quitted their stations and hastened to join in the pursuit, thus leaving the coast quite clear in the direction he was taking.

CHAPTER XXII.

THE FUGITIVE GAINS THE STABLES.—THE SURPRISE.—SATAN RECOVERED.—OFF AND AWAY.—ANOTHER ADVENTURE ON THE HIGHWAY.

SUMMONING up all his powers of speed, Captain Hawk ran on, nor did he pause until he found himself fairly beneath the shadow of some of the outbuildings connected with the Hall.

Here he was compelled to pause for a few seconds to regain his exhausted breath, and he took advantage of the opportunity to look well at the different objects by which he was surrounded.

In the distance the flashing lights carried by his pursuers could be seen, and every now and then a hoarse cry was borne upon the air; but it seemed certain that they had failed to get precisely upon his track.

Before him, gloomy and rambling, was the picturesque old Hall, the outbuildings connected with which were of quite a bewildering extent.

"There is nothing to guide me to the place I wish to find," he gasped. "My only plan will be to examine all the places successively. I must lose no time, for they are coming this way."

Apparently the party in pursuit had once again contrived to get upon the track of the fugitive.

"At last!" gasped the captain, a moment afterwards, as, on pushing open a door, he found himself in a long range of stabling.

But ere he crossed the threshold he heard voices and footsteps close at hand.

"Come on," said some one. "The horses are close at hand. It will not take us a moment."

These few words made it clear that those who were approaching had the stables for their destination.

"Confound it," muttered the highwayman, "they are coming here! What shall I do? Hide, I suppose—and yet——"

He stopped, for there was not another second for deliberation.

Hastily entering the stables, the first thing he came in contact with was the corn-bin. As his hand rested upon it the idea occurred to him that it might afford him a temporary hiding-place.

In a second he acted upon the idea.

He lifted the lid, entered, and let the lid down again with wonderful rapidity; but yet he was only just in time, for two men at the precise instant that the lid descended crossed the threshold.

"Get a light," said one—"we cannot do without."

"Here you are."

"Now come this way. Here is the harness-room. Be quick and provide yourself with a saddle and bridle."

The men passed close by the corn-bin.

Returning speedily from the harness-room, they saddled and bridled a couple of horses, Captain Hawk being in a state of ferment all the time lest Satan should be one of them.

"We were told to pick the best in the stable, mate," said one, "and I think it would be a hard matter to find a better one than this—he's a real beauty!"

"Never mind that—lose as little time as possible."

"Right you are. I am all ready now."

"So am I."

The clattering of hoofs succeeded as the two horses were led towards the door of the stables.

It was with the utmost difficulty that the captain prevented himself from lifting the lid and peeping out, despite the obvious impolicy of doing so; and probably he would not have preserved his restraint but for the arrival of the pursuing party from the park, which now halted somewhere near the stable-door.

"Have you found him?" asked one of the two men.

"No."

"Keep up your vigilance, then. It will not take us long to return with more help. D—n the horse! Here, hold him still, somebody, while I mount!"

The last portion of his speech was uttered with angry impatience.

Captain Hawk raised the lid of the corn-chest to the extent of about a couple of inches.

The stable was empty.

A contention of an extraordinary character, however, seemed taking place outside of it, and after listening a moment Captain Hawk said, mentally:

"That's Satan—Satan for a thousand pounds! That fool of a fellow is trying to mount him, and he might just as well try to fly away on the back of a pigeon!"

"Curse the brute!" continued the man, angrily. "He is not fit to live! D—n you, be still! I never saw a bit of horseflesh yet that I could not mount! Curse you, be still!"

He accompanied his words with a blow.

The sound struck upon Captain Hawk's heart.

He could remain passive no longer.

Despising all danger, he with one bound sprang from the corn-bin, another brought him to the door of the stable, and the third to the side of his incomparable steed, which, after the blow it had received, was ten times more unmanageable than before.

The appearance of Captain Hawk was so very sudden, and so totally unexpected, that all present stood amazed, without knowing what to think of it.

The highwayman did not give them the opportunity to recover from their astonishment.

With one flying bound he seated himself upon the back of his prancing steed.

"Ho, boy!" he shouted, in a ringing voice. "On, Satan! Away—away!"

The gallant creature knew his voice, even if it had not already recognised its master by sight, which was more than probable.

As the words were uttered he reared high in the air, as if to gain additional impetus, and then, striking out his fore-feet, away he went with a swiftness and fury that nothing could withstand.

Not until this took place did one in the crowd find out who it was that had rushed upon them with such extraordinary suddenness.

"Fire!" bawled some one. "That is our man, and that is his horse! Curse his impudence! Fire, I say! Cripple his horse! Stop him somehow!"

But the men either had not their weapons ready, or else hesitated a little before obeying the order.

The words fell upon the highwayman's ear, and no sooner was the barbarous order given about crippling his horse than a deep red flush came over his features, and he tugged at the rein with all his might.

It was no easy matter, though, to check a horse when going at such a rate.

Partially succeeding, however, he with his right hand drew forth that formidable weapon which he had christened by the ominous name of Death.

He had no trouble in singling out the man who had spoken, and after a hasty glance along the brightly-polished barrel he pulled the trigger.

At this moment passion had the complete mastery of him; and, averse as he always was to the needless shedding of blood, yet on the present occasion his intention was to deprive the craven-hearted officer of his life.

But the restiveness of Satan was fatal to the steadiness of his aim, and the bullet, instead of entering the man's heart, struck his elbow, shattering the joint in a frightful manner.

"Base coward!" the highwayman cried. "I will let you fellows know that if it is your duty to apprehend me that it is no excuse for you to practise cruelties upon my steed! Take me who can! But my horse has never offended against the laws, and, by heavens, I will have him respected!"

At the last words he released the rein, and Satan, turning his head, renewed his gallop with all the more ardour from the check which had been placed upon it.

He was out of range before those of his pursuers who were furnished with pistols could make up their minds to fire a volley.

In the excited state of his feelings, the hard gallop at which he was going was very agreeable, and ere long the Hall and its surroundings were left far behind.

There were indications now of the approach of morning, and when the highwayman became calm enough to notice the circumstance he began to wonder where he should look for a place of shelter.

His heart prompted him to return to the lonely inn, and it was more the fear of bringing fresh trouble on Lottie and her father than any dread of his own personal danger that made him relinquish the idea.

A hiding-place of some kind, however, where he could pass the hours of daylight was indispensable.

"I do not care to go very far away," he muttered, as he raised himself in the stirrups and took a long look around and about him. "I have not done with the steward yet. The three hundred pounds I must and will have back again; and what is more, I will baffle him and the squire's unworthy son in their scheme of roguery, and fix the odium of the cold-blooded murder on the right persons!"

While making these resolutions, morning advanced with rapid strides.

Satan still kept up his tremendous gallop, for it seemed as though he, like his master, had been labouring under some unusual excitement for which the rapid motion seemed a vent.

Of those who were, or rather who had been, in pursuit not the faintest trace could be discerned.

But although out of sight, they were most likely upon his track for all that, and if he slackened pace or came to a halt the probability was that they would ere long come into view.

Knowing this made the fugitive all the more anxious that his resting-place should be such a one as his foes would pass by without suspecting for a moment that he was there.

Where to find such a place as this was the difficulty.

It was when the sun was somewhere about an hour above the horizon that the highwayman came upon a scene of such rural beauty that he was compelled to pause and spend a few moments in gazing upon it.

He was all the more inclined to do this because Satan had just accomplished the ascent of a long, toilsome hill, which, after the immense efforts he had made, told rather severely upon him.

But the view spread out before him was one that would have elicited the admiration of the most unimpressionable of beings, so truly beautiful did it appear, especially now while the ruddy morning sun glinted upon every object.

Below, the ground descended rapidly until a valley was reached, through which meandered a glittering, silvery stream.

On the other side the ground rose with even more abruptness, and possessed rather a gloomy look, in consequence of the quantity of dark-foliaged trees with which it was clothed.

In one place the stream widened into a placid pool, the glass-like surface of which reflected the sun's light lustrously.

Then there was what appeared to be an old water-mill, though, so far as could be gathered from such a distant view as Captain Hawk had of it, some time had passed since it had been at work.

Below the mill the water formed a mimic cascade; the splash and roar were just audible.

Then further on the stream subsided into its former calmness of flow, and melted away in the distance.

The air was very still and the sky cloudless, and the effect produced by the beauty of the reposeful scene was so strong that some moments elapsed before the hunted highwayman could shake it off.

"Beautiful!" he murmured—"truly beautiful! When I gaze, I seem in doubt whether the turmoil and danger of existence is not all a dream. In the face of such a scene, it seems incredible that there can be such a thing as man, with his mad, warring passions, to deface it."

Again he plunged into a day-dream, in which many things mingled strangely.

"Enough of this!" he said, giving himself a slight shake "I am growing sentimental—ha, ha! sentimental! Where are my foes? From this elevation I ought to be able to make them out, even if they are some miles distant."

He turned round and looked carefully along the way he had lately come.

His eyes were keen and strong, and had the officers been anywhere within ken he must have discerned them.

"They have given it up, I suppose, for the present," he said, with great coolness. "What next for me?" he added, gazing upon the magnificent panorama below and before him. "Would that old water-mill—for old and ruinous I take it to be—afford me a shelter? I will make the trial, at any rate."

Having thus decided upon his proceedings, Captain Hawk commenced to descend into the valley with as much rapidity as the nature of the ground would admit of.

A few minutes only elapsed before the place he had mentioned was gained, as it was much nearer in reality than it had appeared to be when seen from the eminence.

The closer view showed that the highwayman had been right in his surmises.

For some cause or other, the water-mill was quite deserted, and was fast falling to decay.

"If I am any judge," the captain remarked, "some long time has passed since human foot last trod this place. That promises well for my security during the brief period I want to stay; and there is nothing near that will suggest to my foes the notion that I have chosen this for my halting-place."

He slipped from the saddle as he spoke, and having led Satan a few paces, dashed open a half-crumbling door which communicated with a dilapidated shed, which chanced to be of unusual extent.

Few traces of the roof were left, and the floor was as thickly overgrown with grass as any meadow—and grass, too, of good quality, as Satan proved, for he began to eat heartily.

"These will be comfortable enough quarters for you, old fellow!" said his master, removing bit and bridle, but only loosening the saddle-girths, in case of any sudden emergency arising.

This done, he proceeded to look well about him, for his curiosity was already strongly excited.

His examination brought to light no particular event—there was nothing that would serve as the faintest clue to account for the desertion of the place.

"I will watch for one hour," he said, "and if, at the expiration of that time, my pursuers do not put in an appearance, I shall come to the conclusion that they have abandoned the chase. In the meanwhile, let us look at the paper the squire's son was so anxious to obtain."

He produced the document in question while he spoke Opening it, he found it to contain only a few words.

"'To my only son, George, I bequeath the sum of one shilling sterling. The remainder of my property, of what description soever, to Mark Appleton, absolutely, save and except the legacies as hereinunder mentioned.'

"Duly signed and witnessed by that rascally steward, and his no better son, I'll be bound! It is to the point. I wonder, now, whether a lawyer could have done it better? Never mind. I will take good care of this, and will not rest until I have found out this Mark Appleton. Mr. Steward, you may make certain that you are foiled!"

The hour elapsed, but no more signs were to be seen of the police officers than were discernible on his first arrival.

"I am satisfied; and now for a little rest. I feel badly enough in want of it, and therefore hope that I shall meet with no interruption."

He gave one last look at his steed, and then betook himself to the mill.

Even in the sunlight, the rusty, broken, dust-covered machinery looked strangely gloomy and forlorn, as all things do which tell of man's presence and desertion.

Captain Hawk made his way to the topmost portion of the building, from which he could obtain an extensive view. Some old, blackened straw was in this place, and he stretched himself upon it with a sigh of weariness.

"A little rest now will just put me right," he muttered. "It must be a dog sleep, though, that must enable me to wake up at the approach of danger."

The reader will not feel surprised at Captain Hawk's fatigue, a long time having elapsed since he had taken any proper rest.

The consequence was, that he had not assumed a recumbent posture more than five minutes before he was sound and fast asleep—so sound that nothing short of a pistol-shot could have aroused him.

But the deep silence—which appeared to be one of the features of the place—remained unbroken. It would almost seem as though, from some reason or other, the mill and its surroundings were deserted by all human beings.

Captain Hawk's deep sleep continued for some time after the sun sunk in the west.

Had his enemies known where to find him, he would have been an easy prey.

At length, with a sudden start, he awoke, and looked around him for a few seconds with an air of great bewilderment.

"Confound it!" he exclaimed, "I had forgotten my whereabouts. I fancied I had that villanous steward at arm's-length, and was just about to settle scores with him. That was a dream. How dark it is, but it cannot be night, surely!"

Much to his amazement, and at first incredulity, he found this to be the case—night had fairly set in—a night that promised to be full as glorious as the day which had preceded it.

There was not the faintest or the smallest speck to dim the azure brilliancy of the sky, in which the moon was already shining with silvery radiance.

"A beautiful night—a most beautiful night!" ejaculated the highwayman, looking out at the opening at the top of the mill. "How calm all is around. Well, I will leave this place; but I fancy whenever I have the opportunity I will return to it. I will not linger now, however; I will get Satan ready for the road at once, and be off without delay."

The interior of the mill was very dark, and seemed doubly so after the bright landscape without, on which he had been gazing, and consequently it was with some little difficulty that he made his way to the lower portion.

Before passing through the doorway at the head of a flight of stone steps leading to the ground, he took the precaution to reconnoitre, and instantly had cause to congratulate himself upon having done so.

His eye lighted for a moment upon a dusky object some distance off, so far that he could make out little concerning it, save that it was in motion.

But as he continued to move, and as the dusky object came nearer, it assumed the shape and appearance of a man.

Captain Hawk, upon making this discovery, shrank back a step or two into the shadow of the mill.

"A moment longer, and I should have been too late," he muttered. "Who can he be, and what can he want? Surely he cannot have tracked me? And yet, to all appearances, this deserted mill is his destination. I cannot emerge now without being seen, and so I will draw back and wait. He appears to be alone, and one man need cause me no uneasiness."

That Captain Hawk was right in his conclusions as to the destination of the man there could be little doubt, for he walked hurriedly towards the mill along a little path which, however, had been so long disused that it could scarce be distinguished from the luxuriant herbage which bordered it.

CHAPTER XXIII.

THE SECRET OF THE OLD MILL.—RETRIBUTION.—THE MURDERER'S FATE.—CAPTAIN HAWK ONCE MORE ON THE HIGHWAY.

IRRESPECTIVE of the interest which Captain Hawk already felt in the old, disused water-mill, there was much to excite the curiosity in the appearance of the man who, at this lonely and silent hour, seemed about to pay a visit to the melancholy building.

The moon shining full upon him as he advanced showed that his form, though sinewy, was bowed and withered.

His hat was drawn as far as possible over his eyes, and a few straggling locks of silvery-white hair escaped from beneath it and fluttered in the wind.

What was strangest of all—or, rather, what most strongly excited the highwayman's attention—was, that he kept continually gesticulating with his arms, as though carrying on an animated conversation with some one, and opening and shutting his bony hands with a convulsive, spasmodic movement.

"If not so completely alone—as he certainly is," muttered Captain Hawk—"I should judge that he was expostulating very warmly. And hark! Surely that was his voice which I heard!"

He listened, and a murmuring sound floated to his ears, proving that the new-comer was speaking to himself, though the words he uttered were not distinguishable.

On—on he came till he reached the foot of the flight of stone steps of which we have spoken, and there he paused.

He turned back, looking across the fertile valley, doubly beautiful now that it was bathed in moonlight.

Then he made many strange gestures, as though of mingled fury and despair.

While watching his approach, Captain Hawk had by slow degrees retreated further and further into the mill, until he reached the crazy ladder communicating with the upper story.

After a brief pause the stranger came on again—the steps were ascended, the threshold crossed.

Then he spoke.

For the first time the unsuspected listener caught the purport of his words.

"Just such a night—oh, just such a night!" he exclaimed, in a voice that trembled with unutterable anguish. "The moon was shining then as now, and all was still around. Alas—alas! When will my breast know stillness and peace again?"

He interrupted himself with a deep groan, and then shuddered from head to foot.

Creeping further on, he paused near the wall; Captain Hawk wondered for what purpose, until he heard the creaking of a bolt, immediately after which a kind of wooden shutter was flung back upon its hinges, admitting the moonlight in one brilliant flood, and threatening the hidden witness with discovery.

But the old man—for old he was—appeared to be too much engrossed by his own thoughts to pay much attention to the objects around him, and with which he seemed wonderfully familiar.

Walking straight to one particular spot, where, to the excited fancy of Captain Hawk, the moonlight was brighter than elsewhere, he abruptly paused.

"This is the place," said the old man, moaning out his words rather than uttering them—"this is the place. Here they stood, side by side, with the moonlight silvering everything as it does now. God of Heaven! it seems as though only a few minutes have elapsed since that time, and yet they tell me it is years—many—many many years."

The last words were pronounced falteringly, and at the conclusion of the sentence he passed his hand several times across his brow, as people often will do during any temporary suspension of their mental powers.

Then he abruptly broke forth again.

"How beautiful she looked," he said, half regretfully, half bitterly—"how more than beautiful! I see now the smile which hovered on her lips! Oh, the dire bitterness of knowing that smile was intended for another—not for me! Curses on him for winning from me my dearly-cherished prize! But he perished, as all such should perish, only she went down to destruction with him, and I was left here alone—alone! Oh, if I could only recall that moment! The mill was prosperous then. The wheels went round, and the gushing waters made a pleasant music which she told me many a time she loved to listen to. Oh, those happy days! The wheels are rusty now, and the water which turned them is diverted from its course. Can I set them going once again? If I could it would indeed bring back old times. I will do it—I will do it!"

He quitted the mill with more suddenness than the captain had anticipated; but having no clear idea as to his intention, and knowing nothing of the time he might be absent, he did not venture to move from his hiding-place.

It was lucky he adopted this course, for the old man returned.

"It is done," he cried, in a louder voice, and exhibiting more frenzied excitement than hitherto—"it is done! Hark—hark! I hear the water gurgle—it is rising! A few more moments and the old mill wheels will strike again!"

He stooped down and appeared to move or adjust some portion of the machinery.

The rushing of water followed.

It grew louder and louder, until the wheels began to move, slowly at first, and then with dizzy rapidity, while the dilapidated, tottering erection seemed to shake and tremble with the unwonted din.

And as the fury of the water increased, so did the excitement under which this singular old man laboured grow greater and greater.

His gestures became more furious and extravagant, and his voice grew louder and more cracked in tone.

"Yes, here they stood," he screamed rather than said—"here, on this narrow plank, with the water bubbling and boiling around them. His arm encircled her, while she rested her head against his breast, and looked up into his hateful countenance with that old trustful smile which so maddened me, and which I have seen ever since—yes, ever, ever since!"

Again he paused, for his further utterance seemed to be impeded by a gasping sob.

But he went on, more excitedly than ever:

"How I hated them then—how I hated them both! The demon took possession of my soul. Their dream of happiness was short. Like a shadow cast by the cold moonbeams I crept behind them. Wrapped up in their own thoughts of love, they neither heard nor saw me. Then bending down he kissed her. Once, and once only, their lips met—the next instant they were struggling with the boiling, seething mill-stream, and I was standing here—here, on this very spot—alone—alone! The heavy, oaken, iron-bound floats on the old wheels struck them swift, death-dealing blows. That beauteous face which had been the destruction of us both was in a second red with blood, and the next stroke converted it into a hideous, shapeless mass. Then they both vanished, and the red-stained water, flowing on, soon became calm again."

He clasped his withered, skeleton-like hands over his face.

But only for a moment.

Removing them, he cast another glance upon the white, foaming water, and as he did so he started back as though his eyes had encountered some horrible object.

"No, no!" he cried, with an awful, yelling shriek—"no, no! Do not sear these poor old eyes again! Begone! Off—off, I say! Why is your face so like it used to be in the years long ago? It is calm, beautiful, and smiling as ever. Do not look at me like that!—do not—oh, do not! Ha!" he continued, bending lower down—"she extends her arms—she invites me to join her—she smiles again! Margaret, I come—I come!"

With the last words thrilling on his lips, he plunged headlong into the mill-stream, in pursuit of what he fancied he saw there—a fair, girlish face, with golden curls, and eyes of heaven's own blue.

Had Captain Hawk for a moment suspected the old man's intention, he would have taken effectual measures to prevent it; but before he could move a step, the murderer was struggling with the swift-flowing stream.

Round went the remorseless wheels; the heavy wooden floats cut short the death-scream which thrilled from the lips of the poor wretch, and in a moment afterwards there was nothing left to show what had taken place, save a ruddy tint in the water, which grew fainter every moment.

"How horrible!" murmured the highwayman, turning away as soon as he saw he could be of no service; "and yet, judging by what he said, his fate here must be an awful retribution. The double murder of which he speaks may be the occasion of this place being left thus to ruin and decay."

The awful fate of the old man had such an effect upon Captain Hawk as to make him feel the interior of the mill to be insupportable, and a sensation of indescribable relief came over him when he once more found himself beneath the canopy of heaven.

"Not a moment longer will I stay here," he muttered, as he made his way to the shed where he had left his steed.

On pushing open the old door, he found Satan comfortable enough.

Hastily slipping on the bridle and tightening the girths, he led him forth and mounted.

"Who would have thought," he murmured, as he rode away and gave a last look around him, "that this beautiful and peaceful spot should have been the scene of so dire a tragedy? Bah! I shudder to think of it; and yet surely he deserved his fate."

But even this reflection could not dissipate his unpleasant thoughts; but he consoled himself by thinking that as soon as the steep side of the valley was ascended he would indulge himself with a hard gallop.

The very moment, however, that he reached the high-road, his quick ear caught the sound made by some one approaching.

He stopped, and for the present abandoned his design.

"A single horseman," he muttered. "Who can it be, I wonder? Ha!" he exclaimed, listening with more attentiveness as fresh sounds came upon his ears—"others are coming, and from the opposite direction. I can hear two distinctly. If I remain where I am I shall be on the spot where they meet each other."

This circumstance caused him a moment's consideration.

The travellers came on at a rapid rate.

"I am scarcely in the mood to interfere with anyone at present," muttered the highwayman. "I will draw aside—the black shadow of these trees will serve well to conceal me—and continue my journey afterwards."

He at once rode behind a dense clump of trees which fringed the wayside, and which, from their density, promised to conceal him effectually from any passing observation.

As the travellers were not far off when he heard them first, he had not to wait long before they came in sight.

From the left came a couple of horsemen, mounted on indifferent steeds, which they urged onwards in the best manner they were able.

From the right came a well-mounted man, who, judging by his manner, looked with rather uncomfortable feelings upon those who were advancing towards him.

This became more decided when the two riders, having got within a few yards of him, stopped their horses and abruptly called upon him to halt.

The traveller had no resource but compliance, as it would not have been possible to have forced a way past those who blocked his path.

But he was not deficient in courage nor inclined to yield without making some resistance, for while with his left hand he reined in his horse, with his right he drew forth a pistol.

"Put up your weapon," cried one of the two travellers. "You have no occasion for its use, as we mean you no harm. We merely wish to ask you a question."

"Speak on!" said the one who had been stopped, and who, despite the assurance he had received, still held his pistol in readiness.

"We wish to know whether you have met with a strange-looking old man upon the high-road?"

"Describe him."

"He is tall and bowed—the wreck, indeed, of a powerful and sinewy man. His hair is long and white, and while he walks he has a strange habit of gesticulating wildly and muttering incoherent words to himself."

The traveller shook his head.

"I have not seen anyone," he said, "who in the remotest way corresponds with the description you have just given."

"Have you come far?"

"About twenty miles."

"And if he had been on the high-road you would, of course, have seen him?"

"Certainly. I could not have passed by such a one unnoticed."

"Then we may assume he has gone no further than this."

"May I ask who this person is of whom you are in search?"

"An escaped lunatic. For many years he has been confined in an asylum, where he has needed constant attention. From morn till night he did nothing but make those furious gestures and rave about some horrible murder committed in a mill!"

"A mill?" said the traveller. "I saw one down in the valley yonder. I would recommend you to go there. His delusion may have carried him to the spot."

"A good thought, sir! We will act upon your suggestion. Good night!"

"Moreover," continued the traveller—"though perhaps you may be aware of this——"

"Say on, sir!" cried the others, pausing.

"Why, I have heard that the mill I mentioned a moment ago is a forsaken place, and has been for many years, in consequence of a barbarous murder committed there. Hereabouts the place is always called the Haunted Mill, and such is the popular terror that few will venture near it even by daylight."

"Thanks, sir! Being strangers to this part of the country, we were unacquainted with the circumstance. Once more, good night!"

The traveller returned the parting salute and continued his journey.

It was not until both parties had got to a considerable distance that Captain Hawk emerged from the shadow of the trees.

"That, then, is the solution of the mystery," he exclaimed. "I might have guessed it. A lunatic! Well, perhaps so, but I have my opinion of his madness. He deserved his fate. About that there can be little doubt. He will be found, and those who find him will have little difficulty in coming to a correct conclusion as to how he met his fate."

So saying, Captain Hawk rode leisurely along the highway until he came to a cross-road, down which he turned without hesitation, though he had not the least idea as to whither it led.

"Now for a gallop!" he cried. "Away, Satan—away! My blood is chilled. When I feel it once again dancing in my veins I shall think differently of these occurrences from what I do at present."

His horse needed no other incentive to rapid motion than that which his master's voice afforded.

Away he went almost like the wind itself.

Hedges, trees, gates, and other rural objects flew past them with bewildering rapidity—so swiftly that one could barely be distinguished from the other.

And as he rode thus madly onwards the captain, by the spirit-stirring accents of his voice, inspired his matchless steed with double vigour.

As if by magic all those disagreeable images which filled his mind were chased away, and he experienced that peculiar elation of spirits which nothing but a good gallop can produce.

And when this was accomplished he gradually drew rein.

Then at last he waved his hat, and cried, in loud tones of exultation:

"Hurrah—hurrah for a life on the road! What can equal it? Nothing in the world with such a steed as thou art, Satan! Woa, then! Gently—gently! Have you not galloped enough yet? Steady now—steady!"

Satan, hearing his master speak, seemed at once to wish to continue his former speed.

"No—no!" said Captain Hawk. "But, come what may, the next thing that comes this way will have to pay a liberal toll. Then, after that, I will try to have my reckoning with the steward. I must not lose sight of him. And Lottie, too—what an age it is since I saw her last!"

The mention of this name called up a train of very pleasant recollections, and, probably in order that he might indulge them freely, he pulled up.

But his reverie was quickly broken in upon, and by anything but an unwelcome sound.

This was the distant rumbling of wheels—so distant and so faint that none but a highwayman's ears could have detected it.

But, practised as Captain Hawk was, he could not for a moment or two make out what kind of vehicle was approaching.

"It travels slowly—very slowly. And now," he muttered, "I could almost fancy it was receding. No—now the sound is plainer than ever. What can it be?"

He listened attentively, but some moments elapsed before he could decide upon the point.

The tinkling of little bells, however, came at last upon his ears with a pleasant sort of music.

The highwayman smiled as he heard it.

"As I live," he cried, "it is a waggon! Perhaps it carries passengers—most likely such is the case. But whether or not, I will be as good as my word, and compel it to come to a standstill. I have taken a good booty from a stage waggon before now, and who knows but that I may do so again?"

CHAPTER XXIV.

CAPTAIN HAWK STOPS THE WAGGON.—A MERRY COMPANY.—THE BOASTING LAWYER.—THE HIGHWAYMAN IS SMITTEN WITH A FRESH BEAUTY.

The lumbering old waggon came on so slowly that it afforded Captain Hawk abundance of time to get his weapons in readiness for service.

Indeed, after this was done, the clumsy vehicle seemed so far off that his impatience would not allow him to await its arrival where he then stood, and therefore he walked his horse slowly forward to meet it.

In these days it must seem strange indeed to read not only of a waggon being the object of a highwayman's attack, but that such a slow-travelling vehicle should ever have been made use of as a conveyance to get from one place to another.

Yet such was the case in some parts of England up to a very recent period, and at the time of which we write it often happened that this was the only public means of conveyance that was at hand, unless a post-chaise was ordered, which we need scarcely say was an expensive mode of travelling.

For the most part, the stage-coaches only ran on the high-roads, and as there were many places of considerable size lying out of the main route, the inhabitants had to content themselves with such accommodation as an empty waggon could supply them with.

Then there were two classes of persons who generally travelled by waggon from choice, not from necessity.

These were those who, although well able to pay stage-coach fare, were too penurious to do so, and went by waggon because it was so much cheaper—this last consideration quite outweighing the intolerable length of time taken by a journey, the rate being generally under three miles and a half an hour, so that they were often three weeks going from one place to another when the stage-coach would have carried them in three days.

The other class consisted of those who, having to travel for some distance with a large sum of money in their possession, chose to do so by waggon, as holding out more chances of safety, as they were not so likely to be stopped on the high-road as a stage-coach.

THE ATTACK UPON THE WAGGON.

Presented Gratis with No. 8 of the New Re-Issue of the Black Highwayman, by the Author of Black Bess.

[HOPKINS ON THE TRACK OF THE BLACK HIGHWAYMAN.]

We were induced to give this explanation lest the reader should consider it unreasonable that people with money should be found riding across the country in a waggon.

But Captain Hawk well knew that there was a strong probability of his being able to secure a tolerable amount.

At length the lumbering old vehicle came in sight.

It was drawn by a team of four huge, heavy horses, who took each step with the regularity of some well-made piece of machinery.

The four horses carried several little jingling bells upon various parts of their harness, and as they walked and nodded their heads these bells made a tinkling sound which in the quiet country could be heard for a long distance.

The waggoner trudged on beside his team with equally monotonous regularity—every step was of equal length, and his hat and long-thonged whip nodded in perfect unison.

The air was very still, and as the highwayman did not wish the inmates of the waggon to be aware of his presence until he was actually upon them, he checked his steed and waited.

The moment he stopped he caught the sound of voices engaged in conversation.

Apparently the subject was a pleasant one, for a peal of laughter was carried to his ears.

Little did they think that so redoubtable a personage as Captain Hawk was so close at hand, who waited until the waggon was near enough, and then stopped it in a fashion of his own.

This was simply by seizing the bridle of the fore horse, who no sooner felt the check upon his progress than he came to a dead standstill.

The other horses, after bumping against each other,

No. 8.

GRATIS with this Number, The ENGRAVING of THE ATTACK UPON THE WAGGON.

stopped also, and then a scream came from the interior of the vehicle.

But the most surprising and amusing circumstance was that the waggoner, who plodded on by the side of the vehicle much like a machine, continued to trudge forward, being quite unconscious that the team was no longer by his side.

The shrill scream, however, and the tremendous hubbub which succeeded it aroused him, and the startled manner in which he gazed around him was ludicrous to behold.

But in the meantime Captain Hawk made his way with as little delay as possible to the back part of the waggon, and at once drew back one of the flaps of tarpaulin, which, hanging down from the roof, formed a protection from the weather.

He was greeted with a general cry of dismay, which had scarcely died away before a couple of pistols were discharged in rapid succession.

"I fancy I had the villain then!" said a voice. "There is nothing like being a little beforehand with such gentry!"

"Indeed!" cried Captain Hawk, quietly, who had not been in the least injured by the double discharge, though the shots had whistled past him with unpleasant closeness. "You are very likely right, sir; but, you see, it comes to the same thing in the end."

This speech was followed by a loud yell.

The man who made this hasty attack dropped his pistols, and then plumped down heavily to the bottom of the waggon.

"Mercy!" he groaned—"mercy! Oh, have mercy upon me!"

"Stop there," cried the captain, suddenly changing his position, "and I will soon put an end to this part of the business."

The moonlight shone very brightly on the glittering barrel of the highwayman's pistol.

"Oh, sir," said a young girl, pleadingly, "let there be no bloodshed! Pray spare him and spare us all! Take what I have and let us ride on unhurt."

"Yes—yes," cried the man who had fired, "take what she has, and you will have no room to find fault with your booty. Take it, and let us go!"

"I shall take what I please," rejoined the highwayman; "and certainly full satisfaction from you will be one of them."

"No—no! Have mercy and spare me!" he cried, abjectly. "You don't know what wealth she has! Take her money and spare the rest of us!"

A most contemptuous expression came over the captain's face when he heard this speech.

The young girl, however, said, seriously:

"You shall have what money I carry with me—I can afford to lose it; and I shall not regret it if you spare the rest, who are not so fortunate as I am."

"That speaks volumes for the goodness of your heart," said Captain Hawk, who was touched at once by this exhibition of self-sacrifice. "And as I am not destitute of all feeling, I promise you that not one farthing of it shall be touched by me. One kiss from your lips is all I crave."

"Then you will never have it."

"You will force me to take your money?"

"I have already promised it, and told you you are welcome."

"Laura—Laura," said an elderly lady, who sat next to the young girl, "don't, for pity's sake, make such a ridiculous exhibition of yourself! You will learn to value your wealth properly when you no longer have any of it! Don't hesitate to preserve the large sum you have with you when the terms are so very light!"

"You may think so, aunt, but I do not. As for that gentleman who is hiding himself under the straw, he has done nothing but boast the whole of the journey that it would be a bad thing for a highwayman if he chanced to show his face, and that he did not care for a thousand such. Now look at him—I do believe he is more frightened than anybody."

While the foregoing was taking place, Captain Hawk had not noticed that one of the passengers had stealthily quitted the waggon at the other end.

He pushed his way between the tarpaulin, and so got on to the shafts, after which he stealthily crept across the roadway until he had concealed himself under the shadow of the hedgerow.

His next proceeding was to draw a pistol, which he cocked so quietly that the sharp clicking sound was unnoticed.

Then, holding the weapon with both hands in order to steady the barrel and take aim more effectually, he levelled it deliberately at the head of Captain Hawk, who happened to have taken up such a position as made him the best mark in the world.

"Ha, ha!" he chuckled. "Bang! Who killed Cock Robin? Ha, ha!"

He pulled the trigger as he spoke.

The report was terrific, for the weapon had been heavily charged.

Captain Hawk shook in the saddle.

He was hit.

He knew that, and felt tolerably sure that the injury was a serious one.

Like lightning, however, he turned in the direction from which the shot had been fired.

The blue, curling wreaths of smoke slowly ascending in the calm night air formed an unerring guide.

The man who had fired still retained his crouching posture, with the discharged pistol still in his grasp.

But the moment he saw the highwayman turn towards him he guessed his danger, and, with a wild cry of fear, sprang up, and, heedless of all personal consequences, dashed himself through the hedge.

Captain Hawk no sooner perceived this movement than he fired his pistol, but with what result he could not tell, for the man disappeared almost instantly.

His first impulse was to follow him, but the pain of his wound, which now began to make itself felt, caused him to change his mind.

As for the passengers in the waggon, it was by no means an easy thing for them to tell whether the highwayman had been wounded or not.

When they found him renew his demands with as much calmness as ever, they concluded that such could not be the case.

But Captain Hawk, with wonderful stoicism, made up his mind to conceal his injury, if such a thing was any way possible.

There was a dull, heavy aching about his brain, which increased each moment in intensity, strive as he would against it.

"Quick!" he said. "Your money, purses, and rings! I can wait no longer. I will begin, sir, with you!"

He addressed himself to the man who sat nearest and immediately opposite to Laura.

He began some ejaculatory excuses, but the highwayman speedily cut them short.

With many heavy groans and almost with tears, the man surrendered at length a very heavy purse.

From the boaster, also, he succeeded in obtaining an excellent booty, by which time he felt his wound increase so much in pain as to make him conscious of how unwise it would be to remain any longer.

"Here, sir," said Laura, trembling—"here is my money. Now depart."

But Captain Hawk only leaned forward suddenly and pressed his lips to hers.

A loud shriek followed, which the next moment was echoed by the young girl's aunt, who had caught sight of a few spots of blood.

The captain turned swiftly and urged his steed to motion.

For once, however, the noble animal refused obedience to the rein.

His master touched him with the spur.

It was to no purpose.

Not one step further would he advance.

There was now a dreadful dizziness about the highwayman's brain, who was just conscious of what was taking place, and only just.

Faintly came upon his ears a clattering sound, which seemed to come from far, far away.

With an effort, he looked before him, and then, with the swiftness of a lightning stroke, perceived his danger.

A troop of police officers were coming along from the direction in which a moment before he had endeavoured to urge his horse.

But for Satan's sagacity his capture would have been as absolute certainty.

There was a film, however, before the highwayman's eyes.

He saw certain objects, it is true, but he saw them as it were through a haze, dimly and indistinctly.

At this moment, by mere accident, he dropped the reins, and the horse no sooner found them loose about his neck than, with a snort and sudden bound, he started off and sprang over the hedgerow into the meadow like a feather.

The officers, who were very close at hand, at once fired after him.

It was a thousand wonders that the highwayman retained his seat when his horse came down heavily in the meadow; but after swaying dangerously from side to side twice or thrice, he recovered his balance, for long-continued practice had made riding a kind of second nature.

Seeing him stagger thus, and unaware of the hurt he had formerly received, the officers jumped to the conclusion that he had been wounded by the discharge of their volley, and commenced the pursuit with unusual eagerness and vigour on that very account.

It would really seem that Satan comprehended not only the dangerous condition of his master, but also that unusual efforts were required of him.

Never before had he put forth his powers of speed as he did on this occasion—the rate at which he went was absolutely incredible.

Every moment, however, it seemed as though Captain Hawk would fall from the saddle.

He had lost completely all power of retaining a perpendicular position.

His head bent forward over his horse's head, and his hands were entangled in the long, flowing, waving mane.

In this strange fashion, then—knowing nothing save that he was being carried with terrific rapidity over the meadows, and that his sole chance of escape lay in his being able to retain his perilous position—went Captain Hawk.

His pursuers gave vent to occasional loud cries of triumph as they hurried on, but the object of their pursuit heard them not.

Upon Satan's ear, however, the sounds seemed to come with preternatural loudness, and each time he would gather himself up for greater efforts.

The pursuing officers were well mounted, as was evidenced by the rate at which they came; but yet, despite all their endeavours, the distance between them and the flying horse grew greater and greater—slowly at first, and swiftly afterwards.

Miles and miles of open country were crossed.

The number of those in pursuit had dwindled down to less than one-half of the original number, but those who remained seemed possessed of an extraordinary amount of determination.

But it was only occasionally and in the far distance that they caught sight of the wounded highwayman.

At last both horse and rider vanished.

Still they did not despair.

The moon was still shining brightly—so brightly that they were able to distinguish with perfect ease the trail of blood which the fugitive had left behind him.

"We must have him!" they kept saying to each other, in order to keep up their animation. "We cannot fail to have him if we persevere for a little while. He will swoon and fall off his horse before long, and when that happens we shall find him without difficulty, because we have this well-defined blood track to guide us to the very spot."

These words seemed to carry conviction along with them, for what other termination would the pursuit be likely to have?

But the officers were not long in finding that they were not able to make such good speed now that their prey had ceased to be in view.

Every now and then they had to pause and look about them for the track, which kept getting less marked and continuous.

Their horses, too, were beginning to show very evident marks of the violent exertion they had been compelled to make.

Yet they saw no reason to despair.

They calculated that they must without doubt ere long come up with the wounded highwayman, and the prospect of making him a prisoner so easily was in the highest degree agreeable.

Away, then, they went, spurring their horses vigorously, for though they persuaded themselves that there was no need for hurry, their impatience would not allow them to go very slowly.

Their expectations soon after began to suffer a little abatement, for the track of blood became fainter still.

At times it was completely lost, and was only found again at some distance off.

"We must push on," said the leader, who by no means felt the degree of confidence he had experienced a short time before. "We must push on, or we may have trouble yet. It may be that he has recovered sufficiently to bind up his wound. But if this should prove to be so, don't let it dismay you," he added, hastily, perceiving the effect which his words had produced among his weary followers. "I need not tell you that after a man has lost such a quantity of blood as he has, he cannot travel very far. Forward—forward! Don't spare the horseflesh!"

CHAPTER XXV

SATAN BY HIS SAGACITY SAVES HIS RIDER'S LIFE.—THE RECOVERY.—THE LONELY INN.—CAPTAIN HAWK THINKS OF A NOVAL PLAN FOR STOPPING THE MAIL-COACH.

Leaving the police officers to push on in the best manner possible, we will turn our attention to Captain Hawk, whose situation it need scarcely be said was one of no common danger.

Satan, as we have already seen, galloped on until the police officers were completely lost to view, nor did he relax his speed until very many miles had been travelled over.

That Captain Hawk should have preserved his position in the saddle is indeed wonderful, but it almost seemed that the motion assisted him.

At any rate, it is quite certain that the moment Satan stopped his ability to keep his balance was lost.

He swayed twice from side to side, and the third time he fell heavily to the ground, where he lay as though completely deprived of life.

Satan, after a start and a loud snort of alarm, stood perfectly still.

He turned his face towards his master's, and remained as though watching it in anxious solicitude.

Nearly half an hour elapsed before the wounded highwayman made the slightest movement.

He opened his eyes languidly and looked up at the moonlit sky seemingly without being aware of his situation, or conscious of what had happened.

The powers of recollection, however, speedily reasserted themselves, and he was soon able to form a tolerably clear notion of what had happened to him.

"I shall have the officers upon me ere long," he murmured, faintly.

As he pronounced the words he strove to raise himself, and was glad to find that he succeeded much better than he could have ventured to anticipate.

But his head throbbed with a violent aching pain, and every object upon which his eyes rested seemed in rapid motion.

"Is it a bad wound, I wonder?" he asked himself. "I fancy not, or I should scarcely be living now and feeling so little of its effects."

In fact, each moment the captain found himself getting better and better.

This, upon examination, was fully accounted for.

To his extreme satisfaction, he discovered that the pistol bullet had done little more than plough up the skin half way round his head, carrying away the top of one ear in its course.

Such a wound as this was just such a one as would bleed profusely.

But the hemorrhage had nearly ceased, and had done for a long time.

"A wet bandage now," he said, in a stronger voice, "would, I fancy, almost put me right. There must be water somewhere close at hand, and I will strive to reach it."

He found it by no means easy to move, for he had been bruised by his fall.

The bubbling of a brook close by, which could be heard distinctly, acted as an incentive for further efforts, and by a deal of perseverance he dragged himself in the required direction.

Soaking his neckcloth in the limped stream, he applied it as a bandage.

The coolness was inexpressibly grateful.

For a few moments he was quite free from pain.

It was during this interval that he turned his attention to his horse, who had followed him to the brink of the brook with all the docility of a dog.

"Brave boy!" he ejaculated, in as inspiriting a tone as he could assume—"brave boy! You have saved my life this night beyond all doubt. But for you I should by this time have been in the power of my foes. Ha! What is that? Have they hurt you too?"

The last words were uttered in a tone widely different from those which had preceded them.

They were caused by the sudden discovery that Satan had received a wound.

There was an ugly-looking furrow on the animal's flank, from which the blood was oozing, though very slowly.

His first emotions, of course, were full of the liveliest alarm, and it was through being under their influence that he was enabled to spring to his feet.

No words, however, can possibly convey the least idea of the sensation of joy which he experienced upon making the discovery that the injury was a very slight one—so slight as to set at rest all apprehension.

It had bled freely, it is true, but not sufficiently to impair to any appreciable extent the strength of the noble creature.

The revulsion of feeling was almost more than he could bear.

"This wound must have been inflicted just as we left the waggon, when the officers fired that volley after us. Thank Heaven it is no worse, though I wish a thousand times I had received it instead of you."

The reader will now have no difficulty in understanding how it was that so easily-followed a trail of blood should appear upon the ground.

Had the whole quantity escaped from Captain Hawk's veins, as the police officers fully believed it had, he must have been reduced to the last stage of exhaustion; as it was, he continued to feel severely the effects of so great a loss of the vital fluid.

A liberal application of cold water made Satan's wound change in appearance to a scratch.

"We must be off now, old boy. Not too fast. But yet we will quit this spot, to which no doubt the officers will easily find their way. It will puzzle them, I fancy, to tell which way we have gone."

When he attempted to mount, however, Captain Hawk became better sensible of the extent of his weakness.

He had to make several attempts before he succeeded.

At last, having seated himself, he made his way in a direction that would almost carry him back to the spot from which he had started.

His object in doing this was in order that he might baffle the officers all the more easily, for he judged that they would continue to push straight on in the direction which he had all along been taking.

He was still very weak, and his head so dizzy that it was with great difficulty that he could decide whether his pursuers were within sight or not.

"I think all is well," he murmured, faintly. "My brain whirls, until all objects are inextricably mixed up. Forward, boy! Gently, now, for there seems no urgent need for haste, and I must make up my mind what I am to do. I fear this wound will change my plans a little."

Satan made his way onwards at a canter—a pace which suited his rider better than almost any other—and yet got over the ground with tolerable rapidity.

It was not long before the highwayman's thoughts reverted to one who was very often present to his mind.

This was Lottie, the daughter of the landlord of the lonely inn.

"I cannot be such a long way from the old place," he said. "Whether I shall succeed in finding it while in my present state seems almost doubtful. I will try, for if I gain the shelter of that roof I shall feel that I am safe; and a short time indeed of rest will make me myself again. I shall be keeping near the Hall, too. Come what may, I will be even with that steward. He shall suffer dearly for all his villany!"

With his brain in such a state of confusion, it would have been the easiest matter possible for the captain to have missed his way, and it is a thousand wonders that he did not.

Good fortune, however, would appear to have been his guide, and long before daybreak he found himself within sight of the house he so much desired to reach.

But by this time he was terribly fatigued.

"I have seen nothing of my foes," he murmured, as he cast a last look behind him, "and to the best of my belief I have left no mark behind me by which I can be followed. I trust I have not. If I thought I had I would turn my back upon this place, for I would not for all the world bring fresh trouble upon its inmates."

But everything around was very calm—so calm as fully to justify the highwayman in believing that none of his enemies were near.

The old inn presented a perfect picture of repose.

After a momentary hesitation, the captain knocked at the door—gently at first; but finding his summons disregarded, he availed himself of the butt-end of a pistol.

The din thus made quickly had the effect of arousing the landlord, who thrust his head out of one of the upper windows in a state of great surprise, as it was a most unprecedented event for anyone to seek shelter at such an early hour.

"Let me come in," said Captain Hawk. "I would not trouble you but for the fact that I am wounded."

"Good Heavens! It is the high—I mean Captain—that is, my benefactor!"

"Just so. I never thought to have exacted anything in return for what I have done, but I must entreat admittance."

"You shall have it; though I tell you frankly I should yield it much more readily but for one circumstance."

"Indeed!" said the captain, quickly, of course expecting that some mention of Lottie was about to be made.

"Nevertheless," he continued, "I cannot forget what you have done, and therefore you are free to enter."

"But to what do you allude?"

The landlord hesitated.

"Do not be afraid to tell me, but speak."

"I was alluding to the events at the Hall."

"What of them?"

"The squire was a bad man, I know, and yet I think the steward more to blame. At any rate, he did not deserve——"

"What?"

"To be murdered in cold blood."

"It was an atrocious deed!"

"Can you so characterise it?"

This question amazed the captain for a moment.

But immediately afterwards a light broke in upon his mind.

"You have been told, then, that I committed the guilty act?"

"I have. It is on the lips of everyone throughout the country."

"Yet I am innocent. I take Heaven to witness that I am wholly and solely innocent!"

"I will believe you," said the landlord, "and I no longer hesitate to admit you."

"I will satisfy you I am guiltless," continued the highwayman. "Fortunately, I have a proof of it."

An entire change in the manner of the landlord now took place, and he hastened to admit his early guest.

Satan was accommodated with the best stall in the stable; and, despite Captain Hawk's great fatigue, he did not quit his steed until he had seen him well fed, and his hurt, which was really little more than a scratch, properly attended to.

Then, and not till then, would the highwayman enter the house.

His own wound being but a superficial one was speedily dressed, and the landlord comforted him with the assurance that in twenty-four hours' time it would cause him scarcely any trouble.

Some refreshments were then brought, and during the time he was discussing them the highwayman made the landlord acquainted with the facts just as they occurred at the Hall.

"It is an unfortunate thing for you," said the landlord, "since everybody believes you guilty. And I am afraid you will have no little trouble in bringing the crime home to the right party."

"I anticipate trouble, but I shall do it for all that. Be sure, for your own sake as well as for mine, to drop no hint of my presence here."

"You may rely upon my fidelity."

"I will seek out this Mark Appleton and tell him all. His exertions will aid me not a little. In the meantime, I hand over to your safe keeping the old squire's singular will. If I retain it there is great danger of the document being lost. Keep it safely till I demand it of you."

The landlord readily promised.

"I am glad you have taken the trouble to acquaint me with all the particulars," he said. "To my mind there is nothing so very criminal in the act of stopping a person on the highway, since he has every chance to defend himself. It is a very different matter to a cold-blooded assassination."

"You are right."

Captain Hawk now was thoroughly worn out, and it was with a sensation of the greatest relief that he laid himself down to sleep.

He closed his eyes in perfect confidence, having no fear of any harm coming to him unawares.

Although nothing had been said between them on the subject, he was certain that the landlord would give him timely warning of the approach of any danger.

But the day passed over in perfect silence.

Not a single human being came near the old inn—a thing that often enough happened, in consequence of the successful machinations of the steward.

As night approached the captain rose, and was glad to find that, with the exception of a dull headache, nothing ailed him.

A liberal application of cold water went far towards assuaging this; and having paid as much attention to his toilet as circumstances permitted, he made his way downstairs.

Descending, he met with Lottie.

She recognised him instantly, and became covered with confusion.

Captain Hawk would willingly have detained her for a few moments, but this he found impossible.

Hastily murmuring a few half-inarticulate words, she drew aside and bounded up the staircase like some wild fawn.

The landlord accompanied him to the room he had previously occupied.

His first question was concerning the safety of his horse.

"He is as right as you could wish, captain," was the reply. "That was the merest scratch in the world which he received."

"He will suffer no inconvenience from it, then, you think?"

"None at all."

"And be fit for the road to-night?"

"Yes. But you will not want him?"

"Indeed, but I shall. As soon as the darkness deepens I shall be off. Nothing torments me like tranquillity and rest; besides, I may chance to meet with the steward."

"You may; and yet I scarcely think you in a condition to cope with him. He is a powerful man."

"And a coward."

"He must be."

"He is. And now tell me where shall I be likely to find this Mark Appleton?"

"I cannot tell you. Many years have elapsed since he was last seen about these parts. The steward made this part of the country unendurable to him."

"And he has disappeared?"

"Yes. Some say he went for a sailor; how true the report may be I know not."

"That is awkward. But I will find him; and when I make up my mind for anything it is rarely indeed that I fail."

He rose as he uttered these last words, and accompanied the landlord to the stables.

No time was lost in getting Satan ready for the road; but when he was led out his rider failed to display his usual agility in mounting.

"Farewell!" he said. "It is possible that I may return ere long."

"You will be always welcome," said the landlord. "I shall never forget that but for you at this moment my wife, my child, and myself would have been homeless wanderers beneath the canopy of heaven."

Captain Hawk said nothing, but merely waved his hand and rode off.

The personal resentment which he now felt against the steward was ten times stronger than before.

"What will Lottie think of me?" he murmured. "She must believe the report which that rascal has spread abroad, or she would never avoid me as she does. Yes, yes—that must be it. But I will know no rest or peace until I have compelled him to retract his words!"

He set forward at a swift pace as he spoke.

It was easy enough to make this determination, but difficult to a degree to carry it out.

He laboured under every disadvantage in trying to clear himself of the charge, and there seemed every probability that the odium of this base crime would affix itself to him in spite of all his efforts.

And although he spoke in such terms of confidence he had not settled any plan of operations in his mind.

As usual, he had thrown himself entirely upon his good fortune, and was prepared to act just as chance might direct.

It was not long before he found himself upon the high-road at no great distance from the Hall.

Having reached this point, he paused to think.

Scarcely, however, had he reined-in his steed before he heard some vehicle approaching him.

As it would seem, instinctively he turned his face in the direction of the sound.

But he could see nothing, for by this time the darkness was intense.

"Whatever it may be," he said, as he drew back, "I will allow it to pass by. It seems against the natural course of events, but I will do so, for I must not lose sight of what I have in hand. At any rate, I will have a look and see what kind of vehicle it is."

These last words did not promise very well for the maintenance of his resolution; but he drew back as far as he could, and as in this part the high-road was bounded by a rather steep embankment there seemed every probability that he would remain unseen.

CHAPTER XXVI.

CAPTAIN HAWK PUTS HIS PLAN INTO EXECUTION.—A NOVEL WAY OF STOPPING A STAGE COACH.—THE ALARM.—THE HIGHWAYMAN WISHES THE TRAVELLERS A PLEASANT JOURNEY.

Having taken up this position, Captain Hawk once again turned his eyes towards the approaching vehicle.

A couple of gleaming lights immediately arrested his attention.

"Can it be the mail coach?" he asked himself. "If it is, I shall repent the resolution I have come to."

Just as he spoke, the vehicle whirled past him with a rumble, a rattle, and a cloud of dust.

The last almost hid everything, though it did not prevent Captain Hawk from ascertaining the nature of the conveyance.

"As I live," he ejaculated, "it is the mail-coach, and I do repent it!"

He gazed wistfully after the cloud of dust, which was all that remained visible.

"Let me think," he exclaimed, apparently struck by a fresh thought. "Their next stopping is many miles off. Fast as they go, Satan, I know, can carry me easily at double the pace. It would not take me long to get past them. Come what will, I will do it, and play them such a prank as shall make them ever after hold my name in remembrance. Ha, ha! It is a good thought—a very capital thought indeed!"

Captain Hawk's temperament truly merited the name of mercurial in more senses than one.

It seemed scarcely likely that he should be so ready to engage in a fresh adventure when he had so many matters on hand.

But he did not pause to reflect.

As usual, the moment he arrived at a decision, he set to work to carry it into execution.

At a swift gallop he urged Satan along the high-road, as though his intention was to give direct chase to the stage coach.

But it soon appeared that this was not precisely what he meant to do.

On coming to a large white gate communicating with some meadows, he drew up somewhat suddenly, alighted, and opened it.

Leading his horse through, he closed it and remounted.

"The road winds a little, too," he said; "and that will be all the better. I shall make my way in a straight line. Ha, ha! The guard will have something to talk about the next time he comes to a halting-place. It is an excellent plan. The more I think of it the better I like it."

What Captain Hawk's plan was it is unnecessary to say here, because his actions will declare it.

Satan seemed to understand that it was necessary for him to put forth his utmost powers of speed.

He held his course in a straight line, overleaping every obstacle which presented itself in a manner that would have thrown a foxhunter into ecstacies.

This wild gallop across the open country did not fail to exercise its full influence upon the highwayman, who quickly found that every unpleasant recollection was banished from his mind.

One would have thought that he had never before looked forward to an adventure with so keen an interest and with so much impatience.

Looking over to the left, his eyes by chance rested on two tiny starlike lights, apparently gliding along the tops of the hedgerows.

"There is the coach!" he cried, in a voice of exultation. "Hurrah! I shall accomplish my purpose easily. Steady, boy! Away—away!"

Satan increased his speed, and the two twinkling lights soon ceased to be visible.

The highwayman held to the direction he had all along been pursuing, and after rather more than a quarter of an hour's hard gallop he halted somewhat suddenly before a hedgerow of unusual height.

"There is the high-road," he exclaimed; "and I fancy I have reached this spot at least a quarter of an hour before the coach. Woa—woa!"

So saying, he alighted with all possible rapidity.

"Now, Satan, old fellow," he exclaimed, "I am going to let you have your liberty for a little while, but it will be on the express condition that you obey my signal to recall you without delay. I will make things as comfortable as I can for you. This is really a beautiful meadow!"

With these words, he unbuckled the steel bit and removed it from the horse's mouth, leaving him at full liberty to graze upon the sweet grass all around and yet not removing the bridle.

This being done, he patted his steed fondly, and ran as rapidly as he could to a gate, which formed a means of communication with the high-road.

Satan followed him with the docility of some faithful dog.

Captain Hawk climbed over the gate, that being less trouble than meddling with the fastenings.

Satan looked as though he intended to go over too.

"No—no! Be off!" cried the captain. "I don't want you at present. Be off, I say, and avail yourself of the nice bit of turf you find yourself upon."

Satan seemed to comprehend that he was not desired to follow his master but would not go into the meadow.

He remained with his head over the gate looking wistfully after him.

Captain Hawk only gave one parting glance behind him.

Then set off at a brisk run in the direction in which he expected the coach would come.

Apparently, it was his intention to stop it, not merely single-handed but on foot.

Why he should think of adopting such an extraordinary and unlikely course will be quickly seen.

He was a good runner, but on the present occasion he found the severe exertion rather trying to his wound, and therefore was not long before he subsided into a trot which enabled him to make tolerably good progress.

A few minutes afterwards he caught sight of the twinkling, starlike lights in the distance before him.

They rapidly increased in brightness.

He ran on some distance further and then paused.

He was slightly out of breath, but by the time the coach got close to him he had quite recovered his calmness.

The coach came rolling on in splendid style.

The horses that were harnessed to it were really first-class animals.

Captain Hawk heard the coachman crack his long-lashed whip, and immediately afterwards, despite the rattle of the wheels, distinguished the murmur of conversation.

In one more moment the coach would have passed him, but he raised his arm and cried:

"Hoi! hoi! there! Pull up, if you please! A passenger! Have you an inside place vacant?"

It was not a very common thing for the mail-coach to pick up travellers on the road, but it so happened that on this particular night there was one inside place vacant.

With a great deal of flourish and trouble, the coachman brought his mettlesome horses partially to a standstill, and, having done so, he placed one hand above the rim of his hat, in order to have a better look at the traveller.

"Where for, sir?"

"London," replied Captain Hawk, in a moment.

"All right, sir—we have one inside place vacant. You are fortunate. Woa! woa!"

After an infinite deal of swaying to and fro, the mail-coach was stopped.

As usual, the windows were let down by the inside passengers, who were full of curiosity to know what was taking place.

The guard opened the door.

"Here you are, sir. Be quick, if you please!"

In the calmest and most matter-of-fact manner that can by any possibility be conceived, Captain Hawk entered the vehicle.

Surely this was carrying audacity to its fullest extent.

Bang went the door, and the highwayman found himself rather bewildered by the light that was burning in the roof of the carriage, and which seemed of dazzling brilliancy when contrasted with the darkness in which he had been for so long.

As usual, the passengers showed but scant ceremony, in making room for a fresh-comer, and the vehicle was actually in motion before the captain could seat himself.

"Pray excuse me," he said, crushing into a corner.

Of course, all eyes were fixed upon him.

A long ride in a mail-coach was a very tedious affair, and when anything occurred to vary in the least the monotony of the journey a most disproportionate amount of interest was immediately displayed.

The bold highwayman did not show to particular advantage on the present occasion.

His face was pale, and the bandage round his head gave him a very ghastly look.

Silence was maintained for a few moments, but was at length broken by a gentleman who was seated immediately opposite to our friend.

"A dark night, sir," he said. "May I ask whether you have met with an accident?"

He glanced at the bandage while he spoke.

"Yes," answered the captain; then leaning forward and sinking his voice to a whisper, which he took care should be loud enough to reach the ears of every person in the coach, he added:

"An affair of honour, that's all, sir. You understand! I winged my man, and I had a narrow escape myself. But it is nothing—the merest scratch in the world. Looks a little ugly, that's all."

"Very ugly," said the traveller. "Another half-inch and the bullet would have entered your brain."

"Yes, I suppose it would," answered the captain, with the same air of profound indifference. "But I trouble myself more about the things that are than those that might be."

"And a very good philosophy too, sir."

Captain Hawk had kept a good look-out along the side of the road, and now found himself close to the field where he had left his horse.

He foresaw that some time would elapse before he could effect his purpose, and so determined upon signalling to Satan at once, as circumstances might arise to make it necessary that he should regain his position on his back without loss of time.

Accordingly he let down the coach-window, and, thrusting out his head, gave a peculiar whistle, which he repeated twice.

He knew Satan could not fail to hear the sounds, and

was also certain that he would follow the coach for any distance.

Having accomplished this, the captain drew in his head and closed the window.

The proceeding was one that aroused the doubts and fears of the passengers in a moment, and on sitting down again he found himself regarded with universal looks of suspicion.

"Don't be alarmed," he exclaimed—"it was only my dog!"

"Your dog, sir?"

"Yes; I thought it was my dog—a splendid creature! I fancied I caught sight of him by the side of the road, and so I whistled. I must have made a mistake, though."

"Oh, indeed!"

"A most valuable dog," continued Captain Hawk. "I travel about a great deal, but while I had my dog with me I should never fear a highwayman."

"A highwayman!" ejaculated an old lady at the other end of the seat, and who was slightly deaf. "Oh dear me! What did you say about a highwayman?"

"Nothing that can cause you the least apprehension, madam."

"Oh dear me! I am glad to hear it! How glad I shall be when this dreadful journey is over, to be sure!"

"Don't be alarmed, ma'am," said the gentleman who had first spoken to Captain Hawk. "As I told you, in case the coach should be stopped—which I don't think very likely, by-the-bye—all you have to do is to sit still and retain your presence of mind. All then will be well."

"I for one shall not fail to resist," said Captain Hawk, touching his pistols significantly.

"Pho—pho! My dear sir, if you are at all wise you will think of no such thing."

"Not resist?"

"Certainly not."

"But why?"

"Take my word for it, you could do nothing worse."

"What do you advise, then?"

"Do you carry property of value with you?"

"I do—of great value."

"Then let me recommend you to secrete it somewhere; and then, should you be stopped, fein a good deal of reluctance, and hand over your purse. Mind there is not too much in it. If we all agree to do the like the highwayman will be satisfied and ride off."

"An excellent plan," cried Captain Hawk, enthusiastically—"a most excellent plan! Allow me to congratulate you upon it."

"And you will avail yourself of it?"

"Certainly, if the rest of the passengers agree."

"Oh, sir, it is quite agreed. I do not mind telling you that at the present time I am travelling with an unusually large amount of money, which I should not think at all safe only I have hidden it in my boots, where you will admit no highwayman would dream of looking for it. Should a demand be made, I have my purse ready, with which the villain will ride off, no doubt, well enough satisfied."

"The probabilities are that he will do so," said Captain Hawk. "And, after all, it is not wise to run the risk of sacrificing one's life for the sake of a few guineas. The loss of the one we do have the chance of replacing, but the other is impossible."

"Just so," said the traveller, who experienced to the full the pleasant sensation caused by feeling his advice approved of and acted upon.

"And I," said a sanctimonious-looking individual, who was scrupulously attired in black, and who wore a white neckcloth of alarming dimensions—"I have followed this gentleman's practical and sensible advice. Ahem! I am now on my way to London, for the purpose of purchasing some ornaments for our church. The subscription has been slowly mounting up, and now, as it has reached the requisite amount, I am off to make the purchase—ahem!"

"Indeed!" said Captain Hawk, with unfeigned interest. "And you have the money with you, I suppose?"

"Oh yes; here in this brown-paper parcel. I have abstracted five guineas, and put them ready to deliver to the highwayman, should we be attacked. Ahem! That will be charged, of course, in the travelling expenses."

Captain Hawk smiled, but said nothing.

He was anxious to hear some more revelations.

He was fast getting to the opinion that of all the ways ever devised for laying the passengers in a stage-coach under contribution this was the best.

"I hope we shall meet with no interruption," said the lady, who has been mentioned before as being slightly deaf. "The very sight of a highwayman would cause me to faint; and, as you all know, I am travelling to London with my niece's marriage portion, so that I would not for all the world be stopped. I should regret the loss ten times as much as I should if it was my own."

"My dear madam," said the traveller opposite to Captain Hawk, "as I said before, you have only to retain your presence of mind, and make the rascal a suitable offering, and all will be well."

"It's all very fine to hear you talk of your money in that way," exclaimed a military-looking individual. "It's enough to make anybody wild, that's what it is, and I beg that you won't say another word upon the subject. Here am I, poor devil, with nothing but my pay to depend upon."

There was only one other person in the coach, and this was a gloomy, sullen-looking man of middle age, who had propped himself up in the corner, and drawn a huge fur travelling-cap over his face, which made it hard to say whether his eyes were shut or whether he was furtively watching the countenances of those present.

He said not a word, and apparently it was not his intention to join in the conversation.

The military-looking individual, however, turned round and addressed him.

"You seem to take all this uncommonly quiet, Sir John. But, then, you are one of those lucky fellows that a few pounds more or less makes no difference to."

A growl was the only response that Sir John condescended to make.

A pause now ensued.

Captain Hawk rubbed his hands slowly over one another, in token of the satisfaction he experienced at what he had heard.

He considered himself sure of a good booty.

The travellers, for the most part, occupied themselves in watching him, and in a short time they had plenty to occupy their attention.

In the most deliberate manner possible, he drew forth a pistol, the priming of which he carefully examined.

Having done so, he restored it to his pocket and produced another.

He went through the same operation.

Then produced his favourite weapon, the singular appearance of which instantly attracted general notice.

"You are well armed, sir," said the traveller opposite to him, on whom as well as the rest some impression had been made by this exhibition of firearms.

"Yes—I take care always to travel so," answered Captain Hawk; "and just at the present moment I feel all right, as they are in excellent condition, and in readiness for instant use. By-the-way, ladies and gentlemen, I suppose you have heard of Captain Hawk?"

"The highwayman?"

"Yes."

"What of him?"

"Nothing particular," was the response, accompanied with a low bow. "I merely wish to announce myself as that individual—Captain Hawk—entirely at your service, ladies and gentlemen!"

CHAPTER XXVII.

CAPTAIN HAWK FINDS HIS ADVENTURE WITH THE MAIL-COACH END MORE DISASTROUSLY THAN HE ANTICIPATED.

It is open to question whether any other combination of words could have produced so electrical an effect upon the travellers in the mail-coach as the speech which Captain Hawk had had the audacity to make.

Absolute consternation and incredulity for a second or two made everyone speechless and motionless, and the stillness which prevailed was most remarkable.

But it was not of long continuance.

The rather deaf lady uttered a shriek.

The clever traveller clapped both hands to his boots with an air of ludicrous dismay.

The military gentleman rapped out an oath.

The Parson groaned and turned up his eyes, while he

gripped the brown-paper parcel as a vulture might grip its prey.

Sir John dashed his fur travelling-cap back from his face, and sprang to his feet with a louder oath on his lips than had been uttered by the soldier.

And while all these people were manifesting in such different ways their alarm and dismay, the causer of all the tumult sat and looked at them all with an air of perfect composure.

"Ladies and gentlemen," he said, with an affectation of extreme politeness, as soon as ever there seemed a chance of his being able to make his voice heard, "let me entreat you to calm yourselves! This exhibition of alarm is most unseemly and uncalled for, and all because I took the simple liberty of introducing myself to you."

"Liberty—the devil, sir!" said the soldier. "Do you mean what you say?"

"Do you wish to insult me, sir?"

"Fiddlededee! Are you in earnest?"

"I am; though why you should be in such a fume about it I can't guess, since, according to your own showing, you have nothing to lose."

"Well, I have heard and seen a few examples of matchless impudence in my time—very many, but nothing approaching this."

Captain Hawk bowed.

"You flatter me," he said. "But excuse me for reminding you that time is passing. I must attend to business. I have to thank you all for the charming frankness concerning the good things you carry with you, and I shall have the pleasure of troubling you for them in succession."

"But, confound it!" said the clever traveller, "do you suppose for a moment that we shall all tamely submit to be robbed by one man? Why, we are four to one! Ha, ha! Mr. Captain Hawk, you have overshot the mark; and rely upon it, decidedly the best thing you can do is to yield yourself up a prisoner at once. You must see the absolute folly of resistance. This seems like a case of the biter bit, doesn't it? Why, gentlemen," he added, turning to his fellow-travellers, "if you will only stand by me, this adventure will turn out most profitable to us. Instead of losing what we have with us we shall actually obtain the reward offered for this rascal's apprehension, and I know it must amount to such a sum as to make it worth striving for."

The highwayman's composure was not in the least degree ruffled by this speech, though many a bold man would have felt no slight amount of uneasiness.

He calmly drew forth one of the pistols which they had seen him so carefully examine a short time before.

The sight of the weapon, and still more the careless and indifferent manner in which it was handled, produced an instantaneous effect.

The deaf lady seemed to swoon away at once.

"Really, now," said Captain Hawk, addressing himself to the traveller who had just spoken. "I am surprised to hear you speak in so unwise and unphilosophical a way. Surely you must have forgotten what you were saying to me a few moments ago. Don't be so foolish as to risk your lives for the sake of your money. You will remember I fully applauded the wisdom of such a course of action.

The traveller muttered some bitter execrations.

"We should be more foolish, I take it, if we sat here and allowed one man to despoil us of our property when we might net a good sum ourselves and do society a service by taking him a prisoner."

"Wait a moment," said Captain Hawk, still playing with his pistol in a way that was dreadfully significant. "Just consider the risk you run. Three of you are sure to lose your lives—the fourth will probably take the whole reward; but it is most uncertain. Abandon the thought at once; and with as little loss of time as possible hand over your wealth. I will begin with you, sir. Pull off your boots. You had better do so yourself—if you leave it to me you will probably find me rougher than is agreeable."

The traveller glanced hopelessly at his companions, not one of whom seemed to possess the amount of courage requisite to make an attack upon the highwayman.

On the contrary, they seemed capable of doing only one thing, and that was looking after their own property and lamenting its prospective loss.

In the meanwhile, the mail-coach continued on its journey in the most placid manner, those on the outside little guessing the nature of the scene which was taking place within.

There was nothing in the world to make them aware that there was anything unusual going on.

The guard was asleep, and not dreaming of danger.

The coachman was in the middle of one of his most interesting stories with which he was wont to beguile the time of those privileged persons who occupied a seat on the box beside him.

"Come, sir," said Captain Hawk, "off with your boots! I will wait no longer! If you have ill-usage to complain of there will be no one to blame but yourself!"

"Will you not combine—will you submit to be——"

"Come—come, no more of that! Do you not see that your fellow-passengers have been wise enough to follow your good advice? Really, your conduct is too inconsistent! Off with your boots, I say!"

With a deep-fetched groan the traveller began to pull off one boot.

But never was anything unpleasant done half so unwillingly.

"It's all very fine, but when it comes to their turn——" he muttered.

Captain Hawk interrupted him.

"Make haste!" he cried. "Don't you see that you are keeping all the rest waiting? Be quick, I say!"

With a groan he pulled off one boot.

Captain Hawk in a moment pounced upon the money it contained, though he was not a little disappointed at finding that it was for the most part in the shape of bank-notes.

"Now the other, sir. No more delay."

It would now seem that the traveller had made up his mind to resign himself to circumstances since it seemed utterly hopeless to think of controlling them.

The military individual sat next, and addressing him, the highwayman said:

"I will take your word that you have spoken the truth. Do not fear that I shall think of taking from you any trifle you may have. A soldier is scandalously underpaid; and I am too fond of the profession to think of doing one of its members the least injury. All I require of you in return is that you remain quite neutral, and leave me to deal with your companions in the manner I may fancy."

"I shall not interfere," said the soldier, "and thank you for your consideration. What little I have I can afford to spare less than any of the others."

"No, no," said the traveller, who, having apparently resigned himself to the loss of his money, was busy putting on his boots again. "If we are to be robbed, let it be all round. Share and share alike, and no favour shown."

Of this speech Captain Hawk took no notice; but addressing himself to the parson, he said:

"I will trouble you for that little brown-paper parcel and the purse you had reserved especially for me."

"Ungodly villain! Are not the revenues of the church to be held sacred? If you touch them, the curse of the sacrilegious will rest upon you!"

"All right! I will bear the burden of that. No more words—learn the wisdom of making a virtue of necessity."

The wealth was with many dolorous groans handed out.

"Now, ma'am," said the captain, raising his voice, in order that the deaf lady should be in no doubt as to what he said, "I will trouble you for that wedding portion you speak of—you will have the consolation of knowing it has fallen into the hands of one who will make good use of it."

"No—no, sir. You will not deprive the dear girl of her right. Surely you are not in earnest? Bad as you are, you will not touch that?"

"Indeed, madam, but I must have it. And in taking it I consider I am rendering the young lady a service of the utmost value. When it is known that she is to be a dowerless bride, she will have the opportunity of testing the truth of the affection of the person who has sought her hand. If he breaks off the match, she will have the unutterable satisfaction of discovering that she has escaped the clutches of a fortune-hunter and a life of perfect wretchedness."

[CAPTAIN HAWK'S PARTING WITH THE LANDLORD'S DAUGHTER.]

"But," said the old lady, "he is rich. It cannot have been her wealth that he sought her for."

"The less need, then, for her to have any dower. If they love each other they will not find the loss of it any bar to their happiness. And now, having shown you that it must be to the advantage of all concerned, please to hand the money over to me!"

At this there was a general laugh, except that the lady did not join in it.

She was the only one that did not think the captain's reasoning excellent.

With sighs and tears she requested to be allowed to retain it.

But the highwayman was inflexible.

"Now, Sir John," he cried, "I have to deal with you, and then I will rid you of my presence, and allow you to ride comfortably on your journey. A gentleman of your

rank and position I shall, of course, expect to give me something handsome."

"Confound your impudence!" cried Sir John, who had witnessed the despoilment of his companions with infinite complacency. "I think you ought to be well satisfied with what you have got. Be off with you, and think yourself lucky to escape so easily!"

"Thank you!—but I cannot go without receiving my contribution from you. I could not be guilty of such a flagrant mark of disrespect as passing you over would be. Come, Sir John! Make no bones about the matter—you cannot help yourself. Your money, watch, rings, and other valuables—I must and will have them!"

It was, however, with the very worst grace in the world that Sir John surrendered these objects; nor would he have done so as readily as he did, but for the influence exerted by the sight of the captain's pistol.

No. 9.

GRATIS with this Number, The ENGRAVING of THE BLACK HIGHWAYMAN LEVIES A CONTRIBUTION ON THE PRINCE OF WALES.

"Now, gentlemen," he said, "I will wish you all very good night! Of course you will all remember this adventure. You will also know that never was contribution levied by a highwayman in a pleasanter fashion. As to what I have taken, you will easily make it good; and it might have fallen into the hands of those who would have ill-used you into the bargain—which strikes me as another advantage, since it frees you from this danger. Again good night!"

He accompanied the words with the politest bow in the world; and certainly, if anything could have reconciled the travellers to the losses they had sustained, the captain's behaviour would have done so.

He now let down the window, and again gave his signal whistle.

After that he cried out:

"Hi! hi! Coachman—guard! Stop—stop a moment—I must alight!"

Hearing the voice of one of the inside passengers, the coachman, fancying something was amiss, pulled up.

Captain Hawk had the door open in a twinkling.

But just as he was stepping down he heard a loud explosion.

He fancied for the moment he was shot.

He experienced then a smarting, burning sensation in his neck.

Springing out into the road and placing his hand on the spot, he found that a pistol bullet had made a round hole in the collar of his coat, and that the burning wad had set his neckcloth on fire.

"A close touch," he said, "but a most dastardly shot! I did not deserve it. Ha!"

There was a sudden rushing sound, and then he found Satan by his side.

He sprang into the saddle instantly.

Then rode towards the coach door, not heeding the danger there was that some one else would try a shot at him.

The coachman, the guard, and all the outside passengers were in a state of the greatest possible bewilderment.

They looked at each other without being able to form the remotest notion of what was the matter.

"I know not who it was that fired that shot as soon as my back was turned," said Captain Hawk, looking into the coach—"nor do I care to trouble myself much to find out. It is one of you, and I take the opportunity of calling him to his face, before you all, a base coward—a poltroon—a wretch unfit for the companionship of his fellow-creatures!"

Not a word was spoken in reply to this.

The explosion of the pistol appeared to have put out the light—at any rate, the lamp was now extinguished, which prevented Captain Hawk from judging by appearances who it was that had committed so treacherous a deed.

"It's a highwayman, Joe," bawled the guard—"I'm blest if it isn't! Wait a moment until I have got my blunderbuss ready! I'll let him know the London mail is not to be stopped and robbed!"

The guard made furious efforts to get his weapon ready for use as quickly as possible, and of course his haste defeated its own object.

Captain Hawk heard the words, and drew back at once, feeling no inclination to run the risk of receiving injury from so desperate a weapon.

"Cover him with it, Bill," cried the coachman—"cover him with it! And if he offers to stir, pull the trigger and blow him to bits! Only keep him a moment, for here come the officers!"

This was the first intimation the captain received of the vicinity of the officers, but immediately he heard a loud trampling of horses' feet close at hand.

Glancing swiftly in the direction of the sound, he caught sight of a considerable number of his foes.

How they had contrived to get so near unheard he knew not, nor did he trouble himself to speculate upon the point.

He merely uttered a cry of contempt, and then, waving his hat, he, in defiance of the guard's blunderbuss, touched his heel against his horse's flank.

Satan's bound forward was a sudden one indeed, and in another second he was flying along the highway with his accustomed speed.

The rapidity with which this was done flurried the guard to such an extent that he could not pull the trigger just at the right time.

But he banged away for all that, and so much at random that the troop of pursuing officers narrowly escaped destruction.

Captain Hawk and his steed escaped unhurt.

Still, the officers were dangerously close behind; and having so poor a start, it seemed that Satan, despite his matchless powers of speed, would find it no easy matter to distance them.

But Captain Hawk was full of high spirits in consequence of the excellent booty he had obtained.

Several shots were fired after him, but he heeded them not, knowing full well that he was out of range.

"A sharp touch will do it, Satan my boy!" he exclaimed, addressing himself to his steed. "On, my boy—on! Let me see you once again put forth your powers, and then before we have passed over many miles the officers will be far behind!"

The rate at which Satan had before been going was surprising, but after these few words from his master he seemed literally to fly over the ground.

Away—away along the broad high-road—away in absolute darkness, save when at distant intervals the horse's hoofs would strike upon a flint-stone and produce a momentary gleam: away—away at a speed which it was ridiculous for the officers to hope to equal.

Yet they held on with sullen determination.

They might not be able to overtake the fugitive, but they might be able to keep on his track till daylight, and then summon fresh assistance to their aid to hunt him down.

There was just the possibility, too, that the highwayman's headlong speed would bring about some accident—and from any delay which might arise, no matter how trifling, they had everything to hope.

At length Captain Hawk reached a point where the road sloped abruptly downward.

So far as he could tell, the descent was regular and the road smooth. He did not hesitate, therefore, to let his steed have his head freely, because he knew that much time would be gained by riding swiftly down.

But, alas! he soon had cause to regret having adopted this course.

It was with feelings of which we cannot hope to present even a faint idea, that he found Satan suddenly fall lame.

So painfully did he limp that it seemed all but an impossibility for him to place one foot to the ground.

For at least a minute Captain Hawk sat like one stupified.

"Good Heavens!" he at last ejaculated, with a heavy groan, "what am I to do? It seems impossible for him to move. Fool that I was to run so great a risk! What is to be done?"

Just as he asked himself the question, the distant clatter of horses' feet came upon his ear, telling of the approach of his persistent foes.

CHAPTER XXVIII.

THE POLICE OFFICER IN THE WOOD.—THE HUT.—THE KNEELING FIGURE.—SUSPICIONS.—A TERRIBLE TRAGEDY, AND A FRESH MYSTERY.

We go back now to Hopkins, the police officer.

The reader will remember that we left him in the wood to which the Black Highwayman had been tracked.

His courage had failed him somewhat, and to a certain extent he had succeeded in raising his spirits by swallowing copious draughts of brandy.

Then his attention had been attracted by a tiny glimmering light, which started suddenly into existence among the trees, and then remained fixed as a star.

It will be recollected, too, that strange, superstitious thoughts were tugging at the heart of this police officer—feelings which he had never experienced before, and for which he could only account by supposing them to be engendered by the loneliness of his position.

It is quite certain, however, he was dimly conscious that some great peril threatened him—that he was about to meet with some misfortune—but the sensation was too vague to enable him to form any notion of the kind of danger which menaced him.

Shaking off and despising these inward monitions, as he was able to do by blunting the edge of his feelings with the fiery spirit, he had crept cautiously and silently forward.

Ere long, however, he felt himself irresistibly compelled to come to a halt, while a voice seemed to whisper among the soughing branches of the trees: "Turn back—go no further!"

Hopkins improved the occasion by another appeal to his brandy-flask, after which he appeared to be considerably fortified.

"I will get the better of this weakness," he exclaimed, "or else it will prevent me from doing that which I am determined to perform. That I am on the track of this Black Highwayman, who has for so long and so successfully kept up the mystery respecting his actions and identity, I feel certain; and I should be a fool indeed if, under such circumstances, I was faint-hearted enough to give up the pursuit. No—no, it shall never be said that I turned tail in that manner!

"How steadily the light burns, to be sure," he added, after a brief pause, during which he had been gazing most intently. "I must and will know its origin. Come what will, I'll not pause again."

With increased determination perceptible in every movement, the officer moved forward.

Apparently by this time he had managed to

"Screw his courage to the sticking place,"

for, save when for a second he stopped to listen, he never once hesitated about his course.

So deep was the darkness that reigned among the trees that it was not until he had gone a much greater distance further that the light in any way altered its character.

"It's from a window," he exclaimed—"I would wager my life it came from a window; and what window can there be here unless in that woodman's hut? In a few moments I shall see."

As he crept slowly on he found the darkness gradually diminish, owing to the trees growing less densely together, until at last he was just able to distinguish the dusky, half-blurred outlines of some rude, straggling building.

There was something so peculiar about the appearance of the place that, partial as was the view he obtained of it, he had no difficulty in recognising it as the hut to which he had paid a visit in company with his superior officer, Peterson.

"It is the woodman's hut. There is not the least doubt about it now. I must be out in my reckoning, for I could have declared it lay in just the opposite direction. But it is here. It is impossible to entertain a doubt about it now."

As he came nearer to the hut, his progress was marked with additional circumspection, but not by the least display of timidity.

It was fortunate for his purpose that the ground about the hut should be free from underwood, and covered with soft, springy turf, because it enabled him to approach with what may be termed perfect noiselessness.

At last he came within arm's-length.

He held his breath.

The first thing he noticed was that the window was small, and that it consisted of many little diamond-shaped panes.

In an ordinary way, this window was protected by a heavy wooden shutter, which, when closed, would effectually have concealed every trace of light from the inside.

But now, from negligence or some other cause, this shutter was standing open. Perhaps proper care had not been taken with the fastenings, and the wind had blown it back.

The officer listened a moment or so before he ventured to take a peep through the window.

He was aware that he ran a very great risk of discovery by doing this, and he was most anxious to remain unseen.

But the perfect silence which prevailed encouraged him—a silence that could not have been more profound had the hut been untenanted.

For aught he knew, this might be the case.

Cautiously edging closer and closer, he resolved to satisfy himself upon this point.

The window was rather low, and he had to crouch down close to the earth so as to get beneath it.

Having accomplished this, however, without making the least approach to an alarm, he slowly, inch by inch, raised himself until his eyes were on a level with the window-sill.

Just a little higher permitted him to take the peep at the interior for which he had longed so anxiously.

The first glance was not very satisfactory.

Although when seen from the distance and viewed in contrast with the surrounding darkness the light had seemed a very bright one, yet on looking in it was apparent that the interior of the hut was but dimly illuminated.

Consequently, all that he saw at first was a portion of the smoke-blackened roof, which, with its beams and rafters, had a picturesque appearance rather than otherwise.

The officer raised himself a little higher, and then beheld the source of the light which had attracted his notice.

It was only a thick tallow candle stuck into the neck of a bottle.

But it is always easy to look from darkness into light, even though that light should only be of a very partial character.

Consequently, by the aid of the flickering gleams of this one candle, the officer was able to make out in succession the various objects which the place contained.

Furniture there appeared to be none, save one rudely-made chair and a still ruder table.

But the next moment Hopkins discerned something on which he fixed his eyes with all the intentness he was capable.

It was dark, was this something, very dim and undefined, and it was rather by instinct than by actual visual power that the officer concluded that it was a human form.

But what was this dusky form about?

Who was it?

Could it be the Black Highwayman?

The police officer's breath came thick and fast as he mentally asked himself this question.

His excitement and anxiety made him forget some portion of his former caution.

He raised himself still higher.

This action, and the fact of his becoming more accustomed to the gloom, enabled him to make out that beyond question the dusky object was a man, and that he was kneeling down in the farthermost corner of the place.

His hands were moving, and the next moment Hopkins saw that before this man was a large wooden chest, some articles in the interior of which the man was evidently arranging.

Still, as the man's back was turned towards the window, Hopkins could make out but little that was of a decisive character concerning his personal appearance.

"If—if that was only the Black Highwayman!" he said to himself—"if I could only make sure that it was him, and no other, how easily I could shoot him from here! One touch on the trigger, and there would be an end of the business. Oh, if he would only move!"

When he expressed the last words, he little thought that his wish would be so speedily complied with.

The man rose.

From head to foot he was attired in dark costume.

He wore a sword, for the hilt could be perceived faintly glittering.

His face was turned towards the window.

Fearful of discovery, Hopkins crouched down again.

When he again ventured to take a peep, the unknown tenant of the hut was in the position in which he had first seen him.

But his suspicions now were stronger than ever.

Transient as was the glimpse he had obtained, yet it was sufficient to make him almost certain that it was indeed the Black Highwayman, and no other.

"Would I could be sure!" he whispered. "I dare not venture to shoot him now, lest it should after all prove to be some one else. Let me think a moment. Ah! I have it—that will be the plan. So much better too—so much surer, and so much more credit to myself!"

He gave one more peep inside, and finding the figure in its former position, he glided slowly and silently away.

His old attack of apprehension again came over him.

Again he had recourse to the brandy-flask.

This time he did not remove it from his lips until he had emptied it.

The quantity of raw spirit which he had now drunk was very considerable, yet to all appearance it had not produced the trace of an intoxicating influence upon him.

"If I can find the door," he murmured, "and enter silently, I believe I can make sure of the rest. By what I can see, he appears to be alone—quite alone. If so, and I take him at unawares, I shall be more than a match for him."

And certainly, when the officer's burly form and muscular development were duly taken into consideration there seemed every indication that he was able to cope successfully with any ordinary man.

"If it should be the Black Highwayman, and I overpower him, not only will the immense reward be mine without any division, but I shall be certain of promotion as well—certain of it. It is worth a little risk. How odd it is that I should have such nervous feelings come over me to-night!"

While these words were passing through the officer's mind, he was not idle, but engaged in looking round the premises in the hope of finding the doorway.

The building exteriorly was of such a rambling character that this would have been far from easy had he not enjoyed the advantage of having paid it a former visit.

He came upon it at last, and crept towards it with limbs which he vainly strove to keep from trembling, though probably intense excitement was the cause as much as anything.

With white lips, he whispered to himself:

"If I open the door silently—very silently, and if I find him still upon his knees, with his back turned towards me, surely—surely it will be easy for me to rush forward and overpower him! Yes—yes, nothing could be more simple. What a fool I must be to hesitate! And yet even at this moment I feel tempted to find out what I can and then rejoin Peterson, according to arrangement. But in the meantime this man may go, and I may be unable to follow him. No, I must run the risk."

By thus speaking to himself, and counting on the success which he was likely to meet with, the officer doubtless thought he should raise his courage, and to a certain extent he was right.

But that disagreeable presentiment recurred to him with additional force the moment he raised his hand towards the drop-latch.

Again the mysterious voice seemed to whisper in his ears, and bid him depart.

Resolved to disregard what he considered as the most childish folly, he gently pulled the string that undid the fastening of the door, which in a moment yielded.

With the swiftness of thought, the officer crossed the threshold.

But slight as was the noise, it certainly was enough to attract the notice of the mysterious occupant of the building.

He turned round, and then, with an ejaculation, sprang to his feet.

Hopkins drew forth a pistol.

All his irresolution was gone now.

He was full of courage; but it was courage of that dogged, desperate nature which is exhibited by some wild animal at bay.

He was, too, rendered more determined by what he saw.

The figure which sprang up and turned towards him was that of the Black Highwayman himself.

Much plainer could he be seen now than on any other occasion.

At a glance, the officer took in his appearance from head to foot.

There was the long black coat, apparently of velvet, or some such rich material, the sombre hue of which was only made more manifest by the narrow edging of silver lace which it had upon it.

There was the huge vest, with its row of glittering silver buttons, and the tight-fitting small clothes, all of the same sombre hue.

The countenance was clearly cut, and an eminently handsome one; no one could have called it otherwise.

It was a youthful face, too; and though it bore upon it unmistakable traces of continual dissipation, yet it retained that peculiar impress which is the distinguishing mark of noble birth and education.

All this, which has occupied some lines to describe, Hopkins saw at a glance.

And more than this, he perceived that the chest before which the Black Highwayman had been kneeling was filled with rich costumes.

Particularly his attention was fixed by a richly-embroidered coat of the kind then worn by most young men of high birth or wealth.

"Surrender!" cried Hopkins, boldly, and placing his pistol on full cock as he spoke—"surrender, or by the heavens above us, I will shoot you where you stand!"

Apparently the sudden appearance of the police officer took the Black Highwayman greatly by surprise, for he never moved, but stood with his arms folded, in an attitude as calm and unconcerned as can be imagined.

"Did you hear me?" cried Hopkins, raising his voice, for he gathered additional courage from the aspect of affairs—"did you hear me? Surrender, I say, or your death be on your own head!"

The Black Highwayman, with the same unruffled demeanour, deliberately raised his arm and pointed to the officer.

But he said not a word.

The action and his manner were, however, so peculiar and so at variance with the officer's experience in such matters as to make him feel far from comfortable.

"Surrender!" he cried again, advancing several paces towards the centre of the hut.

But his progress was suddenly arrested by one word, which came upon his ears with the suddenness of an explosion:

"Hold!"

That was the word.

It was spoken by the Black Highwayman.

It was, according to common rumour, the first time he had been known to utter a syllable.

Mechanically, Hopkins obeyed.

But the moment after, ashamed of the hesitation which he thus evinced, he raised his pistol and came on again.

"Hold!" cried the Black Highwayman, in still more commanding accents. "I warn you that if you advance three steps from where you now stand your death is certain and immediate—nothing can save you!"

Situated as the police officer was, no one could have heard those words pronounced without awe.

Again he stopped, although, strange as it may seem, he did so against his will.

But he quickly recovered himself.

"Pooh—pooh!" he said. "You are my prisoner! Don't think you can frighten me away in this fashion! I say again you are my prisoner! If you attempt to resist a bullet will settle the business!"

The Black Highwayman laughed lightly and scornfully.

"I your prisoner," he said—"I surrender! Never! You stand upon the brink of the grave! If you make the least act of aggression against me your doom is sealed!"

Despite his uncomfortable feelings, the officer affected to laugh at the highwayman's threats.

He was encouraged to do so because the strange being before him produced no weapon.

He stood with his arms folded, showing as much unconcern as ever.

His sword was by his side, but he made no attempt to draw it.

"You will not impose upon me by such tricks!" he exclaimed. "I say again you are my prisoner, and again I call upon you to yield quietly, otherwise it will be the worse for you!"

"And I tell you once more if you advance nearer you are a dead man! If you choose to despise my warning no one will be to blame but yourself."

Hopkins uttered an indignant cry, and, pistol in hand, rushed forward, intending to precipitate himself upon the highwayman and overcome him with a sudden attack.

The Black Highwayman never moved.

An awful shriek thrilled from the lips of the police officer as he felt the flooring of the hut suddenly give way beneath his feet.

The pistol dropped from his nerveless grasp.

There was another scream, more terrible than the former one, for it seemed to raise a thousand dismal subterraneous echoes.

A rushing sound—

Then a heavy splash, as of some weighty object falling from a great height into water.

Mingled with this was another cry.

It came from the lips of a man who suddenly made his appearance at the doorway of the hut.

CHAPTER XXIX.

THE BLACK HIGHWAYMAN AND HIS ACCOMPLICE.—THE ABYSS.—A TRANSFORMATION.—THE WOODMAN'S HATE.

"Hush!" said the Black Highwayman, addressing himself to the man who had so suddenly come into view. "Hush! It is done. The danger is over."

"Good Heavens!" cried the man—"what has happened?"

The Black Highwayman moved his foot, and then it became apparent that he had been bearing all his weight upon a certain part of the flooring only a few inches square, for this portion was much lower than the planking which surrounded it.

The moment the pressure he had been exerting was removed, the small square piece of the floor slowly rose into its proper position, and as it did so the trap door, which had given way with such awful suddenness beneath the officer's feet, closed of itself, leaving no trace of the direful tragedy which had just been enacted.

The Black Highwayman's pallid countenance exhibited no signs of remorse for the deed, but retained that calmness and immobility which seemed natural to it.

The man, who was no other than the woodman interrogated by Peterson on the night of the robbery of the Bishop of Oxford, now with every sign of fear and horror crossed the threshold.

He closed the door behind him, and essayed to fasten it; but his hands trembled to such an extent as to make this impossible.

Aghast, he turned round to his companion.

"Who was it?" he gasped.

As he asked the question his very lips were white.

"A meddling fool!" was the stern, pitiless reply. "One who was warned, but who would not listen. He has met his fate."

"A police officer?"

"Yes."

"I thought so, by the glance I had. How came he here?"

"I ought to ask you that question!" cried the Black Highwayman, with an angry frown. "After all these pains the secret guarded so carefully is discovered. Where were you, on whose watch I so thoroughly depended?"

"I—I was watching," answered the woodman. "I could have sworn that no one could have come near the place without my knowledge."

"Behold the proof of your carelessness! How and by what means I know not the wretch found out the secret."

"And it has cost him his life."

"Yes; there was stern necessity to take it. If the knowledge rests only with himself I may yet go on undetected."

"Shall you remain here?"

"No; the place must be deserted."

"For——"

"You know where, without naming it. Take the horse with you, and leave this hut and all that it contains to its fate. I could never rest here again."

The man received the orders of the highwayman as some slave might have received those of an absolute monarch.

The bond of union which bound two such dissimilar beings to each other must have been a strange one, and must have been brought about by strange circumstances.

What these circumstances were we have yet to disclose.

One thing was evident, that while the woodman exhibited every token of deep concern for the death of the unfortunate police officer, the Black Highwayman was profoundly indifferent.

"That awful place!" he murmured, more as though speaking to himself than addressing his companion. "Never have I had the courage to lower the awful trap—never dared to tread near it. Are you certain that—that——"

"Certain of what?" said the Black Highwayman, who had again turned to the chest.

"That he is dead?"

"Quite. He falls forty feet, and there is an untold depth of water below that. Escape is impossible."

The woodman shook like an aspen leaf.

The calm indifference displayed filled all his veins with horror.

Involuntarily he bent his head towards the trap-door.

But from the hideous depths which it concealed no sounds whatever came.

The Black Highwayman had doubtless spoken truly.

The officer had perished.

In the meanwhile this singular being busied himself in making a complete change in his apparel.

Every article belonging to the Black Highwayman's costume he threw aside, and appeared dressed as a man of rank and fashion attired himself in those days.

A remarkable change was the result, for a greater difference than existed between the two costumes could scarcely be imagined.

His coat was of a deep crimson cloth, richly trimmed with broad gold lace, and studded here and there with gems of considerable value.

His vest was of blue satin, with large pockets and lapels, while his legs were encased in white leather breeches and silk stockings.

Upon his feet were shoes, on the top of which were large ornamental buckles, which were of great size and literally encrusted with jewels.

And that air of courtly breeding which we have before noticed became much more conspicuous; and no one could have guessed that so aristocratic and fashionably-dressed a personage could have anything in common with the Black Highwayman.

"Remember what I have said!" he cried, in tones of stern command, throwing on his cloak and preparing to leave the hut.

"And—and when may I expect you?" asked the man, with a submissive bow.

"At any moment. Farewell!"

He walked direct to the door, and then paused, as if a fresh thought had suddenly occurred to him.

"Stay!" he cried. "Before I leave it will be as well for you to reconnoitre. For aught I know, or you either, more officers may be lurking in the wood. Be quick, and ascertain!"

With another inclination of the head, the woodman glided forth.

During his absence, the Black Highwayman paced rapidly up and down.

His brow was contracted slightly, his lips compressed.

Who shall say what thoughts were occupying his mind?

More than once his eyes sought that part of the floor which had fallen beneath the officer's weight, and which could in no way be distinguished from the woodwork around it.

"Suppose," he muttered—"suppose that he should not have perished! No, no—escape, I know full well, is impossible—quite—quite! I will trouble myself about it no more."

But apparently the thought was not banished quite so easily from his mind.

"How long he is!" he murmured, impatiently. "Perhaps, now, I should be able to satisfy myself by one peep into the abyss. Satisfy! Yes, that is the word. I should be better satisfied if I took but one peep, though I am fully persuaded that there is no necessity for it—not the slightest!"

So saying, he again approached the chest.

He pressed upon the small square piece of wood, and immediately the terrible abyss in the middle of the hut flooring yawned open.

In some way he contrived to fix the trap-door open, for when he moved his foot the square beneath it did not rise as on the former occasion.

Going, then, to the rude mantelpiece, he took the candle, and, approaching the hideous depth, knelt down on the verge, and held the light down to the full extent of his arm.

The dark, moist, shining walls of the excavation were revealed to him, but little more, save a faint, star-like glimmer which was caused by the reflection of the candle in the water far below.

"All is still," he murmured, after having listened for some moments—"all is still as the very grave itself! He has perished, and the rash fool well deserved his fate!"

The opening of the door at this moment caused him to spring to his feet.

It was his associate who had returned, and who, when he saw the trap-door again open, stopped at the threshold of the door, and refused to advance another step till it was closed again.

This was soon done, for the Black Highwayman was anxious to depart.

"Have you seen anyone?" he asked.

"Not a soul."

"Of course you have looked well?"

"I have reconnoitred most carefully."

"Enough. Attend to my directions without delay! Even if this place is not permanently abandoned it must be for a time, that is quite certain. Take care of Phantom."

The man again bowed low, and the Black Highwayman took his departure.

The woodman followed him to the door.

He watched him until he saw him disappear among the trees.

It was in less than a moment that the darkness swallowed him up, and when he was no longer in view the woodman shook his clenched fists after him with savage gestures.

"How I hate him!" he ejaculated, in tones which testified to the earnestness and fervency of his feelings. "How I should like to bring this life to an end! Had I guessed that he was hanging half way down the trap I would have entered so silently as not to have disturbed him. One sudden push would then have sent him headlong down to keep company with the police officer! My servitude would have been over then."

He interrupted himself to pour out curses upon his own head for not having entered more quietly.

"But there," he ejaculated, with greater calmness of manner, "that chance is over now, so it is useless to think about it. I must wait. And so I am to abandon the place! 'Tis well, for after what I have seen to-night I should like to know who could pass such long, solitary hours in the hut as I do? If I could betray him! But no—no. My own safety's sake will not let me do that. I must banish the thought. Curse him—curse him, I say!"

Once more he broke out into imprecations more horrible than those which he had before made use of.

Whether the Black Highwayman was aware of the sentiments of his subordinate time alone can determine.

In order to clear up the events of this particular night it is necessary for us to turn our attention to the proceedings of that astute officer, Peterson, after his parting with Hopkins in the way we have recorded.

It was not many minutes after the separation that he paused and listened.

"I fancied I heard something then," he said. "What is it?"

But, apparently, the only audible sound was that of the wind as it careered furiously over the Common.

Just as he was about to continue his journey the sound came again.

It was a deep groan—such as would have been given by some one suffering extreme bodily pain.

The sound was borne but faintly to the police officer's ears; but he had no doubt about its character for all that.

"Ought I to try and find out what that is?" he said, irresolutely. "There is time, I think, and I ought to allow nothing to escape my notice. The sound came from that direction, I think."

From these last words it will be seen that he had made up his mind to turn aside.

He proceeded slowly and cautiously, for the ground beneath his horse's feet was of more than ordinary roughness.

Before he had gone many yards, however, the groan came again upon his ears.

"I am going right," he cried, for the sound was now much more distinct than before. "What does it mean? Has the Black Highwayman been at his work again, I wonder?"

The darkness was very perplexing; but in spite of it the police officer presently discovered the form of a human being lying in a strange, huddled-up mass at the bottom of a gorse-bordered hollow, into which he himself had a very narrow escape of falling.

Dismounting, he placed the stranger in a more comfortable position, though, judging from the loud, continued groans which escaped him, the process was attended with no ordinary pain.

Peterson then displayed his lantern.

By the aid of its light he discovered that the stranger was richly attired, and that he evidently was a member of the upper ranks of society.

"Can you speak, sir?" he said. "Because, if so, let me know your name in order that you may be carried to some place of safety."

The stranger evidently heard these words, for he opened his eyes languidly.

"You are a police officer?"

"I am."

"I have seen the Black Highwayman."

"Ah!"

"I pursued him across the Common, for I saw he was making for yonder wood; but my horse foundered, and here I am."

"Then you know no more?"

"Nothing."

"And how long is this ago?"

"I cannot tell—some hours I should think."

"And your name? You haven't told me that."

"Tracy—Lieutenant Tracy, in his Majesty's navy."

"Have you any friends hereabout?"

"No nearer than London."

"I am afraid you are too much hurt to be carried as far as that."

"So I am."

"What is to be done, sir? I am ready and willing to assist you in any way I can."

"If you could take me to some inn," said the lieutenant. "Surely there must be one not far off, and then I could obtain the services of a surgeon."

"Just so. There is an inn on the high-road, near the beginning of the Common."

"Yes, yes—I noticed it."

"We are not far from there. If I assisted you to mount my steed, and walked by the side of you, do you think you could manage to reach it?"

"I fancy so—at any rate, you shall be well rewarded for your trouble."

Peterson was by no means sorry to receive this assurance, though he professed to desire no other reward than that of doing his duty.

With no little difficulty the unfortunate lieutenant was raised on to the back of the officer's steed, and afterwards led to the inn which had been mentioned.

Here he was shown every attention, and Peterson left after announcing that he would call again the next time he came that way.

Just as he was passing out of the front-door some one clutched his sleeve.

He turned round in a moment to see who this could be.

It was the traveller who had been robbed of the three hundred pounds in gold, and who had been told to wait at the inn until Peterson called.

"Have you caught him, sir?" he said, wildly. "Have you got him—that is, have you got my money?"

"I have got neither one nor the other," said Peterson, shaking off his detaining grasp. "You ought to think yourself lucky."

Lucky!" echoed the traveller, in incredulous amazement.

"Yes."

"Lucky—me lucky! Oh dear!"

"Yes—you have only lost your money, while the

gentleman I have just brought has well-nigh lost his life. It will be many a day before he can be moved from here, so you are better off than he is."

Peterson clambered into the saddle, and struck his horse sharply with the spurs.

He rode towards London swiftly, without anything occurring to attract his notice, until he heard the whirl of rapidly-revolving wheels behind him.

He stopped to see what was coming along at such a furious rate.

He had not long to wait.

To his inexpressible surprise he caught sight of Lord Harcliffe's never-to-be-forgotten white horse, and the light gig with the very large wheels.

"Again!" ejaculated Peterson. "Why, I only saw it going the same way at the beginning of the evening. He must have turned back. What does it mean?"

The last question was more than he could answer.

On the present occasion there were two persons in the gig.

That they were Lord Harcliffe and Pharoah there could scarcely be a doubt.

But the vehicle dashed by so quickly that Peterson was not able to make sure of it.

"Confound it!" he said. "Am I to be continually bewildered in this fashion? Surely I am on the right track! What should he want riding about in this fashion for at night? Never mind, we shall see!"

He spurred his horse savagely, his intention being to keep close behind the gig, and, if possible, be in time to see its occupants alight.

In a very little time he became sensible of the folly of attempting this.

The white horse went two yards to his one, and long ere Tyburn Gate was reached all trace of it was lost.

This additional disappointment by no means improved Peterson's temper.

On reaching Bow Street he found himself so thoroughly fatigued that he was compelled to seek a few hours' repose.

Towards noon he set out to make his inquiries respecting the singular individual who declared himself on secret service.

Considerable address was requisite in the endeavour to find out whether this was correct or whether it was an audacious trick.

But Peterson managed pretty well.

He contrived to find out what he wanted to know without letting slip a word which might give a hint of the circumstances of the case and his reason for making the inquiry.

He esteemed himself fortunate in having managed so adroitly.

The result was that no such person had been commissioned by the Secretary of State, and consequently that Hopkins was correct in his suspicions.

With a boldness and audacity quite inconceivable, the Black Highwayman or one of his accomplices had played this part, and so contrived to get the police officers out of the way.

"I shall have him," he exclaimed, "in spite of all his audacity! Some day he will go a step too far. I must be patient and keep a good look-out. Oh, if night would only come! for if the Black Highwayman entered the wood, as the lieutenant says he believes he did, Hopkins will have some information for me."

Little did Peterson think what an awful fate had befallen his coadjutor, and that he should never meet him again in this world.

CHAPTER XXX.

RETURNS TO CAPTAIN HAWK, AND RELATES WHAT A NARROW ESCAPE SATAN HAD OF FALLING INTO THE HANDS OF THE POLICE OFFICERS.

When, after Satan fell dead lame, Captain Hawk heard the approach of his foes behind him, he imagined his difficulties had reached their culminating point.

A moment afterwards, however, he discovered that a fresh and greater danger assailed him.

At first he refused to credit the evidence of his own senses.

But it was not possible to do so for long.

Down the hill and no very great distance off he could hear another body of horsemen coming towards him.

To be sure he did not know that they were police officers, though probably such was the case.

It was rarely indeed that any other assemblage of mounted men were found travelling along the high-road by night.

Thus hemmed in, as it were, between two foes at a moment when it was impossible for his horse to move at any considerable rate of speed, Captain Hawk's position did indeed seem to be one of extreme danger.

For a moment, accustomed to perils as he was and in the habit of thinking so lightly of them, he sat like one stunned and bewildered.

He could see no sign of escape or safety.

Flight was out of the question, and if he remained where he was destruction was inevitable.

To attempt to fight while surrounded by so many foes would have been nothing short of madness.

But the chief cause of the paralysing sort of horror which had seized upon the captain's faculties was the circumstance of his priceless horse having sustained so great an injury.

Satan to him was almost as much as life itself.

And he had failed.

The highwayman gave himself a good shake.

"It is madness to stop here!" he exclaimed. "Action of some sort or other must be taken! How is it that all my powers of invention and strategy have deserted me?"

Determined to break the spell which had seized upon his bodily energies, he slipped from the saddle, and hastened to examine his steed's injured leg.

He had no trouble to find which it was, for the poor creature held it bent as though unable to rest it on the ground at all.

The cause of the lameness was revealed by the presence of a sharp and jagged stone which had wedged itself very tightly just inside the rim of the iron shoe.

So tightly, indeed, that it almost defied the captain's efforts to dislodge it.

When this was at length done, he led him a pace or two, but, to his dismay, saw no signs of the lameness abating.

This no doubt was owing to the pain from the jar the whole limb had suffered, for of course a stone could not have been wedged in so tightly as we have described without extreme violence.

Just when the captain made this unwelcome discovery, the sounds made by the hoofbeats of both the parties that were approaching had become so distinct as to make it certain that after the lapse of a few more seconds they would be in sight.

Captain Hawk grew desperate.

Satan could afford him no aid.

Having had that disagreeable fact forced upon him, he resolved nevertheless to obtain the safety of his dumb companion if such a thing was at all possible.

With this view he led him gently towards a gate which opened on to the high-road, and on the other side of which stretched a meadow of considerable extent.

No sooner did he stop at this gate for the purpose of unfastening it than he heard a low neigh, and immediately afterwards the rush of a horse's feet.

"Be off!" said the captain, waving his arm, for the horse already the tenant of the meadow seemed strongly inclined to escape out of it into the high-road.

At this very instant like a flash of light the idea darted into the captain's mind that there was a means by which the safety not only of his horse but of himself could be assured.

Like all good plans, it was a simple one.

Had it not been so he would never have had time to carry it out

"There is one horse in this field already," he muttered, "and why should there not be two? What will the officers know of it? Nothing. I will just slip off Satan's trappings and turn him loose—he will begin to graze, and if the officers chance to see him it is a thousand to one whether they recognise him."

Captain Hawk was always very nimble in his movements, but never had he been so dexterous as in the present instance.

In the twinkling of an eye, as one may say, Satan was divested of saddle and bridle.

"Off and away, boy—away—away!"

It only needed those words, uttered by his master in a tone little above a whisper, to send him limping across the field after the other horse.

With a gush of joy the captain saw that his lameness had diminished.

It now behoved him to be very speedy in his movements.

But little time had actually been consumed by the incidents which we have been compelled to relate at some length, still the officers were so near that one party had already commenced the descent of the hill.

With the saddle over his shoulders and the bridle over his arm, Captain Hawk ran to the hedgerow.

When he reached it he was overjoyed to find a deep, dry ditch on one side of it.

It was literally filled with rank vegetation.

Into this the highwayman flung his burden with very little ceremony, and then jumped in himself.

He was not a moment too soon.

Yet he was in time, and a sensation of deep thankfulness came over him.

"If they find me amid all this vegetation now that they have not the least suspicion I am here, and while there is not the faintest trace to lead them to my hiding-place, they will be clever fellows—ten thousand times more clever than I take them to be."

He ceased, and bent all his attention to a careful observation of the events about to take place.

It must be understood that when Captain Hawk came to his forced standstill on the hill, the two parties of police officers approaching from opposite directions were about equidistant from the highwayman, and as they were coming on at about the same rate of speed, it follows as a natural consequence that they must meet somewhere very near to the spot where the captain now lay concealed.

Captain Hawk soon became aware of this, and, so far from feeling any uneasiness in consequence, prepared to listen with the utmost interest to what might be said on both sides.

He had scarcely time to settle himself comfortably against the sloping bank of the dry ditch and choose a place where he could see between the interstices of the hedge before the party which had pursued him from the coach came in sight.

They mustered very strongly, for he was able to count no less than fourteen of them.

Just then the second troop appeared.

They were about the same in numerical strength, only their horses looked in better condition.

A mutual surprise manifested itself on both sides, which was convincing proof that the meeting was by no means premeditated.

By common consent, and without the interchange of a syllable, both parties came to a halt.

They pulled up almost opposite to the very spot where the highwayman was concealed.

But nothing was further from their thoughts than that the object of their pursuit actually had his eyes fixed upon them, and was waiting to catch the first words which fell from their lips.

"Hullo!" said one of the first party, riding forward a little in advance of his companions. "How many miles have you come along the high-road?"

"About a dozen," was the reply.

"A dozen!"

"It may be more. But why do you ask?"

"Have you seen anything of a single horseman mounted on a jet-black steed?"

"A highwayman?"

"Yes. Have you seen anything of him?"

The officer interrogated shook his head as he replied:

"Nothing at all."

This answer seemed not only to cause surprise but deep vexation to the one who had asked the question.

"Who are you after?"

"Captain Hawk."

"The devil you are! So are we! Have you seen him?"

"Yes. He robbed the mail-coach about half an hour ago. We missed him by the merest trifle. If we had arrived a couple of moments sooner we must have had him."

"And what did he do?"

"Rode off like the wind. We gave immediate chase, but do all we could it was impossible to keep up with him. The sound of his horse's hoofs grew fainter and fainter until at last we could not hear them at all."

"Where has he gone?"

"That is the question. By the way of him I should have guessed his intention to be to keep along the high-road; but he cannot have done that, or you must have seen him."

"Certainly. We could not fail to have done so."

"Then he must have taken to the meadows."

"Likely enough. He may have become aware that we were on the road before him, and that would cause him to change his course."

"Of course it would; and I suppose that is what he has done; but as there is no means of finding out whether he has gone to the right or the left, I suppose we shall have to abandon the pursuit and wait for a fresh opportunity, though I assure you it goes sorely against the grain to do so."

"I am afraid you cannot help yourself, for——"

The rest of the officer's speech was quite drowned by the loud neigh which his horse gave at this moment.

The creature had scented out the presence of some of its own kind in the adjoining field.

The shrill sound was responded to in a moment by Satan.

When Captain Hawk heard this he clenched his teeth and gave himself up for lost.

"Hullo!" cried one of the officers, as soon as there was silence. "What does that mean?"

"That there is a horse in the next field, I suppose."

"But suppose our man should be hiding there?"

The officer, upon hearing this supposition, raised himself up in the stirrups in order to see over the hedgerow, which was of a good height.

All the members of both troops followed his example.

The night was dark, but yet the obscurity was by no means so great as to prevent them from seeing with tolerable plainness all over the meadow.

They caught sight in a moment of the two horses, who were standing together with their heads and the tips of their ears pointed to the roadway.

"No such luck," growled the first officer. "A couple of horses turned out to grass, that's all."

"So it appears. You may depend that Captain Hawk, so far from being hidden anywhere, is at work putting as much distance as he can between himself and this place."

"I suppose he is. But just look. What a beautiful fellow that black horse is yonder—do you see him?"

"Yes—yes. He is a real beauty and no mistake."

Captain Hawk, in spite of his habitual carelessness, felt himself go suddenly chill all over.

He made up his mind that discovery was certain now.

Satan would be recognised, and then the officers would make sure of finding him not far off.

"I never saw one more to my mind," continued the officer who had first spoken. "He looks as though he had some mettle about him. As for the miserable screw I am riding now, he is only fit for the knacker's yard."

The other laughed.

"You had better make an exchange if he takes your fancy so much," he said. "You are on the King's service, and empowered to take him in case of necessity."

"I'll do it," was the answer. "You might travel many a mile without catching sight of a beast like that."

"Yes; if his powers of going are only equal to his looks he will be a prize indeed."

"He can go—don't be afraid of that. You never saw a horse of such a stamp as that which could not. At any rate, I'll have him."

The reader perhaps may be able to form some idea of Captain Hawk's feelings while listening to the foregoing conversation.

"I should think he heard you," said the officer. "Look, he's off! By Jove," he added, in a startled tone, "who would have thought it! Why, your fine horse is as lame as a cat. Look at him now. Why, if he had any weight on his back you would not get him a dozen yards."

Just as the officer had spoken, Satan, as if he understood an attempt was about to be made to capture him, turned round and trotted off

[CAPTAIN HAWK HAS A PEEP AT THE POLICE OFFICER'S MEMORANDUM BOOK.]

His lameness then became most strikingly apparent.

To a certain extent, then, it seemed fortunate that he had received this injury, for it put an end to the officer's ideas of appropriation.

"What a pity!" he ejaculated. "But for that the horse would have been worth anything."

"That accounts for his being turned out in a meadow," said the other. "But for that you would not have seen him left out like this. Never judge a horse by his looks when he is standing still again."

"I shall not. But what is to be done? I don't like giving over the chase in this manner."

"I am afraid we shall only be fatiguing our horses to no end if we ride away," answered the other. "No one knows where he may be by this time. However, as he has been hereabouts so lately, and as he must have gone on one side of the road or the other, suppose I take one way and you the other? It is possible we may be able to hear something of him."

"Anything would be better than tamely giving in," was the reply. "Since you are agreeable, let it be done."

Without any further discussion, this arrangement was carried out.

One party of the officers went over the hedge—which was low and full of gaps—while the other rode through the very gate through which Captain Hawk had led his steed such a short time before.

The highwayman noiselessly crouched down until he was completely hidden beneath the rank vegetation.

Another moment or two would decide whether he would escape or not.

"Poor fellow!" exclaimed the officer, as he rode past Satan. "It is indeed a world of pities to see you thus. But come on—come on! Captain Hawk's horse is black

No. 10.

Gratis with this Number, The ENGRAVING, AN AWFUL SHRIEK THRILLED FROM THE LIPS OF THE POLICE OFFICER AS HE FELT THE FLOORING OF THE HUT SUDDENLY GIVE WAY BENEATH HIS FEET.

and may be a better looking fellow than you are; but I doubt it. Come on!"

With these words, the whole troop rode across the meadow, and presently disappeared in the darkness.

Captain Hawk waited some time before he ventured to emerge from his hiding-place.

He could hardly believe that after so many narrow escapes of discovery the officers had ridden away and left him the field quite clear.

"If they could but have guessed it!" he muttered. "But no—no. How could it occur to them? But still, if at any time they should happen to find out that the lame horse was no other than Satan, and that I was hidden in the ditch all the while listening to every word they said, what a state of frenzy they will be in, to be sure!"

Whatever amount of pleasure the captain might have derived from these reflections was completely damped by the remembrance of his steed's condition.

In spite of his good fortune, his position was very far from being a safe one, and more especially as he relied more upon his steed than upon himself.

Taking up the saddle and bridle, he walked a little way, and then gave that signal which always had the effect of bringing Satan immediately to his side.

"He is not half so lame as he was," the highwayman muttered, in tones of great satisfaction. "If he goes on like that it will soon be all right again. He must have sprained himself slightly. The injury can be nothing more—that is certain!"

Satan rubbed himself caressingly against his master's breast, evidently much rejoiced at the reunion.

After a momentary hesitation, the captain put the saddle and bridle on again, considering that to be as easy a way as any of carrying them.

"A nice pool now," he said, "is the place I want; or a good running brook would be still better. Let him stand half an hour in that, and ten to one the lameness will wholly disappear. At any rate, I hope it will. If it does not, the injury is of a more serious nature than I at present take it to be."

So saying, he slipped the reins over his arm and walked on, Satan walking, with his usual docility, behind him.

It so happened that the captain had not far to go to find what he sought.

Running brooks are common enough in England, and one rarely goes far across the country without meeting with a pretty running stream.

Captain Hawk walked along the brook for some distance, until he came to a place where the water was deeper and ran with greater swiftness than elsewhere.

He made his horse walk into the middle of it, and there kept him standing for more than half an hour.

The water was intensely cold, and reached above the horse's knees.

But the captain knew there was no better treatment for a slight sprain than this in all the world; and the event proved clearly enough that he was right.

On leaving the water, Satan's lameness had so far diminished as to be only just perceptible.

Finding this to be the case, the highwayman did not scruple to mount.

"You shall go gently, old boy," he said, "and be well nursed until you have quite recovered from the mishap. Motion may do as much as anything towards carrying it off entirely."

He seated himself as he spoke, and then looked around him, as though in no little hesitation as to the direction he should take.

"I suppose," he said, "I cannot do better than make my way back to the high-road, because I know that is deserted by my foes. Gently, now—gently, boy! The night is young, and we have plenty of time before us."

CHAPTER XXXI.

CAPTAIN HAWK FINDS HIMSELF EMBROILED IN FRESH DIFFICULTIES.—THE STRANGE COMPACT.

NOTWITHSTANDING the lameness, Captain Hawk had some little difficulty in subduing Satan's tricksiness: he seemed as impatient and full of fire as ever.

But his master insisted upon allowing him to go no faster than a walk.

In this way the meadow was crossed, and the captain had to take the trouble to close the gate to prevent the other horse following them.

The very moment that the highwayman found himself on the high-road, he heard a single horseman approach.

He half drew back, as though intending to conceal himself, and then he changed his mind.

He caused Satan to take up a position in the very middle of the road, and there to stand like some black marble statue.

The traveller came on swiftly, and by the time Captain Hawk had looked to the primings of his pistols he was in sight.

The highwayman prepared to stand firm, and waited till the horseman was within a few yards of him.

Then raising his voice to loud, commanding tones, he cried:

"Halt—halt! Pull up, if you value your life!"

Almost by instinct, the stranger drew the rein and slackened his horse's pace; but he recovered from his confusion instantly.

"Stand aside!" he exclaimed, in a voice that was quite as stern and commanding as the highwayman's. "Stand aside, or, by Heaven, I will ride you down!"

"If you have a grain of wisdom, you will neither think of nor attempt to do anything of the kind."

The stranger took no further notice of the captain's words than to utter a derisive cry.

At the same moment he spurred his horse savagely with both heels.

The animal, maddened by pain, came on at a terrific tearing gallop.

His rider said something in a loud tone, but the din of hoofbeats made it inaudible.

But Captain Hawk sat firm.

He knew that there was not one horse in a thousand that would submit to being ridden against another.

When, however, he saw the fury with which this steed came on, he was half inclined to flinch.

Luckily, he did not; and the frantic horse, when within a couple of feet of him, suddenly stopped, swerved, and almost unseated his rider.

Before he could recover any command, Captain Hawk was by the traveller's side.

"You feel that?" he exclaimed. "It is the muzzle of a loaded pistol. Submit! for you are wholly at my mercy!"

"What do you want?"

"Your money and valuables."

"A highwayman?"

"If you like. But I must have the things I ask for!"

"Hark ye!" exclaimed the stranger. "At one odd time or another I have heard strange, romantic tales of you knights of the road, as you are pleased to call yourselves How true they are, I know not; but I have been told that you not unfrequently go out of your way to succour the oppressed, and to aid those whom you may consider worthy of your assistance."

"And what of that?"

"What of it? Why, are you one of those knights I have been speaking of, or a common craven-hearted robber?"

"Judge by events," said the captain. "I shall not return a verbal answer to that question."

"Humph! Indeed!" said the stranger, apparently very little, if at all, discomposed by the pistol, which was within a couple of inches of his brain.

"Come sir!" continued Captain Hawk. "It is no part of my business to stand and answer questions on the high-road. I have better use to make of my time."

"Very likely," answered the stranger, with an indifference that challenged the admiration of the highwayman. "Still, if you are inclined to listen to a few words I have to say, I shall look upon it as a favour."

"That is another matter entirely."

"You grant my request, then?"

"Certainly."

"Then," said this mysterious personage, speaking in slightly changed tones, "I think I may say that there is no one at this moment in all England who more requires the aid of a strong arm and willing heart than I do, and no one who is so badly situated for obtaining what is so urgently required."

"And you want me to assist you?"

"That was the request I was about to make, after I had

given you a little necessary explanation. If you consent, I will reward you to the best of my ability. I cannot promise so much as I could wish, or so much as the service would justly claim. Still, to the utmost extent of my power I will reward you."

"That is a secondary matter with me—quite. The main thing is, the nature of the service. Until you tell me what it is I cannot answer you."

"Then listen. The service is to aid me to remove from the power and custody of those who contemplate a cruel wrong to her—a young girl."

Despite the indifference which the stranger had formerly displayed, his voice now gave unmistakable tokens that he was sensible of some deep emotion.

"There is no enterprise I would more willingly engage in," replied Captain Hawk. "But proceed."

Upon receiving this assurance, the stranger seemed to throw off all restraint, and to take his companion wholly into his confidence.

"You must know first," he said, speaking with considerable rapidity, "that I am by profession a sailor. I took to it partly from necessity and partly from choice; but there is no occasion to waste time by going into my early history. Before I left England, though then a very young man, I had fallen deeply in love. Do not smile at the confession. The attachment has been a lasting one—at least, on my side. Vows of constancy were exchanged before my departure. We parted, and we have not seen each other since."

"But you have heard?"

"Yes, I have heard. Lilian—for that is her name—is an heiress; but as she is under age, and her parents are no more, she is under the custody of a guardian. I suppose the hardness of resisting temptation is the reason why so many guardians are bad ones."

"And hers is a bad one?"

"You shall judge. Lilian is now within a very few days of being of age. On my return, for some time I could hear nothing of her. Her guardian, finding out who I was, refused me admittance; and all endeavours to see my betrothed, or to find out her whereabouts, were unavailing. At last by the merest accident I discovered—I will not stay to enter into particulars—that her rascally guardian has had her carried to some religious place of refuge, where she is kept like a prisoner in a dungeon, while she is continually threatened that there she shall remain, unless she chooses to purchase her freedom by bestowing her hand in marriage upon her guardian."

"And this she refuses to do?"

"Most steadfastly.'

"Then she is true?"

"As true as a compass needle."

Captain Hawk smiled at the enthusiastic and delighted tone in which these words were spoken.

The young sailor noticed it.

"You smile!" he said. "But you know not what the feeling is like when you receive the assurance that, after years of absence, the one to whom you have plighted your troth has stood the hard test of separation, and is anxiously looking forward to a reunion."

"It is agreeable enough, no doubt; but, as you have truly said, I have not had the pleasure of experiencing it. But go on, sir: your narrative interests me much, and I strongly desire to hear the rest of it."

"I am still further informed, then, that to-night or to-morrow at the latest a stronger attempt than ever will be made to coerce Lilian into doing that which her soul abhors. That attempt I am resolved, at all risks, to prevent."

"And have you laid down any plan of operations?"

"Nothing very definite at present."

"You know the place of her incarceration?"

"Oh yes! I am now on my way to it, and doubtless should have arrived there by this time but for our meeting."

"Then it is not far off?"

"No; close by."

"And what is its character?"

"Well, there you puzzle me. If I happened to be in any other country than England, I should say at once a convent. It is some kind of religious house—or rather assumes to be; but it seems clear that it is only a cloak adopted to hide their nefarious doings."

"There are many strange places, and this appears to be one of them."

"It is. I am informed that the building is well protected by a stone wall of unusual height. Its object is stated to be that of enabling the pious inmates wholly to seclude themselves from the world; but from what I hear it serves a widely different purpose."

"That of screening their villany?"

'Just so."

"And is the building a large one?"

"I think so."

"And well defended?"

"Beyond doubt."

"How, then, shall you find out in what part of it your affianced is imprisoned?"

"The chamber has been described to me by my informant, who is no other than Lilian's own attendant, a young girl who has a sincere attachment to her."

"And this is the source of your information?"

"Yes."

"Where is she now?"

"I hope with her mistress. She told me she felt almost sure she could obtain admission. If possible, she would remain all night, in the hope of being of real assistance. At any rate, I am to expect to find a small light flickering in one of the windows."

"And that will direct you to the chamber you wish to reach?"

"Yes; and if I can only rescue her, as soon as eight o'clock strikes in the morning she will be my bride; and when once Mrs. Appleton, she will be able to bid her rascally guardian defiance."

Captain Hawk started when he heard this name pronounced.

"I beg your pardon!" he cried—"but what name was that?"

"Appleton."

"That is your name?"

"Yes."

"And what is your Christian name?"

"Mark."

Captain Hawk started again—this time so visibly as to attract the young sailor's notice.

"One would think my name was well known to you."

"I have heard it before, I confess, or one that sounded strangely like it—but never mind now. Let us turn our attention to the matter in hand. When we are in action you will find the time between this and daylight will speedily pass away."

"Yes, yes—it is growing late, I know. But you speak as though you had quite made up your mind to grant my request."

"I have."

"Then here is my hand; and I shall be more inclined to believe what I hear about you knights of the road than I have been. One might think easily that the days of chivalry had come again."

The captain merely bowed in reply to this speech.

"Come on!" said the young sailor. "Since we so well understand each other, we can finish talking as we ride along."

"I shall be glad to do so, for, unfortunately, my horse is slightly lame, and I do not want to push him on at all rapidly if I can help it."

"I will not permit it. Go at what rate you think proper; I will accommodate my horse's pace to yours."

"Then lead the way."

The young sailor with whom Captain Hawk had been so strangely thrown in contact set forward as these words were pronounced.

"You may ask me," he said, "why I have not availed myself of legal redress in this affair, and think it strange I should attempt to take the law into my own hands. But we sailors have rough-and-ready ideas of justice, and can ill abide the law's proverbial delay. Besides, I should not stand a ghost of a chance, as before even the preliminary steps could be taken such pressure would be brought to bear upon her as she could not hope to resist. It would be madness to defer."

"You are right. I approve always of the straightforward course myself, and therefore shall not object to your decision. I never felt more inclined to a thing in all my life."

"Give me your hand again! I heartily approve of your spirit!"

Captain Hawk and the stranger shook hands warmly and continued their journey.

For some time nothing was said.

As for the highwayman, he was deeply plunged in thought.

The events which had just occurred were eminently of a character to provoke reflection.

"There is something more than a chance in this," he said, mentally. "Here is the young man I intended to seek, and who has not been heard of for so long literally thrown in my way. I will render him this service first, and afterwards make that disclosure which he cannot be displeased to hear."

Little did the young sailor guess the nature of the thoughts that were passing through the mind of his companion.

He was solely intent upon the object he had in view, which was pretty certain to absorb his entire faculties.

"That, then, is the place," he exclaimed, breaking the long silence and pointing forwards as he spoke.

The captain immediately caught sight of a long wall of great height which effectually shut out from view whatever might be behind it.

"You are sure you are not mistaken?"

"Quite sure. There is no other place in the locality at all resembling this."

"Then we shall be right. Come on! Do you know what force we shall probably have to cope with?"

"I do not."

"That is unfortunate. But we must reconnoitre."

The place to which Mark Appleton had pointed was not very far off, and consequently it was soon reached.

When Captain Hawk said he should have to reconnoitre he pulled up almost immediately.

They were then beneath the shadow of some tall trees.

"It will be an awkward matter to peep over those walls," said Mark. "How is it to be done?"

"Wait a moment, and I will show you."

So saying, Captain Hawk, dropping the reins, placed both his hands on the pommel and sprang into an upright position with his feet resting on the saddle.

This was rather a ticklish balance to preserve, but he seized the branch of a tree and steadied himself.

At this elevation, of course, there was not much difficulty in drawing himself up into the tree, which he did with so much dexterity and ease that the young sailor could not help giving audible expression to his admiration.

"I can see now capitally," cried the highwayman, shading his face with one hand while he clung tightly with the other. "It is a large place."

"Yes. Can you see a light?"

"I can see two."

"Two!" ejaculated Mark. "Are you sure you can see two?"

"Quite certain."

"The deuce!"

"How are we to tell which is the right one?"

"That, my friend, is more than I know."

"Ha!"

"What now?"

"One is out."

"Then, depend upon it the one I want to see is that which remains."

Captain Hawk waited a few moments longer, but finding that the second light did not reappear, descended.

"It is quite certain," he exclaimed, "that there is some one about, and that our task will be all the more difficult on that account."

Mark was silent.

"But do not on any consideration give way to dejection," said the highwayman; "there is no need for it. If she is there we will have her free before we are an hour older."

The confident way in which the captain spoke—as though such a thing as failure could not happen unless they chose to allow it—of course produced a wonderful effect upon the young man.

"What shall we do next?" he said.

"Get a little closer. We are yet too far off to be able to decide upon our future proceedings."

Captain Hawk did not draw rein until he was fairly beneath the shadow of the high wall.

"So far very good," he exclaimed. "Now for the next step."

"We must surmount this wall," said Mark. "And look, there are some trees yonder, growing close by, which will enable us to reach the top of it without much trouble, for I am no bad climber."

"I suppose not," said the highwayman. "But how shall we descend? We might drop the distance on the other side without coming to much harm. A prudent general, however, always weighs the capabilities of retreat. Supposing us down—how shall we get back again?"

"That must be considered, certainly."

"It must. Let us leave our horses here and walk round the walls. It may be that we shall find something that will serve us as a guide."

This suggestion was promptly carried out.

Taking care not to make any more noise than could be helped, the pair began their examination of the wall.

They first of all came to what were evidently the principal entrance gates, and here they stopped.

CHAPTER XXXII.

CAPTAIN HAWK'S STRANGE ADVENTURES WITH THE YOUNG SAILOR.—LOVE AND DEVOTION.

"HERE will be a starting-point, at any rate," said Captain Hawk. "It will be in vain to seek admission by so well-protected an entrance as this. We must travel on."

Apparently there was some kind of lodge-keeper's residence near these great gates, but if so, and darkness and silence could be taken as any guide, it was unoccupied.

In a short time they came to the angle of the wall.

Passing round this and going a few yards further, Captain Hawk discovered a small doorway, and instantly came to a halt.

"Here is the very thing I was looking for and expecting to find. My experience tells me that there are very few places of this character that are not furnished with a small side entrance similar to this, affording a ready means of ingress and egress."

"But the door is fastened, is it not?"

"Sure to be; but yet there will be no one near to look after it, or who would give an alarm upon the occurrence of anything unusual. The fastenings will cause little trouble."

The captain shook the door, or rather attempted to do so, for, despite his strength, it remained as firm as the wall itself.

His next action was to take from his coat pocket three pieces of steel, each somewhere about a foot in length.

These he screwed together, and the young sailor, who had watched all his strange companion did with much interest, saw at once that the instrument thus formed was intended to be used as a crowbar.

One end was sharpened, and this the highwayman inserted in the crevice of the door.

A gentle pressure now produced a slight cracking sound, which was succeeded by a sharp snap.

"There goes the lock," cried the captain.

But somewhat to his disappointment, the door remained as firm as ever.

Seeing this, the sailor began to look rather blank, but Captain Hawk showed no signs of being cast down.

"It must be held by bolts," he said; "and if so, we shall have little trouble in removing them. I shall merely want you to remain where you are."

Just while he spoke he had noticed a tree with wide-spreading branches, which was growing close by, and up this he began to climb with great agility.

"Where are you going?" asked Mark. "What are you about to do?"

"Remain there a moment, and you will see."

The tree was a chesnut, and therefore very easy to climb.

In less time than it has taken us to write it, Captain Hawk had ascended sufficiently high to answer his purpose, and then he began to creep forward horizontally.

The branches of the tree projected right over the wall, and the highwayman was soon enabled to pass over this obstruction.

The distance to the ground was considerable, but he

let go unhesitatingly and alighted with a smart shock, the ground being composed of well-trod gravel.

Hastening to the door, he found that his conjecture was correct, and being now on the inner side, nothing could well be easier than to draw back the bolts.

As soon as this was done, Mark pushed open the door and entered.

"It is not fair," he said, "that you should run all the risks and go first into danger."

"Pooh—pooh! We will not talk about that. We must think ourselves lucky at having succeeded so well. We have now a ready means of retreat that we can avail ourselves of."

"Right. But would it not be better to bring our horses as close as possible to the little door? and we shall have a better chance of getting away should an alarm be raised."

Most certainly. That must be done at once."

The horses were fetched, and tethered under the chesnut tree.

As speedily as possible they re-entered the grounds.

They had some distance to go before the light was perceptible, as the little door was situated in that part of the wall which skirted the side of the edifice.

"It is there," whispered Mark, at length. "There is the signal upon which my eyes have so longed to look. Thanks to you, sir, my Lilian will soon be in safety."

"I trust so; but excuse me for saying that the less we speak now that we are near the house the better."

Captain Hawk was right enough about this, and their approach was now marked with the utmost circumspection.

There was a question on the tip of the highwayman's tongue which he much wished to ask, but he hesitated, and while doing so the necessity passed away.

The question was concerning what means had been decided upon for letting the prisoner know that her friends were near.

But it was quickly evident that their approach was seen, for the window from which the faint light glimmered was silently opened.

Two pale faces could then be indistinctly seen.

With a fast-beating heart the young sailor advanced a step or two.

"Pray be silent," he said, just loud enough for those he addressed to hear. "All is well! Escape is straightforward and simple. All you have to do is to descend."

Just then he looked around, and was astonished to find his companion had disappeared.

Where he had gone to he could not conceive, and he was beginning to have some anxious thoughts, when, to his infinite relief, he saw the captain appear.

The latter was carrying a short ladder such as is often required for garden operations.

"I guessed you would want this," he said; "and I felt sure that it would be found somewhere near. This will save both time and trouble. Ascend," he added, placing the ladder against the wall, below the window. "Be as quick as you can. I will remain here and keep guard."

Mark was too full of impatience to waste time by any reply, and ran up the ladder with the agility of a sailor.

It was much too short to answer the purpose required very comfortably; but still it was much better than nothing at all.

Apparently the keepers of this mysterious abode relied more upon the height of the surrounding walls for the security of their prisoners than any particular fastenings upon the windows.

At any rate, the one in which Lilian was confined was not barred; nor was there any other kind of impediment to egress.

"Come, dear one," cried Mark, a little louder than was at all safe. "Trust yourself with me, and fear not. In a few minutes you will find yourself in safety."

"I will trust you, Mark," said a sweet female voice. "If you prove false I shall care not what becomes of me."

"Do not speak like that, dear one. Come—summon up your courage! The descent is a little awkward, but by no means dangerous. There—that is it!"

While speaking, he assisted Lilian through the window, and clasping her by the waist, fairly carried her down.

"Did you not say that the lady had a companion?" said Captain Hawk.

"Martha?"

"Yes, if that is her name. Where is she?"

"I am here!" said a voice above. "But do not mind me—leave me. Fly—fly! You are already much too late! In a few moments the watchman will appear, making his round, and then such an alarm will be raised as will make your escape impossible."

The words were uttered with rapid, anxious earnestness.

"But we cannot leave you there. Stay a moment, Lilian," said the young sailor. "Do not tremble so; believe me, all is well."

"No, no!" said the girl above. "All is not well! Fly—fly, I beseech you!"

"Never—and leave you here. That would be both a base and ungrateful return to make for your services."

"Go—go! Do not encumber your flight with me. On the morrow, or whenever the escape is discovered, they will not harm me. I have done nothing—I am beyond their power. Fly—fly, I say!"

"Never, while I am here!" exclaimed Captain Hawk, and as he spoke he sprang up the ladder.

But even then the girl refused to descend; and it was not until the highwayman pointed out to her that her refusal would produce more delay and danger than compliance that she yielded.

The delay thus caused, however, though trifling, was attended with serious results.

Suddenly a small starlike light appeared.

It was the watchman's lantern.

At the same moment a rattle was sprung most vigorously, and the hurried trampling of feet became heard.

"Quick!" said the captain, as he reached the bottom of the ladder with his burden. "Fly—fly at once! Follow your mistress! I will settle this fellow!"

The watchman little thought what kind of foe it was that he had to contend with, and so came on with a great deal of valour.

The captain, however, resolved to astonish him.

Accordingly, he seized the short ladder which had been of such service to them, and throwing it into a position similar to that in which a lance would be held, he with this novel weapon charged at the lantern with all his might.

The shock from this novel weapon was very severe.

Not being prepared for anything of the kind, the watchman was taken at a great disadvantage.

Before he could form the least idea of what was going to happen, he felt himself borne to the earth with a force which not only deprived him of his wind, but also made him feel as though every bone in his body was broken.

Having done this execution, Captain Hawk hastened to rejoin the fugitives, who were now rather more than half way to the little door in the wall.

What had just happened, however, had clearly been sufficient to arouse all the inmates of the building

Lights were flashing from window to window.

Then came the loud report of a firearm.

Captain Hawk felt a whole cloud of missiles dash past him.

"My friends," he cried, "haste—haste! Are you hurt?"

"No; are you?"

"Not at all. Forward—forward! Everything now depends upon the rapidity of our movements!"

The inmates of the house were of a desperate character, for another shot was fired after the fugitives.

Many footsteps, too, became audible.

It was no easy thing to reach the little door in the wall.

Lilian was in a half-fainting condition from terror, and had to be carried by her lover.

The girl who had shown such a rare spirit of self-sacrifice led the way, turning round every moment in the endeavour to cheer her mistress.

Just as the threshold was reached, those who were in pursuit came to a halt and fired a volley.

Captain Hawk and the young sailor both felt that they were slightly hit.

The girl Martha, too, had uttered a faint scream, but whether this was from fear or pain there was no time to ascertain.

Mark was in an agony of doubt, for Lilian was now quite insensible, and might have received a serious injury without giving any token of it.

No sooner was the threshold crossed than Captain

Hawk dashed the door shut in a moment, and putting forth all his strength, determined to hold it fast.

"Now," he cried, "be quick and mount! I must soon quit this position. Still, it gives you a chance. Quick—quick!"

The sailor was not slow to comprehend the advantages which this gave him, and he improved the occasion to the utmost.

Lilian being so perfectly helpless, made mounting a most difficult process; but it was accomplished much more speedily than could have been expected.

The girl Martha untied Satan's rein from the branch of the tree.

But before she could do this the party in pursuit arrived at the door; yet such was Captain Hawk's strength and determination that their united efforts failed for a moment or so to force it open.

"Fire!" said a voice. "A pistol shot will remove this obstruction, I'll warrant."

Hardly had the last word escaped his lips when a bullet came crashing through the woodwork, passing very close to the captain's head.

But he saw now, on looking back, that all was in readiness for instant flight.

Relinquishing his hold, then, he ran with all speed to Satan, and at one spring seated himself in the saddle, to the great admiration of his companion.

"Now, Martha," he cried, "give me your hands. Now spring! There—that will do. Off and away now—off and away!"

While speaking, he swung the girl into the saddle before him, and set the example of dashing off at full gallop.

The young sailor kept up with him tolerably well.

As for the pursuers, as they appeared to be unprovided with horses, their efforts went for nothing.

They only fired a few impotent shots, and then they were lost sight of altogether.

Nevertheless, the fugitives did not relax their speed until they had placed at least half a dozen miles between them and the place of their adventure.

"My friend," said Mark, "you said something to me about your horse being lame, and your incapability to go at any great speed in consequence; but if this is a specimen of a lame pace, I should like to know what you call a good one."

"Will you believe it," said the captain, "that the excitement caused by what we have been about made me forget all about my horse's lameness?"

"Then I should say he has forgot it too."

"It seems like it. The sprain was slight, and the consequences of it appear to have passed completely away."

"I am glad of it. And now—as I daresay you are tolerably well acquainted with the locality—can you tell me where we shall find an inn? Lilian has never moved. I do not think she is hurt," he added—"only insensible from terror."

"This poor girl has been injured, I am afraid," said the captain. "She does not speak, nor does she appear to understand one word I say to her."

"I trust she is not badly injured," answered Mark, with great agitation. "Can you not direct me to an inn?"

"I cannot direct you," was the reply, "but I have little doubt that if we travel on a little further and make good use of our eyes we shall meet with one."

"I trust so. Let us renew our speed."

At a canter the little party resumed their interrupted progress.

Captain Hawk's prediction was very quickly verified.

After going only a few hundred yards further they came to an inn, all the windows of which were plunged in darkness.

The time was somewhere about an hour before daybreak.

"We are not likely to find anyone up," he said. "But we shall soon be attended to for all that."

He rode direct to the front-door of the inn and hammered away at it with the butt-end of a pistol with great vigour.

Such a clatter as this produced could hardly fail to wake the soundest sleeper, and in less than a moment a night-capped head appeared at one of the windows.

"We want accommodation," cried Captain Hawk, without waiting for any questions to be asked; "and we will pay handsomely for it if you will make haste and let us have the best of everything the place affords."

"All right, gentlemen," answered the landlord, in a voice very different from that he had intended to adopt when he first sprang from his warm bed with the terrific knocking ringing in his ears—"I will be down in a moment."

He was almost as good as his word.

"We had better wait until we have some assistance," said Captain Hawk; and the young sailor, despite his impatience, could not help seeing that this was the best plan.

Fortunately, he was not kept long in suspense, for, as we have said, the landlord speedily appeared.

His astonishment was very great upon finding that his unseasonable guests each carried what appeared to be a lifeless female form.

"They have only fainted," cried Captain Hawk. "Help my friend there, and he will dismount."

The landlord obeyed.

Just then the ostler put in his appearance.

He performed for the highwayman a similar service.

More inmates of the inn now came forward, carrying candles.

The light from these fell upon Martha.

The ostler immediately gave utterance to a shriek of dismay.

"Help—help!" he cried. "Murder! There is somebody murdered!"

"Silence, fool!" said the highwayman, angrily, taking the form of Martha from his arms. "Let me have your attention," he added, as he strode to the inn-door—"I was afraid she had been hurt."

This filled Mark with the utmost alarm, for he at once feared Lilian was also dead or badly hurt, for she showed not the slightest signs of life.

Having alighted from his horse, he took her in his arms, for he would suffer no one to carry her into the inn save himself.

Then, to his unmistakable joy, he heard her sigh faintly, after which she opened her eyes languidly.

"She lives!" he exclaimed, in tones that thrilled through all who heard him—"she lives!"

He sprang up the steps before the inn-door as he spoke.

Captain Hawk had been deeply touched by the devotion shown by the girl Martha—so much so that it made him disregard his own danger entirely.

Having placed her upon a sofa, he inquired eagerly for a medical man.

There was an expression on her face which he feared to look on.

Having been directed, he mounted Satan and rode off, leading Mark's horse by the rein for the doctor's use, thus avoiding all unnecessary delay.

The time occupied by his errand was short indeed.

The surgeon, by good fortune, was just returning home.

He was on the doorstep when the captain arrived, and he mounted the spare horse which had been brought for his accommodation in a moment.

On the way back he made his inquiries; but he received very vague replies, the captain thinking it much better that Mark Appleton should answer questions instead of himself.

The doctor's report was waited for with great anxiety.

It came at length.

Mark's worst fears were set at rest.

Lilian was safe and uninjured.

But poor Martha had met with her death.

A bullet from one of the pistols had passed through her chest.

The shock was great to both.

"Poor girl!" said Captain Hawk. "She deserved a better fate. Would that I could have saved her! But I feared it—I feared it!"

A few moments afterwards he beckoned to Mark to follow him out into the inn-yard.

"What is it?" asked the sailor, eagerly.

"A few words about us both," answered Captain Hawk, seriously, "and to which I must request your attention. I chose this place because we are less likely to be overheard here; and besides, for my own safety. You must not forget my real character."

CHAPTER XXXIII.

CAPTAIN HAWK COMES TO AN UNDERSTANDING WITH THE LANDLORD OF THE BLEEDING WOLF.—THE PARTING.

"It is not likely that I shall do so," answered Mark Appleton, in a tone of peculiar significance. "You have shown yourself in your true colours to-night. There is no one for whom I have more admiration and respect. I wish I could repay the obligation."

"Do not name it, for I am about to confer a greater."

"A greater?"

"Yes. You remember that I started upon hearing your name pronounced?"

"I do."

"You were surprised, of course?"

"I was. I fancied you recognised me."

"Not exactly that; but I heard your name under very peculiar circumstances, and if you will only listen you will find that what I have to communicate is of the greatest importance to you."

"You may command me to a much greater extent than the mere claim of attention to what you say, especially when I have your word as to its importance to me."

Captain Hawk then, in as few words as possible, made Mark Appleton acquainted with all the strange occurrences which had taken place at Pemberton Hall.

The auditor listened with horror.

"I am bound to believe you," he said. "And so this is the actual account of the case?"

"It is indeed—I pledge you my solemn word."

"The villain—the monstrous villain!" he exclaimed. "I heard of the squire's death; but the information was that he had been brutally murdered by one Captain Hawk, a desperate robber who has of late infested that part of the country."

"In other words, myself!"

"You!" ejaculated Mark, starting back several paces in his intense surprise—"you Captain Hawk?"

"Hush—hush! It is not prudent to pronounce my name in so loud a tone of voice: the reward offered for my apprehension is very large."

"Pray pardon me! But my absolute amazement——"

"I can easily understand it. But you know now the real author of the odious crime. You are the rightful heir to the late squire's wealth and possessions."

"And the will?"

"I have placed it in the custody of one who, when you show yourself, will hand it to you."

"And that person?"

"The landlord of an inn not far from the Hall—an inn that once stood on the high-road."

"You mean the Bleeding Wolf?"

"I do."

"He is an honest fellow."

"He, then, has the will. I must leave it to you to fight your own battle—you will have great trouble, no doubt; but should circumstances arise to make you think that I can be of any benefit to you, do not hesitate to call upon me."

"And where shall I find you?"

"You will hear of me at the Bleeding Wolf."

"I shall not forget that."

"And you will promise to call upon me, if needful?"

"I will."

"Enough, then—we must part. I hold my life very insecurely, and after what has lately happened I dare not show myself much by daylight. My nearest place of shelter is far from here, and therefore it is time for me to be gone."

"I will not offer to detain you, since you tell me that your safety is in question. Farewell! and when you go take with you my best thanks for what you have done in my behalf. It will go hard with me if I do not find some method of recompensing you. At any rate, it will not be long before we meet again."

"I shall be glad to see you once more," said the highwayman, as he returned the warm pressure of the other's hand, "chiefly in order that I may receive the assurance of the consummation of your happiness. There are a few other questions relating to what I witnessed at Pemberton Hall that I should be glad to have replied to."

"Enough. Farewell! Do not jeopardise your safety by remaining longer. Again farewell!"

The warm pressure of their hands was renewed, and then, suddenly separating, Captain Hawk sought the stable.

He had previously given instructions that no part of the trappings should be removed, so that now there was no delay in starting.

Springing into the saddle with his accustomed ease and grace, he waved his hand and galloped off.

Morning now was coming on very rapidly, but the captain knew very well that a sharp gallop would take him to the Bleeding Wolf in a very short space of time.

This was his destination, and he no longer hesitated about making his way thither, since he had so good an excuse for a visit.

"Fair Lottie," he murmured, "I shall see you once again! How is it that my thoughts so often revert to her, and that I look forward to this meeting with so much pleasure? I must get the better of this feeling: it is the indication of a lasting attachment—a very unwise thing for me to form."

If he really thought so, his best plan would have been to find some other means of making his communication to the landlord, but this was a thing he never once thought about.

But the day had fairly begun before the picturesque old inn presented itself to his view, despite the excellent speed which Satan made.

No words can tell how overjoyed he was at finding that of the lameness that had so terrified him scarcely a trace remained.

Early as was the hour, the landlord was up and standing in a thoughtful attitude at the front-door.

He started when he caught sight of the captain, as though he had been the subject of his thoughts.

"Good morning!" he said, apparently with some constraint of manner.

The captain returned the salutation, and alighted.

"I have to request shelter for the day," he said—"at night I have business which calls me far away. I should not have troubled you now but that I have something of importance to communicate to you concerning the squire's will."

The landlord judged from these words that his visitor had noticed his coolness, and, ashamed of having shown it to one to whom he was so largely indebted, he came forward and took hold of Satan's rein.

"This way, captain. I am glad to see you. Come! You know the way to the stable!"

"I do. And now prepare yourself for a piece of intelligence that will startle you."

"Indeed! What is it?"

"I have found Mark Appleton."

"What, already?"

"By the merest chance in the world; but in time you shall know all."

"You amaze me!"

"Very likely. He will come here to claim the will, which of course you will hand over to him."

"Certainly."

"I only trust that he may defeat the steward's infamous machinations, and that he may do so my help shall not be wanting."

On re-entering the house, Captain Hawk, at the eager importunity of the landlord, related the adventures of the preceding night—that is, as far as Mark Appleton was concerned.

"You have done three good deeds, captain, to my knowledge," answered the landlord, as soon as the highwayman had concluded, "and in my opinion they will go a long way towards palliating your other offences on the road."

Captain Hawk was not so thoroughly recovered from his wound as not to feel any unpleasant sensations from it, and he was glad enough to respond to the landlord's invitation to have a quiet doze in one of the upper chambers.

"Be under no alarm," he said—"sleep soundly and peacefully. You need not fear interruption; and should danger show itself, you may depend upon having timely warning from me."

"Many thanks; I am truly weary."

"That is your wound. A few hours' rest will make you feel all right again."

"I hope so."

"I am sure of it. This way."

The landlord conducted his guest to one of the best sleeping chambers in the inn, and there left him.

A very few hours' sleep sufficed to recuperate the exhausted energies of the highwayman—or rather his impatience would not allow him to slumber any longer.

He was longing to see Lottie once again, and his heart whispered to him that he should never have a better opportunity than the present.

He paid, therefore, on rising very particular attention to his toilet, and when he descended the stairs and made his appearance in the old inn kitchen there could be no disguising the fact that his appearance was strikingly prepossessing and handsome.

His manners, too, were characterised by an air of ease and courtly grace which indicated with tolerable plainness that his proper sphere of life was, as had been, very different from that in which he now moved.

It was afternoon, and the kitchen was occupied only by Lottie and the landlord's wife, both of whom rose to welcome him with a smile.

Whatever amount of embarrassment they may have felt the captain speedily put an end to.

Lottie's cheeks had flushed crimson, and, after once meeting the highwayman's gaze, was unable to raise again her eyes to his, but sedulously bent them upon the needlework she was engaged with.

The conversation between the trio had in it nothing sufficiently interesting to make it worthy of being placed on record, consisting chiefly of the expressions of gratefulness which the landlord's wife poured forth on account of the old inn being preserved them.

At length she arose for some purpose, and then Captain Hawk had the opportunity he had been so anxiously waiting for.

He was alone with Lottie.

For a moment or two both were silent.

The captain was engaged in furtively watching his companion.

He could see the colour deepen on her cheek, while her head bent lower and lower over her work.

The casual remarks he made at first were responded to only by monosyllables.

But in the embarrassment which the young girl displayed, Captain Hawk saw the revelation of the fact that he was far—far, indeed, from being indifferent to her.

And on his own part he could not help thinking that never had he seen a more perfect or more beautiful specimen of rural loveliness.

His annoyance may be conceived when, just as he was about to improve the occasion, the *tete-a-tete* was broken in upon by the entrance of the landlord.

There was a deep frown upon his brow, and his teeth bit his lips convulsively, as though something had happened to distress his mind excessively.

As the captain thought, he spoke to his daughter with unnecessary asperity, and bade her quit the room.

He was obeyed instantly, but her father's unwonted manner caused her eyes to fill with tears.

No sooner had the door closed than the landlord sat himself moodily down in a chair, and thrust his hands deeply into his pockets.

Then turning his frowning gaze upon the fire, he exclaimed:

"Hark ye, Mr. Captain: I am deeply indebted to you. Don't feel afraid that I shall forget the obligation."

"Nay. But I——"

"Hush! hear me out. I say I am deeply beholden to you, and so I am. But still, what you have done for me does not in my opinion give you the right to destroy my happiness."

"Destroy your happiness?"

"Yes. Do not feign astonishment. I can tell plainly by your manner that you understand well enough what I mean. You too well understand me when I tell you that the sum total of my earthly happiness is vested in my daughter. Without her, you understand, life would be a blank—I should not care to live."

Captain Hawk was silent.

"It has been my pleasing task up to now to shield her from all harm. I have succeeded. My jealous eyes are quick to perceive. I can tell that your appearance and the gratitude she is bound to feel have created a favourable impression on your behalf upon my daughter, while you, too, show only too plainly that you have been smitten with her beauty."

"Well," said Captain Hawk, endeavouring to assume an air of indifference, "supposing this to be the case, what then?"

"What then?" echoed the landlord. "Why, ten thousand times sooner would I have lost this place and let the steward triumph—even though we had to beg our bread from door to door—than that the feelings between my daughter and yourself should be any further developed!"

"I hold myself accountable to no man for my actions," said the captain, "still less to you. I shall do as I think proper."

"Then I can see that the opinion I formed of you was a better than you deserved."

Captain Hawk rose.

"As you please," he said. "I should have preferred that we remained friends."

"And that I should quietly submit to be deprived of my dearest treasure!"

"That is your own assumption, and made, so far as I can tell, without just and reasonable grounds."

"Will you say that my suspicions are unfounded?"

"I decline now to answer that question."

The landlord smiled scornfully.

"Let me have my horse!" continued the highwayman. "I will depart. I am a fool, or I should have known how much dependence could be placed upon the generosity of anyone!"

"You wrong me—you know you wrong me! No one detests ingratitude more than I do—but I cannot forget my child!"

"You shall see how much ground you have for your suspicions," said the captain. "Let me have my horse at once at the front-door!"

Strangely enough, the landlord hesitated to obey this order.

But the captain repeated it with angry sternness.

The landlord then began to wonder whether he had not allowed his jealous love to carry him too far—whether what he dreaded was not more imaginary than real, and whether, after all, he had not done more harm than good.

But Captain Hawk was imperious, and he had no resource but to obey.

During his absence on this errand, the highwayman paced up and down the room with rapid, irregular strides.

What his thoughts were, who could tell?

The landlord at length returned.

"Is the horse ready?"

"It is; but are you really in earnest about departing by daylight?"

"Yes; upon no consideration whatever would I remain another five minutes beneath this roof!"

"Consider your danger."

"Never mind that. Here is a guinea—you can take the reckoning out of it, and keep the change."

"I want no payment."

"I choose to make it—that is sufficient. Some day you will know me better."

He strode across the room as he spoke.

The landlord seized him by the arm and detained him.

"Captain," he said, earnestly, "if I have misjudged you, you ought to make allowance for the feelings of a father, and not be mortally offended in consequence."

The highwayman attempted to shake him off.

"Supposing you should plead, in justification of yourself, that your intentions are honourable, what satisfaction would that be to me? I should die at the bare thought of my daughter meeting such a fate as becoming the—the——"

Captain Hawk shook him off, and prevented him from finishing his speech by hurrying off.

He was in an angrier mood than he could remember ever having experienced before.

On gaining the front-door, however, his features softened.

He saw before him his matchless steed, and holding him by the bridle was the cause of the dispute between himself and the landlord—the fair Lottie.

[THE BLACK HIGHWAYMAN'S ADVENTURE IN THE VAULTS.]

She was patting Satan's glossy neck, and apparently was unaware that the highwayman had reached the threshold.

Captain Hawk did not speak, but sprang into the saddle.

Lottie regarded him with looks of surprise.

"Farewell," he said, sinking his voice. "It may be long—very long before we meet again. Farewell!"

Lottie was too much agitated to speak.

"A stirrup-cup," cried the highwayman, who at that moment caught sight of the landlord—"fetch me a stirrup-cup, Lottie. I will not bid you farewell with dry lips. Quick—quick! A stirrup-cup, I say!"

The sudden alteration of his manner, which was an abrupt transition from sadness to hilarity, increased her surprise.

Catching sight of her father's gloomy face only made her embarrassment the greater.

The simplest thing seemed obedience to the order she had received, and she hastened off to execute it.

She was not a moment away.

She carried in her hand a good-size flagon filled with foaming ale.

"Come," he said, "bring it to me. I will say farewell!"

Near the horse-trough were three large pieces of stone arranged so as to form three steps.

They were placed there for the convenience of persons mounting on horseback, and were chiefly used by ladies as an easy means of gaining the saddle.

Close to these steps Captain Hawk now stood, and according to a custom that was common then, Lottie ascended these steps in order to place the flagon in the hands of the rider.

"Thanks," he said. "I drink confusion to all ingrates and suspecters! Happiness, the greatest that earth can afford, to the beautiful and good, and a health to friends and foes alike!"

He quaffed deeply when he finished.

Lottie was still more astonished at his words.

To her they were in the highest degree enigmatical, for, of course, she had no means of guessing what had taken place between her father and the highwayman.

"And now, Lottie," he added, resuming his former tenderness and sadness of tone, "the time has come when I must bid you farewell. We may never meet again. But whether we do or not, your image will never be effaced from my heart. I shall always look back to the last few days as the pleasantest time of my existence; I shall never forget you, and shall even hope that you will always keep me in your remembrance. For the last time, farewell!"

He drank again and returned the flagon.

At the same moment he flung his right arm around Lottie's shoulders, and, despite the resistance which she offered, drew her to him and impressed half a dozen burning kisses on her lips.

Then releasing her suddenly, he gave his horse the rein, and set off at a gallop which quickly carried him out of sight.

He did not once trust himself to look behind, nor did he allow his horse to pause until he had passed over many miles.

"I will leave this part of the country," he said, determinedly; "and I fancy it will be long, very long before I can return to it. The landlord was right. I feel it now—I felt it then. My best plan is to keep away, and I will do it. I must not forget the charge which poor Dick gave me with his last breath. London—yes, yes, I will go to London, and make better speed than I have done hitherto. There is nothing now to keep me here of particular moment, for, sooner or later, I and the steward will meet again."

As he spoke, he urged Satan once more into a gallop.

Away—away he went, until the picturesque old inn was more than twenty miles behind.

Then he stopped.

The exertion made Satan's lameness show a little.

"We will stop a little while at the next inn we come to," he said. "I will not run the risk of injuring you. Ah! and here is the very place I want!"

Just at this moment he saw, a few yards to the left, the roof-tops of an inn of more than usual extent.

CHAPTER XXXIV.

CAPTAIN HAWK AMUSES HIMSELF AT THE EXPENSE OF A VERY CELEBRATED POLICE OFFICER.

Judging by the exterior, the inn, upon a closer approach, seemed to promise more comfortable accommodation than usual for man and beast.

The very moment that Captain Hawk pulled up the landlord and ostler both came forward with the intention of assisting him to alight.

But the highwayman, with his usual agility, slipped out of the saddle before they could reach him.

"Good evening, sir!" said the landlord, rubbing his hands briskly one over the other. "Glad to see you and bid you welcome to the Old Cross Guns! Going to stay the night, I suppose? A nice bit of horseflesh you have there, sir—upon my word he's a beauty!"

"Yes," said the captain, proudly—"I fancy you would go a very long way without meeting with his equal. I have had the misfortune to lame him a little; but it is nothing—still, I should like to see to him after my own fashion."

"Certainly, sir—certainly. I always say, remember the old proverb: 'A merciful man is merciful to his beast.' Jacob will show you the way to the stables. I ought to alter my sign and call the place Liberty Hall, for I always allow my guests to do as they like, if it is in reason."

Captain Hawk hastened to follow the ostler to the stables, glad to escape from the chatter of the loquacious landlord.

He soon found that Jacob knew well how to attend to a horse in a case like the present; and in a very little while, by their united exertions, Satan was left as comfortable as could be wished.

The captain then, with a sad, melancholy feeling about his heart, crossed the inn-yard and entered the house.

The landlord ushered his guest into a little parlour with a sanded floor.

"A bottle of your best wine," the captain said; "and let it be good, for I sha'n't be particular to a shilling or two in the price."

"All right, sir. You could not come to a better place—though I say it—to have a bottle of genuine wine. I have got some down in my cellars equal to the best in the land."

"Then let me have some, and as quickly as you like," replied the captain, who in his present mood felt anything but inclined to listen to his host's garrulity.

No sooner had he left the room than the highwayman allowed his face to sink between his hands, and thus, with all external things shut out, he gave himself up to a melancholy reverie, which would have lasted much longer than it did but for the entrance of the landlord.

With a great deal of display, and with an extraordinary expenditure of talk, the bottle was placed on the table and the cork drawn.

"This is the stuff, sir!" he exclaimed, enthusiastically. "Allow me to pour you out a glassful. There—look at that! As clear as a bell and with I don't know how many beads all round it! And look at the colour too—as pale as a straw!"

The wine really was excellent, and the captain, in accordance with what was then a universal custom, asked the landlord to drink with him, though in the present instance he would gladly—very gladly—have dispensed with his company.

"Ah!" he said, "my grandfather bottled that wine, and laid it down in one corner of the cellar, and there it has remained, without having been touched, ever since. By-the-way, sir, I forgot to ask whether you would like a bed here?—we have the best accommodation."

"I had scarcely made up my mind," was the answer. "I suppose you are safe enough here," he added, more from the desire to say something than any other cause—"no robbers or highwaymen?"

"Safe!" ejaculated the landlord, seizing upon the one word—"safe! I should rather think we are, sir! A little more than safe I should be inclined to say just at the present time! I should like to see the highwayman or robber that would show himself within a dozen miles of the place!"

"Indeed!" said the captain, smiling for the first time. "And what is there about the place that has so terrifying an effect upon them?"

The landlord sunk his voice to a confidential whisper.

"Why, sir," he said, "you must know that I have staying in the house just at this present time no other than the great and celebrated Mr. Hogg!"

"Hogg!" said Captain Hawk. "Who the deuce is he?"

"Is it possible you have never heard of him?"

"Never to my knowledge. What is he?"

"A Bow Street runner."

"A what?" ejaculated the highwayman, with a sudden start, for no announcement could have come more unexpectedly upon him.

"The great and celebrated Mr. Hogg," repeated the landlord, giving an oratorical flourish with his arm, "is a Bow Street runner—the greatest and most celebrated of all the Bow Street runners!"

"I never heard of him," answered the captain, who by this time had thoroughly recovered his composure, and was also prepared to be interested in what might follow.

"I wonder at that! He is really a great man. He is the one to whom all particular cases are given; and so clever is he, that if he takes up anything in which everybody else has failed, he is sure to succeed."

"And what brings him so far from London, may I ask?"

"An errand of more than usual importance."

"What is its nature?"

"I see no reason why I should not tell you, sir."

"Is it a secret, then?"

"I believe Mr. Hogg wants to keep his business quiet."

"But you know what it is?"

"Oh yes!"

"Then drink another glass of wine. That is it! And now oblige me by gratifying my curiosity."

The landlord tipped off the glass of old wine with particular gusto, and then said:

"Mr. Hogg has been sent down here specially to capture that highway-robbing scoundrel who has the audacity to call himself Captain Hawk."

"The devil!"

"It is a fact, sir, I assure you."

"I don't doubt you for a moment. I was only a little surprised, that is all."

"I see. Well, then, that is the great Mr. Hogg's business in these parts; and such being the case, you may make sure of one thing."

"And pray what is that?"

"Why, that before many more days are over, Captain Hawk will be safely lodged in prison."

"Time will show," said the highwayman, with a smile.

"Yes; and the result will be as I have said."

"This Mr. Hogg, then, must be a very great man."

"I believe you. He has fathomed out things which everybody else would give up as hopeless. He is so quick, too—he seems to see through everything at a glance."

Captain Hawk enjoyed this conversation mightily.

So great was his interest that for the time he quite forgot all those unpleasant things which had thrown such a damp upon his spirits.

His mind, in fact, became intent upon one thing, and that was to cause the officer with so great a reputation to sustain some striking, overwhelming defeat, as well as be thoroughly hoaxed into the bargain.

"Do you say he is in the inn at the present time, landlord?"

"Yes, he is here."

"Then I must request a favour at your hands."

"Pray name it, sir."

"I want you to take my compliments to the great Mr. Hogg, and tell him that a gentleman is here who would feel highly honoured by having a little conversation with him over another bottle of this excellent wine of yours, landlord."

"Thank you—but I am afraid——"

"Afraid of what?"

"That you cannot have the company of the great Mr. Hogg just at present."

"Why not?" said the captain, quickly, and with an air of manifest disappointment.

"Because when he came here he had ridden a great many miles—over sixty, I think—and his horse and himself were both thoroughly knocked up. After a little refreshment, he asked leave to go to his bed-room, where he has been asleep these two hours."

"Oh indeed! I regret the circumstance, for it would have given me much pleasure to see him."

"No doubt, sir. It is not every day that one has the good fortune to have a talk with a truly great man."

"Very true."

"But I would not disturb him on any account."

"Oh no, no—certainly not; don't think of such a thing for a moment."

"I know Captain Hawk will shake in his shoes when he hears of it," said the landlord, highly pleased. "It does me good to think about it."

"No doubt. But a strange thought has just occurred to me."

"Indeed!"

"Suppose just for one moment—but I daresay you will tell me that the thing is too unlikely to be entertained as a supposition even for a moment—still, suppose that instead of this great Mr. Hogg capturing Captain Hawk, the highwayman should play him one of his pranks—one of the sort you have often heard about?"

"Ah no, sir—there's no good in thinking of such a thing! Lor' bless you, there's no need to knock a round out of a ladder to let the great Mr. Hogg see daylight on the other side—oh dear no, not at all. Captain Hawk, if for the first time in his life, will really find that he has met with his match."

"And you think that no long time will elapse before his capture?"

"I feel certain of it."

Captain Hawk poured out the remainder of the wine.

"I suppose I shall have the chance of seeing this great man in the morning, providing I stay here all night?"

"In all probability, sir, if you are an early riser, for Mr. Hogg announced his intention of getting up in good time."

"I should be sorry not to catch sight of him."

The landlord was silent for a moment, as though thinking over something, and then he said:

"I'll tell you what, sir, since you seem so very anxious to see the great Mr. Hogg, I am happy to say that I think I can put you in a fair way of gratifying your inclination."

"How so, landlord?"

"I must explain. Of course, when a great man honours my poor house with his presence you would naturally expect that I should put the best room in the house at his service?"

"Certainly."

"But it unfortunately happens that on the present occasion my very best room is engaged, so Mr. Hogg could not have it. The second best room is a double-bedded one."

"And is that where you have bestowed him?"

"It is."

"Well, but I don't see——"

"Of course you don't; but you will in a moment. If you like you can have the vacant bed in Mr. Hogg's room, and then you may feel sure of not missing him in the morning."

This was a proposition for which Captain Hawk was unprepared.

How he would have decided upon the spur of the moment is hard to say; but just then, by a lucky accident, the landlord was summoned from the room.

"Sorry to quit your company, sir," he said, departing, "but business, you know, must be attended to. I will be back in a minute or two."

No sooner did the door close than Captain Hawk sprang to his feet.

Then, deliberately pacing the room, he muttered:

"What shall I do? Having obtained this information, who can doubt but that my wisest and most prudent course would be to get as far away as possible? But when did Captain Hawk suffer himself to be swayed by such considerations? Never! No—no, I will not go away."

He remained silent a moment, and then continued:

"But to contemplate going up into the bed-chamber of a police officer with a great reputation, and there passing the night, seems something beyond even Captain Hawk. But no matter, I will do it—I will follow out the adventure to the end, and avail myself of every opportunity that falls in my way. I will go up to this double-bedded room, and if something does not follow from it that will form a gossip subject for every tongue it is very odd to me."

At this juncture he was interrupted by the appearance of the landlord.

"Well, sir," he said, "what do you think of the double-bedded room?"

"Why, I have made up my mind to pass the night there, and am much obliged to you for having thought of it."

"Oh, don't mention that."

"One thing that helps to decide me is the thought of how very safe I shall be while actually breathing the same air as the great Mr. Hogg. I am not very rich, but what little I have I can ill afford to lose; and I shall sleep soundly, knowing that for this night, come what will, what I have will remain untouched."

"You may make sure of that, sir," the landlord said, with great confidence. "So great is the terror caused by the bare mention of the name of Hogg that not a thief would venture within a dozen miles of where he happened to be."

"Unless it should happen to be Captain Hawk."

"I do not even except him."

The highwayman shook his head.

"I am rather afraid you are wrong there, landlord. Captain Hawk has so profound a disregard for that which others would call danger that, ten to one, he would get as near as he could to this Mr. Hogg instead of running away from him."

The idea seemed so truly monstrous that the landlord could not help laughing heartily.

"What a notion!" he ejaculated. "Why, if that could be I should really think the world was coming to an end!"

Captain Hawk joined in the merriment with right good will, though his companion little thought what he was laughing at.

"I don't care how soon I retire now, landlord," he said. "I am very tired, and have a long day's journey before me to-morrow."

"I trust you will have a good night's rest."

"I have little fear about it. I will just go and have one peep at my horse and I shall be ready."

The landlord very officiously volunteered to light the highwayman across the yard; but this was not permitted.

Captain Hawk alone found his way to the stables with very little difficulty, and awoke the ostler, who was fast asleep up in the loft.

"Your horse is all right, sir," he said, "and so you'll say when you've seen him. I have seen many an out-and-outer in my time, but never anything like him. And so quiet too—he's like a lamb!"

The captain found the ostler had spoken the truth.

Satan was as right and comfortable as a horse could be wished to be.

"Here, Jacob," he said, "take this crown-piece and drink my health. If you look well after my horse I shall not forget you in the morning when I leave."

The ostler was not a little amazed at this unbounded liberality; but he pocketed the coin in silence, and stood ready for further instructions.

Just then the captain's eye happened to light upon a gray horse, apparently of great strength and good breed.

"Whose horse is that?" he asked.

"The great Mr. Hogg's, sir," was the reply—"the celebrated Bow Street runner from Lunnon."

Hearing this, Captain Hawk stopped to examine the animal more particularly.

There was little that he could find fault with.

The animal was evidently one that had been selected because he possessed several qualifications.

He was up to a great weight, rapid in action, and possessed of rather unusual powers of endurance.

"Not a bad sort, sir?" remarked the ostler.

"By no means," was the reply.

Going to the stable door, Captain Hawk looked up at the back of the inn.

From one of the upper windows there came a feeble glimmer of light.

The ostler saw the captain look up, and said:

"That is Mr. Hogg's window, sir—the light comes from the fire that he's had put in the room, sir."

The highwayman looked at the window with no ordinary attention.

Then, bidding the ostler good night, he made his way back to the room where he had left the landlord.

After a short delay a candle was brought and he was shown upstairs.

"This is the room," the landlord said, "and I should feel obliged if you would make no more noise than you can possibly help—it would be a pity to break the great man's rest."

The captain, with a smile, assured his host that he would not make noise enough to wake a cat, and after this he was left to himself.

Having closed the door, he first full shot a bolt into its socket, and, having done so, stood for a moment listening intently.

The deep, regular breathing of some person reached his ears distinctly.

"My friend is asleep," the captain murmured, "and I don't think it will be long before I follow his example. Who would believe, now, that I should deliberately choose to sleep in the same room as one who is intent either upon my death or capture? How will the adventure end?"

On tiptoe Captain Hawk now crossed the room.

He paused just at the foot of the bed occupied by his foe.

"I will just have one peep," he said. "I wonder what sort of a looking fellow this great man is?"

The curtains were apart a little at the foot of the bed, and, shading the candle with his hand, the highwayman gazed for a second or two upon the slumbering form.

He was not able to make out very much concerning Mr. Hogg's personal appearance, beyond that he was thin and tall, and had little gray whiskers reaching from the lower part of his ear to his chin.

Going to the dressing-table, the captain's attention was immediately attracted by some glittering object.

Upon a closer examination this turned out to be a pair of handcuffs.

He took them up and looked at them attentively.

"Intended for my accommodation, no doubt," he said, as he balanced them in his fingers. "I wonder whether I shall wear them?"

His attention was now diverted from the handcuffs to a couple of large pistols, placed rather ostentatiously one on either side of the looking-glass.

He found that the weapons were carefully loaded and primed.

"These might be dangerous," he said, mentally. "I will reverse the charges for him, and he will wonder what on earth is the matter."

The captain's inherent love of frolic had now got full sway.

He drew the charges out of the pistols, and replaced them reversed—that is, he put in the bullet first and rammed it as tightly down as he could without making too much noise, and then put the powder on the top.

"There," he said, as soon as he had completed the operation, "that will astonish him a little bit. Hullo! what have we here?"

As he spoke, he placed his hand upon a box of polished wood.

A key was sticking in the lock.

He turned it, and lifted the lid.

Four more pistols of a smaller size were disclosed.

These he treated in precisely the same manner, and then locked the box as before.

He was about to turn away, when he happened to perceive a rather large-sized memorandum or pocket-book.

The reason it had escaped his observation hitherto was that it had been partially pushed under the looking-glass.

"Now," said Captain Hawk, "I should say it is extremely likely that this pocket-book contains matters of no ordinary interest. At any rate, here goes to see."

So saying, he opened the book.

The first words upon which his eyes chanced to fall caused him to give a great start.

CHAPTER XXXV.

CAPTAIN HAWK MAKES A MEMORANDUM IN THE POLICE OFFICER'S POCKET-BOOK.

The wick of the candle had by this time attained a portentous length, and consequently it gave forth but a feeble illumination.

Before perusing any more of the officer's pocket-book, Captain Hawk trimmed the light.

The book seemed to be a kind of diary, wherein the great Mr. Hogg entered the most important events occurring during a day.

The entry to which the captain had chanced to open read as follows:—

"'According to arrangement, waited on the S. S.——'

"'S. S.!'" repeated the captain. "What the deuce does he mean by 'S. S.?' However, I will go on—perhaps the meaning will appear presently.

"'And received from him full instructions and authority respecting the notorious highwayman, Captain Hawk. Was promised double the amount of the rewards now issued, provided he is tried at the next sessions and executed out of hand. Gave my word it should be done—told the S. S. to make himself quite easy, and to look upon the thing as done.'

"Indeed!" was the highwayman's comment. "It strikes me, Mr. Hogg, that you will have just a trifle more trouble than you at present anticipate. But let us see what comes next:—

"'From certain information received, arranged to start for Yorkshire without delay. Travelled sixty miles the first day'

"Not bad work, by any means, Mr. Hogg," said the captain, "though I should hardly have thought so great a man as yourself would have taken the trouble to register such a trifle. But what comes next:—

"'Succeeded in reaching the Old Cross Guns Inn before nightfall. According to my information, I ought to expect to see Captain Hawk before long, as he is certainly in this part of the country. Shall commence a look-out the first thing in the morning.'

"Oh, indeed! And rather an odd look-out it will be, I'll be bound!"

This was the last entry in the book, and doubtless it had been made just before the officer retired to rest.

At one end of the book was a kind of pocket, and this was quite filled with folded papers.

Captain Hawk had a look at these also.

Several were handbills offering rewards for his own apprehension, and giving particulars of various robberies, accompanied in all cases by a tolerably accurate description of his personal appearance.

These papers he replaced just as he had found them, and then, taking the lead pencil from its resting-place, he wrote the following words in large letters:—

"Captain Hawk begs to assure the great Mr. Hogg that he has derived a great deal of amusement and satisfaction from a peep at his pocket-book, and also that he thinks Mr. Hogg will be disappointed. As for Captain Hawk, he will, as a rule, always be found where he is least expected. While Mr. Hogg reads these lines, the probability is that Captain Hawk will be very close at hand indeed."

This done, he put the pocket-book where he had found it, and took care to leave everything on the table in its proper position.

After that he took off part of his apparel, and flung himself upon the bed, wrapping himself up in the coverlet.

He must have had a poor opinion of the great Mr. Hogg's abilities, despite his extraordinary reputation, for, incredible as it may appear, Captain Hawk closed his eyes, and in less than five minutes afterwards was slumbering as calmly as an infant.

Perfect unconsciousness followed, for his sleep was undisturbed by dreams.

He was aroused by something, he knew not what.

Opening his eyes, he was surprised to find that it was quite light.

So perfect and sound had been his sleep that it did not seem to him as though his eyes had been closed for more than a moment.

He remained perfectly still, and was not long in ascertaining that the noise which had aroused him was made by the great Mr. Hogg attiring himself.

He was cursing and swearing in the most violent manner.

Lifting his head, Captain Hawk saw that his companion was busy putting on his boots—or rather attempting to do so, for the task seemed almost beyond his power.

But by dint of much tugging, swearing, and stamping down the heel, this unpleasant part of the toilet was finished.

Mr. Hogg chanced to look up, and gave quite a melodramatic start of surprise upon finding the second bed was occupied.

"Good morning, sir!" said Captain Hawk, screwing up his face in a peculiar way, and thereby materially altering its appearance.

The great man growled out something by way of a reply.

"I am delighted," continued the highwayman—"extremely delighted to have the opportunity of making an acquaintance with you, Mr. Hogg."

"You know me, then?"

"Who does not?" asked the captain, with well-affected surprise. "And I trust you will not be offended with me for saying that I am one of the many thousands of persons who have the highest opinion of your talents and ability; and I shall always consider myself singularly favoured in thus being afforded the opportunity of telling you so."

Mr. Hogg smiled and looked very gracious after hearing this speech.

"I am much obliged to you, sir," he said. "I endeavour my best to do my duty—that is all."

"Oh!" ejaculated the captain, admiringly. "You may always know true talent and true genius by a delightful diffidence. When last night the landlord told me you were here I requested him as a particular favour to allow me to share this chamber with you. I the more wished it because I carry a good round sum with me, and I knew there would be no fear of losing it with you."

It is hard to be entirely proof against flattery.

Mr. Hogg was softened.

It is not wonderful that he should immediately form a very favourable opinion of his new companion.

"I am much obliged to you, sir, for your good opinion," said Mr. Hogg, "but I really cannot help having the vanity to think that any property is perfectly safe when I am near."

"There is not the least doubt of it. The bare pronunciation of your name would make a robber tremble."

Mr. Hogg smiled, and looked as though he quite believed it.

"Talking of robbers," continued the captain, passing his hand over his forehead, "reminds me that I have had a dream—a most singular dream—a dream concerning no less a personage than the notorious Captain Hawk."

"Indeed!" ejaculated Mr. Hogg. "And what may the dream be? I am interested in everything about this Captain Hawk, his capture being the identical business which has brought me into this part of the country."

The highwayman bowed as though aware of the fact, and then said:

"Like many dreams, it is almost too preposterous to be told, and yet every part of it is so vividly before me that I am half puzzled to think whether it is a dream or reality."

"You excite my curiosity," said Mr. Hogg, settling the tie of his cravat.

"I will allay it, then. My dream simply was that in the night Captain Hawk came into this room——"

"Preposterous indeed!" interrupted Mr. Hogg, with a guffaw. "If he knew I was here he would be off at full speed, I'll warrant."

"Well, in my dream he seemed to take matters very coolly, for he actually peeped through the curtains and had a good look at you while you were asleep."

The idea of such an occurrence as this so tickled the police officer that he had to sit down and give vent to his laughter.

Captain Hawk joined in with hearty good-will.

"Pray go on," said Mr. Hogg, with tears in his eyes. "Do let me hear the rest. I can't remember ever having heard anything half so amusing."

"I don't recollect just what followed," said Captain Hawk, admirably simulating the manner of one who is endeavouring to recall something to his remembrance, "but I know I saw him standing close to the dressing-table yonder—that is in my dream, you know."

"Of course—of course!"

"I saw him take up what appeared to be a book, look at it for some time, and I fancy after that he wrote something on one of the pages, and afterwards left the room."

"Capital—capital! A more unreasonable or unlikely thing could not have been thought of."

"But these dreams, you know, always go by contraries."

"Oh, yes—yes—of course!"

"By-the-way," added the captain, "does there really happen to be a book on the table?—because if there should be it will be strange indeed."

"Oh yes, there is a book: this one—my own private diary and memorandum-book"

"How singular"

Mr. Hogg had the book in his hand.

He opened it, and immediately rapped out an oath.

"Death and the devil! What is here?"

"Good gracious!" cried the captain. "What is the matter?"

"Matter—the devil! Why, your outrageous dream could not have been a dream after all."

"Not a dream?"

"No, not a dream!"

"What do you mean?"

"Why, somebody has been writing in my book!"

"Impossible!"

"Look for yourself!"

The officer, of course, displayed what the captain had written.

"Well, well," the latter ejaculated, after the lapse of a moment, as though it took him that length of time to recover from his astonishment, "this passes everything. What are we to think of it?"

"I don't know," said the great Mr. Hogg, looking remarkably confused and puzzled.

"It is incomprehensible!"

Mr. Hogg stared blankly at the straggling letters.

"Surely—surely, Mr. Hogg, this Captain Hawk cannot have come into the room?"

"Oh dear no—no—no! I am sure he would not venture so close to me!"

"Then how do you account for this writing?"

"I can't account for it just at present, but rest assured I shall before long."

"It is fairly bewildering."

Captain Hawk played his part so naturally that Mr. Hogg never once had his suspicions roused to the fact that his companion was the author of the hoax, or that it was a hoax at all.

"I must inquire into this," he said. "Shall I have the pleasure of seeing you downstairs?"

"Yes. I will rise at once."

Mr. Hogg, having finished dressing, quitted the room and went stamping downstairs.

Captain Hawk leaped out of bed and dressed himself in a remarkably short space of time.

After that, with all the confidence in the world, he marched down after Mr. Hogg, who chanced to be the first person he met.

"Well" he said, "is the mystery any clearer?"

"Not at present, but it soon will be, I think."

"I hope so. In the meantime I feel that a little breakfast would be acceptable. Do you?"

"Decidedly."

Captain Hawk fancied that Mr. Hogg bent a searching, not to say suspicious, gaze upon him.

But he took no notice of it.

Breakfast was ordered.

The strangely-assorted couple sat down to the meal together.

"Landlord," said Captain Hawk, "may I trouble you to ask the ostler to saddle and bridle my horse for me? as I shall have to be off."

"And do the same for me, landlord."

"Very good, gentlemen."

The landlord departed to execute his errand.

Captain Hawk now could not help noticing that his companion was watching him very closely.

"I must take care," he said, mentally. "I would wager any amount that he suspects who I am."

Then in a loud voice, he said:

"Mr. Hogg, I am afraid you are not doing justice to the good things before you—your appetite fails you."

"It is because I can't come to a clear understanding about what took place. On one point only am I certain."

"And what is that?"

"That yours was no dream."

"No dream?"

"No, not a bit of it—it was reality."

"But do you think——"

"I have my opinion. It may turn out wrong, and it may turn out right."

The captain went on eating his breakfast with perfect composure, and evidently thoroughly relished every mouthful that he swallowed.

It was no doubt this that baffled Mr. Hogg.

Such extraordinary calmness was out of the pale of belief.

Suddenly the clatter of a horse's hoofs became audible.

By common consent both parties turned their eyes to the window, and were just in time to see a man ride past.

Mr. Hogg jumped up and ran to look out, but by the time he reached the window the rider had disappeared.

His ears told him, however, that he had stopped in front of the inn.

At this moment the door opened, and the landlord came in.

"Mr. Hogg," he said, "a messenger has just arrived, who says he must see you upon urgent business."

"Where is he?"

"Outside. He would not dismount."

Mr. Hogg snatched up his hat and ran out.

As soon as he had gone, Captain Hawk said:

"What man is it, landlord?"

"The messenger?"

"Yes."

"A police officer, I should say."

"Very good. You need not take the trouble to make out your bill. Here are a couple of guineas. You can keep the change until I call for it. Good morning!"

The landlord stared.

He was amazed, and well he might be at such munificence.

"Are you really going, sir?"

"Yes, I am off. Good morning!"

Captain Hawk, taking care not to exhibit any hurry in his movements, made his way with all possible speed to the back of the premises, and quickly gained the stable.

"Jacob," he said—"my horse, quick! Oh, he is all ready—that is well. Here is a guinea for you, and if you like to do me a little service you shall have another."

"Lor', sir!"

"What do you say? Make haste! Minutes are precious!"

"I'll do anything I can to oblige such an out-and-out gent as you are, sir."

"Enough! Find me a spur—an old one will do."

The ostler, wondering much, went to a shelf and took down the instrument asked for.

While he was doing this, Captain Hawk had hastened to the side of Mr. Hogg's horse, which was also standing in readiness for instant use, and unbuckled the saddle girth.

"Now, Jacob, the spur, quick!"

"Here it is, sir."

"Well, do you see what I am going to do with it?"

"Lor', sir, what's that for?"

The ostler might well ask the question in a voice of the utmost astonishment.

Captain Hawk had taken the spur and fixed the two ends of it in such a way under the tree of the saddle that the moment anyone attempted to mount, the weight would cause the rowels to sink to the head in the horse's back close to his withers.

When the captain had rebuckled the girths, it could be seen that he had fixed the spur so cleverly under the padding that a cursory examination would fail to show that the saddle had been meddled with at all.

"Lor', sir," exclaimed the ostler, again, "what is it for?"

"Why, Jacob, I think it very likely that when I start Mr. Hogg will be in a great hurry to follow me. But as I don't think his company agreeable, I have devised that little contrivance to delay him a little, that's all."

"But, sir——"

"No more. Here are two guineas instead of one. All you have to do is to keep quiet and plead entire ignorance. If you are found out to have any share in it that will be your own fault."

The ostler pocketed the coin with an air which seemed plainly enough to say that he considered the payment quite sufficient to compensate for any disagreeable consequences that might follow.

All that we have just described took place with extraordinary rapidity.

Captain Hawk jumped on to Satan's back, and feeling then perfectly secure, had the matchless effrontery to walk him round to the front of the inn.

He had his eyes well about him though.

He saw Mr. Hogg listening earnestly to something which the messenger was telling him.

Judging by the animated gestures made use of, the communication could have been of no ordinary character.

His face was turned so that he could not fail to catch sight of Captain Hawk the very moment he appeared round the angle of the building.

He uttered an ejaculation.

The messenger turned swiftly.

"By Jove!" he exclaimed, "that's the man!"

"Never!"

"It is! That is Captain Hawk!"

Amazement and rage mingled together had such an effect upon the great Mr. Hogg that he could not move.

He looked as much astonished as any ordinary individual could have done under such circumstances.

Just at this moment, in accordance with orders given to the landlord, the Bow Street runner's horse was brought from the stable by Jacob the groom

Captain Hawk pulled up.

But he held the rein in such a manner as would enable him to turn Satan in a second in any direction he wished.

Mr. Hogg drew a pistol.

"Captain Hawk," he said, "I know you now. I forgive you for the fun you have had at my expense. You are a much braver fellow than I gave you credit for being. Still, for all that, you must yield yourself my prisoner. I should be sorry to do you a hurt; but if you refuse or resist you are a dead man!"

"Mr. Hogg!"

"Well?"

"I am really surprised that a great man like yourself should speak in such a fashion."

Mr. Hogg was short-tempered.

Captain Hawk could not have said anything that would have raised his choler sooner.

He gave utterance to an odd kind of snorting sound.

Then with great rapidity he drew a pistol, and, raising it to a level, pulled the trigger.

Captain Hawk never flinched.

There was a puff of white smoke; but nothing more.

With a bitter oath the Bow Street runner cast the useless weapon from him, and in the twinkling of an eye raised another, and again pulled the trigger.

The same result followed.

"Ha! villain," he yelled, as the truth flashed upon him, "you have tampered with my weapons! I ought to have guessed it. But, dead or alive, I will have you my prisoner!"

So saying, he rushed headlong to his horse.

The ostler, knowing what was about to ensue, could hardly keep his countenance.

The animal winced the moment Mr. Hogg seized the rein, for the spur was so placed that the weight of the saddle galled him slightly.

The Bow Street runner, however, took no heed of this.

He lifted his foot, and thrust it into the stirrup-iron.

The pressure of his foot at once caused the points of the spur to sink into the horse's back.

As a matter of course the animal swerved, and Mr. Hogg, wholly unprepared for any such event, went head-over-heels to the ground, where he rolled and rolled until, in some inexplicable manner, he rolled on to his feet again.

The messenger, by promptly stretching out his hand, had been just in time to arrest the half-maddened horse's flight.

"D—n the jade!" cried Mr. Hogg, as he lifted his foot and kicked the poor creature viciously in the ribs. "Stand still, can't you!"

Terrified by his violence, the animal stood as still as its trembling limbs would allow it.

Mr. Hogg again essayed to mount.

But in vain, though, being prepared, he did escape a fall this time.

"What on earth ails the beast? I never knew him like this before. Hold him, some of you, can't you? Why do you stand like stocks and stones? Hold him. When once in the saddle I shall be all right."

The landlord and ostler hurried forward

By their united efforts the horse was held.

The great Mr. Hogg prepared himself for a feat of horsemanship which should astonish everybody.

But he was doomed to be astonished himself.

Retiring a few paces, he gave a sudden run forward and a spring.

The act was really very cleverly done, for, without touching either saddle or bridle, he vaulted into his seat in the saddle.

Of course he came down with considerable force.

Of course the spur was rammed more violently than ever into the poor horse's back.

And of course, as such excruciating pain was not to be endured, Mr. Hogg performed a most extraordinary flying somersault.

Not by his own free will, though.

But the horse flung out in such a way that no rider living could have kept his seat.

With a prodigious splash, Mr. Hogg alighted in the very middle of a little duck pond near the sign post.

As this pond happened to contain more mud than water, he emerged in a very insalubrious condition indeed.

But his fury was unabated.

He was plastered with mud from head to foot.

He wiped the slimy stuff from his eyes, and looked around.

"My horse!" he yelled. "Where is my horse?"

He was not in sight, for this time, thoroughly maddened, he had started at a headlong gallop along the road.

Captain Hawk remained in his former position, enjoying mightily the great man's complete discomfiture.

Mr. Hogg screamed with passion.

"I will be the death of you for this!" he said.

But the highwayman only laughed the more.

Mr. Hogg rushed to the messenger.

"Get down, you d—d idiot—get down! Let me have your horse! Are you a stock or a stone, that you remain like this?"

The messenger, grumbling out some sort of reply, dismounted.

A more pitiable spectacle than Mr. Hogg now presented could hardly be conceived.

He was drenched with foul water from head to foot.

His apparel was streaked with green of various shades, for the pond into which he had had the good or the ill fortune to fall was by the general voice pronounced to be "the nastiest place in the parish."

The Bow Street runner's rage, however, made him deaf and blind to all ordinary affairs.

He climbed into the saddle.

"I will have your life!" he yelled, shaking his clenched fists in impotent wrath. "I say I will have your life! and I will—I will! I swear it! I will be your death! I will cling to you like your shadow, Captain Hawk—you are a doomed man!"

But the object of his denunciations merely took off his hat, waved it, and turned his horse's head round.

In another second he was going at full gallop.

But Mr. Hogg, with a burning heart, came thundering on at his heels.

CHAPTER XXXVI.

PETERSON EXPLORES THE MYSTERIES OF THE WOODMAN'S HUT.—THE LONELY RIDER.—THE MYSTERIOUS RESIDENCE NEAR STAINES.—AN UNEXPECTED RECOGNITION.

THERE is doubtless a strong desire felt to know how Peterson got on when the night came following the one upon which Hopkins had met with so awful a fate.

Having ascertained beyond all possibility of doubt that it could not have been any emissary from the Secretary of State he had had the singular interview with, Peterson naturally looked forward with the utmost impatience to the coming of night, making sure that his companion would have important intelligence to communicate.

In anticipation of this, he provided himself with six picked men on whom he felt he could rely.

They had proved their courage in many a desperate encounter

He took care to see that they were all well armed and mounted.

Then, with himself at their head, he set forth early in the afternoon, and made his way to Ealing by taking a very circuitous direction.

He arrived on the outskirts of the little village somewhere about an hour before sunset.

There was time for a brief rest to refresh both horse and rider, and as he knew not what events the night might bring forth, he very gladly ordered it.

But as the time drew near when he had appointed to meet Hopkins, his anxiety and impatience became so great as scarcely to be restrainable.

Almost before the hour he had his men mounted and in readiness.

Then he set forward for that extremity of Ealing Common which was nearest to London.

This, too, he reached in a very circuitous manner, and

on arriving experienced a pang of disappointment upon discovering that his companion was not there before him.

With what patience he could command he prepared to wait.

Half an hour, then an hour, elapsed.

Still Hopkins came not.

It was now intensely dark.

"I will wait half an hour longer," said Peterson, to his men. "Probably something has occurred to detain him a little longer than he expected."

But though he said this, he did not for a moment think it.

A dim kind of foreboding overshadowed him.

He seemed in some strange way inwardly conscious that some evil had happened to his comrade.

But he waited.

The half-hour came and went.

As a forlorn hope, he said:

"Let us give him a fair chance. We will stay only a few moments longer, and then, if we are unable to discern any signs of his approach, we will go into the wood and seek for him."

In this way, another half-hour dragged its tedious length away.

By this time it was verging closely upon midnight.

"He does not come."

"No," said Peterson, gloomily. "As you say, he does not come."

"Some misfortune must have happened to him, then."

"I fear so."

"Shall we proceed?"

"Yes; follow me. I will lead you to the wood, where I trust we shall find some clue to his whereabouts."

With these words, Peterson, with a mind still more ill at ease, led the way to that portion of the wood that we have had such frequent occasion to make mention of.

He found the place without much difficulty, for he had noted it carefully.

Keeping steadily on as well as the darkness would permit, he made his way as nearly as possible in the direction he had formerly taken.

All around was not only as dark but as silent as the grave.

The wind had dropped, and now scarcely a leaf upon the trees rustled.

The intense silence made its impression upon all.

The wood was not of any very great extent—in fact, it scarcely merited so important a designation, and as Peterson's party was a large one they were not long in trampling over nearly every part of it.

But they found no trace of Hopkins, nor any clue to direct them to where he might then be.

At length, quite by accident, they stumbled on the woodman's hut.

There was no glimmering light to guide them to it now.

The hut was as dark as the trees by which it was surrounded.

"A light—quick!" cried Peterson.

The men all had their lanterns, so that this order was not long in being complied with.

The building was quickly examined exteriorly.

All seemed as it should be.

There was nothing whatever provocative of suspicion.

The place seemed well secured, and, as no one appeared in answer to their knocking, they rightly enough surmised that the hut was empty.

"I have my suspicion of this place," Peterson said, at length. "Knock again, and if the summons is disregarded we will break open the door."

The usual adjuration to open in the King's name was then made.

But it was to no effect.

"Down with it!" exclaimed Peterson. "Break it open!"

The door was strong, but such a job was quite in the way of these officers, and so, despite its strength, they in a very short time forced it from its hinges.

The inside of the hut was, if anything, less calculated to excite suspicion than the out.

But Peterson clung to the notion that this place, peaceful and ordinary-looking as it was, yet had some connection not merely with the disappearance of the Black Highwayman, but with the disappearance of Hopkins as well.

This was why he bestowed more scrutiny upon it than the circumstances would seem to warrant.

The large chest at one end of the hut attracted his attention sufficiently to cause him to lift the lid

He was going to let it fall again, believing the box to be empty, when the glitter of something caught his eye.

"What is that?" he said, to the man standing nearest to him. "Pick it up."

The man obeyed.

The something proved to be a small piece of narrow silver lace, and attached to it was a strip of black velvet.

Peterson's breath came thick and fast.

"By Heaven!" he cried, "I was right! Look—look! Here is indisputable evidence of the presence of the Black Highwayman in this place. We shall not be long in getting completely to the bottom of the mystery now."

All crowded round.

The fragment did indeed appear to be torn from some part of the highwayman's attire.

A more rigid search was now instituted.

In the adjoining chamber, one of the men, stamping heavily on the boards with his riding-boots, declared the ground to be hollow beneath.

This soon became evident.

"We will find that out. Depend upon it, we have got on to the right scent at last."

In the excitement he felt upon making this discovery he almost forgot all about the mysterious absence of his comrade.

But although the narrowest search was made for some means by which the underground chamber could be reached, they failed to discover it.

Peterson's patience was exhausted.

"Tear up the flooring!" he exclaimed—"that will be the easiest and quickest way of finding out what is beneath!"

The floor was only composed of rough planks rudely nailed down, and these were pulled up without much trouble by the united efforts of half a dozen strong men.

Their suspicions were verified.

There was a chamber beneath.

But a chamber differing greatly from what they had expected.

It was neither more nor less than a stable.

And there were abundant signs to show that no very long time had elapsed since it had last been occupied.

"And this is where the Black Highwayman keeps his horse, depend upon it!" cried Peterson, exultantly, as he leaped down on to some straw.

His men speedily followed his example.

But the place contained nothing of an unusual character.

The most interesting discovery was that there was a sloping passage leading up from the floor of this underground stable to the surface of the earth outside.

The passage terminated in the trunk of a hollow tree, and was admirably concealed.

Re-entering the hut, they came to the flooring in the principal chamber.

Remembering the former result, they tried that too.

In one part, an unmistakably hollow sound was returned to their blows.

"Another cellar!" cried Peterson.

Again the boards were torn up.

But an ejaculation of horror broke forth

Trembling and aghast, they all shrank back from the edge of the hideous chasm.

A small log of half-burnt wood was lying on the hearth, and this one of them flung down.

Breathlessly, all waited to hear it strike the bottom.

There was a dull splash.

"Water!" ejaculated one.

Recovering from the first shock of surprise, several now ventured nearer, and, holding their lanterns in a convenient position, peeped down.

But they could only see the slippery, shining walls.

Convinced at length that that there was no further discovery of importance to be made in this direction, and having not the least idea that they had been peeping into their companion's untimely grave, they turned away.

Nor did they afterwards find anything worthy of special notice.

[LIEUTENANT TRACY RECOGNISES THE BLACK HIGHWAYMAN.]

"We must never quit this place," said Peterson. "Sooner or later the Black Highwayman will return to it, and then we shall nail him with ease."

"But where is Hopkins?" said one.

The question was followed by silence.

"We must find him," said Peterson, at last; "but in the meantime this hut must be closely guarded."

This was done accordingly.

But though both parties stayed till daylight — one watching for Hopkins and the other guarding the hut—nothing whatever occurred to reward them.

While they were thus engaged, however, other events were taking place in an opposite quarter of London, to which it is necessary to direct the reader's attention.

As nearly as possible at the time when Peterson gave up looking for Hopkins, a man, mounted on a powerful horse, and wrapped from head to foot in a long horseman's cloak, was making his way along a narrow, miry country lane that branched off from the high-road near Staines.

This man was unattended, and sat upon his steed with an air of ease and confidence that showed him to be a thorough master of the by no means easy art of riding.

By his manner, too, he appeared to be thoroughly acquainted with the road he was taking, though the night was so dark that it was as much as he could do to discern the hedgerows on either side of him.

At length he stopped, and rode quite close to one side of the lane.

"I am right," he ejaculated; "here are the boundary palings. Now for a leap in the dark!"

He backed his horse a little way as he spoke, and then touched him sharply with the spur.

In the darkness, it did indeed seem terrible to attempt

to leap a horse over the high wooden, spike-topped palings.

But the gallant creature went over like a gazelle, descending upon the soft turf on the other side with scarcely a perceptible shock.

At a walking pace, this mysterious rider now made his way onward.

He had to pick his way carefully among the trunks of stout old trees; but in this he seemed to trust more to the sagacity of his horse, while he turned his chief attention towards escaping a concussion with any of the horizontal low-lying branches.

His ear presently told him that his horse had passed from the turf on to a gravel pathway.

Immediately upon making this discovery he changed his course, following the trees and windings of the avenue—for such it was.

A short time afterwards he reached a spot where the trees grew less thickly, and where consequently he could see better about him.

Massive and grand, in front of him rose up a building of very considerable extent, the many gables, turrets, and twisted windows of which could be faintly descried against the cloudy sky.

The horseman paused a moment to look up at the building, and during that moment he seemed to be deeply moved by some reflections which the sight of the dark place had appeared to conjure up.

What those reflections were cannot now be told.

Recovering himself from them, he again rode forward.

As he approached, the grandeur of the old building became more manifest.

But judging by appearances, however, the old mansion was uninhabited and deserted, for even in the darkness the traces of neglect on every hand were visible.

When the solitary horseman gained what had once been a smoothly-shaven lawn, but which was now nothing but a mass of ill-looking weeds, he turned abruptly to the left.

This brought him to a shrubbery—no doubt in years long past a place where the choicest plants had displayed their full perfections.

Now, however, in no way it differed from a piece of tangled undergrowth in a forest.

Through this the horseman threaded his way with a facility which proved how familiar he must have been with the whole locality.

Presently he came upon a sheet of stagnant water thickly overgrown with a kind of slimy moss.

At one extremity of this was a little building—a rustic summer-house—a place which, in spite of the ravages of decay, looked charmingly picturesque.

This little building seemed to be the solitary horseman's destination, for, upon arriving at the door, he drew rein and then leaped lightly from the saddle to the ground.

The door was locked; but a key was produced by which he effected an entrance.

He led the horse in after him, and once more closed the door.

The darkness within the ruined summer-house was now profound.

But the horseman produced a bottle of phosphorus, by the aid of which he ignited a small piece of wax candle.

The twinkling, star-like light only partially illuminated the place; but still it did so sufficiently to indicate its principal features.

The lighted piece of candle was then placed in a lantern, which was taken from a bracket near the door.

The power of the light was now much increased.

The stranger now unclasped his heavy cloak, and threw it over his steed's back.

The light now falling full upon him, disclosed a lithe, symmetrical figure clad in a tight-fitting costume

The features were regular, but strangely pale—perhaps they appeared all the more so from the contrast they afforded to the piece of black crape which, worn as a half-mask, covered the upper portion of his countenance down to the cheek-bones.

Once seen, that face and form could never be forgotten.

Doubtless our readers have recognised this late-riding horseman.

It was the Black Highwayman.

No sooner had he fixed the candle in the lantern than he turned to that part of the summer-house immediately opposite the door, and where apparently at some time or other a fireplace had existed.

Few traces now remained of it, and the likeness almost ceased when the Black Highwayman, pressing upon a hidden spring, caused the back of it to fall back, disclosing a dark, gloomy-looking recess.

But the Black Highwayman passed through this doorway unhesitatingly, and by a sudden pull effectually closed up the secret entrance again.

He was now standing at the top of a flight of steps, down which he began to make his way with an air which plainly enough showed that he had descended them at least once before.

About a dozen steps brought him to the bottom.

He paused and gasped once or twice for breath.

"What is this?" he exclaimed, in a half-whisper. "What ails me?—or is it something unusual in the place? Pah! It smells more like a charnel-house than aught else."

Just at the bottom of the flight of steps was a door.

When this was pushed open so sickening and overpowering an effluvium gushed forth, that the Black Highwayman was fain to ascend several of the steps again.

"What can this mean?" he said. "Surely there must be something strange in this! Let me think—how long is it since I was last in this place?"

He considered attentively a moment, and then said:

"It must be close upon two years now. How the time flies! Had I been told that so long a period had elapsed I should have been incredulous. But it does not admit of doubt. Well—well, only too well do I remember the occasion of my last visit. I—I——"

He broke off abruptly, and a slight shudder shook his frame.

It must have been a reminiscence of no common kind to produce so great an effect upon his iron nerves.

But the effect was only transitory.

"Bah!" he exclaimed, as he descended the steps rapidly "I am growing weak and childish. I must banish those remembrances: I thought I had done so. To return to them would be to court madness."

The overpowering odour which had forced him to retire was now much diminished.

"It must be from the fact of being closed up for so long a time," he said. "It must be that and nothing more. In a few moments it will doubtless become imperceptible."

But so far from this anticipation being realised, the sickening, grave-like smell only became the more apparent.

"There is something more than I expected in this," he ejaculated. "What can it be?"

While speaking, he held the ends of his voluminous neckcloth to his mouth and nose.

This rendered his progress less uncomfortable.

The light from the lantern shone with a dim and flickering radiance upon the walls of this subterranean passage.

It showed them reeking with unwholesome moisture, while here and there in the cracks and fissures could be seen strange specimens of plants of the fungus species.

No doubt a great length of time had elapsed since the place was formed.

Its strength must have been immense.

For the most part, the walls, floor, and roof were composed of solid stone, while here and there additional substantiality was given by means of an archway.

Suddenly, the Black Highwayman paused.

One would almost have thought that the hand which held the lantern slightly shook.

A strange sound had come to his ears.

He at once arrested his footsteps, and stopped to listen, in the hope that he could ascertain its character.

The sound came again.

"Good Heavens! What is that?"

An odd, rushing, pattering noise succeeded.

It was shortly followed by a squeak.

"Rats!" he exclaimed. "I might have known or guessed what it was. But why should they be here in such numbers? There must be a whole army of them."

All was silent now.

The animals, terrified at his approach, had hastened to conceal themselves in their various hiding-places.

But before the intruder's feet strange, loathsome-looking reptiles crawled— creatures of that kind never seen upon the surface of the earth.

But the Black Highwayman strode on, apparently determined to get to the end of the disagreeable passage as speedily as possible.

All at once, however, he stopped, as though he had by some invisible power been suddenly deprived of motion.

In the sudden shock the lantern almost fell from his grasp.

Recovering himself a little, his first involuntary impulse was to step a pace or two backwards.

Then he drew his sword, and held it before him in an attitude of defence.

"Merciful powers!" he exclaimed—"what is it?"

He raised the lantern, and, bending forward a little, turned his eyes towards the hideous object upon which he had come with such startling suddenness.

But from the distance at which he stood it was impossible to see with any degree of distinctness.

All he could discern was that some black object occupied the centre of the passage some paces off.

It cost him a momentary struggle to overcome his repugnance and advance a little closer.

But in order to resolve his doubts it was absolutely necessary that he should do this.

With the sword well projected before him, then, he advanced.

The dark object became more distinct.

It could be seen that it was suspended from the roof or ceiling of the vault.

Gradually—slowly but surely—this object took the form of a human being.

The outlines could not be mistaken.

The Black Highwayman's amazement increased.

His manner made it quite clear that he had not expected to find such a hideous spectacle in this gloomy place, the very silence and solitude alone of which was more than enough to strike a chill to a stout heart.

Steadily he came on until he stood within sword's-length.

The light of the lantern, insufficient as it had seemed, now revealed with horrible distinctness what it was depending from the roof.

It was indeed a human being—or, to speak more correctly, what had once been one, for all signs of life had long since passed away.

Alone in such a place, the most courageous might expect to feel his spirits quail.

A more terrible object could not be imagined.

The half-decayed apparel, which seemed as though the slightest touch or breath of wind would be enough to reduce to powder, made it palpable that the remains were those of a man.

The stout cord by which he was suspended passed round his neck.

The face was ghastly to look upon through the ravages which decay had wrought.

The hands were entirely fleshless, while here and there, through rents in the clothing, the white bones could be seen glistening, thus showing that the cord suspended nothing more than a skeleton.

The Black Highwayman was compelled to avert his eyes.

But as if ashamed of this manifestation of weakness, he the next moment bent upon the loathsome spectacle a more scrutinising glance.

"And so," he said, in half-suppressed tones, "this was the end—this the secret—this your fate! The long-hidden mystery is at last revealed!"

CHAPTER XXXVII.

THE PRISONER.—A MYSTERY EXPLAINED.—THE BLACK HIGHWAYMAN LEVIES A CONTRIBUTION ON THE PRINCE OF WALES.—THE COMPACT.

FROM these last words it was tolerably evident that the Black Highwayman recognised these last relics of human life.

It must have been the clothing that enabled him to do this, for the face had so far gone in dissolution that scarcely one feature could be traced.

"Would I had known this earlier!" the Black Highwayman continued. "But such hopes as those are vain—the past cannot be recalled. The only satisfaction I have is that I know the end."

An invincible repugnance made him hold back as long as possible from passing the body.

The passage was narrow, and he would have to pass in most unpleasant proximity to it.

But there was no alternative.

With a sudden effort, then, and with averted gaze, he strode onward swiftly, nor did he look before him for at least a dozen paces after the dreaded object was left behind.

"I must have it moved," he said, shuddering, "or it will make this passage insupportable. And yet why should I? Ought I not to hold myself superior to all these childish fears and follies? I ought—I must, for should any prying officer discover this retreat, the sudden coming upon such a grisly object will be enough to scare him into madness. It shall remain. This unwonted nervousness shall be checked at once."

By the time he had finished the utterance of this speech he found himself at the foot of a flight of winding steps, the appearance of which did not greatly differ from those he had descended.

He mounted without a moment's pause.

Gaining the top, he struck three sharp blows with his sword-hilt upon the woodwork.

A momentary delay took place.

Then a door was opened.

Across the threshold there seemed to be a perfect blaze of light.

But this was owing to abruptly coming from such a deep darkness.

The Black Highwayman stepped forward.

The door had been opened by the man who had held charge of the woodman's hut.

"Your light seems brilliant," said the mysterious highwayman, in stern tones. "Are you sure that every crevice is so well stopped that no tell-tale beam will find its way out into the night air, and so betray the fact that the old place is again inhabited?"

"I have been careful," returned the man, with his usual sullenness; "but if a light should be seen it will matter little, I think."

"Matter little! What do you mean? Are you mad?"

"Not in the least."

"What do you mean, then? To show a light would only be to court discovery."

The man shook his head.

"You don't know the evil name this place has got," he said—"not that it is worse than it deserves. And to think that I am doomed to stay in this horrible dwelling for an unknown period! What slavery could be worse? I——"

"Hold!" cried his master. "Not another word like that, or—— But I will not waste by breath in threats."

The man ground his teeth savagely together.

"Quick! Tell me what you have heard about this place?"

The man dared not disobey.

"Its reputation is worse than ever," he said; "and for ten miles round there is no one to be found who, by daylight even, would venture within a hundred yards of Harcliffe Hall!"

"So much the better, then—so much the better!"

The man's eyes gleamed with suppressed anger; but he went on:

"Horrible stories have been told of the frightful sights and sounds which have been seen and heard about the place. All believe that it is haunted. And in the village——"

"Well, what is in the village?"

"A boy, or rather a young man: he is mad—stark, staring mad!"

"And what of that?"

"He was fool-hardy, and some time ago made a wager that he would go by night to Harcliffe Hall. Whether he kept his word or not cannot be told, for no one would venture to accompany him. But the next morning——"

"Go on, curse you! Why do you make these pauses?"

The man took no notice of the question; but simply said:

"The next morning he was found."

"Where?"

"Some distance from the Hall."

"And what had he found?"

"That no one knows," said the man, shuddering.

"Why was he silent?"

"Because he was mad—raving mad; and so he has remained ever since. He must have come face to face with some horrible spectacle, which had such an effect upon him as to deprive him of his reason."

"It may be so," returned the Black Highwayman, thinking of his own adventure in the vaults. "The security is all the greater."

"And you would have me stay here?"

"Why not, Martin? Surely you are above all such foolish ideas as these?"

Martin was silent.

"Look here," continued the Black Highwayman—"you know our compact. If you do not fail me I will perform my part of it to the very letter. I have, in one sense, been fortunate of late, and——"

"But when will this serfdom end?"

"Soon—soon. The time will quickly come when I shall have to change my course. Till then be content."

"Content? You know not what it is to pass the long hours alone——"

"Alone? How can you say alone? You forget your prisoner."

"I wish I could forget her," was the still more gloomy response. "I prefer solitude a thousand times to her society."

"Is she so very violent?"

"You shall hear."

Martin—for so we may as well call him—opened a door in one side of the vast apartment, and then drew aside a curtain which had hung behind it.

"Hark!" he said.

Just as he pronounced the word a wild and thrilling shriek came upon the night air.

Those who heard it would know at once that the sound issued from female lips.

The shriek was long-enduring, but changed into a mournful wail, which was succeeded by a peal of horribly-discordant laughter.

As he listened a deep frown settled upon the features of the Black Highwayman.

"Close the door," he said, abruptly. "Is she often thus?"

"Continually."

"It must be seen to; and yet, if such sounds came upon the ears of any prying fools, ten to one they would only serve to give colour to the rumours already current."

The door and curtain must have been well contrived for destroying sound, for when they were restored to their former state all was still—not a murmur could be distinguished.

"We will see more to this, Martin," said the Black Highwayman, in more gentle tones than he had yet made use of to his dependant. "But to-night I cannot spare the time—I have business of importance on hand now. Where is Phantom?"

"Below."

"Safe and well?"

"Quite."

"Then I will leave at once. Take up the light and lead the way."

Martin silently obeyed.

Quitting the room, the strangely-assorted couple found themselves in a wide and lofty hall, evidently the principal entrance to the mansion.

Passing down this, they paused before a door, which Martin opened by means of a key he carried with him.

A flight of stone steps then appeared.

Down these they went carefully, for the damp had made the staircase slippery and treacherous to the feet.

On reaching the bottom, they traversed a long passage, from the extremity of which opened a door.

This led them into a vaulted chamber, which, however, gave evident signs of having been rudely and hastily converted into a stable.

One horse—as jetty black as Captain Hawk's steed Satan—occupied it.

The Black Highwayman, with an impatient step, strode forward, and then stood for some moments caressing the noble animal.

It was indeed a splendid creature, such a one as scarcely had an equal for beauty.

But its powers of speed were still more extraordinary.

The Black Highwayman, and not without good reason, believed them unequalled.

It was for this he prized him; and, next to that, for his unusual sagacity.

The horse, too, knew his rider, and evinced the pleasure it felt at this meeting in a hundred different ways.

"Come, Phantom," the Black Highwayman said, taking hold of the bridle, "we have a night of adventure before us."

The name Phantom was an appropriate one, as regarded the strange stories told about the abrupt manner in which this steed appeared riding noiselessly by the side of some late traveller.

"He is all ready for the road," said Martin, "except his feet; it will not take me a moment."

The Black Highwayman stood aside.

Martin then, from a small chest, produced what at first sight looked almost like four black driving gloves.

They turned out to be, however, four outer shoes or cases, which he proceeded to fit over Phantom's feet.

The horse was well accustomed to the proceeding, for he stood perfectly quiet.

These shoes were composed of leather, or some such material, and were secured round the coronet of the hoof by means of a small but strong strap.

The contrivance was a simple one, and yet how materially it had assisted in sustaining the supernatural notions that were rife respecting the Black Highwayman and his spectre steed.

So closely did the casing fit round the hoof that it would have required a second glance to have perceived that there was anything unusual.

"All is ready now," said Martin, as he rose to his feet.

The Black Highwayman led his horse a little way over the stones.

But so well protected were his feet by this elastic covering that in his progress he made scarcely an audible sound.

"Open the door, Martin, and expect me to return at any moment; it is impossible to say how soon I may be back."

Martin complied in silence.

The door which he now threw back upon its hinges communicated with a subterranean passage, the size of which was sufficiently large to allow him to lead the horse down it easily.

Its length was considerable, and for some time it had a gradual upward tendency.

At last he emerged on the side of a precipitous hill, that from top to bottom was thickly overgrown with dense bushes and stunted trees.

A narrow, zigzag path, scarcely discernible, afforded a means by which the descent could be accomplished.

The Black Highwayman did not mount until he reached level ground.

He then directed his course at a gentle rate over the meadows until he gained the high-road.

"It must be somewhere near the hour now," he said. "I fancy his Royal Highness must be leaving Windsor at about this time. How fortunate it was that I should receive a hint of this incognito visit! It is just what I require. With only a few—perhaps no attendants—my task will be an easy one. I wonder whether a reconciliation has been brought about?"

At the time of which we are writing, the Second George occupied the throne.

Between himself and his eldest son, Frederick, the Prince of Wales, there had been a complete estrangement.

Many attempts had been made towards a reconciliation, but the effect of them had only been to widen the breach they were intended to bridge over.

The present was one of these occasions, and the Black Highwayman was intent upon turning it to his advantage.

"I shall win my bet and accomplish my purpose much sooner than I had expected. But when this is done I will hold back a little until popular excitement has subsided. Otherwise the discovery of my secret is almost certain—and discovery would be fatal to all my future plans."

So saying, he made his way out of the meadow on to the high-road leading from Windsor to London.

A hasty inspection of his weapons was then made.

Before he finished, the distant rumbling of carriage-wheels came upon his ears.

"That is the prince for a thousand pounds!"

Driving close under the shadow of the hedgerow, he awaited the arrival of the approaching vehicle.

His patience was not put to any great trial, for the well-poised carriage was being drawn with great swiftness along the smooth highway.

"I would wager anything," said the highwayman, "that to-night's visit has been attended with no more success than those which have preceded it. Otherwise he would not be on his way to London so soon after his arrival."

At this moment the vehicle became visible to the Black Highwayman's piercing eyes.

It was drawn by four beautiful gray horses, that were tearing along in a way that would elicit the admiration of anyone.

"His Royal Highness is angry and impatient," said the highwayman, "or he would never travel at such a pace as that."

In another moment the carriage whirled past him.

It was just at this juncture that the Black Highwayman rode out swiftly in a diagonal direction from the place where he had concealed himself.

Despite the swiftness with which the prince's carriage was being hurried along—the four horses harnessed to it were going at a gallop—Phantom was able to keep up while going at a trot.

In his left hand the Black Highwayman held a pistol.

As soon as ever he was in a line with the door of the carriage, the window of which was open, he thrust in his head.

A glance told him that the vehicle contained one person only.

"Your Royal Highness," he said, riding in what appeared to be most dangerous proximity to the wheels—"your Royal Highness need be under no apprehension. I mean no harm."

"Harm! The devil!" ejaculated the royal voice. "Who are you to know who I am?"

"That matters not. Give your coachman orders to proceed more slowly. I have a few words to exchange with you."

"Insolent!"

"Perhaps so."

"Suppose I refuse?"

"Then," said the Black Highwayman, as he rattled the barrel of his pistol upon the sill of the carriage window, "should your Royal Highness be so unwise, your son will have a better chance of being the next King of England than he has at present."

"Villain! Do you threaten my life?"

"Not at all; but it will be prudent for you to tell the coachman to drive more slowly. What I have to say is of importance, and while going at this rate your Royal Highness might have a little difficulty in distinguishing what I said."

The pistol was rattled again.

This produced the desired effect.

The prince leaned forward and pulled the check-string.

The coachman turned round, and to his amazement, not to say horror, he saw a mounted man riding along by the side of the carriage, when a moment before he would have firmly declared that he had the road entirely to himself.

His consternation was so great that he uttered a cry of dismay and whipped the horses vigorously

But it was to no purpose.

Phantom kept up his pace as easily as before.

"The devil!" the coachman ejaculated, dropping his whip and crossing himself. "It's the devil himself!"

"Your Royal Highness," said the Black Highwayman, "I must and will be obeyed—the consequences of refusal will be serious."

The check-string was again pulled violently.

This time with its due effect.

The horses were reined-in.

"Drive gently," said the prince, in a gruff voice.

When this command was obeyed the Black Highwayman had little or no difficulty in continuing a conversation with the inmate of the carriage.

"Your Royal Highness," he said, "believe me, I regret very much this interruption to your journey——"

"Bah!"

"I assure you of it."

The contemptuous exclamation was repeated.

"Really, your Royal Highness——"

"This comes of my own folly in travelling without an escort. It serves me right. Another time I shall know better."

"But, your Royal Highness——"

"Well, what have you to say?"

"I regret having approached you at such an unfavourable moment, but——"

"I suppose you want my purse and money? That is the long and the short of it. Were I King, there would be few of your race left to trouble passengers."

The prince was in a terrible state of chagrin.

Things had gone wrong with him that night, and this incident had completed his discomfiture.

"Your Royal Highness, then, has doubtless heard of the Black Highwayman?"

"And what then?"

"I have the honour to be that individual."

"The honour!"

"And at least one of the most sincere and devoted of all your Royal Highness's adherents."

The prince was silent.

Owing to his own equivocal position at the time—having the King, his father, and most of the influential personages of the realm arrayed against him—he could not afford to despise anyone who professed himself a friend.

All acquainted with the history of the period must be aware of the difficulties and dilemmas into which he was thus thrown.

"Why do you stop me, then?" he said, at length. "What is your errand?"

"I regret to state it; but I made a heavy wager that the next time your Royal Highness went abroad I would stop your carriage and levy a contribution upon you as I would upon any ordinary traveller."

"You are an impudent scoundrel!"

"And one willing to serve your Royal Highness at the same time."

The prince was again silent.

"Your Royal Highness," continued the Black Highwayman, "it is not my intention to despoil you, though, as I find you quite unattended, nothing would be easier than to strip you of every valuable you carry with you; but, nevertheless, I must request you to hand me your purse with a few gold pieces in it, and your watch or some other trinket which may easily be recognised. This, if you want it back, you can have in a few days by offering a trifling reward. What does your Royal Highness say to that?"

"Why, that it is the coolest and most impudent speech I have ever heard in my life!"

"But at least you will admit that I have treated you with forbearance?"

"How so?"

"I have the power, yet do not use it."

"Why not?"

"Simply because I am attached to your party."

"And yet you would rob me!"

"Nominally only, and merely that I may be able to win the wager."

The prince was again silent.

The Black Highwayman trotted unconcernedly by the side of the carriage.

"Look here!" he said at last. "Supposing that I comply with this outrageous demand of yours?"

"It will be decidedly best for you to do so."

"But suppose I do?"

"Well?"

"Why then I shall exact a condition."

"Of what nature?"

"That when I call upon you you shall render me a service."

"Agreed!"

"Will you swear to do so?"

"I will give you my word, which is the same thing."

"And you will not refuse?" said the prince, in a suppressed voice. as though some dark project was hovering in his mind.

"What is the nature of the service?"

"That I cannot tell you now. Will you promise?"

"If it is nothing that cannot be done by a man of honour."

The prince gave a short and scornful laugh.

"Once more," he said, "will you promise?"

"I will."

"Enough, then. Take my purse—it is here."

"Thanks! Your watch!"

"It is here; and also a ring. No one will dispute whether that belongs to me or not."

"Many, many thanks, your Highness. If the service you ask for is one that requires an unflinching determination, a strong arm, and a stout heart for its execution, I will perform it."

"Those are the very qualities. And when shall we meet again?"

"That is hard to say."

"But a time must be appointed."

"Your Highness, on the third night from this I will send a confidential messenger to Lancaster House. He will bring with him your watch and ring. They will be his credentials. Do not fear to tell him the nature of the service."

"Is he to be so much trusted?"

"He has my entire confidence. My life is always in his hands."

"Agreed, then!" said the prince. "If I cannot name the service then, I can at least appoint another place of meeting."

"Just so, your Royal Highness."

"Farewell till then!"

He raised his hat, and pulled the rein.

In a moment he disappeared in the darkness, and the prince angrily bade the coachman drive on.

What desperate idea it was that crossed his mind will soon be known.

Doubtless his impression was that he should find the Black Highwayman one of those unscrupulous persons who would commit any enormity so long as they were urged to it by a prince.

England has need to be thankful that George the Second's eldest son never became King.

The truth of the old proverb which says "A man is known by the company he keeps," was never better exemplified than in his case.

In the meantime, however, the Black Highwayman had made his way in the direction of the mysterious dwelling from which he had set out, as though it was his immediate purpose to return there.

But just when about to quit the high-road the distant clatter of a horse's hoofs came suddenly upon his ears.

He paused at once.

"Who comes?" I wonder.

The clatter grew louder.

"I will go on," he said. "Ten to one if it is worth while to wait."

Yet he lingered.

"He rides well," he ejaculated, mechanically feeling for a pistol. "He shall not pass me unchallenged."

Having come to this determination, he, as on the former occasion, concealed himself close to the hedge-side.

One would have thought that the approaching traveller was in more than usual haste.

The pace he came along at was most unusual.

A turn in the road concealed him from the view of the highwayman until he was within a hundred yards.

On he galloped at the same unabated speed.

The Black Highwayman, watching his time, dashed out just as the traveller was passing.

Phantom's well-covered hoofs made no sound, and the suddenness with which he appeared made it seem as though he had either dropped from the clouds or risen from the ground.

The traveller was aware of the presence of his strange companion almost instantly.

He pulled up.

He did it so abruptly that his horse reared high in the air, and for a moment seemed in danger of falling over backwards.

The Black Highwayman pulled up also, though he could not help shooting a little ahead.

But he turned back immediately.

The stranger showed no inclination to retreat.

"At last," he exclaimed, in tones that unmistakably bespoke the utmost exultation—"at last we meet! Ha!"

While speaking, he leaned forward, and by a sudden movement snatched away the half-mask which had so effectually concealed the features of the Black Highwayman.

CHAPTER XXXVIII.

LIEUTENANT TRACY RECOGNIZES THE BLACK HIGHWAYMAN.—THE SECRET PRISONER AT THE HALL.

THE reader probably has not forgotten Lieutenant Tracy, who met with so serious an accident on that eventful night when he gave chase to the Black Highwayman.

He was carried by Peterson to an adjoining inn, and being there, he received every attention.

This was no doubt in consequence of the well-filled purse which he displayed before the landlord's eyes.

Medical assistance was called in.

The report was more favourable than could have been expected.

No bones had been broken.

He had been severely shaken, and had received some ugly bruises, but nothing more.

His escape from death must have been little short of miraculous.

Under these circumstances, of course it was not long before he was able to move about unaided.

Then, his profession was one that had made him familiar with hard knocks, and no doubt, on this very account, he got over his injuries much sooner than any-one else would have done.

His failure, too, just at what he believed the moment of success, filled him with impatience to get upon the road again.

Not only that, his leave of absence was about to expire, and he was afraid it would do so before he had accomplished his firmly-fixed purpose.

This will explain how it was, then, that almost before he had recovered himself sufficiently to make any violent exertion prudent, he insisted upon having his horse and setting out upon his mission.

In vain the landlord and the doctor endeavoured to dissuade him from his purpose.

He was resolved.

As soon as dusk set in he took his departure.

His adventures during the earlier part of the evening and night were uninteresting.

At last he gave up in despair of meeting with the daring depredator.

He was about to turn his horse's head towards London when he chanced to remember that he had an old school friend living in the neighbourhood of Windsor, and as he happened to be nearer to the latter town than to the metropolis, he determined to pay him a visit, and ask his opinion concerning the matter in hand.

Directly after this, the carriage occupied by the Prince of Wales whirled past him.

He fancied he recognised the vehicle, but was not quite certain.

But his doubt made him remember what had happened on that memorable evening at Lord Harcliffe's mansion.

"I do believe," he said, "that that was the Prince of Wales's equipage; if so, I may reasonably hope to catch a sight of this Black Highwayman, for, by all that I can learn, he is almost certain to do it if the opportunity presented itself."

With this he quickened his horse's pace.

What followed, the reader is already aware of.

It was Lieutenant Tracy that the Black Highwayman had laid in wait for.

The young sailor was full of exultation at finding himself at last side by side with the mysterious robber he had used such exertions to meet.

The Black Highwayman uttered an oath and raised his pistol.

For a moment or so Lieutenant Tracy remained like one thunderstruck.

"Good heavens!" he ejaculated, "can it be possible? Lord Harcliffe the Black Highwayman!"

"Fool—meddling fool!" said the latter, in hasty tones of suppressed passion—"those words are your death-warrant! The secret you have discovered is my life, and self-preservation compels me to prevent it going any further. Take a good look around you—it will be your last. I would a thousand times rather have death than discovery. I would willingly spare you if I could; but you were warned, and you must take the consequences of your folly, for I know well it would be quite useless to bind you down to keep my secret."

"I will have no conditions or compact with such as you. Once again I call upon you to surrender. If you refuse, I will shoot you down where you sit, with as little compunction as I would shoot a mad dog."

"Then I do refuse," said the Black Highwayman, bringing his pistol to a level. "I would willingly spare you if I could, but my own safety demands your death. You have no one to blame but yourself. Take your fate!"

As he spoke he pulled the trigger.

Precisely at the same moment Lieutenant Tracy fired also.

The explosion of the two weapons produced but one report.

For a second or two a perplexing haze of blue smoke hung around.

But the gentle breeze wafted it away.

One horseman only remained seated in the saddle.

This was the Black Highwayman.

Poor Tracy lay upon his back in the roadway, without motion.

His horse, filled with terror, galloped off.

The Black Highwayman calmly wiped his pistol and restored it to his pocket.

"The meddling fool well deserved his fate," he exclaimed, looking down at the prostrate form of his foe; "and yet nothing else than my own self-preservation should have induced me to fire upon him. But one of us was doomed, and he has turned out to be the one. How still he lies!"

He gazed intently at the young sailor, and then, after a momentary hesitation, dismounted.

"Quite dead," he said, placing his hand upon the lieutenant's heart. "I thought my hand did not tremble. Well—well, I am sorry for him."

He dragged the body to one side of the road, and then, mounting again, rode slowly away.

There was a marked expression of regret upon his features.

"It was necessity," he said, at last—"stern necessity. I could not have acted otherwise."

At a smart gallop he rode towards Harcliffe Hall.

He made his way back in the same manner as he had left it.

Martin was waiting for him in the stable.

The man looked as sullen and gloomy as before.

But his master took no notice of it.

With as little delay as possible, he made his way into the upper chamber

"Tend your prisoner well, Martin. Remember that."

"Will you not see her?"

"Not to-night."

"I will mind her—there is no fear of that. Terrible as her company is, it is better by far than solitude."

"I may not be here for some days," continued the Black Highwayman, passing over his remarks without further notice; "but keep expecting me every moment. Above all, be careful."

"And is that all?"

"Yes. I have had a narrow escape to-night, which will make me doubly cautious for the future. Open the door."

Martin obeyed, and the Black Highwayman, passing through it, made his way to the ruined summer-house where he had left his other horse.

When he had gone, Martin's face assumed a truly diabolical look.

"Is there never to be an end?" he said—"am I so wholly in his power? Can I not by any means extricate myself? I must think it out."

He closed the door again, and stirring up the fire, which had smouldered low, sat himself down moodily.

But finding it impossible to retain this position long, he sprang up and paced the room.

"I could betray him easily enough, but then I should bring destruction upon myself. But surely, if I could only think of it, there must be a means of delivering him to his foes and securing my own safety at the same time. I distrust him. Some day or other he will be found out, and perhaps I should suffer too."

He was silent then for some moments.

"If I could only make terms with the officers," he said, "and bring them here, how easy it would be to seize upon him. He would be so taken by surprise that he would be deprived of all power of resistance. Surely for such a service as that I ought to obtain immunity for the past. At any rate, come what will, it shall be tried."

Little did the Black Highwayman think of the tremendous danger impending over him.

He had to place an absolute trust in Martin; and judging by what had happened, he believed he could do so with perfect safety.

He relied on the power which he held over this man to make him faithful.

But for a long time the desire to put an end to the present state of things had existed in Martin's breast.

He brooded upon it night and day, and the idea occupied his mind to the exclusion of all others.

And now seating himself near the fire, he drew out of his pocket a packet of papers.

They were bills relating to the Black Highwayman, and offering various rewards for his apprehension.

While engaged in looking them over for the hundredth time, he was startled by a subdued shriek.

No doubt it was a shrill and piercing one—it must have been, or it would never have reached his ears through the door which so perfectly shut out all sound.

"How awful!" he said. "He has that to answer for which I should be sorry for. I will go to her, poor thing—it must be dreadful for her to be thus!"

So saying, he arose, replaced his packet carefully, and went towards the door which we have before mentioned.

When he opened it all was still.

Crossing the spacious apartment with which the door communicated, he emerged into a broad corridor.

On the opposite side of this was a door with fastenings on the outer side.

The bars were up, the bolts shot into their sockets.

Near the centre, too, was a huge lock.

Martin took a brightly-polished key from his pocket.

Just then the sound of some one weeping and sobbing came faintly to his ears.

"Poor thing!" he ejaculated, in tones of compassion. "Her paroxysm is over now—there will be no more shrieks and screams for a little while."

He seemed half in doubt as to whether he should enter.

Overcoming his hesitation, however, he slowly undid the fastenings, and then opening the door, passed through swiftly, and closed it after him, as though he feared that the prisoner might make a sudden dash and attempt to get past him.

But the fear was groundless on this occasion, at all events.

The chamber was wrapped in gloom.

High up near the ceiling an oil-lamp hung, suspended by a chain.

But the illumination it gave forth was of the feeblest and most uncertain character.

At the first glance, one would have taken the room to be untenanted.

But in one corner of it crouched something in a strange, huddled-up position, which would have been found to be a human being.

Now that Martin had entered, the sobbing and weeping had ceased.

As he advanced towards the lamp his feet made no sound.

The floor, as well as the walls to a height of more than five feet, was thickly covered with some kind of soft padding.

Martin's manner, as he approached, was a strange mixture of respect and familiarity.

"Is there nothing I can do for you?" he said.

There was a pause.

Then the crouching figure in the corner said, in low, sad tones:

"Yes, there is much that you can do for me, but you will not."

"I wish I could help and serve you; but, alas! I cannot."

"You can—you can!"

Martin shook his head.

"Will you listen to me? Surely you ought not to refuse me that slight favour. I am calm, am I not?"

"You are—calmer than ever I have seen you."

"Who can command calmness when smarting under such injuries as mine? You see, I cannot make this slight mention of them without my voice rising to a higher pitch. But I will try my best not to grow excited."

The crouching figure rose and came towards the lamp.

Involuntarily Martin stepped back.

The prisoner perceived the movement and paused.

"Do not fear me," she said—"I will come no closer."

As she now stood, she was partially revealed by the flickering light.

At the first glance it could be seen that she was still young, though grief and violent sorrow, with probably confinement as well, had left their traces upon her cheeks.

Her form was so emaciated that it was painful in the extreme to look upon it, and she moved as though she had barely strength sufficient to support the weight of her own body.

Her hands, which she extended in a supplicating manner towards her jailor, were well-nigh as fleshless as those of a skeleton.

Her eyes were deeply sunken and surrounded by broad, livid circles.

But the eyes themselves were unnaturally large and brilliant.

There were few who could support their gaze.

"Listen to me, Martin," she said—"do listen to me! I will promise to be calm—quite calm. Will you listen?"

"I will."

"Thanks, Martin—thanks!"

"But I cannot aid you."

"You shall hear. Will you promise to wait till you have heard me?"

"Yes."

"You think I am mad, and, Heaven knows," she said, clasping her hands over her forehead, "sometimes I think I am or have been! Perhaps I am going mad."

She stopped then.

Martin saw the tears roll down her cheeks.

"There is no madness about me now," she continued, in a choked voice. "I am as sane as you are at this moment, and I will prove it by my words. But tell me—do you really think that I am mad?"

Martin made no reply.

"I know what your silence means, but you are deceived for all that. I must be free, and by your aid, Martin—I must gain my freedom through you. Once outside this terrible place, do not fear that I shall want for friends or for money to reward you for your services. I can make you a rich man, Martin, if you do not continue blind to your own interests."

Martin shook his head doubtfully.

"I am almost afraid to trust myself to speak about the causer of all that I have suffered for so long—I dread that my calmness will give way and that you will take my excitement for a return of madness. Some day, not only you, but all the world shall hear the story of my wrongs; but while I am kept here I have no choice but to submit."

"You forget his power."

"Forget it? How can I? Is not my imprisonment in this place enough to force the fact upon me?"

"And his position and influence."

"I forget nothing, his downfall will be complete."

Martin listened attentively.

There was a coherence and a method in what she said that seemed to prove her sanity.

Never before had she so addressed him.

For this reason, then, he listened with eager interest to every word that fell from her lips.

"Tell me, Martin, for what sum you would consent to set me free?"

"I would do so without reward," he said, "for I pity you from the bottom of my heart."

"Thanks—thanks for that assurance," she cried, springing forward and clasping his hands, though he made an effort to prevent it.

"Be calm," he said—"remember you promised to be calm."

"I will not forget. I know you will aid me now, Martin—I feel sure of it."

"I will if I can."

"Then you shall be a rich man, for I repeat that when once I can recover my liberty I shall have the means of making you one. As for the villain who——"

Insensibly her voice rose to a high pitch.

Martin held up his hand warningly.

"Oh, if you only knew how hard it is to keep this restraint!" she cried, piteously. "And yet, unless I exercise this superhuman command, you will think me mad, and refuse to listen to me."

Tears choked her utterance.

"Listen to me," said Martin. "I have something to tell you if you will promise to keep it secret."

"I promise faithfully."

"And you will keep your word?"

"While I live and breathe. What is it, Martin?"

He glanced about him apprehensively, as though afraid to speak.

Sinking his voice to a low whisper, he said:

"I, too, am determined to put an end to my servitude and odious bondage. I am resolved to brave his power, great as it is. His race is over. You know not what I know of him; if you did——"

He stopped abruptly, and turned ghastly pale.

A slight noise had reached his ears.

He turned round swiftly towards the door, for he saw the prisoner was gazing as if spellbound in that direction.

A gasping cry escaped his lips when he saw standing upon the threshold the subject of his conversation—the Black Highwayman.

CHAPTER XXXIX.

CAPTAIN HAWK CALLS TO MIND HIS PROMISE TO DICK TURPIN.

"Upon my life," said Captain Hawk, as he pulled up after galloping a few hundred yards—"upon my word, I never enjoyed anything better in all my life! It was capital! Ha, ha!"

He stopped in order to indulge in a good peal of laughter.

"Mr. Hogg will not forget me for some time, I'll be bound. Ha! here he comes. How wild he does look, to be sure!"

The great police officer did in good truth present a remarkable appearance.

His hat had been left behind in the duck-pond when he scrambled out of it, and so had his wig.

He was absolutely reeking with the unsavoury mud, the accumulation of many a year.

His face was streaked here and there like a wild Indian, or as if he had been streaked with some strong pickle.

He foamed at the mouth, like the animal whose name he bore.

Upon seeing Captain Hawk stop, his fury redoubled.

All coolness and discretion had completely disappeared.

Although nothing like within range, he drew a pistol, but as this one, like all the rest, had been manipulated by the captain, he could not discharge it.

His oaths were frightful as he flung the weapon from him.

He goaded his horse savagely, and came on at a breakneck rate.

Captain Hawk aggravated him by allowing him to get quite close.

Then giving Satan the rein, away he went at at least double the rate the great police officer's horse was capable of going at.

Then, when he had placed a sufficient distance between them, he stopped again.

[CAPTAIN HAWK INQUIRES THE TIME OF DAY.]

Mr. Hogg came on more madly than ever.

"Never mind," he bawled, "your triumph will be short—I will follow you like a shadow! You may outdistance me, but you cannot shake me off. I will never—never leave you!"

"Very good," replied the captain—"I have no objection."

This derisive treatment was enough to make any man desperate under the circumstances.

"As for this cursed jade," continued Mr. Hogg, expending some of his spare fury on his unfortunate horse, "I will ride her to the next town at the top of her speed, if she drops down dead when I get there! You don't know the man you have to deal with!"

One would almost have thought that the horse both heard and understood what its rider said, and that it had an objection to going so far as he intended, for there happening to be an awkward hole in the road, it took advantage of the circumstance by putting one foot into it.

This ended the pursuit at once.

Down went the horse on his knees, and the great Mr. Hogg for the last time fell ignominiously to the earth.

The fall was both awkward and severe, and he remained just where he had fallen, giving no signs whatever of vitality.

The whole happened so quickly that Captain Hawk could hardly believe what he saw.

"Is he dead, I wonder? If so, his fate is awfully sudden. I will go and see."

Without a thought of danger, he rode swiftly to his prostrate foe, and when within a pace or two, stopped to look at him.

A slight movement instantly attracted his attention.

He had just time to draw a little to one side when the air rung with the discharge of a pistol.

"Another narrow escape," said the highwayman, coolly. "I shall trouble myself no more about you. Doubtless you fully expect me to retaliate upon you for the cowardly act of which you have been guilty, but know that I consider you unworthy of it. My intention was to assist you as far as was in my power if I found you seriously hurt. Now stay where you are, and do the best you can for yourself."

Mr. Hogg cursed and swore bitterly.

He was much enraged at finding that his treacherous shot had been an unavailing one, and still more so at the captain's contemptuous manner.

"I will be your death!" he said, with bitter malignity. "Don't think much of this. I give you leave to enjoy your triumph all you can. It won't last long—mind that!"

A sharp twinge of pain caused him to give a howl of agony, which put a stop to what more he might have been about to say.

Captain Hawk waited no longer, but rode away.

He went slowly, for he had no immediate danger to apprehend from Mr. Hogg, and he wished to think over his future plans a little.

He was by no means decided as to where he should go and what he should do.

His thoughts, of course, reverted to the squire's villanous steward.

"I must have my reckoning with him," he said, "but it seems as though I should be compelled to put it off for a time. Never mind; my revenge will keep. I will get away from this locality. If I do not, Mr. Hogg will soon make it too hot to hold me. His power, no doubt, is great, and there is not the least doubt he will exercise it to the uttermost. The best way to disappoint him will be by riding clear away."

Having come to this resolve, he, as usual, proceeded to act upon it.

A slight slackening of the rein was all that Satan wanted to let him know that his rider wished him to increase his speed.

Away he went at full swing in a moment.

Captain Hawk remained plunged in reflection, and so absorbed by his thoughts that he altogether forgot that it was broad daylight, and that the numbers of people he passed looked back after him in great amazement.

At length, becoming sensible of it, he moderated his horse's speed, and took the opportunity of turning down the very next lane he came to.

A few yards only sufficed to conceal him entirely from the high-road.

The lane was a picturesque and beautiful one even under its winterly aspect.

"I had almost forgotten my purpose," he exclaimed, at length. "It is the occurrence of so many strange events which has caused me to do so. I ought to have remembered it. Poor Dick! Well—well, there is ample time to carry out your last wishes even now."

He was silent for some moments.

A pained, saddened expression settled itself upon his features.

He was thinking of his parting with Dick Turpin at York Castle.

The subject of his comrade's fate affected him so deeply that he always refused to dwell upon it—making an effort to direct his thoughts into other channels.

But on the present occasion he could not recover his composure for some time.

Presently, drawing his hand across his eyes, he exclaimed:

"What is the good of grieving thus? I cannot recall what has passed; if I could, it would be different; I cannot bear to think of him, and yet never to bestow one moment upon his memory seems ungrateful to a degree. But what I have promised I will perform."

Again he rode on in thought.

"Why should I linger?" he said. "I may as well make my way with all the speed I can to London. I have nothing to prevent it. That shall be my plan. I am almost open to the accusation of forgetting you, my best friend, but I have not. With as little delay as I can I will seek out old Matthew at his house in Drury Lane. My task will be a painful one, but I will keep my word to the very letter. I will let him know every fact connected with Dick Turpin's untimely fate."

The thought of this saddened him extremely.

What his feelings would be when he came to speak at full upon the painful topic would be hard to realise.

His head sunk down upon his breast, and assumed so great an appearance of dejection that those who had known him in his merrier moods would have found it difficult to believe him the same person.

In all probability his melancholy reverie would have continued much longer than it did had he not at last been aroused by the sudden downfall of a torrent of rain.

Many heavy premonitory drops had fallen, but they had not proved sufficient to excite his notice.

But when the rain came down in a perfect shower, deluging everything like a cataract, he awoke to a consciousness of what was going on around him.

"Confound it!" he exclaimed, "I shall be wet through to the skin."

His first impulse was to urge Satan to a gallop, and the next to look about him for some place of shelter.

But no human habitation—not so much as a shed—could he discern in any direction.

A little further on, however, was a large evergreen tree, which spread out its branches widely in every direction.

"It is better than nothing," cried the captain, as he at once rode under the boughs.

He was agreeably surprised to find that the tree afforded much better shelter than he had anticipated.

Only a few pattering drops occasionally reached him.

He shook off the wet as well as he could, and then, with what patience he was able to command, waited for the storm to pass away.

Of this there seemed little token at present.

Indeed, if anything, the rain fell faster.

Just as the highwayman had made up his mind that he should have to remain in his present quarters for some time, he heard the clatter of hoofs.

"Somebody else caught in the wet," he ejaculated, "and somebody else making haste to a place of shelter."

Just as he said this, he caught sight of a stout, elderly-looking individual mounted on a stout, strong cob, who required continual belabouring with the stock of a riding-whip to get beyond his usual shuffling trot.

No sooner did the old gentleman catch sight of Captain Hawk under the tree than he immediately rode towards him.

"Goodness gracious!" he exclaimed, "whenever did it rain like this? I am wet through, I declare!"

"Such a shower makes the shelter of a tree agreeable," said the captain, looking attentively at the new-comer as he spoke.

He was a man, probably, of middle age, and by his appearance it was clear that he had lived thus long without experiencing many of the cares of life.

His brow and his cheeks were smooth and unwrinkled, and the circumference of his waist was such as would make any bodily exertion very trying.

Riding on horseback at the unusual rate he had just been doing had caused his face to flush and his heart to pant.

"Dear me!" he said, "I don't know that ever I went along the road at such a pace before! Just look how it comes down now!"

Captain Hawk saw, too, by the peculiar cut of his companion's costume that he was a dignitary of the church.

He seemed in comfortable circumstances, for the plain broadcloth of which his costume was composed was of the best and finest quality.

He now took off his hat, disclosing a very bald head by the operation, and taking his handkerchief, wiped from his face the mingled rain and perspiration that was upon it.

But what attracted the most of Captain Hawk's attention was a massive gold chain, hanging below the worthy parson's waistcoat.

At the end of this chain was a bunch of seals of proportionate massiveness.

Captain Hawk at once resolved that they should be his, together with the no doubt equally massive watch concealed in the fob.

"I think the rain comes down faster if anything," remarked the highwayman. "Who would have thought now, that this old tree would have afforded such excellent shelter?"

"Excellent indeed!" returned the clergyman, who seemed the embodiment of gossip and good humour. "I little thought when I started that such a sousing was in store for me. That looks a capital sort of horse you have, sir," he added.

"Yes," said the captain, "I think if you travelled to-day till you met with his fellow you would be very tired before you reached the end of your journey."

"Very likely. And of course he's a great favourite of yours?"

"Very great indeed."

"I thought so. I cannot see a white hair about him."

"He has not a speck."

He patted his steed as he spoke.

This made him prance about slightly, to the discomfort of his rider.

"Woa—woa!" he exclaimed. "Quiet, Satan—quiet."

Upon hearing this name, an expression appeared on the parson's face which mightily amused the highwayman to look upon.

"My dear sir," he exclaimed at length, "what was that you said?"

"What?"

"Why, either my ears deceived me, or else I heard you pronounce the name of the d—— I mean the prince of darkness."

"And so I did," returned the captain, laughing.

"But what for, young man? Excuse me for taking the liberty of saying that your levity is very wrong and unseasonable."

"Levity!" echoed the highwayman. "What do you mean?"

"Nay, what did you mean?" asked the parson, with increased gravity. "Why did you adjure Satan to be quiet?"

"Because he was just a little more tricksy and unruly than I thought agreeable—that's all."

"All!" ejaculated the parson, whose amazement now changed to absolute horror.

"Yes," cried the captain, bursting out into a hearty peal of laughter, which he was unable longer to restrain. "Excuse me, sir, but you seem in a mist. You don't appear to know that Satan is the name that my horse answers to."

The parson sat still for a moment.

Then shook his head in a very slow and solemn manner.

"My young friend, I cannot forbear saying that you have chosen a highly improper name for your horse. The bare idea of such profanity—I can't use a milder word—makes me shudder from head to foot. Let me improve the present occasion by——"

Here the captain, being able to give a shrewd guess as to what was coming, interrupted him.

"It don't rain much," he said, in commonplace tones. "I think we may venture to say the storm is over. Such being the case, I must get on my way, for I am behind-hand already."

"But, my dear young friend," said the parson, appealingly, "if you would only——"

"Would you oblige me with the time, sir? I perceive you carry a watch with you; my own happens to be out of repair just at the present time."

With a faint groan, the clergyman proceeded to pull out his watch.

This was no easy matter, for not only was his fob a deep one, but his breeches very tight indeed round the waist.

With a tug, however, the watch was at length brought to light.

It was a very large one, the face being such as might serve for a moderate-sized clock.

"My young friend," he said, "this watch brings to my recollection a little circumstance wonderfully bearing on the present case, and I must beg of you to hear it."

"Oh, certainly! But what is the time?"

"Half-past ten to a moment. You may depend upon the time being correct. The watch is always right. A very valuable watch, and one that I am proud of. It was given to me, my young friend, by my parishioners, as a token of their good will and esteem. You will see all that expressed in more flattering terms than I should like to employ if you will glance at the inscription engraved on the back of it."

"Indeed!" exclaimed the captain, with an air of wonderful interest. "I should much like to see it."

"It is here, sir."

The highwayman extended his hand and received the watch, which the parson confidingly placed into it.

He examined it attentively.

"It is a magnificent watch—a very valuable one, I should——"

"Ahem! Well, yes, especially with the chain and seals."

"To be sure—to be sure. Were they included as part of the gift?"

"Oh dear, no; I bought them myself."

"Ah, I thought so! And you say it goes well?"

"Excellently. No piece of machinery can go better."

"Than it has done," added Captain Hawk.

"Why, yes, than it has gone."

"Because," continued the captain, "it will now go very much better, because it will go altogether."

As he pronounced these words he coolly slipped the watch into his pocket.

The parson looked the picture of bewilderment.

Captain Hawk retained the same good-tempered smile upon his lips.

A moment elapsed before the parson could recover himself sufficiently to make use of his voice.

"I do not understand you, my young friend!" he ejaculated at last. "What do you mean?"

"Just simply what I have said—that no matter how well your watch may have gone hitherto, it will now go better, since it will go altogether."

"There is only one construction I can place on those words," said the parson, growing alarmed. "But this must be some kind of jest, though I assure you I fail to see the point of it."

"Believe me, it is no jest. Your watch has gone."

And as if to intimate that it was irrecoverable, Captain Hawk buttoned up his pocket.

"But—but——" gasped the parson, and then he stopped.

Captain Hawk smiled.

"But what?" he said.

"You—you do not, cannot mean to say that you intend to keep my watch?"

"Indeed but I do! It has changed hands now, and I should say that the chances are against your ever catching a glimpse of it again."

"Nonsense! You cannot be in earnest. I am sure this is some joke."

"None at all, I assure you. Look! the rain has cleared off nicely now, and I think we can venture to quit our place of shelter. Good morning, sir!"

The clergyman was dumbfoundered at the highwayman's coolness and audacity.

"Stop—stop!" he cried. "Stop, I pray you!"

Thus adjured, the highwayman turned round.

The parson came eagerly towards him.

There seemed to be tears in his eyes.

"Come, come—let there be an end of this. Give me back my watch."

"Impossible!"

"Why impossible? Surely you are not a robber? And if you are, surely you would not have the impudence to rob a man in this barefaced manner by broad daylight, and within half a mile of his own home?"

"Yet you see it is so."

"Oh, young man, pause—pause a moment and reflect! Think upon the sacrilege which you are committing. Your crime would be bad enough perpetrated upon an ordinary individual, but upon a minister, unworthy as I am, it is absolutely heinous!"

"That I can't help," said the captain; "nor can I spare the time to stay any longer here. Therefore, once more I must beg leave to wish you good day!"

"Good day, the devil! and with my watch in your pocket!"

"Stop—stop, sir! Such language ill befits your station."

"Station be d—d! Who can use temperate language when he sees another man riding off with his watch in his pocket?"

"Don't get in a passion, reverend sir. It will do no good. Make up your mind to the fact that the watch is gone."

"No, no—give it back to me! You cannot be so depraved. Ah, young man, let me exhort you to pause and reflect! Do not add this act to the list of your sins, or it will weigh heavier than all the rest. Repent—repent, or you well know what will be the end. Begin the work of grace by giving me back my watch."

"So far from doing so," answered Captain Hawk, "I shall now require your purse, as recompense for the delay and trouble you have caused me."

Every particle of colour now forsook the clergyman's face.

"Come!" said the captain, "hand it over quickly, or I shall increase my demands."

"Give me back my watch!"

"Be a sensible man. Your purse—quick, and we will part company."

Just as these words were spoken, the parson, to the inexpressible surprise of Captain Hawk, clapped his hands together, as though something had occurred to overjoy him.

At the same time his countenance assumed a delighted aspect.

"Ha, ha!" he cried. "Now, you rascal, I am level with you! We shall soon see whether you will give me my watch back again or not. This way, gentlemen! Help—help! I have been robbed—help, help!—of my gold watch, with the chain and seals!"

Captain Hawk for once was slightly taken by surprise.

Looking behind him, he saw approaching four or five mounted men.

It did not need a second glance to show that they were police officers.

The captain had been so intent upon his adventure with the parson, which had amused him mightily, that he never heard the sound of horses approaching.

This circumstance is all the more easily accounted for by the fact that the officers had been coming along very gently, and were riding at the side of the lane, where a quantity of long grass was growing.

No sooner did they hear the outcries of the clergyman than they spurred forward.

Captain Hawk knew very well that he could not cope successfully with five men, and so he abandoned his attempt upon the parson's purse—that is, supposing he had been in earnest about taking it.

"You may bid your testimonial watch farewell," were his parting words. "It will go direct over to Holland: there is no difficulty in getting a good price for such things there."

So saying, he rode off.

"Gentlemen—gentlemen!" bawled the parson—"after him—after him quick! He has taken my watch—which cost a hundred and fifty guineas—and the chain and seals—which cost almost as much more! Seize him, and bring the watch back to me, and I will give you a hundred pounds out of my own pocket! Seize him, I say! If you are quick, you will be in time."

The parson uttered these words with great rapidity and energy.

But the police officers were fully alive to what he said, and the prospect of an additional hundred pounds to the reward stimulated them very greatly.

In the meanwhile Captain Hawk had taken matters very quietly.

He had only been solicitous to get his horse out of the range of any pistol bullet, and then stood in readiness to make a sudden start whenever required.

"Surrender!" cried one of the officers. "We know you, so you had better give in at once. Captain Hawk, yield yourself a prisoner!"

"No," said the captain. "I think it's scarcely reasonable of you to expect that. If you want me, gentlemen, upon my word I must really trouble you to take me."

"Oh, d—n it!" said the officer. "Words are wasted upon him. He would like nothing better than to stop there and chaff us. Come on at once!"

The officers all struck spurs into their horses simultaneously.

But if they had for a moment thought that they should be able to come up with Captain Hawk, they were grievously mistaken.

He just gave Satan the rein, according to his wont, and away he went at a rate that must have astonished the parson much more than the loss of his watch had done.

In less than a moment the wide-spreading, sheltering tree was left behind.

Some moments elapsed before Captain Hawk could recover his gravity.

His clear, triumphant laugh rang for a long time in the ears of his pursuers, tantalising them beyond all power of description.

Growing calmer at length, he said to himself:

"I will shake off these fellows completely, and at once. It will only require a slight effort on Satan's part to do it. Otherwise, if they follow me far, they may bring that persistent Mr. Hogg upon my track again."

So saying, he slackened the reins, and uttered an inspiriting cry.

Nothing more was required.

The rate at which Satan had up to then been going was astonishing, but now he seemed rather to fly than gallop.

In the twinkling of an eye almost the end of the lane was reached.

Here five cross-roads branched off in different directions.

Captain Hawk took one almost at random.

He was satisfied by seeing that it led him southward.

At the same terrific speed Satan pursued this fresh direction.

For an hour did he continue it undiminished, nor did he exhibit more than ordinary tokens of distress.

How much longer he would have maintained it is hard to say.

But his master now drew rein.

Of course by this time not the ghost of a sign could be seen of the officers in pursuit.

"That is all right, I think," said Captain Hawk at last, "and very nicely, too, it was managed. We will take it easy now for awhile, old boy. You did that bit in first-class style. I wonder where we are?"

As he asked himself this question, he glanced around him with very great interest.

What place he was in he had not the remotest idea.

Of one thing he was quite certain.

He had never been there before.

The scenery all around was very charming.

Not far off he could see the square tower of a village church.

Close to this he could distinguish the straggling street, and at its extremity a windmill, the long sails of which were fanning the air languidly.

"How happy," said the highwayman, with a half sigh—"how peaceful—how content! What a contrast to my own violent and turbulent career! But there, I must not think of that. Such reflections would do no good—on the contrary, they would unman me. I am what I am, and it is too late to change. I am a highwayman. I cannot be worse, nor will the world now permit me to be better, so I must continue my old course. But no more repining—not another word. I have chosen my line of life, and I will abide by it."

He gave himself a good shake as he pronounced these words, and pursued his slow, onward course.

Somewhat to his surprise, the cross-road he was pursuing wound round through the village, and past the church and the windmill, though no one, from the distance, would have guessed that it would go in that direction.

The village was one of those quiet, inaccessible places which were much more easy to be found in Yorkshire a century and a half ago than they are now.

Probably it was but rarely anyone rode past on horseback, for the captain's appearance seemed to cause a great sensation.

The inhabitants, old and young—who seemed as though they had all been born very tired, they moved about so deliberately—sidled to their front-doors, and, leaning against the frame, gazed after the horse and rider with feeble interest.

Captain Hawk did not increase his pace.

"I cannot be seen any more than I have been at present, so I may as well take things easy."

As the village was not of any very great extent, the captain, although travelling at so leisurely a rate, was soon clear of it, and the open country again lay before him.

He was still no nearer about knowing his whereabouts, nor did it appear very easy to obtain the required information.

"To be sure," he said, "I might, while passing through the village, have inquired the name of the place, but then, if I had been told it, I question whether it would have advanced my knowledge very much. I will travel on. I know I am going southward by the sun, and therefore I must be getting nearer to London."

He travelled on gently all that afternoon.

He had certainly got into a very lonely part of country, for though he journeyed many miles he did not meet with a single fellow-creature.

With this state of things he was by no means in the humour to grumble.

He passed several dwellings, but for the most part they were situated some distance back from the road, and it did not appear that any of the inhabitants noticed him.

"They will have some difficulty in tracing where I have gone, I rather think. Even the great Mr. Hogg, with all his supernatural cleverness, cannot fail to be at fault."

Soon after this he reached another point where several roads branched off.

Here some one had been good enough to fix up a finger-post, which, however, had apparently fallen into disuse.

The woodwork was cracked, and thickly incrusted with green.

The letters were barely distinguishable.

But by dint of perseverance, the captain made out the greater portion of the word "London."

There was no sort of doubt as to which way the finger pointed; and being at ease on this score, the highwayman resumed his journey at an accelerated pace.

"When one comes to think of it," he said, "it is rather a bold thing for a man with a reward of five or six hundred pounds on his head to ride about the country by broad daylight, as I have done. But boldness often means safety."

The sun was now getting low down in the west.

The sky, except in this portion, was covered with dense black clouds, so that the effect was rather singular, but very picturesque.

The sun shone redly upon every object, but from the south-east came frequent gusts of wind.

"I fancy it will turn out a roughish night. Well, no matter if it does. I am beginning to grow tired of the saddle, and Satan, too, would be all the better for a rest. We will find some comfort-promising place, old boy, and there we will pass the night."

Satan knew his master spoke to him, and that the tones of his voice were encouraging, and so he showed himself pleased accordingly.

Just then the captain felt a scud of rain upon his cheek.

At the same instant the dark heavy clouds dropped over the sun's disk.

The change in the appearance of things around was truly wonderful.

It seemed almost like the effects of magic.

The wind howled with a dismal, melancholy sound, and the tree-tops clashed violently together as the sudden gusts of wind forced a passage among their branches.

"I don't care how soon I am under cover," was the captain's remark. "The storm will break forth in a very few moments now."

To his great joy, the next bend in the cross-road brought him in view of the broad highway.

"Hurrah!" he said. "Nothing could have suited me better. I may make sure of getting to an inn before long now."

He increased his speed, and soon had the satisfaction of feeling the hard high-road beneath his horse's feet.

The first object he met with was a mile-stone, and, out of curiosity, he stopped to see the number of miles he was distant from the metropolis.

So suddenly had the darkness come on that he could not ascertain this without alighting.

"One hundred and sixty-six miles," he said. "Somewhere about the distance I expected. It will take me some time to reach my destination."

A still heavier scud of rain came down at this moment.

It was the precursor of the torrent that was about to follow.

He mounted hastily.

"On, boy—on! We must get shelter now, or we shall be too late!"

This was true enough; and had he not met with a comfortable-looking hostelry only a few hundred yards further on he would not have escaped a severe drenching, for the storm now fairly broke out.

No one appeared at the front of the inn, and so, without any hesitation or delay, the highwayman rode through the black gates at one side of it, and made his way direct to the stables.

As the yard was paved, Satan's hoofs made a great deal of clatter.

This had the effect of producing the ostler.

As he emerged from the stable door, he held up his hand.

"Woa, sir—woa! No further, if you please. This is the way, sir."

Captain Hawk pulled up at once, and slipped from the saddle before the ostler could make up his mind whether he should take hold of the bridle or not.

"That's a fine nag you've got, sir," he said, casting a critical glance upon Satan. "You'll excuse me being so bold as to go for to say so, but when I see a piece of good horseflesh I am pleased—there."

"So am I. I think this a fine nag myself, and that makes me particular about seeing that he is well attended to; so I will just see the corn put into the manger before I go indoors myself."

"All right, sir. Come this way."

"I know I give an extra bit of trouble," continued the highwayman, "but then I don't mind paying a trifle for it. Here, take this half-crown to start with; and if I am satisfied with what you do, I sha'n't feel disinclined to open my purse, I assure you."

"Lor', sir!" ejaculated the ostler, looking at the half-crown with a comical air—"why, this here's somewhere about a week's wages!"

"Then you will think yourself a rich man in the morning if you will only do as I tell you."

Of course, the ostler solemnly promised obedience.

He bestirred himself actively, and Captain Hawk soon had the satisfaction of knowing that his constant and faithful companion was as well attended to as he possibly could be.

When he saw this was the case, he crossed from the stable to the inn.

By this time night appeared fairly to have set in.

The rain was coming down at a rapid rate.

This, and the fatigue he felt, made the interior of the inn appear all the more comfortable and inviting.

The landlord, having heard that a traveller on horseback had arrived, was waiting to accost him.

He greeted the captain with a profusion of bows.

"Can I have a private room, landlord?"

"Certainly, sir—certainly! Pray follow me."

The landlord went a few steps along a passage, and then threw open a door.

Captain Hawk crossed the threshold.

A lamp was burning dimly in this room, which somehow had a dull and cheerless look, and this was increased by the circumstance of there being no fire in the grate.

"Here you are, sir," said the landlord.

"Then, as I am a man of candour, I may as well say at once that I don't like the quarters."

"You don't?"

"I certainly don't."

"But you can have a fire lighted in a moment, sir."

"I know that. But how long will it take to warm the room? Why, dear me! it feels as though it had not had a fire in it for a fortnight."

"Fancy, sir—fancy! We had a fire here yesterday."

The captain did not contradict this statement, though he did not believe it for all that.

The room had a particularly damp, musty, disagreeable smell, such as all unoccupied apartments invariably have.

"You see, sir," said the landlord, apologetically, "trade is so bad, that at this time of year we cannot afford to keep fires always burning in the private rooms—indeed we can't; but in the public room, where there are only a very few respectable people at the present moment, you will, I assure you, find every comfort that heart can wish for."

Captain Hawk hesitated a moment between the discomfort of the chilly apartment in which he now stood and the risk he might run of sitting down in another which would be free for anyone to enter, and where the chances of recognition were much increased.

But the reader knows enough of Captain Hawk to feel quite sure how he would decide.

He resolved to take the chance of the public room.

He signified his decision to the landlord accordingly, and that individual, with no end of bows and apologies, led him along the passage.

Opening a red baize door, he ushered him into an apartment which certainly merited some of the encomium which had been bestowed upon it.

Not more than half a dozen persons occupied it, and they were all seated round the spacious chimney, up which the red flames went roaring and flickering in a way that would have done one's heart good to see.

As a matter of course, the entrance of a stranger of so distinguished appearance as Captain Hawk did not fail to excite immediate and profound attention.

But the assembled guests showed their civility and hospitality by drawing their chairs close together and edging round in such a way as to allow the stranger a place to put his chair in a comfortable position.

Captain Hawk acknowledged this civility with a low bow, and, sitting down, ordered a bottle of the best wine.

At this the frequenters of the inn exchanged glances.

It was not often that the public room was honoured with the presence of anyone who ordered a bottle of wine.

They all prepared, therefore, to treat him with a great deal of deference and regard.

"A miserable night, sir," said the one who chanced to occupy the seat nearest to him—"a truly miserable night."

"It is indeed, and I esteem myself fortunate in having fallen in with such good company."

"Travelled far to-day, sir?"

"Yes, some twenty or thirty miles—not more."

The conversation was now interrupted by the entrance of the landlord with the wine.

What further questions might have been addressed to Captain Hawk is hard to say had not universal attention been distracted from him by the appearance of another traveller, who was also a stranger.

Everyone, the captain himself not excluded, turned round on his entrance.

All then beheld a tall figure which had an unmistakably military air.

His face was scarred and sunburnt, and eloquently bespoke hard and dangerous service in foreign lands.

He bowed rather haughtily to the company.

Captain Hawk offered his chair.

But the military stranger, after expressing his thanks, declined to accept it, but seated himself in one which the landlord officiously brought forward.

Another order for a bottle of wine followed, and the landlord, with feelings of deep gratitude towards the weather which had sent him two such good customers in one night, departed to execute it.

There was something frigid and restraint-inspiring about the bearing and manner of the new-comer that had the effect of checking the general flow of conversation.

For some moments after his entrance silence was maintained.

Perhaps those present were waiting in the expectation that the stranger would first of all address himself to them.

But they waited in vain.

Knitting his brows, and drawing the skirts of his coat over his knees, he stretched out his feet towards the glowing fire, and gazed frowningly at it.

This was the state of affairs when the landlord came in.

"You will find that, sir," he said, "to be as good a bottle of wine as you can reasonably expect an innkeeper to produce from his cellar."

The stranger merely bowed.

The landlord, walking round to the fire, seated himself in an arm-chair in the chimney-corner which was always kept vacant for his use.

Of course now he was present the conversation was soon set going again.

But it ran upon subjects which apparently possessed not the slightest interest for either Captain Hawk or the stranger, and therefore the reader will care nothing about its omission.

At length, however, a remark uttered by one of the company caused the military stranger to look up with a sudden start.

CHAPTER XL.

CAPTAIN HAWK HAS SOME MOST SINGULAR ADVENTURES AT THE INN.

"Excuse me," he said, "but I thought I heard you mention a name then that was familiar to my ears. Would you oblige me by repeating it?"

"Certainly, sir. The name must have been Lucy Gray."

"I fancied so, but I was busy thinking, and not listening to the conversation, when the name arrested my attention."

"You have probably heard something of her, then, sir?"

"Yes, I have, though not within the last half-dozen years or so during which I have been abroad."

"Oh, indeed!"

"What was the exact nature of the remark?"

"Why, that it would soon be seven years since the mysterious disappearance of Lucy Gray."

"Yes," said the stranger, slowly, with the air of one who was calling up the half-forgotten past, "I remember that event exceedingly well, and the sensation it caused all about the neighbourhood."

"You are right, sir—nothing else was talked of."

"And has she never been heard of?"

"Never, sir, from that day to this."

"How very strange!"

"It is strange. All manner of inquiries were made, but without result. Had she melted away into air she could not have vanished more completely."

"And was no motive found?"

"None whatever."

"And was anybody suspected of having spirited her away?"

"Yes, sir, more than one, but, as it turned out, without sufficient grounds. The mystery was as great then as it is now, which is just the same as saying that the mystery was as great as it well could be."

These remarks somewhat stirred the curiosity of Captain Hawk, who, noticing at this moment a lull in the conversation, said:

"I beg your pardon, gentlemen, but it seems to me I am the only member of the company who is entirely unacquainted with the subject of the conversation. Might I trouble you to tell me who was this Lucy Gray?"

"You can know that in a very few words, sir. She was a native of the village hard by, and up to the time when she vanished so strangely I cannot find that anything happened to her but what might have befallen any other maiden in the land without attracting remark."

"She was a good girl," said another, "and, according to the notions of this place, a rich one. She was an orphan, and her parents, when dying, left all that they possessed to her."

"And did she inherit this property?"

"No—she disappeared just before her twenty-first birthday."

"And what has become of the property?"

"It is in the hands of the trustees still. They scarcely know what to do with it; but they have no proof of her death, though popular opinion is quite against any belief that she is alive."

"I remember," said the military stranger, "that the will stated that in case his daughter should die before she attained her majority the property should all go without reserve to one Luke Ford. I remember, too, that some ugly rumours about him were current at the time—with what foundation I cannot pretend to say; but then, he was the person most interested in the young girl's decease."

At this point the landlord rose.

He had sat for some time like a man ill at ease.

He left the room.

"You have touched upon a tender topic, sir," said one.

"Indeed! How so?"

"After what you have said, is it possible that you do not recollect the landlord here?"

"No, that I do not. To the best of my belief, I have never seen him in my life before."

"Dear me, you surprise me."

"Who is he?"

"Luke Ford!"

The military stranger pushed his chair back several inches in astonishment.

"That Luke Ford?"

"Yes, that is Luke Ford."

"How wonderfully he has altered, then! I have a pretty good memory of faces, but I never should have recognised him."

"Very likely not. As you say, he has altered wonderfully. I don't know how it was this subject was brought up, for he never cares to have it talked about, not that ever I knew him so discomposed over it as he seems to-night."

"Nor I—nor I," murmured many voices.

"I am sorry," said the stranger; "and yet I assure you I meant no harm. What I said was spoken innocently enough, goodness knows."

"Well, sir, the long and the short of the matter is," said an old man, sinking his voice to a confidential whisper, "people were ready enough to accuse Luke Ford of knowing more about Lucy Gray than anyone else, because, you see, he was the only one that could receive any advantage from her death."

"It would be only natural."

"Luke, sir, as I daresay you know already, was Lucy's cousin; and some have said that he was not well pleased at finding nothing had been left him in the will; then others declared that he made love to Lucy, but that she rejected him, and that it was after this rejection that she vanished."

"I see," said the stranger, "it is only natural that he should be the object of suspicion. No foundation was found, however, I suppose, for all these rumours?"

"None at all, or next to none."

"It is a very strange affair," remarked the stranger. "Poor Lucy! I am sorry for her. I recollect her well. She was a beautiful girl, and one would have thought was in a fair way of passing through existence happily. How hard it is for anyone to form an opinion regarding the future!"

"Hard indeed!"

"And so the landlord is rather sensitive upon this point, is he?" persisted the stranger. "Well, perhaps, after all, that is only natural too. It must be very disagreeable to become the object of everybody's supicions."

"And then, from his boyhood upwards, Luke Ford never bore the best of reputations. Not that he ever did anything actually bad, but his temper was an evil one, and after any slight he never rested till he had revenge."

"I trust you will excuse the liberty I am going to take," interposed the old man who had before spoken, "but, unless I am greatly mistaken, I remember you."

The stranger frowned, as though this intimation was anything but a welcome one.

Still he said nothing, but he bit his lips angrily.

"I may be mistaken; but I should be glad to know, sir, whether your name is not Frederick Chambers, the same who left these parts a little while before the occurrence of these events?"

"Your memory has not failed you," said the stranger, with an air of one who makes a reluctant admission. "I am somewhat surprised, for I believed that my very long residence in foreign climes had so altered me that recognition was well-nigh impossible."

"I thought I was right," said the old man, delighted with his sagacity—"I thought so! And now I remember me, it was, I think, after the disappearance of Lucy Gray that you took your departure."

Captain Hawk half expected that this remark would embarrass the stranger, but, apparently, he had regained his original composure.

He showed not the least signs of agitation.

"It was somewhere very near the time, and I think after it, though not long."

"And you have not been to England since?"

"Never."

There was a silence.

During it, the stranger finished drinking his wine.

The wind howled without; and now that the conversation had lulled, the rain-drops could be heard pattering against the windows.

"A disagreeable night for anyone to be abroad in," said the stranger, as he finished his draught. "Might I trouble one of you to ring the bell? I have travelled far to-day, and feel completely worn out with fatigue."

This request was promptly complied with.

The summons was replied to by the landlady.

"A candle, if you please," said the stranger. "I am ready to retire."

Lights were soon brought, and the military stranger—or, as we may as well call him, Frederick Chambers—gravely bade the assembled company good night and left the room.

As soon as he had departed, the conversation flowed with redoubled vigour.

"I thought I knew him," said the old man, chuckling—"I fancied I was under no mistake. Dear me! It seems but yesterday that he was a wild, harum-scarum lad."

"I have heard of this young Chambers," said another.

"Yes, his name was brought up at the time. Some said that he had made love to Lucy, and that she had rejected him, and that it was in consequence of it that he went off to foreign lands to be a soldier, for he was very fond of her."

"But the suspicion against him soon died out," said another; "for it was shown that he had spoken about leaving some time before Lucy's disappearance, though he went almost immediately after it."

More conversation followed; but as no additional circumstance of the least importance was brought forth, it is needless to report it.

Captain Hawk paid a visit to the stables.

The night was pitchy dark.

The wind had dropped, but the rain came down very heavily.

"I ought to be thankful for having so good a shelter to-night," he said, as he hurried across the inn-yard.

He found Satan perfectly comfortable.

His mind at ease in this respect, he resolved to retire to rest.

Accordingly he was shown upstairs.

"Not that room, sir," said the landlady. "I forgot for the moment that the other gentleman is there. This is your room, sir—the one next to it."

The door was opened, and the captain entered.

"Good night," he said. "I shall want to be leaving early."

"You will find some of us up, sir."

He locked his door.

Then carefully examined his pistols.

Being assured that they were all right, he placed them were they would be readiest to his hand.

"I do believe I am safe here," he said—"I might say I am certain of it. At least, as safe as I can ever hope to be. No one beneath this roof has the remotest suspicion of who I am, and there is scarcely any chance of anybody else arriving before daylight that can do so."

The highwayman did, indeed, seem to be more than ordinarily secure.

It was in consequence of this feeling of security that he resolved upon indulging in a luxury, which was a night's rest—one worthy to be called such.

In a general way he was content to throw himself down without removing much of his apparel, and to snatch a brief repose in the best way that he was able

On this night, however, influenced by his feeling of safety, he fairly retired to rest.

But, somewhat to his disappointment, although he felt

so fatigued, he found it a matter of impossibility to close his eyes in slumber.

In vain he sought for a reason for this.

His brain was unnaturally active, and, while it continued so, to hope to sleep was simply ridiculous.

His thoughts ran a great deal upon what he had heard talked about that evening, and after awhile, as might be expected, his mind ran into strange confusion.

Young Chambers, the landlord, the unfortunate Lucy Gray and himself were mixed up in the strangest and most bewildering manner that can be conceived.

At length he unconsciously sunk off into a troubled slumber.

How long this lasted he knew not, but all at once he started wide awake.

To his great surprise he saw the room was full of light.

It came from the moon, which was shining in at his chamber window with particular brilliancy.

This showed that a great alteration in the weather had taken place.

The storm was over.

Just as he had had time to notice this much, a faint sound came upon his ears.

It was so very faint and so very indistinct that he could not at first take upon himself to say whether it was a sound at all.

His doubts, however, were speedily put to rest by hearing it repeated.

"What is it?" he murmured. "Is some one near me? It sounded like a long, deep-drawn breath—I might say a sigh."

The sound came again.

He started up in bed.

So great was the power of the moonlight that he was able to distinguish almost every article of furniture the room contained.

But he saw nothing resembling a living creature.

"Can my fancy have deceived me? No—surely, no. I am wide awake. What was it?"

No answer to this query suggested itself.

Can it be the gentleman in the next room?

He was about to lie down again, fancying he had hit upon the true solution of the difficulty, when he fancied in one corner where the obscurity was greater than elsewhere that he detected a slight movement.

He drew aside the curtains and strained his eyes.

The movement was repeated.

And as he continued to gaze the obscurity grew less—or rather his eyes became more accustomed to it.

His surprise may perhaps be conceived when he at length made out the outlines of a female form.

There could be no mistake about it.

If there was he could never trust his eyes again.

She was sitting with her back turned towards him, and with her head bent down over a little table.

To say that the captain remained perfectly cool and composed would scarcely be to speak the truth.

His heart fluttered a little more than usual, and his breath came short and quick, as it will under circumstances of great excitement.

But he continued to gaze.

The figure became more distinctly revealed.

He could now see how she was engaged.

She was writing.

He saw her put down the pen.

He saw her fold up the piece of paper.

After that she seemed to look at it wistfully.

Then pressing it to her lips, she concealed it in her bosom.

To perform this last action she rose to her feet.

As she did this, she turned round so as to face the window.

Her face was then visible, and so indeed was her whole form.

Captain Hawk had never seen anything more distinctly in his life.

And what a beautiful face it was!

A very pale face, and yet the features were so delicate and so regular that not even the most fastidious could have found fault with them.

Her form was that of a young girl just ripening into womanhood—the time when a woman's charms are at the full.

She clasped her hands over the letter in her bosom, and with a slow gliding movement came a few paces nearer to the bed.

But a feeling of deep awe, such as he had never before in all his life experienced, came over Captain Hawk as he noticed that her movements produced not the faintest possible sound.

His own heart beat so hard that to his excited ears the din seemed overwhelming.

The figure paused.

It gazed intently upon Captain Hawk, and as it did so an expression came over the face which unquestionably denoted great bodily or mental anguish.

She raised one hand, and made a beseeching gesture.

Then she turned towards the door.

But she only went a step.

Turning back, she repeated the gesture.

There could be no mistaking the meaning of it.

She wanted him to follow her from the room.

A struggle took place in his breast.

Then utter forgetfulness and unconsciousness succeeded.

The next thing of which he had any recollection was that he was standing in a place of singular appearance—certainly a place that he had never seen before, because its features were so remarkable that they could not be forgotten.

But what was strangest of all was that the sun was shining with a rosy light upon every object.

It was day, and he himself, in his ordinary costume, was standing near the trunk of an old tree.

This tree was situated in a kind of rocky dell, the sides of which were so thickly overgrown with shrubs that the rock-work only peeped out here and there.

Across this dell a huge tree, growing near the top, had fallen.

It seemed as though some violent wind had laid it prostrate.

But the roots had struck deeply into the cliffs and fissures of the rock, and had defied the power of the wind to dislodge them.

Consequently, although the tree had fallen to a horizontal position, yet it continued to grow, and to send out branches in all directions.

These branches were covered with leaves to such an extent that the bottom of the dell was always in deep shadow.

It was this downfallen tree that gave the place so singular an appearance, and which made Captain Hawk feel certain that he had never seen it before.

While gazing in surprise, he all at once perceived the same figure that he had beheld in the bed-room.

It gazed upon him with the same beseeching look, and made the same earnest gesture for him to follow.

But, although willing to do so, he found himself unable.

His feet seemed riveted to the ground.

In the meanwhile the figure glided on.

Then it stopped before the tree growing in the centre of the dell, turned back once more to look at him, repeated the beseeching glance, and again beckoned to him to follow.

But, as before, he found this impossible.

The figure turned again, and continued to walk on until, which was stranger than all, she reached the trunk of the tree.

And there she vanished.

It seemed as though the bark had been as yielding as water, and that she had walked through it.

After that the captain saw her no more.

The singular-looking dell faded altogether from his view.

Unconsciousness came again.

Yet it only seemed a moment after he had last seen the dell that he opened his eyes again.

This time he was in his chamber.

It was morning.

The sun was shining, and on a spray of ivy that stretched before the window sat a little bird which poured forth the most delightful notes ever uttered by a feathered songster.

Captain Hawk for several moments was very much confused.

He could hardly make out where he was or what had happened.

[LIEUTENANT TRACY DENOUNCES LORD HARCLIFFE AS THE BLACK HIGHWAYMAN.]

He closed his eyes and opened them several times.

But on each occasion he saw the same objects, while the trilling notes of the little bird never ceased to vibrate upon his ears.

"I am awake now," he said at last, "and in proper possession of my senses; but whether I have been so all the night is more than I can take upon myself to say. What is it all about? I will lie back again and have a quiet think."

The result was that he came to a very reasonable and natural conclusion.

He had been dreaming, and the events which had presented themselves during slumber had received their shape and colouring from the conversation he had heard on the preceding evening, and the details of which last occupied his thoughts before falling into his uneasy slumber.

Having settled the matter thus, he rose, and, dressing himself carefully, went downstairs.

Still, in spite of the conclusion he had arrived at, he could not help fancying more than once or twice that the occurrences of the past night were something more than a dream.

In the breakfast-room he found the military stranger, who had evidently risen for some time, as his morning meal was almost finished.

He bowed gravely to Captain Hawk on his entrance, but did not speak.

The highwayman ordered breakfast, and being of a sociable turn of mind, he was rarely in company with anyone very long before he succeeded in getting up a conversation.

"I have had but a bad night's rest," he said, warming himself before the fire. "Try as I would, I could not sleep for thinking about the subject of the conversation last night, and even when I did drop off the same subject pursued me in my dreams."

Little did Captain Hawk anticipate what sort of an effect his words would produce.

The stranger dropped his knife and fork as though he had been suddenly smitten with paralysis.

"Dream!" he gasped. "What did you dream?"

"It would almost trouble me to tell you," was the reply. "But you seem agitated. What is the cause?"

"A coincidence—nothing more. But tell me as well as you can the nature of your vision."

"I have been more than once in doubt as to whether it was a vision at all; but you shall hear, and then you will be able to draw your own conclusions."

The stranger prepared to listen with the utmost attention.

Captain Hawk then, with tolerable clearness, recounted those particulars which have already been laid before the reader.

As he went on the agitation of the stranger rapidly increased.

But, to the highwayman's surprise, no sooner was the narrative brought to a conclusion than, with a countenance ghastly pale, he started from his chair and quitted the room.

He was gone before our friend could make the least attempt to oppose his departure.

"I would wager any money," he ejaculated, "that this stranger is in some way connected with the disappearance of Lucy Gray. I will mention it to the landlord at all hazards."

But he was prevented from carrying this design into execution, for the landlord never made his appearance.

As soon as breakfast was over Captain Hawk went over to the stable.

He had not quite made up his mind whether he should remain at the inn during the greater part of the day, or whether he should resume his journey at once.

He found his favourite all right, and perfectly content.

The ostler had not had his palm oiled for nothing.

A powerful iron-gray horse was standing saddled and bridled in the next stall.

It was a powerful, well-built creature, and had several points which called forth the highwayman's critical admiration

"Whose is this?"

"It belongs to the military gentleman who came late last night."

"He has not taken his departure yet, then?" ejaculated Captain Hawk, in some surprise.

"No, sir—not yet. He came into the stable not long ago, and told me to get the saddle and bridle on."

"And where is he now?"

"He walked out."

"Can you show me which direction he took?"

"Oh yes, sir! He followed the little bridle path that runs round by the back of the stabling."

"And where does that lead to?"

"Oak Tree Dingle."

"Oak Tree Dingle!" said the captain, repeating the name.

"Yes, that is what we call it. It is a rocky dell not very far away, which has a large and singularly fine oak tree growing in the centre of it."

"Is it an old tree?" asked Captain Hawk, with sudden interest.

"Yes. Perhaps you would like to pay the place a visit. Many do on account of its appearance, which is very singular."

"I will," answered the captain: "not only for this reason, but because I should like to have a word or two with the military gentleman."

So saying, he quitted the stable.

The ostler obsequiously followed him to the door, and then pointed out the road he had been speaking of.

Captain Hawk at once strode off along it.

The path was a pleasant one, being clean and well kept, and wound pleasantly about among several scattered clumps of trees.

As he advanced a singular feeling came over Captain Hawk.

He was thoroughly under the impression that he had at some time or other been that way before.

But when he reached the dingle he fully understood this feeling.

His amazement and incredulity can be imagined when he saw that the rocky dell below him was just the place he had seen during the still, lonely hours of night.

The brief conversation he had held with the ostler had in some degree prepared him for it—but for this his bewilderment would have been overpowering.

Involuntarily he paused.

Everything was perfect and complete.

There were the half-covered rocky sides—there was the strange-looking tree which grew slantingly across it, and at the bottom, in the centre, the umbrageous oak from which the dell received its name.

"This was the place," he said, "and nothing more is needed to make it precisely like it was when I first saw it than the melancholy form of the young girl."

As he spoke, a faint rustling sound reached his ears.

Glancing in the direction of it, he saw the military stranger.

"Come what will, I will speak to him," he said, "for I feel convinced that he has something to communicate if he will only speak."

He began the rather difficult and precipitous descent as he spoke.

The noise he made in doing so was heard by Frederick Chambers, and he at once looked up.

A frown settled upon his features as soon as he caught sight of the captain.

But the highwayman was not one to be easily daunted, so he quickened his pace.

The other turned, and seemed about to quit the spot.

"Stay one moment, sir," said the captain—"I have one word to say."

The young man paused.

"I want to tell you," said the highwayman, "that in this place I recognise the dell which I described to you as having seen in my dream. Here the figure of the young girl walked—here she paused, and looked at me beseechingly, while she beckoned me to follow; and that is the tree into which she seemed to fade away."

The young man's agitation was very great while Captain Hawk thus spoke.

His lips moved convulsively, but he uttered no articulate sound.

"Is there not something more than strange in this?" said Captain Hawk. "Ought I not to look at what I saw as being something far more than a dream? Imagination could never have produced a place like this, and I am certain that never in all my life have I seen it before."

The stranger seemed as though he wished much to speak to Captain Hawk, but as though some strong consideration kept him back.

He struggled with it for a moment, and then, with a sudden effort, he came to a decision.

"I know not who you are," he said—"I own you are an utter stranger; but in spite of that I will tell you of some circumstances bearing on this subject. I shall leave you to form your own opinions concerning them."

The captain bowed.

"I will first tell you, then, that last night, while sleeping in the room adjoining yours, I had precisely the same visitation as you have described. I can scarcely bring myself to call it a dream as you do."

"I am unwilling to think it anything else."

"That may be. But do you not think it more than strange that at the same time, or nearly so, the same visitation should have come upon us?"

"It is, to say the least of it, most strange."

"What shall you think of it, then, when I tell you that the figure you describe was the exact counterpart of Lucy Gray?"

"I know not what to say."

"I was much disturbed by what I saw," continued the stranger, "and the extraordinary coincidence agitated me to such a degree that I knew not what I was about. By your manner I could tell that you did not recognise the figure, and that you were unaware of the existence, close at hand, of just such a spot as you described."

"You are quite right about that."

"While still influenced by this great agitation I started off to walk to the Oak Tree Dingle. In my young days I was in the habit of visiting this place very frequently.

and I felt irresistibly impelled to look upon it once again."

His voice faltered

But clearing his throat, he continued:

"I will tell you all. I loved Lucy Gray—no one save myself can tell how truly, how devotedly. I showed my affection in a thousand ways. Here, on this spot, under the shadow of this old oak tree, I told her of my love. I besought a return of affection; but she coldly refused me. I begged—I entreated; but it was all in vain. On this spot I left her. I never saw her again."

These memories of the past profoundly affected the young man.

Captain Hawk looked at him with a puzzled air.

He had had strong and grave suspicions against him; but his demeanour now by no means seemed like that of a guilty person.

His emotion passed away.

In a solemn voice, and holding his right hand upwards, the young man said:

"I firmly believe that the finger of Heaven is in all this! I believe that the time has come when the disappearance of Lucy Gray will cease to be a mystery."

"And for what reason?" asked the captain, greatly surprised by his change of manner.

"Because of the occurrences of the past night. I consider there is but one inference to be drawn from it. My belief is that the letter we both saw her write was intended for me, and meant that her sentiments had changed; and I believe that this dell is the place where she disappeared."

CHAPTER XLI.

THE DISCOVERY OF THE FATE OF LUCY GRAY.—CAPTAIN HAWK RESUMES HIS JOURNEY TO LONDON.

THE young man pronounced the last word with a considerable amount of hesitation, and in such a manner as would lead to the inference that he had intended to make use of a stronger word.

Then he paused, and again gave way to his emotion.

"Chance, sir, has thrown us together," he said, at last. "Who you are I have not the least idea. But as I have begun to tell you of the past, I will no longer hesitate to give you my entire confidence. After that you will be fully able to judge for yourself."

Captain Hawk bowed.

"I will begin by telling you," continued the young man, "that my firm belief is that poor Lucy's disappearance is attributable only to one cause, and that is death: not by a fair death either, but by foul, unnatural murder."

"You have some sufficient reason for thinking this?"

"I have, and I will tell you what it is. What Luke Ford may be at this time I know not, but those who are able to remember him in his young days will tell you that he was hot-tempered and revengeful."

"But would he have any interest in the girl's death? What benefit has it been to him at present? The money is all in the hands of the trustees."

"Wait a moment, sir! You will find that I shall arrive at a consideration of those points presently. I wish you to understand what kind of young man Luke Ford was at that time, not that he is an old one now."

"Very good."

"You have been told already that Luke Ford was annoyed to find that all the property had been left to his cousin Lucy, and none to himself—that is, none unless she should happen to die. You have been told, too, that the rumour ran he had made love to Lucy."

"Yes, I remember that remark being made."

"I, then, happen to know as an absolute fact that he did make love to her. The motive for his affection is transparent. If he could only persuade his cousin to marry him all would be well, the coveted wealth would be his."

"But Lucy refused to listen to his advances."

"I have positive evidence of that also. She indignantly declined to listen to his proposals. It is possible that she may have been conscious of the motives which swayed his conduct. At all events, I have good reason to believe that the way in which she refused him was such as would be likely to sting him almost into madness. They parted."

"And what more is known of the unfortunate girl?"

"Nothing. From that moment she vanished. With subsequent events I am but imperfectly acquainted, as you might surmise from the questions which I asked last night."

"Not the least extraordinary part of the affair," said Captain Hawk, "is that you should have failed to recognise Luke Ford."

"Could you form the least idea of the alteration which has taken place in him your wonder would entirely cease. He is more unlike what he once was than you are able to conceive."

"And what is the nature of the alteration?"

"You shall judge. When I left here his hair was of jetty blackness and covered with short crisp curls. Now you see that it is almost white and very thin. Then his face was of a ruddy-brown tint; now it is, as one might say, unnaturally pale, and everywhere crossed with furrows and wrinkles."

"And what caused the change?"

The stranger looked at Captain Hawk for a moment, but returned no direct answer to the question.

"One would almost take him to be an old man, some fifteen or twenty years older than myself."

"I should indeed."

"And yet there is hardly any difference in our ages."

"You surprise me!"

"No doubt I do, but you cannot any longer wonder that I did not know him again."

"Certainly not."

"You must already have come to the conclusion that the circumstances were not ordinary ones which effected this alteration."

"One would think not. But there is one question which I should like to ask."

"What is it?"

"The reason why you left the neighbourhood just at the time you did?"

"I am glad you asked me that. I ought to have told you. As you see, however, I follow the military profession, and just at the juncture you named I was summoned off on foreign service. I had expected the event for some time, and I have often fancied that the reason why Lucy refused me was because of the horror she felt at the idea of becoming a soldier's wife."

"It is possible."

"I went off, however, with an angry heart, and with much bitterness of spirit. I resolved to banish from my mind every recollection of this place. Need I tell you how much easier it was to form such a determination than to adhere to it? Yet I succeeded indifferently well."

He sighed as he spoke, in a way that showed how much mental anguish the attempt had cost him.

"The lapse of time, however," he continued, "diminished the intensity of my sorrow, and to this the change of life and the exciting nature of the events through which I passed not a little contributed. I returned as you have seen, but should not have put up at this place had it not been for the violence of the storm compelling me to take shelter. In that circumstance, as in all the rest, I can trace the finger of Providence. I firmly believe I am destined to unravel the mystery."

"Although you have not precisely said so," exclaimed Captain Hawk, "it would be idle for me to pretend that I do not understand who you believe has been instrumental in Lucy's disappearance."

"I have not said who it is, but you must be able to surmise it."

"I can easily. But where is your proof?"

"I have none at present—nothing more, in fact, than a conviction that overweighs everything. I cannot tell you why it is that I feel as it were upon the threshold of the mystery, but I do feel it. Wait a moment, and you will see what I am about to do."

As he spoke he turned towards the oak tree which we have mentioned as standing in the centre of the dingle.

From beneath his ample cloak he next produced a small hatchet, such as is used for the purpose of cleaving firewood.

"I borrowed this of the ostler at the inn," he said.

"What are you going to do with it?"

"Behold!"

He struck the tree a heavy blow.

The sharp edge of the weapon sunk deeply into the bark.

A dull but unmistakably hollow sound was evoked

"Is the tree hollow?" asked the highwayman.

"It seems like it; but we shall soon see."

A rapid succession of blows followed.

The splinters of wood flew about in every direction.

He worked as though for the time being he had been endowed with supernatural strength.

Hearing a slight sound in the rear, Captain Hawk looked behind him.

He then caught sight of several men, who, by their attire, were evidently farm labourers.

Their attention had been attracted by what the cloaked stranger was about, and they paused, gazing open-mouthed and wondering what it all meant.

But the young man himself was so intent upon what he was about that he remained wholly unconscious of their presence.

A few minutes enabled him to make a breach completely through the tree, which was hollow to within an inch of the bark.

No sooner was this done than he paused.

He wiped away the drops of perspiration from his forehead.

Then an ejaculation burst from his lips.

Quick as lightning, he plunged his hand through the opening.

He withdrew it as quickly.

Everybody then saw that a small fragment of something was fluttering in his fingers.

"What is that?" asked Captain Hawk, who had been watching these proceedings in the utmost suspense.

"The proof!" he cried, in thrilling tones. "Did I not say so? Behold, here is proof incontestable! I will swear that this is a portion of Lucy Gray's dress."

The words, uttered in an exalted tone, reached the ears of the rustics who had paused on the brink of the dingle.

Having heard them, they rushed down tumultuously.

In a moment the young soldier found himself surrounded by an eager, excited throng.

The name of Lucy Gray was familiar to all of them.

The little piece of torn apparel was eagerly gazed at by every one of them.

Most recognised it.

At this point the young soldier became so overcome by his feelings as to lose all power over his muscles.

The axe which he has just been wielding so vigorously slipped from his strengthless fingers.

A deep groan escaped his lips.

But the others present were not so affected.

The hatchet was seized upon instantly.

"Stand aside, young sir," said one. "You are exhausted. Allow me. We will soon see the bottom of this."

The speaker was a man of powerful and sinewy build.

The axe, too, was an implement with the use of which he was familiar.

The progress therefore that he was enabled in the course of a few minutes to make in cutting away the tree was wonderful to see.

As to Captain Hawk, seeing the condition of poor Chambers, in whom he was much interested, he rushed forward in order to lend him the assistance of his arm.

It was well that he did so.

He was only just in time.

But for the timely assistance thus rendered, the young man would certainly have fallen to the ground.

"Be calm," said the captain to him, earnestly. "Try to compose yourself. Look, the trunk of the old tree is almost demolished now."

With an effort he rallied and looked up.

Just as he did so, the man with the axe desisted from his labour.

He stood aside.

A loud ejaculation of horror escaped from every breast.

Young Chambers pressed both hands before his face to shut out the horrid spectacle presented to his view.

In a strange, huddled-up position that was of itself terrible to think of, were the remains of a human being.

About that there could be no doubt.

Decomposition had almost accomplished its dreadful work; but though the bones of a skeleton showed here and there, yet sufficient fragments of apparel still remained to enable all to pronounce with certainty that the remains were those of a female.

"Here ends the mystery," said the man, throwing down the hatchet. "We know what has become of Lucy Gray now. But," he added, glancing with suspicion at Captain Hawk and the young soldier, "how comes it that you have been able to find her so easily?"

Young Chambers had not yet recovered sufficiently from the severe shock he had sustained to return an answer to this question.

And now a fresh arrival appeared upon the scene.

This was no other than the landlord, Luke Ford.

What had induced him to come there—what business had brought him to the spot none could tell.

But his appearance betokened the utmost disorder of mind.

There was an air of wildness, too, observable in all his movements.

No sooner, however, did he perceive that part of the trunk of the tree had been hacked away and the horrible sight that it had so long concealed brought to light, than, with fixed eyes and trembling limbs, he stood horror-struck and helpless.

A cold perspiration started out at every pore.

Then starting all at once, as though he had suddenly been brought into contact with a galvanic battery, he turned to fly.

"Seize him!" cried young Chambers, in a voice that rang through the calm morning air like a blast upon a trumpet—"seize him! Seize the murderer! Let him not escape! Are you all paralysed? I tell you to seize Luke Ford, the murderer of Lucy Gray! Quick, or he will escape!"

Before he had finished the utterance of these words at least one-half of those assembled started off in pursuit.

To have looked at Luke Ford's apparently aged and decrepit form no one would have believed that it lay in his power to make such extraordinary speed.

He bounded up the rugged, rocky sides of the dingle like an antelope.

But those who were in chase were one and all burning with the desire to avenge the murder of poor Lucy Gray, who in her life had been the general favourite of everybody far and near.

They put forth their utmost powers.

But in spite of their exertions they were not capable of getting over the ground as quickly as the guilty man, to whom terror had lent a superhuman power of fleetness.

How the pursuit would have terminated is hard to say.

Possibly he might have held out long enough to baffle his pursuers entirely.

An accident occurred, however, which prevented this.

His speed was what might truly be termed blind haste.

Right before his path was part of the root of a tree, which had pushed itself an inch or two above the level of the ground.

Against this obstruction Luke Ford caught his foot.

At the rate he was running, a fall was inevitable.

He struggled desperately after he stumbled, but failed to recover his footing.

Down he went, and with so much force that the impetus carried him several feet.

Before he could scramble on to his feet again his pursuers were upon him.

With shouts of triumph mingled with execration, he was seized in a dozen places, and lifted into an upright position.

He tried hard to break loose, but his strength seemed ebbing now, for the effort was abortive.

"Bring him on," cried the foremost of the throng—"bring him on! We will force him face to face with his victim, then let him deny his guilt if he can."

This proposal was received with universal acclamation.

The prisoner, however, had the utmost aversion for this, and renewed his struggles to break away.

But, as before, they were fruitless.

Those who held him were determined that at all hazards they would keep him safe.

"Come on," they cried—"none of that, or it will be the worse for you! We are resolved to bring you face to face."

Despite his desperate struggles, then, they led or rather dragged him down the dingle side.

As he drew nearer to the dreadful spot he uttered the most abject supplications for mercy, and begged hard to be released, or, at all events, not to be forced any closer.

But his appeals might just as well have fallen upon deaf ears.

Relentlessly they dragged him on, heedless of the many injuries they inflicted while so doing.

At last the tree was reached.

From this young Chambers had not stirred.

It seemed as though he considered himself in some way the custodian of the spot.

When they approached they saw that there were traces of tears in his bright black eyes and upon his swarthy, sunburnt cheeks.

Captain Hawk stood near him.

He had contented himself by remaining nothing more than a spectator of what took place.

Had there arisen any circumstance that would have rendered his interposition necessary, the reader need not be told that he would have readily come forward.

A still larger opening had by this time been made in the trunk of the tree, so that its grisly contents were perfectly revealed.

But the prisoner would not lift his head.

His captors strove hard to make him look, but this was beyond their power.

"Do you deny your guilt, wretched man?" said one. "Confess—confess! Who was it murdered Lucy Gray?"

"Yes—yes, confess—confess!" echoed the others.

The wretched prisoner, with trembling limbs, still stood with downcast looks.

"Bring him closer!" was the cry—"bring him closer! Then let him deny his guilt if he can."

But any closer proximity to the old tree was too horrible for the shrinking wretch to endure.

With a sudden and terrific effort he got his right arm at liberty.

Before it could be seized again, he, with incredible rapidity, drew a long sharp knife from his breast, and plunged it several times into his bosom.

Then the weapon was wrested from him, and he was once more held firm prisoner.

"I have conquered now!" he cried. "My death is certain! Thank Heaven I have succeeded in avoiding the hangman's touch! Don't try to stanch the blood. It is useless; I can feel that the wound is mortal."

His voice already showed signs of growing weaker, and those who held him, being unaccustomed to such scenes, grew faint with horror.

A deep silence ensued.

It was eventually broken by young Chambers, who said:

"Luke Ford, in the old time there was but little love between us; I ever held you to be a bold, bad man. I was right, it seems. Your guilt is so transparent that it will be utterly vain for you to seek to deny it. Make, therefore, all the atonement in your power by confessing the motives which led you to the commission of this awful crime."

The villain's lips moved convulsively, and all thought that he was about to do as he had been bidden.

But when he did speak, nothing but a volley of bitter curses escaped his lips.

"I defy you," he cried, at length—"with my last breath I defy you; and my last curse will be upon the head of him who brought about this discovery!"

While speaking, it was evident that he only preserved an upright position with a great effort; and now, all at once, he shrunk up together, as though completely deprived of life.

"He is helpless now," said one. "Let him lie down."

"And run for the doctor," added another. "We ought to have thought of that before. It will be a thousand pities if he cheats the gallows."

A messenger was accordingly despatched in all haste for a surgeon.

Young Chambers was now stern and calm.

He went close up to the tree without saying a word, and gazed for some moments into its interior.

"Poor girl!" Captain Hawk heard him murmur at last. "It is hard indeed to think that this was your cruel fate. I can scarcely bring myself to believe that these grim, mouldering relics can be all that remain of you. Heaven help me! My grief is greater than I can bear."

A deep sob convulsed his breast

Luke Ford noticed his mental anguish: but he gloated over instead of pitying it.

"Fred Chambers," he cried at length, "I will tell you that which will cause you many a bitter pang: Lucy Gray loved you, and would not have denied your suit but for my machinations! Ha, ha! It was myself, and no other than myself that turned her heart from you!"

The young soldier made a step forward, as though he intended to inflict summary chastisement upon the shrinking wretch; but he recollected himself just in time, and paused.

"I made sure," continued Luke Ford, "that I had only to succeed in the accomplishment of this, and then the task of winning her for myself would be an easy one. But I was mistaken; she spurned me, and with so much contempt and disgust that at the moment I swore to have revenge. It was no idle boast. You see I have kept my oath."

The villain was now growing so weak that his voice, which had been gradually sinking, now failed him altogether.

After the lapse of a few minutes, however, he appeared to recover.

"Fred Chambers," he continued, "I have not yet told you all. Lucy repented her rejection of you; and going home, she wrote a letter to you, entreating you to see her once again before your departure abroad."

"Well—well?" said the young soldier, whose agitation was terrible to witness.

"You never received that letter; I took good care of that. And as for Lucy, the pretext by which I lured her to this place was that she might see you here. I again urged my suit—she refused me. Then I remembered my oath—I had my revenge!"

These admissions excited young Chambers to such a degree that he had no longer any mastery over himself.

He sprang forward, and had not Captain Hawk held him back he would have trampled out what little life yet lingered in Luke Ford's carcass.

"This is bitter knowledge," he said. "I took the letter intended for you and tore it into a thousand fragments. After that my passion cooled a little, and I began to wonder how I should escape the consequences of the deed I had committed. My first impulse was to dig a grave. That notion I abandoned upon casting my eyes upon the old oak tree. I knew the trunk was hollow; but believed that not many knew it save myself. You can guess the rest. With infinite trouble I raised her into the branches of the tree, and let her fall into the hollow trunk. The hiding-place was never discovered, and I—I——"

He stopped abruptly; and his head, which had been slightly raised, fell back as though life had fled.

A ghastly change came over his face—a change that was the sure indication of the coming of the destroying angel.

He fought and gasped desperately for respiration; but every breath grew fainter than the one which had preceded it.

The young soldier kept his face buried in his hands.

But looking up, and seeing Captain Hawk close to him, he cried:

"My friend—for so surely I may call you—what think you now of the events of the past night? Can you take upon yourself to say that what you saw was all a dream? Was I not right in declaring that the finger of Providence was in all this?"

"It is hard to offer consolation in such a case as this," continued the captain; "but yet you ought to be able to derive some satisfaction from the thought that though this is certainly dreadful, it is infinitely better than suspense, and also from the knowledge that the author of the crime is known, and has confessed his guilt."

"The consolation is but slight," he said. "What will recompense me for the loss I have sustained? Heaven help me! When I think upon what has happened I feel as though I could not control myself—that I must commit some desperate act."

"But calmness is imperative," said Captain Hawk, placing his hand upon his shoulder. "I must leave you in a moment or so, at the most," he added. "The business which I have on hand will admit of no more delay."

"Must you leave me?"

"I must indeed."

"I regret to hear it, for I feel that I never required the services of a friend more than I do at this moment. Will you not remain, at least, a few moments longer, so as to see the termination of the affair?"

"I will not refuse you that slight favour," answered the captain. "Look, here comes some one!"

"It is the surgeon."

An elderly man now came forward.

It was plain that the intelligence he had received had produced a powerful impression upon him.

On reaching the side of Luke Ford, he stooped down and made a hasty examination.

"The wound is a mortal one," he said, gazing intently upon the features of the dying man. "The mystery is, how he can have survived so long."

The words reached the ears of Luke.

It seemed certain that he heard them with satisfaction, for a slight smile wavered upon his lips.

"This is terrible indeed," said the surgeon, deeply affected. "I can scarcely believe that what I have heard and see can be true. I trust the magistrate may be in time to take his deposition. He ought to be, for I told him the case was urgent."

The words were uttered as though said more to himself than those around him.

But they reached the ears of Captain Hawk.

"A magistrate and myself," he said to himself, "will never breathe the same air together."

Then, turning to his companion, he added:

"Believe me, sir, I much regret having to part with you; but I can stay no longer. My business is indeed most urgent, or I would remain. Farewell!"

"Farewell, sir, since it must be so, though I much regret your departure."

Captain Hawk wrung his hand, and turned to leave the spot.

But before he could take half a dozen paces he became aware that the top of the dingle was surrounded by armed men.

He stopped.

Then a loud voice cried:

"Captain Hawk, yield yourself a prisoner! You are known! You are covered by the muzzles of twenty pistols! If you offer to move they will all be discharged! Surrender, or you are a dead man!"

CHAPTER XLII.

MARTIN RESOLVES TO BETRAY THE BLACK HIGHWAYMAN TO HIS FOES.

When the man Martin, suddenly turning round, caught sight of the well-known form of the Black Highwayman standing on the threshold of the prison chamber, he seemed like one afflicted with paralysis.

A wild and piercing cry thrilled from the unfortunate prisoner's lips.

Then, throwing up her arms, she fell back totally insensible.

The Black Highwayman, with that aspect of unnatural calmness which he so frequently exhibited, remained standing on the threshold, gazing alternately from one to the other.

Fortunately the light in that dismal apartment was not sufficiently brilliant to discover very plainly the signs of confusion and dismay which Martin exhibited.

If such had been the case the Black Highwayman could not have failed to suspect his dependant, no matter how much he might have been impressed with his fidelity

Martin, however, though confused for the moment, was not long in recovering his self-possession.

Resuming his usual manner. he advanced towards the door.

"What is all this?" the Black Highwayman said at last. "What is the meaning of it?"

His manner and his tones were slightly indicative of suspicion.

"Her cries were so terrible," answered Martin, pointing to the prostrate figure, "that I came here in the hope of calming her."

"And you succeeded?"

"No—she raved, and offered me untold wealth if I would but put her in the way of gaining her freedom."

"And you?"

"I," answered Martin, not without a little hesitation, "told her that it was impossible."

The Black Highwayman gazed at him searchingly.

So searchingly that Martin was obliged to lower his eyes beneath it.

"Come," he said, "follow me!"

"But look," said Martin, turning towards the prisoner. "She has swooned!"

"What of that?"

"You would not leave her thus?"

"Why not? Come on, I say. She will recover sooner or later, depend upon it."

This callous indifference seemed to take even Martin by surprise.

He said not a word, however, but followed his master from the room.

"Put up the bar!" was the next order.

It was obeyed in silence.

"Martin," he said, as they made their way towards the apartment we have already described, "but for the knowledge of the power that I have over you, I should be almost inclined to suspect you. I am, however, so persuaded that you fully comprehend your own utter destruction would follow the discovery of me and who I am, that I overlook many things which, otherwise, would not be passed by in silence."

Martin did not speak.

"Let me again impress it on you," he continued, as calmly as though he had been speaking about the most indifferent matter in the world—"let me again assure you that my safety is your safety—my destruction your destruction. As things are, it cannot be otherwise. Do you admit that?"

Martin only emitted a kind of growling sound by way of a response.

"If you have been foolish and thoughtless enough to encourage the idea that you might betray me and yet secure your own safety, rest assured that you are mistaken."

Martin muttered some protestations of fidelity.

"I take all that for just what it is worth, Martin. I know you well enough to feel certain that nothing would afford you greater satisfaction than the accomplishment of my destruction; but yet you do not long for it so earnestly as to be willing to sacrifice yourself as well. That is how the case stands. You know my power, and beware!"

A gloomy silence followed.

"Now bring me a change of clothes," continued his master. "Make haste! I had almost left the place before I recollected what costume I wore. Moments are precious. Quick, I say!"

The Black Highwayman hastily commenced throwing off various portions of his attire.

In the meanwhile, Martin, darting into an adjoining room, brought forth a complete change of costume.

The highwayman's preparations were soon completed, and when this was the case he again enveloped himself in his ample cloak.

"Beware, Martin!" were his parting words. "Let what I say sink deeply into your mind. This period of servitude under which you chafe so much will endure only a little time longer. When the end is reached you will have no reason to complain; but if you betray me, or attempt to do it, your doom is sealed. You are wholly and utterly in my power."

He strode out of the room by means of the secret door, which he slammed violently after him.

Martin stood with his brow wearing a gloomier aspect than before.

"Utterly in his power!" he repeated. "Well—well, we shall see about that soon. I have hesitated too long already. Had I been as resolved at first as I am now, he would have had no power. What should I care?—why should I? The worst is but death, and that is likely enough to be my portion when the time arrives that I cease to be of any use to him. If he takes my life he will be sure then that I can never breathe a word of his guilty secrets. Yes, yes—if I am foolish enough to submit that will inevitably be my fate."

He paced the room in much agitation.

It would seem as though more than once he had wavered in his resolve.

But at last he paused near the centre of the vast apartment, and when he did so a glance at his compressed lips would have told anyone that his mind was fully made up.

"I am determined!" he said "I swear that nothing shall make me swerve from my course—nothing—nothing! Even though ten thousand torments followed the commission of the act I will not hesitate! I will tell all, and trust to receiving mercy. If he could hear me say that he would think that it was his turn to beware!"

In the meanwhile, the Black Highwayman made his way rapidly along the subterranean passage, never thinking that such desperate thoughts were passing through the mind of his dependant.

Yet his mind was distracted by anxious thoughts.

"Curses on this delay!" he muttered, as he strode forward impatiently. "I ought by this time to have been miles upon the road. If I am not speedy I shall have some meddling fool or other upon my track."

A moment or two afterwards the deserted summer-house was gained.

His horse was there safe enough, and saluted him with a low neigh as soon as he made his appearance.

Leading him forth, he mounted, and then made his way back again through the neglected grounds to the place where he had previously leaped his horse over the park palings.

This leap was again safely performed.

A dim gray light was now beginning to steal over the face of nature, and this circumstance caused the Black Highwayman to push his horse forward at the utmost speed he was capable of making.

Hedges, trees, cottages, and all those objects which compose a landscape flitted by him with wonderful rapidity.

There was no mistake about the quality of the horse, though for all that he could not be compared to Phantom for a moment.

He never drew rein until he saw before him a small, yellowish light that appeared to be struggling for life with the coming daylight.

"Tyburn Gate!" he ejaculated. "All is well now. A few more moments and my journey will be at an end."

CHAPTER XLIII.

LIEUTENANT TRACY PROCLAIMS LORD HARCLIFFE THE BLACK HIGHWAYMAN.

Two nights after the events which we have just related, every window in Leicester House was ablaze with lights.

At the time of which we write this building was occupied by the Prince of Wales, then a man of middle age.

It was tolerably well known that the prince was by no means on good terms with his Royal father.

With the cause of their differences we have nothing to do here; let it suffice to say that they existed.

The consequence was that the Court was split up into two parties, one of which visited St. James's and the other Leicester House.

But it is also well known that the singular conduct and behaviour of the prince, and the questionable character of some of his companions made it difficult for him to retain the bulk of his adherents, who professed themselves attached to his cause.

From time to time, then, entertainments were got up on a scale so extensive that they rivalled those of St. James's; and these regal displays were supposed to assist in keeping his faction together.

The night in question was one of these, only the entertainment about to be given had been planned upon a scale of more magnificence and lavish splendour than any of those which had preceded it.

At an early hour all the reception rooms were thronged, and by the time midnight arrived the crowd was so great that motion from one point to another was a matter of extreme difficulty and discomfort.

The strains of music floated through the perfume-laden air; there was the hum of conversation, and an occasional burst of silvery laughter.

In one corner, watching the crowd of dancers, stood Lord Harcliffe.

He was magnificently attired, and had around him a small group of young men, who all wished to be considered as men of the highest fashion.

Lord Harcliffe was, as it were, the sun round which these lesser luminaries ever circled.

Many and many were the glances cast upon the prodigal young nobleman, for his career had been so marked, so much out of the common course, that wherever he went he was gazed upon.

And although conscious that he was the object of universal attention, Lord Harcliffe preserved an air of the utmost indifference, bowing and smiling, as occasion required, with the utmost grace and self-possession.

Just as the hour of midnight was chimed forth by one of the silver-toned timepieces, he was observed to raise his hand in a peculiar manner.

"Harcliffe, my boy," said a pale, effeminate-looking young man, "what the deuce do you mean by that?"

"Mean by what, Sidney?" was the calm and unembarrassed question.

"Why, that signal you made a moment ago."

"Signal?" he echoed, in marvellously well-assumed surprise.

"Yes—you raised your hand as though you intended to beckon somebody."

His lordship laughed.

"My dear Sidney, your over-anxiety to note all *I* do has made you construe an accidental—I might say involuntary—movement into a signal. Believe me, it was nothing of the sort."

A fresh arrival to the group changed the current of the conversation.

But it was rather strange that, just after midnight had been proclaimed through the saloons, his Royal Highness Frederick Prince of Wales found himself confronted by some one who was an entire stranger to him.

The prince had at the moment stepped into a kind of recess half concealed by a crimson velvet curtain.

In this recess was a magnificent sideboard, covered with wines of the choicest kinds, and liqueurs such as would have delighted a connoisseur.

Something apparently had taken place to disturb the mental equilibrium of his Royal Highness, for, with a trembling hand and a stealthy glance around him, he poured out half a gobletful of pale brandy and placed it to his lips.

It was just at this juncture that he found himself confronted by the stranger we have mentioned.

Where he had come from he knew not.

The first idea he formed upon the point was that he must have been in the recess at the moment he (the prince) entered it, but that the massive fold of the curtain had concealed him from his view.

"Your Royal Highness," said the man, with a low bow, "I am sorry to intrude upon and discompose you, but——"

The prince, having recovered himself a little, poured a considerable quantity of the brandy down his throat.

"Well," he cried, drawing a long breath—"your business? Quick! What is it?"

"I have the honour to carry with me some trifles which I believe belong to your Royal Highness."

"Ha!" ejaculated the prince.

"Some which your Royal Highness lost a night or two back."

"Let me see them."

"They are here."

The man drew back his ample cloak, and produced a watch and ring.

He held up both, so that the prince could see them plainly.

"They are mine," was the answer.

He accompanied the words by stretching out his hand to receive the jewels.

The man surrendered them without uttering a syllable.

Evidently he expected that the prince would speak; but, finding that he remained silent, he at last murmured:

"I had been led to believe that your Royal Highness had some special commands."

A deep frown settled upon the prince's brow.

"Are you, then, the man who dared to stop me on the highway?"

"I am not Believe me, I am nothing more than his humble messenger."

The prince gazed at him for a moment or two.

Then, probably with a view of escaping from his embarrassment, he emptied the goblet of brandy at a draught.

"Tell your master," he said, sinking his voice, "that what I have to say is of such great moment that it cannot be confided to the ears of a third party. Tell him that he has nothing to fear. On the contrary, should he not fail to serve me in this matter, I will pledge myself that all his past actions—terrible as they may have been—shall be wholly pardoned and forgiven."

The messenger heard these words with an amount of surprise so great that he could not prevent it from showing in his features.

"Enough," said the prince. "Leave me. All you have to do is to deliver the message to your master."

After this dismissal he could not linger.

With a low bow he quitted the recess, and, gliding in among the crowd of idlers, was almost immediately lost to view.

What thoughts were now uppermost in the mind of the misguided prince we know not.

Certain it is that some moments elapsed, and he had to renew his attentions to the decanter of brandy, before he could recover his composure sufficiently to show himself again in the saloon.

In the meanwhile Lord Harcliffe, surrounded by his little knot of admirers, continued to lounge in the corner where we left him.

The hum of conversation grew somewhat louder.

The crowd was at its height.

The last arrival had taken place, and the hour for departure had scarcely come.

"By-the-way, Harcliffe," exclaimed one of those human butterflies, "have you heard the news about poor Tracy?"

"No," said his lordship, coolly, regaling himself with a pinch of snuff. "I want to see him, though. You remember the wager that was made. The Prince of Wales has been stopped on the high-road by the Black Highwayman, and has had his purse, watch, ring, and other things taken from him."

"Impossible! You jest!"

"Nay, it is no jest at all."

"Is it really a fact?"

"I am credibly informed so."

"Then should such turn out to be the case you will have won the wager fairly enough. But as for poor Tracy——"

"Well, what of him?"

"You know well that he announced his resolution of discovering the identity of this Black Highwayman."

"I do, and endeavoured to dissuade him from embarking in any such rash enterprise."

"I remember it well, but he took his own course."

"Has he, then, met with another accident?"

"Yes; scarcely had he recovered from the terrible fall from his horse than he started off again upon his mad errand."

"Indeed! And what was the result?"

"He was shot by somebody—by whom no one can tell."

"And is he dead?"

"I fear so."

"Poor fellow!" ejaculated his lordship, who chose this juncture to take another pinch of snuff.

"He was found just at daybreak, three mornings ago, lying on the Windsor Road. His horse had gone, and has not been recovered, while he lay bleeding profusely from an ugly pistol wound."

"Did you say it was a mortal one?"

"Not immediately so, though I am told there is little or no hope of his recovery. The last I heard of him he was lying speechless and literally at the point of death."

"That comes of foolish rashness," said Lord Harcliffe. "I feared from the first that this would be the end. How true that old proverb is which says, 'A wilful man will have his own way!'"

Just at this moment an unusual commotion seemed to be taking place in one of the outer saloons.

The noise grew louder, and it appeared almost as though some contending persons were forcing their way towards the prince.

There was a general movement of all the guests towards this spot, and Lord Harcliffe, animated by the same feeling of curiosity, joined in it.

Those who were near caught sight of a young man whose countenance was deathly pale, and who carried with him the proof that he had recently been severely wounded.

His apparel was disordered, and he walked with difficulty, as though the effort he was making was very far indeed beyond his strength.

Nevertheless, he struggled onwards through the glittering throng, not one member of which showed any disposition to make room for him.

"The prince," he said, feebly—"I must see the prince. I have important news for him!"

But this announcement only increased the difficulty of his progress, for everybody at once became anxious to remain near him, so as to hear what it was that had caused the appearance of so strange a messenger.

"Why, my dear Tracy," said one at last, recognising the new-comer, "you must be mad to think of venturing out to night. It will cost you your life!"

"Where is the prince?"

"Close by. But let me beg of you to retire, and not to think of presenting yourself before him in that plight."

"No—no—never! Let me go to him, I intreat you! Be speedy, or my strength will be exhausted."

He pressed his hand to his brow as he spoke, as though his brain was not properly under command.

"Take my arm," said the one who had questioned him. "You stand badly in need of assistance, I am sure. Make way, ladies and gentlemen, if you please. It is important that the lieutenant see the prince at once."

The speaker apparently was some one of importance, for his request was attended to with tolerable readiness.

As it happened, the prince was close at hand.

"What is it?" he asked, in his well-known peculiar voice—"what is it?"

Like magic the crowd separated right and left, allowing his Royal Highness a full view of the lieutenant, who bowed low.

Every sound was hushed in expectation.

There was not one present who did not wait with the utmost eagerness to hear the next words pronounced.

"I trust your Royal Highness will excuse this interruption," he said, in a languid voice, "but——" and here his voice became so faint that what he said was only heard by one or two, "I have discovered the identity of the Black Highwayman. The doing so has well-nigh cost me my life."

"Well," said the prince, with an air of indifference, not to say displeasure, which greatly astonished everybody, "and why do you come to me above all others? Why not make your discovery known to the proper authorities?"

"Your Royal Highness, part has been done. I have communicated with the authorities. The police officers are here in strong numbers."

"But why here?"

"Because, your Royal Highness, this same Black Highwayman of whom I speak numbers one of the guests in these saloons this evening."

Those who heard this announcement received it with a shout of mingled dismay and incredulity.

"The Black Highwayman in these rooms?" gasped several.

The lieutenant bowed.

"I came here, your Royal Highness, because I have been informed that you are a sufferer by this man's depredations. If so, you will have an opportunity of regaining possession of your own."

"It is true I did lose something," returned the prince, coldly, "but everything has been returned."

Still more astonishment was manifested at the manner of the Prince of Wales.

No one could understand it.

All that we have just described was unheard—nay almost unseen—by Lord Harcliffe, who, in consequence of the density of the throng, could not get near enough to recognise the lieutenant.

But an opportunity to press forward presenting itself, he availed himself of it, for his curiosity was strongly roused.

It was at the same time that Lieutenant Tracy, fighting hard against the languor which spread its influence over him, glanced around.

[THE CAPTURE OF CAPTAIN HAWK.]

His eye rested on the pale countenance of Lord Harcliffe.

The recognition was instantaneous and mutual.

"He is there!" cried the lieutenant. "Behold him!"

"Who—who?"

"Lord Harcliffe!" he cried, raising his finger and pointing with it. "I denounce Lord Harcliffe as being the Black Highwayman, who has so long been a terror to the road! The source of his vast wealth is now laid bare. I repeat it—Lord Harcliffe and the Black Highwayman are one! I met him in the latter character on the highway three nights ago, and snatched the black mask from his face!"

It is quite impossible to convey by any words the least impression of the tremendous confusion which followed this declaration.

Swords were drawn on every side, while the oaths of the gentlemen and shrieks of the ladies drowned every voice.

Lord Harcliffe was the first to draw his sword.

He was lucky enough to get it into a position for defence.

He tried hard to make himself heard; but what he said was undistinguishable in the terrific uproar.

He raised his voice to a shout, but it was equally unavailing.

And now fresh confusion was created by the advent of a strong party of police officers, who, with Peterson at their head, forced a passage into the saloon.

"There he is," cried Peterson, pointing to Lord Harcliffe—"there he is! Seize him—seize him! There is your prisoner!"

The fashionably-attired guests shrank back from the by no means gentle contact of the police officers, who concentrated all their attention upon the object they had in view to the exclusion of everything else.

Lord Harcliffe again waved his sword, and strove still to obtain a hearing.

Finding himself as unsuccessful as before, he turned round with his sword drawn, and a look of deep desperation on his face.

"Stand aside, gentlemen," he cried, "or it will be the worse for all of you! This matter must be settled! But I shall not surrender myself a prisoner for all that! Stand aside, I say!"

CHAPTER XLIV.

RELATES WHAT BEFEL CAPTAIN HAWK AFTER HE FELL INTO THE HANDS OF THE POLICE OFFICERS.

If a bombshell had suddenly exploded in the very midst of Oak Tree Dingle, Captain Hawk could not have been more taken by surprise than he was upon finding himself environed by his foes.

The very peculiar nature of the events which had occurred in and around that spot probably had the effect of distracting his mind somewhat, and depriving him of that coolness which was one of his most prominent characteristics.

Amazed and startled, he paused.

The next moment a sudden flush came over his face.

His hand sought his breast, from which he drew a pistol.

But before he could do more his foes were upon him.

The little dell seemed to be literally alive with them.

Down the rocky sides they poured with a precipitation which showed they were utterly regardless of all personal consequences.

Captain Hawk was a prisoner.

He made one effort to free himself from the many hands that were laid upon him.

But it was in vain.

The other persons who had occupied the dell were, if possible, more astounded than the highwayman.

Their quiet lives had for the most part been so undiversified by any incident of a startling character that these two remarkable events succeeding each other with such rapidity fairly bewildered them.

"Captain Hawk," said the leader of the police officers, with a voice so trembling with excitement that he could scarcely be understood—"Captain Hawk, you are a prisoner, and if you are wise you will now attempt no resistance, because you can only bring harm instead of good upon yourself by so doing."

Captain Hawk remained silent.

His eyes were turned slightly towards the ground, but the expression upon his countenance afforded no indication of what might be passing in his mind.

"Be reasonable," continued the officer. "You will find that I am disposed to treat you as well as I can consistently with my duty. It will be the better for you if you give your word that you will make no attempt to get free."

To this highly pacific speech Captain Hawk also declined to make a reply.

At this moment young Chambers came forward.

He was quite unable to believe that his companion could be a highwayman.

"What is all this?" he said, on coming forward. "This gentleman is a friend of mine. What is it, I say?"

"You had better not interfere," said the chief officer, gazing suspiciously upon him.

"But there must be some mistake."

"There is no mistake," was the reply. "This is Captain Hawk, the famous highwayman—let him deny it if he can."

"Impossible! Release your prisoner!"

"Oh, I daresay! If you interfere I shall take you into custody; I have half a mind to do so now."

Captain Hawk now opened his lips for the first time since his capture.

Ignoring altogether the presence of the officers, he turned to the young soldier, and said:

"Let me entreat you to trouble yourself no more about me. If you do, you will only get yourself into danger. Forget we have ever met."

Chambers still looked incredulous.

"Bring him along," said the officer to his men. "We will not wait any longer. Bring him this way"

"But won't you have him handcuffed, sir?"

"Of course I will! I made sure that you had already done it. Clasp the darbies on at once."

"Surely," said the highwayman, "you might spare me that indignity. There are enough of you to keep me secure without the help of handcuffs. I protest against it!"

"Look here, captain," said the chief officer, in the same conciliatory tones that he had before adopted, "I bear you no grudge or ill-will, and don't want to be disagreeable. Give me your word that you won't attempt to escape, and the handcuffs shall not be put on!"

"It is too unreasonable on your part to expect me to do that. You know very well that if I passed my word you would have no more trouble. You have got to earn the reward. Your duty is to take care of me, and mine to use every exertion I am able to get away."

"Very well. Since that is the way in which you are disposed to treat my friendly advances, I will begin by doing my duty to the letter. On with the darbies, Jarvis, and just slip a little bit of cord through his elbows. If he resists, we will adopt some additional means of security."

Captain Hawk knew very well that it would be perfectly futile to oppose the officers in what they were about.

Their united strength so far exceeded his that he was absolutely helpless.

It was not very likely, however, that he would pledge his word in the manner the officer had so coolly requested him to do, his determination being to allow no chance of recovering his liberty to escape him.

The handcuffs were accordingly adjusted

The captain, though, had a knack of swelling out the bones and muscles of his wrists in such a way as to make them seem much larger than they were in reality.

The consequence was that the first pair of handcuffs produced were found to be too small.

"Come, come," exclaimed the highwayman, with a smile, "if you will persist in adorning me with this jewellery, don't hurt me with it. Hold—hold! I say! I can't bear it!"

He made a wry face, as though the fastening of the handcuffs had inflicted great pain upon him.

"What's the matter there?" said the one in command—"what's the matter?"

"Mr.—a—— I have not the pleasure of knowing your name."

"Pearson," said the officer.

"Well, then, Mr. Pearson, if you think fit to accommodate me with handcuffs, I don't see that you are justified in letting your men use them for instruments of torture."

"What do you mean?"

"Why, that they are much too small, to be sure."

"Well, then, if that is the case, you shall have a pair that will fit. Just see to it, Jarvis."

After this, to the highwayman's great satisfaction, the handcuffs were removed and another pair substituted that seemed large enough to allow him to draw his hands through them, provided he did not mind losing a little skin in the process.

"Are you ready?" said Pearson.

"In a moment, sir. I have just the bit of cord to arrange."

"Be quick, then."

Not content with the handcuffs, the officers now passed a piece of rope through the prisoner's elbows, and thus pinioned his arms behind his back.

Any attempt to get free without the aid of a confederate seemed impossible.

But Captain Hawk was not in the least cast down.

To speak the truth, he was just at this time thinking far more about his horse than himself, and suffering some anxiety on his account.

He was wondering whether these officers had secured Satan as a preliminary step towards capturing his rider; and if they had not, whether they would make their way to the inn and do so.

He had to control his impatience to be informed on these points as well as he could, and to await the issue of events.

Having learned that the prisoner was for the time being quite safe, the chief officer began to take cognizance of what had happened in the dell just before his arrival.

His inquiries were soon responded to, and he quickly comprehended the case.

Calling aside three of his men, he gave them instructions what to do in the matter.

At any other time, probably, he would have considered this alone a most important business, but when taken in comparison with the capture of Captain Hawk, it almost sunk into insignificance.

"Follow me!" he said. "Keep strict guard! Remember what you have to expect if the prisoner gets away from you."

The officers practically replied to this by closing more densely round the highwayman.

At a slow pace they followed their chief up the side of the dell.

The assembled people—young Chambers included—seemed to hesitate whether they should remain in their present position or see the result of the important capture.

Captain Hawk's name was well known to them all, and they seemed as though they should never be tired of gazing at him.

The wavering did not last more than a moment.

In a body they followed the officers.

Young Chambers, still scarcely able to believe in the reality of what he had just seen and heard, followed also, with a vague idea in his mind that he might be able to render some assistance to one whose hand he had grasped and called friend.

The officers directed their steps towards the inn.

Captain Hawk, when he observed this circumstance, felt his heart sink within him.

He made sure that his horse was to be taken too.

"Had they only spared him," he said, mentally, "I could easily make light of this accident. Impossible as it may seem now, something will turn up that will enable me to elude these fellows; and then if I only had Satan I should laugh at all their future efforts."

The nearer he went to the inn the more did his spirits sink.

His dejection was plainly visible to everyone.

All wondered at it, but not one guessed the cause.

The young soldier especially wondered at seeing him so downcast.

At last the inn was reached.

Here, of course, nothing but confusion reigned, though the scene was not so distressing as it would have been if the landlord had left a wife and family to deplore his loss.

"Now, ostler," bawled Pearson, "out with the horses as quick as you like."

"Very good, sir."

Jarvis, who was the second in command, sidled up to his superior.

"Ahem!" he said.

"Well, Jarvis, what is it?"

"I was wondering, sir, what plan you had thought of adopting in order to keep the prisoner secure."

"I was thinking of it," was the reply. "We will walk apart a little and consider it over."

"Very good, sir."

"It will never do to lose him now we have got him so safely in our clutches."

"Certainly not."

"That would be a shame and disgrace that I should never be able to survive."

"We won't think of it, sir; and if you would excuse me for making a suggestion——"

"Oh, of course—of course!"

"It is presumption, I know——"

"Not at all—not at all! I shall be very happy indeed to listen to what you have to say."

"I have been thinking over two things, sir."

"What are they?"

"One is, how we can keep our prisoner best."

"Yes—yes! And the other?"

"The other is, what we are to do with him now we have got him?"

"What we are to do with him?"

"Yes, sir. Of course, there is no occasion to remind you that we are a long way from London."

"Yes, we are—a very long way."

"Well, then, Mr. Pearson, it strikes me that we shall run a great many risks while making such a long journey."

"But how is it to be avoided?"

"I am not quite clear upon that point. But I was wondering whether there was any Justice of the Peace close at hand."

"Why do you want to know that?"

"Because if there is I should advise that we go there with the prisoner and get a warrant signed that will authorise us to deposit him in the nearest county jail."

"I see."

"If we can once manage that, Mr. Pearson, all will be well. The responsibility will be off our shoulders the moment we lodge him in the prison, which will be a very different thing from going all the way to London with him."

"You are quite right, Jarvis; and I am quite inclined to try whether it can be done."

"If so, sir, it will save us every one a great deal of trouble, and will be, in a manner of speaking, making sure of the reward."

"Certainly—certainly! And what next?"

"Why, that was concerning the safest way to take him to the magistrate's—that is, of course, sir, making so bold as to suppose that you are going there."

"Well—well?"

"I hardly like to push my notions forward."

"Oh, pho—pho! you are a great deal too considerate, Jarvis—you are indeed. Pray what were you going to say?"

Pearson was quite affable and gentle, as he always was when anyone behaved to him like Jarvis did.

"Then, sir, my suggestion, you will see, is very simple."

"I am impatient to hear it, Jarvis."

"Do you see that old cart, sir?"

"The one under the shed yonder?"

"That's it, sir."

"Yes, I see it. But what of that?"

"That cart, sir, gave me my idea."

"Indeed!"

"I will explain, sir. Now that the landlord here is dead, or next thing to it, I suppose we shall have no trouble in borrowing that cart for a time."

"But what do you want with such a tumble-down thing as that? It looks as though it would fall to pieces before it was taken half a mile."

"It would have been better stronger, sir. But I think it will hold together, and I expect there will be no chance of getting hold of any other vehicle."

"What do you want it for, Jarvis?"

"For the prisoner."

Pearson shook his head.

"Look here, sir: Suppose we harness one of the horses to that cart, and that we bind the prisoner hand and foot, and lay him at the bottom of it."

"Well?"

"Then suppose that two or three of us get into the cart as well, and that one drives, while all the rest form a circle round, and ride as close to the cart as they can."

"I should suppose in that case, Jarvis, that the prisoner would be about as safe as we could hope to make him."

"Just so, sir; that's what I thought. Perhaps you will turn it over in your mind and decide?"

"I will. Just give an eye to him for a moment."

The plan suggested by Jarvis was such a good one, and so well calculated to answer the end in view, that one would have thought it did not require a moment's deliberation.

Pearson, however, like plenty of men in command, was an incompetent blockhead, who could have done nothing unaided, and considered it wrong to manifest his approval all at once.

On the contrary, he wanted to be quiet for a minute or two, in order that he might hit upon some means of making a minor alteration or two in the plan, by which he would be entitled to lay claim to having done a very clever and successful thing.

Everybody must have come into contact with one of these people.

"Confound it," he said, "that's a very capital idea! I don't mind admitting it to myself, though I shouldn't like to let it go any further. It must be a capital idea, for I don't see how I can alter any of the arrangements without spoiling the whole. And to think that that old cart should have suggested it! Why, I should have looked at a thing like that for a month without its suggesting anything whatever to me."

Mr. Pearson scratched his wig, but he could not think of any change that might be made, unless it was clearly a change for the worse, and he valued the safety of the prisoner too much to feel inclined to run any risks.

While in this state of indecision, the ostler approached. He seized eagerly upon him.

"Tell me," he said, "do you know of any reason why I should not have that old cart yonder for a day or two?"

"No, sir, I don't, unless it be that the probability is that the shafts will break or the wheels come off, or something of that kind, before you get very far with it."

"Is it so unsafe as all that?"

"Well, perhaps scarcely; but I know the man who belongs to it, and I feel sure he would part with it for a trifle, because it is of no manner of use to him."

"But don't you know that his Majesty's officers of police when in the execution of their duty are empowered to take anything that, for the time being, will further the ends of justice?"

"That may be," said the ostler, "and I am not going for to dispute it—not at all; only I should *raycommend* you not to try anything of that sort on with the owner of the cart, or you'll find him precious disagreeable to deal with, I can tell you."

"How much does he want for the cart?"

"That I don't know."

"But you have an idea, perhaps, of how much he would take?"

"Yes."

"How much?"

"Nothing under a couple of guineas."

"Are you sure?"

"Certain; and it's cheap enough for that. Lor' bless me, look at it! Why, I do believe it would almost fetch the money broken up into firewood!"

This was an exaggeration doubtless, but we leave our readers to imagine for themselves what kind of vehicle it could be that was purchasable for two guineas.

After some hesitation, Pearson resolved to buy it, believing that when done with he could sell it without sustaining any material loss.

"I'll call the man, sir," said the ostler; "I saw him not a moment ago."

He called him accordingly.

The bargain was soon struck and the money paid.

In the meanwhile, the officers' horses were brought out and got in readiness for travel.

Captain Hawk had not been able to overhear the confidential conversation between Pearson and Jarvis.

An occasional word spoken in a higher tone than the rest had reached his ear, but that was all.

There was nothing that would let him into the light of their intentions.

He had observed them once or twice looking at the old rickety cart under the shed; but he could not think how that concerned him.

Young Chambers afterwards came forward, and, addressing him, inquired whether there was anything he could do for him.

Fain would he have whispered something about his noble steed; but the proximity of his foes prevented anything of the kind.

Nor did he like to see the young man compromise himself by holding communication with him.

"My dear sir," he said, "I can only thank you for your kind, well-meant attentions, and ask you to leave me to my fate. It matters little to you; and any attempt at interference will only bring suspicion, and perhaps serious trouble, on yourself. Fare you well, sir. You have my best thanks."

But the young soldier would not be thus rebuffed.

He had taken a strong liking to Captain Hawk, and was resolved to aid him whether he would or not, and in spite of any personal danger to himself.

But finding how firm the highwayman was in his determination to hold no further conversation with him, he drew back with the intention of watching the progress of events.

The old cart having been brought out, was, by means of a wisp or two of straw, roughly cleaned of the dust and mildew which had accumulated upon it.

This being done, one of the horses was put into the crazy shafts, after which the ostler declared all was ready for a start.

"Stop a moment," said Pearson, drawing the ostler on one side. "I want you to tell me whereabouts the nearest Justice of the Peace resides."

"Well, sir, there doesn't happen to be one anywhere very near."

"But where is one?"

"At Crogsdon."

"Where the deuce is that?"

"Close to Gorsebrook."

"Thank you for nothing. I mean, how far is it off?"

"Not more than eleven miles, sir."

"Confound it! that's a long way."

"Well, it is, sir, for that cart to go certainly; but if you are careful it may hold out."

"I'll try."

"Very good, sir; all is ready now."

"And what is the name of this Justice of the Peace at Crogsdon?"

"Fielding, sir."

"And how shall we find the place? I have not the least idea which way to go to look for it."

"That's easy enough, sir."

"How?"

"You can't miss the road. You go on along the high-road towards London till you reach the second mile-stone; and just beyond that you will find a turning to the right. Go down there. It's a bad road, though. There's no other, so you are obliged to take it."

"Well, well—and how far are we to go down this turning?"

"Till you come to a finger-post at the four lanes, and on one of the arms you'll see, '*This way to Crogsdon.*' Go straight on then, and you will see the squire's house on the top of the hill. You can't miss it, because it is very large, and built of white stone."

"Very good," said Pearson. "It strikes me I shall find the way easy enough."

Captain Hawk was still in a state of anxious suspense and excitement.

Every moment he expected to see Satan led forth.

What the cart was intended for never struck him, and nothing he had heard had in the least tended to enlighten him.

But every preparation being now completed, Pearson came towards him.

"Don't be offended," he said, "because we are going to make use of a few extra precautions; but the fact is, we have had a great deal of trouble in catching hold of you, and now that we have you fast, we don't intend to let you go. You understand that, don't you?"

The captain nodded.

"Just allow my man Jarvis here, then, to make you comfortable, and then we will be off."

"What do you mean?"

"You will see in a moment," said Pearson, with a smile.

Jarvis came forward, with a piece of strong cord hanging from his arm.

Before Captain Hawk could have prevented him, even supposing him desirous of doing so, the cord was slipped in a running noose over his legs just above the ankles, and pulled tight.

"I hope you have me secure enough now," he said, with a smile.

"Rather!" said Jarvis.

"Into the cart with him, then!" cried Pearson. "Just lend a hand there, two or three of you."

The highwayman was now totally incapacitated from resistance; and the police officers, by their united strength, lifted him into the cart, and laid him upon the bottom of it with no more trouble than they would have had with a sack of grain.

"Capital," exclaimed Pearson, rubbing his hands together in a perfect ecstasy of delight—"it's really capital!"

Three officers got into the cart, seating themselves on the sides of it, and looking down at the prostrate form of their totally helpless prisoner.

"How will you ride, Mr. Pearson?"

"I will drive, Jarvis," was the reply. "I would not

miss that treat for worlds. You can ride my horse by the side."

Jarvis obeyed with his usual docility.

The ostler grinned when he saw the extraordinary number get into the cart.

"Go it!" he muttered to himself. "Why don't a few more of you try?—you will only break it down the sooner. My eye, what a spill it would be to be sure!"

The ostler chuckled away at a great rate, and was evidently mightily pleased; but he took good care not to let the officers see it.

After a little more delay the cavalcade set forth, and most assuredly a more remarkable one never left any inn yard.

First went a couple of police officers, as if to clear the way.

Then came the cart with its heavy load, and a couple of police officers on each side of it.

The rear was brought up by two more of them, so there was no mistake about the captain being well guarded.

His chances of escape could not well have been less than they were at this juncture.

The horse harnessed to the cart had to pull well, for the wheels had grown rusty and stiff for want of use.

As for the vehicle itself, it creaked and rumbled in the most alarming manner.

Pearson, however, was so over delighted with Jarvis's clever expedient, and the complete success which had hitherto attended it, that he overlooked every minor consideration.

One would have thought that under the circumstances Captain Hawk would have felt it extremely difficult to experience any kind of consolation or satisfaction.

Such an idea, however, was very far from the case.

So consoling were his thoughts that he lay at the bottom of the cart with a placidity which astonished his captors.

Satan was safe.

The dreadful dread which had been pressing on his heart was now quite removed.

Pearson's delight had made him altogether forgetful of the highwayman's horse, which, however, he had previously determined to claim as a perquisite.

The high-road, however, was reached in safety, and this emboldened them all to proceed with a little more confidence.

"My eye," ejaculated the ostler, as he stood at the gate and watched the party out of sight, "this here is a blessed go, and no sort of a mistake! Brimstone and blazes, what a spill there will be! I think I can see it!"

This idea amused the ostler so much that he was obliged to return to the stable to laugh it out.

When there his eyes fell upon Satan.

"And so that is Captain Hawk's steed, is it? Well, he will be safe enough in my care, I will answer for that; and if what I have heard about him is true, it won't be long before he is back here again, and then, when he finds what I have done, he will make this a capital night's work."

Thus highly satisfied with himself, the ostler gave Satan an extra feed of corn.

It would have been immensely satisfactory to Captain Hawk could he but have heard that his much-prized steed was in such capital hands.

Of the friendly intentions of the ostler he, however, knew nothing.

At first the horrible jolting of the cart set anything like thought at defiance.

Bump, bump, bump it went, as though quite destitute of springs.

It was most uncomfortable to all, but especially the captain, who could not move hand or foot to steady or save himself from the continual blows the jolting inflicted.

To speak, he knew full well, would be worse than useless, so, very wisely, he held his tongue.

The faster they went the worse the jolting became, until at last, out of consideration for his own seat of honour, Pearson was obliged to decrease the horse's speed.

Moreover, the crazy cart every instant threatened dissolution.

"We must go very carefully," he said, "or the horrid thing will never hold out; and if it broke down we should be in a regular fix, that's certain."

But even at a walk the bumping was something alarming, for the second mile-stone being passed they had turned down the cross-road, agreeably to the ostler's instructions.

When he said this road was bad, he certainly confined himself to the truth.

At the present day it would be almost impossible in any remote district to find a by-lane so ill-kept as this road was.

Here and there heaps of stones had been placed, as though for the purpose of improving its condition; but these had only been roughly strewed about, without any attempt to obtain a level surface.

It was no uncommon thing for one wheel of the cart to be six or eight inches higher than the other, and then, with alarming suddenness, the wheel which had been highest would sink and the other abruptly rise, so as to threaten the overturning of the cart altogether.

Captain Hawk was rolled from side to side unmercifully, and when by chance he happened to come in contact with his foes he was saluted with a sly kick, which piece of petty spite delighted them amazingly.

To complain would have been ridiculous, so the captain had to content himself with muttering vows to pay them off in kind as soon as ever an opportunity presented itself.

The journey was inexpressibly tedious.

Nine miles, however, were accomplished in safety, though almost three hours were consumed.

How in the world the cart held together was a most extraordinary mystery, and one that defies all elucidation.

"Come, come," said Pearson, shifting about uneasily upon his seat—"after all, this is not so bad as it might have been. We have come so far safely, therefore I think we ought not to complain.

"Come up, will you!"

The horse struggled on.

The road was dreadfully trying for a horse, especially with such a load behind it.

"We shall be there in something like half an hour, sha'n't we?" continued Pearson.

"And," growled one, "we may have to go eleven miles more before we meet with a county jail."

"Don't meet trouble half-way," was the philosophic answer. "If it is so, we must have a rest, that's all."

Captain Hawk listened to this with a sigh of delight.

The uncomfortable ride and the kicks bestowed by the officers had made him one mass of bruises from head to heel.

"What place is that?" said Jarvis, who had been looking about him for some time, and now caught sight of a white building in advance. "Do you see that mansion up above the trees yonder?"

"That must be the squire's house."

"Not a doubt of it," said Pearson; "it answers exactly to the description the ostler gave of it. Upon my word, now, this is capital!"

Pearson was much elated upon finding himself within view of his destination; but his joy quickly met with a reverse.

Just as he uttered the word "capital," the cart gave a more ominous creak than it had done hitherto, and, without further warning, down it went in the road.

The crash was terrific.

No one at all was prepared for any such catastrophe.

When they first started all kept on the look-out; but having come so far in safety had induced a false feeling of security.

From the very first it had seemed most extraordinary how the cart had held together, and now one would fancy that some particular screw must have secured the whole, for it lay in the road an absolute wreck.

There was not any part of it left unsmashed.

The wheels lost their tires and spokes, and fell together in a heap, while of the body of the cart no fragment could be found that was more than a foot square.

Pearson had been perched up in the front of the vehicle, and at the time of the downfall away he went, as though he had been some projectile hurled by a piece of ordnance.

His aerial gyrations were wonderful to view, and when he alighted it seemed to him as though the force of the fall had been sufficient to make an indentation in the stony roadway.

All the breath was, of course, knocked completely out of his body.

He was capable of no other movement than that of opening and shutting his eyes.

Captain Hawk, too, was thoroughly taken by surprise.

The officers who sat around almost all fell upon him—either accidentally or purposely, it is hard to say which.

They and the portions of the cart remained for a moment or two a confused heap.

By degrees, however, they separated themselves.

Just as they succeeded in doing so, Pearson, after many trials, found himself able to use his voice.

"The prisoner!" he gasped—"on your lives see to the prisoner! Don't let him escape!"

"All right, sir," said Jarvis; "I have got my eye upon him."

Those officers who formed the escort, having recovered from their astonishment, dismounted to render assistance.

Pearson was picked up and placed on his legs.

The same service was performed for Captain Hawk, as he was quite unable to rise unaided.

The fall of the cart, though by no means an unexpected event, had not contributed in any way that he could see at present to his freedom.

A great deal of breath, in the shape of cursing and swearing, was wasted by the police officers, and when they had somewhat eased and soothed themselves by this process they began to think of holding a consultation.

The confusing blow which Pearson had received on the side of his head made him less than ever capable of concocting any plan of operations.

Jarvis, however, was equal to the occasion.

His superior called him aside.

"Dear me," he said, "I feel very bad after that fall. What an acceptable thing a glass of brandy would be, to be sure."

"You are right, sir. And when we get to the squire's house, you may depend we shall be hospitably treated."

This was an encouraging prospect, but Pearson kept to the matter in hand.

"D—n that cart," he said, "and the man who sold it! What a wreck it is now, to be sure! What the devil are we to do with our prisoner now?"

"We must consider a moment or two, sir, as to what will be the best plan we can adopt."

"What do you think, Jarvis?"

"I have thought of several things," was the answer; "but I don't know which will be best."

"Stop a moment!" said Pearson, putting his finger to the side of his nose. "I have an idea."

"The deuce you have!"

"Yes, I have indeed!"

"I shall be delighted to hear it."

"You shall have that pleasure. I daresay you have heard of Mazeppa, Jarvis?"

"Oh yes—a fellow that was tied on the back of a wild horse."

"Just so; and as far as I am able to learn, very secure it kept him."

"Oh yes, very secure; there can be no question about that."

"I thought not, Jarvis—I thought not. We will treat our prisoner Mazeppa fashion, Jarvis; and, rely upon it, we shall get safely to the Hall."

"But——"

"What objection have you to make?"

"None at all, sir. I was only thinking about the prisoner."

"And, pray, what about him?"

"It struck me that he would consider it a very harsh punishment."

"And what the devil!" broke out Pearson. "Do you think I am going to trouble myself about the prisoner, and what he may consider? Nothing of the kind, sir. I shall do what I think proper to keep him safe."

Former experience had taught Jarvis that it was quite useless to attempt to reason with his superior officer when in his present mood; so he wisely forebore irritating him by making the attempt.

The order accordingly was given that Captain Hawk should be bound securely on the back of one of the horses.

The officers received this proposal with acclamations.

It was just such a piece of practical fun as would delight them, and they set about carrying out their orders with the utmost alacrity.

As for the highwayman, he burned with indignation upon learning the kind of treatment to which he was to be subjected.

He even raised his voice and protested against it.

He was not long in finding, however, that he might just as well have addressed himself to the winds.

But he was resolved not to submit with perfect tameness.

Unfortunately, though, the resistance he was able to make was so slight as to be of no avail.

By main force he was lifted up and flung with no gentle force upon a horse's back.

Then cords were rapidly thrown over him, and tight knots tied here and there.

In less time than it has taken to write it he was bound on the horse's back so tightly that he could not move a single joint.

Two officers then rode at each side, holding the rein in such a way as to guide the horse, which immediately afterwards was surrounded by the troop.

In this strange fashion, then, the journey was resumed.

But for the consciousness that he was submitted to a very great indignity, the captain would not have minded so much the circumstance of being bound on the horse's back.

Compared with his bumps and knocks received in the cart, it was quite an agreeable and comfortable means of locomotion.

The men, as they rode on, amused themselves by cracking jokes at his expense, and it required all the self-control the highwayman was master of to prevent him from replying in some way or other to the taunts levelled at him.

Luckily, the distance to the squire's house was not great, and they journeyed much more rapidly than before, so that the highwayman's mortification was not very long enduring.

But as they approached the Hall, its inmates, amazed at the extraordinary sight which presented itself, turned out in a mass.

When the officers got closer still they were overwhelmed with questions as to the meaning of the strange-looking cavalcade.

The news that the strongly-guarded prisoner was no other than the much-dreaded Captain Hawk, who had been for so long the terror of the road, quickly flew from mouth to mouth.

Not a little alarm was manifested, in spite of the strength of the cords; but when at length the youthful and gentlemanly figure of the highwayman was brought into view, loud cries of "Shame!" were raised, and terror gave place to pity.

Of course Pearson checked these manifestations as well as he could.

Just as they halted before the principal entrance, an individual came forth, whom the officers at once recognised as the squire.

He was an oldish man, short and very stout.

His florid face was surrounded by piebald whiskers, which lent a strange aspect to it.

His mouth was drawn down at the corners, and his eyes were almost hidden beneath a penthouse of grizzly hair.

"What the devil is all this about?" he said, in a growling voice, and with an air such as some petty monarch might have put on. "Explain it—explain it!"

Pearson had seen a good deal of the world, and his experience at once told him how he ought to comport himself to this individual.

Putting on all the humbleness and servility he could, he said:

"Your worship, I am one of the principal officers at Bow Street, and to-day it is my pleasant duty to bring to you a prisoner no less a personage than Captain Hawk, the highwayman."

"Is that the man yonder?"

"It is, your worship."

"And why have you tied him like that?"

"To keep him secure, that is all. If you only had the least idea of what a desperate character he is, you would not wonder at my taking these precautions. We have had a world of trouble to capture him, so that now it would be doubly vexatious if we permitted him to escape, and so lost the reward."

"Humph! I see. But why have you brought him here?"

"Simply in order that your worship may furnish us with a warrant to lodge him in the nearest county jail."

"Why not take him to London?"

"I had thought of that, your worship, and such was my first intention, but I am afraid I could not keep him in safe custody for so long a journey, and therefore think the ends of justice will be most effectually secured by handing him over to some prison officials without any avoidable delay."

"Well, well—perhaps you are right. But what evidence have you to offer that will warrant me in committing him?"

This was a poser for Pearson, and he had to consult with Jarvis.

"I humbly imagine, your worship," said this individual, "that if one of the bills offering the reward is produced, and that two of us swear that to our certain knowledge the prisoner is the man we want, that will be sufficient."

"Oh, quite—quite!"

"Then you will grant me the warrant?"

"Certainly."

"I am much obliged to your worship."

"But everything must be *pro forma*, you understand."

"Oh, certainly—certainly!"

"Then release the prisoner from the horse, and bring him into the justicing-room. You will find me there, ready to receive the depositions."

With these words, the squire turned on his heel and re-entered his house.

A very animated scene now ensued.

The unbinding of Captain Hawk was felt by all to be a very ticklish operation; and even the squire's servants, who were not immediately interested in the result, closed round more densely, in order not to miss any part of what might follow.

Captain Hawk had found some consolation in pondering over the reprisals he should make upon the officers for their treatment of him.

There did not seem any bright prospect of carrying any scheme of revenge into effect, but the captain did not despair.

It was no little relief to be lifted off the horse, for the ropes and the quick motion had galled him sorely.

When he found himself standing again upon the ground, he felt ever so much nearer freedom.

The calm, unruffled demeanour which he assumed, and the unabashed manner in which he looked around him, elicited much admiration.

"Bring him along!" said Pearson, full to the brim of importance. "Take care how you come. Don't let him get away. Recollect, he is as cunning as a fox and as slippery as an eel."

"All right, sir! We'll look after him, never fear."

The officers pressed round very closely, and, under the guidance of one of the domestics, they all made their way to the justicing-room.

This was a large, gloomy-looking apartment, rarely used except on such occasions as the present.

At one end were a couple of desks, raised one above the other.

The lower one was occupied by the justice's clerk—the upper one by the justice himself.

The last-named individual kept Pearson and the prisoner waiting for something like a quarter of an hour.

At last the great judicial functionary assumed his seat.

He settled his wig in what he considered a dignified and imposing way.

"Now, fellow," he cried, "stand forward!"

Captain Hawk took no notice.

"Stand forward, I say!" bawled the magistrate.

"Now, then, move a little closer, can't you?"

Captain Hawk's legs were no longer tied, so when the police officer who spoke roughly jostled him forwards, he retaliated by giving him such a kick upon the shins that he was obliged to dance about for more than a minute, while tears of agony streamed from his eyes.

"I don't approve of kicking," remarked the prisoner—"it is too Frenchified to suit me; but you must not expect a man to put up with everything simply because he has handcuffs on his wrists and his elbows tied behind his back."

The officer muttered an oath, and rushed forward, with the evident intention of inflicting some severe personal injury upon the captain.

But he had yet to learn the nature of the man he had to deal with.

With astonishing rapidity, the captain bent forward, presenting his head like a battering ram.

The officer rushed on with his fists up, intending, no doubt, to deliver two blows on the prisoner's face.

He saw his adversary stoop; but not soon enough for him to pause.

On he came, and his stomach came into violent contact with the top of Captain Hawk's head.

A sound not unlike the smashing of a bonnet-box followed, and the next thing the spectators beheld was the officer lying breathless on his back, extended at full length on the floor, while Captain Hawk remained in his former position, not showing by the quiver of a muscle that his calmness had been in the least ruffled.

It was certainly the first time that such a scene of violence had been enacted within those walls.

Hitherto the very aspect of that huge, cheerless apartment had been sufficient to strike terror to the heart of every depredator who had been brought before that dreadful double desk.

Absolute amazement petrified the magistrate and his clerk.

Neither could speak; and it would not be going too far to say that neither would have been at all surprised if the end of the world had followed there and then.

Some such event did seem to threaten, for a sudden darkness swept over the sky.

On a bright day the justicing-room looked sufficiently gloomy, but now such a dubious twilight prevailed in it that the outlines of different objects could not be very well discerned.

The officer was lifted up, but he made no attempt to renew the conflict.

That battering-ram blow was a settler.

"Hallo!" ejaculated the justice, who was about to make some other remark. "What the deuce is the matter? Is it night, or what?"

"Or what, I should say, your worship," said Captain Hawk, with mock gravity.

"Hold your tongue, fellow!" said the magistrate, in what he intended should be tones of withering scorn.

"I fancy we are going to have a storm, your worship," answered Pearson. "And by the suddenness of its coming on, and the great darkness, I imagine it will be a severe one."

He was proved right in his supposition by a faint, rattling peal of thunder, which at this instant came upon the ears of those assembled.

This was succeeded by a few spots of rain, which fell with a sullen splash against the windows.

"It will be a storm," said the justice. "Francis, ring the bell for candles. We shall not be able to finish this business without them."

This order was obeyed by the clerk, and the fact of candles being found requisite will give the best idea of the extent of the obscurity.

Captain Hawk fidgeted with his handcuffs.

He felt sure that he could slip them over the back of his hands, and but for the cord through his elbows, doubtless would have done so, and, favoured by the gloom, have made a bold dash for escape.

He clenched his teeth with vexation.

"I must wait," he said to himself. "Something is sure to turn up, and any rashness now will spoil all."

Just as he arrived at this very proper conclusion, the doors were opened, and a footman, carrying a couple of tall wax candles, came in.

These were placed before the magistrate.

By the time, however, that this was done and the doors closed again, darkness, equal to that of night, set in.

The two wax candles were, of course, miserably insufficient to illuminate an apartment of such large dimensions, and, to use a common phrase, they seemed only to make the darkness visible.

"The Court is open," said the justice; "let no time be lost. Prisoner, come forward."

His words were followed by a clap of thunder of such terrific violence that the house seemed shaken to its foundations.

It was succeeded by a perfect deluge of rain.

It came down in a sheet, and with such violence as to rebound from the stones in the court-yard without as though it had fallen from a cascade.

"God bless me!" said the justice, "was the like ever known before!"

"I think we got here just in time," said Pearson, and the officers mightily congratulated themselves upon escaping from such a drenching.

A flash of lightning, which inflicted a momentary blindness, and seemed to put out the wax candles entirely, now followed.

The next moment a louder peal of thunder than the former burst upon their astonished ears.

"Come, come," said the justice, "the business in hand need not occupy us many minutes, and I shall be glad to get to some other part of the house."

"Would your worship like to adjourn the case for an hour or so?" suggested the clerk, with a trepidation that he vainly strove to conceal.

"No, no!" said the magistrate, who was scarcely more at ease. "Let us get through with it. Prisoner, I say, come forward!"

A couple of officers gently pushed the captain forward, and, as they abstained from roughness and violence, he submitted quietly.

"Now, fellow," said the magistrate, in his most disagreeable manner, "what is your name?"

Captain Hawk was silent.

"Speak, sir, or I will commit you for contempt!" said the magistrate, furiously.

Captain Hawk resolutely closed his lips.

"Never mind, your worship," said Pearson—"it don't at all matter. Here is the handbill. Just glance at the description, and compare for yourself."

The justice glared over the tops of his spectacles at the police officer as though about to resent this interference.

But if he had designed to do so, his mind was changed by another brilliant flash of lightning, which brought all things into view with painful vividness, leaving a double darkness behind.

The lightning flash was followed without the lapse of a moment by another terrific crash of thunder.

CHAPTER XLV.

RELATES THE STRANGE ADVENTURES WHICH BEFEL CAPTAIN HAWK AT SQUIRE FIELDING'S.

THE storm by this time seemed at its height.

The downpour of rain was incessant, while the lightning and thunder followed almost without intermission.

At times it was impossible for those in the justicing-room to make their voices heard at all.

The magistrate sat for some moments resolutely spelling away at the bill.

He had not troubled himself much about education—indeed, prided himself upon being no scholar, and therefore any reading was a tedious process to him.

But as he spelt over the description word by word, he looked up and nodded, as he noted how exactly what was printed corresponded with the appearance of the prisoner before him.

"There's no doubt about it," he said at last, folding up the paper. "Who swears that this scoundrelly fellow is Captain Hawk?"

"I do," answered Pearson, readily; and Jarvis stepped forward also, so as to be in readiness if called upon.

"Very good. Swear them, Francis."

This was done when the lulls in the storm would permit.

Francis, the clerk, was as white as a sheet, and devoutly wished himself in some other place.

"That's enough, Francis," said the justice. "Now draw up the commitment, and I'll sign it."

This was done accordingly.

"Excuse me, your worship, but I should be glad to know how far it is to the county jail?"

"Only twenty-seven miles."

"Only! the devil! I beg pardon, your worship," stammered Pearson, who now looked decidedly crestfallen. "But I thought—that is, I made sure—there was a county jail not far off where this very troublesome prisoner could be lodged."

"So there is, man—so there is."

"But don't you call twenty-seven miles far off?"

"It's the nearest."

"That may be, your worship, but d—n me if I wouldn't sooner take him all the way to Newgate. There would be a proper end of the matter then."

"Just as you like," said the justice, rising, "I have done as you asked, and yet you seem to throw the blame upon me."

"Not at all, your worship—not at all. I trust—very humbly trust—that your worship, out of your abundant goodness, will be so kind as to pardon me. It's my unfortunate temper."

"Oh, very well—very well! You have the commitment you asked for, and now you can pack off with your prisoner as soon as you like, and go where the devil you choose."

"I am truly sorry," said Pearson, affecting to be very contrite, "to find that I have so deeply offended your worship, for——"

"Well, sir?" said the justice, pausing on his way to the door.

"I was going to say, your worship, that but for this unfortunate disagreement I was going to ask you—being as it is a night not fit to turn a dog out in——"

"Well, well—to the point."

"Then the point is, your worship, I hoped that you would give us all shelter for an hour or two, until the violence of the storm be overpast."

"Well, well—I don't mind doing that. Francis, see to it. You are welcome to what you like to eat and drink."

Pearson poured out his thanks.

The magistrate cut him short by asking a question.

"And while you are feasting and sheltering, what you intend to do with your troublesome prisoner?"

"The best we can to keep him secure, your worship"

"Of course!"

"Had your worship a suggestion to make?"

"There is the strong room," he said. "Francis has the key of it. It is plated with iron all over the inside; and if you bind him well, and lock the door, he will be tolerably safe, I should think."

"I am much obliged to your worship. It shall be done."

The justice left the room, banging the door violently after him.

Francis, glad to escape, seized one of the wax candles, and led the way out.

The storm showed no symptoms whatever of abatement.

The lightning still flashed, and the thunder rattled as before, while the rain came down faster, if anything.

"Lead the way to the strong room first, Francis," said Pearson.

"All right! This is the way."

"All right! Have you the key?"

"Here it is."

He produced one of formidable size as he spoke.

With this in one hand and the wax candle in the other, he marched on, followed by the throng.

Captain Hawk's hopes rose a little when he heard mention made of the strong room.

He thought nothing of the circumstance of its being plated with iron, but only of the fact that he should be for a short time certainly separated from his captors.

That, he told himself, could hardly fail to prove an advantage to him.

He made, then, not the least opposition to being led from the justicing-room.

He assumed, however, an air of dejection for the purpose of throwing the officers as much off their guard as possible; but while so doing he was careful to note everywhere he went, and every object that he passed.

He was not a little curious to know where this strong room could be situated, and wondered for what purpose it was generally used.

He was most careful, however, not to manifest this in any way.

On quitting the justicing-room some stairs were

[CAPTAIN HAWK'S MYSTERIOUS VISITOR.]

ascended, which at the top communicated with a corridor of considerable length.

Along this Francis marshalled them, nor did he halt until the further extremity was reached.

Here a ponderous iron door was situated, and here Captain Hawk told himself was the entrance to the strong-room.

Francis thrust the key in, and then gave the wax candle to Pearson to hold, for it required the united strength of both hands to shoot back the bolt.

When this was done a small square space was disclosed.

Another iron door was then visible.

This inner door was well secured by bars and bolts; but there was no lock upon it, that on the outer door being, doubtless, deemed sufficient.

These fastenings were soon drawn back.

Crossing the threshold, the officers found themselves in an apartment about twelve feet square.

It was very remarkable, but nevertheless a fact, that the floor, walls, and ceiling were all composed of strong plates of iron, so cleverly placed together that the joints could scarcely be seen.

On one side, opposite the door, and as high up in the wall as it was possible to place it, was a grated opening, which we suppose was dignified by being called a window.

The atmosphere in this chamber was very chill.

It struck instantly into the breasts of all.

The rain, too, had happened to beat against the grated opening we have spoken of, and this materially added to the discomfort of the place.

The wax candle flickered and threatened to be extinguished, so that Francis had to shade it with his hand

"There," he said, with chattering teeth, "your prisoner cannot fail to be tolerably safe in here when we have locked and barred the doors."

"As safe he can be anywhere, I should think," said Pearson.

"But I would make doubly sure by binding him well," said Jarvis; "and when we have done that pleasant bit of duty, I don't care how soon we have something to eat and drink."

Captain Hawk submitted to having his feet tied together without so much as a murmur.

But when this was done, he spoke.

He had preserved silence so long that all were anxious to listen to his words.

"Look here, Pearson," he said; "but for one thing I should look upon you as being a very decent and good sort of a fellow, considering you are a police officer, and I never expected you would serve me thus."

"Ha, ha!"

"You laugh, but you don't understand me."

"What do you mean, then? Be quick—we want to be off."

"Well, then, Pearson, without blaming you at all for any extra precautions for keeping me safe, I still didn't think you would shut me up here without a crust, while you and the rest feasted below."

At this reproof Pearson hung his head.

"You have yourself to blame for it," interposed Jarvis, hastily. "If you had passed your word not to try to get away, you would not have had that disagreeable ride in the cart, or have been tied on to the back of the horse."

"To be sure not," said Pearson. "You must blame no one but yourself, captain. If you will give your word now you shall come down and eat with us."

"Now, Pearson, does that strike you as being at all a reasonable thing? Of course it doesn't—it can't! But I have a small favour to beg of you, which you can grant or not, just as you think proper."

"I bear you no ill-will, captain, and anything short of putting you in the way of getting off I wouldn't mind doing for you."

"Very good."

"What do you want?"

"Why, as I have been out with you so long, and have had neither bite nor sup, I am as famished as you are. All I want is, for you to bring me some of your good cheer up here and leave me to enjoy it in the best way I am able."

"That's only fair, is it, Jarvis?"

"Oh, fair enough. We are not justified in starving a prisoner to death."

"Very well, then," said Pearson, magnanimously. "I will give you no reason to alter your good opinion of me, if that is all you want."

"And you will let me have a meal?"

"I certainly will."

"Then I am much obliged to you."

"I will send it up at once."

"Many thanks."

Pearson walked round his prisoner and looked at him scrutinisingly.

Satisfied that he was quite secure, he told Francis he was ready to depart.

The magistrate's clerk was a very nervous young man, and it seemed as though the strong-room had even greater terrors for him than the one below.

With great alacrity, then, he crossed the threshold.

Pearson and Jarvis between them saw to the fastening of both doors, as they considered that business too important to be left to any of the subordinates.

"There!" said the former, as they made their way back along the corridor. "If Captain Hawk is clever enough to get out of that, I'll forgive him."

Francis conducted the party to a large plainly-furnished room.

The officers were delighted to see that the large table in the centre was covered with materials for making a very substantial repast.

Without exception, they were as hungry as a pack of wolves.

There was a good deal of confusion before they got settled in their seats; but when this was accomplished, Pearson said:

"Now, then, we will serve the prisoner first, and then that matter will be off our minds."

There was a huge joint of cold roast beef close to the chief police officer, and off this he cut a couple of terrific slices.

One of the large home-baked loaves was then divided into two portions, and a flagon of the fine old ale poured out.

"Now, Jarvis," cried Pearson, "you can be carver, and you, Thompson, come with me upstairs. I will take the prisoner his meal myself, and then I shall be sure that he will be left all right."

The next moment he quitted the room, carrying the key.

Thompson walked behind him with the viands.

"We will be careful how we enter," said the former, when the door of the strong-room was reached. "I have heard some surprising things related of him; and there's nothing like being prepared, and on the safe side."

To this maxim Thompson made no demur.

The doors having been opened, the redoubtable prisoner was found in just the same position he had been left in, but looking, if anything, a trifle more dejected.

Pearson's spirits rose accordingly.

"Here, captain, is a meal fit for a prince; and I hope you will be just enough to say that I have done well by you."

"There are many worse in the world than you, I can see, Pearson."

"Well, here you are! I hope you will enjoy yourself. Put the victuals down on the floor, Thompson, and we will be off."

"You are not going, are you?"

"Yes; why not?"

"Don't you see?"

"See what?"

"Why, you have brought me something to eat and drink, to be sure; but how am I to get bite or sup to my lips, eh?"

Pearson was puzzled.

"I can't loose you," he said; "and that's a fact."

"But am I to starve?"

As usual when in a dilemma, Pearson looked round for Jarvis; but, of course, that useful individual was not this time at his elbow.

"Not loose me!" ejaculated the captain. "You don't mean that, surely?"

"I daren't do it."

"Nonsense! Why not? Surely this place is strong enough to keep a dozen men secure."

"But not a dozen like you, captain."

"Thank you for the compliment. But look here—be reasonable."

"I can't."

"But you must."

"Must?"

"Yes, unless you are resolved to starve me to death, for of course you must see that though the eatables are here they are no good to me."

Pearson uttered something in which the name "Jarvis" was alone distinguishable.

"Stay a moment," continued Captain Hawk. "Without going so far as asking you to set my limbs at liberty—though, mind you, I think that no more than you ought to do under the circumstances—I will only just ask you to slacken the rope that goes through my elbows. If you will grant me that slight favour, I think I can contrive to find the way to my mouth, despite these confounded handcuffs on my wrists."

Pearson, for want of some one better to appeal to in his difficulty, looked at Thompson.

"I don't think there can come much harm of that, do you?"

"No, sir, I don't. He must have something to eat."

"Well, release him. You can take the rope off altogether; but leave the handcuffs on."

Captain Hawk found it no easy task to conceal the satisfaction which this announcement gave him.

But he managed tolerably well.

"I am much obliged to you, Pearson; and rely upon it that those who have treated me best during my captivity will be the best off."

"What do you mean by that speech?"

"Never mind; time, perhaps, will show."

Pearson did not feel very comfortable.

But having issued the command he did not like call it.

Thompson felt decidedly uncomfortable.

He was one of the officers who had ridden in the cart, and he was the first to begin the little pastime of kicking the prisoner in the ribs.

He dreaded the captain's threat all the more on account of its vagueness, and it was most reluctantly that he undid the cord.

Captain Hawk's heart swelled, as well it might, for he knew now he had the command of his limbs

Pearson looked at him musingly; but the captain, in order to appear more at his ease, and to make it seem that he was really hungry, commenced a vigorous assault upon the bread and beef.

This reminded Pearson that the claims of his own appetite were still unsatisfied, and so, without any more hesitation, he quitted the strong-room.

Most particular was he with the fastenings; and when with his own fingers he had made every one secure his spirits revived.

By the time he had reached the room below he found that his men had made a terrific inroad upon the provisions.

"Is all well?" said Jarvis, with his mouth full.

"Yes."

"How does he manage to eat with his elbows tied?"

"We have been obliged to untie the cord."

"But you have not removed the handcuffs?"

"Oh dear no!"

"He's safe enough, then?"

"I hope so."

"At any rate, we will go up every now and then so as to make sure that he is up to none of his tricks."

"Yes; if we do that we need not feel any alarm, I think."

Pearson now, considerably relieved, sat down.

"I am afraid I have gone a little too far," he said.

"No—no. You have not lost your appetite Mr. Pearson?"

"Not a bit of it," replied Jarvis, with a grin. "He means that he feels as though he could eat just twice as much."

There was a general laugh at this; and in the same merry humour they continued their meal.

Ere long, however, Jarvis declared that he would go to look at the prisoner; and as Pearson was anxious to satisfy his inward cravings without interruption, he was allowed to go alone.

In the meantime Captain Hawk had been carefully considering his position.

Some time after the door was closed he continued calmly eating, grumbling, however, at the inconvenience of having no knife and fork, for, of course, such dangerous implements as these were not allowed to find their way into his hands.

"They may be watching me through some little place that I know nothing at all of; and if so, I will try to disarm their suspicions. Besides, I ought for another reason to make a good meal while I have the chance of doing so, because if I am to escape—and that is what I have made up my mind to do—I shall want to make use of all my strength."

After this, Captain Hawk went on eating with a composure and deliberation quite wonderful to behold.

While thus engaged, his thoughts were very busy, and from time to time he cast anxious glances around him in the hope of being able to perceive something that promised him a chance of getting away.

Nothing but the almost perfectly smooth iron walls met his view, and in them he was not able to find the least encouragement.

The terrible storm which had been the primary cause of his being placed in the strong-room was now almost over.

The muttering of the thunder could occasionally be heard in the distance, and more rarely came a feeble flash of lightning.

And as the storm abated the light increased, although the day was fast drawing towards a close.

A slight noise at the door suddenly made the captain start.

He went on eating, however, and then Jarvis made his appearance.

"Oh, you are all right and comfortable, are you?" he ejaculated. "That's all right."

Bang went the door shut again, and Jarvis was gone almost before Captain Hawk was perfectly aware of his presence.

"What the deuce, now," he said, "does he mean by that? Oh, I know! It's plain enough. They are frightened to death now that they know my arms are no longer tied, and they will keep peeping in upon me at frequent intervals until it is time to go."

This occurrence was simple enough, and might have been expected.

But it disconcerted the prisoner greatly, because he had not happened to think of it.

He saw, of course, how much it would interfere with any plan of escape that he might form.

"My chances now are not so good as I fancied them," he said, a little dejectedly.

But he shook off this feeling immediately, and continued:

"No matter: I will make the best of things as they are. My motto is 'Never despair!'"

He now took a deep draught at the flagon; and having done so, proceeded to make a close examination of his prison.

Unfortunately for him, this did not last long, and nothing rewarded his exertions.

In no place could he find the least break or unevenness in the iron walls.

The door was so heavy and so firmly fixed, that after putting forth all his strength he was unable to shake it in the least in its setting.

One thing remained, and that was the grated window.

But this was so high up, and apparently so strong, that he could not derive any hope at all from this direction.

The strong-room contained but one object that might be considered of a movable character.

This was an iron chest or safe, such as are in use for the safe stowage of plate or valuable papers.

Casting his eyes upon this, the captain thought that if he managed to drag it along the floor until it was beneath the window he might be able to reach the bars.

He made the attempt to do so, and his disappointment may be imagined when he found that so great was the weight of the box that it would have required the united strength of two or three men to move it a single inch.

"Never mind," he said, "I may be able to get a peep out for all that."

Running towards that portion of the wall where the opening was situated, he gave a sudden leap upwards.

This enabled him to catch hold of the grating; and having done so, an exertion of strength enabled him to raise his body until he was able to peep out.

The first glance satisfied him that escape in this direction was impracticable.

The wall apparently was of great thickness, and on the outer side another and still stronger grating had been placed.

With a faint sigh he released his hold.

He had not been able to perceive anything save some trees on a bit of rising ground in the distance.

Baffled thus at every turn, a feeling very closely resembling despair—though he would not have admitted it—took possession of the captain's breast.

"Confound their precautions!" he said. "It seems that I am doomed to remain their captive some time longer, and that this halt, which I felt so sure would result in something to my advantage, will do nothing of the sort."

He bit his lips to restrain himself.

"I will slip my hand through the handcuff again," he said, "for fear some one should enter suddenly, and in the meanwhile I will think a little."

Captain Hawk found the process of replacing the handcuff more difficult and painful than drawing it off.

Relieved of the pressure, his hand had swelled a great deal.

But at last the manacle was replaced.

Then sitting down on one corner of the strong box we have mentioned, he allowed his head to sink between his hands, and covering his face, he gave himself up to anxious thought.

"What am I to do?" he said. "Something must be determined on; and yet I am obliged to confess that I do not see the least chance of getting free. Stop a moment, now—I fancy that at the last moment I have got an idea."

He paused

"Yes—yes," he added, with additional spirit, "that idea is worth thinking of. Does it afford me a reasonable chance? I think so. At any rate, I will try."

Captain Hawk's idea is easily explained.

He judged that before very long Jarvis would pay him another visit. so as to make sure that he was in safe custody.

When he did come, the captain wondered whether he could not suddenly spring upon him and make him a prisoner.

The suddenness of this attack would doubtless aid much in its successful termination.

When that was done, a hasty flight through the squire's abode might enable him to get clear off before the officers exactly comprehended what was the matter.

Few persons save Captain Hawk would, we imagine, have given such a desperate, hazardous scheme as this a moment's consideration, or have ventured to believe that there was a chance of success.

But the prisoner, who felt certain that he could not by any means make his position worse, resolved to try it.

The first step, of course, was to pull off the handcuff which he had been at so much pains to replace.

Before, however, he could so much as stir the iron fetter, he heard sounds which told him plainly enough that he was about to receive another visit.

He clenched his teeth hard together, for he had the mortifying thought to bear up against that he was a minute or so too late.

He was only just able to compose his countenance tolerably when the door opened.

This time he had two visitors.

As may be expected, they were no other than Pearson and Jarvis.

"There you are, sir," said the latter, in an elevated voice—"just as I told you, sir: as safe as a church tied to a hedge."

He finished with a loud laugh, and then slapped his superior officer upon the back with so much force as to bring on a violent fit of coughing.

"Ugh—ugh—ugh!" gasped Pearson, trying to recover his breath. "What the devil did you do that for? Ugh—ugh! Don't try it again!"

"Beg pardon, sir!"

"Oh, all right!" answered Pearson, with a hiccup.

Captain Hawk now noticed that they were both partially intoxicated.

They had been paying their respects rather freely to the magistrate's ale, which probably was more potent in its effects than they had imagined it to be.

And if the two chiefs—for so Pearson and Jarvis might be considered—were in this condition, it was only reasonable to presume that the rest were a great deal worse

CHAPTER XLVI.

CAPTAIN HAWK HAS A MYSTERIOUS VISITOR IN THE STRONG-ROOM.

This discovery at once revived the captain's hopes.

Not once had he dared to indulge in the supposition that his captors would throw such a facility in his way as this could hardly fail to be.

But the truth was, the officers were one and all half intoxicated with joy before they began to taste the ale, so that their inebriation was speedily completed.

"Very good, captain," stammered Pearson, who was still half choked by his cough. "We won't keep you in these uncomfortable quarters much longer. We shall be all ready to start very soon now."

With these words the door was again closed.

The fastenings were carefully replaced.

Then silence again followed.

"I shall never have a chance like that again," exclaimed the captain, despondingly. "Had I only been in readiness for an attack, I could doubtless have vanquished both. Then, with a lot of half-tipsy fellows only to contend with, my escape would have been almost a dead certainty."

It was not Captain Hawk's practice, however, to give way to regrets.

Sinking his head in his hands once more, he set to work to think how he should act in the present altered condition of affairs.

There seemed hardly a chance that he would have another visit paid him, except the final one, when, most likely, all would come, in order to lead him forth.

Some other course of action must then be thought about.

His reflections made him for a time unconscious of where he was.

Suddenly, however, he looked up with a start.

While plunged in his reverie, he all at once felt a hand placed upon his shoulder.

If one of the iron walls had suddenly dissolved, his surprise could hardly have been greater.

There had been no warning sound.

He was indeed confident that, however great might have been his abstraction, the iron door had not been opened.

Whose hand was it, then, he felt touch lightly upon his arm?

If he had felt some slight superstitious terror upon looking up it would have been almost excusable.

What he saw, however, on raising his eyes, increased rather than diminished his astonishment, yet at once put an end to the slightest sensation of alarm.

The captain's amazement may, however, be imagined when we state that his uplifted eyes fell upon the form of a young and handsome lady.

She was standing within a couple of paces of him, and her calm, unruffled face showed no signs of trepidation at being alone in such a place.

She was wrapped from head to foot in a simple cloak, but, nevertheless, Captain Hawk could see that her apparel was composed of the richest materials.

Her hand, too, he saw, carried many glittering rings, the aggregate value of which must have been considerable.

But the face, though eminently handsome, was not a pleasing one to look upon.

There was a cold, hard glitter in her eyes, and her lips were compressed in a manner that indicated she was possessed of no ordinary share of determination.

She remained gazing earnestly at the captain for a moment or so after he looked up, as though she was striving to read his character.

Recovering himself from the intense astonishment into which he had been thrown by this unexpected and inexplicable visit, the captain rose and bowed profoundly.

The lady drew back a step, and, gathering her cloak more closely around her, said:

"Do you want to be free?"

Her voice had a hard metallic ring which to the ear sounded just the reverse of musical.

But it was in accordance with her eyes and mouth.

The question so amazed the prisoner that he was unable to reply.

The lady repeated the words, accompanying them with an impatient gesture.

"Do I want to be free?" reiterated the captain.

"Yes—yes! Surely you are not so dull-witted as not to comprehend me?"

"I do understand you, lady, and I trust you will pardon me," he said, with a bow, "but your appearance was so sudden and extraordinary that——"

She cut him short by another hasty wave of the arm

"I know all about that. Do you want to be free?"

"Do I want to live?"

"Enough! You can be set at liberty."

The captain's amazement increased.

"Am I the sport of some dream?" he muttered.

"No. It is reality. I am willing to set you at liberty."

"Upon what condition?"

"That you shall know presently."

"Let me know now."

"Impossible! Hark! Can you not hear!"

The sound made by the approach of the whole troop of police officers could be distinctly heard.

"Quick!" she continued, with considerable excitement. "Another moment and the chance will be for ever gone!"

"It must be too late now."

"No—no! I tell you it is not too late. Do you consent? Choose between liberty and freedom. Are you decided?"

"I am. I must be free!"

"This way, then."

She seized him by the sleeve of his coat and hurried him across the iron room to the door by which he had entered.

This, he now for the first time noticed, was standing ajar.

To pass through this took but a second.

"Quick! Put up the fastenings," she said, in an anxious whisper. "If you make the least sound you are lost."

Captain Hawk did her bidding well.

He was now standing in that square place which we have described as being situated between the two iron doors.

On the outside of the other door Captain Hawk could hear his foes.

He was unable to think what was the reason they were so long.

The fact was, however, all were deeply under the influence of the squire's ale.

Pearson had insisted upon carrying both key and candle.

He had to make many attempts before he could find the keyhole; but, succeeding at last, he held out the candle for some one to take.

He relaxed his hold upon it a moment too soon.

It fell to the ground, and was extinguished in a moment.

The man who ought to have taken the candle made a sudden dash in the hope of catching it, but in trying to do so he came with considerable force against Pearson, who, being anything but steady on his legs, went sprawling on to the ground in a moment.

Cursing and swearing, he seized hold of something to get up by.

The first thing that came into his hand was the skirt of Jarvis's coat, and, as that worthy was no surer upon his feet than his commander, the drag caused him to overbalance, and the confusion was redoubled.

The others now bawled for lights, and raised such an intolerable clamour that all the inhabitants of the mansion came rushing to the scene, making sure that nothing less than the violent escape of the prisoner could have happened.

Lights were procured by the command of Squire Fielding, who felt that he should be greatly rejoiced when his troublesome visitors had taken their departure.

The iron door was now safely unlocked, and the strong room entered without the occurrence of any misadventure whatever.

But no sooner was the door pushed back upon its hinges—no sooner was the threshold crossed—than a shout of dismay came from every throat.

The prisoner had disappeared.

Pearson at first could not credit the evidence of his own eyes.

"Jarvis—Jarvis!"

"Yes, Mr. Pearson?"

"Am I blind?"

"I think not."

"Is the prisoner gone?"

"I cannot see him."

"Done—done, by ——!"

Pearson uttered a howl of agony, and tearing off his hat and wig, flung them violently upon the floor

The others hastily rushed in and dispersed themselves over every corner.

But no trace of the prisoner could be found.

"What's all this?" asked the squire, amazed. "The prisoner gone? Impossible!"

"I hope it is, sir," said Jarvis, lugubriously.

"Was the door fastened?"

"Both, your worship, as you saw."

"Then how could he have gone?"

The officers could only stare blankly at each other

No mystery could be more complete.

Again they peeped and pried into every corner.

Of course with the same result.

"Well, but this must be seen into," said the magistrate, with considerable agitation. "Such a thing as this must not take place in my house and remain unexplained. He cannot have made himself air."

This discovery had chased away all the ale fumes from Pearson's brow.

He was sober enough now.

"Your worship," he said, speaking with more calmness and deliberation than he had done hitherto, "I will take my oath I saw him sitting on that iron chest only a few minutes ago."

"So did I—so did I!" cried Jarvis.

"He can't have got into it and hidden himself there, can he?" ejaculated Pearson, seizing eagerly upon this very unlikely supposition.

He darted across the strong-room at full speed.

But it was only to find out that which he might have been told.

The iron chest was strongly secured by several locks.

"He is not there," said the squire. "I would defy anyone to open that plate-chest without the proper keys."

"But where is he, your worship?"

"That we must find out."

"But how?"

"I leave that to your sagacity."

Pearson dashed his fists against his head in his despair.

"Your worship," said Jarvis.

"Well—well?"

"Are you sure there is no means of leaving this strong-room?"

"None but that by which you have entered.'

Jarvis was in despair too.

"That inner door was just as you left it?"

"It appeared to be so."

This caused a fresh examination to be made.

But nothing peculiar could be seen.

To all appearance the door had been untouched—certainly not one of the fastenings had been tampered with.

The squire's bewilderment was very great; and after gazing all around the iron-plated walls, he gave up all attempts to solve the mystery.

Pearson, however, and Jarvis too, gradually recovered their ordinary calmness.

The loss of the prisoner had a very sobering effect upon the whole body of officers—the way in which the influence of the ale had subsided was wonderful to see.

"Mr. Pearson," said Jarvis, "let me have a word with you."

"Speak on. But it can matter little what you say."

"Don't give way too much to despair, sir. Recollect how short a time it is since we both saw him here."

"And what consolation are we to find in that?"

"Does it not make it certain that he has not got far away?"

"You revive my hopes."

"I wish to do so."

"Go on—go on!"

"It's my belief, and, right or wrong, I may as well let you know it—I say it's my belief that he is in hiding somewhere close at hand, and that he will make no attempt to leave these premises until after we have done so."

"The latter part of your speech seems likely and reasonable enough; but as to the first——"

"Well, sir?"

"Where the devil can he be hidden? that's what I should like to know!"

"I can't tell you, sir; but it's my belief for all that."

"But there is nothing like a hiding-place to be seen."

"Granted, Mr. Pearson; but what more likely than that there is some secret recess in connection with such a place as this?"

The supposition was greedily seized upon.

"If there is," continued Jarvis, "how likely Captain Hawk would be to find it out!"

"But how are we to tell?"

"Let us ask the squire. It is hardly possible that there can be any secret recess without his being cognizant of it."

Pearson took the hint.

"Ahem!" he said, sidling up to the magistrate. "Excuse me, your worship, but is there no secret recess in connection with this place which the prisoner may have been sharp enough to find out, and in which he has concealed himself?"

The squire hesitated a moment, and then, in rather a stammering voice, he replied:

"To the best of my knowledge there is no such place in this room."

"Will your worship allow us to make the attempt to find out?"

"Most certainly. How shall you set about it?"

"Sounding with the butt-end of a pistol will do it, I fancy. Just try, Jarvis."

With great willingness the police officer drew forth a large pistol.

With the brass-bound butt of this he tapped sharply against the wall in a systematic manner, so that no space of more than a foot square escaped his examination.

This consumed much time, and unfortunately produced no result.

A uniform sound was returned by the wall wherever it was struck, giving no indications of hollowness whatever.

"It's no go," said Jarvis, with a groan. "He is gone, and I am afraid we shall see him no more."

"There is no probability of his having found a way through the grating?"

"None whatever; that would be a perfect impossibility."

The officers were now at a dead lock.

Jarvis, however, was busily cudgelling his brains.

"Stop," he said—"not so fast! My brain seems muddled. Let me think the whole matter over again. Only a few minutes ago I saw him with my own eyes sitting on the edge of that box yonder. He had the handcuffs on then, I am certain, for I saw them. Well, now we come in and he is gone, and we are satisfied that he is not hidden in the walls. The conclusion is clear—I see it now."

"The devil you do!" said Pearson. "Just enlighten me, will you?"

"Yes. The conclusion — the inevitable conclusion is——"

"What?"

"That Captain Hawk has some friend beneath this roof."

"Impossible!"

"I say he has either a friend or an accomplice, and that person, whoever it may be, has unfastened the door and let him out."

This was quite a fresh view of the case to the rest, and they were astonished accordingly.

But Pearson only sighed, and gloomily shook his head.

"What is the matter?"

"You forget that I held the key of the door in my hand all the time. I never once relaxed my grasp upon it."

"But there may be two keys," suggested Jarvis. "Perhaps his worship will inform us."

"There is but one."

"Only one?"

"And no means of gaining admittance to the strong-room without it?"

Again the squire hesitated.

"Your supposition that Captain Hawk has an accomplice here is most unreasonable and absurd!" he said.

"But excuse me, your worship—not impossible."

"It is not one of your number who has set the prisoner at liberty, is it?"

"Certainly not," said Pearson. "I can answer for that."

"Very well, then: I will answer for all my household. I am confident no member of it would do anything of the kind."

"It is an unfortunate business," pursued Jarvis, "and you must not blame us if, in sifting it to the bottom—as we are bound by our duty to do—we put you to a little trouble and inconvenience."

The squire muttered some reply.

"As well as I remember," Jarvis went on, "your worship did not give an answer to my last question."

"What was it?"

"Whether there was any means of gaining admission to this room without the key which Mr. Pearson kept in his safe custody?"

The squire did not reply for some moments.

Jarvis waited in the direst suspense to hear what he should say.

At length, with great reluctance, the magistrate said:

"If I answer your question truthfully," he said, "I can only do so by the revelation of a secret which has been zealously guarded for many years, and which I am consequently not certain whether I am bound to reveal."

"That's it!" cried Jarvis.

"What do you mean?"

"Captain Hawk has discovered the secret."

"I can scarcely think it possible," said the squire, thoughtfully. "However, I am determined not to rest under the least imputation of obstructing the ends of justice, therefore the secret shall be made known."

The curiosity and interest manifested after this speech was uttered made Captain Hawk for the moment forgotten.

The squire walked towards the door.

He crossed the threshold, and stood in the little lobby—for so we may term it—between the two doors.

There was an anxious and suspenseful pause.

"You observe," said the squire, overcoming the last lingerings of reluctance—"you observe that there is no lock upon this second or inner door, and the fastenings are all upon this side."

"Yes," said Jarvis, excitedly; "and anyone standing where we now stand would have no sort of difficulty in getting admission to the iron room."

"None whatever. The fastenings would have to be removed, that is all."

At this all the officers exchanged glances.

"And you mean to say, your worship, that there is a way of getting to this lobby without passing through the door I hold the key of?"

The squire inclined his head in token of assent.

"Then, your worship, you may make yourself perfectly assured that some one else in this house knows of this secret, and that some one has liberated Captain Hawk."

Squire Fielding looked deeply troubled, but he said:

"I cannot and will not believe it. However, I will show you this other way, and leave you to make what you can of it."

So saying, he pressed heavily upon the wall at one side of the lobby.

It gave way bodily before the pressure, disclosing a narrow, dark, and dusty passage.

"There it is!" he said. "I have never before confided this secret to a soul, nor do I believe that anyone in the house so much as suspects the existence of such a place. If you will follow me, I will show you where it leads. Why it was constructed matters not. It must have been done when the house was built, and that was a hundred years before my birth."

The exploration of such a place as this was of itself interesting, but how intense must have been the feelings of those who entered it under the present circumstances!

The light of the candle was more than ever needed in this place; in fact, its yellow, sickly beams were scarcely sufficient to reveal the smooth, dust-covered walls.

Apparently, the secret passage followed the angles of the different rooms, for every now and then the party came to an abrupt corner.

Its total length was probably about a hundred feet.

But as first of all there were steps leading upwards, then others leading downwards, and then more going upwards, it was exceedingly difficult for those who traversed it to come to any clear conclusion as to whether they were on the ground floor or up at the top of the building.

At length, however, another secret door was pushed open, and the officers found themselves in an octagonal chamber, which seemingly had at some previous time been used as an oratory.

From this chamber there was to all appearance but one mode of egress, and that was by means of a small oak door, the blackened wood of which formed a contrast to the unrelieved whiteness of the walls.

"He is not here, you see," said the squire, "nor is there the slightest trace of his presence."

"And is there any way of getting out of this place save by that door yonder?" said Pearson.

"None at all."

"You are quite sure of that, your worship?"

"Quite sure."

"Very good. Then be kind enough to tell us where that door leads."

"It communicates with my wife's apartments."

"Are they occupied?"

"They are. My wife is unfortunately so afflicted with nervousness that she is a complete invalid, and it is only on the rarest occasions that she quits these rooms."

Pearson and Jarvis exchanged glances, as though both

had something they wished to say, yet hesitated to give their thoughts utterance.

At a sign from his superior the latter spoke:

"Beg pardon, your worship — we are very sorry, but——"

"You wish to see these rooms?"

"We do."

"Surely you do not think my wife the accomplice? That would be too absurd."

"It would, your worship. Yet if we were to enter, it is possible that we might obtain some information of importance."

"Perhaps so, too," answered the squire, "for, unlikely though it may be that Captain Hawk has made use of this passage at all, yet if he has done so he must have passed through the adjoining room, and that he cannot have done without being seen by my wife."

"And your worship will kindly allow us to enter?"

"Certainly. I long to find him quite as much as you do. I could not rest with the suspicion haunting me that he was concealed somewhere about the premises."

"It would be most unpleasant."

"It would indeed. All I have to ask of you is, that you will be kind enough to remember my wife's invalid condition, and abstain from violence of any kind."

The assurance was readily and promptly given; and then the squire, stepping forward, knocked at the oaken door.

The faint sound of a voice was just audible.

The squire raised the latch and entered.

The officers, with their curiosity rather increased than otherwise, saw that the room with which the door communicated was not of any great extent, nor furnished with particular luxury.

There was a thick carpet on the floor.

Opposite to them was another door, standing partly open, through which could be perceived a much handsomer apartment.

It was occupied by a lady, who was stretched at full length upon a massive couch.

She was holding a handkerchief to her face, so that her features could not be very well distinguished.

The paleness of her countenance, however, amply bore out what the squire had said respecting her invalid condition.

The chamber was loaded with some powerful perfume.

No doubt it emanated from the handkerchief.

Turning her eyes languidly towards the door, she raised her eyebrows in token of surprise, but gave no other manifestation of astonishment at this visit.

The squire, however, advanced quietly, as though afraid of doing anything to increase her discomposure.

But Jarvis, who was keener-sighted than most men, fancied that the lady shrank back as the squire advanced, as though she would, if possible, have sunk into the soft cushions on which she was reclining.

Jarvis also saw that the squire was older than his wife by considerably more than a score of years.

"My dear," he said, "as I daresay you must have heard, the notorious Captain Hawk has been brought here to-night and locked up in the strong-room, from which he has mysteriously escaped."

"Lucy has just told me so," was the reply, given in a nervous, agitated voice, "and it has so distressed me that I have been obliged to send her for a stimulant. Oh dear!"

The lady looked very much as though she was about to faint.

"These police officers from London," continued the squire, "have reason to suspect that he has come this way."

The lady screamed, and, opening her eyes, manifested the keenest sensations of fright.

"Fear nothing," said Pearson, with a low bow. "No harm can possibly come to your ladyship while we are by. But we wish to know whether our suspicions are well founded."

"Your suspicions?" repeated the lady, starting, and speaking with more clearness than she had hitherto done.

"Yes, your ladyship. We fancy he has come this way and wish to make a thorough search of these rooms."

But her ladyship sank off into her former half-fainting condition, and made no reply.

At this moment a young girl entered the room

This was the lady's personal attendant.

She carried in her hand a small salver, on which was a bottle filled with some dark-coloured liquid, and also a wine-glass.

"Quick, Lucy!" said the squire. "Your mistress is fainting! You ought to have known better than cause her so much alarm."

The young girl received this rebuke in silence.

"Do your duty quickly," said the squire, to Pearson; then, turning to Lucy, he added:

"How long has your mistress quitted her rooms today?"

"Not at all to-day, sir," was the answer. "She has been so very much worse that she has not been able to stir from the sofa."

"And have you been with her all the time?"

"Very nearly, sir."

"And you have seen nothing of Captain Hawk in these apartments?"

"Heaven forbid!" ejaculated the young girl, her eyes dilating with terror.

"You see," said the squire, "it is impossible for him to have come this way. However, satisfy yourselves by searching, but be as speedy as you can."

Pearson and Jarvis alone advanced.

After what they had heard it seemed quite useless to think of making a search at all.

But they resolved to satisfy themselves by a look around, so as not to leave the least room for a doubt.

The room in which her ladyship was, revealed nothing.

The adjoining chamber was a bedroom, and into this they only gave a glance.

It presented every appearance of quietude.

Baffled now completely, and deprived of their last hope of finding their prisoner, they, after many apologies, withdrew into the oratory.

"Lucy," said the lady, rising quickly, and speaking with surprising animation, "you can leave me now. I shall not want you for some time. When you return, I shall expect you to give me a full account of what takes place."

The girl bowed and departed.

CHAPTER XLVII.

CAPTAIN HAWK IS MADE ACQUAINTED WITH THE NATURE OF THE SERVICE REQUIRED OF HIM.

When Captain Hawk was standing in the lobby between the two doors of the strong-room, with his mysterious visitant beside him, and heard the noise made by his foes without, he gave himself up for lost.

And but for the accident we have related, which retarded the opening of the door, there can be little doubt that he would have been discovered.

But before he could recover from his uneasy sensations, the cloaked lady seized him again by the sleeve and dragged him forward.

"Silence!" she whispered, energetically. "Not a word, or you are lost!"

A very faint sound followed, like the closing of a door that moved stiffly upon its hinges.

The loud voices of the officers and the sound of scuffling then came very distinctly upon their ears.

"Follow me," said the unknown. "Never mind the darkness. Step forward confidently, yet quietly. The path is clear."

Captain Hawk, his brain still in a whirl, complied with these directions.

Every now and then his invisible guide would pronounce the word "Steps," adding "up" or "down," as the case required.

At length the octagonal room was reached.

Into this a few faint beams of twilight penetrated.

But, viewed in contrast with the pitchy darkness of the passage, it seemed like absolute daylight.

The captain glanced inquisitively at his companion.

But she allowed him no opportunity to gaze at her.

Opening quickly the oaken door, she beckoned to him to follow.

Then crossing the ante-room, they paused in the apartment where the invalid lady had been found upon the couch.

"You must hide," said the lady, to Captain Hawk. "It is quite possible that they may trace you here. At any rate, the house is almost certain to be searched as soon as your disappearance is discovered."

Captain Hawk glanced around him rather apprehensively.

"For my sake you must not be found," she added—"so compose yourself."

"I am composed enough," was the answer, "but puzzled to know why this extraordinary interest in my welfare is taken by one who appears an entire stranger to me."

"You shall know all about that in good time. In the meanwhile, it is absolutely necessary for you to carry out my directions to the very letter. Look—here is a hiding-place that will serve you for the present. Enter."

"But——"

"Be quick, or you will be too late. Leave all to me, and, no matter what takes place, do not move a muscle. If you do, you will destroy not only yourself but me."

While speaking these words, the lady had lifted the lid of a large chest, which had been covered and made up so as to resemble an ottoman.

But Captain Hawk scarcely liked the idea of confining himself in such a place.

The lady stamped her foot impatiently.

Then came a faint tap-tap at the door.

Captain Hawk started, and his hand, by the mere force of habit, was plunged into the breast of his apparel.

"Hush!" said the lady. "There is no cause for alarm. Be still."

Then, in a louder voice, she said:

"Is that you, Lucy?"

"Yes, my lady."

"Be quick—fetch me a bottle of my stimulant immediately!"

"Yes, my lady."

"That is over. Now, once for all, will you enter?"

"I will; but——"

"Never mind any reservations. Restrain your curiosity. I tell you again you are safe if you remain still, and that you shall know all in good time."

Captain Hawk no longer hesitated, though it must be stated that it was with far from comfortable feelings that he suffered the lid to be shut down upon him.

When this was done, however, he resolved to abide by what the lady had said to the very letter.

The lady, then, going to a side-table, poured from a richly-cut bottle a quantity of liquid into her handkerchief.

The odour was very powerful, and speedily saturated the whole atmosphere of the room.

Extending herself then on the couch, she awaited the coming of her maid.

Before the squire and the police officers reached the door she had had time thoroughly to recover her composure.

What ensued the reader is already aware of

The feelings of Captain Hawk, however, when Pearson and Jarvis began their search, we cannot describe.

But, faithful to his promise to the lady who had played so incomprehensible a part, he neither moved nor made a sound.

Some moments elapsed, after the second departure of Lucy, before the lady ventured to rise from the couch.

Her first proceeding was to cross stealthily to the door and listen.

Satisfied that no one was near, she shot a small bolt into its socket, so as to secure herself from any sudden interruption.

Before raising the lid of the chest in which she had hidden the highwayman, she seemed deeply stirred by inward emotions.

With a faltering hand she poured out a glassful of the liquid which the girl had brought, and swallowed it at a draught.

The effects of it were immediately visible.

Her eyes burned, and her cheeks flushed.

All tokens of agitation passed away.

She raised the lid of the chest.

Captain Hawk gladly enough sprang forth.

"Hush—hush! Silence is required, above all things. Sit down. You need not fear an interruption."

The captain complied, and then occupied himself in more attentively surveying the lady than he had yet had the opportunity of doing.

But he saw little that was remarkable.

Her lips were ruddier and she drew her breath quicker than before.

Resuming her seat upon the sofa, she paused for a few moments, as though making up her mind how to frame her thoughts into words.

"You may guess," she said, "that I should not have taken all this trouble and run so much personal risk to save you from your enemies, had I not some powerful motive for doing so."

The captain inclined his head

"I shall tell you what service it is that I shall require you to perform for me; and when it is done you will be enabled to leave this house secretly and in safety. Is that reasonable?"

"I should have no hesitation in replying," answered the captain, "could I but form some idea of the nature of the service which is required of me. As it is, I am completely in the dark."

Captain Hawk spoke with considerable uneasiness, for he felt that he was now to a very great extent pledged to do whatever might be the lady's bidding, and however repugnant it might personally be to him.

This, then, was the chief reason of his anxiety.

"You must first listen to something I have to tell you," the lady began. "It will serve to pass away the time, for it would not be safe for you to leave the house now, nor has the time arrived when you will be able to do my bidding. Will you listen?"

"Most certainly."

"Suppose, then, that, by a series of cruel circumstances and unwearied persecutions, a young girl was forced into a marriage which for many reasons was most odious to her, should you not feel full of compassion for her unhappy fate?"

"Unquestionably."

"And supposing, too, that this young girl had set her affections upon one who loved her sincerely and devotedly, and that she was parted from him, never to see him again, while her husband's age was double hers, his thoughts and feelings entirely at variance with her own, and his very presence absolutely hateful—should you not think there was a still stronger claim upon your sympathy?"

"I should indeed," murmured the captain, wondering greatly to what this prelude would lead.

"Can you conceive a fate harder than this, or an existence more unendurable?—to know that death alone could put an end to all this wretchedness? Should you think that such wrongs could be tamely borne and submitted to?—should you blame that hapless victim of a disgusting, enforced marriage, if, instead of resigning herself to her hateful lot, she cast about her for some means of putting a period to her misery?"

Captain Hawk did not make a direct reply to this question, but said:

"Am I to infer that the situation you have so vividly portrayed is your own—that you are the victim of which you speak?"

"And what if I am?"

"You have my sincere commiseration."

"But that is not what I want. I require something more—your co-operation, your aid, to free me from this hideous bondage, and I depend upon you to do it."

Her excitement was now terrible to witness.

Her eyes burned like coals of fire, and her whole frame quivered like an aspen.

"But how?" said the captain, in a deep voice, and fixing his eyes upon her as he asked the question.

"Surely," she said, "you are not so dull as to be unable to suggest the means by which my freedom is to be obtained? You know there is but one way."

"And what is that?"

"You force me to speak out. But I will not flinch *The one way is the removal of my hated husband!*"

The last words sounded more like the hissing of some venomous serpent than the accents of a woman's voice.

"What! murder him?" said the captain, with a thrill of horror.

"Hush—hush! Do not pronounce that awful word in so loud a tone. I did not say it."

[CAPTAIN HAWK'S STRUGGLE WITH THE MASTIFF.]

Captain Hawk felt his blood turn cold as the next words, calmly and evenly uttered, fell upon his ears.

"The service I require in return for securing your freedom is the death of my husband, Squire Fielding. Do not shrink; but remember that but for my interposition you would at this moment have been in the hands of your foes. Your daily life is nothing but one unvarying scene of violence. Bloodshed can be no fresh thing to you, and nothing for you to shrink from. Let me, then, hear nothing of conscience and compunctions · such feelings must be strangers to your breast."

The captain was about to make some violent reply; but by an effort he restrained himself.

He was conscious, too, that what the lady said was neither altogether unreasonable nor absurd.

"Hear me out," she went on, perceiving his inclination to speak. "When I have done you can give me your reply. What I require can be done without any risk or danger to yourself, and without any circumstance to cast suspicion upon me. I can so arrange it that my husband shall come in and find you here. Self-defence will compel you to attack him in order that you may secure your own escape; then one blow, and all is over. I shall clear myself without difficulty, for I shall say that you, by threats of instant death, compelled me to keep secret your presence. Then I shall be free—free—once more free, and this terrible life—than which the most abject slavery in a foreign land would be preferable—will be at an end! I shall be free!"

The last words were repeated with thrilling intensity.

Despite the horror with which he was filled while listening to the words of this terrible woman, the captain could not help experiencing the deepest compassion for her unhappy fate.

But what he had heard filled him with so many conflicting emotions that now, when the time came for him to speak, he felt that he could not command his utterance.

The lady went on with an ever-increasing excitement:

"What I have suffered since the consummation of this unholy union no words, however powerful, can convey more than a feeble idea. By simulating this indisposition —which is not all unreal—I have been able to keep myself more out of my husband's company than I could have done otherwise. But I cannot endure it. My only hope is in you."

"But if I refuse?"

"Refuse!" she ejaculated, as though the bare possibility of such a thing had never once entered her thoughts —"refuse! No—no! You cannot think of refusal. That would be too base even for a highwayman!"

"But suppose it?"

"For what reason?"

"Merely suppose that I refuse to execute your purpose."

"What should I do? I should call in the officers instantly, and consign you to your well-merited fate. Pah! But say no more on such a foolish topic. Do you wish to make me believe that you, who would not scruple to take a man's life on the highway for the sake of what few shillings he might have in his purse, would yet refuse to do no more in order to purchase your liberty? If it is gold you wish to exact in addition, name the sum which will remove your scruples, and you shall have it."

Captain Hawk was silent.

He found himself in a delicate position, and one of peculiar difficulty.

At any time it would have been hard for him to come to a rapid conclusion upon such a matter; but now that he was harassed by the dangers of his own situation it seemed well-nigh impossible.

The lady could see that some kind of inward struggle was going on in his breast, and clasping her hands rigidly together, she endeavoured to ascertain his thoughts by watching his features.

Captain Hawk was much shocked and surprised at what had fallen from the lady's lips, though when he came to reflect he could not help admitting that her position was a most dreadful one, and her fate hard enough to drive her into absolute madness.

He could tell she was growing impatient.

Yet how to answer her he knew not.

All he could think of was to make the attempt to turn her from further contemplation of her dreadful purpose.

Fixing his eyes upon her, he said, in deep, low tones:

"Are you in earnest?"

"Earnest!" she repeated, her eyes flashing suddenly. "What do you mean?"

"In what you have just said."

"About my husband?"

She shuddered at the name.

"Yes."

"Why do you ask so idle a question? My wrongs have now worked me up to such a pitch that nothing but an immediate termination of this life of worse than serfdom can appease me."

"And should I consent," said the captain, "what guarantee should I have that you would not betray me to my foes?"

"I will give you any that you wish to name; and if it is money that you want, name your price and you shall have it."

Captain Hawk bent a gaze upon her which she could scarce withstand.

"It is not that," he said. "No amount of money would tempt me. Do you not know that were this deed committed you would be as guilty as myself, and that you——"

She waved her hand imperiously for silence.

"I will take upon myself the responsibility of my own actions. But can it be really possible that I have taken all this trouble for a coward? Can popular report be so far from the truth?"

"Those who know me," answered the captain, "will be able to tell you whether I am a coward. If to shrink from committing murder is cowardice, then I plead guilty to the accusation."

The lady looked at him contemptuously.

"I made mistake," she said. "I took you to be a man resolute and fearless; I know you to be neither, or you would at the first have refused me."

"I should have done so but for the sense I had of the obligation I was under to you."

"Then you have the common honesty to confess that I rendered you a service?"

"A most inestimable one, lady, and that is why I hesitated. Had it laid in my power to do your bidding there would have been no need to utter another word. All I ask now is, whether you will listen to me for a moment."

She made a sign to him to proceed.

"Your lot is hard enough to bear, no doubt," he began; "but even you at this moment, in the midst of your distress, must be infinitely happier than you can be with the weight of your husband's murder on your soul."

"No sermonising," she interrupted. "What can be more out of character coming from a highwayman? It is absurd!"

She laughed again that sharp ringing laugh which had sounded so unpleasantly in the captain's ears.

"Tell me," she added, "if I do not adopt the means I have mentioned, how am I to gain my liberty? My endurance has been pushed to its furthest limit—I can bear it no longer. I must and will be free!"

"There must be many methods," said the captain. "Why not fly—why not leave this roof for ever? You would then remain crimeless."

She appeared to be struck by this remark, and remained a moment or so in silent reflection.

"Alas!" she said, "I have nowhere to go, and I fear it would be impossible to leave this place without my husband's knowledge; or if I did, he would infallibly overtake me before I had gone many miles. I should then have more to suffer than I have now."

She poured out another glassful of the powerful aromatic mixture, and drank it at a draught.

That this liquid, whatever it might be, had the quality of producing intense excitement was quite manifest.

Her eyes and cheeks again burned, and her respiration became hurried.

The captain, as he gazed upon her, felt himself moved to commiseration.

It was indeed saddening to note the result of this unhappy marriage.

"Listen," she said. "Flight is impossible! The idea must be renounced at once. There is one way, and only one. I must be rid of him for ever. Shrink no longer. Pity me, and tell me what amount in money, joined to the service you have rendered me, will induce you to do my bidding."

"Alas! lady," he replied, "I would to heaven you had left me in the strong-room to my fate! I do indeed pity you! I feel that it is ungrateful to make you no return for the risk you have run. But I cannot: it is impossible! Bad as I am and have been, my hands have never yet been reddened by murder!"

"No more words—no more words! You must now choose your own fate. Either consent to what I demand, or I will summon the officers to this apartment."

"I cannot consent," was the answer. "Summon the officers if you will."

He folded his arms as he spoke.

The lady, who had put her hand upon the bell-pull, paused irresolutely.

She was struck, as well she might be, at the extraordinary calmness the highwayman displayed.

"I will give you another moment to reflect," she said. "If I once pull the bell it will be too late."

"I have reflected," he said. "Nothing will change my determination."

"But, remember," she urged, "it is not actual murder. When he comes in, he will try to seize you. There will be a struggle, and in that struggle he must fall."

But Captain Hawk shook his head.

"In any other way you can command me," he said. "I am full of anxiety to requite the obligation I am under to you. On my part, I ask you to reflect."

"Alas—alas! miserable creature that I am," she exclaimed, releasing her hold upon the bell, and bursting into tears, "I have betrayed myself, and all to no purpose! I am now in your power."

"Fear not that I shall make use of my knowledge to your prejudice," he replied. "That I will never—never do. But abandon the dreadful thoughts that now hold possession of your mind. If this life is, as you say, insupportable——"

"It is—it is."

"Then leave it. There is the opportunity now for you to make your escape, if you will but avail yourself of it."

"How so—how so?"

"I will aid you. I have little doubt that I can get you away in safety; and having done so, I will accompany you whither soever you choose, nor will I leave you until you say that you are in safety."

"What?" she said, scornfully. "Must I for that wretch's sake debase myself so far? Elope with a highwayman? What would be said of me then? No—no! That is impossible. That is a disgrace which I could never—never survive!"

"Would it not be better than murder?"

"I tell you it is not murder."

"And I maintain that it is, and in your own heart you must be conscious of the sophistry your lips utter. Look! Night has already set in. No one need know that you depart in company with me, or that I have been in any way instrumental in your flight. I will solemnly declare to leave you whenever you think proper to command me."

It was quite evident that the captain's urgings were not without their effect.

But the unhappy woman had brooded so long over her husband's death that she was unable for some time to divest herself of the idea.

There was a long interval of silence, during which the captain listened attentively.

Occasionally the uproar made by the officers in searching the mansion floated to his ears.

"Hark!" said the lady. "While such a vigilant lookout as that is maintained, what chance can there be of escape?"

"It will be best to wait a little while. But these officers are dunderheads, and will almost let a prisoner walk away under their very noses."

The lady was thinking still.

Captain Hawk could tell as well as if she had said so, that she was debating whether she should accompany him or not.

That for more reasons than one she should shrink from doing so he could easily understand.

It was certain, too, that if she decided to accompany him, it would much multiply the difficulty of escaping.

But this he cared not for.

He was deeply grateful for the service which she had performed, and, as he had told her, was most anxious to requite it.

At this juncture there was an interruption in the shape of a faint knocking at the door.

"It is only my girl Lucy," said the lady. "You need be under no apprehension."

"But I must hide?"

"Oh yes! Conceal yourself behind that curtain. As there will be no search for you, that will be a sufficient hiding-place."

Captain Hawk at once took the hint, and placed himself behind the massive folds of the window curtains.

The door was opened, and the girl entered.

Captain Hawk, by a slight movement, was enabled not only to hear but to see what took place.

He was wondering whether Lucy was in the secrets of her mistress.

The question she asked, however, led him to infer that she was not.

"Have they found him, Lucy?"

"No, my lady."

"Have they searched the house?"

"From top to bottom. There is not, I believe, a corner they have not pried into."

"And without result?"

"Quite."

"And what do they say?"

"The mystery baffles them all."

"But what opinions have they formed?"

"They fancy by some means or other he must have got out of the building and made off."

"Indeed!"

"Yes; but master says that is impossible, and that he is certain the robber is in the house somewhere."

A deep frown settled upon the lady's brow.

"He has had a close watch set all round outside, so that no one can leave unseen," continued Lucy; "and he has declared that he will search every inch of the premises but what he'll find him. Isn't it dreadful, my lady, that such a character can be under this roof?"

"Very dreadful, if such is the case," answered the lady, impatiently.

"Then do you think he has got off?"

"There can be but little doubt of it. It is ridiculous to think he could escape such a search."

"That's just what the officers say; but master sticks to his opinion."

"Very well. You can leave me again, and don't interrupt me unless you have something very important to tell me."

"Yes, my lady.

The girl, evidently without the remotest suspicion that Captain Hawk was so near her, quitted the room again.

The lady, as before, took the precaution of slipping the bolt into the socket.

"There!" she cried, turning round. "You see how it is. It is impossible to escape. He must die!"

"Not by my hand. And as to escape, believe me, I have managed things far more difficult than this."

"And do you think it possible to get away?"

"Quite possible. There is time yet. Make up your mind whether you will avail yourself of the present opportunity."

"I will go. I am almost distracted. Heaven forgive me if I am wrong; but this existence is unendurable!"

"You have chosen rightly," said the captain; "and paradoxical and ridiculous as it may sound to your ears, you will find that in this matter a highwayman will conduct himself as carefully as a man who prides himself upon his honour."

The lady smiled, but was silent.

"When will you make the attempt?"

"Now if you wish it."

"Nay, I will leave you to arrange everything. When you are in readiness for the attempt you will find I shall not keep you waiting."

The lady was one of those who, having made up their minds to the adoption of any course, cling to it steadfastly.

"Enough!" answered the captain.

As he pronounced the word, he crossed the room to the window.

The curtains were drawn completely across it, and he was careful to draw them aside in such a manner as would prevent him from being seen by anyone without.

The recess between the curtains and the window was almost dark, so he had but little difficulty in looking out.

The window he found commanded a view of a kind of yard, the floor of which was between ten and twelve feet below him.

This was almost all he was able to make out with the window closed.

He watched for some time; but seeing nothing move, and hearing no sound, he gently undid the fastenings of the window and allowed the casement to open a little way.

He was now able to decide that not one of his foes happened to be in the yard, and the obscurity was so great that there was little fear of his proceedings being visible from any of the other windows.

Turning round, he was surprised to find the lady at his side.

He was about to speak to her when a succession of loud knocks upon the outer door startled both.

CHAPTER XLVIII.

CAPTAIN HAWK FINDS HIMSELF IN FRESH PERIL.—THE STRUGGLE WITH THE MASTIFF.

For a second the lady stood like one paralysed.

Even the blood forsook the cheeks of Captain Hawk when the clamorous summons for admission first came upon his ear.

"What is to be done?" he asked,

Almost before he had put the question, the lady had recovered her wonted calmness.

"Close the windows silently," she said, "and follow me."

The captain obeyed instantly.

She raised the lid of the false ottoman.

"Quick, for your life's sake!" she said. "No remarks. Once there, I tell you you are safe."

Captain Hawk by no means felt assured of this.

But there was no resource for him save compliance with the lady's dictates, and, though it was most unwillingly, he entered.

She shut down the lid, and replaced the cushions on the top.

They presented not the least sign of having been disturbed, and it would have required some one with an acuter intellect than the police officers possessed to have guessed that it was a hiding-place.

All that we have just described took place with wonderful rapidity.

The knocking had been discontinued, but now it recommenced.

"The delay, slight as it is, will prove awkward and suspicious, I am afraid," murmured the captain. "I wonder how she will account for it?"

But the lady had no such anxiety on her mind.

The very moment the lid was shut down, she put on that outward appearance of complete nervous prostration.

It was so much like what was simulated, that the doctor had been completely deceived.

With a languid step she crossed the room.

Her strongly-perfumed handkerchief was held to her face.

On gaining the door, she pretended to make several efforts to speak, but took care that the attempts were loud enough to reach the ears of those outside.

"Who—who is there?" she at last faintly stammered.

"Open the door!" cried the squire, impatiently. "What the devil do you mean by keeping us waiting like this?"

With a trembling hand, the lady drew back the bolt.

No sooner was this done than the squire pushed the door open with great violence.

His wife leaned for support against the doorpost.

Either from real or pretended terror, or else through the influence of the subtle drug which she had inhaled, her countenance was ashy white.

She seemed as though on the very point of fainting.

"God bless me!" ejaculated Pearson. "How bad the lady looks! She is about to faint. Look—look! She is as white as a ghost!"

The words attracted the squire's attention more particularly to his wife.

"D—n this nervousness! She is always like this when the least thing happens out of the common way."

"You terrified me so!" she gasped. "I made sure the highwayman had come at last."

"Why, you foolish woman," said the squire, contemptuously, "could you for a moment think the fellow would make such a noise as that?"

"I was too frightened to think," she answered, trembling violently. "The sudden noise deprived me of all sense and motion. It was cruel in the extreme to make me suffer so!"

Conscious that this rebuke was just, the squire lowered his tone.

"Come," he said, advancing and taking her hand, "let me lead you to a seat. There is no need for fear. You are quite safe now."

The lady affected to be somewhat reassured, though she could hardly repress her loathing at his touch.

She went no further than just over the threshold of the inner room.

There was the ottoman, and on this she sank, apparently because it was the nearest seat, but in reality to make the captain's hiding-place more secure.

"Why are you here?" she gasped. "What has happened?"

"If you will promise not to distress yourself, I will let you know."

"Do so; I shall be more composed then."

"Well, then, we cannot find this fellow anywhere, high or low, and where he can have got to I cannot think. I won't believe that it is possible he has left the house unseen. My firm conviction is that he is hidden somewhere."

"Have you searched well?"

"In every nook and corner."

"And could you find no trace?"

"None at all. The only place which has escaped the most rigid scrutiny is this suite of rooms; and although you and everybody else may tell me it is impossible he can be secreted here, yet I will not be persuaded of it until I have had every corner pried into."

These words caused the lady to grow pale with real fear.

She dreaded that the ottoman would not be an effectual hiding-place.

The captain shared her fears.

Indeed, he gave himself up for lost.

He was compelled to inaction.

No movement that he could make would have the least effect in bettering his condition.

It was most unwillingly that he remained so still.

"Let the result come," he said, mentally; "I am prepared for the worst that can happen."

"You have no occasion to look so terrified," said Squire Fielding; "I am out of all patience with this perpetual terror. The rooms can be searched without disturbing you."

"And we can begin at once, sir?" said Pearson

"Certainly."

Under the direction of their leader, the officers now separated themselves over the three apartments.

The search they made was narrow indeed.

The fact was, they were one and all perfectly assured that Captain Hawk was not in any other portion of the habitation.

Their only hope lay in finding him in one of these rooms, and if they failed to do so, they would have to give up the affair as an incomprehensible mystery.

The most unlikely places were scrutinised, but as they did not happen to look into the ottoman, of course they did not discover what they wanted.

The lady reclined almost at full length, and was unceasing in her applications to the pocket-handkerchief.

"Can you not find him?" she inquired at length, when the officers, with crestfallen looks, gathered round their leader. "Do not tell me that, or I shall be haunted with a perpetual dread."

"Don't distress yourself, my lady," said Pearson. "We cannot find him, it is true, but we are perfectly certain that he is not anywhere within the building."

"It is most perplexing and unaccountable," said the squire. "Even now, in the face of all this evidence and searching, I cling to my former conviction that he is hidden in the house."

"I think we may safely assure your worship that he is not," said Jarvis. "And now, with your consent, we will have a look on the outside of the premises. If we do not find him there, I am afraid we must give it up as a bad job."

He spoke the concluding words with a very wobegone air, while Pearson cursed him inwardly for having suggested such a thing as a halt at all.

Of course this was not right, but then, if all had turned out well, Pearson would have appropriated all the cleverness to himself, which would not have been right either.

A few more words passed, and then, to the infinite relief of the lady and Captain Hawk, they quitted the room.

The latter for some time could hardly believe in the reality of his escape.

Lucy had entered after the officers, and now stood awaiting the commands of her mistress.

"I shall not want you again to-night, Lucy," she said. "You can go to bed. I do not suppose that we shall meet with any more interruption. Good night."

"Good night, my lady."

She left the room.

Throwing off all her assumed languor, the lady ran hastily to the door, fastened it, and then released the highwayman from his place of confinement, which was much too limited in extent to be borne comfortably for any great length of time.

"The danger is over," she said. "You will not be troubled again. We have only to wait a little while, and then we shall be able to take our departure in safety."

"For your sake I trust so, lady; and for the same reason, I should be glad to avoid all unnecessary risks."

"Alas—alas! How hard is my fate! Compelled to fly at night in a manner and with a person that must destroy my reputation for ever!"

"It is not too late to retract," said the captain.

"What do you mean?"

"If you feel you can endure your late existence for some time longer, it is not too late for you to say so."

"No—no, anything is preferable to that."

"Enough, then. It will be best not to give encouragement to any vain regrets."

Her tears, however, could not be controlled.

"It will be best to leave her to the indulgence of her grief for a time," said the captain, mentally. "In the meantime I will try to form some idea of what my friends are doing without."

In the same cautious manner as before, he approached the window.

He did not attempt to open it, however, but contented himself with looking through the panes.

It was not long before the flashing of lanterns met his view.

Dark shadows moved here and there with apparent aimlessness.

"Their search cannot last long," he muttered; "but when it is ended it is a question in my mind whether they will conclude that I have really got away."

"What was that?" said a voice near him.

Turning round, he saw the lady had, unperceived, placed herself by his side.

She now seemed perfectly composed.

Her lips were compressed with determination.

Captain Hawk noticed, too, that she had attired herself in readiness for a journey.

"I was merely thinking over our position," he said.

"Is it safe to start?"

"As safe as ever it will be, I think," he replied.

"Why?"

"They have searched this part without, and have found nothing, so I should say the chances are ten to one whether they come here again."

"Let us not have another day here."

"No—no; I should be loth indeed to stay till morning. Now or never, rely upon it, is the time for the escape to be attempted."

So saying, he now ventured to open the casement noiselessly.

Apparently, the ground below was paved: if so, the shock of falling upon it would be severe.

For himself, however, the captain did not care—he was wondering how his companion would accomplish the descent.

"Could you drop down yourself," she asked, "without sustaining any injury?"

"I think so. But how shall you descend? It is that which puzzles me."

"If you can go first," she said, "you will find the garden ladder hanging against the wall. I think it is long enough to reach the window."

"If so, nothing could be better. I will see at once."

Captain Hawk reconnoitred carefully, and having satisfied himself that the coast was clear, he cautiously lowered himself through the window.

When he hung down from the window-sill at the full length of his arms, his feet were not much more than five feet from the ground.

Such a distance as this could be dropped easily.

He came down, however, with great force on the paving stones.

At the same moment, he heard a low and savage growl close to him.

Almost before he could regain his feet, an immense mastiff sprang upon him.

The animal made no other sound save the low growl we have spoken of, but flew direct at the captain's throat.

It was well that the highwayman was used to sudden surprises, or he would inevitably have fallen a victim to the attack made upon him.

But he caught the savage creature by the throat, and a furious struggle immediately ensued.

How it would have terminated is hard to say.

But the lady above, who was much longer in recovering from her astonishment than the captain was, now cried out:

"Down, Nero—down—down! Quick, I say!"

The words were uttered in a suppressed voice that would not be sufficient to raise an alarm, but yet which would reach the ears of the huge dog.

"You may venture to let go your hold now," she said. "He will not injure you."

Captain Hawk did not relax his grasp without feeling a great deal of misgiving.

The dog growled, and after panting once or twice seemed strongly inclined to resume the conflict.

The sound of the lady's voice, however, proved sufficient to restrain him.

"Now," she said, "the ladder. Quick—quick! Down, Nero, I say."

The dog did not seem to approve of Captain Hawk being allowed to touch anything.

The ladder was found without much difficulty, and reared against the window.

It was just long enough.

"Wait a moment," whispered the captain. "I will ascend and assist you."

Without his aid, the lady would have had very great difficulty in getting on to the ladder.

The highwayman's strength and coolness, however, made all easy.

At this moment, the fortitude displayed by the lady appeared to forsake her.

She trembled so violently that but for the captain's arm she must have fallen.

"Compose yourself," he said, in reassuring accents. "Be calm now, and all will be well."

But her agitation was too great to be controlled.

"Come," he said; "stand firm a moment. I will replace the ladder, and then there will be no clue to our flight. You can lean against the wall for support."

"Yes—yes!" she said, faintly.

The ladder was soon restored to its original position.

"Now," cried Captain Hawk, "all depends upon the rapidity of our movements. You are better now?"

"Oh yes! much better."

"That is well. Now lean upon me again, if you have no objection to doing so, and show me which will be the best means of getting free from the premises."

"Oh yes! I ought to know."

The manner in which the words were pronounced made the reply seem a strange one.

Captain Hawk looked at her inquiringly, but the obscurity was too great to permit him to see her features very distinctly.

"Which is the way, then? Do not forget I am an utter stranger to every object."

"This is the way."

"Remember, my object is to get clear of the premises as speedily as possible."

"You will see a gate a little further on," she said. "You will be able to open it easily, and then we shall be in the paddock."

"Ah!" said the captain, with a sigh of relief, "that last word sounds like freedom indeed!"

The little gate was soon reached.

To this point the dog followed closely at their heels, but as the captain by no means wished to have such a companion, the squire's wife sent him back.

The first thing they did on passing through the gate was to glance keenly and apprehensively around them.

Their confidence increased when they saw no one was near.

Captain Hawk, with that boldness that characterised all his actions, struck off in a straight line across the paddock.

But in doing this he was over bold.

His dismay may be conceived when he heard a rough voice close at hand utter an exclamation.

This was succeeded, without any perceptible pause, by the report of a pistol.

The lady uttered a piercing scream.

"Speak—speak!" said the captain. "Tell me that you are not hurt!"

A gasping sob was the only reply, and his companion slipped from his grasp on to the turf an inanimate mass.

Despite the danger of his position, he stopped.

To leave her, he felt would be base.

The man who had fired came rushing on, evidently intent upon capture.

He was alone, being one of the sentinels set to watch the premises.

The captain thrust his hand into his breast, and then suddenly recollected that he had no weapons.

"Cowardly wretch," he exclaimed, as he met the fellow in full career, "take that for your reward!"

He dealt a terrific blow with his clenched fist as he spoke.

It was a blow which no one could have borne up against.

The sentinel fell down on his back as though he had been struck with lightning.

The report of the pistol, and the lady's shriek, had of course spread a general alarm.

Lights could be seen flashing in all directions, and the hoarse cries of many voices and the trampling of footsteps came quite plainly upon their ears.

But Captain Hawk never once thought of attempting to secure his safety by immediate flight.

Bending down over the prostrate form, he cried, appealingly:

"Speak—oh speak! Tell me quickly if you are much hurt."

A faint groan was the only response.

Bending down still more, he was able to perceive that which literally made him go sick at heart.

The bullet from the pistol had made a frightful gash on one side of her head, from which the blood was streaming.

"Dying!" he said, with a groan. "No one could survive such a hurt as that."

The unfortunate woman was indeed insensible, and now, even as the captain spoke, a slight convulsion shook her frame.

Then all was still.

She was dead!

The suddenness of this event had a paralysing effect upon the highwayman.

He knew his foes were approaching, yet he did not move, but remained with dilated eyes gazing upon the terrible spectacle before him.

"Dead," he murmured—"quite dead! How awful! Poor thing, bad as she was, I grieve for her. Perhaps, after all, this death blow is a mercy and a kindness to her. Her troubles are over now. I can render her no service by remaining. My own life I am bound to preserve, and I will not lose it without an effort."

So saying, he sprang to his feet and ran with full speed across the paddock.

A shout let him know that he was seen, and immediately afterwards a rattling volley was discharged.

But the pieces were aimed too hastily to do him any damage.

He bent all his energies, then, to running swiftly, so as to get a good distance before his foes were able to reload.

The discovery of the squire's wife lying dead on the turf delayed them for a moment.

"Good Heavens!" cried Pearson. "What mystery is this? What can this mean?"

"We shall never know from her lips, that is certain," answered Jarvis, who carried a lantern, and who had directed a beam of light upon the mutilated countenance.

"Never mind her—let us look after our man!" cried Pearson. "By Heaven, we shall lose him!"

"Let half of us follow him on foot, and the other half follow with the horses—we shall be almost certain to have him then."

"Good! You see to that, Jarvis."

Pearson rushed on.

The figure of Captain Hawk could be just distinguished in the gloom, but that was all.

The paddock was bounded by a broad quick-set hedge little less than five feet in height.

Over this the captain took a flying leap.

He came down awkwardly on the other side, but he did not care for that.

He was on his feet again in a moment, and running at the same headlong speed as before.

He counted upon the hedge being a serious obstacle to his foes, and so it proved.

Pearson made a valorous effort to clear it, and stuck half-way.

The force with which he came down seemed to defy all extrication.

Sharp thorns were sticking into him in ten thousand places.

The more he struggled the more his pain was increased.

"Murder! Help—help! The devil! Ten thousand curses! Help me out!"

His men were in duty bound to assist him, and by their united aid he was dragged out.

But the process was infinitely more painful than jumping in.

He was torn and scratched frightfully.

No sooner was he liberated, however, than he cursed his followers for not keeping up the chase.

It was in vain they declared that if they had tried the terrific leap they would have fared the same as he did.

"Force a way through, then! D—n it, after all this trouble do you think we are to lose him because a few thorns happen to be in the way? Ten thousand devils! Out with your cutlasses—you will soon make a gap then!"

The hint was promptly acted upon and a gap made.

But just as they were about to push through, Jarvis arrived with the horses and the second party.

"On with you!" cried Pearson. "Straight ahead he went! Never mind us—we will follow you as soon as we can scramble into the saddle!"

The opening made allowed those who were on horseback to get out of the paddock easily.

The delay, however, slight as it was, enabled Captain Hawk to get a wonderful start, for he never once relaxed his speed in the least degree.

Panting painfully for breath, he kept on leaping recklessly over every obstacle that crossed his path.

He knew that he was flying for his life, and it is wonderful what an incentive this is for exertion.

It is not to be supposed, however, that even under the domination of this feeling it was possible to keep up for any great length of time such a rapid rate of running, or that he could hope to outrace the horses that were in pursuit of him.

In a short time, therefore, Captain Hawk very unwillingly pulled up.

He panted so fearfully that he could hardly breathe.

He glanced behind him.

His pursuers were not visible in the darkness, but he could hear them.

They were coming in a direct line to the spot where he stood.

The first thing necessary, then, was to change his course, and the darkness favoured him wonderfully in doing this without the officers being any the wiser for it.

Just as he had congratulated himself upon having eluded them, though, the other party came upon him.

Unaware that his enemies had separated into two companies, he was taken greatly by surprise, and had a narrow escape of being seen.

Fortunately, however, there was a wide dry ditch close by, and in this he concealed himself.

This ditch lay right across the path taken by the police officers, and they leaped their horses over it at only a short distance from where the captain had hidden himself.

The loud cries to which they gave utterance came clearly upon his ears, though they were gone too quickly for him to make out what they said.

He remained profoundly still, listening to every sound and watching every movement.

The darkness soon swallowed them up.

As they went on after the first party, and as they passed by the spot where the highwayman was hidden, it follows that no success could by any possibility attend them unless they turned again.

Pearson was fully impressed with the notion that the prisoner had pushed on in a direct line to get away.

He went some distance before he would be persuaded that he was wrong.

Just when he pulled up in hesitation, Jarvis arrived.

"It's no good, sir," he said—"not a bit. We have missed him."

"But we must find him again—he cannot have gone far."

"That may be true, sir, but how in the world are we to find him on such a dark night as this, now that he has once got out of our sight? He has had plenty of chances to conceal himself in a tree, or half a dozen other places."

"Never mind, he must be found."

"But how?"

"Why, by looking for him, to be sure."

"Now, look here, Mr. Pearson, I have an idea."

"D—n your ideas!"

"Eh—what?"

"I say, d—n your ideas! If it hadn't been for them I shouldn't have been in this fix. It is all owing to your cleverness."

"Never mind, Mr. Pearson. It don't matter, of course, but I know this much: if you will hear what I have to say you will have no further trouble about the prisoner. I do think I can take you to the very place he has made for."

"Indeed, Jarvis!—that is a very different affair altogether. Where do you think it is?"

"Don't you think I should be a fool to say, and then be abused afterwards for my pains?"

"Come, come—think no more about that. You should not attach so much importance to a few hastily-uttered words."

"That's all very well, Mr. Pearson. Just say what you are going to do, and I am here along with the rest ready to obey orders."

"Don't be so unreasonable, Jarvis. Just pass over what I said. Consider it as not spoken. Tell me your idea."

"Well, I will; but I shall do no more than tell it you."

"What do you mean?"

"I sha'n't use any arguments to persuade you to act upon my suggestion. That I shall leave entirely."

"Very good; only please not to keep us in suspense any longer, and recollect you are wasting valuable time."

"Well, Mr. Pearson, the question I asked myself was this: what would be the most likely thing for the prisoner to do on recovering his liberty? Where would he be likely to go?"

"Well—well?"

"I soon found an answer to those questions. I may be wrong, of course. You will hear them, and you will know how they impress you."

"Yes—yes. But, confound it all, man! why don't you come to the point?"

"I am coming to it as fast as I can. The first thing the prisoner would do, you may depend upon it, Mr. Pearson, would be to get into some hiding-place or other, and then wait until he fancies we were far enough away from him, and then off he would go."

"And where to?"

"Ah! that's it. Does no particular place suggest itself?"

"London?"

"No, no—guess again."

"I can't guess, and I'll be d—d if I try. Either tell me, or let it alone."

"Don't you recollect," said Jarvis, who enjoyed his triumph mightily—"don't you recollect that when we got to the public-house where Captain Hawk had been staying that his horse was there?"

Being suddenly reminded of this made Pearson give a great jump.

"By Jove!" he said, "I forgot the horse."

"And a good thing we did."

"A good thing?"

"Yes—because it puts us on his track at once. He knows where the horse is, and, rely upon it, as soon as he can be off he will hasten to the public-house to recover possession of it. What is your opinion, Mr. Pearson?"

CHAPTER XLIX.

CAPTAIN HAWK FINDS HIMSELF AT THE BEGINNING OF FRESH DIFFICULTIES.

JARVIS asked this question in a very triumphal tone indeed.

"There can be only one answer," replied Pearson. "Of course he will make direct to the stable where we were forgetful enough to leave his horse. How I came to overlook it I cannot think."

"You have need to congratulate yourself upon having done so. Nothing could have been more fortunate. In my opinion, our course of action is most simple and clear. All we have to do is to gallop as hard as we can to the inn."

"And abandon the pursuit?"

"Yes, there will be no good in keeping it up, for as we are on horseback and he is on foot we must reach there first; then all we have to do is to wait his arrival, and as soon as he shows himself to nab him."

"There is a very great deal in what you say, Jarvis; and whether or not, I am determined to have his horse. I will tell you what I will do."

Jarvis prepared to listen.

"You and four of the men shall remain here and keep a good look-out, holding yourselves in readiness for pursuit if a chance should arise, and I will go back with the rest to the inn."

This was evidently most disagreeable to Jarvis.

But he said nothing.

Pearson, as usual, bent on appropriating all the cleverness to himself, gathered his men around him, and started without delay.

On his departure, Jarvis let fall some very dreadful oaths and curses.

"If I had known," he said, "I would have bit the end of my tongue off before I would have spoken. I will wager anything now that he misses the road, and that the captain gets clear off. Never mind, I hope he does. Another time I may have a chance of working on my own account."

"Then what are we to do, sir?" asked one of the men.

"Do? Why, obey orders, to be sure."

"I should pretend to chase him to the inn," said another. "We can easily say he was in front of us all the way; then if we arrive before the other lot we shall be certain to nab him."

"I'll do it!" cried Jarvis. "Come on—I am certain I can find the road!"

Before he had gone very far, however, he found this a much more difficult matter than he had anticipated.

The darkness was intense, and quite prevented him from ascertaining his exact whereabouts.

After the manner in which he had spoken, however, he would not suffer his hesitation to be seen.

For the present, however, we will leave the two parties of police to get on in the best manner they were able, and return to Captain Hawk, whose doings must possess a much greater amount of interest.

With some care he emerged from the dry ditch, and feeling tolerably certain that there was no immediate danger to be apprehended from his foes, he quietly set to work to think what steps he should take.

It would have been a great advantage to him could he but have overheard the conversation which passed between the two police officers.

Unfortunately for him, however, he was quite ignorant of it.

He was not long in coming to a decision, and the first words which sprang to his lips showed how very near Jarvis had been to the mark in what he said.

"My horse," he said—"I must have my horse. Without that noble companion I can do nothing. But what a long journey it is from here to the inn where he was left. How shall I perform it?"

It was rather strange that the idea did not occur to him that the officers might not start for the inn as well.

But the fact was, he was by no means certain that he should find Satan where he had left him.

His anxiety, indeed, upon this score was most acute.

He knew nothing of the ostler, and had not been allowed a single opportunity of making known his wishes.

Nevertheless, it was clearly his best plan to make his way direct to the inn with as little loss of time as possible.

It was some time before he could make out which was the direction he ought to take.

The journey from the inn to Squire Fielding's had been made in a manner that allowed him little or no opportunity of taking notice of surrounding objects.

He relied mainly on the directions of the ostler.

When he heard them given, he was particularly careful

to treasure them up in his mind, so as to be able to make use of them when needful.

Now they served him well.

After looking about him for some time attentively, he decided upon which direction he ought to take.

Having done this, he set forward without delay.

The captain was a good walker; but yet, as he thought of the distance and looked up at the sky, he feared he should be overtaken by daylight before he could reach his destination.

He glanced around perpetually, and when he had gone about half a mile he came to a halt.

"Yes," he said, "I feel sure this is the entrance to that execrable lane that jolted me so as the cart was driven along it. If I meet with no interruption it will be all plain and easy sailing now."

No sooner had he said this than he heard the clatter of a horse's feet.

He drew back, making sure that some of his pursuers were at hand.

If so, his situation was full of peril, for, as the reader is aware, he was totally unprovided with weapons.

A moment more of listening relieved him from his worst apprehensions.

Mingled with the clatter of the approaching horse's feet was the rattle of wheels.

"Some chance traveller," the captain ejaculated. "I will remain where I am and let him pass."

Dark as the night was, Captain Hawk had been so long out in it that his vision had become quite accustomed to the gloom.

He was able to discern all objects at a moderate distance, though of course his perception of them was dim.

It was not very long before he caught a glimpse of the approaching vehicle, which proved to be a very high gig, drawn by a powerful, light-coloured horse.

Despite the inequalities of the roadway, the horse came on in capital style.

"Both driver and horse must be well acquainted with the road," was the captain's mental remark, "or they would never be able to push along it in this manner.

As the gig came nearer, he said to himself:

Why not ask this man for a ride? He would hardly refuse me, I should think; and if he only takes me a mile on my road, it will be a clear gain, and well worth trying."

Just as he arrived at this conclusion, the gig got close to his side.

"Hoy!" he cried. "Pull up, sir, if you please. I am a poor unfortunate fellow, lost in these lanes, and if you will give me a ride a little way I shall be extremely obliged to you."

Captain Hawk hardly ventured to hope that the traveller would pull up.

Most persons, knowing the insecurity of the roads, would, on hearing themselves so addressed, have urged the horse onward at the top of his speed.

Agreeably to the captain's surprise, however, the driver tightened the rein.

"Hallo!" he cried, in a gruff, cheery voice. "Who are you? What do you say?"

Captain Hawk came forward.

"Will you oblige me with a ride? If you are only going on for a mile I shall be deeply grateful."

"It is a slight favour enough. Jump up."

There was evidently no fear about this man.

Captain Hawk squeezed himself into the gig, which was barely large enough to hold two, and no sooner had he done it than away the horse went at the same rapid rate.

"A rough part of the country this, sir," said the stranger, to Captain Hawk.

"Very indeed. It seems alarming to go at such a pace along a rough road, so dark as it is now."

"Why, the fact of the case is, I leave the matter almost entirely to my nag. He is a rare old fellow. I don't believe there is a square inch of country for twenty miles round here that he does not know. That's the way, sir. Why, if I tried to drive him we should come to grief in less than a moment."

Captain Hawk looked out a little apprehensively.

He expected every moment that the vehicle would be overturned.

The driver, however, seemed to have every confidence in the ability of his steed.

"I daresay it seems strange to you, sir," he said, addressing Captain Hawk; "but I have been in the habit of coming up and down these lanes at all hours, ever since I was a boy; so, you see, I am thoroughly familiar with it."

"So it appears; and, believe me, I am much obliged to you for your kindness in giving me a lift."

"Tut-tut!—don't mention it."

"Many a one would have driven on, fearing an attack."

"Very likely; but then I never fear anything. I have been looking out for some one to beat me for a good many years now, but I have never found him."

Owing to the roughness of the road, the gig jolted and rattled so fearfully that it was anything but pleasant to carry on a conversation, so ere long complete silence reigned.

Captain Hawk's mind was full of anxious thoughts, and it seemed to him that the nearer he got to the inn the more did his impatience increase.

His reverie was interrupted by the gig being brought to a standstill.

"Here we are!" said the stranger. "I am happy to tell you that I am at the end of my journey."

Captain Hawk looked about him, but he saw no signs of any human habitation.

"You can't see the house from here," he said, "though it is not far off."

"This is your house, then?" said the captain, as he alighted.

"It is; and if you are willing to accept of my offer, I shall be very glad if you will step in with me. You know what the accommodation of an old farm-house is like, I daresay; and we can make you comfortable till daylight if you like to stay."

"Many thanks!" returned the captain. "At any other time I should have embraced your offer very gladly indeed; as it is, you have my best thanks."

"Is your business, then, so very urgent?"

"It is—it will admit of no delay."

"Very good, sir. Then I have the pleasure of bidding you good night!"

"Good night!"

"There is only one thing I should be glad to know."

"What is it?"

"The distance from here to the high-road."

"Not more than a quarter of a mile."

The farmer drove through a narrow gate that was standing open, and Captain Hawk resumed his journey at a sharp run.

Before he could reach the high-road, however, he heard numerous hoofbeats in the rear.

He had by this time quite concluded that he had got out of the way of his foes entirely.

He was by no means certain that they were his enemies he could hear behind him, but the probability was that they were no other.

Without a moment's hesitation he availed himself of the hiding-place which had served him so well on the former occasion.

The ditch was not quite dry, however, but it was wide and deep, and so overgrown with bushes that it would have made an effectual hiding-place even by daylight.

He had only just time to settle himself when a troop of horsemen passed by.

They were going at a tolerable speed, and, owing to the awkward position the highwayman was compelled to assume, he was not able to speak positively as to whether they were police officers or not.

He remained without moving until the faintest and most distant clatter of their horses' feet had died away.

"They have missed me," he said; "but then, how on earth could they have guessed that I came in this direction?"

Strange to say, the real answer to this question did not suggest itself to him.

Emerging from the ditch, he continued to make his way along the lane until he gained the high-road.

Here he stopped to listen, but hearing nothing of the horsemen, went forward with renewed hopes.

At that hour it was a great chance indeed whether anything would be found upon the road.

"If I only find him safe," he said, "no words will be

[LORD HARCLIFFE'S DESPERATE LEAP.]

able to express my satisfaction. Once let me find myself upon his back, and I can laugh to scorn all the police officers in Christendom."

But his spirits sank as he drew nearer.

"Courage—courage!" he kept repeating to himself. "In a short time now I shall know the worst."

His anxiety and impatience made him almost insensible of fatigue.

He walked along the smooth high-road as briskly as when he had first started.

At length the inn appeared in sight.

No sailor ever experienced greater thankfulness at finding himself in safe harbour than the captain did now.

For a moment his emotion almost overcame him.

His horse Satan was almost the only thing he loved and prized upon earth, and he sickened with dread as he thought of the probabilities that some danger had befallen him.

Suddenly, when within about a couple of hundred yards of the inn, a dark figure glided out from one side of the roadway.

"Hist, captain!" said a low voice. "Is that you?"

Captain Hawk stopped short with amazement.

"Who is that?" he asked.

"Hush—not so loud! Don't you remember me? I am the ostler."

"Oh yes! I recollect you now. And—and—my horse?"

"Safe, captain, and as right as a trivet."

"Take my best thanks for that assurance."

"Be quiet—be quiet! One would think you did not know your foes were almost within earshot."

"I did not know it. Is it a fact?"

"It is. They are at the inn yonder. They have not arrived very long. Do you guess their errand?"

"Never mind—tell me."

"They expected to find your horse there, and calculated you would come to fetch him. Don't you see, they meant to nab you easy."

Notwithstanding the knowledge that he had escaped a great danger, the captain felt a sharp pang of alarm upon hearing this intelligence.

"What is to be done now?"

"Easy does it, captain. I made sure you would be here before this; but when I found you did not come, something seemed to strike me that the officers would be after your horse, so I determined to move him."

"And you have done so?"

"Oh yes!"

"Thanks—thanks! You will find this the best and most profitable bit of work you ever did in your life."

"That's just what I said to myself, captain. I knew you would not forget me."

"Rest assured that I will not, no matter what occurs. But where is he?"

"In a shed—not far from Oak Tree Dingle. You recollect the place."

"Oh yes—yes!"

"I will show you the way."

"And where are the officers?"

"I left them at the inn yonder."

"Did they see you?"

"No, but I saw them, though, and took good care to keep out of sight."

"Will they not wonder at your absence?"

"They may do so; but I have given up the job, you understand, now master's dead. I have been doing nothing but look after Satan. You will find him in splendid condition."

"I am burning with impatience to behold him. Lead the way; I cannot control myself any longer. We can converse as we go along."

The ostler, however, found leading the way was a task of no little difficulty, for no matter how fast he walked, the captain kept a pace or two ahead of him.

"I have been watching for you all the time," he said; "and just before the officers came I was almost ready to think that it was all over with you—that I should never see you again."

"I have had a narrow escape, that is certain. You are sure the officers cannot find him?"

"Oh, make yourself quite contented about that!"

"How far is it from here?"

"We shall be there directly. Take it easy, captain. I tell you it is all right."

But this assurance was unheeded.

Nothing less than actually seeing his priceless steed would content him.

"Do you see that black mass yonder?" said the ostler.

"I do—I do. Is that it?"

"It is."

No sooner was the reply pronounced than Captain Hawk bounded towards the shed at the top of his speed.

His footsteps must have been heard, for he was greeted by a loud, shrill neigh.

"Confound it all," gasped the ostler, endeavouring to keep up with the highwayman—"that's a very bad job! The officers will hear that, safe as rain, and now they will be down upon us."

But Captain Hawk was too much intent upon seeing his horse to pay any attention to what the ostler said.

With one blow he dashed open the frail little door, and the next moment Satan's head was placed caressingly upon his master's breast.

This unexpected—nay, unhoped-for recovery of his steed affected the captain deeply.

The revulsion of feeling was so great, that several moments elapsed before he could comprehend what the ostler was saying to him.

"Captain—captain," he cried, in the utmost anxiety, "are you mad, or in a dream? Can you not hear me? I tell you the officers are coming; they will be upon you in a moment! You must be speedy if you wish to save yourself."

But it was not until he took hold of the highwayman by the arm and shook him somewhat roughly that he succeeded in attracting his attention.

"Well, well—what is it?" he added, at last, with a long-drawn sigh.

"I tell you the officers are upon you!"

"Officers! Upon me! And I unarmed!"

"Quick—quick, captain! Shake off this dreamy feeling, and all will be well."

Captain Hawk was fully aroused now, and needed no urging to make haste.

Satan was caparisoned in readiness for the road, and taking hold of him by the bridle, the captain led him forth.

"One moment," said the ostler: "the girths want tightening, but nothing else. There you are—it's all right now. Be off, and good luck to you!"

The next moment Captain Hawk was in the saddle.

The officers were coming on at full speed now.

They saw him, and, what was more, recognised him, as was proved by the loud shouts which they immediately set up.

"Be off, captain! Don't wait another moment."

"All right; but what shall you do?"

"Never mind. Depend upon it, I am capable of taking care of myself."

"But I must reward you for this, though, of course, just at the moment I have not a farthing towards doing it."

"I know that. The officers would take care not to leave you with any spare cash."

"Listen. I am going to London. In three days' time, or thereabouts, I shall be at the Greyhound, an inn three or four miles this side of the town."

"Lor' bless you, captain, why I know that old crib as well as you do."

"I shall be there, then. Let me see you. If you ask quietly for me, the landlord will let you know where I am. I cannot stop to say more. You shall be well paid for what you have done."

As he spoke, he let the reins fall loosely upon Satan's neck.

That was enough.

The gallant creature had been chafing ever since her rider mounted, and it was with the utmost difficulty that the hurried conversation had been carried on.

No sooner was the pressure upon his mouth removed, however, than he darted off like an arrow from a bow.

It was only just in time.

The police officers had approached dangerously close.

Their disappointment upon seeing their prey suddenly bound off when they were close to him may perhaps be imagined.

Under the influence of their vexation, they all discharged their pistols in a straggling volley, upon the bare chance that one of the bullets might bring either horse or rider down—they did not care much which.

The ostler, the moment the captain started, dropped flat down upon the ground.

At first the officers were too much intent upon the highwayman to think of him, but when reflection did come to them he was nowhere to be found.

"We can consider ourselves fairly done now, Mr. Pearson," cried Jarvis, for both parties of officers had arrived at the inn. "We might just as well set on and milk he-goats in a sieve, as try to catch him now."

Pearson swore savagely for some moments.

But his fury being expended somewhat, he cried:

"I don't care! I heard him say that he was going to London. That, too, is our destination. We will follow in his track. It is rarely indeed that I fail when I set myself upon a thing, and, come what will, I will lodge Captain Hawk in Newgate or die in the attempt! I swear it!"

"Very good," said Jarvis. "I only hope you will, that's all."

"I shall not look to you for any assistance," was the reply. "If I had trusted to myself instead of listening to your foolish suggestions I should have had him safe now."

Jarvis retorted, and a recriminatory conversation was carried on for a long time, which, however much it may have amused the officers who listened to it, is not worth being recorded here.

Leaving the officers to do the best they could, we will follow in the footsteps of the highwayman.

When Satan bounded off in the manner we have mentioned, such a feeling of exultation took possession of the captain's heart that he could not restrain himself from shouting aloud.

"Hurrah!" he exclaimed. "On—on, brave steed! We will show them what a little bit of riding is like. I feel free now, and care not a rush for my foes, nor should I were they ten times as numerous. That is it, old boy! Away—away!"

Never before, Captain Hawk thought, had Satan made such wonderful speed.

He literally seemed to fly over the ground without touching it.

In such a race, what earthly chance could the police officers have?

Satan was perfectly fresh and in wonderful condition after his long rest.

The horses of the police officers, on the other hand, were all but knocked up.

They had been ridden at a furious pace along bad roads from Squire Fielding's residence, and exhibited every symptom of distress.

Pearson and his followers, however, were not the men to trouble themselves over much about this.

Whenever the poor animals flagged it was only a signal for the more liberal use of whip and spur, and the horses, in madness caused by the pain, forgot for a little while their exhaustion.

Not for long, then, did Captain Hawk hear anything of his pursuers.

But as Satan was inclined to go, he let him have his head, in order that the greatest possible distance might be placed between himself and his foes.

At length, however, when the rapid respiration and the flecks of foam flying from his mouth testified that further hurried riding would be injudicious, he drew rein.

All around him then was as silent as though he was the only human being in all the world.

"Bravo!" he cried; "that was well done. Twelve hours ago who would have thought that I should so soon be again upon the back of my gallant horse, and in perfect freedom? Yet here I am. The only question is, what shall I do next?"

Just as he asked himself the question he found he was at the foot of a long, steep hill.

He made up his mind at once that Satan should climb this at a walk, and that while he was doing so he would take the opportunity of considering over his prospects and ultimate proceedings.

"I told the ostler I was going to London, and so I have been for some time past, only one accident or another seems to hold me back; but I will lose no time now. I have been absent for so long a time that I quite yearn to look upon the great metropolis again. I will go; and when there, the first thing I do shall be to seek out old Matthew."

He paused a moment in thought.

"But even now I see a hindrance in the way. The service the ostler rendered me unasked is one that no amount of money can pay for, yet that is the only way that I can recompense it; and such being the case, I will take care that the reward is an ample one."

A moment or two of further reflection served to show him that he was more than usually worse off as regarded the accomplishment of his design.

He had no weapons.

Where to obtain others from he knew not.

"I must have them somehow," he exclaimed. "Yet, stop: let me see—I ought to have a good brace of pistols in the holsters here, and shall have, provided no one has removed them."

He hastened to ascertain, and an ejaculation of satisfaction escaped his lips when he discovered the pistols were not only safe but ready for immediate use

"Capital!" he cried. "I will accept of this as an augury that Fortune means to befriend me. Between here and the Old Greyhound at Huntingdon I shall doubtless have more than one opportunity of making a good booty, and what I obtain the ostler shall have every farthing of!"

A moment or two after he had thus announced his decision, he stopped on the brow of the hill.

"Morning cannot be far off, I fancy," he exclaimed. "At any rate, this has seemed a long night to me. Ha! yes, there is a feeble gleam yonder. Now I shall have no difficulty in making out where I am."

The faint light in the eastern sky rapidly increased.

The approach of morning brought other considerations into the captain's mind.

It was necessary that he should gain some place of shelter, not merely because it was unsafe to show himself by daylight, but because he felt rather acutely the effects of all that he had recently undergone.

"There is little chance of making a good booty during the day," he said; "and I ought to be in perfect readiness for action on the approach of night. I must have rest. The question is, where can I obtain it?"

This was a matter of no ordinary difficulty.

"I will not go to an inn," he said, "because, if I do, the officers will have the opportunity of finding out more about my movements than I care for them to know. I will ride on a little way. I shall be able to see about me better in the course of another half-hour, and then it is quite possible I may light upon a place that will exactly suit me."

In this hope he descended the hill at a small trot.

Morning came on with great rapidity.

Although only a dim twilight prevailed, yet the air was vocal with the twittering of numberless birds.

By the time the level road was gained the gray light in the east had given place to a ruddy tint, proclaiming that the sun was not far off.

Captain Hawk again looked round.

He saw nothing, however, that held out the slightest prospect of answering the purpose he required, save a wood of considerable extent, the nearest point of which was more than a mile off.

While gazing hesitatingly upon it his attention was attracted by the movements of his steed.

"What is it, Satan? Can you hear something?"

He listened for a moment, and then the rumbling of wheels came upon his ears.

"What is this, I wonder?" he ejaculated. "Shall I remain here and endeavour to discover, or shall I make haste and place myself where I cannot be seen?"

There was not much time for deliberation, for the approaching vehicle came on at a very unusual speed, though a sharp angle in the road not far off effectually concealed it from view.

CHAPTER L.

LORD HARCLIFFE IS CAPTURED AND CONVEYED TO NEWGATE.

We go back now to that night when the grand assembly was held at Leicester House.

The reader will no doubt remember how Lieutenant Tracy, pale as a ghost, and so weak as scarcely to be able to stand, had worked his way among the guests, and then had denounced Lord Harcliffe as the Black Highwayman—that mysterious being who had been for so long the terror of every traveller, and who had hitherto defied all attempts at capture and identification.

Amazement and incredulity filled the breasts of all present.

There were many, however, to whom the denouncement came like a revelation.

These were the persons who had always been unable to make out from what source Lord Harcliffe had obtained that wealth which enabled him to live at so prodigal a rate.

As for the young nobleman himself, he carried matters with a high hand.

He held his drawn sword before him in a manner which threatened death to the first man who ventured to lay a hand upon him.

"Seize him!" yelled Peterson. "Upon him! Down with him! Make him your prisoner!"

"Hold!" cried Lord Harcliffe. "Stand back, I say! I will be heard! That poor young man yonder must be in the delirium of fever, and says he knows not what! He must be mad to make so ridiculous an accusation! Can it be possible," he added, turning to look upon those surrounding him—"can it be possible that any here believe for one moment there can be the least truth in this odious charge?"

The appeal produced a clamour of tongues; but the majority of voices proclaimed a total disbelief in the fact of Lord Harcliffe being the Black Highwayman.

"Silence—silence!" screamed Peterson. "It is my

turn to be heard now. True or not, he must come with me! I have here a properly signed warrant for his apprehension, and, mad or not, Lieutenant Tracy has sworn to the truth of the charge which he has made. Surrender, Lord Harcliffe! I call upon you in the name of his Sovereign Majesty the King!"

"Never!" was the reply; and his lordship, as he spoke, flashed his sword around him in a manner which made those immediately contiguous to him shrink back with precipitation. "Never will I suffer the indignity of being made a prisoner by a common constable!"

"Then the result of resistance be on your own head! You have heard, and you are warned. Either surrender yourself quietly to us, or abide by the result of a refusal."

"I will abide by it. I will not yield! Never—never!"

One of his old companions approached, apparently with the intention of acting the part of a mediator.

"My lord," he said, "of course this is a ridiculous mistake, for which those who have been guilty of it will have to pay dearly. Lay aside your sword and submit. I will see that no unnecessary indignity is offered to you."

"Never!" cried Lord Harcliffe, as, with a sudden bound, for which no one was prepared, he leaped upon one of the refreshment tables. "Stand back, I say! The man who touches me does so at mortal peril!"

The confusion and uproar in the saloon may now be said to have reached its height.

"I call upon you again, by virtue of this warrant, to submit yourself a prisoner!" bawled Peterson. "If you refuse the third time, my orders are to fire!"

"Then do so. I would rather face a hundred pistol bullets than suffer any of you to lay a finger on me! Gentlemen, good night! I will not be taken!"

Before anyone had time to recover from the astonishment which this singular speech produced, Lord Harcliffe, with a sudden bound, sprang off the table through a large latticed window, against which it had been placed.

Before the crash of glass had ceased he was off.

A dead silence followed this unexpected act.

Peterson was the first to speak.

"Just what I expected," he cried. "I guessed we should have no little trouble, and I took my precautions accordingly."

A succession of cries from below and the sound of struggling came at this moment distinctly on the ears of all those who were in the saloon.

There was the clashing of steel, followed by one sharp, ringing report of a pistol.

"This way!" cried Peterson to his men. "Follow me now, all of you, and assist in making him secure!"

With a general rush, the police officers departed.

The guests, fearing their rudeness and violence, shrank back, and allowed them free passage.

Those who were nearest to the window through which the accused nobleman had taken so desperate a leap pressed towards it, in the hope of being able to distinguish what was going on below.

The window was one of a long range looking out upon the gardens attached to Leicester House.

In all probability, Lord Harcliffe was aware that he had nothing harder than garden mould to fall upon.

Nevertheless, as the distance was considerable, he alighted with so much force that he could not immediately recover his footing.

Just as he was about to rise, some half-dozen men flung themselves upon him.

With desperate and extraordinary strength, Lord Harcliffe, despite their efforts, struggled to his feet.

The conflict was sharp but short.

In accordance with instructions given, one of the officers fired off his pistol, which was the agreed upon signal for all the others to hasten to their assistance.

Before Peterson arrived, however, the prisoner had been secured.

"My lord," he said, with a bow, for, despite the circumstances, he could not forget his prisoner's undoubted rank, "in one sense I regret what I am about to do. But duty is duty."

His lordship maintained a sullen silence.

"This warrant which I hold in my hand, and which you can examine if you choose, authorises me to use every possible precaution to keep you in safe custody, and, in order that all fear of escape may be lessened, I am to convey you to the prison of Newgate prior to your examination before a magistrate."

But his lordship showed himself in no way moved, or even interested in this speech.

"Bring him along," said Peterson, "if that is his humour. We will let him know that he is a prisoner, even if he is a lord."

The subordinate police officers, however, could not help feeling and exhibiting no little degree of awe; but, inspired by the reward which they had undoubtedly gained, they kept a firm grasp upon him.

Peterson had made all his arrangements very completely.

We have seen that he had men posted as sentinels outside, in case the prisoner should attempt an escape.

Close by, too, was a hackney-carriage, which he had hired in readiness, so confident was he this time that he should be successful.

This vehicle the prisoner was compelled to enter.

As many police officers as the conveyance could possibly accommodate crowded in after him.

More then climbed on to the top.

Peterson seated himself beside the driver.

"Now then," he cried—"to Newgate. Go slowly, so that these men can follow easily on foot"

The last injunction was superfluous.

The two miserable bundles of skin and bone harnessed to the wheezing old coach could never in the most desperate emergency be pushed forward at a faster rate than three miles and a half an hour.

The police officers who remained now surrounded the hackney-coach at every point, and with drawn swords escorted it to Newgate.

The distance was rather great, and those people who were about could tell at a glance that a prisoner of more than usual importance had been captured.

Then, in that magical manner which can never be explained, it became generally known that this carefully-guarded prisoner was no other than the Black Highwayman.

There was no one unacquainted with his exploits, and long before half the journey to the great City prison was accomplished, the streets were filled up with so dense a crowd, that Peterson began to have serious apprehensions whether his men would be able to force a passage.

According to his instructions, about a dozen had placed themselves in front.

One man with a drawn cutlass led the way.

The others, also with their cutlasses drawn, placed themselves so that they formed a compact body wedge-like in shape.

In this manner, slow progress was made.

Fortunately the hour was such a late one that the streets were scarcely occupied with anything else.

What made Peterson more serious was, that the nearer they got to Newgate the denser did the crowd become.

No indication of meditated violence was, however, perceptible.

The prisoner, with a moody frown upon his countenance, leant back upon the seat as far as he could, so as to escape as much as possible the gaze of the gaping crowd.

He made not the slightest attempt at resistance, but sat like one who feels that the worst has happened, and that nothing remains for him to do but to submit to his fate.

Perhaps he saw that no effort that he might make would have the slightest chance of restoring him his liberty, and only bring ill-usage upon him.

It was, however, very hard to say what thoughts were passing through his mind.

His particularly pale face exhibited no symptom of emotion, nor did its expression afford the least index to the state of his mind.

"Push on!" said Peterson, as the phalanx in front came to a standstill. "If they will not give way, compel them with your weapons."

Every member of the assembled multitude was most anxious to catch sight of the notorious highwayman; but yet not enough so as to render them inclined to risk receiving a serious wound.

The threatened use of the cutlasses had, then, the desired effect.

The journey was resumed, and though their progress

was necessarily slow, no further halt or interruption took place until they arrived opposite to the vestibule of the prison of Newgate.

The news of their coming had preceded them, and on their arrival they found the interior of the prison in a state of unwonted bustle and excitement.

The coach, with some difficulty, was driven close to the little flight of steps leading up from the street to the door of the vestibule.

A space of only about a couple of feet was left for the prisoner to traverse, so that the huge crowd had hardly any opportunity of seeing him.

The officers, indeed, took hold of the prisoner in so many places that he was bodily carried in.

"Shut the door," cried Peterson, in a voice full of anxiety—"shut the door, I say!"

The heavy portal closed with a clang.

Lord Harcliffe admirably preserved his impassiveness.

Indeed, of all those present he seemed the least interested and concerned in what was taking place.

The Governor came forward, looking flurried and anxious.

Only a vague report had reached his ears coupling the identity of Lord Harcliffe and the Black Highwayman together.

But he could not believe they were the same.

He knew Lord Harcliffe well by sight, and started with surprise when he saw him strongly bound and held like a common felon.

He immediately bowed low.

Lord Harcliffe acknowledged the salutation by a cold and distant nod.

"Surely," said the Governor, turning to the triumphant Peterson, "here is some terrible mistake."

"None at all," replied Peterson, puffing and panting, and wiping the heavy drops of perspiration from his face. "It's correct enough, I assure you, and no sort of mistake whatever!"

"But I don't understand."

"Read that," replied Peterson.

He roughly thrust the warrant, as he spoke, into the Governor's hands.

"Yes, yes—extraordinary!" ejaculated the Governor, as he glanced down the document. "Still, for all that," he concluded, "I am sure there is some dreadful mistake which will be found out before long."

"Whether that is the case or not," said Peterson, "I imagine your duty is clear before you; and let me advise you to be more than ordinarily particular, as any carelessness will inevitably cost you your situation. You understand?"

"I know my duty," said the Governor, addressing himself half apologetically to his lordship, "and, as a matter of course, I must fulfil it, no matter how individually disagreeable it may be."

"Very good. Just write out a receipt in due form, Mr. Governor, and I will depart. Thank goodness that part of the business is over, and when I have your signature my responsibilities will be at an end."

Peterson spoke as though this would be no ordinary relief to him.

The Governor had hardly recovered from his surprise as yet, and Peterson had to repeat his application before it was attended to.

The Governor then wrote out the receipt according to the usual form.

Peterson folded it up, and placed it in his pocket with an air of extraordinary satisfaction.

"Now, Mr. Governor, you can do with your prisoner just whatever you choose. My part is over. I have warned you to be careful, and that is sufficient. In the morning I suppose we shall be here to take him before the magistrate at Bow Street."

So saying, Peterson took his departure.

When the door had closed, the Governor looked hesitatingly towards his prisoner.

"Really, my lord, this is a most unpleasant, and, I may add, incomprehensible affair. Still, I am quite sure your lordship is the victim of some extraordinary mistake."

Lord Harcliffe slightly inclined his head.

It may be that the Governor thought circumstances were enough to warrant a little more condescension and affability upon his lordship's part, for when he spoke again the tones he made use of indicated that he was offended.

"Nevertheless, my lord," he said, "I have my duty before me. In this place we can make no distinction between one man and another. Therefore, however disagreeable it may be to your lordship, and however painful it may be to me, I have no alternative, but must place you in one of the strongest cells."

Still was Lord Harcliffe silent, and the Governor, thoroughly displeased that his amicable advances should be received in such a manner, cried:

"Now, then, Jenkins, bring a light this way, and the keys! I will see that the prisoner is safely bestowed myself."

At these words there was an immediate stir among the crowd of turnkeys and other officials, with whom the prison vestibule was thronged.

The one who had been specially addressed came forward, and said:

"Here I am, sir! Quite ready."

"Enough! Lead the way. You others, except the man on the lock, had better follow, and bring the prisoner with you."

Lord Harcliffe made no objection to crossing the threshold, and entering upon the dark, dismal passage which communicated with the innermost recesses of the prison.

"Which cell, sir?" asked Jenkins.

The Governor considered for a moment.

"No. 17 is occupied, is it not?"

"Yes, sir."

"And 11?"

"Yes."

"Which is the next best, do you think?"

"No. 31 is strong, sir, and light, and dry, and clean—one of the best cells in the prison."

"Right!"

"Shall that be the one, sir?"

"Yes—lead on."

The direction in which they had been going was changed.

Lord Harcliffe showed himself just as indifferent about this as he had been before.

The door of No. 31 was not far away, and so the whole party quickly halted before it.

The cell into which it led was of tolerably large dimensions, though its interior was not very well revealed by the dark lantern which the turnkey carried.

"There you are, my lord. Be good enough to enter."

"You will remove this cord, of course?" he said, haughtily, making use of his voice for the first time.

"Certainly, my lord, and anything else compatible with duty which I can do shall be done."

No sooner was the cord removed, however, than Lord Harcliffe strode into the cell.

"That is all I shall require to-night. Leave me!"

"Would your lordship like——"

"Nothing," he answered, interrupting him.

"Then I have the honour of wishing your lordship good night!"

This salutation he did not condescend to reply to.

"D—n his pride!" muttered the Governor. "It will have a fall, though, I'm thinking."

Then, in a louder voice, he added:

"Make the door secure, Jenkins; and it will be your duty to remain here on guard. Do not leave watching it a moment, as you value your place. You shall be relieved in a couple of hours."

With these words all departed, save Jenkins, who prepared to make himself as comfortable as his situation would allow.

On reaching the vestibule, the Governor, who had been in deep thought for some moments, turned to the two men who were nearest to him.

"Go you," he said, "out into the courtyard, and fix your eyes upon the window of No. 31. If you see anything that should not be there, raise an immediate alarm. We must not omit any such precaution as this, for should he escape, rely upon it we shall all be turned out at a minute's notice."

The men did not seem to go very willingly to their duty, but seemed somewhat more content when promised that they should be relieved in an hour.

After that the interior of Newgate resumed something like its ordinary appearance.

The various officials congregated together and discussed the strange events which had taken place, speculating whether Peterson had made an egregious mistake or not.

Gradually even this ceased, and the wonted calmness of night reigned beneath the vast roof of the City prison.

Jenkins yawned at his dreary and silent post.

"I don't care how soon the relief comes," he muttered. "I wonder what he's about?" he added, glancing towards the cell door and alluding to the prisoner. "How wonderfully quiet he is, to be sure! I should think he has never so much as stirred."

Hardly had these words escaped his lips when his ear caught a faint tapping sound.

"Hullo!" he cried. "What is it?"

"Open the door!" said the prisoner, in a deep voice.

"Not if I know it!" was the reply.

"I want to speak to you."

"All right! So you shall! The Governor did not say I was to hold no communication with you."

But if the prisoner had expected to see the cell door opened he was deceived.

Jenkins made his way to a kind of little wicket in the middle of the door.

The opening was less than a foot square, and was very strongly protected with iron bars.

Nearly all the cell doors were provided with these *guichets*, as they afforded a ready means of inspecting the prisoners.

"Here I am, your lordship. What do you want?"

"To hold a few words of conversation with you."

"Very good—the Governor never said a word agen that."

"But why not come in?"

"Because I prefer to stay here. If you have anything to say you can come a little closer to the grating, and I shall be able to hear every word."

There was a pause.

"I wanted to ask you a question," said the prisoner, at length.

"I am waiting to hear it, my lord."

"What wages do you receive?"

The question was so very different from what Jenkins had expected that all he could say was:

"What wages, my lord?"

"Yes, how much a week are you paid?"

"Well, my lord, leaving out my reg'lars, I should say eighteen shillings."

"And how much are your reg'lars, as you call them?"

"Well, when things are good, my lord, about as much more."

"Ah! not so bad! But you have a wife and children, I suppose?"

"Yes, my lord."

"And is this the mode of life you like best, Jenkins? If you had your choice, now, is this what you would like to be?"

"Well, no."

"I thought not. Surely at some time or other you must have said: 'There, that is the life I should like! Why wasn't I born with money enough?'"

"You are as good as a conjuror, my lord."

"Then you have had some such thought?"

"I have."

"Well, what is it now?"

"Well, if your lordship must know, though I don't see how it can at all signify to such as you——"

"Never mind about that. Go on!"

"Well, then, I think if there is one life more delightful than another, it is to be the landlord of a quiet roadside inn."

"Ah!"

"It is truly delightful, my lord. Just think of getting up every morning with the beautiful trees and fields to look at—plenty of the best of everything around you, only waiting for you to take the trouble of putting it down your throat. Then across the yard would be your stable, with a capital fast-trotting pony in it that you could go off for a ride round the country with whenever you felt inclined to do so, and—— But there, don't let me say another word, or it will make me wild enough to go and knock my head against the stone wall, that it will."

"Ah! What a strange thing it would be, Jenkins, if you were to find yourself nearer to realising your dream than you have ever been before!"

"What do you mean, my lord?"

"How much would it cost now, do you think, to carry out your little plan?"

"A very great deal—more than ever I shall have. I am nothing better than a thundering fool for thinking about such a thing!"

"Nothing of the sort; but just name the sum to oblige me."

"Why, three or four hundred pounds, I should say," replied the turnkey, with a sigh at the magnitude of the sum.

"Indeed! Now, what should you think if you were to find yourself in the way of earning six times as much?"

"Six times!"

"Six times as much as three hundred pounds."

"There's never no fear, my lord," was the emphatic rejoinder.

"Nay; there, now, you make a mistake—a very great mistake. Will you listen to me for a few minutes?"

"Certainly, my lord."

"Well, then, I will give you two thousand pounds in money if you will only consent to do what I ask."

"Two thousand pounds?"

"Not a shilling less."

"You are joking, my lord."

"Not I—I never was more serious."

"Then you must want me to set you at liberty, and that is beyond my power. So we had better say no more about it, as it will only make me wretched."

"Nay—nay, Jenkins, you are too hasty. You will not wait to let me finish what I have to say."

Jenkins shook his head despondingly.

"You are not very wide of the mark," continued Lord Harcliffe. "What I wanted you to do was only to assist me to escape."

"It's no good, my lord. It's impossible—it is indeed."

"But I am of a different opinion."

"So you may be, my lord, but I am right after all."

"Don't make too sure of it."

"I can't help it. There's extra precautions taken in the prison, and I know Peterson too well to think he will give you the ghost of a chance. I'll warrant you the outside of the prison is so well watched, that not so much as a mouse could leave it unseen."

"Never mind," said his lordship, "I will run the risk of that."

"How so?"

"All I want you to do is to liberate me from this cell. If you will do so you shall have the money, no matter whether I make my ultimate escape or not."

"Do you mean that, my lord?"

"I do."

"But it would be only robbing you. I assure you it is impossible for you to get away. And I—— But hush—hush! Some one comes!"

Jenkins hastily slammed the little wicket, and all was still.

To his annoyance, he found it was the relief guard, which such a short time before he had been longing for so earnestly.

Had he possessed the power, he would have sent the man back who had come to replace him.

His dismay may be conceived when he discovered that the Governor formed one of the approaching party, and the first words that fell from his lips were:

"What have you been saying to the prisoner, Jenkins?"

"What have I been saying?"

"Yes! Let me have no prevarication!"

"I have said nothing particular, sir, I am sure."

"Then why did you open the wicket?"

"Merely to see that he was quite safe, sir—nothing more."

"But I heard you talking."

"Yes, sir, the prisoner asked me what I wanted."

"You are too officious by half, Jenkins! Just lend me your lantern a moment."

Jenkins complied.

The Governor took it, and, opening the little wicket, directed the rays through the aperture.

The broad, bright beam of light falling through the bars disclosed the prisoner instantly.

The Governor was satisfied at the first glance that all was right.

"Excuse me, your lordship. I am obliged to take all these precautions for my own sake. I feel the responsibility of having you a prisoner very deeply indeed."

He paused a moment or two as if expecting a reply; but finding none came, he closed the wicket again.

"Now, Robinson," he said, addressing the turnkey he had brought to take Jenkins's place, "under no pretext open that wicket; but if the least thing unusual occurs give the alarm. Smith will be within call; and if I find you have disobeyed me, or held communication with the prisoner in any other way, you will be discharged in the morning."

So saying, the Governor turned on his heel and departed.

Jenkins followed him.

He was occupied all the way in contrasting his present life with the jovial existence of the landlord of a roadside inn.

But the chance of embracing the offer of Lord Harcliffe was at an end, and it was useless to think of it further.

Whether the prisoner had overheard the instructions given by the Governer or not is hard to say.

Certain is it that the other turnkeys who kept watch outside during the remainder of the night heard nothing of him.

In the morning, as soon as the regular duties of the day had commenced, the stir and bustle in Newgate was prodigious.

The Governor could not rest until he had paid a visit to his important prisoner.

An audible sigh of relief escaped his lips when he found him safe.

Lord Harcliffe looked but little the worse for his night's incarceration.

"I suppose you would like breakfast?" said the Governor, by way of saying something. "There is not much time to lose, because it is necessary you should be early at Bow Street."

"You seem a reasonable man——" begun the prisoner.

The Governor bowed low to the compliment.

"Tell me, then," continued his lordship—"is there no possible means by which I can escape this morning's ordeal?"

"You mean the examination before the magistrate?"

"I do."

"I fear not, my lord. But really, when you come to think of it, it is nothing. Ten to one if the proceedings altogether occupy more than a quarter of an hour, and then you will be brought back here safely enough."

"Are you quite sure that this proceeding is inevitable?"

"I am, my lord. However painful it may be to you, it cannot be avoided."

"Enough, then. Let us say no more upon the subject," he said, with a moody frown.

"But your lordship will take some refreshment?"

"What appetite can you expect me to have?"

"Not enough to make you relish our prison fare. But I need hardly tell you that the same thing which procures delicacies elsewhere will not fail to do so even within the walls of Newgate."

His lordship smiled.

"Leave me," he said. "Send me what you like—I care not."

His behaviour puzzled the Governor.

"I don't know what to make of him," he said, mentally, as he went out. "Last night I believed that there was some astounding mistake; but now, judging by what I see and hear, it seems more likely that Peterson is in the right. Any way, we shall see what the next few days will bring forth. I will wager any money that at the worst he will fare all the better for having possession of a title."

Nevertheless, he gave orders for an excellent breakfast to be served, wisely thinking that he could scarcely be a loser by doing so.

But the delicacies failed to tempt the prisoner's appetite, and the meal went away almost untasted.

A few moments afterwards the officers appeared who had been instructed to carry him to Bow Street.

Of course it was a very unusual thing for an uncommitted prisoner to be sent in the first instance to Newgate; but it was judged expedient by the authorities to depart from the ordinary course on the present occasion.

Peterson, of course, was at the head of those who entered; and, considering the immense amount of trouble he had had, and the great stake he had yet depending on the result, nothing could be less wondered at.

CHAPTER LI

LORD HARCLIFFE HAS A STRANGE AND UNEXPECTED VISIT PAID TO HIM IN THE NEWGATE CELL.

The few necessary preparations for conveying the prisoner to Bow Street were quickly made.

Lord Harcliffe remained as impassive as it was possible for any human being to be.

When Peterson proposed to pinion him for greater security, not a word of objection escaped his lips.

Then the gloomy passages—gloomy even now, when the bright sun was gilding the interior of the prison—were passed through.

As on the previous night, a hackney-coach was drawn up and in waiting close to the entrance of the vestibule.

Into this conveyance the prisoner was hurried, and, escorted as before by an overwhelming body of police officers, carried to Bow Street.

The hour for opening the Court had not yet arrived, and his lordship was taken to the police station on the opposite side of the way.

Here some formalities, which, strictly speaking, ought to have been gone through the night before, were complied with.

The charge was duly entered by the inspector in the book appointed for that purpose.

During the whole of this scene, Lord Harcliffe preserved his former air of utter indifference.

As soon as all these preliminaries had been gone through, the inspector, addressing Peterson, said:

"I would advise you to get across to the Court now without any further delay. This job is sure to get blown about, and if you stay you will have more trouble to force your way across than a little."

Peterson acted on this suggestion immediately, and found that he was not a moment too soon.

The intelligence that Lord Harcliffe was about to be brought up for examination diffused itself abroad, and the consequence was that the roadway was already thronged with idlers.

Still, not enough people had assembled to make it difficult to cross over.

"Thank goodness that is done!" said Peterson. "If we had stayed any longer we should have had ten times more trouble."

Some time had yet to pass away, nevertheless, before the hour came for opening the Court.

Accordingly, they were all shown into a small apartment.

The numbers of the officers were quite enough to prevent the slightest hope of escape, and Lord Harcliffe, doubtless being fully impressed with this fact, did nothing but sit in gloomy silence.

The officers seemed rather ill at ease in his society.

Those jokes and quips which would have fell readily enough from their lips had he been an ordinary prisoner, were unheard.

What conversation passed, took place for the most part in whispers.

At last, after what seemed an age, the welcome intelligence was brought that the Court was at length open.

Immediately upon this intimation, the prisoner was led into that inconvenient, dingy chamber where the presiding magistrate metes out justice.

On the present occasion the narrow limits of the Court were crammed to suffocation point by a crowd that seemed more than usually anxious to become acquainted with what was going on.

Several gentlemen occupied seats on either side of the magistrate.

Proceedings were opened in due form.

The charge was read over, and the prisoner, when called upon to plead, said, amid a death-like stillness in the Court:

"Not guilty."

His tones were firm and clear.

"It is my purpose," said the counsel for the prosecution, "only to lay just so much evidence before your worship as will justify the prisoner's commitment to Newgate, and, therefore, I will first call the gentleman towards whom the public is under so deep an obligation—I mean Lieutenant Tracy."

Amid a slight hum and confusion, the naval officer was placed in the witness-box.

No sooner was this done than every noise was stilled in expectation.

"What is your name?" asked the magistrate.

"Tracy."

"What are you?"

"A lieutenant in his Majesty's navy."

"Look at the prisoner at the bar. Do you know him?"

"I do."

"Who is he?"

"Lord Harcliffe."

"And under what other character have you known him?"

"As the Black Highwayman."

The words, firmly uttered, produced an immense excitement in the Court.

"Are you sure that you are not mistaken?"

"Quite sure, your worship."

"How came you to make the discovery?"

"On the eighth of the present month I was on the Windsor Road, and was stopped by a man on horseback, whose features were concealed by a black mask."

"And what did you do then?"

"I resisted his demand, and, leaning forward, suddenly snatched the mask from his face."

"Well?"

"I recognised him instantly."

"And who was it?"

"Lord Harcliffe, the prisoner at the bar."

The magistrate now looked across the Court, and said:

"Have you no solicitor in attendance?"

"None, your worship. This monstrous and unfounded charge has taken me wholly by surprise. If your worship commits me, as in the face of the testimony just given I suppose you cannot help doing, of course you will accept of substantial bail?"

The magistrate shook his head.

"The charge is not a bailable one," he said. "Unless you can show me that it is some great mistake—and I confess I feel that there has been a mistake somewhere—I shall have no alternative but committing you to Newgate till the next assizes; the hardship of this will not be so very great, as the sessions will commence in a day or two."

"But," said Lord Harcliffe, with well-manifested surprise, "does your worship really contemplate committing me to Newgate?"

"I regret to say I have no other alternative, unless such evidence is brought before me as will completely clear you of the charge."

Lord Harcliffe was silent, and Peterson was next called into the witness-box.

He deposed to the capture of his lordship, and, with many exaggerations, related what took place at Leicester House.

Then he produced the different bills that had been issued, offering various rewards, and containing descriptions of the daring highwayman.

"Those are all the witnesses I propose to call on the present occasion, your worship," said the counsel for the prosecution.

The magistrate then turned to the prisoner, and said.

"What have you to urge by way of defence? Have you no witnesses to call?"

"None at all, your worship. I can only say that the charge against me is utterly false and wholly without foundation. I am not prepared with my defence, however. I can only say that this is the first unravelling of a base and villanous conspiracy against me."

"Then, my lord, however much I may regret it, I have but one course to pursue. It is to commit you in the usual form to take your trial at the ensuing assizes."

The prisoner inclined his head with the air of one submitting to an inevitable fate.

The witnesses were then bound over to give their evidence when called upon, and the prisoner was removed.

This was a more anxious and difficult matter than bringing.

But ultimately, by the exertions of large bodies of the officers, it was done, and the gloomy portals of Newgate again reached.

After numberless precautions, the prisoner was once more conveyed within the prison walls.

"Committed for trial, then?" said the Governor, in accents of surprise, as though he had not expected such an event.

"Yes; and I would advise you to look carefully after him. Should he escape, your place would not be worth a penny."

"I am ready to take the responsibility," was the reply. "I would stake any amount of money he does not escape, so confident am I in the excellence of the plan I have devised for keeping him securely. It will entail a great deal of trouble upon myself, but then I do not care for that."

What the Governor's plan was, about which he expressed himself so confidently, will very shortly be seen.

The same cell—that is, No. 31—was again chosen for the reception of the prisoner.

The Governor saw him safely placed in it, and watched the bolting and locking of the ponderous door attentively.

Satisfied that all was well, he retired to his own apartments.

In half an hour afterwards, however, the prisoner was disturbed from a fit of gloomy meditation by hearing the *guichet* flung open.

Looking up, he saw the Governor's face flattened against the grating.

"Oh, all right!" he said, and immediately closed the little wicket again.

In another half-hour the same ceremony was gone through.

"Oh, that's his little scheme, is it?" cried Jenkins. "Well, it is an odd thing to me if he does not get tired of that caper before he has paid many visits. What a nice pleasant life he would have if he just looked after every other prisoner in the same way!"

Despite Jenkins's disparaging remarks, there could be no doubt that the Governor had actually hit upon the best and easiest plan of keeping a prisoner in safety.

It was better by far than trusting to bolts and bars.

The only question was whether, after a certain time, he would not get tired of following it up.

This peeping and prying was excessively annoying to the prisoner; but in his present situation it was useless for him to think of making any objections.

He determined at last not to gratify the Governor by looking up when he paid his visit, and so resolutely kept his face buried in his hands.

The next time, however, the door itself was opened.

Still he took no notice of it, believing it only to be the Governor on his ordinary errand.

It was not until the words, "A visitor," had been several times pronounced that he looked up.

His fingers had been pressed upon his eyes for so long that at first he could not see who had entered.

But he felt some one take him by the hand, and the accents of a familiar voice fell upon his ear.

"Why, Colonel Swift," he said, "who would have expected that you would have paid me a visit?"

"Yet here I am, you see; and, as the Governor will tell you, I am entitled to half an hour's private conversation with you."

"Yes, that is the case," said the Governor, who looked far from pleased.

"Very well, then," said the colonel. "Be good enough to lock the door and leave us to ourselves."

No sooner was this done than Lord Harcliffe, with an expression of great surprise and curiosity upon his face, said:

"My dear colonel, what is the meaning of this?"

"Wait a moment, and you shall know all. That confounded Governor is doubtless within hearing, and I don't wish him to have the least idea of my business."

"Come further back. In this corner of the cell, close to

[LORD HARCLIFFE HAS A VISIT FROM THE GOVERNOR OF NEWGATE.]

the window here, I don't believe that anyone can overhear a syllable."

"Very well. In the first place, I suppose you will not have much trouble in guessing who has sent me?"

"Sent you? Then you have not come of your own accord?"

"No," said the colonel, with a laugh. "I confess I have not."

"But who can have sent you?"

"Try, now, if you can exercise your ingenuity sufficiently to hit it."

"I am puzzled."

"Come, now—who should you think most likely?"

"I know not, unless it should be—— But no—no: he would not trouble himself so far."

"Who? Name—name!"

"The prince."

"You are right, my boy!"

"The prince sent you to me?" ejaculated Lord Harcliffe, in a way that showed how much the intelligence astonished him.

"Yes, my boy."

"And for what purpose?"

"You shall know anon. What I have to say is very confidential indeed."

"Do not keep me in suspense."

"I will not. Of course the prince at first was a good deal amazed at what took place last night, and a good deal annoyed as well."

"Why annoyed?"

"Because he would gladly have saved you if he could."

"Does he believe that there is any truth in this charge made against me?"

"I think he does."

"You think he does?" said Lord Harcliffe, almost with a shout.

"Quietly—quietly, my dear fellow! What if you have cried 'Stand and deliver!' a few times on the King's highway? It is no more than many a one like you has done before when running short of supplies, and no more than many a one will do again. Tut! man, where is the harm in it?"

Lord Harcliffe made no reply.

He was busy, trying to surmise the meaning of this extraordinary and unlooked-for visit.

Colonel Swift was well known to him.

He was one of those doubtful and by no means reputable characters that Frederick Prince of Wales was too fond of having close to his person.

He was well known for a swaggerer and inveterate gamester, a duellist, and a few things more redounding still less to his credit.

"Pshaw, man!" he said. "You think too deeply of it. What more is this than a mere escapade?"

"It seems that I am likely to suffer dearly enough for it, whether or not," replied the prisoner, interrupting him.

"No, no—not a bit of it, believe me."

"How? What do you mean?"

"Why, supposing that this accusation is really well founded—and it seems absurd to doubt it—I have the power to set you free."

"You are dreaming, colonel."

"Not I, believe me."

"You are really in earnest?"

"I am."

"Explain yourself, then."

"I will; but do you admit first the truth of the accusation?"

"I will not admit that to any living soul!"

"Will you deny it?"

"No—nor deny it either."

"Enough: I understand you."

"Beware how you draw a false conclusion!"

"Listen. This Black Highwayman, whoever he may be, is under an obligation to the prince already. He has promised to render him a service when called upon."

Lord Harcliffe bowed.

"Well, supposing that, in order to support your jolly life, you have sometimes played this character, his Royal Highness will free you from the consequences of all that you have done, and set you at liberty in less than twelve hours."

"Is this really so?"

"I answer you upon my honour."

The prisoner smiled at the assurance given him.

"What do you say?" continued the colonel.

"What are the conditions, supposing it done—for of course there are conditions?"

"You are as good as a conjuror, my dear fellow; there is a condition."

"Name it."

"Supposing the prince to be right in his surmise that you have played the character of the Black Highwayman, he will set you at liberty and gain you a free pardon——"

"On condition that?"

"On condition that you take a solemn oath that you will, when called upon by him, perform a certain service."

"What service?"

"That I cannot tell you."

"Cannot you give me any idea of its nature?"

"I might do so, but dare not."

"Can you tell me whether——"

"I can tell you nothing. If you have got confidence enough in the prince to swear to do his bidding at the time when he requires you, you will be got out of this scrape without the slightest trouble and danger to yourself."

"But it does not lie in his power to pardon me."

"Not now it does not," said the colonel, in a way that showed his words had a peculiar signification, "but some day it will. Life is uncertain: who can say how soon he may not ascend the throne?"

The prisoner remained in deep thought.

"And you will tell me no more about this mysterious service?"

"No—I have told you too much already."

"How too much? You have told me nothing."

"But if you have not guessed my meaning you are duller witted than I could have conceived was possible."

"And suppose I refuse?"

"Why, then you will have to get out of your fix as best you can. Let me tell you you will meet with no mercy. Your rank will not shield you in the least. You are well known as being one of the adherents of the Prince of Wales, and the King's party will be only too anxious to get you out of the way. Rely upon it, your only chance is taking the oath the prince requires."

But Lord Harcliffe was silent and undecided.

The colonel looked at him in amazement.

"I am rather surprised, Harcliffe. I should have thought you would have jumped readily at such a chance as this. Be quick! Decide ere it is too late."

Just as he uttered these last words the cell door was opened, and the pertinacious Governor appeared.

"The half-hour allowed for the visit has expired. Come!"

"Do you decide, Harcliffe?"

"How long can I have to consider?"

"Three hours."

"No longer?"

"Not a moment."

"Leave me till then."

"Enough!" said the colonel. "Mr. Governor, oblige me by showing me the way."

The Governor bowed with a great deal of respect as he said:

"This way, colonel, if you please."

Most people treated the prince's adherents with the greatest deference, because, in the natural order of things, it seemed certain that before very long the Prince of Wales would ascend the throne.

The Governor fancied himself a politic man, and though he openly professed to belong to the King's party, yet he was ever careful not to do or say anything that might lead to his dismissal when the prince came to the throne.

He was careful, therefore, not to do anything to displease the colonel.

"I am sorry I broke in upon your conference, colonel," he said, with a very apologetic air, "but I have received such particular orders about the safe keeping of the prisoner, that I am obliged to do my duty to the letter."

He said this while he stood watching the turnkey secure the door.

When this was done, and he was satisfied that the prisoner had no chance of getting out, except through the treachery of some person in the prison, he conducted his visitor along the gloomy passages.

"In three hours," said the colonel, "you will see me again."

"But—but I am sorry to inform you that in three hours' time the visiting hours will be over."

"Never mind about that. I am no ordinary visitor, understand, and shall come fully provided with authority."

The Governor made a wry face, but said nothing.

He was terribly distrustful about all this visiting, and feared somehow that it would end in the loss of his prisoner.

These misgivings, of course, he was too prudent to make visible to Colonel Swift, who, on leaving the prison, stalked down the Old Bailey with his usual swaggering air.

That the interview which had just taken place had had a disturbing influence on the prisoner, the turnkey on guard was certain.

Although the ponderous door was shut and fastened, yet so great was the silence that reigned in the dismal building that the turnkey could hear the prisoner pacing up and down his cell with rapid and irregular steps.

He was thus engaged every time the Governor paid his visit of inspection.

"Something is going to happen," he said, feeling more uncomfortable than ever. "I must be doubly vigilant. Confound the colonel! I wish I had never seen his face."

It would be quite impossible for anyone to be in a more dreadful state of anxiety than the Governor was.

Punctual to the moment, Colonel Swift, at the expiration of the three hours, showed himself at the entrance to the Governor's house adjoining the prison.

He brought with him a letter, which he placed in the hands of the Governor.

"I hope that is authority sufficient."

"Quite," said the Governor, with a bow—apparently to the letter.

"Then be good enough to conduct me to the prisoner without delay."

"I am ready," was the reply, given with a half-suppressed sigh.

"And please to observe," continued the colonel, "that not a word is said about the duration of the interview."

"How long do you expect it to last?"

"I can't say. Perhaps not many minutes; but, at any rate, if it is not over in half an hour, do not interrupt us."

As may be supposed, the result of this speech was to make the Governor more uncomfortable still, and his heart grew heavier at every step he took towards the cell.

The colonel, however, was, as usual, in the best of spirits.

He was one of those beings to whom depression of the mind is a thing unknown.

Lord Harcliffe was still at his restless walk when they opened the door.

At their entrance, however, he stopped short and wheeled round suddenly towards them.

Not a word was spoken, however, until the Governor withdrew.

"Come, Harcliffe," said the colonel, tapping the lid of his gold snuff-box, "have you made up your mind yet?"

He calmly took a pinch of the highly-perfumed snuff, and then held out the box to his companion.

But it was rejected with a hasty, angry gesture.

"You feel this too deeply—indeed you do, Harcliffe. Come, be a man, and answer my question."

Lord Harcliffe's eyes flashed.

But subduing his resentment, he said, in a calm, determined voice:

"I must know the nature of the service before I can pledge myself to perform it."

"And is that your decision?"

"It is."

"Then our interview will be much shorter than I anticipated. The Governor's satisfaction will be great. As for you, my boy, you must just use your own exertions to get out of this delightful abode."

So saying, he turned on his heel, as though about to depart immediately.

But Lord Harcliffe restrained him.

"Stay," he said; "let us have a clear understanding. Will you not give me a hint as to what it is I shall have to do?"

"No more than I have given you already."

"But consider the unreasonableness of such a condition!"

"Say, rather, consider the unreasonableness of one who, in your position, hesitates to adopt a ready and simple path to freedom!"

Lord Harcliffe resumed his hurried walk.

Colonel Swift leered after him with an expression that would have done credit to Mephistopheles.

"What would you give to be free, Harcliffe?"

"Anything."

"I thought so. I am mistaken in you. I believed that you would, as I told you before, have jumped at such an opportunity."

"But, colonel, what is it but taking a desperate leap in the dark? Would you pledge yourself to such a matter?"

"Would I? Had I been in your situation, I should have been free by now. Bah! Such scruples sicken me."

"Colonel, you know that I am in a desperate condition."

"You are. Without the prince's aid you will as surely swing by the neck at Tyburn as the sun will rise to-morrow."

"Once more," he said, "will you tell me what I shall be required to do?"

"I cannot and dare not, and, what is more, if you refuse now, the chance will not again be offered to you."

"Then I consent," he said, with the manner of one who, by the force of circumstances, is compelled to adopt an unwilling course.

"That's right. Although you spoke in so determined a way, I could not bring myself to believe that you were serious in your refusal."

"I consent most reluctantly," was the reply.

"Now—now! Come, no hesitation! Here is my sword. Take it. So! Now swear upon the hilt that you will, when the time arrives, perform the service the Prince of Wales requires without scruple and without shrinking."

For a moment Lord Harcliffe seemed unable to speak.

But at last, half-maddened by the taunts of the colonel, he said:

"I swear to do the prince's bidding in anything that he may require of me."

"Enough!" cried the colonel, sheathing his sword. "Now only think how much better it would have been had you made up your mind in the first instance!"

Of this speech Lord Harcliffe took no sort of notice, but merely said:

"When shall I be free?"

"Before daybreak. I will leave you now, for I have much on hand. When I see you again, you will be once more at liberty."

Colonel Swift knocked sharply at the dungeon door.

The turnkey opened it cautiously, and allowed him to pass out.

Remembering his way, the colonel hastily walked through the various passages.

"I want to see the Governor," he said, to the first turnkey he met. "Where is he?"

"In his own room, sir, I think."

"Take me there, then."

The man complied, and, as he had stated, the Governor was sitting down in his private room, looking very restless and haggard.

His countenance showed how much the colonel's visit surprised him.

"Sit still, Mr. Governor. I will take this seat. I shall not detain you long."

What passed between the two no one ever knew, though many were the guesses given as to the import of the interview.

It lasted nearly an hour, and when the Governor opened the door to allow the colonel egress, his face was as white as ashes.

"You will not fail," were the colonel's parting words, spoken in a tone that almost sounded like menace. "Do not shake so, man, and look so white; people will wonder what ails you. Rely upon it, all will be well."

The colonel then assumed his nonchalant air, and ran nimbly down the steps into the street.

The Governor stood like a man in a dream, and for a moment or so forgot that the door was open.

Closing it hastily, he staggered rather than walked back to his room, and going to a cupboard, produced a bottle of brandy.

A great quantity of this fiery beverage he swallowed at a draught.

"Heaven help me!" he said. "How this matter will end I cannot tell. I have as good as got a noose round my neck already—I feel I have."

He shivered in spite of the potent draught he had just taken.

Then drawing a chair close up to the fire, he plumped down upon it, and then covering up his face with his hands, sat immersed in thought.

The clock of St. Sepulchre's Church struck the hour of eleven.

Still he stirred not.

But when the hour of midnight was pealed forth with clanging notes, he started up and looked around him nervously.

"Twelve o'clock!" he gasped. "The hour has come! What I have to do must be commenced. But I must have more brandy first, or my nerves will fail me."

Another draught, much larger than the first, was poured out and swallowed.

"I must do it," he said, with desperate resolution. "Come what will, I must do it. There is no loophole of evasion—none—none."

With a heavy sigh he replaced the brandy, and from the cupboard produced a small dark lantern.

So excessive was his agitation that for some moments he could not ignite the wick.

At last all was right; and throwing a cloak over his shoulders, he opened the door of his room cautiously, and peeped forth.

The passage with which it communicated was as dark and silent as the grave.

While remaining thus in a listening attitude, another attack of irresolution came over him.

But it ended as before.

Shutting his door behind him, he strode silently tow... as the double doors which formed the means of communication between his own private apartments and the main body of the prison.

On the outer threshold he again paused.

A cold, chilling air came sweeping up the arched stone corridor—so cold that his blood seemed to turn to ice.

Again advancing, he made his way in a direction that rendered it tolerably certain that his destination was No. 31.

CHAPTER LII.

RELATES THE STRANGE EVENTS ON ONE NIGHT IN NEWGATE.

THE Governor now seemed to have got the better of his fear and irresolution, for he walked on without pausing until he reached the door of the cell in which Lord Harcliffe was imprisoned.

The change of guard had taken place at twelve o'clock, so that the man now on guard could not have occupied his post many minutes.

It proved to be Jenkins.

He exhibited no signs of astonishment at seeing the Governor at so late an hour, expecting, no doubt, that he had merely come to make his usual inspection.

But when he was ordered to remove the fastenings he began to wonder what was afloat.

The Governor's countenance was inscrutable.

"Be quick!" he said. "And when I go in, close the door after me."

"And fasten it, sir?"

"Yes, and fasten it. I will knock when I want to leave."

The door being opened, the Governor, raising the lantern in his hand, crossed the threshold

Lord Harcliffe, who had been anxiously wondering what means would be adopted to secure his freedom, looked up inquiringly.

The Governor, however, did not attempt to open his lips until the door had been closed and fastened after him.

Then he glanced suspiciously around, and finally beckoned Lord Harcliffe to a distant corner.

"What is the meaning of all this?" he asked.

"Hush—hush!" exclaimed the Governor, unable to conceal his trepidation. "If you speak so loud we shall be overheard!"

"What is it you have to say?"

"I have seen Colonel Swift!"

"Ah!"

"Yes," continued the Governor. "And though I know I might as well go and put a noose round my neck at once as attempt to carry out his commands, yet I dare not refuse."

"And what are his commands?"

"To set you at liberty."

"But how?"

"He would not trouble himself about the means; he said he would leave that to my discretion."

"And you have been promised some recompense for this?"

"Yes; but no one knows how long it may be before I receive it, or what may happen between now and then."

Lord Harcliffe's countenance gave token of the amount of surprise he felt.

"And you will really set me free?"

"I dared not refuse."

"Strange that Colonel Swift should have such extraordinary power over you!"

"Hold—hold! Not a word about that—not a word!"

"Listen to me a moment."

"I am all attention, my lord."

"There are a variety of reasons why I wish to get away from here with secrecy and speed. I cannot bear to contemplate being the object of any further judicial proceedings."

"Then—then you are——"

"Never mind what. Listen to me."

"Certainly, my lord."

"You must understand that, although I so urgently desire my freedom, yet I do not want the slightest service rendered me to be unpaid for; therefore, whatever arrangement you may have made with Colonel Swift I shall take no notice of, but if you aid me to escape I shall pay you liberally for so doing."

Hearing this, the Governor brightened up a little.

"Do not speak so loud, my lord," he said, cautiously; "the turnkey outside may hear us."

"Enough. We now thoroughly understand each other, I think; and what I now want to know is how you intend to get me out of the prison unseen and unsuspected?"

"It will be difficult, my lord—very difficult."

"But you have thought of some plan?"

"Oh yes!"

"What is it, then?"

"There seems to me to be only one way."

"Let me hear it."

"I will take you to my private apartments in the prison, and when we are sure the coast is clear you can slip out of my front-door into the street."

"An excellent one and an easy one, or rather would be but for the man outside. You seem to have forgotten him."

"No I do not, my lord—that is just the difficulty. I could curse myself now for my extra care. But, then, who could have guessed this would happen? And I dare not do away with the guard now, because if I did I should at once be suspected of having connived at your escape."

"You would."

"And that, my lord," said the Governor, with feverish anxiousness, "is the one thing that I want to guard against."

"Just so."

"But I don't know how it is to be managed, unless I send Jenkins off to some part of the prison, and then, as soon as he is gone, allow you to make your way to my apartments."

"Well, and what shall you do when Jenkins comes back?"

"I shall step out of the cell, pretending to speak to you, and take care to close the door before he has time to look inside; I would then follow you to my rooms."

Lord Harcliffe shook his head.

"Don't you like the plan, my lord?"

"I do not."

"Nor I; but I cannot devise anything better."

"Something else must be thought of," he cried—"that is quite certain. Suspicion would inevitably fall upon you; and, besides, I do not know the way to your private apartments, so ten to one I should meet some one by the way."

The Governor was in despair.

"I don't know how it is to be done."

"Wait a moment: I have a plan in my head which will get us out of our difficulties entirely."

"Indeed, my lord!"

"Yes; I feel sure it will answer. Did you not say Jenkins was the man on guard outside?"

"Yes, my lord."

"Very good; then we may depend upon his co-operation."

"Would you take him into confidence in the matter?"

"Certainly. He is to be trusted."

"You have been holding some communication with him, then?" said the Governor, interrogatively.

"Never mind about that. I will give you my plan in brief. I will make it appear that Jenkins entered the cell for some purpose, and that I then seized upon, bound, and gagged him, first taking his coat.

"Well, I should then accompany you to your apartments as you proposed, and take the first opportunity of slipping out."

"But——"

"You will find," continued the prisoner, interrupting him hastily, "that in the morning when my disappearance becomes known you will never be suspected, and Jenkins will not have anything more serious to fear than a reprimand."

"But how shall you induce him to take his part?"

"Believe me, I shall have not the least trouble about that. If you have no objection to the plan, call him in at once."

The Governor hesitated a little while under the fear that Jenkins might make an undue use of the power this secret would give him.

Unable, however, to see any better way to accomplish that which he was obliged to perform, he gave his consent.

Jenkins was accordingly called in.

On his entrance he attempted to put on such a look of extreme ignorance and surprise that Lord Harcliffe at once came to the conclusion that he had overheard some portion of the conversation.

The latter part of it, indeed, had not been carried on in so low a tone as to render it impossible for anyone at the door to catch the import of what was going forward.

"Jenkins," said the prisoner, "you remember the conversation we had together?"

"I do, my lord."

"Of course you have thought a great deal about it?"

"Not so much as you may think," was the gruff rejoinder. "What was the good?"

"You shall hear. If you are willing now to do what I asked you then the reward I named shall be yours."

Jenkins was, in spite of what he might have overheard, not a little amazed at hearing such a speech as this made in the presence of the Governor of the prison.

"But how is it to be done, my lord?"

"It is only necessary to explain to you your part of the business. You must allow me to bind and gag you, and leave you on the floor of the cell; I shall then lock the door and depart."

"But what must I say when I am found here—how am I to account for your disappearance?"

"You must say that you came into the cell at my earnest entreaty, and that no sooner had you entered than I set upon you, overpowered you, and then bound you secure."

"Will they be satisfied?"

"The Governor will take your part, and, as he will tell you, the most that you will have to fear will be a severe reprimand. Now do you consent?"

"I do."

"And you will promise to observe profound silence in relation to this affair?" said the Governor, most anxiously.

"I will."

"Then the reward I named shall be yours if you will apply to my house for it to-morrow. You will find my attendant there."

With this assurance Jenkins was satisfied.

Lord Harcliffe then pulled off the turnkey's coat, and, having done so, bound him tightly with his neckcloth and pocket-handkerchief.

"You know what you have to say?" cried the Governor, when all the preparations were complete.

"Never fear me: Peter Jenkins is quite equal to such a little matter as that."

"I can trust him," said the prisoner. "Come on, we have lost too much time already."

The pair, after one more glance around them, quitted the cell.

It was with feelings of peculiar satisfaction that Lord Harcliffe assisted the Governor to replace the fastenings on the door.

"Quick!" said the latter. "There is but little chance of one meeting with anyone in the corridors, but still, the sooner we are out of them the better."

With this Lord Harcliffe thoroughly agreed, and at a rapid rate they made their way to that part of the prison which was appropriated to the Governor's especial use.

The door of communication between them was reached in safety, and when he closed it behind him the Governor drew a long breath of relief.

"A few more moments at the most, my lord," he said, "will, I hope, see you beneath the canopy of heaven—no more to your relief than to mine. You must enter this room first, however, while I ascertain that the coast is perfectly clear outside."

Lord Harcliffe inclined his head in token of consent, and followed his conductor into the apartment where the mysterious interview with Colonel Swift had taken place.

The fire had burnt low, but the Governor stirred the embers, not only so as to diffuse warmth, but also so as to furnish them with as much light as they required.

The Governor hastened to pour out two glasses of his favourite spirit.

Lord Harcliffe gladly accepted the brandy, which he swallowed at a draught.

"Now," he said, "the sooner I am off the better. I have much to do before daybreak. Let me know whether the coast is clear."

"I will, my lord," answered the Governor, whose courage was a good deal fortified by the draught of brandy.

Accordingly he went to the front-door, and opening it to the extent of about a couple of inches, peeped forth.

Not a soul was to be seen.

He waited for some moments, and then, finding that no one appeared, gently closed the door again.

"Is all well?" asked Lord Harcliffe.

"There is not a soul to be seen."

"Excellent! I will be off without further delay. As to the reward I promised you, it will be left in a small parcel addressed to you in the course of the next day or two."

"Many thanks, my lord. Your liberality in this affair will be much appreciated, for I feel almost certain that I shall be dismissed."

"The contents of the parcel will compensate for the worst that may happen. Now show me to the front-door."

But just as he pronounced these last words a loud knocking made itself heard.

"What is that?"

But the Governor was too much taken aback to reply.

He stood like one stupified.

The knocking was resumed with redoubled clamour.

"Recover yourself!" cried Lord Harcliffe. "Don't stand like that! It is probably only some chance visitor."

"A chance visitor at this time of night? Oh no!"

"Well, then, whoever it may be," said Lord Harcliffe, impatiently, "open the door! I will screen myself behind this curtain. If it is some one you are obliged to invite to enter, take no notice—my presence will not be suspected."

The Governor was rallied a little by the energetic way in which Lord Harcliffe spoke, and he moved towards the door just as the other concealed himself behind the long, heavy curtains with which the window of the room was furnished.

The hiding-place was a good one, and would remain undetected unless suspicion should be roused and a search made; but this was not likely.

By the time he had opened the front-door, the Governor had recovered his composure tolerably well.

Standing on the doorstep was a tall, cloaked figure, which pushed rudely in without staying for the ceremony of an invitation to enter.

"Why the devil did you keep me waiting so long?" said the new-comer, fiercely. "Is a King's messenger to be kept waiting by the d—d Governor of a prison?"

"King's messenger?" gasped the Governor, whose courage evaporated as he heard the, to him, dreadful words.

"Yes. Which is the way to your room? I am the bearer of a special and important message from the Secretary of State."

Trembling in every limb, the Governor led the way to the room where the prisoner was hidden.

"It's very cold," he stammered, in order that his trepidation should not excite suspicion. "I really believe I had fallen asleep in my chair when your knocking startled me."

"Never mind about that," said the King's messenger, who happened to be one of those consequential, arrogant fellows who generally obtain such situations. "All I want you to do is to listen to me."

The Governor bowed, and wondered what was coming, though his heart whispered and suggested the nature of the communication he was about to hear.

"You have a prisoner of unusual importance now under your care?"

"Lord Harcliffe?"

"The same; and I have come here to inform you that it has reached the ears of his Majesty's officers of state that there is on foot a cunning and deeply-laid plan by which his escape is to be effected."

The Governor put on a look of well-affected astonishment.

"There is, I think, little doubt about the truth of the information received," continued the King's messenger, "and I have come to tell you that you are to take every precaution for the frustration of the attempt; and if, after this warning, it should be effected, the consequences will be serious to you."

"I will do my best, of course," stammered the Governor. "But can you not give me an idea of the nature of the plan of escape you speak of?"

"Nothing is known about it, I believe, and it was considered sufficient to warn you."

"It is a heavy responsibility," groaned the Governor, "and I shall not care how soon I am clear of it."

"Never mind: do your duty, and you will have nothing to fear. On the contrary, you will doubtless receive a substantial recognition of your services provided all goes well."

The Governor groaned.

"What's the matter with you, man?" said the messenger. "You look as melancholy as a condemned man! The prisoner is all right now, I suppose?"

"Oh yes—he's all right!"

"When did you see him last?"

"At midnight."

"Not long ago; but, now I think of it, I will trouble you to conduct me to the cell, in order that I may satisfy myself by ocular inspection that he is now quite safe."

"Were you instructed to do this?" asked the Governor, with a countenance from which every particle of colour had fled.

"Well, no, not exactly."

"Then I have to inform you that this is not the hour for allowing visitors to see the prisoners."

"Never mind about that. This is a special business, and you ought not to require telling so. Moreover, I am invested with full powers, and I insist upon being shown to the cell at once!"

The Governor was now in a dreadful dilemma.

So dreadful, indeed, did it appear to him, that his wits almost deserted him.

He knew that if he refused the King's messenger's request he would be laying himself open to suspicion.

On the other hand, if he visited the cell the discovery of the escape would be made—and be made, too, before Lord Harcliffe would have the opportunity of getting far from the prison.

The next words uttered by the King's messenger decided him.

"Beware how you refuse me and despise my power!" he said. "I tell you I must and will see the prisoner!"

"If you must you must, then. My lamp is lighted."

"Then I will follow you at once. Lead the way."

It was no easy task for the Governor to support himself.

But he knew what must be the inevitable result of the visit, and he summoned all his fortitude to his aid in the hope that he should be able to manifest the utmost astonishment when the fitting time for doing so arrived.

In another moment they left the room.

Lord Harcliffe, who had never moved and scarcely breathed during the conversation we have just set down, now ventured to draw the curtain aside a little.

But until he heard the door closed which formed the means of communication between the Governor's house and the prison, he did not move.

No sooner, however, did the welcome sound strike upon his ear than he strode swiftly across the room.

Just as he was about to cross the threshold his eye caught the cloak belonging to the King's messenger, which, upon his entrance, had been thrown by that individual across the back of a chair.

"I will take that," he muttered; "it will assist to disguise me. Perhaps, even if there is anyone outside, I shall be taken for the King's messenger."

Without further delay—for he knew many more minutes could not elapse without the discovery being made—he opened the front-door and glided forth.

The night was a very dark one.

Just as his feet touched the pavement a voice said:

"Here you are, sir! All right! I have only been walking him up and down a little."

He shrunk back at first in alarm.

A moment, however, served to show him that a boy was standing near, holding a horse by the bridle.

"The King's messenger's for a thousand!" ejaculated his lordship, mentally. "What a fortunate mistake! My escape will be ten times easier than I could have hoped for."

Almost before these words had passed through his mind he sprang into the saddle.

"Here, boy," he said, as he threw him a coin. "Good night."

The boy uttered a yell of dismay.

Lord Harcliffe's voice was so very different from the King's messenger's that he could not help being struck by it, and experienced a dreadful shock upon discovering that he had given up the horse he had been left in charge of to a wrong person.

He started to run, but before he could get half a dozen paces the horse had disappeared round the corner of Snow Hill, and the clatter of iron hoofs alone reached his ears.

"Capital!" said Lord Harcliffe, in a voice that was full of exultation. "I am free—free at last! And now I care not what ensues. I shall never be a prisoner again!"

He rode at a headlong rate down towards the Fleet Bridge.

Just as he was crossing over, the loud tolling of a bell came upon his ears.

"So soon?" he cried. "They have found me out! But what matters that? I am free, and being so, they have my free permission to ring the bell till doomsday if they like."

The tolling of the bell was heard by others besides himself, and an immediate stir was observable around, where but a moment before all had been perfect silence.

Up Holborn Hill he rode, at the utmost speed the horse was capable of making.

But just as he reached Holborn Bars a body of police officers came sweeping round the corner of Gray's Inn Lane.

Even at that distance the sonorous clanging of the bell could be distinctly heard.

"Quick—quick!" cried Lord Harcliffe. "You are wanted at once at Newgate. The Black Highwayman has escaped! I am off to Bow Street for further help!"

He shouted these words at the top of his voice, and was off before the officers could recover from their astonishment.

"Confound him!" said the one in command. "I wish I could have stopped him. He ought not to be going this way to Bow Street, the fool! But come on to Newgate—that is the only thing we can do!"

Lord Harcliffe's presence of mind had served him admirably.

What might otherwise have been a serious danger was by it completely avoided, for the officers were, in the innocence of their hearts, riding directly away from the man they so much wished to capture.

Lord Harcliffe's triumph increased.

At the same furious rate he directed his course towards his mansion in Piccadilly.

There was extreme danger in doing so; but it was a peril that had to be incurred.

"If I do not go now," he said, "I shall never have such another chance."

The further west he went the quieter and more deserted he found the streets.

When, at length, he pulled up in front of his mansion his horse was covered with foam from head to foot.

Slipping from the saddle before the creature had fairly stopped, he flung the reins over the iron palisades in front, and pulled the bell.

Exertion and excitement together had almost deprived him of breath.

The interval which elapsed between the ringing of the bell and the opening of the door seemed an age.

But just as he was about to repeat his summons, the

noise made by the removal of bars and bolts came upon his ear.

Another second and the door was gently opened.

"Is that you, Pharoah?"

An ejaculation of astonishment followed the inquiry, and before it was over Lord Harcliffe had crossed the threshold and closed the door behind him.

It was indeed Pharoah who had answered the door, and his lordship, bending down his head, whispered rapidly and energetically into his ear for some moments.

Pharoah listened in silence and made no attempt at interruption.

"Where are the servants?" Lord Harcliffe asked, at length.

The question was probably suggested by the intense silence within.

The house was like a house of the dead.

"Gone!" answered Pharoah, in his peculiar deep voice.

"All of them?"

"All."

"They are best gone. And, now that you have the place to yourself, take care that you allow no one to enter."

"And you?"

"I cannot say where I may be during the next few days. Do nothing save remain here till you hear again from me. I dare not stay longer. I expect every moment to hear the officers upon my track."

Pharoah opened the door with his former caution.

"Close it instantly after me," said his master, in a rapid whisper. "Don't remain to watch my departure."

He was obeyed.

No sooner had Lord Harcliffe descended the steps, however, than he found himself in the grasp of a man who bounded suddenly upon him out of the darkness.

The attack was so sudden and unexpected that it is a wonder he was not hurled to the ground.

Recovering himself by a great effort, he put forth the whole of his extraordinary strength to master his antagonist.

But this was no easy matter, for the man was tall, and powerful, and strong.

Determined not to lose his prey if he could help it, he raised his voice and bawled aloud for aid.

Nor were the shouts unavailing.

Windows were speedily thrown up, and footsteps could be heard hurrying to the scene.

Lord Harcliffe grew desperate.

By putting forth all his powers, he succeeded for a moment in getting free from the clinging grasp of his assailant.

Clenching his fist, he struck out with all his might.

The blow was enough to fell an ox.

The man tumbled headlong backwards, and lay upon the stone pavement motionless and insensible.

But by this time the whole neighbourhood had become aroused.

Watchmen came hurrying towards him with all the speed that age and the cumbrousness of their apparel would permit.

They sprung their rattles vigorously, however, and thus materially assisted in spreading the alarm.

But having disposed of his antagonist, Lord Harcliffe made a dash towards the spot where he had left his horse.

Just as he removed the reins from the palisade two more men rushed upon him.

But shaking them off before they were able to obtain a firm grasp, he sprang nimbly into the saddle.

He did not wait to thrust his feet into the stirrups; but striking vigorously with his heels, caused the horse to break into a gallop.

He was only just in time, for a party of police officers now came in sight.

Being mounted, they gave chase at once.

But Lord Harcliffe was an incomparable rider; and having obtained a good start, he contrived to keep it, for the horse belonging to the King's messenger was one of no ordinary character.

The escaped prisoner made his way towards the open country.

Trees and hedges flew past with a rapidity that was absolutely alarming.

Lord Harcliffe had neither whip nor spur; but he called aloud in excited, animated tones, and the intelligent animal hearing them, was induced to put forth his utmost powers of speed.

Further and further the police officers fell to the rear.

At last they became invisible, and, finally, the hoof-beats of their horses inaudible.

As soon as this was the case, Lord Harcliffe struck across the country in quite an opposite direction from that which he had been pursuing.

Although there did not now appear to be so much urgent necessity for great speed, he would not allow the horse to relax his pace.

It soon became evident that the fugitive had some particular destination in view, and that he was straining every nerve to reach it in the shortest possible space of time.

Regardless of almost every object, he made his way across the country as a bird wings its flight through the air.

Not once did he hesitate or turn aside.

At length some moss-grown park palings could be dimly seen in advance.

The leap was a high one; but he put the horse to it fearlessly.

Over he went like a gazelle; and when he alighted on the other side, Lord Harcliffe drew the rein as he said:

"Well done, brave fellow—well done! There are few better than you to be met with, I am sure. The race is over now. We are safe—safe!"

At a walking pace Lord Harcliffe made his way towards that lonely and apparently deserted building which we have formerly described.

When he paused before it on this occasion there was a faint tinge of daybreak in the eastern sky, and the cold gray light falling upon the crumbling walls and roof of the old Hall, made the place look still more gloomy and forlorn.

CHAPTER LIII.

RELATES WHAT BEFEL CAPTAIN HAWK ON HIS ARRIVAL AT THE GREYHOUND INN.

We last left Captain Hawk listening to the approach of a vehicle that was rolling along the high-road towards him at an unusually rapid rate.

He was undecided how to act.

Concealment seemed impossible, for the ruddy light of the rising sun was diffused around.

"I will let Satan walk on quietly," he muttered, just as the vehicle appeared round the bend of the road. "I will try to assume the manner of an ordinary traveller."

With admirable coolness, then, and self-possession, Captain Hawk walked on.

"If they do not interfere with me," he added, "I will not interfere with them. I am hardly equal to an adventure this morning."

Considering all that the highwayman had recently gone through, this is not to be wondered at.

The approaching vehicle proved to be a rather small travelling carriage drawn by a couple of first-class horses, who, being put upon their mettle, tore away at a great rate.

A man, closely muffled in a top-coat, and wearing a hat drawn closely over his brows—perhaps to keep off the cold—held the reins, and who, although the horses were going at full gallop, smacked his long whip over their ears at frequent intervals, which prevented them from relaxing their exertions in the least.

The rapid motion caused the carriage to jolt fearfully, and Captain Hawk fancied that since the driver had caught sight of him a greater inclination than ever was shown to keep the cattle at the top of their speed.

True to his expressed resolution, however, Captain Hawk rode on without making the least attempt at interference.

He noticed that the windows were closed and the blinds drawn down.

Just as he was in the act of passing, he fancied his ear caught a faint ejaculation, and immediately afterwards there was a sudden crash.

Turning round swiftly, he saw that one of the windows had been shattered to atoms.

"What does that mean?" he asked himself, checking his horse instinctively.

But before he could recover from the surprise into which he had been thrown, the carriage had got a considerable distance, as the driver, after the occurrence of this event, was no longer content to crack his whip, but lashed the high-spirited horses he had under command with it in a most vigorous manner.

"There is something going on there which should not, and now I know it I should never rest if I did not try to find out what it is."

No sooner had he said the words than he wheeled Satan round, and set off at full gallop after the carriage.

It was now more than a quarter of a mile in advance of him; and as the horses harnessed to it were such good ones and going at full gallop, the chase promised to be a long one.

This, for Captain Hawk, was diagreeable and dangerous, because it was taking him directly back to the officers he had been at so much pains to get away from.

Fortunately, Satan was in splendid condition.

The intelligent creature seemed at once to realise that the vehicle in front was the object his rider desired to overtake, and so he put forth to the very utmost those extraordinary powers of speed which we have so often had occasion to make mention of.

The distance intervening rapidly grew less.

In vain the driver used his whip—Satan flew on with the velocity of a racehorse.

When within about twenty paces of the carriage, however, one of the windows was let down with great violence, and a head projected.

It was drawn back instantly, but only to appear again without a second's delay.

This time a hand came with it, and this hand held some object on which the morning sun shone glitteringly.

Before Captain Hawk had time to do more than notice this, there was a sharp report and a wreath of blue smoke.

Simultaneously the highwayman uttered a cry, and after swaying to the right, fell backwards over the crupper of his horse.

He reached the ground with a tremendous shock, and then lay like one deprived of life.

Satan now well displayed his extraordinary sagacity, for he stopped immediately, and turned his head round towards his rider.

"I had the villain then!" said the man who had thrust his head out at the window so suddenly. "Serves him right—he should not interfere with a gentleman's private business! He will not do so again, I'll warrant."

Then turning and addressing himself to the driver, he said:

"Curse you! Drive on, will you! Don't spare the whip! Drive on, I say!"

So saying, he withdrew his head, and closed the window with a crash.

How long Captain Hawk remained lying motionless in the middle of the road he knew not.

When his faculties came back to him he lay without attempting to move, gazing unconsciously up into the blue sky, and having but a vague recollection of what had happened.

"I remember now," he murmured, at length. "I was shot. Is the wound serious, I wonder?"

It was only natural that, after asking himself this question, he should set about finding out the reply to it.

He sat up, and the first thing he saw was his horse, who rubbed his head against him with evident gratification.

"I feel no pain," he ejaculated, "and there are no signs of blood. What can have fetched me down, I wonder?"

This seemed more mysterious than ever, for he was able to rise to his feet without difficulty.

But happening to draw a long deep breath, he felt an acute pain in his lungs.

Placing his hand instinctively upon the spot, he found it to be near the upper edge of his sword-belt, which during his hasty ride had got somewhat shifted from its position.

But there was no wound, and no perforation of his apparel, as there would have been had the bullet entered.

The mystery was complete until he noticed that the top part of the buckle which secured his sword-belt was deeply indented.

"That is it," he said. "What a wonderfully narrow escape! I can only account for it by believing that that bullet did not carry my billet. What a dent! The bullet must have glanced off, and it must have been the sudden shock which caused me to fall."

Just then he remembered all about the carriage.

The particulars of the adventure had not recurred clearly to his mind until this moment.

On looking around him, however, no trace of the vehicle could be perceived.

"I am afraid," he said, "that that rascal's shot has been in one sense effectual, for, doubtless, the carriage is so far off as to make pursuit quite useless. But something more than usually atrocious must be in hand, or he would never have gone to the length of shooting a man on the high-road rather than be discovered."

Quite sure now that he was unharmed, and had no cause whatever for apprehension, he mounted his horse.

He remained for a moment irresolute.

"I must follow up this adventure as best I may," he said. "If I do not it will haunt me to my last hour. There may be no hope of success, but yet I shall not be content until I am quite assured of it."

A word to Satan was enough, and away he flew along the road again at a pace that promised to overtake anything, no matter how good a start it might have.

A little way further he reached a spot where he could see the high-road stretching out for a great distance before him.

Not a trace of the carriage, however, could be discerned.

The worst of it was, too, that Captain Hawk had no idea how long his insensibility had continued, though he fancied it could not be more than a few moments at the most.

Despite the little encouragement held out, he kept on at the same rapid rate, though he made sure that every moment would bring him in sight of his foes.

Nothing but the actual occurrence of this event would have been sufficient to cause him to abandon the enterprise.

"There seems no one on the road that I could make an inquiry of," he said, "though it would be a little dangerous to ask anyone—no more dangerous than to ride back upon my foes. What is that yonder?"

Some object by the wayside attracted his attention; but, as the sun shone into his eyes, he could not for the moment make out what it was.

"An old man breaking stones," he ejaculated. "There can be little danger in asking him a question; and whether there is or not, I shall risk it."

He pulled up as he spoke, and the old man, noticing the cessation of the sound, looked up.

"Tell me," said the captain—"have you seen a small travelling carriage, drawn by a couple of horses, pass this way?"

"Yes, I have."

"How long since?"

"Not three minutes."

"Were they going fast?

"At full gallop."

"Did they keep straight on?"

"No; they turned down the green lane yonder, on the right."

"Many thanks."

Captain Hawk put his hand into his pocket, intending to reward the old man for his information, but he found he had no money.

"Thanks," he cried. "I shall not forget you."

Off he went again, at the same headlong rate, though he took care to keep a good look-out for the green lane the old man had spoken of.

The fact that the carriage had had such a short start of him increased his ardour and impatience.

The green lane was not far off.

The name was appropriate, for apparently there was so little traffic along it that the grass had overgrown it in nearly every part.

[CAPTAIN HAWK SCALES THE BALCONY OF THE OLD MANSION.]

The lane was cut into two deep ruts, but the space between them was hard and well trodden, so that the captain was able to make his way along it at a very slightly diminished speed.

But he saw that the nature of the ground was such as to form considerable impediment to the progress of the carriage.

He listened from time to time in the hope of catching the rumbling of the wheels, but no such sound came to his ears.

But if his information was correct—and he had no reason for thinking that the old stone-breaker had spoken falsely—the vehicle could not be far ahead.

Suddenly among the tree-tops he caught sight of the pointed gable roofs of a house of considerable size.

This discovery and the circumstance that he could not hear the slightest sound made him come to a standstill.

"I do believe that is where the carriage has stopped," he said. "What could be a more likely destination than this lonely house? And apparently the road leads nowhere else. I will reconnoitre."

He now advanced, but with a much greater degree of caution than he had before made use of.

The object that presented itself to his notice consisted of a pair of massive wooden gates.

At one time no doubt they had borne a very handsome and ornamental appearance, but now neglect and the damp and dry of many seasons had completely disfigured them.

The elaborate carving could only here and there be traced, while nearly half-way up the woodwork grew a yellowish slimy-looking moss, such as never seems to show itself save in deserted places.

These gates stood back some twenty or thirty yards

from the lane, and the little bit of roadway leading up to them was nothing but a tangled mass of weeds and gorse bushes.

It appeared, however, that Captain Hawk was not quite right in his supposition that the lane led only to this old building, for as far as he could tell it went on almost in a straight line.

Determined to see to this, and being unable to discern a sign of a human being, he pushed on with the same amount of cautiousness.

It proved, however, that the lane did not go more than fifty yards further, and the continuation of it only formed a means of communication with the rear of the mansion.

"I wonder, now, whether I shall do any good by attempting to look further into this affair? After all, what have I seen? The window of a carriage broken. An unusual event: I do not recollect such a one. It might have been accident, but I am strangely mistaken if it was not design. Then there was that hasty shot. Surely no man would have fired it unless there was something that he greatly feared to have discovered. Yes, that decides it. I won't leave this place until I have learned all, and, what is more, it shall go hard with me if I do not have a reckoning with the fellow who fired that treacherous shot!"

Captain Hawk, having arrived at this conclusion, began to look around him in order to decide what he should do next.

"Satan will be of little service," he said, "and so first of all I will try and find a place where he will be not only safe but also within my reach. I will see to that first, and fix upon my next proceeding afterwards."

The lane seemed to terminate abruptly at the side of a plantation of considerable extent.

This was fenced round, but age had so rotted the woodwork that it required scarcely any trouble for Captain Hawk to make a gap large enough to allow Satan to pass through easily.

As the vegetation was dense, there was no need to penetrate far into the recesses of the plantation for his steed to be effectually concealed from observation.

It luckily happened, too, that sweet herbage was abundant, and Satan began cropping it with great satisfaction.

"Stay there, old fellow," said his master, patting him fondly. "Wait there till I call for you."

He left him without attempting to tether him in any way.

The excitement and curiosity produced by the late events made Captain Hawk quite forgetful of his bodily fatigue, although he had felt it so strongly such a short time before.

Now that he was on foot, he was, of course, able to make his way towards the mansion with the utmost secrecy.

A little examination of the roadway leading up to the back gates convinced him of the truth of his supposition, for he could make out unmistakable signs that a vehicle had recently passed that way.

The rear of the premises was well defended by a red brick wall, which would be troublesome to surmount, even if there was no fear of being seen.

"No, no," said the captain, shaking his head; "I must look a little further and find a place that offers easier entrance."

He skirted the wall rapidly, making sure that he was secure from observation, while the distance from the house was too great for any trifling sound to betray him.

He had quickly reason to congratulate himself upon the course he had adopted, for before going very far he discovered that the wall was succeeded by a hedge.

This, through thorough neglect, had almost lost its original character, for it grew up like so many independent tall trees, and scarcely intertwined its boughs at all.

To push aside the twigs and force a way through occupied not a moment.

He paused, but seeing nothing stirring, proceeded to look a little closer around him.

He now found himself in the garden, or rather what had once been a garden, for few traces to show what it had been now remained.

It was nothing but one mass of tangled vegetation, presenting a scene of desolation that was absolutely painful to look upon.

Captain Hawk's thoughts, however, were too intently occupied with the immediate business of the moment to think much about this.

A better cover to enable him to get close to the mansion unperceived could scarcely have been wished.

He now saw that the building was of even greater extent than he had before imagined it.

In former times it must have been a place of unusual importance.

Crouching down almost to the ground, Captain Hawk threaded his way among the trees and shrubs until he reached the border of a grass plat.

There was no further cover between himself and the house which reared its walls at a distance of only a few yards.

Feeling certain in his own mind that the old grand-looking mansion before him contained the persons who had occupied the travelling carriage, Captain Hawk ran his eye over every object before him in the hope of being able to detect something that would be absolutely convincing of the fact, and put an end to supposition altogether.

But fortune was not going to favour him so far as this.

Although he gazed in succession at every window, he failed to catch the least sign of the presence of human beings.

"I must enter in order to satisfy myself," he said, with all the coolness that can possibly be conceived; "and I think if I climb up on to yonder balcony it will be the easiest way to do it."

Just before him was a crumbling stone balcony which ran completely along one side of the building.

No doubt at one time this was a beautiful feature of the place, but now decay had imprinted its ineffaceable marks deeply upon it.

Ivy trailed over it here and there, much adding to the appearance of general neglect that was everywhere observable around.

Upon this balcony a long range of windows opened, and it was through one of these Captain Hawk contemplated effecting an entrance.

Had it been night instead of broad day, nothing could well have been easier, for the panes were broken in many places.

Now, however, there was the great risk that in leaving the concealing shadow of the trees where he stood, and crossing over to the house, he would be seen by some one or other of its inmates.

"If I wait here for an hour," he concluded, "I shall not lessen that danger. The risk must be run, and it had better be at once. A rush will do it best, and here goes."

Just as he pronounced these words he darted suddenly out of his hiding-place, nor did he pause until close against the wall of the mansion.

The point to which he had directed his course was, he believed, one that would effectually prevent his being seen from any window.

He waited now for several seconds.

A little bird with a great fluttering of its tiny wings perched itself upon an adjoining tree and began to warble melodiously.

That, however, was the only sound which came upon Captain Hawk's ears.

The balcony above him was not so high but that he should by a good spring be able to get a good grasp of it; and this was all he wanted, for he knew he had power enough in his arms to draw himself completely over it.

This was his next proceeding, and it was accomplished with the same good fortune which had attended his former efforts.

But just as he was drawing himself over the crumbling balustrade the first sound which could be called an alarming one came upon his ears.

Instinctively he paused.

"What was that?" he asked.

But the sound was not repeated.

"It sounded like the sudden opening and shutting of a door," he said, as he hastened to leave his present exposed position. "Can it be that I have been seen, or that my presence here can be suspected?"

But he could gain no information upon these points, and finding that the silence remained unbroken, he crept towards the window nearest to him.

Most of the panes were shattered to atoms, so that when tolerably close he had no sort of difficulty in making an examination of the interior of the room.

His satisfaction may be imagined when he ascertained beyond all doubt that it was empty.

By introducing his hand he was able to undo the fastening, though it had remained so long untouched that at first it resisted his efforts.

"Safe!" he ejaculated, as he cautiously stepped in. "And now that all is well so far, let me try if I cannot arrive at some conclusion respecting what I have seen."

The room was empty in the strict sense of the term.

Not only was it unoccupied by persons, but not so much as a vestige of a single article of furniture could be perceived.

Indeed, the air of desolation which had been the characteristic of the place from the very first was now more painfully apparent than ever.

There was nothing in the apartment to induce him to linger, and so he went at once to the door.

When he placed his hand upon the knob he felt some misgiving as to whether he should be able to go further.

But it yielded easily to his touch.

Another apartment of much larger dimensions, and furnished with a large stained-glass window, through which the sun was shining in such a way as to make it seem that the dust-covered floor was covered with checkered tiles, appeared beyond.

Across this he glided silently.

The door opened upon a broad and noble corridor.

Here he stopped, for he fancied the sound of voices came upon his ears.

But this proved a fancy merely, for after listening for several minutes he found all was still.

At the extremity of the corridor was the grand staircase—a magnificent place, the area it covered being more than sufficiently large to allow of the erection of a large house.

By peeping over the massive carved balustrades, Captain Hawk could see down into the hall below.

The sun was shining in at the staircase window, but all was still.

"Shall I descend?" he said.

Just as he mentally asked himself the question he heard unmistakably the faint tinkling of a bell.

The sound came from somewhere below; and having recovered from the slight state of surprise into which he had been thrown, he remained anxiously waiting to know what would happen next.

Almost immediately a door was opened.

"Hannah—Hannah!" said a voice. "Where are you?"

"I am here," was the reply, given in trembling tones, as though the age of the speaker was great.

"Has she recovered?"

"No; she is the same."

"Leave her safely, and then try to get some boiling water. Be quick!"

The reply was so faint that it did not reach the ears of the unsuspected listener.

The door below was closed again violently.

Captain Hawk then made a discovery.

The first voice which had spoken was unquestionably a masculine one.

About the sex of the other speaker there could be no sort of doubt; but what Captain Hawk discovered was, that she had leaned over the balusters just below him when she gave her reply.

By slightly shifting his position he was able to see her.

It was an old, a very old, woman, and about as hideous a specimen of feminine humanity as could well have been looked upon.

Her form was attenuated to the extremest degree, so that she far more resembled a skeleton than a human being.

Her eyes were red and bleared, and deeply sunken in her head, while the skin hung about her throat and neck in huge yellow folds.

A slight fit of coughing attacked her, but suppressing it, she opened a door and peeped into the chamber with which it communicated.

She withdrew her head almost immediately, and then after several futile efforts succeeded in turning the key which was sticking in the lock of the door.

Having done so, she tried to withdraw the key, but it resisted all her efforts.

"I must make haste," she mumbled, with her toothless gums—"I must not lose a moment. The door will be safe enough, I daresay, if I leave it as it is. How am I to get boiling water, I wonder, in such a place as this?"

Mumbling and muttering, and shaking her grisly head to and fro with a kind of palsical movement that was inexpressibly hideous, she descended the remainder of the staircase.

Captain Hawk from his point of vantage above watched her until she reached the foot, and then saw her cross over the stone flooring.

After that the profound silence which had before prevailed now reigned around.

"I am beginning to understand the state of affairs now, and my original guess as to what all this meant is not, I'll warrant, very wide of the mark. As to the person about whom that fellow inquired—who, by-the-bye, is the person who fired at me, I dare swear—she is of the female sex, and confined in that room yonder."

Captain Hawk could see the door of this room with perfect plainness.

He stood gazing at it for some moments in silence.

"I shall never have a better chance of effecting an entrance than the present," he said, at last. "If I am quick I shall be able to get inside before that old hag returns with the hot water. I must and will know all."

Having thus expressed his resolution, the captain stole swiftly yet silently down the staircase.

On reaching the door, he turned the key with anxious solicitude, as he was particularly desirous to avoid a premature alarm.

But just as the key turned in his hand a fresh thought occurred to him.

"This is all easy enough," he said; "but when I get inside, how am I to lock the door again? It's impossible. Yet, if it is not done, the old woman's suspicions will be at once awakened."

He could not see his way out of this difficulty; and as he knew his danger was very great if he remained where he was, he cautiously opened the door, and, having crossed the threshold, closed it after him.

Looking round, he found himself in a chamber so dark that at first, having stepped out of the bright sunlight into it, he could not make out anything in it.

By degrees, however, he discerned the outlines of one of those massive bedsteads in which our ancestors so much delighted, with four huge posts, and massive plumes of feathers above.

He also made out the situation of the windows in the room.

Either the shutters had been closed, or else the massive curtains had been closely drawn, for the light only found its way in by long slanting pencils.

The very silence of death was in this chamber.

Captain Hawk strained his sense of hearing to the utmost, but not the slightest sound could be detected.

CHAPTER LIV.

CAPTAIN HAWK BECOMES ACQUAINTED WITH THE RAMIFICATIONS OF A NICE LITTLE PLOT.

But for what he had heard and seen, Captain Hawk would have arrived at the conclusion that this apartment was untenanted.

It would never do, however, to stand hesitating.

He could not count upon the old woman being absent very long, and so he stole gently towards the bed.

The curtains closely shrouded it everywhere.

His hand shook a little as he drew them cautiously aside.

By this time the obscurity of the chamber caused him no difficulty, and therefore at the first glance he beheld some dark object on the bed.

Looking closer, he saw that it was a young girl who, judging by the imperfect light, could not have been more than sixteen.

She had been thrown on the outside of the bed apparently with very little ceremony—not even her travelling garments had been removed.

She was dressed entirely in black.

Her face was ashy pale, but yet, for all that, full of the most touching beauty.

Her hair was long and of a rich golden hue.

It had escaped its fastenings in some way, and now trailed over the dusty pillows and down her shoulders in wavy masses.

Captain Hawk for a moment or two could do nothing save gaze in silent admiration.

Then he started, for the traces of blood met his view.

"Was she dead?" was the startling question which instantly sprang up in his mind.

The pallor of her countenance pointed to this being the case.

But on a nearer examination he discovered that the sanguine stains proceeded from several small cuts on her right hand, from some of which the blood was still oozing.

Then he comprehended all.

"I know now," he said. "This was done when she smashed the carriage window, in the hope of attracting the attention of who ever might be passing by. Poor girl," he added, "you have at your side a more powerful friend than perhaps you dared to hope for. It is no ordinary villany which has brought you here, and there will be all the more need for a strong hand to protect you."

He ceased, for a sound resembling a faint sigh seemed to come from the lips of the unconscious creature.

Captain Hawk drew back, fearing lest she should open her eyes, and in her sudden alarm at seeing him would utter a cry that would have the effect of bringing her foes upon the scene.

But the fear proved groundless.

She made no other sound or movement, and the captain began to think it was high time he adopted some expedient whereby he could remain in the room without the old woman being aware of it.

This was a task, however, that seemed to set his powers of ingenuity completely at defiance.

Seeing a door opposite to the one by which he had entered, he made his way towards it.

Being unfastened, it yielded to his hand.

It communicated with another large apartment, which had a door opening from it in such a position that the captain felt almost certain it led on to the staircase.

If this should prove so, his difficulty would be at an end.

He hurried towards it with considerable impatience.

It was both bolted and locked on the inner side, but as the key happened to be in the lock these fastenings were soon removed.

On opening the door, he saw the staircase just as he had expected.

"I am all right now," he said, as he crossed the threshold. "I will turn the key in the other lock again, and then the old woman will never have the remotest suspicion of what has happened."

He did this without delay.

He was none too soon, for the tinkling of the bell once more came upon his ear.

He did not wait to attempt to ascertain the result of it, but retreated through the second door.

This he secured by means of the bolt, merely so that he should be able to beat a rapid retreat if necessary.

When he had done this he made his way into the sleeping apartment again, for he fancied a faint cry had reached his ears.

He was not mistaken, for on nearing the bed he saw that the young girl's eyes were open.

Tears were upon her cheeks, and she trembled violently from head to foot.

She regarded Captain Hawk with the utmost affright, and seemed as though on the point of screaming out.

Evidently she took him for one of her persecutors.

He hastened to undeceive her, and also to convey the assurance of his friendship.

"My poor girl," he said, in tones so kind and gentle that they could not be mistaken, "do not fear me. I am not one of those who have had a hand in bringing you to this place."

"Then you will save me, sir?" she said. "You will not let them harm me?"

"Hush—hush—not so loud, or we shall be overheard! Believe me, I will save you, and no one shall harm you while I am by."

The young girl's tears started out afresh.

The captain made no attempt to check their flow, for he knew they would be the means of giving her breast relief.

"You must be careful," he said, "not to let anyone know that I am here. When the fitting time comes I will show myself. If you are not careful in this respect, you may only bring destruction on me, and do yourself no good."

"Cannot you take me away at once? Oh, I shall die if I remain here!"

"Not now this moment I cannot," was the reply. "It is day; were it night it would be very different."

"Day!" ejaculated the girl. "The room is very dark!"

"True; but it is a darkness artificially produced. Outside those windows the sun is shining brightly."

"Alas—alas! What dreadful place is this? Why—oh! why have I been brought here?"

"I was in hopes you would be able to answer me those questions."

"Alas! I cannot."

"You are now in an old mansion, the name of which I know not; but from its appearance I should imagine it has not been inhabited for very many years."

"I remember nothing of coming here," she said, clasping her hand over her brows. "What has happened? Ah, yes! now I recollect. As we were riding at that furious pace along the high-road I caught sight of a mounted traveller; just then an opportunity presented itself of making my case known, and I availed myself of it."

"You broke the window, did you not?"

"I did. I dashed my hand with such force against the glass that I shivered it to atoms."

"And you hurt yourself, too. Look at your hand."

"Yes. I do not mind that," she said. "And were you the traveller I saw?"

Captain Hawk replied in the affirmative.

"Heaven bless you, sir, for seeking to aid me! Had I been alone I shudder to think what might have befallen me. Breaking the window is the last thing I can recollect," she added. "I must have been insensible when they brought me here."

"Hush—hush!"

"What is the matter?" the girl ejaculated, starting up in the utmost terror.

"Compose yourself—pray compose yourself! The old woman who apparently has been appointed to tend you is about to enter. Once more let me entreat you to be calm, and, above all, do nothing and say nothing that will lead to the belief that I am anywhere at hand."

Captain Hawk uttered these words very rapidly—so rapidly, indeed, that the young girl hardly caught their purport.

But there was no time to be lost; and having thus spoken, he glided swiftly across to the door communicating with the adjoining room.

This he shut almost close, but not quite.

He was deprived of the sight of what went on; but he could hear distinctly.

The old beldame had some little difficulty in unlocking the door, but succeeding at last, she made her way straight to the bedside.

"Oh, you have thought proper to come to yourself, have you?" she croaked. "And a fine, pretty creature you are, I must say, to make all this fuss about! Faugh—bah!"

A violent fit of coughing interrupted the old beldame's further speech.

Indeed, so severe was the paroxysm that Captain Hawk began to think that she would really fall down in a fit and die at once.

But the hideous creature had a much firmer hold upon existence than he was aware of.

By degrees, she regained possession of her breath.

But before she could speak again the young girl addressed her:

"Oh," she cried, in accents so tenderly appealing that one would have thought them capable of producing an impression even upon a heart of stone, "as you are one of my own sex, let me entreat you to save me! Do not abandon me to the dreadful fate which is intended for me! Do not be an accomplice against me! Save me—oh, save me! Let me go free!"

"Hoity-toity!—here's a fuss indeed! Marry come up! Save you indeed! From what, I should like to know, except making a fool of yourself? Here, drink this; it has cost me trouble enough to make it, I can tell you; and let me have no more such foolish speeches as those which I have just heard! Save you indeed! Why—— Ugh, ugh, ugh!"

Another fit of coughing cut her short, to the captain's great relief, for it made his blood so boil with indignation to hear her speak that he could hardly control himself from rushing out.

The young girl, thus rebuffed, wept bitterly.

Her sobs indeed were terrible to hear.

"There, there—no more of that noise! Be quiet, I say, and drink this."

"Never—never!"

"You had better obey me, or it will be the worse for you!"

But the young girl firmly persisted in her refusal.

The old woman grew terribly incensed.

Volleys of abuse poured from her lips, and she was really about to proceed to vengeance, when the door leading to the staircase was dashed open.

"Ah! Jezebel!" ejaculated the new-comer in a furious voice, "is it thus that you obey my orders?"

He seized her violently as he spoke, and whirled her aside with so much suddenness that it was only after a great struggle that she succeeded in keeping her feet.

"Begone!" cried her assailant, with undiminished anger—"depart, I say! Come near no more!"

The old woman was too much terrified to dream of disobedience, and so slunk towards the portal.

In the meanwhile the new-comer advanced to the bedside.

The young girl shrieked aloud for help as soon as ever she caught sight of his countenance.

It was to Captain Hawk that she appealed, though her persecutor failed to understand.

"Hold—hold!" he cried, in a voice so loud that hers was completely drowned. "Hold—hold! It is in vain—perfectly in vain for you to cry for help: there is no one near to attend to or even hear your supplications! You are in my power, wholly and utterly, and the best thing you can do is to obey, and make a virtue of necessity."

The stentorian tones of his voice completely terrified the young girl into silence.

"Listen to me," he said, speaking more gently. "There is no occasion for the manifestation of so much terror. Inexorable circumstances compelled me to act as I have done. If you will now command yourself to listen to an explanation, so much the better—the sooner your captivity will be over."

"Are you in earnest in what you say?"

"Certainly I am."

"Speak, then."

The speaker affected to clear his voice, as though scarcely prepared with what he had to say.

"You must remember the time," he said at length, "when you became my ward?"

"Shall I ever forget it?"

"Never mind about that," he cried; "it is sufficient at the present moment that you do recollect it. Your father's death taking place so suddenly scarcely allowed him time to make a will; however, something having the semblance of one was drawn up and witnessed, leaving you sole inheritor of what be had, and appointing me your guardian."

"Yes, I remember that painful time too well. But surely there was no need for you to bring me here to tell me this?"

"No; that, as you may suppose, is only part of what I have to say. Time went on. Your father's sudden death took place at a time when his affairs—I mean his monetary affairs—were in a state of the greatest possible confusion. The popular impression was that he had died a very rich man; in this case, as in many others, the popular impression was a fallacy. Your father had money; but he was scarcely so rich by three-fourths as he was currently represented."

"But——"

"One moment more, and I have done. I have told you more than once that I love you."

A slight cry of aversion involuntarily escaped the young girl's lips.

Her companion ground his teeth with rage.

But subduing his anger, he cried:

"Enough! Since the subject is so extremely distasteful to you, I will no longer put it in the light that I have hitherto done. You recollect, no doubt, also, that the will stated that in case you should die before your marriage or the attainment of your majority, the whole of the wealth, what there was, reverted to me?"

"I do recollect it, and I know well the amount of wretchedness which that provision has cost me."

"Nothing of the kind, foolish girl—none save that which your own imagination has vainly and foolishly conjured up."

"Alas! I know too well that it is not imagination."

"Listen to me."

"I am compelled to do so."

"Well, then, having explained matters thus to you, I will tell you what I intend to do. My words will be plain and to the point—there will be no further beating about the bush. Do you hear me?"

"I do."

"Then I am going to present two things before you—I shall leave you time to consider over them. You will have to make your choice. You understand that?"

The young girl inclined her head.

"The first of these things that you have to choose between is, to become my wife."

"Never! I defy you to the last! Never—never!"

Captain Hawk was surprised to hear one who seemed so fragile speak with so great an amount of energy and determination.

But it was plain that the bare utterance of this proposal filled her with the extremest aversion.

"If you refuse that," continued her villanous guardian speaking in low, determined tones—"if you refuse that, your only other choice is to die!"

"To die?" she gasped, for the idea of passing from life to death presented itself with the utmost terrors to her imagination.

"Yes," he continued, speaking more like a fiend than a human being—"you can be at no loss now to understand why I have brought you to this lonely place. I am certain that there is no one near save my own faithful dependants, who will stand by me to the last. No one is aware of your absence—no one will suspect that even I knew anything of it. If you refuse to become my wife, your death is certain and immediate! You have no escape—no hope; and let me assure you that my plans are so well laid that it will be impossible for suspicion to attach itself to me: no one will for a moment guess that I had the least share in your death."

The way in which these words were uttered was appalling.

The young girl seemed overcome with horror—so much so as temporarily to render her oblivious of the fact that she had a powerful friend near her.

"It is death and life you have to choose between," continued her persecutor, "and your decision must be given shortly. I leave you entirely free to decide. It would be idle for me to say that I am indifferent which way you answer me. Painful and repugnant as the circumstance seems to you, yet I avow again that I love you. Be mine, and a life of happiness is yours to look forward to. I will gratify your every wish—lay at your feet an adoration that all women would sigh for. If you refuse this, there is nothing but death."

"Death? Then let it be, a thousand times!" she cried, with the energy she had formerly employed. "I know only too well the treatment I should receive if I once promised to be your wife. I should then be doubly in your power—I should be yours then, body and soul! But such a monstrous thing will never be permitted to take place."

"Listen."

"No—I have listened, and the time is gone by. It is your turn to listen now, and you shall hear me. There is a Heaven above us——"

The assertion was received with a low, mocking, scornful laugh.

"I say there is a Heaven above us," she repeated, "and

I will never believe that its all-seeing eye will permit the perpetration of such iniquity as you contemplate."

He interrupted her again with his derisive laugh, and cried:

"My dear girl, that sort of thing is all very well for childhood; but when you grow older you will become wiser—you will find that Heaven only helps those people who help themselves."

"Silence, scoffer! Impossible as you in your fancied security may deem it, I believe that, rather than suffer you to triumph in your wickedness, Heaven will raise me up a friend even in this solitary and forsaken spot, and that he will frustrate your heinous schemes."

The boldness with which she spoke and the amount of reliance she displayed produced a sensible effect upon her rascally guardian.

"I know full well the villanous motives which have driven you to this course. You know well that my father died a wealthy man—you also know that you have made away with much of the money entrusted to your charge: so much that you dread for the amount to become known. By wedding me or compassing my death, your defalcations will be covered. I can easily understand that you would prefer the first, because the risk would be infinitely less to yourself. But your schemes will be baffled!"

"Cease—cease! I will listen to you no more! Cease, I say! Make up your mind! If your aversion to me is so great, you can only escape me by embracing death! I tell you your struggles are as vain as those of a tiny fly entangled in a spider's web. You must be mine or Death's. Choose!"

"I will not! Even now I defy you!"

"Insensate girl! you know not my power! A little while, however, will render you sensible of it, and until then I shall leave you. You are safe—close watch will be kept on every point. In a day or two your mind will be greatly changed."

"Never—never!—not if it were my unfortunate fate to remain here for twenty years!"

"It is not my intention to run the risk of keeping you here for twenty days. If you persist in your refusal to become my bride, you will be food for worms long before then! But I will hear no more. I will leave you to ponder upon my words."

He turned abruptly upon his heel as he spoke, and quitted the apartment, taking care to lock the door carefully after him.

In the silence which filled the huge, deserted building, his heavy footfall on the staircase was distinctly audible.

The hapless prisoner listened to it breathlessly.

Then a door was violently closed, and all was still.

Captain Hawk opened the door cautiously, and crossed the threshold.

"Why did you not save me as you said you would?" she said, in reproachful accents.

She could say no more.

The fortitude which up to this point had supported her suddenly gave way.

She broke out into a fit of hysterical weeping, which Captain Hawk vainly attempted to repress.

But by degrees it exhausted itself by its very violence.

"I was afraid to show myself," he said.

"Afraid?" she exclaimed, as though in doubt whether she had heard aright.

"Yes, afraid."

"Of what?"

"Not of myself, certainly," he responded, for he fully understood her.

"Of what, then?"

"Of you."

"How of me?"

"Need I tell you that your guardian is a desperate man?"

"Alas! I know it well!"

"You have good cause to know it. He would stick at no atrocity. Your death or silence is vitally essential to him. Do you know what I feel certain he would have done had I come forward to interfere, as I felt most strongly tempted to do?"

"No; what?"

"Finding himself discovered, his first act would have been to slay you; and, as I saw he carried firearms, I feared he might do this before I had power to prevent him—that kept me back. It would have been a poor consolation to me had you perished."

"But do you think he really would have murdered me?"

"From what you know of him, do you believe that he would hesitate a moment about doing so?"

The young girl made no reply.

"Your silence is quite sufficient answer," continued the captain. "It was this I dreaded, and so long as he refrained from offering you any personal violence, so long did I determine to remain without interfering. It was hard for me to restrain myself; but, now that all is over, I am most glad that I did so."

"You were right, my friend—quite right! I must beg of you to pardon me for speaking so hastily as I did."

"Do not name it. You could not guess my motives."

"But what am I to do?" she cried, imploringly. "How am I to escape him?"

"Remain calm—that is the most essential thing. Leave the rest to me, and then, rely upon it, all will be well."

"But you will give me some idea of what you purpose doing? It will relieve me of infinite suspense."

"It was my design to tell you. In such cases as this, craft must be met by craft. What I propose is that, if possible, you should remain here until nightfall."

The young girl shuddered at the idea.

"The time will seem very long and wearisome," he said, "but you must endeavour to bear that."

"And the danger?"

"There will be no danger. I shall be close at hand all the time, and, rely upon it, no harm shall come to you. I do not believe any will be offered. Your guardian will think that, after you have spent some hours in this melancholy place, your spirits will be so far broken that you will accede to anything which he requires."

"He does not know me, then!"

"He will discover his mistake," said the captain, with a quiet smile.

"You said, wait till nightfall?"

"Yes."

"And what are we to do then?"

"Escape."

"How?"

"If possible, unperceived."

"Is there any hope of doing so?"

"I believe there is. If we only wait for the coming of darkness, I believe that I shall be able to lead you from this place in perfect safety, and conduct you to any place you may think fit to name."

"And you would do all this for a perfect stranger such as I am?"

"Most willingly."

"And when you have done all this, what will be your reward?"

"I shall care for nothing save a word of thanks."

"But why this extraordinary interest? Why this readiness to take my part?"

"Lady," answered the captain, unconsciously infusing a tone of solemnity into his reply, "I am one who, though young, yet happen to be old enough to have committed many wrongs and done much which I wish could be undone. But the past is irrevocable. It is my fancy, however, that any such deed as this is a kind of atonement or set-off against my evil actions. And now, lady, having said that much, I must ask you to question me no more."

This evident mystery greatly stimulated the young girl's curiosity.

The captain did not give her time to speak again.

"If you will take my advice," he said, "you will endeavour to get all the rest you can, in order to fit you for the inevitable fatigues of the coming night. Do not fear to close your eyes. Remember that I shall be watching you, and that you will be in greater safety than you have been for a long time past."

The young girl was deeply touched by the tenderness of his behaviour, and it was in a voice choked by tears that she poured forth her thanks to him for what he had done.

But as early as he could the captain interrupted her.

"Do not thank me now," he said. "Wait till I have

done something worthy of the expression of your gratitude. Let me beg of you to compose yourself. Hark! that hideous woman again approaches. Be careful that you do not give her cause to guess that I am near, or the peril will be much increased."

There was no time to utter more, for the key could be heard rattling in the lock.

Captain Hawk, after one hasty parting glance, glided over the thickly-carpeted floor like an apparition.

He had just time to resume his former position when the door was once more opened, and the old woman made her appearance, looking a thousand times more ugly and malevolent than before.

CHAPTER LV.

CAPTAIN HAWK BIDS FAREWELL TO THE YOUNG HEIRESS.

THAT something had occurred to ruffle the old hag's temper, one glance at her countenance was enough to testify.

Her features were literally convulsed, and had upon them an expression that would have well befitted a demon.

On entering she took particular care to fasten the door behind her, and then muttering under her voice, she approached the bed.

What she said could not be comprehended, but she dashed aside the curtains with such violence as to terrify the already overwrought girl.

"So, there you are, my fine miss, are you?" she screeched. "And so you are to come here and cause all this fuss, and I am tamely to submit to anything! No, no, my fine creature, I will spoil that beauty of yours for you! You shall not have the cause to think so much of it as you do very long, I'll warrant! You are in my power now! The door is fast, and the master is too far off to interfere in time. I will be revenged—I will be revenged, if I die for it!"

"Good heavens!" ejaculated the poor girl—"what ails the woman—are you mad?"

"No, but I will be revenged—I will not suffer tamely. I tell you again, I will be revenged!"

"Revenged, and upon whom?" asked the girl, so terrified by the old woman's menacing manner that she could scarcely speak.

"Upon you!" was the answer given, while the speaker fumbled in the breast of her apparel.

"Upon me; and why should you be revenged on me? What have I done to injure you? You must be mad!"

"Mad? Ha, ha! I am not mad!"

"You must be to think that I have injured you."

"Injured me? See what I have had to bear through you! But you shall die! I will be revenged!"

As she repeated the words, she withdrew with all the fury of a maniac the hand wherewith she had been fumbling in her breast.

She raised it aloft to strike.

The young girl caught the glitter of the steel, and shrieked aloud.

At the same time she sprang up and called for help.

Captain Hawk of course was not an idle spectator of all this.

But the unexpectedness of the incident took him greatly by surprise, and being so unprepared made him undecided how to act.

He did not wish to show himself, because of his desire to keep his presence there a profound secret.

If once he was seen there was an end of this, and most probably all end to his escape as well.

"If I could only terrify her," he murmured, struck with a sudden thought, "that would be the best. Ha! and this is likely enough to do it. I can but try."

The table in the centre of the room in which he stood watching was covered with a large snow-white cloth.

Quick as thought he seized this, folded it about him so as to conceal the whole of his apparel, and glided into the other room.

He entered just at the moment when the young girl made that sudden start to escape the beldame's murderous knife.

The bed was now between the two, and this obstacle for a moment baffled her.

But, perfectly blind and mad with passion, she darted round, only suddenly to find herself face to face with the disguised highwayman, whose altered appearance added not a little to the terror of her he came to save.

The old woman dropped the knife.

Her jaw fell, and she tottered back a step.

In the semi-obscurity, Captain Hawk looked appalling indeed, and it is no wonder that she should be so much overcome.

A strange sound issued from her open lips.

It was not a shriek nor a groan, but something which seemed made up of both.

It was a sound that must have made itself heard over the whole mansion.

Then, foaming at the mouth, she fell down in a fit of strong convulsions.

At this juncture some one tried to enter the room, but the old woman's precautions rendered this impossible.

Then a loud voice, which the captain immediately recognised, demanded admittance.

Captain Hawk hastened to the girl.

"Compose yourself if you can," he said; "the immediate danger is over now—there is nothing to fear. Remember I shall be at hand to protect you, and, above all, do nothing to make my presence here suspected."

The girl's guardian, finding no attention was paid to his demands, grew frantic with passion, and commenced a violent attack upon the door.

Captain Hawk meanwhile, divesting himself of his strange covering, took up his former position.

"Admit him," he whispered.

But the order came too late.

With a crash the door was flung open, and the guardian came in.

His face was the very picture of surprise, and, as well as the darkness would permit, he glanced around him.

But what he saw tended very little towards an explanation.

Gazing at the terrified girl, who was now crouching down close to the window curtains, he said, angrily:

"What is the meaning of all this? Speak, girl—speak!"

Terror and danger seemed to have sharpened the faculties of the poor young thing.

Captain Hawk was terribly afraid that as soon as she spoke she would betray his presence.

But, to his surprise, it was in a tolerably firm voice that she replied:

"I know not what this means, sir, unless it is some further portion of your diabolical plan against my happiness."

"Part of my plan?"

"Yes; that hideous hag came into the room in order to murder me. Look! there is the knife close to her grasp! It was Heaven which interfered to save me, for she fell down there as though stricken by lightning."

This intelligence served to rouse all the fury which had existence in the man's nature.

Raising his foot, he dealt the old woman a couple of heavy kicks that were enough to deprive her of existence.

They served, instead, to bring her back to consciousness.

No sooner did her eyes open than she began to rave about the apparition which she fancied she had seen.

This increased the brute's impatience and fury.

Stooping down, he seized her by the shoulders, and, uttering the most awful curses all the while, dragged her from the room.

Reaching the top of the stone staircase, he gave her a push which sent her headlong to the bottom.

Captain Hawk was so full of resentment against the old woman that he could not help looking upon this as a righteous punishment for her iniquity, and he made not the slightest attempt to interfere.

The young girl, however, upon her knees, begged hard of her guardian to spare her, but her supplications might just as well have been poured out to the wind.

When he returned from the execution of this bit of punishment, the anger in his face had sensibly abated.

"Foolish girl," he said, "why did you not cry out for assistance, the moment you became aware of her intentions?"

"I did so."

"Then why did you not admit me?"

"I wished to do so, but was too terrified to move."

This seemed credible enough, for she trembled so excessively that she could not move even then.

"Well, this will not occur again, nor would it have happened now but for your own insensate stupidity. You have only yourself to blame. Had you given the promise I require, you would have been in safety and in peace."

"It is in vain to speak to me of that now," she said.

"Now," he repeated, catching eagerly at the word—"now! Am I to infer from that, that the time may come when you may take the matter more fully and favourably into your consideration?"

"I cannot say," she exclaimed, piteously. "I am distracted. I know not what words I use. If you have any regard for me, leave me for awhile in peace."

"Willingly; and you must look upon my willingness in doing so as a proof that I shall gladly accede to any of your requests that come at all within the bounds of reason."

He waited, as though in expectation of receiving some reply to this speech; but finding none came, he retreated, as though full of fear that he should lose his fancied gain.

He remained for some time at the door, for, having burst it open, he was not able to fasten it securely.

Succeeding at length in making it tolerably fast, and apparently having little fear that his prisoner would attempt to escape, he again descended the staircase, still muttering curses against the hapless old woman, who remained motionless at the foot of the staircase.

As on the former occasion, Captain Hawk ventured to show himself soon after the sound of footsteps had died away.

Now that the danger was to all appearance over, the young girl's fortitude no longer buoyed her up, and the captain had no little difficulty in reviving her spirits.

But the confident manner in which he spoke of effecting an escape insensibly produced an impression upon her, and after awhile her eyes brightened.

"Now," said the captain, "sleep if you can. In your present state an hour or two's slumber would do you more good than anything else in the world. Try if you can obtain it. Have no fear of closing your eyes. I pledge my word that you shall be unharmed."

"I fear it is hopeless," she said, with a sad and weary smile; "but I will try to follow your advice."

"Do so—do so. Remember that when nightfall comes, and the attempt at escape is made, the chances of success will be ten times greater if you have partially recovered your lost strength. That consideration alone ought to have the greatest power over you."

"It has—it has."

"Then I will leave you now; and once more receive from me the assurance that you will be quite safe."

As he pronounced these words, Captain Hawk retired to the adjoining room and pulled the door after him.

That silence which we have before had several times occasion to mention again filled the mansion; and the captain, as he threw himself upon a couch, could scarcely bring himself to believe that the building contained any other living creature save himself.

It was sheer fatigue which had tempted him to lie down; but when he assumed the recumbent position on the couch it was with the firm determination that he would not on any account close his eyes.

But by insensible degrees his lids weighed themselves down more and more.

He was much exhausted, and now such a feeling of lassitude crept over him that he was powerless to resist it.

All at once recollection of everything faded from him.

His mind became a perfect blank, and so it remained until some slight sound awoke him.

He started up in no little confusion.

He could not all at once remember just where he was and what had last happened.

"My protector!" he heard a voice cry, in low, faint tones, but unmistakably the tones were those of alarm—"my protector—my friend, where are you?"

Those words were quite sufficient thoroughly to recall the captain's wandering recollection.

"I am here!" he said, as he slipped from the couch.

But when about to make his way to the door of communication he became aware that the obscurity had very materially increased.

But he managed to grope his way to it without encountering any obstruction.

"Have you slept?" was his first question, when he found himself near the young girl.

"I fancy so; and so have you, or I am much mistaken. Is that the way you guard me from harm?"

Captain Hawk hung his head abashed.

But the young girl lightly rested her hand upon his arm as she said:

"Pardon me—I meant it as no reproach. I know that you, my generous preserver, stood in need of repose even more than myself, and you were quite right to take it."

"It was a light slumber," stammered the captain, who was more annoyed with himself than he could have described.

"And yet I had to call you several times before you awoke," she said, with a smile, "and each time louder than before."

"I ask——"

"No apologies—I will not listen to them! We are safe, and all is well."

"All shall be well," said the captain, in a determined voice, "in the course of a few minutes at the most—that is," he added, "if the darkness is sufficient."

"I fancy it is—night seems fairly to have set in. Look! This window will enable you to judge."

She led him to one of the windows from which she had partially withdrawn the curtains.

Night had indeed fairly set in, and it was with great surprise that Captain Hawk discovered it; indeed, he could hardly believe his eyes.

"I must have slept long and soundly," he muttered; "but as things are I ought rather to rejoice than regret it."

"Do you think the time has come?" asked the young girl.

Her voice and her whole form trembled with anxiety.

"It has come," was the reply. "Be firm, and I will answer for all the rest. There is no need for nervous tremors. I assure you again that you are safe."

"But should we be discovered?"

"Never mind about that. My conviction is that if you can only retain your presence of mind we shall get away unperceived by anyone. Perhaps we shall be miles off before your flight is discovered."

But it was in vain that the young girl tried to steel herself into calmness.

She had too much at stake to have control over her emotions.

There are few indeed who, placed as she was placed, could have retained their firmness.

Captain Hawk, however, inured to situations of danger of every conceivable description, presented by his immobility a remarkable contrast to the young girl's agitated demeanour.

His calmness had one good effect, however.

It inspired the young girl with a firm belief in his powers to protect and save her, no matter how great the danger might be.

"All seems still," the captain whispered. "I am rather surprised no visit has been paid you ere this. But," he hastened to add, observing her distress, "I can at least save you from that infliction, and I will do so."

"And you will really go now?"

"Yes, if you are quite ready, and feel that you have the power to perform your part."

"I am ready," was the quick answer, "and rely upon it I shall do my best."

"Enough. Give me your hand. So! That will do. Now accompany me without hesitation. Have no fear or question about where I shall lead you."

The young girl promised obedience.

She clasped her protector's hand tightly.

The captain noticed, however, that her hand was as cold as marble.

Upon this, however, he made no remark, but led her to the door which led from the adjoining room on to the staircase.

He had already made up his mind pretty nearly as to what steps he should take to get away.

When he opened the door, the poor girl at his side

[CAPTAIN HAWK'S ARRIVAL AT THE GREYHOUND INN.]

trembled so violently that she seemed to have great trouble in remaining on her feet.

"Courage—courage!" whispered the captain. "Remember how much there is at stake! The effort must be made now. Courage—courage!"

The staircase was plunged in the profoundest darkness, but the captain's eyes were tolerably well accustomed to it.

Very dimly he could see the feeble gleaming of the white stone steps.

Both listened.

No alarming sound, however, floated upwards.

"All is well," the captain said, in a low, reassuring whisper—"all is well now, believe me. I remember the way out perfectly, and a few minutes at the most will see us fairly beneath the blue canopy of heaven."

No assurance could possibly have been more welcome to the young girl than this.

But now that she found herself on the verge of liberation from her terrible danger her agitation increased beyond the power of control.

Her trembling limbs almost gave way beneath her, and doubtless would have done so completely had she not clung tightly to the captain's arm.

He could support her weight easily; and when they came to the steps which had to be ascended, he half carried her.

The silence in the house remained unbroken.

"They have not, depend upon it," he said "the slightest suspicion of what is going on; and so, if you can only preserve your calmness for a little longer, our safe escape will be rendered certain."

"I will try," she whispered—"I will try my best."

"Enough; we have only a few steps further now to go."

As he spoke he opened the door which led into the room with the large stained-glass window.

The position of this could only just be discerned, yet it indicated to the captain the way he ought to take.

The next moment his hand was on the knob of the second door.

No sooner had he opened it stealthily than a rush of cold air came most gratefully upon their faces.

It to some extent revived the young girl from her half-fainting condition.

"Come," he said, "one more effort, and we shall be in the garden. After that nothing will be easier. I have a horse close by, and if we can once get upon his back we shall be able to laugh at all pursuit."

Upon reaching the dismantled window the captain paused, for he happened to remember what the villainous guardian had said about the close watch that was kept everywhere around the building.

This might or might not be the truth, but it was best to be on the safe side.

His opinion was that it was a pure fabrication, invented only in order to deter the young girl from making the attempt to set herself at liberty.

To have kept watch upon every part of so vast a building would have required a great many men—more, he felt certain, than could have been brought in the travelling carriage.

But, more than all, the captain had managed in broad day to make his way into the building unseen and unheard.

How reasonable, therefore, seemed the prospect of leaving by the same way when they had darkness to shroud their movements!

Unable to see or hear anything, he opened the window and stepped at once upon the balcony.

"Depend upon it," he said, "the quicker we can be now the better. Trust to me. There! You are over the parapet now. Fear nothing, but release your grasp. You will alight in perfect safety on your feet. The ground is only a few inches beneath you."

He let go as he spoke, and in less than a second flung himself over the balcony and stood at her side.

"Now, then, forward! Summon up what energies you can."

But at this moment a loud, shrill whistle broke the intense silence of the garden.

"Discovered!" ejaculated the captain.

Had there been any doubt about this, it would have been dispelled by the loud shouts which were now given forth.

"Help—help, there!" cried some one. "An escape—an escape!"

The trampling of footsteps succeeded.

Captain Hawk quietly pulled out a pistol.

The next moment he caught sight of a man hastening towards him.

Releasing his hold upon the now almost swooning girl, and grasping the pistol lightly by the barrel, he rushed forth, and struck the man a violent blow upon the head with the butt-end of it.

The attack was so sudden and unlooked for that the man had no time to think of resistance.

The captain did not bring his hand down very lightly.

The sharp blow could have been heard a long way off, and the man immediately fell down like a log of wood.

This done, the captain, with the same rapidity of movement, made his way back towards the spot where he had left the girl.

She was crouching down, her strength not being sufficient to enable her to stand upright.

Without a moment's hesitation, he slipped the pistol in his belt, and raised her in his arms almost with as much ease as if she had been no more than a child.

But by the time he had accomplished this and taken his first steps towards the garden, indications were visible that the alarm had become general.

Lights flashed here and there, voices and footsteps could be heard.

Captain Hawk, however, apparently took no notice of all this, but bent all his energies to making the utmost speed he could.

Suddenly a loud voice cried:

"Hold, villain—hold, I say! Take that as a reward for your interference!"

A couple of pistol shots followed in quick succession.

A hot flush swept over the captain's face, for he fancied himself slightly hurt.

His position was full of embarrassment.

If he attempted to continue his flight more firearms would be discharged, and both the girl and himself might fall beneath the bullets.

On the other hand, if he paused and faced the danger, there was the probability that he would be overpowered by numbers.

What was worst of all was that there was no time for him to consider his way out of the dilemma.

It was, therefore, without thinking, that he deposited his now quite senseless burden upon the ground and turned round to defend himself.

He was only just in time, for his assailant was close to him.

Captain Hawk recognised him in a moment.

It was the young girl's guardian.

A feeling of additional resentment infused itself into the highwayman's mind upon making this discovery.

"Treacherous villain!" he cried. "Stand back, or this moment shall be your last!"

A laugh was the only reply.

Captain Hawk saw the villain in the act of drawing a pistol.

He waited to see nothing further, but, bringing his own weapon to a level, pulled the trigger.

Speedy as he was, two reports were heard.

But when the smoke curled upwards the villanous guardian was stretched upon the ground.

Captain Hawk was unhurt.

This was enough.

Rightly thinking that the other men would pay more attention to their master than keeping up the pursuit, Captain Hawk stooped down, picked up his unconscious charge, and ran across the garden at the top of his speed.

One shot was fired after him, but only one, and that was from such a distance as to make it totally ineffectual.

The fall of the chief actor in this atrocious drama filled all the subordinates with dismay, and they crowded around the senseless form unable to decide what to do.

This irresolution was just what the captain wanted to favour his projects.

Before the men had recovered from it he had dashed through the neglected hedge.

When here, he did not delay to give utterance to the signal which he knew would have the effect of bringing his horse Satan to his side.

Then taking a better hold upon his insensible burden, he hurried on with accelerated speed.

The next moment, however, a clear ringing neigh was heard, and then, with a sudden bound, the noble jet-black horse stood before him.

Captain Hawk's heart swelled with delight.

"Safe now," he said—"all is safe! What else they may do I care not. Quiet, now! Steady, old boy! Stand still!"

Satan seemed inclined to be playful; but these few words from his master seemed to subdue him.

Tenderly and gently, the captain laid the fragile form of the young girl before the saddle, and then, not without a little difficulty, mounted.

Then, flinging his left arm around her, he placed her as comfortably as the nature of the place would allow.

"Now, Satan boy, off with you!" he cried, as he seized the reins. "Away—away, I say!"

It did not seem as though the horse was at all conscious that he carried a double burden.

He flew off at a speed which in the darkness seemed absolutely terrific.

The highwayman, however, well knew from long experience that he could safely trust to the sagacity of his horse, and that there was no fear of coming in contact with any obstacle.

The lane was quickly gained, and keeping in the middle of it, the captain urged his horse to go still faster.

The high-road was reached in an incredibly short time.

Before emerging from the lane on to it, however, he paused.

In a moment the distant clatter of horses' feet reached his ears.

"Ah," he cried, "they have begun a pursuit! Well, well—let them come on; they will be tired before long, I'll warrant!"

He took the opportunity of looking at his charge.

But she showed no signs o flife whatever.

"Can she be dead," he asked himself, with a sharp and sudden pang—"can she be dead? One of those bullets may have pierced a vital part! What shall I do?"

He was not long in finding an answer to this question.

He resolved to ride on rapidly in the direction of London for several miles, and then on coming to any water, make the attempt to revive her.

No sooner was this sudden resolution taken than he turned Satan's head in the required direction, and urged him forward by every means in his power, for his impatience was now a hundredfold greater than it was before.

CHAPTER LVI.

CAPTAIN HAWK FINDS THE OLD GREYHOUND INN TO BE BY NO MEANS SO COMFORTABLE A SHELTER AS HE THOUGHT IT.

More than half a dozen miles were passed before Captain Hawk drew rein.

He listened; but he heard no longer the hoofbeats of those who had been in pursuit.

The spot he had chosen to pause at was just at the foot of a very steep bridge, which spanned a river of considerable width.

There was a little path leading down to the water, and along this he made his way.

On reaching the banks he again halted.

The continued insensibility of the young girl made his dread that she was mortally wounded increase.

That she was not yet dead he was certain.

He had thought, however, that the long, hard ride which they had taken would have brought her senses back to her.

It was therefore with deep misgiving that he alighted and gently placed her on the river's bank.

This done, he sprinkled her face and bathed her temples with cold water.

For some time all this seemed ineffectual; and it was, indeed, just when he was about to abandon the attempt in despair that he noticed her breast heave with a faint, convulsive sigh.

This made him renew his efforts more vigorously than ever, and in a few moments he had the inexpressible satisfaction of seeing her eyes open.

She gazed round at first in absolute bewilderment, evidently unable to think where she was and to remember what had happened.

The voice of Captain Hawk falling upon her ear quickly had the effect of calling back the recollection of past events.

She uttered a faint scream of terror.

"All is well," said the captain, calmly—"that is, if you have not been wounded. We have escaped, and are now safe beyond the reach of all pursuit."

Most welcomely did this intelligence fall upon the ears of the persecuted girl; and, despite the captain's protestations, she insisted upon giving expression to her deep sense of thankfulness for all which he had done in her behalf.

Tears ran down her cheeks; but though her utterance was impeded, she still gave voice to her gratitude.

"Enough—enough!" the captain interrupted. "Let us now talk of other things. Remember that you have not yet told me where you wish to go. Let me know your desired destination, and I will conduct you to it in safety."

"And that will add still more to my heavy debt of obligation."

"Never mind about that. I am determined to see you in safety."

"Alas!" she replied, weeping afresh, "I know not where to go! I have no home save at my guardian's house, and I cannot go there."

"No, certainly not—that must not be thought of for a moment. But surely you have some relations?"

"I have only one."

"And that one?"

"Is an aunt. I have never seen her, for she lives in London."

"In London?"

"Yes."

"And have you never been there?"

"Never."

"But you know this aunt's address?"

"Oh yes! I have often written to her, though sorely against my guardian's wish, for she is my father's only sister, and has not scrupled to say what she thought about the misappropriation of her brother's wealth."

"Then, rely upon it, you could not make your way to a better person. Take my advice; go to her with the least possible loss of time, and then do not hesitate to make her acquainted with the whole particulars of what has happened. She will then be able to compel your guardian to account for all his actions."

"And how shall I reach London?"

"We must think about that. Gladly would I, if I could, take you under my protection during this long journey; but circumstances render it impossible for me to do so. Instead of being a protector to you, I should only be the means of involving you in difficulties from which you would scarcely be able to extricate yourself."

These words filled the young girl with surprise, and increased her wonder as to the nature of the mystery which enshrouded her protector.

The reader must not lose sight of the fact that she knew nothing as to the captain's real character.

Nothing had occurred, indeed, to lead her for a moment to suspect that he could be a highwayman.

She only knew there was a mystery, and mingled with this knowledge was the consciousness that he was no ordinary man.

Captain Hawk remained in thought for some moments.

"When I passed the carriage," he said, "I was even then on my way to London, and it is my intention to continue my journey very shortly; but, as I told you, circumstances render it impossible for me to accompany you. I have, however, thought of a plan by which you can make the journey in perfect safety."

She looked up into his face with eager inquiry.

"Before very long," he said, "the coach from York will pass over yonder bridge. What I propose is that when it arrives I hail it and secure for you a seat inside. You will not be afraid to ride alone?"

"Oh no—no!"

"You will then be safe enough until you reach your journey's end. I shall never be far away from the coach, though probably I may reach London first. When you alight in the inn-yard I will be at hand to render you assistance should you require it."

"Many—many thanks! How kind it is of you to take all this interest in me!"

The captain laughed.

"Once under your aunt's protection all will be well; but if events should turn out wrongly, and you think the services of a strong and willing arm are required, I will write down the name of the place where something may be heard of me if I am in London."

"Here are my tablets," she said, handing them to him quickly. "I may not want you for the purpose you have mentioned, but I should like to have the power to communicate with you if I wished it."

"Enough! This, then, is the place where you can hear of me when you wish, and, strange as it may sound, there are many who would give no less than a thousand pounds for the information. But no matter. Hark! I can hear the coach."

The hideous notes of the guard's tin horn broke upon the stillness of the night.

Then the rumbling of the huge vehicle could be heard and its streaming lamps perceived.

"Come!" he said. "Accompany me along this little path—it will lead us to the foot of the bridge, and there we can hail the coach."

The girl obeyed without a moment's hesitation.

Indeed, her mind was in such a state of bewilderment that she found it much the easiest to comply with what her companion said—indeed, to allow him to think for her.

On the arrival of the coach near to them, Captain Hawk bawled aloud:

"A passenger—a passenger! Pull up, I say!"

The driver partially arrested the progress of his vehicle, and then bawled out:

"All the places full! No room!"

A sharp cracking of the whip followed, and away rolled the stage-coach at its former rate.

The young girl seemed a good deal disappointed at this result.

Captain Hawk felt himself in another dilemma.

"When does the next stage-coach pass?"

"Not before to-morrow night."

"And what is to be done till then?"

"I scarcely know. We cannot remain here. But hark! Unless my ears deceive me, I hear something else coming!"

The young girl, whose breast was full of fears of pursuit, clung to the captain in terror.

But he quickly reassured her.

"It is a waggon," he said. "Hark! you can hear the little bells tinkling on the horses' heads."

"Yes, I hear it now."

"And that suggests a thought. Should the waggon chance to be empty, let me recommend you to secure a seat in it. Do not disdain such a means of conveyance: it is very likely to suit you better than the stage-coach, because no one will think of looking for you in a carrier's waggon."

"And should I be safe there?"

"Perfectly safe. As I told you, I am going to London, and as time is no object with me it will afford me much pleasure to keep a look-out after your safety and comfort, and also when you arrive I will see to you again."

"You are very, very kind. I will be guided entirely by your directions; you shall be the judge of what is best."

"Then should this waggon be empty and proceeding only a portion of the way to London, I shall recommend you to take a place in it. Afterwards you may complete the journey by stage-coach."

The waggon came on at a very snail-like pace.

The young girl had relied so much upon the captain's protection, that she felt low-spirited and sad at this prospect of parting.

Silence for some moments reigned between them.

Then the waggon came up.

The rumbling it made was truly alarming, and by the nature of it the captain was sure the vehicle was empty.

The driver was perched up in a little seat in front.

"Ahoy!" bawled the captain. "Stop, I say! Ahoy!"

But the man took not the least notice.

"I see what it is," cried the highwayman—"the fellow is asleep. But if I stop the horses that will wake him, I'll warrant."

So saying, he took several hasty steps, which brought him in front of the team.

Then taking hold of the rein of the fore horse, he put his mouth close to the animal's ear and bawled:

"Waugh—whaup!"

The horse shook his head and stopped at once.

The other three, who walked in a line behind him, followed his example, so that the waggon of necessity came to a standstill.

As the captain had foretold, the sudden jerk and the cessation of the motion woke up the driver.

"I have a passenger for you," cried Captain Hawk—"one that will pay liberally for a ride on the road to London. How far are you going?"

This was a great deal for the man's intellect to grasp all at once, so a moment or two elapsed before he made a reply.

"I be agoin' a matter o' fourteen mile beyond Huntingdon, if that's any good t'ye."

"It will do exceedingly well. And if you attend to the lady's comfort, you will find this about as profitable a night's work as you were ever engaged in."

Captain Hawk now led the girl to the back of the waggon, and assisted her to enter it.

He was glad to find that the bottom was covered with a quantity of new straw, and that there were plenty of empty sacks lying about.

He was thus enabled to make her a comfortable sort of couch, on which she could either sit or recline as she chose.

"I will not say farewell," the captain said, "because I shall be sure to see you at least once again. If you do not catch sight of me, do not infer on that account that I am not near. I will give you my word you shall be safely watched over."

Again she thanked him, but the captain would not stay to listen.

Laughing lightly, in order to cheer her spirits to what extent he could, he jumped down into the road.

"Here," he said, as he thrust a crown-piece into the hand of the astonished driver, "take that to drink the lady's health with, and I will settle with you when you get to the end of your journey. Now start on."

As soon as ever the waggoner could recover from his intense astonishment, he cracked his whip, and the horses resumed their ordinary pace of about three miles and a half per hour.

The young girl crept to the back part of the vehicle and looked out wistfully.

It was quite clear that she was by no means willing to ride alone in this manner.

Captain Hawk waved his hand, and watched the waggon until it was out of sight.

As soon as it was hidden from his view, he called his horse.

The faithful animal was instantly at his side.

"It is not very late," he said, "so I will ride back a little way in order to find out whether they are making any pursuit after the girl or not. Then I will ride across the country to the Greyhound. If I am speedy, I shall be there by daybreak or soon after."

Suiting the action to the word, Captain Hawk rode down the high-road in the direction he had just come.

He put Satan upon his mettle, for time was precious, and he wished to set the point at rest with as little delay as possible.

"I shall not have to ride far," he said, "because, from the length of time which has elapsed, they must have got almost as far as I am now, even if they rode slowly."

Determined, however, to put his mind at rest, the captain rode rather more than three miles further.

But when he had done so, he found no more signs of the approach of anyone than at first.

"All is well now, I feel sure," he said, "and that old waggon is about the last place in the world they will think of looking into for her."

But even now he lingered a few minutes.

The silence remaining unbroken, however, he at length turned back, and, by his voice, quickly urged Satan into a pace that few would have relished riding at, especially when so dark as it then was.

But the highwayman knew no fear in this respect.

"I will get to the old Greyhound with all speed," he said. "I know I can make sure of a welcome there, and, what is more, of a safe shelter. When once beneath that rare old roof I can quietly think over what I have next to do. Satan, too, after all this, needs a little extra attention."

Just as he had finished making these mental remarks, the highwayman quitted the high-road.

The point he wished to reach was a very long way off, but he happened to be well enough acquainted with the district to know that by riding over the country he should save several miles as well as be in less danger of being either seen or recognised.

In the open country the darkness seemed absolutely greater, but he held on bravely, except when occasionally a piece of heavy land presented itself.

Despite all these drawbacks, however, he got in a short time a long way upon his journey.

Streams were forded, hedges and ditches leaped, and hardly any obstacle turned away from.

Satan seemed in no way distressed by his exertions, and bounded on as freely and vigorously as at first.

And so without interruption the ride was continued until the clouds banked upon the eastern horizon began to be flushed with light.

"Courage, old boy," cried the highwayman, enthusiastically, for his headlong ride had raised his spirits to the utmost pitch—"courage: we are almost there!"

The accents of his voice were quite enough to cause Satan to increase his efforts.

Indeed, it almost seemed as though he knew what his master had said to him, and was rejoiced to learn that their destination was at hand. Half a mile further on he came to a high hedge, along which he rode until he came to a tolerably wide gap.

On the other side, at a little lower level than the field, was the broad, well-kept high-road.

"Over!" cried the highwayman, and at the word the docile creature leaped through the gap and alighted in safety on the other side.

"The place will be quiet enough at this lonely hour, I'll warrant," he said, "and I shall get to the Greyhound before many people are abroad. I should be glad to cross the threshold unseen by anyone if I could."

He rode along swiftly, though no longer at a gallop.

The light rapidly increased, the sky assuming every moment ruddier tints.

On turning a corner in the road, he looked behind.

"Yes," he cried, as his eye fell upon a cluster of roof-tops and the steeples of several churches, all looking doubly beautiful in the gentle morning light—"yes, there is old Huntingdon once more. I have skirted the town nicely. Its inhabitants, I daresay, are all fast asleep, and I might have galloped down the High Street unrecognised; but having come this way, I am sure no prying eye has seen me. Now, Satan my boy, three miles more, and we shall be as far as I intend to go at present."

As before, the horse seemed quite to understand this.

His speed was increased immediately.

His rider made no attempt to check him.

A very little over ten minutes brought him in sight of the steep, red-tiled roof of some building that stood a few yards back from the main road.

"There we are at last!" he cried, tightening the rein. "Old Beckford will open his eyes a little when he sees me. But I said when we last parted that we should meet again when least expected."

He trotted gently up to the building we have mentioned.

This proved to be one of those ancient and picturesque hostelries for which the highways in England were once so famous.

The old pole which supported the old swinging sign was quite a wonder to look at, and well worth coming to see.

Then the greyhound that was limned upon it was not very true to nature, but no doubt as good as the rural artist could produce for the money.

Underneath the representation of the dog was painted, in straggling letters, "Tom Beckford."

No sooner had Captain Hawk brought his panting horse to a standstill than a loud cheery voice cried out:

"Well, well, and so the captain has turned up at last! You are as welcome as the sun in harvest time!"

Directly afterwards there appeared in the doorway of the old inn one of the stoutest men that could be seen in a journey from London to York.

It looked very strange to see him emerge from his domicile, because so great was his rotundity that he had to stand sideways, and to work himself through the portal by degrees.

But when once this difficult feat was accomplished, he was active enough in his movements—that is, bearing in mind the size of his body.

Like some great overfed duck, he waddled to the horse-trough, close to which the captain had pulled up.

His huge round, red face, which was irresistibly suggestive of a rising sun in a fog, was beaming all over with unmistakable delight.

Thrusting forth his hand, he seized hold of the highwayman's fingers, and crushed them as though in a vice.

"Glad to see you, captain—heartily glad to see you, captain! My old eyes have been longing for this treat for many a day."

"You speak loudly, Tom. Are you sure there are no Philistines in the land?"

The landlord shook his head.

"Bad luck to all such gentry, say I! Thank goodness, there happens to be none near the old Greyhound at the present time!"

"That is welcome news. And now, Tom, I want to put up here for a day or two."

"Just as long as you like, my boy—just as long as you like. You don't want me to waste my precious blood by telling you that you are welcome."

"No, there is no need for that," said the captain, releasing his hand at length from the landlord's iron grasp, which he had borne without flinching. "Just perambulate that great paunch of yours towards the stable, and I will lead my horse after you."

"I'll see to him, captain—I'll see to him. Why, lor' bless me, I can see by the animal's eye that he knows perfectly well he is at the Greyhound, and that he is heartily glad of it."

It was perfectly certain that the landlord was highly delighted.

He led the way through a variety of passages and open yards until he paused before one particular door.

This he pushed open with his foot.

"Now, captain," he said, "just let go of him, will you, and see if he does not go straight through the door and up to the manger like a Christian."

Captain Hawk immediately complied.

Satan seemed perfectly at home.

With a quick, springing step, he entered the stable, and, just as the landlord had foretold, walked directly up to the manger in a way that proved how familiar the place was to him.

Of course ability to groom and tend a horse properly was not possessed by the old landlord, so Captain Hawk very readily and willingly took those duties upon himself.

It was much better to do so than to take the ostler into their confidence.

Half an hour saw Satan as comfortable as any horse could wish to be, and when the captain closed the door, locked it, and, in accordance with unvarying custom, slipped the key into his pocket, he felt thoroughly content and at ease.

"He is safe now, captain," gurgled the landlord—he was much too fat to articulate with any degree of distinctness. "If the Philistines arrived they would ten to one miss him if they made a search of the place. No one would think of finding a stable there."

The outbuildings connected with the old inn were so extensive and were erected in so perplexing a manner, that it would have been very hard for any strangers to the place to have made certain that no structure had escaped their scrutiny.

"Come along now, captain," continued the landlord; "let us get indoors. I am sure after all this early travelling you must be badly in want of your breakfast. I'll get something nice ready for you. The fire is lighted."

"Many thanks," answered the captain. "I can assure you there are few things more welcome than a breakfast will be."

"I should think not indeed! Why, look at me. I have had nothing to eat since yesterday, I assure you, and to-morrow will be the third day."

Captain Hawk laughed as he followed his conductor into the house.

The kitchen at the Greyhound was about as comfortable a looking place as anyone could wish to see.

A huge fire was blazing in the capacious grate, and it could be seen that some preparations for breakfast were already in progress.

"I was getting things together a bit, captain, you see, when all at once I heard a horse coming. That's the captain, said I to myself, and off I went to the door, where sure enough I found you."

The landlord while he spoke bustled about with more alacrity than would have been expected from so unwieldy a personage.

He reached down a huge ham that was hanging from the ceiling, and cut two immense slices out of it.

These he put over the fire, and in less than a quarter of an hour there was a breakfast spread that would have tempted an epicure.

As for Captain Hawk, the sight of these rich viands stimulated his appetite surprisingly, and made him remember how long it was since food of any kind had passed his lips.

Consequently, he did full justice to the meal.

The landlord was in excellent spirits, and chatted away without ceasing.

"And so you have not seen the Philistines lately, Tom?"

"No, not for a good while. I shall begin to look out for them now, however."

"I suppose so. The old turret-chamber is not occupied, I suppose?"

"Now, captain, don't you know perfectly well that I always keep that on purpose for you, and that I never allow anyone else to enter it? When you want to go there, just say the word."

"It will be very shortly, Tom, for I do not know that ever I remembered feeling so tired as I do now."

"A good rest there will put you all right. I should advise you not to come down till dark. In the meantime, you know you will be safe."

"Yes. But for all that, should any danger threaten, no matter how trifling, let me know it. Don't keep me in ignorance."

"Very good. Your wish is law always."

"Then I think you shall lead the way, Tom."

Captain Hawk was completely worn out by fatigue.

Indeed, so overpowered was he that had his foes presented themselves at that moment he would have had scarcely any power to resist them.

The landlord noted his condition and rose at once.

"When I see you again," he said, "I must get you to relate some of your adventures; there have been things of rather an unusual character going on latterly, I'll warrant."

Captain Hawk yawned out a reply, and stumbled up the dark old staircase after his conductor.

The interior of the Greyhound Inn seemed as complicated as the buildings outside.

The numerous passages, with here and there little flights of steps—now up, now down—were quite enough to perplex anybody.

"Here you are, captain," said the landlord, at last. "You will excuse my going up the ladder. I don't think it exactly up to my weight. Here is the key."

They had paused on a small, dark landing-place, which must have been familiar to the captain, or he would never have made his way about it so readily.

Taking the key from his friend's hand, he ascended a short ladder placed against the wall.

When at the top, he thrust the key into what was apparently the ceiling, but in reality it was a trap-door.

CHAPTER LVII.

THE POLICE OFFICERS MAKE A THOROUGH SEARCH OF THE GREYHOUND INN.

Having turned the key, Captain Hawk put out his strength and pushed the trap-door upwards.

When raised to a certain height, there was some contrivance for preventing this from falling down again.

As soon as it was secured, the captain ascended the remainder of the steps and stood on the floor of a room of such limited dimensions that the trap-door which he had raised occupied half its area.

"Now, Tom," he said, "you can take the ladder away and hide it. When it is time for me to get up, come and call me. Rest assured that I shall sleep till then."

"Just as long as ever you like, captain."

"But if there is danger, fail not to make me acquainted with it instantly."

"Very good. Don't trouble your head about it. I will answer for it that you are safe; and now, good morning. A pleasant sleep to you."

So saying, the landlord removed the ladder for the purpose of secreting it.

When this was done, there was nothing to be seen, when the trap-door was closed, that would lead anyone to suppose that there was a chamber above.

Captain Hawk remained watching until the landlord had disappeared, and then he gently lowered the trap-door into its place, and locked it on the inner side.

The chamber which he now occupied was of a very singular appearance.

In shape it was quite round, and the roof rose up conically to a point, so that it bore a strong resemblance to the interior of an extinguisher.

In the walls were several small loopholes, which were so placed that a view on every side could be obtained from them.

As this turret chamber was higher than any other part of the roof of the old inn, it follows, as a matter of course, that the look-out was very good.

Had he done nothing but keep watch, the captain could have been aware of the coming of his foes when they were a mile off.

He did not on the present occasion, however, contemplate doing anything of the kind.

He had the utmost trust and confidence in the landlord, and knew that after what had passed he should be secure from all harm.

He just looked in succession through all the different openings, but finding no sign of the approach of anyone from any direction, he threw himself down, dressed as he was, on the bed, which was about the only article of furniture the room contained.

For some time back the highwayman had had the greatest possible difficulty in keeping his eyes open, and so it is not surprising, especially when it is remembered what fatigue he had gone through, that as soon as he had assumed a recumbent posture sleep should descend upon him.

In a moment everything was as completely forgotten as though he had passed out of existence in reality.

The beams of the sun streamed successively through the narrow loopholes, and fell upon his face.

But the warmth and brilliancy of the rays failed to wake him, and so he slumbered on until the coming of nightfall.

He sprang up with a start, and for a minute or two gazed about him confusedly.

"Confound it all!" he exclaimed, chafing his neck with both his hands. "So it is nothing but a dream after all! I trust I may never have such another."

He shuddered in a way that plainly indicated some very terrible images had presented themselves to him during his slumber.

He gave himself a good round shake, so as to rid himself from these feelings, and then moved cautiously towards one of the loopholes, for now the turret chamber was involved in deep obscurity.

The night was clear and fine.

There was no moon; but the sky was studded everywhere with brightly-shining stars.

"I do believe now that I have outstripped my foes!" he exclaimed, when, after listening for some moments, he failed to catch any alarming sounds. "I shall have a little rest from them now, depend upon it. I wish old Tom would come; I am tired of being cooped up here, and I am sure there is no occasion for it."

He unlocked the trap-door and looked down.

But the profound darkness prevented his eyes from penetrating an inch into the abyss.

"I had better not call, perhaps," he said. "Surely he will be here before long."

Turning back again, he once more placed himself at one of the loopholes, and looked out.

But there was nothing to disturb the quiet of the scene.

"Let me see," he said, "I had almost forgotten an important obligation I am under. That young girl, and all the strange events which have happened since the carriage window was broken yesterday morning, have driven everything else out of my mind. I am glad I thought about the ostler in good time. I will keep my word at all hazards."

These few words will suffice to make the reader acquainted with the subject of the highwayman's thoughts.

Up to that moment, however, he had forgotten all about his promise to reward the ostler for the service he had so faithfully performed for him.

The remembrance of this made him still more anxious for the landlord to make his appearance.

"Ten to one," he muttered, "if I shall have a better chance of effecting my purpose than there will be tonight. Confound him, why don't he come?"

He waited for some moments longer with undisguised impatience, and then, unable to stay any longer, walked to the trap-door with the firm intention of calling out.

No sooner had he reached the edge, however, than a slight sound made him pause.

The sound increased in loudness.

Some one approached.

The captain remained still, lister'

The gleam of a candle could now be detected, and the next moment the landlord, carrying a candle in his hand, came into view.

"Ah!" he exclaimed, "are you there?"

"Yes, I am here, as you know very well; and I have been wondering where the devil you could have got to."

"I have a little bit of news for you."

"Quick!—let me know it!"

"Don't be in such a desperate hurry."

He put down the candle, and proceeded to draw the ladder from its hiding-place.

"That's right!" cried Captain Hawk. "I am waiting to come down."

"I fancy you will have to go up again."

"Why?"

"Because I have heard that the police officers are about. They have managed to get scent of you somehow."

"But how?"

"You ought to know that much better than myself. There is little doubt about the correctness of my information."

"But do they guess I am here?"

"No, not exactly that. They have merely an idea, I think, that you are somewhere in the neighbourhood."

"Ah, well, it cannot be helped! I have business on the road to-night."

"Then you had better put it off."

"Just because the officers are on the road?"

"Yes, for they are in great force, I assure you. I have been thinking the matter over, captain, and there is something I want you to do."

"Name it, and if it is at all in reason you shall not want in vain."

"Very good. I want you to disguise yourself."

"Why?"

"In order that the Greyhound may be searched. Depend upon it, now that the officers have an inkling that you are somewhere about here, they will not be very long before they pay the Greyhound a visit—in fact, I expect to hear them ride up to the door every moment."

"The deuce you do!"

"Yes, it is a fact; and, if you will only leave matters to me, I will undertake that they shall turn out all right."

"What do you want on my part?"

"In the first place, I want you to disguise yourself."

"How?"

"If you will have patience I will tell you."

"Patience! It's all very well for you down there to talk about patience. How should you like to be cooped up in this extinguisher sort of a place?"

"It won't be for long, and you ought not to despise it."

"No, far from it. But pray go on."

"Well, this disguise that I propose is an excellent one. You need have little fear it will be detected."

"And you want me to wear it while the officers come in and search the place, I suppose?"

"Just so."

"And do you for a moment think it would be good enough to escape their penetration?"

"I do. If I didn't, I shouldn't ask you to try the experiment."

"Well?"

"Then after the search is over the officers will depart, and, having once satisfied themselves that you are not here, what better hiding-place could possibly exist than this will be then?"

"I quite understand you."

"And am I not right?"

"Unquestionably. The only thing I see in the way is the difficulty of disguising myself."

"Then just listen to my explanation."

"I am paying every attention."

"You must know, then, that for some time past I have had an uncle of mine staying here in the house with me. He is a very queer old fellow, and is well known by everyone who comes to the place.

"Well, at night there is always one seat that he occupies in the chimney corner, and if he does not happen to be present no one else ventures to take it."

"But what the deuce——"

"Don't I tell you not to be impatient?"

"Impatient! I should like to know how on earth I could be otherwise when you are so long in coming to the point!"

"But I am at the point. My uncle is about your height and make, only, of course, very much older; and to-night I have persuaded him to go to bed—he is not very well—and to let me have his clothes. Now do you understand?"

"It's getting clearer. But go on with your explanation in your own way; I shall be better able to judge then."

"All right. I shall take pains to disguise you like my uncle, and when I have done so you will walk downstairs and take the accustomed seat in the chimney corner. That's clear enough, isn't it?"

"Quite so."

The landlord nodded his head complacently.

"My uncle is a very surly old chap, and will often sit the whole of an evening without saying a word to the company. If he is asked a question that he can't get out of replying to, he gives a grunt."

"That will make the part all the easier to play."

"Of course it will; and it is not half so difficult as you now think it. Everybody knows my uncle; and as he is known to be rich, all put up with his whims and fancies without a word of complaint. When a guest enters he will be sure to speak to you."

"And what am I to do in such a case?"

"Why, nothing more than lift your head up a little way and give a half-grunt, half-growl by way of response."

"I see."

"Well, now, when you are there, and the ordinary guests seated around, suppose the officers come in?"

"Yes."

"All you must do is to sit quite still—nothing disturbs my uncle. Take no notice of the officers. They will look at you, I daresay, and if a question is asked, everybody in the room will be ready to say who you are."

"I see."

"Is not the plan good?"

"Very good."

"Do you see anything to prevent it from being successfully carried out?"

"Nothing at present."

The landlord rubbed his hands together, while his face beamed all over with satisfaction.

"Come down the ladder now, then, and we will get on with the disguising. If we stay long we may lose the chance altogether."

Captain Hawk descended the ladder, and having done so, resolved to trust himself entirely into the landlord's hands.

The more he thought over the proposal that had been made to him the better he liked it, and the greater seemed the chances that it would answer the end in view.

He followed the landlord, without another word and without another moment's delay, through the long winding passages, until finally he pushed open a door that led into a bed-room.

"Here you are," cried Beckford, as he closed the door. "Now then, on with these things as soon as you can. All that you are able you had better wear over your own apparel."

He pointed to a pile of garments on a chair.

Captain Hawk quickly set to work to effect an exchange, and he was aided by the landlord, who lent him material assistance.

At length all preparations were complete.

The captain had to sacrifice some of the long waving locks of hair of which he was so proud, in order to make the uncle's wig fit him; but when this was done, the alteration which this one article made was wonderfully greater than can be imagined.

When all was ready, Captain Hawk's personal appearance may be summed up as follows:—

On his head, as we have said, he wore a wig which allowed no signs of his own hair to be visible.

And a very dirty, grotesque-looking wig it was too.

Round his neck was a neckcloth almost as large as a blanket, which enveloped the lower part of his face, being worn by the uncle in that way, because, as the landlord said "he suffered with rheumatiz in the face so bad.

The coat was of vivid blue cloth, of most ample cut, and garnished in every possible place with huge double-gilt buttons.

The waistcoat was white—the smallclothes of corduroy.

These buttoned closely at the knee, and beneath them were bright-blue worsted stockings, and shoes with huge buckles.

"Excellent!" said the landlord. "Why, bless me, if I came upon you on a sudden I should take you for my uncle myself."

"I am glad to find the alteration so great," said the captain, surveying himself as well as the old cracked mirror would permit. "Now shall we go down?"

"Yes," answered the landlord; "I think all is ready."

"Is there anything more in the shape of directions?"

"Nothing. Just bear in mind what I have already said."

"Never fear."

"Follow me down, then; and when you get to the kitchen, walk straight to the unoccupied three-cornered elbow chair, and sit down in it. Take care not to look either right or left as you cross the room, and stoop a little, with your shoulders bent round like a cart wheel."

Captain Hawk promised obedience; and feeling not a little curious to know how the adventure would terminate, followed the landlord in silence.

"There is one thing," he thought to himself, and the reflection gave him great satisfaction, "if, when I enter, the people in the kitchen do not notice the change, I may be sure the officers will not recognise me."

He was about to communicate this thought to his companion, when just at the moment both were startled by a sound which they knew perfectly.

It was caused by a number of horsemen suddenly drawing up in front of the inn.

The pair exchanged glances.

"Hush!" said the landlord.

He put down the candle, and pushed the door open that communicated with the kitchen.

Captain Hawk was well acquainted with the whole interior economy of the inn, so he knew how to make his way to the fireplace without exhibiting the awkwardness and hesitation of a stranger.

On his way to the seat, he affected to have a bad cough, and by putting up his hand to his mouth he still more concealed his features.

There was no light in the kitchen save that which the huge pile of logs on the hearth emitted; and it so happened that at this juncture the blaze had sunk low for want of attention.

Thus all things conspired in the highwayman's favour.

"I hope you are better to-night, Mr. Beckford?"

The captain grunted as he had been told.

"Dear me!" added the speaker, in quite a changed tone of voice. "What an awful clatter! What on earth can be the matter?"

These words were caused by a most furious knocking, which caused every nook and corner in the old inn to resound.

"God bless me!" ejaculated the landlord, with an affectation of ludicrous dismay. "It's the French! We are invaded at last!"

Absurd as this fear was, it was caught up directly, for it happened to be the point upon which the public mind was most anxious and alarmed.

The knocking was resumed with double vigour.

The landlord moved slowly to the door.

He was anxious to give Captain Hawk time to compose himself.

But this was unnecessary.

The captain was quite prepared.

"Who's there?" bawled the landlord, with the full power of his stentorian lungs as soon as he got near to the front door.

"Officers of police!" was the reply. "Open in the name of his Majesty the King!"

The landlord let fall the bar with a prodigious clatter, and opened the door.

He then saw that the open space between his front door and the horse-trough was filled up with horses.

At the head of each animal stood an officer.

"Now, landlord," said the one who had the command, "we have received information that the notorious Captain Hawk is not far off. If you can tell us anything of his whereabouts let me advise you to do so. If we search the house and find him, you will be in more than usual trouble, I can tell you!"

"Enter, gentlemen! You are quite welcome to do your duty. I know nothing of the man you want, and if he is in the house it is without my knowledge."

"Very good. Morris, look to the horses. Half a dozen enter the house with me! The rest keep a close look-out on every part of the building, so that no one can have a chance to leave unseen."

"All right, sir."

Having settled matters so far, the commanding officer entered the inn, followed by the half-dozen he had mentioned.

The landlord led them straight into the kitchen.

"Here are all the guests I have in the house at the present time."

"Oh indeed," said the commanding officer, looking around him with preternatural keenness—"oh indeed!"

The rustics who were present were awed into silence by the presence of these legal emissaries.

"And pray how many strangers do you happen to have in the company, landlord?"

Old Tom pretended to look very carefully around him before he replied:

"As I live," he ejaculated, "it is a most strange thing!"

"What—what?"

"Why, although I am honoured with so numerous an assemblage to-night, I can't see one strange face amongst them."

"Oh, that is it, is it?" said the chief officer.

"Yes, that is it."

"But you have strangers sometimes?"

"Oh, very often! See, this being a roadside inn, people are always dropping in promiscuous-like, and I assure you it is a very great wonder indeed not to see two or three strangers among the company."

The landlord's words produced a little consternation among the assembly, and each one turned quickly to look into his neighbour's countenance with an anxious desire to be recognised.

The well-known figure sitting in the shadow of the chimney corner with the grotesque wig, the blue coat with the double-gilt buttons, and the thick home-made worsted stockings, was known by everybody."

Not one suspected for an instant the imposition which had been practised, as, indeed, why should they, when there was absolutely nothing at all to suggest such a thing to their minds?

"You appear all to know one another perfectly well," said the commanding officer, who, with a quickness of vision upon which he much prided himself, had noted the interchange of glances—"that is, all but the old gentleman in the chimney corner."

"Oh, that is Mr. Beckford, the landlord's rich uncle!" cried everybody in chorus, for, now that the danger of being taken for the notorious highwayman was over, each was anxious to speak.

"Oh, indeed!" said the officer, as he turned away, for there was nothing in the appearance of the figure to suggest the remotest resemblance to Captain Hawk.

"Eccentric and rather deaf," whispered the landlord, confidentially. "I would not have him offended for all the world. He is as rich as a Jew, and has no one nearer of kin to leave his money to than myself."

"Ah, very well! Now then, let us have a look about the rest of the house. I shall then be able to make a decided and satisfactory report."

"Certainly."

"You have no objection?"

"None whatever. You will want lights."

"Yes. Can you supply us with some?"

"Oh yes!"

"Very good. Then please do so."

The landlord went out to fetch the candles, and as soon as he was at a safe distance he indulged in a good laugh to himself.

"Only think now! The bare idea! What a joke to think of searching such a place as the Greyhound by candlelight! It's rich! But they don't dream what kind of a place they are in. Why, I could hide a regiment of men nearly if they were only searched for by candlelight."

[LORD HARCLIFFE REGAINS POSSESSION OF HIS STEED.]

The landlord got the candles, and hastened back to the inn kitchen, where the police officers were still standing. He made a great display with the candles, and professed a fabulous amount of willingness to assist them by every means in his power.

The officer seemed to be completely deceived.

"Now, gentlemen," he cried, as he took one of the lighted candles himself, "I am quite at your disposal, and most willing to conduct you all over the place. Will you please to signify whereabouts you would like to begin?"

"Up at the top," said the commanding officer, after a moment's consideration.

"Very good; then I will take you direct up into the attics at once."

"Yes; and then we can take every place in rotation as we descend, and then we shall be sure of not having missed anywhere."

The landlord was so tickled at this idea that he had to simulate a dreadful fit of coughing in order to smother his laughing.

As soon as he had recovered a little, the chief officer said:

"Smithson, just run out to those who are watching outside, and tell them to keep a doubly sharp look-out, because we are going to commence the search. Tell them to take notice whether we disturb anybody. Then follow us upstairs."

"Yes, sir."

The man departed.

"Now, then, landlord, up you go!"

"I think we had better wait."

"Why?"

"Till the man comes back."

"Pooh—pooh! He can follow us up the staircase fast enough. There is no need to wait."

"Well, sir, I daresay you know best, and I daresay you ought; but if anybody thought it worth while to ask my opinion, I should say just the reverse."

"Indeed! Why?"

"Because he would be in danger of losing us."

"Losing us while going upstairs! What on earth does the man mean?"

"Will you allow me to explain?"

"Oh, certainly!"

"Well, then, I must begin by telling you this is far from a regularly-built place. Indeed, it is about as irregular as any place well could be, even if half a dozen fellows sat down to contrive it. You see, in former times a large farm-house, with cottages and numerous outbuildings, stood here, but it was turned into a public-house and all the lot knocked into one. It's most confusing, I assure you, till you happen to become acquainted with the ins and outs of the place. There's steps up here, then steps down there, then a lot of rooms opening one out of the other, and all on different levels; and then long passages—— And I declare here comes Smithson back again before I have finished my explanation."

The officer muttered something between his teeth, for dimly the idea came over him that the landlord was humbugging him.

A glance into Tom Beckford's countenance, however, seemed more than sufficient to dispel any such idea.

It looked so remarkably serious and well-intentioned.

"Lead on," he said. "If there is any truth in what you say, this house must be more like a rabbit warren than a human habitation."

"You will have an opportunity of judging directly," was the reply as he led them up the staircase.

But by the time they had, in accordance with the officer's wishes, reached the topmost story, all were impressed with the belief that there was not much exaggeration in the landlord's description.

He brought them right under the trap-door communicating with the room in which the captain had enjoyed such a sound slumber.

He took care not to direct the light of his own candle upwards any more than he could help.

But now that the ladder was removed there seemed no trace of there being any communication aloft.

"And so this is the top, is it, landlord?"

"Yes; we are here at last. Pooh—hooh! What a job this getting upstairs is, to be sure! I can't manage it now like I could one time of day. Oh dear me!"

The landlord puffed and blowed like a porpoise, and wiped the perspiration from his face with a pocket-handkerchief not much smaller than an ordinary table-cloth.

CHAPTER LVIII.

CAPTAIN HAWK'S POSITION BECOMES MORE CRITICAL THAN EVER.

The landing beneath the trap-door was so small that the officers had some little ado to squeeze themselves on to it.

The landlord knew there would not be much room to move about, and so, with prudent foresight, took care to place himself close to the place where the ladder was concealed, so that there should be less danger of its discovery.

The police officers looked around as well as the aid of no better illumination than candlelight would allow them; but they saw nothing whatever of a suspicious character.

Their leader happened to be one of those men who are profoundly impressed with the sense of their superior sagacity.

This sagacity led him to the conclusion that Captain Hawk was not at that time an inmate of the Greyhound Inn.

The search which he was instituting was merely a matter of form, and made for the purpose of removing all doubt from the minds of those of his followers who might not be of the same way of thinking.

Had not this been the case, it is probable that the turret chamber would have been discovered.

As it was, the one in command said:

"All right, landlord. Now show us the way down; and if you will take us into the different rooms in succession we shall be satisfied."

"Very good," replied Tom. "Be good enough to come this way."

The officers followed him; but as we know that their search through the different rooms in the inn must be without success, there is no need to describe their doings in detail.

Tom Beckford admirably assumed an air of wonderful sincerity, and seemed anxious to a degree to aid the officers as far as possible in the execution of their duty.

The chief officer did not know him very well, or he would not have been imposed upon so readily.

Nothing worthy of special mention occurred in searching any of the rooms until they came to one upon the first floor.

The door of this room was shut, and the landlord knocked at it.

"Who's in there?" asked the chief officer, whose original suspicious were re-aroused by this circumstance.

"Why, gentlemen," said Tom, in a subdued voice, "you must know that my poor old father-in-law is in this room."

"Your father-in-law?"

"Yes. Poor old man! he is almost past doing anything now, and yet I can remember the time when——"

"There, there—that will do. I have had enough of your long-winded stories. Open the door at once!"

Contrary to the expectations of the sagacious officer, the landlord opened the door without the least show of reluctance.

Nevertheless, the chief officer pushed in hastily.

"Hush—hush!" said Tom. "Don't make a noise, for the poor old fellow's sake."

The first glance showed that the apartment was an ordinary bed-chamber, and some powerful nasal sound unmistakably proclaimed the fact that the bed was occupied by some one who was slumbering profoundly.

"Don't wake him if you can help it," added Tom, with difficulty making his voice heard above the snoring. "You will soon see that the man you want is not here."

The curtains were pulled aside, and the light of one of the candles thrown upon the bed.

On the pillow lay a head that was protected by a huge conical scarlet nightcap.

The glare of light disturbed the sleeper, and, rolling over, he opened his eyes in stupid bewilderment, as people will when suddenly awakened from deep sleep.

It was a palpable fact that the occupant of the bed was a very old man.

His cheeks were deeply sunk, and a few straggling locks of gray hair could be seen beneath his nightcap.

The most sceptical and suspicious must have been convinced that this was not the highwayman they sought.

The examination of the rest of the room was soon made.

Of course nothing was discovered.

When the search was all but over a heavy step was heard upon the staircase close to the head of which the whole party was standing.

"Who's that?" said the landlord, advancing a step.

"Wait a moment; we shall soon know."

Just as he spoke, one of the police officers who had been put on duty outside of the inn made his appearance.

"What is the matter?" asked his leader, anxiously.

"Why, don't you see, sir, I am dripping wet?"

"Well?"

"It isn't well at all, sir—leastways, you wouldn't think so if you had to stand outside. I am not like a cow, fond of standing to be rained on."

"Does it rain?"

"Does it? Oh my! Why, haven't you heard it?"

"Heard it? No."

"Well, we have felt it. There is not one of us that is not wet to his shirt, and the rest have sent me to know whether they can get under cover?"

"I will let you know in a moment. The search is all but over, and I hope the rain will not be sufficient to keep us from getting on with our duty."

The man muttered something in a grumbling tone, and retired.

"Nothing would please them better than to find an excuse for staying here half the night."

"Nor me either," said the landlord. "Though I say it, you will find here as good accommodation as you can wish, and it will afford me the greatest pleasure and satisfaction to wait upon you, gentlemen."

"Oh, no doubt—no doubt! Have we any more rooms to see?"

"Only this one."

"Then he is not here. And now let us get down and ascertain the state of the weather."

On gaining the front door, the rain was found to be very much worse than anyone had anticipated it.

One could not say that it came down in drops, but in perfect streams.

It was certain that no one could be exposed to it for a couple of moments without getting wet through to the skin.

"Confound it all!" cried the chief officer. "Who would have thought of this? It promised to be a beautifully fine night. It's as dark as pitch, too!"

"So it is," said the landlord, concealing his annoyance, for when he spoke as he did before he was very far indeed from meaning what he said, and now he felt certain he should have the company of the officers for a much longer time than was agreeable to contemplate.

This unexpected downpour of rain placed Captain Hawk in greater danger than ever, for, of course, everything was to be dreaded if the officers should make a lengthened stay.

It is comparatively easy to keep up a deception for a few minutes, but very difficult when it comes to an hour or two.

The horses and men outside could not be discerned, so very great was the darkness.

But the latter could be heard cursing and swearing most vigorously.

"We must shelter for a little while at all events, landlord," said the one in command. "Ten to one if the men would follow me if I ordered them to start now. One thing, it can't keep on raining like this very long; it is only a shower."

"Well, gentlemen, you are welcome to stay," cried the landlord, with well-affected cordiality. "Shall I call out and tell them to put the horses under cover and to come inside?"

"Yes."

The landlord did so.

But the officers had already tied their horses under a long wooden shed, where they were quite protected from the weather.

The consequence was that the order to enter was obeyed with wonderful promptitude.

In they rushed like so many drowned rats.

The others had to stand aside quickly to escape their violence as they entered.

Oaths and curses broke out on every side.

The front door was shut, so as to prevent the rain from beating in any longer.

After that, all without exception made their way to the inn kitchen.

The assembled guests looked up in surprise.

"Turned out 'nation wet, gemmen," said one, anxious to conciliate these minions of the law.

"Here, take my seat; it's close to the fire, and you're very welcome."

The offer was accepted without any mock hesitation; and the others, following the example thus set, allowed the officers to come up close to the fire.

That is, all but the supposed uncle.

Captain Hawk sat perfectly still, though he inwardly cursed the chance which had caused the officers to stay.

He thought once of getting up and leaving the kitchen.

But believing from what he had heard that this was just what the landlord's uncle would not think of doing, he had the presence of mind to retain his seat.

It was no comfortable thing, however, to have the officers so close to him, especially when, in order to obtain more heat to dry their clothes, they poked the fire until the blaze made the interior of the kitchen as light as day.

But Captain Hawk, with a composure that few could have maintained, sat at the fireside, drinking occasionally from a large can of ale, and keeping his eyes almost constantly fixed upon his knees.

Those officers who were wet, however, were much too busy drying their apparel to take the least notice of him; while as for the others, they were already more than satisfied that the man they wanted was not beneath that roof.

The landlord's mind was far from being at ease, though he managed to conceal it from all present.

No one could have had a livelier sense than himself that Captain Hawk was in imminent danger of discovery, and that if the highwayman was detected, he (the landlord) would find himself in a very ticklish position indeed.

There was nothing to be done, however, save to watch and abide by the course of events.

Certainly, if one man more than another was to be trusted in an emergency like the present it was Captain Hawk.

And as minute after minute elapsed without the much-dreaded discovery taking place, the landlord's apprehensions abated.

He was busily occupied now in attending to the wants of his guests.

Without exception, all clamoured for hot rum-and-water, that being the beverage best fitted for the occasion.

"Upon my word," cried one, as he supped at his steaming glass, "this is not so very bad, after all."

"Not for you it isn't," cried one of his companions; "but if you had been outside with us, instead of searching the rooms, you would not have found it half so pleasant."

Emboldened by the satisfaction which was universally expressed upon the countenances of the police officers, the ordinary guests of the inn kitchen attempted to join in the conversation.

"And so," said one, half hesitatingly, for he did not know how his remark would be received—"and so you have not been able to capture this celebrated Captain Hawk, after all?"

"No," answered the chief officer, with an affectation of indifference he was far from feeling. "We have just missed him; but it does not signify much."

"Oh, indeed, sir!"

"You seem surprised to hear me say that."

"Well, yes, sir, I am."

"I will explain."

An immediate manifestation was shown to listen eagerly to the next words.

"You see," said the chief officer, sinking his voice to a confidential tone, "we are more anxious to drive him towards London than actually to make him our prisoner, although we should not let slip an opportunity of doing so if one presented itself."

"I suppose not."

"But why not be anxious to capture him?" said another. "I can't quite see that."

"Why, you see, if we did so we should have to convey him to London, and that would be about as difficult a task as anyone could undertake, because the length of the journey would give him such continual opportunities of getting away."

"And so you are driving him before you?"

"Yes; and we have not had much difficulty in doing so at present."

"Of course."

"What we are most anxious about is passing him on the road. Should we be unlucky enough to get first it will be very awkward."

"And you don't think you have the start of him now?"

"Oh dear no! I have certain knowledge of his having been very near this place indeed."

"I wonder whether he has any notion, now, that what you want to do is to drive him before you?"

"He may suspect it, yet I hardly think so. He will find, however, that as soon as ever he gets near to London he will be made a prisoner in earnest."

"You are sure of catching him then?"

"Oh yes! I have a plan ready which cannot fail to be successful."

At hearing these words, Captain Hawk looked up swiftly.

But just as quickly he resumed his old indifferent attitude.

No words can tell, however, how strongly he was

tempted to ask the nature of this plan about the result of which the chief officer expressed himself so confidently.

It was with almost ungovernable impatience that he waited for one of the company to put the question.

As a matter of course, the villagers wanted to know by what means the capture of the great highwayman could be insured.

"The plan is one," replied the chief officer, "the success of which depends upon it being kept a profound secret. If once it got to the ears of Captain Hawk, there would be no hope of accomplishing it; he would take such measures as would defeat it entirely."

"But how can it get to Captain Hawk's ears," said one, "if you satisfy our curiosity by telling us what it is? I am sure no one of us is in communication with him."

"That may be," replied the chief officer; "but I am compelled to be extremely cautious."

"But how is Captain Hawk to know?"

"That I can't say; but you cannot fail to see that if I disclose the scheme he will have a much better chance of hearing of it and providing against it than he will have if I keep my mouth shut."

"Yes, of course—that's true enough," assented several.

"Besides," added the officer, "I do not mind acknowledging that this plan is my last card. If I play it and lose, all hopes of success will vanish."

"Well, then, gentlemen," said one of the guests, "it seems all we can do is to wish you good luck. When the time comes we shall hear all about it, and until then we shall have to rest content."

And in this easy manner the subject was dismissed, though there were a few of a more inquisitive turn of mind who renewed the attack.

But it was in vain.

The chief officer seemed to imbibe firmness along with his rum-and-water, for he persistently refused to disclose his secret.

This was tantalising to a degree to Captain Hawk, who perplexed his brain in a vain endeavour to guess what the officer had in contemplation.

"It's getting late," said one of the guests, as the old clock in the corner finished striking the hour of eleven. "How is the rain now, landlord? Does it come down as fast as ever?"

"I can't see much difference," replied Tom. "I have just been to the door, and by the way it comes down now one would think it never intended to leave off."

"I hope it will do so in less than another hour," said a farmer. "If it does not, I shall hardly get home to-night."

"Let me go and see," said the chief officer. "As for the landlord here, I know he would only be too glad if we would sit drinking here till sunrise; but I want to be out on the road looking after my man, and a few drops of rain ought not to stop any of us."

So saying, he quitted the room.

Very few minutes elapsed before he returned.

"Come on," he said. "Drain your glasses."

"Has it left off?"

"Well, not exactly left off, but it is giving over; and by the time we are ready to ride away I'll warrant there will be no more than a spot or two falling."

The men grumbled a little, but they dared not refuse obedience to their chief.

The glasses were emptied, though with manifest reluctance.

Then ensued that bustle which is inseparable from the departure of many persons.

Not only the officers but the majority of the guests prepared to go, for already the hour was past when they set out for their homes.

Old Beckford made no opposition to the departure of anybody.

In fact, he was chiefly anxious that all might go, in order to allow him the opportunity of conversing with the captain.

As for the latter, he preserved his composure and kept up his assumed character to the last.

Three-quarters of an hour, however, elapsed before all had left.

The landlord then closed the door.

As soon as he entered the kitchen, Captain Hawk sprang to his feet and cried:

"Have they all gone?"

By way of reply, the landlord made a rapid signal with one hand, and placed a finger of the other on his lips in token of silence.

Captain Hawk sank down again.

He comprehended that he was not out of danger.

What special form peril was going to take next he could not tell.

Beckford glanced behind him, and then advanced to the fire, repeating his signals for the highwayman to keep silent and seated.

"Don't be alarmed," he said, as he bent over the blaze.

"What is the matter?"

"The officers are suspicious."

"Of what?"

"That you are here."

"How?"

"Sit quiet, and I will tell you. Don't forget for a moment the part you are playing."

"Be at ease about that. Tell me what has occurred."

"Why, when the officers entered the inn I counted them."

"Well?"

"There were eighteen wet. Six went with us about the rooms upstairs, the one in command counting one more. How many is that in all?"

"Twenty-five."

"Very good. Well, when they left, I took the precaution of counting them again."

"And how many were there?"

"Twenty-four."

"Are you sure you counted right?"

"Yes."

"Then where is the other?"

"That is just it."

"What is your opinion?"

"The same as yours, captain."

"That one has been left behind?"

"Yes. I can see through it all well enough. The chief thought it would be easy enough for one of his followers to secrete himself without anyone knowing it, and so it was, for had I not taken the trouble to count them I should never have been the wiser."

"Then they suspect I am here?"

"I don't know that exactly."

"Then why should one stay?"

"From the idea that if you were not here just at the present moment you might be ere long, and the one who was on the watch would be able to give timely notice of your arrival to his companions."

"What is to be done?"

"Nothing in a hurry."

"Still, we must decide."

"Wait a bit. Supposing the man here—and there can be little doubt of it—the first thing to be done is to find out where he has hidden himself."

"And how do you propose to do that?"

"It will not be very difficult, and especially to me—I am well acquainted with all the likely places."

"And when you have found him, what are you to do then?"

"I should like to put him out of the power of doing further mischief. But not to trifle with you any longer, and keep you in this dreadful suspense, I may as well say that I guess he has hidden himself in the front parlour."

"And suppose he has?"

"I will keep him safe," answered the landlord, with a chuckle. "Wait a minute or two, and I will see that all the doors and windows are properly fastened."

So saying, he left the captain in anything but a comfortable frame of mind.

"Confound the fellows!" he said. "What a nuisance they are! Here I had determined to have a night of adventures on the highway, and they have spoiled everything! What does Tom mean to do with the spy, I wonder?"

A few more minutes afterwards the landlord entered.

"There," he said, "I will forgive him now if he gets out of the house unawares to me."

"You have made all safe, then?"

"Yes, every loophole."

"Good! And now what next?"

"Come with me into the parlour."

Captain Hawk rose with all the readiness in the world.

"But look here, Tom: I don't want to get you into trouble on my account, and it will be serious trouble if it is found you have secreted me."

"Pooh, pooh!"

"It's all very well to say 'pooh, pooh!'—but——"

"Captain, look here: all you have got to do is to leave me to take care of myself; and after having lived so long in this dreadful world, I think I ought to be capable of doing it."

Captain Hawk could not help laughing at the comical way in which the landlord spoke.

Without attempting to expostulate any further, he followed him into the parlour of the inn, which was an apartment set aside for the better class of visitors who might chance to call.

The landlord opened the door quickly, and lost not a moment in closing it after him.

At the same time he shot a little bolt into its socket.

He shaded the candle with his hand, and signed to the captain not to speak.

That done, he walked to the fireplace, and taking a key from his pocket, he stuck it into what appeared to be a crevice in the brickwork.

A strange rushing sound followed, succeeded by a suppressed cry.

Then all was still.

"That's it!" said the landlord, as he turned the key. "Just what I thought. It's all right now."

"But please explain?"

"Didn't you see?"

"Yes; but I don't understand."

"I will make all clear directly."

"It's a perfect mystery now."

"Well, then, from what I saw I came to the conclusion that the man who had been left behind had hidden himself in this old closet."

As he muttered the words, the landlord flung open an antique-looking door at the side of the fire-place.

The light of the candle then disclosed a recess with a shelf near the top, and large enough below to allow a man to conceal himself easily.

But now the closet was empty, nor were there any signs visible that it had lately been occupied.

"You see that?"

"Yes."

"That's enough for the present, then. Now come with me, and I will make all clear."

The landlord shut the closet door again, and led the way out of the room.

Captain Hawk followed him, feeling a little mystified.

But in the kitchen the landlord proceeded to explain himself.

"You must know," he said, "that this old house, being part of a farm homestead, has many queer places about it. One of them happens to be under that cupboard."

"Is it a well?"

"Not exactly a well, though something very much like it. The depth is not very great. At the bottom is a kind of arched subterranean passage, large enough to allow the passage of a man."

"And that is where you have let him down into?"

"Yes."

"But you have not killed him?"

"Killed him? Oh dear no! It would take a great deal more than that to put an end to an officer, I can assure you!"

"Where is he now?"

"Somewhere about half smothered, I should think, for the place is filled up with rubbish that has been accumulating for generations. Some of it is not very savoury, because I know how unpleasant it is in wet weather; but then I can't help that."

"And there is a means of exit from it?"

"Oh yes!"

"Then when the officer gets out he will alarm his companions."

"Yes, I daresay he will; but you need be under no apprehension, for I think he will be a little while groping his way to the entrance. It is not very easy to find the way out even with a candle."

"How is that?"

"It twists and turns about so."

"And where is the exit?"

"Just beyond the back of the sheds."

"But what shall you say to-morrow, when the officers come again?"

"Just nothing at all. I shall tell them I knew there was a board loose at the bottom of the closet, but that I did not know what was below. I can make out a clear case, never fear me."

And the landlord chuckled in anticipation of the pleasure which the morrow's events would give him.

"And in the meanwhile, where shall I be?"

"Why, if you like, you may make sure of being safe in the turret chamber."

"Do you think so?"

"I do."

"And Satan?"

"He is all right."

"I must see him now," said the captain. "Nothing but actually setting eyes upon him will make me believe that he is in perfect safety."

"Come along, then. There is a little risk about it, but if it's your whim I will not balk you."

CHAPTER LIX.

IN WHICH CAPTAIN HAWK MEETS WITH SOME PROFITABLE ADVENTURES ON THE HIGH-ROAD.

Captain Hawk showed how pleased he was to hear this by springing at once to his feet.

When he saw that, the landlord thought no more of opposition.

Sticking the piece of candle into an old lantern, he prepared to lead the way to the stable where the highwayman's steed was standing.

Some idea of the rambling nature of the inn buildings may be formed when we say that this stable was reached without once emerging into the open air.

The captain expressed his amazement.

"Ha, ha!" cried the landlord. "The chief officer compared the old place to a rabbit warren! And he was somewhere about right, wasn't he?"

"He was indeed."

Captain Hawk's heart was full of joy upon positively ascertaining the fact that his matchless steed was in perfect safety.

He patted him many times, and testified his satisfaction in every way conceivable.

As soon as his transports abated he pulled out his watch.

"What is the time?" asked the landlord.

"Just a quarter to one."

"I thought that was about it."

The saddle and bridle had been put close by, and Captain Hawk now seized the first named of these articles, and clapped it on to the back of his steed.

"Stop—stop!"

"What's the matter?"

"What are you doing?"

"Can't you see?"

"Yes, I see; but—but——"

"But what?"

"Why, surely you don't think about going out to-night?"

"Indeed, but I do, and I am quite resolved upon it. I knew if I mentioned it inside it would have led to a discussion which, if it had done nothing else, would have lost valuable time, and so I thought I would come here direct, and tell you afterwards."

"Ah! it's too bad, captain—that's what it is! Here have I been trying all sorts of things to keep you in safety, and directly I have done you go and rush headlong into danger again."

"I can't help it, Tom."

"Yes, but you can help it."

"I say I can't!"

"Why?"

"Because time presses so. I have entered into an engagement, and am bound to requite the obligation."

"That's a grand way of putting it, captain, but I can tell what you mean, for all that."

"Very well, then," answered the highwayman, as he finished buckling the bridle, "that ends the matter. And now, as I am quite ready and waiting, perhaps you will be kind enough to open the door and to show me the way out."

By this time the landlord clearly saw the folly of attempting to contend, and so, with nothing more than a shake of the head, he lifted the latch.

"Mark you," he said, "I won't be answerable for any danger you may run into. For aught either of us knows, some of the officers that have just paid us a visit may be waiting and watching outside."

"It will be bad for the one I find at it," was the carelessly-uttered rejoinder. "Business calls me forth to-night, and I don't intend to come back again until my pockets are replenished. No matter what adventure may befall me on the road, I will not allow it to turn me from my purpose for a single moment."

"Very good; and when may I expect to see you after this?"

"Not before to-morrow night."

"All right."

"I expect a man to call here for me. Should he come before I arrive, put him somewhere out of the way to wait. He saved my horse lately from falling into the hands of the officers."

"And you are going to reward him for it, I suppose?"

"That's just it. You know I never allow anyone to do a service for me without making them all the better off for it. And now farewell for the present—I cannot linger any longer."

"Good luck to you, and I hope we shall soon meet again!"

Captain Hawk waved his hand, but made no verbal response to the landlord's good wishes.

The next moment he passed through a little gate into a paddock that adjoined the inn.

Tom Beckford had thought it best that he should leave in this direction, as the officers would be more likely to keep a look-out in the front.

The highwayman had his pistols ready for immediate use, and took care to glance everywhere around him.

The night was dark, for though the rain had ceased, the leaden-coloured clouds still overhung the sky.

Not a trace of his foes could be discerned.

On the paddock turf, now it had been so recently moistened, the hoofbeats of Satan were inaudible.

This would make it all the more difficult for anyone, even if set to watch, to be aware that some one was quitting the premises.

"I am in a strange costume to play the part of a highwayman," he muttered, as he glanced at the double-gilt buttons on his coat. "That matters little. My weapons, I know, are in perfect readiness for instant use, and I shall be less likely to be recognised or suspected in this garb."

The captain was obliged to say this in order to reconcile himself to his present appearance.

Neither of the considerations he mentioned had much weight with him.

The fact was, he knew changing the disguise would occupy more time than he could spare.

Even as it was, morning threatened to overtake him before he had the chance of accomplishing much.

But as soon as the vicinity of the inn was quitted he urged Satan to make all possible speed across the meadows.

"I shall soon come to the high-road," he said; "and though the hour is late, I shall be surprised if I do not make a good booty. That rain would drive all passengers to seek the first shelter they came to, and now it is over they will be resuming their journey."

This seemed probable enough.

How far Captain Hawk was right in counting upon it will be quickly seen.

A few moments more brought him to a low hedge which skirted the high-road leading from London to Huntingdon.

Here he remained and listened.

"Ah! Satan, my boy, do you hear something? So do I. Let us hope that it is good booty."

A slight touch with his heel made the obedient horse leap over the hedge.

Drawing then close to one side, he waited for his prey.

The sound told him that a couple of mounted men were approaching.

"This promises sport," he said. "They would only be abroad on such a night as this from necessity, and they are almost certain to carry money."

The travellers seemed as though they had been hindered on their journey, and were anxiously endeavouring to make up for lost time.

Their horses were going at full gallop, and every now and then the sounds of their voices as they shouted to each other could be heard.

Captain Hawk selected a light piece of roadway, and planted himself in the middle of it, for, as the travellers were approaching at such speed, he would have a difficulty in preventing them from dashing by him if he did not adopt this course.

In another moment now he dimly caught sight of their figures in the distance.

It was just about the same time that they beheld a dark figure standing immovable in the middle of the road.

The natural impulse upon making this discovery was to draw the rein.

The horses seemed willing enough to moderate their speed.

Finding they stopped so quickly, Captain Hawk rode towards them.

"I shall not detain you long, gentlemen," he said, with overwhelming politeness, "nor shall I offer you the least violence, provided you comply with my reasonable demands."

"You are a cool customer, I must say!" cried one of the travellers. "What the devil do you stop us on the highway for? Are you a highwayman?"

"Do I look like one?"

"Curse me if I know or care what you look like! What do you want?—that's the question."

"You are right," said the captain, in the same tone "that is the question."

"Well?"

"I want your purses."

"Cool—very!"

"Do you refer to the weather?"

"No, the devil, sir! but to your demand."

"Oh! then I will just trouble you to comply with it, and you are both free to ride on. It will be no one's fault but your own if you sustain the least personal injury,"

"Well, Westbroke," cried the traveller who had spoken, to his companion, who had not once opened his lips, "what do you think of this fellow, eh?"

"It does not matter what I think, I suppose?"

"What is to be done?"

"Give him our purses and get rid of him."

"A wise resolution," cried the captain. "I applaud it! Here is my hat. I shall trouble you no further than I said. Throw in your purses and ride on."

"But, Westbroke, are the pair of us to suffer ourselves to be robbed by one man without so much as raising a hand in our defence?"

"You can do as you like," was the phlegmatic rejoinder. "Here is my purse, and here, likewise, is an end of the matter."

"Then, if that is the way you look upon it, I will follow suit. The loss of a purse of money won't matter much to either of us."

"Not so much as a serious or, perhaps, a mortal wound," replied Captain Hawk, as he slipped the purses into his coat pocket and replaced his hat. "I have the honour and the pleasure to wish you both good night, gentlemen."

"Egad!" cried Westbroke, "the fellow was in earnest. I am glad now I took him at his word."

Captain Hawk waved his hat and rode off, disappearing almost instantly in the darkness.

But he soon drew rein again.

"A fair commencement," he remarked. "But I must have more than this to achieve my purpose. Will this good fortune continue to attend me?"

Hardly had he asked the question when Satan pricked up his ears, as he always did upon catching any faint or distant sound.

Directly afterwards the highwayman heard it too.

"Some one else comes," he said. "Surely, I am in luck's way to-night. I must give the storm credit for all this."

Captain Hawk was fully prepared for whatever might come, and waited contentedly enough.

It was a vehicle that was approaching him this time, and judging by the lumbering sound produced it must have been one of no ordinary weight.

"Better and better!" remarked the captain. "I'll be bound it is some one substantial who rides in such a vehicle as that."

Just as he spoke, the glimmer of distant lights became visible.

There was now no time to be lost.

Captain Hawk held his pistol ready.

"A summary proceeding will be the best," he said.

What he meant by a summary proceeding was soon seen.

A moment or so before the carriage came on a level with him he elevated his pistol and pulled the trigger.

When doing so he took care that there should be no danger of the bullet inflicting any injury upon the coachman.

The report was prodigious, and the flash of light for a second made every object distinctly visible.

Mingled with the report of the pistol came an oath and a shriek.

The former issued from the lips of the coachman, who at the same time pulled up his horses.

The latter proceeded from the interior of the vehicle, and certainly came from female lips.

"Stop!" cried the captain to the terrified coachman. "If you attempt to stir again you are a dead man! Depend upon it I shall not miss you twice!"

The man's fright now became so great that it swallowed up everything else.

Without loss of time the highwayman then made his way to the side of the carriage.

One touch with his hand sent the glass window down with a sudden crash.

"Mercy!" gasped a faint, stifled voice inside. "Oh, good Mr. Robber, pray have mercy upon me—spare my life, and take what I have. Mercy—mercy!"

"Be under no alarm," said the captain, in the gentlest tones, for he now saw that the carriage contained only a female form, which was crouching in the furthest corner —"be under no alarm," he repeated, finding that his words produced very little effect. Had I guessed that a lady travelling alone occupied this vehicle no consideration should have tempted me to cause a moment's terror or uneasiness."

"Oh, mercy! You will spare my life?"

"It is in no danger."

"Thanks for that. Now take what I have, and allow me to resume my journey."

"My dear madam," said the captain, still more gently than before, "you are quite at liberty to depart this moment. I take shame to myself for having been the means of creating so much apprehension in your breast."

"Are you not a robber, then?"

"Do I behave like one?"

"Not now; and that is why I asked the question. Yet why stop my carriage?"

"Be content with what you know already, lady. Farewell!"

He heard something said, but would not stop to listen to it, from the fear that it might entangle him in some adventure that would interfere with his immediate purpose.

"Let us hope for better luck the next time," he said. "Captain Hawk never has robbed a lady, and never will. If the next travellers are not speedy in making their appearance I shall have daylight upon me."

But though he rode on towards London at a sharp trot for nearly an hour, he heard no sound to indicate a traveller's approach, and, what was still more extraordinary, without seeing anything of the police officers.

"I will go no further in this direction," he said, reining in his steed. "If no one comes I will seek a place of shelter before daylight, and take up my station again as soon as ever twilight sets in."

Having expressed this resolution, the highwayman occupied himself with looking to the priming of his pistols.

He had scarcely made an end of this, however, before the grinding of wheels upon the miry road became audible.

"Ha!" he said. "Good fortune has determined not to abandon me. What can be coming? I should say a gig or light spring cart."

He was pretty near the truth in his guess, for the vehicle turned out to be the latter.

His brow clouded, for this did not promise him any very great booty.

Nevertheless, he determined not to let the light spring cart pass by unquestioned.

It came in sight a moment afterwards, and there was by this time light enough in the sky to make him aware that it contained two persons.

About the sex he could form no opinion: both were muffled up so closely for protection from the cold.

The captain rode right up to the side of the cart with his loaded pistol in his hand.

"Hold!" he said. "Pull up at once!"

The man who was driving, instead of taking any notice of this, suddenly lifted his right hand.

Before the highwayman was aware of his danger, the sharp report of a pistol was heard.

At the same time the man exclaimed, in an exultant and self-satisfied tone of voice:

"That is the way to treat such gentry as those; and if everyone had the firmness to act as I have done the roads would soon be free from these pests. Come up, will you!"

These last words were addressed to the horse, and accompanied by two or three vigorous strokes with the whip.

The man evidently believed that he had settled Captain Hawk's affairs so far as this world was concerned.

But he was destined to find himself egregiously mistaken.

Nevertheless, the highwayman had a fearfully narrow escape.

So narrow that it can only be accounted for by believing that he was not doomed to die just at that juncture.

The wad from the pistol struck him on the face, and this for a second made him believe that the bullet had entered his brain.

How it had missed doing so was an unaccountable mystery.

His bewildered, staggered feeling only lasted for a moment, yet that brief interval of time had enabled the man in the cart to get a good way along the road.

"I think I wanted something just to stir my blood and give me a little excitement," he cried, rubbing his cheek vigorously. "Confound the fellow! He shall smart for this!"

Away he went at the fullest speed Satan was capable of making.

He was up with the cart in a very little time.

The man heard him coming, and made frantic efforts to increase the speed of his horse; but this was not to be done—he was then exerting himself to the utmost.

"Hold!" thundered the highwayman. "If you do not pull up, this moment shall be your last!"

Terrified by the tones, the man obeyed.

"I suppose I may as well submit to my fate," he said, sullenly and doggedly. "I can't help myself, for I have no more firearms."

"Then you did a very foolish thing. You made a treacherous attempt upon my life. Do you think I am going to pass it over without taking any further notice of it?"

"Oh, sir," said the other occupant of the cart, and who now turned out to be a woman, "forgive him and spare him for what he has done—do sir, I entreat you! And after all, if you were attacked, would not the first thing you would do be to defend yourself?"

This was a question that did not admit of a very ready reply.

Observing his silence, the man cried:

"Hold your tongue, wife! I must abide by the consequences of what I have done."

"What do you expect?" asked the highwayman.

"You will take my life, I suppose," he said, with the same sullen air. "I tried to take yours. You will call that fair, I suppose?"

"It was a treacherous shot."

"Oh, sir," said the wife, renewing her appeal, "for my sake do not take his life! If it is money you want, you can have it. But, oh! spare—spare his life!"

"Hold your tongue about the money, can't you? What

is it to do with you? Hold your tongue, I say! You will only make matters worse."

"I do want money," answered the captain; "give me what you have, and I will look over the attempt upon my life."

"Never—never!" cried the man, fiercely; "you shall take my life first! I have not much wealth, and I will not be deprived of my all!"

"He is mad, sir, and knows not what he says!" interposed the wife. "He has money more than he can live to enjoy, and what little he has with him now he can never miss. Take it, then, and welcome, but spare his life. The one loss can be made good—the other cannot."

These words so incensed the man that for a moment he was deprived of speech and motion.

But when his faculties returned to him, he would, beyond all doubt, have had some personal vengeance upon his wife had not Captain Hawk taken care to prevent it.

"Desist!" he cried, "or, so sure as you are a living man, I will make it impossible to repeat your brutality! Desist, I say! Your wife's words are dictated by common sense. Do as she suggests, and we will willingly part company. If you refuse, the consequences will be upon your own head."

"Oh, John—John!" moaned the poor woman, "give him the bag that you have with you."

"Wretched woman! you would ruin me."

"No, I would save you. You know full well that the loss of that bag and what it contains would not ruin you, nor even if the amount was treble what it is."

"Silence!" he shrieked, hoarsely.

The woman cowered down, sobbing and crying.

Captain Hawk was disgusted to behold such an exhibition of sordidness.

Roughly thrusting the muzzle of his pistol into the man's neck, he said:

"Give me the bag of money your wife makes mention of."

"Never! Curse her! I——"

"Hold! not another word!"

The highwayman's stentorian tones drowned the man's voice completely.

"Hark ye!" he said. "You feel my pistol. I will count six deliberately, and if, when I have done so, you do not hand over the bag of money peaceably and quietly, I will pull the trigger, and your death is certain."

"No—no!" screamed the woman.

"Can you plead for such a wretch?" cried the captain, in surprise. "I should think the greatest service I could render you would be to put him out of the world."

"No—no, sir! Pray do not think of such a thing! He is my husband."

There was a world of pathos in the utterance of those last words.

"I wish him no harm," added the highwayman, "but after what I have heard, I am determined not to go away until I have had the bag of money."

"I am ruined, lost, undone! Wretched woman, it is all through you!"

"Enough!" cried the captain. "I will hear no more. Remember what I have said. One!"

The woman uttered a wild shriek for mercy.

"Two!"

"Kill me!"

"Three!"

"Kill me, I say!"

"I shall not shrink from my word. You have but little time to decide. Four!"

The woman threw herself down at the bottom of the cart, and clasping her husband's knees, wildly implored him not to bring death upon himself by his sheer obstinacy.

But he disregarded her.

"Five!"

The cold way in which the highwayman pronounced the numbers convinced the woman that he was thoroughly in earnest.

The imminency of the danger rendered her desperate.

Changing her position, she, with the suddenness of thought, tore open her husband's coat, and, before he could prevent her, dragged the bag of money from his breast pocket.

"There!" she screamed—"you have it now. Take it and leave us!"

Captain Hawk seized the bag instantly.

The weight was considerable, and should the contents be gold the booty would be more than sufficient to make up what was required.

But the man, undeterred by the captain's pistol, and fully prepared to sacrifice his life rather than part with his much-loved gold, was furious with rage.

In the midst of his passion, however, he seemed to be fully sensible that now the bag had once got into the hands of the highwayman, it was hopeless to attempt to recover possession of it.

Without making the least attempt in this direction, then, he seized hold of the reins and the whip, and with the latter belaboured his horse vigorously.

This no doubt was a very great relief to his pent-up feelings.

Captain Hawk turned round and watched his progress.

"The miserly wretch!" he muttered. "I hope, however, that he will not visit his spleen upon his wife, and ill-use her for the part she took in the matter. Such a thing, however, is far from being unlikely—it is just what I should expect of him."

He continued to watch for a moment or two longer, until, in fact, a turn in the road hid the light cart and its occupants from his view.

"It cannot be called exactly morning yet," he muttered, as he glanced around him at the rolling mists. "Shall I have time to get to the old Greyhound? I think, perhaps, I had better not attempt. Most likely some one would catch sight of me, and I do not want to be driven from there to-night. I must look out for a shelter somewhere."

Just as he uttered these words, a piercing shriek broke the silence which reigned around him.

The shriek was followed by two others, which came in quick succession.

"Curse the fellow!" cried the captain—"that is just what I feared. The cowardly villain! He thinks now that he has got his wife to a safe distance, and is ill-using her for saving his life."

The highwayman's anger was extreme, and it was while he was under the influence of it that he set off in pursuit.

He knew that it could not take him long to overtake the cart, yet in his excited state the time was exaggerated tenfold.

And the woman's screams, which were now incessant, completely maddened him.

The sound of blows, too, was distinguishable, and it was certain that the man was behaving with the utmost violence.

Faster and faster yet Satan was urged onwards.

"At last!" the captain cried, as he caught sight of the light spring cart drawn up under a large tree at one side of the road.

He had eyes for nothing else.

The man was standing up in the cart, looking more like a maniac than a sane being.

He held the whip aloft in readiness to strike.

The woman, to escape his violence, had crouched under the seat.

"Come out!" he screamed—"come out, I say, or it will be worse for you!"

"Mercy—mercy!"

"Oh yes—lots and lots of it!"

Down came the whip, and at the same time the brute uttered a yell, for he felt a vice-like grip at the back of his neck.

Captain Hawk's resentment knew no bounds, and, having got this firm grip, he was not satisfied till he had dragged the fellow over the side of the cart.

Then the highwayman released him, and he fell with a crash into the roadway, close to the wheels.

Scorning to take further notice of him, he turned his attention to the woman.

"My poor creature," he said, "this is what I feared. I told you the best service I could render you would be to rid you of him. You would have been spared this."

The woman was in such an hysterical condition that at first she could only draw her breath in gasps when attempting to speak.

Yet her first utterance was not of complaint or of pain

[CAPTAIN HAWK INVITES HIS FOES TO A PURSUIT.]

but consisted of a renewed appeal to the highwayman to spare her husband.

He looked at her in admiration.

"Such is woman's love!" he murmured. "Alas! that it should meet with no better return."

But raising his voice, he cried:

"It is in vain for you to plead; I am determined that he shall suffer retribution for his actions! He shall not escape!"

He took hold of the riding-whip as he spoke, and slipped quickly from the saddle.

The man either was or else pretended to be so much bruised by his fall as to be unable to rise.

The first stroke of the whip, however, dealt with the full force of the captain's arm, produced a magical effect.

Up he sprang, with more nimbleness and agility than a well-trained harlequin could have displayed.

But quick as he was, the captain was quicker, and he had a couple more strokes the while.

Then he turned to flee.

Another stroke.

The whip was long in the lash, and had a strong, pliable handle.

It twined round the man's body like a snake

"You shall know a little better than you do what pain is like, and you will think twice before you inflict it on anyone! Take that, and that!"

The man ran with all his might; but he could not escape Captain Hawk.

Worn out at length, he stumbled and fell, nor did he try to rise again.

Captain Hawk used the whip until sheer exhaustion compelled him to leave off.

When that happened, all that remained of the whip was a small piece of stick little more than two feet long.

The highwayman went towards the cart, where the woman sat trembling with dread.

The man raised his aching, smarting body, and between his clenched teeth swore to have revenge.

Just then the clatter of horses' hoofs reached his ears.

He looked up.

Officers were at hand.

Oblivious of his agony, he started to his feet, and, waving his arms frantically, screamed out:

"A highwayman—a highwayman! This way—this way!"

CHAPTER LX.

LORD HARCLIFFE QUITS THE HALL, AND RECOVERS POSSESSION OF PHANTOM.

The strange adventures befalling Captain Hawk have had the effect of leading us away from one chief personage of this narrative, to whom it is now necessary that we should return, in order that successive events should be properly understood.

No doubt the reader well remembers when and where we parted company with Lord Harcliffe.

It was when, by the aid of the horse belonging to the King's messenger, he managed to shake off his foes and reach the mouldering front of Harcliffe Hall without, as he believed, having been seen by anyone.

On arriving here, he paused and looked up at the crumbling walls, now looking more than usually forlorn with the cold gray streaks of early daylight falling upon them.

It was with a strange commixture of feeling in his breast that he thus stood and gazed for some moments silently on the old and massive pile.

Then shaking himself as though he could by that physical process clear his mind thoroughly from all incumbrances, he walked his horse towards the rear of the mansion.

He drew rein in what had once been the well-kept and productive kitchen-garden, but which now looked the most desolate, uncultivated spot of all.

The trees grew round so thickly that he had nothing to fear from observation, so he dismounted and left the horse to go whithersoever it chose, making certain, after its long, hard ride, it would not be willing to stray far away.

This done, he walked quickly to one of the shuttered windows.

A heavy stone smashed the rusted fastening, and another blow enabled him to push back the old-fashioned casement.

When this was done, the way into the Hall was clear and plain before him.

Ere he stepped in, however, he leant forward, and for some moments remained in an attitude of intense listening.

But had that old ruined mansion been nothing but a tomb consecrated for ages to the sole reception of passed-away humanity, the silence could not have been more profound or more impressive.

"Am I right in believing that there is no one here?" he said. "All seems quite still. Are my suspicions well-founded? Is it that villain who has betrayed me and wrought my ruin? I shall soon see now."

There was evidently the weight of some unusual depression upon Lord Harcliffe's mind, and from his manner it seemed equally certain that he had more than a presentiment before him that he had a painful and dangerous discovery to make.

Reassured apparently to some slight extent by the continuance of the profound stillness, he stepped over the window-sill into the room.

His acquaintance with the interior of the old building must have been a minute one, for, despite the darkness, he made his way across the flooring with a firm, unwavering tread.

With little trouble, he found the handle of the door.

Turning it, he made his way into a darkness deeper still.

"A light would be most agreeable and satisfactory," he said; "but as I have not the means of procuring one, I must grope my way as well as I am able to Martin's room."

But when he said this the misgiving seized his mind that he should find Martin had departed.

Keeping free from contact with any obstacles, Lord Harcliffe reached at length that room which we have formerly described.

But now, as his lordship fully anticipated, it was empty, though there were traces visible that showed that no long time had elapsed since it was vacated.

A few dull embers were smouldering on the hearth, apparently on the verge of extinction.

A little trouble, however, had the effect of causing a tiny blaze to shoot up afresh, which enabled Lord Harcliffe to light a lantern which he took from the shelf above.

Thus provided, he could see tolerably well all over the extensive apartment.

"He determined not to leave anything of value behind him," was the bitter comment made as his lordship glanced around the walls. "Perhaps the villain has not quitted the building. Should that prove to be the case, I will exact a terrible retribution from him."

Taking that route which we have formerly described, Lord Harcliffe now made his way towards that apartment wherein the mysterious lady was confined.

There was a profound anxiety visible upon his countenance, and this manifestly increased at every step.

At last the door was reached.

He raised the lantern.

An exclamation escaped his lips.

The door was standing wide open.

"This is what I expected," he said, clenching his teeth hard. "She is gone! They have gone together. But no matter; after what has happened this cannot affect me very greatly, much as I regret it. I am a fool to suffer so much on this account. Nevertheless, Martin shall pay dearly for his share in the transaction."

As he spoke, he strode into the deserted apartment.

On every side were indications of how hastily it had been quitted.

Lord Harcliffe remained for some moments in gloomy meditation.

Then, turning on his heel, he made his way back to the other room.

Extinguishing his lantern, he removed the old folding shutters from one of the windows.

He expected that a good stream of light would find its way into the interior, but he was disappointed.

It will be remembered that when he arrived in front of the Hall a gray, rusty light was beginning to steal over every object.

But since the dawning a dense, heavy fog had descended, obscuring all outdoor objects even more than the darkness of night itself.

It was only those huge patriarchal trees which grew nearest to the window that could be discerned, and their leafless boughs looked like spectral arms pointing and stretching out in all directions.

Lord Harcliffe next opened the window.

A gush of cold air came on to his face.

He seemed to inhale it gratefully; and the way in which it struck upon his heated brow seemed to relieve in some degree the oppression both mentally and bodily under which he laboured.

It was only for a few fleeting moments, however, that he remained in this quiescent attitude.

A slight sound caused him at once to start and raise his head.

He seemed then like some statue suddenly inspired with life by the touch of a subtle magician's wand.

He did not utter an exclamation, but leant forwards, as though deeply anxious that the sound should once more float to his ears.

He strained his eyes.

But it was in vain.

The vapour was by far too dense for human eyes to pierce for any distance.

The sound had come from the ground below, and it was towards this point that all his attention was directed.

A moment afterwards he heard a voice.

There could be no mistaking it; and what was more, the voice was close at hand.

The accents were subdued, yet he heard every syllable distinctly

But he could see nothing.

"Hush!" said the voice. "Advance quietly. How dense the fog gets! It almost baffles me."

Lord Harcliffe knew the voice.

As he caught its well-known tones his hand clenched as it were involuntarily, and his brows contracted into a deep frown.

"Are you sure you are right?" said another voice.

"Oh yes, I am right enough so far. About that I have no sort of doubt whatever. But don't speak so loud."

"Why not?"

"It will be better not."

"Who is to overhear us?"

"I know not," was the reply, given with considerable trepidation; "but I like always to be on the safe side."

"Enough—enough! Lead the way. Do not dally any longer."

"I will not. But you understand our terms?"

"Yes, yes."

"An equal portion of everything valuable that we can lay our hands on here, and also an equal share of the reward offered for his apprehension. I tell you he is sure to come here, and, as he will not expect officers to be within the place, you will make him your prey easily."

"Yes, yes," said the other, impatiently; "I thought we had settled all that beforehand."

"Still, it is best to be sure that we have a clear understanding."

"Certainly; and I hope you have got it and are satisfied."

But by his manner, the speaker seemed hardly satisfied, and yet appeared to lack the boldness to speak out further.

It was as though he had the dread upon him that an attempt would be made in some shape or other to deprive him of the spoil.

"Yes—yes," said Lord Harcliffe, mentally, "I can guess your fear, Martin, just as easily as I can see through your plot. As for the latter, that will be in great danger of failure, because I have the singular good luck to get here before you. Retribution is nearer at hand than you expect."

The tramp of feet was the next sound which reached the apparently impassive listener at the window.

Few men would have stood so quietly under the circumstance.

The heaviness and regularity of the footsteps' tread upon the gravel told him that the body approaching was a numerous one, and that it consisted of partially-disciplined men.

Yet Lord Harcliffe never moved, nor did the expression of his countenance show that he was in the least way unnerved.

"This way," said Martin. "It is not far now."

"Be quick, then," said the other, who appeared to be the leader of the rest. "We ought to have been here much sooner. Luckily, the fog hides us, or we should never have gained this place unseen, which is the most important thing of all."

"True—true."

"Once more, then, lose no time. Even then I felt a puff of wind, and there is no telling how soon the fog may lift and clear away."

The puff of wind spoken of did lift the fog a little, and rendered it partially transparent, inasmuch as Lord Harcliffe caught a transitory glimpse of a throng of persons all closely huddled together.

"Officers, as I thought, and sure, no doubt, of making me a prisoner; but they will all find the old Hall will be a hornets' nest to them."

The next moment what looked like a dense wave of fog rolled in, and once more hid all things from his view.

He continued to listen; but no sound came save that caused by the stealthy closing of a door.

Lord Harcliffe turned away from the window.

Could anyone have seen him at this juncture, the last thing that his countenance and manner would have suggested was that he was in the slightest danger.

His pale face was perfectly composed, and he crossed the room as though he felt himself to be master of the situation, and consequently void of all sense of peril.

"The fools!" he murmured. "They will have to find that in dealing with me they have no ordinary being to contend with, and therefore ordinary means will be of no avail. Something of this was in my mind, and caused me to enter the Hall as I did instead of by the usual method. I had a presentiment that Martin had laid a trap for me."

He went to the door of the room and opened it.

No sooner had he done so than sounds were carried to his ears which convinced him that his foes were already within the mansion.

"There is not much time to lose," he said; "but, then, my preparations will not take very long."

As he spoke he relighted the lantern.

By this time the fog had found its way into the room through the open window, so that it was as difficult to see within as it was without.

The wax candle in the lantern glimmered dimly.

With great rapidity, and yet most quietly, Lord Harcliffe piled together against one wall of the room a number of the lightest articles that the apartment contained.

When this was done, he tore down from a window a pair of old crumbling curtains.

They were very old, and excessively dry.

These he pushed under the whole.

From a shelf where several articles were kept he took a bottle filled three-parts full of some dark-coloured fluid.

A small quantity of this he poured upon the pile he had erected, and finally taking the candle out of the lantern, applied the flame to one corner of the old curtains.

As if by magic a sheet of flame shot up, and in less than a moment every object he had so skilfully piled up was burning fiercely.

The wall, too, against which he had erected these combustibles, was lined with massive oaken wainscoting.

This, from its extreme age, had become as dry as tinder itself, and the fire communicated itself to it with a rapidity that no one would have credited.

"Surprise the first!" murmured Lord Harcliffe, as he strode to the inner room. "Unless they make the discovery quickly, and remember perfectly well which is the way out, they will have a trifling difficulty in escaping from the burning pile alive."

There seemed every probability of this, for a dense and pungent smoke now filled the room, which, mingled with the fog, not only made it almost impossible to see but to breathe.

In the next room a similar course was taken. and the next and the next.

Although there was not the slightest appearance of hurry observable, yet the rapidity with which one heap of combustibles after another was set fire to was surprising.

"The fire has a firm hold," he said, at length; "and if I am any judge, it is far beyond all human power to check its progress. Hark! what was that?"

He listened, but the terrific roaring of the flames prevented almost anything else from being heard.

"That was a cry," he said—"a shout given by many voices. The fire is discovered; but long ere they can recover from their alarm I shall be miles away. Now for my faithful steed. Once upon Phantom's back, all will be well."

With hasty strides, Lord Harcliffe now made his way towards that singularly-constructed stable which we have already described.

Had he not been desirous of being speedy in his movements, the fire would have made it necessary, for the fierce element, finding in every direction fresh food for its voracity, came on as though instinct with the spirits of ten thousand demons.

To see the long tongues of red flame dart forth, one might fancy that the fire's sole purpose was to seize upon the one who had called it into being.

And the greater the hold the flames took upon the old, deserted building, the more rapidly the conflagration spread, until when Lord Harcliffe reached the top of the steps leading to the stables, the whole of the mansion was one sheet of flame from floor to roof.

Closing the door after him, so as to check a little the progress of the devouring element, he made his way to the secret stable.

And now came the first moment when he had suffered his countenance to show the slightest token of emotion

A sinking dread came over him that made him pause with his hand upon the latch, and deprived him of the power to raise it.

A sudden effort however, recalled his wandering faculties.

He dashed the door open.

No sooner, though, was the threshold crossed than a cry, which was unmistakably one of deep despair, came from his lips.

The stable was empty.

For a moment after making this, to him, truly appalling discovery, he did not move a muscle.

"The villain!" he cried—"the cursed villain! I ought to have expected this, and been prepared for it," he ejaculated. "But a reckoning in full shall come! If he escapes his fate now, the time will quickly come when I will have vengeance upon him for his treachery. Now what is to be done?"

It is clear that up to the last moment Lord Harcliffe was fully persuaded that he should find Phantom in safety in the stable.

His unlooked-for absence at such a moment disconcerted all the plans which he had laid.

He was irresolute.

With ever-increasing loudness the roaring of the flames came upon his ears.

"The place burns bravely," he said, with a grim smile. "A moment ago I could have wished that traitorous villain perishing in the midst of it; but now I trust he may escape in order that I may have a fuller revenge upon him."

He came back to the stable-door.

A gush of hot air came upon his cheek.

"I must go," he said. "There is but one way, and I must trust to my good fortune to befriend me. If I hesitate another moment I shall be too late."

The roaring grew louder still.

Along that gloomy subterranean passage which we have formerly described, he made his way with rapid steps.

The lighted lantern which he still carried afforded him material aid, for without it his progress must of necessity have been much slower.

A very short time sufficed to take him clear of the mansion, so that he was speedily free from any personal apprehension respecting the fire.

Suddenly he caught sight of a dim gray pencil of daylight.

"There is the end of the passage. I will extinguish the lantern now, for it will be of no further service. Another moment, and I shall be free!"

The passage terminated on the face of a steep declivity in the park—a place where no one would have imagined it possible for a horse to find a foot-hold.

The entrance was thickly overgrown with bushes, so carefully and cleverly arranged as to make it impossible for any but the closest search to discover there was any opening at all.

Through the interstices of these bushes the dull gray light of morning dimly shone.

It would scarcely have appeared like light had it been viewed anywhere but in contrast with the dismal darkness of the subterranean passage.

As he drew nearer to the entrance, Lord Harcliffe advanced with greater caution.

There was no immediate necessity for haste.

He quickly had good reason to congratulate himself upon the course he had adopted.

Just when about to push aside the bushes and emerge the faint sound of a footfall came upon his ears

He held his breath.

Nearer and nearer came the step.

Could it be possible that his foes had ascertained his precise whereabouts?

Exercising extreme caution, he leaned a little further forward.

The fog still prevailed, though it had lost much of its density.

Another second, and he caught sight of an advancing human form.

The heavy vapour exaggerated its size almost threefold.

But, notwithstanding this distortion, Lord Harcliffe could tell that it was a police officer.

On he came, with a regular and stealthy step.

Nearer and nearer to the entrance he came.

Lord Harcliffe clenched his fist and prepared for an encounter.

But the officer, without bestowing more than a casual glance upon the bushes which covered the secret entrance to the subterraneous passage, passed on.

But Lord Harcliffe did not move.

He waited in the full expectation of seeing something more which would serve to make clear to him the meaning of what he had already beheld.

He did not wait in vain.

Fainter and fainter grew the receding steps, until he fancied they were lost to hearing altogether.

But just then they began to be more and more audible, until finally the man walked by the entrance as before.

"I have it now," murmured Lord Harcliffe—"all is quite clear now. No doubt those fellows have taken care to set a sentinel watch all round the place. It is either so, or else this man has been set to watch about this spot in the expectation I should make my appearance here. In either case my course of action will be the same."

What it was that Lord Harcliffe had decided upon doing will very speedily be seen.

He waited until the man reached the extremity of his beat, and turned again.

Just as he did so, Lord Harcliffe stealthily drew aside the bushes and crept forward until he was in such a position that he could dash out swiftly and easily.

Nearer and nearer came the man.

Little did he dream, as he walked composedly onwards, what was in store for him.

From where he stood the topmost portion of the old Hall could be discerned.

This was now wrapped in fire, and as he walked he gazed upon this with the fascinating interest which a conflagration on a large scale excites in every breast.

Calm and composed as ever, Lord Harcliffe remained upon the watch.

The man came in sight.

Half unconsciously he muttered:

"How grandly it burns! Confound this fog! I wish——"

Those were his last words.

His speech was interrupted by a gasping cry.

Lord Harcliffe, with the suddenness of a tiger, had sprung from his place of concealment and, with his clenched fist, gave one well-directed blow.

Down went the man like an ox struck down at the shambles, and then with awful suddenness disappeared.

The path was narrow, and no sooner did he fall upon it than he rolled over and over into the abyss.

The fog hid him from view instantly; but a dull sound told when he reached the bottom of the declivity.

CHAPTER LXI.

LORD HARCLIFFE AVENGES HIMSELF UPON MARTIN, AND REGAINS POSSESSION OF HIS STEED.

Lord Harcliffe glided forth without delay.

He looked down, but could neither see nor hear anything of the sentinel police officer.

Then he paused a moment to vent some imprecation upon Martin's head.

"Curse him!" he cried. "Had I but found Phantom in the stable, as I had expected and fully counted on, how easy would have been my escape! It is in vain to think of that now. I must get away, and to do so it is necessary I should have a horse."

A loud crash at this instant caused him to turn his head.

The greater part of the roof of the old Hall had just fallen.

For a second the fury of the flames was checked; but soon the blaze shot up with redoubled brilliancy.

"So perish all remaining secrets connected with the place!" he said. "The work of destruction is complete. Now then for a horse! It is odd to me if all the officers are not intent upon watching the progress of the flames."

So saying, he walked with singular audacity and coolness towards the Hall.

The fog favoured him greatly.

Its density was now, if anything, increased for there

being no wind to carry off the smoke, it spread along the ground.

This, added to the perfect knowledge which Lord Harcliffe possessed of the surroundings of the Hall, made it comparatively easy for him to gain the neglected kitchen garden unperceived.

So little noise had been raised during his brief encounter with the officer, that no alarm had been given, and no one had witnessed what had taken place.

On approaching the blazing building, however, he discovered that the brilliancy of the blaze and the great heat made the fog more transparent, while the thick black smoke hung like a canopy above.

He glanced hastily around.

The trees and rank, luxuriant weeds in the neglected garden were scorched and withered.

Where was the King's messenger's horse, which had already rendered him such good service?

Terrified by the heat and the flames, it had doubtless galloped off no one could tell whither, and in the present condition of the atmosphere it seemed utterly hopeless to think of commencing a search.

It was just at this juncture that he was made sensible of a fresh danger.

A loud shout was raised.

Turning quickly in the direction whence the sound had come, he just caught a glimpse through the rolling smoke of a dense cluster of his foes.

They, too, saw him.

"There he is!" cried a voice, which Lord Harcliffe recognised at once as being that of his faithless follower. "There he is! Quick—quick! Fire upon him, or he will escape!"

A close volley followed, but the smoke rolling in again in denser volumes than before, made the officers unable to ascertain immediately what damage had been inflicted.

A slight cry of pain escaped Lord Harcliffe's lips.

He had been hurt, but not seriously.

He turned at once to fly.

Under cover of the fog there was every probability that he would be successful in making his escape.

On he rushed towards the ancient park, with every tree in which he could almost claim acquaintance.

Its area was great, and there were hiding-places within its boundary which would baffle more than police-officer sagacity to discover.

The palings were at no great distance, and on reaching them he hastily scrambled over.

In doing so he noticed that the topmost portion of the woodwork had been recently torn away.

He looked closer.

"One horse at least has been this way," he said, "and very lately too. Jumping short, he has broken the palings. Can I hope to find him?"

But beyond what he had just seen there was nothing whatever to indicate in which direction the animal had gone.

It would never do to linger there, and that Lord Harcliffe knew full well; yet before he plunged into the recesses of the park he tied his handkerchief tightly over the wound in his arm, from which the blood was flowing.

It took but a moment; and when the operation was completed, he exclaimed, in tones of satisfaction:

"They will have some little trouble to track me beyond this spot."

So saying, he darted at once among the dense-growing trees.

He was none too soon, for hardly a moment elapsed before Martin appeared at the palings.

He was surrounded by officers.

"We shall lose him," he said, in a voice of deep disappointment. "Even with a clear light to aid us it would be no easy matter to discover him in this park. He is familiar with every twist and turn."

"Never mind," cried the officers, "we can but try."

In the meantime, Lord Harcliffe, by dint of keeping steadily in one direction, got a long way from the Hall.

Once or twice he fancied he heard a slight noise in advance of him, but he could not stay in order to make sure whether he was deceived, or to ascertain its character.

Large heavy drops of rain now began to fall pattering upon the leaves of the gigantic trees.

"So much the better," muttered his lordship, as his apparel more closely around him: "all these things favour my chances of escape."

The fall of the rain increased, and as it did so the fog partially cleared away.

Behind him he could occasionally hear sounds which testified that his foes had contrived to keep tolerably well upon his track.

He was now in comparatively an open space.

Trees were growing upon it to be sure, but by no means closely enough together to shelter him from observation.

He had some distance to go, too, before the vegetation grew denser, and every moment it was getting lighter, for a faint breeze which had sprung up seemed as though it would carry both fog and rain before it.

He was about to glance behind him in some little dubiety, when his eye caught sight of a large, dim-looking object on one side of him.

Gazing more attentively, he made out the outlines to be those of a horse, though they were so blurred and magnified as almost to defy recognition.

"If that, now, should prove to be the horse belonging to the King's messenger," he said, "I should look upon my safety as assured. At any rate, I will endeavour to ascertain."

So saying, he changed the direction in which he had been going.

At his approach the horse raised its head, and projected its ears as though ready to start off upon the least provocation.

By dint of approaching carefully and speaking soothingly every now and then, however, Lord Harcliffe managed to get within a few yards of it.

Then, with a gratification he could not conceal, he saw that this horse was indeed the one which had already performed such excellent service in his behalf.

This discovery increased his confidence, and the animal upon its part seemed actually to recognise him, for it suffered him to get quite close without making the slightest movement to get away.

Suddenly reaching out his hand, Lord Harcliffe seized the rein.

The next moment he was in the saddle.

No sooner had he gained this position than, despite the extraordinary self-control which he always exercised, a cry of exultation forced itself from between his lips.

He could now laugh his foes to scorn.

He was somewhat surprised, though, to find they were so close behind him, but just when he urged his horse onward he caught sight of the whole troop of his foes emerging from the trees.

They were all mounted, though the mist made them look strangely ghost-like.

The fact of their being provided with horses at once accounted for their being so close upon the track of the fugitive.

"It is in vain to struggle with so many," murmured Lord Harcliffe. "I must fight my enemies in detail. My sole course now is instantaneous flight."

He turned round as he spoke, but did not get many paces towards the trees before those in the rear perceived him.

Their first act was to spur their horses in order to make them put forth their utmost speed.

But Lord Harcliffe had the start, and, what was infinitely of more importance, he knew every step of the way that lay before him.

The horse which, for the second time, had fallen so strangely into his hands, was of first-class quality.

It was indeed a picked animal, and there were very few horses to be found to match it for symmetry, swiftness, or endurance.

Therefore, slight as the start was which Lord Harcliffe had, he turned it to good account, and he was not long in having the satisfaction of finding that his foes had dropped considerably in the rear.

Still they held on with a persistency which indicated how firmly they had resolved to succeed in their purpose.

"I can outrun them, I am certain," he said; "and when I have done so I will pause and reflect upon my future proceedings; but until I have shaken them off I can think of nothing."

As he spoke he made yet further efforts to accelerate his horse's speed.

Those efforts were gallantly responded to.

The limit of the spacious park was reached, the palings overleaped, the high-road gained.

Along this he rode more swiftly than ever.

But his foes were most unsparing in their exertions, and he found more difficulty in shaking them off than he could have imagined.

One especially kept well before the rest of the troop.

His horse must have been of a character vastly superior to the others, for after riding in advance for some time, he would turn round and call out to those behind as though urging them to make greater speed.

It was evident, however, that they were coming as rapidly as they were able.

Lord Harcliffe noticed this, but the mist was too dense for him to see with any degree of distinctness.

Now, however, there seemed every probability that the sun would break forth.

He watched its doing so with great impatience.

At length the golden beams triumphed over the dense vapours opposed to it, and sent them rolling off in fleecy masses.

The effect was magical and beautiful.

In an instant every object was clearly defined in the ruddy morning sunlight.

Lord Harcliffe hastened to look back.

"By Heaven!" he cried, "it is as I expected. That one in front of the rest, and urging them to follow him, is no other than the villain Martin! I guessed it. And the reason why he is able to maintain that prominent position is, that he is bestriding my matchless Phantom. That is past endurance. My vengeance craves for satisfaction, and it shall not be delayed."

It was with increasing impatience that the unusually impassive nobleman pronounced these words, and there was an ominous glitter in his eyes which boded evil to his treacherous dependent.

His hand sought his belt.

"Ha!" he ejaculated. "I had forgotten what has occurred to me. I am unarmed. Is the villain again destined to elude me?"

Just as he uttered these words his eyes happened to fall upon the holsters of the saddle.

Previously he had not noticed them.

"A King's messenger," he said, "would hardly travel unarmed. Shall I be fortunate enough to find myself in possession of weapons now that I have so much need for them?"

His hand trembled so with excitement that he could scarcely undo the straps.

A moment afterwards he uttered a cry of joy.

His hand had encountered the butt-end of a pistol.

Drawing the weapon quickly, he hastened to throw up the pan.

The priming appeared to be in perfect order.

"Now then, treacherous rascal that you are," he said, "you shall receive the reward which your actions so richly deserve. I will soon change your exultant manner. Your doom is sealed. I could have forgiven almost everything else had he not taken my steed. He knew full well, however, that Phantom would not permit anyone to remain upon his back save himself and me. The faithful creature does not comprehend the business of his rider, or he would long since have bit the dust."

The part of the high-road upon which the pursuers and pursued chanced to be was perfectly straight for more than a mile, so that both parties were in full view of each other.

The main body of officers was distant about half a mile from Lord Harcliffe, or perhaps it might be a trifle more.

Martin was now somewhere about a hundred yards in advance of the foremost officer.

He was tugging violently at the reins, and evidently experienced no little difficulty in keeping Phantom back.

And every moment this difficulty increased, so that it actually encouraged the idea that the faithful horse was in some way cognizant that his master was on the road before him.

"Come on!" bawled Martin. "Curse me if your horses are worthy of their name! If you cannot make better speed than that, give in at once; you must see that it is hopeless to attempt to overtake him."

"Go on with you!" growled the chief officer, whose temper was by no means improved by the course events had taken. "Go on, I say, and leave us to do our duty. Trust us for doing it!"

It was just at this moment that Lord Harcliffe, having got his pistol in readiness, whistled shrilly.

The sound was clear and distinct, and the morning air transmitted it without the loss of a note.

It was faint by the time it reached Phantom's ears, but yet, nevertheless, loud enough not only for him to hear it, but also to recognise it as the signal which his master had with so much care taught him to obey.

The signal meant that he was to place himself without loss of time at his master's side.

Phantom pricked up his ears.

Martin seized a rein in each hand, and pulled with all his might.

Then the whistle came again, this time being, if anything, a trifle louder than it was before.

It was in vain for Martin to pull in any longer.

Disregarding altogether the pressure upon his mouth, Phantom galloped forward like a greyhound.

The officers were amazed.

But their astonishment was destined to be increased.

Martin, dropping one rein, seized the other with both hands, and strove to pull his horse aside or turn him round.

But this proved as vain a proceeding as the other.

Phantom bent his head round towards his shoulder, but, nevertheless, continued to gallop on in a straight line.

A mortal fear then took possession of Martin.

He seemed to know that he was on the very threshold of death.

His face grew white, and his whole body shook like one in an ague fit.

The officers for the life of them could not understand the meaning of what they beheld.

But they saw that the object of their pursuit had checked his career, and consequently they pressed onwards in the hope of overtaking him at last.

In the meantime Phantom galloped on.

Going at such a tremendous speed as he then was, it took but a few moments for him to come close to his master.

By mere instinct alone, Martin continued to tug the rein.

His mental powers were overcome by the knowledge that he was being hurried towards the master to whom he had behaved so treacherously.

He knew well also that that master was implacable, and that it would be folly to expect mercy or to beg for it.

As soon as he was within speaking distance, he heard Lord Harcliffe say:

"Villain that you are, you shall now receive the reward which you so richly merit! You have betrayed me! But as I told you, in doing so you have compassed your own destruction! Die, villain!"

As he spoke, with eyes flashing with resentment, he pulled the trigger.

Martin's death-scream mingled with the report; and the officers, altogether unable to account for his seemingly incomprehensible conduct, saw him fall headlong to the ground.

At the very same moment Lord Harcliffe dismounted.

He gave the animal he had been riding a smart blow with his hand, which made the frightened creature start off at a gallop.

Then, without pausing or deigning to cast a glance upon the prostrate and bleeding form, he vaulted on to Phantom's back.

"Away—away!" he cried. "Let those who will pursue me now; I fear not the result. I feared I had lost you, my brave steed, and never ventured to hope that I should so soon regain you. Away—away, I say!"

The tones of his voice, if not the very words, were understood; and now no longer being under any restraint, Phantom flew off at a pace that was breathless to look upon.

But rapid as Lord Harcliffe had been, yet sufficient time had elapsed to enable the wondering police officers to get within a very short distance.

So short, indeed, that when they heard the fugitive speak to his horse they thought it worth while to discharge their pistols after him in a volley.

The bullets flew thickly round the fugitive, but not one

touched him, which is not surprising when the rate at which he was going is considered.

Finding this to be the case, and seeing him pass round a bend in the road and get out of sight, the police officers thought fit to abandon the pursuit.

"It's not one bit of good to go a yard further," said the one in command. "It is more like a demon than a horse that he is upon now, and not one of our animals could go more than one mile to his two. Let us see how this poor fellow is; perhaps we can do something for him."

But on dismounting to make a narrower examination, it became evident at once that Martin was past having anything done for him in this life.

He was quite dead.

The bullet from Lord Harcliffe's pistol had passed through his brain, tearing away the skull at the back in a frightful manner.

"He is dead enough," said one. "What an awful shot! What shall we do with him?"

After some discussion it was decided that Martin should be carried through a gate that was close at hand and deposited on the soft turf in the meadow, under the charge of two of the men, until further necessary steps should be taken.

In the meanwhile, Lord Harcliffe rode on as though he had a thousand fiends in his rear.

Whether the officers were continuing the pursuit he never troubled himself to ask or ascertain.

His only object was to get as far away as he could in the least space of time.

At length he suddenly pulled up, for before him meandered the silvery Thames.

Being many miles below Windsor, the stream was proportionably narrow.

He paused a moment in deep thought.

"Which way shall I go?" he said. "I don't want to get far away from London if I can help it, for I have much to do. Let me see: if I cross here I shall be able by making a considerable detour to get to the north of London somewhere near Hampstead or Hornsey. That shall be my course. No one will suspect me of having doubled on my course like that. The distance is great, but we can accomplish it."

He patted his steed fondly as he spoke.

Only one object lay between him and the carrying out of his purpose.

This impediment was the river.

There was no bridge; and to have made his way to the next ferry would only be to leave a clear and easily followed clue behind him.

"A bath will not hurt either of us, old fellow," he said, addressing himself to Phantom. "The stream is narrow here, and apparently not deep. We will try it."

So saying, he walked his horse deliberately into the river.

The water was shallow—in fact, it was only just in mid-stream that they were submerged.

In a few moments they were on the opposite bank.

A good shake then put all things right.

"Now for a gallop, old boy, and that will free us from this moisture as well as help us on our journey. Off and away!"

Only those words were needed.

The cold water seemed to have had a wonderfully invigorating effect upon the horse, and the way in which he now stretched across the low-lying meadows was beautiful to behold.

But by this time it was something like nine o'clock, and at every step he went he found more and more signs of people being abroad.

He noticed, too, that in a general way these people looked after him with inquiring and suspicious glances.

"This will not do," he said. "If I ride by day the officers will be upon my track immediately. I will seek some inn, and stay there until dusk, and then resume my journey. Phantom, too will be all the better for rest and food."

So saying, he at once began to look out for such a place as seemed likely to suit him.

"Wait a moment," he cried. "I was very near forgetting that I had a sojourn in Newgate and that the officials had taken all my cash. Before I can stay at an inn I must have the wherewith to satisfy the reckoning."

He plunged his hands into his pockets, but not a single coin could he discover.

"It would have been awkward had I not made the discovery till later."

He pulled the rein until his horse reduced his speed to a walk.

Just as he had done so and examined the pistols in the holsters, he looked up and uttered a low cry of satisfaction.

Some little distance before him on the high-road appeared a mounted man.

The sun shone full upon him, and therefore Lord Harcliffe could see him with peculiar distinctness.

There was much to attract the notice of anyone in the appearance of this new-comer.

He was attired in a singular costume, which glittered and spangled everywhere, reflecting the sun's rays in a hundred places.

Coming closer, Lord Harcliffe saw that he wore some kind of uniform.

Of what precise kind it was he knew not; all he could be certain of was that it had an immense amount of ornamentation about it.

"Who on earth can he be?" he ejaculated. "He looks almost like some Eastern prince. At any rate, his outward appearance seems to promise that he carries about him sufficient to pay for a breakfast for myself and steed."

The stranger, seeing some one advancing, seemed to put on an air of additional grandeur and importance, as though he wished to create the most profound impression.

Little did he guess what was passing in the mind of Lord Harcliffe as he rode towards him.

When within about twenty yards it could be seen that the richly-dressed stranger was a very young man.

He was very slim in his build, had small girlish features, and on his upper lip was a little fluffy down, which could not possibly by any exaggeration be called a moustache.

What surprised Lord Harcliffe most of all, however, was the manner in which this young man sat in the saddle.

He must have been a novice in the art of riding, for, though his horse was only going at a showy walk, he seemed in imminent danger of falling to the ground.

At his side was a long sword, with a brightly-polished scabbard.

This weapon seemed to cause an infinity of trouble both to himself and horse, for, fidget as he would, he could not keep it in its place.

His attire was decidedly of a military cut, though there was nothing military about the wearer of it.

Lord Harcliffe was puzzled more and more.

"I can't think what he is. Surely it must be some ridiculous masquerade. But no matter for that, I will proceed to business without delay."

Phantom advanced.

The stranger, who could not have been more than eighteen at the very most, assumed a most supercilious air as Lord Harcliffe approached.

He intended to pass him by with the utmost disdain, as though fully impressed with the notion that his position was immeasurably above everybody else's.

Lord Harcliffe made a profound bow.

This flattered the young fellow exceedingly, and puffed up his self-importance ten times more.

He only condescended to notice Lord Harcliffe's salutation by a very slight and haughty nod.

But, unfortunately for the effect which it was intended to produce, it caused his large gold-laced cocked hat to fall over the bridge of his nose.

This imparted to him a most ludicrous aspect.

"Ha! how now, fellow!" he lisped, in most affected accents. "What are you laughing at? You ought to know your plaith better!"

"My dear boy——"

The young fellow's face crimsoned with indignation.

The bare idea that anyone should think of so addressing him was most hurtful to his feelings.

"Do you know——"

"My dear boy," said Lord Harcliffe, with even more than his usual imperturbability, "if you had only the remotest idea of how ridiculous you look you would not be surprised at anyone making you a laughing-stock."

This dreadful speech almost annihilated the poor fellow.

"You are a ruffian," he gasped, after making several attempts to speak—"you are a ruffian! There now!"

"Well, and who may you be?"

"Who may I be, fellow?"

"Yes."

"Don't you know me?"

"I have not that honour. Will you be kind enough to enlighten my ignorance?"

This change of address had rather a soothing effect.

"If you must know, fellow," he said, with unabated pomposity, "I am the colonel of the Loyal Berkshire Yeomanry!"

Had he been Emperor of all the Russias he could not have spoken with greater pomp.

He expected that his querist would be almost ready to sink into the earth after hearing this announcement.

How great must have been his annoyance and disappointment when he found it was greeted only with a shout of laughter!

"You're a low ruffian!" he said. "Stand aside and let me pass!"

But Lord Harcliffe disregarded this request altogether as he said:

"And what sort of a body must the Loyal Berkshire Yeomanry be if you are the colonel of it?"

"Fellow, ride on! I will listen to no more of your insulting remarks! I won't be spoken to by you—there now!"

"My dear boy, now don't—pray don't make a bigger fool of yourself than you have done already!"

Hearing this, the gallant colonel uttered a howl of rage, and clapped his hand upon the hilt of his sword.

"There—there," cried Lord Harcliffe, "pray don't touch that plaything—you might chance to hurt yourself with it, and that would be a terribly bad job."

"You shall insult me no longer!" he said, almost with the tears in his eyes. "I won't be badgered by you—there now! So go away!"

"Presently, colonel—presently. But I wished to know whether you were a gentleman."

"A gentleman? What do you mean?"

"Just what I say."

"Can't you see?"

"Yes, I can see."

"What more do you want, then?"

"Only some kind of proof of it."

"Look at my horse!"

"A fair nag."

"My clothing!" said the boy, almost bursting with pride.

"Magnificent! But then, I happen to believe in the old proverb that says, 'It is not the fine coat which makes the gentleman.'"

"What more do you want?"

"A gentleman should carry a purse, and a heavy one, too. Have you one?"

"Of course!" was the supremely disdainful answer. "Look here!"

And, actuated by that same vanity and love of display which had made him set out attired in such a manner, he thrust his hand into the breast of his military coat and drew forth a large purse.

Like everything else which he possessed, it was richly ornamented, and through the meshes of the bead and silk work Lord Harcliffe could see the edges of a goodly store of guineas.

"Ah!" he exclaimed, suddenly reaching out his hand.

He had hold of the purse in a moment, for the gallant colonel, never once suspecting what was going to happen, held it daintily between his finger and thumb.

"I was mistaken," said his lordship, as he consigned the purse to the safe keeping of an inner pocket.

"Murder!" cried the colonel, in a far more natural and unaffected voice than he had hitherto made use of—"murder and thieves! Oh, oh! Dear me! What shall I do?"

"If you ask me for advice," said Lord Harcliffe, "I should say at once, make haste home and tell your mother!"

This was the cruellest and unkindest cut of all.

Tears rushed into his eyes.

"It's too bad!" he whimpered. "Who would have thought I should be robbed on my own father's ground, and in the broad light of day? Oh! Murder—murder! What shall I do?"

His distress was very great, and in a schoolboy would have been right enough, but shown by a colonel in the Loyal Yeomanry it was absurd beyond all powers of description.

"My dear boy," said Lord Harcliffe, resuming this insulting mode of address, "you have brought all this on yourself by your own egregious folly. If this proves to be a lesson to you, it will be very cheaply purchased. Go home now at once, like a good child, and never make a fool of yourself by dressing yourself up in those clothes again."

"You are a mean, low robber, and I tell you so to your face; and it serves me quite right for condescending to speak a word to such a clod of dirt as you are. If you had the pluck of a man you would fight me. I dare you to combat! Ha, ha!"

It would have been hard for anyone to say whether the last exclamations were to be properly called a laugh or a cry.

"Don't—don't," said Lord Harcliffe—"don't make me laugh any more, I beg of you! My sides ache already. Do go home now, and mind you don't forget to tell your mother all about it."

With this dreadfully withering remark, Lord Harcliffe rode on, leaving the gallant colonel in the middle of the road with feelings, as the novelists say, which may be imagined and not described.

He had some trouble to control his tears; but, partially succeeding in this, he drew his sword and made many gestures of defiance and hatred.

This helped to recover him greatly.

But Lord Harcliffe, turning round and seeing how he was engaged, resolved to complete his discomfiture.

Turning his horse round swiftly, and assuming an air of great menace, he made a feint to ride towards him.

The gallant colonel's courage sank at once into his boots.

A dreadful panic took possession of his breast, and he endeavoured to find safety in instant flight.

But, unfortunately, his horsemanship marred all.

Before his horse had taken twenty steps, down the poor fellow tumbled into the road.

To add to his troubles, he cut his finger with his sword.

He sat down in the middle of the dusty road, a doleful picture of ludicrous distress.

CHAPTER LXII.

IN WHICH CAPTAIN HAWK REQUITES HIS OBLIGATION TO THE OSTLER.

CAPTAIN HAWK, to whom we now return, had been so intent upon punishing the cowardly rascal in the light spring cart, and afterwards in looking to the victim of his brutality, that he never once heard the noise made by the approaching officers, nor would he have been conscious of their proximity but for the man's frantic cries.

Turning swiftly, he saw that the danger which menaced him was serious.

The officers were not many yards off—a few moments would bring him within the range of their bullets.

But he did not allow the sudden shock of surprise to deprive him of his presence of mind.

"Fear nothing now," he said to the weeping woman. "Circumstances compel me to leave you now; but should accident bring us together again, rely upon it I shall make it my business to thrash your husband if he so much as raises a finger against you."

With these words he rode off, before the woman had time to utter her fervent thanks.

Her husband in the meanwhile forgot, in the hope of retaliation, all the pangs and smarts which the castigation with the long-lashed whip had caused him.

More like a madman than aught else, he ran towards the officers, yelling and shrieking:

"A highwayman! There he is! Take him, and I will give you a hundred pounds out of my own pocket!

[THE ARRIVAL OF THE POLICE OFFICERS AT THE BLACKSMITH'S FORGE.]

h, how I ache and smart! I would give a hundred pounds to see the villain hung!"

By this time the officers discovered what they had not previously been aware of, namely, that the mounted man such a short distance before them was no other than the redoubtable Captain Hawk himself.

This discovery caused them to make every exertion, and, very much to the man's indignation and surprise, he found they took no notice of him.

"Surrender, or we fire!" cried the foremost officer.

Captain Hawk only replied by a laugh.

Checking his horse's speed and looking behind him, he cried, tauntingly:

"Gentlemen, if you feel inclined for a ride to-night, I am both ready and willing. Come on! Let him catch me who can!"

He waved his hat derisively as he spoke, inviting the officers to follow him.

If they had any doubts before about the identity of the fugitive, those doubts were at an end now.

And if one thing was calculated more than another to fill the breasts of the police officers with annoyance it was to find that they and their efforts were only laughed at.

"Never mind," cried the one in command. "We will make him laugh on the other side of his mouth. We have the game fairly started now, and, as I explained to all of you, we have only to hunt it down."

The officer alluded to his plan of driving Captain Hawk before him until close to London.

Captain Hawk by no means allowed Satan to go at his full speed, but merely went fast enough to enable him to preserve a respectful distance between himself and his foes.

For some moments, then, as the road was perfectly straight, the chase was an exciting one.

There was another circumstance from which the officers drew abundant gratification.

This was, that morning was rapidly approaching.

The long night of exciting adventures was at an end, and from the eastern sky there came a faint but ever-brightening tinge of light.

Captain Hawk, however, was still so full of his last adventure, that some time elapsed before he actually took cognizance of this fact.

"Hallo!" he cried, in astonishment. "I was scarcely prepared for this. Why, it will be daylight directly, and here are the police officers not a couple of hundred yards behind me! I must take care to alter this state of things."

But on no side could he see the least signs of being able to effect any alteration.

"I remember now, too," he said, "what that confoundedly clever officer said in the inn kitchen. He talked about driving me to London, and, egad! I am just letting him do it in capital style. I never thought of that. Confound that brute! I do believe he has driven everything else clean out of my head."

Captain Hawk looked around him once more.

But he was unable to see any means of escaping from his enemies.

The country for miles around was particularly flat, and offered no apparent chance of his eluding them.

And in the east the gray light of dawn had given place to the ruddy lines which betoken the uprising of the sun.

He grew desperate.

"I must end this somehow," he said. "I shall be so far away soon that it will be quite impossible for me to gain the shelter of the old Greyhound by nightfall. There is but one way: it is to urge Satan to the utmost extent of his powers and get so far away that my pursuers can neither see nor hear me. When this is the case I shall be better able to decide what to do than I possibly can be now."

Taking all things into consideration, this certainly seemed the very wisest course he could adopt.

The highwayman did not waste a moment in weighing the matter.

One touch was sufficient.

Away went the noble creature like a racehorse.

The officers, amazed at the sudden change, whipped and spurred their own animals most furiously.

But it was to little purpose.

Strive as they would, they could not prevent the object of their pursuit from getting further and further away.

When at length he got quite out of sight, owing to the serpentine character of part of the roadway, they were filled with dismay.

Their hopes revived somewhat upon catching sight of him speeding up a hill in the distance.

"Pooh—pooh! Take no notice of this," said the leader, to his men. "It's only a spurt, and will soon be over. His horse can't keep up that kind of thing very long."

But when another quarter of an hour elapsed without so much as letting him get one single glimpse of his prey, he began to lose a great deal of his confidence, though he strove his best to conceal this from his followers.

In the meanwhile, Captain Hawk, having, as he believed, got to a safe distance, pulled up, for he observed that Satan showed some signs of distress.

Besides, it was by no means his desire or intention to go one yard further than he could possibly help.

"I shall do now," he said; "and, upon my word, I should like to play the officers a trick. That would repay me for all. Come what will, I'll try it."

Close to the side of the road where he had halted there grew a very dense clump of trees, which formed part of the boundary of a gentleman's estate.

"Nothing could suit me better," muttered the captain, when he noticed this. "Now, then, I will serve them such a trick as will almost drive them to madness when they find it out."

So saying, he leaped Satan over a low stone wall, which skirted the high-road, and afterwards made his way behind the clump of trees.

The vegetation was so dense that he had to look several times before he could find an interstice through which he could see into the road.

"Now," he cried, "I will wait here and let them all ride past. They cannot have the least reason to suspect that I am hiding here. On the contrary, they would think that I should get much further away. They have not been able to hear Satan's hoofs for some time, so the fact of their not being able to hear me in advance will count for nothing. When they are comfortably in advance I will either work quietly round to the Greyhound, or else seek a place of concealment until sunset."

Knowing the anxiety the chief officer had to drive him towards London, and his fear lest he should miss him, made Captain Hawk chuckle mightily over the prospect of getting them in front instead of behind him.

"If all goes well," he cried, "they may go on for miles before they discover I have cheated them. Ha, ha! And then from their spy they will afterwards learn that I have got back as far as the Greyhound. Ha, ha!"

Of course, now that the highwayman was acquainted with the officers' tactics, he would take care to plague them, and make their task as difficult and tiresome as possible, notwithstanding the anxiety he felt to deliver Dick Turpin's last message.

Satan very much appreciated this bit of rest.

A quarter of an hour or thereabouts elapsed.

At the end of that time, Captain Hawk assumed an attitude of attention.

"Yes," he said, after listening intently for a moment, "my ears did not deceive me: they are coming."

But the sound was so faint that probably no one save a highwayman could have detected it.

By regular and perceptible degrees, however, that which was at first only a murmur like that of some tiny insect became a definite, regular clatter.

"They make good speed," was the highwayman's comment. "I only hope they will keep it up. What a satisfaction it will be to see them riding off at that speed after nothing, and making such exertions to increase the space between us instead of to decrease it!"

Louder and louder grew the rapid beats of the horses' hoofs.

Captain Hawk kept Satan well in hand.

"Quiet now—quiet, can't you, for a minute or two!" he said, for the gallant creature was chafing impatiently to get at the soft sweet grass that grew around his feet. "Be still. If you make a movement you will betray me."

With some trouble, the horse was made to hold his head up and stand still.

The officers were now very close at hand, but, somewhat to the captain's disappointment and uneasiness, he discovered that they were slackening speed.

For what reason he knew not, and all he could do, circumstanced as he was then, was to remain still, and trust to his good fortune for the result.

But the nearer the officers came to the clump of trees, the slower and more irresolute did their pace become, until, just when about opposite to the highwayman's place of concealment, they stopped altogether.

Captain Hawk held his breath, and heartily wished his horse had the sagacity to do the same.

What was going to happen?

Through the leaves and boughs, the captain could see the foremost officer.

He was wiping the perspiration from his brow.

He looked anxious and uncomfortable.

"I'm d—nably afraid," he said, with extraordinary emphasis, "that we have overshot the mark!"

"What do you mean, sir?" asked the man next to him.

"I mean that I am afraid we have passed him somehow. We must have done so, or else we should be able to hear something of him by this time."

"But think what a wonderful horse he has."

"I don't care if—— But what the devil's that?"

The sound which had attracted the officer's notice and caused him to stop short in what he was about to say, was made by Satan.

It was a kind of cough and sneeze, such as horses will frequently give.

The cause most likely was the way in which the captain had been making him hold up his head.

"A horse!" cried a man, in reply to his chief's question—"that's a horse somewhere close at hand."

"Suppose it should be our man?"

But this supposition seemed too wild a one to be worthy of being entertained.

The moment after, however, another cried:

"By Heavens, it is! Look, there he goes yonder—under the trees!"

All looked in the direction towards which the man excitedly pointed.

There could then be no sort of doubt about the matter.

The figure of a rapidly-retreating horseman could be plainly seen, and beyond all doubt that horseman was Captain Hawk

In fact, the moment when Satan coughed and sneezed, he knew that a discovery was unavoidable, and also had the presence of mind to be aware that the very best thing he could do was to get away without the loss of a single moment.

He was terribly annoyed at the miscarriage of his plan. Of the danger, which was great, he thought nothing.

He was lucky, too, in getting off as well as he did; but the nature of the ground was such that he could not get many yards without a discovery taking place.

He heard the cry given utterance to by the man who saw him first, and from that instant became aware of the futility of attempting concealment any longer.

"It is your fault, old fellow," he cried, "and you must take the consequences of what you have done. You might have had a rest for some hours had you chosen to keep quiet. Now you must put out what powers of speed you have left."

Anyone would almost think the gallant creature perfectly well comprehended what was said to it, for, without any further urging on his master's part, away he went at really a faster gallop than he had before gone at.

Captain Hawk was delighted.

"A little of this will do wonders," he cried, in an enthusiastic voice, which he well knew would have an animating effect upon his steed. "The officers will quickly be behind, and then we will seek out a rest."

A few moments afterwards, Captain Hawk found himself in a leafy, pleasant lane.

The hedge was too high for a leap to be attempted with safety, and so he followed the twists and turns in the road.

A few moments after he emerged on the high-road.

"This will do," he said, after a moment's consideration. "A gallop along this for a mile or so will put me quite out of their hearing."

But ere he had gone half the distance he contemplated, Satan gave a kind of stumble, and immediately afterwards a ringing sound was heard.

Captain Hawk had heard that sound too many times to be in any doubt as to what it meant.

His horse had knocked off his shoe, and on looking down he saw the piece of iron rolling along the hard and stony road.

He could do nothing but pull up at once.

"Cursed mischance!" he cried. "How am I to remedy this misfortune?"

He looked down ruefully at the bright piece of iron lying in the roadway.

Then, after a momentary hesitation, he dismounted, and picking it up, examined it closely.

The shoe was a good one, and how it had come to be detached was not a little mysterious.

For some seconds he gazed at it blankly.

The sound of his pursuers in the distance aroused him.

"It is folly to linger here," he said, giving a sudden start. "How am I to remedy this misfortune? It is in vain to think of it."

He was about to fling away the horse-shoe in hopeless despair, when a second thought induced him to change his determination.

"There may possibly be a blacksmith's forge not far off, and if so, and I can manage to reach it in time, it will only take a very few moments to put the shoe on again. Yes—yes, I will take care of it."

Before he remounted he looked closely at Satan's foot.

But he could not perceive any signs of injury; and as every nail had been drawn out with the shoe there was little fear of lameness resulting, provided he had not to go far to find a forge.

It was, however, very despairingly that he looked around him after having again seated himself in the saddle.

In the morning air all objects looked clear and bright, and could be distinguished at a great distance.

But though he looked keenly everywhere, he could not detect among the trees the thinnest wreath of smoke that would indicate the position of the place he wished to find.

He rode on slowly, and in the meanwhile examined his weapons, and got them in readiness for instant use.

There was a look of firm and settled determination on his face.

Under the circumstances, it seemed most probable that an encounter would take place between him and his foes.

The contest would be a terrible one, for Captain Hawk was not the man to yield easily, no matter how many enemies opposed themselves to him.

"They come," he said, as the trampling of his pursuers reached his ears with more and more distinctness—"they come! But they will find their victory will be by no means so easy as they think."

CHAPTER LXIII.

CAPTAIN HAWK HAS A NARROW ESCAPE OF CAPTURE AT THE OLD SMITHY.

Captain Hawk, however, could not shut his eyes to the fact that in the contest that seemed imminent he could not fail to be the worst off, and that the officers by sheer force of numbers were almost certain to be the victors.

The reader may depend that there was no inclination on his part to fall into the hands of his enemies if he could possibly help it, and so, notwithstanding his preparations, he continued to keep keenly on the look-out for any little thing that might turn out to his advantage.

His pursuers were not yet in sight.

On one side of him was a meadow of great extent, only divided from the high-road by a very low, dilapidated hedge.

"The turf must be the best for your foot, old boy," he said; and no sooner did he pronounce the words than he turned Satan's head towards the hedge.

He went over easily enough.

The grass in the meadow was quite soft, and could not possibly injure the unprotected hoof, so the captain did not for a moment scruple to let fall the rein.

It was all that was needed.

Over the broad expanse went the noble horse like a greyhound.

The speed was one that could not fail to leave the officers far behind.

The highwayman's heart throbbed with excitement.

Then a cry of satisfaction escaped his lips.

Not far off, nestling on the hill-side, was a small red-tiled building, which, even from that distance, he felt almost sure was a blacksmith's forge.

There was no smoke curling upwards, however, and this circumstance a little damped the joy which he would otherwise have felt.

However, he hastened onwards, for should his surmise prove correct, there seemed at least a chance that he should be able to get away from his pursuers, notwithstanding the advantages on their side.

A closer approach showed Captain Hawk that he was not mistaken with respect to the nature of the building which he had seen.

It was indeed a blacksmith's forge.

"On, boy!" he cried. "Every moment saved now is of vast importance!"

Faster than ever Satan flew on.

The highwayman pulled up suddenly.

"Hilloa there!" he cried. "Is there anyone within?"

A growling sound made itself heard from within.

Directly afterwards, a burly fellow, whose eyes seemed scarcely opened, came to the smithy door.

"Well?" he cried, staring stupidly at the new-comer.

"I want you to put a few nails in this shoe for me."

"Very good," he said, with a yawn. "You are in no hurry, I suppose?"

"Indeed I am! It is most urgent."

"Ah well! it will be all the same."

"How the same?"

"Peter hasn't come yet."

"D—n Peter! What has he to do with it?"

"I have got none of my tools, and the fire isn't lighted yet. There's no help for it. You must wait."

Then raising his voice to its highest pitch, he bawled:

"Peter—Peter! Confound your carcass, come this way!"

Captain Hawk flung himself out of the saddle full of impatience and anger.

But the man stood quite composed.

"You must know, sir," he calmly explained, "that measter got married yesterday, and last night every one of us got a drop too much. Even that imp of the devil, Peter, got drunk, and that's the reason he hasn't come yet and lighted the fire."

"Listen—listen," said the highwayman, taking a handful of silver from his pocket. "The matter I am upon is of life and death. There must not be the delay of a single moment. Take this, and in return all I want you to do is to fasten this old shoe on again."

The man, who seemed himself scarcely to have got over the deep potations of the preceding evening, shook off his lethargy when he saw as many glittering coins waiting for him as he could obtain by a week's toil.

"Come in, sir," he said, in quite a different tone of voice, "and though I say it myself, yet I give you my word that there is not a man in the country who could do this job in such a little time as I can."

This assurance was welcome enough to Captain Hawk, who at once led his horse into the forge.

The man, by his way, seemed to prove that his words were something more than an empty boast.

He set about his task with the utmost alacrity.

Captain Hawk handed him the shoe, and then began to breathe a little more freely.

But much time had already been consumed, and he fancied that if the officers had been clever enough to follow closely in his footsteps they must be somewhere near at hand.

The gaze which he bent upon the man was consequently a most anxious one.

While this is going forward, we will just give a glance at the proceedings of the officers, because rather a peculiar occurrence had taken place.

By one of those odd coincidences which sometimes happen, it chanced that the chief of the troop of officers met with the same accident as the highwayman—that is to say, his horse lost a shoe.

No sooner was he made aware of this disagreeable event than he poured out some very hearty curses, which, however, only wasted his breath without mending matters in the least.

What added to the difficulty was the fact that this horse was infinitely better than any other in the troop.

To proceed for any distance along the road would be, he felt certain, seriously to injure the animal, and this he by no means wished to do.

Yet to abandon the chase was what he could not bring himself to think of, and yet, at the same time, he was conscious that it was no good to continue it without his favourite horse.

He was beginning to give way to despair, when he happened to catch sight of a man advancing towards him.

This man was driving a quantity of sheep.

"Hoy!" cried the chief officer. "Can you tell me of a blacksmith's hereabouts? My horse has cast his shoe."

"Oh, ay!" was the reply, "there's one *anunst* the hill yonder. Go on a bit, and turn to the left. You'll soon see it."

"It's not far, then?"

"No, not much more than a mile."

This intelligence was most welcome, and the chief officer's countenance brightened immediately.

"Push on!" he cried. "Going such a short distance as a mile without a shoe won't hurt him."

The men prepared to obey this command, but ere they could do so he cried.

"Hold—hold! Hi! My man! Another word with you."

"Well, what now?"

"Have you seen anything of a man riding on a black horse?"

"What, a little while ago?"

"Yes."

"Oh, yes! I saw one."

"Where was he?" asked the chief officer, eagerly.

"He was riding wi' might and main across Stubbs's meadow. Thinks I to myself that's trespass!"

"Stubbs's meadow!—which is Stubbs's meadow?"

"Eh, I thought every fool knew which was Stubbs's meadow. It lays over beyond there, on the left, afore you come to the hill; you can't miss it."

The chief of the police officers was very glad of this information, the correctness of which he did not for a moment doubt.

It made him more than ever anathematise the accident that had befallen his horse.

Clearly, however, he had no resource but to make his way without loss of time to the forge, and then resume his pursuit.

Little did he dream that the very man of whom he was in pursuit was actually at the place he so much wished to gain.

Throwing a shilling to the sheep drover, the chief police officer set off at full gallop, followed by his men.

An old farm labourer they met soon afterwards pointed out Stubbs's meadow, and also, in the distance, the red-tiled roof of the old smithy, which was quite a conspicuous object among the trees.

Thus, by the strangest accident in the world, the police officers, without knowing it, got upon the highwayman's track.

What was stranger, too, was that the commander, seeing that he should have to make a considerable detour in order to reach the forge by the road, decided to take a cut across the fields for the double purpose of abridging the distance and having a softer kind of ground under his horse's feet.

From this it follows that the whole party got quite close to the smithy before there was the least sound heard indicative of their approach.

It was with great suddenness, then, that they dashed up to the narrow door.

The forge was rather dark within, but the foremost officer could detect two human forms and a horse standing within, while all could hear the sharp clink of a hammer striking upon iron.

Captain Hawk no sooner became aware of their closeness to him than he stepped back quietly, close to his steed.

"Have you nearly done?" he said, in tones scarcely above a whisper.

"This is the last nail."

The blacksmith was in the act of driving this when the whole troop pulled up in front of the shop.

Captain Hawk's position now seemed critical indeed, for the police officers were quite numerous enough to block the doorway up completely.

But he evinced no signs of consternation; and when the blacksmith delivered the last blow upon the nail, and looked up, he did not for an instant suspect that the newcomers had anything to do with his liberal customer.

Captain Hawk, however, for all his coolness and apparent indifference, was fully prepared.

Just as he took hold of the rein, however, one of the officers stretched out his arm and cried:

"Blow me to bits, if he is not there! Look—look—yonder by the anvil! Seize him, blacksmith—seize him, and you shall have a hundred pounds reward! That is Captain Hawk, the highwayman!"

A scene of confusion far beyond the powers of any description now ensued.

The blacksmith, as well he might be, was so bewildered by the uproar and the suddenness of the whole affair, that for a moment he was incapable of doing anything, and stood like one thunderstruck.

The other officers, scarcely able to credit for the moment that their companion spoke the truth, all eagerly looked through the grated aperture which served for a window.

Captain Hawk was there sure enough.

Their pistols and cutlasses were drawn, and loud cries came from every throat.

They dismounted with frantic haste, and rushed into the smithy.

But they were one second too late.

Just while the blacksmith had been completing his operations Captain Hawk detected a small door close to where Satan's head was tied.

This door was composed of nothing save a few old planks very roughly nailed together.

There were plenty of chinks and crevices through which Captain Hawk could see.

He beheld the green fields and the waving trees, and knew that the door formed a direct means of communication with the open air.

Unperceived, he had drawn back the iron bolt, which was the sole fastening the door could boast.

Just at the moment, then, when the officers rushed in he kicked open this side door and darted through it.

He held Satan by the bridle, and the docile creature followed him with the utmost alacrity.

They were out in the twinkling of an eye.

"Fire!—fire!" shouted the chief officer, mad with rage at being thus disappointed when he fancied he certainly had the highwayman secure. "Fire, I say; and kill one or both of them rather than let him slip through our hands again!"

A hasty volley followed.

Before the smoke died away, however, Captain Hawk had not only managed to swing himself up into the saddle, but also to get to a good distance.

So far as the officers could tell, both horse and rider were unhurt.

The one in command was more furious than ever.

"He seems to have a charmed life," he cried, as he flung away his discharged pistol. "I aimed at him most carefully, and could have sworn it was impossible for me to miss my mark; and yet off he goes as though nothing at all is the matter."

"What is to be done, sir?" asked several anxious voices.

"Done?" was the impatient answer. "I think the best thing would be to go home at once. We are no good here.

"Blacksmith," he added, in a louder voice, and turning round as he spoke, "put a shoe on my horse as quickly as you can. But for the cursed accident of losing it I should, ten to one, overtake him!"

He forgot at the moment that had it not been for the occurrence of the accident he regretted so deeply he would not have got to the smithy at all.

"Then let me tell you," said one, "that I don't intend to wait here, losing valuable time! There is always something to prevent us from following up the chase! There's the reward, and I mean to have it!"

"What do you mean to do?"

"Ride off after him alone—that is, if none of the rest will follow."

"And leave me here alone?" yelled the chief, almost black in the face with passion.

"Yes, certainly! Just because your horse has met with an accident, do you think it reasonable we should wait and lose our chance? I don't, for one, and I am off without any further argufying of the matter!"

So saying, the man, who had already hastily scrambled into the saddle, dug his spurs into his horse's flanks and galloped off after the highwayman.

There were one or two others who seemed rather more than half inclined to follow his example.

But while they hesitated the chance was lost; and besides, the fury of their superior officer terrified them into submission.

In the meanwhile, the one who had had the boldness to act independently for himself, and the courage to pursue the highwayman single-handed, continued to make his way at full gallop.

As to his courage, however, it must be stated that he fully calculated his spirited example would be more than sufficient to induce the greater portion of his comrades to accompany him, and when he galloped off he was entirely under the impression that two or three at least would follow him.

But this did not prove to be the case, and so he had no resource but to carry out his rash enterprise single-handed.

No one could have felt its rashness more strongly than he did, and in his heart he wished a thousand times over to turn back.

But then he knew full well that if he did this he would be subjected ever afterwards to the ridicule of his companions, who would never suffer him to have a moment's respite from their taunts.

And thus in a manner he was forced to gallop on.

This was not the kind of spirit in which to cope with such a man as Captain Hawk.

But as he rode on, that species of courage which is produced by sheer desperation took possession of his breast.

He clenched his teeth hard, and hissed out:

"I care not for myself—I will either have him or perish! I will get as close behind him as I can, and then when within range I will take careful aim and put a bullet in his back!"

This seemed a very reasonable and easy method of putting an end to the affair, and the officer's courage rose still higher.

But there were a few trifling difficulties in the way of doing what he had marked out.

It so happened that the horse he bestrode was about the best in point of speed and endurance in the whole troop, and had it not been necessary for the whole to keep together, he would have got closer to the highwayman long before.

Now, however, animated by excitement, and having nothing in the world to keep him back, he made wonderful speed.

Presently a cry of joy issued from his lips.

Some distance off he could perceive the figure of Captain Hawk.

The highwayman was allowing his horse to go slowly up a piece of rising ground.

The officer, who quivered all over with excitement, redoubled his exertions to get his steed along.

Very soon he had the satisfaction of seeing the distance between himself and the object of his pursuit greatly decrease.

It was some time before Captain Hawk turned to look back.

When he did so, and saw only one police officer riding after him at so furious a rate, he could scarcely credit his own vision.

"Is the man mad?" he said, "or does he imagine he can take me single-handed? At any rate, I will push on for a mile or two, when I shall doubtless lose sight of him altogether."

As he spoke, he let the reins fall upon Satan's neck, and, to the officer's infinite chagrin, he found the distance increase much more rapidly than it had decreased.

For all that he would not be discouraged, but kept on at unabated speed.

"If I conquer, the triumph will be mine," he said—"if I fail, I shall never hear the last of this! I will try my best—such a chance will never happen again."

But, despite all his exertions, Captain Hawk got further and further away, until finally he disappeared altogether.

The officer tried hard to stifle his annoyance.

It was some relief to his excited feelings to spur and belabour his horse, and he did so most unmercifully.

So time passed on.

But he saw nothing of the highwayman, nor did he until just at the moment when he despaired of ever doing so and was about to give up the chase.

The captain, who imagined that he had rid himself of his foe, had reduced Satan's speed again, while he occupied himself in looking around for that place of concealment and shelter which he had been seeking for so long.

When the clatter of hoofs behind him came upon his ears he was incredulous.

But when he caught sight of the selfsame single officer a little more than a quarter of a mile off, he felt that some more energetic measures than those which had been taken at present would be required to get rid of him.

"This will never do," he said. "The fellow does not intend to attack me, I can see, but thinks to keep well upon my track, in order that his companions should not miss me. As gentle means will not do, I must try to spoil his game in some other way."

As for the officer, his long ride had enabled him to recall his reflective powers a little, and he began to see more and more the absolute folly and insanity of the enterprise in which he had so hastily plunged.

He wished himself well out of the scrape he had so rashly got into.

He tried his best, however, to stifle the suggestions of reason in his breast.

"I have come so far," he said, doggedly, "and I will have him! At any rate, I will not turn back until I have had a good try at putting a bullet into his back!"

Just as he arrived at this determination his courage received a shock.

To his dismay, the object of his pursuit not only halted, but turned round.

Almost unconsciously the officer slackened his horse's speed.

"What is he going to do?" he asked himself, with fast-increasing misgiving.

Captain Hawk had resolved to put a decided stop to the pursuit, and he hit upon rather a strange means of doing it.

"I do believe the fellow is a coward," he said, "notwithstanding the audacity he has shown in pursuing me alone. At any rate, I shall quickly prove what kind of metal he is made of."

Speaking thus, Captain Hawk drew a pistol and cocked it.

This he held in his right hand.

Then, taking the reins in his left, he cried:

"Now, Satan, boy! Ahoy—ahoy! Off and away—away!"

With a snort, the horse galloped back.

This was an action for which the police officer was not prepared, and the terrific rapidity with which Captain Hawk approached him struck such a panic into his breast that he was deprived of all motion.

This made Captain Hawk think the officer was calmly awaiting his attack, and he was just about to reduce Satan's speed, when his adversary, with a cry of terror, recovered sufficiently to pull the rein.

But his horse, already wearied by the incessant exertions he had been forced to make, did not start off very briskly.

It was with additional alarm that the officer became sensible that in a few moments at the most the famous highwayman would overtake him.

This made him resolve upon the adoption of another expedient.

At a point where the road turned off abruptly was a hedge, over which he determined to leap his horse, so that at least there might be some impediment between himself and his pursuer.

He urged his horse towards the hedge at a brisk gallop.

When at the right distance, he uttered a shout and raised the rein, fully expecting that the horse would jump.

But he was deceived.

Whether the animal felt that the leap was beyond its powers, or whether it determined to take the opportunity of ridding itself of its troublesome rider, cannot be known.

Certain it is that just at that point where he ought to have made his spring he stopped short as though by some magical process.

The consequence of this simple act was that the officer was projected forwards with great violence over the animal's head, and after describing a most singular curve in the air, descended with immense force into the deep and wide ditch on the other side of the hedge.

Captain Hawk's enemy was disposed of.

Seeing that such was the case, the highwayman suddenly pulled up.

The ludicrous termination of the affair caused him to give vent to a loud burst of laughter.

When this ceased, a prodigious splashing reached his ears, as though his foe was making the most strenuous efforts to escape from the ditch.

He did not trouble himself any further about him; but after another roar of laughter, restored his pistol to his pocket, and wheeled his horse round.

"Surely," he said, "I may now venture to think that I have in good earnest put an end to the pursuit. And not before it is time, for I never felt more inclined for a rest in my life. And besides, if I do not quickly get under cover somewhere, I shall certainly be seen."

The day was, in fact, advancing with rapid strides.

But that he should actually get free from his enemies without further trouble could scarcely with reason be expected.

The fact of its being broad daylight gave the police officers an immense advantage in carrying on the pursuit, while the same circumstance was, of course, a corresponding disadvantage to the highwayman.

Of this, though, it must be said Captain Hawk thought little, and his chief solicitude was to find some place where he could rest himself and his horse and remain in security for the rest of the day.

"I despair of finding a place," he said, glancing around for the thousandth time. "There looks to be a small clump of trees yonder; but I fear the extent is not sufficient for me to stand any chance of remaining undiscovered. I can do nothing better, though, it seems. I will go there, and make a closer examination."

The clump of trees to which he alluded was some distance off, and he had to change his course entirely in order to reach them.

The ground also had an upward tendency; and as Satan was fatigued, everything conspired to make him longer in reaching this point than he otherwise would have been.

At length, however, he arrived, as he believed, without having been observed by any individual whatever.

An agreeable surprise awaited him.

The clump of trees which, seen from the distance, had seemed so small, was really the outlying portion of a wood of considerable extent.

Into this Captain Hawk plunged without delay.

The trees grew very densely together, so that he was speedily lost to view.

"If I have only been fortunate enough to reach here unseen," he said, "I think I may venture to consider myself safe for a time, as I have left no track that the officers will be clever enough to follow."

Just as he came to this conclusion he dismounted, having penetrated so far into the forest that further progress on horseback became impossible.

But by walking in advance, and holding the rein, he was able to make his way for a considerable distance further.

Finally reaching a dense thicket, the entrance to which was only just wide enough to allow of a passage, he agreed to come to a halt, feeling certain that no one could come upon him very quickly to take him at unawares.

The path widened a little, and Captain Hawk chose the end of it for his temporary halting-place.

Everywhere around him save the narrow path, then, was nothing but a dense mass of thorny vegetation, through which neither horse nor man could have forced a way.

CHAPTER LXIV.

IN WHICH CAPTAIN HAWK IS THE AUDITOR OF A VERY MYSTERIOUS CONVERSATION.

Seeing all this, Captain Hawk felt tolerably content and safe.

His first proceeding was to remove some of the trappings of his horse, and to loosen the remainder.

This being done, he threw himself wearily down upon the grass, which was so long as to conceal him almost entirely.

In the sky, the sun was shining brightly, but his beams did not much illuminate the gloomy recess of the old wood in which the highwayman then was.

It was pleasant enough, however, to be extended at full length, watching the gentle waving of the branches, listening to the rustling of the myriads of leaves, and observing the glittering of the patches of sunlight among the tree-tops.

The silence was profound.

How long Captain Hawk remained in this position he knew not, but by degrees he was drawn off into a deep slumber.

Satan for some time busily occupied himself in cropping the sweet grass, but at last he, too, laid down at full length, and became as motionless as his master.

After so much fatigue, the silence of such a place as this was well calculated to make slumber long and refreshing.

Gradually the sun declined until his rays only pierced the trees in a horizontal direction.

Still Captain Hawk slept on, heedless of the coming darkness as well as of the moaning of the wind, which seemed to betoken the speedy coming of a storm.

Just before the sun quite sank out of sight, however, Captain Hawk rolled over and opened his eyes.

The first object upon which his eyes chanced to fall was his horse.

Some caressing words immediately escaped his lips, and he seemed as though about to reclose his eyes in slumber, when all at once he started.

"Can it be so late?" he said. "My slumber has lasted twice the time I could have believed. Satan, my boy, we must be up and off, for we have much to do, and the distance from here to the old Greyhound is no trifle."

The highwayman was on his feet in a moment, and without loss of time Satan followed his example, and seemed by his manner as if he desired to show he was quite ready and willing for a departure.

The trappings were soon placed in readiness, and then taking the bridle as before, Captain Hawk made his way along the narrow path.

He advanced with caution, for, having been so long asleep, he was unable to guess what might have taken place the while; and besides, on all occasions it behoved him to err on the side of over cautiousness.

It was, therefore, more from habit than aught else that he paused at every few steps, and listened intently.

Just when he was within a few yards of the entrance of the thicket he had good reason to congratulate himself upon having had the prudence to act in this manner.

While listening, he felt certain that a distant but perfectly distinct sound came upon his ears.

He patted Satan gently, in order to keep him from moving, and listened more intently still.

The sound came again.

"Unless I am very greatly mistaken," said the highwayman, mentally, "the sound which I can hear is produced by some person forcing a passage cautiously among the underwood. Who is that so likely to be as one of my foes, for who else would be likely to be here, taking such pains to approach unheard?"

Captain Hawk's supposition was a very reasonable one indeed.

It was hard to think that there was anyone else besides his foes who had an object in creeping stealthily among the trees.

The sound made was very slight, and had not the highwayman been listening most intently, he must have missed hearing it.

Still stroking Satan, he stood waiting for what should happen next.

He was not long in coming to the conclusion that it was the approach of one person only that he heard, and this fact enabled him to await the course of events with less anxiety than would otherwise have been the case.

The man came on steadily.

He paused once or twice, as though to remove some impediment from his path, and then came on again.

From the sound, the captain concluded that the new-comer must be making his way direct towards him.

Still the highwayman did not stir a step, though his right hand found its way into his pocket and gripped a pistol.

After that he stood like a statue.

Satan, too, could hear the sound, for he stood with his ears projected in the direction of it, while his eyes were more than ordinarily dilated.

Captain Hawk had again the fear that his faithful friend would betray his whereabouts, and stroked him continually, in order to keep him quiet if possible.

The footstep grew quite distinct, and then paused, certainly within twenty paces of where the highwayman stood listening in anxious expectation.

There was a pause of deep silence.

Then, in deep tones, a voice said:

"It is the hour!"

After that all was still again.

Those few words, simple as they were, served to change the whole current of the highwayman's thoughts.

The new-comer was not one of his foes, he felt almost confident, or he would never have uttered such words in such a tone.

It seemed tolerably clear, on the contrary, that it was some unknown person who had sought that place in expectation of meeting some one with whom he had appointed a meeting.

That was the idea which suggested itself immediately to the captain's mind.

Whether it was a correct idea or not could only be shown by time.

To move from his present position, no matter how much he might have wished it, would have been impossible without instant discovery.

So far as his sense of hearing could be trusted, the position taken up by the new-comer was somewhere very near to the end of the path, by means of which the thicket could alone be left.

Captain Hawk's curiosity, too, was not a little aroused by the few words he heard, and he waited most impatiently to know what should happen next.

The first thing he heard was some one pacing up and down the piece of open ground close to the end of o path leading into the thicket.

The steps were all stealthily taken, but they were nevertheless rapid and irregular.

Then they ceased suddenly, and the voice pronounced again the self-same words:

"It is the hour!"

No more was said for a moment, and then the sa. voice continued, somewhat hastily:

"Why comes he not? He cannot have mistaken the spot. Curses on him! Can any foolish scruples have assailed him, and induced him to forego the enterprise to which he stands pledged? If he comes not soon I shall begin to think that such is the case."

After this the stealthy pacing up and down, which was irresistibly suggestive of some wild and dangerous beast, was renewed.

What had been said did not enlighten the unsuspected listener very much, but it served to confirm him in the conclusion to which he had immediately come.

This man, whoever it was, knew nothing of him, and could not even guess his presence there.

"Hark!" said the voice, suddenly. "What was that?"

Captain Hawk held his breath, for he fancied that some slight movement on the part of himself or his steed might have reached the ears of the listener.

But this fear was baseless, for at this moment Captain Hawk heard a faint and distant sound.

But it grew plainer with wonderful rapidity.

The first comer uttered a faint cry of satisfaction, and by some means or other emitted a whistle, which sounded more like the call of some crepuscular bird than aught else, and, heard in the depths of a wood, it would certainly have been taken for this.

Even Captain Hawk was half in doubt until he heard the same sound repeated, and directly afterwards another voice said, in suppressed accents:

"I am here."

"Yes," said the first; "but you are late. How comes it that you are so much behind your time?"

"It cannot be more than a few minutes."

"But there should have been no delay."

"It was unavoidable."

"What was the cause?"

"As I was coming here—of course taking every precaution to escape being seen by——"

"Yes—yes!"

"I came upon a large troop of officers."

"Officers!" ejaculated the other, in tones that seemed to indicate that this intelligence not only surprised him, but also caused him some little uneasiness.

"Yes, officers!" repeated the other.

"And where were they?"

"Close by here."

"And—and their errand?"

"Does not concern us."

"You found it out, then?"

"Yes."

"What is it?"

"They are in pursuit of the celebrated Captain Hawk, who has been seen close by, and is suspected of being in hiding somewhere near here."

"In this wood, perhaps?"

"It may be so. If he is, rest assured he is tolerably safe. It would be no easy task to search it."

"No- -no. But let us return to our own affairs."

"Well?"

"Have these officers seen you?"

"They have not."

"Are you sure?"

"Quite."

"That is well."

"I was aware of the necessity for secrecy, and took every precaution."

"And is that the sole reason you were behind your time?"

"Yes. What else did you suspect?"

"Never mind now—precious moments are flying. Have you made all inquiries?"

"Yes."

"And you are satisfied?"

"Perfectly."

"Then let us be off at once. The less delay there is the better."

"Nay—nay!"

"How?"

"It is impossible to-night."

The other uttered an oath.

"It is annoying, but unavoidable."

"Are you sure of it?"

"I am certain. It would only be to court failure to make the attempt to-night; and you must know that when we try we must succeed, or we are ruined for ever."

"Yes, yes—that is true enough."

"Then all thoughts of to-night must be abandoned."

"But explain why."

"Come closer. Walls, they say, have ears, and so may trees for aught I know."

"Go on—go on!" cried his companion, impatiently.

"Never mind that."

The other then spoke energetically for some seconds.

But he had manifestly got near enough to whisper in his comrade's ear.

It was in vain, then, that Captain Hawk strained his sense of hearing to the utmost.

Nothing but a low murmur reached him.

Not one single syllable reached his ears until the man slightly raised his voice and said, in conclusion:

"Is it not best to postpone the attempt?"

"I fear I must admit it. And to-morrow?"

"To-morrow the difficulty will not exist."

"And you think it can be achieved safely then?"

"I do."

"To-morrow be it."

"You know the old Greyhound of which I speak?"

Captain Hawk's astonishment was so great at hearing these unexpected words that it is a thousand wonders he did not betray his presence.

But, restraining himself, he now waited with tenfold the amount of curiosity to hear more.

"I think I remember it."

"You must do so—it is an old, straggling inn, just at a convenient distance from the town, and not very far from the church."

"Hush—hush!"

"It is right enough. Do you know it?"

"Yes; the place is of ill repute, is it not?"

"It is; but it is none the worse for our purpose on that account—I might go so far as to say it was all the better."

"And what time do you say we had better be there?"

"Any time in the evening. Till then I propose that we separate as usual."

"And we will meet there?"

"Yes, if you consent."

"I am willing, for I am unable to think of any other place that will suit us better."

"Or half so well."

"Well, agreed. You will, of course, in the meantime take every pains to see that all is right?"

"Yes; should anything threaten to go wrong I shall be aware of it in good time, I'll warrant. But I think there is no need to be apprehensive."

"It will be necessary for you to quit the wood unseen by the officers."

"Yes, trust me for managing that. I shall make my way out at the opposite side—it will be further out of my way, but then I can almost reckon for certain upon being unseen."

"And that is of paramount importance."

"It is. Ahem!"

"What now?"

The expenses are great, and I shall have to spend freely at the Greyhound if we expect the rascally old landlord of it to keep his tongue between his teeth."

"Any excuse for money! Here, take this purse, and rest assured I shall not part with another farthing until the business is completed."

"That will be to-morrow night, then. You had better take this plan—I shall not want it between now and then, and you can familiarise yourself with the details."

"As you please."

"Is the plan correct?"

"To the very best of my belief."

"Enough, then. We will part now."

"To-morrow, then, at sunset, I shall be waiting for you at the Greyhound."

"You will have a private room?"

"Oh yes!"

"Farewell till then!"

"Farewell!"

The sound of retreating footsteps followed these words.

Gradually they died away, and the profound silence of the forest again reigned.

But even after this, Captain Hawk waited some moments before he emerged from his hiding-place.

There was a puzzled look on his face.

"I would give much to have the key to what I have heard to-night. I can learn nothing from the conversation, save that some game of villany is on foot. How more than strange it is, however, that they should make a rendezvous at the old Greyhound! There is one thing about the matter—I have but to control my impatient curiosity for a little while, and then I shall be in a fair way of knowing all."

With a thoughtful look on his face, Captain Hawk emerged from the narrow path, and stood in the open space before the thicket—the very spot which had such a short time before been occupied by the two men.

"There is another thing I would give much to feel certain of," he added, "and that is the way the one has gone who spoke about being able to get away without fear of being seen by the police officers. That is what I want to do, if I could only see my way to manage it. So far as I can trust to my ears, he went this way, and as I have no other or better guides, I suppose I can do nothing else than follow them."

But even supposing he had not been mistaken, and that he actually started in the direction taken by the man, it was next to an impossibility for him to keep at all upon his track.

Convinced, however, that there was no choice in the matter, Captain Hawk, holding the rein, plunged without hesitation among the trees.

He had no little difficulty in forcing a passage, but feared to make a detour to avoid any obstacles lest he should grow confused and miss the direction in which he ought to keep.

After more than an hour of painful struggling through brushwood and tangled brake, he came upon a more open ground, which inspired him with the hope that the boundary of the wood was almost reached.

He was not mistaken.

Soon after he could perceive between the trunks of the trees glimpses of the open country, now faintly illuminated by the rays of a young moon.

With more caution, Captain Hawk now approached the boundary of the wood.

The deep silence, however, was most assuring.

Failing to hear a single sound save the low moaning of the wind, he ventured to emerge.

The prospect before him was an extensive one.

Far and wide stretched field after field of richly-cultivated land, with masses of trees here and there, which agreeably diversified the view.

Seen by the moon's gentle radiance, the scene was one of exquisite beauty—one upon which the eyes could ever linger without tiring.

At that time, however, Captain Hawk felt but little inclination to admire the beauty of nature.

His eyes roamed over the fair prospect, it is true, but not in order to note its many beauties, but to ascertain if possible whether his enemies were anywhere within sight.

The result of his scrutiny was most encouraging.

"There is some little consolation," he said, "in les

[THE POLICE OFFICERS ATTEMPT TO CAPTURE THE BLACK HIGHWAYMAN.]

ing that they are not very close at hand. I can venture to ride forth without any dread; and I must trust to my own quickness to keep out of their way."

He sprang into the saddle as he spoke.

"Come, Satan," he said, in inspiriting tones, "we have both of us had a long rest. A gallop ought not to hurt you now; and as for myself, I never felt more in the humour to enjoy one than I do now. Off and away, then, old fellow! It is far from here to the old Greyhound, and we ought to be there already. Make your best speed, my boy; for when you arrive a comfortable stable will be your quarters for some hours at least—that is, provided those confounded officers will let us remain in peace for a little while. Now then, soho, boy! Away—away!"

With an impatient snort, as though he fully understood every word which his master had just said, and felt to the full as anxious to reach the Greyhound speedily, Satan bounded off.

Over the gently sloping ground he flew with all the vigour and elasticity of movement observable in a wild horse who has never known what it is to carry a rider on his back.

Away—away without a moment's pause.

Over brooks and brawling streams—over hill and dale—past tree and meadow—away, away like two shadowy phantoms of the night.

It was almost a straight line that Captain Hawk made towards his destination.

And all the time, while going at this headlong speed, he kept a sharp look-out around, lest he should unexpectedly run foul of any party of his foes.

But not a trace of a police officer showed itself throughout the whole journey.

This event, together with the inspiriting effects of his long gallop, filled the highwayman's breast with exultation.

In his excitement, a wild cry would ever and anon escape his lips.

This reaching the ears of his incomparable steed, would make him fly like the wind itself.

At last the captain began to draw the rein.

"Gently—gently!" he said. "We shall soon be there; and if the officers do not learn in some way that I have doubled thus upon my course, they will have some trouble to find me. And how can they tell but what I have gone in the direction of London? They cannot tell that I have any business to bring me here to-night. Yes, yes—I begin to think that I shall certainly be able to enjoy a rest of four-and-twenty hours at the least beneath the hospitable roof of the old Greyhound. Gently, now, my boy! We shall arrive there in good time, after all."

Such was the speed that had been made that only a little more than an hour's riding had brought the captain close to the place he wished to reach.

"I have little to complain of," he continued. "I have had rather more adventures than I bargained for; but then I have in my pocket the means of requiting the ostler for the great service which he rendered me. Then when that duty is performed, I will take care that Tom Beckford does not go unrewarded, while the next thing I mean to busy myself about is the clearing up of what I have heard to-night. Perhaps by the time I have done that, my enemies will have got as far as London—imagining that I must be before them. If so, my journey to the metropolis will be a pleasant one. I would give much, however, to know what the plan is about which the officer expressed himself so confidently."

It was in vain, however, for Captain Hawk to speculate upon this point—there was not the slightest circumstance to guide him in coming to a conclusion.

"Unless chance throws some information in my way," he said, "I must abandon all thought upon the subject, and wait with what patience I can until time reveals the mystery."

His attention now was fully required in looking around him, for the closer he got to the old Greyhound the greater need was there for him to observe circumspection in all his movements.

His satisfaction much increased, however, when he found himself unable to discern any more tokens of them than he had done already.

This almost convinced him that if they had any idea that his intention was to return to the old inn, they had abandoned it, and that they were, on the contrary, fully impressed with the belief that he was making his way with all possible speed to London.

Nevertheless, he did not allow this conviction to deprive him of any of his circumspection.

But suddenly he checked his speed.

He carried his hand to his forehead as he exclaimed:

"By Jove! I had forgotten that. Perhaps now I am too late. How odd it seems that any succession of events should have driven from my mind all recollection of the helpless creature I promised to befriend! Who can say, during this interval, what danger may not have assailed her on her dreary journey?—or how often she may have looked longingly for succour? and, placing dependence on my word, have hoped to see me to the last. What could be more unfortunate? How can I repair my negligence?"

The reader will have no sort of difficulty in divining the subject of the captain's thoughts.

He was reproaching himself for having forgotten for so long a time all about the fortunes of the poor girl to whom he had been of so much assistance, and in whom he felt so warm an interest.

When, however, we bear in mind the number of strange occurrences which had followed hard and fast upon his parting with her, his forgetfulness will not appear to be so very strange after all.

But after making every allowance for the slowness of the waggon's progress, he could not help fearing that it had long since reached its destination, which, it will be recollected, was about fourteen miles beyond Huntingdon and towards London.

"Had I but kept to the high-road on my return journey," he said, regretfully, "I should in all probability have met with her. But it is useless to regret that now. But let me think: I shall at least be able to know whether the waggon has passed the Greyhound. With that crown-piece in his pocket, the driver would not be able to resist the temptation of calling."

Captain Hawk was a good deal satisfied with this reflection, and he accordingly resumed his way to the inn, though he went slowly and thoughtfully.

But it was only by keeping a firm pressure upon Satan's mouth that he moderated his pace, for the sagacious creature seemed fully aware that its resting-place was near, and was full of impatience to reach it without loss of time.

Captain Hawk, however, when within about a quarter of a mile of the inn, turned off to the left, so as to reach it in a circuitous manner.

He made, indeed, a complete circuit of the building, but nowhere could he see any more signs of his enemies than he had done after leaving the shelter of the wood.

He paused close to a low wall at one side of the premises, on the other side of which was the stable-yard.

Before he had stopped a moment he heard a footstep, and directly afterwards Beckford, the landlord, made his appearance.

The night was dark, but yet not so obscure as to prevent the highwayman from recognising the portly form of his friend.

"Here I am, Tom!" he said, in a low voice. "Is all well?"

By the sudden jump the landlord gave it might be inferred that he was greatly taken by surprise at finding the highwayman so near.

But recovering himself directly, he said:

"Yes, all is well, my boy, and you are most welcome, as you always are."

"That is good news. Can I get to the stables without going round to the front?"

"Of course you can; that wall is low enough. Jump your horse over it."

"What is on the other side?"

"Only a dung-heap. That will be soft enough. Come on."

Captain Hawk had very little trouble in getting Satan to jump the low wall in front of him, and in less than another moment the highwayman and the landlord were standing side by side.

CHAPTER LXV.

CAPTAIN HAWK LEARNS SOME VERY STARTLING INTELLIGENCE AT THE GREYHOUND INN.

"Now, then, Tom," cried Captain Hawk, in cheery tones, for he had reached the inn with a thousand times more ease and safety than he had dared to hope for, "show me the stable, for I don't care how soon my horse crosses the threshold. We have been many miles together since we left here, and he stands doubly in need of rest, for, unless I am much deceived, there will be more business on hand before long."

"Of what nature, captain?—the old game, eh?"

"You shall know anon. But I cannot enter into explanations now. Has anyone been here inquiring for me?"

"Yes; the ostler of whom you spoke."

"Good. He is a faithful fellow; and I am glad he has arrived, for I have the means now with me of rewarding him liberally for his services."

"Then you have been successful, captain?"

"Tolerably so. And what has happened at the old place since I left it?"

"Nothing of importance."

"You have not seen any officers, then?"

"Not one."

"That is more than you expected."

"It is indeed; and there was only one way in which I could account for it."

"And how was that?"

"Why, that they had got uncommonly well on your track, and your long absence encouraged the idea."

"It is not very far from the truth."

"But, I suppose, now you are here, they will find it out in some mysterious manner, and be turning up before long."

"I don't see how they are to find it out. I doubled upon them well, and, though I have kept the closest look-out, I have not seen anything of them since. My belief is that they are still riding towards London."

"If so," said the landlord, "they must, before very long, be quite certain that you are not before them, and then they will turn back."

"If they do, they will be some time reaching here."

"So much the better."

"But you said just now you had not seen one officer."

"I have not."

"How about the one you dropped down through the flooring?"

"Oh! as for him, strange as it may seem, I have seen nothing of him."

"I suppose he crept out."

"I have not been to see; but it is only reasonable to suppose he has. Anyway, as he has not troubled us, it does not seem worth while for us to trouble about him, does it?"

While this conversation had been taking place, the reader must not suppose the speakers had been standing still.

Satan had been placed in the stable and attended to according to his master's wishes, and the landlord and the highwayman, after having locked the door to make all secure, made their way to the house.

Captain Hawk knew he might enter without any sort of fear whatever, and so crossed the threshold with perfect confidence.

Tom Beckford led the way to a private room—an apartment which he reserved for his own especial use.

A voice welcomed the captain in a moment, and a man came forth to greet him.

It was the faithful ostler.

Captain Hawk was not the man to think lightly of any service rendered, and he knew how to estimate aright the one which this man had performed for him.

He took his hand and wrung it warmly.

The simple action greatly gratified the man, as could be seen by the flush of colour that came over his face.

"Captain," he said, "I shall prize that hearty grasp, and think more of it than aught else. I want no more reward for what I have done—it is sufficient."

"But, my faithful fellow," was the reply, "I do not intend to let the matter pass over in any such manner. Here is something much more substantial, and something which will do you infinitely more good."

As he spoke he drew forth the bag of money which he had taken from the man in the spring cart.

"Why, goodness, captain," said the ostler, "how much is here?"

"Never mind. I have no means of judging save by the weight."

"You are too generous——"

"There, there—not a word more about that."

"There is but one thing I should like to say, and yet——"

"Do not hesitate. Speak freely, I beg."

"Well, captain, you see—I—— But, there, I will out with it at once. I want you to take me with you—I want to join my fortune with yours. No, no—that's not it. But I want to share your dangers; and I want to be your faithful companion—nothing more. I will keep out of the way; and, humble as I am, ten to one there will come a time, perhaps, when I shall be of great use to you."

This proposal was received in silence.

It was not that Captain Hawk was weighing over the expediency of availing himself of this offer of an ally, but considering in what way he should reply to the faithful fellow before him so as not to appear unkind.

Perceiving his hesitation, the man, with an earnestness that could not be mistaken, added:

"You hesitate, captain. Don't refuse me. Let me entreat you to take me with you as a very humble but very faithful servant. You will not refuse now, will you?"

There was something in the earnest pleading of this man, rough and rude as he was, that Captain Hawk could not resist.

And yet, if he gave his consent, he did not see how the proposal could be carried out.

The man would be faithful beyond all question, and he would, no doubt, make the many lonely, solitary hours that the captain was compelled to spend less irksome, though he was by no means the companion he should have selected for the purpose.

Therefore, although he could not see his way clearly into the future, Captain Hawk, unable to refuse, gave his consent.

When the faithful fellow first heard the permission given, he was so intoxicated with delight that he could scarcely believe his ears, and would insist upon having the words repeated over and over again.

When finally convinced, his gratitude took a most boisterous tone, and he capered about like a schoolboy.

Captain Hawk felt more moved by this simple episode than he cared to acknowledge.

There was something to him deeply affecting in this man's devotion, and he insensibly felt himself drawn towards him, great as was the difference between them in every way.

"You are a witness, landlord, to what the captain said," cried the ostler. "He gave his consent! Hip—hip—hurrah! I shall be happy at last!"

"I have only one thing to say," said Captain Hawk, and somehow the tones of his voice, as soon as he began speaking, told the ostler something unpleasant was coming, "and that is, that I intend to make my way to London with all speed, as soon as I have concluded a little business which I have on hand in this neighbourhood. My rapid journey there will make it difficult, if not impossible, for you to accompany me, and so you had better go on in advance, and then we can decide upon what is to be done in the future, for at present I have no idea what my movements may be."

"What! go to London by myself?" said the ostler, with a very crestfallen air.

"Yes; I do not see how it is to be arranged otherwise."

"And where shall I find you in that great place?"

"I will give you the requisite directions, never fear; and when you have them you must be careful to keep the knowledge to yourself."

"Trust me for that, captain!"

"I believe I can safely do so. And now, if you wish to commence your career of usefulness, begin by playing the part of a scout outside, and be sure you give me warning of the approach of danger. I shall rely entirely upon you."

The contrast in the man's face upon hearing these words was wonderful to see, and without the loss of another moment he started off with pleased alacrity to perform the service that was required of him.

In the meanwhile Captain Hawk closed the door of the little private room, and as he did so he said to the landlord:

"I believe that we can now look forward to exchanging a few words together in comfort."

"It seems like it," was the reply. "And before we go any further we will try some of this."

While speaking, Tom Beckford went to a kind of cupboard there was in the room, and from which he produced a cobweb-covered bottle and some glasses.

He placed these on the table, and seated himself at the table opposite to the captain.

"Now then," he said, "help yourself to some of that wine, and if you don't say it is better than any that can be had at any roadside inn in England, you shall never have bite nor sup in my house again."

"You need not threaten me," said the highwayman, tasting the wine. "It is really first-rate."

"It is, and no mistake," assented the landlord, as he smacked his lips with extraordinary relish. "And now we can't begin our talk better than by you giving me an account of all that has befallen you since you went away from here."

"It will take too long."

"Not a bit of it. I am determined to hear all; and until I do, I will neither stir from here nor utter a word."

"You are very arbitrary."

"Never mind about any of those long words, captain. When I want a thing in reason, you ought not to say no to it."

Captain Hawk saw that it would be useless to attempt to deny the landlord's request, so he wisely made a virtue of necessity.

In as few words as possible he recapitulated those events which have already been laid before the reader.

The landlord was a most attentive listener—he did not lose one single syllable.

But it was when Captain Hawk came to the adventure

in the wood that his greatest amount of curiosity was manifested.

The captain, as nearly as he could remember, repeated every word of the mysterious conversation which had passed between the two men.

"And so they appointed to meet at dusk to-morrow at the Greyhound?" he said, musingly, when the highwayman had finished.

"Yes, I am sure that was the place; and it made me start a little, I can promise you, when I heard them say it. There is no inn of the same name anywhere about, is there?"

"Not one."

"I thought not, for I have never heard of it; and they spoke, too, of being near the church, though what that had to do with it puzzles me to think."

"And me also," said the landlord, in a brown study. "Confound it! I sha'n't be able to feel contented till to-morrow night comes. I could almost wish you had not told me."

"Then that serves you right. But, seriously, there was something in the manner of the two men which irresistibly made me suspect that it was a scheme of no ordinary villany which is afoot."

"You are very likely to be near the mark there, captain; but still, the whole thing bothers me. And to think they should have pitched upon this place, too, above all others!"

"I am very glad of it, for it gives me the opportunity of frustrating their schemes should I find it necessary."

"Yes, that is well enough. The worst is, there is no knowing what trouble they may bring me into."

"I had not thought of that."

"It is a serious matter."

"We will try to prevent anything unpleasant. And now we must leave the subject, for if we talk from now till to-morrow we shall get no nearer the mark."

"The church!" repeated the landlord. "What the deuce has the church to do with it?"

"Or rather, what have they to do with the church?—that, I take it, is a great deal nearer the mark."

"It is all one."

"Is there more than one church near?"

"No, there is only one."

"The one with the square, ivy-covered tower?"

"That's the one."

"I have noticed it many times, being always struck with its peaceful beauty. Do you know of anything taking place there that would throw a light upon the matter?"

The landlord pondered for some moments, and scratched his head, but was finally compelled to admit that nothing whatever out of the usual course of events had taken place.

"It's very strange," replied the highwayman; "but we shall have the key to the riddle before long."

"I might go so far as to say that, so far as the church is concerned, only three events have taken place during the past month, and they are of regular and usual occurrence."

"What are they?"

"One marriage and two burials."

"Is that all—everything?"

"Old Hunkers, a miserly old farmer, was married to his housekeeper, as miserly as himself; poor Tom, the well-sinker, was killed by the falling in of some earth, and buried three weeks ago; and the day before yesterday there was a largely-attended funeral."

"There seems nothing in any of these events."

"Nothing at all that seems to form a connection with what you overheard. The last funeral had many circumstances of interest."

"Indeed! How?"

"It was the burial of young Mr. Kingsbury up at the Hall yonder. You know it?"

"What! the large white mansion at the top of the hill?"

"The same. Poor thing! Everyone was sorry. Only twenty-one and a day or two, and heir to about the most splendid estate in the whole county."

"And he is dead?"

"Yes, dead and buried; and never was more genuine and wide-spread sorrow exhibited at any interment as at his. All mourned him like a near relative. He was so gentle, so kind, so good—the most exemplary young man in all the world."

"And his parents are much distressed, I suppose?"

"Parents? They were both dead. I thought you knew that. His mother died in his infancy; and his father—the old squire, as we used to call him—was carried off eight or nine weeks past, leaving this young man, his only child, the whole of his immense property."

"His enjoyment of it was short."

"Very short. The attainment of his majority was not kept on account of his illness. What ailed him, no one knew. The doctor here was puzzled, and sent off to London for more advice; but on the very morning when these physicians arrived he was found dead in his bed."

"And did they discover his disease?"

"They professed to do so, and gave it some long name that I could not pronounce even if I remembered it. Had it been any common person, there would have been an inquest and a *post-mortem* examination, and all that kind of thing; but the doctors agreed between them about what he died of, and so he was buried without any such unpleasant inquiries."

"Quite a romance," said Captain Hawk, who had listened to the foregoing particulars with a degree of interest for which he was quite unable to account.

He remained in thought for some moments after the landlord had finished speaking, and then said:

"And now that the young heir is dead, into whose hands does the property fall?"

"A nephew of the late squire's—a young man of thirty, but who looks much older. He has travelled much in foreign parts, and they say that has aged him. But little is known of him about here—indeed, his existence was unheard of until a few days ago."

"And he is now in possession, I suppose?"

"Oh yes! And he has shown already by a few things that he intends to have some wonderful alterations. We shall feel the change of masters."

This ended the subject, Captain Hawk then being no better able than before to arrive at any conclusion respecting what he had heard.

At this moment the recollection of the young girl he had promised to protect recrossed his mind, and he at once asked the landlord whether he remembered having seen such a vehicle pass by.

The reply was a negative.

"But it might have passed without your knowledge?"

"It might; but I scarcely think so. Where do you say he was going?"

"Fourteen miles beyond Huntingdon."

"On the London side?"

"Yes."

"What sort of a man was he?"

"It was too dark for me to take particular notice of him."

"Or of the waggon?"

"Yes. I only know it was one of the usual kind, with a tarpaulin covering."

"Stop a minute. It's Old Hunkers's place that's fourteen miles off about, and I don't know anywhere else near where a team is kept. One of his waggons did go northward some week or so back. Did you notice the horses? Were they not three piebald ones, and wonderfully alike?"

"They were," ejaculated the highwayman, rather surprised at the landlord's earnest manner; "though, if you had not mentioned the circumstance, I should not have remembered it; now I recollect perfectly."

The landlord shook his head, and, in a very serious tone, said:

"He has not been by here on his return journey."

"But what do you look so solemn about?"

"I fear there is good reason for it."

"Tell me your thoughts. Don't keep me a moment in suspense."

"Is the girl quite unprotected that you placed in his waggon?"

"Quite," said the captain, a vague sense of alarm rapidly creeping over him.

"Was she young and pretty?"

"She was more—she was beautiful."

"And had she articles of any value about her?"

"Nothing much. I think, as well as I can remember, she was attired with great plainness. But what is your reason for asking all these questions? Tell me at once—do not keep me a single moment in suspense."

"I don't want to alarm you needlessly——"

"There, there," said the highwayman, quivering with excitement, "I want no preface!"

"Well, then, I regret to tell you that Jack Battersby, the driver of that waggon——"

"Yes—yes!"

"Is about the most ferocious and unscrupulous fellow that could be found within ten miles of the place. I don't believe he would stop short at any atrocity. He is a brute in human shape."

"How comes it, then, that he has respectable employment?"

"Old Hunkers likes him. He keeps him up at his lonely farm-house yonder, and looks upon him much as I should a bull-dog or a mastiff. He believes he would defend the property he has got hoarded up and is too miserable to enjoy, and so when Master Jack gets into any scrape, which he is always doing, Old Hunkers gets him out of it."

Captain Hawk rose, and paced the room impatiently.

"You feel a great interest in this young girl?"

"Can you doubt it?"

"Well, then, I am sorry. I do not want to alarm you; but it would be false kindness to hide the truth, and you would be the first to blame me for it."

"Well—well?" said the highwayman, whose anxiety now was all but insupportable.

"Then I do not exaggerate when I tell you that you might as well trust a lamb with a wolf in a hut all night and expect to find all safe in the morning as to leave a young girl at the mercy of such a monster as Jack Battersby."

"Good Heavens!"

"He would think nothing of maltreating her in the worst way possible. You understand me, captain? Or if she had articles of value about her, he would not scruple a moment, when he had the opportunity, about murdering her, and putting her body where no one would find it."

As these last awful words rung in his ear, Captain Hawk uttered a deep groan, and, completely overwhelmed sank into a chair, where he remained, unable to move.

The landlord was not a little alarmed at the result of his communication.

"Come, come," he said—"perhaps things are not so bad as I have made out."

"Hold—hold! No more of such delusive consolation as that! Good Heavens! To think I should have placed her so wholly in the power of such a fiend, and then have broke my promise of keeping watch and ward over her! I feel the worst has happened. A presentiment comes over me, the force of which is irresistible, that she is lost, and I—I am to blame: it is my fault!"

"No—no, captain, don't say that. It wasn't your fault. How were you to know what kind of man he was?"

"No more—no more. My horse — take me to my horse!"

"No—no. You are mad!"

"I shall be if you obstruct me."

"But you know not what you say. You would rush upon destruction."

"No matter. I may be too late—I feel that I am; and yet I will not miss the chance of saving her At any rate, I can have vengeance upon the dastard who has dared to lay a finger on her."

Captain Hawk's vehemence greatly alarmed the landlord, who had never before seen the highwayman in anything like such a state of excitement.

Indeed, some species of madness seemed to have taken possession of him.

"My horse!" he said, furiously. "Where is my horse?"

"Listen to me."

"I will not listen to a word!"

"But the time!"

"Yes—yes, it is hours too late."

"You are right. The night has gone. In two hours it will be daylight."

"I did not mean that. But I will delay no longer. Since you will not move, I will find the horse myself."

"Calm yourself!" cried the landlord, who saw that any further opposition would be unavailable. "Subdue this terrible excitement, and act more calmly."

"Calmly, man! How can you stand there and prate to me of calmness? To the stable, I say—to the stable!"

The landlord pushed his portly body through the door with inconceivable alacrity.

The stable was reached in a few moments.

The highwayman's impatience increased rather than abated.

It was by far too great to allow the landlord to put on the trappings, and the haste which he made himself in caparisoning Satan only defeated its own object.

Still, in a wonderfully short space of time the gallant steed was in readiness for the road.

Captain Hawk led him to the low wall over which he had leaped on his arrival, and here he mounted.

As full of fire and spirit as many a horse would have been who had had a week's rest in the stable, Satan cleared the obstacle before him.

A faint cry arose.

It came from the ostler, who was amazed at the captain's sudden departure.

It might well astonish him.

The highwayman heard the sound and knew its meaning; but could not stop a moment for a word of explanation.

He had but one idea before him, and that was the rescue of the young girl.

In imagination he saw her struggling with the villain to whose charge he had been unfortunate enough to consign her.

The thought was maddening.

He felt that he was responsible for any harm that might happen; and if any befel her, he should never cease to blame himself.

But these reproaches, however severe, would not undo the mischief when once committed; and it was with a vague and only half-entertained hope that if he made haste he might yet be in time that caused him to urge Satan along the high-road at the full stretch of his extraordinary powers.

His own danger, great as it was, he quite unheeded.

It was submerged utterly in his intense excitement.

Dawn was breaking, but he recked not for this. Had it been broad daylight, he would not have swerved from his course one jot.

One idea occupied him to the absolute exclusion of all others.

But still, as he galloped onwards, something like calmness and reason came over him, and he first of all began to be conscious that he was not taking the best and most sensible course to achieve his end.

This feeling grew stronger and stronger, and, influenced by it, he drew in the rein more and more.

But just when he had succeeded in moderating Satan's headlong speed, a loud and thrilling shriek came upon his ears.

CHAPTER LXVI.

THE OFFICERS MAKE A DESPERATE ATTEMPT TO CAPTURE THE BLACK HIGHWAYMAN.

The ludicrous adventure the Black Highwayman had had with the valiant colonel of the Berkshire Yeomanry served to chase away from his mind many of the melancholy and angry feelings which had possessed it.

When he witnessed the total discomfiture of the gallant young man, another burst of laughter came involuntarily from his lips.

"Come—come," he said, "I think this will do. I will not push matters any further; and besides, for Phantom's sake, I wish to keep out of sight just now, in order that he may have a rest."

After one glance at the young man, he again turned round, and, at a rapid rate, rode along the high-road.

The morning by this time was so far advanced that it is greatly to be wondered at he did not meet more people on his way, but this was accounted for by the fact that he was in a very thinly-populated part of the country.

Still, he looked out for some means of quitting the main road; and coming presently to a cross-road, he at once availed himself of it.

"If this should lead to a retired inn, now," he said, "I

should begin to consider that Fortune was favouring me indeed."

But he rode on for a long distance without passing anything save trees and hedgerows.

His impatience was great; but he consoled himself with the fact that since he had turned down the cross-road he had not met with a living creature, and therefore the officers would be more than ordinarily sagacious if they got upon his track.

It was soon after this that he came upon the object he so wished to see.

This was a roadside inn—a very dilapidated structure, composed entirely of wood, but so old that it seemed as though every moment it must fall bodily forward into the road.

In the distance, on the summit of some rising ground, could be seen a tapering spire, and a little to the left of this the huge arms of a windmill.

"I am not far from a village," muttered the highwayman; "but this place seems lonely and quiet enough in all conscience. I may go very far before I find a place more likely to suit my purpose."

The beat of his horse's feet must have been heard; and, judging by the fact that the whole household turned out at the front-door to observe his arrival, it may be inferred that it was but rarely that such a spectacle as a mounted traveller was to be observed.

Lord Harcliffe, without the least hesitation, rode at once up to the horse-trough and paused.

The landlord, who had not expected such a piece of good fortune as this, was so confused that for the moment he could neither move nor call out to the shock-headed urchin whose multifarious duties comprehended that of ostler.

But recovering himself, he rushed forward, at the same time bawling out lustily to the boy.

Lord Harcliffe descended from the saddle, and as he did so he pointed towards the sign-post, saying:

"I see by that that you profess to have good accommodation for man and beast. I want to stay here for a few hours; but before I enter I will go with you to the stable just to see what accommodation you can give my steed."

The landlord made a very low bow at the end of this speech, and then, in most respectful tones, he said:

"Be kind enough to follow me, sir. I will lead your horse myself."

He took hold of the bridle as he spoke, and led the way to a small wooden shed, only a trifle less dilapidated than the inn itself.

Nevertheless, on entering, the Black Highwayman found the place to be by far more comfortable than he had expected to find it, and Phantom was soon at his ease.

"A private room," said Lord Harcliffe; "and bring me a bottle of the best wine you have."

"Certainly. Be good enough to step this way. You see, the Stranger's Rest looks but a poor place from without, but you will find it better than you expect inside."

Lord Harcliffe found himself ushered into rather a dark but neatly-furnished room, where everything appeared to be scrupulously clean.

The landlord quickly produced the bottle of wine, and while he was drawing the cork Lord Harcliffe said:

"This appears to be a very quiet spot. You don't have many passers-by, I suppose?"

"Only on market day, sir, and we are tolerably busy then. On other days sometimes we go for hours without seeing a soul go by. Is there anything more I can do for you?" he added.

"Nothing more," was the reply. "I shall probably wait three or four hours, in order that my horse may rest himself, and during the time I should wish not to be disturbed."

"No one will intrude upon you, sir; and if you will only slip the bolt when I go out, you can then guard effectually against any interruption."

On the departure of the landlord, Lord Harcliffe at once took advantage of this hint, and then went to the window.

This looked out upon the road in the front of the inn, and on the window-sill so many climbing and flowering trees were growing in little red earthenware pots as to form a screen dense enough to enable anyone within to keep a good watch outside without the least fear of being seen.

Here he remained for some time, but as he saw nothing but trees and fields he flung himself into an antique and capacious easy-chair.

Leaning his elbow on the arm of the chair, and half covering his face with his hand, he gave himself up to deep and anxious thought.

Who can say what strange reflections occupied his mind?

They were of no pleasant nature judging by the anxious expression of his countenance and the contraction of his brow.

But the quiet which reigned around him insensibly drew him off into a slumber.

Many hours had passed since he had closed his eyes, and all those hours had been full of exertion.

No wonder, then, that, thoroughly overcome and overpowered, he should sink off to sleep.

Entire oblivion existed for some time, but as his fatigue wore off his mind began to renew its activity, and frightful dreams invaded his slumbers.

Then came a distorted repetition of his adventure with the young colonel, who, finally waving his sword, conjured up a troop of armed men, who at once prepared for action.

Then Lord Harcliffe felt as though some insensible power held him to the ground, preventing him from making the slightest movement to escape.

Closer and closer his foes closed round him, until at length, with a sudden start, he awoke.

He was much confused at first, for the room was involved in semi-darkness, and he could not precisely remember where he was and what had last happened.

Moreover, an unusual stir was going on somewhere close at hand.

As he recovered possession of his faculties more and more, Lord Harcliffe could distinguish voices engaged in a loud dispute.

Cautiously rising, he crept carefully across the darkened room in the direction of the door.

He listened.

"I tell you," said a voice, "that the squire is just like a madman; and as for his son, I think he has done nothing but blubber ever since. Don't you think things have come to a fine pass, landlord, when a squire's son is robbed and ill-treated by broad daylight on his own property?"

"No doubt about it."

"Well, as I told you before, the squire has offered a hundred pounds out of his own pocket to whoever will capture this daring robber and bring him before him."

"And you are going to try to earn it, eh, Stephen?"

"Yes; myself and these I have with me. We all think the reward quite large enough to stand dividing, and as we are not short of pluck we ought to be a match for one man."

"Yes—yes! What sort of a man was he?"

"Why, the young colonel can only describe him as a pale, thin gentleman mounted upon a black horse."

"A black horse you say! Whew!"

The landlord indulged in a long whistle, but before he could well get to the end of it, he and the rest all started, for a desperate clatter came upon their ears.

"Goodness above! What's that? It can't be the French come at last, can it?"

In a body the whole party went to the door, and no sooner did they reach it than a large troop of horsemen pulled up with a sudden dash.

This was an event such as had never before been witnessed at the Stranger's Rest, and the landlord was so amazed at it that he forgot all about what he was going to say, namely, that a tall, thin gentleman, who had arrived on a black horse, was at that moment seated in one of the private rooms.

"Hullo, there! Where's the landlord?" cried one of the new-comers, in a very loud and commanding tone of voice.

"Here I am!" said that individual, pushing his way forward. "What is wanted?"

"Let us have some hay and water for our horses, and be quick about it, for we have no time to lose—not a single moment!"

"All right. Bob—Bob, you villain! Come this way with a truss of that new hay out of the loft; and as for water, I'll soon supply you with that."

There was a long horse-trough in front of the inn, and at one end of this was a pump.

To the handle of this the landlord applied himself vigorously, and the trough was soon full.

"Now for some ale; and while we are drinking it, just answer a question or two, will you?"

"I will if I can, with all the pleasure in life," replied the landlord.

"Very good. But just look at this bill. Mind, it is wet, for it has not long been printed. You had better hang it up inside the house, in the most conspicuous place you can think of."

"What's it about?" asked the landlord. "I am no sort of a scholar. It would take me a week to spell through all this."

"Well, you see 1,000*l.* at the top, don't you?"

"Oh yes."

"Well, that is the reward offered for the capture of the celebrated Black Highwayman, who has been found out at last, and who has had a narrow escape of capture."

"The Black Highwayman!" said the landlord, in mingled interest and alarm. "He has not been seen anywhere about here, has he?"

"Indeed, but he has, though; and I should advise you to keep a sharp look-out upon all travellers. He is very likely to try and find shelter at an out-of-the-way place like this."

"You don't say so?"

"Yes—nothing is more likely. And, in order that you may not fail to recognise him, should he come this way, I will briefly describe him to you as a perfect gentleman, with a particularly pale face, which is almost expressionless. In his manner he is as quiet as a tiger; and he rides an unusually large, magnificent black horse, such a creature as is only seen about once in a lifetime."

The landlord staggered back until he went bump against the pump.

His jaw fell, and he seemed on the point of saying something without having the power to articulate.

"What ails the fellow?—what does he mean?" asked the principal officer.

"A thousand pounds!" gasped the landlord.

"I say," cried the man Stephen, who was a stalwart fellow in the garb of a gamekeeper—"blow me if this Black Highwayman fellow is not the same that robbed the squire's son on the high-road yonder, and by the broad light of day, too!"

"What—what is that you say?"

The landlord in the meanwhile, although too excited to speak, pointed frantically to the window of the room in which his strange guest was.

But no one understood his motions; and Stephen, the gamekeeper, repeated almost word for word what he had said to the landlord.

"By Heaven!" cried the officer, "that is our man—there cannot be a doubt about it. My lads, we are in luck's way!"

"Yes, yes!" screamed the landlord, whose tongue now was suddenly unloosed. "I have seen him—I have seen him!"

"Where—where?"

"Here!"

"Here?" cried the officers, in chorus, and drawing their pistols the while. "Which way did he go?"

"He is in there," he replied, pointing to the window. "I peeped through the keyhole not many minutes ago, and saw him fast asleep in the arm-chair."

The explosion of a bombshell right in the midst of the party could scarcely have caused more astonishment than the landlord's speech.

A moment elapsed before the officers were fully able to realise what they had heard.

Then, with a general shout, they flung themselves from their saddles, and dashed towards the door of the inn.

A cry from the landlord again arrested them.

"Look—look! There he is! He has got out somehow! Quick—quick, or he will be off!"

The landlord was pointing with his finger, and, of course, all looked in that direction.

Ejaculations came from every throat.

There was the Black Highwayman beyond all shadow of doubt.

He was in the yard at the side of the inn, close to the stable door, and in the act of securing some portion of his horse's trappings.

How he had contrived to get there seemed not a little mysterious.

The room in which he had been sitting had but one door, and as the window was close to the horse-trough it was impossible for him to have escaped through that.

But the explanation of this seemingly wonderful occurrence was simple enough.

The Black Highwayman, upon hearing the clatter of so many horses' hoofs, at once hastened to the window, and saw at a glance that an unusually large party of police officers had arrived.

He did not linger at the window an instant, but returned to the door.

All appeared still on the other side, so he opened it carefully.

He then saw that all the inmates of the inn, without any exception whatever, had hastened to the front door, in order to be auditors and spectators of what was going forward.

Such being the case, it was the easiest thing in the world for Lord Harcliffe to step out of his room into the passage and close the door after him.

This done, he with rapid strides made his way to the back of the house.

He was not without the hope that he should be able to reach the stable in time to caparison his steed before the officers knew anything of his presence.

In this he was very nearly successful.

When the landlord caught sight of him and attracted the officers' attention, he was in the act of tightening the girth.

When the police officers saw him, they rushed forward with the utmost impetuosity.

But the buckle was secured, and the highwayman, quick as lightning, put his left foot into the stirrup.

Before he could do more, the officers were upon him.

The foremost seized him tightly round the waist.

This made the act of mounting impossible.

Lord Harcliffe knew it, and wisely removed his foot.

He knew then if he escaped it must be by some sudden effort performed before the whole body could pounce upon him.

With an ease and strength for which his captor was not prepared, the highwayman wrenched himself free, and then clenching both his fists, by a couple of well-directed blows, delivered almost simultaneously, stretched two of his enemies upon the ground.

But there were others near, intent upon making him their prisoner.

One held Phantom's rein tightly in his grasp.

Another of those terrific blows disposed also of this adversary, and then Lord Harcliffe cried out to his steed:

"Away—away!"

With a sudden plunge, the animal bounded forward, the highwayman meanwhile clinging tightly to the saddle.

One officer attempted to hold on, but a heavy kick, which must have demolished no inconsiderable number of his teeth, sent him sprawling backwards.

At the same moment that he reached the ground, the Black Highwayman vaulted into the saddle.

"Fire—fire!" cried the one in command. "Fire—fire! If you can't hit him, cripple his horse—we are sure to have him then!"

Those words reached the ears of Lord Harcliffe, and they raised such a tempest of fury in his breast as cannot be described.

His eyes seemed to flash with fire, and his usually impassive countenance was distorted with rage.

Turning half-way round in the saddle, he drew the remaining pistol from the holster, and aiming it at the coward who had spoken, pulled the trigger.

The highwayman's aim did not waver in the least.

The sharp report of the firearm followed, and the chief officer, with a smothered shriek, fell helplessly forward on to the neck of his steed.

The other officers, who had held their pistols hesitatingly in their hands, now discharged them.

A rapid change of position, however, at that instant effected by the highwayman, rendered all the bullets quite useless.

"Me you have a right to hunt," he cried, in clear,

ringing tones, that were distinctly heard by everybody; "but beware how you touch my steed!"

He slackened the rein as he spoke, and away the gallant creature flew.

Horse and rider seemed instantly to be swallowed up by the darkness.

On the part of the officers there was no little confusion and terror.

The unlooked-for fate of their leader alarmed them all, and they crowded around anxiously, as though more interested in knowing whether the injuries were fatal ones than pursuing the highwayman.

Of course Lord Harcliffe made the best use he could of the time thus given him.

He had but little trouble to urge Phantom forward, for the noble animal was well refreshed by the long rest it had had, and covered the ground more in the manner of a greyhound than a horse.

Lord Harcliffe was a splendid horseman, and sat in his saddle like a rock while going at this tremendous pace.

It was not long, therefore, ere he got quite out of the reach of his enemies, who, when they recovered themselves sufficiently to commence a pursuit, had not even the clatter of the horse's hoofs to guide them.

Feeling himself at a safe distance from them, Lord Harcliffe reined in, for it was by no means his wish to distress his steed unnecessarily.

"Now, then," he said, "to work my way towards London. Pharoah I must and will see at once. If I allow time to elapse, it may become impossible. Besides, those fellows would never guess that I should take this direction."

At a rapid trot, which, however, he knew Phantom could keep up for a long time with very little exertion to himself, Lord Harcliffe made his way in a tolerably direct line towards the northern outskirts of the metropolis.

The night was unusually dark, and at frequent intervals the chilling wind that was blowing would bring upon its wings a dash of rain, which made it most unpleasant to be abroad.

Consequently, on this night the roads were all but deserted.

Presently, however, Lord Harcliffe caught a faint sound, which caused him to pull up and listen intently.

"As I expected," he ejaculated, as soon as a lull of the wind took place. "I fancied I could hear horses' feet. Who is approaching?"

The squally gusts in which the wind blew made it very difficult to listen with any amount of precision.

But before many moments had elapsed, Lord Harcliffe had arrived at the conclusion that a large party was approaching, and that the men who composed it were well mounted and armed.

Whether they were police officers, or whether their presence in that spot had anything to do with himself, he could not decide.

At any rate, he judged it expedient to pause.

"If I could only see some suitable place handy, where I could stand with Phantom," he said, "all would be well. Then, even if they were seeking me, which is doubtful, they would pass on without having the least suspicion of my being near at hand."

This was probable enough.

But it became quite certain that if he was to conceal himself at all, it would be necessary to do so without loss of time, for the horsemen were coming along at a smart pace, and in between the gusts of wind they appeared to be alarmingly close at hand.

Close to where Lord Harcliffe paused, a cross-road ran at right angles along the highway.

His first thought was to go down a little way either to the left or right, and wait there, but almost immediately afterwards he reflected that the horsemen might be going in one of these directions, in which case he could not fail to be discovered.

The only other course that lay open to him was to enter a meadow by the roadside, and conceal himself behind the hedgerow.

Accordingly he did so.

The meadow was gained by means of a gate, which he closed carefully after him, and then, with Phantom's bridle over his arm, walked as closely as he could to the densely-planted hedge.

This was quite enough to conceal both from any but very close observation, and this was not what he had to fear.

At the same time, the boughs were not so closely grown as to prevent him from seeing partially into the roadway.

Keeping as still as possible, he looked in the direction from which the horsemen were coming.

For some reason or other, they had moderated their pace, and came on either as though they were inclined to make a halt or else felt doubtful as to their further course.

Lord Harcliffe grew rather more anxious, and leaned still further forward, for he was aware that a conversation was being carried on.

As yet, however, they were not near enough, and the wind was too blusterous for him to catch a single syllable of what they said.

They came closer.

The first words he heard distinctly were these:

"We must be close upon the cross-road now, sir, that I was speaking to you about. I don't think it can be twenty yards further."

"And it is a good deal used, you say?"

"Oh yes."

"Then I think that, upon due consideration, the best thing to do will be to act upon your suggestion. I did not like the idea of dividing our force, nor do I now, on account of the desperate character of the man we have to deal with. Still, we had better divide than lose the chance of finding him altogether."

"Oh, I think it will be all right, sir—I don't feel at all afraid. You see, all the roads from here to London are so well patrolled that it is scarcely possible for him to make his appearance at any point without being seen."

"Well, well! Recollect, all of you, that when any discovery is made an immediate alarm is to be given, so that we can concentrate our forces."

This was assented to, and the whole party, which walked by the hedge behind which the highwayman stood, passed on until they reached the cross-road that we have already mentioned.

Here they came to a halt, and there was a little confusion about effecting a division.

Lord Harcliffe now had good cause to congratulate himself upon not having obeyed his original impulse of riding along the cross-road, because had he done so his danger would have been imminent, while now he looked upon it as all but at an end.

That it was himself to whom they alluded he had not the smallest doubt, although they had not once mentioned his name.

He remained profoundly still.

The division into four parties was at length made.

One portion went to the left, another to the right, a third went straight on, while the fourth retraced their steps, riding for the second time past the highwayman's place of concealment.

Nothing, however, occurred to lead them to suspect that anyone was near.

Neither Phantom nor his master stirred, while the darkness was by far too profound to enable them to see more than a dozen paces in advance.

Gradually the sound of their horses' feet died away in the distance.

"So they are determined to have me, are they?" muttered the Black Highwayman, as he slightly shifted his position. "Well, we shall see! To London I am determined to go, though if all the roads are watched in anything like this manner, it will be a task of no little difficulty. I can scarcely think the watch is so close as this, because—— Ah!"

The last ejaculation escaped his lips with great suddenness, for he felt a heavy hand laid with no little force upon his shoulder.

CHAPTER LXVII.

THE BLACK HIGHWAYMAN FINDS HIS PERILS AND PERPLEXITIES INCREASE AT EVERY STEP.

If one event more than another was calculated to disturb anyone's equanimity this was. Yet such was the command that Lord Harcliffe habitually exercised over himself, that he did not for a moment [illegible] his self-possession.

[CAPTAIN HAWK'S ENCOUNTER WITH THE WAGGONER.]

That the person who had seized him was one of his foes scarcely admitted of a moment's doubt.

How he had managed to come upon him so quietly was more than he could surmise.

"So I have caught you at last, my fine fellow, have I? Don't make a fuss; your little game is stopped, and you may as well take it easy as not. Master will make an example of you, make your mind easy about that."

"Your master?" said Lord Harcliffe, quietly, for he felt assured there was some mistake. "Master? For whom do you take me?"

"Come, come!—that's good! I like that much! Here, Bill, show the light, and let us have a look at our customer!"

No sooner were the words uttered than a dark lantern was produced, the full glare of which was turned upon him.

"Hallo!" cried the first speaker. "Blow me—here's some mistake! But, come! what do you want in the meadows at this time of night? Don't you know you are trespassing?"

The light of the lantern, though puzzling at first from its great brilliancy, now showed Lord Harcliffe that the men who had stolen upon him at unawares were two gamekeepers.

"You took me for some poacher, I suppose?" he said. "But you are convinced of your mistake. It may be, however, that you will be questioned whether you have seen me. Divide that among you, and say no."

As he spoke, Lord Harcliffe threw at the feet of the two men the heavy purse of gold which he had taken from the valiant colonel.

The action surprised the men not a little, for by the aid of the lantern they could see the glittering of the gold coins.

Before they had time to recover from their amazement,

Lord Harcliffe, with that peculiarity which he had more than once displayed, swung himself into the saddle and galloped off over the meadow, for his quick ear had caught sounds which indicated the approach of one of the patrolling parties.

No doubt their attention had been attracted by the exhibition of the light.

"If those fellows will only hold their peace about me, and merely say they are looking for poachers," reflected the fugitive, "that little accident may turn out very favourably to me indeed. But that is almost too much to expect. I must make the best use I can of my time."

After what he had heard, the Black Highwayman came to the conclusion that it would be wisest to avoid all roads as much as possible, and make his way towards London across the open country.

He believed that he was familiar enough with the country to be able to do this with tolerable certainty, in spite of the darkness of the night.

"They must be aware, by all these precautions, that I am no longer in London," he said; "and if I can once run the gauntlet of all these armed parties, I shall doubtless be able to get to my own mansion without difficulty. They would never believe in the probability or possibility of my returning there; and so I question whether I shall have a guard of any sort to contend against."

One would think the motive was a very strong one that made his lordship willing to encounter the many dangers that lay before him in his enterprise of reaching his house in Piccadilly.

How far he was right in his surmises about the guard time alone can show.

He was startled by the sharp report of a couple of pistols fired almost simultaneously.

Then the roar of voices came to his ears, and he saw the lantern waved furiously.

"Those fellows have betrayed me," he said; "and those pistol shots are doubtless an agreed-upon signal for all the others to make for that spot with the utmost speed. But no matter, I have an excellent start; and if I do not fall foul of any other party all will be well."

He glanced somewhat anxiously before him as he spoke.

It was no trifling matter to ride at such a rapid rate through the darkness, depending for safety entirely upon the sagacity of his steed.

"Confound it!" he cried, suddenly. "A newly ploughed-up field! This will never do. To cross it would fatigue him more than an hour's hard gallop on the high-road. We must avoid this somehow."

To do so on so dark a night as this was no easy matter; but after straining his eyes for a moment, he made out the position of the hedge, towards which he hastened with all speed.

Here, as he fully anticipated, he found the earth to be much firmer, though still Phantom's feet sunk in deeply at every step.

"You shall walk," he said, as he pulled the rein; "it will make but little difference, and this will be quite as formidable an obstacle to my foes as to myself. One thing is certain—if they attempt to ride fast across it their horses will founder, and there will be the end of the chase."

It was without question Lord Harcliffe's best policy to keep his horse only at the walk while crossing the ploughed field.

This proved to be of rather unusual extent.

A narrow brook, to which he came at length, divided it from a meadow; and when this obstruction was leaped over, the highwayman's progress became easy enough.

He turned his head to ascertain the whereabouts of his pursuers.

As they carried lighted lanterns, there was no trouble about this.

The lights could be seen flashing here and there as though they were tracking the highwayman by his horse's footmarks, which, of course, they were easily able to do.

"I need trouble myself no further about them," Lord Harcliffe said, as he loosed the rein. "It is in vain for them to think of overtaking me. All I have to be careful of is not to run across any other party."

Keeping entirely to the fields held out at least the hope that he would be able to do this.

His pace was now terrific.

Never had the extraordinary powers of his matchless steed been exhibited in greater perfection than on this night.

In an incredibly short space of time his pursuers with their lanterns were wholly lost sight of.

Away—away he went, with a recklessness which no one would have displayed in a less desperate state than his.

An hour elapsed.

During the whole of that time he never once drew rein, nor did his horse show the least signs of exhaustion.

How many miles were passed over in this interval would be hard to say; but when he pulled up, the lights of London could be seen twinkling dimly in the distance.

"Well done, brave boy!" he cried, patting Phantom's neck, now slightly wet with perspiration. "Bravo, old boy! That was well done! Our pursuers are distanced, the other officers avoided, and here we are within sight of London! Well done—well done!"

There is no animal except the dog that knows so well as a horse does when words of encouragement and satisfaction are spoken to it; and Phantom now seemed ready to fly off at full speed again, in order to earn the reward of a few more syllables of praise.

But his master kept a firm hold upon the bridle.

"Quietly!" he said. "Steady, now! The remainder of our journey requires even more circumspection than the former. Gently—gently!"

Not without a little difficulty, the Black Highwayman succeeded in reducing his horse to a trot—that magnificent trot which in so many cases had been proved to be a more rapid rate than ordinary horses could gallop at.

Away—away, still over the open country, preserving almost a straight line, only diverging from it indeed when there was some such object as a dense plantation in the way.

Every now and then he would come upon the high-roads and lanes; but only to cross them, disappearing almost as soon as seen.

The lights of London grew plainer still.

The success which had attended him in his efforts to avoid his foes—a success so much greater than he had dared to hope for—had a most inspiriting effect upon him, and encouraged him still more to try well to carry out the perilous plan of operations he had laid down.

The conviction was very strongly impressed upon his mind that he should find London the safest place to be in.

The officers, as was known to everybody, had chased him many miles into the open country, and all would rely upon the patrolling parties to keep him away from London, should he attempt so unlikely and suicidal a thing as to enter it.

Whether the Black Highwayman was or was not right in thinking no particular look-out would be kept up for him in the metropolis, succeeding events will quickly show.

He was now very close indeed to the huge city.

His nearest and best means of gaining admittance to it was by passing through Tyburn Gate, and he once thought of taking that direction.

But feeling the importance of keeping out of sight of everyone, he made a considerable detour; and then, by riding at random over the gardens attached to the few houses then standing in and near the Oxford Road, he managed to get almost in a straight line to Piccadilly.

It was only just at dusk, as the reader will remember, when he started from the public-house, and now that he was fairly in London it was no more than nine o'clock.

A century and a quarter ago, except in summer weather, the streets of London were all but deserted at that hour, for there were scarcely any lamps even in the most important thoroughfares, and the darkness afforded such facility for the execution of robberies and deeds of violence of all kinds, that no one ventured to stir abroad after night had fairly set in except under the protection of an escort.

This was a state of affairs very favourable to Lord Harcliffe, who made his way along the silent streets with even less difficulty and danger than he would have experienced in traversing one of the country lanes.

He went on quietly, for he had not yet decided what to do with his steed.

It was running no slight risk to trust him out of his hands at all; but for this there was no help—it as unavoidable.

Such being the case, then, he was most anxious to select some place where, to the best of his knowledge, Phantom would be safe, and where he could, if necessary, place his hand upon him at a few moments' notice.

The most obvious place was some livery stable not far distant from his house; but then there was a strong probability that some person or other about the premises would recognise him.

"I must run that risk," he said; "it will be worth while to do so. I can make a few trifling alterations that will baffle an ordinary observer, and then I shall not be likely to be suspected, simply because no one will believe in my presence in London, and, least of all, so near this spot above all others."

The reader will not fail to observe how much importance the Black Highwayman attached to this circumstance; it was, he considered, the greatest element of success.

It chanced that there was a livery stable close to the spot where he had been making these reflections, and as he had quite decided upon his proceedings, he rode up to the gateway and rang the bell.

Dismounting, then, he pulled his hat well down over his eyes, and bent forward, so as to assume a stooping gait, which was strikingly at variance with his usually erect attitude.

The next moment half of the gate was opened.

"I want to leave my horse here for a few moments," he said to the ostler, and taking care to speak in an assumed voice.

"Very good, sir," answered the ostler, touching his hat, for, dark as it was, he could see that the horse was a costly animal.

"Do not remove either saddle or bridle," continued the highwayman, as he reluctantly surrendered the rein. "Just wash his mouth out, and then expect my return, as my business, I expect, will not occupy many moments. I shall not forget to reward you for your trouble."

So saying, Lord Harcliffe, still taking care to preserve his stoop, walked quietly away.

How great an effort it cost him to put on this air of indifference, and never once to look back to where he had left his steed, no one could tell save himself.

He was glad to turn round the first corner that presented itself, in order to be out of sight of the gateway.

"I don't believe the fellow suspects me," he murmured; "and Satan there is hardly any fear he will recognise, for I have never brought him to London before. If he will only obey my injunctions, all will be well."

The clock in the old Palace of St. James's chimed half-past nine.

"I must be moving," he said, as the jangling sounds came upon his ear. "There is much to do, and time flies fast."

He walked on a little faster; but to have seen him exhibiting so much outward calmness, no one would have believed that there was a reward of a thousand pounds hanging over his head.

The narrow street down which he was walking led into Piccadilly, and emerged on the side opposite to the one on which Lord Harcliffe's mansion was situated.

"There cannot be much risk in walking past," he said, "and I shall then have a good opportunity of reconnoitring."

But he saw nothing to recompense him for his trouble.

From top to bottom, the dwelling was plunged in profound darkness.

This seemed to make him hesitate as though he had expected that the building would present a different aspect.

He walked on some paces irresolutely.

But suddenly coming to a determination, he said.

"No matter—no matter. My original plan, I feel assured, is a good one, and I will not allow this appearance—which, after all, may be deceptive—to turn me from it. No—no. What I had intended, I will perform to the letter. There cannot be a safer course."

Without appearing to do so, he cast a glance up and down the wide thoroughfare.

But, save a solitary watchman in the distance, who was bawling out the hour, not a human creature could be seen.

"All is well," he said. "Fortune favours me."

As he spoke, he crossed the road, and then turned down the first turning that he came to.

Along this he did not pass more than twenty yards before he again turned.

The street which he now entered was narrow and silent, and ran parallel with Pall Mall.

By walking on, he knew that he should pass the back of the mansion.

CHAPTER LXVIII.

LORD HARCLIFFE ACQUIRES SOME IMPORTANT INFORMATION FROM THE LOQUACIOUS BARBER.

In all this street, though it contained many shops, there was only one window in which there appeared a light, and even this twinkled dimly, despite the conspicuousness which it obtained from being the only light within view.

Lord Harcliffe knew that little shop well, though he had never crossed its threshold or paused a moment to look in at the window.

But that house happened to stand exactly at the back of his own mansion, and it was this circumstance which had brought it under his notice.

"He is not closed yet," he muttered, as he strode more rapidly towards the twinkling light. "In a little while longer, though, I should have been too late."

He came to this conclusion because he observed as he drew nearer some one was putting up the shutters.

Walking past, he pushed open the door and entered the shop with all the ease and indifference in the world.

No one, to the best of his knowledge, had seen him enter, and this increased his confidence wonderfully.

The shop was a hair-dresser's and barber's—at that time a more important trade than it is at present, in consequence of the almost universal use of wigs by men and of elaborate head-dresses by ladies.

Lord Harcliffe calmly took off his hat, and seated himin a wooden arm-chair, opposite to a looking-glass.

The barber, who had given over expecting any more customers that night, had already retired to his snug little parlour behind the shop; but now he emerged, all bows and smiles.

"Good evening to you, sir!" he said, rubbing his hands briskly together. "Glad to see you—very. Would you have the kindness to excuse me a moment while I light another lamp?"

Now, there was quite as much illumination in the shop as Lord Harcliffe cared about, and he by no means desired that it should be increased.

By the languid way in which he spoke, it was hard to think the point was of so much importance to him.

"Pray do not on my account," he said. "I feel sure the light is quite sufficient to enable a practised artiste to do what I require."

"Well, I—a—yes. In a manner of speaking, I think I am; only, you see, sir, most young bloods who come here are so over particular about every trifle, and are never satisfied unless the whole place is ablaze with light."

"You will not find me so unreasonable and exacting, then. All I want you to do is to rid me of this stubbly beard, which I have been obliged to neglect for a day or so."

"Just so, sir. Fortunately, my water is still hot, so I shall not have to keep you waiting a single moment."

"I have only just come up to London from a long way in the country," said the Black Highwayman, observing that the barber stared inquisitively at his apparel, which was much travel-stained, "and what has got me into this trouble has been a brush with a highwayman."

"A highwayman! Good gracious, sir! You don't say so?"

"I assure you it is a fact, as the pickle my clothes are in will testify. But I flatter myself the rascal for once in a way met with his match. He demanded my purse, but, though he rolled me in the dirt, he did not obtain it."

"You were more fortunate than most people are," said

the barber, flourishing his razor. "Surely it could not have been the Black Highwayman, about whom all London is just now ringing, that attacked you?"

"Black Highwayman!" repeated Lord Harcliffe. "I don't know about that. But whoever he may be, his tricks will be stopped for a day or two, for the wound I inflicted upon him, though probably not mortal, will lay him up for a day or two beyond doubt."

Upon hearing this account, which was given so quietly as to convey at once an impression of its truthfulness, the barber drew back a little, and looked at his guest with much more respect than he had hitherto done.

"It is to be wished that you had settled him altogether, sir. There have been fine doings in London, sir. I assure you I don't recollect the town ever being in such a state of excitement before. But of course you have heard all about it?"

"No; on the contrary, I have not heard a syllable. I have come from a considerable distance, and no town news whatever has reached me."

"Ah! then, sir, you will find the place all agog, sir. You must know that for a long time past all the principal roads leading out of the metropolis have been visited by a highwayman, who succeeded in robbing everyone he attacked; and there was a wonderful deal of mystery, too, as to where he came from and where he went to. But, as I had all along expected, the mystery came out one day; and who do you think this great highwayman turned out to be?"

"Really," said Lord Harcliffe, as he wiped the lather off his chin with a towel the barber handed him at the moment, "I have not the slightest idea."

"Why, sir, then you will hardly believe it when I tell you he turned out to be a lord."

"A what? Nonsense, man—you are jesting!"

"I never was more serious in my life, 'pon honour. You will find on every side my words will be confirmed. There is no doubt about it. The mysterious highwayman and this young lord have been proved to be one and the same."

"But what on earth could make a lord turn a highwayman?"

"There, now, sir, you have asked me a question indeed."

"What do you mean?"

"Why, the real cause for such a thing is not at present known; but, as you may suppose, there is plenty of conjecture, all of which may be very wide of the mark."

"What is your opinion?" asked Lord Harcliffe, who fancied it might be possible to obtain information of some importance from this man.

"Ahem!" said the barber, stroking his chin with an air that implied that he could say a great deal if he pleased. "You must know, sir, that I am peculiarly fitted to express an opinion on this engrossing subject, and—ahem!—I believe I am very near the mark."

"Indeed! You interest me greatly. Suppose you have a try to restore my wig to something like order; and while you are doing so I should be glad to hear what you have to say."

The barber was, of course, delighted.

By this time it should be stated that the shutters had all been put up by the boy, who now stood waiting.

"You can close the door," said the barber to him, "and go downstairs."

He then set himself to work upon Lord Harcliffe's wig, which, considering the state it was in, promised to require no slight amount of attention.

With more interest than the barber supposed, his late customer waited for the expression of his opinion.

"In the first place, sir, I must tell you that the house—or I suppose I ought to say mansion—lately in the occupation of this highwayman lord is precisely at the back of my house."

"At the back of your house?"

"Yes; the houses stand back to back, and are only separated by a narrower space than you would imagine. The mansion fronts Piccadilly; my humble shop fronts this narrow, dirty back street."

Lord Harcliffe received this perfectly well-known piece of intelligence as though it had been the greatest novelty in the world to him, and waited for what was coming next.

"Consequently," continued the barber, "it not only has happened that I have been situated so as to see a little, but also to hear a great deal."

"Just so."

"Well, I used to wonder at one time—long before anything of this kind came out, you know—I say I used to wonder where all the mint of money came from that this young lord used to lavish. You observe, sir, I say lavish—not spend: lavish is the word."

"He was very extravagant, then?"

'Extravagant! I assure you that word is very ill-chosen to express the idea of his expenditure, yet I can't think of a better. The English language is short of a word, sir."

The barber's tedious and diffuse way of telling what he had to say was supremely tiresome to Lord Harcliffe, who had to exercise all his self-control to overcome his impatience.

"The waste and riot that went on is extraordinary. Money only seemed to be looked upon and valued as the commonest dirt. Thinks I to myself that won't last long, though I confess I was far from thinking events would at all take the turn which they have."

"You did not guess he could be playing the part of a highwayman?"

"Lor' bless me, no! That I should have thought as too wildly improbable. That serves to show how careful we ought to be in judging of things. Well, what was oddest to me before the crash came, was that I had ascertained that Lord Harcliffe's father—the earl of something or other—was a very poor nobleman, living for the most part on the Continent in a very penurious fashion, so I was certain that it could not be from him that this prodigal young lord derived his wealth, and I was puzzled to think where it did come from."

The barber paused; but his customer did not make any remark.

"Well, sir, you understand it all now. This needy and impoverished young nobleman, in order to keep up his position and live like those in his own station of life who were not short of cash—he took to the road, and levied contributions on them; and very cleverly he managed it to remain not only undiscovered but absolutely unsuspected for so long."

"And what has become of him now?"

"If I could only lay hands upon him, sir, it would be just one thousand pounds in my pocket."

"Is that the amount of the reward?"

"Yes."

"He is still at large?"

"Yes, though his capture is expected every hour. It can't be very long delayed, I am certain of that."

"Why?"

"Because of the extraordinary precautions which have been taken. If he does elude the authorities, I shall be quite ready to believe he is more than mortal."

A mocking smile appeared for a moment at the corners of Lord Harcliffe's mouth.

He was wondering what would be thought of all the boasted precautions taken should it come to be known that he had actually returned to his residence.

But Lord Harcliffe had now greater need still to be well upon his guard, for all that the barber had said previously was no news to him; now all that further fell from his lips would be entirely fresh.

He could hardly trust himself to speak.

"Not the strangest part of the affair is, that this highwayman lord, as I suppose I must call him, was captured once and conveyed to Newgate, from which prison he vanished in the most mysterious and incomprehensible manner. It has set afoot all kinds of superstitious tales; but those who are likely to know a good deal about such a matter say that his escape was brought about by connivance, and a certain high personage, whom it would be very unwise for me to name, has been implicated in the affair in a manner very discreditable to him. What truth there may be in this part of the affair I am not in a position to say."

"And that is all?"

"Yes, that is all. And here is your wig, sir—finished so far as I can finish it to-night. It wants a thorough dressing, which service I hope to have the pleasure of performing at any future time that may suit you."

"Very good," said his lordship, rising. "And what

about this house? I suppose the officers have taken possession of it?"

"Oh yes, sir, I believe you! That was done at once."

"And—and," said his lordship, with just the least unsteadiness in his voice, "and what have they discovered?"

"That I should be glad to know, sir; but for some reason or other that I am not acquainted with, the utmost secrecy is observed."

"Indeed!"

"Yes. That very active and highly-intelligent police officer, Mr. Peterson, was in my shop this morning. He is in possession there, sir; but though I used all my arts, not a word of information could I get out of him anyhow."

Lord Harcliffe was deeply disappointed.

He had thrown out the supposition about the police officers, not that he expected such was the case, but rather to lead the barber on with the subject.

Therefore the intelligence came upon him as an unexpected shock.

A moment, however, enabled him to recover his composure.

He would have given much to have inquired what had become of his faithful ally, Pharoah, but dared not do so, because the mere fact of asking such a question would clearly show that he was not such a stranger about the matter as he professed to be, and consequently suspicion would be at once aroused.

This fact, and the disturbance caused by learning that Peterson was in possession, rendered him unable to think of an excuse for remaining longer.

The barber bowed him to the door with an amazing amount of deference.

"How very dark!" he ejaculated.

"Yes, dark indeed! This street always does seem doubly dark when my shop is closed. Being a stranger, sir, I make bold to hope that you have not far to go, for London streets are anything but safe after dark."

Lord Harcliffe glanced up and down the dark, deserted street, and hesitated.

CHAPTER LXIX.

LORD HARCLIFFE CARRIES OUT HIS DESIGN, AND HAS SOME PERILOUS ADVENTURES ON THE HOUSE-TOPS.

"I AM a perfect stranger," said Lord Harcliffe; "and now you speak of it, I remember I have often heard how people from the country have entered the City, and have never been heard of again."

"Yes, sir; and there are, no doubt, terrible traps into which the unwary may fall. But, of course, you have decided where to pass the night?"

"Indeed I have not," was the reply.

"You have not?" ejaculated the barber, in great astonishment.

"No. You see, I have come up to London on a very peculiar errand. I have a gentleman to see in the morning; and to-night I intended to pass at some respectable lodging-house. But for that confounded highwayman, I should neither have been in this pickle, nor half so late!"

The barber stroked his chin.

"Perhaps you can assist me in my difficulty," added Lord Harcliffe, "for I can assure you I have not the least idea which way to turn. Do you know of any lodging-house near?"

"Yes," was the reply, "I know of several; but just at this time of the year they are almost certain to be full."

"But is there any neighbour who would accommodate me for a single night? I will pay liberally—— Or, stay, you may have a room in your own house that you can spare for one night?"

"Ahem! sir—well, really, I have not."

"You have not," said Lord Harcliffe, his voice unmistakably expressive of deep disappointment—"you have not?"

"Not one that I should like to offer to a gentleman like yourself."

Lord Harcliffe drew in his breat as though his heart had been lightened of a heavy load.

"You will not find me at all particular," he said, with an impatient gesture. "Anything in the shape of a room will do for me; and rest assured I shall not overlook the value of such a favour, for I know how to estimate the security and comfort of sleeping under a respectable roof."

"Then, sir, if that is the case, pray come in."

Lord Harcliffe willingly obeyed.

The shop-door was closed and fastened.

"The greater part of my house is let out in apartments," explained the landlord; "but we have one poorly-furnished little back attic. Into this myself and my wife will go, and you can have our room."

"Not upon any account! I will not consent to such an arrangement for a moment. Rather than do so I would wander forth and take my chance of finding a shelter where I can."

"But——"

"Let me have the back attic which you mentioned; no matter how small or how poorly furnished it may be, it will do for me. You appear to be an honest man, so I do not mind telling you that I carry a large sum of money with me, and it is most important to me that it should be safe."

"It will be all right here," said the barber, anxiously. "And since you wish for the back attic, why the back attic you shall have."

"I am deeply obliged to you."

"You will only permit me to place it in order a little?"

"No—nothing of the sort. I do not wish any preparation. Besides, I am half dead with fatigue; and if you will show me up at once, I shall esteem it a very great favour."

"Your wishes in this respect, as well as in any other, shall be attended to," said the barber, respectfully.

"Many thanks. I have travelled many miles, and I think nothing in the world will keep me from sleeping like a rock."

Lord Harcliffe was quick sighted enough to perceive that the barber's manner had changed somewhat since he had mentioned the money, as though his cupidity had been excited thereby.

But to this his lordship attached but little importance, for a reason which will presently be seen.

"Then you will not require any refreshments to-night, sir?"

"No—none whatever: I am too weary."

"Then since it is your wish, I will show you at once upstairs."

Lord Harcliffe eagerly prepared to follow the barber, for much more time than he had anticipated had already been consumed.

That he had some ulterior object of great importance in taking so much pains to obtain lodging in the barber's house the reader of course feels certain of.

What he intended to do will very speedily be seen, for the barber without further delay lighted a candle and led the way to the upper rooms.

The house was a high one, and as the barber was not of very active habits, he had to pause more than once to gain breath.

At last the attic was reached.

A miserable place, in good truth, it was, and the barber might well hesitate to offer it to any guest.

There was only one place where it was possible to stand with anything approaching to comfort.

The barber broke out into more apologies.

But his guest cut him short.

"Believe me," he said, "this will suit admirably. Safety is my chief concern, and that I feel assured of. Good night."

Thus addressed, the barber could do nothing save respond to the salutation and take his departure.

Lord Harcliffe watched him as far down the staircase as he could under the pretence of lighting him with the candle, and as soon as he was hidden from view he turned round and fastened the door.

The only means of doing this was by the aid of a couple of strong bolts, which were perhaps almost as effective as a lock could have been.

Great rapidity now characterised all Lord Harcliffe's movements

His first act was to extinguish the candle.

Then hastening to the window, he opened it silently.

At the very moment he did so he heard a clock begin to strike.

He paused to listen.

"Eleven o'clock," he said, when the last of the jangling sounds had died away on the night air. "I almost thought it was later, though that, no doubt, was the effect of my impatience. I am now in capital time, and unless my luck changes all will be well."

The night was dark and disagreeable, and looked particularly so from where Lord Harcliffe stood.

The sky was covered with leaden-coloured clouds, and the wind howled dismally among the gables and chimney-pots, while every now and then a few drops of rain would come dashing down.

At first he had some difficulty in making out the objects by which he was surrounded, but it was not long before his eyes got accustomed to the obscurity

"It is there," he said, as his eyes rested upon the pile of building in front of him. "The question is, how shall I make my way across the chasm?"

The problem was a difficult one, and yet Lord Harcliffe did not hesitate very long.

He watched first of all most carefully in order to make out if possible whether there was any person who could observe his movements.

But all seemed still.

"Unless there should be some confounded officer of police lurking about, all will be well enough, for on such a rough night as this is, all the people would take care to keep indoors."

Yet he watched.

The clock he had heard strike now chimed the quarter-past.

"Time flies," he said. "Now is the time to take the first step towards the accomplishment of my design."

The barber would have been greatly surprised had he seen his weary guest quietly and adroitly draw himself through the little lattice casement, and then cautiously slide down the steep tiled roof until he reached the low parapet wall.

Here he paused again, but only for a moment.

Crouching down so as to avoid all possibility of being seen, he rapidly crept along, surmounting in a moment the wall which divided the barber's house from the one next to it.

On reaching the third house he came to a stop.

The fourth was in course of repair, and a great quantity of scaffolding had been erected.

Of the existence of this he had not previously been aware, and he considered a little before proceeding further.

Looking closer, he saw that the back wall of this house had been propped up, and that in order to keep it still more secure in its proper position, two huge beams of wood had been extended almost horizontally from it, and wedged tightly against the wall of one of the opposite mansions—the next but two, indeed, to the one occupied by Lord Harcliffe.

Upon making the discovery of the beams, he murmured:

"The question is, shall I carry out my original intention of creeping along to the end of the street, and then making my way over the roofs where they are connected by the hotel, or shall I run the risk of creeping over one of these beams? I think I can do it."

But the feat which Lord Harcliffe so calmly contemplated was one that most men would have hesitated to attempt.

The beam of wood was not more than twelve inches square, and it might not be fixed with sufficient security to bear his weight.

Besides, the depth to the ground was something awful to behold—enough to make the head swim, even when protected from falling by the parapet wall.

How, then, must it be to attempt to cross a narrow piece of wood with nothing for a side support, and with a wind that every now and then seemed to blow with force enough to sweep him from the perilous position?

Lord Harcliffe thought of all this, and the more he thought the more inclined did he feel to make the venture.

In making his way over the roofs of so many houses, he ran the serious risk of being heard by some of the inhabitants.

On the beam, supposing he made the passage in safety, he would only be exposed to view for the space of a few moments, and it was almost a question whether his dusk form could be perceived from the ground below.

"Come what will," he said, as the clock now chimed half-past—"come what will, I will lose no more time, but make the trial."

The top of the beam was something like six feet below the edge of the parapet wall, and the only means by which it was practicable to gain it was by going cautiously feet foremost, over the parapet wall, then, holding tightly to the coping, lower himself down until his feet rested on the narrow bridge.

And this was the feat which Lord Harcliffe set about accomplishing.

As calmly and quietly as though within a couple of inches of the ground instead of more than fifty feet, he bestrode the wall, and then, drawing both feet to one side, safely let himself down until he felt the beam beneath his feet.

As soon as this was the case he, with unspeakable daring, released his grasp upon the edge of the coping stone.

His position now was dangerous in the extreme.

There was but little more room than he required to stand upon, and yet, while at that giddy elevation, and without anything to hold by with his hands, he had to turn completely round, for, of course, as he now stood his back was turned in the direction he wished to go.

But even this was safely done, and but for the darkness and the violence of the wind he might have walked in an erect position across the fearful abyss.

Very wisely, however, he crouched down on his hands and knees, and then, grasping the edges of the beam firmly, he crept on.

But once when he endeavoured to look beneath him, a faint sound having reached his ears, his brain reeled, and he all but lost his balance.

After that he took good care to keep his eyes steadfastly fixed upon the beam at a point about six inches in advance of his hands.

And so he crossed over in safety.

The heavy beam, partly owing his weight and partly to the furious wind, swayed and creaked alarmingly.

But it kept its place.

When the wall of the opposite house was before him, Lord Harcliffe managed to get once more upon his feet.

Then holding his arms at full stretch over his head, he found himself just able to grasp the coping stone above.

It was a perilous thing, too, to trust his weight in this manner to a piece of stonework which had doubtless been exposed to the weather for many a year.

But Lord Harcliffe, apparently without giving this a thought, put forth his strength and gradually drew himself up until able to fling one leg over the summit of the wall.

When that was done he felt that he was safe, and drew a long breath of exquisite relief.

"My hope is," he said, "that I shall not have to find a road back that way. I do not think I could run such an awful risk again."

He shuddered from head to foot, for at this moment, happening to look down, he formed a better estimate of the distance to the ground.

"No more of this," he said. "It is a weakness, and I must not give way to it. Let me confine myself to what I have to do."

So saying, he turned his head, and adopting the mode of progression which we have formerly described, he made his way along the gutter until, after the lapse of a few moments, he had the roof of his own mansion beneath him.

At this point he paused to listen, in order to make sure that it was safe for him to go further.

CHAPTER LXX.

CAPTAIN HAWK IS JUST IN TIME TO RENDER THE HEIRESS ANOTHER SERVICE.

When that loud and awful shriek came upon the ears of Captain Hawk all the blood in his veins seemed to turn to ice, and while the shriek lasted his heart stood still.

But when the shriek came again, as it did a few moments afterwards, the effect produced upon him was entirely different.

His blood seemed literally to boil, and, uttering a startling cry, he just touched his heels against Satan's flanks.

But the cry to which he had given utterance was enough to inform the intelligent creature that something was amiss, and no sooner did he feel the slight pressure we have mentioned than he bounded off at full gallop.

Where the shriek had come from Captain Hawk could hardly tell, except that it was somewhere in advance.

His doubts upon the point were quickly set at rest, for, upon quickly turning a corner of the road, he beheld a sight which filled him with the utmost fury.

Drawn up to one side of the road was a huge waggon.

Three piebald horses were harnessed to it, and the highwayman immediately recognised the vehicle as being the one in which he had persuaded the young heiress to ride to London.

At the back of the waggon was the driver, and struggling in his arms was the young girl.

She was not screaming now—it seemed that she was too exhausted and too terrified to utter another cry.

All her energies seemed to be concentrated in one act, which was clinging tightly to a round upright bar of iron that was fixed at the back of the waggon.

The grasp she had taken was the tenacious one of despair, and, despite the wonderful strength possessed by the man, he was unable to tear her away.

Moreover, the thundering clatter of Satan's hoofs came upon his ears, and caused him to look up irresolutely.

Captain Hawk came on like a whirlwind, and before the man could make up his mind what to do he flung himself from the saddle and rushed forward.

He disdained to make use of any other weapons than those with which Nature had furnished him.

Clenching his fists, then, he, with greater suddenness than was expected, delivered such a blow upon the waggoner's ear as to make a thousand stars dance before his eyes.

Then, before the effects of that were anything like recovered from, another on the opposite ear was dealt, if possible with greater force than the first, and a third alighting on his nose laid him prostrate.

Captain Hawk was victorious, not having sustained the slightest injury, while his adversary seemed as though some time would have to elapse before he was able to rise.

The young girl was so maddened by extreme terror that at first she did not recognise her preserver.

Captain Hawk, however, without loss of time hastened to her side.

He was just in time to receive her fainting form in his arms.

She had held out to the last moment, and now, when she found that she was really saved from her brutal opponent, her feelings gave way completely.

Captain Hawk was rather alarmed at her condition, and could not all in a moment make up his mind how to act.

"Let me think," he said. "The distance from here to the Greyhound is a mere trifle. Can I do better than get her before me on the saddle as soon as possible and ride back to the inn at full speed?"

After a very brief consideration the highwayman concluded that as things stood this was the best thing he could do.

The young girl's weight was a mere nothing to him, and, raising her in his arms, he laid her—though, it must be confessed, rather awkwardly—across the front part of the saddle.

Then, mounting, he placed her head to lean against his shoulder, and clasped her tightly round the waist with one arm.

Away they flew, Satan seeming to be quite unaware that he carried a double burden.

But Captain Hawk was rather deceived about the distance he had to go.

In his excitement he had taken no heed of distance, and in returning, when every yard seemed three, this was the more apparent.

At length, however, the roof-tops of the old hostelry met his view, though when they did so it was fairly daylight.

But Captain Hawk's thoughts were so entirely absorbed by his charge that he never once gave it a thought that it might be possible for some prying police officer or other to see him.

The young girl had not once made the slightest movement.

Her eyes were closed, and her appearance was just as it would have been had Death really claimed her for his own.

The first person the captain saw on gaining the vicinity of the inn was the faithful ostler.

He had learned some particulars concerning the highwayman's errand from the landlord, and therefore he exclaimed, in tones that were indicative of the utmost satisfaction:

"So you were in time, captain?"

"Yes, as you see. Is the coast clear?"

"All is well, captain. I'll guarantee that at the present minute there is not a police officer within half a mile of the place."

"That is well. Where is the landlord?"

"Here I am!" said Tom Beckford, making his appearance. "But what's the matter? The poor young thing is not killed or even hurt, I hope?"

"No, I think not; only fainted from excessive fright. Just assist me while I dismount."

The landlord sprang forward, and by his aid the highwayman was quickly on the ground.

But he would suffer no one to touch the young girl save himself.

Raising her tenderly in his arms, and leaving Satan to the sole charge of the faithful ostler, he cried:

"Lead on, landlord! Move that carcass of yours with what speed you can! The sooner we are inside the house the better!"

For more reasons than one, the landlord thought so too; and it was truly ludicrous to observe the efforts he made to get over the ground quickly.

"Where's your wife, Tom?" cried Captain Hawk. "I have not seen her yet, but forgot to inquire after her health."

Tom Beckford uttered a groan as he replied:

"Ah! captain, she was away on a visit when you were here before; but now she has come home, and you must expect to find things somewhat different."

He spoke in tones of comical distress.

"Oh, never mind, Tom! Your better half and myself have always been on the best terms up to the present moment, and I daresay we shall continue to be."

"Well, we shall see," answered the landlord, with a doubtful air.

"What do you mean?"

"She encourages the green-eyed monster; and when she sees that tempting little creature, lor' bless me! there's no saying what she will do."

Just at this moment the inn-door was gained, and Captain Hawk crossed the threshold with his insensible burden in his arms.

"Hoity-toity!" cried some one, in tones that were wonderfully like the screeches of a Scotchman's old bagpipe. "Marry come up! Here's fine doings indeed! What's the meaning of all this? Get out!"

"My dear madam——" said Captain Hawk.

"Don't madam me! Get out, I say!"

"But——"

"Get out, I tell you! I won't have nothing of the sort in my house, so I tell you plump to your face, without going behind your back to say it!"

"But this is Tom Beckford's house."

"Oh! is it? I should just like to see him come forward and say so! Tom Beckford's house, forsooth! Where is the great skulking hippopotamus? Let him come forward and show his nose if he dare!"

But Tom Beckford, so far from coming forward, only shrunk back, and tried to conceal and shelter himself behind the highwayman.

There could be no doubt about his dread and alarm, and there was something so truly ridiculous about it that, although Captain Hawk was in anything but a merry mood, he could not refrain from bursting out into a loud peal of laughter.

Tom Beckford could not have been much under six feet in height, and must have measured something like the same round the waist, while his shoulders were so wide that there were very few doorways through which he could walk without turning sideways.

His arms were of enormous size, and his hands not much smaller than an average-size shoulder of mutton.

He was indeed a perfect giant; and, as often happens when men outgrow their natural dimensions of human nature, he was as gentle and simple as a child, and never thought of contending for mastery in anything.

His invariable practice was to submit—it was so much less trouble than opposition, and he hated everything in the shape of worry with a most cordial detestation.

But then his wife—what a wonderful contrast she presented to him in every particular!

It has often been remarked that we are attracted by our opposites, and a greater confirmation if the statement could not have been seen than by simply placing the landlord and his wife side by side.

They were opposite in every way.

Mrs. Beckford was unnaturally spare and thin, and measured no more round the waist than her husband did round the wrist. She was at least eight inches below the average height of her sex, and was the most restless, fidgety being in all creation.

She was here, there, and everywhere with unquenchable supervitality, or, as her husband expressed it when sure she was not within hearing, "like a parched pea in a porridge-pot."

She was the main-spring of the whole establishment, and most absolute master over her bulky husband.

"Ah! you may well hide yourself!" she continued, perceiving that Tom showed no signs of coming forward. "You know very well you are down-right ashamed of yourself!"

Tom Beckford did not deny it, nor would he have denied anything else she might have thought proper to say.

But Captain Hawk, who was exceedingly anxious concerning his charge, took the first opportunity he had to put in a word.

He knew he would have to be conciliatory, for if the little lady thought fit, there would be no stopping there for him.

"Mrs. Beckford," he said, "I have always noticed that, superior to the rest of your sex that I have fallen in with, you have always been willing to listen to reason."

This adroit speech mollified the landlady considerably, and she prepared to listen somewhat graciously to whatever else her guest might have to say.

"You see this poor young thing," he continued. "Is it not sad to think that she is worse than alone and friendless? The one who ought to be her protector and second parent is her bitter foe, and would take any desperate step to deprive her of life. He has almost succeeded once, and would have done but for me. But you see the state to which the poor thing is now reduced. She stands badly in need of that assistance which none but one of her own sex can render her. I know you have not an unfeeling heart, so tell me where I can place her so as to receive your attention?"

The landlady was impressed by the captain's manner; but her voice was just as sharp as ever when she said:

"Take her upstairs, and leave her to me—you know the way."

Captain Hawk did not need twice bidding.

The dark old staircase was rapidly ascended; and kicking open the first door he came to, he placed her in a large arm-chair.

"Now leave her to me," said the landlady, pushing him from the room, for the captain would fain have lingered until she showed some signs of returning consciousness.

"Remember, she's quite a lady," he said, as he crossed the threshold, "and the heiress to much property. You may depend she will not forget those who lend her a helping hand in her present circumstances."

The landlady was not a mercenary woman, yet we must state that she was by no means displeased to hear that there was a reasonable prospect of reaping some substantial reward for her efforts.

"It's only a swoon," she said, banging the door in the captain's face. "I'll soon bring the young madam out of it pretty quick, never fear!"

But the captain departed perfectly satisfied.

He knew that her roughness of manner was only seeming, not real

He found Tom Beckford at the bottom of the stairs, rubbing his huge hands together and looking amazingly delighted.

"Egad! captain, I'd give a pound of my flesh if I could only manage my wife like you can. But, mark me, captain, there's no mistake about it, she's a wonderful woman. I know it. That's why I am so fond of her, and that is what makes me do just what she says, and makes me let her have her own way in everything."

"Tom," said the well known shrill voice, "how dare you stand there talking such rubbish when there are so many things to be done? Be off, you great mountain of flesh—be off at once!"

As meekly as a lamb, Tom Beckford retreated, and when he entered a room he closed the door behind him, so as to make perfectly sure of not being overheard.

"Captain," he said, "we shall be able to have a little talk now, I think."

"I hope so," answered the highwayman, laughing.

"You don't know how much I have been thinking about what you told me of the appointment you overheard made here by those two fellows in the wood. And, captain——"

"Well?"

"May I never taste ale again if I can make it out a bit!"

CHAPTER LXXI.

THE TWO STRANGERS KEEP THEIR APPOINTMENT AT THE GREYHOUND.

Captain Hawk laughed at the landlord's perplexity and impatience.

"Control your curiosity," he replied. "If you cudgel your brains ever so much, rely upon it you will get no nearer to the truth than we are at present."

"I fear not."

"There is one comfort, however, which is, that we have not a very long time to wait."

"Several hours."

"Yes; and that reminds me that just at the present moment nothing in the world would be so acceptable as a bit of a rest."

"I daresay not, captain; you must want it badly enough. Come along with me, and, rely upon it, I will make you comfortable. Isaac the ostler will give timely warning of danger, so you can go to sleep with a contented mind."

Captain Hawk knew that this was nothing more than the truth, and never could the assurance of such safety have come more welcomely upon his ears than on this occasion.

Now that all excitement was past, a kind of faintness would seize upon him at frequent intervals, which threatened to terminate in a swoon.

Tom Beckford saw his condition and understood it, so, without delay, he conducted the captain upstairs.

"You had better try the old turret again," he said. "It is not the most comfortable chamber in the household—that I know very well; but it is the safest."

"Yes—yes," said the captain, languidly. "Just where you please."

The little square landing-place was soon reached, and then it was as much as Captain Hawk could do to ascend the ladder.

But at length the trap-door was shut down and locked, and the ladder restored to its secret hiding-place.

"If I had a mind to play false with him," murmured Tom Beckford, as he slowly descended the stairs, "there would not be much trouble about it now. But he is safe with me—quite safe. I would not have one hair of his head injured for all the world."

His thoughts reverted then to the mysterious appointment, and he quickly became helplessly involved in hopeless speculation.

He placed himself at one of the front windows of the inn, and, lighting his pipe, awaited with what patience he could the coming of the mysterious guests.

In the meantime, Captain Hawk, too much exhausted to remove a single article of his clothing, no sooner locked the door than he threw himself upon the bed, and, closing his eyes, fell instantly asleep.

How long his slumber might have continued is hard to say; probably many hours longer than it did had he not been interrupted.

[PERILOUS POSITION OF THE BLACK HIGHWAYMAN.]

It was just about sunset, when a loud and vigorous knocking coming faintly upon his ears, and mingling with his dreams, caused him to turn over and over uneasily.

The knocking was persistently continued—if possible, with increased loudness.

But some time elapsed before Captain Hawk realised that the troublesome knocking was intended to arouse him.

The thought of danger caused him at once to start up and gaze around with only a very confused idea of where abouts he was.

"Captain—captain," said a voice, which sounded as though it came from the bowels of the earth—"captain—captain! If you don't answer me, I'll break the door open! Awake—awake, I say!"

The highwayman recognised the voice of Tom Beckford, and that helped him more than anything else to a remembrance of where he was.

"Coming—coming!" he said. "What the deuce is the matter?"

"Why, enough, I should think! Confound it, man! if the police officers had arrived, and I wanted to warn you ever so, how on earth could I do it?"

"Do you say the officers are here?"

"No, no. But suppose they were! Just unlock the door, will you? I have something to say. And mark me, I will take particular notice, another time, to keep the key myself, and then I'll wake you, I'll warrant!"

"No more grumbling," said the highwayman, as he raised the trap. "Now tell me what you want! It was too bad to disturb such a sleep as that without good reason."

"Sleep, do you call it? Well—well! But never mind. Don't you see how dark it's getting?"

"Yes—yes!"

"And have you forgotten——"

"What?"

"Who we expect here this evening?"

"Oh! confound them!"

"Yes; so say I, for my poor brains ache with thinking over the matter."

Captain Hawk laughed.

"Come on down, do; and then we shall be prepared."

"It is too early to expect them yet."

"I don't know about that. There is nothing like being prepared. Besides——"

"What?"

"Why, that young lady—for she is a young lady, I can tell you that——"

"Well, what of her?"

"She has been asking for you."

"Asking for me?"

"Yes."

"Where is she now?"

"Down in my own sitting-room, sitting there like an angel waiting for you; while you, forsooth, must needs be snoring up here, like a great boy."

"Never mind. I am coming. But look here, Tom—I do hope that you have not let fall a single word or hint that would lead her to suspect who I really am?"

"No, that I have not; but it has been because I have never thought of it."

"Well, since it is not too late, let me give you the caution. She has not the least suspicion of my identity, nor would I let her for worlds."

"Enough. And there is one other person you might—ahem!—just drop a delicate hint to. Do it carefully, captain, in your own style."

"Who do you mean?"

"Why, Mrs. B., to be sure."

"Oh, ah! Do you think she has mentioned it?"

"I can't tell. You had better speak as soon as you have the chance."

Captain Hawk now had very serious misgivings that his secret was a secret no longer.

While the little conversation we have recorded was in progress, Captain Hawk had been very busy at work making such improvements and alterations in his toilet as circumstances permitted.

A few minutes made a wonderful difference, and then, with an unaccustomed fluttering of the heart, the highwayman followed the landlord down the stairs.

"Is Satan all right?" he whispered.

"Yes; make your mind easy about him."

The next moment a door was opened, and Captain Hawk saw the young girl reclining in a comfortable arm-chair close to the fireside.

No sooner did she catch sight of him than, with a flush of colour suffusing her countenance, she rose, and taking him by the hand, poured forth her protestations of gratitude.

Captain Hawk was so overcome with confusion that he was not able for a moment or two to interrupt her in what she was saying.

"You magnify the service I have performed," he said.

"No, no," she answered, warmly, "I do not magnify it, nor the danger in which I was when you arrived so opportunely. Words are too poor to thank you, my preserver; nor shall I ever forget how much I owe you."

"Lady," said the captain, with the profoundest respect, "you have said already too much, even had the services I was so fortunate as to have the opportunity of rendering been twice as important as they really are."

"No—no; I cannot, and will not think that. Oh! if you only knew what I have suffered from the villain from whose grasp you rescued me!"

"Nay, do not thank me for that."

"Not thank you!"

"No; for I am to blame. It was my neglect that caused it all. I ought to have been at hand."

"I am glad things are as they stand, for had you seen me earlier you might have been impressed with false ideas of my safety."

"Indeed, lady—how?"

"Do not call me lady. Surely you, although I know you not, have done enough to warrant you in addressing me less formally. Call me Blanche."

"I—a——"

"I ask it as a favour."

"Then I cannot refuse."

"I must tell you," she added, with a simplicity and grace charming in the extreme, "that after you had left me, I felt, oh! so lonely and so miserable! A thousand fears beset me, and in every trifling sound I fancied I could hear my guardian in pursuit, and I trembled from head to foot with terror, for I knew I should be helplessly in his power."

"I was to blame for all that."

"No—no. It was unreasonable—most unreasonable upon my part to think that you could devote yourself entirely to my service. You had already done a thousand times more than I had a right to expect."

Captain Hawk made a gesture of dissent, and said:

"May I ask what it was that might have given me a false impression of your safety?"

"Why, before you had left me very long, a man called out to the waggoner, in the same way as you did, asking him for a ride, and offering to pay him liberally for it.

"The driver, after a little hesitation, stopped, and the new-comer crawled in at the back of the waggon. I felt timid and terrified, and he seemed a good deal surprised at seeing me."

"But he was a stranger?"

"Oh yes—a man who looked as though, at some time, he had been well off, but that he had met with misfortunes and become poor. He took off his hat respectfully, and hoped that I should not find his presence an intrusion."

Captain Hawk was deeply interested in this narrative.

The young girl only paused a moment for breath, and then went on:

"His manner was full of deference, and I soon lost my terrors, for I felt that in the event of any danger he would side with me. He told me that he was an actor, that he had been unfortunate, and that he was working his way towards London, where he had hopes of obtaining an engagement. His story brought tears to my eyes more than once. He told me he was too poor to travel by the stage, but that he should be able to pay the waggoner for his lift as far as Huntingdon, in which town he hoped to earn a little before he resumed his journey."

"And did he leave you at Huntingdon?"

"Yes. I was sorry to part with him, but did not like to ask him to remain. However, out of my slender purse I paid for his ride, but I could not prevail upon him to receive a farthing. His pride prevented him from accepting alms. The waggoner was by when I took out my purse, and what took place afterwards reminded me of the strange look which I saw come over his face."

Captain Hawk's fists involuntarily closed tightly.

How he wished he had got that rascally waggoner within reach!

"Go on," he murmured.

The young girl observed his agitation.

"We left the town," she continued. "And when I remembered that the man had said he was only going a few miles further I began to look out for you, my preserver, and to wonder how it was so long a time had elapsed without seeing you. I looked out continually, and my heart sank when I saw you not."

The young girl paused, and Captain Hawk could tell that she had reached the critical point of her story.

"We travelled slowly on until, at length, towards morning, we reached a lonely, solitary spot. To my dismay, when in the darkest and loneliest part of all, the waggon stopped and the driver descended. He drew aside the canvas at the back, and said, roughly:

"'Come, miss, you must get down here.'

"'Down here? Are you going no further?'

"'Not a yard. Come on!'

"I was so terrified I knew not what to say and how to act.

"I murmured forth something about seeing you.

"The fellow only answered by a curse that made my blood run cold, and rudely demanded my money.

"I thought he wanted nothing save what I promised to pay, and I reached forth my purse.

"But before I was aware of his intention, he snatched it from me, and consigned it to his own pocket.

"I begged—I entreated—I implored him to give it back, telling him that it was all I had, and that if he took it from me and left me on the road, I knew not what would become of me.

"But he answered only with a brutal laugh, and demanded, in addition, all the articles of value that I had about me.

"Oh! how I longed to see you, my generous preserver! I feared that you had fallen a victim to my uncle's violence, for in no other way could I account for your absence after the assurance that you gave."

Captain Hawk was overwhelmed with remorse.

"I refused to comply with his demand," she went on, "and then he threatened me with violence.

"But seeing, as I thought, an opportunity of escaping from him, I sprang suddenly from the waggon into the roadway, and darted off with all the speed I was able to make. But it was in vain. He was fleeter of foot than I was, and seized me with such violence that I almost fainted with pain and fright.

"By an effort, however, I recovered myself, and screamed aloud, in the hope that the sound would reach your ears.

"But all was still.

"I now implored him to release me, and offered to give him every trinket and jewel I had; but he only laughed a horrible, brutal laugh, which almost deprived me of all power.

"He told me he would take them when he wanted them, and, in spite of my struggles, dragged me back towards the waggon.

"He was stronger than I, and he succeeded.

"Then he tried to force me back into the vehicle; but I saw the piece of iron at the back, and clung to it with convulsive energy.

"He tried to force me away, but I determined rather to let him tear my hands off. It was then that I heard a horse approach, and my heart told me who it was. That redoubled my strength. The rest you know. It is to you and you only that I owe my escape from a fate a thousand times worse than death."

"To me!" said Captain Hawk. "Instead of thanking, rather blame me for being the cause of all this mischief. I shall never—never——"

At this moment some one tapped lightly at the door.

The next moment the landlord showed himself, his whole frame quivering with excitement.

"Captain—captain," he said, in a suppressed voice, "there's one of them come!"

CHAPTER LXXII.

CAPTAIN HAWK'S PLAN DOES MORE HARM THAN GOOD.

BLANCHE seemed a good deal surprised at the landlord's manner and at the strange words to which he gave utterance.

She glanced up at Captain Hawk, and saw that the interruption had caused a deep frown to settle upon his brow.

"Come now," continued Beckford. "Don't lose a moment, I beg of you—come—come!"

"Pray pardon this interruption," said the highwayman, smoothing over his looks as well as he could. "I cannot stay now to explain matters, as I gladly would; but on my return——"

"You will not be long?" she said, with anxious eagerness.

"No; a very short time, I assure you. In the meanwhile, remain here, and rest assured that beneath this roof, it will not be possible for any harm to come to you."

The girl could plainly see that there was a mystery of some kind afoot; and her heart readily yielding to terror, told her that in some way it concerned herself.

Captain Hawk's words, therefore, failed to reassure her, and she witnessed his departure along with the landlord with the utmost depression of spirits.

Tom Beckford closed the door.

"Sorry to break in upon you, captain," he said. "I did not know you were quite so agreeably engaged."

"Hold—hold! No more of that."

"Well, well, you ought not to mind what I say; and, lor' bless me! how can I help having eyes in my head, I should like to know?"

Captain Hawk did not vouchsafe any answer to this question; and the landlord chuckled as though he had said some very witty thing indeed.

"Where are they?" said the highwayman, turning round suddenly.

"They? Don't I tell you there is only one of them come!"

"Well, and where is he?"

"He asked for a private room, so I have put him into the oak parlour; and then he asked for a bottle of wine."

"You took it him?"

"Yes."

"And what sort of a looking man was he?"

"Well, captain, when he first came I was a little bit flustered at seeing him, and didn't take particular notice. I only saw that he was well wrapped in a travelling-cloak."

"You did not recognise him?"

"No. I feel almost certain he is a stranger in these parts."

"And what next?"

"When I took him the wine, I spoke about bringing lights, but, in a deep, hoarse voice, he said it was light enough for him, and that for the little time he was going to stay he should prefer to sit in the dark.

"He only begged if any stranger called, to show him in without delay."

"And is that all?"

"Yes. I could not find any excuse for lingering after that, so came and disturbed you. You don't mind it now, I can tell; and you can finish your——"

"Silence—no more!"

"No offence, captain—no offence."

"Then let us keep to the business under hand. The man is in the oak parlour, you say?"

"Yes."

"And the other has not arrived?"

"Not at present."

"And he told you if a stranger came, he was to be shown in to him?"

"Yes."

"And was that all he said?"

"Yes."

"He gave you no description of the person he expected?"

"None at all."

"Then I will have a look at this stranger, and very likely interchange a few words with him."

"Gracious powers, captain! what do you mean?"

"You need not look so scared, man."

"Yes; but what do you mean? To force yourself in upon him would spoil all."

"Not a bit of it. You have only to introduce me as a stranger just arrived, asking for one with whom he had an appointment here this evening."

"And what then?"

"Why, your guest will find out that I am not the person he expected to see. I shall make an apology for intruding upon him, and there will be an end of the matter."

"But what will he say to me?"

"Not a word of blame, certainly. Don't you see, it is quite possible for two parties to have appointments here to-night."

"And what special advantage shall you gain from this?"

"I shall have the opportunity of getting a tolerably good look at this mysterious stranger, and perhaps I may discern something that may put me on the scent of their intentions, about which I am just as much in the dark as you are."

The bare possibility of being able to bring to a close the horrible suspense he had endured for so long was more than sufficient to remove any objections which the landlord might have had to the highwayman's proposed course of action.

"Come on," he said, "and don't stay long."

"Why not?"

"For fear the other should come."

"That is just the event I should like to happen, because then I should be able to see them both face to face."

The landlord could not understand the captain's boldness, and trembled very much for his safety, but his desire to have the mystery cleared up rose paramount to all.

"Come on," he said. "I will introduce you. Don't ask me to do any more; I am not accustomed to this sort of thing, and might make a terrible botch of the matter."

"I want you to do no more; and to favour the deception, in case the individual in the oak parlour should be watching at the window, I will go out at the back and make my way round to the front-door, where you can meet me."

The landlord uttered a sigh, and wiped the perspiration from his brow.

The present business taxed his brain severely, and probably never before had he undergone such severe mental exertion.

He hardly saw his way clear yet; but he had such faith in the highwayman's abilities, that he was quite willing to leave all to him.

In the meanwhile, Captain Hawk took down from a peg a voluminous cloak belonging to the landlord.

From its huge size he was, of course, easily able to envelope himself completely.

"That is disguise enough, I think."

With these words on his lips, he passed out at the back-door of the inn.

He crossed the yard swiftly, and then paused.

"Now I am here," he muttered, "I may as well satisfy myself that Satan is all right, in case I should want to make use of him in a little while."

The distance to the stable was so short that the delay that might be caused by paying a visit to it was not worth while taking into consideration.

Moreover, he had the key in his pocket.

On entering, he found that Satan required some little attention in order to fit him for the road.

"Now comes a chance for the ostler to make himself useful," he said, "and no doubt he will be glad enough to embrace it."

He closed the door, but did not lock it.

On reaching the low brick wall we have had occasion more than once to mention, he heard a low voice say:

"Captain! Is that you, captain?"

"Yes; I am here."

The darkness was increasing each moment, and as the ostler had stood in the shadow of one of the numerous outbuildings, the captain's eyes, keen as they were, failed to detect him until he stepped forward.

"Is all well, Isaac?"

"Not a mouse stirring."

"You have kept good watch at all points?"

"I have."

"Well, then, go now to the stable and see to my horse. Get him in readiness for the road, so that, should I have occasion for him, I shall not have to wait a single moment."

"Enough, captain; you may depend upon that. Don't trouble yourself to give a second thought upon the point."

The highwayman nodded, and lightly sprang over the wall.

"He is faithful," he said. "I cannot mistake it—treachery could never assume such a manner. Who shall say of what importance he may be to me some day?"

The ostler, on his part, was highly delighted by the duty which had been assigned to him.

"This is better than going on to London by myself," he said, rubbing his hands together gleefully. "It is to be hoped that the captain will reconsider his intention."

Drawing the cloak well around him, and pulling the hat a trifle more over his brows, Captain Hawk, having reached the high-road at a point a few yards below the inn, walked forward with surprising ease and boldness until he arrived at the front-door.

He gave a glance towards the windows of the oak parlour, and fancied that he could just detect the outlines of a face pressed against the latticed panes.

It was too dark for him to be sure about this. Besides, he did not want to appear to be looking in that direction at all.

The landlord was standing at the door, for, not thinking the highwayman would be so long in simply making his way round, rendered him somewhat anxious.

Captain Hawk, fully impressed with the belief that the stranger in the oak parlour was watching him, stopped on the threshold, and looking in the landlord's face, said:

"You have a gentleman in a private-room waiting here for me, have you not?"

"Yes," answered Tom Beckford, almost involuntarily.

"Then show me to him at once."

The landlord obeyed.

He knocked upon the panel, and without waiting for permission to enter, threw open the door.

Captain Hawk crossed the threshold hastily.

"My dear Frederick," he said, rushing towards the dusky-looking figure at the window, "I have kept you waiting, I know; but such a cursed mischance——"

"The devil, sir!" said the other, in tones which the captain recognised at once as being those of the man who had received the money—"the devil, sir! This must be some mistake."

"Mistake!" echoed the captain. "What can be the meaning of all this? Landlord, a light! D—n you! what do you mean by standing there and causing your guests to make mistakes in the darkness?"

"Hold—hold!" said the other. "There is not the least occasion for a light. It is by my wish that this room is in darkness. It is quite plain already that there is a mistake. I certainly expected a visitor."

"And I to find a dear friend, from whom I have long been separated," said Captain Hawk. "He promised to be here early this evening, and to take a private room, as we have business of great importance to transact with each other."

"It is an odd coincidence," said the stranger; and Captain Hawk fancied that he spoke like one ill at ease —"very odd indeed. But you are quite convinced that I am not the person you hoped to meet?"

"Oh, quite—the voice alone is more than sufficient to dispel any doubts."

Captain Hawk lingered in the hope that the second comer might arrive.

But the other was determined to bring the interview to a close, so that the highwayman, much against his inclination, had to withdraw after making an apology, which he took care should be long enough.

"That will do, sir," said the other. "I have the honour of wishing you good evening."

"Good evening," said the captain; "and I repeat that I very much regret such a mistake should have occurred."

So saying, he departed, and the landlord closed the door.

The pair then hastened to the apartment in which their former conversation had been held.

Captain Hawk threw off the huge cloak, and laughing, said:

"I managed that little bit tolerably well, don't you think?"

"Wonderfully—wonderfully! What a nerve you must have!"

"That is nothing, Tom—I——"

He was interrupted by a loud peal upon a bell.

"What is that?"

"The oak parlour bell. Wait a moment; I will go and see what the gentleman wants."

Tom was not long away.

But when he returned, his countenance had upon it a very serious look indeed.

"What's the matter?"

"Your experiment is not so successful as you imagined."

"How so?"

"You have alarmed the bird. He is off."

"Off?"

"Yes; he has just asked me for his bill. He says the time is so much gone by that he appointed for seeing his friend, that he feels sure he will not come to-night."

"Think you there is any truth in that?"

"You ought to be the best judge."

"But what is your opinion?"

"Why, I think that he has taken the alarm, and come to the determination not to run the risk of staying any longer."

"Depend upon it, you are right, Tom. I am sorry for this. He will go outside, and meet his friend somewhere else, so that the chances are ten to one whether we find out what there is between them."

This put the landlord into a perfect fever of regret.

"Don't say that, captain. I should go wild, I know I should, if I failed to learn what brought them to appoint a meeting here."

"Well, we shall see. Go now with the bill for the reckoning, or he will wonder what makes you so long."

Tom Beckford waddled off; and the highwayman's brows contracted in a way which showed how annoyed he was at the turn affairs had taken.

The reckoning between the landlord and his guest

did not occupy many seconds, for the parlour-door was almost immediately thrown open, and the latter crossed the threshold.

The moment he did so, Captain Hawk, muttering the words, "I ought to have thought of that before," made his way out into the yard, before the landlord had time to ask him where he was going.

As he drew near to the stable, Captain Hawk called the ostler in a suppressed voice.

The faithful fellow was on the watch, and showed himself instantly.

"What is it, captain? Do you want Satan? He is all ready."

"No, no. Listen to me."

Captain Hawk then hastily described, as well as he could, the appearance of the stranger who had just quitted the oak parlour.

"Follow him, Isaac," he said. "Don't lose sight of him on any account. But don't let him suspect you are at his heels. You will have to be cautious in the extreme. If I mistake not, he is half alarmed already."

CHAPTER LXXIII.

CAPTAIN HAWK SUCCEEDS IN GAINING ADMITTANCE TO THE OLD CHURCH.

"I MUST track him to his destination, I suppose?" said the ostler.

"Yes."

"And how shall I let you know where he is? If I leave him, perhaps I may not be able to find him again."

"A good thought. I will follow you at a safe distance; and when anything of a particular nature occurs, whistle to imitate the cry of some night bird. I shall hear and understand it."

"All right."

"Now be off."

These words had been exchanged with very great rapidity indeed, and the ostler now disappeared instantly in the gloom.

Much less time had been consumed in the doing of what we have just described than one would be apt to imagine; and when Captain Hawk re-entered the inn, which he did immediately upon parting with the ostler, he found the landlord still standing at the front-door, apparently gazing after the departed stranger.

"Have you seen Isaac?" was the highwayman's first question.

"Yes, there he is."

The captain could dimly distinguish a dusky form.

"Did you point out to him the way the stranger took?"

"No."

"Then do so now, but do it quietly."

A very suppressed call had the effect of attracting the keen faculties of the ostler, and he turned round at once.

The landlord then extended his arm in the direction taken by the stranger.

Isaac waved his hand and disappeared almost instantly.

"I must follow him," said the captain to the landlord. "I am determined to probe this mystery to the bottom."

"And how shall I know anything about it?"

"You will have to wait till my return."

"Confound it!"

The landlord's anxious suspense about this matter was quite amusing.

"Can't I come with you?" he said, laying a detaining hand on the highwayman's arm.

"By no means."

"I might be useful, you know."

"You will be useful—most useful, but not in the way you think."

"How then?"

"While I am away you must remain here, and on no account quit the premises. In your charge I leave that young girl and my horse, and should any harm befall either of them, rely upon it you will suffer. Promise to do this, and I will take care to let you know everything on my return."

The landlord was obliged to acquiesce, though he did so with a very ill grace.

Captain Hawk did not stay to exchange any more words with him, but started at once after the ostler, of whom he was afraid of losing sight.

The direction he had taken led almost in a straight line towards the church.

Captain Hawk had not gone much more than a hundred yards when a low whistle reached his ears.

"That is Isaac's signal, I'll be bound."

He quickened his pace, though he took care to advance without making any more noise than he could possibly help.

"Hush—hush, captain!" said a voice, in a low whisper. "Take care."

"All right. I am here"

As he spoke, he found his faithful ally standing at his side.

Isaac sank his voice to the lowest whisper and said:

"Be very cautious—he is just here."

"Where?"

"Among those trees. If you listen, you will hear him pacing backwards and forwards."

Captain Hawk could hear distinctly the peculiar sound caused by anyone walking heavily upon a gravelled path.

"Enough!" said the highwayman, a few seconds afterwards.

"You hear him?"

"Yes."

"And what can I do next?"

"Return to the inn and keep good watch, so that on my return you can warn me of danger should there be any."

The ostler seemed anything but pleased with this arrangement, and hesitated about obeying.

He had been indulging in the hope that he should be allowed to share in the highwayman's adventure.

"Perhaps if I go back," he said, "that fellow will hear me, and so take the alarm again. If I remain somewhere here, I may be able to be of more service to you than at the inn."

A moment's reflection made Captain Hawk come to the same opinion; besides, he did not like to disappoint his faithful companion, to whom, despite his roughness, he was fast growing more and more attached.

"Remain here," he said; "I will advance a few paces, and endeavour to find out what he is about."

As he spoke, the captain crept forward with an amount of cautiousness and silence that elicited the utmost admiration from the ostler.

The trees among which the stranger was walking proved to be a kind of grove, shading a broad piece of road leading from the highway up to the churchyard gates.

It was as dark and lonely a spot as could have been found within a mile or two of the Greyhound.

Listening intently, the highwayman made out that the stranger walked about twenty yards or so, and then retraced his steps, much after the fashion of a sentinel on duty.

The captain took advantage of the moment when the stranger was at the further extremity of his beat—for so we may term it—to advance still nearer to the trees until he fairly stood beneath their boughs.

Then he leaned his back against the massive trunk of a grand old elm, and it would have taken an eye of more than human keenness to have distinguished the outlines of his form.

The stranger approached.

Not only was he walking up and down, but muttering to himself.

The captain assumed an attitude of intense listening.

"Have I taken the alarm unnecessarily?" were the first words the highwayman caught—"have I been scared away by a mere nothing? No—no, I will not think that. Better—far better to be on the safe side. Oh, if he would but come!"

He paused now, having reached the extremity of his beat, and looking down the avenue, he appeared to be waiting impatiently for some one.

"How lucky it was that I prepared myself for this contingency!" he said, at length, though in tones so low that, had not the listener been very close at hand, he would not have overheard them. "As it is, all will be well. Surely—surely he will not be long."

Relapsing into silence, he resumed his restless walk, while Captain Hawk, whose sense of hearing now was morbidly acute, heard the ostler creeping closer and closer up behind him.

He was afraid to attempt to check his progress lest in doing so more noise should be made than was occasioned by his approach, so he awaited his coming in an agony of dread.

To his great relief, the ostler came to a halt about a dozen paces in his rear.

But now, most unmistakably, sounds were heard, which indicated that a new-comer was approaching the scene—one who took no particular pains to approach unheard.

"He comes," said the one who had been waiting—"he comes at last!"

He paused for the other to advance.

"You are here, then?" said a voice, which, though suppressed, was recognised by Captain Hawk in a moment.

"Yes; it was as well we took this precaution."

"Why? Have you been to the Greyhound?"

"Yes. But, as I found we could not have the place all to ourselves, I thought it best to keep away entirely. I will let you know all the particulars presently."

"It is quite as well," said the other. "I have been thinking since that it was needlessly running the risk of recognition. This is just as good a meeting-place."

"True. But then you must remember we are much too early for us to be safe in beginning our undertaking; and how is the intervening time to be spent?"

"Are you sure it is too early?"

"I think it is."

"Have you seen anyone about?"

"Not a soul."

"Then, depend upon it, it is none too early. The darkness is profound, and it will be odd if anyone should come here at this hour. People generally give country churchyards a wide berth at night."

"That's true enough. What do you think of doing?"

"Why, let us gain the interior of the building without delay. When once there, we must be safer than we can be anywhere else; and we can wait for a suitable hour to commence our operations."

"Very true."

"Lead the way, then, at once. You have not examined the place to see what facilities there are for entering?"

"I have not. But with such tools as I carry with me there would be very little trouble in getting into a place secured ten times better than this."

"Enough. The sooner we are away from here the better."

Without further interchange of words, the two worthies, whose errand and intentions were now as great a mystery to Captain Hawk as at first, walked rather rapidly along the gravelled road.

About a couple of hundred yards brought them to the churchyard gate.

"We will get over this," said one. "It will be little or no trouble, and there is no one at hand to observe us."

The gate was prettily made of rustic woodwork, and evidently had not been constructed with the view of keeping anyone from entering.

The bars were as easily climbed as a stile, and, without any perceptible delay, the strangers were in the churchyard, and hurrying along the pathway leading direct up to the church itself.

Captain Hawk, who had followed silently in their footsteps, felt, on coming to the gate, that he had reached a difficult point, for it would be hard to surmount the gate without exposing himself more to the view of those in front than was either safe or prudent.

Fortunately, however, a tree in the churchyard path hid the two men from his view, and this was the moment he chose to cross the obstruction.

Isaac was over after him in a second.

"Be careful," said the captain

"All right. If we walk on the turf here at the edge of the pathway, there will be scarcely any fear of their hearing us."

Captain Hawk took the hint, and was able to proceed almost with absolute noiselessness.

There now seemed no doubt whatever that the destination of these two men was the peaceful-looking, ivy-grown old church.

It was equally certain that their errand to it was an unlawful one, or they would not have chosen such an hour as the present, or taken so many precautions for secrecy.

Captain Hawk came to a halt.

The two men, having reached the shadow of the church walls, paused to reconnoitre.

"What is that?" said one, in tones that made the captain shrink back a pace or two, for he felt sure he had been seen.

"What—what?" said the other, quickly.

"That light yonder?"

Captain Hawk breathed again.

"Oh, that does not concern us. It only comes from one of the windows in the parsonage."

"Are you sure of that?"

"Oh yes! There is no cause for alarm whatever."

"Then show me where you intend to enter the building, because the sooner we are under cover the better I shall be pleased."

"There is no better spot than the window, then. It is only secured by a very common fastening which I have only to break a pane and draw back."

"Do it, then, at once."

There was a certain air of command about the second comer which showed him to be the chief personage in this undertaking, though the other, familiar from a knowledge of his crimes, spoke as though there was little if any difference in their social positions.

The crackling of glass speedily followed, and after the lapse of about three minutes, one of the little latticed church casements was thrown back, leaving the way free for the two men to enter the sacred edifice.

The sill was some distance from the ground; but the one who had broken the pane showed himself possessed of considerable agility, and, having effected an entrance, assisted the other to follow him.

Having thus gained the interior of the church without, as they believed, any human eye observing their motions, the two men fastened the window again, and passed both out of the sight and hearing of the unsuspected watcher

Captain Hawk now found himself rather at a loss how to act.

To attempt to follow the men through the window without attracting their notice was, as he well knew, a totally impossible feat.

At this instant the ostler glided up to him.

"They are inside, ain't they, captain?"

"Yes."

"What are you going to do next, then?"

"I can hardly say. I must and will find out what it is that brings them on a secret errand to the old church at such an hour as this. It may be that I shall be able to frustrate some villanous design that they have in contemplation."

"Very likely, captain. But what I want to know is, how you are going to get inside the building without them knowing of it?"

"I must gain an entrance at some other point. Do you remain here while I look round the building. Don't move on any account whatever until I come back to you."

"All right, captain. You may depend I shall keep good watch and ward."

The highwayman knew this very well, and so, as silently as possible, he crept along the exterior of the church, so as to make his way to that part of the building which was most distant from the broken window.

The church was not a very large one, so he was not long in reaching the tower, which happened to be at the further extremity.

Captain Hawk had often noticed the old tower with admiration.

It was almost entirely overgrown with ivy, which must have been growing for centuries, so dense was it and of so great extent.

"Let me see," said the highwayman. "If I remember rightly, there are loopholes in the sides of this tower, and I am greatly deceived if they are not wide enough to allow me to pass through. They lead into the belfry, no doubt; and if I can only get up to them, that will be an excellent way of getting in, for if I am in the upper part of the church I shall stand a much better chance of observing what is going on in any part of it."

This was all right enough, but the trifling difficulty stood in the way that there was no apparent means of gaining these loopholes, which were at a distance of something like five-and-twenty feet from the ground.

But Captain Hawk knew that old ivy, like that which clung about the tower, furnished almost as easy a means of ascent as a scaling-ladder; and so what, perhaps many would have considered an insuperable obstacle, he made no difficulty of whatever.

He listened.

All was still.

The clouds overhead were drifting rapidly, and when every now and then they became less opaque, the moon sent down a faint glimmer of light.

Slight as it was, it proved of great service to the captain, who, in total darkness, would have had a good deal of trouble in executing his task.

As he fully anticipated, he found that the old ivy afforded ample hand and foot hold, while the clinging boughs were so strong that his weight disturbed them scarcely more than the wind would do.

The highwayman ascended with great rapidity, and only a few moments elapsed before he reached the first loophole.

This proved to be much larger than he had expected, so that it was the easiest matter in the world to pass through it.

But the interior looked repellingly dark, and it is no wonder that he hesitated before he ventured to go any further.

Fortunately for him, at this juncture the moon shone forth with much more brilliancy than she had done before that night.

Her beams streaming through the loophole showed the captain that he had indeed gained the old belfry, for he could see the massive beams of blackened timber and the dust-covered bells themselves.

How far it might be to the floor of the belfry, however, he was unable to ascertain.

But he judged that it could not be very far below the level of the loophole, and so, with a great deal of confidence, he lowered himself through the aperture until he hung down at the full length of his arms.

But then, contrary to his expectations, he was unable to feel any signs of the flooring, and he felt afraid to drop lest the noise he should make in alighting should reach the ears of the two men and give them the alarm.

CHAPTER LXXIV.

CAPTAIN HAWK IS A WITNESS OF A STRANGE SCENE IN THE VAULT BENEATH THE CHURCH.

It was impossible, however, for him to remain for any length of time where he then was; and as he had no possible means of discovering the depth, he had no resource whatever but to let go.

He did so with great misgiving; but immediately discovered he had been giving himself a great deal of unnecessary apprehension.

Although out of reach, yet the flooring was not more than a couple of inches from his toes, so that he descended absolutely without making any sound whatever, for the flooring was covered with a thick coat of dust.

He had to wait a moment, however, before he could quite recover himself.

"How ridiculous!" he muttered. "But I ought not to complain. I cannot have caused any alarm yet, and now what I have to do is to find the way to the head of the staircase.

The belfry was very dark; but yet there was glimmering enough from the night sky to enable the highwayman to guard from running against any obstruction.

It was no easy matter, though, for him to find the stairs; but at length, pushing open a little door which his hand encountered in feeling round the walls, he discovered them, and without more ado began to descend.

He was conscious that a great deal of time had already been consumed, and felt that it was quite time for him to be present in the main portion of the church.

In comparison with the narrow winding stairs, down which he cautiously made his way, the belfry above was absolutely light.

Captain Hawk had literally to feel his way down, and he had to trust himself entirely to this one sense, none of his other faculties being of the slightest service to him.

Suddenly he stopped.

His hands, which had all the while been passing over smooth stonework, encountered wood.

A very brief examination told him that this was a door.

"No doubt," he said to himself, "this is one way by which the upper part of the church can be reached. If the door is not fastened, all will be well."

He was fortunate.

The door had no fastening save a heavy iron latch, which he raised in a moment.

Such a bright light appeared on the other side of the threshold that, involuntarily, he drew back.

But the light was only bright when viewed in contrast with the pitchy darkness of the staircase.

Captain Hawk soon found that the light, which was soft and gentle, found its way through the various windows in the sacred edifice.

The moon appeared to be shining rather more brightly, too, than it had before been on this eventful night.

Reassured after a moment's pause, Captain Hawk advanced.

He left the door behind him unclosed, for fear an alarm should be raised by the slight noise that would unavoidably be made by shutting it.

Moreover, the faint murmur of voices came upon his ear, and this increased his anxiety to find out what was going on without any more delay.

The little door through which he passed brought him out into the gallery at the side of the organ, and just opposite to the altar window.

Through the stained glass panes of this the moon was shining with a very beautiful effect.

The silence was profound.

Captain Hawk began to have his doubts whether he should be able to make the slightest movement without attracting attention.

This was all the more annoying because where he then stood he could neither see the speakers nor distinguish their voices from a loud continuous hum.

But circumstances again favoured him.

The floor of the gallery was covered with carpet, or some similar substance, and this enabled him to advance with absolute noiselessness.

The church was not a large one, so a few steps brought him to the edge of the gallery.

Cautiously peeping over, he was unable for a moment or so to see any signs of the two men.

Presently, however, he saw that they had secreted themselves in one of the old-fashioned pews.

"There," said the first, speaking in rather louder tones than he had hitherto done, "did you hear nothing then?"

"Nothing whatever," was the reply, given in a way that seemed to indicate the speaker wished to appear at ease but could not.

"Where are your ears?" said his companion, with evident trepidation. "I am quite sure that I heard something then."

"Pooh—pooh! You are nervous. If you get yourself into an excited state, you will imagine all sorts of things in a place like this."

"But it was no imagination," persisted the other. "I am certain I heard something then, as I did a few moments before."

"Perhaps some slight accidental sound. Large buildings at night are always full of strange noises. Think no more of it. Here is another drop of brandy; drink it, and let us begin our work."

The two men were both very ill at ease, that was perfectly clear, and a very little thing would have served to scare them away from their design altogether.

Had this been Captain Hawk's object, he would have accomplished it easily; but he was anxious to know the nature of the work to which they referred.

For some moments now all was still.

The two men were engaged in partaking of copious draughts of brandy, by which they hoped to enkindle a spurious kind of courage in their breasts.

The words he had heard made Captain Hawk aware that, careful as he had been in all his movements, a still greater degree of caution would be required in order to avoid discovery.

"Come," said the one who appeared to have control of the affair; "I tell you it is idle to wait here longer, expecting that a more favourable opportunity will arise. What more can be wished for than we have now?"

"It would be better later," said the other. "Any little thing that we do now might bring about discovery; but after all the villagers have retired to rest there will be little fear of it."

"And if we wait till then we may as well wait till doomsday. I'll tell you what it is, Ralph—your courage is fast oozing away, and if we wait much longer there will be none left at all."

To this imputation Ralph made no reply.

The one who had spoken rose, and, pushing open the pew-door, stepped into the aisle.

Ralph followed him, though with manifest reluctance.

"Come on!" said the other; "nerve yourself to the task. It must be accomplished; and the sooner it is over the better."

Ralph gave himself a good shake, and followed his companion along the aisle towards the altar.

But from his post of observation, Captain Hawk could see that as the fellow advanced he continually cast apprehensive glances around him, as though each moment he was beset by the fear that he should see some dreadful sight.

With a real or assumed boldness, however, the other walked on; nor did he pause until he reached a massive tomb that occupied a conspicuous position near the chancel.

Even from the distance Captain Hawk could see that this tomb showed many signs of ancient grandeur.

The solid stonework was protected by a ponderous iron railing which surrounded it.

Ralph, following the example of his leader, stopped at the rails.

In obedience to a hastily-uttered command from his companion, he drew from his pocket something which the highwayman quickly made out to be a bunch of skeleton keys.

Ralph was expert in their use, for without the occurrence of scarcely any delay he contrived to open a little gate in the tomb railings.

"Now for the next, Ralph. And if you are as speedy as with the last, I shall add something to the reward which I intend to give you."

"But," said the other, grumblingly, "you promised to let me into the light of the whole affair, and tell me just what you expected me to do."

"You shall know that all in good time, Ralph."

"So you have told me."

"And I mean it; and, moreover, the time is very close at hand now. When you have opened this stone door we will descend, and then we can converse without fear of being overheard."

"But why not here?" stammered Ralph, who was anything but pleased with this proposition.

"Because it is my will to confide the secret to you when we get below, and not before. Surely that is reason sufficient. Open the door, and let us have no further bother."

Ralph said something in an undertone—words of remonstrance, no doubt, but not uttered with sufficient distinctness for Captain Hawk to hear them.

It would seem, however, that Ralph was well aware it would be futile to attempt to dissuade his companion, for without another syllable he set to work to open the door, that was apparently situated in one end of the tomb itself.

But from some reason or other this proved a much more difficult and tedious task.

Eventually, however, the huge block of stone rolled back, and a black chasm was brought into view.

Up to this point the two men had found the illumination afforded by the moon to be quite sufficient for their purpose; but now that they were about to descend into the vault, Ralph produced a small but well-constructed lantern, which he ignited by means of a splinter of wood and a bottle of phosphorus.

"All is well now," he said, with an apprehensive glance behind him as though he was far from feeling that all was so well as he had said.

"Yes, all is well, of course. Give me the lantern—I will lead the way, and you can follow."

Ralph acquiesced instantly, and his accomplice, who certainly seemed unaffected by the fears which would naturally strike into any breast upon such an occasion, boldly began to descend the steps which commenced at the threshold of the stone door.

Ralph followed as closely at his heels as he was able.

"You will not close the door, I suppose?"

"No—there cannot be any necessity for it; and, moreover, we might have a good deal of trouble in getting it open on this side on account of the weight."

"All right!" said Ralph, and as he uttered the words the two speakers passed altogether out of the captain's view.

Their disappearance seemed to have the effect of removing some kind of spell that had weighed upon him, for he gave himself a good shake and drew a long breath.

"Confound it all!" he said. "Am I never to get to the bottom of this business? Things look awkward; but, come what will, I will have a try to hear what those two worthies have got to say to each other. It must be something of no trifling interest and importance, or they would never choose such a place and such an hour as this to hold a conference. But still, if I have come here merely to hear them plot together, I shall regret the pains I have taken."

While these words were passing through the captain's mind, rather than finding utterance on his lips, he glided rapidly along the carpeted floor of the gallery.

Of course, his object now was to gain the main body of the church in the shortest possible space of time.

To attempt to find a way by any of the staircases would occupy an indefinite period of time, and might result in his not making his way after all, so that, very wisely, he at once looked out for some readier means of effecting a descent.

He was not very long in fixing upon this.

The pulpit occupied a position not very far distant from the gallery, and was not much beneath it.

"I can manage that," he said; "and what is more, I feel pretty sure I can do it so quietly that those two rascals cannot hear me."

So saying, he crossed the parapet, if so we may term it, of the gallery, and then, with a little trouble, managed to get one foot on the reading-cushion.

After that, it was easy enough to descend.

Captain Hawk experienced a strange sort of sensation upon finding himself for the first time in a pulpit.

But on the present occasion he could not spare the time to give way to his feelings, so, opening the little door, he ran nimbly down the steps into the aisle.

Three cautious strides brought him to the iron gate in the railings, and, having got so far, he could see the faint glimmering of a light below.

He had made such good use of his time that really a very few seconds had been occupied by his making his way out of the gallery.

He was now getting upon ticklish ground.

And now, had any observer of the singular doings in the old church been asked whether it was possible for Captain Hawk to have got any nearer to the two men without being discovered, an answer in the negative would certainly have been given.

But the captain was quite of a different opinion, for with great caution he pushed himself through the opening into the interior of the tomb.

As soon as he felt his foot touch the topmost stone, he nodded his head, as though to express that he felt great satisfaction, and then he moved immediately with more confidence.

The fact was, he had found, as he had fully expected, that the steps were covered to a depth of several inches with sawdust, which absolutely and completely deadened every sound.

With the light of the lantern below to guide him, Captain Hawk had confidence in his ability to descend unheard.

Nor was the confidence misplaced, for the bottom step was actually reached without any alarm having been given.

Probably few persons could have been found who would have placed themselves in a position of so much peril as the captain's was without taking some consideration about the matter.

The fact was, however, that, though there were two men, he was so assured of his own power to defend himself, that he never once thought to trouble in the least about what might be the result of an encounter.

[CAPTAIN HAWK WATCHING RALPH OPEN THE COFFIN.]

He took every pains to remain undetected, but that was not on account of any personal fear, but merely in order to listen to what conversation passed between the two.

Perhaps what had contributed not a little towards his being able to approach them so very closely without being heard, was the circumstance that Ralph was listening most intently to what his companion was saying.

On reaching the foot of the steps beneath the tomb, Captain Hawk found that there was another door communicating with a vault of considerable extent.

This door was partially closed, and Captain Hawk, by gliding up to it, was able to peep through the crevice between the door and the door-post.

The scene that presented itself to his view was a strange one.

In the centre of the vault were three or four wooden tressels, doubtless placed there in readiness to receive a coffin as soon as it was brought down into the vault.

On one of these tressels the lantern had been placed, and the light which it sent forth enabled the highwayman to see the countenances of the two men with great distinctness.

Let him see them again wherever he might, he felt certain he should not fail to recognise them.

They were sitting on the wooden tressels, facing each other, and with the lighted lantern between them.

Upon Ralph's face was an expression which was unquestionably one of horrified amazement.

"Now, look here: there must be no flinching; and remember that such an oath as you have just taken is not to be broken with impunity."

Ralph's lips moved, but no sound came from them

"Now then to tell you what you have to do. As you have more than once said, you know your power over me. You are aware that, through your knowledge of my secrets, you can compel me to do almost anything you think fit. But now the time has come when I am determined an alteration shall be made. I will have a little power over you. You have kept clear hitherto; but what you shall do to-night will implicate you to such an extent that a syllable breathed against me will involve you in utter destruction. That is the sum and substance of it, Ralph."

"But—but——"

"But what, Ralph?"

"Suppose I should refuse?"

"You would not be so foolish.

"I don't know about that."

"Well, then, you see this pistol! It is carefully loaded. I know you are unarmed. If you hesitate a moment about doing my bidding, I will blow your brains out as sure as you are a living man!"

CHAPTER LXXV.

CAPTAIN HAWK FOILS A DEEP-LAID SCHEME OF VILLANY.

THERE was so much cold-blooded determination in the tones of this man's voice that it was impossible to doubt whether he would be as good as his word.

Ralph felt, and so did Captain Hawk, that he would not scruple to fulfil his threat.

There was little at present that had shown itself in Ralph's character to make him an object of compassion, nor did the captain feel much inclination to take his part; but now affairs had reached their present crisis he thought it as well to draw forth one of his pistols, which he knew to be in readiness for immediate use.

The change in his companion's manner evidently took Ralph greatly by surprise.

On recovering himself, the first thing he did was to turn his eyes in the direction of the door, as though he meditated making a sudden dash in that direction.

But the other had adroitly contrived to take up his position on the tressel so as to be between Ralph and the entrance of the vault.

He saw the hasty glance, and understood it.

"Don't think for a moment you will be able to escape. You may be rapid in your movements, but the bullet from this pistol will be quicker still. You may reach the threshold, but it will only be to fall over it a corpse!"

Whiter and more ghastly still grew Ralph's face.

"Surely—surely," he said, with a wonderful amount of submission in his manner, "you have not enticed me to this place to—to murder me?"

"No. Such was not my intention," was the emphatic answer. "But remember that you *are* here, and if I chose I could easily free myself from you without your fate being guessed at by anyone. I know, of course, that your presence here to-night is a profound secret from everyone. Now can you see that you are in my power?"

Large drops of perspiration broke out upon Ralph's brow, and rolled down his swarthy visage.

His eyes were fixed open to an unnatural width, and his lower jaw hung down like that of a corpse.

He was now the abject dependant.

When Captain Hawk had heard their previous conversations, he fancied that there was not any great difference between them in rank.

It did not strike him that the familiarity was attributable instead to companionship in crime—the thing which more than any other sweeps away the barriers of social distinction.

But now the richer and more educated villain had the sway, and having gained it, there was little fear that he would lose it again.

It was evident, too, that he enjoyed his triumph over his presumptuous accomplice.

"Take it easy, Ralph," he said, with a mocking laugh. "As we have begun with explanations we will continue them before we attempt to take in hand the business which must be done to-night."

Ralph glared at him as though he scarcely comprehended what he said.

"Understand this," said the other. "If my purpose only was to rid myself of you, I should not have the slightest trouble or hardly any risk in doing it. A bullet would settle the business in a moment, and I should effectually conceal your body by forcing it into one of those coffins yonder. No one would think of looking there for you, and the sawdust that lies here so thickly would conceal every trace of your fate."

He paused a moment, in order that these words should sink deeply into Ralph's mind, and produce their due effect upon him.

"Don't be dismayed," he added, afterwards. "I will relieve your mind by saying that I have no thought of doing anything of the kind—that is, not unless you drive me to it. Do you understand that?"

Ralph nodded.

"In order that my future designs may be carried out, an assistant is absolutely necessary, and, of course, I would rather have all my secrets confided to one breast. You understand me?"

"Yes, yes," murmured Ralph, partially recovering the use of his voice—"I understand you."

"Very good. Hark!"

Very faintly, as though proceeding from a great distance, the sound of the church clock striking came upon their ears.

The hour was twelve.

Captain Hawk, like the two men, counted every stroke.

When the last one had died away, a profound silence reigned for several seconds in the vault.

Ralph shivered, and the movement, slight as it was, aroused his companion from the kind of fit of abstraction into which he had fallen.

"The hour has come," he said, "and there must be no more lingering. Very few words will be required to make all plain to you.

"Are you paying attention, Ralph?"

"Yes."

"Then, before going further, let me be sure that you understand that if you refuse to accede to my demands the alternative is death, and never fear that I shall flinch."

"Tell me what you want?" said Ralph, in an agony of dread and suspense. "Don't keep me any longer."

"I will not."

Captain Hawk leaned forward, deeply anxious to catch every syllable of what might follow.

The man, lowering his voice, said:

"You know well enough, Ralph, how it was that chance threw into my way the papers and other things which enabled me to pass myself off as the nephew of old Squire Kingsbury—you recollect what became of the real nephew, too, don't you, Ralph?"

Ralph only replied to the interrogation by a groan.

"Everything succeeded as though under the immediate hands of Fate itself. The old squire passed away—the only person who could have raised the least question as to my identity—and then young Mr. Kingsbury died on purpose to make room for me. There he lies, with smaller possessions than he looked forward too, while I—I—by a little cleverness, am already master of one of the finest estates in the kingdom. That's it, Ralph."

When he spoke about the young squire's possessions, he pointed scornfully towards one of the coffins.

"Yes," said Ralph, "I know all that; and you know that if I chose I could drag you down again to your old level."

"Just so. I don't dispute that. It is an absolute fact. But I mean to disarm you, Ralph; and what is more, I mean to do it to-night. I am going to deprive you of the power of holding such an instrument of terror over me, and if you thought for a month you would not be able to guess how I shall do it. In one hour from now, no matter how much you wished to do so, you would be unable to betray me."

Ralph gazed at his companion with a more wondering expression still.

He was evidently at a loss to understand what was about to ensue.

"You can't see it, Ralph; and I'll give you my word that if time was not so urgent I should like to enjoy your wonderment for a long while."

"I can't bear it," said Ralph. "Tell me what you have to say—anything would be better than this suspense."

"No doubt—no doubt. But I will ease your mind now. You are a clever fellow, Ralph; yet you have been deceived just like all the rest of the world."

"In Heaven's name, what do you mean?"

"You believe the young squire is dead."

"The young squire?"

"Yes, I say you, in common with the rest of the world, believe that he is dead."

"And he is dead," said Ralph, drawing the sleeve of his coat over his streaming brow. "You know full well that he is dead."

He was replied to only by a mocking smile.

"Did I not see him placed in his coffin?" cried Ralph, with increasing excitement—"did I not follow him to the grave, or tomb rather?—and does he not lie in yonder coffin?"

"I can say yes to all your questions, Ralph."

"And yet you tell me he is not dead!"

"I do."

"What do you mean?"

"Can you be at a loss to understand that? No, no—you are by far too quick-witted for that."

These last words were accompanied by a wonderfully expressive glance.

It was understood by Ralph, who, shrinking back upon the tressel, held up his hands before him as though to defend himself from an expected blow.

"I see you catch my meaning," cried the other, at length. "The young squire was buried, and now lies strongly screwed down in yonder coffin; but he is not dead for all that."

Captain Hawk felt a strange sensation thrill through his frame when he heard these words pronounced.

The revelation had taken him wholly by surprise.

Ralph, too, although to some extent prepared, was greatly overcome, and for some moments he could neither move nor speak.

How long he might have remained in this motionless condition is hard to say had not the other rose and took up the lantern.

That made Ralph give an inquiring glance.

"What now?" he said.

"Come, stand up!"

"Why have you brought me here to-night?" he asked, hoarsely.

"That you will quickly see. Get up, I say!"

Almost mechanically Ralph obeyed.

"Now, then," said his companion, with more and more of authority in his tones, "where is that crowbar I told you to be sure to bring?"

"It is here."

"Produce it, then."

A child could not have been more obedient.

From an inside coat pocket Ralph produced two pieces of iron, which, when screwed together, formed a crowbar of a formidable kind.

"What is it for?" he asked, with chattering teeth and rolling eyes. "What am I to do with it?"

The other, raising his lantern, pointed to the coffin which had last been carried into that dismal place.

But Ralph shrank back.

"Off with the lid!" said the other, sternly. "It will not take a moment."

"And what must I do next?"

"Cannot you guess?"

"I—I cannot."

"You must put yourself into my power, Ralph."

"Your power?"

"Yes; you will see that, when the coffin lid is raised——"

"Yes—yes!"

"The fresh air—such as it is in this vault—will have the effect of rousing the young squire from the death-like trance in which he has remained for so long—that trance which was brought about by the skilful administration of that Indian drug. You chose to jump to the conclusion that it was poison, Ralph, and at the time I failed to see any good reason for undeceiving you."

"Not poison?"

"No, but a cunningly-prepared drug, which once mingling with the pure and wholesome blood would produce effects precisely similar to death itself. Its virtues are proved."

"And that is the drug which you administered?"

"It is, Ralph."

"Heaven help him, then!"

"Hush—hush! None of that! Heaven has nought to do with us or with our business."

Ralph groaned.

"Raise the coffin lid."

"I—I cannot."

"But you must. I insist upon it!"

Ralph trembled in every limb.

"The time has come," continued his companion, "when the subtle drug will cease to exercise its power over the springs of life. Consciousness will return, and the victim will be no more aware of what has taken place than if he had slept peacefully and dreamlessly for one night only."

"But—but——"

"Speak on! What would you say?"

"Well, then, if what you tell me is the truth——"

"Dare you doubt it?"

"No—no, but I——"

"What thought is in your mind? Let me know it at once."

"Then, if he is safely screwed down in that coffin, why not leave him to himself? Should he revive, the confined air, which will with difficulty find its way into his lungs, will quickly deprive him of his new-found vitality. What good can be served by breaking off the lid?"

"I have my reason, depend upon it, and not the least of it is what I said about placing yourself as much in my power as I am in yours."

"I do not understand," faltered Ralph.

"Well, then, in the first place it does not suit me to remain in a state of doubt as to what becomes of the young squire. I must feel assured of his death before I can feel that I am safe and secure in my possessions."

"Then——"

"Do not interrupt me. I can guess that you were about to ask me why I did not administer a poison instead of this narcotic drug. The answer is simple. Had I done so, ten to one an examination would have been made that would have brought the truth to light; and if once it had been known that the young squire had been poisoned, no pains would have been spared to find out the author of his death. That is so, is it not, Ralph?"

"It is—it is."

"Very good. You begin to see now the excellence of my plan. I run little, if any, risk. The appearances of natural death were perfect, you see—perfect enough to deceive them all, and to consign him to this vault. But suppose foul play had been suspected—suppose they judged that poison had been given to the young man—what would have happened then?"

"I know not."

"Why, dull-pate, at the first stroke of the surgeon's scalpel—and, as you must know, the poison, if any, could only be discovered by the use of such an instrument—I say at the first stroke of the surgeon's scalpel it would have been plainly seen that the young man still lived. A trance would then be suspected. Remedies would have been tried for his recovery; and had they all been unsuccessful, time alone, in due course, would have brought him to his senses."

"But," said Ralph, whose mystification was still considerable, "suppose this had happened, how would it have fared with you then?"

"Why, that was the only risk I ran. I should not have been suspected—that was impossible. My position would have been just what it has always been. I had everything to gain by the attempt, and nothing whatever to lose."

Ralph was a villain; but as these revelations of horror fell from the lips of the speaker, he recoiled step by step until one of the stone pillars in the vault prevented him from going further.

By the malicious and triumphant gleam in the other's eye, it could be seen how much he enjoyed this scene.

"Why talk of this, Ralph?" he said, at last. "It does no good—it cannot do any, because the time for speculation is past. The result is achieved—it is certain—it is here."

Again was his finger scornfully and triumphantly pointed at the coffin.

"But," cried Ralph, the words seeming rather to burst from his throat than to be uttered by his lips, "you tantalise me, and you do not tell me what it is that you have brought me here to do."

"Then you shall not have that to complain of any longer. You will force open the lid of yonder coffin, and when you have done so you must deal the inmate such a blow as will prevent him from ever returning to life again."

The crowbar dropped from Ralph's nerveless fingers, but as it fell upon the thickly-sawdusted floor of the vault it made no sound.

Although he might have guessed what the reply to his question might have been, yet the utterance of it paralysed him with terror.

"No—no!" he said. "Were it for my life I could not do it!"

"It is for your life," said the other, in menacing accents, as he stepped towards him—"I tell you it is for your life!"

He raised his arm, and Captain Hawk saw the loaded pistol was still in his grasp.

"Listen!" he said. "You have now your choice to make, and whichever way you decide I care not. Either obey my commands or else refuse."

"And if I refuse?"

"Then you do not survive the utterance of that refusal for one single moment. You know that is no idle threat. This bullet would bury itself in your brain."

Ralph uttered a deep groan.

"But if you consent," continued his tempter, "you shall be as free as myself to enjoy all the comforts, and the luxuries, and pleasures of my new possessions. There is much more to do, and in the execution of it all you shall be my right-hand, my trusted instrument. Think well of that, Ralph. Weigh all well over in your mind ere you pronounce your refusal."

"Alas—alas! Heaven help me!"

"Help yourself."

Ralph looked at him fixedly.

"Why appeal to me in such a case?" he said. "Why not do the deed yourself?"

"Can you ask why? That would be only to place myself in your power more and more. No—no. By your hand must the last blow be dealt, and then I shall have the power over you. Do not fear that I should exercise it to your prejudice," he added. "It is only to protect myself. Come—come! No shrinking! This is not the first ugly business you have gone through with to my certain knowledge. Drive away, then, all the scruples that beset your breast, and let the reflection nerve you that upon your aim depends the safety and security of our future life. Let us have no more words. Your choice, I can see plainly enough, is already made. Take up the crowbar."

With the air of one who does something entirely opposed to his inclination, Ralph seized the bar.

No sooner was it in his grasp than the touch of the metal seemed to urge him to do the awful deed blindly in haste, and before reflection should set in.

Almost with the air of one who hurries to his death he made his way to the coffin, and inserting the point of the crowbar, raised up the lid.

CHAPTER LXXVI.

REVERTS TO THE PROCEEDINGS OF THE BLACK HIGHWAYMAN.

It is, we confess, with the very greatest reluctance that we break off the narrative of Captain Hawk's adventures at this point in order to return to the Black Highwayman.

But the reader will remember that the last-named personage was left in a position of much greater peril—namely, on the roof-tops of his mansion in Piccadilly, at a time when he had certain knowledge the police officers were within.

For a brief space, then, Captain Hawk must be left in the vault beneath the old church, and the mystery connected with the two men left unrevealed.

After, then, fairly reaching the roof of his own house, a kind of revulsion of feeling came over the Black Highwayman.

A species of reaction from the violent excitement he had recently undergone set in, and, clasping his hands over his eyes, he remained quite motionless for several minutes.

How long this state of semi-unconsciousness would have continued, had not the striking of the palace clock again warned him of the flight of time, is hard to say.

Rousing himself with a start, he whispered to himself:

"Tush—tush! this is mere childishness, and such as I should never have believed myself capable of being guilty of. I must be firm and bold—with nerves like steel itself. This weakness I must shake off at once."

He shook himself as he spoke, as though he could by that means rid his mind of the feelings which weighed it down.

One would almost have been ready to think that the means was really successful, for he set about the execution of the remainder of his task in a manner similar to that in which he had commenced it.

"The trap-door is fast, no doubt," he murmured. "I will try it, for if, by chance, it is not, I shall be saved much trouble."

It was, however, only as a kind of forlorn hope that Lord Harcliffe made his way to that trap-door in the roof with which most London houses are provided.

Consequently, when he found himself quite impossible to move it in the least, he experienced no feeling of disappointment.

"Quite fast," he said; "and now to try those means which I provided so long ago, under the conviction that a necessity like the present must sooner or later arise."

Crouching down on his hands and knees, he then cautiously climbed up the tiles in the direction of the principal stack of chimneys.

The distance was not great, and he paused at the foot of the brickwork.

Then producing a strong knife, he counted the bricks until he paused at one near the centre.

This he removed from its setting by means of the knife.

It was evidently constructed for this purpose, as the removal caused him no trouble whatever.

Thrusting his hand into the small and dark-looking recess, he drew forth the end of a piece of strong rope.

With this in his hand, he cautiously slipped down the roof to the parapet.

The rope came easily through the opening, and as soon as his feet rested in the gutter, he pulled the line until it tightened.

He tugged at it two or three times, as though to make himself quite certain of its security.

Apparently satisfied about this, he nimbly formed the end into a kind of slip-knot, into which he thrust his right foot, and then pulled the cord tightly.

This done, he chose a certain portion of the parapet close by, over which he threw the rope, so that, being fastened at both ends, it hung down in the manner of a loop.

This was all done with rapidity, and yet with perfect coolness and self-possession.

He listened.

But no sound came upon his ear to indicate that it would be unsafe to proceed with his enterprise, and without any more delay he set about doing that from which most men would have shrunk in deadly fear.

This was to lower himself from the top of the house by means of the rope which he held tightly in both hands.

But he seemed quite convinced that there was no fear the end fixed above would give way in the least.

When about six feet from the top of the parapet, he reached the extremity of the rope.

The way in which his foot was secured in the loop furnished him with a kind of standing-place.

Before him was a small window, which, to all appearance, was constructed so as not to open.

But this was only in appearance, for, upon pressing on a certain portion of the framework, the window opened like a door.

It opened, too, with perfect noiselessness.

All was dark within, and, after listening for a few seconds, Lord Harcliffe satisfied himself that all was silent too.

"All is well," he said.

As he pronounced these words he placed his left foot cautiously upon the window-sill and liberated his right from the loop of rope.

After that he found the task of entering comparatively easy.

In view of some such contingency as the present, thick carpeting had been placed beneath the window, and on this he descended without raising any sound audible at more than a few paces.

Having achieved thus much of his daring design, the Black Highwayman drew a long breath of relief.

Despite the fact that the house was occupied by police

officers, he evidently considered that the most difficult and perilous portion of his undertaking was over.

His first act was to close the window, and, after having done so, he stepped forward in the darkness with an amount of confidence which showed he must have been wonderfully well acquainted with the interior of the dwelling.

When he paused it was at the top of a flight of stairs.

Carpets seemed to be spread in all directions, and in his progress from the window to this point he had been all but as noiseless as a shadow.

Leaning upon the massive balustrades, he looked down.

At first all appeared darkness, but by-and-by he perceived far below him a very feeble glimmering of light.

"So they are there, are they?" he said. "Chance in such matters is most perverse. I would lay a wager to any amount that I shall find them seated in the one particular room which I want to enter—which I must enter," he added.

Down the staircase he stole swiftly, disregarding all things on his way, and apparently only intent upon reaching the foot in the shortest possible space of time.

The light grew stronger.

It came from one of the rooms on the ground-floor, the door of which was only partially closed.

In the profound silence which filled the mansion, Lord Harcliffe could distinguish the faint hum of conversation.

The foot of the staircase was reached.

The partly open door was within a few paces of him, but he could not see into the interior.

On gaining the level of the ground-floor, however, instead of going nearer to this door, Lord Harcliffe strode along the spacious hall until he reached a doorway fixed almost at its extremity.

He passed through instantly.

This room would have been plunged in utter darkness but for a few fitful straggling rays from an iron lamp fixed swinging in the street.

But the illumination which came from it through the spacious windows would have been quite inadequate to enable anyone less familiar with the apartment than Lord Harcliffe to make his way across it.

He, however, with even more confidence than he had before displayed, advanced to the recess that was at one side of the ample fireplace.

Here stood a small side-table, the white marble top and gilt legs of which could just be distinguished from the general gloom which hung upon the objects surrounding them.

Agile as a harlequin, Lord Harcliffe gave a spring and stood upon this table.

Then, after feeling for a moment against the wall, he pulled open a kind of door.

That this was the entrance to some secret passage there was little doubt, and still more certain was it that this doorway was so constructed as to be concealed, when closed, from the view of any persons in the room, although now it was not light enough for anyone to see whether this was the case or not.

Having opened this little door, Lord Harcliffe remained standing on the table for a minute or two.

It was very strange, but now the murmur of voices could be heard almost as distinctly as when he reached the foot of the staircase, which proved that the secret passage must form a communication of some kind with the chamber in which the police officers were sitting on guard.

The result of the listening appeared to be satisfactory, for now, with the same noiselessness and rapidity which had characterised his movements ever since he entered the mansion, Lord Harcliffe passed through the opening in the wall and drew the door after him, though he did not quite close it.

When he had done this, the darkness was profound indeed.

Nothing more appeared before his eyes than would have done had a thick black cloth been covered over his face.

Notwithstanding this, he made his way very slowly forward, only taking the precaution to keep his arms stretched out to their full extent.

No doubt he was impressed with the conviction that it would have been most dangerous to show a light.

At every step, too, it became more and more necessary that he should absolutely make no sound whatever in his progress, for the voices of the police officers came more plainly upon his ears.

But every precaution had been taken to prevent discovery.

The sides and floor of the secret passage were thickly covered with some substance resembling felt, which effectually deadened every sound.

After going about twenty paces, Lord Harcliffe came to a halt.

A short distance in advance of him were two small points of light, which bore no slight resemblance to the glittering orbs of some wild beast of prey.

It soon became evident, however, that these points of light were nothing more than two holes pierced in the end of the secret passage.

They were not more than two inches apart and half an inch in diameter.

Through them came two streams of light.

Lord Harcliffe listened.

"Did you say pour out another glass?" he heard a voice say which seemed startlingly close at hand. "Thank you, sir. Really, if it was not for this splendid wine, which I had the good fortune to find down in the cellars, I don't know what I should have done all through the night."

"Peace!"

"Oh, yes—certainly, sir! I will be quiet as you wish it. But really, after being so long silent, it is cheering to hear a voice, even if it is one's own—it is indeed, sir."

No reply was vouchsafed to this remark, but the noise made by some one drinking awkwardly and greedily from a glass then followed.

Lord Harcliffe came quite to the end of the passage.

The two small holes that we have mentioned were just about the height of his eyes above the level of the floor of the passage.

Without apparently the least dread of being seen, he applied his eyes to the aperture and looked through.

The scene was a strange one.

The large and luxurious apartment in which had been passed so many hours of riotous dissipation was now a perfect wreck.

Articles of all kinds were tumbled about and strewed in all directions on the floor.

The place, indeed, bore the appearance of having been thoroughly ransacked.

It was lighted by a large fire, which was crackling and blazing brightly, and by three or four wax candles irregularly placed against the walls.

One of the tables had been drawn near to the fireplace, and on this stood a goodly collection of bottles and glasses, tobacco and pipes, which showed that, after their fashion, the police officers had been vastly enjoying themselves during their vigil.

In a crimson and gold chair on one side of the fireplace sat the highly-intelligent police officer, Mr. Peterson, his face wearing an appearance suggestive of a certain amount of obfuscation of intellect.

Sprawling opposite was another officer, whose face and form were quite unknown to the unsuspected observer.

The brows of Lord Harcliffe knitted together in an angry frown when he saw the waste and destruction around him, though he was about the last man in the world who would trouble himself about anything of the kind.

The room in which the two police officers had chosen to take up their quarters was, however, one of the finest in the whole mansion, and the one in which in former times his lordship habitually sat, because he preferred it to all the others.

Ranged completely round its walls were paintings of full-length figures, each one surrounded by a massive frame.

By a certain amount of resemblance and by the different changes in costume, it was evident at a glance that these were portraits, or professed to be such.

We must explain that it was behind one of these that Lord Harcliffe stood, so that he was only divided from the room by the canvas.

The two holes through which he looked were really the eyes of the portrait behind which he stood; and unless something of the kind was suspected it would have required an eye of more than ordinary keenness to have made out that there was anything unusual in the picture.

This we ought to state was the portrait of a man in complete armour, the panoply being of that kind which was worn by knights in the reign of Richard the Lion Heart.

The steel armour had been most cleverly represented by the painter, and in some parts actually seemed to reflect the glitter of the firelight as it played upon it.

This picture was behind Mr. Peterson, but considerably to one side, so that Lord Harcliffe was able to obtain a tolerably good view of the police officer's countenance.

The other sat exactly facing him, so that he was able to see his features with particular distinctness.

It was, however, either fancy or reality on the watcher's part, but this second police officer seemed to fix his eyes with almost suspicious persistency upon the portrait of the man in armour.

And while he kept his gaze fixed he fidgetted about in all manner of ways upon the chair, and every now and then raised to his lips the glass of rich wine which he held carelessly in one hand.

Mr. Peterson seemed to have all his attention concentrated upon the fire, the blaze of which appeared to possess a wonderful amount of fascination for him.

As Lord Harcliffe gazed upon this scene his brow grew darker and darker.

Involuntarily, as it were, his hands wandered towards his pistols.

But if for a moment he had contemplated bringing about the deaths of the two police officers from the secure position where he stood, he abandoned the idea.

Perhaps he was governed by the reflection that there might be, and probably were, other police officers within hearing of the sound of a pistol-shot who would immediately rush upon the scene.

And yet, while the two police officers remained in their present positions, how was Lord Harcliffe to enter that room, and obtain from it a certain package? for that, after all, was the motive which had brought him back to the dangerous proximity of his own dwelling.

Again his hands wandered to the butts of his pistols.

But he did not draw them.

Little did those two men think, as they sat so very comfortably by the fireside in those luxurious chairs, that they were really so near to death.

And yet such was the case.

But whatever Lord Harcliffe might have been about to do was checked by the next words which fell from the lips of the police officer who sat facing him.

That worthy moved about in the chair with more and more uneasiness.

"Mr. Peterson," he said, "I do wish you would let me hear the sound of your voice: after sitting here in the silence for so long it would be a downright treat if you would curse me well, that it would."

"There is nothing to talk about," said Mr. Peterson, emptying his glass. "The silence suits me best to think over my plans."

"But it does not suit me a little bit, because I have no plans to think about, you see, sir."

"And because you have not, is that any reason why I should keep up a senseless chatter, eh?"

"But the silence is what I don't like, Mr. Peterson. Just think of this great house, and no one in it at this lonely hour but ourselves! If you talked I should not think so much of it, but to sit here like this without a word is more than I can stand. I get fancying all kinds of things, Mr. Peterson."

"Bah!" was the contemptuous exclamation. "How I do hate to hear people talk about fancy and imagination, and all that rubbish!"

"But, Mr. Peterson, as I am a living man and sitting here, I can't get rid of the notion that that portrait yonder has got living eyes."

And he pointed to the one behind which Lord Harcliffe was standing.

Peterson received this statement with a stare of amazement, which changed into a loud laugh of derision.

"A portrait with living eyes!" he ejaculated at length. "This comes of imagination! Thank goodness, as I have often said before and as I say again, I never was troubled with any."

"But would you just turn your head and look at the picture I mean, Mr. Peterson? It is that one of the knight in complete armour, don't you call it?"

Peterson did look up.

But it was only with a casual and contemptuous glance, and so he failed to see anything peculiar in the portrait.

Lord Harcliffe had the presence of mind to stand perfectly still, not even attempting to remove his eyes from the orifices in the portrait, because he felt certain that by the firelight, and at the distance the portrait was from the ground, it was all but an impossibility for the deception to be discovered.

CHAPTER LXXVII.

LORD HARCLIFFE EFFECTUALLY ALARMS THE POLICE OFFICERS, BUT IS PURSUED ON TO THE HOUSE-TOPS.

"DON'T make a fool of yourself, Bryan!" said Mr. Peterson to his subordinate. "A portrait with living eyes indeed! I wonder what imagination will come to next?"

But the man's superstitious fears were in the ascendant, and what had just been said produced no effect at all upon him.

"I don't care, Mr. Peterson—I can't help it, and I can't stand it. I tell you again that portrait has got living eyes! I have seen them roll from side to side ever so many times; and even now the firelight is shining upon them quite brightly."

But Mr. Peterson would not turn his head in the least.

"Do you think I am going to make as great a fool of myself as you are? Hold your row, I say! I will have no more of your foolery!"

Hereupon silence remained, and Lord Harcliffe was rather in doubt as to what he should do next.

Had Bryan been by himself, or had he been accompanied by almost anyone rather than Peterson, the task of frightening them out of the room by playing upon their superstitious terrors would have been an easy one.

But with Peterson—a man who made a boast of having no imagination, and who had never under any circumstances showed the least symptoms of fear—Lord Harcliffe felt very doubtful as to the result of any experiment he might try to this end.

The most likely termination of it would be the discovery of his presence; and though he felt his chances of escape were good in such a case, yet there would be an end to all hope of accomplishing his important errand.

Time, too, was flying.

Up to the present moment his adventure had occupied him more than four times as long as he thought it would, and there seemed but very little probability just then of bringing it to a speedy termination.

"I have but one course," he said, mentally, "and were the risk ten thousand times greater than it is, I should be compelled to do it. I must contrive to scare them from the room. Could I but succeed in doing that and securing their absence for a few minutes only, all would be well. The question is as to how it can be done."

This was a point which required an immense amount of consideration.

He taxed his inventive powers for some moments without result.

In the meanwhile, the man Bryan sat stupidly staring at the portrait, as though the eyes, like those of a rattlesnake, had completely fascinated him.

More than once he opened his mouth, as though about to make some remark to his chief, but the manner of that redoubtable individual made him change his purpose.

"A groan," said Lord Harcliffe, "or even a faint sigh, coming from behind this portrait, would effectually serve to rid me of Bryan, but upon Peterson it would be worse than useless. He would be more likely to dash his cutlass through the canvas than anything else."

Suddenly, however, just when Lord Harcliffe was about to give up the problem in complete despair, the long-looked-for idea darted suddenly into his mind like an inspiration.

"I have it!" he said, almost too loudly to be exactly safe—"I have it! Nothing could be easier or better. Success is certain."

So saying, he left the secret panel, and retraced his steps, as rapidly as he could, to the point where he had entered the hidden passage.

Three seconds served to bring him to the room, through the window of which the rays from the oil lamp still feebly struggled.

Thrusting his hand into his pocket, Lord Harcliffe drew forth a large holster pistol.

It was one of those which had been thrust into the King's messenger's saddle.

He cocked it quickly.

There was not light enough to enable him to see whether the priming was all right or not.

He believed it was, and in this belief pulled the trigger.

A tremendous report followed.

In the confined area of that apartment it sounded almost like the explosion of a cannon.

Several of the window-panes were shattered, and fell jinglingly on to the pavement outside.

The moment he had fired, Lord Harcliffe flung the smoking pistol into the middle of the room, fearing that if he took it into the secret passage with him the subtle vapour should betray him.

The very instant that this was done, he closed the secret panel after him with a sharp snap, and hastened back to his former position behind the portrait.

So swift was he in his movements that when he peeped through the eyeholes again he found that neither of the officers had quitted the apartment, though both had sprung to their feet, and were looking as though they hardly knew what had happened.

Bryan showed every possible symptom of intense fright, and his first act, upon partially recovering himself from the shock of astonishment, was to rush upon his chief and cling fast to him, as though he felt that by so doing he should be securing his own safety.

Even Peterson was a little bewildered, for of all sounds that he expected to hear in the empty mansion, a pistol-shot was the last.

But the action of Bryan enraged him greatly.

"Let go, you fool!" he said, struggling furiously and vainly to release himself from the other's frantic grasp. "Let go, I say! Don't you hear me? Let go, I say!"

"Murder—murder!" cried Bryan, who, quite out of his senses with intense fear, so far from heeding what Peterson said to him, only clung the tighter.

"Let go, I say!" thundered Peterson. "Didn't you hear that pistol-shot?"

"Pistol shot!" roared Bryan. "It must have been an earthquake. Why, it was louder than the Tower guns fired all together; and I ought to know, for I have heard them times enough."

Peterson swore most awfully.

Then by dint of a vigorous effort, in which he put forth all his strength, and aided by the effect of his thick-soled shoes upon Bryan's shins, he got free, and with an oath dashed out of the room.

Lord Harcliffe was doubtful whether the other would be able to follow.

Placing his lips close to the canvas, he said, in deep and hollow tones:

"Bryan—Bryan—Bryan!"

"That's me," yelled the officer, with his hair bristling and his eyes rolling. "I'm one of them—only one!"

"Begone—begone!" said the same awful and sepulchral voice.

No command could have been more delightful.

Gathering himself up in some mysterious manner, he dashed out into the hall.

As soon as this was the case, Lord Harcliffe, fully sensible that he had no time to lose, pressed upon the spring close to which his hand had been resting in anxious speculation.

The panel opened instantly, and before it had done swinging back upon the hinges he was standing in the room.

His first act was to hasten to the door through which Bryan had just passed, to close it, and slip a bolt into its socket.

When that was done, he felt that, for a minute or two at least, he had a clear field for his operations.

Peterson was in great doubt as to where the pistol-shot had come from, and on gaining the hall of the mansion he was unable to discern the faintest signs of recent disturbance.

Suddenly there came upon his ears another sound which, though of an ordinary enough character, yet nevertheless at first filled him with almost as much confusion and dismay as the pistol-shot.

This other sound was a succession of loud and violent knocks upon the outer door of the mansion.

Upon realising this, Peterson drew a long breath of exquisite relief.

"Ah!" he said, "some of my men! All right now!"

As he spoke, he went without hesitation to the front door and flung it open.

As he fully expected, he [illegible] the doorsteps two of his men.

"Ah!" he said. "I thought it was you."

The men looked rather surprised.

They had evidently expected a very different greeting.

"What's the matter, if you please, sir? We thought we heard firearms."

"Yes, and so did I. But I can't find out where they were used."

"Somewhere in the building, sir. Shall we come in and help you search?"

"Yes—that is, no. Now I come to think of it, you had better double your watch on the outside. Bryan and myself will search the interior of the mansion, and as soon as you hear my signal hasten to my assistance, as I shall not give it except under the strongest necessity."

"There's the glass broken in one of the front ground-floor windows," said the officer, as he closed the door. "The glass is lying all over the pavement."

Peterson carried a wax candle in his hand, which he had snatched from its resting-place after escaping from the clutches of Bryan, and, aided by this, he commenced his explorations.

As fate would have it, the very first room into which he entered was the one in which the pistol had been discharged.

Of this, the wreathing masses of blue smoke and the pungent smell of the burnt gunpowder would have been certain evidence.

But not only that, the wind came whistling in through the broken panes of which the officers outside had spoken.

Peterson marched boldly enough into this room, and Bryan, too frightened to stay anywhere alone, followed him.

But the stillness of death itself prevailed in this room, and though the wind made the wax candle whiffle fearfully, yet it showed that there was no living creature in the room.

Nor was there apparently any other mode by which the room could be left than that where Peterson had entered.

Despite the boldness of the chief officer, a strange kind of feeling began to creep around his heart.

Fear, it is well known, is infectious, and, perhaps, some of it communicated itself to him from his trembling companion, Bryan.

The mystery was inscrutable.

But as he crossed the apartment, in order to make quite sure that it was empty, his foot came into contact with some loose object lying on the floor.

Stooping and picking it up, he found this to be the pistol which Lord Harcliffe had flung there.

At the first glance he saw this weapon had been recently used.

A thin wreath of smoke was curling from the muzzle, and upon throwing open the pan the smoke made its exit there also.

"As I live," he cried "this is the pistol!"

"Murder!" yelled Bryan, making a sudden dash towards the door.

But he stopped on the threshold, afraid to go any further, while he watched the further movements of his chief with widely distended eyes.

Peterson, however, felt all his customary courage and astuteness return to him.

His first act was to go to the window.

One cry brought the watching officers before him.

"The pistol has been fired off in this room," he said. "Are you sure no one has escaped by this window?"

"Quite."

"Redouble your vigilance, then. I shall find all out now very soon indeed."

But though he looked very carefully round the by no means large apartment, he failed to make any discovery.

Not a single article, so far as he could tell, had been shifted from its place.

There were no signs of confusion or derangement anywhere.

"Strange!" he said. "But I will not yield to the mystery yet. Come what will, I will unravel it."

Convinced, however, that no discovery was to be made there, he approached Bryan, who, encouraged by the quiet which had succeeded, was fast recovering the use of such faculties as he possessed.

"I must have my lantern," said Peterson, as a puff of wind from the broken window almost extinguished the candle he was carrying. "I ought to have brought it at first. But never mind, it is not too late. Come on, Bryan."

Bryan came on.

Not that he by any means wished to do so, but he preferred accompanying his resolute chief anywhere to remaining alone by himself for a single moment.

In the meantime Lord Harcliffe had been busily engaged.

After stepping through the secret panel that the portrait of the man in armour formed, his first exclamation was:

"It is just as I suspected. They guessed at what I have, and have been busily looking everywhere. But the hiding-place has foiled them beyond doubt. Once let me get the precious packet of papers in my possession, and I shall leave this place almost without one pang of regret, notwithstanding the very many pleasant hours I have spent here."

"I must lose no time," he added. "Ten to one if many moments elapse before Peterson and his companion return."

The loud knocking at the front door, the meaning of which is well known to the reader, now came upon his ears.

He stood listening, in order to form some idea of what amount of new danger threatened him.

The result was reassuring.

No sooner was the front-door closed again than he set himself seriously about the business of the night—that business which had met with so many interruptions.

Over the lofty, massive mantelpiece was a curious piece of woodwork richly carved.

Time had so blackened it that it would have required no ordinary judge to state of what kind of wood it was composed.

But its outlines were sharp and clear as ever, and the carving represented some ancient feat of arms.

This was the object upon which Lord Harcliffe's eyes became in an instant riveted.

It was out of his reach as he stood; but the table covered with bottles and glasses stood near, and he had only to draw it a little nearer to the fire to make it serve his purpose.

Mounting nimbly upon it, he leaned forward.

The carved woodwork was then just within his reach.

Pressing upon a certain part of the exterior moulding, the centre-piece flew open like a little circular door, showing a small black space behind it.

That this was a receptacle chosen by Lord Harcliffe for the safe custody of those articles which he most prized was quite certain.

With considerable rapidity, he transferred to his pockets several small articles, and finally he produced a dust-covered packet of papers.

This he put carefully into an inner breast pocket.

Then finally shutting the little circular door again, he dropped lightly to the floor.

"It is done," he said—"it is done! That little hiding-place, cleverly constructed as it is, will some day, no doubt, be found, but it will be a barren discovery. What they would so much like to handle will be elsewhere."

These words were pronounced with a vast amount of satisfaction; but the next moment, as the young man gazed around him at the defaced grandeur of the room, and reflected that he was about to leave it for ever, a feeling of deep melancholy stole over him

But it did not last for long.

Shaking it off, he said:

"No more of this! Time presses, and the sooner I am off the better."

He gave one glance around, and then, in a half-choked voice, pronounced the word:

"Farewell!"

The next moment, and he stood within the dark passage.

When there, he was about to close the portrait door, but a sudden thought restrained him.

"If yonder door is found fastened by Peterson when he returns," he said, pointing to the one which he had fastened by slipping the bolt into its socket, "his suspicions will be at once aroused. He will know some one has been here, and I shall probably be subjected to a closer pursuit than will be at all desirable. To unfasten the door will not take a second, and then when I depart there will be absolutely no trace whatever left of my presence here."

This decided him, and he stepped into the room again.

He said it would not take him a moment to unbolt the door.

And he was right.

But there are times when one single moment is of more vital import than an hour, and this was one of them.

Just at the very instant when he withdrew the bolt, Peterson placed his hand on the knob at the other side of the door.

The reader will be aware that he was returning for the purpose of fetching his lantern, which he had neglected to provide himself with in the first instance.

The bolt which we have mentioned was a small brass one, near the lock, and as it was well made it was either pushed or withdrawn without making scarcely an audible sound.

Peterson was too excited to hear it had it been ten times louder than it really was.

He pushed open the door with great violence, and strode into the room.

Lord Harcliffe had the presence of mind to do the only thing which promised even a ghost of a chance of safety. He stepped back nimbly over the soft carpet, and the door being flung open to the full extent, concealed him.

He stood without daring to breathe.

Up to this moment Peterson had not the faintest suspicion of the true state of affairs.

Bryan, as before, came no further than the threshold.

Peterson was intent wholly upon seizing, as quickly as possible, the lantern he had come on purpose to fetch.

It was Bryan who first saw that, instead of the mysterious portrait of the man in armour being in its accustomed place, there was a black yawning space instead.

Horror and fright prevented him from making a sound or movement to acquaint his chief with the startling discovery he had made.

At last Peterson, having found the lantern and lighted it, turned round.

He was struck in a moment by the unnatural appearance of Bryan's face,

"I told you so," said the latter, after several gasping efforts to speak—"I told you so!"

"What—what?" said Peterson.

"The portrait had got living eyes; and now look! See—see, the man in armour has stepped down out of his frame!"

CHAPTER LXXVIII.

IN WHICH THE BLACK HIGHWAYMAN ESCAPES DEATH BY A HAIR'S BREADTH.

"Get out, you fool!" said Peterson, without deigning to turn round, and intent only on leaving the apartment as quickly as possible. "Terror has driven you mad!"

"No—no!" repeated Bryan, more energetically. "Turn—look—judge for yourself!"

Thus adjured, Peterson followed with his eyes the direction of Bryan's arm.

When he saw the black open space, he was so confounded that he almost let fall his lantern.

"Now, wasn't I right?" said Bryan, triumphantly. "Come away — come, or who can say what will follow?"

[LORD HARCLIFFE REACHES THE STABLES JUST IN TIME.]

'Come away?" echoed Peterson. "Bah! Follow me. I see it all now plainly enough."

In spite of this assertion, we are of opinion that, with all his acuteness, Peterson did not see so very plainly after all.

In the meantime, Lord Harcliffe, shrinking as closely as possible to the wall, did not venture to draw his breath.

While the door remained in its present position—that is, thrown wide open—he might consider himself safe.

But should an attempt be made to close it, nothing on earth could prevent his discovery.

What his feelings were during the few moments that elapsed who can pretend to describe?

It was wonderful indeed to think he had so much presence of mind as enabled him to keep perfectly still while threatened with so much danger.

But, as we have said, he did not stir a muscle—a statue could have been more motionless.

Peterson drew his cutlass.

"Come on, Bryan!" he cried. "Shake off your fears! Come on, I say—follow me!"

So saying, he with surprising boldness rushed towards the open space.

"It's a secret passage," he cried, as he gave a bound up the kind of step that led to it. "Come on, Bryan, I say!"

The latter seemed equally balanced between his dread of remaining where he was and his fear of following his chief, for he stood stock-still.

But when he saw the form of Peterson disappearing, he felt that he could not remain, and so with a sudden dash he followed him.

The disappearance of both was instantaneous.

Lord Harcliffe remained with his back against the wall, unable to believe in the reality of his escape.

But the next moment a heavy sigh issued from his lips.

Then he started into life and activity.

He knew if he was speedy in his movements that all might yet be well, despite the untoward turn events had taken.

While Peterson and his colleague were poking about in the passage, he fancied surely he should have time to ascend the staircase and make his way out on to the roof.

This was what he instantly attempted to achieve.

Running first to the portrait panel, he closed it with as much silence as he could.

The click was, nevertheless, audible.

Whether Peterson heard it he did not stop to attempt to inquire, but satisfied with having placed this additional impediment between himself and his foes, he darted from the room.

The foot of the staircase was immediately opposite.

Up he went at break-neck speed.

At every step his hopes of ultimate escape increased, and thus he was stimulated to make more and more exertion.

In an incredibly brief space of time he reached the window through which he had so cleverly effected an entrance.

But before he had time to press upon the secret spring, he heard voices and footsteps on the staircase.

Incredible as it seemed, Peterson must in some way have been sagacious enough to arrive at a tolerably good notion of the real state of affairs, for he was making his way to the top of the house with all speed possible.

Still, he was not in time to observe the proceedings of the Black Highwayman.

No sooner was the window open than, seizing the rope that was hanging down from above, he swung himself over the sill.

Then supporting all his weight with one hand, he closed the window again, and after that began to ascend the rope with an amount of agility that would have done credit to a sailor.

He seemed altogether to forget that he was at such a dizzy height from the ground—or if he did not, it is certain that it produced no effect at all.

Reaching the parapet, which, as we have said, was only a few feet above the window, he had by far the most difficult task to perform.

But he surmounted the obstacle with rapidity and safety, and having reached the gutter, he crouched down in order to recover himself a little from the effects of his violent exertion.

After that, his first act was to draw up the rope by which he had ascended, so that there should be no fear of Peterson seeing it.

But in this he was just too late, for that active and intelligent officer, having reached the top of the staircase, chanced to look through that particular window, and was just in time to catch a transient glimpse of a looped piece of rope just disappearing above the topmost panes.

He needed no more than that to make him aware of the route taken by the disturber of his watch.

Of course he could have no idea of who it was that he was chasing; but we may safely venture to assert that in his wildest surmises upon the point he never came near to guessing that it might be Lord Harcliffe himself.

He did not pause, however, to indulge in any speculations.

Indeed, all his actions consequent upon what he saw were characterised by a precision and rapidity which did him great credit.

On first taking charge of the house, he had been most careful to examine it as thoroughly as he was able.

It was in consequence of the knowledge thus gained that he lost no time in attempting to open the window, but made his way direct to the ladder communicating with the trap-door on the landing.

The disappearance of the rope told him that the object of his pursuit had reached the roofs, and the readiest way to gain them was by means of the trap-door, which he had taken good care to see was properly secured.

Still trembling in every limb, and only following in his footsteps because it was judged to be a lesser evil than being left behind, was Bryan.

Peterson, carrying the lantern in one hand and his cutlass in his mouth, ran up the little ladder, and with wonderful speed drew back the bolts of the trap-door.

This he removed by pushing against it with his head while he ascended.

But upon emerging upon the house-top he discovered that, quick as he had been, yet he had afforded the fugitive time enough to get out of sight.

With an oath he called out to Bryan to keep close behind him, and then fairly stepped out upon the roof.

He drew himself up to his full height, and looked around him as well as the obscurity would allow.

By this time, however, it was by no means so dark as it had been.

Day had dawned, and the cold, misty morning rays brightening each moment, kept bringing into view objects that were more and more distant.

A cry escaped Peterson's lips.

On the next house but one he caught sight of what was surely a human form.

He gave chase at once.

It was indeed Lord Harcliffe that Peterson, by his energetic movements, had been able to catch sight of.

The reason was that Lord Harcliffe, not anticipating that the officers would get so quickly upon his track, had paused when near the beam across which he had made so perilous a passage.

Now that the dim gray light of dawn was beginning to show itself upon every object, the achievement of such a feat seemed ten thousand times more terrific than before.

Naturally enough, then, Lord Harcliffe shrunk from adopting such a means as this of getting to the ground.

"And yet," he said to himself, "how else am I to think of getting away? I cannot hope to enter one of these houses at such an hour as this, and reach the front-door without being seen and most likely recognised. And then if I did, are there not officers outside who would pounce upon me the moment I showed myself in the street? No—no. At all hazards the risk must be run. I have performed the journey once in perfect safety, and why should I not again?"

There was no reason except the fear that he would be unnerved by the better knowledge which he now had of the actual extent of his danger.

His hesitation was cut short by hearing the cry which escaped Peterson's lips as soon as he made the discovery of his whereabouts.

"Confound the fellow! It is to his accursed perseverance that nearly all my misfortunes are attributable. I must be speedy."

Now, of course, Peterson had no idea of the means by which access had been obtained to the mansion, and consequently his astonishment knew no bounds when he saw the fugitive suddenly slip over the edge of the parapet and disappear.

But resolved not to lose sight of him if possible, Peterson scrambled over the roofs with great apparent recklessness.

Never once did he move his eyes from the spot where Lord Harcliffe passed over.

On gaining it, and looking down, he stood petrified with amazement.

He tried to cry out, but he could not, and had his life depended upon it he could not have made the slightest movement.

Lord Harcliffe was by this time nearly half-way across the abyss.

He was crawling along upon his hands and knees.

Of course he was within pistol shot; but Peterson was so breathlessly interested in what he beheld that he never once thought of resorting to his weapons.

As he gazed with widely-distended eye he expected to see each moment the swaying, crawling mass fall headlong to the ground.

There was a dreadful feeling of dizziness about Lord Harcliffe's brain, for, strive as he would, he could not keep his eyes from occasionally seeking the ground below.

Some horrible species of fascination seemed to draw his regards in this direction, although he knew full well that it was essential for his safety that he should forget his elevation altogether.

Of Peterson's presence behind him he knew nothing

whatever, but suddenly he felt the beam give way alarmingly.

An odd creaking noise followed, which was succeeded by a loud shout.

The cry evidently came from many throats.

It made Lord Harcliffe look up suddenly—almost too suddenly for safety.

Then it did indeed seem as though all hopes of escape were at an end.

Nothing but the absolute certainty of capture stared him in the face.

To return, even if Peterson had not been on the roofs, would have been impossible.

To advance seemed worse than useless.

Who can conceive his dismay when he perceived the empty ruined house which he was striving so hard to reach suddenly become alive with his foes?

The moment he perceived them he was able to account for their presence, and wondered how he could have forgotten to think of it before.

There was now light enough to enable most things to be discerned with tolerable clearness.

Those officers who had knocked at the front-door of the mansion had caught sight of him on the beam, and, with what reinforcements they had been able to obtain, had gained admission to the half-demolished dwelling.

A feeling of overwhelming despair now took complete possession of Lord Harcliffe's heart.

He was trapped, and the only chance left to him was whether he preferred sudden death by dropping to the ground below to falling into the hands of his enemies.

The police officers could hardly contain themselves for exultation.

Incredible as the fact appeared, yet their own eyes assured them that the person on the beam was no other than the Black Highwayman himself.

But seeing him pause gave them a little misgiving.

"Surrender!" cried one of them—"give us your word to surrender, and we will assist you! If not, we will make sure of your capture by a volley of pistol-shots, for our orders are to take you dead or alive!"

A mist floated before Lord Harcliffe's eyes.

His heart ceased to beat, and a feeling of numbness pervaded every joint.

He fancied that he was no longer able to hold on to the beams: all sensation had left his fingers.

"Surrender!" said the police officer again. "Be careful, or you will be—— Ah!"

There was a sudden crash, mingled with shrieks and cries from many lips.

The beam had given way.

Either it had not been fixed with sufficient firmness to bear Lord Harcliffe's weight, or the violent wind which had been blowing for so many hours had loosened it from its hold, for, with a hideous crash, down it went.

Or, what was more likely, the catastrophe had been brought about by so many police officers having collected on one of the tottering walls.

But of the house which had been propped up so carefully there remained in about the twinkling of an eye nothing but a heap of bricks and dust.

The beam being one of the chief supports, of course, in giving way, caused the walls to fall—if indeed it was not, as some had said, the walls of the house gave way first and so caused the beam to fall.

Peterson and Bryan, on the opposite house-tops, saw the catastrophe, though the latter was not yet sufficiently recovered from his superstitious terrors to be able to comprehend it thoroughly.

All happened with a suddenness that made him fancy he was the sport of some delusion of the senses.

But the next moment the groans and cries coming from the confused mass below assured him that the awful sight which he had beheld was indeed a reality.

"Come," he said, tearing himself away from a contemplation of the scene only by a very severe effort—"come, we must descend. We can be of no assistance here."

In the meantime, how had Lord Harcliffe fared?

When he felt the beam sinking beneath him, he suddenly started into life and activity.

There was no time to think—no time to adopt any expedient to secure his safety.

All that remained for him was to obey the immediate impulse he experienced to cling as tightly as he possibly could to the massive wooden beam.

Fortunately for him his fingers did not release their grasp.

It was with the clutch of death that he held on.

But before any appreciable space of time elapsed, he found himself at the bottom of the descent.

There was a terrible jerk, which shook his fingers from their firm grasp, and then ensued complete forgetfulness.

But his insensibility did not last more than a moment, and on recovering himself he seemed to comprehend most fully all that had taken place.

He was alive, and, so far as he could tell at present, absolutely unhurt.

How such an extraordinary event could have happened—how it was he was not dashed to pieces, his first glance upwards was enough to show.

The beam in its descent had caught against a projection of the brickwork when within about ten feet of the ground.

The sudden shock had compelled him to let go, and though slightly hurt by falling upon the *debris* beneath, yet he escaped all injury from anything falling upon him.

Then darted into his mind the recollection of his great danger.

The consciousness struck him that, if he was only speedy enough in his movements, there was yet a chance of escape remaining, though only a moment or two ago he felt so certain that such could not be the case.

To feel this was, of course, to try it.

By a violent effort he scrambled to his feet.

A groan escaped him, for he was beginning to feel the effects of his fall more acutely, and no doubt would continue to do so.

A wild uproar reigned all around.

The whole neighbourhood was, of course, aroused by the occurrence of such a tremendous catastrophe, and people were hurrying to the scene of ruin from all directions.

The groans of the unfortunate police officers filled the air.

Scarcely one of them had escaped serious injuries, for, from their position, most of the *debris* had fallen upon them.

Lord Harcliffe, however, was not likely to waste a thought upon their condition.

A formidable heap of ruins lay between him and the street, but receiving strength from desperation, he scrambled on, and before Peterson could reach the spot he had all but got clear of the ruins.

But a police officer, who had chanced to receive only slight injuries, saw the highwayman attempting to escape, and, springing up, endeavoured to prevent him.

Lord Harcliffe let him come quite close.

Then turning round suddenly, he clenched his fist and struck the unfortunate man a terrific blow upon the ear, which laid him senseless at once.

But the action had been observed by one of the first arrivals at the scene of the accident, and guessing that something was wrong, though he knew not what, he endeavoured to stay the fugitive's further progress.

But better—far better would it have been for him had he foreborne all interference whatever, for a second sledge-hammer blow, delivered with the same precision as the first, stretched him likewise senseless on the ground.

At the same moment the Black Highwayman, hardly yet able to believe in the fact of his escape so far, made a sudden dash into the street.

CHAPTER LXXIX.

IN WHICH CAPTAIN HAWK RESCUES YOUNG SQUIRE KINGSBURY FROM THE TOMB.

RALPH'S sudden outburst of frenzy took Captain Hawk entirely by surprise.

So far from being prepared for such an event, he had been firmly persuaded that, when the supreme moment came, Ralph would have refused to commit the barbarous deed that was required of him.

But Captain Hawk was far from knowing all the guilty secrets that were locked up in those two callous breasts.

But, as the reader must feel perfectly aware, the highwayman had determined that at all risks to himself he would interfere in time to prevent the consummation of the skilfully-laid plan of personation, fraud, and murder.

And this sudden violence which Ralph so unexpectedly displayed raised in his breast the fear that the villain would, by two or three heavy blows upon the head of the ill-used heir, put an end to his life before there was time for reflection to set in.

Certain it is that such an awful deed could not be perpetrated in such a place in anything like cold blood.

There could be little doubt that Ralph, made thoroughly conscious that he was in the toils, and could not escape, resolved to commit the deed in the fury of sudden desperation.

A sardonic grin contorted the countenance of his companion when he observed the sudden change.

Slipping the loaded pistol into his pocket, he hastened to the side of his accomplice.

Ralph was strong, and possessed of skill in the use of the weapon in his grasp.

A crackling sound was quickly heard, and then, by the assistance of the other, the lid of the coffin was thrown back.

Captain Hawk could remain quiescent no longer.

Pushing the door further open, and thrusting in the hand that held the loaded pistol, he cried, in startling tones:

"Accursed villains! what is it you would do?"

No words, however powerful, could convey anything like an idea of the amount of dismay that the pronunciation of these words produced.

Exclamations of horror and fear burst from the lips of the two men.

Ralph, with a hideous cry that was enough to wake the very dead, dropped his crowbar and turned to fly.

But, in his blind fear, he forgot all about the tressels that were placed so awkwardly between him and the door.

Down he went with a terrific crash.

Then he made many attempts to rise.

But his terror and his desperate haste prevented him from performing this simple action, and he lay grovelling in the sawdust of the vault as though grappling with some invisible assailant.

The other seemed paralysed.

He was so absolutely certain in his own mind that they had the church all to themselves, and that no human being was aware of his intentions, that he could not divest himself from the horrible idea that the interruption came from some of the dead around him.

It was a thought likely enough to be engendered in a guilty breast on such an occasion, and surely a thought terrible enough to sear the brain with madness.

He shuddered from head to foot, and then let the lantern fall from his strengthless hand.

Captain Hawk, by darting forward suddenly, was just in time to catch it as it fell, otherwise darkness would have been added to the horror of the scene.

It was just at this moment that the lid of the coffin—which had fallen down again as soon as Ralph and his companion had released their hold upon it—was thrown back with great force against the wall of the vault.

Its occupant started up suddenly into a half-sitting posture.

His winding-sheet, and the white bandage round his head gave him an awful and ghastly aspect.

His eyes, which were opened to an unnatural extent, rolled round the vault with wonderment and terror.

Such an awaking must, in good truth, have been an awful one.

With a second horrible cry upon his lips, Ralph, having partially recovered an erect position, half rolled, half crawled out of the vault.

The young man in the coffin, unable to comprehend his situation and to recollect clearly what had last happened to him, incautiously leaned forward so much as to overbalance the coffin as it laid upon the narrow shelf.

The other's fears exaggerated this into an attempt upon the part of the dead to seize upon him.

It galvanised him into life.

With one bound he reached the door of the vault, and the next moment was scrambling with Ralph up the dark and narrow staircase.

Captain Hawk, who was just a little bewildered by the rapidity with which the events had taken place, strode towards the door, lantern in hand, as though his intention was to pursue the two villains.

But changing his mind instantly, he turned back.

"I shall know them," he said; "and I can be of more service here."

So saying, he endeavoured to raise the prostrate form of the young squire.

The sudden shock, or else his fall, seemed to have been too much for his feeble powers.

He was insensible.

By main strength, however, Captain Hawk extricated him from the coffin, and raised him to a sitting position, resting his back against one of the stout stone pillars.

Then recollecting that he had in his pocket a small bottle of Tom Beckford's very best brandy, he produced it, and poured a small quantity into the unfortunate young man's mouth.

The result of this was at first rather alarming, for it seemed as though the ardency of the spirit would deprive him of life.

But soon a different effect was produced.

His eyes opened, his breath came more vigorously, and he essayed to speak.

"All is well now," said Captain Hawk, reassuringly. "Be under no apprehension—you have nothing whatever to fear."

The young squire looked amazedly at his surroundings.

"All will be clear to you in a short time. Do not perplex your brain about anything just at present."

The young squire responded by a grateful smile.

"If you would allow me to leave you for a moment or two, I will send for help. I shall not be far away; and in the meantime you will be out of all danger."

He nodded.

Apparently, however, he was not conscious that he had been in any peril at all; but the fact was, at the present moment he was not sufficiently recovered from his swoon to be in full possession of his senses.

Captain Hawk, on receiving this permission, hastily left the vault.

He did not take the lantern with him, but left it for the young squire, though he would almost have been better without it, as its effects, so far from dissipating the gloom, only served to bring the horrors of the place into stronger relief.

But, despite the darkness, Captain Hawk rapidly made his way to the ground-floor of the church above, and from thence down the aisle until he reached the window outside of which he had placed the ostler on guard.

He had now good reason to congratulate himself upon having been accompanied by the faithful fellow on the present expedition.

Captain Hawk found him in a great state of agitation.

"Captain—captain, whatever has happened? Do you know that those two fellows have left the church, and have gone galloping off as though the devil himself was at their heels?"

"Yes—yes! Attend to me, Isaac."

"Yes, captain."

"Make all the speed you can back to the Greyhound. Tell the landlord to come here with what help he can, and to send word up to the Hall that the young squire is not dead, but has just awoke from a trance, and is now in the vault. Quick! Be off! There is not time to exchange a single word."

Isaac looked terribly bewildered, but as he understood well enough what the captain had said, he departed to deliver the message, much wondering the while what it could all mean.

Having done thus much, he hastened to the vault, where, doubtless, the young squire was awaiting him with the utmost impatience.

He found him in a state of great mental anxiety, not to say alarm.

"Tell me," he said, "what is the meaning of all I see? Why am I here? Can it be that, after all my attempts to satisfy myself upon the point, I am, nevertheless, only the victim of some vision?"

"Do not distress yourself, sir," said Captain Hawk. "At the same time you must prepare yourself for a severe shock."

"What—what? Speak to me: relieve my doubts and

fears. Tell me anything rather than keep me in this awful suspense."

A very little consideration, however, sufficed to make the highwayman aware that it would be better not to tell the young squire all just then.

"The simple fact is," he said, "that in your illness you fell into a trance, which was so much like death itself that they actually placed you in this vault; but in a way that I will explain to you at a more fitting opportunity, the discovery was made that you were alive!"

The young man drew his hand across his brow, on which the chilly dew of perspiration stood thickly.

"And—and," he said, with unmistakable horror pervading every tone, "*I have been buried alive!*"

The words were accompanied by a shuddering glance round at the coffins which filled every niche.

Of this remark and the glance, Captain Hawk did not think fit to take any notice.

"Do you think," he said, "that you are sufficiently recovered to ascend the steps which lead up into the church? You will be much better on the cushions in one of the pews than you can be here. Will you try?"

"I will."

"That is well. But drink first a little more of this brandy. You will find that it will render you less susceptible of the cold."

The young man trembled like a leaf.

But despite his weakness and the cramp in every joint, he, by a vigorous effort, succeeded in gaining an upright position.

Captain Hawk then half carried rather than led him from the vault.

The steps were ascended in safety, but both felt it a relief to enter one of the old-fashioned pews.

The young squire seemed about to fall into another fit of insensibility, but another draught of brandy averted the attack.

"Tell me," he then said, "who you are, and how you came to be here to-night? I have been looking at you as well as this faint light will permit, but cannot remember to have seen you anywhere before. Are you a stranger?"

"I am."

"Then satisfy my curiosity"

"I would do so gladly; but do you not think it will be better for you to wait until you have to a greater extent recovered yourself from the shock?"

"No—no! Believe me," he said, earnestly, "I feel that anything would be better than the dreadful state of perplexity and suspense in which I now find myself."

"If so, then, of course I will comply with your request. Still, I should have thought——"

"No—no!"

"Well, then, the account so far as I know is simply this: After your father's death you were taken ill. Do you remember that?"

"Yes—yes!" was the feverish answer.

"Well, then, it seems that one who represents himself to be your father's nephew, but who is really an impostor, administered to you some foreign drug, which produced effects exactly similar to death. Your medical attendants were deceived by it, and, as I have said, you were buried here for dead."

"But," said the young squire, with a half-stupified air, "why a narcotic? Why not a poison?"

"Ah! you may well ask. But there lies the most diabolical portion of the whole business."

"How so?"

"Had you been poisoned, your murderer would have been discovered almost to a certainty. But, having taken this drug, and being only under the influence, the first touch with the surgeon's knife would have shown that you were alive—that is, supposing foul play had been suspected. Your trance would have been passed over as coming from natural causes, and your would-be murderer would have had patience for another trial."

The horror of this recital was so great as to be almost past the young squire's power of endurance.

"Then," he said, "I understand now. Having had me consigned to the vault, they afterwards repaired thither in order to complete their hellish work."

"That is it—precisely it."

"And you?"

"A chain of the strangest and most fortuitous circumstances brought me here. What I have told you I have gathered from what fell from the lips of the pretended nephew and his accomplice, Ralph."

"Ah! the villain!"

"You know him, then?"

"I do."

"Enough! Then let me beg of you not to distress yourself further."

"No, no—I am calmer now—much calmer, and I am now conscious that I owe to you a deeper debt of gratitude than I shall ever be able to repay. But for your presence and courageous interference, I should by this time have fallen entirely a victim to their hellish plans."

Captain Hawk was silent.

The young man's vehemence rendered him uneasy.

To pass through such a horrible ordeal without some effect being left upon heart and brain was not to be expected, and he dreaded lest an attack of insanity should be brought on.

"Heaven bless you, sir," he said, taking one of the highwayman's hands and pressing it between his own, which were now of such corpse-like coldness that they sent a thrill through the captain's entire frame—"Heaven bless you! I know not who you are; but from this day forth you shall be my dearest brother. Never—never shall I forget what I have escaped through your assistance; and you will find that I am one who knows how to be grateful for it."

"Be calm," said the captain—"pray be calm! What I have done for you is no more than I would have done for anyone else. Your thanks are grateful to me; but I am one not used to praises."

"Then you shall grow accustomed to them, my generous preserver. I will not allow you to pass over this service so lightly. But let me think. Where are the two villains who have planned and executed all this fiendish villany?"

"Escaped."

"No, no—not escaped—do not say escaped!"

"At any rate, they have fled from the spot; and I could not pursue them without abandoning you."

"But I must be avenged. Such a deed must not go unpunished."

"Ah! I see you are better."

"Why?"

"Because you are thinking of vengeance."

"I am—I am; and I will have it! I had forgotten for the moment that the two villains are known. My faculties are not quite so clear as usual. I will set on foot such a well-organised pursuit that it will be impossible for them to escape me long."

These words showed that the young man, despite the fearful ordeal he had gone through, was beginning to recover his wonted vigour of mind.

Turning more, so that he could see the captain's face, he said:

"You have told me already that you are a stranger; now add to that knowledge by letting me know your name. Rely upon it, I shall never forget to think of it with gratitude."

"You will be good enough to excuse me if I decline."

"What?"

"To pronounce my name."

"But why?"

"I have reasons for wishing to keep my identity a secret."

"Yes, but——"

"Pardon me, sir; surely that is sufficient ground for me to decline."

"But to withhold your name——"

"It may savour of suspicion, and no doubt does so. Still, I can only rest under any such imputation."

The young squire did not reply.

But his countenance assumed an expression of determination, which could have been easily interpreted by anyone to mean that he would not rest until he had penetrated the secret.

At this moment a subdued roaring sound made itself heard.

"What is that?" said the young man, with a start of alarm.

"Help coming, no doubt," answered the captain. "I can distinguish voices and footsteps. Wait a moment—I will look."

As he spoke, he hastily quitted the pew, and made his way to one of the latticed casements of the church.

Coming up the avenue, he could distinguish a dense crowd of persons.

Many carried lights, and not a few had armed themselves with whatever defensive articles had happened to come first to hand.

"Yes," he said, turning back; "it appears as though all the neighbourhood had been aroused. In a short time you will be beneath the roof of the old Hall, and you will forget the disagreeable adventures of to-night."

"Never—never," was the firm reply—"never while I breathe; nor shall I forget those who have done me this foul wrong; nor the one to whom I owe my life."

At this moment a loud uproar and clamour of voices informed them that the approaching throng had reached the door of the church.

"Now, then, Mr. Bootles," said some one, "come forward as fast as you can, and unlock the door, will you?"

"Yes—yes," replied a wheezy voice; "here I am, sir. Well, who would have thought of such a thing as this here happening at the blessed church where I'm the *beetle?* I——"

"There—there—that will do. Open the door first, and then you can chatter as much as you like."

"Ah, ah!" responded the beadle, sighing, and inserting the ponderous key into the huge keyhole. "It all comes of losing respect for *beetles.* It's growing, sir, this disrespect of *beetles*, and of what the *beetles* says. But, mark my words, it will be a sad and sorry day for England when respect for *beetles* is altogether lost. Ah me! —it will—it will!"

Groaning and sighing, Mr. Bootles turned the key.

The bolt of the massive lock went back with a sudden snap.

CHAPTER LXXX.

THE POLICE OFFICERS RECOGNISE CAPTAIN HAWK IN THE OLD CHURCH.

The door was flung open in a moment by the pressure of the crowd without, and there was anything but a decorous rush into the church.

The lanterns cast a dim and partial illumination around.

The utmost excitement was exhibited by every one of the new-comers.

With the most marvellous rapidity the account of what had taken place had spread itself over the village.

The Hall was not very far distant from the church; and nearly all the servants, headed by the old butler, had come down, bringing with them anything which they thought might be at all useful in the emergency.

It was the butler who, trembling in every limb, first approached the lantern which Captain Hawk had again taken in his hand.

"Good Heavens, sir!" he cried, "what is all this? I hear——"

"Fear nothing," interrupted the highwayman, instantly: "here is your young master safe and well. Make haste and wrap him up warmly, and convey him with all speed to the Hall, or he will catch such a cold as will probably cause his death."

"Yes—yes, sir, I have provided myself for that; but still I can hardly believe that my young master is really not dead after all."

"But you can believe it now, can you not?" said the young squire, rising and grasping his hand.

The greater part of those assembled witnessed his appearance in the grave clothes with a shout of horror, and retreated several paces towards the door.

How far they might have gone is hard to say, had not their progress been arrested by the foremost of a large troop of police officers, who had just entered the church.

The one who had the command of the party strode forward with an air of great authority.

"Come—come," he said, in loud, pompous tones—"what is the meaning of all this? I must have the whole matter explained before I permit anyone to leave the church. We are in pursuit of a daring highwayman, and I should not be in the least surprised to learn that he has had something to do with the business."

The villagers shrank back with a great deal of awe from before the troop of police officers, who made a very formidable display with their drawn cutlasses, the blades of which reflected the rays from the lanterns with a great amount of brilliancy.

"Gentlemen," said the old butler, "this is my young master, the squire: he fell into a swoon, and was buried for dead; but he has recovered."

"Yes; I am here," said the young man, who seemed possessed of a more than ordinary amount of courage and determination. "Wrap a cloak around me, and then I shall do well enough until I have said the few words I wish to utter."

Of course, an ample cloak was instantly thrown around him.

All present waited in breathless silence to catch the next words which fell from his lips.

To the majority it seemed like a voice coming from the jaws of Death himself.

"Do I not see officers of police here?" he said, in the way of one who is accustomed to command.

"Yes—yes!" replied many voices in chorus.

"Let the one in command stand forward, then."

"I am here," said the chief officer.

"Very good. Then I inform you that a base attempt has been made upon my life by the man who passes himself off as my father's nephew, and his accomplice, Ralph Garret. They have fled. Pursue them—capture them, and I will give two hundred pounds reward!"

The chief police officer who, in obedience to the young squire's order, had come forward, fixed his eyes in a moment upon the form of Captain Hawk, where they rested as if fascinated.

The highwayman knew his danger.

A sensation of alarm came over him at the moment when the officers first entered.

But he had the presence of mind to stand still.

He felt that his only chance of escape was that, in the dim, uncertain light which filled the church, his foes would fail to recognise him.

He was certain that any attempt to withdraw would only have the effect of directing special attention towards him.

But when he saw the fixed look which the police officer's eyes assumed, he knew he was detected.

His uneasiness was increased by the knowledge that he was surrounded by a dense throng of persons, who, at a word, would close together so as to prevent his further progress.

And even had this not been the case, long before he would have been able to gain the window the officers would have had time to fire upon him, a thing which former experience had made known to him they would not scruple for a moment about doing.

He knew all this not by reflection but by intuition.

And so, as it turned out, he did the wisest and best possible thing under the circumstances—that is to say, he stood still.

The young squire was amazed at the chief officer's strange manner.

"Don't you understand me, man?" he said. "I tell you that my life has been sought and almost taken by the two villains I have mentioned. Don't I tell you that they have fled? Why do you not pursue them?—why stand there like a stone?"

"Because," said the chief police officer, with very great deliberation, and drawing forth a pistol while he spoke—"because I see before me the man who it is my special business to capture. Beyond a doubt he is one of the accomplices."

Then, amid the intense amazement and silence of everybody, the police officer continued, in loud tones:

"Captain Hawk, you are recognised! Flight or resistance are equally vain and out of the question. Surrender, then, quietly into our hands, for our orders are to make you prisoner at all risks, alive or dead!"

So saying, he pointed the muzzle of the pistol at the highwayman.

Hearing this made the young squire give a start of surprise, but it was so slight as to escape the notice of everyone.

With wonderful sagacity he understood all at once, and with still more wonderful promptitude he determined to make an attempt to save him.

He understood Captain Hawk's singular manner now,

when his identity was mentioned, and perfectly comprehended how it was that the captain had saved him from his awful fate.

In return he resolved to throw around him the shield of his protection.

He cared not for the fact that his preserver was a highwayman.

He had only known him in the former character, never in the latter.

Accordingly, he assumed an air of great surprise, and, haughtily drawing himself up to his full height, he advanced a step forward, by which means he interposed himself between the captain and the muzzle of the officer's pistol.

"Are you in your senses?" he said to the chief officer, who stepped back like one thunderstruck. "You don't know the meaning of what you say? What strange hallucination possesses you?"

"Hal—hal——" gasped the officer.

"Yes; for this person you call Captain Hawk is my best and dearest friend, and no highwayman. Some accidental resemblance or the dim light of the lanterns must have deceived you."

Captain Hawk drew a long breath.

Not for one moment had he expected such an event as this.

He had some doubts, however, as to the success of the stratagem; but then he did not know the influence which the young squire exerted on all around him.

The chief officer was staggered, as well he might be.

But as he stepped back, he again caught sight of the captain's countenance, and this time he felt certain it could be no fancied resemblance that had deceived him.

"Excuse me, sir," he said, somewhat recovering himself, "but I assure you the mistake is on your side. I have seen the highwayman too often, and studied his description too well, to make any mistake about the matter. Captain Hawk, I once more call upon you to surrender yourself quietly, and without causing strife and bloodshed in this holy place!"

Captain Hawk now at once took the cue which the young squire had given him.

Putting on a look of the utmost surprise that was well mingled with indignation, he said, haughtily:

"I don't know quite what is the meaning of this; I cannot bring myself to believe that you would make so great a mistake. Is this some premeditated insult? I can call fifty witnesses who will prove I am not the man you take me to be; and surely the words of Mr. Kingsbury himself ought to be sufficient guarantee."

The officer got bewildered, and knew not how to choose.

On the one side there were his own faculties, which assured him that the individual standing near the squire was Captain Hawk, the highwayman.

On the other hand there was the squire himself declaring that the officer must be mistaken, for the supposed highwayman was his friend.

But the chief officer was not disposed to discredit so readily the evidence of his own senses.

If he did, he should hardly know what to believe again.

He beckoned one of his companions to his side as though about to confer with him.

But the young squire interrupted.

"I will stay here no longer," he said. "You can adopt what course you please."

"Then," said the chief officer, determinedly, "I will at all hazards make that man my prisoner."

"Nay—nay! Let there be no rashness! You will be sorry when you find out what a mistake you have made. He will accompany me to the Hall. I will vouch for his safety, and will undertake to prove that he—he is not the man you take him to be. Surely my word ought to be enough to vouch for that."

Loud murmurs began to come from the assembled villagers.

They had been in the habit of considering the young squire's authority as absolute; and as he never used it unjustly, they did not relish the idea of having it called in question by a police officer.

"Remember," added the young squire, in a threatening tone, "I shall not forget to make my report of what has taken place; and I shall charge you with wilful neglect of duty. I have told you there has been made an infamous attack upon my life, and I have offered you a reward out of my private purse if you would overtake the miscreants. You disregard that altogether, and stupidly maintain that an intimate friend of mine is Captain Hawk, the highwayman. It's monstrous! As I said before, I will answer for him, and surely that ought to suffice. Is the carriage ready, Gibson?" he added, turning to the old butler.

"It is, my dear young master. Oh! I fear that this night will be the death of you after all! This church alone is like a grave. Come, sir—come!"

And he held out his arm for the resuscitated young man to lean upon.

But the squire was in no need of such a support.

Naturally he was of an unusually robust disposition, and the little excitement which had succeeded to his recovery had the effect of benefiting rather than of injuring him, for it kept his mind from dwelling too much upon the horrors of the vault.

No doubt a time would come when all the terrors of that grisly place would present themselves to him with terrific force; but the longer the time that elapsed without anything of the kind taking place the better.

"Come!" he said, placing his hand upon the captain's arm. "Despite your refusal a little time ago, you shall now accompany me to the Hall, and in the morning, when the officers bring me the real culprits, I will satisfy them of the ridiculous mistake that they have made. Come!"

Of course Captain Hawk readily accepted this invitation, though he took care not to display the slightest anxiety.

The chief officer gnawed away at the butt-end of his pistol, not knowing what to say or how to act.

He looked after Captain Hawk much as some half-famished cat might glare after a plump and highly desirable mouse when being escorted from her fangs.

In spite of all, he could not divest himself of his first impression; but, on the other hand, he could not believe that Squire Kingsbury was the accomplice of a highwayman.

The reader will fully understand his perplexity.

Yet he felt that he dared not interfere.

Instances of mistaken identity had frequently come under his notice; and supposing that he was in error after all, he knew that there would be no pardon for the offence.

He glared after them, then, as they departed, and afterwards, turning to the man whom he had called to his side before, he said:

"Gibbons, what do you make of all this?"

"I don't know what to make of it."

"That is just my difficulty."

"I can assure you, sir, that I would take my oath anywhere any minute that that is Captain Hawk; and yet it is impossible, for the young squire would never get himself into trouble by attempting to screen such a one. I'm afraid, sir, it's a case of mistaken 'dentity."

"Well, Gibbons, I tell you what we will do."

"Very good, sir."

"Captain Hawk or not Captain Hawk, we won't lose sight of him."

"That's the policy."

"It is, Gibbons; for if it should turn out we are mistaken there is no harm done, while, on the other side——"

"We shall be prepared," said Gibbons, finishing his chief's speech, and accompanying the words with a very satisfied nod.

"Then I will leave that to you."

"All right, sir."

"I cannot refuse to go in pursuit of these two men—doubtless I shall speedily capture them. In the expectation of that event, you must watch the person we suspect."

"You can safely trust me to carry out that little affair, sir."

"I know that, Gibbons. Come along."

While this whispered, hasty colloquy between the two police officers was taking place, the young squire and Captain Hawk reached the church porch, where the old family carriage was waiting in readiness to convey them to the Hall.

As for the highwayman, he could hardly believe in his escape so far.

It seemed an impossibility that he should quietly walk

out of the church, leaving the officers in the building behind him.

Yet he could not deny such was the actual state of the case.

Not for a moment, however, did he give way to the idea that he was out of danger yet.

Such a notion, he knew full well, would be wholly illusory.

But there was the strong probability that he would be able to escape them.

As may be supposed, it was with strange and varied feelings that he took his seat in the luxurious vehicle.

As it rolled away from the ivy-grown tower of the old church, he glanced out at one of the windows in the hope of catching sight of Isaac the ostler.

But no signs of his faithful follower were visible, and it was almost with a sigh of disappointment that he leaned back against the cushions again.

No sooner had the carriage got through the churchyard gates than the young squire, leaning forward, said:

"Tell me, is there any truth in what the police officer said? Fear not to answer me. You will be in no danger at my hands."

But Captain Hawk remained silent.

It was not on account of a disinclination to speak, but because his feelings so far overpowered him that he was unable to do so.

The young squire seemed intuitively to understand him, for he said:

"You may wonder, perhaps, why I acted as I have. I confess it was solely upon impulse. But I seemed to feel that if there was truth in the accusation, I should have the means of showing my sense of the obligation I am under to you by screening you from your foes. On the other hand, if there was no truth in it, I should be able to save you from the annoyance to which such a charge would subject a stranger."

Captain Hawk took one of the squire's hands, and pressed it warmly and gratefully between his own.

"It is rare," he said, in a voice that was almost choked with emotion, "to find so much sense of generosity existing. I——"

"Enough. I understand fully what you are about to say: I understand that the police officer was not mistaken—that you are——"

"Captain Hawk."

A silence followed, during which the squire gazed at his strange companion as well as the semi-obscurity of the carriage would permit.

"I have heard much of you," he said, at length, "and much of what I have heard I should be glad to believe untrue; but for all that——"

"I am a highwayman!" said the captain, with considerable bitterness in his tones.

"True—you are."

"And I shall remain one."

"Nay, for——"

"I can understand what you would say, and fully comprehend the friendly feeling which dictates it. You would ask me to quit my present course of life, to fly, and in some other place bury my identity."

"Exactly."

"I have thought of it; but it is impossible. I am what I am, and the world will not suffer me to be anything else. I should be hunted from place to place. They would not be content that I should quit my course of life, and so, you see, I should be compelled to turn round in self-defence."

"I see—I see."

"Never—never, though, shall I forget your kind generosity in rescuing me from my perilous position. I could hardly have escaped those officers alive."

"Think no more of it. Could I do less for the one who had saved me from so awful a fate? It seems that I have not yet had time to realise its full horror. But you will escape now, will you not?" he added. "The police officers may be suspicious, and a second time I might fail in my efforts to screen you."

"I am afraid that the officers are suspicious now. From what I saw I feel certain that this carriage is closely watched."

"Do you think so?"

"I could almost stake my life upon it."

"What is to be done?"

"Do not let the consideration of that be the means of giving you the slightest uneasiness. Believe me, now I shall find it the easiest matter in the world to secure my own safety."

The squire looked at him in incredulous surprise.

"I have one favour to beg, however," said the captain, speaking with a good deal of hesitation.

"Name it."

"It is not for myself, but for another."

"It is granted."

"Many—many thanks! Will it take us long to reach the Hall?"

"Not more than a quarter of an hour. It would not be so long, only there is a steep ascent which can only be accomplished at a walk."

"Enough—enough," said the captain. "That will afford me abundance of time to tell you what I have to say."

"It is, then, a confession you have to make?"

"Nay, scarcely that; and yet I trust to enlist your full attention."

"There is no fear of it. Say on—I am listening."

And in a way which showed how intense was the interest he felt, the young squire waited for the next words which should fall from the highwayman's lips.

CHAPTER LXXXI.

THE BLACK HIGHWAYMAN SUCCEEDS IN REGAINING POSSESSION OF HIS STEED.

When, after felling his two assailants to the earth, Lord Harcliffe succeeded in getting free from the ruins of the fallen house, and dashing into the street, he fancied that his escape was accomplished.

This event was so much beyond what he had dared to anticipate that it had an overwhelming effect upon him; and on reaching the opposite house he was fain to steady himself by clinging to a projecting doorway.

For some seconds every object whirled around him in frantic gyrations.

He felt his eyesight growing dim, and then it seemed as though he sank down—down into the centre of the earth.

The horrible consciousness came over him that he was about to swoon, and the knowledge sent such a pang to his heart that it rallied his failing spirits, and caused the blood to flow freely in his veins.

The first thing of which he was sensible after this was that a loud uproar was going on around him.

Crowds of people were hurrying to the scene. Some with a tolerably accurate knowledge of what had taken place, others merely conscious that some accident had occurred.

Lord Harcliffe drew his breath short.

All the neighbourhood was of course in a state of great commotion, and he knew that he should yet have a hard struggle to reach the stable where he had left his horse.

And until he did that, he could hardly take upon him to say that he had escaped.

With the adjoining streets thronged with people, how was he to hope to make his way undetected?

Moreover, what was more appalling still, was the consciousness that as every minute passed away his weakness increased with frightful rapidity.

He would not be able to defend himself successfully should he be attacked as he was before.

And in every limb and joint he began to feel the most excruciating pain, and, to make matters worse, that pain rapidly increased instead of abating in violence.

At first no doubt he was so far stunned as to be incapable of feeling his bruises; for, notwithstanding that he had clung so tightly to the beam, it was not possible for anyone to fall from so great a height without being seriously hurt.

And now his eyes cleared a little, and he saw that the people who arrived all collected round the ruined house, apparently paying no attention whatever to the side of the street he was on.

This kindled in his heart the hope that he might be able to steal away unnoticed.

Without more delay he set to work to try.

The distance of one house was passed without the least notice being taken of him, and he might have g

[PHANTOM CLEARS TYBURN TOLL-GATE.]

further unperceived but for the recovery of the police officer he had stretched upon the ground.

This was the person upon whom several of those who arrived bestowed their attention, and after dashing some water in his face and half choking him by pouring some brandy down his throat, the police officer opened his eyes.

He glanced about him for a second, as though unable to remember what had happened.

Then recollection suddenly returning, he started up to a half-sitting posture, and cried out:

"Where is he?—where is he? Which way did he go?"

"Who?—who?" clamoured twenty voices in chorus.

"The Black Highwayman."

The words were repeated with intense astonishment, for the popular belief was that the mysterious highwayman had succeeded in getting many miles away from London.

"Yes—yes! I almost had him!" said the officer, wildly, and making the most furious struggles to rise—"I almost had a thousand pounds! But he felled me with a blow which makes my head sing now just for all the world like a Methodist chapel."

With these last words the officer stood upright.

It chanced that he was on a heap of rubbish, which enabled him to see over the heads of the people who surrounded him.

His piercing glance swept round instantly, and almost the first object he beheld was the staggering form of Lord Harcliffe.

"There he goes—there he goes! Yonder—yonder! He is hurt! Hurrah! we shall have him now!"

Those cries sent a pang of alarm through Lord Harcliffe's heart, but, fortunately for him, he just then reached a corner, round which he turned as hastily as his benumbed and aching limbs would allow.

This took him momentarily out of the sight of his foes, so that when the people looked round after the officer called out they failed to catch sight of anybody.

Consequently they stood irresolute, not knowing which way to run.

That momentary irresolution unquestionably saved the highwayman.

The officer forced his way through the throng.

It did not take him many seconds, but still the fugitive was out of sight.

"Come on!" he cried. "Follow me if you wish to earn a share of the reward!"

"Where is he?"

"He must have turned the corner; but he cannot have gone far, I am certain. Come on—come on!"

The officer reached the turning just in time to catch a fleeting glimpse of the highwayman as he vanished round another corner about a hundred yards distant.

"This way—this way!" cried the police officer, with renewed excitement. "I have seen him!"

The others ran on pell-mell.

They made much better speed than Lord Harcliffe could.

But then the fugitive had the start, and that was a great matter.

He knew he was close to the stables, and that nerved him to make more exertion than he could have done without this incentive.

Could he but reach the place where he had left Phantom, he felt that all would yet be well.

The careful instructions he had given about his steed being in readiness, and the liberal reward he had promised in case those instructions were complied with, made him feel sure that he should have nothing to fear from a delay.

Once on the back of his steed, he would have an immense—nay, an immeasurable advantage—for, as all his pursuers were unmounted, it followed that he must get a long way before they were able to procure horses.

It was just at this moment, then, that Lord Harcliffe stopped before the entrance of the stables.

He was about to summon assistance by ringing the bell, but just as he laid his hand upon the handle, he perceived that one of the huge doors was standing ajar.

To push this open was the work of a moment, and the first thing he caught sight of was Phantom standing all ready caparisoned in the gateway, with the ostler patting him upon the neck.

A thrill of delight shot through the highwayman's frame, and so powerful was it that it made him momentarily forgetful of the frightful pain which racked his limbs.

And that calmness which we have so often mentioned as one of his characteristics now resumed its sway, and no one, to have looked at him now, would have guessed what he had so recently passed through.

"I am late," he said, taking a plain, strong riding-whip from the ostler's hand. "I did not imagine I should be detained so long."

"I was almost tired of waiting, sir," said the ostler, hastening forward with the horse so that Lord Harcliffe might mount him easily. "But it's all right now, I suppose."

"Yes; it's all right," was the calm reply.

At this moment, the silence which usually prevailed at that early hour was broken by loud shouts and the trampling of heavy, hasty footsteps.

"Goodness gracious!" ejaculated the ostler. "What's up now, I wonder?"

"Something or other. But stay; you have carried out my instructions faithfully, and in case I should come here again here is something that will induce you to do the same another time."

He accompanied these words by slipping a couple of guineas into the ostler's hand.

The man looked at the glittering gold coins as though unable to believe the evidence of his own vision.

"Into your pocket with them," said Lord Harcliffe, gathering the reins in his hand; "and the less you have to say to anybody the better it will be for you."

The ostler knew that something greatly out of the common way was going on, though what it was he could not imagine.

But this did not prevent him from pocketing the money.

The next moment he rode out of the gateway into the street.

By this time the nearest of his pursuers were very close at hand indeed.

They greeted his appearance with a howl of disappointment and dismay.

Lord Harcliffe, guessing that a bullet would probably enough be sent in pursuit of him, turned Phantom's head quickly, and set off at a gallop.

Those who were on foot pulled up at once.

To continue to pursue a mounted man they knew would be perfectly useless.

The officer was foremost in the chase, and his rage knew no bounds.

He could hardly believe that the object of his pursuit could have found a horse so quickly.

Just as had been anticipated, the moment he made the discovery he stopped and drew his pistols.

He fired both off in quick succession.

But the rate at which he had been running and the excited state of his mind were fatal to correctness of aim.

The bullets sped after the highwayman, but they fell harmlessly, and ere the smoke had blown away both horse and rider had vanished round a contiguous corner.

But Lord Harcliffe was not fated to get clear away from the scene of his perilous adventure with quite as much ease as he had anticipated.

Turning the corner was indeed a most unfortunate act, for, before he was aware of it, he found himself well in front of a mounted body of police, who were making what speed they could to the scene of the catastrophe.

A loud shout was the first intimation the fugitive had of this fresh danger.

But, luckily, he realized it in a moment, and without pausing to think he turned his horse round again, almost throwing him down in doing so.

The officers were quite as much taken by surprise as he was, only they did not recover themselves quite so quickly.

But when they did discover what had happened, they commenced a determined pursuit.

The very slight start the highwayman had got made them feel almost certain of success, and they would no doubt have felt quite confident as to the result had they but known how seriously he had been hurt.

The excitement of the moment, however, rendered the highwayman insensible to pain.

His course he now directed towards the open country.

He was by no means blind to the dangers which confronted him in this direction, but then it was his only hope.

At that amazing speed, then, which Phantom was able to put forth when required, he rode along one broad, long street.

But while compelled to pass continually from one street to the other, Phantom was not able to obtain so decided a victory over those behind as his rider had supposed.

His sole anxiety was, however, to get free from the streets and into the broad high-road, for he could not tell how soon he might be intercepted by some other party of his foes.

Strive, therefore, as he would, he could not get out of sight for more than a few moments together of those who were in pursuit.

Their horses were fresh, and had been specially chosen for the service they were upon, and neither whip nor spur was spared to make them exert themselves to the utmost.

Lord Harcliffe began to grow less anxious.

The continuous lines of houses were beginning to be broken.

Dwellings stood apart, and the further he went the greater was the distance between them.

Triumph and exultation filled his breast, and it was only by an effort that he suppressed the cry which rose to his lips.

But a fresh danger awaited him.

All at once another body of horsemen appeared, and it did not require a second glance to enable him to ascertain that these, like those behind him, were police officers.

The horses which they rode were worn and jaded, for they chanced to form one of the parties that had been sent out to patrol the roads,

As to actual pursuit, then, from these new-comers, Lord Harcliffe had nothing to fear.

But they were capable, nevertheless, of vastly increasing his peril.

As soon as they were near enough to comprehend the state of affairs, they, at the command of their leader, pulled up, and arranged themselves across the roadway —which chanced to be somewhat narrow—in such a manner as to make it impossible for the fugitive to force a way through them.

This act was followed by a simultaneous drawing forth of their pistols.

Lord Harcliffe was obliged to pull up.

It was most reluctantly, however, that he did so.

But he saw at once that to go another step more forward was only to place himself still more in the power of the officers and diminish his chances of escape.

A succession of shouts from the rear let him know that his pursuers were aware of what had occurred.

At last they thought the highwayman who had given them so much trouble would surely become their prisoner, for escape seemed out of the question.

Shouting, then, to those in front to stand firm and not to fail to fire the moment he came within range, they, with a wonderful accession of courage, hope, and vigour, urged their horses forward.

The position of Lord Harcliffe was a trying one, but then, by comparison with what he had passed through, it seemed little more than a temporary difficulty.

At one side of him was a stone wall, garnished at the top with pieces of broken bottles and other fragments of glass, so as to deter anyone from scaling it.

The wall was rather formidable as regarded height, and was still more so with the innumerable sharp, jagged points.

But in spite of all this it soon became evident that Lord Harcliffe was about to make the desperate trial of jumping his horse over it.

The difficulty was increased by the narrowness of the road, which permitted no preliminary gallop.

But Lord Harcliffe could see that unless he adopted this course he had no chance, and he had faith in the ability of his steed to clear the obstacle.

A few encouraging words were all that were needed, and over Phantom went in the most beautiful style conceivable.

His hind-hoofs just struck against some of the projecting points which were higher than the rest, but that was all.

No damage at all was done, and the gallant creature alighted safely and easily on a soft garden bed.

Obstacles now showed themselves to the highwayman on all sides.

He was in the garden of a house of no very great extent, and over another but lower wall he saw a kind of paddock.

This was gained without much trouble; but he found it fenced with strong wooden palings in its turn.

But he did not pause.

One after the other these obstacles were surmounted, but the highwayman saw that it was too much to expect his horse to keep up these tremendous leaps.

His only means of extrication from his present quarters was by getting out on to the road again.

The police officers, too, who were in pursuit, showed that they were much better acquainted with that particular neighbourhood, for, by riding down a kind of back way, they contrived to reach the paddock almost as soon as he did.

But, by a succession of jumps, the highwayman kept out of their reach, and managed to gain the road again at a point some few yards above the spot where the officers were stationed who had hoped to intercept him.

The officers were almost ready to give way to despair.

But their leader rallied them.

"Come on!" he said. "Let us have one more good try before he gets fairly into the country. When he does that, I am afraid our chances are over."

"He leaps like a deer," said one. "What is the good of thinking of following him?"

"He may take just one leap too many, and then we shall have him. There must be a limit to a horse's powers of jumping in that fashion. Come on, I say!"

With renewed determination they continued the pursuit.

The highwayman had made his way now in a direct line for the Western Road.

Momentarily he was out of sight; but they soon had him in view again, but he had got by no means as far as they had expected.

The reason was that Lord Harcliffe had encountered a large drove of horses, which were doubtless on their way to some market.

They filled up the roadway entirely, and, strive as he would, several precious moments were lost in forcing a way through them.

By the time the officers arrived, the horses had passed, so that they avoided this delay.

Of course the circumstance animated them greatly, and encouraged them to hope for the best.

"There's the gate!" cried one, suddenly, as the old toll-bar at Tyburn came into view.

"Is it closed?"

"I cannot see from here."

"Wait a moment—we shall know directly. If it is shut we shall have a double chance."

"He will leap over it."

"If he does," said the chief officer, "I will forgive him. The thing can't be done! Push on—push on!"

They rode at an increased speed; and then suddenly one cried, in tones of despair:

"The gate's open!"

A glance showed that such was the disagreeable fact.

"No matter. Push on all the harder!" said the chief. "We may be in time to call out and get it suddenly shut in his face. That will throw him out a bit."

There was some hope in this, but not much.

The officers, however, were one and all in a very angry state, and as they had no reason to be careful in sparing the horseflesh, they found it rather a relief than otherwise to their feelings to bestow a liberal application of whip and spur upon the foaming beasts.

It was probably the prodigious clatter they produced which had the effect of causing the toll-keeper to emerge from his narrow domicile.

It was not often that so many horses were heard thundering along at that very early hour in the morning.

"As I live!" he cried, as he beheld Lord Harcliffe coming at full speed with the officers behind him, like a party of ardent huntsmen after a fox, "it's a highwayman! Snigger me if it ain't!"

At this moment a loud and confused shout from the police officers came upon his ears.

None of the words could be distinguished; but yet he comprehended their purport.

The gestures, however, of the pursuing party were almost enough to make known what they wanted.

Lord Harcliffe, too, was aware that they wished the toll-keeper to shut the gate.

In his turn he called out, offering a handful of guineas if he would leave it open.

But in the uproar his words were quite drowned.

Nor did the toll-keeper seem inclined to favour his escape, for, with an alacrity rather wonderful to witness, he shut the great white gate, though he did not stop to attempt to lock it.

A cheer came from the officers behind.

Now, they doubted not, they had their prey secure.

If anything had been wanting to make Lord Harcliffe determine upon a desperate course, that cry would have more than sufficed.

Clenching his teeth, he resolved upon the hazardous achievement of jumping the gate.

Had Phantom been fresh he would have thought but little of it.

Now, however, he was exhausted with the many leaps he had been compelled to make, and there were very reasonable grounds for entertaining some misgivings as to the result.

But for all that he did not hesitate.

Patting his horse's neck, and doing all he could to encourage and inspirit him, he rode at full speed towards the toll-bar.

CHAPTER LXXXII.

THE BLACK HIGHWAYMAN, BY THE ADOPTION OF A CLEVER STRATAGEM, THROWS HIS PURSUERS OFF THE SCENT.

THE toll-keeper, having closed the gate, stood with his legs wide apart, and his hands thrust deeply into his breeches pocket as though he was mightily delighted with his own quickness and cleverness.

Not for a moment did he imagine the highwayman would be desperate enough to hazard the leap, especially as the top bar of the gate had recently been raised with a view to render impossible any such exploit.

In his mind, then, the capture of the highwayman was quite a settled matter; and he prepared to watch the sport from the safe side of the gate he was upon.

But he was quickly undeceived.

On came the Black Highwayman's famous steed at a pace that was absolutely appalling considering the nature of the obstacle in front,

But just at the moment when, to all appearances, both horse and rider were to be dashed to pieces, Phantom rose in the air as though lifted up by some wonderful invisible power.

Then down he came on the opposite side lightly and easily.

"Mudder," cried the toll-keeper, when he witnessed the performance of this (as he believed) impossible feat —"mudder! That's no natural horse, I'll swear!"

He drew back only just in time to escape a blow with the butt-end of the riding-whip which Lord Harcliffe levelled at him.

He was furious to think that he should have closed the gate as he did, and hoped to teach him to behave differently on another occasion.

But the tollman's quickness of movement saved him.

The officers gave vent to cries of rage, which were, however, it might have been unconsciously, mingled with admiration.

Phantom descended easily and safely on the hard road, and the next moment had reached a slight turn in the road.

"Come on!" cried the commanding officer. "Hang me if I give in even now! Open the gate there," he added to the toll-keeper; "and be quick about it! Don't you know that every moment is of the utmost importance?"

But the toll-keeper shook his head as he leisurely advanced.

"You may as well take it easy," he said. "It will make little or no difference. There's none of you going to catch him, take my word for that!"

But the chief officer was in such a state of aggravation at being again disappointed that, whether or not, he would persist in continuing the pursuit.

Lord Harcliffe had, however, obtained an excellent start, though an unfortunate accident made it of little account.

While galloping along at so wonderful a rate, Phantom suddenly picked up a stone, which wedged itself in a moment tightly inside the shoe.

The discovery of the lameness at first made the highwayman's heart stand still with dread; but instantly guessing the cause of it, he lost not a moment in dismounting.

By the aid of a pebble he managed to dislodge the stone from its position, and then Phantom was all right again.

Now, although this had occupied such a very little time, yet when he turned round to remount, he saw that the police officers were in sight of him, and apparently pushing on with greater resolution than ever.

But unless some other untoward event occurred, he felt that he could set them at complete defiance.

The only thing that gave him uneasiness was his knowledge of the fact that the roads everywhere round London were patrolled by parties of men who, by means of agreed signals, could easily communicate with each other.

If he could keep clear of these, all would be well.

A gallop of no very great duration would take him sufficiently far from London to enable him to find some place of shelter until the friendly shadows of night again settled upon the landscape.

The necessity of getting somewhere under cover was obvious, for, as it was fast getting broad day, he could not fail to be seen by many persons whose information would enable the officers to follow him up without trouble.

Glancing again behind him where the road extended itself in a straight line for a considerable distance, he looked for some signs of his pursuers.

A faint cloud of dust, invisible, perhaps, to almost every eye save one trained like his, just served to show whereabouts the police officers were.

"Easy, my brave fellow," he cried to his steed; "there is scarcely a necessity for you to strain yourself. Easy! We shall shake them off, I have no fear."

He moderated Phantom's speed a little as he spoke, and then looked earnestly forward.

A faint ejaculation escaped him when he beheld what he had all along expected to see—namely, another party of his foes.

The discovery was made on both sides at the self-same moment.

But although the officers numbered six or seven, yet, as they had been out with their horses all the night, it was scarcely to be supposed that they would be in anything like fitting trim to give successful chase.

But for all that, they made the trial, perhaps in the hope that they might drive the highwayman before them until he encountered one of the many other patrolling parties that were out upon the road.

Lord Harcliffe was aware of this, and at once left the high-road, making his way at a rapid rate across the flat meadow ground, which reached as far as he could see.

The officers at once left the high-road also, and made their way towards him in a diagonal line.

The superiority of Lord Harcliffe's steed, notwithstanding all it had accomplished, was manifest in an instant.

Strive as they would, the officers could not near him, although their position gave them every advantage.

But the open character of the country which prevailed for many miles enabled them to keep him in full view, and there was hardly any hope that in the daylight he would be able to get far enough away to escape their observation before falling in with some other patrolling troop.

In the night, or even at dusk, it would have been another matter, but the day chanced to be an exceptionally fine one.

The transparent atmosphere enabled all objects to be discerned at a much greater distance than usual.

Everything was in favour of the police and against the highwayman.

But he held on determinedly and unflinchingly.

"Let me but once get quite out of their vision, and I shall doubtless be able to hit upon some stratagem that will rid me of them altogether. While they can see me it puts that out of the question."

Suddenly he came upon a broad and well-kept lane, which was fringed on both sides by hedgerows.

Insufficient as this cover was to conceal him from his foes, yet he gladly enough availed himself of it, and he immediately changed his course.

But almost immediately the clatter of hoofs came upon his ear, and turning back, he caught a glimpse of a third party in the distance.

That they also had commenced a pursuit was evident, and with a savage cry Lord Harcliffe let the reins fall slackly upon Phantom's neck, and urged him to still greater exercise of his powers.

But now the hedgerows on each side of him began to be higher and denser, the surface of the country to be more undulating, and the trees more abundant.

All these things were in his favour, and before another couple of miles had been passed over not any trace of his pursuers could be seen.

As soon as he was aware that this was the case he gradually reduced Phantom's speed, so that, should any of his pursuers be within hearing, they should not be aware that he had come to a stop.

Phantom evinced signs of being a little exhausted by the efforts he had made, and therefore willingly obeyed the slight pressure upon the rein.

The gallop became a canter, the canter a trot, and then, by rapid degrees, the trot subsided into a quiet walk.

"I rather think," he said, again patting his steed's neck, "if any of those fellows were within earshot they would be not a little puzzled to know whether I have gradually pulled up or whether the sounds have died away in the distance. So far, then, all is well."

Phantom showed the pleasure his master's caresses gave him by neighing somewhat shrilly.

"Quiet, now—quiet! None of that, or you will make them acquainted with our whereabouts, and then a long gallop is again before me. Let me think," he added, passing his hand over his forehead. "What stratagem can I invent and adopt to throw these fellows off the scent for a time at least, so that I may have a little leisure for rest and thought?"

He glanced about him, but without being able to catch sight of any object that held out any promise of serving his purpose.

But in the midst of all these difficulties and dangers there was one circumstance for which he felt most deeply grateful.

Contrary to all his expectations, the pain arising from his fearful fall had passed off, so that, beyond a general dull, aching sensation, he had nothing whatever to complain of.

As the horse walked forward now, Lord Harcliffe kept his head bent down upon his breast, and it was easy to see by the expression of his face that he was in deep thought.

"The idea eludes me," he said, looking up after the lapse of a few moments. "What is to be done? I can hear them again now. How pertinaciously they keep at my heels! If I do not shake them off, I shall be running foul of another crew of them."

The clatter of horses' hoofs behind him proved plainly enough that the officers were upon his track, and much nearer to him than he had believed it possible for them to get in so short a space of time.

And the sound, borne upon the clear morning air, rapidly became more and more distinct.

"They are pushing on as fast as whip and spur will urge their beasts, while I seem no nearer to what I want than before. No, no—surely not that," he added, hastily. "With plenty of cool impudence, I may be more than a match for them yet."

These words were called forth by his suddenly catching sight among the trees of the twisted chimneys and gables of some dwelling, which, from its situation among the trees and other indications visible at the first glance, seemed to be the residence of some person of high social position.

On every side could be seen traces of the most careful cultivation—neatness and order prevailed everywhere.

Some plan was now floating in the Black Highwayman's brain in connection with this dwelling, though at present it was dim and undefined.

Nothing was wanting, however, save some chance circumstance to give it shape and consistency.

It was for this reason that, ignoring the alarming sounds of pursuit behind him, he bent all his attention upon the objects which now surrounded him.

The lane, he quickly found, took a capricious turn, which brought him round much nearer to the old-fashioned building among the trees, so that he was able to make out many of the windows, and also the broad terrace, which formed a conspicuous ornament to its front.

Directly afterwards, he saw among the shrubs and bushes on the open space before the building—half-lawn, half-garden—the figure of a hale and hearty old man.

He was dressed in the deepest black, which made his white wig show out in strange contrast beneath his cocked hat; there were snow-white ruffles, too, upon his wrists, which, when his arms hung down, fell over the tips of his fingers.

The Black Highwayman was now in full possession of the idea which had so long eluded him.

A stratagem had darted into his mind, and without considering it in its details, he set about its execution.

He saw that the old gentleman in the garden was a perfect stranger to him, and that he was busily employed in tending some rose-bushes, which, just bursting into bloom, formed objects of the greatest beauty.

It was easy to see that the cultivation of these flowers was the old man's hobby, and by the manner in which he attempted to assist the gardener at his side, the interest he felt was of the keenest possible kind.

He had just given some finishing touches to one of the fine bushes, and stepping back a pace or two, plased his hands behind his back, and stood in an attitude expressive of the utmost admiration.

"I have it!" said Lord Harcliffe, under his breath. "Nothing could be more simple. Gentlemen," he continued, turning in the direction of his foes, the clatter of whose horses' feet was now alarmingly distinct—"gentlemen, you will find that you have had all your pains and trouble for nothing."

What the Black Highwayman was about to do will now very quickly be seen.

Just in front of him was a little iron gate, forming a kind of private entrance to the garden.

Dismounting from his steed, he slipped the bridle over his arm, and with all coolness conceivable walked to the gate, opened it, and led his horse on to the gravel-path beyond.

Before going further, he was careful to close the gate again.

Round about this entrance shrubs had been trained to grow thickly, in order to screen the garden from the gaze of every passer-by, so that before he had gone many paces Lord Harcliffe was delighted to discover that his horse occupied a position which rendered him invisible from the lane.

As soon as he made this discovery, he transferred the bridle-rein to a broken branch conveniently near, and then, without pausing, walked as rapidly as he could across the grass-plot towards the old gentleman, who was too much absorbed in a deep consideration about his favourite flowers to be aware that anyone was approaching him.

The first intimation he had of Lord Harcliffe's visit was the sound of his voice, and upon first hearing it he jumped back suddenly on to the gardener's toes, for he was fully persuaded he was quite alone.

"My dear Sir Roderick," said Lord Harcliffe, his countenance beaming with smiles, and expressive of the greatest delight—"my dear Sir Roderick!—this pleasure—so great, so unexpected! Really, I am at a loss how to express myself! But I recognized you from the distance, and obeying the first impulse which sprang up in my breast, I hastened to greet you, and to express my thanks for your kind exertions in my behalf."

While speaking, Lord Harcliffe extended his hand, and taking the old gentleman's, shook it warmly.

As for the old gentleman, he was so overcome by the suddenness and strangeness of the whole affair, that he could neither move nor speak.

The gardener's jaw dropped in amazement.

But Lord Harcliffe acted his part so well that the old gentleman was bewildered.

At last, however, he managed to gasp out:

"Really, sir—I must say—that—in a manner of speaking—decidedly there is an error."

"An error," exclaimed Lord Harcliffe, with a start—"an error?"

And as he repeated the words he pretended to look more closely into the gentleman's face.

As he did so, a well-simulated air of confusion became visible, which increased rapidly, until his embarrassment was painful to witness.

"I beg ten thousand pardons!" he said at last, with even greater confusion still. "How can I excuse myself? What can I say in explanation? I have made a mistake, I find, and with your permission will take my leave at once."

But the gentleman began to recover his self-possession a little, and said:

"Stay, sir—stay one moment, I beg! Let me request you to explain this singular affair."

Lord Harcliffe, who appeared as though full of anxiety to quit the grounds, paused upon hearing these words, and then, with well-affected reluctance, retraced his steps.

"I can hardly explain myself," he said; "indeed I am sure I cannot, unless you pardon me for this foolish and unwarrantable intrusion."

"Sir," said the gentleman, "I pardon you for that very willingly indeed."

"Then my explanation is, that when in the lane yonder I caught sight of you among these bushes. I did not see your face, it is true, but your figure was so familiar to me that I jumped at once to the conclusion that you were my estimable friend and second father, Sir Roderick Grandison."

"Grandison—Grandison."

"Yes, that is the name of my more than patron. He has the same commanding presence as yourself—the same benevolent countenance. I perceive the difference now," he added; "but could you see him, you would find him so much your counterpart that you would cease to wonder at the mistake I have made."

"It is very singular."

"Very indeed, for what convinced me that you must be Sir Roderick was seeing you thus employed."

"Is he, then, fond of flowers?" said the old gentleman, with the eager air of one meeting with another having a liking for the same object.

"His fondness amounts to a perfect passion, especially where roses are concerned."

The gentleman gave a gasping cry.

His delight was too great to be expressed by articulate sounds.

"Yes," continued Lord Harcliffe, admirably keeping up the character he had so readily assumed; "and as the greater portion of my life has been passed in his company, it follows, almost as a matter of course, that I have imbibed much of his liking for these objects, without having, however, much of his knowledge and good taste."

The old gentleman had not been so delighted for many a year as he was that moment.

Seizing Lord Harcliffe's hand with both his own, he pressed it with great warmth, as he said:

"Oh, how I rejoice at the accident which has introduced you to me—I am delighted! I must make the acquaintance of this Sir Roderick you mention. In the meantime, let me beg of you as a great favour to remain here a short time. William," he added, turning to the gardener, "be good enough to take this gentleman's horse up to the stables, and have him properly attended to."

Lord Harcliffe made a movement as though about to object to this.

But his new acquaintance said, hastily:

"Not a word—not a word! I am determined upon it! You must stay with me for a short time. You will allow me to show you my small and poor collection. Perhaps your description of it will induce Sir Roderick to pay me a visit. Come, come—no denial—no denial whatever!"

While uttering these words, with a vast amount of volubility, he took Lord Harcliffe by the arm and led him among the bushes, while William made his way at once to the stables.

It was just at this moment that the old gentleman heard a body of horsemen approaching.

He looked up in natural curiosity; and Lord Harcliffe congratulated himself upon the fact that he was tolerably well screened from the view of anyone on the road by the numerous shrubs and trees.

"Good gracious!" he said. "What a morning of adventures, to be sure! I wonder what is going to happen next?"

Hardly had the words passed his lips before the foremost of the police officers came in view.

Believing there was nothing to direct their attention or suspicions to the spot, Lord Harcliffe naturally enough expected that they would ride past.

In this very agreeable anticipation, however, he was doomed to be disappointed, for, with a prodigious clatter and dash, the whole body of police officers pulled up before the identical little iron gate through which the highwayman had entered.

When he saw this he gave himself up for lost, as he naturally enough suspected that some person must have observed his actions and communicated with his foes.

He drew back a little more among the bushes, not so much with a view to conceal himself as it was to look after his weapons.

The old gentleman, who had never in the whole course of his life seen such a formidable-looking body of horsemen in the lane, was filled with astonishment, and had eyes for nothing else.

Even his favourite and much-prized rose-trees were for the moment forgotten.

The horsemen all collected in a dense throng, and no sooner had they done so than some one looked over the hedge, and shouted out:

"Hoy—hoy! Come forward there from among those bushes—come forward at once, I say!"

But Lord Harcliffe never moved a muscle.

CHAPTER LXXXIII.

CAPTAIN HAWK'S FAREWELL INTERVIEW WITH BLANCHE IS SUDDENLY CUT SHORT.

YOUNG Squire Kingsbury was full of curiosity to know whatever it could be that Captain Hawk had to disclose to him, and waited most impatiently for the first words to fall from the highwayman's lips.

Stranger as he was, he could not make out what he could possibly have to say to him.

In his wildest guesses he would never even have approached the truth.

"I have to ask your protection," were the captain's first words, "on the behalf of one who sorely needs it."

"My protection?"

"Yes—you may well echo the words in those accents of surprise; but if you feel that you remain under the slightest obligation to me—that I have the faintest claim upon your gratitude, it will be cancelled—annulled, if you will grant this favour."

"Consider it as done," said the young man, with that warmth and fervour which characterised him. "But do not keep me any longer in my present state of suspense."

"I will not, for moments are precious. I cannot enter into any explanation, so fully as I could wish—time will not permit it. I must content myself with saying that chance threw me in the way of a young girl——"

"A young girl?"

"Yes—you can hear all the particulars at another time. I have learned that she is an heiress. Her father dying, left her in charge of his brother."

"As guardian?"

"Yes; and now, for some cause or other, he seeks her life. The poor girl was wholly in his hands. She had not the power to save herself in the least. By good fortune, however, I was near, and rescued her."

The young squire nodded, and said:

"Proceed."

"Wholly unprotected, she was glad enough to trust herself to the guardianship of such a one as I am."

"Did she know your character?"

"No."

"What happened after?"

"I secured her a passage in a waggon, thinking by that means she would be more likely to escape any search that might be made after her."

"And where is she now?"

"At the Greyhound, temporarily, under the charge of the landlady. As of course you must know, they are not in a position to aid her in the way she wants. She has but one other relative, a lady in London."

"And what is it, then, you want me to do?"

"I want you to communicate on her behalf with the proper authorities, in order that her wealth and possessions may be restored to her. I have all the inclination in life to serve her, but any connection with me, however slight, would be terribly damaging to her cause; but with you to take it up, the result would be entirely different."

"And you are sure her chances are good?"

"I am. But it will be the simplest matter in the world for you to satisfy yourself."

"How so?"

"All you have to do is to call upon her at the inn. If you are willing to have one interview with her, I will take care to inform her of it, and advise her to confide in you without reserve."

"I accept the trust gladly," was the unhesitating response. "If I find that wrong has been done, rest assured I will know no rest until it has been set right. But I thought that it was something for yourself you wished to ask."

"No. I am able to take care of myself tolerably well," was the careless response.

The young squire gazed at the strange being before him with mingled wonder and admiration.

"Decidedly," he said to himself, "that man is worthy of being something more than a mere highwayman."

Captain Hawk, having arranged this matter to his satisfaction, looked out of the window of the carriage.

To his great satisfaction he found the darkness as profound as he could wish.

"Tell me," said the young squire, "how you expect to escape if there is, as you say, some of your foes watching you?"

The captain smiled.

"I may not be followed."

"But I will soon find out," said the young squire.

So saying, he pulled the check-string, and opened the little window at the back of the coachman's box.

The worthy old butler turned round, full of anxiety, to know what was the matter.

"All is well," said young Kingsbury. "All I want to know is, whether you have noticed anyone on the road behind us?"

"Yes."

"Who are they?"

"Police officers."

Captain Hawk uttered a faint ejaculation.

"Are you sure?"

"Yes, quite. I saw them when we were in a lighter part of the roadway. Confound their impudence! Things have come to a pretty pass indeed, when a squire's word is to go no further than anyone else's!"

"There, that will do."

"Shall we drive on?"

"Yes—yes."

The squire closed the little window again.

When he looked again at Captain Hawk there were traces of great care and anxiousness upon his visage.

"Tell me," he said, "what are you to do?"

The highwayman smiled.

"Do you know your danger?" was the astonished question.

"Perfectly."

"How, then, shall you escape?"

"The thing is simple enough. I have been in positions of so much peril that I look upon this as a mere trifle."

"But what shall you do?"

"You observe," said the captain, "that this part of the road is very dark, owing to the trees which grow so thickly on both sides of it."

"Yes—yes!"

"Well, then, I shall open the carriage-door quietly, and, without troubling your coachman to pull up, shall alight. The officers, if I know anything of them, will keep in the rear, their object being merely to watch the carriage."

"But will they not see you?"

"No. If they do see me descend, they will have better vision than I give them credit for possessing. And now, sir, let me bid you farewell. I have only time to say that I shall never forget your generous treatment of me to-night. Do not fear that your two miserable assassins will escape. If the officers fail, I will find them."

He did not wait to hear any more; but the very moment he had done speaking, he opened the carriage-door quietly and to the extent of a few inches only.

As they were ascending the hill of which the young squire had made mention, the horses were not going very quickly, so that Captain Hawk readily slipped into the roadway.

Keeping close to the vehicle for a moment, he refastened the door, and then, watching his opportunity, sprang into the darkness among the trees.

He only went just far enough to conceal himself, lest the slight sound he should make in his progress should reach the ears of the police officers, for he could now very plainly hear they were approaching.

Another moment brought them within half a dozen yards of him.

These words came distinctly upon his ears:

"It may be fancy, as you say," cried one of the officers; "but it is very odd to me if the carriage-door did not open."

"It is so confoundedly dark that one cannot see," said the other, grumblingly.

"But had we not better make sure? If the door opened, and I believe it did, it was to allow him to alight."

"How can we make sure?"

"What could be simpler? Ride to the door of the carriage and look in. If you find all right it will be easy to make our excuse for doing so; and if not, we shall get all the blame, make your mind up to that."

Gibbons, to whom this affair had been entrusted, knew this perfectly well.

"Keep about here," he said. "Come what will, I will ride forward and make sure. It is no good to follow the carriage if the man we want is not in it."

"Not a bit."

"Then take my advice and make sure."

Gibbons did not hesitate about doing this any longer, but, touching his horse with the spur, rode swiftly towards the carriage.

And all this took place so close to where Captain Hawk stood that not only was he able to hear every word, but he was compelled to hold his breath lest the slight sound should betray his whereabouts.

To reach the side of the carriage took Gibbons hardly a moment.

Drawing a lighted lantern from beneath his coat, he directed its beams full into the interior of the vehicle.

No sooner had he done so than he uttered a cry, which was unmistakably one of terror and alarm.

At the first glance he saw that one person only occupied the vehicle.

This was the young squire, whose energies had succumbed at last.

Just when Captain Hawk left him, he was seized with a death-like sensation of faintness which he strove in vain to shake off.

He leaned forward to seize the check-string so as to make his faithful dependant aware of the change in his condition.

But the effort was beyond him, and he fell in an awkward, huddled-up posture, partly on the floor of the carriage, and partly on the opposite seat.

"Help—help!" cried Gibbons. "He has murdered the squire and escaped!"

What he saw was calculated to raise such an opinion in his mind.

The other officers no sooner heard it than, acting under the impulse of ungovernable curiosity, they rode forward.

At the carriage, of course, they were of no assistance whatever.

They ought to have looked about them at once for the highwayman.

Of course, Captain Hawk was not slow to avail himself of this unexpectedly favourable opportunity to get out of his present position.

Yet, before he had taken many steps, he paused.

He thought of the words Gibbons had spoken, and, although able to give a pretty good guess as to the actual state of affairs, yet the remaining for a moment under the imputation of having murdered one who had behaved so generously was so odious to him that some wild thought of returning to refute it took a momentary hold upon his imagination.

Hardly any reflection, however, was required to show him the uselessness and insanity of any such attempt.

"No matter," he said; "I will look to my own safety. The charge cannot be maintained against me, so what need have I to care?"

He continued to run swiftly in the direction of the Greyhound.

But pausing as he drew nearer to the inn, lest he should find it surrounded by his enemies, he bethought himself of the faithful ostler, Isaac.

"Where is he now?" he murmured. "Were he here all would be well; but to attempt to find him would, perhaps, only be to render it impossible to exchange a few parting words with Blanche, and, come what will, I will do that—yes, in despite of all the officers in the kingdom!"

But a feeling of melancholy immediately stole over him, and he found that this parting with the young girl he had saved showed him how great was the interest he already felt for her.

"We must part," he said, "and the sooner the better I shall only be a curse and a trouble to her. She will speedily forget me, no doubt; but I shall find the task of forgetting her by no means so easy."

He sighed as he spoke.

In the distance dimly outlined against the dark night

sky, he could see a portion of the irregular pile of buildings of which the old Greyhound was composed.

But nowhere could he see the least signs of Isaac.

"No doubt he is searching everywhere for me," he said. "But if he has left Satan here all will be well. He will be sure to rejoin me sooner or later. But if, thinking to facilitate my escape, he has taken my steed, I shall be awkwardly placed indeed."

This anxious consideration made him approach the inn with even more quickness than was consistent with caution.

Luckily for him, however, none of his foes appeared to be lurking in this direction.

As soon as ever he had gained the shadow of the straggling mass of outbuildings, a sensation of tolerable security came over him.

Keeping as close as he could to the wall, so that it was next to impossible for the faintest glimpse of his figure to be obtained, he made his way to the stable, where he hoped to find Satan standing, though he greatly feared he should not.

He reached in safety that little piece of low wall which we have so often made mention of, and, after listening intently for a moment without hearing any sound of an alarming character, he ventured to scale it.

Alighting upon the dungheap, which effectually deadened all sound, he then, in a crouching position, directed his steps towards the well-known stable.

The door was speedily reached.

He found it locked.

Unthinkingly, he put his hand into his pocket for the key, forgetting for the moment that he had relinquished possession of it to the landlord.

To force an entrance without making much more noise than was consistent with prudence was impossible.

"I must give that up; and yet I must satisfy myself whether or not Satan is here. If he is, all will be well."

But to see into the stable was an impossibility.

Tom Beckford had taken care to guard effectually from all fear of discovery by peeping and prying.

Only one resource was left.

This was to give his well-known signal.

He did so.

To his joy, it was responded to instantly by a sudden movement and then a neighing sound, which to his ears sounded alarmingly loud.

"Quiet, boy—quiet!" he said, in suppressed tones. "I am here. All is well."

There was silence.

"So far, then, I can rest content," said the highwayman. "Now, then, to speak those words of parting, which I know will well-nigh choke me in their utterance, and then off and away, and the officers can do their worst."

Rapidly, yet silently, he made his way to the back-door of the inn.

He was wonderfully well acquainted with the premises or he would never have been able to make his way in the darkness as he did without encountering a single obstacle.

Just as he reached the door, and was about to open it, some one from within lifted the latch.

He had barely time to place himself flat against the wall before the door was pushed wide open.

Then, whatever alarm he might have felt for the moment was now dissipated, for this turned out to be no other than Tom Beckford himself.

The portly landlord looked well all around him, though no doubt the darkness was much too great to allow him to see anything.

Then he closed the door.

When the latch fell, Captain Hawk advanced a step, and in a voice little louder than a whisper, said:

"Tom."

Had the landlord been then and there shot, he could not have given a more sudden start.

"Murder!" he ejaculated.

"Hush!" said the captain, striding up to him, and placing his hand over his mouth. Not another sound, if you wish to save me!"

Tom Beckford struggled, and despite the pressure of the highwayman's hand, gasped out:

"The captain!"

"Yes, I am here. Take care not to make my presence known."

"Trust me. I was just then going to the stable to see to Satan, and hoping that you would not be long in getting upon his back and riding off."

"Ah! that is well! You have the key?"

"Yes."

"My mind is at ease on that score."

"Come with me, then. If you are speedy, all may yet be well."

"In a few minutes, Tom."

"Few minutes! Are you mad?"

"I hope not"

"Come away, then—come away without the delay of a single moment!"

"I cannot," said the captain, taking a step towards the door the landlord had just closed.

Tom Beckford viewed this proceeding with the utmost dismay, and, by moving as rapidly as he could, he just managed to lay hold of the skirt of the highwayman's coat.

"Stop—stop! Goodness above! what would you do?"

"Enter."

"Impossible!"

"Why?"

"The officers!"

"Are they there?"

"Well, not exactly there, but they will know in a moment if you enter."

"Listen to me then, Tom."

The landlord gave a groan of assent.

"I missed the officers well on the brow of the hill yonder, and have made my way here without, I am sure, one of them guessing which way I have taken."

"Well—well?"

"I have spoken to Squire Kingsbury about the young girl, and he has promised to take her under his protection."

"Very good. Then, if you have arranged things so well as all that, let me give you a word of advice."

"What is it?"

"Don't lose a moment, but come with me to the stable, mount Satan, and be off."

"Bah!"

"It is your only chance of escape."

"Listen to me, Tom. You are wasting precious moments by this profitless discussion."

"It is your fault."

"Not at all. Let the danger be what it may, I cannot leave here without seeing Blanche, and letting her know what I have done in her behalf. No more now. You know my determination, and once taken you also know it to be irrevocable."

Tom Beckford groaned again.

"Don't make that noise," said the captain, laughing lightly; "but just attend to my wishes, and leave me to take the consequences of them."

"I suppose I shall be obliged to do so," said the landlord. "But don't say I did not warn you. Don't blame me for what I am certain will happen."

"You may be sure I shall do nothing of the kind."

"Very well, then. You will live to repent neglecting my advice."

"Nonsense—nonsense! What I have to say to Blanche will occupy but a very few moments indeed. While I am saying it, go you to the stable, get Satan out, and lead him as close as you can to that little wall. You know which I mean."

"Perfectly well," responded the landlord, groaning still.

"If you can get him on the other side of it, why, so much the better. I shall make my way there, and expect to find him."

"And you will have to make a great deal more haste than you imagine just at present, mark my words if you do not!"

"Never mind, Tom—that part of the risk I take upon myself. And now another word, in case I should not have another chance of speaking."

"Well, what now?"

"Where is Isaac?"

"I don't know."

"Well, should he turn up, as doubtless he will—"

"Trust him for that."

[ISAAC SAVES THE LIFE OF CAPTAIN HAWK.]

"Tell him I am off to London, and bid him follow me with all speed. I shall be on the look-out, so there will be little fear of his missing me."

"Very good; but it strikes me he will not give you the chance of riding off without him."

"Perhaps not. But where are the officers?"

"Everywhere," was the landlord's comprehensive answer.

"Are there any inside the inn?"

"I don't know."

"Were there any when you came out?"

"I think not."

"That is enough, then. I am quite prepared. Now start for the stable, and be sure that, no matter how quick you are, you will not have Satan close to the wall a moment too soon."

Tom Beckford knew that it would be useless to utter the remonstrances that were at his tongue's end, and

equally vain to make the least attempt to dissuade him from the course he had resolved upon.

"The sooner it is over the better, I suppose," he said; and then, with more activity than he would have displayed for anyone else, he made his way towards the stables.

CHAPTER LXXXIV.

THERE IS A RUDE INTERRUPTION TO THE CAPTAIN'S INTERVIEW WITH BLANCHE.

At the same moment Captain Hawk, turning round, crossed the small space which intervened between the building and where he stood, and, reaching the door, placed his hand upon the latch and raised it.

Had he but reflected, this was a most rash action for him to commit.

But Captain Hawk did not reflect.

He was only intent upon carrying out his purpose.

For all he knew, the moment he pushed open the door he might come face to face with a body of his foes, for, as the police officers had indubitable evidence of his presence in that locality, they would naturally look upon the Greyhound as being his head-quarters.

But Fortune favours the bold, and certainly she favoured Captain Hawk in this instance.

On opening the door, he confronted some one, but it was a friend, not a foe.

In was, indeed, no other than the landlord's decidedly better half.

"Where's Tom?" she said, the moment she beheld Captain Hawk. "Have you seen him? The great fat, idle, good-for-nothing creature, to go sneaking off while the house is full of people, leaving me with more work than one pair of hands can get through with! Wait till I get hold of him, that's all!"

"My dear madam," said the captain, in his blandest and most persuasive manner, "if you can possibly spare the time, I have a few words of the greatest importance to say to you."

"Come in here, do!" she answered, opening the door. "What do you think of yourself, coming in here, and running the risk of getting us into such trouble? I am ashamed of you! Be off to my husband! You are just a pair, and only fit for each other's society!"

Captain Hawk knew just how much importance to attach to the landlady's words.

Indeed, her own actions were sufficient to show that she was far—very far—from meaning a word she said, for, having pushed the highwayman into the room, she carefully closed the door after her, so that he should be in no danger from an interruption.

Captain Hawk could not repress a smile.

"Tell me," he said, "are there at this moment any police officers in the house?"

"Not to my knowledge," she answered; "but then this is such a place: they might easily be here almost a thousand strong without me or anybody else knowing the least bit about it."

"Enough. Then I hope to get away before any of them show themselves. Where is Blanche—the young girl I brought with me? I have a few words of the gravest importance which I must say to her, and as soon as I have done that I am off for London."

"Oh, indeed!" said the landlady, smoothing down her apron, and looking very demurely out of the corner of her eyes. "I suppose it would be quite impossible to guess what this important business is, wouldn't it?"

"I can guess your meaning," said the captain, quickly; "but you are very far from the truth. The fact is, I have made young Squire Kingsbury acquainted with the story, and, in return for the service I have been fortunate enough to render him, he has promised to exert all his power and interest in her behalf."

"You have done this?"

"I have."

"Then you deserve to be something better than what you are. Wait here a moment, and I will send her to you. It will be a thousand times better than for you to make the attempt to reach the room where she now is."

Captain Hawk acquiesced in this at once, and prepared himself to wait with what patience and coolness he could command for Blanche to make her appearance.

There was an odd flutter about his heart while he stood there, not caused by his proximity to the officers, and his great danger in consequence, but by the thoughts which this parting interview called up.

Captain Hawk had an impressionable heart, and Blanche's loveliness and friendlessness had touched him very deeply.

It was not without a pang that he contemplated resigning the task of achieving the restoration of her rights

After a moment a better feeling came over him. and he was able to shake this off.

"I am a highwayman," he said, half bitterly, half regretfully. "What can I be to her? Should she know me as I really am, how sudden and complete a revulsion of feeling would follow!"

Just as he finished murmuring these words the door opened, and Blanche entered.

She had nearly, if not quite, recovered from the shock she had sustained, and now that she presented something like her ordinary appearance he was more than ever struck with her exceeding beauty.

Mrs. Beckford closed the door, and Blanche, after a momentary hesitation, advanced towards the captain with an air half of timidity, half of familiarity.

The colour upon her cheeks deepened, and the charming embarrassment she displayed enhanced her beauty a thousand times.

Captain Hawk took the tiny hand which she frankly extended towards him, and pressed it warmly.

But he checked himself as he thought how different would be her behaviour could but one word of the truth be whispered in her ears.

The reflection caused the words he was about to utter to die away unspoken on his lips.

Blanche, with confiding trustfulness, looked up into his face, and noted its troubled aspect.

In a moment her own countenance clouded as she murmured, half brokenly:

"It is, then, the truth which I have heard. You are about to leave me—we are about to part!"

There was so much anxiety and distress expressed in the tones of her voice that there could be little doubt her feelings towards her preserver were something stronger than mere gratitude for the services he had rendered.

And that such should be the case is nothing to be wondered at.

Captain Hawk's fine open countenance and sparkling eyes, his well-knit, muscular, yet lithe and elegant form, were in the highest degree calculated to challenge the admiration of the fair sex.

And Blanche in her life had known so little what kindness meant, that the captain's manner and behaviour towards her affected her more than she could express or was aware of.

It was only after an effort that the highwayman responded to her question.

Even then his voice had lost all its usual clearness and firmness.

"Yes," he said, "it is quite true."

"That we must part?"

Even so."

"But why?"

"I cannot tell you now. There may come a time when you may learn all. But with every wish on my part to guard and protect you from all harm, to assist in the restoration of your wealth, circumstances unfortunately arise which interpose an insuperable barrier to my doing so. That is all the explanation I can give on that point. Let me hasten with what I have to say, for it is necessary that my departure should be final."

"And—and are we never to meet again?" asked Blanche, in a manner that sent a thrill to the captain's heart.

"I hope so—I trust so," he answered. "But it is accident alone that can bring us together."

"But how strange this is!" she said. "What have I done that you have ceased to care for me?"

"You mistake," he said. "I have not ceased, and never shall. But the circumstances I speak of are imperative. Some day you will perhaps know all; but never—never from my lips. I can only say that by associating myself with you in this matter I should be doing you a life-long and irreparable injury, and that is what I can never consent to do."

Blanche did not speak.

But her features expressed eloquently enough the intense surprise which these mysterious words had raised in her breast.

"Injure me?" she said at length, perceiving that the highwayman did not speak.

"Yes—injure you; though Heaven knows I cannot help it! But, as I have said, we must part. I have told your history to one who not only has the will but the power to see you protected. He has given me his word that he will do so."

"And who is this?"

"Squire Kingsbury. The landlady here will tell you all about him. To his charge I leave you, and I feel satisfied that you will be safe—and—and happy."

"And you," she asked, tears which she could not suppress showing themselves in her eyes—"and you—what shall you do? Where are you going?"

"To London," was the answer. "I have promised to do something there for a friend who is now no more. Let me entreat you, however, not to trouble yourself about my doings. Forget me. Farewell!"

"It is unjust and unkind on your part to ask me to forget you," she said, with great emotion. "You have done so much for me—you, to whom I owe my very life!"

Captain Hawk's agitation increased.

The words which this young girl spoke touched him more keenly than any which had ever fallen upon his ears.

But he felt that to prolong this scene would not only increase his pain but his peril.

Again taking her hand, which she surrendered willingly enough to him, he repeated his parting words.

"I will not forget you—I cannot! Whether you——"

"Rest assured that I shall never—never forget," answered the captain, in tones coming from the bottom of his heart, "and——"

"You will grant me one favour, will you not?" she said, anxiously.

"You have but to name it."

"Then tell me who you are, and why this mystery shrouds all your doings. In remembering you, let me at least have a name to remember you by. You will not refuse me—will you?"

Captain Hawk had not expected to hear these words, so he started and drew back with evident pain and annoyance.

"Forgive me!" cried Blanche, hastily. "I can see that I have offended you."

"No, no—not so," he answered, with equal quickness. "Your request took me by surprise. I had expected—that is, I thought—that it would be something different."

The words were stammeringly and confusedly spoken.

"And cannot you tell me?" she said, mournfully. "Am I to have nothing by which to remember you?"

A great struggle was evidently going on in the captain's breast.

At one moment he felt tempted to make abruptly the dreadful disclosure of who and what he was.

The thought, however, of the manner in which the communication would be received stifled the words.

But Blanche, with a woman's tact, forebore to press him any further.

Taking from her finger a plain but costly ring, she pressed it upon his acceptance.

"Take this," she said, "and keep it always for my sake. If my other request was painful, you will not at any rate refuse to accept this souvenir."

"Refuse you?" he said, warmly. "Never—never! While I have life this shall be my inseparable companion. Be assured that you will never—never be effaced from my remembrance, and that I shall always look back to our brief companionship as the happiest moment in my stormy life. And now let me hear you pronounce the word farewell, for I must be gone—indeed, I incur great personal danger by remaining here."

At the words "personal danger," Blanche's cheeks grew white with terror.

"How unkind," she said, "to allow me to keep you here! Why not have told me earlier? Should——"

"Do not be too much alarmed. I——"

But before he could finish his sentence there was a sudden crash.

Blanche, whose fears were already in the ascendant, accompanied the violent noise by a shrill scream, which penetrated to every corner of the straggling dwelling.

It was the door communicating with the passage that had been thrown open with terrific violence.

On the threshold appeared a dense body of police officers.

All were armed.

"Captain Hawk," cried one, triumphantly, "we have found you at last! Attempt no resistance! The game is up! You are in our power! If you venture to stir from where you now stand you are a dead man!"

These words proved a terrible shock to Blanche.

In common with everyone else, the name of the famous highwayman was familiar enough to her ears.

Her first emotion was incredulity.

But in the face of such circumstances as the present it was impossible for this feeling to continue.

One glance alone into her companion's face was enough to satisfy her upon the point.

Another shriek came from her lips, almost drowning the last words spoken by the police officer.

Her countenance grew even more ghastly worse; and then, unable to bear up any longer against the horror and anguish which this discovery carried to her heart, she sank down senseless.

By stretching out his arms suddenly, Captain Hawk was just in time to prevent her from receiving the consequences of a heavy fall.

For a fleeting instant he held her in his arms, and then, overmastered by the tumult of his spirits, he pressed a fervent kiss upon her lips.

Then gently released his hold, and stood erect.

All this happened so rapidly that the police officers had not had time to make any further movement.

The highwayman noticed that the greater part of them held their pistols pointed at him, and they seemed content while they thus kept him at bay.

"Come, captain," said the one who had first spoken, now advancing, pistol in hand, into the room, "you must see that we have the advantage of you, so you may as well escape a serious wound as not."

Captain Hawk did not need a second glance to convince him of the gravity and imminency of his danger.

But he was not disposed tamely to submit himself for all that.

His only hope—and no one knew better than himself how slight it was—consisted in getting out of the inn with all speed.

Once outside its walls, he felt that all would be well.

He knew also that it was next to impossible for him to quit the room without falling a victim to the officers' pistols.

Clumsy and ill-adapted for their purpose as the weapons were, and blunderingly as they might be used, it was still by far too much to expect that he should be unscathed by so many fired at him from so short a distance.

There was another means of leaving the room—a means which, to the best of his belief, was at present unguarded: the door through which Blanche had passed.

This door only led to the interior of the inn; but the captain felt that, could he only succeed in passing through it, he should be able, by his intimate acquaintance with the place, to gain the exterior very quickly.

But then, with all these weapons levelled at him, with the fingers of the police officers encircling and pressing upon the triggers, how was he to be quick enough to open the door and cross the threshold without meeting his death in the attempt?

It was impossible, and he knew it.

His only chance was to throw his enemies off their guard.

All this, which has occupied us so many lines to express, passed through his brain while rising to his feet.

It was, too, without any perceptible pause after this act that he proceeded to carry a stratagem into execution.

Placing both his hands together, and extending them before him, as though ready to have the handcuffs clapped upon his wrists, he advanced a step or two towards his foes.

On his face was a look of deep humiliation, as though he was fully persuaded that it was utterly in vain to make the least attempt to escape.

The officers were quite deceived by it, and took the seeming for the real.

But then it seemed so natural that, under the present circumstances, the highwayman should abandon all hopes of saving himself, and were not surprised that he should be inclined to surrender quietly, since surrender was inevitable.

Captain Hawk's heart beat quickly.

He saw that already the police officers were thrown off their guard by his demeanour.

They made sure now that the affair would be quickly brought to a termination.

"Upon my word," said the chief officer, sticking his

pistol into his belt, and drawing a pair of bright handcuffs from his pocket, "this is handsomer behaviour than I expected of you, captain—it is indeed! But let me assure you it will be none the worse for you on the——"

The police officer uttered a cry, and dashed the handcuffs to the ground.

Captain Hawk, suddenly altering his manner, turned round and darted to the door, through which he felt certain lay the way to escape.

So quick was he, and so unprepared were the officers for such a movement, that he had his hand upon the latch before they could realise what had happened.

"Fire—fire!" bawled the chief officer, drawing his own pistol hastily from his belt, and cocking it. "Curse you all! why don't you fire? He will escape!"

But the officers, believing their pistols would no longer be wanted, had ceased to level them at the highwayman.

But they raised their arms quickly again, and fired a straggling volley.

As might be expected, though, they were too hasty and too flushed to take anything like an aim.

The report from the discharge of so many pistols in so confined a space was prodigious.

In an instant nothing was visible but a dense cloud of blue smoke.

"He's hit—he's hit!" cried several. "He can't escape. Come on—come on!"

But whether the statement about the highwayman was correct or not, it was quite certain that he had succeeded not only in getting through the doorway, but out of sight.

The hasty rush of footsteps was heard for a moment, and then followed a tremendous crash of broken glass.

"He's through a window!" cried the foremost, catching sight, a moment afterwards, of a shattered casement. "Quicker—quicker, or we shall lose him after all!"

The officers came on with all the speed they were able to make.

Captain Hawk had cleared the road so effectually that there was no trouble in following him.

One after another they leaped through the dismantled window.

A hasty glance then showed them that they were at the back of the inn, but the darkness had increased so much that they could scarcely tell exactly where.

As before, however, the hasty rush of footsteps enabled them to get upon the track of the fugitive.

"Shoot him the moment you see him!" said the chief officer. "Our instructions are to take him dead or alive! Don't give him the chance to deceive us a second time. We ought to have made sure of him at first."

The others responded with a growl, and made their way, as well as they were able, among the intricacies at the back of the old inn.

"There he is—there he is," they cried, as they got clear of an irregularly built outhouse—"there he is! Now we have him!"

At this moment a flash was seen, and the report of a pistol heard.

"Hurrah!" cried the commanding officer. "It's all right, after all. Hickman is watching yonder, and he has shot him! Hurrah! Come on—come on!"

And with a good deal of exultation, the chief officer, followed closely by his men, hurried to the spot from which the flash of the pistol had proceeded.

CHAPTER LXXXV

ISAAC THE OSTLER SAVES THE LIFE OF CAPTAIN HAWK.

THE officer who had cried out that Captain Hawk was hit was perfectly right.

But notwithstanding the fact that in flying from the room he had received an ugly wound from one of the many bullets fired at him, Captain Hawk felt that he had been successful beyond his most sanguine expectations.

Once through the doorway, he felt that he had something more than a chance of ultimate escape.

He knew just whereabouts he should find his horse, saddled and bridled ready for the road, and all he had to do was to make his way quickly towards that point.

We have already seen that he did so.

Instead of going further to the door that led out into the inn yard, and where, for aught he knew, an officer might be stationed to interrupt his flight, he leaped through the little lattice casement.

The lead of which the casement was composed yielded readily before his weight; and by drawing his hat as low down over his face as he could, he escaped with only a few scratches of such a trifling character that he thought nothing about them.

He alighted easily upon his feet, and, without pausing, ran direct to the little wall.

But ere he could quite reach it, a man rushed suddenly out of the darkness and seized him.

There was not time to elude him; and Captain Hawk felt that the grasp which had been taken was too tight a one to be easily shaken off.

But, without a moment's delay, this man cried:

"Captain Hawk, you are my prisoner! Dead or alive, I will have you!"

The highwayman made a vigorous effort to be free.

But this police officer, whose name was Hickman, determined to act up to his instructions—which were to take the highwayman dead or alive—drew a pistol quickly, and, holding it within a few inches of the captain's face, pulled the trigger.

Captain Hawk did not see his danger until it was too late to do anything to elude it.

He was too close to the muzzle of the pistol to have the least chance of escape.

But the flash which followed the act of pulling the trigger showed him the figure of a third person.

The terrific report almost stunned him, and the combustion of the gunpowder singed his lips and cheeks.

He staggered back, fully believing that he was mortally hurt.

Then he saw the third person strike the officer a tremendous blow, which laid him prostrate at once.

Then he heard a voice say:

"Too late—too late! I was just too late! The captain is no more!"

The voice was a familiar one.

It was Isaac who spoke.

In a second after, Captain Hawk, beginning to realise that he had in some most mysterious way escaped serious consequences from the discharge of the pistol, staggered forward a few paces towards his preserver.

"Are you dead, captain?"

"Not quite," gasped the highwayman, faintly.

"But badly hurt?"

"No—no. I—I——"

"What—oh! what?" asked Isaac, anxiously.

"I do believe that I am not hurt a bit."

"Then I was just in time after all. I was afraid not."

"What did you do?"

"I saw the blackguard with the muzzle of the pistol pointed to you, and with his finger on the trigger, so I sprang forward and knocked up his arm."

"And saved my life."

"I hope so, captain."

"You have unquestionably," said the highwayman, who was fast recovering himself.

"It was a close touch, though," said Isaac. "Another half second would have done the business. Look at your hat."

Captain Hawk did so, and saw that the bullet had torn away a great piece of the brim.

"An awfully close touch!" he said, with a shudder which he could not repress.

"But come, captain, quick—quick, or there will be more of the rascals down on us than we can compete with!"

And, in fact, the loud trampling made by the approach of the main body of police officers could be heard with alarming distinctness.

"Yes — yes!" Captain Hawk cried. "Where is Satan?"

"In the stable."

"Nay, I hope not. If he is, good-bye to all escape."

"No—no!" cried another familiar voice. "He is here. Mount quickly and be off! You deserve to be taken for running such unnecessary risks."

It was Tom Beckford who spoke.

His hand was on Satan's bridle-rein.

The sight of his noble steed so close at hand when he

was just despairing of reaching him in time infused a marvellous amount of vigour into the highwayman's limbs.

Seemingly unconscious of all that had recently taken place, he gave one bound, which seated him in the saddle.

Then, without waiting either to thrust his feet into the stirrups or to take hold of the reins, he urged Satan onward by a slight pressure of his heels.

Away went the gallant creature like a race-horse

"Help—help!" cried the landlord and Isaac in chorus, and both pretending to run after him. "Help—help! Here he is! Quick, or he will get away after all!"

The officers came rushing on; but when they found that the object of their pursuit had actually mounted and ridden off, they stopped and gnashed their teeth with rage.

The most horrible imprecations came from their lips.

Disappointment for a second time, just when they had told themselves the moment of success had arrived, was more than they could bear.

Isaac and the landlord both kept up their pretended pursuit.

But running was precisely one of those things which Tom Beckford could not keep up for any length of time, so he was shortly constrained to come to a standstill.

"Make your way back to the inn unperceived if you can," gasped Isaac. "I will continue to run on. I shall find the captain sooner or later, I'll warrant."

Tom Beckford retraced his steps, taking a detour in doing so, however, which he imagined would keep him out of the way of the police officers.

Whether he really eluded them or not time alone can show.

For the present, we must be content to follow Captain Hawk.

For some moments he suffered Satan to carry him at a headlong pace, without being exactly able to realise his good fortune.

But, by degrees, the agreeable consciousness came over him that he had once more succeeded in defeating his foes.

"Well done, old boy!" he cried, enthusiastically, to his priceless steed. "Well done—well done! But gently now. Let me put myself a little more comfortable than I am at present."

Docile as a spaniel, Satan at once reduced his speed; and Captain Hawk thrust his feet into the stirrups, and, taking hold of the reins, settled himself comfortably in the saddle.

This done, he pulled up altogether, in order to listen.

But though he stretched his sense of hearing to its fullest limit, he failed to catch any sounds that indicated a commencement of pursuit.

"No—no," he said. "It seems as though their disappointment and aggravation were too great to allow them to try further. Well, so be it. I have only the danger of meeting with other parties to contend with."

This was right enough.

"I am as likely to elude them here as anywhere," he said—"more so, indeed, for by going in any direction I might only get in closer proximity with some of them, while if I go no further than this there is just the possibility that the faithful fellow Isaac will rejoin me. I should be glad to see him, and to thank him, for certainly had it not been for him I should have been a dead man this night."

So saying, the highwayman took off his hat, and looked again at the ugly, jagged rent which had been made by the bullet.

It was impossible for anyone to contemplate such a thing as this unmoved.

Indeed, it was at this moment that the highwayman best comprehended the extent of his danger and the awfully narrow escape he had had.

He was aroused from the reverie into which he was unconsciously thrown by hearing sounds which unmistakably boded danger to him.

Satan was full of impatience to be off again.

But before releasing the rein, his rider resolved to listen a second longer.

The sound before had been faint, now it was unmistakable.

"A large party of horsemen," the captain said. "Well—well. It is no more than I ought to expect. They are police officers doubtless, for I know there is more than one party out on my track this night. I can elude them, no doubt. But how am I to meet with Isaac?"

This was a question that presented no ready solution.

But he was by no means certain that his faithful dependent would find him there; or that, if he did, he would be able to accompany him in his flight.

"But I will not abandon him," he said. "Humble as he is, he has established the firmest claim upon my friendship; and he will find that I am the one to appreciate it. I will get clear of these fellows at once, and when the heat of the pursuit has died away somewhat, I will make my way back to the neighbourhood of the Greyhound—that will be the best. I have yet something in the way of a farewell to say to Tom Beckford. Yes—yes—after a brief rest I will push on direct to London, and will take the Greyhound on my way."

With these words upon his lips, Captain Hawk turned his back upon his pursuers, and dropped the reins upon Satan's neck.

Away—away he flew through the darkness, heedless of all the obstacles that lay in his path, and only intent upon getting out of hearing of the horses' hoofs in the shortest possible space of time.

Fainter and fainter grew the ringing sound of the horses' iron-bound hoofs upon the hard high-road until, to the captain's great satisfaction, they ceased altogether.

He pulled up and listened.

But all was still.

"Have I really shown them a clear pair of heels so soon? I will make sure, at any rate, before I go any further."

So saying, he slipped quickly from the saddle, and leaned down until his ear was within an inch or two of the ground.

Then he again listened.

This time for several moments.

But, at the expiration of the time, no more sounds indicative of pursuit reached his ears than at first, and so he prepared to mount leisurely enough.

It was not often that Satan had been in better condition for the road than he was at the present moment, and the temptation came very strongly over Captain Hawk to make his way to the metropolis without delay.

But one or two considerations swayed him.

He wished to meet with the landlord and the ostler; but what was most important was that the morning now showed unmistakable signs of being very close at hand indeed.

"No—no," he said, "it is not to be thought of, great as the temptation seems. With the country all alive with men on the look-out for me, it would be impossible for me to get more than a mile or so by daylight without being recognised by some one. My only course seems to lay clear enough before me."

But for all that it seemed by no means agreeable to the highwayman.

Well enough, however, did he know that what he ought to do was to seek out some sequestered spot where he would be in little danger of being disturbed, and there remain until the friendly shadows of night began again to fall upon the landscape.

By the aid of the faint light which was fast beginning to creep over all objects, Captain Hawk set about looking for some place which held out any promise of answering his expectations.

But, as was commonly the case under such circumstances, nothing of the kind presented itself.

Clearer and brighter grew the morning light, and the captain, as minute after minute passed away without his being able to see anything resembling what he sought, grew more and more impatient.

"If I go much further," he said, "I may as well set out upon my journey at once. There can hardly be more danger in travelling in one direction than in another."

Just at this moment he came in sight of an object which had the effect of immediately arresting his attention.

This was a small, rudely-constructed hut.

So small, and so rudely constructed that one could hardly believe that it had been intended to serve for a human habitation.

It was more than halt buried in trees and tangled brushwood, which grew about this lonely and deserted spot with singular luxuriance.

As far as the eye could reach no traces of any other dwelling presented themselves.

On the side of a distant hill, however, the highwayman's keen vision detected several small spiral wreaths of smoke, which, from their appearance, he could tell came from the chimneys of some cottages.

"That hut," he said, as he gazed upon it, "is surely a deserted spot. It cannot be that it is used as the dwelling-place of anyone. Years ago it might insufficiently have answered that purpose; but surely—surely not now."

The appearance of the place was well calculated to bring Captain Hawk to this conclusion.

The lonely dwelling was almost roofless.

Tufts of half-decayed and blackened thatch clung here and there to the rotten beams and rafters, and formed the sole means of keeping out the violence of the weather.

The two windows which the wretched hovel boasted were battered in, and the door hung insecurely by the topmost hinge.

Take it for all in all, it was as vivid a picture of utter desolation as could well be seen.

And as if nothing should be wanting to complete the desolateness of aspect, a green, slimy pool surrounded it on three sides.

The silence was oppressive, for the morning was one of those unusually still ones which arrive once or twice during that season of the year.

There was not even wind enough to make a rustle among the upper branches of the tall trees which grew everywhere around.

The low-lying situation of the hut, too, caused the ground all around to be soft and swampy.

Like snow almost, it yielded an impression of every one of Satan's footmarks; and when the captain became aware of this, he looked around him still more narrowly in the hope of being able to discover by this means whether anyone had recently been near.

But all around the ground was smooth, and showed no trace.

"It is enough to give one the horrors," he said, "to think of spending even a day in such a place. What would a night be? But no matter. What I have to consider is, whether it is safe, and, judging by what I can see at present, there could not be a place that will suit us better."

This was likely enough, for it was easy to imagine that a place of this appearance would be carefully avoided by those whose occupation brought them into the neighbourhood.

Yet, despite all the advantages which the hut, as a place of temporary shelter, held forth, the highwayman seemed strangely reluctant to approach more nearly than he then was.

But the ruddy beams of the rising sun, which were now beginning to show themselves among the tree-tops, warned him of the imperative necessity there was of getting out of sight.

"I suppose there is no getting out of it," he murmured, half aloud, "though I would fain have chosen some other abiding-place. But why think of it? I ought only to remember that it is safe."

It was hard, however, for one to bring himself to forget the cheerless aspect of the scene; and the impression it produced upon the highwayman grew stronger and stronger the more he gazed at it.

But nerving himself by an effort to draw nearer, he directed Satan's head towards the dismantled doorway.

But ere he had taken more than half a dozen paces he suddenly pulled up.

"What was that?" he said, his voice unconsciously becoming strangely hushed in tone.

All was still.

"What was that?" he said.

But though he listened after asking this question, his ears failed to catch any sound.

"I could not have been mistaken," he said, at length—"my fancy cannot have misled me to such an extent as that. No—no. If ever I heard any sound in my life, I heard a feeble groan. But it was distinct, and it came from somewhere close at hand. How strange it is not repeated! I——"

He checked himself abruptly.

Again there came upon his ears the sound which had caused him to bring his horse to a standstill.

It was a groan—a hollow, dreadful sound, which surely could only have been wrung from mortal lips by more than mortal pain.

"Good Heavens!" he ejaculated, involuntarily. "What an awful sound—what a world of suffering that one sound summed up! What can it be suffering so much woe?"

All was still again.

"What is it?" cried the captain, in louder tones than he had hitherto made use of. "Who is it? What is the matter?"

Another dismal groan was his sole response.

But he was prepared for the sound this time, and knew from what direction it came.

"That was from the hut," he cried. "After all, then, this dismal, foot-forsaken place is tenanted by some poor wretch in an extremity of suffering. I have done much harm," he added; "perhaps now I shall have the opportunity of doing good."

As he spoke, he urged his horse towards the door.

When within a few paces of the threshold he alighted, and, unable to restrain his curiosity, hastened forward and pushed open the door.

This was no easy task; but when it was performed he beheld such a picture of squalor and destitution as had never before come within his experience.

The interior of the hut was even smaller than he had judged from seeing the outside.

The floor was composed of nothing save masses of leaves and little branches of the trees which had been drifted by the wind through the numerous open spaces in walls and roof.

A damp and sickening odour pervaded the whole dwelling—an odour like that of the charnel-house itself.

So powerful was it that it caused Captain Hawk to retreat half-way to the door, where a purer atmosphere prevailed.

While so doing he took in with his eyes the general aspect of the place.

The walls were roughly composed of brick and timber, and the two materials seemed vying with each other as to which should decay the fastest.

There were huge gaps here and there, so that had it not been for this extensive communication with the open air the stench would have been overpowering indeed.

Up above through the roof the sky could be seen in half a dozen places, though some wide-spreading trees which grew near cast the shadow of their branches over it, thus forming a slight additional protection from the rain.

Had Captain Hawk but given a hasty and casual glance into the interior of the hut and then departed, he would have gone away with the notion that it was uninhabited.

What he had heard, however, induced him to look closely, and then in the furthest corner he saw a slight movement among a mass of the leaves and vegetable *debris* of which we have spoken.

This movement was almost immediately followed by the groaning cry which had first attracted his attention.

This time there could be no doubt but that it proceeded from the mass of leaves in the corner.

"Who is it?" asked the captain, as, overcoming his repugnance as well as he was able, he made his way into the interior of the dwelling. "Who is it? What do you want? Speak, for aid is near."

A long-drawn, heavy sigh followed.

Then ensued a still greater amount of agitation among the decayed leaves.

Captain Hawk stepped nearer still.

"Speak," he cried, pausing when near the centre—"speak! Why do you remain silent?"

"Help—help—help!" responded a stifled and half-strangled voice.

CHAPTER LXXXVI.

CAPTAIN HAWK HAS A HORRIBLE ADVENTURE IN THE RUINED HUT.

THE moment those articulate sounds fell upon the ear of Captain Hawk, all his hesitation and irresolution vanished.

He thought no more about the soul-chilling appearance of the old hut, but, with an expression of determination upon his face, he walked quite close up to the heap of leaves.

Then, and not till then, was he able to discern who was the inmate of that wretched bed.

A face, pinched and gaunt with famine, hollow cheeks, and white, fleshless lips, was presented to him.

But for the fact that the chin was covered with a dense mass of stubbly gray hair, he would have had some trouble in deciding upon the sex of this wretched object—truly wretched in every sense of the term.

Care and want had doubtless done much to impart an air of premature old age; but after making every allowance for this, it seemed next to certain that this miserable being had almost lived out man's allotted span.

The glassy, leaden-coloured eyes were deeply sunken in their orbits, round which a broad and livid circle spread itself.

Clothing, this poor outcast seemed to have little, if any.

One skeleton arm alone was visible above the mass of leaves, and that was bare up to the shoulder, the bone of which seemed almost through the skin, that hung upon it in rugose folds.

The long, attenuated fingers, resembling more the claws of some wild animal than aught that was human, had closed themselves upon a handful of leaves, which they pressed with convulsive tightness.

Captain Hawk was struck by the resemblance which this man had to a huge, formidable bird of prey—a resemblance which was heightened by the large hooked nose, that stood out in horrible relief from the rest of his emaciated face.

The highwayman, as he gazed, though he had been witness of many a scene of unusual horror, could not help shuddering from head to foot.

His first impulse was to turn and fly from so horrible a spot, and endeavour to erase from his brain the recollection of the horrors he had beheld.

But a feeling of compassion and humanity for such a ghastly object as that extended before him made him linger where he was.

By the ever-increasing light of the new day he could see that a strange gleam had come back to the man's lack-lustre eyes.

It was a gleam which seemed to have almost the power of speech.

Captain Hawk gazed upon those eyes with growing fascination.

The skinny and retracted lips moved twitchingly, as though the man desired to speak, yet lacked the power of articulation.

His breath came and went in hard and fitful gusts, every one of which seemed to rend his chest.

"Miserable man," said the highwayman, at last recovering sufficient command over himself to use his voice—"miserable man, how comes it that you are in this wretched plight so far away as you are from your fellow-creatures? If you have the power, speak—tell me what I can do to mitigate your sufferings?"

By the still brighter gleam visible in those spectral eyes, Captain Hawk could tell that his words were both heard and understood.

The efforts that the wretch then made to gasp out some sound were terrible to look upon.

"What is it you would wish to say?" asked Captain Hawk, who had watched the movement of his lips attentively. "Is it water that you would ask me for?"

Again that wild and vivid gleam in the horrible eyes, which expressed an affirmative as plainly as the tongue could have done.

"Enough," said the captain, hardly able to suppress his loathing—"you shall have it."

But he looked in vain for any vessel which would serve to carry the wished-for liquid.

But happening to look back towards the animate heap, he saw that the gleaming eyes were fixed upon one point.

He turned in that direction and saw a broken, dirty piece of platter, which looked like the fragment of a dish.

But it would hold a little drop of liquid, and picking it up, the captain sallied forth.

The first thing he beheld was Satan drinking out of a very narrow brook, which apparently supplied the pool which we have mentioned.

"That will do," he said. "I can't say it is water I should like to swallow myself; but if it is good enough for you, that poor wretch inside won't object to it."

So saying, he filled the broken dish as full as he was able, and hastened back with it.

Just when he reached the heap of leaves, the captain bethought himself of the bottle of brandy in his pocket.

Drawing it forth, he mingled a small quantity of the spirit with the water.

Then conquering his aversion as well as he was able, he knelt down and moistened the man's lips.

The sip—for it was nothing more—was swallowed greedily.

Small as was the drop of brandy administered, its effects were visible almost instantly.

The efforts to speak were renewed, and of course with much additional vigour.

The tip of the blackened tongue touched against the still more blackened teeth.

"T—t—t——"

That was the sound.

Evidently it meant that the man desired to pronounce some word beginning with the letter T.

What this word could possibly be greatly raised the captain's curiosity.

He would never have guessed it.

At last, and only half articulately, the sufferer gasped out:

"Ten—ten—ten——"

He repeated the word as though unable to pronounce the next, until all at once there burst from his lips with startling suddenness and clearness:

"Thousand pounds!"

Then the eyes closed as though complete exhaustion had followed the effort.

"Ten thousand pounds!" repeated the highwayman.

Of all the words he had expected to hear, those surely would have been the very last to suggest themselves.

The horrible eyes opened again and emitted that responsive gleam.

The captain was right.

The man had mentioned the sum of ten thousand pounds.

And what a horrible and dismal mockery it seemed to hear this large amount mentioned by such a being!

His whole worldly possessions at that moment could only, by a liberal estimate, have been judged worth a millionth part of this immense sum.

What could such a miserable outcast have to do with ten thousand pounds?

"It is a mockery," said the highwayman—"a horrible mockery!"

But though temporarily exhausted, the utterance of these few words had seemed to unlock the outcast's tongue, for now, though feebly and indistinctly, he breathed out:

"Water—water! Give me more of that water!"

This was a request to which Captain Hawk could not give a refusal, so once more picking up the broken dish, he fetched more water.

This time he mingled it with a larger dose of brandy.

It was swallowed with the utmost conceivable greediness; yet such was the dreadful state of weakness to which this object was reduced that it almost choked him.

After a furious battle for his breath, he gained the victory.

But for a moment he could do nothing but gasp pantingly.

Then with a wild shriek, that seemed to ring through the captain's brain, and with a degree of frenzy indescribable, he repeated his former words:

"Ten thousand pounds!" he screamed. "Do you hear me?—do you understand me? Ten thousand pounds!"

"I hear you," said Captain Hawk; "but such a sum can have nothing to do with you. Waste not the little breath you have left by such vain remarks, but rather tell me what I can do in your behalf."

"Vain remarks!" shrieked the outcast, convulsed with

impotent fury. "What has it to do with me? I tell you it has everything to do with me! Vain remarks! Ha, ha! I like that vain remarks!"

The exertion almost prostrated him.

Captain Hawk, unable to move his eyes, gazed at him with mingled disgust and pity.

But a moment or two served to recruit to some extent the powers of the old man, or rather the spirit he had swallowed begun to exert its influence by infusing a factitious strength into his limbs.

With a sudden start, as though his muscles had been brought into contact with a galvanic battery, he sprang up to a sitting posture.

As he did so, the black decaying leaves fell from him, and showed that he was only dressed in the veriest rags.

How they held together was a mystery.

Having assumed this attitude, he remained for some seconds gazing into the countenance of Captain Hawk.

It was not until this moment that he seemed to awake to the knowledge that it was a stranger who stood near.

"I don't know you!" he gasped, wildly, pushing back the tangled locks of gray hair from his temples. "Who are you? What have I said? Not breathed the secret? No, no! Not even whispered the secret? No, no, no!"

He repeated the last words half assertingly, half interrogatively.

"I am a stranger," said Captain Hawk. "Chance alone has guided my footsteps to this most desolate place."

"But what have I said — what have I said?" he screamed, with an anxiety almost amounting to anguish.

"You have uttered the words——"

"Yes—yes!"

"Ten thousand pounds."

"And what else—what else?"

"Nothing more."

"Would you deceive me?" he said, still more wildly. "But no—no, it does not matter. I may have said that the vast treasure is buried—I may have said that. It would have been no harm if I had."

"But you did not say it."

"I care not—I care not! I may have said that it lies snugly under the old tree, but those who find it will have to look cunningly among the roots. Ha, ha! It does not matter."

And so saying, he fell back again upon his rude couch, the stimulant having expended much of its power.

Captain Hawk now very reasonably came to the conclusion that he was listening only to the raving of a maniac.

The wild gleams which had come into the eyes of the miserable wretch must have been indicative of the fire of insanity that was burning in his brain.

"Perhaps, after all," he said, "I have done harm instead of good. Without my interference Death would doubtless by this time have seized his victim, and to lengthen such a horrible existence must be opposed to humanity."

While the captain was making these reflections, the old man was trying his utmost to recover a portion of his wasted strength.

His eyes opened, and this time it was with a calmer expression that he gazed around him.

"Where's Martha?" he said, faintly. "She has not abandoned me? No, no! Surely she would not leave me here to die alone. Martha—Martha, where are you?"

"To the best of my knowledge," answered the captain, "there are no human beings near this spot save ourselves."

"She has left me, then: she is gone—gone! But I can disappoint her yet. I am yet able to revenge myself for this last act of cruelty!"

"Do you know that you are on the point of death?" said Captain Hawk. "Ought you not to occupy your mind with other thoughts? What has one in your position to do with revenge?"

"Ten thousand pounds, I tell you!" shrieked the old man, with even ten times his former violence—"ten thousand pounds, I say! You may think me mad—ha, ha! But I know—I am not. What has she lost? Wealth—wealth! Such wealth as in her wildest dreams she has never thought of! Ten thousand pounds!"

The captain tried to speak, but the old man prevented him.

"I tell you that the treasure is buried. Oh, it is securely hidden! I am not afraid that chance will ever discover the precious deposit. More water—more water, and the secret shall be yours."

And so saying, he fixed his gaze with an indescribable expression upon the countenance of Captain Hawk.

The latter, after a momentary hesitation, again took the broken dish.

It was not that he was influenced by the old man's words, for he believed them to be only insane ravings; but because he did not like to refuse him the last favour which probably he would be able to ask for on earth.

That there was an unusual degree of mystery about the whole affair Captain Hawk knew well enough; but not from the lips of the poor outcast did he hope to obtain any elucidation of it.

But with a degree of rationality and calmness, which the highwayman was far from expecting, the old man said:

"You will find that the most profitable action that ever you have performed. Quick—quick! or you will be too late; for already I feel the chill damp of death about my heart and brain. Quick—quick, I say!"

He ended much in his former excited manner.

Captain Hawk again placed brandy-and-water to the sufferer's lips.

The same results were produced.

But the end was different.

The utmost fury and incoherence characterised the old man's speech.

He strove to rise; but his strength was too feeble for that.

Curses, the most horrible that ear ever heard, poured like a torrent from his lips.

His anathemas were all directed against some one that he called Martha.

"She has deserted me in my last moments," he said, with a little more calmness of manner—"she has left me here to die alone! Little does she think what she has lost—little does she think what she has lost! But I will be revenged!"

Then with a sudden and startling transition of tone and manner, he cried, wildly:

"Hark—hark! Did you not hear that? I mean that faint clanking sound. You hear it now? The gibbet is at hand. How the winds sport with the murderer's bones! The birds of prey circle around! See them—see them now!"

"Hush!" said the captain, drawing nearer. "Compose yourself. There is nothing here that you rave about."

"Not here! Look—look!" And, starting up with great suddenness, he seized the highwayman by the waist.

His bony grasp was like the pressure of an iron vice.

"You can see it now!" he screamed, with his distended eyes fixed on vacancy. "Look at the moon: her light is now almost like the sun's. Now you can distinguish every stock and stone—the grass and bushes on the heath. And there is the gibbet! Look at the long shadow which it casts!—how grotesque!—how far it stretches itself across the broken ground! You see it now?"

"I see nothing save these miserable walls."

"Nothing? But you must. Look at that poplar: how high it raises its head above the rest of the vegetation, as though rejoicing in its conscious pride! Look at the shadow of that: clear, dark, and well defined! Away—away it stretches! How far—how far! Look, there it crosses something! Another shadow: the shadow of what? The shadow of the gibbet! Ha, ha! That is it! All right now—all right! See where the two black masses cross each other! Mark the spot well: it is there—it is there! Don't I tell you—ten thousand pounds!"

And this time, wholly exhausted, the old man, panting and labouring for his breath, fell back upon the leaves.

Captain Hawk was so filled with surprise at hearing these last words that some seconds elapsed before he could recover himself sufficiently to release his wrist from the old man's iron grip.

This was by no means easily done; and the action seemed to bring the old man back once more to a dim and confused knowledge of what was passing around him.

"What have I said?" he asked, in low, feeble accents.

[CAPTAIN HAWK STOPS JUDGE NORTH'S CARRIAGE.]

which formed a vivid contrast to the shrieking tones he had just employed—"what have I told you? Ha! She comes—she comes! Too late—too late! The secret is disclosed! Ten thousand pounds all lost—all lost!"

It was not until the old man thus spoke that Captain Hawk became aware that another person had entered the hut.

But now he saw that a girl, who, perhaps, was not more than eighteen years of age, though she appeared much older, had crossed the threshold and advanced to within a few paces of his side.

Her apparel was of the scantiest description, and hung in tatters about her.

In her manner there was an unusual amount of boldness and effrontery; and so far from exhibiting any shame on account of the condition she was in, she gazed at the captain with a bold, defiant leer.

"Well," she said, boldly, "and what do you want with the old man?—what do you want here, peeping and prying and listening to his secrets? Off—begone! We want you not!"

"No—no!" exclaimed the old man, vehemently. "Don't leave me with her—pray don't! Protect me—save me! She would murder me for my secret; but—ha, ha!—I shall balk her yet!"

"Pay no attention to his ravings," said the woman—girl we cannot call her, though her years entitle her to that appellation—"they mean nothing. Leave us to ourselves. He is mad."

"Mad, am I?" asked the old man, catching at the words. "Should you think me mad if I began to tell you about the ten thousand pounds? Ha! your eyes light up, do they? But no, no—you will be disappointed yet. My lips are sealed. The treasure will never be yours!"

While he was thus speaking, the woman, who in appearance was even more loathsome and repulsive than the man himself, displayed signs of the deepest agitation.

She seemed wavering between her hope and desire to hear more, and her dread that the words should fall upon stranger ears.

"Silence!" she said, fiercely; and then turning to Captain Hawk, she again told him to begone.

He seemed half inclined to obey her, for what he had beheld sickened and disgusted him.

But somehow, in spite of himself, he felt disinclined to leave the helpless old man to the tender mercies of this abandoned creature.

A deep groan coming from the rude couch caused him to turn round.

At the first glance he could see that a great change had come over the old man's features.

It was a change that heralded the approach of death.

And fearful indeed was his face to look upon.

"No—no!" he said, moaningly. "Away—away! Don't look at me like that! Oh! those dreadful eyes! Away—away, I say! Help—help! Save me from you! Why do you glare at me so—why those threatening gestures? I did not kill you. You cannot say the deed was mine. Mercy—mercy! What, nearer and nearer yet! Off—off! I can struggle yet! Mercy—mercy!"

And the old man writhed and rolled about as though struggling with some powerful assailant.

But the struggle did not last long.

Gradually his strength left him; and then, with a horrible rattling in his throat, he fell back upon the heap of leaves quite dead!

CHAPTER LXXXVII.

CAPTAIN HAWK ENDEAVOURS TO PENETRATE THE MYSTERY OF THE HUT.

An intense stillness followed this event.

Even the woman, despite her brazened hardihood, could not help feeling impressed by the singular and mysterious old man.

But this feeling was only transient.

Darting swiftly to the heap of leaves, she rudely seized the dead man's shoulder and peered into his face.

"Is he dead?" she said. "Am I balked after all? No—no! he must live long enough to make me acquainted with the secret he has so zealously guarded! Is all my time and attention to have no reward? Look up—look up! You must and shall tell me where the treasure lies!"

While she spoke she shook the inanimate mass roughly, and with more disregard of all Christian feeling than the captain until then believed a woman could be guilty of.

But that mysterious power called the soul which had animated the body of the horrible old man had quite departed.

Nothing remained of him save a senseless lump of clay.

"Woman," said the highwayman, as soon as he was able to master his feelings sufficiently to speak calmly—"woman, have you lost all sense of decency? Can you not see that Death has claimed his own?"

No sooner had he spoken than she turned upon him like a tigress.

"Who are you?" she asked. "What do you here? I was a fool for leaving *him!*" she said, pointing to the corpse. "You have come in and learned that which I have been years and years waiting to listen to—I who have endured at his hands every species of indignity—I who have obeyed his every whim—followed him from place to place—suffered hunger, cold, and every ill which waits upon homeless, shelterless humanity. And all that I might, some time or other, learn the important secret. But he guarded it well. But with his last breath I quite expected that the secret would be mine. Now you have learned it; but I will wrest it from you!"

The woman seemed to be completely carried away by her extreme disappointment.

Fire flashed from her sunken eyes; and as she finished speaking, she sprang at the highwayman with all the suddenness and fury of a famished tigress.

But Captain Hawk was accustomed to attacks, and on the present occasion was very little taken by surprise.

The furious disappointment which she displayed told him that she was ready to commit any act, no matter how desperate.

In the twinkling of an eye she drew from the bosom of her dress a glittering, formidable-looking knife, and before the captain was aware that she carried weapons at all, she gave a wild and vicious stab with it.

Captain Hawk put up his left arm to avoid the blow.

He was wounded; but the next moment he had wrested the weapon from her and left her defenceless.

"Stand back, woman!" he said, having disengaged himself from her grasp. "Approach me again at your peril! Your actions are almost enough to make me doubt your sex. Take care you do not compel me to forget it altogether."

The woman had evidently relied much upon her knife, for now that she was deprived of it she seemed completely cowed.

Most probably, too, her attack was made at a moment when she was blind to reason.

She stepped back; and the captain flung her knife through an opening in the wall, into the stagnant pool of which we have made mention.

"Wretched being!" he said. "You have confessed that you have followed this poor old man from the most mercenary and sordid of motives. That you have been disappointed at the last is no more than you deserve. For myself, I have nothing more to do at this place, which I have reached by the merest chance."

So saying, he turned upon his heel, determined to run any risk rather than seek shelter beneath that humble roof.

But the woman Martha witnessed these movements towards a departure with the utmost alarm and dread.

From the poor inanimate object among the leaves she could not hope to gain the slightest information now.

Firmly persuaded that the secret had been confided to Captain Hawk, she endeavoured to summon up what art she could to induce him to make the disclosure to her.

"Don't leave me," she cried, piteously—"don't go away—pray do not! Think of my wretched state. Poverty and my dreadful sufferings have almost driven me mad. A little while ago I knew not what I said or what I did. Do not leave me—pray don't!"

Surprised at the remarkable change in her manner, Captain Hawk arrested his steps upon the threshold, and turned round.

Martha, encouraged by the success she had met with, endeavoured to be doubly blandishing.

But her efforts only produced disgust instead of the feeling she hoped to call into existence.

"Alas!" she said, trying hard to force some tears into her eyes—"alas! If I was only able to give you some description of what I have suffered, you would be sorry for me—you would pity me—you could not fail to do so. Listen—listen—only for a moment—listen!"

Captain Hawk was about to pronounce a fierce refusal, but a second thought induced him to alter his determination.

That thought was that it was possible by constraining himself to listen to have some light thrown upon the extraordinary scene which he had witnessed.

That he should feel the utmost amount of curiosity concerning it is nothing to be wondered at.

And to stand still a moment and listen seemed a trifling thing indeed.

"You will hear me, will you not?" said Martha, imploringly. "If you will only listen, I will tell you all."

Captain Hawk did not reply, and gave the woman no more encouragement to speak than by stopping where he was.

"If you could only guess what I have put up with from him! And now he has died without giving me that reward to which I was so justly entitled. You must see that, though chance has made you the recipient of the secret, you are not entitled to reap all the benefit from it—you who have done nothing for him—you who have only seen him such a short time ago; but make me acquainted with that which was surely intended for my ears alone, and you will find that I shall be generous beyond your expectations."

And in her intense excitement the woman's form seemed to dilate, her eyes sparkled, and she drew her breath in sudden and irregular intervals.

Captain Hawk had stood in the same position, listening attentively to the words which poured from her lips.

And now she stopped, expecting him to make her some reply.

But her impatience was too agonising for her to remain waiting for an answer very long.

"I will conceal nothing from you," she went on. "You will wonder, doubtless, by what means such a wretched-looking object as that which lies on the leaves yonder obtained the sum he raved about: you have wondered, have you not?"

Captain Hawk inclined his head.

"Well, then," she replied, "the mystery will be solved when I tell you that he was all his life a miser. You can tell his age was great—how great I know not. He has always been hoarding up his wealth and denying himself, for fifty years at least, every comfort and almost every necessary of life, and not hesitating to stoop to any meanness in order to keep adding to his hoard. And despite all the privations he has undergone, you see, his iron constitution has enabled him to live to a great age. He has outlived all his relatives and friends; and when I met with him he was quite alone in the world. You understand me, do you not?" she added, perceiving the captain did not speak.

"Perfectly," he replied.

"Enough, then. For years, now, he has supported himself by wandering up and down the country and begging from door to door—aye, and not only supported himself, but contrived to add more and more money to his secret hoard, which he has many a time told me was little short of ten thousand pounds."

"Is it possible?" the captain ejaculated, almost involuntarily.

"I have no doubt he spoke the truth—in all probability the amount is even greater than he said. Often and often has he told me that he would show me where this treasure is deposited; but he has never done so. I know from what he has said that it is buried in the earth. I fancy it cannot be far from this spot, for we were on our way to it when this mortal sickness struck him down. It has been in the hope of one day possessing myself of his wealth that I have followed him many hundreds of weary miles—that I have given up everything for; and now at the last I am disappointed—bereft of all, and through nothing but a brief absence from his side. Oh, I ought never to have left him—not even for a single moment!"

And in the paroxysm of her disappointment, the wretched woman wrung her hands and wept bitterly.

"Tell me—tell me," she added, with increasing vehemence—"tell me where it is that all this treasure has been buried! Do not be so selfish as to think of taking it all yourself. Give me one half of it, and I will be content. Refuse me, and I will never, never leave you—I will haunt you through your life like a shadow."

"Stand back!" said the captain, observing that she was about to approach more closely to him. "Stand back, I say! Your disappointment is a true and just punishment for your mercenary conduct!"

"Then you will not tell me where it is that the wretched old man has buried his treasure?"

"I shall not tell you, because I do not know."

She received this declaration with a wild and mocking laugh.

"Not know!" she repeated. "Ha, ha! Not know! Think you that I am such a shallow fool as to be deluded by such a statement as that? You do know, and when you leave here you will go direct to the spot."

"You are mistaken," said the captain, with a calmness and evenness of utterance that almost forced the woman to believe in spite of herself that he was speaking the truth. "The old man's secret died with him. Just before his death he raved out something about a buried treasure. He mentioned that it was near a gibbet and a poplar tree, and that when the moon caused the shadows of these two objects to cross, the point of intersection would indicate the spot where the treasure lies."

"Yes—yes!" she said, pushing back her hair with feverish eagerness.

"That is all."

"All?"

"Yes," he said; "no more. Where these two objects are, I neither know nor care; and I make the revelation to you simply because it will be to you a punishment and a curse."

"Punishment—curse!" she ejaculated, unable to comprehend him.

"Yes; for those words condemn you to be a restless wanderer on the earth to the last day of your existence. You will seek this treasure——"

"I shall find it!" she said, resolutely.

Captain Hawk smiled.

He saw that he was right in his conjecture.

"Yes," she cried, almost with a scream, "with half such a clue as you have just given me, I shall find the prize. A gibbet, said you? I will visit every one in England with a poplar tree growing near. I shall not forget it. The money will at last be mine!"

Then suddenly the thought darted into her mind that Captain Hawk had only told her this in order to get rid of her while he himself set out upon the important expedition.

"You know more than this," she said, between her clenched teeth.

"I do not. I will even take the trouble to swear that that is all I know of the matter. Be assured I have something else to do than to set out on such a hopeless errand."

Martha clasped her hands over her face, and broke out into a passionate burst of tears.

"I cannot—cannot believe," she said, "that this is to be the end—that I have endured so much and toiled so hard in vain! No—no! If you have told me the truth, the ten thousand pounds will yet be mine!"

"I have told you the truth, and I repeat it. Seek and find, and then you will have sufficient punishment for your mercenary conduct."

With these words Captain Hawk turned suddenly upon his heel, and made his way with a rapid step towards the spot where he had left his horse.

The woman called after him in the most frantic manner.

But disregarding her altogether, he quickly made his way to his steed, and sprang into the saddle.

The woman seemed more than half inclined to commence a mad pursuit.

But if ever such an idea did cross her brain it was banished almost immediately, for Satan, who seemed no less impatient to quit that dismal spot than his master, started off at one of his amazing gallops.

Just before losing sight of the hut, Captain Hawk looked behind him.

He saw her throw her arms up wildly in the air.

The next instant the sound of a piercing shriek came upon his ears; and ere the cry had ceased to vibrate upon the air, he saw the wretched creature fall senseless to the earth.

"Gold—gold!" murmured the highwayman, as he moderated his horse's speed somewhat. "What has it not power to do? Witness those two wretched creatures in that hut. What a picture of humanity! And no doubt the influence will be strong enough upon her to make her a weary wanderer during the remainder of her life. And how faint is her chance of success! How can she hope to discover the secret hoard guided only by what I have told her? What is wanting is the season of the moon and the hour, or else the shadow will not be in the right place. No—no, she will never find it."

Captain Hawk no doubt would have indulged in much more speculation upon this strange adventure had not his mind been so busily engaged with the consideration of other important matters.

He was satisfied to some extent with regard to the mystery which at first had so much troubled him.

The discovery that the old man was a miser accounted for all that had before appeared so strange.

Having gone some distance from the hut, and having taken care to avoid the village, in the vicinity of which he stood, Captain Hawk paused to reconnoitre.

He was more induced to perform this important action by finding himself at the highest portion of some gently-rising ground, from which a very extensive prospect of the surrounding country could be obtained.

The scene was brilliantly lighted up by the glorious sun.

The strong wind which had been blowing for some hours left the air remarkably transparent, and far and wide all objects were visible with a very unusual amount of distinctness.

Shading his eyes with his hands, Captain Hawk looked long and scrutinisingly in every direction.

"This is much better than I had dared to hope for!" he cried, as soon as he had finished his survey. "Not a single officer within miles of me; or if there is, so well under cover as to be out of sight. It is certain that there are none of them upon my track. Bravo, Satan!" he added, patting his noble steed fondly on the back. "It is in vain for officers to try to pursue me while I am on your back: as well might they try to overtake the wind!"

While looking so carefully around, Captain Hawk had noticed at no great distance a plantation of great density and extent.

As there was no one near to observe his actions, there was nothing which would furnish a better shelter for himself and his horse than this.

Many hours would have to elapse before the coming of night; and it was fortunate such happened to be the case, for, after the exertions he had made, Satan was sadly in need of a rest.

Now there was every chance of his having one, for his master, without any more delay, directed his steps towards the nearest point of the plantation that we have mentioned.

On his way thither, Captain Hawk's mind was occupied with many reflections.

"I was too hasty," he said, "in deciding upon starting at once for London. At all hazards, I will find Isaac. With him by my side, I know that I shall have one that I can trust, and to whom I can refer when I find myself in doubt. Surely, the likeliest way to find him would be to ride back again to the Greyhound. But that would be not only to involve myself in great peril, but old Tom Beckford as well. Confound those officers! If I could but think of some plan of getting rid of them!"

Captain Hawk performed the rest of the distance to the wood in perfect silence, and with an expression of deep thought and anxious consideration upon his face.

He was not able to penetrate very far into the plantation while seated in the saddle; and a straggling bough striking him rather a sharp blow across his face aroused him from his reverie.

"Confound it all!" he cried, slipping quickly from the saddle. "Who would have thought of that now?"

He did not take the trouble to hold the rein, for he knew his faithful dumb companion was sagacious enough to follow wherever he might lead, and so the result proved.

"It is hardly necessary to go very far," he said to himself. "I know the officers are not very close at hand. I think just where I am will do as well as anywhere."

He had reached a small open space, where, owing to the trees being further apart, the grass grew more luxuriantly.

"This will suit you, old fellow. Let me make you as comfortable as I can."

So saying, he removed all Satan's trappings, and placed them on the sward.

"Now, then," he said, "for a rest and a little calm reflection. I must get to the Greyhound somehow, and I must also get the officers away, so that my visit may be made in peace."

As the reader must know, it was no easy task which the captain had set himself; but not for one instant did he despair of accomplishing it.

With singular sophistry, he tried to persuade himself that his principal if not his sole reason for resolving upon paying a visit to the Greyhound was to meet with the faithful Isaac.

He kept back even from himself what was his main motive for wishing to make his way back to this dangerous quarter.

Although he would not admit it to himself, it was with the hope that he might once more see Blanche.

The impression which she had made upon his susceptible nature was a very deep one.

He was anxious to know how she was affected by the discovery of who and what she was, and experienced an insatiable longing to know what effect it would have upon her behaviour to him should they meet again.

This was a point upon which he could not bear to reflect with the slightest amount of patience.

"Anything—anything would be better than this feeling of suspense upon the subject!" he cried, starting to his feet and pacing up and down the little glade. "I will know it," he said. "The worst cannot be so bad as the doubt and uncertainty which I now feel."

Had Captain Hawk been asked what probable good for either was likely to accrue from this meeting, he would have been puzzled to reply.

Surely he must have known that for Blanche's peace of mind it would, at any rate, have been better for him to stay away.

But Captain Hawk would not, or at least did not, look at the matter in this light.

All he seemed to think about was ascertaining what effect the revelation of his identity had produced in the young girl's breast.

And with a continuation of the same self-hypocrisy, he tried to cover over his real purpose with another motive.

"There is Tom Beckford, too," he said. "How much he has done for me! How can I ever recompense him sufficiently for what he has done, and the risk he has run in my behalf? At present I have done nothing in return—absolutely nothing; but it will be a strange thing to me if I do not make him a worthy recompense."

He paused again in thought, and then broke out again suddenly into the utterance of his thoughts aloud.

"The officers know I am going to London," he cried. "If I could but hit upon some expedient to make it appear as though I was miles and miles on my way, and then when they were, as they believed, hard upon my track, I could be making my way back again towards the inn! Is such a thing beyond the powers of my invention? I should think not. It ought not to be. At any rate, I will try to think."

Captain Hawk remained in anxious consideration for several moments.

Then his brow began to clear, his mouth to lose its stern expression, and his eyes to brighten.

"At last—at last!" he cried—"at last! I have it! Ha, ha! What could be simpler or more effectual? Ha, ha! My purpose will be gained exactly, and the police officers will discover that, clever as they are, it will yet be an easy matter for me to deceive them completely. Ha, ha! It is a good plan!"

CHAPTER LXXXVIII.

IN WHICH CAPTAIN HAWK DEVISES AND EXECUTES A SCHEME TO DISAPPOINT AND ENRAGE THE POLICE OFFICERS, AND STOPS CHIEF JUSTICE NORTH ON THE HIGHWAY.

Captain Hawk was highly delighted with the plan he had just thought of, and manifested his joy in every way possible.

"An excellent plan!" he continued, rubbing his hands briskly together. "How fortunate it is in every way that I should have thought of it! I shall secure a brief interval from this ceaseless persecution. I don't care now how quickly night comes."

Already there were evident signs of night closing in; but it was doubtful whether the highwayman's impatience would suffer him to wait until dusk had fairly set in.

"Let me see," he said, pausing reflectively. "It will be best for me to consider over the details of the affair. At present it is only the outline of an idea. It will require careful filling in. In the first place I will, as soon as it is dark enough, leave this copse and ride across the country for a dozen or sixteen miles in the direction of London, taking care to remain unobserved. Good. I can manage that. Then I will go to some well-known inn on the roadside, and there refresh myself. Before leaving, I will take care to let them know who I am—that is, if they don't find it out without my doing so. I will also say something about my intention to ride post haste to London. To favour this I will ride off at a gallop; but as soon as I am at a safe and convenient distance I will turn off and take to the open country again. Thanks to Satan, I shall be able to get to the Greyhound long before morning. Yes, yes—that is it."

Captain Hawk was more delighted than ever with his

plan. In fact, the more he considered it over, the more practicable did it appear, and the better calculated to answer his purpose.

"Bravo!" he said, in great glee. "I can just imagine a troop of police officers riding up to the front of the inn after I have left it. The landlord will be called, they will question him about me, and of course he will be fast enough to say that I galloped off along the road towards London at such a time, and that he heard me saying I was going to make the journey at full speed. Ha, ha! How they will swallow that, and how they will be deceived! Why, it's worth any risk to play them such a trick."

Captain Hawk grew so outrageously pleased, that he could not make up his mind to wait there any longer, so he began to caparison his steed in readiness for the adventure.

After that he looked to all his weapons, and by the time he had completed these preparations there was a considerable degree of darkness prevailing among the trees.

Accordingly he slipped the bridle over his arm, and began to make his way into the open country.

Before emerging from the trees, however, he took care to look well all around him.

To his great satisfaction he found that the coast appeared to be perfectly clear.

"Good!" he said. "I can see that fortune intends to favour me in this adventure. How I shall enjoy it! I would not miss it on any consideration."

Having satisfied himself, as well as the fast gathering shadows on the landscape would permit, that there was no one to observe his motions, he vaulted into the saddle in a manner which showed how light-hearted he felt.

Then with surprising boldness he rode out from the place of friendly shelter.

"I noticed by daylight how lonely this part of the country seemed, so that I shall have little to fear in riding on my way. Besides, these shadows are almost as perplexing and confusing as intense darkness. At any rate, here goes to chance it."

A moment's consideration served to let the highwayman know which way he ought to take in order to go in the direction of London, and, having settled this important point, he allowed Satan to go at a sharp gallop, for the noble animal appeared to be quite fresh, and just in the humour for the exercise.

For half an hour this pace was continued; and though at the end of that time Satan discovered no signs of fatigue, yet a very considerable space of ground had been passed over.

"Bravo!" cried the highwayman, with greater glee than ever, for the exercise had caused his heart to beat rapidly and every vein to tingle, "that was well done, old boy! We will take it easy for a few moments, and then another half-hour like the last, and I shall have gone far enough to answer my purpose. Gently, now—gently."

But the horse's blood was up, and the highwayman had no little trouble in keeping him anything like steady.

But a fresh idea in furtherance of his plan now crossed the highwayman's brain, and he compelled his steed to go slowly, in order that he might follow it out with the more ease.

"Yes," he said, at length breaking the silence, for when quite alone Captain Hawk generally uttered his thoughts aloud—"yes, there are several weighty reasons why I should do it, and I cannot, for the life of me, think of one why I shouldn't. We may consider, then, that is decided."

Captain Hawk stroked his chin reflectively, and continued his chain of thought.

"Yes, yes—that is exactly it. All is quite ready, and the delusion of the officers will be complete. I cannot be far from the high-road, and I will make my way to it with all speed. Then, taking up a convenient station, I will wait for the first traveller who comes up riding towards Huntingdon. I will stop him, and then let him know who has done it. He will be full of fury if his loss is considerable (and I hope it will be), and, without doubt, will look after one of the troops of officers. He will inform them of the adventure, and then, should my enemies be in doubt or ignorance, that will serve to set them in pursuit. Decidedly this must be it. If I omit it the whole business will be in danger of miscarrying."

Captain Hawk interrupted himself to chuckle heartily over the nice little discomfiture he was providing for his foes.

"My inventive powers are in good order to night," he said, as he changed the direction in which his horse had been going—"there can be no doubt at all about the fact. Oh, what a glorious triumph this will be!"

His distance from the great Northern Road was not very considerable, so that a gallop of a very few minutes brought him up to it.

He looked over the hedge which divided him from the dusty highway.

There was nothing to be seen, and after listening for a minute or two he came to the conclusion that there was nothing to be heard either.

"There's plenty of time," he said, "and so I won't risk doing any harm to Satan by jumping over this hedge, low as it is; I sha'n't go far along the meadow without finding a gate, I'll be bound."

In this conjecture he was perfectly correct.

About a dozen yards further on was a large white gate.

On dismounting he found that it was secured only by an ordinary catch.

As he threw the gate back upon its hinges he happened to look overhead, and perceived that some wide-spreading trees threw quite a shadow over this spot.

"Stop a minute," he said—"let me think. If I prop this gate open, and stand here in wait, I shall have an excellent place of concealment. Unless I choose to show myself, no passers-by would be aware of my presence. That would be a very desirable thing indeed. When I am ready, nothing will be easier than to ride forward; while, should I be compelled to fly, the open gate will furnish me with a ready manner of getting into the open country. Most decidedly this is the place where I ought to take up my station."

So saying, he went as far as the road.

But all remained still as before.

Returning, he mounted his steed, and so was in readiness for an adventure as soon as one should present itself.

Five minutes, or thereabouts, elapsed.

"I hope I shall not be kept waiting long," he said, impatiently. "But I can't be: such a road as this cannot remain unoccupied for many moments together."

Just as he spoke he heard the tread of a heavy footstep, and directly afterwards he became aware that the person approaching was whistling some lugubrious air or other.

Captain Hawk drew further back under the trees.

The foot-passenger approached, until in a moment or two he reached the gate.

Captain Hawk fully expected that this man would walk on without taking any further notice.

But he was mistaken.

Suddenly the whistling and the footstep simultaneously ceased.

"Dang it all," he cried, in a very loud voice, "if this gate bean't open again! I wish I was behind the chap that left it open! I'd help him on his way! Here's all manner of things comes straying over the meadow, and I get the blame for it. Why, bust me, if this don't cap all! Impudence has come to something, I think! Thrash me if they haven't propped the gate open!"

With many impatient angry exclamations, the man removed the little piece of wood which Captain Hawk had taken the pains to fix very cleverly to keep the gate from swinging shut, which it had a tendency to do.

He looked across the meadow, but the shadow cast by the trees was by far too dense to enable him to distinguish the forms of the horse and rider standing there.

Grumbling and swearing, he fastened the gate, and then trudged off, beginning his whistle again at the very same note where he left off

Captain Hawk waited until he had passed quite out of hearing, and then, with a cry of impatience, set to work to prop the white gate open again.

"He will be a little mystified when he comes in the morning and finds it propped open in precisely the same manner, I'll be bound. Hush! what is that?"

He stopped suddenly, and listened.

"Wheels!" he said, with an exclamation of satisfaction "My waiting is over at last."

He made haste to remount his steed, so as to be in perfect readiness.

It was not until he did this that he discovered another disappointment awaited him.

The vehicle he had heard was going from Huntingdon in the direction of London.

"It won't answer my purpose to stop it, whatever it is," he said. "And yet it will be a hard matter to let it go by. Let me remember, however, that if I interfere with it it will quite derange the plan I have laid for the amusement of the officers."

This reflection was quite enough to enable him to overcome the powerful temptation he felt to ride forward and stop the coming vehicle.

On it rolled, at a very rapid rate indeed, and, after listening for a moment or two longer, Captain Hawk ejaculated, in tones much too loud to be prudent:

"As I am a living man, it's the stage-coach!"

After this it seemed for a few seconds doubtful whether he would remain constant to his purpose or not.

But before he could decide upon spoiling the capital plan he had thought about there was a flashing of lights, a roar of wheels, a clatter of horses' hoofs, a confused sound, a cloud of dust, and the stage-coach whirled by.

"Oh, how I wish it had been coming from London instead of hastening to it!" exclaimed Captain Hawk, in tones of the deepest vexation and annoyance. "I would have given them all something to talk about at the next stopping-place! But never mind—it would be foolish to spend a world of regrets upon that. I must wait."

Captain Hawk did wait until the noise made by the York coach died away into the faintest possible hum.

By degrees this seemed most inexplicably to grow louder until Captain Hawk, with the utmost delight, discovered that this was attributable to the fact that the stage-coach had passed some other vehicle, and that this other vehicle was now rolling towards him with considerable rapidity.

"Now, then, all will be well," he exclaimed. "My patience is about to be rewarded—my vengeance on my foes is about to be complete."

Captain Hawk was so delighted with the prospect he now had that he quite forgot all the disappointment he had experienced regarding the stage-coach.

His weapons he knew were all ready, so that he had nothing to do but to await a favourable opportunity of riding forward.

This did not put his patience, or, more correctly speaking, his impatience, to a very severe trial.

"It is a carriage," he ejaculated, at length—"a private vehicle. No doubt it belongs to a personage of some considerable importance, for it bowls along in capital style."

One more minute, and the time came for Captain Hawk to execute his project.

Riding into the road, he discharged a pistol over the coachman's head, and as soon as the sound of the discharge had ceased he called out, in a voice of thunder:

"Pull up, coachman, or, as sure as fate, you are a dead man! It's no idle threat! The least disobedience or attempt at resistance will be the unfailing signal for your death!"

The coachman showed that he comprehended these awful words by uttering a cry of terror, and then suddenly becoming as quiet as a mouse.

This little preliminary matter having been got over thus agreeably, Captain Hawk went to the side of the carriage, which was a close one.

He was about to let down the window with a crash, when some one within saved him the trouble.

The carriage lamp then enabled Captain Hawk to perceive that the carriage was occupied by an old gentleman, who exhibited a good deal of consternation which he made the most vigorous efforts to conceal.

"Good heavens!" he cried. "What monstrous thing is this? What am I to understand——"

"Simply that Captain Hawk is on the road to-night. I presume that is sufficient."

The gentleman's face assumed an expression of the most extraordinary incredulity.

"And if that detestable depredator is on the road," he said, after a long pause, "do you mean to tell me he would have the indescribable audacity to stop a judge in his own private carriage?"

"I have every reason to believe that he would stop not only a judge in his own private carriage, but anybody anywhere, no matter who."

The nonchalant manner in which these words were uttered seemed to make the gentleman slightly in doubt as to whether this strange-looking horseman was in jest or earnest.

"And is it, then, a fact," continued Captain Hawk, in the same sprightly, airy tones, "that I have the honour of conversing with so high a judicial functionary as a judge?"

The gentleman's face began to assume a bluish tinge.

But he said:

"You have. It is to Judge North that you address yourself."

Captain Hawk took off his hat and made a very low bow.

"What the devil, then, is the meaning of this masquerade?" said the judge, losing all patience.

"I have merely the honour to state," continued the highwayman, in precisely the same tones as before, "that I must request you to hand over to me, without any reserve whatever, all the valuables you may happen to have about your person and in your carriage at the present moment. I trust your lordship will see the advisability of obeying my demands forthwith, because by that means you will prevent me from losing my temper, and also do away with all fear of bodily injury."

The judge's face grew bluer than ever.

He opened his mouth.

But he could give utterance to no sound.

"Oh, papa—papa," said a gentle voice at this moment, making Captain Hawk aware for the first time that the judge was not alone in his carriage, "give the dreadful man what he wants, and let us make haste to get away from him!"

"Very sensible advice," remarked Captain Hawk, "for to have all your valuables I am determined."

"Silence, girl!" said the judge, angrily. "How dare you presume to interfere in matters that you know nothing about!"

A slight movement made the highwayman aware that the young girl, who had spoken merely on account of her father's danger, shrank back abashed.

This little circumstance, had anything been wanting, would have made Captain Hawk determined not to spare the judge in the least degree.

"Come, my lord," he said, "no more harshness to your daughter—she only obeyed a natural impulse when she spoke. Quick! for I have no time to lose. Once more your money, watch, rings, and all valuables whatever."

The judge drew back.

Captain Hawk guessed for what purpose, and held himself prepared.

The next moment a pistol was discharged in the interior of the vehicle.

"Take that, you villain!" cried Chief Justice North, who no doubt firmly believed he had put a period to the highwayman's career—"take that, you villain!"

"Willingly," said Captain Hawk; "but upon the condition that I shall return the fire. My aim will be steadier than yours, my lord, because, you see, I am more accustomed to such encounters as these. Now——"

"No, no, sir!" said the young girl, leaning forward, and clasping her hands piteously together—"no, no! You must not think of carrying out your cruel purpose! Spare him—spare him, I entreat you! To defend one's own property is justifiable, but you are about to commit the worst of crimes—murder. Spare him, I entreat you! Do not stain your soul with the guilt of the awful crime you are about to commit."

Captain Hawk stood motionless.

Not that he had any thoughts of turning a deaf ear to her appeal, but merely that he might feast his eyes upon the vision of loveliness which now appeared before him.

Captain Hawk's heart was most susceptible to the influence of female beauty; and numerous as had been the lovely faces it had been his good fortune to gaze upon, never—never had there been one which could compare with the noble and patrician beauty of the judge's daughter.

He gazed like one entranced—fascinated.

"You do not plead in vain, lady," he said, his voice involuntarily sinking to a respectful and serious tone. "I will not fire, but for all that I must have my demands complied with."

"Yes, yes—you shall! Father—father, do not you value your life as being worth infinitely more than the trifling sum you have about you?—for, though great, it is trifling when compared with what you possess. Give it him, and let him begone."

The old judge remained sullenly silent.

But his daughter, terrified to death lest any injury should befall him, set busily to work to collect together the various valuable articles they were travelling with.

The judge looked on in silence, neither giving her permission nor making any demur to what she was about.

As soon as she had as much as her hands would hold, she held them for the highwayman to take.

He did so, and then, leaning forward suddenly, just managed to touch her cheek with his lips.

The impulse to do so was irresistible.

The young girl drew back with a deeply-offended air, and immediately afterwards burst into a passion of tears.

"You rascal!" cried the judge. "Is this the return you make? But rest assured I will have you punished! I am powerless now; but I have been attentively perusing your countenance, and, no matter when the day may come, I shall always be able to swear to your identity—ay, and I will do it, too! I swear that your career of villany shall be speedily cut short! You may rejoice and triumph now, but the day of your downfall is at hand, and I will know no rest until you meet with the fate that you so richly merit!"

CHAPTER LXXXIX.

CAPTAIN HAWK CREATES A GREAT SENSATION AT THE GOLDEN BALL INN.

The judge's threats, which were uttered with a great deal of vehemence and fury, produced no other effect upon Captain Hawk than a smile, while he went quietly on with his occupation of putting away the valuables he had acquired.

When he had finished, he turned quietly towards the judge, and said, with admirable calmness:

"I have only one question to ask your lordship; and if you will answer it, I shall always consider it in the light of a personal obligation."

The judge's curiosity was so much inflamed at once, that he felt sure he could not rest until he knew what it was the highwayman wished to say.

"Well?" he said, sternly.

"The information I shall be glad if you will accord me," replied the captain, with an affectation of the greatest politeness, "is the place of your destination to-night. I have a particular reason for desiring to know how far you may be journeying?"

The judge was so enraged at the captain's cool impudence that he could not speak.

But his daughter, fearing that after all her pains some misfortune might yet befall her cherished parent, answered quickly:

"We are on our way to Lincoln. Now be satisfied, and let us ride on in peace."

"Many thanks, lady. I am deeply grateful to you for the information. I want nothing further. You are now at perfect liberty to ride on."

But the judge, who seemed at first inclined to be angry with his daughter for having spoken so hastily, now turned to the captain and said:

"As things appear to go by turns to-night, perhaps you will oblige me with an answer to a question?"

"Certainly, my lord. It is always a pleasure to be able to oblige anyone, but especially a high judicial functionary like yourself. Let me hear your question?"

"It is, then," said the judge, with difficulty suppressing his pride and anger sufficiently to speak with any degree of calmness—"it is to know your reason for wanting to be made acquainted with our destination?"

"The answer is a simple one, my lord."

The judge waved his hand.

"It is," answered Captain Hawk, "because I feel justly terrified after hearing the terrible threats to which you have given utterance, and I want now to get into some part of the country where you will not be."

The judge only looked half satisfied with his reply.

"I can at least look forward a little longer to the continuance of my career now that I know you are on the way to Lincoln. I am off to London, where I hope to be before daybreak to-morrow morning. And now, after that explanation, let me bid you farewell. Hey—hey—for London!"

He just touched Satan with his heel, and away the gallant creature went, in its usual beautiful style, along the high-road in the direction of the metropolis.

"If I live," said the judge, vindictively, as he witnessed the captain's departure—"if I live, I will be the death of that fellow—I will have him hung! To London, does he say? And, by the powers, he seems to be in earnest! If he keeps up that pace he won't be long in getting there. He laughs at my power, but I will make him dread it. I will have him hung—hung!" he added, with increasing rancour, "and if it costs me my fortune and my life! I would go to the uttermost ends of the earth in order to be present at his trial and execution!"

He ground his teeth furiously, and there could be no mistaking the fact that Captain Hawk made that night a bitter, uncompromising foe, and, what was most of all, a powerful one.

But the captain, with his usual disregard and defiance of danger, rode along the highway in the best of spirits.

Every now and then he would give vent to the exultation which filled his breast by uttering a loud shout.

"Hurrah!" he cried—"hurrah for a gallant life on the highway! It has been no common booty that I have made to-night; but, more important still, I have managed matters so that a tremendous outcry shall be raised about me. It will be impossible for the officers to be in doubt as to where I am. They will be after me before long a thousand strong. But just when they feel assured that they are really getting on my track, and that there is something more than a usual prospect of capturing me, I shall be riding back to the Greyhound, and increasing the distance between us at a double rate. Hurrah! It is capital—that it is! How delighted Tom Beckford will be when I explain the affair to him!"

Filled with these pleasing anticipations, Captain Hawk rode on for yet some distance further along the high-road.

But presently, espying a favourable opportunity, he turned his horse's head towards the meadows, and made his way onwards with redoubled speed.

Fields, brooks, hedgerows, open spaces, were rapidly crossed, until the scene of his adventure with the judge was left far behind.

As before, he continued his wild gallop for something like the space of half an hour, and then he gently slackened speed.

"There," he said, stroking his horse's neck with great fondness—"there, you can take it easy now. We are quite far enough from the old Greyhound at Huntingdon for my purpose to be answered. All will be well now. But before I commence my return journey you shall have a rest and a good feed of corn, even though I run some extra risk by it."

Satan seemed quite to understand this promise on his master's part, for he immediately displayed the strongest inclination to start off again at his former speed.

But this it did not suit the highwayman to allow.

"Gently—gently!" he said. "There is time yet and to spare for what we have to do. Quietly, then, can't you?"

But in spite of all the captain could do, he could not bring his horse down to a quiet, steady walk.

And all the while he had been flying across the country at this rapid rate, the highwayman had been most careful in observing his direction.

"If I have made no mistake," he said, "I ought to leave the high-road something within half a mile of me on the right here. Let me see. How lucky I have been: I have not met with a single soul, so that there is little fear the officers will have the least chance of guessing the trick I am going to play upon them."

Captain Hawk chuckled again for the success he had met with was far greater than he had dared to anticipate

Changing his course now, and going almost at right

angles to the line he had been formerly pursuing, Captain Hawk set about ascertaining whether his calculations about his position were well-founded.

"All is well!" he cried. "I thought I could rely upon my knowledge of this part of the country. Here is the highway, just as I expected to find it. Yes; and I shall be strangely disappointed if I do not find about half a mile further on the well-known old hostelry of the Golden Ball. That shall be my temporary resting-place—that shall be the scene of my triumph and the officers' discomfiture!"

Taking the same precautions as before to make sure that there was no one in the way, Captain Hawk, on finding all was quiet, rode out on to the high-road.

Then, at a gentle trot, he urged Satan towards London.

It was not many moments before he caught sight of some twinkling lights in the distance.

"Right again!" he cried, with the utmost satisfaction. "There is the Golden Ball. Now for the crowning triumph!"

Drawing nearer, Captain Hawk found that the old inn before him evidenced every sign of doing a brisk business.

In fact, there were few inns or coaching-houses of greater importance than the Golden Ball.

And it must be also borne in mind that so great was the speed which the highwayman had made that by the time he reached the old inn the night was by no means far advanced.

It was, he found, on reference to a massive gold repeater which had lately belonged to the old judge, precisely half-past nine.

This allowed him plenty of time for all that he proposed to do that night.

"Now to put a bold face on the matter," said Captain Hawk, when within a few yards of the Golden Ball. "My doings to-night will be talked of for many a night to come, I'll be bound."

During his ride, Captain Hawk had had ample time to arrange all the details of his plan.

He had made up his mind just exactly what he should do, provided nothing occurred that he was not prepared for to derange his plans.

As he drew nearer, then, to the inn, he settled himself more firmly and stiffly in the saddle, for long practice had got him into the habit of riding in rather a negligent fashion.

The change at once imparted to him an appearance of authority very foreign to his ordinary manner.

Then cantering up to the open space in front of the inn, he pulled up very suddenly, and cried out:

"Hi—hi, there! House—house! Is there no one at home? What the devil do you mean by keeping an inn in this fashion? Hi—hi! Curse it! am I to be kept here all night?"

These words were pronounced in the most swaggering, hectoring tones that can be imagined.

He raised his voice to the highest pitch possible, so that all around firmly rung with its tones.

A more noisy way of riding up to a place of public entertainment could not be imagined.

But Captain Hawk had a part to play.

It required an immense amount of audacity and boldness to carry it through; but those were the qualities the highwayman excelled in, so there was not much fear that it would fail through any falling off on this account.

But still it appears well-nigh incredible that anyone so well known as Captain Hawk, with so many people on the watch and ready to pounce upon and capture him, and with such a large reward over his head, should have the heart to act as he had done.

But then he actually relied upon the course he was pursuing forming a safeguard.

People would be so little prepared to see him arrive in this manner that they would hardly believe in the reality or possibility of it even if told.

It was, he argued, the best possible way of disarming suspicion and escaping danger, and within certain limits there can be hardly any question that he was right.

His vociferations, the like of which were not often heard at the Golden Ball, produced a prodigious commotion.

Out rushed the ostler.

Out rushed the landlord, and behind the two a crowd of stable boys, guests, and other persons connected with the place.

And when they saw the captain sitting so very erectly in the saddle, and looking around him much in the manner that a general at a review might do, and when they saw the splendid quality of the steed which he bestrode, one and all jumped to the conclusion that he must be a person of very great importance indeed, despite the fact that he appeared to arrive without any retinue.

"Quick—quick, you lazy varlets!" he cried, to the ostler and stable-boy who were hurrying towards him. "Is it your custom to keep every visitor waiting at the door in this fashion? Where's the rascally landlord?"

"May it humbly please your worship," said the latter, bowing low at every word, so that he advanced in a very odd, doubled-up fashion—"may it very humbly please you, I am here."

"Bah! Time you were! Now then, fellow," he added, to the stable-boy, "hold the stirrup while I alight!"

His domineering, bullying way produced just the effect that he had calculated upon.

Had they all been his abject slaves they could not have flown to execute his behests with more alacrity.

But then, Captain Hawk had often seen the effect produced by behaviour of this description.

Having reached the ground, he gave a glance all around him, which implied how vastly inferior everything and everybody was to himself, and then, addressing the ostler, said, imperiously:

"Take him round to the stables carefully. Attend to him well. When he is treated to my satisfaction, I always give the ostler a guinea and the helper a crown-piece."

This was not spoken quite so loudly as the rest, but nevertheless sufficiently so for the landlord to hear, as well as the ostler and boy.

The effect which it produced was greater than anything yet.

The ostler took hold of the lock of hair which hung down over his forehead, and pulled it so reverentially that it is a wonder it did not come out by the roots.

As for the boy, he could only stand and stare with unmitigated amazement.

The landlord thought his guest must be a duke, or a prince, at the very least.

If he was so liberal to the ostler and his assistant, what might not he, the landlord, expect to receive?

His brain was almost turned; and with another succession of bows, he walked backwards towards the house.

But arriving at the doorstep a little sooner than he expected, or else, perhaps, in the elation of his spirits forgetting all about the existence of any such obstruction, he staggered, and then sat down with a violence that almost drove all the breath out of his body; and, what was worse, gave him a terribly undignified and ridiculous aspect.

Gaining his feet again as quickly as possible, and trying to conceal his annoyance by a laugh, he ushered his distinguished guest into the best room in his house.

Had Captain Hawk been Emperor of all the Russias he could not have behaved more autocratically.

Decidedly, he mistook his vocation: Captain Hawk should have been an actor, not a highwayman.

"What will you please to take, your worship?" said the landlord, more humbly than before.

Captain Hawk smiled in a peculiar and affected manner at the title by which he was designated—

A smile which said plainly enough that he was entitled to a much higher distinction.

He answered the landlord's question in a voice which could be, and was, heard all over the house.

"A couple of roast fowls, properly served, broiled ham, and devilled kidneys, with a bottle of your best wine! And be quick!" he bawled, yet louder still. "And let me have none of your paltry excuses! Begone, and execute my commands at once!"

These last words were uttered because the captain saw that the landlord was about to protest that it was impossible to execute the order so peremptorily given.

Thus commanded, the landlord backed out of the room before he could recover himself or find time to think.

When he had departed, and the door had been closed

[CAPTAIN HAWK ENJOYS THE MAGISTRATE'S DINNER.]

behind him, Captain Hawk indulged himself with a quiet laugh.

"Only to think, now, what effect a haughty and overbearing demeanour will produce! This is an excellent farce! Why, if anyone said now that I was Captain Hawk, the highwayman, he would stand but a poor chance of being believed."

Again he laughed.

"I won't carry it too far," he said. "But Satan shall have a rest, for all that. I shall soon learn whether any of my enemies are very close at hand. But whether or not, I will take good care that before I leave they shall be convinced of my real identity."

At this instant there came a faint tapping at the door.

"Ha, ha!" he said. "The landlord has recovered himself sufficiently to be able to come back and say that he cannot execute my commands."

In obedience to his permission, the door was opened.

The landlord appeared upon the threshold.

"May it please your worship——" he said, as though he hardly dared speak.

"Well?" exclaimed the captain, in a way that made him jump again.

"May it please——"

"Do you come to say I cannot have the wretched fare that I have ordered—that I am to wait—or order something else? If that is your excuse, out with it at once!"

"No—no, sir—I mean your worship," said the landlord, more terrified than ever at his guest's violence. "The fact is——"

"Why don't you speak? Am I to be kept here in suspense half the night?"

"I hope not, your worship."

"Well, then?"

"If your worship would only condescend ——"

"Bah!"

"To allow me to explain."

"Speak, I say—speak!"

"I have on the spit, and ready for serving, just exactly the things your worship has been good enough to order."

"You have? Then, curse you, why don't you put them on the table instead of keeping me waiting?"

"I wished to say, your worship, that those same viands had been expressly ordered to be ready for one of the chief magistrates from Bow Street, London, who is coming down by to-night's coach, in order to make arrangements for the capture of Captain Hawk, the terror of the road."

The captain strode up to the landlord.

There was so much fierceness in his manner that Boniface, putting up his hands before him for protection, shrank back several paces.

"And do you mean to tell me," roared Captain Hawk, looking as though he would certainly annihilate the hapless landlord—"do you mean to tell me that I am to be kept waiting just for a pitiful, paltry, dirty, money-earning Bow Street magistrate? Do you mean to say that, eh?"

"I—I——" stammered the landlord.

"Silence, sir! Not another word! Obey my orders! Serve the dinner at once!"

"But the magistrate!" expostulated the landlord. "If I obey your worship's command, which I should be glad to do, it would be the ruin of my house."

"Do you hear?" roared the captain, in more stentorian tones than ever. "Serve the dinner; and as for the magistrate, leave me to deal with him. Begone!"

The landlord, terrified out of his wits, felt that he dared not disobey.

"You shall have it, sir," he said, with a grievous sigh.

"And an apology, too," roared Hawk, "or, as soon as I get to town, I will give the Golden Ball such a character as will prevent any person of consequence from ever calling here in future!"

This was an alarming threat, and the landlord vanished instantly.

When the door closed Captain Hawk in a second became himself again.

"Ha, ha! Capital! Another revenge! And so they have thought fit to send down a Bow Street magistrate to look after my capture. Just as if there will be any good in doing that! What a satisfaction it will be to me to devour his dinner! Ha, ha! I never had such an extraordinary appetite in my life. I really feel as though I could eat an old spade. Ha, ha!"

Captain Hawk was immeasurably delighted at the idea of eating the sumptuous viands which the Bow Street magistrate had ordered.

"I rather think that this will turn out to be one of the most notable and eventful nights the old Golden Ball has ever witnessed. But I must not stay too long, though. I was forgetting my original design."

And his face suddenly grew serious; for all at once Blanche had vividly presented herself to his mind.

CHAPTER XC.

CAPTAIN HAWK EATS THE MAGISTRATE'S DINNER, AND IS RECOGNISED BY THE GUARD OF THE YORK COACH.

THE somewhat sad reverie into which the highwayman now fell would probably have lasted for some time had it not been interrupted by the opening of the door.

Across the threshold appeared the servants bearing the dishes.

The odour which saluted the captain's nostrils was of the most appetising description.

With considerable celerity the table was spread with a repast that would certainly have tempted the appetite of an epicure.

But Captain Hawk was most outrageously hungry, so that it was quite certain he would do full justice to the good things before him.

Indeed, he could hardly control himself sufficiently to wait until the table was properly laid.

But as soon as this was the case, he sat down and commenced a most vigorous onslaught.

All the things that the magistrate was no doubt already feasting his imagination upon vanished with most wonderful celerity.

"Upon my word," the captain said, when the keenness of his hunger was somewhat subsided, "it is not every day that I have the chance of sitting down to a meal of this sort, so I ought to make the most of it."

And he did make the most of it.

The landlord all the while was in truly a pitiable frame of mind.

He kept fidgeting backwards and forwards to the front door, and looking up the road in momentary expectation of the stage-coach.

"Where on earth can it be?" he said, for about the dozenth time. "In all the years that I have kept the Golden Ball I never yet knew it to be so much behind its time. Certainly something must have happened to it!"

Captain Hawk himself, having finished his sumptuous repast and swallowed all the wine, began also to wonder what could have happened to the stage-coach.

That an accident of some kind or other had befallen it, he considered as absolutely certain, though of what nature he could not of course guess.

"I should not at all wonder, now," said the landlord, "if it has not been stopped and robbed by that double-dyed villain, Captain Hawk."

"I shouldn't wonder, now," answered the captain, who was now in that comfortable state of body and mind which a good dinner ought to produce.

"He's a villain!" said the landlord. "I only hope I may catch sight of him some day or other, that's all!"

"Why, what would you do?"

"Why, settle his bacon, that's all."

"Indeed!" murmured the captain, with a smile.

"I'd put an end to his career pretty quick if I could only see him, the villain!"

"He has done you some bad turn, I suppose?"

"Bad turn? I should rather think he has!"

"Of what kind?"

"Why, he has half ruined my trade."

"Is it possible!"

"It is not only possible but perfectly true."

"But how—how?"

"Why, now that he is on the road all the best people—I mean those who carry any worth about them—do not travel at all—that is, not unless they are compelled by some very urgent business. There was a time, sir, when the Golden Ball did an excellent trade; but that was before that scoundrelly villain, Captain Hawk, took to robbing on the Great North Road."

"Ah, well! perhaps he will come some day and make up your loss. But just let me have the bill, will you? Or stay, I can save you the trouble. If you intend to charge me more than five guineas for this dinner, I sha'n't pay it, so take the money and be thankful."

Captain Hawk accompanied these words by drawing out of his pocket a very elegant purse, which he had taken from Judge North.

It was well filled with gold.

He threw down five guineas on the table.

The landlord regarded him with a stupified air.

He had intended to come it rather strong with the dinner, and had actually some notion in his brain of charging a guinea and a half.

But this extraordinary munificence on the part of his strange guest overwhelmed him with surprise.

Captain Hawk pretended to mistake his confusion.

"There—there!" he cried, "don't look so straight down your face. If you had charged me any more I should not have paid it; so put the coins into your pocket at once, and say no more about it."

"Really, my lord," stammered the landlord,—"that is, your highness—I——"

Captain Hawk cut him short.

Much as he enjoyed the scene, he felt that he ought not to prolong it—that he ought to be getting on his way towards the Greyhound.

"Be good enough," he said, "to show me to the stables. I will be starting now, but I always like to have a look at my horse before he comes out of the stable."

"Very good, your highness," said the landlord, obsequiously. "I am sure that any wishes you may have shall be instantly gratified in my house—that is, if they are within the power of your very humble servant."

Of course, such a stir as Captain Hawk had made could not have failed to attract the attention of every person within the building.

Consequently when, with the same assumption of

arrogance and importance in his mien, he stepped out of his room, there were many anxious faces turned towards him, all burning to see so extraordinary an individual.

The landlord felt that some of the importance ought to attach itself to him, and he exhibited, by his pompous walk and the manner in which he bowed continually, to indicate the direction his guest ought to take.

As soon as they had passed through a door communicating with the back part of the premises, Captain Hawk assumed an air of familiarity.

"I daresay you wonder, now, what is the business which has brought me to this place?"

The landlord smiled at the bare idea of so great a personage having anything to do with such low and vulgar matters as business.

"The fact is," said Captain Hawk, lowering his voice to a whisper, "I am the Secretary of State. Hush—hush!"

"What!" gasped the landlord. "Lord Malmesbury?"

"The same."

"He was almost ready to sink into the earth."

"I tell you this," said the captain, only preserving a serious face by a very great effort, "because I can see that you are a person of discernment and discretion——"

"Oh, my lord, you are too good!"

"And because I don't want you to get into any trouble on account of having placed before me the meal ordered by the magistrate."

"Oh, my lord—my lord," the perspiration bursting out from every pore in his skin, "don't mention it—pray don't mention it!"

"Oh yes; it is no more than just. Mark you, my business in this part of the country is of a very private character, as you may guess by my riding unattended. You will, then, jealously keep secret who I am?"

"Trust me, my lord."

"I merely make the revelation to you in order that you may let the magistrate know, on his arrival, how it is that he has met with so great a disappointment. You will find that the disclosure will appease him at once."

"I should rather think it would, my lord."

"Enough, then. Here we are at the stables, are we not?"

"Yes, my——"

"Hush—hush! Don't forget what I have said."

"You may trust me."

On reaching the stable, they found the utmost excitement prevailing there.

That attention and curiosity which in the house had been displayed towards the rider was in the stable shown to the horse.

Never had Satan undergone so close an examination.

But on the part of all those who beheld him there was but one opinion expressed, which was that the like of him had never before been in the stables of the Golden Ball.

He was universally pronounced to be, in every way, all that a horse could be.

On knowing that his illustrious master was waiting for him, there was a tremendous stir in the stable immediately.

Many hands went to work, and, in a very short time indeed Satan was led out in perfect readiness for the road.

A great curiosity was manifested by all the stable hangers-on to see the start, for there were not wanting those who declared that the promise which had been made was nothing but moonshine.

Accordingly Satan was led to the front part of the inn, followed by an excited and anxious throng, and the cynosure of every eye within the hostelry.

Captain Hawk mounted with his usual lightness and address.

Then seating himself comfortably in the saddle, he gathered up the reins.

Thrusting his hand into his pocket, he took forth a guinea, which he placed in the expectant ostler's extended palm.

But while in the act of feeling for a crown-piece for the boy, a noise in the distance became heard.

All eyes were now instantly turned in this direction.

A horseman then appeared in view

Even when far off they could see that he was labouring under great excitement.

He was riding without a saddle, and the horse he was upon was encumbered with harness.

Nevertheless, he came on at a hard gallop.

"Help—help!" he cried.

"What's the matter?" cried every voice.

"Something has happened to the York coach!" cried the landlord. "I knew it—I knew it!"

"Yes," said the stranger, who, on coming nearer, was recognised as being the guard of the coach in question, "I rather think something has happened!"

"What—what?"

"Why, it has been stopped and robbed!"

"Stopped and robbed!" echoed everybody, aghast.

"Yes; and now it lies on the road a perfect wreck. The horses are gone the devil knows where; and the wretched passengers are sitting in the cold, waiting for help."

"How far off?"

"A couple of miles."

"Of course," said the landlord, "it is that accursed Captain Hawk who has done it!"

"Some say so—some say not. But it's all one for us and the passengers. D—n all highwaymen, say I! Look here: behold me!"

The guard flung himself from his foaming horse as he spoke, and then it became manifest that he was a good deal the worse for the adventure.

His face was scratched and bleeding—his clothes were plastered all over with mud, and his coat was slit up the back as far as his collar; and as these two monstrous tails fluttered behind him in the road they imparted to him a most ludicrous aspect.

Captain Hawk had listened to what this man had said, as well he might, since it made him aware there was some one else out on the same errand as himself upon the North Road that night.

A moment before, too, he was wondering how he could contrive to make them all acquainted with his identity, so that the police officers might be set upon his track.

Now he saw that he had no need to perplex his brains any further on this point, for the guard, if he chanced to look, would be almost certain to recognise him.

And with wonderful calmness he awaited the occurrence of this event.

"And what is to be done?" said the landlord.

"Why, get some conveyance, to be sure, and fetch the passengers as far as the inn. There they can rest and recover themselves while we, in the meantime, get the stage-coach ready for the road again. But—eh?—what—hullo! Can I believe my eyes?"

"Why, what's the matter?" asked everybody.

"No—no! But yet—— Yes—yes, it must be! Why, this surpasses all belief! Do you see who stands there?"

He pointed to the captain as he spoke.

"Chut—chut!" cried the landlord, in a suppressed voice, and making many mysterious signs for the guard to be silent.

"Why, what ails the man?"

"Here—here!"

"Well, what now? Are you all mad?" cried the guard. "Don't you see that man on the horse? That is Captain Hawk, the highwayman?"

At the same moment our old friend made Satan walk backwards for a few steps.

The landlord hurried to the guard.

"You are bewitched," he said—"confound you! You will ruin me."

"Ruin you? Why, d—n it all! you must be mad!"

"No—no! It is you labouring under some extraordinary delusion."

"The devil a bit!"

"But you are!"

"I tell you that is Captain Hawk, the highwayman, for all he appears to stand there so quietly, but don't you see he is ready to start off the moment there is danger?"

The landlord threw up his arms in despair.

"Dunderheaded idiot!" he cried. "I tell you that is the Secretary of State—Lord Malmesbury!"

"Lord Fiddlestick!" roared the guard, in a furious passion. "Do you think I don't know him?"

"No—no! you are mistaken!"

"Bah! I have seen him a hundred times, and would swear to him from among ten thousand! Lord

Malmesbury indeed! May I be double d—d if it is not Captain Hawk, the highwayman!"

At this point, the captain, feeling that the joke had been carried far enough, and that his purpose was fully answered, now tossed the crown-piece to the stable-boy and took off his hat.

Then he made with it a very profound and circular kind of bow, which he intended should comprise all those who were so admiringly looking on.

"Gentlemen," he said, "the guard is perfectly right. I have the pleasure and the honour of bidding you farewell. Landlord, don't forget to remember me to the magistrate from Bow Street. Tell him he need not have come so far from home to look for me, for I am off to London at full speed. I don't mind giving him the information, for I shall be there before daybreak to-morrow morning."

So saying, he made another circular bow, after which he put on his hat, and caused Satan to wheel round suddenly.

Another second, and he was off and away.

The landlord at this moment realised the degrading fact that he had been most shamefully and outrageously hoaxed.

A dolorous cry came from his lips; and then, his legs seeming to collapse, down he sat on the doorstep with a tremendous bang.

As the guard graphically remarked, he brought his latter end to an anchor with such force as to drive all the breath clean out of his body.

The utmost astonishment and confusion now prevailed.

Indeed, no words at all could possibly convey an idea of the terrific tumult which followed the highwayman's departure.

A good many were of opinion that the guard had been misled by some accidental resemblance.

"If it was Captain Hawk, and you knew it, why didn't you seize him?" they asked. "And why don't you pursue him now?"

"Do you take me for a fool?" roared the guard, passionately—"for a regular-born natural? I have rather more sense than to ride single-handed after a highwayman, and a desperate fellow like him! Some of you had better try it on. He would wait until you were near enough, and then quietly turn round and put a bullet through you. Did you think I was born yesterday? Why didn't you catch him yourselves?"

The guard was in a great state of wrath and exasperation, as well indeed he might be.

The landlord was too much overcome to do anything but gasp for his breath.

But leaving them to recover as best they may, we will hasten to follow in the steps of the highwayman.

No sooner had he got a short distance from the inn than he broke out into a fit of the most irrepressible laughter.

"Good—good!" he cried, with the tears rolling down his cheeks. "Who would have thought that things would turn out like this? Everything has gone in my favour—every chance has turned to my advantage. But," he added, subduing his merriment a little, "who can it be on the high-road to-night? Some one possessed of something more than common boldness, or he would not have attempted or executed what he has done to-night. I must find that out. But gently—gently! What was that?"

Captain Hawk had pushed along at a good rate, and now at this moment there came upon his ears a faint, far-off sound, seemingly of so singular a nature that in a moment he pulled up in order to listen to it more attentively.

He then heard distinctly a strange moaning noise, the like of which had certainly never before floated to his ears.

"Goodness gracious!" he ejaculated, his face suddenly expanding into a smile. "I could not for the life of me think what that could be. Why, it must be the passengers sitting in the stage-coach and calling out for help in a dismal chorus."

Captain Hawk laughed long and heartily at this idea, and then, in order to find out whether he was right, set off at a hard gallop.

This quickly brought him to the scene of disaster.

And a scene of disaster it certainly was.

The stage-coach had been drawn all to one side of the road, and the fore-wheels were embedded in the ditch bank in what appeared to be a very dangerous manner.

Of the horses not a vestige remained.

It was pretty clear that the highwayman had cut the traces and started them off, so that no doubt they were on their way back to their stable as fast as their legs could carry them.

The passengers were all lamenting in various ways the misfortune that had befallen them.

Some found ease and consolation in pouring out oaths and curses; others groaned, and abused the Government for allowing such things to take place at all.

Then others screamed and wept; but the effect was just the same.

Their position was not altered in the least.

But upon hearing Captain Hawk approaching, something like silence followed; for they were one and all filled with the delusive notion that the sounds meant immediate succour.

As for Captain Hawk, he did not fail to see how even this chance circumstance might be made to turn to his advantage in the scheme he had on hand.

A dismal outcry set up as soon as he got near to the intercepted vehicle, for each person was anxious to relate the story of his own particular individual sufferings.

"What has happened?" cried Captain Hawk, pretending to be in perfect ignorance.

Every passenger tried to tell him at once, so the result was rather confusing.

"Do you mean to tell me the coach has been stopped?"

"Yes—yes! Don't you see?"

"But by whom?"

"Why, Captain Hawk. If you know anything, you must know that he is the terror of every traveller on the North Road."

"Captain Hawk!" he ejaculated. "How very extraordinary!"

"Extraordinary! Why——"

"Was he anything like me?" asked the captain, riding to a certain spot where the light from the one coach lamp that was burning fell full upon him.

A deep silence followed.

There was something in the general aspect of Captain Hawk, and more especially on the present occasion, that marked him out as being something more than an ordinary man.

He repeated the question.

"Yes, something like," said one.

And there was an immediate chorus of voices to the effect that there was not the slightest resemblance whatever.

Captain Hawk laughed, and waited until silence was restored.

The passengers, warned, apparently, by some species of intuition that something was about to take place of an extraordinary character, looked inquiringly at him, and forgetting for a moment their own uncomfortable condition, waited patiently for him to speak.

"On one point, at least," he said, in gay, clear tones, "you are mistaken"

"Mistaken! How so? In what way?" were the questions instantly put.

"And it is possible you may be equally mistaken in others."

"What do you mean?"

"You tell me you have been robbed by Captain Hawk. Now, I happen to know that that is an impossibility."

"An impossibility! Why?"

"Simply because this is the first time I have been near this spot to-night."

"You—you?" was the general cry, in tones of the utmost amazement. "What the devil have you got to do with it?"

"Nothing further," was the quiet response, "than that I happen to be Captain Hawk—that is all!"

CHAPTER XCI.

CAPTAIN HAWK MAKES A FAIR START FOR THE GREY-HOUND INN.

These words were received with a dead silence.

All the travellers seemed to be by far too much overwhelmed with amazement to be able to say a word.

The idea that a highwayman should present himself before them and calmly proclaim his identity was so outrageous an idea that a minute or so elapsed before any of them could realise the possibility of it.

"Don't look so dreadfully alarmed," said Captain Hawk, with a merry laugh. "Since some one has been beforehand with me and robbed you all, what have you to fear from me?"

"But—but," said a thin, grey-headed little man, thrusting his head out of the coach window, "this unparalleled assurance—this shameless audacity——"

"Well, sir?"

"It's monstrous! That's what it is."

"But you see, sir," said the captain, with much gravity, "I have my professional reputation at stake. The night-flyer that you have taken for me might have done something decidedly wrong and disagreeable; and if so, I could not bear to rest under the imputation of it."

"Oh, this is too gross!" said the little old gentleman. "Hang me if I can stand it! The idea of a highwayman being jealous of his reputation! It would be a good joke if it was not for the ridiculousness of the thing."

"Have I the honour of addressing the worthy magistrate from Bow Street?"

"The devil! You know me, then?" cried the old gentleman, with a start of astonishment.

Captain Hawk bowed profoundly.

"I have only to say, sir," he continued, "that the dinner you ordered was excellent. It was done to a turn. I never enjoyed a meal more in my life."

The magistrate appeared at first a little bewildered.

"W—what, what!" he said. "Do you mean to tell me that you have had the astounding—the unmitigated—the unparalleled impudence to—to——"

"To eat the dinner you ordered. Just so, and excellent I found it!"

"Now this is beyond all! Dastardly wretch! How dare you to presume!"

But Captain Hawk laughed so loud, so long, and so outrageously, that he could not continue.

"Thank goodness!" he said at last, when the highwayman's paroxysm had somewhat abated, "there is the comfort of knowing that your race will be short!"

"Very good," answered the captain; "though you have done a foolish thing by coming into the country to look for me. You ought to have stayed at home. I am now off to London as fast as this good horse of mine can carry me; and, notwithstanding all the delays that I have had, I still hope to be able to get there before daybreak. Good-bye, ladies and gentlemen all! Don't fall into the mistake of believing that it is Captain Hawk who has robbed you! I see the guard is coming at last, with assistance from the inn. Once more, farewell! Hey! now for London!"

He turned round and rode off with these words upon his lips, pursued by the oaths and exclamations of the passengers, who were now getting more into their ordinary frame of mind, and beginning to realise the daring joke that had been played upon them.

But long before the guard came up with such assistance as the Golden Ball Inn could afford, Captain Hawk was not only out of sight, but out of hearing.

But no further did he go.

Mindful of his purpose, he turned off into the open fields, so as to make his way back to the Greyhound.

"Capital—capital!" he cried, with the utmost exultation. "After this I shall have faith in what the most consummate impudence can accomplish. It is odd to me if, after all that I have done, there is not such a hue and cry after me as far as London as has never been before."

In this no doubt he was perfectly right; for such a succession of daring events would, of course, be the theme of universal discussion.

That the officers might discover he had doubled on his course before they got anything like so far as London was probable enough; but if they did, it would not be until they had got to such a distance as would make it perfectly safe for him in the meantime to pay his projected visit.

Coming to rather a stiff piece of ground, he allowed Satan to go at a more gentle pace.

The noble steed had served him well that night.

Without his aid he could not have accomplished those events which were destined to make his name talked about for many a day.

The captain's thoughts reverted to the stage-coach and the pitiable condition of the passengers.

"They will be rather longer on the journey than they expected to be, I'll be bound! And what a furious passion the old magistrate will be in when he finds that I have in good truth devoured his dinner! Ha, ha, ha! I shall never forget it! How Tom Beckford will enjoy it when I come to relate to him all the particulars!"

He paused, and his countenance assumed a rather more serious expression.

"I wonder, now," he said, "who in the world it could have been who stopped the coach? The job was done neatly enough, that is certain; and so far as I could judge, the passengers seemed not only deprived of all their pelf, but of their weapons also. Am I to get the credit of it, I wonder, and so the real doer of the deed remain unknown? I hope not; for I would give much to make his acquaintance, whoever he might be."

It was, of course, quite in vain for Captain Hawk to speculate as to who the mysterious, unknown highwayman could be.

Yet, vain as it was, he could not help his thoughts dwelling upon this point for a very considerable period.

At last, however, with a sudden start, he roused himself from his reflections.

"I must trust to time to find it out for me," he exclaimed. "Come, Satan, old boy, there is firm, springy turf beneath your feet now! One more effort, then away—away!"

That was all the splendid creature wanted.

The rest, brief as it was, and the attention he had met with at the Golden Ball Inn, seemed quite to have recovered him from the fatigue produced by his exertions on this most eventful night.

He bounded on now as though he had had the advantage of two or three days' rest.

Captain Hawk's heart swelled with pleasure.

He patted the gentle steed upon his neck, and spoke encouraging and caressing words to him continually.

And Satan showed his intense delight by bounding on, and every now and then uttering a low, neighing cry of satisfaction.

But in carrying out his scheme much more time had been consumed than the captain calculated upon.

Still, by making an effort, he thought it possible to reach the Greyhound before dawn, though he would certainly have to remain there during the day—if not only to avoid being seen, at least to give Satan the repose which he so well deserved.

"How blank Tom will look, to be sure, when he sees me!" he exclaimed. "What a way he will be in! How apprehensive for my safety!"

Captain Hawk quite enjoyed the prospect.

Away—away he went.

There was no more light to guide him on his way than that which the glittering stars afforded.

Yet such was the clearness of the air that, though no signs of the moon were visible, yet the night could not have been called a dark one.

And the captain's eyes had become so accustomed to the obscurity that he could see tolerably well.

As regards keeping clear, however, of any obstacles which might obstruct the path, he trusted himself entirely to Satan's sagacity.

He knew the noble creature's finer instinct would easily enable him to avoid whatever was dangerous.

And so, on—on went horse and rider, over fields and meadows that seemed interminable.

At such an hour there was scarcely the least fear that he would meet with anyone, or, if he did, it was scarcely likely he would be in any danger through it.

But at last the objects which he passed began to grow more and more familiar.

The end of his journey was at hand.

Satan bounded on as lightly and freely as before.

Not the least symptom of exhaustion or fatigue did he display, although for a considerable distance the ground was of a heavy character.

At length the straggling roof-tops of the ancient inn came into view; and just as the highwayman reined in, close to the low wall, he perceived in the eastern sky a faint flash of light, which indicated that the new day had just begun.

He glanced around him.

In and about the old inn an unusual quiet seemed to reign.

All the windows were plunged in darkness, and it would have required no great stretch of the imagination to believe that the quaint old building was deserted.

"We must find some one," he said, after a pause. "It will never do for us to linger here. Over, boy—over!"

The slightest touch of the rein was sufficient to make Satan leap over the little wall which he had cleared so often.

"If the door is only unlocked," said the highwayman, as he slipped from the saddle, "I will put you in the stable without saying a word to anybody, and then look after Tom Beckford afterwards."

Captain Hawk hardly dared venture to believe that he should find the stable-door unlocked, but to his great joy he discovered that such was the case.

"Where is Isaac, I wonder?" he said. "Perhaps asleep somewhere close at hand. I will call him."

He did so in a suppressed voice.

But he had no reply, nor could he, by listening with the utmost intentness, distinguish the faintest sound.

"He is searching for me, then," concluded the captain. "Now to make my brave steed comfortable, as he deserves to be."

By the time he had finished rubbing down his horse, and had given him some corn, which he knew where to find as well as Tom Beckford himself, objects out of doors began to be dimly revealed.

The silence which on his first arrival had struck him as being profound, still prevailed.

"Now," he said to himself, as he looked out into the deserted yard, "I wonder which will be the best thing for me to do: to go up to the house and arouse the landlord, or remain where I am?"

He glanced back at the abundance of clean white straw with which the stable floor was covered.

"I could make myself as comfortable here as in a palace," he said; "and perhaps I shall be as safe as if I strove to place myself in some extra secure spot. At any rate, I will try it. I shall have Satan for a companion, and I am weary enough to go to sleep anywhere."

With these words on his lips, he stepped back into the stable, closed the door, and felt for some fastenings on the inner side.

But he could find none.

His next proceeding was to collect a quantity of the new straw, which he piled up in a great heap against the door.

"There," he said, when he had finished, "if I lie down on that, I rather think it will be a difficult thing for anyone to get in without my being aware of it. How my bones ache, to be sure!"

The reader will not feel in the least surprised at hearing that Captain Hawk felt dreadfully fatigued.

After all the exciting adventures he had had, and the exertion he had gone through, it is not wonderful that he should feel as though he could throw himself down and fall into a state of complete insensibility.

And, in fact, something like this did occur.

No sooner had his body assumed a recumbent position than exhausted Nature demanded her due.

His eyes closed, his body became inert, and, for the time being, he was completely dead with respect to past, present, and future.

But when the first loss of strength had been repaired, his sleep became more unquiet.

He rolled over and over, and by the exclamations which escaped his lips, it was tolerably clear that he was enacting over again some of the violent scenes through which he had just passed.

It seemed to him as though a police officer was endeavouring to push him out of the saddle, while he (the captain) was unable to do anything more to prevent or resist his foe than oppose the dead weight of his body.

But he soon became aware that, in spite of all his efforts, he was being gradually pushed out of his position.

At length, however, he gave a sudden start.

He fancied he heard some one calling out in a loud voice.

He opened his eyes.

Then he saw that the dream he had had was not all a dream.

Some one in the yard outside was trying to push open the stable-door, which, owing to the precautions he had taken, was by no means an easy matter to accomplish.

"Confound it all! What does it mean?" said a well-known, friendly voice. "Open—open, can't you? Are you wounded, or what?"

It was Tom Beckford who spoke

With no little difficulty he had managed to peep through the little barred aperture which served as the stable window, and then he beheld not only Satan, but Captain Hawk lying against the door.

To say that this discovery caused him a great deal of astonishment would only be to convey a very feeble idea of his feelings.

Finding himself quite unable to arouse the highwayman, he naturally enough jumped to the conclusion that he must be wounded.

The alarm caused by this supposition was so great that, disregarding the caution which he had hitherto exhibited, he pushed at the door with all his might, and called out in tones quite loud enough to reach the ears of the officers, provided they happened to be within anything like a reasonable distance.

That this had the effect of awaking the captain we have already seen.

Still, several seconds elapsed before he could shake off his slumber sufficiently to recollect just where he was, and what had last happened to him.

But as soon as he had driven these vapours from his brain, he sprang to his feet, and hastened to admit his faithful friend.

"Powers above!" ejaculated the landlord, "how came you here? When I peeped through the window, and saw Satan in the stall, you can't imagine what a turn it gave me!"

"Oh yes, I can, though. But never mind that. Are there any Philistines at hand—eh, Tom?"

"Ah! It's very fine for you to come here and make yourself comfortable in this fashion, and then coolly ask the question afterwards!"

"I know what that means. All's well."

"And if it is, what brings you back again here? One would think you would consider you had made the place hot enough."

"Oh, I have something to tell you, Tom—something that will make you shake those old sides of yours. You will laugh more when you hear what has happened to me than you have done for many a day, or will do again."

This, as a matter of course, put the landlord in a perfect fever of impatience, for there was nothing in the world he enjoyed so much as to hear Captain Hawk recount his adventures.

"Don't keep me in suspense," he said,—"now, pray don't! I can't bear it!"

"Answer my question, then."

"What question?"

"Is the coast clear?"

"I think I may venture to say quite."

"What happened after my departure?"

"That you shall know presently, but not until you have given me the treat you promise."

"Well—well, I suppose I shall know no peace."

"You certainly will not."

"Then I had better begin at once."

"Yes, do; and you can't have a better place for it than this. There is no fear that we shall be overheard."

Captain Hawk was of the same opinion.

"Just a little drop of your ale to wet my lips with," he said, "before I begin, for I feel as thirsty as a thatcher."

"Wait half a moment, then."

It was truly ludicrous to see the hurried manner in which Tom Beckford waddled out of the stable and across the yard towards the house.

The captain laughed heartily at him.

He was absent only for a very short space of time indeed.

The foaming flagon which he carried with him was indeed welcome to the highwayman, who drank heartily.

Then, without further preface or delay, he related rapidly all those occurrences which have already been placed in full before the reader.

That Tom Beckford roared with laughter until his sides ached again, and rivers of tears poured down his cheeks, the reader need not be told.

At those parts which most took his fancy he would make the narrator stop, and then go back and tell it all over again.

In vain did the highwayman object.

The landlord was inflexible.

And in this manner a considerable time was spent.

At last, however, worthy Tom laughed his full, and then Captain Hawk ventured to mention the matter which had all the time been uppermost in his thoughts.

He had been burning to do so from the first moment of his arrival, but a feeling which he had never experienced before made him hesitate to speak.

When quiet was restored, however, he affected to say, in a very offhand and unconcerned tone:

"And the young girl, Tom, what of her—Blanche, I mean?"

"Ah, captain, when I heard how you had acted in that affair you can't think how you rose in my estimation."

"Yes, but how is she?"

"Well, for aught I know——"

"For aught you know," cried the captain, vainly attempting to conceal the amount of interest he felt—"for aught you know?" he repeated, hastily. "What do you mean?"

"Don't put yourself about, captain; she's all right."

"But where is she?"

"Why, where should you think, after the arrangement you had been kind and sensible enough to make for her?"

"Is she at—at Squire Kingsbury's, then?" he stammered, with a faltering voice, and with deep disappointment smiting at his heart.

"Yes, she is," said Tom. "But one would think, by your manner, that you repented what you had done, and that you feared she had again fallen into bad hands."

"No—no," said the highwayman, dejectedly; "it is not that."

"What is it, then?"

"Why, in simple truth, I wished to speak a few more words to her. You remember, we were interrupted by the officers breaking in."

"Oh!" said Tom, drily.

"That, indeed," continued the captain, his voice showing how great was his vexation, "was the principal reason why I made my way back here instead of following out my original plan of going direct to London."

"Well—well, worse things than that might have happened," said the landlord, philosophically.

"And when did he send down?" asked the highwayman, with impatience.

"Do you mean the squire?"

"Of course I do."

"Why, yesterday, early."

"And she was glad to go?"

"To be sure."

"And—and she left no message for me?"

"None."

Captain Hawk turned round suddenly, and, walking to the stable-door, looked out into the yard.

Here he stood for some moments, and probably would have stood longer had not the landlord approached and touched him on the arm.

"Captain," he said, "you will excuse me for speaking frankly to you, I know——"

"Well—well?"

"Take an old friend's word for it, that the less you think about that young girl the better it will be for both of you. There, don't turn away and be offended! It may be a bit of a disappointment to you just at present; but you will soon get over it. You know I am right."

A pause followed.

Captain Hawk turned and looked at Satan as though contemplating quitting the vicinity of the inn at once.

But Tom Beckford, who had watched him narrowly, said:

"Come—come, captain, be yourself. Just wait where you are for a minute or two, while I go and see whether the coast is as clear as it was a little time back. There may be some suspicious fellow or other lurking about. When I come back I will tell you what happened at the inn after your escape; and I'll warrant you will say it is worth listening to."

Captain Hawk did not make any reply.

Tom Beckford made his way towards the house, and as he went, he muttered:

"He is best left to himself a bit. He will soon get over it."

CHAPTER XCII.

IN WHICH LORD HARCLIFFE MEETS WITH A SURPRISE.

It is quite time now that we returned to the adventures of Lord Harcliffe, whose situation was particularly critical.

It will be remembered that after having succeeded so well in gaining an asylum in the garden where the old gentleman was trimming his rose trees, he had been startled by the police officers stopping near the little iron gate, instead of riding on, as he fully expected they would do.

Luckily, however, he was so surrounded by bushes and evergreens, that but little could be seen of him from the road; and by taking one step backwards he was able still further to conceal himself from view.

The officer who had called out was, no doubt, the one who had command of the troop, and it was with a great show of authority that he stood up in the stirrups and looked over the hedge.

The old gentleman remained silent.

Lord Harcliffe thought because he was too astonished to speak.

The officer repeated his command in a still more offensive manner.

The old gentleman drew back, manifestly offended.

He was always in the habit of being treated with a certain amount of deference, and what was more, he would exact it.

Never before had he been addressed in such a manner as by this police officer.

Lord Harcliffe, with wonderful quickness of perception—he was able to read almost anyone's character at a single glance—understood all.

Completely altering the tones of his voice, he said, coldly and haughtily:

"When you know how to address a question to a gentleman, you will probably have an answer!"

The keen, cutting manner in which these words were spoken made an impression even upon the obtuse faculties of the police officer.

He grew very red in the face, and sat down again in the saddle with a bang.

"Precisely!" said the old gentleman, nodding and smiling at his young friend.

Then turning towards the officers, he said:

"You will get no reply from me unless you alter your tone!"

So saying, he drew himself up to his full height, and looked round him with a very dignified air indeed.

The officer bit his lips, and then, with a clumsy attempt to be polite, he said:

"Then, perhaps, sir, since you are so very particular, you will answer me a question?"

"If properly put, certainly I will."

"Very good. Then I want to know whether you have observed a well-dressed man on horseback ride down the lane?"

"Not while I have been here with you, my dear sir," said Lord Harcliffe, quickly, and thus preventing the old gentleman from giving the reply which was on the tip of his tongue, and which, if made, would probably cause the officers to have their suspicions.

"No—as you say," he assented, "no one has passed while you have been here."

"I suppose," said Lord Harcliffe, in the same feigned voice, and affecting to be busily engaged in tying one of the rose trees—"I suppose you are all after some criminal or other?"

"We are," said the officers. "And if you have seen nothing of him as he passed by here, I am puzzled to think what has become of him."

And the officer, as he finished speaking, looked curiously and mysteriously around.

But he saw nothing whatever of a suspicious character.

Phantom was by this time safe in the stable, and secure from his prying gaze.

"And who may it be you are in quest of?" the old gentleman said, pompously.

"The Black Highwayman."

"Good heavens!" he ejaculated, his countenance assuming an expression of such intense alarm, that it was ludicrous to behold it. "You don't mean to say that desperate villain is anywhere in this part of the country?"

"I have certain knowledge that he was close here a short time since, and where he can have vanished to is a mystery."

Had not the old gentleman been so carried away by the abject terror which the bare mention of the Black Highwayman produced, he would probably have been struck by the arrival of his strange guest just a few moments before.

It is questionable, however, whether he would have believed that the great highwayman could have such a smooth and gentlemanly address, and, above all, take an interest in flowers.

But the worthy man was of too simple-minded a disposition for any such thoughts to spring up in his mind.

"You have not seen him, then?" said the chief officer.

"No, that I have not, and hope I never shall. But are you really in earnest about having seen him so near?"

"Quite, I assure you. He must have hid himself in some place or other. I am almost certain he has not gone on."

The old gentleman's distress grew greater and greater.

"Dear—dear me!" he said. "What is to be done? How shall I protect myself? Suppose he intends to make an attack on my house!"

"Nothing is more likely," said the chief officer, enjoying the old gentleman's alarm.

It was a sort of revenge upon him for the manner in which he had behaved at first.

"Good morning!" he said, pretending to ride away.

"No—no! Stop! Good gracious! Stop! You would not think of leaving me at the mercy of such a scoundrel as that, should you?"

"But how can we help it?"

"Help it? Come in—come in, all of you, and beat all the covers! If he is here, he must be found. Come and search the place thoroughly."

These words were unwelcome ones enough to Lord Harcliffe, and yet for the moment he hardly saw his way to preventing them.

"My dear sir," he said, calmly, and keeping his back turned towards the road, "I hardly think there is good ground for so much alarm. The fellow these officers are after is, no doubt, only intent upon getting away. I should hardly expect him to make an attack or even show himself, because that would bring the police at once upon him."

"I don't know about that," said the chief officer, who was delighted to see the old gentleman so terrified. "I need hardly tell you, I suppose, that he is a most desperate and unaccountable character, always doing the thing which people would think most unlikely. But good morning! You had better beat your covers yourself. We are off to look elsewhere. If you find him he will be worth the trouble, for the reward against him has just been doubled."

And with a loud laugh, the police officer rode away.

So far as inclination went, he would gladly enough have made a search of the whole premises, but then to have done so would have set the old gentleman's mind at rest, and that was what he could not bear the idea of.

"He'll be more respectful another time when he sees an officer, I'll be bound," he muttered. "At first we were hardly good enough to be spoken to; but now he would not mind how much he said. It serves him right."

So saying, the officer, more satisfied than ever about the revenge he was taking for the fancied injury he had received, quickened his pace.

But ere he had got many yards, he met with an old man, who was engaged in mending the hedge.

"Hi! you fellow there! Have you seen a man on horseback ride past here lately?"

"No; there's been nobody down t'lane this morning."

"And who lives up in that big house yonder?"

"Why, maister."

"Who's he?"

"Why, Squire Cockeram, to be sure. Didn't you know that he is the richest man in all the county?"

The officer did not reply, but turned to his companions.

"It seems pretty certain," he said, "that our man has not gone this way, so we can only retrace our steps and look well around us the while. He is hidden somewhere, and we must unkennel him."

"I am afraid," said the second in command, "that if he is in hiding, the moment we pass by he will quit his place of concealment and ride off in the opposite direction."

"And if so," replied the chief, "he cannot fail to fall in with the other parties who are looking for him; so come on."

With these words, the horses' heads were turned in the opposite direction, and they again rode past the old gentleman's grounds.

But though they looked narrowly around, they could see nothing of him nor his companion.

The fact was, that Lord Harcliffe, hardly able to believe in the reality of the escape he had just had, had contrived to lead the squire towards the house.

He judged that nothing was more likely than that the officers would make their way back again, and another time he might not be so fortunate as to deceive them.

At any rate, he thought it not worth while to run the risk.

A pretext for leaving that part of the grounds readily presented itself.

"What a disagreeable interruption!" he said to the squire.

"Disagreeable indeed, my young friend!" he replied, glancing uneasily around him. "If the Black Highwayman, as he is called, was to——"

"I think," said Lord Harcliffe, with a smile, "that you are alarming yourself unnecessarily."

"Do you indeed? And what reason have you for thinking so?"

"No very particular reason. But it does not seem to me to be in the least probable that the highwayman would venture upon any aggressive act when he must know how close at hand the officers of justice are. His detection could hardly fail to follow close upon the commission of the deed."

"There is some consolation in that, to be sure," said the squire, appearing to be somewhat reassured; "but, nevertheless, it is confoundedly annoying to be haunted by the notion that a fellow like that is lurking about the premises!"

"Very true. And if I might venture to make a suggestion——"

"Speak freely, my young friend—speak freely."

"It is that you should go up to the house, and have as many of your workmen collected together as possible."

"Yes—yes."

"Let them well arm themselves, and then, under the guidance of your steward or bailiff, let them make a careful search all about the grounds."

"But do you think we shall find him?"

"Nay, I don't know about that; and I don't know it is so particularly your object to find him as to drive him away; and that, if the search is properly conducted, you cannot fail to do, supposing, of course, that he is anywhere near."

"My dear friend, give me your hand. I am delighted with you, and very much obliged. Will you oblige me by going up to the house, and let me have the assistance of your arm? for the shock upon my quiet life has unnerved me quite."

The squire trembled a great deal, and Lord Harcliffe wondered at his agitation.

He could only account for it by supposing that he had some very valuable things at the Hall, and that he greatly dreaded the loss of them.

By the aid of Lord Harcliffe's arm, however, he walked with tolerable firmness as far as his dwelling, and then gave immediate instructions for the carrying into effect of the suggestion that had been made to him.

Thus it happened that Lord Harcliffe was out of sight when his foes again passed by.

"It will be better for you not to accompany the

[CAPTAIN HAWK'S ADVENTURE WITH THE BLACK HIGHWAYMAN.]

searchers," he said to the squire, with a consideration that was not altogether simulated. "From some of the many windows here we shall doubtless be able to see all that goes on with sufficient plainness."

The squire acquiesced; and, holding Lord Harcliffe's arm, ascended the steps leading to the principal entrance of the mansion.

It was a magnificent building in the Elizabethan style; and Lord Harcliffe, turn which way he would, could not help seeing objects that elicited his utmost admiration.

The door stood open; and on gaining the topmost step a young girl, charmingly attired in white, came bounding forward with a cry of pleasure on her lips.

But when she saw the squire was accompanied by a stranger she stopped short, and stood looking the very picture of pretty bashful confusion.

The age of this girl could not have exceeded sixteen, and she presented a type of a beauty of very high order.

Lord Harcliffe was charmed.

"That is my niece, Rose," the old gentleman said, with a smile of affection which showed how dear she was to his heart.

"And the Rose of which you are not the least fond, I'll be bound," said Lord Harcliffe, with a low bow to the girl.

But she, unused probably to strangers, and not yet having recovered from her embarrassment, turned round and fled, vanishing in a moment up the grand old oaken staircase.

"Ha, ha!" said the squire, forgetting all that had lately occurred to disturb him. "There she is, truly as timid as a fawn!"

"And as graceful," said Lord Harcliff

"Yes—yes, as you say, as graceful. But come, come, we are forgetting the errand that has brought us to the house. This way—this way."

He crossed the wide hall, and, opening a door led the way into a room of spacious dimensions.

The furniture, though antique, had a comfortable and luxurious look.

On the wide hearth a huge fire of wood-logs was blazing, diffusing a most agreeable warmth around.

From the huge old-fashioned bay-window an extensive view of the grounds could be obtained.

A little distance off a group of servants had collected.

They were all armed, and apparently were only waiting to be joined by more, in order to commence a vigorous search.

Lord Harcliffe's eyes did not rest upon them more than a moment, but wandered off into the distance, where he thought he might perchance catch a glimpse of his foes.

But he saw nothing; and he began to draw his breath more freely than he had done yet.

He considered it was very possible, if he showed himself adroit, that he might remain under the shelter of the squire's roof until nightfall.

If so, there was little doubt about his ability to elude his foes, who would give up by that time all idea of finding him in that locality, and would be looking elsewhere.

At this moment there came a tap at the door of the apartment.

"Breakfast is waiting, sir," said the servant who appeared upon the threshold.

"Bless me! Yes, breakfast!" ejaculated the squire. "I'll declare if I had not forgotten all about it; but now I am reminded I do feel as though I wanted it."

Lord Harcliffe laughed.

"I shall be glad to join you at the meal," he said, carelessly. "It was very early indeed when I partook of my scanty breakfast."

"I shall be delighted," said the squire—"you know I shall. Come—come!"

Never did Lord Harcliffe obey a summons more willingly.

Many hours had elapsed since he had been able to partake of any food, and more than once a giddy, sickly feeling came over him that made him fear he should faint.

But by the strength of his will he bore up well against this sensation.

It was a most substantial and tempting breakfast which was spread upon the table, and he felt that he should do full justice to it.

"There is nothing like the morning air to give me an appetite," he said. "Now I see these tempting viands before me, I feel just as though I had had nothing to eat for a month."

"Glad to hear it," said the squire. "My appetite is generally good in the morning; but what has just occurred seems to have upset me completely."

Lord Harcliffe looked around, naturally expecting that Rose would make one at the table.

But she did not appear, and he forebore to make any remark upon the subject.

From where they sat they could see the servants dispersing about the lawn; and by the way in which they commenced, it was quite clear they intended the search should be a thorough one.

The squire, notwithstanding the upset he had had, got on capitally with his breakfast.

Perhaps he was encouraged by the example his guest set him.

And as minute after minute swiftly passed away, Lord Harcliffe began to feel more and more secure in his situation, and to think that he should certainly have no trouble in remaining there till night.

The old squire seemed every moment more and more delighted with his society, and all promised well.

But events were quickly destined to take a turn which Lord Harcliffe little dreamt of.

"By-the-way," said the squire, carefully buttering a piece of toast, "I daresay you must have been a good deal surprised to witness my alarm as soon as the name of that dreadful Black Highwayman was mentioned?"

"I thought it only natural," was the calm response "He seems to me to spread terror on every side."

"Just so. But then I thought you would have guessed that I had some special and particular cause for my fear."

"No, in good truth, I did not."

"But I have," said the squire, shaking his head.

"But what—what?" said Lord Harcliffe, with anxious eagerness. "The Black Highwayman has never injured you?"

"Not personally," was the reply, "but he was very near being the death of one I hold very dear to my heart."

"Indeed!" said Lord Harcliffe, biting his lips, and vainly endeavouring to remember to what the squire could possibly allude.

But he had to give the attempt up in despair.

He could think of nothing.

There was a pause, during which the squire quietly ate his piece of toast.

Despite his iron self-control, Lord Harcliffe could hardly maintain his calmness.

"I must explain," continued the squire. "Of course I need not tell you that for a long time the identity of this Black Highwayman was an impenetrate secret, and all attempts to find out who he was signally and successively failed."

Lord Harcliffe assented by inclining his head, and, in order that his countenance should not be observed too closely, sipped gently at his cup of coffee.

"And, of course, you must also have heard that at last it was found that he was no other than a certain prodigal reputed young nobleman, who had been the talk of the town for two seasons?"

Again Lord Harcliffe signified his assent by a nod.

"Then he was taken to Newgate, and escaped. But, perhaps, knowing all this, you may not be aware through whose exertions his identity was discovered."

"By one Lieutenant Tracy, was it not?" said Lord Harcliffe, with wonderful calmness and evenness of utterance.

"You are right," said the squire. "More than once the impetuous young fellow came near to losing his life in the achievement he had imposed upon himself; but he vowed to tear the mask from the Black Highwayman, and he literally did it."

"Yes, so I have heard," said Lord Harcliffe, who, dreading lest some slight change or working of his features might lead to suspicion, perhaps detection, rose as he spoke, and advanced towards the window. "How goes the search?"

"Energetically enough," he replied; "but as yet it seems without result."

"Ah, well! let us hope it is so. But, as I was saying, this young Lieutenant Tracy——"

"A lieutenant in the navy, was he not?" asked the fugitive, endeavouring to appear perfectly at his ease.

"Yes; and as brave a young heart as ever trod a deck. He used to be an intimate friend and constant guest of this Lord Harcliffe, though he little suspected what the character of his entertainer was."

"And making the discovery as he did," said Lord Harcliffe, an amount of bitterness unconsciously tinging his voice, "was it not base on his part to be so anxious to betray him?"

"I don't pretend to judge about that; but I don't think he would have done it had not Lord Harcliffe at the time of his discovery tried to slay him. But you shall hear all the particulars, and for the matter of that, his defence from his own lips."

"His own lips?" repeated Lord Harcliffe, mechanically.

"Yes. As I was about to tell you, he is my nephew."

"Your nephew?" ejaculated Lord Harcliffe, in tones of such startling loudness as made the old squire jump and drop his coffee cup with a great clatter into the tray. "Your nephew?" he added, more gently.

"Ye—ye—yes!" stammered the squire. "How you startled me! I'll declare I am quite nervous this morning!"

"I was, in truth, surprised," said Lord Harcliffe, who was fast recovering his self-possession. "How strange a coincidence!"

"Yes. It was knowing that that alarmed me so much as soon as I heard of him being in the vicinity."

"Ay, truly so. And this young Lieutenant Trac 's your nephew?"

"Yes," said the squire, proudly, as he wiped some of the spilled coffee from his white frilled shirt. "Rose, that you just caught a glimpse of when you entered, is his sister."

"How very singular!"

"Singular, indeed, I thought it, and deucedly unpleasant into the bargain! But, as I was saying, you shall hear the account from his own lips. I am never tired of hearing it."

"I—I——"

The squire proceeded without heeding Lord Harcliffe's interruption, which was, however, too slight to be taken notice of.

"He has almost recovered from his serious hurts, though still an invalid. He promised to be here this morning to see me. Bless the dear boy's heart! Where's his letter? Oh, ah! here it is. 'Dear uncle,—Expect me at nine in the morning, prompt.—Your's truly, Jack.' Ha! he'll be here, I know, to the minute."

Just as the squire pronounced the words, the antique timepiece on the cabinet struck the hour of nine.

CHAPTER XCIII.

THE BLACK HIGHWAYMAN IS DISCONCERTED BY LIEUTENANT TRACY'S ARRIVAL AT THE SQUIRE'S HOUSE.

Lord Harcliffe still kept his face half turned towards the window, as though deeply interested in the proceedings of the servants on the lawn.

As he stood, the long damask curtain cast a shadow on his features, and concealed the flush of colour that had overspread his usually pale countenance.

Besides this he exhibited no sign whatever of agitation.

He knew the worst now.

He had felt the shock, and now each second that elapsed enabled him still more to recover his wonted calmness of demeanour—that calmness which only some most extraordinary circumstance could shake.

And in the present instance the shock was most severe.

To think that perverse fortune should fool him so by seeming to bring him to a place of safety, but in reality face to face with the one he now looked upon as his deadliest and bitterest foe.

To remain, of course, was impossible.

Yet how could he get away?

What plausible pretext could he make to the old Squire? and, above all, how should he keep himself from the view of those police officers whom he knew to be perilously close at hand?

All this passed through his brain with lightning speed.

Before he had time to decide, to think, or even to speak, a sound came upon his ears which immediately engrossed all his attention.

This was a shout from the body of servants.

For some reason they all paused, and waving their hats, cheered lustily.

The cause of this proceeding was in a moment explained.

The grinding noise made by the revolution of carriage wheels upon a gravel path next became heard, and almost instantly afterwards a close carriage, drawn by a pair of horses, came in sight.

The ringing cheer had brought the old squire to the window; and no sooner did he catch sight of the vehicle than he manifested the most extravagant delight.

"Hurrah—hurrah!" he cried. "Here is my boy! Hurrah! How glad I feel! Hip—hip! I must go out to meet him!"

And so saying, with his eyes sparkling with joy, and every limb trembling with excitement, he caught up his hat and dashed from the room like an impetuous schoolboy.

The door through which he passed was hung upon self-closing hinges.

Lord Harcliffe was alone.

He took one step from the window.

The carriage whirled by.

"Now is my time," he said, in a low, deep voice. "To stay here would be madness. I should be overpowered instantly. If I can only find my way unseen to the stables all will be well."

But this promised to be no easy matter, for he had not the least idea of where the stables were situated.

He gave a rapid glance around.

He then saw that there was another door opening from the breakfast-room besides that through which the old squire had rushed so hastily.

Through the latter was doubtless Lord Harcliffe's best way, and one most likely to lead him to freedom.

But there was the difficulty that, the moment he crossed the threshold, he should be in full view of the front-door.

It was impossible to get to the stables unobserved by taking that route.

It was, then, with a feeling of the greatest relief and satisfaction that he discovered the existence of the second door.

To reach it did not take a second.

He placed his hand upon the knob and turned it—not without a certain amount of trepidation, for he knew not where the door might lead.

Upon pushing it open, however, he experienced instantaneous relief.

The adjoining room was magnificently fitted up as a library.

The walls were lined with shelves loaded with books, and here and there were choice specimens of sculpture.

It was empty.

Quickly closing the door behind him, Lord Harcliffe stood for about a second in a state of irresolution.

"The moment I am missed, search will be made," he said; "therefore I must be speedy. My only hope is that the squire will be so full of his delight at his nephew's return that he will forget my existence for a minute or two."

With these words passing through his mind rather than being uttered by his lips, Lord Harcliffe strode swiftly across the oak-polished floor towards the door which he observed at the extremity of the library.

On passing through this he found himself in a picture gallery, of dimensions much greater than are ordinarily found in a private dwelling.

This, like the library, was vacant; and without pausing to bestow a passing glance upon the numerous works of art, Lord Harcliffe turned to the further end.

Here the door led into another room, which, in its turn, communicated with a conservatory.

Towards this last he made his way with quickened steps, under the belief that he should very shortly find himself in the open air.

He was not mistaken.

A glass door led from the conservatory on to a broad terrace, the same which he had first caught sight of among the trees.

All around seemed quite deserted.

No doubt all the occupants of the Hall had left their accustomed stations in order to testify their delight at the safe return of the young sailor.

"By the course I have taken," said Lord Harcliffe, "I must certainly be at the rear of the Hall; and, therefore, at no great distance I ought to see something of the stables. Where can they be, I wonder?"

Again he hurried forward, being now in momentary expectation of hearing a cry raised for him.

After crossing a beautiful miniature flower garden he caught sight of some outbuildings surrounded by a high wall.

"There, surely, must be the place I seek," he said; and as he spoke the words he hurried on once more.

He was right.

But the stables, like everywhere else, seemed perfectly deserted.

"So much the better," he muttered. "I can saddle Phantom more quickly than any of the old squire's servants, who have never within their lives, perhaps, had to make haste."

This was probable enough; but yet a guide would have saved him many precious minutes.

The stabling attached to the Hall was extensive, and he had to look through several doors in succession before he found the object of his search.

And even then he met with another delay.

The saddle and bridle had been removed.

Good luck, however, quickly guided him to the harness room, and there he picked up the first trappings he could lay his hands on without pausing to consider whether they were his own or not.

And with still greater speed he ran back to the stable, saddled and bridled Phantom, and led him into the yard.

But despite all the speed which characterised his movements, the reader will not require to be told that a considerable space of time had altogether been consumed—more than enough for his sudden absence to be noticed, and inquiry made for it.

In fact, just as he was in the act of putting his foot into the stirrup he heard some persons approaching.

About his ability to escape from them he had no doubt; but what he wanted to do was to get away without leaving a trace behind him by which he could be followed.

All hope of doing this at once fled when he rode out of the stable yard.

The first person of whom he caught sight was the old squire, looking anxious, puzzled, and alarmed.

Close to him was Lieutenant Tracy.

The young man looked pale and ill; and well he might, for the wound he had received was a severe one, and he had been by no means careful to take care of himself.

At the first glance, too, it was a matter of certainty that he recognised Lord Harcliffe.

A deep flush of colour suffused his ashen face, and in an angry voice he cried out:

"It is as I expected, the villain! But this time, at least, he shall not escape the hands of outraged justice!"

As he thus spoke, he, with great suddenness, raised his right hand, in which, though Lord Harcliffe had not noticed it, he held a small pocket-pistol.

No sooner was his hand raised than the weapon exploded.

Lord Harcliffe, by retaining his presence of mind, was just able to make a sudden movement to one side.

By doing so he unquestionably saved his life, for the bullet whizzed close past him without inflicting the slightest injury.

For about half a second it seemed as though the Black Highwayman meditated some vengeance for this attack.

But if so, the feeling was only momentary.

Turning Phantom's head round, he set off at a hard gallop before any of the squire's domestics were sufficiently recovered from their consternation to make the least attempt to stop him.

Tracy fired another pistol; but, though he was rapid in his movements, Lord Harcliffe had got out of range.

But the clear and loud reports of those pistols echoed far and wide over the silent fields.

"Confusion seize him!" the Black Highwayman cried. "That sound will be certain to reach the ears of the police officers, and they will, of course, hurry in this direction to see what has happened. But no matter. Phantom is swift, and, despite the daylight, I shall escape them all."

But, unluckily, he had not yet got clear of the squire's grounds, which were not laid out in a manner favourable for a horse making any great speed.

Impediments presented themselves at almost every step.

At length a more formidable object than any presented itself.

This was a high brick wall, doubtless belonging to a garden.

The height of this made leaping it quite out of the question; and, as it lay quite across his path, he had no alternative but to change his course.

A loud cry of triumph from the pursuing servants told him plainly enough that he had made some mistake, and that they were in consequence full of the hope of being able to arrest his flight.

It was therefore very anxiously that the Black Highwayman kept a look-out in front of him, for he knew not how soon he might come upon a serious obstacle.

In less than a moment afterwards he comprehended why it was that the servants had given utterance to the cry of gratification.

On reaching the end of the high wall which had compelled him to turn aside from his course, he found that it was flanked by another equally as high.

For a moment he thought he should have to turn round and make a fight of it.

But in one part of the wall, a little further on, he saw there were some wooden gates.

Of course, as ill-luck would have it, they were closed, and their height was such that probably no one would have thought of attempting to leap a horse over them.

But Lord Harcliffe had great faith in Phantom's wonderful powers, for without a moment's hesitation he rode straight at them.

The manœuvre was witnessed by his pursuers, who could not refrain from uttering loud cries.

"We have him now!" cried the groom, who happened to be foremost in the chase. "There's no horse living that could clear those gates. Black Bess might have done it, but no other. Don't go closer, or you will have him on you."

The opinion thus confidently expressed by the groom was fully shared in by the rest, and they pulled up accordingly.

But without faltering, Lord Harcliffe rode Phantom to the gates.

The noble creature gave a tremendous spring.

The groom shook his head.

But instead of recoiling, as he was quite sure the horse would, what was his astonishment to see him clear the gates!

Phantom's iron hoofs struck against the top part of the gates, it is true, and split the woodwork in all directions.

But he alighted in safety on the other side.

"That's a wonder!" cried the groom, rubbing his eyes in order to make sure that his vision had not deceived him. "He deserves to get clear after that. It was truly a leap for life or death."

But Lieutenant Tracy, in whose breast burnt the fiercest fire of resentment against the highwayman, was of quite a different way of thinking.

It was his hand which removed the fastenings and flung the gates open.

But all hope of pursuing the highwayman was at an end.

He had gained the open country, and Phantom was flying across the meadows like a race-horse.

The lieutenant was furious with rage and disappointment.

But suddenly he uttered a cry of gratification.

"Look—look!" he cried. "The villain will not get off quite so easy, after all. Oh, for my former strength, and a good horse, that I could join you in the chase! Look—look, they ride well! If they persevere, they may yet succeed in running him down. In the broad daylight it seems hardly possible that he can elude them."

These words were called forth by his perceiving a strong body of well-mounted police officers riding at full speed in pursuit.

Whether they were the same that had called over the hedge, the distance was too great to determine.

But they had the highwayman in full view, there could be no doubt about that; and by the unmerciful manner in which they applied whip and spur to their poor horses, it appeared equally certain that they were determined to effect a capture.

Lord Harcliffe could not help experiencing great annoyance at finding his foes so very close at his heels; and yet, after all that had occurred, it was no more than he might with absolute certainty have calculated upon.

"Curses on that Tracy!" he cried, grinding his teeth. "But I will be even with him for it ere long! But for his cursed appearance I should now have been comparatively safe, with no greater anxiety upon my mind than that of waiting for the approach of night. Now, under the bright sun, how am I to elude my enemies? At the first road I come to the probability is that I shall encounter another party."

The wonderful speed that Phantom was now making ought to have inspired him with some encouragement.

But there were special reasons why this pursuit was unfortunate for him.

It had been his intention, could he but have stayed at the squire's in quiet until nightfall, to have made his way back towards London.

The uncertainty he was in with respect to the fate of his faithful companion, Pharoah, filled him with anxiety, and, moreover, there were the strongest reasons why he should communicate with him without delay.

His escape from present capture, was, however, the greatest consideration, and he could see but one plan that held out to him the faintest and most distant chance of success.

This was to keep Phantom's head steadily in the direction of the open country, and trust to his extraordinary powers of speed to enable him to keep out of reach of his foes.

By this course he stood the chance of getting clear of those detachments of officers who held possession of all the roads.

But this could only be the case within a certain distance of the metropolis.

Therefore, ill suited as it was with his plans, he had to trust to this as his only chance.

When he had once decided upon it, it is wonderful what a difference it made to his progress.

There was no faltering or hesitation now.

Having determined what line of action to adopt, he kept his horse's head steadily in the required direction, and urged him to make the greatest speed of which he was capable.

"The sooner I can shake these fellows off," he said, "the better will be my chance, and then I must endeavour to shape my course in such a manner as to avoid seeing anyone. Otherwise, all my exertions will be in vain. I must leave no clue by which they can follow me."

While these thoughts were passing through his mind, the speed which Phantom made was absolutely terrific.

It was in vain that the officers made every exertion to keep up with him.

Further and further they fell in the rear, though the flat, level, open character of the country they were in enabled them to keep their prey in view when at a long distance off.

"Fortune smiles upon me," said the Black Highwayman, mentally, as, after looking searchingly in every direction, he failed to see and signs of human beings or even habitations. "I hardly dared to hope that I should ride so far without running against some other party of my foes. It would have been different, I suppose, had I not kept so constantly to the open country."

This was a probable enough conjecture.

The officers were, no doubt, engaged in patrolling the various high-roads and byways, and not in scouring over the country.

Far behind him, however, and undiscernible by any eye less piercing than his own, were those officers who had followed him from the Hall.

But the great distance they had dropped back made the highwayman feel certain that if no outward event occurred, in half an hour at least he should be completely lost to their senses of sight and hearing.

Such being the prospect, it became doubly imperative that he should keep the strictest watch that there should be no one to observe his movements.

But his restless gaze brought nothing to his sight save those inanimate objects which form a country landscape.

"All is well!" he cried at length, unable to refrain from uttering his thoughts aloud. "At last I have rid myself of them altogether. Now, then, to change my course. Yet stay! I——"

"Here's wishing your honour a hearty good *moorning!*" said a voice at this moment.

There was no mistaking the rich brogue in which these words were pronounced.

The sound came from somewhere very close at hand; and as the Black Highwayman was fully persuaded that he was quite alone, he experienced so sudden a shock, that he bumped himself seriously against the pommel of the saddle.

Just before giving vent to his felicitations, he had, to ease his horse, reduced his pace to a walk.

He was the more moved to do so because for some distance their way lay over ploughed land.

It was in order to save Phantom from unnecessary fatigue, too, that he took him close to a high, thick-set hedge that divided one field from another.

The voice which had so startled him came from the other side of this hedge; and on looking in the right direction, Lord Harcliffe saw the figure of a man, who, with a billhook in his hand, was standing in a gap in the hedge.

It needed but one glance into the open, merry countenance and dark, twinkling eyes, to make anyone aware that he was one of those good-tempered labourers who are so often found at farm-houses.

Even Phantom looked a little scared at seeing this sudden apparition; and before Lord Harcliffe could recover from the state of astonishment into which he had been thrown, the Irishman, with a loud laugh, added:

"And bedad, your honour, it's *meself* that's thinking you and your horse, begorra, are just the laste bit surprised at the seeing of me. Bad luck to meeself for scaring a jintleman! I'm sure I axes your pardon, sir. You see, I was but just a repairing this bit of a hedge here. Bad cess to old Grumper's sow! We niver can keep her out of it; and masther, he says to me, 'Murtough Macgillioray,' he says—says he, 'just take your brumhock, and mend that hedge again,' says he. And here I am, axin' your honour's pardon, I'm sure."

CHAPTER XCIV

LORD HARCLIFFE AT LENGTH SUCCEEDS IN OBTAINING A PLACE OF TEMPORARY SHELTER.

A MORE trivial incident than the foregoing can hardly be imagined, yet how fraught it was with dangerous consequences to the Black Highwayman!

Just at the time when he had, after so much difficulty and exertion, outdistanced his pursuers, up popped this man, who would, of course, out of the bluntness of his nature, give all the information to the officers he possessed.

And how to get himself out of this difficulty, Lord Harcliffe could not for the moment see.

That the police officers would keep on in a straight line after him as far as he then was amounted almost to a certainty.

A deep frown settled upon his features.

But all at once, like an inspiration, a thought crossed his mind which suggested a means of turning this untoward event into a fortunate occurrence.

At any rate, his idea seemed to offer so feasible a plan by which he could turn the officers off the track altogether, that he determined to try it.

As yet he had not spoken, but now he made a gesture of impatience, and said, in a tone and manner so different from his ordinary manner, that one could hardly believe it was indeed the Black Highwayman:

"Bad luck to you, then, Murtough Macgillioray!" he exclaimed, in an Irish brogue, so well simulated that it deceived the person he addressed. "Bad luck to you for a thafe of the world! What y're doing there?"

"Sure, masther, and it's meeself that's——"

"Hold your tongue, you spalpeen! Sure it's yourself that has ruined me intirely?"

"Ruined ye?" cried Murtough, in ludicrous bewilderment. "Ruined ye, is it? Och, now! by the powers, and how could meeself do that any way?"

"Don't I tell ye ye have!" said the Black Highwayman, with a vexation that was not all feigned. "Bad luck to your ugly old carcass!"

"Oh, what's that you say, masther?" said the Irishman, with an air of pitiable distress. "Is it meeself, then, that's ruined a jintleman of the ould country?"

"Troth, and ye have—ye have!"

"Then, begorra, masther, I'm mighty sorry, though how I've done it I don't know at all, at all."

"Why, ye blundhering thafe, didn't ye jump up in the gap in the hedge and look at me?"

"Sure, masther, and I did."

"Very well, then."

"And, och! now, is it that that's ruined ye?"

"It is, Murtough, and I'm mightily sorry for it. Ye see, I was off as fast as my baste could carry me back agin to the ould country; but, ochone! it's you that's prevented me intirely."

The Irishman took off his well-worn hat, and scratched his head vigorously.

All this was sadly beyond his comprehension; and the more he thought upon the subject the more hopelessly involved did his ideas become.

"Masther—masther," he said, "do tell me how I have done it, for, faith! it bothers me quite altogether."

"Well, Murtough Macgillioray——"

"Sure and faith, and that's me, masther!"

"Didn't you jump up and see me going quietly by; and don't you know there's them spalpeens of English officers hard at the back of me; and when they come here, they'll see you, and ask you 'Where is gone the man on the black horse?' And isn't it you that will be afther saying, 'Straight down the leasow there, and up the hill beyant?'"

"What," said the Irishman, with that shrill cry so often given by those of his race when powerfully excited —"what, is it me?—is it Murtough Macgillioray that'd do that same?—is it me that would be afther giving them dirty spalpeens the office against you? Och, no! Sure it's some other thafe of the wurrld! it isn't Murtough Macgillioray!"

An imperceptible smile curled the lips of the Black Highwayman as he received this assurance.

He fully expected, on account of the confidence he had, that he could imitate the brogue of an Irishman so well as to deceive anyone.

And he knew further, that the warm-hearted Irishman, once impressed by the notion that it was one of his own countrymen in trouble, would die rather than betray him.

"Get along wid you, Murtough!" he cried. "Don't ye know very well that you're a blundhering omadawn! Two or three questions would draw all the particulars out of you."

"Whisht there, masther—whisht! Not another word! Sure it's no danger you're in from me at all, at all! And it's no need you have to wish you had never seen me! Oh, wirra! that a jintleman from the ould country should ever say them words!"

"Now, Murtough, my boy, will ye just listen to me?"

"Troth, and I will! Go on, masther; I'm payin' every attention."

Lord Harcliffe looked behind him.

The position he occupied commanded tolerably extensive views in every direction save that he was about to take, and there a steep hill hid all things from his view.

No trace, however, of his enemies could he behold.

Then, sinking his voice, he said to the mystified Irishman:

"Murtough, my boy, it's my life they're afther!"

"Your life, masther?"

"Yes: nothing less will satisfy them. They're afther me with all their might. But if you are true to me, Murtough, I shall get to the ould country yet, and then I am safe."

"Me be true!" said the Irishman, excitedly. "Now, masther, do you think it's me that would think of betraying you? No, no—the divil a bit!"

"But there's the reward, Murtough."

"The what?"

"The reward."

"Sure, now, and what's that?"

"Why, the money, sure, the dhirty thaves will get that either take me or shoot me down like a dog."

"Och, now! and do you think I'd touch any of their dhirty money? No—no! May the divil roast me if I touch a ha'penny of it!"

"But it's a dale of money, Murtough."

"And what do I care, now, how much it is? Faix, now, don't say another word about it."

"Then you will not say a word about having seen me?"

"They shall pull my tongue out by the roots first."

"Give us your hand, then, Murtough; and it's greatly I'm obliged to you; and you sha'n't go unrewarded either. Here, take this."

Lord Harcliffe thrust his hand into his pocket, and drew forth a handful of guineas, which he forced into the man's hand.

"There, now," he said; "put them in your pocket, Murtough, and be satisfied with the good day's work you've done."

"Oh, jabers!"

"Those spalpeens that are coming after me may promise you ten times as much; but there's a difference between promising and doing, and that you ought to know very well."

"Trust me—trust me, masther. But it's not your money I want; and if you'd take it back, sure, it's quite content and delighted I'd be to save you for nothing."

"No—no, Murtough, that's but a poor reward for your fidelity. But I must go now; and, remember, when the officers come up you must say you have seen nobody."

"Oh, I know all about it; and if when you get over to the ould country, now——"

"What, Murtough?"

"If you should ever come to Ballynamara——"

"What then?"

"Sure, if ye'd call at the ould mud cabin there that's just over the iligant wooden bridge and ask for the Widow Macgillioray——"

"If ever I come there, Murtough, I will call and tell her everything, and give her something worth her while. But good-bye to ye now, Murtough. I have stopped too long. But I trust my life in your hands, Murtough."

"And you can do it without being afeard. Good morning to your honour: more power to you, and confusion on the dhirty blackguards that's afther you!"

Lord Harcliffe waved his hand, and set off as fast as the rough nature of the ground would permit.

He did not pause or look behind him until he reached the summit of the hill which we have mentioned.

Upon looking back, he saw Murtough standing in the gap, by no means sufficiently recovered to go on with his occupation.

He made a gesture of recognition.

But Lord Harcliffe's gaze wandered further and further away to the utmost point his vision would reach.

"Is not that a cloud of dust?" he said to himself, and shading his eyes with his hand. "Yes—yes, it is! How faint—how distant! It is caused by something in motion. It may not be the troop of police; but the probability is that it is no other. While so far off as that, however, and having so faithful an ally as Murtough, surely I have little to fear."

He gathered up the reins as he spoke; and then, in encouraging tones, he said:

"Now, Phantom, my brave boy, once more away—away! Safety and rest are before us. Away—away!"

The descent on the other side of the hill was easy, and the slope extended for some distance.

The ground, too, was firm and good, so that for some distance Phantom flew on at a very wonderful rate indeed.

His rider was breathless.

"Not quite so fast," he said, at length. "Such a speed as that would knock you up too soon, my brave friend. Easy—easy!"

It was not at a very gentle rate, however, that the next half-dozen miles were passed over; but at the end of that time Lord Harcliffe reduced Phantom to a canter, which he could maintain with comparatively light exertion to himself.

"Can I believe that I am at last secure and safe?" Lord Harcliffe said, as he glanced around him. "I have seen no one—not a soul. I can trust to Murtough—that is, I think I can. His will to screen me is good enough. The only fear is, that he will be a little over anxious in doing it, and so cause that suspicion which he would try all he knew to remove. In that quarter there is only one thing to do, which is, to hope for the best."

Again he looked around him keenly and scrutinisingly.

But, as before, he saw nothing to excite his apprehension.

Well-cultivated fields picturesquely broken in upon by masses of trees surrounded him on all sides.

It was now growing fast toward mid-day

Lord Harcliffe looked up to the meridian sun, and said:

"If, now, I could find somewhere in these solitudes a cottage, or some place where both Phantom and myself could have food and rest till nightfall, all would be well. There is scarcely any fear that those behind will track me so far as this; while by going further on I may only encounter some other troop, in which case all my difficulties would commence again — with this difference, that Phantom is tired instead of being fresh."

Lord Harcliffe felt that he was suffering most acutely from the want of sleep.

Very many hours had elapsed since he had taken any repose whatever; and he now felt certain that unless he slumbered very quickly he should be altogether incapacitated from further exertion.

But it was not until he had gone at least two miles further that he perceived, at some distance, a small, humble dwelling.

It was densely surrounded by trees—so much so that, had not Lord Harcliffe been very keenly on the look-out, he would have passed it by unseen.

No sooner did his eyes rest, however, upon the ivy-covered front than he turned Phantom's head towards it.

For some moments he fancied that the place must have been unoccupied; but the noise made by his horse's hoofs brought a woman to the cottage door.

In her arms was a child, which manifested so much terror at Lord Harcliffe's approach, that he at once came to the conclusion that the visits of strangers to that lonely spot were of very rare occurrence.

This was a pleasant enough discovery to make.

"My good woman," said Lord Harcliffe, raising his voice to rather a high pitch, in order to make it heard above the crying of the child, "I have unfortunately lost my way in the country here, and in trying to find it have wandered so many miles that I have completely tired my horse. Can you tell me the nearest place where we can find a rest for a few hours?"

By this time the child had got over much of its alarm, so the woman was able to reply:

"There is no place near this, sir—that is, not nearer than four miles, and that is only a little cottage no better than this, where you would be able to find no more accommodation than there is here."

Lord Harcliffe listened to the statement respecting the solitary situation of the cottage with a gratification which he could scarcely conceal.

"It is useless for me to go further, then," he said. "If you will permit me to rest for a brief time beneath your roof, I will reward you liberally."

But the woman, after some hesitation, said:

"My husband is not at home, sir."

"Well, what of that?"

"He is such a strange man, sir. Ten to one he would be very angry with me for allowing a stranger to cross the threshold."

"Pooh—pooh! you must suffer me to take the risk of that. Do not fear but that I shall make things all right with him. I will guarantee beforehand that he is contented rather than displeased."

"If that is so, then," answered the woman, "I assure you on my part I am glad to place at your disposal such poor accommodation as this wretched place affords."

Lord Harcliffe could not help being struck in an instant by the woman's language, so different from what might have been expected from the lips of one in her apparent situation.

"You have not always been used to such a place as this, then?" said Lord Harcliffe, dismounting.

"Indeed, sir!" said the woman, quickly, and with a hot flush suffusing her face the while. "How did you know that?"

"I merely surmised it from the way you spoke."

The woman gave a sigh, apparently of relief.

"Where is your husband?"

"Away from home, sir."

"And when do you expect him?"

"I do not know when. His return is quite uncertain. He generally makes his appearance when he is least expected and least wanted."

Lord Harcliffe was conscious that there was something unusual in the woman's manner; but he was by far too weary and too heavy with slumber to make any attempt to solve the mystery.

He noticed that at the back of the cottage there was a roughly-constructed shed, which he fancied would be just about large enough to contain his horse, and towards this he led Phantom as rapidly as his stiffened joints would permit.

The woman raised no objection.

On gaining the interior, Lord Harcliffe found that there was a tolerably abundant supply of hay and straw, but there was no corn.

"No matter, old fellow," he said, patting Phantom on the neck; "you must do as well as you can with the fare before you. After all, it is rest that you want most."

Phantom nibbled away at the hay as though he enjoyed it, and so his master closed the door of the shed and left him to his own devices.

The woman was standing outside, looking anxious and alarmed, as though she almost wished she had peremptorily refused shelter to the stranger.

"Come—come," said Lord Harcliffe; "if you will only show me a place where I can lie down for an hour or two and sleep, that is all that I require. The moment I am rested, I shall want to rejoin my friends."

He fancied the woman looked keenly at him, as though she half suspected that he was not telling her the truth.

"When I depart," he continued, "I am certain you will not regret what you have done. Come! lead the way."

With palpable unwillingness the woman led the way to the door of the cottage.

The humble dwelling contained but two rooms, both of which were on a level with the ground.

The woman walked to the rude door communicating with the inner chamber.

"There," she said, "make yourself as comfortable as you can, and I hope that your departure will take place before my husband's return."

"Wherefore?"

"Never mind!"

"Then you will add to the obligation I am already indebted to you if you will keep good watch outside and give me timely warning of his approach, or the approach of anyone else, for that matter," he said, with well-assumed indifference.

The woman gave him another of her penetrating glances.

"They may be the friends from whom I separated looking for me," he said.

"Enough. I understand you."

"Understand me?"

"Yes."

"How?"

"You are a fugitive! Nay, don't start, nor attempt to deny it!"

"Woman! I——"

"I am not easily deceived," she said, "and feel quite certain that I am not in the present instance."

Lord Harcliffe was silent.

"Don't be uneasy," she said. "You have nothing to fear from me. As I said before, make yourself as comfortable as you are able, and trust that my husband does not return before your departure."

She closed the door as she spoke, and went out of the cottage.

For a moment Lord Harcliffe seemed about to follow her.

But changing his intention, he flung himself upon the miserable bed, which was about the only article of furniture the room contained.

He closed his eyes, expecting, of course, that he would instantly be visited by slumber.

To his astonishment, however, he could not sleep.

His thoughts were busy, and, strive as he would, he could not prevent them from dwelling upon the woman and her singular behaviour.

"If I could fathom this mystery—for some mystery, I am sure, exists—I think then that I should be more content. As it is, it baffles me."

He turned over and over continually.

But despite his fatigue, he could not rest.

When he once began to think, he had no lack of materials for reflection.

All the anxieties of his own position presented themselves.

It troubled him to find that he was so far away from London at a time when it was necessary for him to be so near to it.

Of the fate of Pharoah he was in absolute ignorance.

For aught he knew, his faithful associate might be at that moment a prisoner in Newgate—lying in his cell waiting for help to be released.

The more Lord Harcliffe reflected, the more ungovernable did his impatience become.

Unable to remain lying down any longer, he slipped from the bed, and going to the one small window that the place boasted of, looked out.

He was able to see for a considerable distance among the trees; but he was unable, after waiting for some moments, to discern anything calculated to arouse his apprehensions.

From the window he went to the door

The latter was composed of nothing better than a few old planks rudely and hastily nailed together.

No pains had been taken to make these planks fit closely together, so that there was many a chink through which it was easy enough to reconnoitre.

At the first glance he saw the outer room was empty.

The strange-behaving woman was seated in a chair outside the door, rocking the child and singing to it in a low tone.

While so doing, she was also apparently watching stealthily all around her.

Lord Harcliffe remained gazing for some moments, but finding all so calm and peaceful he at length flung himself upon the bed.

This time he was more fortunate.

Hardly had he stretched himself out at full length before he fell fast asleep.

His slumber was profound, and no wonder that it should be so, for he was doubly exhausted.

Hours passed.

Lord Harcliffe knew it not, but the sun sunk down low in the west, and shining through the ill-glazed casement, sent a ray like a fiery dart full into his face.

Lower still it sunk until no trace of it remained, and absolute obscurity prevailed.

It was not likely, however, if the present silence con tinued, that the wearied-out highwayman would awake until his exhausted energies had been thoroughly recuperated.

CHAPTER XCV.

CONTINUES TO FOLLOW THE FORTUNES OF LORD HARCLIFFE.

At last Lord Harcliffe became vaguely and dimly aware that the long-lasting silence was broken in upon.

For some time he was content to remain knowing this, without troubling to inquire either what the sound was, or whether it concerned him.

But the sound grew louder, and then with electric suddenness he knew that the sound was caused by voices.

He sprung up.

It did not require one single moment's listening to tell him that the voices were disputing.

Another second enabled him to shake off the leaden influence of slumber altogether, and he listened eagerly to what was being said.

He recognised without difficulty the voice of the woman.

The other speaker (and there were only two), was undoubtedly a man.

His voice was harsh and angry.

"You can say what you like!" were the first words that Lord Harcliffe distinctly heard. "You can say what you like, I tell you; but I have my doubts! You know that well enough!"

"Alas! I do know it," said the woman, wailingly. "But never was a man doubtful with less cause for being so. You have no cause, however—not even the shadow of a pretext!"

"You can say what you like, I tell you!" repeated the man, in still fiercer tones than he had before employed. "But some day I shall find out all my suspicions verified. I've got a feeling that comes over me that says so as plainly as if words spoke it. You did not expect me back just at the present time, now, did you?"

"Indeed I did not!" said the woman, vainly struggling to repress her tears.

Her husband—for, as Lord Harcliffe thought, he could be no other—received the admission with an exultant laugh.

"Stop your snivelling!" he cried. "I have had enough of it! Stop, I say! You'd better not have me speak twice!"

"I did not expect you," said the poor wife, "because I have long learned to look for your appearance at any minute."

"Ha! it is so, is it? You are clever in your deceit; but I shall catch you some day. I have only to wait with patience."

"I practise no deceit," protested the woman—"Heaven knows I do not!"

"Bah, woman!"

"One would have thought," she continued, "that in this lonely, out-of-the-way place you would have had no grounds for your absurd and jealous fears."

"Silence, I say!"

"I will be silent no longer. I have been too much your slave. I ought to have asserted my rights more vigorously long ago. It was only the belief that I should hear no more of your miserable jealousy that I consented to a living burial in this place, so far removed as it is from all human habitations. And now that I have yielded to your foolish whims so far you are only ten times worse!"

"So you are going to try and carry things off with a high hand, are you, my lady? You had better not try it on, perhaps, though" (and here he ground his teeth savagely) "you have one of your lovers not far off, who you think will come forward to your assistance."

"Oh! Ned, how can you say such things?" A tinge of alarm perceptible in her voice. "I——"

"It had better not be so," he said, wrathfully. "It would be bad for the man that I found anywhere near this place!"

"Ned—Ned, if it were not that I feel that you are upon this subject completely dead and deaf to all reason, I should speak, but I have lost all heart in doing so."

The man growled something inarticulately, and by the sound which Lord Harcliffe next heard it would seem as though he had flung himself heavily and recklessly into a chair.

"Oh, Ned," said the unfortunate woman, after a pause, "if I could only persuade you to cast off this causeless, foolish jealousy! You see how it poisons and embitters the lives of both of us! Think of the past, and what we were then—think of the present, and behold what we are now!"

"And whose fault is it, I should like to know?"

"Not mine."

"You lie, woman—it is yours! You with your everlasting glances at the men—you with the palpable attentions you paid others, even before my face, drove me completely mad!"

"Oh, Ned, you know that you are not justified in laying the blame on me! I have been, and am still, a true, tender, loving wife to you! Yes, in spite of all the hard treatment and little kindness that I have met with at your hands. Will nothing cure you of this jealous feeling—will nothing convince you that I am wholly yours?"

The man was silent.

Lord Harcliffe was wondering what would be the best step for him to take.

But the next words uttered by the man had the effect of arresting the whole of his attention.

"Susan," he said, "I will believe you—I will cast off this mad jealousy for ever."

"Oh, Ned!" said the woman, with a moan of overwhelming joy.

"Yes, for ever. Do you understand me?"

"I do, Ned—I do."

"But there is a condition."

"Name it, then—name it."

"I will."

The man rose.

Lord Harcliffe crept like a shadow to the door and peeped through the chinks.

He saw the husband reach down from a shelf a square thick book, which he placed on the table close to where the woman was.

She had sunk down upon her knees close to the chair from which her husband had just sprung.

Her face had an unquiet look.

She was wondering what the strange actions of her husband portended.

"Ha, ha!" he said, with a discordant laugh, which subsided with startling suddenness. "I sha'n't be jealous any more—oh no!—never any more—that is——"

He checked himself abruptly.

"What, Ned—what?"

"If you stand the test," he said, significantly.

"The test?" faltered the poor creature. "Alas! What do you mean? What test?"

"You shall see," he answered, with grim calmness. "Give me your hand."

She extended it to him mechanically, helplessly, and made a slight movement as though about to rise.

[THE OATH OF FRIENDSHIP.]

"No," he cried, suddenly, "remain where you are and as you are. So."

He then opened the book at random, somewhere near the middle.

The woman gazed at him affrightedly.

"You know what book this is?" he said, vehemently. "It is the Bible: your mother's Bible. You remember it?"

"I do. What of it?"

"Place your hand upon the open page. That is it."

The poor woman trembled in every limb now.

An awful dread seemed to hold possession of her heart.

Her husband's eyes glowed like those of a demon.

"Now, then," he cried, in cracked tones, "I am about to be satisfied now—I am going to be jealous no longer. How strange it will be, now, if I have been mistaken all these years, and done you so great an injustice!"

"You have been mistaken," said the wife. "You have done me an injury—believe me, you have."

"I shall believe you soon—very soon now. Pay attention to what I am going to say."

"Indeed, I am listening intently to your every word."

"Then, with your hand upon that open Bible, swear to me that during my last absence you have spoken to no man—that no man has been here. Swear that, and kiss the sacred page afterwards, to seal your oath, and I will believe you: I will never be jealous again—I will never doubt you any more."

The woman seemed to grow as rigid as stone.

"Come—come!" he said. "Why do you hesitate? You have ever been full of your protestations when I have never felt inclined to listen to them or to attach any importance to them; now, when I put you to the proof, you shrink back. What does it mean?"

The poor woman was silent.

"Come!" cried her husband, raising his voice more and more. "Swear—swear, I tell you! unless you want my jealousy to continue."

"Will you hear me, Ned?"

"Will you swear?"

"Will you listen to——"

"I will hear no excuses. Once more I ask you, will you swear?"

"I will."

"Come, then."

"I will swear that you have ever been jealous without a cause, and that I have never given you reason for being so."

"Cunning devil!" he cried, shaking with suppressed passion. "So you would palter with the oath, would you? But I am not to be so easily cajoled! I will reword the oath."

"You need not."

"You remember my words, then?"

"Perfectly."

"In one word, will you swear?"

"Not just what you propose."

"Enough!" he shrieked, rather than said, and closing the Bible violently the while. "I am satisfied now, and satisfied in the way that I expected. I was wondering whether you would damn your soul by swearing to so black a lie!"

"Oh, Ned!"

"Don't Ned me, you baggage! Off—off! For shame! I knew well enough that men did visit the cottage during my absence from it. And do you think me so great a fool that I should not know their reason for doing it? Foul wretch, begone!"

The woman sprang to her feet.

She had been a poor, yielding creature up to this moment; but now that so foul a wrong was accumulated upon her, she stood like some animal forced at bay.

Her attitude was splendidly demonstrative of injured innocence.

Her air of dignity was sublime.

Even her blinded husband was moved by it.

He stepped back a pace, and regarded her without speaking.

"You have trodden out the love in my heart, Ned—trodden it out with your cruel words!"

He greeted the words with a mocking laugh.

"Remember," she said, "I love you no longer. I shall never have the least respect for you again. I have loved and suffered much; but the time for endurance is over now."

"Love, eh?—endurance! Come, come, I like that—like it much. But if you think you are going to brazen out your shame you are deceived. Impudent creature, quit my roof! You shall not remain under it another hour!"

"I have done very wrong by remaining under it so long," she answered; "I ought to have left it long ago. I can see my error now, and can tell what it will cost me."

"Begone," cried her husband, now quite beside himself with rage—"begone, I say! Under this roof you shall not stay another moment! Do you hear me? Begone—begone, I say!"

With a faltering voice, and with her whole frame convulsed with sobs, the poor victim of jealousy moved towards the door.

But the husband, starting suddenly, as though he had just remembered something which he had well-nigh forgotten, cried:

"Stay—stay! Go not yet! You shall not leave until your shame and guilt are made complete! Your guilty lover—who I am convinced is secreted here, and is too great a coward to show his face to the man he has so deeply wronged—shall go with you!"

He advanced towards the door communicating with the inner room.

Lord Harcliffe still remained listening.

He was so surprised at what he saw, and at the strange complexion that could be placed upon his visit, that he felt himself unable to summon up sufficient effort to interfere.

But now the crisis was at hand.

That in the frenzy of his jealousy the man would attempt some deed of violence was likely enough, and so he prepared himself for an encounter.

But it was just at the moment when the man placed his hand upon the latch that sounds arose which arrested his attention.

But although so taken by surprise as to be unable to raise the latch, yet he did not remove his hand from it.

The wife, too, started and looked terrified.

"Good Heavens!" she cried. "What noise is that? What does it mean?"

It was a sudden rushing sound which had at first come upon their ears.

But now the trampling of footsteps and the murmur of voices became audible.

"What can these men want?" exclaimed the woman.

Some heavy blows were dealt upon the door as she pronounced the words.

Lord Harcliffe was the one least taken by surprise by this occurrence.

He had no need to ask himself a single question, or speculate for a moment as to who these new-comers might be.

His heart told him that it was his pursuers, who had tracked him to his resting-place.

How they had done so was beyond his comprehension.

But they were there, and being there, he had but one course to adopt.

That was to turn the whole of his attention to flight.

And yet it was, as the reader can imagine, most unwillingly that he turned away from the rudely-made door.

Never was he more unwilling to fly.

But his life demanded it.

He was anxious to try his best to disabuse the man of the opinion he had formed, and if he had thought there was only a reasonable prospect of success he might have run some risk of capture.

Knowing, however, full well there was not, he made his way noiselessly to the window, and reached it just at the moment when the officers, impatient at no response being given to the summons, opened the door of the cottage.

The attitudes and the flushed countenances of the husband and wife were quite enough to attract immediate attention, and the officer paused upon the threshold without speaking.

The woman uttered a cry of terror.

Her husband turned a lowering gaze upon the intruders and said, angrily:

"Well—well, what want you here? What is your business?"

"If you will take my advice," said the foremost officer, advancing, "you will keep a civil tongue in your head."

"What for?"

"It may serve to keep you out of trouble, that's all."

"Trouble! What trouble? What do you mean?"

"Come—come, you must understand all about it. You know as well as anybody what we are here for."

He looked amazed.

But the officer, attributing his behaviour to a very different cause from the real one, continued, though he spoke in a much lower tone of voice than he had hitherto employed:

"Come, now," he said, "let us have no beating about the bush. You may as well make a good thing of this as not."

"What do you mean?" asked the man, with an amazement too great to be feigned.

"We want the Black Highwayman."

"The Black Highwayman!"

"Yes; and we have tolerably certain knowledge that he is here or somewhere close at hand. Put us quietly upon his scent, and you shall have a hundred—that is, I mean fifty pounds out of the reward."

"Reward!—highwayman! I do not understand you. Do you mean to say that——"

The officer uttered an angry exclamation.

"I see we have only lost time here," he said, addressing his companions. "Come, now, then, be quick: let us search this place!"

"Search it for what—for whom?" asked the man, going to the door of communication and looking as though he was half inclined to bar the progress of anyone.

"For the Black Highwayman!" repeated the officer. "Stand aside there! Obstruct us in our duty at your peril!"

The poor woman, who, overcome by all that had occurred, had sunk upon a chair in a half-fainting state, now lost consciousness altogether, and fell heavily to the floor.

But her husband never stirred a step, or made the slightest motion towards going to her assistance.

The only notice he took of it was shown by a darker contraction of his brows.

"Why, man, what is amiss?" asked the officer. Would you let her lie there unaided?"

"Curses!" he said, bitterly. "She can lie there and rot for all I care! Curse her, I say!"

"Well, you seem a pleasant couple! But come on, my lads; we have something more important to do than attend to domestic squabbles."

He opened the door as he spoke, for the man, overawed by the authoritative manner of the officers, made no opposition to his doing so.

No sooner was the door opened than a gush of cold night air came upon the officer's face.

At the same instant the window was heard to close violently.

"May I be d—d," cried the officer, "if the bird has not flown! I would stake a thousand pounds upon it!"

With more angry curses upon his lips, he dashed across the sleeping-chamber.

The window was a latticed one, with a swinging casement.

This was unfastened, and flapped backwards and forwards in the wind.

"It's small," said the officer, as he pushed it open. "One would hardly think a man could have got through so——"

He was interrupted by a voice outside.

"Help—help," cried some one, in loud tones—"help, I say! Quick—quick! He is here!"

The night which had set in was an unusually dark one; and about the lone cottage the obscurity was unusually great on account of the dense masses of trees by which it was surrounded.

Therefore this officer, though he looked through the window immediately upon hearing the voice, failed to see anybody.

"Quick!" he cried to his comrades. "Round to the back! We ought to have gone there first. I am afraid we shall be too late now."

The officers hardly waited to hear what he said, but rushed out of the cottage precipitately.

The one in command looked at the window, and seemed half inclined to get through it because unquestionably the nearest way to the point he wished to reach.

But he possessed too much rotundity of body to make a passage through that particularly narrow casement at all practicable, and with a sudden dash he rushed after the others.

As the reader has seen already, Lord Harcliffe had contrived to leave the inner room.

The window was small, but he was slim and agile, and therefore with very little difficulty and loss of time he forced his way through it.

"How fortunate it should be so dark!" he said, as he glanced around him. "How they have tracked me here passes my comprehension entirely; but with such a gloom as this hanging over all things, surely Phantom will be quickly able to elude them."

Every movement that the Black Highwayman made after forcing his way through the window was characterised by the utmost caution.

That some of the officers were watching the exterior of the cottage he considered a matter of certainty; and his only wonder was that he should succeed in getting through the window at all without being observed.

It was well, too, that he carefully noted the position of the shed in which he had left his horse, otherwise he would have had no little trouble in making his way to it.

But when once he had passed through the door without the least outcry having been raised by his enemies, he felt himself secure.

But dark as it was outside, the obscurity was nothing when compared with that which filled the shed, for it was not provided with any opening through which a glimmer of light could enter.

But Phantom, glad to find his master near him, neighed softly, and the next moment Lord Harcliffe felt the noble creature's head against his breast.

The expectation of being suddenly surprised had caused him not to remove any of the trappings.

All he had done was to take out the bit, without removing the bridle, and to let out the girths.

It was easy enough, despite the intense darkness, for him to put these things right.

Only a few seconds, too, were consumed in these proceedings.

Pushing open the door of the shed, he waited a moment before he ventured to emerge.

But the deep darkness and the intense silence were reassuring, and so, without any further hesitation, he crossed the threshold.

"What on earth can they be doing?" he asked himself. "I do believe that, unlikely as it seemed a few moments ago, I shall be able to get away unseen."

But this anticipation was destined to disappointment.

No sooner had he got a couple of paces from the shed when he heard the hasty rush of feet.

"Discovered!" he ejaculated.

But all he did was to prepare to mount with all possible speed.

His foot was in the stirrup when he felt himself seized by some one from behind, who immediately called out for help.

Lord Harcliffe released his foot from the stirrup, and struck out with it with such force that the man who had seized him went reeling back half a dozen paces, uttering dismal groans as he went.

Before he could recover himself from this totally unexpected attack, Lord Harcliffe had fairly seated himself in the saddle.

But he was not a moment too soon.

Had his contest with the man been at all prolonged, he would have had the whole body of police officers upon him.

As it was, he was ready to ride away just at the moment when they came rushing round the corner of the cottage.

But they were on foot, and Lord Harcliffe testified his exultation by giving utterance to a loud laugh.

"Defiance!" he cried—"I defy you all! Now, Phantom, away—away!"

With a snort, Phantom dashed off at a gallop.

His rider, however, kept some check upon the rein, feeling certain that there was no necessity for extraordinary speed.

Not only was the darkness greatly in his favour, but he knew that his enemies would have to mount, and this with them was by no means a trifling matter.

The time consumed by it would, he calculated, give him a sufficient start to elude them altogether.

"Confusion on them!" he cried at length. "How pertinaciously they keep upon my trail! I would give much to know by what earthly means they could have discovered my whereabouts. I fancied that I had left behind me no trace which they could follow up. What am I to think of it?"

The circumstance was one well calculated to plunge him into serious thought.

It made him aware that it would be by no means so easy as he fancied to shake them off.

He might take every precaution again in the present instance only to find in the moment when he was most congratulating himself upon his security that they were close at his elbow.

He ground his teeth with angry, impotent rage

"It is so unfortunate," he exclaimed. "Were it for myself I should not care; but there is my faithful ally, Pharoah, in want of aid. He will rely upon me, and his reliance, preventing him from taking any vigorous steps on his own behalf, will prove his destruction."

This was a thought maddening in the extreme to Lord

Harcliffe, and one that he could not bear to dwell upon.

But his reflections were suddenly broken in upon by an unexpected occurrence.

From the time he had left the cottage Phantom had been going at a sweeping gallop across the country.

Seeing that there was nothing but open meadows surrounding him, Lord Harcliffe allowed Phantom to exercise his own instinct.

But suddenly, and without giving his rider the least warning, Phantom came to a dead stop.

CHAPTER XCVI.

THE OFFICERS IN PURSUIT OF LORD HARCLIFFE MEET WITH A MISHAP.

So very unexpectedly did his horse come to a standstill that Lord Harcliffe felt himself bumped very unpleasantly upon the saddle.

A less practised rider would certainly have been sent flying over the horse's head, for even he only saved himself with difficulty.

"Why, Phantom," he exclaimed, "what ails you, boy?"

Phantom stood still with his forefeet planted closely together in a way which seemed very resolutely to express his intention of not going any further.

"I ought not to have given myself up so much to anxious thought," the highwayman said. "I have had a narrow escape, and no doubt I owe to my horse's sagacity an immunity from a still worse accident."

So saying, he leaned forward upon Phantom's neck so as to see what there was in advance; for that there was an obstruction of some sort or other in his path he felt certain.

Phantom stood without manifesting any sensations of terror.

The darkness was intense, and it was not until the highwayman had strained his eyes for some moments that he was able to make out what it was in front of him.

At length, however, he discovered that his horse had halted on the brink of some water, the extent of which he could not make out.

"What can it be," he said—"a pool, or stream, or what? Not a pool, I'll be bound, or Phantom would have skirted it."

From the position he occupied in the saddle it was impossible for him to come to a correct conclusion on this point, and so he dismounted.

But just as his feet touched the earth he heard a sound which had the effect of enchaining the whole of his attention.

He remained for some seconds quite motionless.

"They ride hard," he said. "Surely they must have some mysterious means of following in my trail. But let them ride," he added, with a scornful laugh. "If they come on as far as this, unless they are better riders than I take them to be, and unless their horses are as sagacious as Phantom, they are likely to be treated to a cold bath."

Considering the narrow escape the Black Highwayman himself had had, this seemed to be a very probable occurrence indeed.

Turning now towards the water, he tried to make out its character.

His first discovery was that Phantom had stopped just at the right point.

Another step in advance, and he could not have saved himself, for he had paused on the very brink of a steep bank.

So precipitous was it that the highwayman had no little difficulty in descending it.

On reaching the bottom he took a long and careful look about him.

"This must be a river," he said at length, after several seconds' careful observation; "and, so far as I can tell in this darkness, a wide one too. A river. Let me think. What part of the country can I be in?"

But he was unable to come to any satisfactory conclusion upon this point.

But the more he saw, the more cause did he find to congratulate himself on possessing a steed that had so much sagacity.

A fall down that steep, shelving bank into the wide river, at a moment when such an occurrence was anything but expected, would have been a very serious matter.

"I shall not venture to cross over by this dim light," he said; "I might get carried down the stream, or else reach a point where the bank is as steep as this, in which case it would be impossible to get Phantom out. Besides, if I keep on this side of the stream I shall not be going quite so far from London; and, after all, that is about as important as anything."

But he found the task of scrambling up the stony river's bank much more difficult than descending it, and before reaching the top his foot slipped dangerously twice or thrice.

"Brave boy!" he said, patting Phantom's neck. "I shall not forget this good service. It is one more to the long account I——"

He checked himself, for the sound made by his pursuers came more and more unmistakably upon his ears.

They were, indeed, much closer at hand than he was aware of.

For a second or so he stood hesitating whether he should follow the course of the river to the left or the right.

At length he decided upon taking this direction.

No sooner was this determination made than he mounted and put it into execution.

"I will go only at a trot," he said. "The ground is soft, and it is hardly within the bounds of possibility for them to hear me, and the darkness puts seeing effectually out of the question."

The highwayman's reason for lingering will be easily comprehended.

He was curious to the utmost degree to know how the officers would fare upon gaining the river's bank.

His own confident anticipation was that the foremost of them at least would get a good ducking.

He was anxious to know this, not merely on account of the satisfaction it would give him to find that his foes had met with such a mishap, but because he would know that it must result in an interruption to the pursuit.

Slower and slower became his trot, until at length he stopped his horse altogether.

This was on the banks of the river, and, as he judged, not so far off the point the officers were making for as would render what took place inaudible to him.

On they came.

As he listened to the regular beat of their horses' hoofs he could hardly repress a chuckle.

If anything, they were making greater speed than they had been a few moments previously.

"I can account for that," said the highwayman, mentally. "They have ceased to hear Phantom's feet, and have grown fearful I have outdistanced them. How hard they ride! Nothing can save them—nothing. I had feared that some one among their number might be sufficiently well acquainted with the geography of this part of the country to put them on their guard. But it does not seem that such is the case. No—no. They come—on—on—faster and faster yet!"

The air was very still, and the highwayman's acute sense of hearing enabled him to judge very exactly the position of his foes.

At frequent intervals the cracking of the dog-whips which they carried could be heard, and oftener still the oaths and curses which they bestowed upon the poor beasts they were urging to the very utmost extent of their powers.

Nearer—nearer still they came.

Lord Harcliffe held his breath.

"Nothing can save them now," he said—"nothing! Ah!"

A strange succession of sounds now smote upon his ears.

It then became quite certain that the police officers knew nothing whatever about the broad sluggish river that lay right across their path.

The horses, urged on to their utmost speed, and half maddened by the cruel treatment they had received, almost without exception dashed into the flood.

Those who did pause upon the brink stopped so suddenly and so awkwardly that the riders were propelled from the saddle almost as though they had been discharged from a cannon's mouth.

Such a splashing and uproar succeeded as baffles all description.

Lord Harcliffe's triumph was almost too great for him to restrain it.

Never was discomfiture more complete.

"Surely—surely," he said to himself, "I shall have no further trouble with them to-night. Now is the time for me to gallop off; and yet—and yet I feel that I cannot tear myself away until I have learned a little more about the condition they are in."

That the Black Highwayman ought to have embraced this unusually favourable opportunity of riding off is unquestionable.

But his desire to ascertain how his foes fared triumphed over all feelings of safety or even of discretion.

Instead of turning Phantom's head either in the direction of the open country or else of the metropolis, he deliberately set to work to retrace his steps.

The danger of doing so was no doubt great, but yet not so great as might be at first supposed.

The officers, without exception, would be too busy in looking after their own safety to be able to bestow much attention upon any slight sound which they might hear.

From this cause it happened that, by exercising a little caution, Lord Harcliffe succeeded in walking Phantom very close to his enemies indeed.

Dismal cries filled the air, mingled with the snorting of the horses as they struggled furiously to regain a footing on the bank.

Had the river in that part not been so shallow as it was, there is little doubt that the adventure would have had a tragical termination.

But it was wide, and even in mid-stream not more than five feet deep, while near the banks the depth would be reckoned by inches.

But there was water enough to cause a prodigious floundering to take place.

The current was so slight as to be scarcely perceptible.

One by one, then, the officers managed to crawl to the shore, where they stood dripping, shivering, and swearing, and looking more like drowned rats than human beings.

So intent was Lord Harcliffe on observing all their motions that he did not hear so soon as he should have done some sounds which would have warned him against tarrying any longer.

Those sounds were caused by the approach of a body of mounted men.

It was, indeed, one of those troops which within the last few days had been appointed to patrol the roads.

The tremendous uproar which had followed the fall of the officers into the river had reached their ears, and the sound was quite enough to make them aware that something of a very unusual character had occurred.

Anything was agreeable as a change from the monotony which they had experienced hitherto, and, guided by the din, they made their way with all speed to the spot.

Their horses were quite fresh, and of pretty good quality, so that they were not long in gaining the scene of action.

So absorbed was Lord Harcliffe that it was not until they had approached to within a distance of not much more than a hundred yards that he became aware of their presence.

The discovery of them so very close at hand came upon him like a clap of thunder.

The shock deprived him of his usual presence of mind, and he remained without moving a single muscle.

"Hilloa there!" cried the foremost of the new-comers, reining-in his panting steed. "Hilloa there, I say! What the devil is the matter? Cannot any of you speak?"

No articulate reply followed, and the darkness, of course, was too dense to enable them to form anything approaching an accurate view of the case.

"Out with your lanterns!" said the one who had before spoken.

His command was obeyed instantly.

Seven round globes of light were immediately displayed; and the Black Highwayman knew by that he had at least eight more of his foes to contend with.

Still, he did not move.

For one thing, he was aware that, being quite out of the sphere of light cast by the lantern lenses, there was much less likelihood of the officers seeing him than there was before.

But the lights were a great advantage to him, inasmuch as they enabled him accurately to determine the position of his foes.

"By jingo!" cried the same commanding voice, "here is a set out! What the devil does it mean? Have none of you a word to say? Speak, some of you!"

"Speak!" said one of the soused officers, in a spluttering voice, for he had no more succeeded in ridding his stomach of water than he had succeeded in wringing his clothes. "Who the devil could speak, I should like to know! Look here—wherever I stand there is a lake in a moment!"

The ludicrous manner in which this complaint was made caused the whole troop to burst out into a roar of laughter.

And, indeed, the mere spectacle which these officers presented to the eye was quite sufficient to excite the risibility of the gravest breast.

Without exception, they were not only hatless, but wigless, and the deprivation of this last article of attire gave them a most ludicrous appearance.

Lord Harcliffe could see this even from the distance, and he had no little trouble in restraining himself from joining in the hearty laughter of the police officers.

"Why, how the devil," cried the commander of the fresh troop, after stifling his laughter somewhat—"how the devil came you all to ride into the river? for that seems to be what you have done."

The question aroused the ire of the unfortunate men.

"The devil! D—n the river!" they exclaimed, in chorus. "We were hard after the Black Highwayman! How were we to know the river was there, or to see it, such a damnably dark night as this is!"

"The Black Highwayman!" echoed the leader of the second troop, becoming all gravity and attention in an instant. "Do you mean to say that he is anywhere about this part?"

"About this part!" repeated the other, scornfully. "If you were at all fit for duty you would have known all about it, and not be grinning there like a death's head on a mopstick!"

"Come—come, none of that! Do you mean to say that you pursued the Black Highwayman to somewhere near this point?"

"Of course we did; and we were in the fairest way possible of capturing him when this cursed mishap occurred."

"Tell us, then—tell us, then. If he is near we will be after him at once, if you will but give us a hint of the way we ought to go; and you may depend if we are successful that we sha'n't object to giving you a share of the reward."

The officers who had been soused in the river, so far from being discouraged in their enterprise, only burned all the more to accomplish it.

The feeling they had against the highwayman had increased tenfold.

To him they attributed the dreadful discomfiture they had met with, and burned to have their revenge upon him for it."

They were now quite raised above the inducement which a reward held out.

It was with a personal feeling of hatred that they were now animated.

"After him, then, at once!" they cried. "He can't have got far. You have not passed him on the road, have you?"

"No," said the leader; "I will answer for that."

"Well, then, he has either crossed the river or gone along its banks to the right."

"That's the most likely. Come on, comrades; we will have a try what we can do. At any rate, we shall warm our blood a little, and even that will be agreeable."

"Go on, then. But, in the devil's name, where are we? We must get shelter somewhere. We are every one soaked to the skin!"

"This is the river Ouse."

"We are near Huntingdon, then?"

"Yes, within a few miles of it."

"And — and," said the half-drowned officer, with chattering teeth, "where is the nearest place of shelter where we can dry our clothes and get a drop of something to drink?"

"The nearest place to here," answered the other "is the old Greyhound Inn."

"And where is that?"

"Just across the river. Go down a little way, and you will come to a ford. You won't have much trouble to cross over."

"And then?"

"Why, then, if you use your eyes, you will see a small twinkling light among the trees; make your way to that, and you will be right."

"A thousand thanks."

"We have been here on the look-out for Captain Hawk."

"Any success?"

"Nothing but disappointment."

"Come then, my lads," said the crestfallen officers, "it seems we can do nothing but get under cover, and leave the chase to our friends. Good night to you; and may you have better luck than we have met with!"

"If he is anywhere near, we shall have a good chance of capturing him. Our horses are all picked, and in capital condition."

"Off you go, then!"

Lord Harcliffe listened thus far with the most eager interest.

But now he felt that he had listened quite long enough.

It was time for him to be gone if he was to have the least chance of safety.

As regarded getting away from where he was unheard by his foes, circumstances greatly favoured him.

The ground near the river was so soft and muddy that Phantom's footsteps were almost inaudible.

At first the Black Highwayman allowed him to go only at a walk, by degrees increasing his pace as he got further and further away, until at length he was going at full gallop.

"In search of Captain Hawk," he said to himself, the while, thinking of the latter part of the conversation he had overheard. "The name is familiar to me: I have heard something of his exploits. I wonder whether accident will ever bring us face to face?"

But the exigencies of his situation were too great to allow him to continue vain and unprofitable speculations.

Having learned that the officers who were on his track were furnished with horses of superior quality, it behoved him to give the whole of his attention to getting away from them as speedily as possible.

Favoured by the darkness, however, it was not long before he succeeded in getting out of the way of them, and, though he paused several times to listen, not the faintest sound was carried to his ears.

"All is well now," he said at last, when the most attentive listening prolonged for several moments failed to bring to his ears the faintest sound indicative of the coming of his foes. "At length surely I may congratulate myself that I have got rid of them. Now what am I to do? If I am to believe the officers, I must be within a few miles of Huntingdon. I could scarcely have believed they had driven me so far from London. How am I to get back? That is the point which demands my closest attention."

He remained for several moments in deep thought.

"The worst of it is," he said at length, for he found it some relief to utter his thoughts aloud—"the worst of it is, I am all but unacquainted with this part of the country, and which way to turn I scarcely know. Could I only make sure of the direction in which London lies, I would at all risks take it. As I am placed, I am more likely to go wrong than right; and to inquire the way would only be to furnish the police officers with a clue to get upon my track."

Thus, turn as he would, Lord Harcliffe found himself beset by difficulties.

Yet anything was preferable and more endurable than inactivity.

Accordingly, he once more set his steed in motion, though he was absolutely without a guide.

"Chance alone can aid me," he concluded, "and so I will give chance every opportunity of doing so."

He was fully in earnest when he spoke, and so let the reins fall quite slackly upon Phantom's neck, so that he could proceed just in what direction he thought proper.

It was a wild but exhilarating ride.

The spirited horse, finding that his master exercised no control over him, galloped on at a race-horse speed.

Lord Harcliffe kept what look-out he was able, so that he might have warning of the presence of any obstacle.

But Phantom held on until a broad and well-kept road, which looked almost like the highway, was reached.

Here Lord Harcliffe came to a halt.

All around him was quite still.

"If, now, I only knew which way to turn, he said, "this road would be likely enough to take me in the required direction. How shall I decide it? Ha! what is that?"

A tall white object, two or three feet from him, attracted his attention.

Going closer, he found out what it was.

"A finger-post!" he ejaculated. "Now, if I have only the means about me of procuring a temporary light, all will be well. Should I speak the truth if I said Fortune was not my friend?"

The circumstance was a strange one, and, but for the fact that the finger-post had been newly painted, Lord Harcliffe would never have seen it at all.

CHAPTER XCVII.

LORD HARCLIFFE STOPS THE STAGE-COACH, BUT IS STILL FOILED IN HIS ATTEMPTS TO REACH LONDON.

TRIVIAL as this occurrence may be deemed, it produced a very marked effect upon the highwaymen.

He looked upon it as a favourable omen, and suffered his mind to be filled with the pleasing notion that henceforward he would have fewer objects in the way of carrying out the purpose he was bent upon.

Under the influence of this feeling, he slipped lightheartedly from the saddle, and set to work to procure a light, without which it was not possible for him to avail himself of the information contained upon the finger post.

He was unfurnished with any of those phosphorous matches which were at that time just creeping into use, and known, as they were for many years after, as "thieves' matches."

Nor had he any tinder-box; but he had a pistol and gunpowder, and by this means he hoped to attain his object.

The covering of the packet of documents which had cost him so much trouble to procure furnished him with a kind of torch.

Placing it upon a stone, he covered one end of it with a small heap of gunpowder.

The latter he ignited by means of the flint of his pistol.

There was a flash and a puff.

The paper was not properly alight; but with a little trouble he got it to blaze freely, and as soon as this was the case he hastily re-mounted his horse.

As the night was a particularly calm one, the paper was not extinguished.

He was only just in time to reach the post, however, before it was consumed.

Not until he had managed to make out the words "To London," and noted the direction in which the arm pointed.

"All is well now," he said, with an air of ease and confidence which seemed strangely at variance with his real situation. "This must be the high-road; and if I can only keep out of the way of those troublesome police officers, it will not take me so very long to reach London."

Full of these hopeful and pleasant feelings, he started off at a trot—a pace which he knew full well his horse could keep up for a great length of time without much exhaustion, and which got over the ground very rapidly indeed.

He was not destined, however, to go very far uninterruptedly.

Before he had left the finger-post a dozen miles behind him, his sharp sense of hearing told him that there was something approaching.

Immediately upon making this discovery, he pulled up in order to ascertain what this should be.

The ringing sounds of horses' hoofs could first be distinguished; but a peculiar although very faint rumbling sound with which they were accompanied informed him that a vehicle of some importance was coming.

"Four horses!" he exclaimed, after listening for a moment with deep attention. "If it is so—and I feel certain I am right—it must be the York coach which is approaching. I shall know directly by the lights."

As he finished speaking, he fell into a fit of deep musing.

His thoughts were very absorbing, for by his manner it almost seemed as though he had forgotten all that had just occurred.

He roused himself with a sudden start, and looked towards London.

In the distance two twinkling and scarcely discernible lights could be perceived.

"It is the coach!" he cried. "And now, then, what am I to do? The time for deliberation is short. I must decide."

He passed his hand over his brow thoughtfully.

"In my enterprise," he said, speaking very deliberately, as though carefully weighing every syllable, "money is essential, and money, too, of considerable amount. Without it I can do little or nothing. Not anticipating that the crash of discovery would come so soon, I made no provision, as I ought to have done, for a reverse of fortune. But the means by which I filled my purse then is still open to me. Why should I hesitate?"

He paused again.

"It is only the extra danger and delay," he concluded. "And what is the first? Is not my position already so perilous that it cannot be made more dangerous? And as for the delay, that cannot but be trifling. At any rate, it shall be done."

He came to his resolution only just in time.

The York coach was now within a very short distance of him indeed—so short that it seemed scarcely possible for him to carry out his intention.

As well as he could, he inspected his weapons, and put them in readiness for use.

After that, as soon as he had gathered the reins tightly in his hand, the coach was upon him.

The course of action he pursued was rather singular, but highly successful.

Instead of calling out to the coachman, and attempting to bring the vehicle to a standstill by threatening him, he turned Phantom's head towards York, and, keeping close under the shadow of the hedgerows, urged him onwards at a gallop.

As he had fully anticipated, the darkness was too intense for the driver to discover that there was any-one on the road in advance of him.

It must be understood that Lord Harcliffe by no means allowed Phantom to go at full speed, but managed so that he kept just in advance of the fore horses harnessed to the coach.

Then, gradually drawing in the rein and getting more towards the centre of the highway, he contrived to get abreast with the first horses.

By stretching out his hand, he, by a dexterous movement, caught hold of the reins.

It was not until this moment that the driver became aware that anything of an unusual character was taking place.

He uttered a strange cry—obviously one of alarm and dread, for he could not make out just what was amiss.

Then, ere he could recover from the first shock of his surprise, he was almost flung from his seat by the suddenness with which the coach was brought to a stand-still.

Lord Harcliffe had contrived to do this with all the neatness conceivable.

Keeping a firm grasp upon the rein which he had so adroitly seized, and guiding Phantom with the other hand, he compelled the foremost horse to wheel quite round, and the others who were harnessed to him of necessity followed his example.

He continued tugging at the rein until the stage-coach was broadside across the road; and when he stopped, one of the front wheels had run very dangerously some distance up the ditch bank, where it remained firmly imbedded in the soft soil.

Scarcely, however, had the vibration of the vehicle ceased than the traces were cut; and the horses, thus freed from all control, and much alarmed by what had happened, started off at full speed along the road as though they were bent upon getting to their well-known stable at the earliest moment.

All this happened, as we may say, in the twinkling of an eye.

But now a tremendous uproar ensued.

The guard discharged his blunderbuss, but he was too hasty and flustered to do any execution with it.

The passengers on the roof, indeed, were in the greatest danger, for that seemed to be the direction which the greater portion of the storm of missiles took.

The highwayman and his horse were untouched.

The discharge of the cumbrous firearm doubled the confusion.

Nevertheless, Lord Harcliffe raised his voice to so high a pitch that what he said was audible above all other sounds.

"You are at my mercy," he cried, "and resistance will only bring death. If you accede to my demands you know the worst which can befall you. If you refuse, the consequences will be yours, not mine."

"Perhaps, then," said a voice, "you will take that in full of all your demands, you infernal scoundrel!"

The words were accompanied by the discharge of a pistol.

Lord Harcliffe at the same instant felt that he was shot, though he felt almost certain the hurt was not a serious one.

This incident had a wonderful effect upon all the other passengers.

They became as silent as death.

No doubt they fully expected to see the highwayman fall headlong into the roadway.

But there he sat, calm enough, and apparently quite unharmed.

"I never fail to return a shot," he exclaimed, in tones that sounded strangely clear amid the peculiar silence; "and what is more, I never fail to hit my mark!"

He advanced to the coach door as he spoke.

He had noted who had fired, for the light at the side of the stage-coach happened to fall full upon his face.

Lord Harcliffe, with apparently an utter disregard for personal danger, thrust the barrel of his pistol through the window, and pressed the muzzle against his assailant's breast.

"Death is certain," he said, "yet I give you one moment before I pull the trigger. But at the least sign of resistance, you die as surely as you are now breathing."

Lord Harcliffe's resolute and determined manner seemed to produce a paralysing effect upon everybody.

Each person, without exception, felt that he was at the mercy of the highwayman.

Fear prevented Lord Harcliffe's would-be destroyer from moving or uttering a single syllable.

But finding that no one made the slightest movement towards extricating him from his unpleasant position, he contrived to gasp out:

"Help—help! Surely you will not all sit there and see me murdered in cold blood! Help—help, I say!"

"He will be an unwise man who makes the slightest attempt at interference," cried Lord Harcliffe; and the way in which he spoke fully convinced every one of his hearers that he meant what he said.

Finding this appeal in vain, and seeing that the highwayman's countenance still expressed invincible resolution, his cheek turned pale, and he trembled from head to foot.

Vain as he believed it to be, the impulse of self-preservation compelled him to make an appeal to the highwayman.

"Surely—surely," he exclaimed, "robber and outcast as you are, you would not slaughter me in cold blood for merely endeavouring to preserve my property!"

"You have heard my determination," said the highwayman, in cold even tones, which sent an additional thrill through the hearts of those who heard him.

"And have you no mercy?"

"None."

"Alas!"

"There is one and only one way in which you may save yourself."

"There—there is an alternative, then?" And by the

manner in which he spoke it was tolerably plain that he had given himself up for dead.

"There is."

"Name it—name it!"

"If you refuse or hesitate a moment your fate is sealed. By common fairness, I am entitled to return your shot."

"Name your condition."

"It is that you exert your influence to persuade your fellow-passengers to part with their purses. I want nothing else. Let me have them, and no further violence shall be offered to a soul."

"But—but——"

"Do you object?" said Lord Harcliffe, cocking the pistol.

The sharp click was decisive.

"No—no; I will do your bidding. Come, my friends," he added, "we are helpless; he is the master of the situation. Give him what he demands, and so secure yourselves from further hurt."

"Let there be no demur," said Lord Harcliffe, resolutely, "or I swear I will not depart until I have wrested from you every article which you possess. Do you decide?"

The passengers were almost too terrified to make any movement whatever, and the slight hesitation which they showed arose more from dismay than disinclination.

"Only your purses—only your purses," said the trembling traveller. "Remember, you are to lose nothing else."

"And you are to save your life," growled one.

"And which is of the most value?"

"That depends."

"Give me your purses," he continued, in an agony of terror. "Can you be so mad as to hesitate? I will make good the total loss."

The last words were uttered in suppressed tones.

But they were not so faintly uttered as to be inaudible to Lord Harcliffe, who, however, affected not to hear them.

This assurance produced a wonderful effect.

The passengers, glad to get off so cheaply, vied with each other in pulling out their purses.

The passenger collected them hastily, and thrust them into the highwayman's hand.

"Enough," he said—"I am content."

"And we are now even?"

"Quite; and you will see I am as good as my word. A slight delay is all you will have to put up with. Good night!"

"And I will be as good as my word. If you are who I suspect you to be—and no one save Captain Hawk could have acted in this daring fashion—your race is short. I have come down from London with express orders for your arrest; and I here swear that I will never know a moment's peace until you are swinging at a rope's end on Tyburn Tree."

The only notice Lord Harcliffe took of this menacing speech was to utter a scornful laugh.

The next moment he had gone, leaving no trace behind save the clatter of his horse's feet.

But this last speech will let the reader know that the individual who had been in such mortal fear was no other than the magistrate whose dinner Captain Hawk had devoured with so great a relish at the Golden Ball.

Lord Harcliffe had noted that all the purses he had received were tolerably well filled, and therefore he congratulated himself upon having netted a considerable sum—quite enough, he thought, to supply his immediate wants.

But what impressed him most was the second occurrence on the same night of the name of Captain Hawk.

"There seems to be as close a search and as great a hue-and-cry after him as there is after myself," he cried. "But for the pressing nature of my present business, I would do my best to meet with him, for he must be one gifted with no common courage; as it is, I must get to London without delay."

But Lord Harcliffe was doomed to find that events which he could not control again arose to frustrate his intent.

The excitement which his late adventure produced even in his phlegmatic breast made him forgetful of a circumstance which should have been uppermost in his remembrance.

He ought to have recollected that the nearer he got to the metropolis the more closely the roads would be watched and patrolled.

To have reached London undisturbed, he ought to have made his way across the country, and followed the most unfrequented route that he could possibly discover.

Instead of that, he galloped for some distance along the highway.

It is most wonderful that he should have got so far as he did without being interrupted.

All he thought of was, however, the importance of reaching his destination speedily; and as the road was in fine condition, Phantom got over the ground wonderfully.

Suddenly, however, recovering his calmness, he discovered, with a slight pang of dread, that he was within fifty paces of one of the largest troops of officers he had yet encountered.

And, what was more, they were fully aware of his presence, and spurred their horses on most furiously.

There was but one thing which Lord Harcliffe could do, and that was so repugnant to his inclinations that he almost felt inclined to dash headlong among his foes than adopt it.

The latter course would only have secured his instantaneous destruction, and so he abandoned it and turned round.

To leap the hedge on either side was a feat beyond even Phantom's powers.

Yet how repugnant it was to his feelings to be obliged to retrace his steps the reader can fully realise.

But there was no help for it.

Alive he could serve his attached dependant, but dead he would be useless.

Setting his teeth hard, then, he struck his horse sharply in the flank with both his heels.

The gallant creature, unused to any such treatment, darted off as though maddened.

To have seen him, no one would have credited that he had travelled so many miles already.

"Fool—fool that I was!" Lord Harcliffe kept repeating to himself. "Idiot—insensate fool! Now all my difficulties are renewed!"

The speed which Phantom made, however, was such as no other horse probably could equal, so that, in spite of the slight start which he had had, he was not long in distancing his foes.

But Phantom very soon displayed such manifest symptoms of exhaustion as filled his master's breast with a greater dread than he had yet known.

He pulled up gradually, and began to look about him for some means of quitting the high-road.

"Cursed mischance!" he said. "But, Phantom, my brave fellow, you must do your best to-night. My only chance, I see still plainer now, is to shake off these fellows by riding into the country. I must not attempt to enter London with any of them at my back, or there will be such a hue-and-cry after me as will prevent me from doing one single thing. No—no. I must devise some means of getting there unperceived."

It was all very well to announce a resolution of this kind; but something very difficult to carry it into execution.

At the present moment all his energies were required to extricate himself from pressing difficulty.

To his great joy he was not long in finding an opening in a hedge, through which Phantom forced a way with little difficulty.

Already he was out of hearing of his foes; and unless by some mysterious means they found out where he had branched off, the pursuit would be for the present virtually over.

And well it was that such was the case, for Phantom every moment showed how severely he felt the strain that had been put upon him.

A gallop for any distance was far beyond his powers.

"You must have a rest," said the highwayman, despairingly. "Despite my expectations, it seems as though Fate was against my reaching London. At every step I

[THE BLACK HIGHWAYMAN DISCOVERS SATAN RIDERLESS.]

find myself foiled. But much of the night is spent now; and what I must do is to get to some place where my horse can rest."

He went now only at a walk.

Although it must have been growing towards morning, yet the darkness showed no signs of dissipating.

So intense was the obscurity that the highwayman failed to see a dense mass of trees in front of him, nor did he become aware that he was in a kind of plantation or wood until he found himself among the trunks of the trees.

"Perhaps this will afford us the shelter needed," he exclaimed. "I would rather put up with it than trust myself at present beneath any roof."

As he spoke he dismounted, and putting the bridle over his arm, walked onwards cautiously.

At every step the gloom increased, and as he narrowly escaped once or twice coming into contact with a tree, he exclaimed:

"I rather think that the officers would have some little diff[illegible]ty in finding me even if they saw me enter this wood, which I am quite certain they did not."

In order to make sure if he could of not being disturbed, he penetrated yet further into the leafy recesses of the trees, until at length gaining a spot which he imagined sufficiently secluded, he came to a halt and relieved his horse of his trappings.

This done, he left him to follow his own devices and go whither he chose, feeling certain that he could at any moment bring him to his side by giving the well-known signal.

Lord Harcliffe himself was sensible of considerable fatigue, and began to wonder where he should look for that rest which was so necessary to him.

Some time elapsed before he could make up his mind, but finally he decided to climb into one of the trees and ensconce himself as snugly as he could among the branches.

There was some difficulty and a great deal of discomfort in doing this, but then there was the greater amount of safety to be secured, and this reconciled him to the disagreeable nature of the situation.

And so he remained until the thick and heavy darkness had completely rolled away, and until the sun shone brightly among the tree-tops, and the air became vocal with the song of birds.

"I must make up my mind to wait here until night," he said, "and then I will make one final effort to accomplish my design. But I must try to find some more comfortable place than this. The officers have most certainly lost all traces of me, or I should have heard of them before now. If I could contrive to make a couch among some bushes by means of the dry leaves that have fallen from the trees, I think I could venture to snatch a few hours' sleep."

After a little more deliberation, he decided upon the adoption of this course.

Dry leaves were to be had in plenty, and by collecting them together he was soon able to form a tolerably good substitute for a bed.

The place he selected too, was so surrounded by bushes and underwood of the most tangled description, that, supposing the officers penetrated into the wood, it was next to an impossibility that they should find him.

It was with a sensation of the most profound relief that he stretched his limbs at full length upon the bed of leaves; and scarcely had he done so than, wholly overcome by fatigue, his eyes closed, and he became unconscious of everything.

The deep silence which prevailed in that place—a silence broken only by the twittering of the birds as they flew from spray to spray, and the drowsy rustling of the leaves—was well calculated to make the highwayman's slumber a profound one; and when, with a sudden start, he opened his eyes and looked about him, he saw that the day was well-nigh spent.

Turning his head, the first object upon which his eyes rested was his faithful steed.

A glance sufficed to show how much the better he was for the long rest he had had.

"And now," exclaimed the highwayman, as he rose slowly to his feet, "unless I am pursued by the same evil fortune, a few more hours will see me in London. Yet how am I to contrive it? Every avenue seems guarded so closely as to make it next to an impossibility for me to go far unseen. I must think—I must think."

But an hour's reflection brought him no nearer to the solution of his difficulty.

Deeper and deeper grew the gloom, until at length all traces of daylight had departed.

Lord Harcliffe took advantage of the last few moments before the actual close of day to make a careful examination of all his weapons, and also to recaparison his horse.

This done, he again slipped the bridle over his arm and sought to make his way out of the wood.

But owing to the dense darkness which prevailed when he entered it, he found himself unable to remember in which direction he had come.

Nor was there any object visible which would serve to point out in the least which was the way he ought to take.

Therefore, although he spent some moments in consideration, it follows that he took his course quite at random through the wood.

A very little while brought him to the unwelcome conclusion that he had missed his way.

The further he went the denser did the trees become, and the more he got entangled among them.

But at length, having the good fortune to emerge into a glade, he made his way along it, rightly judging that this was the likeliest means to get clear of the mass of trees.

He was nearer to the boundary than he had dared to hope.

"At last," he said, when he could just discern among the myriad trees and branches some signs of the open country that lay beyond—"at last I am clear. Now, then, to consider which shall be my route."

He mounted now, for there was ample room for him to ride among the trees.

But on going a few yards further he discovered that the wood was fenced in by some unusually high park palings, on the other side of which was rather a broad cross-road.

To think of leaping over this fence was quite out of the question, and luckily there was no need for it, for only a few yards off was a place where an opening had been made.

Through this Phantom picked his way readily enough.

"I fancy to the right is the course I ought to take," he said, after a little consideration. "At any rate, I will go in that direction until I see a chance of getting fairly into the open country."

The cross-road we have mentioned was bounded on both sides by this high wooden fencing, so that the highwayman, however much against his inclination it might have been, was compelled to keep along the road.

But by all that he could see, the way seemed a most unfrequented one.

It was not yet so dark as to prevent him from observing that the grass grew luxuriantly all over the road, except near the centre, where there were two deep ruts made by heavy cart-wheels.

"Now for a trot," he said, "until the end of this paling is reached. Away—away!"

Phantom was off immediately; but just as he started Lord Harcliffe fancied he heard the faint and distant ring of a horse's hoofs.

But not hearing the sound repeated, he fancied it must have been the echo of Phantom's own hoof-beats.

In a very few moments more, however, he heard the sound again, and this time it was unmistakable.

Lord Harcliffe pulled up and listened.

"Only a single horseman!" he exclaimed. "Some chance passenger probably, from whom I have nothing to fear. Certainly not one of my foes. Still, I wish to escape the observation of everyone; so now for a gallop, Phantom. It will not take many moments to get quite out of his hearing."

Phantom galloped off freely enough, being apparently in pretty good condition, although he had had no corn during his rest.

The trees flew past like shadows; and when this rapid pace had been kept up for a few moments, the highwayman reined-in his steed again, feeling quite confident that his object was achieved.

But what words can express his astonishment when he found that the hoof-beats of the rider behind him could be heard with greater distinctness than ever!

For at least a moment, Lord Harcliffe remained motionless and speechless.

He could hardly believe in the evidence of his own senses.

"What!" he cried, "has my steed, who I thought matchless, lost his marvellous powers of fleetness? What am I to understand by such a circumstance as this? What horse can it be, and why should his rider pursue me? He is coming on like the wind itself!"

He paused to listen, and the rapidity with which the hoof-beats smote the earth proved that he had not practised any exaggeration.

Even in the space of one brief moment the increased loudness of the sound showed how much progress had been made in that trifling interval of time.

"Wonderful!" he cried. "But never yet was the horse seen by me that could compare with Phantom for fleetness, and I will try whether I have found such a one at last. No—no," he added, confidently, "it is impossible. A few moments will leave him behind."

But the short time which he had remained had enabled the rider in the rear to approach much more closely, and very little more waiting would certainly bring him into view.

By all the means in his power, Lord Harcliffe incited his horse to make the utmost speed.

But somehow, he was conscious that Phantom did not respond to the tones of his voice as he was wont.

A feeling of anger and rage first filled his breast; but a moment afterwards he felt how unreasonable it was.

"He is out of condition," he said. "The change in his life has told upon him more that I thought. The

Phantom who set all other steeds at defiance, and contributed so much towards keeping up the mystery, is now almost as much changed as his master."

Unconsciously, his words became tinged with sadness and regret.

But any feeling of despondency he felt ought to have no home in his breast, and so, by a sudden and violent effort, he dismissed the unpleasant thought.

A revulsion of his ideas took place.

He was now desperate and determined.

"Whoever it is behind gains upon me. There is no doubt about it, despite Phantom's furious speed. Alas! that it should ever be so! But no more of that—no more of that."

It was only by another strong effort that he repressed his feelings of bitterness.

"He shall not triumph," he added. "Come what will, he shall not triumph! I will try speed with him no longer; but I will find out not only who and what he is, but why he makes these strenuous efforts to overtake me."

So saying, Lord Harcliffe pulled up his horse with dangerous suddenness.

There was a compression of his lips and a contraction of the brows that indicated his state of mind was none of the pleasantest.

No sooner had Phantom stopped than he wheeled him round, and made him stand with his head turned to the direction from which he had been coming.

Clearer, sharper, and louder became the rapid hoof-strokes.

Most certainly the wonderful speed was unabated; and it was with increased curiosity and interest that the Black Highwayman waited for the mysterious rider to come in sight.

CHAPTER XCVIII.

RETURNS ONCE MORE TO OUR OLD FRIEND, CAPTAIN HAWK.

The worthy landlord of the old Greyhound Inn was perfectly right when he said that Captain Hawk would be best left to himself for a little while.

The disappointment which he had experienced was a very bitter one indeed—more bitter than any which he could remember.

He was angry and enraged with himself, and all the world as well.

"Confound them all, and that Tom Beckford too! It is more his doings than any other person's, I'll be bound! Gone—gone for ever! How am I to hope to see her again now that her circumstances are so changed? I have seen her for the last time!"

It was with the deepest dejection that these words were pronounced, and for several moments he remained with his eyes fixed upon the ground.

Suddenly he looked up.

"I will banish all such thoughts," he said. "And as for Tom Beckford, I can make him feel keenly what I think of the way he has acted in this matter. No matter what the peril may be to myself—the more the better, perhaps—I will leave this place: now at once, and for evermore. Nothing shall induce me to pass another hour beneath that roof. Tom Beckford, from this hour we part company for good."

So saying, he turned into the stable.

But for all his resolution, and in spite of the determination he had come to, his heart was heavy and his chest swelled.

He determined to direct his thoughts into other channels, but learned that to do so was beyond his powers.

Still, the occupation which he had set himself brought him some relief, and he endeavoured with what success he could to concentrate all his energies upon what he was about.

As the reader may suppose, his task did not occupy him very long.

No sooner had he finished than, strong in his purpose, he took Satan by the bridle and led him to the stable door.

But on the threshold he was confronted by Tom Beckford.

The landlord's portly form filled up the doorway completely.

His face was expressive of the utmost amazement.

"Why captain—captain!" he exclaimed. "Whatever is in the wind now? What on earth are you a-going to do? Just tell me that, will you?"

Captain Hawk endeavoured to push by without speaking and without looking his old friend in the face.

But the accomplishment of any such feat was a total impossibility.

As the landlord stood exactly in the centre of the doorway, he left not so much space on either side of him as would have allowed the thinnest mortal to squeeze by.

And he was not only huge but ponderous, and when he once planted himself in any position, it required a very considerable amount of strength to move him from it.

"Now, captain," he said, in tones of mock entreaty, "don't go for to——"

"Stand aside!" said the highwayman, with the utmost fury of tone and manner.

Indeed, he was highly delighted just then at having the chance to vent his spleen upon anybody, and more especially the landlord, who, he considered, had done him a serious wrong.

As for Tom Beckford, however, he took things as usual, in a very calm and philosophic way.

"I shan't stand aside," he said, "and that's flat! Put your horse back again."

"Don't talk to me!" cried Captain Hawk, more furiously than ever—"don't talk to me!" he repeated. "Best get out of my path. If you do not, it will be the worse for you!"

"All right. Let it be the worse, then, for I don't intend to stir just at present."

"Don't tempt me to violence, Tom Beckford!" continued the captain, clenching his fist menacingly—"don't tempt me to violence, I say, or you will repent it!"

"So I should think."

"Beware, I say! You have already caused me to think of you no longer as my friend—a little more will make me forget that I owe you any respect at all; and then, as I said, you would repent it!"

"But, captain——"

"Stand aside, I say!"

"Be reasonable!"

"Let me pass!"

"I will not!"

"You will not?"

"I will not! That is plain English enough, I hope. You can forget or remember, just what the devil you like, and try what you think proper; but until you are calmer and more reasonable than you are now, you don't go out of that stable!"

"Insolent fool!"

"Oh, go on—I don't mind that a bit! I will take as many hard words from you as you can find in the dictionary—and without giving you one back either."

Captain Hawk lost all patience.

Summoning up his strength, he made a sudden effort to get out.

But he might just as well have cast himself against the wall.

The landlord merely placed his hands against the door-post, and stood the shock without flinching.

Captain Hawk finding himself thus foiled, suddenly lost all that fury which had hitherto characterised his movements.

But it was only by exciting the whole of his strength of mind that he succeeded in maintaining his calmness.

"Tom Beckford," he said, in suppressed tones, by using which he alone contrived to retain his composure—"Tom Beckford——"

"That's me," returned the landlord, with comical gravity, "or, as the man in the play says, 'Had I three ears, I'd hear thee.'"

"Bah! I am determined to leave this place without another moment's delay, and without listening to a single word which you have to say; and I give you fair warning that unless you choose to stand aside and allow me a free passage, I will force my way without regard to what the personal consequences may be to yourself. Now I have been explicit. Have the common sense to stand out of the way."

"Captain Hawk," said the landlord, admirably imitating the highwayman's tone and manner, "I have listened patiently and calmly to what you have to say."

"Yes; but I don't intend to show the same consideration towards you, so do not attempt to speak; it will be in vain."

"I shall speak. You are acting now from blind passion, and I am certain that in a short time you will repent having acted as you now wish. If I am no longer your friend, I am sorry. Yet all I ask you as a favour is that you will take five minutes for calm reflection. If at the end of that time you are in the same frame of mind as you are now, I will give you my word that I will make no attempt to oppose your departure."

Captain Hawk's frenzy was beginning to abate.

The reader might have judged such to be the case by his listening to the landlord's long sentence without interruption.

And but for the shame he felt at letting his feelings so far outrun his discretion, he would have stated that he already repented of his rash determination.

But to admit that he was so grossly in the wrong went sadly against his proud spirit.

"I will indulge you," he said; for he fancied he could do that without much derogation. "But as soon as the time is up I am off."

The landlord merely inclined his head, without speaking a single word.

Captain Hawk, who wished at that instant to ask his old friend to pardon him for his foolish behaviour, took his watch out of his pocket with a great show of resolution, as though his determination was just as strong as ever.

As second after second flew by, however, in perfect silence, he could not help feeling how rashly and how wrongly he had acted.

At the end of the third moment he returned the watch to his pocket, and giving a kind of gulp, as though swallowing some particularly unpleasant morsel, said:

"You have conquered, Tom. Here is my hand, and I must ask your pardon——"

"Nothing of the sort—nothing of the sort! Not another word!" cried Beckford in his usual jolly tones. "Bless your life! do you think I have lived all these years without knowing perfectly well what that sort of thing's like? Give me your hand, I say."

He shook hands warmly with the highwayman as he spoke, and then led Satan back to the manger, and slipped off the bridle.

"I don't know what you will think of me, Tom, for——"

"Captain!"

"Well?"

"One word."

"A hundred if you like."

"Then you will confer the greatest possible obligation upon me if you won't say another word about that business. I don't want to hear a single syllable of it."

"Just like you, Tom. Generous to the last degree! It only makes my conduct show out worse and worse!"

"Tut—tut! Nothing of the sort! You were deeply disappointed—that is it! I don't wonder at it, because it is only natural; but the sharpest pang of it is over now."

"It is—it is," said Captain Hawk, though he could not help his words being tinged with a certain amount of sadness.

"Very well, then. Drop the subject, and let us turn to other things. I can assure you I have got something to tell well worth the listening to."

"I am all attention."

"Very good."

"But shall we not go into the house?"

"Well, if you will put up with the stable, I think it will be as well."

"Why?"

"Simply because there are so many of the grabs on the look-out."

"What, now?"

"Now."

"Then if I had gone as I wanted to?"

"By this time you would either have been a dead man or else a prisoner."

"Are you serious?"

"I am indeed."

"Then how much do I not owe you!"

"Now, remember!"

"But I won't be silent."

"You must on that point."

"How can I when I find how much I owe to you?"

"Well, listen, and I can promise you as singular a tale as ever you listened to."

"About the officers?"

"Yes; and that is why I want you to remain here instead of going into the house."

"Indeed!"

"Yes. I do believe that your presence here is unknown and unsuspected at present, and it is less likely to be found out if you do not show yourself."

"There can be no question about that."

"Very well, then. In going across the yard from here to the house there is just a chance of your being seen; and then, of course, there is an end of your stay."

"Tom, my boy, this stable will do perfectly well for me. I don't desire to leave the place. Of course, with me safety is the primary consideration."

"Very good then; as that point is settled, in order to make quite secure I will shut the stable door; and if you have no objection, we will go up into the loft overhead to finish our conversation."

"For what reason?"

"Because not only is it more comfortable on account of the quantity of clean straw which is up there, but because from the window of it we can keep a tolerably good look-out upon the movements of the enemy without any fear of being seen ourselves."

Of course Captain Hawk made no objection.

But as he knew that the only communication with the loft overhead was by means of a ladder, he was not a little curious to see how the bulky landlord would achieve the feat of climbing up.

To his surprise, however, Tom Beckford managed it with far greater dexterity than he could have believed possible.

To Captain Hawk, lithe, strong, and agile as he was, the feat was nothing.

The straw lay thickly all over the floor of the loft.

Tom Beckford made his way towards the circular window at one end of it.

The opening was partially covered by a wooden shutter.

"Come on, captain. Don't speak too loud, for fear of listening ears."

Both looked out carefully and silently.

But beyond the buildings which formed the inn and its outhouses there was nothing to be seen.

"There are no officers here now," Tom Beckford said, "and if we remain where we are we shall have timely intimation of their approach."

"Very good. And now will you be kind enough to appease my curiosity? I think I have shown a great deal of patience."

"Well, you have—that is true enough."

"I can only ask you to begin at the beginning, and to let me know what took place after I got away so cleverly?"

"Ah! you may well say that. It was an awfully narrow escape."

"I am used to them."

"So it seems."

"But to your story, man. Will you never make a commencement?"

"I will without further preface. You must know, then, that when you rode away I ran after you, and pretended to be in pursuit."

"Yes, and Isaac also."

"You are right. But you may depend I did not keep up that violent kind of exercise very long; it's past my powers."

"And what did the officers say when they came up to you?"

"I told them that you were only just ahead, that you could not get far, and if they were only speedy they would recapture you. They seemed to think it likely, and so, instead of questioning me as to what I had been doing, bent all their energies upon getting their horses ready for immediate service."

CHAPTER XCIX

IN WHICH CAPTAIN HAWK MAKES ACQUAINTANCE WITH THE BLACK HIGHWAYMAN.

"That happened very fortunately for you, Tom."

"Most fortunately. But I showed all possible alacrity, and got their horses ready in a much shorter space of time than they could have done without my aid."

"And Isaac—what became of him?"

"I know no more than you."

"How? Have you not seen him?"

"Not since."

"Where can he be?"

"Looking for you somewhere. But don't trouble yourself in the least degree about him. Rely upon it, he is well able to take care of himself, and will turn up sooner or later."

"He is a faithful friend."

"He is. But for his presence of mind you would certainly now be numbered among the dead."

"Don't talk about it; it makes me uncomfortable."

"I don't doubt it."

"What else happened?"

"Well, to tell you the truth, I was for some hours in a considerable state of fidget—not on your account, for I made sure with such a start as you had had you would get clear off; but because——"

"Because what?"

"Why, I feared I should be suspected of the part I had taken in securing your escape, and that, consequently, I should be deprived of the power of helping you another time."

"You are a rare good fellow, Tom—there cannot be two opinions about that; and when I think of the way I behaved to you a little while ago——"

"Now—now, leave off, do! Will you never be content to drop that subject?"

"I shall never forget it."

"Pooh—pooh!"

"But this is not what you were going to tell me?"

"No—no."

"What on earth is it, then?"

"Oh, I have kept the best till the last, and so you will say. Ha, ha! When I think of it I can hardly contain myself, that's a fact."

Hereupon the landlord opened his mouth very wide, in order to indulge in a very hearty laugh.

But to this the captain objected for two reasons.

The first was, that he was impatient to know what the landlord had been so long tantalising him with; and the second, that he feared the sound of his merriment might reach unfriendly ears.

He took effectual measures.

Seizing suddenly a handful of straw, he doubled it together, and thrust it with no gentle force right into Tom's mouth.

His laughter was choked in a moment.

But the dreadful coughing and sputtering that he made in ridding his mouth of the unexpected morsel made almost if not quite as much noise as the peal of laughter would.

"Be on your guard," said the captain. "Remember what you told me about the police officers lurking about."

"Right, my boy. But I wish you had taken more gentle means to remind me. Fuff! Achew! The devil! I shall never get my throat clear again, I believe."

An application to the flagon of ale which he had brought soon served to put him right, and then he said:

"Last night—something after twelve, I should say—all the place being very quiet, and no one seeming to be about, and the old house quite empty of guests——"

"Yes, yes, confound you!"

"I went to bed——"

"Wonderful!"

"So you will say in a moment. According to custom I left a light burning at the little side window, so as to serve as a beacon to any chance traveller, and went to sleep."

"What then?"

"I had hardly closed my eyes before there came the most d—nable knocking at the front-door that ever you heard in your life. It was just like a shock of an earthquake, that it was."

Captain Hawk laughed.

"I sat bolt upright in bed."

"'Sure enough' said I, 'the house is on fire. I thought it could be nothing less.

"But soon I heard the sound of voices clamorously demanding admission; so I slipped on my things, and went down; and when I got to the door, who do you think I found outside?"

"How on earth should I know?"

"Well, of course you could not, only it's my way of telling a tale, you understand."

"And a confoundedly long-winded way it is—that is all I can say!"

"Your patience won't be tried much longer then. When I opened the door, lo! and behold! who should it be but a party of officers."

"After me, of course?"

"By the powers, no!"

"Not after me?"

"No, no," said the landlord; "they had had enough to satisfy them for one night, I can tell you."

"What was the matter?"

"Why, they were every one drenched to the skin. You never saw such a lot of miserable objects in all your life. There was not one with a dry thread on him, and they had every one lost hat and wig. It was quite a treat to behold them, I can tell you."

"But," said the captain, now deeply interested, "what could have happened? What did it all mean?"

"Ha, ha! I told you I had something to tell that was worth hearing."

"Pray go on, then, in your own style. I daresay I shall get to know the particulars all the sooner."

"Well, they came in, leaving their horses to shift for themselves; and what was oddest too, was that the horses were dripping wet also. What they *had* been up to, captain, I couldn't think."

"But you found out?"

"Oh yes. Well, cursing and swearing most frightfully, they made their way into the kitchen, and then cursed at me for not having a fire. I told them that we had let it out for safety's sake before going to bed, as we had not expected any more guests that night."

"Well, what did they say to that?"

"Why, they were as deaf and as blind to all reason as you were, captain, a short time back—forgive me for saying it. Well, I raked the ashes together and made a bit of fire. Then they all called out for brandy; and then such a quantity as they tilted down them would have made you stare to see. They never ought to be cold any more, not if they went to the North Pole—that's my opinion."

"But keep to the point more—keep to the point."

"I am—I do. Can't you see it's all point, every word of it? They were just wet! Before they had been standing in the kitchen ten minutes you would have thought, to look at the floor, that ten buckets of water had been thrown upon it!"

"Draw it mild, Tom!"

"I'll assure you it's a fact. The next thing they did was to declare they would go to bed."

"And did they?"

"Every man Jack of them; and they put their clothes out on the stairs to be dried in the morning."

"And when was this?"

"Last night."

"And where are they now?"

"Why, I left them all upstairs, fast asleep and snoring away like pigs."

This announcement came upon Captain Hawk so suddenly and unexpectedly that it caused him to give a very great jump.

The landlord enjoyed his consternation mightily.

"And are they in the house now?" asked Captain Hawk, unable to realise such a thing.

"They are."

"Then, why the devil didn't you tell me of it the very moment I came?"

Tom Beckford put his finger by the side of his nose

and shook his head backwards and forwards in a very knowing and cunning manner.

"Now, captain," he exclaimed, with indescribable drollery, "can you ask me that question?"

"Can I ask it, you old sinner? Of course I can! You ought to have made me acquainted with such a state of affairs the moment I arrived."

"What! and spoilt the cream of the joke? And what sort of a tale should I have had to tell you, then, I wonder? Why, the best part of it would have been lost entirely."

"D—n your tale!" said the captain, who, despite his annoyance, could not help laughing. "And so that is the reason you did not want me to go in the house for? A nice pretty fellow you are to trust one's safety to! How could I have remained here a moment had I known that?"

"Leave things to be managed by those who know best how to do them, my boy. If you will take my advice you will wait here quietly until they have all gone, and then you will have the satisfaction of knowing they are before you instead of behind you."

"Yes, that is all very well. But supposing they were to take it into their heads to search the premises before they left?"

"I should see to that, never fear me. While you are here, captain, be assured you are safe, and be assured also that I will give you timely warning of the approach of any danger."

"I know that, my friend," said Captain Hawk, taking the landlord's hand and pressing it warmly. "You will forgive me for what I said?"

"Oh, don't trouble yourself to mention it."

"But I could not help feeling a certain amount of annoyance upon finding I had been kept in the dark, and that is the truth."

"Very likely; but it was all for the best."

"But to go back to these officers."

"Well?"

"Won't they be getting up pretty soon? The day is considerably advanced."

"It is; but when I was up at the house a short time ago, lor' bless you! they were all sleeping like ancient Britons."

"But when they wake?"

"I have made arrangements to be informed the moment one of them shows signs of stirring."

Captain Hawk lapsed into deep thought.

"But, I say," cried the landlord, "what is the matter with you?"

"Why?"

"Because you don't ask me how it was the officers came to be in the deplorable condition that I described to you."

"Do you know?"

"Oh yes; I could not have rested if I had not found out."

"Well, how was it?"

"I can promise you it is the most amusing part of the whole affair."

"How came you to be acquainted with the particulars?"

"Why, there was one of the officers who seemed to take his drenching more patiently and philosophically than the rest of them; and instead of breaking his neck upstairs like the rest of them, he sat and waited till the fire burnt up a little; and I gave him some more brandy, and mixed a glass for myself."

"And by that means got all out of him?"

"Yes. It seems that the whole party of them had been in hot pursuit of the Black Highwayman——"

"The who?"

"The Black Highwayman."

The captain repeated the words musingly.

"It is possible you have not heard of him," cried the landlord. "Why, he has made all the country ring with the fame of his exploits."

"It has been since I have been in this part of the kingdom, Tom."

"Very likely. I forgot that you had been northward for so long."

"You have excited my curiosity though, Tom. Let me know all about him."

"All about him? Why, that would furnish me with talking matter for a month."

"But who is he? and why is he called by so strange a name?"

"I can tell you that much. He was always seen attired in the deepest black, and his horse was the same colour. He appeared suddenly, vanished incomprehensibly, and defied alike all attempts to capture him and discover his identity."

"You interest me greatly."

"You would be interested if you only heard a tenth part of the wonderful tales that are told about him."

"And he must be somewhere in this neighbourhood."

"It seems like it."

"Have you ever seen him?"

"Never."

"And how came the officers to miss him?"

"Ah! that's what I want to tell you. It seems that they had an unusually good chance of getting hold of him; but the night was most frightfully dark——"

"You are right. I really think it was the darkest night that ever I can remember."

"So the officers said, captain, for all they rode on at full speed after the Black Highwayman, who led the way as confident across the open country as though he could see a mile before him, and then——"

"Well, then?"

"Then they lost him."

"How?"

"Nobody knows. They all went galloping on at full speed, and trusting to their horses, I suppose, to take them right, when all at once souse they went into the river!"

"But——"

"You don't understand. Wait a moment, and I will make all clear to you. I daresay you will remember that at the foot of the hill yonder, where the river winds round, the water is very wide, but shallow?"

"Do you mean by the ford?"

"Yes; to the east of it."

"I know the place."

"Then, beyond doubt, you will recollect that the bank on the opposite side is very steep and precipitous?"

"I do."

"Well, then, the officers knew nothing about it. In the dark they saw nothing of the water—or if they did, it was not till too late—and over the bank they went into the stream!"

Captain Hawk laughed long and loud.

"Excellent indeed!" he said. "That is about the neatest finish to a pursuit that ever I heard of!"

"Yes, horses as well as riders fell into the flood. It was lucky the water was not deep, or there would have been an end to a good many of them."

"Then they never found out what became of this Black Highwayman?"

"No. Just after the accident I have spoken of, up came another party of officers. Indeed, their attention had been drawn to the spot by the terrific uproar."

"What happened then?"

"This troop happened to be the one in search of you, but they went off on the fresh track, while the poor half-drowned wretches made their way to the Greyhound."

"And that is the end of the story?"

"Yes, and as good a story, too, as you have listened to for many a day."

"I hardly think we are at the end of it yet, Tom. We are a great deal too close together for things to be pleasant. Stop, now—I'll be bound it was no other than this said Black Highwayman who stopped the York coach last night."

"Stopped the coach! You must tell me all about that."

"It is not much I have to tell."

Thereupon Captain Hawk related what had happened to him at the coach; but as the reader is already possessed of the full particulars of the adventure, it is not worth while to repeat what he said.

"You may make a dead certainty of it," said Tom, "he is somewhere close by. I wonder what brings him into this part of the country? Always before he has kept himself tolerably close to London."

"I know no better than yourself. But what is that?"

"Oh, that's my friend whistling 'Rule Britannia.'"

"Good Heavens! I thought somebody was filing a saw."

"I must be off."

"What for?"

"That's the signal."

"What, that the officers are stirring?"

"Yes."

"What am I to do?"

"By no manner of means stir from where you are. Make yourself quite happy and comfortable. I pledge you my word that I will either come myself, or else send some one in ample time to allow you to get out of danger."

So saying, Tom Beckford, with all the haste he could, descended the ladder into the stable, the door of which he locked, so that he might make sure that Captain Hawk should not spoil all by an untimely attempt to leave.

There was no time for remonstrance or expostulation, though the reader may guess that it was with anything but easy sensations that the highwayman watched the landlord cross the yard and enter the inn.

"Confound his firmness, or rather his obstinacy I ought to call it! I am now obliged to trust myself entirely to him, whether I like it or not."

Captain Hawk had a great deal of faith in Tom Beckford, but yet he scarcely felt comfortable under present circumstances.

Planting himself close to the circular opening, but taking care not to allow any portion of his body to be visible, he waited to see what might happen next.

But all remained profoundly still.

The ordinary tranquil air which pervaded that spot seemed to reign with double intensity.

To the highwayman the time which elapsed seemed endless.

In vain he asked himself over and over again whatever it was the officers were doing.

In vain also he wondered why on earth Tom Beckford did not take an earlier opportunity of relieving him from his anxiety.

Could he but have seen what was going on inside the inn, his apprehensions would have been allayed.

The officers were all terribly tired out, and what with the cold bath they had had and the potations of brandy they had swallowed, slept very soundly indeed.

When they awoke it was the after part of the day, and naturally enough they were no sooner dressed than they were assailed with the keenest pangs of hunger.

A violent outcry was made for the landlord, and on Tom presenting himself he was given instructions enough to have lasted him an hour to carry out.

However, he set about providing food for his ravenous guests, and in a short time the officers were all at work as if for their lives upon a huge dish of broiled ham and eggs.

Seasoned by appetite, the meal was pronounced excellent.

As for Tom, he was almost incessantly employed in going up and down the cellar to fetch the ale, the consumption of which was the greater on account of the somewhat over-saltness of the ham; but then, perhaps, that was only cunning on the portly landlord's part.

And while time was passing thus pleasantly indoors, Captain Hawk was fretting away in the loft and picturing events occurring quite different from those that were really taking place.

After their meal was over the police officers elected to have a smoke.

Pipes and tobacco were brought in accordingly.

Then dismissing Tom Beckford in anything but a polite manner, they set about discussing their plans of action for the future.

About their plans Tom cared very little.

He was by far more anxious to go and speak to the highwayman.

A more favourable opportunity than the present could not be conceived.

Making sure, however, that his movements were not observed by anyone, he crossed the old inn yard.

The officers had consumed so much time in eating and drinking that already a dimness was beginning to spread itself over all things.

When Tom unlocked the door he found Captain Hawk standing close to the threshold.

"Now, Tom," he said, "don't you think of locking me up again, or as sure as fate I will do something desperate that will bring both of us into trouble."

"Now, there's no occasion for threats. Be quiet for a moment, can't you?"

"What are the officers doing?"

Tom Beckford explained.

"Upon my word they take things very easy."

"They do; but depend upon it they are only waiting for darkness to set in."

"It is likely enough."

"I feel certain that as soon as night comes they will be off. They think they cannot be much good until then; and not only are they resting themselves, but their horses also; and goodness knows the poor beasts stood badly enough in want of it."

"Well, then, Tom," said Captain Hawk, "I will bid you adieu. Already it is beginning to grow twilight, and long before the officers think of rising from their chairs I shall be miles away."

"I shall leave you free to do as you think proper, but if you will listen to my advice——"

"I shall stop longer."

"Just so. The officers will ride off; you will be able to watch which way they go, and then what could be easier than for you to take the opposite direction? It is in vain for you to say there is any pressing need for haste. I know perfectly well that there is nothing of the sort. Still, as you don't seem to like my friendly control, all I can say is, please yourself."

Captain Hawk could tell by the way these words were spoken that the worthy landlord was quite offended.

"I will please myself, Tom," he said, "and in so doing I will take care to please you."

The landlord's face beamed all over with smiles immediately.

"Then you will stop?"

"Yes, until it is fairly dark, and then, if there are no signs of the officers departing, I shall consider myself at liberty to leave."

"Agreed on! And I feel sure that you will have good reason to rejoice at the choice you have made."

"All right, then; and if, in the meantime, you could let me have some fodder to amuse myself with——"

"I have been preparing something for you, my boy, and a drop of the finest ale you ever tasted. I only tapped it the other day; and by the time you have done justice to what I shall bring you, it will be time enough for you to be off and away."

"I hope so!"

"And now I will leave you. I don't like to be away too long, lest they should grow suspicious."

"Have you heard them mention my name?"

"Not once."

"Strange, isn't it?"

"Not very, for, you see, they are after the Black Highwayman. They are a strange lot altogether, and I am certain know nothing about the events which have lately happened here."

"So much the better, then."

"Farewell for the present."

Tom Beckford returned to the inn.

But he found the officers still in solemn conversation.

The door of the room they were in was shut, and outside of it they had stationed an inferior member of the troop, so as to guard at one and the same time against eavesdropping and interruption.

Finding this to be the state of affairs, Tom Beckford busied himself in getting in perfect readiness the meal which he had been preparing for the highwayman.

It was a repast of a very sumptuous and enticing nature.

"It's well there's enough for two," he ejaculated. "I'll declare the very smell makes my mouth water to such a degree that I don't know what to do with myself."

CHAPTER C.

RELATES HOW A COMPACT WAS MADE BETWEEN CAPTAIN HAWK AND THE BLACK HIGHWAYMAN.

After making sure that the police officers were still busily engaged, Tom Beckford carried all the good things into the stable, where, despite the scanty accommodation there was in the place, they made together a very hearty and convivial meal.

It was rarely, in the restless, wandering life he led, that Captain Hawk had the opportunity of partaking of such a repast as the present; and what gave it a great additional zest was the circumstance of his foes being within so short a distance of him.

"Ah, captain," the landlord exclaimed, after having taken an immoderate draught of the ale, "I shall never forget these doings—never—never! What has been going on lately will serve me to talk about as long as I live—it will indeed."

"All has gone well so far certainly," said the highwayman. "I wonder how long it will be before I show myself in this part of the world again?"

"Not very long, I hope, captain," said the landlord, earnestly. "I cannot bear to think about parting with you, and that's a fact."

"What says the old proverb: 'the best of friends must part,' and we must succumb to the general rule."

"You must—you must," answered the landlord, with a heavy sigh. "But if ever you are in extreme danger—if ever you are hard pressed, or if you are near the Greyhound, remember there is some one beneath the roof of the old inn who would—— Confound it! there's 'Rule Britannia' again! The officers want me. I must be off."

So saying, he scuttled hastily out of the stable.

Captain Hawk could not help laughing at the odd manner in which worthy Tom's protestations had been interrupted.

"I know it's all right," he said; "and it warms my heart to find that there is at least one human being in the world strongly attached to me."

He had no inclination to proceed with his meal after his friend had left him.

Not only was his position too full of anxieties to allow him to sit calmly anywhere long together; but the last words he had uttered had served to bring Blanche vividly back to his recollection.

He had been trying valiantly to forget all about her, but he now discovered that so far all his efforts had been quite in vain.

His face became clouded with an expression of deep melancholy, and he gave full play to his sad reflections, until a considerable bustle and noise taking place outside roused him from his reverie.

It was now quite dark.

When he looked through the stable window he saw that objects outside were beginning to grow confused in their outlines.

The flashing of a lantern next attracted his notice, and then he discovered that the officers were positively about to take their departure.

With how much interest he observed all their movements the reader will not require to be told.

Much less time, however, was consumed than he had anticipated, and at length, after much grumbling and swearing, the whole party mounted and rode away.

Tom Beckford took care to stand and watch them until they got to a safe distance, and when he felt quite sure that there was nothing to fear from a sudden return on their part, he went to the stable.

But he could hardly make up his mind to part with his favourite.

Captain Hawk's recent thoughts, however, made him extremely anxious to be off.

Therefore he cut short much that the landlord was about to say.

"Now, look here, Tom," he said—"I know that with you my safety is a paramount consideration. You must know perfectly well that so favourable an opportunity as the present is for me to take my departure can hardly be hoped to occur again. So let the parting be over briefly."

"Perhaps it will be best," said Tom, endeavouring to make light of the matter, and most lamentably failing to do so.

"It will, old friend. This parting is as sad to you as to me; but I promise you that no long time shall elapse before I pay you another visit."

"Thanks for that assurance, then," said the landlord, wringing the captain's hand—"a thousand thanks for it."

While these few words were being exchanged between them, Captain Hawk had led Satan out of the stable, and brought him close to the often-mentioned low bit of wall by which he ordinarily left the premises.

"Once more farewell, Tom!" he said, springing into the saddle. "I shall never forget all your kindness towards me!"

"Farewell, captain! The word must be said, though it well-nigh chokes me to utter it. If you would not be offended, I should like to say something."

"Say it, then, without any such fear."

"It touches on a tender point, captain. I wanted you to give me a promise that you would think no more of the girl Blanche, and that you will never make the least attempt to see her again."

Captain Hawk, at a loss what to say, forced a laugh, which he intended should serve as an answer.

"It is for your good that I make the request," said the landlord, impressively. "Promise me, and I will be content."

"We will talk it over another time, Tom," was the response, uttered with apparent carelessness. "It will take too long to discuss it now. Farewell!"

"One moment!"

"No—I am off!"

Even as he said the word, Satan, in obedience to the slight impulse he had received, flew over the wall like a greyhound.

"Stop—stop!" bawled Tom. "One word, I say! Isaac!"

It is questionable whether anything else save the utterance of that one name would have induced the captain to turn back.

"What of Isaac?" he said.

"Should I see him, what must I say?"

"Tell him to follow me."

"For London?"

"Yes."

"And which road?—not the high?"

"No."

"If you will take my advice, you will make your way by the old cross-road; it will save a mile or two, and you are less likely to be interrupted—the road now is so little travelled."

"Well thought of, Tom. I will go that way. Farewell again!"

He waved his hat as he spoke, and rode off.

In less than a moment he was lost to the landlord's view.

Captain Hawk directed his course with great certainty. He knew full well the cross-road which had been mentioned, and he was convinced that he could not possibly take a better way.

The road was bad, but then safety was the all-important consideration.

But as he went, Captain Hawk found his inclination to go to London became weaker and weaker.

An irresistible fascination seemed to draw him to Squire Kingsbury's house.

"Pshaw!" he said, "she cares nought for me now that she knows who and what I really am. The remembrance of the service I rendered her is quite effaced. I will think of her no more. Where is Isaac?—he at least is true as steel, and likes me because I am one of the night-riders. Hark! What did I hear?"

It was the clatter of a horse's feet on the road before him which had struck upon the acute listening faculties of the highwayman.

"Perhaps that is Isaac," he said; "at any rate, Satan shall have a gallop forward. If it is not Isaac, it is some traveller, and when I overtake him I will ease him of his purse, if only to help to banish the unpleasant reflections which, in spite of me, keep crowding into my mind."

No sooner did he express this resolution than he carried it into effect.

Hitherto he had with some difficulty kept Satan down to a trot, but the noble creature was full of mettle and spirit, and was in the highest degree impatient to make a display of his speed.

The slightest slackening of the rein was sufficient.

Away he went at a gallop, which the captain believed to be of unparalleled swiftness, for it fairly deprived him of his breath.

[THE POLICE OFFICERS DISCOVER THE INSENSIBLE BODY OF CAPTAIN HAWK.]

At such a rate he expected to make short work of overtaking the horseman who was on the road before him.

What words can express his surprise, however, when he found that the rider in front, whoever he might be, possessed a steed of wondrous quality, for he kept ahead marvellously.

Nevertheless, he could tell that, however fast the traveller was going, he was slowly and surely losing ground, so that the question of overtaking him was one of time merely.

"On, Satan!" he cried. And the noble steed gave some wondrous bounds that made the trees by the roadside fly past like magic, while sparks flew continually from his thundering hoofs.

Still, the manner in which the unknown rider contrived to keep ahead surprised him exceedingly.

"I thought there was only one steed in the world capable of such a gallop as that," he said; "and but for the fact that I know well she is under the ground, I should be firmly persuaded that it was no other than the bonny Black Bess before me."

Still, Captain Hawk became every moment more certain that he was gaining on the traveller with great rapidity.

This knowledge, of course, was highly satisfactory.

His surprise, however, may be imagined when the rider in front put an abrupt termination to the chase by all at once stopping his horse's headlong career.

"What!" exclaimed the captain. "Stopped! Yes, by Heaven, he has pulled up!"

For the moment he could hardly believe that he had heard aright, so totally unexpected was the event.

Instinctively he checked Satan's career.

"Who on earth can he be?" he exclaimed, with tea

times more curiosity than he had yet felt. "No ordinary traveller, that is quite certain. But no matter: at all hazards I will find out who he is."

The intense interest produced by this unprecedented occurrence made the captain for a brief space forgetful of those events which had so much depressed his spirits.

Again at a swift gallop he urged Satan onward

It was not long before he perceived before him in the middle of the roadway a dim and dusky mass, which he could never have recognised for what it was had he not been aware of it already.

But without checking his steed in the least, he rode at once full in front of the unknown.

From what has been already written the reader will be at no loss to know who this mysterious rider was.

There was nothing in the world, however, to inform Captain Hawk that it was no other than the Black Highwayman who was so calmly awaiting his approach.

So great was the speed at which he came on, that Lord Harcliffe fancied it was his intention to ride past.

This by no means agreed with his determination, so he made a sudden movement, by which further progress was rendered impossible.

Captain Hawk pulled the rein so suddenly that Satan rose on his haunches and pawed the air with his fore feet.

Then, before he could recover himself, he heard the unknown say, in resolute tones:

"Hold—hold! Not another step if you value your life!"

By the time the last word was pronounced, Captain Hawk was in possession of his ordinary *sang froid*.

"I am going no further just at present, my dear sir," he said, in those light, airy tones which he loved to employ on an occasion like the present. "You have saved me a little trouble, and, therefore, I don't mind showing you a little extra consideration."

It is perfectly certain that no words could have astonished the Black Highwayman more than these did.

The address was something so different from what he had expected that he was only able to echo in great astonishment:

"Save you trouble?—show me consideration?"

"Exactly, my dear sir, if you will permit the familiarity," answered the captain, with the same sprightly air.

"The devil! What do you mean? I——"

"I allude to your pulling up. You have a capital nag. I don't mind admitting it; and it was wise of you not to distress him unnecessarily, for I can promise you that, let him have gone at what speed he might, I have a little bit of horseflesh here that would have overtaken him before long."

The Black Highwayman's amazement increased.

"But come," added the captain, "time passes; and since you have been so kind and considerate to await my approach, I will——"

Lord Harcliffe drew a pistol from his breast and levelled it at his companion's head.

"No more of this!" he cried, in his cold, stern tones. "Your money and valuables! Hand them over quickly, for I have but a slight stock of patience! If you value your skin, you will not exhaust it."

"What!" ejaculated Captain Hawk, in tones that made all the place ring again—"what! Has the time come when Captain Hawk should have his purse coolly demanded from him on the highway? Ha, ha! Capital—capital! Sir, I congratulate you on your wit and presence of mind. The joke is a good one—a capital one, as I said before; but yet not good enough to get you out of your difficulty."

Lord Harcliffe no sooner heard the name Captain Hawk pronounced than he gave a sudden start and uttered an ejaculation of surprise.

"What," he cried—"what name was that? Do you say you are——"

"Captain Hawk, at your service," was the reply, accompanied by the politest of bows. "But, as I said before, time passes; and as I have satisfied you so far, hand over your purse, and permit me to continue my journey."

Lord Harcliffe deliberately replaced his pistol in his breast.

"A wise action," said the captain, approvingly. "Upon my word, I like your self-possession vastly. Now for the purse!"

But Lord Harcliffe only extended his open hand.

"Captain Hawk," he said, "I have heard of you often, and your name was on my lips not very long before. Give me your hand. I am pleased to make your acquaintance; and some strange feeling comes over my spirit which convinces me that we are destined in the future to become firm friends."

It was now Captain Hawk's turn to be astonished.

But, prompted by a sudden impulse, which he did not for a moment attempt to resist, he put out his hand, and closed it with a friendly grip.

"You know me?" he said at length.

"By name and reputation only."

"And you," said the captain, endeavouring to pierce the thick obscurity—"you should be no other than the Black Highwayman."

"Your surmise is correct—I am no other."

"Give me your hand again then," he cried; "for I, too, share your feeling to the full!"

Again was the friendly pressure of hands exchanged.

"My life," said Captain Hawk, "has made me acquainted with many strange vicissitudes, yet it is certain that this is the strangest of them all."

"I might say the same," returned Lord Harcliffe; "and with perfect truth add at the same time that it is the pleasantest I can remember—that is," he added, "if you feel inclined to join your fortunes with mine."

"Nothing would delight me more," said Captain Hawk, his voice unconsciously becoming tinged with a tone of sadness. "Companionship is the one thing I have longed for with the utmost ardour since the occurrence of an event which I cannot bear to think upon."

"And I the same," said Lord Harcliffe, who, since his miraculous escape from the mansion in Piccadilly had suffered much from being cut off from all human society.

"The chance is a most fortunate and happy one, and never could it have occurred more opportunely. At some other time I will acquaint you with much you ought to know about, but which would consume too much time to tell now."

"And I the same; but if it is agreed that for a time we unite our fortunes, let us ratify the agreement with an oath of friendship."

"With all my heart!" said Captain Hawk, whose liking for and interest in the Black Highwayman increased every moment. "I swear by that which I hold dearest to be for ever your friend until such time as you shall grow tired of the companionship!"

"Which will never be," said Lord Harcliffe, as he again clasped the hand of Captain Hawk; "and I repeat your words with all heartiness and sincerity!"

CHAPTER CI.

IN WHICH THE TWO HIGHWAYMEN MAKE A VOW TO BE FAITHFUL TO EACH OTHER UNTIL DEATH.

It would in good truth be hard to say which of the two highwaymen was the most delighted at the occurrence of this meeting.

And what was, perhaps, strangest of all was the fact that the event had by no means been unanticipated by either of them.

Each in a dreamy way, upon hearing the other's name mentioned, had felt that there was at least a chance that Fortune would at some odd time or other throw them together.

And in having this unconscious feeling—for so we may term it—both had felt that should a meeting really take place it would be the prelude to a long-lasting intimacy and friendship.

And, as the reader will remember, just at the present juncture both the highwaymen had keenly felt the want of some friend who would share the perils and fascinations of their hazardous career.

From all these circumstances, then, it follows that a feeling of the warmest possible description sprung up between them—so warm as to have appeared scarcely natural and reasonable but for this.

After the Black Highwayman, in a solemn voice, had pronounced the words with which the last chapter concluded, a silence of several moments' duration ensued.

But it was a silence full of the busiest thought, and a silence, too, that was most impressive.

Lord Harcliffe was the first to break it

"Come," he said, "we will not linger here; let us push on into some place less obscure; for though I have heard your voice, yet I have not as yet had an opportunity of discerning your features."

"With all my heart," said Captain Hawk, whose gay, light-hearted manner formed a strong contrast to his new friend's grave deportment. "When once clear of these thick-growing trees we shall be able to see much better."

"True. But your destination — have you one in view?"

"Yes, London."

"London!" repeated the other, in tones which declared that he was not so much surprised as delighted to receive this assurance.

"Why did you repeat the word?"

"Simply because I was struck by the strangeness of the coincidence."

"You, then, are bound for the same place?"

"I am."

"That happens fortunately indeed. The business that takes me there—though through one cross accident or another, I have been long enough in executing it—is to deliver the last dying message of my dearest friend, Dick Turpin."

"You are much affected."

"I am indeed."

"Wherefore?"

"Because I cannot acquit myself of the reproach that in some measure I was the cause of his untimely fate. Some day I will tell you all—I cannot now."

"Do not attempt it if it causes you pain. We shall have so much in the shape of confidences to share with each other that we must look for opportunities to present themselves."

"That is true," said Captain Hawk, still sadly, for he was thinking of the times past when he had ridden by the side of gallant-hearted Dick, the Prince of Highwaymen.

Lord Harcliffe adopted the readiest means of arousing him from his sad reverie.

"My business in London," he said, "is of the most urgent nature conceivable; and yet such has been my unlucky fate that, strive as hard as I would, events perpetually occurred to hinder me."

"That is a strange coincidence as well."

"It is; but your business, I take it, is of such a character as not to suffer very seriously by delay."

"That is true enough."

"Mine, however—and deeply it pains me to say it—is a matter of life and death. While I have been here riding in all directions across the country, hunted implacably by my foes, my faithful accomplice and associate—the one who has served me from the first—has been in the most extreme danger."

"And is so still?" said Captain Hawk, interrogatively.

"And is so still," said Lord Harcliffe, almost frenzied with excitement, "unless, indeed, he has been put beyond the reach of all mortal help."

"Do you mean by death?"

"Yes."

"How is that?"

"I fear that, by inexorable circumstances, my arrival in London has been hindered so long that there has been time to hurry him through all the judicial ceremonies, and to hang him at Tyburn like a dog, on account of his fidelity to me."

Rarely indeed was it that the Black Highwayman manifested so much excitement as on this occasion.

His eyes gleamed, and his whole frame shook with intense emotion.

Captain Hawk observed it, but did not think it so strange as he would have done had he known his companion better.

"Let us hope for the better," he said. "There is, of course, only one thing for us to do, and that is to get to London without a moment's delay. Our horses are both good ones; and it ought not to be any ordinary event that should be able to stay our progress."

"But you forget——"

"Forget what?"

"Or is it possible you do not know?"

"Explain yourself."

"How long is it since you were in London last?"

"Some months at least."

"Ah! then you are unaware of what has happened, and can know nothing of the elaborate and extraordinary precautions taken by the police officers."

"That is quite certain. But do not keep me any longer in suspense. Relieve my anxiety without delay."

"I must tell you, then, that in their anxiety to effect my capture, they have caused every avenue and outlet from London to be jealously guarded by troops of men, who succeed each other at frequent intervals."

"And is their vigilance so great?"

"It is excessive. I have been foiled in every attempt to get nearer to the metropolis—in fact, all my exertions only thrust me still further into the country; for upon meeting with my foes, I have no resource but instant flight; and I am compelled to turn my horse's head towards the open country. To ride towards London would only be to bring about my instant destruction."

"I see—I see," said Captain Hawk, with unaccustomed seriousness.

"Let me assure you," added Lord Harcliffe, "that never stood I in more need of friendly assistance and advice than I do at this moment. How to act puzzles me."

"At all hazards," answered Captain Hawk, "your faithful associate must be rescued."

"But how—how?"

"That demands a little resolution and consideration too."

"You are right."

"The first thing is to devise a means of gaining London unseen and unknown by the officers."

"Which I fear is an impossibility."

"Nay, stay a little."

"No; rather should I pronounce those words. I had forgotten. I have no claim upon you to cause you to share in the dangers of the enterprise I have now in hand. It is of a private nature altogether, and therefore I feel I ought not to embroil you in fresh difficulties."

Captain Hawk looked a little surprised at this speech.

"I have sworn friendship with you," he said, "and when I do that I do not do it lightly. When I join with one, I join heart and soul. What is my friend's enterprise and danger is mine too, and I feel that it is my right to share it."

"Captain Hawk," said the Black Highwayman, "give me your hand once more. I feel quite persuaded now that our intimacy, so strangely begun, will long continue. You speak in the right spirit."

Captain Hawk held out his hand frankly.

"I began to think," he said, "that you had some private reason for wishing me not to join with you in this affair."

"No, no, my dear friend; on the contrary, I assure you that I felt it was wrong on my part to expect you to take part in an affair so fraught with danger."

"Danger!" cried Captain Hawk, with a contemptuous air. "It is the one thing I delight in—it is the very breath of life to me. So that when you speak of danger you only increase my desire to take an active part in the affair."

Lord Harcliffe regarded him with the utmost admiration.

"This hearty co-operation," he said, "and thorough friendliness delights me more than I can express. But you will find that I shall follow your example should the time ever come when you will require a like favour of me."

"I believe you," answered Captain Hawk; "so that we understand now that the friendship which subsists between us is thorough."

"Yes," replied Lord Harcliffe, catching a portion of his enthusiasm. "It is a friendship to the very death. I will at any time lay down my life for you."

"And I the same," said the captain. "Such a friendship as this is a friendship worth having."

For some moments after this they rode on in silence.

From time to time they glanced towards each other, but as yet there was not light enough to discern each other's features.

"Come," said the captain, "let us go back to the business we have in hand, and endeavour to bring it to a conclusion."

"With all my heart!"

"You have certain knowledge, I suppose, of the position of your comrade?"

"Nay; that, strictly speaking, I have not. All I know is that he was taken prisoner."

"He may, then, have escaped by his own exertions?"

"I fear not."

"Why?"

"Because he would rely altogether upon me, and would not raise a hand in his own behalf, feeling confident that I should have the power to set him free."

"That is unfortunate."

"Truly so."

"The only hope is that he may have heard of your own difficult position."

But the Black Highwayman only shook his head.

"I can derive no consolation from that suggestion," he said. "Too much anxiety would be shown and felt to compass his destruction to allow him even the ghost of a chance to escape by his own exertions."

"You know all the circumstances better than I do," said the captain, "and that of course will make a great difference. But for this, however, I should say that you take altogether too despondent a view of the business."

"I trust so," he said. "My satisfaction then will be so much the greater should I find that all is well."

"True."

"But, on the other hand, if the authorities are powerful enough to hinder me, despite my every effort, from entering London, how easy it would be to make his detention in prison perfectly secure!"

This was rather an unanswerable argument, and so Captain Hawk found it.

"For my part," he said, "when I have an enterprise of this kind to carry out, I never allow any such thoughts to trouble my mind."

"You confine yourself to action, then?"

"Exactly; and that is what I should recommend we should do in the present case. Let us take for granted that your friend is in the prison of Newgate. In the first place, we must rescue him; and having decided so far, we can think of what is wanted next. It is always part of my plan not to try to look too far into the future, because ten to one something will happen to render all your planning nought."

"You are perfectly right," said Lord Harcliffe; "and as I have up to the present signally failed myself to accomplish the least good, I shall be glad to submit myself to your direction."

"Nay, that would not suit me either. There must be an equality between us. But do you know what I consider the first essential requisite?"

"I do not."

"And it is not only first but last," said Captain Hawk. "We want but one thing, and that thing is money."

CHAPTER CII.

IN WHICH CAPTAIN HAWK CARRIES OUT HIS BOLD DESIGN AND MEETS WITH A MISHAP.

DESPITE the great anxieties that were pressing upon his mind, the Black Highwayman could not suppress a smile when he heard his companion's reply. It was different, very different indeed, from what he had expected.

Captain Hawk laughed as well; but presently subsiding into seriousness, he said:

"But tell me how stand the funds, for after all it is quite impossible to do the least thing without an ample store of cash."

"That was my thought."

"Then you are well provided?"

"Not so well as I could wish."

"That is unfortunate, for just now my purse is at a low ebb. Still, you are most heartily and entirely welcome to all I have."

"Alas!" said the Black Highwayman, with a sigh of deep regret. "Would that I had possessed prudence and foresight enough to provide against the coming of such a day as this! But I went on secure and careless: prolonged success had made me over bold. Of to-morrow I took no thought, and so I heedlessly squandered more than ten times as much as I now want to set Pharoah at liberty."

The words were spoken in accents of the greatest remorse.

Captain Hawk, who was too light-hearted or else too philosophical to grieve about that which was past and beyond help, looked at his new friend with great surprise.

"Come—come," he said, "no more of that. It only does harm instead of good. The ill is one which can easily be repaired."

"But I ought to have expected that the time would arrive when discovery was certain to take place. I ought to have provided myself against that contingency."

"And so ought I, for the matter of that; but I have never done so—never even thought of it. Why make life a toil? I live only for the present; and that, if mankind did but know it rightly, would prove the summit of all happiness."

"I am at a loss to estimate how much I may be possessed of," said Lord Harcliffe.

"Does it consist of the booty taken from the York mail?"

"Ah! how did you know of that?"

"Never mind now. It will take too long to tell: you shall know another time. Is there any more?"

"No more of moment."

"Then I may as well tell you that it is nothing like enough; and, as I have no secret hoard to take you to, our only course is——"

"What?"

"To levy contributions on our way."

"But that seems madness."

"How?"

"The way to certain destruction."

"How?"

"We shall have all the whole pack of officers at our back."

"Pooh—pooh! nothing of the sort. I know too well how to deal with them. Once do anything out of the ordinary course of events, and they are flabbergasted immediately."

"You surprise me."

"You will find what I tell you to be neither more nor less than the truth, and experience will very shortly prove it. Do you know that when I resolve upon the execution of any course, the very last thing I think about or trouble over in the least is how it will affect the officers."

Outrageous as the captain's words seemed, yet there was in them a very great amount of truth, and there can be no question that it was more owing to his reckless audacity than aught else that he succeeded so well and for so long in setting at nought all attempts to capture him.

"Then," said Lord Harcliffe, "you are really in earnest in your intention to stop some travellers?"

"I will assure you that I was never more in earnest in my life."

"Then you amaze me. You will forgive me for saying that I think what you propose to do is neither more nor less than inviting capture."

"Let the event prove it, then."

"Agreed! I will not oppose you. I will only say that should you prove mistaken, and that you fall into any great peril, I will either save you or perish."

"I will give you the same assurance, with the same amount of fidelity and good faith. How confoundedly dark it is, to be sure!"

There was no doubt about the truth of this remark.

So far from the obscurity lessening, as they had fully anticipated, it grew greater and greater, rivalling even the deep, impenetrable gloom of the preceding evening.

It was only by an effort that the two friends kept each other in view at all; and it was no easy matter to decide whether there were trees growing by the roadside or not.

"It is dark," said Lord Harcliffe.

"Just right for our enterprise," said Captain Hawk. "It deprives us of the pleasure of looking into each other's faces, but that is a pleasure to come, and one we can afford to wait for with tolerable patience."

Lord Harcliffe was much amused by the captain's manner.

It was something so very different from what he had been accustomed to.

"Are your weapons in good order?" was Captain Hawk's next question. "You will have to decide in the best way you can, for to see is a thing altogether impossible."

An examination was, nevertheless, made on both sides, though by no means so satisfactory a one as they could have wished.

"Just in time," cried the captain, again. "My ears deceive me, or else there is some one coming along the road."

"I heard nothing."

"Listen!"

Both did so.

A very faint sound then became audible, which, however ambiguous it might have proved to unpractised ears, was by no means so to the highwaymen.

"You are right," said Lord Harcliffe. "Some one comes."

"Yes," replied the captain, who had been listening with all conceivable intentness. "Two persons on horseback are approaching us, and they are well mounted too."

"Are they our foes?"

"You may depend they are not. They would be in greater force. But be they whom they may, we will stop them, and not leave them until we have possessed ourselves of all they carry."

Jauntily as the captain spoke, yet Lord Harcliffe had no difficulty in seeing that a vast amount of resolution underlaid his words.

"As you will," he said. "I am with you."

"Enough. And you will find that this little affair will do more to disconcert and perplex our enemies than anything else we could hit on if we tried for a month."

Lord Harcliffe was by no means assured as to the result of all this; but he firmly determined that, come what might, he would allow his new friend to follow out his own devices without a breath of opposition; and not only that, he was determined to second all his endeavours to the utmost.

The sound made by the approaching horsemen now became more and more distinct, insomuch that it was no longer possible to entertain the least doubt as to who it was coming.

"Hurrah!" exclaimed Captain Hawk, enthusiastically. "Something seems to tell me that Fortune will favour us—that we shall make a good booty to-night."

"I hope so. But how shall we act?"

"What do you propose?"

"Nay, I wish to leave that to you."

"Very good. There is no time to strain courtesy about it, so I can quickly tell you what arrangements I should make."

"Speak, then."

"Listen. If you will stay here where you are, I will ride a little furthor along the road and conceal myself under the hedge, which there will be no trouble in doing to-night."

"Not a bit."

"While there I will allow the travellers to pass by unmolested, for it is just ten thousand to one whether they will espy me."

"Very good. And I?"

"When they come to you, you must ride out suddenly, and boldly bid them stand. At the self-same moment I will ride up behind and bid them stand likewise."

"A good plan."

"I think it will prove so. Seeing themselves surrounded, they will have the good sense to surrender what they carry with them without thinking of the least resistance."

"Very good. Take up your position. They are close at hand now."

There was no time to be lost, and the two highwaymen, having settled their plan of operations, proceeded to take up their positions as they had agreed upon.

They had barely time to settle themselves when the travellers came up.

For some reason or other they had slightly slackened their speed, and as they came on they talked to each other in a manner which, as the captain thought, betrayed a considerable amount of apprehension.

The only words he heard were those uttered just as they passed by his place of concealment.

"Confoundedly dark!" was all he heard with perfect plainness.

The other traveller made some response; but only a confused sound reached the captain's ears.

All that then took place gone with extreme rapidity.

No sooner had they passed by than they were confronted by the Black Highwayman.

The suddenness with which he sprang out of the darkness startled the travellers considerably.

Before they could recover themselves in the least they heard their assailant cry, in tones which were full of menace:

"Hand over your purses quickly, and you may resume your journey without injury or opposition! If you refuse, the consequences will be on your own heads!"

"Stand!" cried Captain Hawk, riding forward the moment his companion had done speaking—"stand! You are surrounded! Resistance is vain!"

Hearing this, the travellers seemed indeed to give themselves up for lost.

One produced a purse, and Lord Harcliffe instantly snatched it from him.

At the same identical moment a voice cried, in tones of superhuman excitement:

"Now, my lads—now you have them both!"

"Fly," exclaimed Captain Hawk—"fly! Good God! We have fallen into an ambuscade!"

The utmost confusion followed these words.

Captain Hawk had no sooner spoken the warning than he set his own good steed in motion.

But a sharp volley of firearms succeeded his outcry almost instantly.

Lord Harcliffe, realising the danger of his position, immediately took to flight to save himself.

Not one of the bullets which had been fired had touched him.

"Captain," he cried, as he turned to his comrade, "are you hurt?"

"On—on!" was the reply. "Don't spare your horse! Urge him to the utmost! Rest assured I shall be able to keep close behind you!"

By this time the officers were in full pursuit.

They seemed mad with fury on finding that the discharge of their weapons had been of no effect, and they came on as fast as the incessant application of whip and spur would urge their horses.

But with all their efforts, they stood but a very faint chance of overtaking such steeds as the two highwaymen possessed.

But Captain Hawk on this occasion had not been attended with his usual good fortune.

He had been hit.

He felt the bullet strike him.

The sensation was precisely as though he had been struck with a switch.

But he believed that the injury he had received was not of a serious nature, and so, as we have seen, he was able to ride away, and also to speak in his accustomed manner to his comrade, who never for a moment suspected what was amiss.

CHAPTER CIII.

LORD HARCLIFFE FINDS CAPTAIN HAWK'S STEED WITHOUT A RIDER.

It was, however, only by a stern and stoical effort that Captain Hawk bore up so well against the consequences of the hurt he had received.

He had purposely evaded the question the Black Highwayman had put to him.

The effort to speak at all, however, was well-nigh too much for him.

He felt his brain reel, and then for some seconds he experienced a dreadful sickening sensation, which made him feel as though he was helplessly slipping away from everything.

By a sudden start he then seemed to recover his faculties, his eyes cleared, and he was able to understand that the Black Highwayman was going at full speed in front of him, and that the officers were much closer behind than he had expected.

He hardly realised to the full the peril in which he had so short a time before been placed.

That he had fallen into an ambuscade of his foes flashed into his mind like an inspiration.

It was strictly true.

The police officers, wearied and out of patience with the numerous defeats they had sustained, began to despair of ever accomplishing their object while they continued to use what they called fair and open means to do so.

Stratagem was then called into their aid, and, after much deliberation, a plan was adopted of a nature so well calculated to answer the purpose they had in view, that it is a thousand wonders it did not succeed better than it did.

The sole reason of this, however, was their stupid, blundering way of carrying their conceived design into execution, and which, just at the critical moment, spoiled everything.

A few words will suffice to let the reader fully into the light of all their schemes.

It will be recollected that on rising late in the day at the Greyhound Inn, they had, after satisfying their bodily wants, sat down to hold a consultation as to what should be the next step taken.

The reader will remember also that the officers while talking over their plans did all they could to secure themselves from being overheard by stranger ears.

At any other time than that, no doubt Tom Beckford would have taken some trouble to hear what they had to say to each other, and if he had tried, there is very little doubt he would have succeeded.

But he was by far too much intent upon enjoying the society of Captain Hawk for as long a time as he could to think in the least about them or their plans.

Yet had he listened instead, who can say how great a difference it would have made to the current of after events?

Many things were proposed by one member and another of the troop, but each one was pronounced as unsuitable.

At last, one man, named Barclay, who was the most reserved and taciturn member of all the lot, was induced to admit that he had something to suggest.

An immediate curiosity was felt, and, after a great deal of difference and hesitation, this man proposed the following scheme:—

Two of the officers were to disguise themselves as ordinary travellers, and ride in company along the high-road.

The other officers, keeping in the fields, at each side, and adopting what precautions they could to remain unheard, were to follow at as little distance as was compatible with the perfect success of the plan.

He had no need to explain himself any further.

The idea fixed itself firmly in the minds of every one of his hearers; and Barclay, with apparent relief, resumed his usual listless attitude.

The details was speedily arranged.

They gave no trouble at all.

The excitement of the officers almost exceeded all bounds.

They were frantic; and they looked upon the capture of the Black Highwayman as a dead certainty.

"It seems pretty clear that he wants to get back to London," said the one in command; "and so I propose that we select the London Road as the first place in which to try our experiment. If we don't find him to-night, we shall before we are much older, you may rest perfectly convinced of that."

There was not one dissentient present.

All, too, were impatient to carry their design into execution.

How nearly it succeeded, and what a narrow escape the captain had, the reader knows well enough.

It was the unexpected sight of the two highwaymen together which disconcerted the officers and prevented their plan from succeeding as it otherwise would have done.

To catch one, they had deemed the very summit of their desires; but to take both at one swoop so excited them that they were unnerved.

But to expect that under such circumstances they would be able to preserve their ordinary coolness was by far too much to be expected.

Thus it was that the volley they fired failed to do as much execution as it ought to have done.

There was another thing, too, which conspired to cause this.

In firing they had to take care not to injure their companions, who had rendered them such good service by consenting to take the dangerous part of playing travellers, and without whom the scheme could not have been carried out at all.

The real truth was, however, that they were all too much carried away by excitement to take anything which could be called an aim.

The bullet which had struck Captain Hawk, and which was very near indeed to inflicting a mortal wound, was entirely a chance shot.

What rage and mortification all the officers felt at finding this well-considered plan of theirs miscarry the reader probably will be able to imagine much more easily than we can describe.

Indeed, such words as rage, fury, and despair, are all too weak to employ on the occasion.

The poor horses, as usual, came in for the worst effects of their passion, for they lashed and spurred the poor animals in the most unmerciful manner.

The speed at which the two highwaymen were now going was absolutely terrific.

Such a thing as the interchange of a single syllable of conversation was an utter impossibility.

On they went through the darkness with a swiftness that seemed more than mortal.

Bending down in the saddle, Lord Harcliffe could hear continually the thundering hoofbeats of Satan close behind him.

No matter how fast Phantom went, Captain Hawk's horse never fell behind a single pace.

But the rider?

How fared he in this headlong ride—a ride whose swiftness would have well tried the abilities of the most practised horseman?

Alas! must we say it!

It was only by the greatest wonder in the world that he kept his seat at all.

A thousand times he seemed upon the point of falling to the earth.

From side to side he swayed in a manner which, could but the officers have perceived it, would have given them great hopes of being able to secure one prisoner at least.

Indeed, it almost seemed as though it was nothing else but the swift motion which retained him in the requisite position.

And Captain Hawk, as he rode in this strange manner, was not quite unconscious, but nearly so.

In a dim and dreary manner he seemed to feel that he was flying from his foes at the swiftest gallop Satan was capable of accomplishing.

He knew, too, that he was wounded, and that he was in great danger of falling off.

It was influenced by this knowledge that he shifted the position of his feet in the stirrups somewhat, so that, should he chance to fall, he would at least escape being dragged along the high-road at his furious courser's heels.

For now that Satan's mettle was up so much, and while Phantom continued to gallop on in front, there would be no hope of stopping him.

And so the terribly exciting pursuit continued.

Lord Harcliffe, coming suddenly to a turning branching off to the left, thought fit to avail himself of it in preference to continuing his straight course along the high-road.

He uttered a loud shout at the very top of his voice—a shout which he felt certain would reach the ears of his new friend, and apprise him what it was he meant to do.

And under ordinary circumstances this would have answered its purpose.

But Captain Hawk, though still contriving by some mysterious means to retain his seat upon his horse, was nevertheless beyond hearing or understanding any shout, no matter how loudly it might be uttered.

But Lord Harcliffe was not situated so as to have the remotest idea of this.

So far from thinking his new friend in such extremity

he believed him to be as free from all personal hurt as he was himself.

He slackened speed a very little, and then swept round the corner of the lane with prodigious swiftness.

Satan, who had long been without feeling the least guide upon the rein, and who had done nothing save follow in the track of the other horse in front, prepared to turn the corner too.

The sudden sweep was more than his rider could support.

Swaying quite to one side, he made a wild and desperate attempt to recover his balance.

But the attempt was vain.

Down he went with a hideous, heart-sickening sound—

A dreadful sound; but one that was completely drowned in the terrific clattering of horses' hoofs.

Owing to the precaution he had taken, his feet disencumbered themselves from the stirrups, and he lay just vaguely conscious that he was living, and that he was in imminent danger of being trampled to death beneath the hoofs of the officers' horses, which were coming on with undiminished speed.

He tried to move, making in the attempt efforts sufficient, as he thought, to shift a mountain from its base, but in reality it did not raise his head the space of half an inch.

Then he tried to shout, so as to make his comrade aware of his desperate situation.

But all that came from his lips was a low murmur that would have been inaudible a couple of paces off.

In the meanwhile, Satan, too excited by the chase to be able to display any of his accustomed sagacity, seemingly forgot or was unconscious that he had lost his rider.

Round the corner he went, intent upon following the other horse.

The Black Highwayman as he went turned round and uttered a cry.

It was not responded to; but he thought nothing of that, fancying that any responsive shout his friend might give would be drowned by the thundering din of the horses' feet.

Nor was he indeed certain that his own cry was audible.

To see was impossible, for the darkness, intense as it was before, was now redoubled.

The narrow lane down which he was galloping at such an awful rate was thickly fringed with huge, dense-foliaged trees, which effectually shut out the very faintest glimmerings of light.

But Lord Harcliffe could hear, and therefore was quite certain that Captain Hawk's horse still preserved the same position in the rear.

That he should be without a rider never once struck him, nor was this at all surprising when the whole of the circumstances are borne in mind.

The lane was a long one, and wound about deviously.

It was not until at least three miles had been passed over that Lord Harcliffe bethought himself to listen whether his foes were still upon the track.

He listened.

But all was still.

No sound, save the clatter of Satan's hoofs and the rustling of the tree-tops, smote upon his hearing.

He began to slacken his pace.

The darkness was still undiminished, so that even now, although he looked back continually, he did not make the dreadful discovery that was awaiting him.

"At last," he said—"at last we have distanced them once more."

In order to make sure of this, he stopped his horse altogether.

The place where he reined up was scarcely so dark as the remainder of the way.

To him, having been so long accustomed to the gloom, it seemed actually light.

And by slow degrees the darkness dissipated.

Morning was dawning.

Yet all remained as before calm and still.

He turned round once again to address his comrade, whose silence at this moment struck him as being somewhat strange.

That he should not have done so before is natural enough, for events had been too stirring and exciting to leave thought a chance.

Satan, too, seemed at the same moment to miss the accustomed weight from his back.

The light increased.

Then an ejaculation of amazement blended with the direst horror came from Lord Harcliffe's lips when he saw that his friend's horse was riderless.

For some moments he remained gazing at the empty saddle like one bestraught.

And well indeed might he be incredulous—well indeed might he remain glaring in amazement like one half stunned by receiving a sudden, terrible, and unexpected blow.

CHAPTER CIV.

DESCRIBES WHAT THE OFFICERS DID WITH CAPTAIN HAWK WHEN THEY FOUND HIM LYING INSENSIBLE IN THE ROADWAY.

CAPTAIN HAWK, however, now demands the whole of our attention, and so for a time we will leave Lord Harcliffe to realise the terrible catastrophe which had occurred.

Helplessly he lay in the middle of the roadway, and that dim consciousness of peril and existence which we have made mention of rapidly faded away, leaving him altogether inanimate.

What took place afterwards was to him a perfect blank.

The very last thing of which he was sensible was the dull and muffled sound made by the hoofs of the fast-approaching horses.

The officers as they came on of course were as far from expecting what had taken place as the Black Highwayman himself, though as far as they were concerned the surprise to them would be agreeable enough.

Still urging their horses on with the same disregard for mercy, they all the time bitterly cursed their ill luck for having failed so egregiously in accomplishing their intention.

But they derived some little consolation from finding that traces of the break of day were beginning to appear; and as they had the game fairly afoot before them, there really seemed as reasonable a prospect as they could hope to have that they should be able to keep up the chase successfully.

But these indications of coming day were so faint that they were altogether invisible to Lord Harcliffe as he galloped down at full speed past the trees.

Nor did he dream that morning was anything like so close at hand; but in the conversation which he had had with Captain Hawk time had passed with more than usual rapidity.

Still this light, although every moment it increased, was not sufficient to enable them to discern the body of the highwayman lying extended on the road.

It was the horses who, by their finer senses, first gave notice to their riders that something of an unusual character had occurred.

The one ridden by the leader of the party manifested every sign of intense terror and alarm, and this, as by some species of magnetism, speedily spread itself through all the rest.

The repugnance which most horses have to passing anywhere near a place where human blood has been freshly shed is a fact well known.

Quite a broad stream had flowed from Captain Hawk's terrible wound; and the keen scent of the horses made them aware of it, although the darkness was so perplexing.

The horse belonging to the chief officer came to a dead stop.

The others, as though only waiting for his signal, stopped likewise.

Then, of course, came a great deal of cursing and swearing from their riders' lips.

Vainly, however, was it that they well plied whip and spur.

The more the poor creatures were goaded to advance the more firmly they kept their forefeet planted on the ground.

The only one who was at all unmoved under existing circumstances was Barclay.

Although the scheme which had been so highly applauded had turned out so disastrously, his usual phlegm did not desert him.

On the present occasion, he waited silently, and to all

appearances indifferently, until the abuse of his companions was exhausted.

Not a bit of good had been done by it, for the horses remained just in the same position, resolutely resisting every effort to urge them on.

A dead silence succeeded, which was, however, broken by Barclay.

"I strikes me," he said, in the coolest and most matter-of-fact manner in the world, "that there is something in the road."

"Something in the road?" repeated the chief.

"Those were my words," returned Barclay, with the same impassibility; "and I think also that we had better go and see what it is."

"But the horses won't move!"

"Dismount, then."

"Never!"

"Oh, very well!"

And there he ended the discussion.

It was supposed that his stock of patience would hold out as long as anybody's, and so the event proved.

The chief at last, finding that it was impossible to have things his own way, and feeling sure that this delay was likely to prove fatal to the success of the pursuit, thought fit to follow his subordinate's advice.

But by this time morning had come on with great rapidity, and most objects that were within a distance of a few yards could be readily enough distinguished.

"By Jingo!" cried one of the officers, in tones of excitement which contrasted oddly with Barclay's quiet manner—"by Jingo! It's right! There's something in the road after all! Look there!"

All followed the direction in which his finger pointed.

All eyes then beheld a dark mass of something lying in the middle of the roadway; but from the distance, and in the dim morning light, it was impossible to say what.

Strange to say, the horses now lost some portion of their former terror, for they suffered themselves to be forced several paces further.

When they stopped again it was so near to the body of the wounded and insensible highwayman that there was no longer any possibility of doubting what it was.

But the discovery came upon the police officers so unexpectedly—it was something so different to what they had anticipated—that it struck them all dumb and motionless.

What they saw seemed too impossible to be real; and when they had a little recovered from the first shock of their amazement, the first thing they did was to glance into each others' faces and ask whether they were the sport of some fantastic delusion.

As before, Barclay was the one to speak first.

"Never tell me again," he said, with all the composure imaginable, "that the luck is all on their side and none on ours. What do you think of that for a slice of luck now?"

Hardly ever had the taciturn officer been known to say so much at once before; but in the general intense interest which was naturally excited by their discovery, this was overlooked.

"Can it be possible?" said the chief officer. "It cannot be real; it is too good! It must be some delusion—some trick!"

Barclay said nothing more; but, dismounting, walked leisurely towards the prostrate form.

By this time the light was tolerably clear.

He kicked the body lightly in the side with the toe of his heavy riding-boots.

But Captain Hawk neither moved nor spoke.

Had he been really and truly dead he could not have lain there exhibiting greater show of inanimation.

"He's here, sure enough!" said Barclay, no more unmoved than before. "Our task is over, so far as he is concerned."

The others now, shaking off their amazement, came nearer to satisfy their curiosity.

"Who is it?"

"Captain Hawk."

"So it is!"

"Is he dead?" said another voice.

"Yes, I'll warrant him. Look! there's a nice hole he has got in his side; and there is blood enough about to float a ship!"

The ground round about where the poor captain lay did indeed present a terrible appearance.

His wound had bled very profusely, and it was in consequence of this great loss of vital fluid that he had swooned away—not because the wound itself was serious or mortal.

And the rapid ride which he had taken had, of course, contributed to make the blood flow still faster than it would have done.

This ghastly appearance which so deeply impressed all the officers was more seeming than real.

The dull gray morning light, too, served to make the highwayman's countenance appear more ghost-like than it really was.

Thus it happened that all his foes came without hesitation to the conclusion that he was no more.

The bullet had pierced the captain's side just below the ribs. One inch more to the right, and he would have escaped untouched; but it was not so to be.

Finding him lie still, the officers one by one dismounted, all being anxious to lay a hand on the man who had given them so much trouble for so long.

"It's lucky," said one, "that the reward was offered for him alive or dead, otherwise we should have been done out of our money and had all our trouble for nothing."

"True enough," said the one in command; "but it would have been in every way much more satisfactory and agreeable if we had secured him living. But we must be content to take things as they come."

While these words were passing, Barclay had knelt down by the side of the prostrate highwayman and made an examination of his wound.

He possessed skill enough in surgery to be able to come to the conclusion at once that the wound itself was not sufficient to cause death.

He thrust his hand, too, into the breast of the captain's apparel and placed it above the heart.

His movements were watched with a great deal of attention, especially by the chief.

"Well?" said the latter, with some anxiety perceptible in his tones.

"He is not dead a bit," said Barclay.

CHAPTER CV.

THE OFFICERS CAN HARDLY MAKE UP THEIR MINDS WHAT TO DO WITH CAPTAIN HAWK.

So firmly persuaded were the officers that Captain Hawk was indeed no more, that the intelligence of his being yet in life caused them almost as much astonishment as did the circumstance of finding him there at all.

"Not dead!" ejaculated the one in command, at the very top of his voice. "Do you say not dead?"

"I not only say it, but mean it," answered Barclay.

"Are you sure?"

"Quite. But at the same time, if he does not receive speedy attention I would not give much for his chance of recovery."

"We will do what we can for him," said the chief. "It is no ordinary night's work that we have done tonight, and I should like to make the best of it if I can. I would a thousand times rather deliver him up living than dead."

"Lend me a scarf, then," said Barclay, who, while this was passing, had cut away a portion of the captain's clothing. "I will bind up the wound so as to stanch the bleeding for a time. But I will not answer for the result."

A scarf was immediately handed to him, and the manner in which he set about folding it showed that he had been used to such a job before that day.

The bandage was applied tightly, and then in reply to a question from the one in command Barclay pronounced the captain still alive, though hovering as it were upon the very brink of death.

"Confound it!" said the chief, "we must not have all our trouble for nothing. Can you not do something else for him?"

"A little cold water would be serviceable."

The chief ran off to fetch it himself.

He soon returned with a pretty good quantity of the wholesome fluid, which for want of some better utensil he carried in his hat.

With this Barclay drenched the captain's countenance

[LORD MARCLIFFE SEEKS TIDINGS OF CAPTAIN HAWK.]

very liberally, and he had the satisfaction in a very short time of seeing him move slightly.

A faint, struggling sigh followed, and then the eyes opened.

It was easy enough, however, to perceive that the captain was quite unconscious still of where he was and who they were who stood around them.

He drew his breath a few times in fitful gasps, and then, in spite of the application, he lapsed into insensibility again.

Barclay shook his head.

"You think badly of his state?"

"Yes; the sooner we can get him off our hands the better."

These words caused the chief to assume an attitude of deep reflection.

At the time when the ambuscade was first proposed, the question was raised as to what they should do with the highwayman after they had caught him.

But this was too much like reckoning without their host, some said, and so by general consent the discussion was postponed.

Now the difficulty had to be met, and the commander of the troop found no little difficulty in coming to a decision.

Very wisely, he asked the opinion of Barclay, who had recently risen very much in his approbation.

"What shall we do with him?" he said.

"Get him off our hands without delay."

"Yes, that is easily said. But how are we to do it?"

"Take him to the nearest jail that you think strong enough to hold him; there ought not to be much fear of his getting away while in such a state as you now see him."

"Yes, I know all about that, and admit the force of it. But our instructions are to take him to London——"

"If possible," interposed Barclay.

"Why, yes, as you say truly enough—if possible."

"Very well."

"But——"

"I can't see a but in the case. I can only see that up to the present all attempts to get him so far as London have signally failed. This is not the first time he has been captured, recollect."

The commanding officer scratched his head in perplexity.

"The job bothers me," he said, "and that is the fact."

"I don't see why it need do so. Don't take him to London, that's all. There's my advice: I have done. Take it for what it is worth."

After that Barclay turned aside as though to intimate that he did not intend to waste any more words on the subject.

"One more question, Barclay."

He turned round, but did not speak.

"If we don't take him to London," said the chief, "where the devil shall we take him?—that is what I want to know. Will you tell me?"

"I will."

"Where then?"

"To Huntingdon."

"Huntingdon?"

"Yes. How surprised you speak!"

"I had never once thought of it."

"There is a stone box there strong enough to hold him or a hundred such."

"Oh yes," chorussed the others, "and it is so close at hand too. We might make sure of getting him there safely; and once inside the prison, it would be just as well as to take him to London."

But the chief did not appear to be at all decided.

"I have a last word to say," cried Barclay, "and that is, if he is not seen to pretty quick it will be a case with him."

"To Huntingdon!" was the general cry. "It will be a hundred times the best; and it would be a shame, too, that, after doing all this, the gallows should be cheated of its due!"

This was a feeling which all the officers shared in with wonderful unanimity.

"Let it be so, then," said the commander. "I am not quite reconciled to it, mind you; but under the present circumstances I think it will be a great deal the best."

This point being so settled vastly delighted the men, to whom the prospect of taking their prisoner in safety to the town of Huntingdon was much more agreeable than the perils and anxieties of a long ride to London.

But no sooner was this difficulty got rid of than another presented itself.

Barclay started it.

"And how are you to get him there?" he said.

"Get him there?"

"Those were my words."

"The best way we can," said the chief, perhaps with a desire to imitate his companion's laconism.

"Oh, very well!" said Barclay.

And as he spoke he turned aside with an affectation of great indifference.

"Why the devil did you ask?" cried his superior officer. "What do you mean by your words?"

"You want to deliver him up alive, don't you?"

"Of course I do!"

"Very well, then. I was merely going to tell you that unless you exercise a great deal of care in conveying him, he will be cold mutton before you get there."

"Curse the fellow! he is nothing but a trouble! How heartily glad I shall be to get rid of him!"

"And finger the reward."

"Oh yes!"

The officers were all most anxious to find out the means of conveying Captain Hawk to Huntingdon in the best manner.

Not for a moment, howeve must the reader be allowed to fall into the error of supposing that this was through any motives of humanity on their part.

On the contrary, all they had in view was their own selfish and personal benefit.

While the discussion was proceeding, without much signs of a satisfactory conclusion being arrived at, the attention of the whole troop was arrested by the sound made by the approach of some vehicle.

So absorbed had they been in their discussion that it was not until the light cart—for such it was—was close upon them that they were at all aware they had not the road completely to themselves.

It was now quite light enough to enable them to perceive that this cart was occupied by one man only, who, of course, was driving.

He had on a coat of light blue, which at once enabled the officers to know his trade.

"A butcher off to market," said Barclay—"the very thing for us, if we can only persuade him into the job, and induce him to turn back. I'll be bound his horse is a good one; and if we once got Captain Hawk in the bottom of his cart we should be in the front of Huntingdon Jail in no time."

"I'll insist upon it," said the chief.

On came the butcher at that slashing rate which has become proverbial.

It was only a pony that was harnessed to the cart; and, though the driver was no inconsiderable weight, the way he stepped along was something astonishing.

He drew rein a little upon perceiving the officers, for they formed a group which stretched across the road and blocked it up entirely.

The predominant expression upon his countenance was one of amazement, though as he came nearer it was plainly enough to be seen that it was largely mingled with dismay.

"Hoy!" said the chief officer, a moment afterwards. "Pull up, will you!"

The butcher obeyed.

But he looked more uneasy than before.

The commanding officer spoke in sharp, clear, domineering tones.

"Come a bit closer. We have a wounded prisoner here, and we require you to drive him to Huntingdon Jail."

"I'll be d—d if I do! Get somebody else. Stand out of the way! I am off to market."

The officer pulled his staff of authority from his pocket, and, striding up to the cart, flourished it about in an imposing style.

"Do you see that, Mr. Butcher?"

"Yes, I see it."

"And you understand it, I suppose?"

The response was no more than a growl.

"Very well—that is sufficient. I call upon you in the name of the King to aid and assist us like a good man and true, and if you refuse you know what the consequences will be."

These words were not without their effect, for, of course, it would have been a serious thing for anyone to set the King's authority at defiance.

"It is a d—d shame, then, that a man should be taken out of his business and made to lose his money by an affair like this! Let me go on. There will be some one else passing by before very long, and you can call upon them."

"Oh dear, no!" was the reply.

The chief took hold of the pony by the bridle while he spoke, and led the cart close to the inanimate body of the highwayman.

While so engaged he said:

"We prefer taking you, my friend. You see, the arrival of some one else is quite uncertain; and I notice that you have got a very fast-trotting pony, and our business is of so much importance that it will not admit of a single moment's delay."

The butcher grumbled; but he had to submit.

The back of the cart was taken down, and then, by the united strength of several men, Captain Hawk was raised and placed gently and carefully on his back on the bottom of the cart.

"To Huntingdon Jail did you say?" asked the butcher, with a twinkle in his eye which, if the chief officer had seen it, would have convinced him that mischief of some sort or other was intended.

"Yes."

"And you are in a hurry?"

"We are. You will have to make that pony of yours step out, I can tell you."

The ghost of a grin appeared upon the butcher's good-humoured-looking face; but by drawing down the corners of his mouth he managed to conceal it.

"She can step," he said.

"And she will have to!"

"All right, then; here goes!"

So saying, the butcher leaned forward in the cart, and doubling the reins at the same moment, he administered a sharp blow to his pony.

The result was rather surprising, especially to the officers.

Away went the pony, at a rate which no one would have believed him capable of.

Round went the wheels with incredible velocity; and before the officers could recover themselves enough to mount, the butcher and his cart, with its precious contents, had vanished in a cloud of dust.

CHAPTER CVI.

IN WHICH IS RELATED WHAT TOOK PLACE ON THE ARRIVAL OF CAPTAIN HAWK AT HUNTINGDON JAIL.

Never had the police officers made so fine an exhibition of their cursing and swearing abilities as they did upon this present occasion.

Assuredly, if curses had been possessed of mortal powers, the butcher would have been a dead man before he got half-way to his destination.

"D—n it all!" said Barclay, going as near to losing his temper as anybody had ever seen him. "It is worse than useless to stop here. Let us mount this moment and pursue him."

As for the chief, he was simply furious; and when we have said that we have said all which it is in our power to say.

He vowed the direst vengeance upon the audacious butcher's head the very moment he should catch sight of him.

The butcher, when he started off in the manner which we have described, had no intention whatever of conniving in any way at the highwayman's escape.

But he was annoyed at the way in which he had been treated; and as he was a man who dearly loved a joke, he determined to have his revenge.

What decided him was the sneering tones in which he fancied the chief officer spoke of his pony.

"I'll let them to know," he said, doubling up the reins preparatory to administering another blow—"I'll let them to know that there's chaps as knows a thing or two out here in the country, though they do come from Lunnun! Now, my lass!" he added, addressing his pony. "Sail away! I should not be afraid to lay a thousand pounds that not one of their long-legged animals can come within two or three miles of us."

There seemed a strong degree of probability about this, owing to the excellent start which he had obtained, while the pony rattled along in the mysterious manner of which a butcher's pony alone is capable.

And all this time poor Captain Hawk continued to lay completely insensible in the bottom of the vehicle.

The present kind of locomotion seemed by no means to be that which his condition required.

The great rate at which the butcher's pony went made the cart jolt awfully, and the helpless highwayman received many terrible bruises in consequence.

But the butcher himself was so much delighted at the nice little trick which he was playing the officers that it drove all recollection of the condition of the wounded man out of his mind.

He stopped several times to look behind him, but not once did he catch a glimpse of the police.

Just as he was entering Huntingdon, he began to think that carrying out his impulse in the way he had was an imprudent thing to do, to say the least of it.

"Confound it all!" he said. "Here most likely I shall get into no end of trouble through this affair! What a fool I am to be sure! And I have lost the market into the bargain!"

The butcher, however, was gifted with too easy a temperament to grieve long about anything, and before he had gone much further he had come to the conclusion he could not do better than let things take their course and make the best of them.

"I should think," he said to himself, "if I take this fellow, whoever he is, and leave him safely at the jail I can't get into much trouble; but whether or not, it is the only thing I can do now."

Arrived at this philosophic conclusion, he gave his fast-trotting horse another good cut, and in a few seconds afterwards he pulled up with a jerk in front of the jail.

Alighting nimbly, he knocked with more vigour at the entrance than probably anyone had dared to do before.

The door was opened by a warder to whom the butcher was perfectly well known.

"Good morning, Mr. Bones!" he said. "Who would have thought of seeing you here at this time in the morning!"

"I shouldn't have thought of it myself a few minutes ago," replied the butcher.

"What is the matter, then?"

"I have brought you a prisoner."

"A prisoner?"

"Yes; you will find him safe and sound at the bottom of my cart. There does not seem to be much chance of his getting away."

"A prisoner in your cart! What next, I wonder!"

"Come and see him."

The warder called out to another man in the vestibule of the prison to pay attention to the lock, while he walked across the small paved courtyard to where the butcher's cart was standing.

The warder looked in; but as he had no suspicion as to who the prisoner was, he did not recognise him.

"Good Heavens!" he cried, catching a glimpse of the blood-stained condition of the captain's apparel. "What can all this mean? You must have made some mistake, Mr. Bones," he added, looking at the butcher with some little suspicion.

"A mistake! What do you mean?"

"Mean! Why, that you ought to have taken the poor fellow to the hospital, and not have brought him here."

"Oh no, nothing of the sort! I have made no mistake, I can promise you that."

"But who is he?"

"I am sure if you don't know I can't tell you."

"Know!" said the warder, beginning to get suspicious in good earnest. "How should I know? I have never seen the man before in my life!"

"No, more have I," said Mr. Bones.

"And yet you bring him in this bleeding and wounded condition to the door of the jail!"

"Certainly."

"What has he done? What is the charge against him?"

"I don't know."

"Your conduct is very suspicious, Mr. Bones."

"Hold—hold!"

"I say it is. And though I don't want to be guilty of any act of disrespect to a townsman, yet I must really say that I am in duty bound to retain you here until I can learn a little more of the particulars of this mysterious affair."

"Pooh—pooh!"

The warder turned round and called out to the man he had left at the door, and who was gazing at what was going on with wide-open eyes.

"Call the Governor, Gutch!" he said. "Curse me if I understand this! And I don't intend to run the risk of getting myself into trouble."

"Nonsense—nonsense!" said the butcher, with more apprehension than he could conceal, for he wanted to get off if he could before the officers arrived. "It's all right, I tell you. Carry the man inside, and let me be off."

"Now, do you really think, Mr. Bones, that we could receive a prisoner in any such way as that? No—no."

"I don't know anything about prisons and prison regulations," was the retort. "I want to be off."

"And I can't permit it. It would not be right for me to do so. Thank goodness, here is the Governor at last!"

A fussy little individual, whose whole attention appeared to be absorbed in fitting an eye-glass to his eye, now came with a mincing step across the courtyard

"Aw! Baldwin," he said, "what is it? Aw—what's amiss?"

"If you please, sir," said the warder, "Mr. Bones has brought a dead man in his cart, and wants to leave him here a prisoner."

"A dead man!"

"Well, sir, I don't exactly mean that, though he looks as though he had got very little life in him. I thought at first he had mistaken the jail for the hospital."

While this little conversation was going on, Mr. Bones was in a state of mind very hard indeed to be described.

More than once he felt inclined to start off and run for his life; and, indeed, the only thing that restrained him was the conviction that he should not be able to get away.

The Governor, with an air of vast importance, walked up to the cart and looked in.

"Gracious powers!" he ejaculated, and becoming oblivious of his eye-glass from that moment. "Mr. Bones, where ever did you get him from?"

The butcher was almost afraid to open his mouth, lest something should come out of it that would make his situation worse than it was.

The Governor, however, repeated his question in such a commanding manner that refusal was an impossibility.

"I was told to bring him here by a party of police officers, who turned me back as I was on my way to market."

"A party of police officers? But where are they?"

"Coming, sir."

Just at this moment the whole troop of officers swept round the corner into the street where the prison was situated.

They were all in a terrible state of wrath, and made at once up to the cart.

The first anxious glance was, of course, cast into it.

"Oh, thank goodness," said the chief, "he is here! Well, it is more than I expected."

The officers clustered round the cart in a dense throng for the double purpose of taking a peep at their prisoner and for keeping him secure.

The Governor coughed very loudly, to call attention to the fact of his presence upon the scene.

The officer in command made a very low bow.

"I presume, sir," he said, "that you are already aware that I have brought you a prisoner of unusual importance this morning?"

"I am not aware that you have brought one, sir; I rather think Mr. Bones has done that service."

The butcher had kept out of sight up to this moment, as well as he had been able.

But the chief officer now turned round upon him, with his face inflamed by fury.

"Villain—rascal—wretch!" he cried. "What did you mean by starting off in that way? I have a great mind to give you into custody on the charge of seeking to procure the escape of the notorious highwayman, Captain Hawk!"

At hearing this much-dreaded name pronounced, the butcher's jaw fell, and he staggered back.

How far he would have gone is hard to say had he not been suddenly brought to a standstill by forcibly coming into contact with the prison wall.

But his whole aspect was so wonderfully expressive of ludicrous dismay that the chief officer was compelled to burst out into a laugh.

"C-Cap-Captain Hawk!" ejaculated the butcher. "Do you mean to say that I have been riding with Captain Hawk in my cart? Oh, lawk! and I have got my purse in my pocket!"

Mr. Bones either was or pretended to be in a dreadful state of fright.

"Come, come," said the Governor—"let us proceed to business in a regular manner. I must understand this. As to suppose that Mr. Bones, who is one of our most respectable and influential tradesmen, would think for a moment of conniving at the escape of Captain Hawk is absurd."

"Very good, sir; but I must inform you that he went the right way to let him get off, as I will explain to you presently."

"You are sure there is no mistake?"

"I am perfectly certain of it."

"That's all right then. I fancied that I recognised him at the first glance."

"He is a prisoner at last, sir," said the officer, with a triumph which he could hardly contain within reasonable bounds. "But such is his obstinacy that I should not be surprised if he cheated the gallows after all."

"As how?" said the Governor, at length, refinding his eye-glass. "What do you mean?"

"Why, I should not be surprised at him dying, just on purpose to spite us."

"He is not dead yet then?"

"Oh, no—that—that is, I think not. At least, he was not when we lifted him into the cart."

The officer spoke hurriedly and anxiously, for he was by no means sure that the prisoner had not expired on the way.

"I thought he looked uncommonly like a corpse when I peeped at him; but, then, he may only be insensible."

With a view to ascertain whether this was the case or not, the Governor and the chief officer made their way hurriedly to the side of the cart.

But Captain Hawk, though in so great a strait, was worth a great many dead ones yet.

While the above conversation was going on he had to some degree recovered his senses.

Where he was, of course he could not tell; but he knew that he was in no ordinary danger.

This feeling was so strong that, despite his weak state it gave him strength to start up and glare wildly around.

The first objects on which his eyes lighted were the faces of the Governor and the chief police officer.

CHAPTER CVII.

A CELL IN HUNTINGDON JAIL IS EXPRESSLY PREPARED FOR CAPTAIN HAWK.

But the strength which had enabled Captain Hawk to do this much speedily departed, and with a kind of groan he sank back in the cart, striking his head so sharp a blow against the woodwork as to deprive him of all consciousness once more.

"Hurrah!" said the chief officer. "He isn't dead!"

"Aw—that's true enough," responded the Governor; "but he looks as though he was not long for this world."

"Never mind," was the business-like answer. "I have brought him here alive. There can be no dispute about that; and the reward, when divided, will make just a nice little sum apiece. Mr. Governor, I'll just trouble you for your receipt."

"Aw—yes. But I don't know whether I should do right by admitting him."

"Oh, but you will. It's all right."

"You ought to take him to Newgate."

"He would die on the way. And not only that, my warrant authorises me to lodge him in the nearest place of security."

The paper alluded to was produced; and the Governor, after one glance, was satisfied that it would be in vain for him to raise any more objections.

"Help him out, then," he said, with a sigh. "Bring him inside. I know I shall have no end of trouble with him. But it's a good job he is as he is. Things might have been a great deal worse."

And comforted by this piece of practical philosophy, the Governor led the way into the interior of the prison.

The officers were all highly delighted at the prospect of getting rid of their prisoner so speedily, and manifested it by the alacrity with which they set about getting the unfortunate captain out of the cart.

A stretcher was brought from the interior of the prison, and on this the highwayman was laid and carried in, being all the while in happy oblivion of what was being done to him.

A great anxiety was manifested by every one of the officers to have a hand upon the stretcher and assist in carrying the prisoner.

Perhaps this was because they feared that unless they did this they should not be able to make such a good claim of having taken part in the arrest.

There was one personage who noticed this more than anyone else, and upon whom it produced the greatest effect.

This was Bones, the butcher.

The dread he had of the consequences of what he had done made him shrink back as much as he could out of sight.

The attention of the officers had been so taken up with Captain Hawk that for the moment they entirely forgot all about the individual upon whose head, as they rode to Huntingdon, they had vowed such bitter vengeance.

But the butcher was watching his opportunity of getting off.

The very moment he beheld the officers enter the building with their burden, he emerged from the corner where he had squeezed himself, and made all speed to his cart.

Up into it he scrambled with marvellous rapidity.

How on earth he did so was one of those things which for the life of him he could never remember.

But he seized hold of the reins and off he went like a shot, at a pace his fast-trotting pony had never performed before, and which he felt certain would set at defiance any pursuit which the officers might attempt.

He was out of sight in a moment.

But, in real truth, he had very little grounds for apprehension.

The officers were too much delighted to think they had succeeded in lodging their troublesome prisoner safely to care much for matters of minor moment.

The whole of their attention was engrossed, for they now looked upon the reward as being as good as though in their pockets already.

The stretcher was deposited upon the floor of the vestibule—

A careful examination of the prisoner made so that the Governor might have no fear or doubt as to his identity, and then the receipt was signed.

The chief officer clutched the precious paper with hawk-like avidity.

"Let us hope," he exclaimed, in tones of the utmost excitement—"let us hope this is only an earnest of our future success."

"What do you mean?" inquired the Governor, in no little surprise.

"I mean that we were as near as could be in capturing the Black Highwayman at the same stroke. But we shall have him ere long: perhaps soon enough to have them both tried next sessions."

"You will have to be quick, then."

"When do they begin?"

"In a fortnight from this very day."

"That's ample time. If we don't nab him by then we will give the job up altogether."

"He's a coming-to now, sir," said one of the warders at this moment—"he's a coming-to. Hear him groan!"

Captain Hawk did begin at this moment to evince some signs of returning vitality.

Whether it was merely from the struggles of nature, or whether the pleasant warmth of the huge wood fire burning in the vestibule which caused his heart to beat again, we know not.

Apparently his pain was great, for deep groans came from his throat—groans which grew louder and more awful to listen to as he gradually recovered his lost strength.

"Aw—ah!" exclaimed the Governor, contemplating the prisoner through his eye-glass, which by some mysterious means he had managed to fix in its right place—"aw—we must send for the surgeon. It won't do to have him die here after all this trouble—aw—no! That would be too bad! Oh, d—n it!"

The last exclamation was caused by his troublesome glass, which again dropped out of his eye.

"No," said the chief officer, bending over the scarcely yet conscious form, and regarding it with the closest attention, "he must not die. That would be a complete swindle. There's one comfort, though, to be drawn from his condition."

"And—aw—what is that?"

"You will not have so much to dread from an escape."

"I'll forgive him if he gets away."

"Don't be over-confident. We shall keep good watch for our own sakes, and I shall at once let the Secretary of State know all that has happened."

"Aw—very good. Oh, here comes the surgeon."

A grave elderly man entered at this moment.

His face looked graver still the moment his eyes rested on the form of the highwayman.

But without asking a superfluous question, he proceeded to make an examination of the wound.

"Who put on this bandage?" he said.

Barclay stood forward.

"I did, sir."

"Then you may have the satisfaction of knowing that you have saved his life. But for the skilful manner in which it was bound on he must by this time have bled quite to death."

He called for several things that were essential to dressing the wound properly.

The anxious group standing around watched all his movements in intense silence.

Captain Hawk continued to moan and to move about uneasily.

But although alive to pain, it did not seem as though he was at all aware of where he was.

Not until the surgeon had finished bandaging the wound did the chief officer speak, and then in tones which, though suppressed, proclaimed how intense was the interest he felt, he said:

"Do you think he will recover, doctor?"

"I can hardly take upon myself to give a direct reply to that question."

"The wound is a serious one, then?"

"Yes, in one sense it is very so. Not that it has touched any vital part, but because so much blood has been lost. If inflammation and fever do not set in he will soon get over it, but that is hardly probable."

Captain Hawk sighed and closed his eyes.

The doctor looked vexed. In speaking as he had he had fully believed the wounded man was unable to understand what he said.

But by his manner it really seemed as though he overheard the last words.

"Aw—but, doctor," said the Governor, who, having fixed his glass, felt something like himself again—"aw, doctor, what are we to do with him?—aw!"

"Do with him!" echoed the doctor, in considerable surprise at the question being put to him.

"Yes—aw," replied the Governor—"what are we to do with him?"

"He requires the closest and most careful attention," he said, "and unless he gets it his life is not worth a straw."

"He must have attention," said the chief officer—"he must not be allowed to die."

"Aw—doctor," said the Governor—"aw—you see he is a desperate character—I ought to say a most desperate character—and although—aw—he looks so helpless as he does now—aw—yet we must adopt proper precautions to keep him secure. If he can't get out himself, there is the danger that some of his accomplices will come and fetch him—aw!"

"If they do," said the doctor, "his death is certain."

"I shall be on the safe side, doctor: I always keep on the safe side—aw—aw—yes, the safe side."

"Do what you please," said the doctor, shrugging his shoulders. "It is your province, not mine. I have nothing to do with it."

"Aw—of course—just so—d—n it!"

Down came the eye-glass again.

The doctor looked at his new patient with fresh attention.

"To look at him," he said, "no one would think him very desperate. Are you quite sure you have made no mistake?"

"Quite certain, sir," said the chief officer, who could not endure that the least shadow of a doubt should be entertained for a moment. "We caught him, sir, in the very act—in the very act, sir."

"And who is he?"

"Captain Hawk."

"This Captain Hawk?" said the doctor, with the manner of one who finds something too hard to be believed.

"Yes. And if you feel any doubt, take this paper, and compare the written description."

"You amaze me! I had pictured this desperate highwayman, about whom I have heard so much, as being a very different man indeed."

"If you only knew what he is capable of, sir!" said the chief officer. "Sometimes it seems to me to be a thing not to be believed."

"But what do you intend to do with him?"

"He must be kept in absolute safety, that is certain," said the police officer, "and if it would not be taken as amiss on my part to make a suggestion——"

"No—no—aw—decidedly no. Glad to hear it."

"Then I should propose that one of the strongest cells in the prison be fitted up in the most comfortable manner the place will admit of, and the prisoner, or patient, whichever I ought to call him, be there kept under safe guard."

"And a very good suggestion too," said the doctor, "and so far as I am concerned I should recommend that it be carried out."

"Aw—yes—to be sure: let it be done."

Instructions were given for the cell to be put in readiness, and while this was being done the surgeon endeavoured by various methods to restore the wounded highwayman to complete consciousness.

For some time all his efforts were perfectly fruitless, and it was not until he had well bathed his patient's head and applied some very pungent essence to his nostrils, that he succeeded in evoking any tokens of returning consciousness.

Captain Hawk opened his eyes languidly to their full extent.

His gaze rested upon the countenances of those by whom he was surrounded; but it did not appear that he knew where he was.

But the eyes soon brightened, and a wondrous change was speedily visible in his countenance.

After a violent effort, he spoke.

But the tones of his voice were so low and indistinct as to make what he said almost inaudible to those who were standing close by.

"What place is this?" he whispered. "What has occured? Where—where is——"

"You must not speak," said the doctor, interrupting him, "nor must you attempt to do so. Keep perfectly calm and still; by these means only can you hope to recover yourself."

Captain Hawk closed his eyes.

Not doing so, however, to express acquiescence in the surgeon's words, but because he felt the effort to keep them open any longer was too much for him.

"It looks serious," said the chief officer.

"Very," was the doctor's answer. "Something unusual must have happened after he received the wound—something which has caused the loss of blood to be ten times greater than it would be under ordinary circumstances."

"Well, yes," said the chief officer, with a grin, "something of an unusual character did happen—that is right enough."

"What was it?"

"Why, he rode on horseback like a demon for a matter of a dozen miles before he fell out of the saddle."

"Good heavens! And did he apply no bandage?"

"No—no; we were too close to him for that."

This intelligence seemed to astonish the doctor exceedingly; and he questioned the officer closely as to every particular.

The preparations in the cell were quickly made, and a warder now entered the vestibule to say that all things were in perfect readiness.

Under the doctor's superintendence, the highwayman was carried into his cell, and placed upon a rude but tolerably comfortable bed.

Although partially aware of what was going forward, the unfortunate captain was not able to make the slightest movement, or even so much as utter the faintest whisper to protest against it.

CHAPTER CVIII

CAPTAIN HAWK RECOVERS HIS CONSCIOUSNESS, AND FINDS THAT HE IS THE INMATE OF A PRISON CELL.

One of the turnkeys was appointed to share the cell with Captain Hawk—not only as a protection against his escape, but also to perform to some extent the duties of a nurse.

The Governor, who was full of anxiety that his prisoner should be kept quite secure, climbed up to the grated aperture in the wall, by which light and air were admitted, and made sure that the massive iron bars were quite firm in their setting.

Most scrutinisingly he looked around, and pried into every corner.

Then, with a last glance at the prisoner, he crossed the threshold.

With his own hands he made the door secure, and, having locked it, pulled out the key and placed it in his pocket.

"There," he said, complacently, "I shall now be able to feel quite sure that no one will be able to hold a communication of any kind with the prisoner without my knowledge. Doctor," he added, "when you want to pay your next visit come to me."

"That will be in about three hours' time."

"I shall be in readiness to attend you then."

We ought to mention that the Governor even took the precaution to station one of his best and most reliable men outside the cell door, and another in the yard just under the grated opening of which we have made mention.

With three guards like this, one might consider Captain Hawk to be tolerably well taken care of.

The officers who had brought him were particularly well satisfied, though they vowed and declared that not one unnecessary and superfluous precaution had been taken.

The Governor was quite puffed-up with conceit, and had the vanity to think that if no one else could succeed in keeping the redoubtable highwayman in safe custody he should have no trouble about it.

The officers then took their departure, having no pretext for remaining any longer.

"You will take care to let me know when the prisoner is likely to be carried before the magistrate," were the last words spoken by the chief, as, followed by his men, he strode into the courtyard.

"Aw—certainly—to be sure—yes! Aw!"

The Governor was conscious how much additional dignity would be imparted to his whole appearance if he could only get his refractory glass to remain fixed in his eye; but he had to give it up as a bad job.

No sooner had the officers departed than the great door was closed, and the prison resumed its ordinary still, tomb-like aspect.

People, however, rapidly began to collect around the outer gates, for with marvellous rapidity the intelligence was spread abroad that the celebrated Captain Hawk had been brought a prisoner to Huntingdon Jail, and securely lodged in one of the strongest cells in the prison.

As a matter of course, the most exaggerated and ridiculous rumours respecting the capture were freely circulated, anything like the plain and simple truth being too tame to be endurable.

Poor Captain Hawk continued insensible for more than four-and-twenty hours.

At the expiration of that period he looked around him for the first time with eyes that informed his mind what was his actual condition.

He did not speak.

The turnkey, who was sitting on a small stool, with his back to the door, knew nothing at all about his recovery, but remained whistling dismally, while his eyes were riveted upon the grated window.

Captain Hawk made no movement.

Quietly his eyes passed from one object to another around him.

What had happened last he could not remember very well; but it was with an icy-cold feeling about his heart that he concluded that he could be nowhere else but in a strong stone prison cell.

He knew that he was weak, faint, and sick.

He had not the energy to move one of his limbs, nor did it appear strange to him that he should remain where he was without making a single effort to rise.

He closed his eyes again, for the light which came into the cell, though by no means brilliant, yet caused him intolerable pain.

He tried then to think, though his brain whirled and throbbed in such a way as well-nigh to set all thought at defiance.

But by slow and painful degrees he was able to recall what had occurred.

He remembered vividly stopping the two travellers.

He recollected the wound that had been inflicted upon him.

At this point he put his hand to his side, which was the first movement he made.

While doing so, the conclusion flashed upon him that he must have fallen from his horse and then have been taken prisoner while in a state of insensibility.

But of all this he had no recollection, not even so much as a dim and indistinct remembrance.

He was badly hurt—he was sure of that; for even moving one arm had caused him much anguish.

But he could not think that the wound was a mortal one—he would not think of it.

The next anxious consideration that presented itself to his mind was the question as to where he was

Again he glanced around, while he noted every little detail of the things surrounding him.

His lips moved slightly as he asked himself the question:

"Am I in Newgate?"

The sullen-looking face of the turnkey on guard, the massive iron-studded door, the solid stone walls—everything he beheld seemed to furnish an affirmative answer to his question.

Then he wondered what had become of his new friend.

Of course, as the reader knows, he had no idea whether he had escaped, or whether he had shared a similar fate.

The position in which he lay was irksome to him, and by a powerful effort he rolled himself over on to one side.

The noise he made in doing so was very slight, and yet sufficient to attract the observation of the turnkey, who removed his eyes from the window on which they had been so persistently fixed, and favoured the prisoner with a good long stare.

"Why, captain," he said, "come-to at last, have you? Blest if I didn't think you meant to give Jack Ketch the go-by after all!"

"I'm a prisoner?"

"Rather, I should say! Have you only just woke up to that funny fact? Eh, captain?"

"Is—is—this——"

"What, captain?"

"Newgate?"

"No; we're a precious long way off that 'ere beautiful place. I wishes I was there this minute, I do."

"Not Newgate?" said Captain Hawk, in great astonishment, for he made sure the first thing his capturers would do would be to convey him without loss of time to the great metropolitan prison.

"No, captain, you're at Huntingdon—that's where you are."

The prisoner was more surprised still.

Desperate as his position seemed, yet this unlooked-for piece of intelligence from the warder had the effect of causing hope to inflame his breast.

Yet why he hoped was a thing which would have puzzled him to tell.

"Huntingdon!" he repeated. "Why on earth did they bring me here instead of taking me direct to Newgate?"

"Why, you see, captain, they was so awfully considerate—so werry partikler humane—that they couldn't think of it."

"But why not?"

"Because they could not bear the idea of thinking that you might cheat Jack Ketch; and since you have been here they have taken such pains to get you round as no tongue could tell. One would have thought they were a saving of your life for some very important purpose, that they would."

"And I am better, then?"

"Rather."

"And I have been in very great danger?"

"Rather, I tell you again. How do you feel now?"

"Not like myself."

"But you're going on, captain, for all that—I know you are going on most wonderful and partikler well."

"Indeed! How is that?"

"Why, I heard the doctor say it the last time he was here. Says he, 'This young man has got a constitution more like a horse than a human being. He's getting well all one way.'"

"Did he say that?"

"Rather!"

Captain Hawk's hope increased.

And it was truly wonderful to see what a difference these words made to him.

Having heard the doctor's opinion, he felt sensibly better already.

"Why, captain," continued the man, who no doubt found it an uncommon relief to speak after having been compelled to maintain silence for so long—"why, captain, he said that the wound was a mere nothing, and that but for the loss of blood there would never have been anything the matter with you."

"Many thanks for what you have just told me. Feel assured that I shall not forget to reward your kindness."

The turnkey shook his head dubiously.

"Your time's very short," he said.

"Short! What do you mean?"

"Why, they are most anxious to have you taken before the magistrate and have you examined, so that you could be formally committed here to take your trial."

"Oh, I see."

"But the doctor is very firm, and won't listen to anything of the sort being done. Do you know why they are so anxious?"

"No; why is it?"

"Because the sessions will come on in rather less than a fortnight from now, and they most partikler wish to have your trial on then, so that you can be scragged comfortably without any more bother."

"I am infinitely obliged to them, but if you will tell me one thing you will add very much to the amount of obligation I am already under to you."

"Out with it, captain. Fire away!"

"I want to know whether anyone else was captured with me or soon after me!"

"Do you mean one of your pals?"

"I do."

"Then there hasn't."

The captain's heart gave a bound, for he had all the time been expecting to hear that Lord Harcliffe had been captured as well as himself.

It was only from the dread he felt of having his worst fears realised that he forbore for so long from putting the question.

"You seem glad, captain, to think as we don't enjoy the werry great honour of having any of your pals under this hospitable roof."

But the exertion of talking so much, and the excitement caused by the knowledge that Lord Harcliffe was not captured proved too much for his weak powers.

He drew a long breath and fainted.

When he recovered he found that several persons occupied his cell.

The friendly turnkey had disappeared.

In fact, the Governor and the doctor had arrived just in time to catch a few words which convinced them he had been talking to the prisoner, and as that was directly against the rules he was rudely banished.

But the doctor, having restored the captain to consciousness, proclaimed him to be wonderfully better, in spite of the shock which some exciting conversation or other had given him, and which would probably retard his recovery for a day or two.

The Governor vowed vengeance upon the turnkey.

Gladly would he have precluded the possibility of the recurrence of such an event by leaving the cell without anyone in it as guard.

But he had great dread the prisoner would somehow contrive to escape if he omitted this precaution.

Another warder was summoned, and the strictest injunctions laid upon him that he was not on any pretext to enter into conversation with the prisoner.

The doctor asked the captain whether he wanted anything.

An affirmative answer was given in a moment.

"What is it?"

"Liberty."

"For that you will have to ask in vain."

"You will at least allow me to send to my friends?"

"We will talk of it to-morrow."

That was all the satisfaction he could get.

When they had all taken their departure, Captain Hawk remained for a long time silent, plunged in busy thought.

Then he began to give furtive glances at the countenance of the new turnkey, so as to come to a conclusion, if he could, as to what kind of disposition he had.

The result was so far encouraging that it induced the captain to speak.

"I have heard what has been said," he whispered, "but it does not seem natural that we should spend so much time here together without opening our lips. At any rate, I cannot be silent, so that if you cannot join in the conversation, you must listen."

"Well, captain," said the man, after a cautious glance around, and sinking his voice to as low a tone as he could, "I am sure I would do anything I could to oblige you."

"That's right! I thought so by the look of your face."

"Ah well! Do you know what I have been wondering?"

"What?"

"How you could be such a fool as to get better."

"How—what?"

"Why, if you recover you will only be scragged; and surely it would be better to die comfortably in bed."

But the captain gave a disdainful smile.

Already the thoughts of escape had taken a firm hold upon his imagination.

"You won't have a ghost of a chance, that is very certain!" said the turnkey. "You have made yourself too great an enemy."

"Indeed! Who is that?"

"Sir Thomas Walker, the celebrated Bow Street magistrate. He is down here on a special commission to apprehend and convict you. He declares you robbed and insulted him, and vows to have revenge—not to be satisfied, indeed, till he sees you dangling at the end of a rope.

CHAPTER CIX.

LORD HARCLIFFE SEEKS TIDINGS OF CAPTAIN HAWK FROM THE WOOD-CUTTER.

For a time, however, we must be content to leave Captain Hawk in his cell at Huntingdon while we devote a little space to the doings of the Black Highwayman.

It will no doubt be recollected that when we saw Lord Harcliffe last was at the terrible moment that he discovered that Satan was riderless, and that his new comrade was nowhere to be found.

We have said that, after making this terrible and wholly unlooked-for discovery, he had remained staring at the empty saddle like one bereft of all faculty of reason.

But that incredulity which he had first felt soon passed away.

The direful, awful truth was palpably before him.

"Good heavens!" he exclaimed, in tones of the utmost agony. "I have been riding all this way with a riderless steed! Why—oh! why did I not turn back sooner and see that he was no longer with me? I shall never be able to reproach myself enough!"

Lord Harcliffe did indeed feel that he had been most terribly to blame; and yet when we calmly consider the whole of the events we shall see that his censures upon his own conduct were not altogether just.

But he would not suffer himself to be comforted in the least by any such consolatory thoughts.

Captain Hawk, however, had called out to him and bidden him ride on with all the speed he was capable of making, assuring him he should be able to keep close at his heels.

And Lord Harcliffe did not even know that his new friend had been so much as scratched, for Captain Hawk under-estimating the injury he had met with, and anxious to avoid any delay, had returned an evasive answer when questioned on the point.

"Had I known that he had been hurt," the Black Highwayman said, in tones of the most poignant distress—"could I but have guessed at it—how very different would have been the result!

"I should have looked back continually to see that he was all right; but when I heard his horse behind me coming on so regularly, I made certain all was well."

Lord Harcliffe was perforce compelled to remain where he was, giving audible expression to his deep and sincere regret.

At length, however, he shook off the heaviness of his spirit.

Now, when he looked around him, all objects were well illuminated.

Morning had fairly dawned, and in a very little more space the sun would begin to show himself above the horizon.

"I have been wrong," he exclaimed, striking his forehead a sharp blow with his open palm. "Instead of remaining here idle and motionless, giving vent to vain regrets, I ought to have put myself in action: I ought to have commenced a search for him without delay. But it is not yet perhaps too late."

Animated by this hope, Lord Harcliffe directed his panting steed nearer to the captain's noble horse.

The gallant creature seemed full well to comprehend that something of a most distressing character had taken place.

His eyes glared, his nostrils dilated, and he seemed more than half inclined to dart away at a wild, headlong gallop.

Lord Harcliffe was full of dread lest this additional misfortune should take place.

It cost him, however, an effort to put on a show of outward calmness, and to speak soothingly and caressingly to the terrified animal.

By doing so he succeeded in taking a firm grasp upon the rein; and as soon as he had done this he set about the accomplishment of the task that he had set himself.

The saddle was stained with blood; and one stirrup had completely lost its original colour.

Down Satan's foam-covered flanks, too, the sanguine stream had flowed.

"Alas—alas!" said the Black Highwayman, as he observed these indications of a prodigious loss of blood, "he has surely perished! I shall find him lying in the roadway dead. That is," he added, "if the officers are not first upon the spot to find him."

It was just at this moment that he comprehended how it was the officers had so soon and so completely given up the pursuit.

"They *have* found him!" he ejaculated, in tones of deeper anguish than had yet passed his lips. "It comes upon me now with the irresistible force of conviction: they have found him on the roadway either dead or senseless, and have made him their prisoner; that, and that only, is the reason why they have abandoned the pursuit of me."

Nothing but positive proof to the contrary could have shaken Lord Harcliffe in the belief which he now held.

Without another moment's pause he urged his exhausted steed into a gallop.

Satan at first seemed half inclined to refuse to bear him company, but after a few caressing words and a steady pull upon the rein, he followed easily at his side.

But though Lord Harcliffe made such good speed, it seemed to take him an endless time to reach the point where the lane debouched upon the high-road.

In the darkness, and in his excitement, he had indeed gone quite twice as far as he could have believed possible.

And what made the way back seem to him doubly long was that, at every tree which he perceived before him, he expected to see the termination of the lane.

More than once he began to doubt whether he had not fallen into some unaccountable error—whether he had not mistaken his way.

But the freshly-made marks of horses' hoofs on the soft road convinced him that he was indeed retracing his steps.

But, as all things must have an end, the high-road was gained at last.

But by the time he emerged upon it, the sun was shining brightly in the eastern sky, and in the distance could be seen men working in the different fields, showing that the new day had fairly begun.

Lord Harcliffe was now quite satisfied upon one point.

Captain Hawk had not turned the corner of the lane.

So far, then, at all events, he had been riding alone

[LORD HARCLIFFE'S ENCOUNTER WITH ISAAC.]

How much further he had been doing so he had yet to find.

If the captain had fallen off his horse in that narrow lane there must have been indisputable evidence of the fact upon the ground.

But there was nothing of the kind—nothing but the impression made by the flying hoofs of the two horses.

Lord Harcliffe rode out into the highway.

His eyes were turned in the direction from which he had fled.

At the self-same moment a dolorous cry escaped his lips.

"My worst fears are confirmed," he said. "This is what I dreaded, though I tried my best to bear up against it—to close my eyes to it. The very worst has happened now."

His remorse for a moment was overwhelming.

In the middle of the high-road, and close to the spot where the road turned off, was a great pool of blood, and the unmistakable marks of many footsteps.

Lord Harcliffe then knew that Captain Hawk had fallen off his horse at that spot, and the officers had found him there, and carried him away.

There was no other probable conclusion to be drawn from what he saw.

He had no little ado to calm and control the horses, and the repugnance which they displayed to the fresh-shed blood was so great that Lord Harcliffe could not, try as he would, get so near to the fatal spot as he wished.

But yet, for all practical purposes, he was near enough.

He looked around.

An unusual amount of calmness appeared to prevail.

A little bird perched on the outside of a huge tree poured forth his notes of harmony.

But beyond this there was no sound to be heard indicative of the presence of any living creature.

Lord Harcliffe looked wistfully up and down the road, first towards Huntingdon and then towards London.

But he could see nothing.

As far as his view extended, no human being was in sight.

He listened as well as the restlessness of the two horses would allow him.

But no sound reached him to give any indication of which route the officers had taken with their prisoner.

Nor did the ground afford him any clue as to which way they had gone.

It was uniformly trampled in every direction.

"What am I to do now?" Lord Harcliffe asked himself.

The question was a puzzling one on more grounds than one.

To start with, he had a divided duty to perform.

Strictly, he was bound not to relax his efforts to reach London and ascertain the precise amount of Pharoah's danger.

But then he was at least equally bound to find out what had become of Captain Hawk, and the more so because he believed himself to be inexcusably to blame in the whole transaction.

"Oh, for some clue, however slight!" he said. "Oh, for some means of knowing which way I ought to take! Now, being absolutely without a single thing to guide me, if I take one way it is certain to be the wrong one, and I shall only be going further away from him instead of going to his assistance."

Lord Harcliffe was almost ready to give way to despair.

And considering how unfortunate he had been in all things lately, this is hardly surprising.

"There is but one thing I can do," he said, "and that is to ride on for a certain distance in one direction, and then if I can learn nothing I will turn back and try my fortune in the opposite direction. It may be a loss of time, perhaps, but anything would be preferable to remaining here."

For a moment he hesitated as to which way he should take first.

But after weighing the matter over, he resolved to go towards London.

What made him come to this conclusion was the apparently strong probability that the officers would without loss of time convey their important prisoner to the metropolis, and not risk confining him elsewhere.

How erroneous this conclusion was the reader knows already.

When once he got the horses past the place where Captain Hawk had fallen, they went on freely enough.

But as he went he saw so little indications that his foes had been this way before him, that, in defiance of all probability, he resolved to try the opposite direction.

Now, from all that has been written the reader must be aware that Lord Harcliffe must have reached the end of the lane only a very short time after Captain Hawk had started away.

Indeed, if he had only had the least idea of the true state of affairs, he might perhaps have been able to overtake his friend before he got as far as Huntingdon.

But it was not so to be.

Turning at length, however, as we have said, he rode towards Huntingdon.

It was not until he had galloped three or four miles that he met with a single living being.

But his attention being attracted by a succession of rapid ringing blows, he looked keenly before him, and saw a man at work with a huge axe, cutting down a tree that grew by the roadside.

"A woodcutter; and I should say, judging by appearances, he has been at work for some length of time, so that he will be able to inform me for certain whether Captain Hawk has been carried past."

The hope of having his doubts set at rest to some extent encouraged the Black Highwayman to accelerate his speed.

But so intent was the woodcutter upon what he was about, that he never noticed his approach.

Lord Harcliffe pulled up at what he considered to be a safe distance, and called out to him.

The man looked up with a sleepy, vacant stare

"I must quicken his faculties," said the highwayman mentally.

With a view of doing this he took from his pocket half-a-crown, which he threw to the man.

"There," he said—"put that in your pocket and just answer me a question or two."

It was surprising to note what an effect the silver coin had.

"What do you want to know, your worship?" he asked, touching his hat. "I shall be glad to tell you what I know."

"Very good, then. I want you to tell me whether you have seen a party of police officers ride past?"

"Yes, I have."

"You have?"

"Oh yes—thirteen or fourteen of them."

Lord Harcliffe tried hard to retain his calmness.

"Had—had—they anything with them?"

The woodcutter stared.

"I don't know, sir," he said. "What sort of a thing might it be?"

"A—a prisoner."

The woodman shook his head very emphatically.

"They had no prisoner?"

"Oh dear no!"

"You are sure of it?"

"Quite certain of it, your honour."

Lord Harcliffe struck his breast with his clenched fist

"The man was insensible if he was with them."

"No; they were all by themselves on their horses, and the reason I know it so particularly was because they all stopped to speak to me, or else if it had not been for that I should not have taken much notice: I don't generally."

"Stopped to speak to you?"

"Yes, they did."

"And what did they say?"

"Asked me whether I had seen a butcher go by driving a cart at a very sharp rate; and I told them I had."

"A butcher in a cart!" said Lord Harcliffe, much surprised, for, of course, this information did not in the least serve to enlighten him with regard to the true state of affairs.

It was impossible he should know anything about the captain being in the butcher's cart. He had somehow jumped to the conclusion that they would be certain to convey their prisoner on horseback.

"And how long ago was this?" he said.

"Not very long. I don't justly know, for, you see, your honour, when I'm at work I don't generally take much notice. It might be an hour ago—perhaps more, perhaps less. If it was to save my life, your honour, I could not tell."

CHAPTER CX.

IN WHICH THE BLACK HIGHWAYMAN HAS A MOST SINGULAR ADVENTURE.

LORD HARCLIFFE gave a sigh of vexation and regret.

His disappointment was all the greater because he had felt himself to be on the verge of hearing something important.

What connection there could be between the officers and the butcher's cart puzzled him to conjecture.

The only reasonable conclusion to which he was able to come was that the whole affair had got nothing whatever to do with him or the captain either.

"And you have seen nothing else?" he said, addressing the woodman with a kind of forlorn hope that he might chance to hear something after all.

"I have not, your honour," was the reply.

"Then be good enough to say nothing about our meeting; and as an encouragement for you to do so, take this other half-crown."

He tossed him the coin mentioned as he spoke, and rode slowly away towards London once more, at every step he took doubling the distance he was from his new yet much-valued friend.

The woodman looked after him in silent astonishment.

At length, as he took up his bright axe preparatory to renewing his attack upon the noble tree, he ejaculated:

"Now, I should not at all wonder if something uncommon is not taking place this morning. However, it doesn't matter to me. I never take any notice. I have five shillings more than I thought to have safe in my pocket—I know that, and that's enough."

The woodman, who was without knowing it as great a practical philosopher as ever lived, renewed his attack upon the tree, never once troubling himself to give a glance after Lord Harcliffe's retreating form.

Insensibly as he rode on, the Black Highwayman fell into a deep and melancholy reverie.

He was startled from it rudely.

Without knowing that there was any human being near him, he heard a gruff voice say suddenly:

"Hullo, you there! Hullo, I say! Hoy—hoy!"

Hearing these shouts, Lord Harcliffe looked up, and the moment he did so he caught sight of a man on horseback who was standing in a gap of the hedge and looking as though he was strongly inclined to jump over.

Lord Harcliffe's first act upon the impulse of the moment was to rein up.

The man who had called out to him jumped the gap at the same moment.

Placing himself close to the highwayman, and assuming an aggressive attitude, he cried:

"Before you go any further, I want you to tell me how you came by that horse."

While speaking, he pointed to Satan.

The Black Highwayman was astonished.

So great was his surprise, that for a second he found himself incapable of either moving or speaking.

All he could do was to keep his eyes fixed upon his assailant.

He was unable to form any clear notion, however, of what this man really was; but certainly he was not a police officer.

He was mounted on a gray horse of great power and symmetry of form—such an animal as one might expect to see beneath a gentleman when on his way to the hunting field.

But, incongruously enough, the rider who sat upon his back was decidedly a rough specimen of humanity.

His clothes were rough and coarse, and in many places had great rents in them.

Altogether, in fine, he looked a singular combination of poacher, gamekeeper, and stable-helper.

As he might be either of these, so he might turn out to be neither of them.

While observing thus the form of the new-comer, Lord Harcliffe was exposed to a very attentive scrutiny.

He was the first to break the silence.

When he spoke again his tones were even more authoritative, not to say insolent, than before.

"I want to know how you came by that horse," he said. "And, mark me, I don't intend to let you go a step further until you tell me! He accompanied the words by drawing from the breast pocket of his coat a horse pistol of formidable dimensions.

But Lord Harcliffe was the very last individual in the world to be intimidated by any such display.

Besides, he could see that this man was labouring under some very deep and suppressed emotion, the cause of which did not appear.

He was certain also that this man was not one of his foes.

Had he been he would have acted in a far different manner.

All these things, joined to the fact of the evident interest which he felt in Captain Hawk's steed, made Lord Harcliffe conclude that there was more in this meeting than appeared at the first glance.

"Suppose I refuse to take any notice of your demands —what then?" said Lord Harcliffe, with a return of his usual coolness.

"I shall compel you!"

"That is easier said than done. I demand to know why you ask the question?"

"And I refuse to answer."

"You do?"

"I do."

"Who are you?"

"Who are you?"

"Never mind, fellow! Don't try me too far, or you may feel the consequences of your insolence!"

But the man, so far from appearing moved by this threat, only uttered a scornful laugh.

"I claim that horse," he said; "and now I give you warning that unless you surrender it to me or answer my questions, I will put a bullet into your skull, and take it by main force!"

However little Lord Harcliffe might have been disposed to regard the threat which had just been uttered, yet there could be no doubting the fact that the rough-looking man fully meant what he said.

There was a degree of resolution not only about the tones of his voice, but also in his deeply-set black eyes and in the compression of his lips.

Lord Harcliffe, however, never for a moment lost that wonderful self-possession of his.

Indeed, after the man had spoken so menacingly, he looked just as calm and unconcerned as he would have done had a remark been made of the most trifling character.

Had he not felt that there was something unusual in the affair, his demeanour would have been very different.

Certainly he would not have permitted the man to address him with so much insolence.

The man on his side was not a little astonished at the deportment of his opponent.

His extraordinary calm indifference puzzled him.

Finding that no notice was taken of what he had just said, and seeing no signs that he was about to make any reply, he cried, with additional fierceness:

"Are you deaf?—or what is the reason you pay no attention to my words? Do you not see the muzzle of this loaded pistol? Don't think I shall be afraid of carrying my threat into execution!"

"Have you done?" said Lord Harcliffe, in quiet tones, that were all the more remarkable on account of the contrast they formed to the other's furious manner.

"Done?" echoed the man—"done? What do you mean?"

"I ask you whether you have made an end of your foolish speeches?"

"Foolish speeches?"

"Yes, worse than foolish.

"I——"

"If you think to produce the slightest effect on me by such behaviour you are mistaken."

The man, more staggered still, could not answer for a moment.

Yet when he did speak again there was marked humility in his tones.

"I want that horse," he said. "If you are disposed to give it up quietly, why, as I said before, well and good. I claim it."

"So do I," answered the Black Highwayman, if possible in a more unruffled manner than before.

"But——"

"Let us cut short this discussion. You hear I claim this horse—you see it is in my possession; and now take my assurance that I will relinquish it to no one."

"And I am determined to have it!" said the man, doggedly. "I give you a moment. If you persist in refusing at the end of that time, this bullet will be lodged in your brain."

"Fool!" said Lord Harcliffe. "You will force me to lose patience with you. There! Perhaps now you may feel inclined to carry on the conversation in a more reasonable tone."

While speaking these words, Lord Harcliffe, by a sudden movement for which the man was quite unprepared, snatched the formidable-looking pistol from his grasp, and flung it over the hedgerow into the adjoining field.

The man looked aghast for a moment, and then his right hand sought the breast of his coat, as though his intention was to produce another weapon.

"Hold!" said the Black Highwayman. "Make another movement on peril of your life!"

He held his own pistol within a few inches of the man's breast.

"Now," he said, "be reasonable and speak civilly. I will listen to whatever you may have to urge respecting your claim; but you will do nothing with me by threats or attempts at force."

The man began to see this, and wondered into whose hands it was that the horse had fallen.

"But if I tell you," he said, sulkily, "how am I to know that I shall be any nearer to getting possession of him than I am now?"

"To speak frankly," Lord Harcliffe continued, with the

same evenness of utterance, "I don't think you will be any nearer—no, not a bit."

"You don't?"

"I don't."

"Then what the devil is the good of my saying a word?"

"Not much that I can see. I have the best of all possible claims upon this steed; and rather than relinquish him to anyone save his owner, I would sacrifice my life a hundred times over!"

If the man had not already reached the utmost degree of amazement possible, these last words must have surprised him beyond all utterance.

A moment elapsed before he could open his lips at all, and when he did speak it was to say, stammeringly:

"You—you know the owner, then?"

"Know him? Of course I do! Do you?"

The man seemed quite unprepared for this reply, and appeared to be on the point of saying something but with a sudden effort he choked the words, and said instead:

"I know the horse as well; and, what is more, the horse knows me, as I can quickly prove to you."

"Let me see your proof."

After a momentary hesitation, the man consented.

"Hoy—hoy, there!" he cried. "Satan—Satan, boy! Aha! you know me now, don't you? I was sure you would. Aha!"

Satan neighed loudly, and exhibited every sign of being highly pleased, while at the same time he made every endeavour to break away from the Black Highwayman's detaining grasp.

"Are you satisfied?" said the man, whose triumph showed itself in every tone and gesture.

"I am satisfied, so far as that goes; but I am no more inclined to part with the horse than I was before."

"But at least you will tell me who you are?"

"Yes; since you put the question civilly, I shall have no hesitation in doing so."

"Well, sir?"

"Well, then, I am a friend of the owner."

"A friend of the owner?"

"That is it."

"And I prefer the same claim."

"So you may; but that does not incline me to give up the horse to you."

"But, sir, whoever you are," cried the man, "I feel somehow bound to believe that you are in good truth master's friend; but——"

"Your master—Captain Hawk your master?"

"Yes—yes! But bear in mind you mentioned his name first."

"Come, now," said Lord Harcliffe, "let us understand each other. You may depend it will be best for you to speak freely."

The reader no doubt has already guessed who Lord Harcliffe's strange opponent really was.

"Then, if I must tell all," he said, "though I don't know that I am right in so doing——"

"Rest assured all will be well so far as that is concerned."

"Well, then, Captain Hawk is my master—for such I will have him to be—though he declares I am his friend."

"Well—well? Go on."

"His last orders for me were, when he left the Greyhound, that I was to join him on the London Road without delay, as he was anxious to get to his journey's end."

"And where was that?"

"London."

This answer went a long way towards freeing Lord Harcliffe's mind from any doubts, because it tallied exactly with what he himself knew of the captain's movements.

"You may guess, sir," continued Isaac, "that when, after being told to do that, I happened to see you leading Satan by the bridle, I should feel sure something wrong had occurred."

Lord Harcliffe nodded.

"And I felt, too," continued Isaac, "as Satan was particularly my charge, no one ought to have him in his possession but myself."

"If I was quite sure that all you say is the truth——" said Lord Harcliffe, with a little hesitation.

"I will swear gladly to every word of it."

"Very likely."

"I would, sir, indeed!"

"I don't doubt it for a moment."

"Come with me to the Greyhound, then," he urged. "If you know anything at all of Captain Hawk, you must be aware that that is where one of his best friends lives."

"A good thought," said Lord Harcliffe. "We will go to the Greyhound. Come with me—come at once."

Lord Harcliffe seized very readily at the idea of paying a visit to the Greyhound, where he made sure he should be perfectly safe.

The anxiety he had felt as to how he should dispose of the captain's steed was removed at once.

Nowhere, he felt certain, could be better than in the charge of honest Tom Beckford.

It was also with a vague hope of hearing some information that he turned Phantom's head in this direction.

Hardly had they gone a dozen yards, however, before Isaac said, in tones of the deepest entreaty:

"You have not told me yet who you are, sir; and, if you like, you can keep that knowledge to yourself; but let me beg of you to tell me where he is and what has happened? How is it that, after the instructions he left, I found you leading his horse, and such a short distance away, too?"

While speaking, he had fixed his eyes upon Lord Harcliffe, whose countenance kept growing graver and graver at every word.

Isaac noted the changing expression.

"How is it?" he asked, with still more interest—"how is it? Don't tell me anything has happened to the captain! You shake your head! Don't tell me he is dead, or—or—I am sure I shall go mad!"

CHAPTER CXI.

LORD HARCLIFFE LEARNS SOME IMPORTANT INTELLIGENCE FROM ISAAC THE OSTLER.

THERE was something in the way in which Isaac spoke and in his actions that would have convinced the most sceptical of his sincerity.

It was impossible that such behaviour as his could be feigned, and Lord Harcliffe no longer felt the slightest doubt of his honesty and fidelity.

"You seem strongly attached to Captain Hawk."

"Seem!" repeated Isaac, with something very much like scorn in his accents—"seem! I am——"

"I beg your pardon," said the Black Highwayman, deeply touched by Isaac's earnestness. "I should have said you are strongly attached: no one could doubt it."

A grateful smile appeared upon the ostler's lips.

"I am glad you have said that, because I think you will not keep me in suspense any longer."

"I will not."

"What, then, has happened? Something has—I feel certain of that from your manner. Let me know it. The very worst could not be so bad as the suspense that I now feel."

"Well, then, the captain has met with a misfortune. I had hopes I should be able to learn something from you respecting him; but I can see you know nothing."

"No, no—nothing."

Lord Harcliffe then made Isaac aware of all that had occurred, from the moment when their strange meeting took place up to the time when he had discovered Satan riderless.

During the recital deep groans came from Isaac's lips.

His head sunk down upon his breast, and he said disconsolately:

"The worst has happened! I knew it—I felt it!"

"You think the officers have him, then?"

"There can't be two opinions about it. And now they have got him, they will keep him secure—never doubt that."

"They will try, certainly."

"And they will succeed."

"Perhaps."

"I tell you there is no room for hope—not the slightest. The captain's hours are numbered: he has taken his last ride on the highway."

"You take altogether too despondent a view of things."

"No, no, I don't—it is because I know. I have heard the officers talk over the matter, and I am quite certain from what they have said that it would be all over with the captain if he was once so unlucky as to fall into their clutches."

"But we must do our best for him."

"We will!" said Isaac, bringing his hand down with angry violence upon his breast. "They won't keep him, and drag him to the scaffold very easily! They will have to take my life to do so!"

"And mine, too!" said the Black Highwayman, with his usual quietness, but with no less amount of resolution.

"Still," said Isaac, lapsing into his former despair, "what can we do against so many? I tell you—and you may take my word that it is correct—now that they have once laid hold upon Captain Hawk, they will cling like grim Death himself. He has eluded them so many times, that now they have him they will make sure of him."

"Let us take a more hopeful view of things, Isaac: at any rate, until we have more certain knowledge than we at present possess. All may not be as bad as you imagine even now."

"I don't see the least signs of a gleam of hope," replied Isaac. "But we are not such a long way off from the Greyhound now; and when we get there we shall be certain to learn further intelligence."

Filled with this anticipation, they rode onwards at an accelerated pace.

But Isaac's countenance seemed to became gloomier still as they approached the old well-known inn.

"I wonder if Tom Beckford knows anything of this," he muttered. "I am afraid that hardly time enough has elapsed for the news to be diffused abroad very much."

"We shall soon see now, shall we not?"

"Yes; we shall soon be in sight of the old place. I little thought I should be back so soon when I set out a short time ago."

Although not able to know so well as Isaac, yet Lord Harcliffe could not help being aware that the situation of his new comrade was one of no common danger.

Judging from what had happened in his own case, he could tell that no effort would be wanting on the part of the officers to carry out their designs.

Satan seemed to know where he was going just as well as Isaac; for he testified his satisfaction in a hundred ways, and it required no great stretch of the imagination to fancy that he expected to refind his master in his old quarters.

"It seems rather a bold proceeding to ride up to the inn like this by daylight," said Isaac. "The captain's steed is well enough known even if you are not. But," he added, as a thought suddenly occurred to him, "if they have power to take the rider, I question if they have any claim upon the horse. At any rate, it will be bad for them to try it on."

Until Isaac spoke, Lord Harcliffe never once thought of the grave danger he was incurring by thus riding abroad during the daylight.

So great was the anxiety he had felt upon the captain's account, that it had completely submerged all other feelings.

But the mere fact of his having been successful in riding so many miles as he had without creating the least remark emboldened him to ride on with considerable confidence now that their destination was almost in view.

The event proved that he was perfectly right in doing so.

The front of the old inn was reached without the slightest molestation having been offered him; nor, indeed, despite the fact that he led so noble-looking a horse by the bridle, was much attention bestowed upon him.

"Now, sir," said Isaac, as soon as they halted, "if you will be content to follow my advice you will leave all three of the horses in my care. Rest satisfied they will be safe and where they can be obtained in a moment if wanted. While I am making them comfortable, explain everything to the landlord. Look—here he comes!"

Lord Harcliffe turned and saw Tom Beckford's portly form advancing towards him.

In Isaac he had now the most absolute trust, and so he surrendered the horses to him without hesitating a single second.

Isaac noted this proof of confidence, and mentally determined that it should never be found to be misplaced.

Tom Beckford looked considerably astonished upon seeing the Black Highwayman.

Of course, he had no idea of his identity—never having, to the best of his belief, seen him till that moment.

But he saw not only Isaac, but also the captain's horse, and that filled him with anxiety—not merely to know what had happened, but also to find out who this new-comer was.

"Good morning!" he said, bowing as well as his obesity would allow him. "Unless my eyes deceived me more than they usually do, that was Captain Hawk's horse that you led up to the front door?"

"You are right," said Lord Harcliffe, gravely—"it was."

"What has become of him—what has occurred?"

"Then do you know nothing?"

"Know nothing!" gasped the landlord, beginning to feel very uncomfortable. "What do you mean?"

"I will explain myself. But you must see that this is not a proper place to choose for such a purpose."

"No—no, that's right enough. As you say, this is not the place."

"I should suggest a private room."

"Follow me, and I will lead you to one."

Poor Tom Beckford was in a state of mind which fairly defies all attempts at description.

But he did not need informing that something of an unusually serious nature had taken place, so that, despite all his anxiety, he dreaded to hear what it was.

This feeling made him, after he had ushered Lord Harcliffe into the private room, go into the bar, ostensibly for the purpose of fetching a bottle of brandy and a couple of glasses, but in reality in order that he might compose himself a little and be somewhat prepared for the disclosure which was about to be made.

Closing the door behind him, he poured out with an unsteady hand a couple of glasses, and then said, huskily:

"Speak, sir, after you have tasted that. I know you bring bad news, and I shall be better prepared to hear it."

Lord Harcliffe did not hesitate a moment to respond to this invitation, for really just then a drop of brandy was about as acceptable a thing as could have been offered to him.

"Now, sir," said Tom Beckford, "I shall take it as a favour if you will put what you have to say into the fewest words."

But Lord Harcliffe chose to be explicit.

As when he gave the account to Isaac he commenced with the singular meeting in the cross-roads, so he did on the present occasion.

Tom Beckford listened with all conceivable eagerness.

But notwithstanding what he had said about being prepared, he suffered a severe shock when Lord Harcliffe related first how he had found Satan riderless, and then afterwards the pool of blood on the highway, with the many impressions of footmarks around it, which was, he felt certain, the place where the captain had fallen and been found by the police.

Tom Beckford could not speak for some moments.

He let his head fall upon the table in silent grief, and in this position he was found by Isaac, who, having disposed of the horses to his entire satisfaction, now peeped into the room.

"What!" he cried. "Do I see you down like that, Tom? Come—come, look up! Depend upon it this is the time for action, not for the indulgence of grief."

"You are right," said Lord Harcliffe, in those calm tones which would have made one who did not know him thoroughly feel in doubt whether he experienced any emotion or not.

"It is well, no doubt, for you to speak so," said Tom Beckford, who was hardly able to command his voice. "But then you do not feel as I do. He was not the same to you as he was to me. Had he been my own flesh and blood—my own son—I could not have loved him more;

no, nor half so well. I knew this evil day would come at last, and it has come sooner than I expected."

He let his head fall upon the table again, and gave unrestrained flow to his grief.

"It will be best to let him have his fling," said the ostler. "I will leave you with him to finish talking over the affair."

"Where, then, are you going?"

"To try and pick up some information."

"It will be well."

"If the body of the captain has been found on the high-road at a point so near as you describe, rest assured that I shall speedily hear something about it."

"Be quick, and return as soon as you have anything to communicate. You ought to know what suspense is, and think how we shall be till you return."

"Right," was the answer. "The moment I learn anything you may depend upon seeing me."

So saying, Isaac departed, but not until Lord Harcliffe had obtained from him the assurance that the horses were safe and well.

Some time elapsed before Tom Beckford was able to look up.

Even then he had to imbibe several glasses of brandy before he was able to say anything.

"I have tried hard," he said, "to think that this day would come at last, and have tried to get courage and nerve to face it, but now I feel how little I have been able to do towards it."

Poor Tom's grief was genuine, and therefore Lord Harcliffe respected it.

But when he saw that the landlord was gradually getting better able to understand what was said to him, he remarked:

"Perhaps even now matters are not quite so bad as we have thought. Remember, we have no certain evidence that he has fallen into the hands of the officers at all. Indeed, all I was able to learn pointed to quite the opposite conclusion."

"That's the only hope, then."

"How—what do you mean?"

"Why, that the only hope is that he has not fallen into the hands of the officers."

"Why?"

"Because I know so well that if they have once fastened upon him they will never relax their hold till they see him on the scaffold. You have no idea what a strong personal feeling there is against him in the breasts of every one of the police officers. They hate him; and to see him on the scaffold would only be to put the crowning piece upon their revenge. And if you know as much of humanity as I do, and especially police-officer humanity, you will be able to guess what sort of chance the captain would stand when he was once in their clutches."

Lord Harcliffe was obliged to admit the truth of all this, but yet did not feel inclined to take entirely a gloomy view of the matter.

"If they have him," he said, "we must try what we can do to get him away; and I know well how much determination and resolution can accomplish, even when a few are banded among the many. I feel that I am in no small degree to blame for all that has happened, and it will not be for want of a determined effort if he is not set free."

But Tom Beckford could not derive much hope from this.

"Poor fellow!" Lord Harcliffe added. "If we do not aid him he will stand but a poor chance, for he cannot help himself, and——"

He was interrupted by the opening of the door.

Both turned round and beheld Isaac standing on the threshold.

He was in a state of the utmost excitement, and it became quite certain that he had something to communicate of more than ordinary importance.

CHAPTER CXII.

TOM BECKFORD ENDEAVOURS TO OBTAIN A CONVERSATION WITH CAPTAIN HAWK.

"Your news?" said the Black Highwayman. "Shut the door, and let us know the intelligence at once."

Isaac obeyed without hesitation.

"Prepare for a surprise," he said.

"Has he been captured, then?"

"He has."

Tom received this confirmation of what his fears told him was the worst with a deep groan.

"Was he found by the officers?"

"Yes."

"On the roadway where I described?"

"Yes."

"They made him fast prisoner?"

"They had but little difficulty in doing that. When they found him he was quite helpless and insensible."

"That was as I feared."

"But the surprise has yet to come," said Isaac, with a countenance that looked so bright and encouraging that the wildest hopes were raised by it.

"Speak—speak!" said Lord Harcliffe. "Do you mean to tell us that by some miracle he has escaped?"

"No—no—the news is not so good as that, though better than I expected."

"Explain yourself."

"Well, when they had made him fast prisoner, they, in order to make sure of him, as they thought, carried him to Huntingdon Jail, where he is at this present moment."

"Huntingdon Jail!" repeated Lord Harcliffe and Tom Beckford, in one breath.

"Yes."

"Are you sure?"

"I have not been there to see, for no sooner did I hear it than, according to agreement, I made haste back to you."

"How strange they did not take him to London!"

"No more strange than fortunate," said Isaac. "If he is in Huntingdon Jail, be sure it will not be very long before we set him at liberty."

"Huntingdon! How can they have got him there? I made inquiries on the road which convinced me he had not been taken that way."

"I will tell you how it happened."

Isaac then related how it was that the insensible body of Captain Hawk was put into the butcher's cart, and so conveyed to the prison.

A light dawned upon Lord Harcliffe's mind instantly.

"Oh!" he said, "this only adds to the poignancy of my regret. To think that, had I but known, I should have been able to get him out of their clutches by my own unaided exertions!"

Under the circumstances there could hardly have been a more mortifying piece of intelligence to the Black Highwayman than this.

"It is vain to bestow any regrets upon the past," said Isaac. "On the contrary, I feel that we ought to be full of thankfulness at finding things are so much better than we could have dared to hope."

"I don't see it," said Tom Beckford. "The prison is a strong one; and there will be such close watch and ward kept within and without as to defy all attempts at rescue or escape."

"I don't know that," said Isaac. "When I heard that bit of news I made up my mind that I would have him out if I had to pull the jail down stone by stone."

"Wait a moment," said Tom. "It's now my turn."

"Your turn? What do you mean?"

"Why, I must go to Huntingdon at once. The stage-coach will pass here in a few minutes."

"But what do you want to go for?"

"To see him, and to find out all about it. Let me assure you it is something which I can do better than anyone else."

"No—no," said Isaac—"let me go."

"Not on any account."

"Why not?"

"I should advise you to keep under cover. You seem to have forgotten that the officers already know you as one of the captain's friends, and the law would empower them to arrest you and have you tried; while, as for myself, they cannot touch me."

"Is this correct?" asked Lord Harcliffe.

"It is."

"Then I have no hesitation in saying that Isaac could not do a more unwise thing than leave the inn."

But Isaac would not hear of this.

"Stay," said the Black Highwayman. "What we each and all desire is the welfare of Captain Hawk."

"It is—it is."

"Then what we have to do is to consider what will be most likely to answer the end we have in view. Is not that right?"

Isaac was reluctantly compelled to admit that it was.

"Very well, then," said Lord Harcliffe. "Tom Beckford, I want a word with you."

"As many as you like, so that you don't attempt to turn me from my project."

"Nothing is further from my thoughts."

The landlord gave a wonderful sigh of relief.

"I want to know whether you are acquainted with anyone of position and standing at Huntingdon?"

"Oh, yes—with several."

"Then that settles it."

"How, sir—how?"

"When going there your object must be not to come back without having seen the captain."

Tom's eyes glowed at the bare idea.

There will be some difficulty about it, you may be sure, but you must not allow yourself to be daunted by it, however great it may be."

"I will not. If it is possible for mortal man to accomplish it, I will."

And as he spoke he buttoned up his coat in a manner which expressed the extent of his determination wonderfully.

"What you must do," continued Lord Harcliffe, "is to apply to the most influential friend you can think of, and get from him an order of admission. If you can once manage that the rest will be easy enough."

"Then," said Tom, "just look upon it as done. We have come to our resolution only just in time, for hark! here comes the mail."

Just as the landlord spoke, the clear, ringing notes of a post-horn became distinctly heard.

"Yes, here it comes, sure enough," said Isaac. "But don't you think it will be best for me to accompany you? Who can say what may happen to make my presence useful?"

But the Black Highwayman at once protested against anything of the kind.

"No—no," he said. "It may fret you as well as myself to remain inactive at the present juncture; but you must be content to reserve your strength until a better occasion arises for making use of it."

Isaac, however, did not seem to be much impressed by this argument.

"Besides," added Lord Harcliffe, "your presence in company with the landlord would just do the very thing which it is most important we should avoid."

"And what is that?"

"Why, give the alarm to our foes. If the officers saw you and Tom together, they would jump immediately to the conclusion that your object was the rescue of their prisoner, and they would double their precautions accordingly."

"Yes, Isaac, rely upon it that such will be the result. I don't see how it can be otherwise. If I stay to argue the point, however, I shall lose the coach."

"And don't do that by any means," said Lord Harcliffe "Isaac will stop—that is decided."

But the ostler grumbled a great deal at the way things were brought to a settlement, though he was obliged to confess that all was for the best.

It was rather an unusual event for Tom Beckford to go very far away from home, his bulk not rendering him adapted to locomotion to any great extent.

When, therefore, he made his appearance at the horse-trough in front of the inn with his broad-brimmed Quaker-looking hat on his head, his brass-buttoned coat buttoned tightly up to the chin, and a thick walking-stick in his hand, the driver of the stage-coach uttered an exclamation of surprise.

"Whips and spurs!" he exclaimed. "Why, what will happen next? I do believe that the landlord here is about to start off on a journey!"

"Not for far, though," said Tom. "I'm only going to Huntingdon."

"Very good. You will have to scramble up to the top somehow, for the inside is quite full."

It was a feat of no ordinary kind for a man of the landlord's weight and bulk to mount to the top of a stage-coach; but after much puffing and blowing he accomplished it.

The only vacant seat was the one next to the driver, and no sooner had he settled himself than the vehicle was set in motion.

His departure was watched by Lord Harcliffe and Isaac, though they took care to screen themselves so that they should be in no danger of being seen.

They remained gazing from the window long after the coach had disappeared.

Neither seemed inclined for conversation.

Isaac was vexed to think it had been decided that he should not go to Huntingdon; and, in order that he might recover his spirits somewhat, went out to the stables.

Lord Harcliffe did not regret his absence, for it gave him the opportunity of indulging in his meditations without restraint.

First taking the precaution to secure the door, he paced up and down the room in anxious thought.

There was much to furnish him with food for thought, and as he gave full sway to his reflections his brows contracted and his lips moved uneasily.

Up and down—up and down he paced, only resting now and then at the window, when he would look anxiously in the direction in which he expected Tom Beckford to come.

But time elapsed without bringing any signs of the landlord.

Wearied out at length, not only by his harassing thoughts, but by bodily exhaustion, he flung himself upon the rude sofa, and before he was aware of it fell fast asleep.

How long his slumber lasted he could form no idea.

It was deep and dreamless.

It was interrupted by a sound which he could hardly understand.

But as it was repeated, he started up.

At first he glanced around confusedly.

For his life he could not tell where he was.

With a sudden rush, however, all the events of the past four-and-twenty hours surged upon his brain.

He knew that the sound which had so puzzled him was caused by some one knocking at the door of the apartment.

"That must be the landlord. Thank goodness, his return will relieve me from suffering any more suspense!"

So saying, he rose and felt his way across the room, for during his sleep the day had waned, and now all objects were beginning to be wrapped in the obscurity of evening twilight.

On turning the key and throwing open the door, he saw that his conjecture was verified.

Tom Beckford was standing on the threshold; but even in the semi-darkness Lord Harcliffe could discern that Tom's countenance wore an expression of unusual gravity.

Behind the landlord stood Isaac the ostler, who betrayed the most ungovernable impatience to become acquainted with the result of the landlord's errand.

In silence the two entered.

Lord Harcliffe, with that self-command we have so often mentioned, sat down and waited without evincing the least eagerness.

Not so with Isaac, however.

No sooner had he shut the door than, approaching the landlord, he cried:

"Oh, Mr. Beckford! put me out of my misery at once! What I have suffered while you have been away no tongue can tell save my own! Let us know all that has happened, whether the news is good or bad!"

Tom Beckford was much moved, and despite the urgent appeal which had just been made to him, did not speak, though he made several efforts to utter something.

"The news is bad, then?" exclaimed the ostler, with a foreboding of the truth.

Tom nodded.

"Speak out, man!" said Lord Harcliffe, sternly. "If your courage fails you, drink that."

Tom gladly enough swallowed the glass of brandy which was proffered him.

"It is worse than I feared," he began, as soon as the last drop had passed his lips.

"He is not dead?" said Isaac.

"No—no. He lives."

"Then where there is life there is hope."

But Tom Beckford only shook his head.

"I will tell you," he said. "I have learned from the best authority that he is badly wounded—so badly that the surgeon will not give a decided opinion concerning him."

"Yes—yes."

"But for all that they have immured him in a prison cell, where he is guarded with the utmost rigour."

"You have seen him, then?"

"No."

"Not seen him?"

"It was impossible."

"How?"

"All the authorities are afraid that a desperate attempt will be made to wrest the prisoner from them; and so great is this fear that they are resolved not to let anything take place which they consider is likely to lead to it."

"Well—well?"

"Consequently they have expressly prohibited any person whatever from having an interview with the prisoner, or making any sort of communication with him whatever."

Lord Harcliffe received this intelligence in dead silence.

Isaac was not so undemonstrative.

He poured out a volley of oaths.

No one attempted to check him.

He was relieved at the end of a few moments, and then ensued a long pause.

Tom Beckford broke it.

"What's to be done?" he said. "From all the inquiries I have made to-day, it seems quite certain that it is impossible for anyone to see the prisoner with the permission of the authorities."

"Then we must see him without," said Isaac, boldly.

"That's all very well," returned Tom Beckford; "but how are you to do it? I thought I would not come away until I had learned all I could."

"Quite right," said Lord Harcliffe.

"I found that his cell was almost in the centre of the building. It is shared by a turnkey, who watches his every movement. There is another stationed outside the door, and another just below the grated window looking out into the prison yard. The Governor pays him frequent visits, being fully alive to his responsibility; it is said should the prisoner get free the Governor will lose his situation. In the face of all this, just let me ask you what earthly chance there is that we shall be able to exchange a single syllable with the captain, let alone effect his release?"

The question was one which did not admit of an immediate or direct reply.

Isaac and Lord Harcliffe did the only thing that remained in their power, which was to stare blankly and helplessly at each other.

CHAPTER CXIII.

RETURNS TO CAPTAIN HAWK IN THE PRISON CELL.

LEAVING the trio in the old inn parlour to get over their difficulty in the best manner they were able, we will pay another visit to Captain Hawk in his prison cell.

It will be recollected that we left him soon after the introduction of the fresh turnkey to watch over him.

It was from the latter he had heard the somewhat alarming intelligence that the magistrate appointed to hear his examination had a personal feeling of revenge against him.

The wounded highwayman's mind, however, was far from being in a sufficiently clear state to allow him to recollect everything properly.

Therefore it was that when the turnkey had concluded his very emphatic speech, Captain Hawk turned towards him with a look of listless wonderment.

"What is that you say?" he asked. "Sir Thomas who?"

"Sir Thomas Walker."

"Who is he?"

"Is it possible you do not know?"

"You might judge as much from the mere fact of my asking the question."

"Well, yes, captain, I suppose so; but it seemed such a very odd thing. That's what made me speak as I did."

"Explain, then. I want to know who and what this Sir Thomas Walker is?"

"Well, captain, he is one of the chief magistrates from Bow Street, if not the very chief. However, I don't know about that; but I do know that he has been sent down here by the express orders of the Secretary of State."

Captain Hawk had just a confused notion in his mind that he had heard something of this before, but when and where he could not precisely remember; therefore he said:

"Sent here by the Secretary of State! And for what purpose?"

"Why, to apprehend you, to be sure. Only when he arrived he received the pleasing intimation that you were a prisoner already."

Captain Hawk remained some moments in silent reflection.

"And did you not say that he had a personal feeling against me?"

"Yes."

"And for what?"

"Why, captain, your wits are wool-gathering!"

"Perhaps they are: my brain does feel dizzy. But don't keep me in suspense."

"Very good, captain—I'll oblige you. Excuse me for saying, though, that it does tickle me a little bit to think you should ask such an innocent question as that. But I suppose these little jobs are so much in your line and of such frequent occurrence that they easily slip off your memory."

"What on earth are you talking of?" said the captain, in unmistakable surprise.

"Well, as you don't seem to know, I'll tell you. But it's rich, that it is! Ha, ha!"

The man was so much amused that he was obliged to have his laugh out before he could go any further.

"Now, what the magistrate has against you," he said, at length, "is neither more nor less than this: Not many nights ago, as he was on his way down here from London—in fact, you stopped the mail-coach in which he was travelling."

"What?"

"You stopped the mail-coach."

"It is a mistake: I did nothing of the sort."

"Ah, captain! your mind is still just a little bit deranged. It is no good for you to go for to deny it: the evidence is conclusive."

"But I repeat," said Captain Hawk, "that I did not stop the mail-coach. And don't think my brain is in such a whirl as to make me forgetful of such a thing as that."

"Well, that passes me, captain. There's any quantity of witnesses ready to come forward and swear it."

"What! that I stopped the coach?"

"Yes, to be sure."

"They will swear to a lie, then. I didn't do it."

"Will you let me refresh your memory a little?"

"Certainly—by all means."

"Very well. After you robbed the stage-coach——"

"But I didn't rob it."

"Listen to me a moment."

"Go on."

"I say, after you robbed the mail-coach and had cut the traces and sent the horses off so that the passengers were obliged to remain in the middle of the road—I say after you had done all that, you rode on to the inn where the magistrate had purposed making a halt, and where, in consequence, he had ordered a sumptuous dinner to be got ready against his arrival."

"Oh yes!"

"Ah! you recollect that now?"

"Oh yes; I remember that very well."

"I am glad your memory is coming back to you."

"Go on."

"When you got to the inn you put the landlord in bodily fear for his life; and having done that, compelled him to serve up the magistrate's dinner, which you devoured to the last scrap. Do you plead guilty to that, captain?"

"Oh yes: I won't deny the truth."

"Very well. Now I will just ask whether you had not done enough to content any ordinary man? But no. Nothing would do but you must ride back to the coach where you had left the magistrate."

[CAPTAIN HAWK ON HIS WAY TO THE SESSIONS HOUSE.]

"No, no—I had not left him there."

"But you had!"

"Oh, very well!"

"Now, why deny it?"

"I should not were it the truth. I encountered the mail-coach in the middle of the road. Some one had been beforehand with me in robbing it. All the passengers were quite cleared out. The job was done neatly enough to satisfy anybody."

"That's your tale. Now, the magistrate's is different; and whichever is true, I know which one will be believed."

"Let me hear it, then."

"I will. He says that after you had finished the dinner you came back to the coach, used all manner of insulting expressions: called him a fool—defied him to the teeth, and added that you were off to London, and that if he wanted you he was to come there to find you."

"So far as that goes, that is true enough. And this is why the magistrate has a personal feeling against me?"

"Yes. He swears he will have no rest until he has had his revenge upon you. You have no idea how he frets over this illness of yours. He has been here half a dozen times."

"I don't remember seeing him."

"No, captain, you were not in a condition to know anyone."

"Oh, that's it!"

"Yes, that's how to account for it."

"And he is full of impatience, you say?"

"Yes; he is most anxious for your recovery. I should not be surprised to see him here in the course of a minute or two—this is somewhere about his time."

Captain Hawk moved uneasily.

As may be supposed, although wonderfully better, I

was hardly in a condition to support the excitement of a continued conversation.

"Take it easy," said the turnkey.

The highwayman was silent.

But though his lips were still and his eyes were closed, he was busily engaged in thinking upon what he had just heard.

He was able to arrive unhesitatingly at the conclusion that, if before he had had the slightest hope of getting acquitted at his trial, there was not the slightest chance of it now.

His condemnation he looked upon as an already settled matter, and all his thoughts were directed to the one point of making his escape.

And as for this, one would have thought that he could have seen but slight prospect of accomplishing it.

He was so weak that it was only by the greatest exertion and at the penalty of considerable pain, that he was able to make the slightest movement on his bed.

But in his hopeful, sanguine imagination he already saw himself perfectly recovered and in possession of his usual strength.

Nor was this altogether unreasonable on his part.

Aware that excessive effusion of blood had alone made his wound dangerous naturally brought him to the conclusion that his recovery would be a rapid one.

In the meantime, the turnkey, in accordance with the instructions which had been given him, poured out a small glassful of medicine which had been prepared by the surgeon.

This he held to the captain's lips, who swallowed it without hesitation or inquiry.

But the results very speedily manifested themselves.

The drug must have had some very cordial properties, for almost immediately the captain felt a warm glow pervade his whole form.

His heart beat with a firmer and more regular pulsation; and when he opened his eyes again he discovered that he was able to look about him with much greater ease than before.

"That's wonderful stuff, captain," said the turnkey—"blow me if it isn't! But, as I said before and as I say now, I can't see what on earth is the good of taking all this trouble to bring you back to life and to restore your strength only to be taken before the beak afterwards, and then scragged. You're a fool, captain, that's what you are, or you would never take any of the confounded stuff!"

"Perhaps I shall get off," he said.

"Never think it," he cried—"never think it; and to have the least idea of escape is more ridiculous still!"

At hearing this, a faint smile curled the captain's lips.

But it was so faint as to escape the jailer's observation.

The effect of the draught, so far from making the captain down-hearted and causing him to regard the future with dismay, only strengthened the hopes which had already found a resting-place in his bosom.

From the fact, too, that the Black Highwayman had not been captured he drew the most favourable conclusions.

He knew full well that after what had passed between them he would strain every nerve to set him free.

Altogether then, desperate as his situation might seem to a casual observer, Captain Hawk was able to find abundant comfort in it.

But another thought recurring to his mind, he turned to the turnkey and said:

"Has no one called to see me during all this time?"

"No one at all that I am aware on, captain."

"Strange!" ejaculated the highwayman. "I suppose it is known abroad that I am a prisoner?"

"Oh yes—all the town is alive with it."

"And yet no one has called. That puzzles me."

"I can easily account for it, captain."

"How so?"

"Because the strictest orders have been issued that no one should see you—not even your nearest relations."

"And why not? Surely that is not fair."

"I can't altogether say as how it is, captain. But, you see, they are most desperately frightened that you will make your escape; and they don't intend to run the least risk in doing the slightest thing that they think might tend towards it."

"How over-cautious!"

"They mean to be, captain. They are uncommonly fond of your company, and prize it very highly, I can assure you. They won't let you go, make your mind up to that."

"And when am I to be taken before the magistrate?"

"Very shortly, I expect. They would have had you up before this, only your desperate condition prevented it. However, they will soon think you well enough now, I fancy."

"That will do, my friend. Many thanks for all that you have told me. I feel now as though a little slumber would be about the most acceptable thing in the world."

"All right."

"When I recover, I shall have another favour to ask you."

"Name it, captain."

"It is to tell me just how it was that I was brought here, with all the particulars of my capture."

"Don't you recollect anything about it?"

"Nothing at all. Everything is a blank to me from the moment after I fell from the saddle into the roadway."

"Don't let that distress you then, captain, for I happen to be acquainted with the exact facts of the case—I will tell you all."

"Many thanks."

With these words Captain Hawk turned over on his bed.

His joy may be imagined when he found that he could accomplish the feat with much less exertion than on the preceding occasion, and from this he derived the keenest hopes as to the rapidity of his recovery.

He was much exhausted; and before he had been comfortably extended many minutes he was sound asleep, and as completely oblivious of all events past, present, and to come, as he would have been had he dropped out of existence altogether.

In this unconscious state he remained for many hours.

But this calm, sound sleep was doing wonders as regards his recovery.

Sir Thomas Walker came, and the Governor and the surgeon.

But Captain Hawk obliviously slept on.

The doctor, when he saw the condition of his patient, gave peremptory orders that the cell should be vacated immediately, for any disturbance would tend very greatly to retard the prisoner's recove[illegible]

This was what [illegible] the Governor and the magistrate were most anxious to avoid, and so they withdrew.

They solaced themselves, however, with a few glasses of wine in one of the Governor's private rooms.

The latter was quite as anxious, though from a widely different motive, that Captain Hawk should be got before the magistrate with the least possible delay, on account of being relieved from the responsibility which the captain's abode in the prison occasioned him.

"We must lose no time," he said, with a resolute effort to secure his refractory eye-glass. "The sessions are getting alarmingly close at hand. I am afraid he will disappoint us after all."

"We will try to prevent it," said the magistrate. "It will never do for his case to remain over till next assizes. As soon as ever he is sufficiently recovered to bear being placed in the dock, he shall go through the form of being examined and committed."

"Aw—yes—that's very good; and we must really contrive to do it somehow. That confounded surgeon of ours is so awfully strict in his notions of duty—aw—and what's right and proper, that—aw—aw—demme, we could do no good with him at all!"

"My dear sir," said the magistrate, leaning forward in his chair, "what conclusion am I to draw from your words?"

"Why—aw—your worship, just this: You see, if we had got some one for surgeon who was not so cursedly scrupulous—aw—we could persuade him to give the prisoner some powerful drug—aw—that would for a time exert a very strong effect—aw."

"A good notion! You are right. You mean, you would have something administered that would fill his frame with a temporary and factitious strength, and when the medicine was at the highest point of its power, have him taken before the magistrate?"

"Exactly."

"The examination won't take very long," said the magistrate, slowly, rubbing his hands together. "By Jove! I think it can be managed. There would be plenty of time for him to recover and get up his strength in time to have his trial."

"Aw—yes. It would be an excellent thing."

"I will see to it. It will go hard with me if I cannot get it done. I have sworn to know no rest until this fellow is disposed of, and as surely as we are sitting here I will fulfil my oath."

The words were uttered with an intensity which proved how much in earnest the speaker was.

And his rancour is not to be so much wondered at, for the events which had occurred having oozed out, had caused him to be the butt of almost every person he met, and the continual jokes that were cracked at his expense drove him almost to the verge of desperation.

He was continually asked when he intended to find another dinner for a highwayman; and he felt that he could only free himself from the ridicule which faced him at every turn by bringing the matter speedily to a tragical termination.

The hint which the Governor had thrown out took a firm hold upon his imagination; and after having a few more words with the Governor he took his departure, with his mind firmly made up that he would go to any length to have the experiment tried.

CHAPTER CXIV.

CAPTAIN HAWK REGAINS HIS STRENGTH RAPIDLY, BUT FINDS THERE IS NOT SO MUCH PROSPECT OF ESCAPE AS HE HAD THOUGHT.

It was not until early on the morning of the following day that Captain Hawk awoke from his long and refreshing slumber.

The difference which it made in him is a thing which can scarcely be conceived.

As the turnkey said, and with perfect reason, he was not like the same person.

"You will surprise the surgeon, I can tell you. When he comes he won't expect to find you so far recovered as you are, I'll warrant."

"I feel wonderfully better," was the answer, "and if you have another glassful of that physic anywhere, I shall be glad to take it. There cannot be two opinions about its wonderful effects."

"All right, captain—here you are; though, as I said before, what you want to get better for at all, to have your neck stretched, I can't make out. But here you are. Drink it off, and much good may it do you."

Captain Hawk swallowed the draught with very great satisfaction.

He only smiled at the turnkey's words, for his mind was filled to overflowing with anticipations of liberty.

As we know, the object of all parties in the prison was to get his strength restored in the shortest space of time possible, and in order that there might be every chance of this, all kinds of nourishing things were provided for his especial use.

When he had taken the draught, the turnkey set to work to prepare a light but tempting and strengthening repast.

He set it before the captain in a very short time, who, we need scarcely take the trouble to say, did full and ample justice to it.

Already a faint tinge of red could be detected in the captain's cheeks—already there was apparent an increased vigour of his whole frame.

Every morsel of the breakfast was devoured, and then the captain, assuming the easiest position he could, prepared to listen to the turnkey's account of his capture.

But this we have no need to place before the reader, to whom the precise facts are sufficiently well known.

Of course the jailer dressed up the narrative a little according to his own ideas, but in the main he stuck to the truth.

The captain was deeply interested.

What puzzled him most was how it had happened that the Black Highwayman did not discover he was in the butcher's cart, and contrive to rescue him.

The only plausible reason he was able to think of was that Lord Harcliffe must also have been wounded; and when once this idea took hold upon him, it was easy enough for him to picture his comrade in a condition not greatly differing from his own.

This would account for everything.

There was only one point he wished to be satisfied upon, and that was, whether anyone had applied at the gates to see him.

This the turnkey promised to find out, and the result of his inquiries was that no one whatever had made a single inquiry

This unexpected circumstance made the captain's spirits sink a great deal.

He made sure that some one would at least have made an effort to pay him a visit.

He did not know that Tom Beckford had made inquiries in the town which had convinced him of the uselessness of making application at the prison gates.

"Don't be down, captain," said the turnkey. "Your friends must have known that the strictest orders were given that no one should be admitted."

But Captain Hawk would not believe that any orders would be sufficient to prevent his friends from making at least the attempt to see him.

Something out of the ordinary course of things had certainly occurred, but what it was puzzled him to conjecture.

Nor was he allowed any great length of time to indulge in his speculations without being interrupted.

His quick ear soon caught the sound of footsteps and voices in the corridor.

They grew louder until they ceased on the threshold of the cell.

Then the fastenings were carefully removed, and the door cautiously pushed open.

Captain Hawk, with a mingled feeling of vexation and curiosity, turned his eyes to see who was entering.

They were all strangers to him, or nearly so, for he had not a clear recollection of one—not even the Governor, who was of course a member of the little party.

He was accompanied by Sir Thomas Walker.

The surgeon, with his brows contracted, brought up the rear, and by the manner in which he paused it seemed as though he was half a mind not to come in at all.

The fact was, the magistrate had been urging his little scheme upon him, and, as the Governor had foreseen, he set his face dead against it.

The magistrate, however, affecting not to notice his disinclination, was most importunate.

And he was powerful.

None knew the extent of it better than the doctor, who, though a conscientious man, was unfortunately a needy one.

The remembrance of this, and the knowledge that if he lost his prison appointment he should be a ruined man henceforth, made him smother his repugnance and enter the cell.

The condition in which he found his patient filled him with peculiar satisfaction.

"There will be little need, I think, to adopt any unusual measures," he said. "One more day's rest like the last will do wonders: he will be all but in possession of his usual strength."

"Do you really think so?"

"I do indeed."

The magistrate was satisfied with the assurance, for he knew full well that what he said could be depended upon.

Captain Hawk, wondering what could be meant by this, fixed his gaze steadily and inquiringly upon the magistrate, who bore the scrutiny as long as he was able, and then cried out:

"Well, villain, why do you stare? What is it?"

"Hush — hush!" interposed the doctor, who saw instantly the flash which faintly suffused the highwayman's countenance. "I must forbid all excitement; it will undo all that has been done."

This threat was powerful enough to make Sir Thomas choke down his resentment.

Up to this moment Captain Hawk had been silent, and now when he spoke immediate attention was given to his words.

"I demand permission to communicate with my friends," he said.

"Demand as much as you like," said the magistrate. "You will not be allowed to do so. We have got you safe—and goodness knows, we had trouble enough over it—and now we have you we will take care to keep you."

"But I protest against it!" said the highwayman. "You have no right to refuse me this demand."

"All right: have your own opinion; it will not alter facts in the least degree."

"We shall see," said the captain.

And having uttered these words, he became silent, nor could anything induce him to utter another syllable.

"Doctor," said the magistrate, as soon as they were in the corridor again, "I insist upon what I say being done. Of course, you can refuse if you like; but at the same time I hope you will not do so until you have well weighed the consequences of your refusal. On the day after to-morrow I insist upon his examination taking place."

The surgeon bowed without replying.

The turnkey waited until all was silent, and then said:

"I told you just how it was, captain, didn't I? You must give up. I can only compare you to some nice chicken that people have taken particular pains about fattening in order that he should be roasted—that's you, captain. And as I said before, if I had been you I should have preferred dying quietly in my bed."

"You are a very worthy fellow," said the highwayman, "and one of the first things I shall do after my recovery will be to reward you handsomely for the kind way in which you have treated me. Now, mark me, I shall be as good as my word."

"Well, captain, I do admire you, and that's a certain fact! That's good, that is, captain—the best joke that I have heard of for many a day! And you keep such a capital face on all the while—that's the cream of it! Ha, ha! It's capital!"

Hereupon the turnkey laughed enormously.

"I don't see anything funny," said Captain Hawk, calmly.

"You don't?"

"I really do not."

"The idea of you talking about what you will do! Why, I'll bet you a wager of what you like that on the Monday morning after the end of the sessions you will be past praying for."

"Very good," said the captain. "You are at liberty to have your own opinion—quite; and so am I. Now, on the Monday you mention, if you will meet me on Hampstead Heath between midnight and sunrise, I shall have much pleasure in giving you the reward I mentioned."

Hearing this, the turnkey manifested every token of ludicrous and outrageous fright.

"No, captain," he said. "Don't—don't!"

"Don't what?"

"Why, don't talk in that horrid way, to be sure! Meet you on Hampstead Heath on the night after your execution! No, not for a whole globe of gold! Why, the bare idea of such a thing is enough to drive all the sleep away from a body for a month at least!"

"You don't understand me," said Captain Hawk, with more seriousness than he had yet employed. "There comes a feeling over me so strong—so overpowering, that I cannot resist it."

"And what may that feeling be, captain?"

"Why, that I am far—very far from having reached the end of my career as yet. I feel that there's much yet for me to do, and that it will far surpass all that I have yet accomplished."

The manner in which these words were pronounced was so impressive that even the turnkey was sensibly affected.

"Well—well, captain," he said, "I will allow you to know the best; but I shall have my opinion for all that."

"You are quite free and welcome to do so."

"But, mark me," he added, "if things don't turn out as I think they will, I shall never look upon any object as certain any more—that's all."

Here the subject ended.

Captain Hawk, feeling drowsy, shortly fell off into another of those sleeps which refreshed him so marvellously.

Its duration was even longer than any which had preceded it; and when he awoke it was with a proportionately increased amount of strength—not only of body but mind.

The wound was healing up with great rapidity; and this is not wonderful, for it was really, as the doctor had said, a trifling affair; and if the highwayman had only well bandaged it immediately after the injury was inflicted he would have experienced but little future inconvenience from it.

Or if the hemorrhage had not been promoted by the violent exercise there would have been little amiss.

We mention this because really it did not take long for him to repair the loss of blood his system had sustained.

The doctor came and went without disturbing him.

As he left the cell he muttered:

"After all, there will be little need of the stimulant spoken of, and still less fear that the reaction from it will be productive of any serious consequences."

So much better did the captain feel that he insisted upon rising and dressing himself, and this he did without wanting much assistance from the turnkey or feeling any extreme degree of exhaustion afterwards, such as might reasonably have been expected.

There was only one subject which gave him uneasiness and anxiety, and this was the continued silence and absence of his friends.

It was almost in despair that he told the turnkey that by some means or other he must communicate with his friends outside.

"Captain," was the reply, "anything that is in the power of mortal man I'd do to serve you; but no one can accomplish impossibilities, and what you ask me to do for you is neither more nor less. You have no idea of the strictness of the watch which is kept. Not so much as the weight of a pin could by any means be smuggled in or out of the prison. You might just as well think of making your escape. The one would be no harder than the other."

"I am glad to hear that."

"Hear it? Why?"

"Because I have made up my mind to escape, and from what you say it seems it will not be so difficult as I had expected."

"Well, that's the best yet! Not so difficult! Captain, I admire your style of talk—I really do! Not difficult! Why don't you ask me to put Huntingdon Jail into my waistcoat pocket?"

"Wait and see the result," was the captain's calm reply—so calm that it staggered the turnkey's opinions in spite of himself.

"It's all very well," he said, at last; "but for all that I wish you would listen to a little reason, captain, and try to realise what your position is actually like."

"I do."

"But I say you don't."

"How so?"

"Shall I tell you?"

"By all means."

"Will it be any good?"

"Let the result prove."

"Well, then, here goes."

"I am all attention."

The turnkey cleared his throat, and then spoke, in a very solemn, deliberate tone of voice:

"Captain, just look here. You'll admit that you are inside Huntingdon Jail, won't you?"

"I am sorry to say I am obliged to do that."

"There you go again. But stop a minute, and I'll make your position clear to you. Understand, then, first of all that all the time you are here either myself or some other turnkey will be locked up inside the cell along with you."

"Well?"

"Well do you call it? I should like to know, now, whether you think that alone is not enough to put the stopper on to all hopes of escape?"

"No, I don't."

"You don't?" echoed the turnkey, who had made so sure of his position that he could scarce believe he had heard aright—"you don't?"

"No, certainly not. I regard it as a trifling difficulty to be got over—that's all."

"Oh, very well! Regard it how you like—the fact remains the same."

"Pray go on!"

"I will. Further than that, there is on the outside of the door a man constantly on guard, whose instructions are not to hesitate a moment about raising an alarm should anything at all of an unusual character come to his ears."

"Very good. That is another trifling obstacle in the way."

"But there's a clincher to come."

"What's that?"

"Why, outside, down in the yard, there is a man whose eyes are constantly fixed on that grated opening there. If he saw you there attempting to get out, he would make an alarm; and if he could only prevent you by the means of the blunderbuss he carries, he would favour you with the contents of that; and I know from the way the barrel is loaded that it would be certain to bring you down as dead as a nut."

Captain Hawk, hearing this, looked more serious.

In good truth, he hardly thought the precautions taken to guard against his escape were so elaborate and complete.

It did indeed seem that unless he possessed the faculty of rendering himself invisible he would stand not the ghost of a chance of getting away.

The turnkey enjoyed his triumph.

"That's capped you, I rather think!" he cried, exultingly. "But over and above all I have told you, there is another difficulty greater than all."

"Name it."

"Why, it's the officers who have captured you, and who cannot handle the whole of the reward until you are fairly tucked up. Between them they keep up a constant guard round the prison night and day. Not so much as a mouse could leave it without their knowledge."

CHAPTER CXV.

CAPTAIN HAWK IS TAKEN BEFORE THE MAGISTRATE.

The turnkey wound up his catalogue of difficulties with a triumphant chuckle.

Captain Hawk remained silent.

When vaguely thinking and resolving upon his escape he had not taken any of the details into consideration.

Of course, if he had been in a clear-headed enough condition to think the whole matter calmly over from first to last, he would naturally have been brought to the conclusion that precautions of a far more than ordinary character would be taken by the authorities, so as to preclude all possibility of his escape.

Nevertheless, it was but for a moment that he suffered himself to be cast down and dismayed by the obstacles in his path.

His natural lightness of heart speedily asserted itself; and the turnkey was considerably taken aback upon finding how slight was the impression which his formidable list of obstructions had produced.

"There will be a little trouble," the captain said; "but then there will be all the more credit in effecting an escape. I should think it an insult to be allowed to walk out of a prison without having to take any pains."

"Oh, you're a rum 'un, you are, captain!" said the turnkey, with great admiration—"no one can't go for to dispute about that! You're game, you are, and it's my opinion game you'll die!"

"Mind you keep your appointment," returned the highwayman. "Rest assured I shall be there."

"I'll take particular notice I'm not, though; so just oblige me by dropping the subject, will you, captain?"

"I am quite in earnest, and you will find that I shall reward your services and kindnesses to me liberally."

"Oh, don't mention it—pray don't! I assure you all I have done for you, captain, you're very welcome to. Pray look upon it all as being done free, gratis for nothing. Please to recollect that."

Captain Hawk laughed, for he could see that the prospect of meeting him on Hampstead Heath produced the most uncomfortable feelings in the mind of the turnkey.

Soon afterwards the conversation ended, and as before, many hours were passed by the prisoner in the oblivion of sleep.

But his slumber was no longer dreamless.

His mind, pondering continually upon the absence and silence of his friends, played him strange pranks when his eyes were closed, and all manner of fantastic visions flitted through his imagination.

His recovery was wonderfully rapid, and had the magistrate possessed the least stock of patience, Nature would soon have recovered the captain sufficiently to undergo his examination.

But he had fixed his mind upon the administration of the stimulant, and the hesitation evinced by the doctor only strengthened his determination.

Accordingly, on the following morning, an alteration was made in the captain's medicine.

What drug it was that the surgeon employed for the accomplishment of the much-wished-for purpose we know not.

All we can say is that the captain, having drunk it, without, of course, having the glimmering of an idea about it, suddenly felt a remarkable amount of exhilaration and vigour.

The turnkey, too, who was not let into the secret, was much amazed at the effects apparently produced by the last dose.

The highwayman felt he had only to give a bit of a spring, and he should be able to fly through the ceiling of his cell.

He rose and dressed himself with probably as little trouble as ever he had had in his life.

There was an odd kind of feeling at the back of his head and just over his eyes, though it was so slight and so peculiar that it would have puzzled him to describe it.

Immediately upon finishing his toilet, he made a hearty breakfast.

He declared to the turnkey that he had never enjoyed anything so much, or felt in such good spirits, in all his life.

He had not finished his meal when the door opened and gave admittance to the same party that had visited him before—namely, Sir Thomas, the Governor, and the surgeon.

"Now, doctor," said the former, crossing the threshold of the cell with a very authoritative air, "just let me have your report, though, if I am any judge, I should say he is quite strong enough."

With a look on his face which showed clearly enough how repugnant all these irregular proceedings were to him, the surgeon made a brief examination of his patient.

Captain Hawk, although he was at a loss to think what all this meant, and wondered greatly what was coming next, remained profoundly silent.

"Well," repeated the magistrate, "what is your opinion? Is he able to take his examination this morning?"

"I think so," was the answer; "though I cannot be responsible for the consequences which excitement may produce."

"I will take the responsibility of that upon my own shoulders," said the magistrate.

Then turning to the captain, he said:

"Prepare yourself to be taken before the magistrate for your preliminary examination. You will be wanted in the Court in about an hour's time."

Captain Hawk merely bowed his head and turned aside.

The magistrate, after lingering a few moments, left the cell in order to make the necessary preparations for the event upon which his mind was so anxiously fixed.

"I will take care there is no hitch or breakdown," he said, confidentially, to the Governor.

"That's right, your worship—aw—aw! After all these pains and trouble, it would be—aw—too bad, curse me! for there to be a flaw in the evidence."

"I will guard effectually against that."

"Can you make sure of that?"

"I will enter the witness-box myself; and after that if he is not committed for trial, it is a strange thing to me."

Matters having been thus satisfactorily settled, the precious pair parted.

In the meantime the turnkey, as on the occasion of the former visit, remained silent until he was tolerably certain that the late visitors were out of earshot.

Then, looking the prisoner full in the face, he said:

"Can't you see that what I told you is coming to pass as fast as possible? Mark my words if it does not all turn out to be true to the letter. And what sort of an examination do you think you are going to have to-day? Why, a mere matter of form, which might just as well be gone without, only custom is opposed to it."

"We shall see," said Captain Hawk, if possible with greater confidence than he had yet displayed.

The reason of this was because he looked forward to his interrogation before the magistrate with feelings of the greatest satisfaction.

If his friends had been prevented from visiting him in his cell, they would at all events contrive to be present at his examination.

One glance into the face of any one of them would, he felt, be worth anything, and consequently he was full of impatience for the time to come when he should be summoned forth.

The time was short, and yet to him it appeared endless.

The potion he had swallowed was now beginning to make its effects more manifest, and, under the influence of it, he paced up and down his cell with rapid steps.

It was in vain the friendly turnkey spoke to him.

He would not listen to his prediction that, by thus exerting himself, he should be prostrated when the time came for him to require his utmost strength.

In the irritated state of his mind, anything resembling rest and repose was unendurable even to think of.

In less than an hour the Governor made his appearance, accompanied by several of the prison officials.

"Prisoner," he said, "the Court awaits you."

"I am ready," was the calm response.

"Let me caution you against the least show of resistance or the faintest attempt at violence, because the consequence will only recoil upon your own head. Every precaution will be taken to prevent your escape, and so I bid you beware."

To this speech Captain Hawk did not think fit to make answer of any kind.

The men he had brought with him formed into a kind of procession.

Two parties of two placed themselves before the captain, and two similar parties in the rear.

At a signal from the Governor, two more placed themselves on each side of the prisoner.

It was noticeable that these were the strongest and tallest of the whole party.

"Are you all ready?" asked the Governor, taking a general inspection of the whole group through his eye-glass.

A murmured assent was given.

"Follow me, then. Officers, secure your prisoner. Those in the van and rear keep good watch and ward—aw!"

Down came his eye-glass, and marred somewhat the Governor's imposing appearance as he stalked majestically from the cell.

At the words he had just uttered, those men who stood beside the captain took each a firm grasp upon him.

Simultaneously the prisoner felt himself seized by the wrists, while a firm grip was taken upon each side of the collar of his coat.

His first impulse was to struggle to release himself, but a second thought convinced him that it would be the best policy on his part to keep quiet.

Any show of resistance just at that juncture would not only be useless but unwise.

It was in consequence of feeling a conviction of this kind that he pretended to be quite listless and unconcerned respecting what was going forward.

The Governor glanced back and seemed surprised to see the prisoner so quiet.

The men, however, who had him under their care had been duly cautioned against being thrown off their guard by any behaviour of the highwayman.

The Governor looked harassed and vexed, and was more vigilant than a Tom cat after a mouse.

In perfect quietude, however, the singular procession made its way along the various corridors of the jail until they emerged into one of the paved yards.

Crossing this, they entered a large room which had been temporarily fitted up for its present purpose in order to avoid the risk of taking the prisoner through any of the streets of the town.

Even as he went and as he found that he was not to be examined in the ordinary place appointed for the purpose, Captain Hawk felt his spirits sink.

He could not shut his eyes to the fact that while this superhuman vigilance was exercised and care used it would not be in the power of any living man to gain his liberty.

There was another thing, too, which caused the captain to experience a great sinking of the heart.

This was the fear that his friends should be excluded from the Court during the time of his examination.

This was a thing it had never occurred to him to think upon until the present moment.

He had but little space, however, allowed him for reflection.

The doors of this outer room had been thrown open, and he was hurried swiftly towards the portal.

As he advanced he distinguished that strange murmuring sound which is always heard when people are congregated together in any large numbers.

His hopes revived as he heard the hoarse murmur, for it told him that his worst forebodings were not realised—the public had not been shut out of the Court-room after all.

The sudden revulsion of feeling which followed upon this discovery rendered his remembrance of the events which followed somewhat indistinct.

But he was perfectly conscious of being thrust forward among the people until he was hoarsely bidden to stand still.

As we may say, mechanically he obeyed this mandate, and at the moment when he did so a sharp quick sound came upon his ears.

It was caused by the turnkeys closing the door of the square box-like place in which he stood.

The sound seemed to arouse him, and raising his head, he gave a hasty but searching glance around him.

The many upturned faces all bent upon him caused him to feel a momentary confusion.

He could see nothing distinctly.

Then he heard a sonorous voice cry:

"Call Captain Hawk."

"He is here, your worship."

On receiving this assurance, the clerk read over the charge against him.

Of all the over and over again repeated details Captain Hawk heard little.

He was scanning furtively the many faces by which he was surrounded, and endeavouring to discover one the lineaments of which were familiar to him.

But at present he looked in vain.

He was recalled to the reality of what was passing around him by hearing the clerk say, in a loud voice:

"Prisoner at the bar, do you plead guilty or not guilty?"

"Not guilty," he said, amid a universal silence.

The plea was duly recorded.

"Produce the evidence."

Captain Hawk looked to see who it was that had pronounced these words.

Guided by the sound, his eyes settled themselves upon the countenance of a man who occupied a high seat exactly in front of him.

This he knew at once to be the presiding magistrate.

His face was quite unknown to him.

Not so was that of the individual who occupied the seat next to him.

This was Sir Thomas Walker, who, even as he sat there upon the bench of justice, was unable altogether to conceal the animus he had against the prisoner.

There was now a stir about the body of the Court, and Captain Hawk once more gave a hurried glance around him.

But still he saw not what he looked for; and in spite of the determination he had come to to preserve his stoicism to the utmost, a sigh of disappointment came from his lips.

But the manifestation of feeling was only transient.

In less than a second he was perfectly calm.

It was embarrassing, however, to find himself the cynosure of so many eyes—not one of them expressive of the least sympathy for his position

It was some relief for him to fix his gaze upon the magistrate; and while doing so he endeavoured to be unconscious of all else that was going on in the crowded Court.

The chief of the party of police officers was the first witness called upon.

He stepped into the witness-box in a business-like, off-hand manner, which showed that the proceedings of the present morning were familiar enough to him.

While the little door was closed in front of him he affected to adjust his wig just to show everybody how much at home a truly great man can be under difficult circumstances.

Then he glanced around him in a jaunty, self-satisfied air; and having favoured the prisoner with a hard stare, he turned his face towards the magistrate's desk, and by a look said as plainly as if he had spoken that he was in readiness to answer any questions that might be put to him.

The clerk turned his papers over until he found the document he required.

As soon as this was the case a profound stillness prevailed in the Court.

CHAPTER CXVI.

THE POLICE OFFICERS GIVE THEIR EVIDENCE AGAINST CAPTAIN HAWK.

"Is your name Nicholas Twigg?" said the presiding magistrate.

"It is, your worship."

"An officer of the police?"

"Yes, your worship?"

"Be good enough to look at the prisoner at the bar. Do you recognise him?"

"I do, your worship."

"What is his name?"

"I can hardly say that, your worship; but he is generally known as Captain Hawk."

"Very good. In default of further knowledge we will presume that that is his name. Now tell the Court what you know of him."

"I know him to be a highwayman, and guilty of various acts of robbery with violence in various parts of the kingdom."

"Yes. Go on."

"Warrants have long been out against him, but he has eluded capture—partly because of the number of accomplices he has, all of whom have been faithful, and partly on account of a horse of great swiftness, which has often aided him to get clear off when pursued."

"Very good. That is quite clear."

"Yes, your worship."

"A reward has been offered for his apprehension, of course?"

"Yes, your worship—it is here."

Accordingly the officer pulled out of his pocket a folded paper, which he first opened, and then bending over, placed it on the clerk's table.

The clerk in his turn handed it up to the magistrate, who sat at a desk above him.

That worthy, having adjusted his massive gold spectacles, looked very knowingly at the paper.

He was but a very indifferent scholar, and knew more about hunting and shooting than he did about the niceties and intricacies of the law.

But then that was all right.

Had he understood the law himself, he would not have required the services of the clerk, and to abolish that official would be very unconstitutional indeed.

Law was dealt out to his satisfaction; and as they were mostly persons in the lower sphere of life who came before him, few complaints were heard about the injustice of his decrees.

Still, he was not so great a dunce as to be unable to make out from the large letters at the top of the bill that it offered a reward of five hundred pounds. But the comparison of the captain's appearance with the description given beneath was a feat entirely beyond his power; so, after shaking his head very wisely and profoundly, he handed the paper to his colleague, Sir Thomas Walker.

The latter availed himself of the opportunity which the comparison gave him to dart some looks of withering hate upon the prisoner

"There can be no doubt about the rascal's identity," he said, as he handed back the paper—"not the shadow of a doubt. The officer who has captured him deserves to be congratulated for having seized the villain at last."

At this compliment the officer bowed very low, and looked highly gratified.

But the people in the body of the Court took a different view of the matter, and an audible hiss arose.

Sir Thomas turned purple with passion.

The presiding magistrate glared around and said:

"I—I give notice that if any disorder is shown in the Court, I will have it cleared at once. Understand once for all, if there is any manifestation for or against the prisoner, I will insist upon clearing the Court."

These words produced silence.

Those who were present knew full well that the magistrate had the power to turn them all out if he chose to exercise it.

Therefore the hissing ceased, for the desire to witness the proceedings from first to last was infinitely stronger than that of expressing their opinion audibly.

"Silence!" bawled the usher, although no one was speaking a word; but after that little formality the magistrate was enabled to resume his inquiries.

"Ahem!" he cried, in a loud voice, and then he fixed his spectacles on his nose in a manner that was highly expressive of his determination to persevere in his intention at all hazards.

"Now, Mr. Twigg," he said to the chief officer, who responded instantly with a very deferential bow, "I want you to inform the Court how and where the prisoner at the bar was captured and safely lodged in prison?"

"May it please your worship," said the chief officer, preparing to make a speech, "from information I received, I got my men together on the evening of the twelfth of the last month, and rode to a certain place on the London Road."

"Yes. Very good. Whereabouts was the place you mention?"

"Rather less than twelve miles from here, your worship."

"Twelve miles," said the magistrate, affecting to make a note, but only dropping a huge blot on the paper instead. "Hum! ha! Twelve miles."

"A little less than twelve, your worship."

"Yes; thank you. I consider that very material."

And in order to testify to it, he made a long tail to the blot, which caused it to bear a strong resemblance to a comet; after which, looking doubly wise, he said, profoundly:

"Proceed, Twigg—proceed!"

"May it please your worship, I disposed my men on each side of the road behind the hedge, so that there should be no danger of us being observed by any chance traveller passing. The night was so dark, however, that if there had been no hedge to conceal us we should have been invisible."

"A dark night. Yes. Go on."

"When all was ready, I directed two more of my men to ride down the road like ordinary travellers."

"Were they disguised accordingly?"

"They were, your worship."

"And what took place then?"

"As I fully expected, the prisoner at the bar rode up to them, and called upon them to stand and deliver upon pain of instant death."

"You heard that, Twigg, and will swear to it, of course?"

"Oh yes!"

"How far off were you at the time?"

"Not a dozen paces, your worship."

"Was the prisoner alone on the occasion we are speaking of?"

"No, your worship."

"Who was with him?"

"Another desperate highwayman."

"And where is he?"

"He managed to escape, your worship."

"Have you any further particulars of him?"

"I have."

"Name them."

At this Captain Hawk looked up with a much greater amount of interest and curiosity than he had yet manifested in the proceedings.

"Excuse me, your worship, but I feel it necessary, in the interest of justice, to ask leave to keep to myself whatever information I have received, because, as the man is not yet in custody, it will interfere with the plans I have laid."

"Oh, of course—quite right. You are perfectly at liberty to be reticent. Go on, please, confining yourself to the prisoner at the bar."

How great the disappointment was that the captain felt we need not tell our readers.

Had he not known the character of the police officers so well, he would have suffered great anxiety on account of his comrade, but, as he rightly enough judged, Twigg was silent simply because he had nothing to tell.

"Well, your worship," he continued, "as we had fully expected, from the information we had received, to see the prisoner at the bar alone, we were just at the moment a little flurried at discovering such was not the case"

"What happened then?"

"According to arrangement, the two men who personated the travellers gave up a purse containing the sum of sixteen shillings in silver, in order that we might be able to swear to the actual committal of a robbery."

"Very good—very ingenious!" said the magistrate, making another huge blot in token of his delight. "Be good enough to state what followed."

"Finding it impossible to capture the prisoners without having recourse to firearms, I gave the order for the men to fire. I had previously instructed them to take care to do no more than wound the prisoner, and on no account to slay him outright."

Of course the reader knows that this statement was in direct opposition to the truth.

But even in those days police officers were not over-particular as to what they swore to when the strengthening of a case was the object they had in view.

"And you wounded the prisoner at the bar?"

"Yes, your worship, though we could hardly believe it at the time, because he rode off after his companion at full gallop as though nothing at all was the matter."

"And what happened after that?"

"We lost no time in commencing a pursuit, your worship, which we kept up until just about daybreak."

"And then you found the prisoner insensible in the roadway, did you not?"

"Barclay will depose to what followed, your honour."

"Very good."

Then turning towards Captain Hawk, the presiding magistrate said:

"Prisoner at the bar, have you any questions you wish to ask this witness?"

Captain Hawk shook his head and replied in the negative.

But his voice was so low and faint that his answer would have been inaudible but for the expectant silence which prevailed in the Court just at that juncture.

The fact was, the captain's strength was beginning to fail.

How great the effort had been for him to maintain an erect posture for so long a time no one had the least idea but himself.

Now, however, such a sensation of deadly faintness came over him that he was compelled to clutch at the iron spikes in front of the dock for support.

His condition would have been unnoticed and unsuspected but for the prison surgeon, who saw the condition to which his patient was reduced.

But he judged rightly—any appeal to the humanity of the magistrate would have met with a prompt and stern rebuke, so, instead, he very wisely called for a glass of water and a chair.

These articles were furnished without causing much delay, and without meeting with any opposition from the magistrate.

Into the glass of water the surgeon dropped a small quantity of a stimulative essence.

Captain Hawk thanked him with an earnest glance, and swallowed the potion gratefully.

It was, however, an exquisite relief for him to sink down into a seat.

The fact of his being fatigued so soon served to show him very forcibly to what a state of weakness he had been reduced.

After this little episode Barclay was called.

Those who were acquainted with the man's ordinary manner felt not a little curious to know how he would behave himself under present circumstances.

"Is your name John Barclay?" said the clerk, who now took up the questioning in order that his master should have a rest.

"Yes."

"Look at the prisoner at the bar. Do you know him?"

"Yes."

"Where have you seen him before?"

"Lying like one dead."

"Where?"

"In the road."

"Well, go on," said the clerk. "It's as bad as drawing water from the bottom of a deep well to get anything out of you."

Not a muscle of Barclay's countenance moved.

"Go on with what you know," said the clerk.

"I bound up his wound."

"What else?"

"That's all I did."

"Did you not put him in the cart?"

"No."

"Who did?"

"The others."

"Then we will try whether there is not one a little more able to speak. Yet, stay: you must first say who the prisoner at the bar is."

"Why, Captain Hawk, of course. He's been sworn to; and you can't make him anything else."

There was a general laugh at this, in the midst of which Barclay beat a retreat from the witness-box before Captain Hawk was asked whether he had any questions to put to him.

Another officer, named William Jones, was called.

The same formula was gone through with him as with the former witnesses.

All he did, however, was to relate at some length those circumstances which must be quite fresh in the reader's remembrance.

He declared how the captain's body had been found, how it was placed in the butcher's cart, and finally how it was delivered safely to the Governor of the jail.

The evidence was complete.

On being asked, Captain Hawk said he had no questions to put to the witness.

Mr. Bones, the butcher, was next called, to his very great annoyance and no little alarm.

The evidence he gave was simple enough.

Captain Hawk, of course, had nothing to say to him, never having, to the best of his belief, set eyes upon him until that moment.

Mr. Bones therefore beat a very hasty retreat, glad to get off so easily, though what harm he had anticipated would befall him it would be hard for us to say.

Captain Hawk felt that, despite the power of the drug he had swallowed, he was fast getting weaker and weaker, and as he gazed at the sea of faces surrounding him he found himself idly speculating as to where he was and why he should feel so strangely.

The murmur of voices around him reached his ears, but failed to penetrate to his mind.

He was just dimly aware that another officer, who answered to the name of Sampson Clark, was brought up against him.

This was one of those who had so well personated the characters of passengers on the highway, and who were, in fact, the mainsprings of the scheme.

He swore positively to what he knew as well as anybody else was an absolute falsehood.

He declared that it was the prisoner at the bar, Captain Hawk, and no other, who had called upon him to stand, and to whom he had handed the purse.

The reader knows, of course, that it was the Black Highwayman who had done all this—Captain Hawk, by preconcerted arrangement, riding up behind them.

In the way in which this man gave his evidence, however, it made the case against the prisoner very complete and conclusive.

Sir Thomas was in ecstasies.

He could see there was abundant evidence to warrant a commitment without his taking the trouble to come forward.

[LORD HARCLIFFE AND ISAAC ON THEIR WAY TO LONDON.]

He resolved to wait until the day of trial, when he expected that his testimony against the captain would prove overwhelming.

"That is the case, your worship," said Twigg, stepping forward, and looking blander and more jaunty than ever.

"Oh, very good!" said the presiding magistrate, as he flung down his pen. "Prisoner at the bar, have you anything to say?"

The question roused Captain Hawk.

By a vigorous effort he shook off to some extent the lethargy which weighed him down.

He stood erect, though he had to steady himself by holding tightly to two of the iron spikes that were bristling before him.

CHAPTER CXVII.

IN WHICH CAPTAIN HAWK IS DULY COMMITTED TO TAKE HIS TRIAL AT THE FORTHCOMING ASSIZES.

On the part of every person present in the densely-crowded Court the greatest curiosity was felt to hear what the celebrated highwayman had to say.

The many romantic stories with which his name had been mixed up had invested him with far more than an ordinary degree of interest.

But the weakness which had seized the prisoner was so great that he had to make more than one effort before he was able to speak.

"Your worship," he said, "the greater part of what the last witness has said is false."

A faint murmur of applause followed this declaration, but it was promptly stopped.

"Have you anything to say in your defence?"

"I demand the aid of a solicitor," was the reply. "I have been denied communication with everyone; but it is my right to be defended, and I claim my right!"

Here the applause was more unequivocal.

Sir Thomas Walker frowned and looked deeply vexed.

"It is not right to hang me off like a dog," continued the prisoner. "And up to the present moment all that has taken place is a mere sham—an absolute mockery! I am innocent, and I desire legal assistance to make that innocence known."

"No one thinks of depriving you of it," said the magistrate. "Of course, you are entitled to hold communication with your solicitor."

"I am satisfied with that assurance," said the captain, with a low bow.

"What more have you to say?"

"I can say nothing. I have no one to defend me."

"Then," said the magistrate, drawing a long breath, "it is my duty to tell you that you are duly committed to take your trial at the assizes next following."

Captain Hawk bowed again, and really it seemed as though he was slipping away from life.

It was at this moment that a voice in one corner of the Court suddenly pronounced the words:

"You shall have a lawyer."

The tones of this voice, more than the actual words uttered, seemed, like a shock from a galvanic battery, to bring the prisoner back to life.

He stood erect, and glanced around him, as though in full possession of his usual mental and bodily vigour.

The magistrate started up to his feet in passionate amazement.

He was almost choked with rage.

"Who was that spoke? Bring the fellow before me, and I'll commit him! Where is he, I say?"

But the words were spoken so suddenly, and attention was so universally fixed at the moment upon the prisoner at the bar, that no one seemed able to take upon himself to say where the voice had sprung from.

"Officers," yelled the magistrate, in a frenzy, "am I to be defied in my own Court like this? I insist upon having the person who spoke brought before me!"

But if his frenzy had been ten times as great it would have been all the same.

Innocent persons were accused of the heinous fact, and in the course of about two minutes the confusion in the Court was increased tenfold.

The magistrate was standing up, gesticulating like a madman.

His face was absolutely purple, and terribly suggestive of apoplexy.

He was, no doubt, speaking; but that conclusion could only be arrived at by seeing that his lips were moving as though words were issuing from them.

But in the tremendous hubbub which prevailed around him his speech was just as inaudible as if he had been silent.

He banged upon the desk before him with both his clenched fists with frantic violence.

Sir Thomas Walker, who sat next to him, was scarcely less desperate

And what was more, he was apprehensive.

Not exactly on his own account; but at that moment the idea seemed to strike him that he would not be very safe if he fell into the hands of any of the captain's friends.

The great dread about his heart was that all this would only prove a colour and pretext to assist in rescuing the prisoner.

He would scarcely have been surprised if in the midst of the turmoil he had seen the captain carried bodily through one of the windows into the street.

We need not tell the reader, however, that this was an exaggerated fear, and that no such extraordinary event actually took place.

Indeed, in the whole crowded Court there was but one [illegible] person, and that person was Captain Hawk.

His demeanour did indeed present a wonderful contrast [illegible] the rest.

The effect produced upon him by the sudden sound of the [illegible] had not yet vanished.

He knew the voice.

Hardly any accents could have been more familiar to his ears.

The gush of feeling which came over him when he thus found that he was not, according to the discouraging anticipations in which he had indulged, forgotten by his friends was almost overpowering.

It was Tom Beckford who had spoken.

He knew that he was running some risk in saying such words; but, then, had the risk been ten times as much, he would not have held his peace.

What a reward it was to him to see the effect his voice produced upon the prisoner we need not attempt to describe.

Tom, as we have said, had chosen his opportunity with great tact.

At the moment when he opened his lips no one was prepared in the least degree for any interruption.

And attention was universally absorbed in gazing at the captain, for every person present felt the keenest interest in the prisoner's slightest movement.

And then Tom had only spoken five little words, so that as soon as anybody was aware of the interruption he was done.

And having escaped the first search successfully, there was little fear that he would be detected now.

Captain Hawk, however, at the moment the words were spoken, turned round like lightning, and caught a transient glimpse of his old friend's face.

But it was gone almost immediately, for the people in the Court gave a great surge, which can be likened to nothing else save the swell of the sea, and Captain Hawk saw his friend's face no longer.

The magistrate, finding the confusion increase, and discovering that all his efforts to obtain a hearing were vain, quitted his position, leaving the Court by a little side door close to his right hand.

He was beginning to fear that the confusion would end in a rescue.

Sir Thomas Walker hastily followed him.

"The Court must be cleared," said Sir Thomas—"at whatever cost, the Court must be cleared!"

"It must. I have left the bench for that purpose."

"Good! Lose not a moment, or depend on it the end will be a rescue of the prisoner."

"That is my fear."

The two magistrates were in a dreadful state of alarm, and with all haste gathered as many turnkeys and police officers as they could together.

These they admitted by means of the small side door we have mentioned.

The instructions were short and to the point.

They were to clear the Court, no matter at what hazard.

These men, forming themselves into a compact body, charged the tumultuous crowd.

An impression was made upon them.

The outer doors were opened, and the steady pressure being kept up from the rear, the angry crowd was by degrees forced into the yard outside.

In less than ten minutes the Court was clear, excepting, of course, the officials belonging to the prison.

Captain Hawk felt how weak he was, and yet the feeling of weakness was by no means so deathlike as it had been before.

The reason was because his heart was lighter.

Hope had once more found a dwelling-place in his breast.

When he had continually cast his eyes round and round the Court without finding one of the familiar faces he hoped to see, he had grown sick with disappointment.

Now all was changed.

The words which had been spoken were expressive to him of something more than the mere promise of legal assistance.

He knew that if that failed other means would be resorted to, and that he should not be suffered to perish on the scaffold if human efforts could avert his doom.

As soon as ever ordinary tranquillity was to some extent restored, a strong guard was formed around the prisoner.

There might not have been the actual need to support the captain's steps so much, but probably for security's sake so many officers clustered around and held him, that it might be said he was carried back to his cell rather than that he walked.

After what had happened, the highwayman felt it even a comfort to be taken back to the cell; and no sooner had he crossed the threshold, and been released from the grasp of the prison officials, than he flung himself at full length upon his bed.

Here he remained, silent and motionless, for more than an hour.

The turnkey who had behaved towards him in so friendly a manner throughout, watched him with the greatest interest and solicitude.

With much persuasion, he induced the captain to swallow another dose of medicine.

Not the stimulating draught which had been administered before, but a strengthening potion which the surgeon had prepared in readiness, and into which he had introduced such ingredients as would be best calculated to disarm the stimulant of its depressing after results.

The captain was not long in feeling the benefit of it, and, as usual, it threw him into a deep slumber.

This lasted longer than usual, for it was not until the following morning that he awoke.

When he opened his eyes and glanced around him he was sensible instantly that he was wonderfully better.

He seemed to behold surrounding objects with an additional amount of distinctness.

His heart beat with more vigour than he had felt for many days.

And, as a matter of course, his spirits were lighter and better, and the obstacles which interposed between himself and freedom no longer seemed so formidable as before.

As may be supposed, the first thing to which his memory reverted was Tom Beckford's promise.

"A lawyer!" he said to himself, thoughtfully. "How will that avail me? I cannot deny my identity, and no forensic power would make the judge believe that I am other than I am. No, no—I fear but little good will be done in that way. If I am to be set free it must be by means of much stronger measures."

But, as before, Captain Hawk took the words to mean much more than they actually expressed, and the inference he derived from them was that his friends would strain every effort on his behalf.

The great misfortune was that time was so short.

In seven or eight days at the furthest he would be placed upon his trial and made to go through what was nothing better than a formal mockery.

Up to this moment the captain had not moved upon his narrow bed, so that the turnkey was not aware that his prisoner's slumbers had ended.

But the instant the captain shifted his position slightly the turnkey was at his side.

"Ah!" he exclaimed, "you look ten times better than I expected to find you."

"Yes, thanks to your attention, my friend, I am much better. I shall show my gratitude, never fear."

"Oh, don't mention it, captain, I beg!" was the hasty response. "All I do is done with hearty good will."

"I am well aware of it, and that is why I feel all the more determined that your behaviour shall receive due recognition."

"Now, do oblige me, captain, by not saying a word about it. I want to give you just a little bit of advice."

"I am anxious to hear it."

"I have a capital breakfast here quite ready for you, and you'll oblige me if you will do justice to it before you attempt to get up."

"Breakfast?"

"Yes."

"Can it be possible that I have slept the whole of the night?"

"Such is the fact, captain. There was something extra strong, I take it, in that last dose I gave you."

"There must have been."

The turnkey did not wait for the prisoner to say whether he would take his breakfast in bed or not, but hastened to spread the meal on the coverlet.

The sight of the viands made the captain feel that he was somewhat languid for the want of food, and as he found everything he tasted excellent, he made a wonderfully good repast.

Then, while dressing afterwards, he was conscious of a very great accession of strength.

"You don't seem much put about by the result of your examination before the magistrate, captain."

"No; all turned out just as I anticipated."

"Oh, you are a cool hand, you are, as I have said before! Do you know when the trial will be?"

"No; do you?"

"Not the exact day, but I could give a pretty good guess."

"Let me know, then."

"Why, the assizes will begin on Monday next. They are sure to last three or four days, and I fancy yours will be about the last case heard."

"I have not many days for preparation."

"No, captain; and if you had, the result would be just the same."

"How?"

"Now, can you ask the question? You must know just as well as I do that your fate is decided upon already. They are sure to put you through the form of a trial because the law requires it. But for all the difference it will make to you, you might as well be tucked up without either judge or jury having a word to say about it."

"I don't know that, my friend; and if we live long enough we shall see."

"So we shall. But if you build any hopes upon being able to get off on your trial you will be wofully disappointed—that's all I can say."

"We shall see," said the captain again.

"You'll be disappointed. Lor' bless me, captain, know just as well what the end will be as though it had already taken place. I am sorry for your sake, captain, because I like you. It's a pity you should come to such a bad end."

"I have not come to it yet, my friend, nor can I get rid of the conviction on my mind that I am as yet nowhere near it."

The turnkey shrugged his shoulders, while his own manner said plainly enough that he had arrived exactly at an opposite conclusion.

Captain Hawk walked quietly up and down his cell.

He felt that this was what he ought to do in order to make the recovery of his strength more rapid.

The exercise was fatiguing at first, but by taking rests and persevering he was ultimately enabled to go through an amount of exertion which otherwise would have been quite impossible.

The only diversity to the day's monotony consisted of the customary visit of the Governor.

He came, as usual, accompanied by Sir Thomas and the surgeon.

Captain Hawk felt that there was nothing he could say to either of these men that would advantage him in the least, so he remained perfectly silent, save and except the monosyllabic replies which he gave to the surgeon's questions.

Sir Thomas and the Governor were quite content to see that their zealously-guarded prisoner was as secure as they could hope to see him, and also that there seemed no fear that he would be unable to be put on his trial at the coming sessions on account of his insufficient recovery from his wound.

With this comfortable knowledge they departed, Sir Thomas being especially delighted at the prospect there was that the vengeance he had sworn to have would not be long delayed.

CHAPTER CXVIII.

ISAAC HAS SOME ADVENTURES AT HUNTINGDON.

It is necessary now that we should take a passing glance at the captain's friends, in whose proceedings it is only reasonable to suppose the reader is deeply interested.

Long were the conferences which the landlord, Lord Harcliffe, and Isaac held together

But they produced no result.

Try as they would and tax their brains as they might, they could not see themselves any nearer towards releasing the captain from his critical position.

When they separated in this unsatisfactory manner Isaac could not rest.

He paid a visit to the stables, and having seen that Phantom and Satan were as comfortable as horses could wish to be, he turned to attend to the one upon which he was riding when Lord Harcliffe saw him first.

From what place this valuable and handsome horse had been procured, and in what manner, were secrets confined to Isaac's own breast.

It was his intention to have made this horse like the rest, comfortable and safe for the night, but on reaching its side he was assailed with so violent a temptation to ride to Huntingdon that he could not resist.

Nor was much time consumed in the struggle.

"I must be quick," he said. "Ten to one if either the landlord or the Black Highwayman do not come to see whether things are all right, and if they found me on the point of starting they would do all in their power to hinder my departure."

His dread that this would occur seemed to increase every minute, and caused him to make practical proof of the truth of the old proverb which says "More haste less speed."

Had he taken matters quietly he would certainly not have been so long.

Very few seconds however, were lost, although his impatience seemed to increase the lapse of time a hundredfold.

Springing into the saddle, he rode direct to that low part of the wall over which Captain Hawk had so often made Satan leap.

The gray horse cleared the obstacle in a manner which showed that he was far from being deficient of jumping powers.

When once on the other side of the wall it did not take Isaac long to gain the high-road; and having done so, he rode at full gallop towards the town.

The few intervening miles were speedily passed over.

But Isaac put up his horse at the very first inn he came to on the outskirts of the town.

The man to whose charge he consigned it eyed him very attentively, not to say suspiciously.

Certainly Isaac's appearance by no means agreed with that of the gray horse.

He seemed to read the man's doubts at a glance, and with admirable presence of mind he said:

"Take care of this horse. I expect master will come for it; but at any rate have it ready at a moment's notice."

He did not wait to utter a word more, or to listen to what the man into whose charge he gave it might have to say, but turned at once upon his heel and strode off towards the jail.

It was now getting somewhat late.

Many of the shops were closed, and the streets generally had a deserted appearance.

A disagreeable, drizzling rain was falling, and this had served very much to keep pedestrians indoors.

Isaac, however, was quite regardless of any such trifle as this.

Had anyone asked him what was his immediate purpose in thus visiting the town, he would have been puzzled to return a satisfactory reply.

He had acted merely upon the impulse which restlessness had created.

Anything he felt would be better than remaining at the Greyhound, where it was not possible for his knowledge of the captain to receive the smallest addition.

Now there was at least just a chance that he should learn something which might serve to guide them out of their embarrassment.

Isaac bent his steps in a direct line towards the jail.

Not that he applied at the gate, or had the least intention of so doing.

He was well enough aware that at that late hour no attention would be paid to his summons.

His destination was a small, old-fashioned public-house, which chanced to be the nearest habitation to the prison.

Here he knew perfectly well the officials who were connected with the jail were in the habit of repairing in the evening when the time and turn came for them to be off duty.

That he should be more likely to glean here the intelligence he longed for was reasonable enough.

To make his way there at all, however, was entirely an after thought, his first intention—if it can be said he had one—being merely to take a walk round the prison walls in the expectation that he might be able to single out the window of the captain's cell from all the others.

Now that his mind was made up, he quickened his pace.

"Would that I had thought of this a little earlier!" he said. "I am afraid now I shall only get there about closing time."

As he might have thought, however, the present was a very unusual occasion, and that more than a common interest would be felt in their conversation, which was certain to result in keeping the house open to a later hour.

This public-house was of a very mean exterior.

A miserable light flickered over the fanlight, and through the rents in a large red curtain which had been drawn across the window could be seen the flaming light of an iron lamp.

All around was dark, and on that present night the dim outlines of the prison roofs made the spot look unusually dismal.

Without stopping to pause, however, for any purpose, he pushed open the door and crossed the threshold.

The moment he did so his ears were greeted by a chorus of voices.

Guided by the sound, he pushed open another door, and found himself in a room of much larger dimensions than one would have expected to see when judging from the exterior aspect of the dwelling.

It was but rarely that this inn was frequented—especially at night—by any but prison officials; and the entrance of a stranger was always looked upon as an intrusion.

No sooner did Isaac make his appearance than the conversation, which had been going on so briskly before, dropped as if by magic.

This seemed to promise him less success than he had been hoping for, and when he sank down upon the nearest seat it was with a feeling of deep disappointment.

But concealing his feelings to the best of his ability, he called for a tankard of ale.

"A wretched night," he said, speaking in a broad country accent, which was very unlike his ordinary voice, but which suited his appearance admirably—"it is a wretched night, my masters—a main wretched night! This sort of rain wets a body."

He spoke with great apparent seriousness, so much so that the officers were completely deceived by it, and grinned at what they thought was the countryman's simplicity.

Still, for all that, his presence was a complete check upon the conversation.

Captain Hawk's name was mentioned once or twice, but little of importance was said concerning him.

Isaac was burning with curiosity to put a question or two, but the manifest impolicy of so doing restrained him.

What he gathered was merely a confirmation of what Tom Beckford had told him.

To his vexation, the turnkeys and other jail officials rose one by one from their seats and quitted the public-house.

He could tell by the glances that were cast upon him that he was considered an interloper; but he preserved a stolid indifference of manner which, though it might have deceived the warders pretty well, yet did not induce them to lay aside the reserve which his presence had been the cause of their assuming.

Yet clinging desperately to hope, he waited and waited until he had the room entirely to himself.

With a sigh of disappointment he finished drinking his ale, and, convinced that nothing more was to be learned in that quarter, he made his way out into the street again.

The discomfort of the night had in the meantime much increased.

The rain came down with a sullen persistency which showed no symptoms of cessation.

"What a night for an escape!" he said to himself. "Would that I possessed a little more knowledge! But I will not despair even yet."

So saying, he approached still more closely the prison walls.

He looked up at them; but their smooth, unbroken surface did nothing more than impress him with the great amount of difficulty there would be in scaling them.

With a slow and steady step, he made his way for a distance of some twenty yards, when he was all at once confronted by some person, who sprang out of the obscurity with so much suddenness that it would have puzzled anyone to say where he did come from.

"Hullo!" he cried, in a gruff voice. "Who are you?"

With a ready thought, Isaac counterfeited intoxication.

He seemed to know instinctively that the man who had addressed him was one of the officers Tom Beckford had spoken of as keeping strict watch round the prison.

He pretended to be very drunk indeed.

"Hic—hic!" he said, with a lurch forward and several attempts to preserve his balance—"hic!—what's it to you, I should like to know?"

He ran the words all together with so much art as to create immediately the conviction that he was very far gone in inebriation indeed.

"Come—now then!" said the officer. "Hold up! We don't allow any prowlers round here at night. Turn your head the other way, and mind you don't fall."

"What's that, Willis?" said another voice close at hand. "Who are you talking to?"

"Here's a drunken man here."

"Detain him a moment until I can see who he is."

The light of a dark lantern became immediately visible.

Isaac felt his danger.

His first impulse was to make a run for it.

But the probabilities of capture were too great to make it worth while for him to run the risk, so he wisely determined to try his utmost to keep up the character he had assumed.

"L—l—look here," he said, addressing the officer who had been called Willis, and affecting to steady himself by holding to his arm while he spoke—"look here! Ain't this free-born England, I should like to know—hic!—and can't a man go where he likes?"

As he finished, he released his hold upon the officer's arm, and then pretended to try to catch it again.

Instead of doing so, however, he fell heavily to the ground.

Isaac's motive for this was, that the mud, which chanced to be unusually plentiful just about that spot, would do much to disguise him.

When down, he made no attempt to rise, but began to sing some ditty or other, not one word of which, however, could be detected.

"He seems very drunk, Willis," said the officer with the lamp; "but then we must take care that it is not a sham. We ought to be careful."

"Shall I help him up?"

"Yes; try to get him on to his feet."

It was well the officer said "try," for the task was by no means an easy one to perform.

By dint of many efforts Isaac was at last made to stand tolerably erect.

"Lem me be, can't you?" he cried. "What are you doing? Watch—watch! Here's thieves! Let me go!"

So saying, he broke loose from the officer's hold, and staggered away for several paces.

So unsteady was his gait, however, that the two deluded officers kept expecting to see him fall headlong to the ground at every step.

But Isaac staggered on, his object being to get away from his dangerous quarters with the least possible delay.

Yet he took care to go in a devious direction.

"What shall we do with him, Willis?"

"I don't know. If we take him up, perhaps we shall find it only a plant to get us away from our posts. If it should be, we should be blamed, you know."

"So we should, Willis—so we should. There's not the ghost of a doubt about that."

As he spoke, he held the dark lantern in such a way that the beams fell upon Isaac's reeling form.

"We'll watch him to a safe distance, and trouble ourselves no more about him. I think that will be wisest."

"So do I. If you find him attempting to approach again, we will make him a prisoner at all hazards."

Isaac was quite near enough to hear these words; and of course he took care to receive them as a caution.

Breaking out with his song in louder tones, he continued to stagger away; nor did he venture to change his manner of going until quite sure he was at a safe distance from the prison.

"I may think myself lucky in having got out of that scrape so well," he muttered. "I was very near to being lost, I fancy."

But his thoughts were too busily occupied concerning the captain to allow him to think much of himself.

So far the result of his expedition had been very discouraging; nor was he able to see that he should achieve any good by lingering or by making an attempt in any other direction.

On the contrary, there was the fear that he should get noticed, and so be recognised, should necessity cause him to come a second time to the spot.

"I will go back," he said. "The officials are too vigilant for anyone to have the ghost of a chance. I will go back; the matter requires further consideration. Perhaps in a little while, if the officers find that no attempt is made to approach the prison, they will abate their vigilance."

This, however, was but a very poor and frail hope.

Yet, such as it was, Isaac, for default of a better, was obliged to content himself with it as he best could.

"I think I hardly needed to splash myself so much," he said, as he paused to remove some portion of the mud from his apparel.

In this he succeeded tolerably well; but still he was in a lamentable plight when he made his way back to the inn where he had left his horse.

It was not without much misgiving that he drew near.

He fully anticipated that the man into whose charge he had given it would make some remark or other.

The danger was one, however, which could not be avoided; and so, knowing this, Isaac boldly prepared to meet it in the best manner he was able.

He avoided the inn altogether.

Going direct to the gateway at the side, he made his way at a rapid pace towards the stables.

He was guided by a dim light which flickered from a half-open doorway.

When about a dozen paces from it, a man emerged.

"I want the gray horse," said Isaac, resolutely. "Be quick—there is not a moment to be lost!"

"Look here, my fine fellow," said the man: "I have my doubts of you!"

"You are welcome, so long as you make haste."

"Oh, I daresay! But I tell you what it is—I don't intend to give that horse up to you unless you show me very good reason why I should do so."

"I'll soon do that," said Isaac, quietly.

CHAPTER CXIX.

TOM BECKFORD SUGGESTS AN EXCELLENT PLAN OF OPERATIONS.

The manner in which he spoke deceived the man completely.

Not for a moment did he expect what was in store for him.

Isaac, without another word, and without losing a moment, clenched his fist, and struck out with it with all his might.

The blow alighted just between the man's eyes.

A very faint cry escaped his lips, and then down he sank as though he had been felled by a pole-axe.

After the accomplishment of this deed Isaac did not trouble himself so much as to cast a glance at his adversary, but striding over his prostrate form, entered the stable.

By the aid of the huge lantern which was hanging on an iron hook he perceived his horse in the stall nearest to him.

The bridle was slipped on and the saddle fastened in a moment; and the steed being thus in readiness, he proceeded to lead him forth.

It was only by a great deal of trouble that he got the creature past the body of the ostler, who showed signs of recovery from the hard blow he had received.

"Serve you right, you fool!" was Isaac's remark, as he saluted the fellow's ribs with a parting kick. "Let it be a caution to you to mind your own business on another occasion, and let other people's alone."

As he finished, he mounted and rode away.

He was glad when he was clear of the gateway and once more fairly on the way to the Greyhound.

The rain still fell heavily; and it was no doubt mainly owing to this circumstance that he was able to reach his destination without being interrupted.

As he fully expected, however, he found Tom Beckford awaiting his arrival.

The landlord stared at him without speaking.

"Well," cried Isaac, "cannot you believe that you see me back at last?"

"Where have you been?" the landlord managed to ejaculate.

"To Huntingdon, to be sure."

"I guessed it. And what mischief have you done?"

"Why do you ask that?"

"Because I am certain that you cannot have done any good."

"You shall judge," was the answer. "Where is Lord Harcliffe?"

"Indoors."

"Is he sitting up?"

"Yes."

"Then wait a moment, and I will tell you both."

It did not take Isaac long to put his steed all right for the remainder of the night; having done which he followed Tom Beckford into the house.

He found Lord Harcliffe pacing up and down the room, looking harassed and vexed.

"So you are back!" he said, sternly. "You had no right to take your departure in secret. What ought to be done ought first to be considered by us all."

"I was wrong," said Isaac. "Yet listen to me and I think you will find that not only have I satisfied my own mind, but my ride has been worth the trouble it gave me."

So saying, Isaac proceeded to give an exact relation of all the night's adventures.

"You see," he concluded, "that I have learnt one important thing, which is, that the captain's position is much more serious than we had thought it. I mean," he added, "that the authorities are more vigilant than we could have conceived."

"It seems so," said Lord Harcliffe.

"How we are to set him free," said Isaac, "I can't think. At present it seems neither more nor less than an utter impossibility."

"I am distracted!" said Tom Beckford, stroking his bald head with ludicrous dismay. "I can't tell what to do!"

"We must give it the most anxious consideration possible," answered Lord Harcliffe. "We have yet two or three days which we can give up to reflection entirely; and perhaps at the end of that time not only may a good idea have occurred to us, but the authorities may have begun to grow tired of such perpetual watching."

With this hope, poor as it was, they were obliged to remain content; and so they again separated without being in any better state of mind than on the former occasion.

But before Isaac was suffered to depart the second time, he was required to promise that he would not again attempt to carry out anything on his own responsibility.

All three felt the absolute necessity of rest: and they felt it was wise to take it while they had so good an opportunity as at present.

But their minds were too full of anxious thoughts for sleep to visit their eyelids very readily.

On the following day and on the one after that Tom Beckford made journeys to Huntingdon, but on neither occasion did he gain any addition to his former stock of knowledge.

They felt that matters were growing desperate.

On the next day they learned, however, that the captain had so far recovered from his wound as to be in fit condition to be brought before the magistrate for his preliminary examination on the ensuing morning.

No sooner was this intelligence received than all three of the captain's friends determined to be present during the trial.

The impolicy of all going, however, was so manifest that a consultation was held to decide who should stay away.

In this there seemed not the faintest likelihood of any agreement being come to, until the landlord proposed that they should draw lots, and that the result of the drawing should be unanswerable.

By no other means probably could the question have been settled amicably.

Fortune favoured the landlord.

When the lots were drawn, it was found that the much-wished-for permission had fallen to him.

Their feelings were too deeply interested for either the Black Highwayman or Isaac to conceal their disappointment, or for Tom Beckford to refrain from manifesting his joy.

"Depend upon it," he said, "things could not have been arranged better. I do not run a tithe of the danger that either of you would; and I shall be as well able to relate all that passes as anyone."

With what happened at the examination the reader has already been made aware.

The landlord was much distressed when he beheld the captain's terribly altered appearance.

But fearful that the prisoner would make some movement or utter a cry that would attract the suspicion of his janitors, Tom took good care to keep quite out of sight, though, while doing so, the intention was in his mind of showing himself at the last moment, no matter what the consequences were of doing so.

The words which the captain had chanced to speak at the close of his interrogation suggested an idea to him.

Then it was that, carried away by excitement, he had uttered the words which one might almost say brought Captain Hawk back to life at the moment when he was swooning.

But when he spoke he little dreamed that his action would produce such tremendous consequences.

In the uproar and confusion which followed, he suffered much from the crush; but he would have borne a thousand times as much with the utmost cheerfulness for the sake of the captain.

Before he quitted the precincts of the Court he took care to make himself acquainted with the day on which the trial was likely to take place.

With what anxiousness and impatience he was waited for by Isaac and the Black Highwayman no pen could describe.

"He is committed, of course," said Tom, not giving either time to ask a question. "You must have expected that."

"Yes—yes. Did you see him?"

"Yes."

"And how did he look?"

"Like one risen from the grave."

"Is he much altered?"

"You would scarcely know him. His sufferings must have been frightful."

Lord Harcliffe struck himself sharply on his breast as he said, half aloud, in reproachful accents:

"My fault—all my fault! But mine shall be the atonement."

"Wait a moment," said Tom, who had now recovered his breath somewhat—"just oblige me by waiting a moment. I have something more to say."

"What is it? Speak quickly."

"I have thought of the best way in which you can serve the captain."

"You have?" roared Isaac, springing to his feet.

"I have. But don't be violent."

"Be quick, then; I am full of impatience."

"Well, then, you must go to London and find some clever lawyer who will come down here and undertake the captain's defence."

"I had thought of that," said Isaac, much disappointed, "only I did not think the idea good enough to be mentioned."

"I had thought of it before," said Tom Beckford; "but it never struck me as it did this morning; and now I come to remember, I can call to mind plenty of cases where a clever London lawyer has got a prisoner off when everybody knowing the case would have declared he must be found guilty."

"The suggestion is worth consideration," said the Black Highwayman. "There seems little chance of our being able to get at him in his cell, and for seven days we have absolutely nothing to do unless we decide upon this."

"Yes," said the landlord, rubbing his hands in a satisfied manner, "that is just what I was thinking myself. The law is a very funny thing, especially if you can coax it with plenty of money."

"True," said Lord Harcliffe. "And what is more, I think I know just where to find the very man we want for the purpose."

"That is fortunate."

"I should not be afraid to say," continued Lord Harcliffe, "that if he was not able to pull a prisoner through an ugly business no one would."

"Then," said Tom Beckford, more and more delighted, "he is the very man we want."

"But do you think there's any chance he will be got off at his trial?" said Isaac, with a very dubious air.

"Well, if there isn't there can be no harm in making the provision. If we prepare for it we shall be in readiness for whatever may occur. If he is cast we shall only know the worst, and we shall have the satisfaction of knowing that we have not left that means untried."

"You are quite right," exclaimed Tom Beckford. "And if you will be only guided by me, you will not lose any time, but start off to London at once and see the lawyer you speak off."

"I will do so," said Lord Harcliffe, resolutely. "You are quite right. We have everything to gain and nothing to lose by adopting this course."

"Is that really your opinion?" asked Isaac.

"It is. Main force, you may depend, will be the very weakest weapon we can make use of, and we must not resort to it until every other means has failed."

"Then in that case the captain is certain to remain in the prison until after his trial?"

"Yes. The time is short; and what is more, I very much question whether the captain would be able to escape now even if he had the opportunity."

"If you had seen him when he stood before the magistrate to-day you would have thought so," said Tom. "He almost fainted away once."

"I am glad you have thought of it in time," said Lord Harcliffe, "for I have business of hardly less urgency in London, and I can do both at the same time."

"But suppose you are captured," said Isaac, who had been misgiving all along—"suppose you are made a prisoner—what is the captain to do then?"

"I am obliged to take my risk of that," was the calm, almost unconcerned reply.

"But you will be most careful," said the landlord—"you will think how terrible would be the consequences should you fall into the hands of the officers as well."

"Rely upon me," was the answer; and somehow the self-possessed manner in which it was given contributed wonderfully towards setting the landlord's mind at ease.

"But there will be great danger, will there not?" said Isaac, "in the mere attempt on your part to get towards London?"

"Yes, there will be peril certainly; but not more than I have encountered many a time, and escaped from without very serious consequences. I don't think you have need to be alarmed on that point."

"Shall you go to-night?" asked Tom.

"Yes, as soon as ever darkness sets in sufficiently to give me a chance of remaining unseen."

Then, turning towards Isaac, he said:

"Phantom is in perfect readiness, is he not?"

"Yes—never was better for a ride, I'll be bound."

"Enough."

"But," said Tom, "as we have a little time to spare let us continue our talk."

"Have you something to propose?" asked Lord Harcliffe.

"Well, I have."

"I shall be glad to listen to it, then."

The attentive manner in which the Black Highwayman prepared to listen to what he had to say was most flattering.

And not only flattering but embarrassing as well: and to hide his confusion the worthy landlord had to cough twice or thrice.

"I was considering," he said, "how far a disguise would be likely to serve you."

"A disguise?"

"Yes. Won't your foes be on the look-out for you, and expect to see you attired and mounted in your usual fashion?"

"Yes, I suppose they will."

"Very well, then; it seems to me the first thing you have to do is to consider how you can change all that from beginning to end."

"You are once more right," said Lord Harcliffe. "And not only so, I feel sure you would not have suggested thus much unless you had something more to say."

"You have guessed rightly."

"Speak, then, without reserve. As for myself, I am so perplexed with respect to the awkward conjunction of affairs at the present moment that I hardly know what to think."

"Well," said the landlord, "now we are agreed so far, I should begin by thinking how I could make a total change."

"Explain yourself."

"I mean in this way: Your foes will expect to see you on horseback."

"Yes—no doubt."

"Then I should go in a vehicle of some kind or other."

"Good! And what else?"

"No doubt your horse is quite as well known and would be almost as easily recognised as yourself?"

"Well, yes, I suppose so."

"Then, in that case," said the landlord, "I should reduce the chance of discovery by leaving him in the stable."

But at this proposal Lord Harcliffe shook his head in a very decided manner.

"No—no," he said. "Whatever you may think, I could not listen to such a thing as that. Phantom has carried me out of danger too many times for me to be able to think myself safe anywhere else but on his back."

"Stop a moment," said the landlord. "You can hear me out, and then make up your mind as you think proper."

"Yes, certainly. Pray go on."

"I was going to say neither more nor less than this; and I may as well put my speech into a few words as not."

"Nay—nay. Let us know all your reasons."

"Well, then, you will admit that the gray horse which Isaac has is one of a quality far superior to any you often see?"

"Quite true," assented Lord Harcliffe. "It is a noble creature, and no doubt is capable of making wonderful speed."

"That's just it," said the landlord, slapping his thigh; "now you have it exactly! Now, you must know that I have in one of the sheds at the back of the house here an old chaise cart. It has not done any work for many a day, but yet I think it is good for a great many journeys yet. I should recommend you to put Isaac's gray horse into the shafts, that you should both of you make what changes you can in your apparel, so as to render the fear of recognition less; then, when you have done that, it would not surprise me in the least if you were to start off and ride through all the troops of officers between here and London not only undetected but unsuspected. Think it over for five minutes, and then at the end of that time I will ask you your opinion of the plan."

So saying, Tom Beckford leaned back in the great arm-chair, in which he sat with a very complacent air.

CHAPTER CXX.

IN WHICH LORD HARCLIFFE AND ISAAC START FOR LONDON IN THE CHAISE CART.

A DEAD silence was preserved for rather more than the time mentioned by the landlord.

Lord Harcliffe and Isaac were both busy in weighing over the suggestion which had just been made.

As the reader may readily suppose, the more they reflected upon it, the more did it reconcile itself to their minds.

Lord Harcliffe began to perceive clearly that unless he adopted some scheme or other of this kind, he should be most likely frustrated in all his efforts to break through the circle of officers.

"Have you any particular facilities for disguising us, landlord?" he asked.

Tom's eyes twinkled.

"Let me know what you think of my plan?"

"Why, I don't see how there could possibly be two opinions about it. The idea is excellent; and I seem to feel a conviction that it will be successful."

"I am glad to hear it, and very proud at the same time."

"Nay—nay, our best thanks are due to you for taking so much genuine and practical interest in our affairs."

"Pooh—pooh! not a word of that! I want Isaac's opinion, and then I am ready to answer any questions you may feel inclined to ask me."

"My opinion is, that no better plan could have been thought of if we had puzzled our brains for a week."

"That is comfortable. And now you want to know what are the means I possess of disguising you?"

"Yes—that is it."

"I am sorry to say that I am by no means so well provided as I could wish; still, I will do the best I can, and that will show that I am willing at any rate."

"And it is quite time we began to see about them," said Isaac—"that is, if we are to get far on our journey to-night."

"I would not lose a moment of time for the world!" said Lord Harcliffe, springing to his feet. "It is almost dark," he added, "and our preparations will, of course, take some time."

"Not so long as you may think," said the landlord. "Just wait where you are for a minute or two, and I will bring into this room all the things that I think you will require."

Lord Harcliffe expressed his thanks, but Tom Beckford would not stop to listen to them.

"It's an excellent plan," he said to Isaac, as soon as the door was closed. "Unless we had thought of something of the kind, we should never have reached our destination."

Isaac assented.

But it was easy to see that he did not enter into the scheme with any particular amount of ardour.

As to reaching their destination, he felt little doubt about their ability to accomplish that much in safety.

But what he failed to see was the ultimate good that was likely to arise from making the visit at all.

He thought, however, that, as he was placed, it would be better for him not to give audible expression to his thoughts, especially as he had nothing better to propose in the captain's behalf.

His own deliberate conviction was, however, that no amount of cleverness on any lawyer's part, no matter how clever he might be, would induce the authorities to let the captain off after they had had so much trouble to lay their hands upon him.

How far Isaac was right in his ideas will very speedily be seen.

The landlord was only absent a very short time.

When he made his appearance he was laden with various articles of wearing apparel, from which he speedily relieved himself by casting the whole on to the floor.

The first object he produced from the mass was a very large light-brown smock-frock, a kind of garment then more frequently worn than at the present day, except in some remote corner of the country where old-fashioned notions are preserved.

"Now," he said, "there's no article in the world that can come up to this in making a complete transmogrification in anybody."

The Black Highwayman looked at the garment with a degree of repugnance which he could not repress.

And certainly the garment in question was not very well calculated to win upon him.

It showed obvious marks of having received hard usage, and the odour which exhaled from it was just the very reverse of agreeable.

"You don't want me to put that on, do you?" he asked, retreating a step.

"Yes, I do. And I must insist upon it if you want to escape undetected. It smells just a wee bit musty like, but the fresh air will soon take that off."

In spite of a slight annoyance which he felt at having such a garment presented to him at all, the Black Highwayman could not help smiling and being amused at the very cool manner in which Tom Beckford treated the whole affair.

"Think yourself lucky," he said, "at having such a capital thing found you. On with it, and in a little while you'll be as used to the feel as though you had never worn anything else."

Lord Harcliffe did not see very well how he could refuse, nor was he blind to the fact that such a garment would serve to disguise him far more effectually than any other."

No one certainly would dream of looking for the aristocratic Black Highwayman attired in such a garb.

Summoning up his courage for the sacrifice to the best of his power, he suffered the landlord to slip the smock-frock over his shoulders.

"Now that's over the worst is done," said Tom, who rather enjoyed this part of the affair. "To complete your disguise all you have to do is to wrap yourself up well in this old brown coat, and muffle it well round your throat, and you'll be right."

After the smock-frock, the brown coat, though old and greasy, was tolerable.

"Oh, I forgot the hat," cried the landlord, diving among the heap of old clothes. "You must have a hat, and you will say that this is the very identical ticket—a regular long-sleeved one this is."

The hat which he produced was as remarkable a piece of head-gear as ever Lord Harcliffe had beheld—Petruchio's copatain hat was nothing to it.

Still, as a means of disguise, there could be no doubt about its efficiency, for when on it shaded Lord Harcliffe's features completely.

Isaac was next treated in a somewhat similar fashion.

But as the garments now provided for his use were just a trifle better than those which he wore usually, he was more delighted than otherwise with the alteration.

"Now," said the landlord, stepping back to regard his handiwork with an admiring gaze—"now you both look like what I intended you should, namely—a couple of countrymen on your way to market. If you could only speak in a good broad dialect, you would have little to fear if you had to answer the questions of a troop of officers at every mile on your way."

"I hope we shall escape such an ordeal as that."

"So do I. But it isn't likely you will. Come on. Time is passing more quickly than you are aware of."

The landlord was right.

Time indeed had slipped by while the disguises were being tried on; so that now it could be said that night had fairly begun.

"Never mind," continued Tom; "very likely it's all for the best. There's not so much risk of your being seen leaving the premises; and I can venture to say that the horse, when he once starts, will bowl along at a rate that will quickly make up for lost time."

So saying, he led the way out of the apartment where the foregoing scene had taken place, and conducted the strangely-attired pair to the stables.

Lord Harcliffe came on very clumsily, and once or twice narrowly escaped a fall.

The smock-frock was a garment to which he was altogether unaccustomed; and as it reached far below the knees, it interfered with his locomotion a great deal.

"You'll soon get used to it," said the landlord. "Come along. Shut the door, Isaac."

On reaching the stables, Lord Harcliffe set to work to harness the gray horse, because it was of the utmost importance every moment should be saved.

While he was thus occupied, the landlord and Isaac proceeded to drag the old chaise cart from under the shed, where it had reposed in rest for many a long day.

The spokes in the wheels rattled ominously as soon as there was any motion; but the landlord affected to make light of the circumstance.

[LORD HARCLIFFE DISCOVERS PHAROAH.]

"I will warrant it for lasting the journey."

The scene in the inn-yard was a curious one, and certainly such as any police officer would have taken the greatest amount of interest in watching.

By the light of the one lantern which illuminated their proceedings, the three figures looked for all the world like phantoms gliding hither and thither.

The night was a dark one; and they had a little trouble in getting the gray horse into the shafts.

It was easy to see the fine-looking creature was full of fire, and most impatient to be off.

It took all the landlord's strength to keep his head anything like steady while Lord Harcliffe and Isaac got into the cart.

"Right!" said the former, the moment he had the reins.

"I had better lead him," said the landlord. "It is an awkward place."

"As you like."

The horse was glad enough to start; and though he was held in as much as possible, he went at a pace that the ponderous landlord would not have been able to keep up very long.

But the distance to the gateway through which they had to pass was short, though it required one very familiar with the premises to avoid bumping up against some object or other.

"Away you go!" said Tom, as he gladly let go the rein. "Mind what you are about. If——"

The Black Highwayman and Isaac had no chance of hearing the end of his warning.

No sooner did the horse feel his head at liberty than away he went in magnificent style.

"It's confoundedly dark!" said Lord Harcliffe. "Are you familiar with the ground hereabouts?"

The chaise shook awfully, and no doubt the slightest obstacle in the world would have overturned it.

Luckily, the high-road was smooth and clear of all impediments, so they went on with perfect safety.

It was not long before they were convinced that the police officers were fast falling into the rear again.

Lord Harcliffe's satisfaction at this, however, was not so great as it would have been had he not felt so certain that he must ere long encounter another patrol.

He was full of surprise that he had not done so already.

Still, whenever the encounter did take place, he could not hope to get away without the interchange of some few sentences, and that, he feared, would take long enough to enable the hoofs of his pursuers' horses to become audible.

Then, of course, there would be almost an end of their further safe progress.

From this it will be seen that, although he had distanced his pursuers so rapidly, yet his mind was occupied by anxious thoughts.

Nevertheless, he could see clearly that his best chance consisted in keeping the gray horse going at the top of his speed until, at all events, he encountered the next party of men on guard.

About this there did not seem to be much trouble.

The horse apparently was at present quite insensible to fatigue.

What he had yet done he looked upon as nothing.

Ten minutes of anxiety elapsed.

"Can you hear them now?" Lord Harcliffe asked.

"Not a bit."

"Are you sure?"

"Yes. But if you would only pull up for a moment it would do the horse no harm, and we should be able to make quite certain."

By degrees the reins were drawn in, and the panting, steaming steed once more arrested in his headlong flight.

Yet even now, despite his efforts, he was full of mettle, and would hardly be restrained.

Both, then, listened with all possible intentness.

"I can hear nothing," said Isaac at length.

"Nor I; and yet to think that they have abandoned the chase already seems hardly reasonable."

"It seems like it, at any rate," said Isaac, after listening for some seconds longer.

"It does."

"At any rate, we'll sail on again, and trust to our good luck."

Lord Harcliffe said nothing, but set the gray horse once more in motion.

But though the rate at which he now went was a fast one, yet it was slow when compared with the pace at which they had latterly been going.

Lord Harcliffe, however, was anxious that there should be nothing unusual visible to excite the suspicions of the next patrol he might encounter.

From what he knew of the arrangements of the police officers, he expected every moment that an interruption would take place.

The high, gusty wind had now almost subsided, and in consequence the rain which it had held in suspension began to fall in a smart shower.

This, although disagreeable to them, could not be called unwelcome, for it increased the likelihood of their having the high-road pretty nearly to themselves.

The obscurity became, if possible, still denser than before.

Suddenly a voice cried, in loud and distinct tones:

"Halt!"

Lord Harcliffe and Isaac both looked around them, but they could see no one.

"Halt!" said the voice again. "Pull up, will you, or it will be the worse for you!"

At this instant a light appeared.

It evidently came from a dark lantern, the beams of which were fully directed towards them.

But this light, so far from making them any the better aware who these persons were, only made them still more invisible, for the light dazzled the eyes of those on whom it fell.

The chaise cart was stopped, and then the light rapidly approached.

The tread of horses' hoofs was distinctly audible, and in another moment our two friends were able to make out the dim and dusky forms of two or three mounted men—they could not be certain which.

"Who are you?" said the one who carried the lantern, as he placed himself close to the side of the cart, "and where are you going?"

"To Lunnon," said the Black Highwayman, with the same assumed voice. "We ha' been stopped afore, and they told us to say so."

"Oh, indeed! But what was that? Hark, all of you, a moment! I thought I caught the clatter of horses' feet!"

CHAPTER CXXII.

THE POLICE OFFICERS COME VERY NEAR TO ACHIEVING THEIR PURPOSE.

Of course there was an instantaneous dead silence.

Then there came to the ears of every one a sound, which, though faint and coming from afar off, was nevertheless unmistakable in its character.

"There's no doubt about it, sir," said another of the police officers, respectfully. "It's the clatter of horses' hoofs sure enough."

"What can it mean? Rely upon it, something unusual has taken place."

"Not the least doubt of it, sir. The game must have been started at last."

"We shall know more about it shortly, that is very certain. Hark how plain the sound is now."

It was indeed plain, so much so as to lead the listeners to suppose the horses were much nearer than they really were.

But then the sound died away again, as such sounds will according to the variations in height and direction that the roadway takes.

So deep was the interest taken in this circumstance that the officers seemed to forget all about the cart and its occupants.

How anxious the latter were, and how great the effort was to retain their self-command we need not say.

Both, however, succeeded in preserving the semblance of perfect indifference.

Yet every moment that so rapidly flew by was fraught to them with indescribable danger.

Suddenly the police officer who had the other two under his command seemed all at once to awake to the knowledge that the cart was there.

"Didn't you say you had been stopped by another party of officers?"

"Yes; a good way back."

"And what did they say?"

"Asked where we came from and where we were going."

"And they were satisfied and let you come on?"

"Oh yes. They said they were on the look-out for highwaymen, so that they could not want us."

"And have you seen no one since?"

"Divil a soul!"

"H'm—it's odd! Are you quite sure you have seen no one? Remember this is a serious matter, and any holding back of information on your part will be attended with serious consequences to you—take my word for it."

Lord Harcliffe, struck by a sudden thought which seemed to offer him at least a chance of getting off, affected to hesitate.

"Come, now," said the officer, who prided himself upon being a more cunning fellow than any of his companions, and who thus continually laid himself open to being deceived. "Confess at once."

"I dare not."

"Then you have seen some one?"

"I dare not tell."

"Why not?"

"I dare not."

"But you must!"

"I dare not."

"Then if you don't I will take you into custody at once, and have you severely punished."

"Well, then," said Lord Harcliffe, pretending to make a desperate effort to summon up his courage, "will you hold me free from the consequences?"

"Yes."

"Then I'll tell you."

"Be quick."

"We saw some one who threatened with most awful oaths to be the death of us if we dared so much as breathe a word that we had met with him."

"Our man for a thousand pounds!" said the officer. "Describe him."

"It was too dark for us to see him very well, your honour; but he seemed to have a kind of cloak on that looked as black as his horse."

"There's no doubt about it now," said the officer, immensely delighted. "All is explained. Hark! they are in full pursuit of him now. Get ready, my lads. We shall have him upon us directly, and as soon as ever he shows himself don't stop, but remember the word—pop! down he goes!"

The officers examined their pistols, whereat Lord Harcliffe pretended to be dreadfully alarmed.

"Do you want us to stay?" he said, with chattering teeth.

"Not that I know of."

"Because if you are going to use them pistols I should like to be off. Besides, if it is the highwayman, as soon as he comes he will know we have told what he forbid, and our lives won't be worth twopence."

"Oh, don't be alarmed about his threats: he will have no chance of carrying them out. It will be all over with him in a very few moments now."

"Then we can go?"

"Yes; be off."

"Thank you, your honour."

Although hardly able to believe that he had passed through this difficulty, Lord Harcliffe set his horse in motion.

But notwithstanding his strong desire to get away as quickly as possible, he took a lesson from his former experience, and was careful that there should not be anything to excite suspicion a second time.

Isaac, who had preserved a profound silence throughout, did not venture to speak yet.

Neither knew it, but the chief officer from whom they had just parted was slightly delighted in getting rid of them; and by sending them off in the way he had, he thought he had done a very clever thing indeed.

"Now, my lads," he said, in a suppressed voice, "we have it all our own way. Think yourselves lucky in getting rid of those louts in the cart. If they had stopped to be present at the capture they would, ten to one, have insisted upon receiving an equal share of the reward."

To lose any portion of the amount offered was a dreadful idea to the minds of all police officers, and more especially when any sum had to be bestowed on one who did not belong to their own ranks.

It was, therefore, with the utmost satisfaction that all three listened to the receding wheels.

By degrees Lord Harcliffe accelerated his horse's speed, and it was not very long before they were going at full swing.

In the meanwhile the officers just left may be said to have fixed their attention exclusively upon the horsemen approaching.

The darkness was very baffling and confusing.

"It's very odd we see nothing of him," said the chief officer, dubiously. "There don't seem to be anyone galloping in front. I could almost swear they were all riding together."

This alarming idea gained strength every moment, until at last it deepened into a certainty.

"Confusion! Can they have missed him? Or"—and here the chief officer poured out a string of fearful imprecations—"have those fellows in the cart misinformed us? Death and the devil! we ought to have detained them!"

He glanced down the road; but by this time the chaise cart had got completely out of hearing.

It was vain to think any more of that neglected opportunity.

He was obliged to t[illegible] in the opposite direction for comfort.

But the only consolation he met with was the by no means cheerful fact that in a couple of minutes at the most the horsemen would reach the spot where he was waiting, and when of course an explanation could be obtained.

The time quickly elapsed, and then the new-comers, attracted no doubt by the lantern which was still burning, pulled up their smoking cattle.

It needed not a second glance to show how desperately hard they had been riding.

The poor beasts seemed ready to sink to the earth.

The riders were covered with flakes of mud; and for a second not one could speak.

At last the commander bawled out:

"Have you seen——"

"No—no," said the other, thinking, of course, he must refer to the horseman described by Lord Harcliffe. "He has not come so far as this. You must have missed him somewhere."

The officer had to give a great gulp to swallow down the rage which came swelling to his lips.

"Will you hear me out?" he roared.

"Yes. But I know——"

"Shut up! Tell me! Have you seen two men in a cart?"

"Oh yes."

"Oh yes! D—n you for a one-eyed son of a cook! I know what's coming now! Ten thousand devils! Where are they now?"

And the officer, as he asked this question, gave force to his emphasis by flinging his hat down into the mud.

"Why, gone, to be sure!"

"Gone!" shrieked the other—"gone! Just what I expected!"

"Have you gone mad?"

"Did you see the men in the cart?"

"Yes; don't I say so?"

"Did you stop them?"

"Of course we did."

"And yet let them go again?"

"What earthly excuse had we to keep them?"

The officer, in his desperate despair, pulled off his wig and flung that down into the dirt after his hat.

"They told us," continued the second officer, whose ire was fast rising too—"they told us they had passed you."

"Yes, curse them!"

"They also said they had seen a horseman on the road, who, from the description given, must be our man."

"Oh, ten thousand curses!"

"And when we heard you galloping this way we made sure you were in pursuit of him, and prepared to stop him from going on any further. Now, what explanation have you to give? and why ought we to have stopped the cart?"

It was quite in vain to ask questions of the officer in command of the first patrolling party.

All he did was to pour out curses with a volubility and variety of utterance which proved he could have few compeers in that accomplishment.

At last, however, he tamed down sufficiently to speak with a little reason.

"Was ever anyone so stupidly — so egregiously deceived? Fools—dolts—idiots that you are!"

"And how much the better are you?"

"Not much."

Following upon this admission came another volley of imprecations.

"And now what about the cart and the men in it?" said the second officer, as soon as he found the other stopped for breath.

"Why, I have my suspicions about them. I have every reason to suppose——"

"What?"

"That one is the Black Highwayman in disguise."

This took the second officer aback for a moment.

He was dumbfoundered.

But recovering himself, he said:

"No—no—that can't be—the supposition is too absurd! I had them here talking to for several minutes. I feel quite sure they are what they seem."

"Oh, are you? And pray did you notice what kind of horse they had with them?"

"Yes; a gray one."

"And what else did you notice?"

"Nothing particular."

"Well, then, if you had half an eye you ought to have seen that it was not the animal you would expect to find in a cart of that description."

"Well, and how was it you didn't find it out and stop them instead of letting them pass by?"

"We did not know till too late," was the humiliating rejoinder.

"Then don't find fault with us," said the second officer, who at once perceived he had the advantage. "Why couldn't you up and say all about it in a few words? We might have been after them by this time."

"It's none too late now."

"Yes, but it is though. If there is the least ground for your suspicion, rely upon it they are far enough off by this time. They have had the best of chances to give us the go-by."

By common consent all the officers paused to listen.

But though they strained their hearing to the utmost, not the faintest sound resembling the rumbling of the chaise cart could they hear.

While listening, the officer who had command of the second party was also reflecting.

The result of his deliberations was to come to the conclusion that the other officer's suspicion was perfectly baseless.

"What grounds had you for supposing that the Black Highwayman was in the cart?"

The other hesitated.

"Was there anything besides what existed in your own fancy?"

"And what if there was not?"

"I don't believe there is any ground for it."

"Why?"

"Why? Because when I told them to stop they pulled up in the most unconcerned manner; and before they went they were quite willing to stay if we wished it. No—no. Rely on it, had the Black Highwayman been in the cart, he could not have sat there so calmly and collectedly as he did."

"Pooh—pooh! You don't know the man. He has nerves of steel."

"I don't care what his nerves are made of. There never was a man in his peril who could sit and talk like he did! It's monstrous—impossible!"

The decided way in which these words were uttered shook the other's doubts.

But he carried it off well.

"You can do as you like about it," he said. "I have communicated my suspicions to you, and you can act upon them or not, just as you think proper. Of course, you will have to abide by the consequences."

"Why don't you pursue him yourself if you think it worth while?"

"Can't you see that our horses are blown? We could not do the least bit of good. It is your place to continue the pursuit."

"Then I don't think there are sufficient grounds for it."

"Oh, very well! Of course, should any inquiries be made, I hope you will find your answer sufficient."

The officer hearing this, felt rather uncomfortable.

He knew that a threat lurked under the words.

All knew the necessity there was for over caution.

"I'll tell you what I'll do," he said. "Gardener here has the swiftest horse of the lot of us."

"Well?"

"He shall ride on as far as the next troop, and inquire whether they have seen the cart."

"Very good. I don't want to interfere with your actions, or take any responsibility on to my shoulders. I have made the pursuit thus far, and I turn it over to you. I'm going back to my post at a quiet rate."

After a great deal more fruitless discussion, in which much precious time was lost, Gardener was started off.

His instructions were to catch up with the chaise cart if he could just about the time when it would reach the next troop. Then, by giving the alarm, he would be able to procure the arrest of the vehicle.

"But mind, Gardener," said his superior officer, "don't attempt anything against these two men by yourself."

"Oh, trust me!"

"Remember, we have nothing better than suspicion to go upon. Still, if there was to turn out any truth and foundation in it, you would find yourself awkwardly situated with two such fellows—so mind that."

"You can trust me," said Gardener. "Shall I start now?"

"Yes; I see no reason why you should stay a moment longer."

"Off and away, then!"

"Come back as soon as you can!" bawled his leader.

He was by no means sure he had been heard, for hardly had the words left Gardener's mouth before he was flying along the road at the topmost speed that his horse was capable of.

Judging by appearances, there seemed something more than a chance that he would be able to overtake the chaise cart before it reached the point which had been mentioned.

Of course, this entirely depended upon the chaise cart keeping on the high-road.

Strangely enough, the contingency that it might turn off in some other direction never occurred to one of the police officers.

CHAPTER CXXIII.

IN WHICH ISAAC SETS A TRAP FOR THE POLICE OFFICERS.

No doubt the reader will be well enough content to leave the police officers to carry out their plans in their own bungling fashion while we devote ourselves exclusively to the exciting incidents which befel the Black Highwayman and Isaac on their ride to London.

As we have said, their departure had been marked by caution; but as soon as he had felt himself to be a safe distance away, Lord Harcliffe pushed the gray horse along at the fastest speed he was capable of making.

Isaac sat for some time in silence.

But if his tongue was still his thoughts were busy.

"I'll tell you what," he broke out, suddenly, "it won't do to go on like this."

"Why not?"

"Why, we shall have the officers after us like bucks; and if we should be so lucky as to keep well in front of them all the way we should enter London with such a hue and cry at our heels that it would be quite impossible for us to do anything."

"That has been my fear all along," said Lord Harcliffe, "and the worst of it is I cannot see any means of rectifying it."

"We must dodge 'em," said Isaac—"that's our only plan."

"But how?"

"Let us look around a bit. We shall see something to give us an idea no doubt. What is that yonder?"

"Where?"

"That faint light."

"It looks like the coming dawn."

"And that's what it is. We shall have morning upon us soon; and I mean to say we have made a capital night of it."

"We should have been further but for those confounded interruptions."

"Perhaps we should; but not much. Now I'll tell you what is my idea."

"I am listening."

"Of course, we can't get to London before sunrise. That's impossible, isn't it?"

"Quite."

"Then, as you must be well aware, it won't do for us to go driving along in the daytime. Our disguises might pass muster at night, but in the daytime it would be too risky."

"Do you think so?"

"I am sure of it. Besides, the horse must have a rest."

"Then what do you propose?"

"To stop somewhere all the time it is light."

"I thought as much. And where?"

"That we must see. What I want to do at the same time is to bother the officers as much as possible."

"I should like to know how to do it."

"I have it."

"You have, already?"

"Yes; listen. In a short time we shall come to a turning of some kind; let us take it, and make our way across the country until we reach some out-of-the-way place which holds out the promise of concealing us without fear of interruption."

"But is such a place to be found?"

"Plenty of them, never fear for that."

"Then that shall be the course of action; for, of course

you intend now to make your way into London at another point?"

"We can do as we like about that. You have made up your mind to turn off the high-road?"

"Yes, certainly."

"Pull up a bit, then. While flying along at this rate it would be hard to say when we came to a turning or did not."

"Right."

Lord Harcliffe tightened the reins.

"I suppose it does not matter, Isaac, whether we turn off to the right or the left?"

"Not in the least that I know of."

"Very good; then I will keep a look-out on my side as well, for I begin to think the sooner our course is changed the better."

Isaac was quite of this opinion, and gave the whole of his attention to the attempt to discover whether there was an opening between the trees or not.

But, as ill luck would have it, on neither side could any signs of a turning be seen.

No doubt their impatience made the distance seem very much longer than it really was; still, a long time elapsed before Isaac cried out:

"Halt!"

Lord Harcliffe pulled up as quickly as possible; but he was not able to avoid overshooting the mark a little.

"Turn back," said Isaac, "and you will see just the place we want; and we have found it just in time, too. Only look how light it's getting!"

Morning was coming on with great rapidity.

Lord Harcliffe drove round the corner of the lane, and was about to put the horse to good speed again, when Isaac said:

"Wait a moment; it can't make much difference to us."

"But why stop?"

"I should just like to know whether our friends are on the road behind us; and if so, how far they are off."

"It will be well to manage that if possible."

"Stop the cart, then, and I'll soon do it."

Isaac leaped nimbly to the ground, and, running to the centre of the roadway, flung himself at full length, with his ear resting on the earth.

He remained thus for several seconds.

Rising at last, he made his way towards Lord Harcliffe with a look of importance on his face.

"There's somebody coming," he said.

"Only one?"

"That's all."

"Your ears must have deceived you."

"Not a little bit. One horseman, and one only, is on the road, and he is coming along at a desperate gallop."

"Who can it be?"

"That is the question I asked myself while I lay on the road."

"What is your opinion?"

"Why, very close to the truth, I think. You may depend this one horseman is the best-mounted officer of the lot, and he has been sent on in advance to pass us if possible, and give warning further ahead that we are coming."

"What on earth could have put such an idea into your head?"

"It did not want any putting—it came there in a moment, like a flash of lightning. I just asked myself what the officers would be likely to do in such a case."

"And that was your thought?"

"It was."

"It may be so; and in that case the sooner we are out of sight the better."

"No, I don't think so."

"Why?"

"Because we ought to try to intercept the fellow if we can; and I believe we could do it just as easy as nothing at all."

"You have a plan ready, I suppose?" said Lord Harcliffe, with a smile.

"Yes."

"I thought it."

"Shall I tell you what it is?"

"There can be no harm in doing so."

"Harm? I should think not indeed My plan would be very simple. Let us both get out of the cart, and leave it just at the corner of the lane here, letting the horse nibble a little at the grass growing on the ditch bank."

"And what then?"

"We will secrete ourselves in the bushes close handy, and you will find that cart a most excellent man-trap."

"Go on—I like your plan."

"It will be just getting light enough to see dimly, and the officer won't fail to observe the cart at once. That will at once excite his attention and curiosity, and he will come closer. All we shall have to do will be to wait for the most favourable opportunity to be down upon him."

"Make him a prisoner?"

"Yes."

"What shall we do with him then?"

"Why, really, I don't know yet. It will be time enough to decide about that when we've got him."

"Right."

"Come, then, it is quite time we began our preparations. He will be here very soon now. What a rate he is coming at, to be sure!"

The preparations were quickly made in exact accordance with Isaac's suggestions.

It happened that some unusually high and dense bushes grew just at the corner of the lane, behind which they had no difficulty in concealing themselves.

The horse, just as Isaac had said, began to nibble at the grass.

By the time all was in readiness, the quick clatter of the horse's hoofs could be heard very plainly.

"Now, how nicely we shall do their nice little plan!" said Isaac, rubbing his hands together, and feeling highly pleased with himself for the cleverness he had displayed. "Here he comes, like a blessed babby running to have his goose cooked!"

"Hush—hush! No more! Let us watch in silence."

"All right! But mind, when the time comes, what we've got to do is to nab him."

Lord Harcliffe nodded his head to intimate that he fully comprehended.

The next minutes that ensued were anxious ones.

Every second it seemed as though the single horseman would come into view.

As for Lord Harcliffe himself, he was by no means certain that it was a police officer who was approaching.

His doubts were speedily put an end to.

The horseman came in sight, and an officer he proved to be, sure enough.

"Didn't I say so?" muttered Isaac, with a chuckle.

Lord Harcliffe placed his hand over his mouth.

Of course, to ensure the successful accomplishment of the scheme perfect silence was essential.

The high-road was perfectly straight for some distance, so that they were able to observe the coming officer very narrowly.

It was not long before they were convinced that he saw the cart, for he began to use vigorous efforts to arrest the flight of his horse.

When about twenty yards distance he came to a dead stop, and rubbed his eyes vigorously, in order to make sure that he saw aright.

"Why, split me!" he ejaculated, "there's the d—d identical cart drawn up under the hedge! What can that mean, I wonder?"

He looked for a moment very steadily at the horse and vehicle, and then glanced in the direction from which he had just come.

Isaac was in an agony of fear that he was about to ride back to his companions, in which case his scheme would have failed most ignominiously.

Some such thought did cross the officer's mind; but his curiosity got the master of it.

"Where on earth, now, can those two fellows have gone?" he said. "And what do they mean by abandoning the cart in that fashion? I must find out something more about it."

With these words, he directed his horse towards the chaise cart.

But he came at a cautious walk, and, by his manner, seemed as though he felt some kind of inward, indistinct misgiving.

The silence, too, was most oppressive; and the faint

gray light of early morn gave a ghastly look to all the objects on which it fell.

The officer came nearer still.

All was so calm as to do away to a great extent with all sensations of fear, and yet he shrank from a too close approach.

Summoning up his courage, however, by a palpable effort, he rode right to the side of the cart.

"Why, there's no one here!" he said.

A slight rustling close by attracted his attention.

Turning like lightning, he saw Lord Harcliffe with his arm extended over the hedgerow, presenting a pistol within a few inches of his head.

At the selfsame moment he heard the stern, coldly-uttered words:

"If you move a muscle you are a dead man!"

Intense surprise deprived the officer of the power of immediate motion.

Recovering himself, his first thought was, in spite of the threat, to fly.

But just as he was about to carry his resolve into execution a hand was laid heavily upon the bridle, and a gruff voice said:

"No, you don't—not a bit of it! Keep still, now, and don't go for to be violent!"

The officer found that he was caught; and when Lord Harcliffe hastily forced his way through the bushes he gave himself up for lost.

Isaac, slipping the rein over his arm, took hold of the officer's leg with both his hands.

"Now," he said, "are you a sensible man, or are you not? If you'll just answer that question I shall know what to do."

The officer stared at him, as well he might, upon hearing such a question asked at such a time.

But he did not speak.

"Look here, now," Isaac continued, with the same show of friendliness, "you must see that we are two and you are one, and consequently in any struggle you must come off second best. Do just save us all the trouble you can, and yield yourself quietly into our hands; it will be best for all parties. We intend to have our own way at any cost, only we prefer the quiet way, you understand."

"I give in," said the officer, with a sigh, after having given one helpless, hopeless glance around him—"I give in."

"And a good thing it is for you that you have sense enough to say so, for you have saved yourself not a little ill-usage, I can tell you."

"Dismount!" said Lord Harcliffe, who was beginning to grow impatient.

"Obey orders promptly!" observed Isaac. "That's the way! Capital!"

The officer slipped down out of the saddle.

When his feet touched the earth, Isaac fancied he was half inclined to run away, and took measures to prevent it.

Although nothing had been decided as to what should be done with the officer after he was captured, Isaac seemed to have made up his mind on the point.

He produced two pieces of rope from his pocket, with which he bound the officer's elbows and ankles very securely.

Thus fastened, the poor fellow was perfectly helpless.

"Now," said Isaac to Lord Harcliffe, "if you'll just lend a hand we'll heave him into the cart, and when we have got him with us we shall know he is safe."

Lord Harcliffe said nothing, but showed his approval by doing what Isaac had said.

The officer was not a very bulky fellow, yet for all that it was by no means an easy task to lift him into the cart.

"And what shall we do with the horse?" asked Lord Harcliffe.

"We will take that with us," answered Isaac, promptly, "and then we shall be sure to have that safe, too."

"Let us be off, then, without further delay. In another minute or two it will be broad daylight."

"That it will. Suppose you drive the cart, and I will ride behind on the horse, so as to make sure all is right."

Lord Harcliffe assented, and in another minute was driving along at a frightful pace, considering the deep ruts in the lane.

Isaac quickly mounted the officer's horse, and rode two or three yards in the rear.

For some time not a syllable was spoken.

Both were on the look-out for the place in which they were to secrete themselves while daylight lasted.

What the officer thought of the whole affair is hard to say.

He remained quite silent, and uttered no complaint, although the jolting of the chaise cart over the ill-kept road almost shook all the breath out of his body.

Something like half an hour elapsed before they caught sight of a shelter of any kind.

Isaac was the first to point out some ruins in the distance, which looked like the remains of some old barn or other farm building.

"That's the very place for us," he said, "if we can only manage to reach it unseen, because when once there no one will be able to pounce upon us at unawares."

"Right!" said Lord Harcliffe. "But how are we to get to the place?"

"Drive on till you come to the next gate," said Isaac, "and we'll make a short cut across the fields."

CHAPTER CXXIV.

ISAAC IS DEAF TO THE SUPPLICATIONS OF HIS PRISONER.

This seemed the only means by which the building in question could be reached; and Lord Harcliffe therefore did not hesitate to stop at the next gate, which happened to be only a few yards further on.

Isaac slipped nimbly from his horse.

The first thing he saw was that the gate was secured with a padlock.

But this obstacle did not daunt him a moment.

Putting forth his strength, he lifted the gate completely off its hinges, and held it so as to allow Lord Harcliffe to ride through.

"That's what I call fortunate, now," said Isaac, as he restored the gate to its former position.

"What?" asked the Black Highwayman, wondering for the moment to what it was that he alluded.

"Why, this gate being locked, to be sure. Anyone coming by now and seeing it fastened would never think we had come this way."

The field into which the gate led was a fine bit of old turf, which was so firm and closely grazed that the track made by the cart-wheels was hardly visible.

The old ruined building was reached without any more difficulty, though when they arrived both Isaac and Lord Harcliffe were surprised at what they saw.

At some former time a farm-house, with all its out-buildings, must have occupied this position, for the traces of the dismantled walls were everywhere visible.

The only part, however, which boasted anything in the shape of a roof was the barn-like building which had first attracted Isaac's notice.

All around was perfectly still, nor were they able to see a human creature, although the spot was elevated and commanded views in every direction.

One leaf of the large double doors leading into the barn still hung frailly upon one hinge.

As the opening was wide enough, Lord Harcliffe drove right inside, so that the whole party was hidden in a wonderfully brief space of time.

Isaac bustled about and managed to do a great deal in a very little time.

The officer's horse he tied up at one end of the large building, and then, by the aid of his companion, the captive officer was half lifted, half rolled on to the ground.

Leaving him there, his next care was to take the gray horse out of the shafts.

"We have comfortable standing room for him," said Lord Harcliffe, patting the noble steed's neck, "and plenty of straw for a bed; the pity is, we have no provender."

"Haven't we, though," said Isaac, with his peculiar chuckle of satisfaction. "Just as if I should be likely to forget the poor animal in that manner!"

"Do you mean to say you have some, then?"

"Rather."

"Where?"

"Didn't you see me slip this bag into the back of the

[PRICE AND HIS ASSISTANT ENTREAT THE BLACK HIGHWAYMAN TO SET THEM FREE.]

cart just before we started? Here's enough to last him for three days at least."

While speaking, Isaac pulled out from the back of the cart a good-sized sack pretty nearly full.

"I shall be able to spare the other animal a feed," he said; "but as for ourselves, we must do as well as we can without."

"It is chiefly rest that I require."

"And that we must take in turns, one keeping vigilant guard. Make yourself comfortable on that straw there. It's not over clean; but it will serve if you are tired."

"You will let me know the moment anything unusual happens?"

"Depend upon me."

"And whether or not, wake me up in three hours' time."

"All right."

Then, turning to the officer, he said:

"And the best thing you can do is to go to sleep and forget your troubles. You can feel assured by this time that we mean you no injury. All we want is to keep you out of the way of doing mischief."

The officer was helpless.

But he disdained to make any reply to Isaac's speech.

"Very well, old fellow; I don't want to force any conversation on you if you don't like it. I daresay you do feel a great deal aggravated; but, then, put up with it, man. It might have been a great deal worse."

Isaac carefully removed the trappings from both horses so that the animals should be quite at their ease, and then going to the barn door, commenced his look-out for the approach of danger.

There was little to fear in the shape of being pounced on at unawares, for, the country being open, he could see well around.

Lord Harcliffe, despite his weariness, tossed and tumbled about on his by no means comfortable couch.

But sleep eluded him.

So fatigued was he just before getting out of the cart that he felt he could fall asleep instantly.

Now, however, the attempt to close his eyes was a vain one.

All the many anxious thoughts which the present aspect of affairs could not fail to call up perplexed his brain, and made slumber impossible.

Suddenly, however, consciousness left him, and he fell into that profound slumber which follows exhaustion.

Time passed.

Isaac was weary.

But he stuck to his post unflinchingly.

No one came near to disturb him.

He saw men ploughing in the distance; and towards nine o'clock a boy drove some cows into the next field to that in which the ruins stood.

But this boy was too intent upon whistling some doleful ditty to observe anything around him.

Three hours elapsed.

But at the end of that period Lord Harcliffe was sleeping, if possible, more soundly than ever.

Isaac made no movement towards disturbing him.

"Let him sleep," he said—"that is what he wants. I can have a nap in the cart if that's all."

And with this reflection he patiently resumed his watch.

He gave a glance once or twice at his prisoner.

But the officer's eyes were closed as though asleep.

Whether real or feigned, Isaac did not trouble himself to ascertain.

His thoughts were with the captain.

He could picture his master just as he would be sitting at that moment.

And the more he thought, the more terrible did his anxiety become.

Every moment seemed to be one more hope taken away from the captain's release.

Weigh the matter over as he would, he was not able to derive any satisfaction from this journey to London.

It was, as he considered, only so much pains and time completely thrown away.

But then, in the face of the extraordinary precautions taken to keep Captain Hawk a safe prisoner, he could suggest no other plan.

Noon came; and it was just about the time when the sun was at his highest point in the heavens that Lord Harcliffe gave a sudden start and awoke.

He gazed around him with the air of one unconscious of his whereabouts.

The sight of Isaac recalled him to himself.

Strange fantastic visions had been flitting through his brain.

"I have slept past the time I mentioned," he said, sternly—almost angrily.

"I thought it a pity to arouse you from such refreshing slumber."

"You should have obeyed me; you would have spared me unpleasant dreams. But no matter. Seek your own repose now, and leave me to watch."

In good truth, Isaac was very weary, and therefore glad of the opportunity to stretch his limbs upon the straw, old and mouldering as it was.

Lord Harcliffe, with rather more anxiety imprinted on his features than could usually be seen there, walked to the threshold of the barn.

There he stood, watching and thinking deeply.

It was not long before there was an end to any doubts he might have felt whether his humble companion was asleep or not.

A succession of tremendous snores, which seemed to threaten destruction to the crumbling roof, fully testified to the fact that he was fast asleep.

The officer muttered several execrations about the noise; and had he been able to move he would unquestionably have awoke Isaac in a very little time.

And so the hours passed tediously away until the welcome shades of evening began to steal over the landscape, blotting out distant objects one by one.

Isaac awoke just about twilight, and immediately set himself assiduously to work to get the gray horse in readiness for the remainder of the journey.

As soon as he had done this, Lord Harcliffe, who in the meantime had been looking carefully to his arms and ammunition, drew him aside, so as to be out of hearing of the police officer.

"Have you made up your mind what you are going to do with yonder fellow?" he asked.

"I——"

"Speak in a whisper. I don't want him to overhear us."

"All right. I was going to say there seems to me to be only one way of settling it."

"And how's that?"

"Why, leave him where he is. He cannot get loose, and the chances are a thousand to one whether he dies of starvation."

"Do you think so?"

"Yes. He is a decent sort of fellow, considering he is a police officer, and has behaved himself uncommon well. I'll tell you how we can do it. No time will be lost, and we will call here on our road back."

"Agreed. I did not think of that."

"Then shall we be preparing to start now?"

"Do you think it dark enough?"

"Oh, yes; and will be by the time we are fairly off."

"Get ready, then."

The officer had tried his best to make out what passed between Lord Harcliffe and Isaac; but, in spite of all his attempts, he could not catch a syllable.

He viewed Isaac's preparations for departure with perfect equanimity.

No doubt he thought that he should be stowed away in the cart as before.

When he really learned that it was their intention to leave him deserted and alone in that horrible place he became frantic with despair.

He howled, threatened, entreated, prayed, and swore.

But all to no use.

Those to whom he appealed shut their ears to his supplications, and rode away.

But for some distance the howlings of the officer were audible.

"That's good!" said Isaac. "If he'll only keep up that sort of thing all night none of the country folks would go within a hundred yards of the barn for a Chancellor's pension; they would set it down to ghosts or magic."

The further they receded the more unearthly and terrible the sound of the officer's voice became.

The night promised to be as dark a one as that which had preceded it; but as yet the obscurity was not so great as to hinder them from making their way over the fields.

"I have been thinking," said Isaac, "that if we follow the course we are now taking we shall in a short time find ourselves in a cross-road that will answer our purpose very well."

"I will trust myself wholly to your guidance. I need not tell you that the saving of time is the most important thing now."

"I know it well."

"At what time do you think we shall reach London, provided we make tolerably good speed and meet with no unlooked-for interruption?"

"Certainly before midnight."

"If we can get there an hour before I can make sure of finding the man I want to see; but after that all is uncertain."

"You must push the horse, then, that's all. You needn't fear to do it. He is as fresh and strong as though he had not been a mile."

Judging by the horse's manner, what Isaac said did not seem far off from being the truth.

A little time was lost in traversing the fields which lay between them and the cross-road; but after that their progress was rapid—too rapid by far for safety.

The road was not smooth like the highway, but miry, and full of ruts in many places.

Yet, in a mysterious way, the old chaise cart wheels bumped on until at a signal from Isaac Lord Harcliffe tightened the reins.

"What is it?"

"So far we have managed well, and have come off better that I dared to hope. If we keep on like this we shall be there a good two hours before the time."

"So much the better."

"But in a moment or two you will reach the point where the cross-road joins the highway—that is why I wanted you to go steadily."

"You think that our troubles with the officers will be renewed?"

"I fear so; but we must remember the lesson we have had. I feel no fear of the result, for, depend upon it, no communication has been made."

Lord Harcliffe, however, was by no means sure of this, and he looked apprehensively around him.

But when the turn into the high-road was made, all seemed so still that he began to think he had perhaps broken through the cordon which his foes had made around London.

The smooth state of the road, too, so different from that which they had had, enabled almost double progress to be made.

The swift motion inspired him with hopeful thoughts and anticipations.

But suddenly, without giving the least warning of his intention, the gray horse came to a dead stop.

So suddenly was it that Lord Harcliffe and Isaac had some ado to save themselves from being pitched out.

The darkness was too great to enable them to see the ground distinctly.

That something had alarmed the horse was certain, for he now wheeled round and started off in the direction from which they had been coming.

CHAPTER CXXV.

LORD HARCLIFFE MAKES AN UNEXPECTED DISCOVERY.

FORTUNATELY at the moment Lord Harcliffe had a firm grasp upon the reins.

But for all that he could not immediately check the horse's career; though by speaking to him he succeeded in moderating his speed, and at length in turning him round again.

"What can have scared him like that?" Lord Harcliffe said. "It was strange, was it not?"

"Very," said Isaac. "Depend upon it there is something in the road which frightened him."

"But what could it be to produce such terror as that?"

"We shall see in a short time, I have no doubt. Take care, or he will be round again."

The horse showed great signs of restiveness, and seemed inclined to go in any direction but straight on.

Isaac saw that urgent measures were needed, so he jumped out of the chaise cart, risking an awkward fall.

He was at the horse's head immediately.

Holding on by the bridle, he patted the creature's neck, and used all the art he knew to pacify it.

By dint of much trouble he managed to lead him about twenty paces.

But beyond that distance he resolutely refused to go a single yard.

Isaac peered all around him in the darkness.

He could see nothing.

Nor was there any sound borne upon his ears.

"Can't you coax him further, Isaac?"

"Not a yard. It's no good trying any more."

"But what is to be done? We can't turn back again."

"No. There is but one thing to be done: we must find out what the object is that terrifies him, and remove it. He will go on then all right enough."

"I had better alight then?"

"I think so."

Lord Harcliffe descended.

"I'll tie him to a tree," said Isaac. "There is a branch here which seems made on purpose."

"But will he stand quiet?"

"Yes; I think so. We can but try."

With the remainder of the rope which had proved so useful in binding the police officer Isaac secured the horse to the branch of the tree.

In the meanwhile, Lord Harcliffe did all he could by voice and action to appease his terrors.

He succeeded even better than he expected.

"He will stand now." said Isaac. "Wait a moment while I light my lantern. It is so confoundedly dark that we sha'n't be able to find anything without it."

"I did not know you had one."

"I take care never to be without that necessary."

Isaac produced a dark lantern, and lighted it.

The horse seemed satisfied to remain where he was; but by the dilation of his eyes it could be seen that he was watching the movements of the two men half in interest and half in terror.

The lantern burned brightly, and Lord Harcliffe, taking it from Isaac's hand, flashed it around him in every direction.

"There's something there," said Isaac.

"Where?"

"Yonder. Something dark and shadowy—just against the ditch bank there."

Lord Harcliffe perceived the dusky-looking object pointed out; and, after giving one last glance to see that the horse was secure, he walked towards it.

Isaac followed eagerly.

Keeping the broad beam of light full on the object they were approaching, they soon made it out to be a human form.

Something in the outlines of it struck Lord Harcliffe as being familiar to him, and giving a sudden start, he advanced more quickly than before.

"It's a man," said Isaac. "I wonder if he has been wounded, or whether he's only drunk?"

Lord Harcliffe interrupted him by an ejaculation.

"Good Heavens!" he cried. "Can it be possible? What on earth can be the cause of his presence here? and in such a plight, too!"

"Do you know him?" Isaac asked, with an amazement which may be, perhaps, conceived.

"Know him! Why, this is the Pharoah about whom I have spoken to you!"

"The friend about whose safety you were so alarmed?"

"The same."

"How comes he here?

"I am at a loss to think. Hold the lantern. He is hurt! I will see the extent of his injuries."

Lord Harcliffe was deeply affected by this unexpected event—so much so that he could not for a moment make the examination he intended.

"He seems in a deep swoon," he said. "I cannot think it death, though without aid death may follow."

"Is he wounded?"

"I can see no signs of blood whatever. Perhaps he has been stunned by a fall or heavy blow."

"We must wait to hear that from his own lips. But what shall we do?"

"Let me think a moment. This occurrence is so totally unexpected that my ideas seem deranged."

"Shall I give a hint?"

"Yes, certainly; you should not hesitate to speak."

"Well, then, let us put him in the cart, and take him carefully to the nearest cottage. By a payment of money we can doubtless secure him good attention, and we shall lose but little time. Remember, we must not delay."

"No—no," said Lord Harcliffe, hurriedly. "And yet——"

"Yet what?"

"I feel distracted. I know not how to act for the best. A few words from Pharoah would relieve me from my difficulty."

"But why not act on my proposal?" said Isaac, who considered Pharoah and his condition of vastly less importance than Captain Hawk's release from prison.

"Because," was the reply, "he may for aught I know have had great difficulty to elude his foes. If we leave him at a cottage how easy it will be for the officers to recapture him."

"You think he has broke prison, then?"

"It is almost an absolute certainty."

Isaac scratched his head, as though that operation would help him out of his perplexity.

"We can only know by asking him a question or two," he said at length; "and as to that, whatever we do we ought to bring him round to his senses before we attempt to move him. Just try the effects of a little drop of this."

So saying, Isaac drew out of his pocket an enormous black bottle.

"What is it?"

"Brandy."

Lord Harcliffe took the stimulant gladly, and cautiously administered a small portion of it.

Its effects soon showed themselves.

Pharoah opened his eyes; but his gaze was a vacant one.

Besides, the strong glare of the lamp dazzled and bewildered him.

Lord Harcliffe spoke; and no sooner was his voice raised than Pharoah seemed to start at once into life and full possession of his ordinary intelligence.

"I am here," said the Black Highwayman. "Have no further dread—no harm can reach you now."

"Thanks," he said, drawing a long breath. "This meeting is more than I dared to hope for. Some brandy! Quick—quick! I faint!"

The bottle was held to his lips, and a tolerable quantity poured down his throat.

"Better now," he said. "And now tell me how it is that you have found me?"

"By accident. But I want to know how you came into this plight?"

"The story is a long one; and——"

"And must be postponed," interrupted Isaac, speaking with all the firmness and resolution that he considered the occasion demanded. "What we have on hand is too important for any time to be lost."

An angry reply rose first to Lord Harcliffe's lips.

But he repressed it, for he could not blind himself to the fact that what Isaac said was just.

"I am too weak to speak many words," said Pharoah, faintly. "If you could only convey me to some cottage where I could rest for a few days I should recover, for I am but slightly hurt."

"And your foes?"

Pharoah smiled.

"I am clear of the police."

"Clear of the police? How?"

"My strength will not let me tell you now. Personally, I say, I am free from them. Take me somewhere to rest, and I will tell you all."

He closed his eyes, as though the effort to say as much as he had had been almost too much for him.

Isaac drew a long breath.

"I am glad to hear there is an end of that dread," he said. "Now, surely we shall be able to give all our attention to the one who stands so badly in need of it."

Lord Harcliffe made no reply to this speech.

What Pharoah had said, so far from having satisfied him, had only piqued his curiosity to the highest pitch.

How on earth Pharoah could be free and without fear of recapture by the officers, passed his comprehension.

He began to fear that the wits of his faithful friend were disordered.

Isaac, finding Lord Harcliffe in this reverie, said nothing; but went back to the tree to which he had tied his horse.

Releasing him, he took a firm hold upon the bridle, and led the animal towards the prostrate figure.

He had much less trouble than he had looked for.

It seemed strange, but nevertheless it was a fact, that the horse had lost much of his former terror.

He even suffered himself to be led close to where Pharoah lay.

"Come," said Isaac, "let us lift him in now, and the first likely place we come to we will stop at and leave him. On our return we can call for him, and take him with us to the Greyhound. He will be all right there, I'll warrant you."

"Yes," said the Black Highwayman, "if we can manage that I shall indeed be content—all will be well."

"There is no difficulty about it that I can see. Help me to raise him into the cart."

To the surprise of both, Pharoah was able to help himself tolerably well, so that by the aid of his friends he was quickly placed in the bottom of the cart as comfortably as circumstances would permit.

Then, mounting, Lord Harcliffe again took the reins.

"One moment," gasped Pharoah, faintly. "The officers are here. They are tracking me *because they think I shall be sure to join you sooner or later*. If you meet with a troop don't let them know I am with you."

"Right," was the reply.

The horse once more started.

Lord Harcliffe's mind was full of busy speculation as to what possibly could have occurred.

Isaac, fretting and fuming at the loss of time, crossed his arms and remained silent.

Hardly had they gone a hundred yards, however, before they became aware that several mounted men were hastening to meet them.

"Drive steadily, and take no notice," said Isaac, in suppressed accents.

And turning round to Pharoah, he added:

"Don't speak a syllable or move a muscle till I give you leave to do so."

There was no time to say more.

A loud, commanding voice cried "Halt!" and the Black Highwayman, with a suppressed curse upon his lips, perforce obeyed.

The usual questions were then put, to which Lord Harcliffe answered boldly and indifferently as before.

"From Huntingdon. Then you have been met before?"

"Yes, confound it! I ought to have got to London a couple of hours ago."

"Never mind that," said the officer, who certainly was altogether unsuspicious as to the true character of the persons he addressed. "But you ought not to mind it."

"Why not?"

"Because we are sure to rid the road of a pest. But stay: as you have come so far, there is a piece of information which you will no doubt be able to give us."

"What is it?" asked Lord Harcliffe, with a curiosity that was by no means feigned.

"Have you seen a well-mounted man lately, riding at a headlong pace?"

"A highwayman, do you mean?"

"He may be, but certainly he was the accomplice and associate of one of them. Have you seen him?"

"No," was the firm answer, "you may take my word that no such person is now on the road. I could not have failed to see him."

"But we have absolute traces of him as far as this."

"Then he must have turned off somewhere near. He has not passed us."

The officer was completely deceived by Lord Harcliffe's manner.

"Drive on," he said. "If the information you have given us is correct you have done the world great service; but if I find it false I will spare no pains to find you again and make you suffer for it dearly."

"I am not afraid," said Lord Harcliffe, as he drove off. "Good night, and good luck to you!"

"There must be something excellent in our disguises," said Isaac, as soon as they had got to a safe distance. "I could never have believed that they would have stood the test over and over again like this."

"It is wonderful," said Lord Harcliffe, "and yet as I take it, the cause is simple enough."

"As how?"

"It lies in the absence of all suspicion. Had they but the barest idea, the least glimmering of a notion that I should be trying to get to London in this fashion, the disguise would fail were it ten times better than it is."

"You are right, no doubt, but yet it seems as wonderful as ever to me. But stay. Who was it they inquired for?"

"Pharoah."

"I guessed as much. Circumstances seem to point that he has fallen from his horse."

"That must be it."

"Well, there is one comfort—they are quite convinced in their own minds that they have not passed him, and so his presence at any little cottage where we may leave him will not be suspected."

"I hope not."

"It is our only course; and for my own part, if we are to trust to what he says there can come no harm of it."

"Yes, that is just it. Can we trust him, or is his mind wandering?"

"I should say not. So far as I can tell, he was calm and contented enough."

"That is just my impression."

"Look, then—there is a light. If it comes from a cottage shall we leave him there or take him further?"

Lord Harcliffe hesitated.

So far as his own inclinations were concerned he would have preferred taking Pharoah with him to his journey's end, but he saw the impolicy of this too well to think of naming it.

Isaac answered for him.

"He is best left here, rely upon it. In going further we may meet with another troop of officers, and it does not follow that we shall pass through them like the rest."

"No: but you will admit there is a strong probability of it. Besides, you don't know that twinkling light yonder does come from a cottage, or if it does that it will suit our purpose."

"No, I am assuming that; but we shall be resolved about it in a very few seconds now."

The distance between them and the glimmering light lessened very rapidly.

"Yes, it's a cottage," cried Isaac, who had been peering through the darkness in his anxiety to catch a first glimpse of it—"yes, it's a cottage and so far as I can see, is just the very place."

Lord Harcliffe smiled grimly.

Of course he could see through Isaac's anxious desire to get rid of Pharoah, so that their journey could be resumed without the loss of further time.

He, too, felt that if he was to make use of that night he should have to make a vigorous effort, and another day's delay might be fraught with ruinous consequences.

For these considerations he resolved—though somewhat reluctantly be it said—that if this place held out any reasonable prospect of serving the purpose required, he would leave Pharoah there if he could by a liberal offer of money induce the inhabitants to render him the assistance he required.

Accordingly he pulled up at the little white wicket gate at the roadside.

Isaac had jumped to the ground and knocked at the little door beneath the ivied porch almost before the wheels of the chaise cart had ceased to go round.

CHAPTER CXXVI.

LORD HARCLIFFE PLACES PHAROAH IN SAFETY, AND HAS A STRANGE INTERVIEW WITH MR. MARCHANT.

The door was opened after what seemed to Isaac an unreasonable delay by an old lady who carried a candle, and who had upon her nose a pair of the most extraordinary-looking horn spectacles ever beheld.

In a few words Isaac explained what was required.

But the old lady hesitated.

"Our friend," he said, "has only been bruised or stunned by being thrown from his horse. He wants nothing but rest, attention, and quiet. We shall call for him in a day or two, and rest assured you will be paid very liberally for your trouble. If you consent I can promise you five guineas to start with."

The lady's astonishment on hearing this sum named was so great that she almost dropped the candle.

"Mercy on us!" she ejaculated.

"What is it, Betsy?" said a piping voice from within. "Why don't you tell me what it is?"

"A poor gentleman," said the old dame, becoming wonderfully pathetic all of a sudden. "He has been thrown off his horse and wants to rest. Bless the Lord! Let us be charitable. Do as you would be done by! Bless me! five pounds—no five guineas! Bring him in—bring him in!"

The old lady's cupidity brought a smile to Isaac's lips.

But no sooner had he received the much-wished-for permission than he hastened to the cart.

That Pharoah's hurt was nothing serious was proved by his condition now, for, despite the jolting of the cart, he was manifestly much better.

He got down out of the vehicle almost unaided, and walked easily towards the house by the support which his two friends gave him.

The room of the cottage into which the old woman ushered them was about as comfortable a one as could be wished for or expected.

Among the other articles of furniture it contained was an antique sofa

On this the patient was placed.

No sooner was it done than Isaac was in a fidget to depart.

It seemed as though, upon second thoughts, the old lady had grave doubts about the reward offered; but when the Black Highwayman placed the sum on the corner of the table her scruples vanished.

She overwhelmed them with such a profusion of courtesies and expressions of thanks that Lord Harcliffe felt it a relief to cross the threshold.

He had little fear that his faithful associate would be all right till his return.

Isaac's delight was great.

"There!" he said, as he set the example of getting into the cart, "I consider that job is managed about as well as an affair of that kind could be."

"Yes, we have been singularly fortunate."

"We have. At what time do you think we shall get to London now?"

"We have lost much time."

"Shall we be there by midnight?"

"It will require an effort."

"The horse is able to make it."

"Yes; push him on: don't spare him."

The horse wanted very little pushing.

He kept up a surprisingly fast trot until the thousand lights of London became visible in the distance.

No interruption of any kind whatever had taken place.

Contrary to their expectations, the troops of police officers were not closer together as they neared the metropolis.

The fact was that the police had for some time past had a tolerably good idea as to where their men were to be found, and consequently their forces had collected into that point.

From this Lord Harcliffe and Isaac both argued that their greatest danger was over, and that their presence in London would be deemed on all hands such an improbable event that no one would be on the look-out.

How far they were correct in this notion events will quickly show.

Just as they were entering the City they were challenged by the last patrolling troop, and by them it was done merely as a matter of form.

As had been previously agreed upon, Isaac stopped at an old inn with which he was acquainted, situated in Bishopsgate Street—a widely different place in those days.

The inn was such a one as could hardly be found in the most outlying district in all England now, yet it stood within a very short distance of St. Paul's.

Isaac agreed to remain with the horse so as to be in readiness for any emergency, leaving Lord Harcliffe the task of seeking out the man of law alone.

But before starting, the Black Highwayman doffed the smock-frock, retaining only the overcoat, which effectually disguised him.

Great as was the speed they had made during the latter portion of their journey, yet now it was verging upon midnight.

At a rapid walk, Lord Harcliffe made his way in the direction of Newgate.

The course he took was almost a straight one, and the manner in which he threaded alley after alley without being for one second at fault, showed how wonderfully familiar he was with the whole of the City.

Just as the solemn-sounding clock in the church of St. Sepulchre struck the hour of twelve he turned the corner of the Old Bailey.

The black, gloomy, frowning prison of Newgate was close on his left hand.

But the sombre building evoked no emotion.

He did not even turn a second glance upon it.

The building had for him no vague terrors.

Despite all that he had gone through, his nerves seemed to have lost none of their steel-like quality.

Passing rapidly by the front of the prison, he arrested his steps at a tavern that was situated exactly opposite the front-door of the Governor's house.

Late as the hour was, business at the tavern seemed to be in full swing.

Passing down a long, narrow passage, Lord Harcliffe came to a bar window, at which stood the landlord.

Passing him by, however, without taking the least

notice, though Lord Harcliffe knew him well enough, he made his way towards another door, that, from its situation, appeared to communicate with the back part of the premises.

"Hi! stop there!" cried the landlord. "You mustn't go there!"

"Oh yes, it's all right," was the answer, excellently given in a broad country dialect.

"I tell you you can't go there! That's the gentlemen's private room."

"I know it is; but I have come to see Mr. Marchant, the lawyer, on very particular business."

"Did he tell you you would find him here?"

"Yes; if I came before twelve."

"Go in, then. He has not left yet, though twelve is his time."

Lord Harcliffe opened the door in a moment, and closed it as quickly as possible.

At first he could see nothing at all, owing to the dense cloud of tobacco smoke with which the apartment was literally filled.

All eyes were turned instantly upon the new-comer.

His aspect was so grotesque that a loud, sneering laugh went round.

It would have taken much more than that, however, to have disturbed Lord Harcliffe's equanimity.

Piercing the reeking cloud, he at length perceived the person whose assistance he required.

He was a tall, burly man, with a florid face, puffed cheeks, and a cast in his left eye, which served to heighten the low, cunning look that his features habitually wore.

Lord Harcliffe crossed the room and sat down at the same table.

As he did so, he made a slight and rapid sign.

It was as near being imperceptible as could be.

Yet Mr. Marchant saw it, as was evident by his start of surprise, followed by a searching gaze.

But it failed to inform him who his late visitor was, though he prided himself upon his cleverness in piercing disguises.

The other persons present were all connected, nearly or remotely, with the legal profession.

The Old Bailey sessions were about to commence, and consequently their gathering was unusually strong.

Of all that gazed upon the rough, dirty-looking countryman not one suspected that he was really the man who had made himself the terror of nearly every high-road in the kingdom.

"I want to speak to you in private," he said at last, bending over to Mr. Marchant. "Where can we go? We have all eyes bent upon us here."

"No matter for that. Who are you?"

"That you shall know presently."

"Look—there is that table in the corner quite vacant, no one even sitting near it. Let us go there, and we shall be just as well as though in the middle of a wood."

After a glance Lord Harcliffe consented.

Refreshments were then called for, and as soon as they had been served Mr. Marchant, with more curiosity in his manner than he ordinarily displayed, leaned forward, and said:

"Now, then, your business. What is its nature?"

"Important."

"Well?"

"Urgent."

"Come to the point."

"And if performed, *liberally* paid for."

Lord Harcliffe laid a peculiar stress upon the word "liberally," and accompanied the utterance of it with a significant glance.

"Well? Now let me have some details. Drink."

Lord Harcliffe obeyed, and then simply said:

"Captain Hawk."

Mr. Marchant did not move or speak.

He merely expressed his surprise by elevating his eyebrows until they became almost mingled with his shaggy hair, and puffed out his cheeks.

"Enough!" said Lord Harcliffe. "You know now that the business is of no common order."

"And who are you?"

"That you shall know in good time. Now that we have come to the point, let us keep to it."

"Very good."

"You know what's wanted?"

"He's at Huntingdon, isn't he?"

"Yes."

"Strongly guarded?"

"Of course."

"What do you want me to do?"

"Get him off."

"By legal means?"

"Certainly."

"Can't be done!"

"The price paid," continued Lord Harcliffe, passing over the last response as though it had not been uttered —"the price paid for obtaining his acquittal will be five hundred pounds—half the money down at this minute."

Mr. Marchant sat staring for some moments without speaking.

"I know," pursued his client, "that if any man in England can do this thing, you can. The question is will you?"

"The pay is good."

"Will you take the half now?"

"Gently!—not so fast! Don't you know that the Government is determined, now they have got him, to hang him?"

"Yes; but——"

"Very well. An uncommonly strong effort will be made, I can tell you. I'm afraid it's no go."

"Never mind your fears—take the money."

Mr. Marchant sighed.

Lord Harcliffe pulled a bag from his pocket.

"Here," he said, "take this. Let the event be what it will, you will see I'm in earnest."

"You are a man of business."

"Follow my example, then, and settle the bargain."

"I will."

"I'm satisfied."

"When is the trial?"

"In a day or two."

"Confoundedly short notice!"

"Which can't be helped. May I rely on you?"

"You may."

"You'll pull him through?"

"I will. Now, who are you, and where shall I find you?"

"Be satisfied with an answer to your last question. You will find me at the Greyhound, a well-known inn about seven miles on this side of Huntingdon."

"I have heard of the place."

"When there you shall know all."

"Very good. I shall start to-night."

"So shall I—I have no other business to detain me."

"At least, when I say to-night, I think the mail-coach starts at six, and I shall have to set things in proper trim."

"Then don't let me waste any more of your time. You know what you have to do, and we should be no better off if we stopped talking till daylight."

"True. The Greyhound. I shall not forget."

"Should not I be there from any cause, the landlord is wholly to be trusted, and you can confer with him just as you would with me. He knows all."

"Then there is no fear of loss of time."

"None. Once more good night!"

"Good night!"

Lord Harcliffe rose and left the room, followed by as many curious eyes as had greeted his arrival.

The landlord stared after him as he passed the bar, but said nothing.

"So far, then, all goes well," he muttered. "And yet I fancy it would require some one to know the man as well as I know him to rest satisfied with the bare assurance that he gave. But I would take his word for twice as much. Captain Hawk is as good as free."

"What's that you say about Captain Hawk?" cried a voice, suddenly.

Lord Harcliffe started.

At the same time a man started out of the gloom, and grasped him by the arm.

"What's that you say about Captain Hawk?" he repeated.

"Nothing that concerns you or anyone else save myself Let go!"

"Nothing of the sort, my fine fellow! You must come

along with me, and answer a question or two. I have my doubts of you."

By the dim flicker of an adjacent oil lamp, Lord Harcliffe saw that it was a man in the garb of a police officer who thus opposed his progress.

"Do you hear?" he said. "Come along! I tell you I have my doubts, and will have them set at rest before I part company with you."

"With all my heart!" was the reply.

It is questionable, however, whether the officer heard it, for just then Lord Harcliffe gave a sudden bound, and seized him by the throat with both his hands.

Such was the fierce suddenness and unexpectedness of the attack that the officer lost his balance and fell backwards.

Lord Harcliffe could not help falling, too; but he took care that his grasp should be none the slacker on that account.

The officer's head reached the paving stones with a violence that made all the silent street resound with the blow.

Lord Harcliffe was bruised and shaken, and this served to increase his ire against the police officer.

"Take that!" he said, as he shifted his grasp from his neck to his hair; "and that as well! Are all your doubts satisfied now?"

All was profoundly still.

When Lord Harcliffe pronounced the words "Take that!" he accompanied them with the action of lifting the officer's head about six inches from the ground, and then bumping it down again with all his might.

He was now quite insensible; and when satisfied on this point, Lord Harcliffe rose, and made his way back to Bishopsgate Street at a rapid pace

So little time had been occupied, and so little noise made by his encounter with the officer, that no one was aware of what had taken place.

As soon as the corner was turned, he felt that he was safe.

Taking the same direct route as before, he made his way to the inn in Bishopsgate Street.

Just before he reached it, he heard the clock of St. Paul's send forth the hour of two.

"A short rest for the horse," he muttered; "but yet it will not do to lose precious time. He can rest afterwards."

No sooner did he reach the gateway leading to the stables than a dark figure glided out towards him.

Despite the obscurity, he knew in an instant who this was.

It was Isaac.

CHAPTER CXXVII.

LORD HARCLIFFE HEARS SOME STRANGE THINGS FROM PHAROAH.

"ALL is well then?" he said.

"Yes," replied Lord Harcliffe. "Have you been disturbed or suspected?"

"Not at all."

"That is well."

"Have you seen him?"

"Yes; and he says he will get him off. You can trust to that—he will do it."

"Humph!" said Isaac, dubiously.

"How is the horse?"

"All right. When must we start back?"

"Now—at once."

"He has had hardly time to rest."

"That cannot be helped. It is important we should get back to the Greyhound with the least possible loss of time. I have promised to meet the lawyer there."

"When?"

"Before midnight."

"It will be hard; but if the officers don't interfere with as we can manage it."

"Be quick, then. I needn't tell you how important it is not to delay a moment."

"No. Stay here, and I will soon have the cart ready."

Lord Harcliffe stood just under the gateway at a spot where the shadow concealed him completely.

"There has not been much time lost as yet," he muttered. "But there's the return journey: I have my doubts about that. After I have called for Pharoah at the cottage we must take our further proceedings into careful consideration."

He fell into a deep reverie as he spoke, nor did he rouse from it until he heard the sounds of wheels behind him.

"Jump up," said Isaac, at the same moment. "All is in readiness."

Lord Harcliffe did not hesitate an instant.

What was his surprise, however, to find that the chaise cart was loaded with something.

"What is that?" he asked.

"Meat," answered Isaac.

"What?"

"I will explain when we have started."

Isaac climbed into the cart as he replied; and Lord Harcliffe drove off as soon as he was seated.

"Now, then," he said, "explain the meaning of this cargo we are carrying."

"It is some carcasses of meat from Leadenhall Market."

"But for what purpose?"

"Why, the officers who challenged us saw us with an empty cart, and would naturally expect we should not return without bringing something with us."

"Not a bad thought. But I question whether it will prove sufficient to satisfy them."

"We shall soon know."

"True. If the device only serves until we reach the cottage where we left Pharoah we shall be fortunate."

"That was my idea."

Isaac then began to question his companion about the interview he had had with the lawyer.

The reader is, of course, well acquainted with Isaac's sentiments, and therefore it will occasion no surprise that the replies only made his dubiety increase.

He made no attempt to disguise his impressions, though he said not a word.

Lord Harcliffe observed it with some little impatience.

"It seems scarcely reasonable," he said, "that you should have so many doubts. I wonder what arrangement would be sufficient to satisfy you?"

"Don't be angry. My anxiety for the captain's safety won't permit me to be otherwise than I am. If you only knew what my feelings were you would not be surprised at my manner."

"Perhaps not; and yet I feel you are wrong to think so lightly of such an excellent arrangement. I have the strongest faith in Mr. Marchant, because I know he never positively says a thing without performing it."

"And does he say positively he will get the captain off?"

"He does."

"By legal means?"

"Certainly."

"Well, he may; but at the same time, judging by what we all know, it seems absolutely impossible for any living man to accomplish it."

"We shall see. If this fails—and I don't think it will—still, if it does, it will leave us free to try other remedies."

Isaac was silent, but not convinced.

Strive as he would, he could not think of anything strong enough being brought forward at the trial to have the least effect in getting the captain off.

Two troops of officers were passed through without difficulty.

They recognised the cart returning, and appeared quite satisfied when they saw what it contained.

They were now nearing the cottage where Pharoah had been left, and on the part of both much anxiety was felt as to whether they should encounter another troop.

Luckily for them, this was not the case.

But at that hour the cottage was enveloped in darkness, and both dreaded that a dangerous delay would take place.

Isaac clamoured loudly for admission.

On being allowed to enter, they found Pharoah was fast asleep.

He had recovered wonderfully during the few hours that he had been left, and professed himself quite well and strong enough to accompany them.

The old woman, who had felt many misgivings in the meanwhile, had all her fears and doubts put at rest by receiving the full amount which she had been promised.

Pharoah at first seated himself in the cart beside Lord Harcliffe, and in this way they drove away from the cottage.

But when at a safe distance from it they pulled up under the shadow of some trees to hold a consultation.

Isaac, on being appealed to, gave his opinion very promptly.

"I think," he said, "that Pharoah ought to conceal himself under the meat, and then, when we encounter any officers, we shall not have his presence to account for."

This was at once agreed to.

"Then, in the second place, I think it would be neither more nor less than perfect folly to attempt to make our way back by the road we came."

"I fear so, too," said Lord Harcliffe; "yet what other way can we take that will hold out a reasonable prospect of safety? and more especially now that every moment is of so much importance."

All this, of course, was very enigmatical to Pharoah.

But he had been so much with the Black Highwayman that he had imbibed much of his taciturnity and self-command.

He could wait until an opportunity for explanation came.

"We cannot help it," said Isaac, decisively. "I have thought the matter over, and I feel sure there is only one thing for us to do."

"What is that?"

"To take to the lanes, and make our way to the Greyhound in a roundabout direction. There will be no loss of time, rely upon it."

"Are you well acquainted with the country?"

"Pretty well so; and what is more, I think I should be able to take you for many miles through a district so little frequented that we could venture to drive by daylight."

"Then I will hesitate no longer. Take the reins and drive. In the meanwhile I must have some necessary explanations with Pharoah."

Isaac had been itching to have the reins all the time, and so took them now without raising the faintest murmur of objection.

Before starting, however, Pharoah concealed himself to a partial extent.

The position he took up was one which, while it allowed him to hold converse with Lord Harcliffe without much restraint, was nevertheless such that he could have hidden himself in a couple of minutes should the necessity arise.

"Now tell me," said Lord Harcliffe, turning to him, "all that has taken place since our parting. I am full of impatience to hear the details. How it is you are free I cannot think. It baffles me completely. I should have freed you had I been able to reach London."

"It is fortunate you did not make the attempt."

"How fortunate?"

"The officers have been playing a deeper game than you are aware of."

"Explain."

"I will; but first of all I must tell you that I tried to save things at the mansion, and succeeded to a slight extent. I stuck to my post, but was made prisoner by an overwhelming force."

"And carried to prison?"

"Yes."

"What next?"

"I was duly examined and committed to take my trial at the sessions."

"On what charge?"

"That of being the accomplice of the Black Highwayman."

"And how did the trial terminate?"

"In my acquittal."

"Your acquittal?"

"Yes. You may well speak in accents of surprise, but you cannot be half so surprised as I was myself."

"Then it was through no extraordinarily clever legal aid that you had?"

"Not at all."

"How on earth, then? Surely there was evidence enough to have brought you in guilty?"

"So there was."

"Well, then?"

"But they would not produce it."

"Not produce it? You amaze me more and more."

"I am not surprised."

"Go on with your tale."

"Never was there a case more weakly and badly made out against a prisoner."

"And you were acquitted, you say?"

"Yes. Had the feeling against me been ten times stronger than it was it would hardly have been possible to find a jury in the land that would have convicted me."

"But why should not the officers have made out their case?"

"Because they were intent upon a deeper game."

"A deeper game?"

"Yes. They did not want me: they wanted you. Do you understand?"

"Not exactly."

"Well, then, their scheme was to set me free—or rather cause me to be set free by bringing no evidence against me—and then, when once out of the prison walls, not to lose sight of me."

"But when did you learn all this?"

"I was not long in doing that. I quickly found that turn where I would—look where I would—a police officer was at hand. It puzzled me at first, for I thought what can they want with me after letting me off? Then the truth flashed upon me."

"Are you sure you are right?"

"Yes, subsequent events placed it beyond a doubt They thought to make me the instrument whereby you would be captured—they wanted to make me your destroyer. Can't you see their calculation was that my first action on finding myself out of prison would be to rejoin you? They judged they had only to keep an eye on me to make sure of finding you in a little time. Does it not come home to you with the force of a conviction?"

"It does—it does. I wonder a thing so likely and so simple did not strike me at the first. How is it that you have avoided them?"

"It would take too long to tell you all the attempts I made, and all the schemes I tried. Time after time I failed, and when I felt most sure I had eluded them I should be sure to find myself face to face with one or more of them."

"But you seem to have succeeded at length."

"Yes; and how truly fortunate that it should be just at the time when I met with you."

"It was a most wonderful chance. How came you in the insensible condition in which we found you?"

"I had obtained a horse—a vicious and almost unmanageable creature. My object in getting him was to ride away at such a distance as to weary the officers in following me; then afterwards to disguise myself, and do the best I could to rejoin you unperceived."

"A good plan."

"It was the only one I could think of that held out the slightest chances of success. Before I had gone far, however, the brute threw me. I recollect leaving the saddle, but nothing more until, to my unbounded surprise, I found you gazing at me."

"You shook them off sooner than you anticipated."

"That was thanks to your presence of mind in putting them on the wrong track. That has unquestionably saved us all."

"Steady now," interrupted Isaac, at this moment. "I am going to turn into a lane with some deep ruts in it, so expect a bump or two."

The caution was by no means a superfluous one.

Although the pace of the horse was much reduced, the jolting was well-nigh sufficient to shake them out of the cart.

"If this goes on far," said Lord Harcliffe, "we shall soon lose the wheels off this crazy affair."

"It's only for a short distance," said Isaac. "The cart will stand it, and you may feel sure we shall meet with no police officers in this direction."

Although morning was approaching, it was still very dark, and Lord Harcliffe vainly stared about him in the hope of finding out where he was.

Isaac, however, drove on fearlessly, and in a short time as he had said, the road became passable.

It was now Pharoah's turn to ask questions.

[CAPTAIN HAWK IN THE CONDEMNED CELL.]

There was much in what he saw to amaze and mystify him.

But Lord Harcliffe, in a few words, gave a rapid outline of his adventures, and described his meeting with Captain Hawk and the events which followed it.

To all Pharoah listened attentively.

By the time the recital was concluded day had fairly broke forth.

The country around had a rugged and gloomy appearance.

Huge hills rising on every side limited the view to a few hundred yards.

No signs of human beings could be perceived anywhere, and the only things living were countless sheep grazing on the hill-sides.

"We may drive on yet for some hours," said Isaac. "We are going quite out of our proper direction; but I shall bend round, and have little fear that I shall be able to reach the Greyhound unperceived."

"If you can do that all will be well."

"Yes, if the horse holds out."

"As you say, if the horse holds out. Such a journey is trying him severely."

"It is. My proposition is that we stop to rest during the middle part of the day, and then if we start as soon as he has recovered himself we shall be at our journey's end two or three hours on the right side of midnight."

Without anything to interrupt them, they continued on their way.

It seemed quite evident that they had got quite clear of the police officers, though of course they could not tell how soon they should come in contact with them again

Isaac halted in a part of a winding green lane that was well shadowed with trees.

"We shall do better here than anywhere," he said. "All we have to do is to take the horse out of the shafts and let him have his feed. It is not once a week, I'll be bound, that anyone comes this way; and should we chance to see a labouring man, it is a thousand to one if he will know anything of us."

CHAPTER CXXVIII.

THE RETURN TO THE GREYHOUND.—ISAAC HAS RATHER A POOR OPINION OF MR. MARCHANT.

WHEN the travellers had time to glance around them, they found that the spot at which Isaac had chanced to halt was possessed of rare picturesque beauty.

But attractive as the scene was, it had but few charms for them.

Their minds were wholly absorbed by anxious doubts and fears, and when they glanced up at the bright sun, which shone so gloriously among the tree-tops, it was only to wish that they could accelerate his journey to the western horizon.

Long, therefore, and tedious to the last degree were all the hours that passed, although they contrived to lessen the interval by sleeping in turns.

As Isaac had said, no human being appeared to disturb them.

The horse, having eaten his fill, stretched himself at full length upon the turf.

That he was very weary could be seen easily, and it was out of consideration for his condition that they governed their impatience and waited longer before they made their start than there was absolute necessity for doing.

"Rely upon it," Isaac said, "that we could drive till nightfall without fear of meeting with a soul. As for the officers, I am quite convinced that we have got out of their track."

"It seems so; but yet it is best not to make too sure. Let us restrain ourselves a little longer, for it would not be much good if we reached the Greyhound before midnight."

Isaac rather reluctantly acquiesced; but as soon as ever the sun dipped behind the long bank of clouds on the western horizon he replaced the horse in the shafts and made every preparation for a start.

In a few moments afterwards they were rolling along at full speed, the horse having apparently quite recovered himself from his fatigue.

As before, the direction of the vehicle was left entirely to Isaac.

He drove on for some distance without venturing to alter his course, but at length diverged in a way that would bring him circuitously to his destination.

The night was fine, but there was no light save that which the twinkling of myriads of stars afforded.

This was more than sufficient for Isaac.

At length, in tones of satisfaction, he exclaimed:

"At last—at last! Look there—look there!"

"Where?"

"At that twinkling light."

"Yes—I see it now."

"That is the Greyhound."

"Can it be possible?"

"It is indeed. Now surely we may make sure that all is well?"

"Be cautious!"

"Trust me for that!"

Both Pharoah and Lord Harcliffe now concentrated all their faculties upon keeping a keen look-out.

For aught they knew, danger for them might be lurking near Tom Beckford's abode, and so it behoved them to act with the utmost caution.

Luckily for them, whatever apprehensions they might have felt proved to be vain ones.

The back part of the old inn was reached without the slightest interruption being offered.

Under the guidance of Isaac, the stable was quickly gained, and no time was lost in getting the horse out of the chaise cart.

Tom Beckford, though not immediately visible, had evidently been on the look-out for their arrival.

He came forward now with a stable lantern in his hand.

He manifested the utmost joy at seeing them back again.

"You will never know what I have endured in the shape of suspense while you have been away. But never mind that now—it's past. Have compassion on me, and let me know how you have got on."

"As well as could be wished."

"You have seen the lawyer?"

"Yes; and he gives his word to set the captain free."

On hearing this news, the landlord felt a strong inclination to send the lantern spinning in the air.

By an effort he restrained himself, and then somewhat soberly, he asked:

"But what reliance can you place on this man's word?"

"The utmost: when he has given his word you may depend upon the performance."

"Excellent! Now I begin to breathe again."

"Show the light, then."

Tom raised the lantern aloft, and then, for the first time, perceived that the party consisted of three instead of two.

Lord Harcliffe observed his astonishment, and, without giving him time to ask a question, said:

"I forgot. Here is another favour Fortune has shown us. This is the faithful friend I spoke to you about, and concerning whose safety I was so ill at ease."

"That was fortunate indeed."

"In the name of Captain Hawk I must ask you to extend to him the safe shelter that you have done to myself. Rely upon it, should the chance arrive, he will be as ready as anyone to come forward and secure his freedom."

"You are heartily welcome!" was the landlord's unhesitating response. "And whatever lies in my power to do you may depend will be done."

"That was my conviction," said Lord Harcliffe, "or I should not have ventured to bring him here."

"Well—well! Get all things square as soon as you can, for the quicker we get indoors the better it will be, I can tell you. Hallo! What in the name of all that's wonderful have we here?"

The landlord, having drawn a little closer to the chaise cart, perceived the cargo of meat.

His first sensation was that of extreme affright, for he jumped to the conclusion that some unusually desperate deed had been performed.

"Don't be alarmed," said Isaac, with a good laugh. "You need not have that fear. We thought you might fall short of provender, and so have brought you two or three joints of splendid beef."

"But what on earth does it mean?"

"You shall know all about it, and plenty more besides, as soon as we get inside. You will be interested in every word, I'll warrant."

"I am quite sure of that. Don't lose another moment. Come on!"

He started off at once towards the inn.

The others followed.

"How far is it from midnight?" was Isaac's next question.

"Something like an hour and a half."

"Good. We shall just have time to take a bit of a snack before the lawyer comes. It's but little we've had all the time we have been away, I can tell you."

"I have something already prepared for you, as you will find. I quite guessed what state you would be in."

It was a most agreeable surprise to all three of them to find that there was a very substantial and appetising repast awaiting them.

Never were viands sat down to with a sharper hunger or keener relish.

For several moments, despite the close questioning of the landlord, it was impossible to extract a single syllable from one of them.

But when the keen edge of their appetites had been taken off, they satisfied their friend's curiosity as fully as time would permit.

"What time will the coach call here, Tom?"

"Twelve to the minute."

"Then we may expect our guest very shortly; and as I daresay he will be sharp set on his arrival, there will be no harm in leaving the table just as it is."

"None in the world."

Hardly had the words been pronounced when the clear, ringing notes of a post-horn broke the stillness of the night.

"Here he comes, then," said the landlord. "You remain just as you are—don't venture to stir until you see me return."

So saying, he left the room.

The notes of the horn were heard again; and governed by an impulse which they could not resist, all three went to the window.

To their disappointment, they found it was impossible to obtain a glance at the coach, for the landlord, with a view of keeping away all prying eyes, had closed the shutter without and fastened it securely.

Returning to their seats, they controlled their impatience to what extent they were able.

They heard the coach stop—even the murmur of voices was borne to their ears.

Then the rumbling of wheels succeeded as the vehicle started off again.

But the interval which elapsed between this and the opening of the door of the room in which they sat seemed more intolerably long than any other.

But Mr. Marchant showed himself behind the rotund figure of the landlord.

"Here I am, punctual enough, you see," he exclaimed, in thick, unctuous tones. "Ha!" he added, as his eye fell upon the viands remaining on the table, "that is well thought of. Landlord, we will have a little knife-and-fork play before we go any further."

Accordingly he divested himself of the outer garments he had donned to protect himself from the cold, and lost not a moment in making a vigorous attack upon the eatables.

While thus engaged he seemed so intently employed as to be quite oblivious of the presence of everyone.

As the greatest curiosity was felt concerning him, the present afforded a favourable opportunity for him to be regarded attentively.

One conclusion was silently and unanimously come to.

This was, that Mr. Marchant's countenance was far from being prepossessing.

The cast in his eye gave to the whole of his features a terribly sinister look, which was heightened by the manner in which his black shaggy eyebrows overhung his small, glittering, rat-like eyes.

He ate gluttonously, and as though he was in fear that many hours would elapse before he should have the chance of making a meal again.

The quantity of ale, too, which gurgled down his throat was something to be wondered at.

At last he pushed away the plate from before him, and as he did so he breathed a deep sigh, and exclaimed:

"Now then, gentlemen, to business, for, of course, all I have the pleasure of seeing before me at the present moment are concerned in the business under hand?"

Lord Harcliffe hastened to give him this assurance.

"You may venture to speak freely," he said. "Have no hesitation in expressing yourself."

"That makes matters comfortable," said Mr. Marchant, settling himself in his chair. "And to begin with, I have an important question to ask."

"Let us hear it."

"Then," he said, fixing his gaze piercingly upon Lord Harcliffe, "I want to know who you are?"

"A friend of Captain Hawk's."

"I am aware of that; but I require something more definite."

"Is it possible you do not penetrate my disguise?"

"If I did I should not trouble to ask the question."

"You have heard of the Black Highwayman?"

Mr. Marchant started.

Then holding out his hand with the utmost show of cordiality, he ejaculated:

"I know you now, and shall be proud and happy to serve you. I am accustomed to many strange things," he added, after a warm pressure of the hand had been exchanged, "but if I had lived till Doomsday I should never have expected to find you in such a guise as that."

"Ah! just so."

"It is that that does it. I congratulate you upon your self-command in wearing such attire."

"It wants an effort, I confess; and though growing more accustomed to it by use than I could have believed, yet I shall gladly seize the first opportunity of throwing it aside. But never mind that. Let us keep to the point."

"With all my heart."

"What is the first thing you want to know?"

"Why, I want you to give me as concisely as you can a complete account of Captain Hawk's capture up to the present moment. But in trying to be brief, mind you do not omit any little circumstance which may chance to turn out of importance."

"I will do my best to avoid that."

"Proceed, then."

It would be taxing the patience of the reader too far to lay before them the summary which Lord Harcliffe gave. The events that occurred must be too clearly remembered to afford the least reason for it.

Mr. Marchant took a few hasty notes from time to time.

All the time the narration continued, his countenance was watched with the utmost closeness.

It was observed that its expression grew more and more serious.

"It's an ugly business," was his final comment.

"But you will not fail us?"

"No; I have given my word, and if I have to move heaven and earth, I'll keep it."

"But how?" said everyone, excitedly.

"That you must excuse me for telling you just at present. Are you sure this is all?"

"Quite."

"Very good; then I know what to prepare for. It will be no easy task."

"We know that, or we should not have sought your aid. But strain every nerve. You shall not have anything in the shape of a reward to complain of."

"I will not fail you. But as there is no time to be lost, I will be off."

"Whither?"

"Never mind. If I am to succeed you must leave me to follow my own devices unwatched and unquestioned."

"You will find us ready to agree to all your terms and conditions," said Lord Harcliffe, answering for the rest. "There is only one thing that I have to ask of you."

"Name it quickly."

"It is that you will, with as little loss of time as you can, pay a visit to the captain in his cell."

"I——"

"Nay, hear me out. So zealously has he been guarded that we have not been able to hold the least communication with him. For aught he can tell, he is being wholly neglected. I want you to assure him that there is a reasonable prospect of his release."

"It shall be done. Is there anything more?"

"Nothing whatever."

"Then," he said, rising, "our interview is at an end. I have much to do in little time. But you may depend upon seeing me back here again before very long. Good night, gentlemen all!"

So saying, he resumed his outer clothing and his hat and departed.

After the door had closed behind him, a profound silence reigned for several moments.

The landlord left the room along with Mr. Marchant, in order to show him the way out.

Not until his return was a single word said.

"Well," said Lord Harcliffe, in tones of great and unmistakable satisfaction, "you have seen him and heard him—now let me know your opinion."

"Would you like to know mine?" said Isaac, doggedly.

"Most certainly."

"Well, then, if that is the man you depend so much upon, I can promise you I would not trust him to the length of my arm."

CHAPTER CXXIX.

THE MORNING APPOINTED FOR CAPTAIN HAWK'S TRIAL AT LENGTH ARRIVES.

Lord Harcliffe frowned, and seemed on the point of making some disagreeable remark

It was not the first time Isaac had offended him by his blunt, straightforward way of speaking.

The landlord perceived in a moment that there was just a little ill blood, and with admirable tact took part in the discussion.

"I must say his appearance was anything but encouraging; but then we ought not to trust to such an uncertain guide as that. After all, it is what a man says and does that is of importance, not how he looks."

"You are right," said Isaac; "and I can feel that I was wrong. I have only one excuse to make for speaking as I did, and that is the strong affection I have for the captain, and the terrible dread I have that he may somehow fall a victim. If that happened I——"

"Wait a moment. There is no need to consider that just at this moment," said the landlord. "I am quite as anxious as you are, but yet I try to control myself, and find what consolation I can in thinking that we shall not be kept long in suspense."

"What do you mean?"

"Why, the closeness of the time for his trial."

"Is the day fixed?"

"Well, I cannot say that it is exactly, because there happens this time to be rather more cases than usual, and it is hard to say just how long they will take."

"I see."

"Still, there is the possibility that the trial will begin on the day after to-morrow, or on the day following at the very furthest."

"As you say, the time is very short. I suppose you have heard this since our departure?"

"Yes. Business has been brisk, and, as you may think, there has been but one topic of conversation."

"Captain Hawk?"

"You have hit it. Of course, there have been all sorts of tales flying about—mere idle rumours: I was able to make sure of that."

"The time is fearfully short," said Pharoah, speaking for the first time. "Mr. Marchant has much to do; and I confess that, did I not know what I do of him, I should be doubtful and apprehensive as to the result."

"And now you are not?"

"Not in the least."

The confidence expressed and felt both by Pharoah and Lord Harcliffe of course did not fail to make a deep impression on the landlord and Isaac.

The discussion was prolonged until the first flush of light began to show itself in the east.

All three were fearfully fatigued, and their looks fully showed it.

"If you will take my advice, you will all three spend the day, as far as you can, in sleep. Leave me to answer for all being safe and well. No harm shall come to you without timely warning of it."

"Sleep and rest will be very welcome," said Lord Harcliffe, languidly, "for I have had little of either lately."

"I know it: and what you ought to bear specially in mind is that, no matter how events may turn out, the probability is that the time is not far distant when all your strength and energy will be required, and you ought to provide for it accordingly."

It was impossible to gainsay this, and so it was agreed that the landlord's proposition should be carried out.

Lord Harcliffe had not known the landlord of the Greyhound very long, and yet quite a sufficient time to feel certain that he was to be absolutely trusted.

After what Tom Beckford had said, then, not the shadow of misgiving dimmed his mind.

Ere long he was, like Pharoah, slumbering profoundly, for his mind was at rest that so far he had done all that lay in human power towards the achievement of his purpose.

Not so with Isaac, however.

He was by no means so assured that the best had been done; and the anxiety of mind he suffered was quite enough to drive sleep away.

His inclination to rise, slip out, and discover what Mr. Marchant's movements were was almost irresistible.

One thing, and one thing alone, enabled him to govern the impulse.

This was the fear that by so doing he might contribute to the overwhelming of the captain in fresh difficulties, and perchance make his liberation impossible.

This was a consideration quite sufficient to make him hold back.

But his torment, nevertheless, was not much diminished, nor did it lessen during the long hours which elapsed between then and nightfall.

Wearily the time wore away—interminable hours they seemed; and when at length evening came Isaac's excitement was all but ungovernable.

The noise of an approaching footstep attracted his attention, and the next moment the landlord entered.

His appearance aroused Pharoah and Lord Harcliffe.

"What is it?" was the immediate question.

"All is well," returned Tom. "All I want you to do is to come down quietly. Mr. Marchant is below. He has something to state."

That was sufficient.

Up they all three started, and followed him with all possible speed.

Mr. Marchant they found employed in warming himself before the huge fire which the landlord had specially prepared for the accommodation of the three friends.

"Let us have your news quickly," said Lord Harcliffe as he entered.

"I have not much to tell," was the disappointing answer. "I merely called to relieve you of any anxiety you might feel."

"Have you seen him?" was the next question.

"I have."

"In his cell?"

"In his cell. The Governor was present, so was a magistrate from Bow Street, whom I know very well. It seems he has a special commission concerning the affair."

"Well—well?" said Lord Harcliffe, impatiently.

"The turnkey was present also, so you will see that I had not much chance to confer with my client."

"Do you mean to say they remained within earshot all the time?"

"During the whole of the interview."

"Then what could you contrive to say?"

"Not much, certainly; but yet, in spite of their cleverness, I managed to convey the intimation to him that the steps we had taken and were about to take would result in his free release."

"You are sure they did not hear you?"

"Trust me for that. Captain Hawk showed wonderful firmness and self-command. He never started or showed the least surprise; on the contrary, it seemed the message was just exactly what he expected to receive."

"And now he will rely on us?"

"Certainly he will. I could have wished that it had been in my power to have entered a little further into explanations; but then again, I think it will be the best as things are. You can tell him all about it afterwards."

"And how did he look?" asked Isaac, whose self-restraint would hold out no longer—"well?"

"Tolerably so for a prisoner, and one that has been wounded, too."

"Could he walk about without assistance?"

"Oh yes, and, it seemed to me, with perfect ease."

This item seemed to give Isaac wonderful relief.

By the movement of his lips, he seemed to mutter something to himself, but no sound was audible.

"And the trial—will that take place to-morrow?"

"No; make yourself content on that score."

"Do you know, then?"

"Yes. It is almost certain to be the day following."

"And," said Lord Harcliffe, fixing a penetrating gaze upon the man of law, "I suppose nothing has occurred since we last parted that will increase the difficulty of what you have to do?"

"Nothing at all," said Mr. Marchant.

The words were accompanied by a peculiar smile—a smile which Isaac by no means liked.

His doubts and suspicions renewed themselves with tenfold force.

In spite of all that had just taken place, and which had gone far towards removing his misgivings, his doubts concerning Mr. Marchant's good faith grew stronger and stronger.

What an awful calamity it would be should his friends be lulled into a state of false security by this man he could realise perfectly well.

The contemplation of such an event made his back seem as though suddenly turned to ice.

Then he looked at the rest.

He could see that they took every word for granted, and made themselves quite content with the belief that in a day or two all would be well.

Yet, as before, Isaac found himself in the unpleasant and well-nigh unendurable position of not being able to do anything.

"And now," said Mr. Marchant, as he prepared to take his departure, "you can understand that my hands are about as full as a man's hands well could be; and I should not have come here to-night but that I feared unless I gave you some such assurance your impatience might have induced you to take some step as you might think for the best, but which in reality might ruin all I have done."

"No," said Lord Harcliffe. "The fear was groundless. I had trust enough in you."

"That is well; or I was about to ask you to pledge yourselves not to make a single movement or do one thing until after the trial is over. If I could persuade you all not to stir from here it would be so much the better."

But this was coming it too strong for Tom Beckford to stand it.

"No," he said. "Come what will, I shall be there for one; and if I must speak my mind, I should say I feel sure that could not interfere with your arrangements in any way."

Mr. Marchant was silent; but, as may be supposed, Isaac warmly seconded what the landlord had just said.

"I will yield the point since you seem so anxious about it," said Mr. Marchant. "And now you must not expect to see me again until after the trial, or during the time it is on. But mark these words, unless you remain perfectly passive, rely on it you will do mischief. Whatever temptation there may be to interfere, resist it; if not, I will not answer for the result."

"I think you are needlessly alarmed," said Lord Harcliffe. "At any rate, we will do nothing until the trial comes on; then the probability is that we shall all be in Court."

Mr. Marchant shrugged his shoulders.

"It will be quite your own look-out," he said, "and the consequences, whatever they may be, will have to be borne by you."

"Certainly."

"My undertaking is to free Captain Hawk, and if you find the money I will do it."

"You shall have the money," said the landlord. "Ask about me, and you will find I am worth a few more pounds than that."

"I am satisfied; and now let me finish by asking you to think over all that I have said. Good night!"

With these words, Mr. Marchant took his departure.

After he had gone, Isaac's face wore such a gloomy look that the others were obliged to notice and comment upon it.

"What ails you?" said Lord Harcliffe, somewhat impatiently. "It is strange you should be so dissatisfied when the arrangements that have been made are so excellent."

"I cannot help it," he replied, rising, and pacing up and down the room, as though that would subdue his agitation. "I do not mind speaking my mind, and my opinion is that Mr. Marchant is not to be depended upon."

"In what way?"

"Why, I believe that in the end he will play us false."

"But," said Lord Harcliffe, more impatiently than before, "what possible grounds can you have for such an opinion? Don't I tell you that the man is not a stranger to me as he is to you, but well known, and to Pharoah also."

"No matter. I distrust him, and I am one that can form a pretty good opinion of either man or horse at the first glance."

The Black Highwayman uttered an ejaculation of contempt.

"Look here," said Isaac, with deep earnestness, and trying hard to keep calm, "you cannot deny this: Mr. Marchant has agreed to set the captain free, has he not?"

"Of course he has."

"And what has induced him to do so? Why, the promise and part payment of a large sum of money."

"Well?"

"Well! I don't think it is well! You know the feeling of the authorities in the matter—their determination to hang the captain, let what will befall?"

"Yes, we know all that well enough. Why repeat it?"

"Because," said Isaac—and here he shook like an aspen leaf—"because, suppose they should offer Mr. Marchant double the money to keep away—to wash his hands of the affair—than we shall give for him to carry it out: what then?"

"What then?" said the Black Highwayman, who was not ruffled in the least. "Why, I think such an unlikely and improbable, not to say impossible, event is not worthy of a moment's consideration."

Isaac had so little expected that this would be the result of the communication of his dread that he could say no more.

He sank down in the nearest chair, and, covering his face with his hands, remained profoundly still.

The landlord fidgeted about.

"Confound it, Isaac!" he said, after a long, uncomfortable pause. "What could have put such an idea into your head? You ought to have kept it to yourself. I shall have no more peace now. I was just beginning to get resigned."

"It is a pity if it causes you much uneasiness," said Lord Harcliffe, "because there is no foundation for it whatever. I will pledge myself that Mr. Marchant will not play us false."

"You ought to know, of course," answered Tom, but yet the terrible doubt Isaac had suggested rankled in his mind and would not be appeased.

Beyond this nothing of any moment or importance occurred until the morning of the day appointed for the trial.

The whole party was up betimes, for it was determined that all should be present at the Court.

The landlord's aid was again called in to disguise them, and this having been done, they departed singly to their destination.

Lord Harcliffe was the first to arrive.

The doors were not yet open, but a dense crowd had assembled, and it was evident that already more people had collected than the Court could hold.

The others came up soon afterwards, and, according to a preconcerted arrangement, tried hard to get close to each other.

Then the doors were opened.

The rush was terrific.

But of all present none were so deeply anxious to gain admittance as our friends, and the efforts they made in consequence enabled them to overcome the resistance of the others.

The doors were speedily closed again, but not until the whole of Captain Hawk's friends had succeeded in gaining admittance to the building, and, as they believed, without the least suspicion of their identity having been excited.

CHAPTER CXXX.

CAPTAIN HAWK IS BROUGHT TO TRIAL, FOUND GUILTY, AND CONDEMNED TO DEATH.

EAGER indeed were the glances which the four friends cast around them as soon as ever they found themselves fairly within the precincts of the Court-house.

The building was densely packed, save and except those places which had been reserved for the administrators of the law and their assistants.

The business of the Court would not commence for something like another hour.

The time seemed long, and it was a positive relief when the first lawyer made his appearance.

This was about half an hour before the opening of the Court.

One by one the various officials dropped in and took up their stations.

The jury was brought and duly marshalled into the jury-box according to form.

Finally the judge, accompanied by several other persons, emerged from an adjoining room, the entrance to which was covered with a red curtain.

A deep silence fell on the whole multitude

Then the usual ceremonies which accompany the opening of the Court were gone through.

In the meanwhile, need we say with what anxiety Captain Hawk's friends watched the entrance of every person into the Court?

They were looking for Mr. Marchant, but up to this moment he had not put in an appearance.

Isaac looked grim and gloomy, as though he was fully prepared for such an event.

Tom Beckford was harassed and anxious, while Lord Harcliffe, despite the confidence he had expressed and felt, could not subdue a slight sensation of uneasiness.

What, he thought, if some of the authorities, having got wind of the affair, had taken violent means to remove Mr. Marchant?

Such an occurrence as that he considered was far more likely than the supposition Isaac had made.

He was aroused from these unpleasant speculations by hearing the prisoner called for.

An anxious pause followed, and then Captain Hawk made his appearance in the dock.

Lord Harcliffe was much struck by the alteration in his companion's appearance, though now he looked actually well compared with his looks when examined before the magistrate.

But although the prisoner was thin and looked ashy pale, yet it could be seen that he stood firmly and was in no need of assistance from others.

Lord Harcliffe noticed that his first act was to glance round the Court.

His eyes ranged swiftly over the dense mass of faces upturned towards him, but it did not appear that he recognised one of them.

If he did, no sign of it showed itself on his pale features.

His next proceeding was to scan the faces of the various lawyers sitting and standing round the table in front of the judge's seat.

It seemed as though he was looking for Mr. Marchant, and a palpable look of disappointment settled upon his face when he discovered that that gentleman was not present.

Sir Thomas Walker was accommodated with a seat on the bench at no great distance from the judge.

No words can describe the look of malignity which he bent upon the prisoner.

And mingled with that look was an expression of triumph for which neither Captain Hawk nor his friends could exactly account.

There was, however, but little time for consideration upon this or any other subject.

The business of the Court began.

It would be tedious to describe with minuteness all the formalities gone through on an occasion like this.

In the usual manner the prisoner was called upon to listen to the indictment as read by the Clerk of the Arraigns, the only intelligible portion of which was the concluding words.

"Prisoner at the bar," the clerk said, as he folded up the parchment which he had been reading, "do you plead guilty or not guilty?"

The silence in the Court was profound.

In a clear voice, which had not the slightest tremor perceptible in any of its tones, Captain Hawk replied:

"Not guilty."

The plea was duly recorded, and then the Clerk of the Arraigns sat down.

A momentary pause succeeded, during which the counsel for the prosecution arranged his papers and prepared to deliver his address.

But still there were no signs of Mr. Marchant.

Lord Harcliffe felt a painful tugging at his heart which all his stoicism and firmness could not keep under.

The absence of the lawyer at this juncture was most inexplicable and embarrassing.

In spite of himself, the dreadful supposition started by Isaac rung in his ears like a death-knell.

What if it should be true?

What a terrible false position they were in!

After neglecting so much precious time, what possible hope would there be of effecting the captain's release?

As before, these speculations were cut short by the inflexible course of events.

It was some relief to him, too, to fix his attention as far as he was able upon the events which were occurring around him.

The counsel for the prosecution settled his gown with an imposing and self-sufficient air.

"My lord and gentlemen of the jury."

These were his first words after he had taken a comprehensive glance around him.

The tones in which he spoke were flippant to a degree, as though the matter on hand, however important it might seem, was to a man of his abilities the merest trifle in the world.

He cleared his voice after the utterance of the preliminary words, and resumed:

"It would be idle for me to suppose that the prisoner at the bar is not known to you, and therefore any attempt on my part to describe him, or enlarge upon the enormities he has committed in the course of his long career would only be tedious and an unwarrantable loss of time.

"You must know full well from common and general repute who and what this Captain Hawk, as he is called, really is.

"Without any description from my lips you must know him to be about the most daring depredator of modern times.

"The crimes which he has committed are beyond all power of enumeration, but I may make bold to say that there are several persons in reach of my voice at this moment who have sustained serious money losses at his hands, besides having been put in bodily fear of their lives.

"It is not my purpose, however, to dilate upon this point, because, like a description of his crimes, it would only be to repeat that which you all know already.

"But, gentlemen of the jury, it often happens that there is a miscarriage of justice when such a prisoner as the one before you is placed upon his trial.

"The very multiplicity of their offences creates the difficulty.

"It becomes frequently well-nigh a matter of impossibility to bring home to them one distinct charge.

"What a dreadful thing it would be, gentlemen of the jury, if such a thing as this were to happen with respect to such a character as the prisoner at the bar! Suppose from some defect of evidence he was to be set free again after such trouble and expense, not only of money but of life, as there has been to capture him!

"I only mention this to you, gentlemen of the jury, that you may reflect upon it.

"I am happy to say I am in a position to remove from your breasts all apprehension of the occurrence of such an event as this. There is not ground sufficient for the smallest amount of alarm.

"Thanks to the intelligence and foresight of the individual through whose exertions this 'captain' has been brought to justice, we have a charge against him of so clear a character that not all the legal acumen and ability in the land would be able to throw the faintest shadow of a doubt upon it."

Having uttered these triumphant words, he settled his gown, which somehow would persist in getting awry upon his shoulders.

"My lord and gentlemen of the jury, I feel that I have already said more in the shape of introduction than there was occasion for. But let that pass.

"What I have to do now is something much more simple: it is to relate to you how and under what circumstances this 'Captain Hawk' was captured, and afterwards to call the various witnesses, who will depose on oath as to the truth of all that I allege."

From the deep and visible interest which these words created it would seem as though the circumstances preceding and attendant upon Captain Hawk's capture were but imperfectly and uncertainly known to the world at large.

The counsel for the prosecution, probably with the idea of contributing additional impressment to what he said, affected to refer to the voluminous parchment in his hand.

It was in the silence which reigned during this operation, and while all eyes were bent upon him, that Lord Harcliffe heard a hoarse voice whisper in his ear:

"*Who was right about Mr. Marchant? Where is he now?*"

He had no need to turn round to ascertain from whose lips those terrible words came.

It was Isaac who had spoken them.

He had borne his anxiety until it had become absolutely intolerable, and then, with extreme difficulty, had contrived to force a passage to the spot where Lord Harcliffe was standing.

So intent was every person upon what the counsel for the prosecution was doing, and so desirous of catching the next words that would fall from his lips, that no notice was taken of the whispered communication.

A deep frown settled upon Lord Harcliffe's face.

"*Where is he, I say?*" whispered Isaac again.

"Have patience," was the angry answer. "Fool that you are! Do you want to ruin everything, and bring destruction upon us all?"

Thus rebuked, but by no means satisfied, Isaac shrank back, for he had all along been suffering from the morbid dread that he should say or do something that would imperil the captain's cause.

Tom Beckford, however, who had also noted the non-appearance of Mr. Marchant, suffered the most agonising suspense conceivable.

But he was so placed that he could not move a single step, though, if this had not been so, it is questionable whether he would have run the risk of addressing the Black Highwayman.

Moreover, everything that took place at the trial from first to last had for him a terribly fascinating and absorbing kind of interest.

Amid a profound and deathlike stillness, the counsel for the prosecution continued his address:

"My lord and gentlemen of the jury,—

"It must be tolerably well known to you how strenuous and increasing the efforts of the authorities have been for a long time past to capture and bring to justice the notorious prisoner at the bar.

"The result that continually and perpetually waited on their endeavours was defeat; but in spite of that they continued their exertions, being stimulated rather than dismayed and put out of heart.

"But all would not do.

"Try as they would, this highwayman, aided by the fleetness of his steed, eluded them, and at last it was felt that the only means by which they could hope to succeed was by the adoption of stratagem.

"Stratagem therefore was employed; and now I come to the most interesting portion of the whole narration.

"The police officers assembling together, thought matters over from first to last, and they planned the following scheme:—

"Two police officers disguised themselves as travellers, and rode along the high-road where the highwayman was expected to appear.

"The remainder of the troop, keeping behind the hedges on both sides of the road, followed their two disguised comrades wherever they went.

"At last their trouble was rewarded.

"But instead of one highwayman, they were attacked by two.

"For this they were quite unprepared, and no one will feel surprised at hearing that it slightly embarrassed them and deranged their excellent plan.

"However, the prisoner at the bar, riding up to the two travellers, as he thought they must be, cried out to them to stand and deliver upon peril of their lives.

"According to agreement, a purse was handed over, and no sooner was this done than an instant attack was made.

"But from what I have said, and from causes which will appear more fully in the evidence, the attack was not so immediately successful as had been anticipated.

"The fact was, that the officers, like the well-known sportsman in the fable, wanted to bring down both birds, only, more lucky than he, they brought down one of them.

"The prisoner at the bar, as you will hear, was slightly wounded in the scuffle; but now I am informed he has completely recovered from his hurt, and that it is questionable whether he was ever better or stronger in his life.

"You will not have failed to observe, gentlemen of the jury," he continued, "that the scheme adopted makes the guilt of the prisoner a fact beyond all possibility of doubt: no sophistry whatever could make it less apparent. In the most imprudent manner conceivable he took the purse, and consigning it to his pocket, rode off with it.

"Now I don't know whether I need inform you that the peculiar circumstances under which this was all done makes no difference to the fact of the committal of the robbery. In these cases we must look at the motives which actuate the conduct of the offender, and all present cannot fail to be well aware of what those motives were. And now, gentlemen of the jury, I feel that in a case so clear as the present I should only be insulting you were I to dwell any more upon the details of it. I should not have spoken to so great a length as I have done already but for the unusual amount of interest and notoriety appertaining to the prisoner at the bar. My parting words, however, will be the expression of the hope that no false notions of romance, no prompting of sentiment, should contribute towards the averting of justice from the man who has by the enormity and number of his crimes made himself a terror to every road in England."

Having brought his rambling and flippant address to a conclusion, the counsel for the prosecution sat down with a self-satisfied smile upon his lips.

There was then a general buzz in the Court, which continued without much diminishment in spite of the vociferations of the crier.

Up to this moment even Lord Harcliffe had not lost his faith in Mr. Marchant.

But at the same time he was wholly unable to account for his conduct in thus absenting himself.

It was simply inexplicable.

Isaac was in despair, and looked as though he had in contemplation the perpetration of some more than usually desperate deed.

But his despair was mingled with that kind of triumph which everyone is apt to feel on finding that one's own opinion was really right.

As for Captain Hawk, he maintained his calmness in a manner that was most surprising to all those unacquainted with the circumstances.

He had barely had patience to listen to the rodomontade delivered by the prosecuting counsel.

His only anxiety consisted in his wonder of what could have become of Mr. Marchant.

But it did not seem that he looked upon his absence with any particular dread.

The fact was, he felt satisfied with the assurance he had received that he should be rescued.

As for the trial, he had all along believed that it was but an idle form, and that it could come to but one conclusion.

CHAPTER CXXXI.

ISAAC VOWS TO HAVE HIS REVENGE ON MR. MARCHANT.

It is not our purpose to relate at length the depositions of the various witnesses.

They had all well learned by heart what they had to say, and their responses were as nearly as possible in the same words as had been used in the preliminary examination before the magistrate.

As the first witness was about to leave the witness-box, the prisoner was requested to say whether he had any questions to ask.

He replied in the negative.

One after another the others appeared, until at length the counsel for the prosecution rose and said:

"My lord and gentlemen of the jury, that is my case, and I hope you will not flinch from the duty you have before you of ridding the country of one of its greatest pests."

The judge then, with somewhat indecent haste, commenced the summing-up.

Many noticed that he never once inquired whether the

prisoner had any legal adviser, nor did he, as was often done, single out some barrister at the table to conduct the defence in the ordinary manner.

Nor was the animosity he displayed towards the prisoner less remarkable, and his delivery could only be characterised correctly by the word abusive.

He concluded in the usual manner; and the usher of the Court, with a nasal twang, bade the jury consider their verdict.

This was no less a form than the rest, for even before they had taken their seats they had made up their minds to pronounce the word "Guilty."

But, for credit's sake, they did just turn round and whisper to each other.

Then the foreman, sitting down, looked hard at the judge.

"Gentlemen of the jury," said the Clerk of the Arraigns, "have you considered your verdict?"

"We have."

"Do you find the prisoner at the bar guilty or not guilty?"

"Guilty."

The words were followed by a kind of suppressed sob.

The sound was caused by each one of the spectators in the Court drawing in his breath with a strong inspiration.

Captain Hawk was observed to close his fingers with a tighter grasp upon the front of the dock when the verdict was pronounced, but he manifested no other symptom of emotion.

The Clerk of the Arraigns recorded the verdict; and then, turning his gaze full upon Captain Hawk, he said:

"Prisoner at the bar, you have heard the verdict just pronounced by twelve of your countrymen. Have you anything to say why judgment should not be pronounced upon you according to law?"

The silence which reigned while these words were spoken was most intense.

The judge cleared his voice, and was about to proceed, when Captain Hawk's voice checked him.

The prisoner spoke in clear, rich tones, which vibrated to every heart.

His piercing eyes were fixed upon the judge.

"I have this to say," he said: "I protest that I have not had a fair trial, and that judgment should not be pronounced. What the witnesses have sworn to to-day is essentially false. I assert that I did not stop the disguised police officers, nor did I take any purse!"

The judge made an effort to interrupt him at this point; but the captain raised his voice, and went on:

"I was promised legal aid," he said, "but I had no opportunity of conferring with the legal adviser who came to see me. From some cause, I know not what, he is not present to-day, and I am found guilty undefended. Not that I regret this much, or that I consider it will make the least difference; but the truth should be known, and I wish my words to go forth to the world. I say, then, that this trial is a mockery and a farce, and that the determination to hang me in spite of everything was come to beforehand, and that——"

But here not only the judge but the Clerk of the Arraigns and the usher interrupted him, and what further words escaped his lips were inaudible.

As soon as anything like order was restored, the judge commenced his summing-up.

Captain Hawk folded his arms and stood in disdainful silence.

"Prisoner at the bar," said the judge, with much asperity of tone, "the remarks you have just made can only be regarded by any right-minded person as an aggravation of your numerous offences. I maintain that you have had a fair and impartial trial, and for my own part I must say that I never had less trouble, and never felt more satisfaction, in pronouncing sentence than I do at this present moment. Your crimes have been manifold and patent to all the world. You have made it almost impossible for any of his Majesty's subjects to travel with the least degree of safety along any of the high-roads in these dominions; and in dooming you to the death you so righteously deserve, I feel that I am doing society an inestimable service by exterminating you as we should any creature that proved noxious to us. The sentence of this Court upon you is, that you be taken back to the prison whence you came, and thence to the place appointed for your execution; and I hope you will make the best of the short time that yet remains to you on earth to come to a better frame of mind; and may Heaven have mercy upon you."

They were fearful words.

They seemed to ring in the prisoner's ears, and sear both heart and brain.

He gave an appalled glance around.

Was it possible he was taking almost his last look of humanity, and that in a short period of time he should cease to form part and parcel of this living, breathing world?

The feeling which oppressed him at this moment is one which can neither be described nor felt.

The jailer behind tapped him on the arm.

He gave another glance round.

His lips opened as though he was about to speak.

But the officials behind him, fearful probably of the effect which his words would produce, began dragging him away.

It was just then that Isaac, who, as one may say, had stood like one half stunned during the latter part of the proceedings, felt himself irresistibly compelled to speak.

"Don't despair yet!" he said, in tones that rang through the Court. "All are not lost who are in danger!"

The confusion which followed upon this was something awful.

In the midst of it the officials succeeded in dragging the prisoner down the narrow, winding steps by which communication to the dock was had.

The doors of the Court were thrown open, and there was a general move towards them.

Lord Harcliffe cursed Isaac in his heart for having spoken out as he did.

But it could not be helped; and as it was over he only hoped that they would all be able to pass out at the doors unrecognised.

Lord Harcliffe, too, was terribly annoyed at the result of what he had done, and his vexation was increased by the triumphal air which he was certain Isaac would assume.

That Mr. Marchant, too, should prove so utterly base amazed him beyond expression.

In spite of all that he had seen and heard, admitting, as it did, of no sort of doubt, he was nevertheless incredulous.

He could not bring himself to believe in the reality of the events which had taken place around him on that eventful morning.

Slowly but gradually the crowd carried him towards the door, and the nearer he approached the greater his uneasiness became.

Should he be recognised and seized, it would indeed be farewell to any hopes of extricating the captain, even if it were not so already.

The injudicious words uttered by Isaac might have had the effect of putting the officials on the alert.

But the door was passed in safety, though, even after he had crossed the threshold and fairly gained the open street, he was unable to believe in the reality of his good fortune.

But at the first opportunity he dived down a narrow turning, so as to get out of sight as quickly as possible, and then made his way towards the Greyhound.

More than one curious glance was cast upon him; but he was allowed to go on unchallenged.

Of his companions he knew nothing.

He could only hope that they had been as fortunate in getting away as he had himself.

It was quite dark by the time he reached the old inn, which, somehow or other, notwithstanding the short time he had known it, had become wonderfully familiar to him.

When within a hundred yards of the door he was overtaken by Pharoah.

Lord Harcliffe's first act was to inquire of him if he knew how the other two had fared.

A negative reply was given.

But then it had been agreed upon that they should separate immediately upon issuing from the Court, and that they should make their way in different directions to the inn.

[ISAAC OFFERS HIMSELF AS MR. PRICE'S SUBSTITUTE.]

"I heard nothing in the shape of disturbance," Pharoah answered; "and no doubt they will rejoin us shortly."

Hardly had he spoken the words when they heard a voice not far off exclaim:

"Halt a moment, and I will be with you. Confound it! how you step out!"

They recognised the voice as being that of the landlord; and upon hearing him speak they at once came to a standstill.

There was a look of deep distress and concern upon the landlord's countenance; and when he spoke again the tones of his voice betrayed how deeply he was moved.

"What a disastrous termination to our plan!" he said. "Who could have thought now that Isaac's suspicions were so near the truth?"

"Do you know where he is?"

"No; I have not seen him since we left the Court; but no doubt he will rejoin us ere long."

"I don't know that."

"Why?"

"Because he has been itching all the time to take the control and direction of things into his own hands; and because we have not suffered it is the real secret of his discontent."

"And do you think that he will take this opportunity of trying to do something on his own account?"

"I do; I think he would be glad to feel himself free from us."

The landlord was hardly prepared to judge Isaac so harshly as this.

But he said nothing, for just then they entered the inn.

The landlord walked in boldly, for he fully believed that all his customers would be at Huntingdon discussing the business of the day.

The old inn was void of guests.

He led the way towards the room they had habitually occupied, and in which he had ordered a repast to be spread in readiness for them on their return.

Despite their cares, they had fasted quite long enough to make the substantial delicacies acceptable.

"If you will take my advice," said the landlord, "you will sit down and make as good a meal as you can. After that we shall be in a better condition to talk over what is to be done."

"You are right," Lord Harcliffe answered. "We cannot assist the captain by neglecting ourselves."

"Certainly not. And so I propose that we don't mention the subject till the meal is over."

This was agreed to.

Ere they had done much more than make a commencement, Isaac entered.

When he saw how they were engaged, the frown which had contracted his brows deepened into a scowl.

"Ha!" he said, with extreme bitterness. "Feast away—drink away! No doubt you are satisfied with what you have done. The captain now may help himself or not, just as he pleases. Bah! But I have done."

What Lord Harcliffe would have said to this speech is doubtful.

He paused as though to command himself before he did speak; and Tom Beckford took advantage of the pause to interfere.

"Isaac," he said, "you will admit that you are no truer a friend to the captain than I am; nor are you any more anxious for his safety and escape than I am. That we should have been unfortunate hitherto is a misfortune—not a fault. But there is time yet. Make your mind easy—the captain will be free."

"But I am not to be fobbed off with easy words," was the surly rejoinder. "I take such speeches for what they are worth. Misfortune indeed! A rare misfortune, truly! I call it a wilful fault! And you have lost time which you can never recover."

"If it were not for the oath of friendship I have sworn with Captain Hawk," said Lord Harcliffe, with a coolness and calmness that seemed all the more remarkable from its contrast with Isaac's excitement—"if it were not for that," he repeated, "I should either wash my hands entirely of the affair, or else insist that you should be excluded from our councils."

The landlord interposed again.

"Isaac," he said, "don't be blind to reason. Keep your feelings a little under sway. Answer me at least one question: Are we likely to help the captain by quarrelling among ourselves?"

Isaac was silent.

"Since you will admit that, do be content to follow my advice. Sit down with us, and take that nourishment which is necessary to enable us to carry out any plans. After that we will give ourselves up exclusively to the consideration of what we can do for the captain."

Isaac at first refused.

But after a few more words from the landlord he consented to sit down and join them, on conditions that nothing should be said until the meal was finished.

But Isaac was too full to swallow half a dozen mouthfuls.

To him it seemed as though the captain was as good as out of the world already.

"It's no good," he said, as he pushed away his plate—"I can't eat. It don't seem right to be sitting down so comfortable at such a time. There's one thing: if they do hang the captain, I shall want them to hang me too."

Isaac's devotion and attachment to his master commanded the respect of all present.

"You are a worthy, faithful fellow," said Lord Harcliffe, extending his hand, which, after a momentary struggle, Isaac grasped.

"Now," he said, "we are all friends again, and rely upon it, it will be best in every way for us to discuss this matter quietly."

"Very well. But as for that Mr. Marchant, I'll——"

"Don't condemn him too hastily."

"Why——"

"Be calm, my friend. My faith in him is unshaken."

"What! after——"

"Yes, after all that has happened."

"How, then, do you account——"

"I believe his absence was caused by his being kept out of the way by the authorities."

"I don't," said Isaac, hotly—"I don't and can't think that. He has sold us. I feel it—I know it! And only just let me catch sight of him once again, and I won't leave him till——"

Isaac was interrupted by the opening of the door, and then, lo! who should enter the room but Mr. Marchant himself.

CHAPTER CXXXII.

RELATES WHAT FOLLOWED THE ARRIVAL OF MR. MARCHANT.

It was not until Mr. Marchant had shut the door behind him that Isaac recovered himself sufficiently from his shock of surprise to be sure that his eyes had not deceived him.

But when he felt certain Mr. Marchant veritably stood before him, he uttered a howl such as one might expect to come from the throat of a hungry and infuriated wolf.

At the same time he sprung forward and seized the astonished lawyer by the throat.

"Villain—wretch!" he yelled, "who could have believed your impudence would have carried you so far as this! But you shall suffer dearly for the trick you have played us! You need not struggle, for I don't intend to loose you till I have well bruised every bone in your body!"

Isaac, we need hardly tell the reader, was thoroughly in earnest, and but for the vigorous and speedy interference of the others he would have mauled Mr. Marchant very severely.

With some ado the panting combatants were parted, and Isaac, by the main strength of the other three, pushed back into an arm-chair and held there.

As for Mr. Marchant, the attack upon him had been so sudden and unexpected that it had not given him a chance of defence, and he now stood puffing and blowing like a huge grampus.

"Curse it all!" he gasped, at length. "What does that blackguard fellow mean? Is this the way you treat a friend?"

The utterance of this last word exasperated Isaac to such a degree, that it was as much as ever they could do to retain him in his seat.

As soon as comparative tranquillity was obtained, Lord Harcliffe said, sternly:

"Remember you have your behaviour to account for, and you will have to give a wonderfully good explanation to satisfy us."

"You won't satisfy me, so you need not think it!" bawled Isaac.

"If he speaks again," said Lord Harcliffe to the lawyer, "just ram my felt hat into his mouth."

"I won't be quiet," said Isaac. "I am determined to make that scoundrel suffer for his rascality! He has deceived us all! He has taken your money under false pretences, and has put an end to all hope of saving the captain!"

It was rather strange to see how little moved Mr. Marchant was when these vituperations and accusations were heaped upon him.

Certainly there was nothing in his aspect that denoted a guilty man, or even that he had done anything for which he could be blamed.

Having recovered pretty well from the attack, he now approached with Lord Harcliffe's hat tightly and conveniently rolled up.

Isaac, to save himself, closed his teeth savagely.

"That will be just as well," said Mr. Marchant. "And now, if you will only have patience and give me a little time, I will convince you that you have nothing at all to complain of, and that your project is in a fair way of being accomplished."

At hearing this, Isaac could not contain himself.

"Oh, monstrous!" he cried. "Nothing to complain of—nothing to——"

Mr. Marchant made a vigorous thrust at him with the rolled-up felt hat, and Isaac only closed his mouth just in time.

"It sounds extraordinary, I know," said Mr. Marchant, with the same unruffled air. "But, then, how often it happens that those things which appear the most difficult are the easiest of solution; and never was there a better instance of it than the present."

"I must say," remarked the Black Highwayman, "that my dependence on your good faith was never once shaken."

"Thanks for that."

"But at the same time, had I not known you so well, I should perhaps have had the same suspicions, and have been just as violent as our friend Isaac here."

Isaac gnashed his teeth, but as Mr. Marchant made a threatening gesture with the hat, he remained silent.

"I had my fears," said Lord Harcliffe: "my dread was that some of the officers, knowing your intention, had laid violent hands upon you for the purpose of keeping you fast confined until all danger of losing their prisoner was over."

Mr. Marchant's eyes glittered and twinkled while Lord Harcliffe spoke.

"No," he said, "it was not so bad as that. I did not even dream of that danger, or I should have taken certain precautions. No matter, though. All is one so far as that is concerned."

"But your explanation?" said Harcliffe. "How, after what you said to us, can you justify your absence from the Court-house to-day?"

"Yes; do that if you can!" said Isaac, starting up from his chair. "But I defy you! No lying will serve you! I defy you, I say, and——"

He was thrust back into his seat again, and, as before, compelled to preserve silence by the felt hat being held close to his lips.

"Now that we are silent once again, I will show you that I both can and will justify my conduct. I admit that my intentions have changed; but you won't be at all astonished when you hear all; and I promise you I am going to make a clean breast of it."

"We shall be glad to hear all," said Lord Harcliffe, seriously; "for those who do not know you would feel but slight satisfaction, I fancy, in all that has taken place up to this moment."

Having treated Isaac with another menacing gesture, Mr. Marchant replied:

"As I told you on a former occasion, I paid a visit to Captain Hawk in his cell. What passed between us you, of course, remember perfectly."

"Yes."

"Well, there I stopped—that is, I mean, I did not tell you any more. But I mentioned, did I not, about a certain Bow Street magistrate, sent down here with a special commission to settle the captain's hash?"

"You mean Sir Thomas Walker?"

"I do; but at the same time, excuse me for remarking that I think it by far the more prudent not to mention names."

"Perhaps so; but proceed."

"I can reproach you also with a want of candour; and if I wanted anything to plead in justification of what I had done I should make use of it."

"To what do you allude?"

"Why, you never told me what a trick this precious captain had played the worthy magistrate, and that in consequence he had imbibed a deadly hate for him which could only be appeased by his death on the scaffold."

"Well?"

"Well, I say you never told me a word about that. Perhaps it's as well you didn't, for if you had said the magistrate has a personal feeling against the prisoner, and that nothing but death can appease the cravings of his revenge, I should have backed out of the affair, as I should have considered getting the captain off as an impossibility."

"Let me hear further."

"Oh! how can you have patience?" said Isaac.

As before, though, he was summarily silenced.

"It is quite as well," continued Mr. Marchant, "that we should not know everything always. I shall ever remember the present instance."

"So you may," said Lord Harcliffe. "But don't you think you are an unreasonably long time in coming to the point?"

"No, I was not aware I was tedious."

"Time is short," said Lord Harcliffe; "and we shall be none the less pleased if your explanation is compressed into a few words."

"Very good."

"What your caution had kept quiet I was speedily made acquainted with. On leaving the cell where I had exchanged those few words with the captain, I was accosted by no less a personage than Sir Thomas Walker himself."

"Indeed!"

"You may well be surprised. We knew each other perfectly well, though we had never had any conversation before. I need not repeat word for word what passed; it will do if I give the substance of it, I suppose?"

"Yes—yes. Go on."

"Then he began by saying he supposed he was correct in supposing that it was not through any feeling of personal friendship that I had come forward on Captain Hawk's behalf, but that I was induced to take up his defence on the chance of earning a considerable sum of money."

"And what did you tell him then?"

"As I wished to know what it was he had to say, I told him that his surmise was perfectly correct."

"And what followed?"

"He merely said that as it was purely a pecuniary matter he should have no trouble in arranging matters satisfactorily, and ended by making an appointment."

"And did you go to it?"

"Certainly I did."

"You ought to have let us know this."

"Nay, pardon me—I am of a totally different opinion."

"Well, it can't be helped now. Go on."

"I went at the hour specified; and then, having taken care to see that we were entirely private, he came close to me, with a confidential air:

"'Now,' he said, 'I am about to ask you a plain and straightforward question, and all depends upon whether you give me a plain and straightforward reply.'

"I told him of course I should be most happy to be perfectly frank with him.

"'Then,' said he, 'I want you to tell me what confidence you feel in your client's case. Do you feel any amount of certainty that you will be able to get him off?'

"'Yes,' I said, 'I am about as sure of that as a man well could be of anything which has not actually come to pass.'

"'You are?' he said.

"I assured him I spoke the truth.

"'You have had a good large retaining fee, I'll be bound,' he said, after a pause, 'or you would never have come forward in the affair at all.'

"'I don't deny that.'

"Then he paused again, as though he had got something he wanted to say to me, but hardly knew how to utter it.

"I am a man of the world," added Mr. Marchant, with a chuckle, "and I have seen a thing or two in my day. I guessed to a trifle what the nature of his communication would be, and resolved to help him along with it.

"'Your worship,' I said, 'must be well aware that a case of this sort is a commercial speculation. I am furnished with a very capital defence—one which can hardly fail to secure the acquittal of the prisoner.'"

"You said that?" ejaculated Lord Harcliffe, in great surprise.

"I did, I assure you."

"And what then?"

"I told him that the amount offered was very large, and that the two had quite won me over, though I wound up by saying that my inclinations went quite another way.

"He guessed my meaning pretty well.

"'You mean to say, then,' he said, 'that the payment of a sufficiently large sum of money would induce you to throw up the case?'

"'Precisely,' said I; 'because, in the event of such an unlikely thing happening, I should be saved a great deal of trouble, and escape being brought into bad odour by appearing in Court as his defender.'

"'Just so,' he replied. 'You have put the case fairly. Now there are certain personal reasons which make me determined to have this man's life. I must and will have my revenge satisfied! I could never know rest again if he lived after what has happened to me.'

"I professed a great deal of astonishment, and assured

him it was always my greatest pleasure to place myself in his service.

"'May I trust you?' he asked, anxiously

"'The highest bidder has my exclusive and most faithful services,' I replied. 'I never allow feeling or sentiment to interfere with my business.'

"'That is right,' he said. 'Now tell me what sum you have received for this case?'

"I told him.

"'Then,' said he, 'if you will keep away from the Court, I will give you a cheque for double the amount. As things are, I am certain as to the way in which the trial will terminate. Are you agreeable to do this? If so, say the word.'"

"Well?" exclaimed Lord Harcliffe, in loud tones, "and what reply did you make?"

"I told him I was perfectly agreeable," answered Mr. Marchant; "and so, without further demur, he wrote me a cheque and gave it me."

After this, it no longer became possible to keep Isaac in check.

He broke loose from those who held him, and commenced another desperate onslaught upon Mr. Marchant.

But that gentleman was not taken by surprise, as he was on the former occasion, and so he snatched up a chair and defended himself vigorously.

The others were in some doubt as to whether they should interfere or not.

It seemed at the first that Isaac was only doing what was just and right.

Lord Harcliffe, however, on a second thought, saw that Mr. Marchant had yet something in the background, or why should he have come there at all?

And it may be that the grudge he felt against Isaac had some influence with him.

Mr. Marchant used the heavy wooden chair with great resolution, and once brought it fairly on to Isaac's head with force sufficient, one would have thought, to stun an ox.

Isaac only shook himself, though it was quickly apparent that he felt the force of the blow rather severely.

The consequence was that the others were enabled by their united strength to force him down on to the chair again.

"Stop now!" said Lord Harcliffe, in commanding tones. "There has been enough of this, and I insist that Mr. Marchant may be allowed to finish his explanation without being again interrupted in any way."

"If you had insisted upon that in the first place," said Mr. Marchant, "I should have brought my narration to an end long ago."

"Well, proceed now."

"I consider, then, strange as it may seem at present, that I was quite justified in what I did. I took his cheque, got it cashed, and, true to my bargain, kept away from the Court. So you see that I am all that much the richer, and no one but the worthy magistrate any the worse off."

"You forget the captain."

"No, I don't; and I maintain that his position has not altered one bit."

"How! not altered?"

"No; for no matter what had been done or said at the trial, the result would have been the same, and Sir Thomas was a fool for having any doubts about it."

"Then how can you think of being able to keep your promise to us?"

"I am able, and I mean to do it."

"But you said by legal means."

"Truly did I," replied Mr. Marchant, with a chuckle; "but then, being a member of the legal profession, any means I adopt must be legal means, mustn't they? Ha, ha! You didn't think of that!"

CHAPTER CXXXIII.

MR. MARCHANT SATISFACTORILY VINDICATES HIS EXTRAORDINARY CONDUCT

Mr. Marchant laughed.

But he had the laughter all to himself.

Lord Harcliffe looked gloomy and vexed.

There was something too much like trickery and jugglery in the whole transaction to be satisfactory and pleasing to him.

"I see," said Mr. Marchant, reading his thoughts, "that you are not very well pleased, but I will undertake to change your opinions totally in the course of a very few moments if you will only have the patience to listen."

"I doubt it."

"It's only reasonable you should," said Mr. Marchant, calmly. "But now, then, to effect a magical change in your sentiments; for what I have to say"—and here his eyes twinkled with a brightness that was wonderful—"what I have to say will even make a convert of my violent friend in the arm-chair yonder."

Isaac gave a suppressed howl indicative of derision.

"Never mind. Just wait, that is all. You are surprised that I should make any terms with Sir Thomas; but you ought not to forget what I told you—namely, that my aim and object was to make as much money as ever I could out of the transaction."

"Go on—I am listening."

"Then before I made these terms with Sir Thomas I had quite satisfied myself that there was no earthly possibility of any human endeavours causing a verdict of not guilty to be brought in; but I deny I was obliged to tell Sir Thomas that. He was foolish enough to offer me a large sum of money merely that I might keep out of Court during the trial; and as I was positive I could do my client no good by being present, I should have been the biggest fool of the lot to have refused the money."

"Then," said Lord Harcliffe, "am I to understand that your plan for setting the captain at liberty is in no way affected by what has taken place up to the present minute?"

"Not in the faintest or slightest degree," was the emphatic answer. "Indeed, I had based my calculations upon circumstances turning out just as they have—excepting, of course, the additional profit Sir Thomas was kind enough to put in my way."

Despite the distrust which was now pretty generally felt towards Mr. Marchant, what he had last said produced a deep and very visible effect.

He saw this, and, like a politic general, resolved to increase it.

"Bear in mind," he said, "I have faithfully performed for Sir Thomas all that Sir Thomas required of me. It is important that you should not lose sight of that. Now, with you, I have promised, in consideration of a certain sum to be paid by you to me, to set Captain Hawk at liberty. That's right, isn't it?"

"It is."

"Very well, then—mark my words: *I'll do it!*"

"You will?"

"I will; and here's my hand upon it."

Lord Harcliffe took the extended palm, and then said:

"Now, Mr. Marchant, I have one thing to say to you which I feel sure will be shared in by all present. It is that you should be a little more explicit and comprehensible as regards your intentions, for we have all of us a very decided objection to working in the dark."

"Hear, hear!" said Isaac, whose feelings would not allow him to say more, so deeply excited had he become upon hearing there was a means of liberating the captain after all.

Breathlessly he waited for Mr. Marchant to unfold his scheme.

"I will take you entirely into my confidence," said Mr. Marchant; "you shall not have that cause of complaint any longer. At the same time, I think you will be inclined to acknowledge that it was much the best that I should keep you in the dark as to my real intentions, as I have so far."

"Why?"

"Because if I had laid out my plan at first there would have been probably at that time no end of discussion about it, all of which I have saved; and what is of more importance still, I have effectually prevented all fear of any of the particulars leaking out; and I must now inform you that one indispensable and requisite condition for the success of my plan is secrecy and silence."

"They are promised."

"Very well. This is my scheme: Captain Hawk is, as you know, condemned. He is watched over in his cell with even greater strictness and closeness than he was before. You must dismiss from your minds all hope of being able to get him out of the prison."

"How—what?"

Mr. Marchant held up his hand.

"Allow me my say," he said. "As you cannot get the captain out of prison, you must wait till he is brought out, which, I ought to tell you, will be on Thursday morning next: that is the day appointed for the execution."

Hearing this, a shiver ran through all Isaac's frame.

"Now, Price the hangman and his assistant will be sent for to-morrow. How they will travel I don't know; but they cannot avoid night overtaking them upon some point of their journey. You must watch your opportunity. You must make those men prisoners, and keep them securely so for four-and-twenty hours."

"I——"

"Wait a bit; you have not heard all yet. We will suppose that done. They will have Captain Hawk all ready for the ceremony; but there will be no hangman to be found: that will be difficulty and obstruction the first to the carrying out of their plans."

"But by no means an insuperable one."

"Perhaps not. But you have not heard all yet. Any way, the non-arrival of the hangman at the time appointed is certain to cause a great deal of confusion, and a great point will be gained if we can throw the authorities off their guard."

"I admit that; but you must not think that you can procure the postponement of the execution by this scheme. When they find the hangman does not come they will look out for a substitute; and as there are always men to be found ready to do anything for money, they will quickly find one."

"Perfectly true, and just what I look forward to and expect," said Mr. Marchant. "If we can reckon upon that, all will be well."

"Explain yourself."

"Well, then, one of you—the most skilful in disguises, and the one having the most nerve—must go to the jail on the morning of the execution, and offer to be the substitute hangman."

Isaac started up in an agony of wild impatience.

Mr. Marchant went on calmly laying down the details of his plan.

"This we will suppose to be done, for I don't see anything to hinder it. The journey to the place of execution will be commenced, Captain Hawk, strongly bound and guarded, will be placed in the cart——"

"Go on—go on!" said Lord Harcliffe, for even he was in a shiver of excitement. "Why do you pause, man?"

"In order that the details may make a proper impression on your minds."

"Then don't pause again for that reason, I beg."

"We will suppose the place appointed for the execution is reached—all around, we will suppose, orderly and still, except that as close as possible to the scaffold are a couple of men on horseback. One must be a friend of Captain Hawk's, and mounted on a good horse—say his own; the other must be seated on the captain's own steed, and be prepared to vacate the saddle the very instant it is found necessary. Do you understand that?"

"Pretty well; but finish."

"The other friend, who is acting the hangman's part, must contrive in a whisper to give the captain some idea of what is about to happen; then, at the critical moment, while pretending to be busy about the pinioning, he must have a keen knife in his hand, the bonds must be severed at one stroke, and the prisoner at the moment he finds himself free must make a desperate spring over the side of the cart. His mounted friends must do the rest. One must slip out of the saddle and quickly get the rescued prisoner into it—the other must accompany him in his flight. That is the plan."

While Mr. Marchant was speaking the silence had gradually been getting more and more intense, and it was not broken when he finished by saying:

"That is my plan."

A pause of some moments ensued.

The tremendous boldness and daring of the scheme took away all their breaths—paralysed them, in fact.

Oddly enough, Isaac was the first to recover himself—the first to make any movement.

Going straight up to where Mr. Marchant was sitting, he cried:

"Do me a favour—take up your chair again and give me another tap on the head with it."

"What for, man?"

"Because I'm a d—d fool, that's all! Give it me, and I shall be satisfied."

"No, no—I will satisfy you without that."

"How?"

"Just tell me you are sorry you judged so hastily, and promise not to jump to conclusions so readily another time. If you will I shall be content."

"Shall you? Then you are a ten times better fellow than I took you to be, and I am the d—der idiot—so that's settled agreeably."

"You like my plan, then?"

"Immensely."

"You think it will succeed?"

"I am certain."

Isaac's enthusiasm and confidence knew no bounds.

Turning to Lord Harcliffe, who had sat silent hitherto, he cried:

"Come, sir, what do you think of it?"

Lord Harcliffe paused before he answered:

"There is only one word by which I can characterise the scheme," he said.

"And what word's that?"

"Outrageous."

"Outrageous?"

"Yes—beyond all example and precedent."

"Then," said Mr. Marchant, "in those words you admit of its excellence. Everyone will be astounded. Such a thing has never been heard of before, and ere their amazement is over the bird will be flown—the prisoner will be gone. They will be all too paralysed to move a muscle."

Mr. Marchant expressed himself with great animation.

"I know a little about Captain Hawk," said the landlord, who had been a patient listener up to this point, "and I can safely take upon myself to say that if such a plan had been submitted to him he would have agreed to it at once."

"And I can vouch for the same," said Isaac.

Pharoah, who, according to his wont, had abstained from taking any part in the discussion, now, upon being appealed to, declared that he considered the plan appeared to have in it every requisite for success, and that he had little fear of failure if things turned out according to expectation.

Lord Harcliffe then spoke.

"I have purposely kept back the expression of my own opinion," he said, "from the fear that it might influence that of others in an undue manner. But now you have all spoken, I am free to speak my thoughts."

Mr. Marchant fixed his rat-like eyes upon the highwayman.

In point of fact, he valued Lord Harcliffe's opinion far before that of any of the others, and he was now deeply anxious to catch the next words that fell from his lips, though he tried hard to conceal it.

"My deliberate opinion," Lord Harcliffe said, "is that if the plan is tried success is certain."

"Hurrah!" cried Isaac—"hip, hip, hur——"

Mr. Marchant all through the long conversation had not laid down the hat, and now, just at the moment when Isaac's mouth was stretched open to its utmost extent, he stuffed it between his jaws.

His voice was choked in a moment.

"Excuse me for informing you," said Mr. Marchant, "that you were speaking more loudly than was discreet, and don't forget the old proverb of holloaing before you are out of the wood."

Isaac coughed violently for some moments, and could not say a word.

The efforts he made, however, not only brought the tears into his eyes, but made them roll down his cheeks.

Grasping Mr. Marchant's hand, he set to work shaking it in a way that would make one think he never meant to leave off.

"I am glad you are all pleased," exclaimed Mr. Marchant. "I am glad, of course, but not surprised. Such a scheme as that is worth a fortune, and whatever you may think, I will make bold to affirm that when Captain Hawk is made acquainted with all the details, and comes to know how his enemy, Sir Thomas, has been served, he will be delighted, and would hardly have had that missed for his chance of escape."

After this the conversation became so general and rapid, that it would be totally impossible to report it.

At times they would all be talking at once; but notwithstanding that, they would all understand each other in a most wonderful manner.

Perhaps this was because they were so very unanimous.

The more the plan was talked of, the more sanguine they were about its entire success.

Of course, it was much to count upon the whole of the authorities being taken so wholly by surprise as they undoubtedly would be.

And about the whole affair there was such a boldness and rapidity of action, that it did not seem to offer the slightest chance for resistance to be made.

Therefore it was resolved that the plan should be carried out to the very letter.

"Listen," said Mr. Marchant, endeavouring to obtain general attention: "I will undertake to learn when Price will start, how he will travel, and probably where will be the place best suited to the attack. Until you know that you must remain quite still where you are—the stiller the better. Never fear that I shall fail you: I sha'n't. Not only that, you will find that you will have something to do to talk over and arrange the minor details of the whole scheme. Every little particular must be settled beforehand. That is essential, and all I have done has been to chalk out the main outlines of the scheme.

CHAPTER CXXXIV.

THE HANGMAN AND HIS ASSISTANT ARE MADE SAFE PRISONERS BY CAPTAIN HAWK'S FRIENDS.

HAVING thus spoken, Mr. Marchant rose.

Lord Harcliffe, on behalf of himself and the rest, promised that all the suggestions made should be thoroughly and properly carried out.

"Then," said Mr. Marchant, "as the time between now and next Thursday morning can easily be counted by hours, you may suppose I shall have enough to do to gather the information I spoke of. Still I don't despair of doing it. To remain here any longer, though, would serve no good end. Consider the plan from first to last, and get what rest you are able, for you may look forward to having plenty of work before you to-morrow night."

After a repetition of his cautions and directions, and after a renewal of the promise made by all present not to stir until they saw or heard from him again, Mr. Marchant took his leave.

"I am downright ashamed of myself, that I am," said Isaac, "to think I should have harboured the suspicions I did against him!"

"Those regrets are useless now," said Lord Harcliffe. "Let us make use of the short time between now and morning in laying our plans."

The landlord would not allow this to be commenced until a fresh store of refreshments was laid in.

Then drawing up round the fire, they sat for hours conversing in low, anxious whispers.

It is not at all necessary to lay before the reader what they said.

The resolutions to which they came will be sufficiently apparent when we come to relate the incidents in the order in which they occurred.

It was a great satisfaction to all of them, however, to find that the lawyer's plan was one that worked out remarkably well.

The more they pondered over it, and the further the minor details were arranged, the stronger appeared the hopes, not to say certainties, of success.

Wearied out at length, they were all glad enough to avail themselves of the opportunity of snatching a few hours' repose.

This time even Isaac slept.

It may with safety be affirmed that to none of the others did the plan appear in such attractive colours.

The idea was one which he could fully grasp at and see his way towards carrying out.

When once their eyes fairly closed in slumber, it was pretty certain they would not awake for a considerable time—in fact, they did not until close upon sunset.

Then they were busy in making hasty preparations.

Isaac saw that the horses were all in proper order and condition for the road.

The noble creatures all looked improved by the rest they had had.

On re-entering the inn, Isaac found that Mr. Marchant had just arrived.

"All is well," he said, bending over the glowing fire and rubbing his hands briskly together. "Fortune favours our design in a manner I could hardly have dreamt of."

"How—how? Think how impatient we must all feel to hear your news!"

"The first thing is, I have learned that Price the hangman, accompanied by his assistant, started from London alone without any escort."

"Can it be possible?"

"Yes. It seems the foolish old fellow thinks he is more likely to get to his destination unseen and unsuspected by travelling in this fashion than any other. He used to go at one time by the stage-coach; but he was so often tormented by the passengers that he gave that up."

"And how is he travelling now?" asked Isaac, with feverish interest.

"It seems he has an old, tumble-down sort of a cart, drawn by a white mule. In this he sits, muffled up in no end of coats, while his assistant drives."

"We may make sure of nailing him, then," said Isaac, in great glee. "What a noddy he must be to run a risk of that sort! Why, we shall have no trouble at all."

"Let me advise you not to undervalue it," said Mr Marchant, seriously. "Price is a desperate man. He always carries arms, and is not wanting in courage to use them. Moreover, his companion is a desperate fellow, who would stick at nothing."

"Grant that," said Lord Harcliffe, "we should then be three to two."

"Oh, I am not afraid that you will fail in it. And now let me ask you whether you have arranged the details?"

"We have."

"And satisfactorily?"

"Quite so."

"That is all right. I shall not be able to show myself in the affair, you know; but still, if I can lend a hand I shall not hesitate to do so."

"Many thanks! And should the expedition meet with the success which we think it cannot fail to procure, your reward shall exceed by far the sum we promised."

"I leave that to your generosity entirely. I only want to know one thing."

"Name it."

"When all is over, what place shall we appoint for a settlement?"

"This very room, if it is agreeable to you," said the landlord, promptly.

"It is quite sufficient. I desire nothing further."

"One moment," said Lord Harcliffe. "Do you know for certain whether Price will drive along the high-road?"

"I am all but certain of it."

"Is it his custom, then?"

"Yes; and I am sure nothing has occurred to induce him to change it."

"And what time do you think we had better make a start?"

"As soon as you think it is dark enough for you to venture forth."

"That will soon be, then," said Isaac, who was standing near the window. "Even the weather seems inclined to favour us, for the clouds have come up so black and thick that darkness has set in half an hour sooner than it did yesterday."

"There is no doubt you are lucky. Every little circumstance seems to point to a favourable conclusion of the design."

"Let us depart, then," said Lord Harcliffe. "There is no good in remaining here any longer."

"None at all; but have you made up your minds where you shall bestow your prisoners?"

"No, truly, we have not, because——"

"Then excuse me for saying that you ought to have done so. There's no point so trifling as to deserve being overlooked."

"We will consider of it; and now, Isaac, will you get the horses in readiness?"

"That will I—never fear me. You could not set me about a more welcome task. I shall be ready in five minutes."

Isaac had made all the preparations he could beforehand, and now hurrying out, he succeeded in getting the three horses ready within the time he had named.

Patting the gray horse, he said:

"I shall have to give you up for to-night, old fellow. It grieves me a little to do so, but it can't be helped. Being three of us, and only three horses, Satan must be used; and it would not do for anyone else to be on his back than myself."

Just as he pronounced the words he heard the others approaching.

Mr. Marchant came along with the landlord to see them start.

Lord Harcliffe vaulted on to Phantom's back in a moment.

"I suppose this gray is intended for me?" said Pharoah. "Curse it! The one that threw me was just such a creature as we want; his fleetness was wonderful."

"You won't think so much of it after you have tried him," said Isaac, confidently.

He carefully seated himself on Satan's back as he spoke, and then, at the word from Lord Harcliffe, the whole party rode off.

After a momentary discussion, it was agreed that, out of consideration of his intimate knowledge of the locality, Isaac should be permitted to lead the way.

How proud the faithful fellow felt about it, and how very important he believed himself to be, the reader will not require to be told.

The keenest look-out was kept from the first moment, for, judging by the hour, they fully expected to meet Mr. Price without riding very far.

The horses were in magnificent condition; even the gray had thoroughly recovered himself from his fatigue.

The weather was about as uncomfortable as weather could be.

From time to time the moon would dimly show her face through the rifts of driving clouds.

There was a peculiar denseness in the air, which Lord Harcliffe remarked upon.

"That means snow," said Isaac. "I have studied the weather among other things, and I can tell we are about to have a heavy fall of it."

"What, now?"

"Certainly before morning."

"It's cold enough in all conscience. Push on a little faster, so that we can warm our blood a little."

"Wait a moment," answered Isaac. "The wind may have deceived me; but unless I make a very great mistake, I heard wheels approaching."

"Let us halt, then. Should it prove the persons we want, the rencounter could hardly have occurred in a better spot."

This was correct enough.

The high-road on one side was bordered by a dense plantation, composed for the most part of evergreens, so that in spite of the season of the year the foliage was dense in the extreme.

It was under the shadow of these trees, then, that the three horsemen pulled up in order to listen more attentively.

It did not take them a moment to come to the conclusion that Isaac was right.

Some light vehicle was coming from the direction of London.

The wheels rattled in an alarming manner, yet it did not seem that any particular progress was made.

"There's the conviction on my mind," said Isaac, in a suppressed voice, "that this can be no other than the very thing we want."

"Be silent and patient, and we shall soon know."

"Remember Mr. Marchant's caution about the old fellow's firearms," whispered Pharoah.

"Right. Silence!"

All three now almost suppressed their breathing.

Slowly and tediously the vehicle crawled on.

Presently the moon broke out with greater clearness than she had done hitherto.

At precisely the same time they caught a glimpse of the expected vehicle, and the first glance showed them that the animal in the shafts was a white one.

All doubt was now considered to be at an end.

As the mule came on at a kind of a shuffling walk, and as the moon still remained unobserved, the watchers were able to see the occupants of the cart very distinctly; and not only that, the vivid description Mr. Marchant had given of Price and his assistant made the recognition as certain as it was rapid.

Both men were smoking, and the one who drove occasionally uttered a peculiar grunt, which he accompanied by a smart stroke with a whip.

Neither seemed of any use so far as accelerating the speed of the mule was concerned.

The long-eared creature shogged on as before.

As for Price himself, he was so enveloped in overcoats that hardly any semblance to a human form was left.

Isaac commenced the attack.

As soon as the favourable moment came he dashed out from his place of concealment, and seizing the mule by the bridle, abruptly brought the cart to a standstill.

So sudden was the stoppage, that the two men were quite disconcerted, and before they could recover in the least Lord Harcliffe had seized the one and Pharoah the other.

"Don't resist," said the Black Highwayman. "If you do, it will be the worse for you. Keep still, and you will come to no hurt. Do you hear? If you resist, there is nothing but death."

"Och! murdher now! Help—help! Murdher! The divil!" bawled Mr. Price's assistant, whose strong brogue betrayed his nationality the moment he opened his lips. "Wirra now, Mr. Price, and what did I tell ye!"

A suppressed curse came from the hangman's lips.

But he made no attempt at resistance.

Doubtless he could see the folly of making the least attempt at it.

"Silence!" said Pharoah to the Irishman. "If you don't shut up that great gob of yours, I'll make you."

The threat was effectual.

"Now, Isaac," said Lord Harcliffe, "be quick with the ropes. If we linger here the chances are we shall be interrupted."

"All right. This blessed cross-bred Jerusalem pony will stand quiet enough, I know."

Isaac had been careful to provide himself with a quantity of strong rope, which he now produced, and by the aid of which he made Mr. Price and his assistant as helpless as a couple of logs.

"Now what shall we do with them?" was his next inquiry.

"Why, the quickest way will be to take them, cart and all, into the plantation as far as we can, and we will see about the remainder afterwards."

"Very good. As they are in the cart already, I daresay it will be the easiest. It will be a joke to get this four-legged creetur along, I know."

Pharoah, however, drew his sword, and pricked the mule in the flank with it.

The animal's first act was to fling out behind in a very vicious manner.

Then, after shaking its head two or three times, as though feeling that was no use, jogged along at a tolerable pace.

They did not plunge directly into the plantation, but skirted it as far as they were able, for it so happened that on one side it was bounded by a turf field, over which they made their way without any difficulty whatever.

Choosing at last a point where the saplings did not grow so closely together, the cart was fairly led under the branches of the dark-foliaged trees, and so lost to view entirely.

Guided by Isaac, the cart was led on for a considerable distance, nor indeed did they pause until a small open glade was reached, which seemed far enough removed from the high-road to be out of hearing.

The two prisoners were then rolled on to the greensward with very little tenderness, and when down suffered to scramble up as well as they were able.

Both got in some mysterious way on to their knees, and while in this abject position roared most dismally for mercy, and begged and prayed to be released.

But they might just as well have entreated the trees around them as have addressed their supplications to the three men before them.

"Shut up," growled Isaac, "can't you? It will do you no good and nobody else to be howling in that fashion. Won't you listen to what we have to say?"

It was some time, however, before they could be made to pay attention.

"Hark!" said Lord Harcliffe, in tones which could hardly have failed to attract attention. "We are friends of Captain Hawk's!"

The announcement was received with a dolorous groan.

"We know you, and know your errand; and though our shortest, easiest, and surest way to deal with you would be to treat you with five or six inches of cold steel, yet we will be merciful. Your lives shall be spared, and you shall not even be injured, provided you choose to act with the smallest amount of reason."

"But if you don't let us go," whimpered the hangman, "I shall be ruined. Don't you know it is important that this Captain Hawk should be tucked up without delay?"

"We don't intend to allow anything of the sort," was the answer—"you may be quite sure about that."

CHAPTER CXXXV.

THE PRISONERS ARE MADE SECURE, AND ISAAC STARTS TO THE JAIL.

Lord Harcliffe spoke in such a resolute manner that it was not possible for anyone to have a doubt about his being thoroughly in earnest.

The hangman broke out into a howl of grief which had really something comic in it.

"I shall be ruined," he said—"ruined and undone! Oh, alas! I am a ruined man—a——"

"Hold your row!" interrupted Isaac, impatiently. "Instead of yelling like that, you ought to be thankful that any life is left in your miserable old carcass!"

"No—no! Better dead than ruined! I shall lose my situation after this—I know I shall, and then what is to become of me?"

"That's no business of ours," said Isaac; "and as we have plenty to do just at present, don't be so unreasonable as to expect that we should concern ourselves about it."

It was quite in vain, however, for Isaac to speak any words of this sort.

The hangman continued to pour forth his lamentings.

As for his companion, when he found that he was in no danger of his skin he became quiet enough, and professed himself perfectly willing to do whatever his captors required.

In the meanwhile the three friends drew close together and consulted in low whispers.

They could not make up their minds where to bestow their prisoners.

To leave them bound in the plantation was the first suggestion, but the obvious impolicy of doing this became at once visible.

"We must be most careful," said the Black Highwayman. "Should the least rumour arise of what we have done it would destroy the plan utterly even at the moment of fruition."

"I can see but one way of making all secure," said Pharoah, "and with your permission I'll speak."

"Do so—pray do so without the least reserve."

"Come a little further away, so that we may be sure that neither of those fellows can overhear us."

They retreated a few paces; and then Pharoah whispered:

"My idea is that, as we are so short a distance from the Greyhound, we should take them there."

"But the landlord——"

"I don't think he would object; because I should recommend that, in addition to being securely bound, they should be well blindfolded, and deposited in a stable or some other outbuilding."

"And what then?"

"Why, afterwards it would be easy enough for you or us to go there to-morrow night, and convey them to a distance and leave them."

"In that case it does not seem as though there would be any great danger in their discovering the place of their imprisonment."

"So I think. And as there does not, why not adopt the plan?"

Lord Harcliffe seemed to hesitate; but when Isaac pronounced in favour of it, he signified his entire approval.

It was far from uninteresting to see how dreadfully anxious the two prisoners were during this discussion.

As soon as they saw a decision had been come to, and that their captors approached, they renewed their dismal outcries.

"Wait a moment," said Isaac. "I had thought the easiest plan would be to put them into the cart again; but now I see that would be too likely to leave such a clue as would lead to our discovery. No, no—we must think of some other way of taking them; and it will also be necessary to hide the cart, because if that is found it will speedily lead to a discovery."

"It would be best to hide the cart," said Lord Harcliffe; "but I am afraid you will not be able to manage it."

"Why not?"

"Why, such a bulky thing is not easily concealed."

"Well, you just see, then; for just as I spoke I was struck by an idea, and if you will have patience for half a minute I'll let you know what that idea is."

Isaac did not wait for any response, but, hastening to the cart, unharnessed the mule.

He removed every portion of the harness and threw it into the cart.

Then, giving the animal a sharp cut with the whip, he sent it adrift.

"There," he said—"I don't suppose you will be found by anybody. If you are, you will prove a rare find. Ha, ha!"

The moon at this moment shone forth with a little more brightness than it had done hitherto.

"Ah!" ejaculated Isaac, "I thought I was not deceived. Just look through the bushes, and you will see the very thing we want."

Lord Harcliffe and Pharoah pushed forward, for the curiosity they felt about Isaac's proceedings was very great.

They were very much surprised when they caught sight of a sheet of water of considerable extent.

"Why, it's a pool, Isaac!" said the Black Highwayman. "What are you going to do with that?"

"Hide the cart in it," was the answer, accompanied by that peculiar chuckle the ostler always gave when highly delighted.

"But how?" said Lord Harcliffe, with difficulty mastering his inclination to laugh. "It's a thousand to one whether the water is deep enough to conceal the cart."

"Wait a minute. You just help me through these bushes, and I will show you something that you never saw before."

The hangman meanwhile had groaned dreadfully about his mule being turned adrift; but now when he saw that the destruction of his cart was imminent, he grew almost frantic.

He might just as well have been silent, however, for not the slightest attention was given to his vociferations.

Lord Harcliffe and Pharoah both came forward readily enough to Isaac's assistance; and by their united strength the cart was pushed over some bushes that skirted the pool.

From this point the ground sloped rapidly to the water's edge.

"Now hold it a minute," said Isaac; "I don't want it to slip down yet, and I have something to do."

What that something was speedily became visible.

Going to both wheels in succession, Isaac removed the pins by which they were secured to the axle-tree.

This done, he hastened to the shafts.

"That will do," he said to his companions; "you can look on now, and you will see the cart vanish like magic."

So saying, he pushed it down the bank with all his might.

[SIR THOMAS EXAMINES THE CAPTAIN'S BONDS.]

The wheels performed a few revolutions without showing any inclination to come off.

Right down to the water's edge Isaac pushed it, and then let go.

The wheels went round once or twice more in consequence of the impetus he had given it.

Then they fell off at each side, and in an instant every sign of the cart had gone.

"There!" said Isaac, with another chuckle. "I consider that cart well hid, because we shall always know where to find it."

"The water must be very deep," said Lord Harcliffe. "There is not a trace of it left."

"No; it is swallowed up as completely as I could desire; and now if we can only manage the other part of the business as well I shall be thoroughly content."

On going back to the hangman, they found him almost out of his mind at the loss of his cart.

He soon found, however, that Fate had something still worse in store for him.

Both himself and his companion were first of all gagged and then tightly blindfolded.

They could now neither speak, move, nor see, so that it would be hard to conceive anyone in a much more helpless state.

What horrible fears they had no tongue can tell; but that they were extreme may be surmised by the faint moaning which they incessantly kept up, and which was, in fact, the only sound they were able to make.

"Now," said Isaac, "I will take the one, and let Pharoah take the other. We can manage with them across the front of the saddle, I think, for the distance not being great, we can go slowly."

"Very good," said Lord Harcliffe. "If that arrangement suits you, I will go on first and reconnoitre."

"Do so—do so by all means, for it is most important of all that no one should see us."

With no more concern than they would have shown to a couple of sacks of flour, Mr. Price and his assistant were lifted bodily from the ground, and placed across the horses' backs.

Isaac and Pharoah then mounted; and while they used one hand to guide the rein, they employed the other to hold their prisoners secure.

"Are you all ready?" said Lord Harcliffe.

"Yes. Lead the way," answered Pharoah; "we had better lose no more time."

"Follow quietly and at a safe distance, then."

"You need not feel alarmed that we shall make too much speed," said Isaac; "the task is not such an easy one as you might think, I can tell you."

Lord Harcliffe now led the way out of the plantation.

On emerging from the trees, he manifested the utmost caution.

Fortunately for the success of their plan, it was unnecessary.

Not a soul could be seen anywhere.

That peculiar thickness in the atmosphere that Isaac had remarked upon as being a prognostication of coming snow had increased.

The wind blew steadily, and every particle of it seemed loaded with chill vapour.

Ere they had gone many paces from the plantation, Lord Harcliffe came to a standstill.

Then in a low voice he called to the others to draw nearer.

"I have something to say," he remarked; "but I cannot utter it until I have given you a caution."

Both Isaac and Pharoah wondered what was coming.

But the caution the Black Highwayman had to give was an important one and by no means superfluous.

"You must not for one single moment," he said, "lose sight of the fact that if you have bound your two prisoners hand and foot and deprived them of their vision, yet the sense of hearing still remains to them; and when you are speaking either of your destination, or of any person, you must be most careful how you do so, or the consequences will be disastrous."

Both thanked him for the utterance of this caution.

It might not have injured themselves individually; but then they had the safety of others to look to even more than their own.

"Now," added Lord Harcliffe, "let me finish what I was about to say. You, Isaac, no doubt, can find your way to the place we want to reach without going near any roads?"

"Yes, I can; and what is more, the distance is nothing at all to speak of."

"Then you shall do it. Come closer, and surrender your burden to me. Then ride on in advance, taking the straightest course you are able. As for myself, it is useless for me to pretend to take the lead, for I could only find my way back by the high-road."

"And the farther we keep away from that," said Isaac, "the better for all parties."

"I quite think so. Steady now. That will do very well."

It was Price the hangman himself that Isaac had taken under hand; and as he was by no means such a burly individual as his assistant, the exchange of burdens was effected with tolerable ease.

Isaac then, without the least hesitation, struck off across the fields, though the darkness was quite sufficient to have confused anybody.

Isaac, however, certainly possessed the faculty of finding his way easily from place to place.

In the present instance he never once faltered about his route; and in so short a space of time that Lord Harcliffe could hardly believe it possible, he brought them to the rear of the old inn.

"Now," he said, turning to his friends, "not forgetting your caution, I think I had better go now, and have a few words with a certain person, in order to get his consent to what we want to do."

"Cetainly. Remember to be careful."

Isaac had not gone many paces before he was confronted by the person he wished to see.

The fact was that the landlord was as deeply interested as anybody in the success of Mr. Marchant's plan, which seemed to grow more and more enticing as he continued to ponder over it.

For about the hundredth time he had walked to the extreme boundary of his back premises in the hope of seeing or hearing something further, when he met Isaac.

He was rather surprised, not to say alarmed, at the manner the faithful fellow greeted him.

"Whatever you do," he whispered, "don't raise your voice. You mustn't speak any louder than I am now."

"But why not tell me that first?"

"Because the sound would fall upon ears which we would fain keep from hearing anything of the kind, for the simple reason that an unpleasant recognition might take place. You understand me? We want to prevent disagreeable consequences."

As briefly as possible, Isaac then made Tom Beckford acquainted with what they had done, and what they wanted further to do.

As the faithful fellow had foreseen, the landlord so far from raising the slightest possible objection, was only too glad to be of assistance.

"Nothing could be better," he said, emphatically.

"And you don't mind incurring the extra risk for the captain's sake?"

"Risk! Why, bless my life, I can't see any risk about it—that is, provided we are only moderately careful, which we easily can be."

"Very good; then we won't lose any more time."

"No, do not."

A low whistle had the effect of bringing the other two forward.

The two prisoners by this time were now in a dreadful state of alarm,

They trembled from head to foot. They were bound too tightly for there to be the possibility of any further movement.

They continued to moan incessantly, and in doing so they were either more vigorous in their efforts, or else the gags had given way slightly, for they managed to emit a very peculiar but quite indescribable sound.

With scant care they were lowered from the saddle on to the ground, where they lay as they fell, just as helpless as logs.

It was deemed that for the moment, at any rate, they would be safe, and so the horses were first of all attended to.

When they were comfortably disposed of, they came back to the unlucky hangman and his assistant.

It had been agreed by all three that the more they could mystify their prisoners as to their precise whereabouts the better it would be.

Tom Beckford was not long in deciding which one of his numerous outbuildings should have the honour of holding the captives in safe custody.

This was a disused hay-loft over a stable that stood apart from the others, and which, from its inconvenient approach and situation, was very seldom occupied.

In order to raise them into the loft, Isaac thought of an expedient which he confidently asserted would bother them entirely.

This was by slipping a rope under their armpits, and by that means drawing them up from the floor of the stable to that of the loft above.

Here they were left for some time while the four friends descended to hold a further deliberation.

As soon as they were securely seated, Isaac craved leave to speak.

Permission having been accorded to him, he said:

"I hope there is not one of you who will say a word against my being the one to play the pretended hangman's part to-morrow morning?"

"I should not have a single objection to raise," said Lord Harcliffe, "provided you were only just a little less excitable, and were able to keep your feelings somewhat more under control."

"Don't be afraid about that—pray don't. You have not the slightest real ground for dread. For the captain's sake I could do anything, no matter what; and as I know his life would actually be in my hands you may depend I shall maintain proper command."

"Then in that case no one could be better qualified for the task, because you are not so well known to the authorities as Pharoah and myself. Self-command will be everything."

"Have no fears."

"I will not. Let us consider the point as settled. At the right moment you will see Pharoah near the gallows mounted upon Satan's back, while I shall be at hand prepared to accompany his flight and cover his retreat."

"That is it," said Isaac, whose suppressed excitement made him shake like an aspen—"that is it! I can see it all as plainly in my mind as though it was really taking place."

"But stay a little," said Lord Harcliffe. "Supposing all we have arranged is done, and the captain rides clear away ——"

"Yes—yes!"

"Then what is to become of you?"

Isaac scratched his head.

"Well, now," he cried, "if you had not mentioned it, I should never once have thought about it. And no matter now. What becomes of me is of no consequence. I can shift for myself."

Isaac was fully in earnest; but as he spoke Lord Harcliffe mentally determined that he would take such steps as would enable Isaac to escape from the consequences of the part he had taken in the affair.

"Don't bother about me," Isaac repeated. "I had an idea in my head just as you spoke, and you can't think how near I was to losing it again."

"What was it?"

"Why, I have been thinking about the way in which I shall present myself at the prison as Price's substitute."

"Well?"

"It occurred to me that his Irish assistant would be tolerably well known."

"Oh, no doubt he is."

"Very well, then. Now, it struck me that if I could only get hold of that fellow's clothes, I could disguise myself in them, and on reaching the jail could pass myself off for him."

"It is possible."

"I have heard him speak, and feel confident that I could imitate his voice so well that it would take an uncommonly good judge to tell the difference."

"But what should you say when you got there?"

"Why, give them an account of what had happened."

"How?"

"I should tell them that Mr. Price and myself had been attacked on the road, but that I had escaped, and should be willing to do the job for my master."

"A good plan that," said Tom Beckford.

"Yes," assented Lord Harcliffe; "I think it far more likely to succeed than if he went there as a total stranger and asked for the job."

"You may safely depend upon it," said Isaac.

"But you must mind what you say."

"Trust me for that. I am quite easy on that score. Impatience is all that troubles me. I want morning to come now."

"You will have some hours to wait."

"Yes; but not so very many, as I shall walk to Huntingdon; that will take me at least two hours, and then I ought to be there an hour or so before the time appointed for the start."

"I don't know about that," exclaimed the landlord.

"Do you think, then, that it would be better to keep them waiting a little longer?"

"I do."

"And so should I," answered Isaac, "if it wasn't for one thing."

"And what's that?"

"The fear that they might get some one to do the job immediately."

"No," said Lord Harcliffe; "I feel certain that they would be sure to wait a reasonable time before they took any step whatever."

"That is my opinion," said Pharoah. "Being a delay, they would think it quite likely for Mr. Price to arrive."

"Which we must take particular care not to let him do," said the landlord; "and for that reason I think we had better go and take a peep at them."

"Nothing would be more agreeable," responded Isaac, "because I want some of that fellow's clothes. He is just about my height and build. Oh, rely upon it, I shall take him off to perfection!"

At these words, all rose and repaired to the loft.

On entering it, they found their prisoners quite safe, and just as they left them.

Indeed, unless aided by some third party, it seemed a moral impossibility for them to move an inch.

They were still moaning.

Perhaps, hearing some one approaching, they had endeavoured to call attention to their luckless plight.

Of Mr. Price no notice was taken.

His assistant, however, was cautiously unbound, though the bandage was not removed from his eyes.

Isaac, with great dexterity, possessed himself of sundry portions of his apparel, giving up his own instead.

In something like an hour the transmogrification was complete.

So far as outward appearance went, it would have required some very intimate acquaintance to tell the true from the false.

Then, as for the voice, Isaac was quite at ease about that, and during his solitary walk he would have plenty of time to con over what he intended to say.

His impatience would not suffer him to stay after six o'clock.

As soon as the hour was struck, he started off, leaving his companions to fulfil the parts assigned to them.

CHAPTER CXXXVI.

DESCRIBES HOW CAPTAIN HAWK SPENT HIS LAST NIGHT IN THE CONDEMNED CELL.

The current of events has now for a long time quite carried us away from Captain Hawk's cell, and therefore we doubt not that the reader will very gladly accompany us thither.

Not that there is much to be related of him, for he has appeared as the chief actor in several recent scenes, and the termination of the trial is already known.

Still, for all that, no doubt great interest will be felt in coming once more face to face with that gallant heart which, disdaining danger for so long, is now surely in as perilous a strait as one can well conceive.

By the care of the doctor the captain's wound was healed, and on the morning of his trial he felt something like himself again.

The turnkey had given him the gloomiest reports.

The visit of Mr. Marchant, which we have elsewhere described, sent a warm glow to the prisoner's heart, and already he began to feel himself at liberty.

Those few words which Mr. Marchant had been able to whisper in his ear unheard by others were most encouraging.

The good effect which they produced, however, was abated by the turnkey's forebodings.

"Now, captain," he said, "you may not think it, but I am very fond of you. I am sorry for you—I am from the bottom of my heart."

"Thanks for that assurance, my friend. I fully and entirely believe it."

"So you may, captain—so you may. And it's out of the regard that I've got for you that I try my best to save you from the bitterness of a cruel disappointment."

"Pho—pho!"

"Ah, I know," said the turnkey, shaking his head. "Now that you have had that lawyer fellow here, and he whispered a few words into your ear on the sly, you make sure you are going to escape; but you're mistaken, captain—I tell you you're mistaken, and I say so for your own good."

"I don't doubt it, my friend," said Captain Hawk, with a smile; "but my firm and unshaken conviction is that in a few days more I shall be free."

"Yes, free of the world and all its cares, no doubt. If you call that being free, why, of course, I give in."

"No—no, man. You know full well such is not my meaning. You wilfully misunderstand me. I tell you I have powerful friends—friends so powerful that were my situation ten times more desperate than it now is, I should not despair."

"And you depend on them, then?"

"I do. I have just had the assurance sent me that I need fear nothing."

"It may be so. Perhaps they think to get you off by swearing a good alibi, do they?"

"I cannot tell."

"Well, if it's that, it is no better than nothing at all. They have made up their minds to hang ye, captain, and, by the powers, they'll do it, no matter how you strive against it."

"Then," answered Captain Hawk, smiling still at the turnkey's dogmatism, "you will at least admit that until the event takes place my word is as good as yours?"

"No, I won't."

"You won't?"

"No, I won't."

"And why not?"

"Because, captain—and don't treat what I say so lightly—you ought not to do it, because the result of the trial is just as well known and arranged as it could be if it had taken place."

But Captain Hawk did not show himself much dismayed at this.

His confidence in the will and ability of his friends to aid him was very great; and though he had remained so long in his cell without any communication from them, yet his faith was not shaken in the least.

The assurance which Mr. Marchant had given was, nevertheless, none the less welcome on that account.

The words employed were vague enough; but yet the captain gathered from them that events would somehow take such a turn on the day of his trial that he should be set free."

This was, of course, irreconcilable with the turnkey's statement; yet on the morning of the trial, as we have already said, it made him feel much disappointed when he found that Mr. Marchant did not so much as put in an appearance.

It is needless to recapitulate in this place any of the events which took place at the trial.

It had only been by the strongest and most powerful effort that Captain Hawk had been able to shake off the stupor which settled upon his spirits when the verdict was pronounced.

But he did recover himself sufficiently to utter those few words of protestation against the manner in which his trial had been conducted.

Then he was, in spite of himself, crushed by the dreadful words in which the judge pronounced his doom.

At that impressive and appalling moment it required more self-possession than he possessed to stand undaunted.

Then the well-known tones of Isaac's voice rang in his ears.

But ere he could recover himself from the surprise into which he had been thrown, the warders hurried him out of the dock.

With as little loss of time as possible, he was consigned to one of the condemned cells.

No fetters were placed upon his limbs, the Governor still trusting more to a close supervision.

The cell itself was quite as strong as the one which he had before, but darker, damper, and more cheerless altogether.

The turnkey took an early opportunity of reminding the prisoner how exactly his predictions had been verified.

"Bless you, captain, I knew you did not stand the least bit of a chance. You ought to give me the credit for being up to a thing or two. Do take my words to heart."

"Never—never!" was the answer. "In spite of what has taken place to-day, I will hold on to hope to the very last. I am certain my friends will aid me."

"I don't doubt their willingness for a moment, captain, but I do their power. They may be able to accomplish much; but think how great is the force which is opposed to them."

In spite of the confidence which he not merely expressed but felt, such words as these could hardly fail to produce a deep effect upon the prisoner.

He strode up and down the narrow limits of his cell for some time in gloomy silence.

How fervently he wished that his friends could have contrived in some way to make him acquainted with their intentions!

Feeling the impossibility of this, he strove to shake off the depression under which he laboured.

"It is foolish to give way thus," he said. "I must overcome so great a weakness. Let me try to summon up what fortitude I can, and wait with patience for the occurrence of those events which I can neither alter, advance, nor retard by giving way to gloomy notions."

It was all very well for Captain Hawk to reason thus; but he found the task of acting in accordance with his words a very difficult one.

His long confinement, his wound, and all those depressing events with which the reader is acquainted, had deprived him entirely of that vivacity of spirit which in former times used to be his chief characteristic.

And so, alternately swayed by hope and dread, the time between his condemnation and that appointed for his execution passed away.

As usual, he was visited by the prison chaplain.

But as that functionary chiefly exerted himself to procure a confession from the prisoner, his visits were not productive of much benefit.

Once, and once only, Sir Thomas Walker came to exult over the condition of the condemned man.

But he saw there was an angry light gleaming in the captain's eye, and as he valued his personal safety above every earthly consideration, he withdrew rather hastily, and showed himself no more.

Even the Governor seemed to take a hint, for after this he was very careful not to approach his prisoner too closely.

How anxious a time this was for the Governor, and how impatiently he looked forward to the coming of the day of execution no tongue can tell.

The interval of time was short, and the evening before the last day speedily arrived.

Captain Hawk was calmer.

Now that things had gone so far, he believed he could guess at his comrades' intentions.

They had made arrangements, he thought, either to rescue him while on his way to the gibbet, or else to do so at the moment of his arrival at the fatal spot.

With this conviction firmly rooted in his mind, he preserved an amount of coolness and self-command which absolutely amazed the turnkey.

That individual had confidently asserted that when the last night came then the difference would be visible in the captain's manner.

He was forced, however, to confess that he never made a greater mistake in all his life.

Towards midnight the captain threw himself down on the miserable pallet provided for his accommodation, and almost immediately fell asleep.

The turnkey watched him with the closest attention.

Ere long it could be inferred that the prisoner's slumbers were disturbed by unpleasant dreams.

He rolled from side to side, and uttered indistinct sounds, as though his mind was deeply agitated.

With a sudden glance he awoke, and looked around him for a moment or so with an air that showed plainly enough he hardly remembered where he was.

The familiar tones of the friendly turnkey's voice recalled him to himself.

"Ah, captain," he said, "I have always noticed no one can sleep well on their last night: the dreams are always unpleasant."

Captain Hawk looked around more calmly.

The dim oil lamp, which gave out the whole of the illumination the place possessed, revealed to him the cheerless walls of his dungeon, the few articles it contained, and lastly, the turnkey, who was leaning against the wall in an attitude of deep meditation.

With a sudden bound, the prisoner sprang from the pallet.

"Easy does it, captain—easy does it! What is the matter now?"

"Don't be alarmed; I sha'n't be violent."

As he spoke, he seated himself in a careless manner upon the only chair the cell afforded.

"You don't look comfortable," said the turnkey. "Was I right about the cause?"

"You were. But think no more of that. I shall not, for dreams are mere idle nothings."

"Very good, captain—just as you like. But if you'll take my advice you won't try to go to sleep again."

"To-night I shall not," said the captain, with a perceptible shudder.

The turnkey grinned.

"To-morrow night he will be past troubling about sleeping, I'll warrant."

But he did not venture to make this remark aloud.

For some moments the captain sat with his eyes moodily fixed upon the ground, with his chin resting upon his arms, which he had placed on the back of the chair in which he sat.

"Cheer up, captain!" exclaimed the turnkey. "You ought not to take a dream so much to heart."

"No, no—I was not thinking so much about that as of other matters."

"Indeed?" said the turnkey, doubtfully.

"Yes. I want you to answer me a few questions."

"With all my heart! It will be most agreeable to do so, I can tell you, after sitting here in silence for so long. What do you want to know?"

"Why, first of all, tell me how far it is from here to the—to the——"

"Place of execution?"

"Yes."

"Why, I should say somewhere about three parts of a mile?"

"So far?"

"Yes. Do you know Ling Heath?"

"I do. Is that the place?"

"It is. I only learned it a few hours ago, and was, above all things, strictly charged not to convey the intelligence to you."

Somehow this piece of news had a cheering effect upon the captain's spirits.

He went on with his questions.

"Has the scaffold been erected there, then?"

"By this time I have no doubt it has."

"And what is the time appointed for leaving the prison?"

"Eight o'clock is the proper hour, but somehow or another it is rarely kept to. The earliest I know of didn't leave till half-past."

"And what is the time now?"

"Just four—I heard a clock strike not ten minutes since."

"Four more hours!"

"Yes, captain. I shall be sorry to part with you, for you are the best companion I have had for many a day I sha'n't forget you."

"And how will the journey to the common be performed?"

"Oh! you will be accommodated with a cart, which is always kept in the prison for that particular purpose. You would be surprised, too, if you knew what a wonderfully strong guard that Sir Thomas Walker has got together. He is determined you shall not have the ghost of a chance."

The captain's heart fell a little at this intelligence.

But he recovered himself almost immediately.

"Ling Heath!" he said, mentally. "Surely there is something strange in this, and I may draw from it a favourable conclusion. How well I know the spot! It could not be better placed for any attempt my friends may make."

"May I make so bold as to ask what you are thinking about, captain?"

"About Ling Heath, that is all."

"Ah! I daresay you know the place very well, and little thought it would be the spot above all others where you would take your last look of the sky."

"No, I never did think so—you are quite right there."

A silence of some length followed.

Busy thoughts filled the prisoner's mind, and the turnkey, as he watched the changes of his countenance, hesitated to interrupt him.

Suddenly the captain started.

"What was that I heard?"

"The striking of the prison clock."

"And the hour?"

"Five."

"Time flies!"

"It does. It will soon be eight o'clock. I've ordered a first-rate breakfast to be served at a quarter-past seven."

"Breakfast?"

"Oh yes! we could not think of turning you out for such a ceremony with an empty stomach: you might feel faint and queer, you know."

Captain Hawk rose, and again paced up and down his cell.

Then, tiring of the exercise, he reseated himself.

"Captain," added the turnkey, "I have no fear of you—I know you will be game to the very last."

The prisoner smiled faintly.

Had he betrayed no symptoms of emotion in an emergency like the present he must have been more or less than human.

It would be hard to imagine anyone in a condition of so much anxiety.

Six o'clock soon struck, and, as it seemed to the prisoner, after a still briefer interval the hour of seven was pealed forth.

The clanging notes awoke him from the reverie into which he had fallen.

"Now, captain," said the turnkey, springing up, "prepare for breakfast."

But the bare thought of food to one in the agitated condition of the prisoner was insupportable.

Gladly enough, however, he bathed his head and face in the water the turnkey brought him, though its temperature was very little above freezing point.

But the sudden shock braced up his nerves wonderfully.

Then, with what means he possessed, he attended to his toilet.

He had not finished when he heard a faint tapping at the cell door.

"Breakfast, I'll warrant," said the turnkey, briskly.

The door opened, and one of the warders of the prison appeared carrying a huge tray before him.

The opening of the door revealed to the captain's gaze the forms of the men on duty without.

The latter, as soon as their companion had crossed the threshold, closed the door and secured it with scrupulous care.

When the repast was spread, it proved to be of such a tempting character as to excite in the prisoner's breast some faint cravings of appetite.

He invited the two men to seat themselves and eat.

A small portion was taken by the prisoner, who, however, did not swallow more than half-a-dozen morsels.

The man who had brought the tray was one of those individuals whose greatest pleasure is to be chattering on some subject, no matter what.

His loquaciousness was temporarily subdued by the consumption of the good things before him.

But his enforced silence did not continue half-a-dozen moments.

"You have not looked out, I suppose?" he said, addressing himself to the turnkey.

"Looked out! What do you mean?"

"Why, to see what the weather is like."

"No, that I have not. Here it makes no difference whether it is storm or sunshine."

"Ah! it is a morning, I can assure you."

"How? What do you mean?"

"Why, for the last three hours the snow has been coming down in such a style as I never witnessed before. Such flakes!"

"And does it snow now?"

"Faster, I think, than ever."

Captain Hawk heard this intelligence with strange emotion.

Instantly he turned his eyes towards the narrow grated aperture that was fixed high up in the wall.

But such was its situation that no opinion could be formed of the state of the weather without.

"Then," said the turnkey, "there seems every probability of a continuance of the snow-storm?"

"Rather, I should say. Why, it lies at least two feet deep now. In all my time I never knew an execution in a snow-storm. It will be something to memorise the event, captain."

"But not to delay it," said the turnkey.

"I don't know about that," returned the warder.

"How? Do you mean to tell me after all the trouble there has been, and the lucky way in which things have been carried so far, that they will put off the execution merely because snow happens to be falling? Pooh—pooh! It's absurd!"

The turnkey, having all the time expressed himself so confidently that the execution would infallibly take place that morning, could not with common patience endure the idea of a delay.

"Patience, man—patience, man! You should wait and hear what a man has to say."

"You spoke plainly enough."

"Yes, perhaps rather too plain, considering who is present." And he accompanied these words with a glance at the prisoner.

"Don't mind me," said Captain Hawk. "At least, let me ask you as a favour to speak plainly before me. If you think there is a probability of the execution being delayed, pray say so, and give us your reasons for such an opinion."

The warder looked undecided.

"Yes, speak," said the turnkey—"the captain won't be able to ask us many more favours; and as he is certainly the very best fellow that ever sat in a cell, I think we ought not to deny him this one."

The warder glanced around him apprehensively.

"Confound it!" he exclaimed. "My long tongue will be the ruin of me some of these days: I had no business to have dropped the slightest hint about it."

"Why not?"

"Because I was expressly told to keep it secret."

The great reluctance to say anything which the man manifested only served to increase the captain's anxiousness to know all the particulars.

"If Sir Thomas Walker," now said the warder, with another terrified glance around—"if Sir Thomas Walker only knew I had let my tongue blab, I should be kicked out of my place at a moment's notice."

"My good fellow," said the turnkey, "make your mind easy: there is not the least cause for you to be so dreadfully distressed."

"Oh yes, there is."

"Nothing of the sort. You have only to sink your voice, and then it will be quite impossible for anybody outside to catch a syllable; and as for the captain and myself, you might make sure that not a word shall ever escape our lips."

"Will you promise me that?"

"Yes, faithfully promise it," said the captain.

"And so will I," added the turnkey. "Now then; don't torment us any longer by keeping us in such suspense, but let us know what ground there is for fearing that the execution will be put off?"

The warder, who seemed to be inwardly cursing himself for his want of caution in alluding to the matter in the first instance, drew closer to the two others.

Then in low tones he said:

"Sir Thomas Walker is here along with the Governor, and has been all night."

"Well—well?"

"They are both in a dreadful state of anxiety."

"What about?"

"Mr. Price."

"The hangman?"

"Yes."

"Hasn't he arrived?"

"No, he has not—or, at least, had not when I came in."

A profound silence followed the communication of this piece of intelligence.

Somehow or other an inward conviction seemed to steal over the captain's mind that this was in some way connected with the efforts of his comrades in his behalf.

In silence he waited to hear more, for he felt he could not command himself sufficiently to ask a single question.

"But this is something very strange," cried the turnkey, after drawing a long breath. "He ought to have been here seven hours ago."

"He ought."

"But surely he *will* come. He must have been detained on the road by some accident."

"That I know not."

"But even should he not arrive," said the turnkey, "I don't believe the execution would be put off."

"You don't? Why not?"

"Because every effort would be made to find a substitute to do the regular hangman's duty; and if a good sum is offered, there won't be much difficulty about it."

Captain Hawk still sat passive.

He knew not what conclusion to arrive at respecting what he had just heard.

CHAPTER CXXXVII.

ISAAC IS BROUGHT TO THE PRISON, AND OFFERS HIMSELF AS SUBSTITUTE FOR MR. PRICE.

For a brief space we will leave Captain Hawk in his cell, to think over what he had just heard and to recover from his surprise as best he might, while we take a glimpse at the other occupants of the prison on this eventful night.

Sir Thomas Walker, now that the time was so close at hand when he would not only acquit himself of his commission, but also gratify the feeling of personal hatred and revenge he had against the bold highwayman, was so much a prey to anxiety and restlessness as to prevent him from retaining the semblance of calmness even for a moment.

Such a feeling as this is certain to be infectious; and he had not been long in the prison before he had reduced the Governor to the same uncomfortable state of mind.

According to the arrangements made, Price the hangman ought to have arrived at the prison at midnight or very shortly after.

As this hour approached it would be hard to say who suffered the most exquisite tortures of suspense, the Governor or Sir Thomas Walker.

Sleep to both was a thing so wholly out of the question that they had never once made the least mention of retiring.

They were both seated at a table in one of the Governor's private apartments.

Glasses and decanters were within easy reach, but little attention was given to them.

Both kept their eyes fixed upon the slow-moving finger on the dial.

At length the hour of twelve was struck.

"Now I hope our suspense will soon be over," said Sir Thomas, rubbing his hands together, for, despite the brisk fire that was burning, his anxiousness made him feel chilly. "Fill up the glasses, and we will drink to the speedy arrival of Mr. Price. Twelve o'clock was the time, I think you said?"

"Ah, yes, Sir Thomas, that is the hour when he generally arrives—sometimes sooner, sometimes later. The obstinate old fool will persist in driving all the way in an old crazy cart drawn by a mule, and with no one but a stupid Irish fellow to protect him."

Sir Thomas rose and paced up and down the room for some moments.

Then, suddenly stopping short, he exclaimed:

"We have been remiss and careless now to an unwarrantable degree. How could we have overlooked it?"

The Governor said nothing, but glared upon the magistrate with dismay very visibly imprinted on his features.

"You don't seem to comprehend me; but I can see now that we have been elaborately careful in every direction save one, and in that most thoughtless and forgetful."

"You—ah—no—no, you don't think we have omitted anything, Sir Thomas?"

"Yes, I do—I feel sure of it."

"What—what?"

"We ought to have had the hangman sent for by a strong guard of trusty men, and escorted by them from London, so as to make an absolute certainty of his arrival here at the proper time."

"Is that all?" gasped the Governor, with the air of one greatly relieved.

"All! It is everything."

"I don't think there is excessive need for alarm."

"Where is he now, then?"

"He will be here before long."

"How can you speak so positively?"

"Because up to now he has never failed to put in his appearance at the proper moment; and why should this time be an exception to a never-varying rule?"

Sir Thomas was silent.

Not because he was unprepared with a reply, but because he felt an absolute dread of giving his thoughts utterance.

In restless wretchedness another hour passed.

The clock struck one, and no sooner had the clear, bell-like sound ceased than the Governor summoned an attendant.

"Go now," he said, "and bring me word whether the hangman has arrived."

The man bowed and retired.

During his absence a profound silence was preserved.

But the message he brought back gave them neither satisfaction nor relief.

Price had not come, nor had any tidings been heard of him.

The Governor, on his part, began to feel some of those dreads that had for nearly an hour been tugging at the magistrate's heart.

Like him, he was afraid to hint at what he feared.

"Let us be as calm as we are able," cried Sir Thomas, at length, and throwing himself into a chair while he spoke. "We will wait one more hour, and then——"

"Then what?"

"We will have a few men assembled, and send them on the road to London. It is just possible that they may not only fall in with those we want, but be of assistance."

"Assistance in what way?" asked the Governor, pretending to be ignorant of his companion's fears, though he knew them as well as if they had been spoken.

"Fools that we are!" was the angry rejoinder. "We ought to have remembered what unscrupulous and powerful companions this Captain Hawk has."

"Then you fear that they might attempt to seize upon the hangman and forcibly detain him?"

"Attempt! If they try at all, there is nothing in the world to prevent them from succeeding."

"But, after all, why should they do this?—what could they gain by it? They must feel that the non-appearance of the hangman will not prevent the execution altogether."

In his excitement, the Governor forgot all about the foolish lisp and stammer in which he delighted to indulge.

"No, no—I admit the truth of that, but cannot find any consolation in it."

"Why not?"

"Because they would be satisfied if they caused delay and produced confusion. To them time is everything. Rely upon it, but for the vigilance used and strict precautions taken, a desperate and perhaps successful attempt at rescue would have been made."

"It is certain," said the Governor, more as if pursuing the thread of his own reflections than answering the magistrate—"it is certain that if the hangman does not appear at the proper time, it will cause great confusion and much delay."

"No, no—not much delay," exclaimed the magistrate, excitedly. "I will take special care that it does not cause much delay."

"May I ask in what manner?"

"Yes. If no one else can be found to do the hangman's business at the appointed hour, I will not shrink from taking the duty upon myself! Anything rather than give the prisoner's friends the slightest chance of accomplishing their desire."

"Anything would be better than delay certainly," responded the Governor; "yet I did not fancy there will be need for the adoption of such a disagreeable duty as you mention."

"But if the need does come," asserted the magistrate, "I will not shrink. I have sworn that Captain Hawk shall be hanged this day, and I will move Heaven and earth but what I will fulfil my oath!"

He brought his clenched hand down with great violence upon the table as he spoke.

In such-like conversation as this the specified hour was passed.

No sooner had the clock struck than the magistrate rose and went to the door of the room, his intention being this time personally to inquire whether the hangman had made his appearance.

Not that he expected for a moment that the question would be other than an idle one; but then he had his after resolve to carry out.

Of course, no hangman had come.

Indeed, he was at that very moment safe in Isaac's power.

A few chosen men were then hastily called together, and instructed to ride off towards London with the least possible delay, and to endeavour to learn some intelligence concerning Mr. Price.

When this was done, Sir Thomas was more content, and once more returned to his quarters in the Governor's sitting-room.

But this temporary ease of mind did not last more than an hour.

By this time the Governor was compelled to admit that it was almost a certainty some strange accident had befallen the hangman, and there was no more likely supposition than that he had fallen into the hands of the prisoner's friends.

Nor up to seven o'clock was anything heard of the troop of officers.

Outside the prison the hum of the multitude could now be heard.

The deep fall of snow did not appear to have influenced their numbers in the least; and though the fleecy shower was still descending heavily, they stood with all imaginable patience, waiting for the prison gates to be thrown back upon their hinges.

How it had got abroad no one could precisely tell, but the assembled crowd were perfectly aware that the hangman had not put in an appearance according to custom, and that the circumstance had already caused no little anxiety and consternation within the prison walls.

Various were the speculations in which they indulged, and keen and close indeed was the look-out they kept for his arrival.

But the hour of eight arrived without anything having occurred, and then popular excitement and curiosity seemed at its highest pitch.

Not five minutes after the hour had been given forth, however, the cry was raised that the troop of police officers was returning.

Then the commotion was tremendous.

In answer to the question whether Mr. Price accompanied them, both negative and affirmative replies were given, so that the desire to know the actual truth increased each moment.

Those who were nearest to the gloomy portal had their doubts resolved when the troop pulled up before it.

Mr. Price was not with them.

Yet the officers of police did not return empty-handed.

They had with them a person who, judging by the close guard kept upon him, should surely be a prisoner.

Whether he was or not could not with any certainty be determined, for with all possible speed he was hustled through the doorway and hidden from vulgar gaze.

But as it is no part of our plan to keep the reader in the same state of doubt and uncertainty as the assembled crowd, we will state at once that this apparent prisoner was no other than Captain Hawk's stanch friend, Isaac.

How it was he came to be in this condition is quickly told.

Having carefully disguised himself and well considered the part he had to play, he set out on his perilous expedition.

By the careless manner in which he walked on through the snow—which came down in a blinding, bewildering shower—no one would have guessed that he was concerned in an enterprise so fraught with danger.

When within a short distance of Huntingdon, however, he fancied he heard sounds behind him, and this was the first thing that had occurred to break the monotony of his journey.

Looking back, he perceived a troop of mounted men riding at full speed.

Whether they were after him or not he knew not, but the point was one which would quickly be decided.

The horsemen formed the troop sent out by Sir Thomas, who had ridden far along the road in quest of information.

In vain, however, was it that they pursued their inquiries.

Not a trace of the hangman could be found, and so in sheer despair they turned back to deliver their report.

On seeing the figure of a man plodding through the snow they quickened their pace, determined on coming up with him to put the oft-repeated question, but without much hope of a satisfactory result.

The sight of these police officers produced anything but pleasurable feelings in Isaac's breast; and his sense of security was by no means heightened when at the word of command they abruptly pulled up and closed around

But in a wonderful manner the faithful fellow preserved his presence of mind and maintained an outward calm.

With wonderful readiness, he made up his mind how to act.

He did not wait for a single question to be asked him, but hobbled to the side of the chief officer's horse.

"Och, now! an' by the howly powers," he exclaimed, with distress so well feigned that the officers all took it to be genuine, "tell me now if ye are the blessed police officer, or do my eyes desave me?"

"Yes, we are police officers. But what is the matter with the man?"

"Och, wirrasthru! and why didn't ye come before? Oh, ye spalpeens! and where is it ye were when ye were wanted! Och! murder—murder!"

The officers now began to think that they had made a discovery at last.

"Speak—speak, you blundering Irish blockhead!" said the commanding officer. "Let us know what it is that has happened! Speak quickly, I say, for time is precious!"

"Blundherin' is it! Is it the likes of ye that call me blundherin'? Bad cess to the lot of ye! Where was ye, I ask?—tell me that—where was ye?"

"Will you tell us what has happened?"

"Tell ye, is it? And a moighty lot of good it would be if I did tell ye. No—no, I'll get on to the jail beyant and tell 'em there. Ye're no good, bad luck to ye! What do ye, or the likes of ye, care whether my poor old masther's dead or not?"

"Once for all," bawled the chief officer, furiously, "will you tell us who and what your master is?"

"Faix now, and did you think that I was going for to go to deny that same? Och! murder! Out and alas! Boohoo!—boohoo!"

The officer, in his desperate fury, would no doubt have done something terrible had not one of his men pressed forward and whispered:

"Unless I make the greatest mistake in the world, sir, that Irish lout is no other than Price's assistant."

"Can it be possible?"

"I am well-nigh certain of it. Something has happened, and he is almost distracted. Leave him be. He will soon out with it all."

This little conversation was not lost by Isaac, who was keenly alive to what was going on, yet so well did he play his part that the officers without exception believed him to be distracted by grief, and dead to everything.

Taking his cue from what the officer had just said, Isaac wiped his face with the cuff of his coat.

"And poor Moses, too!" he moaned, wringing his hands. "Och! the poor baste——"

"Who the devil's Moses?" bawled the chief officer.

"Sure, and isn't that the mule? Did you think I was going to deny him as well as masther?"

Glances were instantly exchanged by the officers, who, after hearing this, made no sort of doubt at all about their having got hold of Mr. Price's assistant.

Where the hangman himself could be, however, they were most anxious to know.

Accordingly the chief officer bawled:

"Where is your master?"

"By all the powers, now," said Isaac, "and can ye ask me that question? How should I know where he is, unless he is drawn and quartered?"

"Drawn and quartered! Why, who would harm him?"

"Captain Hawk's friends, to be sure. If you would but be quiet for half a minute I'd tell ye all about it, but ye make it onpossible for a poor man to spake. Oh, I'd be ashamed not to look after him better!"

"Will you tell us, or will you not?"

"Ain't I a tellin' ye, now? Sure, ye'd know all if ye would but listen. Don't I say that as we were ridin' along in the cart, and I was a smokhin' my poipe, and—and thinkin' about that thafe of the wurrld, Dennis Mac——"

The chief officer interrupted him with a howl of rage and impatience.

"I suppose," he yelled, "that you were attacked and stopped?"

"There, now, and see he knows all about it, and ye he'd ax me to tak it down again me! Oh, bad luck to the wurrld if I say another word!"

"Why, you double-distilled idiot, can't you see we are friends of yours and your master's too?"

"Friends? Och, now, I like that! The divil keep me from such friends! I tell ye my poor masther's murdered. Tak me to the jail, and it's myself that'll tell the Governor all about it; but divil a word more do you get out of me. Belike now I've said enough to ye to cause my own ruin."

"Oh, confound the fellow for the biggest fool alive!" cried the chief officer. "Take him up behind you, one of you, and we will gallop to the prison, where they will soon make him speak. It is loss of precious time to stop here questioning him ourselves."

Isaac, so far from making any objection to the course proposed, readily complied, and professed himself most anxious to be taken to the jail at once.

Off they went at full gallop, and, despite the character of the road, they got on with considerable swiftness.

The way took them past Ling Heath, where every preparation had been made for the execution.

It was indeed with singular feelings that Isaac looked upon the scene.

But no sensation of fear oppressed his heart.

The way in which things had gone up to the present moment gave him the greatest ground to hope for future success, and he determined that if a continuance of playing his part as well as he had done at present was alone required, that nothing should make him fail or forget himself.

The snow lay very thickly on the newly-erected scaffold and upon all the surrounding objects.

But the view which Isaac had of it was only transient.

The troop swept on at the same hard gallop, nor did they once relax their pace until they reached the prison walls.

What followed then is known already.

As quickly as possible Isaac was hurried into the vestibule.

The Governor and Sir Thomas were instantly sent for.

Both were in a terrible state of anxiousness, as were also the sheriffs and other officials concerned.

Sir Thomas was urging upon them the necessity and importance of obtaining a substitute immediately when the news was brought that Mr. Price's assistant had been found, and was at that moment beneath the prison roof.

Out they all sallied with the utmost precipitation, all being most eager to listen to what the supposed assistant had to say.

The situation now was one which would have made Isaac falter had he not possessed the strongest nerves.

But the thought that on him depended the captain's life was enough to make him do or dare ten thousand times as much, if that were possible.

Sir Thomas Walker stood forward from the rest, taking upon himself the direction of affairs.

He fixed a keen and scrutinising glance upon Isaac, who avoided his continued gaze by bowing almost to the ground.

And having once assumed this submissive attitude, he retained it.

"Now, fellow," said Sir Thomas, haughtily, "let us hear in a few words what you have to say. Where is your master? How is it he has failed in his appointment?"

"Faix, your honour, and it's through no fault of his at all, at all. Oh, help him—help him! But it's too late now, I'll be bound: he's kilt already."

"Speak plainly, man, and to the point. Understand, we have no time to spend in idle chatter. Speak, I say."

"May I make a clane breast of it, your honour?"

"Of course you must do so, only don't use too many words over it, or it will be the worse for you."

"Long life to your honour's honour!" said Isaac, with a lower bow than before.

His personation of an Irishman was in every way perfect: that it was may be inferred from Sir Thomas being completely deceived.

"Go on," he said.

"Well, your honour, if ye'll belave me, the journey was made right enough till within a dozen miles of this place."

[CAPTAIN HAWK'S DESPERATE LEAP.]

"Tell us quickly what happened then."

"Why, as we was ridin' along in the cart as quiet as could be, and never thinkin' of harm, what should happen but a whole gang of blackguards rode out into the road and stopped Moses."

"Who's Moses?"

"The mule, sir."

"Go on."

"They drew their swords, bad cess to them! and their pisthols, and swore to have both our lives, but we begged and we prayed, and so they bound us and gagged us instead."

"How is it you are here, then?"

"I'll tell ye in a moment, your honour. You might guess poor two of us could do nothing agin more than twenty. So they carried us away into the woods."

"And what said they?"

"That they were friends of Captain Hawk's, and that they had sworn his execution should not take place."

"I thought as much," muttered Sir Thomas, glad to find that his penetration had not been at fault. "Your master ought to have travelled well protected."

"Och! sure, sir, and he ought, but he'll want protection no more: the dhirty blackguards are thirsting for his life, every man of them."

"Go on with your tale."

"Faix, sir, and they threw us across their saddles like a couple of sacks, and away they went like the wind. Miles and miles we went into the woods, and then they threw us down on the ground bound and helpless, your honour."

"What next?"

"They swore to serve masther as he deserved: he should have the same as he meant for the captain. So they began to put a rope over a tree."

"To hang him?"

"Faix, yes, your honour. But they left me; and I found my bonds were not over tight, and slipped my hands out of them, and then I rolled into the wood. They were all round masther, and didn't mind me, so I up and run for dear life."

CHAPTER CXXXVIII.

CAPTAIN HAWK COMMENCES HIS RIDE TO THE SCAFFOLD.

THE tale which Isaac told tallied so exactly with what Sir Thomas fancied had taken place that he gave immediate credence to it.

Besides, Isaac had the advantage that his tale was not very far removed from the truth, which gave to the whole narrative an air of truthfulness which it would otherwise have lacked.

"And so you deserted your master, then, did you?" said the magistrate, sternly.

"Faix now, sir, don't be too hard upon a poor fellow!" Isaac whimpered. "Sure, and I did it all for the best. I couldn't help him by stopping, and as there was a chance of getting away myself I thought I should be a fool not to take it."

"Were you pursued?"

"They were afther me in a minute like so many wild cats, your honour, but I was running for dear life."

"And so you escaped?"

"Yes, I did, your honour, and here I am. Oh, it's a sorry day! And a kind good masther he was too! And now he's gone."

Isaac gave a horrible howling yell, expressive of his great grief for the loss of his master.

At this moment the Governor advanced a step or two and touched the magistrate lightly upon the arm.

"Sir Thomas—Sir Thomas!" he said.

"Well?"

"It seems your suspicions were thoroughly well founded."

"It was just what I feared."

"But yet I think there won't be much to complain of."

"How do you mean?"

"Why, as to Price, I consider it is no more than right that he should reap the reward of his own obstinate folly, because he has brought it all on himself."

"And not only that," interposed the sheriff, "but put us to all this dreadful delay, inconvenience, and anxiety."

"You are both right," said Sir Thomas. "The old man is to blame, and fully deserves all he will get."

"Just so. But what I was about to observe," said the Governor, "is that we have reached the end of our troubles, and the delay is not much more than often takes place."

The magistrate bent upon him an inquiring glance.

"This Irishman," he said, "will be glad enough for the sake of a small fee to do his master's duty."

"Has he ever done so before?"

"Not that I know of; but then he has been with Price quite long enough to know how to do it on an emergency."

Meanwhile Isaac had appeared to be thoroughly swallowed up by his grief, but in reality he was straining his ears to the utmost to hear what the Governor and Sir Thomas were saying.

As they spoke in whispered tones, it was only an occasional word that he was able to distinguish.

Still, he heard enough to let him know that they were about to propose to him the very thing he was so anxious to solicit.

"Harkye, fellow!" said Sir Thomas.

Isaac bowed down to the ground.

"You know what was wanted of your master this morning, don't you?"

"Faix, an' I do."

"Very well, then. As the execution cannot be delayed, you must prepare yourself to take your master's place."

Isaac bowed again, but did not trust himself to speak.

"If you do the job neatly and quickly," said Sir Thomas, "I will give you five guineas out of my own pocket, and I daresay the Governor will arrange matters so that you shall receive your master's fees in full."

"It all depends how he acquits himself."

"Acquits is it, your honours? Don't be afraid of me, then. Is it likely I'd be with the masther all this while and not know a something about the purfession? Sure, the captain sha'n't have to complain of any want of iligance in tucking him up."

Sir Thomas glanced at his massive gold repeater.

"It will be after nine before we are off."

"Not a moment shall be lost," said the Governor, bustling about quickly. "Oh! how thankful I shall be when we are once rid of the fellow! He has been more trouble to me than all the prisoners under my charge."

Calling to one of the warders, the Governor instructed him to take a couple of men and conduct the condemned prisoner to the pinioning-room, whither they would immediately repair.

The warder departed, and as soon as he had gone the Governor turned to Sir Thomas and the sheriffs, saying:

"Now, gentlemen, if you will come with me we will make our way to the pinioning-room without delay. The prisoner will not be long in coming."

"With all my heart!" exclaimed the magistrate.

The sheriffs and other officials also pressed eagerly forward.

"Bring him along, Watson," said the Governor to another turnkey—"show him the way."

Watson took hold of Isaac by the shoulder, and pushed him after the retreating throng.

The pinioning-room was quickly reached.

Isaac's heart beat high.

He was in a perpetual dread that Watson or some of the others would perceive his perturbation.

The efforts he made to preserve an outward calmness were tremendous.

The prisoner had not yet arrived though his appearance was looked for every moment.

The warders who had been sent to summon him found Captain Hawk pacing up and down the cell.

He was impatient and anxious.

It was easy to see that his feelings were very fully shared in by the two men by whom he was attended.

"What news, Gibbons?" cried the turnkey who had shared the captain's cell so long—"what news? Has the hangman come?"

"No."

"Not come?"

"No; but his assistant is."

"Where is Price?"

"That nobody knows, I fancy. The assistant is to do the job for him, so there won't be much delay after all."

"Is all ready, then?"

"Yes—everything; and the Governor has sent me to tell you to bring the prisoner to the pinioning-room at once."

"One moment," said Captain Hawk. "Tell me, if you can, what is supposed to be the reason of Price's non-appearance."

"I dare not say anything," was the answer. "And why do you ask? I'll be bound you know as much about it as anybody."

Captain Hawk could tell by the resolute look on the man's face that it would be in vain to attempt to draw any information from him.

Moreover, he felt to have scarcely control enough over himself to keep up a lengthened conversation.

Without attempting the least show of resistance, he followed the men from the cell.

He gave a glance round at its naked, desolate walls, for his heart told him he was taking his farewell look at them.

The pinioning-room was situated at the end of a long corridor.

Sir Thomas Walker's face brightened into an exultant grin when he beheld the hated form of the prisoner appear.

"Now is the consummation of my revenge at hand," he said. "At last I shall be satisfied."

Captain Hawk was pale, and outwardly calm and composed.

Isaac felt that he dared not take one single glance at him, not fearing so much a recognition and the consequences of it as he did the strength of his own self-command.

Captain Hawk's eyes roamed quickly over the whole assemblage.

It rested upon the bulky, ungainly form of the pretended hangman.

As it did so, his heart thrilled strangely, but in a manner for which he was unable to account.

Sir Thomas was determined no more time should be lost.

"Come, fellow," he said, addressing Isaac, "be quick with your duty."

Still with his head bent down, Isaac walked behind the captain, who instinctively shuddered at his approach.

A rope was produced, and with it Isaac bound the prisoner's elbows after the usual fashion.

His hands trembled, despite himself, all the time that he was thus engaged.

Then once, while he was bending down so as to make one of the knots beyond all question tight and secure, he murmured in the faintest possible whisper:

"Courage!"

The prisoner heard it.

A sudden start, which no mortal man could have avoided giving under such circumstances, sufficiently testified to this.

With ready wit, Isaac took care to prevent this from exciting any suspicion.

Confident that the whispered word had reached only the ear for which he intended it, he cried:

"Och, sir! And was it just a leetle too tight? Be aisy now."

An extra tightening of the cord might easily have produced such a movement as the prisoner gave.

The attention caused by this remark enabled him to keep his composure undisturbed.

But what a bewildering whirl his brain was in the reader may be able to form some dim and inadequate conception.

That the prisoner should exhibit emotion and confusion at this moment was so natural and usual that it excited neither suspicion nor remark.

"All's right now, sir," said Isaac, still counterfeiting an Irishman's accent with wonderful fidelity.

"Then we will start, if it pleases you, gentlemen?" said Sir Thomas.

"One moment," said a voice.

It was the chaplain who spoke.

He stood forward now with an open book in his hands.

"The delay will be inconsiderable," he said, with an apologetic bow to those assembled, "as it is not fitting that this hardened sinner should go forth to his death until I have once more assayed to make an impression upon his obdurate heart."

"If you mean by that," said Captain Hawk, "that you have not yet so stultified me as to make me confess myself guilty of that which I declare myself innocent, you have indeed assayed in vain; and I would not advise any renewal of the attempt, for you will only lose labour."

"Hardened criminal!" said the chaplain, with fervent indignation. "But the time is at hand when your base and contumacious career will be cut short, and when you will have to answer for the manifold villanies which lay to your charge."

"No matter what I have done," said Captain Hawk: "I here again declare what I have many times asserted, that I am entirely guiltless of the crime for which I am condemned."

The chaplain closed his book with a smart clap.

"Come on," said Sir Thomas. "As one might have supposed, your holy ministrations are thrown away upon this thrice-hardened sinner. Bring him along. He ought to have been treated to a shorter shrift than he has had."

But Captain Hawk continued to grow more hopeful and reliant.

The first shock of his surprise had passed away; and now he began to believe what he had suspected when the intelligence that a delay in the arrival of the executioner had occurred.

His friends had some deep-laid plan on foot, the object of which was his preservation; and he kept himself on the alert, so as to derive intelligence from every source.

The man who had bound him was a friend.

That admitted of no doubt; but yet he was very far indeed from suspecting his identity.

But now there was a general movement.

To some extent the plan which had been laid was successful.

It had caused hurry and confusion within the prison walls at a time when calmness and order were most requisite.

That this alone would go a long way towards making any sudden attack more likely to be successful than otherwise it would be cannot be doubted.

Isaac by many manœuvres contrived to keep all the time at the back of the prisoner.

He was terribly anxious that no action on his part should have the effect of jeopardising the captain's safety.

His dread was that the captain, on piercing the secret of his identity, would betray so much emotion as would make all present suspect that there was more in the matter than they were aware of.

In this manner the outer courtyard of the prison was reached.

Here the cart usually employed for conveying the condemned prisoners to the place of execution had long been waiting, as well as a chosen body of officers, who, under the directions of Sir Thomas Walker, were to keep strong and safe guard round the cart so as to prevent all possibility of a rescue of the prisoner.

The din of the people without was heard with great plainness, and the sound had so much of impatience and anger in it that even Captain Hawk started back a pace, while he felt his cheek suddenly grow white.

Promptly mastering these sensations, he looked upon all that surrounded him with an unquailing eye.

He was struck at first by the thick mantle of snow which enveloped every object, for the exciting nature of his situation made him forget all that he had heard about the snow-storm.

The cart was half filled up with the fleecy drift, and it lay piled thickly on the empty coffin provided for the reception of his corpse.

This object was painted black, and showed out in all the more ghastly contrast on account of the snow which was piled upon and around it.

The feathery shower still came down, but not with that amount of violence that it had done on Isaac's arrival at the prison.

Sir Thomas and those who were with him vented sundry curses upon the uncomfortable state of the weather.

It was now for the first time that Captain Hawk was enabled to take a tolerably good look at the new hangman.

More and more was he struck with the familiarity the form displayed, but yet so excellent was Isaac's disguise, and so well did he perform his part, that complete recognition eluded him.

By what means he was to be rescued of course remained a profound mystery to him.

But there was no longer any dejection in his breast, though, for fear of exciting the suspicions of his foes, he subdued as well as he could all signs and manifestations of the hope which thrilled his heart.

The men who had been waiting in the courtyard so long looked completely frozen up by the cold, and as they rubbed their blue benumbed fingers together they muttered deep curses upon the delay and the occasion of it.

Nor did the final appearance of the prisoner serve to cheer their spirits very much, though they gladly began to bustle about so as to complete their preparations.

Some huge hackney carriages had been provided for the accommodation of the Governor and the other officials, including Sir Thomas.

These were now brought forward, for it was deemed advisable to form the procession as far as possible before starting.

The crowd that had assembled round the courtyard gates was something unexampled in its magnitude.

Some hint of what was going on appeared to have

come to the knowledge of those without, for the din was increased tenfold.

As he heard the sound and glanced at the forms of the half-frozen escort that had been provided, Sir Thomas Walker felt some slight uneasiness, and wished that still further precautions had been taken.

This was now too late, and he was forced to content himself with thinking that all was right enough, and would prove so in the end.

Captain Hawk was roughly bidden to advance.

As he knew resistance would be futile and ridiculous, he made a virtue of necessity by complying quickly.

As his elbows were securely pinioned at the back, it was of course no easy matter to enter the cart.

To facilitate this some short steps were provided and placed in a convenient position.

He mounted at once; but when he stood in the cart the snow came up over his ankles.

"Where shall I sit?" he said.

"On the coffin, or where you like."

"But surely you do not expect me to sit down on that snow?"

"Why should you be so over-particular?" said the Governor, with a loud chuckle. "You won't have to put up with the inconvenience long, so you might resign yourself to putting up with it."

This treatment made Isaac's blood boil, and in the height of his resentment it is ten thousand wonders he did not say or do something to betray himself.

To master his anger at all, he was obliged to stoop down and affect to busy himself in clearing off the superincumbent snow from the coffin-lid.

"Thank you, my brave fellow!" said the captain. "One often finds a friend in the most unexpected and unlikely quarter. But I'll not forget you for it."

"Come—come, enough of this!" said Sir Thomas. "It seems as though you had made up your minds not to start to-day! Bring a truss of straw here, somebody—there must be something put in the cart. Be quick, now!"

A truss of straw was quickly produced from the prison stables and thrown into the cart.

This seemed all that was needed to complete the preparations and put them in readiness to start.

But what with one delay and another, the magistrate found, on referring to his watch, that the hour was half-past nine.

"An hour and a half late!" he exclaimed, with the utmost vexation. "I would not have had this occur on any account!"

"It is better than I hoped for," said the Governor, with a yawn. "I shall be glad when it is over, so that I can have a few hours' comfortable sleep, which is a thing I have never enjoyed since that confounded fellow has been in the jail."

The truss of new straw made the inside of the cart tolerably comfortable.

It was usual for the chaplain to ride in the vehicle along with the prisoner, reading prayers by the way.

On the present occasion he was glad enough to make an excuse to ride in one of the covered vehicles, where he would be protected from the inclement weather.

"Not that I mind it for myself," he said, with a hypocritical sigh. "Could I see but a reasonable prospect of doing good, gladly—oh! gladly would I bear ten times as much! But, alas! I have proved that all my holy efforts are unavailing. He is one that will preserve his contumaciousness even till the last minute."

The chaplain was almost affected to tears.

"Oh, get into the hackney-coach, of course!" said Sir Thomas. "You might know that all your pious eloquence would be thrown away on such a hardened wretch."

The chaplain groaned, and then complied.

He had salved his conscience, and was content.

This was another sign that Fortune had determined to do her utmost for the bold highwayman.

The cold, uncomfortable morning turned out a disguised blessing for him.

But for it the chaplain would certainly have ridden in the cart, and while seated there uttering his prayers it would have been a matter almost beyond possibility for Isaac to make the necessary communication with the captain.

Even as it was there were grave obstacles in the way, but they had lost so much of their importance by being viewed in contrast with others of far greater magnitude, that Isaac thought nothing of them.

At last the officers were marshalled in due order.

At last the huge folding gates that secured the prison yard were thrown back on their massive hinges.

No sooner was this done than a deep and death-like silence fell upon all the vast assembly.

The uproar ceased as though suddenly suspended by the spell of some all-potent magician.

Each person in the crowd was suddenly governed by the desire to catch a glimpse of the prisoner who had been so long and patiently waited for.

A clear space had been kept round the prison gates, and into this the officers who formed the head of the procession now marched.

Isaac seated himself in the cart close to the captain, and took hold of the reins.

All had gone so unexpectedly well up to the present that he was most sanguine as to the ultimate result.

The police officers, according to their instructions, formed a dense, close guard round the cart, and marched in exact step with the horse that drew it.

The hackney-coaches in which sat Sir Thomas, the Governor, the chaplain, and the sheriffs, then followed, and the rear was brought up by another body of officers, so as to keep the crowd from pressing forward.

It was with most singular and altogether indescribable feelings that Captain Hawk passed out into the open streets.

The enormous mass of human faces, all turned towards him, and all as hushed and motionless as if in death, had an effect that can only be described by the word appalling.

Captain Hawk instinctively shrunk as it were within himself.

The silence only lasted for a moment.

Then came a general buzz, which quickly deepened into a roar that could only have been surpassed by the sea itself.

Then all was commotion and confusion.

The crowd wanted to accompany the cart to its place of destination.

The frost-bitten police officers glanced at each other with visible disquietude, and closed closer together.

With steady but regular force they pushed their way onward through the dense, swaying mass.

Sir Thomas thrust his head and half his body out at the window of the hackney-coach, for he could not bear the idea of losing a glimpse of the prisoner.

But he was quickly warned that this was an impolitic proceeding.

A huge cabbage in an advanced state of decomposition was hurled at him with unerring aim.

Had he not moved very quickly, the blow must have proved very severe.

As it was, the damage he sustained was far too great to be endured patiently.

He drew in his head with great precipitation.

No sooner had he done so than a roar of delight from the mob greeted his ears, and increased his ire beyond all measure.

With the most bitter imprecations, he put up the window and threw himself back on the carriage seat.

But the triumphal roar of the populace still rung in his ears.

CHAPTER CXXXIX.

LORD HARCLIFFE INGRATIATES HIMSELF WITH THE CHIEF POLICE OFFICER.

Let us now avail ourselves of the opportunity of taking a retrospect of the proceedings of those true-hearted friends of Captain Hawk without whose aid his condition would have been desperate indeed.

The reader will remember that every arrangement had been duly talked over and decided on, so that now all we have to do is to describe with all possible briefness what it was that they actually performed after the time when Isaac took his departure from the Greyhound Inn.

They had learned from Mr. Marchant that Ling Heath was the place appointed for the execution.

Had the authorities consulted them on the occasion they could not have selected a place to suit them better.

"Oh, if I could but take some active part in the remainder of this enterprise!" said Tom Beckford, with a sigh. "But, alas! it is not to be thought of!"

"You are right enough there—it is not; so banish the regret from your mind at once. Even to show yourself would only be to bring down destruction on your head."

"And then that would deprive you of a safe resting-place at times."

"Look at it in that light if you think that will enable you to reconcile yourself to stopping away," said Lord Harcliffe, warmly. "And whatever you do, keep a good watch over the prisoners during our absence, for I do not want you to get into trouble on our account."

"Trust me," said the landlord, with a twinkle in his eye; "I will keep them safe enough."

"And now," said Pharoah, "don't you think it would be prudent for us to start? Remember, a dense crowd will certainly assemble round the scaffold, and if the plan is to be properly carried out we must take up particular positions."

"Yes," said Tom Beckford; "and in my opinion it is quite time you thought about starting."

"Very true," said Lord Harcliffe to the landlord. "And now tell me whether you have provided that other horse we spoke about?"

"Yes; he is now in the stable ready for immediate service. I am not afraid that he will give you satisfaction."

"Very good. And have you found a boy for the purpose required?"

"Yes; he is now in the kitchen. Don't be afraid of his fidelity."

"You have managed things excellently," said Lord Harcliffe.

Tom Beckford made a low bow, and looked embarrassed.

"Excuse me," he said at length, "but I should feel better satisfied if we could just run over my duties again."

"Certainly, if you wish it."

"Tell me, then, if I am right."

"Go on."

"You and your friend will start, you on your own horse, and your friend on Captain Hawk's?"

"Just so."

"When the captain makes his leap you will assist him, and your friend will vacate the saddle?"

"Right again."

"Isaac and your friend will then have their personal safeties to look to."

"Yes; and, as you know, they feel that they can look to themselves sufficiently well if the captain and myself ride off without troubling about them."

"Of course," said Pharoah, "because any delay will prove fatal. The very moment Captain Hawk is in the saddle flight must be instantaneous."

"We agreed to all that," said the landlord; "and now for the remainder of my duties."

"That is the point."

"Be sure, then, that I am right. It behoves us all to exercise the extremest care. The most trivial thing might make the enterprise miscarry, and I don't want any blame to rest on my shoulders."

"If you are only careful," said Lord Harcliffe, "all will be well."

"I will try my best. After you have started I shall send the lad I spoke of with the two horses—the gray and the new one."

Lord Harcliffe nodded.

"The horses will be saddled and bridled carefully ready for immediate use, and the boy will take them in a roundabout direction to the small clump of trees close to the north-west corner of Ling Heath."

"You remember and understand your instructions perfectly," said Lord Harcliffe; "and if you will only have them carried out accordingly there is no fear of the enterprise failing in that particular."

"I think I can make sure of that. The boy will wait, and not surrender the horses until Isaac and your friend appear."

"Exactly."

"All that, then, will be performed, you may rely on it," said the landlord.

With this assurance both were perfectly satisfied; and without any more words they set about completing their preparations for a start.

Pharoah and Lord Harcliffe both disguised themselves with the utmost care, in which operation the landlord was of the utmost service.

At length, all being ready, they started on their dangerous mission.

"How right Isaac was about the snow-storm coming!" said Lord Harcliffe, as he seated himself carefully in the saddle.

"Yes; and we may consider that as a favourable augury, I should think; for however anxious the people may be to be present at the execution, such inclement weather as this must have the effect of thinning their numbers."

"It is just possible."

"Let us hope so," said Tom Beckford, who had overheard the remarks. "For my own part, I am doubtful."

"Doubtful? Why?"

"Because I never yet knew the weather bad enough to keep the people away from such a sight as they think to have to-day."

"I fancy you are right, Tom," said Lord Harcliffe. "And now farewell. When I come back again it will be in company of our old and trusty friend Captain Hawk."

"Farewell; and good luck go with you!" said Tom, with tears in his eyes; and as he spoke the Black Highwayman and Pharoah started off at a canter.

About the former there was that air of calm determination which had so distinguished him of old, and which had carried him so successfully through so many perilous shifts.

Not a nerve trembled, and to all appearances he was as calm and composed as any human being could possibly be.

The snow continued to fall with tolerable steadiness and swiftness.

All around as far as ever the eye could reach the white mantle was spread on every object.

A dim, strange light was in the air, and there were no signs visible that the storm was about to cease.

"Be careful of your own safety, Pharoah," said Lord Harcliffe, after a long pause, during which he had been thinking deeply. "To speak the truth, I am scarcely satisfied now I come to reflect upon the arrangements that have been made in that respect."

"Why not?"

"I fear you will be in a dangerous strait."

"Do not distress yourself about that," said Pharoah; "rely upon it, Isaac and myself will be right. The pursuit would be made after you and the captain, not us; and if they divide their forces to look after both, they are almost certain to have neither."

Lord Harcliffe was silent, and seemingly content with what his faithful attendant had said.

They had some little trouble in keeping the fiery-blooded horses down to the moderate canter at which they started.

But even at this pace they were not long in reaching the spot appointed for the execution.

Tom Beckford was proved to be the best judge about the effect the weather would have upon the assemblage of the multitude.

Already many hundreds of people had assembled, and, having taken up favourable positions round the scaffold, waited with wonderful patience for the arrival of the victim.

"We are here none too soon," Lord Harcliffe murmured, in tones just loud enough to reach his companion's ears.

"Almost too late, are we not, to take up the position we had determined on?"

"No, I think not," said Lord Harcliffe, "provided we can obtain the means of communicating with the officer in charge."

Pharoah was so used to the extraordinary things his master was in the habit of saying or doing that he made no answer to this most extraordinary remark, though it caused him to give an inquiring stare.

"I have just thought of a little stratagem," said Lord Harcliffe, "by means of which I feel tolerably sure we shall be able to get as close to the scaffold as we desire."

"What is it?"

"Why, our being disguised as country gentlemen or well-to-do farmers just enables me to think of such a plausible tale that I feel sure the officers will be imposed on by it."

By this time the outskirts of the crowd had been gained; and Lord Harcliffe, rising in the stirrups, was able to catch a glimpse of the police officers who were engaged in the chilling and unpleasant duty of keeping a clear space round the scaffold."

As the Black Highwayman had fully expected, the arrival of himself and his companion had been duly noticed by the officers and commented upon, so that when he rose in the stirrups in the way we have just mentioned he had no trouble at all in catching the eye of the officer in command.

Lord Harcliffe then made a beckoning gesture, which had so authoritative an air that the officer immediately sent one of his men to know what it was the two horsemen wanted.

This man forced his way through the crowd without much difficulty, for the crowd opened into a kind of lane to allow him free progress.

On his gaining the side of Phantom, Lord Harcliffe bent down to whisper in the man's ear.

At the same time, unperceived by anyone, he dropped a guinea into his palm.

It was wonderful to see what an effect the touch of the precious metal had.

The officer was all attention, and prepared to listen with all eagerness to what Lord Harcliffe had to say.

"I want you to go back to your chief, and tell him that two gentlemen want to have a few moments' speech with him."

"Very good, sir. I have no doubt he will come."

Lord Harcliffe nodded.

The man hastened off.

"Whatever is it you have in contemplation?" asked Pharoah, with fast-increasing wonderment.

"Hush—hush! You will understand all in a moment or two."

The officer delivered his message, which was received at first with a great deal of distrust.

But the gift of the guinea made the subordinate officer so eloquent that he prevailed over the disinclination the chief at first felt to leave his post at all.

"He's coming," whispered Lord Harcliffe to Pharoah, as soon as the officer started. "All will be well now, trust me."

Pharoah could not make out what was going to happen.

But he was not kept in suspense for many moments.

The chief officer came close to Lord Harcliffe.

There was something in the latter's appearance which made the officer salute him respectfully.

"I understand, sir," he said, "that you wish to speak to me."

"I do," was the reply, "if you are the officer in command of the guard round the scaffold."

"I have the honour to be that individual," was the reply.

"Then, hearing that that notorious rascal and vagabond, Captain Hawk, was going to be executed this morning, myself and friend determined to ride over and witness it."

The chief officer bowed, and waited for Lord Harcliffe to explain himself a little further.

"The confounded villain," he continued, "once stopped us within half a mile of home, and robbed us of every shilling and article of value we carried. I never was more exasperated in all my life, and I swore then that I would ride a hundred miles, if required, in order to see him make the acquaintance of Jack Ketch."

"Yes, sir—I can quite understand you; but——"

"You were going to say you can't think what it has to do with you."

The officer bowed again, probably thinking that was a respectful and delicate manner of giving an affirmative reply to a somewhat embarrassing question.

"I can explain myself in half a dozen words," continued Lord Harcliffe. "You see, we have come somewhat late, and as I don't want to put up with a distant view of the ceremony, I want you to find us a place close to the scaffold."

"I'm afraid, sir——"

"Now, don't say it can't be done, because I have something here which smoothes away all difficulties."

So saying, he pushed a purse into the officer's hand.

"There," he said, "that contains twenty guineas. Put it into your pocket, and say nothing."

"But——"

"Now, I am too impatient to take up my position to hear any objections. Put it into your pocket and lead the way."

The officer complied, but, as it seemed, almost against his will.

"Ten to one," he muttered, "if I sha'n't get into trouble over this. But never mind," he added, "twenty pounds will form a tolerably good plaster."

The people, of course, had to make way for the return of the police officer, though a few grumbled a good deal at having to make room for the two horsemen.

Pharoah was amazed and vastly delighted, too.

He could hardly have believed that so bold a scheme would have succeeded so admirably.

But even now he trembled a little for the consequences.

Under the guidance of the chief officer, it took them but a very few moments to reach the scaffold.

The police officers were drawn up round it so as to keep a clear open space.

They gazed at Lord Harcliffe and his companion with a good deal of curiosity, but, of course, did not venture to raise any question concerning what their commander had done.

"It's a great wonder you were not too late altogether," said the chief, as soon as Lord Harcliffe and Pharoah had taken up such positions as they judged would be favourable to their design.

"Why?"

"The hour is long past when the prisoner should have been here. Something of an unusual character has happened."

"You don't think the villain has escaped?" cried Lord Harcliffe, with well-affected dismay.

"No, no—little fear of that. I dare be sworn that is not the reason of the delay."

"I hope he will come soon," said Lord Harcliffe, "or I shall be frozen to death."

"It's awfully cold for certain," replied the chief, as he shook the masses of snow from his apparel.

Tom Beckford had taken care to stow into the pockets of Lord Harcliffe's coat and Pharoah's too, a large flat bottle, filled with the best brandy procurable.

The former thought about this, and at the same moment felt that he should never have an opportunity of making better use of it.

All the officers were perfectly blue with cold, and stood shivering and beating their hands against their breasts.

"It is awfully cold!" said Lord Harcliffe.

He drew forth the quart bottle as he spoke.

"Here is something that will drive the cold away pretty well," he added.

It was truly amusing to see how all the officers' eyes glistened when the bottle of spirits was produced.

"You are quite welcome to share it among you," said Lord Harcliffe.

A suppressed cheer instantly followed, showing how welcome the announcement was.

"After you, sir, if you please," said the chief officer to Lord Harcliffe, though his mouth watered to such a degree that he could hardly speak at all.

Lord Harcliffe was by no means sorry to avail himself of the opportunity of quaffing deeply of the spirit himself; and having taken the first draught, he handed it to Pharoah, who did not fail to pay his respects to it most liberally.

Then it came to the chief officer's turn.

He grasped the bottle, and then the way in which the brandy gurgled down his capacious throat was a wonder to see.

It was only when compelled by sheer lack of breath that he left off.

The officer next to him snatched away the bottle, observing very little ceremony in his mode of action.

But it was snatched away from him by the one who

stood nearest before he had taken half the quantity he intended to imbibe.

In this manner the bottle promptly circulated; and, owing to the quantity and the rapidity with which it passed from one to the other, each man had his share.

As may be expected, a great amount of good-fellowship was produced by this politic gift on Lord Harcliffe's part, and the whole of them chatted and laughed together as though they had been intimately acquainted for years.

Not one compunctious thought about the fellow-creature who was doomed to perish before their eyes in so short a space of time troubled their minds.

Although not much given to tender emotions, Lord Harcliffe was disgusted at the callousness they manifested, though, of course, he was compelled to disguise his feelings.

And so the time passed on, but still the condemned man came not.

"Something has happened," said the chief officer—"there can't possibly be two opinions about that. What it is I can't think. If anybody but Captain Hawk were in the case I should say that a reprieve had come."

"And you think it impossible in his case?"

"Oh yes—I'd wager my life upon it. Have patience, and you will see the procession make its appearance ere long."

And now, as minute after minute passed, the huge crowd which had assembled began to get more and more turbulent and unruly.

They showed their impatience in various rough ways, and the chief officer began to grow apprehensively anxious as to what might ensue.

The still-falling snow made it most unpleasant for those who were wedged tightly in the living mass, and every person present felt that he was being badly used because the show did not come off punctually at the appointed hour.

Lord Harcliffe observed the growing discontent with great anxiety.

He had calculated very confidently upon the people at large readily joining in to give their assistance the moment they saw there was a chance of the captain being snatched from the hands of his foes.

But now there was the terrible fear that the ever-fickle mob would feel incensed against the captain, and for that reason be unwilling to separate until the sentence of the law was fully carried out.

All these doubts and fears Lord Harcliffe was obliged to keep rigidly locked up in his own breast, and, besides, pretend to be quite differently disposed.

An hour passed, and the procession seemed just as far off appearing as the snow-storm was from ceasing.

The gravest fears now filled the hearts of Lord Harcliffe and Pharoah, and the only conclusion they could come to by way of explanation was the unpleasant one that something or other had occurred to mar Isaac's scheme.

Every moment seemed to increase the certainty of this supposition, and it was just as they were fairly resigning themselves to despair that a roaring sound on the outskirts of the crowd proclaimed that the long-delayed procession was at last in sight.

CHAPTER CXL.

ISAAC PAYS A PENALTY FOR HIS DEVOTION.

We go back now to Captain Hawk and his escort.

For a moment or two after the cabbage had been hurled at the head of Sir Thomas Walker, a general apprehension was felt that this missile was but the commencement of a regular attack upon the guard.

But this fear proved groundless.

The people all laughed at the ludicrous suddenness with which the magistrate drew his head back out of danger, and then they one and all pressed forward as though their impatience to witness the much-delayed execution outweighed every other consideration.

But there was one who did not fail to avail himself of the opportunity which this chance occurrence gave him to carry out his intentions.

This was Isaac.

He had carefully noted everything, and when the cabbage was thrown he felt that the identical moment had arrived for him to make his communication to the captain.

The precise manner of doing this seemed not a little difficult.

But without stopping to think, Isaac said, in his natural voice:

"Captain!"

The tones in which he spoke were suppressed, yet not so much so as to prevent the word from reaching the prisoner's ears with perfect plainness.

"Beware," added Isaac, hastily, and still in the same low tones. "Don't start—don't move—don't let anyone perceive your emotion. Take my word for it, captain, you are saved."

How welcome and how pleasantly such words as these would sound in the ears of a condemned man it would be vain for us to attempt to describe.

The reader can imagine what a thrill shot through the form of Captain Hawk while Isaac spoke.

We cannot go so far as to say that he manifested no emotion.

On the contrary, had he been observed with the least closeness, it must have been seen that a communication of an important nature must have been made to him.

But Isaac had chosen his time well.

Whatever emotion the captain showed was unnoticed for at the instant no one had eyes for any other object than the magistrate's carriage.

Isaac gave a hasty glance.

He saw that the attention of the guard was still distracted so in yet hastier tones he continued:

"Don't ask a single question, captain, or we shall, ten to one, all be lost. Do just precisely what I say at the very moment when I tell you, and all will be well."

"But——"

"Hush—hush! I see that I can say no more just at this moment without fear of detection. But as I go on I will pretend to be singing half aloud, and you must gather what else is necessary for you to know as well as you are able."

Captain Hawk bent his head to show that he perfectly understood and fully agreed to this arrangement.

Isaac was right.

By this time all fear that there was about to be an organised attack on the procession passed away, and it would have been highly dangerous had he attempted to carry on the conversation.

Captain Hawk accepted the assurance that he was saved in perfect good faith.

But of what was to follow he was unable to form the slightest conjecture.

The whole seemed to him like some extraordinary and incomprehensible delusion.

But notwithstanding the whirl of his thoughts, he collected himself sufficiently to lean forward and give an attentive ear to the monotonous, half-articulate chant which his faithful friend commenced without the loss of another moment.

Of course, had the chaplain been in the cart it would have been almost, if not quite impossible, for Isaac to have done thus much.

As it was, such a means of communication was very far from being satisfactory.

Nevertheless, after bestowing much attention, Captain Hawk comprehended that at the moment when the cart rested beneath the scaffold Isaac would pretend to be engaged in tightening his bonds.

Instead of this he would with the sharp knife he had in his hand sever the cords at one stroke.

Then the captain was to look out for the Black Highwayman, and, summoning up all his energies, make a tremendous jump towards him.

There he would find Satan, and what he would have to do would be to fly for his life.

That was the plan.

Fain would the captain after he had heard it have asked one or two of the thousand questions that came thronging to his lips, and with so much force that he could scarce restrain them.

His first thought was, how should Isaac be saved?

For his own part he could see no means by which he could elude the vengeance of his foes.

Yet he could not bring himself to believe that the

sacrifice of Isaac for his sake formed part and parcel of the scheme for his release.

If so, he would never consent to it.

But in the present stage of affairs little or no discretion had been left him.

Isaac chanted a few more words.

Captain Hawk listened to them with even greater eagerness than any which had preceded them.

What Isaac said was merely to the effect that upon no consideration was the captain to hesitate or ask a single question—that such a course would be full of peril, and that every arrangement had been carefully made and planned up to the minutest detail.

With such an assurance as this, he was of course compelled to rest content.

But still, when he came to think of what was actually to be done, a kind of shudder overspread his whole frame.

Most certain is it that no one under less desperate circumstances than his own would have dreamed for a moment of trying so hazardous an experiment.

But then the captain's life was already forfeit.

His foes already laid claim to and intended to take all that they were able.

Consequently the slightest chance was to him likely to be of benefit.

And with regard to the scheme which Isaac had dimly shown to him, even if it failed, he could but lose his life after all, so that it was impossible for him to be in the least degree a loser by such an attempt, rash and desperate as it was.

Slowly, very slowly, the procession in the meantime moved on.

The nearer they came to the spot where the scaffold stood the more difficult it became to force a passage through the dense assemblage.

It was not, however, until fairly upon the heath that Captain Hawk was enabled to catch a glimpse of the hideous apparatus of death, in consequence of the road they took skirting a dense plantation of trees, which formed an impenetrable screen.

He was warned by Isaac when to look out.

"Now, captain," he said, "in half another moment I hope you will be able to see your friends and your own faithful steed."

Captain Hawk looked up quickly.

But the violence of his emotions was so great as to bring a blinding mist over his eyes.

Strive as he would, he could see nothing

Gladly would he have dashed the troublesome moisture away, but his tightly-pinioned arms prevented it.

He hung his head, and by a great effort recovered his self-command.

When he raised his head and looked round again, it was with a fearless and unquailing gaze.

Despite the fine, driving snow, which was borne onwards with great violence by the blast, he was able to discern all.

He saw the excited, far-reaching crowd.

He saw the black, hideous-looking uprights which supported the fatal beam.

He saw, too, the officers, half smothered in snow as they were, who had been keeping guard so long round the scaffold.

Then, last of all, he saw distinctly what Isaac had told him he would see.

His heart gave a great bound, and again he all but lost his self-possession.

The desire to look again, however, to make sure that his eyes had not deceived him, was strong enough to rise paramount over all.

He did look again.

All remained unaltered.

He could see Lord Harcliffe.

Despite the disguise in which he had attired himself, Captain Hawk readily recognised the familiar outlines of his friend's form.

He saw Pharoah, too, though, of course, who this was he had no means of knowing.

But what affected him most of all was the certainty he felt that the horse this unknown friend bestrode was no other than his matchless steed Satan.

At this moment such a desperate desire for liberty filled all the highwayman's frame that he felt that he could have burst the bonds that bound him like so much flax.

Wisely, he forbore from making any such attempt.

"Oh," he murmured to himself, "could I but once lay my hand upon my horse's bridle I should indeed feel that I was saved! I should laugh to scorn all the efforts of my foes, and boldly defy them to do their worst."

Of course, this was just the frame of mind for Captain Hawk to be in when about to dare the accomplishment of so tremendous an undertaking.

There was no shrinking, no quailing, no fearfulness as to the result.

He would do it, or fling away his life in the attempt.

On his part, Lord Harcliffe was scarcely less affected.

When he saw his comrade appear, and when he saw him approaching so closely to the scaffold, his excitement became so great that he almost betrayed himself.

The crisis had arrived.

What would be the result?

Never had the enterprise presented half the danger of appearance that it did now.

It seemed really impossible that anything so rash and venturous should succeed.

But suspense would soon be ended.

There was another person, too, who must not be omitted from mention, because the excitement under which he laboured was not at all inferior to that felt by the persons we have just mentioned.

We allude, of course, to Sir Thomas Walker.

As the scaffold was approached his excitement grew so ungovernable that he felt he would endure any ill-usage rather than keep his eyes off the prisoner whom he regarded with so deadly a hate.

Again there was not only his head but half his body thrust out at the carriage window.

Now no one seemed to notice.

The huge multitude appeared unable to bestow a single glance on any other object than the prisoner, whose firmness and fearlessness of demeanour so far was the theme of every tongue.

Sir Thomas Walker gave a keen and comprehensive glance around.

It was with feelings of satisfaction which cannot be expressed that he found nothing whatever of a character calculated to excite the least apprehension in his breast.

Fain would the Governor have used the same means as the magistrate to ascertain the actual condition of affairs, but then he had a due regard for his own person, and knew pretty well what sort of treatment he should be most likely to receive from the mob if he afforded them such an opportunity.

So he was forced to content himself with remaining inside.

From time to time he tugged hard at the stiff skirts of Sir Thomas Walker's coat, but it was in vain.

His colleague was by far too much engrossed to pay him any attention.

As Fate would have it, Sir Thomas Walker was unable to see from his side of the carriage that part of the scaffold close to which Lord Harcliffe and Pharoah were standing.

Had he perceived them it is just possible that his suspicions would have been aroused.

The crowd, however, was so unusually orderly and silent, that he felt no fears.

A more energetic tug than ever at his coat skirts caused him to withdraw into the carriage.

The Governor was all anxiety.

"Well," he said, "what is your opinion?"

"I see no cause whatever for apprehension," he said. "We have been suffering a great deal of needless alarm, I think."

"Let us hope so," said the Governor. "For my own part I have seen a great deal of crowds, and I place no dependence in them. The very quiet which reigns this morning I take to be a bad and dangerous sign."

No sooner had he heard this than up jumped Sir Thomas, and out went his head again.

The hangman's cart was very near indeed to the foot of the scaffold.

Two seconds at the most would only have to elapse before it would reach the spot where it ought to pause.

Sir Thomas watched it stop.

[THE DEATH OF ISAAC.]

No sooner had the wheels ceased to revolve than, utterly heedless of consequences, he dashed open the carriage-door and sprang to the ground.

He was scarcely within the carefully-guarded circle, but, with a continuation of the desperation of behaviour he had just displayed, he elbowed his way through the throng until he reached the uprights of the scaffold.

The Governor followed his example, and after him came the chaplain.

The fact that no opposition was offered to their progress, and no attempt made to ill-use them, was probably owing to the absorbing interest which was felt in the prisoner.

Perhaps, too, those who stood nearest were particularly anxious that the execution should take place without further delay, and so allowed all the officials to pass unimpeded.

Isaac was rather disappointed and disconcerted by the promptitude of action which Sir Thomas Walker displayed.

It made the task he had to undertake far more difficult, for he had hoped to enable the captain to make his leap while the cart had no other occupants than themselves.

This was impossible, for, with a continuation of the same almost supernatural alacrity, Sir Thomas Walker climbed into the cart.

Then, and not till then, did he venture to breathe freely.

He was now within reach of the object of his vengeance, and his dread of the accomplishment of an escape was much allayed.

Captain Hawk was in a fever of impatience.

The sight of his trusty friends so close to him, and, above all, of his matchless steed, made him feel that he could do more than any other man.

It was only with difficulty that he restrained himself from making the attempt to burst his bonds by main force, and, such was his excitement, that he felt that if he made the attempt his strength was sufficient to insure success.

It was only the dread of endangering the success of what his friends had arranged to do that enabled him to hold back.

Meanwhile, the officials took up their usual places in the cart.

The chaplain, opening his book, began to read aloud; but what he said was not only rendered unintelligible by the dinning tone in which he spoke, but also by the hum which the huge multitude gave forth.

Isaac's heart beat high.

The critical moment had arrived.

Unperceived by anyone, he had contrived to get an open knife concealed up his sleeve, with the handle conveniently turned towards his hand.

Most particular had he been to sharpen it until it might have vied with the sharpest razor for keenness of edge.

One stroke and he felt that the cords which bound the prisoner could be cut completely through.

All being now nearly ready for the consummation of the expected tragedy, an intense silence fell upon the assembled multitude.

There was no humming now.

The silence could only be accounted for by the supposition that every individual spectator was holding his breath.

Sir Thomas was so intent upon the prisoner that up to this moment he had not noticed the presence of two horsemen in such close contiguity to the scaffold.

He was satisfied that the crowd should show such an appearance of perfect calmness, and had began to lose a great deal of the alarm which had oppressed his heart.

But now the Governor, who had fixed his eye-glass properly, glanced around, and, as a matter of course, his attention was instantly fixed upon Lord Harcliffe and Pharoah.

Who could they be?

That was the question which, with quite alarming suddenness, sprang up into his mind.

His immediate act was to pluck his coadjutor by the sleeve in order to call his attention to it, and receive his opinion.

Isaac at the same moment felt that the crisis had come.

Seizing with one hand the rope which hung dangling by the cross-beam, he made a feint of hanging his weight upon it, so as to test its security.

The people seeing this sent up a faint cry.

Precisely at the same moment, Isaac said:

"Now, captain—now! Jump for your life!"

He accompanied the words by a vigorous stroke of the knife.

The ropes parted as though they had been merely thread.

Captain Hawk was fully prepared.

Summoning up the whole of the energies he possessed, he gave one terrific spring.

The action was accompanied by a dreadful yell which came from the lips of Sir Thomas Walker.

At first he could hardly believe in the evidence of his own vision; and after emitting that sound he stood for some seconds as though deprived of all animation.

Having turned to the Governor at the instant when Isaac severed the bonds, he was utterly at a loss to imagine by what mysterious means the prisoner had contrived to get free.

The officers who were keeping guard were not less overwhelmed by amazement.

Certainly they were incapable of immediate action.

Captain Hawk's mad leap was successful.

No one had anticipated the occurrence of any such thing, and we need not point out how very much this told in his favour.

He half fell — half-alighted beside Lord Harcliffe's steed.

Both the prisoner's friends were thoroughly prepared, and wonderfully swift in action.

Pharoah was out of the saddle in an instant, and before the captain was able to recover himself sufficiently to know just where he was, he found he was bestriding his own noble steed.

But when this knowledge did come upon him it produced so overwhelming an effect—the reaction was so great—that the well-planned scheme was in danger of failure even at the very moment of success.

A couple of words clearly pronounced by the Black Highwayman luckily had the effect of bringing the captain to himself.

"Make way—make way!" Lord Harcliffe cried, urging his horse forward, but still retaining his hold upon Satan's bridle—"make way, I say, good friends all, and let the Governor be cheated! Three cheers for Captain Hawk!"

Who has not witnessed the vacillation and inconstancy of an English mob?

The people had assembled for the express purpose of seeing an end put to the daring highwayman's career.

That they had more than a common inclination for this, the length of time they had waited would sufficiently prove.

Yet, with extraordinary and incomprehensible inconstancy, no sooner did they see the captain at liberty than they with one accord tried their best to perfect his escape.

Right and left they parted, leaving a lane, which closed up rapidly as soon as those for whom it was made passed by.

"Courage!" said Lord Harcliffe. "Things go better than I anticipated. Courage! A few more minutes and we may almost consider ourselves out of danger."

Captain Hawk's brain was in a terrible state of confusion; and, indeed, who can wonder at it?

He heard the words which his companion pronounced; but it was more by instinct than aught else that he preserved a proper position on Satan's back.

With so much suddenness did all this take place that before the magistrate was able to make use of either limbs or voice, Lord Harcliffe and Captain Hawk were more han half-way through the mob.

"Stop them—stop them!" were the first words that struggled from his lips. "A hundred—I mean five hundred—no, a thousand pounds' reward to the man who stops them!"

It was not until these words were uttered that the police officers recovered from their amazement.

But it was too late.

Vain now were any of their efforts to overtake the flying horsemen.

The crowd having taken the captain's part so far, remained consistent, for they did all they could to obstruct the progress of the police.

Beholding this, drove Sir Thomas almost frantic.

"Charge them!" he cried. "Down with them! Cut them down if they oppose you! Charge, I say!"

The officers were enraged at the turn affairs had taken, and so without hesitation they obeyed the order which the magistrate gave them.

But a more injurious mandate could not have been issued.

The mob up to that point had been content merely to resist.

Now by a personal feeling of resentment they grew aggressive.

They attacked the officers.

Their great numbers made this a serious matter.

Sticks were flourished, and heavy stones thrown.

The officers, of course, had the advantage so far as weapons were concerned.

But their cutlasses, although used with a hearty good will, failed to produce any marked effect.

Still the people shrunk as well as they could to avoid the furious lashes which were dealt, and when the cry was raised that the fugitives were fairly off, they gave up the contest.

Just like so much chaff scattered by a sudden and violent puff of wind, they dispersed over the extensive common.

To think of beginning any pursuit seemed nothing less than ridiculous.

Yet this was what Sir Thomas hoarsely commanded should be done.

In the meanwhile, how had Isaac fared?

After the daring act he had committed he stood for some seconds like the rest, profoundly still.

He was breathlessly anxious to know whether the captain would succeed in achieving his escape.

So much was he interested in this, that he became

entirely oblivious of the fact that he stood in great danger himself.

Pharoah endeavoured to attract his attention.

But in vain.

The latter, solicitous about his own preservation, followed as closely as he could after the heels of the horses.

As we know already, what Isaac ought to have done was to have made his way as quickly as he could to the clump of trees where the boy was waiting with the two horses.

The voice of Sir Thomas brought him to himself.

He leaped to the ground.

So intent was the magistrate upon watching the retreating form of Captain Hawk that he forgot all about Isaac.

That is, he forgot him for the moment.

"Way for the friend of Captain Hawk!" cried a voice. "Make way for the friend who set the gallant captain free!"

A cheer was immediately raised, and a way made for the pseudo hangman to pass through.

But the police officer who was in command, determined that all engaged in this outrageous proceeding should not escape scot-free, drew his pistol and fired at the fast-disappearing form.

At first it was thought that the bullet was an ineffective one, for Isaac continued his flight uninterruptedly, and gave vent to no cry expressive of pain.

Again the officer fired.

This time the bullet lodged in the breast of one of the bystanders, who with a gasping sob dropped down dead.

In this particular quarter the animosity against the police officers was much intensified.

But as the general body of the crowd thought fit to disperse, those who were at this particular point were compelled to follow their example.

Isaac ran on.

His eyes were intently fixed upon the little clump of trees where he did not doubt for a single moment the horse was waiting for him.

Could he but reach it then all would be well.

But unluckily, Isaac had been hit, and badly too.

With wonderful stoicism he had passed it off, deceiving everybody.

But he knew that if the officers once became aware that he was injured they would redouble their efforts to capture him.

And so pressing his hand against his side where the ball had entered, he closed his teeth hard, and calling up all his fortitude and resolution, increased his rate of running rather than decreased it.

For the first few moments he experienced no sense of pain.

He was conscious of a benumbed feeling, but nothing more.

In his inmost heart he knew that he was severely injured.

But he tried his best to blind himself to the fact.

Instead of suffering his thoughts to dwell upon it, he fixed them upon the clump of trees.

Nearer and nearer they grew, though as he approached they seemed to swim before his eyes in a manner which made it very doubtful whether he would reach them.

The wound had not bled much outwardly owing to the tight pressure he had kept upon it from the very first.

But his rapid motion forced some portion of the life fluid through his fingers, and ere long the discovery was made that as he went he left a trail of blood behind him.

The police officers became aware of it, and redoubled their efforts.

For their credit's sake they felt they must secure one prisoner.

In obedience to instructions issued, the officer who was the first to get within reach of the wounded fugitive raised his pistol and fired.

The ball struck Isaac full in the centre of the back.

The agony it caused made him throw up both his arms above his head and give utterance to an awful heart-thrilling cry of mortal pain.

He staggered on a few more paces.

Then with another cry, but much more frantic than the first, he stumbled and fell down face foremost on the snowy ground.

He did not move once.

In less than a moment afterwards the officers surrounded him.

"We have nailed that one, at all events," said the one who had fired, and putting his yet smoking pistol into his pocket. "This affair has been so sudden that I hardly know whether I stand on my head or my heels."

"The same here," added the man who stood next to him; "but of this I am certain, there is more in this matter than we can comprehend at present."

"Is he dead?" said the commanding officer, who at this moment arrived upon the scene.

"I think he is, sir; but I'll roll him over on to his back and see."

He suited the action to the word.

But it only required one glance to assure all the onlookers that he was quite dead.

His jaw had fallen, and his eyes were glazing fast.

Poor Isaac!

He had paid a heavy penalty for his intense devotion to Captain Hawk.

CHAPTER CXLI.

SIR THOMAS WALKER RESOLVES TO LEAD AN EXPEDITION AGAINST THE HIGHWAYMEN.

All must have appreciated the fidelity of Isaac and admired him for it, so that his death now must cause a sensation of deep regret in every breast.

Whether the first bullet would have proved fatal in its effects is something more than could be told.

Yet that he should perish at the moment he did seems doubly terrible.

Pharoah, who, having had the start, had been more fortunate, had been successful in reaching the place of rendezvous.

His first act was to mount the horse which had been provided for him.

Then grasping the bridle of the gray horse, he stood ready to be of service to Isaac.

But alas! as we have seen, too late.

On seeing him fall, Pharoah rode towards the spot, determined to rescue him if possible.

But the officers were too close for him to have the slightest chance, and the fate which had overtaken his companion warned him to keep out of pistol-shot.

He could not save or serve the faithful Isaac, but he could perish with him.

For this he saw no necessity, though he hovered about as near as he dared so as to be perfectly satisfied in his own mind that his comrade had perished.

Of this he did not long remain in doubt.

He was not near enough to catch the precise words that were uttered by the police officers, but what he saw was more than sufficient to remove the last lingerings of doubt.

After this he stood for a moment uncertain what to do next, and doubtful which way to turn.

He was warned of the danger he was in by this irresolution by hearing a cry set up by the police officers.

He was not a little embarrassed by the second horse.

How to dispose of him was more than he could tell.

The first thought that presented itself was to ride back to the trees and return it to the boy, and as there was no time for consideration he acted upon the suggestion without a moment's pause.

The officers commenced a pursuit, but as they were on foot and Pharoah started off at a hard gallop they quickly gave up the chase as useless.

To surrender the gray horse to the boy only occupied a moment.

"Take it back," was all Pharoah stopped to say, and then off he set across the heath in an opposite direction.

By this time Sir Thomas Walker and the Governor had both reached the spot where the body of Isaac lay extended.

It would be hard to say which of these two individuals was in the greatest state of fury.

Probably it was some relief to his feelings to bestow upon the senseless clay half-a-dozen heavy kicks.

"I can see it all now!" he exclaimed. "I've got the details of the d—d plot as fully in my mind and as clearly as though I had contrived them all myself! Fool—fo is that we have been! All our precautions are of no avail through leaving that one weak place in our defences!"

Here Sir Thomas went off into a fit of furious curses.

He did not relinquish this delightful occupation until fairly out of breath and almost black in the face.

The Governor showed himself to be possessed of a certain amount of good sense.

"There's not a bit of good in standing here cursing and swearing over a dead body."

"But——"

"I know what you are going to say. Still, what is done can't be helped. It is some satisfaction to see that this villain has reaped the reward he deserves for the part he has taken in the outrage."

"Yes, but——"

"That's it," interrupted the Governor. "We must repair the mischief done in the best manner we are able."

"What are we to do?"

"Why, we will with as little loss of time as possible get together a well-mounted troop of police officers and commence a pursuit."

"But what will be the good?" asked Sir Thomas, dejectedly. "Think of the start they have got."

"Yes, that is bad, I admit; but ten to one if they go far when they find they are not pursued. Captain Hawk cannot fail to be in a very weak condition, and they will be obliged to halt somewhere."

At this faint gleam of hope Sir Thomas snatched like a drowning man at a straw.

"You are right," he said—"quite right; and come what will I will rest no more till I have all this gang in custody. I will lead the troop of officers myself."

Having taken this resolution, he felt much better, and at once made his way towards the town.

Much as he regretted the delay thus caused, he consoled himself by the reflection that it was unavoidable.

Moreover, he was especially taken with the idea of conducting the enterprise in person.

Now that he had resolved upon this course he felt that all the unfortunate occurrences of the morning were in a fair way of being retrieved.

But by the time he reached the Governor's house the pangs of hunger began to make themselves felt with unpleasant force.

Yet such was his impatience that he would probably have set out without satisfying these cravings had not the Governor suggested that there would be plenty of time to take a snack while the horses and men were being got ready.

"After all," he said, "now that matters have gone so far, a few minutes one way or the other cannot be of much moment."

Sir Thomas was so dreadfully hungry that he at once assented to this proposition, though it ill accorded with the state of impatience he was in.

A hasty meal was prepared, to which he did ample justice.

In fact, he did not offer to rise from the table until the Governor informed him that the officers were all ready outside.

Hearing this, Sir Thomas lost not a moment in sallying forth and leaping upon the back of the horse which had been provided for his accommodation.

In the whole affair there was but one drawback, and that was a serious one.

Sir Thomas Walker was but an indifferent equestrian.

In fact, he had arrived at that age when a canter becomes the only pace endurable.

But the burning feeling he had against the highwayman, strong as it had been, was now increased tenfold.

As he gathered up the reins in his left hand preparatory to starting upon his expedition, he shook his tightly-clenched fist and mentally poured out a string of horrible oaths and vows of vengeance.

The Governor, no doubt, had he consulted his feelings, would have been glad enough to form one of the party, but then he had his prison duties to attend to—duties which, of course, could not be neglected.

"Are you all prepared?" shouted Sir Thomas to the men who formed the troop.

"Yes, your worship, all ready."

"Come on, then!" he cried, furiously.

The whole party started off at quite a terrific pace, and, doubtless under the influence of his all-absorbing passion, Sir Thomas kept his seat wonderfully well, though the awkward manner in which he rode provoked many a jeer from the spectators.

It must be understood that up to this moment he had by no means decided upon a precise plan of operations.

It was more by chance than anything else that he started off towards Ling Heath.

Having once taken this direction, he preserved it, and owing to the speed they made the place appointed for the execution was quickly reached.

The sight of the unoccupied scaffold made the magistrate's fury greater than ever.

"I would have parted with all I have," he muttered, between his tightly-clenched teeth, "rather than this confounded chance should have happened! How I shall be laughed at! How I shall be ridiculed and mocked in every quarter for suffering myself to be worsted and undone in so gross a manner! But there is only one way of restoring my credit, and I will do it—I will be revenged!"

The officers seemed to think it quite natural and right that Ling Heath should be the first place to which they should repair.

But on gaining this spot, the one who would have had the command of the troop had not Sir Thomas chosen to appoint himself head officer, thought the proper time had come for some kind of consultation to be held as to their further proceedings.

Sir Thomas was brought back from his dreams of vengeance by the voice of this man, who said, civilly enough:

"I beg pardon, your worship, but I thought I would make bold to ask you whether you had quite made up your mind where we are to go, and whether there are any instructions which you may think proper to confide to me?"

Sir Thomas did not reply for a moment or two, but sat glaring at the officer with looks that threatened to devour him.

But apparently changing his intention about what he had to say, he answered, in quite a calm voice:

"If you have any suggestion in your mind, or any proposal you may wish to make respecting the matter we have in hand, I shall be very glad to listen—pray speak freely."

The officer bowed almost to the pommel of the saddle upon hearing this gracious speech.

"No, your worship," he replied; "only I thought no harm could come of asking the question. It seems to me that about the only thing we can do is to ride in the direction which we saw them take, and make inquiries of everyone we meet."

"Precisely—of course," replied Sir Thomas, with all the effrontery that can be imagined. "That is just precisely what I had made up my mind to do. As you justly enough remark, it is the obvious course to be pursued. I fancied you might have thought of some other plan of operations."

The officer did not relish being treated in this kind of way, for he had a conviction amounting almost to the force of a certainty that Sir Thomas had never had any such idea at all until it was suggested to him.

The magistrate rode on now with a much greater degree of complacency.

"Yes," he muttered, "that fellow behind me is right. There is but one course to pursue—that's obvious enough. Strange that it did not occur to me too. Still, that don't matter. I consider the way in which I took the credit to myself was very adroit indeed."

With still greater satisfaction at his own cleverness, Sir Thomas rode on.

"Yes—yes," he said, "I can see it all plainly. I have but to be persevering, and I shall pounce upon them at the moment when they least expect it. They could not possibly ride away by broad daylight without being seen by many persons. There will be no trouble in getting on their track."

Sir Thomas Walker's state of self-congratulation continued until the boundary of the heath was reached.

Having arrived at this point, he was compelled to pause in a little irresolution.

He looked about.

But over the broad expanse of snow not a single person could be discerned.

The snow-flakes did not fall now, but they had done for some time after the two highwaymen had performed their daring flight, so that all marks made by their horses' feet were completely effaced

The principal officer observed Sir Thomas Walker's embarrassment, and grinned.

"Let him find out what he can by his own acuteness," the officer said to himself. "Curse me if I open my mouth to fill his mind with ideas again!"

The magistrate waited some moments, doubtless expecting that the officer would speak.

But just then, as good luck would have it, his eyes encountered the chimneys of a house that was situated some little distance off to the right.

"That's the place," he muttered. "I'll ride there first and try whether I can obtain any information."

No sooner said than done.

"Follow me," he said, gruffly.

Then as soon as he spoke he put his horse in motion.

The space between where he had stood and this habitation was very quickly passed over.

On a closer approach it was perceived that the building in question was a farm-house.

It was a place of considerable extent, and seemed to have quite a little village of outbuildings attached to and around it.

But by making his inquiries in this quarter, Sir Thomas reaped no satisfactory results.

The inmates of the farm were all too intent upon the various duties they had to perform to trouble themselves about what was taking place around them.

They had seen nothing, and heard nothing, nor could Sir Thomas by dint of the closest and most vexatious questioning contrive to elicit one solitary scrap of information.

The principal police officer was obliged to gnaw hard at the bone handle of his riding whip to keep his exultant grin from being seen by his leader.

Cursing the stupidity of all farm people in general, and the inhabitants of this homestead most particularly, Sir Thomas rode away.

But ere he had gone many paces he came to a halt.

"In cases of this sort," he said, with a very pompous and imposing air, "I have always found it best to hold every now and then a kind of council of war, when our position may be considered and talked over."

"Which in plain English," muttered the officer, "simply means 'I don't know what to do. What do you advise?' A fine leader truly!"

"What was that you said?" asked Sir Thomas, who had imperfectly caught the last words—"what was that?"

"I merely said, your worship, that were I leader I should push on still further. It is almost too soon to make inquiries yet. I have no doubt they would ride straight on for a little distance. A little further on we shall doubtless learn something worth while."

CHAPTER CXLII.

RELATES WHAT BEFEL CAPTAIN HAWK AFTER HIS ESCAPE FROM THE GALLOWS.

Leaving Sir Thomas Walker and the police officers to carry on their search to the best of their capabilities, we will return to the Black Highwayman and Captain Hawk, about whom the reader doubtless feels a more than ordinary interest.

It will be remembered that we said Lord Harcliffe retained his hold upon Satan's bridle.

It was well that he took this precaution, for Captain Hawk had not sufficient control over his faculties to be able to direct his horse himself.

Indeed, before they had gone very many yards, Lord Harcliffe began to have serious doubts whether his comrade would be able to retain his seat in the saddle.

There was a look of deathlike faintness upon Captain Hawk's face; his eyes seemed half closed, and his body leaned forward or swayed from side to side.

Every moment it seemed he would overbalance and fall to the earth.

"Courage—courage," Lord Harcliffe said, in clear and inspiriting tones—"courage, I say! Remember now that all is well, and nothing more is wanting than a mental effort on your part. Courage—courage, then, I say!"

Captain Hawk heard the words, and they seemed to have the effect of causing him to throw off a portion of his deep depression.

"I am saved, I think," he said.

His voice was languid and weak.

"You are," his comrade answered. "Be of good heart."

"Are we pursued?"

Lord Harcliffe looked searchingly behind him before he replied.

"No," he said, "we are not"

"How fortunate!"

"It is doubly so."

"But why have not the officers ridden after us?"

"That is more than I can answer. Among them there seems to be nothing but confusion and dismay. They were completely taken by surprise."

The captain smiled faintly.

Lord Harcliffe felt certain he was fast relapsing into his former condition.

Seeing that there was no one near to do them any injury, he pulled up after calling out to the captain to do the same.

Satan, however, seemed to stop more from his own instinct than because there was any particular pressure on the rein.

Without a moment's loss of time Lord Harcliffe produced what brandy he had left, and handed it to his companion.

"Drink that," he said, "and you will soon feel something like new life in your veins."

Captain Hawk took the bottle gladly, and drank deeply of its contents.

The effects of the draught were very quickly apparent.

"That is like new life," the captain said, drawing a long breath, "and yet when I look around me all objects seem in motion; there is a mist before my eyes and a confusion about my brain such as I have never felt before."

"I do not wonder at it," said Lord Harcliffe. "But these disagreeable sensations will quickly pass away, and you will be yourself again."

Captain Hawk shuddered from head to foot, and then he replied:

"No—no, not myself: I can hardly believe that one who has gone through what I have could ever be the same again."

"Tut—tut! These are gloomy feelings produced by nothing else but weakness. You must shake them off."

"I will try. I do feel better even now. It is the sudden reaction I have been suffering from—the change from captivity to liberty."

"Think no more about the past. Remember only that you are free. Try to fix your mind upon that sole idea."

Captain Hawk passed his hand twice or thrice across his forehead.

"Stay," he said—"there is a question I ought to have asked before, and I take shame to myself for not having done so."

"What is it?"

"Why, where is Isaac? What has become of the faithful, honest fellow? What arrangements were made for his safety?"

"I don't think you need trouble yourself about him. By this time he is no doubt out of the reach of his foes."

"Explain—explain."

"I will; but first of all let me hear your advice as to what we had better do."

"In what way?"

"Why, you see it is broad daylight, which makes travelling awkward, for beyond doubt the first thing the officers would do on recovering from their confusion would be to organise a pursuit."

"Yes, yes—there can hardly be two opinions about that."

"So I think; and as I have said, being daylight, they will have but little difficulty in getting on our track."

"How are we to help it?" said the captain, looking around him in a helpless way that deeply grieved Lord Harcliffe to look on.

"Do you think you feel strong enough," he asked, "to take a good gallop across the country? If you do, I have no doubt we shall be able to do away with the fear of being speedily overtaken."

"I will try," said Captain Hawk. "I feel weak and faint, but yet riding is such a second nature with me that I believe I can keep the saddle."

"I am glad to hear it. Come—brace up your energies as well as you are able. At the earliest moment possible we will call somewhere and try to snatch a few hours' rest."

Captain Hawk assented.

Weak as he was, yet he was evidently getting the better of the shock he had sustained.

For the first time he seemed thoroughly to wake to the fact that it was his own noble matchless steed that was beneath him, for he uttered those caressing words which had so often been made use of in former times.

Satan showed his appreciation of the notice that was taken of him by neighing and prancing.

Meanwhile Lord Harcliffe, standing up in the stirrups, took a searching and comprehensive view all around him.

The snow no longer fell so as to obscure his vision, though the air was thick and misty, making it impossible to see to any considerable distance.

With the weather, on this account, it was not likely that the highwayman would complain, for the same mistiness which hid the officers from his view would likewise serve to conceal him from them.

"The present is a favourable moment, captain," he said. "I cannot see a human being in any direction, so I propose we avail ourselves of so good an opportunity of quitting the high-road."

Captain Hawk of course gave an immediate assent.

"Over this hedge, then," said Lord Harcliffe. "Sit steady. That will do bravely! I can see you are much better."

The hedge over which the horses leaped was but a low one.

Still Captain Hawk took it in capital style.

Lord Harcliffe urged Phantom into a gallop, and Satan instantly adopted the same pace.

At this rate a good many fields were rapidly traversed.

Lord Harcliffe had no very clear idea about where he was going, nor did he consider that it much mattered.

His only aim was to keep in one straightforward direction.

From time to time he glanced at his companion, and it caused him a very considerable degree of uneasiness when he saw how deathly pale he was, and how great were the efforts he had to make to be able to retain a secure seat in the saddle.

As well as he could he encouraged him with words, and Captain Hawk made superhuman endeavours to get the better of his weakness, for he felt that that at least was owing to the friend who had ventured and done so much in his behalf.

Few words were said now.

Lord Harcliffe was anxious to push on as far as his friend's weak state would permit, so as to diminish the danger of pursuit to the very smallest amount.

Captain Hawk gradually fell into a strange dreamy condition.

He was aware that he was on horseback, that his friend was by his side, and that he was being carried away from danger.

But whenever he tried to bring his thoughts beyond this, nothing but vagueness was produced.

He was aroused at length by the tones of his friend's voice, which seemed to reach his ears as though the sound had come from miles and miles away.

How far they had actually travelled, or in what part of the country they chanced to be, or whether there was danger at hand, he knew not.

But giving a sudden start, he seemed to rouse himself in a great measure.

He fancied that evening was coming on.

But such was not the case.

The effect was produced partly by his failing vision and partly by the density of the air, which seemed to portend a further fall of snow.

"What is it?" he said, as firmly as he could—"what is it?"

"Nothing—at least, nothing that need cause you any alarm."

The captain gave a sigh of relief.

"I was only about to observe that we seem in the vicinity of a small out-of-the-way village. The place boasts an inn doubtless, and I was wondering whether it would be best to halt there for a time."

"I will leave you to judge that,' responded Captain Hawk. "You are much fitter to do so than I am."

"If you leave it to me, then, I should recommend a halt. So far as safety goes, there can be no question that the best way to attain it would be to keep straight ahead. But then there are other things to be taken into consideration."

"Never heed me. Let safety come first."

"Nay—nay, I fancy you hardly understand me. What I mean is, that, after you have had an hour or two's rest, you will not be like the same man."

"But do you think we should run much extra risk by taking it?"

"No, I candidly think we shall not. We have already travelled many miles—certainly more than I had ventured to calculate upon."

"We have left no trace by which we can be very easily followed; and therefore I think we may reasonably look forward to remaining for several hours undisturbed."

"I am truly glad to hear it, then, for it has required more fortitude and determination than you are aware of to enable me to keep the saddle so long."

"I know it; but continue your efforts for a short time longer. I don't think we have more than a couple of hundred yards to go, and all will be well."

This assurance, as we may be sure, sounded most gratefully in the ears of Captain Hawk.

But though the distance was really so short, yet to him it seemed interminable.

As Lord Harcliffe had stated, they were at no great distance from a small village, or rather hamlet, the name of which, however, was quite unknown to him.

He was right in his surmise about the inn, for he quickly caught sight of one of those glorious hostelries which in olden times used to gladden the eyes of the weary traveller.

As good luck would have it, this inn was situated at the end of the village nearest to them, so that they were enabled to avoid a great deal of curious observation.

Lord Harcliffe rode directly to the gateway that communicated with the stables.

Indeed, had he known the place all his life, and been in the habit of staying there continually, he could not have made his way to the stable-door with greater confidence.

The noise caused by the arrival made the ostler quickly show himself.

He seemed somewhat surprised when he discovered that the two horsemen who had ridden so boldly into the inn-yard were strangers.

Lord Harcliffe prevented him from making any remark, for he said, in sharp, clear tones:

"Just let us have your best attention, will you? It will be something in your pocket—mark that!"

The ostler touched his cap.

"Now help my friend to dismount. He has been taken suddenly ill on the road, and has only managed to get as far as this with much difficulty."

"All right, sir."

Captain Hawk really stood in need of aid, for had he tried to dismount unassisted, he would have sustained a heavy fall.

When placed upon his feet he had not power to stand.

"Lead me inside the stable," he said, faintly. "I must sit down before I can go any further."

"There's an old corn-bin just inside the door," said the ostler. "That will do capital well for the poor gentleman to sit down upon."

"Nothing could be better," said Lord Harcliffe. "Lead him in."

This was done, and as soon as Captain Hawk was seated, he felt immediately better.

The horses were now seen to, and, owing to the circumstance we have just named, the captain was able to see with his own eyes that his favourite steed was properly attended to.

As soon as this was thoroughly done, he expressed his satisfaction, and, in answer to their inquiries, said that with their assistance he should be able to cross the yard to the inn.

This was done without more delay.

The landlord, who had heard of their arrival, was waiting at the door to receive them.

He afforded a good type of his profession.

He had a huge rotundity of his person, and his nose showed signs of the most careful cultivation, the tip of it more closely resembling a bunch of mulberries than aught else.

In a few hearty words he bade his guests welcome.

He saw at a glance that one of them was suffering from indisposition, so, without being requested to do so, he opened the door of his best private parlour and ushered them into it.

Captain Hawk was glad enough to sink into a chair.

"Has your friend met with an accident, sir?" said the landlord to Lord Harcliffe.

"No, not an accident; but he has been taken suddenly ill."

"We have a doctor, who lives only a few miles off, and who——"

"Many thanks! I don't think his services will be required. My friend has been ill, and in riding out to-day has overtaxed his new-gained strength. It is nothing more. A couple or three hours' quiet will put him quite right again."

Captain Hawk's appearance admirably bore out his friend's little fiction.

It never occurred to the landlord to doubt it for a moment.

At Lord Harcliffe's request, some tea was prepared, together with some easily-digested food.

There was a bonny fire blazing in the grate, and the warmth of this, and the state of rest in which he was, made the captain recover with wonderful rapidity.

The tea was brought, and as soon as the tempting repast was before him he began to be sensible of the cravings of appetite.

As it was more physical exhaustion that ailed the captain than aught else, it is not surprising that he should recover quickly.

Before the meal was done, he had overwhelmed the Black Highwayman with questions, for much that is quite familiar to the reader was perfectly incomprehensible to him.

But Lord Harcliffe firmly refused to satisfy him on one single point.

"My friend," he said, "don't fall into the mistake of tasking yourself too far. Rest assured with the knowledge that you will know all soon. In reality, there is no need for feeling much anxiety or suspense about it. All is past, and no single incident can be recalled. Be content."

Captain Hawk smiled as he said:

"It is all very fine for you to be easy in your mind concerning it now you know all."

Lord Harcliffe pointed across the room.

"Do you see that couch, captain?"

"I do."

"Then follow my instructions."

"What are they?"

"Stretch your limbs upon it, and try to get a couple of hours' sleep. I will watch during the time; and never fear but that I shall awake you as soon as there is a distant intimation of danger."

Truth to tell, Lord Harcliffe's advice sounded very welcome in the weary highwayman's ears.

He raised but a feeble plea against it, and ended by stretching himself upon the couch, which was almost large and wide enough to serve for a bed.

As might be expected, he had not assumed a recumbent position very long before his eyes gradually closed, and then his deep and regular breathing proclaimed that he slept.

For some time Lord Harcliffe stood with folded arms, watching his comrade attentively.

"How strange it seems!" he said. "Here is the man safe and sound who this morning stood upon the very threshold of death—and how deathlike he seems now! It is hard to believe he only sleeps."

A slight movement, accompanied by a deep-drawn sigh, at this moment testified that the captain lived.

As Lord Harcliffe continued to gaze upon him he could not help noting how great was the effect his illness and confinement had had upon him.

Literally the captain was now nothing more than the mere shadow of his former self.

His eyes were deeply sunken, and surrounded by livid circles; his cheeks had lost their roundness, while his hands were so wasted that they were irresistibly suggestive of the talons of a bird of prey.

"It is well he sleeps," Lord Harcliffe added at length, as he turned towards the window. "How dark it grows! Shall we have more snow?"

The day was drawing to a close; but in the natural order of things at least a couple of hours more daylight could have been counted on.

Now the air was so murky that objects no further distant than ten or a dozen yards looked blurred and indistinct.

"Will they track us?" he continued—"will it be possible for them to find out just which way we have come? I cannot think it—I can find no way by which they could obtain the requisite information. Be it how it may, however, it is quite certain that I can have no warning of their approach. My first intimation of their presence will only be received when they are within a few yards of me."

At the expiration of two hours, Captain Hawk was still sleeping, but evidently not so soundly and heavily.

Lord Harcliffe resolved not to disturb him unless circumstances should render it compulsory.

By this time it might be said that night had fairly closed in.

Without all was profoundly dark.

All was still, too.

The landlord had inquired whether his guests wanted candles.

Lord Harcliffe replied in the negative.

The fire, he said, would be quite sufficient. His friend was better, and slept; and he did not wish him to be disturbed.

The landlord bowed, and promised to take the utmost pains that perfect silence should be procured.

After he had gone, Lord Harcliffe stirred the fire, so as to make it send forth a bright and cheerful blaze.

Then, seating himself in the large arm-chair, he fixed his eyes upon the flames, and gave himself up to thought.

How long his reverie lasted he knew not.

He fancied he must have dropped off into a kind of doze.

A slight noise, however, attracted his attention.

The spell was broken.

He started up with much pecipitation, and for the moment seemed as though he was apprehensive of coming danger.

But the sound came from Captain Hawk.

He was not awake, though his slumber now was anything but peaceful.

His breast was heaving, while every now and then his arms would wave wildly above his head.

Then a suppressed cry escaped him.

When Lord Harcliffe saw this, he did not hesitate a moment about waking him.

Touching the captain on the face, he said:

"Awake—awake, my friend! What is it ails you?"

Captain Hawk started up as though he had suddenly been electrified.

His hair was damp, and the perspiration streamed down his face in huge drops.

For a moment he stared about him with so wild an air that it was quite evident he knew not where he was.

Lord Harcliffe hastened to let him hear the sound of his voice.

"My friend," he said, "what has happened? You seem in deadly fear."

"What place is this?"

"All is well. You are quite safe. Come, come—arouse yourself. You have slept sufficiently. Shake the vapours from your brain."

Captain Hawk slowly rose to his feet.

He looked about him now with a far more rational gaze.

But he shook from head to foot; and it was evident that he was very far from having recovered his composure.

"What is it?" asked Lord Harcliffe again. "What ails you?"

"You may well ask that question," was the reply. "What I have suffered is more than mine or any other tongue could tell."

"You have been dreaming."

"Yes; and such dreams as will make me fear to close my eyes again in slumber. I——"

"Hush—hush! Remember that they are dreams, and derive what consolation you can from the knowledge that they are nothing more. Do not dwell upon them."

Captain Hawk said nothing, but sank heavily into a chair.

"Cheer up—cheer up!" said his companion. "I could never have believed in the possibility of your being so deeply affected."

"You can form no conception of what I have gone through," said the captain. "Heaven knows whether I shall ever recover my firmness and courage again."

"Recover! Of course you will. Take my word for it that what you are suffering from is nothing more than a temporary depression of spirits. Quite natural, of course; and yet in an hour or two, when you come to look back, you will blame yourself for having given way so far."

Captain Hawk shook his head.

Lord Harcliffe said not another word; but rang the bell.

The landlord made his appearance with great promptitude.

"Let us have a bottle of the best port wine you can find in your cellar; but remember it must be the best."

"I am not afraid of your finding fault with my yellow seal. It was put in the bin more than twenty years ago, and there it has remained ever since."

So saying, the landlord withdrew, and soon after returned, bringing with him a bottle which, so far as outward appearance went, seemed to bear out the assertion he had made about its age.

"Now, my friend," said Lord Harcliffe, as soon as they were once more alone, "let us try whether the warm juice of the grape will have the effect of raising your fallen spirits. Nay, don't refuse. I know best what you should have. No more."

He poured out a couple of glassfuls as he spoke.

Captain Hawk took up his with a wan and weary smile.

But, out of complaisance to his friend, he drained it to the last drop.

Lord Harcliffe drank his bumper with great relish.

"This landlord is a worthy fellow," he said, as he put down the glass. "But come: in order that this excellent wine may have a good chance to work its proper effect, I will relieve your curiosity by making you acquainted with all that has passed since our separation."

"It will in good truth be a satisfaction for me to hear it," was the answer. "My curiosity is indescribable."

"Listen, then."

"You think we are safe here?"

"Oh yes; and in order to be quite secure, I will only raise my voice just sufficiently to enable you to hear what I have to say."

Captain Hawk signified his assent by a bow; and Lord Harcliffe then proceeded to make him acquainted with all the manifold events that had taken place.

With how much eager interest the captain listened there is no need for us to say.

But his impatience to hear the whole story was so great that he did not once attempt an interruption.

When all was told, he drew a long breath, and sat for some moments in thoughtful silence.

It was a desperate scheme, he said — a truly desperate one—so desperate that he knew not which to wonder at most—that they should have tried it, or that it had been successful.

About Isaac, however, he was of course unable to give any precise information.

"And what arrangement have you for a future meeting?" was the captain's next question.

"I thought it vain and foolish to make any," was the reply, "since it was utterly impossible for either of us to predict precisely what turn affairs would take."

"I see—I see. I ought to have known that without asking."

"The understanding between us, of course, was that we should do what we could to rejoin with as little delay as was possible; and ere very long I have no doubt we shall meet."

Captain Hawk took Lord Harcliffe's hand, and pressed it warmly between both his own.

"My friend," he said, "you will think me ungrateful and remiss; but my confusion of mind must plead my excuse. I ought long ere this to have thanked you for——"

"There—there, believe me you have said enough. And if you wish to please me, you will not add another syllable. You remember our compact—I have but fulfilled its conditions as you would have done had I chanced to fall into the hands of our foes."

"Yes—yes. But all that does not to my mind tend in the least to lessen the obligation that I feel, and which I ought to feel, not only to you, but to those who have laboured with you to the same end."

Lord Harcliffe then gave a more detailed account of the fidelity and anxiety which Isaac had manifested from first to last.

The account of the faithful fellow's devotion affected the captain deeply.

"He has rugged outside," he said, "but a true and generous heart. Come what will, his faithful services shall not go unrewarded."

"He wishes for no other reward than the privilege of serving you," was Lord Harcliffe's answer.

The conversation, as might be expected, naturally occupied some time.

But as the Black Highwayman had foreseen, the interest which attached the recital served to draw away the captain's mind from the unpleasant thoughts and objects upon which it had been dwelling.

He had now recovered some portion of his former manner, and when he looked about him his eyes had not that scared look which had been so observable in them hitherto.

"Wonderful," he said—"all is truly wonderful! Surely never before has there been known such a singular combination of circumstances."

"No; you are right there. Come, drink this one more glass, and the bottle will be empty. There cannot be a doubt as to the efficacy of the medicine. Not the least wonderful thing is the change which it has wrought in you. I am beginning to recognise you now."

"Bear with me a little longer," said the captain, as he emptied the glass. "A short time back I could never have believed that I should have experienced such a return to my former condition. My best thanks are due to you, my friend."

A warm pressure of the hand was exchanged between them.

"And now, captain, I have one more thing to ask: Do you think you feel strong enough and well enough to ride some miles further to-night?"

"Do you think it necessary for our safety to do so?"

"Yes, I do."

"Then that is enough."

"But not if you are unequal to the task."

"I feel that I am in better trim for it than I was this morning."

"Then let us decide upon ordering the horses. Depend upon it, it will be best not to stay too long in any one place."

"I think so too; and having been successful so far, it does indeed seem a world of pities that we should suffer a little to endanger us again."

"That is settled, then."

Lord Harcliffe rang the bell.

When the landlord appeared, he ordered the horses.

This command evidently took the worthy host greatly by surprise.

He was wonderfully well pleased with both his guests, and apparently had entertained the hope that they would remain at his house for a couple of days at least.

"To-night, gentlemen?" he said—"surely you are not in earnest in thinking of continuing your journey to-night? Excuse me, but I must make bold to say that it's nothing else but absolute madness."

"I can't help that," was the firm rejoinder. "I'll assure you that it's with anything but pleasant feelings that we leave such comfortable quarters as these."

The landlord bowed.

"But," continued Lord Harcliffe, "our business is of the extremest urgency; and if any proof were wanted of it, the mere fact of my friend travelling at all before he

[PHAROAH ON THE LOOK-OUT.]

had completely recovered his late illness would be quite sufficient."

This was an unanswerable argument, and the landlord, unable to think of anything further that he could urge against his guests' departure, left the room to carry out the command which had been given him.

As soon as the door closed behind him, Lord Harcliffe set himself busily to work to examine his arms and ammunition.

He had taken care to provide himself with a good store of weapons, and so was able to supply the captain with these very necessary articles.

By the time this was done, the landlord put in his appearance.

"Beg pardon, gentlemen, but I have ordered the horses, though I must make bold to say that you are running a very great risk in thinking of travelling to-night. Believe me, you won't save any time by it. Let me persuade you to stay till morning."

But, as may be supposed, the two highwaymen were perfectly deaf to any such expostulations as these.

"What is the special danger?" said Lord Harcliffe, as he drew forth his purse.

"Why, it's pitch dark, for one thing, and the snow is so puzzling and bewildering, and the roads about here are so bad, that you'll lose yourselves, or else meet with some accident—I am certain of it."

"I hope not," said Lord Harcliffe, drawing forth a couple of guineas. "At any rate, we must venture. An hour saved after the time we have lost will be of great value to us. I assure you."

The landlord gave in, seeing that it was useless to remonstrate any further.

"I won't trouble you to write out a bill," Lord Harcliffe added, as he flung down the two glittering coins. "I fancy that will settle the score."

The landlord bowed to his knees, and was prodigal of thanks.

The munificence of his guests made him regret their departure more and more.

The two friends now left the room and made their way into the open air.

Both shrunk back a little on their first contact with the night air, and no wonder, for the night was such as would force almost anyone to seek a shelter.

But the reflection that the very inclemency of the weather would contribute to their security enabled them to overcome their first shrinking sensations.

Captain Hawk, too, before he had drawn in half-a-dozen inspirations of the frozen atmosphere felt himself most wonderfully invigorated.

In a word, he once more felt like himself.

The horses were in readiness, and on hearing their approach the ostler brought both the noble creatures forth.

Phantom and Satan both seemed to recognise their masters and to look forward with anything but displeasure to their night ride, for they neighed loudly.

Captain Hawk experienced such a sudden elation of spirits that he was able to mount unaided.

Lord Harcliffe was in the saddle in a second, and with a loud "Good-night" to the ostler and landlord the two highwaymen started off.

CHAPTER CXLIII.

THE TWO HIGHWAYMEN HAVE A VERY SINGULAR ADVENTURE, AND CAPTAIN HAWK IS RECOGNISED AT A PLACE WHERE HE MADE SURE HE SHOULD BE UNKNOWN.

"Now for a good gallop, captain," Lord Harcliffe cried. "Rely upon it, nothing will bring your spirits up to the mark sooner. Away—away!"

Captain Hawk responded by a shout, and following his friend's example of allowing the reins to fall loosely on his horse's neck, the next moment after they were flying over the snow-covered ground with reckless speed.

It was bitterly cold, but the exercise of riding so quickened the circulation, that the chilliness had nothing more than a bracing effect upon their nerves.

For more than half an hour this headlong pace was continued, and then coming to some rougher and heavier ground they proceeded only at a gentle trot.

This was a pace that allowed them to converse with tolerable ease.

Lord Harcliffe had been greatly exhilarated by his gallop, and his first question to his friend was to ask what effect it had produced.

"I no longer feel like the same," the captain answered —"the difference is wonderful—far greater than I could have believed would have taken place in so short a time."

"I am heartily glad to hear that. I assure you I began to have great dread about the effect this adventure would leave behind it."

"Don't name it," answered the captain, unable to repress a shudder. "Luckily, all that is past is beginning to seem to me like nothing but a dream."

"It will soon become less and less vivid."

"I trust so."

"It will—it will; and in order to aid in bringing about that good result, let us turn our attention to other topics."

"What do you propose?"

"Well, the first thing to consider will be our future movements."

"True. It is quite time they were decided on."

"Have you any particular engagement on hand?"

"I might say I have not. True it is I want to visit London. I have a visit to make there in order to fulfil the last dying wish of an old, much-loved comrade."

"I recollect you mentioned it before."

"It is long, very long since those words were poured into my ear, and I promised faithfully to lose no time in delivering the message. But somehow or other Fate seemed to have opposed itself to the carrying out of this commission. Try as I will, I cannot accomplish it."

"And I should advise you," added Lord Harcliffe, "that now so long a time has gone by, you will let it get a little longer. To enter London now would be most perilous."

"Probably it would. There is no immediate hurry, and yet I shall be better content when the charge is off my mind."

"Certainly—certainly."

"I have promised some day to make you acquainted with the occurrences of the past, and will take an early opportunity of doing so. In return I shall expect the like confidence at your hands."

Lord Harcliffe did not return any direct answer to this, but after a moment's pause he said:

"I fancy the first thing we ought to do is to make sure we have eluded the officers, and then next to endeavour to rejoin Isaac and Pharoah."

To this Captain Hawk most warmly assented.

His desire to see Isaac and to thank him for his devotion was stronger than any other feeling in his breast.

"All seems quiet enough now," he said. "We appear to have distanced them completely."

"It does appear so, but yet the chances are they will be turning up before long."

"It is strange, is it not, that we have met with none of those troops that seemed to be on every road?"

"You mean the patrols."

"Yes."

"I think they are now all withdrawn, but after what has now taken place I fancy they will be sent out again, and that they will be doubly vigilant."

This idea was probable enough.

"I should propose," continued Lord Harcliffe, "that we should ride on till somewhere towards morning, and then seek again some place of shelter where we can remain during the rest of the day. We shall be able to judge better then whether we have really eluded the officers or not. If we have, they will have some little trouble in getting on our track again—that is, if we are only moderately careful."

"I can think of no better plan of operations. To-morrow night, doubtless, we shall be able to commence our search for our two friends."

"Just so; and during the day it will be necessary to consider several things."

"What are they?"

"First, you must not lose sight of Mr. Marchant, to whom is due all credit for devising the scheme which has set you at liberty. I confess I should never have thought of it myself."

"No—no. He must be paid at the time appointed.

"Then, of course, you know what that means, captain?"

"Yes, a return to the old profession. Well, well—it seems long since I had an adventure of that kind."

"It will be necessary for us to have a good many very profitable ones in order to obtain the amount of booty which we shall certainly require. The sum altogether will be large."

"It will; and as you know, I am at the present moment totally unprovided with cash."

"I am almost in the same predicament."

"And then there is the landlord of the Greyhound.

"Ah! true."

"Such a friend as he has proved himself to be is well worth the having, and what is more, is not often to be met with."

"You are quite right there."

"He ought to have something more in the shape of an acknowledgment than mere thanks—I mean a substantial recompense."

"I am glad you are of such an opinion. Need I say that I am entirely of your way of thinking?"

"I know that he professes not to work for money. Indeed, I believe he would very willingly pay Mr. Marchant the balance of money due to him out of his own pocket."

"I believe he would," said Captain Hawk. "He is, I know, deeply attached to me. I trust that he will get into no trouble on account of Price and his assistant."

"I do not think there is much to be feared on that score. Pharoah promised faithfully that his first act should be to attend to them, and I have confidence enough in him to feel sure that he has done so."

This was of course a great relief to the captain's mind though still he could not help feeling that he should feel much better satisfied if he could see for himself that all was really well.

But he thought it best not to make any remark on this head.

He did not wish his comrade to think that he had the least doubt about everything being done as it should be.

Just then the turnkey entered his mind.

"There is another person," he said, "who has a strong and lasting claim upon my gratitude."

"Who is it?"

"The turnkey who shared my cell."

"And you would wish to reward him too?"

"I should; and yet, believe me, I don't know how I am to manage it."

"In what way can there be a difficulty?"

"He was so convinced during the whole of my imprisonment that I could not escape death, that he would not listen to any propositions for meeting him and handing him a suitable reward. He shrank from the idea in terror, making sure that it would only be my ghost that he would see."

Lord Harcliffe laughed as he said:

"You must wait for the opportunity to arise to give him what he deserves. There is no immediate hurry about it."

"Very true; and the fault is entirely his own."

"Come, then, what say you to another gallop? The way seems clear and fair before us. We might make the next dozen miles easily and speedily."

"With all my heart."

The horses were once more urged into a gallop, and at a rate of very little less than twenty miles an hour they galloped over the snowy landscape.

Although riding, he scarcely knew whither, having no definite destination in view, yet he was careful not to double on his course.

He had been going in a westerly direction after he had left the inn, and in this way he continued.

Morning came at last and found them still in the saddle.

As the day dawned they looked about them with very great curiosity and interest.

There was just a possibility that the dawn would bring some familiar object or other before their view.

The morning was clear and bright, with a keen north-east wind blowing, which made their cheeks smart and tingle.

When the sun rose they were able to see all round for a very great distance.

But though they looked carefully, not one single thing could they perceive which they could recollect having beheld before.

They seemed to have just entered upon a broad open tract of land, either a moor or heath—they could not tell which, in consequence of the concealing snow.

"There is no place of shelter visible here," said Lord Harcliffe, "and, so far as I can judge, no signs of any."

"Nor are there any signs of human beings," added the captain, "and as the hour is such an early one, and our horses still undistressed, I think we cannot do better than push on for some miles further."

"That was precisely my idea: my only dread was whether your strength would stand so great a tax."

"I think there is no need for apprehension on that score," was the reply. "That dreadful weakness which oppressed me so fearfully I now feel nothing of."

Lord Harcliffe was indeed glad to receive this intelligence, and when he glanced at the captain's cheeks, now glowing with the exercise he had taken, he felt there was no longer cause for any apprehension.

But not to distress their horses too much, they continued on their way at a steady trot.

It was a pace which both animals could maintain for a considerable length of time without exhaustion.

On their way the two highwaymen were especially careful to keep a keen look-out.

But they saw nothing whatever of a nature to excite alarm.

The spectacle which nature spread before them was truly grand.

There was not a single cloud visible, while the sky bore that peculiar blue tinge which is often observable when the frost is severe.

The sun's rays glinted over the wide landscape with almost summer power, but scarcely any warmth could be felt from them.

Yet the whole aspect of nature on that morning was particularly cheerful—at least, it seemed to be for Captain Hawk, who had been for so long a time cooped up within the narrow limits of a prison cell.

So great was his joy, that every now and then he would give vent to a sudden cry expressive of his intense gratification.

Still pursuing a straight line, they rode on for a great distance before they found any signs of a change taking place in the general appearance of the landscape.

But stunted leafless trees began to show themselves here and there, and finally, some little distance to the left, they discerned what appeared to be a human habitation.

Lord Harcliffe was the first to perceive the structure, and he immediately directed his companion's attention to it.

"If that should prove to be a cottage," he said, "I should recommend that we pass the remainder of the day there."

"I scarcely think it can be inhabited," said Captain Hawk, after a long and earnest glance at the building. "In such a lonely spot as this who is there that can exist?"

"That is hard to say; but still, should it prove to be an inhabited dwelling, it will be of all others the one best suited for us."

"True."

"The inmates of such a place cannot by any reasonable supposition be likely to know anything of us, or of the events which have taken place at Huntingdon. We can satisfy ourselves that there is no other dwelling within two or three miles, and while there, owing to the open nature of the country, it would be impossible for the police officers to pounce upon us and take us by surprise."

"Yes; it has all you say in its favour," said Captain Hawk, "and even more. My fear is that we shall find it unoccupied."

"And if we do, it will not matter very much. I'll warrant we can make it serve the purpose that we require of it."

Captain Hawk assented, and slightly changing the direction which they had steadily maintained for so long, they rode towards the dwelling.

"It is inhabited," cried the captain, suddenly. "Look there!"

As he spoke, he pointed to a thin wreath of faint blue smoke which came curling up from the roof of the building.

"Strange, is it not," he added, "to find people dwelling so far removed from all association with their kind?"

"It is; but there is no accounting for the freaks of human nature."

These thoughts filled both the highwaymen with curiosity to ascertain what kind of building the cottage was, for by this name we suppose we must call the habitation, though in reality it was little better than a half-ruined hovel.

The nearer they came to it the more forlorn and wretched was the aspect it presented, and both said that never before had they beheld so desolate and melancholy a looking place.

Even when within a few yards of the place they found no notice taken of their approach.

In two minutes afterwards they pulled up near the door, which seemed to stand partially open.

They waited a moment.

No notice was taken of their arrival.

Lord Harcliffe called out in loud tones.

Still no notice.

"Depend upon it," said the captain, "the people who live here have gone out and left the house to take care of itself."

This seemed a likely enough supposition, and Lord Harcliffe no sooner heard it than he slipped from the saddle and hastened to take a peep at the interior.

This, owing to the door being only partly closed, he was easily able to do.

Captain Hawk followed him, though more slowly, for

on attempting to move he found his legs were very stiff.

The first object that met Lord Harcliffe's view was a fire of wood logs that were spattering and smoking, but sending forth very little warmth or flame.

The interior was very gloomy, but nevertheless the Black Highwayman was also able to discern the form of a human being bending over the smoking wood, and apparently so intent upon the task of watching it as to be oblivious of everything else.

A more searching gaze showed him that the form was that of an old woman.

"Look!" he said to the captain. "Who would credit that anyone could be so absorbed? The old creature evidently has no idea of our arrival."

"I fancy her age must be great," answered the captain, after looking closely at the crouching figure. "Doubtless she is deaf."

"If she is, that will account for all. At any rate, we will soon ascertain."

So saying, he knocked loudly with the butt of a pistol against the crazy door.

The din was terrific.

The old woman turned round, and half started from her seat.

But she sank down again, and looked with manifest terror towards the doorway.

Without waiting for any further permission to enter, Lord Harcliffe crossed the threshold.

"My good woman," he said, in loud tones that made all the place ring again, "we have unluckily lost our way, and, as we are very tired, we want you to give us shelter for a little time. For so doing, rest assured I will pay you well."

The old woman appeared not only to be very aged and infirm, but also to be suffering from paralysis, for her head moved tremulously and her arms twitched for some moments before she could say a word.

"I'm not so deaf, sir, as you may think," she mumbled, in tones so inarticulate that Lord Harcliffe had much ado to comprehend her. "I'm not so young as I was, that is all; and what with the *rheumatiz* and the *'lytic*, I can hardly do anything."

"But you don't object to earning something worth while by just letting us have the shelter we want, do you?"

"Oh no, no!" she mumbled—"that is, if you don't stay long—you mustn't stay long."

"A few hours' rest is all we require."

"Rest—rest? Yes, that's it—that's what I want—that's what I'm always seeking after! Rest—rest!"

The last words were scarcely audible, and while they trembled on her lips her head sank down on to her breast, and she seemed fast relapsing into the state of living death from which Lord Harcliffe's terrific knocking had temporarily aroused her.

Lord Harcliffe looked at her irresolutely.

He hardly knew whether to trouble the old creature any further, or to take her at her word.

It was quite certain that she would never interfere with them.

In the meanwhile, Captain Hawk, taking it for granted that the required permission would be accorded, led the two horses round to the rear of the cottage.

Then, loosening the girths and taking the bits out of their mouths, he tethered them by means of the reins to a couple of stunted, dead-looking trees.

The animals then, with wonderful sagacity, after sniffing at the snow, pawed it with their feet until the grass beneath was disclosed.

"It is but poor fare for you," the captain said, "but it is the best you can have at present. We must see what more can be done."

So saying, he turned back to the only door by which admission to the hut could be obtained.

On the threshold he met his comrade.

"All is well, I suppose?" he said, interrogatively.

"Well, yes, I think we may consider so—the old woman seems only just about half alive."

"But did she give permission?"

"Yes, if we did not stay long, and after that she dropped off into the condition in which you see her now."

Captain Hawk looked at the old woman with a wonderful amount of interest.

"It is very strange, is it not," he said, "to see one so close to death and yet alive?"

"It is. But the most surprising thing is that she should be here alone. One would think she could scarcely have made that fire herself."

"It seems impossible—she looks to be perfectly helpless."

"I believe she is; yet look at those logs—they are large, and would require much more strength to move them than she apparently possesses."

"And, what is more, the fire is only recently kindled."

"Some one must have been here lately—that is the only solution of the mystery."

"That is probable enough; and perhaps it is because she expects that other person to return that she said we could only stay here for a short time."

"We can easily satisfy ourselves upon the point"

"How so?"

"Why, if anyone has left the cottage lately, we shall easily be able to trace the impression of footmarks in the snow."

"Certainly. Until you spoke, that circumstance escaped me. As you say, that will be susceptible of easy proof."

So saying, the pair at once went outside the hut.

They made a careful examination all around the premises, but not a single trace of a footmark could they find.

"It is very mysterious, captain."

"Very."

"I don't feel half comfortable about it."

"Neither do I. I thought we were certain to have some hours' peace, but now——"

"Why, now we cannot make ourselves content because we know events are going on which we cannot comprehend."

"Just so."

Both looked vexed.

Situated as they were, they never felt safe unless they were able to understand everything.

"Stop a moment," said Captain Hawk. "It is just possible that there may be some other person now within the hut."

"I had thought of that; but if there is, that person must be practising voluntary concealment. Just think of the blows I delivered! Why, they might have been heard half a mile off."

"We will satisfy ourselves, at any rate," said Captain Hawk. "That there is mystery about this place I firmly believe, and I will try my best to find out what it is."

"I am willing to assist you as far as I can, for I assure you your curiosity is no greater than mine."

On their way back to the hut door, the two highwaymen renewed their examination of the surrounding snow.

But the white sparkling surface remained everywhere unbroken, save and except of course those places where their own horses had trodden.

The old woman was still in the crouching attitude in which they had first found her.

A second and more careful inspection of the rude apartment failed to bring before their notice anything more than they were already acquainted with.

There was one door apparently conducting to an inner chamber, and this the two highwaymen, after having finished their careful survey, did not hesitate to open.

Their conjecture was verified.

The room, however, was furnished in the plainest and scantiest manner.

One object alone challenged their admiration.

This was something that seemed wholly out of place.

It was a painting of a young girl, whose age might have been between seven and nine.

It was a sweet, innocent face, and delineated with wonderful skill.

The large dark-blue eyes seemed instinct with life; and indeed there was about the whole portrait a much closer resemblance to reality than is often seen, except in the works of the great masters.

For some time the two highwaymen stood looking at this picture in silent and rapt attention.

Captain Hawk was the first to speak.

"Another mystery," he said. "What on earth can bring a work of art like that into such a squalid place?"

This was an unanswerable question.

The frame in which the portrait was inclosed looked new, and the gilding upon it seemed to show like a horrible mockery against its surroundings.

It was in vain to speculate about this fresh mystery; and having gazed their fill, the highwaymen again looked round the room in order to make sure that nothing had escaped their former scrutiny.

"There is nothing more here," said Lord Harcliffe, "save and except that old crumbling staircase in the corner yonder."

"That evidently leads to the upper rooms," returned the captain. "Come on—let us see what discoveries await us there."

The staircase was not mounted without considerable misgiving, for it creaked most portentously beneath their weight.

But without accident they gained the room above, into which it led directly, there being neither door nor landing-place.

But whatever hopes they had of making discoveries in this quarter were soon put an end to.

There was but one room, and about the only object this contained was a bed.

The sight of it reminded both that they were weary.

"My friend," said Lord Harcliffe, "it does not appear as though there was any other discovery for us to make. For the present I think we have no need to apprehend danger. Let us avail ourselves to the utmost of the shelter, such as it is. Rest is imperative. Throw yourself on that bed, and get a little sleep, and in the meantime I will keep safe watch and ward."

Captain Hawk was too fatigued to think for a single moment of gainsaying a word of what his comrade had said.

"I will try to sleep for three hours," he said, "and then you shall take my place; for although you have said nothing, I can see that you are terribly exhausted."

CHAPTER CXLIV.

THE TWO HIGHWAYMEN BECOME UNEXPECTEDLY ACQUAINTED WITH SOME OF THE MYSTERIES OF THE OLD HUT.

"I AM weary but not exhausted," said Lord Harcliffe. "And you must bear in mind that I am in a better condition to withstand the effects of fatigue than you are. Sleep as long as you are able. I shall have no trouble in keeping awake for some hours to come."

"And you will keep a sharp look-out on all that may occur in and about this mysterious place?"

"I mean to make that my principal occupation. And now no more. Close your eyes without dread. I will guarantee that you shall have timely warning of the approach of danger."

"Many thanks!"

Lord Harcliffe could plainly perceive how thoroughly dead-beat his comrade was, and so, without another word, he made the best of his way down the rickety staircase.

Before he reached the foot, Captain Hawk was fast asleep.

Lord Harcliffe, on descending, found all perfectly quiet.

After another look round the room, and an attentive gaze at the young girl's portrait, he passed through to the outer chamber.

The old woman was rocking herself backwards and forwards with a gentle swaying motion, and chanting some monotonous tune.

She took no more notice of Lord Harcliffe's entrance than she did on the last occasion.

The highwayman stood looking at her for some moments.

Then, fancying a slight sound reached his ear, he hastened out into the open air.

But he found nothing to disturb the intense quietude of the dreary and melancholy scene.

The two horses were making the best of their scanty meal.

In prying into the different corners of the old building, he next found some hay; but for some reason or other the animals would not touch it.

As may be supposed, the time while Captain Hawk lay sleeping hung very heavily upon Lord Harcliffe's hands.

He fidgeted about—now here, now there—half listlessly, and half with the manner of one who feels that he has something to accomplish.

Such was the bleak and exposed situation of the hut that he could see for several miles in every direction.

Every few minutes he attentively scanned the horizon, and though he fancied he saw small moving objects in the far distance, yet they came no closer, and therefore he concluded that his fancy had deceived him.

The hour of noon drew near.

About this time, the old woman displayed some slight signs of life.

On returning to the hut, after having been absent from it for a short time, he saw that an iron pot had been suspended over the fire.

Already its steam was sending forth a savoury smell, which for a moment roused the highwayman's appetite.

But when he saw the manner in which the miserable old woman was preparing the food, and beheld her bending close down over it, his stomach turned, and he felt that had he been suffering the sharpest pangs of hunger, he could not have touched a mouthful.

It was not long after this that Captain Hawk came down.

He declared that he was greatly refreshed by his sleep, and felt wonderfully the better for it.

His first question was to ask whether he had made any further discovery, and whether there was any symptom of danger.

Lord Harcliffe returned a negative reply, and then the captain said:

"Come, my friend, do not try to conceal your fatigue. With the same readiness as I showed, I must now ask you to snatch a brief repose; and I can only repeat your assurance to me that you will be perfectly out of danger while you sleep."

Lord Harcliffe felt himself too badly in need of rest to think of raising the slightest opposition.

Besides, he knew that a considerable time might elapse before such an opportunity presented itself again.

He firmly believed that for some hours at least the hut would continue to afford them a secure asylum.

As soon as he had ascended the stairs, Captain Hawk turned to pay a visit to his steed.

To his surprise, however, as he was making his way towards the outer door he heard the old woman mumbling.

He paused instantly to listen as best he could to her half-intelligible gabble.

"Time passes," she said. "You have had shelter, and it is your own faults if you have not had rest likewise. Where is the other?"

By the "other," the captain knew that the old woman must mean Lord Harcliffe, so he replied by uttering the one word "Asleep."

"Will you share a dinner with a poor body?" she asked, in whining, half-entreating tones. "It is not much, you will say. But still it is the best there is, and you are welcome."

At first Captain Hawk was disposed to accept of the invitation, but just at this moment the old woman dipped a large mug into the pot and produced a portion of the contents.

The sight of this mess of pottage affected Captain Hawk even more than the preparation had Lord Harcliffe, and muttering a confused refusal of her invitation, he hastily made his way to the exterior.

"There's some mystery about this hut and the inmate or inmates of it, that is certain," he said, as he ran his eye carefully over every object. "What it is baffles me, but yet I hope we shall be able to discover something before the time comes for us to take our departure."

The time passed by, however, very much in the same manner as it had during his comrade's watch, until at length the sun began to hide himself behind the bank of clouds which rested on the western horizon.

Gradually the daylight faded away, and the limit of the captain's vision across the snowy waste became every moment more and more contracted.

It was just when twilight might be said fairly to have commenced that Lord Harcliffe awoke.

So profound had been his slumber, that it seemed to him as though not more than a moment had elapsed since he closed his eyes.

His surprise may therefore be imagined when he discovered that the room was filled with obscurity.

And even when he awoke he felt as though two or three hours more slumber would be most acceptable; but shaking all weight of sleep from him, he hastened to descend.

But just as he reached the bottom of the staircase he heard the sound of voices.

On listening he found that the speakers were the old woman and Captain Hawk.

"My son," she was saying—"my son! How long he stays! Surely now the time is past and gone—long, long past and gone. Stephen—Stephen!"

Her voice rose to an unnatural screech as she pronounced the name.

"Who is he?" asked Captain Hawk. "Why not speak more plainly? What is this secret of which you speak?"

But the old woman seemed to be quite exhausted by her exertions.

Panting and gasping for breath, she sank down into her old attitude, and became dead to all that was taking place around her.

"What is that she has been saying?" Lord Harcliffe asked, stepping forward.

"Nothing that I can make much of. It seems certain that she is quite alone here at the present time."

"How strange for one so aged to be in such utter loneliness!"

"I gather from her words that she has a son who visits her at frequent intervals, but that a long time has now elapsed since he was last here."

"And is that all?"

"All. So it seems we are almost certain to leave here without being much wiser about its mysterious occupant."

"Hark! what is that?"

Both became suddenly silent.

Then they heard with unmistakable plainness the dull beat of a horse's hoofs upon the snow.

Moved by one impulse, the two highwaymen hastened to the door.

But ere they could cross the threshold, a single horseman pulled up with startling suddenness exactly in front of the hut.

And almost before the horse had come to a standstill his rider flung himself precipitately from his back.

Unheeding or els not seeing the two highwaymen, he rushed into the humble dwelling and flung himself down on his knees close to the old woman.

The latter knew nothing of his approach until he touched her.

Then a loud scream thrilled from her lips, and she ejaculated:

Stephen—Stephen! My boy—my own boy, you have come back at last!"

The two highwaymen drew back a pace or two and listened with breathless interest to the words which followed.

"Yes, I am back," he cried, speaking as if only by a most painful earnestness. "Mother—my poor mother—I have come back to die!"

The last words were pronounced with a rude pathos which no language can describe or do justice to.

"Die!" she shrieked. "No—no, Stephen, I must talk of dying!"

"No—no, mother!" he added, with a heartrending groan, and almost grovelling on the ground as he spoke. "No—no, I tell you! There is death in my veins!"

At this juncture the large wood fire broke out into a blaze.

Contrasted with the gloom which had formerly prevailed, the light seemed brilliant.

By it everything could be distinctly seen.

But the object on which the gaze of both the highwaymen was riveted was the form of the new-comer.

The ruddy light shone upon his features.

Horrible indeed was the expression that they bore.

His countenance was distorted and convulsed, and had besides stamped upon it so peculiar and so indescribable a look that the two unnoticed watchers took it to be a confirmation of what he said about his approaching death.

"Speak—speak again, Stephen!" said the unfortunate creature. "Tell me that I have not heard aright—tell me that I have mistaken your words!"

"No, no—it is no mistake—I tell you I am doomed! I have made my way here to—to die! And it is nothing more than the stern determination to do so that has enabled me to survive so long."

He flung himself now at full length upon the floor near the hearth, and writhed about like some wounded reptile.

Deep groans came from his lips, while the perspiration of extreme agony poured from his brow.

The mother gave the wildest expression to her grief for some moments.

Then, suddenly collecting her faculties in a manner which nothing but her present horror would have enabled her to do, she cried:

"Speak—speak, Stephen, and explain yourself! What do you mean? How do you know you are so near death?"

"*Because I am poisoned!*"

The terrible words sent a thrill through the forms of all who heard them.

"Poisoned! How? Who has poisoned you?" exclaimed the poor old mother, as soon as she could recover the use of her speech.

"I am a specimen of royal gratitude," he said, "After having done all that I have, this is my reward! Oh, Margaret—Margaret, never more shall I look into those clear blue eyes! Help! Mercy! Help!"

He was silent; and the two highwaymen were just about to rush forward to aid him when he caused them to change their purpose by suddenly springing to his feet as though under the influence of a galvanic shock.

"Margaret—Margaret! If I cannot see her in life, I can at least have the semblance of it! Margaret—Margaret!"

So saying, he groped his way forward blindly and like a man in a dream.

His eyes seemed to have lost their powers of sight; and yet with wonderful precision he made his way to the inner door.

He passed through it; and after an absence of less than a moment returned.

He held something frantically to his breast.

When he got closer to the fire they saw that it was the mysterious portrait of the beautiful child.

"Margaret—my own, my sweet one, my darling—you for whom I have toiled—you for whom I have run all these frightful risks! Oh! if I had but been successful, I should have been well content; but now I have not that to fall back upon for consolation. You, Margaret, who ought to have been rich, will be no better than a mere beggar."

And with a passionate burst of grief that was dreadful to witness, he pressed the insensible portrait to him, and imprinted a thousand wild and burning kisses on the senseless face.

For some moments his grief was like the onward rush of a torrent.

But by degrees—perhaps more from sheer weakness and pain than any other cause—he grew calmer.

"Heaven help me!" he murmured, faintly. "I can feel the hand of death upon my heart! I die—I——"

He sunk suddenly forward; and both the highwaymen concluded that he had breathed his last.

Nevertheless, they hastened forward to his assistance.

By their aid he was quickly raised, and then they found that life was not quite extinct.

What to do then for his relief they were at a loss to know.

Not only were they ignorant of poisons generally and of their antidotes, but they were without any information as to what kind of poison he had taken.

"Hold him a moment," said Lord Harcliffe.

"What would you do?"

"Pour some of this brandy down his throat," he answered producing from his pocket a bottle of the spirit that he had taken care to provide himself with before leaving the inn.

"Brandy?"

"Yes."

"Brandy for poison?"

"Yes. I believe it to be a sovereign remedy for many things. At any rate, we will try it in this case, for be it how it may, it does not seem as though we should be able to make him any worse, poor fellow."

While these words were being exchanged, Lord Harcliffe was engaged in extracting the cork, and as soon as ever this was done the brandy was poured copiously down his throat.

At first the result seemed very alarming.

He gasped and struggled like one in a deadly conflict

His face grew first purple, then black, until finally a tremendous fit of coughing succeeded that seemed violent enough to rend his entrails.

But after that he grew calmer.

He drew his breath in something more like regular inspirations, and at last after a heavy sigh he raised his head slightly and looked about him.

"What is all this?" he said, almost in a whisper. "Do I really live?"

"You do—you do," said Lord Harcliffe. "Are you not better?"

"I—I think I am."

"I feel sure you are. Now speak more calmly, and let us know what has happened."

"But who—who are you? I know you not."

"Let it suffice for the present that we are your friends, and quite ready and willing to assist you by any means in our power."

"Ah! It is well! Perhaps in all this there is an overruling Providence. Who shall say?"

"You speak in riddles."

"You will quickly comprehend my meaning. I shall want you before I disclose anything to swear that you will be faithful to me, that you will execute the charge I shall leave to you. If you will your reward shall be ample —nay, vast—vast beyond all your expectations."

The exertion of speaking so many words consecutively deprived him of breath, and he had to wait a moment before he could utter any more.

In the meanwhile he again took hold of the portrait, which had slipped from his grasp.

"Here," he said, "press your lips to that fair face, and swear to do justice to my child."

"We will swear," said both. "Whatever we undertake to do, make sure it shall be faithfully performed, no matter how many obstacles stood in the way."

A gratified look came over the man's face.

"Listen to me," he said. "I feel that I have not breath enough left to say many words. I shall try to be as brief as I can. But be sure that you forget nothing."

"We will not. We will promise to pay thorough attention to every syllable."

"Enough; I am content. First kiss the portrait."

Tears thronged thickly in his eyes as he held the painting towards the two highwaymen to kiss.

Both gratified his humour, and then the lips of this singular being were unsealed.

Never before had either the Black Highwayman or Captain Hawk felt so anxious to hear a narrative as on this occasion.

They were absolutely breathless, and would almost have promised anything rather than miss hearing the recital.

"I can give you a key to the whole mystery in a few words," he said; "and I make this avowal to you because I cannot resist the conviction that there was something more than mere accident in our meeting here to-night. I recognise in it the finger of Fate itself."

"It is strange."

"Now listen. I have for a long time past been secretly employed by the King on special secret service."

"Secret service?"

"Yes. I have been making him a secret treasure-chamber."

The interest which the highwaymen had felt up to this point was now redoubled.

"Are you in earnest?" Lord Harcliffe asked.

"I am not surprised that you should ask that question. Such a statement must in good truth sound incredible."

"I can hardly believe that I have understood you aright," continued Lord Harcliffe. "Do you really mean to say that you have been constructing a secret treasure-chamber for the King of England?"

"I have, I repeat it."

"And is the task completed?"

"It is," he answered, with a deep groan.

"Well?"

"I was known to have no common skill in the construction of such places, and the King himself in person having summoned me to a private audience, promised me a large reward if I would make for him a secret chamber that would defy all attempts at discovery."

"And you promised?"

"I did. The largeness of the reward tempted me; not but what I had my doubts at first of the King's good faith."

"You had doubts?"

"Yes, and if you were only acquainted with the history of my life you would not be surprised to hear as much. I have done such jobs before to-day, and have had many a narrow escape of my life in consequence."

"How in consequence?"

"Is it possible you do not understand?"

"We do not."

"Why, cannot you see? When these places are constructed they want the secret to be locked in their own breasts alone, and in order that it may be so they try to take the constructor's life"

"I see—I see. It is an awful risk that you must run."

"Truly an awful risk, because you see the temptation to destroy me is so great."

"It is—it is. But you have escaped."

"Yes, as you see. I bought my life once by the sacrifice of a hand. See."

As he spoke he held up his left arm, and showed the wrist was nothing but a mere stump.

"I had to choose between the loss of a hand and the loss of my life. It would take too long to tell that story now. But you can guess which way my decision would be."

They nodded.

"That hand was caught fast in a trap," he said—"fast beyond all power of extrication save by the means I told you of. When I saw how things stood I took out my knife and unjointed the wrist."

Used as they were to strange things, the highwaymen could not help shuddering at the recital of this grisly deed.

The glance which they bent upon this singular man had, too, no little amount of admiration in it.

None were better able than themselves to estimate and appreciate the fortitude that would be required for such a dismemberment.

"So I escaped," he said, "and my foe was baffled. Then he made every attempt to slay me; but I eluded him, though I have had to pass my life in nooks and corners—even in such a place as you see this is."

Again he paused.

Lord Harcliffe saw that he was exhausted; and encouraged by the good effects produced by the administration of the former dose, he again proffered the bottle.

"What is that?" said Stephen.

"Brandy."

No sooner were the words pronounced than he seized the bottle, and drank an alarming quantity of the contents.

After the draught he lay profoundly still for full two minutes.

The highwaymen feared that it had been too much for him.

The old woman, whose grief had subsided into her usual state of torpor, now arose, and broke out into terrible wailings and lamentations.

Her outcries seemed to have the effect of arousing the man, for, looking up, he entreated her to be silent, in order that he might speak.

It was not without great difficulty that he prevailed upon her; and then turning to the two highwaymen, he said:

"Let me try if I can keep a little closer to the matters under hand. I think I shall be able to do so—I feel so much better now."

"Perhaps you overrate the danger that you are in Your countenance no longer looks like the same."

A ray of hope gleamed from his eyes.

But it faded out immediately as he shook his head and said:

"No—no. I feel—I *know* that I am doomed! Nothing on earth can save me. And now listen to my last dying declaration."

Lord Harcliffe and Captain Hawk drew yet a little closer, so intense was their eagerness to hear further.

"As I told you, notwithstanding the many narrow escapes I have had, I resolved to run the risk of making a secret treasure-chamber for the King. I doubted him; but yet I felt that to be forewarned would be to a certain extent to be forearmed."

"Well?"

"I undertook the task. But I had yet another reason, and one more powerful than all the rest. I have a daughter. You see that painting: the one that you have kissed: it is her portrait."

The two friends exchanged glances.

This was at least one mystery cleared up.

"It seems strange to see such a thing in this place. That painting cost me three hundred guineas. Saw you ever anything to equal it? Is it not like the life itself?"

"It is a gem of art."

"I am hunted to death, and that is why I am compelled to resort to such dens as these. Well, that is my daughter. You have the evidence of the portrait that she is beautiful, and beautiful in no ordinary degree. I love her: she is more than my life: and *I want her to be rich as well as beautiful!*"

He pronounced the last sentence with great emphasis.

"But I am ruined," he said, in anguished accents—"ruined and undone! The labour is performed—all is finished. I am denied my reward—the large sum that I was promised—and I have been made to swallow a dose of poison instead. But stay! Does my fancy or the flickering light deceive me? No, no—it is so: you are no other than Captain Hawk!"

CHAPTER CXLV.

THE SECRET OF THE KING'S SECRET TREASURE-CHAMBER IS REVEALED TO THE TWO HIGHWAYMEN.

THESE last recognitory words were spoken in tones that seemed strikingly loud when compared with those that he had hitherto made use of.

There could be no doubting, either, how great was the astonishment the discovery caused him.

And it was astonishment mingled with satisfaction.

As for Captain Hawk, the reader will doubtless easily be able to imagine how extreme was his amazement at being recognised in such a place and at such a time as this.

Indeed, the whole affair seemed to him more like the vagaries of some unusually vivid dream than the occurrences of sober reality.

The man had made a chance movement, and just as he had done so a particularly bright ray from the fire fell on the captain's face.

It was then that the recognition was proclaimed.

To have denied his identity would have served no useful purpose—and besides, the man spoke in a manner so positive as to make a denial a mere waste of words.

As may be supposed, however, the declaration made Captain Hawk a thousand times more anxious to hear further than he was before.

And Stephen, having made this declaration, kept his eyes fixed upon the captain's countenance.

"And what if I am Captain Hawk?" said the highwayman, at length. "What then? How is it that you recognise me? Where have you seen me before?"

"I fear that would take too long to tell you now," he answered. "I have so much that must not be left unsaid; and I can feel that my minutes are numbered."

While he spoke, both highwaymen fancied they could see in his face indications of a reaction.

"If I have time," he said, "I will, when I have finished my declaration, tell you how it is I know you. For the present, it must suffice that I can trust you, and that there is hardly a being on earth to whom I would have made this disclosure with half the willingness and satisfaction that I shall to you."

"But yet——"

"I know what you would say, and can well understand your curiosity. Still, you must understand I must disclose my secret first, and after that, if my breath lasts long enough, I will put you at ease on the other point."

This was too reasonable to be gainsaid, and so, despite the disappointment that he felt, Captain Hawk bowed his head in acquiescence.

Lord Harcliffe was of opinion that the secret ought by all means to be communicated first, because he could see now plainer than ever that the hue of death was in the man's face.

"Let us go back to the treasure-chamber. I told you that it was in consequence of the fame I had acquired in constructing these places that caused the King to search me out. Then, in an interview which he took care should be unwitnessed, he told me he had occasion for the utmost skill I could put forth.

"I told him that if the reward was sufficient he might depend on my ability to construct a place that would be absolutely safe, and that I would keep a sacred secret the fact of its existence, and so I would," he added. "Not all the engines in a torture-chamber should have wrung from me a whisper of the secret—nothing but the base and treacherous part the King has played would have forced me to unseal my lips to a living creature."

"And you undertook the task?"

"I did; and he promised that during the work I should have all my expenses defrayed, and on the completion my reward was to be five thousand guineas, on the condition that I not only kept the secret, but also left England for ever."

"I see."

"The labour was immense, for the chamber to be constructed was of unusual magnitude, and, as secrecy was the most essential thing, it follows that I had the whole of the work to do myself: to have employed an assistant would simply be to have divulged the secret.

"But I wanted no help: I toiled on willingly—gladly, my mind all the time fixed upon—upon——"

He was so affected that he could say no more for several moments.

There was no need for him to mention the object of his thoughts.

The highwaymen knew full well that it was his daughter.

"I must not give way thus," he said, recovering himself, "or I shall never be able to bring my narrative to a conclusion. I can feel that I am already much weaker."

This was strikingly perceptible in his voice, which was now little more than a deep, hoarse whisper.

"I must not go into details," he said. "Let it be sufficient to say that the chamber was constructed, and, though I say it, yet so skilful was the arrangement that detection is next to impossible, so that in that sense the object sought for must be considered as fully accomplished."

"But you have not told us the situation of this chamber," said Lord Harcliffe, perceiving that the man paused.

"No, I have not. Hush! It is an important secret. It is at Kew."

The last words were uttered in a whisper only just loud enough to reach the ears of those he addressed.

"Kew?" said Captain Hawk, in the same cautious tones, and asking the question in order to make absolutely certain that there was no mistake.

The man nodded.

"At the old palace there?"

He nodded again.

Then immediately after, with great excitement, he continued:

"When I saw the King and showed him the whole secret, he professed himself thoroughly satisfied, and, requiring me to take an oath of secrecy, he said he would fetch me the amount promised.

"I gladly enough, as you may suppose, consented, and felt a great load taken from my heart upon discovering, as I then thought, that my doubts of the King's sincerity were baseless.

"'Sit down there, Stephen,' he said. 'Drink a glass of wine, if you like. I will be back again in a moment with the money.'

"He quitted the apartment as he spoke.

"For a few seconds I sat still, dreaming over my future

[CAPTAIN HAWK AND THE BLACK HIGHWAYMAN ON THEIR WAY TO KEW.]

prospects, and exulting in the accomplishment of my desire.

"Then my eyes rested upon the splendid glittering decanter on the table before me.

"'That is rare wine,' I thought.—'wine for a King.'

"I was weak and faint.

"After a momentary hesitation, I poured out a glass.

"'There can be no harm in drinking this,' I said, as I held it up to the light and noted its transparent straw-like colour. 'He does not care whether I drink or not. If he had pressed it on me in any way I should have been suspicious. No—no: he means me well; and I have wronged him by having such doubts of his good faith.'

"I drank the wine.

"I swallowed it greedily, though, luckily for me, the glass was a small one.

"As I tasted the last drop I was conscious of a peculiar bitter flavour—not unpleasant, but I was certain that the wine had been poisoned—ay, just as certain as if I had seen the noxious drug poured in."

The highwaymen were breathless with interest.

"For a moment after making this appalling discovery," continued Stephen, "I sat like a man overwhelmed by some crushing mental blow.

"My brain reeled, and a kind of delirium seized me.

"Then I thought of my daughter.

"At first that thought was madness.

"But soon it calmed me.

"I knew I had a duty to perform.

"'Fool—fool that I have been!' I said, 'to be trapped so easily? Oh, what a deep design! The King left me here, calculating that I should not be able to withstand the temptation of tasting the wine in his absence. He judged rightly. But stay—is there no hope?'

"I clasped my hands over my head, which, either from the effects of the drug, or else excitement, throbbed unendurably.

"I tried to think.

"Was there nothing that I could take that would nullify the poison?

"Yes, I remembered at last one thing—oil. A very deadly poison it might prove useless against, yet it might mitigate its virulence. At any rate, there was hope in the thought.

"I looked around.

"Then I remembered a small can I had had along with my other tools.

"To reach it was my next action.

"But little oil was left: but what there was I drained to the last drop. Never was the choicest elixir relished half so well.

"But there was not enough—I mean to be of much service, my only hope was that it would ward off the instantaneous effects of the drug.

"I judged that it was of no ordinary kind, and doubtless would be proof against all antidotal remedies.

"A slight noise now attracted my attention.

"The King came in.

"I saw his eyes light upon the decanter and glass instantly.

"He saw that the wine had been taken, and such a change came over his countenance as satisfied me that I had made no mistake.

"'The wine is strong,' he said, in his detestable broken English. 'Let us hope it will have no ill effects.'

"'Villain!' I cried, 'it is poisoned!'

"As I uttered the words I made a dart forward, intending in my rage to have inflicted some bodily injury to him.

"But he took the alarm just in time, and retreated towards the door with more energy and precipitation than he had made use of for many a year before.

"'I was,' he said, 'just in time.'

"Dashing through the portal, he closed the door and slipped a bolt into its socket.

"I made no attempt to force the door, as I might have succeeded in doing.

"My calmness had returned in some degree, and I was able to see the utter folly of any such attempt.

"What should I do?

"Fly.

"That was the readiest answer that came to my lips.

"Fly, and use what strength remained to me in getting clear of the palace.

"Speed I knew was everything.

"The King, of course, would do all he could to oppose my departure, but I calculated that he would wait outside until the poison had done its work.

"There was only one way by which I could hope to leave the room.

"This was by the window, which opened upon a small space of carefully cultivated ground.

"It might have been fancy, but yet I believed I could already detect some impediment to the pulsation of my heart; and full of the most bitter anguish, I slipped hurriedly through the window

"I must be brief.

"In leaving the palace I had no difficulty worth speaking of.

"In order that my work should be performed effectually, the King had given me a pass which enabled me to go where I chose about the building.

"This precious document I had not yet surrendered, and by means of it I not only succeeded in getting away, but also in obtaining one of the best horses that could be found in all the royal stables.

"Mounting, I rode away, and from then until you witnessed my arrival I never drew rein.

"More than once such a strange giddiness and numbness came over me that I felt as though I must fall headlong to the earth.

"But the one strong impulse enabled me to triumph over my weakness, and I am here."

For the last few moments the doomed man had been speaking with extraordinary volubility, and now he was compelled to stop for sheer want of breath.

It almost seemed, too, as though he availed himself of the opportunity to collect his thoughts a little.

Captain Hawk and Lord Harcliffe exchanged significant glances with each other, but did not speak.

They were more than ever impatient to hear the conclusion of the narrative, and were afraid to make any remark lest they should lose some portion of it.

The man after a heavy sigh and a slight change of position spoke again.

The tones of his voice were remarkably even and calm, and he pronounced each word with a particular emphasis.

His delivery was so strange that it produced the deepest effect upon the minds of his listeners, which was precisely what he intended.

"You will remember," he said, "that I told you at the first that I had my doubts of the King's good faith.

"Not that I thought he would go to such a length as taking my life; my fear was that he would devise a subterfuge to deprive me of the reward he had agreed to give.

"Against such a contingency I took care to defend myself, and now I rejoice that I had so much foresight. It will now stand me in good stead."

Had their lives depended upon it, the two highwaymen could not have guessed to what it was that he alluded.

"Now pay special attention," he continued. "My plan was, that if the King shuffled out of his promise, to devise such means as would enable me to pay myself. Do you see that?"

"We do, perfectly. Proceed."

"I managed this by constructing a second secret mode of entering and leaving the treasure-chamber, so that I should be able unknown to everyone to enter and help myself to what extent I thought proper."

The highwaymen were now in a perfect fever to hear the rest.

The man was much weaker, and the fear was great that he would expire before entrusting them with the important secret.

The revelation produced strange feelings in the minds of both, and with that rapidity of which thought alone is capable, a long train of ideas flitted across their brains.

The singular man now drew every breath with extreme pain and difficulty.

"Listen," he said—"I feel that I have only just life enough left to make the disclosure. No doubt, however, you pretty well comprehend what I mean."

"Go on—go on."

"I will tell you how you can gain safe and easy admission to the treasure-chamber; and what you must do is to take from it the five thousand guineas which the King promised me for performing my contract. As to your own trouble, you must estimate the value of that between yourselves, and obtain the payment from the same source."

This was a golden vision indeed for the two highwaymen.

"In return for the impartment of this priceless secret," said the dying man, "you must swear to deliver the five thousand guineas to my daughter, who is entitled to it by every law of right and justice."

"Clearly so," said Captain Hawk; "and our foreign King will be justly punished for his treachery."

"You are right—you are right. And now, Captain Hawk, I will tell you the reason why I experienced so much satisfaction at finding you were here, and what I meant when I said that I would sooner confide the secret to your ears than to those of any other human being."

"I should indeed be glad if you were to satisfy me upon that head."

"I will do so. Do you remember the landlord of the Old Chequers at York?"

"Remember him? Of course I do!"

"He is a friend of mine—a distant relative, in fact—and it is from his lips that I have heard much concerning you. From him I knew that you could be trusted if once you gave your word."

"He said rightly."

"Then there was another reason why I had occasion to rejoice that you were here."

"Name it."

"I was certain that no scruples would arise in your mind about paying a visit to this secret treasure-chamber."

"Scruples! I never thought of such a thing!"

The man smiled faintly.

"Listen once more," he said. "I have to tell you where to find Margaret, and how to gain admission to the treasure-chamber."

"True: that is well thought of."

"My daughter is at school at Guernsey, under the care of Madame Desaques: you will have no trouble in finding it."

"No; that promises to be an easy matter."

"Now for the secret; and when I have told that I have done."

Lord Harcliffe produced a slip of paper and a pencil in order to write down the instructions.

"The Old Palace at Kew must be well enough known to both of you."

"It is to me," answered Lord Harcliffe. "I——"

"What were you about to say?"

"Nothing of importance."

"Let me hear it, then."

"Simply that I have been there many times."

"If so, then, so much the better," answered the man, whose eyes, despite the close approach of death, glittered with excitement—"so much the better: you will be able all the more easily to make your way to the required spot."

"I am all attention."

"Make your way, in the first instance, to the south wall of what is called the Old Garden. Do you know it?"

"I do."

"Good. The wall is high, but yet not unscaleable. First of all reconnoitre carefully; but if you chose a late hour you are almost certain to meet with no one in that quarter."

"What next?"

"You must scale the wall. It is difficult, and there is some risk to be run; but it is infinitely the best."

"The scaling of a wall, no matter how high, would not be a very formidable undertaking to us, I fancy," said Captain Hawk.

"True. I had forgot for the moment that you were accustomed to making your way into strange places."

"Proceed."

"When in the garden, which is but of limited extent, you will see before you a portion of the palace, probably thirty feet in width."

"Not more?"

"I think not. Almost on a level with the ground you will see a row of five narrow windows. In between three of the windows are brick buttresses—put, of course, more for ornament that actual support."

Lord Harcliffe wrote down the details.

"Go to the centre buttress and count four courses of brickwork from the bottom."

"Right."

"The bricks on the fifth course are loosely set, though to all appearance as strongly fastened as the rest. Any sharp-pointed instrument—a knife, for instance—will dislodge them easily and quickly. You will soon find how many you can remove in this manner: a hole will be left about, large enough for you to crawl through."

"And what then?"

"Enter the opening fearlessly, and make your way along it; you will find nothing in the shape of difficulty or obstruction, and the passage will gradually grow larger as you advance."

"So far all is perfectly clear. What next?"

"At the extremity of the passage you will find a large stone, in which is set an iron ring."

"Is the stone level with the floor?"

"No, no—you will find it facing you."

"Good. And then?"

"You must seize the ring and draw it towards you with your whole strength. When you have once stirred it, it will come easily enough. Put the stone aside, and you will find there is a square opening just large enough for you to crawl through."

"And does that lead into the treasure-chamber?"

"It does. You will see that the stone you have pulled away is one of those of which the chamber is built."

"Your plan is ingenious. If the stone fits closely and you have not employed much thickness of mortar, discovery must be impossible."

The secret-chamber maker smiled faintly.

"You will find everything just as I have described it to you," he said. "Secure the amount I named to you, and as to what else you take away you have no one to regard and consult but yourselves."

"Right."

"Swear once more that you will do ustice to my daughter, and I shall die content."

"Willingly."

Again the life-like portrait was kissed, and no sooner was the ceremony over than the man sank back exhausted and almost lifeless.

More brandy was given him, and though the draught he took was a large one, yet it failed to produce the same reactionary effects as before.

No doubt what made a great difference was that now he had the feeling that he had disclosed all and done everything that laid in his power for the benefit of his idolised child.

His eyes closed, and he lay stretched at full length on the floor of the cottage as though in a deep swoon, nor could the utmost efforts of the two highwaymen arouse him.

His mother—for such the helpless old creature evidently was—now became frantic in her grief.

She called upon him by his name time after time.

A slight movement, however, and some inarticulate sounds alone responded to her wild appeals.

The scene was most painful, and the two highwaymen, whose minds were in a state of confusion impossible to describe, could do nothing save remain helpless spectators of the scene.

The man was dying fast.

It would seem as though the oil he had swallowed had been sufficient to retard the action of the poison, but not enough to counteract it.

He was sinking fast.

Every breath seemed to be drawn more painfully than the one which had preceded it.

One word, and one only that could be distinguished, escaped his lips before Death set his everlasting seal upon them.

That one word was the name of his daughter:

"Margaret."

After that there was a convulsive spasm of all the limbs—his jaw fell.

Then all was over.

Captain Hawk touched his comrade on the arm and made a sign to him to walk to the door.

As soon as they were on the outside of the building, the captain said:

"Let us now lose no time in quitting this dismal spot. At present I hardly know whether we ought to feel pleased or vexed at what has occurred."

"We can do no good by remaining," said Lord Harcliffe, "and yet——"

"I know what you would say, but don't let that stand in the way of our departure. We ought to be off. To stay would only be to incur needless peril."

"Let us go back for a moment and see whether life is quite extinct. If so, we will depart without more delay."

"I am sure all is over."

But Lord Harcliffe re-entered the hut and satisfied himself that the unfortunate man was really dead.

The poor old woman, too, was so distraught that it was impossible to make her comprehend anything, and after repeated trials Lord Harcliffe had to give up the attempt in despair.

He was then forced to admit that his longer presence there would be of no service, and so without a murmur followed his comrade to the back of the premises.

Here they found their horses perfectly safe, but of course not in such condition for service as they could have wished.

To get them ready for the road occupied a few moments only.

CHAPTER CXLVI.

PHAROAH SETS MR. PRICE AND HIS ASSISTANT AT LIBERTY.

Before following any further the incidents which befel Captain Hawk and the Black Highwayman, we feel that we ought to devote a brief space to the proceedings of Pharoah.

It will be remembered that we left him last in a situation of some little difficulty.

After having disposed of Isaac's horse, he was pursued by a portion of the police force.

But the excellence of the steed which he bestrode quickly enabled him to get both out of sight and hearing.

When that was done he paused.

For some moments he remained plunged in anxious consideration.

His inclination prompted him to try all he could to rejoin the Black Highwayman.

But he remembered the part he had to perform with respect to Mr. Price and his assistant, and that consideration enabled him to get the better of his desires.

"I must not neglect the landlord and get him into trouble," he said. "That would be a base return to make for all that he has done. No—no. Hard as it is, and much as it goes against the grain, I must conceal myself in some nook till nightfall, and afterwards make the best of my way to the Greyhound."

Pharoah spoke the truth when he said it went against the grain to come to this decision; and besides, the weather was not such as to make remaining in concealment anywhere a pleasant thing to look forward to.

The idea once crossed his mind of going direct to the Greyhound, and it was not any dread of personal consequences that prevented him, but merely the fear that doing so might compromise Tom Beckford.

With any but pleasurable sensations he scanned the snow-covered landscape, but without being able to perceive any place that held out the faintest chance of answering the object he had in view.

But no foes were in sight, and consoling himself with that he rode on at a gentle rate.

The country in every direction presented a particularly deserted aspect.

With the snow lying so very thickly upon the ground it was impossible for any of the ordinary agricultural operations to be carried forward, and so it happened that, though Pharoah rode many miles, he did not meet with a single person.

This was, of course, very fortunate for him under the circumstances in which he was placed.

Soon after mid-day he found himself not far from a village inn, and, after much doubt and indecision, he rode towards it.

The inn was one of that sort which seems to thrive either with or without customers.

On his arrival there was not a single guest in the place.

No alacrity was shown to attend upon him—indeed, from the landlord downward every person seemed to think he was conferring some great favour by what he did.

Annoyed at first, Pharoah soon came to the conclusion that it was lucky he had entered such a dwelling, because of the little fear there was that he would be disturbed.

Having seen to his steed, he seated himself before the fire in the private room he ordered, and in a short time, lulled by the deep silence and worn out by fatigue, he insensibly dropped off into a heavy slumber, from which he did not awake until an hour or so after darkness had set in.

"So late!" he exclaimed, only rousing himself by an effort. "There is no time to lose now. I must be off."

The reckoning was paid with a liberality that compelled the churlish landlord to put on some semblance of civility.

Without loss of time he departed, and rode at a brisk trot towards the Greyhound.

Yet it was not until midnight that he reached his destination.

The whole of the ancient inn was plunged in darkness, and seemed uninhabited.

As a matter of precaution, however, he made his way round to the back.

The moment his horse came to a standstill, a voice cried:

"Who is there?"

He knew the voice in a moment, and all apprehension vanished.

It was Tom Beckford who had challenged him.

"All is well," he said. "It is I—Pharoah."

"You are most welcome," returned Beckford, stepping forward. "Bring your horse this way, for first of all you must give me a full and authentic account of what has happened."

Pharoah felt that this demand ought to be acceded to, and so without remonstrance he surrendered his steed and made his way towards the inn.

Here in one of the private rooms he sat with the landlord for more than two hours in deep consultation.

How much Tom Beckford would regret the untimely fate which had befallen Isaac the reader does not require to be told.

"I had heard of it, of course," he said, "but resolved not to believe it to the very last. Poor fellow!"

"Captain Hawk is as yet unaware of his unhappy fate," returned Pharoah.

"His grief will be great and sincere when he does hear of it," answered the landlord. "He was a rough but honest and true friend, such as would be sought vainly for elsewhere."

"And now, having satisfied you so far, tell me whether the prisoners are safe?"

"Yes; they have not had the ghost of a chance of getting away, or of raising an alarm even."

"That is well."

"I shall be glad enough to get rid of them though, for all that."

"You will soon see the last of them, I trust."

"And then your next act will be to rejoin the captain?"

"Yes."

"But do you know in what direction to look?"

"I have hardly an idea: I shall have to depend upon my own sagacity, and I much question whether it will fail me."

"If it does, you can at least make sure of rejoining them here at the time appointed for paying Mr. Marchant."

"True; I am glad you mentioned it."

"Had you forgotten?"

"I was unaware of it for the moment, but in such a whirl of ideas it is not to be wondered if some things are forgotten."

"I trust the captain will not be forgetful."

"There is no fear. I'll warrant he won't rest much until he has seen you and thanked you."

"I don't want to be thanked, but I do want to see him, and I heartily hope that no long time will elapse before he is here."

Pharoah emptied his glass.

"I dare not stay any longer," he said, rising; "I have much to do, remember."

"Shall you be able to dispose of them both?"

"I think so, by taking them singly; but lead me to where they are."

Taking up the lantern from the table, Tom Beckford led the way to the outbuilding in which the hangman and his assistant had been placed.

As the landlord had said, they were found safe enough.

They turned their weary, bloodshot eyes upon their visitors and began moaning to be released.

Adopting the same means as before, Price the hangman was lowered through the hole in the loft floor and deposited safely in the stable.

Then placing him across the saddle, Pharoah mounted.

"Wait for me," he said. "I shall return before very long."

So saying, he set his horse in motion.

In spite of all the threats Pharoah could make use of, Price kept groaning in a most doleful manner.

Before his arrival Pharoah had made up his mind just how he should dispose of his two troublesome customers, so without hesitation he rode across the fields in the direction of Huntingdon.

When about half-way to the town he turned off at a right angle, and pursuing this fresh direction, he quickly reached the high-road.

Crossing over, he rode about half-way across a meadow, and then slackening speed somewhat, he relaxed his hold and allowed the hangman to find his way to the ground in the best way he could.

He alighted without sustaining much of a shock, the snow being deep enough to break his fall.

Before he could roll over, however, Pharoah was out of sight.

The country round appearing to be thoroughly deserted, he did not hesitate to ride direct to the Greyhound.

"Well," were the landlord's first words, "have you disposed of him?"

"Yes, quite comfortably."

"How?"

Pharoah explained.

"Comfortable for you, no doubt. But how about the old man?—he will freeze to death."

"Not he: his moans will be heard before long, I'll warrant."

"And shall you serve his assistant just the same?"

"Such is my intention. Help me down with him, and I will bid you farewell for the present."

"Shall you not return again?"

"Not to-night. When I have got rid of my burden I shall try to place a good few miles between Huntingdon and myself."

"It will doubtless be wisest to do so. May good luck attend you."

In the same way as before the Irishman was let down.

Owing to his bulk, however, it was found a much more difficult matter to get him across the horse's back.

"I sha'n't take you far," said Pharoah, mentally. "I must devise some other means of getting rid of you."

His farewell to the landlord was briefly spoken, and then off he set at a steady trot.

Pharoah had rather a fertile imagination, and he had not gone far before he saw his way towards getting rid of his encumbrance neatly and safely.

Pausing in the middle of a field of considerable extent, and the surface of which, like the whole face of the country, was covered with snow, he slackened the gag, which, to speak truth, had been secured with more tightness than was really necessary.

"If you speak a single word or make the least sound," said Pharoah, with terrific emphasis, "that very moment will be your last!"

Of course, the Irishman commenced an appeal for his life—that is, as well as the gag would permit him.

"Silence! Don't I tell you that being silent is your only chance?"

He let him down to the ground as he spoke, and alighting at the same moment, he stooped, and with a couple of strokes of his clasp-knife severed the bonds which secured the man's ankles together.

Restoring his knife to his pocket, he drew forth a pistol.

"Now, you rascal," he cried, "get up!—rise! Do you hear me? Get up, I say!"

"Mercy—mercy!"

"I shall not speak many times in vain. If you want to save your life, stand up!"

Thus adjured, the Irishman, after several ineffectual attempts, succeeded in gaining a standing posture.

From having been bound and being kept in one position for so long, his limbs had all grown so frightfully stiff that he had hardly any use left in them.

Probably nothing but the conviction that his life was at stake enabled him to recover his vigour.

His eyes were still blindfolded and his elbows tightly pinioned behind his back.

"Listen to me," said Pharoah. "Can you hear what I say?"

"Ye-ye-yeez!"

"That's enough. I've just drawn a pistol."

"Och, murdher! Now don't, sir!"

"Silence, you blockhead, or your life won't be worth a pin! Hark! I tell you, I am going to cock the pistol."

Terror made the Irishman quiet.

The quick, jarring sound produced by putting a pistol on full cock reached his ears most unmistakably.

"That's done," said Pharoah. "And I've just two or three words more to say: I am going to take aim at your back."

"Murdher!"

"I say I am going to take aim at your back; but before I pull the trigger I shall count twelve aloud. That will give you a chance."

"The blessin's of Saint——"

"Hold! While I count, you can run; and it all depends upon yourself whether you place yourself out of range."

"Murdher! No, sir, you don't mean it!"

"One!"

"But I'm blindfolded!"

"Two!"

"And my legs have got no use in them!"

"Three!"

The cold, steady manner in which Pharoah went on counting was something more than could be endured.

With a wild howl, which was really something wonderful, considering that the gag had only been slackened, not removed, the Irishman made a desperate plunge forward.

But his limbs were so benumbed that he had the narrowest escape in the world from falling.

In some mysterious and totally inexplicable manner, however, he succeeded in keeping his feet, and went bounding over the snow-covered ground with so many odd contortions of body that Pharoah had no little difficulty in keeping from bursting out into loud peals of laughter.

Before Pharoah had counted twelve, he was out of pistol shot.

Evidently he was not aware of it, however, for he went bounding on as before.

But a slight inequality of the ground brought him to grief.

The efforts that he made to recover his balance were no less surprising than ludicrous.

All was in vain, though, and with a most dismal yell he fell headforemost into the snow, into which he grovelled with the instinct of an ostrich, as though by so doing he should be able to protect his body from the bullet.

Pharoah's laughter was now unrestrainable.

Of course he knew better than carry into effect his threat of firing the pistol.

He had no wish to wound or slay the Irishman; and the report of the fire-arm would possibly have brought his enemies about him.

Letting down the hammer to half-cock, he replaced the fire-arm in his pocket, and mounted.

But before he rode away he looked doubtfully and hesitatingly around him.

The task which he had in view was one of no ordinary difficulty, and most would have abandoned it in despair.

With no more clue than he possessed, it did indeed seem impossible that he should be able to rejoin Captain Hawk and the Black Highwayman.

But the indecision he had exhibited very quickly passed away.

A slight touch with his heel put his horse to an easy gallop; and across the open country he directed his way in such a manner as to pass the scene of execution a little on his left hand.

As he neared Ling Heath, his vigilance increased, for naturally enough he expected that in this vicinity he should be almost certain to find officers of police.

But no alarming discovery was made, and he continued his ride beyond this point utterly at random.

He knew that the two highwaymen had certainly gone in this direction; but what capricious turns and bends choice or necessity might have compelled them to make he had no means of guessing.

He rode on until the gray dawn of the winter's day could be discerned in the east.

Up to that moment he had not been able to increase his knowledge one jot.

Knowing the danger of attempting to travel by day, and also being perfectly conscious that his horse could not continue his journey without reasonable rest and proper food, he put up at a small inn, the retired situation of which seemed to hold out a strong prospect that for some hours he could reckon upon remaining there undisturbed.

He was the more encouraged to take up his quarters in this place on account of the good fortune which had attended him on the preceding day.

The people were civil, and promised him the best of accommodation.

Less curiosity was displayed than he could have reckoned on, and altogether things looked as satisfactory as he could hope for.

In this way the day was spent.

No incident whatever occurred calling for special mention, and, of course, so soon as ever the obscurity was sufficiently great for him to feel safe, Pharoah was in the saddle.

And now, although he had carefully considered the subject during the whole of the day, he felt himself at a greater loss than ever to decide upon the route he ought to pursue.

The snow still covered the ground, and as all around seemed so entirely safe and still, he determined to venture upon taking the high-road.

The advantage that this was to his horse we need not say was very great.

Owing to the firmness of the ground that lay beneath its white covering, he was able to make good speed without much distress.

But ere long Pharoah was conscious that some one was on the road before him.

The distance and the snow combined made the sound very indistinct.

Yet to his well-trained sense of hearing it was unmistakable.

For a minute or two, however, he could not decide whether the sound was growing nearer or fading away.

Nor could he tell whether it was one horse or several, though the former seemed more likely.

He listened for some seconds longer.

"Be it one or more, the sound certainly grows plainer. What shall I do?"

The question was one which could hardly be answered in a moment.

Of course it was very important that he should, if possible, avoid encountering anybody.

To retrace his steps was not in accordance with his designs, and to strike off across the country would not only be attended with the disadvantage we have just named, but also the risk of being noticed by whoever chanced to be approaching.

Not many yards in advance the road was bounded by some high fragments of precipitous rock, through which apparently the roadway had been cut.

Their appearance and arrangement were peculiarly rugged.

Pharoah decided in a moment that here would be a chance of concealing both himself and horse from those who were approaching.

Accordingly he rode direct towards the spot and found that the rocks were much better adapted for concealment than he had first imagined.

Some rather extensive quarrying operations had been evidently carried on since the formation of the road, and owing to this he was able to back his horse into a recess where there was little fear of his being noticed by a casual passer-by.

Not only was the night a dark one, but the shadows fell with particular blackness in the recess.

"I seem to be covered up completely," he said, as he placed his horse to his satisfaction. "Now then to see who is coming. It is ten thousand to one, knowing nothing of my presence here, if they are able to discern me."

Pharoah said "they," for he was now convinced that more than one horseman was approaching, though the snow made things very confusing.

He was not to be kept long in suspense, however.

He had just time to draw his pistol and place himself in readiness for immediate defence, should he be discovered or attacked when the foremost horseman came in sight.

The reader must understand that Pharoah's first glimpse was anything but a distinct one.

In less than a moment he was able to recognise the horseman, and never before probably had he felt so strong a desire to discharge his pistol as on the present occasion.

The rider was Sir Thomas Walker.

He was riding at full gallop, and behind him came a straggling but yet rather large party of police officers.

Their horses were not equal in fleetness to the one bestrode by Sir Thomas, whose ardour in the chase had not abated a single jot.

Pharoah's finger encircled the trigger of his pistol.

He was more than half determined to fire as the magistrate dashed past.

But the certainty that this would bring the officers upon him made him hesitate, and the chance was lost.

The next moment the straggling troop swept by.

Not one saw Pharoah.

Indeed, their whole attention appeared to be absorbed in watching the flying form ahead of them.

Five minutes after the last had gone by, Pharoah rode out into the road again.

The troop was not only out of sight, but owing to the snow, out of hearing too.

"A narrow escape!" Pharoah said as he gave himself a good shake and then resumed his onward journey.

CHAPTER CXLVII.

THE TWO HIGHWAYMEN COMMENCE THEIR JOURNEY TO KEW WITHOUT DELAY.

We go back now to Lord Harcliffe and Captain Hawk.

The reader will recollect that we left the two highwaymen busily engaged in caparisoning their horses.

The operation was performed quickly and in silence.

As soon as ever it was completed they vaulted into the saddles and rode round to the front of the hut.

Here they paused a moment.

But Captain Hawk manifested every anxiety to be off.

"Come," he said, "why should we linger? We can do nothing, and the old woman is best left to herself. Come, I say—come!"

"One moment," answered his companion. "I cannot go thus."

To the captain's surprise, he slipped from the saddle and re-entered the frail dwelling.

In a moment afterwards he heard him calling.

Unwillingly enough, the captain entered.

"Look," said Lord Harcliffe, who had caused the fire to burn brightly—"it is as I fancied, and I could not go away with the doubt unsatisfied."

"What is it?"

"Behold!"

As he uttered the word he pointed to the form of the old woman, which lay at full length on the hearth and partly across her son's corpse.

"Is she dead, poor creature?" the captain asked.

"She is."

"It is better so."

"You are right. After what has happened what had she to live for?—what pleasure could existence have? Now I depart content. Come—I am quite ready now."

He hastened to the exterior as he spoke, and a very brief time indeed elapsed before the highwaymen were again in the saddle.

When the horses started both riders could tell that the animals had not recovered very much from their fatigue.

"We shall have to go gently, Harcliffe," said the captain, "or they will never hold out."

"What, the horses?"

"Yes."

"I am afraid you are right."

"Besides, I don't see that there is any need for violent exertion just at present."

"There is not. It is a hundred to one whether we fall foul of our enemies now."

"They must have missed us—there can be no doubt of that."

"And are hardly likely to find us now."

"Still, we must be careful."

"True."

"What I propose is that we shall ride on, but not at such a pace as to make it difficult for us to converse together."

"I am quite agreeable to such a course."

"A canter, with a walk now and then, will suit us."

"Right."

Up to that moment they had been going at half gallop—a rate which would have made talking almost impossible to the generality of riders.

But the reins were tightened, and a word from the riders brought the horses down to the required rate.

It was now quite dark.

The white mantle of snow could be seen stretching before and around them to a considerable distance.

But neither moon nor stars shone forth.

A dark thick cloud covered the whole firmament.

With every confidence, however, the highwaymen rode on, though the road was anything but familiar to them.

As may be supposed, the first subject that was brought forward was that of the strange events that they had witnessed.

"Now I think of it," said Captain Hawk, "all that has occurred since nightfall seems so strange and unreal that I can hardly help taking the whole to be no more than a dream."

"It is indeed more than strange," answered his companion. "Never before has so singular an adventure befallen me."

"I have seen many things, yet I could almost venture to say the same."

"The question is, can it all be true?"

"You may well ask the question; and yet after all we have seen and heard there seems no room for doubt."

"At such a time, and so near death as he evidently was, one can hardly think a man would give utterance to a long string of falsehoods."

"No, no—I will not believe that. Depend upon it, what the man said was true. There was too much coherence in the whole narrative for it to be taken for the insane ravings of a madman."

"It seems quite certain."

"The question which arises is the use we are to make of the secret so strangely confided to us."

"What do you mean?"

"What amount are we to abstract for our own use and advantage?"

Captain Hawk laughed.

"There will be little scruple in my breast against taking away all that I can conveniently carry."

"I say the same. And what is not less singular than all the rest is that this revelation should be made to us at so opportune a time."

"You are thinking now of the arrangement made with Mr. Marchant?"

"Yes."

"It is indeed opportune in that respect, for if all is true——"

"And all goes well."

"Surely if all goes well we have no further occasion to trouble ourselves about the means of obtaining this sum of money."

"None in the least. And there is another idea which crosses my mind."

"What is it?"

"Perhaps I had better not name it."

"Nay, do not hesitate."

"Then, since you insist——"

"I do."

"Then my thought was, that we might be able to secure such an amount in jewels and other valuables as would enable us to live for some considerable time at least in another land."

"What! and quit the road?"

"Why not?"

"Never."

"I thought you would not agree with me, and yet after what you have just escaped, one would have thought you would have gladly seized upon an opportunity of freeing yourself from so much danger."

"No—no," returned the captain; "I am afraid, Harcliffe, that you have not yet realised the glory and excitement which belong to the vocation of a knight of the road."

Lord Harcliffe shrugged his shoulders as he said:

"I ought to know something about it by this time."

"You ought. But I am afraid it is little. To you, perhaps, there is no further object than the obtaining of a good booty. But with me it is quite different."

"I know your notions."

"It is not the purse that I crave," continued the captain: "it is the excitement of adventure, the glory of a gallop by night along a well-kept road or across a heath, to say nothing of the many things that are to be heard and seen which are beyond the experience of all other persons. It is that which makes me cling to the highway and renders me insensible to any temptation or inducement to abandon the highway."

"That is all very fine," said Lord Harcliffe, "but my opinion is that a change for a time would be anything but disagreeable. Wealth will work wonders in other countries besides England, and——"

"I know what you would say. You would like to persuade me that it will be best to take such a sum from the treasure-chamber as would enable us to live in plenty abroad and forsake the road altogether."

"Let us say for a time. You cannot help confessing that our enemies are now so powerful and vigilant as to take off a great deal of the charm of the occupation."

"It may be so. But yet, after all, what we are saying is but idle talk. Let us wait till we have the treasure: it will be time enough then to decide what to do with it."

"Truly; and so let us quit the discussion for the present."

"Are you offended?"

"Not I! I did but speak the thought that sprang into my mind. Since it don't please you, let us say no more about it."

Notwithstanding the way in which Lord Harcliffe spoke, the captain could tell that he experienced not a little vexation.

But passing over the subject altogether, he reverted to the claim which the man's daughter had upon them.

"Never doubt me," said Lord Harcliffe, with a fervency and earnestness which left no doubt of strong purpose. "I will do all that I have promised. No matter what may happen or how great the personal danger may be, she shall have the sum mentioned—ay, and more too. The King will doubtless feel very keenly any injury that we may do him through his money-bags."

"It seems strange to me that he should think of making such a place. What can be his fear?"

"Many would answer that question readily enough. He feels and knows that he is not popular, and that the Prince of Wales has a powerful band of unscrupulous adherents."

"I understand you. But now that we have come to a high-road, let us consider where we are and determine which way to take to get to Kew."

As the captain spoke, he reined-in his horse close to a low wooden fence, on the other side of which could be faintly discerned the course of the high-road, for here the snow, instead of presenting an unbroken surface, was much cut up and trampled.

"It is quite time we thought about it," said the Black Highwayman. "It seems more and more certain that we have given our foes the slip, and now I should like to make my way towards Kew with as little delay as possible."

"So should I. Have you any idea what part of the country we are in?"

"Certainly no definite knowledge; but so far as I have been able to judge we are not very far out of our required direction."

"But we must be many miles from it?"

"Yes—I should say fifty at least."

"So far?"

"Yes—you may depend it is no less than that."

"It is quite a certainty, then, that we shall have to look out for some place where we can give our horses good food and proper rest."

"Yes, I have been thinking of that. I am always uneasy when I know my horse is not up to the mark, and just at the present moment I question whether we should have much of a chance if a party of officers pursued us."

"Do not bring forward such uncomfortable ideas, for, gently as we have come, I have felt Phantom flag more than once."

"What do you propose, then?"

"I think, as we have come so far, that we had better ride gently onwards till towards dawn?"

"Along the high-road?"

"Yes. At this lonely hour it is a great question whether we shall meet a living creature."

No sooner was this said than they forced the horses to clear the fence.

As the height of this was inconsiderable, they alighted in the road without much effort.

Lord Harcliffe turned to the left, and Captain Hawk did so likewise without question.

The snow in the middle of the road was trampled sufficiently to make it much better for the horses to travel;

and for several miles they kept up their former pace without half so much appearance of distress.

For the most part the road had been bounded on one side by an extensive wood, while on the other nothing but open country could be seen.

The locality was particularly lonely, for though continually on the look-out for an inn, they did not see one—no, nor even a labourer's cottage.

But the increased vigour shown by their horses made them less inclined to find fault with this circumstance than they would have been.

Just when objects were beginning to grow distinguishable one from the other, Captain Hawk called his friend's attention to the dusky outline of some building in advance.

Just as they looked, a light appeared, which, from its situation and general character, they could tell came from one of the windows.

"The inmates are stirring early," was Lord Harcliffe's remark. "Depend upon it that is an inn—perhaps a place where the coach horses are changed."

"In that case, it hardly seems likely to be the place for us."

"I don't know that: it may actually be safer than a more obscure resting-place. Surely our foes would never form such a high estimate of our audacity as to think that we should take up our quarters at a well-frequented inn, such as I am sure this is?"

"Let us try it."

"I am quite willing, for I have many a time found security by doing a similar thing."

They rode forward only at a walking pace, and as they proceeded they saw light after light appear at the different windows of the inn, showing that in a short time most of its inmates would be astir.

"There is something unusual going forward, depend upon it," said the captain, "or they would never be moving at this very early hour."

"If so, we shall soon find what it is then."

A few more minutes brought them to the front of the inn.

The building was larger and much more imposing than they had imagined.

The stabling and other outhouses all abutted upon the high-road, and from various portions of them lights glimmered.

What all this bustle could portend the highwaymen were at a loss to imagine, and they became immediately curious to be enlightened on the subject.

Their arrival had not been unnoticed, for an ostler came out of one of the stables and accosted them.

"Morning, gentlemen," he said. "Going to bait a bit? Your horses look as though they wanted a little rest."

"Yes. We thought of staying if we were sure of having good accommodation here."

"That shows you are strangers to this part of England anyway, or else you would know that at the Cumberland Arms here there is better entertainment to be had than at any other place in the kingdom."

"The Cumberland Arms, eh? And do you always open as early as this?"

"Twice a week, sir, when the mail-coach goes by; and that reminds me if you want your horses attended to you had better have them put in the stable at once; if you don't, they won't stand a very good chance when the coach comes."

The arrival of the coach was evidently matter of very great importance at the Cumberland Arms, and Captain Hawk gave a rapid, inquiring glance at his companion to make sure that he still held to his intention of staying there.

Lord Harcliffe nodded and alighted.

Captain Hawk imitated him, and while asking various questions accompanied the ostler to the stables, where, in the course of a few moments, they saw their horses made as comfortable as they could desire.

It would have been easy enough for them to have remained in the stable for some moments longer had they wished it, but they desired to get into a private room before the coach came, as they would then have a better chance of being unobserved.

Lord Harcliffe and Captain Hawk were both quite certain that the ostler neither recognised them nor had the least suspicion of who they were.

This made them all the more confident when they accosted the landlord.

To the best of their knowledge they had never been in this part of the country before, and so it was indeed scarcely likely that they would be suspected or known.

"We must have perfect quiet and seclusion," said Lord Harcliffe, in a manner so commanding as forced the landlord to be more than ordinarily respectful. "Bring us the best you have to eat and drink in the house, and lose no time, for we are in a hurry."

"You shall be served before the coach comes, gentlemen. Luckily, I am well provided with eatables, for the travellers generally make a practice of taking a snack here."

"Good—that will do; now show us to the best room you have, but it must be wholly private, mind."

"Certainly, gentlemen—certainly," replied the landlord, bowing low at every word. "Be kind enough to follow me this way. It is not very far—at least, it is on the first floor. Perhaps you may have an objection to it on that account?"

"None—none at all."

"Thank you, gentlemen."

"That is provided it has a window commanding the road: I hate a dull room."

"Then this will suit you, sir, exactly."

The landlord went upstairs in a high state of flutter.

He was well enough experienced in his trade to feel certain from what he heard and saw that the guests who had arrived that morning were profitable ones, and his thoughts already ran upon the amount which he should charge them for what they had.

The upstairs room was soon reached, and was certainly a very comfortable apartment.

It was well furnished, and brightly lighted by a blazing fire.

"There, gentlemen," the landlord exclaimed, with an air of great satisfaction, "I hope you will be contented with your quarters."

"Yes; and now let us have the refreshment we ordered."

"Certainly, gentlemen: that will not occupy five minutes."

As soon as the landlord left the room both highwaymen hastened to the window.

They found they had a capital view of all in front of the inn, and every moment as the day advanced they were better and better able to distinguish surrounding objects.

Apparently the view from this window was a very fine one, and no doubt it was invariably reserved for special guests.

In less than the time that had been mentioned the landlord appeared, bringing with him a very tempting collation indeed.

There was cold fowl, temptingly laid out with ham, tongue, and other delicacies, together with the whitest and finest bread anyone could wish for, with a couple of bottles of those light wines which were so generally in use in England a hundred and fifty years ago.

"There, gentlemen," cried the landlord, complacently, "were you princes you could not be treated better. You must excuse me for not waiting upon you, but I expect the coach here every moment, and that will take the whole of my attention."

"We can very well dispense with your services."

"Thank you, gentlemen. And should there be anything you require, just ring the bell, and I will take care you are attended to forthwith."

Having uttered this promise, the landlord beat a hasty retreat, for he fancied he caught the distant sound of the guard's horn.

"The coach is late, master," said the ostler

"It's the snow that's done it. Not much behind after all. Here she comes."

The clear ringing notes given forth by the post-horn were now heard distinctly in the still morning air.

The spirit-stirring strain served as a signal to set all the people at the inn in motion.

The general bustle had something extremely pleasing and interesting in it; and no sooner was the horn heard than the two highwaymen posted themselves at the windows.

[CAPTAIN HAWK TAKES A PEEP INTO THE OLD GARDEN AT KEW.]

They took care to do so in such a manner as would enable them to see without much fear of being seen.

Lord Harcliffe opened the window a little way.

"We shall hear something worth listening to, ten to one," he said; "and we shall be able, perhaps, to glean something of the actions of our foes."

"It is most likely. But let us be silent now."

"I hope the landlord will be silent too."

"That is my principal source of uneasiness. If he gets talking about us it is just possible he may get us into danger."

"There is that risk to be run. And we cannot help ourselves: we must abide by the result, whatever it is."

Both now were silent.

The coach was at length in sight.

There was another sonorous blast upon the guard's horn, and then, with a whirl, a dash, and a clatter, the four foaming horses were pulled up and the huge vehicle brought to a standstill.

The scene in front of the inn then became as animated as it was picturesque.

The hungry passengers, every one chilled to the bone by their long night ride through the cold, hastened to alight.

Shivering and trembling, they one by one darted into the inn, where the huge fires that were burning ready for their reception looked doubly tempting and comfortable.

The halt was but a brief one, for almost directly after the jaded horses were taken into the stable the fresh ones were brought out in their stead.

Captain Hawk opened the door and stood at the top of the stairs.

A chorus of voices alone reached his ears.

Not one word could be distinguished from the rest.

He could gather, though, that the conversation was principally, if not wholly, composed of orders for refreshment of various kinds.

Nothing arose to lead them to believe that they were menaced by the slightest danger.

"Time's up!" the guard cried at length; and then the confusion and uproar became doubled.

It was at this point that the highwaymen directed the whole of their attention to the windows.

The new horses were already harnessed, and stood champing their bits and fretting at their detention.

The driver, enveloped in his many coats, had taken his seat.

Then one by one the passengers came forth.

On their return to the vehicle the highwaymen were able to observe them with much greater closeness than on their arrival.

It was with a breath of relief that they learned there was not one who would be likely to be even remotely connected with the objects of the police.

But just before the moment of departure a remark let drop by the coachman arrested their sole attention.

The words were addressed to the landlord, who, according to custom, had advanced as far as the pump at the end of the horse-trough in order to witness the departure of the coach.

"Have you heard the news from Huntingdon?" the driver asked.

"News?—what news? What has happened?"

"There has been the devil to pay," was the rejoinder, "and no hot pitch ready."

"How—how?"

"They were to have hung Captain Hawk on Ling Heath."

"Yes—yes! Haven't they done it?"

"No, I should rather say not. The captain's got off."

"Got off?"

"Yes; and they've killed Price the hangman, set fire to the jail, hung the chief magistrate, and made the Governor run the gauntlet through the crowd so that it has all but been the death of him!"

The landlord, hearing all this, drew a long breath and turned as white as a ghost, as well he might at hearing such a catalogue of horrors.

"And—and this confounded Captain Hawk—the terror of the road—what has become of him?"

"He's got clear off."

"You don't mean that?"

"It is a positive fact. He's away with his companion, but where nobody can tell."

"But they are in search of them?"

"Of course they are. I thought I had better let you know what was stirring in the world, so that if you should happen to see two strangers, soldier-like-looking fellows, arrest them: there is a reward of more than a thousand pounds to be earned by whoever does it."

By the time the driver had uttered this warning the last passenger had taken his seat.

The guard once more blew his horn, and with a loud crack of the whip away the equipage rolled over the snowy ground.

The driver's last words of course brought his two new guests to the landlord's mind, as it could hardly fail to do.

The idea flitted across his mind that they might be no other than the two desperate highwaymen spoken of.

The bare supposition gave him such a dreadful turn that he could neither speak nor move.

So ludicrous was the expression of dismay which settled upon his features that, despite their vexation at what had just happened, the two highwaymen could not help smiling.

He stood gazing after the coach as long as it was visible, and then, with a troubled air, he walked to the front door.

"Curse it!" said Lord Harcliffe. "If that confounded driver had but kept his mouth shut, we should have been all right till nightfall. Now ten to one whether we shall have a moment's peace. I am certain the landlord's suspicions are excited."

"Then we must do our best to allay them, that is all I can say. Let us sit down to the table as though we were quite at our ease."

This was too good a suggestion not to be complied with.

Scarcely, however, had they settled themselves in their seats when they heard the landlord on the stairs.

He opened the door and gave a look at the table and the viands, upon which he showed how great his uneasiness was.

"You have got rid of your customers, then," said Lord Harcliffe, with a perfectly unconcerned and unruffled air.

"Ye—ye—yes! As you say, they have, in a manner of speaking—that is to say, gone."

"Just so. It is rather strange, but at the moment you entered, we were talking about you."

"A—a—about me, gentlemen?" the landlord gasped, looking more uneasy than ever.

"Yes. Just oblige us, now that your bustle of business is over, by taking a chair and a glass of wine, for you are doubtless in a position to give us the information we need."

Somehow or other the idea that his two guests were no other than the two highwaymen grew stronger and stronger in the landlord's breast.

To have refused or to have shown any hesitation would, he thought, be equivalent to signing his own death-warrant.

He sank down, and as he did so the perspiration started out in great beads on his forehead.

In the hope of concealing his confusion, he took out an enormous pocket-handkerchief and wiped his face with it.

That operation over, he glared at the two highwaymen in a manner which showed how terribly ill at ease he was.

"Taste the wine," said Lord Harcliffe, "and then we shall take it as a favour if you will give us your best attention."

"Certainly, gentlemen," said the landlord, licking his lips, which were parched by fear.

"Very good. It is necessary, in the first place, that I should acquaint you with the errand which has brought my companion and myself to your house."

The landlord made a clumsy bow, but he could not speak.

"We are on the look-out," continued Lord Harcliffe, "for a little shooting, and it struck us that you would be almost certain to know whether there was anything of the kind to be had in the vicinity. The number of acres is an unimportant matter: all we want to be assured of is that the sport is good."

CHAPTER CXLVIII.

THE TWO HIGHWAYMEN PERFECTLY SUCCEED IN DUPING THE LANDLORD.

"A—A LITTLE shooting, sir!" gasped the landlord, in a way that proclaimed his terror had undergone no abatement. "What—what sort of shooting was it you required?"

The landlord planted his feet on the floor and pushed his chair back a couple of feet as he asked this question.

Lord Harcliffe laughed.

"Why, dear me," he said, "you don't seem just the thing, landlord."

"No, no—I am not."

"What is the matter?"

"Nothing—nothing. I am better than I was."

"But you seemed terrified."

"No—no, gentlemen, I assure you! Be kind enough to go on with what you were saying."

"About the shooting?"

"Yes."

"Why, you must understand we are both very fond of a bit of sport, and latterly we have had a great deal of trouble in getting it."

He accompanied these words with a glance at Captain Hawk, who smiled to show that he was quite sensible of the double meaning which attached itself to almost every word his friend said.

"You mean pheasant shooting, I suppose, gentlemen?"

"Yes, and anything else in the shape of game. Last year we bought the right of shooting over a thousand acres, and we were most awfully taken in. There was hardly a bird bigger than a sparrow to be found on the whole place."

The landlord felt he ought to say something when his guest paused, so he faltered out that very useful word in such cases:

"Indeed!"

"It is a fact, I assure you; and in order not to be so deceived another time, we determined not to entrust the matter to an agent, as we have done hitherto, but to take the business into our own hands. Up to this moment we have found nothing to suit us, and my friend suggested an appeal to you as being the most likely person to know whether there was anything of the kind to be met with in this neighbourhood."

Lord Harcliffe spoke in so calm and collected a manner as to completely deceive the landlord, who felt it to be impossible to entertain his suspicions any longer.

"Well, gentlemen," he replied, and giving a long-drawn sigh of relief as he spoke, "it happens you have addressed yourself to the right person."

"I am delighted to hear it; and any extra trouble that you may be put to in the affair we shall be very happy to reward you for."

"Don't name that, sir. I never think anything too much trouble if it's to serve a guest as is a gentleman."

Lord Harcliffe bowed gravely to this compliment.

"You must know, sir, that there is not far from here just the very thing you require. Such covers could not be matched in the whole of the county!"

"Capital! And not far from here, you say?"

"Close at hand."

"Then we shall be able to make your inn our head-quarters. That will be glorious!"

The landlord was highly gratified at the prospect of having two such guests during the shooting season.

"There's about fifteen hundred acres that you could have the right to shoot over, and, I assure you, for a nominal sum—merely a nominal sum. Could I persuade you into going with me? We can have a look at the place at once."

But, as the reader knows, it did not by any means suit the highwaymen's plans to leave the inn till nightfall.

All they wanted to do was to free the landlord's mind of the suspicions which the coachman's words had put into it.

This had been done tolerably well up to this point, and therefore it behoved them to be doubly cautious not to lose the good effect which had been produced.

"We should be very glad to do so, but we are dreadfully fatigued with riding so far as we have. I suppose it would make no difference if we were to defer our visit to a later hour in the day?"

"Oh, no difference at all, gentlemen—not the least in the world! It was very inconsiderate of me to propose it just now."

"Oh, no matter! Suppose we say some time in the afternoon?"

"By all means—just as you please; and if in the meantime you should feel that a snooze would be agreeable, all you have to do is to open that door and you'll find yourself in the best bed-room in the inn."

The two highwaymen expressed their thanks; and then the landlord, highly delighted with himself and everybody else, began to remove the remains of the repast from the table.

As soon as this task was completed, and the room only occupied by themselves, Lord Harcliffe indulged in a peal of laughter, to which, however, he could not give free vent for fear the sound should reach the landlord's ears.

"You managed that capitally," said Captain Hawk. "I must congratulate you upon your address and readiness of wit."

"Do you think his suspicions are removed?"

"I feel sure of it."

"Then our end is gained; and I think we can venture to look forward to remaining here in peace during the remainder of the day."

"But what shall you do when he comes to take you to view the shooting ground?"

"Devise some excuse, that is all. But there is plenty of time to think about that."

"Had you any idea of acting upon his suggestion about the bed-room?"

"I had."

"It will be best for one to watch."

"Most certainly. It is impossible to say what half an hour may bring forth."

"Then we will draw lots to settle the matter."

"Agreed."

It fell to Captain Hawk's lot to keep watch during the first two hours.

Lord Harcliffe merely took off his coat and boots, so as to be in readiness in case of alarm.

He had not thrown himself upon the bed for a couple of minutes before he was fast asleep.

Partly screened by a curtain, Captain Hawk spent the greater part of the time in looking through the window.

As the day advanced, many passengers passed by.

But no officers appeared; nor was there anything to suggest the approach of danger.

As the sun rose the snow melted; and at noon there was a general thaw, which made travelling just about as disagreeable as it well could be.

It was about this time when Lord Harcliffe awoke from his dreamless sleep: and on looking out he was of course much struck by the entire alteration which had taken place in the scene.

"It does not bid fair for a very pleasant ride," he said. "But I suppose we must make the best of it."

"Even so. And you will keep guard now?"

"Yes. Sleep, my friend—you look thoroughly worn out."

"I am weary; but ere long I shall no doubt recover my wonted strength."

"Oh yes."

"Rouse me at the end of two hours."

"All right. And as for the landlord, don't you trouble your head about him. I will put him right."

Without another word Captain Hawk made his way to the inner room.

The exertion he had undergone since his escape had indeed told most fearfully upon him; and now his exhaustion was so great that, after tumbling headlong upon the bed, he lay just as he fell, not once making an attempt to rise.

The landlord, who all this time had been in a state of dreadful fidget, now came upstairs and tapped at the door.

He had been waiting for an hour or more expecting that his guests would ring and summon him; but, finding they did nothing of the sort, he waited till his impatience would not suffer him to wait any longer, and he ascended and knocked.

As Lord Harcliffe opened the door, he made an imperative gesture for silence.

"My friend sleeps," he said. "He will awake soon, no doubt; but I would not disturb him for the world."

"Certainly not, sir. You will excuse me for intruding, I hope."

"Oh, of course. I am, in fact, much obliged to you for your attention. If you would only see that the horses are all right——"

"I will attend to them, rely upon it."

With these words the landlord went downstairs again.

Lord Harcliffe, with all the patience he could command, waited until the captain awoke, which was not until close upon sunset.

Captain Hawk felt vexed to think he had slept so long, and chid his friend for not having awakened him at the expiration of the time agreed upon.

But he could not deny feeling much refreshed and rested—to being more like himself than he had been since his capture.

"I knew sleep was the best restorative you could have," Lord Harcliffe said; "and the result proves that I was quite right, does it not?"

"It does. And now what shall be our next step?"

"Another meal. We can call the landlord, and though he may be impatient for us to visit the covers, yet he will not be able to refuse serving another meal."

"Certainly not."

The landlord was summoned accordingly.

He declared he had anticipated their wishes, and had prepared a repast which should give them satisfaction and do justice to himself.

After this flourish he descended.

He was not long in laying upon the table a very substantial meal, to which, as before, the highwaymen did ample justice.

Towards the close of it Captain Hawk said:

"Would it not be a capital idea, now that we have so good an opportunity, to stow away some portion of these good things? The time may soon come when they will be both useful and agreeable."

"You are right. That is an excellent thought."

The two highwaymen then packed up some cold fowl, ham, bread, and other things, and stowed them away.

The landlord would no doubt fancy they had prodigious appetites, unless he should divine the truth of the matter.

Just as they were concluding the meal they rang the bell and summoned the landlord.

"It is getting late," said Lord Harcliffe, "but yet I think we shall have plenty of time to look at the covers."

"Impossible!" said the landlord. "You will be obliged to wait till morning."

"Yes, to make a thorough examination, no doubt we shall; but just the attempt to find out the situation of the place and a general look around will be a pleasant exercise and just serve to fill up the time agreeably."

Lord Harcliffe spoke in such a way that the landlord, who in his vocation had had much experience, felt it would be worse than useless to offer any opposition.

He went down then and ordered the horses.

"What are we to do about paying him, captain?"

"What do you mean?"

"Why, if we ask for our bill or offer to pay him, he will know there is a deception in the whole affair."

"He is sure to make that discovery sooner or later."

"The later the better, then."

"Well, perhaps so."

"And as he has treated us in really a capital manner I should not like to run off leaving the score unpaid."

"No—no, we won't do that."

"How are we to help it?"

"Put a couple of guineas under that tankard there—he will be sure to find them, and now we shall be able to depart contented."

Not waiting for the landlord to come to say that the steeds were ready, they went down to the back door, which opened direct upon the paved yard where the stables were situated.

The ostler was just in the act of leading the horses through the doorway, and the landlord was looking on importantly.

The eyes of the highwaymen lighted up with satisfaction when they saw how differently their horses looked from what they did on their arrival.

The noble creatures now seemed full of fire and vigour.

Rarely indeed had they appeared to be in better condition for a long ride across the country.

"You have deferred your visit until a very late hour," said the landlord, glancing up at the sky while he spoke. "I am afraid it is but little of the covers you will be able to see."

"As the distance is not great we shall soon be there."

"As you like, gentlemen."

"Be good enough to put us in the way."

The highwaymen, while these few words were being exchanged, made a hasty examination of the trappings of their horses.

Having found all secure and satisfactory, they vaulted into the saddles in a way that not a little astonished the landlord and the two ostlers.

But, beyond letting the surprise he felt appear in his face, the landlord did nothing.

Advancing to the front part of the inn, he proceeded to give his two guests very precise and particular directions as to the way they ought to take to reach the preserves.

As they did not intend to pay a visit there at all, the two highwaymen were not very particular about listening.

Their satisfaction was considerable when they found the shooting ground lay in the direction that they wished to take.

A very great detour was thus saved; and after the exchange of a few more words they departed.

Never was any man more completely taken in than the landlord.

Nothing was further from his thoughts than that he was taking his parting glimpse of his two guests.

Such was the case, however, and the two highwaymen, as soon as they got to a safe distance, chatted merrily about the capital way in which they had managed matters.

That they should be in excellent spirits is no more than might be expected.

Everything had gone well.

To the best of their belief they had been successful in throwing their enemies completely off the scent.

Their horses were fresh, and there was every prospect that their adventure would be successfully carried out.

What ultimate effect the gaining possession of so large an amount of treasure would have it was impossible to tell.

Time only, the unfolder of all mysteries, would be able to clear it up satisfactorily.

As they rode darkness came on with surprising rapidity.

To have kept the high-road would only have been to increase their danger very greatly.

As soon, then, as they were certain they were completely out of sight of the inn they availed themselves of a cross road.

After the change in the weather it was utterly out of the question to ride across the open country: their horses would have sunk knee-deep at almost every step.

The state of the cross-road was bad enough to make travelling it a very serious matter.

Captain Hawk's first question was as to the distance.

"It cannot be less than forty miles," was the reply.

"Well, the hour is early, we are rested, and our horses are fresh. We ought to do it."

"It is worth the effort."

"Most certainly it is."

"Do you think we could manage to accomplish the journey and pay a visit to the treasure-chamber as well?"

"What, between now and daylight?"

"Yes."

"That is another matter. I am afraid not, and yet I hope we shall accomplish it. It will be advantageous in every way."

"Let us make the attempt, then. 'Nothing venture, nothing win.'"

"True. And we ought to accomplish the first twenty miles in very little over an hour."

"Off and away then! How astonished the landlord will be when he finds no sign of our returning!"

Both laughed at this, and then the next moment the two horses were stretching along the road at a gallop that would have delighted anyone to have witnessed.

The rapid motion increased still more their exhilaration of spirits.

The night set in particularly dark, but the highwaymen were the very last who would grumble at that circumstance.

Lord Harcliffe made an excellent guide, not once appearing to be at fault.

The roads were almost deserted, and in the first hour the only vehicles they passed were waggons on their way back to the homesteads.

They only halted once during the whole of the hour's ride, and that was to give their panting steeds a little breathing time.

It took but a few moments, and then away the horses started with as much vigour as at first.

The distance of twenty miles was performed in very little over the time mentioned.

"Here we are, then," Lord Harcliffe said, as he brought Phantom down to a trot. "We will cool them down a little."

"A wisp of straw, a mouthful of water, and a good rub down would be just the thing for them now."

"Is it possible for us to obtain it?"

"I think so. We shall be certain to reach an inn before very long, and we could venture to make a halt in front of it without running much risk."

"Certainly there would be no need for us to go indoors, and on such a dark night as this one would think we should have little to fear in the shape of a recognition."

"Rely on it, we need not alarm ourselves on that score. It is almost impossible there should be any of our enemies hereabouts."

"Then, as you are willing, we will ride gently on, and cool our horses by so doing, while we keep sharply on the look-out for what we want."

Hardly a minute after he had spoken the distant twinkling of a little light became visible.

"Is that an inn, think you?" asked Lord Harcliffe.

"We shall soon see, for, according to all appearances, the light comes from some building on the road-side."

They trotted on in silence after this, and in the space of a few minutes found themselves in front of a small public-house, which, as far as they could judge in the darkness, did not hold out any particular good promise of comfortable entertainment for man and beast.

The clatter of horses' hoofs was heard, and a man came bustling forward.

"Stop all night, gentlemen?"

"No—no. Be quick—we are in a hurry!"

"What do you want, gentlemen?"

"A wisp of straw, a little water, and a good rub down for the horses."

"Right."

The two highwaymen alighted.

"Shall I take the horses into the stable?"

"No; rub them down where they are."

"Would you step inside the while, then? You will find the landlord there, and a good fire, which looks pleasant enough at this time of the year."

After a brief consultation the two friends resolved to enter the inn and try a little brandy.

They were the more induced to do this because, judging by all visible indications, the house did not boast of any guests.

Such was found to be the case.

They were accommodated with a seat in a warm, comfortable room, in which sat the landlady and no one else.

She seemed to have no suspicion as to their character, and the two highwaymen did not stop long enough to allow her to note their appearance minutely.

By the time they reached the outside the horses were ready, and really looking very little the worse for the journey they had accomplished so far.

This renewed the highwaymen's good spirits, and after a liberal tip to the ostler they were off.

It was not likely, however, that the remaining distance would be accomplished in anything like a similar time—that is, not without knocking their horses up a great deal more than they had any intention of doing.

"I do believe we shall manage it," said Captain Hawk, "though a couple of hours ago I should almost have thought it impossible."

"So shall I; and now as we are going at this steady rate, we may as well satisfy ourselves that all our arrangements are made."

"It will be decidedly best to do so."

"To begin with, then, you must see plainly enough that, if we can manage to get the treasure before daylight, we might almost reckon upon reaching our destination in three days."

"Certainly we should."

"And what is most owing to this post haste, we shall be down at the sea-shore almost as soon as the robbery is discovered, or any notion is formed as to our whereabouts."

"There is one thing that we may safely reckon upon, my friend."

"What's that?"

"Why, as soon as the loss of the treasure is discovered—that is, assuming we shall succeed in abstracting it—such an outcry and uproar will be raised as this country has never yet witnessed."

"I know that full well; and therefore, I say, as soon as ever the treasure is ours, the sooner we are out of the country with it the better."

"Then we are agreed as to that; and I am more than ever inclined to think that we shall be in time."

After this they rode on somewhat more swiftly.

But, as the fact turned out, they were just a little bit too easy about the matter, and rather too sure that they should reach Kew in ample time.

A little miscalculation upset all.

How it was it was impossible to tell, but somehow or other Lord Harcliffe missed his way.

It was an easy enough thing to do, one would have thought, considering the darkness of the night.

The error was soon discovered; but yet the total amount of time lost to them in consequence could not have been much under two hours.

That of course materially altered the complexion of affairs; yet so intent were they upon carrying out their original intention, or rather so impressed were they by the benefits that would accrue by doing so, that they resolved to make a vigorous push at the last, rather than be vanquished.

The two hours lost, however, was just the time they would have wanted for their enterprise.

From what the man had told them they were quite convinced that if the adventure was successful it would occupy but a short space of time.

"Forward, then!" said Captain Hawk. "Our misfortune cannot be helped, nor the time that has been lost be regained. Yet we may be able to repair the mischief. Forward—forward! I am certain our horses are equal to the effort."

CHAPTER CXLIX.

THE TWO HIGHWAYMEN HAVE SOME PECULIAR ADVENTURES NEAR THE PALACE.

Despite all their exertions, the two highwaymen were considerably vexed at discovering that they did not reach the vicinity of Kew Palace until the night was so far advanced as to render the carrying out of their enterprise unimpracticable.

"We must put up with it," said Lord Harcliffe, "though I own to being more disappointed than I could express."

"And so am I."

"Still, I think we have no resource save submitting to circumstances."

"Perhaps it will be for the best," responded the captain.

"It is not easy to see it."

"I don't know that. Some time must necessarily elapse before day dawns."

"Oh yes."

"How much?"

"Two hours or more."

"That will do."

"Do for what?"

"Why, let us push on. The time you mention will be just about sufficient to enable us to reconnoitre."

"Good. That is well thought of."

"It is rather surprising we did not make the arrangement from the first."

"Yes; but the fact is, we have allowed our ardour to outrun our discretion."

"That is it. Fortunately, we are not too late to repair our error."

"We have good time, and by making a careful inspection of the place and its surroundings, we shall be able to get through with our enterprise in half the time."

"It is unquestionably our best proceeding. Come."

The two highwaymen again urged their horses to a trot—not a fast one, because they were most desirous not to attract attention to their movements.

Lord Harcliffe was, as he said, perfectly familiar with all the approaches to the Old Palace at Kew.

Years had elapsed since he had paid his last visit to the place, but he felt sure he could rely upon his memory.

For some time they rode on without exchanging a single syllable.

Presently Lord Harcliffe drew up.

The night was a dark one, but yet they had been riding for so long that they could dimly distinguish large objects even when at a considerable distance off.

"Why do you pause?" asked Captain Hawk. "What is amiss?"

"Nothing; only from this point we ought to be able to catch a glimpse of the Old Palace."

"Is it not too dark?"

"No, I think not. Look over yonder. Can you not see among the trees a dark mass of something which is just a trifle darker than the night sky above?"

Captain Hawk looked long and anxiously; but some seconds elapsed before he was quite sure that he could see what his companion described.

"I can see something in the shape of a pile of building."

"That, then, is it; and now we will make our way to the Old Garden."

"I think you said you knew its situation."

"I do. I have seen it more than once, and yet I am not certain that I should be able to make my way to the boundary wall of it without any hesitation."

"Proceed, then, and, above all, be cautious."

"Trust me. I feel too deep an interest in this matter to run any risk of endangering the success of it."

Captain Hawk fancied he knew what meaning lurked under his companion's remark.

But he passed it over, affecting to take no notice of it.

Their pace now was reduced to a walk, being the most silent mode of progression; and besides, it was hard to say now how soon they might encounter some person or persons belonging to the royal dwelling.

But they passed on without meeting with any interruption whatever.

No doubt the hour was one at which very few persons in that locality were stirring.

The roofs and chimneys of the picturesque old building became every moment more and more distinguishable.

Faint lights, too, could be seen glimmering from some of the windows, though the light was much subdued, as though it made its way through the crevices of shutters or thick curtains.

Lord Harcliffe took such a course that they passed round two sides of the edifice, though of course he was careful to keep at a safe distance.

During the whole of the time, however, all was profoundly still.

"The silence is encouraging, is it not, and looks like success?" remarked Lord Harcliffe.

"It does; but I suppose on a nearer approach we shall discover sentinels guarding the walls."

"I expect so. Will you believe it?—until you spoke the sentinels slipped my memory altogether. Of course there will be soldiers patrolling."

"I thought so."

"It will be awkward. At present I don't see how we are to scale a wall unseen by them."

"We must go closer and try our best to ascertain whereabouts is the garden wall that was described to us."

"We are now as nearly as can be opposite to it. Shall we advance?"

"I think so; but we must use all imaginable caution."

"Of course we must."

"Lead the way, then."

"On horseback?"

"I fancy it will be best, because, in the event of any accident, we shall be able to make a rapid retreat."

"Well thought of, though I think it will be a difficult matter for two horses to approach the wall very closely without being heard by the sentinel."

"We must try. For one thing, we may calculate that the duty of patrolling is performed in a very careless, mechanical manner: there is so little apprehension of danger that they could hardly help being negligent."

"There is a great deal in what you say, and it will apply more or less to all the officials in the palace."

"No doubt of it."

"That will be unquestionably of great aid to us. But now, above all things, let us be careful how we speak, for I know from experience how far voices will travel when the air is still like it is now."

From this point all their conversation was carried on in whispers.

No inconsiderable portion of their attention was requisite to render the approach of their horses as noiseless as possible.

The nature of the ground they were upon chanced to be very favourable for this, so that without much delay they were enabled to approach within about fifty yards of the garden wall.

To their eyes this was distinct enough, as well as the portion of the main building which could be seen over the top of it.

For at least two moments they remained gazing in perfect silence.

During that time there came not a single sound upon their ears, which almost served to convince them that this portion of the exterior of the palace was unguarded.

At length Captain Hawk ventured to whisper:

"Fortune does indeed favour us."

"It seems like it. Can it be possible that wall is not guarded by a sentinel?"

"It appears so."

"It does."

"One would have thought, had there been any truth in what the man alleged, that his Majesty would have been particularly careful to have the approach to his treasure-chamber well protected."

"I don't know about that. He may rather have chosen to keep guards away. Certainly if it has been the custom for no sentinel to guard here the King would hardly venture to appoint one, because curiosity would be aroused by it. His motive would be sought for, and that might perchance give a clue to the discovery of the whole matter."

"That is very likely indeed, and there is yet another reason why he should leave this place unsentinelled."

"And what is that?"

"In order that he might be able to get his treasure away easily and unseen."

"Just so; but—— Hush—hark! What's that?"

Both were silent instantly.

A slight sound was then just audible to both.

It was a sound that grew plainer each moment.

They recognised it as being caused by the steady tramp, tramp of a sentinel on guard.

The man was coming steadily towards them.

As soon as they fairly realised this fact, the two highwaymen glanced at each other as though they would have said:

"There is an end to all our speculations, for here comes a sentry, after all."

Such was the case.

By straining their eyes, Captain Hawk and the Black Highwayman were just able to make out the dusky form of a man advancing.

It was not very easy to detect his figure, however, on account of the black background which the wall formed.

Indeed, had he not been in motion he must have been undistinguishable.

On he came with a steady, regular pace, which told how well drilled he was in the duty he was then performing.

The faint gleam of his accoutrements followed every movement.

He walked on right past the place where our two friends were standing.

It was quite evident the sentry was wholly unaware of their presence.

Most eagerly was he watched by the two highwaymen, who up to this moment could not make out how it was they had not seen him before.

There seemed but one plausible reason to be found for it, which was, that the man had been lingering or sleeping at his post.

The point they had now to ascertain, however, was the extent of his beat.

Upon this point they were quickly set at rest.

On gaining the end of the garden wall he stopped, and after having looked about him for a few seconds, wheeled round and retraced his steps.

This time there was more vigilance observable in his manner, and the two highwaymen began to fear that they had better have drawn still further back under the shadow of the trees.

It was too late for that now, however, and all they could do was to abide by the result.

Standing profoundly still, and fervently trusting that their horses would make no movement to betray them, they watched the sentry's advance.

For the life of them they could not resist the impression that he was looking at them.

This became almost certain when they saw him come to a halt.

Whether he really was looking at them or not they could not ascertain.

The scrutiny was continued rather longer than was agreeable, but finally he faced about and continued his march.

The two watchers never once took their eyes off him.

Fainter and fainter grew his form, then his footsteps grew more and more indistinct, until finally they became inaudible.

When this was the case, Lord Harcliffe ventured to breathe and then to speak.

"What do you think of that, my friend?"

"At one moment I gave myself up for lost."

"So did I. How do you account for his long absence?"

"I can think of only two reasons."

"What are they?"

"Either that he has only to pass here a few times in an hour, or else that he has been sleeping in his box."

"The latter is likely enough."

"It is. Can you hear him now?"

"No, all is quite still."

"Then let us endeavour to have a peep over the wall."

"How shall you manage it?"

"I think it will be simple. Will you keep guard?"

"Certainly."

"Come, then; I know I can depend on Satan for the service I require of him. It is not the first time he has done the like."

Lord Harcliffe hardly seemed to understand what it was his friend meant to do, but without wasting time by more words he followed him to the wall.

Captain Hawk rode as close as he could to the brick wall, and then cautiously removing his feet from the stirrups, knelt in the saddle.

"Steady, now," he said, in low tones, to his horse —"steady, now, will you? Quiet, I say!"

Satan seemed perfectly to understand what was wanted of him, and stood as though carved in stone.

With considerable dexterity and agility Captain Hawk changed his position from a kneeling to a standing one.

It was, of course, no easy matter for him to preserve his equilibrium while standing in this manner in the saddle, but then he knew how thoroughly his steed was to be depended upon.

Besides, at the very next moment he was able to grasp some of the ivy with which the Old Garden wall was partially covered.

This steadied him wonderfully.

As he had fully anticipated, he now found that he was, by reaching up with his arms, just able to peep over the top of the wall.

To anyone whose eyes were less accustomed to the gloom than his own, there would have been but little advantage gained by this proceeding.

Captain Hawk, however, could see tolerably well.

Lord Harcliffe came closer.

"Can you see, my friend?" he asked, in cautious tones.

"A little."

"Of course, the Old Garden is deserted?"

"Yes; and, what is more, it looks neglected, too. But are you sure you are keeping good guard?"

"Yes. Continue your reconnoitring. Rest assured that at present all is well, and that I will give you timely intimation of danger."

"Enough."

"Can you see the windows that the man mentioned?"

"Yes."

"And the buttresses?"

"I think so. Yet, knowing they are there, my fancy may deceive me."

"Look again, and tell me whether you think there will be much trouble in scaling the wall?"

"No; on the other side the ivy is most luxuriant. It will doubtless be almost as easy to get down by it as by a ladder."

"Good. Now descend, and as speedily as you like, for I can hear the sentinel returning."

"The deuce you can!"

"There is no sort of doubt about it."

Captain Hawk waited to hear no more, but descended with such precipitation that he narrowly escaped an awkward fall.

In less than a moment afterwards, however, he was in the saddle.

"Gently—gently!" his companion whispered. "We must retreat with all possible silence and caution, though there is no time at all to be lost."

Acting upon this, the two highwaymen retreated.

As soon as they had gone a sufficient distance to be out of sight, Lord Harcliffe proposed a halt.

"If we continue on our way," he said, "the sentry is almost certain to hear us, while here we are safe."

Captain Hawk assented without a word.

As soon as the horses were still he listened intently to the steady beat of the sentry's footsteps as he came towards them.

This time he walked right on to the point where they had previously seen him pause, and when there he began to retrace his steps.

By his manner it seemed absolutely certain that he was not apprehensive of anything in the shape of an alarm.

At a steady rate he passed the spot opposite to which our friends stood.

The watchers were now able to conclude that it was the duty of this one sentinel to guard the garden wall; but, having a long beat, several minutes elapsed before he reached it.

From what had happened, they were sure that if they watched their opportunity they would be able to scale the wall and get into the garden without his knowledge.

This, to start with, promised well for the further success of their plan.

"We may venture to speak now," said Lord Harcliffe, when his ear satisfied him that the soldier was at a safe distance.

"We are in luck's way, that is certain," said the captain. "It will not be half so difficult as I expected to gain admission to the garden."

"What made you sigh then?"

"Did I sigh?"

"In truth you did. And it seemed so strange just at this moment, and so ill accordant with your words."

Captain Hawk was silent for some moments before he made a reply.

"Then," he said, "what I have just done has so forcibly reminded me of the past."

"To what do you allude?"

"Why, to standing on Satan's back."

"You have done so before, then?"

"Oh yes."

"I thought so from your manner. And when was this former occasion, and where?"

"At York."

"York?"

"Yes. It was just before the execution of Dick Turpin."

"You knew him?"

"I feel proud to say he reckoned me a comrade and true friend; and yet I cannot help feeling that I was a good deal to blame, and even assisted his fate instead of hindered it."

These reminiscences affected the captain deeply, as they always did, and that was why he constantly endeavoured to banish the remembrance from his thoughts.

But the time would come, however, now and then when the recollection of all that had happened would be forced upon him.

The present was one of these occasions, and, as we have seen, his emotion was so great as to attract his companion's notice.

"You must at some time give me the particulars of all these events," said the Black Highwayman. "I feel the greatest amount of curiosity concerning them."

"I have promised to do so, and some day or other I will fulfil my word. But not now—not now: I could not bear it now!"

"It touches you deeply."

"It does, because I cannot look back to that part of my career without feeling the keenest remorse. Oh, it was a terrible sight that I beheld!"

"Do you mean the—the execution?"

"No—no! Something that was to me even more horrible! You must understand that every arrangement was made for an escape. By a clever stratagem, which I will not stay to describe now, a long cord was conveyed secretly into his cell, which, for security's sake, had been situated at the top of the keep—the distance from the ground was terrific."

"Well?"

"It was far from well. Night came—the night on which the escape was to be attempted. I was outside the prison wall, and, in order to reconnoitre, I stood upon Satan's back, as you saw me do a short time ago."

"And that brought all back to you?"

"It did. It seems now as though not more than a moment had elapsed since then. The night was a glorious one—the moon shining with such power as almost to rival daylight. I saw the figure of my comrade at the grating—I saw the rope lowered—then I saw him force his way through the aperture. Down he came—slowly and gently, and to all appearances unmoved by the awful depth beneath him. How eagerly I watched no words of mine could describe. More than half the descent was accomplished safely; then from some cause—I know not what exactly—the cord gave way at the top, and down he came: the crash with which I heard him reach the flagstones in the courtyard rings in my ears even now!"

Captain Hawk shook with the violence of his emotion.

The Black Highwayman himself was much moved by the recital, and it was not until they had ridden forward several paces that he was able to command himself sufficiently to speak.

"And the fall did not kill him, then?"

"No. Wonderfully enough, he survived the awful injuries he received. The rest you know, or if you do not, I can go no further."

Captain Hawk's utterance was now quite choked, and his companion could hear sobs, or rather groans, of anguish issuing from his breast.

For some time they rode on without speaking.

Their pace was a gentle one.

As for Captain Hawk, he seemed to be quite unconscious of what he was about.

It was not possible, however, under such circumstances as those in which he was placed, for a reverie of this kind to last very long.

With a sudden start he awoke to the remembrance of where he was and what was going forward.

He looked around, and the first thing which attracted his notice was the faint light of early dawn.

"Morning will soon be upon us, my friend," he said, in low, sad accents.

"It will; and therefore it is quite time we made up our minds as to how we shall dispose of the time between now and midnight."

"We must keep somewhere carefully out of sight. But where? Can you not suggest a place?"

"What say you to seeking out some roadside inn?"

"No. I think it will be most prudent for us to avoid being seen by anyone at all in this vicinity—that is to say, if it lays in our power to prevent it."

"You are right, Hawk. I confess I was thinking more about comfort for ourselves than positive safety."

"We must take up with far less comfortable quarters than a village inn could give."

"Have you any place in your mind?"

"Not at present. And yet stop. Now I think of it, are there not some extensive gravel pits not far away?"

"Yes—or rather what used to be, but they have been worked out many a year ago. They were dug for the purpose of forming the paths and roads about the palace."

"Yes, those are the places I mean. Are you well enough acquainted with the geography of the spot to lead the way to one of them in the dark?"

"Yes, for I should think we cannot be more than a couple of hundred yards distant from one of them."

"Fortunate again! Really, I shall begin to think that luck is determined to befriend us on this occasion!"

"Were you thinking, then, of finding a shelter in the gravel pits?"

"I was. You may not like the notion very well, but I think you will become reconciled to it when you think how likely we are to be neither molested nor observed if we take up our quarters there during the day."

"Yes, we shall be safe enough, no doubt, and I fancy that is the only recommendation the place can possibly possess."

"Well, we shall see: I have been contented with worse places many a time."

"How still it is all around this spot!"

"It is, and especially would be at this hour."

"It is my opinion it is but rarely visited by anyone at any time. There is nothing to bring people this way."

"So much the better for us; and now whereabouts is this first gravel pit you spoke of?"

"Advance cautiously now, for we must be somewhere close upon the brink, and I know full well there is no sort of protection to save us from falling in."

This was enough to make both look about them with the extremest care; and well it was they did so, for they discovered that a belt of gorse bushes a yard or so in width alone separated them from the margin of the excavation.

Having made this discovery, they paused.

Although no long time had elapsed since Captain Hawk had first perceived the gray glimmer on the eastern horizon, yet now a faint bluish light fell on all objects, and they were just able to make out their surroundings with certainty.

Every moment, however, increased the amount of light in a wonderfully rapid manner.

Captain Hawk looked around him with much interest, for that precise spot happened to be one which he had never before visited.

So absorbed did he become by it that he forgot all those unpleasant thoughts which had been crowding like an incubus on his mind.

"How rugged, and yet how beautiful!" he said. "Surely there can be no other hour when it wears such an aspect as it does now."

CHAPTER CL.

THE HIGHWAYMEN MAKE A HORRIBLE DISCOVERY IN THE OLD GRAVEL PITS AT KEW.

Wild and grand indeed was the scene that now spread itself out before the two highwaymen.

The ground in every direction was broken up by mounds of earth and deep excavations which were as irregular in shape and as unlike each other as chance could make them.

So many years had elapsed since labour of any sort had been employed there, that it began to assume more the appearance of Nature's handiwork than man's.

Brake and ferns, gorse bushes and thistles, and indeed every species of such vegetation as shows itself in neglected spots was visible in profusion.

In some places, indeed, so luxuriant was the undergrowth as to make it wear the aspect of some thicket in an ancient forest.

The sides as well as the bottom of the gravel pit were completely covered with verdure of some kind.

A place better adapted for purposes of concealment could scarcely have been imagined.

Every moment, too, the changing light imparted an additional picturesqueness of appearance to the scene.

But it was when the sun rose sufficiently high to cast the rosy light of his first beams over the expanse that it wore the grandest and most beautiful aspect.

It even evoked an expression of admiration from the apathetic and indifferent Lord Harcliffe.

But they soon remembered that, situated as they were, it was unwise to give themselves up to a contemplation of the beauties of nature.

"It is beautiful!" said Lord Harcliffe. "There cannot be two opinions about that. But since we are to take up our quarters here, just show me how we are to get down to the bottom."

"That is well thought of," was the reply, "for I confess I was myself so much entranced as to be almost forgetful of the purpose that brought us hither."

"It is well I reminded you, then."

"It is."

"How are we to get down?"

"We shall have a little trouble with our horses, no doubt; but we must look around us for the best means of descent."

"Do you think it possible?"

"Well, I do."

"But why? The sides seem everywhere almost as steep as walls."

"Yes, they do; but you must remember these excavations were made for the purpose of getting the gravel to the surface; and if there is a way for carts to get up, that must serve to allow our horses to go down."

"You are right. I wonder how it was I did not think of such an obvious thing as that myself?"

"It often happens that what would be thought the most obvious thing is really the hardest to see."

"I did not see that certainly."

"Come, then, we will make our way round, for the way down most certainly is not just about where we stand now."

"It will be necessary to keep a sharp look-out."

[THE HIGHWAYMEN ENCOUNTER SOME ROUGH WEATHER IN THE CHANNEL.]

"It will, because, owing to the length of time that has elapsed, the downward road will have become so overgrown with weeds as to become almost invisible."

"That is almost sure to be the case."

"Then all we have to do is to make the best use of our eyes; and having found the road, why, the more difficult it is to discover the better it will be for us, and the greater our security."

This could not be denied; and in order that they should not miss what they sought owing to their attention being distracted, no more words passed between them for several moments.

Believing their search could be better conducted on foot than in the saddle, they dismounted, and just passing the reins over one arm, they led their horses at their heels.

In this way they skirted a considerable portion of the excavations without, however, discovering what they searched for.

Everywhere the sides of the gravel-pit were characterised by precipitousness.

Luckily for them, there seemed little fear of their being seen by anyone, for, turn which way they would, the country seemed deserted.

At last Captain Hawk cried:

"Unless I make a very great mistake, there is the way down we seek."

"Where?"

It was not until the captain pointed that Lord Harcliffe was able to see something that was in the shape of a zigzag path.

"I think it very doubtful whether we shall get our horses safely down there."

"There will be little trouble, I fancy. Both creatures are docile enough, and will follow us readily. And left to themselves, they would pass over in safety a rougher place than that."

"Let us try, then," said Lord Harcliffe, "for even were we pursued I don't believe the officers would dream of looking for horsemen down there."

"So much the better for us, then, as I said before. Shall I lead the way?"

"Yes, certainly."

Captain Hawk began his advance very carefully, for, of course, he was unacquainted with the nature of the ground that might be beneath their feet.

But he soon gained confidence, and his horse, encouraged by his example, followed him without showing signs either of hesitation or alarm.

Seeing that the descent was really practicable, Lord Harcliffe followed.

It was no easy matter to lead a horse down such a place.

A slip, though ever so slight a one, would have had serious if not fatal results.

But alarming as it looked, the descent was performed safely, and the bottom of the excavation reached.

From this point surrounding objects looked even more picturesque than before.

There was a charm about everything on which the eye rested which nothing but Nature can give.

The ground at the bottom was firm for the most part, though the vegetation was so dense and so tangled that they had much trouble in forcing a way through it.

"We must look out for some spot which is screened as much as possible from the view of anyone who might chance to stand above and look down."

"But where are we to look for such a place?"

"Why, don't you see they have hollowed out the ground below into numerous caverns? In one of these, if we can find one large enough, we might be able to make our horses comfortable as well as ourselves, besides being out of sight of anyone above."

This was plausible enough, and therefore the next thing done was to see whether any such place could be found.

Their search was speedily rewarded.

Close at hand was a wide and deep indentation in one of the precipitous sides of the gravel pit.

The gravel had been removed to as great an extent as was compatible with safety.

Some blackened and seemingly rotten uprights still supported the roof.

"Upon my word this is a more comfortable spot than I could have hoped to look for in such a place," said Lord Harcliffe, as he glanced around. "We shall be well protected from the weather; and these heaps of dead leaves will make an excellent bed for our horses."

"And for ourselves, for that matter. But what do you say to breakfast first?"

"I am most agreeable. There is nothing like an early ride on horseback to create an appetite."

"I am sharp-set myself, and feel particularly pleased to think we had the foresight to preserve a meal."

While these few words were being exchanged, Captain Hawk produced the ham, tongue, and fowl, which, when laid out on the white dinner napkin in which they had been brought, looked particularly tempting in their eyes.

A long beam of wood, which had apparently at some former time been one of the supports for the roof, served them both for a seat and a table, and when Lord Harcliffe produced an unopened bottle of wine they declared that nothing was wanting to make their repast as agreeable a one as could be desired.

Hungry as they were, it would have given them neither trouble nor inconvenience to have devoured every morsel.

But bearing in mind that another such meal would be no doubt very acceptable towards nightfall, they restrained themselves, and put what was left away.

This done, they went to the opening of the cave, for such it might be called, and had another look about them.

The intense stillness which yet prevailed was wonderfully suggestive of safety; and indeed as they continued to gaze at the rugged yet beautiful scene before them, they experienced an amount of security to which they had been strangers for a very long time.

The day had now fairly begun.

The sun was shining with unclouded splendour, and his warm rays gilded every leaf and spray with magic beauty.

By no very great stretch of the imagination, it would have been easy enough for the two highwaymen to fancy themselves on some uninhabited island.

In a moment or two the silence was broken by a strange whirring sound.

Anywhere else it would have been disregarded; but the two highwaymen turned their eyes instantly in the direction from which the sound seemed to come

But they saw nothing.

"What was that?" Lord Harcliffe asked, in tones of surprise.

"It sounded like the flight of some large bird, but there's not a moving creature to be seen."

The sound at this moment was repeated, and though they were still unable to see what had caused it, both now had no doubt that Captain Hawk had assigned to it its true cause.

The irregular shape of the gravel pit prevented them from seeing anything like the whole of it, and the noise seemed to come from a part that was screened from their view by a piece of earth which jutted out to a considerable distance.

"We must see what it really is," said Lord Harcliffe, after a short pause. "Placed as we are, I consider it is imperative we should not allow anything to pass by us without the attempt, at any rate, to ascertain what it really is."

"I quite agree with you; and as the place is so lonely and still, there cannot be much extra danger incurred by emerging from our present place of concealment."

"None worth speaking of."

"Not that I think we shall have any trouble in coming to a conclusion about the character of the noise we have heard on this occasion."

"Still, there will be the satisfaction of feeling that there is no room for doubt."

"Just so."

With these words the highwaymen, after a careful glance around, stole gently out of the cave.

In order to diminish the risk of being observed as much as possible, they kept close against the side of the jutting piece of earth that we have mentioned.

On reaching the point they looked round cautiously.

The excavation extended for a considerable distance.

No one was visible, but no sooner had they arrested their footsteps than the strange sound was heard again.

They were now convinced what was the cause.

Some dozen or more large black birds rose in the air.

They flapped their wings heavily, as though they were almost too heavy to fly.

And as they rose they made a melancholy croaking noise.

"What birds are they?" said Lord Harcliffe—"and what can bring them to this place? Are they ravens?"

"I think not," answered the captain, with a strangely altered voice and manner.

"What then?"

"Carrion crows."

His companion started.

Then bent his gaze upon the birds, whose purplish-black feathers reflected the sun's rays almost like polished silver.

The birds, though disturbed, did not seem in any way frightened.

They wheeled round and round in airy circles, hovering over the spot from which they had risen, and seemingly in doubt whether to fly away or to alight again.

Lord Harcliffe now quite comprehended the change in his comrade's manner.

"Shall we go further?" he said.

"It will be a horrible sight."

"No doubt of that, but yet perhaps not so horrible as it may now seem to be in our imaginations."

So soon as the two friends knew that the birds were carrion crows they were quite convinced that they had disturbed them from one of their loathsome feasts.

Strangely enough, both the highwaymen seemed convinced at once that the remains upon which the odious birds were feasting were those of some unfortunate human being.

Should this surmise be correct, it would indeed be an awful sight for human eyes to look upon.

On the other hand, it was just possible that the remains might be those of some large animal.

It was the bare chance that this latter supposition might be correct that urged them to set at rest all possible doubts upon the subject.

"Come," said Captain Hawk, "let us not linger any longer, but ascertain what it is that lures those birds to the spot. Certain knowledge will be far better than doubt."

"You are quite right. Viewing the worst would not be so bad as remaining in a state of suspense, for, strive as we would, we should not be able to banish the subject from our minds."

Thus agreed, the two highwaymen made their way towards the spot from which the birds had risen.

It was easy enough to fix upon the exact locality, for the birds still kept wheeling round and round above it.

They noticed the approach of the two men, and uttered incessant harsh, discordant cries, while they flapped their wings with greater swiftness than hitherto.

At one time their actions and outcries seemed actually menacing.

"Be on your guard," said Captain Hawk. "The ferocious creatures seem as though they would attack us rather than suffer themselves to be driven from their prey."

Lord Harcliffe drew his sword, and waved it round about him.

The birds, thus threatened, flew back further, but their cries, which now seemed to express rage and disappointment, increased.

Unheeding this, the two highwaymen pushed aside the densely-growing brushwood, until their eyes fell upon something which made them quail with horror.

A moment or so elapsed before either could recover sufficiently to look on it again.

When they did turn their shuddering gaze upon the ground their faces were half averted.

And in good truth it would have required nerves of iron, or rather more callousness than exists in the most unfeeling being, to have looked on so awful a spectacle unmoved.

Half concealed by brake and fern lay the remains of what once had been a young girl.

Whether beautiful or not, who could say now?

The rapacious birds had so torn and disfigured the poor face that description would be impossible.

All there was to guide them towards identifying the deceased was the clothing that was left.

By the appearance of this, it would seem as though the body had lain there for some time—perhaps several weeks.

Every article of raiment was saturated with wet, and looked as though at the slightest touch it would crumble to fragments.

The highwaymen were too much affected by what they beheld to be able to speak.

At last, however, Captain Hawk, making a violent effort to shake off the depression which weighed upon his spirits, said:

"Surely, my friend, there has been foul play here—as dastardly a crime committed as ever was brought to the light of day."

"I fear it is impossible to come to any other conclusion," was Lord Harcliffe's rejoinder.

"Depend upon it, what you see is no accident. And the perpetrator of this crime is now no doubt beyond the reach of justice."

"And identity, too, seems all but impossible, or will be very soon."

"I am not so sure of that. Look there!"

As he spoke, Captain Hawk pointed to something glittering.

Overcoming his repugnance in the best way he could, Lord Harcliffe turned his face fairly towards the awful sight, and bent forward a little in order to make out the nature of the object to which his companion had called his attention.

"It looks like a small gold locket set with stones."

"You may depend it is nothing else."

The position of the glittering ornament was almost sufficient to decide this point.

It would seem as though the locket had been worn round the girl's neck, but covered by her clothing, which now partly decayed, and partly torn by the birds of prey, allowed it to be seen.

Seeing this one trinket naturally made them look closer in the expectation of seeing others.

But either the girl had worn no other ornament, or else whatever else she had had about her had been taken away.

Judging by what they saw, the two highwaymen came irresistibly to the last conclusion.

"It is a case of robbery as well as murder," said Captain Hawk, "or else I am altogether at fault."

"It is hard to think otherwise. What the poor girl had about her has either been taken for its intrinsic value, or else in order to prevent identification."

"In either case the locket, worn out of sight, as it evidently was, would easily escape observation."

"Yes."

After this both remained gazing silently.

It was Lord Harcliffe who said:

"I have been thinking that we ought not to allow that locket to remain where it is."

"Such were my thoughts," said his companion; "only I did not like to give utterance to them: I shrink more than words can express from approaching any closer to the body; and to touch it——"

The shudder he gave was far more expressive than words.

"My feelings are the same, but yet for such a purpose the requisite effort ought not to be wanting. I——"

He did not speak; but stooping forward, he put an end to the discussion by suddenly picking up the locket.

It had been secured round the young girl's neck by a ribbon, or something of that kind.

The resistance it afforded was very slight, yet it affected Lord Harcliffe so deeply that the locket almost slipped from his fingers.

The next moment he was standing with his back to the loathsome sight.

"Come away," he said—"come away—I can bear it no longer. The very air hereabouts seems to choke me."

Captain Hawk was willing enough to retire.

Yet, as he had not sustained such a shock as his companion had, he gave a last glance before he departed.

If it was hasty it was comprehensive, and he was almost prepared to swear, should need be, that no other article of an identifiable nature lay upon or near the mangled remains.

"It seems horrible," he said, as he followed his companion towards the hollow in which they had taken up their quarters—"horrible in the extreme to abandon the corpse of a fellow-creature to those ravenous birds!"

"Right. Yet it is an idea merely. The poor girl, whoever she chanced to be, feels nothing, knows nothing, of that senseless mass of clay."

"I grant that; but the thought is most repugnant to me. Look: the horrible creatures are preparing to swoop upon their hideous repast again!"

This was true enough.

The carrion crows, who had held aloof while our friends stood near, now returned, and, floating round in circles with their wings extended, they seemed equally prepared to alight or fly.

The sight so enraged the captain that, heedless of consequences, he drew a pistol and placed it on full cock.

Lord Harcliffe saw him only just in time to prevent him from drawing the trigger.

"Hold!" he cried. "Hawk, are you mad?"

"I am nearly so. See: another moment they will all be down!"

"Then let them be. Put up your pistol: to discharge a firearm as near to the palace as we are would have the effect of bringing some of the guards upon us immediately, and then farewell to our plans."

Reluctantly Captain Hawk returned his pistol to his pocket.

"No matter," he said, half angrily. "Something must be done to stop them at their disgusting work."

This behaviour on his comrade's part enabled the

Black Highwayman to overcome the shock to his own feelings.

But he continued his way to the cave, that being, for obvious reasons, the best place for them to stand and converse in.

His first care was to wipe the locket perfectly clean.

When this was done he was hardly able to retain his composure while looking at it, so powerful were the recollections which it called up.

Very soon, however, all other sensations were absorbed by the act of looking at the locket itself.

Many rare and beautiful trinkets had at various times passed through the hands of the highwaymen, and they were tolerably well acquainted with the value of such baubles, and they both felt that never had they looked upon anything more beautiful.

Its value must have been immense.

The locket itself was composed of solid gold, though there was but little of the precious metal left visible.

It was literally encrusted with gems of large size and unrivalled brilliancy.

On one side was a diamond of a size much larger than any which they had ever before seen.

This alone must have been of immense value.

Some time was occupied in looking merely at the outside of the locket.

When their curiosity was satisfied in this respect, they opened it, though less experienced hands would have been thrice the time in discovering the secret of the fastening.

When open, the portrait of a gentleman, whose age could not have been more than five-and-thirty, was disclosed.

The execution of the miniature was in accordance with the richness of the locket in every other respect.

There was a look about the face which told them that the owner of the portrait was unquestionably of foreign extraction.

He was represented, too, by a long, flowing black beard and moustachios, then very rarely, if at all, seen upon the face of an Englishman.

The eyes were of such a nature as to impart to the portrait an expression of sad tenderness that was truly fascinating to look upon.

CHAPTER CLI.

RELATES WHAT SUCCESS THE TWO HIGHWAYMEN MET WITH ON THEIR VISIT TO THE TREASURE-CHAMBER.

"SURELY this will form a clue to the perpetrator of this hideous crime."

"A strong clue, I should say. The thing which puzzles me is how it came to be left upon the body."

"It is singular."

"Very so, because if robbery had been the motive of the deed, care would have been taken not to leave anything so valuable."

"No matter what the motive might be, the circumstance is just as singular. The only way of accounting for it is that the locket was concealed in some way by the clothing, and only the destructiveness of the birds of prey could have brought it into view."

"It has fallen into strange hands," said Captain Hawk, with a light laugh; "yet, were the value ten times as great, nothing would induce me to part with it."

"Nor me either. And I will keep it in my mind, and try my best to pierce the secret."

"It is in vain to speculate further on the point," said Captain Hawk; "we might go on surmising for a week and yet come no nearer the mark than we are now."

"Very true."

"Place the locket, then, in some safe place, and let us turn our attention to the consideration of our enterprise."

It was not without reluctance that Lord Harcliffe obeyed the injunction of his companion.

There was indeed much for them to arrange with regard to the business they had on hand for the coming night.

It will not be necessary, however, for us to enter verbally into all their deliberations.

It will indeed be sufficient for us to follow them when the time comes for setting out, and relate just those events which took place.

So long a time had now gone by without even the symptoms of any disturbance or interruption occurring that they began to consider themselves as being in perfect safety, and quite out of the reach of their vindictive pursuers.

They took every pains to have their firearms in such a condition that they could be fully depended upon for instant use, though, of course, they did not imagine that any necessity would arise for making use of them on the occasion of their visit to the Old Palace.

Yet it was well to be prepared for all emergencies.

At last all was done that lay in their power, and when this was the case the time till nightfall seemed insufferably long.

In their impatience, which grew greater and greater every moment, it seemed as though darkness would never come.

But when their patience was upon the very verge of exhaustion, the welcome shades of evening began to creep over the precipitous sides of the gravel pit.

Rapidly these shades deepened, until a general gloominess pervaded all things.

Then the two highwaymen emerged from the cavity in the rock which had afforded them such secure safety.

They had taken pains to note particularly the different turns and winds in the ascent, and so, notwithstanding the obscurity, they made their way to the surface of the ground in safety.

In fact, the act of ascending seemed not to be beset with half the perils of the descent, and both were surprised at the facility with which they accomplished the feat.

"Caution now must be our watchword," said Captain Hawk, as he vaulted with something like his usual agility into the saddle.

"You are right, my friend, and we must not allow any circumstances, no matter of what character, to make us forget it."

Lord Harcliffe, having adjusted the saddle girth, now mounted likewise.

At a steady walk they then directed their course towards that portion of the wall over which Captain Hawk had peeped.

It would be hardly possible to exaggerate the magnitude of the danger which in every way beset the enterprise which they had now on hand.

From first to last it was surrounded with difficulties and perils, from which anyone save those two daring spirits would have shrunk back appalled.

But they advanced with a steadiness and coolness which showed that not the slightest amount of dread found a resting-place in their hearts.

As they drew nearer to the palace wall, however, their progress became proportionably cautious.

As on the former occasion, the weather was all that they could desire.

The sky was completely overcast with thick black clouds, which threatened every moment to discharge their watery contents upon the earth.

The wind howled and rustled among the trees, and swept fiercely over the ground in a manner that would effectually deaden all slight noises.

"Shall we take this as an omen of our success, Harcliffe?" said the captain. "Does not the weather favour us to the utmost?"

"It does. It is disagreeable enough, in all conscience, but just such a night as we want for carrying out such an enterprise as we have in hand."

"Just so. And somehow a feeling seems to come most forcibly over my mind to the effect that we shall find the accomplishment of it much easier than anyone could reasonably anticipate."

"That we shall soon see now."

"We shall indeed. Wait a moment. I fancy we are already as near to the palace as it will be safe for us to go with our horses."

Both reined-in their steeds.

Then, as well as they were able, they took a long and steady look about them.

It was not much that they were able to discern, but they came to the conclusion that it would not be wise to approach any nearer while mounted.

Their next care, then, was to look out for some place which held out a reasonable prospect of keeping their horses in safety during the remaining part of their expedition.

It was necessary that this place should be one which would enable them to get at their horses with readiness, should circumstances arise to make a hasty retreat imperative.

It was not long before they were able to suit themselves in this matter.

Close at hand was a small plantation of trees, into which they rode as far as the dense-growing vegetation would allow them.

Then, dismounting, they unbuckled the rein from one side of the bit, and secured it to a stout, low-lying branch of a tree.

The length was then sufficient to allow the animals to graze for a short distance round the tree.

This they began to do without any delay or hesitation, though the grass was coarse and rank.

"They seem inclined to make themselves tolerably comfortable during our absence," the captain said.

"So much the better," replied his friend: "it gives all the more hope that we shall find them here when we return."

"I do not for a moment think they will attempt to stray away."

"Come, then. Time is passing, and remember we cannot tell how long it may take us to accomplish what we have to do."

"You are quite right. Lead on—I am ready."

After a parting glance at their steeds, which assured them they were all right, the two highwaymen made their way out of the plantation with rapid strides.

On gaining the open ground they found that the weather had by no means improved.

The clouds could be seen flying swiftly across the sky, while all the time the wind howled in a most dismal and melancholy manner.

At frequent intervals, too, a mass of watery particles would be borne upon the wind and dashed violently into the faces of the two men.

Certainly if any night was calculated to keep people indoors this was.

Nothing but the sternest necessity would tempt them to go abroad.

"I can put up with the discomfort cheerfully," said Captain Hawk, in reply to an impatient exclamation made by his companion, "because I know how much it will facilitate our operations. Depend upon it, the sentinels will be more inclined to avail themselves of the shelter of their sentry-boxes than to be particular in making every round at the time specified."

"There is certainly a great deal in that, but still it is so confoundedly unpleasant to have such a keen wind cutting through one that a little grumbling seems irrepressible."

"It is," exclaimed his friend. "Nothing but the important affair we have now under hand would enable me to put up with it at all."

A more violent gust of wind than any which they had experienced served to put a stop to their further conversation.

Pressing their hats closely over their brows, they struggled on.

So great was the noise produced by the swaying branches of the trees clashing together that it seemed next to an impossibility that any sound they might make could be heard at a distance greater that a few feet.

It was not long before they were able to discern before them the dark mass of the old garden wall.

As soon as they made this discovery they halted.

The wind about this part seemed to blow with much greater fury than elsewhere.

In vain they looked up and down for the sentinel

Not the faintest sign of him could be either seen or heard.

"Rely upon it," said the captain, placing his mouth close to his friend's ear, "we should find him snugly ensconced in his sentry-box if we only knew where it was situated."

"And if we did it would hardly be worth the trouble to ascertain."

"That is my opinion."

"Let us wait here, then, for a few moments longer. If at the end of that time we are unable to hear any more than we can now, we will boldly make the attempt to scale the wall."

"Agreed."

The intervening moments were anxious ones, and therefore passed very slowly.

But all remained profoundly still.

"Come," said Captain Hawk, "I consider it would be a mere waste of time to wait any longer."

"True. If we had gone boldly to the wall at once, we should have had abundance of time to gain the interior already."

"We should—we should."

"Tread softly, and do not speak too much. It is impossible to say what might contribute to betraying us."

"We cannot be too careful."

Up to this moment the two highwaymen had been standing under the cover of a clump of trees.

The shadow which these trees cast, coupled with the deep obscurity of the night, made it next door to an impossibility that they could be seen by anyone.

When they emerged from these, however, and made their way across the open ground towards the wall, there was hardly less fear of observation.

Nevertheless, by instinct, as it were, they crouched down and hastened towards the wall in a stooping posture.

In reality there was of course no necessity for this.

The moment they reached the wall they felt that they were indeed for the time being safe, as the shadow which it cast was of so deep and dark a character that it was impossible to see anything.

"So far all is well," said the Black Highwayman. "I begin now to be of your opinion that Fortune intends to favour us wonderfully in this business."

"Hush—hush!"

"Can you hear anything?"

"By Heaven I can!"

"So can I."

"It is the sentry."

"It is, beyond a doubt."

"Close at hand too."

"Hush—hush! for our lives—not another syllable!"

The discovery so suddenly made was alarming enough.

The sound told them that the sentry could not be many yards off.

They would not have had any idea of his approach at the time they did but for the fact that the wind lulled suddenly and allowed the tramp of his feet to reach their ears.

The dilemma they thus found themselves in was a very serious one.

The discovery of the sentinel's proximity being made at the moment when they were felicitating themselves upon their good fortune was most embarrassing.

For the moment they could not tell what course to adopt.

But the least bit of reflection told them that to attempt flight would only be to compel their discovery—perhaps death—and certainly put an end to all their hopes of being able to gain admittance to the garden.

Captain Hawk was the first to recover his self-command.

Gripping his companion's arm tightly, he said:

"Press yourself against the wall, and stir neither hand nor foot—it is our only chance. Not another syllable!"

"If he discovers us," said Lord Harcliffe, in low tones, "we must run him through before he is able to give the alarm."

Repugnant as it was to both of them to take the life of a fellow-creature, yet the present occasion demanded that they should not shrink even from assassination in order to secure their own lives.

On came the sentinel.

Little knew he of the danger that was at hand.

Equally far was he from thinking that his life hung trembling in the balance, and that upon the occurrences of the next two or three moments depended his life or death.

On he came.

His manner was unconcerned enough.

By straining their sense of vision to the utmost, the

two highwaymen were just able to make out the dim outlines of his advancing form.

It was quite clear from the man's careless manner that nothing had occurred to excite his vigilance.

Beyond all doubt he was merely going his round in that dull, mechanical way to which he had been accustomed for years.

He came on at a steady tramp, tramp.

The two anxious highwaymen now no longer dared to breathe.

Would he discover them?

That was the important question.

They were not doomed to be kept for any long space of time in their state of indescribable suspense.

As the sentry came closer they wondered whether his gaze would be directed towards the wall or towards the open country.

If the former, the discovery of the two highwaymen seemed almost inevitable, as the sentinel's eyes would most probably be even more familiar with the darkness than their own.

The dark background of the wall, however, was of great assistance in concealing them from view.

The sentinel seemed to look neither to the right nor to the left, but straight on.

He passed them.

It was several seconds, however, before Captain Hawk and the Black Highwayman could realise that they were indeed safe—that the danger which had seemed so menacing had really passed away.

Yet such was the case.

The sentry continued his walk unembarrassed, unconcerned, and evidently having not the remotest suspicion that strangers were so near.

But the danger was hardly over yet.

They were only a short distance from the extremity of the sentinel's beat, and they were only able to recover their breaths by one long, deep inspiration when the soldier grounded his musket.

The clattering sound which this produced seemed unusually loud and alarming, for just then there was another sudden abatement of the wind's violence.

They then saw that the man, having rested the butt-end of the musket on the ground, was leaning on the muzzle of it in a thoughtful attitude.

His eyes seemed fixed on some object in the far distance, but whether they were so or not, or whether he was merely plunged in deep thought, was entirely out of their powers to say.

It was not for long, however, that he remained thus.

With a sudden start, as though awaking from some absorbing reverie, he shouldered his piece and retraced his steps.

But now it could be almost surmised with certainty that his thoughts were very far away indeed from his occupation.

He marched past, his eyes seemingly fixed on vacancy, and not once catching sight of our two friends.

Eagerly they watched his receding form until it was entirely swallowed up by the darkness.

It was not until his footsteps were inaudible that the highwaymen ventured to move.

"Thank Heaven that danger is over!" said the Black Highwayman, with a long-drawn sigh of relief. "At one moment I gave myself up for lost, unless we adopted that means of safety which my soul shrunk from."

"We are truly fortunate! But we must not lose a moment in congratulating ourselves: time is everything."

"What is the next step?"

"Follow me."

So saying, Captain Hawk ran rapidly along close to the wall in a direction opposite to that in which the sentinel was now going.

A few yards brought them to a bend in the high brick wall, and here they paused.

On his former reconnoitring expedition, Captain Hawk had observed that some old ivy grew very thickly and strongly up this part of the wall, and from its appearance he felt pretty certain that by its aid alone they would be able to gain the top of the wall.

When there, he proposed to make the descent—not by dropping down into the garden, which would have been easy enough, but by means of a rope that they had brought with them from the lonely hut.

This last not only made the descent easier and safer, but also provided them with a ready means of escape in case they should have to retreat hastily.

"Keep watch a moment," said Captain Hawk, "while I ascend. I am a lighter weight than you are, and the ivy is consequently more likely to bear me. Then, if it will not support you, I can secure the rope to the top of the wall, and you will be able to ascend by means of that."

"Good."

Captain Hawk reached up and took a firm grasp upon the ivy.

Then he drew himself up until he was able to find a resting-place for one foot among the numerous interlacing branches.

The ivy seemed to come away a little, but it did not yield much.

Shifting his grasp, he in the same manner drew himself up still further, until he was able to place his hands on the top of the wall itself.

When that was the case, it was comparatively easy, by means of the assistance which the ivy boughs afforded, to raise himself so high that he could sit astride it.

Then, while unwinding the rope from about his waist, he said, in tones only just loud enough to reach his friend's ears:

"Is all well?"

"Not the least sound."

"Join me, then, as quickly as you can.

"Do you think the ivy will support me?"

"Yes—yes! Be quick!"

It was not, however, without a certain amount of misgiving that Lord Harcliffe committed his weight to what seemed to him so very frail and insufficient a support.

To his surprise, however, he discovered that the old ivy spead over so large a space and clung so tightly to the brickwork as to sustain him easily.

Finding this was the case, he in less than a moment placed himself by the side of the captain, who still sat astride the wall.

The fact was, the securing of the rope to the top of the wall presented a problem of considerable difficulty.

At last, however, he hit upon the idea of tying one end of the rope very firmly to the interlacing branches of the ivy.

At first sight it seemed as though enough support could not by this means be obtained, but in reality it was found that the tenacious plant held them as well in one way as the other.

To test it, Lord Harcliffe first descended into the garden, Captain Hawk in the meanwhile still remaining upon the top, so that in case the rope gave way he should be able to refasten it.

It stood the strain, however, most admirably.

"All is well," he said; "and just in time: here comes the sentinel."

So saying, he slipped down with a suddenness that rather astonished his companion.

Both then were profoundly still.

The wind had almost ceased to blow, and in its stead came a light but regularly-falling rain.

Consequently, the sentinel's footsteps were almost as distinctly heard on one side of the wall as the other.

As in the former instance, the soldier on guard failed to discover that anything of an unusual character was going on.

It was not until they had again heard him retire towards the other end of his beat that the two friends ventured to stir from where they were, though doubtless they would have been able to cross the soft mould in the garden without making an audible sound.

The time thus occupied was not entirely wasted, for both busied themselves in endeavouring to find out just where the buttress was situated which the dying man had described.

But the obscurity was too great for this, and so they simply directed their steps towards the mass of building, which could, of course, be plainly seen.

In one of the upper windows a light was burning, and only one.

This did not threaten any probable discovery, for the

illumination was of the dimmest character, and seemingly only such as would proceed from a night-lamp burning in the chamber of an invalid.

The soil in the old garden was soft, and yielded easily beneath their feet.

But around the building itself was a broad strip of gravel, on which they came somewhat abruptly and unexpectedly.

The first intimation they had was the crunching noise beneath their feet, for in the darkness the lighter coloured gravel could not be discerned from the soil.

They stopped at once.

The three quaintly-fashioned buttresses could then be seen standing out from the mass of brickwork.

With cautious steps they glided to the one which had been described by the dying man.

During the day Lord Harcliffe had while in the cavern read over the memorandum he had made at the time.

Consequently there was a greater amount of precision and confidence about his movements than there could have been had he trusted to memory merely.

It was easy enough, guided by the sense of touch as well as vision, to count the required number of courses from the bottom of the buttress.

Then selecting the particular brick which had been indicated, they found it yield readily to the point of a knife.

Upon making this discovery their hearts beat high with hope.

Up to this point there had been just a faint suspicion of a doubt that there was little more in what they had been told than the incoherent ravings of a dying man.

But this singular confirmation of all that he had said convinced them that his secret was indeed real, and that they stood within a few feet of the secret-chamber which England's monarch had been at so much trouble to construct, and which, as we may say, he had endeavoured to cement with blood.

Surely what was now about to happen could only be looked upon as a righteous retribution for his wickedness in taking away the life of the faithful dependant who had laboured so sincerely and so heartily in his service.

Having removed the brick, the highwaymen paused to listen, but the perfect silence which continued encouraged them to proceed.

CHAPTER CLII.

CAPTAIN HAWK AND LORD HARCLIFFE FIND THEIR ENTERPRISE CROWNED WITH SUCCESS.

As Stephen had told them, as soon as the first brick was taken from its setting it was easy enough to remove a sufficient number more to make an opening large enough to allow their bodies to pass through.

It was at the moment when the last of these bricks had been dislodged and carefully laid aside, that a clock somewhere in or near the palace gave forth the hour of two in clanging, sonorous sounds.

"Time passes swiftly," the captain whispered. "We ought to be speedy in what we have to do."

"We shall have time, I think. Will you enter first?"

"If you are willing."

Lord Harcliffe stood aside, and Captain Hawk, who was in reality fired with impatience to probe the mystery to the very bottom, made no more ado, but sinking on his hands and knees, crawled quickly through the opening.

He disappeared almost immediately, for, agreeably to the instructions he had received, he found no impediment whatever in his way.

Lord Harcliffe, feeling tolerably satisfied that no one was near, and that there was little likelihood of the opening in the buttress being discovered, followed his companion.

The darkness inside that confined space was something terrific.

In less than a moment, however, he found himself close to his comrade.

"Hist!" he said. "Is all well, Hawk? Let me hear the sound of your voice in this detestably dark place."

"I am here. All is well."

"Are you at the end of the passage?"

"Yes."

"It will do to show the light then, now?"

"It will; but be careful of it. I cannot find the ring."

"We shall soon find whether there is one or not."

Lighting a lamp was not in those days the rapid and easy process that it is now.

Still Lord Harcliffe was not very long in lighting the small dark lantern he produced.

This lantern had been provided by Tom Beckford, and never could it have proved more useful.

When the slide was closed the amount of light which it sent forth was very limited.

But though the lens was small, yet it made up for the deficiency by the concentrated brightness which it shed upon every object to which it was directed.

Almost the first thing upon which the tiny beam fell was the very thing of which they were in search.

The iron ring was there just as had been described to them.

But it was higher up than they had anticipated, and this was how it was Captain Hawk had failed to find it with his hands.

"All right," he said; "there is the ring."

"Pull it, then. Try if your strength will suffice: I will hold the light."

Captain Hawk took a firm grasp of the iron ring with both hands, and pulled it steadily towards him.

At first little or no impression was made, but by continuing the pulling the stone gradually came towards him

"Stephen was right," said Lord Harcliffe. "I cannot help these doubts; but the whole thing seems too much like some wild dream to be the truth."

"Here is positive truth, though," said Captain Hawk. "Put the lantern down on the floor for a moment, and assist me in removing the stone."

Lord Harcliffe complied instantly.

In order that no alarm should be raised, it was necessary that the stone should be lifted carefully and placed on the floor.

This, by their united strengths, they were perfectly successful in doing.

A black space now lay beyond them.

The stone was of such a size that the hole from which it had been removed was just large enough to allow the passage of a man's body.

"As I have gone first hitherto," said the captain, "let me continue to do so. I will crawl through first, and then you can hand me the light through the opening."

"Agreed."

No sooner was the word pronounced than the action was performed.

Strange indeed were the feelings of the highwayman upon finding himself standing in such a place, and it was with the utmost impatience that he stretched out his hand for the lantern in order that he might take a first glance at the mysterious chamber

This he was soon enabled to do.

The result was very disappointing.

And yet if he had really given the subject a moment's attentive consideration he must have formed an idea of a place very similar to what he beheld.

In shape, the chamber was circular or nearly so.

Its walls were uniformly composed of masses of stone carefully and regularly laid, each piece exactly resembling the one which they had removed.

The top rose up into the shape of a flattened dome.

At the outside the place could not have exceeded six feet in diameter, though, of course, considering the use to which it was to be put, this was abundance of room.

By the time Captain Hawk had gone thus far in his observations, he found that his friend had had time to pass through the opening and stand beside him.

"Does the place accord with the idea you had formed of it, Harcliffe?"

"Open the slide of the lantern—we shall be able to see better then."

This was done.

The light was not of the brilliant character it had been hitherto, but its more diffused nature enabled a much better notion to be formed of the general appearance of the place.

"I can scarcely say it does; but where are we to find the treasure?"

This was a serious question.

After looking all about them they found but one object of a portable or even movable character.

This seemed to be nothing more than an old cask, such a one as might be used for the conveyance of spirits.

"There's nothing but that cask, and that I should say, judging by its appearance, is empty."

"If not empty, it seems too old and frail to contain any amount of valuables."

There was deep disappointment expressed in these words.

Considering the short time which had elapsed since the treasure-chamber had been made, there seemed a strong probability that at present no use had been made of it.

"My friend," said Lord Harcliffe, in tones of deep dejection, "we have made a great mistake. Somehow I have feared all along that something would occur to dash our glittering dream to fragments."

"What is the mistake?"

"We have been premature. We have assumed that the King would make immediate use of this place. If we had given the subject a moment's proper consideration we must have seen that it was most unlikely the King would be in so great a hurry to confide his valuables to this place."

Captain Hawk could not help feeling and admitting that there was a very great amount of truth in what his companion had said, and was quite unable to think how it was that such an obvious consideration had escaped them."

But he was not inclined to be so despondent as his friend.

"What you say is likely enough," he said. "But yet there is one hope."

"What?"

He pointed to the cask.

"That," he said, "is a very unlikely object to have been left here by carelessness or neglect. The question is, how comes such a thing to be in the place at all?"

"There is just a bare chance in that."

"Come, then, let us see. It will not take long to ascertain whether the cask is empty or not."

Captain Hawk was right enough there.

The object in question was within a few feet of them, and they at once made their way towards it.

The cask was not empty.

This was decided immediately.

When that was found to be the case, there was reasonable ground for the revival of hope.

"Here is the treasure, my friend, depend upon it. Just try the weight."

Lord Harcliffe did so, and found that, despite its small size, the cask was just as much as he could lift.

"It is there," cried the captain, in tones of mingled joy and triumph—"it is there. What more likely than that the King in his cunning should choose some such object as that in which to stow his valuables? He would think that such an object as that would pass unquestioned almost anywhere."

"I think you are right, Hawk, after all. I can think of hardly anything but gold that would be as heavy as this is."

"But how shall we ascertain the nature and value of the contents?"

"I am afraid we shall have to trust to our good fortune: it won't do to break it open here."

Up to this moment Captain Hawk had held the lamp, but now he placed it down on the stone floor of the treasure-chamber, and felt the cask with his hands.

"The contents are not liquid, that is quite certain," he said, after having rolled the cask about and shaken it as well as he was able.

After listening, Lord Harcliffe became of that opinion.

Yet to carry away the cask upon the mere chance that it contained gold, and when they were almost without anything in the shape of evidence upon the point, seemed running too great a risk.

To open it, however, would only have been to render the task of carrying away the contents difficult, if not impracticable.

"Run the risk," said Captain Hawk. "If we fail to take that, there is nothing else; and I cannot bear the idea of leaving empty handed. Think is it for a moment likely that a cask containing anything else but valuables should be left in such a place?"

"We shall be compelled to open it, at any rate."

"Why?"

"Because it is very odd to me if that hole in the wall yonder is large enough to allow the cask to pass through it."

"I don't believe it is," was the reply, as the highway men compared together the size of the cask and the opening in the wall from which the stone had been removed.

The advantages of removing the treasure in its present condition were so many and so obvious that they would not be persuaded of the impossibility of the thing until they had tried it.

"Come, Harcliffe," said the captain, "it will not take many moments—let us set our hearts at rest."

"I fear it is useless."

"Try."

They did try, and found the opening so nearly large enough that it seemed as though the keg might be forced through.

But after repeated trials they were obliged to abandon the attempt as being altogether impracticable.

"There's no help for it—open the cask."

Both much regretted the time which had been lost, but instead of bewailing it they set actively to work to break open the cask.

This, owing to the strength of the materials, was a formidable undertaking.

By the aid of such weapons and articles as they had about them, however, they eventually succeeded in removing a portion of the top.

After that the remainder was easy.

The first object upon which they came was composed of dark-blue cloth.

On drawing it forth this proved to be a roquelaure cloak.

The highwaymen, with a disappointed, angry gesture, flung it to the ground.

Underneath was a piece of silk, which, on being cast aside, disclosed to them a number of small packets.

"Stephen was right!" Captain Hawk ejaculated, in tones much too loud to be prudent, considering the place they were in. "This is the treasure!"

And as he spoke he with eager fingers took up one of the packets, and, tearing off the brown-paper covering, disclosed within a pile of glittering guineas.

Such a discovery was startling indeed.

Considering the weight of the cask, and reckoning it to be filled with guineas, the value must have been immense.

"Quick!" said Lord Harcliffe, recovering himself. "Stow as much of this about you as you can. Lose not a moment, for after having been so far successful, it would be hard indeed to be interrupted now."

The rapidity with which the rolls of guineas were transferred to the various pockets in the highwaymen's apparel was really wonderful.

Yet it was five minutes at least before they had reached half-way down the cask.

"What's this?" said the captain. "Here is something large. What is it?"

The object to which he referred was a square package, which, like all the others, was tied up in brown paper.

"No matter what it is," was his comrade's rejoinder —"I'll guarantee that it is valuable."

"But we have neither of us a pocket that could contain so bulky an object. And see—here is another of them."

In fact, the highwaymen's pockets were well-nigh filled to repletion.

Yet the idea of leaving any portion of the treasure behind was such a dreadful one that they could by no means reconcile themselves to it.

They were not forgetful, too, that time was flying fast, and that probably every moment they lingered increased the difficulty they would experience in getting clear away with their booty.

It was just at this moment that Captain Hawk bethought himself of the roquelaure cloak which had been cast so contemptuously to the ground.

"Here is the very thing we want," he said, taking it

[THE HIGHWAYMEN ARE ATTACKED BY A PRIVATEER.]

"It will be an easy enough matter to make a bundle with this which shall contain the greater part, if not the whole, of what the cask now holds."

"A good thought. Spread the cloak upon the floor, and we will speedily make a trial of it."

Captain Hawk complied, and then the Black Highwayman, tipping the cask over on to its side, poured out the remainder of the priceless contents.

By a little packing, it was clear the cloak could be made to hold the whole, and though the bundle might be a little unwieldy, yet there were no particular obstacles in the way of carrying it.

As well as they could they made it secure, and as soon as this important operation was over Lord Harcliffe glanced around, and said:

"Now let us leave this place without another moment's delay. We have stopped too long already."

"I am quite ready. Let me go first."

As he spoke, Captain Hawk passed himself through the opening in the wall.

The bundle was then handed to him, and he dragged it for some distance down the passage.

Lord Harcliffe followed, and then between them they with every imaginable care replaced the stone in its setting.

"His Majesty will be somewhat surprised when he discovers the disappearance of the treasure. How mysterious it will seem to him."

"It will," said Lord Harcliffe; "but we need not trouble ourselves much on that account. No—no; our business now is to ascertain whether the coast is clear for our retreat."

They had by this time reached the spot at which they had entered, and the cool night air blew upon their foreheads, that were flushed and heated with the excitement caused by the sudden possession of so much unexpected wealth.

"Phew!" exclaimed the captain, but in a low tone, "it's devilish hard to be without the circulating medium, but at the same time it's no joke to carry all your capital under your arm."

His friend laughed.

"We want his Majesty here to lend us a hand," said he.

"Or rather to deprive us of one. Remember that poor poisoned wretch that left his hand behind him in the trap."

All being perfectly quiet, they went out.

The first operation to be performed was to replace the bricks carefully, exactly as they had found them.

This they did.

All that now remained to do was for them to retrace their steps to the spot where they had left their steeds.

This they were not long in accomplishing.

They crossed the garden with cautious steps.

The rain still fell, but the wind was becoming more boisterous, and the monotonous footfall of the sentinel was less distinctly heard than before.

When they reached the wall, however, they waited quietly for the "tramp—tramp."

It seemed longer than usual.

When at length sounds did reach their attentive ears, it was more than one footstep they heard.

For a moment a shade of anxiety crossed their features, though being dark, neither was cognisant of the expression of the other.

An involuntary whispered "Hush!" alone broke from their lips.

Not that they had anything to fear from the most vigilant sentinel in their present position.

However, there was no resource but to wait.

The sounds increased in volume and explained themselves.

It was a body of soldiers going to relieve the sentinel.

They heard the rattle of their muskets as they came to a halt, and in a few seconds, to their great satisfaction, their ears were greeted with the sound of their departure as they left their comrade to wear out the remainder of the night in his solitary vigil.

Their horses were unnoticed.

"All is safe," said Captain Hawk.

They waited a few moments till the new sentinel turned on his beat, and then as before the captain ascended to the top of the wall by means of the rope.

Lord Harcliffe, having first secured the treasure to the end of the rope and seen it drawn up by his companion, speedily followed himself.

In another moment they were safely landed on the opposite side.

They hastened to their horses, which were still cropping the not particularly savoury herbage, and having unloosed them, mounted into their saddles and rode quietly off, making as wide a circuit as possible, and keeping on the grass to deaden the sound of their horses' feet.

They soon emerged into the London Road; and having now no further occasion for their former caution, they went along at a brisk rate, Captain Hawk carrying the golden spoil in front of him.

Their future course of proceeding now became a subject of consideration.

What should they do with the money?

Was it safe to carry so large a sum about with them?

"I am inclined to think," said Captain Hawk, "that as we have pledged ourselves to convey this money to poor Stephen's daughter, the sooner we start the better."

"For Guernsey?"

"Yes."

"I am ready."

"To-night?"

"To-night—that is, if we can find a vessel to take us."

"I do not apprehend any difficulty about that: money will overcome every obstacle; we shall doubtless drop upon some means of transport."

"The shortest way to find what we require will be to go at once to the docks and make inquiries."

"Agreed. And to tell you the truth, I think our temporary absence will have the double effect of recruiting our health and frustrating the kind intentions of our friends in Bow Street."

"Ha—ha! how they will fret when they find they've lost us! I should like to have seen Pharoah before starting, but it is of no material consequence."

"You can write to him—you know you can trust him—and he will keep his eyes and ears open during our absence."

"Since I have spoken of this intended journey, I quite long for a trip by water. Are you a good sailor?"

"I think I could accommodate myself to circumstances. At all events, I am a good swimmer."

"And I."

With these and other remarks they enlivened their journey to town.

All pursuit and inquiry appeared to have ceased.

The escape of Captain Hawk from the very foot of the gallows had been a nine days' wonder, and the fact was already almost forgotten.

Their first care on reaching London was to seek out a livery stables, where they lodged their horses, despatching a note to Tom Beckford, the staunch landlord of the Greyhound, to send for them, and look to them till their return.

They then proceeded on foot to the docks.

The money accompanied them, carefully wrapped up in the cloak.

CHAPTER CLIII.

CAPTAIN HAWK AND THE BLACK HIGHWAYMAN EMBARK FOR GUERNSEY.—THEY MEET WITH ROUGH WEATHER IN MORE WAYS THAN ONE.

In the docks there was the usual crowd of vessels, but at first sight there did not appear to be any craft that would be likely to run them over to the Channel Island.

There were plenty of seafaring men, too, hanging about—some who were on the eve of starting for long voyages, and others who had just returned.

Captain Hawk and Lord Harcliffe scrutinised the countenances of those they passed, and appeared to be much interested in the bronzed and weather-beaten features of the sons of the ocean.

But without finding the class of man they fancied would assist them in their design.

"We must make some inquiries," said Captain Hawk, "or we may wander about here for a month without being any nearer the point we aim at."

"What point's that, your honours?" inquired a good-tempered, broad-shouldered man, of an unmistakable nautical cut, and redolent of the wholesome odour of tar, touching his hat as he spoke.

"We wish to run over to Guernsey," answered Captain Hawk. "Would such a trip be in your line?" he inquired.

The sailor shook his head smilingly.

"No, sir," said he, "not exactly in mine; but there's a brother of mine as owns the Saucy Sally, as tight a little yacht as ever won a sailing match; she'd run you over there, and not be out of breath at the end of the journey I warrant."

"Where is your brother?" inquired Lord Harcliffe.

"I'll find him for you, gentlemen, in a brace of shakes," returned the sailor, as he departed to seek his relative, who, he had a tolerable presentiment, he should find at the Blue Anchor smoking his pipe and drinking hot rum-and-water.

Such was indeed the fact.

But Ben Breezely held to the maxim, "Bus'ness is bus'ness," and gulping down the grog at one gulp, he started to his feet, threw his pipe under the grate, and at once proceeded in company with his relative to speak to the gentlemen.

A bargain was soon struck.

In fact, the offer on the part of the captain and his friend was so munificent, that there was nothing for Ben to do but to acquiesce at once.

"We shall not remain long at Guernsey," said Captain Hawk, "so if you like you can wait while we are there and bring us back again."

Ben consented joyfully.

"When shall you be wanting to start, gentlemen?" he inquired.

"As soon as you are ready," was the answer; "directly if possible."

"We shall have the tide in a couple of hours, your honours, and we can go out with that."

At this moment the wind rushed past in a tremendous gust, causing the masts and tackle of the numerous vessels to vibrate audibly and quiver like so many reeds.

"We shall want the tide to-night," remarked Ben, "for the wind's dead against us. My eyes!" he continued, as another blast, if anything stronger than the former, swept by, "there'll be some ugly weather at sea to-night."

"Foul or fair," returned Lord Harcliffe, "we start to-night."

In a little more than two hours after the foregoing conversation, the Saucy Sally was picking her way through the crowd of vessels and going down the river with the tide.

It was blowing tremendously hard, and the little craft, that rode on the surface of the water like a cork, seemed to feel the influence of the wind tremendously.

Deptford, Greenwich, Woolwich, were passed in turn, and in time she was off Gravesend.

Here, where the river widens, the decided motion of the yacht told that they were rapidly approaching the sea.

The marine odours also borne upon the wind assailed the nostrils of the travellers, and bore witness to this fact.

The swell was tremendous.

The gale increased.

There was at intervals thunder and lightning.

The yacht, under a full press of canvas, seemed to fly through the water, dipping as she rose and fell, and to the eye of the inexperienced gazer, threatening to capsize every moment.

Ben Breezely was in ecstasies, and pointed out the beauties of his pet vessel to his passengers.

Both were inclined to be silent.

Both were impressed by the scene.

Both were accustomed to dangers on land, but they had had no experience of the perils of the deep.

As the night gradually passed away, the morning came in dark and lead-coloured.

The gale gave no symptoms of abating, but still the vessel sped gallantly on.

"There's something terribly exciting in this, is there not, my friend?" said Captain Hawk to his companion.

"There is," replied the latter; "there's something, in spite of the wildness and the roughness of such a scene, that seems to speak of freedom. Look at the waves how they rise before us as though they threatened to overwhelm this tiny bark!"

"Lor' love yer, sir," chimed in Ben, "there's no more fear of the Saucy Sally being overwhelmed by a sea like this than there is of St. Paul's being blown down and lying in ruins. I'd go anywhere with her."

"She seems a well-built vessel," remarked Captain Hawk.

"She's a real beauty!" cried Ben, admiringly. "Three cheers for her."

He raised his voice as he spoke in a hearty hurrah, in which the entire crew, consisting of two men besides himself, joined.

Their voices sounded but feeble when opposed to the mightier voice of the wind, that seemed to mock all human attempts to rival it.

The sea, lashed into fury by the fierce element that tore over it so furiously, stirring it as it were from its very depths, was clouded with sand, and looked angry and ominous.

The swell seemed to increase each moment.

The waves rose higher and higher.

"I said we should have ugly weather," remarked Ben to an old mate who guided the helm.

"Ay," replied his companion, "it's seldom we see a storm like this so near home."

"Where are we now?" inquired Captain Hawk, who with his friend the Black Highwayman kept the deck, holding their valuable booty under his arm.

"Well, your honour," answered Ben, "if the wind doesn't shift we shall sight the North Foreland in half an hour."

Strange to say, the wind, as though out of sheer opposition, shifted at that moment, causing the Saucy Sally to become very frisky all of a sudden.

But these little freaks were but momentary.

"Haul in!" shouted Ben.

The sails were shifted instantly, and the effects of the change in the fickle element counteracted.

The tight little craft, however, laboured more heavily than before.

Suddenly she made a dash and cut clean through a tremendous wave that swept her deck from stem to stern.

The two highwaymen, who were standing in the fore part of the vessel, were drenched to the skin, but beyond that they suffered no further damage.

Ben evidently seemed to have an idea that Sally was capable of receiving suggestions, and had acquired the habit of speaking aloud to his vessel.

At the last-mentioned freak he shouted out:

"Avast there, beauty! Look before you leap! Remember we've got passengers aboard who mayn't be quite so fond of salt water as you are! So take it easy, sweetheart—take it easy!"

Captain Hawk and his friend smiled at the master's fanciful style of addressing his craft.

Ben glanced towards them with a kind of apologetic smile on his features.

"That was what I call taking us unawares, gentlemen," he said. "I'm afraid it's given your clean linen a soaking," he added, glancing at the parcel that Captain Hawk so affectionately nursed under his arm.

"Oh," replied the captain, laughing, "this is a species of linen that salt water cannot damage."

"Still," remarked Lord Harcliffe, with a shudder, his teeth chattering audibly, "not being accustomed to those sudden immersions, I think a warmer berth than our present one would not be without its advantages."

"There's a snug little cabin below deck," said Ben. "Your honours 'll get as dry there as a couple of herrings in half an hour."

The precise amount of happiness such a state of dryness might be supposed to confer, Ben did not enter upon; the idea was, however, sufficiently suggestive to induce our two friends to descend immediately, and to remain there for some considerable time.

In the meantime the Saucy Sally kissed the gale, that blew, as Ben expressed himself, "right down her throat."

There were no signs of the weather abating, and a sharp fall of sleet was added as a kind of garnish to the general *melee* of the elements.

And so in course of time they rounded the North Foreland.

They passed Ramsgate and entered the Downs.

"We've got plenty of sea room if we ain't got nothing else," remarked the old helmsman to Ben. "I don't see a craft about anywhere."

"Lor' bless yer," said Ben, "it wants a vessel that's used to it, to enjoy this sort o' weather. Now here's Sally here, though she does creak a trifle, enjoying it all the time—ain't yer, old gal?" he called out loudly, so that she should be sure to hear.

"P'r'aps it's as well as we've got this weather, though, arter all," suggested the helmsman; "it'll keep those d—d piratical Frenchmen out of the channel; it wouldn't be healthy for us to fall in with one of those varmints."

"D—n the Frenchmen!" exclaimed Ben, indignantly. "What have they to do with us? I should like to catch any of the lubbers laying their claims on the Saucy Sally: we'd give 'em a run for it, wouldn't we, beauty?" he cried, again appealing to the yacht, every timber of which was creaking and groaning as though she'd had almost enough of it.

Suddenly Alec Burr, the helmsman, uttered an ejaculation.

"Talk of the devil!" he cried. "Look there, Ben!" pointing straight ahead as he spoke.

Ben looked with all his eyes, and then exclaimed:

"Well, and what of it?"

"What do you make of her?"

"Merchantman, from this distance—collier, perhaps."

"I don't think she's either: I think there's something a leetle suspicious about the cut of her jib."

"Well, whatever she is, I s'pose we shall know before long, for she seems to be bearing down straight towards us."

"Rather *too* straight, I fancy."

"Psha! Even if it was Blackbeard or Captain Kyd himself, we're not worth stopping."

"Perhaps not; but who's to know that till we're searched: the most valuable treasures sometimes lie in the smallest compass."

"I'll be d—d if I'll be searched."

"Maybe, after all, they'll pass us without taking any notice."

"We shall see."

The two vessels, the large and the small craft, gradually drew near each other.

The stranger, though only of moderate size, was, as the distance lessened and she could be more distinctly discerned, larger than either Ben or Alec had anticipated.

They were now near enough to discern the crew upon her deck.

Ben was busy with his telescope.

"Any guns?"

"None that I can see, or, if there are, they're masked."

"We'll give her a wide berth. I don't care about being stopped with these gentlemen aboard."

The yacht's course was altered, and she bore away to the starboard, intending to make the distance between them at passing as great as possible.

This manœuvre was noticed by the other vessel, who did not appear to approve of the Saucy Sally's independent behaviour, and who took the earliest opportunity of telling her so.

The hollow boom of a gun rose above the roaring of the elements.

A shot fell wide of the yacht with a terrible plunge.

"Hallo!" cried Ben and Alec in a breath.

"What the devil's the meaning of that?" followed up Ben.

"It's no more than I expected," muttered the helmsman.

"It's a considerable deal more than I did," growled the master, highly indignant at this indignity offered to his beloved Sally. "Oh for a ten-pounder loaded to the muzzle, and a lighted match in my hand, just to let 'em see I'm not afraid of the varmint, whoever she is."

At this moment the two highwaymen ascended the deck.

"Was not that the report of a gun?" inquired Captain Hawk.

"If it wasn't, your honour, it was the best imitation I ever heard," answered Ben, sulkily.

"What is the meaning of it?" asked Lord Harcliffe.

"It means, sir," replied the master, "that that craft there," pointing to the vessel, who had altered her course, and was now edging inwards in her approach, "expects that the Saucy Sally's a going to stop to be questioned. Very likely indeed! They must catch her first."

As he spoke he ran up another sail, which, instantly catching the wind, caused Sally to roll and pitch under the additional pressure tremendously.

"I see," said Captain Hawk, who was getting interested at the movements of the two vessels, "you mean giving my friend yonder"—alluding to the strange craft—"the cold shoulder."

"I believe you, your honour," answered Ben, with a knowing shake of the head and a bright, twinkling smile. "I'll let 'em know what sort of timber Sally's composed of."

The stranger appeared desirous of testing this point in her own way without any assistance from Ben, and, divining from the tactics of the yacht she was desirous to make a bolt, took measures to prevent her.

Again a white cloud of smoke belched forth from the porthole of the on-coming vessel, and the heavy report of a cannon again fell on the ears of all on board the Saucy Sally.

This time the aim was truer.

The ball, ploughing up the angry waves, plunged hissing into the waves at a distance of about thirty yards from the yacht.

"I say," said Alec, "this looks like business."

"Does it?" growled Ben, evidently perplexed. "D—n such business, say I! It's an infernal cowardly attack upon such a female!"

"Is it not strange," said Captain Hawk, whose face was flushed with excitement, "that wherever we go, we are certain to be the subjects of some adventure?"

"It certainly does appear so," answered his companion, "but I suppose it is our destiny, and who can resist or control the powerful grasp of Fate?"

"Ah, who?" echoed the captain, with a sigh.

He, however, checked his emotion, and pointed out the vessel to the Black Highwayman.

She was rapidly drawing near.

She had an ugly, vicious look about her.

No men were visible on her deck.

Suddenly Ben shouted out, as he removed the telescope from his eye:

"Why, there's the union-jack, and she's English after all!"

There was no doubt of it.

There was the English flag quivering in the breeze plainly enough.

Alec gave a grunt of relief.

He had begun to think things were growing rather too warm to be pleasant.

Whether our friends the highwaymen had been longing for some "moving accident by flood" to match the innumerable ones they had encountered in the "field" and on the road, and were disappointed at the prospect of a quiet termination to what had a little before promised to be rather serious, were feelings known only to themselves.

The only remark made was:

"So there will be no adventure after all."

This came from Captain Hawk.

"So it appears," replied Lord Harcliffe; "and perhaps it is no matter of regret considering the formidable odds there would have been against us. Remember the treasure we hold."

"True—true!" acquiesced the captain—"you are perfectly right—perfectly!"

At this moment the vessels were within hail.

A man, supposed to be the captain, shouted through a speaking-trumpet:

"Haul up alongside—I must speak with you!"

This order, though somewhat imperative, was spoken in pure English.

Ben's doubts had been at once dispelled.

He was a good-natured fellow, and to serve a brother sailor would have plunged into the sea at any moment, raging even as it then was.

"P'raps," thought he, "they're in distress, and want some help—who knows?"

With this idea he set himself to bring the yacht up alongside her more massive sister.

This was by no means easy.

The swell was tremendous.

The wind blue a hurricane.

"Move on!" seemed to be the order of the element

Repose was an utter impossibility.

At length by patience and some skilful seamanship on the part of the crews and commanders of both vessels, they were brought sufficiently close to enable a rope to be flung from the deck of the larger vessel to that of the yacht.

This having been accomplished, the rest was easy.

In a few moments they were alongside.

It suddenly flashed across the mind of our heroes that *they* might, somehow or the other, be the objects of their search; but then a moment's reflection told them that this could not possibly be the case, the large vessel having come from an entirely opposite direction.

This was a comforting thought, and so Captain Hawk, still nursing his precious charge, waited patiently for what was to come.

CHAPTER CLIV.

THE PIRATE CAPTAIN ASKS A VARIETY OF IMPERTINENT QUESTIONS AND RECEIVES HIS ANSWER.—CAPTAIN HAWK AND THE BLACK HIGHWAYMAN LOSE THE TREASURE.—MELANCHOLY FATE OF THE YACHT.

THE person of the individual who had first hailed them through the speaking-trumpet was now distinctly visible.

That is to say, as much as a thick frieze pilot coat, with the collar standing upright to his ears, a formidable pair of whiskers, and the waning light of a very gloomy day would permit.

He now stood on the deck close to the side, and applying the speaking-trumpet once more to his mouth, commenced questioning the captain of the yacht.

"What craft?"

"Saucy Sally—yacht."

"Where from?"

"London."

"Whither bound?"

"Guernsey."

"What cargo?"

"None—we're only taking a flying trip to accommodate these gentlemen."

Ben, who was the speaker, pointed out Captain Hawk and Lord Harcliffe.

The individual with the coat and whiskers threw his eye over the collar very scrutinisingly at our heroes, who returned the compliment with the utmost *sang froid.*

"Humph!" muttered the questioner, reflectively, glancing again over his collar at our friends the highwaymen "they *look* somebody—Government agents perhaps."

He roused up suddenly, and bawled through the trumpet:

"Give me the names of those gentlemen."

There was a pause.

The owner of the whiskers looked at Ben, who could not give the desired information for the best of all possible reasons, because he didn't know.

All he could do was to look at Captain Hawk in a manner implying, "What am I to say?"

The captain did not appear to care anything at all about the matter, as he made no reply, but simply turned towards his friend, Lord Harcliffe.

Their eyes met.

A smile stole over their features.

There was a tendency to the comic about the whole proceeding—at least, so it impressed them.

As if instigated by a kindred spirit, they simultaneously looked up at the man with the whiskers.

He appeared to be growing indignant at the delay.

"I'm waiting!" he roared through the trumpet.

"Eh?" exclaimed the two gentlemen, in one breath

"Eh, indeed! Can't you hear?"

"Not in the least."

"Are you deaf?"

"No!"

"I say I'm waiting!"

"Oh!"

"Waiting for your names."

"Oh!"

"I suppose you have names?"

"Oh yes!"

"Let me have them, then, without delay. Yours, sir, first!" he cried, addressing himself to Captain Hawk.

"My name," replied the captain, very deliberately, "is —ah—Jones—Count Jones."

"Oh! Count Jones, is it? Don't believe a word of it!"

This last clause was uttered in a tone too low to be audible.

"Now *your* name, sir—yours?" he continued, impatiently, to Lord Harcliffe.

"Certainly," replied his lordship, in a bland voice. "My name is Baron Brown."

This was uttered in the most serious manner possible, but it failed to impress the inquirer as to its truthfulness.

However, as there were no further means of ascertaining this fact, he was forced to accept it as he received it.

He had not, however, done yet, for turning once more towards Captain Hawk and his friend, he said:

"Have you anything valuable on board?"

"In reply to your exceedingly impertinent question, I may say I have *something* immensely valuable, and so has my friend."

The eye twinkled eagerly over the wall of collar as the owner inquired:

"What?"

"*Ourselves.*"

The man with the whiskers was becoming gradually alive to the conviction that he was being played with, and the idea had an unpleasant effect upon his equanimity.

"You'll have the goodness to give straightforward answers to straightforward questions!" he shouted, irascibly.

"Don't lose your temper, my friend: it's the very worst thing a man can do to give way to passionate emotions," suggested Lord Harcliffe.

"I'm not——"

"Oh yes, you are," dropped in the captain, "and entirely without cause. Our answers are most straightforward and correct: what property is half so valuable to mankind in general as precious self?"

"Oh, psha!"

"To prove it, suppose I were to mount on to your vessel's deck, and, taking you by the back of the neck—an operation which, by-the-by, you richly deserve for your confounded impertinence—were to hurl you headlong into the sea, would any earthly sum be considered too great, when death stared you in the face, to purchase your life? And what is *life* but *self?*"

This was such an exceedingly practical way of putting the case that Whiskers, Collar and Co. was silenced.

But matters were by no means settled yet.

Just as the discomfited subordinate with the speaking-trumpet stepped on one side, another took his place.

Not, however, a subordinate.

This was no other than the captain of the vessel.

Captain Hector Louloupe.

This important personage was attired in uniform, but, owing to the roughness of the weather, his diminutive legs were encased in a pair of ample sea-boots, one of which would have been large enough to have contained his whole body with the greatest ease.

He was a man of about the middle height, but looked smaller than he really was from the excessive spareness of his figure and the meagreness of his face.

But in order to atone for this, he cultivated an enormous moustache that curled up formidably towards each ear.

He was determined to be remarkable for something, and he had his desire in this particular gratified.

As he approached, long before anything else belonging to him was visible this formidable appendage stood forth bristling in the distance with fierce distinctness.

When those who knew his peculiarities wished to please him particularly, they would speak of him in his hearing as "Captain *Moustaches.*"

Then this great little man was satisfied.

Such, then, was the personage who now took the place of the man with the speaking-trumpet.

He looked down upon the occupants of the yacht with profound contempt.

Not that anyone knew precisely what he was looking at: he squinted so frightfully that the particular point on which his vision rested was always a profound mystery.

It might have been here, or there, or round the corner: no one could tell.

Suddenly he looked up to where the union-jack was fluttering furiously.

"Let down zat rag!" he cried, in a tone of scorn and in foreign accents.

Everyone on board the yacht looked surprised, and that surprise increased when in the place of the English ensign the French flag was hoisted.

"Now, zen!" cried the little captain. "I have listen to ze questions my firs lieutenant have ask you, an' I do not see any inclination on your part to answer zose questions, zerefore I am resolve to come an' see for myself."

Immediately upon speaking he blew a shrill whistle and shouted:

"All hands on deck!"

In a moment the deck was filled with sailors, armed with cutlasses, waiting only their captain's signal.

The passengers and crew of the Saucy Sally were aghast.

Alec, the helmsman, groaned inwardly.

"D—d if I didn't expect summat o' this sort!" he muttered.

Captain Hawk and Lord Harcliffe felt seriously uneasy —not on account of themselves, but for the treasure they held in their keeping.

The little captain, too, squinted down upon them horribly—or at least they fancied so—as though he would have pierced with a glance into the very interior of the bundle.

Ben Breezely—Captain Breezely, we will call him—was the first to speak, in a blunt, dogged, English kind of manner.

"Look here, mounseer," said he, "what did you mean, since you're a Frenchman, by hoisting the union-jack, and causing us to believe we were hauling up alongside an English vessel—eh?"

"Ha, ha!" grinned the captain, looking horribly like Mephistopheles, as he twirled his formidable moustaches. "I did zat to give you confidence, *mon cher*. I fire at you firs to try you, an' vhen I see you vish to get avay from me, I knew you vas afraid, so I run up ze English flag to bring you under my paw. Do you see, *mon garcon*?"

Ben was furious with passion.

He was a brave man, and he felt he had been duped.

Captain Hawk, too, and the Black Highwayman, as they listened to the sneering tones of the braggart Frenchman, found their hands wandering involuntarily into their pockets and grasping the handles of their pistols.

"Then, after all," roared out Ben, "who and what the devil are you?"

"I have ze honour to be Captain Hector Louloupe, commander of the privateer Redoutable; and I have ze plaisir to hold you in my grasp like so many poor flies in ze veb of ze spider!"

Having delivered himself of this speech in a tone half polite, half sneering, he squinted in a manner so positively sardonic that it drove the honest sailor well-nigh mad.

"You the captain of a privateer!" he shouted, with bitter contempt—"*you!* More likely a rascally Malay pirate! You're a pretty captain to swoop down upon a little cockle-shell like this, and fire at her, when one shot, had it struck, would have swamped her! Pah! Captain, indeed! Pooh!"

The small captain began to grow indignant.

His moustaches began to work rather convulsively.

"*Sacre!*" he bawled. "Hole you tongue, mistare, or I shall tie you up, an' give you vot ze English call ze cat viz ze nine tail!"

This put the finishing stroke to Ben's wrath.

His features worked, his lips quivered, and his face was crimson with passion.

"You—you—you'll g-g-give me th-th-the cat?" he at last contrived to gasp out, his limbs trembling, and his fingers moving convulsively. "Why, you d—d frog-eating French lubber, what d'ye mean? I should like to see you give me the cat! You couldn't hold it, you miserable, unhappy-looking, squinting, half-bred apology for a shadow, with more hair on your upper lip than flesh on your cheeks or brains in your head! If there'd been anything about you as the wind could a taken hold on, you'd 'a' been blowed overboard long ago!"

This was what might be called strong language, and, under the circumstances, not exactly what strict prudence would have suggested; but in his then exasperated state Ben had lost all control over himself and hardly knew what he was saying.

This was not, however, the case with Captain Louloupe. He had made a note in his memory of every single expression Ben's angry tongue had uttered, and as he was both malignant and revengeful, the probable consequence would be that at the first convenient opportunity Ben would have to pay for his words.

At present, however, Captain Moustaches had other business, so he contented himself by scowling at the master of the Saucy Sally, and, having thus let off a little of his superfluous irritation, he turned with a bombastic air to the captain and Lord Harcliffe.

"You two gentlemen say you have no luggage on board? Vat is zat you carry viz so mosh care under your arm?"

He looked very hard at Captain Hawk as he spoke, but the helmsman had a very strong impression he was gazing at him.

Captain Hawk, from motives of prudence and policy, answered, in a perfectly natural and offhand manner:

"I really, captain, can hardly admit your right to question me so pertinaciously, but since you insist upon knowing, I may inform you that this parcel consists simply of a change of linen—nothing more."

"Aha!" sniggered the cunning little captain, with a terribly incredulous smile upon his puckered features. "Is it so?"

"It is indeed!"

"I see: vun shirt, two pair of stockin', vun nightcap. Yes, yes—of course!"

"It's all right," thought the captain—"the ugly scoundrel believes me."

But the captain was deceived.

It was *not* all right, neither did the ugly scoundrel believe a syllable he (the captain) had said.

The little man had remained muttering for a few seconds, as if talking to himself: "Yes, yes—of course!" when suddenly he looked hard at the captain, and in his old cunning, satirical tone, said:

"I really sink your linen moss be of ver mosh vorth for you to keep him tuck so safe ondair your arm—eh?"

The captain and his friend felt their hearts beat a little quicker than usual.

They felt that their persevering, suspicious questioner had made up his mind to have the parcel.

At the same time they were as equally determined not to relinquish it.

The little captain was getting rather cold and impatient.

"Come, gentlemen, I am in a hurry!" he said. "Have ze goodness to oblige me viz a sight of ze inside of your parcel—jess for my own satisfaction."

"I most decidedly refuse," replied Captain Hawk. "And I look upon your request as a piece of most unwarrantable impertinence!"

"Oho!" screamed the little captain. "You do? Ver good! Zen instead of making a request, I shall make a demand!"

He inflated his chest, and puffed himself up to look as terrible as possible, and then exclaimed, in what he intended to have been an appalling tone, but which sounded very cracky and meek:

"Hand over zat parcel!"

"I'll see you at the devil first!"

"Oho! you vill, vill you? Ahoy, men!"

A dozen sailors rushed forward.

"Fetch me zat parcel at vonce!" cried the little captain, pointing to the bundle Captain Hawk still firmly grasped.

The sailors, without more ado, in obedience to their superior's orders, dropped over the sides into the yacht like a swarm of bees.

The moment for action, a little postponed, had come at last.

The sailors expected no opposition, and merely cried:

"Now, then, hand it over!" several stretching out their hands to grasp it.

They were not a little taken aback, then, when Captain Hawk and his friend, drawing back a step, drew from their pockets a pair of splendid pistols, with barrels as bright as burnished steel, and, presenting them full at their heads, the former exclaimed, in a voice of stern determination:

"The first who stretches forth a hand to touch the parcel I hold shall receive the contents of this in his skull!"

"And if that should be insufficient," Lord Harcliffe continued, "here is another at his service."

This prompt and decided act, and the calm and self-possessed manner of the highwaymen, staggered the sailors.

They paused and looked up somewhat wistfully at Captain Moustache, who stood grinning like a baboon on the deck of the other vessel.

Ben came up alongside at this juncture with Alec; each was armed with an iron bar.

"We've no firearms, your honours," said Ben, "but these are not bad at a pinch."

"You're a couple of brave fellows," exclaimed Captain Hawk, "and I'll not forget your services, depend on it!"

The tide of affairs had by this time considerably changed.

Captain Louloupe, enraged at being thus thwarted, shrieked loudly for a gun or a pistol.

One was brought him.

He grasped it firmly, and prepared for a sudden and speedy revenge.

All at once, however, he observed the pistol of the Black Highwayman raised in a direct line with his head.

His intentions suddenly altered.

He felt he had been rash.

He would take another and a deadlier vengeance.

He lowered his pistol, and shouted:

"Zen you refuse to deliver up ze parcel?"

"Certainly!"

"We'll see you at Old Harry first, and then we won't!" cried Ben.

"Zen look out for yourself: I shall blow you right clean out of ze vatair!"

"Coward!" cried Captain Hawk. "You are no better than a set of dastardly wreckers, who would plunder a poor drowning wretch for the sake of a few coins! You are outraging the laws of nations! We are peaceful individuals, travelling on private business; but whether or not, we have gone through too many perils in the course of our lives to be daunted by the threats of a dastardly pirate, backed by an equally dastardly crew!"

At this moment the captain was aroused by a loud exclamation from Ben, and at the same moment he felt the parcel suddenly snatched from under his arm by some one behind.

He was off his guard, haranguing the villains before him, and this was the unfortunate result.

In an instant, before he had time to prevent it, so instantaneously was it performed, the bundle was passed from one to the other and thrown over on to the deck of the larger vessel.

With a cry of despair, he turned and fastened upon the treacherous scoundrel who had been the first to seize the parcel.

It happened to be the man with the whiskers.

In a fury of impatient despair he grasped him by the throat, and having shaken him till he hardly knew whether he was dead or alive, he threw him violently from him.

The wretched man staggered back against the side of the yacht, where he oscillated for a moment, desperately endeavouring to make good his footing.

The impetus was too violent, and with a cry of terror he disappeared over the ship's side, and sank like a lump of lead in the dark waters.

In the prevailing excitement he was scarcely missed.

Captain Hawk, burning with anxiety to regain the precious bale that had been so treacherously snatched away, whispered to his companion:

"We must have that parcel at any price."

"Undoubtedly."

"I would as soon lose my life as that."

"Follow me, then; we must board the other vessel."

He whispered a word to Ben and Alec hastily, and the next instant all four were scrambling up the ship's side in their efforts to gain the deck of the Redoubtable.

The confusion now became general.

The crew of the pirate vessel—for she deserved no better name—attempted to drag them back, but in vain.

All their efforts failed against the resistless energy desperation gave to the four staunch allies.

They gained the deck.

But neither the bundle nor the captain was to be seen.

They rushed wildly in all directions in search, but in vain.

"Fate fights against us," cried Lord Harcliffe.

"Alas! yes!" sadly returned Captain Hawk.

The disappointment was so severe, the reaction so intense, that their energies seemed almost to forsake them.

A body of men rushed upon them—their arms were pinioned behind them.

They beheld poor Ben and Alec treated in the same ruthless manner.

They gave up all as lost.

Suddenly the captain appeared—with his villanous squint, and the parcel under his arm—and as suddenly vanished.

The sight of that, so far from depressing, supplied them with fresh vigour; but, alas! the chance was lost.

They were too securely bound and must submit.

Borne down by foes, their arms cut by the tightness of the cords that bound them, what other resource had they?

What was to be their fate?

Were they to remain prisoners on board the pirate vessel?

If so, Fortune might still open the way for them to regain possession of their lost prize.

All doubts as to their future destination were speedily set at rest.

Once more the little captain appeared on deck, looking more atrociously evil than ever.

He looked at them askant, and then called the first mate.

During all this time the fettered prisoners were making constant but imperceptible efforts to loosen their bonds.

They heard the venomous Louloupe give his order:

"Let the guns on the starboard side be loaded instantly and manned!"

"Ay, ay!" said the mate, looking towards the prisoners with a malicious grin, that appeared to be a reflection from the face of his villanous master.

Captain Moustaches strutted up to Captain Hawk, and looked with triumphant insolence in his face and that of Lord Harcliffe.

"Count Johne, an' you, Baron Brown, I have a treat in store for you—oh, sosh a treat! aha! *parbleu!* You shall see presently."

He skipped away with a malicious, impish kind of spitefulness, as though his fiendish nature exulted over the villany he was about to execute.

In a few moments he returned.

He approached Captain Hawk.

"Count Johne," he said, with a diabolical leer, "I have examine ze parcel—I have look ovair ze linen—aha! It is ver good—ver fine—beautifool fine!"

He then sidled round to Lord Harcliffe.

Grinning in his face, he went on:

"I have also examine *your* linen, Baron Brown: it is as good as your frien's—ver fine! It moss have cost I don't know how many souzand pound—ha, ha, ha!"

And the skinny wretch rubbed his hands one over the other until his knuckles cracked again.

At this juncture the first mate approached.

"The guns are loaded, captain," he said.

"Zat is right!" cried the villanous commander, exultingly. "Now, zen," he continued, "take zese lying English dogs an' throw zem into zere own boat, zen cut her adrift, an' when zey are a few yards off—mind, not more than a few yards—fire a broadside into zem an blow zem all to ze devil!"

A shudder of horror ran through the breasts of the bound and helpless victims at this atrocious and cold-blooded order.

But it was but momentary.

There were no cowards there.

It was not a craven fear of death, but simply a sensation of loathing indignation at the pitilessness of this semi-demon.

He glanced at Ben, who returned his malicious sneer with interest.

"Ha, ha! you shall call me name again, shall you? Ve shall see vot you vill do vhen ze cannon go off."

"I shall die," returned Ben, boldly, "thankful that I shall no longer belong to a world that holds such an unmerciful, heartless miscreant as you are!"

"Ha, ha! ver' pretty—ver' nice indeed—ze last dying speech. And have you nosing to say, too—eh?" he inquired of the two highwaymen.

"Only this," Captain Hawk answered; "and though anything I might say to you I should only consider waste of breath, I think it may do you good to let you know that I look upon my fate as by no means certain."

"Don't you? Zen I do; zat is ze difference."

"I believe," continued Captain Hawk, "that the time of my death is fixed, and that your puny and malicious efforts can neither hasten nor defer it a single moment. If I am to die to-day, I shall die; if not, be sure of one thing: we shall meet again when you least expect it."

He spoke this solemnly; and, as his thoughts reverted to the strange circumstances that had led himself and his comrade to their present position, he exclaimed, in a sad tone:

"Poor girl! after all you will be deprived of your just

rights—of all that has been purchased at the cost of so much suffering."

The four victims had barely time to bid one another farewell when the shrill, harsh voice of Louloupe fell upon their ears, issuing the ominous command:

"Man the starboard guns!"

A sailor stood by each gun with a lighted fuzee in his hand.

'Throw the prisoners into zere boat!"

This order was instantly and remorselessly obeyed.

They were hoisted unceremoniously over the ship's side on to the deck of their own as though they had been so many cattle.

At this moment Captain Hawk whispered to Lord Harcliffe:

"The rope that binds me is getting looser."

"So is mine," answered his friend.

The harsh voice of the pirate sounded again.

"Cut her adrift!" was the stern command.

The axe fell and severed the rope that held the Saucy Sally alongside.

Released from her moorings, the wind once more filled her sails—alas! in vain: she was not a dozen yards off when the demoniac Louloupe, who stood gloating over the painful sight, shouted:

"Make ready!

"Fire!"

A deafening report and a dense cloud of smoke followed.

When it cleared away, not a vestige either of the vessel or her crew was to be seen.

CHAPTER CLV.

SHOWS HOW THE KING VISITS HIS TREASURE-CHAMBER, AND WHAT HE FINDS.—AN AWKWARD MISTAKE.

Of all the kings that ever sat upon the English throne, George the Second—if history is to be accredited—was one of the most parsimonious if not the most avaricious.

He was incessantly bent upon hoarding money, not—so says history—to benefit others, but himself.

Our readers will remember the confession of the unfortunate Stephen—what he did, and for whom—how he died, and through whose instrumentality.

They will remember that he built the King's treasure-chamber, and that he—

Died by poison!

Administered by the hands of—— But no, let us not make such a fearful charge against one who has long since passed away to receive the reward of the good or the punishment of the evil he committed in this life.

It was on a fine summer afternoon that a heavy-featured, clumsily-built man was seated in a luxurious arm-chair in a chamber in Kew Palace.

His countenance was devoid of intellectual expression—in fact, the animal predominated, as might have been inferred by the massive, fleshy neck and double chin, whilst the broad, large face and the light eyes attested most incontestibly that he belonged to the true German type.

This man was George the Second, King of England.

The room in which he sat was comfortably but not magnificently furnished—the King had no idea of magnificence: he rather preferred saving money than spending it.

His Majesty had just dined alone, mutton chops being the regal repast of which he had been partaking.

The dinner was over and removed, a bottle of port and a decanter of brandy being alone left behind; but even here the King sipped the port sparingly, as though he almost grudged himself the luxury.

He had made, however, altogether a very substantial meal, and now began to feel a little drowsy.

He accordingly dozed off into a light slumber.

Presently a gentle tap came at a door that was evidently private, and masked by a curtain.

No answer save a rich and very mellow snore, so the applicant knocked again louder than before.

The King started from his sleep.

"Who's dat?" he cried, in a somewhat startled manner, speaking with a foreign accent and in broken English, the proper pronunciation of which he had neither the desire nor the application to attain.

He was not fond of learning himself, and either despised it or affected to do so in others.

The knock being for the third time repeated, his Majesty, being now thoroughly awake, cried:

"Come in."

The door behind the drapery opened noiselessly, the curtain was pushed aside, and a young man—whose light hair and blue eyes proclaimed him of German origin—entered.

This was Ernest Von Helm, who, though holding no higher position than the King's valet, was nevertheless a man of considerable attainments and much tact, and had contrived so to ingratiate himself with the monarch, that he had become his prime favourite and adviser.

"Well," said the King to his confidant, as he stood before him, "did you show the ring to Dutch Moses?"

"I did, your Majesty."

"And what did he say to it?"

"He said your Majesty must be an excellent judge of precious stones to have thought so highly of the ring I showed him in its present state."

"He is a sensible man—very sensible; I am a goot judge of gems. An' dish diamond is of value, did he say?"

"He did not make any particular remark about its value, sire."

"It is of value—it most be of value. It vas given to me by der young Lord Edward Gordon; and he vould not give his King dat vich vas vort noting."

"Certainly not, your Majesty."

"Dish Moses is a clever man in his vay, but den he ish a Jew, an' it ish a vay der Jews have to depreciate any article dey vish to purchase."

"So I believe, sire."

"No doubt he tink I vant to sell dat ring."

"I can hardly suppose that, your Majesty—kings do not sell diamond rings."

"Yes, dey do—dat is, ven dey vant money like odere people. I have heard of kings dat vould sell dare teeth out of dare head for gold."

"Perhaps so, sire, but you are not one of those."

"Yes, I am——"

The King checked himself suddenly.

"No, no, no—of course I should not sell my teeth, because I have gort none to sell."

These last words were rather thoughts than words.

"You brought der ring back wid you?"

"It is here, your Majesty."

He took a small case from his pocket as he spoke and handed it to the King.

George the Second seized it eagerly, and opening the case, took out a ring and held it up to the light in various ways, breathed on it, and watched the cloud gradually disperse from the surface.

"Oh yes," he chuckled to himself, "it is a valuable ring, and most be vort at least tree tousan' poun'—I tink more. Did der Jew say he should come to ask me any question about der ring?"

"He did say he hoped to have the honour of speaking to your Majesty about it."

"Yes, yes, of course he did—I understand vot dat mean—he shall nevare be easy till der ring is his."

"I should think so valuable a ring would be beyond his means of purchase, however much he might desire it."

"Dat is because you do not know dese Jews—dey all look poor—at least, all sosh Jews as Moses: it is part of dere trade."

"And does your Majesty think he is rich?"

"I feel sure of it—he is more rich dan he vould like to say."

"And do you also think he would be desirous of purchasing this ring, sire?"

"I daresay he would if he should get him for nothing, bot I shall nort sell him for dat."

"I should think it must have been an heirloom in Lord Edward's family."

"Ver like, and der silly fellow give me der ring to make him von of der page in mein household. Vell, he vould insist on my takin' it—bot I did not vant it: it is more than probable I shall give it back to him some day."

Had his Majesty put a candid question to himself he would have acknowledged that the idea of giving anything back was not one of his weaknesses.

[THE HIGHWAYMEN RE-APPEAR AFTER THE PIRATES' VOLLEY.]

"No money returned" would have suited him as a motto.

His real intention was to sell the ring, so that the proceeds might add to his stores in the treasure-chamber.

Moses seemed a most likely person to buy it.

"I should tink he would come to-day," said his Majesty, in a tone that implied a strong hope that he would come.

"Has your Majesty any further commands for me at present?" inquired Ernest.

"No, nort a present," answered the King; "you can go till I send for you."

Availing himself of the royal permission to depart, Ernest bowed himself out.

He had not been gone long when one of the pages in waiting presented himself.

He held a card between his fingers.

The King's eyes fell upon it, and he cried, eagerly:

"Vot ish dat?"

"The bearer waits for an answer, your Majesty," said the page.

The King glanced at the card, and an exclamation of joy burst from him.

"It ish he—it ish he!" he cried. "Bring him here."

The page departed, and returned speedily, bringing with him the Jew, Moses Goltz.

The page having conducted the old man into the chamber, departed instantly.

The Jew advanced humbly, with the highest possible respect in his manner and deportment, and sank on his knee before the King.

"Your gracious Majesty will pardon this intrusion, but I have taken upon myself to come to point out to you de faults in de ring."

"It has no faults, you lying scoundrel—it ish a lovely ring, an' vould be a fortune for anybody. Vort should you tink it vas vorth?"

"Vell, I should think it might be worth a tousan' pounds."

"No more? Den I must keep him meiself, for von thousan' pouns shall never buy him."

"Vell, dat ish of course as you please."

"It certainly is a lovely ring."

"What should you expect, your Majesty?"

"Tree tousan' at der very least."

"Vot a sum! how could I, poor as I am, afford to pay so mosh?"

"I don't believe you are so poor, Moses."

"Oh yes, I am—indeed I am: I can't even afford to keep a cat, your Majesty."

"A very fortunate thing too—especially for the cat," muttered the King.

"Then vort is der lowest sum you will really take for dish ring, your Majesty?"

"I vill not part vith it under tree tousan' poun'," said the King, decidedly.

"Oh! it ish too mosh, your Majesty—it ish soch a large sum!"

"Well, den, if it is so mosh don't buy der ring. I do not compel you to make der bargain against your vill."

"No—no," cried the Jew, in apparent agony, lest a gem so magnificent should slip through his fingers.

"Vell, have you make up your mind now?" inquired the King, who was as fearful the Jew would decline as the latter was that the King would be too exorbitant.

"Vould you allow me just to look at the ring once more?"

"Certainly," replied his Majesty, who was perfectly unsuspicious that his ring was in the slightest peril. "Dere he is."

He handed the case as he spoke, and Moses appeared to be examining it with the most scrutinising attention.

He turned away from the King and held up the precious gem to the light.

His Majesty sat waiting very patiently until this investigation should be terminated.

A close observer might have observed the Jew slip his hand into his pocket and withdraw it again rapidly.

Then there followed a little kind of legerdemain performance, during which the Hebrew's hand again visited his pocket in a stealthy but most rapid manner.

Why was this?

What was he doing?

There must have been some reason.

The King seemed to think it was almost time his eyes should be feasted with another sight of the ring.

"Come, Moses," he said, "you are a long while making your investigations."

"Yesh, your Majesty," replied that personage, in a tone rather flurried, "but ve're obliged to be particular—so particular—ven ve're purchasing precious stones, and for large sums."

The King's eyes twinkled at the idea.

"He vill be a buyer," he said to himself; and then continued: "If you vere not a Dutchman, Moses, I should nort care to let you hold dat ring in your hand so long, mein friend, but I trust you because I tink you are honest. I tink all der Dutch are honest."

"Oh, your Majesty, you are so goot to say so," replied Moses, trying to screw out a blush, but failing signally, and making instead a hideous grimace that seemed to be a compound of all kinds of villany from petty larceny to murder.

"Den you decide to buy der ring?" inquired the King.

The Jew opened his eyes and shrugged his shoulders very expressively.

"I should be so happy, your Majesty. It ish soch a beauty—soch a real beauty! But it ish soch a sum: tree tousand pound is a very big lump of money. Where could I get it? I am only a poor man——"

"Don't tell lies," said the King, bluntly. "Honest men ought nort to tell lies—I hate liars."

"So do I, your Majesty, but I shpeak the truth—upon my soul I do! I vouldn't tell a lie for the vorld."

"You tell von now, Moses," cried the King, who was out of temper at the prospect of the non-completion of the barter, and who spoke sharply in consequence. "Every von knows dat you are a rich man."

"No, your Majesty—no," returned the Jew, earnestly; "everyvun ish mishtaken. I vork hard for vot I get, but in my pushiness it'sh not all profitsh. I don't vaste my monish—I don't lend exshept on goot security. I'm sure I never give, and yet I don't get rich."

"Den you mean to tell me," asked the King, impatiently, "you cannot afford to buy der ring?"

"I am sorry to say, your Majesty, I cannot, though it breaksh my heart to let it go—upon my soul it doesh!" said the Jew, with every appearance of regret.

"Teifel! Vat did you keep me here den for, talking about your poverty?" the irascible and vulgar monarch exclaimed. "Vhy didn't you say vort you meant at vonce?"

"I couldn't find it in my heart, your Majesty, dat'sh a fact."

"Bah! you mean you couldn't find it in your pocket—dat'sh der fact, more likely. Never mind, return me der ring: I shall find a customer, I daresay."

"Not a doubt, your Majesty," said the Jew, humbly, handling the case that contained the costly trinket to the King.

The avaricious monarch clutched at it as a miser would have grasped at a restored treasure, and having opened the case and taken a hasty glance at the jewel to assure himself that it was positively there, closed it again with a snap, and consigned it to a pocket in the breast of his coat.

"Dere," said he, "dat ish safe dere vonce more."

His eye then fell upon Moses Geltz, the honest Dutchman, who stood rubbing his knuckles apologetically, waiting the royal permission to withdraw.

This came speedily and somewhat abruptly.

"You can go," said the King, bluntly. "I thought you vas gone long ago."

"I vash vaiting for your Majesty's permission."

"My permission? Donder unt blitzen, you have it—get out!"

And with this unregal dismissal the monarch pointed a fat finger to the door, ringing a hand-bell at the same moment.

A page entered.

"Show this man out!" was the command issued.

The man was shown out instanter.

There must have been something more than ordinary that influenced the internal machinery of Moses Geltz as he shuffled after the page.

It might have been expected that he would have been deeply chagrined at having to let so rich a bargain slip through his fingers.

The diamond, priced by the King at three thousand, was worth considerably more.

He acknowledged to himself he could have got eight or ten for it.

His inability to negotiate the purchase was therefore a dead loss to him.

And yet his eyes literally glared with exultation.

He went along, mumbling to himself, and rubbing his shrivelled hands, keeping, however, the upper part of his arm tightly pressed against the breast pocket of his coat.

Why was this?

The page having conducted him a short distance, turned him over to a lacquey, who, looking upon Moses as a very contemptible personage indeed, simply indicated by a motion of his head that he was to follow, and led the way to the gate.

When the Jew was fairly outside, he gave vent to the emotions he had been compelled to restrain in the palace.

"Oh, mein Gott—mein Gott!" he exclaimed, in a kind of ecstasy. "Can it be possible? The King, too, not to suspect—not to detect—ha, ha! ha, ha, ha! To ask me tree tousand, an' to let me have it for—— Ah! vell—vell!" he cried, patting his own forehead with his hand with a chuckling, cunning laugh, "after all it is de brains dat do it. Moshes, Moshes, you are a vonderful man!"

The King in the meantime was chafing at the loss of the three thousand he had expected to receive for the magnificent diamond.

He did not value it for its beauty, however.

He estimated it simply at what it would fetch.

The hand-bell rang again impatiently.

The page entered.

"Send my valet to me," exclaimed the King.

The page disappeared, and the valet Ernest entered.

"What is your Majesty's pleasure?" he asked.

"That stingy old Jew vill not buy my diamond," said the monarch, in a growling tone.

"Indeed, your Majesty!"

"No, he vill nort. He tells me he is too poor; but no matter, let him go: it is of no consequence. I should not vish to sell der ring at all, only I have no love for jewellery, and I tink I could do mush more goot vith der money."

The good his Majesty contemplated was very questionable, and resolved itself into the selfish act of adding the amount the ring might realise to the sum he had already—or rather imagined he had—secured in the treasure-chamber.

"Ernest, you must, amongst your connections, be acquainted with some von who traffics in dese baubles," the King continued—"some von who vould nort object to buy for ready cash dat vich is vort nearly double der sum I ask."

"Well, sire," replied Ernest, "since your Majesty appears anxious to dispose of this ring, I may confess that I did show it to one other person besides Moses Geltz."

"You did right, mein friend—quite right," said the King, a gleam of satisfaction lighting up his heavy features; "and he—dis man dat you speak of—will buy der ring, eh?"

"I cannot positively answer that question with any certainty, your Majesty. All I know is that he admired it exceedingly."

"Who is he?—vort is his name?" inquired the King, eagerly.

"Michael Willis, sire: he is a dealer in gems, and I believe he would give anything in reason for the ring in question; but he is an Englishman."

"Teifel! Vort do I care for dat? He should have it if he vas a Turk—dat is, of course, providing he can pay for it."

"Of course, your Majesty," answered Ernest. "Had I been left to select a purchaser, I should certainly have chosen Michael; but it was your Majesty's particular wish that Moses Geltz should have the first offer."

"Yes, yes—I know—I know. I was a fool for my pains. Dish Moses is an idiot; but den he is a Dutch Jew, an' all de Dutch Jews are idiots."

"Thinking it possible that your Majesty might not agree with this Jew about the price, I requested Michael Willis to attend at the palace," said Ernest.

"You did right—you did right," cried the King, in a tone of evident pleasure. "Vhen vill he come?"

"He is here now, sire."

"Aha! dat is goot!" the delighted monarch exclaimed. "Go — go, mein friend, and bring him to me at vonce."

Ernest left the apartment.

The King rose in a state of exuberant expectation and paced to and fro, rubbing his hands joyfully together.

Suddenly he paused, hearing footsteps approaching, and reseated himself in the arm-chair as the jeweller, preceded by Ernest, entered the room.

Michael Willis was a tall, handsome man, and in every way the exact opposite to the cunning Moses.

He bowed to the King as he entered.

George the Second was too absorbed to attend to courtesies at that moment, and went straight to the point at once.

"You have seen my ring?" he asked.

"Yes, sire."

"It is very beautiful, is it nort?"

"Nothing could possibly be finer."

"Aha!" chuckled the King. "Dish is a vise man—he knows a bargain when he meets von."

He spoke this to himself, and then went on:

"If you like to buy dish ring, you shall have him ver cheap—almost for nothing."

"At what price does your Majesty estimate this ring?"

"Tree tousand pounds."

"It is worth that sum," said the jeweller.

"It is vorth double dat som," echoed the King. "See," he continued, producing the case from his pocket and opening it—"look how it sparkles—see vot a lovely ting it is!"

He took it from the case as he spoke, and held it towards the jeweller.

Michael took it, and regarded it with the earnest eye of a connoisseur.

"What did your Majesty say was the price?" he inquired, looking up.

"Tree tousand pounds. It ish as cheap as dirt."

The jeweller looked at the King, and actually had the audacity to smile.

"This would be enormously dear, your Majesty, at that price," he said, holding the ring between his finger and thumb.

"Vot do you mean?" cried the astonished King.

"That it is not worth three thousand farthings."

"Mein Gott, fellow! It is von d—n lie! Did you not say just now it vas vorth tree tousand pounds?"

"The ring to which I alluded *was* worth that sum, your Majesty," replied the jeweller, calmly.

"Vell, and dat ring is dere, in your hand."

"Pardon me, sire, for presuming to contradict you, but this is not the ring I saw this morning."

"Nort der ring?" almost screamed the incensed King. "But I say it ish der ring! You are mad!"

"Indeed I am not, your Majesty—I speak the plain truth."

"Oh, bah!"

"I will give you a proof, sire."

As he spoke, the jeweller took from his pocket a small steel hammer, tapered at the extremity of the handle to the form of a small chisel.

He then applied this to the ring between the stone and the setting, and in an instant the former shot from its socket into his hand.

The King at this ruthless treatment of his valuable ornament started up in his chair.

"Villain! you are destroying it!" he shouted. "Ernest, do you see vort he is doing? Do you know vort you do yourself?" he cried, furiously, to Michael.

"I am about to disabuse your Majesty's mind of an error, and to prove that you are labouring under a delusion."

And with these words he tapped the fictitious gem lightly with the hammer, and it shivered into half a dozen fragments in the palm of his hand.

The King was frantic.

"You villain—you d—n dog! I will hang you for dis!" he shouted. "You have destroyed my splendid diamond dat an emperor might have worn!"

"I assure you, sire, you are quite in the wrong. Had this been such a jewel as you describe, the light blow I struck would not have injured it in the least; but it is not. So far from being a diamond, it is nothing more than a piece of simple glass, not worth a crown-piece."

George the Second fell back in his chair aghast.

The jeweller spread the fragments on the table before him, and pointed out their peculiar appearance.

As the conviction that the worthy tradesman was perfectly right flashed across him, another mortifying suspicion started up to enrage him—that was, that the *honest* Dutch Jew was at the bottom of the mystery.

"Der d—m scoundrel has changed der ring!" he cried. "He has gone off wid mein diamond, and left me glass instead! I vill hang him—I vill hang him, der Jew tief!"

But Moses did not give his gracious Majesty the opportunity of exalting him in this manner.

Whether guilty o not, he certainly gave a colour to suspicion by his abrupt disappearance.

On the arrival of the private detective sent by the King to arrest him, the Jew was nowhere to be found, and it was supposed he had left the country.

George the Second went about growling and chafing like an angry bear as the official departed on his mission.

In order to calm his agitation and soothe the irritability of his mind, the King resolved to pay a visit to the treasure-chamber.

A glance at his gold would surely revive him.

The sight of what he possessed would in some degree compensate him for what he had lost.

He accordingly proceeded thither.

Placing a key in the lock, the massive door opened noiselessly.

The wax taper the King carried cast a sickly light around.

The first thing that attracted the monarch's attention was the cask lying on its side instead of standing as he had left it, in an upright position.

"Who de devil have move dat?" murmured he, apprehensively.

He did not waste any unnecessary time in surmisings, but pounced upon the cask like a hungry hawk.

Falling upon his knees, he grasped it with both hands.

A dreadful expression passed over his face as he felt how light it was.

A terrible foreshadowing of some impending blow clouded his features.

He lifted it to an upright position.

Summoning his resolution, he looked in.

What meant that dark vacuum?

Was it—could it be possible that—— No—no! Such a ruinous idea was but the suggestion of some mocking fiend.

Desperately he plunged his hand into the cask.

A loud cry—or rather yell—burst from his throat.

"Mein Gott! it is empty!"

To describe the emotions of the avaricious monarch would be impossible.

He raved—he stamped—he swore—and dashed his ring upon the ground in his frenzy.

"Oh, mein Gott—mein Gott! Mein treasure!—der gold dat I have save month after month—year after year—gone—all gone: stolen from dis chamber dat I had built at a cost of——"

He paused suddenly in the midst of his ravings.

A thought crossed him.

The chamber had cost him nothing, for he had not kept faith with the builder—*he* had never been paid.

Then came a darker recollection.

Where was the busy brain that planned that structure?

Where the hands that built it?

The reader knows.

So did the King.

At that moment the groans of the dying victim's agony seemed to pierce the King's ears.

Conscience, with its still louder tongue and its sharp goading sting, forced him to remember the guilty past.

Like the mysterious finger that traced the handwriting on the wall before the licentious Belshazzar, an outstretched hand pointed to an accusation that seemed to blaze in characters of fire—

Poisoner!

The narrow chamber appeared to whirl round.

The walls flashed in its rapid revolutions with a myriad glaring colours.

Light, sense, thought, and feeling became bewildered in the furious race.

Through all this there fell like a dead weight upon the monarch's soul the stern conviction that this was—

The retribution of Heaven's justice!

The King gasped—a choking sensation rose upwards from his heart to his throat—his face grew purple, and with a shriek of horror he fell senseless upon the stony floor.

What became of Moses Geltz, the *honest* Dutchman? The means he took to secure the ring, where he went, and what was the eventual destination of the jewel, we must leave to a future opportunity to narrate

CHAPTER CLVI.

IN WHICH IT APPEARS THAT CAPTAIN HAWK AND THE BLACK HIGHWAYMAN ARE STILL IN EXISTENCE.—THEIR ADVENTURES ON BOARD THE PIRATE VESSEL.

Not a vestige of the vessel or the crew was to be seen!

Such was the melancholy announcement made at the termination of the chapter but one preceding this.

Where, then, were they?

Alas! the cruel broadside from the guns of the pirate had completely annihilated the taut little Saucy Sally, and all that remained of her were some shattered planks, with here and there some remnants of cordage attached, floating helplessly upon the turbid waters.

Poor Ben Breezely, Alec the helmsman, and another, had found a grave in the depths beneath, whose hollow murmurs chanted their requiem.

But our friends—the gallant Captain Hawk and his friend, the Black Highwayman—what had become of them?

Had they shared the fate of the ill-starred yacht and her crew?

Had such been the case, we might have dropped the curtain at once upon this adventurous life drama, and proclaimed it finished.

But fortunately no such disastrous effect had taken place.

When the thick cloud of smoke caused by the pirates' volley had cleared away, two figures might have been seen holding on to the sides of the boat, that floated tethered by a rope to the stern of the pirate vessel.

Their next act was to hoist themselves over its bulwarks, where, drenched with wet and chilled to the marrow with cold, they sat for a few moments to recover their breath.

There was nothing very cheerful in their prospects.

They had escaped immediate death certainly, but they were still within reach of the grim monster, and as it were under the very jaws of their enemy.

They looked somewhat ruefully at each other.

But they were two spirits that could not easily nor for any long space of time be greatly depressed.

Gradually a smile, rather faint perhaps, but still a smile, stole over their features as each gazed upon the other.

Captain Hawk was the first to speak.

"It's perfectly true," he said, his teeth chattering with cold.

"What?" inquired his companion.

"Those who are born to be hung will never be drowned."

"Well, I hardly know what to think," said Lord Harcliffe, looking round upon the dreary waste of waters over which the night had cast her gloomy mantle. "I shall not consider myself quite secure from such a fate till I find a more substantial lodging than the present."

"Any port in a storm, as the sailors say."

"How the boat rocks, and the spray dashes over her and us without the slightest compunction!"

"Take a pull at this," said the captain, handing a flask to Lord Harcliffe, who, benumbed as he was with cold, received it with grateful eagerness, and took a long draught.

"That puts new life into my veins," he cried.

"Yes," returned his companion, following his example, "brandy in these situations is invaluable. Ah! it does warm!" he cried, as he removed the flask from his lips.

"And now," continued Captain Hawk, "what is to be our next move?"

"It would not be a bad idea to cut the rope and take our chance of getting to land," said Lord Harcliffe.

"I have no objection at all to get to land," answered the captain, "but I have a very strong objection to leave our treasure behind us."

"Ah, true, the treasure! I forgot that," said his lordship. "The cold has stagnated my memory, but the idea of leaving such a sum in the hands of that rascally pirate is not to be endured."

"And to think, too, that at this very moment it may only be a few yards off."

The captain glanced up as he spoke.

The stern cabin windows were just over his head.

A light was in the cabin.

Could their features have been discernible in the darkness, it would have been seen that some particular idea had just struck them.

Captain Hawk spoke.

"Would it not be a triumphant termination of our adventures if we could make our way into this den of cut-throats and carry off our prize?" he said, eagerly.

"The same thought crossed me," answered Lord Harcliffe, in a tone of equal interest.

"It is a bold step, and requires coolness, caution, and courage."

"I think," suggested the Black Highwayman, facetiously, "that we are in admirable condition for displaying the first of these attributes at least, for I declare for my own part I'm half frozen."

"The idea of laying my hand once more upon the treasure has warmed me," cried Captain Hawk, "and I long to make the attempt."

"I'm with you!" his companion eagerly exclaimed.

"And these murderous scoundrels shall find that in courage and strength——"

"Resolution and daring," joined in the captain, "they have more than their match."

What could be more improbable than a successful issue to so wild a scheme?

Yet, wild as it was, it suited the reckless natures of the men who proposed it.

Theirs was a temperament that courted the excitement of danger; and like some plants that bloom and flourish in frozen latitudes, they throve in the midst of peril.

The sea was rolling beneath them, and the small boat in which they sat rose and fell and swayed to and fro at the will and pleasure of the mighty waves as it dragged along in the wake of the pirate ship.

It was lucky it was dark.

In this fortune favoured them.

"Come, then," cried the captain, "since we are resolved to make the attempt, the sooner we take the first step in the adventure the better."

"I am ready," said Lord Harcliffe.

They grasped each other's hands by a mutual impulse.

It was the silent but expressive determination of two brave hearts to stand or fall by each other.

"I will ascend by this rope and endeavour to reconnoitre the interior of the cabin," said Captain Hawk.

He grasped the rope as he spoke.

It was wet with salt water, and slipped through his fingers as he essayed to mount.

"Humph!" he cried, in a perplexed tone, "but it will never do to give up thus."

He poured a small quantity of brandy into his palm and rubbed his hands briskly together.

He then seized the rope again.

This time with much better success.

The brandy had imparted a stickiness to his hands, and he could retain his grasp.

"Bravo!" he cried. "Now for it: sink or swim, here goes!"

He then commenced ascending, hand over hand, until he had mounted sufficiently high to look into the cabin.

To his great joy it was perfectly untenanted.

From its appearance, and the style of its furniture, it was evidently the captain's cabin.

His heart bounded as he came to this conclusion.

Extending his foot, he pressed it carefully against the strong wooden frame of one of the windows.

He felt it open inwards.

He withdrew his foot, rejoicing that his end was gained, and slid down again into the boat.

"What success?" asked Lord Harcliffe, eagerly.

"The best," answered his friend. "I would wager anything we have lighted on the captain's cabin at the very outset."

"Is the coast clear?"

"Yes."

"Let us ascend, then, at once and enter."

But this was not so easy as it at first sight appeared.

It was not like a rope suspended against a perpendicular wall.

The stern inclined to a considerable angle inwards, and the boat dragging at the rope caused it to stretch to an equal angle outwards, so that there was a great difficulty in getting near to the window.

This had not struck them hitherto.

"How is this to be surmounted?" inquired Lord Harcliffe.

Captain Hawk was silent for an instant.

"I think I have hit upon a plan," he said. "I will enter first, and then I can assist you—that is, if my efforts prove successful."

The captain once more pulled himself up by the rope, and finding the cabin still empty, he applied his foot sharply to the window-frame.

The window swung open on its hinge, and remained so.

"So far, so good!" muttered the captain

He then extended his leg till he found his toe able to hook itself in the upper part of the opening.

He then, by a powerful muscular effort, contracted his limbs, and bringing this force gradually to bear upon the boat, it drew nearer.

This having been accomplished, he suddenly thrust forth his legs into the interior, preventing their subsequent withdrawal by bending his knees, which formed a powerful means of arrest.

He then with a final exertion of strength pulled the boat as near as it was possible, and then suddenly releasing the rope and throwing himself forward, he shot as it were completely into the cabin.

He was no sooner in than his head appeared looking out again, as he called in a low tone to his companion, who had watched him with a considerable deal of anxiety:

"All safe!"

At this announcement, the Black Highwayman essayed to follow his companion.

The fact of Captain Hawk's attempt having proved successful greatly facilitated the operations of his friend.

The captain could and did assist him materially, and in a very few moments the enterprising pair stood side by side in the pirate's cabin.

Having landed them therefore safely there, our readers may not be unwilling to leave them for a few instants whilst we explain the secret of their escape from the murderous fire that destroyed the yacht and its crew.

It was comprised in two words—*promptness* and *decision.*

They heard the captain of the pirates give the order to man the guns.

From the perception of his character which they had arrived at during their previous conversation with him, and from the cool, sarcastic, sneering tone of his remarks, they recognised a man who with a meagre and weak physique could, without appearing so, be a bloodthirsty and remorseless wretch.

They therefore divined the rest.

No sooner, then, had they reached the deck of the yacht than Captain Hawk quietly released his arms from the rope that bound him, and immediately cut the thongs with his knife that bound his friend.

Then when the fatal command "Make ready!" was heard, they coolly lowered themselves over the side of the yacht, and disappeared beneath the surface.

The pirate Captain Louloupe and his crew were too intent upon the coming sport to notice their disappearance.

Ben Breezely and his men were too absorbed in the impending fate that awaited them to heed aught else.

The light of day also was waning, and objects were becoming indistinct, so that by the time the dread order came to "*Fire!*" our heroes, who were both excellent swimmers, rose to the surface near the stern of their enemy's ship.

The boat attached offered them an asylum: the rest is known.

The contrast between the dark tempestuous ocean, lashed by the chilling blast, and the light and warmth and comfort of the cabin they had gained with so much perseverance, was so great that for a few moments they could only luxuriate in the agreeable sensations they experienced.

The pirate ship was a French vessel, and partook somewhat of the luxury and taste of that nation in the decorations and appointments of, at least, the cabin in which they stood.

It was carpeted, and the walls were ornamented with various trophies, the angles and edges being inlaid with gilt beading.

There was besides a stove grate glowing cheerfully on one side of the cabin, and before this our friends warmed their half-frozen limbs.

It certainly was a great temptation to a state of forgetfulness.

The captain was the first to shake off this feeling.

"We are in the enemy's citadel," he cried, "and must work with our weapons between our teeth, so as to be ready at the first signs of attack."

"You are right, my friend," replied the Black Highwayman. "That reminds me that our pistols need looking to."

Of course, from their immersion, these weapons were perfectly useless, their charges being soaked with seawater.

These were the first objects to which the highwaymen directed their attention.

They wiped and dried the firearms, and with a little oil from the lamp that hung suspended from the low roof they lubricated the springs of the hammers and triggers.

This was a work of paramount importance; but there was an operation of equal necessity yet to be performed.

This was to load them.

"If we could light upon some powder," said Captain Hawk, "our bullets would do again."

"This seems a likely place for such a thing," observed Lord Harcliffe, indicating a small cabinet that stood against the wall, and opening it at the same time.

"Behold!" he exclaimed, triumphantly, holding up a richly inlaid powder-flask.

"Quick, then! we will load."

This operation, to men accustomed as they were to the use of firearms, occupied no more than a few moments.

"I feel more at ease now," remarked the captain.

"Decidedly," joined in Lord Harcliffe; "and if my coat was a little drier, I should feel my pleasurable sensations increased."

"Let us take them off, and hang them near the stove."

This was immediately done, and the steam began to rise from them in vaporous clouds.

In the meantime they took a rapid survey of the cabin.

A large chest stood in front of the windows.

"This," said the captain, "would not be a bad post of observation: it commands the whole room."

"It would be also a capital kind of house of detention unless we remove this," Lord Harcliffe observed, quietly taking the key from the keyhole.

"A good precaution, Harcliffe," said Captain Hawk, who was regarding the powder-flask affectionately. "By-the-by, is there anything in the chest?"

"Ocular demonstration will be the best means of ascertaining that," replied the Black Highwayman, raising the massive lid.

They looked in.

Nothing met their gaze but a few swords and several articles of wearing apparel.

"There is plenty of room for us both there if need be," remarked Lord Harcliffe.

They continued their investigations.

In the course of these, their attention was attracted to a piece of massive drapery that fell in thick folds from the ceiling to the ground on one side of the cabin.

"What have we here?" cried Captain Hawk, pulling aside the curtains, which divided in the middle and disclosed a recess of considerable extent, which was occupied by a luxurious bed.

"The pirate has an eye to his own personal comfort," said Lord Harcliffe, as he pressed his hand upon the yielding mass.

"If the vagabond had his deserts, he should be smothered in it," replied Captain Hawk.

"An hour or two's repose on a bed like this would be paradise," soliloquised the Black Highwayman; and as though anxious for a brief realisation of such bliss, he threw himself on to the bed.

He had no time to expatiate upon its delight, for at the instant his wearied body sank down half buried in the feathery luxury, a hideous yell from beneath the coverlet caused him to start on to his feet with the utmost expedition.

"What the devil's that?" he cried, in a startled tone.

The question was answered as soon as asked by the sudden appearance of a small monkey, who was a pet of the captain, and who was quietly and peacefully coiled up beneath the bed-clothes, and whose slumbers his lordship's sudden visitation had abruptly terminated.

Hissing and chattering in the peculiar malevolent and spiteful manner common to their race, the animal crouched down in as remote a corner as possible, with the evident intention of keeping a sharp look-out for himself.

"Let the brute go," said Captain Hawk, as they continued their researches.

Presently they came upon a small cupboard in the panelling of the wall.

"The wine-cellar, by Jupiter!" exclaimed Captain Hawk, as he opened the cupboard and disclosed a goodly array of bottles of all sorts of shapes and sizes.

"Bacchus be praised!" cried Lord Harcliffe, seizing upon a bottle labelled "Brandy." "Fortune is evidently favouring us to-night."

He poured out a couple of glasses of the *brave Cognac*, and mutually pledging each other, the highwaymen drank them off at a draught.

"Our flasks want replenishing," suggested Captain Hawk; "let us help ourselves."

This was accordingly done, and the flasks transferred to the pockets of their coats, that were by this time dry.

"We have found everything we require," said Lord Harcliffe, "but the treasure, the most important of all."

"Ah!" sighed Captain Hawk, "that precious treasure! Depend upon it this piratical miscreant dares not trust it from his sight. If we are to regain it, we shall have to wring it from him by main force."

At this juncture the voice of the captain was heard shouting some farewell order.

"He is coming below," cried the Black Highwayman.

"Let him come, and welcome! We are ready for him now. Pray Heaven he bring the gold with him!"

There was no doubt about the captain's approach.

Footsteps were heard descending.

"We must conceal ourselves."

"Where?—in the chest, or on the bed?"

"The chest, I think, affords the best view."

"In we go, then. Hark! He is almost at the door."

Hastily snatching up their coats, the two highwaymen ensconced themselves in the chest, leaving the lid a little ajar, so that they could see all that passed without being visible themselves.

They had hardly established their position when Captain Louloupe entered the cabin.

The gale had slightly abated in its fury; and the pirate, having seen all snug on deck, had retired to the warmth and comfort of his luxurious cabin.

He appeared in the very best of tempers, and carried his valuable prize under his arm.

Nothing would have induced him to relinquish that.

He placed it on the table with a hideous grin of triumphant self-congratulation.

Little did he deem that four anxious eyes were intently fastened on it besides his own.

"There it is," whispered Captain Hawk to his companion, exultingly; "the sight of it gives me new life."

The pirate, having contemplated his prize for a moment, went to the cupboard, and brought from thence several bottles of different liquors, a bundle of cigars, and a bag of biscuits.

These last he began to devour with great relish.

"How I wish the rascal would choke himself!" thought Captain Hawk.

Having satisfied his hunger, Louloupe removed a heavy coat of frieze he wore and hung it up to dry.

He also took off his sea-boots; and being now *en deshabille*, evidently gave himself up to enjoyment.

The monkey watched his opportunity, and very shortly after the coat had been placed in the position it occupied when off duty, the animal sprang up and sought an asylum in one of the pockets, where he sat snug enough, with his face peeping out at the aperture, watching his master as he chewed his biscuit, probably wondering when a piece would come to his share.

But Louloupe on this particular occasion was very neglectful of his pet.

He was absorbed in the contemplation of something far more valuable.

"Aha!" he cried, "I sink I have got a prize to-day—a prize that shall make me happy all my life long!"

"Don't be too sure of that," thought our friends in the chest.

The idea so pleased the pirate that he drank off two glasses of wine immediately on the strength of it.

He then proceeded to feast his eyes upon the treasure

As rouleau after rouleau met his gaze, he became uncommonly elated.

He started up, clasped his hands, shouted, "*Vive la France!*" and sat down again.

The monkey, being disgusted at the neglect with which he was treated, began to chatter to himself rather loudly.

The sound attracted the captain's attention.

He turned round and spied his favourite.

"Aha, Jack, zere you are, are you, you old rascal!" his master cried. "Come here! Poor Jacko—pretty Jacko!"

He held out a piece of biscuit between his finger and thumb, and chirped to the animal.

Jacko, thus tempted, sprang from the pocket and

hopped nimbly to the captain, who presented him with a biscuit, which he sat and nibbled with profound gravity, on his master's knee.

The captain watched him for a few moments.

"You are a rascal, Jacko," he said, at length; "you do not know vat is good for yourself. You eat ze biscuit. but you do not drink ze brandy."

He filled two glasses, one of which he drank off.

The monkey, in the spirit of imitation common to its tribes, seized the other, and tossed the fiery liquor down his own throat.

A sensation scene was the immediate result.

"Phzz—phzz! Wr-r-r-r-r-r-r-r-r!" and an additional combination of strange sounds attested the anguish the unfortunate monkey endured from the fiery draught he had swallowed.

"Aha!" cried the brutal Louloupe, "he svear at ze brandee. Don't svear—don't svear, *mon cher!* Come here, pretty boy! Drink—drink—try again!"

But the pretty boy declined the favour with evident horror, and made a precipitate retreat into the first available asylum, which happened to be one of the captain's sea-boots.

Louloupe then devoted himself to the contemplation of his prize.

"Ha—ha!" he cried, exultingly, as he unfastened the rouleaux, and scattered their glittering contents upon the table. "You sweet creatures—you pretty, darling creatures! Oho, ze *brave Anglais*, vot a pity I had to blow zem to pieces! But, zere—zere—no mattair for zem, I have got ze money—ze gold, zat is not blown to pieces—no—no! It is here! Oh you bright, beautifool darlings," he cried, with increased enthusiasm, "let me embrace you!"

As he spoke he threw his arms around the glittering pile, thrust his hands through the golden heaps, scooping up the precious metal, and then opening his fingers and allowing it to fall through with a ringing sound that went straight to the heart of Captain Hawk and the Black Highwayman, who were watching intently from within the chest.

The pirate captain was a profound worshipper of Mammon.

He could not sufficiently adore his golden treasure.

Visions of luxury and splendour floated before him.

"I shall be rich!" he shouted. "I shall build a palace. I shall have slaves to vait upon me—lovely vomans to kiss. Ha, ha! vot a great man I shall be!"

He poured out a glass of brandy, which he drained, and then having sufficiently glutted his sight and touch with his golden heaps, he began to grow weary.

"I have had enough of you for the present," he said, addressing himself to the senseless dross; "so I shall tie you up and put you avay snug in ze chest."

He drank another glass of brandy, and then carefully packed up the coins in their original covering, the cloak.

While this was doing, our friends, the highwaymen, were holding a council of war in the chest.

"What will be the best plan of disposing of this scoundrel?" said Captain Hawk to Lord Harcliffe, in a whisper.

"It would not do to blow his brains out; the report of the pistol would alarm the crew."

"There is only one thing to be done: the moment he raises the lid we must seize him, and before he can recover from his astonishment, we shall be able to bind and gag him—the rest is plain enough."

"I long to clutch the rascal by the throat. My grasp once upon his windpipe, I shall feel strongly inclined to strangle him outright for his infernal brutality."

"Do as you please."

By this time the gold was made up in a compact parcel.

"Diable! it is heavy!" remarked the captain, as he approached the chest and laid his hand upon the lid.

Little did he guess the two lively *Jacks-in-the-box* that were inside, waiting to spring up the moment the lid was raised.

"Are you ready?" whispered Captain Hawk.

"Quite!" was the reply.

Their preparations were, however, for the present thrown away.

Captain Louloupe appeared suddenly to change his mind.

"I will not put him zere," he soliloquised; "if any of ze crew knew dat I have so moch money, it might tempt ze rascals to steal, and I vish no vun to share viz me: I must have all—all to myself."

Louloupe once more seated himself and placed the parcel of guineas before him on the table, again applying himself to the brandy-bottle.

He began to get drunk and convivial.

He chanted snatches of songs. One in particular pleased our heroes.

It ran thus:—

"I am a captain bold: zey sink
I seek my country's vealth;
But all ze time ze only sing
I seek for is myself.
La, la, la, my motto is myself!

"Vhene'er I meet a spanking craft
Zat promise moch of pelf,
I cry 'my country's prize!' and laugh,
And take ze prize myself.
La, la, la, I take ze prize myself!

"I scour ze sea by night and day,
It echo wiz my gun;
But all ze time I fire avay,
I fire for nombair vun.
La, la, la, I fire for nombair vun!"

The captain's throat was dry at the conclusion of this ditty, and required moistening with more brandy.

"Oh, vot a genius I am!" he soliloquised, thrusting his hands in his pockets and lolling back in his chair in a state of semi-inebriation—"vot a beautifool voice I have got!—vot a clevair brain I have in my head! Anyvun but me vould have believe zose two Engleeshmans about ze shirts—ha, ha! I vonder vhere they are now, my friends ze Count Johne an' ze Baron Brown?—ha, ha! Vot funny names, to be sure! Johne—Brown! Ha, ha!"

This struck the captain as so particularly droll that he chuckled and laughed to himself in a confidential and boosey manner, soliloquising at intervals.

He had by this time arrived at a state decidedly favourable to the plans of our two friends in the chest.

The moment had arrived for action.

The unsuspecting Louloupe still continued to laugh and talk to himself.

"Ha, ha! ze idea to try an' make me sink ze gold vas shirts! No—no, my friend Brown; no—no, my friend Johne, you did not know ze man you have to deal wiz; an' vhat have you got by it? Ha, ha! Nozing! You have lose all, an' ze littel fishes shall pick your bones—ha, ha, ha, ha!"

The convivial pirate, in the intensity of his mirth, opened his mouth to the widest possible stretch.

It may therefore easily be imagined that he was considerably astonished when on attempting to close it, he found a decanter stopper thrust half-way down his throat, a cloth tied tightly over his mouth, and his arms pinioned firmly behind him.

All he could do was to sit winking and blinking in a drunken manner, watching the movements of the two highwaymen, who at a certain moment had darted from the chest and secured the captain in the height of his drunken exhilaration.

To cry out was impossible—to move was equally so: all that remained to him was the power of facial expression, and that he indulged in to the greatest possible extent.

He looked as much like Jacko's elder brother as it was possible to conceive.

Captain Hawk coolly surveyed him with quiet contempt for a few seconds.

"If you were worthy of such an honourable dismissal, I'd spit you with this, you bloodthirsty scoundrel!" he said, drawing his sword and pressing the point against his ribs till the pirate winced and rolled his eyes with horror; "but you are not. To take your life would but disgrace a brave man's weapon—you deserve only contempt."

And as the most expressive way of exemplifying this feeling, he seized the pirate's nose between his finger and thumb, and pulled it in a most decided and efficient manner.

The great man with the clever brain plunged and kicked and looked unutterable things under the operation.

Captain Hawk having pulled till he was tired, turned him over to his friend.

"I look upon you," said Lord Harcliffe, "as the cruellest, the most ravenous of sharks, you cowardly, murderous villain! You will meet your punishment one day; but for the present I agree with my friend as to the fitting course of treatment—contempt!"

Again the piratical nose was seized and soundly pulled.

At this second application to the captain's proboscis, he made a terrific demonstration with his legs, but that was all he could do.

The highwaymen took no further notice of him.

They utterly ignored his presence.

"You will take a glass of wine, my lord?" inquired Captain Hawk

"With much pleasure," answered his lordship.

The wine was poured out.

"Your health, my lord!"

"I thank you—yours."

"Capital wine!"

"Another?"

"If you please."

The bottle was emptied.

The Frenchman grinned and grunted horribly as he saw his wine disappearing down the throats of the remorseless Count Jones and his friend Baron Brown.

His grins and his grunts were alike disregarded.

The gallant highwaymen had achieved the purpose for which they entered, and now Captain Hawk, placing the precious parcel in its old place under his arm, said to his companion:

"We have stayed here long enough—it is time we were gone."

"I am ready."

To be obliged to sit there, bound and gagged, and witness the departure of the glittering treasure that had caused the pirate so much exultation, was the severest blow of all.

He groaned and spluttered, kicked and plunged, and finally, losing his balance, fell over, chair and all, on his back.

Our friends took not the slightest notice of him.

"There is only one way of escape," said Captain Hawk.

"And that is——"

"By the rope. As we came in so we must go out."

"'Tis a desperate venture!"

"'Twill not be the first."

"Nor the last."

"Whatever it may be it is our only chance; and I would be dashed to atoms on a rock, or find a grave in the waters that roll beneath us, rather than that this scurvy, hypocritical ruffian should enjoy a single farthing."

The scurvy individual alluded to, who was lying on his back with his heels in the air, would have ground his teeth had he been able; as it was, he could only clench his bony hands in impotent despair.

Captain Hawk glanced towards him and turned towards the window.

The blast howled furiously, and the sea heaved and swelled under its influence.

"We have no police officers here dogging our steps," said Captain Hawk—"nothing but the winds and waters all around us."

"Have you the treasure?"

"It is here."

"Come, then, while the way of escape is open to us."

As the Black Highwayman spoke, he looked out of the cabin windows.

A sudden exclamation from him aroused his companion.

"What is the matter?" he cried, hastily.

"I no longer see the boat."

"Gone?—you can't mean that—your eyes must surely deceive you!"

"Look, then, and judge for yourself."

Captain Hawk looked out upon the dark waters.

It was a melancholy fact—the boat *was* gone.

He uttered an exclamation almost of despair.

"Alas!" he cried, "it is!"

He glanced upwards.

"No," he cried, suddenly—"not gone: it has only changed its locality. Now, instead of going *down* to the boat, we must go *up* to it."

Lord Harcliffe looked upwards.

It had been hauled up, and now hung suspended exactly over their heads.

There was a short pause of silence.

Captain Hawk soon came to a conclusion.

"One thing is certain," he said, "the boat cannot possibly come to us, we must go to the boat."

"That is impossible—at least, from this window!" said Lord Harcliffe.

"Decidedly."

"That is pleasant, then. Here we are caught like two rats in a cage: to remain is destruction—to depart is the same."

"I hope not."

"What do you propose?"

"A disguise."

"Disguise?"

"Yes."

"In what?"

"That!" pointing to the captain's heavy frieze coat.

"Yes—yes!" cried Lord Harcliffe, who caught at the idea. "It is our only possible chance."

"Fortune favours the bold, they say. We have experienced her smiles during the last twelve hours; surely she will not forsake us till we stand clear at least of this accursed vessel?" said Captain Hawk.

This plan, quickly conceived, was as quickly executed.

Captain Hawk in a moment enveloped himself in the pirate's thick pilot-coat.

Lord Harcliffe made free with another of similar texture that hung from a peg against the wall.

Two broad-brimmed waterproof hats completed their transformation completely.

The captain of the Redoubtable had yielded to the influence of the brandy and slumbered.

Clutching the treasure firmly, which he would have died rather than relinquished, Captain Hawk and Lord Harcliffe left the cabin, locking the door after them and taking the key.

They groped their way along in the dark and clambered upon deck.

All was dark there also.

The vessel rolled and pitched tremendously.

The wind, which had lulled a little a short time before, had burst forth with renewed fury, and now swept howling like a wild demon over the foaming waters, and made the masts and timbers of the pirate vessel shiver and creak like so many fragile reeds.

It was blowing a heavy gale.

The sailors on their watch did not evince any surprise at the appearance of the highwaymen on deck, owing to the darkness and the disguise they wore.

They were taken to be the captain and the first mate, consulting together as to the prospect of affairs on that terrible night.

All so far went well with them.

"Have you your knife with you?" asked Captain Hawk of his companion.

"Yes, but why?"

"Good! you will want it presently."

"For what?—what is your plan?"

"To pass the helmsman and clamber over the stern of the vessel into the boat."

"I see. And then——"

"When I give the signal we must cut away the ropes that hold the boat, and trust to Providence for its safe descent into the waves beneath."

Whilst this conversation was taking place on deck, the discomfited Louloupe had aroused from his lethargy, and by dint of great struggles had freed himself from his bonds.

Whether he swallowed the decanter stopper or not remained a matter of doubt; at all events it had disappeared from the captain's mouth.

The first use he made of his recovered freedom was to utter a yell of vindictive fury.

"Hang zem!—seize zem! Ovairboard vis zem! Ye

[CAPTAIN HAWK IS DISCOVERED SENSELESS ON THE SHORE.]

grands voleurs, ye dam robbairs! *Sacre milles tonnerres!*" he shouted. "Vhy ze devil don't some vun come?"

He rushed frantically to the door.

Of course it was locked, and the key in Captain Hawk's pocket.

"Diable! is it a mutiny zat I am lock in in zis vay? Ahoy, zere, vhere is my boots?"

He pounced upon his heavy sea boots like a hawk on its prey.

Seizing one, he pulled it on with a revengeful jerk, nearly crushing the unhappy monkey, who was curled up fast asleep, dreaming of cocoanuts, at the farthest extremity of the boot.

Whether or not Jacko took the captain's toe for a cocoanut we are not able to say, but certain it is that in return for the awful crunch he received, the monkey fastened upon it with a tremendous gripe.

"Oh, diable—*sacre bleu!*" roared the pirate. "Vot the devil is here?"

He drew out his foot from the boot, howling with pain, with the indignant Jacko firmly fastened to the end of it.

The captain kicked the monkey off furiously to the other extremity of the cabin, and threw the boot after him.

Then seizing a gun barrel that happened to be near, he dashed it repeatedly against the door till he burst it open.

It was only the louder tempest of the wind and sea that prevented this sound from being heard.

As soon, however, as the door gave way he raised his voice to its highest pitch, screaming:

"All hands on deck, you lazy scoundrels! All hands on deck, for your lives!"

This summons by some means or other contrived to reach the ears of the crew.

In ones, and twos, and threes, they came tumbling up from their berths, rubbing their eyes and blessing the captain.

Louloupe himself, surmising some daring attempt on the part of our heroes, rushed at once on to the deck, and hastened abaft, where the very first sight that presented itself to his view, aided by the light of the ship's lanterns, was the helmsman remonstrating with Captain Hawk and Lord Harcliffe upon the dangerous and peculiar post they desired to occupy.

Of course he knew nothing of their reasons for such a wish, and loudly condemned so insecure a station on such a stormy night.

The pirate recognised them at once as he approached.

"Hold zem! seize zem! Zey have rob me, ye *voleurs!*" he shouted, excitedly.

The crew, entirely ignorant as they were of the events that had occurred, most of them just aroused from their slumbers, and all of them literally in the dark owing to the obscurity of the night, looked here, there, and everywhere for something to seize, in a very hopeless manner, when just at the precise moment the monkey, Jacko, half scared out of his wits at the rough treatment he had received, made a desperate rush between their legs, over their shoulders, hissing and chattering frightfully, and finally taking refuge in the rigging.

The sailors catching sight of the terrified animal, at once concluded he was the object to be captured, and immediately gave chase.

Away flew Jacko up the rigging, and after him went the sailors, heartily cursing the unlucky pug, and vowing to wring his neck and throw him overboard the moment they caught him.

The captain seeing them disappear so suddenly, was in a fever of despair.

He quickly seized upon a sailor who was passing.

"Vhy ze devil don't you seize zese rascals?" he shouted, alluding to Captain Hawk and his companion.

"All right, your honour, we shall soon have him now," said the man, cheerfully, "but monkeys are slippery customers," and with these words he ran off.

Louloupe was in despair.

"You dam blockhead! It is not ze monkey zere, but ze monkeys here, I vant you to catch!"

But his words were swallowed up by the wind before they could reach the sailor.

Louloupe turned and glared upon Captain Hawk and the Black Highwayman.

He saw by the glance of their eyes they looked dangerous.

What was to be done?

He shouted to the helmsman.

"Barbelais, come here and help me to seize zese d—n Engleesh!"

But the man, who was struggling to keep the ship in her course during the terrific gale, dared not leave his post.

"I daren't leave the helm, captain, or if I do I will not answer for the ship," he said.

"Curse the ship!" roared the enraged pirate. "Do as I ordair you!"

The man left the helm, and at the same instant the vessel, unchecked, swung round with the hurricane.

There was a crash heard, mingled with a cry of terror.

The foremast had snapped in half like a stick of glass.

The helmsman, pale as death, that seemed now to hover over them, returned to his post and grasped the wheel in defiance of the captain's orders.

"I must remain here, captain," he cried, "or the ship will be lost."

Louloupe was tolerably convinced of this; but desperately resolved not to give up his prize without a struggle, he suddenly threw himself upon the Black Highwayman, who grasped him in return with an expression of intense scorn upon his features.

"It is no use your attempting to escape from me," cried the pirate, in a tone half blustering, half agitation.

Lord Harcliffe uttered a quiet laugh, and felt inclined to drop him over the vessel's side.

"Deliver up ze money you take from my cabin!" demanded Louloupe, in a fiercer tone, encouraged probably by the undemonstrative behaviour of his lordship.

But he was soon undeceived on this point, for the Black Highwayman suddenly shifted his hold from the collar of the pirate's coat to the throat of that personage.

"Hark you, miscreant!" he hissed in his ear: "If I were to tighten my grasp I should consign you to a fate you richly deserve, and save the hangman his labour; but at the present time we appear to listen to a mightier voice and to be reconciled by a mightier power than mine, that seems to hush the puny sounds of human strife and drown them into silence! Though you deserve punishment, I do not care to inflict it: the hour of retribution will come soon enough!"

Having uttered these words, he flung him from him as he would have done something utterly vile and worthless.

The pirate rolled over like a skittle-ball, and disappeared in the darkness.

Captain Hawk said to his friend:

"If we are to go at all, we must go now."

"Yes, confound it!" cried Lord Harcliffe. "But my knife has slipped by some means between the lining of my pocket and the coat itself, and for the life of me I cannot get at it."

"Every moment we remain here diminishes our chance of escape. Hark!" continued Captain Hawk, as the wind howled past in furious gusts. "Let us begone!"

The crew had by this time cut the broken mast clear from its tackle, and it now fell over the ship's side.

The captain, having partially recovered himself from the effects of the heavy fall he had received, staggered on to his feet, and shouted to the men.

"Come here, you rascals!"

The order was promptly obeyed.

"Zose men," cried the pirate, furiously, "have robbed me! Seize zem—put zem in irons!"

The sailors were about to advance, when the stern voice of Captain Hawk fell upon their ears and caused them to pause.

"Take my advice, and remain where you are! If you come nearer, you rush upon your own destruction!"

"Obey me!" screamed the captain. "And I ordair you to advance!"

But in spite of this not a man stirred.

The reason was obvious.

By the light of the ship's lantern every one of them clearly perceived the dark bulk of one of the stern guns, with its mouth pointed towards them, and Captain Hawk standing close by its side with a slow match in his hand.

During the pirates' absence they had dragged the formidable weapon from its usual resting-place.

It now interposed between the pursuers and the pursued.

"Remember," cried the captain to Louloupe, "you have set us the example. Remember the yacht—remember the poor fellows who fell beneath the fire of your murderous guns! Would it be more than common justice if I were to apply the spark I hold in my hand to the powder here, and scour the deck clear from such a band of water-rats?"

"You dare not!" cried the pirate. "You are a boaster—nothing more!"

"Try to approach me, and you'll see."

Nobody tried to approach.

If the truth must be told, most of them would gladly have retired.

"You are wise," continued Captain Hawk. "And now mark me: my friend and myself intend to leave this vessel, taking with us our property; and I warn you, if you in any way interfere with our intentions, you do it at your own cost."

He turned to Lord Harcliffe, and said, in a low tone:

"Have you found your knife?"

"Yes," was the reply.

"Then off we go!"

Captain Hawk dashed the lantern on the deck as he spoke, and all was darkness.

"Now, then, for the boat!" he shouted.

They clambered up, and in a few seconds found themselves swaying to and fro in the frail receptacle, with the treasure between them.

Their knives were open and firmly grasped.

"Stop zem!—zey vill escape!" roared the captain. "You d—n cowards, do you hear? Pouchelot—Beaudois, stop zem!"

Two sailors rushed forward and clambered up in a somewhat indefinite manner to arrest the departure of our heroes.

"Stop!" they cried. "It's the captain's orders that we seize——"

They had no time to utter another syllable, for the clenched fists of the highwaymen, delivered at random, sent them rolling back much quicker than they came.

Howling with pain, they fell down upon the deck.

Others advancing trod upon them as they lay, whilst some tumbled over their companions.

The confusion was general.

The wrath of the captain was tremendous.

The sailors, having nothing better to do, began to quarrel with one another, and their shouts and execrations mingled with the roar of the elements.

In the midst of this a calm, clear voice cried:

"Now cut away for dear life!"

There was a simultaneous slash from the two knives.

The ropes were cut, and the detached boat, descending, floated on the dark bosom of the waters, whilst the pirate vessel dashed onwards, leaving them in a few moments far behind.

CHAPTER CLVII.

CAPTAIN HAWK AND THE BLACK HIGHWAYMAN EXPERIENCE A GALE.—THE DEAD FACE IN THE CHEST.—A DISASTROUS TERMINATION TO A PERILOUS NIGHT.

AND there they were alone.

Alone in that small boat, beneath the black sky, and environed on all sides with boisterous and foaming waves!

They had neither mast, sail, nor oar.

The elements appeared to sport with and mock them.

They were like two little children in a rushing crowd.

Powerless—helpless!

But neither *hopeless* nor *despairing*.

It was so dark that neither could see the other's features.

But they had a kind of instinctive consciousness that each was looking at the other, so they sat face to face in the boat.

"Here, my friend," said Captain Hawk, who was the first to speak, offering the brandy-flask, "drink!"

Lord Harcliffe took the bottle, and the draught warmed and strengthened him.

There was great need of such support, for the night was bitterly cold.

The voice of the captain was cheery and firm, however, as he said:

"Well, Harcliffe, we tricked the pirate after all."

"Yes; he will have cause to remember us."

"The scoundrel! It was almost a pity to leave him without a token of regard in the shape of a bullet in his brains."

"It is of little consequence, and certainly not a matter of regret."

"You are right. There is always a peculiar retributive destiny hanging over the heads of such atrocious scoundrels."

"The treasure is safe?"

"It is here at my feet at the bottom of the boat."

"Safe, then, for the present—where it may be before the morning, who can tell?"

"Ah! who?"

Neither attempted to answer that question, though it is not unlikely that each could have formed a very probable opinion.

"It would be a pity, after all the vicissitudes we have gone through, to lose it, would it not?"

"It would, especially since the loss of the treasure implies the loss of something still more valuable—our own lives."

"I do not despair."

"Nor I: a small boat has been known to weather a heavier storm than this."

"Would it were morning! We should then be able to see better what our prospects are."

But there wanted many dreary, tedious hours ere the cold, gray dawn would steal over the angry sky.

The tempest-tossed men felt this.

An involuntary sigh broke from their lips.

"Phew!" exclaimed Captain Hawk, blowing his fingers, that were benumbed with cold. "I feel terribly hungry!"

"These cold winds, clear and fresh, are tantalising friends: they promote hunger, but provide nothing to eat."

"Stay!" cried the captain, as a hard substance in the pocket of the heavy coat he still wore struck against his leg. "What have we here? A bag of sea biscuits!" he exclaimed, joyfully.

Such was indeed the agreeable fact.

It is needless to add that the teeth of the famished highwaymen were speedily in motion.

In spite of their hardness and unsavoury quality, never were biscuits more delicious.

Having satisfied the cravings of hunger and applied themselves once more to the brandy-flask, they felt their courage revive.

They were nerved to endure.

And, indeed, they needed no little patience and resignation at that moment.

But highwaymen as they were, they were not without conscience.

Their daring and, to some extent, reckless life, though it had rendered them fearless and inured to personal danger, had not brutalised their feelings or hardened their hearts.

In that dark hour there came a voice within that made itself heard above the roaring of the storm as it whispered:

"*The hand that guides the furious elements is over and around you: whatever happens will be under its all-powerful control.*"

They felt this as they rose and fell with the swelling waves.

They had no idea of their destination.

The small boat was tossed this way and that in all directions.

The gold at the bottom and the weight of the two men acted as ballast and proved an advantage.

But for that it would infallibly have been upset at once.

"We have no resource but patience," said Captain Hawk, who was usually the first to break up the reveries into which they were continually falling. "That must be our motto."

"We shall drift eventually, I suppose, to land," remarked his friend. "If the storm abates we shall be safe, but to be driven on to a rocky coast on a night like this would be inevitable destruction."

"You are perfectly right, but in that case our best consolation would be that we lose our lives in a good cause—the effort to restore the orphan's right."

They looked out anxiously in all directions over the troubled waste, but they could see nothing.

The prospect was like eternity; no faint boundary line of horizon gleamed forth in the gloom on which their straining eyes could rest: all was darkness—thick darkness.

Above, below, around.

But suddenly a light appeared at some distance.

It was dim at first, and seemed like a red meteor miles and miles away.

"What can it be?" said Lord Harcliffe.

"I cannot imagine," replied the captain.

"It grows fainter—it has disappeared."

The disappearance was, however, only momentary.

Again the luminous object shone forth in the darkness.

"See, it is there again!"

The colour of the light seemed to deepen.

At first it had worn a copperish hue; now it was crimson.

The two solitary voyagers fastened their eyes upon this (to them) strange sight.

As they gazed, the meteor, or whatever it was, grew gradually brighter.

Was it fancy, or did they discern a kind of vaporous cloud that ascended from and surrounded it like a halo?

Each moment it increased in brightness.

Smoke was now apparent mingled with the light.

As if by mutual consent, they exclaimed together:

"It is a fire!"

"Or if not," remarked Captain Hawk, "it is some phenomenon—some *ignis fatuus* of the deep."

Their doubts were speedily set at rest.

As a strong gust of wind swept with renewed fury across the watery waste, a bright jet of flame and a shower of sparks shot upwards in the air.

There was no longer any doubt as to the cause of the sudden illumination.

The pirate ship was on fire.

The highwaymen recognised this fact at once.

As the flames increased in volume, the terrible reality was clearly revealed.

The bright light brought out into vivid distinctness like a picture in a dark frame the extent of the disaster.

The vessel might have been a mile away.

Her dark hull was distinctly defined, her port-holes and windows glowing as with a red-hot furnace within.

Her masts and tackle had not yet been attacked by the ruthless invader, that was now with rapid strides combining with its brother elements to consign to destruction this floating mass of iniquity.

"Her retribution has come upon her swiftly," cried the captain, as he watched the progress of the conflagration with intense interest, not unmingled, however, with some natural emotions of pain and regret.

"That captain was an unmitigated scoundrel," said Lord Harcliffe, who had entirely forgotten the perils that surrounded them in the contemplation of the scene.

"He was," returned Captain Hawk. "If it were he alone who was to suffer it would be no more than he deserves, but the other poor wretches——"

It was probably the sight that now presented itself that suggested this idea.

On the deck of the vessel, that now appeared much nearer than at first, the crew could be distinctly seen hurrying to and fro in great confusion.

"They will miss the boat," cried Captain Hawk, in a tone of regret.

He was by no means an unfeeling man, and had his power been equal to his will he would have guided the frail bark in which they rode under the very hull of the burning vessel.

He would have tried to save some at least, pirates as they were.

But that was impossible.

Both he and his companion were entirely at the mercy of the winds and waves.

The confusion on board seemed to increase.

Now a dense mass of smoke enveloped the ill-fated bark.

Gradually the red glare appeared through the thick vapour and consumed it.

They could almost fancy they heard the cries of the unhappy wretches.

What form was that gesticulating wildly on the deck?

Was it the pirate captain?

So our heroes thought.

They were not deceived.

Suddenly a dense volume of flame and sparks shot upwards in the air.

And at the same moment a wild ringing cry, an appalling heart-shriek, burst from the lips of the doomed victims.

There was no mistake about this.

Far above, or rather so widely different from the roar of wind and wave, was this despairing burst of human nature in its agony, that it forced itself upon the ear.

"What a fearful cry!" exclaimed Captain Hawk, with a shudder. "And see,"—pointing as he spoke where the liquid flames, having ascended from below in eagerness to complete their work of destruction, now seized upon the masts and rigging, up which they darted with eager avidity.

Ropes, masts, spars, blocks, all appeared instantaneously transformed into bright and burnished gold, and then as suddenly to fade away into black nothingness.

The appearance of the vessel at this moment was that of an immense tower of flame.

The conflagration had now reached its height.

The next instant a gust of wind came full upon the burning mass.

For an instant it seemed to struggle against the blast rebelliously, and then to topple over.

This was the mast falling.

Then came another dense mass of smoke, and after that a terrific report and a blinding flash of light, as a mingled shower of flame and sparks rushed up madly through the air, scattering their reflection far and wide across the waters, and then—

All was over.

There was nothing more to come.

The pirate ship was utterly annihilated

All was dark as before.

During this scene the feelings of the highwaymen had been considerably excited, and now the termination of the dreadful tragedy they had witnessed could but produce in their breasts a reaction that was unusually depressing.

The gale had in nowise abated, but still raised its ominous voice to chill their limbs and alarm their apprehensions.

"Would the morning were come!" was their repeated cry.

But alas! the night looked blacker than ever.

How helpless they felt!

If they had had an oar to have been able to make some kind of effort to progress, or even a compass to indicate the course in which they were being driven, it would have been some alleviation.

But to be thus compelled to, as it were, await their fate, whatever it might be, without a single struggle—to be passively driven unresistingly onwards they knew not where—was beginning to be unendurable.

At this juncture, however, the moon, by dint of a great effort, began to peer through a gap in the clouds at intervals.

The appearance of this luminary was in perfect harmony with the surrounding scene.

Her light was pale, faint, and sickly, and served if anything rather to add new terrors to the desolate waste than cheer it by her rays.

She seemed to the two highwaymen, as they gazed upon her melancholy light, to be quite a different moon altogether from that bright planet that had so often lighted up the bright summer nights and spread a heavenly beauty over the landscape, as they galloped along the high-road in quest of adventure.

Now she tinged the turgid waves with her cold light as though she took a malicious pleasure in displaying the cheerless prospect in its most depressing details.

They looked round on all sides.

Nothing was to be seen.

Not a single craft struggling in the distance.

"We seem to be alone in our distress," remarked Lord Harcliffe.

At this moment a wave dashed over them and almost capsized the boat.

"Phew!" gasped Captain Hawk, at the sudden shock, "I thought we had received our death-warrant then."

The thick coats in which they were enveloped proved highly serviceable under these unexpected assaults from the turbulent waves.

They at least kept them dry and comparatively warm.

Suddenly Lord Harcliffe called to his companion:

"Look! what is that?" pointing as he spoke to a dark object that seemed to be drifting towards them.

"I cannot discern at this distance," answered the captain.

"Is it a boat?"

"I hardly think so."

"It is nothing living—that would be impossible."

"And yet it seems to me I can see something moving."

"Could it be some poor, half-drowned, mutilated wretch from the pirate vessel? If so we must take him in, whatever befalls us."

"Decidedly."

The floating object, whatever it might be, still continued to approach.

They appeared to be in similar currents, and in their course to threaten to run foul of each other.

As the distance rapidly grew less and less, they began to be able to form an idea as to what it was.

It appeared to be a large chest.

"It *is* a chest," cried Captain Hawk.

"Undoubtedly," returned his companion; "and if I mistake not, the identical one in which we concealed ourselves."

"And what is that perched on the top?—is it an eagle or a vulture?"

The floating article was now within a few yards of the boat, and there was just sufficient light to prove that the highwaymen were right in their conjectures.

It was the chest, partially filled with water, and floating in an upright position, whilst the living object was none other than poor Jacko the monkey, who hung on, to use a poetical expression, *like grim death*, looking horribly frightened, shivering with cold, and chattering spasmodically.

The poor animal presented a very pitiable appearance, as though he had gone through a process of singeing, an operation by no means improbable considering the conflagration he had just escaped.

As the chest neared the boat the monkey appeared to be divided between his fears of its living occupants and of the waters that surrounded him.

However, as Captain Hawk spoke to him in a coaxing voice out of pity at his forlorn condition, and moreover held up a piece of biscuit, Jacko decided upon the boat, and as soon as he was sufficiently near, leaped on board, and greedily seizing the proffered biscuit, disappeared beneath the seats and nibbled it with great relish.

The chest was now alongside.

It floated backwards, the hinges being next to the boat.

The lid was partially open, some object interposing itself to prevent its shutting to.

What this was they soon discovered.

On turning the chest round, to their great horror they discovered the ghastly hindrance was a human head.

Its identity was unmistakable; it was the head of the pirate Captain Louloupe.

The body was in the chest, the head only protruding, and the lid had closed upon the neck and held it fast there.

It was livid with the unsightly hues of death, and the distortion of the features, the glaring eyes and protruding tongue, proved that it had been a violent one.

The highwaymen looked upon the horrible sight with far less emotion than they had previously upon the burning vessel.

"He has but met the fate he has doubtless often awarded to others," remarked Captain Hawk. "He was a cruel wretch, and I can but think his punishment was merited."

The exact means by which the pirate came to be in that position—or in the chest at all—were matters of surmise.

He might have been thrown overboard by the crew when all hope of saving the vessel was lost; or he might have seized upon the chest as a sanctuary for himself, the boat being gone, and have been seized with a faintness as he leaned over the side, in which case the lid closing as it did would have held him there, and speedily terminated his existence.

But whatsoever was the cause, *death* was the *effect*.

The man of clever brain was dead, and all that remained of him was a ghastly face and an enormous pair of moustaches, that bristled forth as if in mockery at the sardonic features they garnished.

The sight was not a pleasant one.

It was too suggestive of a violent and sudden death.

"Let us get this horrible object out of sight," said the captain; and as he spoke he with some effort raised the lid of the chest.

Thus released, the dead body fell down within the chest, never more to rise till the last dread judgment.

The lid then closed, hiding the wretched spectacle in its dark interior.

Captain Hawk, with a thrill of horror and disgust, thrust the chest from him, and it once more floated away with its unsightly burden, and was seen no more.

The moon, too, as though scared away by the pirate's ghastly face, veiled herself once more in the clouds.

It seemed now darker and more dismal than ever.

The tempest again burst forth in all its rage.

The wind thundered across the bosom of the sea with a fury nothing could resist.

"Heaven help us and all at sea this terrible night!" murmured Captain Hawk.

"Amen!" joined in his friend.

The awful peril of the moment evoked this petition.

A blinding shower of sleet, driven by the gale, dashed down like a legion of tiny arrows, so sharp and stinging was it as it assaulted the face and hands of the tempest-tossed.

Fresh agents, too, added their horrors to the scene.

The lightning flashed athwart the dark horizon, lighting up and appearing to pierce the foaming, angry waves, whilst the hollow thunder lent its voice to the elemental strife as it rolled through the vaults above.

The scene was frightful.

The small boat was dashed hither and thither with a fury that threatened utter destruction at any moment.

Its occupants evidently were making up their minds for the worst.

Throughout the whole of their tempestuous voyage they had not experienced anything like this climax of violence.

Clinging to the seats, it was as much as they could do to prevent being dislodged by the violent and sudden shocks they received.

"We shall never live through this night, Harcliffe," said Captain Hawk to his friend, in a subdued tone.

"I am afraid not," replied his lordship, in a voice equally serious. "I could never have imagined anything so tremendous, except, perhaps, on the wide bosom of the Atlantic."

"Well, we have done all we could. The responsibility is now out of our hands, and if our time has come we must meet it ——"

Ere he could finish this resigned apostrophe, Lord Harcliffe arrested his attention.

A white object floating on the surface of the waves was approaching.

What could it be?

At that time every event seemed to carry with it a certain significance.

They waited anxiously till the white object floated within reach.

They stretched forth their hands and grasped it.

It proved to be a piece of a broken yard with a remnant of drenched sail and rope attached.

"Of what use is this?" cried Lord Harcliffe, who was inclined to release his hold and let it float away.

"Do not let it go," said Captain Hawk. "I have had enough of this infernal floundering about, and I think I see in this a means of moving at least."

By his direction they dragged the timber on board the boat.

It was light, and occupied but little room.

They then wrung the water from the dripping sail as effectually as they were able, and then Captain Hawk said:

"I think we may be able to mount a sail, after all."

On examining the seats of the boat, they found a round hole in one towards the head, with a socket below, which had been made expressly for the purpose of rigging up a mast and small sail if occasion required it.

"This will do," cried the captain.

They accordingly, not without some difficulty, for the fierce wind seemed to throw all kinds of obstacles in their way, contrived to thrust the yard through the hole in the seat and lodge the extremity in the socket at the bottom of the boat.

To their great joy it stood firm.

At this moment Lord Harcliffe placed his foot on the toes of the monkey, who uttered a sharp yell.

"Confound it! What's that?" cried his lordship, who at the moment had forgotten their fellow-voyager. "Oh! the monkey! Poor Jacko! Never mind! Here, old fellow!"

The "old fellow" was chattering away and rubbing his damaged toe, but Lord Harcliffe made matters right by another piece of biscuit, which caused Jacko to subside into a state of placidity, and leave off rubbing to commence nibbling.

The sail flapped to and fro furiously, and for some time obstinately refused to be caught.

At length, however, this was accomplished, and the corners of the sail made fast to two pieces of rope that had been attached to the yard.

The spiteful wind had now something to work upon, and blew upon the sail with all its force.

The boat felt it immediately, and began to go—not onwards, but *round*.

Captain Hawk smiled.

But at that moment a heavy gust took the sail, and one of the corners tore away.

It was fortunate it did so, or the boat would have inevitably capsized.

The captain's smile terminated in a sigh of disappointment.

Both he and his companion understood the nature of horses far better than the conduct of a boat.

"I wish we were on dry land, my dear friend," he said, "mounted on Satan and Phantom: we should know how to manage them."

"Ah!" uttered the Black Highwayman, with a responsive sigh.

"Well, we must try again, and bring a little common sense to bear upon the case," said the captain, grasping the corner of the sail that had torn away, and pulling it in while he fastened it once more to the rope, the end of which he still retained in his hand.

Again the boat moved—*round*.

It seemed like a skittish, playful nag, if such a term may be used in connection with a scene so fraught with danger.

Round and round they went.

But that was the only result—they made no onward progress.

A sense of the ridiculous even at that moment seized upon the highwaymen.

"Hang it!" cried Captain Hawk. "This will never do! We cannot go on describing circles all night in this manner."

They both laughed—positively laughed.

The captain paused a moment reflectively.

He had on one occasion been brought into the company of nautical men, and remembered some of their expressions.

"We must get her head to the wind," he said at last, in an assumed tone of professional conviction.

"What is that?" inquired Lord Harcliffe.

"I'm not exactly prepared to explain what it is, but we must do it," was the answer.

"It seems to me," remarked Lord Harcliffe, who was rather amused—or at least as much as he could be under the circumstances—"that she has her head to the wind, and her tail too, for that matter—in fact, there seems nothing else but wind everywhere."

The captain laughed outright.

The Black Highwayman joined him.

"Let us fortify ourselves with a sup of brandy."

The suggestion was immediately acted upon.

"Now, then, let us see what we can do in the art of navigation," said the captain, tightening the rope and pulling in the sail, which bellied out in the wind.

Again the circular motion was imparted.

"We must get the wind more behind us."

"One should take the rudder: I believe much depends on that."

"True; that shall be your post."

Lord Harcliffe at once shifted his seat and grasped the tiller, keeping it perfectly steady.

This step had a powerful influence upon the boat, which no longer indulged in pranks or described circles, but darted forwards, as though relieved to be once more in motion.

But whatever sensations the boat might have experienced, it is certain those of our heroes were extremely joyful.

It was comparative happiness to be scudding along over the foaming billows as though they were running a race, instead of lying passively and helplessly to be knocked about just as they thought proper.

Like an arrow from a bow, the tiny craft bearing our two navigators sped onwards.

"This is delightful!" cried Captain Hawk, exultingly.

The jaded spirits of these adventurous men rose with the excitement, and made them for a time forget the sense of weariness and exhaustion that was beginning to creep over them.

"If we go on at this rate, we shall certainly reach somewhere before long," remarked the Black Highwayman.

The indefinite *somewhere* rather grated on Captain Hawk's ears and suggested something unpleasant.

"I should like to know where we are going, though," he remarked, looking out upon the dark waste. "We must be in the Channel, I should think, undoubtedly."

"I think so too. Well, we shall have the daylight here before long, and may then be able to judge."

At this moment a violent gust caused the frail mast to bend and quiver as though it would have broken.

It resisted bravely, however, and almost simultaneously a vivid and prolonged flash of lightning blazed across the entire firmament.

The glare lighted up the scene with terrible distinctness.

The character of the waters appeared changed.

Dark objects, more solid and opaque than the gloomy sky, appeared to rear their heads upwards.

The sounds of the dashing waves appeared altered, being less hollow, as though they met with some solid resistance.

They could also discern, when the next flash afforded them the opportunity, that the waters at no great distance were covered with foam as white as snow.

They had heard of rocks and breakers, those terrors of the mariner, and it struck them as a passing thought that they might be near the shore, and that the white foam they had seen was caused by the dashing of the angry waves against the rocks.

Still onward they sped, borne by the furious wind, not at all alarmed at their supposed proximity to the land.

They felt assured, because they knew not their peril.

It seemed a pleasant idea, after buffeting the waves through that long, dark, boisterous night, to feel they were near their kindred element once more—perhaps within hail of the sound of a human voice.

Had they known *where* they were at that moment—had their eyes have been opened to a sense of their perilous position, they would rather have exchanged it for one miles and miles away, out of the reach of—

"Merchant marring rocks."

Still, no mishap had as yet occurred.

Again the lightning overspread the scene, causing a loud cry, not of terror, but joy, from the lips of Lord Harcliffe.

"A ship yonder!" he cried, pointing to the starboard.

His companion sprang up, clinging to the mast to steady himself; and by the light of another electric flash plainly descried a vessel, as his lordship had intimated.

She appeared to be a schooner, and was evidently labouring under the violence of the gale, as she was lying-to under bare poles.

The two highwaymen shouted at the top of their voices, and before long they were answered by a solitary gun.

"That is the signal that she hears us," said the captain, grasping the hand of his friend, the tears almost starting to his eyes, so strong was the revulsion of feeling.

The Black Highwayman cordially returned the pressure.

The crew of the schooner had observed them with their night glasses, but dared not venture nearer in shore on that rock-bound coast, and the swell was so tremendous they hesitated to launch a boat.

The vessel lay to their left, and presently sent up a rocket to guide them.

"We must try and reach her," cried the captain.

Lord Harcliffe endeavoured to the best of his judgment to guide the boat, and so far succeeded that the frail machine was leaving the shore and in a fair way of reaching the schooner.

But at this moment bright torch-lights were seen flashing on the shore, and that seemed to promise a nearer and a safer shelter.

They could discern figures — honest fishermen, no doubt—looking out to render their assistance to some poor shipwrecked castaway.

They heard their cheering shouts.

They shouted in return.

The schooner was forgotten.

They turned the boat's head towards the shore, and approached rapidly, bounding over the crested waves safely and triumphantly.

"This will be a night to be remembered," said the captain, who still stood upright in the boat waving his hand towards the shore.

"I never thought to have looked again upon the face of the bright sky or that of my fellow-man," answered Lord Harcliffe.

"Yohoy—hoy—hoy!" came from the shore.

"Do you hear that? We're safe now. Yohoy--hoy—hoy!" cried Captain Hawk, exultingly, in return.

That was the last word spoken, for scarcely had the exclamation died upon his lips when, with a frightful crash, the boat ran headlong on a rock, shivering into twenty fragments.

The collision was fatal—the destruction complete.

There was a faint cry heard.

After that a voice gasping, and another voice answering, and then silence, save the roaring of the wind that kept on its wild yells as fiercely as ever.

CHAPTER CLVIII.

THE WRECKERS.—CAPTAIN HAWK IS DRIVEN ASHORE.—THE GUARDIAN ANGEL.

"Come now, Morna dear, why don't you answer me?"

"I have answered you, Dan. What more would you have me say?"

"I would have you say that you love me, Morna!—love me as I would wish to be loved—love me as I love you!"

"Ah! you want me to say so much—you forget women have the privilege of thinking more than they speak."

"I know—I know; if I did not, I should be the most miserable of men, for since you never tell me you love me, I am obliged to comfort myself with the hope that, at all events, you do not hate me."

"Hate you, Dan?"

"Well, perhaps that is a strong word; but then I don't acknowledge intermediate expressions. I only know of *two* words—love and hate—and I judge by myself. With me, if it is not one, it is the other."

These words were spoken by a powerfully-built young man to a girl as she lingered on the threshold of a poor cabin on the coast of Cornwall.

The locality was not very far distant from Penzance, and situated between the Lizard Point and the Land's End.

They were evidently lovers.

Though from the manner of the girl it would seem that the affection that existed between them was somewhat one-sided, being stronger in the breast of her companion than her own.

Daniel Macorrie was a young man of about five-and-twenty years of age, dwelling with his father in a cabin in the vicinity.

Born and bred upon the wild coast of Cornwall, and early inured to face the drenching spray and the strong winds that blew from the sea, his complexion, though healthful, was bronzed and tanned by exposure to the elements.

He was not more than about the middle height, but exceedingly muscular, his frame being modelled after the statue of Hercules rather than Apollo.

There was, however, a pleasant expression in his features, unless when irritated or vexed, and then they wore, in addition to the frown of anger, a dogged sullenness that betokened a spirit within capable of brooding over an injury and perhaps resenting it.

Still, on ordinary occasions, his well-shaped head, joined to a pair of broad shoulders by a neck powerful and muscular, and a profusion of crisp auburn curls that contrasted well with his light bluish-gray eyes, gave him favour in many a quarter amongst the young girls of his class.

But he cared for no woman's smile save that of Morna Trevellyn.

Morna was in every way different from her ardent, Herculean young suitor.

She, too, like him, had been as long as she could remember accustomed to the wild rocks and the constant murmur of the restless waves as they dashed upon the perilous shore of the Cornish coast.

But her father, Hugh Trevellyn (Black Hugh, as he was called from the darkness of his hair and eyes) had not always lived there.

He had suddenly appeared on that uninviting spot some twelve years before, bringing his only child Morna, then five years old, and a mysterious history of the past, with him, on which all in the neighbourhood commented, but of which none knew anything definitely.

But Hugh was different from those rude, rough spirits by which he was surrounded.

His manner, language, and bearing all evinced one who had seen better times and moved in a very different sphere.

There was that about him that claimed superiority and gained it.

He was an educated man, and being of a kind though reserved temperament, he soon acquired the respect as well as confidence and love of his neighbours.

In many points resembling her sire—especially in the dark eyes and hair—Morna grew and flourished in the humble cabin where she dwelt, and sprang up from a pretty child into a lovely maiden.

For miles round all the young men swore by the black eyes of Morna, whilst she, unconscious of the wondrous charms she possessed—which ignorance added to them considerably—had reached her seventeenth year with her heart entirely untouched by the blind urchin's dart.

Above the middle height, her limbs had that charming roundness, and her step that graceful elasticity, that health and exercise alone can give; whilst her pure white skin, rendered still fairer from the contrast with her raven tresses and dark eyes, soft and dreamy in their expression, would often incline the casual beholder, as she stood on some rocky crag gazing out upon the sea, to fancy he looked upon some being of another sphere.

She, like her father, was superior to her companions.

Hugh Trevellyn was no mean scholar, and he had taken much pains to cultivate his daughter's mind, so that, in addition to her stately beauty, she held the pre-eminence that education alone can give.

Between Hugh Trevellyn and Andrew Macorrie, the father of Daniel, there had grown up a close intimacy. Their ostensible occupation was that of fishermen; but as the boats were often high and dry upon the beach at the very time when the fishing season was at its height and the wind most favourable, ill-natured people hinted that smuggling was far more profitable than fishing, and that very little of the goods landed at certain times in the narrow creek had paid duty at the Custom House.

There were also darker rumours afloat.

It was said that these men, on that isolated spot, followed the barbarous trade of wreckers.

It was averred that many a gallant bark had been lured on to the formidable rocks by their false lights, and that remorseless murder and rapine had completed the fatal picture.

But even were this true, no one who gazed for an instant on the wondrous spiritual loveliness of Morna would have thought of accusing her of connivance in such nefarious and horrible deeds.

Purity, gentleness, and truth were written on her fair brow, and, what was better still, enshrined in her heart.

No wonder, then, that Daniel Macorrie, the son of her father's friend, loved her, or that he looked upon her with a jealous eye that threatened evil to any daring rival who should attempt to oppose him.

Morna received his attentions passively, because she believed her father approved them.

But there was no emotion in her feelings for Daniel. Whatever she felt for him had been of quiet, gradual, imperceptible growth, and had become one of those matter-of-course circumstances that yielded no excitement.

Morna beheld her lover approach without a blush, and bade him farewell without a sigh.

His presence caused her no unusual pleasure—his absence created no regret.

This was strange.

Surely a being so far beyond ordinary women in her great beauty could not be so far beneath them in the feelings of the heart!

It was impossible she could be always so cold and passionless as she appeared.

More than one jealous rival had not scrupled to accuse her of hypocrisy, cunning, and deceit.

But it was not so.

Morna was as free from these detestable vices as truth itself could be.

In fact, it was her natural self that spoke in her manner.

Had she been a hypocrite, she might have feigned a passion she did not feel.

If she did not show her love, it was because she was a stranger to its power.

That this was the case may be inferred from her replies at the commencement of this chapter.

Far different was it with Daniel Macorrie.

His heart burnt within him beneath the sunlight of her beauty.

She was the "god of his idolatry"—the guiding star he worshipped.

His rough, fierce, jealous nature would have clasped the gentle blossom in the strong arms of his love, and been at rest could she have returned it.

He had wooed her now for three years, and was beginning to grow weary of courtship.

"Come, Morna," he continued, after a pause, "there's never any good comes of these long courtships. Why not let us name the day?"

"What day?"

"Our wedding-day, of course! What other day could I mean?"

"Oh!" cried Morna, with a slight laugh, "there's no need to hurry for that."

Daniel was displeased at this remark, and bit his lip till the dark, angry flush covered his face.

"But there is need!" he exclaimed, passionately. "I can't go on loving and waiting month after month and year after year as you do! Our natures are different: you are all ice—I—I am all fire!"

"I thought you were getting rather hot all of a sudden," said Morna, quietly. "But don't be angry, Daniel: icy as I am, I daresay I shall do my duty if I ever become your wife."

"If you become? Of course you will!"

And in the great delight this prospect afforded him, the young man threw his arm round the maiden and kissed her.

Morna offered no objection—she never did.

"Ah!" continued Daniel, "if you loved me a thousandth part as well as I love you, how happy I should be!"

"Happy!" screamed a shrill, harsh voice near at hand—"happy! Ha, ha, ha! What happiness can there be for him who is a murderer himself, and in whose veins runs the blood of murderers? Happy! Ha, ha, ha!"

The young man started and turned pale.

Morna noticed his sudden pallor.

"It's only poor Mad Cassy—don't heed her," cried the young girl.

"Ah, girl, you're right: it's only poor mad Cassy; but mad people speak the truth sometimes in spite of their madness."

The speaker advanced as she uttered these words.

She must have been between seventy and eighty years old.

Her hair, white as snow, hung in elf locks over her shoulders.

Her features, wan and attenuated by age and suffering, looked sharp and ghastly.

Her back was bent, so that she could not stand upright, but stood leaning upon a staff, turning her head on one side, in order to address those to whom she spoke.

She now fixed her large gaunt orbs upon the young man with fierce intensity.

"What have you to do with such as her?" she cried, pointing towards Morna with an arm and finger almost withered to a skeleton. "Would you poison the purity of her thoughts—would you mingle her bright blood with the foul stream of yours? Begone, thou son of a murderer—begone!"

Daniel Macorrie looked as though, had he been unwitnessed, he would have struck the old woman dead at his feet.

It is not at all improbable he would have done so, but he dared not give vent to his passion in the presence of the woman he loved.

He ground his teeth, however, as he growled, harshly:

"Begone, mad fool! you know not what you say!"

"Do I not?" shrieked the old creature. "Do you think, then, that memory is quite dead within me? It is you who are mad, if you say that! Years—long, dreary years have passed since that night; but I remember it as distinctly as if it were yesterday. I had a beloved husband then, and a darling son, and I was young and beautiful. Ha—ha! Where are all these treasures now—where's my husband, child, youth, beauty? Gone—all gone! And I alone remain to mourn for them. But I'll mourn no longer," cried the old woman, hurriedly: "it will not bring them back—neither the dead nor the past can ever return again to me; but there will come a day of reckoning for you and yours," shrieked the hag, glaring fiercely at Daniel. "Your hands are red with blood, so are your father's. Avoid him—avoid him! There's a curse upon his house—his path—his life; and he will bring the curse down upon the heads of all who join him! Away—away—away!"

With these words uttered at the top of her voice, the crone hobbled away in the darkness.

Daniel remained looking after her, muttering curses "not loud but deep."

"That old witch has lived too long!" he said, mentally.

"The words of poor old Cassy have disturbed you, Dan," remarked Morna; "but you know they are the words of one distraught. You must forget them."

"Oh, I don't heed her mad ravings," cried the young man, with an affectation of carelessness. "If it does her good to vent her imprecations on my head, it does me no harm."

At this moment a gun echoed from the sea.

"A signal!" he murmured, to himself.

"Good-bye for the present, dear Morna," he said.

"Good-bye, Dan. It is a rough night. Be careful!"

"I would if I thought it made any difference to you."

"I would not have any harm come to anyone if I could help it, much less to one I—" she paused suddenly, and then continued—"who is to be my husband."

This thought seemed to reassure Daniel Macorrie.

He pressed her hastily to his breast, and kissed her fervently.

"God bless you!" he cried.

The next minute she was alone.

"I wonder whether she cares for me?" he soliloquised, as he went along. "I don't think she does much."

This conversation was going on at the very time when Captain Hawk and the Black Highwayman were tossing on the waves in their frail bark.

It was the gun fired by the schooner that had attracted the notice of Daniel Macorrie and taken him from the side of his beloved.

It was, as our readers are by this time well aware, a fearful night at sea—it was also a boisterous night on land.

Morna stood alone in the old cabin (her father was away), listening to the fierce wind and the distant roar of the angry waves, mingled with the thunder over her head.

The lightning flashed brightly in at the window enough to have appalled some delicate young ladies.

But Morna was accustomed to nature in her angry moods, and so instead of burying her face in her hands, or going into hysterics, she stood for some time watching the electric fluid as it lighted up the heavens with its dazzling glare, and then calmly heaped fresh fuel on to the hearth ready against her father's return.

She heard the distant shouts of the men upon the beach.

"What is the matter?" she thought. "It is a wreck, I fear. Poor creatures!"

She turned again to the window, thinking what a ter-

[THE ATTEMPTED MURDER OF CAPTAIN HAWK.]

rible fate it must be to be exposed to the ocean's fury on such a fearful night.

Just at that moment a bright blue light shot up in the air. It was the schooner's signal.

"It *is* a wreck!" she cried. "Oh! would I could save them!"

A knock was heard at the door.

She opened it at once.

Old Cassy, her white hair streaming in the wind, stood on the threshold.

She entered at once, without ceremony.

"Did you hear?—did you see?" inquired the old woman.

"I did," answered Morna, sadly.

"It is the night of fifty years ago come back again! If so," continued the hag, wildly, "I shall see my husband and my boy! They'll be much changed in fifty years: my Richard's hair will be white—white as mine; and my pretty, fair-haired boy will be a man. Ha, ha! They will not seem the same to me—no, no!"

She paused abruptly.

"What am I saying?" she cried, pressing her hand to her forehead. "If I rave thus, I shall begin to think I am as mad as people say I am."

"Be calm, Cassy," said Morna, gently.

"I am, darling—I am now," the old woman answered, in a subdued tone. "It is only at times I cannot control myself."

She crouched down by the glowing hearth and warmed her hands.

A loud peal of thunder crackled and rolled over their heads.

The old cabin shook again.

"There is a wreck to-night, isn't there, Cassy?" inquired Morna.

"Ay, my child," the old woman answered, sorrowfully, "more than one — much more. Many a poor mother's heart will ache because of to-night; and the hungry sharks will rejoice in the prospect of their dainty meals."

"It must be dreadful to be wrecked at sea," said the young girl.

"It is dreadful! To see the waste of waters all around you—death—cold death—above, below, everywhere—to know that as the ship breaks up, plank by plank, each one brings you nearer to your doom!"

'Horrible!"

"But there is a worse fate—a more dreadful destiny than that!" the hag continued.

"What can be worse?" asked Morna.

"It is worse," replied the old woman, glaring upon her questioner with strange intensity, "to escape the fury of the winds and waves—to reach the shore, thanking Heaven for your safety, to find a band of murderers, far more pitiless than rock or storm, waiting to take the life Heaven's mercy has preserved!"

"Murderers?" echoed the young girl, on whose ears the ominous word had fastened.

"Ay, murderers!" shrieked the old woman—"such murderers as are now there!"—pointing, as she shouted, from the window in the direction of the beach—"murderers like old Andrew Macorrie—murderers like his son—murderers like them all!"

Morna uttered a cry.

The idea was insupportable.

"You are mad, old woman!" she exclaimed, fiercely. "No more! I do not believe you!"

"Go, then—believe your own eyes, though you do not my words. Go—go—in darkness and in silence! You will believe me ere you return."

"I will!" cried Morna, desperately, as she rushed from the cabin into the dark, tempestuous night.

Loud shouts rang out along the dreary shore.

Fierce, rough-looking men congregated upon the slippery rocks, holding on to the craggy points and flashing their torches over the sea.

The scene was one of terrible sublimity.

Close in shore was a mass of snow-white foam, boiling and bubbling like the scum of a cauldron.

Beyond this, like dark, discoloured fangs, rose the sharp, jagged rocks, over and between which the sea rushed and dashed with sportive ferocity.

As far out as the eye could reach was a mass of swollen waves.

Dark leaden clouds hung over it like a pall.

At quick intervals this vast canopy appeared to be rent asunder and ripped into fragments by the electric fluid, which the thunder followed with its deafening ordnance. The shouts of the men on the shore appeared like the faint cries of children in comparison.

Amongst these were Andrew Macorrie, his son Daniel, and—must we say it?—Hugh Trevellyn.

Yes! It was, alas! too true.

Their present positions and employment left no doubt as to the fatal nature of their terrible trade—

WRECKERS!

They were anxiously watching the schooner—

Praying impiously in their hearts that she might run upon the rocks.

It was at this moment the boat came in sight that contained Captain Hawk and Lord Harcliffe.

Their proceedings and the destruction of their boat have been already described.

With feelings of horror and anguish no tongue could express Morna, shrouded in the shadow of the rocks, heard sufficient to prove the truth of poor old Cassy's accusation, and the fearful and guilty traffic in human life in which her own father—that father who had educated and tended her so carefully, and who had always led her by his precepts to choose good and reject evil—and her future husband were engaged.

She witnessed with an agony of horror the destruction of the frail boat, and at that moment, breathing a fervid prayer to Heaven that she might be able to gratify the strong yearnings of her compassionate nature by saving even *one* life, she hastily flew rather than ran back to the cottage.

The old woman still crouched over the blazing faggots. She looked up as Morna entered.

"You are right, Cassy—you are right!" cried the agitated girl. "They are, as you say, all m-murderers!—father!—lover!—all!"

She spoke with hesitation, in short gasps, and then burst into an agony of tears and sobs.

"Don't weep, poor child!" said old Cassy, gently, "you may save some—*you* may!"

"Ah, yes!" cried Morna, recollecting her errand and dashing away her tears. "I must—I will save one at least. God grant I may!"

She seized a torch composed of pitch and rope, that stood in a corner of the cabin, and lighting it at the fire, hurried out.

Down to the rocks she flew like an angel of mercy to avert the fell blow of the destroyer!

Trembling in every nerve with the intense desire to preserve human life, yet fearless for herself, the intrepid girl sprang boldly from rock to rock.

Staggering, slipping, gasping, clutching the wet, slimy crags, she held her beacon light over the foaming waves.

But, alas! without success.

No struggling swimmer met her gaze.

She raised her voice and called aloud, but no voice answered in return.

"They are lost! — they are lost!" she cried, despairingly.

At this moment, a dark form, that resembled a human body, appeared, driven and hurled by the billows towards the shore.

A cry of hope burst from her lips.

"Was it indeed a human being?"

"Yes."

Nearer and nearer it came—ruthlessly impelled forwards till at last the foaming tide drove violently on to a ledge of rock beneath her feet the drenched and lifeless body of a man.

"Thank God for this!" she cried, sinking upon her knees—"thank God!"

CHAPTER CLIX.

CAPTAIN HAWK IS TAKEN TO THE WRECKERS' CABIN.—LOVE AND JEALOUSY.—THE CAPTAIN RECEIVES A MIDNIGHT INTRUDER AFTER HIS OWN FASHION.

Her prayer was brief, for it was now a time for action.

Cautiously descending to the spot on which the senseless form rested, she gazed for a moment anxiously on the pallid features.

In the flickering light of the torch, shaken and broken as it was by the wind, the lineaments appeared convulsed.

One moment they seemed to smile in sarcastic mockery, the next they wore a dark, heavy frown.

But this was fancy merely, kindled into existence by the excitement of the young girl's brain.

The unfortunate Captain Hawk was at that moment past either smiling or frowning.

He lay perfectly passive and motionless, his handsome features very pale, with dark, drenched hair, tangled and matted with sea water, falling over his brow, from which a thin stream of dark blood oozed, the wound having been caused by contact with the merciless edges of the sharp rocks.

"Poor fellow!" ejaculated Morna, "how handsome he looks, even in his wretched plight! He still lives, I think—pray Heaven he does! He must be removed from here, but I have not strength, and if I ask help from those who——"

She paused and looked round anxiously.

What she had seen and heard that night made her fatally apprehensive.

She grasped the captain's arm, and exerting all her strength, dragged him some distance further on to the piece of table rock that formed his cold resting-place.

"At all events, he will be safe here for a few moments the waves will not wash him back," she cried.

Her mind seemed to have settled on a course of action, as, with a parting glance, she retraced her way to the beach.

The wreckers were there still, looking out like vultures scenting blood in the atmosphere.

They had seen the boat dashed to pieces against the rocks, but they gave little heed to that.

Two human lives were to them nothing.

It was the schooner on which their eyes were fastened.

They had hoped by the light of the torches they carried to have lured her on to the rocks, but they were deceived.

"Will she move?" cried the elder Macorrie.

"I doubt it," answered another.

"She has cast anchor where she rides: there is good anchorage there: she knows a trick worth two of running in among these rocks," joined in a third.

The wreckers were evidently chagrined at the perfect comprehension the schooner appeared to have of her position.

"You may make up your minds," said Hugh Trevellyn, who had not yet spoken, "you'll get nothing out of her."

A growl of discontent followed this announcement.

It had not died away when Hugh felt a light but nervous pressure on his arm.

He turned.

"Father!" exclaimed a voice, in a low, hurried tone.

He recognised it at once.

"Morna——"

"Hush! do not let them hear! Come with me now, this moment!"

Constraining her father with gentle force, she drew him away to some little distance where a cluster of rocks interposed themselves.

"You here, my child, at this hour! What brings you?"

"A matter of life and death, father," interrupted Morna. "Here is a poor man thrown on to the rocks; he lives still, I think; but if he be left in his present state, must soon die from cold and exhaustion."

"He would not be the first who has perished on these rocks," said her father, coldly.

"But he must not be allowed to perish—that would be very cruel while it is in our power to save him."

"What can we do?"

"Much—much! At least, let us do what we can!"

She spoke earnestly, and clasped her father by the arm.

"Come and judge for yourself," she cried. "From his appearance he is no ordinary person."

At these words, Hugh accompanied his daughter.

They soon reached the rock on which the Captain lay.

Hugh knelt down, and by the light of the torch his daughter held over his head, examined the unconscious stranger.

He raised his head and placed his hand upon his heart.

"He is dead," he said, quietly; "nothing can be done."

"No, father," exclaimed Morna, "he is not dead—or if he be, let us at least give him decent burial."

A frown overspread the face of Hugh Trevellyn.

"My dear child, you should have remained at home," he said; "you are unaccustomed to such spectacles as this. The sight of this pale face has awakened a feeling of interest in your young heart which can neither benefit yourself nor the object of your solicitude."

"Oh, father, but to leave him lying there!" she cried, pleadingly. "Oh, help him, for my sake!"

"For your sake? Why, what is he to you?"

"Nothing certainly, but—— Well, then, father, for the sake of charity, that you have often told me is the greatest of all virtues, let us help this poor man."

The parent was embarrassed at this home pleading.

He could not in his practice utterly give the lie to what he had by precept so endeavoured to instil into the heart of his beautiful child.

Besides, he began to feel a sentiment of pity stealing over him as he gazed on the prostrate form.

Morna saw that he was moved, and hastened to follow up the advantage she had gained.

"How happy it will make you, dear father, to see this poor young man revive under your roof," she said.

"My roof?"

"Yes. We must remove him there."

"You consider that a sanctuary—a place of safety?"

"Yes, father."

"Alas! she little knows——" murmured Hugh, with a sigh.

Morna heard his words.

"I *do* know," she quickly ejaculated. "Oh, father, I have this night learnt the fatal secret, that makes me doubly, trebly anxious you should save this stranger. It would be a comfort to you—a balm to your conscience—to feel that he owed his life to you."

"I fear," he thought, rather than spoke, "I should but imperil him. Better to let him die here where he lies, than restore him to meet perhaps a second death from the remorseless hands that—— And yet it is a pity too!"

"This young stranger may have parents," continued Morna; "he may be the hope of a fond father, the idol of a loving mother. Even now they may be awaiting his coming. Oh, father, let them not hope in vain!"

She threw her beautiful arms round her parent as she spoke.

The dark, stern man was moved.

A tear stood in his eye. He remembered, years back, when it pleased Heaven to remove his only son, and what a blank that loss left in his heart.

Morna saw the tear, and knew then that mercy had not forsaken her parent's bosom.

She felt that her point was gained.

Hugh Trevellyn passed his hand across his eyes rapidly to dash off the rising tears.

"He shall not die if I can save him," he uttered, in a broken voice; and then, as if to himself: "But how to convey him to my cabin unseen by the others? Well, I must make the effort at least."

Steadying himself on the slippery rock, he leant down and raised the captain's head, then gradually drawing the body towards him, so that the upper portion hung over his shoulder, he grasped a jutting crag and dragged himself on to his feet.

It was a most critical position.

Encumbered as he was with the weight of the highwayman, it required almost superhuman strength to keep his footing on the slimy rock, much less to step from point to point till he reached the level shore.

However, he summoned all the energies of a strong will and a powerful frame to the task, and in a short time he stood with his heavy burden in a place of security.

His companions, occupied with their scrutiny of the anchored schooner, had not noticed his absence.

It was necessary his present undertaking should be kept a secret if possible.

"Extinguish your torch, Morna," he said. "In the darkness we may pass on unnoticed."

Morna instantly obeyed, but at the moment the moon broke forth from the clouds, and lighted up his path. No shout or voice of recognition hailed him, however, and he went on as rapidly as possible, followed by Morna, whose eyes were fastened on the stranger's dark, tangled hair and white hand as it swayed to and fro with the impetus of her father's footsteps.

At length the cabin was gained.

Old Cassy still crouched over the fire, mumbling to herself.

"Ha, ha!" she screamed, excitedly, as they entered, "he has come at last! Did I not say he would?"

She watched anxiously whilst Morna spread a thick rug on the ground before the fire and placed a pillow for the head of the stranger, who was now placed in a recumbent position on this hastily-constructed but not uncomfortable couch.

She then peered anxiously in his face.

"No, no—this is not my husband!" she cried. "My dreams deceived me: he will never come back—never! never!"

"Cease these ravings, Cassy," said Hugh; "we wish the presence of this stranger to be a secret."

"From the rest?"

"Yes."

"I understand."

"You will be silent, will you not, Cassy?" asked Morna, gently.

"Silent as the grave!" answered the old woman. "Wandering as my wits are at times—mad as they say I am—I know how to keep a silent tongue, or I had not been here at this moment. I'll be quiet—I'll be quiet."

Having uttered these words, she glanced once more at the pale features before her, and went out.

Hugh, having placed a bottle of strong Highland whisky on the table, and given some directions to his daughter, followed.

Morna was alone.

It would be impossible to define the exact nature of her sensations as she gazed upon the placid features of the captain as he lay there unconscious, in a state that appeared neither death nor sleep, but a mingling of both.

Certain it is her countenance wore an expression of profound solicitude.

A smile passed over her lovely face—a smile of hope like a sunbeam—as she fancied the features on which she gazed looked less pinched and ghastly than before.

She carefully and tenderly washed the clotted blood from the captain's face, and wiped his drenched hair.

Then pouring some spirit into a glass, she raised his head and allowed a little to trickle down his throat. She then bathed his temples with the same liquor, and chafed his cold hands between her own to endeavour to restore circulation.

This attention and the genial warmth of the fire were successful.

The colour came into the pallid cheek.

By slow degrees consciousness returned; but the captain's brain was weak, and as yet incapable of recalling the past distinctly.

His mind wandered—he was as one in a dream.

"Harcliffe," he murmured, "look! do you not see the beacon lights? I see them!—there—there! How the boat darts through the waves! We are close on shore! Keep clear of that rock! So—so!"

"He fancies he is still on the treacherous sea," soliloquised Morna; "but he lives, and will recover."

Suddenly, with a cry, he started up and glared around him wildly.

"Where am I?" he exclaimed, in a tone of terror.

"In safety," answered the soft, assuring voice of Morna.

Those gentle tones seemed to quiet him.

His eyes grew less wild in their expression, and he sank back upon his pillow with a sigh of relief, murmuring the word, "Safety—safety!"

He had closed his eyes, but after a few moments opened them again, and fixed them inquiringly upon Morna.

The young girl almost shrunk beneath the earnest scrutiny.

"Yes, yes," he cried, "I know now I am in safety—I am in Paradise, and you are my guardian angel."

"No," she replied, shaking her head, "I am no angel, neither is this poor cabin Paradise."

"It seems to be so to me," he replied.

"Alas! it is but a poor resemblance to so bright a region."

Our hero, whose ideas were becoming stronger each moment, had a kind of comprehension that he had never gazed on anything half so beautiful as the wrecker's daughter.

He accordingly kept his eyes fixed upon the lovely prospect till the maiden blush overspread the pale surface of her cheek.

But of this he was unconscious.

"How came I here?" he inquired, after a pause.

"Do you not remember?"

"I have a faint recollection of the raging sea—the roaring wind: I fancy I can hear them now!"

"Nothing else?—the boat in which you sailed?"

"Ay, true," he continued, slowly, pressing his hand to his forehead as if in the effort to recollect. "Yes, yes, I remember now—the crash, the cry, the rush of waters, the sharp rocks, the blinding foam: I remember—I remember!" and he sank back again on his pillow. "The boat is lost," he continued, slowly, after a pause. "And my friend, where is he?"

"Alas!"

"Is he lost too?"

"I have seen no traces of him, and I fear the worst. It is a miracle your own life was preserved."

"Poor Harcliffe!" murmured his friend, in a faltering voice; "after passing unscathed through so many perils, have you found a grave in that stormy sea? Alas—alas!"

He covered his eyes with his hands to conceal his emotion.

"The treasure, too," he murmured—"that precious treasure for which we endured so much—all lost—all!"

And as these painful thoughts pressed upon him in his present weak and depressed condition, the tears trickled down his cheeks—he wept.

"Had you a treasure with you in that small boat?" inquired Morna, in a tone of deep sympathy.

"Yes, an immense treasure—a poor orphan girl's legacy. That, too, is swallowed up—all the bright gold engulphed by the ravenous waves."

"Hush!" cried Morna, in an admonitory tone—"speak lower!"

"Why?—are we in danger?"

"No," answered the young girl, with some hesitation; "but you might be overheard."

"By whom?"

"Those who love gold more than they value human life."

The captain looked at her with a perplexed expression on his features.

"Of whom do you speak?"

"Do not ask me—I cannot tell you; but you will be safe here."

"May I not ask your name?"

"Morna Trevellyn."

"Have you no parents?"

"My mother is dead, but my father——"

"Where is he?"

"After seeing you in safety here, he went out. It was he who bore you on his shoulders from the beach."

"What is his occupation?"

"He is a fisherman—they are all fishermen here," Morna said. She dared not confess the truth.

"A hard but honest calling, at all events," remarked Captain Hawk; "but, from the remark you made just now, I should fear they are not over scrupulous."

"They are poor, sir, and poverty is always a temptation."

"You are right," returned the captain, remembering how often he had extorted a traveller's purse under the same plea. "But surely," he continued, "these men would not assail a half-drowned fellow-creature as poor as themselves?"

"Not if they were assured of that; but any mention of gold, or a suspicion that you possessed it, would inevitably excite their rapacity. It was this that made me caution you to speak low."

"You do indeed deserve the title of a guardian angel," cried the captain, warmly; "and whatever my fate may be, I shall always hold you guiltless of the designs of those by whom you are surrounded."

He took her hand in his as he spoke.

"One so fair and compassionate as yourself deserves a better fate and a more congenial soil than this. Believe me, sweet Morna, I envy your companions as much as I pity you."

He pressed his lips to the soft symmetrical hand he clasped as he spoke.

At the same moment, a tanned, weather-bronzed face peered cautiously in at the window.

It was Daniel Macorrie.

His pale blue eyes gleamed fiercely and vindictively as he witnessed the stranger salute with his lips the hand of the woman he loved.

Morna, too, made no attempt to withdraw her hand.

With one knee bent to the ground by the side of the invalid, her cheeks flushed, and her bosom palpitating with new and strange emotions, she appeared to forget all besides, and to yield herself to the fascination of the moment.

Nor was the highwayman less inspired.

Weak as he was, there was a charm about the beautiful girl who tended him that seemed to revive and give him a new existence.

The mutual satisfaction each one felt in the society of the other was too manifestly evident in their actions and the expression of their features to be mistaken by one as jealous and vindictive as Daniel Macorrie.

As he stood without, shrouded in the shadow, looking into the interior, in which every object was perfectly distinct from the bright glare of the fire, he ground his teeth and clenched his hands furiously.

"The false, jilting wanton!" he muttered, fiercely. "But I'll be revenged for this!"

All this time those within were utterly unconscious of the evil demon that was writhing without at the casement.

For a brief space all other thoughts were banished.

But suddenly the captain's brow became overcast.

He sighed, and his head sank upon his breast.

"You are thinking of your friend?" Morna inquired.

"Yes."

"You must not give him up yet as entirely lost, it is possible he may have escaped."

"Possible, Morna, but barely probable; and then the treasure——"

"Take courage—that may be recovered."

"I dare not hope it; I fear I shall never see it more."

"Nay, I am not so sure of that. At the spot where your boat went to pieces it is not deep, and when the tide is low the rocks there are quite dry, so that anything lost could be regained."

"Do you really say so?" asked the captain, joyfully. "Oh, pray Heaven such may be the case!" And in the contemplation of such good fortune, he again kissed the fair hand he still held in his own.

Again the malignant eyes of Daniel Macorrie gleamed with deadly menace, but this time there was a mingled expression of exultation in his face.

Not a word had escaped his quick ear.

He gathered the fact that there was a treasure lost, and that there was a prospect of finding it.

He mentally resolved that that should be his task, and his alone; then if he gained it he would be independent for life.

That would gratify his avarice, whilst by the destruction of his rival he would glut his revenge.

With these thoughts running wildly through his brain, he leant heavily on the projecting window sill, which gave way with a slight crash.

It reached the ears of those within.

"What is that?" cried Captain Hawk, starting partly up.

"I will see," said Morna, rising hastily in some confusion, with a consciousness that she was perhaps a little more familiar with the handsome stranger than prudence would have advised.

She approached the window and looked out, but there was nothing to be seen.

She opened the door and called, but with the same result.

"It must have been the wind," she said, as she recollected it; "it makes sad havoc with this crazy old dwelling."

At this moment footsteps were heard.

She listened.

"It is my father's step," she cried.

The words were hardly uttered when her father stood upon the threshold.

He had entered hastily, not expecting to find the man, whom he had carried so short a time back senseless and bleeding to his cabin, so far restored.

He almost started at the sight.

Whether with pleasure or disappointment, he alone knew.

The captain observed his peculiar look, and watched him as he spoke in a low tone to his daughter.

"They are coming here," said Hugh Trevellyn.

"Who?"

"Andrew and Daniel Macorrie."

Morna's countenance betrayed some anxiety.

"When?" she asked.

"In the course of half an hour."

"Do they know we have given shelter to this gentleman?"

"Not from me. I do not see how they can know it; and yet from something in their manner I am half inclined to think they suspect."

"It would be better that our guest should remove to the adjoining room," said Morna.

"Yes, and as quickly as possible."

Turning to the captain, who had partly overheard the above conversation, he said:

"I am glad to see you so much recovered."

"I thank you for your good wishes and for your hospitality," said Captain Hawk, "but for my speedy recovery I think I am indebted to your fair daughter."

Morna blushed at this praise, and approaching the captain, whispered:

"There are others coming here whom I would rather you did not meet. It will be better you should retire into the adjoining chamber."

"If you wish it, certainly."

"I will kindle a fire there," said Morna.

"I am entirely at your disposal," replied the captain; "one room is the same to me as another—that is, provided I see you sometimes in it," he added, gallantly.

Again the colour flushed on the young girl's cheek.

Love's spark was beginning to blaze into a flame.

It took but a few moments to make the exchange with a guest so tractable and accommodating as the captain.

The fire was lit from some logs from the larger apartment; and the captain, who had made a very tolerable supper of dried fish and home-baked bread moistened with a stiff glass of whisky toddy, had, nothing loath, betaken himself to the humble pallet prepared for him.

Morna saw him covered warmly with the thick rug; and, with a parting assurance that "he was safe," whispered in his ear, which gave the captain an opportunity of throwing his arm round her white neck and imprinting half a dozen kisses on her willing lips, she left the room and the captain to repose.

The fatigue he had undergone—the pleasant warmth of the fire, the reflection of which danced and flickered cheerfully on the opposite wall—the fumes of the whisky, and above all the complacent sense of enjoyment he felt in thinking of the fair girl who took so evident an interest in his welfare—all conspired to induce a delicious drowsiness that partook more of a waking dream than slumber; but he felt at that moment perfectly free from unquiet thoughts—perfectly happy.

Morna had hardly returned to the apartment where her father sat moodily over the fire when the latch was lifted and the Macorries, father and son, entered.

Andrew Macorrie was not a pleasant old man to look upon.

Age, that imparts benevolence to some faces as gray hairs approach, had brought with it a scowl to Andrew's face.

His features were sharp, and his brows wiry and overhanging.

His son Daniel has been already described; and the feelings that now oppressed him, though he endeavoured to conceal them, overspread his face with a sullen gloom.

Andrew went straight to the whisky-bottle, half filled a tin drinking-cup, and emptied it at a draught.

He then looked towards his son.

Daniel followed his example, first pausing and looking towards Morna, who was sitting listlessly, her head resting on her hand.

"She's thinking of him, d—n him!" he thought.

He was perfectly correct; she *was* thinking of him.

"Good health, Morna!" he said, in a peculiar tone.

Morna started from her reverie, and coldly replied:

"Thank you, Daniel."

But she felt his words conveyed with them almost a menace.

"You look tired, Morna. You had better go to rest," suggested Hugh Trevellyn.

"I am quite ready," replied she, too glad to be alone.

She kissed her father, and extended her hand to Daniel, who, after a fierce glance expressive of a variety of feelings, coldly took the proffered hand, and as coldly dropped it again.

"Good-night, Andrew Macorrie," she said, as she passed her lover's sire.

"Good-night," answered the old man, curtly.

Morna ascended the narrow creaking wooden staircase, and entered her chamber.

For a few moments after her departure there was a dead silence.

Hugh appeared uneasy, Andrew and his son dogged and sullen.

They had lit their pipes as a relief to their feelings, and smoked in silence.

Andrew Macorrie was the first to speak.

"What stranger is that you brought here to-night Hugh Trevellyn?" he asked, in an abrupt and peremptory tone.

The dark eyes of the person addressed flashed, and the swarthy cheeks flushed, as he answered:

"One to whom I have promised protection."

"You forget the rules and regulations of our brotherhood," said Andrew, still in a tone that Hugh Trevellyn could ill brook.

"No. I remember them too well. The accursed motto is:

"'*Live for yourselves: spare none, neither young nor old: the dead reveal nothing!*'"

"Well! and are you obeying this rule?"

"No. For once I am obeying the dictates of compassion."

"Compassion! Ha, ha!"

"Yes! Compassion! I found this stranger wounded and senseless on the rocks. Something whispered in my heart that I should give him shelter."

"I understand exactly: he is rich!"

"No, you misunderstand: he is poor!"

"Then why the devil didn't you let him die on the rocks where you found him?"

"Because I pitied him and wished to save his life."

"How kind! And what are you going to do with him?"

"Keep him here till he is restored to health and strength, and then let him depart."

"And do you think our mates will agree to this?"

"I do not think at all about them. I do not bow to their opinion. I bring whom I please beneath my own roof without asking permission of any man."

Daniel, who had restrained his passion for some time, now burst forth with irrepressible wrath.

"It is all false!" he cried, fiercely—"utterly false! It was Morna found this stranger: she was attracted by his dark hair and pale face! It is to please her you at this moment give him shelter!"

The dark, keen eyes of Hugh Trevellyn blazed for a moment upon the angry speaker; but he restrained his anger, and said, coolly:

"Boy, leave my daughter's name out of this."

"No, I will not!" shouted Daniel. "You are blind, Hugh. This very night I saw this stranger—this wonderful animal—kiss your daughter's hand, not once, but repeatedly, and she permitted him! Take care—take care!"

"Are you in earnest?" cried Hugh, not so much annoyed at the information as at being compelled to hear it from such a source.

"I am—I'll swear it!" cried Daniel.

"I shall ask my daughter," briefly replied Hugh.

"You doubt my words!" bitterly returned the young wrecker.

"Oh!" joined in his father, "let him alone: he'll hug the snake till it stings him."

"I'll crush the snake myself before he has time to sting!" exclaimed Daniel, fiercely. "I allow no man to kiss the woman who is to be my wife!"

"She is not your wife yet," calmly remarked Hugh; "and if many such words drop from your lips, the chances are she never will be."

"She must—she shall!" cried the young man, fiercely. "She has been promised to me, and death alone shall step between to sever us!"

"Your passion gets the better of the little sense you have," said Hugh, in a tone of profound contempt. "You had better go home and sleep upon your words."

"I will go!" exclaimed Daniel, roused to fury by this cool advice, and starting up—"I will go at once! Come, father!"

The old man rose at this summons.

Father and son reached the door.

Daniel turned.

"Mark me, Hugh Trevellyn," he cried, "you have sealed the fate of the man who sleeps beneath your roof to-night!"

All was silent in Hugh Trevellyn's cottage.

Captain Hawk had passed from his intermediate state of semi-oblivion into a sweet and sound sleep.

He had certainly been conscious of hearing voices, and that they spoke loudly and—he thought—angrily.

He had also an indistinct idea that he was the subject of some altercation; but even this was insufficient to rouse him from his agreeable lethargy; and soon voices, sounds, thoughts, all disappeared, and he slept profoundly.

Everything was very still.

The wind had dropped, and came now at intervals, and then only gently.

The moonbeams streamed in at the window and lighted up the peaceful chamber.

But suddenly a dark shadow came across the pure light.

It approached slowly but certainly, like a spreading cloud on the face of the summer sky.

A figure stood without the window.

Silent—motionless—it remained for a brief space.

There was no mistaking the broad outline of the midnight intruder—it was Daniel Macorrie.

He glanced furtively into the chamber, and then opening a clasp-knife, cautiously inserted it between the window and the frame on which it rested, and slipped back the button.

It gave way with a slight snap.

But that was sufficient to break the captain's slumbers.

He started up and listened.

There was little necessity for exercising the imagination as to the cause of the noise.

The window was open, and a man was entering.

The pallet on which he lay was in shadow, so that he could see without being seen.

The captain's nerves were, as it may easily be imagined from what he had undergone, not in the strongest condition.

He felt his heart beat.

He was in a strange place.

He remembered the words of his fair nurse—

The whispered conversation of her father.

The voices he had heard also occurred to him, and he began to feel he was in peril.

Still, there was only one man.

But might there not be more without?

All these thoughts passed through his brain like lightning.

He lay perfectly still, with his eye fastened on the intruder, who was entirely unknown to him.

Daniel held the open knife in his hand, and glanced towards the bed.

"Psha!" he soliloquised, in a low tone, "there will be no need to spill a drop of blood. This elegant gentleman is weak—exhausted; a strong grip upon his windpipe will do the work as effectually, and leave no unpleasant traces. I will strangle him in his sleep."

Slipping the knife, open as it was, into the breast pocket of his coat, he cautiously advanced to the bedside.

After a moment his eye became accustomed to the darkness, and he perceived that his victim lay in a position particularly favourable to his design.

The head was thrown back, and the throat exposed.

Nothing interfered to thwart him.

Certainly he was not aware that a hand with the palm turned outwards was ready under the coverlet, on the alert to arrest anything intrusive that might chance to come in the way.

Neither did he think that the captain was at that moment slumbering with one eye open.

He was therefore completely taken by surprise when, as he was about to make the fatal grip, he found a strong grasp fasten on his wrist and another on his throat, and to hear a stern voice cry out:

"What seek you, fellow?—why are you here?"

It might have been thought that Daniel, with his jealous fury in his heart, would have turned fiercely upon his unexpected assailant; but the tables were so completely turned upon him that he was bewildered, cowed, and unfitted for immediate action.

"What do you want?" repeated Captain Hawk.

"I—I belong here," stammered Daniel. "I thought I heard a noise, and came to see what it was."

"Why, then, if you belong here, did you not come by the door instead of the window?" asked the captain.

This was a poser; but Daniel, who was beginning to recover his presence of mind to some extent, found an answer.

"I was locked out, and I did not wish to knock anyone up, so I entered by the window. This is my room."

explained the baffled Daniel, in a dogged, sulky manner.

"I believe you are hatching a whole nest of lies!" said the same stern voice. "You had other motives for your visit here."

"What motives could I have?"

"You sought my life, and would have taken it had you dared!"

"How could you think so?"

"Your guilty looks—your cautious, stealthy tread—your trembling limbs—all proclaim you a cowardly midnight assassin! But go! I despise you too much to fear. Begone! or you may find yourself, not the destroyer, but the destroyed."

As he spoke these words, he threw the astonished Daniel from him.

The miscreant, thus released, cautiously slipped his hand into his breast pocket and grasped the open knife; then making as though he was about to depart by the window, he suddenly turned, and bounded like a tiger on to the captain, who, though totally unprepared for such an attack, caught him fortunately once more by the wrist.

But the impetus of Daniel's assault overpowered him.

His superior weight bore him back, and he fell heavily from the bed, dragging his enemy with him.

Weakened from recent circumstances, he had not sufficient strength to overthrow the stalwart form that held him down and pressed his knee upon his chest.

A subdued growl of exultation rose in the throat of the wolfish Daniel.

"You'll kiss the hand of Morna Trevellyn, will you? Curse you! take this!"

The knife was raised, and descended with frightful and deadly impetuosity, piercing, not the captain's body—for he, by a quick motion, eluded the blow—but the floor, in which it was buried up to the hilt beyond the power of extrication, whilst at the same moment the chamber door flew open, and a hand fell upon his shoulder.

He turned in a scared manner, and encountered the flashing eyes of Morna.

"Wretch!—cowardly murderer! For shame!" she cried.

The guilty Daniel glared at her for an instant with a mingled look of terror, rage, and disappointed vengeance, and, with a wild yell of despair, darted through the window and disappeared.

CHAPTER CLX.

THE BLACK HIGHWAYMAN IS TAKEN ON BOARD THE SCHOONER.—AN UNEXPECTED ARRIVAL.—LORD HARCLIFFE PENETRATES A DISGUISE, AND ASTONISHES MOSES GELTZ.

OUR readers will doubtless be anxious to know what became of the Black Highwayman when the fatal collision took place that separated him from his companion.

He, finding himself engulphed in the raging waters, but still unwilling to succumb without a struggle, struck out desperately, but, as he thought, almost hopelessly.

Fortunately for him, however, in the confusion of the moment, he swam from instead of towards the shore.

This saved him.

The crew of the schooner had seen the annihilation of the frail vessel that carried our heroes, and compassionately resolved to make an effort for their preservation.

They therefore lowered their boat and proceeded towards the perilous shore, but cautiously.

Lord Harcliffe, in the meantime, was coming towards them, although unconscious of the fact.

But he was rapidly growing exhausted.

No one could have contended against such a sea.

He grew faint—dizzy—his senses were leaving him.

He seemed to be rambling through bright green fields, and listening to strange, sweet music.

It was just as all had become a blank that the coxswain of the boat, who was looking out for him by the light of a ship lantern, stretched forth his arm and grasped him.

He was conveyed on board the schooner, and, under the influence of restoratives, rapidly recovered his consciousness, the only clouds that rested on his memory being the loss of the valuable treasure, and the still greater loss of his friend, who, he felt confident in his own mind, must have perished.

He was, however, treated with great hospitality by the captain, who was a jolly, red-faced, good-humoured, bluff sailor, with a devil-me-care, offhand manner that was not displeasing to the Black Highwayman.

Lord Harcliffe would have gone ashore to seek tidings of his companion, but the captain dissuaded him.

"If," said he, "your friend has survived, which is almost impossible, you will meet again; if not, you will risk your own life by going amongst the wild beasts who traffic on those shores in human life, to no purpose."

His lordship yielded to this view of the case, and gave up the idea, remaining on board the schooner.

His distinguished appearance and courtly manner impressed the captain that he was some one of consequence; and when Lord Harcliffe gave him the fictitious name of Lord Ramilies, his attentions were mingled with profound deference.

There was, however, something rather mysterious about the vessel in which he found shelter.

At least, so he thought.

She remained anchored there day after day.

The crew made mysterious visits to the shore.

When they left the vessel, the boat was laden with casks; when they returned, it was invariably empty.

And this continued for some days.

What did it mean?

The Black Highwayman surmised on that account, and from the excellence of the brandy that found its way into the captain's cabin, that the schooner was a smuggler.

And he was perfectly right.

A more audacious defier of the excise duties than Captain Jecks did not exist.

He had a large cargo on board, and he lay quietly under the shelter of the rocks till it was entirely discharged, and the liquor conveyed in carts overland to his various customers, the majority of whom were honest, respectable licensed victuallers, but who, nevertheless, preferred the captain's prime cognac without duty more than they did the same article after it had passed through the customs.

Captain Jecks was known personally to most of his customers; and when he took a holiday, as he would occasionally, his rambles through Cornwall, Devon, Hants, and numerous Welsh counties on the other side of the Bristol Channel, were looked upon quite as events by some score of thriving landlords, who looked out anxiously for the hearty voice and the red, jolly, weather-beaten face of the smuggler captain.

There were rare revellings at those times.

The best the larder and cellar could furnish was brought out, and the captain feasted and imbibed to his heart's content, and delighted his hosts with his sea adventures and hairbreadth escapes, of which he had always a large stock on hand that was continually increasing.

It is not to be wondered that the Black Highwayman took a great liking to this jovial individual.

There was something in his frank, open, daring face, his reckless manners, and his stalwart frame, that almost commanded acknowledgment.

He was a man everybody liked, his crew included, which was saying a great deal.

Between him and Lord Harcliffe a mutual friendship sprang up.

It almost seemed to the highwayman that Heaven in depriving him of one friend had sent him another to supply his place.

His lordship had informed him of the loss of the treasure, without explaining how it had fallen into his hands.

The crew of the smuggler had examined the rock at low water, but without success.

The captain, too, had altered his position; he had weighed anchor and drifted round a rocky promontory, where he took up his quarters in a snug little creek, out of the sight of prying eyes, and protected from the assaults of wind and wave.

The schooner was no longer visible to the wreckers as they stood on the shore.

"The d—d sharks!" cried Captain Jecks, warmly, speaking of these marauders; "if I had my will I'd keel-haul every mother's son of the vagabonds, and hang 'em to the yard-arm to dry, with a rope round their necks, afterwards."

That was his opinion of them.

Lord Harcliffe had ventured a remark touching the kegs and casks that he had seen go ashore in the boat.

Captain Jecks's eyes twinkled, and then he laughed aloud.

"I don't think your lordship is a Custom House officer in disguise, so I may as well tell the truth and make a clean breast of it," he said. "Those casks are brimful of brandy, schiedam, and hollands, that never paid duty and never mean to."

"I thought as much," laughed the Black Highwayman.

"Yes; I'm a smuggler, and I don't care who knows it," went on Captain Jecks: "the excise officers would like to grab me if they could, I know; but I don't give 'em the chance. Bah! what a nuisance officers are!"

"I agree with you, my friend!" exclaimed Lord Harcliffe, warmly.

"What! have you had them after you, then?"

"Occasionally," answered the Black Highwayman, with a smile.

"Not for smuggling?"

"No—for debt."

"Oh!"

Lord Harcliffe did not acknowledge his profession to the smuggler; he thought it better not.

But the captain having opened his heart to his companion, amused him with many a wild tale of peril, both ashore and afloat.

The Black Highwayman was delighted.

He was half inclined to reveal himself to the captain, and renounce the road for the sea—a highwayman's career for a smuggler's.

But he restrained himself.

Several weeks passed away.

The smuggler vessel had discharged all her cargo.

The captain had received in exchange a large sum of glittering coin.

"See," said he, jingling the bag musically in the captain's ears; "this is the way we lay up for a rainy day."

He lifted a small plank in a corner of the cabin, and stowed it away by the side of some other bags of about the same appearance.

"You must be growing rich," said Lord Harcliffe.

"So I am," answered the smuggler; "and such is the power of wealth, that when I settle down, as I intend to one day, on some rich estate, no one will question the source from whence I gained the property."

"Certainly not," acquiesced his companion. "Gold is the greatest blinder of the sight in the world, and the greatest destroyer of the sense of hearing: spread it before the eyes, jingle it in the ears, and the world becomes blind and deaf immediately."

"Ha ha! beautiful! How splendidly you talk! Let's drink the world's health."

The captain went to a small cupboard in the wall, and took from it a peculiar long-necked bottle and two glasses.

"Hock?" cried the Black Highwayman.

"Yes, my friend, hock!" answered the smuggler. "We can't go on drinking cognac for ever—we'll pledge the world in something a little more aristocratic."

He drew the cork and filled the glasses.

"The world!" cried Captain Jecks, raising his glass; "but may neither you nor I ever be at its mercy!"

"I echo you!" exclaimed Lord Harcliffe.

They drained the glasses.

The captain refilled them.

"I'll give you a toast," cried the Black Highwayman: "May the friends of our prosperity be the friends of our adversity!"

"Ay, ay!" responded the smuggler, as he tossed off the wine.

At this moment voices were heard.

It was the boat coming alongside with some of the crew, who had been transporting the last cargo of brandy ashore.

With them came the second mate, who had just returned from Plymouth, where he had been leaving a mysterious quantity of bottles at one of the principal hotels.

He descended to the cabin as soon as he got on board, and tapped at the door.

"Come in," cried the captain.

The sailor entered.

One that anyone would for a moment have taken him for a son of the waves, save perhaps from the healthy brown tinge that lighted up his complexion.

He was attired in the habiliments and bore the appearance of a commercial traveller.

"Well, Roderick," said the captain, "all safe?"

"Quite safe, captain, and here is the money."

He placed a small leather purse on the table as he spoke. "Any fresh orders?"

"Plenty."

He took a list from his pocket and handed it to the captain.

The smuggler glanced at it with a complacent expression, and transferred it to his own pocket.

"A glass of wine, Roderick?"

"Thank you, captain."

"Have you anything further to say to me?" inquired Captain Jecks.

"Only that I've brought you a passenger, captain."

Lord Harcliffe looked at the smuggler—the smuggler looked at Lord Harcliffe.

"A passenger?" echoed the captain.

"Yes; I tumbled across an old foreigner—a German, I think he is—at Plymouth. He seems very anxious to get over to Holland, and as he promised to pay handsomely, I thought you might as well have the money as anybody else."

"Certainly. Is he on board?"

"No, captain; he is in the boat—I wouldn't bring him on board without your orders. He's a Jew, I fancy."

"A Jew! Well, we sha'n't offend him with any salt pork, not having any on board," laughed the captain. "On board with him: he can come, Jew or Gentile—it is immaterial so long as he can pay."

The mate disappeared.

There seemed some little trouble in getting the new arrival on deck.

He was evidently unused to the sea, and seemed to suffer considerably from a dread of it.

"Oh, mein Gott—mein Gott!" he was heard exclaiming as the sailors urged him to mount the ladder that was thrown over the vessel's side. "I shall fall—I shall be drown! Oh, oh!" he roared; "hold me, some vun—it ishn't shafe—I'm sure it ishn't!"

These exclamations reached the interior of the cabin.

The tones of the voice seemed to strike the Black Highwayman as familiar to his ear.

"Ah, dere! I am gone!" shrieked the terrified Jew without, whose foot had slipped from the rail of the ladder, to the great amusement of the sailors.

"Surely," murmured Lord Harcliffe, "I have heard that voice before!"

The captain was listening with considerable interest to the sounds on deck, and did not notice his lordship's abstraction.

"Who can it be?" his thoughts rambled on.

"Let us come and see how this Israelite enjoys his sea trip—probably the first he has ever taken in his life," said the captain, rising, and rousing Lord Harcliffe.

"With all my heart," answered his lordship, anxious to have a sight of the speaker whose tones had so impressed him.

They went upon deck.

The Jew having made several abortive attempts to ascend the ladder, owing to the rocking of the boat and the timidity he felt, had, after the last slip, fallen back between the seats, firmly believing he was going to the bottom, and refused to make any further attempt.

"Oh, mein back—mein back!" he cried, as his spinal vertebræ came in contact with the sharp edge of the seat. "Dish d—n boat will be de death of me!"

The Black Highwayman had a good opportunity of observing the Jew as he lay groaning in the boat.

His hair and beard were perfectly white.

Lord Harcliffe looked perplexed.

"Were it not that he looks too old, I could have sworn it was Moses Geltz," he muttered to himself.

At this moment the Jew's voice was again heard.

"How am I to get out of dish d—n boat?" he cried.

"There is only one way, and that is by the ladder," answered Captain Jecks, looking over the ship's side.

"No, no!" exclaimed the Jew, in a tone of horror, "I'll be d—d if I do! Do you vant to kill me?"

"Aha!" laughed the captain, "you are not used to seafaring; but since you don't like the ladder, I can only

[THE JEW OFFERS TO SELL THE KING'S RING TO LORD HARCLIFFE.]

suggest one other plan, and that is to fasten a rope under your arms and sling you up on deck."

"Vat! tie a rope round my vaist, an' hoist me up like a horse or a svine: no, no, I should be cut in halfsh!"

"Oh no," replied the captain; "it's a very expeditious method of getting over a difficulty."

"Don't see it at all meshelf," answered the Jew.

"Well, then, in that case I shall order you to be put on shore again—we can't be kept here all night," said the captain.

This threat did not appear to suit the Israelite at all.

"I don't vant to be put on shore again," he cried.

"Very good, then you must submit to be hoisted on deck."

As there appeared to be no other resource, the Jew reluctantly acquiesced.

A rope passed through a double pulley, with a noose at the end, was thrown to him.

"Place it over your head beneath your arms," directed the captain.

The Jew did as he was told in a very dubious and uncertain manner.

The crew, four or five of whom grasped the rope ready to haul away, looked brimful of delight.

It seemed to them a capital joke.

"Are you quite ready?" called out the captain.

"Yesh, quite! No, shtop! I—I'm not quite ready," the Jew shouted.

Prospective visions of hanging, ducking, and other unpleasant operations rushed into his mind as he clutched the rope.

But there was no other way.

"Now then," cried the captain: "ready!"

"Vait a minute—vait a—— Oh, oh! Mein Gott!" he roared, as, at the signal of the captain, up he flew in the air. "Let me down—let me down! You're taking me up to de cloudsh!" raved the Jew "I don't vant to go dere."

After allowing him to hang suspended, to his inexpressible horror, for a few moments under the pretence that the rope was entangled, they allowed the Jew to come down with a run to the deck.

"Oh, you d—n rascals—you unmerciful brutes—you vicked sinnersh!" vociferated the Jew, who was frightened out of his wits as well as half shaken to pieces. "I'm smashed—I know I am!"

Finding, however, that he was on the deck at last, the Jew calmed down a little.

"You had better come below into the cabin," said the captain.

"Yesh—yesh, by all meansh!" acquiesced the Jew, fervently, glad to escape from the derision of the crew.

The captain descended, followed by the old man, leaving Lord Harcliffe, who had scrutinised his features with the most earnest attention, more perplexed than ever.

"Surely, it must be!" he soliloquised. "In voice and features he is the exact counterpart of Moses Geltz; but his hair and beard were not white."

It was no wonder Lord Harcliffe was puzzled.

Our readers will remember that Moses Geltz, seized with an insatiable desire to possess the magnificent ring shown to him by the King's valet without paying five thousand pounds for it, had by a clever but rascally deception tricked his Majesty out of his costly trinket.

The means he employed were very simple.

While the ring was in his possession, he made a hasty sketch of its appearance, and took note of its weight.

He then had one made of baser material: the diamond being represented by a piece of cut-glass.

When he took the jewel from the King's hand, it was the fictitious—not the real—one he returned to his Majesty.

The remainder of the adventure, the discovery of the cheat, and the fury of the king, the reader knows already.

Moses Geltz, having got the ring in his possession, wisely concluded that the sooner he got out of the way the better.

He therefore resolved to leave England for a time, and pay some of his honest Dutch relatives a visit.

He accordingly, in order to render recognition, as he thought, impossible, disguised himself in a white wig and beard.

But he could not disguise his voice.

On inquiry he found there was no vessel likely to sail for Holland for some days.

He was afraid to wait.

Having business at Plymouth, he proceeded thither, and resolved to sail from thence.

It was the venerable appearance caused by his disguise that for the moment mystified the Black Highwayman.

But only for a moment.

He knew well enough that the Moses Geltz of his acquaintance was by no means a model of honesty—rather the contrary.

Something very near the truth began to dawn upon him.

"Yes—yes," he murmured to himself, "the old rascal has been up to some of his tricks, and wants to get out of the way till the hue and cry is over, I suppose."

He was singularly correct in his suspicions.

"I wonder what it is he has been doing? Is it robbery, or forgery, or what? Well, I daresay I shall be able to discover. Though we have met on one or two occasions, I hardly think he will recognise me; or even if he did, it will only be for me to coolly ignore all knowledge of the old scoundrel, and to tell him he's mistaken."

And with a slight laugh, Lord Harcliffe descended to the cabin.

Moses Geltz was already there.

Captain Jecks was by no means prepossessed by the Jew's appearance.

The sharp, cunning features, and the restless, ferret-like eyes of the Jew were in total opposition to the taste of the smuggler captain.

"Yes—yes, my Hebrew friend," thought the latter. "I don't particularly like you. What you want while you're here I'll take care you shall pay for."

The Jew was cold and ravenously hungry.

The sea air had sharpened his appetite tremendously.

He would at that moment have even devoured a pork chop, or two, without the slightest compunction.

But there were no such luxuries.

He looked wistfully at the hock bottle and the glasses.

The captain poured out a glass, and drank it with the utmost coolness.

He did not, however, offer any to our friend Moses.

"Vot a dam pig he ish!" muttered the Jew, fidgeting in his seat.

"Did you speak?" abruptly asked the captain.

"Oh, mein Gott, no!" cried the Jew, with a start of alarm, lest that personage had heard him.

"Oh, I thought you did."

The Jew bore his internal gnawings till he could bear them no longer.

"Mishter Captain," he said, at last.

"Well?"

"Can I have something to eat?"

"Certainly!"

"You're a gentlemansh! I'm very moch oblige—let me have it quick!" the Jew exclaimed, hurriedly.

"Of course you'll have to pay for it," remarked the captain, coolly.

"Pay?" echoed the Jew, blankly.

"Undoubtedly!"

"Vell, vell, I sh'pose I shall: ve don't get thingsh for nothing in dish vorld," responded the Jew. "Ve musht eat, and anything in reashon of course I shall pay. Only be quick—I'm shtarving."

The captain quitted the cabin, taking the lock with him, a mischievous smile, which Moses did not see, starting over his face as he went out.

"Vell I never!—dere now!" exclaimed the Jew. "Did anyvun ever see anything like dat?"

He had fondly hoped to have had a pull at the bottle the moment the captain's back was turned.

His chagrin may therefore be imagined.

"De dam unbelieving Gentile hog!" he grunted, between his teeth. "Bah! de vorld'sh a bad vorld—it'sh full of pigsh—greedy pigsh!"

Having thus vented his spleen in this widely-spreading opinion, his hungry eyes ran round the room.

They fell upon the cupboard in the wall.

He crept to it noiselessly.

It was locked.

He uttered a Hebrew execration.

Once more his eyes roamed hither and thither—

Those prying, inquisitive eyes that were never at rest.

Suddenly, however, they became stationary—

Fixed on one particular spot.

Why was this?

What had attracted his attention?

It was the small plank which the captain had removed from the floor close to the side of the wall, and which he had replaced somewhat carelessly.

He had not trodden it quite home.

But what was this to excite the old Jew's attention so particularly?

One would almost fancy that his keen eyes would pierce the flooring and fasten upon the money-bags beneath.

Accustomed himself to hide property away in holes and corners, the Jew divined that he had lighted upon some secret receptacle.

He approached hastily.

Hunger and thirst were forgotten.

He hooked up the plank with his nail, and raised one end.

He inserted his hand, and drew it out grasping a bag of gold.

He almost uttered a cry of joy.

Fortunately he restrained himself.

The proximity of the gold bewildered him.

He feared to take it—he could not bear the idea of parting with it.

"Oh, mein Gott—mein Gott!" murmured the wicked old man, "vot can I do wid this? An' I deresay dere's some more."

He thrust his hand into the aperture as he spoke.

"Oh, yesh—yesh!" he cried, greedily: "vun—two—three—four—five—— Oh, mein Gott—it ish de Bank of England!"

He felt inclined to drag forth the whole.

In his lust for gold he thought it would have been delightful to hug it all in his arms and plunge with it over the vessel's side, but this was madness.

He suddenly remembered where he was—

That he was on board a strange ship.

That if the captain should return and discover his present employment, he would stand a very probable chance of a lift out of the cabin window.

He hastily replaced the money-bags, and restored the plank to its original position.

"I must leave it now," he cried; "but I shall come again at night when all ish quiet. I must have some of it—all if I can; but some, at leasht."

His soliloquy was interrupted by the sudden opening of the door.

The Jew was on his knees still, and the sound caused him to turn.

He looked up, and encountered the gaze of Lord Harcliffe, who stood looking down upon him.

The Jew trembled inwardly with guilty confusion.

Some strange suspicions floated through his lordship's mind.

"What are you doing on your knees, Jew?" he exclaimed—"are you at your prayers?"

"Yesh—yesh!" cried the Jew, hastily, glad of having an excuse he would never have thought of put into his mouth. "I vas returning thanksh for my comfortable quartersh, upon my shoul I vas!"

He rose from his kneeling posture, and glanced curiously at Lord Harcliffe.

He fancied he had seen him somewhere before.

At this moment one of the crew entered, bearing a tray, which he placed upon the table.

The savoury odours of a delicious steak, with onion accompaniments, floated under the nostrils of the hungry Jew.

"Aha!" he cried, rapturously, smacking his lips—"dish ish beautifool!"

Captain Jecks entered.

"Now, my friend," he said, addressing Lord Harcliffe, "I hope you are ready for your dinner."

"I am indeed!" was the answer.

"So am I!" cried Moses.

But the captain did not appear to hear

He sat down at the table.

So did Lord Harcliffe.

And—so did Moses Geltz.

"Amongst the various dishes that are concocted to please the palates of epicures," remarked the captain, "there are few to excel, if equal, the one before us."

"I quite agree with you," answered his lordship, warmly. "It is one of those good old English dishes that are always acceptable."

"It smellsh delicious!" wound up Moses.

Captain Jecks helped Lord Harcliffe and himself, and then quickly placed the dish-cover over the meat.

As for the Jew, he appeared to be forgotten entirely.

This was a little too much for human nature to endure.

He looked on wistfully as he witnessed the transfer of floury potatoes and brocoli sprouts from their respective dishes to the plates of the eaters till he could bear it no longer.

The captain and his lordship were enjoying their dinners immensely.

"You haven't served me!" he at length burst out.

"I know that," said the captain, with his mouth full.

"But I ordered dinner, didn't I?" cried the Jew, irritated by his ravenous appetite and the captain's coolness. "I vantsh my dinner!"

"Well, then, pay for it," coolly suggested the captain.

"So I vill vhen I've had it," answered the Jew.

"That won't do here," replied Captain Jecks. "We have a rule that all visitors who dine on board this vessel pay in advance."

"Pay in advansh?" echoed the Jew. "Vell I never!"

"Perhaps not, but it's a fact," said the captain, in a decided manner.

"Vell, there, then," growled the Jew, disentangling a solitary shilling from his pocket and throwing it on the table in a very bad humour; "let'sh have a shilling's vorth."

"Ho, ho, ho!" laughed the captain, at this very innocent remark on the part of the Jew. "Ho, ho, ho!"

"What are you laughing at? Don't laugh," cried Moses, "but help me to some shteak, and don't forget the onionsh: give us a good shilling's vorth!"

"You're as ignorant of our prices as our rules," answered the captain.

"Vhat d'ye mean?" inquired Moses.

"A shilling's no use at all here."

"No use? Vhy, I can get a shplendid dinner for a shilling in London—lotsh of gravy!"

"Very likely; but you're not in London now, but on board my vessel, and being so, you must abide by my rules."

"D—n de rules! Vell, vhat are they?"

"To begin with, you place two guineas in this bowl."

The captain pushed a small japanned basin towards him as he spoke.

"Oh, mein Gott! two guineas! D'ye vant to ruin me?" cried the Jew, excitedly.

"Oh dear no!" said the captain; "there is nothing compulsory whatever in our arrangements. You are not obliged to eat at all unless you please; but if you *do* eat, you must pay."

"It'sh a d—n shvindle!" roared the Jew. "You know I musht eat—I can't shtarve—and you're putting on the price, you know you are!"

"Well, then, do without eating, and then you'll have nothing to pay. A piece more, my lord?"

"Thank you."

Moses's mouth watered at the tempting slice that went on to Lord Harcliffe's plate.

He had reached that pitch of hunger when everything else was forgotten.

"I shall die of shtarvation if I don't eat," he cried.

Lord Harcliffe felt inclined to die with laughter, but he restrained it.

There was a brief pause, and then the two guineas rattled in the bowl.

"That will do," remarked the captain, "to begin with."

"To begin vith?" faltered the Jew. "I don't undershtand."

"You soon will," answered Captain Jecks, cutting off a piece of steak and putting it on a plate.

"I'll take shome gravy," said Moses, eagerly.

The gravy was added.

"And some potatoesh and shproutsh."

The vegetables were served.

"Dat'll do for de present," cried the Jew, making a clutch at the plate, which the captain very skilfully removed beyond his reach.

"What are you doing?—can't I have it now?" groaned the famished Israelite.

"Not till it's paid for."

It was a study to watch the Jew's countenance.

"It ish paid for," he cried.

"Oh dear no! The two guineas was merely a kind of entrance fee," the captain explained.

"Vell, den, vhat elshe ish dere to pay?" exclaimed the Jew.

"A mere trifle: only three guineas."

"Three guineash?"

"Exactly. A guinea for steak—a guinea for potatoes—a guinea for sprouts—total three guineas."

"Dere, den—dere'sh de money; and now let me begin to eat," cried the Jew, with an expression of intense misery on his features.

"Certainly!" said the captain, pocketing the guineas and passing the plate to Moses.

The latter, having got it once in his hands, commenced the work of destruction immediately.

He devoured the food like a voracious cannibal or a hungry dog.

"Can I have shomething to drink?" he cried, in the first pause his appetite would allow him to make.

"Of course you can," replied the captain. "What will you take?"

"Brandy-an'-vater," answered the Jew.

The captain unlocked the small cupboard and took thence a brandy-bottle.

He then poured out a glass.

"Thank you," said Moses, putting forth his hand to take it.

"A guinea first, if you please."

"I von't pay any more guineash—I'll be d—d if I do!" roared Moses.

"Very well—please yourself. Only remember, no guinea no brandy."

"Oh, mein Gott! you'll ruin me altogether!" growled the Dutchman. "Dere—dere ish de guinea!"

The money being paid, Moses snatched the glass, and emptied its contents at a draught.

"Another?"

"Yesh."

"Another guinea first."

The Jew growled like an angry bear, but he threw down the money.

"You're beginning to grow used to our ways," smilingly remarked the captain.

Moses grinned a dreary, ghastly smile, and then applied himself to his steak.

"Delicious! is it not?" inquired Lord Harcliffe, who had enjoyed the proceedings and his dinner at the same time.

"It'sh ash tough ash old leather," grumbled the angry Jew.

The captain and his lordship burst into a laugh.

"It'sh all very vell to laugh!" he cried, savagely; "but never mind," he added to himself in an inaudible tone, "I shall pay myshelf back out of your own money-bagsh."

This reflection dropped like balm upon his wounded spirit.

In fact, it had such a soothing effect upon his system altogether, that he became quite lavish and reckless, and dropped his guineas and drank his brandy in a manner that would have made any of his ancestors' hairs stand on end.

But he still kept his designs screwed down to one point: he would pay himself back again.

As Moses gradually became more and more comfortable, the idea that Lord Harcliffe's features were familiar to him grew stronger and stronger.

His lordship also became quite convinced that the white-haired Jew, Jansen Spraager—such was the name by which he called himself—was no other than Moses Geltz.

Each resolved to be assured at the first opportunity.

Captain Jecks, having moistened his steak with a glass of brandy, went upon deck.

No sooner had he left the cabin than Moses turned to Lord Harcliffe familiarly, and, with a cunning expression on his features, said:

"You'll excuse me; but I tink I've seen you before."

"I doubt it—I fancy you're mistaken," answered Lord Harcliffe, coldly; "but your features are very familiar to me."

He fixed his eyes scutinisingly upon the Jew as he spoke.

At another time Moses would have felt uneasy at this; but under the influence of the brandy he had drunk, it did not alarm him.

He continued:

"Yesh—yesh! I certainly have seen you before, only den your name vashn't Lord Ramiliesh—it vash Lord Harcliffe."

"And your name," returned his lordship, "was not Jansen Spraager, but Moses Geltz."

Moses, in spite of his brandy, started slightly.

Lord Harcliffe observed it.

"Ve musht both be mishtaken den," he cried, wishing to change the subject. "Ha, ha! how strange dat we should both take each other for somebody elshe, ishn't it?"

"Very! But mistakes will occur occasionally."

"Yesh," replied Moses, emptying Lord Harcliffe's glass instead of his own.

"It seems, then, Mr. Mos—I beg your pardon—Mr. Jansen Spraager, that you are leaving the country?" remarked the Black Highwayman.

"Vell, yesh—yesh, dat'sh a fact, I am."

"On business, I presume?"

"Of course on bushiness, yesh—yesh."

"I thought so: you seemed so anxious not to be left behind."

"No vun likesh to be left behind, does he?"

"No, it's dangerous too, sometimes, isn't it?"

"Eh?"

"I say it's dangerous—people that stay behind get caught occasionally, don't they?"

"I don't quite understand what you mean," said the Jew, in as innocent a tone as he could possibly assume.

"I'll endeavour to explain: Suppose, now, for instance, you had stolen something——"

"Vell, but I haven't—I haven't—upon my shoul I——"

"I'm merely supposing by way of illustration. And suppose the police officers were after you—they in the rear and the sea before you—if you couldn't get a boat, they would overtake and inevitably capture you: that's what I mean."

"Oh yesh, I see," said the Jew, looking rather foggy. "I understand—you're quite right; but I haven't stolen anything. I vish I may die if I have!"

This was a strong assertion to make, but the Jew made it, not that it took any effect upon his listener, who knew very well that his whole life had been one long felony.

"Your destination is Holland, I believe?" Lord Harcliffe proceeded.

"Yesh; all my relativesh live dere; I shall see dem, and unite bushiness with pleasure."

"I presume your calling is mercantile?"

"Yesh, decidedly it'sh mercantile," said the Jew, drinking another glass of brandy. "I'm a dealer in precious stones."

"Indeed!" exclaimed Lord Harcliffe, with agreeable surprise. "I take a great interest in gems—in fact, I spend thousands yearly in the purchase of them."

"Do you, though?" the Jew returned, eagerly.

The thought suddenly struck him that he might have lighted upon a customer for the diamond ring.

"And so you're fond of precious stonesh?" he inquired.

"Amazingly."

"Of courshe you're a judge?"

"Undoubtedly."

"You could tell a good diamond if you saw one?"

"Certainly: the bulk of my jewels is in diamonds."

The Jew pulled his chair closer to Lord Harcliffe.

"I shuppose if a very fine diamond vas offered to you for sale, you'd feel dishposed to buy it, eh?"

"That depends upon its quality and price."

"Shuppose, den, it vas de finesht you ever saw, an' dirt cheap, what den?"

"Why then I should be a purchaser, of course."

The Jew's eyes sparkled with expectant eagerness.

"I have got such a vun!" exclaimed Moses, in a sharp, exultant whisper.

"A diamond?"

"Yesh: such a diamond ash you never saw—fit for the crown of an emperor."

The curiosity of the Black Highwayman was excited.

"Have you this precious gem about you?" he asked.

"Yesh, yesh!" eagerly replied the Jew. "I never let it out of my sight—I wouldn't for the world."

"As a probable customer, I suppose, you will allow me to examine it?"

"Yesh, yesh—of course a customer: dat makesh all de differensh."

"I am anxious to examine it."

The Jew slid his hand rapidly into his breast pocket and took thence a morocco leather case.

Opening this, he drew forth the diamond ring and held it up before the eyes of the Black Highwayman.

It needed but a single glance from a connoisseur like Lord Harcliffe to tell him that the Jew had spoken the truth respecting the gem.

It surpassed anything he had ever seen.

As the nervous and trembling fingers that held it shook and quivered, so did the cold pure rays of the diamond scintillate before the eyes of his lordship.

The prismatic colours—orange, blue, green, violet and crimson—mingled their lovely tints in gorgeous profusion.

"It is indeed a lovely stone," said Lord Harcliffe, with real admiration.

"Ishn't it a beauty?" exclaimed the Jew.

"And what price do you set upon it?"

"Couldn't take a farthing under ten thousand—an' dat'sh like giving it away," the Jew answered.

"How unfortunate!" ejaculated the prospective purchaser.

"What's unfortunate?"

"I lost twenty thousand pounds within the last few weeks, or I would have purchased it on the spot," said Lord Harcliffe. "Allow me to take it in my hand."

Moses with evident reluctance relinquished the ring, which his lordship carefully examined, weighing it in his palm.

Strange thoughts appeared to pass through his mind as he performed this operation.

The most prominent of these would naturally be how a gem so princely and valuable should have found its way into the hands of Moses Geltz.

That worthy individual sat looking on nervously on thorns till he should feel the ring in his hands once more.

Having scrutinised it sufficiently, Lord Harcliffe returned it to the Jew, who received it with a gasp of relief, and instantly transferred it to his pocket.

"It is indeed a magnificent gem!" his lordship remarked—"so magnificent that, even if I felt disposed to be a purchaser, I should first ask you a question."

He fixed his eyes earnestly on the Jew as he spoke.

"Vhat qvestion?" echoed Moses, winking and blinking like an owl in the sun.

"How it came into your possession?"

"Vell now—dere—to hear dat!" cried the Jew, with affected surprise. "In trade ve're not expected to say vhere ve get everything we sell."

"In your case it's of little consequence, since if you told me I should not believe you."

"Ha—ha! dat is funny—you are joking!" sniggered the Jew, rather complimented than otherwise. "But we all have our little secrets—you, for instance, call yourshelf Lord Ramilish, when it strikesh me you're Lord Harcliffe. Ha, ha! I've found you out," he grinned, as he saw the person he addressed frown and bite his lip.

Lord Harcliffe started up angrily.

"Whether I be Lord Harcliffe or Lord Ramilies," he cried, sternly, "I am beyond the *espionage* of a sordid rascal like yourself; but lest you should imagine you are deceiving me, I will give you a convincing proof to the contrary."

And advancing a step as he spoke, he dropped one hand upon the head of the astonished Jew, and grasped his beard with the other.

"What d'ye mean? Are you going to drag my hairsh out by the rootsh?" cried the alarmed Moses.

"Out by the roots!" cried his lordship, as with a jerk he snatched off the venerable wig and beard, and disclosed beneath the wrinkled cheeks, the puckered mouth, and grizzled locks of Moses Geltz.

"There you are, Moses, in *propria persona*. I knew you from the first; and more than that, I believe you stole that diamond!"

Anger, horror, and confusion were strongly manifest in the quivering lips and trembling features of the Jew.

But under the circumstances, he thought it better to treat the affair as lightly as possible, especially as matters were beginning to look so truthful and serious.

"Ee, ee, ee!" he sniggered (it was too faint an attempt for a laugh). "You are so droll—so clever to dishcover dat I vore a vig—ee, ee, ee!"

"Moses," said Lord Harcliffe, impressively, "I shall not give you into custody on suspicion of this robbery—because, after all, it is only suspicion on my part—but if you have become possessed of that ring dishonestly—if you have stolen it" (he emphasised the two last words very emphatically), "you will never keep it. Justice will send her messenger to claim it when you least expect it."

"Vell, vell; den when Justice sends for it she shall have it," cried Moses, considerably relieved, and fancying that if he waited for such a messenger, he should keep it a long time.

The brandy he had drank, and the excitement he had undergone, began to tell upon the Jew, who gave unmistakable symptoms of drowsiness.

Captain Jecks descended from the deck and came into the cabin.

"Well, my worthy Israelite," he said, observing him yawning tremendously; "there's a bed ready for you—of course on the usual conditions."

"Another guinea, I supposh," answered Moses, sleepily.

"Two guineas for a bed," the remorseless captain informed him.

The two guineas were paid, and the Jew was ushered into a little box about six feet square, very near to the captain's cabin.

He threw himself upon the couch prepared there, and in a few moments was in the land of dreams.

Lord Harcliffe and Captain Jecks remained in close conversation for more than an hour, and then they likewise retired.

The dreams of Moses Geltz were a compound of money-bags and enormous diamonds, as large as pigeons' eggs.

He appeared to be surrounded by them on every side.

They rolled on to him with crushing weight—he could not breathe—he gasped, struggled, and awoke.

"It'sh dat d—n tough shteak," he said, to himself, "or de brandy—I don't know vich."

Moses Geltz was usually a light sleeper—like a cat.

Had it not been for his unusual potations, he would not probably have slept at all.

He could form no idea how long his sleep had lasted.

He listened.

All was silent. It was quite dark.

He felt eagerly in his pocket for the diamond ring.

It was safe.

The messenger of Justice had not paid him a visit as yet.

His thoughts reverted to the money-bags in the captain's cabin.

The fumes of the brandy had worked off.

He was himself again.

He would obtain as much of that money as possible.

One awkward thought crossed him.

When he had got the money, what was he to do with it—where could he hide it?

No matter: in his cravat, pocket, boots—anywhere.

He crept from his bed.

The night air was chill, and made him shudder.

He groped his way to the door, which, from the smallness of the room, was but a short distance.

At last he found it.

He turned the handle softly; the door opened, creaking slightly as it did so, and throwing the Jew into a fever of nervousness.

No one, however, appeared to take any notice.

All was as quiet as before.

Moses peered out into the darkness, and was not a little perplexed as to the course he was to take to reach the captain's cabin.

Presently his eyes discerned a faint light on the ground at some few yards' distance.

It seemed to come from under a door from a light within the room.

He advanced, but hesitated as he found it was so.

If that were the captain's cabin, the captain would be there, and what excuse could he make if he were found there?

He resolved to ascertain whether or not the room was empty before venturing in.

He tapped cautiously at the door, having previously resolved to say, if the captain's voice answered him, that he had come for a guinea candle, being tired of the darkness.

No answer was, however, returned.

He tapped again.

Still there was silence—not even a snore in response.

He opened the door and looked in.

It was the captain's cabin; but it was empty—the captain was not there, having gone on deck to examine the state of the weather and see all safe.

A lighted lamp hung from the ceiling and diffused a dim light around.

The Jew's heart beat rapidly as he contemplated the tempting prospect before him.

He hastily crossed to the corner where the captain kept his money-bags.

He raised the planks and eagerly thrust in his hand.

Oh, joy! there they were—there were the money-bags!

With trembling hands he withdrew two, which he transferred to his pockets.

He yearned to take them all, but he dared not.

He replaced the plank and departed as rapidly as possible, taking the gold with him, and closing the door after him.

He regained his chamber in safety.

Thus far all was well, he thought.

No one had seen him enter the cabin—no one had seen him depart.

He returned once more to his bed, and crouched down in it.

His heart warmed and glowed as he clasped the purloined treasure dotingly to his heart.

He was more than ever resolved not to part with it.

He would sew every guinea, piece by piece, in the lining of his garments.

"Oh, you darling guineash!" he ejaculated—"you pretty creaturesh! I von't leave vun of you behind!"

He was terribly appalled to hear a deep voice answer in the dark:

"*Yes, you will leave all behind!*"

Moses Geltz, with his guilty conscience, plunged beneath the coverlet of the bed.

He trembled with undefined apprehension.

The perspiration oozed from every pore.

"Oh, mein Gott! it'sh the devil come for me! Oh, misherable shinner dat I am!" he groaned.

He listened, and fancied he could hear the regular breathing of some one in the room.

He would have given the world to have looked forth, but he dared not.

The suspense was unbearable.

Cautiously he looked up.

The room was no longer utterly dark.

A dim, shadowy light was dispersed throughout it.

Just sufficient to render objects visible, and no more.

He started with a loud cry.

What was it he saw that froze him with a nameless horror?—

That made his eyes glare intensely, as though they would burst their sockets, and caused his grizzled hairs to stand on end

"Like quills upon the fretful porcupine?"

It was, that in the centre of the room stood a tall, gloomy, silent form, shrouded in impenetrable black from head to foot, wearing a mask of the same sable hue upon its features.

Yes, there it stood! awful in its silence! terrible in its repose!

The Jew glared at the apparition without the power to speak or to remove his fascinated eyes.

If it would but have spoken to him!

But no! it preserved a rigid, unbroken silence.

"Who art thou?" the Jew at length managed to gasp out.

"*The messenger of Justice!*" replied the deep, stern voice.

CHAPTER CLXI.

MORNA DISCOVERS THE MISSING TREASURE ON THE ROCKS. —DANIEL MACORRIE DEMANDS HIS SHARE, AND RECEIVES IT AT THE HANDS OF CAPTAIN HAWK.—THE ATTACK ON THE CABIN.

HUGH TREVELLYN entered at the same moment.

"Do not mistake me, young sir, or think that I am a conniver in this dastardly attempt," he said, in a frank, bold voice. "You may perhaps be more inclined to take my daughter's word than mine; and she will tell you I am incapable of such a deed."

"Oh yes, sir—indeed, indeed he is!" said Morna, earnestly.

"I believe you from the bottom of my heart," cried Captain Hawk, warmly. "I need but to look in your face, sir," he continued, addressing himself particularly to Hugh Trevellyn, "to tell me of one who has moved in a better sphere, but who in his downfall has not left the feelings of honour and humanity at the top of the hill from whence he descended."

The wrecker sighed.

"You are right, sir," he replied, "in your estimate of me. I was not always what I now am: peculiar circumstances conspired to throw me amongst these rude, lawless men; but I have no sympathy with their actions, neither do I owe my livelihood to deeds of cruelty and bloodshed."

Captain Hawk assured him, with a warm grasp of the hand, that he fully acquitted him of all participation in their nefarious pursuits; and being much refreshed by the profound sleep he had enjoyed, the captain proposed that they should adjourn to the adjoining apartment.

This being agreed to and acted upon, some dried wood was thrown upon the still smouldering embers, and on the top of that fresh logs; a cheerful blaze soon diffused its light and warmth through the chamber.

Morna's fair hands prepared breakfast; and Captain Hawk felt that he had never more heartily enjoyed that invigorating meal.

The morning came in cold and gray.

The wind had lulled, and the clouds were breaking but the gale had been so violent that the sea was still turgid and angry under the fierce lashing of the past night.

It was still early when Morna, intent upon the recovery of the captain's treasure, left her father's cabin.

She went alone, however, at her own request; for though the highwayman offered to accompany her, she would not hear of it, declaring that his life would be imperilled.

"My daughter is right," said Hugh Trevellyn. "Fear not for her—she will be perfectly safe; but with you it would be different. Remain here."

Thus cautioned, the captain had no resource but to submit.

He accordingly remained indoors.

Morna hastened to the beach.

The tide was rapidly receding.

She stepped hastily from rock to rock, till she reached the vicinity of the spot where the catastrophe occurred.

There she waited patiently, and as the ebbing tide allowed her to approach nearer and nearer, she looked anxiously upon the moist sand and the dripping, slimy rocks in the hope of descrying the missing treasure.

But no such sight rewarded her anxious search.

Whilst thus engaged, the sound of approaching footsteps fell upon her ear.

She crouched down behind a rock, and listened.

In a few moments the form of Daniel Macorrie appeared.

He scrambled hurriedly over the rocks in an excited manner; and having approached within a few yards of where she was concealed, he commenced searching, with his eyes bent upon the sand in the same manner as she herself had previously done.

"Can it be possible that he has got some clue to this treasure?" she thought.

She watched narrowly, keeping herself screened from observation by the numerous rocks—an operation of no great difficulty, owing to the absorbed state of him she sought to avoid.

She observed his hurried, anxious gestures, and heard his exclamations and execrations of disappointment as he failed to find that for which he was seeking.

She watched until, wearied with his fruitless search, he retired.

Then, and not till then, she left the rocks.

Captain Hawk awaited her return anxiously

The first glance he took at her face assured him her search had been unsuccessful.

"Well," the captain remarked, philosophically, after thanking Morna for her exertions in his behalf, "I suppose, then, I may make up my mind that this gold is lost beyond the hope of recovery. Let it go, then; all the regrets in the world will not restore it."

And having thus expressed himself, he, with the elasticity of spirit peculiar to himself, dismissed it from his mind, and turned to the bright eyes and fair face of Morna—objects eminently calculated to banish everything else from the memory, for the time at least.

And so day after day passed away.

Daniel Macorrie had not shown himself at the cabin since the night of his murderous attempt.

The reasons for his absence were obvious.

The man he looked upon as his rival—perhaps with some reason—was still there.

To meet him would have been particularly embarrassing.

Besides, he had a vivid recollection of the captain's iron grip upon his wrist and throat, and did not particularly care about a repetition of these feats of strength upon his own person.

Then, he felt he had disgraced himself in the eyes of the woman he loved, and that was the hardest blow of all, and made him go to and fro like an outcast, enduring the gall and wormwood of jealousy and disappointed hate.

The captain, like a caged bird, began to pine for liberty.

Sometimes he would apostrophise as though speaking to his horse.

"Oh, Satan! would I were astride your back, my gallant steed, with a prospect of a good twenty-mile gallop before me!"

He began to chafe under the close confinement day after day; and though he had yielded, more in compliance with the entreaties of Morna than from any fears for his own personal safety, to this enthralment, he felt that he would rather encounter all the wreckers on the coast singly than remain a prisoner much longer.

He longed to make some inquiries respecting his friend and companion, Lord Harcliffe.

He little imagined that that friend was on board the schooner that was lying snugly in her nest behind the rocks, out of sight, but almost within gunshot.

Equally ignorant was the Black Highwayman that Captain Hawk was alive and well, and separated only by a little water and a few rocks.

One fine morning, when the bright sun lighted up the face of nature with a genial smile, Morna betook herself to the rocks, as she was wont to do, still clinging to the hope that the waves might eventually wash up the lost treasure.

"It was heavy," she argued with herself, "and would resist the action of the water."

"I will go once more," she cried, "and for the last time."

The captain watched her departure with longing eyes, yearning to inhale the fresh sea breeze, of which he had had so lately such a boisterous experience.

He kissed his hand to her gallantly from the window, and that action, trifling as it was, sufficed to bring the glow to her cheek and set her heart beating.

Poor Morna! She was feasting her hopes with airy food, but it was a sweet dream to her while it lasted.

She reached the rocks.

The tide was very low on this particular morning.

More so than she had ever noticed it.

Rocks a long way out, whose bases she had formerly noticed covered with water, were now perfectly dry to their extremities where they joined the sand.

She set to work to search eagerly with renewed spirit.

It seemed as though she had never sought with so much spirit or with such a hope of success.

But still, hour after hour passed, and nothing had been discovered.

Suddenly she came upon a mass of seaweed wedged firmly in a narrow aperture between two rocks.

At least, so it appeared to her.

She would have passed it, had it not appeared to be of more consistency than such masses usually were.

She bent down and removed a portion of the slimy vegetable.

This operation revealed to her sight what appeared to be a bale of cloth tied round and round firmly with rope.

"A relic from some disastrous wreck," she exclaimed, "but not what I seek."

Something, however, prompted her to detach it from its position.

This was not so easy as she had anticipated.

She had to put out all her strength.

At last she dragged it from its narrow prison on to the sand.

It was evidently a parcel of cloth.

Cleansed from the brine with which it was encrusted, it might be useful.

She essayed to lift it.

It was tremendously heavy.

"What can it be?" she exclaimed, aloud.

The answer came almost as quickly.

"The treasure—the treasure!" she cried, exultingly, with a kind of inspiration—"I know, I feel it is, by the strange joy I experience!"

With trembling, agitated eagerness, she unfastened one corner, and shaking it gently, several guineas, that had escaped from the saturated paper in which they were enveloped, rolled out.

Her most sanguine hopes were now confirmed.

With a wild shout of joy, the generous girl thanked Heaven, that had permitted her to be the instrument of recovering that which would gladden the heart of the man in whom she had taken so deep an interest.

Summoning all her energy, she grasped the parcel and raised it from the ground.

It taxed all her strength to lift it.

"How heavy it is!" she ejaculated, almost breathlessly. "What an immense sum there must be here!"

"And what are you going to do with it, Morna?" cried a voice in her ear that made her start.

She turned her head, and encountered the fierce eyes of her lover, Daniel Macorrie.

This was the first time they had met since she interposed between him and his prey.

"It's too heavy for you," he said; "you'd better let me carry it."

"No, thank you, Daniel Macorrie," answered Morna, in a cold tone, mingled with contempt. "I don't intend to let this go out of my hand to anyone."

"And what are you going to do with it?"

"Restore it to its rightful owner," she answered.

"To the cursed intruder who is stealing away your heart from me, I suppose you mean?" he said, bitterly.

"I do not understand you," she exclaimed, with proud dignity.

"You had better say you won't understand me," cried Daniel, growing more and more incensed.

"I can say what I please and do what I please, sir, I presume, without being accountable to you either for my words or actions. Let me pass!"

He stood right in her path, defiantly, and did not heed her command.

"How do you know it belongs to this handsome gentleman?" he said, with a sneer.

"I am sure of it," she replied, firmly.

"You are breaking the rules of our community."

"What rules?"

"Why, that all property found on these rocks is to be shared equally by all."

"No one shall share this, Daniel Macorrie—neither you nor any of your gang; of that you may be certain!"

"Save and except your father and yourself," he said, sneeringly. "I suppose you consider yourselves as belonging to us?"

"No!" cried the young girl, indignantly. "I should blush to think that we had anything in common with men who live upon the lives of their fellows!"

"And do you really suppose I'm going to let you walk quietly away with the contents of that bale? If so, you never made a greater mistake in your life."

Never did Daniel Macorrie look so little in her eyes. She had never loved him—now she felt she almost hated him.

He had displayed himself in his true colours,—sordid—cruel—revengeful.

He, too, knew he had gone too far, and this thought added to his spleen and malice.

"You think, because this fine gentleman has condescended to smile upon you, you may venture to look down upon your former friends as so much dirt; but you'll come to your senses when it's too late."

"And so will you! I'll take good care it shall be known to every one of our mates what you say of them, and how you think to rob them of their rights."

"Do so—tell them all, and see how they'll applaud a lover who, out of spite, tries to bring evil to the very threshold of the woman he professes to love."

"I can't keep on loving where I receive no love in return."

"It is all your own fault."

"My fault?"

"Yes. Who can love a man so full of dark and vindictive thoughts as you are?"

"Who can give a heart to one man when she has given it to another?"

"You are mad! Let me pass!"

"You're welcome to go whenever you please, but you leave your treasure behind you."

"Do you mean to say you will take it by force?"

"I swear I will, unless you give it up of your own free will!"

"That I will never do—neither do I acknowledge any further acquaintanceship with one so rude and heartless!"

She made a step forward, when the young wrecker—with flashing eyes, and dark, stormy brows—laid his hand upon the parcel.

Morna, already fatigued with the weight, could not support this additional impetus.

The treasure fell to the ground, and he placed his foot upon it.

"I told you," he said, in his bitter sneering tone, "you had better have let me carry it."

"Coward!—villain!" exclaimed the beautiful girl, her fair face crimson with indignation.

"Rail on!" cried Daniel. "What you say now comes straight from your heart, I know: it doesn't trouble me. So long as I have the gold you may keep your love!"

He delivered this with much bitterness, and stooped to pick up the treasure, when Morna threw herself upon it.

"You shall not touch it!" she cried, fiercely.

With a savage yell of rage, the wrecker dragged her up by the wrist, and flung her passionately to some distance; at the same moment a strong arm grasped him by the collar of his coat.

Daniel recognised his assailant with a startled oath.

"Scoundrel!" shouted the captain. "Do you attack women as well as men? I feel half inclined to batter your thick head against these rocks!"

Daniel's hand glided involuntarily into his pocket.

Captain Hawk noticed the action.

"You'll look in vain there for your murderous weapon," he said. "You forget you left it buried in the floor of my room," he cried.

"Weapon or no weapon," shouted Daniel, madly, "I'm a match for you any day in the week."

As he spoke these words, he fastened his strong grasp upon the captain's throat.

But he was deceived in his estimate of his opponent's strength.

He had had a slight specimen on the occasion of their first encounter.

But then the captain was comparatively weak.

Now he had recovered his strength.

The wrecker had hardly made his seizure when he felt his own throat gripped as though by the sudden compression of an iron band.

It appeared to him that he was being quietly strangled.

By a desperate effort he disengaged himself, and then returning to the charge with all the desperation of vindictive hate, he closed with the captain.

Both were powerful, active, and good wrestlers.

But Daniel, being a Cornish man, and accustomed to that sport, he might perhaps claim some superiority.

It did not appear, however, of much advantage to him.

The great activity and energy of the captain, quickened as it was by the sight of his recovered treasure and the presence of Morna, was more than equal to the emergency.

Clasped in a close hug like two angry bears, they swayed to and fro in their efforts to throw each other, sending the sand flying in all directions.

Morna looked on apprehensively.

She feared a fatal termination to the affray.

She was more than half inclined to run hastily and summon her father; but she feared what might happen during her absence, and she remained.

There were no signs on the parts of Daniel or the captain of fatigue.

The desperate struggle continued, until, in their rapid evolutions, Daniel stumbled over a piece of projecting crag, and fell heavily, dragging the captain with him, and striking his own head so severely against a jutting rock, that he lay stunned and motionless.

Captain Hawk leapt up lightly to his feet.

"Is he killed?" cried Morna, apprehensively, advancing towards her prostrate lover.

"Oh no," replied the captain, "he is only quieted for a time: he will come to his senses soon. I think we may congratulate ourselves on being well rid of an intolerable nuisance. How fortunate it was I came after you!"

Morna did not seem prepared to dispute any of these assertions, but remarked:

"Had we not better return? We can then, perhaps, send some one to his assistance."

She pointed to Daniel, who, by a movement of the arm, proved that his consciousness was returning.

The captain seized his treasure with joyful eagerness, and, with Morna walking by his side, threaded his way through the rocks towards the shore.

Fortunately, they met with no interruption, and reached the cabin in safety.

They were scarcely out of sight when the discomfited Daniel returned to his senses.

"Curse him!—d—n her!" he exclaimed, hoarsely, between his closed teeth. "He's got off scot-free this time; but I shall have my turn yet on him, and on her too. She sha'n't play with me for nothing! I'll be revenged—I'll have his life yet!"

He placed his hand to his head, as a dull, heavy, throbbing pain told him he was wounded.

He withdrew it hastily, and uttered a cry of mingled rage and horror as he found it besmeared with clotted blood.

The sight of the crimson fluid stirred up the angry, vindictive spirit within.

"Curse him!—d—n him!" he reiterated, fiercely "Blood will have blood, and, by hell, I'll have his for this!"

He strode forward, as though he would have rushed after his antagonist to inflict an immediate vengeance; but he had lost more blood than he was aware of, and he staggered from faintness, and leant for support against a rock.

At this juncture, some of his companions—rude, rough, strong young fellows like himself—had sauntered down to the beach, and came, leaping from rock to rock, to the spot where he stood.

He was leaning his head upon his arm.

"Hollo, Dan! what ails thee, lad, moping there? Art thee love-sick?" cried one.

"Has pretty Morna been giving thee hard words?" inquired another.

"No, that's not it; she wouldn't kiss him this morning, would she, Dan?" proposed a third.

"D—n her!" growled Daniel, in a fierce, hoarse voice.

"What! Morna?" they cried, with surprise. "The wind's changed, isn't it?"

"I say again d—n her! the false jilt!" continued the young wrecker, bitterly; "and harkye, don't you let me hear you joking me about it, or maybe some of you'll repent it!"

His companions, looking at him more attentively, saw that he was very pale; and as their eyes fell on his blood-stained hair, and the dark pool that had trickled on the rocks and the sand where he fell, they were at once aware that a contest of some kind had taken place, though with whom they knew not.

"What blood's this?" asked one.

"It's my blood!" he cried, fiercely. "We struggled together here, my foot caught the rock, and I fell undermost—the infernal rocks almost crushed in my skull!"

"Who didst thee struggle with?" inquired half a score of excited voices.

"Who? Why, that d—d stranger—that fine gentleman Morna Trevellyn found upon the rocks here!"

"Oho!" murmured his companions, in a peculiar tone.

"Ever since he came here," continued the young wrecker, furiously, "with his pale face and his woman's hands, she has no eyes nor heart for me—he has stolen all, curse him!"

"What do he want here?" demanded those by whom Daniel was surrounded—"he don't belong to us."

"To tempt the woman I love with gold!" was the fierce answer. "He is rich."

"Rich! Have he gotten gold?" asked all the voices in one breath.

"Heaps and heaps! I found it here in the rocks—this stranger claims it, and says it is his."

"No—no!" cried his companions, in excited tones, roused in an instant at the mention of the gold. "Whatever's found here is ours."

"So I said," continued Daniel. "It was the gold for which we struggled. If I hadn't tripped over the rock and been knocked senseless, I'd have strangled him!"

[CAPTAIN HAWK IS RESCUED FROM THE DEATH PILLAR BY THE BLACK HIGHWAYMAN.]

"And what have he done wi' the gold?" cried the wreckers.

"That's safe enough in Hugh Trevellyn's cabin by this time," returned Daniel.

"We'll soon have it out then if it be there, though we batter down the walls or burn it."

"Ay, ay!" chimed in the whole party.

"You're with me, lads, in this?" asked Daniel Macorrie, appealing to his party.

"Back and edge!" they cried.

Captain Hawk and Morna had long since reached the cottage, and related the encounter with Daniel Macorrie on the rocks to Hugh Trevellyn.

The countenance of the latter grew darker and more serious as he listened.

"I am sorry for this," he said. "He is vindictive, and in revenge will spread the news that you have found this treasure far and wide. As surely as I now say it, you will find it harder work to retain than you did to recover it. You do not know these men."

"They shall take my life before they touch this!" cried the captain, in a tone of determination.

"They will take your life, and think nothing of it, if they do not share it equally," was Hugh's quiet reply.

"The plundering scoundrels! By what law or right do they pretend to claim one penny of this money?" Captain Hawk asked, indignantly.

"By the laws they have made for themselves—by the rule of might over right," answered the wrecker.

"I do not acknowledge such laws, and their might shall not prevail over my right. They do not know me!" cried Captain Hawk, his heart swelling with indignant defiance.

"But should they come down upon us, as it is certain they will, how can we stand against the resistless force of numbers?"

"That we must consider. It will not be the first time I have resisted with as heavy odds against me."

At the prospect of danger, the captain's spirits mounted.

He had been inactive too long, and almost yearned to hear the report of a pistol and to smell powder once more.

"First," he said, "we must conceal this treasure in some spot that will baffle all search. If the worst comes to the worst I should die comparatively content with the knowledge that it was safe from these marauders' hands; not that I anticipate such a fate or am tired of life."

Morna reflected for an instant.

"I think I know a place of security," she went on. "At the back of our cabin stands a tree, the trunk of which is hollow, with an opening in its side large enough to admit the body of a man. Without a moment's delay bury the treasure in the earth in the interior of this trunk—they will never think of looking there."

"I will do so at once," cried Captain Hawk, eagerly. "There is no fear, I suppose, of their taking me by surprise while I am at my task?" he inquired.

"None. The tree is at the rear of the cabin, and if they come they will be sure to approach from the opposite direction. I could give you intelligence, and you could gain the interior before they discovered anything," said Morna.

"Quick, then, my fair monitress! Have you a spade?"

Hugh Trevellyn handed him the required implement, and, guided by Morna, the captain approached the tree.

The aperture in the side was so small that it was with the utmost difficulty the captain squeezed himself through it.

However, having done so, he found the interior of the trunk roomy enough.

In a short time he had dug a hole sufficiently deep to contain the valuable deposit; and having taken from it a sum sufficient for present exigencies, he placed it in the ground, and battered the earth firmly down upon the top, throwing out the superfluous mould, which Morna threw upon the beds of a small garden that was near.

The work being accomplished rapidly and secretly, they returned to the cabin.

"Now, then," said Captain Hawk, "we must prepare for our defence, and strengthen our citadel. This doesn't appear like a place calculated to stand a siege," looking round and smiling as he spoke at the crumbling walls.

"You're right," answered Hugh: "one good volley would, I think, bring it down about our ears."

"Well, we must do the best we can, then—no one can do more."

Captain Hawk examined the windows and tried the fastenings.

They were old and rusty, and ought to have retired on a pension long ago.

The hinges and locks were in the same debilitated condition.

Fortunately, to both doors and windows, back and front, there were strong bars that fitted in sockets on each side of the wall, and kept them secure from the wind.

The windows were also provided with shutters; but they were all afflicted with the rickets and the worms.

"At the first signs of attack," said the captain, "these shutters must be closed, and these bars put up. And now, what firearms or defensive weapons have we? Let us see."

Morna's pale cheek flushed as she heard the man she so much admired go into these matters with such extraordinary coolness.

She was proud, without knowing why she should be so, of his cool self-possession.

What could he ever be to her?

The transient colour, however, yielded to the pallor of anxiety as she saw him draw forth a pair of handsome pistols, with polished barrels, which he quietly placed on the table.

Hugh Trevellyn, in the meantime, had brought forth the whole of the artillery he possessed.

This consisted of a pair of old muskets, and a brace of pistols, which, from their corresponding rustiness and antiquity, looked like their younger brothers.

Hugh placed them on the table by the side of the captain's arms.

He then fetched powder and a bag of bullets.

To clean and load them occupied some little time.

At length, however, all was ready.

"It is an acknowledged fact," said Captain Hawk, "that a country is never so thoroughly fitted to enjoy peace as when most prepared for war."

"I believe that," answered Hugh Trevellyn.

"Then," returned the captain, "being ready for war, let us for a few moments enjoy the blessings of peace, and drink success to the issue of this day in a glass of your incomparable whisky-punch."

He felt that such a stimulant at that moment would have a good effect.

Hugh willingly assented; and Morna, whose spirits rose at the *sang froid* of the captain, hastened to prepare the beverage.

It is needless to add that the person she was most anxious to please pronounced the fragrant compound delicious.

Nor must my readers think the less of the fair Morna, that when the captain proffered his glass, she sipped a little.

The fact was, there appeared to be an ordeal approaching that must be passed through, and the warm and exhilarating spirit nerved them to look danger in the face calmly and cheerfully.

They had not long to wait.

Hardly were the glasses empty when a confused murmur of voices in the distance reached their ears.

"Hark!" cried Morna, listening anxiously. "Do you not hear them coming?"

Her father after a pause exclaimed:

"Yes! they are on their way without a doubt."

"Well," said the captain, rising, "let them come; so far as our means will admit, we are ready for them.

"And now, before we begin"—his tone became at this moment more serious—"give me your hands."

He took the hands of both father and daughter in his own.

"Of course," he continued, "we know not what the issue of this broil may be. It may terminate harmlessly; on the other hand, chance bullets are awkward things: they are like secret enemies—we know not where to expect their blows, and life may be sacrificed."

"Good Heaven forbid!" murmured Morna, fervently.

"If so, believe me I shall deeply regret it, since I shall be the cause."

"You must not think of that," interrupted Hugh, pressing the captain's hand.

"But I cannot help it. If any harm comes of this day's strife, I pray you hold me guiltless."

"We shall do so."

"If I should fall, there is an orphan girl who by right is the owner of a portion of the treasure I have just concealed—a dear friend of mine is entitled to a further sum. Promise me that in this case you will seek them out, and pay them for me."

"I promise faithfully—that is, if I am alive myself," said Hugh, in an earnest, solemn voice.

The captain gave him a letter as he spoke.

"This letter," he continued, "contains full instructions to guide you; and after you have carried them out to the letter, there will still remain a large sum, which you will keep for your trouble."

"I require no reward," said Hugh.

"You must take it, or it will go unclaimed," urged the captain. "It will serve as a dowry for your fair daughter."

Morna's face became suddenly overcast at these words.

The idea of marriage seemed distasteful to her.

"Of course," said the captain, "I am only imagining the worst that may occur. If we get off with only a few knocks, and I can contrive to leave this place with a whole skin, I must still trouble you to bring the treasure to me to the address which I will send you."

"All shall be done," promised Hugh Trevellyn.

"Then now we have nothing to do but to receive our guests," remarked Captain Hawk, "and to stand by each other like stanch friends to the last gasp."

He pressed the wrecker's hand warmly and released it.

"Sweet Morna," he whispered, turning to the fair girl, whose cheeks were pale as the lily, whilst her eyes swam with tears, "don't be offended"—he pressed his lips to hers—"this may be my last keepsake."

Further conversation was prevented.

The enemy was at the gate.

Loud and angry voices were heard without.

Then followed a heavy hammering at the door.

"Close the shutters and put up the bars, Morna," whispered Captain Hawk. "I think from their numbers and the angry sound of their voices they mean mischief."

Morna, who had not anticipated so strong a demonstration, obeyed with trembling eagerness.

"Hugh Trevellyn!—Hugh Trevellyn!" shouted a dozen voices without, accompanied by the heavy battering at the door.

"What do you want?" cried Hugh.

"Open the door! We want to speak to you!"

It was Daniel this time that spoke alone.

"Speak, then—I can hear," answered Hugh.

"No, no—that won't do! We can't speak in this manner. Why, in h—ll's name, do you keep friends outside?"

"If you came like a friend, peaceably and alone, you would be welcome, as you always have been; but when you come in numbers, with sticks and staves, yelling round my house like fiends, I prefer you on the outside!"

"D'ye mean to say you won't open the door, then?"

"I do!"

"Then, by h—ll, we'll burst it open!"

"Be wise, Daniel!" said the stern, deep voice of Hugh Trevellyn. "You will be sorry for this day's work! What do you want?"

"A fair division of the gold that was found on the rocks this morning."

"It is in the hands of its lawful owner. You have no right to it."

"But we'll have a right to it, and we'll have it!"

"Not a farthing; therefore begone!"

A loud yell of execration followed this speech.

"Batter in the door!"

"Fire the cabin!"

"Raze it to the ground!"

Rose on the air in wild confusion.

Some heavy missiles were dashed against the frail and time-worn barricade, causing it to creak and groan audibly.

"Down with it! Smash it in!" thundered the voices.

Captain Hawk, who was waiting calmly, grasped a pistol.

"Beware!" cried Hugh, in a warning tone. "We are armed!"

"So are we," shouted Daniel; "you'll find we have something else in our hands besides sticks and staves."

And as if in proof of his assertion, the report of a gun followed.

The bullet came crashing through the door, struck the wall on the opposite side of the room, and rebounded on to the floor.

"He was a fool that fired that shot," remarked the captain, coolly. "I should like to have seen him when he pulled the trigger: I'll swear he shut his eyes."

There was a slight pause after the gun had been discharged.

The assailants expected probably to hear a cry or a groan, but no such sound followed.

Daniel spoke again.

"You see we've got firearms!" he cried.

"But you don't know how to use them. The next time you fire, fire round the corner," called out Captain Hawk, derisively

The assailants yelled with rage.

"Oh, don't incense them!" murmured Morna, appealingly.

"We hear you, my fine spark!" shouted Daniel, in reply to the captain's taunting advice; "you'll change your tune before the sun goes down."

"To the 'Rogue's March,' you vagabonds! to send you all skulking home!" returned the captain, nothing daunted.

Again the insurgents raised their angry voices; heavy blows fell upon the door.

Another bullet pierced it, and found its way into the cabin.

"This will not do!" exclaimed Hugh Trevellyn, apprehensively; "I must go out and speak to them."

"Not on any account," said Captain Hawk: "'tis madness!"

"It is my only chance of bringing them to reason," replied the wrecker.

"Well, then, if you insist on going, I shall accompany you."

"Not for the world! your presence would but exasperate them, and frustrate all my efforts."

"'Tis true, sir," interposed Morna. "My father understands these lawless spirits better than you do; he will be safe. Suffer him to go alone."

Silenced, but by no means convinced as to his host's safety, the captain gave up the point, though his blood stirred within him, and he longed sword in hand to hurl defiance in the face of the whole lawless crew.

The above conversation had been rapidly carried on, and in a low tone.

"Once more," shouted Daniel Macorrie, "do you intend to open the door?"

"Batter it in!" roared a score of voices.

"Close the door after me as I go out," whispered Hugh Trevellyn to Morna and the captain.

The wooden bar was raised, and as the rioters were about to carry out their resolution, the door opened suddenly, and the irate mob found themselves confronted by the calm face of Hugh Trevellyn.

They fell back as they caught sight of his tall form and fearless eye.

He took advantage of their surpise to speak first.

"Are you not ashamed," he cried, "to assail my quiet dwelling more rudely than the storms that blow over it?"

"Why don't you give us our rights, then?" exclaimed Daniel, who was the mouthpiece of the party. "Divide the treasure found amongst the rocks equally amongst us, and we shall be satisfied; if not—right or wrong, friends or foes, fair or unfair—however you may look upon us, by G—d we'll have the cabin down about your ears, and seize upon the treasure by main force!"

"Ay, ay!—down with it!" they yelled.

There was a general movement as though they would proceed at once to the work of destruction; but Hugh, drawing himself up to his full height, with a look of fierce determination in his stern features, prepared to oppose the rushing tide.

"Are you mad?" he shouted—"you, Andy Morris, and you, Dick Gaskill, and above all, you two, Andrew and Daniel Macorrie, father and son—are you going to join in this act of violence?"

"We are—we are!" was the wild response.

"Harkye!" continued Hugh, still endeavouring to turn them from their purpose. "This stranger is my guest; the property you claim is his; I have given him shelter, and pledged my word for his protection and safe departure."

"You had no right to do so—you are breaking your word to us. You know our covenant—equal division."

"I do not recognise the accursed covenant of blood!"

"We'll make you, by helping ourselves!"

"You gang of murderers, you shall not cross this threshold save over my lifeless body!" cried Hugh, desperately.

"Your life then be it—his life—the lives of all, rather than go away empty-handed. Down with him!"

Yelling like savages, they were again about to advance, when Hugh, raising the gun he carried to his shoulder, pointed the barrel deliberately at the head of Daniel Macorrie.

"Hold!" he cried, with awful sternness. "I would not harm any one of you without cause, much less sacrifice a human life, but as surely as my finger now rests upon this trigger, so surely shall the first advance ring your death knell, Daniel Macorrie!"

"D—n your threats!" shouted the reckless young man. "Never mind me—forward!"

Hugh pulled the trigger, but the weapon, disabled by rust and disuse, missed fire.

A derisive shout heralded the failure; and the barrel was instantly grasped by three strong hands.

Hugh struggled with all the tenacity that a strong frame and iron sinews could offer in a contest so unequal.

The weapon was violently wrested from him, and he himself dashed to the ground.

Furious and pitiless, the wreckers in their insane rage would have sacrificed their more honourable comrade before his own threshold, when, quick as lightning, Captain Hawk darted from the door—which opened instantaneously and then closed behind him—and bestriding the prostrate form with flashing eyes, firmly-compressed lips, and an attitude of indomitable resolution, confronted the assailants sword in hand.

"Cowards!—bloodsuckers!" he cried, with bitter indignation—"wretches who would take a human life for paltry gold!—it is not this honest man on whom you should wreak your spite, but on me—me, the lawful owner of the treasure you seek to appropriate!"

"Give us that, and we'll depart quietly," cried one.

"I'd rather be hacked piecemeal, or riddled with the bullets from your rusty pistols, here where I stand!" answered Captain Hawk, defiantly.

"So you shall be!" was the reply.

"Stand back!" shouted the captain, whirling the sword with a tremendous sweep over his head, and drawing from his belt one of the handsome, bright-barrelled pistols that had done good service on many previous occasions. "Beware!" he cried, "this weapon is accustomed to deal with obstinate enemies, and never misses fire!"

As he spoke, he slowly waved the pistol to and fro, as though ready to drop upon the first that stirred.

The ruffianly mass were somewhat cowed by the unflinching courage of one man.

It gave the captain time as they fell back a little to raise the prostrate Hugh.

At the same moment a weapon was discharged from one of the marauders.

The bullet struck nothing but the door, which it pierced, and was followed by a shriek from Morna from within.

Both Hugh Trevellyn and Captain Hawk uttered an involuntary cry of apprehension.

The next instant the man who had fired the shot received the bullet from the bright-barrelled pistol in his brain.

A wild yell of resistless fury arose at the sight of their dead comrade, and the fate of the two brave men who stood at such fearful odds would have been inevitable, when at a slight tap from the captain's heel—a signal previously agreed upon—Morna raised the bar, the door opened, and before the savages without had time to prevent it, their prey was once more out of their reach, and the door barricaded.

But the wild fury of the wreckers had reached its height.

Blows fell like hail upon the door and the window shutters.

The crashing of glass and the yells of the assailants told the ominous tale that a protracted resistance was impossible.

Morna, pale as death, grasped the captain's hand.

"You must not be sacrificed," she said, with tender earnestness. "There is one way of escape: come with me, and I will lead you to it."

"And your father?—yourself?" inquired Captain Hawk.

"Think not of us; we shall be safe," she replied, with intense anxiety. "It is you, not us, they want."

She knelt down and opened a trap that the captain had not observed till that moment, it fitted so accurately in the floor.

A flight of narrow wooden steps led to the cellar beneath.

"I cannot—I will not leave you to encounter these ruffians alone," cried the highwayman.

"Oh yes, you must fly—you will for my sake, for your own: it is your only chance of preserving your life or ours!" she exclaimed, in hurried, trembling accents.

"If I thought you would be safe——"

"We shall—we shall—they know not of this trap. We have kept it a secret from all but ourselves. Oh, come! Hark! Merciful Heaven! in another moment they will be here, and it will be too late!"

Another deafening shout rose in the air—the door and shutters began to crack and splinter.

Captain Hawk looked towards Hugh Trevellyn.

"Go, my friend," said Hugh. "It's your only chance."

They grasped each other by the hand in silence.

Morna with desperate energy seized the captain's wrist and almost dragged him to the trap.

"Come!" she cried, hoarsely. "It is for life or death."

They descended, and the trap closed over them not a second too soon, for the next instant, with one united crash, door, shutters, windows yielded to the assaults of the invaders, and Hugh found himself surrounded by this incensed mob.

But in vain they sought the captain—he was gone, and Morna with him.

Whither the reader knows.

The wreckers were not so enlightened.

Like howling wolves disappointed of their prey, they vented their baffled wrath in oaths and curses.

Daniel was the fiercest of the angry troop.

"You have aided the escape of this fine gentleman," he shouted, furiously—"this lavender-water scented captain!"

"You did not find him such," retorted Hugh, who, now that his daughter and his guest were safe, cared little for himself.

There was a provoking irony in his tone that added fresh fuel to Daniel's jealous wrath.

"We understand it all, Hugh Trevellyn; but woe betide him when he falls into our hands, though he is your daughter's paramour!" continued the incensed man.

The dark brow of Hugh grew darker, and his cheek flushed at these words as he grasped one of the heavy pistols on the table.

"But that I think passion and the blind thirst for gold has rendered you insane," he said, "you should pay for your foul aspersion with your life; as it is, I treat it with contempt, and simply tell you you lie!"

"Where is he?" thundered Daniel.

"In safety," was the calm reply.

"Oh, d—n him and her too!" cried a voice. "Let them go! Where's the money?"

"Ay, ay!" echoed the whole body.

"Let's ransack the cabin!—pull it down!—burn it, so that we get the gold!" they shouted.

"Ay! go on! commence your demoniac work!" cried Hugh. "Pillage—burn—destroy like ruthless savages as you are! and when your labours are completed, you will be as rich as you are now. The treasure, like its owner, is beyond your reach."

"But revenge is within our reach!" yelled Daniel Macorrie, white and ghastly with rage; "and, by h—ll! we'll have it! Now, boys, lash that honest fool to the beam yonder," he cried, "and then tear down and root up every plank in this rotten cabin! If we don't find what we seek, we'll fire the den, and leave its owner to roast among the ashes!"

Hugh Trevellyn was surrounded in an instant like a noble lion bayed by a pack of hungry bloodhounds.

Resistance was impossible, and he was bound to one of the massive upright beams that supported the roof of his dwelling.

The work of destruction then commenced.

The planks were torn down from the walls, and the flooring in many places pulled up.

Hugh smiled grimly as he observed that the part where the lid of the trap reposed escaped their fierce investigations.

The cupboards and recesses in the walls were emptied of their contents in a few moments, but with no satisfactory result.

The planks inside these receptacles were madly wrenched from their fastenings; but still no glittering treasure poured out its golden stream to allay their fury.

They were mad drunk with rage.

"Fire the d—d place!" raved Daniel Macorrie.

Torches flashed and smoked through the cabin, and this atrocious order would have been at once carried into execution had not a few hurried words from one of their number caused a general pause.

"Hist! I hear the tread of soldiers!"

There was an instantaneous silence.

The regular, monotonous tramp, tramp, of a body of troops fell upon their ears distinctly.

Daniel looked cautiously from the window, and beheld a small body of foot soldiers, accompanied by a sergeant and another person, who walked by his side.

They appeared to be coming in the direction of the cabin.

"King's troops," he said, in a low voice. "We'll give 'em a wide berth and settle with Master Hugh Trevellyn at another time."

Daniel fixed a scowling look upon the bold features of the wrecker as he spoke; but the other condescended no reply.

In a moment the whole party had made good their exit by the windows in the rear.

In the meantime the soldiers—twelve in number—came steadily forward towards the cottage.

It appeared at first as though they would have passed it; but at a sign communicated by the individual who walked by the sergeant's side, the latter cried·

"Halt!"

The soldiers drew up at the door of the cabin.

"Humph!" remarked the sergeant, as he glanced at the shattered door, "there appears to have been warm work here."

Without further remark, he and his companions entered.

Inside the wreck was but too manifest.

Torn planks, shutters wrenched from their hinges, a few rusty firelocks, and the entire *debris* of the late devastation spoke for itself.

Last, not least, Hugh Trevellyn bound firmly to the beam, like a martyr awaiting his execution, completed the picture.

"We appear to have arrived at the right moment, my friend," said the sergeant, drawing his sword and severing the thongs that bound the wrecker.

"A little earlier would have been better for the welfare of my homestead," answered Hugh, with a melancholy smile, as his eye swept over the ruin.

"What has been the matter?" inquired the sergeant's companion, whose appearance and costume betokened him more civil than military.

Hugh, who had no suspicion whatever that Captain Hawk was not what he appeared to be—a gentleman of substance and position—related the facts as briefly as possible.

The person in the private clothes quietly took notes during this.

When the wrecker had finished, he asked:

"Where is this gentleman now?"

"I cannot say with any certainty," replied Hugh. "He had to fly for his life, and is, of course, in some place of concealment."

The questioner looked very hard at Hugh as he gave this answer.

While he is looking, it may be as well to inform our readers that this personage is Roland Gregson, the detective, and that his companion is Sergeant Crank, and that they are scouring the country perseveringly to endeavour to discover a clue to the lost treasure of his Majesty King George II., and the whereabouts of the honest Dutchman, Moses Geltz.

Roland Gregson had discovered that an old Jewish-looking man had inquired at the docks for a vessel sailing for Holland, and that those inquiries were unsuccessful; he had also traced him as far as Plymouth, but there he had lost the scent.

He had also arrived at the fact that two gentlemen had started for Guernsey in the Saucy Sally; but that ill-fated vessel never having arrived at her destination, she was supposed by the agents despatched to the Channel island to have foundered in the fearful gale that has been previously described.

If so, vessel, treasure, and its purloiners were safe from pursuit at the bottom of the sea.

But the account given by Hugh Trevellyn had impressed the detective with the idea that the stranger and the treasure might possibly be the precise objects he was anxious to light upon.

At the end of a long and scrutinising gaze, Gregson remarked to Hugh Trevellyn:

"You are sure you are not deceiving me?"

"Why should I?" said Hugh. "Truth needs no concealment."

"No, no—of course not," acquiesced the detective. "Speak the truth and shame the—— Ahem! You understand? And when do you think it probable you will see this stranger again?" he inquired.

"His concealment is only temporary," said Hugh. "He may possibly return to-night."

"Humph!" returned the detective, thoughtfully. "To-night! Then to-morrow, I suppose, I could see him? I have an important message to deliver to him from a friend, and should wish to speak to him for a few moments. By-the-by, what is his name?"

Hugh was perfectly ignorant of this, never having taken the liberty to ask, and therefore could not gratify the officer.

It, however, seemed to the latter a fresh cause for suspicion.

"This stranger will probably be lurking somewhere near at hand," he remarked, in a low tone, to the sergeant. "It will be as well to search the neighbourhood."

"If you think it necessary, certainly," answered Sergeant Crank, who had had almost enough searching, and who would have preferred a slight refreshment and a pipe of tobacco at some roadside inn.

"I do think it necessary," was the decided reply.

"I shall probably look in to-morrow," remarked Gregson to Hugh Trevellyn, and with this brief information he and the sergeant quitted the cabin.

The wreckers were nowhere to be seen.

"Who could those men be?" thought Hugh, after their departure. "They seem very curious. Soldiers, too! What could they want with our guest? And the handsome stranger, who was he?—*who?*"

CHAPTER CLXII.

MOSES GELTZ FINDS THE MESSENGER OF JUSTICE A HARD CUSTOMER.—THE JEW SEEKS GOLD AND FINDS STEEL.—HE STARTS FOR HOLLAND IN A NOVEL VESSEL.

THE Jew's heart sank within him.

"I have come for the diamond ring of which you are the unlawful possessor," continued the same stern accents.

The Jew groaned pitifully. Had his heart been demanded he could scarcely have made a more sorrowful response.

"Deliver it to me this instant!" the solemn tones enjoined.

"I can't give it up: I haven't got it!" cried Moses.

"Oh yes, you have!" cried the voice.

"But I can't part vith it—I von't part vith it! I'd rather give up my life firsht, upon my shoul I vould!"

"Your life!" returned the cloaked figure, contemptuously. "What would be the value of the life, body, bones, and all, of a miserable old wretch like yourself? But since you hesitate to obey my commands, I shall not only take the ring, but the life you deem an equivalent, into the bargain."

As he spoke he drew from beneath his cloak a pistol with an awfully polished barrel, which flashed in the semi-obscurity, and placed it against the Jew's temple.

Moses, feeling the unpleasant chill caused by the cold end of the barrel pressing against his flesh, began to have very uncomfortable sensations.

In the first place, the pistol was probably loaded; the finger of the mysterious stranger was on the trigger: he could see that with his own eyes.

If the cloaked visitant were in a moment of forgetfulness or excitement to pull that trigger, the beautiful pistol with the bright barrel would infallibly go off—it looked as if it would—and then where would he be?

All things considered, was it worth risking his life for a diamond ring?

Could all the rings in the world bring him back to life again if he were dead?

This train of mental questions was suddenly put a stop to by the voice of the Messenger of Justice.

"You are keeping me waiting," it cried.

"I vish I could—you should vait long enough," thought Moses.

"Are you prepared to deliver up the ring?"

"No, I'm not. It'sh a d—n robbery!"

"You would rather die?"

"No, I vouldn't!"

"You said as much."

"I didn't mean it."

"You must give up the ring or your life. Which do you choose?"

"Neither: I vantsh 'em both!"

"You must part with one or the other; so make up your mind, and quickly."

The messenger gave the pistol an admonitory screw as he spoke.

"Oh!" roared the Jew, "vot 're you doing? you're boring holesh in ma head!"

"I shall bore a deeper hole presently," cried the figure,

in a stern, decided manner, as though he were getting out of patience. "Come, hand over the ring, and thank your stars you can get off so easily."

"Eashily! Ten thoushand poundsh!" murmured the Jew. "Eashily! Mein Gott!"

"The ring!" thundered the figure, "or——"

Click, click, went the hammer as the ominous being placed it on full-cock.

"No, no, no, no!" roared the Jew, at this very definite proceeding. "I'll give you the ring!"

"Be quick!"

"Yesh, yesh!" groaned the Jew, as his trembling fingers fumbled in his pocket for the gem.

He soon found it.

What would he have given if he could have tricked the Messenger of Justice as he had done the King!

But there was no chance of that.

"Here it ish!" he groaned, as he held it towards the sable form, whose outstretched hand immediately grasped it.

"You'll undershtand," cried the troubled Israelite, "I give dish ring under compulshion, but I looksh upon it ash a dead robbery!"

"You can look upon it how you please," returned the appropriator, as he placed the ring in his pocket.

"Vell now you've got vhat you vantsh, you can go avay an' leave me to go to shleep," said Moses.

"Don't be in a hurry, old fox," returned the visitor; "I haven't got all I want yet."

"No?"

"No!"

"I've got nothing elshe, and I'm shleepy."

"Oh yes, you have!"

"I tell you I haven't; upon my shoul I haven't!"

"Don't stake your soul upon a lie!"

"I vish I may die if I have—there!"

"Take care, lest your wish come true! Think—reflect!"

"I can't—I'm dead ashleep!"

"I'll assist your memory. If you place your hand under the coverlet, you'll find two bags of gold!"

The Jew almost leaped up in the bed.

"Two bagsh of gold!" he almost shrieked.

"Two bags of gold," was the calm reply.

"Vhat d'ye take me for? Vhere should I get two bagsh of gold from?" gasped Moses, trembling with apprehension.

"I take you for a lying, thievish old scoundrel," replied the figure, confidently, "and the bags of gold to which I allude were taken by you from beneath the floor of the captain's cabin."

This was a staggerer for the *honest* Dutchman.

"I—I found 'em quite by acchident, under a looshe plank," stammered the Jew; "an' I took 'em to prevent anyvone elshe for getting hold of 'em; I vosh goin' to give 'em to the captain to-morrow—I vosh, upon my shoul I vosh!"

"I'll save you the trouble. Hand them over to me."

"I'll shee you d—— I mean, blesht firsht! How do I know vhat you're going to do vith 'em?" raved the Israelite, to whom excitement and despair gave a temporary boldness. "You may be ash big a tief ash I am myshelf!"

The reproduction of the pistol, and its cold muzzle tickling the old rascal's ear, quickly dispelled his courage.

He shuddered.

The strong wrist of the figure gave the weapon a sharp screw.

Moses yelled.

"Oh, mein Gott, you're pinchin' me!"

"Quick! the money-bags! If you hesitate or refuse——"

"But I don't heshitate or refushe! Dere'sh von, an' dere'sh de other!"

As he spoke he handed the bags to the cloaked stranger.

"That will do for the present," he said, as they disappeared from the longing eyes of the Jew under the cloak. "And now, for the present, I shall take my departure. And remember this, that whenever you deviate in future from the strict course of rectitude, you may always look for a visit from the Messenger of Justice."

With these words the mysterious stranger glided away and disappeared

In the dim light it was not very perceptible where he made his egress.

Through the wall, Moses thought.

"He'sh the tefil—he musht be the tefil! The d—n rogue robbing a poor old man of his hard earningsh!"

The Jew lay down on the bed; but though all was dark and quiet, he could not sleep.

Diamond rings and money-bags haunted him; ugly-looking pistols with long bright barrels came of their own accord, and intruded themselves into his ears.

Gigantic figures in black cloaks came and sat down upon him.

He started up in a kind of horror.

It would seem he had dozed off into a troubled slumber, and from the perturbation of his thoughts, nightmare was the result.

But he was now awake; and with the reviving of his reflective faculties, his loss came vividly before him.

It would not bear thinking of: it must be some horrible dream. But no—the unpleasant fact remained: the ring was gone—the money-bags also.

There was no denying this.

Suddenly it occurred to him that there was more gold snugly stowed away under the plank in the captain's cabin.

"Vhat a fool I am," he cried, "to be a losher, vhen I have a chance of getting back more than I've losht! If de tefil robsh me, it's quite fair if I robsh some von elshe!"

And, as this argument appeared quite satisfactory to the old scoundrel, he crept once more from his bed.

There was no doubt that Moses Geltz had the phrenological bump of *acquisitiveness* inordinately strong.

He was in truth a most incorrigible old thief.

He would have robbed his father—he would have robbed his mother—he would have robbed his uncles, aunts, sisters, brothers—nay, his whole family, if he had had the chance.

One would have imagined his adventure with the mysterious visitor, and the parting warning he had received, would have had a salutary effect upon him; but it was not so.

The Messenger of Justice had hardly departed before the Spirit of Avarice banished from the mind of Moses Geltz all recollection of his admonition; and now nothing would satisfy the reckless old sinner but another visit to the money-bags in the captain's cabin.

"Tefilsh or no tefilsh, I'll remunerate myshelf for my losshes."

Once more he stole softly from the narrow cell he occupied, and guided by the light, cautiously opened the door.

The cabin was still empty.

He glanced from the window.

Faint streaks of light were beginning to appear in the distant east.

But what cared he for that? his mind and thoughts were fixed upon sordid gold.

He approached the well-known spot, removed the plank, and inserted his hand with feverish eagerness to grasp the coveted coin.

As he did so, he fancied he heard a sound such as a person might make under a violent effort to restrain a sudden burst of laughter.

"Vhat'sh dat?" he exclaimed, in a startled tone, looking round but seeing no one. "It musht have been fancy."

Without further comment, he once more thrust in the hand he had withdrawn so quickly.

Suddenly there was a sharp click heard like the snapping of a clasp or a handcuff, and then a terrific howl from Moses Geltz.

He had thrust his hand into a rat-trap.

The steel arm furnished with a sharp, saw-like edge had descended on his wrist, and he was caught fast.

"Oh, mein Gott! Murder—murder! I'm killed—I'm killed! De tefil'sh got hold of me vid his teeth! he'sh biting off my handsh! Murder—murder!"

Thus yelling, and by dint of great struggling and kicking, he at last drew forth his imprisoned wrist with the instrument of his torture firmly fastened to it, cutting him to the bone.

But he could not release himself, and the blood flowed copiously.

To make the matter worse, Captain Jecks quietly showed his face from under a coverlet at the further corner of the cabin (his berth), and politely asked him what he was making that d—d row about?"

"My wrisht'sh cut in half!" roared the Jew. "Oh—oh! Take it off—take it off!"

"Oh dear no!" replied the captain. "I bought that trap expressly for rats, and, I think, this time it has caught a very fine one."

"But I ain't a rat!" yelled Moses. "I'm a poor old man dat'sh—— Oh—oh—oh!" he roared, suddenly, in the extremity of his anguish.

Lord Harcliffe entered.

"Hallo!" he cried, with a pleasant smile. "What's the matter, Mr. Jansen Spraager?"

"I shall be a corpsh in five minutesh, if you don't take off dish d—n rat-trap!" screamed Moses.

"Dear me!" said his lordship, raising his eyebrows in the most unconcerned manner possible. "You've very little time to lose then."

"Oh—oh—oh!" yelled the Jew, rolling on the floor in agony.

"Don't die till you've made your will," his lordship continued; "and be sure and leave me that diamond ring as a legacy."

"I haven't got it!" roared the tortured Moses. "It's de d—d ring vhat'sh got me into all dish trouble!"

"How so?"

"I can't talk—I've got such horrible painsh!"

"Never mind the pains: pray explain!"

"Never mind! Oh—oh! I vish you had 'em inshtead of me!"

"What had the ring to do with your present sensations?"

"De tefil came and shtole it! Oh—oh!"

"Ah! now I understand," cried Captain Jecks, joining suddenly in the conversation: "his satanic majesty stole the ring, and you thought to replace it out of my money-bags. You felonious old rascal! you're justly served, don't you think so?"

"Oh, yesh—yesh!" shrieked the Jew. "I feelsh I'm a misherable shinner; but I von't do it again—I von't, s'elp me Moshes! Only take off dish infernal machine, an' I'll turn honesht—upon my shoul I vill!"

As the avaricious old man had been severely punished by the teeth of the formidable instrument, Captain Jecks, at a sign from Lord Harcliffe, rolled himself out of his berth and approached the Jew, who lay writhing, kicking, and groaning by turns upon the floor.

"Come, be quiet," he cried, "and let me see what can be done."

He bent down as he spoke, and appeared to examine the instrument of torture attentively.

The Jew had great difficulty in restraining his groans and plungings.

"Ah!" ejaculated the captain, very seriously, "I don't see how I can possibly release you without amputating your hand at the wrist."

"Vhat! cut off mein hand? Oh, mein Gott! Oh—oh!" groaned the Jew. "It'sh almost cut off already!"

"A little patience then, and I daresay it will drop off quite," remarked Lord Harcliffe, in a comforting tone.

"I can't be patient! Who de tefil can be patient vid a saw cuttin' 'em to de bonesh?" roared Moses. "Try it yourshelvesh!"

Neither the captain nor the Black Highwayman cared for this experimental effort.

But stooping down, the smuggler, assisted by Lord Harcliffe, raised the steel arm of the trap, and set the Jew's wrist at liberty.

"Oh—oh—oh!" he cried, nursing his wounded limb as though it had been a sick child, and staggering to the nearest seat, into which he dropped thoroughly exhausted with pain and chagrin.

"Get me some brandy!" he groaned.

"Nonsense! Brandy! D'ye want to die of inflammation?" said the captain. "No—no; I'll give you something better than that!" And, beckoning to Lord Harcliffe, they quitted the cabin together.

The Jew remained uttering lamentations over his wounded wrist, and anathematising steel traps vociferously.

"I believe I've been shvindled after all!" he cried. "The cloaked figure vash dat Lord Ramiliesh—I'll take my oath of it! I recognised his voice. It'sh he dat'sh got de ring, de d—n tief!"

Further soliloquy was cut short by the sudden entrance of two of the men.

"You're wanted on deck, mister," they remarked, pithily.

"Vell den, you'll have to carry me," answered the miserable Moses, sulkily.

"We'll soon do that," said one of them. "Catch hold of his legs, Dick."

This was immediately done; and the speaker grasping the Jew by his coat collar, and hoisting him out of his seat, he was by their joint efforts carried up on to the deck.

Moses Geltz glared round upon the crew, who were all assembled, in the highest possible spirits, evidently ripe for mischief.

"Now, my lads," cried the captain, "this honest, worthy old gentleman is anxious to get to Holland; and being very impatient to reach there, prefers starting by himself rather than to wait our time. That being the case, I've fitted him out a boat all to himself. Bring it aft," he called, beckoning two of his men.

"But I don't know anything about boatsh!" exclaimed the Jew.

"It's high time you began to learn something, then. Roll it here," continued Captain Jecks.

Two sailors immediately appeared, rolling a large empty cask along the deck.

"Vat'sh dat?" asked the Jew, apprehensively.

"That's your boat," answered the captain.

"It ishn't a boat at all, it'sh a cask," responded Moses.

"I say it is a boat, and a very tight, snug little craft too of the sort; I call it the 'Roundabout.'"

"But you don't mean to say you're goin' to send me to sea in dish?" exclaimed the terrified Jew.

"Yes, I do," said Captain Jecks. "Now then, boys, in with him!"

No sooner said than done, and Moses Geltz was in the cask, with his head appearing over the top, grinning and chattering like an antiquated ourang-outang.

"You find it very comfortable, don't you?" politely inquired Lord Harcliffe.

"No I don't, you villainsh! You vantsh to drown me, dat'sh vhat you do! Take me out!—I von't go!—I feelsh sea sick already!"

The crew set up a laugh of intense enjoyment.

"Now then, over with him!" cried the captain. "You've all heard of 'Love in a tub?' You now have the opportunity of seeing a Jew in a tub, and if the bottom happens to come out, good luck to him!"

Ropes in the meantime had been fastened round the barrel, and in spite of the yells, entreaties, and execrations of the Israelite, it was hoisted over the vessel's side into the waves beneath.

The weight of the luckless Moses caused it to float upright in the water, which rose to about a foot from the top.

With his hands clutching the edge of the cask, and his face expressive of the horror he felt, he began to drift away, swayed and tossed to and fro by the waves.

"I shall be drowned!" he shouted—"I shall go to de fishes! Murder—murder! you d—n villainsh! I'll look you all up for dish! Oh—oh!"

A wave at that moment playfully splashed him, and filled his mouth with salt water.

"Good-bye, Moses Geltz!" cried Lord Harcliffe, waving his hand. "A pleasant journey to Holland!"

"It strikes me he'll find himself at another place before he gets there," remarked the captain.

The barrel with its freight was now some distance from the ship.

It was getting indistinct as it went on bumping and tossing amidst the restless waves.

The Jew's legs had given way under him, and he had sunk down at the bottom of the roundabout

"Good-bye, Moses Geltz!"

CHAPTER CLXIII.

MORNA CONDUCTS CAPTAIN HAWK BY THE SUBTERRANEAN PATH TO THE CAVERN ON THE ROCKS.—WHAT BEFEL HIM THERE.—HIS TERRIBLE PERIL.—THE DEATH PILLAR.—HIS HAIRBREADTH ESCAPE.

THE cabin of Hugh Trevellyn being near the rocky coast, the foundation on which it was built partook of the same character, so that when the captain descended by the trap-door, he found himself in a kind of cellar formed by a natural excavation of the rocks.

It was quite dark, and the fierce clang of angry voices that reverberated above, sounded muffled and indistinct to the ears of Morna and the captain.

"Is there any outlet here?" he inquired.

"You shall see. Give me your hand," she said, in a low tone.

This agreeable suggestion was immediately complied with, and by means of that gentle guidance she led him across the dark cavern to what appeared to be a recess in the perpendicular rock.

Here she paused.

"You must stoop now," she cried; "there is a cavity here that we must enter."

The fair speaker bent her head as she spoke: Captain Hawk did the same.

By some singular accident their lips met.

Was it strange if the captain took advantage of the occasion?

But strange or not, he did; neither was there any opposition offered by his fair conductress.

This so encouraged the highwayman, that the moment they were able to assume their upright position, he threw his arms round her yielding form and embraced her passionately.

"You have saved my life, beautiful Morna! How can I ever repay you?" he earnestly inquired.

Morna, if her fluttering heart spoke truly, could have answered, but her tongue was silent, and she sighed.

"Was that sigh for me?" asked the captain, who was beginning to feel a tenderer sentiment than mere admiration stealing over him towards the young girl.

"I am apprehensive for your safety," she replied.

"But are we not safe here?"

"So long as the trap remains undiscovered; but should any mischance reveal that, it would be as easy for them to descend as for us."

This was a self-evident fact, and the captain saw it at once.

"We must continue our subterranean path," continued Morna, "for some distance; I will not leave you till I place you in a spot that shall baffle pursuit."

She took his hand once more in hers, and led him along a narrow rocky passage not wide enough to admit two abreast.

At the termination of this she paused.

"Here is our outlet of escape," she said.

As she spoke she applied both her hands to the apparently fixed and solid rock that confronted her.

It swayed round with the force applied as though on a pivot, leaving a narrow space sufficiently large for entrance, through which a stream of cool air rushed.

From its saline odour, it was evident it came from the sea.

"I comprehend," said Captain Hawk. "We shall emerge from this upon the sea-shore."

"Yes," replied Morna.

Having pushed the oscillating rock back to its original place, Morna continued her course, still holding the captain by the hand, till at length a gradually increasing light told that they were approaching the opening of the passage, and in a moment more they came out in a large cavern, that was formed at the base of a gigantic overhanging cliff, from the entrance of which the sea was visible.

The tide was out, and the entrance to the cavern was, as it were, masked and barricaded by a natural breastwork of sharp, slimy rocks.

"Here you will be safe till I return to fetch you," said Morna.

"Safe enough," returned the captain; "for even should any intruder venture here, there are nooks and crannies enough in this rude chamber to hide twenty men, much less one."

"You will remain here, then, till I come to you, will you not?" asked Morna.

"Fixed as fate!" replied Captain Hawk. "I shall not be dull, since I shall pass the intervening time in thinking of you," he added, gallantly.

Morna smiled, and left him; but his last words warmed her heart as she threaded her way back again to the cellar from which she had first started, making her dark pathway light with love.

Captain Hawk, whose excitement and the novelty of his situation had raised his spirits wonderfully, strode up and down the spacious cavern, thinking of the strange events of his chequered career, and the beautiful girl who had taken such a hold upon his imagination, if not his heart.

The captain loved the society of women, and treated them always with a chivalrous gallantry mingled with respect, which, in addition to his dashing figure and handsome face, made him a universal favourite with the susceptible sex.

But though this was by no means the first time he had received unmistakable signs of feminine approbation, he never remembered one instance in which the prepossession had been so cordially returned as in the case of the beautiful Morna Trevellyn.

There was no doubt that in a short space of time he would be desperately in love with her.

But just then a keen north-west wind was blowing from the sea; and love, however ardent, will not warm frail humanity for ever.

The captain began to feel cold.

"Ugh!" he cried, shuddering, "a fire would not be unacceptable here."

There was a quantity of loose wood lying about, probably the accumulation of the wrecks that occurred on the coast, and which the tide had washed up.

"If I had but a light now!" thought the highwayman.

With a sudden recollection he felt in the pocket of his waistcoat.

A radiant smile broke upon his features.

It was his phosphorus box and matches, so carefully closed as to be impervious to wet.

"'Richard's himself again!'" he quoted.

He then collected a sufficient quantity of wood for his purpose, and in an incredibly short space of time a cheerful fire glowed in a snug recess of the cavern.

The brandy-flask in his pocket was still unemptied, and a draught of its contents brought him to a state of calm content, in which happy condition we may leave him for a short time whilst we return to the fierce body of infuriated men whom the arrival of the soldiers had sent scudding off like hares at the baying of the hounds.

They did not separate and seek their homes, but took their way to the beach as affording an easier means of escape had it been necessary.

They had been thwarted in their work of vengeance, and disappointed in their search for the gold, and with moody brows, flushed, angry looks, and bitter imprecations, they congregated together on the rocks, vowing they would never rest till their full revenge was consummated in ruin and bloodshed.

They little knew how near they were to the man they would have been so rejoiced to have held in their power.

And yet not a hundred yards separated them.

The mystery of Captain Hawk's escape hung over them like a cloud.

They could not comprehend it.

He could not have retreated by the back windows, for they were strictly watched.

He was not concealed in the capacious chimney, for several of the party—Daniel included—had looked there on first entering the cabin.

Where, then, was he?

Daniel Macorrie, his thoughts quickened by love—as he called it—hate, and jealousy, suggested a subterranean exit as the only possible means of accounting for the mysterious disappearance.

But, then, where was the trap?

They had never heard of or seen such an outlet in Hugh Trevellyn's cottage.

The reader knows it had been kept a profound secret.

But this idea—this clue once seized upon—they would not relinquish it.

"It must be a trap," cried Daniel; "and the artful old fox, Hugh Trevellyn, and the wanton Jezebel, his daughter, have kept it to themselves. But we'll find it, boys, and before long we'll be on their track, curse 'em!"

Just at this moment a wild, whirling scream rose in the air; and as the wreckers looked round to ascertain the

[CAPTAIN HAWK SHOOTS DANIEL MACORRIE.]

cause, a flock of sea birds flew out from under the cliffs at no great distance.

They appeared startled, and flew round and round, uttering harsh, discordant cries.

"Something has alarmed them," cried one of the wreckers.

As the speaker uttered this remark, a light blue smoke was distinctly seen ascending from one of the cavities in the cliff.

"Look there," cried Daniel, pointing to the spot where the vapour wreathed itself into a snake-like form, "d'ye see that?"

All answered in the affirmative.

"Some one is in that cavern," said Daniel Macorrie.

This was sufficient to arouse the interest of the whole body.

Some shipwrecked party seeking shelter would have been an acceptable restorative to their wounded spirits.

They thirsted for plunder.

At that juncture, the mysterious escape of Captain Hawk, and the fire from whence the smoke proceeded, suddenly associated themselves with singular accuracy in the mind of Daniel Macorrie.

"There must be a trap in the cabin that we know nothing of, leading to some underground passage, and by that our prey has escaped us," he cried, in a tone of strong conviction. "But if he should be there now, nothing can save him."

The next moment, the whole party were rapidly making their way towards the chasm whence the smoke issued.

Not a word was spoken.

Each one felt intensely anxious.

Daniel most of all.

They sprang quickly but cautiously from rock to rock.

The entrance to the cavern was gained.

They paused at its mouth. All within appeared silent.

But a light blue vapour floated over the roof.

They had, therefore, gained the spot they sought.

But not the man.

The cave appeared empty, but upon a closer examination it was seen to be supplied with several recesses.

From one of these at a remote corner, out of the reach of wind or wave, a flickering light was perceptible.

"Follow me!" said Daniel, in a whisper.

They advanced with noiseless steps, till, guided by the glowing embers of the fire, they beheld with savage exultation the object of their search, Captain Hawk.

But how did they find him? With his back against the solid rock, and his heel firmly planted on the ground, with stern eye and compressed lip, looking defiance as he awaited the death struggle with his foes?

Not so; but under entirely different circumstances.

The genial warmth of the fire acting upon the excitement he had undergone had induced drowsiness, which, in the full consciousness of safety, he made no effort to throw off.

He had yielded to the resistless lethargy, and now with his head resting on his arm and a calm smile upon his lips, he slumbered as peacefully as a little child.

But his defenceless state awakened no compunction in the breasts of his foes.

The first impulse was to plunge their knives into his breast as he slept.

But then the treasure—how could they obtain that? Where was it concealed?

That must by some method be extorted.

And what could be so powerful an incentive to confession as the fear of death?

They were decided how to act.

One of the party was despatched for a rope.

The remainder, clutching their open knives, watched the unconscious sleeper with hungry eyes, like a pack of vultures waiting some poor victim's death, that they might commence their feast of blood.

But the captain still slept on; and in a short time the messenger returned, bearing with him a coil of strong rope.

This was speedily unrolled, and a strong noose made at one end, and they then proceeded to carry out the horrible plan Daniel Macorrie had proposed in low whispers while they were waiting the arrival of their comrade.

All being prepared, Daniel approached in company with another, and each seizing an arm of the sleeping man, forced them down to his side. A third then threw the noose over his head, and drawing it tightly, wound it rapidly round and round his body.

This was done so rapidly, that when the captain burst from the trammels of his deep repose, it was to find himself effectually pinioned and helpless in the midst of a savage body of ruffians, glaring at him fiercely, whilst he himself could offer no effectual resistance.

Foremost amongst the throng were the sunburnt features and the pale vindictive eyes of Daniel Macorrie.

"So we've got you at last, d—n you!" he exclaimed, in a brutal tone, not loud but deep; "and now we'll see if we can persuade you to tell us where you have stowed away that gold so cleverly—eh, boys?" he added, turning to his companions.

"Ay, ay!" they cried.

"You may spare yourselves all further trouble, then, you cowardly scoundrels!" replied Captain Hawk: "that gold shall never fall into your murderous hands! And I rejoice to be able to tell you that it is at this moment in a place of perfect security, and quite beyond your reach!"

A growl of fierce disappointment burst from a score of angry lips.

"You mean to say," inquired Daniel, in a voice that trembled with passion, "that you don't mean to confess where you have hidden the gold?"

"No!"

"You're quite resolved?"

"Quite!"

"Do you know the consequence of your refusal?"

"No, neither do I care to know!"

"Are you tired of life?"

"Not at all!"

"You act as though you were. Don't you see your life is in our hands?"

"Presumptuous fool!" the captain burst out, with irresistible contempt, "my life is in the hands of Heaven alone; and though I am now here, tied and bound, and with such disproportionate odds against me, I feel confident that I shall not die one instant before my appointed time."

"Won't you? You'll see shortly how you're mistaken. We'll teach you a lesson you'll never forget, my fine gentleman!" Daniel hissed in his ear, with bitter rage at his coolness. "Bring him out!" he shouted.

Captain Hawk was dragged up rudely on to his feet.

Of course, he expected no mercy or consideration; he asked none—he received none.

He was dragged to the mouth of the cave.

The tide was flowing in rapidly.

Sharp rocks rose up like ugly black teeth.

One in particular reared itself above the rest, and had a formidable, spiteful appearance.

To this Daniel Macorrie pointed.

"We call that rock," he said, in a tone of fiendish malignity, "the *Death Pillar!* Do you wish to know why?"

The captain preserved a contemptuous silence.

"Oh, you're sulky, are you? Then I'll tell you: it's because so many have died bound to its slimy side!"

Still the highwayman made no reply.

"We shall serve you," continued Daniel, with increased spite in his tone at his victim's cool indifference, "as we have served many before: we shall bind you to that rock, and the waters will rise and rise higher and higher, and you will see them coming—ha, ha!—and try in vain to escape them. You will be compelled to swallow the salt water draught after draught till you loathe it and are still compelled to swallow, till at last it pours in in a torrent and you can't breathe! You struggle desperately, but no escape. Your life is bursting out of you—you'd give your treasure a million times over for me to be at your elbow to cut the rope, but it will be too late; and with one strong, last convulsion, all will be over, and you'll be dead, you d—d fool!"

"Free, you mean!" calmly returned the captain.

"When the moon shines to-night upon that rock it will shine on your dead face!"

"And yours!" suddenly exclaimed Captain Hawk, as he pointed to a mass of slimy matter that had fallen from the roof of the cavern upon Daniel's face and marked it as with a streak of blood. "I believe in omens. That is your death token! Ha, ha! how pale you look!"

Daniel Macorrie made an effort to shake off the superstitious feeling his victim's words created, and in a hoarse voice shouted:

"Away with him to the rock!"

At this command the helpless man was ruthlessly dragged from rock to rock, often splashing kneedeep in water, for the tide was now coming in rapidly, till the *Death Pillar* was reached.

There he was bound and gagged with his back to the stony mass, and there they left him.

Alone!—to die!

Little did poor Morna know the horrible position of the man she had already learnt to love.

It was a terrible position—it was indeed the bitterness of death.

Coolly to see the grim monster gradually approaching.

To feel the surging waves rising by slow degrees, to hear them singing their melancholy, monotonous death song as their cold arms encircled the victim.

Captain Hawk was a brave man, but he needed all his courage to bear the horrors of his position.

His eyes strained with desperate intensity across the watery waste, but nothing—not a spec—appeared in sight.

"Good Heaven!" he thought—he could not speak, the gag prevented him—"wilt thou permit these wretches to triumph in this cold-blooded scheme? Shall I perish here that they may return at ebb tide to mock and perhaps insult my lifeless clay! Oh, surely no! Thou wilt preserve me!"

In the strength of this unspoken prayer his spirit revived, but the waters had now risen breast high, and little time remained.

He seemed to fall into a kind of stupor.

Suddenly he was aroused by a voice.

"Oh, mein Gott—mein Gott!" he cried.

He looked up and beheld a floating cask with a pale, terrified old Jew's face peering from the top, drifting towards him.

He would have cried, "Help me!" but he could not.

Moses Geltz could, however, and he did lustily.

"Oh, help me—help me!" he roared. "I vantsh to get out!"

The unfortunate captain would have liked to get in even to that old cask.

But it was impossible—both cask and Jew floated rapidly away.

All hope now was gone.

Higher and higher rose the waters.

They encircled his throat.

The waves dashed over his face and blinded him.

Daniel Macorrie had truly depicted his awful fate.

Higher and higher!

That horrible nauseous draught!—another—another!

No escape!

The water poured in at his mouth—his ears.

With one last groan of agony his eyes opened wildly ere they closed for ever, to see——

Heavens!—was it possible?—did his senses mock him?

No!—it was a boat within a few yards of him, and in that boat the face and form——

Oh, surely this must be a vision from the dead—of his dear friend and companion, Lord Harcliffe.

He heard the wild cry of that friend as he recognised him, he had a confused remembrance of feeling his arms at liberty and a power to breathe, and then he remembered no more.

He had fallen into a dead swoon.

CHAPTER CLXIV.

CAPTAIN HAWK AND LORD HARCLIFFE RETURN TO THE CAVE.—LORD HARCLIFFE GOES IN QUEST OF A JEW AND GETS INTO DIFFICULTIES.

After Lord Harcliffe had seen the pilfering, terrified old Jew fairly launched in his cask, he began to reflect that a joke was all very well in its way, but that it was possible to carry matters a little too far.

He was not an unfeeling man, and he considered the punishment Moses had received in the deprivation of his stolen property, from the sharp teeth of the rat-trap, and his subsequent horror in the "roundabout" or barrel, was almost sufficient.

He accordingly requested the boat might be lowered that he, in company with two oarsmen, should go in search.

It was while on this benevolent errand that he came suddenly upon the sight that both horrified and delighted him.

His friend bound and helpless to that ghastly rock.

Of course, it is needless to say that Moses Geltz and his barrel were at once forgotten.

With eager haste he severed the cruel rope and dragged the body of his friend into the boat.

The wreckers had stood watching with greedy eyes the gradual rising of the tide that was to engulph their victim.

Already they had exulted as the in-coming waves mounted to the breast and washed over his shoulders.

The wretches were now longing for the final catastrophe when the surging waters should reach the seat of life and roll over his head.

But ere this last dread consummation could be accomplished, they caught sight of the same body of soldiers as had previously alarmed them; and being suspicious of the redcoats, they made a precipitate retreat into crevices of the cliff and behind jutting rocks till the soldiers had passed, and then skulked away further down the coast.

This prevented them from witnessing the rescue of Captain Hawk, and when they *did* return the rock was covered—all was over.

In the meantime, Lord Harcliffe had chafed the hands and bathed the forehead of the captain with brandy, with which he was fortunately provided.

He had also poured some down his throat.

The result of this was to produce an immediate attack of vomiting, which was of inestimable service, inasmuch as it relieved him of the large quantity of salt water he had been compelled to swallow.

It also contributed to his speedy recovery.

Almost the next moment he opened his eyes and smiled faintly.

Captain Hawk seemed instinctively to comprehend that he was in safety, and that he owed that agreeable position to Lord Harcliffe.

"My friend—my dear friend," he said, extending his hand, which his lordship grasped firmly, "I was right—I knew I should not die an instant before my time."

"Die! You've many good years before you yet, old fellow!" returned the Black Highwayman, in a cheering tone; and dropping his voice, he added—"many a brave moonlight gallop yet for both of us!"

Captain Hawk at that moment felt that he had a true friend; he threw his arms round his stanch companion, and embraced him.

Tears stood in both their eyes—they had passed through so much together.

The captain briefly explained the past occurrences

Lord Harcliffe urged an immediate return to the smuggler vessel, but Captain Hawk opposed it, remembering his promise to Morna to await her return in the cavern.

"But you are drenched to the skin!" remarked his friend.

"There is a fire in the cave yonder," pointing as he spoke; "I shall soon be dry again."

"You may fall once more into the hands of your kind friends," remarked Lord Harcliffe.

"There is no fear: the ruffians think me dead long before this, and will not look for me."

Finding his friend was fixed in his determination, he ordered the men to pull to the shore, where, having disembarked, the boat returned to the lugger.

The fire still smouldered in the cavern, and by dint of coaxing and piling up fresh wood, it soon revived and diffused a cheerful light and warmth around.

"This is delightful!" cried Lord Harcliffe, as he extended his limbs luxuriantly in the genial heat.

"Very!" returned his friend, who was steaming like a wet blanket, as the fire drew the moisture from his garments. "I think," he added, with a smile, "if I go on giving out moisture like this I shall soon be dry."

"The sooner the better," remarked Lord Harcliffe.

Having stretched themselves before the fire, and lit a couple of cigars, with which the jolly smuggler had supplied the highwayman, Captain Hawk amused his friend with a full account of his adventures since their separation.

It was with the most unbounded enthusiasm he received the news of the recovery of the treasure.

"It is," he cried, "one of the greatest triumphs ever recorded."

Having congratulated his gallant companion on the happy issue of his vicissitudes, he related his own, not, we may be sure, omitting the crowning triumph—the acquisition of the diamond ring.

Captain Hawk laughed heartily as he listened to the nefarious attempts of *honest* Moses, and particularly at the farce of the barrel.

"By-the-by, I remember now," he said, "while I was bound to that infernal rock, in momentary expectation of death, the old fellow passed me, cask included, but unfortunately neither of us could help the other. I wonder what became of him?"

"Ah! what?" exclaimed Lord Harcliffe. "I was going in search of the poor old wretch when I encountered you, and then I thought no more of him."

"The poor devil may be drowned, or at least jammed up in his cask amongst the rocks, utterly unable to extricate himself."

"He's a most incorrigible old rascal," remarked the Black Highwayman.

"Perhaps so; but 'live and let live' is my motto, and so I vote we go in search of him," generously proposed Captain Hawk.

"Not for the world! After what you have related, your policy is to keep out of sight. What is the life of an old vagabond compared with yours?"

"Every man's life, Harcliffe, is valuable in his own eyes. I remember how I felt when I was tied to that rock."

"Well, then, if a search is to be made, I will make it, but I will go alone," said Lord Harcliffe.

"I think it would be as well just to reconnoitre close in-shore under the cliff, for a hundred yards or so. The barrel may have drifted in."

"Very well; and in the meantime you remain here."

"I will."

The soldiers, accompanied by Sergeant Crank and Roland Gregson, the detective, were at that moment performing a precisely similar operation, and for a like purpose to that contemplated by Lord Harcliffe.

In due course of time they came upon the somewhat unusual spectacle of a large barrel standing bolt upright among the rocks.

The tide had washed it nearer and nearer to the shore, till at last, after many cracks, and bumps, and thumps, it was arrested by a little nest of small rocks, and could go no further.

The sergeant and Roland Gregson, stepping carefully from rock to rock, approached the cask.

Peeping in, they beheld, to their unbounded surprise, the terrified old Jew, huddled up, nose and knees together, at the bottom, like a periwinkle.

"Hallo!" cried the sergeant.

"Who'sh dat?" answered Moses, in a doleful voice. "Oh, mein Gott! who'sh dat?"

It was quite a study to see how the detective opened his eyes and pricked up his ears at the Jew's tones.

"We're particular friends," he answered.

"I've got no friendsh here," groaned Moses; "every von here's a set of d—n svindling tiefs!"

"You're wrong, I assure you. We're your friends. We wouldn't have you lost for the world," continued Gregson, who was growing quite facetious, and chuckled at the drollness of his idea.

"Vell, den, if you are my friendsh indeed, jusht get me out of dish infernal barrel—it'sh broke my back and knocked all de shkin off my jointsh," cried Moses.

"We'll get you out fast enough," said the detective.

Without the least attempt at ceremony, the barrel was suddenly pulled over with a jerk, and the honest Moses shot out with a splash into the water, which was more than knee-deep, as though he had been discharged from a large cannon.

"Oh, oh, mein Gott!" he roared, as he went souse into the salt water on his hands and knees.

Being raised from his bent posture, Moses was assisted to the shore in a most decided and efficient manner by Sergeant Crank, who clutched him firmly by the back of the collar and dragged him on to the beach, where he dropped him.

The shivering Jew, who was dripping with wet, groaned and growled, and called upon all the patriarchs to help him; but none of them appeared to answer, or take the least notice.

He then sat up, and became conscious that he was surrounded by soldiers.

This fact made him still more uncomfortable.

His teeth chattered more than ever.

He glanced up wistfully at the serjeant and Roland Gregson, who had his eye fastened on him like a gimlet.

"So, Mr. Moses Geltz, you've given us a pretty chase!" he remarked.

"I ain't Moshes Geltz—it'sh false!" remarked the Jew. "I'm Mishter Jansen Spraager."

"Oh, indeed!" said the detective, with a most provoking sound of unbelief in his tone. "Then I'm sorry to tell you you're so like an old scoundrel of the name I mentioned that I'm in search of, that I shall hold you on suspicion till I can find your double."

"I don't undershtand a vord of vhat you meansh," cried the Jew.

"Or, rather, you won't understand," followed up Roland Gregson.

"Vhat d'ye vant vid dish Moshes Geltz?"

"I want him for robbery. I'm a detective officer, on private service for his Majesty King George, accompanied by a military force to back me," said Roland.

Moses felt very uncomfortable, and almost wished himself at the bottom of the barrel once more.

"Vhat's de poor old—I mean de dam tief been shtealing?" he whined.

"A valuable diamond ring from the King, valued at thousands," stated the detective, as a clincher.

"I haven't got it now, upon my shoul I haven't—dat's ash true ash my name's Moshes!" cried the Jew, excitedly.

"Oh, then, you are Moses Geltz, after all?"

"Yesh, I am," he answered.

He felt he should be sure to be discovered, and therefore made a virtue of necessity, and acknowledged himself.

"Then, although you have not the ring now in your possession, you have had it?"

"Yesh, yesh!—I have—I have!"

"And you sold it, of course?"

"No, no—vorse luck! I vish I had!" cried the Jew, in a tone of deep regret. "No, no—it vashn't dat! I'll tell you how it vash. I got into bad company—fell in vid a d—n dishonest tief, an' he shtole it."

"Then he is its present possessor?"

"Yesh—I'll take my oath of dat."

"And where is he now?"

"He's on board a vesshel lying off——"

He suddenly broke off, crying excitedly, and pointing to an elegant gentleman, who had approached hastily almost close to him:

"No—no! Dere he ish!—dat'sh him!"

At a signal from Roland, which the new-comer did not observe, the soldiers quietly drew near and surrounded him.

"Lay hold upon him! He callsh himshelf Lord Ramiliesh; but I know better: he'sh Lord Harcliffe, *aliash* de Black Highvayman, an' I'll shvear he'sh got my ring!" shouted the Jew.

"In the name of the King I arrest you!" cried Roland Gregson. "Seize him!"

The Black Highwayman, unprovided with weapons, and surrounded by twelve armed soldiers, could offer no effectual resistance; he therefore made a virtue of necessity, and quietly surrendered himself.

He would not have been in his present plight at all but for the very man whom he was seeking to serve.

From a distance he observed him gesticulating to Roland Gregson, and taking him for one of the wreckers, perhaps threatening the old man's life, he hastened forward, unsuspicious of danger and not noticing the soldiers, who were masked by a projecting rock, till he found himself surrounded by them, and then retreat was impossible.

One thought, however, comforted him wonderfully.

He had left the ring in charge of his friend, Captain Hawk, who was at that very moment in the cavern, sipping from his brandy-flask.

Oh, had he known his friend's peril, how eagerly would he have flown to his rescue!

Lord Harcliffe determined upon a desperate attempt at freedom as he passed the cave.

But his intention was utterly frustrated, for at only a few yards' distance a narrow fissure or defile was pointed out in the cliff, ascending almost perpendicularly by rude steps to the top, and by this the detective determined to proceed.

This decision being acted upon, they did not repass the cavern, and thus all hope of communicating his danger to his friend was cut off.

The soldiers marched along with Lord Harcliffe and the Jew both pinioned in their midst.

Moses Geltz grunted and grumbled as usual; Lord Harcliffe, on the contrary, preserved a dignified silence.

At the first inn they came to, they were rigorously searched.

But the missing ring was nowhere to be found.

The detective frowned and bit his lip, and then looked at the Jew, who looked at Lord Harcliffe, who looked at no one, but appeared enveloped in a mantle of proud, insulted majesty.

The Israelite broke the silence.

"I'll take my oath he'sh got it for all his innoshent looksh!" he cried.

"What have you to say to this?" demanded the detective of the Black Highwayman.

"Nothing beyond this," he replied: "that I am a gentleman, and that you will have to answer for this treatment!"

"I am only doing what I consider my duty," returned Gregson, "and duty needs no apology, neither does it recognise position. You will accompany me, with your accuser, to London, where, if the charge is found to be false, every recompense will be made you, I am sure."

Gregson would gladly have continued his journey, in spite of the suggestions of Sergeant Crank, who pleaded the fatigue and the requirements of his men with an earnestness that suggested his being the kindest and most unselfish of human creatures, and then went to the bar to order refreshment for the troops.

However, as the barmaid was pretty and the sergeant thirsty, he became absorbed in old ale and flirtation, and forgot all about the hungry soldiers who waited anxiously for their dinners.

It was not till the voice of Gregson was heard gruffly wondering "where the devil that fellow had got to," that the sergeant remembered he had been commissioned to order an unlimited quantity of steaks and ale for his Majesty's troops on private service.

This order was at length attended to; and the prisoners having likewise refreshed themselves—Lord Harcliffe demanding a table to himself and a bottle of wine, both of which he had, and both of which he paid for—a council of war was held: what was to be done with them?

It was at length decided that they should be locked up in separate rooms, with a sentinel posted at each door within, and beneath each window without, to guard against any possibility of escape.

This was accordingly done, and Lord Harcliffe, who but a short time before was exulting over a union of fortuitous events, now found himself a prisoner, watched and guarded on all sides.

He glanced up the chimney: that was too small to admit his body.

He listened at the door: he heard the deep breathing of the sentinel outside.

He placed his hand upon the handle and softly turned it.

"Leave the handle alone!" growled the soldier.

"How infernally wide awake they are!" murmured the Black Highwayman.

He glanced cautiously from the window, but there stood the sentinel with his eye on it fixed as fate.

"Go away from the window!" he bawled.

"Go to the devil!" ejaculated Lord Harcliffe, as, tired, perplexed, and disgusted, he threw himself upon the bed.

The detective had, before retiring to rest, another duty to perform, and that was to retrace his steps to the cabin of Hugh Trevellyn, and endeavour to meet the stranger, the account of whom and his treasure had awakened his suspicions.

"I shall make a good night's work of this if I mind what I'm about," he soliloquised; "but I should like to have got hold of that diamond ring though. Come, sergeant, it's time to be up and doing."

Sergeant Crank groaned inwardly.

"I've been up since six this morning, an' I've been a *doin'* all day. Baugh! there's no rest in this world!" he grumbled.

CHAPTER CLXV.

THE SPIRIT OF THE DROWNED CAPTAIN.—A FIGHT IN THE DARK.—CAPTAIN HAWK EXPLORES THE SUBTERRANEAN PASSAGE AND MEETS WITH AN ADVENTURE.

Captain Hawk waited and waited the return of his friend, but he came not.

As the dreary hours wore away, he began to grow impatient.

He wondered what had become of his companion.

The fire had burnt low, the flask was empty, and the captain felt chilled and dispirited.

Soon his wonder changed to anxiety.

He feared some mischance had befallen his gallant comrade.

He tried to calm himself by rapidly pacing to and fro, but this would not do.

His apprehensions so tortured him that he could no longer endure the silence and enforced captivity of the cavern.

He approached the entrance and looked forth.

To his dismay it was night, and the moon had risen.

He looked eagerly to the right and left, but no sign of living creature met his gaze—no sound reached his ears but the monotonous, ceaseless murmur of the waves as they dashed against the rocks.

He would have liked to have raised his voice and shouted, but this would have been dangerous.

He wished to go in search of his friend, but in that uncertain moonlight, what little chance was there of his finding him?

Then again, Morna might come in the interim, and his absence would fill her with apprehensions.

It seemed strange, too, that she remained away so long.

He sat down on a piece of rock and tried to compose himself by thinking of her.

As for Morna, the captain had never once been absent from her thoughts.

Had she been guided by her own feelings she would at that moment have been by the side of the man she loved.

But by her father's advice, and in order to lull suspicion in case the wreckers had returned, she had been constrained to leave the object of her solicitude in his solitary rock-bound chamber till the evening.

There was, however, much to do during the day.

Hugh had to the utmost extent in his power repaired the shattered doors and shutters, and removed the torn and splintered planks that lay heaped in all directions.

It was not till nightfall that the cabin began to look a little like itself.

By that time the fire burnt cheerfully on the hearth, the shutters and doors were replaced and barred, and a savoury stew bubbled in an iron pot that hung suspended over the flame, dispensing its ambrosial odours through the apartment as often as fair Morna's hands stirred it in the progress of cooking.

She was not one of those delicately-minded young ladies who ignore the idea of eating as gross and material.

Having a good appetite herself, she wisely judged that the captain after being immured the greater part of the day in a cold, damp cavern, would probably be very nearly, if not quite, ravenous by night.

She therefore employed all her skill in compounding the savoury meal that she anticipated enjoying with him and her father at supper-time.

Of course it is needless to state she knew nothing of what had transpired, or the deadly peril in which the man she loved had been placed.

It was a merciful ignorance, for had she known it she would have been distracted.

She therefore applied herself diligently to her task, looking forward with pleasurable anticipation to the time when she should once more conduct her hero through the dark subterranean passages to the light and warmth of her hospitable fireside.

Captain Hawk still sat moodily on the rock in melancholy meditation.

Suddenly he was aroused by a sound that caused him to start to his feet.

It was a human voice.

His friend must have returned.

"Thank Heaven!" he ejaculated, gratefully.

A shade of disappointment stole across his features as he uttered the thanksgiving.

He listened attentively.

It was *not* the voice of his friend.

There were several speaking, and footsteps appeared to be drawing near the cave.

The moon now shone brightly and lighted up the entrance, but within all was thick darkness.

Captain Hawk retired a little on one side, where he was effectually shrouded in the shadow but perfectly able to see and hear what passed.

It was a party of the wreckers, but Daniel Macorrie was not with them.

They appeared to be waiting for him, as they came into the cavern and remained in groups at the entrance.

Their presence seemed in Captain Hawk's opinion to bode no good.

They were evidently plotting some evil.

Should Morna come while they were there what might be the result?

Yet how could they be got rid of?

These thoughts passed rapidly through his mind.

But the voice of one of the speakers caused him to listen.

"We shall see him when the tide's out," he said.

"They mean me," thought the captain.

"What a d—d fool he must have been to die," said another, "when a lump o' gold would ha' saved his life!"

"I don't know about that," remarked a third. "This captain, whoever he was, was a tremendous plucked 'un, and if he had handed over the gold, it strikes me he'd ha' lost his life all the same."

This had been precisely Captain Hawk's opinion.

"You see," continued the last speaker "Dan Macorrie hated this stranger like blazes—first because he was jealous of him with his sweetheart Morna, and next because the stranger didn't care a d—n for him, and I know he wouldn't ha' been satisfied with anything less than his life, an' that he's got safe enough."

"But what about this trap he speaks of?" asked one.

"Why, he sticks to it there's a secret trap-door somewhere in Hugh Trevellyn's cabin that leads out by some underground path, and he swears he'll never rest till he's found it."

"Then I s'pose he thinks it was by this trap our prey escaped us just as we thought we'd trapped him?"

"Just so."

"And the girl being away, too, of course he makes up his mind they went together."

"Ha, ha! Yes. It isn't a very pleasant idea for a lover—his sweetheart, and a handsome fellow like this captain, cuddling one another in a dark place underground, all by themselves."

A coarse laugh followed this remark.

"Then as we found the fine gentleman here, Dan's made up his mind that the passage from the trap in the cabin leads somehow to this cavern."

"A very likely thing too. Well, if it is so, as Morna doesn't know how much salt water her lover's been drinking, she's sure to come here to look after him."

"Ha, ha! What a capital joke! Ha, ha!"

"You infernal scoundrels!" muttered the captain, between his teeth.

His anxiety grew painful as he contemplated the poor, scared, anxious girl encountering these lawless men.

"I can't help laughing, for the life of me," cried the last speaker. "What a surprise it'll be for the young witch when she comes pit-patting along with her delicate feet, expecting to see her captain's pretty face, and finds herself cheek-by-jowl with our pretty faces instead! Ha, ha, ha!"

This was so excellent a joke that they all guffawed vociferously.

The captain, as he stood in the dark, would have given a large sum for the pleasure of knocking all their heads together, had it been possible.

Another of the party went on:

"Dan swears he won't be satisfied till Morna Trevellyn's looked upon her lover's dead face. He'll drag her down to the rock, and make her look! D—n me! if I don't think he'd tie her up as well, and leave her there to follow him into t'other world for two pins!"

"P'raps his ghost'll come an' pay her a visit by her bedside to comfort her," said one.

"Ghost! Bah! Do you believe in ghosts?"

"A trifle. Don't you?"

"Devil a bit!"

"There may be such things for all that!"

"I don't believe in 'em. The only spirits as ever haunts me is whisky and brandy, an' I wish they'd make their appearance a little oftener."

There was another laugh.

"You may laugh," remarked the believer in ghosts, "but my old grandmother——"

"Oh, blow your old grandmother!"

"You may blow her for twenty years—she wouldn't take much notice where she lies. But she declares she saw grandfather's spirit sittin' in his arm-chair by the fire the very night after he was buried in th' old churchyard."

"Ah! the old boy felt cold, an' came back to have a warm," remarked one of the irreverent gang.

"Well, and what did he say?"

"He said, in a solemn voice: 'Nancy—Nancy! I've come to tell you that we shall meet again in a month!' That very day month old granny died. What d'ye think of that?"

There was something in the impressed tone of the speaker that affected the whole body more or less, and a silence followed.

The previous speaker went on:

"Suppose now the spirit of that poor drowned wretch yonder was suddenly to appear before us, don't you think you'd believe in ghosts ever afterwards?"

"Seein's believin'," replied one of the most incredulous of the party. "But till I do see, d—n me if I'll believe!"

"Ah well—wait till you hear the voice of a spirit, you'll never forget it."

"Bah! Spirits aren't got voices, and if they had, all they could say 'ud be——"

Here the daring speaker imitated a deep groan.

But what was their horror when, as the imitated sound died away, another groan much deeper reverberated through the cavern?

The rude, rough men were like timid children in a moment.

They all crowded closely together.

"Good Lord! what's that?" cried the most hardened, in a terrified whisper.

Another groan, and then a louder one was the reply.

"The d—d place is haunted!" faltered several.

"Ah! see!—look there!—there—there!" shrieked one of the terrified ruffians, as he pointed with his trembling finger to the entrance of the cavern, where, in the pale moonlight, ghastly pale, with rigid attitude and fixed stony eyes, the form of the murdered victim stood gazing upon them.

Several shrieked aloud, whilst one voice above the rest growled out:

"*The Spirit of the Drowned Man!*"

The spectre, after contemplating them for a moment, took a gliding step forward.

This was sufficient.

The whole party uttered a tremendous yell of horror and fell back into the darkness.

When they ventured to look again, the spirit was no longer to be seen.

Captain Hawk hit upon this plan to drive away the intruders, and took advantage of their confusion and terror to retreat into the shadow of a projecting rock, where he resumed the coat he had taken off before playing the spectre, in which performance his white shirt had added much to the effect.

But he had not done with them yet.

He was burning to teach them a lesson.

Daring as was the attempt, he resolved to risk it

He cautiously, with light footstep, glided by a slight circuit through the darkness to the spot where the trembling scoundrels were congregated.

He commenced operations by making as nice a calculation as possible, and saluting the one he happened to be next to with a sharp blow on the ear.

"Oh d—n it!" yelled the man to his neighbour. "Why don't you mind where you're putting your elbow?"

"I didn't touch you!"

The words were hardly out of the speaker's mouth when he received a smashing blow on that feature, that loosened all his front teeth, and made him howl like a baited bear.

"I'll be the death of you!" he shouted, striking out in the dark, hitting nothing, and receiving in exchange a smeller of a most stinging quality.

"Oh, my nose!" he yelled, and determined to hit somebody, he struck out at random, but successfully.

He did hit somebody in the eye, who in his turn hit again, not the one who had struck him, but another—a blow on the jaw that almost threatened dislocation.

The conflict in the dark now became general.

From being first terrified, they now became madly vindictive.

Rolling over on the ground, grappling each other, cursing and swearing like wild demons, they smashed, fought, scratched, and bit one another to their hearts' content.

They were fighting, they didn't know who, for they didn't know what.

Captain Hawk, delighted at the success of his scheme, glided about superintending the whole without being seen himself—stirring up the fire of wrath by judicious applications of his fist and feet.

Administering a blow to one, a kick to another, till he was tired.

How long this would have lasted it was impossible to

say, had not the voice of Daniel Macorrie been heard without.

"Where are you all?" he cried.

This question put an end to the affray, and in a state of great disorder they scrambled on to their legs, as Daniel, carrying a lighted torch in his hand and a bundle of links under his arm, entered the cavern.

As he entered, Captain Hawk, in the smoke and glare of the torchlight, slipped out.

Daniel glared with surprise at the sight that met his gaze.

Black eyes, noses from which the vital fluid was running in copious streams, mouths filled with the same crimson liquid, hands tightly grasping lumps of hair pulled from some friend's cranium, ugly, incised eyebrows, gashed cheeks, ominous frontal protuberances like inflamed egg plums, faces pale with rage, and so transformed that their own mothers would not have recognised them, completed the startling picture.

"What the h—l's the matter with you all?" he shouted. "Are you going mad?"

Then the angry tongues broke loose afresh; everyone talked at once, and a mixture composed of devils, and spectres, and haunted caverns, left Daniel as much in the dark as ever.

But he was not in the humour to endure this.

His brow contracted, and from having by his strength and daring earned a pre-eminence amongst his fellows, he asserted it now.

Striding up to one Mick Sorrell, who with a smashed nose and a dripping, gory mouth, might have been more appropriately termed Dick Mangle, he seized him by the collar, and fiercely demanded an explanation.

This was given at once, and by no means contributed to restore the inquirer's equanimity.

"You set of d—d idiots!" he exclaimed, with fierce contempt, "let there be an end to this! There's something to be done, remember, before to-morrow morning!"

There *was something* to be done!

He little guessed what.

Throwing down the links on the ground, he called out, "Light these!"

In a moment the cavern was brightened up with the yellow glare of a dozen torches.

"Now, then," he shouted, "follow me!"

They carefully, under the guidance of their leader, explored the recesses of the cavern, till at length they came upon that by which Morna had conducted Captain Hawk, who was at that moment cautiously watching.

A shout of triumph heralded this event.

"Here it is!" cried Daniel.

All animosities were forgotten in a moment by the party—that is, by all but Daniel.

He gnashed his teeth like a hungry bloodhound as he hurried along the narrow, rocky passage.

"We must reach it soon!" he cried.

At this moment they turned a somewhat abrupt angle in the path, and found their progress stopped by what appeared a dense block-up of rock.

It was a decided case of *No Thoroughfare*.

A growl of disappointment was hurled at the rocky barrier, of which the rock took not the slightest notice.

In vain they tried to remove it.

The passage on the side on which they stood was so narrow that only the force of one could be applied.

This would have been sufficient; but, then, they did not know *how* to apply it.

Had they done so, the strong hands of Daniel Macorrie would have caused the rock to open its portals more easily than the weaker ones of Morna Trevellyn.

As it was, they were obliged to come to a full stop.

Angry, baffled, spiteful, Daniel called out fiercely to them to return.

They retraced their steps, and with angry execrations and threats of vengeance they left the cavern.

Captain Hawk was once more alone.

But he was by no means tranquil in his mind.

What did those brutal men contemplate?

He had had a tolerable experience of what they would do when they could, and he shuddered with uncontrollable horror as he contemplated the peril to which Morna and her father would be exposed if it was against them their rage was directed.

He heard their wild shouts ringing along the shore as they departed, and then considered what would be the best course to pursue under the circumstances.

His mind, prompt to decide, was soon made up.

To follow these ruffians would be to give them the advantage—since they had the start—of reaching the cabin before him, or even before he could warn its inmates of their approach.

It was of every importance that he should be there first.

He had waited patiently for some hours, and still Morna had not returned.

His plan, then, must be to thread the subterranean path, and endeavour to penetrate to the trap-door.

It was perfectly dark in the interior of the cavern, and it took the captain some little time to grope his way to the entrance of this path, there being several that promised such a continuity, but which stopped abruptly at about thirty yards' distance.

At length, however, he felt he had discovered the right track, and the uninterrupted progress he was enabled to make convinced him that it was so.

His heart bounded within him at the prospect of being able to confront the ruffians—if indeed they contemplated any outrage on the dwelling he held as almost sacred—to confront them, too, as one alive from the grave to which they had doomed him, and to let his enemies no less than his friends see what one brave heart and one determined arm could effect.

Carefully but quickly threading his way along the dark and narrow defile, he came speedily to the opposing rock that formed so effectual a barrier to the progress of the wreckers a short time before.

Here he was compelled to stop.

"I wonder now," thought he, "whether I am in possession of the *Open Sesame* that can cause this rock to turn upon its hinge?"

He applied his hands to the ponderous mass, but without effect.

He pressed against its centre, against its sides, on the right and on the left, but in vain.

The rock remained fixed and immovable as though rooted to the spot on which it rested.

He paused a moment to recover his breath and wipe away the drops with which his exertions had bedewed his forehead.

His chagrin was great.

He would have sworn he could have moved the stone easily.

"Umph!" he cried, "there is some secret which I have yet to learn, I suppose, and the danger may be imminent. How cursedly vexatious!" he continued, in a tone of deep anxiety. "Even now, perhaps——" He listened, but no sound was audible.

All was silent as the grave.

"I will make one more attempt," he said, firmly, all his energy returning as he applied himself once more to the task of opening the stony portal. "It is in vain!" he exclaimed, as he found all his efforts unavailing, "and I have no resource but to follow in the track of those bloodhounds."

He turned with impatient eagerness, as though he would have flown through the dark, narrow space, and came in violent contact with one who was coming in the opposite direction.

Quick as lightning the muscular fingers of the captain were gripping the throat of the one.

"D—n it!" cried he, in a choking voice, "is this the way you welcome a friend in the dark?"

"Who are you?—what do you want here?" cried the highwayman, in a disguised voice.

"Don't choke me and I'll tell you," gasped the man.

"Speak!" said the captain, relaxing his gripe a little.

"Dan Macorrie sent me to keep watch here."

"Oh!"

"Yes."

"Why?—for whom?"

"Well, you see, he and a lot more of our mates are going to hunt out some parties as hasn't behaved square to 'em."

"Well, but those parties are not *here*."

"I know that as well as you. They're in a cabin up yonder, but Dan's got scent of a secret trap, by which they could make a clear run and get away, d'ye see?"

"Ay! I suppose then this trap you speak of leads to some subterranean outlet?"

"That's just it, and this ere place where we're standin' is the outlet; that's why I'm here to cut off their retreat."

"Whose retreat?"

"Hugh Trevellyn an' his gal. As for her fancy man, the captain, we settled him offhand."

"Indeed! How?"

"Tied him fast to a rock and let the tide run over him. Ha, ha! gave him a salt-water bath!"

"Is he there still?"

"Of course he is, as full as a tub."

"I should like to see him."

"So you can when the tide's out—but it's high water at present."

"Never mind that: show me the spot."

"But I'm to watch here."

"No, you're to obey me, and I order you to show me the rock where this poor man met his fate."

"Well, but——"

"Go forward!"

"Not at your orde——"

The captain gripped the man's throat with a pressure like a vice.

"Oh!" he yelled. "I'll go!"

The highwayman released his hold.

He was behind, the man in front.

The latter had conceived an idea very near the truth, that he had "caught a Tartar," and consequently made as rapid a "bolt" as he could in the dark.

But the captain's quick hand was on the back of his collar in an instant.

The jerk nearly pulled him on his back.

"Don't be in such a devil of a hurry!" said the captain, coolly. "Now then!"

In this position they reached the termination of the winding path.

The air blew cool and fresh.

"Now," cried Captain Hawk, "show me where you gang of murderers sacrificed their victim!"

As he spoke, he dragged the man, who was becoming more and more apprehensive, to the entrance of the cavern.

Then, in a deep voice, he said:

"Men are sometimes permitted to destroy the living; but the dead are beyond their power."

Then in his own voice, he cried:

"I am the man who perished at yonder *Death Pillar!*"

He stepped into the full moonlight as he spoke, dragging the terrified wrecker with him.

"Behold me!" he shouted.

The conscience-stricken wretch glared at the pale features and flashing eyes of the captain, and with a scream of terror, fell senseless at his feet.

"I think," said the highwayman to himself, "he will hardly dare to follow me again—I am sure he will not, if he consults his own safety."

With these words, he returned to make one last effort at the impervious rock.

He felt convinced he was pressing it in the right direction.

Still it moved not.

Suddenly he saw, or fancied he saw, a light glimmering from the other side.

Fully expecting to see the rock swing open, he remained perfectly still.

But no such result followed, and the light disappeared.

He called Morna by her name, but no answer.

Then came a confused murmur as of many voices.

"Good Heaven!" ejaculated Captain Hawk. "Those demons are there, and I not by her side!"

With desperate, fierce impetuosity, he dashed himself against the opposing rock. Suddenly his foot struck against a piece of stone, and the cause of the non-oscillation of the door was apparent.

This stone having a sharp edge had become wedged into the ground, and pressing firmly against the bottom of the rock effectually hindered its yielding to the pressure, which only secured it more firmly.

He hastily kicked it away, and to his great joy the rock swung round upon its pivot.

The road was open.

"Thank God!" cried the captain, fervently, as he rushed through.

CHAPTER CLXVI.

MORNA HEARS TIDINGS OF THE CAPTAIN'S FATE.—A CRISIS.—CAPTAIN HAWK ARRIVES JUST IN TIME.—THE PROPHECY FULFILLED.—ARRIVAL OF THE DETECTIVE.—UNEXPECTED RESULT OF HIS VISIT.

THE wreckers having left the cottage of Hugh Trevellyn at peace since the morning, and no other attack having been made, Morna began to indulge hopes either that the appearance of the soldiers had alarmed them, or else that their fierce passions had subsided.

The distant clock had struck nine of the night.

The supper was cooked.

All they waited for was their guest.

"I think I may venture now, father," said Morna.

"Yes, my child, I think we have nothing to apprehend, at least to-night."

Morna accordingly lighted a torch, and raising the trap, descended, with a heart palpitating with fond expectation, into the cellar beneath.

Soon she would be in the presence of the man she loved.

She hastily reached the pivot stone, and, as usual, pressed against it with her hands.

This time, however, it refused to move.

What did this mean?

With a heart sickening with undefined apprehension, she hastily retraced her steps, and ascended to the cabin.

It was the light from her torch the captain saw from the other side.

She found her father listening at the half-open door.

"Father—father!" she cried, in an agitated voice.

"Have you not found him?" he inquired.

"I cannot move the rock: it is fast!" she answered, excitedly. "I feel so anxious—so terrified! It never happened so before. Should any harm have come to him——"

"I will go and see!" exclaimed Hugh.

"You may spare yourself the trouble!" shouted the fierce voice of Daniel Macorrie, whom jealousy, hate, and disappointed cupidity had rendered more like a fiend than a man, and who now, with twenty of his ruffianly crew, poured in at the door Hugh had forgotten, in listening to his daughter's words, to close.

Morna, with great presence of mind, terrified and anxious as she was, hastily closed the trap.

But she was too late for concealment, and a wild shout announced the exultation of the rude gang at its discovery.

"Ha, ha!" shouted the ruffian, "didn't I say there was a trap? I knew it—I was sure of it!"

"And how long is it since I was first supposed to account to you for what I have in my own house, Daniel Macorrie?" asked Hugh, sternly, throwing his arm around his daughter, and confronting the fierce assembly.

"Since that wanton jilt, your daughter, took to making herself cheap to strangers," answered Daniel, bitterly.

"You lie, villanous slanderer!" returned the incensed parent. "My daughter is a good and honest girl; and it is your bad, jealous heart that poisons the words that come from your lips: that stranger is nothing to her."

"No," cried Daniel, in a peculiarly strange and meaning tone, "he is nothing to her *now!* nor to anyone. We all know that!"

His manner of speaking was so marked and deliberate that the sensitive mind of Morna instantly apprehended evil to the man who was now her heart's hero.

She appeared suddenly to throw off all fear for herself as she disengaged herself from her father's protecting arm.

"Daniel Macorrie," she said, in a tone of enforced calmness that was almost desperation, "what do you mean by those words?"

The brutal man gazed at her quivering lips and pallid cheeks, and laughed like a fiend.

"Speak! Do not mock me! or if you do, beware!" she spoke, in hurried, gasping accents, as though her emotion stifled her.

"Your words," she continued, "seemed to imply harm to our guest; you have seen him perhaps since I have."

"Seen him! Ha, ha!"

"If you have injured him, if you have harmed a hair of his head, you shall pay for it deeply—bitterly!" she almost shrieked.

[CAPTAIN JECKS IS SHOT BY A SENTINEL.]

"He is safe—the gallant captain is safe," returned Daniel, mockingly—"out of harm's way: isn't he, boys?" appealing to his companions as he spoke.

"Oh yes, quite safe—quite!" was the ironical reply.

"Where is he?" fiercely demanded Morna.

"Come and see for yourself!" was Daniel's answer.

"Let me know where he is, I command you!"

"Well, then, you shall know. I found him very much in my way; he fell into my hands, he refused to confess where his gold was stowed, and so I had him lashed to a rock till he altered his mind."

Morna's colour went and came like intermittent lightning flashes as she gazed upon the dogged, stern, remorseless features of the speaker.

"Cowardly, unmanly wretches," she cried, "thus to degrade a gentleman! But my own hands shall release him! Lead me to him!"

"You'd better take a coffin with you!" said the brutal speaker.

Morna glared at him as though she did not quite grasp his meaning.

"A coffin!" she echoed, in a strange whisper—"that is for the dead, not the living."

"Well, why didn't you hear me out?"

"Speak—speak!"

"I told you I tied your fine captain to a rock till he altered his mind."

"Yes—yes!"

"Well, he never did alter his mind, so the tide rose and rose, and at last it flowed over his head!"

"And is—is he d—dead?" oozed from her trembling

lips as she fixed her mad-looking eyes upon the face of her torturer.

"He is dead! and a d—d good riddance too!" shouted Daniel Macorrie.

"Infernal villain!—murderer!" cried Hugh.

As for Morna, she stood mute, rigid, motionless: had she been transformed to stone, she could not have been more fixed.

This lasted for a moment, and then one wild, unearthly cry burst from her lips.

It was so terrible that it almost curdled the blood in the veins of the hearers.

Daniel Macorrie alone remained unmoved.

The more emotion the woman he wished to torture evinced, the more he exulted.

"You wished me to lead you to him—I will do so," he said, in the same sneering tone he had lately assumed; "and we will descend by the trap, and you can show us the short road to the cavern as you did him."

A few hysterical, spasmodic gasps were Morna's only reply.

"No more of this, ruffian," cried Hugh, terrified at the symptoms his child evinced—"you are killing her!"

"So much the better," answered the wretch; "she will then be able to follow her darling captain into the land of spirits."

Then approaching the horror-struck girl, he almost hissed in her ear:

"Fool! you were his worst enemy. Had you been with us instead of against us, you couldn't have served us better: you led the prey into the snare, and left him in the very claws of the hunters! But come," he added, "first let us explore the subterranean path, and then we'll go together to the Death Pillar; the tide will be out, and you shall look once more upon the face of your paramour."

As he spoke, he seized her by the wrist roughly.

She uttered an exclamation of pain, and her father, unable longer to restrain his wrath, struck him a sharp blow upon the muscle of the arm, and compelled him to relinquish his hold.

But the next moment Hugh was hurled by his companions violently into a corner of the hut.

They were too strong for the old man.

Again the fierce grasp encircled the fair wrist of Morna, but the second time she turned upon him like a she-wolf robbed of her cubs.

"You think to terrify me—to compel me to obey you," she cried, with scornful indignation; "but you know me not! If I feared, it was not for myself, but for him whom you now tell me your cruel hands have destroyed. Since he is dead, I defy you! Do your worst, butchers as you are, but from me expect nothing but loathing and contempt!"

"We shall see!" shouted Daniel, furious at her defiance. "You shall do as I order you, or, by h—ll, I'll serve you as I served your gentleman lover! Come now, at once descend that trap and show us the way!"

He dragged her towards it as he yelled out these words.

"Open it, and descend!" he shouted, pointing to it.

His action was so menacing and violent, that, had it been open, it seemed probable he would in his fury have precipitated her headlong into the cellar below.

"Open it!" he shouted again to one of his companions.

One of the men stooped down to obey the order, when with a sudden impetus from beneath, the trap flew violently up and knocked him backwards.

At the same moment, Daniel Macorrie felt his legs swept from under him, and he fell with a crash to the ground.

Half stunned and dizzy, he looked wildly for the cause of his fall, and there halfway up the trap was the form of the drowned captain!

His companions, still oppressed with superstitious fears, fell back, and glared at this unexpected apparition, whilst Morna, restrained partly by joy and partly by shame, remained with clasped hands and riveted eyes, unable to move a step.

"Murderous villains!—dastardly wretches!" cried the highwayman. "Did I not tell you I should not die a moment before my time? Your blanched cheeks tell me you fear me *dead:* let my tongue tell you you should rather fear me as I am—*alive!*"

With a yell of rage at this announcement, Daniel Macorrie, who had cautiously drawn a pistol from his pocket, discharged it full at the captain's head.

A scream—a fall was heard, and Morna Trevellyn, bathed in blood, lay prostrate in front of the trap.

She had rushed forward and received the bullet intended for the captain.

Almost at the same instant, a second report rang through the cabin, and with a loud cry the fiendish Daniel leapt up wildly in the air, and fell back wih a dark crimson stain in the centre of his forehead—dead!

Morna was avenged—Captain Hawk's bullet had pierced his brain.

For a moment there was silence.

The astonishment of the wreckers, the grief of Captain Hawk, and the agony of Hugh Trevellyn, formed a painful picture to be imagined, not described.

The moon, too, as if curious to know what was going on, peered through the round hole in the upper part of the shutter.

Her beams fell upon the features of Daniel Macorrie.

Captain Hawk's prophecy was fulfilled.

The moon *did* shine that night upon his dead face!

The wreckers remembered this prediction being uttered, and appalled in spite of themselves at their leader's fate, they seemed scarcely capable of retaliation.

They were scared, paralysed.

Captain Hawk had in the first burst of his passionate regret raised the poor girl who had so nobly sacrificed herself in his defence, and supported her in his arms.

But seeing the wreckers still lingered, he relinquished his fair burden to her father, and then peremptorily ordered them to quit the cottage.

They paused, shuffled, hesitated, and finally obeyed, taking with them the dead body of Daniel Macorrie.

A bright-barrelled pistol which the captain drew from his pocket had doubtless a considerable share in producing this prompt obedience.

Morna was not dead.

At the departure of the ruffians she revived from the deadly faintness into which she had fallen, and glanced languidly towards the captain, who, as tenderly and delicately as possible, had opened her bodice, and was examining the wound, to ascertain if possible its character.

To his great joy it appeared the bullet had not injured the lungs, although it had ploughed up the flesh of her shoulder, and he feared shattered a portion of the collar-bone.

She smiled a sweet, faint smile, and said to the captain:

"You are alive and safe, thank God!"

He bound up her wound as skilfully as he was able, and then, having placed her on the pallet he had formerly occupied before the fire, he yielded to the entreaties of her father and herself to take the refreshment he so much needed.

The meal was soon despatched, and a tumbler of Hugh's whisky greatly invigorated the captain in mind and body.

Morna appeared to suffer little, and was inclined to sleep.

Captain Hawk reloaded his bright-barrelled pistols.

Hugh then related the circumstance of the arrival of the military, to which he attributed the preservation of his own life.

He detailed the information the detective had given him, and the information he had afforded the detective.

As he explained this, Captain Hawk evinced evident signs of annoyance.

Hugh noticed it.

"I am afraid," said he, "I have not done right in saying so much to these officers."

"You have not done wrong," cried the captain, recovering himself in a moment. "It is always best to tell the truth when you can, and I did not tell you to withhold it."

"They promised to call to-morrow," continued Hugh.

"Which means to-night, I expect," answered the captain.

"They *said* to-morrow."

"To throw us off our guard, probably. You see, my kind but simple friend—I mean in these matters—detectives, from constant experience, learn that if they wish to find those they seek, they generally have to drop upon them at the precise time when they are *not* expected.

"But this person only had to deliver an important message to you—nothing more."

The captain smiled.

"That's a very stale reason," he said; "in fact, the more I consider the matter, the more I'm inclined to think that this important message is nothing more or less than a quiet invitation for me to accompany them to London for the purpose of having a little quiet conversation with his gracious Majesty King George, respecting this treasure——"

A tremendous crash at this moment completely burst in the shutter, and the rubicund face of Sergeant Crank appeared looking in, with his musket raised and directed point blank at Captain Hawk, who instinctively shut one eye and calmly looked down the muzzle.

"You're an uncommonly good guesser, Captain Hawk!" cried Roland Gregson, popping round the corner and leaning over the window-sill, at the same time keeping the captain in countenance by presenting a formidable pistol in the same direction as the musket.

Morna raised her head, being roused from her sleep, and looked at them with a scared expression.

Hugh contemplated the scene in a state of utter bewilderment.

"Come," said Roland, "we needn't have any more row in this place; I think there's been enough of that to-day, so just put on your hat captain, and let's make a start."

"There's a guard of honour of six of his Majesty's soldiers waiting to escort you—all picked men," said Sergeant Crank, in a tone of enthusiasm proportionate to the occasion. "If you was an earl or a dooke you couldn't be better attended."

Captain Hawk, who had evinced no emotion whatever at the sight of his Majesty's representatives with their respective weapons pointed at his head, replied, in a tone of the utmost coolness and suavity:

"I feel sensibly the honour his gracious Majesty does me in sending such distinguished escorts as yourself, Mr. Gregson, and six of the flower of the British army, attended by their gallant sergeant, to conduct me; at the same time, I feel rather fatigued, and therefore beg to decline travelling a single step to-night."

Having thus expressed his determination in the most unconcerned manner possible, the captain quietly folded his arms, still looking blandly at the distinguished individuals who were still on full cock at the window.

It will readily be supposed that it was by no means the kind of reply they expected.

It had the effect of making them both open their eyes very wide and raise their eyebrows very high.

"It's not a matter of choice whether you come or stay," said Gregson, assuming a tone of authority.

"Not by any means," added the sergeant.

"The fact is, you *must* come!"

"Decidedly!" wound up Crank.

"I have a duty to perform," continued the detective, who began to foresee a little difficulty in persuading the captain it was to his interest to surrender himself to the tender mercies of his guard of honour—"I say, a duty to perform; and if you resist, I shall of course——"

"Stay!" remarked the highwayman, in a calm, unruffled voice, although there had been a slight agitation of the musket and pistol that confronted him. "How do you know you may not have been too precipitate? How are you certain I am the man you seek?"

"Oh! I know you well enough," answered the sergeant. "You are Captain Hawk—that's sufficient for me. His Majesty has been robbed. You, by the confession of that man," pointing to Hugh as he spoke, "have in your possession a large sum of money answering to the description given, and therefore I arrest you on suspicion."

"Very good; but you come upon me at the close of a day of intense excitement——"

"I've been pretty well excited myself," remarked the detective.

"So have I," echoed the sergeant.

"Very likely," continued the captain; "but I'm quite knocked up—exhausted; and when you burst in upon me in this sudden manner, with deadly weapons pointed at my head, and command me to rise up and follow you, you mustn't be surprised if I argue the point a little. Business is business—duty is duty; but we needn't be butchers over it."

There was something so exceedingly mollifying in the smooth tones of Captain Hawk, that both Gregson and the sergeant were thrown off their guard.

"We don't wish to use any unnecessary violence, provided we're not resisted," said the detective, in a merciful voice, lowering his pistol, and giving Sergeant Crank a private intimation to do the same, in the shape of a sharp nudge in the ribs with his elbow, which made that individual gasp suddenly, and point his musket precipitately downwards.

But no sooner had this taken place than Captain Hawk, quietly slipping his hands into his pockets, drew forth, in the most unconcerned manner in the world a pair of glittering, long-barrelled pistols, and presented them at the two heads that protruded through the open window.

Sergeant Crank and the detective were considerably startled at this manœuvre on the part of the captain.

They convulsively grasped their weapons, and made an instinctive movement to raise them again, but the highwayman's voice stopped them.

"Don't—don't, my dear friends!" he cried; "your firearms are in a much more agreeable position as they are now than when pointed at my head, and if you value your precious lives, don't attempt to raise them!"

"But this conduct——"

"Is a—a——" stammered the sergeant.

"The only conduct likely to be effectual under the circumstances," coolly remarked Captain Hawk; "therefore don't be rash. Take my advice. Remove your heads from that window, and go home to bed—you require rest; if not, I shall be reluctantly compelled to administer a pill apiece you'll find it hard to swallow."

This was desperately provoking.

To be braved thus by a single man—one, too, whom they had congratulated themselves a few moments before on having trapped so cleverly.

Gregson frowned and hesitated.

Sergeant Crank, with his mouth open, winked and blinked at the terrible instrument with the bright barrel, that seemed intent upon shooting him right in the eye.

Matters were becoming desperate, when suddenly the detective shouted, at the top of his voice:

"Ho! soldiers, advance!"

At that very instant, by some unseen power, he felt himself pitched headforemost in at the window, and Sergeant Crank, by a similar agency, found himself on the top of his brother agent.

The soldiers, roused by the detective's cry, rushed forward in a straggling manner, and scrambled in at the window.

"Seize him!" roared Gregson, who had scraped the skin off his forehead against the rough floor.

"Seize him!" yelled Crank, whose nose had come into violent contact with the detective's heel.

The six picked men, slightly bewildered, looked six ways at once for something to seize, and at last, as the most available object, pounced upon Hugh Trevellyn, who had not moved from his daughter's side.

"Hold the rascal fast!" growled the sergeant.

"Bah!" shouted Gregson, as he scrambled to his feet, in a very irritable tone. "Where are your eyes? You've got the wrong man!"

But where was the *right* man?

He had disappeared, and was nowhere to be found.

CHAPTER CLXVII.

THE SMUGGLER CAPTAIN TAKES A JOURNEY OVERLAND.—HE PAYS A VISIT TO THE CROWN AND SCEPTRE.—GAINS SOME IMPORTANT INTELLIGENCE.—LORD HARCLIFFE RECEIVES AN UNEXPECTED VISITOR.—A STARTLING EVENT.

A GREAT reverse following like a thunderclap upon a supposed triumph has a tendency for a time to depress the strongest and the most energetic.

It was in precisely such a state of mind—a state of despondency and depression—Lord Harcliffe found himself, as, surrounded by difficulties—a strongly-locked door, a sentinel without, and another stationed beneath the window, keeping strict watch—he threw himself despairingly on the bed.

Still, however, as might naturally be expected, sleep fled from him.

The revulsion of feeling was too strong, and banished sleep from his eyelids.

He lay wondering what was to be the end of this last misadventure.

Then his thoughts turned towards his comrade and friend whom he had left in the cavern.

He pictured what his anxiety would be when he did not return.

It was almost impossible that the captain should, in his rocky concealment, receive any intelligence of his capture, and consequently, from his ignorance of his position, could take no steps to offer him any assistance.

Could he have communicated with his friend in any way, it would have been an immense relief to his chagrin, as in that case he would have been assured of one thing—that Captain Hawk would have left no stone unturned to effect his liberation.

The only comforting reflection he could indulge was that he had consigned the precious gem he had compelled the old scoundrel, Moses Geltz, to disgorge, to his friend's keeping.

He knew that was safe.

While his thoughts thus rambled on, his attention was arrested by a peculiar sound.

He listened, and could almost fancy some one was in the chamber he occupied besides himself.

He sat up in the bed and looked around, but saw nothing to indicate the presence of any living creature.

He sank back wearily on his pillow, supposing it had been merely fancy.

Still the strange sounds continued—a kind of pattering, scraping sound, something like that of the feet of some four-footed animal on the floor.

"It must be a dog, or a cat, perhaps, beneath the bed," thought his lordship; and leaning over the side, he swung his hand beneath to endeavour, if possible, to unkennel the intruder.

This had not the desired effect, but, on the contrary, he was conscious that something had returned his demonstration by patting the back of his hand, as if playfully.

His curiosity being excited, he launched the pillow beneath the bed with a sudden swing.

This was attended with a more successful result, since in the dim light of the lamp which was expiring, he observed a small dark figure, something human in shape, dart from beneath the opposite side, and make a rapid circuit round the chamber.

The Black Highwayman followed the singular form with curious eyes.

What could it be?

"Is it one of Satan's imps sent to mock me?" he murmured.

A peculiar hissing and chattering convinced him that his mysterious visitant was nothing demoniac.

He lay therefore quietly watching it.

The strange creature seemed to be in a frolicsome mood.

It dragged a piece of linen drapery from beneath the bed, and wrapping himself in it, appeared to enjoy in its own mind either the additional warmth it imparted, or the comicality it added to its personal appearance.

It also appeared in some sort to desire to attract Lord Harcliffe's attention by constantly looking towards him, as though it was performing its little eccentricities for his lordship's especial amusement.

The lamp at this moment shot up with a sudden bright flash, and Lord Harcliffe during that brief illumination was enlightened as to the character of his strange companion.

It was a monkey, in whom his lordship recognized, or fancied so, a fellow sharer of the perils of his friend and himself on the night of the fearful tempest that had so nearly cost them their lives.

He looked at the animal on that account with peculiar interest; and as if to test whether his supposition were correct, called in a coaxing voice:

"Jacko—poor Jacko!"

This was evidently what poor Jacko was waiting for; he hopped forward and took the outstretched hand of Lord Harcliffe—or, at least, one of his fingers—in a most friendly manner; and thus having broken the ice, sprang up on to the bed and located himself by his lordship's side, chattering in a manner indicative of much satisfaction at seeing him again.

Lord Harcliffe was fond of animals, and this little event, trifling as it seemed, diverted his thoughts from more serious matters, and did him good.

"Why, poor Jacko," he said to the monkey, "I thought you were at the bottom of the sea!"

Jacko looked at him like a very wise old monkey, as he doubtless was, but made no remark on the subject but a few chirps.

He, however, seemed instinctively to remember the friend that took him into the boat, and seemed very glad to see him again.

Poor Jacko on the night when our heroes were struggling with the fierce waves, had his share of struggle and salt water too.

His poor little body was, being light, carried on the crest of a wave and lodged among a nest of rocks.

Jacko improved the position by clambering as far upwards as possible; and thus out of reach of the water, he waited, shivering and chattering, till the ebbing of the tide left the rocks dry, when he made the best of his way to land, where he was found in the high road by the landlord of the Crown and Sceptre, who took him home and adopted him as a curiosity.

The sagacious animal had caught sight of Lord Harcliffe as he ascended the stairs and slipped up surreptitiously to renew his acquaintance, hiding himself under the bed to prevent a summary dismissal.

His lordship indulged Jacko by allowing him to remain by his side; and as if to set his friend an example, the monkey nestled close to his side, and went to sleep.

The Black Highwayman, who had perhaps learnt a lesson of philosophy from the poor little animal, began to feel sensations of drowsiness, and gradually yielded to them; thought and remembrance past and present became dreary and indistinct, and he slept profoundly.

* * * * *

When the boat that had conveyed Lord Harcliffe and his friend ashore, returned to the smugglers' vessel, and Captain Jecks was informed of the circumstance that had occurred, he inwardly resolved to go ashore after dark and proceed to the cavern to make a third to their two.

Accordingly at that time he ordered the boat to be manned, and ran her to land as near to the cavern as possible, ordering the men to await his return.

Loaded with a bottle of choice cognac and a pocketful of cigars, the smuggler entered the rocky precincts that had been the scene of such varied occurrences only a few hours before.

Much to his chagrin, however, no traces of the person he sought were discoverable.

"Surely," he soliloquised, "he cannot have taken his final departure without a farewell or a shake of the hand?"

Then a confused idea—that had been floating in his mind from certain expressions that the Black Highwayman had let fall that he had been accustomed to a wild and adventurous life—seemed to gather strength and to shape itself almost into a real truth; and from this it suddenly occurred to him that his elegant guest might have got into some trouble ashore, though what the trouble was, or on what account it was likely to arise, he was alike ignorant.

It was merely surmise.

Of the Jew's fate he was utterly reckless, save as the cause to which he attributed his lordship's departure in the first instance.

"The rascally old shark!" he muttered, as he stood anxiously scanning the dark rocks in the hope of catching a glimpse of his friend. "Why didn't he let the son of a bitch go to Davy Jones, barrel and all?"

However, as his lordship showed no signs of appearing, he resolved to remain on shore that night and institute a search, not doubting he should be able to gain some tidings of him.

He accordingly dismissed the men, and proceeded along the rocks till he reached the ascent in the cliff.

He took this route, and wandered on till by some singular fatality he reached the cottage of Hugh Trevellyn, near the door of which he beheld the soldiers posted.

Keeping clear of these, he strolled round to the side where Detective Gregson and Sergeant Crank were *doing their duty* at the open window.

It struck the smuggler that his lordship might be there, and under cover of the darkness he drew near, and listened to the conversation related in the previous chapter.

He could see quite distinctly into the cottage, and appreciate the cool courage of Captain Hawk as he sat with a pistol in each hand laying down the law to his would-be captors.

Little did he guess how nearly he was connected with the man he sought; little did he imagine that the handsome man with the pistols would have been as rejoiced to see Lord Harcliffe as he himself.

However, it was sufficient for the smuggler, seeing one man beset by two, one of whom wore a military uniform, to divine that the captain was in some kind of danger; accordingly he drew nearer and nearer the window, and when the detective raised his voice for the soldiers, he seized him and his companion by the legs and performed the feat the result of which appeared at the end of the last chapter.

So rapidly and neatly was this executed that neither of the victims had the least idea how it was brought about.

Sergeant Crank declared it was the wind blew him in, but this was doubted.

Having thus rendered Captain Hawk's intrusive visitors *hors de combat*—at least, for a time—he made good his retreat in the darkness, and directed his course along the road till he came in sight of the Crown and Sceptre Inn, the landlord of which was one of his customers.

As he drew near he was a little surprised to observe a sentinel walking to and fro on a very short beat, and occasionally looking up at one of the windows.

Without exactly knowing why he did so, the idea crossed his mind that this sentinel was in some way connected with the absence of Lord Harcliffe.

He stopped suddenly, and instead of pursuing his present path, leapt over the hedge, and crossing a field at an angle, reached the inn by the rear instead of the front.

Jonathan Riggs, the landlord, was smoking his pipe in the bar parlour in a state of solitary enjoyment.

The rest of the household had retired to rest, but Jonathan, who had worked himself up to a state of considerable excitement from the fact of having a prisoner who had robbed his Majesty, under his roof, felt it incumbent on him as a loyal subject to sit up all night in case of any attempt at escape.

He was moistening his clay with diluted draughts of Captain Jecks's cognac, and indulging in a kind of mental struggle with the prisoner above stairs, whom he had pictured making a desperate struggle for liberty, and he (the landlord) gripping him at the top of the stairs, and rolling to the bottom, and eventually dashing out his brains with the iron scraper, and receiving for this astounding feat the honour of knighthood from the hands of his Majesty himself.

He had just knelt down in this waking dream, and was waiting for the final tap with the sword, and the order —"Arise Sir Jonathan Riggs!"—when instead there came a tap of another description at the shutter without.

This dispelled the castles in the air immediately, and caused the landlord to start to his feet.

"That's Captain Jecks's tap," he cried.

After listening a moment he heard a slight scraping of the gravel from the smuggler's heel.

This was an understood signal, and Jonathan instantly unfastened the shutters.

There on the outside sure enough stood the portly figure of Captain Jecks.

In an instant the window was raised softly, and the smuggler stepped in.

"Good evening, or rather good morning, friend Jonathan!" he said. "I suppose you didn't expect to see me at this hour, eh?"

"I should as soon have expected to see old—ahem! I mean my old grandmother," answered the landlord, correcting himself and closing the shutters. "And what brings you ashore, captain?" he continued—"going to pay some of your old friends a visit, I suppose?"

"Well, no, not exactly; but come, talking's dry work: let me have a pipe and a drop of hollands, and I'll tell you all about it," said the smuggler.

The hollands and the pipe were placed before Captain Jecks, and in a very few moments, by the united efforts of himself and the landlord, the small parlour was in a dense fog of tobacco smoke.

"Oh," ejaculated Jonathan, "this *is* comfortable! And now let's hear what you're up to. By-the-by, the last lot of hollands I had of you is nearly used up."

"We'll finish it to-night, and I'll send you in another cask."

"As soon as you like; it's good stuff, and sells well. But we can settle that presently—I want to know what brings you here."

Captain Jecks then related to the landlord the circumstance of his rescuing Lord Harcliffe from a watery grave —how he had remained on board his lugger—made Jonathan laugh till the tears ran down his cheeks at the adventures of the Jew in the barrel, and finally that it was the prolonged absence of his lordship that brought him to the Crown and Sceptre that night, or rather morning.

Jonathan listened with great attention, and screwed up his mouth to a point, as the narrative proceeded, for it struck him he could give a pretty good clue to the whereabouts of the missing lord.

"You see, friend Jonathan," said the smuggler, as he wound up his history, "I've taken a great liking to Lord Ramilies" (that was the name by which he had called himself aboard the lugger); "and when I lose a friend I never rest till I find him. But as I came in sight of your inn, I noticed a soldier patrolling up and down before it; that's why I came round to the back. What's the meaning of it?"

It was now the landlord's turn, and he gave Captain Jecks a full account of the arrival of the soldiers with the two prisoners, the circumstances under which they were taken, and the crime of which they were suspected.

"And I'm sitting up here like a loyal subject of his Majesty, so that in case of any attempt at escape or rescue I may be ready to do my duty—to do my du——"

The words were not out of his mouth when, to his great surprise, Captain Jecks started up.

"D—n me! if one of your prisoners isn't the very man I'm looking for; and the other's that rascally old Jew!" he cried, slapping Jonathan on the shoulder.

"From what you told me, I thought as much," returned the landlord.

The smuggler raised his glass to his lips, and emptied it at a draught.

He then filled it again, and resuming his pipe, sat down, fixing his eyes upon the host.

He looked at Jonathan—Jonathan looked at him.

There was a pause of several moments as they puffed their pipes in silence.

"We're friends, are we not?" inquired the captain, at length.

"Certainly!" answered the landlord, a little dubiously.

"Stanch friends?"

"I hope so!"

"The charge against this gentleman is false!"

"Gregson the detective says its true!"

"Then he's a lying hound, and you're a fool to believe him!" replied the captain, in a manner that had only its excessive frankness to redeem it.

"We're bound to believe the agents of the law!"

"Bah! bound to believe!—agents of the law!—bosh! humbug! I'd as soon believe I could guide my craft without rudder or compass. They're a set of lying, unscrupulous scoundrels—in nine cases out of ten a d—d deal worse than the thieves (as they call 'em) they're sent to lay their grappling irons upon."

"The old Jew made a very clear statement, and Gregson says it quite justified him in seizing this Lord Ramilies, who it appears is suspected not to be a lord at all, but a knight of the road, known as the Black Highwayman."

Captain Jecks looked thoughtful as the landlord thus expressed himself.

He had more than half suspected his lordship was one of those dashing adventurers.

"The Black Highwayman!" he repeated, slowly. "Well, and what if he be the Black Highwayman?" he burst out, suddenly, "or the Brown Highwayman? or the Green Highwayman? He's a d—d fine fellow, whatever his colour! But mine's true blue, and, by G—d! highwayman or not, I'll never see a friend placed in limbo, and carried off by a parcel of landsharks, while I've got a hand to grasp such a weapon as this!"

So saying, he drew out a heavy pistol, and placed it before him on the table.

The landlord, who was of a somewhat cautious, timid disposition, did not share in his companion's enthusiastic admiration of the prisoner.

He did not object to a little quiet traffic in Captain Jecks's contraband brandy and hollands, but with respect to the nobleman embarred under his roof, he felt his character as a respectable member of society was at stake, and he would not—could not entertain the idea of conniving at his escape at all.

"Don't you see, my friend," he said, in a kind of mild tone, which had in it something of stolidity, "that this highwayman——"

"Gentleman!" broke in Captain Jecks.

"Well, then, gentleman, if you like—is accused of robbing his gracious Majesty himself——"

"His gracious Majesty be ——!"

"Oh, really, captain, no—no! That's treating the crown with disrespect!" protested Jonathan.

"Well, there—go on."

"And if he's accused of robbing the king, it would be treasonable to say he hadn't robbed him, wouldn't it?"

"Bah! D—d landlubber's nonsense! Robbing the king! Why, we all know old George is as big a land pirate as ever cruised between St. James's and Wapping."

"My dear fellow, how you talk!" cried Jonathan, aghast at the smuggler's utter want of reverence for the ruling power.

"Yes," replied the captain, "and I can not only *talk*, but *act!* Now look here, friend Jonathan," he added, dropping his voice, and leaning over confidentially to the landlord; "you're not a bad sort of fellow, but you've lived ashore all your life, and you're timid."

"Me!" said the landlord, indignantly, tossing off his brandy-and-water, and throwing himself back in his chair, with his rubicund cheeks puffed out like the frog's in the fable—"me timid! and sitting up all night alone to watch a prisoner—I like that!"

"Well, then, if you're not afraid, prove it by assisting me to set him free."

"Oh, impossible, my dear fellow—quite impossible—can't be done! I should be ruined! the king would hang me as a conniver! I daren't—I really daren't," exclaimed Jonathan, in a tone of great perturbation.

"What d'ye mean, then, by asserting you're not timid?"

"I mean under ordinary circumstances, where——"

"Where there's no danger, Jonathan—that's what you mean," said the captain, in a tone of contempt; "you're brave enough then."

"A man *must* study his own interest a little; besides, this gentleman is no friend of mine," urged the landlord.

"But he is of mine!" bluntly replied Captain Jecks, "and for my sake you ought to help him."

"Very sorry, upon my word, my dear boy, to refuse you anything, but——"

"There, there—I want no excuses. Look here!" continued Captain Jecks, in a firm but angry tone. "Suppose I were to give information to the excise officers that you're in the constant habit of vending illicit spirits, that wouldn't be very good for your health, would it?"

"Oh dear no!" exclaimed the landlord, apprehensively. "But you'd never do that?"

"Perhaps not; but if I did?"

"You'd ruin me, and lose a good customer."

"D—n your custom, or the custom of anyone who values a little personal risk more than the life and liberty of a brave man!"

"Well, don't get out of temper," whined Jonathan.

"But I will get out of temper!" exclaimed the smuggler, bending over him. "I've too much contempt for your cowardice even to betray you; but I could take other means equally effectual to compel you to render your assistance."

"Other means?" gasped the landlord, glancing suspiciously at the heavy pistol that lay so near him on the table.

"Yes! I could tie you to your chair, and placing that pistol to your head, I could blow out your brains, if you dared to move or utter a cry. Or I could lock you in that cupboard under the same conditions; and while you were thus imprisoned, I could release the prisoner. What is there to hinder that?"

"It's impossible, my dear captain—it's impossible."

"Why? To a determined man nothing's impossible."

"There's a sentinel with a loaded musket posted at the door of the chamber inside the house, and there's another under the window outside."

Captain Jecks looked rather blank at this information.

Jonathan Riggs noticed his look and followed up the impression he had made.

"Of course," he continued, "if it hadn't been for the sentinels we might have managed it, but as it is——"

Captain Jecks sternly interrupted.

"As it is, sentinels or no sentinels, my friend shall be rescued!" he cried, emphatically.

"Oh, good heavens, you're mad—you must be mad!" groaned the distressed landlord.

"Then take care how you oppose me: madmen are very dangerous customers to thwart."

"B-b-but what in the world are you going to do?" stammered Riggs.

"My friend is confined in one of the bed-rooms, you say?"

"Yes."

"The oak chamber, I should think, judging from the direction of the sentinel's eyes when he looked up at the window."

"You're right; that's the strongest room in the house."

"Yes, I know—I slept in it once."

"Ah! then you'll remember it had iron bars to the windows?"

"Yes; and I remember it had something else besides iron bars to the windows."

The landlord winced at this remark.

"What d'ye mean?" he inquired, in a subdued tone.

"It had a trap in the floor. I'm fond of taking the bearings of every cabin where I sling my hammock, and in overhauling one of the cupboards I came upon this trap-door. For curiosity's sake I raised it, and saw a flight of wooden steps descending to the apartment beneath. As I was in an exploring mood, I went down these steps, and found the chamber to which they had conducted me led into a passage, at the end of which a door, half glass, opened into the very apartment we now occupy."

Jonathan Riggs fell back in his chair and looked hopelessly at the stalwart smuggler as he stood over him and poured this unsavoury intelligence into his ear.

"So, you see, my friend," continued Captain Jecks, "we're quite independent either of the restraint of iron bars, or the scrutiny of sentinels: the trap will do the business effectually."

"It will do mine," thought the landlord.

"His lordship can descend by that trap; the window by which I entered will afford a safe egress, and you'll have the satisfaction of having saved a brave fellow's life——"

"And of knowing that I've put my own neck into a halter," groaned Riggs.

"I'll secure you from this," said Captain Jecks.

"How can you secure me?"

"By tying your arms behind you and shutting you up in that cupboard, as I said before."

"I can't bear being shut up in a close place; and tying my arms would give me the cramp!" expostulated Jonathan.

"But it is positively necessary that you give evidence of having been rendered powerless in order to ward off suspicion that you were an accomplice in the prisoner's escape."

"So it is—so it is! Oh dear!" whimpered the landlord. "You won't tie my arms very tight, will you?"

"Not tighter than is positively necessary," answered the captain.

"I promise you I'll remain perfectly quiet."

"On that condition, then, the cord shall be left perfectly loose. And now, as time is getting on, where is there a piece of rope?"

"You'll find sufficient in the cupboard," said Jonathan Riggs, in a melancholy tone of resignation.

The rope was found, the landlord pinioned—in consideration of his promise to remain quiet—very loosely, and he himself locked in the cupboard.

"Now, then," said Captain Jecks to himself, "for an agreeable surprise for my friend."

So saying, he took the light from the table and left the room.

Lord Harcliffe and his bedfellow, Jacko, had had some hours' calm and uninterrupted repose.

Suddenly his lordship awoke with a start.

The lamp had gone out, and the apartment was quite dark.

As soon as his consciousness was fully restored, he heard a peculiar sound that denoted the drawing back of a bolt.

He listened, wondering what it portended.

It seemed to come from the cupboard, and presently a bright ray of light shot from under the door.

He watched intently.

Was it a friend or an enemy that was to meet his gaze?

His anxiety was soon at an end, for the door opened cautiously, revealing to his unbounded surprise an open trap in the flooring of the cupboard, and the cavity filled by the head and shoulders of the last man in the world he expected to see at that moment: the smuggler, Captain Jecks.

At one bound he sprang from the bed.

The captain placed his finger on his lips.

"Hush!" he whispered, "the least sound may betray us."

It is useless to say the Black Highwayman was still as death in a moment.

The captain ascended from the trap, and fearing the light which he had kept shaded with his hand might attract attention, he extinguished it.

He then cautiously proceeded to the window, and peeped out from behind the curtain.

The sentinel slowly plodded to and fro on his monotonous and lonely vigil.

He was evidently tired out, and looked anxiously along the road for the arrival of the sergeant and the rest of the men anticipating then the "relieve guard."

"Go on, my friend," muttered the captain; "you won't interfere with our proceedings in the least."

He then turned to Lord Harcliffe, and with unfeigned pleasure silently embraced him.

His lordship returned the fraternal welcome with equal sincerity.

His hopes revived in a moment; he felt that he was saved.

"My friend," he whispered to the smuggler, "your presence here gives me new life; it is a foretaste of freedom."

"I have no time to explain now," said Captain Jecks, in a low tone, hurriedly. "You shall hear all when we are in a place of safety."

The Black Highwayman pressed the hand of his newly made but stanch ally firmly.

"We must depart by the way we came," Captain Jecks remarked.

At this crisis an ominous sound reached their ears.

It was the trap closed suddenly, and the bolt drawn underneath.

The smuggler darted to the closet.

His worst fears were confirmed.

The trap was fast, and escape that way was impossible.

CHAPTER CLXVIII.

THE BLACK HIGHWAYMAN PICKS THE PADLOCK OF THE IRON GRATING.—JONATHAN RIGGS GIVES AN ALARM.—THE SMUGGLER CAPTAIN RECEIVES A WOUND AND FALLS INTO A FRIEND'S ARMS.—A NIGHT OF EXCITEMENT.

As soon as the key was turned in the lock, and the room was vacated by the smuggler, the first act of Jonathan Riggs was to release his arms, which, being very lightly secured, was easily done.

His next step was to put his knee against a panel of the cupboard door which he knew was loose, and force it out.

This done, it was easy to reach the key, which was left in the lock, and let himself out of his prison.

With cautious steps, trembling in every limb, like a traitor as he was, he crept after the track of the smuggler, and quietly ascending the wooden ladder, closed and bolted the trap, thus securing two prisoners instead of assisting in the escape of one.

But having performed this magnanimous feat, he paused as to the next best step to take.

Should he return to the cupboard, and shutting himself in, call "Murder!" or should he alarm the sentinel?

He felt perplexed.

His conscience quietly informed him he had been guilty of a very dirty, treacherous act.

He felt also he had made an enemy of Captain Jecks, but altogether he preferred that rather than to be implicated in any way with the escape of a prisoner and the chance of a rope round his neck.

To assist his deliberations he returned to the parlour and drank two glasses of brandy, and then it struck him it would be better to go at once to the sentinel that mounted guard at the door of Lord Harcliffe's chamber and inform him what he had done.

He knew the trap was safe, and the windows being strongly barred, he apprehended no danger of any escape in that quarter.

The bed-room door, then, was the particular point that required extra vigilance.

Captain Jecks and Lord Harcliffe paused for a moment at finding their retreat thus unexpectedly cut off in something like dismay.

"It's the work of that chicken-hearted coward, Jonathan Riggs!" muttered the smuggler, between his teeth.

"One thing is certain," said Lord Harcliffe: "now there are two of us we must make an attempt at least to get away."

"Ay, though we have to fight a way over the bodies of these lubberly guards of ours," returned the smuggler.

Their mode of action was quickly decided upon.

It was resolved to try the window first.

Having reconnoitred below, and seeing no one, Lord Harcliffe cautiously opened the casement.

Then came the obstacle of the iron bars, which were fixed in a frame of the same metal and swung on a hinge, being secured at the opposite side by a hasp and padlock.

Captain Jecks eyed this formidable obstacle ruefully.

"We shall never be able to open that d—d grating," he said.

The Black Highwayman smiled, and taking from the sleeve of his coat a piece of wire, he bent it at one end, and applying it to the padlock, it opened as if by magic.

The smuggler was lost in admiration, and felt inclined to give a sailor's cheer, but he restrained himself and grasped Lord Harcliffe's hand instead, crying, in a tone a little more enthusiastic than prudence would have suggested:

"You're a conjuror!"

"No, only a good locksmith," replied his lordship, smiling.

As he spoke he gently pushed open the iron grating.

It opened outwards, and creaked as it swung.

The two prisoners clenched their hands and held their breath with anxiety.

They feared it would alarm the sentinel without.

However, as it happened, the poor soldier, tired to death with his long duty, had fallen fast asleep with his back against the inn wall just under the window.

But this they did not know.

The only individual the noise aroused was the sentinel outside the bed-room door, who was indulging in forty winks, perhaps fifty or sixty, at his post.

There was a sudden rattle of his musket, and then a deep voice called out:

"What are you doing, prisoner?"

The prisoner condescended no reply.

"Why don't you answer?"

Still silence.

This was too much for the sentinel.

"I must see what you're after," he cried; and suiting the action to the word, he hastily turned the key, and opening the door, rushed into the room.

"What's the meaning of——"

He had no opportunity of uttering another sound, for, while Captain Jecks pounced upon him from behind and gripped his arms, the Black Highwayman thrust a linen cloth that Jacko had been playing with, tightly rolled up, into his mouth, and both vowing if he uttered a syllable or made the least resistance, they would blow his brains out on the instant, the soldier suffered himself to be thrust into the cupboard as quietly as a lamb—perhaps a little quieter—where the key was turned upon him.

Just about this time—these events having transpired much more rapidly than we could describe them—the landlord, powerfully refreshed with brandy, arrived at the foot of the staircase leading to Lord Harcliffe's apartment.

Not, however, seeing the sentinel at his post on the landing, and hearing a very suspicious scuffle going on inside the room, he instantly divined that some catastrophe had occurred to the unfortunate man.

"They're murdering the poor devil," he hiccuped.

It never struck him that if this were the case, the *poor devil* would have been thankful for a little assistance.

But his haste would not admit of such an interruption.

He felt sure the prisoners were trying to escape, and it was his duty to prevent it.

He accordingly unbolted the front door, and staggered out. He had had a great deal more brandy during the last few hours than he dreamt of, and was very unsteady on his legs.

He reeled to the slumbering sentinel, and grasping him by his cross-belt, shook him violently.

The soldier, suddenly roused from his sleep, and finding himself grappled by—as he supposed—an escaping prisoner, let fly with his right fist, and caught the drunken Riggs such a smashing blow on his frontispiece, that he rolled over like a log.

The soldier, however, speedily discovered his mistake, and raised the landlord, who hiccuped something that was almost inaudible.

"Pris-ss (hic!) 'scape, (hic!) sen'l (hic!) mur-r!" pointing vaguely up to the window.

The sentinel looked up, and seeing the iron grating open, took the alarm.

He rushed to the door, but the wind had blown it to.

He hoisted Jonathan on to his feet, and demanded a ladder.

That personage happened to comprehend the request; and being somewhat sobered by the cool air and the blow, staggered off, and presently returned dragging the required article.

The sentinel placed it against the window, and Jonathan, who was now past fear, boldly volunteered to ascend and reconnoitre the interior.

He accordingly pulled himself together, and with some difficulty mounted step by step.

No sooner, however, was his head on a level with the window-sill, than a strong arm seized him by the back of the neck, and he was hoisted into the room, where, in less time than it takes to write it, he found himself in the cupboard on the top of the sentinel.

"Now," cried the Black Highwayman to Captain Jecks as he turned the key of the door, "we must make a rush for it. You go first."

The smuggler hastily planted his foot upon the ladder, and was in the act of descending, when a loud and peremptory voice cried:

"Halt there!"

The moon was shining at this time full upon the window, but the lower portion was in deep shadow; consequently, though they could hear the voice, the speaker was concealed from view.

"If you move another step, I shall fire!" repeated the voice.

This came from the sentinel beneath, who, with his musket on full cock, raised to his shoulder, his finger on the trigger, was quite ready to carry out his threat.

Death was staring the smuggler in the face, but he did not see it.

"Fire, and be d—d!" he shouted, in his usual reckless manner.

The soldier's finger tightened on the trigger of his musket, when a heavy blow from an unseen hand descended with tremendous force on his skull, and laid him stunned and helpless on the ground.

"Ha, ha!" laughed Captain Jecks, on the ladder. "Why don't you bite as well as bark?"

The words had scarcely passed his lips, when the report of a musket rang through the surrounding silence, and the smuggler fell from the ladder without a word into the arms of Captain Hawk, who as silently let him hang across his shoulder, and by an effort of almost superhuman strength, bore the dead weight of the gallant seaman away from the spot.

Lord Harcliffe had heard the report of the musket; but ignorant of what had taken place below, was about to follow, when the flashing of several links threw a light upon the surrounding objects; and to his dismay he beheld the foot of the ladder encircled by Gregson, Sergeant Crank, and the picked men.

It was a moment of desperation; and urged by the intense desire he felt for liberty, he essayed a leap from the ladder.

But the impetus was so violent that the spoke on which his feet rested snapped like a piece of glass, and he was precipitated headlong into the midst of those he was most anxious to avoid.

Everything seemed to have gone wrong.

The order of the day appeared to be mystery and confusion.

Detective Gregson had a forehead from which the skin had been peeled.

Sergeant Crank had a nose, which he insisted was a nose no longer, but a mashed turnip.

Hard by, the unfortunate sentinel was found bleeding and senseless.

On rousing the slumbering inmates of the Crown and Sceptre, other mysteries of a most unsatisfactory nature developed themselves.

Gregson, accompanied by Sergeant Crank, proceeded at once to the oak chamber, on the outside of which he expected to find the sentry (asleep).

But no such individual being to be found either asleep or awake, his absence suggested all sorts of unpleasant ideas in the brain of the imaginative Crank.

"Something out o' th' common's happened, depend on it," he remarked to the detective, who, trying the door, and finding it locked and without a key, called up one of the soldiers and bade him break it open with his musket.

This being effected, they entered the dark chamber, the window of which stood wide open, with the ladder still placed against it.

It suddenly struck the detective it might be as well to send for the landlord, and orders were despatched to summon him, but he was not to be found.

At length a peculiar nasal sound was distinctly heard in the cupboard, and the door being opened, the missing host and the lost sentinel were discovered snoring in utter oblivion in each corner.

They were with some difficulty roused from their slumbers, and when, after various shakings and toe applications, they were compelled to awake, like the "sleepy grooms" in Shakspere's tragedy of Macbeth—

"They stared and were distracted."

As for Jonathan himself, he was only to be distinguished by his striped stockings, the blow he had received from the sentinel having raised such a protuberance on his forehead, and tapped such a profusion of his claret, that he looked like nothing human.

His remarks, too, when aroused were very strange and incomprehensible, and to this effect:

"Loy'l sujjec' (hic!) grac's maj'st' (hic!) six scoun'ls (hic!) pis'ls—tie (hic!) rope—cub'd (hic!) pris'n's—trap (hic!) sen'l—lad'r (hic!) blow nose (hic!)" And then he fell asleep.

Far different was it with Lord Harcliffe.

Surrounded by a body of men with loaded weapons, he was too painfully alive to his position.

He would have been too glad to sleep; but sleep, alas! fled from him.

The soldiers who guarded him could willingly have slept for themselves and their prisoner into the bargain; but they dared not close their eyes lest he should escape.

After the occurrences of the night, it was thought advisable, all things considered, to continue their journey without further delay.

It was now broad daylight, and, tired as the men were, they were compelled to yield obedience to the sergeant's orders to march.

And accordingly march they did, accompanied by Lord Harcliffe and Moses Geltz, who growled like an angry old bear at being robbed of his natural rest.

[CAPTAIN HAWK STARTLES THE KING.]

The only one left behind was the unlucky wight who received the blow from the butt-end of Captain Hawk's pistol.

* * * * * * *

We left the captain a short time since bearing the senseless body of the smuggler on his shoulders from a spot where, but for him, he must have fallen into hands he would gladly have avoided had he been conscious enough to have expressed any opinion at all.

It was a most singular coincidence, the interchange of good offices between these two men, who were quite unknown to each other.

Captain Jecks had a few hours before facilitated the escape of Captain Hawk, and now Captain Hawk was doing a precisely similar good turn for Captain Jecks.

The smuggler was a powerful man, and very heavy, and Captain Hawk, with all his muscular energy and power of endurance, began to feel it a physical impossibility to carry his burden much further.

Having therefore borne the wounded man beyond the immediate presence of danger, he left the road and took to the fields, where, being utterly unable to proceed a step further, he placed his wounded companion in a small wooden thatch-roofed building he happened to light upon, which had the appearance of a cow-house.

There was a heap of hay in the corner, and on this fragrant couch he deposited the wounded man, and then taking his flask from his pocket, he administered a draught to the smuggler captain.

It had a decidedly beneficial effect, for the patient opened his eyes, and gazed with a kind of dreamy earnestness at his companion.

It was now broad daylight, and the day streamed through the crevices of the building.

"You are better?" inquired the captain.

"Yes, I feel much better," answered the smuggler. "I shall cheat those land rats yet."

"Are you much hurt?"

"I think not; but I am conscious of having lost a great deal of blood, and I feel faint in consequence. Give me another draught of cognac."

Captain Hawk immediately complied, and then said:

"Allow me to examine your wound: I am a little skilled in such matters, and may be able to do you good."

"Examine, then, my friend, by all means," said the smuggler; "and if you look upon it as fatal, don't keep it from me: let me know the worst: I'm not afraid to cross the dark ocean, or to make the dead reckoning."

Captain Hawk then proceeded to investigate the nature of the wound.

He found the ball had injured one of the ribs, and ripped open the flesh in an alarming manner; but he did not express his full sense of the danger.

One circumstance was in the smuggler's favour: the blood had congealed over the wound, and stopped the flow of the crimson stream, and it was this circumstance that enabled Captain Hawk to see a chance of saving his life.

"I will procure you medical assistance to-morrow, and I doubt not you will soon be yourself again," said the captain.

"I shall do very well without doctors, with their pills and potions," answered the smuggler. "I am only anxious to learn whether my friend escaped—I mean my fellow-prisoner."

"I am unable to afford you any definite information on that point, having had enough to do to carry you out of harm's way," replied the captain.

He little thought who the prisoner was to whom the smuggler alluded.

But gradually as Captain Jecks grew stronger, he recognised the features of his preserver, and then he told him the share he had had in upsetting the friendly arrangements of Messrs. Gregson and Crank.

They shook hands warmly upon this discovery, and by degrees, one thing leading to another, Captain Hawk became pretty well convinced that the luckless prisoner, Lord Ramilies, was no other than his dear friend Lord Harcliffe, and when the title of the Black Highwayman was named, he sighed deeply.

"Poor Harcliffe!" he murmured, "he, then, is in the hands of the hawks, and I—but I have done my duty, at least.

"Once let me see you in a place of safety, then I shall leave you, trusting to meet you completely restored at some more fortunate period, and depart to seek my comrade."

It was yet early morning when footsteps were heard approaching the shed where our adventurers had taken shelter.

Presently came the scraping of a dog's foot against the door, and that peculiar, impatient whining noise, accompanied by a short sharp bark, as though the animal was fully conscious of the presence of intruders.

"Why, Snap, what be th' the matter wi' you this mornin'?—do 'ee smell out some vagrants in th' old shed, eh?" exclaimed a comfortable sort of fat voice, without.

Almost immediately after, a hand was laid on the wooden latch, and the door opened.

The person who entered had the appearance of a middle-class farmer, and was a hale, round, red-faced man, who looked as though he fed upon nothing but sunbeams and fresh air, his complexion was so ripe and rosy.

He started as his eye fell upon Captain Hawk and the wounded smuggler.

Snap also made a slight demonstration, and showed some ugly teeth, viciously, growling at the same time very ominously.

"Hollo!" cried the man, "who be yow? and what be 'ee doin' there in my shed, a lyin' on my hay?"

The speaker being startled, spoke perhaps a little more peremptorily on that account; but Captain Hawk, who could never endure to be addressed in a tone of command, looked up at the farmer with a kind of quiet contempt, and merely remarked:

"Before I answer your impertinent question, so insolently put, have the goodness to call off your dog."

"The dog knows well eno' what be his dooty, an' he knows yow be trespassin', an' 'e be showin' 'is teeth to give you notice to quit."

Snap wound up this harangue by a succession of barks and growls, and seemed half inclined to make an attack.

"Didn't you hear me tell you to call off this brute of a dog?" asked the captain, sternly.

"Ees, 'a did!"

"Then do as I order you, and at once! If not——"

One of the bright-barrelled pistols made its appearance at this juncture.

The rosy face blanched a little.

"Why, 'ee wouldn't go to shoot th' poor animal?"

"Not if you remove him; if not, I promise you I shall not stand particular. I've no wish to hurt your dog, but at the same time I decidedly object to his injuring me or my friend."

The captain looked so very much as if he meant what he said, that the farmer called the dog to his side, and held him by the collar.

"An' now," said he, "p'raps yow'll answer my question; p'raps yow don't know as this is my shed, an' that's my hay yow're a layin' on, an' besides that, that yow're on my ground, an' trespassin', eh?"

Captain Hawk looked up at the round face that had seemed to promise so much good nature, and noticed that the forehead was low and narrow.

"Ah!" he thought, "this fellow is not better than one of his own fat pigs."

"Bean't yow goin' to answer, measter?"

"If you had a grain of sense, or even common perception, you'd have known that our being here is the result of accident; but it seems to me your head is wood, and your heart stone, and both these being difficult to touch, it will scarcely move you when I tell you my friend is wounded."

The smuggler turned over, and raised himself on his elbow, with an expression of pain.

No sooner was his face towards the countryman's than a mutual exclamation broke from both their lips.

"Tom!"

"Captain!"

The state of affairs was changed immediately.

"Good Lard!" cried the countryman, in a tone of glad surprise, "who'd ever a thout of its bein' yow? Why didn't 'ee sing out at once? It be a wonder Snap hadn't been on to 'ee—'e would 'a been if Oi 'adn't a' been 'ere."

"He ought to thank you sincerely for saving his life, for, as sure as fate, if he'd offered to use his teeth, I should have given him a bullet in his head," answered the captain.

"Well, well—there," said the farmer, feeling that he had offended Captain Hawk. "You must coome down to th' farm; an' Captain Jecks can lay up there for a bit. Ye see, I wur taken rather aback like, when I found yow furst, an' when that be the case it do make a man speak a bit sharp; but Lard bless 'ee, Oi don't mean no offence at all—the cap'n knows that."

Captain Hawk was mollified in an instant, and retracted in his own mind the opinion he had formed respecting the head and heart of Tom Stacks.

Without entering into particulars, Captain Jecks informed Tom that he had been wounded in a casual affray, and that he wanted to keep out of sight till he was well enough to join his ship.

"Oi've got the very room to suit yow; it be joost over our orchard. Yow can put 'ee 'and out o' winder, and pick th' apples from the trees, if 'ee loike."

Captain Jecks expressed his thanks.

"Oi'll bring th' cart oop presently wi' a bed at the bottom for 'ee to lie on, and then Oi'll run over to Alec Ball, the horse doctor."

The smuggler smiled faintly.

"You're very kind, Tom," he said, "but I'm not a horse."

"No, Oi know that; but 'ee be joost as good wi' men; 'ee be wonderful clever wi' cuts, an' sprains, an' bruises, an' sooch loike."

"Oh, well then, let him come."

"Ay sure! he'll put 'ee to rights in no time."

In less than an hour Captain Jecks was conveyed to Tom's farm; Alec was summoned, and bound up the smuggler's rib, which was broken.

This accident necessitated repose for some days; and

Captain Hawk having seen his friend in as favourable a state as possible, departed to make inquiries respecting his comrade, Lord Harcliffe

He was not recognised at the inn as having been in any way mixed up in the recent *fracas;* and received from the landlord, Jonathan Riggs, a distorted and inflated account of the whole affair, which made the captain strongly inclined to knock him over and tread on him.

But as such a proceeding would not have benefited his friend, he contented himself with despising the landlord profoundly, and making him fully aware that he did so.

It was with a heavy heart that he listened to the intelligence that Lord Harcliffe had been taken a prisoner to London.

Though on consideration he was glad to hear that his friend was escorted thither by soldiers—not police officers.

And then with that buoyancy of temperament which could not long be subdued by fortune's reverses, he came to the following resolution:

"My comrade is a prisoner; my duty is to discover his prison, and to *set him free!*"

CHAPTER CLXIX.

KING GEORGE HOLDS AN EXAMINATION IN HIS PRIVATE APARTMENT AT KEW PALACE.—HIS MAJESTY LEAVES OFF AS WISE AS HE BEGAN.

Return we to the palace in Kew Gardens.

King George rejoiced and chuckled greatly when he heard of the capture of Moses Geltz and Lord Harcliffe.

He ordered them to be brought secretly to the palace, and lodged in some underground apartments that were quite as strong, gloomy, and dispiriting as any dungeon could possibly be.

The king complimented the detective in his broken English highly for his skill and perseverance in effecting these captures, and when in addition he was given to understand there was a clue to the discovery of the missing treasure, the avaricious monarch's joy was unbounded.

"You are von clever man, Gregson, by Gott!—you are von clever man, an' I shall not forget you," he cried.

This, coming from the King of England, was flattering, certainly, but not very substantial.

Had he said, as a wind-up, "Gregson, here are a hundred pounds for your services," the detective would have understood his Majesty much better.

The loss of the king's treasure and his diamond ring was not made public.

The search was conducted privately, and came under the head of *Secret Service.*

The fact was, the king's conscience smote him as he remembered the unfortunate Stephen, who had constructed his treasure-chamber, and how he had rewarded him.

He remembered the fatal poison draught he had placed in his way instead of the five thousand pounds he was justly entitled to.

Then, again, the diamond ring had been almost extorted from a young nobleman to purchase a post at Court.

Thus the loss of both these treasures appeared to be almost like a judgment on their guilty appropriator.

But though the king ardently longed to recover his property, he would not have had his loss made a subject of public notoriety for the world.

Not that he felt any remorse on account of what he had done; but the whole of the circumstances wore an ugly aspect, and therefore they were kept secret.

This, so far as it went, was in favour of the prisoners, inasmuch as it did away with the chance of a public trial.

But still this was by no means a guarantee for their future liberty.

The king had them in his power, and would no more have hesitated to condemn them to a secret but perpetual incarceration, than he would have hesitated to sign their death warrant for Tyburn Tree.

They were very nicely under his royal thumb at that moment—Lord Harcliffe, Moses Geltz, and Hugh Trevellyn, the last having been sent for as a witness in the matter of the treasure.

The king had resolved to hold a grand kind of inquisitorial examination of these parties, on both counts, in his own private chamber; where, with the assistance of Ernest Von Helm, Michael Willis, and Roland Gregson, he hoped to be able to arrive at the truth.

Accordingly, on the day appointed, the stout little king might have been seen seated in his arm-chair, in his private chamber at Kew, preparing himself for his judicial investigation by blowing a cloud of German tobacco, and drinking sundry bumpers of the good *Rhein* wine.

At eleven in the morning, Ernest Von Helm entered the apartment.

"Ernest," said the monarch, who was puffing away vigorously at a long German pipe, and looking very red in the face, "I tink I shall get back mein property, after all."

"I trust you will, your Majesty," replied Ernest, "with all my heart."

"Ah! you trost I vill; but do you tink I vill—um?" inquired the king, pettishly.

"I think there is a probability, sire, of such an event, but of course it entirely depends——"

"Bah, bah, bah! Gott dam! dere is alvays someting dat depends! Vhy der teifel don't you say at vonce you don't tink I shall ever see my money or my ring again?—den I shall know vhat you mean!"

"Such is not my impression," answered the young man, respectfully. "I think there is a very probable chance of your property being restored, but it will require all your Majesty's acuteness and perception to arrive at such a result."

"Yes, yes—I know dat! I believe I moss use all my skill in dis matter, an' you may depend upon it dat I shall do so," answered the king.

"The only difficulty would be, that if the ring had passed out of the hands of the thief, it might be difficult to trace," suggested Ernest.

"I shall trace it! I moss—I vill trace it! If nort, I'll hang up dat dam Jew dog, vid a ring troo his nose like a svine!" exclaimed the irritable monarch.

"There is one circumstance greatly in favour of a successful issue to your Majesty's efforts," answered Ernest, quietly, "and that is, that you will conduct the investigation yourself."

"Yes, yes," chuckled the king, "I shall do it."

"When your Majesty demands to know the truth, the culprits, if guilty, will hardly dare deny it. The king's name and presence are always towers of strength."

"Aha! you are right, Ernest; by Gott, you are right!" cried George Rex, with enthusiasm, "dat is joss vhat I tought meinself, an' dat is de reason vhy I shall try dis case. Is Gregson come yet, an' Michael Villis, der jeweller?"

"They have been here for some time, your Majesty."

"Let dem come in."

In a few seconds the parties named stood in the monarch's presence.

The king, anxious to commence proceedings, ordered them at once to their posts.

There were two recesses in the wall masked in by curtains, behind which they concealed themselves.

"Are der prisoners ready?" asked the king of Ernest.

"Quite, your Majesty," he replied.

There were several doors in the chamber in which the progress of our narrative places us, and each of these communicated with a small ante-chamber, which led into the outer passages.

In each of these Lord Harcliffe, Moses Geltz, and Hugh Trevellyn, having been removed from their underground dungeons, were respectively placed.

The passage doors were locked, and bolts prevented any entrance into the king's chamber.

"We'll have der old Jew pig out first," said his Majesty.

Ernest drew the bolt and called:

"Enter Moses Geltz!"

Whatever the Jew might have felt, he had determined upon his course of action, and that was vehemently to protest his innocence.

When therefore he was summoned into the royal presence he was already primed with a good supply of lies, which he began to discharge at the earliest possible moment.

"Oh, your gracious Majeshty," he commenced, as he

entered, cringing and rubbing one dirty hand over the other, "I'm so rejoished to——"

"Hole your tong!" cried the king, bluntly.

"I can't, your Majeshty, upon my shoul! I can't help shaying how mosch I appreciatesh dish——"

"Vill you hole your dam stoopid noise?" shouted his gracious Majesty, furiously.

The Jew was silent.

"Call Michael Villis," said the king.

"Michael Willis!"

The jeweller stepped from behind the curtain.

"Now den," the royal inquisitor commenced, "Ernest Von Helm."

"Here, sire."

"You tell me you give my diamond ring to der Dutch Jew Moses Geltz?"

"Yes, sire."

"Dat'sh a fact, your Majeshty," joined in Moses.

"Be qviet, you scoundrel!" exclaimed the king, and then continued: "He had dis ring in his possession for some hours, did he nort?"

"Yes, your Majesty."

"Exactly tree hoursh and a half by ma vatch," volunteered Moses.

"And then you brought it back to me?" continued the king, addressing Ernest.

"Yes, sire."

"Oh, yesh, I'll take my oath he had it back!" the Jew exclaimed.

"Bote you had it in your dirty hands again in dish room," the king burst out.

"Only for a few minutesh, your Majeshty, and den it vent out of dem again into——"

"Der hands of as big a rascal as yourself!" the indignant monarch cried, finishing the sentence.

"I don't vish to dishpute your Majeshty's vord, but it vash your own handsh it vent into," affirmed Moses, with impertinent acquiescence.

"It's von big dam lie!" roared the king, starting up in a fury, and looking as though he would have liked to annihilate the irritating Hebrew. "I never have der ring again, or I should have it now. Der ring you gave to me vos nort der von I gave to you, you lying son of a pig! It vos glass! Vos it not glass?" exclaimed the angry sovereign, appealing to the jeweller.

"Undoubtedly, your Majesty; here are the pieces," answered Michael, producing the fragments as he spoke.

"Look at dem—look at dem vell!" roared the king to Moses.

Moses screwed up his eyes and peered at the counterfeit relics with a curious expression in his face.

"Vell, vhat do you say to dem, you old monkey, eh?" demanded the furious George.

"Vhy, your Majeshty, it's an imposhture, dere'sh no doubt," stammered the Jew.

"Yes, an' you are de impostor; bote I'll hang you for it!"

"Upon my shoul I never saw de ring after I gave it to your Majeshty! I vish I may die if I did!" asserted the mendacious Moses.

"Ve'll see—ve'll see. Call Lord Ramilies."

"Lord Ramilies!" cried Ernest, as he drew back the bolt of one of the doors.

In answer to this summons, the graceful figure and pale, self-possessed features of Lord Harcliffe appeared.

"Dat'sh him—dat'sh the rashcal!" cried Moses, pointing excitedly to his lordship.

"This is Lord Ramilies," said Ernest, quietly.

"Now, sir," interrogated the king, "vhat do you know about dis ring?"

"Simply, your Majesty," answered his lordship, "that that man," pointing as he spoke to Moses Geltz, "offered me a ring, which from the description given I believe to be your Majesty's, for ten thousand pounds."

"Dere — dere — dere!" cried the king, excitedly. "What do you say to dat, eh? you dog of a Jew!"

"It'sh a lie—a bashe, vicket lie, your Majeshty. How could I show him de ring vhen I hadn't got it?"

"He had it then, sire," continued his lordship; "but believing it too valuable a jewel to have been honestly obtained, I compelled him to deliver it up to me."

"Oh, mein Gott—mein Gott! vhat'll he say nexht!" exclaimed the Jew, in a tone of apparent horror. "He never had de ring from me at all!"

"Den who der teifel did he have it from?" roared King George, perspiring with annoyance.

"I don't know," answered the Jew, doggedly: "it'sh a myshtery I can't undershtand."

"Oh, bah! can't undershtand! You mean you von't undershtand!" the king hastily said. "But no matter; it is enofe; dis gentleman have got der ring, and——"

"Pardon me, sire, I had the ring, but I regret to say it is not now in my possession," explained Lord Harcliffe.

The impetuous monarch, who had held out both his hands in expectation of receiving the jewel, looked terribly disappointed.

"Den where der teifel is it?" he asked, angrily.

"I left it with a trusty friend, who will keep it in perfect safety," answered his lordship.

"I daresay he vill; bote I don't vant him to keep it; I vant to keep it meinself," said the king. "Who is he?"

"Your Majesty must excuse my answering," returned Lord Harcliffe, respectfully.

"But I von't excuse you: I vant my ring!" cried the king, excitedly.

"Then it's impossible you can have it," answered his lordship very quietly and coolly; "and I can still further inform your Majesty, that so long as I am kept here a prisoner, you never will!"

"Den, by Gott, I'll hang you both for a pair of rascal tieves!" shouted the king.

"He'sh telling liesh, your Majeshty!" whimpered Moses. "I believe he ash got it."

"Bah!" growled the king; "take dem avay an' lock dem both op. Dey shall never see der light of day till I get back mein ring!"

Lord Harcliffe and the Jew were removed; the latter groaning dolefully, and protesting that he "vash ash innoshent ash an unborn babe."

This first attempt was decidedly a failure, and the king was in a very bad humour in consequence.

But the missing treasure had yet to be inquired into.

At a signal from the baffled sovereign, Hugh Trevellyn was summoned.

"Who der teifel are you?" politely inquired his Majesty.

Hugh gave his name; and in answer to a very peremptory command, related the facts of Captain Hawk's arrival with the gold as briefly as possible.

His account seemed to impress the king exceedingly.

"Yes, yes," he cried, "dere is no doubt about it: my money vas wrapped op in joss soch a cloak as you describe. An' vhere is it now?"

"I know not, your Majesty," replied Hugh.

"Donder und blitzen!" roared the king, passionately "An' der man dat found it, vhere is he?"

"I am entirely ignorant of that also," Hugh answered

"What?" again shouted the king, who was thwarted at every turn, "you pretend ignorance vhen de man vas in your own house!"

"He was there till the detective and sergeant of your troop insulted him by presenting their weapons at his head, as though he had been a felon instead of a gentleman."

"How dare dey!" exclaimed the exasperated George, who now could only find fault with everybody. "Here, vhere is Gregson?—vhere is Sergeant Crank?"

"Roland Gregson! Sergeant Crank!" called Ernest.

The detective entered, closely followed by the sergeant, who, glowing with military ardour, and proudly conscious that his swelled and inflamed proboscis attested the faithful discharge of his duty, felt that the time for a captaincy or knighthood, or some interesting trifle of that sort, had arrived.

He was therefore all but petrified when the King demanded, in a loud and angry voice:

"What der teifel dey meant by presenting dere veapons at gentlemen's heads?"

Gregson replied humbly that he only acted up to his duty, and did no more than he had done a hundred times before.

The sergeant snuffled and screwed his afflicted nose about, looked a great deal of something, but said nothing.

"You are all a set of d—n blocks!" cried the King, in disgust. "Get out of my sight! Ernest, clear de room."

The order was obeyed.

The royal investigation was over.

There had been much trouble, a deal of passion, plenty of swearing, and after all the King left off just as much in the dark as he was when he began.

CHAPTER CLXX.

SERGEANT CRANK AND THE DETECTIVE RETURN HOME, AND ENCOUNTER A STRANGE OLD GENTLEMAN.—CAPTAIN HAWK FINDS HIMSELF IN THE KING'S BED-CHAMBER.

The trial, or examination, or whatever name it might be called, being over, Lord Harcliffe and the innocent Moses Geltz were conducted to their underground chambers.

Hugh Trevellyn, who could only be looked upon in the light of a witness, was discharged, with orders to hold himself in readiness to answer any further questions his Majesty might wish to put.

As for the King himself, he sat down to smoke more pipes and drink more Rhenish wine, and, to dissipate his chagrin, sent for one of his special favourites, Lady Schulenberg, a very fat, ugly German female, to assist him.

We therefore leave the illustrious pair to their wine and smoke, and continue our narrative.

Roland Gregson and Sergeant Crank, on leaving the royal presence, were pounced upon by one of the royal domestics, and hurried off—not to solitary confinement—but to some mysterious and remote apartment through a great many passages, to take some refreshment.

Having reached their destination, they were introduced by their guide, who was an old crony of the detective's, to a set of choice specimens of regal flunkeyism, with whom they at once commenced making themselves quite as comfortable downstairs as his Majesty was above.

Being at the palace on secret service, was of course an exemption from all other duties, consequently there were no haunting recollections that they were overstaying their time to mar the bliss of Messrs. Gregson and Crank.

They were equally serving the King (so they felt), whether hunting after his Majesty's despoilers, or getting drunk with his Majesty's wine.

They had a sumptuous dinner, in this remote apartment, sumptuous dessert, and plentiful libations.

They gave toasts, sang songs, smoked pipes, and made speeches, did these choice spirits, and altogether passed the jolliest of afternoons and evenings.

But Time, that inveterate "mover on," who hurries us alike rapidly over our jolliest as well as our saddest hours, did not on this particular occasion slacken his pace one jot.

The consequence was, that at ten o'clock p.m., our worthy friends Gregson and Crank, having taken an affecting leave of the other worthies, found themselves in the open air in Kew Gardens, with a very indistinct and hazy notion how they came there, holding on to one another in a state of the most profound and perfect happiness, experiencing a blissful sense of love and good-fellowship to the whole world, their enemies especially.

With these feelings mingled a strong desire—the night being mild and balmy—to lie on their backs and sing "God save the King."

"W-wha' d'liful day we've (hic!) had—hav'n' we?" said Gregson, in a particularly inarticulate tone.

"Glor'us!" replied the sergeant, in a similar state of verbal abbreviation. "Sush day (hic!) man (hic!) nev' f'gets."

Here the ground rose up suddenly perpendicular before him, and he leant against it—which means, he tumbled down.

"Wh're goin', ole (hic!) boy?" muttered Gregson, tripping over his friend at the same time, and feeling as though some fairy hands had lifted him into bed.

Thus they lay side by side on the grass.

"Crank, my (hic!) frien', g'us (hic!) hand."

Crank, who was on his back, swung his arm over and saluted the detective's nose with his knuckles; but that worthy individual was utterly unconscious of the fact, and caught hold of the sergeant's coat-tail, which he grasped and shook with fraternal warmth.

"Crank, m' frien', I (hic!) r'spec's you! (hic!)" he hiccuped—"you're (hic!) man—gall'n (hic!) soj'r."

"I (hic!) r'spec's you, Gregs' (hic!)," returned the sergeant, speaking in the same shorthand kind of manner; "an' if (hic!) fate d'crees sosh'r's (hic!) gory death (hic!) ba'le fiel', n-nev'r (hic!) f'get (hic!) hap—(hic!) mo—mo—m-——"

Here the gallant sergeant became overpowered with emotion, and melted into tears.

The worthy person addressed had fallen asleep several moments previously.

Sergeant Crank now followed his example.

As they lay thus slumbering, a figure drew near.

He must have been a very old man, for his hair and beard were white as snow.

He was enveloped in a large cloak, and seemed to come so directly towards the inebriated pair that one would almost imagine he had been watching them.

Having approached, he bent over and examined them attentively.

"Ah!" exclaimed the old gentleman, significantly. "I thought so."

He then applied his venerable toe with much energy for so aged a personage to the posteriors of Messrs. Crank and Gregson.

"Thankee!" murmured the sergeant.

"Hallo!" cried the old gentleman, "rouse up! Do you know where you are?"

As, however, they appeared to take no notice, the white-haired man shook them till their teeth chattered again.

"Very windy!" muttered the detective.

"Fall in!" cried Sergeant Crank.

"Get up!" urged the old gentleman in the cloak, administering another effective shake.

"God save our grach' King!" chanted Gregson.

"You'll wake his Majesty if you lie howling here!" exclaimed the old man. "Come, let me help you up."

And with another wonderful effort of strength, considering his white hairs, he hoisted the drunken pair on to their feet.

Gregson looked in a particularly oblivious manner at the old gentleman, and being suddenly impressed with the idea that he was his grandfather, staggered to him and embraced him on the spot.

"Hav'n't seen you (hic!) for 'n age," said the detective. "How's (hic!) grandmo'r?"

"Never better," answered the old gentleman, humouring the detective's fancy; "though I don't know what she'd say to see you in this state."

"Glorious (hic!) state!" hiccuped the sergeant.

"Jolly day!" joined in Gregson.

"Splendid!" said Crank.

"Been to the palace—secret service—(hic!)—trial!"

"Oh indeed!" exclaimed the old man.

"Yes (hic!), not word!—quite secret! (hic!) mum, you know!"

The detective tried to put his finger significantly against his nose, but poked it in his eye instead.

"I comprehend," said the old man: "secret service. Very important, of course?"

"Oh yes!—(hic!)—most important (hic)!"

"Trial, I think you said?"

"Zac'ly. Private cham'r — pris'rs— diam's —(hic!)— treas'r—pipes—pots—(hic!)—s' Mash'sty drunk's—(hic!) —pig!"

"Yes, yes; but the prisoners: who were they?" inquired the old gentleman.

"Lord Harcl'—(hic!)—Ram'shs— B-black High'm'n," hiccuped the detective, "an' rasc'lly old (hic!) Jew, Mo-mos's Gel'z."

"Have they gone to Newgate?"

"Newgate? No! (hic!)—all c'fined in (hic!)—palace. Mum, you (hic!) know!"

"Oh, certainly!"

From the twinkling of the old man's eyes it was evident this intelligence gave him much pleasure.

"Come, grandson," he said, linking his arm in that of the detective—"come, sergeant," he continued, hooking Crank in the same manner.

"Take short cut (hic!) for Lond'n Road," said the detective, staggering.

"Decid'ly!" muttered the sergeant.

It will readily be imagined that an old white-haired man, encumbered with the weight of two drunken men, would not make very rapid progress.

But in the case of this old *grandfather*, it was surprising how he shook up one and jostled the other as he gripped their arms firmly against his side and compelled them to come on.

But were they going towards the London Road?

Decidedly not.

The old gentleman was leading them to one of the most retired parts of the gardens, where the foliage was thickest and most plentiful.

Here he allowed the tired drunkards to slip through his arms—not his fingers—and fall on the grass.

Before their heads touched the green turf they were asleep.

The old man smiled as he regarded them.

He then drew from beneath his cloak a piece of strong cord, and coolly pinioned the detective's arms at the elbow and his legs at the ankles.

Having done this, he dragged him close to the bushes.

Then lifting him from the ground, in a most extraordinary manner for his age, and swinging him to and fro far a moment, to gain an impetus, he tossed him crashing into the thick bushes, which closed over the unconscious officer, and he was seen no more.

The gallant sergeant, however, was destined to undergo a different treatment.

The old gentleman, first of all, unhooked his military coat, and took it off.

Then he pinioned his arms, in the same manner as the detective's; after this he took off his gaiters, and pinioned his ankles, then removed his belt and accoutrements, then his hat, and having thus eased him of these superfluous commodities, he did exactly as he had done with the detective—lifted him up, and pitched him headlong amongst the thick bushes, out of sight.

This done, he rolled up the hat, belt, and gaiters in the military coat, and taking them under his arm, proceeded to that part where he and his friend, Lord Harcliffe, had scaled the wall when they secured the treasure.

Having arrived there, he threw the sergeant's uniform, &c., over the wall, and then quickly followed.

Then picking up the bundle, he made his way to that part which, by the removal of the bricks, constituted the entrance to the treasure-chamber.

Here he paused, and after the directions of the builder, the passage stood revealed as before.

This he entered, and having kindled a small lamp he carried in his pocket, he assumed the sergeant's coat, hat, gaiters and accoutrements; then removing the white wig and beard, he revealed the handsome features of Captain Hawk.

He remained there no longer than was sufficient to make this change in his attire, but pulling the stone towards him, entered the treasure-chamber.

All was dark and silent there as the grave.

He groped along the wall till he came to the round knob in a small indentation in the stone work.

He pressed this, and the door swung open, revealing a dimly-lighted stone arch-roofed passage.

Into this he stepped, closing the door after him.

This small and narrow alley led into a much more capacious pathway, in which were numerous doors.

Being a stranger to the interior, the most difficult and critical part of his task was now to come.

There were so many windings in the passages, it was difficult to remember one from the other.

He took particular note of the narrow passage that led to the treasure-chamber, through which he might find it necessary to make good an abrupt retreat, and marked the stone with his knife.

The disguise he wore was most effective; anyone passing him casually would have sworn it was the sergeant himself.

He cautiously proceeded along the passage, listening at all the doors, but not appearing to discover the chamber he desired.

"I wonder now," he soliloquised, "which is the king's apartment?"

He came to a window at the end of one of the corridors, and looked out.

From the outside appearance, he was able to calculate that he was in one of the side wings of the palace.

At this moment, he heard footsteps approaching.

His first thought was, of course, immediate concealment; and he glanced hastily at the doors in the passage without daring to enter any.

The person, too, whose footfall he had heard, suddenly turned from one of the narrow outlets into the broader passage, and came full in sight.

Of course the first object on which this individual fastened his eyes was Captain Hawk.

His gait was rather staggering and uncertain.

This may be accounted for from the fact of his having been one of the festive party given in honour of Gregson and the sergeant.

It was near upon midnight, and he was, as per custom, going his round to see all quiet previous to retiring to rest.

Seeing a stranger in the passage, he paused abruptly and gazed at him, shutting one eye and shading the other with his hand in order to focus his object.

It was a critical moment for Captain Hawk.

He was expecting every moment to hear the man raise an outcry.

To his great satisfaction, he did not, however.

There was only one course to avoid detection, and that was to assume the character of the drunken sergeant whose uniform he wore.

This he did by staggering up against the wall, and hanging down his head in a very helpless manner.

The domestic, who turned out to be one of the head grooms, advanced towards him, and as he drew near—muddled as his brains were—he fancied he recognised the sergeant's coat and hat.

A nearer scrutiny quite satisfied him on this point.

"So it is!" he exclaimed. "By Jupiter, this is astonishing! Why, sergeant, how the deuce did you find your way here? I thought you were at home and in bed long ago."

"We won' go home till morn'!" murmured the fictitious sergeant.

"Good Gad!" cried the alarmed groom—"don't sing, unless you wish to ruin us all! Don't you know the king's chamber is at the end of this passage?"

"God save our (hic!) grach' King!" repeated the captain, in a muffled, drunken manner.

The domestic became desperate.

"Come away!" he cried, trying to lead the supposed sergeant, who gave strong signs of being ready to fall down. "How beastly drunk he is!" muttered the groom, who was verging on the same state himself. "Here," he continued, "take my arm."

Captain Hawk accepted this offer, and suffered the man to lead him away.

They went on a short distance, when the domestic stopped, and opening one of the doors in the passage, suddenly shot the captain into the room.

"You'll find a couch in the corner," said the groom. "Don't make a noise. I'll come to you in the morning."

He then shut the door and locked it.

The captain listened to his retreating footsteps with much satisfaction.

He had now some clue to guide him.

The king's chamber was at the end of the gallery.

Ten minutes after, Captain Hawk had picked the lock and was standing outside the door.

Profound silence reigned throughout the palace.

The captain retraced his way to the treasure-chamber.

The disguise of the sergeant had answered his purpose, and could now be dispensed with, not being adapted to the character he was yet to sustain.

He accordingly removed it, and assumed his own attire, throwing his ample cloak over his shoulders, examining the priming of his magnificent pistols, which he now placed in his belt, and finally putting on a mask of black lace, which effectually concealed his features.

When his peculiar toilet was completed, there was something terribly imposing in the dark, mysterious masked figure.

He felt satisfied in his own mind as to his appearance, and letting himself out of the treasure-chamber once more, he directed his course up the passage.

When he reached the end he paused.

There was no outlet that way but the window, save from the doors on either side.

This was not satisfactory to the captain, who always liked to be prepared for an emergency.

He therefore undid the fastenings, so that in case of an alarm, his retreat would not be hampered or retarded.

"That fellow said the king's chamber was at the end of the gallery," he said to himself, thoughtfully. "But as there are doors on both sides, how am I to know which is the right? It is barely possible I might intrude upon her Majesty the Queen, and that would be an error I would rather avoid."

He stood looking from right to left at the doubtful doors for a few moments.

"I have heard in cases of uncertainty like this, it is good policy to take the right at a venture," he meditated.

Acting upon this rule, he approached the right-hand door and opened it softly.

Waiting a few moments, listening intently, but hearing no sound, he ventured to glance inside.

It was a spacious, lofty chamber, with a velvet pile carpet, massive crimson curtains to the windows, and a stately regal-looking four-post bedstead at the further end, draped also with crimson damask.

A lamp, partially turned out, burnt with a dim light just sufficient to reveal what had attracted the captain's notice.

"This looks like the chamber of a monarch," thought the highwayman.

As his eyes roamed hither and thither they fell on certain articles that confirmed his opinion that he had found the right room.

These consisted of an embroidered coat, a pair of satin breeches, and a white powdered wig.

Another confirmatory sign came shortly in the shape of a prolonged snorting kind of grunt, not unlike what Captain Hawk had frequently heard in rural pigstyes from slumbering hogs.

He was not, however, quite certain whether a king could snore like a pig.

But on listening attentively, it seemed not only possible but a palpable fact.

"It must be the king sleeping in yonder bed," he said, softly; "I'll hesitate no longer."

He closed the door gently and locked it.

Then with noiseless step, like a dark shadow, he glided towards the table where the lamp emitted its sickly rays, and turned the wick upwards.

The increased light spread through the large chamber and falling on the crimson curtains and bed, invested them with a magnificence truly regal.

The highwayman grasped the lamp, and approaching the bed where the King of England lay, drew the curtain aside and allowed the rays of light to fall upon the sleeper.

It was a daring act, but the captain had a purpose to carry out, and he was now fixed, calm, and immovable as a statue.

George Rex had boosed through the afternoon and evening with the fat Lady Schulenberg to his heart's content, and what with the smoke and the Rhenish wine, was in a profound state of fuddle.

In fact, it seemed as if the spirit of Bacchus had been let loose in the palace that day: above and below the drunken god might have exulted at the number of his proselytes.

Captain Hawk stood motionless watching the king, who, with his white nightcap tied firmly on his bald pate, lay with his round, red face peering from out a pile of bedclothes, and his mouth wide open, snoring like a grampus.

The captain could not forbear smiling at the sight.

"Which does he most resemble," he thought, "a king or a parish beadle?"

The drowsy monarch did not at first appear inclined to wake up at all; but as Captain Hawk kept the bright rays in full play on his Majesty's face, he began to exhibit symptoms of uneasiness.

He moved restlessly, rolled his head from side to side, had a fit of sneezing, and finally with a loud grunt awoke and opened his eyes.

The next thing he did, however, was to shut them immediately, being dazzled and half blinded by the bright glare from the lamp.

"Who der teifel put der lamp dere?" he growled to himself. "Take it avay!" he grumbled, in a drowsy tone between waking and sleeping.

But the highwayman stirred not, but kept the lamp still shining steadily on the king's face.

This at last became unbearable; and as his Majesty began to rouse from his lethargy and to recover his faculties, he became aware that the lamp was in a position where he had never seen it before.

It always stood on the table; now it was close to the bed.

The king, in order to investigate this phenomenon, turned himself over sluggishly and raised himself on his elbow.

At the same time the highwayman, who had hitherto held the light in front of himself, now drew his hand aside, and allowed the rays to fall on his sable figure.

At this startling sight the little king became suddenly energetic, and started bolt upright into a sitting posture, where he sat with open mouth and staring eyes contemplating the strange being before him.

CHAPTER CLXXI.

THE MASKED FIGURE TELLS HIS MAJESTY SOME UNPLEASANT TRUTHS.—THE KING LISTENS TO REASON AT LAST.—THE RESULT.

Whatever may have been the faults of George II., cowardice was not one of them.

He was a brave little king, any way.

But to be awakened suddenly from his sleep and confronted by a mysterious masked apparition such as that he now looked upon, was enough to startle the strongest nerved individual.

It had this effect upon the royal George, and caused some of the Rhenish wine he had imbibed to ooze through his pores in the form of profuse perspiration.

But his native courage soon returned, and he exclaimed, in a tone of voice in which there was no trepidation, and in his usual blunt manner:

"Who der teifel are you?"

"A VOICE FROM THE GRAVE!" answered the figure, in solemn tones.

"Bah! Voice from der grave? Don't talk soch damn stoff to me," returned the incredulous monarch, "bote tell me der truth! Who are you, an' vot do you vant?"

"I am one who has a demand to make of the King of England with which the king must comply."

"Most he indeed? Den let me tell you der king of England never allows himself to be ordered by a sobject, mosh less a black-looking midnight robber soch as you are," answered the king.

"Mine is an exceptional case: your Majesty will listen to me," returned the mysterious being, "and obey my orders."

"You d—n villain!" shouted the irascible George. "How dare you talk to me like dis?"

"Let me beg your Majesty not to put yourself in a passion, and I'll explain the motive of my visit."

"I don't vornt to know! Take yourself off an' let me go to sleep, or I'll hang you, you masked villain!"

"There are other masked villains in the world besides myself," said the figure, in a significant tone.

"I know dere are—plenty," acquiesced George.

"Who would think, now, that under the mask of royalty that shrouds the King of England there lies concealed a murderer?"

The monarch fell back as though a snake had bitten him, and turned pale.

"M-murderer!" he gasped.

"Murderer!" repeated the figure. "I came from the martyred Stephen, whom you poisoned!"

"It is false! Mein Gott! dat is von big lie! Who dare accuse der King of England of soch a deed?"

"There are three who accuse you, sire: *Myself*, the *Spirit of the Dead*, and *your own conscience!*"

"Bah! It is all lies—vicked lies! Vhat proof have you?"

"The dying declaration of the murdered victim, written by his own hand, in which he claims five thousand pounds as his legal due."

"Vort for?"

"Constructing your Majesty's *treasure-chamber!*"

"Ha!"

"He bequeaths this sum to his orphan child, and deputed me to see justice done her."

"Five tousand poun'?" spluttered the king, "Vhy, it's enofe to keep all the orphans in England!"

"It's too much to lose; and, as I have your Majesty's promise to pay, signed by yourself, I am here in obedience to the wishes of the dead to demand that sum."

As he spoke, the highwayman held before the king's eyes his own note of hand.

The monarch's red face grew redder with passion.

"It is von d—n forgery!" he cried. "I have been rob of four times dat sum out of der cursed chamber!"

"It was the judgment of Heaven for your crime."

"Vell, den, it is punishment enofe, an' I vorn't pay anoder fardin', you d—n impudent, masked villain!"

"Very well," coolly returned the figure, "then I shall make the whole of this nefarious transaction public: I shall publish the murdered Stephen's dying declaration, and——"

"No, you vorn't!" roared the passionate king, "for, by Gott, you shall never leave dis room alive!"

He made a spring from the bed as he spoke, and made a rush in the direction of a small cabinet, in which reposed several massive pistols.

But the highwayman divined the angry monarch's intent, and anticipated it by taking a rapid step backward, and producing one of his formidable bright-barrelled friends, which he levelled at the monarch's breast.

"Excuse me, but I should recommend your Majesty to remain where you are!" he remarked, with quiet firmness.

"Vort! would you kill your sovereign, you vicked wretch?" the king exclaimed.

"No, sire—Heaven forbid! but on the other hand, I can't allow my sovereign to kill *me*."

"Den vhy do you hold a veapon to mein breast?"

"In self-defence, merely, and to prevent your reaching yonder cabinet."

"Vat has der cabinet to do vid me?"

"Much; and with *me* also; it contains fire-arms, doubtless, and I wish to settle this affair without bloodshed. If your Majesty will get into bed again, I will explain further."

"Teifel! Den be qvick, for I vornt to go to sleep; and with these words the king rolled into bed once more.

"A friend of mine, sire," continued Captain Hawk, "is confined in this palace, and I wish his freedom."

"Vat, Moses Geltz?"

"No, sire—Lord Ramilies."

"Vell den, let dis Lord Ramiliesh give me back der diamond ring he take from that Jew pig, an' he shall go free."

"Let Lord Ramilies go free, and I pledge my word your Majesty shall have the diamond ring."

The king opened his eyes eagerly.

"Vill you take your oath of dat?" he inquired, eagerly.

"I will!"

"Ha, ha, dat is very goot, bote I have only your vord for it," said the king.

"And on the other hand, I have only your Majesty's word for the liberation of my friend," returned Captain Hawk.

"Bote dat is a king's vord, and——"

"Kings do not always keep their promises. You promised Stephen five thousand pounds, not one farthing of which he ever received."

"Bah! Vhy can't you let Stephen rest?"

"Well, then, is it a bargain?"

"But vhen should I have der ring?"

"The moment my friend's dungeon door is open."

The king remained thoughtful a few moments, and then said:

"Come vid me—I vill open der prison doors meinself; bote if you deceive me I vill have you hunted like dogs till you are found, and den like dogs you shall hang ope by der neck."

"You may depend upon me," said Captain Hawk; "I never break my word—I leave that for kings."

"Get out, den, and leave me to dress meinself!"

"Excuse me, your Majesty," answered the captain, resolved not to allow any approach to the cabinet. "You will require a valet; allow me to assist you to make your toilet."

"Go to der teifel!" his Majesty answered, politely; "I can make mein own."

The king, unable to get rid of his attentive visitor, was forced to yield to circumstances, and once more rolled himself out of bed.

He then proceeded, clumsily enough, to drag on his garments, refusing any assistance from the captain, who retired to the cabinet, and stood with his back leaning against it.

The king during his dressing looked ruefully at the highwayman, and wished he had been standing anywhere else, that he might have made a rush for one of the silver-mounted weapons that reposed in the receptacle behind him.

But no such opportunity occurred.

The mysterious stranger kept his eyes, that glittered like live coals through his black mask, fixed upon the king, and the king was obliged to give up all hopes of securing his pistols.

Having dragged on his dressing-gown and thrust his feet into his slippers, his Majesty declared himself "ready."

His nightcap he still retained to protect his bald pate from the night air.

"Your Majesty, being better acquainted than I am with the intricacies of the palace, must be kind enough to lead the way," the captain coolly remarked.

"Bah!" growled his Majesty, "you are von dam, impudent——"

"You will not be offended if I remind you, sire," interrupted Captain Hawk, "that I shall be close at your Majesty's heels, that both my pistols are loaded, and that at the slightest alarm I should unhesitatingly use them, though I should deeply regret to be the occasion of a general mourning."

"Regicide!" growled the king; and grasping the lamp, he opened the door of the chamber and went out, the captain closing the door after him.

The royal guide, with much grunting and many muttered execrations in German, threaded the intricate paths of the palace till he reached the underground cell where the Black Highwayman was confined.

Here he stopped.

Moses Geltz occupied an apartment a few yards distant. He was not asleep, and the sound of the footsteps arrested his attention.

"If anyvon vantsh Moshes Geltz, he'sh here!" he cried, in a dolorous voice.

"Hold your tong, you dam Jew pig!" growled the king, angrily; "no von vants you!"

Then drawing a key from the pocket of his dressing-gown, he unlocked the door.

"Dere!" he said, turning to Captain Hawk, who was at his elbow; "you can go in."

The highwayman smiled behind his mask, at the innocence of this royal remark.

"I am grateful for the privilege of *going in*, sire, but I must be quite sure I have the power of *going out again*," he said; "if your Majesty will enter, I will follow."

The king gave an angry grunt, and appeared dubious.

"Fear nothing, sire, I only wish to secure the liberty of the subject," remarked the captain.

The monarch made no further remark, but opened the door and went in.

The captain followed, and took out the key as he entered.

Lord Harcliffe was asleep, but the sudden light of the lamp aroused him.

He started up, and the shrouded form of his friend met his gaze.

"Harcliffe!" exclaimed the captain.

"My friend, my dear friend!" he cried, recognising the voice at once, and leaping from his couch he threw his arms round his staunch comrade.

"To what do I owe this unexpected visit?" Lord Harcliffe inquired, eagerly, as he caught the flash of the captain's eye through the mask that concealed his features.

"You owe it to the *king's conscience*," replied Captain Hawk, in a tone of solemnity.

"Dorn't talk rubbish!" said his Majesty, abruptly. "You owe it noting of der sort. It is nort my conscience dat bring me here, bote der promise of der ring."

Lord Harcliffe looked with a hasty and inquiring glance at his friend,

"Is it so?" he whispered.

[KING GEORGE RECEIVES THE RING FROM THE MYSTERIOUS VISITOR.]

"Yes."

"Have you der ring with you?"

"No."

"Come," said the king, "I have keep my promise—I have open der prison door; now den keep yours, and restore me der ring."

"All in good time, your Majesty," answered Captain Hawk, as he showed his friend to the door.

"Here, storp—storp—storp!" cried the monarch, as he observed Lord Harcliffe approaching the door, taking at the same time a step forward.

"Stay!" exclaimed Captain Hawk, in a stern tone, interposing himself between the door and his Majesty. 'The anxiety you evince seems to imply a doubt of my word."

"Teifel! I——" growled the king, in an inward, perplexed manner.

"I know your inmost thoughts. You imagine that I have made a promise I do not intend to keep, and you fear that my friend's prison-door being open, the diamond ring may not be forthcoming."

This was exactly what the king did fear, but he was too politic to confess it.

"Oh, no, no, no!" he answered, in a blustering voice, "I am nort afraid of dat—ha, ha! Vort should be der goot for you to get only out of dis prison? Dat is noting. Remember you are nort *free* till you are *out of der Palace Gardens.*"

"That is precisely what I do remember, your Majesty · it is that very idea that causes me to act as I do."

The king looked at the speaker dubiously.

"Give me der ring den. Let me have him in my hands, and I shall unlock ze door and let you out at vonce," he said.

"I have my doubts as well as your Majesty," replied the captain. "How do I know that the moment you hold this ring in your fingers you may not feel disposed to give an alarm previous to unlocking the door?"

"Have I not give my vord?"

"Ah! your Majesty, so you have done before, and—broken it."

"Donder, you d—n impud——"

"Chut! chut! don't put yourself in a passion, sire—it will take no effect whatever," said Captain Hawk; "besides, the game is in my hands now, and it is for me to make terms with your Majesty—not your Majesty with me."

George II. began to look rather purple about the cheeks.

The choleric but courageous little monarch began to feel he was quietly done.

"You dare to talk to me like dis, you d—n infernal rebel——"

"Hush!—your Majesty will do better to be silent and hear me."

"How can I listen to soch an insolent, lying, tieving——"

"I beg your pardon, I am neither, as I shall prove, if you will allow me. Whatever my faults may be, I hold a promise given, whether to friend or foe, sacred!"

"Den why dorn't you——"

"Hush!—not so loud. I promised your Majesty should receive your diamond ring——"

"Yes! dat is vot I vornt. Give it me!"

"Certainly."

"Now!"

"When my friend is free. I mean *out of the Palace Gardens.*"

"Vort? Do you suppose I shall allow you to get out onless I foorst hold der ring in my possession?"

"I do not think your Majesty will be able to help yourself."

"I shall raise an alarm."

"No, I shall prevent that!"

"You vill? Ha, ha! you audacious rascal—how?"

"By gagging your Majesty the moment you open your mouth; though I should be sorry to take such a step unless as a positively last resource."

The king rolled back against the wall, and glared with concentrated fury at the impudent, cool, shrouded figure.

But passion was unavailing, because the strange visitor would not get into a passion.

"Let me hear vort you propose," growled the Sovereign.

"Certainly, sire. It is my intention to lock you in this apartment, in order to secure our safe retreat."

"Bote der ring?" gasped George, in utter consternation.

"You will receive the ring *to-morrow night when the clock strikes twelve!*"

"Bote you are mad to attempt dis!" exclaimed the excited monarch. "All der doors are locked and barred; you can never get out widout me."

"I got in without you, sire!" quietly remarked the captain.

"Bote der sentinel?"

"He's nobody."

"Isn't he? by Gott! I'll hang der rascal for neglect of duty!" raved the irritated king.

"The man did his duty, and you would be unjust to punish him. Were there fifty sentinels, I could walk through them all," said Captain Hawk, impressively.

"Der teifel you could!" stammered George Rex.

"How can a mere man guard against a power which is *invisible?*" continued the captain, in the same solemn, peculiar tone.

The king, though by no means superstitious, was beginning to feel impressed in a most uncomfortable manner.

The hour, the silence, the strange circumstances, and mysterious figure, all conspired to produce this effect.

"You say I shall receive der ring to-morrow night?" he said, in a broken voice.

"Yes, I promise!"

"At twelve o'clock?"

"At twelve o'clock!"

"Who shall bring it to me?"

"*One* who shall be *nameless!*"

"Where?"

"*In your Treasure Chamber!*"

The king staggered to the couch—the dark figure darted through the door, that closed immediately.

"Storp, storp—you villain!" shouted the king.

The key turning in the lock was the answer, and a voice without exclaiming:

"*Twelve o'clock to-morrow night!*"

CHAPTER CLXXII.

MESSRS. GREGSON AND CRANK COME TO THEIR SENSES. A ROYAL PRISONER.—KING GEORGE PREPARES FOR HIS APPOINTMENT.—VISITS THE TREASURE-CHAMBER, AND RECEIVES THE RING FROM ——.

THE gray dawn of morning had gradually crept over Kew Gardens.

His Majesty King George, having first given way to a violent fit of rage, and hammered the skin almost off his knuckles against the door without arousing anyone but Moses Geltz, who, thinking it was his fellow-prisoner, Lord Harcliffe, bawled out to him to—

"Hold 'ish d—d row, an' let honesht peoplesh go to shleep!"

Whatever the king might have thought of this advice, it is certain that he took it, and, as it was in fact the only tangible thing he could do, he threw himself on to the couch, and pulling the rug over him, went fast off to sleep.

The morning heralded a fine day, being misty. The dew hung thickly on the grass and shrubs in the garden as Messrs. Gregson and Crank began to come to themselves in the cool, moist retreat into which they had been thrown.

Both, of course, from the plentiful potations of the previous evening, awoke with racking headaches and a sense of devouring thirst.

They were also uncommonly chilly from their exposure to the night air.

"Stand at ease!" muttered the sergeant, as he opened his bloodshot eyes, winking and blinking like an owl. "No, no, what a fool I am!—I'm not on duty, I'm in bed. Mary, my love, a glass of water."

Just at this moment he became suddenly conscious that this, too, was a delusion; and then he was made aware of the fact that his hands and feet were tied, and that he was lying on his back on the grass, and had never been home at all.

"This is a pretty go!" he murmured to himself. "How did I come here? Oh, my precious coppers!—how drunk I must have been! Where's Gregson?"

As he uttered these exclamations he rolled himself on to his side, and there, a few yards from him, he perceived the worthy detective, who, like himself, had woke from his slumbers, and was puzzling his brain to account for certain restrictions upon the free use of his limbs, which were to him utterly inexplicable.

"Oh, there you are, Crank!" he said, in a very hoarse voice, as the sergeant rolled himself over.

"Yes, here I am," murmured the sergeant, in a very uncomfortable tone.

"Have you any idea where the devil we've got to?" inquired the detective.

"Not the least; I only know I feel awful queer."

"So do I."

"I wonder what Mrs. Crank'll say?"

"Never mind Mrs. Crank."

"She'll be anxious."

"Your'e out on duty—secret service, remember!"

"Yes, I think I shall. Oh my precious head!"

"Why, Crank," cried the detective, "do you know your arms and legs are tied together?"

"Yes, confound it! I've just found it out. Why," suddenly ejaculated the sergeant, "so are yours!"

"So they are! What the devil's the meaning of this?" growled Gregson, struggling to free himself.

"And where's my coat an' gaiters?" exclaimed Crank, —"where's my sword an' cap?"

"It strikes me we've been hocussed," said Gregson, looking fierce, and giving a plunge which burst the ropes that bound his arms.

"I should like to know who tied us up like this," remarked the sergeant; "it couldn't 'a been your grandfather, could it?"

"My grandfather? Psha!—he's been dead the last fifteen years."

"Why, last night you said that old chap with the white hair was your grandfather."

"Eh, old—eh? Did I?"

"Yes."

"Oh no, quite a mistake!" said Gregson, through whose mind, however, an unpleasant idea floated that this same old gentleman was in some way connected with their arrival at their present position.

"Who was he, I wonder?" remarked the sergeant.

"Oh, no one of any consequence," abruptly returned Gregson.

"Sha'n't we get into trouble about this?"

"No! Trouble—what trouble?"

"You haven't lost your coat and hat—your sword and gaiters!" said the afflicted Crank, in a dolorous tone.

"No more have you," exclaimed Gregson, suddenly, pointing as he spoke to a spot close by, where the above articles were piled one upon the other.

It may be as well to mention that Captain Hawk, before departing, had left them there.

"Why," said Gregson, "you took 'em off in your sleep, of course."

"And tied myself up afterwards, I suppose?"

This did not seem very feasible.

The detective was puzzled; so was his companion—very much so; and both had distracting headaches and nauseas.

"It won't do to stay here all day," remarked Gregson.

"Certainly not! Wait till I put on my things."

The sergeant equipped himself, and then cautiously looking about to see that the coast was clear, and finding it was so, these two worthy creatures sneaked out of the gardens, in a manner strongly suggestive of *secret* service, and made the best of their way towards town, stopping at the first public-house they came to for a draught of liquor to quench, if possible, their wretched internal sensations.

Eight o'clock gradually crept on.

This was the hour when the prisoners were appointed to have their breakfast.

It was the duty of Ernest Von Helm to accompany the domestic who carried their meals.

Accordingly at that time the door in which Moses Geltz was confined opened.

"Your breakfast," said Ernest, curtly.

"Any other newsh?" inquired the Jew, inquisitively.

There was no reply, and the door was closed again.

The same operation was performed in the chamber supposed to contain Lord Harcliffe.

"Your breakfast," repeated Ernest.

"Take it avay!—take it avay!" growled a voice, which caused the valet to start and turn pale, and the domestic who carried the provisions to drop the tray and stagger back in a panic.

The crash of crockery annoyed the king, who detested anything that promised an expenditure of money.

"Vort der teifel are you doing, you careless rascal?" he shouted, starting up on the couch and thrusting out his red face.

The scared domestic was ready to sink down with consternation, but the king grasped him by the wrist, and, in an angry but rapid manner, gripping him so tightly that the tips of his finger-nails were blue, said:

"Not a vord dat you have seen me here! Do you onderstand?"

"Y-e-e-es, sire!"

"If you dare to mention dis, I shall hang you, by Gott I shall! Do you onderstand dat also?"

"Y-e-e-es, sire!"

The king threw the alarmed lacquey from him as he concluded, and the man rolled out of the cell.

"Now den, Ernest, you can lend me your arm; I shall go to mein own chamber."

Ernest, who, after the first surprise, was too well trained in Court customs to evince any further signs of emotion, simply bowed and held out his arm.

"Of course you are sopprised to see me here?" the king said, as he arose and took the proffered arm.

"I am—a little, your Majesty," he replied.

"You mean you are a goot deal," answered the Sovereign, forcibly; "or, if nort, you ought to be. Teifel! when a king allows a prisoner to lock him ope, while he go avay free, it is enofe to sopprise anyvon."

With this remark the royal George left the chamber, leaning on his favourite's arm, and returned to his own.

Here he turned into bed again, and saying to Ernest, "Mind, dis is a secret!" he turned over and fell asleep instanter.

Ernest Von Helm considered the matter for a few moments, and then, having come to the conclusion that the king had some private reason for acting as he had done, dismissed the subject from his mind.

King George woke from his slumbers at noon.

He had slept long and heavily.

But his sleep had refreshed him.

After dinner (his Majesty dined alone that day) King George was seated in his own private chamber, puffing away at a long German pipe, and sipping between whiles his beloved Rhein wine.

He could not forget the mysterious visitor of the previous night.

He could not forget the terrible fact that he was acquainted with the crime he had committed, of which the unfortunate Stephen was the victim.

Then there came across him the means he appeared to have of ingress and egress at the palace.

It was in vain he puffed his pipe and drank his wine; neither could assuage the unpleasant sensations that oppressed him.

"Who der teifel can dis stranger be?" he soliloquised. "He seem to me to come in vhen he like, and go out vhen he like, so dat I shall never be sure at any moment dat I may not see him standing before me. Ugh!" he shuddered, as the idea clung to him. "It is evident he know my share in Stephen's death, and he asserted dat he had his written account of de whole affair. Umph! dat would look bad in print. Donder and blitzen! it would look d—n bad!

"Den dere is der diamond ring. Vill he keep his vord about dat? He promise to send it to me to-night; and der place der treasure-chamber!"

The king laid aside his pipe as he uttered these words, and remained silent for some moments.

"How could he, or anyvon beside meinself, enter dere?" he exclaimed, slowly and musingly. "No oder living soul knows of its existence, and yet he promise me to send it dere to me. If I believed in soch tings, I could almost say it vas der teifel himself dat have pay me dis visit. Bah! I must not tink like dat! Bote it is very strange!"

It certainly must have appeared so to the king, whose conscience was not at rest, and who was of course quite ignorant of the fact of the second entrance to the treasure-chamber, which would at once have cleared up Captain Hawk's entrance of all its mystery.

He therefore sat, and pondered, and worried himself during the remainder of the afternoon and evening, keeping himself entirely secluded.

He heard with a kind of longing impatience the hours strike in succession: nine—ten—eleven—half-past eleven—and then the chiming of the quarter to twelve.

At this he started up with a kind of desperate nervous energy, as though he had "bound up each corporal agent to the feat" he was about to perform.

"It is der time!" he ejaculated.

He then lighted a small dark lantern, and after listening and being assured that all was quiet within the palace, he left his apartment, and proceeded at once to the treasure-chamber.

He opened the door as usual, and entered.

A cold damp seemed to chill his marrow as he closed the door after him.

He left the lantern masked.

The gloom of this narrow chamber, with its stone circular walls, its close earthy odour, and hollow sound when a footstep fell upon the stone floor, suggested the precincts of a vault.

It must have required a strong nerve to have ventured there alone at midnight.

But then George II. was just that kind of man to dare such an act.

Had he lived some hundreds of years before, and had his name been Robert instead of George, he would have passed well for a second "Robert the Devil."

He paced to and fro, hugging his lantern to him, the warmth of which was not displeasing in the midst of that chilling atmosphere.

As it drew nearer and nearer towards midnight, his anxiety appeared to increase.

"Vill he come, or has he been making von fool of me?" he muttered.

"He promised to be here at twelve," he continued, as he strode backwards and forwards.

"At last!" he cried, as the clock began to strike with slow, ponderous beats.

He continued walking and counting, wondering what was to occur, and who the messenger was to be, and whether he would come at all.

Nothing, however, appeared.

"Psha!" he ejaculated. "I knew ne vould nort come —I might have been sure of dat! Nine—ten—eleven—twelve!" he continued, counting the strikes of the clock. "He is an impostor—he is von d—n tief, and I shall never see my ring again!"

"False!" cried an awful, deep voice that seemed to come from the ground beneath. "He is here!"

"Vhere?" asked the king, his blood running coldly through his veins as he faltered out the word.

"Here!" the same solemn voice repeated.

Still there was nothing visible.

The incredulous monarch was about once more to stigmatise the expected visitor as an impostor; he unmasked the lantern, when, as his eyes roamed around, he saw that which froze him to the ground with a nameless horror.

From out the solid wall, as the bright rays of light fell upon it, there emerged the upper portion of a dark, cloaked figure, completely shrouded.

Whilst the king stood with eyes widely extended, glaring upon this mysterious appearance, the cloaked figure extended its arm, draped in sable folds, and holding between its bony fingers the much-coveted diamond ring.

"Behold!" exclaimed the voice.

At the same moment the cowl fell from off the head, and revealed the grinning, deathly lineaments of—*a skeleton.*

"There is the ring—take it if you dare!" urged the same hollow tones.

The king's brain seemed to whirl round with the horror of this unexpected sight.

But his avarice counteracted the sickening terror that stole over his heart.

"I'll have der ring, though I snatch it from der claws of Death himself!" he gasped, with breathless intensity.

He staggered forwards, made a violent snatch at the jewel, and felt that he held it in his grasp once more.

His end was gained, his purpose accomplished; and having nothing now in the shape of impulse to sustain him, his courage failed in the presence of the ghastly visitant, and he fell senseless on the ground.

When the king recovered his senses, he felt a cold chill pass over him from head to foot.

The clock struck one.

He had laid in that deadly lethargy an hour.

He rose with difficulty to his feet, with a faint, sickening sensation of bodily numbness and depression. He grasped the ring—that was safe—but the mysterious messenger had departed without leaving any trace of his mode of exit.

The king, with trembling limbs, examined the walls eagerly; but no signs—not the slightest—of any outlet.

He became more and more convinced that he had been the subject of a supernatural visitation.

"It is a being from de oder vorld dat I have seen," he murmured, in shivering accents of terror; "an' my guilt seem to follow me. Der curse of blood is upon dis place!"

With hurried, faltering steps he hastened from the treasure-chamber; and having once more gained his own, he cowered down in his luxurious arm-chair, casting aside the glittering gem as worthless, since it had no power to drive away the horror from his mind, or the remorse from his heart.

CHAPTER CLXXIII.

CAPTAIN HAWK AND LORD HARCLIFFE PAY A VISIT TO THE OLD GREYHOUND.—THEY HEAR BAD NEWS.—THE LOSS OF THE TREASURE.—THE DEATH OF MORNA.—THEIR RESOLVE TO TRY THE ROAD AGAIN.

It was exactly a month from the time our heroes departed for Guernsey in the Saucy Sally, when early on the morning following the events recorded in our last chapter, Captain Hawk and Lord Harcliffe might have been seen seated on the outside of the mail that was carrying them to Huntingdon.

It was a beautiful morning in the month of May, and both our friends were in the highest possible spirits.

They apprehended no danger—they feared none.

They could but smile as they glanced at each other, as the idea crossed them how novel a position it was to be seated on the top of a coach, chatting occasionally to the coachman and guard, to whom it might one day be their fate to cry: "Stand and deliver!"

Their horses being at Tom Beckford's, they preferred this mode of travelling to hiring hacks at a livery stables, that would have had to be sent back to town at the end of their journey.

At about noon the mail stopped to change horses.

The passengers alighted to stretch their cramped limbs, and to indulge in such refreshment as the inn afforded.

This necessary operation performed, and the fresh cattle being harnessed, the passengers resumed their seats, all but Captain Hawk and his companion.

"Ain't you coming on, gentlemen?" inquired the guard, who had taken quite a fancy to our heroes.

"No, my friend," answered the captain; "we stop here: our journey lies cross country, therefore we are reluctantly compelled to quit your very agreeable society."

The guard looked disappointed: he was really quite sorry to part with his gentlemanly companions of the coach-top.

"Never mind, friend," exclaimed Captain Hawk, who noticed the expression on his features, and guessed the cause; "we must all part sooner or later. Accept this to drink our healths."

So saying, he slipped a half-guinea into the hand of the sorrowing guard, whose affliction was considerably alleviated by this potent salve.

"Thank'ee, gen'l'men," said he. "Let's hope we may meet again upon the road some fine day."

"Or some fine night," thought the two highwaymen, "when you've a good cargo of birds inside and out, that want plucking."

"Well, then, good day to ye, gentlemen, if you ain't coming any further," said the guard. "Time's up, an' the 'osses are ready to be off."

"Now, guard!" shouted the coachman.

"Ready!" bawled the guard, as he clambered up into his seat.

The driver uttered his well-known chirp to the horses, that pranced and capered a little in the exuberance of their freshness.

The long tapering thong of the whip, like the line of a fly-fisher, flew lightly through the air, and tickled the ears of the playful leaders, bringing them to their senses.

The guard waved his hand to the highwaymen, who returned the salute, and the vehicle rolled rapidly away from the inn door, a parting solo on the tin horn being wafted to their ears as it disappeared from view.

"That guard seemed an honest, appreciating fellow," remarked Captain Hawk.

"Exceedingly so," coincided Lord Harcliffe.

"Should we ever be compelled to stop the mail he guards, we must endeavour to remember him," said the captain.

"Decidedly! I wonder whether he'll remember us?"

"Yes, with a discharge from his blunderbuss, most probably," answered the captain.

It was now decided that as it was but a short distance from the Greyhound, they should perform the journey on foot.

They accordingly walked along the high-road for some little distance till they were out of sight of the inn, and then turning abruptly up a narrow lane, were soon surrounded by trees and hedges clad in their bright spring robes, and promising a glorious summer.

"This is delightful!" exclaimed our heroes, who, having had a month of intense excitement, were able to appreciate the quiet beauty of nature on this lovely May day.

"Tom Beckford will be half out of his wits with joy to see us," said Captain Hawk, enjoying beforehand in his own mind his honest friend's jovial face expanding like a bright sun as they burst upon his view. "Oh, dear old Tom!" continued the captain. "Do you know, Harence, I love that man as well as if he were my own father."

"I quite believe you," returned his lordship. "No man could have a more devoted friend or stancher pal than Tom Beckford."

In similar panegyrics, and occasional remarks or admiration on the rural beauties that met them as they progressed, the ground was rapidly passed over, and in due course the well-known red tiles and antiquated chimneys of the Greyhound met their view.

"There it is at last!" cried Captain Hawk, exultingly. "One cheer for the old homestead!"

They raised their voices in one heartfelt, earnest "Hurrah!"

Tom Beckford, who had just finished shaving himself and was washing his rosy face, heard it distinctly, and commenced the operation of drying so vigorously, that his good-humoured countenance glowed like a furnace.

Two other animals who were grazing in the field close by, heard the well-known sound, and paused in their meal.

These, it will be readily guessed, were the faithful steeds Satan and Phantom.

"Dash my buttons!" shouted Tom, "if that isn't their voices, I never heard 'em!" And out he rushed, just as he was, to ascertain whether his suspicions were correct.

The two horses, probably under a similar impression, trotted to the hedge, and looked over.

The highwaymen were truly delighted.

"Satan!—Phantom!" broke from their lips simultaneously.

"My old boy!—my beauty!" cried Captain Hawk, clambering up to the hedge and throwing his arm over the neck of his steed. "So you knew your master's voice again, did you?" he continued, stroking his favourite's glossy coat, receiving in exchange sundry rubbings of the nose of the affectionate animal against his face and breast, accompanied by whinnying sounds and short joyful neighings, that testified as plainly as a horse could its joy to see its master once more.

The highwaymen were thus engaged when Tom Beckford suddenly came upon them, minus coat, waistcoat, or hat, with his braces trailing behind him, his shirt-collar unbuttoned, his hair frizzed out, and sticking up like rats' tails, dripping with water.

"Heard your voices!—knew it was you!" he cried, as he ran up and threw his burly arms round Captain Hawk.

"God bless you, my dear boy!" he exclaimed, in a tone of deep feeling, about which there was no mistake, with the tears in his eyes—"God bless you! and thanks to Him for sending you back to us safe and sound!"

He then warmly saluted Lord Harcliffe; and both having cordially reciprocated his welcome, they proceeded to the inn.

A substantial repast was provided, and at that meal few happier parties could have been found than Tom Beckford, Captain Hawk, and Lord Harcliffe.

All questions were by mutual agreement interdicted during dinner; but the cloth being removed, the events that had occurred both to the highwaymen and in the neighbourhood of the Greyhound were freely related.

It was with deep regret Captain Hawk heard of the death of Isaac, not only because he had thereby lost a stanch and faithful ally, but on account of his intense devotion to himself.

"Poor Isaac!" he murmured. "It was for me he sacrificed himself. He deserved a better fate—at least his humble grave shall be surmounted by a tribute to his memory."

Lord Harcliffe inquired whether Pharoah had visited the Greyhound during his absence.

"He came once," said Tom Beckford, "soon after you left, and stayed a couple of days, while the police officers were scouring the roads; but since that time I have neither seen nor heard anything of him."

"Poor Pharoah!" exclaimed Lord Harcliffe. "Can he be dead too?"

Being fatigued with his day's journey, his lordship retired early; and Captain Hawk being alone with the landlord, inquired earnestly after Blanche, who had accepted the shelter of young Squire Kingsbury's roof.

"Oh!" said Tom, "she's been gone to London long ago."

"To London?"

"Yes. When she found you didn't make your appearance at the squire's, nothing could induce her to remain at the Hall."

A smile of satisfaction gleamed in the captain's face for a moment; but it died away quickly.

"So she went to London?" he said.

"Yes: to her aunt's. She came here before her departure, to inquire whether I had received any news of you. When I said 'No,' she seemed quite cut-up like."

"Poor girl!" murmured the captain, almost unconsciously.

"Yes; she did indeed; and then she told me she was going to leave the Hall, and go up to town to stay with her aunt. She left the address written down, with me, to give to you."

"You have it?" eagerly inquired the captain.

"I should think so!" answered Tom, almost indignant at the idea of being suspected of having lost such a treasure. "Here it is."

The captain gladly received it, and read the address as he would have contemplated the casket that contained some precious jewel:—

"*Miss Blanche Allison,*
"*Grove Cottage,*
"*Chelsea.*

"Then," said Captain Hawk, "I may hope to see her in London."

There being nothing more of importance to ask or to answer, the captain followed his comrade's example, and retired to rest.

Tom Beckford, having bolted and barred his substantial doors, also sought his pillow.

Early the next morning our friends were up and out, thoroughly recruited by their sound night's sleep, in company with Tom Beckford, enjoying the freshness of the mild spring air, and getting good appetites for breakfast.

They were lavish in their praises of the manner in which their steeds had been tended in their absence.

And if honest Tom's heart warmed with conscious pride, it was perfectly justifiable, and warranted by the splendid appearance Satan and Phantom presented.

Their rounded symmetrical limbs, the glossy silkiness of their coats, and the fire of their eyes, bespoke them in the highest possible state of health and vigour.

After breakfast, Captain Hawk and Lord Harcliffe sat alone in an upper chamber that overlooked the distant country.

They were evidently not decided upon their course for the future, and appeared to be recapitulating certain events that had occurred.

"You do not blame me, Harcliffe, for setting your liberty at a higher price than the diamond ring that purchased it?" said Captain Hawk.

"Certainly not—let it go. I am free, and we are together again. Liberty is worth all the diamonds in the world."

"So I think; but remember, there is still the treasure buried in the cavity of the old tree near Hugh Trevellyn's cabin."

"Ay, true! I had almost forgotten that."

"There is sufficient there to do justice to poor Stephen's daughter—to remunerate Hugh for the danger he has undergone, and the damage his property has sustained on my account, and still to leave a considerable balance for our own use."

"It is not of much service lying, as it does now, buried in the earth, is it?"

"You're right. I'm thinking what will be the best course to pursue—whether to take another journey into Cornwall, and bring this treasure away ourselves, or write to Hugh and entrust the commission to him?"

Lord Harcliffe was silent for a few moments, and then replied:

"I think, as we have both so lately passed through so many critical adventures on that coast, it would be hardly advisable to show ourselves there again so soon."

"I am of your opinion."

"Why not write to your friend, and ask him to bring the gold to us here?"

"I will do so: it will be as safe in the care of honest Tom Beckford as though it were lodged in the Bank of England."

"Then with regard to Stephen's daughter—how is she to receive the five thousand pounds that she is entitled to?"

"Ah! that requires some consideration, and I rather think we shall have to transact that portion of the business ourselves."

"She is at school there, is she not?"

"Yes; and we shall have to make inquiries, and be assured of her identity, before delivering up so large a sum."

"Decidedly!"

"This being the case, I think another sea trip will be inevitable."

"I trust under more favourable circumstances than before."

Captain Hawk laughed as he said:

"I hope so."

"Our worthy smuggler friend, Captain Jecks, could assist us in this matter: he would run us over to Guernsey in no time, and our business being finished there, we might find it advisable to pay a visit to the French capital. What say you?"

"I am perfectly agreeable, and in order to set matters *en train*, I will write at once to Hugh Trevellyn, commissioning him to join us here at once with the gold."

This was accordingly done, Captain Hawk sending Hugh a most cordial letter, requesting his immediate presence at the Greyhound Inn—not forgetting to inquire most solicitously after the fair Morna, whom he had been compelled to part from so abruptly without being able to inquire how she progressed after the wound she had received in his defence.

Lord Harcliffe also wrote to Captain Jecks, requesting him to forward a *bulletin* of his progress.

The letters being despatched, there was nothing to be done but to wait patiently for the answers.

On the second day, there came a letter from the smuggler captain.

He wrote in excellent spirits, and was getting on, to use his own expression, like a "ship in full sail" under Tom Stack's hands, who was an excellent nurse.

On the third day our heroes were expressing a little surprise at not having heard from Hugh Trevellyn.

It then, for the first time, suddenly struck Lord Harcliffe that Hugh had been summoned to London, and that he had attended the private investigation conducted by the king at Kew Palace.

"That would fully account for the delay," said his lordship. "He may not yet have returned home."

"Well, then, patience is our only remedy," remarked Captain Hawk, "though I trust he will not be long in replying. An inactive life is distasteful to me: I already begin to feel a little rusty, and long to find myself occupied once more."

"If even in dodging a few dozen mounted police officers," smilingly added Lord Harcliffe.

"Ay, even that, rather than the lethargy of continual inactivity," replied the captain. "I would a thousand times die by a bullet in a fair encounter than quietly drop inch by inch into my grave like an old door that falls gradually from its rusty hinges."

It was growing dusk, when a horseman rode slowly along the road, and pausing irresolutely before the Greyhound, which lay back from the highway, looked anxiously towards its antique but hospitable walls, as though soliciting information.

After a few moments' hesitation, the rider appeared to have made up his mind to stop, as he turned his horse out of the road and walked him leisurely towards the door.

There were no pretensions to anything approaching the cavalier about the traveller, nor anything imposing in the steed he bestrode.

Both looked travel-stained, weary, and dusty.

Tom Beckford caught sight of the tired pair as they slowly approached.

Being naturally suspicious of every new-comer, he went out to the door to be quite ready to answer any questions.

"Is this the Greyhound Inn?" inquired the horseman.

"It is, sir," answered Tom. "Couldn't you see the sign as you came up as large as life before you?" he inquired, in a good-humoured tone.

"It is too dark," replied the traveller, "and my eyes are not so strong at seeing between lights as they were forty years ago. But if this is the Greyhound, this is the place I want: I am here to meet a gentleman."

"What name?" asked Tom Beckford.

"Captain Hawk," he answered.

"All right, friend!" warmly returned Tom, as soon as he heard the name. "You, if I mistake not, are Mr. Hugh Trevellyn, from Cornwall?"

"I am."

"I'm delighted to see you, and so will be the captain: he's anxiously expecting you. Off with you, and come in. I'll look to your nag."

Hugh, with some difficulty, dismounted.

He was not accustomed to travel on horseback, and felt his limbs stiff and cramped.

He made the best of his way to the door.

"Lean on my arm, sir," said Tom, who saw the traveller was past the meridian of life. "I don't suppose the horse will run away."

"There's not much fear of that," remarked Hugh, with a melancholy smile: "I think the horse is as tired as his rider."

Captain Hawk's ears had informed him that some stranger was at the door in conversation with the landlord; but he little guessed who it was.

His curiosity prompted him to listen, when, to his great surprise, he recognised the tones of his hospitable host's voice.

He immediately rushed forward, and received Hugh from the hands of Tom Beckford.

"Welcome, my dear friend!—welcome a thousand times!" cried the captain. "This is a pleasure I really did not anticipate."

Hugh pressed his hand warmly in return; but said little.

Captain Hawk led him into the cosy parlour, where a cheerful fire burnt in the grate, when, as he glanced at the old man's features, he saw his cheeks were wet with tears.

"What can they portend?" he thought. It might be emotion at their meeting; but that was hardly sufficient to produce such an effect.

He affected to take no notice, and Hugh being evidently weary, the important duties of hospitality were first performed.

Hugh ate but little: he seemed weighed down by some secret but hidden sorrow.

He had evidently taken the journey from Cornwall in obedience to Captain Hawk's summons; but he evidently, by his silence, shrunk from conversation, and appeared to dread it, being silent, restless, and sad.

But it was necessary that the required information be afforded.

The captain first inquired after Morna.

At the mention of her name, the old man turned pale, his lips quivered, and the tears started to his eyes.

"Alas!" he replied, in a faltering tone, shaking his head mournfully—"alas!—alas!"

"Good Heaven!" exclaimed Captain Hawk, in a tone of alarm. "Surely she is in no danger?"

The old man shook his head.

"She is out of all danger now," he replied, sadly.

"My friend, speak!" cried the captain, with intense anxiety. "Your words alarm me—your silence still more so! You do not—you surely cannot mean that she is dead?"

A groan from Hugh Trevellyn was the only answer.

There was something in his manner that seemed to herald such a calamity more than his words.

"My poor girl is no more!" he said, in a low, broken voice; and then he buried his face in his hands and wept.

"Merciful Heaven!" murmured Captain Hawk, who was inexpressibly shocked. "So young—so beautiful—so very beautiful! Poor girl—poor Morna! It seems as though I brought destruction upon all who love me!" he groaned, under his breath.

Lord Harcliffe watched these emotions with much sympathy.

"When did she die?" he inquired, in a kind, sympathising voice.

"The night before last, at twelve o'clock," answered Hugh. "You, sir," he continued, to Captain Hawk, "were the last in her thoughts—your name was the last on her lips. She loved you, sir—she died for you!"

"She did—she did!" ejaculated the highwayman, in a tone of anguish. "Oh! my friend," he cried, turning to Lord Harcliffe, "she did indeed die for me! She interposed her fair bosom between myself and death, and received the fatal bullet destined for my heart. Heaven rest her soul, for I believe in its bright regions there can be no brighter spirit than that of Morna Trevellyn!"

For some moments there was a mournful silence, broken only by an occasional sob.

But Hugh Trevellyn speedily mastered his emotion.

"This is idle grief," he said. "Tears cannot bring back the loved and lost—besides, they unfit us for our duty."

He was in a short time calm, composed, and quite himself.

"I need scarcely say," he continued, to Captain Hawk, "that it was your letter brought me here. I had scarcely returned from London, whither I was compelled to journey by the king's command, when I found my child dead. I had hardly recovered the shock of that blow, when the summons to attend you was placed in my hands."

"Oh, had I known——" eagerly interrupted the captain.

"You would not have written, I know. But do not regret it—she was dead: I had no one to detain me, and I came."

"It is too soon after such a loss."

"No, no: I am better away, I think. Besides, it was necessary I should come at once to tell you what has happened since our departure. First, I discovered on my return I had not a roof to cover me."

"Good Heavens! But your child?"

"Had been removed to the wretched hovel of poor old mad Cassy, where she died."

"And who had destroyed your humble homestead?"

"The wretches who would have taken your life if they could. Enraged at the loss of the gold they coveted, burning to avenge the death of that brutal Daniel Macorrie, and unable to glut that vengeance on either of our bodies, they in my absence, having, as you know, discovered the secret of the subterranean passage, rolled a barrel of gunpowder into the cellar beneath the cabin, and where that once stood there is now no vestige save a dreary, wide-spreading, waste ruin."

"Well, my friend, take heart: you shall be no loser. The treasure that lies buried beneath the tree shall more than compensate you for all you have lost."

At these words Hugh's countenance fell, and a deep sigh of regret burst from him.

"That treasure!" he ejaculated. "Alas—alas!"

"What of that?" inquired Captain Hawk, with some apprehension.

"You know the tree within which it was buried stood very near to our cottage?"

"Yes—yes!"

"The subterranean cavern extended beneath that tree, and in this fatal explosion its time-worn trunk was torn from its hold and scattered like so much tinder to the four winds of heaven."

"But the treasure?"

"Has shared the same fate. The earth in which it was buried—nay, the very rocks that supported that earth, have been wrenched asunder, and the devastation has been so complete that of the buried treasure not the slightest traces remain—not even one solitary coin."

"Then all is lost?"

"All is lost."

There was a dead silence.

Fate had indeed interposed to mar their plans.

All that they had secured at so much risk—the orphan's legacy, the gold for which Captain Hawk had imperilled his life in the face of the ruthless wreckers, and which had sealed the fate of the beautiful Morna—was gone for ever.

The words of the guilty king seemed to be true, and to admit of amplification.

The curse of blood was on the treasure-chamber and on the treasure it had contained.

Deeply, however, as the highwaymen regretted this circumstance, their regrets were not merely selfish.

They felt for the orphaned Margaret, and found themselves deprived of the power of recompensing Hugh, as they had fully intended doing, for the services he had rendered.

They candidly explained their circumstances to Hugh, who would not hear of reward.

But Captain Hawk assured him that he should be no loser, and that the recompense he deserved should be his at the first opportunity.

The bereaved old man was satisfied; his thoughts were far above the earth, soaring upward to those bright regions whither he believed the sacred spirit of his gentle child had fled.

But he remembered that the cherished clay was still unburied, and on the following day he departed on his journey homeward, taking a cordial farewell of our heroes, and expressing a hope that they should one day meet again.

It may easily be imagined that so many sad occurrences happening almost simultaneously clouded the spirits of our heroes.

But theirs were temperaments that soon recovered their elasticity.

On the third morning after Hugh's departure they had recovered themselves.

"We have lost all, certainly," said Captain Hawk—"all——"

"But liberty," rejoined Lord Harcliffe.

"And that is worth more than all," wound up the captain, with enthusiasm. "We are still free, and there are still people in the world with more money than they know what to do with; the road is still open—there lies our path."

"Yes, we must take to the road again."

"Ay, the road! Hurrah for the road!"

CHAPTER CLXXIV.

CAPTAIN HAWK AND LORD HARCLIFFE DEPART FROM THE GREYHOUND.—THEY PUT UP AT THE SKITTLE BALL INN, AND WITNESS AN EQUESTRIAN PERFORMANCE.—THEY DISCOVER AN EAVESDROPPER, AND PUT HIM OUT OF THE WAY.

Once more a lovely May morning had dawned, when our heroes, mounted on the backs of their respective steeds, rode forth from the stable-yard of the old Greyhound Inn.

Tom Beckford attended them to the gate, and bade them farewell with evident unwillingness.

"D—n it!" he exclaimed, trying to get into a passion to conceal his real feelings, "we no sooner get settled nice an' comfortable together than off you go again like skyrockets. It's too bad, d—d if it ain't!"

"Come, Tom," said Captain Hawk, who understood his kind friend's feelings perfectly, and wished to comfort him, "you know, business is business."

"That's true, captain—so it is," answered Tom.

"We're completely cleaned out, and it is a palpable fact we can't live upon nothing—at least, if you can, I can't."

"Nor I," responded Tom, in a tone of strong conviction—"it wouldn't suit me at all."

"Very well, then," replied the captain, cheerfully. "As we all appear to be of one mind in this matter, we must look upon our parting as an unavoidable necessity; and in the meantime, wishing each other health and fortune, look forward to as speedy a meeting again as possible."

"Good luck and prosperity to ye, my dear boys! Take care of yourselves, and come back as soon as you can—and God bless you!"

Tom delivered this with effort, for his heart was full.

"Good-bye, Tom—good-bye, my dear old friend!" cried Captain Hawk, in return. "Expect us at any moment!"

"Farewell!" called Lord Harcliffe.

"G-g-good b-ye!" gasped honest Tom.

The horses were so eager to be off that it was with the utmost difficulty they were restrained during the foregoing few words, and they now started off like arrows from a bow, and were almost instantly out of sight.

"What a fool I am!" said Tom to himself, as he went back to the house. "But it's always the way when I wish him good-bye—d—d if I don't feel myself a reg'lar baby!"

It was so long since the highwaymen had been seen or heard of that all pursuit had lulled.

They were supposed to have left the kingdom

They were now, therefore, able to traverse the road, and inhale the perfume of the sweet May blossoms, and drink in the fresh, pure air, and rejoice in the warm sunshine, without any apprehension of finding a score of police officers at their heels.

Onwards they flew, and if their pockets were light so were their hearts.

At the end of two hours they stopped.

The fresh air and the excitement of the ride had given them voracious appetites.

"We shall all be the better for a little refreshment," said Captain Hawk; "and then over a glass of wine we can determine precisely where we are going to shape our course and what we are to do."

They were in sight of a small roadside inn, in connection with which a painted board informed them, in very tumble-down letters, that there was *Good Rest for Man and Beast* to be found at the Skittle Ball, kept by Timothy Bunker, who had been better off in times past, but who had now to lament a great falling off in his trade and profits.

This so soured his temper, that, as a rule, he resented the indifference of those who kept away from the Skittle Ball by looking as surly as possible at those who came to it.

There were some exceptions to this rule; but it was few—very few—on whom the blighted Bunker condescended to smile.

The highwaymen were not of that favoured number, and, as they drew near the small inn, could not help remarking the surly, sulky, forbidding countenance of the landlord.

"By Jupiter! the sight of his face in the cellar would turn all the ale sour," remarked Captain Hawk, as they dismounted, and delivered their steeds to the care of the ostler, who stood waiting.

"Let us have some refreshment," said Lord Harcliffe to Timothy Bunker.

"Don't know as there is any," he growled, sullenly.

"Well, then, let us have a tankard of old ale, and show us to your best room," returned his lordship.

"You'll find it straight on," muttered the bearish host. "It's the *best* and *worst*, since there's no other."

Without condescending to take any immediate notice of the impertinence of Mr. Timothy, our heroes obediently went down the passage in the direction referred to, where at the end they came upon a moderately-sized apartment, that looked out upon the stable-yard, where they had a full view of their steeds, and the admiration they excited in the minds of the ostler and several country bumpkins who were hanging about.

"Darn'd if Oi ha' seen a prettier bit o' horseflesh in all my born days!" remarked Dick the ostler.

"Bean't they a pair o' beauties, Measter Bucks?" inquired the same individual of a very conceited, self-sufficient-looking groom who rode into the yard at that moment.

"Um!" replied the groom, condescending to glance at the magnificent steeds as they stood playfully rubbing their noses together. "Thee're not so bad; but then I've seen so many 'osses in my time, I have: it takes a good deal to astonish me."

"Well, so ha' Oi for the matter o' that," returned Dick; "but Oi dain't remember as ever Oi seed two 'osses as black as coals, with coats like them two."

"I 'av'n't no opinion o' black 'osses," remarked the supercilious groom, as he dismounted from his own steed: "they ain't o' no account, as a rule. Now, these animals is too fleshy about here," he continued, letting his hand fall rather sharply on Satan's haunches as he spoke.

The high-spirited animal answered by a sharp kick, which, had it happened to tell on the groom's shins, would probably have tended still further to lower black horses in his estimation.

"Dickens!" exclaimed the ostler, as he witnessed Satan's action; "he be a spirited one, an' no misteak!"

"I don't look upon that as sperrit," answered the groom, contemptuously—"that's wice. If that 'oss belonged to me, I'd soon take 'is kickin' out of 'im."

The windows of the apartment were open, so that the two highwaymen, concealed from observation by the curtains, not only saw all that passed, but heard all that was said.

"The presuming idiot!" exclaimed Captain Hawk, as the groom made his last remark.

"Now, I dessay," said Mr. Bucks, conceitedly, "you'd 'ang back if you was asked to mount that 'oss," pointing to, but not touching, Satan as he spoke.

"I don't think as I should care much about it," candidly confessed the ostler.

"Lor' bless you," returned the other, turning up his nose, which had a natural tendency that way, with a pitying expression at Dick's ignorance, "them sort o' cattle is as mild as lambs when they gets anyone on their backs as knows 'ow to manage 'em."

"Well, Oi tell 'ee what, Measter Bucks: Oi should like to see you mount this 'ere animal," said Dick, indicating Satan, who threw his eye askant in a peculiar manner, as though he understood the conversation, and meant to say, "Try it!"

Captain Hawk and Lord Harcliffe, who had been indulging in some Cheshire cheese and ale, now leant out of the window, smoking their cigars, rather curious to see to what extent this wooden-headed puppy of a groom would carry out his assertions.

Mr. Bucks caught sight of them immediately, and noticing their distinguished appearance, and rather flattering himself that he was, perhaps, one of the model riders of the age, felt his vanity tickled, not only to astonish everybody present, but, being a sporting man, conceived the idea of putting something in his pocket at the same time through the medium of a wager.

"Of course," said he, to poor simple-minded Dick, "you 'av'n't got such a sum as a guinea; but if you 'ad, I shouldn't mind bettin' you that much that I not only mount that black 'oss,"—Satan he meant—"but compel 'im to do jest whatever I please while I'm on 'is back."

"Oi ain't got no guineas to bet," replied Dick; "but Oi be in doubts about you're ridin' that 'ere 'oss."

"Anybody take the bet?" inquired Mr. Thomas Bucks, conceitedly, looking round upon the few yokels congregated in the stable-yard, who gazed at the daring individual in the top-boots with their mouths open in silent admiration.

No one answered; but the groom took care in making his proposition, as he glanced round, to let his eye fall on the highwaymen last of all.

"Take my bet, gentlemen?" he said, with an impudent smirk.

"I never bet with grooms or stable-boys," Captain Hawk remarked, with impressive hauteur; "but if you can mount that horse's back, whose merits you have been so ably discussing, and if, when mounted, you can keep your seat for *one minute*, instead of accepting your presumptuous wager of one guinea, I will *give you* five."

Mr. Bucks, who, firmly impressed with his own equestrian powers, looked upon the captain as decidedly possessed of more money than wit to make such an offer, immediately consented.

"I don't wish to rob yer," he said; "but since yer make the offer, I say done."

"Will'ee gi'e Oi a guinea if Oi can keep on this 'ere one's back for one minute?" Dick inquired of Lord Harcliffe, pointing to Phantom at the same time.

"I'll give you five," replied his lordship.

"Then darn'd if Oi dain't 'ave a try, though Oi break my neck over it!" exclaimed Dick, tempted by the reward of success.

The groom and ostler approached their respective steeds and grasped the bridles.

Both Satan and Phantom, accustomed to the light handling of their masters, were instantly conscious that strangers were meddling with them.

They looked at the intruders with widely-dilated eyes and nostrils.

The expression of each of the animals had in it something particularly ominous and vicious—at least, so Dick thought, and he resolved to try the coaxing system.

"Woho—wo!" he exclaimed, in a tone intended to be winning in the highest degree—"wo!—poor fellow!" he continued, stroking Phantom softly with his rough hand;

[CAPTAIN HAWK AND THE BLACK HIGHWAYMAN DEPART FROM THE GREYHOUND INN.]

but Phantom didn't entertain the association at all, and tossed his head, jerking Dick, who still contrived to retain his hold of the bridle, off the ground at every movement.

Mr. Thomas Bucks, who had remained watching poor Dick's ineffectual efforts to mount with a pitying smile and elevated proboscis, resolved now to go in and crush him at once by showing him how "a man as knew about 'osses ought to mount."

With this idea he tightened Satan's bridle, being resolved to carry his point in a decided manner.

Satan remained quiet, and beyond a slight convulsion that seemed to pass through him, made no motion; but he threw the white of his eye with such an unmistakably spiteful expression at Mr. Thomas Bucks, that, had that eminent horse-tamer been any judge at all of his position, he would have felt it necessary to look out.

No such idea, however, struck him; for in order to make Satan quite easy in his mind that he was in the hands of one who "wouldn't stand any nonsense," he indulged in a sharp "ya-hip!" close to the horse's ear.

Satan considerably astonished Mr. T. B. by launching out his fore feet and drawing his proud head back, and glancing with profound contempt at the groom out of the corner of his terrible eye.

"Oh, that's your game, is it?" soliloquised Mr. Bucks, nothing daunted, as he made a dash at the stirrup with his foot.

But Satan suddenly wheeled round, and Mr. B. had to drop his foot as quickly as he had raised it, and hop round as well.

The highwaymen were highly delighted at the unavailing efforts made by the groom and ostler, and laughed heartily, in which infectious act the spectators joined.

"Well," inquired Lord Harcliffe, in a peculiarly satirical tone, "how much longer are you going to be before you mount?"

"Darn 'is oyes!" muttered Dick. "A woan't gi'e a body a chance! 'E be movin' about all over the pleace!"

"Come, Mr. Groom," said Captain Hawk, "you'll never win your five guineas at this rate; though there's one comfort: if you *do* manage to get up you'll gain the time you've lost by the rapidity with which you'll come down."

Then both the highwaymen said, in a low tone:

"Satan—Phantom!"

At the well-known voices both the steeds stood suddenly still and glanced towards the window from which their masters were looking.

Taking advantage of their temporary quietude, both Tom Bucks and Dick managed to stick their toes into the stirrup nearest them, and launch themselves on to the horses' backs.

They were mounted, but to find the other stirrup for their other toes was an utter impossibility.

The horses plunged, and whirled round and round, and dashed themselves about as though they were bewitched.

It was a moment of intense excitement for the yokels, and of unbounded mirth to the highwaymen.

Both the equestrians tightened their reins, and stuck in their knees, and performed the usual feats common to such circumstances.

"I must have them five guineas!" ejaculated Mr. Bucks, grinding his teeth.

"Darn'd if I doan't!" gasped Dick, who was crimson in the face and breathless.

"Half a minute gone!" cried Captain Hawk. "Hold on another half-minute, and you win."

This was encouraging—highly so—the five guineas seemed almost in their grasp.

Dick pictured himself in a new Sunday suit and a yellow bandana with white spots.

Mr. T. B. was the possessor—in his mind's eye—of a new pair of topboots and a riding-whip, silver mounted.

Alas! vain hopes!

Suddenly Satan and Phantom darted up on their hind legs.

Just as suddenly Satan and Phantom dropped down again, and then, kicking up their heels in the air with desperate impetuosity, sent Mr. T. B. and the ostler flying through the air, the former into the pig-stye, the latter into the middle of the dung-heap.

"Another quarter of a minute, and you'd have won five guineas each," quietly remarked Lord Harcliffe.

Of course all this equestrian business was not gone through without some considerable noise, from the plungings and prancings of the horses on the one hand, and the shouts and laughter of the spectators on the other.

To such an extent had it arisen at last, that the blighted Bunker, the landlord of the sour visage, felt it incumbent on him to shake off the drowsiness that oppressed him, and proceed to the stable-yard to see what was the matter.

He arrived just in time to see Dick sprawling on the dung-hill, and Mr. Thomas Bucks emerging from the confines of the odorous pig-stye, followed by the gruntings and squeakings of a sow and a litter of pigs, into whose domestic circle he had so suddenly intruded himself.

The sour visage of Mr. Timothy Bunker grew sourer still as he observed the prevailing confusion.

"What the devil are you doing?" he growled.

There was a general "haw—haw—haw!" from the yokels, that irritated but did not explain.

"Can't you speak, instead of grinning there like a set of idiots as you are?" cried the landlord.

"Ee, ee, ee!—ho, ho, ho!—haw, haw, haw!" was the only answer.

"What's all this hubbub about?" shouted the landlord.

"Ee, ee!" prefaced one of the joskins. "Measter Bucks an' Dick Ostler ha' been a trying to roide the black 'osses theer, an' they ha' pitched 'em over their 'eads Ee, ee, ee!"

Mr. Bucks, having extricated himself from the pig-stye, now came forward very much shaken and annoyed, and dispersing not exactly Arabian odours as he advanced.

"It's nothing, Mr. Bunker," he explained, in as off-handed a manner as he could assume under the circumstances. "The fact is, I mounted that vicious brute there,"—pointing as he spoke to Satan—"and being full of vice, he plunged and reared till he threw me. The fact is, no one but the devil himself could ride either of those horses."

"They look as though they belonged to some one of that description, they're so dreadfully black," muttered the host. "But," he continued, in more genial tones, to the groom, "what brings you here to-day?"

"I rode on in advance to prepare you to receive Major Bombshell, Mrs. Bombshell, and young Ensign Augustus Bombshell," answered Mr. Bucks.

"Oh, indeed!" ejaculated the landlord, brightening up at the prospect.

"Yes; they are going to town, and will stop here to bait their 'osses. It was the major's express desire that he should have a room to himself—a private room. He's very particular."

"Certainly," replied the landlord. "But, dear—dear!" he exclaimed, fretfully. "Things always happen contrary! Here have I been empty—positively empty—for the last fortnight, and now, just when a British officer and his family are about paying me a visit, the only room in the house fit to receive such distinguished guests is occupied by two strange beings, who seem inclined to stop when I wish from the bottom of my heart they'd go."

"I hope, when they *do* start, those infernal 'osses'll run away with the pair of 'em an' break their d—d necks!" muttered the groom.

"I never saw two such horses in my life. From the look of them, they either belong to two noblemen or else to two highwaymen," remarked Mr. Bunker.

"Well, whoever they are, you'll have to let 'em know who's coming, and get rid of 'em. You know what a out-an'-outer the major is when he don't 'ave ev'rything 'is own way."

"Perfectly well: I know him before to-day. Don't make yourself uneasy, Mr. Bucks—I'll get rid of these uneasy customers. It ain't likely I'm a going to lose the patronage of a military commander for the sake of two poppinjays who only drink ale and eat bread and cheese," said the landlord.

He forgot that he had denied them anything more substantial.

"This is a nice stinking state to be in," remarked the groom, as the pig-stye odours he exhaled offended even his own olfactory organs. "If missus was to scent me she'd faint, and the major would storm the place down or the clothes off my back."

"Come with me," said Timothy, "and I'll pump upon you till you're sweet."

"No thank you, Mr. B.," answered the groom: "I prefers bein' p'ison'd by the odours of your piggery rather than being screwed to death by rheumatics or lumbago."

"We'll purify you," continued the host; and with these words he returned to the house, accompanied by Mr. Bucks.

Dick the ostler, having recovered his faculties—no very great difficulty, considering he had so few—led Satan and Phantom into the stable, where, as he took particular care to handle them very gently, he found them much more tractable than he had imagined from the experience he had had so lately.

He found, to his great satisfaction, that they allowed themselves to be rubbed down and ate their corn in a manner precisely similar to that of other horses.

In the meantime our heroes, having enjoyed the joke exceedingly, were deeply engaged in drawing up a programme of their future operations.

"One fact is palpable enough," said Captain Hawk: "our funds are well-nigh exhausted."

"Unfortunately they are," returned Lord Harcliffe. "I have not more than ten guineas in hand."

"And I scarcely so much."

"And what are twenty pounds between two?"

"A mere trifle—nothing."

"For my own part," continued the Black Highwayman, "I have had so much of rural scenery and the quiet beauties of nature lately, that I confess I long for a little town life."

"I should have no objection at all to that myself. But do you not think, in going to London, we rush into the very hotbed of danger?"

"Perhaps so," answered Lord Harcliffe; "but there is one thing to be considered, that from the absence of all pursuit it is evident enough we are supposed to have left the country; if not, do you think we should be quietly sitting smoking our cigars in peace at this moment?"

"Most assuredly not," said Captain Hawk; "and it becomes a question whether it would be policy on our parts by venturing in broad daylight in the streets of London to risk undeceiving our Bow Street friends in this particular; you know how fond they are of our society, and how perseveringly they seek it."

Lord Harcliffe smiled as he answered:

"I have every reason to wish to avoid London, and yet in spite of the danger, I feel an almost irresistible desire to visit it; you, too, who are usually so reckless of consequences, to hesitate, seems strange to me."

The captain felt this almost as a reproach, and replied, somewhat proudly:

"The fear of what might happen to me personally never yet deterred me from the pursuit of any object on which I had set my mind; and since your wishes lead towards London we will go there."

"I am glad to hear you say this. There is only one obstacle——"

"I know to what you allude—our want of funds; but they must be raised, and I think you will admit there is little difficulty about that when we have such an unlimited quantity of bankers."

The Black Highwayman laughed.

"You are facetious, my dear friend," he answered. "However, there is no doubt our exchequer must be replenished before we enter the metropolis. We might as well attempt to stop the mail without horse or pistol, as go to town without sufficient funds."

"Well, then, let us consider it settled that we first take steps to fill our pockets, and that accomplished, we go to London to empty them."

"Agreed! And now let us have another tankard of old Sour Kraut's ale to drink success to our undertakings."

Captain Hawk rose with the intention of ringing the bell, but some circumstance caused him to adopt a different course.

He hastily advanced to the door, and opening it suddenly with a jerk, Mr. Timothy Bunker, the landlord, who had for some time past been posted outside with his ear to the keyhole, tumbled in in a state of the utmost confusion.

Lord Harcliffe started up from his seat.

The first idea that crossed the minds of the two highwaymen was to strangle Mr. B. on the spot, or else to put him up the chimney out of the way.

But a moment's reflection suggested a different course.

"What were you doing there?" inquired Captain Hawk.

"Nothing, upon my honour, gentlemen!" stammered the landlord, looking dreadfully guilty. "I—I was just list—no, I mean coming to see if the mail—no—dear me! what am I saying?—I mean, if you wanted any more ale, that was all, gentlemen, upon my honour!"

"And I was just coming to order some more ale. What a singular unanimity of ideas, wasn't it?" remarked Captain Hawk, in a peculiarly freezing tone, fixing his keen eyes upon the landlord's face, who didn't know what to do or where to look.

"I'll fetch you some more directly, gentlemen; same as before, I s'pose—a gallon—I mean a quart; but I'm so shaken I don't know what I'm saying."

He was about to sneak out sideways like a cr..., when the captain, seizing him by the back of the neck, pulled him back, whilst Lord Harcliffe closed the door.

Timothy Bunker had two minds about shouting murder, but there was something in the expression of his visitors' countenances that proclaimed the danger of any such attempt.

"Listen to me," said the captain, sternly, "and don't imagine we are quite so foolish as to believe a word you're saying. You were listening at that keyhole."

"No, gentlemen, no—upon my——"

"Psha! no lies. How long were you there?"

"I—I wasn't there at all—I wasn't indeed!"

"What?"

"That is, I mean I was there——"

"I know it."

"That is, I got there just as you opened the door!"

"What made you come tumbling in then like a skittle ball when I *did* open it?"

"I caught my toe in the mat—I did indeed!" faltered the terrified Bunker.

"You're a lying hound!" cried Captain Hawk, furiously. "You have overheard our conversation, and I shall take care not to suffer you to go at large while we're here."

Having uttered these words, Captain Hawk drew forth one of his bright-barrelled pistols.

Lord Harcliffe produced another.

"Mercy, gentlemen—mercy!" groaned the horrified host, falling on his knees, firmly believing his last hour was come.

"Of course you are prepared to die?" inquired Lord Harcliffe.

"No, no—I'm not; nothing like prepared; I've got a great many little things to——"

"Never mind them. Have you repented of your sins? They are not little things."

"No, I'm sorry to say I——"

"Have you made your will?"

"I—I've nothing to leave."

"So much the better; there will be no disputing after your death. Come now, here are two pistols, both loaded with bullets——"

"Oh—oh, mercy!"

"One is for your heart, the other for your head: which will you have first?"

"Neither, gentlemen! Oh, pray be merciful! I won't mention a word of what I heard—I swear I——"

"Oh, then it seems you *did* hear something?"

"No I didn't, not a syllable; I meant what I didn't hear; but I'll never mention it again—I won't as I'm a christian!"

The highwaymen had much difficulty in restraining their laughter, but they did so by a strong effort.

"You're a sneaking scoundrel!" said Captain Hawk. "And were you worth it, I'd blow a hole in your contemptible carcass; as it is, I spare your life on one condition, and on one only."

"What is it?" eagerly inquired the frightened landlord.

"That you ascend that chimney and stay there till I call you."

"Oh lor! but I can't climb!" groaned Bunker.

"You'd better; or if not you'll find this an excellent means of expediting your movements," urged the captain, giving the sneaking host a dig in the ribs with the terrible weapon he grasped.

"Oh don't!—pray don't! I'll try!"

"Be quick, then."

The landlord finding escape utterly impracticable, shuffled to the chimney and looked up it wistfully.

"Oh, Lord—oh, Lord! I shall be smothered there!" he exclaimed.

"Oh dear no—there's plenty of ventilation," said Captain Hawk. "All you have to do is to keep your eyes and mouth shut—the latter especially—and you will find a day or two passed in the quiet retirement of the chimney far from unpleasant."

"A day or two!" groaned the unhappy Bunker. "But how am I to support myself there—there's nothing to sit down upon?"

"Oh yes! You'll find an iron bar, each end of which rests in the brickwork, which will answer the purpose of a seat admirably."

"But suppose they light a fire?"

"Confound it! suppose they do!" cried the captain, with an assumption of impatient irritability, though he was ready to laugh outright. "Why, then you'll be roasted. Now, quick—mount!"

With many groanings and lamentations, and "ohs!" and "ahs!"—slippings and scrapings—the agitated Bunker scrambled up the chimney, and perched himself on the rail, looking like an enormous blackbird, but not uttering such melodious music.

"Now then," finally remarked Captain Hawk, "you'll understand distinctly you're to remain where you are till I call you?"

"Y-es—I understand! Oh! how the bar cuts!"

"If you dare to disobey me, you will forfeit your life!"

Having thus spoken, the captain fixed a chimney-board that stood close by in the cavity of the grate, and his prisoner was secure.

CHAPTER CLXXV.

MRS. BUNKER FINDS THE HIGHWAYMEN RATHER OBSTINATE.—MAJOR BOMBSHELL THINKS HE RECOGNISES CAPTAIN HAWK.

BOTH now found it necessary to thrust their heads out of window, and indulge their risible faculties.

While they were thus engaged, there came a tap at the door; but they were too much occupied to notice it.

A second tap came, and as there was no response to this, the tapper, who happened to be Mrs. Bunker, opened the door and looked in.

One of the most ostensible motives the landlord had for intruding upon our two heroes was to inform them as distinctly as possible that the sooner they were gone the better he should be pleased.

He was most anxious to have the room quite clear, and free from the odour of cigar-smoke, before the arrival of Major and Mrs. Bombshell, and their son the ensign.

It was quite an afterthought that induced him to remain listening at the keyhole previous to opening the door.

As, however, he did not return, his better-half had come to see what had become of him, being half inclined to believe he was drinking with the two strangers.

To her surprise on opening the door, no signs of her spouse appeared—nothing but the highwaymen's backs as they lolled out of the window laughing heartily.

"Ahem!" ejaculated Mrs. Bunker, who was a thin, wiry, little woman, with an expression of feature bordering upon the vixenish—"ahem, gentlemen," she continued, in a louder key, her first summons being ineffectual—"gentlemen!"

"What is it, my good woman?" inquired Captain Hawk, who heard her eventually, and looked round over his shoulder.

"Oh, if you please, gentlemen, would you——"

"Yes, decidedly; another tankard of ale directly; it's the very thing we want," said the captain, and looked out of the window again.

But this was by no means what Mrs. Bunker wanted. However, as she did not object to the money for the ale, she departed to fill the tankard.

When she returned, the two highwaymen were seated composedly, having laughed themselves into a proper state of seriousness.

Having placed the ale before them, and each of our friends having taken a hearty draught, the thin hostess still lingered.

"Do you require anything else, ma'am?" asked Lord Harcliffe.

"I was going to ask you if you had seen anything of Mr. Bunker—I mean my husband?"

"He came in a short time since, but disappeared rather suddenly," answered Captain Hawk.

"Oh, thank you, sir," said Mrs. B. "I thought perhaps he might be here still."

"I daresay he's not far off," remarked Lord Harcliffe.

"Oh no, sir; I shall find him somewheres, I daresay," answered the landlady.

She went to the door, fidgeted, coughed, and then turned back and stood washing her hands nervously, evidently having something to say, but not exactly determined how to begin.

Captain Hawk assisted her.

"Well, my good woman?" he said.

"Oh, I'm sorry to hurry you, gentlemen," she commenced, simpering and screwing her head like a moving waxwork. "But if you're not going to stop here——"

"But we are going to stop here," dropped in the captain, rather abruptly.

"All night?" she faltered out.

"No; but for some hours."

"Oh! I should be very sorry to disconvenience you, gentlemen; but you see this is the only room in the house for visitors, and——"

"It will do for us well enough."

"Yes, gentlemen; but I was going to say that Major Bombshell—of course you've heard of Major Bombshell?"

"Never had that honour?"

"He's a military man—a great commander—that fought like a lion at the battle of somewhere, and lost his leg."

"Oh indeed!"

"Yes, gentlemen, and he's got a cork leg, and he's coming here with Mrs. Bombshell and Ensign Bombshell; and he's sent word beforehand by Mr. Bucks—he's the major's groom, gentlemen—that he's going to stop here, and that he must have this room; and so, gen——"

"Certainly—by all means: we shall be happy to see the gallant major, and his cork leg into the bargain," replied Captain Hawk, cordially.

"You're very kind, gentlemen, I'm sure," returned Mrs. Bunker, licking her lips nervously; "but the major is very particular, and he wants the room to himself."

"Does he? Then he can't have it," said Captain Hawk, decidedly.

"Oh, but, gentlemen, I hope you won't stand in my way!" urged the thin hostess, in a nippish manner that was beginning to be spiteful. "I do assure you he's a very great man, is the major, and——"

"D—n the major!" cried the captain.

Mrs. Bunker uttered a shrill, sharp shriek of horror at this profanity, which reached the ears of her consort on his iron perch.

"Whatever can be the matter," he thought, "to make Mother Bunker scream? Those rascals can't be trying to kiss her! Oh no, it can't be that: no one would care about kissing her."

"If our company is not good enough for this major," said Captain Hawk to the agitated hostess, "you can give him our compliments and tell him he is at perfect liberty to take his illustrious self and his cork leg elsewhere."

"Yes, gentlemen, that's just where it is," screamed Mrs. B.: "I don't want him to go elsewhere: I want him to stop here, and I'm sure it couldn't make any difference to you, for the short time you're going to stop—especially as you only drink ale—whether you sat in the parlour or the tap-room; and so——"

"Harkye, woman!" cried Captain Hawk, starting up indignantly. "If your sex did not protect you, I should feel inclined to behave like a tap-room customer and horsewhip you; but, since you are a woman, I can only order you out of the room at once! Let's hear no more of your impertinent messages; and as to drinking your ale, if all the other liquors you sell resemble what we have drunk under that name, Heaven help those who swallow them! Begone!"

Mrs. Bunker, thoroughly appalled, rolled out of the room and staggered up the passage, feeling inclined to scream, and cry, and go into hysterics, and not decided which to do first.

Meeting Dick the ostler, she seized upon him, and pulled his hair vigorously, which was a great relief to her feelings.

At the same moment the sound of approaching wheels was heard, and in a few moments the carriage containing the major and suite drove up to the door of the inn.

Mrs. Bunker, grinning ghastly smiles, and feeling certain the major would cut off her head with his sword for her dereliction of duty, descended the steps, and stood twiddling the corner of her apron, and bobbing as though she was worked by some secret machinery.

Down jumped Pompey, the black footman, and opened the carriage-door.

The gallant major soon made himself heard.

"Lend me your arm, you black rascal!" he shouted, in a stentorian voice.

The black rascal did as he was ordered, and having safely landed the great man and his cork leg on *terra firma*, performed a similar service for Mrs. B. and the ensign.

Major Bombshell was a very short, podgy, consequential personage, with a very red, bloated face, who had—so it was rumoured—blown off his own leg by getting in the way of a cannon-ball at the siege of some fortress or other in Spain, and been promoted in consequence.

His arrogance and irascibility were enormous, and he

was inordinately proud of his cork leg which supplied the place of the missing member, and which he looked upon as a trophy of his valour and services to his country.

He was arrayed in a scarlet regimental coat, white breeches, and a pair of high jack boots, and his round, red face glowed forth from under his white wig and three-cornered hat like a furnace.

He was certainly to all appearance a very formidable-looking little major.

Even his wife was afraid of him, and the ensign evidently had to be on his P's and Q's in his papa's presence, whatever he did behind his back.

This young gentleman was precisely the reverse of the major, being inclined to be tall and lathy; but he rather liked that, as he considered it imparted a certain elegance to his figure.

Mrs. Major Bombshell was a little woman, who seemed to have been made to order, expressly to suit the major, being short and fat, and in all respects—the cork leg and irascible temper excepted—the very counterpart of her spouse.

Such were the party who now stopped at the Skittle Ball.

"Good day, your honour!—good day, your ladyship! —good day, sir!" murmured Mrs. Bunker, in a perfect flutter of agitation, bobbing up and down at each exclamation.

"Good day, Mrs. Bunker," growled the major, as he jerked his leg up the steps. "Room ready?"

"Quite ready, major," faltered Mrs. Bunker, who felt she must disclose the dreadful secret, but dared not bring it out.

"Quite private, as I ordered, of course?" growled the stout little potentate, interrogatively.

"Well, major, I am very sorry, but——"

"What have you got to be sorry about, Mrs. Bunker?"

"Why, your honour, two gentlemen put up here this morning——"

"Eh!"

"Two gentlemen, major; and, of course, as I've only one room, I couldn't do otherwise, major, than ask them into it."

"Well?—go on."

"Well, your honour, when your message came, of course I went to the gentlemen and told them your honour was coming——"

"That was right; and of course they cleared out?"

"No, major—that's just what they did not do."

"Not?"

"No, your honour; and you can't tell how it's upset me," whined Mrs. Bunker.

"Are they there now?"

"Y-es, major."

"In my private room?"

"Y-es, major; and they positively refuse to go."

"What! refuse to go?" roared the military despot. "Refuse?" he reiterated, as though doubting the evidence of his senses.

"Refused!" repeated Mrs. B.

"Do you hear that, Matilda Jane?" shouted the little major, appealing to his wife.

"Yes, Anthony," she replied.

"Do *you* hear, Augustus?"

"Yes, pa," answered the ensign.

"Refuse to obey my orders—the orders of a man who has lost a limb in the service of his country? Fire and fury! Here, Pompey—Bucks!"

Pompey rushed forward, and Bucks, wafting around him a questionable fragrance, sneaked out of the back parlour.

"Oh my!" exclaimed Mrs. Bombshell, fanning herself with her scented pocket-handkerchief as the odoriferous groom approached.

"Oh dear!—oh! pheugh!" ejaculated Augustus, applying at the same time a small bottle of aromatic vinegar to his nostrils. "What a disgusting effluvia!"

"Come, here, Bucks!" roared the major.

Bucks advanced doubtfully: he knew his master had a susceptible nose.

"Bucks, I'm insulted—I——"

He paused suddenly, and, making the wriest of faces, commenced sniffing violently.

"Why, what in the name of all that's horrible is the meaning of this infernal stench?" he growled. "Gunpowder's nothing to it! Bucks," he shouted, suddenly, as his sense of smell guided him to the right source, "it proceeds from you!"

Bucks looked humbled and abashed, a thing unusual with him.

"I had a little accident, major," he said.

"Accident?—what accident? You're a positive walking cesspool!"

"Fell off my horse into a pig-sty, sir."

You taint the atmosphere, sir! But go—go into that room, and order those two fellows out of it immediately: if your words won't make them move, by G—d the smell of you will, in double quick time!"

Thus ordered, Tom Bucks hastened to the room, where, the door being ajar, the two highwaymen, to their intense amusement, had heard every word that was uttered.

Mr. Bucks presented a very rueful countenance.

"Well, Pegasus," said Lord Harcliffe, "what now?"

"It's Major Bombshell's express orders that you get out of this room," stated the groom, in as definite a manner as he could assume.

"Tell Major Nutshell that we have no intention of moving at present," exclaimed Captain Hawk, in loud, ringing tones, that reached the major's ear, and rendered it necessary for his spouse and the ensign, assisted by Mrs. Bunker, to lay violent hands upon him to restrain his wrath.

"And tell him also," the captain continued, "that if he sends any more of his d—d impertinent messages, we shall not allow him to enter our presence under any circumstances."

The groom, perfectly appalled at such unparalleled audacity, made the best of his way back to the major, and informed that formidable personage of what he had already heard.

"Won't they go?" roared the major, purple with rage. "Fire and fury! We'll see! Unhand me!" he shouted, struggling with the combined forces that endeavoured to restrain him. "I'll see if they won't!"

And with a desperate effort of strength he broke away, and went stumping down the passage in a furious state of passion.

Arriving at the door, he banged it open, and confronted Captain Hawk and Lord Harcliffe, who, leaning back in their chairs, with their legs resting on the seats of two others, sat smoking their cigars with folded arms as coolly as two cucumbers.

"Well, old gentleman," said the captain, in a jocular tone, "what's the matter with you?"

"Fire and fury!" roared the major.

"You'd better send for the parish engine, then," suggested Lord Harcliffe.

"Did you receive my message, you two fellows—eh?" foamed out the major.

"We did, and returned an answer, which was more than it deserved," said Captain Hawk.

"Do you or do you not intend to vacate this apartment?"

"Decidedly not," replied the highwaymen.

"I ordered a private room!"

"And we've taken it."

"Fire and fury! Do you know who I am?"

"Perfectly well: you're Major Nutshell."

"Bombshell, sir—Bombshell!"

"Immaterial, since they're both made to crack."

"I beg your pardon—the difference is tremendous!" spluttered the irascible officer. "When a nutshell cracks it's nothing; but when a bombshell explodes—pheugh! fire and fury!—it—it—it——"

"Explodes," suggested Captain Hawk.

"Yes," continued the incensed major; "it makes a report, and—and scatters destruction on all around."

"We never heed such trifles," coolly remarked Lord Harcliffe.

"Trifles, sir!—d'ye call bombshells trifles? It was by a bombshell I lost my leg——"

"Lost your head?"

"My leg, sir, at the siege of—ahem! No matter, but it was a siege. Fire and fury! Red-hot shot flying in all directions——"

"Oh, Anthony!" exclaimed the major's spouse, rushing in, followed by the ensign. "Don't tell us about it—pray don't!"

"No, don't, pa: you know ma can't stand it," said Augustus.

"That's right—pray don't inflict us with the history of a cork leg," entreated Captain Hawk.

"Cork leg, you villain!" shouted Major B., indignantly. "Is a soldier who has lost a limb in the service of his country to be thus insulted?—is his highly honourable cork leg to be continually thrown in his face?"

"My dear sir, on the contrary, it is not our wish to insult you," said Lord Harcliffe; "but if you persist in throwing your highly honourable cork leg at us, we shall most decidedly throw it back again."

"You're a pair of insolent subordinates!" growled the ferocious major—"insufferable puppies! Were I as young and strong as I was at the siege of——"

"Anthony, pray!"

"D—n it, ma'am, be quiet! I'd, fire and fury!—I'd kick——"

Here his fury reached its culminating point, and expressive of what he would have done under the aforesaid circumstances, he launched out his limb with such a vigorous jerk, that he snapped the fastenings, and with a sharp crack the Kersey inexpressibles rent asunder, and away flew the cork leg across the room.

Where it would have gone to had its course been unchecked, we cannot undertake to say; but as it was, the door suddenly opened, and Pompey, entering with a tray containing sundry decanters and glasses, stopped the flying limb with his nose.

As might naturally be expected, the sudden shock caused the startled negro to drop the entire apparatus, and devote himself to his damaged proboscis.

Pompey danced a *pas seul*, howling with pain, and the indignant little major hopped about like a corpulent robin redbreast on his remaining pin.

Mrs. Bombshell screamed—the thin landlady, finding this an excellent opportunity, went into hysterics, from which—no one taking the slightest notice—she speedily recovered—the Ensign Augustus looked on aghast, and the highwaymen roared till their sides ached.

Altogether the din and confusion were tremendous.

"Don't laugh, you audacious villains!" shouted the hopping major, who was perspiring profusely. "It's gross disrespect to a man who has lost a limb in the service of—— Bring me my leg, you d—d black rascal!" he suddenly shouted, "and let me have something to drink: I'm choking!"

These orders being complied with with the utmost precipitation, the major was a little appeased.

But the storm still raged within.

He was highly indignant with the two cool strangers.

"You're a couple of puppies!" he said, nursing his leg under his arm. "Anyone could see that by the look of you; and, now I come to consider," he continued, looking earnestly at the captain out of a pair gooseberry eyes, "I've seen you before somewhere, I'm certain. Ah! yes, to be sure: you're Captain Hawk, the highwayman. You were tried at Huntingdon—you were hung at Huntingdon—that is, you ought to have been, only you escaped. What have you to say to that, eh?"

Having uttered this, the major leant his elbows on the table, and looked hard at Captain Hawk to watch the effect.

It appeared to take none whatever, as the captain merely glanced at the door and then looked straight in the major's eyes.

"What have you got to say for yourself?" asked the pompous major.

"Nothing at all on my own account," answered the captain; "but with respect to your words, they are only a proof what strange hallucinations seize upon the brains of old gentlemen, and what nonsense they talk. You fancy I am Captain Hawk!"

"Fancy? I am sure of it. I remember your face perfectly well: I was at your trial."

"Poor old gentleman! that bombshell has turned his brain," said the captain, pityingly. "I see now: that accounts for his strange conduct."

"Evidently," added Lord Harcliffe, "he is not accountable for his own actions."

Mrs. Major B. and the ensign opened their eyes rather wider than usual, but said nothing.

"I'll take my oath you're Captain Hawk!" persisted the major.

"How is that possible when it's well known Captain Hawk escaped across the Channel and went abroad?" observed the captain himself.

"Quite true!" joined in Lord Harcliffe.

"Do you imagine for an instant, my dear Major Nutshell——"

"Bombshell, sir!"

"Bombshell, that if I really were Captain Hawk, my kind friends, the police officers, would suffer me to be sitting here enjoying the pleasure of your illustrious society?"

This appeared rather improbable certainly; but the major was in a very irritable, disagreeable temper, and having started the subject of highwaymen, seemed determined to stick to it.

"Well, at all events, if you are *not* Captain Hawk, you ought to be his brother, you're so exactly like him," the major continued.

"Appearances are deceitful," said the captain, quietly.

"Very," returned the major; "these highwaymen, for instance, have the credit of being very daring beings."

"And are they not so?"

"Not a bit of it; they're the greatest cowards in creation. One of the rascals stopped me once on the highway and demanded my purse. That was before the siege of—ahem!—no matter: I mean it was before I lost my leg."

"And this highwayman demanded your purse. Well, and you——"

"I drew my pistol and shot him dead on the spot—fire and fury I did!"

"Excuse me, major—I don't believe you," said Captain Hawk, coolly.

"By guns and trumpets I did!" protested the valiant son of Mars. "And that's the way all such rascals should be served—at least, it's the way I intend to serve all whom I come across."

"Do you know, major, it strikes me that if you did happen to encounter one of these rascals you'd be ready to sink into your boots," observed Captain Hawk.

"I sink into my boots!" exclaimed the major, with profound scorn. "Never! I'm a Bombshell! Courage is a part of my very nature—it runs in the family; my son here, Ensign Bombshell, is as brave as I am."

"He looks like it," was the quiet reply.

"Oh yes," said the graceful Augustus, "I'm never afraid where there's no danger."

"Now there's my friend, Sir Thomas Walker, a gentleman and a justice of the peace, he's never been the same man since the escape of that Captain Hawk," stated the major.

"I'm glad to hear it," returned the captain.

"Glad?"

"More rejoiced, especially as it was very evident the captain was innocent of the crime for which he was condemned."

"Innocent? He was known to be one of the biggest scoundrels unhung."

"Was it known also that Sir Thomas Walker was urged on to desire the death of this Captain Hawk from motives of private malice?"

"Stuff and nonsense! It was for the public good."

"Was it known that Sir Thomas bribed the unfortunate prisoner's counsel not to appear in his defence, and that he had only the mockery of a trial?"

"All false!—utterly false!"

"All true—perfectly true! And but for a few devoted hearts that loved this highwayman, he would have perished on the gibbet."

"Ah! that is true enough," acquiesced the major. "He was rescued by a band of armed ruffians."

"Dreadful!" sighed Mrs. Bombshell.

"Atrocious!" muttered the ensign.

"And now," continued the officer, "I suppose he's prowling about, wherever he is, like a midnight wolf, too cowardly to show his face by day?"

"Well, major, you may one day chance to run against this skulking, prowling wolf; and if you do, be sure you pounce upon him."

"Trust me!" said the major.

"I'll help!" remarked the ensign.

"Two upon one! That's not fair," exclaimed Lord Harcliffe. "Not that I think he'd find much difficulty in disposing of half a dozen such as you."

"The fact is," joined in Captain Hawk, "a highwayman such as you are speaking of only cares to stop those who may be worth plundering, and majors in the army are, as a rule, but needy individuals."

"I beg to say I'm an exception," replied the pompous Bombshell. "Our family is rich. My uncle was a general——"

"Postman, perhaps?"

"No, sir—a military general. He left me his entire fortune and all his trophies."

"Amongst the heirlooms was a valuable bracelet, presented by Queen Anne to the general's great grandmother," explained Mrs. Major B., displaying at the same time the really valuable trinket glittering on her plump wrist.

"Very handsome indeed!" remarked the captain, admiringly.

"This repeater, edged with diamonds, formerly belonged to him," continued the major, drawing forth the massive timepiece, that was almost as large as a turnip, and as thick.

"And this diamond ring was presented to the general by the Governor of Brazil," said the ensign, coming in at the end, and holding out his delicate hand affectedly, on the little finger of which glittered a costly brilliant.

The highwaymen looked with the utmost complacency at these valuable relics, and quietly glanced at each other.

Though no words were spoken, each divined the other's thoughts.

The major was mollified at the evident admiration of the two intruders.

"I hope," he said, "you are now perfectly satisfied that I am not a *poor* major?"

"We are quite convinced of that," answered Captain Hawk, "for without any cash, these costly trinkets are a fortune in themselves."

"Oh," replied Augustus, "there's plenty of cash besides."

"I should hope so," exclaimed the major, in a tone of energetic confirmation; "and it will be a pretty convincing proof to you how little I fear these rascally highwaymen, when I travel with between three and four hundred pounds in my carriage pocket."

The two highwaymen nudged one another gently.

"I think," said Lord Harcliffe, "we have mistaken you, major."

"I'm sure of it," acquiesced Captain Hawk; "there is no doubt in the world you are a brave man."

"You may rest assured of it," responded the major, with conscious pride, beginning to look with more favour upon the strangers, who were so adroitly flattering his vanity, and acquainting themselves with those facts most important to their own interests at the same time.

Having, as it were, sucked him dry of his information, the highwaymen rose.

"You will pardon our running away from your charming society, major," said Captain Hawk; "but time flies, and we must be going."

"We'll take a glass of wine with you first, though," observed Lord Harcliffe.

"Decidedly," responded Captain Hawk.

Two glasses were filled.

"Your very good health, major," cried the captain. "That of course includes your highly honourable cork leg; and as bravery and clemency are usually united, let us hope that should you ever encounter this Captain Hawk, you will season justice with mercy, and spare him."

"Impossible! Perfectly impossible!" replied the major, grandly. "A soldier has a duty to perform to—a—society—to—a—his country—and a—that duty must be to exterminate such pests to society. Don't mention mercy—it's impracticable. If I meet this Captain Hawk I'll exterminate him."

With these words, and a majestic wave of the hand, the corpulent little major emptied his glass, the highwaymen emptied theirs, and bowing gallantly to Mrs Major B., quitted the room.

"Ha, ha!" laughed the captain, as they proceeded to the stables, "it strikes me this *braggadocio* major will encounter Captain Hawk sooner than he expects."

When they reached the yard, Tom Bucks, Pompey the black footman, and Dick the ostler, were fraternising over half a gallon of the landlord's best ale, and puffing clouds of smoke from long clay pipes at the stable door.

"Keep these fellows here for a few moments," whispered the captain to his comrade, as he went out by the gate to the front of the inn, where the carriage stood in solitary grandeur.

No one—not a soul was about, and the captain inspected the hind wheels minutely, especially in the neighbourhood of the axletrees.

This done, he once more returned to the stables, where he found Satan and Phantom ready for mounting.

"Are you prepared to start?" he inquired of Lord Harcliffe.

"Quite," returned his lordship.

In an instant, without any opposition on the part of the noble animals, the highwaymen were on their backs, to the great surprise and admiration of Messrs. Bucks, Dick, and Pompey.

Captain Hawk threw a crown to Dick as they rode out, without condescending to notice the groom, and in a few moments they were once more on the road

CHAPTER CLXXVI.

MRS. BUNKER MISSES HER HUSBAND.—THE MAJOR FINDS HIM.—AND IS ASTONISHED IN MORE WAYS THAN ONE.

MRS. BUNKER began to grow uneasy at the prolonged absence of her husband.

She had sought him high, she had sought him low, but he was nowhere to be found.

A terrible suspicion crossed her that he might, as times were bad, have made a hasty escape from his difficulties by precipitating himself down the well; but of that she had no proof.

Then her imagination fastened upon the two strangers.

Mr. Bunker had certainly entered the chamber where they were; but she had not seen him come out again.

She worked herself up accordingly into a state either of real or imaginary terror, and at last presented herself before the pompous major, who was becoming more and more grandiloquent over the sherry he was imbibing.

"Oh, your honour!" she said, in faltering tones, as she entered—"oh, your ladyship!"

"What's the matter, woman?" inquired the red-faced commander.

"My poor Timothy!" she whimpered.

"Well, what about your poor Timothy?" asked the great Bombshell, roughly.

"I can't find him, sir!" she replied.

"I'm not surprised at it, considering the visitors you harbour in this house; it's a wonder you can find anything!" said the major, with stern emphasis.

"I hope and trust that my visitors, your honour——"

"Bah! Hope and trust! Do you know—are you aware that the two individuals who have been sitting in this room ever since I came here, and goodness knows how many hours before, are neither more nor less than a couple of rascally highwaymen? Do you know that, ma'am?" wound up the major, slapping his hand violently on the table.

Mrs. Bunker uttered a faint scream.

"High-highwaymen?" she gasped.

"Highwaymen!"

"Oh, my good gracious!"

"Yes, ma'am," continued the major, with declamatory energy, "I detected the rascals immediately; though they might have deceived you, they couldn't deceive me: I was not to be done. I let 'em know my opinion pretty plainly, and they sneaked away like a couple of midnight depredators as they are!"

"I hope they haven't taken anything!" faltered Mrs. Bunker.

"You may depend upon it they have if they had the opportunity," remarked the major, in a comforting manner.

"D'ye think they've taken Timothy?" inquired the hostess, as a new light seemed to break in upon her.

"Timothy!" ejaculated the major, with contempt. "Of what use would he be?"

"I find him useful sometimes," murmured the landlady.

"If they've done anything with him, they've cut his throat."

At this horrible prospect the afflicted hostess uttered a shriek.

"You may think yourself highly fortunate that I came

just when I did," continued the major, "or it's my opinion you'd have had all you throats cut."

At this moment a strange noise was heard proceeding from some remote spot, the locality of which was not immediately apparent.

"What's that?" exclaimed Mrs. Bunker, with a look of dismay on her sharp features.

"What's what?" ejaculated the major.

"Did—didn't you hear something, sir?"

"I thought I did," remarked Mrs. Major B.

"So did I," coincided Augustus.

The sound was repeated.

It was something between a cough and a groan.

"Yes, decidedly, there is something somewhere," affirmed the major.

"What can it be, Anthony?" said his wife.

"If you wish for my decided opinion," exclaimed the corpulent little soldier, "I should say it's those two vagabonds, foiled in their attempts below, are committing depredations above."

"Oh—oh, major!" gurgled Mrs. Bunker.

"There, don't stand ohing there, but go and see directly. I'd go myself, only, having lost my leg, I—ahem! well—Why the devil don't you go?" shouted Major B.

"I—I—I'm afraid!" cried the hostess.

"Psha! Augustus, go upstairs and see what's the matter," enjoined the valorous officer.

Augustus hesitated; he did not see the policy of such a step.

"Oh, Anthony," cried Mrs. Major, clinging to her son, "would you sacrifice our child—our only one?"

"I'll go, ma—I'd rather go," exclaimed the dauntless youth, who was fully assured that his mamma, having once got hold of him, would not release her grasp; "I'm not afraid!"

"Brave boy! do you hear him?" sighed the proud but timid mother.

"Somebody must go! Fire and fury, if my leg were not off, I'd——"

Here another dismal "Oh!—oh!—oh!—ugh!" reached their ears.

"I think," said Mrs. Major Bombshell, in an alarmed whisper, "it comes from the chimney."

"That leads to the room above where we keep the spoons and forks," cried the landlady.

"Oh!—oh!—oh!" was again heard.

"D—n it!" exclaimed the major, who had been listening, "it comes from the chimney. The rascals are hiding there, depend upon it."

"Oh, what shall we do? We shall all be murdered!" groaned Mrs. Bunker.

"Where's Bucks?" growled the dauntless officer.

"Call Pompey!" murmured Mrs. Major B.

"I'd better not leave you, ma," lisped Augustus, holding on to his maternal parent tenaciously.

"Dick!—Dick!" gasped the landlady.

"Ah-tch!—ah-tch!—ah-tch!" went a sneezing voice in the chimney.

"If I had but a weapon—if only a cannon!" vociferated the major.

"There's a gun in the bar-parlour over the chimbley," exclaimed Mrs. B., nervously.

"Loaded?"

"Yes."

"Fetch it instantly—this moment!"

"Yes, major."

Away went the landlady on her tiptoes to procure the deadly weapon.

"Don't do anything rash, for Heaven's sake, Anthony!" entreated Mrs. Major B.

"Hold your tongue, ma'am!" answered the valorous major, who was balancing himself on one leg, and trying to remove the chimney-board. "This is nothing—mere child's play! When I was at the siege of——"

Here he overbalanced and rolled over, chimney-board and all, on his back.

"Confound it!—d—n it!" he growled.

At the same moment Mrs. Bunker entered with the gun.

"Lift me up!" shouted the major, "and get me a chair instanter!"

The gallant veteran was raised by the united efforts of the ensign and the two ladies, and placed in a chair close to the fireplace.

"Now, then," he cried, "give me the gun."

The weapon was placed in his hands.

With cool intrepidity he placed the muzzle up the chimney and cocked the weapon.

"Now," he cried, "we shall see!"

The ladies involuntarily shut their eyes and stopped their ears with their hands.

The gallant ensign cuddled his ma.

The redoubtable major compressed his lips firmly and shut *his* eyes.

There was a moment's pause, and then, with indomitable resolution he pulled the trigger.

Whiz!—bang! went the gun.

The women screamed, the ensign sat down instantaneously, as though his legs had suddenly given way under him—a loud and prolonged howl came from the top of the chimney—a dense volume of soot, about half a cart-load, shot out at the bottom—over rolled the major, almost smothered in the dark concretion—and down fell Timothy Bunker from his iron perch, as black as the place he had just fallen from.

The yell was tremendous, and roused Messrs. Bucks, Pompey, and Dick, who thought the house had fallen down, and came running in in a body to see what was the matter.

Great was their surprise at the scene that presented itself.

Mrs. Major Bombshell in a cataleptic state, nursed in the arms of the gallant ensign, who was little less alarmed than his mamma, and had quietly doubled up, and sat on the floor with his back against the wall, looking as white as a sheet.

Mrs. Bunker, the landlady, had become rigid in one corner of the room.

The redoubtable major lay on his back with his one leg in the air, sneezing and growling in a most terrific manner, in an atmosphere composed of gunpowder and soot, whilst the most conspicuous object was the blackened form of the landlord himself, who lay in a heap in the centre of the apartment, gasping and choking, and calling "Murder!" at intervals.

For the first few moments the new arrivals could do nothing but sneeze from obvious reasons; but Mr. Thomas Bucks, having opened the window, they were presently enabled to breathe, and to investigate the cause of the dire confusion that prevailed.

The principal object that attracted their attention and excited their apprehensions was the landlord, who was so thoroughly begrimed with soot as to be unrecognisable.

"What be that?" asked Dick the ostler, timorously, pointing to the sable mass on the floor.

"Him don' know 'xac'ly; but him tink him's de debbil!" returned Pompey.

"Murder!—mur-ur-urder!" shouted the individual in question, at that moment.

"That bean't no devil!" exclaimed Dick: "that be measter's voice, Oi know."

"Of course it's your master's voice!" screamed Mrs. Bunker, recalled to herself by the yells of her spouse, "and there you stand like three dummies with your mouths open! Why don't you pick him up, you set of fools?" she shouted.

"D—n it!" roared the major, "will anyone pick me up?"

"Iss, massa!" shouted Pompey, rushing forward and making a vigorous clutch at the major, who, furious at having been left so long upon his back, seized the unfortunate darkie on the top of his head, not only—as the song says—where the wool *ought* to grow, but where the wool *did* grow, and shook him so fiercely that Pompey yelled out at the very top of his voice.

"Oh lor, massa! don' shake poor nigger like dat! Him got no bref left in him body!"

"Don't talk to me, you d—d black villain! but help me up!" shouted the major.

"Oh!—oh!—oh!—oo!" whined Mrs. Major, who was just coming out of her faint.

"What's the mattah?" languidly inquired the gallant ensign, who was growing tired of sitting with his back against the wall nursing his mamma, and who, seeing there was no danger, thought he might put in a word.

"Matter? you spooney!" roared the incensed major. "The matter is that if we had all been murdered you ought to be arrested as an accessory to the fact. The

[MAJOR BOMBSHELL ENCOUNTERS TWO STRANGE HORSEMEN.]

idea of sitting down like an automaton at such a time, and doing nothing—positively nothing! You're a disgrace sir—a disgrace to the Bombshells!"

"I was doing something, pa!" snivelled the graceful Augustus. "Ma was frightened, and I was attending to her. You were frightened, weren't you, ma? he inquired, appealing to that lady.

"Yes, love!" sighed Mrs. Bombshell. "Gus protected me during this terrible scene, the dear boy!" she exclaimed, with maternal fondness, throwing her arms round the dauntless youth.

"Dear bosh!—terrible fiddlesticks!" roared the furious major. "Will anybody kick that black lump of muck for me?"

This of course alluded to the landlord, who persisted in lying where he was, curled up on the floor like a periwinkle in mourning, gasping "Murder!"

At the major's request, the toes of Messrs Bucks, Pompey, and Dick were vigorously applied to those parts of his person that were available.

The consequence of this was that he very speedily uncurled himself.

"Get up!" shouted the major—"get up!"

But Timothy's ideas were confused.

He still, somehow or the other, fancied himself up the chimney, and he had a vivid recollection of Captain Hawk's peremptory command that he was not to descend without his express permission.

In reply therefore to the major's orders to "get up!" all he did was to inquire earnestly whether he "might come down?"

"You are down, you idiot!—can't you see you are?" exclaimed the fierce Bombshell.

"I'm not quite sure," murmured the discomfited Bunker, sitting up and trying to look around him, a proceeding which the soot in his eyes rendered an exceedingly difficult operation. "Where am I?" he exclaimed.

"You're at home, Timothy!" sharply returned Mrs. B. "How can you act so ridik'lus as to pretend not to know that?"

"If you'd been stuffed up a chimney, as I've been, by main force," spluttered the landlord, "with a long-barrelled pistol follering yer all the way to the top, an' when yer got to the top, obligated to sit on an iron bar till human natur', that can't stand bein' cut in half, couldn't endoor it any longer, I think it's very like you'd 'act ridik'lus,' as you call it, Mrs. B.!"

"Get up then," persisted the major, "and let us hear all about this strange affair!"

The landlord having glanced around, and seeing no signs of the presence of the individual he appeared so much to dread, at length contrived to scramble up on to his feet and drop into a chair.

"And now what the devil's the meaning of all this?" sternly demanded the major.

"It means that we've had two bloodthirsty highwaymen here!" answered the landlord.

"Highwaymen!" ejaculated everybody.

"Yes, highwaymen!" re-echoed Timothy Bunker. "You must know, major, that before you came, two gentlemen—at least, they looked like gentlemen, and you know, major, when—a—gentlemen look like gentle——"

"D—n it all, man! drop the *gentlemen*, and go on!" gruffly interrupted Major Bombshell.

"Well, then, they put up here; and when I came to them very politely, as they were drinking their ale—they drank nothing but ale, major—and of course when people drink nothing but——"

"Go on!"

"Certainly. Well, I went to them, and I said 'Major Bombshell's coming here, and of course he'll want this room all to hisself.' An' what did they say? 'Their compliments to the major, an' he couldn't have it.'"

"Well?"

"Well, of course I told 'em pretty plainly what I thought; and then what d'ye think they did?"

"Go on, and then I shall know!" grunted the major.

"They—that is, one of 'em draws out a pistol from his pocket, a yard long if it was an inch, an' looks at me with a most evil expression of countenance. As soon as I saw that, I knew he was no good—I felt convinced in my own mind he was a housebreaker or a highwayman, or something of that sort, an' I there an' then give myself up for lost. Of course, under these awful circumstances I began to say my prayers——"

"Never mind what *you* said: let us know what *they* did!" said the irreverend soldier.

"Why, the fiend in human form with the long-barrelled pistol said he should put me out of the way. Of course I thought he meant to blow my brains out——"

"Perfectly impossible!" growled the major, with a chuckle at his own wit; "you haven't got any to blow."

"At all events, I've got something that answers instead very well," explained the landlord; "but it turned out I was mistaken, for instead of shooting me, he ordered me get up the chimney."

"Oh, la!" ejaculated Augustus.

"Oh, scissors!" muttered Mr. T. Bucks.

"And you were fool enough to go?" demanded the major.

"What was I to do?" asked the landlord, pitifully. 'You know, major, life's life."

"Bah!" snapped the major.

"It's very sweet to all, though, when it comes to the pint," suggested Mr. Bucks.

"It's more than you are at this moment," exclaimed the commander, whose olfactory nerves had received a passing whiff from the groom, who was still redolent of pig-stye odours. "Get out!"

Bucks instantly disappeared, much to his delight, and retired to flirt with the barmaid.

"And so," continued the major, "you did get up the chimney?"

"Yes, I did, and I sat on the rail till somebody fired up the chimney, and then I—I—don't remember anything more till I found myself lying here on the floor."

"There!—there!—there!" exclaimed the little corpulent major, looking round triumphantly at everybody. "Wasn't I right?—wasn't I, Mrs. B.?—wasn't I, Augustus?"

"Oh, you're *always* right, pa," returned the youth, in a tone that might have been interpreted two ways—"*always!*"

"Of course I am! Didn't I accuse them of their flagitious way of life to their faces? Didn't I say what I'd do if ever I dropped across them?—didn't I, Mrs. Bombshell—eh?"

"You did, Anthony—you did," acquiesced the lady.

"And I'll keep my word, Matilda Jane!" exclaimed the major. "Fire and fury! I'll keep my word!" he shouted, starting up and hopping fiercely across the room. "I only hope I may encounter these scoundrels—this Captain Chalk!"

"Hawk, pa!" corrected Augustus.

"Hawk, then. I'll let him know what a hawk is by the side of an eagle!"

The major having by this time pretty well exhausted himself, and having been hopping about more like a jackdaw than the bird he mentioned, with his highly honourable cork leg under his arm, allowed himself to drop into a chair.

"That's right, Anthony," exclaimed his spouse, finding an opportunity in her husband's silence to put in a word. "I'm sure you must be quite tired of standing on one leg. Do rest yourself! And suppose we have tea? it would be highly refreshing to us all."

The major gave a grunt, which under the circumstances was interpreted into an expression of assent, and tea was accordingly ordered.

Pompey and Dick withdrew; and Mrs. Bunker, having seized upon her begrimed partner, marched him off to the pump, where by dint of vigorous pumpings and scrubbings, she contrived to reduce him from black to a state of whitey-brown, and then having administered a glass of hot rum-and-water, sent him off shivering to bed.

By the time the major and his party had finished their tea, and the former had indulged himself with an extra bottle of Timothy Bunker's port, and a glass of diluted cognac on the top of that, he began to think it time to continue their journey.

Accordingly the bill was paid, the horses led from the stable and harnessed to the carriage, that still remained in solitary grandeur in front of the inn, and the major hopping along, nursing his cork leg, led the way to the vehicle.

At length they were all seated, Pompey grinning and showing his white teeth in the dickey, and Mr. Bucks, who was to act as postillion for the remainder of the journey, in his saddle on one of the horse's backs, into which he had vaulted as gallantly as possible, conscious that Susan, the barmaid, was looking at him through the window.

All being ready for starting, the major gave the word of command, and the ponderous travelling carriage moved on its way towards London.

CHAPTER CLXXVII.

THE MAJOR'S CARRIAGE GOES DOWN THE HILL WITH A RUN, AND COMES TO GRIEF AT THE BOTTOM.—THE MAJOR ASKS A QUESTION, AND RECEIVES AN ANSWER FROM A MASKED HORSEMAN.

It was a beautiful moonlight night, and the cool evening air was redolent with the perfume of sweet may wafted from the hedges.

At a few hundred yards from the inn the road wound round somewhat abruptly, and a short distance further brought them to the summit of a tolerably steep hill, the descent from which lay before them.

Mr. Bucks suddenly became aware of this fact from the increased impetus of the motion of the carriage.

"Um!" he ejaculated, "this is too much for the 'osses; I must have the drag on. Here, Snowball!" he called to Pompey, who was snoring in the dickey, "just put on the drag, will you?"

"Boder de drag!" ejaculated Pompey, who did not relish this interruption to his dreams.

"Get down directly, you lazy nigger!" exclaimed Mr. Bucks. "Do you want to have us all over?"

"What de debbil him care wedder 'em go ober or not?" grumbled the sable footman, descending, however, at the same time as the carriage, yielding to the steepness of the incline, was increasing in its velocity every instant.

"Be quick!" shouted Mr. T. B., who was beginning to feel a little uneasy.

"Gorra! him can't bo quick: dere's no drag to let down at all!" cried Pompey.

"There is—there must be!" called out the *pro tem* postillion.

"Him take him oath dere isn't!" protested the black.

"Then, d—n it all, we're in a pretty pickle!" returned Mr. Bucks, in a tone of anxiety. "Woho—wo!" he cried to the horses; but it was in vain he "woho'd" and "woohoo'ed."

The road was so steep, and the heavy vehicle had rolled itself into such a state of downward velocity, that instead of being drawn by the horses, it drove them.

In vain they hung back and tried to come to a stand by stiffening their fore legs and digging their hoofs in the road.

They were jostled and bumped onwards, plunging and struggling, by the unwieldy machine behind them.

"Stop de 'osses!" roared Pompey.

"Stop 'em yourself, and be d—d!" shouted Mr. Bucks, "I can't."

"'Em all stop when 'em get to de bottom!" said Pompey, consolingly.

The party inside the carriage had fallen asleep, but the jolting and the speed were such, that they awoke Mrs. Major B., who became immediately conscious that something was the matter.

"Good gracious!" she ejaculated, in dismay. "Whatever can be the matter? What a frightful pace Bucks is driving at—down a hill, too!"

Here the coach gave a fearful lurch.

"Oh, we shall all be killed!" she screamed. "Anthony—Augustus," she continued, shaking those individuals violently, "the coach is running away!"

But neither the major nor the ensign woke up to the fact, from the fact of their being too fast asleep.

Bump—bump—roll—roll went the coach, till presently by a particularly energetic jerk on the part of the vehicle, the somnolent ensign was propelled violently forward, his head finding a resting-place in the pit of the major's stomach.

Now, as it happened that this was the one particular portion of the gallant officer's anatomy in which he was particularly sensitive, he at once awoke with a tremendous howl, and clapped both his hands on the ears of his son and heir, which he pulled so vigorously, that the astonished Augustus yelled lustily in concert; so that with the howls of the major, the yelling of the ensign, and the shrieks of his mamma, the din was perfectly bewildering.

"Ugh! Oh, my stomach!" grunted Major Bombshell.

"Oh, my ears!" whimpered Bombshell junior.

"Oh, Anthony—Anthony!" screamed Mrs. B., "we shall all be killed!"

"Eh—why? What the devil is the matter?" exclaimed the major, beginning to perceive that the carriage was progressing at a headlong pace.

"The coach is running away!" shrieked his wife.

"D—n it, so it is!" cried the major, fiercely. "Fire and fury! this is destruction—annihilation!"

"Murdah!" shouted Augustus, looking very pale.

"I'll put a stop to this!" exclaimed the indomitable commander, thrusting his head out of the window, and observing that the trees and hedges seemed to be flying past as if propelled by some magic influence, and dancing and jumping in a most unnatural manner.

"Here—heigh, Bucks, you scoundrel! stop the horses! Dy'e hear?"

Bucks, who, in an intense state of alarm and perspiration, was tugging away at the horses' mouths as though his life depended on it, *did* hear; but, alas! stopping was out of the question.

"It's no good hollering, major," he groaned: "it's not the 'osses, it's the coach—it won't stop."

The major did not hear any of this very distinctly but the two last words, 'won't stop!' and of course he translated them as wilful disobedience.

"How dare you say you *won't* stop, you reckless villain! You're killing the horses, and you'll overturn the coach! Fire and fury! do you hear what I say?"

Not the slightest notice, however, appeared to be taken. The coach still dashed on.

"Call Pompey, Anthony!" entreated the terrified Mrs. B.

"Pompey!" wailed out Augustus.

"Pompey," shouted the stentorian voice of the hero of sieges, "you black rascal, where are you?"

"Him holding on behind, massa, like ole boots!" cried Pompey.

"I'll old boot you, you vagabond, when we *do* stop!" growled the major

This seemed such a very indefinite period, that it did not alarm the sable domestic in the least.

"Can you inform me," roared his incensed master, holding his hand to his mouth to make himself heard, "where we're going?"

"Him can't say for certain," replied Pompey, as he swung along behind, "but him tink 'em all going to de debbil by de fuss post."

Pompey appeared to be right in his conclusion, for as he spoke the two front wheels shot off, and down came the coach with a terrific crash in the middle of the road, the startled horses dragging it along, grinding, scraping and smoking, and its occupants screaming, groaning and anathematising severally.

This continued till the horses, fairly tired out, gave up, and stood perfectly still.

The scene within the carriage was ludicrous in the extreme.

When the grand crash took place, the ensign, who had for some time previously been in a state of collapse, disappeared entirely.

His maternal parent sank down at the bottom of the coach, and the major bounded into his spouse's lap, and sat there.

The object that did not succumb to the shock was the major's 'highly honourable' cork leg, and that coolly maintained its upright position—that is, it leant forward and showed its honourable toe out of the window.

There was a pause of gruntings and groanings.

"Ugh!—phew!—whew!—waugh!" burst from the major at intervals.

"Oh dear!—oh, good heavens!" murmured his lady. "Are we alive?"

"Of course we are!" gasped her husband, gruffly.

"Where's dear Gus?" inquired the anxious mamma.

"Haven't seen anything of him lately," abruptly answered the major.

"Oh dear, dear! what can have become of him? He must be killed—I'm sure he must!"

This supposition was not far from the truth.

For when it is considered that the individual in question was lying on his back at the bottom of the carriage, supporting the united weights of his corpulent relatives, who were seated on his nose, it will easily be imagined that that ornament was squeezed as flat as any nose could have possibly desired, and that the dense weight pressing upon the mouth and chest of the gallant but helpless ensign, he could neither kick, scream, nor breathe.

The only thing he could do was quietly to suffocate, and that he was doing as rapidly as possible.

In the agonies of strangulation, however, his jaws closed with such intensity, that they grasped a mouthful of his mamma's silk dress, and with the silk a considerable portion of a totally different material, which caused that good lady to scream vigorously and make desperate efforts to rise.

"Oh, oh! Anthony—oh! something's biting me at the bottom of the carriage! Let me get up!"

By dint of much pushing and struggling, the major was somehow or other hoisted up.

Mrs. Major B. followed, and the biter was then discovered in the person of the unfortunate Augustus, who was black in the face, and who in a few seconds more would have been "past all surgery."

However, the sudden removal of the corporeal mountain from his burdened chest saved his life, and by dint of shaking and rubbing, and applications of ammonia and eau-de-Cologne, which restoratives the major's lady invariably travelled with, the half-suffocated ensign came to, to the great joy of his anxious mamma and the relief of the major, who, having only one son, thought it might be as well to keep him if possible.

Their apprehensions on this head being allayed, the major's wrath at the catastrophe that had occurred, and which he considered entirely owing to Tom Bucks's reckless driving, burst forth anew.

"I'll cut Bucks and Pompey into mincemeat!" he exclaimed, half drawing his sword and sheathing it again angrily, as though it had been in the bodies of those culprits. "The rascals—the scoundrels!" he continued. "If it hadn't been for my coolness and presence of mind, all our lives might have been sacrificed!"

What the major meant by this boastful speech, or what he had done to avert any additional suffering he and his party might have endured, was not very apparent; however, he looked grand, and nobody contradicted him.

"I'll get out at once, and speak to the villains!" he exclaimed, seizing the handle of the carriage door and giving it an excited twist.

But from some cause or other—perhaps from a jar the concussion had given it—it refused to open.

He tried the other, with no better result.

"There seems to me to be a d—d conspiracy everywhere!" he growled. "Even the carriage doors are mutinous and refuse to obey orders."

Suddenly he remembered the carriage opened at the top.

"Bucks—Pompey!" he cried, as he tried to unfasten the hooks that kept this part of the vehicle together, and found that from want of oil or some other cause they would not move. "Where the devil are those atrocious mutineers? These hooks are as obstinate as the doors—they won't stir a peg!"

The major, thus imprisoned in the coach, looked out as well as he could sideways from the windows, but could see nothing.

He bawled, "Pompey—Bucks!" till he was out of breath; and then, vowing he'd cut off the ears of the delinquents as soon as he got near enough to them, he applied his sword's point to the obstinate hooks, and at last, by dint of wrenching and coaxing, they flew back, and the major, pushing up that part of the carriage roof that opened like a trap-door, managed to scramble up and look out.

To his great astonishment and dismay, however, he found the horses had vanished; neither did he see anything of the culprits, whom he in the heat of his fury had consigned to impalement or the loss of their ears at least.

"The traces have snapped and the horses, frightened, of course have bolted!" growled the major. "Very natural too! I would have done the same, only I was *bolted* in!" he continued, in a grumbling kind of soliloquy. "And now we're left here in this abominable, execrable, aggravating, infernal plight—deserted, too, by those cowardly varlets!"

At this moment his eye glanced to the right, and there, close to a gate in the hedge side, which lay in shadow, he dimly descried the "cowardly varlets."

They appeared to be leaning up against the gate with the utmost coolness, and this sight added fuel to the fire of the major's indignation.

"Come here, you d—d deserters'" he shouted.

They didn't stir an inch.

"Why the devil don't you move?"

"We can't," was the reply.

"Oh! you 'sha'n't,' sha'n't you?" cried the major, who once more misunderstood the word uttered. "Then, by guns and trumpets—fire and fury!—I'll quicken your knowledge of your duty with a bullet, you disrespectful, mutinous scoundrels!"

And as he spoke, he, in the extremity of his indignation, drew forth a pistol from the pocket of the carriage-door, and would have carried his design into execution, when he was stopped in his intent by feeling a hand laid upon his wrist and a voice exclaiming in his ear, which appeared somewhat familiar:

"They would come if they could, major; but as they both happen to be tied to the gate they find it impracticable. You must therefore look upon their compulsory disobedience as their misfortune, not their fault, and be merciful."

The major, startled somewhat at this unexpected address, slipped from his perch and disappeared suddenly inside the vehicle.

It will be remembered that he had kicked off his cork leg, which he had not yet had an opportunity of having refixed; he having, therefore, only one leg to stand upon, was a little more unsteady on his gallant pins than usual—perhaps, also, the port wine and brandy added their influence to produce this result.

But he was excessively annoyed at the slip he made.

In the first place because the suddenness of his descent caused him to scrape his chin violently, the pain of which was sufficiently irritating, and lose his wig; and then his instantaneous disappearance seemed to suggest the idea that he was afraid.

He—the renowned, the dauntless—afraid! The reflection was terrible.

Growling and rubbing his chin, he scrambled up again and looked out, when his sensations were not more gratified to perceive a masked horseman mounted on a coal-black steed quietly looking down upon him.

CHAPTER CLXXVIII.

THE MASKED HORSEMEN INDULGE IN AN HOUR'S AMUSEMENT AT THE MAJOR'S EXPENSE.—BRAVERY OF THE MAJOR AND HIS SON.—THE HORSEMEN CLEAR OUT THE CARRIAGE, AND RIDE OFF WITH THE BOOTY.

"THAT was rather a sudden drop, major, was it not?" inquired the horseman, in a pleasant tone, as though the occurrence was rather a facetious affair than otherwise.

"D—d sudden!" growled the major, surlily.

"Never mind. Accidents will happen to the best of us. I trust you haven't hurt yourself?"

"Bah! hurt myself? I never hurt myself!" returned the irascible warrior, in reply to the courteous question.

"You're a very fortunate man, major; but I fancied I noticed that you had only one leg?"

"I have only one leg," returned the major, holding on to the edge of the carriage top. "The other was lost——"

"In the service of your country," exclaimed another voice from the opposite side of the carriage.

The major turned his head with such a sudden jerk, that he very nearly repeated the slipping casualty.

By a strong effort, however, he retained his hold.

"Fire and fury!" he gasped, as his eye fell on the latter speaker, who was also mounted on a black horse, and masked.

This was undoubtedly a peculiar, if not a trying, position for the dauntless major's nerves.

To be looking out at the top of a damaged carriage, with a couple of masked strangers quietly keeping guard on each side of it, was very unpleasantly suggestive.

At least, it proved so to those inside, for Mrs. Major B., having glanced from the left-hand window, and caught a glimpse of one of these mysterious beings, immediately began to scream.

Whilst the gallant Augustus, who was about to assure her there was "no danger," happening to catch sight of the other masked rider, felt suddenly impressed with the idea that there was a great deal, and assisted his mamma by calling "Murdah!" in a most unsoldier-like manner.

The major, what with the strange sight without, and the doleful lamentations within, was considerably bewildered; but still he would not give in, or own himself in any way alarmed so long as there was anyone else to bully for being so.

The exclamations of his wife and hopeful son afforded him this opportunity, to say nothing of Messrs. Bucks and Pompey, who, tied side by side to the gate, bore their bonds with the stoicism of two Red Indians.

The major, however, turned his anger upon the members of his own family.

Looking down into the carriage, he shouted:

"What's all that infernal hullabaloo about, eh?"

This fierce interrogation had the effect of somewhat quieting the mourners.

The cries died away into faint murmurs and "ohs!"

"Don't let me hear any more of that!" cried the major, who, if he had had his other leg on, would undoubtedly have kicked his son and heir. "Be quiet!"

He then once more presented himself to the mysterious strangers

Our readers will have no difficulty in surmising that these two redoubtable personages were no other than our dear friends Captain Hawk and the Black Highwayman.

Before starting from the Skittle Ball, Captain Hawk had quietly removed the "drag" and loosened the linchpin, knowing perfectly well that these operations would sooner or later, when they began to descend the hill, lead to the present result.

They had waited very quietly in a small plantation near the road at the foot of the hill, and were now enjoying themselves immensely with the pompous little major, and in the prospective possession of a handsome windfall, which their circumstances just now especially needed.

Everything had turned out so propitious, and in such exact accordance with their wishes, that our two friends were in the very best of tempers.

Indeed, such was the mellifluous tones in which they spoke, that the major began to feel inclined to bully *them* as well as those of his own party; and even Mrs. Major and the ensign revived as the honied tones of Captain Hawk and his companion fell upon their ears.

The major addressed the former in an imperious tone.

"You were kind enough to inform me just now," he said, "that the reason why my two rascally servants couldn't obey my commands and come to me was, because they were tied to that gate?"

"I did, major. If you look in that direction and take particular notice, you will perceive they *are* tied," remarked the captain, with the utmost suavity.

"Yes—yes! d—n it! I see they are!" the major growled. "You will doubtless then," he continued, "be able to inform me who had the audacity to tie them?"

"Certainly, major," said Captain Hawk, sweetly: "I had the pleasure of tying one."

"And I the other," added Lord Harcliffe.

"Well I never!" exclaimed the major, turning almost purple in the face with indignation. "No—I never did, not even at the siege of—— Ahem!"

He stopped short—he never got any further than "*the siege*"—and then burst out again:

"And my horses?" he raved. "You pair of rascally"—but he thought better of it, and corrected himself with a great deal of stammering and spluttering—"I mean *my pair* of rascally horses! Perhaps you can tell me where they are?"

"I should be sorry to venture upon too decided an opinion," replied Captain Hawk; "but when I cut the traces on this side——"

"And I on the other," dropped in Lord Harcliffe.

"What, you—you cut my traces?"

"Your *horses'* traces, we did," they replied, with perfect coolness.

The major opened his mouth, and his eyes protruded like the optics of an astonished codfish.

"You—you d—d scoundrels!" he at last managed to jerk out.

"Hush—hush, major! Use better language; remember your good lady is within!"

"Good lady be d——"

"Oh, hush! I really must insist! I cannot allow such unparliamentary expressions."

"But where the devil are my horses?" roared the incensed officer.

"I really can't pretend to say," replied Captain Hawk, indifferently; "and I really don't particularly care."

"Nor I," chimed in his lordship.

"All I know of them is, that they were nearly frightened to death; and that when we released them, they trotted off as fast as they could on the road to London," explained Captain Hawk.

"They'll be lost! My beautiful pair of grays that cost me a hundred guineas!" groaned the major.

"Oh no," said the captain, consolingly; "they'll not be lost; they'll be picked up somewhere or other."

"I'll have you both hung for horse stealing, you pair of scoundrels!" shouted the major.

"Oh no, you will not, my dear sir," quietly answered the captain. "Setting two horses at liberty, is not stealing them."

"But it's detaining me on my journey!" exclaimed Major Bombshell. "When you cut the traces, you had a motive—you must have had a motive!"

"We *had* a motive—you are perfectly right—a very strong motive!"

"What was it?"

"To stop *you!*"

"I was certain of it—I knew it from the look of you!"

"I compliment you on your discernment," answered Captain Hawk.

"Oh yes," continued the blustering major, "you can't get over me. I'm an old soldier, not to be deceived."

"Anyone looking in your face, could detect that fact at a glance," further remarked the captain.

"And from the appearance, and remarkable development of your head, which the absence of your wig renders so discernible," added Lord Harcliffe, "I have no doubt you could offer a pretty tolerable guess *why* we stopped you."

This was an awkward question, and the major felt it so.

"What shall I answer?" he reflected. "If I say that I know perfectly well these two rascals are nothing more nor less than a couple of highwaymen, it will imply a perfect consciousness on my part that I am prepared to be robbed as a matter of course—if, on the other hand, I affect utter ignorance of their motives, it will be little better than courting an explanation, which they will doubtless make as practical as possible. I must adopt a middle course."

These thoughts passed through the major's mind in a few seconds.

"Of course," he said, "I understand all this perfectly well—this practical joking, though I must say I think you carry your jests a little too far when you stop the carriage of an old soldier who has lost a limb at the siege of—— Ahem! Never mind—you know you don't frighten me, but the consequences may be very serious to my wife, who is inside, and—and my son Augustus, who, though naturally inheriting the family courage, is of an extremely nervous temperament."

"Oh, major," replied Captain Hawk, speaking purposely in a tone loud enough to reach the ears of the parties alluded to, "Mrs. Major Bombshell and your son may make themselves perfectly easy, as we never wish to alarm *women* or *children*."

The major's lady was very much comforted at this assurance; but the *child* felt himself insulted, and looked fiercely at his mamma, and made a slight demonstration of getting up, but was pulled down again, and consoled himself with muttered threats, in which the words, "satisfaction," "deadly insult," "honour," "family," "washed out," "blood," and "knocking somebody's head off!" were distinctly heard.

However, he managed by a strong effort to restrain his indignation and remain quiet.

Captain Hawk continued:

"In spite of your natural acuteness, you are not right in your supposition as to the cause of our detaining you on your journey. We are both—my friend and myself—practical men—very practical; but in this case we are not joking."

"Not joking?" stammered the major. "But you must be joking: you can't be in earnest!"

"Be kind enough to listen to me, and I will explain," continued the captain.

"Certainly; and be quick about it, for I can feel I'm catching cold in my head."

Here the major sneezed violently several times in confirmation of this fact.

"You are travelling to town, major," Captain Hawk went on. "Your postillion drives at a headlong pace down hill——"

"I'll break his d—d neck, the vil——"

"Hush, major!—no swearing."

"I can't help it! Some infernal Catiline stole the drag!" he roared.

"All the more necessity, major, for cautious driving."

"I admit that. Well—well?"

"This caution is *not* exercised, and, as a natural consequence, when the carriage reaches the bottom of the hill, off come the front wheels, and down you come with a crash."

"Fire and fury! yes, we did!"

"Well, just at that moment, we—my friend and myself—reach the spot: we find the horses kicking and plunging, to the imminent danger of the carriage-panels and the lives and limbs of the parties within."

"Well?"

"To preserve your lives we instantly severed the traces and released the terrified animals, in all probability saving your lives."

"Oh, thank you, gentlemen!—thank you sincerely!" exclaimed Mrs. Major, thrusting out her head in a burst of grateful enthusiasm.

"Keep your head inside, Matilda Jane!" growled the major.

"Nay—nay," interposed Captain Hawk, gallantly, "don't snub your good lady in that way. You are most welcome, my dear madam, to our unworthy services," he added, bowing to the little woman, who felt quite flattered.

"You're two very decent fellahs!" piped Augustus, who was mollified at the great services they had rendered.

"Thank you, my little man, for your good opinion," returned the captain, pleasantly.

The ensign pulled a long face at the "little man," and felt himself again insulted.

"Well," remarked the major, who felt that, perhaps, all things considered, it would be as well to appear a little grateful, "I am willing to admit you saved our lives by cutting the traces; but what did you mean by tying my two servants—though they're a pair of unmitigated ruffians for bringing us into this plight—to that gate, eh?"

The major wound up with a triumphant tone, as though he had proposed a very knotty question.

But Captain Hawk replied, quite readily and coolly:

"I don't know what your opinion may be, major, but I consider that when two fellows have, by their wanton carelessness, destroyed the property and endangered the lives of their master and his family, they ought not to be suffered to go at large."

"You're right, sir!—by guns and trumpets you are, sir! I'll make an example of those reckless villains: I'll lock 'em up! You did quite right to tie 'em up. I'm very much obliged to you indeed! The rascals shall stay where they are till the police come for them!"

The major uttered this with such volubility that he was quite out of breath.

"So, you see," said Captain Hawk, "that after all we have proved your best friends."

"Yes, yes—I see," echoed the major, feeling, however, at the same time a lurking, uncomfortable presentiment that there was something unpleasant still hanging at the tail of all this.

However, he affected to take it all in good faith.

"I wish," said he, "gentlemen, you'd oblige me by riding to the Skittle Ball—it's not more than a mile hence—and telling them to send me a couple of horses and a blacksmith, or we shall be here all night."

"I think it very probable you will be," replied the captain, with extreme frigidity, "as it is utterly impossible for us to go in the direction you wish: you see we are going to town."

"So are we *going*, though when we shall get there, the deuce only knows at this rate!" grumbled the major.

"It's very awkward—very!" ejaculated Captain Hawk, as though he were talking to himself, pressing the hand of his riding-whip against his teeth musingly.

"It is indeed!" joined in Lord Harcliffe, in the same reflective tone—"dangerous too!"

"What's dangerous?" inquired the major, who wondered what they meant—"what's dangerous?"

"Your remaining here all night."

"Oh, I shall not injure anybody!" remarked the major, with magnificent emphasis.

"I quite believe you are incapable of such a thing," responded Lord Harcliffe; "but some one, on the other hand, might injure *you*."

"Injure me—an old soldier? *Me* indeed! Ha, ha! I should like to know who'd injure me!" laughed the major, contemptuously.

"My dear sir," inquired Captain Hawk, in a tone of the greatest concern, "don't you know, then?"

"Ah-tch!—ah-tch!—ah-tch-ah!" sneezed the major. "I know I'm catching cold in my head!" he cried.

"But haven't you heard?" said Lord Harcliffe, excitedly.

"Ah-tch! Heard what?"

"That Captain Hawk and the Black Highwayman are on the road again."

"The rascals!—the marauding, prowling thieves! as I told those—a—I mean—two individuals I encountered today, and whom I strongly suspect to be friends of this Black Hawk and Captain Highwayman. If ever I met them, I'd—a—a——"

"Well, major," said the captain, quietly, "what would you do?"

"I'd—I'd blow out the brains of the pair of 'em, and rid society and the high-road of such rascally—ah-tch!—banditti!" returned the dauntless, sneezing major.

"You're either wandering in your mind, my very dear sir," went on Captain Hawk, calmly, "or else you have a very indistinct idea of the characters of these gentlemen you propose to exterminate."

"I know what I'm talking about, sir," replied the pompous commander; "and what I promise I'll perform!"

"You're a very inflated, deluded, boasting old man, or you'd know you are boasting of a power you do not possess!" answered the captain, sternly. "Either Captain Hawk or the Black Highwayman, whom you appear to hold in such slight estimation, would think no more of chopping you into mincemeat—that is, if you were worth so much trouble—than they would of telling you to 'get out of the road' if you happened to be in their way."

"Oh, pooh!—pooh! And so you think to frighten me with these tales about the blackguards, eh? I suppose you think if they came upon me—here as I am now—they'd try to rob me?"

"Try?"

"Yes; it would only be a 'try:' I have pistols!"

"Pistols?—psha!"

"Loaded pistols!"

"Ha, ha! Loaded fiddlesticks!"

"I'd pepper their jackets!"

"You mean, they'd dust yours!"

"Wait till they try!"

"Take my word for it, you obstinate, inflated old idiot," exclaimed the captain, who was beginning to lose patience with this egotistical old gentleman, "whenever you come in contact with these redoubtable heroes of adventure, they'll not only try, but in spite of you and your pistols into the bargain, they'll strip you of all they require—nay, they'll take your wife into the bargain if they're so disposed."

A sharp little shriek burst from the major's spouse at this announcement.

"You hear," said Captain Hawk, "how the bare prospect of such an event disturbs your good lady; therefore I am resolved when I depart—and I'm sure my friend coincides with me in my determination—to leave you beyond the reach of molestation."

"That's kind, at any rate!" remarked Major B. "How are you going to manage this?" he inquired.

"I'll explain: these gentlemen never stop anyone on the high-road but such persons as are likely to repay them for their trouble."

"Oh!"

"Now, if you had nothing to lose, it is quite plain they could steal nothing, could they?"

"Decidedly not."

"Very well, then; in order to leave you in perfect security from the assaults of the Black Highwayman and Captain Hawk—in order to reduce it to a positive certainty that even should they stop you they will find nothing—it is our intention to clean you out completely ourselves!"

The major at this announcement released his grasp and disappeared instanter, but almost as speedily he reappeared.

"You'll clean me out, will you?" he spluttered.

"You, your worthy wife, and infant son," explained the captain.

"I won't be cleaned out!" cried the corpulent little matron inside the carriage.

"No more will I!" added the infant.

The major when he disappeared did not return empty-handed: he grasped a pistol, which he instantly levelled and discharged at Captain Hawk.

"Take that, you vagabond!" he cried, as he pulled the trigger.

"And you take that!" said the chivalrous Augustus, discharging the fellow-pistol—which he had taken from the pocket in the carriage-door—at Lord Harcliffe through the window.

There was a great clatter and a prodigious odour of gunpowder; but, to the great surprise and horror of both the heroes—Bombshell and Son—instead of two bleeding corpses, or, at least, two desperately-wounded sufferers lying on the ground, gasping for mercy, the two masked horsemen sat very composedly on their respective steeds just as usual, without evincing the slightest discomposure.

It was a miracle they were able to do so, or how the bullets could have passed by and left them scathless.

So the major thought, and so thought major junior.

It was rather a ticklish situation—a very ticklish situation in the major's private opinion.

When people are fired at, they are apt to get indignant and fire in return; and as it happened, they had exhausted their ammunition, and had now only the butt-end of their pistols and their swords as weapons of defence.

Suddenly a clever *ruse* occurred to the major.

"Ha, ha!" he laughed, with an exuberance that was painfully forced, the more so as the rigid silence of the masked horsemen implied anything but a disposition to joke. "Very droll, wasn't it?—ha, ha!—wasn't it, Gus?"

"Oh, very—ah—highly comic!" returned that youth, who was as pale as a ghost, and was quite at a loss to conceive where the drollery was supposed to come in.

"Ha, ha, ha!" laughed the major, desperately—"thought I'd frighten you—ha, ha!—but two brave men like you are—ha, ha!—not to be frightened at *un*loaded pistols—ha, ha!"

Captain Hawk, in reply to this laboured address, quietly took off his hat and pointed to an ominous perforation in the side.

"*Un*loaded pistols do not make holes like that," he said, with peculiar and freezing calmness.

"Nor like this," remarked Lord Harcliffe, pointing as he spoke to a similar rent in his cuff.

Again the father and son were visibly disconcerted.

The entire position was so exceedingly awkward.

At length, however, Captain Hawk, after a long pause, broke the silence.

"You're the most ungrateful man I ever met in my life," he said to the major.

"And the son equals the father," added Lord Harcliffe.

"We offer to preserve your property from spoliation, and in return you fire at us. But having done so, of course you will not complain if we administer the *quid pro quo*."

As he spoke, he and his companion each drew forth a long, bright-barrelled pistol, that made even the gallant major feel cold all down his back, and set the *infant* shaking like a jelly.

"You—you d-don't mean actually to say that you're going to shoot me—I mean *us*?" gasped the rotund officer, whose indomitable courage was beginning to melt.

"Why not?" said Captain Hawk. "Shot for shot is all fair."

"It is the law of justice, duels, and battles," added Lord Harcliffe.

"But we're in a broken-down travelling-carriage," suggested the major, who failed to see the force of the argument.

"Well," continued Captain Hawk, "I've no positive desire to take your worthless lives, therefore hand over all you have that is valuable, and we may be induced to spare you."

The major grunted and grumbled; but the sight of the bright barrels prevailed, and he dropped once more into the carriage.

There was an immediate fumbling in pockets and rummaging for treasures on the part of the inmates of the vehicle.

In a few moments the various articles were collected and passed out of the window to Captain Hawk.

"Is this all?" inquired he, as his eye fell upon three purses, a silver snuffbox, an eye-glass, and a few rings, but failed to perceive the more valuable treasures he knew from ocular demonstration they possessed.

"Everything, I assure you," answered the major, with an inward chuckle, as he reflected how easily he was going to get off.

"You are quite certain everything *is* here?"

"Quite."

"You are sure you have not forgotten anything?" inquired Lord Harcliffe.

"Oh, positive! You have not forgotten anything, have you, Augustus?"

"Oh no, pa—decidedly not; nor ma either, have you, ma?"

"No, my love," faltered Mrs. B.

"I'm afraid you have all very bad memories, or else you are not speaking the truth," said Captain Hawk, rather sternly.

The major hemmed, and tried to look fierce, but failed.

"What has become of your great-great-grandfather's repeater set with brilliants?" inquired the captain, in the same cool, stern, searching tones.

"I haven't got it with me," answered the major, who was growing terribly fidgetty and red in the face.

"Yes, you have," was the stern reply.

"I assure you!" protested the major, displaying the pockets of his vest, which were, of course, empty. "See!"

"Try your boot," suggested the captain, ironically.

"Oho! my boot: you're too ridiculous real——"

"Try it!" exclaimed the highwayman, turning the muzzle of his pistol full in the direction of the officer's head.

This quickly brought him to his senses, and in a very crestfallen manner the dauntless hero dived into his boot, and ruefully fished up the repeater.

"Thank you," said Captain Hawk, laying his hand upon the costly timepiece, and transferring it to his pocket.

"Come, young gentleman," he continued to the ensign, "I'm waiting for your watch."

"I've left it behind me," stammered the gallant youth.

"You mean you've placed it behind you," answered the captain.

This was literally true, as the interesting youth was at that moment sitting on it.

"You remind me of the goose sitting on her golden egg. Come, Mr. Goose, hand it over."

The unhappy goose gave way at this, and ceased sitting immediately, handing over the golden egg to the highwayman.

"And now, madam," said the captain, in a courteous tone to Mrs. Major B., "I must trouble you for the valuable relic you usually wear on your wrist—that bracelet presented by Queen Anne to your ancestral Aunt Deborah."

The lady uttered a pitiful wail.

"My beautiful bracelet!" she cried: "it's worth two hundred guineas at least!"

"I'm delighted to hear it, my dear madam," returned the captain, coolly. "Don't keep me waiting, if you please."

"Oh, give him the trumpery, and have done with it!" growled the major.

Still there was a pause, and the lady fanned herself and began to assume a very crimson hue.

"I can't get at it, Anthony," she cried, in a faint voice. "In order to hide it from these dreadful men, I put it—that is, it dropped down——"

"Where?" shouted the blunt major.

"Oh dear! I think it's got down to——" Here the lady's voice sank to a whisper.

"Well, then, the sooner you get it up the better," was the major's reply to her whispered words.

There was a silence for a few moments, in which there was a considerable amount of rustling of silk heard, and several tugs, as though sundry tapes were being dragged apart.

At length, however, the lost bracelet was produced from some remote portion of her attire that was not immediately perceptible.

The captain bowed as he received it.

"And now," he continued, in the same imperturbable tone he had used throughout, "there is only one thing more I require."

"There's nothing else, you insatiable cormorant!" exclaimed the major, who was growing furious under his losses. "You've got all there is to have."

"Not quite; I'll trouble you for the notes and gold in the pocket at the back of the carriage," said Captain Hawk.

The major, completely floored at this last request, started up on his one leg, bumped his head against the carriage roof, that knocked him down again, and there he lay, with his eyes and mouth open, glaring at the mask of the captain, through the opening in which a pair of dark mischievous orbs appeared to be enjoying his dismay.

"You—you—you're ruining me, you d—d, unconscionable miscreant!" he gasped.

"Sh! sh! Be cool, major—you'll get over it."

"I shall never get over it."

"Oh yes, you will!" said Captain Hawk. "Be kind enough to throw the light of your lantern this way," he remarked to his companion.

Lord Harcliffe did as he was requested, and in a few seconds the contents of the bag were emptied.

This consisted of a pocket-book well stored with bank-notes, and two bags of gold.

"Now I think we shall do," cried Captain Hawk, in a cheerful tone.

"I should think you would—I should indeed! Ha, ha, ha!" laughed the major, in such a drivelling, idiotic manner, that he appeared as though his losses had disordered his brain.

"What's the matter, Anthony?" cried his alarmed spouse.

"Ha, ha, ha! Ho, ho, ho!" he continued.

"He's going mad—your papa's going mad, Augustus!" she shrieked.

"Don't bother me, ma—he's been mad long ago," was the dutiful reply.

But the major continued his unnatural cachinnation without appearing to heed these remarks.

"Ho, ho, ho!" he roared—"you haven't got all! Ha, ha, ha! Isn't there something else you'd like to take?"

"Well," said Lord Harcliffe, looking across to Captain Hawk, "I think this would be a very interesting memento of the gallant major." And as he spoke, he seized the cork leg and drew it out of the window.

"Ha, ha, ha!" roared the temporarily-demented hero. "Stick to it! Hold it tight! You're very welcome! Charge!"

"And now, major," said Captain Hawk, impressively, "take this piece of advice from me—never behave to strangers in a manner unworthy of a gentleman and a soldier—never boast of your courage, nor, when you are travelling, of the quantity of money you have in your carriage. Lastly, accept the united thanks of Captain Hawk and the Black Highwayman for the valuable information you so freely offered them, for the valuable booty you have so kindly handed over to their keeping, and for the hour's amusement you have been the means of affording them. Good night, major! Madam, your servant!"

Waving their hands to the major, and taking off their hats gallantly to the major's spouse, the highwaymen touched their steeds' flanks lightly with their heels, and galloped off, leaving the carriage and its occupants to recover themselves as best they might.

CHAPTER CLXXIX.

CAPTAIN HAWK AND THE BLACK HIGHWAYMAN RESOLVE TO COUNT THEIR SPOILS.—A NOVEL POSITION FOR THE MAJOR'S CORK LEG.—SIR THOMAS WALKER TALKS TOO FAST, AND LOSES A HUNDRED POUNDS.

OUR heroes, who had retained their masks during the above transactions, removed them as they retreated, and allowed the cool evening breeze to fan their flushed and heated faces.

They were evidently in high spirits, and the expression of their countenances was light and buoyant.

"Fortune has indeed smiled upon us," exclaimed Captain Hawk, joyously.

"Perhaps the fickle goddess pities us for our late reverses, and is resolved to atone to her humble servants," suggested Lord Harcliffe.

"Never in my life did I feel more inclined to be grateful at the acquisition of wealth," continued the captain.

"Nor I," acquiesced his lordship. "In times past I have recklessly thrown my gains into my pocket as a matter of course, not even counting my spoil, and utterly heedless how long it was likely to last."

"That proves the truth of the great poet's assertion:

'Sweet are the uses of adversity,
Which, like the toad, ugly and venomous,
Wears yet a precious jewel in its head.'"

By-the-by, talking of jewels," said Lord Harcliffe, "that diamond-framed repeater must be immensely valuable."

"I am sure of it," returned Captain Hawk. "I price it at two hundred guineas, at the very lowest."

"And then the bracelet?"

"Two hundred more; and young Hopeful's watch, about twenty; the rings and other trifles, I suppose, about ten. Altogether they will realise a sum that will be quite a fortune to us at the present crisis."

"And what should you imagine this magnificent and serviceable piece of machinery would fetch?" inquired his lordship, holding forth the renowned cork leg, with its massive riding-boot, which he had hitherto carried under his arm.

Captain Hawk roared with laughter, and Lord Harcliffe joined him.

For a few moments the comicality of the ideas it suggested prevented any reply.

"I think," said Captain Hawk, at length, "this is an unprecedented incident in highway adventures. I can safely affirm I never before eased a traveller of his leg, though I may have frequently assisted him in running away with his own."

"Ha, ha! it will be something for the gallant major to talk about to the longest day he has to live."

"What are you going to do with it?"

"Well, you shall see presently," replied his lordship. "The extraordinary success we have met with to-night has inspired me with a desire for a little harmless, practical joking; and I think what I am about to do will afford you no small amusement, and probably be the means of restoring the leg to its rightful owner."

"A very good idea, whatever it may be," returned Captain Hawk; "especially since it cannot possibly be of the slightest use to us. While I have my own legs safe and sound, I certainly am not ambitious to mount a cork one."

They had now ridden more than a mile from the scene of their late adventure, and had reached a part of the road where on the right a dense body of trees arose, intimating the entrance to a wood.

One of these trees hung over the road, and projected its branches in a very erratic and straggling manner.

They pulled up here as if by mutual consent.

"I am longing to count the gold and notes," remarked Captain Hawk.

"Decidedly," replied his comrade; "and with respect to the latter, they must be converted into cash immediately, since if the numbers are known, a notice will inevitably be sent to the bank the first thing to-morrow morning, and that wouldn't be altogether a lucky event for him who presents them."

"We'll manage it," answered the captain, "somehow."

As he spoke, his eye rested on the dark mass of trees on the right.

After a moment's pause, he said:

"I think at a very short distance from the road, behind those trees, we shall find a glade lighted by the moonbeams, where we can make our necessary calculation."

Lord Harcliffe was at that moment earnestly contemplating a long straggling branch that hung over the road.

He evidently had some ideas respecting it, as he smiled to himself as he looked at it.

"Are you seeking a convenient branch on which to hang yourself, my friend?" inquired Captain Hawk, jestingly.

"Not exactly," returned his comrade, with a laugh. "I never felt in a mood less inclined for the performance of such an operation."

"I thought, perhaps, from the attention you are devoting to that branch over your head, you might have resolved to take your last swing at once, so that you might be certain of dying in prosperous circumstances."

"Oh no!" laughed Lord Harcliffe, merrily; "I have no such idea in my head. You may rest perfectly assured that whatever use I make of this branch, I shall most certainly not hang myself on it."

"I believe you," said the captain.

"Oblige me," his lordship observed, impressively, "by riding forward to the moonlit glade yonder, and I will follow you in a moment."

"Certainly."

Captain Hawk turned Satan's head towards the hedge,

[CAPTAIN HAWK ASTONISHES SIR THOMAS WALKER]

and with a slight whistle and a touch of the heel, the well-trained animal bounded over it as though it had been no more than a rut in the road, and soon disappeared.

Lord Harcliffe remained behind to carry out his little joke.

He drew a piece of paper from his pocket and a small ink-bottle and pen, and with these he traced certain letters on the paper.

What he did further will be shortly related.

When he joined his friend he found his opinion verified.

There was behind the clump of trees a small, snug glade entirely invisible from the road, into which the friendly moon cast her bright clear light.

Here Captain Hawk was busily engaged in counting the gold.

It was speedily performed—so speedily that neither of our heroes would have complained had this agreeable operation lasted double or treble the time it did.

It was discovered that the bags contained exactly three hundred guineas.

The notes took less time than the gold, and amounted to two hundred pounds.

"Five hundred and fifteen pounds," calculated Captain Hawk, "in gold and notes; and estimating the value of our watches and trinkets at four hundred, we may consider ourselves the possessors of nine hundred pounds."

"A very excellent night's work too!" exclaimed Lord Harcliffe. "A run of luck like this for a few months would enable us to retire. Nine hundred pounds!—a good sum!"

"Rather an odd sum though, is it not?" said Captain Hawk.

"Well, nine certainly is an *odd* number."

"Wouldn't it be a crowning triumph if we could pick up another hundred on our way home, and make it a thousand?" suggested the captain.

"We must try," answered his comrade. 'I see no reason why we should not."

'Nor I. Come, then, let us go forward, and resolve, Fortune favouring us, to reach London with a thousand pounds in our pockets."

"Forward, then!"

In a few moments they had reached the point from which they had started, where the straggling tree jutted out across the road.

The moon was partially dimmed by a light cloud passing over her face.

Suddenly Captain Hawk pulled up Satan, and exclaimed, pointing with his finger as he spoke:

"Look there!"

"What is it?" said Lord Harcliffe, innocently, smiling as he glanced at a dark object dangling from the branch.

"Has some one hung themselves in our absence?" inquired his comrade.

"No, surely not."

"Let us approach and see."

The moon being partially veiled, rendered that part of the road somewhat obscure.

However, as they advanced, the luminary burst from the cloud with all its former brightness, so that by the time they reached the spot, Captain Hawk found himself facing the major's highly honourable cork leg.

"What!" he cried, as he quickly perceived from his comrade's hearty laugh that he had been victimised. "Well, this is the first time I ever heard of a cork leg committing suicide."

The paper affixed to the member in question next attracted his attention.

"What's here?" he said, as he read the inscription.

"'STRAYED AWAY!!—*On Thursday evening, a Cork Leg. Anyone discovering the same, and carrying back the wanderer to Bombshell Hall, will be handsomely rewarded from the toe of the proprietor.*'"

This was too much for the gravity of the captain, who burst into a loud laugh, in which Lord Harcliffe joined.

This had hardly died away when the sound of horses' hoofs in the distance fell upon their ears.

"Hark!" cried Captain Hawk, "is there not some one approaching?"

"More than one," returned the Black Highwayman, after listening a moment.

"We shall net the other hundred now, comrade, if we mind what we're about," the captain exultingly exclaimed.

"Let us stand aside, then, behind this clump of trees."

"And the leg?"

"Will still afford us amusement, and serve our purpose into the bargain."

"How so?"

"The travellers, whoever they are, will be sure to stop at so strange and unusual a sight, in order to examine it. We shall then be able to judge who and what they are, and be gratified with the remarks and comments they may make upon it."

"I see."

The sounds of the approaching travellers grew more and more distinct; and Captain Hawk and the Black Highwayman drew their steeds aside, and concealed themselves behind a mass of dense vegetation, from out the midst of which the straggling branch reared itself.

Onward came the riders—two in number—at a brisk trot, when, as Lord Harcliffe had surmised, as they came within a short distance of the dark object dangling right in the centre of the road, they made a sudden stop.

And this not of their own accord, for the strange apparition startled their horses, which shied, and stopped their course with such abruptness that the horsemen were within an ace of being pitched headlong over their heads.

It may be as well to state that the new-comers were no other than Sir Thomas Walker, who had been trying some cases at some miles distance, and after dining with a brother magistrate, was now returning on horseback, accompanied by his groom.

He had passed a pleasant evening with his old crony, who kept excellent wine, of which Sir Thomas had imbibed a considerable quantity, in consequence of which he was in an excellent humour, and not particularly firm in his saddle.

If his groom had not caught him suddenly by the arm when his horse made his abrupt pause, he would infallibly have been dismounted.

The first thing Sir Thomas did after being once more adjusted in his saddle, was to express his opinion that something had startled his steed.

"A hare, doubtless," remarked the justice, "running across the road. Did you see a (hic!) hare, Jaggers?" he inquired of the groom.

"No, your wushup," answered that personage, "it was not a hare running across the road that frightened the horses, but something hanging in the middle."

"Eh—eh?" inquired the justice, pricking up his ears at the word "hanging"—"who's hanging, eh?"

"It's not a body, your wushup—it's a *thing*," explained the discriminating Jaggers.

"What thing, Jaggers (hic!)—what thing?"

"There, your wushup—see!" he answered, pointing as he spoke to the pendant leg that swayed gently to and fro in the evening breeze."

"It's a body!—a human body, undoubtedly!" exclaimed Sir Thomas, in a decided tone—"an unmistakable case of (hic!) *felo de se* on the king's highway!"

"Excuse me, Sir Thomas," the groom ventured to remark, "I don't think——"

"Hold your (hic!) tongue, sir!" snapped the justice, as sharply as a terrier. "What do you know about it? Mind your own business!"

The extinguished Jaggers relapsed into silence, and meditatively nibbled the end of his whip-handle.

The justice had contrived suddenly to work himself into an ill-temper.

"The idea of anyone presuming to commit suicide in the public thoroughfare!" he ejaculated, indignantly. "If I had my way, I'd hang everyone who dared to——"

He made a sudden pause as the idea occurred to him that to hang an offender who had previously hanged himself, was no great punishment.

"Let me see," said he, "who it is. Perhaps I know the rascal."

After several attempts to adjust his spectacles on his magisterial nose, and a considerable deal of hiccupping, he cautioned Jaggers not to interfere in any way, and approached the disputed *object*.

In the bright moonlight, his harsh, crabbed features were distinctly visible, and Captain Hawk immediately recognised them as those of the man whose vindictive malice had gone so far towards condemning him.

A hot flush passed over his cheek as he gazed upon the magistrate, and his hand involuntarily grasped his pistol.

The past seemed in an instant to roll backwards.

He saw the evil-minded guardian of the public peace tampering with his counsel, and buying him off with a heavy bribe; he seemed to stand once more in a felon's dock with the steel handcuffs on his wrists, gazing upon the malicious and triumphant smile of his enemy as he heard his sentence of condemnation; and now that enemy stood within a few yards of him, unsuspicious of his propinquity, entirely at his mercy.

As he gazed, his hand tightened upon the weapon he grasped, and he drew it from his pocket.

Why should he hesitate to revenge himself upon the old miscreant? Why keep back the bullet that would finish the account at once?

Little did the cross-grained magistrate dream who was so near him.

Little did he imagine there were but a few yards between himself and eternity.

There was an ominous click from the hammer of Captain Hawk's pistol, and there is no knowing what might have been the result, had not the evil spell that seemed to bind him been broken by a hand placed lightly upon his wrist.

It was the hand of Lord Harcliffe, who had watched his comrade narrowly for some time, and who divined accurately the emotions that actuated him.

The touch of his friend at once recalled him and restored his better nature.

He perfectly understood without a word being uttered the intention of that gentle arrest, and he felt grateful for it.

"You have in all probability saved that hard-hearted old scoundrel's life," he said to his comrade.

"He is not worth your bullet," answered Lord Harcliffe.

"You are right, my friend, he is not; but the sight of him acted upon my blood like poison. He may thank you that he still lives."

"It strikes me that his life will be more profitable than his death," whispered his lordship. "Let us put on our masks and listen."

This they did immediately.

In the meantime Sir Thomas had carefully and scrutinisingly examined the strange object through his spectacles, but without having arrived at any definite idea as to what it could possibly be.

But as the justice would persist in going as near as he possibly could, and almost boring his nose into the article he was trying to investigate, it was not surprising that he saw nothing; the wonder would have been if he had.

Jaggers, whose closer approach was interdicted, was in a more favourable position, and he speedily discovered what it appeared to be.

The justice, on the contrary, walked round and round the dark object like a cunning old fish sailing about a suspicious lob-worm, which he was half afraid to touch, yet unwilling to relinquish.

His brains were muddled with old port and brandy, and he winked and blinked like an inebriated owl.

He had forgotten the strict injunctions he had given his groom not to "interfere in any way," and now getting into a passion at his own obtuseness, rated him soundly for not offering to assist him.

"Jaggers!" at last he shouted.

"Sir!" shouted Jaggers, who had fallen asleep, and whom his master's hasty summons startled from his slumber. "What's the matter?"

"Matter!" echoed Sir Thomas, in disgust, "I've been wandering round and round this a—(hic!) infernal machine, and all I can make out respecting it is, that it has somewhat the appearance of a boot."

"Your wushup is perfectly right," replied Jaggers, "it is a boot."

"Who in the world can be mad enough to hang his boot there?" inquired the justice.

"There's a leg in the boot, your wushup, I think," said the groom.

"A leg?—why—eh? yes; I think there is—I'm sure there is!" acquiesced the justice, tapping the boot with his knuckles and finding it quite firm and solid.

"Isn't that a bill affixed to it, your wushup?" inquired Jaggers.

"Yes, there is a bill, certainly. What does it say?"

Here, by the assistance of his glasses, the justice managed to decipher the inscription that caused Captain Hawk to laugh so heartily a short time before.

But it did not strike Sir Thomas as being anything to laugh at in the least.

On the contrary, he frowned sternly.

"This is a cork leg, then, after all," he cried: "my friend, Major Bombshell's cork leg, of Bombshell Hall; and this ridiculous notice is the work of some contemptible practical joker. I pass the hall on my way home; it would not be a bad idea to carry the leg thither, and inquire into the truth of this. It seems to me a very extraordinary occurrence."

"Some one must have hung it there," sagely remarked Jaggers.

"That's a very ridiculous remark," returned the justice. "Of course some one hung it there! Cork legs don't usually hang themselves."

"I wonder who it was, your wushup?" humbly remarked Jaggers.

"It might be the handiwork of some of those highway rascals, those land pirates, that I should like to see exterminated—rooted out! Do you know, Jaggers, between ourselves, I thought at one time it might be a trap, a snare, laid by one of these scoundrels."

"A snare!" faltered the groom, looking rather scared, and glancing round with some apprehension.

"Yes, I thought it was just possible that some of these vagabonds might have got scent of the hundred pounds that old fool of a farmer insisted on giving me to get his son acquitted."

"Ee-ee!—*convicted* he meant."

"Be quiet, sir! I took the money, as he would have me do so; but of course I don't want it; I shall give it to the poor, as I think bribery and corruption are terrible in a justice, who ought to be as true as a correct pair of scales."

"Yes, sir. Well, sir—but about the land pirates——"

"Oh, ah!—yes—you mean the highwaymen vagabonds?"

"Y-es, your wushup."

"Well, Jaggers, it struck me that one or more of these scoundrels might have been informed by some means—by the old farmer himself probably—that I was going home with the hundred pounds in my pocket."

"Oh, your wushup, pray don't talk so loud!" exclaimed Jaggers, in a tone of alarm. "How do we know but what some of these rascals—ahem! I mean gentlemen—may overhear us?"

"Have no fear, Jaggers!—have no fear whatever!" enjoined the justice, in a tone of the utmost assurance. "They know me too well to venture within twenty miles of my shadow if there was any other road for them to go."

"Insolent, shallow-headed braggart!" muttered Captain Hawk, between his teeth.

"Didn't I hang that rascal Hawk?" continued the justice.

"Your wushup would have done, only he escaped," corrected Jaggers, with a shudder at the idea of such a formidable robber being at large.

"True, Jaggers—owing to the exertions and connivance of a large body of ruffians, the vagabond *did* escape; but he has never dared to show even the tip of his nose since. No, no! I gave him a fright he'll never forget."

"And I'll give you a fright you'll never forget before I've done with you," thought the captain.

"Besides," added Sir Thomas, "if I travel with a hundred pounds in one pocket, I take care to carry a loaded pistol in the other. But come, we're wasting our time. Just unhook that cork leg, and you can carry it under your arm till we arrive at Bombshell Hall."

Jaggers, not without some apprehension, approached the pendant member, and was about to detach it from the branch, when a deep and commanding voice, proceeding from he knew not where, exclaimed:

"*Leave that leg alone!*"

Jaggers not only did as he was commanded, but pulled his horse back so suddenly that horse and rider nearly fell over together.

"W-w-w-what was that?" stammered the groom, as soon as he recovered his equilibrium.

"Some more of this ridiculous practical joking!" exclaimed the justice, who had heard the captain, and who put on as fierce a tone as possible, in the firm conviction that the sound of his voice was sufficient to appal anything human that might be within hearing.

"Come out, whoever you are!" cried the doughty magistrate; "how dare you countermand my orders? Mine! Do you know who I am?" he shouted, waxing bold from the silence of the unseen speaker; "my name is——"

"Walker!" exclaimed another voice, proceeding from an invisible source.

"No, scoundrel," shouted the indignant justice, "not plain Walker!"

"*Very plain* Walker!" echoed the voice.

"Sir Thomas Walker! I say—baronet and justice of the peace!" he roared, furious at the disrespectful manner in which *somebody*—or rather, as it seemed, *nobody*—was addressing him. "I'll not be trifled with in this manner!" he continued, in a tone of exasperation. "Jaggers, obey me! Pull down that rubbish instantly!"

Jaggers hesitated, and fidgeted in his saddle, but without obeying his master's orders.

"Pull it down this moment," roared the justice, pointing to the cork leg, "or I'll give you six months for aiding and abetting in a conspiracy."

At this terrible threat, the doubly-alarmed Jaggers approached and grasped the leg, and by a vigorous tug tore it from its pendulous position.

"Now then," said the justice, "put it under your arm, and let us ride onwards; we shall not be home till broad daylight."

Jaggers did as he was commanded, and master and man were about to continue their journey, when Captain Hawk and the Black Highwayman, both masked, suddenly rode forth from their place of concealment and confronted them.

The groom shook like an aspen in the extremity of his terror.

The justice, who was of a more iron temperament, and who would have been annoyed at any opposition to his will, even though it had been the devil himself who opposed him, fell back, and reining in his steed, glared at the two highwaymen.

Captain Hawk spoke first.

"I thought I ordered you not to touch that leg!" he said to Jaggers, who felt strongly inclined to drop his armful and make a bolt of it.

However, he reflected that if he did so it was possible that he might be pursued and overtaken, so he answered:

"I heard your order, and should have obeyed it, but my master told me to pull down the leg, and I therefore pulled it down."

"And pray," joined in the angry justice, with more passion than prudence, "by what right do you claim possession of that cork limb, which evidently belongs to Major Bombshell?"

"By what right do you dispute my claim?" returned Captain Hawk.

"Major Bombshell is my friend, and as it is evident he has been despoiled of his limb by some atrocious outrage, I intend to restore it to him," answered the justice, determinately.

"With my permission," said Captain Hawk, with equal determination.

"Without your permission!" answered Sir Thomas, passionately. "I am a justice of the peace, and I ask no man's permission to act in accordance with my duty."

"Your duty will, in the present instance, be in accordance with my will," said the captain, coolly; "and though I detest justices in general, and have an especial loathing for such contemptible judicial impostors as Sir Thomas Walker, still I have no objection to make use of him as my lacquey."

"Your lacquey, you audacious villain! Who are you who dare to stop me on the king's highway with words like these?" roared the furious justice.

"Do you particularly wish to know?"

"I *demand* to know!"

"I am the dearest friend Captain Hawk has in the world."

"So you are the friend, then, of that marauding highwayman, that pest of society, that—that——"

"Man for whose life you thirsted, and whose blood you would have shed upon the scaffold had not a few gallant hearts risked theirs to save him."

"I shall light upon the scoundrel one of these days," the justice continued, "and when I do he may consider his days are numbered."

"Ha, ha! I like to hear you talk; you remind me of the frog in the fable, who wished to swell himself to an ox, and burst in the attempt. Take care you don't burst."

Sir Thomas swelled, and turned pale with rage.

"You insulting villain!" he growled.

"I shall use you for my own convenience," continued the captain, not heeding the justice's ejaculation; "but first I shall rid you of every superfluous weight, which would but encumber you on your journey."

"What do you mean, rascal?"

"Simply that gold is a heavy metal, and that you will travel more expeditiously without the hundred pounds the old farmer gave you to get his son off, than with it; therefore hand it over at once."

Sir Thomas, aghast at this daring command, thrust his hand hastily into his pocket for his pistol.

But the captain anticipated his intentions by riding forward and placing the muzzle of his own weapon to his breast.

"Not *that* pocket, Sir Thomas; but the other," he said, in a peculiarly meaning tone.

The justice seemed inclined to be refractory, but Captain Hawk spoke very decidedly.

"I know you are feeling for your pistol," he said. "But allow me to say, it is not *lead* I want, but *gold*; and I give you due notice that the first glimpse I have, even of the butt-end of your weapon, I shall fire; therefore, beware!"

There was no escape; the justice was too dangerously close to his enemy to admit further parley.

There was a stern determination, too, about the tone of the masked rider that carried conviction with it; besides, there sat his comrade at a few yards' distance, and he also grasped a pistol; so that between the two, there was not the smallest loophole for escape.

"Come, be quick!" cried the captain, peremptorily; "you are detaining my friend and myself, and we are both in a hurry. Cease playing with your pistol, and hand over the hundred!"

Foaming with rage that left him speechless, the justice reluctantly drew forth the canvas bag that contained the gold, which Captain Hawk immediately appropriated; whilst at the same moment, Lord Harcliffe, who had quietly approached the justice on the other side, thrust his hand into his pocket and drew forth the pistol, thus disarming the wasp of his sting.

"Now, then," cried the captain to the trembling Jaggers, who thought his turn was coming next, "get off your horse!"

The groom was off in an instant.

"Take off your bridle!"

The order was obeyed.

Captain Hawk received it from Jaggers, and at once cut away the steel portion, leaving only the leathern reins.

The justice looked on in frowning amazement at what was transpiring, when just as he was wondering what strange act was in the course of performance, he felt his arms suddenly seized from behind.

He had no time to offer any resistance, before the captain passed the rein rapidly underneath, and pinioned him firmly at the elbows.

He then, with a piece of strong cord, confined his arms at the wrists.

Having done this, and Lord Harcliffe having performed a similar operation upon Jaggers, he compelled the incensed but powerless justice to turn round in the saddle, so that he sat facing the tail instead of the head of his horse, a picture of impotent fury.

The groom's steed was started off to gallop wherever it liked; and the bridle of the justice's horse being placed in Jaggers's hand, Captain Hawk buckled the cork leg to Sir Thomas's back, and all was ready for their departure.

The justice looked very crestfallen, and felt particularly contemptible.

"You are at liberty now," said the captain, permissively, "and thank your stars you escape with your life, Sir Thomas. I shall see Captain Hawk face to face in a few hours, and will tell him what a ridiculous figure you cut on a horse whose head is where his tail should be. Now start!"

Lord Harcliffe, as a parting salute, fired the pistol he had just taken from the pocket of the justice, in such close proximity to his horse's ear, that the startled animal started and plunged in a manner that threatened dire consequences to both master and man.

However, by dint of great efforts on the part of Jaggers to avoid pitching on his nose, and of Sir Thomas to maintain his equilibrium, they succeeded in weathering the storm, and gradually disappeared along the road.

Our heroes turned their horses' heads and galloped on gaily towards town.

"We have got the thousand pounds after all!" cried the captain, exultingly, as they dashed along.

CHAPTER CLXXX.

THE JUSTICE AND THE MAJOR BECOME PARTNERS IN AFFLICTION.—THE ENSIGN CHASTISES POMPEY, AND GETS A LIFT FOR HIS TROUBLE.

It took the gallant major some time to recover from the effects of his heavy loss.

It had produced an effect in him which in a woman would have been called hysterical.

He laughed, cried, and bullied alternately.

Mrs. Bombshell tried her restoratives for a considerable time in vain.

At length the concentrated essence of ammonia set the major off into a violent sneezing fit, the shakings of which, following in rapid succession, were of great benefit; and the major eventually came to himself once more.

His chagrin and fury at the recollection of how he had been treated, and what he had lost, were immense.

The only consolation he could arrive at was in reflecting on the indomitable resolution he had shown under these trying circumstances, and in severely commenting on the pusillanimity of his son and heir, whom he was compelled to look upon as an arrant coward unworthy of his profession.

"If it hadn't been for my coolness and courage our lives would have been sacrificed without the least doubt!" he exclaimed; even the check he had just received not being sufficient to prevent his inordinate propensity to boasting.

"We're very much obliged to you, Anthony," sobbed his lady, who was heart-broken at the loss of her bracelet.

"I don't see it," grumbled the ungrateful ensign. "Pa, with all his coolness and courage, as he calls it, let 'em take all there was to take; so what is there to be obliged for?"

"Oh, Gus," exclaimed his sorrowing mamma, "don't talk like that!"

"I tell you what," burst out the major, indignantly, addressing himself to his son and heir: "if you'd had an atom of the family courage in your composition, we could have defied those scoundrels! What could I do without my leg? As it was, didn't I fire at them? Undoubtedly I did!"

"Yes, and missed them," dropped in the ensign. "I fired too, and missed them as well."

"Oh, if I'd only had my leg, I'd have shown them what I'd have done! Hang me if I think they were human after all!"

"I don't," remarked Augustus: "I'm almost certain they must have been vampires, or warlocks, or demons, or something of that sort."

This idea seemed to afford a sort of negative consolation, inasmuch as a man could scarcely be called to account for not being powerful enough to resist the influence of the devil.

"And we are to remain here for the remainder of our existence!" whimpered Mrs. Major. B., piteously.

"We must wait here, I suppose, till somebody comes to take us away," growled the major.

"Couldn't Augustus walk back to the inn and let them know what a plight we're in?" inquired the lady.

"Certainly he could. He shall too!"

The hopeful made a wry face, and was about to venture an expostulation, but his papa quashed it immediately.

"Not a word, sir!" he cried. "Step out at once and—quick march! Or stay!" he added: "first of all untie those two scoundrels from the gate there, and bring them to me, that I may break every bone in their rascally carcasses!"

"Yes, pa!" acquiesced the gallant youth, eagerly, hoping that that pleasing operation would put his contemplated journey out of his father's head.

He accordingly contrived to scramble out by the window and approach the gate where Messrs. Bucks and Pompey, looking like two strange birds nailed to a barn-door, had fallen fast asleep, and were snoring melodiously.

The youth called them, but receiving no reply, hastened to inform the major.

"They're asleep, pa," he said.

"Zounds!" roared the major—"asleep! Fire and fury! I'll soon wake 'em! No, d—n it! I can't stir without my pin! Here, take my rattan and lay it about their lazy bodies. Lay it on strong, d'ye hear?"

"Yes, pa," answered the youth, chuckling as he grasped the major's cane.

The chivalrous ensign approached the unconscious sleepers, and was just about to commence operations, when the sound of approaching steps reached his ears.

He looked down the road apprehensively, but saw nothing, and as the luxury of torturing two individuals, who were utterly incapable of resistance, was too great to be refused, he commenced with the shins of the slumbering Bucks, who roared vociferously, and was under the impression the highwaymen were cutting him in pieces.

Having had his first innings at the groom, he next applied himself—or rather the cane—to Pompey's woolly head.

After he had hammered away for full five minutes, the black began to have an idea something was tickling him.

"D—n de flies!" he muttered, shaking his head and sneezing. "How de beggars bite!"

The motion of his head caused the cane to miss that particular part and allowed it to fall with considerable impetus on his nose, which was a different thing altogether.

"Oh, gorra!—gorra, massa! Murder!" he roared; and lunging out with both legs at once, he caught the amiable Augustus with his heels clean in the chest, and shot him on to his back in the middle of the road, where he lay with the breath nearly shaken out of his body.

The impetus he imparted to himself also was sufficient to burst his bonds, and he accordingly dropped down on the grass, where he sat ejaculating and rubbing his excoriated nose.

He was aroused from this by his companion, Bucks.

"Is that you, Pompey?" he inquired, in a melancholy voice.

"Iss, dat's me," replied Pompey.

"Are you *quite* dead?"

"Gorra! him don' know jess yet till him see."

"Are those highwaymen gone?"

"Him tink him knock one into de moon jess now," answered Pompey.

"Couldn't you untie me?" inquired the groom.

"Him dessay him could," said the black; and applying himself to the rope that restrained his companion's limbs, he speedily set him at liberty.

At the same moment the horse bearing Sir Thomas Walker, pinioned with his face tailwards, and led by the unhappy Jaggers, also pinioned, and holding the rein with great difficulty, came slowly in sight.

"Oh, gorra! what dat?" exclaimed Pompey, glaring at the strange sight.

"What's what?" groaned Bucks, as he extended his cramped limbs.

"Look dere!" ejaculated Pompey, pointing to the back of the approaching magistrate, with the cork leg attached. "By golly! him tink dere's a man ridin' de wrong end up'ards!"

"It isn't the highwaymen coming back, is it?" suggested the groom, apprehensively.

"Highwaymen coming back?" shrieked the prostrate Augustus, who had just recovered his breath, and heard Mr. Bucks's remark. "Where?—where?"

"Dere, massa!" answered Pompey, pointing, delighted at the terror the dauntless one exhibited.

The ensign stayed to hear no more, but clambering up to the top of the carriage with the agility of a monkey, dropped into his mamma's lap, to her inexpressible terror.

"What the devil's the matter now?" roared the major, who had received the heels of his descending offspring on his bald pate.

"They're coming back!" shouted the terrified ensign, making a desperate effort to get under the carriage seat.

"Who?" bawled the major.

"The highwaymen!" responded the youth.

"The devil they are!" exclaimed the persecuted Bombshell, clambering up and thrusting his head out at the top of the vehicle to reconnoitre.

"Be careful, Anthony," cried his spouse—"don't expose yourself!"

"Don't be a fool, ma'am!" he answered, gruffly. "I think we're all exposed enough as it is."

The gallant major looked in vain for the two masked horsemen; he saw nothing like them; but in their place the form of Sir Thomas Walker seated on his horse, with his back towards him, and his elbows and wrists tightly bound.

A similar spectacle also presented itself in the pedestrian, Jaggers.

The major gazed at the strange sight, and became impressed with the idea that the parties were familiar to him.

"Is anybody there?" he inquired, as a preliminary question.

"Yes, sir," answered the afflicted Jaggers, very sadly; "we're here: me and my master."

"What's the matter?" said the major.

"Everything's the matter," answered the groom: "we've been robbed and murdered—a—that is, almost!"

"So have we," replied the major.

"Yes, that we have, indeed!" joined in Mrs. Major B. and the ensign.

"By two terrible men in black masks?"

"Precisely!"

"Bloodthirsty ruffians!"

"With long——"

"Pistols!"

"Very long, and bright barrels?"

"The very same."

"And they robbed me—that is, my master, of a hundred pounds in gold."

"A hundred pounds? That's nothing: the villains robbed me of *five* hundred pounds, besides watches and jewellery!" groaned the major.

"They stole my bracelet!" wept Mrs. B.

"And my ticker!" joined in the ensign.

"And my cork leg!—the d—d cannibals!" wound up the major.

"They tied my master's arms behind him, and mine too!"

"And who is your master?" asked the major at length.

"Sir Thomas Walker, magistrate and justice of the peace."

Here that worshipful gentleman's patience was thoroughly exhausted, and he growled out:

"Will anyone cut these infernal cords, and rid me of this d—d *incubus* at my back?"

The mention of Sir Thomas Walker's name took an evident effect upon the major.

By a prodigious effort he dragged himself and sat on the roof of the carriage.

"What!" he cried, looking down upon the angry minister of law, "is it possible those abandoned villains have dared to molest my friend, Sir Thomas? Why," he added, as his eye fell on the well-known riding-boot that stuck upright in the air at the justice's back, "I declare—yes! surely that's my cork leg!"

"Then, by all that's infernal and uncomfortable, I wish you'd come and take it off my back!" grumbled the justice.

"Certainly! Here," he continued, "Bucks—Pompey, assist Sir Thomas instantly!"

There was an immediate rush on the part of these individuals towards Sir Thomas, who was almost capsized in their eagerness to release him.

At length, however, he was lifted from his saddle, placed on *terra firma*, and his thongs severed by Mr. Bucks's knife, which also performed a similar service for the tortured Jaggers and the major's cork leg.

The first few moments of recovered liberty were spent in sundry stretchings and rubbings, interspersed with much groaning and complaining.

At last, by dint of mutual assistance, they all began to feel their unpleasant sensations decreasing.

The justice called out to Jaggers for a flask that was packed away in the pocket of his saddle.

The flask, which contained brandy, was produced, and the justice, having taken the first pull, handed it to the major, and subsequently to the major's lady and the ensign, who, having drank, threw the flask at Pompey's head, and struck the devoted Jaggers in the eye instead.

But this was a mere trifle to all but the party concerned, who retired to give vent to his feelings behind the carriage.

The major and Sir Thomas had by this time fully recognised each other, and shaken hands as partners in affliction.

"So it seems, major, you have been roughly handled as well as myself to-night," remarked Sir Thomas, in a tone in which a great deal of pent-up irritation was very discernible.

"Roughly handled?" echoed the major, beginning to bubble again at the bare idea; "they've *taken away* my handle—that is, they've stolen my *cork leg*, the rascals!"

"And robbed you into the bargain?"

"Of everything!"

"Have you any idea who they are?"

"A very strong idea, Sir Thomas."

"I happen to know they're friends of that pest of society, Captain Hawk!"

"My dear sir, is that *all* you know?"

"All!—isn't it enough?"

"Not half enough!" returned the major, excitedly; "they're not only *friends* of Captain Hawk, but one of the vagabonds is actually *Captain Hawk himself!*"

"What! do you mean that he's the Captain Hawk that escaped at the foot of the gallows?"

"The very same; and the other ruffian is the Black Highwayman!"

The justice staggered back with surprise, and his cheek grew ghastly with passion.

"Hang me if I didn't fancy I recognised the miscreant's voice!" he exclaimed; "though that he should have had the audacity to stop me, a justice of the peace—nay more, to rob me—is such an unprecedented outrage that I can scarcely conceive it possible."

"It's perfectly true, depend upon it," answered the major. "I've had the misfortune of enduring the society of these villains at the inn where I stopped on my journey."

"I'll indict the house!" shouted Sir Thomas.

"Oh, the landlord hadn't the least suspicion," returned Major Bombshell—"no one had, till I fastened my eyes upon them, and then my suspicions were aroused, and I accused this Captain Hawk to his face."

"And he admitted your suspicions were correct?"

"Not in the least—he denied the accusation *in toto*; but I wasn't to be deceived. I insisted that I was right; and the end of it was, the two vagabonds sneaked away like a couple of guilty curs."

"I see—I see; and the scoundrels waylaid you on the road afterwards?"

"They did—that is, they came upon us just after the carriage broke down, in consequence of the drag being missing. It's my belief the villains stole it on purpose to break all our necks!"

"Quite possible—quite possible!" returned the scowling justice. "Then it was after they left you that they stopped me?"

"Evidently."

"Let them beware—let them beware! this Captain Hawk and this Black Highwayman! I've set my mark upon them; and I swear if ever they come within the reach of my judicial power, I'll show them no mercy!"

"But what is to be done? We can't stay here in the cold hour after hour," said the major, who was getting very sleepy and chilly.

"The best plan will be for me to ride forward to the nearest inn," suggested Sir Thomas.

"That will be the Skittle Ball."

"Ah, yes! where you first met these rascals. They must send you horses and a vehicle to carry you back, and I should advise your staying there for the night. I think I shall stay there also myself; we can then talk the matter over, and determine on the best course to pursue."

"It seems to me that the best course under the present circumstances will be to go to bed as soon as possible," remarked the major, yawning drowsily.

"Perhaps so, for an hour or two."

"Oh dear!" suddenly ejaculated the officer.

"What's the matter?" inquired the justice.

"It has just struck me that, as *two* out of the five hundred the vagabonds robbed me of are in notes; they will be sure to go to the bank the first thing to-morrow morning to change them."

"Decidedly," acquiesced the justice, eagerly; "and if we mind what we're about we shall catch them there."

"What a triumph that would be, wouldn't it?"

"What a boon to the country! But do you know the numbers of the notes?" inquired Sir Thomas.

"Every one of them: trust me!" answered the major.

"Very good, then—nothing can be easier. You must send two of your servants——"

"Yes, Pompey and Bucks will do very well: they

could identify the rascals—you could, couldn't you?" he continued, addressing himself to those two persons.

"I'm rather inclined to think so," replied Bucks, with an expressive shake of the head.

"Him take him oath him *indemnify* de rascals," said Pompey.

"Well, two of them must be sent to the bank early to-morrow morning, with the numbers of the notes, and an express order, which I will enclose, to detain the party or parties presenting them until our arrival, which must be as soon as possible."

"A very excellent arrangement!" said the gratified major. "I have no doubt I shall get everything back."

"I *trust* you may, and that I may be equally fortunate," returned the justice, in a tone that was not altogether free from doubt.

"You don't think there's any chance of a failure, Sir Thomas?" the major inquired, somewhat anxiously.

"There is no certainty in anything, my dear sir," replied the justice, coldly, "and these vagabonds are as slippery as eels. All you have to do is to take care your servants are at the bank before it opens, and caution them to keep out of sight, so as not to excite the highwaymen's suspicions should they—as it is probable they will—be lurking near."

"I'll take care I'll be particularly impressive in my instructions," said the major, "and both Bucks and Pompey know me too well to dare to disobey my orders. Fire and fury! if they did,"—here he blazed up with his former vehemence—"I'd—I'd—— But they won't—they dare not!"

The major looked very comically grand as he uttered this harangue, and glanced at Pompey and the groom to impress them with a due sense of its vital importance, whilst they, on the other hand, appeared to absorb it in meditative silence.

Suddenly a brilliant idea shot through the major's brain.

"I've got it—I've got it!" he cried.

"The bracelet?" inquired Mrs. Major B.

"No, ma'am—no, but something equally bright and sparkling."

"My ring?" suggested Augustus.

"No, sir: an idea!" exclaimed his father.

"Hold it tight, then," murmured the dutiful son, aside: "you don't have one very often."

"Pompey and Bucks shall go in disguise," said the major, emphatically—"in disguise! then all chance of recognition will be utterly impossible."

The major was quite elated at the brilliant suggestion of his own brain, and looked triumphantly at Sir Thomas Walker, who was mounting his horse.

"I shall order them to send you a vehicle from the Skittle Ball," he said to the major. "Jaggers," he called to his groom, "you can follow on foot as fast as you can."

"Thank you!" murmured Jaggers, as his master galloped off.

CHAPTER CLXXXI.

CAPTAIN HAWK AND LORD HARCLIFFE ARRIVE SAFELY AT LONDON.—THE CAPTAIN MEETS A FRIEND OF DICK TURPIN.—THE HIGHWAYMEN HOLD A CABINET COUNCIL, AND DEPART FROM THE ROYAL GEORGE INN FOR IMPORTANT REASONS.

CAPTAIN HAWK and Lord Harcliffe rode on quietly to town, perfectly satisfied with their evening's adventures, and neither encountering nor seeking any new ones.

They could not forbear smiling as they trotted onwards at the peaceable manner in which they were suffered to proceed.

"A few weeks ago, Harcliffe," remarked Captain Hawk, as they neared the metropolis, "we should not have been allowed the luxury of a quiet ride like this."

"No, indeed," answered his lordship, smiling; "if even we could have forced our way as near to town as we are at present, we should have been at the present moment scudding along with, in all probability, half a dozen police-officers at our heels."

"It strikes me we shall soon raise the hue and cry after us again," said Captain Hawk.

"We won't anticipate annoyances," rejoined Lord Harcliffe. "I confess my heart warms as I draw near London, as though I were about to enter a congenial atmosphere. Ah!" he continued, with a sigh, "shall I ever again taste the luxury of which I have drunk so deeply there? Are such brilliant days—such joyous nights—ever to return to me in the future?"

"Why, I declare you are becoming quite wrapt in your reminiscences, and forgetting to notice the faint glimmering of old London's beacon lights that I begin to discern already," said Captain Hawk.

This was sufficient to arouse his comrade, who looked forth eagerly.

"Yes," he said, "in less than an hour we shall be there"

They galloped on for some time in silence, probably occasioned by the recollections that the great city recalled to the minds of each, and which wrapt them in reflection rather than induced conversation. It was only the clattering of their horses' hoofs upon the paved road that aroused them from their reverie.

"Here we are at last!" exclaimed Captain Hawk, waking up suddenly and looking about him.

"Yes, at last!" echoed his companion. "Welcome to London once more!"

"It now becomes a question where we shall lodge to-night," said the captain. "Shall we put up at the first hotel we come to, or shall we seek one of our old haunts, and inquire what is going on in the great Babylon?"

"I think," rejoined Lord Harcliffe, "that until we have cashed the notes it will be as well to keep ourselves very quiet."

"You are right," said Captain Hawk: "we will stay at an hotel as peaceable citizens to-night, at all events."

This point being determined on, they stopped at an old-fashioned but substantial inn in Holborn—one of those hostelries where, from the quantity of stable room, a traveller might be sure of good accommodation not only for himself but his steed.

Here, then, our heroes came to a halt.

As they rode into the yard, several ostlers came running out, each one as he approached being struck with the nobility of the riders and the extraordinary beauty of the animals they bestrode.

Their similarity of colour, and their almost equal symmetry of limb, gave rise to great surprise, and elicited many remarks from the grooms.

"If Dick Turpin had been alive," remarked an old gray-headed ostler, "I shoul a' sworn that one o' them 'orses was Bonnie Black Bess."

"Oh, she broke her 'eart, poor creetur, over 'er trip from London to York; so it can't be 'er; an' as for poor Dick 'imself, he was turned off at York, so it can't be 'im; so that bein' the case, it can't be either," was the rejoinder of the first speaker's companion.

"Well, never mind, let's look to 'em—we're a keepin' them gentlemen waiting. By George!" he added, "what two fine-looking men! I don't know which is the 'ansomest, the 'orses or the riders."

Our heroes had overheard this conversation, and felt inclined to be very friendly towards the old ostler who spoke so pityingly of the gallant Dick and his luckless steed.

"I should like to have half an hour's conversation with that old fellow," said Captain Hawk. "Who knows? he may have been personally acquainted with my friend."

When the grooms led the steeds to their respective stalls, Captain Hawk followed the old man, under the pretext of seeing that his horse was properly lodged.

The old fellow noticed the captain, and gave him the opportunity he desired by starting the subject himself.

"Do you know, sir," he said, "I was just a sayin' to my mate that your 'orse put me in mind of Black Bess—o' course you knew who she was—Bonnie Black Bess?"

"A valuable mare, formerly possessed by Dick Turpin, I believe," answered Captain Hawk.

"That's right, sir," said the old man; "and as your 'orse resembles Bess, I can't 'elp sayin' as you're like her master, Dick."

"In what way am I like him—in stature or feature?" inquired the captain, smiling.

"No, sir, I don't mean in that way, but in the manner in which you look after your horse."

"Indeed!"

"Yes, sir. I used to be ostler at an inn where Captain Dick—he used always to be called captain—used to put up. Lor' love yer, sir, he'd no more a thought of taking any refreshment himself afore seein' as his 'orse was served than he'd a thought a ridin' out o' the stable yard wi'out giving the ostler a guinea to drink his health."

"It's a good sign, I think," said Captain Hawk, "in any man when he attends to the wants of a dumb animal before his own."

"So do I, too, sir. They say 'a good man's merciful to his beast,' an' if this be true, why then, Dick Turpin was a real, good man, for I think he loved Bonnie Bess as dearly as if she'd been his sweetheart."

"You say you knew Dick Turpin?" said Captain Hawk, who was inexpressibly interested in the old man's words.

"Knew him, sir?—ay, that I did indeed!" responded the old man, warmly. "He was the best friend as ever I had," he continued, drawing his hand across his eyes, to wipe away a tear that had started up unbidden at the recollection of the past.

Captain Hawk, too, felt strangely affected at this unexpected touch of feeling, and found some difficulty in restraining his emotion.

It seemed as though the gallant highwayman had risen from his cold grave in the quiet churchyard, and was near them once more.

"And Dick Turpin was a friend to you, you say?" he inquired.

"Ay, sir, that he was! When my old woman lay on a sick-bed in her last illness, and things were going all wrong, and we were going to lose all our few poor little sticks; when Captain Turpin heard of it, he came to see my poor wife, sir, and talked to her as kindly as if he'd a been her own son, an' when he went away he counted down twenty golden guineas on the table; and they paid our debts, and enabled the poor sick woman to close her eyes in peace with a few comforts around her which she'd never 'a had if it hadn't been for him."

"This is not the first time I've heard of Dick's generosity," said Captain Hawk, with moist eyes.

"He was a good friend to the poor," continued the old ostler; "and though he was condemned to die, and did die upon the gallows, I can't help thinking that Heaven didn't find him half as guilty as the world called him."

"Heaven rest his soul!" exclaimed the captain, fervently.

"P'raps *you* knew him, sir?" inquired the old man, with some curiosity.

"I knew enough of him to be quite convinced that all you say of him is perfectly true, and that he was a noble-hearted, generous fellow. Once more, Heaven rest him!"

"Amen!" said the old man, raising his cap.

These words spoken, and this act performed, though only in a stable, was deeply impressive from the earnestness of the actors.

There was no attempt at display: it was the natural outpourings of two hearts, who had loved the dead of whom they spoke, and who paid this tribute to his memory.

Lord Harcliffe, who witnessed this emotion, wiped his eyes as he turned away.

"And now," said Captain Hawk, throwing off the sadness that had stolen over him, "we have had a long journey, and riders as well as steeds require food and rest."

With these words our heroes proceeded to the door of the inn, where they were received by a buxom, comely-looking matron—the landlady—whose pleasant, smiling countenance still retained much of its early beauty.

"We have just been seeing our horses to their stables, and now we must look to you to provide for the wants of their masters," said Captain Hawk, with an answering smile that prepossessed the good lady in his favour immensely.

"I trust, gentlemen," she said, "you will have no reason to complain of the accommodation of the Royal George."

"We feel convinced of that," returned Lord Harcliffe; "and it is for that reason we have come to test its hospitality."

"Of course, gentlemen, you will require a private room?" inquired the landlady.

"Yes, we should prefer it," answered Captain Hawk.

Our heroes were then conducted by a very pretty chambermaid to a substantial, double-bedded room, the very sight of which seemed to invite repose.

The bright red embers of a fire glowed in the grate, and a couple of luxurious arm-chairs stood temptingly on each side of the fireplace.

Lord Harcliffe relieved the young girl who had conducted them of her candlestick, and relieved himself at the same time of a kiss, which did not seem to alarm the pretty domestic in any way, and then, with a sigh of gratification, dropped into the nearest arm-chair.

"This is delicious!" he exclaimed, closing his eyes, and speaking dreamily.

A tap came at the door.

It was the landlady, to know what the travellers would take for dinner.

"Whatever you please, my dear madam," answered Captain Hawk, "and as quickly as possible, as we are both ravenously hungry."

The door closed again, and the captain followed his comrade's example by sinking into the other arm-chair.

There seemed to be a kind of charm about the room and the chairs, since our heroes remained so quiet that anyone looking at them would have reasonably concluded they had fallen asleep.

And no very wrong conclusion either.

At the end of a short interval the door was tapped at again, and dinner announced.

But no answer being returned, the pretty chambermaid became naturally apprehensive, and having essayed a second tap without eliciting any response, she opened the door and peeped in.

Then the cause of the silence at once explained itself. Both the tired occupants of the arm-chairs were fast asleep.

"Oh dear!" exclaimed Charlotte, but in a whisper. "I declare they're both asleep. How handsome they look!" she thought. "Shall I wake them? I think I'd better," she soliloquised; "they must want their dinner, and the water's getting quite cold."

She accordingly—feeling herself entitled to be the most familiar with the gentleman who had kissed her—commenced by shaking Lord Harcliffe very gently. His lordship, who was a light sleeper, responded immediately by opening his eyes and looking at Charlotte.

"What's the matter, my dear?" he inquired, innocently.

"Dinner is ready if you please, sir," said Charlotte.

"Eh?—why, dinner in the middle of the night?"

"It isn't the middle of the night, sir."

"No?—why—certainly, of course it isn't; I'm dreaming!" exclaimed his lordship, now thoroughly aroused. "Here!" he cried, shaking his comrade, "dinner's ready!"

Captain Hawk started up from his doze, and having hastily removed a little of the dust from their locks, hands, and faces, they descended to the apartment where their meal awaited them.

The appearance of this room was as equally prepossessing as that they had just quitted.

The fire burnt cheerfully in the grate, and comfort seemed vividly depicted in every flicker of its dancing light.

The repast was excellent, and so was the wine, not omitting the cigars.

The slight nap they had had before dinner had refreshed them, and they were now in a state of mind thoroughly to enjoy the comfortable quarters in which they were located.

It was after dinner had been cleared, and a fresh decanter of old port placed before them, that Captain Hawk remarked:

"I am thinking about those notes."

"Strange! I was thinking of the same thing."

"To gain the rest and lose *them* would be only a partial triumph."

"True; and yet to lose all by endeavouring to secure two hundred would not be very satisfactory, would it?"

"You mean to imply there may be danger in cashing these notes?"

"Yes."

"This fact has struck me; at the same time, I think by

[CAPTAIN HAWK AND THE BLACK HIGHWAYMAN LAY THEIR SNARE.]

watchfulness on our parts the notes may be changed without any danger whatever."

"What is your idea of proceeding?"

"I am inclined to think the major would probably hasten to town as soon as he could to-morrow to reach the bank before the notes could be converted into cash—that is, if he knows the numbers, which is most likely."

"Yes—well?"

"On the other hand, should the major be unable, either from fatigue or excitement, or any other cause, to perform the journey in time, he would be certain to send a messenger."

"Yes. The question then arises, who would he send?"

"It would undoubtedly be some one who could identify us—his son, perhaps—or his servant."

"And what course do you think they would adopt?"

"They would give information at the bank that the notes had been stolen, and then watch for our approach."

"I see; and of course the moment we entered we should probably find ourselves encompassed on every side."

"I am not quite so apprehensive on that point. I think we might contrive to fight our way out again."

"It is scarcely worth the risk, is it?"

"My dear friend," said Captain Hawk, "our plan must be to do away with the risk."

"How is that possible?"

"We must consider. I feel in a brilliantly reflective humour to-night."

"This bright fire, excellent wine, and these unexceptionable cigars are certainly conducive to the flight of fancy," rejoined Lord Harcliffe.

"We must endeavour to bring down our fanciful flights to the sterner regions of reality. Can you suggest anything?"

"Well," said his lordship, "just now I confess I am not particularly brilliant; but it seems to me the most important fact to arrive at is, whether the major will perform the office of spy himself, or whether he will entrust it to one or more deputies."

"You are perfectly right—that is the all-important point we must endeavour to ascertain; and to do that——"

"I think I foresee another journey."

"Right again, my friend! We must leave this delightful sanctuary—we must for a time bid adieu to this luscious port and these fragrant Havannahs, and go forth once more to endeavour to gain the information we require."

"And to arrive at that, whither do you propose bending our course?"

"I should suggest retracing the path we have just traversed."

"Good; and then——"

"We must take up our position in some spot that will command a view of all travellers that pass."

"I see. We shall be able to recognise the major and any of his family——"

"Or his domestics."

"Or the worshipful Sir Thomas Walker."

"Umph! I do not apprehend *his* presence."

"I, on the contrary, am inclined to think his indignation would stimulate him to greater exertions than all the rest combined."

"But he knows nothing about the loss of the notes."

"I am not so sure of that; he would be sure to pass the broken-down carriage in the road; the major would assuredly detail his losses, and by this time the justice may be as well informed about the notes as we are ourselves.

"Ah!" said Captain Hawk, thoughtfully, "you are right—that did not strike me. But at all events," he continued, with a laugh, "if his *worshipful* does come in sight, I shall take it for granted his errand is hostile to our plans, and effectually prevent his progress. For the rest, I will explain more definitely as we ride along."

It was with something very much resembling a sigh our heroes rose from their comfortable seats.

"'Tis hard to part!" exclaimed Captain Hawk, sentimentally, as he drained his glass. "And now to business."

And with this remark, he quitted the room, followed by his companion.

The landlady looked particularly surprised when our heroes announced their intention of departing; and Charlotte was quite chagrined.

But Captain Hawk consoled the kind hostess with the assurance of their return shortly; and as a further guarantee of this event, he confided his portmanteau to her care, enjoining her to guard it as the apple of her eye.

This receptacle was fastened by a patent lock, and weighed heavy; so much so, that the good lady at once concluded it contained a large sum of money.

Captain Hawk, to quicken the caution of the hostess, spoke vaguely and mysteriously about the Government, and departed eventually, leaving the landlady quite mystified as to who the gentlemen could be, but strongly convinced that they were a pair of very important personages.

In order to quicken this impression, Lord Harcliffe found an opportunity of slipping a guinea into the pretty hand of Charlotte as a reward for awakening them from their slumbers, and Captain Hawk having gallantly saluted the blushing landlady—who, by-the-by, was a widow—the two highwaymen departed to the stables, where they found the old ostler, who quickly brought out their horses.

The captain did not forget to follow Dick Turpin's example, inasmuch as he placed a guinea in the old man's hand, who felt that the glorious bygone days were come back again.

CHAPTER CLXXXII.

THE HIGHWAYMEN PAY A VISIT TO THE COSTUMIER.—THEY PROCURE DISGUISES.—THEY DROP IN AT MR. SNAGSON'S.—AND PROCEED AFTER SUPPER TO LAY THEIR SNARES

It was growing late as our heroes rode out of the stable yard of the Royal George.

"Half-past eleven!" ejaculated Captain Hawk, as the chime of a neighbouring church clock fell upon his ear.

"We shall have, then, plenty of time to follow out our plans," said Lord Harcliffe.

"Decidedly; that is why I was anxious to tear myself from the hospitable quarters we have just quitted."

"It required certainly some resolution, did it not?"

"Undoubtedly it did; but we shall reap the benefits of our self-denial anon, and then when we have achieved our task, we can devote ourselves to ease and enjoyment like soldiers who have fought their battle and won it."

The highwaymen proceeded at a gentle trot till they reached the shop of a costumier, over the front of which the name of "Abrahams' Masquerade and Fancy Dress Warehouse," figured conspicuously.

There was a bal masque at Vauxhall Gardens on that particular evening, so that the shop was still open, much to the satisfaction of our two friends, who had made up their minds to have had to "knock up" the worthy proprietor either from his bed or from his supper.

Summoning a ragged urchin who stood amongst the stragglers who lingered round the doors of the emporium, to catch transient glimpses of the kings, dukes, clowns, and demons, that from time to time were wafted in coaches from the depot of Mr. Abrahams to the gay and festive scene whither they were bound, they consigned their steeds to his charge and entered the shop.

Mr. Abrahams and his assistants were very busy at that particular moment giving the finishing touch to the false ringlets and moustaches of a party of young bloods who were bound for Vauxhall.

"I thay, Abwahamth, you don't call thethe a pair of mouthtathe: one thide'th twithe ath long ath the other!" exclaimed an affected young gentleman in a long flaxen wig, as he looked with an expression of considerable dismay at the appendages alluded to in a glass.

"I'll put 'em all to rightsh in a minit, ma tear," answered the accommodating Jew, who had caught sight of the imposing figures of Captain Hawk and Lord Harcliffe as they pushed open the door.

"Now gentlemensh, vot can I do for you?" he inquired, as he advanced, bowing and smiling and rubbing his hands.

"Oh, we're in no hurry," said Captain Hawk, carelessly; "you can finish these gentlemen first."

Mr. Abrahams, who was very glad of this permission, returned hastily to the anxious youth in the light wig, and with a pair of scissors reduced the exuberant moustache to the same length as its fellow, and by the aid of a little cosmetique twisted it into a curl, with which the wearer condescended to express himself satisfied.

"There," exclaimed the Jew, as he placed a broad-brimmed cavalier hat on his head, "you looksh quite a pictur, you doesh; your own mother wouldn't know you."

The party being now ready to start, a communication was made to the coachman, and amid the cheers of the spectators without, the masqueraders were driven away.

The Jew now turned once more to the highwaymen.

"Now gentlemensh," he said, smiling all over his face, "you vantsh two dresshes of course?"

"You're quite correct, my friend," answered Captain Hawk, "we do."

"Vot kind will you have? Ve've got 'em of all periodsh, from the Conqvest downvardsh. Here'sh a beauty!" continued Mr. A., seizing upon a dark-coloured velvet suit and spreading it open before his visitors. "Dish ish de identical shuit in vich King Charles the First vash beheaded. Vould you like dat?"

"No," replied Captain Hawk, "we do not require fancy dresses."

The Jew's countenance fell.

He imagined, from the appearance of our heroes, nothing less than something regal would suit them, but he did not give up the case as hopeless.

"Yoursh are jusht the kind of figuresh to shuit fancy dresshes," he continued. "Now here," he added, as he pulled down a black velvet trunk suit elaborately ornamented with bugles; "here'sh a 'Amlet's' dressh, vorn by David Garrick; an' 'ere's a Oliver Cromwell'sh——"

"My dear Mr. Abrahams," interrupted Lord Harcliffe, "we neither wish to enact the character of Hamlet, nor to go back to the times of the Commonwealth; the costumes we require are of a much more modern description."

"Ah, yesh—yesh, I shee!" eagerly cried the Jew. "Look here: here'sh a Court shuit vorn by His Grachious Mashesty George the——"

"No, no, that won't do," said Captain Hawk; "we want something of an entirely different description."

"Vell, vot *do* you vant?" asked Mr. Abrahams, whose good humour was rapidly disappearing.

"Something much plainer."

"Ah, someting cheap, I supposhe!" replied the Jew, in a tone of disgust. "Vell, vot ish it?"

"Let us have the uniforms of two English privates in any foot regiment you please; the older and more faded the better."

"Two old uniformsh?" growled the Jew. "Vhy, vot d'ye take me for? I don't keep any such tingsh in my eshtablishment: you ought to go to a rag shop for vot you vantsh. No von comesh here but dem ash can afford to pay."

"And pray, Mr. Abrahams, who told you that *we* could not afford to pay?" inquired Captain Hawk, grandly.

"Oh, certainly, of courshe I—I didn't mean to inshinuate that *you* couldn't," stammered Mr. A., who began to think he had spoken a little prematurely—"in fact, you looksh as if monish vash no object at all."

"It is no object at all," replied the captain, "and we should have been prepared to pay as much for a ragged uniform as for a Court suit. However, as you cannot supply us——"

"Shtop—shtop! I'll see vot I can do!"

"Oh, don't trouble yourself; we'll try the nearest rag shop," said Captain Hawk, taking his friend's arm, and turning on his heel as though about to depart.

"No, don't—don't! I can't bear the idea of two gentlemensh like you going into such plaches—you might catch feversh an' all kindsh of thingsh. Jusht vait a minit: I've jusht recollected I've got some old uniformsh that'll be just the very tingsh you requiresh."

At this entreaty the highwaymen paused, and in a few moments two faded old uniforms were brought out, with caps and belts to match, that were exactly what they wanted.

"There; will those shuit you?" inquired the Jew, anxiously.

"Admirably," said Captain Hawk. "Now, then, a patch for my eye."

This ornament was speedily produced.

"Of courshe you'll dressh here?" said the Jew.

"No," answered Lord Harcliffe.

"Dere'sh excellent accommodation upshtairsh—shoap and clean towelsh if you vantsh to vash," urged Mr. A.

"You're very kind," answered the captain, "but as we washed our faces before we came out, we shall not require the use of your soap or towels. These uniforms we must take away with us. I suppose you will have no objection to that?"

"Certainly not—dat ish, if you paysh the deposhit," answered the Jew, with some apprehension.

"Of course. What is it?"

"The hire of the dresshes, ash they're old, will be only a guinea each, an' the deposhits will be two guineash more," answered the moderate costumier.

"Four guineas in all."

"Shtop; dere'sh the patch for the eye—dat'sh fivo shillingsh: it'sh made of de besht black silk."

"Four pounds nine shillings."

This seemed an odd, uncomfortable sum to Mr. A.

He couldn't bear the idea of missing the other shilling.

"I haven't got change," he said. "Here, you'd better take another black patch for the odd shilling, an' say four poun'sh ten for de lot."

The money being paid, and the things made up into a parcel, our heroes were soon on their way again carrying their accoutrements with them.

They directed their course towards the neighbourhood of St. Giles's.

When they reached this district they threaded their way through some very narrow and questionable thoroughfares, and at length pulled up in front of a dingy court.

Their horses had scarcely stopped when a peculiar whistle was heard proceeding from this confined locality.

"All right," said Captain Hawk—"Charles is there."

The words were hardly out of his mouth when the individual answering to that name came shuffling up the court bearing a lanthorn.

No one, to look at the new-comer, would ever have accused him of bearing such a baptismal title.

Most certainly he had never been christened, and from his appearance it seemed to admit of a doubt whether he had ever been civilized.

However, we must never judge by appearances; and though Charles, as he was called, was short, broad, round-shouldered and frightfully bow-legged, with a head of coarse red hair, like a door-mat, a pair of large ugly ears, and a yawning cavernous mouth that showed a *chevaux de frise* of jagged, discoloured teeth; still, in spite of all these disadvantages, he was by no means the worst of his kind.

As he emerged from the court, the light of his lantern revealed in his undeniably coarse, ugly features a redeeming expression of shrewd good nature, that preserved them from being brutal; and when he spoke, there was a geniality in his tone that was quite inviting.

"Ah, captain!" he said, grinning from ear to ear, and looking quite delighted to see him, "said it was you; never forgets your signal. Coming in?"

"Yes, Charles," returned the captain, shaking the enormous hand that was held up towards him—that is, as much as he could grasp of it.

"Come to stop, captain?"

"For a while."

"That's the sort! I likes company like yours. Who's that with you—a pal?"

"Of course!" answered Captain Hawk, "and more than that: he's not only a pal, but the dearest friend I have in the world."

As he spoke, the captain extended his hand to Lord Harcliffe, who shook it warmly.

"You might introduce a feller, captain," remarked Charles.

"Certainly," answered the captain. "You've heard of him often, both by name and fame: in this gentleman you behold the Black Highwayman!"

"Are it possible!" ejaculated Charles, waddling round to get at his lordship. "Allow me the honour o' shaking yer by th' 'and," he entreated, in a tone of profound respect. "This 'ere's a honour I didn't go for to expec'."

"I'm very glad to make your acquaintance, Charles," said Lord Harcliffe.

"An' I'm werry proud to make yourn!" returned Charles.

This little interchange of ceremonies occupied but a few moments.

Not that there was anything to fear.

All was perfectly quiet—a score or two of throats might have been cut in that street, and no one much the wiser.

At that period there were no tight-limbed, helmet-tipped policemen, with their staves and dark lanterns, on their several beats in gloomy localities.

The public safety was then attended to by superannuated old watchmen, who did not poke their noses intrusively into suspicious localities a jot further than they could easily draw them back again, and who, in case of a row, very much preferred springing their rattles at the end of a dark, narrow street, than venturing their ancient persons into its recesses.

However, both Captain Hawk and Lord Harcliffe were very hungry, and though the locality in which they found themselves did not appear to promise much, still it was another instance of the folly of judging by externals.

"You'd better get down, gentlemen, and I'll bring the 'orses forrards," said Charles. "There's a prime ham an' a couple o' chickens jest done to a turn, an' I know the guv'nor 'll be glad to see you."

The highwaymen were off their horses in less than no time.

"P'r'aps you'll be good enough to take the lantern whilst I bring the animals arter; prime 'uns they is too!" exclaimed Charles, admiringly.

Captain Hawk readily accepted the proffered light, and led the way, accompanied by Lord Harcliffe, and followed by Charles leading Satan and Phantom.

There was no thoroughfare through this court, which was short and narrow, and which appeared for some little distance to have walls on either side, and no houses; but these came presently.

At the last of the row, Captain Hawk stopped.

Pressing his hand against a small brass plate at one side of the door, a bell was heard to ring faintly within, and almost immediately a click was heard, and the door opened, revealing the features of the proprietor and his wife, who stood in the passage, offering a smiling welcome to the visitors.

Mr. and Mrs. Snagson lived in this mansion—which turned out to be very substantial—in a manner that was not immediately apparent.

It was a private boarding-house ostensibly—some called it a family hotel; in fact, there was an announcement to that effect on a brass plate on the door; but whether from the remoteness and obscureness of the locality, or from its apparently insalubrious surroundings, or some other tangible reason, it was a remarkable fact that no families ever came within a mile of it, which rendered the comfort and prosperity of Mr. and Mrs. Snagson under such circumstances equally remarkable, and perhaps a little suspicious.

However, no one took any notice, or asked impertinent questions.

Mr. Snagson paid his rent and his taxes, and drank the "King's health, God bless him!" and considered himself, and was generally considered, a loyal subject.

The only clue to this mystery was that at certain times—that is, usually before it was light, or after it was dark—sundry gallant-looking, cavalier-like figures, would quietly come and go, gliding like shadows.

Some of these gentlemanly night visitants had been known to remain guests at Snagson's for a fortnight or three weeks at a time.

Snagson had been also known when these gentlemen were short of coin, or otherwise hard up—as what gentlemen are not occasionally?—to lend them money at a trifling interest—say, twenty per cent.; nay, more, he would purchase at a reasonable rate—which meant about one-third of their value—watches, rings, bracelets, or any description of jewellery that were offered him, without making any fuss about it, or asking any embarrassing questions as to where the said jewellery had been obtained.

This slight explanation may help to account for the substantial position of Mr. Snagson, and how it came to pass that he prospered under such seemingly unpromising circumstances.

It will also explain why Captain Hawk should have paid the hotel a visit on this particular night.

"Welcome—welcome, captain!" exclaimed the host and hostess together, as the highwaymen entered. "I do believe you smelt the ham and chicken," added Mrs. S.

Captain Hawk smiled, and introduced his friend, Lord Harcliffe; and this done, the four sat down to supper, to which they individually and collectively did ample justice.

Everything, even to the wine, was of the best quality; and it may be added the best price—in fact, rather better than the best—was charged for the *Snagson luxuries* and invariably paid unhesitatingly by the consumers.

The highwaymen, having satisfied their appetites, rose from the table.

They had, during supper, explained their plan of action to their hosts, and the time had now come to commence operations.

These did not occupy any great length of time, and in about an hour from the time when they had stopped at the end of the court leading to Snagson's, a small cart, drawn by one horse, might have been seen emerging from the same avenue, driven by Charles, and containing Captain Hawk and Lord Harcliffe, both disguised in the uniforms supplied by Mr. Abrahams.

This cart progressed in the exact road by which they had that night journeyed towards London.

When they had arrived at a certain distance, they stopped, and the two soldiers alighting from the cart, the vehicle once more turned towards town.

"I s'pose yer won't be very long, captain, afore yer gets back?" Charles asked, preparatory to making a start.

"I think not," returned the captain; "though *how* long, it is impossible to say. At all events, we shall return as quickly as possible, and shall depend upon your being on the watch. Listen for the signal as we approach."

"All right, captain," answered Charles. And waving his large hand, he drove off.

CHAPTER CLXXXIII.

MESSRS. BUCKS AND POMPEY FIND TWO POOR SOLDIERS. —THEY RECOUNT THEIR MISFORTUNES —AND RECEIVE SOME INFORMATION IN RETURN.—THE DOMESTICS ACCEPT AN OFFER TO BREAKFAST WITH THE SOLDIERS' GRANDMOTHER.—A PLEASING PROSPECT! HOT ROLLS AND COFFEE.

It was a very snug, retired spot where Captain Hawk and his comrade were standing; and it had this advantage: that anyone coming to town must, of necessity pass that way, so that they would have a full opportunity of reconnoitring all comers.

The moon, too, was still bright, and everything favourable to investigation.

All was perfectly still, as through the silence broke the voice of a distant church clock, kindly informing our friends that it was two o'clock.

"Do you know, Harcliffe," said Captain Hawk, "I don't remember ever feeling more anxious in my life for the success of an enterprise than I do now."

"I feel as though we should succeed," exclaimed Lord Harcliffe.

"We must—we *will* succeed!" echoed the captain, with enthusiasm; "and that we may, it will be as well to put the finishing touch to our disguises."

"Ay, true," replied his lordship. "The actors are perfect in their parts, and ready dressed; but they want '*making up*.'"

"It will not take long to do that," said his comrade, who at once commenced that operation.

It was a very simple one.

First, he passed a sponge, dipped in a liquid of a creamy colour, over his own and his companion's face.

This dried in a few moments, and then being lightly wiped with a handkerchief, left each of their countenances of a ghastly yellowish hue.

Anyone would have thought they had just been recovering from an attack of yellow jaundice.

"Now then," said the captain, "I'm going to tie myself up."

Lord Harcliffe smiled, and watched his comrade, who, folding a piece of white linen, fastened it round his face over his head and under his jaws.

He then placed the black patch over one of his eyes.

His lordship could not refrain a hearty laugh at the great transformation he had effected in a few moments in his personal appearance.

"Now, Harcliffe, I must disguise you," the captain said.

"I am ready," answered his lordship.

A little powder applied to his hair, a little chalk to his eyebrows, and a few artistic touches with a pencil, made the Black Highwayman look quite another person, and twenty years older than he really was.

"Now I have only to deprive myself of my arm, and I shall be perfectly ready," said the captain.

In order to effect this, he unbuttoned the soldier's coat he wore, and, slipping his arm out of one of the sleeves, placed it straight down by his side, whilst Lord Harcliffe rebuttoned the coat, leaving the arm empty.

The vacant sleeve was then fastened to one of the breast buttons, and the disguises were complete.

Captain Hawk and Lord Harcliffe existed no longer.

They were transformed into two invalid disbanded soldiers.

"Now I think we may safely defy recognition," said the captain, with a smile which, under the coating of wash on his face, looked ghastly.

"Ay," answered Lord Harcliffe, "there's not an officer in the force would recognise us at present."

"A very pleasing reflection that," said his companion.

Their outward preparations being completed, they passed their time in inventing a little programme of the tale they were to relate to those who should pass them.

This occupied some little space, and by the time their rehearsal was finished the moon had waned considerably, and the light was assuming that diminished brilliance, and gradually fading into that pale cold aspect, that heralds the coming on of early dawn.

The highwaymen began to grow chilly, and not only chilly but drowsy.

But sleep was not to be thought of.

"I think," remarked Captain Hawk, "that a couple of poor invalids like ourselves need a little something stimulating to enable us to endure this chill morning air."

With these words he drew forth a small flask of brandy and passed it to his companion, who, having taken a very tolerable sip for an invalid, returned it to the captain, who followed his example.

At this moment, the sound of an approaching vehicle caught their ears.

But before attending to the coming travellers, let us for a few moments return to the major and his party.

During the time that had elapsed since we left them, a vehicle had been despatched, and they had been conveyed to the Skittle Ball, where, with Sir Thomas Walker, they were staying for the night.

A blacksmith had been despatched to the damaged vehicle; and the wheels having been restored to their proper places, it was brought back to the inn, like a captured runaway.

The horses also, who had trotted on till they were tired, had turned into a field near the roadside, for a feed, where they were found by the owner, who recognised the major's grays, and who, after making certain inquiries, discovered the whereabouts of the major himself, brought back the arrant steeds, and claimed compensation for his trouble, so that altogether it was a decidedly expensive night for the gallant officer.

He, however, cheered by the company of Sir Thomas Walker, and further comforted by several strong glasses of Timothy Bunker's brandy-and-water, became more and more impressed with the idea of sending his groom and footman—both disguised—on to London to keep strict watch at the bank from an early hour.

There they were to remain as much out of sight as possible.

One, if not both of the highwaymen, would be sure to arrive as soon as the bank opened; they—the watchers—were then to follow the depredators into the interior, and on their presenting the notes, to accuse them of the robbery.

This plan appeared very feasible, but Sir Thomas Walker added to it his proposition, which was that Messrs. Bucks and Pompey were to take a note from him to the Inspector of Police, at Bow Street, who would send with them a select body of officers, and thus render the escape of the highwaymen impossible.

As this proposal seemed to render assurance doubly sure, nothing could be said against it.

Accordingly the groom and footman, who were enjoying themselves in the parlour with the landlord and a few visitors, were summoned into the presence of the justice and the major, and informed of the responsible task that was about to be entrusted to them.

Their chagrin may be easily imagined when they heard that instead of a good night's rest, they were about to engage in a lonely drive, perhaps to encounter fresh perils on the road.

Disguised too! Pompey was highly indignant when he understood he was to represent Tom Bucks's better half: that is, he gave vent to his indignation as soon as he got outside the door.

"Nebber!" he protested to Tom Bucks—"him nebber wear de petticoats for nobody—not even for do major; him see him an' him ole cork leg d—n fuss, an' den him won't!"

This was all very well behind the major's back, but when, after much deliberation and research, female attire to the extent of dress, shawl, petticoats, bonnet and cap, were collected, and Pompey ordered to put them on immediately by the major himself, in an authoritative tone, the lion became a lamb, and he obeyed very submissively.

Mr. Thomas Bucks was provided with the only available disguise, which happened to be a Quaker's suit and a broad-brimmed hat.

When they were completely equipped, they were ushered into the presence of the justice and the major to receive their final instructions.

Both these potent personages, who were in what might be called a state of *diluted cognac*, expressed themselves satisfied with their appearance.

A further promise of a reward if they performed their mission successfully, and a bumper of brandy each, sent them off in tolerable spirits.

A chaise-cart had been provided, and in this they mounted; and having been supplied with some creature comforts in the shape of bread and cheese, and ale in a stone bottle, they drove off.

The justice and the major, it was arranged between themselves, were to start for town early in the morning, where the former was to seek an interview at once with Sir Jekyl Judd, the sitting magistrate at Bow Street, and urge the strongest measures against the daring breakers of the laws, Captain Hawk and the Black Highwayman.

The more they talked the more they drank, and the more they drank the more determined they became to protect their country, and the constitution, and root out the highwaymen from the land.

They worked themselves up to a state of ardent loyalty, sang "God save the King" in several keys at the same time, vowed eternal friendship, and finally fell off their chairs and were carried off to bed *dead drunk*.

* * * * * * *

The countenances of the highwaymen brightened considerably as the sound of the approaching wheels drew nearer and nearer.

"Is it they?" whispered Lord Harcliffe.

"We must be prepared in case it should be," answered Captain Hawk; "so now for a pathetic tableau. You will support me on your arm, and remember our *melancholy* history."

So saying, the captain threw himself back in a debilitated manner, keeping at the same time his eye on the advancing vehicle, which had just come in sight.

At first he was rather puzzled as to who it might be, since both the occupants of the chaise presented such a strange appearance.

Mr. Bucks did not loom out strongly in the distance under his broad-brimmed Quaker's hat, which extinguished him; and Pompey—or rather Mrs. Bucks, as we shall call her for the present—was equally undiscernible from the fact of her being occupied with the ale-bottle, which she was applying to her mouth when she came in sight, and which she held there so long that it appeared like a fixture.

At length, however, the bottle was removed, and the round, black face at once informed the keen glance of Captain Hawk who it was that was approaching.

It needed but a single thought from one so fertile in expedients as himself to tell him that the parties advancing were disguised; for what purpose he was yet to ascertain.

The horse, who seemed to belong to that order of the brute creation in which resignation and a fixed determination never to go beyond a certain pace under any circumstances seemed to be the prominent characteristics, came jogging along, much to the disgust of Mr. Bucks, who laboured very much with the whip, and used frequently very *un*-Quakerlike expressions with reference to the eyes and limbs of the said animal.

The slow pace at which they were travelling enabled them to see everything they approached some distance before they arrived at it.

Consequently the figures of the two soldiers were forced upon their attention ere they could make up their minds what or who they were.

"Gorra! what dat?" said Mrs. Bucks, apprehensively.

"What?" inquired Mr. Bucks.

"Sometink red at de side ob de road," replied Mrs. B.

"So there is," said Mr. Bucks, dubiously. "What is it?"

"Him don' know," answered the lady, forgetting her sex for a moment. "Um look like sometink, anyhow."

Mr. Bucks therefore checked the already slow pace of the animal that drew them to a walk, and as they drew nearer the feelings of both were greatly relieved at finding that the *something red* was nothing more formidable than a poor-looking, dusty soldier, supporting his comrade on his arm.

They stopped altogether as they reached the spot where the soldier was lying at the side of the road.

"Hallo!" cried Mr. Bucks—"what's the matter?"

He spoke in a bold, bluff manner, as he addressed only a couple of poor sick soldiers.

A moan from the captain was the only reply.

"Golly, Massa Bucks," whispered his sable partner, "you forgettin' you're a Quaker."

"So I am," said Mr. Bucks, in a self-reproving tone; and then, as if to atone for his forgetfulness, he burst out:

"What aileth thee, my friend?" in a more Quaker-like fashion.

"Oh—oh—oh!" groaned Captain Hawk.

"Oh—oh—oh!" echoed Lord Harcliffe.

And then they uttered a long "Oh!" both together.

"What the devil's the——"

A dig in the ribs from Mrs. B.'s elbow checked him, and he said:

"What are you 'Oh, ohing' about, friends?"

"We've been robbed!" cried Lord Harcliffe, piteously.

"Robbed?" echoed Mr. B. and Pompey.

"Alas! yes—by two ruffians in black masks and riding on black horses," groaned his lordship.

"Oh, gorra, gorra!" murmured Mrs. Bucks, aside.

"These scoundrels stopped us. We of course resisted; but they were too strong for two poor invalids like us, and we got the worst of it. I'm covered with bruises, and my poor brother here is almost dead."

"Oh, golly!" exclaimed Mrs. B. "Did 'em knock him broder's eye out?"

This remark was of course suggested by the black patch.

"No," answered Lord Harcliffe—"that was knocked out before."

The unfortunate soldier with the deficient optic applied his hand to his patch and groaned.

"Wid a cannon ball?" inquired the black lady in the chaise, sympathetically.

"No; with the butt-end of a musket," the wounded man explained, faintly.

"Gorra! 'em poke de gun in him eye!" exclaimed the dark woman. "Here," she continued, "jess catch 'ole o' dis." As she spoke, she held forth the stone ale-bottle.

"What's that?" inquired Lord Harcliffe.

"Dat's prime ale. Hab a drink," replied Mrs. B.

"No, thank you," returned his lordship, with a shudder. "Our state of health is such that we daren't venture to drink anything so strong."

"So thee hast been to the wars, hast thee?" Mr. Bucks inquired, addressing himself to the soldier with the patch over his eye.

"Yes, Mr. Quaker," answered Captain Hawk; "we went out to South America to fight the Spaniards under Admiral Vernon; there we caught the yellow fever——"

"Golly! 'em do look yeller, don't dey?" remarked Mrs. B.

"And then when we came home, we were discharged as sick and incapable of duty."

"Him mean to say it d—n shame to leave two poor debbil——"

"Hush—hush! Verily thou dost forget thyself, Susannah!" exclaimed Mr. Bucks, reprovingly, to his better-half.

"Me know me berry wrong to use sich langige; but me feel *indigent* at de way dey treat de sojers dat fight an' get dere eye poke out for de good of dere country!" returned Mrs. B.

"Ah yes!" said Captain Hawk, mournfully, "it's too true! Our country gets all it can out of us, and then leaves us to starve or die in a ditch."

"Here—don't starve," cried the sympathetic Mrs. B., diving down to the bottom of the cart, and bringing up the half of a loaf, which she precipitated eagerly into the lap of the wounded soldier; "eat dat loaf."

"I've no appetite," murmured he; "I've gone without too long, and so has my brother."

"If thou canst not eat it, friend, I'll trouble thee to pass it back again," said the Quaker; "we shall find it acceptable."

Lord Harcliffe returned the loaf.

"Are you going to town?" faintly inquired Captain Hawk.

"Yes, we are indeed. And verily we must be starting; the business we are on is of the utmost importance," answered Mr. B.

"We were going there, but the injuries we have received, have so crippled me, that I couldn't stand, I'm sure," groaned the captain.

"Dey don't look as though dey'd got a leg between de pair ob 'em," remarked Mrs. B., reflectively.

"So thee was going to London, was thee?" inquired Tom Bucks, struggling manfully with the Quaker dialect.

"Yes," was the mournful reply. "Our poor old grandmother will be expecting us; she'll have the coffee and hot rolls all ready, and we not there to eat 'em. Oh, oh!"

"Poor ole creetur!" observed Mrs. Bucks, in a tone of regret. "What a pity lose all de coffee an' de hot rolls."

"Where does thy grandmother live, friends?" inquired Mr. B.

"Daffodil Court, Bloomsbury," said the captain, faintly.

"I did think, my friend," suggested the Quaker, "that we might call on your grandmother, and tell her what hath befallen thee."

"An' den p'r'aps 'em might 'elp de ole lady eat de rolls, and drink de coffee," whispered the considerate Susannah; "we can't abear waste."

"But that's not the worst," continued the captain, in a doleful voice.

"What is de worst?" inquired Mrs. B.

"Why, we'd saved up twenty pounds between us for the poor old woman, and those rascals in the black masks have robbed us of every farthing! Oh, oh!"

"Golly!" whispered Mrs. B. to her spouse. "'Em seem to be in de same state as ourselves."

"Yes," returned Mr. B., "so it seems. Well, my friends," he continued, "you may comfort yourselves you're not the only persons these scoundrels have assaulted to-night."

"No, d—n if 'em are! Dey 'saulted us an' de major: dey tie us up to de gate, an' dey steal de major's cork leg. Yah, yah, yah!"

A sharp dig in the ribs reminded the gentle Susannah that she was forgetting her assumed character.

The wounded soldier, too, appeared to notice this, for he said:

"Excuse me, but you seem to me to change every few minutes."

Mr. and Mrs. B. nudged one another.

"At one time you speak like a Quaker, and at another like an ordinary person. Then, you, ma'am, at one moment speak like a woman, and now you speak like a man."

"So him am a man!" exclaimed Pompey, with energy.

"And that gentleman with the broad-brimmed hat isn't a Quaker, is he?" inquired Captain Hawk, innocently.

"Not a bit of it!" answered the assumed follower of William Penn.

"So I thought," said the soldier.

"No; him not a Quaker: him Massa Thomas Bucks; an' me Pompey Snowball. An' now de cat's out o' de bag," exclaimed the black, much relieved at being delivered from the burden of the secret, and taking a long swig at the ale-bottle, in which feat Mr. Bucks joined.

"And are you relations of the major?" asked Captain Hawk, with well-assumed simplicity.

"Golly, no!" answered Pompey. "I'm de major's footman."

"And I'm the major's groom," joined in Mr. Bucks.

"And you say your master has been robbed to-night?"

"Yes; by the same two masked men as robbed you."

"What did they take?"

"Everytink dey could find, de greedy debbils!" remarked Pompey.

"Three hundred pounds in gold, and two hundred pounds in notes," said Mr. Bucks, going into the matter more definitely.

"Dear, dear! What a sum!" exclaimed the one-eyed soldier, shaking his head sympathetically.

"To tell you the truth," continued Mr. Bucks, "it's about the notes we're going to town."

"Oh, indeed!"

"Yes. You see, of course stolen notes is no good to a thief, unless they're cashed, because as soon as information is given at the bank of the numbers, away goes all chance of their being changed."

"Certainly. And does the major know the numbers?"

"Every one of 'em!"

"Oh, it's always a good precaution to take the numbers of your notes."

"And what do you think we've got to do?"

"I'm sure I don't know—unless it is, that you're to try and stop the notes from being changed into gold," answered Captain Hawk.

"That's just what we *are* to do," said Mr. Bucks. "And," he added, in a highly confident tone, "between ourselves, we not only mean to *try*, but we mean to floor the vagabonds like a pair of skittle-balls! Don't we, Pompey?"

"Golly! 'em jess do!" replied the black.

"I shouldn't like to be in their shoes," returned Captain Hawk, apprehensively.

"I should think you wouldn't! You'd have to look out for your toes, if you was," answered Mr. Bucks, with a knowing jerk of the head.

"You seem two such clever fellows," continued the captain, "these highwaymen won't have a chance with you."

"Not they. They little guess what's in store for them!"

"But you didn't tell us what you were going to do."

"Well, I've got a letter from Sir Thomas Walker. I s'pose you don't know Sir Thomas Walker?"

"No."

"He's a justice; and these rascals robbed him as well. Fancy robbing a justice!"

"Ah, indeed! What daring chaps they must be to rob a justice! Well I never!"

"An' dey not only rob him, but dey tie him arms behind him, an' stick him in him saddle, wid him nose to de 'orse's tail, and massa's cork leg hanging to him back! Yah, yah, yah!" roared Pompey, who thought this was an excellent joke.

"Wonderful!" exclaimed the captain. "And you've got a letter from Sir Thomas, you say?"

"Yes, to the Inspector of Police, at Bow Street. That's where we're to go directly we get to town."

"Yes. Well?"

"Well, then, we're to give him the note, and——"

"Den de 'spector read the note," continued Pompey, anxious to put in a word.

"I suppose so," added the captain. "And after that?"

"After that, he'll pick out a body of the best men in the force, and we shall go to the Bank of England very early—before it opens."

"I see. And the officers of course will go with you?"

"Certainly."

"Den we're to hide ourselves round de corner, an' keep out ob sight," continued Pompey.

"He means," resumed Mr. Bucks, in an explanatory manner, "that the officers will keep out of sight, while we in our disguises keep watch at a distance."

"Exactly—I understand."

"Then the moment either of the two rascals appears, we know what to do."

"Oh! then you know them by sight?"

"As well as I know my own top-boots."

"Ah! then there's not the slightest chance of their escape."

"Not the slightest. The moment either of them enters the bank——"

"You follow them. I see! What a capital plan!"

"Tremendous, isn't it?"

"Splendid!"

"Then they go up to the counter, and the moment they present the notes to the clerk, I taps my gentleman on the shoulder, an' says, in a voice of thunder:

"'*Them notes is stolen!*'"

"Then of course the accused will make a rush to get away."

"O' course! And then they'll run slap into the arms o' th' officers, as'll be waiting for 'em at the door. Now, if that ain't a plan as ought to be recorded in th' 'istory of England, nothing ought!"

Mr. Bucks had wound himself up to such a pitch of intensity that he already fancied he held those he sought in his grasp.

"You see," he continued, triumphantly, "it's quite impossible they can escape. We shall catch 'em as sure as they're alive!"

"I wish you could get back our twenty pounds," said Captain Hawk, in a doleful tone.

"Ah!" sighed Lord Harcliffe, with equal sadness.

"Didn't you say something about your grandmother?" inquired the groom.

"Ah yes!" sighed the soldier. "Poor granny expects us, and there she'll be, waiting and waiting, as I said before, and the coffee and hot rolls all getting cold, and no one there to help her eat 'em."

"Couldn't your grandfather lend a hand?" inquired Mr. Bucks.

"He'll never eat hot rolls any more—he's dead."

"Him don' like de idea ob de breakfast going begging," remarked Pompey, regretfully.

"Well, then, look'ee here," said Mr. Bucks, as with a sudden thought. "One good turn deserves another: suppose we give you two"—meaning the soldiers—"a lift to town——"

"Or s'pose we take 'em right slap to deir gran'moder's?" suggested Pompey.

"That's what I was going to say," continued Mr. B. "Then we could lend our assistance in getting rid of the coffee, et cætera, and then we'd try an' get back your twenty pounds."

The two poor fellows seemed too overpowered with gratitude to speak.

At last, however, the one with the patch murmured forth his acquiescence.

"Poor granny will be so—so much obliged to you for helping us: she—she's such a dear old woman!"

"Come, then," said Mr. B., "we'll consider that settled. But how are we to get you into the cart? Can you walk?"

"I don't know till I try," answered the captain.

"Lean on me, brother," said Lord Harcliffe.

With great apparent difficulty, the fictitious soldier managed to rise from his sitting posture.

"Poor Peter!—how weak he is!" murmured his brother.

"Jess hoist him up here!" cried Pompey, leaning out of the chaise, and holding forth his arms.

The invalided soldier clasped the strong support thus offered, and by dint of dragging and pushing, he was at length safely landed in the vehicle.

His brother then ascended after him.

"St—st!" hissed Mr. B. to the resigned animal in front, who had made no offer to move during the above colloquy, and who would have stayed there without a murmur till Doomsday if it had been necessary.

"St—st!"

The animal made a move, and being at once convinced of the fact that his load had considerably increased, there and then—like a sagacious creature as he was—resolved to counterbalance the overweight by decreasing his speed in an equal ratio.

It was in vain Mr. Bucks alternately coaxed, threatened, and laid on heavily with the whip: the picture of resignation was deficient in feeling, and appeared to take no notice.

"Oh, d—n it all!" cried the groom, in utter disgust. "We sha'n't get to town in a month like this!"

At this moment the horse, perhaps attracted by a brother quadruped that was quietly browsing by the roadside, stopped dead.

Mr. Bucks ground his teeth, and gave the animal a slash on the ear that would have driven some horses frantic.

"You d—d lazy brute!" he shouted. "You're only fit for cats' meat!"

"Won't the horse go?" moaned the poor soldier.

"No; he's stopped for good, I think—the wretch!"

"And the coffee and hot rolls will all be cold!" exclaimed the soldier, in a melancholy voice.

"The d—d half-bred skeleton's doing it o' purpose!" shouted Mr. Bucks, in a fury.

"Don't put yourself in a passion," quietly remarked the wounded soldier—"it does no good."

"No, but to be kept here like this by a lazy, ugly brute like this is enough to put anyone in a passion."

"Do you know what we used to do when we were on a march and fell short of horses?" asked the soldier.

"What?"

"We used to make use of every horse we came across."

"Did you? A very good plan too!" replied Mr. Bucks, as his eye fell upon the sleek colt that was feeding in the hedge. "That colt looks well—exchange is no robbery, is it?"

"Only in notes."

"Yes, only in notes, of course! D—n me if I don't change too!" exclaimed the groom.

"Shall I help you?" asked Lord Harcliffe.

"Thank you!" answered Mr. B.

And in a moment both were out of the cart.

The first thing they did was to unharness the miserable apology that was drawing them.

And then to secure the strange colt, which might have after all ended in disappointment but for Lord Harcliffe.

Mr. Bucks, whom anxiety and prospective visions of hot rolls and coffee had rendered somewhat impetuous, would have seized the colt by main force.

But Lord Harcliffe suggested milder measures, especially as the animal was beginning to prick up his ears and to look suspiciously at the equipage in the road.

However, his lordship, by dint of using a few coaxing expressions, was permitted to approach close to the colt, when, after stroking his neck and patting him for a few moments, he quietly slipped the bridle over his head and the bit in his mouth, and led him to the chaise-cart.

A few more moments sufficed to harness him, and, this accomplished, the party were, by the energy of the new horse, who stepped out beautifully, carried along the road in such prime style that Pompey, in the fulness of his heart, could not help expressing his opinion that they would "be in time for de coffee an' de hot rolls after all."

A brisk trot of about an hour brought them clattering along the paved roads of the metropolis.

When they had progressed some distance along Oxford Street, Mr. Bucks appeared to be racking his brain to try and imagine where that rural retreat answering to the soldier's description of the place where his grandmother dwelt might be.

"Daffodil Court, Bloomsbury," he said to himself, thoughtfully.

Captain Hawk had his *one* eye upon him, and, divining the cause of his perplexity, said:

"You won't find Daffodil Court on the Bloomsbury side. Grandmother calls it Bloomsbury, but it belongs properly to the district of St. Giles's. If you don't mind giving up the reins to my brother, he'll drive you there in less time than you could make inquiries."

To this Mr. Bucks had not the least objection, and immediately resigned the reins to Lord Harcliffe, who, turning shortly out of the main street, was soon threading the narrow and tortuous approaches that led to the domestic retreat of Snagson's family hotel.

It was now better than half-past three, and broad daylight.

Neither Mr. Bucks nor Pompey had the slightest idea whither they were travelling, the neighbourhood through which they were passing being entirely new ground to them.

Another thing was, they were both particularly sleepy, and the jolting of the cart operated as a kind of narcotic, so that they lost all the beautiful prospect of the squalid neighbourhood through which they journeyed.

They nodded and swayed backwards and forwards in their seats, to the imminent danger of pitching out headlong.

They were now very near their journey's end.

It was then Captain Hawk unbuttoned his military coat, and releasing his arm, which by this time was tolerably cramped, thrust it into the sleeve. He then took a small whistle from his pocket, and blew a rather prolonged, peculiar note.

It roused Mr. Bucks.

"What's that?" he cried, drowsily.

"A man calling his pigeons on yonder roof," answered Captain Hawk, with a mischievous smile.

Mr. Bucks did not hear this reply—he was asleep again.

Three more moments passed, and then the vehicle stopped so abruptly at the end of Snagson's Court that Mr. Bucks saved all anxiety respecting his descent by shooting out of the chaise into the arms of Charles, who stood ready to receive him.

He was handed over immediately to two *assistants* who stood near, and a bandage being passed over his eyes, he was hurried up the court and into the house in the twinkling of an eye.

Pompey was very unceremoniously lugged out of the chaise-cart and treated in precisely the same manner.

All this had been performed so neatly and rapidly that it had the appearance of a dream rather than reality.

Neither of the prisoners had noticed the road by which they had been brought.

Their eyes being blindfolded the instant they were out of the vehicle, they had no opportunity of reconnoitring even the house to which they had been conveyed.

If the possession of the world had depended on it, they could not have given the least information on any of these points.

They were in a state of considerable drowsiness, and when, at the expiration of a few moments, they found themselves in a somewhat gloomy, dingy chamber, it did not appear to strike them as anything extraordinary; they had some sort of an idea that they had arrived at their journey's end, and, under the impression that it would be as well to repose themselves until the arrival of granny with the coffee and hot rolls, shut their eyes and went to sleep again.

In a few moments Captain Hawk and Lord Harcliffe, having divested themselves of their uniforms, entered the room.

For a short time they contemplated the slumbering pair in silence.

"A beautiful illustration this," remarked Lord Harcliffe, laughingly, "of the *Sleeping Beauties.*"

"Or the *Babes in the Wood.*"

"Nothing could have happened more propitiously for our plans."

"Nothing. Success is the order of the day, and I prophesy we shall hold the two hundred pounds in our hands before ten o'clock this morning," said Captain Hawk.

"What is the time?" inquired his lordship.

"A little past four," answered the captain, after referring to his watch.

"I propose, then, a few hours' sleep," said his comrade. "I feel completely worn out."

"I am in much the same condition. We will lie down till eight: we shall then be able easily to reach the bank by nine or a little after."

"And these poor devils?"

"Oh, they will snore away for hours to come, and dream of coffee and hot rolls. We will lock them in and leave them to themselves—they will be safe enough."

So saying, the highwaymen locked the door and sought repose in their own chamber.

CHAPTER CLXXXIV.

CAPTAIN HAWK AND LORD HARCLIFFE PAY A VISIT TO THE BANK AND CHANGE THE NOTES.

At half-past seven o'clock exactly the indefatigable Charles knocked at the door of our heroes' apartment, bringing hot water for their shaving operations, and informing them that it was a fine morning.

The highwaymen had of late had so little sleep that they would both willingly have courted the embraces of the drowsy god a little longer.

But business was business with them, and they struggled against the temptation.

"We have work to do," cried Captain Hawk, as he sprang from the bed.

"Two hundred pounds to win or lose!" exclaimed Lord Harcliffe, following his example.

A few moments sufficed to remove their beards, and a plentiful ablution followed.

In a very short time their countenances glowed with the freshness imparted by the bathing and rubbing they had undergone, whilst their chins shone

"Like stubble new reap'd at harvest-home."

Lord Harcliffe threw open the window, allowing the air—the freshest that was to be procured in that confined neighbourhood—to blow into the chamber, and to admit the twitterings of the birds that sang on the roofs as

[CAUGHT IN A TRAP.]

merrily there as they would have done a hundred miles away in the green boughs of some country wood.

"What a blessing cold water is!" said Lord Harcliffe. "I feel quite revived."

"And I," replied Captain Hawk, who was applying some fragrant pomade to his hair. "Anyone, to see us now, would imagine we were either going to Court or to lay siege to some fair lady's heart."

Lord Harcliffe smiled as the captain, having arranged his locks, proceeded to powder them carefully.

In this operation he was followed by his lordship, and in a few moments they were so effectually sprinkled with the white compound that all traces of the original colour of their hair were effectually concealed.

It took them but a short time to invest themselves in their garments—not, be it remarked, the same they usually wore, but two suits of irreproachable, glossy black, from the extensive wardrobe of the accommodating Snagson.

When their toilet was finished and they descended to the parlour, they looked, in their sable suits, with their powdered hair and spotless white cravats, like two divines or members of the legal profession.

They did not wait for breakfast, taking merely a cup of coffee, into which was poured a small glass of brandy.

During this slight morning refresher, Captain Hawk wrote a note, which having finished and sealed, he, accompanied by Lord Harcliffe, proceeded to the chamber where they had a few hours before deposited the slumbering forms of Messrs. Bucks and Pompey.

There they lay still, in precisely the same position in which they had been placed, slumbering still, and snoring like a couple of pigs.

"They seem particularly comfortable," said Captain

Hawk. "They will most probably sleep on till we return, especially as the room is not particularly light. When we have settled our business at the bank, we will breakfast together—we shall be, I flatter myself, in a humour to enjoy it."

Once more the lock was turned upon the sleepers and Captain Hawk, having left the key of the room in the care of Charles, and given him some directions respecting its occupants, went out with Lord Harcliffe.

All was quiet in the narrow courts and passages they traversed.

Occasionally they encountered a curious-looking customer or two, who looked at the two well-dressed, elegant men with bleared and blinking eyes, and made remarks one to another as they passed.

But no one offered any molestation to the handsome strangers.

Indeed, it seemed, from their upright, well-knit figures, and the firm determination of their steps, that it would not have been altogether safe to have attempted any outrage.

In a short time they had reached Drury Lane.

As they approached the hackney-coach stand, Captain Hawk remarked:

"They say we are never so safe as when under the very noses of those who are anxious to find us, and I begin to think it is true."

"Yes," replied Lord Harcliffe, laughing, "we may consider ourselves in that agreeable proximity at this moment; three minutes' walk would bring us to Bow Street."

"Ha, ha! Courage and confidence can defeat the devil himself. Here, Jarvey!"

"Coach, your honour?" cried an old hackney coachman.

"Come along, old boy!"

The coach drew up alongside the pavement, the waterman opened the door, and our friends stepped in.

"Where to, your honours?" asked the man, respectfully.

"Mansion House," replied Captain Hawk, throwing him a half-crown, to his great delight.

"Mansion House!" he called to the coachman, adding, as the coach lumbered away. "Thank'ee, your honours!" and then shuffled off to indulge in half a pint of purl on the strength of his liberal *tip*.

As for the jarvey himself, he felt persuaded he had got the Lord Mayor or some other important personages for his fares, and stirred up his horses in such an unprecedented manner that they almost galloped.

On being set down at the Mansion House, they paid the coachman liberally, and strolled leisurely towards the Bank.

It was only a little past nine, but business had commenced, though the visitors were but few at that early hour.

They advanced calmly, and entered with perfect soberness and *sang froid*, till they stood in the interior before the counter.

A clerk advanced to the handsome, elegant strangers.

Captain Hawk coolly took out his pocket book, and extracted the notes, that rustled in their fresh crispness.

Lord Harcliffe occupied himself with his eye-glass and a bill on the wall.

"Let me have change for these," said the captain, in a careless tone, to the clerk, as he handed him the notes.

"How will you take it, sir?" he inquired.

"In gold," answered Captain Hawk, indifferently, though his heart bounded exultingly as the clerk began to count the glittering coin.

In a short time it was counted, weighed and tied up in a small canvas bag, which the captain, with extreme *nonchalance*, transferred to his pocket.

He then took a step as if to depart, but stopped, and turned to the clerk again.

"Oh! by-the-by," he said, "I was to have met two friends of mine, Major Bombshell and Sir Thomas Walker, here this morning; but as I find business calls me away earlier than I expected, you will oblige me, on their arrival, by delivering this note to the major."

As he spoke, he handed a note to the clerk, who received it with great respect, and promised to give it to the person to whom it was addressed.

The captain then, with a condescending inclination of his head to the young man, took his friend's arm and walked out.

"We triumph, my friend!" exclaimed Captain Hawk, exultingly, as they passed the Mansion House once more.

"Never was anything better managed," returned Lord Harcliffe, in a tone of equal satisfaction. "I shall eat a tremendous breakfast in honour of the occasion."

A hackney-coach was hailed, and the triumphant pair, after travelling in that conveyance as far as they deemed it prudent, alighted, and, dismissing the vehicle, proceeded on foot to the retired abode of Snagson.

On their arrival, breakfast was ready and waiting.

"Well, Charles," inquired Captain Hawk, "have you received any intimation, during our absence, of the existence of our sleeping beauties?"

"No, captain," answered Charles. "I've been in to look at 'em three times, and they were doing nothing, each time as I went, but sleepin' an' snorin'."

"Well, as breakfast is ready, and as we are ready for breakfast, and as our two visitors showed us some consideration, believing us to be what we appeared—two poor soldiers—we will keep our promise in the matter of the 'hot rolls and coffee;' so you can wake them in any way you please."

Having delivered this message to Charles, the highwaymen retired to their bed-chamber.

The deputy shuffled along to the sleeping apartment of the two domestics, and unlocking the door, entered very quietly.

Still they slept, and Charles stood contemplating them, and wondering how he should wake them.

First he thought of tickling the black's nose with a straw, but this did not seem to promise amusement enough in its results to satisfy him.

Another plan speedily suggested itself.

The sleepers were reposing in chairs side by side, and Pompey's mouth was most invitingly open.

Charles therefore took the hand of the oblivious Bucks, and raising it gently, quietly guided the fingers into this capacious receptacle, that seemed capable of swallowing the entire arm if necessary.

This done, he shouted in the black's ear in a stentorian voice:

"*Hot rolls and coffee!*"

The effect was instantaneous.

Pompey snapped his jaws together with the voracity of a shark, gripping the fingers of the luckless Bucks with such tenacity that that individual started from his downy slumbers, and roared "Murder!" at the top of his voice.

Pompey, who had a confused notion that he had got a hot roll in his mouth that some one was trying to take away from him, kept his teeth closely set.

The more Mr. Thomas Bucks yelled and struggled to free his tortured fingers, the tighter Pompey compressed his strong jaws, till at length the groom's anguish having reached that point which human nature finds unendurable, he clenched the fist that was at liberty, and swung it round with such desperate intensity that, as it came in contact with the biter's nose, he fell over on his back with a crash, and the striker, overbalancing with the impetus of the blow, fell upon him, and there they lay on the ground, scuffling, growling, and striking, to the intense delight of the benevolent Charles, who laughed till he cried at the amusing spectacle.

He was aroused from his delightful contemplation by Mr. Snagson's voice mildly requesting to know whether they were desirous of *quite* shaking the house from its foundations.

He then spoke to the belligerents.

"Hollo!—hollo!" he cried. "What's the matter with you two, eh?"

"My fingers is bit off at the knuckle joints!" growled Mr. Bucks.

"Some 'un's knock him nose down him troat!" cried the black.

"Oh, nonsense! you're been a dreamin'—that's where you're been!" suggested Charles, in a bantering tone.

"No, I ain't!" answered Mr. T. B. "Look'ee 'ere," he continued, holding up his damaged fingers that looked as though they had been scored with some sharp instrument.

"An' look'ee 'ere!" grumbled Pompey, making a most

comically hideous face, and pointing to his nose, from which the sanguinary fluid was falling in large drops. "Him nose droppin' to bits!"

"Oh," said Charles, "I see 'ow it is: you're been a fightin' in your sleep—that's what you're been up to."

The two combatants looked at one another in some perplexity.

"You're a couple o' nice youths, don't yer think yer are?—a comin' out to breakfast, an' then a rollin' about on the floor a punchin' one another!" continued their inquisitor.

The two domestics, who had now thoroughly come to their senses, began to remember the "coffee and hot rolls," and their countenances assumed a penitent and rueful expression.

All this the good-natured individual before them enjoyed immensely.

"D'ye think as yer deserves any breakfast at all after kickin' up all this scrimmage?—d'ye think yer does now?"

"Well, yer see," said Mr. Bucks, apologetically, "it was, as I may say, a sort of a accident."

"Golly! yes, dat it was," joined in Pompey. "Him nebber get punch like dis on de nose for de purpose."

"You've almost gone and frightened the old lady into fits," said Charles.

"Who?—de ole lady?" inquired Pompey, mystified.

"Why, it's them parties' grandmother—them soldiers as we brought in the cart, o' course," explained Mr. B.

"Is dis deir gran'moder's 'ouse?" asked the black.

"Don't you arks no questions, an' then you won't 'ear no stories," remarked Charles, abruptly.

"Well, but where's the soldiers?" inquired Mr. Bucks, who was beginning to grow somewhat impatient with his ugly monitor.

"They're in their skins—don't you fret your kidneys about them," answered the blunt Charles.

"Where's de coffee an' 'ot rolls?" asked Pompey.

"Here they are," said the factotum, as the door opened and a small servant entered, carrying a tray, on which were two quart jugs of coffee and a towering plate of hot rolls.

"Golly! here 'em is!" exclaimed Pompey.

And without further remark on either side, the hungry pair commenced an immediate attack on the eatables.

"Mind yer don't bust yerselves," said Charles, as he closed the door.

In the meantime, Captain Hawk and Lord Harcliffe, having first discarded their sable garments and assumed their own attire, were making an excellent breakfast with Mr. and Mrs. Snagson.

The meal finished, Mrs. S. retired to perform sundry household duties, whilst the highwaymen informed her worthy partner of the magnificent collection of jewellery they had to dispose of.

The placid countenance of Mr. Snagson lighted up radiantly as the captain described in glowing terms the magnificent massive repeater, the ensign's watch, the antique bracelet, the gems by which they were surrounded, and the other valuables that were safely locked up in the portmanteau under the care of the landlady of the Royal George.

"From the description you give, captain, they must be very fine! I've no doubt they are so—you understand these things, and, of course, you are a judge—you must be a judge!" said Mr. S.

"I flatter myself I am," answered the captain.

"There is no mistaking the fire of really fine diamonds," added Lord Harcliffe.

"No, no—there is not!" replied Snagson, eagerly, whose mouth watered at the bare idea of securing the precious gems. "And you say they're left at—— Ahem!"

"At a friend's for the present," said Captain Hawk, without further enlightening his host.

"Ah, yes! of course—very prudent not to carry them about with you," remarked Mr. S. "And—a—what, in your opinion, is the value?—that is, what do you expect to receive for the lot?" he inquired.

"The value I estimate at a thousand, and we cannot take a farthing less than five hundred."

"Five hundred? Dear me! that's a large sum of money—a very large sum!" remarked Mr. S., biting his nails.

"Diamonds usually *do* fetch a large sum," coolly but impressively returned Captain Hawk. "And it is a singular fact," he continued, in a tone almost of reflection, "that although diamonds realise more than any other species of property, they are always the easiest to dispose of."

"Certainly—you are quite right," answered Snagson. "I'd rather buy diamonds—at a price, mind you—at a price—than anything else in the world."

"Well, you can buy *ours* at a price—*half* price is fair for diamonds, is it not?"

"Oh yes—very fair!—that is, in the present instance, since you say the jewels are particularly fine; but, of course, I must see them!"

"Undoubtedly! We do not wish you to make a bargain with your eyes shut."

"I shall be very glad to examine them as soon as possible; and I think you've known me long enough to be quite sure that I give ten per cent. more for what I purchase than anyone else in the—ahem!—trade."

The highwaymen assured him that they were fully aware of this fact, and so the conversation terminated for the present.

Messrs. Bucks and Pompey had also finished their meal. They were both full up to the muzzle, like two overcharged pistols.

The cravings of appetite being satisfied, Mr. Bucks began to be anxious about the business that had brought him and his companion to town.

He wondered first of all at the solitary manner—very suggestive of imprisonment—in which they had taken their morning meal.

Then he wondered where the two military grandsons had absconded to—and whether the dear old soul, their grandmother, of whom they had spoken so affectionately, knew what two important personages had honoured her with their presence at breakfast.

Then came a floating idea as to where the chaise and the colt had been taken to—and lastly there came a desire to get out, and proceed to Bow Street.

He tried the door: it was fast.

"It's d—d rum, their locking us in!" he remarked, fretfully.

"So him tink!" exclaimed Pompey.

"I wonder what the time is?" continued the groom; "I don't hear any noise about, so it must be early."

"Ob course," said Pompey.

"I shall try and make somebody hear, anyhow!" exclaimed Mr. Bucks, decidedly.

"Kick de door," suggested Pompey.

"I will too! I don't quite understand this." And without further preface, he commenced.

"Hollo! hollo! heigh!" he shouted, kicking as he called out. "Open the door!—d'ye hear, somebody? Open the door!"

Pompey assisted in this energetically.

"Hollo! heigh!—anybody!—nobody! open de door!"

And then they both kicked in concert, to the great danger of the panels.

Suddenly the door flew open; and they found themselves, not at liberty, but confronted by Charles, who stood right in the doorway, in a particularly dogged manner, and with an expression on his features by no means conciliatory.

"Now then—now then!" he cried, in a tone of indignation. "Go on! Make a little more row—do! Knock the blessed panels right in whiles ye're about it—I would, if I was you!"

This peculiar manner of expression, and the formidable scowl on the speaker's face, considerably damped the energies of Messrs. Pompey and Bucks; however, the latter ventured to speak.

"What are we locked in 'ere for? We've got business to do, and we want to go and do it," he said.

"Well, then, look'ee 'ere, yer'll jest 'ave to want!" was Charles's reply.

"Where's the two soldiers?" inquired Mr. Bucks.

"Ho, ho!" laughed their grim custodian, harshly.

"Wheer's de ole granny?" asked Pompey.

"Now, look'ee 'ere, you couple o' spoons: jest 'old yer tongues, an' don't bother about other people's business," Charles growled.

"I beg to say as it ain't other people's business—it's *our* business," said Mr. Bucks, with tolerable firmness, all things considered. "An' I want to get out—and, what's more, I will get out! Come on, Pompey!"

"Oh!" ejaculated the grim Charles, who was beginning to look more and more ogreish every minute, but who still blocked up the doorway, with his broad figure as immovable as a statue. "You're quite made up your minds to go, then, is yer?"

"Yes, we have!" answered Mr. Bucks, with an expiring effort of pluck.

"Yes, 'em am!" added Pompey.

"Werry good! That's English, that is! Now I knows what to do," returned the ogre. "Here!" he added, giving at the same time a sharp whistle—"Blazeup! Heigh!"

Immediately two sharp-featured, cunning-looking youths, with pale faces, appeared in the distance.

"Jest step this way, will yer?" cried Charles.

The youths immediately stepped that way.

"What's the little game?" they inquired.

"These two coves ain't well—they're been a trying to knock down the mansion," Charles explained.

"Ah! I see: they wants a little coolin' mixture," said one of the youths with particularly long fingers.

"I don't want any o' this nonsense," Mr. Bucks exclaimed.

"No, I knows yer don't: I said yer wants physic—that's what I said," answered the youth.

Without further ceremony the trio entered the room, pushing back the indignant Bucks and Pompey.

The door was immediately locked.

"This 'ere one fust," said Charles, indicating the groom with his finger, that looked like a saveloy.

In an instant Mr. T. B. was seized by the pale-faced youths, and seated with startling abruptness in one of the wooden chairs.

A rope was then produced and passed round Mr. B.'s body and over the back of the chair, his arms having been previously, in order to keep him quite quiet and composed, placed close to his side.

With this rope he was literally "wound up," nor were his legs forgotten in the general "winding," inasmuch as they were fastened securely to the legs of the chair.

Pompey, who had looked on at the above proceedings with considerable apprehension, was next attended to, and placed in a similar state of restraint.

The victims were now seated side by side.

"You can go now," said Charles, to the pale youths.

The pale youths vanished.

"We shall 'ave some law business over this, I can see," Mr. Bucks exclaimed.

"Ho, ho, ho!" laughed the aggravating Charles. "I do like to 'ear you talk—I do indeed! It is sich a treat!"

"You won't find it a treat!" growled Mr. Bucks. "I'll pull you up for this!"

"Ha, ha! D'ye know where yer are?"

"Of course I do—Daffodil Court, St. Giles's."

"Eh? Daffodil—— Oh lor!—ho, ho, ho! Daffodil Court!"

There was something evidently so irresistibly ludicrous about this locality that Charles roared again.

The reason of this was that Daffodil Court was an invention on the part of Captain Hawk, no such place being in existence.

"It may be very funny to *you*," exclaimed the indignant Bucks, "but I don't see the joke; an' if you don't want to get yourself into serious trouble, you'll jest tell those two soldiers we found on the road as I wants to see 'em."

At that moment a tap was heard at the door.

Charles opened it, and the two individuals in question appeared.

As they entered, Lord Harcliffe whispered to him, and he departed.

The two invalids advanced.

"Ah! there you are," said Captain Hawk.

Both Mr. Bucks and Pompey opened their eyes and mouths in utter and hopeless astonishment as they recognised the features of the two highwaymen.

"I heard you say just now," continued the captain, "that you wished to see the two soldiers you found on the road. Your wish is gratified—here we are."

"You?" gasped Mr. Bucks. "You're not soldiers."

"Not now. Like snakes, we have cast our skins," said Lord Harcliffe, "and here they are!" he exclaimed, as the door opened and Charles entered, carrying a tray containing wine and cigars, and a bundle hanging to his arm.

Having unburdened himself of his load, Captain Hawk said to him:

"Charles, these individuals are oblivious; have the goodness to show them our skins."

Charles, grinning from ear to ear, untied the bundle, and displayed the uniforms, not forgetting the patch.

"And you really mean to say it was you as we found in the road then?" asked Mr. Bucks, in a faltering voice.

"I mean to say it was," replied the captain.

"Oh lor'! oh dear!" groaned Mr. B.

"Oh, golly!" ejaculated Pompey.

"Why, then, it must have been you two gents as robbed my master and Sir Thomas Walker."

"You are quite right; it was."

"Then we've been telling you the very secrets that we ought to have kept from you?"

"Not a doubt of it; much obliged for your information!"

"But the letter I was to give to the inspector?"

"Don't trouble yourself about that."

"The officers that were to come with us from Bow Street?"

"No matter."

"To the bank?"

"Too late! not of the slightest use!"

"Too late? How d'ye mean too late?" gasped the perturbed Bucks.

"I mean that it would be giving those worthy functionaries a great deal of useless trouble, since we have already been there and cashed the notes, and here is the money safe and sound."

As the captain spoke, he held up the bag and jingled it in a tantalising manner in the ears of the victimised domestics, who felt as though the sound was ringing their death knell.

"You see," he continued, "how very much we have benefited by your letting us into the secret of your plans, and it will be a lesson to you to be more guarded in future. I trust, however, you enjoyed your breakfast, and that the '*hot rolls and coffee*' have not disagreed with you!"

"D—n the hot rolls!" muttered the wretched Bucks.

"An' d—n de coffee! nasty muck!" growled Pompey.

"Don't get out of temper," said the captain, sweetly; "it will do you no possible good. Your health!" And as he spoke, pouring out two glasses of wine, he and Lord Harcliffe emptied them.

"I s'pose, then," remarked the groom, "as you've got all you want, we can go?"

"Not just yet, my friend," answered the captain; "we can't allow you to go till you've refreshed yourselves. Here, Charles!" he shouted, "brandy and glasses!"

"You must drink with us!" cried Captain Hawk, as he lighted a cigar, and handed one to Lord Harcliffe.

Charles then entered, smiling, with a brandy-bottle and *et cæteras*.

"This worthy fellow will attend to you," said the captain. "Charles, you will *look after them*."

"All right, captain—I'll look after 'em, never fear!"

And on this assurance the highwaymen departed.

"Yer 'eard th' horders, didn't yer?" said Charles, as he locked the door after them: "I'm to look arter yer; an' afore I begins, I shall just take a sniff at this brandy, to take the dust out o' my eyes."

The sniff was neither more nor less than drinking off two glasses in succession, after which he seemed to grow genial and benevolent.

"Do you know what you're a-goin' to do, you two?—I'll tell yer. Ye're a-goin' to injoy yerselves—ye're a-goin' to drink, an' ye're a-goin' to smoke—'ere!" And he poured out as he spoke two glasses of brandy. "Now, then," he cried to Mr. Bucks, "open yer mouth."

Mr. Bucks opened his mouth obediently, and the glass being held to his lips, he swallowed the spirit.

"Now, then, Mr. Black-Lead, open yours."

Pompey, who felt inclined to resent this misname, looked indignant, but a passing sniff of the fragrant spirit checked him, and he opened his mouth according to orders, and received the contents of the glass.

"Now I'm going to treat you to a smoke," Charles continued, as he took up a couple of cigars and thrust one between the teeth of the prisoners, and then selected another for himself.

"These are prime blazers," he continued, as he lit his weed.

Then turning to the domestics, he flashed the taper before them.

"Have a light?" he cried. "Go on—blaze away!" he added, holding the flame under the nose of Mr. Thomas Bucks in such a reckless manner that that individual roared out:

"You're burnin' my nose off!"

"Never mind your nose! 'Blaze away!' is the horder of the day!" exclaimed the convivial Charles.

"That's all very well," remonstrated Mr. B., "but noses ain't cigars, an' mine ain't used to bein' smoked."

"Got used to anythink in time! Here, Blackey, light up! Here, I'll light it for yer."

So saying, he snatched the cigar from Pompey's lips, and lit it carefully.

"This is a real beauty—draws like a chimney. Open yer mouth while it's in full swing."

Pompey, unsuspicious of evil, opened his mouth, and received the luxury wrong end foremost.

"There, pull away!" cried Charles. But before Pompey had time to pull, he shot the cigar out of his mouth with a dismal yell.

"Oh, gorra! him red-hot, like um d—n kitchen poker!" he roared.

Charles was in such ecstasies that he was compelled to apply once more to the brandy-bottle.

Mr. Bucks then remarked:

"I say, Mr. Charles, considerin' we're to enjoy ourselves, I don't see much enjoyment in bein' tied down in our chairs like a couple o' suckin' babies, to prevent us falling out."

"Oh! but yer see ye're a couple o' sich noisy customers," answered Charles.

"Untie us, an' we'll be as quiet as mice," entreated Mr. Bucks.

Charles, who was growing more friendly under the influence of the brandy, appeared inclined to yield

"Now mind," said he, "if yer begins any o' yer rows when ye're untied, I shall give the pair on yer a good weltin'."

"'Em won't say notink, 'em take 'em oath," protested Pompey.

In consideration of this promise, the prisoners were unbound.

Conviviality then became the order of the day.

Under the influence of the spirit, they forgot all their past annoyances, and were the merriest of the merry.

They smoked cigars and drank brandy till the room appeared to swim round and round.

Under these happy circumstances, let us leave them, and return to the major and Sir Thomas Walker, whom we left in much the same condition, but under less excusable circumstances.

CHAPTER CLXXXV.

SIR THOMAS WALKER PAYS A VISIT TO SIR JEKYLL JUDD.—THEY RECEIVE SUSPICIOUS INTELLIGENCE AT BOW STREET.—THEY PROCEED TO THE BANK, ACCOMPANIED BY THE POLICE.—THE MYSTERY SOLVED BY CAPTAIN HAWK'S LETTER.

When these worthies awoke in the morning, it may easily be imagined their sensations were none of the pleasantest.

Racking headaches and nauseas were the results of the previous night's excesses.

Sir Thomas Walker was the first to rise, and by the assistance of Jaggers—whose head, like his master's, was in a considerable state of muddle—he contrived to get himself on to his feet.

Then, by dint of copious ablutions, and a glass or two of brandy, the justice managed to complete his toilet.

The very idea of a breakfast he shuddered at; and being of course in a very bad humour, he growled out to poor Jaggers, the instant he could dispense with his services, to go and see if his horse was ready.

This being ascertained, Sir Thomas had a few minutes' conversation with the major, who was enveloped in a dressing-gown, and groaning with spasms at every word

It was arranged that Sir Thomas should go at once to the residence of Sir Jekyll Judd, and that the major should follow as quickly as possible in his carriage, and take him up at the magistrate's house, when they were to proceed first to Bow Street to identify the highwaymen, who would of course be in custody by that time, and afterwards to the bank.

The ride in the early morning, although it cost the justice an enormous effort of resolution to prepare himself for the task, was in the end of much benefit to him.

The fresh air cooled his aching head, and the exercise braced his nerves—ditto Jaggers; so that by the time they reached Russell Square, where Sir Jekyll lived, both master and man felt considerably refreshed, and began to look upon breakfast in a more friendly light than they had done at starting.

It was only seven o'clock, a.m., when they reached the magistrate's house.

But Sir Jekyll was an early riser, and had been up and in his library since six.

Consequently, when Sir Thomas was announced, he was ushered at once into Sir Jekyll's presence.

The magistrate was a little spare, wiry-looking personage, who had a sort of sharp, frosty look, as though he lived upon spring water and icicles; he had moreover the misfortune to be very deaf, which perhaps added to this sharpness.

He rose as Sir Thomas entered.

"Good morning, my dear Sir Jekyll," said the justice, as he hastily advanced.

"Good morning—good morning!" answered Sir J., in a bawling tone.

"I daresay you're rather surprised to see me so early?"

"Oh yes," returned the magistrate; "I always rise early."

"I know *you* do, but it is not *my* usual habit," said Sir Thomas.

"Very good habit indeed!" echoed Sir Jekyll, who only caught a word occasionally.

The justice began to foresee some difficulty in making his deaf friend understand, and therefore bawled as loud as he could:

"I've come about Captain Hawk!"

"Oh! come out for a walk? Ah! walking's a very healthy exercise before breakfast."

"No, no, d—n it!" exclaimed the justice, irritably. "You must be aware I couldn't have walked all the way from the country. You misunderstand me."

The former part of this speech was spoken to himself; the remnant only being bawled into the ear of the magistrate.

"I've come about Captain Hawk!" he shouted.

Sir Jekyll *did* contrive to catch the name.

"Oh! ah! Captain Hawk—yes—what of him?"

"Confound him! he's on the road once more."

"Found him in the road, did you? Glad to hear it!"

"No, no! I say he's on the road again! He must be hung!"

"Oh yes; I remember now—so he was—hung at Huntingdon, wasn't he?"

"N—o! he *wasn't!*" roared the irritable Sir Thomas. "He escaped; and he's been committing fresh acts of trespass: he has robbed me, and our friend Major Bombshell; and we must take strong steps for his apprehension!"

The angry justice dug this information so forcibly into the auricular member of Sir Jekyll, that he was compelled to hear.

"Oh!" he said, "I understood you to say you'd found this Captain Hawk!"

"No! that is what I wish to do!"

"Certainly! Oblige me with that speaking trumpet," added Sir Jekyll, pointing to an acoustic instrument on the table.

The justice handed his friend the required instrument; and by its assistance Sir Jekyll was put in possession of the outrages committed by Captain Hawk and the Black Highwayman.

"Dear me—dear me!" exclaimed the little magistrate, who, in the exercise of his functions, was as tough as wire. "Dreadful indeed! We'll have breakfast, and then we'll proceed at once to Bow Street. You may depend on my hearty co-operation in any measure to bring these scoundrels to justice."

Having thus expressed himself, Sir Jekyll rang the bell fiercely, and ordered breakfast, dividing his attention during the matutinal meal between eggs, buttered toast, and his speaking trumpet.

They had scarcely finished when the major's carriage rolled up to the door.

"Here is the major," said Sir Thomas. "We can ride together in his carriage."

"Will he take breakfast?" inquired the magistrate.

The invitation was conveyed to the gallant Bombshell; and in a few moments, a peculiar stumping sound indicated that he *would* take breakfast.

He was ascending the stairs with a considerable quantity of puffing and blowing, and at length reached the door of the library.

"Phew!" he ejaculated, as he entered. "Good morning, Sir Jekyll! I declare your stairs have quite taken the—phew!—breath out of my body!"

"Sit down and have some breakfast, major," answered the magistrate, "and then we'll take immediate steps for the recovery of your property and the arrest of the thieves."

The major, having planted himself in a seat, contrived, all things considered, to make a very tolerable meal."

"You see," he explained to the magistrate during his hasty repast, "we've taken every precautionary measure."

"Quite right."

"Two of my domestics we despatched to Bow Street with a letter from Sir Thomas to the inspector, and I have no doubt by this time the villains are in custody."

"Suppose, then, we go at once and see? Have you quite finished, major?"

"Quite; and I really feel considerably better for your hospitality," answered the officer.

In a few moments they were seated in the major's carriage, which bore them rapidly to the police court in Bow Street.

Here, to their great surprise, there was not the least stir or excitement of any description.

Beyond the usual night cases, nothing had transpired out of the usual course of events.

"It's very extraordinary! What can it mean?" exclaimed Sir Thomas Walker. "We had better get out, Sir Jekyll."

"Decidedly!"

Accordingly, they descended from the carriage and entered the police office.

"Inspector Nutkins!" bawled Sir Jekyll.

"Here, your worship!" answered the inspector, making his appearance instantly.

"Answer Sir Thomas Walker's questions," said the magistrate.

"Yes, your worship."

"Two of this gentleman's servants have called here this morning?" commenced Sir Thomas, in a stern voice, pointing to Major Bombshell.

The inspector shook his head dubiously as he replied:

"Not as yet, Sir Thomas."

"Oh, nonsense! But they have—they must!" cried the major.

"I haven't seen anything of 'em, sir."

"They were disguised: one as a Quaker, the other—my black footman—as a female."

"Not been here, sir."

"What?—why? They had a letter from me to the inspector. You are the inspector, are you not?" inquired the justice.

"I am, Sir Thomas."

"In this letter you were authorised to select a body of efficient officers to accompany them—these domestics—to the Bank of England, there to watch for and take in custody those notorious malefactors known as Captain Hawk and the Black Highwayman."

Inspector Nutkins scratched his head, opened his eyes very wide, and evinced sundry other symptoms of bewilderment.

"Well, Sir Thomas," he at length exclaimed, "I don't for a moment dispute your having wrote the letter, neither do I doubt that you delivered it to this gentleman's domestics; all I say is that I haven't seen either."

At this assertion there was a dead pause.

The inspector looked at Major Bombshell, the major looked at the justice, and the justice looked at the magistrate, who, not having heard a word, looked at everybody.

"Well, have they caught 'em?" he inquired.

"Caught 'em?—they've never been to look after 'em!" shouted the justice.

"Fire and fury!" roared the major. "Where the devil have those villains of mine taken themselves off to? I ought to have known better than to have entrusted such an important commission to such blockheads!"

"They were to have come here before going to the bank, weren't they?" inquired the inspector.

"Of course they were!" answered the justice and Major B., simultaneously.

"Then the only way in which I can account for my not having seen 'em," replied the inspector, sententiously, "is that they must have gone to the bank before coming here."

"How dare they disobey orders?" roared the major.

"People *will* make mistakes sometimes, sir," suggested Mr. Nutkins.

"I don't allow it—I never do!" returned the angry major.

"The directions given were very distinct and explicit," chimed in the justice.

This was not strictly true, inasmuch as when Messrs. Bucks and Pompey received their final instructions neither Sir Thomas nor Major B. was in a condition to be very distinct upon any point; but this we may suppose they had forgotten.

"Well," said the inspector, "we had better, perhaps, send some men to the bank without loss of time?"

"Decidedly," answered Sir Thomas.

This determination having been arrived at, a small body of officers was quickly selected, and, in order to avoid attracting particular attention, it was arranged that they should proceed to the bank in a hackney-coach.

A coach was accordingly called, and the officers selected.

These consisted of Nicholas, Twigg, Sampson, Clark, Peterson, Jarvis, and Jessop.

With this load the coach departed, followed closely behind by the major's carriage, containing the major and the two ministers of justice.

On arriving at the bank and descending from the vehicle, there were no more signs of ferment, confusion, or agitation than there had been at the police office.

Everything and everybody seemed painfully calm and composed.

The major and Sir Thomas hardly knew what to think.

The shortest way was to enter the bank and know the worst.

They accordingly proceeded to the interior, and approached the counter.

It was then about half-past nine in the morning.

Captain Hawk and Lord Harcliffe were there at a *quarter* past, so they must have almost passed each other on their road.

But, alas! they were just a *quarter* too late.

The clerk who had waited upon the highwayman now advanced to attend to the major and his party.

"Have you cashed any notes this morning?" he inquired of the young man.

"Yes, sir," answered the clerk. "I cashed two hundred pounds' worth about a quarter of an hour since."

The major got very red in the face, and clutched the edge of the counter convulsively.

"Do they correspond with these numbers?" he cried, in a thick, agitated voice, as he handed the clerk a piece of paper.

The clerk referred to the notes, and replied in the affirmative.

"Fire and fury!" roared the major. "We're done! What were the rascals like that changed these notes?" he inquired, furiously.

"Two handsome, gentlemanly-looking——"

"D—d infernal thieves!" roared the incensed major,

winding up the sentence himself. "Is this to be borne?" he continued, appealing to Sir Thomas Walker.

"Decidedly not!" replied the justice.

"There's no doubt about it—not a shadow of a doubt —that these scoundrels have had the audacity to change these notes themselves!" exclaimed the major.

"Have they been here?" bawled the deaf Sir Jekyll.

"Been here?" shouted the incensed Bombshell. "Of course they have, and got clear off with the money! Are you aware, sir," he went on, in a bullying tone, to the clerk, "that the parties who changed those notes are two vagabond highwaymen? Are you cognizant of the fact that when you handed over two hundred pounds to those rascals you gave them *my* money—*mine!*—eh?"

The clerk replied in a calm tone that "he was *not* cognizant of the fact"—adding that "the notes were presented, and that he had cashed them in the usual manner."

But the defeated major was not to be appeased.

"You are deficient in discernment, young man," he cried, to the clerk, "or at the first glance you would have seen that those fellows were a brace of vagabonds!"

"There was nothing about them to warrant such a suspicion," returned the clerk, by no means disturbed at the major's insane fury: "their appearance was extremely prepossessing, and their manner and bearing perfectly gentlemanly—much more so than that of *many* of our visitors," he added, emphasizing the adjective in such a pointed manner that the irascible major, feeling the cap fitted him, instantly put it on.

"You are making personal allusions to myself, sir!" he roared to the young man, who, instead of replying, coolly took from a desk the note Captain Hawk had left for the major, and held it towards him.

"What's this?" he growled.

"A note, sir."

"I can see that."

"I thought you could not, since you asked what it was. It is addressed to you, sir."

"Psha! Give it me."

The excited commander snatched the note from the clerk's fingers, and tearing it open, read as follows:—

"*My dear Major,—*

"*We admire your clever plan exceedingly—in fact, it was so well contrived that it ought to have succeeded, although we have reason to congratulate ourselves that it turned out as many equally well-laid schemes have done—a failure. You will doubtless be delighted to hear that the notes are cashed, and the money safe in the pockets of your admiring servants. Compliments to Sir Thomas Walker, who will, of course, join with you in extolling our skill.*

"*Your obedient servants,*

"*The Masked Horsemen.*

"*P.S.—Your worthy domestics are safe, and will, most likely, be visible in a few hours.*"

The major, having read this cool epistle, rolled up against the counter, and held it out to Sir Thomas Walker, who, having adjusted his spectacles, ran it hastily through.

"What unparalleled audacity!" he exclaimed, as he finished it.

"Audacity!" yelled the major—"it's d—nable atrocity!"

"Be calm, major; we must not waste our time in regrets," remarked the justice.

"They shall be hung, drawn, and quartered, the vagabonds!" he shouted.

"Yes, yes; but we must catch them first," said Sir Thomas, drily.

"Of course—of course! I'm aware of that. We'd better get back to Bow Street at once."

"I think so."

Sir Jekyll, to whom a great deal of what had transpired was little better than "inexplicable dumb show and noise," and who, to say the truth, had been almost forgotten in the general excitement, was now shown the note, which partially explained the circumstances, and accounted for the major's ebullition of wrath and excitement.

"Warrants for their apprehension must be issued immediately!" he cried; and in order to put this into immediate execution, the party hastily took their leaves.

Waiting outside, in expectation of some sudden outbreak, were the police officers, like so many hungry cats, ready to pounce upon the mice as they passed.

Their hands in their pockets played affectionately with the handcuffs that reposed there in dark secrecy.

But no mice came, and the cats looked rather sulky.

Their looks were not improved when the magistrate and the major came out.

"Any *noose*, your honour?" inquired Peterson, touching his hat to Sir Thomas Walker.

"No," growled Sir Thomas; "but there ought to be, and those rascals' heads in it!"

"They have been here, then, your honour?"

"Been?—yes, and gone: got clear away with the two hundred pounds."

"Good gracious me!" ejaculated Peterson. "Who'd ever believe such a thing?"

"There—don't waste time wondering, but jump into your coach, and get off all of you to Bow Street. We are going to take extraordinary steps this time. The rascals will not long elude our vigilance."

The entire party was then conveyed back to the police office, where warrants were issued for the apprehension of Captain Hawk and the Black Highwayman.

CHAPTER CLXXXVI.

CHARLES SUGGESTS A PRACTICAL JOKE TO THE HIGHWAYMEN.—MESSRS. BUCKS AND POMPEY MAKE THEIR APPEARANCE IN NEW CHARACTERS.—A SHARP RUN AND THE RESULT.—A NIGHT'S LODGING IN BOW STREET.

IN the meantime, our heroes had paid a visit to the Royal George, and brought from thence the portmanteau containing the valuables they had described so temptingly to Mr. Snagson.

They had also taken a friendly farewell of the buxom widow and the pretty Charlotte, who were both disappointed at the short stay of the handsome visitors.

However, Captain Hawk explained that an unexpected summons on very important duty had altered their arrangements, and necessitated their departure, and cheered them with the prospect of as early a return as possible.

They then returned to the family hotel, where they negotiated the sale of the watches and jewellery for the sum they had stipulated, five hundred pounds.

The friendly Charles, having received an intimation to the effect that the chaise-cart and gray colt were *nobody's* property, had left his friends, Bucks and Pompey, locked up with the brandy and cigars, whilst he quietly drove over to Smithfield, and sold them for fifteen pounds.

He made it his business to pass through Bow Street on his way back, and there he managed to acquaint himself with what had taken place at the bank.

He had crept into a public-house, where several of the police off duty were drinking, and whilst apparently spelling over the newspaper, listened intently to their conversation, the subject of which was the facts with which the reader is already acquainted.

"They won't be at large for long," remarked one of the officers: "we shall all be on the scent, and I shouldn't mind laying something handsome that they're nabbed before the end o' the week."

"All right!" muttered Charles to himself, as he finished his porter and slipped out.

Soon after he reached home, the highwaymen returned; and when they had finished their business with Snagson, Charles had an interview with them, when he detailed all he had heard.

"We've a little excitement before us," remarked Captain Hawk, smiling. "To enjoy the pleasures of the metropolis, and at the same time elude the vigilance of these Bow Street runners, will afford sufficient exercise for all our faculties."

"Well, captain," remarked Charles, "you're pretty well up to dodging these coves; you've had a good innings."

"Yes, my lad, and am not bowled out yet. I don't know, after all, whether we're not safer in London than the country, for the simple reason that they will imagine we should never dare remain in the metropolis, and consequently not think of looking for us there."

"Well, captain, good luck to yer, anyhow!" exclaimed

Charles, who then informed the highwaymen that he had sold the chaise-cart and colt.

"How much did it realise?" inquired the captain.

"Fifteen pounds exactly."

"Keep the money for your trouble," said Captain Hawk, generously.

Charles was overwhelmed with gratitude.

"And now," remarked the captain, "let us pay a visit to our prisoners."

"They're as happy as birds," said Charles—"at least, they was when I left 'em—singin' included."

"Oh! have they been singing?"

"I believe yer, captain."

"Come, then, let us go and look at the vocalists."

It appeared that Messrs. Bucks and Pompey had lost none of their mirth, for as the highwaymen approached the chamber where they were confined, prolonged strains of harmony—of a peculiar kind—were distinctly audible.

When the door was opened, the first object that presented itself was Mr. Bucks, mounted on the table, addressing Pompey, who, with a cigar in his mouth, was leaning back in his chair, listening with evident relish to his oratorical fellow-servant.

The arrival of Captain Hawk and Lord Harcliffe cut Mr. Bucks short in an energetic speech upon the horrors of slavery and the blessings of freedom, and had the effect of making him descend rapidly from his elevated position.

Pompey could not so easily subdue the enthusiastic feelings Mr. B.'s eloquence had excited, and continued to cry "'ear, 'ear!" for several minutes after the speaker had subsided into silence.

"Well, my friends, you appear to be enjoying yourselves," said Captain Hawk, in a cheerful tone.

"'Em jess am!" replied Pompey. "'Em jolly good fellahs, an' 'em don' care a d—n for notink!"

"Oh, captain!" suddenly ejaculated Charles—who had entered the room with them—in a tone of suppressed mirth.

"What's the matter now?" inquired the captain.

"Sich a jolly rum idea's come into my head, all of a sudden!"

"Out with it! What is it? A bad idea is better than none at all."

"But this is a rale good 'un. My heye! what a game it 'ud be!"

"Well, let me hear what it is."

"I was thinking—suppose we could get these two coves mounted and dressed something like you an' your pal, an' start 'em up Bow Street! It'd soon get wind as it was your *own selves* as had passed, an' there'd be sich a precious chiny—fancy, all up Bow Street, into Oxford Street, and right along to Tyburn!"

"By Jupiter!" exclaimed the captain, after a moment's pause, with a merry laugh, "it's a brilliant idea, and I see no reason why it shouldn't be carried out."

"What's that?" inquired Lord Harcliffe.

His comrade informed him of Charles's suggestion.

"Capital!" laughed his lordship. "But will it not open the eyes of these infernal myrmidons to the fact of our being in London?"

"I think not, since I shall take particular care to impress upon the minds of these individuals the fact that they are following *us* into the country," returned the captain.

"What, then, do you intend to lead the way for them to follow?"

"Only *part* of the way; we can give them a lead, and by a sudden turn round a corner, which they will not perceive, we will allow them to pass us, and, in fact, go wherever they please—to the devil if they like—while we quietly remain behind. They'll soon have the hue-and-cry after them, and it strikes me they'll have such a ride as they haven't enjoyed for many a night."

This practical joke being resolved upon, the captain proceeded to prepare the minds of the victims to fall willingly—nay, eagerly—into their plans.

"I'm sorry in any way to interfere with your festivities," he remarked—"you seem to be so particularly happy."

"Never spent a pleasanter day in my life!" exclaimed Mr. Bucks, lighting another cigar.

"No more him ebber did eider," said Pompey, emptying a glass of brandy. "Dis prime stuff warm de cockles of him 'eart."

"I should be too happy to have the pleasure of your society for a few days, but you see circumstances preclude the possibility."

"Oh, *succum*stances be blowed!" remarked Mr. Bucks, in a tone that implied a thorough contempt for consequences—nay, for fate itself—"who cares for *succumstances*?"

"D—n de succumstances!" echoed Pompey

"Nay, my friends," continued the captain, somewhat reprovingly, "you forget how it is you are here."

"No him don't," interrupted Pompey—"him come because he was brought."

"But do you remember you were entrusted with a very important commission," continued the captain, "and that instead of keeping your own counsel, you very indiscreetly blabbed your secret to us, two entire strangers?"

"'Ow de debbil did we know it war you?" inquired Pompey.

"That does not alter the fact that you behaved in a most foolish and indiscreet manner," the captain went on, "and the consequence of this indiscretion is that you have been confined here, while we have been to the bank and changed two hundred pounds' worth of notes that you ought to have stopped."

This was an awkward fact; and as the captain addressed them in a very serious tone, they began to feel uncomfortable.

Charles, also, who stood by, was particularly ominous in his ejaculations.

"Oh, lor'! Oh!—oh!" he dropped out periodically.

"I happen to know," continued the captain, skilfully, "that the major is aware of his loss——"

"Oh, my heye!" said Charles, in a reflective tone of horror.

"Is he though?" remarked Mr. Bucks.

"Yes, he has been to the bank, and I am given to understand his rage was something terrific."

"Oh, gorra!" exclaimed Pompey.

"O——h!" dropped in Charles.

"He swears solemnly," the captain went on, "that unless you can give a good and satisfactory account of your absence, he'll decapitate you the moment he sets eyes on you again!"

"Golly! what dat?—what de meanin' ob decap-i-tate?" asked Pompey, apprehensively.

"Cutting off both your heads!" wound up the captain, impressively.

"Oh, crikey jemmy!" murmured Charles, in a tone which implied a world of unknown terrors.

The groom and the black were by this time verging into a state of considerable alarm.

"Go on, captain!" whispered the mischievous Charles—"work 'em up: they're a gettin' the funks beautiful!"

"In a case of this kind," continued Captain Hawk, "when a loss of property has been occasioned by such palpable neglect as you have shown, you are looked upon in precisely the same light as though you had actually stolen it yourselves."

"You don't say so?" gasped Mr. T. Bucks.

"It's a fact, I assure you!"

"Poor innocent creeturs!" murmured Charles, in a tone of intense commiseration.

"And," continued the captain, "of course you're aware that when persons are found guilty of stealing two hundred pounds, they are *invariably hung*."

Messrs. Bucks and Pompey at these awful words collapsed, and were ripe for any plan that promised escape from Jack Ketch.

"I shall most decidedly b-bolt!" faltered Bucks.

"Gorra, me'll bolt too!" echoed Pompey.

"You forget you'll be watched—the police will be on the look-out for you—your persons described," urged the captain, energetically.

"Couldn't I disguise myself?" inquired the groom, anxiously.

"Well, to tell you the truth, that's your only chance," answered the captain.

"I'll disguise myself as well," said Pompey.

"With that black mug?" remarked Charles.

"Gorra! him forgot him black face," whined Pompey—"dere's no disguisin' dat!"

"Yes, there is," said Charles; "you could be white washed."

[A RIDE TO TYBURN.]

Golly, so him could!" exclaimed the black, in a tone of great relief; "him nebber tink ob dat!"

"Oh, that'll be all right," continued the benevolent one. "I'll undertake to make yer white enough."

This idea appealed so strongly to the risible faculties of the captain and Lord Harcliffe, that they were compelled to turn away to conceal their laughter.

By a strong effort they controlled their emotion.

"Could you disguise us?" inquired Mr. Bucks, anxiously.

"I will see what I can do," answered Captain Hawk. "Though you have got yourselves into this scrape by your own carelessness, I should be sorry to see you dangling at a rope's end for it."

Messrs. Bucks and Pompey involuntarily cuddled their necks with their hands as if to protect them.

Charles snapped his fingers, making a very disagreeable dislocating kind of sound.

"It *must* be awful to be 'ung!" he jerked out, and crack, crack! went his fingers.

"I'll save you if I can," said the captain, after a moment's reflection.

The domestics were brimful of gratitude.

Charles received some whispered directions, and disappeared.

"You had better divest yourselves of your garments," remarked Captain Hawk; "it will save time."

"What! take off him petticoats?" inquired Pompey, somewhat ruefully. "Dat's rader a delicate job for one ob de fair sex."

"Well, if you prefer being hung, you'll find that an operation still *less* delicate," returned the captain, coolly

Pompey, in order to prove his intense horror of this last proceeding, commenced dragging off his feminine attire in the most violent manner possible.

Strings and tags were dragged asunder ruthlessly, and in a few moments he stood in his shirt.

Mr. Bucks was in the same state of undress by his side.

Charles now entered with two suits that had been formerly worn, but were now cast off, by some *gentlemen of the road.*

"There!" he said, as he placed them on the table, "slip into these."

There was a desperate rush for the garments.

"Gently—gently over the stones!" cried Charles, who was in a frenzy of delight as he contemplated Pompey, in his anxiety to change his identity, making desperate efforts to thrust his legs into the arms of one of the coats.

At last, however, they were encased each in a pair of breeches, coat, and vest.

Though the gold lace on them was somewhat tarnished, they still presented a stylish appearance.

Next came two ample white cravats, and a couple of three-cornered hats ornamented with lace and dilapidated feather trimming.

Lastly, their legs were encased in two pairs of worn-out riding-boots without soles; and the disguise, so far as the dress was concerned, was complete.

"There!" exclaimed Captain Hawk. "I defy the major to recognise you now."

"De debbil himself wouldn't know us," said Pompey.

"Wait a little," added Charles. "If your bodies are disguised, remember yer faces ain't."

"Get de whitewash—quick as ebber you can!" urged Pompey, eagerly.

"All in good time," said Charles.

And as he spoke the pale-faced youth with the long fingers entered with a small box and a tin vessel, in which was a brush.

Having placed them on the table, the pale youth departed.

"Now, then," said Charles to the black, "sit down."

Pompey dropped in a chair instantly.

"Now shut your eyes."

Pompey shut his eyes, but at the same time he opened his mouth, and received a brushful of whitewash from his facetious operator.

"Oh, golly!" spluttered the black. "Him don't want to be whitewash inside as well as out."

"You must keep your mouth shut, then," said Charles, who commenced the whitening process.

In a few moments Pompey's sable visage was as pale as that of a plaster image, and he was released with orders that he was to walk about till he was dry.

Charles then attended to Mr. Bucks, whom he adorned with a pair of moustaches, which he fastened with a preparation of gum.

Pompey, as soon as his face was dry, received a similar ornament; and this having been accomplished, they were pronounced finished.

"Admirable!" exclaimed Captain Hawk.

"Wonderful!" ejaculated Lord Harcliffe.

"They looks quite 'ansome—doen't they?" asked Charles, admiringly. "I 'aven't seen sich a pair o' picturs for many a day."

It required no little effort on the part of the highwaymen to maintain the gravity necessary to the carrying out of their plans.

"An' now we're ready, when are we to start?" inquired the groom.

"You'll require horses," remarked the captain. "But there are plenty of livery stables."

"I can't go to a livery stable in this toggery," protested Mr. Bucks.

"Oh yes, you can," said the captain—"I'll provide you with the necessary funds."

The groom, feeling the strong necessity that existed for his speedy departure, offered no further objections; and, having received five guineas from Captain Hawk, he left the house with Charles.

As they descended the steps, Charles quietly knocked Mr. Bucks's hat over his eyes, and, telling him to be quiet, guided him out of the labyrinthian locality towards the nearest livery stables.

When they had got to some distance he kindly informed him that he could "raise his hat if he liked," when Mr. Bucks, who felt as though he "wandered in dreams," found, to his great surprise, that it was quite dusk.

"You see, yer'll get away in the dark," remarked Charles, "an' nobody none the wiser."

The bargain was soon struck at the livery stables.

Mr. Bucks hired a pair of horses on his own account, and Charles hired another pair himself, quite independently of his companion.

They then returned to Snagson's, each riding one of the animals and leading the other.

Charles took care to guide him by such a roundabout way that in the obscurity of the evening Mr. Bucks could never have found his way there again, even had his life depended on it.

Captain Hawk and Lord Harcliffe were ready, and each had assumed a plain, sober suit, surmounted by gray George wigs; and their necks being encircled by ample cravats, no one would have easily recognised them.

They rode on towards the Strand, Charles accompanying them a certain distance, and then diverging towards Bow Street.

He, it must be understood, was on foot, and had his part to play in the forthcoming equestrian performance.

He waited, however, till he saw the horses in the Strand at the bottom of the street.

"Now," said Captain Hawk to Mr. Bucks, "we are going to be your guides to a place of safety."

"Thank'ee!" murmured Mr. Bucks, who was longing to be off. "When are we to start?"

"As soon as you hear me call '*Go on!*' Stop for nothing! We shall be ahead. Ride like the very devil, without looking to the right or left, up Bow Street."

"What! past the police station?" gasped Bucks.

"Past the fiend himself, and *over* him if he gets in the way," returned the captain.

"Make your way into Oxford Street, and on towards Tyburn," he continued.

"B-but couldn't we go some other way besides passing the police office?" stammered the anxious groom.

"Can't 'em go roun'?" asked Pompey.

"No! Don't you see, they'll never think you would dare to pass close under their noses, and consequently they won't be prepared for you there. Don't you see?"

Mr. Bucks endeavoured, but did not succeed in getting a *very clear* view of this arrangement; however, the captain insisted, and there was no further appeal.

"All you have to do is to give your horses the spur and fly past like sky-rockets or the wind."

At this moment Charles appeared in the distance.

"We are going on a little ahead," said the captain.

"Not far, are you?" asked Mr. Bucks.

"Oh no! We're only going to see if the coast's clear. Mind, don't stop to look *at* us or *after* us, as we shall scud past like will-o'-the-wisps. Remember the signal!"

"'*Go on!*'" exclaimed Mr. B., to let the captain know he remembered it.

"Quite right."

And the captain and Lord Harcliffe quietly walked their horses forward almost to the corner of Drury Lane.

It was a ticklish position, that required all the *sang froid* of our heroes to enable them to maintain.

But they were well disguised and muffled up, and they were in a good neighbourhood for a game at hide and seek.

Two police officers passed at that moment in earnest conversation; and Captain Hawk heard one say to the other:

"The warrants 'll be out first thing to-morrow morning, and then I s'pose we shall have a month or so in the country hunting after these foxes."

They peered up rather curiously at the captain and his comrade as they passed, but the highwaymen in their plain attire, ample neckties and gray wigs, had so much the appearance of sober citizens that the officials never dreamt of even suspecting them.

Luckily, however, the men had not long been in the London police; the persons, therefore, of the highwaymen were unknown to them.

Seeing two such respectable persons on horseback, one of the officers could not forbear a little voluntary information.

"Good evening, gentlemen!" said the younger of the two.

"Good evening!" replied Captain Hawk, in a comfortable tone.

"Heard the news, gentlemen?"

"What news?"

"Captain Hawk and the Black Highwayman are on the road again."

"You don't mean to say that!" exclaimed Lord Harcliffe, in a tone of assumed apprehension.

"I do, though, gentlemen," the officer affirmed. "They have been robbing by wholesale these last few nights, and they changed two hundred pounds from notes into gold at the Bank of England this morning."

"Dear, dear!" exclaimed Captain Hawk. "It is really dreadful these continual depredations."

"We shall be after 'em. They'll have to look out sharp if they escape us this time," said the officer.

"Ah!" replied the captain, "it's a great comfort to think that our police are such a vigilant, courageous set of men—it gives us poor citizens confidence."

"Oh, never fear, sir! we've made up our minds to nab the pair of 'em this time, dead or alive!"

"Well, I wish you success! Take care they don't prove too much for you."

"We'll look out for ourselves, depend on it. Good night, gentlemen!"

"Good night!"

With these words, the men slowly proceeded towards the police office, at the door of which a body of the night patrol were waiting with their horses for the signal to mount.

Charles, who had never once removed his eye from our heroes during their brief colloquy with the police, now sauntered past, and exclaimed, in a low tone, as he passed:

"Ready, captain?"

"All right!" was the answer.

Charles continued his stroll a little way in the direction of the Strand, just so far as to enable him to discern Pompey and the groom, who were waiting on thorns for the signal to start.

"They're there safe enough," he said to himself "Ha, ha! poor devils!" he laughed, inwardly.

He passed the captain again.

"Look out!" he cried, softly. "As soon as yer sees a bustle among the police orcifers, give the signal to them poor blokes to come on."

He then crossed over, and suddenly darted across the road again, stopping the first person he met excitedly, and seizing him in a frenzied manner.

"Have you seen him?" he cried, frantically.

"Wh-o?" asked the startled wayfarer.

"Captain Hawk!" shouted Charles; and away he darted, pushing aside the astonished individual whom he had questioned, and who fell into the arms of somebody else, to whom, on inquiry, he could only gasp out the monosyllable:

"Hawk!—Hawk!" and then in a few seconds: "Captain Hawk!"

A small crowd soon collected, and the well-known name flew from mouth to mouth.

"Captain Hawk?—who?—what?—where?"

Charles in the meantime had flown across the road again, and seized upon another personage.

"Did you see him pass?" he cried, shaking the person violently.

"Good gracious alive! who?"

"The Black Highwayman!" roared Charles, in the highest excitement, and ran away to ask the same question of the next person he passed.

The last individual interrogated staggered up against the can of a baked potato merchant, and nearly capsized it.

"Where the devil are yer agoing?" shouted the man.

"The Black Highwayman!" yelled the other, in return, as he ran down Bow Street towards the police office, shouting at the top of his voice:

"The Black Highwayman!—the Black Highwayman!"

Uttering this alarm, he found himself in the midst of the police officers.

Seeing himself thus surrounded, he redoubled his cries.

"The Black Highwayman!—the Black Highwayman!"

"Where?—where?" cried the police, in a breath.

"There—there!" he shouted, pointing excitedly up the street.

"No—no!" bawled a crowd of people who had just hurried across the road, "he's there!"

"Who?"

"Captain Hawk!—Captain Hawk!" cried thirty or forty voices, whilst the same number of fingers pointed *down* the street.

"Why, d—n it!" shouted Peterson, who was there, "which do you mean, Captain Hawk or the Black Highwayman?"

On this point the crowd had now become divided.

Some cried one, and some the other.

Suddenly Charles rushed into the middle of the throng, shouting wildly:

"Here they come!"

"Who?—where?" shouted everybody at onc

"Black Hawk!—Captain Highwayman!" Charles roared, in confusion.

"Where?"

"Here?—down there!—up that way!" continued the frantic Charles, swinging his arms about and pointing every way at once.

"To horse!" cried Peterson. "I s'pose they're somewhere! Stand back!" he roared, to the crowd.

The mass of people congregated, oscillated and fell back.

"Now for it!" said the captain to himself; and going out into the road so as to let Mr. Bucks catch a glimpse of him, he waved his hand, and cried:

"Go on!"

The anxious domestics, wound up to a pitch of nervousness almost unbearable, and fancying they detected the features of Jack Ketch in every passer-by, on hearing this welcome cry, by a mutual impulse dug their spurs up to the rowels in the flanks of their steeds, who, utterly unprepared for such an attack, started and plunged so violently that it was a great wonder Messrs. Bucks and Pompey did not finish their ride before they began it.

However, they were desperate, and held on manfully, still spurring their horses, till they at length, half mad with pain, darted forward up Bow Street at a tremendous pace.

Having started them, Captain Hawk and Lord Harcliffe turned abruptly on one side and shrouded themselves in the obscurity of a narrow turning.

The police officers were mounting their steeds.

Suddenly the sound of horses' hoofs was heard rattling along in rapid motion.

"Here they come!" yelled Charles. "Ya—whoop!" he screamed, as the two steeds, as though pursued by furies with scorpion whips, were seen approaching.

"Here's Captain Hawk!—here's the Black Highwayman!" Charles continued, bawling at the top of his voice.

The crowd clamoured—the women screamed—the police officers swore as they tried to mount their horses, which the hubbub and din alarmed and rendered restive.

"Mount!" shouted Peterson. "D—n you!—stand still!" he cried to his horse. "By jingo! here's somebody!" he exclaimed, as with a sudden effort he swung himself into his saddle.

At the same instant—for all the above had occurred in no longer space than a few seconds—Messrs. Bucks and Pompey, mounted on their furious steeds, dashed recklessly through the middle of the crowd, scattering to the right and left men, women, and children in dire confusion.

"There they are, by gosh!" cried Peterson, whose horse was waltzing round and round as he was endeavouring to get his feet in the stirrups.

"After 'em!" he cried.

Those who were mounted gave chase, and Peterson having at length succeeded in fixing his feet in the stirrup-irons, started too—

The crowd, that had now become dense, also following, screaming and yelling, and quickening the speed of the terrified hacks, who had never been so scared out of their wits in their lives before.

And how was it with their riders all this time?

Following the advice of Captain Hawk, they looked neither *at* nor *after* anything but the end they had in view, and that was to escape the gallows.

As their steeds flew on, they hardly even thought of guiding them; indeed, the terror of the animals was so great, and the punishment the equally frightened horsemen were administering with such unconscious liberality so severe that they were quite beyond control.

As it happened, however, after various narrow escapes of collisions at sharp narrow turnings, they emerged into Oxford Street, and went on at full swing towards Tyburn, enveloped in clouds of choking dust, and with the officers in full chase at their heels, and the yelling crowd like a vast pack of hounds in the distance.

Pompey was by no means an experienced equestrian, and had long since relinquished the graceful for the safe position, and was now stretched forward, with his arms tightly clasped round the neck of the steed that bore him onwards.

Mr. Bucks, bent down in his saddle, appeared to more advantage.

"Oh, gorra—gorra!" groaned the whitewashed black. "'Em goin' to de debbil—him know 'em am!"

"After 'em, boys—after 'em!" from the officers fell distinctly on their ears.

"Dey'll catch us!" gasped Pompey. "Whar's de oder two gen'lemans?"

"There they are!" exclaimed Mr. Bucks, pointing to two indistinct objects in the distance that he imagined must be them.

"Him don' see notink!" groaned Pompey.

Their horses now began to give intimations of being pretty well winded.

They were only hacks, and must have astonished themselves at the speed with which they had travelled, but they now began to relax.

The officers observing this, set up a great shout, and increased their efforts to overtake them.

"Golly, dey'll catch us!" cried Pompey.

"Give him the spur!" shouted Bucks. "Don't spare him!"

Again the cruel goads were unmercifully administered.

The poor hacks, stimulated once more by this infliction, roused themselves and sped onwards.

A drover with a sow and a litter of young pigs was advancing.

The man shouted, and the pigs were refractory.

The fugitives were deaf either to the cries of the one or the gruntings of the other.

They dashed into the middle of the throng helter-skelter.

Over went the driver of the animals—away went the sow, whilst the juvenile sucklings were scattered in all directions.

Still onwards they went, till Tyburn turnpike appeared at no great distance.

"Can you leap a gate?" asked Bucks, in an agitated voice.

"Golly, no," answered Pompey, breathlessly, "unless him go ober head fuss."

The idea was perfectly insane, since neither of the "done-up" animals they rode could have gone over a stile, much less a five-barred gate.

But the idea was pleasant, inasmuch as it spoke of freedom, and the unhappy Bucks somehow clung to it.

"Now then!" he cried, as they drew near to the gate, "get yourself together, keep your horse's head well up, and when we near the gate give him the rein and the spur together!"

Pompey swallowed these directions in a confused—a *very* confused manner—in fact, he swallowed them the wrong way upwards.

He certainly spurred his horse and sawed away with the bit, and he also kept his head well up—so well, that when they reached the turnpike, he shot over the animal's head into the middle of the road on the other side of the gate.

While Mr. Bucks's horse, making a vain attempt at a leap, got his legs entangled in the bars of the gate, and in its struggles rolled over, and shot the groom into the dust, where he lay perfectly blown and powerless.

In an instant the foremost of the police officers had reached the spot and dismounted.

The toll-keeper had made his appearance, and opened the gate, and in an incredibly short space of time our two unlucky wights were handcuffed and in the hands of the officers

"Said we should nab you, my fine fellows!" exclaimed the young man who had spoken to Captain Hawk.

"Oh, lor! don't hang us!" exclaimed Bucks, in a tone of horror. "It was quite a accident."

"No, don't!" ejaculated Pompey—"him nebber do it again!"

At this moment, Peterson, who, having started the game, had allowed his men to run it down, whilst he followed more leisurely, intending to be in at the death, rode up.

"Here they are, Mr. Peterson!" cried the young officer.

"Who?" asked that individual, somewhat sternly, as his eye fell upon Messrs. Bucks and Pompey.

"Captain Hawk and the Black Highwayman!" jerked out the youthful member of the force, in a bumptious tone.

"Black Highwayman be d—d!" growled Peterson, in a tone of profound contempt. "Go an' teach your grandmother to suck eggs! an' don't come talkin' sich rubbish to me."

"What! ain't they the parties as I said?"

"Ain't they the parties as you said?" repeated Peterson, with the most ironical disgust conveyed in his tone "When you've had one brush with Captain Hawk and the Black Highwayman, you'll know better than to mistake two sich 'Jack in the Greens' as these for sich crack gentlemen!"

The youthful official was confounded, and said no more.

Peterson cast his eyes scrutinisingly on the terror-stricken domestics, and became extremely puzzled.

"What have we got here?" he soliloquised—"a couple of tailors? Who and what the devil are you?" he demanded, gruffly.

"I 'ave the honour to be Mr. Thomas Bucks, Major Bombshell's groom," returned Mr. B.

"An' I hab de honour to be Massa Pompey Snowball, Major Bombshell's footman," explained the black.

"And what in the name of all that's disorderly d'ye mean by gettin' up this chase, an' givin' us all this trouble?" growled Mr. Peterson.

"Our horses ran away with us," said Mr. Bucks, mildly.

"Dis 'ere 'oss pitch dis child ober de gate," stated Pompey, ruefully.

"Serve you right!" answered Peterson. "And what do *you* mean," he continued, leaning down and twitching off Mr. Bucks's moustaches, "by wearing these sort of things, eh?—very suspicious indeed!"

Mr. Bucks, in his confusion, murmured something inaudible.

"And you," the officer went on, addressing himself to Pompey, who, with the streaks of perspiration running down his face, looked like a human gridiron, or a semi-decomposed cannibal—"what have you been doing to your mug to make yourself look like a near relation of the King of the Cannibal Islands, eh?"

"Him bin whitewashed!" answered Pompey, boldly.

"Oh, indeed! Well, I think your conducts highly suspicious, so I shall take you both into custody," cried Peterson. "Now then, up with 'em!" he shouted.

Messrs. Bucks and Pompey were instantly hoisted up on to their respective steeds, and safely escorted by an officer on each side. The party returned to Bow street, where they were locked up in separate cells, till their little freaks could be inquired into.

CHAPTER CLXXXVII.

CAPTAIN HAWK AND LORD HARCLIFFE ARE COMPELLED FOR URGENT REASONS TO KEEP OUT OF SIGHT.—THE CAPTAIN COMMENCES THE HISTORY OF HIS YOUTHFUL DAYS.

CAPTAIN HAWK and Lord Harcliffe having seen the frightened domestics started on their wild career, did not follow them, but emerging from their temporary place of concealment, returned to Snagson's.

In due course of time, Charles, who *had* followed the crowd, and seen the unfortunate victims of his facetious plan brought back ignominiously and placed in durance vile, returned and detailed the whole affair for the amusement of the highwaymen.

When, however, their case was called, and it was ascertained that they were the servants of a military officer, and that they had apparently been made the victims of an audacious joke, they were discharged.

The major, it may be stated, as a pleasant wind up to the whole proceedings, had to pay something handsome for the damage done to the hacks on which his domestics had taken their hasty flight.

The warrants were out for the apprehension of Captain Hawk and his comrade, the Black Highwayman; consequently, they were compelled to be circumspect in their movements.

For an entire week they buried themselves in the calm seclusion of the "Family Hotel."

The indefatigable Charles made flying visits in order to obtain every possible information in those quarters where he would be likely to gain it.

It appeared that from the account given by Messrs. Bucks and Pompey, the officers were led to believe that the highwaymen had led the flight with better success, and preceded them into the country.

Consequently, the attention of the officials was directed to the outskirts of the town, as well as to more remote quarters.

Troops of mounted police watched, waited, and patrolled all the suburban approaches to the metropolis, whilst London was left to take care of itself.

All this was elicited and duly reported by the wide-awake Charles.

"I'm growing infernally tired of this confinement!" exclaimed Captain Hawk to his comrade, as they sat smoking their cigars one fine May morning in their apartment, in luxurious idleness.

"Not more than I am myself!" yawned Lord Harcliffe. "This life of inaction following upon the excitement we usually experience, is anything but agreeable."

The windows were wide open, and the merry chirpings of the sparrows struck the enforced captives strongly.

"Hark at those merry little fellows outside," said Captain Hawk. "Unpromising as this locality undoubtedly is, both as regards its situation and atmospheric peculiarities, the birds *will* sing—and why? because they are free. Shut them up in a close room, and they would droop their wings and die."

"The cry for liberty," said Lord Harcliffe, "is nature's voice claiming the greatest boon of Heaven! I do believe that were I condemned to live in a palace filled with all that could delight the eye and charm the taste, it would become loathsome to me if I were forbidden ever to *go out of it*."

"Undoubtedly," returned the captain, warmly. "Give me rather a mud hovel and freedom."

"How much longer are we to endure this confinement?"

"Till this evening only. Our presence in London not being suspected, we may venture forth—nay, we *will*. We have not been to the theatre for some time: let us go to Drury Lane, and see Garrick."

"With all my heart!" acquiesced Lord Harcliffe, eagerly; "and in order to pass away the time till dinner, suppose you relate to me, as you once promised you would, the history of your early life."

"With pleasure," returned the captain; and relighting his cigar, he commenced:

"I shall call this THE EARLY ASSOCIATIONS OF THE NOTORIOUS HIGHWAYMAN, CAPTAIN HAWK!'" he said, laughingly, by way of preface.

"My earliest recollection of home attaches itself to a secluded cottage, about twenty miles from London, and to my mother, a pretty pale-faced woman, with dark eyes and hair, who seemed to me from some cause which then I did not understand to be of a sad temperament."

"She probably had some cause," remarked his lordship.

"Great cause; but we must not anticipate. I remember at this moment, when I was quite a child, how she used to take me on her knee, and kiss me, and call me her 'poor boy,' and 'her darling.' Perhaps before going any further, you will like to see what my mother was like?"

"Have you her portrait?"

"Yes; her miniature painted on ivory. I would not part with it for the world."

As the captain spoke, he unbuttoned his vest, and from a small pocket in the lining, drew forth a small locket, attached to a chain round his neck.

It opened with a snap, and revealed to Lord Harcliffe, who rose to inspect it, the likeness painted beautifully on ivory of a remarkably lovely young woman, in whose features the resemblance to her son was clearly discernible.

"Beautiful!" ejaculated his lordship; "and without wishing to flatter you, my friend, there is no doubt as to your relationship."

Captain Hawk smiled and bowed to the compliment; and having restored the portrait to its usual resting-place, he continued:

"My first remembrance of my father was that of a tall, dark, handsome man, handsomely attired, who used to come periodically, and remain at home sometimes a week or a fortnight, sometimes a month, but rarely so long.

"He appeared devotedly attached to my mother, and she to him; and his arrival always chased away the sadness from her features, and made quite a holiday in our cottage.

"During these visits, my father would frequently have visitors, and I used to remark that they were all fine, handsome, gallant-looking gentlemen, who seemed on the most intimate terms with my father, very polite to my mother, and particularly generous to myself, who was quite rich with the guineas they invariably slipped into my pocket.

"They used to assemble in the parlour, that looked out upon the orchard in the rear of the house, and I used to wonder why my mother never joined the party, and why she was anxious to keep me from doing so.

"At these times they appeared to be very merry, and after I was in bed at night I could hear them laughing and making speeches and singing, till I fell asleep.

"When the morning came, they would all be gone; the chamber they had occupied the night before alone bearing witness to their conviviality, being filled with empty champagne bottles and the remains of other liquors, with pipes and the ends of cigars, that left their powerful odours everywhere.

"This disorder, however, was very quickly set right by my mother; and the windows being thrown open, no traces of the past festivity were suffered to remain.

"One night, during my father's absence, we were aroused from our sleep by a tapping at the door.

"My mother descended, and on opening it, she discovered my father, barely able to support himself.

"She uttered a cry that aroused me, and I hastened downstairs.

"I saw her supporting him into the parlour, which he had no sooner, with great difficulty, entered, than he sank down upon the sofa and fainted."

"I understand," said Lord Harcliffe, much interested.

"You will also understand that, boy as I was, when I saw my father's pallid face, and noticed how motionless he lay, I was very much alarmed.

"I remember saying 'What's the matter with father?'

"'He has met with an accident, darling,' was my mother's answer, and I then noticed that his coat and lace cravat were drenched with blood.

"'Shall I run for the doctor?' I cried, dreadfully alarmed.

"'No, no!' uttered my father, in a faint voice.

"He had revived after drinking a glass of brandy my mother had poured down his throat.

"'I shall do—I am better already. Send that child to bed, Emma,' I heard him say; and this injunction being carried out immediately, I saw no more.

"It was a week before my father was able to leave his room, and nearly two months before he could take his usual journeys.

"He would lie on a sofa with his arm in a sling, my mother's arm supporting his head, and tell me all kinds of wonderful tales.

"I have often heard my mother say that the two months he was confined to that sofa were the two happiest she had ever passed in her life.

"This seemed strange to me at the time, but afterwards I comprehended the truth of her assertion.

"When I was eleven years old I was sent to school at an establishment about twenty miles distant, and there I suppose my mischievous propensities began to develop themselves.

"I soon got accustomed to the company of boys, but there was one in particular for whom I conceived a particular affection, which he returned with equal warmth and sincerity.

"The name of my friend was Will Stanley. He was a year older than me, and no two brothers could have loved each other better or sympathised more in each other's tastes and pursuits.

"There was also one boy in particular, in opposition to this, whom I particularly hated for the simple reason that he hated me.

"From my first entrance into the school, he made a dead set at me. His name was Peter Bollard, and his appearance was as unpleasant as his disposition was cowardly and sneaking.

"He was nearly fifteen years old; and in spite of the disparity of our ages, he set himself to annoy me in every possible way.

"Aggravations, accusations, kicks and blows, fell from Master Peter Bollard on my devoted head without intermission.

"Do I tire you?" asked the captain.

"Not in the least; I am exceedingly amused," returned Lord Harcliffe.

"Doctor Short, the principal, was a kind little man, and very indulgent.

"He appeared to take a great liking to myself and my friend Will Stanley, and this was a great comfort to both of us.

"Not so, however, the French master, M. Adolphe Sanier.

"He, from some inexplicable reason, conceived a violent antipathy to my comrade Will, which extended to me because I stuck to Will back and edge.

"The most unfounded complaints and accusations were laid against us of insubordination and inattention to our studies, which puzzled the worthy doctor, who found us in all the branches in which he instructed us, as forward and attentive as boys usually are.

"But, as 'frequent droppings wear away the hardest stones,' so continual complaints being poured into the doctor's ear, made him at last almost distrust his own powers of perception; and as Master Peter Bollard was always ready to bear witness to any lie of M. Sanier's, and as M. Sanier would perjure himself in the same manner twenty times a day if necessary, we had a great difficulty in getting out of the nets that were constantly spread for us.

"We became fully aware at last of the virulence of our persecutors, and to the extent they carried their malice, in the following manner:

"It appeared that M. Sanier and Peter Bollard were great friends, and that out of school they were almost constantly together.

"Their favourite position was on the trunk of a decayed tree that had been felled, and that lay prostrate in the field that served as a playground.

"This tree was located almost at the edge of a deep, wide, but dry ditch, in which weeds and stinging-nettles flourished prolifically.

"On this trunk our enemies invariably sat, and concocted diabolical plans against the peace of Will Stanley and myself.

"The French master was a great smoker, and he used to light his black pipe with a burning-glass, and when necessary knock out the ashes of the tobacco through a hole—which happened to be near his hand—in the trunk, and which formed a convenient receptacle for the carbonised weed.

"Will Stanley and myself being curious to know what these two evil spirits usually talked about, would occasionally creep along the dry ditch in defiance of the stinging nettles, and under cover of the long grass, close up to the trunk on which they were seated.

"In the garden adjoining the school was a pear tree, which produced pears of a very choice description, of which the doctor was very fond, and still more proud.

"There were also two other persons equally partial to these pears, and they were M. Sanier and Peter Bollard.

"To the doctor's great chagrin, he was continually missing his pears.

"As often as he remarked two or three just on the verge of ripeness, so surely when he looked the next time did he find them vanished.

"He did not believe the birds swallowed pears whole, stalk and all, and he was annoyed and perplexed at the idea of being robbed.

"He called all the boys together, and plainly, like an honest little doctor as he was, stated the case.

"I remember perfectly well his saying: 'Now, boys, it is not the value of the missing pears that annoys me, but the idea that I have any pupils under my charge who would be ungenerous and wicked enough to rob their master.

"Of course no one confessed their guilt, though M. Sanier, fixing his eyes on Will and myself, said:

"I am sorree a charge so heavee should press upon ze whole school, doctair, at ze same time when ve know zat it is only *von* or *two* are guiltee."

"'I am equally sorry,' replied the doctor, without, however, directing his attention, as the Frenchman desired, to us in particular, 'and I trust after what I have said, my pears will be respected in future.'

"It was on the same afternoon we crept to our dry ditch, and there the murder came out.

"The French master and Peter Bollard were seated on the trunk of the tree as usual, and the subject of their conversation was—*pears*.

"'Ha, ha!' we heard M. Sanier say, with a diabolical grin, to his companion, 'ze littel doctair miss his pears: he vould like to catch ze birds zat fly avay viz zem, but ze birds are too clevair!'

"'We must have some more,' replied Peter, 'early in the morning; as soon as it's light's the time. I say,' he added, quickly, 'wouldn't it be fine if we could let those young fools, Hawk and Stanley, in for stealing a dollop of pears?'

"'Ha, ha!' grinned M. Sanier, delighted at the treacherous idea, 'I should like!—I should like!—but how can ve do it?'

"'Easily,' answered Peter. 'I'll get up early to-morrow morning—*very* early—and gather a bag full of pears. Then I'll creep quietly into their bed-room and hide them between the mattress and sacking of their beds.'

"'Oh, *oui! oui!* Zat is good—ver' good!' chuckled the wicked Frenchman.

"'Well, then you will state to the doctor,' continued Peter, 'that you saw two boys under the pear tree at an early hour; the pears found will confirm your story, and fix the guilt upon Masters Hawk and Stanley.'

"'Zat is excellent,' said the Frenchman; 'but you will not put *all* ze pears under zeir beds? Ve shall vant some.'

"'Of course,' answered Peter, 'I shall only put two or three, just enough to convict them—the rest I shall leave in the bag, which I shall stow away in your desk.'

"'Zat is right; no von sall dare to look zere,' said M. Sanier. 'An' you vill do zis to-morrow morning?'

"'Without fail.'

"Having thus gained this important information, we were provided with the means of defence," continued the captain.

"Ha, ha!" laughed Lord Harcliffe, "I declare it grows quite exciting. But don't let me interrupt."

"Well, you may depend upon it we were awake at the earliest dawn of day; and in course of time we heard Master Peter enter the room quietly, and after assuring himself no one was awake, creep quietly to our beds, which were next to each other, and conceal the pears in the spot he had previously indicated.

"He then stole from the apartment, and proceeded to the school-room to place the bag containing the bulk of the stolen fruit in the schoolmaster's desk.

"As soon as he was gone, we hastily collected the pears from beneath the mattresses of our beds, and ascending to the room in which Peter Bollard slept, placed them beneath his own mattress.

"We had hardly accomplished this feat, when we heard him coming back.

"It was an awkward casualty this, but he was quicker than we had anticipated.

"We stood in the lavatory, which interposed between the bed-room and the passage along which he was coming

"Luckily, a shower-bath with curtains stood near the door, and behind this we concealed ourselves.

"We saw Master Peter steal past, munching a pear; and as he disappeared into the bed-room, we slipped out into the passage, and then paying a visit to the bag in

Frenchey's desk, we helped ourselves beautifully, and returned with our spoil to bed.

"It was customary at the doctor's to have school before breakfast, after which the old gentleman would walk a short time in his garden and examine his trees—*the* pear-tree in particular.

"On this morning he discovered to his horror that in spite of his address on the previous day, a quantity of very choice pears had been since purloined.

"The doctor was a very good-natured man, but this loss was too much for him.

"He entered the long dining-room, hastily, looking very flushed and angry, where the boys were at breakfast, and stated his recent loss.

"The boys looked at one another, but no expression of guilt appeared on any of their features.

"As for Peter Bollard, conscious of security and hardened by repeated depredations, he sat as bold as brass.

"'What is the meaning of this?' cried the doctor—"how is it that I am continually robbed in this manner? Who is the thief?' He looked round at the boys as he put this question.

"'I am sorree to be oblige to speak, doctair,' commenced M. Sanier; 'but I cannot allow all ze young gentlemen to be looked upon as guiltee, when I have reason to sink zere is onlee two concern in zis.'

"'Who are they?' inquired the doctor, eagerly.

"'It is Mastair Hawk an' Mastair Stanley zat I mean,' answered the Frenchman.

"'What proof have you?' asked the doctor, who was a just man.

"'Veree airlee zis morning I hear ze garden gate shut,' said M. Sanier; 'but I was half asleep at ze time, an' I take no notice—I go to sleep again. Vell, a little after, I hear ze gate shut again, zen I jumped up from my bed, and look from ze window, when I see two boys go out of ze gate juss as I get zere.'

"'Were those boys Masters Hawk and Stanley?' inquired the doctor.

"'It seem to me it vas them, but I onlee had a glimpse for an instant, an' I could not swear to zem.'

"The doctor turned to us with a severe air

"'Young gentlemen,' he said, impressively, 'are you guilty or not guilty?'

"'Not guilty!' we answered in a breath.

"'Did you not,' the doctor asked, suddenly, of the Frenchman, 'go out to see who the boys really were?'

"'Oh, yes,' answered the lying master, 'but zere was somezing in ze lock which prevent me to open it for some time, and when I get out and go to zeir rooms zey appear to be fast asleep.'

"There was a pause.

"At length one of the boys said: 'Doctor, we don't feel comfortable under these repeated accusations. If there is a thief among us, let every boy's box and locker be searched—nay, bed and bedding—that we may stand a chance of finding out who he is, and that those who are innocent may stand clear in your estimation.'

"'Your proposal, sir, is very much to the point, and is a just way of removing doubts that are very painful to me to be obliged to entertain,' said the doctor. 'Let the search be made.'

"Accordingly, every boy's box and locker were opened and examined, but no pears were found.

"M. Sanier, who was foremost in the cry to be searched, now remembered the beds.

"'Zere is ze beds,' he suggested.

"'Ay, ay, the beds!—the beds!" exclaimed all the boys.

"These were first overhauled in the room where I and Will Stanley slept; but of course no pears were found there.

"We observed that both Peter and the Frenchman looked rather blank at this.

"However, they went on with their search until a loud shout announced the fact that the stolen fruit had been discovered under Peter Bollard's mattress. At the same moment the doctor himself appeared with a bag half full of pears which he had discovered in the Frenchman's desk, which he had taken upon himself to examine.

"The confusion of M. Sanier, whose complexion changed from yellow to green, and from green to blue, at this evident proof of guilt, was greatly enjoyed by the boys, few of whom liked him.

"He grumbled out something about 'conspiracee,' and 'wicked boys,' but he could not satisfy the doctor.

"Neither could Master Peter Bollard—although he stoutly denied the imputation of theft—remove the impression from the principal that he was guilty.

"The affair, however, blew over, and in a short time the doctor appeared to have forgotten it.

"But if he had, M. Sanier and Peter B. had not.

"They were, on the contrary, full of vindictive hate and burning for revenge.

"Amongst our boyish predilections was one in particular common to most lads—a love of playing with gunpowder.

"I and my comrade had quite a collection of small artillery—tiny brass cannons—which we used to load and discharge at wooden soldiers, which we used to denominate as French and English, sticking up two on either side with particularly ugly faces, which we specified as M. Sanier and Peter Bollard.

"We had been complained of several times for indulging in this amusement, which was considered dangerous, and had had several quantities of gunpowder seized upon and confiscated.

"But the temptation was too great to be resisted, and we bought more, and carried on our mimic battles, and demolished castles, and cannonaded cardboard citadels in defiance of M. Sanier, in remote corners of the playground.

"The doctor had been informed of our prepossession in favour of gunpowder, and had lectured us on the danger of firearms in inexperienced hands, but we were on this point incorrigible.

"One evening we were amusing ourselves and our schoolfellows after we had gone to bed by constructing diminutive volcanoes of damped powder, and letting them off outside the window.

"In the midst of a brilliant display, the malignant Frenchman, whose acute nose had detected the smell of gunpowder, entered the room.

"'Ha, ha! I have catch you zis time!' he cried, exultingly. 'You shall blow up ze 'ouse, shall you?' and with these words he proceeded to chastise me.

"After knocking me about till he was tired, he went off to fetch the doctor, leaving Master Bollard behind, who had entered with him, and who began imitating the Frenchman and pulling my ears.

"'You'll make Mount Vesuviuses and fizgigs outside the window of your bed-room, you young scamp, will you?' he hissed out, in his horrible sneering tone, and pulling my already bleeding ear as he spoke.

"Annoyed at being interrupted in my sport, and smarting under the manipulation I was enduring, I forgot the time, place, and the difference of our respective sizes and ages, and clenching my fists, I dropped into Master Peter Bollard right and left. I hit him in the eye, I hit him on the nose, and then in his other eye, and then on the nose again; I hit him in the mouth, and knocked out three of his teeth, which he swallowed; I hit him in the wind, which made him retch violently, and so bring the teeth to light again; I knocked him down, and as often as he got up I knocked him down again, and when he could rise no longer I believe I jumped upon him.

"You will easily credit that by the time the doctor arrived, Master Bollard was completely settled."

"I should think so," said Lord Harcliffe, laughing heartily.

"Of course this attack was an aggravation of the first offence, and I was kept a prisoner in the house for a week

"But this punishment did not satisfy the revengeful Peter and his French ally.

"The former, after the thrashing I gave him, kept very clear of me, but I could see there was some plot hatching as they sat in close consultation on the old trunk of the tree.

"I mentioned my suspicions to Will Stanley, and we both agreed to play the eavesdroppers again in the dry ditch.

"This time we were again fortunate enough to get the clue to a very pretty little piece of villany, which, had it not been frustrated, might have cost us our lives.

"We heard the Frenchman say:

"'Von qvarter of a poun' vould be enough, and I have got moch more zan zat, vhat I 'ave take avay from ze rascal.'

"We wondered what he meant, but the explanation soon followed.

"'Where should you put it?' asked Peter.

"'Undair ze bed in ze tin canistair,' replied the fiendish Frenchman; 'den I should lay a train to ze door, an' vhen dey are asleep ve vould light it. Den it vould only be fizz! bang! crash! an' dese d—n rascals should be blown to ze devil!'

"'And of course,' said Peter, 'all the blame will fall on them, as it will be supposed they have been playing with gunpowder again.'

"'Of course it vill,' returned M. Sanier—'zat is vhere ve shall be so safe.'

"It is needless to state that after hearing this we were very careful to search very scrutinisingly under our beds when we retired to rest, and to keep awake at night as long as we could.

"We had not long to wait, for their revenge was eager.

"Three nights after, when all the boys but ourselves were asleep, we heard a sound of suppressed breathing near our beds.

"We listened, and distinctly heard *something* placed under mine. 'That's the canister,' thought I.

"Then came a sound as of a hand scraping the floor very gently. 'That's the train,' I said to myself again.

"This sound then ceased, and a stealthy step cautiously stole towards the door, which we heard close softly.

"In an instant I was out of bed, grasping the canister, which must have contained quite half a pound of gunpowder.

"I at once detached the canister into which the fuzee was thrust through a hole in the side; and placed it safely under my pillow, feeling assured it could do me no injury there.

"But I felt at that moment I could have immolated the two murderous wretches on the spot, who had contrived this infernal scheme.

"However, we lay quietly, and presently, by the smell, we knew the train was smouldering.

"We looked down between the beds and saw it creeping along the floor in the dark like a fire-fly.

"Not wishing to rouse our companions, we lay perfectly still.

"Hour after hour passed, and we head no more.

"We marvelled, that hearing no report, either the Frenchman or Peter had not suspected a mishap or some casualty, such as the train becoming extinguished ere it reached the powder, and have come to reconnoitre.

"The truth was: they were so confident of the success of their diabolical scheme, that the moment M. Sanier had applied a light to the train, he, accompanied by his ally, Peter, had left the house, having previously obtained the doctor's permission to visit a friend some miles off, where they remained all night.

"They were therefore terribly disturbed when on their return early the next morning, instead of finding the roof of the dormitory blown off, and our mangled bodies tortured with agony, if not dead, to see us quietly sitting at our desks as if nothing had happened.

"The Frenchman looked hard at us, and Peter Bollard made several abortive attempts to draw us out, but could get nothing from us.

"We assumed perfect innocence and unconsciousness.

"One thing, however, we had resolved upon, young as we were, and that was a deadly revenge in kind upon our cowardly persecutors.

"Our plans had been laid and arranged early that morning before their return.

"And they were, so we thought, simple and likely to prove efficacious.

"We had first tied up the canister of powder tightly; I then crawled up the hollow of the tree in the playground, on which the French master usually sat, and placed it safely there, scattering thickly a quantity of extra powder exactly under the hole into which he always knocked out the hot ash of his pipe; taking care that this should communicate thoroughly with the fuzee stuck in the side of the canister.

"This being done, we felt our trap was laid, and we could afford to wait calmly the result.

"All the morning, the Frenchman seemed suspici and ill at ease.

"At length school was over, and Mr. Sanier, having lighted his eternal pipe, repaired to his usual seat on the trunk of the tree, accompanied by his inseparable companion; but little did they imagine what a mine they were sitting on.

"How our hearts beat! We could have roared with laughter, but we were too excited.

"'I'd give the world to hear what they're saying,' said Will Stanley; 'let's try the ditch.'

"'Will it be safe?' I asked.

"'Oh yes, we shall be down in the hollow out of the way; anyhow, I shall chance it.'

"'I'm with you!' I cried.

"Watching our opportunity when the Frenchman was looking another way, we dropped into the ditch, and crept along till we reached our usual post behind the trunk.

"Just as we reached there we heard him say: 'I don't understand how it could have fail?'

"'The fuzee went out, most likely,' suggested Peter.

"'Bote where did ze gunpowder an' ze canister go to?' exclaimed the Frenchman.

"'I hope you'll both find that out experimentally presently,' thought I.

"'Some von moss 'ave got it: it can't have fall into ze 'ands of zose d—n boys—zose wretches!' the professor continued, impetuously.

"'They're as cunning as Old Nick!' remarked Peter.

"'Cunning or not,' replied M. Sanier, 'I shall nick zem ze next time!'

"Here he began to tap his pipe on the trunk.

"We knew what was coming—at least, we hoped so—and crouched down and held our breath, our hearts beating convulsively.

"The Frenchman continued: 'Zose d—n boys shall 'ave a poun' of powdair ze next time—a whole poun'; zough I should give anyzing to know vot became of zat canister.'

"As he spoke, he gave the cue for the answer by shaking the ashes of his pipe through the hole in the trunk.

"It came in an instant, and in his own words.

"*Fizz!—bang!—crash!*—and away went M. Adolphe Sanier, away went Master Peter Bollard, and away went the trunk!

"The two former into the air, whence in course of time they descended, bruised, scorched and seriously damaged.

"As for the unoffending trunk, as that was never seen any more, we concluded it was blown over the hedge, or annihilated

"We crept away from our post of concealment, and I must confess we both rejoiced as we saw our two persecutors carried perfectly helpless into the house.

"This last event terminated all feuds between the professor, Master Peter and ourselves: and as it was near the end of the half year, we shortly after went home for the holidays, our last reminiscences of our persecutors being M. Sanier with a patch over his eye, limping along on a crutch, and Peter Bollard also walking with a stick, and his arm in a sling."

At this juncture, Charles announced dinner was ready.

"A very agreeable interruption," cried the captain to Lord Harcliffe.

"A very *unseasonable* one," returned his lordship. "I never was more amused in my life."

"Well, then," said the captain; "if it does not weary you, I will finish my account at the next convenient opportunity."

And with this, they descended to the dining-room.

CHAPTER CLXXXVIII.

CAPTAIN HAWK AND LORD HARCLIFFE VISIT DRURY LANE THEATRE.—THEY GAZE ON A BEAUTIFUL VISION, AND DISCOVER AN UGLY PLOT.—THEY DROP IN ALSO UPON AN OLD ACQUAINTANCE.

THE repast finished, and after they had sat some time over their wine, they retired to their sleeping apartment, where they proceeded to dress for their contemplated visit to Drury Lane Theatre.

As our heroes were not given to dandyism, and as they

[CAPTAIN HAWK AND THE BLACK HIGHWAYMAN IN NEW CHARACTERS.]

were both endowed with great personal advantages both of face and figure, they neither needed nor attempted any of the impostures of art, Nature having rendered such a step unnecessary.

Their toilet duties were rapidly performed, and when they descended from their bed-chamber, in two rich suits of silk velvet and gold, it would have been difficult to find in all London a more courtly and gallant pair of cavaliers.

When it was time to start, they threw their cloaks around them, and sallied forth on foot until they reached a point where a coach could be procured.

Then delivering their cloaks to Charles, who accompanied them, a very short time saw them beneath the portico of our grand national theatre.

As they were entering, the attention of our heroes was attracted by a very young and extremely lovely woman, who was attended by a gentleman scarcely older than herself, whose uniform bespoke him an officer in the Guards, and whose elegant and at the same time manly bearing seemed to justify the affection with which it was evident his fair companion regarded him.

"I wonder who that lovely creature is?" remarked Captain Hawk to his comrade, as they were waiting to pay their admission money.

"I do not know her by sight," returned his lordship; "but from her appearance and manner, she is evidently of noble blood."

The two highwaymen followed the handsome couple with their eyes as they ascended the staircase, and were about to proceed in the same direction when a young gentleman of fashionable though somewhat rakish appearance entered hastily, and brushing rather rudely past Captain Hawk, without troubling himself to apologise, or taking any further notice, ran hastily up the stairs.

"Humph!—that's civil!" remarked the captain, stooping to pick up his hat which the other had brushed off. "Let us see who this young spark is that treats us so unceremoniously."

They accordingly ascended the stairs, the prominent idea in the captain's mind being to read the young gentleman a lesson on civility.

When, however, they reached the top, they saw the object of their thoughts in the lobby at the back of the dress circle in earnest consultation with another some years older than himself.

Both were handsomely dressed, and there was something in their general appearance that denoted them to belong to the upper ranks of society.

The features of the elder of the two were aristocratic and courtly, though disfigured by a frowning brow, and deeply-marked lines on each side of the mouth, apparently induced by a habit of compressing the lips firmly together.

His companion possessed regular features, but dissipation had spread over his countenance an unnatural paleness and an expression of licentious recklessness that destroyed what might else have been termed handsome.

Captain Hawk would have gone up to him at once to demand an apology for his rudeness, but he was restrained by the words that reached his ear from the young man's lips:

"*She is here*, Sir Richard!"

There was no particular reason why this exclamation should have altered the captain's intention, nevertheless it had this effect.

And the reason was, that the idea crossed him that the remark had reference to the beautiful woman he had been so struck with at his first entering the theatre.

"My niece?" asked the gentleman addressed, in an inquiring tone.

"Yes; and *he*, too, with her—curse him!"

"Hush, my lord—hush!" said the other, reprovingly.

"Oh! can anyone be silent when he sees the woman he loves as madly as I love her in company with a rival, and not only that, but smiling on him—permitting his addresses?" exclaimed the young man, impatiently.

"Try to compose yourself—you may be mistaken. Are you sure 'twas she?"

"I could swear to it. I watched the sedan chair that brought them stop at the foot of the steps. I'll not submit to it!"

"Nay, nay—but be patient!"

"It is impossible! But have I not been patient? When, in order to secure the rank of countess for your niece, you married her to the old Earl of Blacklake, you advised patience then, did you not?"

"I did, and you followed my advice."

"Yes, because I knew Clarissa did not love him, and because the earl was an old man, and I felt that death would, in the ordinary course of nature, speedily annul the ill-assorted union."

"As it has done."

"Yes. A twelvemonth has now passed since the earl's decease, when, just as I was rejoicing in the prospect of paying my addresses to your lovely niece, up starts this beggarly intruder—this penniless captain, who, with a handsome face, insolent assurance, and the King's uniform on his shoulders, dares to thrust himself between me and my most cherished desires."

"Well, but all this passion will not mend matters," remarked the elder, quietly.

"You speak coolly enough, Sir Richard, in all conscience. Do you not wish me to marry your niece?"

"Undoubtedly."

"Such being the case, you are her guardian—she is yet under age, and your authority may be as successfully exerted in my behalf as when you used it to bring about her union with the Earl of Blacklake."

"I fear I am too late. I think she loves this young captain; in fact, I believe it is no new attachment, but that they loved mutually previous to her marriage."

"Then is there nothing to be done?"

"Yes, but, whatever it be, it must be done quietly, without quite the publicity you seem inclined to give to it."

These words were spoken in a manner that implied much more than the words themselves.

The young man looked at the speaker for an instant, and then said:

"What mean you? How am I to understand your words?"

"Thus," answered the old man, as he bent down and whispered in his companion's ear.

Captain Hawk noticed a sardonic expression on the whisperer's features, and a fierce, cruel smile on those of his listener as he drank in the words that were inaudible to any but themselves.

"You have only spoken my thoughts," said the young man, fiercely. "There are some rivals that can only be disposed of in the same manner as you would rid yourself of some noxious animal that annoys you. We do not *fight* with such—we *crush* them."

"What, then, do you propose?"

"They came hither and will return in a sedan chair."

"Well?"

"What more easy than to bribe the chairmen—two Irishmen—to *lose their way purposely*, as they carry them back, and leave them in some obscure court or alley, where, under the cover of night and our cloaks and masks, we can give this troublesome rival his quietus? Dead men tell no tales, neither have they power to stand in the way of the living."

This last speech was spoken so earnestly that Captain Hawk and his comrade heard every word of it.

"I see no reason why your plan should not succeed," said the old man, in reply. "But come, let us take our seats—we may be overheard."

With these words they entered the dress circle.

"A very agreeable arrangement for that handsome young soldier," remarked Captain Hawk, as the door closed upon the pair of plotters, "and one that there would be some credit in foiling."

"I'll join you willingly. We can consider the best steps to take as we sit in our box," said Lord Harcliffe, "and keep our eyes on these cut-throat gentlemen at the same time."

The highwaymen accordingly repaired to a private box, where, by leaning a little forward, they could command a view of the whole interior.

To their great satisfaction, the beautiful creature whom they in their own minds determined to be the Countess of Blacklake sat with her companion in a box nearly opposite.

The performance now commenced.

The play was Shakspeare's tragedy of "King Lear," in which the renowned actor Garrick was soon delighting the audience by his masterly assumption of the persecuted and demented monarch; and our heroes were fully able to enjoy the great poet's masterly creation, and the great actor's skill in interpreting it.

At the same time they could watch the proceedings of the parties in whom they were severally interested.

"I should like to know whether that extremely beautiful woman is really the Countess of Blacklake," remarked Captain Hawk, after the curtain fell at the end of the first act.

This doubt was speedily set at rest by a conversation he overheard from some sprigs of nobility in the adjoining box.

"That beauty in the opposite box, with the golden hair," said one, evidently in answer to some previous question, "puts me in mind of Hebe. Who is she?"

"That is Clarissa, the young Countess of Blacklake."

Captain Hawk and Lord Harcliffe nudged each other to listen.

"A widow, isn't she?" continued the questioner in the next box.

"Yes, and only nineteen."

"Charming age! Would there be any chance for me, think you?"

"I rather fancy not. That handsome fellow by her side, in the uniform, might prove an obstacle."

"Ah, yes! Who is he?"

"Captain Alfred Nugent, of the King's Guards."

"Is he a favoured suitor?"

"Rather! But he's only *one*."

"What! has she more?"

"I believe so. They say Lord Edward Strathern—ah! by-the-by there he is in the dress circle, with the uncle, Sir Richard Chandos—well, they say he's mad after her, but the general opinion is that she does not favour his suit."

The rising of the curtain at this moment interrupted further conversation, but it had informed our heroes of all they wished to know—the identity of the parties in whom they were concerned.

The play proceeded, when, in one of the most quiet portions, the entire audience were startled by a stentorian voice shouting furiously from the dress circle:

"There they are! They're the rascals that stole my repeater! That's the villain that robbed me of my cork leg!"

The highwaymen looked in the direction from whence the voice proceeded, when, to their horror, they observed, standing bolt upright in the dress circle, the portly and incensed Major Bombshell, with the graceful Augustus at his side, both of whom were exclaiming at the top of their voices, and pointing directly towards them.

"D—n it!" whispered the captain to his comrade, without, however, blenching in the least, or losing his presence of mind, "it will never do to be bowled out by a pair of idiots like that!"

He drew back as he spoke, and Lord Harcliffe quickly pulled the curtains across so as to shroud them from view.

The major seeing this, and fancying they would escape, roared louder than ever.

"A madman!" exclaimed several.

"What's the mattah with that old individual?" asked one of the occupants of the next box, leaning over and looking into that occupied by the highwaymen.

"Old fellow out of his mind—fancies he's been robbed of his cork leg," replied Captain Hawk.

"Ha, ha! thank you! Very droll indeed!"

As the major still continued shouting, it caused such a stoppage to the business of the stage, that the audience took it up indignantly.

Loud cries of "Order!" "Turn him out!" from the pit, and "Throw him over!" from the gallery, added to the general din.

"The sooner we're out of this the better, I think," remarked Captain Hawk.

"I am of your opinion," returned Lord Harcliffe.

"Now for it, then," said the captain, as he opened the door quietly.

They emerged from the box, but had no sooner done so than the captain was pounced upon by the gallant Augustus, who in the light and crowded theatre felt sure of immediate assistance, and was consequently full—for the time being—of the hereditary valour of the Bombshells.

"I've got you now," he cried, "and nothing shall induce me to release you—nothing!"

"Oh, pooh!" muttered Captain Hawk, between his teeth.

At this moment the major, puffing and blowing, with his face crimson with excitement, came stumping up.

Seeing his son grappling the captain, he at once threw himself upon Lord Harcliffe.

"You scoundrel!" he shouted, "where's my repeater? Fire and fury!—where's my 500*l.*?"

"Give me my watch!" shouted Augustus.

Matters were now growing rather critical.

There was only one thing to be done.

The door of the box they had quitted stood open.

Lord Harcliffe therefore coolly bundled the major in unceremoniously, who fell with a crash between the seats, whilst Captain Hawk dropped the gallant Augustus on the top of him.

The anxious Mrs. Major B. at this critical juncture hastened forward.

"My boy!—my bracelet!" she shrieked—"where are they?"

"In here, madam," said Captain Hawk, as he opened the box door suddenly and lifted her inside, where she added to the dismay and discomfiture of her beloved relatives by overbalancing and sitting upon them with considerable impetus.

Captain Hawk, in order to gain time, thrust a portion of the playbill tightly screwed up into the lock, so that there was no getting it open.

There was so much shouting and confusion in consequence, that the parties came out of the next box for information.

"What the devil's the meaning of this demmed Babel?" asked a young fop.

"Family of lunatics in this box," remarked Captain Hawk. "Take care they don't bite."

"Oh, demmit!" exclaimed the dandy, retreating precipitately with his friends into the seclusion of their box once more, whilst Captain Hawk and Lord Harcliffe without further delay quietly, and as quickly as possible, left the theatre.

"A narrow escape that!" exclaimed Captain Hawk.

"By Jupiter, I think so!" answered his comrade.

"Let us take this turning," said the captain, as he suddenly branched off down a narrow court.

"And the handsome lady," remarked his lordship, "and those two conspirators? How can we assist her and frustrate their designs?"

"Umph!" answered the captain, reflectively, "it's awkward, certainly. It will be scarcely safe to enter the theatre again to-night!"

"No."

"And yet to leave that fair creature and that gallant young soldier to the treacherous attacks of these wolves in sheep's clothing galls me; we must help them somehow."

"I don't know whether you noticed it, but I remarked that they had left the box before that old idiot recognised us."

"I did not. We must keep our eyes open: we may see something of them outside, and—— Ha!"

The captain broke off suddenly and pointed behind him.

"Talk of the devil," he said, "and he stands at your elbow. See, here are the very persons we were speaking of coming behind us."

"By heaven! I can almost fancy I scent the odour of blood as they approach," said Lord Harcliffe, in a tone of repugnance. "But who are those fellows with them in long cloaks?"

"The chair bearers, no doubt," answered the captain. "Don't you remember hearing them say that they were Irish, and that they must bribe them?"

"True."

"Let us step aside in the shadow, and let them pass. One plot may be good until it is superseded by a better."

As he uttered these words Captain Hawk drew his comrade into a dark doorway, so that they were perfectly unseen as the noblemen passed.

"That's right," murmured the captain to himself. "I always like to see mischief in front of me."

At this moment, however, the party stopped, probably because it was a quiet and obscure spot, where a bit of villany or murder could be safely planned, or, if need required, executed.

Our heroes remained perfectly quiet and listened.

He heard Sir Richard Chandos say, as they came to a stand, "We need go no farther; we can talk here."

"Bedad, your honour," remarked one of the Irishmen, "it's so dark we can hardly see to hear in this place!"

"It will serve our purpose exceedingly well," said Sir Richard.

"An' what is it your honour wants wid us?" inquired the former speaker.

"You brought a lady and gentleman in a sedan chair to the theatre to-night?"

"Sure yer honour's honour an' we did that same. I was afoor, an' Pat he was behint," answered the Irishman.

"Where did you carry them from?"

"Oh, thin, yer honour, wasn't it from a large house in St. James's Square, wid more bricks than windies, an' more windies than doors?"

"Well, now," continued Sir Richard, "we wish to try a little practical joke, quite in a friendly way, with the gentleman, who is a friend of ours. You understand?"

"Is it his brains you're wantin' to knock out, thin?"

"Do you call that a joke? No, certainly not; but we want to test his courage, and for that purpose we should require you, when you convey them home, to take them by some roundabout way, some out-of-the-way spot, where we could rush out upon you, and, under the character of a couple of pickpockets, demand our friend's purse."

"Would ye be wantin' to knock us down, your honour?" inquired the Irishman.

"Not if you remain perfectly quiet—that is, unless you

particularly wish it," said Sir Richard, with an ironical attempt at pleasantry.

"Just as your honour plases," returned the man, "only we'd be having to charge a little more for the crack on our nobs."

"There will be no occasion for that, I think," remarked Lord Edward Strathern, who had not previously spoken. "As soon as we appear you will feign great alarm and take to your heels."

"An' what'll become of the chair, poor crathur?"

"Oh, the chair will take care of itself. At all events, it will not run away, and you can return after a time. It will not then be too late, perhaps, to make amends by carrying the frightened couple home."

"An' if we do this, what'll your honours be afther givin' us?"

"You will receive a guinea each."

"What!" exclaimed the Irishmen, simultaneously—"a guinea!—a rale, bright goulden guinea? Oh, blessed St. Pathrick, it's good ye are to us poor sinners, anyhow!"

"Will that satisfy you?"

"O' course it will, yer honour! Long life to ye!" said Mick O'Donnell, enthusiastically, adding: "Maybe yer honours wouldn't mind givin' us a thrifle afoorhand jest to bind the bargin?"

"Here is a guinea," said Lord Edward, as he placed the coin in the Irishman's hand.

"Thankee, your honour! And whin'll we be expecting to resave the other?" inquired the man.

"I'll place it in your hand when we stop you on your way home," answered the young nobleman.

"All right, your honour. Anything else?"

"Nothing; only remember this—the moment your fares enter the chair, move on as quickly as possible, and under pretence of making a short cut, or with what excuse you please, be sure and take an unfrequented route. Do not stop to look for us—we shall be sure to follow and intercept you."

"We'll be sure to remember, your honour."

This arrangement being effected, the two treacherous noblemen departed once more towards the theatre, first intimating to the Irishmen that they were to wait till they were some distance ahead before they followed them.

"Bedad," said Mick O'Donnell to his comrade Pat, "we'll give 'em a good long start anyhow. Let's come an' have a noggin o' whiskey."

This was, of course, at once acceded to, and the exultant pair were about to proceed along the court in the opposite direction to a low public-house they were accustomed to use, when they were greatly astonished at finding a hand laid with considerable restraining power on each of their collars.

The idea that first suggested itself was that they had fallen into the hands of footpads who had overheard the secret of their newly-acquired wealth, and intended robbery. Of course, under such desperate circumstances, they were resolved to fight to the last rather than yield their money.

"Bad luck to ye!" cried Mick, "is it our gould ye're wantin', ye spalpeens?"

"Silence!" the captain exclaimed, under his breath, gripping Mr. O'Donnell's arm till he winced again; "we do not want to *take* your gold, but to *give* you more."

As Captain Hawk spoke, he slipped a guinea into Mick's hand, whilst Lord Harcliffe performed the same operation upon his companion Pat.

The two Irishmen were electrified.

"I've got another guinea, Pat!" cried Mick, enthusiastically.

"Bedad, Mick, so have I!" returned Pat, with equal fervour.

"Och, tunder an' turf! it's rainin' nothin' but goulden guineas to-night!" Mick continued, and would have gone on apostrophizing had not Captain Hawk cut him short.

"Come," he said, determinedly, "if you wish to earn money you must listen to me."

"We're as dumb as dead lambs' tongues, sir!" exclaimed Mick.

"We have heard all the conversation that passed between you and the gentlemen who have just left you."

"Yes, your honour."

"They wish to play a friend of ours a trick, and in return we wish to play them one—d'ye see?"

"Perfictly, your honour."

"But in order to do that effectually, we must not be known; and of course, as our present dresses would betray us, we wish to——"

"Change clothes wid us," anticipated Mick, eagerly. "Sure, we'll do that same wid all the pleasure in life, an' make an honest penny by the job into the bargain."

"No, no, you are too premature," interrupted Captain Hawk; "we do not wish to exchange clothes with you, but to borrow *your* coats, hats, and cudgels, for which we are willing to pay handsomely."

"Ye can have 'em, your honours," cried the men, "an' the shirts off our backs into the bargain, if ye like."

"No, thank you," remarked the captain and his friend, with an involuntary shudder at the idea. "Take off your coats and hats at once."

These articles of wearing apparel were removed in an instant; and the highwaymen having put them on, Captain Hawk said to Mick O'Donnell:

"Hold your hand."

The hand of the Irishman was immediately extended, and the captain counted into it three guineas.

Lord Harcliffe, as before, paid his comrade.

Their joy was unbounded, but Captain Hawk restrained them.

"Och, but," said Mick, "we've had a guinea ache from the other gintlemen: what are we to do about him?"

"Do nothing. We've outbidden them," answered the captain. "You've received four guineas each from us: go and enjoy yourselves, and leave us to attend to them."

"By the powers, an' so we will!" cried the Irishmen. And with many blessings, and any quantity of "good luck" invoked upon the heads of the highwaymen, the two sons of Erin hastily took their departure, making their way to the nearest public-house for a drop of the crathur; whilst our heroes, in their humble disguises, entered a tavern in the neighbourhood to discuss a glass of brandy, and the probable result of their plan, until the clock admonished them it was time to get to their posts outside the theatre where the sedan chair was standing.

CHAPTER CLXXXIX.

CAPTAIN HAWK AND LORD HARCLIFFE MAKE THEIR APPEARANCE IN PUBLIC IN NEW CHARACTERS.—AN ENCOUNTER IN A DARK LANE.—THE TWO CHAIRMEN SAVE THE LIFE OF CAPTAIN ALFRED NUGENT.

On their arrival they found people talking in a confused manner about some disturbance that had taken place inside.

"What's the matter, me darlin'?" asked Captain Hawk of a bystander, putting on an admirable Irish brogue suitable to his character.

"Well," answered the individual addressed, "I don't quite know the rights of it, but I heard that somebody had lost his cork leg in the theatre, and that he had gone mad about it."

"Oh, is that all, me jewel? Thankee," replied the captain.

Soon after, he put the same question to another, and he was then informed that it was understood that a major somebody had dashed out his wife's brains with his cork leg in one of the private boxes.

"Oh, bedad now, that's bad!" returned the captain, "onless the poor crathur's brains were of the same material as the cork leg—thin p'raps it wouldn't matther so much."

About this time several mysterious personages in *blue* congregated about the front, apparently looking at nobody, but in reality watching everybody.

Our heroes, snugly ensconced in their thick frieze coats, laughed in their sleeves—where, to speak truly, there was plenty of room to laugh—as they observed the acute officers slyly spotting out the various passers-by without appearing to do so.

Presently visitors from the theatre beginning to descend and sundry bawlings for carriages and sedan chairs, announced the fact that the play had terminated.

Shortly after there was a great stumping heard, and the loud voice of the major, laying down the law in his usual pompous manner.

In a few moments he appeared walking by the side of a police officer, to whom he was giving his opinion gratuitously.

"The law!" he exclaimed, in an angry, disgusted tone "Pooh! Law and equity are going post-haste to the devil! Here have I this very night been insulted in our national theatre!—I, a British officer, have been thrown upon my back between the benches; my son has been thrown upon me, and my wife has been thrown upon the pair of us! Justice! there's no such thing, or the dignity of the Bombshells would not be suffered to be so outraged!"

Talking in this manner all the way he went, the major, followed by his insulted wife and son, reached his carriage and was soon driven off.

He had hardly been driven away when the beautiful Countess of Blacklake appeared on the stairs, smiling graciously like the Queen of Night.

She had now a cloak around her, the hood of which covered her fair head, but she looked equally lovely enveloped as she was.

Having reached the door, a firm manly voice cried.

"The Countess of Blacklake's chair!"

"That's us!" replied Captain Hawk, pretending to start up in a hurry.

"You will come home to supper, Alfred!" whispered the fair Clarissa to her companion. "I am quite alone to-night."

We may be quite sure that the young officer did not say no to such a delightful proposition.

He bowed his affirmative, and handed the countess into the chair, the door of which Captain Hawk in his new character of chairman held respectfully open.

As he did so, his eye wandered across the road and fell upon the forms of Sir Richard Chandos and Lord Strathern who, wrapped in their cloaks, stood furtively watching the occupants of the chair.

His attention was directed from them by the sweet voice of the countess as she cried:

"Home!"

The fictitious Irishman closed the door, and when he looked again the watchers had disappeared.

Disappeared, but not departed; they had retired into a doorway to elude observation, and were waiting to see the route the chair would take.

"Well," said Captain Hawk, with a smile to Lord Harcliffe, as he prepared for his task, "we're coming to something at last."

"Yes," whispered his lordship; "this, I suppose is what is termed getting one's living honestly."

"Exactly!"

"I don't think it would exactly suit me," returned his friend.

"Nor me; but never mind, the motive justifies the deed: it is to *serve a lady!*"

With these words our heroes grasped the poles of the sedan chair, and raised it from the ground.

"We'll give these noble cut-throats a run for it," said Captain Hawk to himself. "They wish for a retired spot: they shall have it! Forwards, Pat!"

They hurried along through a portion of Covent Garden Market, and then abruptly branched off to the right, where they dived down some courts of a very suspicious aspect.

Had not the loving couple inside been so occupied with each other, they might have easily observed that they were returning by a very different route from that by which they had come.

As it was, they were wrapped in the sweet mists of "love's young dream," and thought of nothing but love.

The highwaymen knew perfectly well that their pursuers were on their track, for they distinctly heard their footsteps gaining upon them.

They could not suppress a smile of joyful exultation as they contemplated the surprise in store for them.

At this moment they came to a spot where the alley they were in branched off to the left, though there was still a pathway straight on.

Of these, both led into a broader court at not many yards distance.

Anxious to bring the affair to a climax, they took the turning to the left.

As they did so, Sir Richard and his companion passed by, keeping straight ahead, and Captain Hawk distinctly heard him say:

"Now we shall have them," as they hurried on

The highwaymen slackened their pace a little, and as they turned out of the narrow alley in which they then were into the wider path, they were met by their pursuers, who emerged at the same moment from the other footway, and confronted them.

Both were masked, and both cried with one voice:

"Stand and deliver!"

The chair-bearers, in pretended alarm, stopped, and set down the chair, and, according to agreement, Lord Edward took the opportunity of slipping the remaining part of the stipulated sum into Captain Hawk's hand.

"Now, begone—fly!" he cried, with pretended fierceness, to the fictitious Irishmen.

But the men appeared to be suddenly seized with deafness, and did not stir.

He had hardly time to comment upon their conduct, when Captain Nugent opened the door and sprang from the chair.

As he advanced, seeing the masked figures, he laid his hand upon his sword, exclaiming, in a bold voice, that had a considerable deal of indignation in it:

"What is the meaning of this? What do these fellows want?"

"They tould us to stop!" said Captain Hawk.

"And we want your purse!" added Lord Edward, in a feigned voice.

"That you may have if you can get it!" replied the young officer, tauntingly.

"There! didn't I tell you he wasn't worth a crown-piece?" cried Lord Edward, contemptuously, to Sir Richard.

The young nobleman's spleen which dictated this remark had overpowered his prudence, and he had forgotten to disguise his voice sufficiently.

Captain Nugent recognised it at once.

He paused and looked scrutinisingly from one to the other.

He then exclaimed:

"You may disguise your features, but you cannot conceal your voice. I know you now: you are no footpads. It is not money you seek, though I think Sir Richard Chandos and Lord Edward Strathern might find more creditable employment than that of roaming the streets at night in this absurd and inexplicable masquerade!"

And having uttered these words, the young officer, before either of the parties addressed could divine or anticipate his intention, took a rapid step forward and snatched the masks from their faces.

Both brows were dark with bitter rage at this exposure; but the expression on the face of Lord Edward was perfectly satanic in its fury.

He was ghastly pale, and could hardly command himself sufficiently for utterance.

At last his wrath found vent in words.

"By what right, fellow, do you occupy a place by that lady's side?" he raved.

"By the right of her permission," replied the young officer, calmly.

"Which she has no power to give!" added Sir Richard. "The Lady Clarissa is under age. I am her guardian, and her will must be mine."

"This is no place or time to jangle about rights and permission," returned the captain, angrily. "Stand aside, and let us pass!"

"No!" answered Sir Richard; "I intend to remain here. Go you, if you will; the sooner the better; but my niece returns with me."

"Once more, I command you, cease this outrage, and let us go by!" shouted Captain Nugent, fiercely, as his sword flew from his scabbard.

The opponents also drew theirs, when the voice of the countess, in accents of alarm, reached their ears.

"Oh! what would you do?" she cried. "Uncle—my lord—let there be no blood shed on my account, for mercy's sake!"

"Let him depart, then!" shouted her uncle, in a voice hoarse with passion.

"The soldier who would leave his ground at the threats of bullying violence, disgraces the uniform he wears!" answered the captain. "Men," he added, addressing the highwaymen, "take up your charge; if these brawlers attempt to stay your progress, the consequences fall on their own heads!"

"If you attempt to obey," shouted Lord Edward to the chairmen, "I'll batter your thick skulls against the wall."

"Forward!" thundered the captain; and as though to clear a passage, he, in a burst of uncontrollable impetuosity, rushed forward past his opponents, clearing his road by a sweep of his sword.

It was rather a rash movement on the part of the young officer, since it placed his opponents between the sedan chair and himself.

Their bloods were heated, and a contest was now inevitable.

Urged by vindictive jealousy and hate on the one side, and a sense of outrage and insult on the other, the weapons met in deadly clash.

All were good fencers; but two on one were rather disproportionate odds.

The countess, in an agony of terror, wept, entreated, implored them to desist, but in vain.

She was answered only by the clashing of swords and the angry ejaculations of the combatants.

The two noblemen fought side by side, and pressed furiously on the young officer, who parried their blows with a wrist of iron and the rapidity of lightning.

But what skill and hatred appeared unable to effect, Fate did.

The sword of the captain, in striking one of his adversaries' weapons on the flat of the blade, snapped short off at the hilt, and the young officer, unable to recover his balance, sank upon his knee.

Like angry wolves, his bloodthirsty antagonists fastened upon him.

Their arms were drawn back to inflict the fatal death stroke, and the terrified countess, with a cry of despair, covered her eyes to avoid the sickening sight, when suddenly the tremendous ringing thwacks on the heads of the cowardly assailants from the cudgels of the chair-bearers stretched the former senseless and motionless on the ground.

Captain Nugent, at this unexpected deliverance, sprang up and hastened at once to the countess.

"Oh! Alfred dearest, are you hurt?" she cried, in a faint voice.

"No, darling—no! thanks to these brave fellows!" he exclaimed. Then turning to the highwaymen, he said, in a tone of gratitude: "I am indebted to you, my men, for my life."

At this juncture footsteps were heard, and in a few seconds after the chair was surrounded by a body of police officers.

It was a thousand chances to one any assistance arriving in that obscure locality; but it so happened that the stealthy motions of Sir Richard and Lord Edward, while watching the starting of the sedan chair, had attracted the attention of the ever-wakeful but somewhat verdant Jessop.

The reader will remember that this youthful member of the police force had already made a great mistake in the case of Messrs. Bucks and Pompey.

He still smarted under the lash of Mr. Peterson's remarks—which were to say the least uncalled for, if not unjust, since the young man was only doing his duty to the best of his ability—and longed to wipe out the disgrace by some brilliant act.

When, therefore, having mentioned his suspicions to his comrades, they followed cautiously, and observed the noblemen cover their faces with black masks, there no longer existed a doubt as to the work they were engaged upon. They therefore followed, and arrived at a time which but for other and more available assistance would have been just too late.

"Hallo, here!" cried Jessop, importantly, "what's this?" gazing down upon the faces of the senseless men at his feet by the light of his lantern.

"Make it out a case of robbery, your honour," whispered Captain Hawk to the young officer, who acted on the suggestion.

"These men," he answered, "stopped this lady and myself on our way home from the theatre, and we have struck them down in self-defence."

"Um!—ah!" ejaculated Jessop, trying to look profound. "I see—yes—exactly! Who are they?" he continued, examining their upturned faces again.

"Bedad," said Captain Hawk, "if these rapparees ain't Captain Hawk and the Black Highwayman, thin they're their brothers."

At this suggestion there was a general murmur

"There's no doubt about it," said some of them.

"You've seen these fellows, I s'pose?" inquired Jessop of Captain Hawk.

"O' coorse I have, as distinct as I see the nose on your face, an' I must say I niver saw a greater likeness to them than these same spalpeens," answered the captain.

The general opinion seemed to be that the worsted robbers were the notorious highwaymen in question, and Jessop's heart glowed with conscious pride as he reflected that he had dropped upon the right parties at last.

The two senseless men were lifted from the ground, and Captain Nugent, much against his will, had to accompany the persevering Jessop to Bow Street to make the charge.

It was, however, at no great distance, and the journey was soon performed.

The bulk of the work fell on the shoulders of our heroes, the pseudo Irishmen, who did all the carrying.

As they sat on the poles of the chair outside Bow Street police office, they felt strongly impressed with the strange mixture of the terrible and ludicrous, of which their position was composed.

"This is extraordinary, Harcliffe, is it not? Here are we coolly sitting at the very portals that would lead to the scaffold—in sight of the bloodhounds that would worry us—within reach of the hands that long, and that need only to be outstretched, to grasp us, whilst two noblemen are being locked up in our stead."

"It almost passes belief!" replied Lord Harcliffe. "But see, here is the captain returning."

Captain Nugent, glad that the operation was over, hastily descended the steps of the police station, and seated himself by the side of his beloved.

Our heroes were not sorry to get away from a place so unpleasantly suggestive, and, by their united efforts, a very short time brought them to the mansion of the late Earl of Blacklake, in St. James's Square.

Having deposited the countess and the captain safely beneath this roof, the supposed Irishmen were invited strongly to partake of whatever they chose.

The excitement of the past few hours, and the unusual exertion of carrying a sedan chair laden with two inside, in addition to the heat of the freize coats over their own, had produced a sensation of thirst that was almost alarming.

When, therefore, they mentioned the state of their feelings, and the footman brought them a quart tankard of ale, that individual was somewhat astonished to see Captain Hawk empty the vessel at a draught, and then, at his demand, the very next moment, that he should conduct him and his friend to the cellar.

The man felt inclined to remonstrate, but as the chairmen were permitted to order what they liked, he was compelled to obey, though with evident reluctance at such an irregular proceeding.

Having arrived there, Captain Hawk desired to be introduced to the nearest ale cask, which having been accomplished, he and his comrade filled and emptied, emptied and filled, the quart tankard so many times that the footman's hair stood on end, and he at last burst out in disgust:

"Good gad! are you fellers goin' to empty the cellar?"

In reply to which the captain bade him mind his own business, and continued imbibing till they had thoroughly quenched their thirst and revived their spirits.

Then, having received the thanks of the grateful and beautiful countess and the captain, accompanied by a handsome gratuity, which they would have refused if they could have done so, they departed without their disguises being in the least suspected.

But it so happened that as they were leaving the cellar, a projecting nail caught in the captain's freize coat, and pulled it violently aside, revealing to the eyes of the flunkey—who began to think "wonders was never a going to cease"—a magnificent suit of silk velvet and gold, whilst, as Lord Harcliffe stooped down hastily to detach the coat from the intrusive nail, he unconsciously revealed a pair of legs cased in pink silk stockings, and feet with magnificent shoes, with red heels and brilliant buckles; all of which were, he felt, utterly inconsistent with the idea of Irish chair carriers.

But the footman, who answered to the name of Tuppers, was a prudent man, and knew his business, which was to hear, see, and say nothing.

So he kept his own counsel on this occasion, only saying, as he let our heroes out, "Good night, your lordships!" in a most respectful manner, in return for which Captain Hawk slipped into his palm the money he had received in recompense for his services from the young officer.

This settled the business, for as Tuppers, the moment he had closed the door, examined the amount, and found ten guineas in his hand, he exclaimed:

"I was certain of it! I said so! They are lords or dukes, an' nothink less!"

Inspector Nutkins had been out that evening to have a chat with a friend, and as he was returning he was met by one of the force, who informed him that Captain Hawk and the Black Highwayman were taken.

To use his own expression he was knocked quite "topsy-turvy" at the news, and at once, on his arrival at the station, proceeded to the cell in which the prisoners were supposed to be confined.

Opening the wicket in the door, and throwing the light from his lantern into the cell, he was much astonished at beholding a couple of men who had all the appearance of noblemen, being splendidly attired, and of commanding presence, the elder of whom peremptorily ordered him to remove the light from his eyes.

There was something in the very tone that implied a habit of commanding and being obeyed.

Inspector Nutkins became dubious immediately.

Nor were his doubts in any way removed when the stern voice of Sir Richard Chandos exclaimed:

"What is the meaning of this? Why are we confined here?"

"Really can't say, your honour." He checked himself; it was degradingly respectful for an inspector, and said instead: "I s'pose the charge is taken down."

"You shall be taken down, fellow!" continued Sir Richard, in the same stern voice; adding: "Are you aware who we are?"

"I heard—that is, I—a—thought—— Here, Nicholas," he cried suddenly to Nicholas Twigg, who had just entered, and who advanced in obedience to the summons, "just tell me—that is, are those gentlemen in there Captain Hawk and the Black Highwayman?"

"Them?" exclaimed Nicholas, dashing the rays of the lantern through the wicket into the prisoners' faces, who blinked like owls under the glare. "Of course they isn't! Any fool could tell that!" he answered, in a tone of contempt.

"Well, as you're so clever as to know who they're *not*, perhaps you can enlighten me as to who *they are?*" said Nutkins.

"Don't know 'em," remarked Nicholas, shaking his head.

"I can enlighten you on that point," said Sir Richard, in a tone of condensed passion that was ominous in his calmness. "I am Sir Richard Chandos."

"And I am Lord Edward Strathern," added his companion, in an equally stern tone; "and you may depend upon it you will be called to account for this."

This was of course ridiculous, since both these noblemen knew that they had both premeditated an act of assassination.

However, *bounce* in those days was as effective as it is in the present era, and these aristocrats tried it on with Nutkins the inspector, and Nutkins was profoundly impressed by the same.

At this moment Peterson entered.

He also had been out that evening having several cheerful glasses with professional friends, and like Nutkins, had heard floating reports that the *right birds* were caught at last.

Accordingly he had expedited his return to ascertain the truth.

"Well," he cried, as he entered, "have you got em?"

"Got 'em, no!" answered Nicholas, with a growl; "but we've got somebody, an' a pretty mess we're like to get into, I think."

"What d'ye mean?"

"Oh, another mistake!"

"What mistake?"

"Why, 'ere's a couple o' lords an baronights been brought 'ere instead of Captain Hawk an' the Black 'Ighwayman."

"Cuss them two fellers," cried Peterson, "they're the plague of our lives! Whose charge was it?"

"Jessop's."

"He's a d—d idiot!" said Peterson, remorselessly.

"I should say he were," acquiesced Nicholas. "These lords as he's been a collarin' are as savage as crocodiles; they're a goin' to play h—ll and Tommy with the lot on us!"

"That fellow ought to be done up in brown paper an' sent 'ome to his mother by the fust post," said Peterson; "he's a makin' the force ridiklus, an' bringin' it into disrepute."

"There ain't no denyin' that," added Mr. Twigg.

"I must try and settle this business before it grows into a rumpus."

Mr. Peterson, with this laudable intention, approached the cell and opened the door.

Here he either recognised or fancied he recognised that a great mistake had occurred.

"Very sorry, my lords!" he said, in the most respectful manner possible. "I can see at once this is a mistake; but you see you was found lyin' in the gutter stunned and speechless, an' a charge being made, o' course we're obligated to do our dooty."

"You call locking up noblemen, who have been assaulted and knocked down, in these filthy cells, doing your duty, do you?" growled Sir Richard, savagely.

"Very sorry, your lordship—*very!*"

"Call me by my proper title!" cried the angry nobleman, sharply. "I am not a lord, but a baronet."

"Beg your pardon, humbly, Sir—Sir——"

"Richard!"

"Sir Richard."

"Let us out, then, immediately!" demanded the baronet. "The atmosphere of this place stifles me!"

"Certainly, your honours; an' I trust you'll *except* my apology for the mistake as has occurred, but which was entirely a accident."

There was such a profound expression of submission and regret in the manner of the apologetic Peterson, that whatever Sir Richard and Lord Edward felt, they affected to be pacified.

They were not desirous of an investigation of the affair; and as they had been charged as Captain Hawk and the Black Highwayman, which they were subsequently proved not to be, the entire case resolved itself into a casual mistake.

And so they went out free men from Bow Street.

Sir Richard and Lord Edward were of course completely mystified as to the cause of their overthrow.

They remembered feeling themselves struck down by two heavy blows delivered by some persons behind, but who those persons were they had not the remotest conception.

This ignorance, in addition to their ignominious defeat, and the aching of their heads, added increased bitterness to their feelings, and they vowed vengeance, as juries sometimes deliver verdicts, against some person or persons unknown; but Captain Alfred Nugent came in for the accumulated weight of their animosity.

As they expected him to accompany the countess home they bent their steps towards St James's Square.

It was just as our heroes, still in their disguises as chairmen, had resolved to visit Bow Street once more before returning home to see if they could gain any tidings of the prisoners, that they beheld, to their great surprise, those very individuals coming towards them.

Fortunately, the two angry noblemen were too much occupied with their conflicting sensations to have observed them.

Stepping aside into the shadow of a portico, they allowed them to pass, and then watched them as they progressed.

The highwaymen observed that they did not approach the house by the front, but turned round a corner at some little distance from it.

"Let us follow them," said Captain Hawk. "I fancy from the expression on their faces they mean mischief."

Our heroes then with light steps hastened on in the track of Sir Richard and his companion.

When they reached the corner they were not to be seen; but they observed a turning nearly opposite that evidently led to the rear of the houses in the square.

Crossing over and keeping in the shadow of the wall,

they advanced cautiously, and soon descried the objects of their search standing together before a door in the wall, that led into what they supposed would be either a garden or courtyard—at all events, there were trees planted in it.

They drew as near as they could without arousing the attention of the noblemen, and listened attentively.

"If he is with her to-night," they heard Lord Edward exclaim, "I swear I'll so insult him in her presence that he must fight!"

"Oh, he'll fight fast enough, don't fear!" returned the other. "This is an awkward business! D—n the women! they're always the corner-stone of everything that's unpleasant!"

"You have the key of this door, have you not?" asked Lord Edward.

"Yes."

"It will be better to enter here: our presence will be unsuspected, and we can make our appearance exactly at the right moment."

Having found the key, Sir Richard opened the door, and the hopeful pair entered, after which it was immediately closed softly, and locked again.

Captain Hawk and Lord Harcliffe then approached it.

"Humph!" said the former, "we are on the side every unfortunate prisoner wishes to be—that is, the right side to run away."

"An opportunity which, in the present instance, I think we shall not embrace," remarked Lord Harcliffe.

"Decidedly not!" answered his comrade. "We must follow these noblemen, or there may be murder done before morning."

They listened: all was silent.

"The first thing to be done is to gain an entrance into the citadel," said Captain Hawk.

"And the only way to that is by scaling this wall," continued Lord Harcliffe.

"That will not be a very difficult task for us. You remember the last time we scaled a wall?"

"Yes, at Kew."

"This is not so high."

"Come on, then! You help me up, Harcliffe, and I will lend you a hand from the top—that is, if all is safe."

By the assistance of the Black Highwayman, Captain Hawk speedily reached the top.

Then, sitting astride the wall, he leant down, and grasping his friend's hand, in a few seconds they had both gained the summit.

All was perfectly still.

There was no barking of dogs—no sound of footsteps on the gravel beneath—no lights in the windows.

"We had better descend, and reconnoitre from below," said the captain. "Here we may be seen."

Accordingly they dropped down as quietly as possible on to the grass that grew beneath the wall.

The enclosure in which they found themselves was neither a garden nor a yard, but partook of the character of both.

There was a grass-plat edging the base of the wall, and the remainder of the space was gravel, with a paved footpath leading from the door in the wall to that at the back of the mansion.

Some handsome trees gave a little life and verdure to this quiet spot.

The highwaymen stepped lightly across the gravel and tried the back door.

It was fast.

"Egad!" whispered Captain Hawk, "if some of our friends could see us at this game they would vow we had renounced the road and turned 'cracksmen.'"

"How are we to get into the house?" inquired Lord Harcliffe.

"Patience, my dear fellow, and we shall see. Have you your sword safe at your side?"

"Quite—and you?"

"Trust me."

"There seems to be a path here."

"Yes; this enclosure surrounds the house except just at the front. Let us come this way."

They cautiously walked round, scanning every window and outlet as they passed it.

But not the slightest aperture disclosed itself.

They retraced their steps, and went round to the other

Here they were more fortunate.

There was a kind of lawn on this side, and from a window at a short distance from the ground, guarded by a stone balcony, a bright light shone forth.

"See," said Captain Hawk, "here are signs of life at last."

They drew near, the soft turf effectually concealing the slightest sound of their footsteps.

Voices were heard in the room a little above the level of their heads.

"We must mount this balcony," whispered the captain. "But first hoist me up gently and let me reconnoitre."

The result of this investigation was satisfactory.

It proved that the window was open, and that the curtains were sufficiently closed inside the chamber to conceal anyone standing at the entrance.

With great caution, and by considerable effort of muscular strength, the highwaymen mounted the balcony and reached the top of the balustrades.

In stepping down, a piece of plaster was displaced and fell with a slight noise.

It was heard by those within.

"Who's there?" cried the captain.

There was no reply.

"It is nothing, dearest," they heard the sweet voice of the countess exclaim.

"The events of to-night have made me suspicious, love," answered the officer. "With your permission I will see."

The captain and Lord Harcliffe had barely time to enter the window on tiptoe and shroud themselves in the ample folds of the curtains, before the young officer passed between them and looked out from the balcony.

Nothing, however, appeared to excite his suspicions, and he returned.

"You were right, love," he said to the countess, "it was nothing."

At the time this slight alarm took place the lovers were at supper.

Tuppers was the only domestic in attendance.

Of course the presence of a servant was a restraint upon their actions, and forbade that interchange of affection which might else have passed between them.

Still it was evident enough that the captain lavished upon his beautiful mistress all the attention such restraint permitted, offering her the most delicate morsels, and tempting her to sip the choice wines that glistened in the richly carved decanters.

Captain Hawk and Lord Harcliffe could from their place of concealment command a view of the interior, which was a perfect combination of elegance and refinement, from the massive velvet carpet on the floor—the softness of which prevented their detection when they so hastily concealed themselves—to the tiniest piece of fretwork on the carved mouldings of the ceiling.

Vases of the choicest exotics were placed in various portions of the apartment whose delicate fragrance imparted to the atmosphere a quality of luxury and refinement.

The plate and china with which the supper-table was loaded, were of the richest description, and the whole scene appeared to the eyes and senses of the beholder as the home of elegance and beauty.

Tuppers performed his duties with the silence of a mute and the gravity of a mandarin, and with that absorbed air that seemed to convey the idea that he was so entirely engrossed in the exercise of his functions as to have neither eyes nor ears for anything else.

This was, however, on this particular night, not strictly the fact.

Tuppers had not yet got over the astounding paradox of a pair of Irish sedan chairmen wearing silk velvet suits trimmed with gold, and silk stockings, and shoes with brilliant buckles, under their frieze coats; to say nothing of the ten guineas which crowned the whole mystery.

The strange occurrence sat uneasily upon the footman's chest, and he felt oppressed with its weight.

He longed to communicate the secret to his mistress, but did not know how to bring it out.

The captain, to his great relief, unwittingly opened a way for him.

"I can't help thinking, Clarissa," he suddenly remarked, "of this night's strange adventures."

[THE DUEL IN THE GARDEN.]

The countess shuddered slightly as busy memory brought back the whole scene before her.

"I had given myself up for lost," continued the officer, "when my sword broke and my foot slipped."

"Oh, do not speak of that," cried the countess, with a pained expression on her lovely features. "I cannot bear to think of it, it seemed so terrible!"

"I have much cause to thank the two stanch fellows that carried our chair; but for them I believe I should be no longer in the land of the living," said Captain Nugent.

Tuppers at this moment made a dead stop.

He felt himself wrought up to a climax.

He was, as it were, loaded and primed, and had a strong conviction that he must either fire off his information at once, or burst.

So, not desiring to do the latter, he, with a preparatory "Hem!" commenced, in a tone of the utmost solemnity:

"Pardon me, capting!—may I speak?"

The captain and the countess looked at the burdened domestic with evident surprise, and then the captain replied:

"Certainly! Speak!"

"I am going to take a great liberty," continued Tuppers.

The captain, who marvelled what this preface portended, was half inclined to fancy the footman intended inviting himself to supper, and therefore asked:

"What is that?"

"I have made a discovery, and I am going to disclose it, with your permission," replied the solemn Tuppers.

"What discovery?"

"The chairmen that brought home the countess and you, sir, was no chairmen at all," said the footman, with deliberate emphasis.

"What do you mean?" asked the silvery voice of the countess.

"Why, your ladyship, I mean what I says," answered Tuppers. "When I went down in the cellar to give the men some ale, which they emptied one cask entire, their long overcoats blowed a one side, and I see underneath velvet and gold, silk stockings, and brilliant buckles!"

And, having thus delivered himself, the footman drew a long breath, and appeared intensely relieved.

"How very strange!" exclaimed the countess.

"Exceedingly!" added Captain Nugent.

"Who could they possibly be?" continued the lady, evidently much surprised. "From the slight view I had of their features," she went on, "they certainly appeared very unlike porters; yet what could have induced any mere strangers to attempt such a masquerade?"

"It's a mystery that baffles my limited powers of perception entirely," said Tuppers.

"At present I am quite in the dark upon the subject," remarked the young officer; "but perhaps time will fathom it."

Tuppers was prepared for a deep and prolonged investigation, but the countess blighted his hopes at once by saying:

"I shall not want you any more to-night, Tuppers. You can go to bed."

This was a blow the footman did not expect; but he swallowed his chagrin, and, with a solemn, "Good night, your ladyship," glided from the room like a lost spirit in plush breeches.

For a time the countess and the captain puzzled themselves as to who the mysterious chairmen could be, and then gradually forgot them in the sweet consciousness that they were alone together.

The highwaymen felt for an instant something akin to eavesdroppers, but the reflection that their presence there was in no such unworthy characters, but to preserve, perhaps at the risk of their own safety, two loving, amiable hearts from the attacks of jealous hate, they became reconciled to their position.

For some time the lovers sat in silence gazing at each other.

The captain then spoke:

"There are some moments, Clarissa," he said, "in this chequered life of ours, when happiness seems almost to have reached its climax."

"True, Alfred," replied the countess, placing her white hand softly on his, "and I think this is one of them."

"I say *almost*, beloved Clarissa," he continued, "because my joy will never be completely consummated until, holding, as I do now, this dear hand in mine, I can press on it a husband's kiss."

The fair countess blushed and fixed her lustrous eyes lovingly on the face of the man she loved; but she looked her reply and said nothing.

"Oh, how I envied the Earl of Blacklake when I heard he was to be your husband you know not—you cannot conceive!"

"Neither can you, my Alfred. Oh, speak not of it—mention it not! It was an unholy union, at which my heart rebelled even while I spoke the marriage vows. But it was my uncle's doing, not mine. He *sold* me to the earl."

The young soldier bit his lip with indignation, and a hot flush passed over his handsome face as he added:

"But you never loved him?"

"Loved him!" she echoed, in a tone almost of horror. "Can spring love the icy winter? or the northern blast consort with the gentle south? Never! No, my Alfred! I never *did* love him! I never loved—I never shall love any but you! I would not speak against my husband now he is no more, but oh! if you knew how I loathed my false position, my wealth, my rank, my jewels purchased by my sacrifice—you would have pitied me. Let no one envy that which is purchased by the loss of self-respect: nothing is—nothing can be so terrible," she continued, with a shudder, "to a woman who has any feeling left as to be condemned to the galling slavery of an union with the man who in her heart she loathes."

The young officer clasped her in his arms, and embraced her passionately.

"You love me, my adored Clarissa!" he exclaimed, impetuously. "I know it! I feel it! and I glory in the knowledge!"

"And you love me, Alfred, do you not?"

"Love you? That is too weak a word! I worship—I adore you! You are my star—my light—my life! When you are present all is bright as summer; apart from you everything wears a gloomier aspect. Is not this true love?"

The young soldier sank upon his knee, and entwining his arms around the delicate form of the woman he loved, pressed her fondly to his breast.

"You will be mine, Clarissa—my wife, will you not?" he murmured.

"Yes, Alfred—yours for ever!" she uttered, faintly.

"My own darling!" he cried, "you can give me no greater treasure."

Her fair head sank gradually on to his shoulder, and the golden tresses escaping from their fastenings, enveloped him in a shower of delicate perfume; their lips met in love's fond, clinging, rapturous kiss, and in that fragrant bower they forgot the world and all things else in the sweet dream of that halcyon moment.

But these bright visions were soon dispelled, for with an ominous crash the door opened suddenly and violently, and Sir Richard Chandos strode into the room, closely followed by Lord Strathern.

CHAPTER CXC.

A DOMESTIC OUTRAGE.—A RUFFIAN AND A GENTLEMAN.—A CRITICAL POSITION, AND AN UNEXPECTED APPEARANCE.

Clarissa uttered a scream of terror, and started up; her dishevelled locks falling over her snowy neck in wild but beautiful disorder, and her fair cheek crimsoned with blushes.

Her lover also started to his feet, and with flushed face and knitted brows confronted the unceremonious intruders.

The countenance of Sir Richard was dark with anger, that of Lord Edward pallid with jealous rage.

"Abandoned woman!" cried the former, hoarsely, "is it thus I find you? Is this the fruits of the lessons I have taught you?"

"What lessons did you ever teach me?" returned his fair niece, who, conscious of no wrong, felt naturally indignant at this rude interruption. "What lessons," she continued, "but those of sordid baseness?"

"Baseness!" echoed Sir Richard, fiercely.

"Yes, baseness!" she repeated in a firm tone, from which all fear had vanished. "Did you not sell me to an old white-haired, imbecile man with one foot in the grave, for gold which you appropriated, though your ostensible motive for this odious traffic was a title for myself? You did—you know you did! And yet you boast of the *lessons you have taught me!* You should rather blush to think what I might have become had I *learnt* those lessons, and thank Heaven I am still capable of an honest love, which I should not be had I done as you would have had me."

"When did I ever countenance your receiving the visits of any man at this hour of the night?" demanded the baronet, furiously.

"I am mistress of my own actions, and I pass my hours as I please!"

"I am your guardian still, madam, and I exact obedience!"

"I deny your power—I abjure your authority, and refuse to yield to it!"

The baronet was about to utter an angry exclamation, when Captain Nugent stepped forward.

"Allow me, Sir Richard Chandos, and you, Lord Edward Strathern, in order to put an end to this system of espionage, to state that I am the affianced husband of your niece."

"You?" foamed the baronet.

"I! She honours me with her favour, her confidence, her love, of which I trust I am not unworthy."

"You are mad!" shouted Lord Edward, in a voice harsh with rage.

"I fear that title more befits yourself, my lord," returned the young soldier, calmly. "Your base attack of to-night proves to me how far your vindictive passions would lead you. But I seek not to embroil myself in idle quarrels; and I request you will not insult me, or place me in such a position in which I shall be compelled to strike in self-defence."

"Do you threaten, insolent upstart?" raved Lord Strathern.

"Upstart!" repeated the young officer, warmly. "In what, pray, are you superior to myself? My birth and name are equal to your own; and if the wealth and fortunes of my house are not so prosperous as they once were, there is no blot on our escutcheon: we are equals at least, and by virtue of that equality I demand the respect that one gentleman has a right to expect from another."

"A robber deserves no respect!" answered the young lord, furiously.

"Robber?"

"Yes. You knew I loved that lady."

"Did she love you?"

"She might have done but for your cursed intrusion!"

"My lord, your spleen makes you forget yourself."

"You are right, or I should not so long have wasted breath upon a coward, who, like a cur, barks but dares not bite!"

"Dares not? Were we not beneath this lady's roof, and in her presence, I——"

"Oh, of course! Hear the gallant soldier," cried Lord Edward, in bitter mockery, "shelter himself under the lame excuse of not wishing to draw his sword in the presence of a lady. Times are altered since the knights of old were wont to break their lances under the very eyes of their mistresses. It was then the *bravest* who *won* the prize. Who wins it now?"

"Insulting villain!" cried the young soldier, stung by the taunting sneers of Lord Edward, "I cannot talk to you!"

"Then, by hell, you shall fight with me!" shouted the infuriated nobleman.

Captain Nugent, prompted by involuntary indignation, was about to place his hand upon his sword, when the countess darted forward and arrested the action by clinging to his arm.

"Dearest Alfred! heed not his words!" she cried. "For my sake let there be no bloodshed."

At this appeal, though even then it required a strong effort, the young man suffered himself to be restrained.

He allowed his hand, though it trembled with indignation, to be passive in the trembling grasp that held it.

This forbearance afforded fresh fuel to the spiteful venom of Lord Strathern's tongue.

"Ha, ha!" he laughed, with bitter mockery. "Look at him, Sir Richard!—do look!—gaze on the gallant soldier who professes to serve his country, and wears the king's uniform, and yet suffers himself to be held back by a woman! Look at him!"

"Unmanly, uncourteous ruffian!—the foul current of whose slanderous speech not even beauty like this can check—I would to Heaven I had you foot to foot alone!" exclaimed the young captain, in a voice almost inarticulate with rage.

"Psha!" replied the other, contemptuously and sneeringly, "the King's Own are *pacific gentlemen*; they do *not* fight—it is too dangerous a pastime; but since *words* cannot arouse your craven spirit, let us try how *this* will stimulate you."

As Lord Strathern uttered these words, he struck the young captain a sharp blow on the breast with the flat blade of his sword.

The officer's indignation, controlled hitherto by a strong effort in compliment to the desire of the woman he loved, was roused by this last insult to a pitch of irresistible fury.

It was in vain the lovely Clarissa clung to him with all the energy of appealing love: he shook off her grasp with the violence of a madman.

"Miscreant!—coward!" he shouted, "defend yourself!"

He rushed madly forward as he uttered these words, at the same time placing his hand in the direction of the hilt of his sword.

To his chagrin, however, no weapon met his grasp, and he then remembered that his sword had been broken in their previous encounter in the dark alley.

There was, however, no time for pause, neither did the young soldier in his furious impetuosity think of retreat or parley.

Had there been an army of weapons pointed at his breast, he would have gone onward.

"Armed or unarmed, I am your match, Lord Strathern," he cried, as he parried a desperate lunge from his cowardly antagonist, and, closing with him, gripped the hilt of his weapon with resistless tenacity and wrenched it from his grasp.

"Now," he exclaimed, "it is my turn!" And grasping the nobleman by the throat, he pressed him backwards to the ground, and placed his sword's point against his breast.

"Apologize, villain!" he demanded, vehemently.

These words had hardly passed his lips when the weapon was wrested from his hand by Sir Richard Chandos, who, seeing the critical posture of affairs, took this unchivalrous method of restoring their equilibrium. In the effort to regain his sword, the captain relaxed his grasp on his antagonist, who, alive to the favourable opportunity, started on to his feet.

With the rapidity of lightning Sir Richard transferred the weapon he had secured to its owner, and drew his own, so that by the time the rapidity of the passing events allowed the young officer to glance before him, he found himself confronted by two enemies instead of one.

It was a desperate position.

Two naked swords, in experienced hands, against an unarmed man.

He glanced hurriedly round, not seeking an outlet to escape, but some weapon of self-defence.

None, however, in that abode of luxury and peace presented themselves.

Suddenly, with a shout of triumph, he darted to the table, and seizing one of the glittering cut-glass decanters glowing in the light with its golden contents, he hurled it with all his force at his opponents.

The young soldier was too excited, and the effort was wasted, inasmuch as the decanter missing its intended objects, flew from the open window into the garden beneath.

Before he could recover from the impetus he had given himself in casting this missile from his hand, his inveterate antagonists were upon him, and their swords pointed at his throat.

"Hold! inhuman, dastardly murderers!" shrieked the countess, whose senses appeared fast leaving her with terror. "If you harm a hair of his head——!"

Her voice subsided in a convulsive, gasping murmur, and she fell senseless to the ground.

"Now, Sir Captain, it is ours to make conditions!" cried Lord Strathern.

"Renounce this lady!" exclaimed the stern voice of Sir Richard Chandos—"renounce her with your own lips, or we'll pin you to the ground with our weapons as remorselessly as we should a mad dog that crossed our path!"

"Never, cowards!" answered the officer, struggling to rise, but being prevented by the grasp of his assailants and the sharp points of their weapons, that already drew blood from his neck.

"This is no fair contest!—this is murder!" he continued, still endeavouring to elude the swords of his foes.

"You refuse, then, to renounce your presumptuous claim to the hand of my niece?" once more demanded the stern accents of Sir Richard.

"I do!—I would die a thousand deaths sooner!" was the firm reply.

"We take you at your word then!" answered the cold, half-exulting, half-malignant tones of Lord Strathern.

The hands of these deadly foes tightened ominously on the weapons they held, and for the second time on that eventful night their hands were drawn back to strike what would immediately have been a death-blow, when to their great surprise, a sharp, piercing pain on the back of their wrists caused them suddenly to drop their weapons and utter a cry of pain.

No less astonished were they when, after an instant's pause, they essayed to pick up those weapons, to find them vanished, and that the blood was flowing freely from two gashes precisely alike on their wrists.

A cry of mingled surprise and joy that escaped from the lips of Captain Nugent, and an eager expression that seemed to rest on some object behind them, caused them to turn their heads, when, to their utter dismay, they saw standing in the opening of the curtains in front of the window, rigid and silent as statues, two figures completely enveloped in black cloaks and masks.

Their astonishment was so great that they thought no more of their prisoner, who, being released, rose to his feet and silently, in common with his adversaries, regarded these mysterious visitors, whom he nevertheless recognised as friends, inasmuch as they had saved his life.

There was a long pause of silence, the only signs of life in the entire party being the slight motion of the dark cloaks as they waved gently in the breeze that blew in at the open window.

Sir Richard Chandos was the first to speak.

"What intruders are you?" he exclaimed, in a tone not unmixed with apprehension, as the glittering eyes of the masks glared full upon him, "and what means this masquerade?"

The stern accents of Captain Hawk replied:

"You appear to me, Sir Richard Chandos, and you, Lord Strathern, to desire to have all the amusement to yourselves."

"Amusement! What mean you?"

"That you commenced your *masquerading* frolic this evening, and that we simply followed your example; the only difference being that whilst ours is merely a harmless frolic from a good motive, and in a good cause, yours was undertaken from the worst of motives; and from the position of that gentleman when we entered, I should imagine for the purpose of destroying human life." As he spoke, he pointed to Captain Nugent.

"It was—it was!" cried the countess, who had slowly recovered from the faint lethargy into which she had fallen. "Their hideous designs were clothed in the secrecy and silence of night—theirs is indeed the *Masquerade of Death!* But you live—you are safe!" she added, joyfully, throwing her arms round her affianced husband.

"Peace, madam!" exclaimed Sir Richard—"you know not what you say!" Then turning to our heroes, who in their sable disguises still preserved their statue-like immobility, he demanded: "Who are you?"

"We are both lovers of fair play," replied Captain Hawk, in his natural tone; "and wherever my companion and myself happen to be, we always take care to enforce it by every possible means in our power."

"*You* enforce?" echoed Lord Strathern, haughtily. "By what right?"

"By the right of power," coolly returned the Black Highwayman, speaking for the first time.

"And a peculiar tact in adapting the means to the end," added Captain Hawk.

"What do you mean?"

"I'm about to explain. When, for instance, we observed your weapons pointed at that gentleman's throat,"—indicating Captain Nugent, who, with his arm encircling the fair countess, was seated by her side on one of the couches, listening with much satisfaction to the covert vein of irony that ran through the polite manner and quiet words of our heroes—"when, I say we observed this, we at once determined—we are obliged to decide very quickly in such cases—that the simplest and most efficacious means of diverting you from your purpose would be to deprive you of the power of executing it by inflicting a slight gash across the back of each of your wrists."

"So, then, we have to thank you for our wounds," growled Lord Strathern, frowning heavily.

"You have; but don't thank us, for I assure you we do not merit it, since I can conscientiously affirm we never inflicted two wounds with so much pleasure."

"Insolent!" exclaimed Sir Richard.

"But necessary," added the Black Highwayman, "since they caused you to drop your weapons, which circumstance preserved a very valuable life."

The speaker bowed slightly, as he finished, towards the countess, who acknowledged the courtesy by a beaming smile and a graceful inclination of the head.

"By-the-by, where *are* our weapons?" inquired Lord Strathern, looking scrutinizingly on the carpet.

"You may spare yourself any anxiety on that point, my lord," said Captain Hawk: "we have them here safely beneath our cloaks."

"How dare you detain our swords?" angrily demanded the irritable and baffled nobleman.

"It's a part of our system," returned Captain Hawk, in the most unruffled tone in the world. "When we find parties misusing such deadly weapons, we invariably take them away and detain them as pledges for their good behaviour in future."

"What insufferable audacity!" murmured the young lord to Sir Richard.

"Monstrous! I do not understand it at all," he replied. "Pray how the devil did you come here?" he continued, addressing himself to Captain Hawk.

"You're very inquisitive; but since you particularly wish to know, we came over the wall; and I may add, I think, there are some here who will be inclined to admit we dropped in just at the right moment."

An expressive glance from Captain Nugent and the countess attested their assent to this remark.

"Are you aware you are trespassing?" indignantly demanded Sir Richard.

"Trespassing! Nonsense!" laughed Captain Hawk.

"Ay, indeed—absurd!" boldly exclaimed the countess. "These gentlemen are my guests."

"So, madam, I understand," returned Sir Richard, with bitter contempt, "you keep your bullies, do you?"

"If I did, I might be almost justified when I am so persecuted by ruffianly insolence," retorted the lady; "but these gentlemen are no bullies."

"They are—they must be! else why are they here, and thus disguised?" exclaimed Lord Strathern, spitefully.

"Oh! if everyone be a bully who wears a *cloak* and *mask*," answered the Black Highwayman, "the four of us may shake hands as brothers of that honourable fraternity. But the lady is right—we are none such."

"I acquit you, gentlemen, of the charge," said Clarissa. "and Sir Richard and his lordship were wrong to call you so."

"And exceedingly rash into the bargain," remarked Captain Hawk.

"Rash, fellow?"

"Very!"

"Why so?"

"Because the calling us 'bullies' insults us, and whoever insults must fight us."

"Fight *you*?"

"Fight us!"

"We only draw swords upon our equals!"

"There will be no necessity to *draw* your swords: they are *drawn* already, and you must fight!"

"Do you entertain this challenge?" whispered Lord Edward to Sir Richard, in a doubtful, perplexed tone.

"You have no resource," replied Captain Hawk, who overheard the question. "If you refuse, we shall be under the necessity of horsewhipping you!"

The nobleman made an angry gesture of indignation.

"I see you don't relish the idea of that," continued the captain, "so have the goodness to accompany us."

"Whither?"

"Into the garden—it's a delightfully retired spot: the moonbeams invite us, and all is most propitious."

"Psha!" ejaculated the baronet, annoyed beyond endurance at the quietly-aggravating tone of the captain. "We have no weapons."

"Oh dear yes! We will take care you are provided," said Captain Hawk. "Come, lead the way into that snug little garden yonder without further loss of time."

The nobleman, after a brief pause of sulky indecision, had come to the conclusion that there was no escape, and that they *must* fight or be horsewhipped.

It is not, therefore, surprising that they chose the former of these alternatives, and were about to leave the room when Captain Nugent rose.

"Your pardon, gentlemen," he said, addressing himself to our heroes: "this is my quarrel; I cannot allow you to take it out of my hands."

"Yours in return, sir," answered Captain Hawk. "We do not wish to interfere with your arrangements; therefore, when we have *finished our* business with these individuals, we shall be very happy to turn them over to you."

There was a peculiar intonation that accompanied the word "finished" that sounded rather ominous for the two noblemen.

Captain Hawk lowered his voice, and said to the young officer:

"We are going to give these would-be assassins a slight present that they will carry away with them, to remind them of our meeting, and that they will never part with as long as they live."

"I understand," replied Captain Nugent.

"Everything will be conducted on the most rigid principles of justice; but if you doubt it, come yourself, and see fair play."

"I will, though I have every confidence in your word."

With these words they followed Sir Richard Chandos and Lord Strathern into the garden.

CHAPTER CXCI.

THE MASKED MEN MAKE THEIR PREPARATIONS, BUT DECLINE TO REMOVE THEIR MASKS.—DRAWING FOR PARTNERS.—A DOUBLE DUEL BY MOONLIGHT.—OUR HEROES ACCEPT THE INVITATION OF THE COUNTESS AND CAPTAIN NUGENT.—THEY MAKE AN IMPORTANT DISCLOSURE.—AN UNEXPECTED EAVESDROPPER.

It was a beautiful night.

The moon shone calmly and brilliantly down into the garden, lighting up the scene of the approaching contest, and playing upon the features of the parties assembled.

Here and there dark shadows fell wherever the light of the luminary was intercepted either by trees, or some projecting portion of the building, and formed a picturesque contrast and relief to the prevailing pallid brightness.

"Here we are," remarked Captain Hawk, as they emerged into the open air and looked around them. "And I wouldn't desire a pleasanter spot for an *assaut d'armes*."

As he spoke, the gentle west wind murmured past, gently stirring the branches of the trees and causing the shadows to start from their repose into a trembling motion.

"Now, gentlemen, we had better lose no time," said the Black Highwayman; "let us arrange the preliminaries."

These consisted in the act of disrobing, and the choice of opponents.

Captain Hawk commenced by taking off his massive cloak, which he folded and consigned to the arm of Captain Nugent; his comrade in the meantime holding the weapon he had taken from Lord Strathern.

The noblemen were profoundly astonished and mystified at the magnificent and courtly attire that revealed itself to their eyes upon the removal of the cloak.

The prominent question each mentally asked himself was, "Who can he be?" But no satisfactory response came. The handsomely-dressed, elegant cavalier was a mystery.

Captain Hawk then removed his coat, and rolled up the sleeves of his shirt with the utmost deliberation, revealing an arm that combined the qualities of symmetrical grace and muscular power.

Having finished his preparations, he stood calmly leaning upon his sword, which he had drawn from his scabbard, looking at the noblemen, as in a more hurried manner they completed their arrangements, from behind his mask, which he still retained, and which gave a striking peculiarity to his appearance.

"Well, gentlemen, are you ready?" he at length inquired, in a voice that sounded like the deep tones of a bell.

"Quite," was the reply.

"There is only one thing more to be arranged," he said. "We are two to two, and must select our respective opponents."

"It is immaterial," answered Sir Richard, in an impatient tone, as though he wished the affair had been well over.

"Excuse me," replied Captain Hawk, "it is not immaterial, inasmuch as on the choice of opponents sometimes depends the life of *one*, if not *both*, the combatants. My friend and myself are advocates for fair play, even when our game is with edged tools."

"Decidedly!" exclaimed the Black Highwayman. "We will draw lots."

Captain Hawk drew from his pocket a small pocket-book, and tore a leaf from it, on which he pencilled some figures; he then tore the paper in half, and handed it to Sir Richard, who received it in silence. The other half he retained himself.

"What mummery is this?" muttered Lord Edward, between his teeth.

"Now," said Captain Hawk to the baronet, "you will tear the paper you hold in your hand, on which are two numbers, in half, and give one to your friend. I will do the same with the paper I hold. The corresponding numbers will fight together."

This was immediately done, and the four combatants stood each retaining his number.

"Now we will call out our numbers," said the captain.

"Twenty-four!" cried the Black Highwayman.

"Twenty-four!" echoed Sir Richard Chandos.

"Fifty!" called Captain Hawk.

"Fifty!" repeated Lord Strathern.

"That is settled," said the captain, in a business-like tone. "I fight with your lordship."

"The sooner the better," he answered. "I'm tired of standing here without my coat."

"I am quite ready!"

"But my sword?"

"Is here," said the Black Highwayman, advancing, with dignified composure, and presenting the weapon hilt foremost.

The young nobleman eagerly grasped it; and having essayed one or two passes to assure himself that his wrist had not lost its power, lowered the point to the ground.

"Now, my lord, *en garde!*"

"Do you not intend to unmask?" inquired Lord Edward.

"No!" answered Captain Hawk, abruptly.

An angry flush passed over the cheek of young nobleman, and he clenched his sword vindictively.

The weapons crossed.

The combatants made one or two feints, and then the fight began in earnest.

"One!—two!—three!—four! Well stopped!" cried the captain, as he quietly parried a venomous lunge from his opponent. "But your lordship will soon grow tired of that."

"Look to yourself that you are not tired first!" was the angry answer.

"Do you know where I intend to hit you, my lord?" inquired Captain Hawk, with aggravating coolness and confidence, as he toyed with his adversary's blade.

"No, braggart!" furiously replied the young nobleman, his eyes glowing with rage.

"I'll tell you, then," answered the highwayman, in a tone of the most mellifluous quality. "I have no desire to touch any vital part—I shall therefore content myself with running your lordship through the arm about *six inches above the wrist*."

"Silence!" foamed the young aristocrat, white with rage. "I'll teach you! One—two—three! Ah!"

With an exclamation of pain, the weapon fell from his hand as the point of Captain Hawk's sword entered his arm *six inches above the wrist*, and just appeared on the opposite side.

"D—nation!" he hissed, fiercely, as the blood trickled from the wound.

"You see I have kept my word," remarked the captain, coolly thrusting the point of his weapon into the mould at his feet to cleanse it.

Lord Edward was too enraged and indignant to reply.

"You had better wrap a handkerchief round your wrist, my lord," suggested Captain Hawk, in a sweet, persuasive tone. "Young blood flows freely, and loss of blood is apt to induce faintness and exhaustion."

The pallor of Lord Edward's features proved the truth of this remark, and Sir Richard, whilst performing the operation of binding up his wound, whispered to him:

"I will avenge you in the heart's blood of that masked ruffian!"

In the meantime, the Black Highwayman had thrown off his cloak and coat, and had, moreover, caught the whispered words of Sir Richard.

He, however, made no remark at the moment beyond a request to finish his surgical operations as quickly as possible.

"I am ready!" gruffly exclaimed the baronet. "Perhaps one of you masked gentlemen will oblige me with the loan of my own sword!"

"It is here," said Captain Hawk, who had resumed his coat and cloak, and who now handed him with the utmost ceremony his required weapon.

"Come on, then!" cried Sir Richard, in a harsh, gruff voice.

"Come on!" echoed his opponent.

"Where do you intend to hit *me*?" asked the baronet, ironically, as their swords crossed.

"Having no desire for your *heart's blood*," coolly answered the Black Highwayman, emphatically, "I shall content myself with an inferior member of your body and puncture your right ear."

An angry growl from the baronet followed this announcement, and the violence with which he commenced the attack gave evidence of a resolute determination on his part to frustrate if possible the design of his antagonist by forestalling him in the more fatal manner he had promised his friend.

But with all his good intentions he signally failed in their accomplishment.

Every lunge was stopped—

Every thrust parried.

The baronet grew hot and wrathful: the perspiration stood in heavy drops upon his brow.

His masked foe, on the contrary, was perfectly cool and placid, doing what he did apparently without the least exertion.

"Come, baronet," he cried, "I'm waiting for the fulfilment of your promise. Use all your skill! You know on which side my heart lies—the left."

This taunt was sufficient to stimulate the angry baronet to fresh exertions.

Still he was unable to discover a weak point in his adversary's defence, or break through his guard.

There was something, too, that was very aggravating in the indifferent, nonchalant manner in which the latter replied to his exertions.

Another annoying fact that appealed strongly to Sir Richard was, that his wrist was growing tired, and that he was becoming uncomfortably short of breath.

All these indications warned him that it was necessary that whatever he intended to accomplish must be done quickly.

He made, therefore, one last desperate attack.

So fierce were his lunges that the swords as they struck against each other seemed to strike fire.

All, however, would not do, and as his power began rapidly to fail him, he became aware, from the short, dry laugh of his antagonist, that the latter had been merely drawing him on, and suffering him to exhaust himself to no purpose.

"Come, make haste, Sir Richard!" he cried. "You're not half so skilful as I thought you were!"

The taunting invitation was not complied with, since the baronet, so far from "making haste," gradually became slower and feebler in his thrusts, and more unguarded in his defence.

The crisis had now arrived when the grand *coup d'epee* was to be given, and by a quick turn of the wrist the Black Highwayman disarmed the baronet, and passing his sword through the lobe of his ear with unerring aim, pinned him to the tree before which he stood.

The discomfited baronet thus transfixed was perfectly unable to move save at the will of his antagonist, who simply remarking, "Had I laid a wager on this, I should have won *it*," withdrew his sword, and set the baronet and *his ear* at liberty.

"Now, gentlemen," said Captain Hawk, as his comrade resumed his cloak and coat, "we are perfectly satisfied, and we trust you are the same."

It is needless to explain that both the gentlemen addressed were the very reverse of this.

Both were smarting with their wounds, and from the inward rankling of the sense of defeat.

In the utmost recesses of their hearts they execrated their masked victors, though their rage was silent, not expressed.

"We had better leave this place," whispered Lord Edward to the baronet.

"Yes," answered his friend, with an angry frown, as he picked up his sword and sheathed it.

"Do you require anything further of us?" politely inquired Captain Hawk.

"Nothing of *you*!" Sir Richard contrived to articulate, in hoarse tones. "We are not accustomed to contest with ruffians!"

"But with *you*," added Lord Edward, taking up his friend's speech, and addressing himself to Captain Nugent, "it is different! From this time we are deadly enemies. We shall meet again, depend upon it, ere long, and when our swords next cross each other, it will be a *combat to the death!*"

Captain Nugent bowed his head coldly in acceptance of this cold-blooded challenge, and the two friends, arm-in-arm, slowly took their way towards the end of the garden, and departed as they had entered, by the door in the wall.

As soon as they had disappeared, Captain Nugent turned towards our heroes, and extended a hand to each which they immediately took.

"Gentlemen!" he cried, warmly, "I have not the pleasure of knowing you at present by any other names than those of the preservers of my life; but they are sufficient to justify me in desiring to know you better, and in inviting you in my own name and that of the Countess of Blacklake, to enter and take such refreshment as the time permits."

The highwaymen, being somewhat fatigued, and the exercise they had been taking having sharpened their appetites, had a very grateful recollection of the rich wine that they had seen glowing in the cut-glass decanters, and were by no means averse to passing an hour in that luxurious chamber and the society of the beautiful woman who inhabited it; they therefore readily accepted the courteous invitation.

Captain Nugent's eye fell upon the decanter, which was lying unbroken on the turf on which it had fallen after he had hurled it from the window.

He picked it up with a smile.

"This is the first time in my life," he remarked, "that I ever used a decanter as a weapon of defence."

"I think the bottle is oftener entitled to be called a weapon of *of*-fence," replied Captain Hawk, as they entered the house.

The beautiful countess received them with that winning courtesy always so charming in a woman, especially when she is young, lovely, and high-born.

She received them with the frankness and cordiality of a sister, and the best proof of the effect she produced was, that the highwaymen felt at home with her in a moment.

She pressed them to eat, and pointed out the various wines, and our heroes at once accepted her invitation in a very practical manner.

Before they commenced supper, however, Captain Nugent said to them:

"You will not think me impertinent or curious, gentlemen, but, feeling sure you must find your masks hot and inconvenient, will you not like to remove them for a time? We are all friends here, and, even were your features intimately known to me, you need fear nothing—honour would make me blind as Fortune and dumb as the grave respecting your share in this night's adventures."

Without another word, the highwaymen bowed in reply, and removed their masks and cloaks.

Whatever astonishment the countess and her lover might have experienced at the appearance of their disguised visitors, they were both equally, if not more, surprised at the strikingly handsome faces that met their view now their disguises were removed.

So far from being coarse or ruffianly in their expression, they were not even of the ordinary type they might have expected to behold, but intellectual and powerful, and at the same time highly prepossessing.

Of course both the captain and the countess were too well-bred to allow their surprise to manifest itself, and, judging wisely that hungry people cannot well talk and eat simultaneously, they allowed our heroes to commence and continue their repast without interruption.

One action only of the highwaymen struck them as a little strange.

This was that, when they divested themselves of their cloaks and masks, they each rolled up their disguises carefully, and placed them on the ground on each side of the window, covering them with the bottom portion of the ample curtains.

This appeared somewhat significant, and to a suspicious mind might have suggested a *precautionary* measure. And so, indeed, it was, and, as the sequel proved, attested the foresight of our heroes, and how they had learnt by past experience to avoid the least inadvertence that might lead to unpleasant consequences.

And thus divested of the mystery of disguise, and the sable mantles stowed away out of sight, there remained nothing but the pleasing and natural aspect of two fashionably-attired, handsome gentlemen, who appeared indigenous to the elegance and luxury by which they were surrounded.

But although, as has been before stated, the good-breeding of the countess and her adorer forbade them openly to express any astonishment, Captain Hawk and Lord Harcliffe felt perfectly conscious that their elegant host and hostess must be wondering all the time who they were that had made so sudden and unexpected, though *apropos*, appearance in their mansion, and under such mysterious circumstances.

Besides this, they had really done them the highest possible service, inasmuch as they had undoubtedly preserved human life, and the unravelling of the mystery that surrounded them, and the necessary explanations for that end, were legitimate rewards to which they felt themselves entitled, in the same manner that a brave soldier at the end of a battle may be permitted to recount his share in the struggle; or a prisoner who has returned from a foreign dungeon, the means by which he burst his fetters and escaped.

After paying a full compliment to the excellence of the viands and the skill of the cook by heartily enjoying their supper, which they had moistened by sundry goblets of iced wine and water, Captain Hawk led the way to the conversation he felt certain his hosts were longing to begin.

"I have no doubt, madam," he said, courteously bowing to the countess, "you will often recall the events of this night?"

"I shall, indeed," answered the fair lady, shuddering and turning pale at the thought of the perils that had threatened one she loved dearer than life; "and whenever I do," she added, "believe me I shall always associate you with that recollection as the brave instruments of our preservation!"

She bowed gracefully to the highwaymen as she spoke.

"There is one grand principle that may always stimulate a man in his endeavours to assist others," replied Captain Hawk, who, with his comrade, had courteously acknowledged the fair speaker's salutation, "and that is, that the effort, if successful, is in itself a sufficient reward."

"To a generous mind it is," remarked Captain Nugent, joining in the conversation.

"And fortunately such minds are to be found in the humblest of our fellow-creatures," said Lord Harcliffe.

"We have had a proof of that to-night, dear Alfred, have we not," affirmed the countess, "in the persons of two poor Irish chairmen?"

"Are you quite sure they were *Irishmen*?" asked Captain Hawk, pointedly.

"Oh, no doubt of it! The brogue was too decided to admit of any doubt on that point," replied Captain Nugent, with the utmost confidence.

"It is possible to imitate a brogue very accurately," remarked Lord Harcliffe.

"So accurately as to deceive even the ear of an Irishman," added Captain Hawk. "For instance, those two poor chairmen who saved your life, and afterwards took you to Bow Street, and then, having conveyed you home, were regaled with strong ale and rewarded with ten pounds, were no more Irishmen than we are."

The countess and Captain Nugent looked at one another in much astonishment, and then the assertion of the footman, Tuppers, recurred to their memory.

"But are sure of this?" inquired Captain Nugent.

"Positive!" returned Captain Hawk.

"May I ask how it is you are so strongly assured on this point?"

"Certainly, madam," he replied; and then assuming the counterfeit brogue, he continued: "*Share, thin, isn't it Paddy and meself as ought to know, since we was the Irishmen as carried ye wid our own blessed arms?*"

"Is it possible?" exclaimed Captain Nugent, recognising the voice in a moment, and opening his eyes wider than ever with astonishment. "Then you were the chairmen?"

"We were."

"Then to you we are indebted for that service also?"

"Yes. We cannot deny it."

The countess *looked* her gratitude.

"This is most extraordinary—more, it is almost miraculous!" she exclaimed. "It would seem as though Heaven itself had sent you to interpose between us and such a dire calamity as I shudder even to contemplate!"

As she spoke she threw her arms around her handsome lover, while tears of irrepressible emotion arose to her eyes.

"But we are strangers," said Captain Nugent. "How did you learn our names, or the plot against us?"

"We made the former of these discoveries at the theatre, from the casual remarks of some visitors in the private box next to which we sat," answered Captain Hawk. "The latter we gathered from the lips of Sir Richard Chandos and Lord Edward Strathern, who bribed your *honest* Irish chairmen to convey you home through some of the *back-slum* localities, where they might have the opportunity of intercepting you."

"I comprehend. And you?"

"We turned the tables upon these lordly miscreants by outbribing these chairmen, and persuading them to let us have their coats and hats and sticks."

"Excellent! so that when the crisis of the assault arrived——"

"Instead of their weapons piercing your throat, our cudgels broke their heads!"

"And never was a broken head more richly deserved."

"I quite agree with you, captain."

"And you wound up the affair by conveying them to Bow Street, insensible as they were, and giving them in charge as two fictitious characters—two gentlemen of the road, were they not?—Captain Hawk and the Black Highwayman?"

"Exactly; though I confess I think it was paying these gentlemen a very poor compliment to confound them with such cowardly rascals."

"I think so myself," acquiesced Captain Nugent, "but you have not finished. Pray, continue," he urged.

"As we were leaving your mansion, in our capacity of chairmen, we perceived your foes, who had evidently been released from durance, coming towards it.

"We ensconced ourselves in the shadow of a portico, and from what we heard were convinced they meditated an assault.

"Upon this we instantly resolved to follow.

"We scaled the garden wall, mounted the balcony, and discarding our frieze coats, assumed our cloaks that we had rolled up and strapped round our bodies beneath, and shrouded behind these curtains, awaited the proper time to make our appearance. The rest you already know."

The beautiful countess, in the natural impulse of her grateful heart, rose from her seat, and with a beaming smile extended two hands of faultless shape and whiteness to our heroes.

"I can only reward you with my thanks, gentlemen," she exclaimed; "but the service you have rendered me and my future husband is so great that no words can adequately convey the gratitude I feel. May Heaven reward you and send you such help as you have afforded us in the hour of your need!"

Our heroes, whose hearts glowed with conscious satisfaction at the thanks of this fair creature, silently and respectfully pressed her hands to their lips.

"There is only one other favour you can render us," said Captain Nugent.

"What is that?" inquired Captain Hawk, smiling.

"First pledge me in a bumper," he answered.

"Most willingly."

The wine was poured out and the glasses raised aloft.

"In my own name and that of my beloved Clara," said Captain Nugent, "I drink your healths, gentlemen, and wish you all the happiness you can desire yourselves.

This loving cup shall be our pledge that the services you have this night rendered me shall never be obliterated from our memories."

The glasses were emptied and refilled, and Captain Hawk then said:

"And this draught shall be a pledge on our parts of the pleasure we feel at having been enabled to defeat the machinations of cowardice against honour and beauty, and an assurance that the generous manner in which you have acknowledged our humble services, while it affords us the highest gratification, far outweighs the services themselves. In my own name and that of my friend we drink your health, coupled with that of the fair lady at your side."

"And now what is the favour you spoke of?" inquired Captain Hawk of the young officer, after they had drained their glasses.

"I would fain know your names, gentlemen," he replied, "that we may be able to address our benefactors by their proper titles."

There was a slight pause.

Captain Hawk and Lord Harcliffe looked at one another.

It was a glance of mutual inquiry and mutual reply in an instant.

But there was no embarrassment in either.

Captain Hawk spoke.

"You desire to know our names?" he said.

"Greatly!" replied the captain and the countess.

"The knowledge you seek," he continued, "though it might heighten the romance of this night's adventures, would probably lower us in your estimation in a proportionate degree."

"Nothing can ever lower true gentlemen in our estimation," warmly answered the countess, "and most assuredly not yourselves, whom we are convinced *must* be gentlemen."

"You shall learn then, and afterwards judge us as you think fit. We are gentlemen—*gentlemen of the road!* My name is Captain Hawk!"

"And mine the Black Highwayman!"

These words had hardly been uttered when an indistinct sound, scarcely audible, caused Captain Hawk to glance aside.

That glance was sufficient to reveal the figure of a solitary police officer crouching cautiously in the shadow near the open window.

CHAPTER CXCII.

SIR RICHARD CHANDOS AND LORD STRATHERN VOW VENGEANCE ON THE MASKED MEN.—THE OFFER OF £200 REWARD.—THEIR VISIT TO BOW STREET.—PETERSON WAKES UP TO A FACT.—SO DOES JESSOP.—THE RESULT.

We propose leaving our heroes in the elegant and hospitable mansion in St. James's Square, and the crouching official who had so lately made his appearance on the threshold for a time, while we follow the discomfited noblemen, who, with their joint ailments in the shape of bruised heads and their respective inflictions of a pierced arm and a perforated ear, made so undignified a retreat from the back door of the garden.

They had to all intents and purposes been taught a lesson they would probably never forget, viz.: that revenge, delightful as it may appear to some minds, has its sweets as well as its bitters.

Bitter enough were their sensations.

Smarting with pain, in a fever of impotent rage—and in Lord Edward's case, of jealousy—these two baffled gentlemen slowly wended their way homewards.

It was growing daylight, and as solitary wayfarers and roaring peep o'day boys passed them, many a joke was cut on their rueful appearance. Apart from the bitter enmity they entertained towards the young guardsman, and their indignation at the infatuation, as they called it, of the fair Clarissa, there was an ardent longing for revenge upon the masked swordsmen who had administered such retributive justice, mingled with many surmises as to whom or what they could possibly be.

"Some adventurous night-gallants, glad to strike in the defence of a pretty woman," suggested the baronet.

But then the free and easy manner of these intruders, unembarrassed air and their confidence, and the perfect knowledge they appeared to possess of the names of the discomfited noblemen, suggested a different idea.

They might be brother soldiers of the captain; but even this did not appear a satisfactory solution.

It was in vain they tried to force their throbbing brains to think.

The more they tried the more obtuse and muddled their brains became, and the more their wounds smarted and throbbed.

They could arrive at nothing, save that the entire aristocracy of England had been insulted in their persons by two powerful and skilful masked ruffians; but who the masked ruffians were they were utterly at a loss to conjecture.

As they crawled slowly along, execrating everything and everybody, their attention was attracted by a bill posted prominently on a lamp-post.

It had a very official appearance, and this induced them, in spite of the other bill of *pains and penalties* they were then paying in their own persons, to pause by mutual consent and read it.

It ran thus:—

"£200 REWARD.—Whereas, it being credibly affirmed that the NOTORIOUS ROBBERS known as CAPTAIN HAWK and the BLACK HIGHWAYMAN are again on the road, the above reward will be given to anyone who shall deliver them, or give such information as shall cause them to be delivered, into the hands of justice.

"(Signed), WALPOLE, Secretary of State."

No sooner had they perused this official document than the thought flashed across them that their castigators might very possibly be these identical robbers.

"They evidently had the appearance of such vermin," remarked Lord Edward, with a grin of pain.

"Undoubtedly," acquiesced Sir Richard, nursing his perforated ear.

"Their disguises, masks and cloaks are sufficient proofs that they dared not show their faces," continued his lordship.

It was strange that neither of the speakers remembered how short a time had elapsed since *they* had shrouded themselves under similar disguises.

"The throbbing of my arm almost drives me mad, or I would go to Bow Street at once," groaned Lord Edward.

"And if my ear did not burn like a red-hot iron I'd accompany you," Sir Richard remarked, in a fretful tone.

"And yet it would be a salve to our wounds and to the indignities we have endured if we could lay these masked vagabonds by the heels, would it not?" asked Lord Strathern, whose desire for revenge overpowered his bodily pain.

"It would—by Heaven it would!" cordially returned Sir Richard.

"Let us then forget our physical pains in the prospect of handing over our inflictors to the hands of justice," urged the young lord.

"What do you propose?"

"Simply to go at once to Bow Street, state what has occurred, and set the police at the heels of these ruffians."

"Agreed. It will not take long, and we shall sleep all the better from the thought that we have dug a pit into which our enemies have a good chance of falling."

"Let us come, then, at once."

In a few moments they reached the Haymarket, where, having called a coach, they proceeded at once to Bow Street.

When they arrived, they found Inspector Nutkins and Peterson, who were on night duty, and who were solacing themselves with a glass of whisky toddy and a pipe.

Both had had a night of it—both were fuddled with liquor, and as a natural consequence both were as drowsy as a pair of owls.

Great was their surprise when they beheld the faces of Sir Richard and Lord Edward, which, in the half morning light, looked a mixture of ashen and yellow.

The cravat, too, of one, and the bandaged wrist of the other saturated in blood, caused some temporary excitement in the minds of the officials.

But they were used to such things, and after the first few moments they relapsed into their usual indifference.

[FIRING A VOLLEY.]

It was with the utmost difficulty the astute Nutkins or the vigilant Peterson managed to keep their mouths shut and their eyes open whilst the indignant noblemen were detailing their wrongs and suspicions.

The black cloaks and masks certainly appeared to take some effect upon the drowsy officials, but even this spark rapidly died out again.

The two gentlemen, too, who were in a state of incipient fever, and longing to get away, spoke wildly and somewhat incoherently.

The only two points of their narration Peterson positively did hear was, that two men in cloaks and masks, supposed to be Captain Hawk and the Black Highwayman, were at that moment at No. —, St. James's Square, and that Sir Richard Chandos offered a reward of £100 from his own private purse to anyone who should secure them.

Inspector Natkins had taken out his pocket-book as a last effort of expiring nature, and pretending to take notes, had fallen asleep in the futile attempt.

But the noblemen were too much occupied with their own feelings to notice this.

As Sir Richard was going out, he turned to Peterson.

"I have given you the particulars of this affair," he said, "and shall leave it with every confidence in your hands, feeling assured you will leave no stone unturned. You can call upon me after breakfast to-morrow."

"Have 'em both 'fore brex's' 'morr'," murmured the somnolent Peterson, as his informant left the room; and ere he had descended the steps into the street, the P. O. had fallen forward on his desk in a state of blissful forgetfulness.

Somehow or other, though, the masks and cloaks had

—perhaps from habit—fastened themselves on the slumberer's memory.

The reward, too, seemed to mingle with his sleeping thoughts.

He dreamt of tall, dark-robed figures, with bright glaring eyes, looking out of mysterious round holes.

He saw himself counting gold out of a bag labelled "*Reward of Merit*," and as often as he counted, the sum in the bag came to exactly 100*l.*

It was too much for him to sleep upon, and with a start he awoke.

His nap, sharp as it was—not over ten minutes—had refreshed his faculties.

"D—n it!" he exclaimed, stretching his chilly limbs, "I must have a try for that hundred!"

It would be, he reflected, such a grand triumph if he could drop upon these masks with a well-loaded pistol and a couple of pairs of handcuffs, and secure them himself, without any other assistance.

It was a brilliant idea; then the 100*l.* would be *all* his—his alone!

Full of this enchanting prospect, he put a formidable pair of "barkers" in his pocket, not forgetting two pairs of handcuffs, and, without rousing the still recumbent Nutkins, sallied forth.

Almost the first person he encountered was the vigilant, but over anxious and credulous, Jessop.

In the pride of his heart he could not forbear enlightening the verdant member a little.

"You don't know where I'm off to?" he remarked.

Jessop did not, of course—how should he?

"I know where to lay my hands upon Captain Hawk and the Black Highwayman; and I'm going to drop on 'em!" said Peterson, triumphantly, thrusting his hand into his pocket and jingling the handcuffs.

"What! alone?" asked the astounded but admiring provincial.

"Alone, of course! They won't dare to resist me—they know me too well!"

"Because, if you want any help," proffered Jessop, "there's me, and Jarvis, and Clark——"

"Don't want *any* help!" abruptly interrupted Peterson. "I shall drop on 'em like a carrion crow on a worm! I can't mistake 'em—two men in cloaks and masks, at No. — St. James's Square. I'll show you what an experienced officer can do! Now, mark me, Jessop, in less than an hour's time I shall have 'em both here, cloaks and masks and all, and pocket 300*l.*"

"Two hundred pounds," corrected Jessop.

"I say 300*l.*!" persisted Peterson. "Sir Richard Chandos has offered a hundred on his own account, in addition to the Government reward, so it'll be something handsome. This'll be a lesson to you, young man!—a lesson to you!"

And with these words, delivered in a very self-confident style, the *experienced* officer strode away.

Jessop, the verdant, felt crushed and wretched, and went moodily into the police-station.

The first thing he saw was the inspector fast asleep, and snoring as a chimney that required sweeping might have been supposed to snore, had such an event been possible.

He thought how differently he should have acted had *he* been inspector, and then sat down in the office and gave himself up to contemplation.

The silence and the gray light of morning were altogether favourable for such a disposition of mind.

Jessop was alone, save for the presence of the inspector, and there was nothing to check the current of his thoughts but the stentorious breathings of his superior.

He, like Peterson, had received into the storehouse of his memory very carefully the "*two men cloaked and masked*," and the "*reward of* 300*l.*" offered for their apprehension.

He could not banish them thence.

Why should he not make the attempt and secure the reward? Why?

Simply because an older officer in the force had undertaken the job, and he must knock under to him.

It was very annoying to his young ambition, but there was no resource but to wait till he, like his coadjutor, grew older.

There certainly was one solitary chance for him.

Peterson, the vigilant, the experienced, the profound, might possibly make a failure.

Should he do so, then would be the time for the junior officer, who had been snubbed, and derided, and told to go home to his mother, to start forward in full vigour, and walk triumphantly over his ironical superior.

But, then, Peterson being at St. James's Square, and he at Bow Street, how could he know whether failure or success had attended his efforts?

He rose from his seat in a perturbed manner, and then sat down again.

Inspector Nutkins still slumbered sweetly, and snored like a choked gaspipe.

It was no use, he could not restrain his intense longing to see what was going on in the region of St. James's.

He accordingly clapped his hat on his head with a resolution that might have made Peterson tremble had he witnessed it—to say nothing of the unfortunates in the cloaks and masks, who would have considered their death-warrant signed and sealed.

Jessop walked to the door, opened it, and descended the steps.

He looked up the street, and down the street, but there was nothing human in sight but an old man at a coffee-stall at the corner.

His mind was made up; he walked rapidly onwards, and turned into Covent Garden Market.

There was no retreating now—the die was cast!—the Rubicon past!

Jessop was on his road to St. James's Square.

CHAPTER CXCIII.

CAPTAIN HAWK AND THE BLACK HIGHWAYMAN BECOME ALIVE TO THE FACT THAT THEY ARE WATCHED.—AN INTERESTING CONVERSATION.—POLICE-OFFICER PETERSON PLAYS HIS LITTLE GAME, AND IS CHECKMATED.

The sound that caused Captain Hawk to turn his head was so slight that nine out of ten ordinary persons would have taken no notice of it.

But to men like our heroes, who existed from hour to hour with their lives and liberties hanging, as it were, on the turn of a hair, the slightest sound at certain times was sufficient to ring the alarum, and warn them of approaching danger.

Lord Harcliffe had heard this slight sound as perfectly as the captain, but, seeing his comrade turn rapidly towards the spot whence it proceeded, he took no further notice, a glance being sufficient to put him in possession of the fact that they were *watched.*

Not that the watcher had the remotest suspicion that he had been observed.

Such an idea never for a moment entered his head.

Our readers will have no difficulty in divining that this prying personage was the persevering Peterson himself.

He, having aroused to the importance of the undertaking and the magnificence of the reward, was now heart and soul interested in his pursuit.

Thus far he was eminently successful.

He had discovered the house, scaled the garden wall, clambered up the balcony, and actually entered the very chamber where with his own eyes he saw the identical men he wanted.

Being familiar with their persons, there was not a vestige of doubt about the matter.

And all this had been accomplished so quickly and cleverly!

The only little counteracting circumstance was, that the slight noise he made in clambering over the balustrades had given just that *particular* information to certain interested parties within that ought *not* to have been given.

But of this the exulting Peterson was utterly unconscious.

When he scraped the stonework with the toe of his boot, he instantly dropped on his knees, and remained crouched down quietly as a mouse for several moments.

It was in that position Captain Hawk perceived him.

Accustomed to control their emotions and to smile in the midst of danger, our heroes gave no signs at all that anything unusual had occurred.

When Peterson ventured to look up from his prostrate

attitude, he was rejoiced to see that his little accident had not alarmed or startled the parties within.

Oh no—not in the least! There they stood, evidently enjoying themselves, and, from the melodious jingle of glasses, drinking wine.

Peterson's triumphant exultation was unbounded.

He had managed the affair so well!

The 300*l.* seemed to be already in his pocket.

To say nothing of the honour of the thing, which was as good as another three hundred.

As these thoughts bubbled in his swelling breast, his hands wandered longingly to his pockets, and dallied a few moments with the handcuffs he carried.

Then they changed their locality, and caressed the pair of heavy "barkers" in his other pocket.

"I shall have no difficulty about this job," he said to himself, in a kind of mental rapture. "It'd be a pity to have to put a bullet into such furniture as this, or to damage any o' them glasses. I must wait till I see a good opportunity, and then I'll be down upon 'em like a Cossack on a tallow candle."

Having thus given vent to the exuberance of his fancy, the gallant Peterson subsided into silence, and watched.

Our readers will remember that it was just as Captain Hawk and the Black Highwayman had declared their identity that the noise that startled them had reached their ears.

As these names, so familiar from the daring deeds and the desperate defiance of the laws with which their owners were associated, were pronounced distinctly by the captain as the proper titles of himself and comrade, the astonishment of their hosts seemed to have reached its highest point

There was no terror or alarm expressed, however, by either.

Simply astonishment, and this astonishment had the effect of producing a somewhat long pause, during which all the parties present looked at each other.

Captain Nugent, this time, was the first to speak.

"Then you really are what you affirm yourselves to be?" he inquired—"Captain Hawk and the Black Highwayman?"

"We are!" they replied, with one voice.

Peterson, in his place of concealment, tingled all over, from the crown of his head to the soles of his feet, as these words reached his ears.

There was no indignation or excitement in Captain Nugent's voice when he addressed our heroes; the question was calmly put, and in a tone of the kindest solicitation, as though entreating them to be candid on this point.

When, therefore, the answer came in the two brief monosyllables we have recorded, he looked earnestly at the two gallant forms before him for an instant, and then in a tone, the earnestness of which proved its sincerity, exclaimed:

"I must believe your assurance, though had anyone but yourselves told me so, I would not have believed them."

"May I ask why?" said Captain Hawk.

"Because your manners — your appearance — your language, and—and, in short, everything connected with you seems to repel the idea. Knights of the Road!—*Highwaymen!* Oh! it is impossible!"

"Or at least," murmured the countess, somewhat timidly, "most extraordinary!"

"And why, my dear friends?—that is, if you will allow me to call you so *now*,"—asked Captain Hawk, "why impossible—why extraordinary?"

The speakers were silent.

"You have been accustomed, I see," continued the captain, "like the rest of the world, to regard us gentlemen of the road—or highwaymen if you please—as a set of ruffianly marauders, scouring the quiet roads and bye-lanes of the country, and as the great poet observes, 'making night horrible with our depredations'——"

"Nay——"

"Excuse me, captain, but it is so; and as one man often suffers from the faults of another, so we are mixed up indiscriminately by the mass of mankind with every outrage that is committed."

"Pray, gentlemen, do not think so!" the countess eagerly exclaimed.

"My dear madam, it is not what we *think*—it is only what our experience proves to be the fact," continued Captain Hawk.

"At least *we* do not!" she replied, earnestly.

"I freely acquit you, madam," answered the captain, respectfully. "Those who know us best give us the best characters: it is from those who do *not* know us we suffer most. They cannot understand how a chivalrous sense of honour can exist in the breast of a man who defies the law, or how one who cries 'Stand and deliver!' to a rich traveller, and takes from him a portion of that coin of which he has too much, can sympathise with the sufferings of humanity, or feel for those who are poorer than themselves."

"It seems strange," remarked the countess, in a low tone.

"Then, again, with respect to women," the captain went on, "it is affirmed that no woman's honour is safe in our company, or secure from our attacks!"

"Oh!"

"I grieve to say such is the prevailing opinion, and that though men may escape our clutches, women, whether young or old, rich or poor, we never spare!"

"'Tis a cruel slander!" exclaimed the countess, indignantly, her beautiful eyes sparkling with anger.

"It is, madam," echoed Captain Hawk—"cruel in the highest degree, since it makes us appear traitors to every sense of delicacy and manhood, and stamps our characters with an infamy that we have no opportunity of refuting save by our deeds."

"And they, after all, are the best witnesses in the end," said Captain Nugent; "but you may rely upon it, there is no fear of *our* mistaking your characters. Short as our acquaintance has been, it has existed long enough to prove that you are gentlemen in the highest sense of the word, and that your sentiments merit the esteem of all who call themselves by that title."

"I rejoice sincerely to think that Fortune has so far favoured us as to give us the opportuntity of enlisting on our side two such noble and generous advocates!" replied Captain Hawk, bowing low to the great compliment the young officer had paid him, at the same time casting a glance under his own arm at the exulting Peterson, who, feeling that the important time had arrived, was gradually edging along under cover of the curtains, in order to be ready for the final swoop.

All this Captain Hawk, much to his amusement, took in at a glance.

It argues something for the imperturbable coolness of our heroes that the foregoing conversation had taken place wher they were fully assured of the presence of a police officer within a few yards of them, and that he was listening to every word they uttered.

It was, perhaps, this very consciousness that stimulated the eloquence of Captain Hawk.

He commented on the injustice of society for the express benefit of the lurking Peterson.

Not that, all this time, his thoughts were inactive, or that he was not contemplating an attack, and the means of frustrating it.

Far from it.

He had already resolved what to do.

The conversation had become more general.

Lord Harcliffe, at a sign from his comrade, moved towards a magnificent piece of furniture that had the appearance of a couch.

"Pardon my rudeness," said his lordship, "but I cannot help admiring this beautiful couch!"

"It is immensely admired," answered the countess; "and see," she exclaimed, advancing and raising the seat, disclosing a large cavity, "it answers a double purpose, serving both for a seat and for a chest."

"Very convenient indeed," remarked Captain Hawk, laughing to himself very quietly; "it has a lock, too, has it not?"

"Yes," replied the countess, lifting up the fringe at the edge and disclosing a keyhole and key, "it is a very convenient receptacle, and holds more than anyone would imagine. I generally fill it with books."

Captain Hawk was impressed with the idea that it would in all probability be filled very shortly with something of quite a different material, but he did not say so.

But both he and Lord Harcliffe, thinking it was time

to bring matters to a crisis, in order to draw out the cautious Peterson, suggested that it was time for them to take their departure, it being now broad daylight.

"We part as friends, I hope," said Captain Hawk, "despite the unfortunate profession to which we belong?"

"Be sure of that," exclaimed the countess and her lover, warmly; "whatever others may say or think, we shall *always* consider you amongst our chief friends. I trust we shall meet again."

The highwaymen shook hands cordially with their new but staunch acquaintances, and as they did so they distinctly heard the rattle of handcuffs, and the sound of a pistol placed on half-cock, behind the curtain.

The moment for action had arrived.

"Farewell, Captain Nugent! Farewell, madam!" the highwaymen exclaimed; "with your permission, we will return as we came, by the balcony and the back garden door."

"Just as you please," answered Captain Nugent, smiling. "You made a romantic entrance: you will make a romantic exit."

The highwaymen made an advance towards the open window, when, as they fully expected, the burly form of P. O. Peterson presented itself with a heavy pistol in each hand, and forbade their further progress.

"Sorry to contradict you, sir, in your own house," he said to the captain; "but I want these men; they are my property."

As he spoke, he pointed to our heroes with one of his formidable pistols.

An exclamation from Captain N., and a slight shriek of surprise from the countess, had followed the sudden appearance of the police officer.

Peterson was greatly flattered by the sensation he had produced.

That is, upon the parties mentioned: the utter unconcern of the highwaymen looked rather ominous for the success of his plan, as it proved they did not care a straw either for him, his uniform, or his pistols.

They both folded their arms, and looked at him as they would at any other ordinary individual.

At length Captain Hawk, who dearly loved a joke at the expense of his sworn enemies the police officers, threw a gleam of recognition into his immovable features, and exclaimed, suddenly, as though he had just awoke from a dream:

"What, Peterson!—is it? Yes—it must be—it *is* Peterson!"

"Yes; it *is* Peterson," returned that worthy, who was beginning to feel nervous at this kind of dalliance. "Of course you know what I want, so I hope you'll come quietly, and not give me any trouble."

Without replying to this friendly appeal, Captain Hawk turned to the countess, who hardly knew what to make of this strange encounter, and said:

"Will you permit me to introduce to you, madam, one of the most vigilant supervisors of the public peace, Police Officer Peterson."

The countess bowed slightly with some *hauteur;* but caught a glance from the eye of Captain Hawk that implied he had a motive for what he did.

As for Peterson, he bowed to the ground.

"Sorry, your ladyship, to make anything unpleasant," he said; "only dooty, your ladyship knows——"

"Is duty, of course," interrupted Captain Hawk.

"And you may be quite sure that we should never think of raising an *emeute* in a privileged spot like this," remarked Lord Harcliffe.

"That's exactly what I thought," said the police officer, much relieved by an assurance that seemed to promise a pacific realisation of his wishes.

During this, Captain Hawk again caught the eye of the countess, and guided it by a look first to the decanter, thence to Peterson, and lastly to the couch.

The countess, with woman's quick perception, at once divined that the officer was to be asked to take a seat and to drink.

"It's never any good making a disturbance, when things can be done quietly," remarked that individual, feeling with one hand in his pocket for a perverse handcuff that persisted in hiding away in one of the corners. "Now then, gentlemen, if you please," he continued, to our heroes, as he produced the two pairs of steel bracelets, "just for form's sake, you know—nothing more."

The highwaymen were apparently about to hold forth their hands to be thus adorned with all the willingness of obedient children, when the countess, in a silvery voice, said:

"Perhaps Mr. Peterson would like to take a glass of wine before you go?"

Now it so happened that Peterson had been casting sundry longing glances at the glistening decanters, and as the fumes of the whisky toddy had left behind them a considerable thirst, he was not at all unwilling to accept the gracious offer.

But then he was suspicious.

He thought there might be a plot to make him intoxicated or drug him.

But he dismissed the latter of these ideas, and resolved to protect himself from the former by resolutely refusing more than two or three glasses at the outside.

He, however, with a little affectation of modesty—*very* little—endeavoured to excuse himself.

"Very much obliged, your ladyship," he murmured, "but bus'ness is bus'ness."

"Nay," replied the fair solicitor, "I can take no excuse."

And in order to put such an event utterly out of the question, she advanced to the flattered official, and extending her white and jewelled fingers, took him by his hard, coarse, red hand, and actually led him towards *the couch.*

Surely never before was a police officer so honoured!

So Peterson himself thought as he glanced at his beautiful conductress.

He did not observe that a very significant look passed between her and Captain Hawk, who placed his hand upon one of the decanters.

"Do not trouble yourself: I will *open it myself,*" said the fair conspirator, sweetly, to the captain.

"She's going to open another bottle for me," thought the officer.

"Now, Mr. Peterson," she continued, urging the officer with the most winning courtesy to be seated, "pray sit down."

"You're uncommonly kind," said the unconscious Peterson, sitting down upon *nothing,* and instantly disappearing through the body of the couch, the only portion of his corporeal structure remaining visible being his boots, which stuck up in the air.

He uttered a yell of rage; but it was too late.

In an instant Captain Hawk and Lord Harcliffe darted forward, and packing up his legs with more speed than ceremony, slammed down the seat of the couch, which formed the lid of the box, and the vigilant Peterson was quite beyond the reach of doing any further mischief, and with as good a prospect of being suffocated as ever he had in his life.

The officer shouted and hammered with his knuckles furiously, but the sides of the interior were lined and padded, and the carpet was half an inch thick—the sounds, therefore, were of the mildest possible description.

He therefore knocked till he was tired, and then, having nothing better to do, renounced all ideas of the £300, and like a sensible man, went to sleep.

"I thank you sincerely, madam, for your skilful assistance in this manner. I always make a point of treating these fellows in this way," said Captain Hawk, as he shook out the priming of the officer's pistols on the balcony and then concealed the weapons beneath the couch.

"I'll be bound," he continued, "you never expected to fill your couch with such merchandize as it now contains?"

"No indeed," replied the countess; "but what is to be done with him?" she inquired.

"You will be kind enough to let him out when we are gone," replied the captain. "For his own sake he will be glad to keep silence upon the subject of his incarceration."

"And now once more farewell, madam," said Captain Hawk; "it is time we were gone—it is broad daylight."

This was a palpable fact; and the brilliant wax tapers in the apartment had paled before the more powerful glare from without.

"It has just struck me that our services may be needed

by you at some future time. Should this ever be the case, do not hesitate to call upon us."

"But where are you to be found?" asked the countess.

"A note placed in the cavity of the tree opposite your window will reach us," answered the captain. "We will send for it."

"Then in order to facilitate the entrance of your messenger into the garden, here is a passport." And as she spoke she handed Captain Hawk a duplicate key.

Once more the highwaymen were about to depart, when stealthy footsteps on the gravel arrested their attention.

CHAPTER CXCIV.

IN WHICH ARISE FRESH ADVENTURES.—PERSEVERANCE AND PATIENCE ARE REWARDED.—A MASKED RUFFIAN SECURED.—PETERSON COMES TO GRIEF.

THEY paused.

"Did you not hear footsteps?" he inquired of his comrade.

"Undoubtedly," replied the Black Highwayman.

"What can it be?—some more of the Philistines at our heels? Madam," he said to the countess, "will you oblige us with reconnoitring?"

The lady walked quietly to the window and looked cautiously from the balcony, but immediately withdrew, and in an accent of alarm exclaimed:

"Heavens! there are three men in the garden, evidently, from their dress, police officers, in close consultation."

"Be not afraid, madam. Let me see," whispered Captain Hawk.

As he spoke he cautiously approached the window and looked out.

"Umph!" he said, in a low voice to Lord Harcliffe, "they are all new faces to me, and I feel convinced we shall be equally unknown to them."

This was a truth, inasmuch as the trio consisted of Jessop, Jarvis, and Wilkins, the two last of whom Jessop had met on the road and enlisted in his enterprise.

They were at that moment deeply engaged in conversation, and spoke in low tones.

Captain Hawk and his comrade listened attentively to catch their words.

Some of these they heard.

"You are sure this is the house?" said one.

"No doubt of it, according to the number," was the reply.

"Peterson ought to be here, oughtn't he?" asked the first speaker.

"He ought," answered Jessop, with something like contempt in his tone, "but he isn't."

"And what do you suppose is the reason?"

"P'raps he's been here and gone with the two men in custody," suggested one of the three.

This was by no means a palatable idea, and Jessop scouted it accordingly.

"More likely he's made a mess of it," he replied. "He's not everybody, though he did brag that he'd have these highwaymen in custody in less than an hour."

"Those that call out the loudest don't always do the most," remarked Wilkins.

"It's a good stiff reward, isn't it?"

"Rather—£300; that's just a hundred each if we succeed."

"Well, then, the best thing to do in my opinion is to make a beginning," suggested Jessop.

"So I think. Are your pistols all right?"

"Yes."

"D'ye know these men by sight?"

"No; do you?"

"Not in the least; never saw 'em. Jessop does."

"No, I don't. I've collared two or three at different times on suspicion, but they turned out to be the wrong persons."

"That was awkward."

"Very; but there's one comfort, we can't go wrong this time," said Jessop.

"Why not?"

"Because our men wear black cloaks and masks."

"Oh, well, we can't mistake them."

"How are we going to begin?"

"We must enter the house somehow."

"It's early yet; the doors are locked."

"But that window is open."

Jessop pointed up to the balcony as he spoke.

"There's a light in the chamber, isn't there?"

"There's so much light outside I can't distinguish."

"Couldn't we clamber up and see?"

"I think not. Our better way will be to enter by the door if we can; it looks more regular and business-like," Jessop replied, who appeared to be the oracle of the verdant ones.

"Isn't that a door there?"

"Looks like it."

The three men approached the door indicated, and to their no little surprise it was ajar.

"The door is opened," exclaimed Jarvis.

"All the better. Now then, tread light and follow me," ordered Jessop.

"These fellows are as green as grass in their profession," said Captain Hawk to Lord Harcliffe, as the footsteps of the men died away.

"They are evidently coming in at the door," returned his lordship.

"Let them come as soon as they like. We shall have no trouble with them," answered the captain.

"Shall you be able to elude them?" inquired the countess, with some apprehension in her tone. "Three will be more difficult to dispose of than one."

"Fear nothing for us, my dear madam," said Captain Hawk. "Seat yourself with perfect unconcern, and act according to circumstances; you will be guided by us."

"You reassure me," answered the countess.

"Have you any cards?" inquired Captain Hawk.

"Here is a pack," she replied.

"Come, then, let us play a game at whist."

The cards were dealt round and the play commenced.

In the meantime the three officers, ignorant of the locality, and strangers to the subterranean passages of the mansion, had wandered into the scullery and twice into the coal cellar in their efforts to find their way upstairs.

"This door must lead somewhere," sagely remarked Jessop, as he turned a handle and pushed open the opposing barrier that creaked upon its hinges.

This time they had infringed upon the territories of the footman, who slept in the pantry, and who, being suddenly roused from his morning dreams, was impressed with the idea that there were burglars in the house.

The shutters being closed, the room was quite dark.

Jessop turned on his dark lantern and threw the light around, speedily discovering the alarmed Tuppers, who was sitting up in the bed with his nose and knees together, the bedclothes being pulled tightly up to his chin.

His pale face and white night-cap, which had a comical tassel at the end, being the only portions of his outward man that were visible, he presented an appearance that was excessively ludicrous.

"Good gad! gentlemin!" he gasped, "whatever *is* the matter?"

"Nothing," said Jessop, abruptly, trying to imitate his superior, Peterson, whom he abominated while he imitated him.

"Is it burglars?" inquired the agitated flunkey.

"No. Go to bed."

"I am in bed, gentlemin!"

"Then go to sleep."

"I really can't! What's to become of the plate?" groaned Tuppers, in a tone of lamentation.

"Never mind the plate! We're police officers," answered Jessop, proudly, as though that piece of information ought to have been sufficient to allay every lingering doubt as to the safety of the entire establishment.

"Which is the way upstairs?" inquired Jarvis.

"First to the right, second to the left, through the glass door, then straight on, and the stairs is before yer!" answered Tuppers.

"Come on then," said Jessop. "You can lay still and take no notice of anything," he informed the footman as they left the room.

This counsel Tuppers followed by getting out of bed in a fever of apprehension, and listening with all his ears, expecting to be scared each moment by loud cries of murder.

All, however, remaining perfectly quiescent, he

sneaked into bed again and held his head under the bedclothes, more than ever convinced that the police officers were burglars in disguise.

The trio, guided by the footman's description, found the stairs at last and ascended to the parlour door, notwithstanding an obstinate inclination on the part of Wilkins to walk into a cupboard on the stairs.

The door of the room in which the card-players were seated was partly open, and Jessop could distinctly hear what was going on.

After a few moments he ventured to peep in.

What was the sight that presented itself?

A lovely woman and three handsome, aristocratic-looking gentlemen playing a quiet game at cards.

But no signs of any ruffians in black cloaks and masks.

Jessop quickly withdrew his head.

"It's very rum," he remarked, in a thoughtful whisper. "All seems as quiet as death. We surely can't have gone and made a mistake after all?"

It was a most embarrassing contemplation, and he endeavoured to reason himself out of such an idea.

"It's impossible we can be wrong," he continued; "and even if we are, we're only doing our duty."

"Certainly," added Jarvis.

"Besides," chimed in Wilkins, "there's the reward of three hundred to be considered."

"Of course," answered Jessop, in a decided tone, "I *do* consider it, and, what's more, I want to get it, so prepare to follow me."

"We're all ready," answered his companions.

"Come, then."

And without further preface he thrust his head in at the open door, and uttered a preliminary—

"Ahem!"

The card-players ceased their game, and in great apparent surprise turned their gaze towards the door.

Jessop on this felt it his duty to advance.

His companions also followed their leader.

"What do you want?—who are you?" inquired Captain Hawk, with affected languor, of Jessop.

"We're police officers," answered that individual. "I'm Jessop, of Bow Street, this is Wilkins, and this is Jarvis, of the same locality."

"Oh, indeed!" drawled Captain Hawk. "Never heard of you. You'd better go back again there. Whom do you seek here?"

"One of our force—Mr. Peterson."

"Never heard of *him* either."

"We expected to find him here."

"Did you indeed?"

"Yes, my lord. Isn't he here?"

"No."

"But he has been here?"

"Has he?"

"I mean *has* he been here?"

"Not that I'm aware of."

"It's very strange!" murmured Jessop.

"It strikes me you're the victims of some delusion," continued Captain Hawk, in the same affected style. "What do you want with this Peterson?"

"He came here to look after two ruffians in black cloaks and masks."

"Eh?—what? Ruffians cloaked and masked?"

"Yes: two of 'em."

"Haven't seen anything of the kind. You've decidedly come to the wrong house."

"Well, upon my word, I begin to think I—that is—a—I mean——" stammered Jessop, who was so thoroughly floored at the coolness of Captain Hawk's address and the gaze of the aristocratic company who sat at the table, that he hardly knew what he was talking about.

"I rather imagine, my fine fellows," continued the captain, in a bantering tone, "you have been offering up your libations to Bacchus too freely overnight, and are not in the entire possession of your faculties."

Jessops, Wilkins, and Jarvis, who had a very indistinct idea as to the identity of the personage mentioned as Bacchus, protested that they had not been out with anyone of that name.

This caused the company to laugh.

"Take my advice," said the captain—"retire at once to your respective homes, or I shall be under the unpleasant necessity of showing you the most expeditious route from the window yonder."

"Come on, Jess," whispered Wilkins. "We've got into the wrong shop, depend upon it."

Jessop, who now yielded to the same opinion, became very humble, and began to apologise, when some extraordinary sounds were heard from some quarter that seemed everywhere and nowhere.

"Wh-what's that?" Jessop ventured to inquire.

"What's what?" demanded the captain.

"That noise!"

"What noise?"

"Sounds like some one snoring as much as anything," answered Jessop.

"Don't hear anything," said the captain, obtusely. "Do you, my lord?" he inquired of Lord Barcliffe.

"Nothing, duke," replied his lordship.

"Excuse me, my lords," persisted Jessop, "but as sure as a nose is a nose, that sound is caused by somebody snoring."

"It's uncommon like Peterson's snore, too," remarked Wilkins. "There! there it goes again!"

The fact was, the imprisoned police officer was in a happy state of blissful repose—dreaming he had captured his prey, and pocketed the reward—and snoring with all his might.

The sounds, however, coming as they did from such a confined space, had a peculiarly muffled quality.

"You see," said Captain Hawk, "how your senses are unsettled—your minds are wandering. Pray get home as fast as you can, and sleep yourselves into your sober senses, or I shall really be compelled to send for a constable."

This struck Wilkins as such a good joke that he actually laughed.

Jessop, however, who was disappointed and chagrined at the ill-success of his plan, looked anything but mirthful.

"We're perfectly sober," he affirmed, in a tone of injured pride, "and can find our way out, my lord, without any assistance, and p'r'aps, under all circumstances, the sooner we go the better."

"I'm decidedly of your opinion," answered the captain. "However, as you belong to the police force—a body of men I very greatly respect—you must take a glass of wine first."

At this intimation the tyros licked their lips, and touched their heads in token of respectful gratitude.

Indeed, so overpowered were they at the honour done them, that when they essayed to drink, the liquor went the wrong way, and set them all coughing and choking till they were on the verge of strangulation.

It was some time before they could recover their usual equanimity.

"You are excited," remarked Captain Hawk, as they stood with their eyes watering, and their faces very red from the effects of their late choking fit. "You had better try another."

There was no reason why they should not, so they tried another with better success.

"And now," said the captain, "home as fast as you can, and the next time you come out in search of ruffians in cloaks and masks, be sure you go to the right house."

Murmuring some inarticulate and confused excuses, the three brother officers made some straggling efforts to bow to the countess, and after some difficulty backed out in a very humble and submissive manner.

Tuppers, who heard them descend the stairs and leave the house, rejoiced that the burglars had departed, and being somewhat stimulated—now that his fears were removed—by curiosity, hastily threw on his clothes, and followed at a respectful distance, being anxious to see what these strange visitors were doing on the outside of the house.

As he emerged into the garden, he saw the three officials, who looked rather sheepish in the morning light, holding a conference at the back garden-door.

The subject of this appeared to be the best means of getting out.

The door seemed to be the most natural and the easiest; but that was closed, and there was no key.

The only way, therefore, was that by which they had gained admission—over the wall.

Accordingly, by dint of much hoisting and struggling and scraping of boots against the bricks, much to the amusement of our heroes, who were quietly watching their manœuvres from the window, they contrived to scale the wall and gain the other side in safety.

But though they had achieved this great feat, they were by no means satisfied with the result of their undertaking.

Jessop felt confident the house they had visited was the right house, and felt perfectly bewildered at the utter failure of their scheme.

The mysterious snoring also preyed upon his mind.

"Hang it all!" he exclaimed, scratching his head, as he lingered with his companions on the other side of the wall. "If that wasn't Peterson's nose we heard snoring, I never heard it!"

"I'm sure it *was* his nose!" exclaimed Wilkins, with energy.

"I'm blowed if I don't think he was hid away somewhere in the room we've just left, fast asleep!" cried Jessop.

"P'r'aps some one's murdered him!" suggested the former speaker.

"Psha! Murdered men don't snore!"

"No more they do!"

"No. If John Peterson's there at all, he's alive, hid away under the sofa."

This idea seemed to hit the members of the league strongly.

"I've half a mind to go back and demand to make a search. £300 is a good lump of money to miss," remarked Jessop.

"I should say it was!" acquiesced his companions.

"But then if we went back, we're not positive that swell there'd let us look everywhere."

The prevailing opinion at that moment was, that he would not.

"So p'r'aps we may as well leave it for the present?"

"P'r'aps so."

They were about to turn their lingering steps away from the spot that seemed, in spite of themselves, to exercise a kind of magnetic influence upon them, when a confused kind of noise on the other side of the wall attracted their attention.

"Did you hear that?" asked Jessop, eagerly.

"I did," was the reply.

"What can it be?"

"Is it Peterson?"

"Or the fellows with the cloaks and masks, after all?"

"Trying to escape, perhaps—who knows?"

"If so, there's the door, and there's the wall; they must come either through the one or over the other."

There was so much sound, practical sense in this remark of Jessop, that it was accepted at once by his companions.

"No one can see us here. Let us stay and watch for a time," suggested Jarvis: "we shall be sure to drop on to somebody, take my word for it."

This being agreed upon, they took up their posts close to the door and waited, expecting every moment to see some anxious fugitive make his appearance.

They were perfectly unconscious that the anxious Tuppers had caught, in a broken and unconnected manner, fragments of their conversation, and that he had, by putting these fragments together, come to the conclusion that "*somebody was murdered and hid away under the sofa*," and that "*two fellows in cloaks and masks were trying to escape!*"

This was too much for his weak powers to sustain at one time, and he accordingly hastened back to the house in a state of enormous trepidation, to unburden himself of the dreadful intelligence he had to communicate.

The sudden appearance of Tuppers in a state of ghastly excitement, and the dark tale of blood he had to reveal, was another little episode in the facetiæ of the night's adventures.

It, however, suggested to the fertile mind of Captain Hawk a highly affective wind-up to the whole affair.

"You're a very praiseworthy young man," he said to Tuppers, who quite agreed with him. "Return to the garden wall and listen for any further intelligence those rascals on the other side may reveal; when I beckon you from the window, come quickly."

Away went Tuppers, suddenly swelled into vast importance at the responsible part he fancied he was playing in this curious game.

He planted himself close to the garden door and listened, but could hear nothing but indistinct murmurs arising from the low tones in which the parties on the opposite side of the wall spoke.

No sooner was he gone, than Captain Hawk, having reprimed the pistols of the slumbering Peterson, rendered them harmless by extracting the bullets.

He then unlocked the receptacle in which he slept, and allowed him to breathe a little fresh air.

This was necessary, as there were some very apoplectic symptoms on the face of the police officer.

This done, he went out on to the balcony, and gesticulated violently to Tuppers.

The footman hurried to him at the top of his speed.

"What's the matter?" he cried, in a voice full of excitement.

"Quick—quick!" replied Captain Hawk. "Run back to the garden wall and plant a ladder against it, and then cry out loud enough for those on the other side to hear, that the police officer is murdered by the masked men, and that they are escaping."

Tuppers performed his task with considerable ability.

Jessop, Wilkins, and Jarvis heard his agitated remarks and the scraping of his feet on the gravel as he went for the ladder, and their hopes revived.

They felt the £300 was once more within their reach.

In the meantime, Captain Nugent and the countess, instructed by Captain Hawk, who with Lord Harcliffe, kept out of sight, shook Mr. Peterson violently.

"Hallo—hallo! what's the matter? What is it, eh?" he cried, starting from his sleep, and looking round in a scared manner.

"Oh, Mr. Peterson!" cried the countess, in an agitated tone, "those terrible men, since you have been asleep, have robbed us!"

"Robbed?" murmured the officer, who was then only partially awake, "when—where?"

"Oh, don't stop to ask questions; one of them has escaped over the wall, by the assistance of a ladder, the other has strangely disappeared and left behind him his cloak and mask. We thought perhaps that if you disguised yourself in these, and went out hastily by the door in the wall, you would be mistaken by the one lurking there, for his comrade. He would approach under this impression, when you would seize him immediately, without risk or difficulty, and earn a portion of the reward, at least."

"Yes, yes, I'll do it!" cried Peterson. "Excellent!"

In a moment the mask and cloak were affixed, and the bulky Peterson, in a frantic hurry seizing his pistols, hurried off towards the end of the garden.

As he reached the door, he suddenly remembered he had no key.

His eye fell on the ladder; that was the very thing.

He pushed it up firmly against the wall.

The officers without watched its appearance with intense anxiety, and cocked their pistols.

Peterson at the foot of the ladder cocked his.

Enveloped in the cloak and mask, he hastily ascended and looked over the wall.

"Scoundrel! I——"

But ere the sentence was completed, three pistols went off, and a loud shout rose from the throats of Jessop, Wilkins and Jarvis.

Peterson's weapon discharged itself in the air, and he, with a howl of pain, fell with a crash to the bottom of the ladder, carrying with him his three colleagues' bullets—one in the shoulder, and two in his hat—*not* his head.

"Hurrah!" shouted the men. "he's hit! Forward! over the wall!"

And suiting the act to the words, they scrambled over like three monkeys in double quick time.

"The reward's ours! Lay hold on him!" they yelled, excitedly, as they dropped down on to the gravel without even stopping to descend by the ladder.

Like three hungry vultures on a dead carcass, the three men threw themselves upon the *ruffian in the cloak and mask*, who had fainted with the pain of his wound.

With eager haste they tore away the cloak, and

dragged the mask from the features of their prize, when, to their horror, they beheld instead of some strange countenance, the well-known lineaments of the Bow Street runner, Peterson.

In a state of mind which may be easier imagined than described, they raised the body and carried it towards the house, inwardly execrating cloaks, masks, and ruffians in general, of all sorts and sizes.

Tuppers was despatched for the disguises which had been left lying on the gravel; and whilst the officers were attending to their wounded comrade at the back of the house, Captain Hawk and Lord Harcliffe quietly walked out at the front.

The busy world was now astir; and as they felt somewhat exhausted with the long continued excitement which, from various causes, they had undergone, they called the first coach they met, and contrived to reach Snagson's Family Hotel, just about breakfast-time.

The meal being finished, our heroes retired to their chamber, and in a few moments were enjoying the blessings of calm and undisturbed repose.

CHAPTER CXCV.

CAPTAIN HAWK AND THE BLACK HIGHWAYMAN ARE COMPELLED TO LIE CLOSE FOR A TIME.—THE CAPTAIN CONTINUES THE HISTORY OF HIS EARLY ADVENTURES.

It was at a late hour of the day that our heroes awoke from their slumber invigorated and refreshed in body and mind.

Charles, who had been making anxious inquiries abroad, made his appearance, and gave so glowing a description of the excitement their names and acts had created; the feverish competition there was amongst a certain morbid class to gaze upon such extraordinary men; and last, but by no means the least, the stimulant of a large reward to urge on pursuit; convinced the captain and his comrade that a further term of caution and seclusion was necessary.

There was one comfort—they felt themselves safe from the perils that would have environed them had they been anywhere else but at the Family Hotel.

In this sanctuary, then, they resolved to remain until the first burst of the hue-and-cry had somewhat spent its fury.

It was on one afternoon, when they were seated in their chamber smoking cigars, and sipping sherry and water, that Lord Harcliffe suddenly remembered his comrade had not yet fulfilled the promise he had made to continue the relation of his youthful reminiscences.

"Since you appeared to be amused by what I have already told you of my boyhood's days," said Captain Hawk, "I shall have much pleasure in continuing the recital. I am only fearful lest I should grow tedious and wearisome."

"That I am positive you will never do," answered his friend.

"Let me see, where did I leave off in my history?" said Captain Hawk, thoughtfully.

"You were just starting home for the holiday at the end of the quarter, leaving your damaged friends, or rather foes, M. Adolphe Sanier and Master Peter Bollard, with something to teach them better behaviour for the future."

"True, I was. How well you remember!"

"I always remember what interests me."

"Well, then, to continue," said Captain Hawk, "I returned no more to Dr. Short's academy, my father, who was a very excellent scholar, informing me that the remainder of my education he should undertake himself.

"Whether my morals were improved or not by the lessons he taught me I will not pretend to say; I only know he was careful to impress upon my young mind certain truths, the observance of which on all occasions would inevitably stamp my reputation as a gentleman and a man of honour."

"And what were they?"

"Fidelity in friendship, constancy in love, coolness in danger, humility in prosperity, patience in adversity, charity to all."

"Very excellent mottoes, and I think I may add from experience you have practised these precepts."

"I have endeavoured to do so out of respect to my father's memory.

"He had the quality of adapting himself so to my tastes, that whilst he exercised over me the authority of a parent and guide, he seemed more to me like a companion or playmate.

"He seemed to be very fond of me, and by the time I was sixteen years old I was his almost constant companion.

"It seemed to me that the life my father led was the jolliest, merriest life in the world.

"He always mingled with good-humoured, witty, cheerful companions like himself, and never, so far as I could perceive, had to work to provide for his support.

"While I was younger this did not strike me, but as I grew older I found myself very often asking myself curious questions about my father?

"What was his business or profession?—in short, how did he live? were queries I was constantly putting to myself.

"So inquisitive did I grow on this point that I tried in all kind of ways to—as it were—screw the secret out of my father, which he appeared to have made up his mind not to tell.

"At last my curiosity so far overmastered my prudence that I became too importunate, which caused my father to administer a rebuke I shall never forget.

"'My boy,' said he, in a brief but impressive manner, 'I see you are over curious to know all about me; in time you shall do so; but for the present learn to judge me from what I *am to you*, rather than from the line of life I follow.'

"This silenced me; and I went on, knowing nothing further about my father's profession until my sixteenth birthday; and then as we were sitting alone over our wine after dinner in our cottage parlour my father said to me:

"'You were a year or two ago exceedingly anxious to know what profession I followed that brings me in so handsome an income without obliging me to do any work. You were then too young to permit me to enlighten; now, however, as you have reached your sixteenth year, I intend to do so, and have fixed on your birthday to make my revelation.'

"I expressed myself extremely delighted, as indeed I was, at this announcement, and my father, having drank my health as his 'son and heir' in a bumper, commenced:

"'I am by profession what is called a gentleman or knight of the road.'

"'Knight of the road!' I echoed, with surprise. 'I thought there were no such persons as knights in existence now-a-days.'

"My father smiled and explained:

"'Nor are there—that is, no knights errant travelling about cased in armour and armed with spear, helmet and shield for the express succour of young ladies in distress.'

"'Oh, then I suppose you belong to a different order of knighthood,' I remarked.

"'Exactly,' returned my father, with a chuckling laugh, as though I had said a capital thing, though I confess I could not see the joke myself. 'You are quite right; I do belong to an entirely different order.'

"'Being a knight of the road, I suppose you have something to do with the road,' I continued.

"'Yes,' answered my father. "It is there I levy my contributions on the public.'

"Oh!' I exclaimed, 'I understand now. You are a collector of taxes?'

"My father laughed outright at this very innocent remark of mine, which struck me as being very strange, and to speak the truth rather piqued me.

"He observed this, and patting me good-naturedly on the shoulder, said:

"'I cannot explain more definitely at this moment; think no more about it, and to-morrow you shall dine with me and some friends of mine in London; you will there hear some conversation that will probably be sufficiently explicit.'

"We spent that afternoon and evening very pleasantly at home—my father and mother and I.

"The next day, according to promise, I was arrayed in a new suit—my father's birthday present—and as I surveyed myself in the glass when my toilet was com-

[THE HIGHWAYMEN NOTICE THE MYSTERIOUS FIGURE.]

plete, I fancied, in the pride and vanity of sixteen, that I looked the *beau ideal* of a young cavalier.

"I noticed my mother looking at me with a kind of scrutinising, melancholy earnestness, as though she was very proud of me, but for some reason could not find it in her heart to express it.

"I remember, as we stood waiting for our horses to be brought round to the gate, she came to me and threw her arms round me lovingly, and kissed me over and over again; after which, she turned to my father and said:

"'Richard—dear husband—spare me our son! If any harm comes to him it will break my heart!'

"I recollect thinking my mother was very timid, considering I was so skilful a horseman.

"I little deemed that it was to other and far greater perils she alluded."

"And what did your father say in reply to her?" inquired his lordship.

"He laughed in his usual good-natured manner; and kissing her on both cheeks, told her 'not to be foolish, for he would take every care of me.'

"We had a delightful ride to London, during which my father amused me with a series of the most amazing adventures till we reached our destination, which was a large, old-fashioned, dusty-looking house, in a most intricate portion of the City.

"My father rang the bell, which gave no indication of having sounded, save that the door swung open of its own accord, and as we entered, closed again.

"We descended the stairs, when, stopping before a dark, massive-looking door, he gave it a peculiar tap with his knuckles, and that too swung wide open and allowed us to pass through its portal.

"I shall never forget the scene that presented itself at our entrance.

"It was a long, old-fashioned room, with oak panelling and a rather low ceiling.

"At a large table loaded with viands, were seated a party of the noblest-looking, best-dressed gentlemen I had ever beheld.

"I remember asking my father in a whisper whether they were, like himself, connected with the road.

"I think he answered: 'Yes, my boy, all;' but at that moment a cheer of welcome from the assembled guests attracted my attention.

"'Welcome, Dick!—welcome, old pal! Three cheers for Captain Richard Hawk!'

"'So, then, my father's a captain after all,' I remember saying to myself. 'I wonder whether in the army or navy?'

"We had dinner shortly after our arrival; but in the brief space that intervened I discovered the names of the principal guests.

"My father addressed them cordially by name, and grasped their hands with the utmost familiarity.

"He then introduced me to them.

"Many of these I had seen before at our cottage in the country, but never heard them addressed by their distinctive appellations.

"This party comprised names now well remembered and familiar to both of us."

"A jovial crew, I warrant me!" said Lord Harcliffe.

"Yes," returned Captain Hawk, with a sigh of sad remembrance. "There were Dick Turpin, Sixteen-String Jack, Claude Duval, Gentleman George, and Jeremiah Odell, nicknamed Jerry Ode, because he was an author and wrote poetry."

"Ah! those must have been glorious times!" exclaimed his lordship.

"It seemed so to me at the time.

"We had a delightful dinner, and the company was so agreeable I thought I had never been in such entertaining society before."

"In all probability you had not," remarked Lord Harcliffe.

"All the visitors were so perfectly handsome, so well dressed, and so well bred, it affords me real pleasure even now to bring that table and its guests before my mind's eye.

"I remember Dick Turpin calling me to him—poor Dick!"

"Ah, poor fellow!"

"He said to me: 'We are namesakes; so you must come and sit by my side.' What a brave, noble-hearted fellow he was! I little thought what perils we should encounter together!

"Well, he made me drink 'Success to the knights of the road.'

"I thought I might take the liberty of requesting an explanation of this term; I therefore asked him in a low tone what was the real occupation of such a knight.

"I shall never forget the peculiar expression of Dick Turpin's countenance as he fixed his eyes upon me; they seemed to convey three different meanings at once.

"He smiled, however, and taking my hand, said, in the kindest tone in the world:

"'Why do you not ask your father?'

"'I have asked him,' I replied.

"'And he has not replied?'

"'Not so that I can understand it.'

"'My dear boy,' he said, 'your father can explain the term much better than I can when he *wishes* you to *understand it!* I make it a rule never to interfere between a parent and his child.'

"Was not that a lesson worthy of imitation?"

"It was indeed, and worthy of him who taught it."

"But this was not all; for when the dinner was finished and the cloth removed, Dick having somehow taken a liking to me, rose and proposed my health in these words:

"'Gentlemen,' he said, 'I have often had the honour and the pleasure of drinking the health of my dear and esteemed friend Captain Richard Hawk; but on the present occasion I shall substitute in the place of that another toast, at which I am sure he will not be jealous. It is the health of his son: may he,' he continued, 'live to prove himself as stanch, true, and brave a man as the father that begot him!'

"My father rose, and returned thanks in my name and his own, and then made a speech which I shall never forget. It ran thus:

"'The distribution of wealth, and the different opportunities different individuals have of acquiring distinction, are exceedingly uneven and disproportionate——'

"'Hear—hear!' from several guests.

"'One man is born poor, and is told to be content—nay, thankful for his poverty—and to be honest, and humble to his superior brother worms, and not envy them because they are better off than himself.'

"A laugh from Jerry Odell.

"'Now it may happen that a man in such a position has within him a spirit that aspires to the riches, the luxury, and the powers he sees others not more deserving than himself enjoying around him, and he makes a desperate effort to grasp at these; and when resisted indignantly, flouts at and contemns the idea of the monopoly.

"'This, of course, is called by the preachers of contentment (who are invariably rich) an envious spirit supposed to be the offspring of the devil.

"'Well, this poor man, being neither content with nor grateful for his poverty, sets his wits to work to see how he can mend it, and by some means mount the ladder and perch himself by the side of his rich brother.

"'In nine cases out of ten, he begins honestly; and what does he find?—that his honesty, because it is covered with a ragged coat, is met with suspicion, and trampled underfoot by every purse-proud fool he encounters.

"'He learns also that these same persons who make such an outcry about honesty are perfectly unscrupulous in their own dealings.

"'He sees that with his good intentions and his right dealings, he can only barely raise a miserable pittance to keep life and soul together, and he then resolves to *take* from society what it refuses to *give* either to his entreaties or his labour.

"'He joins with kindred spirits; he takes to the road; his pockets become filled; his wit and invention are exercised in the constant effort to elude pursuit.

"'His blood, formerly thin and stagnant, now circulates richly through his veins as he gallops gaily across the moonlit heath.

"'He drinks the best of wine, and can afford to help a poor brother or sister. If he takes from the rich, he gives to the poor; and when he makes his exit from the world, as all must do some day, more blessings than curses follow him; and the best and worst posterity can say of him is that *if he robbed like a thief, he gave like a prince*; and for my part I wouldn't wish a better epitaph.'

"This speech, which was received with loud applause, impressed me greatly, and opened my eyes in some measure to what had before been a mystery.

"I could not get the recollection of it out of my head, and when my father, as we returned, asked me what I thought of such a life, I replied that it was of all others the one I would soonest have selected, from my ardent love of excitement and adventures.

"My father patted me on the shoulder, and said I was a brave lad, and shortly after he proved he had not forgotten my avowed predilection.

"One afternoon he called me to him in the garden, and said:

"'Dick' (I was christened Dick after him), 'you shall make your first experiment on the road to-night, but do not mention it to your mother.'

"I promised I would not, and waited in a state of feverish impatience till the night came.

"The night set in calm and beautiful, the moon being in the first quarter.

"We were mounted on splendid cattle; and as we rode quietly through the green lanes that led by a circuitous course to the high-road, my father gave me some general instructions, which I swallowed with avidity.

"He gave me also a present which I valued still more; a pair of bright-barrelled pistols, which I use to this day.

"At length we reached the end of the lane, and the dusty road was distinctly visible.

"'Now,' said my father, 'for a strong nerve, a bold heart, and a resolution that the devil himself cannot turn.'

"All these I had the modesty to affirm I possessed

"My father smiled.

"'You will need them all,' he said, 'when the moment for action arrives.'

"We had stopped under a tree at the end of the lane that opened on to the high-road.

"My father then addressed me:

"'Do you know what you are going to do?' he asked.

"'Shoot somebody,' I remember replying, innocently, as I observed my father draw one of his pistols and examine the priming.

"'Not exactly,' answered he, smiling, as he replaced his weapon—'that is, unless there is an urgent necessity for such an act. Gentlemen of the road do not shed blood, as a rule, wantonly—in fact, never except in self-defence. It is, however, always as well to see that your pistols are in proper condition.'

"'Then,' said I, 'what am I going to do, father?'

"'You are going to take your first step in your future career,' he answered.

"I felt my blood tingle a little at this announcement.

"'You saw what I did just now: imitate me,' he said.

"I understood what my father meant, and immediately, with a sort of conscious pride, drew the pistols he had given me from my belt, and examined their primings.

"'All right,' said I. I was quite sufficiently acquainted with the use of firearms to know that they were so.

"My father patted me encouragingly on the shoulder as I replaced the weapons in my belt.

"'What next?' I inquired.

"'Nothing else at present,' said my father, 'but to wait until some traveller passes. Stay,' he added, as he took from a breast pocket in his coat two black crape masks, 'it is always as well to conceal your features.'

"He handed me one of the masks, and put on the other himself.

"I followed his example.

"'Suppose no traveller should happen to pass to-night?' I inquired, in a tone of some anxiety.

"'Why, then,' said my father, laughing at the earnest manner in which I put the question, 'you will have to control your impatience till a more propitious opportunity.'

"But seeing that I looked rather blank at such a prospect, he said, in order to cheer me:

"'Don't despair; there's plenty of time yet before us for twenty travellers to pass; we have not yet waited ten minutes.'

"This consoled me, and I then asked:

"'When a traveller *does* pass, what am I to do?'

"'Ride boldly out into the middle of the road, and face him. Point your pistol to his breast, and cry "Stop!"'

"'But suppose he won't stop?' said I.

"My father laughed outright at the drollery of the idea, but answered:

"'He's sure to stop. There's not one man out of fifty would dare refuse compliance with such a reasonable demand, especially when there's a loaded pistol at his breast to back it.'

"'And when he has stopped, what is the next step I am to take?' I asked.

"'Take all you can get,' was the brief reply.

"'Thank you, father,' I answered, exultingly. I felt that I had got my lesson by heart, and that I was prepared to stop the mail with all its passengers, on the spot, had it happened to pass at that moment.

"Minute after minute flew by, until we had waited in our quiet place of ambush over an hour.

"During this period, my father gave me several useful hints, and some general practical instructions, that I was too excited then to pay as much attention to as they deserved, though I have since found them highly valuable.

"I was beginning to feel the suspense unendurable—my very flesh seemed to crawl on my bones, when, just as I was about to anathematise all travellers in a body, for not coming forward boldly to allow me to operate upon their purses, the distant sound of a horse's hoofs fell upon my ear.

"'Hark!' said my father.

'You may be quite sure I *did* 'hark'; no music I had ever heard sounded so melodiously; at the same time, however, I confess a new sensation mingled with my excited feelings.

"This was a sudden and uncomfortable doubt of my own powers. It was excusable enough, I being at the time little better than a boy, and this my first attempt.

"However, my father observed the slight change that had come over me, and laying his hand on my shoulder with an affectionate pressure, whispered in my ear the words:

"'Courage, Dick!'

"Poor father! I have often thought of those words since, and wished he had been as near to me as he was then to whisper a word of hope."

The highwayman paused for a moment, with an uncontrollable emotion, but after a few seconds continued:

"However, those words were sufficient to banish all my doubts.

"The gallop of the approaching traveller's horse was now distinctly heard.

"My nerves seemed braced up like steel.

"'Be bold,' again whispered my father, 'and remember I am here!' he added.

"'I won't disgrace you, father!' I replied, as I drew my pistol and turned my horse's head towards the road.

"Nearer and nearer drew the unconscious traveller; and when he arrived at a proper distance, my father cried: 'Now!'

"Like an arrow from a bow, I darted from my place of concealment into the very centre of the road, and wheeling round, stood fixed and firm as a pillar of stone.

"Then, in as commanding a tone as a boy of nineteen could assume, I exclaimed: 'Stop!' presenting my pistol at the same time.

"The traveller was a round, tub-like, rosy-faced man, evidently one out of the fifty whom the sight of a weapon such as I carried strongly impressed.

"I was much gratified of course to see the roses fade from off the worthy individual's cheeks as he pulled up his nag with the utmost precipitation, almost pitching forward on his nose as he did so, and inquired in faltering accents of evident trepidation, what I wanted.

"This was the proudest moment I ever remembered experiencing, though I have often laughed since at the small chance this poor traveller would have had with his daring opponent, considering my father had stationed himself in a gap in the hedge, with his pistol pointed directly at the little man's head.

"However, of this additional peril the horseman was unconscious—in fact, my presence seemed quite sufficient to thoroughly unnerve him.

"I suppose also the charm of this my first essay and its brilliant success made me forgetful, as, instead of answering the traveller's question, I did nothing but gaze at him through my mask with ferocious eyes, and press the muzzle of my pistol against his chest.

"He appeared to find this suspense unbearable, as in a voice of great anxiety he repeated his question.

"'My dear sir, what is the meaning of this? W—w—w—what *do* you want?'

"'Everything you have about you!' I answered, in a stern voice.

"'W—w—what! e—e—everything?' gasped the traveller.

"'Everything!' I answered, abruptly, giving my pistol a screw that made him wince again.

"'You—you'll sp—pare my l—life?' he inquired, piteously.

"'Well, I don't know,' I answered, in a doubtful manner, as though I hadn't quite made up my mind on that point; 'but if you're quick, perhaps I may be induced to do so.'

"At these words the frightened little man, with many grunts and groans, disencumbered himself of his watch, ring, and purse, which was very well lined, and handed them to me.

"I received them condescendingly, and coolly placed them in my pocket.

"'M—m—may I go on now?' inquired the timid traveller.

"'You *may* go on now,' I answered, grandly, as I drew my horse on one side. 'Ride as hard as you can, and don't look behind you.'

"The stout individual required no second incitement to depart, but digging his spurs into his steed, galloped off as if the arch fiend had been at his heels, whilst my father burst into a roar of laughter, and coming from his place of concealment, shook me by the hand and loaded me with applause for the manner in which I had conducted this my first enterprise.

"These praises completed the charm of the spell that had been some time working, and from that night my destiny was fixed—I became a highwayman.

"Well, about a twelvemonth after this my poor father got into trouble.

"His horse fell lame one night, and he was run down by a body of police officers: trapped at last.

"Every effort was made to save him: his counsel was heavily bribed, a rescue attempted, but in vain.

"The vigilance employed was something tremendous, and frustrated every stratagem to liberate him.

"I being young and unsuspected, was permitted to go with my mother when she went to visit poor dad in the condemned cell.

"Those who unbarred the prison doors little thought the son was already treading in the same path as his father.

"I remember as though it was yesterday the expression of my father's face when we entered.

"He looked very handsome, but paler and thinner from confinement than when I had last seen him.

"My poor mother was almost heartbroken.

"Altogether it was the most affecting scene I ever witnessed.

"My father, who was himself much affected—for I know he loved my mother dearly—endeavoured to cheer her as well as he could.

"'I go out of the world,' he said, 'cheered by the reflection that I leave behind me a son who will keep my name alive amongst my old pals, who will never do a mean or despicable action, never desert a friend, betray a comrade, or turn his back upon a foe!'

"'Never, father!' I remember saying.

"'I am sure you will not!' exclaimed my father, throwing his arms round me, with tears in his eyes.

"Then dashing them away as if ashamed of his weakness, he exclaimed, in a tone of proud exultation:

"'Long after my bones are laid in the grave my shadow shall walk!—the moonlit road shall again echo with the sound of Captain Hawk's steed; the ring of his pistol shall reverberate through the silent night, and his voice repeat the well-known cry: "Stand and deliver!" Ha! ha!' he laughed, triumphantly, '*whilst my son lives I shall never die!*'

"This was the last time I ever saw him; and on the fourteenth of May, thirteen years ago, my father, Captain Richard Hawk, was hung at Tyburn!"

The speaker paused with emotion as the quick memories of the past crowded upon him.

"And your mother?" gently inquired Lord Harcliffe.

"She never recovered the shock of my father's death," answered Captain Hawk, in a low, broken voice; "she faded away like a shadow gradually, and before the next spring had dawned, its flowers grew upon her grave. She died in my arms, with a blessing for me upon her lips, and praying that I might be spared from my father's guilty life, and—and ignominious death!"

As the captain ceased he bowed his head, and tears that he could neither account for nor restrain, fell like a shower from his eyes.

☞ The reader must remember that the course of conduct adopted and the language used by the characters of this history *are not recorded* for *example* or *imitation.* It must never be forgotten that the writer is giving the *sentiments of a highwayman—not his own;* and the tears that trickled down the face of Captain Hawk prove that his heart and conscience whispered to him that his *life was guilty*, and that it was but the forerunner of a *violent and disgraceful end.*

CHAPTER CXCVI.

CAPTAIN HAWK AND LORD HARCLIFFE LEARN THE UNPLEASING INTELLIGENCE THAT THEY ARE ENVIRONED BY THEIR FOES.—THEY HOLD A CABINET COUNCIL.—CAPTAIN HAWK SUGGESTS A PLAN OF ESCAPE.—THEY RECONNOITRE FROM THE TOP OF THEIR HOTEL.—THE STRANGE MAN ON THE ROOF.

THE position of our heroes was just at this time extremely critical.

Messrs. Bucks and Pompey, having come to their sober senses, and recovered the violent shaking they had received from their headlong ride, had given a full narration of their adventures, so far as they remembered them, to the major.

Their meeting with the invalided soldiers, and their ride with them in the chaise-cart, was perfectly clear to their recollections up to a certain point.

But at this point memory failed and became a perfect blank, until they found themselves prisoners in Snagson's hospitable abode.

Then memory broke forth again, and they recollected the coffee and hot rolls, the cigars and brandy, and the other enjoyments of which they had been the recipients.

The hasty and mysterious way, however, in which they had been hustled in and hurried out of Snagson's prevented them effectually from giving any description of the locality or neighbourhood they had visited.

All they could say on that point was that they had been *somewhere.*

Where that *somewhere* was was a secret yet to be divulged.

It certainly did occur to Mr. Bucks that one of the "poor invalided soldiers" had mentioned his grandmother's residence as being at Daffodil Court, St. Giles's; but as upon inquiry no such place existed, it was supposed that the groom's mind wandered, or that he was the victim of a delusion.

Nevertheless, on this fact being reported at Bow Street, the acute authorities, burning to lay hands on these daring defiers of the law, were seized with the idea that the delinquents were concealed *somewhere* in St. Giles's parish.

They accordingly took the most energetic measures to entrap their prey.

What those measures were will speedily transpire.

There were, besides the accounts given by the domestics, the complaints uttered by Sir Richard Chandos and Lord Edward Strathern.

It is needless to say that the bitter invectives of these gentlemen against the highwaymen, and the insufficiency of the police in general, had a far more immediate effect in stirring up the authorities to action than the assertions of two inebriated men-servants.

The noblemen have given an account partly true, but garnished with an infinite quantity of falsehoods.

The duel in the garden—which our readers know had been conducted on principles of perfect equality and fairness—was transfigured into a sudden attack made upon them in the streets by two men armed and masked, whilst they (the noblemen) were unarmed and at their mercy.

They, from motives of policy, withdrew the scene of the encounter from the garden of the countess's mansion, since, taking place upon her premises, it would have brought her name into the affair as a witness, which would have in all probability proved the utter falsehood of the alleged assault, and have implicated the noblemen in other criminalities which they were anxious to avoid.

They, however, were loud in their indignation; and being noblemen and having wealth as well as rank to back them, they were fully prepared to perjure themselves and swear black was white, if necessary.

Captain Hawk and Lord Harcliffe, since the night of their adventure in St. James's Square, had kept themselves very quiet at Snagson's, as they had done before, consequently they knew nothing of what was passing in the world without save through the medium of Charles.

But a life of inaction was not suited to their energetic temperaments.

It was bad enough to be hunted from place to place, but then there was something exciting about that, whilst in the enforced confinement they were then called upon to endure there was none.

There was certainly one pleasant reflection—they were the possessors of £1,000; and there is always a certain amount of solid satisfaction in the possession of a sum of money, which, if it does not bring positive happiness, realises at least a certain amount of negative enjoyment in giving immunity from want.

They therefore, as one way of passing the time, arranged with their host Snagson to forward by a confidential messenger £200 to the bereaved father Hugh

Trevellyn, whose daughter had paid for her love and devotion to Captain Hawk with her life.

The captain also issued strict orders to Charles (the trusty), giving him the key at the same time, to pay periodical visits to the tree in the garden of the mansion in St. James's Square, resolving, with the chivalry of his nature, that should any letter be found there declaring his assistance or that of his friend to be necessary to the countess, no thought of personal risk should deter them from issuing from their place of concealment.

It may easily be imagined that Charles's time was almost entirely taken up in hanging about, watching, and making inquiries for the benefit of our heroes.

Any less vigilant being would have been tired out the first day.

But Charles, with his bow legs, wide mouth, and altogether peculiar appearance, was in his way an uncommon character.

He loved to be on the watch.

Nothing pleased him better than to hang about the bar of the public-house where the police officers were wont to adjourn, and there putting on a simple manner and a stupid, dull look, sit crouched up puffing his pipe, apparently half asleep, but in reality looking out from his half-closed eyes and wide awake to everything that was passing around him.

It was in this way he was a source of most valuable information to the highwaymen, as he was a kind of Bow Street thermometer by which the temperature of the official atmosphere could be arrived at with infallible certainty.

Certainly these gentlemen paid him well, although the reward alone was not the principal stimulant to his exertions.

Captain Hawk, in the heat of excitement, had not thought much of late of the fair Blanche; but now he had no other occupation than to think, she came vividly into his imagination.

The more he thought, the more he longed to see her again, and the more intolerable his deprivation of liberty appeared.

"It really seems to me, Harcliffe," said he, after a pause of moody silence, "that rather than be cooped up for any length of time in this way, I'd a thousand times sooner ride point-blank through an army of police officers, though each one were armed with a pistol in each hand!"

"So would I," returned his lordship, earnestly; "better one crash and the end, than rust out day by day and hour by hour as we are doing."

"And yet if we go forth now it is a thousand chances to one we find ourselves in a few hours in a state of captivity far more galling than this."

"Yes. Here we can drink our wine and smoke our cigars and listen to our friends, the sparrows," said Lord Harcliffe. "Look," he whispered softly to his comrade, "at that daring little rascal!" pointing as he spoke to an audacious sparrow which had hopped in at the open window, and was very coolly picking up some crumbs of biscuit which lay there.

"Brave little fellow!" exclaimed Captain Hawk, admiringly. "It does me good to see him make himself so much at home! Look at him, how he plumes his wings and looks at us, as though he said, 'I know you are two jolly good fellows, who won't take advantage of my confidence.'"

At this juncture, the door opening suddenly, caused the little visitor to fly away to the nearest chimney-pot, where he sat twittering, either in gratitude for his crumbs, or in denunciation of the messenger Charles, who entered at the same moment.

The highwaymen, in order to pass away the time, were smoking some excellent Havannahs and drinking sherry-and-water.

But even these luxuries had grown monotonous, and the appearance of Charles, therefore, was hailed with delight.

"Well, Charles," cried Captain Hawk, what news?"

Judging from the downcast expression of that worthy individual's face, he might have augured unfavourably with reason.

Never had the messenger's countenance betrayed so much dismay.

He looked ruefully at the two highwaymen, who remained quietly waiting for him to open his budget.

But on this occasion, he dropped into the seat to which the captain pointed, and remained silent.

"Come, hang it!" said Captain Hawk, "if you continue this ominous silence, I shall think some very serious catastrophe has occurred. Why don't you speak?"

"Because I ain't got any good news to tell," answered Charles, in a tone that, in another, would have been dogged, but which in him was only expressive of regret.

"Well, never mind," said Captain Hawk. "Let us hear the worst, then. Anything is better than none at all."

"Decidedly!" added Lord Harcliffe.

"Well, then, to begin with, there's the devil's own stir up about you!" commenced Charles.

"That's nothing new," returned Captain Hawk. "We have often produced that effect before now."

"But not like this, captain," replied Charles. "This is what I call a good thick stir up, that there's no getting out of; it sticks to yer like bird-lime."

"Let's hear what it's all about?"

"Well, then, there's two noblemens been a swearin' you attacked 'em with masks on yer faces."

"So we did."

"But they swear it was in a most cowardly manner, when they were unarmed. But, of course, that's a lie!" Charles added, energetically.

"Undoubtedly!" said Captain Hawk. "These noblemen, as they designate themselves — Heaven save the mark!—are a couple of cold-blooded, lying scoundrels! And as for cowardice, I would back them against the most arrant poltroon in this or any other country!"

"I was sure of that," answered Charles.

"The fact is, we twice prevented them from committing murder. I only wish I did not stand obnoxious to the law, that I might charge them with their outrages, and bring the witnesses I could summon to appear against them. But no matter for them. What else?"

"Then there's that swipy pair as we brought here," continued Charles—"I mean the groom and the nigger."

"What of them?"

"They've been a lettin' their tongues run like wildfire in return for the good treatment they received."

"I suppose you are now inclined to think a good horse-whipping would have been more efficacious?"

"I always *did* think so," said Charles. "And if I'd a had my way, I'd a' given it 'em too!"

"Well, what harm could they do?"

"Why, though they couldn't point out this 'ere crib where we're now a sittin' any more than they could fly over the Monument, still, they've got it somehow into their stupid heads that it was in the neighbourhood of St. Giles's."

"Ah!" replied Captain Hawk, "I remember giving them a fictitious address, but the *right* parish. I'm afraid I was wrong in doing so."

"I'm sure yer was, captain," answered Charles, reprovingly; "for the beaks have got hold of it; and they're firmly convinced in Bow Street that you are hiding away in some snug retreat about here."

"They are singularly correct in that particular."

"Yes, worst luck," said Charles. "And so confident are they on this point, that they're determined to tire you out, and unkennel you at last; so, in order that they may succeed in that, what d'ye think the beggars have done?"

"Brought out a battery of cannon, perhaps, to demolish the entire parish of St Giles's," replied the captain, smiling.

"No, they haven't done that," said Charles, very gravely, "but they've done something almost as bad."

"What's that?"

"They've gone and posted police at every thoroughfare leading from St. Giles's, so that it's impossible to go in or out night or day without being dropped upon!" said Charles, with almost spiteful emphasis.

"The devil!" ejaculated Captain Hawk, looking inquiringly at his comrade, who puffed out a voluminous stream of smoke in reply.

"The devil's nothing!" Charles continued, in a tone of contempt. "If he attempted to stop me, I'd cut his tail off, or catch him by the nose with a pair of red-hot tongs, like that old trump, St. Anthony; but these 'ere d—d police officers, all in, one with another, like a swarm of bees—oh, it's outrageous!—infernal! d—nable!" he wound up, stamping his foot with indignation.

Charles, having thus vented his disgust, grew calmer.

"It's devilish awkward!" said Captain Hawk, meditatively, sipping a little sherry to assist his reflections. "Just, too, as we were growing tired of our confinement and were thinking of going out."

"Thinking of going out, captain!" echoed Charles, aghast at the bare idea—"going out! D'ye want to run right bang into the lion's jaws with yer eyes open?"

"Not particularly. I would rather break his jaws," answered the highwayman.

"Yer'd never think o' goin' out if yer knew what a blessed job it is to get back agin!" continued Charles. "Why, even a cove like me——"

"Did they stop you?"

"I believe yer they did too, and asked me all sorts of questions, an' if I hadn't a' answered 'em pretty stiff, I think they'd a' collared me; an' even when they had let me pass they looked after me awful suspicious, as though they was sorry they'd let me go. O' course I was off like a shot; but I didn't think as I should ever 'a got back if I hadn't 'a transmogrified myself into a milkman."

"A milkman?"

"Yes, captain. Yer know, people must have milk. And while I was a comin' along on my road home as full of information as a newspaper, I began to think what I should say to the police to get past 'em again.

"Well, while I was a-considerin' this point, I sees a milkman opposite put down his cans outside a public, while he went in to get a drain.

"A idea came into my nob all on a sudden.

"Now's my time!" says I to myself. "So off I steps it across the road, collars the man's milk cans, and steps it off as bold as brass, singing out 'Milk O!' with all my might.

"I'd taken out my red handkercher an' put it round my throttle, an' pulled my hat over my face so as they shouldn't recognise me; an' on I goes right up to the police.

"They began chaffing me, o' course.

"'Much chalk in that milk?' says one.

"'No,' says I, 'we doesn't use chalk in our business; we leave that for the bobbies behind the bar; there's chalk enough there. This 'ere's the genuine article, fresh from the cow.'

"'Yer might give us a drop,' says he.

"'Ye're very welcome if yer like,' says I.

"So they comes up, an' blest if I didn't milk 'em all round, like a lot o' suckin' babbies!"

Charles laughed at this as an excellent joke; and our heroes, who had a strong sense of the ridiculous, joined him.

"I suppose," said Captain Hawk, "they asked no more questions after that?"

"Not a syllable. Oh, no! they only sent their best respects to the proprietor of the dairy; and I trotted off like a post-horse with my cans."

"And what of the owner of the milk—what will he do?" inquired the captain, laughing.

"Oh, he'll have to go to his cows for some more of the precious beverage. All I know is, I've got the cans, and I means to stick to 'em."

"I advise you to do so by all means," said the captain; "they will be your passport in and out of our stronghold."

"Then, if you want to go out, you might use 'em," suggested Charles.

"They would not, I think, be of much service to us," replied the captain, "unless I could carry out my friend in one of the pails."

Charles did not think that would answer, neither did Lord Harcliffe.

"At all events, Charles, you're a capital scout," said Captain Hawk, "and here's your reward for your information."

He handed Charles a guinea as he spoke.

"For the rest we must consider what is to be done," he continued; "for on one point I'm determined: and that is, not to be hemmed in like a couple of sparrows surrounded by a lot of hawks. I'll have a consultation with my comrade, and when we've arrived at something definite, we'll let you know."

Charles took the hint and vanished.

As soon as he was gone, Captain Hawk laid his hand upon his friend's arm.

"Harcliffe," he said, "we must set our wits to work. Some plan must be thought of to double our watchers, though we go out tied up in coal sacks."

"I'll devote my thoughts entirely to the subject," said Lord Harcliffe, lighting a fresh cigar.

"And I," replied the captain, following his example.

There was a pause of considerable duration, during which neither of the highwaymen spoke; but leaning back in their chairs, puffed out thick clouds of smoke till the room was in a dense mist of ambrosial vapour.

Suddenly, however, Captain Hawk started up.

"I have it!" he cried. "I've hit upon a plan!"

"Of eluding these hounds?"

"Yes, my friend."

"Let me hear it."

"You would never guess."

"Some disguise, of course?"

"None, unless it be the sable mantle of night."

"But they are there night and day."

"There let them remain. We will set them at defiance."

"How?"

"By walking over their heads."

"By an aerial trip in a balloon?"

"No; by an aerial trip over a few hundred housetops."

"A roof scramble! Pray explain."

"Have you not remarked that the houses in this locality lie very close together?"

"Frequently."

"What would be easier than, when night arrives, to mount on to the top of this house, and then, passing from roof to roof, traverse the whole distance till we are quite clear of the radius that contains our custodians?"

"An excellent idea certainly; but you forget the intervening streets."

"No, I do not forget. They are narrow, and may easily be crossed by means of a plank that we could carry with us."

"Certainly, we could."

"Then, having reached a spot beyond the circle of danger, a rope would enable us to reach the ground; and while our hunters imagined they were holding their prey in check, the enfranchised lions will be free and quietly laughing at them."

"Admirable—most admirable!" exclaimed Lord Harcliffe, with undisguised joy at the quick and practical manner in which his comrade had suggested their escape from what was in reality a very formidable ambuscade. "I firmly believe, Dick," he continued "if you were dropped to the bottom of the crater of Vesuvius, you'd find your way to the top!"

"I don't know about that," replied the captain: "all I *do* know is, I should try."

"Well, then, we'll try this; and not only try, but succeed," exclaimed Lord Harcliffe, enthusiastically.

"And when do you propose starting?" inquired his lordship, eagerly.

"To-night."

"By all means. To-night be it, then."

This being determined on, Charles was summoned, and the plan detailed to him.

His admiration and exultation were far more demonstrative than Lord Harcliffe's.

He chuckled, then grinned, then rubbed his large hands together and roared till the extremities of his capacious mouth disappeared altogether behind his ears.

"It's glorious!" he cried, in ecstasy; "it's the out-an'-outest dodge I ever heard of in all my life! Beats the milk cans holler, an' that warn't bad!"

His delight having subsided in some measure, to him was confided the task of procuring a plank of the requisite dimensions—*i.e.*, neither too light nor too heavy—and a coil of rope.

Having received his directions, he departed in a stat of the highest exhilaration to execute his commissions.

The highwaymen dined in their own private apartment this day and after dinner they sat in a state of placid enjoyment, waiting till the time should arrive for them to make their start.

Liberty—freedom—the power to come and go at pleasure—is always a delightful thing to contemplate, and so they found it.

"I began to think I should have had to draw upon you, my friend, for my entertainment," said Captain Hawk to Lord Harcliffe, "and request you to let me hear the history of *your* early days, but I think now I shall reserve that pleasure for some other occasion."

"I received so much pleasure from your own account," replied his lordship, "that I feel myself bound to return the compliment whenever I am called upon."

"I shall not forget to make the demand one of these days."

"Though I promise you beforehand you will not find my experience so peculiarly interesting as your reminiscences."

"That will be for me to say when I have heard them."

In this and other desultory conversation, that would not interest the reader, the day wore gradually on.

It had been one of those bright, glorious English days of life and sunshine, that makes an Englishman laugh when you speak to him of foreign lands and Italian skies, and point upwards to his own, as he says, exultingly:

"That is the sky of my own land! Beat it if you can!"

The afternoon sun had gradually sunk lower and lower behind the distant—not hills—but chimney-pots, and the cool, gray twilight had supervened. That gradually deepened, and at length the moon appeared.

It was yet early, and they sat, as we are often apt to say, "between the lights," enjoying the cool breeze, and not having rung for candles.

"I wonder," said Captain Hawk, at length, "whether there is a trap-door in the roof of this house?"

"No doubt of it, especially in such a house as this, where a sudden necessity for an abrupt exit *might* happen at some time or other."

"It was a foolish question of mine," said the captain; "at all events, I will take the liberty of examining."

The bell was accordingly rung, and lights ordered.

These being procured, the highwaymen took one, and proceeded at once to the top of the house.

As Lord Harcliffe expected, there was a trap-door, and a ladder besides leading up to it.

The trap was bolted; but, as everything at Snagson's had its individual use, the bolt was in perfect working condition—not covered with rust, so that, in case of fire, or any other casualty, you would not have had to lug and tug, and knock the skin off your knuckles, in your frantic efforts to open it.

Snagson was a man who didn't believe in trap-doors that wouldn't open, or bolts that wouldn't draw, any more than he believed in a drawer that wouldn't lock, or a purse with nothing in it.

The consequence was that the bolt shot back by simply touching it, and in a moment the highwaymen were standing on the roof.

The view was like all other views of the same kind, an interminable line of roofs and chimney-pots.

The house on which they stood was considerably higher than the rest, so that, at the very outset of their journey, they would have to bring the rope into requisition.

But this was a trifle.

"We shall accomplish our design triumphantly!" exclaimed Captain Hawk.

Suddenly Lord Harcliffe grasped his arm, and pointed downwards to a roof at some distance.

"Look!" he said, in a low voice. "Do you see?"

"What?" inquired the captain.

"A man upon the roof yonder."

"Where?"

"There!" returned his lordship, pointing in the direction as he spoke.

"I distinguish nothing."

"He is in the shadow. Now—now he is in sight again! Do you not see him?"

"Yes, yes—I see him now distinctly."

"What does he want there, I wonder?"

"Us, perhaps."

"Not unlikely. He seems to be looking for something, or somebody."

"See, how cautiously he proceeds!"

"Yes, he evidently has some motive in his journey."

"Surely he cannot be hemmed in as we are."

"Perhaps he is looking after his runaway wife."

"Or perhaps he's running away from her."

"See, he's about to descend."

"Yes, it's evident he wishes to get to the ground."

"Let us go downstairs again; we can watch him from the window in our room."

The man, whose object was evidently to change his elevated position for one nearer the ground, was now hanging by his hands to the wall of one of the buildings, previous to dropping down.

This was the next step he accomplished, and, having done so, he disappeared for a time from view.

During the interval the highwaymen descended once more to their apartment.

The chamber they occupied was a back room on the first floor, that looked out upon some leads that were encircled by a wall about eight feet in height.

Beyond this the sides of the adjacent houses reared themselves.

Captain Hawk and Lord Harcliffe, whose curiosity had been excited by the appearance of the figure on the roof, stood at the window, shaded by the curtains, fully anticipating his reappearance.

Nor were they disappointed.

In a few moments after they had posted themselves behind the curtains, the man's hands appeared clutching the top of the boundary wall of the leads.

Almost immediately after a figure was seen to draw itself up, and throwing one leg over the wall, to bestride it for the purpose evidently of taking breath.

During this operation he looked scrutinisingly around him, and the watchers observed that he was particularly attracted by the light that gleamed from their apartment.

The spot on which the stranger had posted himself being in shadow, his features were undistinguishable.

They could only judge from his fixed position that he was regarding the window of their room with great earnestness.

"Do you see how he keeps his eyes fixed in this direction?" whispered Lord Harcliffe to his comrade.

"Yes; I am curious to know why," returned Captain Hawk, in a low tone.

"We shall see presently, no doubt."

"Does he strike you as belonging to the police?"

"I am at a loss to judge; I cannot see him with sufficient distinctness."

The man, whoever he was, or whatever his errand, appeared to hesitate as he looked down behind the wall he bestrode.

At length, however, he seemed to have arrived at a decision as to his future operations, for, swinging his leg over the top of the wall, he allowed himself to drop his full length.

Then, relaxing his grasp, he descended with but little noise on to the leads.

Here he paused a few moments, remaining close in the deep shadow of the wall, to assure himself that he had not aroused anyone by his approach.

All remaining perfectly still, he drew near the window, and with the utmost caution looked into the room.

The light now fell full upon his features, and most extraordinary was the effect produced.

No grim police officer was there—no stealthy minion of the law prowling, like a night-wolf, for his prey, but a friend—a true friend—whom one, at least, of the highwaymen felt his heart leap in his breast with joy to see.

There were only two words uttered, and they burst forth with eager spontaniety:

"Pharoah!"

"My lord!"

CHAPTER CXCVII.

UNEXPECTED MEETING BETWEEN LORD HARCLIFFE AND PHAROAH.—THE LATTER EXPLAINS THE COURSE HE HAS ADOPTED, AND THE MOTIVES THAT INFLUENCED HIM.—HE GIVES LORD HARCLIFFE A MESSAGE FROM THE PRINCE OF WALES.—THE HIGHWAYMEN MAKE A START OVER THE ROOFS, AND ENCOUNTER A SLIGHT MISHAP AT THE OUTSET.

Had a being from another world suddenly stood before Lord Harcliffe, his surprise could hardly have been greater than at the appearance of his faithful servant in such a place and at such a time.

Captain Hawk, too, shared his astonishment.

Pharoah, on the contrary, expressed more joy than surprise, the sincerity of his feelings being attested by the tears that trickled down his cheeks.

"My dear master!" he exclaimed, as he pressed his lordship's hand with respectful devotion to his lips; "it is indeed you! I clasp you by the hand once more!"

"Yes, my faithful Pharoah, it is, indeed, myself, not greatly altered in spite of all the vicissitudes I have undergone," answered Lord Harcliffe.

"It must be quite two months since I last had the happiness of seeing your lordship," said Pharoah, still retaining his grasp of his master's hand as though loth to part with it.

At length, his emotion having somewhat subsided, Lord Harcliffe being anxious to know what he had been doing, and where he had been hiding during his absence, put the inquiry.

"Your lordship will never guess," he answered.

"Very likely! Such strange and unlooked-for events happen so constantly that he must be more than human who can shape his guesses with certainty. I shall, therefore, not make the attempt, but leave it for you to tell me."

"I am now in the service of the Prince of Wales," said Pharoah.

"The Prince of Wales?" echoed Lord Harcliffe, with evident surprise.

"Yes, my lord! I was sure you would be surprised. Such a position is probably the last in the world you would have suspected me of occupying."

"It is, I confess," returned his lordship. "And it only proves that in these times we must never be surprised at anything. How did you obtain your post?"

"After your lordship disappeared, I found that neither town nor country was safe for me. Either of these places was *too warm* for me. The police officers had become acquainted with my features, and I found myself hunted from post to pillow, and from pillow to post, till I began to feel like a hunted hare."

"Or like a hunted wolf—which?"

"A little of both, my lord."

"Did you not feel inclined to turn wolfish, and show your teeth to your hunters?"

"I confess I did. I am no coward. And when I found parties of these officers, all well mounted and armed, riding me down, and banging away at me in all directions, I heartily wished on more than one occasion I could have transformed myself into a loaded cannon, and have blown them all to the devil."

"And how did you contrive to elude them?"

"I owe my life to Tom Beckford."

"Dear old Tom!" cried the highwaymen, in a breath, "he's always stanch!"

"He hid me in his cellar; and while these Bow Street worthies ransacked every nook and corner in search of me, I was snugly stowed away in an empty barrel, the top of which he fastened down, so that they never thought of investigating the interior.

"I remained with him till the pursuit was over. And as I was not of the same consequence as either of you gentlemen, it died away in the course of a few days. And then it suddenly struck me that I would go boldly and offer my services to the Prince of Wales."

"And what put that idea into your mind?" inquired his lordship, with some curiosity.

"First, because he knew I had been attached to your lordship's person."

"And next?"

"Because I knew the prince liked to have those around him whom he believed trustworthy."

"Go on."

"Thirdly, because the prince is powerful; and I knew that to be in his service was to be safe myself."

"True."

"And lastly, because I thought that in that capacity I might be able to serve you, if you needed it."

"Four very excellent reasons," said his lordship, smiling.

"But you must not imagine that I had forgotten you all this time, my lord," Pharoah exclaimed, earnestly.

"I do not imagine so," answered Lord Harcliffe; "your last motive for entering the prince's service is a sufficient proof that you had not done so."

"Since I have been in his employ, I have made every possible inquiry without effect. I therefore coincided with the general opinion that you had left the country."

"That opinion was perfectly correct, Pharoah," said Lord Harcliffe. "We have been away, and I assure you the 'moving accidents by flood and field' we have experienced during our absence would fill a volume."

"And how did you hear of our return?"

"It was only a few days since that I heard you were on 'the road' again, that the 'hue-and-cry' was hot after you, and that rewards for your apprehension were posted in every corner of the City, and in every country town."

"Then were you seeking us when we encountered you so strangely just now?"

"I was."

"That seems strange."

"It will not when I explain."

"How did you know we were here?"

"From accounts received at Bow Street, it is strongly suspected you are concealed somewhere in St. Giles's Parish——"

"What d—d keen noses these foxes have!" exclaimed Captain Hawk, with a bitter laugh.

"And the worst of it is, they happen to be on the right scent this time," returned his lordship. "But go on, Pharoah."

"Well, it struck me that you might be run to earth here, surrounded by vigilant guards, and unable to break through, so I resolved, if possible, to find you out, and let you know exactly how matters stood."

"It was a kind thought, Pharoah; and believe me, I'll not forget it," said Lord Harcliffe.

"And how did you manage to drop exactly upon us as you so cleverly did?" he inquired.

"I am indebted to chance for that."

"To chance?"

"Yes. As soon as I heard the report of your being concealed in St. Giles's, I puzzled my brains to think of the best means of discovering you."

"And at last you hit upon this?"

"Yes. The fact of my being in the employment, I may say the *confidence* of the Prince of Wales, made my task comparatively easy."

"How did that assist you?"

"I always carry a letter from the prince in my pocket, certifying that I am in his service, so that in case of any molestation, or recognition, I have only to show that, with the royal seal affixed, when the police, instead of taking me, touch their hats respectfully."

"You are a clever fellow, Pharoah!" exclaimed Lord Harcliffe. "I understand how, armed with this letter, you can traverse this *sanctum sanctorum* of St. Giles's through its breadth and length, as you please."

"Exactly. Well, after wandering about for some time, and scrutinising the various nooks and crannies that abound in this neighbourhood, I fixed upon one house in particular as my starting-point, and took lodgings there."

"Were you guided entirely by chance in your selection of this house?"

"Not exactly; it was rather a curious incident that settled this point for me. Yesterday, as I was approaching the neighbourhood, I observed a somewhat strange-looking individual suddenly pounce upon a pair of mik cans, left by a milkman at the door of a public-house, and trot off with them at a brisk rate."

Lord Harcliffe glanced at Captain Hawk, and they smiled mutually, but Pharoah did not notice the action.

"I was struck with this proceeding," he continued, "and followed, keeping my eye on the man, who stopped shortly after, and taking a red handkerchief from his pocket, tied it round his neck, then pulling his hat carelessly over his face, he continued his journey."

"Did you infer anything from this act?" inquired Lord Harcliffe.

"Yes, my lord; it struck me that it was done to disguise himself; and when I saw the man pass the police and stop, and give them a drink all round, I felt almost certain.

"Well, I followed the man as quickly as possible, but

[PERILOUS POSITION OF THE HIGHWAYMEN.]

being challenged by the police, I was compelled to show them the prince's letter, which occupied some little time.

"When I was able to resume my journey, the man had got on too far ahead to be overtaken; and when I reached the turning round which he disappeared, I could see no traces of him.

"However, something seemed to suggest itself to me that he might be a messenger of yours; and since there was no means of discovering him, I determined to hire a room in a house as close as possible to the spot at which I missed him."

"And you did so?"

"Yes; I managed to secure a back attic, which suited my purpose admirably, inasmuch as it led from the window immediately on to the roof of the adjoining house, from which I could command a view and make a journey over all the roofs in the neighbourhood.

"I took a long and deliberate survey of the scene before me; and as soon as the day began to draw in I commenced my *roof scramble.*"

"We saw you when you stood on the roof of this house," said Lord Harcliffe.

"Guided by chance, I went on and on, peering into several windows as I passed, but seeing nothing of those I sought, till I reached yonder wall, which having mounted, the light in your window attracted my attention; I yielded to the impulse that impelled me to approach, and am rewarded in having once more found my dear master."

Pharaoh once more clasped his lordship by the hand with all the intensity of affectionate joy.

"It is rather singular this affair altogether," said Lord Harcliffe. "You were right in your suspicions as regards the milkman; he *was* our scout, our messenger, our factotum; in fact, I don't know what we should do without him. It is from him we gain all our information; it was he who informed us what excellent arrangements our foes are making for our capture."

"You must not be taken!" exclaimed Pharoah, eagerly.

"Do we look as though we contemplated such an event?" asked Captain Hawk.

"Not at all," he replied.

"Far from it," said Lord Harcliffe. "We have already resolved to deliver ourselves from the surveillance of our would-be captors this very night."

"By what means?"

"The same as those by which you discovered us—by roof scrambling."

"Can I help your lordship?" inquired Pharoah. "If so——"

"No, my friend; in such an enterprise as ours I consider the fewer the better, as being less likely to attract attention."

"And does your lordship expect to be out of this neighbourhood to-night?"

"Undoubtedly. We will meet in Pall Mall at eleven o'clock."

"Oh, my lord! I had almost forgotten in the joy of meeting you again," exclaimed Pharoah · "but the Prince of Wales wishes to see you."

"Indeed!"

"So he informed me. Did you make some promise to him?"

"I did, and I presume now he claims its fulfilment."

"I imagine so."

"Well, if it be anything that a man of honour and a gentleman may perform, I shall not shrink from it," answered Lord Harcliffe.

"Would your lordship object to accompany me to Leicester House to-night?" Pharoah inquired.

"I am not yet free."

"But you are sure to accomplish your object."

"I have no doubt of it."

"May I tell the prince he may expect you?"

"Well, yes," replied Lord Harcliffe, after a pause.

"And you are not offended at my entering the service of the Prince of Wales?" said Pharoah.

"Offended, my good fellow! I applaud you for it. By so doing you preserved your own liberty, and may be able to serve me," answered his lordship.

"Do you require my services again? Because if so, at any moment I would renounce the prince for my old master."

"No, Pharoah. Having no fixed residence, my destination being always uncertain, you are better provided for where you are," returned Lord Harcliffe.

"You wish me, then, to remain with the prince?"

"Yes."

"And if fortune favours your attempt, you will meet me in Pall Mall at eleven to-night?"

"I will."

"And you will then proceed with me to Leicester House?"

"I will."

Pharoah's eyes sparkled with joy at the prospect of seeing his old master beneath the roof of his royal highness, though he little deemed what was the nature of the proposal the latter had in contemplation.

"Come, Pharoah, time wears," said Lord Harcliffe. "But before you start, a glass of wine will serve you for your backward journey."

The wine was poured out in a tumbler, and Pharoah, who was somewhat fatigued with the exertions of his peregrinations on the tiles, and his excitement at the discovery of his master, drained it eagerly, wishing his master and Captain Hawk a safe and prosperous termination to their enterprise.

This draught acted as a stimulant, and both refreshed and restored him; and taking his lordship's hand once more in his, he kissed it fervently.

Then bowing to Captain Hawk, he stepped with a light foot and a light heart on to the leads, and had soon regained his position on the top of the wall.

Then, waving his hand as a parting salute, he swung himself over and disappeared.

The highwaymen stood watching him as long as he remained in sight, and then turned from the window.

"Strange," said Captain Hawk, "that even in our desperate life, when society and the law seem leagued to destroy us, when our hand is against every man's, and every man's hand against us, we can yet find true and devoted servants whom neither threats can intimidate, nor bribes corrupt, from their allegiance."

At this moment the clocks sounded the hour of nine.

"I think," said Captain Hawk, "we may venture to make a start."

"The sooner the better in my opinion," returned his comrade.

"But Charles has not yet provided us with the necessary materials for our journey," said the captain.

"You mean the plank and the rope?"

"Yes; we could not travel far without their assistance."

At this moment a sound was heard on the stairs, and the next instant the personage just alluded to appeared laden with the required articles.

"Here they are, gentlemen," said Charles—"here's a beautiful tough plank, and a rope strong enough to pull down the side of a house."

After thanking their assistant for his efforts, they directed him to take them to the top of the house and leave them there.

"I'll wait till you come, gentlemen," exclaimed Charles, who was anxious to see them start.

"There is no necessity," said the captain.

But Charles, who was enthusiastic about the whole scheme, and who would have liked to have made one in it if he could have done so, was not to be put on one side.

"Oh, let's see yer off, gentlemen," he pleaded.

"As you please," answered Captain Hawk, "only it behoves us to be cautious. Too many on the roof at one time might awaken attention or excite suspicion, both of which I am anxious to avoid."

"I'll be very careful," said Charles: "I'll make myself invisible."

And with these words he proceeded to convey the plank and rope to the top of the landing.

The highwaymen then carefully loaded and primed their pistols, and filled a pocket-flask with prime cognac, which having bestowed in one of their pockets, their preparations were complete.

"Come, Harcliffe," cried the captain, "one glass to the success of our enterprise!"

"With all my heart! Pour out!" replied his comrade.

Raising their glasses, Captain Hawk gave the toast:

"Liberty!" he cried.

"Liberty!" echoed the Black Highwayman.

In a few moments after they were standing on the roof.

Everything was calm and quiet, save the murmur from the streets at a distance.

Captain Hawk glanced rapidly around.

"Our first effort will be to drop on to that roof," he said, indicating the top of a house about ten feet beneath them, and taking from his pocket a bar of steel, about six or seven inches in length.

Touching a spring at one end, there shot out a transverse arm, having a sharp hooked point.

He then fastened the other end, which was supplied with a ring, to the rope, and having first lowered the plank, he placed the steel bar on the top of the brickwork, into the side of which the sharp point penetrated.

All being ready, Lord Harcliffe descended on to the roof beneath.

Captain Hawk then grasped the rope, and swung himself over.

"Good night, Charles," said the captain, as he hung there. "I may have some work for you before long."

"All right, captain," he answered. "Drop us a line when and where, and I'll be there. Good night!" he added. "And may you reach the ground sound in wind and limb!"

This parting benediction reached the captain's ears as the rope glided rapidly through his hands, and he reached his comrade on the roof.

By a jerk of his hand, Captain Hawk dislodged the steel hook from its hold, and coiling up the rope, which he handed to his companion, he shouldered the plank, and gave the word, "Forward!"

They proceeded cautiously, and it will be readily understood that, loaded as they were, such a step was necessary.

slanting tiles not being the most agreeable footpath for a pedestrian.

However, they made considerable progress, when, as they were stepping across a gutter, Captain Hawk accidentally slipped, and dropped the plank with a terrible clatter.

It was a very annoying circumstance, and might have led to the frustration of their whole plan.

It happened too close to a window, and the moment the plank fell a sharp scream within told the adventurers that they had startled some fair one.

Before they had time either to retreat or conceal themselves, a very ancient female visage appeared, in a very ancient nightcap, at the window.

On catching sight of the highwaymen, she uttered a louder scream, and inquired, in sharp, frightened accents:

"Who's there?"

"Ay, who's there?" growled a thick, surly voice from within.

"Don't be alarmed, my dear madam," said Captain Hawk, addressing himself to the old woman in most mellifluous accents, "we are merely looking for—for something we've lost."

"What can you have lost on our roof?" screamed the vixenish old dame.

"What do they want?" growled the voice within.

"We've lost our cat," explained Captain Hawk, with the utmost suavity.

"Shot the cat!" roared the gruff voice inside. "I'll shoot you if you come any of that fun!" and at the same moment a fiery red face, surmounted by a red nightcap, thrust itself out of the window.

"We've got no cats here!" roared the owner, "so jest take yerselves off; we don't sell 'em!"

He was about to continue in the same bullying strain, when Captain Hawk, annoyed at the pertinacity of the man, who had evidently been drinking, said, quietly:

"Harkye, my red-faced friend! Your grandmother——"

A shriek from the antiquity in the nightcap.

"Grandmother be blowed! My wife, sir!—Mrs. Blare! What the devil d'ye mean!" shouted the man.

"I mean this," answered Captain Hawk, "your wife, or grandmother, or whatever she is, asked me a question, which I answered; but if you do not instantly shut your mouth, and go to bed, the chances are I may either give you a pill to compose you, or drop you over the parapet here."

As the captain uttered these words, he just tickled the man's nose with the muzzle of his pistol, and seized him expressively by the nightcap and what hair there was within it.

The sight of the weapon was sufficient, for the blustering individual fell back instantly into the room with the utmost precipitation, and a violent slamming-to and fastening of the window announced that the enemy had beaten a retreat.

"We must be more cautious for the future," said the captain, as they crept away from the spot, and continued their course.

CHAPTER CXCVIII.

SOME EVENTS AFFECTING OUR HEROES OCCUR AT A HOUSE IN THE NEIGHBOURHOOD.—JARVIS, THE POLICE-OFFICER, VISITS AN OLD SCHOOLFELLOW.—THEY SEE TWO FIGURES ON THE ROOF.—JARVIS GIVES CHASE.—HIS SCHOOLFELLOW FOLLOWS.—AND MEETS WITH A MISHAP.

PHAROAH, in a tumult of joy at having discovered his old master, clambered over the intervening roofs, at the imminent danger of breaking his neck, with a rapidity that was perfectly marvellous.

When he reached his own attic, it was a matter of surprise to him how he had accomplished the journey back so much quicker, and with so much greater ease, than when he performed the same distance in search of his master.

However, having arrived, he threw himself into a chair by the window, and lighting a cigar which he moistened with a bottle of claret, gave himself up to the most pleasing reveries.

Pharoah, now a confidential servant of the Prince of Wales, was now what would be called in "good feather."

His pockets were well lined, and he could afford to drink the best claret and smoke the best cigars.

As he puffed the clouds of smoke through the open window, all the adventures of the past seemed to roll back vividly before him.

He saw Lord Harcliffe again the master of his splendid establishment in Piccadilly, the elegant, the admired, the centre of an admiring throng of aristocratic guests, that crowded round and formed a brilliant setting of which his lordship was the jewel.

Then from that his thoughts reverted to the present. He saw the same master, no longer recognised, but, on the contrary, a proscribed, hunted fugitive, seeking by desperate means to elude the strong arm of the law.

Would he succeed? he thought, or would he be detected in his attempt at flight?—would he reach *terra firma* in safety once more, with his comrade, or would a false step, a slip of the foot, precipitate him headlong, a bleeding, insensible mass, into the street below?

As he pondered and rambled in his imaginations, enveloped in a cloud of smoke, and sipped his claret, those thoughts began to grow as hazy as the atmosphere of the attic in which he sat; his head nodded to and fro languidly, and at length sank upon his breast. He slept.

On this particular afternoon it happened that Jarvis, one of the police officers on duty to watch the suspected fugitives in St. Giles's, remembered he had a country friend who lived in that locality.

It was a very hot afternoon, and Jarvis felt particularly hot and thirsty; and the hotter he became, the greater became his desire to see his old friend Peter Stitchem.

Peter was a small tailor, who made up people's "own materials," and "executed repairs neatly"—at least, so the board outside the door stated.

Jarvis was aware of this fact, and as he reached the humble dwelling where Peter vegetated, far from the pure fresh air of his native Berkshire, he asked himself a few questions.

First: Was it perfectly correct for an officer on duty to leave his beat even in the sacred cause of friendship? Secondly: Would Peter be glad to see his old schoolfellow, and would he (a very important point) have anything to give him? Thirdly: Should he ascertain whether Peter was then as Peter used to be, or should he withstand the temptation, and cool his thirst by a drink from the pump?

Jarvis considered all these, but he had an objection to pump water—it never agreed with him; so, as he passed the tailor's lodging, he looked at the board, then up and down the narrow street, and finally knocked at the door.

He was answered by a little nondescript sort of girl, who informed him that if he rang four times, Mr. Stitchem might possibly become visible at the fourth pull.

Accordingly, P.O. Jarvis pulled the rusty bell four times so vigorously that he almost dragged it out by the roots, and so startled the industrious Peter—who was pressing a coat he had turned, up stairs, in his little attic—that he dropped his goose on his hand, and ironed three or four of his fingers, to his very great inconvenience.

"It must be a customer," said Peter to himself; "no one but a customer would ring the bell like that."

In order to ascertain this important point, the tailor thought the best way would be to go and see.

On reaching the door, and beholding a police officer standing on the threshold, a qualm passed over the little man.

Visions of past delinquencies, summonses, cabbage, and other matters, rushed rapidly through his mind as he inquired, in a very mild voice:

"What do you please to want, sir?"

"I want my old schoolfellow, Peter Stitchem," answered Jarvis, in a cheery voice.

"I'm Peter Stitchem," answered the tailor, in a doubtful tone, though he felt relieved at the officer's manner, "but I don't remember that I have the pleasure of knowing you."

"What! not know Tom Jarvis, old Dick Jarvis's the farrier's son, that used to go fishing with you, robbing orchards, and the deuce knows what besides?"

"Lor', are you really Tom—Tom Jarvis—my old schoolmate?"

"Of course I am, only a little stouter and bigger than when we met last," said Jarvis.

"So you are!" burst out Peter. "There's no mistake about it all: I remember you perfectly; how are you?"

"Hearty as a buck, my boy! and as dry as brick-dust!"

There was a prodigious shaking of hands, and a good deal of "dear boying" and "old fellowing" in the passage, and then Peter, whose confidence had now completely returned, was heard in loud accents of invitation.

"Come upstairs, old boy—you must come!" he said.

"Can't, old feller—can't: I'm on dooty."

"Oh, that be bothered!" exclaimed the tailor, who was a convivial and hospitable little man so far as his means would permit. "You must come!"

"Well, but——"

"There now, it's no use your a-talking—you must! We haven't met since I don't know when. There's the primest drop o' beer in the world to be got round the corner, threepence a pot; so you must come up into my top garret—that is, if you don't mind—and we'll have a smoke and a drink, and talk over old times."

Jarvis, who had been vacillating between friendship and duty for some time, at the mention of beer and pipes gave way at once, and grasped Peter's hand.

"I can't refuse you, Peter, old boy! I'll go up. I can find my way upstairs. And go and get the beer, old fellow, for I'm regler choking," said Jarvis.

"All right," answered Peter. "They'll lend me a pewter. I sha'n't be gone a minit."

"I'll go up to the snuggery," said Jarvis, ascending the stairs.

"You can't miss it," cried Peter, calling after him; "go on till you knock your head against the beam at the top, and then turn to the right—that's my room."

Jarvis ascended, and was very particular not to knock his head against the friendly *landmark*, suggested by the tailor, who shortly appeared triumphantly carrying a half-gallon can filled with foaming porter.

"There," said Peter, puffing from the haste with which he had executed his commission, "put your lips to that, and tell me if it's the right sort?"

The thirsty Jarvis complied with alacrity, and having imbibed a quart at least at a draught, declared that it was.

The worthy tailor, having provided his old chum with pipe and tobacco, dismissed all further ideas of work for the remainder of the day, and resigned himself to the enjoyment of beer and friendship.

They smoked and drank, and talked of old times.

Peter related his vicissitudes after coming to London—how he had very nearly been deluded into a marriage with a virgin with four children—and how he had had to work early and late to keep the "pot boiling" and to save a pound or two, whilst Jarvis came out strong with some of his raciest anecdotes of criminal life, to Peter's great delight.

The can had to be filled again, and P.O. Jarvis was in the full swing of a glowing account of the notorious marauders, Captain Hawk and the Black Highwayman, when suddenly Peter started up.

"There they are!"

"Who?"

"The highwaymen!" exclaimed the tailor

"Where?" cried out Jarvis, starting up also, and nearly choking himself with the end of his pipe, which he bit off in his excitement, and which stuck in his throat, and required a strong effort to bolt.

"There!" answered Peter, pointing to the open window, and directing his companion's attention to two figures that were making their way over the distant roofs.

Jarvis had to shake himself, and screw his eyes together very firmly for a few moments to press the beer out of them, before his visual powers were clear enough to make the necessary observation.

He then looked out of the window in a profound and professional manner.

He shaded his eyes with his hand, and gazed intently.

Backed by the clear blue evening sky, the dark figures on the roofs came out with extreme vividness—that is to say, their outlines.

Of course, from the distance, their features were quite undiscernible.

But every movement was distinctly perceptible, as also the plank and rope they carried.

"Are they the highwaymen?" inquired Peter, at length, as he observed the anxiety depicted on the features of the police officer.

"As sure as my name's Jarvis, they are!" he answered.

This announcement, which had originally been quite a speculation on the part of the tailor, now that it was confirmed by his more experienced friend, threw him into a great state of excitement.

Vague ideas of some heroic deed flashed through his brain, already a little excited by his potations.

He had a sudden thought of making his goose red hot, and going out boldly in pursuit of these desperadoes.

But then he reflected that the iron would probably grow cool before he could overtake them.

"There's a reward offered for their apprehension, isn't there?" asked Peter.

"Only £300," replied Jarvis, still keeping his eyes on the figures, who had come to a standstill, and appeared to be considering which course to take.

"Three hundred pounds!" echoed the little tailor. "Why, it's quite a fortin', ain't it?"

Jarvis made no reply: he was just making up his mind that he would secure it if possible.

"I intend to capture these fellows," he said, at length, in a tone of determination that proved he meant it.

"But there's two of 'em," suggested Peter. "You'll want help: I'll come and help you."

This was a magnanimous offer on the part of the heroic little man, but Jarvis did not appear particularly grateful.

Strong as his friendship was for his old schoolfellow, he by no means saw the policy of allowing him to share the reward.

Jarvis was selfish and greedy, and wanted the £300 all to himself.

"You're very kind, Peter," he said, "but you're not used to this sort of work—it's very different from stitching trousers; you'd be no use to me; besides, a puff of wind 'ud blow you over the first parapet you came to."

This was not a very flattering remark, and Peter felt it so.

"I'm a great deal stronger than you think," he remarked to his friend. "Didn't I stop a burglar once that broke into the house and was bolting off with a coat?—of course I did! I tackled him, and stuck to him too, till I handed him over to the police."

He spoke this in a tone of indignation, that Jarvis might see he was in earnest.

"It's all very well talking," replied Jarvis, with professional contempt for his friend's valorous assertions, "but a struggle of that sort's a very different thing from a scrimmage with two desperate characters on a house-top. You stop where you are, and leave me to settle this business by myself; I'm used to it, and know how to set about it."

Having thus expressed himself, the uncivil functionary examined the primings of his pistols, swallowed the remaining drop of beer in the can, and with an abrupt "Good night!" got out of the attic window, and made his way over the roofs.

The figures were still visible, and Jarvis shaped his course in the direction most likely to overtake them.

"Well!" ejaculated Peter, as the officer disappeared, "I don't call that very friendly. He comes in here, drinks my beer, and smokes my bacca, and then when I offer to go shares in helping him to catch these highwaymen, he turns up his nose at me! I believe," he continued, in a tone of vexation, "it's only because he wants to get all the reward to himself."

The little man was ill at ease. He felt he had been snubbed and undervalued by his friend, and his heroic little soul burned within him at the reflection.

"What a go it'd be," he thought, "if I could somehow manage to drop upon these gents before he did! Ha, ha! he continued, laughing to himself, "wouldn't it be glorious?"

Poor little Peter Stitchem! he little knew the characters of the "gents" in question.

It is also a matter of great doubt whether the avaricious Jarvis had any clearer idea on the same subject.

"Dashed if I don't try, anyhow!" exclaimed Peter, at length. "Nothing's done without trying, and if I could only manage to gain the £300, I should be independent for life."

This felicitous prospect so animated the tailor, that he resolved to lose no further time, but start at once.

He therefore locked his door, so that it might be supposed he had gone to bed, and then looked about for some weapon of defence.

"I ought to have a weapon of some sort," he reflected, casting his eyes around his small apartment.

The articles there were essentially domestic, not aggressive.

"If I had but an old sword or a pistol!" he thought.

Suddenly his eye fell upon the heavy iron with which he was wont to press the seams of his coats.

"No," he said, as he lifted it, "this is too heavy; not the sort of thing at all. Ha!" he exclaimed, as his glance encountered the sleeve-board that stood resting against the wall, "this is better—this will do! the rascals will think it's a club."

Having armed himself with this, and flourished it in a terrible manner two or three times over his head, he blew out the light, and imitated his companion by stepping out of the window on to the roof.

The figures had by this time continued their career, and he came to the conclusion that he must use all possible speed.

He listened, and fancied he heard Jarvis's boots scraping along the tiles at a little distance.

But he could only hear him, the police officer being at that moment some distance off.

Peter Stitchem was a wiry little active man, and grasping his sleeve-board firmly, he clambered over tiles and ran along parapets as nimbly as a cat or a monkey.

In fact, so much agility did he display, that by pursuing a path different from that which his quondam schoolfellow had pursued, he had considerably outstripped him.

Jarvis was a thick-built man, heavier and slower in every way than the nervous, wiry little tailor.

Peter made the discovery that he was ahead by happening to look back, in order to—using a nautical expression —"take his bearings," when as he gazed he perceived his friend cautiously mounting with many *slips* and *slides* a steep roof, at some distance behind.

He caught also a glimpse of the figures in front, that now appeared much nearer than before.

Stimulated by this prospect, he could not forbear exclaiming, triumphantly:

"Ha, ha! I'm no use, ain't I? A puff of wind'd blow me over the parapet, would it, Mr. Tom Jarvis? If you don't look sharp, I shall have the £300 now, before you, with all your experience!"

A very slanting roof was before him, but what of that? He gathered himself together, and ran up on his hands and toes, on all fours, like a cat.

Presently he came to the edge of a parapet, and there he paused and looked down.

The roof of the next house was four or five feet lower than the others, and there was a gap of about four feet between.

He could not let himself down There was no resource but to jump.

This was certainly not a pleasant feat to contemplate, but he was resolved at any hazard to outstrip his unconscious competitor.

Still the chasm beneath looked very deep and awful.

No matter; neck or nothing: he must win the prize.

He planted his feet firmly on the parapet, bent down, swung his arms backwards and forwards a few times to gain a sufficient impetus, and then sprang boldly forward.

The leap was admirable.

The chasm was cleared by several feet, as though it had been a mere puddle in the road.

The little tailor's heart bounded with conscious pride as he descended with a prodigious crash on to the opposite roof.

He felt that his heart was strong and firm.

But although his heart might have been in this healthy condition, it unfortunately happened that the tiling on which he alighted *was not*; and the consequence was that after the crash the active little tailor was nowhere to be seen, having gone clear through the dilapidated roof and pitched feet foremost, like a sprite down a vampire-trap in a pantomime, on to a slumbering couple in the top garret.

Now it so happened that the sleepers were the red-faced man with the gruff voice, and the sharp old lady with the night-cap whom Captain Hawk had unwittingly disturbed not a quarter of an hour before.

Of course there was an awful clamour.

One of Peter's heels had descended in the pit of Mr. Blare's stomach, and the other on Mrs. Blare's nose.

The effect upon the former was that of a sudden and violent emetic, whilst the latter shrieked "murder" with all her might.

It may be remarked that the red-faced man, who was given to intemperate habits, was by no means a loving husband, and that after the departure of the captain he quieted his indignation by administering a sound thrashing to his ancient partner.

When, therefore, the catastrophe of Peter's sudden appearance occurred, she being aroused from her sleep and suspecting a renewal of hostilities, declared she "wouldn't be knocked about no more for the best man in the world," and divided her attention between calling "murder" and digging the only two front teeth she had into Peter's leg.

As for Peter himself, all his valour had departed.

The suddenness of the drop, and the horror he—being a moral and well-conducted person—felt at thus plunging into the very bed of a sleeping couple were too much for him, and he himself roared "murder" in concert.

The red-faced man, who was for a few moments a great deal too sick to speak, suddenly recovered his voice, and seeing a hole over his head, and feeling a stranger struggling as he thought with his spouse on the bed under his very nose, shot out with his right, and sent the unfortunate tailor flying into a corner of the room, half stunned and scared out of his senses.

"H—ll and Tommy!" roared the gruff voice, "what is it?—who is it, my love? What the h—ll's he been a-doing of? Why don't yer speak?"

"Oh, John!" piped the loved one—"oh, if I didn't think it was you a paying on to me agin!"

"An' so I will, yer old fool, if yer lays there makin' that humpus!" shouted her amiable partner.

"He's been a scrunchin' my nose!" she whined.

"Who?" roared Mr. B. "D—n my rags!—who?"

"I don' know!" whimpered the ancient female.

"It was an accident—an entire accident!—upon my honour it was!" faltered the unhappy Peter, sitting up ruefully in the corner, where the moonlight kindly lent its assistance to make him perfectly visible.

"Oh, it was, was it?" growled the red-faced Blare, leaning out of bed and glaring at him like an ogre.

Poor Peter's heart beat audibly.

"Upon my word——" he began.

"Shut up!" roared Mr. B.; "we don't want none of your lies! I've suspected this 'ere game for ever so long! I'll teach yer to come after my wife!"

"I didn't—as true as I'm alive I didn't!" gasped Peter, in an agony of horror.

"An' I'll teach you too, yer old image!" he shouted, seizing the unfortunate but slandered female at his side by the few straggling locks she had remaining, and tugging at them with all his might.

"Oh, John!—oh, murder!" she yelled.

"This is awful!" thought Peter. "What ever shall I do?"

"So," continued the red-faced brute, once more fixing his bloodshot eyes on the nervous tailor, "you've come agin, has yer?"

"I was never here before in my life!" answered Peter, earnestly—"I wasn't indeed!"

"It's a d—d lie!" answered the other; "wasn't yer here shooting cats not half an hour ago, eh?—wasn't yer?"

"Shooting cats!" faltered Peter. "I never shot a cat in all my life! The man must be mad!"

"An' d'ye see what yer've done to my ceiling, eh?" shouted Mr. B., pointing to the hole in the roof.

"I'm very sorry indeed; but as I said before——"

"I don't want to know what yer said before, or what yer didn't; but I'll tell yer what I'm a goin' to do, I'm a goin' to take yer by the back o' th' neck and drop yer down into the back yard!" growled the incensed Blare.

This was a terrible announcement, for Mr. John Blare was a sort of a modern Hercules, and poor Peter was a very slight man.

Suiting the action to the word, the strong man rolled himself out of bed.

Peter, who, though nervous and alarmed, was by no means deficient in spirit, and who, conscious of his innocence, did not at all admire the idea of being dropped into the back yard, cast his eyes hopelessly for some weapon of defence.

Suddenly his eye fell on his sleeve-board, which he had unconsciously clutched, and which now lay close to his side.

Here was a friend at least!

He grasped it firmly as the angry Blare advanced in his shirt to seize the shivering little man.

"Now then!" growled the brute, "I'll teach you to come droppin' through people's roofs an' shootin' cats! Come on!"

He stretched forth a large red hand to seize poor Peter, but received instead, to his very great surprise, such a tremendous thwack on his head, that in spite of its thickness the sleeve-board triumphed, and Mr. John Blare rolled over like a pole-axed ox.

Mrs. B. immediately commenced screaming; but Petor was desperate, and seizing the old dame by her arms, he hoisted her out of bed very unceremoniously, and then, placing a table on the bed, he mounted it, and in a moment was once more on the roof.

He did not stop to ask himself any questions. The highwaymen and the £300 were alike forgotten; and he made the best of his way back to his garret, resolving never to go "out on the tiles" again as long as he lived.

As for the discomfited Blare, he in a few moments recovered his senses; and seeing from the table on the bed the way by which the little tailor had made his escape, took the same route to follow him.

"The dirty little rascal," he growled—"I'll have him!"

He clambered up on to the table, that creaked and groaned under his weight, and by dint of great efforts managed to drag himself up through the aperture just in time to find himself face to face with the bull's-eye of a police officer's lantern.

Mr. Blare was so astonished that he dropped down again into his sleeping apartment, as though he had been shot.

Jarvis, in no very good humour at thus being interrupted, looked down upon him through the hole in the roof.

"Stop him!—stop the vagabond!" shouted Mr. B.

His exclamation and directions were abruptly stopped by the police officer, who said, sternly:

"If you don't leave off this drunken nonsense, and go to bed, I'll take you into custody!"

This was sufficient to quiet the choleric Blare, who covered the hole in the roof with a tea-board, gave his wife a parting kick, and once more retired to rest.

Jarvis, growling and muttering a volley of angry oaths at being thus delayed, continued his pursuit of the figures.

CHAPTER CXCIX.

PHAROAH WAKES FROM HIS SLEEP, AND DISCOVERS A SPY ON THE ROOF.—CAPTAIN HAWK AND THE BLACK HIGHWAYMAN CONTINUE THEIR COURSE, AND ENCOUNTER IMMINENT DANGERS.—AN UNEXPECTED FRIEND.

We left Pharoah in a happy state of unconsciousness asleep in his garret, enveloped in a misty cloud of tobacco smoke.

We will now look in again just as he awakes.

He, of course, having been asleep for some time by the open window, feels cramped and chilly; he discovers that his cigar has dropped from his mouth on to the floor, and of course picks it up.

He then takes a few turns up and down the narrow chamber, and throws up his arms in the air to stretch his cramped limbs, and then indulges—not this time in claret—but in a small glass of pale brandy, which he takes from the cupboard.

This warms him and gives him resolution to re-light his cigar.

He discovers by his watch it is ten o'clock; he has therefore been asleep nearly an hour.

He gives himself another shake, and then goes to the window and puffs his cigar, leaning on the window-sill.

While thus occupied, his attention was suddenly attracted by a man who, under shadow of the roofs, was making his way along them as quickly as possible.

It was too indistinct for Pharoah to discern what he was like.

Most certainly it was neither Lord Harcliffe nor Captain Hawk.

Who, then, could it be at that hour in such a place?

The man, whoever he was, must have some motive.

He must either be watching or pursuing some one, or else he must himself be watched and pursued.

His ideas took a more definite shape as the figure emerged suddenly into the full moonlight, and he recognised the uniform of a police officer.

He felt assured that his presence there augured hindrance, perhaps threatened frustration, to the plan of his master and his comrade.

"He shall not succeed if I can hinder him," thought Pharoah, as, without further consideration, he stepped out on to the roof and followed with the utmost caution.

In the meantime our heroes had gone on swimmingly.

Nothing save the little incident that took place on their starting had occurred to hinder their progress.

The only delays had been the times when they paused to reconnoitre, and to judge of the course in which they were progressing.

It was in one of these pauses they had first been discovered by Peter Stitchem.

They had now arrived at a considerable distance from the point from which they had started.

A short interval more, and they looked forward to being able to descend out of the reach of their enemies.

They had found the plank eminently serviceable in crossing the narrow alleys with which the locality was intersected; and though this feat might have been almost impracticable to a person of weak nerves, it was mere child's play to our heroes, whose nerves were like steel, and who, moreover, had freedom, like a powerful astringent, to brace them up for any task of danger in securing it.

They were just crossing a narrow court when Captain Hawk, who was constantly on the watch, fancied he saw a figure watching them in the gloom beneath.

He mentioned his suspicions to Lord Harcliffe, who looked down, but could distinguish nothing.

"It must have been my fancy," said the captain; "but in a journey like this we cannot be too watchful or suspicious. A stray shot, or even a sudden exclamation while we were crossing our narrow plank might be certain destruction."

"These feats and their perils do not bear reflection," replied Lord Harcliffe. "Shall we go on?"

"Yes."

Hardly had the highwaymen turned their backs before a man appeared, almost following in their steps, and looked furtively below.

He held in his hand a paper, in which was wrapped a piece of mortar to give it weight.

This he threw down.

A man below picked it up.

"Hullo!" he ejaculated. "What's this?"

Opening the paper, he read by the light of his lantern the following words:—

"*Look out in the next street, but keep out of sight.*

"*Jarvis.*"

The man having thrown the paper, made a circuit, and was soon out of sight.

In the meantime, our heroes continued their course till they came to a street wider than any they had hitherto crossed, and in which the rays of an oil lamp were distinctly visible.

A parapet of about a yard in height ran along the edge of the houses on which they stood, and on those on the opposite side of the way.

"Humph!" said Captain Hawk. "Will our bridge be long enough to carry us across?"

"The shortest way to arrive at an answer will be to drop it across and try," answered Lord Harcliffe, smiling.

"But should it prove too short," said his comrade, "we shall not only lose our plank, but inevitably cause an alarm by the clatter of its descent into the street below."

"The streets seem quite deserted; depend upon it, our enterprise is entirely unsuspected."

"Perhaps so. Still, I should hardly like to venture any step that might create a disturbance now that we are so near our journey's end," said the captain.

"Nor I," returned his lordship. "So long as we are unsuspected we are safe."

"Still," continued Captain Hawk, meditatively, "we must not remain here. Stay! Hark!" he exclaimed, suddenly, as he bent down and listened intently.

"Do you hear anything?"

"I think so."

"Footsteps?"

"No, voices."

"Whence do they proceed?"

"From the street below, I think."

"How can we ascertain?"

"I will look over. If there is anyone there they will not observe me."

As the captain spoke he cautiously leant over the parapet and looked down.

He found his suspicions were correct.

Close to the houses on the side on which they were was a body of men.

How many he could not distinctly determine, the gloom was too intense.

But the light of the lamp revealed the figures of several.

They spoke in whispers, so that what they said was quite inaudible.

Captain Hawk withdrew from the parapet.

"Our foes are there," he said—"at least, somo of them."

"But do you imagine there is any connection with that circumstance and the figure you fancied you descried in the court behind us?" asked Lord Harcliffe.

"I cannot say, but I should think not. I should judge by their manner they are entirely unsuspicious of our propinquity."

At this moment a solitary footstep was heard in the street beneath.

"Hush!" ejaculated Captain Hawk, as he looked cautiously over.

As he looked, he distinctly saw a man buttoned in a thick great coat emerge from a narrow outlet, and passing under the oil lamp advance close alongside of the houses to the spot where the men he had previously noticed were stationed.

Lord Harcliffe, who had this time looked also, said to Captain Hawk, as he drew back a little:

"Can this be the man from the other street?"

"I think so."

"Can he be come to give an alarm?"

"We shall soon see."

The man remained with his comrades a few moments; but there was no excitement—nothing to imply any stirring information below.

The conversation also was still carried on in whispers.

In a few moments there was a general move, and Captain Hawk counted twelve men as they passed successively under the rays of the lamp and disappeared up the narrow turning.

"They are gone," said Lord Harcliffe.

"Yes; not a single one remains."

"What do you think of this sudden and very quiet departure?" asked his lordship.

"I think one thing," replied the captain.

"So do I: that it looks suspicious."

"Perhaps so; but it leaves the coast clear, and that being what we want, I propose instead of hesitating further, we throw the plank across and chance it."

"Over with it, then!"

The plank was accordingly raised perpendicularly, and then, one end resting on the ledge of the parapet, Captain Hawk lowered it gradually till it rested on that of the opposite house.

The hold the captain maintained upon it during the greater part of its descent was so firm that it made but little noise as it fell.

The highwaymen paused a few moments in order to be quite sure they had not alarmed the men.

All, however, remained quiet.

"It is all right," exclaimed Lord Harcliffe: "they are gone for good."

"We will follow their example."

"Shall I go first?"

"Yes; I will keep the plank steady."

Accordingly Lord Harcliffe mounted on to the parapet, and proceeded cautiously to cross the frail bridge, that quivered and bent beneath the weight.

It was the widest street they had crossed yet, and, of course, the strain upon the plank was greater.

Captain Hawk began to be apprehensive that it was not sufficiently strong.

"Will it bear you, Harcliffe?" he inquired; "if not, return—do not risk it."

"It will bear me," replied his lordship, continuing to move forward.

But a peril they had not anticipated now burst upon them, for as Lord Harcliffe reached the centre of the plank a loud shout rang from below, and a blaze of light from a dozen torches revealed the entire body of police officers, who darted suddenly from their place of ambush.

An involuntary expression of uncontrollable rage broke from the lips of Captain Hawk.

The loud reports of pistols echoed through the night air.

Lord Harcliffe, startled by the sudden shout, the gleam of the torches, and the crash of the weapons, swerved, and lost his balance.

It was an awful moment, that hanging, as it were, between life and death.

In vain his lordship struggled to regain his equilibrium: he had gone too far, and his footing was entirely lost.

"My God! he's gone!" cried Captain Hawk, in an agony, as his comrade fell.

A loud shout, too, from the police officers below announced their exultation at this catastrophe.

They were, however, disappointed as to the result.

They fully anticipated seeing the Black Highwayman come crashing headlong to the ground, instead of which he, finding it impossible to recover his balance, suffered himself to fall, but dexterously clasped the plank in his descent, and supported himself by clinging to it.

"Thank Heaven!" exclaimed the captain. "That was bravely done—it was miraculous!"

"Oh, yes, I am not dead yet!" answered his friend, in a cheerful tone, in spite of his imminently critical position.

"Can you recover your footing?"

"I think so. Hold the plank firmly, Dick!"

"I will, my boy—trust me!"

Captain Hawk grasped the plank with a clutch of iron, and there was every probability that his comrade would have been astride it in a moment, when a second volley was fired from beneath, and a cry from his lordship told that he was hit.

"Are you wounded?" he asked, frantically.

"Yes," said his lordship; "but not seriously, I think—at least, at present."

"The d—d cowardly hounds!" muttered Captain Hawk, grinding his teeth with fury. "Hold on a moment, my dear friend," he cried, "till I can reach you: this is now a matter of life and death!"

"No, no—you must not venture!"

"I must—I will!"

"But the plank will not support two of us. You will not be able to save me, and will sacrifice yourself!" urged Lord Harcliffe.

"Could I lose my life in a better cause than in endeavouring to preserve a friend? Say no more—I shall come and make the effort!"

He glanced down for a moment and saw one of the officers in the act of drawing his pistol.

Quick as lightning he drew one of his own, and as the man presented at his friend, he fired.

The officer fell with a bullet wound in the centre of his forehead.

"So perish all such unfeeling scoundrels!" cried the captain, as he commenced his perilous journey along the plank.

He was compelled to crawl on his hands and knees; but in a moment he had reached his friend and had clasped him with his arm.

It was a most awfully perilous situation—

Beneath, the hard stones of the street and the police officers—

Their only resting-place a frail plank.

It may here be remarked that the torches, though they lighted the street below, did not throw their glare quite to the tops of the houses.

This circumstance had hitherto preserved Lord Harcliffe.

The wound he had received was merely a chance graze, whereas had it been daylight, his fate would have been inevitable, exposed as he was to so many remorseless weapons.

But even without any additional aid the posture of our heroes was one of the most imminent danger.

The plank, having no one to steady it at either end, oscillated and shifted at the least motion.

"Oh, Heaven!" cried Captain Hawk, almost in despair, "after escaping so many dangers, are we to perish thus?"

"You should not have imperilled yourself for my sake, Dick!" said Lord Harcliffe.

"I should have been a base coward, unworthy of the name of man, much less friend, had I not done so! But come!" he suddenly exclaimed. "Courage, Harcliffe! Try and rouse yourself for a moment, and all may be well yet."

This inspiration was necessary, for his lordship showed symptoms of weakness.

One of Captain Hawk's arms was round him; but with the other hand he contrived to reach the flask of brandy.

Unscrewing the top with his teeth, he placed it to his friend's lips, and then took a sip himself.

Small as was the quantity, it revived them both.

"Now, then, my friend," said the captain, "are you able to make the effort?"

"Yes."

"That's right! Grasp me firmly."

The words had hardly passed his lips, as he nerved himself for the effort, when a new and more deadly peril seemed to start forth at their elbow.

Captain Hawk beheld a sight that almost petrified and unnerved him.

It was that of a police officer grasping one end of the plank with both hands, and ready to dash it from the parapet.

A cry of horror burst from his lips.

"Stay, wretch!" he shouted, desperately.

The man looked at him with dull, remorseless eyes; but did not remove his hands from the plank.

"You can never," the captain continued, earnestly, "be such a diabolical coward as to take this mean advantage of our position? My friend is wounded!"

"Serve him right!" said the official. "We know you, Captain Hawk, and your friend, too, the Black Highwayman; and as you won't allow yourselves to be taken fairly, it's fair for us to catch you how we can."

"But listen!"

"I can't. This'll be a capital drop, and will save you a 'drop' of a different sort at Tyburn."

The officer tightened his hold upon the plank.

"Stay!—one moment!" adjured Captain Hawk.

"No! There's a reward of £300 offered for the pair of you, and I'm going to earn it," answered Jarvis.

"I'll give you three hundred—four hundred—not to touch this plank!" cried the captain, desperately.

"Too late!—can't do it: my mates know I'm here, and I must do my duty."

The remorseless and mercenary Jarvis gripped the plank, and the fate of the highwaymen hung upon a hair.

Captain Hawk was about to utter a parting word of defiance to his destroyer, when an exclamation from the man arrested him.

The officer had been gripped by some one behind, and had released his hold on the plank, and turned to face his assailant, who was masked.

No words passed.

One tremendous blow was given, which made the mercenary official stagger.

Another followed, and Jarvis, recoiling from its effects, reeled backwards against the edge of the parapet.

A third blow, delivered with the rapidity of lightning, knocked him clean over.

Jarvis lay in the street below, with his skull fractured, and every rib in his body broken—dead!

He had worked for his reward, and he had received it.

"Now, quick!" cried their deliverer, removing his mask. "I'll steady the plank!"

"Pharoah!" exclaimed the highwaymen.

"Yes, thank Heaven! I just arrived in time. Quick! while you have yet the chance!"

As the necessity for haste was urgent, Lord Harcliffe dismissed the idea of regaining his upright position on the plank; and as Pharoah kept it steady, he contrived, by clasping it with his arms and legs, to work himself across in that manner.

Captain Hawk followed, keeping close to his comrade, ready to stretch forth his hand at the first sign of need.

But it was not required.

His lordship held on bravely, and in a few seconds was with the captain, safely landed on the opposite parapet.

Their first impulse on reaching a place of comparative safety was a softened feeling, that usually in generous natures accompanies an unexpected deliverance from a violent death.

They clasped each other's hands in a fraternal pressure.

"Friend!—brother!"

These words, spoken with deep emotion, were the only two words uttered.

Then looking across to Pharoah, Lord Harcliffe said:

"My faithful Pharoah, you have saved the lives of myself and friend, and, believe me, you shall not go unrewarded!"

"I am rewarded," cried Pharoah, "in having saved my dear master!"

He waved his hand, and crying "Eleven o'clock!" disappeared.

"Come, my friend," said Captain Hawk to his comrade, "though the most vital peril is over, we are not yet beyond the reach of danger; nor shall we be until we stand once more on the solid ground."

"I am quite ready to proceed," answered Lord Harcliffe. "Oh!" he suddenly added, "the rope?"

"'Tis on the other side," said the captain. "These unexpected dangers make us forgetful. No matter, I will fetch it."

"What! cross that treacherous abyss again?" asked Lord Harcliffe, with a look of horror.

"I must; or how are we to reach the ground?"

"Ah!"

"There is no danger now: the street seems clear."

This was perfectly true.

All was quiet, and not a living soul was in sight.

But the calm was only temporary.

The fire smouldered, to burst out presently into a flame.

Captain Hawk stepped lightly on to the plank, and crossed it easily.

The rope lay coiled up close to the parapet.

The captain stooped to pick it up, when, as he grasped it, a man suddenly sprang forth, and threw himself upon him heavily.

"I think I've got you this time, Captain Hawk!" said the man, who was a big, burly member of the Bow Street community.

"Do you indeed?" answered the captain. "I think you'll find yourself mistaken!"

"We'll see!" cried the officer. "Help here—help!" he shouted. "I've caught the rascal: I've got Captain Hawk!"

"Take this, then, as a keepsake!" cried the captain, disengaging his hand, and delivering a blow on the officer's forehead with such terrific force that he staggered several yards backwards, and then fell prostrate, utterly senseless and motionless.

His shouts, however, had aroused his comrades, who arrived on the roof just in time to see Captain Hawk and his companion safe on the opposite side, the plank and the rope walking away with them, and the street between.

[HORRIBLE FATE OF THE TREACHEROUS BEAUTY.]

CHAPTER CC.

THE OFFICERS CONTINUE THE PURSUIT OF THE HIGHWAYMEN OVER THE ROOF-TOPS.—LORD HARCLIFFE KEEPS HIS APPOINTMENT WITH PHAROAH.—THE HIGHWAYMEN VISIT THE "PRINCE'S RETREAT."—THE RED ROOM.

It will possibly be a matter of surprise that our heroes were left so much to themselves during the latter portion of their adventures on the plank.

But it must be remembered that their attention was diverted first by the death of one of their number from the bullet of Captain Hawk, and that within a short space afterwards another of their comrades was hurled, a crushed and lifeless mass, in their midst.

They were partly stunned by these tragical events, partly surprised at their strangeness; and by the time they had recovered themselves and removed their dead, the highwaymen were beyond their reach.

On hurrying to the roof in answer to their comrade's cry for assistance, they fully expected to secure one, if not both the men, whose attempted capture had been attended with such terrible results.

Their chagrin, therefore, when they found that after all their prey had escaped their clutches, may be easily imagined.

All they could do they did, and that was to utter a yell of rage, that as nearly as possible resembled the roar of the wild beasts at the Zoological about feeding time.

But as the highwaymen disappeared, and it appeared very possible they would escape altogether, voices clamoured loudly for a plank, that they might cross as the desperate men they sought had done, and follow in their very footprints.

They were now filled with the most vindictive feelings.

Two of their number had been killed before their eyes, and each felt that in addition to his duty, he had a comrade's death to avenge.

It was in such a state of mind that when, after some delay, a plank was found, they hastily crossed it and followed in pursuit.

In the meantime, Captain Hawk and Lord Harcliffe, having put some distance between themselves and their foes, came to the determination of effecting a descent as speedily as possible.

They paused; and having refreshed themselves by a sip at the brandy-flask, they advanced to where a broad street interposing, their further progress was cut off.

"This is our point," said Captain Hawk; "we must descend here."

"Can we do so in safety?"

"Yes, here is an alley on this side that is quite dark and unfrequented; we will make that the point of our descent—that is, if your wound has not disabled you?" said the captain.

"Not in the least," returned Lord Harcliffe. "The bullet must have barely grazed my arm—I can scarcely feel it now."

"Well, then, let us prepare."

The preparations were very simple, and merely consisted of placing the steel hook so that it would fix itself in the brickwork of the coping stone of the wall, and throwing the rope over.

It was now half-past ten by the clocks.

The alley was a very retired place; and there being no thoroughfare through it, no one was visible.

Being assured the rope was long enough to reach the ground beneath, from hearing it strike against the stones, Captain Hawk said:

"Now, my friend, hand over hand for a moment, and you will once more touch *terra firma*."

"Am I to go first?"

"Yes."

Lord Harcliffe lowered himself over the top of the wall and grasped the rope.

"Farewell, my friend, for five minutes!" he cried, as he commenced his descent.

Hardly had his lordship disappeared when the shouts of the police reached his ears.

"Is there danger?" he cried to the captain.

"Yes! Remain quiet!" returned Captain Hawk, hastily.

He paused and looked round; they were evidently near.

Would it be safe or politic to trust himself to the rope then?

The question was at once decided by the sight of a police officer in the distance.

The man evidently perceived him, and turned to shout to his companions:

"Come on! Here he is!"

Captain Hawk made up his mind in a moment.

He resolved at any risk to put them off the scent and scatter them if possible.

He accordingly bowed himself as near to the ground as he could, and ran forwards in the direction in which the officer was coming till he reached a friendly stack of chimneys that concealed him.

He then waited for the arrival of the impetuous officer, who came blundering over the roof as rapidly as he possibly could.

He was in advance of his companions, and would have passed by the stack of chimneys without noticing Captain Hawk, but that was not the captain's plan.

He wished to decoy the officers away from the point of escape, and it was therefore necessary he should show himself in order to invite pursuit.

As a means to bring about this result, he quietly put out his foot as the police officer passed, and the man stumbling over it, rolled head over heels down the tiles, and was eventually stopped by his nose coming in contact with a ridge at the bottom.

"D—nation!" growled the man. "Who was that?"

"Ha, ha!" laughed Captain Hawk, playfully, on the summit of the roof. "Hurt yourself much?"

The man, looking ruefully up and seeing one of the objects of his pursuit behind him, instead of in front, bawled out, furiously:

"Stop him!—there he is!—after him!" And immediately gave chase.

This was exactly what Captain Hawk desired.

He had now stopped the whole body in their pursuit, or at least turned their course in another direction.

The captain, who was as active as a panther or a leopard, dodged them successfully over roofs and behind chimney-pots.

Occasionally he showed himself just to whet their appetites.

Bang!—bang! immediately went a couple of pistols, seriously damaging a couple of rickety weather-cocks, and very nearly settling the earthly account of an elderly gentleman who put his head out to see what was the matter.

Away went the captain; and away went the officers, stumbling, slipping, and swearing, after him; but he managed to keep them so effectually at bay, that they were no nearer than when they started.

At length, however, fortune seemed to give the officers an advantage.

A gable window stood in front.

Captain Hawk was in full view.

The officers were behind, and coming on at full swing.

Half-a-dozen bullets whizzed over his head.

Their shouts rang in his ears.

He dropped on his knee, deliberately drew one of his favourite long barrels, and fired.

The foremost of the troop came to a sudden stop—a *dead* stop: the bullet had pierced his heart.

The captain rose with the yells of execration ringing on his ears and retreated.

The gable window was open; he paused not, but leapt in, drawing the curtains after him.

"Now we have him!" cried the foremost of the men, as they dashed in after him.

But again they were doomed to defeat and disappointment.

There happened to be a window at the back of the room, which Captain Hawk had remarked, and out of which he had sprung instantly with the agility of a harlequin.

"Follow!" they shouted.

But which way were they to go?

They were quite at a standstill; the object of their pursuit was nowhere to be seen.

All kinds of suggestions were rapidly offered.

"He must be in one of the chimney-pots," said one.

"He's the devil himself!" cried another.

"We're not going to lose the d—d rascal!" exclaimed a third.

But in spite of this confident assertion, it seemed very much as though such an event would occur, since at that very moment, like a hare doubling the hounds after throwing them off their scent, the captain was rapidly making his way back to the very point from which he had started.

Breathless with his exertions, he seized the rope and swung himself from the wall.

"Is all safe?" cried Lord Harcliffe, from below.

"All!" gasped the captain.

"No, it isn't, you scoundrel!" exclaimed a gruff voice; and immediately a burly officer, who had straggled from the rest, rushed to the edge of the wall and looked over at the highwaymen.

Captain Hawk's hand being occupied with the rope, he could do nothing but cast a desperate look of defiance at the officer.

"I'll cure you of this!" said the latter.

As he spoke he drew a sharp clasp-knife from his pocket and opened it with a jerk.

His object was manifest.

He grasped the rope, and prepared to sever it at a stroke.

But 'ere the blade could reach its destination, a sharp report was heard, the knife fell from the officer's hand, and with a stifled cry he rolled over, a lifeless heap, whilst a masked man darted forward, and leaning over the wall, cried:

"Go on, captain! All's safe! We'll be in Pall Mall now by eleven o'clock."

Captain Hawk descended; the man in the mask followed, and both reached the ground in safety.

A jerk of the hand detached the hook from the top of the wall, and the rope fell into the alley beneath.

As the clock chimed a quarter to eleven Captain Hawk,

Lord Harcliffe, and the faithful Pharoah shook hands with each other, and offered their mutual congratulations on their hair-breadth escapes.

The police officers heard the report of Pharoah's pistol, but could arrive at no intelligence whence it came, neither did they know the result of the discharge.

They went straggling about in their search, vexed and dispirited, till at last they caught sight of their comrade.

On examination they discovered that a bullet had pierced the back of his neck and severed the spine.

He, too, was dead.

"That makes four to-night," cried one of their number, in a hoarse voice. "It won't be good for these tiger-cats when we once get 'em into our claws."

No clue, however, led to the "how" or "where" the highwaymen had effected their retreat.

Galling as the conviction was, they were compelled to acknowledge, however unwillingly, that for the time at least their prey had escaped the hunters.

"It's no use wasting our time here!" they cried. "Let us carry this poor fellow away."

So saying, they raised their dead comrade, and left the roofs, to give information of all that had transpired at Bow Street.

In the meantime, our heroes, accompanied by Pharoah, made the best of their way towards St. James's Street, and as the clocks struck eleven they turned into Pall Mall.

"True to our time," said Lord Harcliffe; "but I confess I never experienced so much difficulty in keeping an appointment in my life."

"It will not do to remain in the public streets just now," said Pharoah.

"I was just thinking the same thing," answered the captain.

"Come with me, then," replied the former; "I know a place in the neighbourhood that will afford you a secure asylum as long as you like to stop."

As this was a matter of vital importance, the highwaymen gladly accepted Pharoah's offer.

They branched off down a narrow turning. Pharoah, who acted as guide, led the way till they stopped at a modest-looking private dwelling that carried respectability in every brick that composed it.

The windows were perfectly free from a speck of dust, and the blinds entirely divested of that yellow tinge that the smoke of London chimneys so often imparts to those articles.

Everything about the establishment was quiet and orderly.

The narrow court in which it stood was apparently untrodden by many feet.

No one passing by would have dreamt what scenes were night by night enacted there.

Yet could one have pierced through the impervious walls, one might have seen, after dark, the wildest scenes of revelry and dissipation going on within.

Here the dice box rattled, and the cards flew from hand to hand the livelong night through.

Here some of the noblest blood in the kingdom departed from its nobility, and circulated in feverish excitement till the rising sun must have blushed as it over powered the wax tapers that illumined the revellers.

Here the loveliest and most abandoned women congregated and mingled unreservedly with the opposite sex.

And yet all was done so quietly and respectably, with such a prudent regard to decorum and secrecy, that even the next-door neighbour would have lived in unsuspicious ignorance.

Pharoah gave one gentle tap with the knocker, and was admitted so quickly that it appeared as though the knock and the turn of the lock were simultaneous.

Such was indeed the case.

Tapped in a certain spot, the door opened with a spring.

On entering this unpretending establishment, that promised so little from its external appearance, our heroes—not very easily taken by surprise—were profoundly astonished at the luxurious magnificence and size of the rooms.

Pharoah's first act on entering had been to light several wax tapers.

It was then seen that the interior was more like a palace than an ordinary dwelling-house.

"What do you think of this, gentlemen?" asked Pharoah, with a smile he could not suppress at the evident amazement of the highwaymen.

"I confess I never was more astonished," answered Captain Hawk.

"I thought," said Lord Harcliffe, as his eye glanced at the magnificent mirrors in their elaborately gilt frames, "that I was acquainted with all the splendid haunts of dissipation in the metropolis; but this has certainly escaped my observation."

"That is not surprising," answered Pharoah. "This establishment has only been in existence a little more than a month."

"Oh! then that accounts for my ignorance," returned his lordship. "Having been so much away from town of late, it is not astonishing that I know little of what is taking place there."

"There is no other Elysium like this in London," said Pharoah.

"Which does it most resemble," asked Captain Hawk, "Elysium or Pandemonium?"

"That would be entirely a matter of opinion," answered Pharoah, "and depends on the different aspects under which the scenes that are enacted here, are viewed. They have their dark as well as their bright side."

"Like everything else in nature," remarked Captain Hawk; "but a place like this must cost an enormous deal to keep up," he added.

"You are right, captain," returned Pharoah; "but then there are enormous sums spent here; all the members of this *sanctum sanctorum* are rich men, and each member is bound to contribute an equal share towards its support. I need scarcely tell you that the fair sirens who display their charms so lavishly within these walls are wonderfully clever at preventing the funds from accumulating too rapidly."

"I can perfectly understand that," said Captain Hawk, with a smile. "If a man is at any time overburdened with money, he need only call in the assistance of a beautiful and dissipated woman, and he will feel his burden diminish rapidly hour by hour."

"The truth is," remarked Pharoah, "this is indeed a true Temple of Dissipation, where all the worst vices and passions are fostered and flourish as in a hot-bed. But who do you think was the original promoter of this Golden Hell?"

"Nay," returned the highwaymen, "it is impossible to say."

"His name is Frederick Prince of Wales," answered Pharoah, in a low voice, "and this place is called amongst his associates the '*Prince's Retreat*,' out of compliment to the noble——"

"Or ignoble!" put in Lord Harcliffe.

"Institutor."

"And is it here, then, we are to remain?" inquired Captain Hawk.

"I strongly recommend you to do so," answered Pharoah, "since you can find no place so secure if you were to search London through; and especially since your recent successful attempt in baffling the police officers will be certain to make pursuit after you hotter than ever."

"Undoubtedly; but since we are *not members* of this community, will our presence here be tolerated?" inquired the captain.

"I will arrange that," answered Pharoah; "the arrangements of this place are all left to me, so you see the prince holds me in some confidence."

"He could not trust one more worthy," exclaimed Lord Harcliffe.

"I have the ordering of all that comes into the house," continued Pharoah; "in fact, I am Purveyor-general. I can therefore supply your table with all the luxuries of the season, and the choicest wines, whilst for your lodging there is an apartment at the top of the house which I reserve for myself, to which you are perfectly welcome. It is elegantly furnished, and is one of the pleasantest rooms in the building."

"My faithful Pharoah," warmly exclaimed Lord Harcliffe, who was delighted at the prospect of so secure an asylum, "you have indeed proved yourself a most invaluable friend; we shall never be able to repay you!"

"I ask no reward," returned Pharoah, pressing his late master's hand affectionately to his lips; "it is more than enough to repay me that I am able to serve you."

It was at once decided then that the "*Prince's Retreat*" should for the present be their hiding-place; and Pharoah having conducted the highwaymen through the entire length and breadth of the establishment, and pointed out the peculiarities of the different chambers, at last led them to the topmost story.

During this surveillance, two circumstances struck them as remarkable.

One was, that there was not a single individual—domestic or otherwise—to be seen besides themselves.

The other was that the chamber next to the one they occupied was papered and carpeted with crimson, and that a massive four-post bedstead—which proved that it was used as a sleeping apartment—was also hung with the drapery of the same sanguinary hue—*crimson.*

On seating themselves in the room destined by Pharoah for their reception, Lord Harcliffe made an allusion to these peculiarities.

"It is one of the rules of this establishment," explained Pharoah, "that no domestics are employed; it would not be *safe!* It is my office to see that everything that can minister to the tastes of the visitors is ready to their hands, but that done, each one must help himself."

"And the *Red Room*" inquired Lord Harcliffe—"what is the meaning of that?"

"That is as much a question of surmise on my part as on yours, gentlemen," answered Pharoah.

"What do you infer?" followed up his lordship.

"I suppose, since you seek the truth, that gentlemen sometimes quarrel—sometimes fight; and that the crimson hue of the room being of the same colour as blood——"

"Exactly," interrupted Lord Harcliffe; "that is sufficient. The carpet might be dyed with human gore and yet leave no traces behind."

"I can only imagine that was the intention of such an ominous colour."

Pharoah having spread before our heroes a plentiful and elegant repast and a bottle of choice wine, directing their attention to a buffet in one corner of the room well stocked with a further supply, presented them each with a small key, which would admit them into the house at any hour, whether by day or night.

"I must leave you now, gentlemen," he said. "Draw the bolt when I am gone, and you will be perfectly safe from all intrusion."

Then, addressing himself solely to Lord Harcliffe, he said:

"I will inform the prince that you are to be found."

"You will not let him know we are here?"

"No; I shall simply tell him I can discover you for him if he desires an interview, which I know he does most eagerly."

"Of course that interview would not take place to-night?"

"No, not to-night; you will have enough to do to rest yourself after the excitement you have undergone. Perhaps to-morrow his royal highness may decide to see you."

"Will he be here to-night?"

"I cannot say to a certainty, though I think, as the beautiful Henrietta—who is an especial favourite of the prince—is to be here to-night, it is very probable he will be. But I must go now, for the members will be shortly arriving. For the present, farewell!"

With these words Pharoah departed, and our heroes, with that inward confidence which a sense of security imparts, sat down with good appetites to the tempting supper Pharoah had placed before them.

After the arduous chase they had endured, they felt somewhat exhausted, and as the generous viands disappeared, and the bottle gradually shrank, they were sensible of the great benefit they derived from those restoratives which nature imperiously demanded.

They resolved mutually to attempt nothing that night, but to recruit their bodies with sleep.

Accordingly the wine, inducing an inclination to slumber, they disposed themselves, one in an easy-chair, and the other on a couch, and sank into a profound and tranquil slumber.

CHAPTER CCI.

THE QUIET HOUSE IN THE COURT.—PHAROAH SURPRISES THE HIGHWAYMEN.—HE EXPLAINS THE CHARACTER OF HIS RETREAT.—THEY FIND IT A SECURE HIDING-PLACE.—DOINGS WITHIN THE WALLS.—THE SLEEPING DRAUGHT

PHAROAH, having lighted up the candelabras and chandeliers in the different suites of apartments, and placed wine and liquors with fruit, and a variety of tempting luxuries in the form of a cold collation on the sideboards, not omitting several silver racks filled with the choicest cigars, together with dice and new packs of cards on the tables, returned to the apartment where he had left his old master and Captain Hawk.

He tapped softly at the door, but, receiving no answer, he concluded justly that they had retired to rest for the night.

He therefore did not disturb them, but once more descended to superintend the arrangements below.

The company had now begun to arrive.

They came quietly, but in quick succession, and before the clocks had struck the hour of midnight, between thirty and forty members, male and female, had arrived.

Various were the motives that brought together that mixed assembly.

The passions that actuated them were as different as the persons themselves.

There were infatuated gamblers who came to play with and fleece one another if possible.

They little recked by what means it was accomplished, whether fair or foul, so long as the glittering coin flowed into their purses.

There were also the more grossly sensual visitors—the old hoary-headed voluptuary, as well as the younger of this class, each seeking to bask in the full tide of beauty, and to purchase at any price a semblance of love from the fair courtesans that displayed their half-naked charms before them, which was nothing more than a polluting and hideous mockery.

Then there were the gluttons, who came to gorge themselves; and the wine bibbers, the votaries of Bacchus, who came to lave themselves in the nectarean juice of the grape till they were full to the brim.

All there had their several motives, and they indulged them to the full without restraint.

But though laughter, sometimes light and silvery from some fair frail one, or loud and uproarious from some aristocratic toper, continued to peal forth, it was very remarkable that no sound reached to without the doors.

Nay, when, as would sometimes happen, the shriek of some desperate gambler, maddened by his losses, was howled forth, it fell upon the ear of the passer-by in the corridor like a child's whisper.

Should the reader be curious to know how this state of non-conduction had been arrived at, we reply that the walls of this haunt of vice were coated with a layer of thick padding underneath the paper, so that no sounds within could possibly escape when the doors were closed.

The shout of laughter, the shriek of despair or murder, would have been alike unheard.

Ever and anon some young *débauché*, reeling under the influence of champagne, might have been seen, with his arm encircling the neck of one of the fair Circes, seeking one of the luxurious chambers with his wanton companion to sleep off the effects of his debauchery.

There was not a room or a corner of a room in the entire mansion that would not have blushed to have had its secrets revealed.

The Prince of Wales arrived at about one in the morning.

He had been to the opera and to a ball afterwards, and wound up his evening in this aristocratic Pandemonium.

Almost as soon as he arrived he was joined by the lovely Henrietta.

The beauty was flattered by the attentions of a prince of the blood royal, and for a few days was faithful to him a great feat for her.

The prince retired with this lovely but licentious woman to a private apartment, where, having drank a considerable quantity, he speedily fell asleep, thus releasing his companion from her thraldom, who took advantage of the opportunity to flirt with the young Marquis of Athol, to whom she had a real partiality.

But it is not of the dalliance of the amorous, nor the acts of the drunkard, we would now speak.

Let us betake ourselves to the gambling saloon and see what is transacting there.

There are in it some ten or a dozen players, all eagerly engrossed in their treacherous pastime.

Prominent amongst the throng is a gentleman of elegant figure and strikingly handsome features, evidently a foreigner.

This gentleman is the young Count Antonio Riccioli, and the youthfulness of his appearance proves that he can hardly be more than one or two and twenty years of age.

Still, even in the spring-time of his life he has yielded to the wild infatuation and become a desperate gambler.

Fortune, however, is on his side to-night; he is winning largely.

The players around him, not so fortunate, sit with haggard and anxious looks, expecting a "turn in the luck."

Of course the count, being a great winner, the rest of the players are proportionately great losers.

Fortune seems on this particular night to have laid aside her usual fickleness and to have clung to the young Italian with great tenacity.

At every throw the gold flows into his purse in a fresh shower.

The rival players gnash their teeth and grow more and more pale with rage.

But fortune does not heed them; she still keeps on the side of the young count, whose cheeks are flushed, and whose dark eyes literally blaze with excitement.

The play continues.

Muttered oaths and execrations burst involuntarily from despairing lips at each fresh reverse.

Still the game—the mad infatuation—goes on.

The players grow more and more excited with their losses.

They talk wildly, they start up from their chairs like men possessed, and then sit excitedly down again, cursing the low stakes and clamouring for higher ones.

"A thousand pounds on the next throw!" shouted one.

"Two thousand!—three!"

"Agreed—agreed! Three thousand!" roared some six or eight voices, harsh and unnatural in their tones from intense excitement.

"Six, if you like!" cried the exultant count.

"No, no, three this time!—'tis an unlucky number for a winner, and changes luck!" shouted one of the players.

"Stake your money, gentlemen!"

Gold and notes poured in, in a confused heap, on the table.

A dead silence reigned around.

With bated breath, and riveted eyes, that seemed almost ready to start from their sockets, the players threw in turn.

The light rattle of the dice in the dice-box seemed to fall mockingly on their ears.

Suddenly an universal execration burst from their throats.

The count was once more the winner.

He had cleared at that last sweep 14,000*l.*

Sharp, angry growls, like the mutterings of wild beasts, mingled with curses, not loud but deep, were distinctly heard.

"This is more than chance!" cried one infuriate voice; "the dice must be loaded!"

This was not true, and the hot-blooded Italian started up.

"Who dare make that assertion?" he cried, laying his hand upon his sword, and looking round fiercely.

"No one!—no one!" cried Ashley Fordyce, a banker, who had lost ten thousand, and wished to go on till it pleased Fortune to allow him to win it back again. "It is a mistake!" he cried—"a word spoken in a moment of irritation, meaning nothing! We have perfect confidence in your honour, count, though we might be excused for accusing you of bribing the fickle goddess to-night—she is so d—nably loyal!"

"Shall we go on, then?" asked Antonio, appeased by the banker's words.

Some were for, and some against continuing to play.

With some it was impossible, they being completely cleaned out.

Those who were in that condition rose from their seats moodily, and departed.

In a short time four only of the players remained.

These were the banker, Lord Hubert Mansfield, Sir Slingsby Sleuforth, and the Marquis of Rockleigh.

They continued playing with the count with greater zest than ever.

But the result was always the same.

No matter how they varied the stakes, whether they were little or much, the Count Riccioli was invariably the winner.

When he rose from his seat it was as the winner of 30,000*l.*

He was almost intoxicated with success, and staggered from the saloon.

Seizing a goblet of iced water, he poured it down his burning throat.

Just at that moment the Marquis of Rockleigh might have been seen giving some directions to a beautiful, voluptuous-looking girl, with magnificently bright auburn locks, and a skin white as ivory.

The marquis was concise in what he said, and might have been seen to place a small white packet in her hand.

She laughed, showing a row of perfectly even pearly teeth, and replied:

"I understand, marquis; but I shall expect," she added, in a lower tone, "my share!"

"Depend upon it, *mia cara!*" said the marquis, as he left her side.

The count had scarcely ended his draught of iced water, when the beauty with the golden hair passed him.

"How long has the Count Antonio been a member of the 'temperance society?'" she inquired, looking over his shoulder with a most bewitching smile.

"Ever since Fortune told me she loved me," replied the young Italian, gaily.

The icy draught had calmed his nerves, and restored him in a great measure to himself.

"So, then, the fickle, blind coquette, has been kind to you, has she, count?"

"Oh, most kind: she has never once deserted me throughout the entire evening."

"I feel jealous, count," replied the beautiful Clarissa—such was her name—"that one woman should engross so much of your society; and feel inclined to dispute her pretensions!"

"What! would you quarrel with Fortune, because she has befriended me?" he asked.

"I quarrel with any woman who robs me of—— But there!" she exclaimed, stopping suddenly with a pretty coquettish air, she knew so well how to assume, "I shall make you vain. Farewell, count—I leave you to your new love, Fortune: take care she doesn't lead you into the dark, and lose you there."

She was about to pass on as she spoke, but the young Italian called her.

"Clarissa," he cried, "I want you: stay!"

The beauty returned a few steps.

"What do you want?" she inquired, pausing, and turning her bright blue eyes full upon him.

"I have done with Fortune for to-night," the count said, in a low tone: "I am about to transfer my affections to another divinity."

"To which, Cupid, or Venus, or——"

"To neither, but Clarissa!" he replied, insinuatingly.

"Ho, ho!" she laughed, in a pretty mocking tone. "Sated with one mistress, you come now to me; do you wish me to receive you?"

"I wish you to love me, Clarissa!"

"Our tastes will not agree: I do not always drink the beverage of brutes," she said, laughingly.

"Nor I, my charmer!" said the count. "My brain was on fire, that is why I swallowed this icy draught. Champagne—I suppose you drink that?"

"Sometimes," laughed Clarissa, mischievously.

"Are we friends, then?"

"Of course!"

"Partners?"

"Decidedly!"

"In champagne and—love?" added the count, throwing his arm round his companion.

"Oh, yes, in love, of course! What would the world be without it?" she replied, as she leant her beautiful head upon the young man's shoulder.

"Come, then!" cried the count, drawing the yielding form of Clarissa more closely to him; "let us forget the world, whilst we devote ourselves for the hour that passes over us to Love and Wine!"

As he uttered these words, the young Italian, his arm encircling the white throat of the fair Circe, and her arm thrown around him, disappeared down the corridor and entered one of the private apartments of which each member had a separate one.

The chamber they went into was luxuriously furnished—a couch, bed and bath, being the principal adjuncts to its comfort as well as elegance.

The young count, flushed with his great success at play, was now in the full vein to enjoy a few hours' amorous dalliance with the lovely but dangerous woman at his side; whilst she, like a gilded snake, drew closer and closer till her folds should be securely wound around the unsuspecting victim.

Acting upon the principle already stated as peculiar to this establishment, that each member should wait upon himself, Clarissa inquired softly as the count threw himself upon the couch, whether she should be his Ganymede, his cup-bearer?

"Yes, *belissima!*" he replied. "Let us have fruit and wine."

He called after her as she was leaving the room:

"Don't forget some cigars as well, Clarissa."

The treacherous beauty smiled a honeyed smile, and disappeared.

As she passed along the corridor, she was met by the Marquis of Rockleigh.

"Well, Clarissa, does the fish bite?"

"Yes, marquis; I am going now for the bait; he will be in the landing net shortly," she laughed.

"Good girl!" whispered the marquis, as he passed on.

In a very short space of time, Clarissa returned with two bottles of champagne and a small basket of delicious fruit.

She glided into the room like a Hebe, and her smiles were full of light and love—treacherous beacons, shining but to betray—as she placed the luxuries she had brought with her on the table.

"Now, count," she said, "if I am to be your Ganymede, you must draw your own corks."

She laughed as she spoke, and pointed to the long-necked champagne bottles at the same time.

The count returned her laugh, and rose acquiescently to liberate the inspiring beverage from its confinement.

In a moment a sharp *pop!* peculiar to the opening of a champagne bottle was heard, and the creamy vintage glittered in the glasses.

"To love and wine!" cried the count, as he drained his glass.

"To wine and love!" echoed the false beauty, as she emptied hers.

Several similar draughts followed, and the young Italian, lighting a cigar and lolling back dreamily on the luxurious couch he occupied, gave himself up to the witcheries of his fair companion.

There was a piano in the room, and Clarissa—who was as educated and accomplished as she was abandoned—sang to him with her clear soprano voice some of the choicest operatic *morceaux* till the count was enthralled beneath the spell of melting sounds, and felt as though he had wandered into the regions of Elysium.

Almost unconsciously he had drank the sweet tones of Clarissa's voice and the champagne together.

The bottle was empty, and he was in a delicious halo of happiness without being conscious of the cause.

"Come, Antonio!" cried the enchantress, as she finished a grand *scena* and started up from the piano. "Whilst I have been singing, you have been drinking, and—why, I declare the bottle is empty!" she exclaimed, in a merry tone of surprise. "No wonder you could listen so patiently to my discord with such a composer at your elbow."

"Nay, Clarissa, it is quite the contrary," said the count, warmly; "your voice has charmed me so entirely that I have emptied the bottle in a kind of dream, in which I knew not what I did."

"But what is to become of me?" she inquired, dolefully.

"You forget, sweetheart, there is another bottle."

"True, dearest! How stupid I am!"

How lovely, you mean! But I will atone for my absence of mind," cried the count; and rising as he spoke, he seized the remaining bottle, and after a slight effort, again the *pop!* was heard.

While thus engaged he did not observe his companion quickly empty the contents of a small white paper into his glass.

Again the goblets were filled and emptied.

"I cannot sing any more to night," said Clarissa.

"You have sang enough," said the count. "I should not wish to trespass further upon that lovely voice of yours. Come and sit by me."

Clarissa obeyed; and seating herself on the couch by the count's side, she glided her arm under his head, and supported him much in the same manner as a mother might have sustained her son.

The Italian's eyes seemed heavier in their expression than they had been a few moments before.

"Never be jealous, my Clarissa," he said, in a dreamy voice, "of any man who only courts Fortune. Remember, if he does so, it is that he may share her favours with the woman he really loves."

"I am not jealous, dearest," she murmured, as she pressed her cheek to his. "I did not mean it. But you have been successful—very successful—to-night, love, have you not?" she asked, in a soft, winning voice.

"Yes, dearest: I have won thirty thousand pounds."

"Great heavens! what a sum!" she exclaimed.

"Here," said the count, in a tone that was thick, drowsy, and indistinct, as he with some difficulty took from his pocket a morocco leather case—"here is that which will, I hope, reconcile you to Fortune."

As he spoke, he disentangled a handful of bank-notes from the mass, and thrust them into Clarissa's hand.

He then replaced the case in his pocket.

"They are for you, my fair songstress," he said, "though you deserve much more than that for the pleasure you have afforded me."

"Oh, no!" returned Clarissa, with all the assumed warmth of the liveliest gratitude, "it is you who are so generous—I am far overpaid."

As she spoke, she gazed earnestly at his eyes, from which the consciousness was rapidly departing.

"You are growing drowsy, Antonio!" she said, pressing her lips to his.

"Yes, love; y-es—I—I think I am," he murmured in scarcely intelligible accents. "Phew! the room is hot! I—I——"

"You had better sleep, love!" said the fair snake, pressing another treacherous kiss upon his lips.

"Y-es, y-es—sleep—slee——"

His eyes closed, his head fell forward on his breast, and as the white arm was withdrawn from beneath the young man's head, it lay motionless on the pillow.

The drug had taken effect.

He was utterly insensible.

Clarissa drank another glass of champagne, and then opened the door.

The Marquis of Rockleigh entered.

"Is he quiet?" he asked.

"Still as death! Judge for yourself."

"You have done your work skilfully!" exclaimed the marquis.

"And my reward?"

"Shall be in proportion to your services," he answered.

CHAPTER CCII.

CAPTAIN HAWK AND LORD HARCLIFFE WAKE FROM A STRANGE DREAM.—VOICES FROM THE CUPBOARD.—THE MOVING PARTITION.—THE HIGHWAYMEN FIND THEMSELVES IN THE RED ROOM.—THE STRANGE EVENTS THAT OCCURRED THERE.

Our heroes, tired out with the excitement they had previously undergone, slept profoundly for several hours.

Suddenly Captain Hawk started up as from the influence of some unquiet dream.

He looked around him.

It was becoming quite light.

For a moment he was a little bewildered at the strange place in which he found himself.

But his brains were of that kind that speedily recover themselves, and he immediately remembered all the circumstances that had led them to the shelter of "*the* Retreat."

He rose and approached the window.

It was then, almost at the same moment, Lord Harcliffe also started from his slumber.

Their waking was nearly identical.

It was singular that both awoke with a start.

"Did anything alarm you?" inquired Captain Hawk of his friend, fancying he observed in his countenance some traces of excitement.

"Nothing of any consequence; but still, has anything occurred to excite *your* suspicions?" he suddenly asked, instead of answering his comrade's question.

"Why do you ask?"

"You look scared."

"Perhaps so—I awoke from a disagreeable dream."

"How strange!—so did I."

"What might have been the subject?"

"Death—murder!"

"Is it possible?"

"Yes. It was most vivid."

"And where was the scene of this horror?"

Lord Harcliffe rose, and, laying his hand upon his friend's arm, pointed to the wall of the room, and sinking his voice to a whisper, exclaimed:

"The next room!"

"The *Red Chamber?*"

"Yes."

"This is most extraordinary!" ejaculated Captain Hawk—"it was there the scenes of my dream passed! Were it not now broad daylight, I should think this unanimity in our dreams was ominous."

"You mean that some deed of blood was transpiring within these walls?"

"Yes."

They listened.

All was still.

A distant clock struck three.

Captain Hawk quietly unbolted the door and looked out on to the landing.

The gray dawn of morning did not penetrate there.

The window was closed and barred by shutters.

He cautiously advanced and looked over the balusters.

All was buried in obscurity.

No sounds were heard.

The visitors had either departed or retired to rest.

The profoundest silence reigned around.

Suddenly whispered words fell upon his ear from below.

He listened intently, but, beyond a faint murmur, nothing reached him.

Presently the sound of cautious footsteps was heard.

"Some one is approaching," whispered Lord Harcliffe.

"I think so," said Captain Hawk, in a low tone. "Hush!"

The sounds became gradually more and more audible, and a dim light shot upwards.

"We are not safe here," said the captain; "let us return to our chamber."

They re-entered, and closing the door noiselessly, bolted it.

They were not aware that on the outside of this room no suspicion of there being any door at all would have been entertained by a stranger unacquainted with the fact, so closely did it fit into and assimilate with the adjoining panelling.

Having bolted themselves in, they listened.

But not the vestige of a sound reached their ears.

Every room in the house was rendered *mute* by padding.

While the highwaymen were wondering at the strange silence a voice fell upon their ears that seemed to proceed almost from the cupboard in a corner of the room they occupied.

Captain Hawk hastily approached this receptacle, and quietly opened the door.

The cupboard was empty, but at the bottom of one of its sides a bright ray of light streamed through from the other side.

"See," said the captain, pointing to the light, "there is some one in the next room—*the Red Room.* Is it possible that our dream is going to be realised?"

"We shall probably discover that," returned Lord Harcliffe. "Where light can enter, sound can."

"Let us listen."

The captain threw himself on the ground, and placing his ear as close as possible to the opening at the bottom of the cupboard, found to his great satisfaction that he could hear with tolerable distinctness.

There appeared to be several in the room.

"Phew!" exclaimed one, "he's heavier than I expected."

"Yes," rejoined another—"heavy with our gold."

"Well, never mind; let us place him on the bed—he'll be lighter before long," said a third.

This direction, from the creaking of the bedstead, appeared to have been complied with.

"How drunk he is!" remarked the first speaker.

"All the better," replied another.

"He looks quite apoplectic!"

"He may die in a fit—*people do sometimes!*"

These words were said in a meaning tone, though from the words reaching the ear of the captain in an indistinct manner, he lost their significancy.

"Let him lie there," said one; "he'll be better when he wakes."

"No doubt of it!"

Having uttered these words, the three persons left the Red Room, fastening the door after them.

All was once more silent.

"What think you of this?" inquired Lord Harcliffe.

"I scarcely know," returned his comrade. "It may be nothing more than one of the members—a youthful one probably—dead drunk."

"It is by no means unlikely," replied his lordship. "These youthful scions of nobility are frequently great tipplers."

"If so, then our terrible dreams have been delusive, and have deceived us."

"I should be inclined to think so. Surely in a magnificent establishment like this is, deliberate and cold-blooded assassinations could not take place in the broad light of day."

"This is doubtless some young gentleman who has made too free with the bottle, and who is quietly put to bed to sleep off the effects."

At this moment a peculiar sound reached their ears.

It was not loud, but so striking as to arrest their attention.

It was precisely such a sound as the winding up of a jack or a clock would produce.

"Hark!" ejaculated Captain Hawk, "do you hear that?"

"Yes, distinctly: click—click—click! What does it mean?"

"It sounds like the action of machinery."

The two highwaymen looked at each other.

They had heard of strange contrivances to put people out of the world, and were no strangers to those dark deeds that were enacted at times almost under the very eyes of the world, undetected and often unsuspected.

They did not like this sound.

Suddenly it struck Captain Hawk that from the circumstance of the light appearing underneath the cupboard side, it was possible the side itself might not be a fixture, but that there might be some means of egress through into the next room.

"Light the candle, Harcliffe," he said; "I am quite anxious to see what is going on in the adjoining chamber."

"The *Red Room?*"

"Ay, the Red Room," echoed the captain, as he received the wax taper from his comrade, and proceeded to examine the interior of the cupboard.

There seemed no signs of any opening.

"Is there any outlet?" inquired Lord Harcliffe.

"None whatever," answered the captain.

Still the click—click—click! went on.

The highwayman was about to give up his search as fruitless, when a peculiar round knob, that looked almost like a knot in the wood, caught his eye.

"Ha!" he exclaimed, "what is this?"

"What?" inquired his lordship.

"This knob," answered the captain, pointing to it as he spoke. "I have known very important results achieved by simply pressing a small piece of wood like that with your knuckle."

"Let us see," said Lord Harcliffe, pressing the knob indicated.

"Well, does it move?" inquired Captain Hawk.

"It yields, I think, to my pressure," returned Lord Harcliffe.

"Continue it, then; we shall see what will come of it," said Captain Hawk.

"See, see!" cried his lordship, as the side of the cupboard gradually ascended like a shutter in a groove.

"We have found our way into the Red Room, at least!" the captain exclaimed, energetically "And now to examine its mysteries."

As he spoke, he examined the aperture which had thus unexpectedly disclosed itself.

It was evidently a cupboard.

The cupboard of one room opened into the cupboard of the other.

Captain Hawk entered, bearing the light.

"Is the door fastened?" inquired Lord Harcliffe.

"No," answered the captain, gently, as he turned the handle and thrust it open.

The room was pitch dark, the shutters of the window being evidently tightly closed, and the gloomy hue that pervaded it gave it an ominous and terrible appearance, if only from the associations it suggested.

Suddenly Lord Harcliffe uttered an exclamation.

"See—see!" he cried.

"What?" inquired Captain Hawk, whose eyes were roaming round the room.

"There!—there!" continued his lordship, excitedly. "The sound we heard is now explained!" He pointed to the bed as he spoke, on which lay the senseless form of the Count Antonio Riccioli.

"Good Heaven, yes!" returned the captain, in a tone of horror, as he glanced towards it.

The click—click—click! still continued, and at each sound the top of the bed slowly, almost imperceptibly, but surely descended in its progress towards the unconscious sleeper.

"What d—d villany is this?" cried the captain. "Well may they call this the Red Room! But we'll disappoint these cowardly assassins!"

As he spoke, he advanced hastily, and dragged the unconscious young man from his fatal position.

A few moments more, and he would have been beyond the power of rescue.

He was utterly unconscious, and the captain had time to make a brief examination of this horrible *Bed of Death* before it had quite descended.

The top was solid, heavy, and massive.

The under portion of the top was padded and quilted, so that when it had completely descended it would have been like one bed pressing upon another.

Of course escape for the poor victim between them, would have been utterly impossible.

"Wretches!" exclaimed the highwaymen, in tones of strong indignation.

"I can understand a man killing another in self-defence or under the influence of strong passion or excitement," said Captain Hawk, "and pardon him, but to deliberately condemn a poor wretch to this horrible fate, is more than I can endure to think of!"

"The remorseless fiends!" exclaimed Lord Harcliffe, in tones of extreme indignation.

"At all events, we shall disappoint the expectations of these murderers," said the captain, as he raised the body of the unconscious young man, and carried it into the adjoining room.

The click—click! had ceased, the bed had descended, and the deed of destruction was supposed to be accomplished.

At the end of about a quarter of an hour, the click—click! of the machinery of this infernal engine of destruction was again audible, and slowly the top of the bed began to re-ascend till it assumed its usual position.

The young Italian was still utterly unconscious.

"He is a foreigner evidently," said Lord Harcliffe.

"What motive do you assign for this horrible attempt?" inquired Captain Hawk.

"I imagine gold to be at the bottom of it. This young man, who seems to be of some rank, has either won too much last night, or else he is a pigeon worth destroying for the sake of his feathers," answered Lord Harcliffe. "His wine has evidently been drugged."

"Let us see what wealth he has about him," said Captain Hawk; "it will be safer with us for the present than with him."

It took but a second to abstract the count's leather pocket-book in which were the whole of his winnings, minus the sum (about £500) which he had given to the treacherous Clarissa.

After making a rapid calculation, there was found to be nearly £30,000.

"What enormous sums are staked in these places!" said Captain Hawk.

"Yes indeed!" replied Lord Harcliffe. "The game carried on here is indeed a game of life and death!"

Captain Hawk, having closed the cupboard door in the Red Room and left everything exactly as before, allowed the partition in the cupboard to descend to its former place.

Still, both he and Lord Harcliffe kept their ears open for the slightest sound of approach.

No one, however, came.

The count still continued in his heavy slumber.

His face was pale as marble and his lips were covered with a light froth.

"I don't like the look of this," said the captain.

"Nor I," said Lord Harcliffe. "I wonder whether it is possible to procure a draught of iced water?"

"The attempt must be made. I'll go in search at all events," replied Captain Hawk.

"And in the meantime I'll keep watch," returned his comrade.

The search of the captain through the deserted rooms was successful.

He not only discovered a pitcher of cool spring water, but also a vessel containing ice.

These were invaluable, and were immediately conveyed to the upper story.

By dint of keeping the young man's head constantly bathed with the cool and refreshing liquid, consciousness was gradually restored.

A draught of iced orangeade completed the cure, and the count was able to recall the past with perfect distinctness.

He was then informed by our heroes of the fate intended for him, and how narrowly he had escaped a fearful death.

The young Italian was at first incredulous, but on Captain Hawk presenting him with the pocket-book containing his money, and suggesting the reason of such an attempt being made, the count, reverting to his enormous winnings of the previous night, coincided with him, and warmly thanked both him and Lord Harcliffe for his preservation.

"I should rejoice," exclaimed the captain, "to catch these cowardly murderers in their own trap; and I think, with your assistance," he added, turning to the count, "we shall be enabled to do so."

"Any help I can afford you," answered the young nobleman, "you may rely upon."

"Quick, then!" cried the captain, in his usual practical manner. "Remove your money from your pocket-book and give me the latter."

"Empty?"

"Empty."

This being done, Captain Hawk placed in it scraps of paper until it was of the same bulk and weight as before.

He then returned the pocket-book to the count.

"Place it once more in your pocket, and now go and lie down again upon that bed," he said.

"On that bed?" echoed the young man, in dismay.

"Yes."

"But——"

"Excuse me; I will briefly explain. These wretches will return, of course, expecting to find your lifeless body extended upon that bed. The object of their visit will be to obtain possession of the money you possess."

"Yes."

"Let them take it, or rather let them take the pocket-book—the money will be beyond their reach. Before they can discover their mistake you will be in a place of safety, and then, if the worst comes to the

[CAPTAIN HAWK PLAYS THE OFFICERS A TRICK.]

worst, and they find out you are alive, here are a couple of good swords and stout arms at your service.

Captain Hawk listened, and hastily informed the count that the would-be murderers were returning.

"Quick—quick!" he cried, "we shall not have a moment to lose!"

The aperture in the cupboard was speedily opened, and the count placed upon the bed.

The highwaymen, with their swords drawn, then retired to the cupboard, through the partly open door of which they kept good watch.

Presently the door of the room cautiously opened, and the Marquis of Rockleigh, followed by three others, appeared.

The marquis carried but one light, and as he appeared upon the threshold he gave the taper to one of his companions to hold.

Our heroes were thus enabled from their retreat to catch a distinct view of the faces of these four individuals.

The marquis with a light step approached the bed, and at once proceeded to search for the pocket-book.

This was speedily found.

The marquis uttered an exclamation of satisfaction as he grasped the treasure for which he imagined he had dyed his hands in blood, and was about to return, when he paused, and feeling his way with his hand in the obscurity, he placed his palm upon the count's forehead, which, from repeated ablution with iced water, was as cold as that element.

This also seemed satisfactory, and the party then quitted the room.

At the same moment a noise in the adjoining chamber (their own room) attracted their attention.

"Hush!—be still!" whispered the captain to the count, who was extended on the bed. "I will call you if all is safe."

On entering their apartment, to their surprise they found Pharoah, who smilingly inquired what sort of a night they had passed, and what mysteries they had discovered in the Red Chamber.

"Enough," answered Captain Hawk, in an indignant tone, "to prove that this place, with all its splendour, is nothing more nor less than a den of murderers!"

"Captain!" exclaimed Pharoah, with astonishment.

"It is true, Pharoah," said Lord Harcliffe. "Listen to me."

And he at once gave his faithful friend a rapid and concise account of the events that had lately transpired.

Pharoah listened attentively, and then said to his lordship:

"I hope you acquit me of all blame in this, or of being a conniver at these villanies."

"Perfectly," answered Lord Harcliffe.

"That I suspected something from the red colour of the carpet, walls, and furniture of the adjoining room I admit, but I never suspected the deliberate and deadly use to which it was applied; I did not, my lord, as I hope for mercy!" said Pharoah, earnestly.

"I believe you, Pharoah," replied his lordship, "because I think you too much attached to me to deceive me."

"And the count, then, is safe?"

"Perfectly."

"Where is he now?"

"On the bed in the next room. Not knowing it was you, we advised him to remain there till we called him."

"I think we may release him now from a chamber so full of terrible associations," said Captain Hawk.

"Decidedly!" replied Lord Harcliffe.

Captain Hawk walked towards the cupboard for the purpose of calling the count, when suddenly a sound like the falling of a trap-door was heard, and at the same instant a wild, piercing scream of terror, that almost chilled their blood to hear, burst from a woman's lips in the darkness of the Red Chamber.

"Good Heaven! What's that?" exclaimed Captain Hawk, as he seized the wax taper and rushed, sword in hand, into the adjoining room, followed by Lord Harcliffe and Pharoah.

They rushed towards the bed, in dread anticipation of some dire event, and now a new phase in the catalogue of horrors presented itself.

The body of the bed had entirely disappeared, and in its place was a yawning chasm, or immense well, from which ascended a stagnant and noisome odour.

They stood for an instant with riveted eyes, gazing horror-struck at this unexpected sight.

The fate of the unfortunate young man who had been resting on the bed must have been inevitable.

The bed was in reality a trap by which, the work of death being accomplished, the body of the victim was consigned to the dark abyss beneath.

"But the cry was not that of a man, but of a woman!" remarked Pharoah.

"It was so," said Captain Hawk; "but I am still utterly at a loss to conjecture——"

"I can explain," said a voice at his elbow which he at once recognised as that of the count.

He started back as though a dead man had spoken to him, and turned suddenly.

It was no spectre, but the count himself who stood before him.

"It was a woman's cry you heard," he said.

"What woman?"

"A fair traitress, known as Clarissa, as beautiful as she was abandoned," explained the count. "She laid a snare for me, into which she has fallen herself."

As he spoke, he pointed to the dark chasm in the bedstead.

"Was it she, then, who has met her death thus?" inquired Pharoah.

"It was."

"Still I do not understand," said Captain Hawk "how——"

"I will explain," returned the count. "When the men who sought my life departed, this remorseless woman, who had followed them, entered.

"I guessed her motive—plunder. She had come to drag the ring from my dead finger.

"It was a valuable emerald that had excited her cupidity.

"I heard the door open softly, and recognised her step as she entered.

"I moved noiselessly from the bed as she approached, and heard her breathe deeply and with evident trepidation as she felt for my body.

"Not discovering it as she expected, she stepped on to the bed, and leant over it, in anxious search.

"Just at that moment the trap, worked by machinery below, was loosed from its fastenings, and the miserable wretch met with an untimely but deserved death in the terrible abyss into which she fell with the cry of horror on her lips and hopeless despair in her heart."

"It is indeed an awful doom," said Captain Hawk, "and I feel very much inclined to wish that those four gentlemanly murderers could share a similar fate."

"They would richly deserve it," acquiesced Lord Harcliffe. "But hark!" he exclaimed, suddenly.

They all listened as a grating sound, like the turning of a windlass, caught their ears.

In a few moments the trap began to rise, and in a very short space of time the bed was restored to its original place.

No sign or trace of the awful catastrophe was left behind.

And from that room no passing breath of that awful death shriek had passed beyond its walls.

CHAPTER CCIII.

THE HIGHWAYMEN, HAVING PRESERVED THE INTENDED VICTIM, RESOLVE TO VICTIMISE THE ASSASSINS. — A STRANGE IDEA. — CAPTAIN HAWK AND LORD HARCLIFFE TURN DETECTIVES, AND NET A THOUSAND EACH BY THE UNDERTAKING.

THEY returned to the room they had previously occupied, and then Captain Hawk, drawing Pharoah aside addressed him thus:

"You know that in our profession we look upon mankind as our lawful prey; but with such men as these, who would have first robbed and then murdered this young foreigner——"

"The Count Antonio Riccioli," added Pharoah.

"For such," continued the captain, "I have no mercy. Had I my will, they should be now resting with that miserable woman at the bottom of the well; but since that cannot be, I am resolved they shall pay for their crimes; at the same time I do not wish to compromise you, who have given us shelter in our hour of need; and why I mention this to you is to prepare you for anything I and my comrade may do, so that with your connivance and assistance we may not only secure the safety of the Count Riccioli, but make these cold-blooded gentlemen remember the *Red Room* for the rest of their lives."

"You may depend upon me, captain," said Pharoah. "If I can assist you, command me."

"And you may also depend," said Captain Hawk, "that any assistance you can render us shall never be betrayed."

They were then joined by Lord Harcliffe, and the three conversed together in low tones, the count having fallen into a doze.

We will leave them in close conversation, while we follow the four gamblers after their departure from the Red Chamber.

Their first operation was to loosen the trap, and, as they thought, get rid of the body of their victim, little thinking who it was that had fallen into the stagnant depths.

This done, and the trap restored to its proper position, they returned to the gaming saloon, exulting in the success of their atrocious scheme, to reimburse themselves for their individual losses.

They felt no remorse for their deed, but their features were pale and haggard in the morning light, and they threw themselves listlessly into their chairs, watching the marquis as he drew forth the pocket-book.

"Ha, ha!" laughed that nobleman, spitefully, as he placed the book on the table, "the Count Riccioli must have been intoxicated with his good fortune. He little guessed what his luck would cost him!"

"Divide the money, marquis, as quickly as possible," exclaimed the banker, "and let us get to bed; my head is splitting, and I have an early appointment."

"It will not detain us long," the marquis said, as he unclasped the bulky book.

Every eye eagerly watched as the contents were emptied on the table.

An observer of the scene might have remarked how the riveted pupils dilated at those contents.

"Why, d—nation!" cried the marquis, "what is here?"

"Ay, what?" they all exclaimed, excitedly.

"A mass of old papers!" burst out the banker—"not a note or a cheque, it appears to me!"

"This is some infernal trick!" the marquis shouted, hoarsely, turning pale with rage.

"Or some equally infernal piece of stupidity!" added Lord Hubert Mansfield. "For security's sake the Italian may have concealed the money in his pockets, and stuffed his pocket-book with those counterfeits!"

"And now he has descended into the depths of the well with all his money with him," growled Sir Slingsby Sleuforth.

"And all our labour has been lost!" cried Lord Hubert.

A universal growl of baffled rage burst from the lips of all.

"We ought not to have trusted to that pocket-book, marquis," said Ashley Fordyce; "the body ought to have been searched before it was committed to the well; that was my counsel, only you were so confident."

"Of course now there is not the remotest hope of our recovering our money," Sir Slingsby Sleuforth exclaimed, in a tone of the highest vexation.

"Considering it lies at the bottom of the well, I should think not," answered the marquis, in a spiteful and sarcastic tone at the implied reproaches levelled at him.

"Thirty thousand pounds swallowed up," cried Lord Hubert, wrathfully, "that we might have had for the mere trouble of taking! How cursedly vexatious!"

"Well, gentlemen, if we sit here till to-night execrating our losses, it will not mend the matter in the least," said the marquis. "I therefore propose that we separate for the present, first passing a resolution that the next body we consign to the well be previously searched."

The ironical tone of the marquis served still further to irritate the ruffled tempers of his three companions, and Lord Hubert replied, angrily:

"If you think it a matter of jest, marquis, to lose five thousand pounds, I do not!"

"Nor I—nor I!" exclaimed the rest.

"Psha!" cried the marquis, contemptuously. "Five thousand pounds! what is that to rich men?"

"It is so much that we are quite justified in calling you to account for your obstinate stupidity in loosing the trap before searching the body. It was entirely your fault, and we were fools to be guided by one who is a bigger fool than any of us."

"Ay—ay!" they all vociferated, wrathfully.

"What!" cried the marquis, his brow darkening with passion. "Do you call me fool?"

"We do!"

The nobleman's sword flew from its scabbard.

"You shall maintain your words at your swords' points! I allow no man to call me fool! Lord Hubert, yours was the tongue that first vilified me! Defend yourself!"

Lord Mansfield drew, as did also his companions.

The swords of the noblemen crossed; a fierce and angry light flashed from their bloodshot eyes.

From the vindictive expression on their features, it was probable blood would be spilt.

"Look to yourself!" shouted the marquis, as he lunged desperately at Lord Hubert, who parried his thrust, and in return passed his sword through the sleeve of his antagonist's sword-arm.

This seemed, if possible, to increase their animosity, and stimulate them to continue.

"Come again!" cried the marquis. "*En garde!*"

Once more their swords met.

Thrusts were again given, parried, and returned, when suddenly there came at the door—

Three distinct knocks.

The combatants paused.

Each looked at the other doubtfully and somewhat apprehensively.

And yet the cause of these expressions was simply a knock at the door.

But then there was a great *peculiarity* about the knocks.

They were slow, firm, and impressive.

The banker was the first to speak.

"Who can it be?" he said, in a whisper.

"Let us open the door and see," suggested Lord Hubert.

"No!" exclaimed the marquis, imperiously, "let the knocker, whoever he be, open for himself! We are not lacqueys! Seat yourselves, gentlemen!" he cried.

The tone of the marquis seemed to reassure his companions, and to give weight to his words, as they sheathed their swords and did as he directed.

At this moment the three knocks were repeated louder than before.

"Come in!" called out the marquis.

The door opened instantly, and two men in cloaks appeared upon the threshold.

They entered silently, with a stern, cold expression on their pale features, where determination sat in every line.

One of them coolly locked the door, and, having done this, they advanced with a firm and deliberate step to the table where the four gentlemen, in mute surprise and no little apprehension, sat gazing at them, and wondering what their presence foreboded.

Our readers will scarcely require telling that the new-comers were Captain Hawk and Lord Harcliffe.

They remained for a few moments gazing at the gentlemen in silence.

This scrutiny was unbearable, and at last the Marquis of Rockleigh spoke.

"Who are you?—and what is your business here?" he inquired.

"We are here," answered Captain Hawk, in a stern voice, "to inquire into the particulars of a murder that has been committed within these walls."

Could a spectator have looked into the hearts of the four individuals to whom these words were addressed, he would have seen them contract and throb violently.

Their cheeks grew pale as they echoed, in faltering tones:

"Murder!"

"Ay, murder—here in this house! this very night!"

The marquis, who possessed the strongest nerves of the party, exclaimed, with assumed surprise:

"Murder! I do not understand you; you must be mistaken. This is a private dwelling, not a den of murder. We are gentlemen; all are friends here."

"I suppose, then," said Captain Hawk, "that the contest you were engaged in, and which our knocking at the door put an end to, was a *friendly* contest to attest the love you bear each other?"

"It was a trial of skill, and nothing more," answered the marquis. "There was not a drop of bad blood in the encounter."

"You are not speaking the truth, sir!" said the captain, sternly.

"How? Do you dare to give me the lie?" cried the marquis, angrily.

"I dare to give any man the lie, when he utters a lie," answered Captain Hawk, calmly and impressively.

"You know as well as I do, marquis," he continued, "that the cause of quarrel was a large sum of money which an imprudent act on your part has caused to be lost."

At this piece of information, which everyone present knew to be true, there was an awkward pause of silence.

"Come now, gentlemen," the captain went on, "we want the truth—we must have the truth! Where is the body of the Count Antonio Riccioli?"

There was another pause, whilst Captain Hawk earnestly scanned the countenances of those he addressed.

"The Count Riccioli is not here," said Lord Mansfield, at length.

"He has been here to-night?" remarked the captain, interrogatively.

"I believe he has."

"You know he has."

"At all events, he is not here now. He left the house long since."

"He did *not* leave the house."

"You seem acquainted with every particular that transpires within these walls," said the **marquis**, in a tone of irony.

"I am perfectly acquainted with everything," answered the captain, definitely.

"Who are you?" inquired the marquis.

"You will know in good time; but first let *me* know respecting the count."

"I have told you I know nothing of him."

"Some of these gentlemen—your friends—may."

"No—no!"

No one knew anything of him.

"It seems to me then," continued Captain Hawk, "that I am better informed than any of you, since I can at this moment tell you where he is."

"We are not the count's keepers, neither are we in any way responsible for him," said the Marquis of Rockleigh, petulantly.

"Your ideas, marquis," Captain Hawk went on, quietly, "are peculiar on certain points."

"How peculiar?"

"I suppose you are aware that if a man assists in the destruction of another, he is responsible for that man's death?"

"But what has this to do with me? I have destroyed no one."

"Yes, you have destroyed the Count Antonio Riccioli. For the means you employed, I refer you to the *Bed of Death in the Red Chamber at the top of this house!*"

The countenances of all grew pale at this terrible accusation.

The marquis alone called *bravado* to his aid, and seemed desperately resolved to dispute the crime imputed.

"Do you dare accuse me of murder?" he inquired, loftily.

"I dare accuse you of murder! Your accomplice has betrayed you, marquis. You should never trust a woman."

"A woman?"

"Yes. Clarissa Lafitte has betrayed you. She confessed to me and my colleague that she drugged the count's wine, and that, while in a state of insensibility, he was placed upon the murder-bed in the *Red Room*, from whence, by means of a trap, he was launched into the depths beneath, to wake in eternity."

These words, delivered with the most impressive earnestness, fell like words of fire upon the ears and hearts of the listeners.

They wavered in their seats like drunken men, and reeled as if they would have fallen.

Captain Hawk continued:

"If I had had any previous doubts of your guilt, I should have none now; your own looks are your accusers, and justify me in denouncing you, Marquis of Rockleigh, and you, Lord Hubert Mansfield, and you, Sir Slingsby Sleuforth, and you, Ashley Fordyce, as four murderers whom I and my comrade are here to arrest!"

As the captain uttered these words, both he and Lord Harcliffe drew their pistols.

There was a general panic amongst the guilty party at this announcement.

The four murderers started to their feet, and appeared inclined to make a desperate attempt to escape, but the stern voice of Captain Hawk restrained them.

"Stay!" he cried, in a commanding tone.

Everyone was still.

"At the first attempt on the part of anyone to leave this room, we fire!"

"Do you imagine we shall allow ourselves to be taken quietly by two men, without resistance?" the marquis exclaimed, excitedly.

"Your resistance would be worse than useless," returned the captain. "I have but to give a signal, and you would be overpowered by numbers in a moment."

The gentlemen looked at one another.

The captain followed up his advantage.

"You will find it better for yourselves to make no attempt to hinder us in the performance of our duty," he said.

"And that duty is?" remarked the marquis, gloomily.

"To arrest you. I told you so."

"Then you are——"

"Detective officers from Bow Street."

This was a crisis, and the four guilty gentlemen felt the seriousness of their position.

The banker, leaning over to Lord Mansfield, said in a low voice to him:

"These fellows are mercenary, and will not refuse a bribe. Put it to the test."

Lord Hubert accordingly whispered to Sir Slingsby, who rapidly communicated with the marquis.

During this our heroes appeared to be occupied with examining the primings of their pistols.

As drowning men will catch frantically at straws, so the four gentlemen, thus caught in a net, were ready to adopt any means to deliver themselves from the arm of the law which they felt was suspended over them.

Their common danger had entirely quashed their antagonism, and they were now mutual in their thoughts and desires.

"Gentlemen," at length said the marquis, addressing the highwaymen, after a brief consultation with his friends, "it is not our wish to thwart you in the execution of your duty; at the same time, we can make it very well worth your while to close your eyes. We are all rich men. Do you understand?"

"Perfectly," replied Captain Hawk. "You are willing to pay us handsomely for voluntary blindness."

"We are. What will you take to pass this matter over?"

"What will you give?"

There was a slight pause, and then the Marquis of Rockleigh replied:

"I promise, on my own account and on that of my friends here, that if you will be silent, and take no further notice of this unfortunate affair. you shall both receive from each of us £200."

"That will be £800 each," said Captain Hawk, meditatively.

"Well, do you accept the terms?" inquired the marquis.

"You must make it a thousand, and then I think we can make it a bargain," answered the captain.

It was not a time to haggle over a hundred or so.

Life was sweet, and they were willing to purchase it at the cheap rate of £500 per head.

"We agree," cried the marquis.

"You must let us have your cheques for the amount, and we will take our departure immediately," said Captain Hawk.

"Certainly," answered the marquis; "you shall have them this instant."

A pen and ink were brought from the sideboard, and the requisite cheques were respectively written and handed to the supposed detectives, who placed them carefully in their pockets.

"But," remarked the marquis, suddenly, "this woman—this Clarissa, if she has betrayed us once, she may do so again. How is she to be secured?"

"I can answer for her," replied the captain. "You need be under no apprehensions on her account. I promise you her lips will never again open to betray you, though you were to live till Doomsday."

"Then we may consider the conference terminated?"

"Quite. Good morning, gentlemen."

"Good morning."

With these parting salutations the highwaymen left the room, closing the door behind them.

The four gentlemen remained in their seats, until the banging of the street-door seemed to announce the departure of the officers.

Then, with feelings of intense relief, they rose.

At the same moment Pharoah entered.

He was, of course, supposed to know nothing of what had occurred.

These gentlemen little imagined that when the street-door slammed no one went out of it.

Had they seen the two fictitious detectives quietly ascend the stairs and join the murdered victim in the topmost apartment, they might have been impressed with the idea that in some miraculous manner they had been hoaxed.

No such suspicion, however, occurred to them.

Pharoah's manner was, as usual, perfectly unembarrassed, calm, and attentive.

"Do you require anything, gentlemen?" he said.

The nerves of the whole party had been pretty well shaken, and they felt they required some refresher.

"Yes," answered the marquis; "let us have brandy and soda water all round—let there be plenty of brandy."

"Yes, gentlemen."

The order was quickly executed, and its reviving effects were speedily visible.

The marquis then said:

"Pharoah, there is a traitor in the camp!"

"A traitor, marquis?" echoed Pharoah, who at first imagined he was suspected, and found it difficult to avoid the betrayal of emotion. "Who is it?"

"That fair snake, Clarissa! She must never be allowed to enter the house again."

"She never shall, marquis, I promise you," answered Pharoah.

This was all that passed, and the next moment the four gentlemen took their departure.

The house was empty save of the Prince of Wales and Henrietta ——.

The prince had drank deeply on the previous night, and it would take him till noon on the following day to sleep off his debauch.

He was, of course, utterly unconscious of the events that had taken place, being in a state of drunken lethargy.

At noon, therefore, with the assistance of Pharoah, and sundry stimulants frequently administered, he was enabled to undergo the operation of dressing.

This done, he made an apology for a breakfast.

But though his jaded palate was tempted with every luxury that could provoke appetite, it would not be commanded.

Outraged Nature vindicated her rights, and the prince could eat nothing.

A little dry toast steeped in brandy being the only thing he could endure even to look at, much less taste.

It was at the close of this meal that Pharoah informed his royal highness that if he wished to see Lord Harcliffe, he thought he could find him.

This intelligence seemed to act as an invigorator, for the prince immediately revived.

"I do wish to see him," he said. "When can you bring him to me?"

"I daresay I could contrive a meeting for to-night if that would not be too soon."

"Not at all—not at all!" replied the prince, earnestly. "The sooner the better."

"Shall I bring him here, your royal highness?" Pharoah asked.

"No, no—not here. Bring him to Leicester House. He will be more in my power there."

This last expression of the prince struck Pharoah as strange.

"*More in his power!*"

What did it mean?

However, he promised that the prince's wishes should be complied with, resolving to put Lord Harcliffe on his guard, and to assist him to the extent of his ability, if necessary.

After the departure of the prince and the fair Henrietta in the afternoon, Pharoah apprised his late master of his royal highness's wish to see him that evening if possible, informing him also of that expression made use of by the prince, which he considered suspicious.

"I am glad you mentioned this, Pharoah," said Lord Harcliffe, "since it suggests to me the necessity of being on my guard. I have learnt by experience that it is as necessary to be as equally armed and prepared for the assaults of ruffianism in a palace as in those dark dens where you would naturally expect it."

His lordship seemed to think that the keeping back the secret that the Count Riccioli was alive might be a powerful weapon at a crisis.

The count therefore, grateful to those who had preserved him from a violent and terrible death, willingly consented to immure himself for a time in the upper chamber where they were then located until he had the consent of his deliverers to show himself once more in public.

"Will you go to Leicester House to-night?" inquired Pharoah of Lord Harcliffe.

"I think not," replied his lordship. "The prince will be exhausted and debilitated with his previous night's excesses, and then I think one clear day had better pass before I leave this retreat; besides, there are two thousand pounds' worth of cheques that we must first commission you to cash for us."

"I can do that to-morrow morning," said Pharoah.

It was therefore determined to spend that evening quietly.

This they accordingly did.

Very few members visited *The Retreat* that night, and those who did retired early.

Pharoah took care to supply his guests in the top room with every luxury of the season, and the choicest wines and cigars, and as soon as the last member had departed, he joined his party, and spent with them such an evening as they all remembered long after as a bright green spot in their lives' journey, on which in looking back their eyes could rest with pleasure.

CHAPTER CCIV.

LORD HARCLIFFE DECIDES UPON PAYING A VISIT TO THE PRINCE OF WALES.—CAPTAIN HAWK RESOLVES TO GO TO CHELSEA IN SEARCH OF BLANCHE.—HE MEETS WITH A PERILOUS ADVENTURE ON THE RIVER.

THE next morning Pharoah visited the different banks at which the cheques delivered to the highwaymen were made payable, and returned at noon with £2000 in cash and notes.

The tide of fortune appeared to have turned in favour of our heroes.

Want of money, at all events, was not at this juncture one of their necessities.

In the meantime the hue-and-cry from Bow Street was loud against them.

The police officers who had been so cleverly and desperately baffled a few nights previous, indignant at the loss of three of their comrades, and ashamed and crestfallen that in spite of their superior numbers their prey had slipped through their fingers, were eloquent in their determinations never to rest till they had secured the highwaymen.

It was therefore necessary that in going forth they should be constantly on their guard.

This vigilance, however, they were from habit used to, and they found no difficulty in exercising it now.

They could, if need had so required it, have slept almost with one eye shut and the other open.

One thing was in their favour—they had each a key of *The Retreat*, and that was always open to them, day and night.

If they could only, in the event of pursuit, elude their pursuers, that was a sanctuary where they would be always safe—always unsuspected.

The highwaymen were already on the best of terms with the young Count Riccioli, who seemed quite to enjoy his temporary incarceration with such cheerful and agreeable companions.

But the time was fast drawing on when this happy companionship must for the present be interrupted.

"You have decided to go to Leicester House to-night, have you not?" inquired Captain Hawk.

"Yes," said Lord Harcliffe. "I am rather curious to know what service the prince will have the conscience to require at my hands."

"You will not be kept long now in suspense.'

"All the better—I detest uncertainty; I always like to know the best or worst at once, at any time."

"Then as your destination to-night is Leicester House, I think I shall risk the scrutiny and vigilance of the police, and journey as far as Chelsea; I am longing to look once more upon the fair face of Blanche Allison," said Captain Hawk.

"Well, Heaven speed you!" replied his comrade. "I am almost inclined to congratulate myself that I am still heart-whole."

"Don't boast, Harcliffe: love is a plant of hasty growth," returned the captain—"a single glance from a pair of bright eyes is often sufficient to inflict a wound that nothing but the owner of the eyes can cure."

"Well, when my time comes, I suppose I shall endure it with my usual philosophy," said his lordship, laughing.

It was about eight o'clock at night when Captain Hawk strolled quietly from *The Retreat* down the courts and into Pall Mall.

He hailed the first hackney-coach he saw, and was conveyed by that to the Strand.

No great distance to have walked, but he wished to avoid observation, and there was peril in every yard of distance.

On descending from the vehicle, he paid the man hastily nearly double his fare, and then dived down one of the numerous narrow turnings that led towards the river.

He soon reached one of the piers, where a number of boats lay waiting for a fare.

He was soon caught sight of by the watermen, and "Boat your honour?" was asked by more than one voice.

Captain Hawk was not disposed to be particular as to the craft in which he was about to sail, and consequently stepped into the first he came near.

"Where to, your honour? Row you up the river in style!" said the owner of the boat.

"Chelsea Reach."

"All right, your honour," answered the man, who began immediately to disentangle himself from the shoal of boats by which he was surrounded.

Of course all the watermen considered that the fare might just as well have stepped into one of their wherries, as into that which he had selected, and revenged themselves by chaffing rower, fare, and boat until they were fairly out of hearing.

The evening was delightful.

A mild, refreshing breeze swept over the surface of the noble river on the broad bosom of which he was borne along.

Lying back in the stern, placidly smoking a cigar, he gave himself up to the happiest thoughts, in which the fair face of Blanche Allison occupied a prominent position.

Such moments as these were not of frequent occurrence in the life of the highwayman, where the calms were outnumbered by the storms; they were, therefore, all the more highly appreciated.

Besides, there was a sense of freedom in the rapid motion of the boat, and the splash of the oars, as they impelled her onwards; and as the soft evening breeze met him with its cool and refreshing welcome, he felt that he had never in his life experienced more delightful sensations.

"I wonder," he soliloquised, mentally, "how I shall find Blanche? Well, I trust. She will think I have forgotten her—and no wonder! I must seem sadly forgetful. Yet how can I avoid it? In the roving, adventurous life I lead, each day brings its own thoughts—its own vicissitudes—and I seem to have no time to think of anything but how best to escape the perils of the passing moment. I wonder if I shall ever be permitted to settle down into a peaceful life; and, if so, whether I could make myself content in some quiet country cottage, with Blanche for my wife, and——?"

These pretty "castles in the air" were suddenly dissipated by the boatman's voice.

He said:

"I beg pardon, your honour, for interrupting your thoughts, but it seems to me as if the party in that boat astarn was a following us."

Captain Hawk looked round, and saw that which, in the twinkling of an eye, dispelled the quiet calm he was enjoying, demolished the fairy vista he had created, and aroused him to the painful consciousness that for him there was *no rest*.

He felt at that moment the *felon's brand* was on him, and that peace was not to be his portion on this side the grave.

In the distance, but rapidly gaining upon them, was a boat, rowed by four men, and filled with police officers.

"Curses light on them!" muttered Captain Hawk, between his teeth, as he gripped the stock of one of his pistols

But he controlled his anger, and smiled bitterly and scornfully at his pursuers.

"Is it us they want, your honour?" inquired the boatman.

"*One* of us," coolly replied Captain Hawk, "and that happens to be myself; but as I am quite determined not to be had, you will be good enough to act as I tell you!"

As an incentive to prompt obedience, the captain pressed a couple of guineas into the man's hand.

The sight of the gold was more potent in its effect than a thousand words.

"What am I to do, your honour?" asked the man, eagerly.

Captain Hawk, who had made a rapid scrutiny of every object within sight, had made up his mind what.

"Make for that barge ahead of us," he said, distinctly, "and take care to place it between us and our pursuers, but without appearing to do so."

"Ay, ay, your honour! Do you wish to stop near the barge?"

"Only for a moment."

The waterman, who had never ceased rowing, now redoubled his exertions.

The boat flew rapidly through the water, and in a few moments passed almost under the stern of the barge.

Captain Hawk had an instant previously taken a deliberate view of his pursuers.

Foremost amongst the number he distinctly descried his old acquaintance Peterson, who appeared to sit with his eyes riveted upon him, grasping in his hand what seemed to be a pistol, waiting till he came within range to discharge the deadly weapon.

Cautiously as the captain had proceeded in his progress from *The Retreat* to the Strand, he had been sighted in the Haymarket, as he stepped into the hackney-coach, by a Bow Street runner.

The man had followed, and seen him hire the boat, and start in it, and, having been informed of its destination by the watermen at the pier, who readily volunteered every information, he had at once hastened to Bow Street with the intelligence, and the result was that a body of officers were now in hot pursuit.

The boat in which Captain Hawk was, had now reached the stern of the barge, which was anchored, and waiting for the turn of the tide to continue her progress towards London.

The officers were no longer visible to the captain, neither could the captain's boat be perceived by the officers.

"What the h—ll's he up to now?" growled Peterson, grinding his teeth savagely, and knitting his brows till they almost touched his cheeks, in his unavailing efforts to look through the haze and see what was going on on the other side.

Suddenly the little boat shot out once more into full view.

Peterson uttered a cry of exultation.

"There he is!" he cried, as he pointed to the little craft, in the stern of which, calm and motionless, sat Captain Hawk, wrapped in his cloak, his three-cornered laced hat placed jauntily on his head, not condescending to take the slightest notice.

The man stuck to his work bravely, and the wherry darted through the water, favoured by the tide, like an arrow.

But then the same tide that aided the progress of the captain's boat assisted equally that of his pursuers.

Besides, one pair of arms, however muscular and enduring, could not, for any length of time, perform the work of three pairs.

The consequence was, that the larger boat was each minute rapidly drawing nearer and nearer to the smaller.

A loud shout of triumph from the police officers attested the joy they felt at the prospect of a speedy capture.

The poor waterman, the sole proprietor of the wherry strove hard, with undaunted pluck, to keep his ground.

He was almost black in the face with his exertions, but though he did not relax his efforts, he saw there was no chance for him.

"We're sure to have you!" shouted Peterson, as they

passed the barge, "so you'd better give in! D'ye hear?" he bawled.

The waterman, winded as he was, laughed derisively.

"You must catch us first!" shouted the rower of the wherry, pulling away with all his might.

This defiance on the part of the man irritated Peterson exceedingly, and he fully resolved to take him into custody, as well as the highwayman, for aiding and abetting in his escape.

Certainly it struck him that the waterman might not be aware of the desperate criminal he was assisting to elude the hands of justice.

So he bawled again, at the top of his voice:

"Stop! D'ye hear? D'ye know who you've got in your boat? He's Captain Hawk, the highwayman!"

"Go to blazes!" bawled the waterman, in reply.

"Pull away, my boys!" shouted the exasperated Peterson; "there's a guinea each for you if we capture the rascal!"

The men, stimulated by the promise of reward, renewed their efforts.

A second or two more they would be within pistol-shot.

Peterson grasped his weapon, and knelt up with one knee on the seat.

"If you don't stop, I'll fire!" roared the police officer.

"Fire and be d—d!" politely returned the solitary waterman.

The words had hardly passed from his lips when Peterson, taking the man at his word, discharged his pistol.

Oh joy—triumph! his aim was true! the noble bird was struck at last! the cloaked figure fell forward, shot in the back, prostrate at the bottom of the boat!

A ringing shout from the officers heralded the noble act of the chief, as the four-oared cutter dashed up alongside its slight antagonist, almost capsizing it in its desperation.

Peterson, intent only on capturing his prize, made a desperate clutch at the prostrate figure.

He grasped it boldly and firmly.

"Now, scoundrel, dead or alive, I have you at last!" he cried.

But to his great and utter confusion, it was not the scoundrel he sought; for as the cloak was displaced from the body of the supposed victim, he discovered he had first shot and afterwards seized a tarry sack filled with coal, the material with which the barge was loaded.

"D—nation!" he roared, in a paroxysm of fury and confusion, with a face as red as a turkey cock's. "Escaped again!"

CHAPTER CCV.

SHOWS HOW CAPTAIN HAWK WENT ON BOARD THE COAL BARGE, AND WHAT BEFEL HIM THERE.—HE VISITS GROVE COTTAGE, AND RECEIVES A SURPRISE.

ESCAPED again!

There was no doubt of it; it was such an evident, palpable fact there could be none.

The scoundrel had given the double in the cleverest manner possible, and left nothing in lieu but an old sack redolent of tar.

The indignation and disgust of Peterson and the officials were prodigious.

There were only two or three objects on which these sentiments could be expended.

These were the sack, the boat, and the waterman, who had been honourably beaten in the race, and now sat placidly, with the perspiration oozing from every pore, smiling quietly at the chagrin of the police, every now and then wiping his heated forehead.

To every question, he replied, doggedly, "*He didn't know*," till Peterson was in a state of semi-madness.

"Don't keep telling me you *don't know!*" he shouted. "You must know!"

The boatman laughed.

"You know you must!"

The boatman laughed again.

"Don't keep on laughing like an idiot, but tell me how did the rascal get out of the boat, and where did he go to?"

The boatman placed his finger confidentially along the side of his nose, and *laughed* once more.

"The fellow's a natural!" roared Peterson. "But we'll see if we can't bring him to his senses!

"Lay hold of him, one of you, and lug him into the boat!"

In this they were frustrated, however, for the waterman, as one of the officers leant forward to seize him, suddenly pushed the boat off, the result of which was that the official lost his balance and plunged head-first into the water, whilst the waterman, plying his oars, was soon far ahead.

It took a few minutes to pick up their drenched comrade and get him into the boat, and by that time the man was at too great a distance to make it worth while to chase him.

Peterson was sorely puzzled.

"How could he have given us the slip in this manner?" he thought.

One of the men suggested the possibility of the highwayman having clambered up into the barge as he passed.

"Oh, yes—so he might!" cried Peterson, struck with the idea; "he's cunning enough for anything. No doubt he's on the barge; we shall have him still if we're quick."

Impressed with this idea, he called out to the rowers:

"Pull back to the barge we passed; go as quick as you can! Row like blazes!"

The men turned the boat round and commenced their return; but the tide was now running strong against them, and they did not make so rapid a progress as before.

Still Peterson buoyed himself up with the hope of success, and pictured himself sharing a considerable moiety of the promised reward for the highwayman's apprehension.

Our readers will probably be curious to hear what measures Captain Hawk took to frustrate his pursuers, and though from what has been already narrated they may have possibly formed their own conclusions, still, an exact but brief account of the captain's proceedings may not be uninteresting.

As soon as the boat in which he was, passed under the stern of the coal barge, so as to be out of sight of his pursuers, he grasped a rope that hung from it, and pulled himself up.

The barge was loaded with sacks of coal, and finding a small sack close at hand, he lowered it into the boat he just quitted, and directing the waterman to place it in the stern, threw down his cloak and hat, ordering the man to envelope the sack in the former of these coverings, and to place the latter on the top.

This, as may be imagined, at a distance had much the appearance of a living freight; and as the little wherry continued its course, Captain Hawk had the satisfaction of seeing his *ruse* perfectly successful.

Crouched behind one of the coal sacks, he chuckled to himself as he saw the police in full chase after a coal sack, and laughed in his sleeve at the excited Peterson, who kept his eager fingers on the trigger of his pistol, ready to perforate the insensible object in the stern.

As the four-oared cutter rowed past, the bargemen, aroused by the shouts, were all eagerly looking over the side of the barge, so that Captain Hawk's presence was entirely unnoticed.

However, he felt that he was not yet out of danger.

He was amongst strangers.

The name of Captain Hawk had been shouted by the police.

The bargemen had gathered the fact that they were in pursuit of a highwayman, and doubtless would be aware of the reward offered for his apprehension.

He was surrounded by water.

The only prospect of reaching land was by a boat or a swim.

The idea of going to visit his lady love dripping wet was not congenial to his feelings.

A boat would be preferable.

Should he discover himself to the rough bargemen before they discovered him?

They were not a bad-hearted lot generally, in spite of their want of cultivation.

He was eventually guided as to the course he should pursue by a conversation he overheard after the officers had passed.

"So them constables are arter Captain Hawk, air they?" inquired one of his companions.

"Seems like it," answered the other.

"Who's Captain Hawk?"

"Lor'! don't yer know who he is?"

"He's a horcifer, ain't he?"

"No, a highwayman—a cove as robs the mail, and breaks out of prison, and knocks down the perlice, and plays the very devil!"

"An' these chaps wants him, does they?"

"Yes; and there's a thundering big lump o' money for anyone as 'ud lay their grapples upon him!"

"I wishes as he'd come within arms' length of us; we'd grab him, wouldn't we?"

"Well, I don't know as I should; he never did me no harm; an' as for these highwaymen, it's my opinion they makes em out a great deal worse than they are."

"But look at the reward! Why, it's I don't know how many hundred!"

"Well, that's no reason we should betray a poor devil, is it? If it wur thousands instead o' hundreds, I wouldn't put out my hand to lock up a fellow-creetur in prison, an' p'r'aps hang him, if he hadn't wrong'd me, not if he wur fifty times a highwayman."

Captain Hawk felt his heart warm at the honest bargeman's words.

He knew that a man with such sentiments would never betray him.

The companion of the bargemen evidently felt a little ashamed of himself, and said, a little apologetically:

"Oh, I don't want to do any harm to anyone, only I'm a poor man, with a lot o' young uns; an' a hundred pounds is not to be refused, an' if we could earn it in a honest way by stopping a runaway thief——"

"Hold hard, mate!" cried the other. "In the first place, the money earned by *treachery* ain't *honest*, and no good ever comes of it. All the bread it brings turns sour; and then these highwaymen are the friends of them as are bad off. They robs from the rich, but they gives to the poor. I likes 'em, I do, and I'd never put out a finger to lay 'em by the heels as long as my names Bill Brock, or I've got sense enough to know my right hand from my left."

"You're a noble fellow!" cried Captain Hawk, rising from his place of concealment and coming forward. "You have got the heart of a man and a gentleman under the garb of a coal-heaver!"

The daylight was fast departing, and it may be imagined the two men were somewhat startled at seeing a handsome, stalwart figure, who had suddenly started up as it seemed from nowhere, in their midst.

"Who are you?" they ejaculated, gazing at the captain earnestly, with open eyes and mouths.

"Your friend. Don't be alarmed; you have nothing to apprehend from me. I am Captain Hawk!"

"Darned if I didn't think so!" exclaimed the honest bargeman—a big, burly, broad-shouldered Hercules of a man—who had uttered such generous sentiments a few moments previously.

"Yes, I am the man whom my friends in the boat yonder are now pursuing so eagerly," replied the captain, in an unconcerned, pleasant tone of voice.

"Dash my wig!" said the bargeman, "yer seems to take it mighty cool!"

"Yes; I've sent off one of your sacks wrapped in my cloak, with my hat on the top," continued the captain; "so when they come up with the boat and think they've captured the prize——"

"I see!" burst out the man; "they'll only a' gotten a sack o' coal! Ho, ho, ho!—ha, ha, ha! that be a capital joke!"

The worthy bargeman was so tickled at this that he quite forgot the loss of the coal.

But Captain Hawk did not.

"Here, my friends," he said; "here is a trifle to pay for the sack and its contents."

As he spoke he slipped five guineas into each of their hands.

The men were astounded.

But before they could express their thanks, he captain said, hastily:

"There is no time to be lost. These hounds of the law will return. How can I get ashore?"

"God bless your honour!" answered the man, with grateful eagerness. "I'd take you on my back r than you shouldn't go at all."

"I might as well swim to the bank," remarked the captain, smiling; "but as I am going to visit a lady, I prefer going dry."

"Certainly, your honour. I'll hail a boat," replied the bargeman.

"Do so as quickly as possible," said the captain.

Fortune favoured their wish, for at that moment a boat that was crossing the river from the Surrey side of the water passed in front of the barge.

"Yo-hoy! boat!" sung out the man.

The waterman, who had no fare, altered his course and made for the barge's side.

"Here's the boat your honour," said the bargeman.

"Thanks, my friend. You have rendered me a great service. Here," he added, in a lower tone, drawing the man a little aside, "accept this from Captain Hawk as a trifling testimony to the nobility of your sentiments and the kindness of your heart."

As he spoke, he placed three ten-pound notes in his hand.

"Farewell, my good fellow! If ever you want a friend, call on Richard Hawk," cried the captain, as he lowered himself into the boat alongside.

"And if ever you want a friend, captain, call on Bill Brock," answered the man, warmly, as the boat made for the shore.

This operation took only a few moments, and by the time the police officers reached the barge, the captain had been some time on the land.

Our readers may be pretty well sure that there was not much information to be screwed out of Bill Brock.

He would have had his tongue cut out rather than have uttered a syllable.

Even his more mercenary and less generous companion had been overcome by the five guineas, and would give no information.

There was, however, something in the jeering, ironical manner and words of the bargemen in answer to their replies that awakened a lurking suspicion that they were not speaking the exact truth.

This irritated the police, who revenged themselves by searching the barge and upsetting the coals, which so aggravated the men, that at last, as if by accident, one of them made a sudden lurch amongst the officers, who were sent spinning off the barge into the water like a lot of floored ninepins.

Owing to the gloom that now shrouded the river, the moon not having yet chased away the shades of twilight, this little feat had well-nigh cost P.O. Peterson and three of his coadjutors their lives.

Encumbered as they were with their thick boots and heavy garments, they could barely keep themselves afloat till the boat could pick them up, and they then departed in a high state of wrathful disappointment which even the sudden immersion they had undergone could not cool down.

In the meantime Captain Hawk proceeded in a vehicle as rapidly as possible to Chelsea.

He was in excellent spirits, partly at the recollection of the generous sentiments of the honest bargeman, but principally at the triumphant issue of the trick he had played the police officers, and the crestfallen attitude they would have to assume on their return to Bow Street.

Having dismissed the vehicle, he entered a small but comfortable inn, where, calling for a tankard of old ale, he wrote a few lines to Charles.

He then drank the ale, posted his letter, and proceeded at once to discover the locality of Grove Cottage.

Chelsea was at the period of our history a very different place from the Chelsea of the present day, being more like a little country town.

Grove Cottage was an isolated dwelling, there being no houses near it for a considerable distance.

He had some difficulty in finding it; but at length, by dint of inquiry and searching, he, to his great joy, stood before the gate.

The moon had now risen and shone full upon the cottage.

The unpretending little mansion was surrounded by a wall, save the front, at which part iron railings and a gate were substituted

[THE ABDUCTION OF BLANCHE BY HER GUARDIAN.]

The walls—that is, as much of them as the ivy permitted to be visible—were white.

The old-fashioned gable window and the porch, with its slanting roof, looked quite quaint; and the contrast between the bright white of the side of the cottage and the sombre hue of the ivy that clung to it imparted quite a ghostly effect to the whole prospect.

All was very still.

It was not yet ten o'clock; and though it was such a lovely night, the shutters were closely fastened, and not a glimmer of light was seen anywhere from within.

The captain tried the gate. It was locked.

Surely he must have come to the wrong house?

But no. There was the name on the brass plate—

GROVE HOUSE.

There was a bell to the gate.

He pulled it vigorously, but it offered no resistance when pulled, neither did it return the smallest tinkle in response.

It was evidently broken.

The captain was at a standstill.

"The house looks as though it was deserted," he said to himself. "Surely they cannot have left? But even if it were so, Blanche would have contrived to let me know."

He looked up earnestly at all the windows, but no sign of anything human appeared.

All was close, impenetrable, and unsatisfactory.

The question was, how to make the inmates aware of his presence.

They could hardly have retired to rest at that early hour.

The gate being locked, and the bell broken, his position was somewhat embarrassing.

The captain's patience, too, was becoming somewhat exhausted.

"I think," he said to himself, meditatively, "all things considered, the circumstances justify me in climbing over the gate."

This mental suggestion he at once acted upon.

It was not a difficult task, and the railing spikes had long since ceased to be sharp.

He stood in the little garden in front.

He paused a moment, and scraped his heel along the gravel, thinking he might attract some attention from those within.

But he was disappointed.

No blind hastily drawn up, or window cautiously opened, attested that anyone was at all aware of his propinquity.

Even the glimpse of a nightcap would have been satisfactory.

But no such glimpse was afforded.

"They must be all asleep," he reflected. "Well, as there is no other resource, I must knock them up. I daresay Blanche will forgive me."

Having uttered this apostrophe, he approached the door and knocked.

Not wishing to startle the inmates, it was not a loud knock, but there was an indescribable *something* in the very sound of the knocker that suggested desolation.

It seemed to reverberate through a *deserted house.*

Is there not always something akin to melancholy in a shut-up mansion?

Death—ruin—may have entered there, and rendered desolate and silent the hearth that once echoed with the joyous laugh of love, and life, and happiness!

But we are digressing.

Captain Hawk waited patiently for a time.

He then walked to the gate, looked up at the windows, and walked back again.

He knocked again—this time louder than the first—but still no reply.

"They must be dead!" he cried.

And then there stole across his heart that bitter pang—that almost insupportable sadness that such a thought always awakens.

"At least," he continued, with a kind of eager impetuosity, "if they be alive, they shall hear me!"

And, hardly conscious of his act, he grasped the knocker, and knocked long and loudly.

The hollow echoes within seemed to mock him.

But that was the only answer returned.

He struck the door impatiently with his foot.

He hammered at the shutters with his clenched fist.

Still no notice was taken from within.

Not even a dog barked.

"They must have left!" he exclaimed, impatiently; "and they have left the house to the care of some gin-drinking old woman, who has, perhaps, gone to bed dead drunk. Who knows?"

He seized the knocker again, and kept up a running fire of knocks till the quiet night echoed again.

Most assuredly, had it been at the present era, Captain Hawk would have been locked up as a nuisance.

As it was, the persevering manner in which he plied the knocker, had the effect at last of eliciting some signs of vitality from within.

But even this came very slowly.

A step was heard descending the stairs.

As it drew near, it seemed heavy and unequal, as though the person descending was lame.

The landing of the passage being reached, the approaching footsteps sounded shambling and unpleasant.

"It is not a woman's step," said the captain to himself.

The individual, whoever it was, had now reached the door.

CHAPTER CCVI.

CAPTAIN HAWK EVENTUALLY ENTERS THE DESERTED COTTAGE, AND MEETS WITH AN UNEXPECTED DROP.

"Who's there?" he cried, without opening the door.

"I've been knocking here for the last half-hour!" cried Captain Hawk, somewhat irritably; "and if you imagine I am going to exercise my throat as I have the knocker, by bawling through a wooden partition or a keyhole, you're mistaken. Open the door!"

"Oi shorn't oppen no door for nobody!" answered the person within, in a horribly hoarse, grating voice, that seemed to come from the speaker's throat with a rattle. "Whor d'yer wornt?"

"Miss Blanche Allison."

"She arn't 'ere."

"This is Grove House?"

"Yea."

"It belongs to Miss Esther Allison?"

"It did."

"Does it not now?"

"Noa! She arn't here noo, she's gorn."

"Gone! Where?"

"Whort's that to yow?"

Captain Hawk ground his teeth with passion.

"If I had you outside, my friend," he muttered to himself, "I'd let you know what!"

"Go away, and dorn't storp makin' a row outside. I warnt to go to bed!" continued the voice from within.

"Stay!" cried the captain, who was most anxious to get some definite information; "tell me what I want to know—I can pay you well."

"Can yow?"

"Yes. But I can't pay through a closed door."

"Oi can oppen th' door, but the chairn be oop."

"Then open it at once. I'm hoarse with bawling."

There was a great unfastening of bolts, and then the key turned in the lock, and the door opened about six inches.

"Noo yow can throw the money inside!" cried the croaking voice.

"Not till you've answered my questions," said the captain.

The door was slammed with an angry growl, but the captain had taken the precaution to insert his foot in the aperture, so that it remained still open.

"Now we can hear one another," he remarked.

"If yow dorn't tak' yer futt from atween the door," growled the amiable being within, "Oi'll smash it for yow!"

"If you talk such rubbish to me, you infernal dolt!" shouted Captain Hawk, provoked beyond endurance at the threat and the forbidding voice that uttered it, "I'll burst open the door, and batter in your skill with the butt end of my pistol!"

This threat seemed to have taken an effect, as the man was quieter, and did not attempt to execute his threat.

"Well, go on. But the money?" he inquired.

"You shall have it, as I promised, when you have answered my questions," said the captain.

"Well, ask away, and be quick—Oi'm sleepy."

"You say neither Miss Blanche Allison, nor her aunt, is in this house?"

"Noa."

"Have they given it up?"

"Yes."

"How long since?"

"'Ow do Oi know?"

"Where have they gone to?"

"They didn't tell Oi."

"Do you mean to say you are ignorant of their present residence?"

"Oi arn't supposed to know everything."

"Who are you?"

"Oi'm here to moind th' 'ouse."

"What is your name?"

"Jacob Mawks."

"Not by any means a promising name," thought the captain; "there appears suspicion in its very sound as well as repulsion in the voice that utters it."

However, masking his sentiments, and still keeping his foot firmly wedged between the partially open door he said:

"This extraordinary precaution is ridiculous. Remove the chain and let me in!"

"Oh, ah! noa thankee! Oi wur tould not to let th chean down arter dark."

"Why, you foolish fellow, what do you suspect? Do you imagine I want to murder you?"

"Oi dorn't imagine nort aboot ut; Oi only goes by moi orders; them's all Oi goes by."

"D—n your dogged stupidity!" muttered the captain, between his teeth.

"Noo, then, jest take away yer futt, an' let me shut th' dour, will ee?" growled Jacob from within.

"No; you must answer my questions first," answered Captain Hawk. "I am a particular friend of the ladies I am inquiring after, and——"

"Ee, ee, ee!" grinned the Cerberus, in a horrible croaking tone. "Oi s'pose yow means yow be a friend o' th' young un's!"

"You impertinent scoundrel!" cried the captain, irritably. "If I had your neck between the door instead of my boot, I'd teach you to laugh in another key!"

"Ee, ee, ee!" again croaked the horrible discord. "Yow'll foind yourself grumblin' through the key*hole* afoor long."

As he uttered these words Jacob made a sudden and desperate lunge at the door, but the captain's boot was firm, and it still remained open.

"You dog!" shouted Captain Hawk, exasperated beyond measure at the provoking impudence of the unseen custodian. "I'll—— Ha!"

This exclamation came involuntarily from the captain's lips, as a sharp and extremely painful blow from some invisible instrument fell on the instep that was protruded in the aperture, and caused him instantly to withdraw it.

That act was fatal, for the door was instantly slammed to, and Jacob's harsh voice was heard croaking out his triumph, as he turned the key in the lock and shot the bolts in rapid succession.

The captain, in a frenzy of pain and rage, could only give vent to his feelings by hammering the door with his clenched fist, mingled with some very expressive anathemas on the head of Mr. Jacob Mawks.

That worthy, now that he had placed the barricade of the door between himself and his persevering interrogator, appeared to be greatly amused at his unavailing wrath, and added considerably to the captain's boiling indignation by his sarcastic jeerings from the other side.

"Ee, ee!" he chuckled. "Oi tould yow yow'd be grumblin' outside th' keyhole afoor long. Ee, ee, ee!" he continued, as the captain kicked with his sound foot in addition to striking with his hand, "yow may kick an' hammer—it worn't make no manner o' odds, and it worn't wake me, 'cos Oi sleeps loike a doormouse; soa kick away till yow're tired an' all the paint's off th' dour! Oi'm off to bed: good-night, Measter What's-yer-name!"

And having thus expressed himself, his retreating shuffle was heard along the passage, a heavy, clumsy pair of feet descending the stairs, and all was silent again.

That is, externally; but there was a voice in the captain's heart that was anything but silent.

The pain of the blow on his foot had nearly passed away; the passing feeling of irritation he had felt would have speedily yielded to his own sense of self-respect, but there was a voice whispering within him that with respect to her he sought, all was not right.

The apprehensions that stole over him—undefined, vague, as they were—were yet sufficient to awaken in his breast sensations almost unbearable.

Did he then love her so dearly?

His heart seemed to spring forth with an immediate response as it throbbed tumultuously to the mental question.

Oh yes, dearly—most dearly! dearer than life!

And where, then, was the object of so much affection? —where was Blanche?

That was a question of the wildest surmise.

All the captain knew was that he was on the outside of Grove Cottage, without any clue to guide him to her place of abode or to give him the slightest intelligence of her welfare.

It suddenly struck him in the midst of his moody, thoughtful fit, that cooling his heels on the stone flags was not the speediest means possible of elucidating the mystery that seemed to hang around the place, or of bringing him into the presence of the beloved object he sought.

It was rarely, as our readers are by this time aware, that Captain Hawk lost much time in determining as to the course he intended to pursue.

On this occasion, however, he had just awoke to the conviction that he was in love, and that the loved one was not to be found, and this, too, under circumstances that appeared at least suspicious, if nothing more.

In less time, however, than it has taken to write these few lines, the captain had proved that his love for Blanche Allison had not robbed him of his powers of determination, or of looking a difficulty boldly in the face and grappling with it.

The first evidence he gave of this was his deliberately climbing over the gate.

He now stood on the outside of the enclosure.

Not a soul appeared in sight.

No sound fell upon his ear save the wind as it rustled in the boughs over his head.

"All this is very strange," soliloquised the captain, "and augurs ill for Blanche's happiness. The sound of that fellow's voice, too, fills me with horror. I am ignorant of his features, but if the speech be any index of the speaker, he must be a human ogre, not a man."

The captain moved forward in deep thought as he spoke, almost unconsciously.

"And I suppose that fellow imagines," he continued, stopping without knowing he had stopped, "that because he has locked and bolted the door, he has quietly got rid of me. Well, Mr. Jacob Mawks, ogre as I suspect you to be, everyone has a right to an opinion, and you may keep yours: I also will keep mine."

He took a few more unconscious steps, and then paused again with a sudden outburst of emotion.

"I fear treachery," he cried, clenching his fist fiercely "and though I know not whom to accuse, or at what object to point, there is an instinct at my h[illegible] that tells me Blanche is in danger!"

He looked up at this juncture, and to his surprise found he had wandered on some distance from the cottage, and turned round by the boundary wall that enclosed it.

"I'm determined," he went on, "not to leave this place till I've dragged out—by main force, if necessary —all that that croaking wretch within knows of Blanche's present locality. Yes, I'm resolved, since Jacob Mawks refuses me admission, to enter on my own responsibility and in my own way."

He walked along by the side of the wall some distance, and then stepping out into the road, reconnoitred the back of the edifice with scrutinising attention.

At first all seemed profoundly dark, but at length his long and earnest examination was rewarded by a faint glimmering light that proceeded from the topmost window.

This tiny ray was so indistinct that a casual passer-by would not have remarked it.

It was only the intense and fixed scrutiny which the captain employed that enabled him to discern it.

This solitary beam seemed to open out a fresh channel for thought in his mind.

Might not Blanche herself be there confined a prisoner.

As to the assertion of Jacob Mawks, that the house was empty of all save himself, he attached no credence to his words whatever.

Who was the occupant of that chamber from whence the dim light proceeded.

Not the Cerberus, for the captain remarked particularly that he did not ascend but *de*scend the stairs; and trifling as this circumstance was, it was still sufficient to strengthen, if not confirm, his opinion that that apartment at the top of the house was not untenanted.

His resolution having been formed, he approached the wall.

It was an old wall that had stood the heats and frosts of many a hot summer and cold winter, and was now beginning to show symptoms of decay.

The bricks were in many places broken away.

Into one of these orifices he inserted the toe of his boot, and then springing up, he caught the top of the wall, and in a moment was safely landed on the soft mould of the flower-bed that edged the wall on the other side.

Indistinct as the light was, the moon at that time throwing her rays entirely on the front, he could still after a few moments' investigation, when his eyes had grown accustomed to the obscurity, perceive that the garden was in good order, thus betokening the presence, or at least the recent departure, of the proprietor.

As he peered curiously at the shrubs and flowers, and noticed their well-trimmed, and healthy appearance, he found himself imagining, what was by no means improbable, that the fair hands of Blanche herself might have had something to do in producing such a result.

It, however, made him more determined than ever to penetrate into the interior.

He accordingly stepped lightly across the gravel path on to the centre grass-plat, and walked towards the house.

It took him but a short time to fix upon a spot for his operations.

He screwed together the small steel crowbar which he invariably carried with him.

The door did not appear by any means calculated to withstand the powerful leverage which that apparently slight but really efficacious instrument was calculated to afford.

The captain inserted the sharp edge of the steel bar between the door and the wooden framework surrounding it, close to the lock.

A sharp, cracking noise told in an instant, as plainly as old wood could tell, that in less than no time the door would be effectually broken open.

But, before that consummation of destruction to the property had arrived, the captain was arrested in his work by a window opening violently on the first floor, and the harsh, croaking voice inquiring, in a more unpleasant tone than ever:

"Who's there?"

"You'll know in a moment, fellow!" cried Captain Hawk.

The captain looked up as he spoke, and though the speaker from the first-floor window carried no candle, there was evidently a light somewhere in the background.

This remote illumination was just sufficient to develop the outline of Mr. Jacob's figure.

It certainly appeared to the captain like nothing human.

It might have been a lion's head, or a bear's, or a hideous pantomime mask, but certainly there was nothing about it like the head of a man.

The captain stood looking up for a moment in silent astonishment at the strange apparition the very partial light revealed.

"Oh, it be yow agin, be it?" inquired Jacob Mawks. "You can't get in at the froant, soo Oi s'pose yow thinks yow'll 'a better look at th' back? But yow won't; soa yow'd better go hoam an' go to bed."

"I shall do neither till I'm assured of that which at present I doubt," answered the captain, definitely.

"Dorn't Oi tell yow the gal bean't here?"

"It is not because you tell me that I am compelled to believe you; and, to tell you the truth, I am not satisfied either with your manner or your answers to my questions. In fact, I believe you to be a lying scoundrel!"

"Didn't Oi tell yow as Miss Allurson an' her ornt worn't here?—didn't Oi say as they'd gorne away?"

"But you must know where?—and I demand to know also; and, what's more, I will know before I leave this place!"

"'Ow should Oi know? They dorn't tell me nothen'; Oi'm only a poor marn as is kept here to look arter th' hoose!" asserted Jacob.

"If you are an *honest* man," replied the captain, "why object to open the door and answer my questions, face to face, in an honest manner?"

As the captain uttered these words, he once more inserted his steel lever into its former aperture, and the ominous crackling it caused evidently produced an effect on the nerves of Jacob Mawks.

"Whort be 'ee doin'?" he exclaimed, hurriedly, "breekin' th' door doon?"

"That is my fixed determination," answered the captain; "that is, unless you save me the trouble by opening it."

"Oh, dorn't breek th' door doon!" cried the ogre, in evident anxiety; "yow maun't spile th' property!"

"Then open the door!"

"Oi didn't know yow wur in sich a takin' aboot ut, but since yow seems to wornt the door open soa pertickler, whoy Oi can open it a' course. But yow'll gie Oi th' mooney yow promised?" said Jacob.

"Open the door first, or you may chance to get something you deserve more than money!" cried the captain, in a tone of disgust. "If you hesitate another moment, I shall put my foot through the panel!"

"By goom! yow be a desp'rate k'racter, yow be! But wait a minnit, Oi'll open th' door."

"Be quick, then!"

The head disappeared, and there was a dead silence.

During the interval that succeeded, it struck Captain Hawk that he had never heard so horrible a voice.

There was something in its hoarse, croaking, inhuman sounds that inspired him with an instinctive—not horror—for that sentiment is too closely allied to fear, and the captain certainly did not fear the individual whose presence he anxiously awaited; it was rather a strong loathing, an invincible disgust amounting to hatred for a person he had never even seen.

He began to grow impatient at being kept so long waiting, and clutched his crowbar nervously, as though half inclined to wrench the door from its hinges, when the heavy, slouching footfall of Jacob was heard approaching the door.

Even this act appeared to occupy an unconscionable time.

The captain fancied he heard strange boltings and barrings taking place inside, as a preliminary step to his admission.

What did it mean?

Was the wretch concealing anyone?—and could that one be Blanche?

His blood turned cold at the thought.

At that moment, Jacob reached the door.

Captain Hawk grasped the steel weapon he carried, and had Mr. Mawks observed the significance of this action, and the stern expression of the highwayman's countenance, it is probable he would have been a little less speedy than he was in his operations.

He was now unfastening the bolts; and having done this, he turned the key in the lock, crying at the same time:

"Wait a morment!"

Captain Hawk, imagining there was some other fastening to be removed, waited impatiently till the voice of Jacob called again:

"Push!"

Thus admonished, the captain impelled the door inwards with a startling bang.

The passage was enveloped in semi-obscurity, but what light there was descended from a lamp on the stairs leading to the first-floor, and the rays fell full upon Jacob's face, that individual having retreated several yards, and stationed himself in a position facing the door.

The captain paused involuntarily—not from doubt, or fear, indecision, or any such feeling, but in pure astonishment at the hideous countenance of Jacob Mawks.

Nothing so revolting had ever met his gaze before.

A hideous shock head of sandy hair, that looked more like a lion's mane than the usual covering of the human *cranium*—a pair of wiry eyebrows of the same colour, depending from an unnaturally protruding forehead—a nose almost flat to the face, with broad, spreading nostrils—an enormous, sensual mouth, filled with yellow fangs—and a lank, bristly beard, forming the framework of a cadaverous countenance, the hue of which more resembled that of liver than the human complexion: these, added to a stunted and uncouth figure, completed the picture of Jacob Mawks.

The contemplation of this loathsome object sent so many terrible ideas rushing through the captain's brain, that he felt half inclined to rush forward and at one blow sweep such an abortion from the face of the earth.

He felt he had never hated a fellow-creature so cordially.

Jacob noticed his hesitation, but made a profound mistake as to the cause.

He imagined his appearance had scared the new-comer, and that he required encouraging.

"Noo then," he croaked, "yow made row enoogh befoor Oi oppened th' door, an' naw it be open bean't yow comin' in? What be yow afeard on?"

"Afraid, you dog! Not of you, or any such vile carrion!" cried the captain, as he sprang forward, fully intending to give Mr. Jacob Mawks a preliminary lesson in respectful behaviour by knocking his head against the wall.

But alas! his intentions were entirely frustrated, for

hardly had he advanced three yards when he felt the floor of the passage suddenly give way beneath his feet, and himself fall, with a cry of fierce but powerless rage, through a space which, though it took but a second to traverse, seemed awfully deep till he reached the bottom.

There he lay, breathless, enveloped in thick darkness, whilst the deriding laugh of the monster above rang in his ears as the trap closed up again.

"Yow wornted to git in, an' yow've gort in. Haw, haw, haw!"

CHAPTER CCVII.

CAPTAIN HAWK MAKES THE DISCOVERY THAT HE HAS FALLEN INTO A DARK CELLAR.—HE BECOMES A PREY TO THE SPECTRES OF DARKNESS AND THEIR VISIONARY ILLUSIONS.—HIS HORROR IS DISPELLED BY AN ANGEL VISIT.

If Captain Hawk had been previously inclined to suspect Jacob Mawks of a capability, from his peculiar physiognomy, of any atrocity, his suspicions were now more than confirmed.

He had evidently fallen into the trap laid for him by the treacherous rascal.

As soon as he recovered his breath, after the shock of the fall, he strove with all his powers to penetrate the darkness that surrounded him.

He might as well have striven to have accomplished any other feat that was equally impossible.

His eyeballs ached and throbbed with the efforts he made: strange coloured fires seemed, as it were, to dance in his head—but he saw nothing.

We often talk of the oppressive heat of the noonday sun, of the oppressive glare of the bright luminary on a scorching summer's day, but neither of these will bear any comparison with the oppression of utter darkness.

He had, in the natural instinct of preservation, stretched forth his hands as he fell, and this act had preserved his face at the expense of his hands, which, from the violence of his unexpected fall, had suffered some severe abrasions.

The first thought that suggested itself was the kind of place into which he had fallen.

He rose to his feet cautiously, thinking perhaps the subterranean cell into which he had been precipitated might be low-roofed; but there was no need of such care, for he could stand upright easily without his head coming in contact with any overhanging substance.

He stretched out his hand over his head, but even then he touched nothing; the pit that held him was deeper than he thought.

He sprang upwards, and was just enabled to brush the roof with the tips of his fingers.

He walked cautiously forward till his progress was stopped by a wall; he then walked over to the opposite side, and found that the superficial extent of his prison was about six yards one way.

Having performed the same operation at a right angle, he counted twelve steps, so that he calculated with tolerable correctness that his place of confinement was about twelve yards in length and six in breadth.

The floor of the cell was evidently earth, pressed firmly down till it was quite hard and solid.

From the damp, mouldy odour that prevailed in these dark precincts, it was easy to assume that he had fallen into a cellar.

He had grasped his steel crowbar firmly as he fell, consequently he had it with him.

After some time spent in groping on the ground, he found it.

He picked it up with much satisfaction, it being an invaluable friend either as a weapon of defence or as an instrument of escape.

Rapidly his thoughts rushed forth with painful and almost bewildering velocity.

The strange mystery that seemed to attach itself to the house in which he was—the suspicious silence of the abominable Jacob as to the whereabouts of its occupants—the existence of a pitfall such as that into which he had fallen in a private dwelling—the treacherous means that had been employed to entrap him—and, finally, the fate of Blanche, were a mass of facts that filled his breast with indignation and intense anxiety.

The thought that one so beautiful, so defenceless as Blanche might be in the power and exposed to the malignance of the hideous being, of whose horrible aspect he had had a brief glimpse, was unbearable.

He clenched his hands and teeth, and groaned in the bitter anguish of his spirit, as his own fettered condition came vividly before him.

Of all positions that are calculated to overthrow the philosophy of man, none can be so powerful as that wherein some loved object is in imminent peril, whilst he himself is utterly debarred from the slightest chance of rendering any help.

"My Blanche!" he cried, desperately, in the thick darkness, "where art thou at this moment? Perhaps confined in some dungeon as dark and cheerless as that I now inhabit, but with less strength to endure the horror of such impenetrable gloom! But courage, loved one! —though you know it not, there is one whose thoughts are never removed from you, whose prayers are ever for your welfare and safety, dear girl, and whose arm shall yet, with Heaven's help, save you!"

This soliloquy, which partook partly of the nature of an excited soliloquy and partly of a fervid prayer, had the effect of reviving his spirits.

Still the darkness was horribly oppressive.

"The first thing to accomplish," continued the captain, more calmly, "is to break through my prison walls."

He crossed to the side of the cellar, and tapped at them with the crowbar, listening attentively to the quality of the sound the strokes produced.

They were anything but satisfactory.

Could his features have been visible, a heavy shade of disappointment would have been seen hanging over them like a cloud.

"This dead, non-reverberant sound proves that beyond this wall all is solid earth!" he exclaimed, bitterly.

He repeated the experiment along the entire extent of the four sides, but with the same result.

"Of course," he continued, in a tone almost of despair, "this cottage standing alone, this cellar does not join another, or I should have every confidence of speedily effecting my escape. As it is, how can I proceed? To burrow in the solid earth like a worm or a mole is impossible! There is only one point of attack that promises success, and that is the roof—and how can I reach that? Lost—lost!" he cried, as he dashed down the crowbar in fierce despair, and, sinking in a state of sullen apathy on the ground, buried his face in his hands.

This state of feeling, so different from the usual custom of Captain Hawk, was the result of his position.

In circumstances of the most vital peril—whilst clambering over roof-tops, hanging between life and death from dizzy heights, surrounded by the weapons of his pursuers—he could be calm and self-possessed; there was still a chance—a faint one, perhaps, but still a chance—that he might escape; but in his present state there was none.

His case seemed hopeless, and not only his, but hers he loved better than himself. Was it strange, then, that he sank down in the gloomy torpor of despair, and uttered the sad words—"Lost—lost?"

He was suddenly aroused from this dangerous and unprofitable state of mind by hearing the street-door close with a bang.

He started, and looked up; the very shock had a beneficial effect upon his partially benumbed energies.

Anything was better than that deep, dead silence.

The most horrible yells or the most piercing shrieks could have been more easily endured.

Any restlessness or anxiety was preferable to that leaden, listless paralysis of the soul, that, feeling exertion to be useless, resolves to make none.

He listened attentively, and his thoughts began to work more healthily; they had once more recovered somewhat of their usual elasticity.

It was evident some one had left the house when the door closed.

Who could that some one be but the ogre Jacob?

Then came the question: "Why had he gone out?—for what purpose?"

"Perhaps to return with one or more, more ruffianly and hideous even than himself, to accomplish his destruction!"

"Let them come!" cried the captain, with the fury of

a tiger, gripping the steel bar with the intensity of a vice—"let them come: they shall find it no child's play!"

His eyes flashed fire in the darkness as he spoke; could their expression have been seen, it would have been terrible.

Could he but break from his prison during his jailer's absence—could he but search the house, what would he not have given?

His imagination pictured the fair girl he loved, pale and woe-begone, with dishevelled hair and bowed-down, shrinking form, crouched in some narrow chamber, trembling with apprehension, and perhaps crying out with faltering voice for him to save her.

"Oh, Blanche!—angel!" he cried, "would to Heaven I were near you!"

At the thoughts he had been lately indulging he was as wildly excited as he had been previously deeply depressed.

Every nerve in his body quivered with the strong, yearning desire he had for liberty.

His cheeks were hot and flushed.

He seized the crowbar madly, and struck the solid brickwork that composed the walls of his cell with the fury of a fiend.

Had they not been solid, and backed by earth, they must infallibly have yielded to his impetuous assault.

They were not the blows of a man in the calm exercise of his reason—they were more like the wild, convulsive assaults of a maniac.

Woe to Jacob!—woe to his myrmidons, at that moment, had they stood before his frantic arm!

Captain Hawk paused from sheer exhaustion, and once more sank down, and would again have fallen in a state of apathy deeper than the former, when a sound fell on his ear, that appeared preternaturally acute to the faintest echo.

It is a fact that the deprivation of one sense quickens the action of the rest.

The blind are always exceedingly delicate in the organ of hearing.

Captain Hawk, being temporarily deprived of sight, heard everything with unusual distinctness.

He listened with a new sensation of trembling hope.

The sound was very indistinct, and was of a creaking quality, such as a person's boots might cause when the wearer is endeavouring to ascend the stairs surreptitiously.

They gradually increased.

"Oh surely," he cried, "it is a human footstep, but not the heavy tread of that miserable abortion. No—no!"

Suddenly the sounds ceased.

"Surely they will come!" cried the captain, in an excited tone. "Man or devil, nay, a legion of fiends would be preferable to encounter than this hopeless, horrible darkness!"

As he ceased speaking, the sounds were once more audible.

It was evidently a footstep, and this time undoubtedly approaching the trap over his head.

Though the sound was very faint, he could detect that perfectly.

He listened in a perfect agony of expectation lest the comer, whoever he was, should alter his mind.

But no! there is a sound of the drawing of bolts over his head.

"Thank Heaven—thank Heaven!" cries the excited prisoner, fervently.

This sound is harsh and grating, but no music to his ears ever appeared so delightful.

The operation of unbolting continues, and now a dim light seems to steal through the darkness over his head.

The light widens and increases in brightness; suddenly the trap falls with a crash, and the full rays of the light from above shine down into the gloom.

Captain Hawk uttered a cry of joy as he gazed upwards.

A lost spirit from the depths of eternal woe could hardly have looked more longingly towards the bright regions he might never enter than did the captain at the rays of light that shone upon him.

But what was it that so fixed his attention and for a moment paralysed his tongue?

It was that, with the light falling full upon her fair sorrowful features, and lighting up her rich, golden hair, he gazed upon the object of all his anxiety—his beloved, his adored Blanche!

CHAPTER CCVIII.

BLANCHE RELEASES CAPTAIN HAWK FROM THE TRAP.—THE CAPTAIN MAKES LOVE AND PLIGHTS HIS TRUTH IN THE UNINHABITED PARLOUR.—AN ANTICIPATED FLIGHT FRUSTRATED.—TRUE LOVERS SEPARATED, AND THE CAPTAIN RE-COMMITTED TO HIS PRISON.

"MERCIFUL Heaven!" he cried, "I thank thee! Do you not remember my voice, Blanche?" he inquired, eagerly, as he remarked that her delicate cheek grew paler still as his familiar accents fell upon her ear.

"Captain Hawk!" she faltered, "is it indeed you?"

"Yes, love!" he replied.

"Oh, let me hasten to release you from this horrible snare!" she eagerly exclaimed.

"Yes, dearest! Let me once rise from this living tomb, I can defy your enemies and my own!"

In a moment Blanche had dragged to the trap a small ladder that was near at hand, and that was evidently used as a means of descent.

This she lowered into the cellar.

In an instant Captain Hawk had mounted and clasped his fair deliverer in his arms.

Even the indistinct light of the lamp was sufficient to show that the fair face of Blanche was covered with blushes.

These love-messengers were but transient, and quickly faded from her cheek, leaving it paler than before.

"My Blanche!—my dearest Blanche!" murmured the captain fondly, as he drew her to him.

The beautiful girl permitted this freedom, but bashfully.

She felt that the handsome and ardent cavalier at her side had not made any express avowal of affection.

Then, again, they had not met for some length of time; and now that they had once more met together, it was under peculiar circumstances—at night, in a lonely house—and the result of these reflections was a timid restraint that seemed like coolness, which it certainly was not.

Blanche undoubtedly, had she confessed the exact state of her feelings, loved the handsome highwayman as even he himself, with all his warm, impetuous nature, could have desired; but, like other timid maidens, she required wooing into confidence.

Captain Hawk—whose love, eager and passionate as it was, was pure as the early dewdrop that kisses the blushing rose—was not slow to divine this, and he hastened to remove any doubts or fears she might entertain.

If she had enemies around her that threatened her honour and her happiness, he resolved to convince her that he was not one of them—that in him she might trust.

"Forgive me, sweet Blanche, for this impetuosity!" he said, tenderly, "but we cannot always command ourselves; and if you knew what I have suffered during the last hour on your account, I am sure you would forgive me!"

"Oh, I do forgive you!—I have nothing to forgive!" she replied, sweetly.

But there was something of anxiety in her tone and manner that proved she was not at ease.

"Let us close this trap," said Captain Hawk, "and then we shall be able to collect our thoughts. The sight of that yawning cavity is enough to frighten love away."

The ladder was quickly removed, and the trap made secure.

The captain then took the lamp, and led Blanche into the parlour.

It was empty of furniture, save two old-fashioned-looking wooden chairs.

In one of these he placed the young lady, and seated himself in the other by her side.

He then gently took her hand in his, and looked, with all the tenderness of love's solicitude, in her fair sad face.

Her eyes drooped under this scrutiny, but not painfully; she felt that, with the man who had already risked so much for her, she was safe.

"My Blanche!" he said, fondly, "if I may be permitted to call you so, you are not well—you look pale! You do not fear me?"

"Fear you—*you?*" she exclaimed, eagerly, tightening her grasp involuntarily upon the hand she held. "Oh no!"

"That's right!—you need not. Poor girl!" he continued, "you have suffered much since we last met; I can see you have!"

"I have indeed!" she faltered. "I never thought I should see you again!"

"When I left you at the Greyhound," continued the captain, "I little imagined how many vicissitudes I was destined to undergo until I should again see you. I left you hastily—circumstances compelled me to do so—and, though your image was indelibly impressed on my heart and memory, I had no time or opportunity to tell you how deeply. We met, and parted, and all I dared to hope was that you would sometimes think of me."

"I have thought of nothing else!" was Blanche's comforting assurance.

"You knew what I was before we parted," the captain went on—"you were acquainted with the wild, adventurous career I follow, and the life I lead; and I have sometimes thought, that though any little service I may have been able to render you might have awakened your gratitude, that it would fail to win your love, and that you would despise me!"

"Despise you! How could that be possible?"

"Then I am not an object of contempt to you?"

"Contempt! Oh, how could you think so?"

"Then you do not hate me?"

"No, no!—I love you!"

As she made this confession she buried her glowing face upon the captain's shoulder.

"Then you would not hesitate to link your fate with mine, my Blanche?"

"Oh no! It would be my pride—my joy—my greatest happiness!" she eagerly exclaimed.

"Then hear me, my own love!" cried the enraptured lover—"hear me, my own Blanche, while I swear solemnly, in storm or sunshine, in sickness or health, in riches and poverty, in life and death, to be yours—and yours only! Heaven, that hears my vow, can attest the sincerity with which I make it!"

He sank at her feet as he spoke, and, with his arms lovingly encircling her waist, gazed fondly into the gentle eyes that now sparkled with renewed lustre.

"You accept my vows—and myself?" he inquired, with a loving smile.

"Both, dearest Richard!" murmured Blanche; "and, in return for your generous devotion, accept all I have to offer—my noble heart, my love: a wife's untiring, self-denying devotion, the effort of whose life shall be to prove herself worthy of her husband's love, to share his confidence, to cheer him in sorrow, to nurse him in sickness, and to cling to him alike in prosperity and adversity—even until the end!"

With a long, clinging embrace, that proved all her fears and scruples were effectually silenced, the beautiful and faithful girl set her seal to her vows, and the happy pair, thus strangely brought together, and unexpectedly affianced, sat together in that solitary, unfurnished, dusty parlour, which, in their present frame of mind, seemed to be transformed into a paradise.

So occupied were they in their newly-found happiness, that for a time all explanations of the past, arrangements for the present, and prospects for the future, were entirely forgotten.

Captain Hawk suddenly remembered their position, and the necessity there was for some inquiry as to what had transpired.

"My Blanche," he said, "what is the meaning of the mystery that appears to surround this cottage?—the desolate appearance of the interior?—the absence of furniture?—the presence of the hideous wretch who informed me that your aunt and yourself had gone away? What does it mean?"

Blanche shuddered at this interrogation, and glancing round apprehensively, as though she almost feared to encounter some dreaded object peering through the half-open door, nestled closer to the side of her betrothed, as she replied in a low voice:

"The answer to all may be summed up in two words: *My guardian!*"

"Is he not dead?" exclaimed Captain Hawk. "Then my bullet missed its mark!"

"He was scarcely wounded, but recovered himself," continued Blanche. "No sooner was he convalescent, than he lost no time in discovering the place of my retreat. This was not difficult, inasmuch as he knew my aunt resided in London, and suspected that I should seek shelter there."

"And did he follow you?"

"Yes, and renewed his hateful proposals. Oh, he is not only a heartless, mercenary man, but a remorseless, cruel, bloodthirsty wretch, capable of any act, however atrocious!"

Blanche spoke with a shuddering, intense horror, that proved how deeply she felt the words she uttered.

"And he dared insult you with his hateful addresses?" inquired the captain, indignantly.

"He did," replied Blanche; "but they were met with nothing but contempt from me. I felt that, under my aunt's roof, I was safe, at least from violence, and I defied the villain!"

"My own brave girl!"

"But I repented afterwards that I had aroused the resentment of one so vindictive. I did not know the man I braved. I did not believe him so great an adept in dissimulation, or so audacious in executing his plans, as he has since proved himself."

"What did he do?"

"He was at first indignant at my utter rejection of his suit; but when he found that neither his indignation nor his threats moved me, he changed his tactics."

"In what way?"

"He pretended to believe that I was right, and that he had been to blame, assuring me that his conduct throughout had been influenced by love for me——"

"Love! The old scoundrel!" indignantly interrupted Captain Hawk.

"You may be sure, dear Richard, I received these protestations for what they were worth. Would he had been really penitent! But I knew him to be utterly false and deceitful, and did not believe him."

"And what then?"

"He took his departure. Shortly afterwards a gentleman called and inquired if this cottage was for sale. It was not; but it suddenly struck my aunt that it would not be a bad plan, in order to get quite clear of any future annoyances from my guardian, to sell the cottage, and reside for the future in the country. Accordingly she expressed herself willing to treat with the gentleman for its purchase. The arrangements were soon made, and my aunt was in treaty for a country house, where we were henceforth to reside. It was necessary, previous to deciding upon this house, to visit it, and accordingly my aunt hired a conveyance, and departed, leaving me here alone, promising to return at night. I waited patiently, and—as the hours passed on—anxiously for her return; but she came not, and I was growing seriously alarmed when I heard the sound of the carriage wheels at the gate. The carriage door was unfastened, and the gate unlocked. I hastened to the door, and opened it, expecting to find my aunt standing on the threshold. Judge of my dismay, when, in her place, I beheld the hated form of my ruthless guardian, and behind him the horrible, distorted object who answered your questions and snared you in the trap. The villain clasped me in his arms when I would have rushed out, and forced me back; my screams he stifled by tying a cloth over my mouth."

"The d—d unmanly ruffian!" muttered the captain between his teeth, as he drew the fair narrator more closely within the folds of his protecting arms. "Go on, love," he continued.

"I was so startled and terrified at the violence of my guardian and his frightful assistant that I lost all consciousness; when I recovered, I found myself a prisoner in the topmost room of the cottage; it is a room at the back, overlooking the garden."

"That from the window of which I observed the light," thought the captain.

"My first effort on recovering my senses was to try the door. Of course, as I expected it would be, it was locked the window was barred with iron, and even had it not been, the distance from the ground was too great to permit my escape that way, save with the loss of my life, though even that would have been preferable to the insults of my captor. Thus I found myself a prisoner, entirely at the mercy of a man whom I at first disliked and despised, but whom I now feared and loathed. I was burning with thirst; a bottle of water and a glass stood on the mantelshelf. I dashed some of the cool liquid into the glass unsuspiciously, and drank it eagerly, but hardly had I swallowed it than the room seemed to whirl round in rapid gyrations, and I once more sank down in a state of utter insensibility."

"I understand!" cried the captain, clenching his hand ominously, "the water was drugged!"

"Undoubtedly!" replied Blanche. "How long I remained in the lethargic state it had produced I know not, but when I recovered consciousness I found my persecutor standing at the side of the couch on which I had been placed.

"I shrunk from him as from a poisonous reptile, but the wretch was not to be repelled or avoided, and in spite of my struggles he clasped me in his loathsome embrace, and——"

"Surely he did not dare——" shouted the captain, violently, his face crimsoning with an indignant blush.

"No, no!" cried Blanche, assuringly, "he did not harm me. I felt at the moment he seized me the imminent and critical peril into which I had fallen, and I cried to Heaven for help. My prayer was answered in the renewed strength and resolution with which I felt myself suddenly inspired.

"With a strong effort, every nerve in my body being strung with desperation, I threw off the designing villain, and seizing the glass, I hurled it with all my force into the ruffian's face as he advanced.

"The missile inflicted a frightful wound in his forehead, from which the blood poured in torrents, and he fell prostrate and stunned to the ground, as insensible as I had been a short time previously. I began to fear I had killed him."

"It would have been a fitting punishment for such a dastardly wretch!" cried the captain.

"The noise of his fall aroused his servant Jacob, who came to his master's assistance, and removed him from the room, threatening me with all kinds of punishment for what he was pleased to call my violence."

"The miserable abortion! Let me but encounter him!"

The expression of the captain's countenance, and the nervous working of his fingers seemed to indicate that nothing short of strangulation would have been sufficient atonement for Jacob's misdemeanours.

"From that time," continued Blanche, "I have not seen him. I believe he has been away, but he left his servant behind to watch, who kept me constantly under lock and key."

"And how were you able eventually to effect your escape and release me?" inquired the captain.

"I found a table-knife in the cupboard of the room," returned Blanche, "and with that I contrived to loosen the screws in the lock, resolving to make an effort to escape at the first opportunity. I fancied I heard a voice that was familiar speaking below stairs, and almost immediately after the falling of the trap reached my ears, and I divined there was some treachery afoot.

"Not long after I heard the street-door shut, and, believing it was Jacob who had gone out, I felt the time to attempt my escape had arrived.

"I accordingly removed the screws; the lock fell from its place, and the door opened.

"I hastily traversed the chambers in search of my aunt; but, alas! without success; she was not there. Every room, too, was entirely empty, all the furniture having been removed; and the hollow sound of my own footsteps in the deserted mansion seemed like the echoes of some departed spirit.

"As I descended the stairs with trembling haste, the same voice that had reached my ears from the passage some time before was again audible.

"It seemed familiar, and I listened eagerly.

"I soon discovered that it proceeded from the cellar beneath.

"With mingled sensations of hope and fear, I resolved to open the trap.

"I felt confident that no one imprisoned there could be an enemy of mine—nay, I judged that on that account the prisoner was more likely to prove a friend.

"Little, however, did I think when I drew the bolts who it was I was going to set free."

"Then you did not recognise my voice?" inquired the captain, with a little reproach in his tone.

"No, dearest!" she answered. "Though it appeared familiar, it was too muffled and indistinct for recognition, until the trap was lowered, and I then knew who it was in a moment—it was you, my kind, my brave, my generous preserver!"

As she finished her recital, she threw her arms round the captain, and clung to him fondly, as the ivy entwines its tendrils round the oak, a figurative emblem of weakness clinging to strength for protection.

"Then you are ignorant what has become of your aunt?" inquired the captain.

"Entirely," answered Blanche, "and I am more uneasy at her absence; I fear some danger has befallen her."

"I am inclined to think the gentleman who called about the cottage was an impostor, and the purchase of the house a mere blind," said the captain.

"I think so myself," returned Blanche. "Would that I could see her again in safety! dear, dear aunt!" she exclaimed, warmly.

"You shall see her again, love, and in safety, too, I trust," replied the captain, pressing his lips to hers; "but first let us leave this place."

"Oh yes, let us go. But then," she added, pausing suddenly, a blush of shame overspreading her face, lest her lover should misinterpret her eagerness, "where can I go? at this hour of the night, too!"

"Can you not trust yourself with me, my Blanche?" asked the captain, persuasively.

The fair girl glanced at his handsome features, and confessed to herself that there might be danger even with him; the thought made her sigh.

Captain Hawk divined the cause of that sigh, and said:

"You need not fear to trust me, my own love. Are you not my betrothed wife, and are not your honour and reputation as dear to me as my own? Oh, trust and fear not!"

"I do trust you, Richard! and I fear nothing, under your protection!" she cried, firmly.

"Come, then, darling!" exclaimed the captain, and passing his arm lovingly round her waist, he led her into the passage, and then passing along to the front door, turned the handle and threw it open, uttering a cry of mingled hate and defiance as he found himself face to face with Jacob Mawks.

It seemed as though the sight of him filled the captain from the crown to the heel with the most violent animosity.

"You foul abortion!" he shouted, as without hesitation he seized the ungainly Jacob by his shock head of hair.

"Leave moi 'air aloan, will yow?" growled Jacob, in a surly tone.

"I'll wring your accursed neck!" cried the captain, transferring one of his hands from the fellow's head to his throat.

But the highwayman soon perceived that this frightful object with the hoarse, croaking voice, and the brutal physiognomy, had also a brute's strength.

The ruffianly Jacob evinced a disposition to resist.

He looked at Captain Hawk knowingly from under his penthouse brows, and seeing in his antagonist nothing more than a well-made, handsome young gentleman, not immoderately broad in the shoulders, and perfectly straight in the legs, despised him accordingly.

"Soa," he grunted out, "yow thout yow was goin' to run away, didn't yow? But yow bean't! Soa yow can jess goa back, moi foine gintlemarn!"

Captain Hawk, with profound disgust, tightened his grasp upon his throat, and endeavoured to drag him from his position.

But he found he had mistaken his adversary's powers.

He found that this uncouth, hideous domestic had the strength of an elephant, and that moving him was something like moving a monument.

[THE POLICE OFFICERS MAKE AN UNPLEASANT DISCOVERY.]

He still stood in the way in the narrow passage, entirely blocking it up.

"Ho, ho!" laughed the brute, derisively, "what be th' good o' yow a tryin' to move Oi—a poor, weak boy loike yow?"

This was a little too much for the captain, who, at the first attempt to dislodge the intruder, had not used any great effort; but now, wound up to a pitch of indignant disgust, he concentrated all his forces into one focus, and with a sudden jerk that made all Jacob Mawks's teeth chatter in his head, he turned him round and got next to the door.

"Now, you dog!" he cried, with strong contempt, "you see, in order to be strong, it is not necessary to be entirely out of proportion. Lie there!" he shouted, as, with a tremendous effort of strength, he flung off the misshapen object, who fell with great force, his head coming

in contact with the stairs, that creaked again with the blow.

This had hardly taken place when a startled cry arose from the lips of Blanche, and ere Captain Hawk could inquire or even speculate upon the cause of her emotion, a blow dealt by an unsparing hand behind him descended with crushing violence on his head, and felled him to the ground, utterly bereft of sense and motion.

The door was slammed hastily to, and Grove Cottage was still the prison of Captain Hawk and Blanche Allison.

Blanche, at the sight of the captain stretched insensible on the ground, uttered a piercing cry and prostrated herself before him as though to preserve him from the attacks of further violence.

But Jacob, having shaken himself and recovered the effects of the slight collision between his head and the stairs, darted forward, and seizing her, dragged her away and thrust her into the parlour, the door of which he closed.

He then dragged the insensible body of Captain Hawk to the edge of the trap, and once more drawing the bolts, the lid fell with the usual clatter.

He then lifted up the unconscious captain, and holding him over the dark cavity, dropped him in, with a chuckle of vindictive delight, and then refastened the trap.

There then followed a low whispered consultation between master and man in the passage, which had hardly finished, when a close carriage, drawn by a pair of horses, stopped at the gate.

"Now, then, quick!" cried Blanche's guardian, whom we shall know henceforward as Ridley Massingham.

The two worthies entered the parlour just in time to prevent Blanche, who had unfastened the shutters and unclosed the window, from escaping by that way.

She was immediately seized, a handkerchief tied tightly over her mouth, and she herself lifted into the carriage.

Mr. Massingham seated himself by her side and closed the carriage windows, whilst Jacob, having locked the cottage door and gate, scrambled up into the dickey behind, and the carriage, with its cargo, drove off.

CHAPTER CCIX.

CHARLES FROM SNAGSON'S PAYS A VISIT TO "THE RETREAT." —HE BRINGS A NOTE FROM THE COUNTESS OF BLACKLAKE, AND SOME IMPORTANT INTELLIGENCE.—HE LEAVES "THE RETREAT" AND SUDDENLY RESOLVES TO TAKE A TRIP DOWN THE RIVER.—HE PUTS UP FOR THE NIGHT.

CAPTAIN HAWK had hardly taken his departure from the "Prince's Retreat," when Charles the Trusty, who had been put in possession of the new locality of our heroes by Pharoah, made his appearance there.

He had prudently disguised himself so skilfully that he defied recognition.

Lord Harcliffe had not yet started for Leicester House, and was not a little surprised at the sight of Charles.

"Good evening, your lordship," said the stanch messenger, as he entered.

"Ah, my friend, good evening!" returned Lord Harcliffe. "Come to see if we're alive?"

"Not exactly that, my lord," replied Charles, "since I heerd that from the gent as brought your address. I've come about something else."

As he spoke he held up a note addressed in a beautiful female handwriting to "*Our Two Friends.*"

"Oh, I understand!" said his lordship, smiling; "it is from our lovely countess in St. James's Square."

After gazing at it for a moment admiring the delicacy and beauty of the writing, he broke the seal.

The contents ran thus:—

"*My dear Friends,—*

"*Circumstances have occurred which have decided us upon expediting our marriage. The ceremony will consequently take place at St. George's, Hanover Square, on Friday morning next at 12 o'clock. Relying upon your promise of assistance, should we require it, it is the united wish of my dear —— and myself that you should be present. The carriage will be at the door at half-past eleven. For reasons which you will comprehend, our marriage will be strictly private.*

"*Your Sincere Friend,*

"*C. C.*"

"Certainly," ejaculated Lord Harcliffe, as he finished the note, "there is no reason in the world why we cannot oblige the fair countess with our presence; I will write at once and say she may depend upon us."

"Excuse me, yer lordship," said Charles, "but there's somethin' else as I haven't told yer."

"Out with it, then," replied his lordship. "What is it, eh?"

"Why, as I was quietly creeping along the garden of the mansion in St. James's Square, what does yer lordship think I saw?"

"Nay," he replied, with a laugh, "how can I possibly tell? A balloon, probably?"

"No, your lordship, not a balloon, but a police officer!"

"Oh indeed! And pray what was he doing?"

"He wasn't doing anythin' pertickler, 'cos he'd done what he wanted, an' that was to read that note. I see him a fastening down the edges agin; an' when he'd done that, he pops it into the hole in the trunk agin' just as if it had never been touched."

"And what did you do?"

"Nothing at all but keep quite snug and quiet behind the bushes till he'd passed and gone out of the garden, and then I went and took the note into my charge."

"Then it is very evident this police officer is acquainted with the contents of this note?" remarked his lordship.

"Every word on it, as clear as you are yourself, my lord."

"This fellow is a spy. How fortunate you were a witness to this, Charles! It might else have frustrated the whole affair. By-the-by, did you know this police officer?"

"Very well, my lord, by sight. Let me see, what's his name?" said Charles, reflectively, to himself.

"Peterson?"

"That's him!"

"Yes, yes, I understand; this Peterson is undoubtedly a spy of Sir Richard Chandos, the countess's guardian. How did he become acquainted with this little arrangement? He must have overheard it while he was confined in the body of the sofa. Yes, yes, that is it, there is no doubt of it."

"I s'pose," observed Charles, "now you knows as the officer's read the note, yer'll be able to circumvent 'em."

"Easily, by the simplest plan in the world," replied his lordship.

"May I take the liberty o' askin' how?"

"Why, instead of the marriage taking place at St. George's Church at twelve o'clock, it must be solemnized at St. James's Church at ten. We shall thus throw them off the scent, and get a good two hours' start—d'ye see?"

"Perfectly, your lordship!" answered Charles. "What a capital idea!"

"Oh, it's very simple," returned Lord Harcliffe. "But you will have to take a note, which I will write, to the countess's residence, apprising her of the *surveillance* that has been exercised, and suggesting to her the slight alteration of time and place for the performance of the ceremony."

"Certainly, your lordship, I'll take it, never fear," said Charles, readily.

"The captain has gone over to Chelsea, on a voyage of discovery, this evening," continued his lordship; "I do not imagine he will be late; therefore if you can, I should suggest your remaining till his return, to hear your own recital of this *contretemps*."

"I'll stop, an' welcome!" cried Charles, eagerly. "It's allus a treat to me to see the captain."

Pharoah at that moment entered and informed Lord Harcliffe that the Prince was so indisposed that he would not be able to give him the required interview that evening.

"All the better," said his lordship. "I shall devote this evening then to sherry and cigars in the society of my worthy friend here," indicating Charles, who was immensely flattered.

It was a quiet night at "The Retreat"—in fact, since the awful catastrophe of the "Red Room," and the subsequent shaking the nerves of the guilty parties received at the hands of our heroes, not one of them ventured to make his appearance, and those members who did come retired early.

Pharoah consequently was not very much in request; and having supplied his friends with everything their hearts could desire, he was enabled to pay them flying visits, and at last when the members had departed, to join them and partake their conviviality.

The evening passed joyously and rapidly away.

The clocks struck midnight, and still the revellers sat with their cigars in their hands and their glasses before them.

"Midnight!" remarked Lord Harcliffe, as the horological monitors informed them how time was passing. "I suppose, then, we shall have our friend here presently."

But minute after minute passed, and still he came not.

The minutes increased and multiplied until the clocks again pealed forth one o'clock!

"Umph!" ejaculated his lordship, "I fancy the captain has been successful in his suit: he stays so late."

But Charles, who was anxious to see the captain, whom he held in profound respect, heeded not the lateness of the hour, and would have remained there all night had not Lord Harcliffe, as the clocks once more dinged forth two o'clock, suggested his taking his departure.

There being no particular reason why he should prolong his stay at that late hour, he rose from his seat joyous and exuberant under the influence of numerous glasses of some of the finest wine in the kingdom, and prepared to go.

Having received from his lordship particular injunctions to take his note to the Countess of Blacklake the first thing in the morning, and having promised the most implicit obedience to his wishes, Charles made his obeisance and retired.

Lord Harcliffe attached but little importance to the non-return of his comrade.

Though not in love himself, he was sufficiently acquainted with the manners and customs of persons in that blissful state to know that lovers in the presence of their mistresses had a habit of entirely forgetting to look at their watches, and, in fact, of ignoring the existence of any such antiquated personage as Time altogether.

He therefore quietly resigned himself to another cigar, and dozed over it till the captain should make his appearance.

Charles, however, was not quite so easy in his mind on this point.

He knew the stir and excitement that was boiling up amongst the police authorities, and he became impressed with a kind of vague idea that the captain had got into some trouble.

Certainly Chelsea did not appear to be the very hot-bed of danger like Bow Street; but then at such times as these, and with a reward of £300 to stimulate them, he knew very well that police officers became migratory, and rambled about in all directions after their prey; and why should they not go as far as Chelsea?

This thought so fastened on his mind that he could not shake it off.

So much was he impressed, that instead of proceeding towards St. Giles's, he found himself, as it were, walking on air (the champagne he had drank having made him ethereal) in the direction of the Strand.

He was hardly conscious of the fact, when he suddenly discovered that he had diverged from that thoroughfare, and was leaning against the railings of one of the piers on the banks of the Thames.

It was somewhat singular that he should have arrived at the very point from which Captain Hawk had started on the previous evening.

Stranger still, that he should have been accosted by the very waterman who had rowed the captain up the river.

But facts are stranger than fiction, and it actually was so.

"Boat, sir?" asked the waterman.

"Y-es," answered Charles, somewhat dreamily, as his eye wandered along the river—"y-es."

Now, though Charles said "yes" twice, he showed no signs of moving; the waterman therefore, being impressed with the idea that before he could be of any practical service to his "fare," his "fare" must get into the boat, observed:

"Won't you get in, sir?"

"Certainly!" said Charles, waking up from his reverie and complying with the boatman's invitation.

"Where to?" inquired the man, as he pushed off, and began to pull gently.

"Chelsea," answered Charles.

"Chelsea?" echoed the waterman. "Lor'!"

"What's the matter?" inquired the other.

"It *is* rum, that it is!"

"What's rum?" asked Charles, who was full of champagne, and scouted the idea of any spirit so plebeian and common-sailorish.

"Why, your wantin' to go to Chelsea," the waterman answered. "I rowed a gentleman there last night from this very pier!"

"Well, is that any reason why *another* gentleman shouldn't want to go there?"

"Oh no, but I don't mean that; but this gentleman I speaks of was a rale dashing gentleman, that he was, and——"

Charles began to be indignant, and exclaimed:

"Then I s'pose I'm not a gentleman?"

"I don't mean that neither," answered the honest waterman, who began to think he was somehow or other putting his foot in it; "but it was a reg'ler adventur', that it was!"

"What d'ye mean?"

"Why, I means as I never had sich a chase in all my born days. Talk about rowing-matches, it's nothing to compare to bein' chased by a four-oared cutter full o' Bow Street police.

These words so startled Charles, that he started up in such an abrupt manner as nearly to capsize the wherry and precipitate himself into the water.

"Avast, master! Gently!" cried the boatman, "or we shall all have a ducking!"

Charles dropped into his seat again, exclaiming, as he did so:

"Police officers!"

"Yes, that's a fact. This gent orders me to row him to Chelsea, an' off we starts. We was a goin' along all nice an' comfortable—the tide being with us—when all of a sudden I sees this big lump of a boat, full of police, astarn of us.

"The gent was a sittin' quite quiet, a smokin' his cigar, when I pinted 'em out to him. He looks over his shoulder an' twigs 'em pullin' away for dear life.

"'I wonder who they wants?' says I.

"'I can tell you,' says the gent; 'they wants me.'

"But it seemed as the gent had his own ideas about that, an' had made up his mind as they warn't a goin' to have him, so he slips a couple o' guineas into my hand, an' tells me, in the purlitest way possible, to row like blazes."

"And you?"

"I did row like blazes. I believe yer; I ain't got a bit o' skin left on the palms o' my hands," said the boatman, earnestly.

"And what kind of a gentleman was he as you rowed?" inquired Charles, with equal earnestness.

"A real handsome, dashing, out-an'-out sort o' lady-killer, with a fine gold-laced coat, and a three-cornered hat all over feathers," answered the man; "an' dark eyes as seemed to look bang through yer!"

"It was the captain! It must ha' bin the captain—I'm sure on it!" cried Charles, excitedly.

"What, was he a captain?"

"Every inch of him!"

"I thought as much! And do you know him?"

"A thousand times better than I know you!"

"Lor!" ejaculated the waterman, "only to think of that!"

"But these police officers," continued Charles, in eager accents of inquiry, "they—they didn't take him, of course?"

"Take him! 'Twasn't likely when I was a rowin' him!" returned the boatman, who had got excited at the recollection of his feat of the previous night, and was now pulling so furiously that his face was crimson.

"Then he got away?"

"Clean away!" cried the boatman, exultingly.

"Brayvo!" joined in Charles, triumphantly.

"Such a trick, too, as he played them purlice, too! Ho, ho! yer'd never believe it if yer hadn't a' seed it! I wouldn't!" continued the excited waterman.

"I would," returned Charles. "They must be a clever lot o' blokes as can circumwent the captain. But let's hear all about it."

Upon this the boatman, slackening his speed and wiping the drops from his forehead, gave a full and vivid description, after his own fashion, of the manner in which Captain Hawk had outwitted his pursuers, and effected his escape.

Charles was in raptures; and, having reached Chelsea Reach, he paid the man his fare, with a little additional "tip" for his information, and proceeded in search of the hero in whom he had such a profound belief.

Everything was very quiet, and everyone was in bed, or appeared to be so, since nobody was abroad, which amounted to the same thing.

Not even a dog trotted past to break the quiet monotony of Chelsea at three in the morning.

Charles wandered here and there in search of Grove Cottage, but it seemed to him that the further he went the further Grove Cottage appeared to retreat.

No such place was to be seen.

The effects of the champagne, too, were fast wearing away, and the morning air was chilly, and sensations of drowsiness and weariness began to steal over the senses of the faithful Charles.

"This won't do!" he soliloquised. "I feel quite dead asleep!"

A tremendous yawn followed up this assertion.

"No one's any good for anything when they can't keep their two eyes open," he reasoned. "I feel jest for all the world like a howl."

He yawned again; and looking up, found himself under a garden wall.

He had been walking, as it were in his sleep for the last half-hour.

"I must have a nap," he thought. "I wonder what sort of a place it is on the other side?"

In order to ascertain this, he contrived to scramble up the side and look over.

The house was closely shut up, and had a desolate appearance: probably it was to let; but the garden was in good order.

It looked to his sleepy faculties just the kind of place to take a quiet nap in.

He accordingly dropped over on the inside, and approaching the house, selected a clump of bushes not far from its walls, and instantly assuming a recumbent posture behind the said bushes, as instantly fell asleep.

The chill morning breeze blew over him; but he felt it not. Had a cannon been fired off close to his ear, the possibility is he would scarcely have noticed it.

He was rambling miles away in the fantastic regions of Dreamland.

CHAPTER CCX.

CAPTAIN HAWK FINDS HIMSELF ONCE MORE A PRISONER IN THE CELLAR.—HE HEARS A STRANGE SOUND, AND DISCOVERS A HOLE IN THE WALL.—THE CRY FOR HELP.—THE RESULT.

THE violence of the blow struck by the cowardly hand of Ridley Massingham, and the shock of the subsequent "drop" he received, were such that for a long space of time Captain Hawk lay in a state of happy unconsciousness.

We say happy, because in his insensible state he could think of nothing, and in his present position that was happiness comparatively.

A return to consciousness could only awaken him to a sense of bodily torture, and the conviction that he was once more a prisoner, with the still more agonising remembrance that Blanche was torn from him—most probably in the power of remorseless and unscrupulous hands, without his being in the least able to render her any assistance.

To these miserable truths, however, he was destined at length to awake.

Slowly Nature assumed her sway.

The first symptoms of returning consciousness was a violent, racking headache.

His brain and temples throbbed so strongly and acutely that he could almost—but for the absurdity of the idea—have imagined that a troop of tiny imps or demons had been incarcerated in the interior of his skull, and were hammering with all their might against the sides to get out.

The pain was most intense—so much so that it overpowered for a time, by its maddening violence, every other faculty.

But by degrees, the demons within seemed to hammer less fiercely, and the power of recollection returned.

With this came a burning thirst, so parching and withering, that could he have held the world in one hand and a cup of cold water in the other, with the liberty of choosing between them, he would unhesitatingly have accepted the water, and spurned the world.

But by degrees this terrible sensation abated; and though he still experienced both pain and thirst, there seemed a lull in their intensity.

Then came the same thought that had crossed his mind before, when he suddenly found himself a prisoner in the dark:

"Where am I?"

But there was no voice to answer that question, and the thick darkness all around him rendered ocular investigation impossible.

But his mind reverting to his previous incarceration, suggested the most natural answer to his question, viz: that he had been restored to the same dungeon he had previously occupied.

He extended his hands along the ground on which he lay, and they encountered the steel crowbar, which, in the surprise and joy caused by the sudden and unexpected vision of Blanche, he had forgotten to take with him.

This was, however, rather an advantage, since, if he had taken it away, the probability is he would not have been permitted to carry it back with him, whereas now he held it securely in his grasp.

With some difficulty he managed to rise up and stand upon his feet.

But the effort pained him; he felt giddy, weak, and faint.

In a moment, however, these sensations subsided, and he walked as he had done on the former occasion to the side, and tapped it with the crowbar.

He instantly recognised the same dead, solid sound that a similar act had previously produced.

He walked towards, and in six steps touched the opposite wall.

This almost convinced him that he was in the same place that had formerly held him a prisoner.

He thrust at the ceiling with the steel crowbar, and the end struck the wooden trap.

He now knew for certain where he was.

But this knowledge only suggested other thoughts.

How long was he destined to remain there? Would he ever be released?—if so, who would set him free?

Before it was his own beloved Blanche; now she would be unable to assist him—she would be too closely watched.

What fate might not be reserved for him?

In the close, dark cellar of that solitary house, he might starve over and over again, and no one be any the wiser.

It was a terrible idea! nor was the thought that the poor girl who had been snatched from him might be exposed to the vindictive oppression of an unscrupulous scoundrel, on whom neither her helplessness, her sighs, nor tears, would have any effect, more reviving.

He groaned in the bitterness of his spirit.

"Oh, Blanche—dearest Blanche!" he cried, "it is not of myself I think, but of thee!"

But all his thoughts, his anguish and despair, availed him nothing. He was there, utterly helpless—powerless; and there must he remain, unless the hand of Providence should in some signal manner interpose to deliver him.

Despair again seemed to be settling down in a dull, leaden cloud over his soul, and the thirst that seemed to have been for a time assuaged without drinking, now became raging and intolerable.

"Oh, for a drop of water—oh, for but a drop!" he cried, fiercely.

He dashed his hand madly along the walls of his prison to see if any moisture clung to or trickled down them, but the weather was warm, and the cellar was dry—at least, too dry for that.

Again a prostrating sensation of faintness seized upon him. He made, however, a strong effort to shake it off, but it was too much for him; his legs gave way under him, and he sank down upon the ground, and became again insensible.

He was not long, however, in this condition; and when he revived, he was conscious of hearing a peculiar sound at no great distance from him; nay, it would almost seem as though this sound had been instrumental in arousing him from his lethargy.

He listened with the most eager attention.

At first the hope flashed across him that it might be Blanche, who having eluded her jailors, was coming once more to set him free, but this hope soon died away.

The sound, whatever it was, remained stationary, and

seemed to come from a different quarter, though whence appeared difficult to ascertain.

It was moreover not the sound of a footstep; but something entirely different, and appeared like the respiration of some living animal.

Captain Hawk gazed round him in the dark as though he almost expected to see a pair of tiger-like eyes glaring at him from a remote corner of the cellar; but nothing of the kind met his gaze.

He thought of rats; but he heard no scratchings or squeakings common to such vermin; and besides, the deep breathings could not have proceeded from so small a creature.

The more he listened, the more his acute sense of hearing told him that the respiration that had attracted his attention came from the lungs of a human being.

The strangeness of this was the distinctness with which he heard it.

Here he was, confined in a close bricked cellar, of which he was confident he was the sole occupant, and yet listening to the breathings of a person whose respirations he heard as vividly as though that person had been at his side.

By dint of great attention, he fancied that the source of the sounds was the far end of the cellar.

He approached the wall, and felt satisfied that he was right in his conjecture.

He fancied, too—but that must have been a delusion—that he felt the air fresher at that particular spot.

He passed his hands carefully over the wall in all directions, as far as he could reach, but could discover no signs of any opening.

Not the smallest aperture or grating met his touch.

He raised his hand, and sprang up at short intervals, beginning at the angle of the side.

When he had reached to about the centre of the end wall, he thought, as he sprang up, he felt a stream of cold air blow on to his hand.

He uttered an exclamation of joy at this. But was it so?

He leaped up again. Yes, this time there was no doubt of it; he felt the grateful coolness of the air distinctly.

There must, then, be some aperture.

Grasping the steel bar, and extending his arm, he felt with its point along the top of the wall, till the steel came in contact with a very small iron grating.

It was through this, then, that the air entered the cellar.

All was, however, as dark there as in any other part of the vault.

Not the faintest ray of light shone through.

It was evident, therefore, the aperture did not communicate directly with the exterior; and even if it had, he was more than seven feet beneath it, with no possibility of ascending or gaining any foothold that would have enabled him to wrench away the grating or remove the bricks that surrounded it.

The air, it was clear, reached the interior by means of a pipe or chimney, and it was with a sad feeling of disappointment he came to the conclusion that the respiratory sounds he fancied he had heard were nothing more than the whistling of the wind as it poured through the narrow passage.

But no sooner did he form this conclusion, than a circumstance occurred that quite overturned his opinion.

The sounds suddenly ceased.

"It cannot be the wind, then," said the captain, anxiously; "if it were, I should still hear it; but all now is perfectly still."

He remained listening intently.

"Now I hear it again," he cried, suddenly. "It is, it must be, the breathing of a human being! Help, there! help!—help!—help!"

Still no answer came to his cry, and his parching thirst and his faintness seemed to seize upon him with renewed power.

He made a desperate, despairing, mad effort to fight against it.

He staggered against the wall, and struck it furiously with the bar he grasped, and shouted—screamed:

"Help!—help!—help!"

But he had overtaxed his strength—the words died away gradually on his lips. One last faint effort:

"Help!—hel——" and he lay fainting for the third time on the cellar floor

CHAPTER CCXI.

CHARLES WAKES FROM HIS SLUMBERS SURROUNDED BY SEVERAL SPECIMENS OF ANIMATED NATURE.—HE HEARS A CRY FOR HELP, AND ANSWERS IT.—DISCOVERY OF CAPTAIN HAWK.—SUDDEN ARRIVAL OF THE POLICE OFFICERS, AND WHAT BECAME OF THEM.

Let us now return to our friend, Charles—who, with a small tribe of caterpillars meandering in his thick hair, and wondering, perhaps (if such animals ever do wonder) what new species of vegetation they had discovered, and a snail in each pocket, had slumbered sweetly in the quiet little back garden where he had disposed himself.

His dreams had been of the happiest and most *couleur de rose* description.

He had been up in gorgeous balloons miles high—he had soared in the air on purple-coloured clouds tipped with silver—suddenly they had descended rapidly and alighted on the surface of a noble river, when they suddenly became transformed into boats, one of which he occupied, and that, strange to state, happened to be the very craft in which he had been rowed up the river, with the boatman sitting opposite.

He had hardly time to speak to this man, when there arose a cry for "Help!"

He looked round eagerly, expecting to find some unfortunate struggling in the strong current.

No one, however, appeared, but again the cry reached him:

"Help!—help!"

Charles started up in the boat, like a sky-rocket, threw off his jacket with impetuous haste, and plunged over the boat's side.

Wonderful to state, the water was solid, and on examination he found it was not water at all, but grass.

He looked for the boat, but that had disappeared—for the boatman, but he had become transformed into a lilac bush.

He opened his mouth to exclaim at these strange events; something immediately dropped into it—it was a slug, and nearly choked him.

"Oh, d—n it!" cried Charles, as he sputtered forth the unpleasant mouthful, and opened his eyes. "Why, I declare, I've been dreamin', an' here instead of bein' up in the clouds, I'm a lyin' on my back on the grass under a lilac bush! Well, I never! Dreams is rum things!"

One portion, though, of all this was reality; for though his eyes were open and he was wide awake, he still heard faintly the cry:

"Help!—help!—help!"

Our readers will perhaps divine that honest Charles, seeking for a retired corner where he might take forty winks unmolested, had, without being at all conscious that he had reached the very place he sought, clambered over the wall into the garden of Grove Cottage.

It was therefore with some surprise he heard the cries alluded to.

They appeared to him to come from some remote spot, though where that spot was he could form no correct idea.

He started up, and scratched his head with a vehemence that sent the caterpillars flying in all directions.

He listened, but the cries had ceased.

He walked quietly out a little into the garden, and reconnoitred the windows furtively.

All the shutters were closely fastened.

"This house is to let—it must be," he said to himself, "and they've left some one behind. P'raps it's the cat. No!" he suddenly exclaimed, correcting himself: "cats don't cry 'Help!—help!'"

He had hardly uttered these words, when, as if they were echoed, they were repeated:

"Help!—help!—hel——" and then silence.

This was the last expiring effort Captain Hawk had made, previous to his relapsing into insensibility, that fell upon Charles's ears.

The sound made him feel extremely uncomfortable.

"Goodness grashus! D—n it!" he cried, "where the dooce have I got to? An' who's that a crying help?"

He looked round about, up and down, but arrived at no conclusion as to whence the sounds proceeded.

He cautiously approached the house, and tried the back door.

It was locked and bolted within.

"I'll go round to the front," he exclaimed, "an' see what's to be seen there."

He accordingly scrambled over the wall, and hastened round the corner till he stood before the gate.

This gate was fast, but on the brass plate he read that which made him open his eyes to their widest extent and stagger back several paces.

There it was, as large as life: *Grove Cottage.*

"Why!" he ejaculated, "this here's the very crib as th' captain was a goin' to visit!"

Then another idea flashed across him.

Perhaps that was the captain's voice he heard.

Conviction seized him at once. It was! It must be!

The captain might be incarcerated in some gloomy chamber in that old mansion—wounded—bleeding—dying—*dead!* perhaps, by this time.

The thought was so terrible that Charles rushed back and climbed over the wall again into the garden as nimbly as a cat, making his way as quickly as possible to the spot where he heard the cries.

He listened, but all was silent.

Presently he fancied he discerned a faint moaning.

"Good Heaven! there's summut wrong, I knows!" he murmured.

The moaning continued at brief intervals.

"It seems to come from the bowels o' the earth," he soliloquised, thoughtfully, after a pause of intense listening.

Placing his ear to the ground, he was enabled to follow the sound till he traced it to a small grating some yards from the house, that was concealed from sight by leaves that had accumulated over it.

"Here's the place," he cried, as he swept away the leaves and applied his ear to the grating.

The moans were now distinctly audible to Charles.

"There's some poor wretch down there somewheres!" he exclaimed.

Then putting his mouth to the grating, he called:

"Who's there?"

Captain Hawk replied, faintly, roused by the question:

"Help!—help!"

"Who are you?" inquired Charles.

The captain had just sufficient consciousness to remember that it would not be safe for him to pronounce his name; he therefore only cried, very faintly:

"Release me, for Heaven's sake!"

Charles, who at the first sound of the captain's voice had failed to recognise it, now that his ear was in more direct communication with the cell in which he lay, knew it immediately.

"It is himself!" he cried, eagerly, "there's no doubt on it! Is it you, captain?" he called, putting his mouth to the grating and speaking through that aperture.

An indistinct murmur was the only reply.

"Don't you know me, captain? It's me—Charles!" he continued.

These words fell with perfect distinctness on the ear of Captain Hawk.

"Is it really you, Charles?" inquired the captain.

"Yes, it is indeed!"

"Quick then! release me from this infernal hole, or I shall never come forth alive!" he cried.

"So I will, captain," answered Charles, eagerly. "But how am I to get to yer?"

"This is Grove Cottage, is it not?"

"Yes, captain."

"Have you any instruments with you that will open a door?"

"I believe yer, captain. I've got two chisels, a file, an' a bunch of picklocks."

"Try and effect an entrance, and lose no time, for I'm half dead with thirst," cried Captain Hawk, who was, nevertheless, revived by the prospect of deliverance.

"I won't lose a minute," returned Charles, taking the implements from his pocket, including the two snails that had taken shelter there.

"Make as little noise as possible, so as not to arouse the scoundrels in the house," said the captain.

"I don't think there is anyone in the house," answered Charles.

A pang shot through the captain's breast as the thought suggested by Charles's words flashed across him.

"No one in the house!"

Had Blanche, then, been abducted by her villanous guardian?

The idea was too terrible to contemplate, and he endeavoured to dismiss it, crying to Charles, excitedly:

"Quick—quick, my good fellow! When you have effected an entrance, make your way to a trap-door you will find in the passage. It is in a cellar beneath, that I am now confined."

"All right, captain! I'll be with yer in a brace o' shakes!" answered Charles.

The faithful friend and messenger, after contemplating the back of the house for a moment with the eye of a *connoisseur* selecting the weakest point for attack, at length decided upon the window of the back parlour, in front of which was a balcony.

On to this he stepped; and opening his clasp-knife and passing it from beneath between the upper and lower sashes, speedily forced back the spring "catch" that secured it, and opened the window.

The shutters now remained.

He contemplated them somewhat dubiously for an instant, as though more than half inclined to take some particular step at which he hesitated.

"The captain told me to make as little noise as possible; but as I feels certain there's no one in the house, and as speed's everything when a gentleman's dying of thirst in a cellar underground, I don't think as it's a time to be particular, and so——"

Here Charles, determined literally to "go in a burster," to get inside and chance the consequences at any risk, gathered up his foot and, with a decided and effectual effort, sent it crashing through the shutter.

In a second Charles had followed his foot and was in the room.

He hastened to the door and looked out into the passage, grasping, as a weapon of defence, one of his chisels, which in his grasp looked a somewhat formidable weapon.

He listened, fully expecting to hear a door open, or some voice exclaim: "Who's there?" but all continued silent.

"I was sure there was no one in th' house," he said to himself; "but it's as well to be sure; and now for the captain."

Charles at once went to the trap, which he had some little difficulty in finding, as it was beneath the level of the passage, and the cavity filled by several planks strongly fastened together and fitting in and matching with the rest, just as a fire-board might fit into the aperture of a chimney.

It was only when this planking was removed that the trap and bolts were visible.

However, Charles's senses being tolerably acute, he was not long in discovering the secret of the masked trap.

The bolts were speedily undrawn, and Captain Hawk was once more rescued from what had almost promised to have been his tomb.

But the exhaustion and excitement he had undergone had proved more prostrating than even he himself was fully aware; and when he came once more into the open air and the light of day, he could at first scarcely endure either.

Charles, having seated himself on the steps leading from the back of the house to the garden, ransacked the empty domicile for a vessel of some description.

He at last found an earthenware jug and a glass.

The former of these he filled with clear, cool water from the pump, and brought it to the captain, who received the delicious draught with all the joy and eagerness of a parched traveller in a scorching desert.

Charles then bathed the captain's aching head with the cool element, who gratefully accepted the good offices of the honest fellow.

He knew they were done with hearty good will and from affection to himself, and he prized them accordingly.

Depend upon it, in times of pain and sickness, the gentle nurture, the kind words, the patient endurance, the whispered hope that real love can give, are worth more to us, and do more to restore us, than all the prescriptions of learned M.D's., with the draughts and pills they so liberally supply.

The effects of Charles's attention were speedily manifest.

The captain drank plentifully of the water, and was bathed plentifully with it, and Charles was rewarded by his assurance that the pain had almost entirely abated.

He was soon able to stand and walk about, and before long was—save a lingering sensation of weakness—quite himself again.

Then his anxiety for Blanche's safety revived in its full strength.

He would depart that moment in search of her.

"I cannot rest in this uncertainty," he cried. "I will never relinquish my pursuit until I discover her hiding-place!"

Our readers will quite enter into the captain's feelings when they reflect that he was entirely dependent on his own exertions to rescue the woman he loved from the hands of her persecutors, and on the strength of his own arm to avenge her wrongs.

It must be remembered that Captain Hawk was at this moment himself pursued by the hounds of the law—a hunted criminal, watched and dogged at every turn.

No matter what outrages were perpetrated upon those he loved dearest and best, he dared not summon the assistance of the law in their behalf, for, alas! that law was at all points armed against him.

It was with a bitter heart he was obliged to acknowledge these painful truths to himself.

But while he did so the consciousness did not depress him.

His self-reliance, now that he once more breathed the fresh air, and saw the bright daylight, had fully returned to him, and as hope sprang up in his breast, he felt confident of being able to discover the retreat of his beloved Blanche and inflicting a well-merited retribution on her guardian's head.

Charles, however, had yet to relate what had transpired in the garden of the countess's mansion; and having requested the captain's attention, he detailed the whole affair, and the means Lord Harcliffe had devised for frustrating it.

This was a sudden call to keep a promise when every voice in his heart told him his presence was required in quite another direction.

He bit his lip thoughtfully, and remained a few moments in silence.

"This is Thursday," he at length soliloquised; "the marriage of the countess will take place to-morrow. If I attend the ceremony, as I promised, I must, perforce, lose two days, and when time is so precious too, since it would be useless to commence a search without being able to follow it up. What can I do?"

He remained undecided and perplexed, but at length he determined, in his usual straightforward, honest manner, on his course of action.

"I have given my word to the countess," he cried—"I must keep it! Heaven will watch over my Blanche and preserve her from the assaults of ruffianly violence, till I can reach her! Yes, I am resolved! Come, Charles, my good, faithful friend, let us return to London."

"I'm ready, captain," acquiesced Charles.

The shortest way of getting out was by the garden wall; and they were about to adopt this means of leaving the premises, when the sound of horses' hoofs at the front reached their ears.

There was something ominous in these sounds, especially as the horses appeared to have dashed up at a furious pace to the gate of Grove Cottage, and to have suddenly stopped there.

"What is that?" said Captain Hawk, apprehensively.

"Let me go and see," answered Charles, who did not at all like the idea of horsemen stopping at the gate.

"Do so quickly. I will keep watch here," returned the captain.

Charles disappeared, and quickly returned with an expression of considerable dismay on his features.

"They're police officers, captain!" he cried, in an undertone.

"Ha!" ejaculated the captain, "but it's no more than I expected! Where are they?"

"Outside the gate."

"How many?"

"Only three at present."

"That's fortunate! Keep cool; let us go in, close the door, and lock and bolt it quietly. We can escape by the balcony window, if necessary. An idea has struck me."

These precautions having been taken, and the door made fast, Captain Hawk, followed by Charles, went into the back parlour, where the former, mounting on to one of the chairs, reconnoitred the official trio through the round hole in the top of the shutters

"So, so!" said the captain, quietly, to himself, "Peterson, Nicholas Twigg, and the indefatigable Jessop! Of course they are after me; they have heard by some means that I am confined here, and are come to pounce upon me, just as we might open a trap to allow the poor mouse to run into the jaws of the cat. I fancy, however, they'll be disappointed."

The three officers had dismounted, and, quite confident that their prey this time would be captured without their so much as "turning a hair," were holding a little preliminary conversation, and not putting themselves out of the way in the least.

They were doing what we are all more or less inclined to do at times—reckoning their chickens before they were hatched.

As they talked they, in a business-like way, as much perhaps from habit as anything else, drew out their pistols, pulled back the hammers, gently shook up the priming without looking at it, let the hammers fall again, and restored them to their pockets.

"You see," said Peterson, "there'll just be a hundred each, so we needn't make any bother about that. My gentleman's snugly packed away in the cellar, so all we've got to do is to just drop on to him there, fit him with the bracelets, and hoist him out. Ha, ha! what a treat it'll be for him!"

"What a agreeable surprise!" added Nicholas Twigg.

Jessop simply rubbed his hands and looked knowing.

"Come, then," continued Peterson, "we may as well do the job at once. I feels as though I wanted my breakfast. I thinks we shall be able to afford a rasher o' 'am an' a few eggs apiece out o' this lot, eh?"

His confederates laughed at this culinary jest, and wagged their heads with a roguish confidence that made the captain smile.

The gate was speedily unlocked, and the three men stood on the threshold.

Our readers will probably like to know how these officers gained their information as to the whereabouts of Captain Hawk; so, while P.O. Peterson is fumbling in his capacious pockets amongst a variety of heterogeneous articles for the door-key, we will enlighten them.

When the officers, after chasing the captain on the previous night, and according to custom letting him slip through their fingers, had returned in high dudgeon to Bow Street, it suddenly occurred to Peterson that their prey, having escaped their clutches, and being of a most daring and reckless disposition, would as likely as not continue his progress to Chelsea as coolly as though nothing out of the common way had occurred.

This idea was entirely concurred in by Nicholas Twigg, and it was at once determined between them to start off at once to Chelsea in fresh pursuit.

Jessop, whose incessant vigilance had forced itself upon their attention, they took with them—first, because he was young and enthusiastic; and secondly, because, in case of any struggle or violence on the part of the captain, the gallant Jessop would commence the attack and take off the rough edge of the captain's resistance, after which they could drop in and finish him.

As they were going along they passed the carriage which contained Ridley Massingham and the senseless form of Blanche inside, and Jacob Mawks on the dickey outside.

Peterson called out to the postillion to "stop!"

This personage, with some difficulty, obeyed, for the horses were going at a good pace.

It was a fortunate thing for Ridley Massingham that the poor girl he was carrying off was unconscious at the time, or his plans might have been at once overturned.

As it was, however, the light being indistinct, and the blinds of the carriage down, and the senseless form of Blanche lying back in a corner covered with a cloak, nothing appeared to excite the suspicion of the officials.

Ridley Massingham, when the vehicle stopped, let down the window and thrust out his head.

"What is the matter?" he inquired, pretending he had been just aroused from his slumbers.

"We are police officers," answered Peterson, "and we're in pursuit of Captain Hawk, the highwayman. He has taken this road. Have you seen such a person as you came along?"

"Captain Hawk?" echoed the gentleman in the carriage. "The fellow has made a desperate attempt upon my house to-night! We had a terrible struggle with him, and he is now securely fastened in my cellar! I am at this moment travelling to town for assistance."

A vivid glow of pleasure lighted up the countenances of the police officers at this announcement.

"You needn't fear, sir," said Peterson: "we'll nab the scoundrel, desperate as he is!"

"I shall go on, nevertheless," answered Ridley. "You may want help."

"You can go if you like, sir, and we'll go on too. By the time you get back we shall have him laid by the heels, with the bracelets on his wrists."

"That's right!"

"You say he's in the cellar?"

"Yes; you'll see the trap-door under the boards in the passage."

"All right! But whereabouts is the house?"

"Grove Cottage, about a mile and a half down the road, first turning to the right."

The window was quickly drawn up, and the horses began to move on.

"Look oot sharp for un!" croaked Jacob Mawks from the dickey; "'e be a main desperate un, 'e be! 'E nearly killed Oi!"

"We'll look out sharp enough, never fear!" cried Peterson, as the carriage rolled away.

"Well," said Nicholas Twigg, "if this ain't a bit o' luck, there never was a bit!"

"On we go, then!" cried Peterson.

And accordingly on they went, and in due time arrived at Grove Cottage as has been previously stated.

Peterson, having after some delay managed to disentangle the key from his overcrowded pocket, continued, by dint of a little coaxing and a little swearing, to induce the key to turn the lock, which was rusty.

The officers entered; and the floor of the passage being carefully searched, the planks that masked the trap were soon discovered.

"Here it is!" ejaculated Peterson.

Taking out a large and massive clasp-knife, Nicholas Twigg speedily raised the planks and disclosed the trap with its massive bolts.

"So far, so good!" remarked the senior official.

"Now then," said Peterson, addressing Jessop, "jest see as your lantern's all right, and your barkers."

Jessop performed the necessary investigation, and reported "all *was* right."

"Then 'ere's the 'andcuffs," continued Peterson, handing him the steel retainers; "an' as you're the youngest, you'll go fust, our friend Nicholas 'll follow, an' I'll keep watch 'ere."

It is worthy of remark that Peterson knew his own value, and never put his own nose within reach of the scent of danger, if by any possible chance he could employ somebody else's nose to inhale a little of the atmosphere first.

He had been thirty years in the force, and infinitely preferred *directing* an attack to *making* one.

The bolts of the trap being drawn, the lid descended with a hollow crash, and hung for several seconds creaking on its rusty hinges.

All below was intensely dark, and as far as odour was concerned, extremely musty.

"Show a light," said Peterson, authoritatively.

Jessop obediently cast the rays of his lantern down the abyss.

His brother officers in the meantime made their observations.

Not that they were much the wiser.

The cellar was so obscure that it seemed to extinguish the light.

They were just enabled to perceive that the trap was there and open, but that there was no ladder by which to descend.

Neither seemed inclined to chance dropping down into a dark cellar, of the depth of which they were ignorant.

There was a slight pause—rather an awkward pause, but only for an instant.

Peterson's watchful eye caught sight of a ladder, evidently used for the purpose of descent and ascent to and from the cellar.

"Here we are!" he said, joyfully.

The ladder was lowered in a moment.

"Now then," cried Peterson, "down with you!"

Jessop descended boldly, grasping his lantern in one hand and a pistol in the other.

Nicholas followed with a pistol in each hand.

Peterson took advantage of the opportunity to take a good suck at his rum-bottle.

"Now then!" he cried, as he wiped his lips and looked down, "what are yer doin'?"

He had expected an immediate rumpus, and a severe struggle before the daring highwayman should be handcuffed, and he marvelled at the quietude.

"We're a lookin' for him," called out Nicholas.

Suddenly a faint, moaning noise was heard in the cellar as of a person in pain.

"'E's a dyin', ain't 'e?" inquired Peterson, as the moans reached him.

"I don't know what 'e's a doin' of," answered Nicholas, with some asperity, from below. "I'll ask him when I finds 'im."

"Be quick, then," returned his superior; "you'll find him in one of the corners; I can 'ear 'im a gruntin'."

"'Ow many corners is there? I've been into four already!" bawled Mr. Twigg, indignantly.

"Why the devil don't yer lay 'old on him?" shouted Peterson, who was becoming quite impatient at the tardy operations of his colleagues.

"'Cos we can't find him!" bawled Nicholas.

"Why, d—n it! I can 'ear 'im a groanin' for dear life!" asserted Peterson.

"So can I; but 'earin's one thing, and seein's another. At all events, 'e ain't 'ere."

"Not there? Don't talk sich d—d muck to me!" roared the irate Peterson. "You're drunk or blind!"

"No I ain't, any more than you are yourself!" retorted Nicholas. "An' if you're so clever, the best thing as you can do is to come down and find him yerself!"

At this juncture the groans burst forth in the cellar more audibly than ever, and Peterson took another pull at the rum-bottle.

"There—there—there!" he cried, gasping from the effects of his hasty draught. "What's that?"

"It's Old Nick, or some such person!" bawled his brother officer. "You'd best come an' see!"

"Blest if I don't, too!" cried Peterson, who was now *rum* valiant. "You're a couple of fools!"

As he spoke, the indignant P. O. descended the ladder, very nearly pitching on his nose during that operation.

"Now then," he cried, as the groans again sounded in agonising distinctness, "let me see. Give me the lantern."

Jessop handed the light to his superior, who searched the length and breadth of the cellar, but without discovering the object he sought.

His countenance fell, and the expression became savage and perplexed.

He scratched his head spitefully.

"This 'ere's some d—d 'oax, then, arter all! P'raps there's another cellar. At all events, let's get out of this."

They advanced towards the spot where the ladder had rested, but it was no longer to be seen.

"Why, d—n it! the ladder's gone now!" roared Peterson, holding up the lantern. "Who the devil can ha' taken that?"

"I did!" answered a placid voice from above.

Of course six eyes immediately looked upwards, when, to their horror, they beheld the countenance of Captain Hawk, with sarcastic enjoyment, smiling down upon them.

"You d—d villain! You outrageous unhung rascal!" shouted the furious Peterson.

The next moment three pistols were simultaneously discharged at Captain Hawk.

A mocking laugh was heard, followed by the loud shutting-to of the trap and the shooting of bolts.

The three police officers found themselves fastened in, and almost stifled by the smoke of their own pistols.

[THE HIGHWAYMEN WATCH THE MYSTERIOUS FIGURE.]

CHAPTER CCXII.

THE DOUBLE MARRIAGES.—ST. GEORGE'S AND ST. JAMES'S.—SIR RICHARD CHANDOS GETS DRUNK, AND BEHAVES HIMSELF INDECOROUSLY IN CHURCH.—A GREAT MISTAKE.—DESTINATION OF THE BRIDE AND BRIDEGROOM.

FRIDAY morning dawned bright and beautiful—that day on which Captain Nugent and the fair Clarissa were to plight their troth to each other at the altar.

They had been fully apprised of the plot that had been carried on against them, and readily agreed to the change of time and place for the performance of the nuptial ceremony.

Captain Hawk and Lord Harcliffe breakfasted in St. James's Square on this eventful morning, and the whole party laughed triumphantly as they sat at table in anticipation of the frustration of the schemes of their opponents.

The subsequent arrangement of the proceedings was according to Lord Harcliffe's plan, as follows:—

That the marriage was to take place at St. James's Church, Piccadilly, at ten on Friday morning, instead of St. George's, Hanover Square, at twelve.

Consequently, at precisely a quarter to ten a plain hackney-coach drew up at the corner of the square, and the captain and countess, accompanied by our heroes, entered it.

It must not be supposed that Captain Hawk was in much spirits to enjoy the happiness that seemed to fill the breasts of the lovers.

If he smiled, it was sadly; if he laughed, it was a forced laugh wrung from a heavy heart.

But his disposition was too unselfish to allow him to cloud the atmosphere of this auspicious morning with his own private sorrows; he therefore assumed an outward cheerfulness he did not feel; and when the fair countess rallied him on his pallid looks, he laughed off her gentle *badinage*, whilst at the same moment his heart bled within.

By eleven o'clock the whole party had returned to St. James's Square and were seated at lunch.

The marriage had been quite private, and the happy pair were now united together in those sacred bonds that man, with all his violence and oppression, may not put asunder.

It was the intention of the captain to spend the honeymoon in strict privacy at Windsor, and after that, the duties of his profession calling him to the Court at St. James's, to send his fair bride to his ancestral seat in Cheshire, where she would remain until he could join her.

It was precisely at the same time as the newly-married couple were seated at lunch, that Sir Richard Chandos and Lord Edward Strathern, with a bitter, vindictive light in their eyes, but yet with something of lurking triumph occasionally breaking forth, rose from the breakfast table.

The anxiety and resentment they both nursed in their bosoms were not conducive to appetite, and the morning meal was removed almost untasted.

But what they failed to do in eating, they atoned for by drinking.

Their countenances were flushed with wine, and the sensual hue of over-indulgence inflamed their features, whilst the potent draughts added increased strength to the rancorous hate that devoured them.

As the time drew on for them to start, they buckled on their swords, wishing from the bottom of their hearts as they did so that both weapons could have been buried in the heart of Captain Nugent; and having swallowed a bumper of cognac apiece, they departed for St. George's Church, wishing to arrive neither too soon nor too late, but precisely at twelve o'clock.

But marriages are not in this great city, or in fact any place, very solitary occurrences.

Never a day passes in this world of ours without some one coming into, or going out of it, or without some one being married.

And it so happened that, in addition to Captain Nugent and the Countess of Blacklake, two other parties were to undergo the ordeal of the marriage ceremony at the same time.

These were no other than Mr. Barnaby Bubb, tea dealer and grocer, of Houndsditch, and Miss Matilda Mite, only daughter of Ebenezer Mite, cheesemonger and pork butcher, of Seven Dials.

Mr. Barnaby Bubb was a bachelor of forty-two; the gentle Matilda a spinster of some five-and-thirty.

Neither party was in the first bloom of youth; but legends were abroad to the effect that they had loved one another from childhood, and that their union had been procrastinated and all but negatived entirely by a certain handsome, reckless, shiny-headed, curly-haired cousin, who was a butcher, and who deluded the fair Matilda with perjured vows until her thirty-fourth year, and then ran away to Australia with his first cousin, leaving his ancient flame to the longing Barnaby, who had looked on and loved for some years at a respectful distance, his nose being completely put out of joint by his more audacious and handsome competitor.

But no sooner was the butcher off over the seas than the tea dealer and grocer stepped into his place, popped the question, and was accepted.

In person they were the antipodes of each other; Barnaby Bubb was short and fat, Matilda Mite tall and thin.

It was stated she had fretted after her shiny-haired perjurer, but as no one ever remembered her being otherwise than *lathy*, this was looked upon as a fiction.

Well, it so happened then that at 12 o'clock on Friday these middle-aged turtle doves were to be united at St. George's, Hanover Square.

They arrived in due course in a hired carriage, accompanied by a prodigious number of Mites and Bubbses, also in hired carriages.

The minister, having waited some little time in expectation of the arrival of the other contracted parties, and they not appearing, commenced the ceremony.

There was the usual fluttering and agitation, the usual uncertainty as to the responses, an utter ignorance which hand to take, and how to take it, and when to let it go; with an inclination to profuse perspiration on the part of the bridegroom.

The ceremony had arrived at that point when, in answer to the minister's question whether the perspiring Bubb would "have this woman to be his wedded wife," the agitated grocer, speaking thick and indistinct, as though his mouth was filled with his own plums, had just gasped forth "yes," and wiped his forehead with a rose-coloured silk handkerchief after the solemn monosyllable, when a loud and sonorous voice startled the entire assembly, and appeared almost to shake the church in which they were.

"Never!" it cried. "I forbid the banns!"

At the same moment Sir Richard Chandos and Lord Strathern appeared at the door, and with excited and violent demeanour, and eyes full of intemperate fury, rushed, with sacrilegious indecorum, down the middle aisle of the sacred edifice, even to the altar's foot.

The minister nearly dropped his book, the clerk collapsed, the pew-opener suddenly disappeared in a pew, the bride fainted away on the spot in the arms of the bridegroom, who immediately commenced oozing at every pore till he was wet through, and the entire collection of Mites and Bubbses set up a dismal howl in all kinds of keys—*soprano* to double bass.

Under these circumstances, Mr. Bubb senior felt it his duty, as a father, to interfere, and consequently, in the mildest of small voices, he begged to know why Sir Richard "had interrupted the ceremony?"

"My niece and that man shall never be united!" raved Sir Richard, who was too drunk with rage and champagne to notice his mistake.

"I beg your pardon!" exclaimed the mild paternal Bubb; "but that lady is *not* your niece!"

"Not my niece, you old idiot!" raved Sir Richard—"not my niece! But I tell you she is! Stand aside, old man, and do not interfere with me! As for you, madam, come with me!"

As he spoke, he rushed towards the fainting Matilda, and grasping her wrist with a violence that threatened dislocation, dragged her ruthlessly away, and planted so decidedly vigorous a kick on a certain portion of the corpulent bridegroom's person, that the little grocer disappeared suddenly, as though he had been shot out of a cannon, and was discovered eventually in the vestry in a pool of water that had oozed from him in the form of perspiration.

"Now, madam!" shouted Sir Richard, furiously, "hear me once and for ever, while I swear that, while I can prevent it, you shall never be the wife of Captain Nugent!"

"I don't want to be the wife of Captain Nugent!" whimpered the terrified Matilda. "I want to be the wife of Barnaby Bubb!"

"Barnaby Bubb!" shouted Sir Richard, recoiling at the plebeian name uttered by the sharp voice of Matilda, as though his whole frame had been set on edge. "What is the meaning of all this? and who the devil is Barnaby Bubb?"

"This gentleman, sir," simpered the fair bride, grasping the arm of the perspiring bridegroom. "He is my intended."

Sir Richard stamped his foot with impatient irritability.

"Oh, psha!" he cried, as he turned away in disgust towards Lord Strathern. "Your lordship!" he exclaimed, suddenly.

But his lordship was not to be seen.

Perceiving the parties he sought were not in the church, he had hastily sought the exterior.

Sir Richard then turned once more to the somewhat agitated bridal party.

"This in an entire mistake," he said, in a tone of ill-concealed vexation. "I was excited, and for the moment mistook this antiquated maiden"—alluding to the fair Matilda, who uttered a sharp squeal of indignation at being alluded to as an antiquity—"for my niece. It is very absurd! How I could have been so greatly misled as to mistake one for the other I am at a loss to imagine. Pah!" he ejaculated, as he glanced at the indignant spinster, "she's an old woman!"

With these rude remarks, the angry baronet strode out of the church, leaving the ceremony to be concluded.

Lord Strathern, in a state of considerable mental perplexity and irritation, was standing moodily outside.

Sir Richard hastily approached him.

"This is very strange!" said the baronet, in a low voice to him.

"It is more than strange," replied his lordship—"it seems as if the devil himself was conspiring to thwart us!"

"I cannot account for it. Did we not read the letter written by my niece's own hand, that the ceremony would take place on Friday morning at St. George's Church at 12 o'clock?"

"Most indubitably we did; yet it is now more than half-past twelve, and no signs of their appearance."

"What construction do you put upon these circumstances?"

"I can scarcely control my mind to think; but it seems to me that we are the dupes of some infernally artful plot, —such a plot as women, always treacherous and deceitful, can alone devise."

"I am utterly at a loss to conjecture," responded Sir Richard, in a moody voice: "time will show. The champagne, which would have raised me, had our enterprise been successful, to the seventh heaven of elation, has by this reverse made me heavy and muddle-headed."

"As it has me," answered the young lord, morosely.

"We shall need another bottle to restore our equanimity," said the baronet.

"Another bottle!" fiercely echoed Lord Strathern. "In my present mood I feel as though I could quaff a dozen, though they were filled with liquid fire!"

At this moment there was a stir amongst the few idlers congregated at the church door, and a rumour was heard that the ceremony was over and the bride and bridegroom were about to leave the church.

This was verified bythe beadle, who made his appearance, looking very grand and feverish, and called in a rough, wheezy tone:

"Mr. Bubbses' carriage!"

As that vehicle was stationed exactly opposite the door, no exertion on the part of the coachman was necessary.

All that was needed was for Thomas Deakings, Mr. Mite's head shopman—who, arrayed in a shiny suit of black, and a white necktie of voluminous proportions, performed the office of footman—to open the door of the hired conveyance, and stand respectfully with his hand on the handle, waiting the arrival of the bridal party.

He had not long to wait, for hardly had the carriage door swung on its hinges when the bride and bridegroom, all moisture and blushes, emerged from the church portal, followed by a long line of Mites and Bubbses, who, having as quickly as possible sought shelter from the gaze and criticism of the admiring crowd in their several vehicles, the entire *cortege* drove off.

The noblemen, who had stood aloof, scornfully glancing at the proceedings from a corner of their eyes, uttered a sneer of contempt as the carriages disappeared.

This feeling seemed to be perfectly reciprocated by the crossing-sweeper, who had stood touching his ragged cap with great perseverance to the bridal party, without extracting a solitary copper in return.

The sweeper was highly indignant, as was only natural.

"Not a blessed mag!" he ejaculated. "Vell, they are a measly lot: a gettin' married an' never so much as givin' th' poor crossin'-sweeper a copper to drink their 'ealth! Psh! *she* a bride! Pooh! *he* a bridegroom! Bosh!"

In the extremity of his wounded feelings, he appealed to the crowd.

"It'd be a good look-out for us poor coves if all the married couples was like them! Why, only this morning there was a pair tied together at St. Jeameses, Piccadilly, an' you should a' seed the difference! They *was* a pair, they was! The minit I touched my cap, out come a guinea for me. They wos summat like, they wos—a rale 'andsome couple! As for these, they're all lard an' trotters!"

And with this contemptuous comment, the sweeper shouldered his broom, and was shuffling away, when the noblemen, who had heard his harangue to the populace, beckoned him.

"Heigh! here! sweeper!" cried Sir Richard.

"Yes, your honour!" answered the lad, quickly, advancing as rapidly as an old pair of boots several sizes too large for him would permit. "Want the sweeper, gen'l'men?" he inquired.

"What marriage was that you were speaking of?" asked the baronet.

"A marriage atween a lady an' gen'l'man," answered the lad, quickly.

"So I imagine," returned Sir Richard, "at St. James's Church."

"Yes, your honour; this mornin' at ten o'clock."

The baronet glanced at Lord Strathern. His lordship returned the glance. An idea had struck them both.

"Were they young?" asked Sir Richard, continuing his inquiries.

"I should think they wos too!" answered the sweeper. "Oh, my heye! wosn't they 'andsome neither! An' they give me a guinea."

The gift had evidently increased their beauty wonderfully in the eyes of the crossing-sweeper.

"Do you know who they were?"

"No—that is, not 'xacly. They come in a coach quite private like."

"A hackney-coach?"

"Yes."

"Were they alone?"

"No; there wos two gents with 'em."

"What kind of gents?"

"'Andsome: reg'ler stunnin'-lookin' coves!"

"Tall?"

"Pretty well: dark 'air, 'starchers, an' so on."

"And you know not who they are?"

"No."

"Nor where they came from?"

"Not 'xacly."

"You know, perhaps, where they went to?"

"Yes."

Sir Richard slipped a guinea into the hand of the crossing-sweeper, as he said:

"Perhaps you can tell me, for I wish to know?"

The lad's eyes sparkled at the sight of the gold, which stimulated his perceptive powers immensely.

"I'll tell your honour 'ow it wos. I thought p'r'aps as people's gen'rally gen'rous at marriges, I might pick up summat else; so vhen they drew avay from the church, I 'ung on behind, an' vent vith 'em. Vell, they didn't go far, for they stopped at von o' th' corners of St. James's Square, an' theer they gets out."

The noblemen exchanged significant glances.

"And you saw whither they went?" asked Lord Strathern, eagerly.

"O' course I did! They vent into von o' th' 'ouses in th' square."

"'Twas they!" ejaculated Sir Richard. "They must be there, then, now!"

"No, they ain't, for I stopped an' watched," said the lad; "an' in about a quarter of a hour I see a 'andsome carriage vith four osses an' a postillion draw up to th' door. The 'ole party gets in an' drives off."

"Do you know the road they took?" inquired the baronet.

"Not for certain," answered the lad. "Yer see, it vas unpossible to keep up vith four osses, an' there vas nothin' to 'ang on behind to; but I thinks as I 'eard vun o' th' postillions say to th' other, ''Ve can get to Vindsor by three o'clock.'"

"Thank you, my lad," exclaimed the baronet, hastily. "Come, Edward," he said to Lord Strathern, as he linked his arm through his.

The two noblemen walked hastily away.

"'E might 'ave give me another guinea," soliloquised the sweeper, "for vot I've told 'im!"

But the baronet, having squeezed the sponge dry, kept his money in his pocket.

"They must have gone to Windsor to dally away the honeymoon," growled Sir Richard, as they hastened along.

"Cursed mischance that threw us off the scent!" muttered Lord Strathern. "Did I not tell you it was some infernal plot? I can see through it now! While we were waiting their arrival at St. George's at twelve, they had been married at St. James's at ten. Now all is over!" he exclaimed, with bitter despair.

"Is it? By Heaven, you know little of my temper, if you think so!" cried Sir Richard, wrathfully.

"You cannot annul their marriage," said his lordship, gloomily.

"I'll separate them by some means, though twenty

marriages stood in the way!" answered the baronet, fiercely. "But come, we must not let our spirits flag now; let us recruit ourselves, and then start in pursuit at once. Having got the clue to their retreat, we must never lose it till we unkennel the fugitives."

"I am ready, if necessary, to hunt them even to the death!" replied the amiable Lord Strathern, as they hastened to make preparations for their journey

CHAPTER CCXIII.

CAPTAIN HAWK AND LORD HARCLIFFE, AFTER ACCOMPANYING THE BRIDE AND BRIDEGROOM TO THEIR DESTINATION, RETURN TO TOWN.—THEY PAY A VISIT TO GROVE COTTAGE.—MYSTERIOUS APPEARANCE OF THE LADY IN WHITE.—THEY FOLLOW THE SPIRIT.—A ROMANCE OF REAL LIFE IN A CHURCHYARD.

In the meantime, Captain Nugent and his lovely bride, accompanied by Captain Hawk and Lord Harcliffe, were drawing near the town of Windsor as rapidly as four horses could draw them.

As faithful esquires, our heroes, in accordance with their promise, not only witnessed the marriage ceremony, but accompanied the newly-wedded pair to the town of Windsor.

Here, having seen them safely located at their hotel, our heroes, after dining with them and drinking their health and happiness, returned to town in a close carriage, bearing with them the thanks and best wishes of the happy bride and bridegroom.

In the course of their journey, a close carriage passed them, in which Captain Hawk, from the casual view he was enabled to take of the interior as the vehicle whirled by, fancied he descried the forms of Sir Richard Chandos and Lord Strathern.

The carriage dashed past so rapidly, that the highwaymen, who were at that moment in a contemplative mood, had barely time to catch a glimpse, and it was gone.

Still, brief as that glimpse was, it was sufficient to awaken apprehension.

At any other time they would have at once turned their horses' heads and gone back to ascertain whether or not their suspicions were correct, but at that juncture it was impossible.

Captain Hawk had, in a most self-denying manner, subdued his almost overwhelming anxiety for the fate of Blanche, and kept his promise to the countess.

But that done, he felt he could no longer delay his search after one who, in a few hours, had grown to be the idol of his existence—the life of his life.

"I cannot retrace my steps," said the captain to his comrade. "There is a cry continually ringing in my ears 'Help me!' and the voice that utters it is the voice of Blanche. I fear I have already delayed too long."

"Nay, my friend, there is no need for self-reproach for having kept your promise. Duty sometimes appears a very hard, stern master; but when we follow strictly in its path, the end proves that we have not been losers."

"No, no!" cried Captain Hawk, with somewhat of enthusiasm in his tone; "I do not—I will not regret having done my duty. Heaven will preserve my Blanche till I can reach her side—that is," he added, with a sudden sadness, "if I am ever permitted to do so."

"That brings me to what I was about to remark," said Lord Harcliffe.

"What was it?" inquired the captain.

"That it would have been sufficient if I had returned to Windsor, whilst you proceed to town; but then, I have my appointment to keep with the Prince of Wales."

"An appointment which I advise you by all means not to neglect," interrupted Captain Hawk.

"I should be sorry to do so," said his lordship; "and since I am ignorant at what moment I may be summoned to the presence of his royal highness, I think it wise not to remain away from London."

"Can you form any idea what it is the prince desires you to undertake?"

"Not in the least; but whatever it be, if I can carry out his plans satisfactorily, it will secure us at least a powerful friend; and Heaven knows *we* need a friend who have so many enemies."

"I have every confidence that you will succeed in all you undertake to the prince's entire satisfaction," said Captain Hawk, confidently.

"I believe so too," added Lord Harcliffe; "and I sincerely trust that the commission I shall be called upon to execute may be something a gentleman and a man of honour may undertake; if not——"

"Though the king himself, instead of the Prince of Wales, should propose to you a reprobate deed, refuse the task with contempt, though he should seek to bribe you into compliance at the price of half his kingdom."

"Depend upon it I should do so," replied his lordship.

It was near midnight when our heroes reached "The Retreat," where they found Charles and Pharoah, who, in company with the Count Antonio Riccioli, were making themselves very comfortable.

Dissipation and the gout sadly unfit poor humanity for its various duties; and Pharoah could only report that the prince was too much indisposed to see Lord Harcliffe, and that it was probable several days might elapse before his royal highness would be able to give him an interview.

This was no particular matter of regret, inasmuch as it enabled Lord Harcliffe to assist his comrade, whose anxiety on behalf of Blanche was very great.

Charles had picked up the intelligence that the police officers had been rescued from the cellar by some of their companions a short time after their incarceration, having been directed to Grove Cottage by Ridley Massingham, as he passed them on the road.

Captain Hawk, on reaching "The Retreat" sat moodily, with his head bent upon his breast, a prey to many conflicting emotions.

Suddenly he started up, and beckoned his friend to his side.

"Harcliffe," he said, in a low but intense voice, "I can bear this anxiety no longer. I must commence my search after Blanche."

"To-night?"

"Yes, to-night."

"But whither will you bend your steps? In what direction?"

"I know not. Oh, this suspense is maddening!" he cried. Then, more calmly, he added: "I feel a strange desire to visit the old house at Chelsea once more."

"But Blanche is not there."

"Alas, no! but it seems to me that there—though I know not by what means—I shall gain some clue to the place of her captivity. Late as the hour is, my anxiety will not let me rest. I cannot, after the long journey you have just completed, ask you to accompany me."

"What!" cried Lord Harcliffe, "do you imagine, at a crisis like this, I feel fatigue? But even if I did, it would not prevent me from accompanying you. The woman you love is in danger, and we must endeavour to rescue her."

"I thank you, my friend," exclaimed Captain Hawk, warmly grasping his lordship's hand; "you know your company is always valuable to me. You will come then?"

"Undoubtedly!"

"We will start then at once; and as for sleep, we can take a snooze in the boat as we go up the river."

This idea of Captain Hawk was at once acted upon.

Fatigue and hunger were forgotten, and the two friends departed once more from the only place where they could feel they were safe, and bent their steps towards Westminster.

Fortunately they reaced it unchallenged and unnoticed, and were soon making their way up the Thames as fast as two pairs of oars could propel them.

Overcome by fatigue and lulled by the gliding motion of the boat, both the highwaymen fell asleep almost as soon as the boat left the pier at Westminster, and never opened their eyes till they reached Chelsea.

Their slumbers, brief as they were, were of inestimable service, inasmuch as both on awaking felt invigorated and refreshed.

Having discharged the claims of the boatmen, they proceeded in the direction of Grove Cottage.

It was a beautiful night, and a gentle breeze came refreshingly from the river and stirred the trees as it passed.

This was the first time Lord Harcliffe had visited that particular part of the suburbs of London.

The quiet beauty of the spot attracted him.

"How delightfully tranquil the night appears!" he said to Captain Hawk.

"It does indeed," returned his comrade; "and when the breast is tortured with anxiety, there is some kind of alleviation in a calm like this."

They went on, and gradually the trees in front of Grove Cottage came in sight.

They approached cautiously till they stood in front of the building.

How quiet and still it appeared in the moonlight, as though nothing evil could exist or transpire beneath its peaceful roof!

The trees, as they nodded to the breeze, seemed to unite with the clustering ivy, as it rustled and fluttered, in singing their plaintive and monotonous music.

Both the highwaymen seemed strangely impressed, whilst a deep sadness fell upon the heart and spirits of Captain Hawk.

"I never thought till now," said Lord Harcliffe, as he stood listening to the soft murmurings over his head, "there was so much melody in a few moving leaves."

"It seems as though *she* was whispering to me," said the captain, in a dreamy tone. "If I were superstitious, and believed the dead had power to revisit this earth, it is on such a night, at such a silent hour as this, I should look to behold the sacred, shadowy forms of those we have loved and lost."

"Would not such a meeting be more than we could endure?" asked Lord Harcliffe, in a low voice.

"Perhaps so," answered his friend; "but it seems to me I could have no greater joy than to see again the dear, familiar faces of those I had loved in life, and to hear——"

He paused, for just at that moment a strain of melody, so soft and yet so distinct, stole upon the silent night.

It was a woman's voice, and appeared from its sweetness to belong to the choirs of Heaven rather than to earth.

Almost awe-struck, the highwaymen listened, silent and motionless, as the words of the singer fell upon their ears:—

"Why do I linger?—why?
I watch, I wait in vain;
In vain I weep and sigh—
He will not come again.
My tears the dead can ne'er restore,
And I shall see him—never more:
Never—never—never more!"

The voice died away.

Captain Hawk turned towards his comrade, who, he could see, had been deeply impressed by the words of the singer.

"How strange! How sweet!" he whispered.

"Whence did the sound proceed, and from whom?" inquired Captain Hawk.

"From Heaven it seemed! Such exquisite tones could only proceed from some bright being—— Ah!—look! Heavens!—do you see?" suddenly exclaimed his lordship, pointing to a large, old-fashioned-looking window on the first-floor of the house, where a female figure, robed in white, was distinctly visible.

All within had been dark a moment before, but now the figure was fully revealed by the light she carried.

"Can it be Blanche?" cried the captain, eagerly, but under his breath, lest he should scare away the fair spirit.

This question was immediately answered by the mysterious being, who, turning towards the window, looked from it with a fixed, sad, melancholy stare, inexpressibly touching.

It was not Blanche, though that fair, pale face, with its large, lustrous, dreamy eyes, and the flowing golden hair, that fell in rich profusion over shoulders white as marble, might have challenged competition even with the greatest beauty.

The figure remained gazing from the window for some time, without, however, taking the slightest notice of those who stood without watching her so eagerly.

"This is no spirit," said Captain Hawk.

"No. Observe how fixed is the expression of her eyes!" remarked Lord Harcliffe. "I imagine she must be a somnambulist. Let us be cautious not to wake her."

"Her expression is certainly that of a person asleep," acquiesced Captain Hawk; "but how did she gain access to the interior of this building?"

"The doors may have been left open," suggested Lord Harcliffe.

"They were fast enough the last time I was here But let us see."

The outer gate was ajar, and creaked on its hinges as he pushed it open.

Captain Hawk advanced gently to the front door, and turned the handle softly.

It opened readily; and as he looked in he could see the dim reflection of the rays of the lamp the mysterious figure carried in her hand.

Even the slight noise made by the opening of the door was sufficient to arouse her.

"She is going!" cried Lord Harcliffe, in a hasty whisper, approaching the door.

"Enter quickly, and let us watch this strange but beautiful night wanderer," answered the captain.

Lord Harcliffe had barely time to pass over the threshold and pull the door to after him when the figure appeared at the top of the stairs.

She looked straight before her, and there was no recognition in her fixed eyes.

She descended the stairs slowly, and, pausing at the foot, stood for a moment in a listening attitude.

"Harry—Harry," she cried, at length, in a whispered tone, "you can come now—there is no one here—they are all gone."

She paused a moment, and then continued:

"Why do you not come? It is so long since we met, and I long to clasp you to my heart. Ah, no—no!" she continued, sadly, "I forgot, he will never come again; they tore him from me and sent him far away across the sea; I remember the fatal morning when the letter came edged with black, that told me he was dead. Oh, my Harry!—my love!" she exclaimed, growing more excited as she proceeded, "the wide deep ocean is your grave, and the cold rocks your pillow! Never more in this world will your poor Madeline behold you—never—never more!"

She drooped her head mournfully for a few moments, and then as suddenly raised it.

"Who knows?" she cried, in a more hopeful tone, "he may be still alive! My father hated poor Harry, and may have deceived me. I'll go at once to the spot where we parted and wait till my Harry returns; he will be sure to seek me there!"

And with this strange confusion of ideas—that left it doubtful whether the speaker was under the influence of sleep or pouring forth from a distraught brain fond remembrances of a happy past—she rose, and passing along the passage, opened the door leading into the back garden, and descending the few steps, hastily crossed the grass-plat towards the end wall.

The highwaymen, moved by irrepressible interest and curiosity, followed the fair vision, who proceeded on her way, looking neither to the right nor left.

There was a door in the wall which Captain Hawk had not previously noticed.

Through this the white-robed figure passed.

The highwaymen also entered a garden utterly fallen into neglect and choked with weeds, offering an entire contrast to the one they had just quitted.

The only difference was, that in this wilderness the shrubs grew higher, and had evidently at one time edged the walks where now grass and weeds grew thickly and spoke of solitude and neglect.

One avenue at the side, however, was still perceptible, and down this the fair-haired girl took her course.

Our heroes still followed.

The creaking of a gate on its hinges expedited their movements, and they reached a turn in the avenue just in time to see the mysterious object of their pursuit pass through into the road.

The gate yielded readily to their touch, and they were again in sight of poor Madeline.

The place she sought was but a short distance off.

It was a small churchyard where the dead of several generations slumbered peacefully.

Almost concealed by trees, the unpretending, modest little church reared itself, within whose sacred walls Sabbath after Sabbath the voice of prayer and praise ascended to the Great Creator who does not despise the humblest adoration from the humblest worshipper when offered in sincerity and truth.

The young girl made her way quickly over the grass-covered, crowded graves where—

"Each in his narrow cell for ever laid,
The rude forefathers of the hamlet sleep."

She paused, not till she had reached almost the extremity of the churchyard, where, surrounded by masses of dark cypress and holly, a plain marble slab reared itself, bearing this simple inscription :—

"In Memory of Harry."

Before this she sank down on the grassy turf, and appeared lost in meditation.

At the same moment the majestic tones of the organ within the church swelled upon the silence of the night, producing an effect that sank deeply into the hearts of the highwaymen.

The mournful story of the poor girl seemed to be told by her few significant utterings, and the simple record on the tombstone.

Captain Hawk, whose heart ached for the uncertain fate of his beloved Blanche, found the subdued sorrow of the poor girl he gazed on echoed in his own breast.

They gazed in silence, until their attention was aroused by a footstep on the gravel.

Looking up, they perceived an old white-haired man carrying a pickaxe, and spade, and a lantern.

He was the sexton, and he was now going to dig a grave, preferring the cool, quiet night, to the glare of day for his labours.

He evinced no surprise at the sight of our heroes.

It was no uncommon thing for wayfarers to pause, tempted by the quiet beauty of the spot, to contemplate the sacred edifice and the tranquil burying-place in its solemn moonlight aspect.

The old man appeared, however, to think that his own appearance at that hour needed some explanation.

"Good evening, gentlemen," he said, in a cheery tone; "you see I work when others sleep, and so does our worthy organist. He likes to practise at night. Whilst I dig, he plays, and, listening to his music, I can dig all the better."

"You must be a hearty old fellow," said Captain Hawk, "to be able to endure the fatigue at your age."

"Well, sir, thank Heaven, I am as hearty as here an' there a one, considerin' I'm past threescore and ten year old."

"A great age!" remarked Lord Harcliffe.

"Ay, ay!" answered the old man; "they say grave-digging be unhealthy, but I don't believe it. My grandfather died at eighty-five, my father at eighty, and they were both grave-diggers. I've been sexton here, man and boy, fifty-five years, and save a little touch now an' then of the rheumatiz, I don't ail anything."

"Here, my friend, taste this," said Captain Hawk, handing the old fellow his pocket flask.

"Thankee, sir," replied the sexton, as he immediately complied. "Oh," he cried, after a hearty pull, "that be prime stuff, that it be!"

"The best that money can purchase," returned the captain.

"I know it be better than they sell at the Crown an' Anchor by a long way," said the old man, with a discriminating shake of the head.

It suddenly struck the captain that the old sexton might be able to afford them some information respecting the poor girl, who still sat in a silent, listless attitude before the white marble tablet her love had reared to the memory of the lost.

His inquiry was anticipated by the old man himself, who, glancing at the crouched figure, simply remarked:

"Ah, she's there again to-night, poor thing!"

"You allude to that young girl?" said the captain.

"Yes, sir."

"She has greatly excited our curiosity. Her beauty, her melancholy, and the sweet tones of her voice, have invested her with an almost sacred interest."

"Ah, you may say that, sir," the old man replied, shaking his white head with a mournful sigh. "There never was a more beautiful, kinder, sweeter-voiced young lady than she as now sits there."

"Has she lost her reason?" inquired the captain, with much sympathy.

"Well, sir, sometimes she has, and sometimes she hasn't. It's just as the fit seems to take her. Between you an' me, I think the moon's got somethin' to do with it, for she's allus worse when it's at the full."

"She has, then, experienced some trouble?" remarked the captain.

"Ay, poor girl, she have indeed!" answered the old man, in a tone of deep commiseration. "I thought I'd a had to prepare a place for the poor broken heart to rest in afore this."

"She seems to be mourning for a lost lover."

"Ay, your honour, that's it. It were a cruel piece of business; but no good came of it. No good ever comes o' tearin' asunder two fond young hearts as love each other."

"Your words interest me deeply. May I hear her history?" inquired the captain, earnestly.

"Ay, surely," said the old man: "it's not a long one."

And after another sip at the flask, which appeared to suit his palate immensely, he commenced:

"You must know, gentlemen, that Miss Madeline Wentworth is the daughter of a rich man, who lives in a large mansion not far along the road yonder—that is, he did live there; but he's gone where his riches can't avail him, and where he'll have to answer for his cruelty to the poor child. All that's now left of him lies there."

As the old man spoke, he pointed to a handsome tomb at some little distance that reared itself in massive pride above the humble graves that surrounded it.

"Well," continued the old man, "Miss Madeline, who was the darling of everybody for her beauty and her kind loving ways, fell in love with a handsome young feller named Harry Chester, an' he fell in love wi' her. But Master Harry was poor in comparison with proud Mr. Wentworth; and when the young man declared his affection for his daughter, the old man raved and stormed, and went on like a madman. However, all his threats and passion couldn't prevent the young people from loving each other more than ever. They used to meet by stealth. Many a night have I seen 'em seated lovingly just on the spot where the poor solitary girl sits now; but of course I took no notice, nor did I ever say a word. I was in hopes they'd a got married on the sly; an' so I think they would, only some pryin' busy-body found out that they used to meet, an' went an' told Mr. Wentworth.

"O' course he was furious; but without sayin' a word to his daughter, he watched there behind the trees, and overheard the young people plight their troth and swear to be true to each other till life should end. He hadn't patience to hear more, but rushed from his hiding-place, and after heaping all kinds of maledictions on the head of his daughter and her lover, he dragged her away, and kept her locked up in a lonely room in his large mansion, where the passers-by have told me they could hear her cries and groans."

"Unfeeling wretch!" murmured Captain Hawk.

"So I say, sir," warmly assented the old man, "an' so everyone said; but what did the rich, hard-hearted man care? Not a fig, or a straw! His pride and his gold made him as hard as granite. He carried it in his face."

"But did he keep her thus secluded?" inquired Lord Harcliffe, in a tone of great interest.

"Yes, as long as he could. But love, you know, gentlemen, is full o' expedients; an' Master Harry contrived to clamber up one night to the top chamber where Miss Madeline was confined."

"And did he enter?" asked the captain.

"No; entrance was impossible—the window had been secured by iron bars. But he contrived to whisper into her ear something that comforted her greatly, and after that time her sighs and tears ceased."

"I presume the young man revived her with hopes of deliverance?" said Lord Harcliffe.

"That's jest what he did," returned the old man; "but, as though Fate itself opposed the young lovers, that very night one o' the servants saw him as he was descending the wall, an' told the old man.

"Well, after that night, watch was always kept. But you must know when Master Harry clambered up, he gave Miss Madeline a sharp file; and it was her daily work to file away at the bars till they were nearly cut through on the outside, and could be easily broken away.

"About a week after, one dark night, when there was no moon, Master Harry came, bringing with him a rope ladder.

"He ascended as before, and found poor dear Miss Madeline waiting anxiously for him.

"The window was opened in a moment, the bars wrenched away, and the lovers clasped in each other's arms.

"Well, the ladder was made fast at the top, and Harry descended to steady it for Miss Madeline's descent.

"With trembling limbs, but a stout heart—for she was a brave young lady—Miss Wentworth trusted herself to the fragile rope."

"And she reached the ground in safety?" inquired the highwaymen, simultaneously.

"Yes; to find herself in her father's arms, once more a prisoner!"

"Cruel fortune!" murmured Captain Hawk.

"And the young man?" inquired Lord Harcliffe.

"Was taken by a press-gang that night, no doubt at the instigation of Mr. Wentworth, and has never been seen since."

"Is he dead?" asked the captain, eagerly.

"It is supposed so," answered the old man; "since about twelve months after his disappearance a letter, edged with black, was brought to the great house for Miss Madeline, and from that moment she was never seen to smile; so everyone supposed it brought the intelligence of her lover's death. She almost always carries it about with her; and see," he added, pointing, "she is reading it now."

The sad, pale creature was eagerly perusing the fatal paper that had given her such disastrous intelligence.

"Poor girl!" exclaimed Captain Hawk; "my heart bleeds for her!"

"And this unfeeling father, what became of him?" asked Lord Harcliffe.

"He was punished," the old man replied; "that mourning round the letter served for two instead of one, for on the very day it arrived, and almost at the same hour, Mr. Wentworth was brought home a lifeless corpse to his grand house.

"His horse had taken fright, and thrown him. His neck was broken."

"Serve him right!" cried the captain; "he had broken his child's heart, and richly deserved his fate!"

"After the funeral, the poor young lady was allowed to wander wherever she pleased; and now rarely a night passes that she does not come into the quiet churchyard and sit just where she now is. Sometimes she sings to the organ, sometimes she talks to herself, and sometimes she comes and watches me as I dig, poor girl! Ah, it's a sad thing—a sad thing! You wouldn't believe how she's changed since she heard of her lover's death!"

"But from what she said, she appeared to be uncertain upon this point, and to indulge a kind of wandering hope that he might be alive," said Captain Hawk.

"Oh, yes," replied the old sexton, "she does that. She often tells me he is not dead—that she has seen him in her dreams, and that he has told her so, and that she intends to watch for him every night until he returns."

"And do you think he will return—that these hapless lovers will ever meet again?" inquired Lord Harcliffe.

"Yes; but not until the Day of Judgment!" replied the old man, solemnly.

Our heroes had been so engrossed with the sexton's recital, that they had not observed a solitary figure which, wrapped in a cloak, had entered the churchyard, and after glancing a moment at them, advanced amongst the graves, and was soon lost amongst the tombs and shrubs.

Madeline had evidently caught the old man's last words.

"Day of Judgment!" she murmured—"judgment! That is a long time to wait! Oh, I shall see him before then: I feel I shall—I know I shall!"

"Hark!" cried the sexton, "she has broken from her moody fit, and she will speak now! Listen!"

They drew nearer; and shrouded in the shadow of a cypress tree, they were enabled to hear and watch her.

The subdued tones of the organ fell upon the ear with grateful harmony, and seemed to soothe the poor bereaved mourner.

"Why do I come here, winter and summer, night after night," she cried, "unless with the hope of meeting him? Why is it that such sweet music vibrates through the still air as I watch? I know why; it is to bid me hope! Yes—yes, my Harry will come back to me! Oh, Harry, dearest—loved one! Come to your poor Madeline—oh, come! I believe that we shall meet in Heaven, but not till we have met once more on earth! Oh, come!"

She glanced upwards as she ceased speaking, and as the moonbeams fell upon her features, it was difficult to imagine that her beauty was merely mortal.

She paused a moment, and then continued:

"Dost thou not hear me, dearest? See how I watch and wait! They tell me that you are dead, and that the cold waves wash over your lifeless clay; but I don't believe them! I never will believe them, till your own voice assures me! Oh, speak to me—let me but hear your voice, and then I shall die in peace!"

With eyes dilated and arms outstretched, in the attitude of invocation, the poor girl looked so fixed and statue-like that Captain Hawk was about to suggest that they should speak to her, and endeavour to draw her from the spot, when her voice again attracted him.

"Oh, answer me!" she cried—"Harry, answer me!"

There was a dead silence for a moment, and then a gentle voice, like a whisper, uttered the word:

"*Madeline!*"

Low as the tone was in which that word was spoken, it was still perfectly distinct, and, mingling with the chords of the organ, seemed like the dying echo of some sacred chant.

A deep and solemn awe stole over the listeners.

"Merciful Heaven!" whispered Captain Hawk, "did you hear that?"

"I did, sir," answered the old sexton, under his breath. "That voice never came from this world!" he added, as he wiped the drops from his brow.

"Hush!" murmured Lord Harcliffe—"see!"

The poor girl, who had heard the voice distinctly, so far from being terrified or appalled at the sound, appeared to welcome it gladly.

She started on to her knees, and a radiant smile overspread her features, whilst a crimson flush lit up her pallid cheeks with a transient and almost unearthly loveliness.

"I hear you, darling—I hear you!" she cried, eagerly. "Oh, speak again!"

"Madeline—beloved Madeline!" the voice replied.

The highwaymen glanced at each other excitedly.

"What does this mean?" said the captain to his comrade.

"Let us listen," returned Lord Harcliffe.

"He answers me!—he answers me!" cried the fair girl, in a tone of rapture. "And having heard his dear familiar voice, I am now more than ever assured that we shall meet again. Oh, come Harry! let me see you!"

"Will you not fear, dearest?"

"Oh, no!"

"But have you not heard my fate?"

"I have—I have!"

"Do you expect, then, to gaze upon my spirit?"

"I know not—I care not, so that I once more look upon the face I love!" she cried, vehemently.

"Then look upon me, my own love!" returned a pleasant, manly voice, and at the same moment a handsome young fellow of five-and-twenty, attired in the uniform of a naval lieutenant, emerged from behind an adjacent tomb.

"Madeline!—Harry!" they cried, simultaneously, and the lovers were locked in each other's arms.

Perfectly understanding, and fully rejoicing in the happy termination of this romance, and not wishing to disturb the lovers, the highwaymen quietly withdrew, and placing in the old man's palm a sum it had not held for many a day, they left the churchyard.

Captain Hawk could not repress a sigh at the thought, that while some hearts were rejoicing in the happiness of reunion, he was severed from her he loved so dearly, and that she was surrounded by perils—perils which, like spectres in the dark, seemed more terrible because they were shapeless and unknown.

CHAPTER CCXIV.

LORD HARCLIFFE DISCOVERS A SLIGHT CLUE TO BLANCHE'S RETREAT ON THE WINDOW-PANE.—THEY RETURN TO TOWN AND START IN SEARCH.—FORTUNE SENDS THEM A DINNER.—THEY DEPART.—SIR RICHARD CHANDOS AND LORD STRATHERN STOP THE CARRIAGE OF THE COUNTESS OF BLACKLAKE.

CAPTAIN HAWK and Lord Harcliffe retraced their way to Grove Cottage, from which they had been so irresistibly attracted, and the captain showed his comrade through every chamber of the deserted mansion, not omitting the cellar in which he had been immured, but without discovering any sign to serve as a clue to where Blanche had been taken.

They entered the parlour, where only a few hours previously he had received the confession of her love and promise to be his from the lips of Blanche herself.

Now a solitude like that of a desert seemed to reign in every crevice of the close, dusty chamber.

"I thought perhaps—I hoped," said the captain, in a tone almost of despair, "that Blanche might have left some written word or sign to guide me. But alas! poor girl! perhaps she had no opportunity—and most probably was as ignorant of her destination as I am who seek her."

Every nook and cranny of the house was searched, every cupboard and drawer opened and examined, but without success.

They were about to give up any further investigation as hopeless, when an exclamation from Lord Harcliffe aroused his dispirited comrade.

"See here, Dick!" he cried.

"What have you discovered?" eagerly demanded the captain.

His lordship pointed to the window of the parlour, the shutters of which he had opened.

"Read that!" he answered.

"I see nothing," said Captain Hawk.

"Take my place," returned his comrade: "you will see more distinctly."

The captain took the position pointed out, and observed some letters hastily traced on the glass of the window, evidently with a diamond.

These letters read thus: "Haste Hert——"

The last letter "t" was terminated abruptly by a long scratch on the glass, but beyond that there was nothing.

The two highwaymen stood silently contemplating the brief sentence for a few moments.

"What do you make of this?" inquired Lord Harcliffe, at length.

"I should interpret it thus," answered the captain. "If this is Blanche's writing——"

"It is decidedly a woman's hand, and evidently written with hasty terror."

"Yes. Well, I can only imagine that from some unguarded word dropped by the scoundrels who have carried her off, she gained some clue to her place of destination, and, as the only means of informing me, endeavoured to inscribe it on this pane with her diamond ring."

"But the abrupt termination—the unfinished word?"

"Must have been caused by the arrival of her cowardly persecutors! See, that scratch is an evidence that her arm was violently seized before she had time to complete the sentence."

"*Haste Hert——*" read Lord Harcliffe. "How do you interpret that?"

"'Hasten to Hertfordshire,' I should imagine. Could her trembling hands have finished her directions, they would, I believe, have been, 'you will find me there.'"

"I agree with you," said his lordship.

"Thank the good powers even for this clue!" cried Captain Hawk, and then with a burst of enthusiasm in striking contrast with his recent subdued manner, he exclaimed:

"Dear Blanche, I will find thee, I swear, though I roam the whole country through its length and breadth!"

Having now a point at least where to commence his search, the captain to a great extent recovered his spirits and was himself again.

Lord Harcliffe, who rejoiced at the sudden change, shook hands with his friend and comrade warmly.

"We shall find her!" he exclaimed, in an encouraging tone.

"Yes, yes—hope springs up once more in my breast!" exclaimed the captain. "Dear Blanche! To lose her would be to lose life—love—all!"

The highwaymen reached "The Prince's Retreat" about five in the morning in perfect safety.

They were so fatigued with their exertions, having only had a brief nap during their voyage to Chelsea, that repose was absolutely necessary.

They therefore retired to rest, and for a time the world and its cares and sorrows were alike consigned to the oblivion of "Nature's soft nurse."

* * * * * * *

It was about noon next day when our heroes, invigorated in mind and body from the sound repose they had enjoyed, and still further strengthened by a hearty breakfast, sallied forth to commence their search after Blanche.

Their weapons had been carefully cleaned and loaded, flasks well filled, and every precaution taken by Pharoah to supply them with bodily comforts, as well as means of defence.

As their appearance, mounted on the backs of their steeds, in broad daylight at such a crisis as the present would have awakened an attention they were anxious to avoid, they chose a close conveyance to convey them to the suburbs of London, where Charles, attired as a nobleman's groom, awaited them with Satan and Phantom, well disguised in horse wrappers.

In a few moments our heroes were once more on the backs of their faithful steeds, which had suffered nothing from their confinement, but which testified their delight by sundry neighings and prancings, which might have caused some trepidation to less skilful riders, but which to the minds of the highwaymen seemed only to say: "Let us be off."

"You won't be away long, captain?" said Charles, in a tone of some doubt, as he grasped the captain's hand.

"No, not long," was the reply. "We shall pay you flying visits, so be prepared."

Captain Hawk bent down in his saddle, and said, in a low tone to Charles:

"It is possible my friend, Lord Harcliffe, may be summoned to town on important business. If so, I shall want you to accompany me in his stead."

"Certainly, captain!" answered Charles, a beam of pleasure illuminating his extraordinary physiognomy. "There's nothing I should like better!"

"Very well, then, hold yourself in readiness; for the present, farewell!"

"Good-bye, captain! Good-bye, your lordship!"

And with this parting salutation, our heroes rode off, Charles standing watching them till they were out of sight, when he turned his steps backwards towards town.

"What a wonderful man the captain is! An' so is his comrade, Lord Harcliffe. They're both wonderful men! Ere's 'alf the p'lice in London arter 'em, an' blest if they 'don't slip through their fingers like heels!"

With this apostrophe, he quickened his pace homewards.

The highwaymen paused as soon as they had got clear of the houses, and consulted together for a moment, the horses neighing and pawing the ground, and curvetting, with other signs of impatience.

"The poor animals are fresh," said Captain Hawk, "and want a good run to set them right. I propose, therefore, that we give them a good five-mile gallop; the exercise will be beneficial both to them and us."

"I perfectly agree with you," returned Lord Harcliffe. "It will clear our brains, and fit us for what we have to do."

Accordingly they gave their steeds the rein, touched them lightly on the flank, and the eager animals bounded off with the speed of the wind.

As trees, hedges, and distant farm-houses flashed past them in their rapid flight, they began to feel their old enthusiasm reviving in their breasts.

Though they were not certain that at any moment they might not encounter a body of mounted police, still the exhilaration of their spirits increased as they sped along.

"Hurrah for the road!" cried Captain Hawk, with irrepressible enthusiasm.

"Hurrah for the road!" echoed his comrade.

After an hour's hard galloping, they pulled up their

[THE MANIAC IS TERRIFIED AT THE APPEARANCE OF THE OLD MAN.]

steeds, that were covered with foam, and looked about them.

"Where are we?" asked Captain Hawk, thoughtfully.

"We must be near Harrow, I should think," replied Lord Harcliffe.

"You are right, my friend; see, the milestone informs us we are within two miles of that place."

"How is your appetite, Dick?" inquired his lordship.

"As it always is when I am on the road," answered the captain—"I'm voraciously hungry!"

"Your sensations represent mine exactly. I'm almost ashamed, though, to confess it after the excellent breakfast I made," returned his lordship.

"I really see no reason why we should be ashamed of one of the necessary results of the best gift of Providence—good health," replied the captain; "and as we both seem to be of one mind in this particular, I

think the sooner we put an end to these disagreeable sensations by a substantial meal, the better."

"Forward, then; we will test the quality of the larder of the first inn we arrive at."

The horses were once more urged onwards, and a ride of a very few moments brought them in sight of a commodious, handsome-looking roadside tavern.

"There is our mark," cried the captain, pointing to the hospitable mansion, with its tall signboard swinging flauntingly in front, informing the passing travellers that its sign was the Crane with Three Necks.

"And see," added Lord Harcliffe, "mine host has heard the clatter of our horses' heels, and is waiting to arrest us on our journey."

"We may thank our stars, Harcliffe, that it is not an arrest of a less agreeable description," said his comrade, laughing.

They continued their course towards the inn, at the door of which stood John Tonks, the landlord, who, as Lord Harcliffe had surmised, had recognised their approach, and appeared expectant and ready to receive them.

Nor was the landlord the only individual in waiting.

Two others, in corduroy breeches, stood prepared to hold the heads of their steeds, whilst in the doorway Mrs. Tonks fluttered in all the glory of a silk dress and a cap from which depended a vast profusion of cherry-coloured ribbons.

"Good morning, your lordships!" cried John, respectfully removing his hat; which example was instantly followed by the two ostlers, who tugged at their short crops in front with great energy, after which feat they laid their hands upon the horses' bridles.

"Good morning, landlord," answered our heroes, who were struck with that individual's obsequious politeness.

"I've been expecting you for this hour, your honours," the landlord continued.

"Have you?" said Captain Hawk. "What the devil does he mean?" he thought.

"Yes, gentlemen. Your groom was here early this morning, and left word you were coming."

"Very kind of him!" thought the highwaymen, still inwardly puzzled as to what was meant.

"We're quite ready for your lordships," the landlord exclaimed, in a tone of proud assurance. "Dinner will be on the table by the time you have dismounted and washed the dust from your hands."

"Dinner!" echoed our heroes, more at a loss than ever to comprehend the state of affairs.

"And," continued Mr. John Tonks, "though I say it that shouldn't, your honours will have no reason to complain either of the bill of fare or the cooking."

"Oh, we're not difficult to satisfy," answered Captain Hawk, who thought it might be as well to say something.

"And what have you provided for us?" inquired Lord Harcliffe, who, being desperately hungry, rejoiced at the bare mention of the bill of fare.

"There's a prime piece of salmon, a pair of young pullets, and green peas, and a quarter of lamb, with pastry to follow," explained the landlord, triumphantly.

"That will do, my friend," answered the captain, as he dismounted.

"Admirably!" added Lord Harcliffe, as he followed his comrade's example.

"Give our horses a rub down, and keep them in readiness, so that we may be able to start at a moment's notice," said the captain.

"They shall be attended to," answered the landlord; "fine animals they are, too, as ever I clapped my eyes on!"

Captain Hawk watched the ostlers as they led away Satan and Phantom, and at the same time reconnoitred the position of the stables, and, having done this, he and Lord Harcliffe entered a private room that had been prepared for them, in which the table was laid, and where the atmosphere was fragrant with the odour of freshly-sliced cucumber.

The landlord, having shown them their dining-room, summoned the chamber-maid, who escorted our heroes to a delightful bed-room, where they were left to the enjoyment of such ablutions as they thought proper to make, and of which they were too glad to avail themselves.

By the time they descended, dinner was on the table.

The salmon was delicious, the pullets so delightfully tender that they seemed to melt in the mouths of the hungry travellers; the lamb and peas were in an equal state of perfection; nor, to do the landlord justice, was the wine he put on the table in any way inferior to the rest.

The landlord, who had waited on them personally, withdrew at the termination of the repast, and left his visitors to the quiet enjoyment of their wine.

"Well," said Captain Hawk to his comrade, with that kind of complacent smile that always accompanies a sense of enjoyment, "how have you enjoyed your dinner?"

"Immensely!"

"So have I."

"There is only one droll circumstance connected with it."

"What is that?"

"That I believe it is all a mistake."

"Not the dinner?"

"Oh, no! There was no mistake about that!"

"What, then?"

"I believe the mistake is with the landlord. I feel confident he takes us for some one else."

"Then in that case I presume we have eaten somebody else's dinner?"

"Exactly. It is evident enough dinner was ordered for two travellers who have not yet made their appearance. By a strange freak of fortune we drop in at the right time, the landlord takes us for his expected visitors, and we have quietly eaten their dinner."

"For what I have received I feel truly thankful."

"And I, my friend—much more so than if the expected visitors had devoured it."

"Do you know I felt confident in my own mind that the landlord was mistaken in us."

"I thought so too. But in such cases as this, I think we are perfectly justified in profiting by our host's delusion."

"Decidedly. When two hungry men have an excellent dinner placed before them, my advice to them would be: 'Eat as much as you require, and then, if you suspect any mistake, explain it afterwards.'"

"I do not see any necessity for explanation. My conscience will not trouble me for what I have done."

"Nor mine. I therefore vote that we pay our bill and get onwards before the arrival of the legitimate proprietors of the dinner."

"I am ready."

The bell was accordingly rung, the landlord summoned, and the bill discharged.

The highwaymen had had a delicious dinner, and they paid a *delicious price*.

But they were then flush of money; and had it been twice or thrice the sum, they would not have thought of disputing it.

The horses were brought out, and after all demands, even to the remuneration of the ostlers, had been paid, Captain Hawk bade the worthy host "Good day."

"Good day, gentlemen!" cried the latter, smiling blandly.

"Good day!" cried the captain; "and if the gentlemen on the road enjoy the dinner they ordered as well as we have, who have helped them eat it, they will have no cause to complain. Good day!"

Waving their hands gaily, our heroes galloped off.

There was something in Captain Hawk's farewell speech that somewhat mystified the landlord.

What did it mean?

It seemed very much like one party *ordering* a dinner and another party *eating* it.

The landlord was conscientious in his capacity of host, but he was not a deep thinker; the consequence was, he became utterly confused with the difficulties of the subject, and gave it up in despair.

He had almost forgotten the circumstance, and was quietly dozing over his afternoon pipe, when the sound of horses' hoofs approaching fell upon his ear.

Captain Hawk's mysterious parting words rushed into his mind with redoubled force.

"It must be the gentlemen who were *on the road!*" he soliloquised, in a very perturbed state of mind. "Then I suppose those who have eaten their dinner and gone away are the *somebody elses*. Dear me, what a mistake I have made!"

His meditations were cut short by the horsemen stopping at the door of the inn, and shouting out:

"Heigh! landlord! ostler!"

There was no way of undoing what had been done, or rather of doing up what had been undone.

It was impossible to reproduce the sliced salmon, or restore the mutton, or make the pullets whole; the landlord, therefore, had no resource but to respond to his visitors.

He accordingly went out at the door; and if he had felt some little anxiety previously, that feeling was greatly increased as he gazed at the riders, who were attired in sky-blue velvet coats of the period, thrown up with amber and gold at the cuffs, and the broad flaps over the pockets.

Their long vests were also of amber and gold, and

glittered in the sunlight so magnificently that the landlord's heart sank within him.

"There is no doubt," said John to himself, very secretly, "that these are the noblemen for whom the dinner was ordered."

He, however, so far recovered his presence of mind as to remove his hat and bow very humbly to his aristocratic visitors, whom he observed looked extremely sour and unamiable.

These, in the meantime, had dismounted and resigned their steeds to the ostlers, who led them away.

"You expected us, of course?" remarked the elder of the two gentlemen, as they stood upon the door-step.

"Why a—um—y-es, your lordship!" replied the landlord, in an agitated manner. "I expected you—oh, yes, certainly!"

"My groom called here this morning and informed you that we should be here, did he not?" inquired Sir Richard Chandos, who observed the confusion evident in the host's manner.

"Oh, yes, your lordship!" replied John Tonks, rubbing his hands nervously together, "the groom called certainly."

"And I presume he also informed you what our requirements would be?" asked Lord Strathern, in a voice of sufficient sternness to make the perplexed landlord's heart die within him.

He, however, contrived to jerk out a reply to Lord Strathern's speech to the effect that he perfectly understood that their lordships' honours required dinner.

"Show us to a private room, and after that let dinner be served immediately!" said Sir Richard, in a peremptory tone.

Once more the chambermaid was summoned, and the noblemen were escorted into the very chamber where, not long before, Captain Hawk and Lord Harcliffe had refreshed their respective toilets after their quick gallop.

The only difference was that the former were in an exceedingly good humour, whilst the latter looked as black and lowering as thunder-clouds.

The reader may probably wonder how it is that these two gentlemen, having been the day before travelling post-haste to Windsor in pursuit of Captain Nugent and his bride, should now be dining at a country inn in Hertfordshire.

The reason was this: As they drew near the town of Windsor, after passing the highwaymen on the road, they encountered one of the King's special messengers.

Being acquainted with this emissary, they stopped and exchanged compliments, and from him they learned that he had just been delivering an express summons to Captain Nugent to attend his Majesty at St. James's Palace on the following day.

This, of course, was annoying to the captain, and not less so to his bride; but as George II. was irascible and punctilious, and expected his faithful and loving subjects—especially those about his person—to do precisely as they were ordered, the newly-made bridegroom had no resource but to obey.

He therefore resolved to accompany his beloved wife to town, and, taking leave of her there, that she should proceed to the residence of a relative of his at King's Langley, while he paid his court to his Majesty at St. James's.

This intelligence they contrived to extract from the post-boys; and as no plan could have been better arranged for the carrying out of their plans, they received the intelligence with grim satisfaction, consoling themselves that the countess would in a few hours be once more in their power.

This, then, was the cause of their presence at the "Crane with Three Necks."

Little did the two evil-disposed nobles know who had preceded them and eaten the best part of their dinner.

Little did our heroes imagine for whom the repast they had so much enjoyed had been ordered.

Sir Richard and Lord Edward having refreshed themselves in their private apartment, descended to the dining-room.

In the meantime, John Tonks had communicated his difficulties to the wife of his bosom, and a desperate struggle was going on in the kitchen to endeavour to patch up the eatables, and to render them presentable.

The salmon was pressed together and plunged desperately into boiling water; the remaining pullet was buttered and floured and hung before a blazing fire to induce a tempting brownness, whilst the mutton was reduced to half its original proportions, and subjected to a well-heated oven.

Fresh peas and vegetables were set on the fire; and a cucumber, newly cut from the frame, shed its powerful odours in the dining-room.

The noblemen strode up and down the room impatiently.

Their ride had kindled appetite, and they were in no humour to be kept waiting.

Presently the bell rang furiously, causing much agitation in the breast of John Tonks, who was working hard at some melted butter for the salmon.

He had to relinquish his task to Mrs. T., who was watching the peas as they bubbled in the pot, and probing the potatoes unmercifully with a fork to see if they *ever would* be done.

John, with a beating heart and a very red face, presented himself humbly at the door of the dining-room.

"Your lordship rang?" he said, dubiously, as though he was not quite certain.

His doubts on that point—if he had any—were soon dispelled by Sir Richard Chandos, who turned upon him as though he would have snapped his head off.

"Are we to have dinner to-day, or not?" he growled.

"Undoubtedly, your lordship—I hope so," answered the distressed host.

"Why are we kept waiting?" cried Lord Strathern, in a tone much fiercer than the occasion required.

"I really, your lordship—a—I'm very sorry, but——"

"Psha! no 'buts!'" burst out Sir Richard. "Let us have dinner at once!"

"Certainly, your lordships. It would have been ready before this, but we did not expect you quite so soon," murmured the honest host, in the most apologetic tone he could possibly assume.

"Don't talk, man, but act!" exclaimed the baronet, waving the landlord from him. "We're hungry!"

A very few minutes brought John Tonks and the waiter with the repast.

And now he felt there was another ordeal to undergo.

"One would think you had been cooking a banquet for the Lord Mayor and Corporation!" cried Sir Richard, as he and his friend took their seats at the table.

"I am really very sorry, your lordships!" faltered poor John Tonks, who stood humbly waiting until one of the gentlemen should say grace before he removed the cover.

Neither, however, of the graceless specimens before him appeared to have any feelings of gratitude either towards Heaven or man; and the landlord was suddenly roused to a sense of his remissness by the angry voice of Sir Richard, who shouted:

"What are you waiting for, sirrah? Remove the cover!"

"Ye-s, your lordship!" gasped John. "S-salmon, your l-lordships," he contrived to ejaculate, in the most deprecatory and feeble of voices.

There was an awful pause—a dead silence—that appeared to the troubled landlord to last a quarter of an hour at least.

The salmon—all that was left of it—certainly did look amazingly small.

"What do you call this?" shouted the baronet.

"S-salmon, your honour," answered the host.

"Did you imagine you were providing for men or Lilliputians?" growled Sir Richard. "Salmon! Psha! It requires a magnifying glass to see it at all!"

"It was all the fishmonger had left, your lordship," explained John, driven in his despair to utter an untruth.

The irritable baronet, without condescending to reply, divided the fish at one stroke, and served Lord Strathern.

The fish having been rapidly consumed, there being very little of it, John Tonks removed the cover from the pullet, which looked very much scorched and shrunk.

Again the frown deepened on the baronet's face.

"What's this?" he cried, as he plunged his fork into the unoffending chicken.

"One of the finest pullets, your lordship——"

This exordium was cut short by the angry nobleman, who, in a fit of passion, launched the chicken impaled on the fork at the landlord's head.

"If you call that a pullet, eat it yourself!" shouted Sir Richard. "Now, quick! what else?"

"Lamb!" ejaculated the landlord, who was engaged in wiping his face from the anointment of the fowl, but who darted forward and removed the cover from the meat.

This joint appeared to be more satisfactory than the rest of the banquet.

Sir Richard at once applied himself to carving the joint; and having at last found something to eat, he desired the landlord to bring some wine.

"Sherry, your honour?" he inquired, more hopefully.

"Sherry."

John Tonks departed, blessing his stars that he had got so well out of his difficulty, and feeling assured that his sherry would amply make amends for all former shortcomings.

The wine was speedily disinterred from the dusty bins in the cellar, decanted, and placed upon the table.

Sir Richard drank a glass immediately, and with the air of a thorough *connoisseur*, expressed his opinion that *it would do.*

A few glasses of wine considerably mollified the acerbity of the drinkers' tempers, and they were at length able to discuss their future plans.

"Nothing could have happened more opportunely for the success of our plans than our accidental encounter with the King's messenger," said Sir Richard.

"Nothing," acquiesced Lord Strathern, with malicious satisfaction. "These turtle-doves will arrive in London about noon, I should imagine."

"Not later, since the gallant captain will have to present himself at the palace by two o'clock at the latest."

"Ha, ha! they little imagine when they part how long it will be before they meet again."

"I wish to Heaven it might be never!"

"It should if I had my will."

"Patience, Edward!" said Sir Richard. "It may come to that yet."

"And where do you intend to place the countess?" inquired Lord Edward.

"Where she will be safely taken care of," replied the baronet. "But the first step is to hold her in our hands," he added.

"But surely there is no doubt of our securing her this time?" remarked Lord Edward, eagerly.

"I think not," responded Sir Richard; "but experience teaches us every day that we must never 'reckon our chickens before they are hatched.' So far as I can see, our plans are certain to be successful."

"What can hinder them?"

"Nothing that I can foresee at present, only it is as well not to be too certain about anything. Who would have thought that this handsome braggart—this scented, elegant coxcomb, Captain Nugent, would have twice escaped our swords?"

"Ah! who? and by such strange means!" said Lord Edward. "Do you know, Richard, I often find myself pondering upon those mysterious beings who thwarted us."

"Ah!" ejaculated the baronet, with a short expressive grunt—"ah!"

"I wonder who they were?" continued the young lord.

"Some of Satan's imps, I should infer, since they seem to do as they please, and defy detection."

"I am sometimes inclined to think that those fellows in the masks and cloaks are after all nothing more or less than the midnight marauders about whom so great a stir is made, and whom the agents of the law are so anxious to capture——"

"And whom, with all their skill, they seem as though they never *could* capture. I presume you allude to the scoundrels who call themselves Knights of the Road——"

"Captain Hawk and the Black Highwayman? I do."

"Psha! With all their skill—effrontery I should rather call it—they'll prove too clever for themselves at last."

"It is wonderful, though, how they baffle their pursuers as they do."

"Oh, it is only for a time! But they're always caught at last. These fellows are always dependent on some contingency; a friend—a *pal*, I believe they call it—or a mistress. Umph! Whenever heroes of this class are laid by the heels, it is usually through the intervention of some stanch ally or some loving courtesan, who prefers a few gold coins to keeping inviolate the sacred pledge of friendship."

"Well, I have thought over our past adventures frequently, and positively, if my better reason did not forbid such superstitious notions, I should be inclined to think that the fiend himself has power to assume a human form, and traversed the earth for the express purpose of frustrating our schemes of happiness."

"Ha, ha! Why not say you believe that such *is* the case?"

"Well, they say the devil 'goes about like a roaring lion,' and I'm inclined to believe it."

"You will also, my friend, be inclined, probably, to admit that 'time flies,' and that we must be journeying onwards?"

"Oh yes, I am not altogether metaphysical. I believe that in this world of struggle and opposition, we must not only think, but act—that we must oppose force to force, and that when a sword is pointed at our breast, we need a sword, not a blade of grass, to ward off the stroke. I am ready."

"That's right!" answered Sir Richard. "I thought you were becoming thoughtful and dreamy."

"Not I; I perfectly understand what we have to do," said the young lord, in a tone of pique.

"You will understand, then, that we must be gone from this inn before the Countess of Blacklake arrives."

"Certainly. But I do not apprehend that she will reach here before the evening," returned Lord Edward.

"Probably not. But she will be anxious to arrive at her journey's end; and will in all probability not alight even while the horses are being changed, therefore that is an additional reason why we should be away."

"Well, then, let us depart," said his lordship, "and get to our posts. I suppose you adhere to our original plan of stopping the carriage as it passes?"

"Decidedly."

It took but a short time to pay the bill, in which John Tonks took care to charge for the trouble he had been put to, the anxiety he had suffered, and the personal indignity to which he had been subjected.

This having been accomplished, the two noblemen mounted their horses, and took their departure.

The shades of evening were beginning to fall, when a travelling carriage, drawn by a pair of horses, guided by a postillion, stopped at the door of the "Crane with Three Necks."

All that was required was a draught of water for the horses, which, having been supplied, the vehicle rolled forward on its journey.

Inside the carriage sat the young and lovely Countess of Blacklake.

Newly wedded—wedded, too, for the first time to the man she loved—it was a bitter disappointment, the sudden separation rendered inevitable by the King's summons.

As the beautiful Clarissa sat solitary and alone in the vehicle, her eyes filled with involuntary tears as she thought of her beloved husband, who was all the world to her, and wished him at her side.

But as the carriage rolled rapidly onwards, and as the shadows lengthened and the twilight darkened, and the evening breeze wafted the fragrance of distant hayfields even to the highway, she became more reconciled to her separation.

Anon the moon appeared, and a deep calm stole over her spirit: she felt that, though parted from her husband for a time, the joy would be all the greater when they should be permitted to meet again.

They had now descended a somewhat steep hill, down which the horses had been compelled to walk, and which, when they had reached the bottom, was dark and gloomy from the fact of the trees meeting and forming a leafy canopy over their heads.

The countess, who preferred the open moonlit road, was about to urge on the old postillion, when a harsh voice with which she seemed to be familiar, cried:

"Stop, for your life!"

A deadly sense of peril seized upon her, but she neither fainted nor cried out.

All that she did was to look with much self-possession from the carriage window, to see who it was who had issued the peremptory mandate.

Dusk as it was, she had no difficulty in discerning that the figures clothed in light blue and gold were those whom she had more reason to dread than all the rest of the world combined—Sir Richard Chandos, her guardian; and Lord Edward Strathern, her would-be lover.

She sank back in the carriage almost in despair, and could only beseech Heaven to watch over and preserve her.

She was not long left in peace, for the harsh, angry tones of her uncle were heard as he ordered the old postillion at the peril of his life not to advance a step.

As he backed this order with a loaded pistol, it will be readily believed that the old postboy, who found his brains —such as they were—tolerably serviceable at times, was very particular to remain just where he was.

The baronet then advanced to the carriage and flung open the door.

"So, madam," he cried, with bitter emphasis, "after all the tricks you have played us, we meet again. I felt assured we should do so before long. And now we do meet, what have you to say for yourself?"

"Nothing—to you!" replied the lady, firmly. "I am in no way responsible to you for my actions; I am no longer my own mistress, but the property of another. For what I have done, for any explanation, I refer you to my husband."

"Oh, fear not," returned Lord Edward, sarcastically, "we shall not forget your husband, depend upon it. We owe the gallant captain a heavy debt of gratitude, which we shall pay at the earliest opportunity; but one thing at a time—we must first secure your ladyship!"

"Secure me! What mean you, sir?" demanded the countess, indignantly.

"This gentleman feels, naturally enough, that his feelings have been trifled with and his honest affection trampled on."

"Honest affection!" reiterated the countess, in a tone of sarcastic contempt. "It is the first time I ever knew Lord Strathern capable of such a sentiment."

"Your flattering opinion, madam," returned Lord Strathern, with a scowling brow, "does not in any way turn me from my purpose."

"Your purpose!" exclaimed the countess. "What is your purpose?"

"To force you to obey my will!" was Lord Edward's abrupt answer.

"Force me!—*me*, a countess! on the King's highway? You dare not!"

The beautiful eyes of the indignant lady flashed fire as she spoke.

"Dare not?" continued Lord Edward, mockingly. "You have got to learn what I dare. You have thought fit to trifle with me——"

"Never!"

"'Tis false! I say you have!"

"When have I ever done so?"

"Always; but especially since the plausible Captain Nugent ingratiated himself into your affections. Since then your petted, pampered vanity has led you to magnify your beauty and attractions, and to imagine that men are to be your slaves and to bow down like slaves before you, and then you condescend to place your foot upon their necks and treat them with contempt!"

"Slanderer!"

"I speak the truth! I have felt all this bitterly! I have writhed under your insults, till at last I have the means of repaying them in full!"

The young lord glared upon the woman before him with the malignant cruelty of a fiend.

"Villain!" she cried, "stand aside, and allow me to proceed upon my journey, or the law shall——"

"The law!" laughed his lordship, mockingly. "A fig for the law and all such important agencies. The only law I acknowledge is the law of power—the law of possession, and that I hold to. You are mine!"

As he spoke the young nobleman sprang into the carriage, and seated himself by her side.

"Wretch—monster!" shrieked the countess, shrinking from his contact as from anything loathsome. "You, Sir Richard Chandos, are my kinsman—nay, not only that, my guardian——"

"You forget," interrupted Sir Richard, with sardonic coolness, "you repudiated my guardianship, and disputed my power over you not long since, if you remember."

"I did so, but still I should think your duty as a man and a gentleman would prompt you to protect me from outrage!" she exclaimed, with breathless indignation.

"Listen to me, madam," answered the stern baronet. "Your conduct has been such as to lead me to fear that your reason is in some degree impaired—that you are not capable of judging for yourself upon certain points. I shall therefore treat you as I should any other insane person, and place you in a proper asylum until you recover your reason."

The countess fell back, and looked with an expression of horrid doubt at her uncle, as though she did not clearly understand him.

"What do you mean?" she exclaimed.

"I mean," returned Sir Richard, coolly, "that you are mad; and that I shall place you in safe confinement, leaving it to his lordship here to woo you into a more accommodating disposition of mind."

"She will understand me better when we are left alone," cried Lord Edward, as he threw his arm round the countess.

But Clarissa, provoked beyond endurance at these insults, snatched his arm from its position, and flung the young nobleman violently back on the opposite seat of the carriage.

"Charming!" he cried, with a taunting laugh. "How much I admire spirit in woman! It heightens the bloom of their cheeks, and fires the lustre of their eyes. By Heaven! Clarissa, I never saw you look so lovely as at this moment!"

And as though his passions, excited by her beauty, burst through all restraint, he clasped her wildly to his breast, and covered her cheek and brow with burning kisses.

"Oh, shame! — unmanly miscreant!" shrieked the countess, in whose pure breast every womanly feeling cried out aloud against this outrage. "Sir Richard—uncle—though I can scarcely call you so, you are my father's brother—for my dead father's sake, protect his child!"

"I have no power over you," cried the brutal baronet. "You are his lordship's property; I leave you to his care."

Then addressing himself to the scared postboy, who was in momentary expectation of being despatched to his account, he cried:

"Get forward as quickly as you can drive. Take the first turning on the right, and use your spurs and whip freely. If you disobey me, I'll blow your brains out!"

The postillion, who had no idea of disobedience, gathered himself together—body, whip, and spurs—for a vigorous onslaught on the poor horses—when, with the energy of despair, and before Lord Edward could arrest her, the countess disengaged herself from his embrace and sprang from the carriage into the road, along which she darted with the rapidity of a startled hare, shrieking loudly for help as she fled.

"Follow her!" shouted Sir Richard.

Without needing a second admonition, Lord Edward gave chase to the fair fugitive, whilst Sir Richard, opening a gate in the hedge, ordered the postillion to drive the carriage out of the main road into the field. The baronet then watched the unequal chase, which promised to be speedily terminated.

CHAPTER CCXV.

CAPTAIN HAWK AND THE BLACK HIGHWAYMAN COMMENCE THEIR SEARCH; BUT WITH LITTLE SUCCESS.—THE DARK MANSION IN THE TWILIGHT.—THE NIGHT SHRIEK.—TO THE RESCUE!—THE HIGHWAYMEN ARRIVE IN TIME TO RESCUE THE COUNTESS.—THE TREACHEROUS SHOT.—DEATH OF LORD STRATHERN.

When Captain Hawk and Lord Harcliffe quitted the inn, the sun was descending; and as they rode along, the purple and gold of the horizon blending gradually with the deep blue sky, formed a glowing picture, which could not fail to attract their attention.

However, much as they might have felt disposed to linger over nature's glories, they were conscious that there was a task to perform, and that until that was concluded nothing beyond the rest and refreshment positively necessary to sustain them was to be thought of.

After riding some distance, they paused and looked about them.

"There seems nothing," remarked Captain Hawk, at

length, "that promises any adventure in this monotonous road, with its trees and hedges."

"Nothing!" echoed his comrade.

"Suppose we branch off to the left, then, and see what discoveries kind Fortune may have in store for us across the country?"

"Any way you please, Dick," acquiesced Lord Harcliffe. "Since we must scour the country all roads are alike, and wherever you go I will follow."

"Let us try this path, then," said the captain, as they came to a narrow lane on the left-hand side of the road. "This must lead somewhere, and will be far more likely to bring us where we may glean some intelligence than the open road."

Accordingly they turned into the pathway indicated.

There were hedges on each side and trees as they proceeded.

The lane seemed of considerable extent, and intersected other lanes of a similar kind.

However, as they progressed, the trees increased in number till at last they emerged from the tortuous windings of the lane into a more open space where a body of trees rearing their heads at irregular intervals seemed to indicate the borders of a wood.

Here the chirpings and twitterings of thousands of the feathered tribe preparing to go to roost fell pleasantly on the ear.

The sun had now disappeared below the horizon, and the face of Nature was overspread with that soft bluish gray cast that lingers for awhile until, verging deeper and deeper into the evening twilight, it is finally overshadowed by the deeper veil of night.

It became a matter of consideration whether at that hour they should enter the wood.

"I am half inclined to proceed, and let chance direct us," said Captain Hawk, meditatively.

"I see no reason why we should not," remarked Lord Harcliffe.

"We shall still have a partial light for an hour at least, and then the moon will rise."

"At all events, the worst that can happen would be a night's lodging under these old trees."

"And they are infinitely more preferable to some lodgings I have occupied," remarked the captain, smiling.

"I understand you," replied his comrade, returning the smile; "but to tell you the truth, there is always something in a wood that inspires me with a peaceful sense of happiness and security."

"Why?"

"I can hardly say why. Whether it is the cool luxuriance of its shadows, or the healthy, earthy odour that rises from the ground, or the songs of the birds over my head, I know not: I only know that when I stand in the silence and solitude of a wood in the summer time, I feel as though I could live there for ever."

"If we lived in the times of the heathen mythology, we should have some benevolent goddess taking compassion on you and transforming you into a tree," said Captain Hawk, smiling. "But I quite agree with you—there is something very attractive in the solitude of a forest."

"Shall we proceed, then?"

"Yes."

Satan and Phantom, who had been nibbling the grass as they stood, pressed forward with evident pleasure into the wood, which, as the trees grew closer and thicker, looked dark and gloomy.

But of this the steeds were unconscious; the cool, moist grass was refreshing to their hoofs after the hard, dry, dusty road, and they appeared to understand and enjoy the relief it afforded.

They went on for some time through the wood till they noticed the trees became more straggling and fewer in number.

"We must be drawing near the other side of the plantation," said Captain Hawk.

"Undoubtedly," acquiesced Lord Harcliffe.

Almost as they spoke, they emerged into an open space that extended far on either side.

Before them, at some distance, the wood commenced again.

This space evidently intersected, or cut the grove in half.

They directed their horses to the left, not entering the plantation before them, till in a short time they came to the banks of a beautiful river, near whose verdant banks luxuriant sedges rose, which in the daytime cast their dark shadows over the running stream.

"This must be the Lea, on whose banks good old Isaac Walton spent so many happy hours," remarked Captain Hawk.

"Yes; and from which he extracted such a quantity of excellent fish," added Lord Harcliffe.

"It must seem incomprehensible to men whose hearts are wholly and solely buried in their counting-houses, who go year after year diving into their ledgers till they see Nature only through a medium as yellow as their own guineas, what charm there can be in sitting by the banks of a stream like this all day, trying to tempt its finny inhabitants to take the bait that dangles from the end of a fishing rod?"

"It is so; but in my opinion, no one more thoroughly enjoys himself and his sport than the angler," said Lord Harcliffe.

"Are you partial to the sport?" inquired Captain Hawk.

"In my youth, I may almost say I adored it," returned his comrade.

"And I," said the captain—"I think some of the most truly happy moments I ever spent were passed on the banks of a murmuring trout stream, with an alder switch for a rod, and a few yards of thread obtained from my mother's work-basket, with a crooked pin for a hook."

"There is in the pure air, the bright sky, the early fresh morning, or the calm evening, that always more or less accompany the angler, everything to calm the passions and purify the taste, whilst there is nothing to vitiate. I think angling, for those who love it, the best and purest of all amusements."

The highwaymen, thus conversing, wandered along by the bank, following the course of the river till suddenly their attention was arrested by a solitary building that stood at a considerable distance from them.

It was impossible to judge what was its character, owing to the fading light; but, in strong contrast to the deep blue of the horizon that backed it, it stood prominently forth in bold relief even in the rapidly increasing darkness.

Though there were many dark objects and shadows near it, that gaunt, solitary-looking object was darkest and blackest.

Both the highwaymen fixed their looks upon it for some time in silence.

Neither spoke; each was occupied in his own mental inquiry suggested by that strange and ominous-looking edifice.

"A strange-looking object that," exclaimed Captain Hawk, at length.

"Very," said his companion. "To my mind it has an unsightly appearance, and looks like a blot upon the face of Nature, which is else so lovely."

"What place can it be?"

"I have not the least idea; but ignorant as I am, were I to predict aught respecting it, I should speak of it as a place where *hope never comes*."

As they stood gazing, as though unable to withdraw their eyes from the dark, massive pile, regular streaks of dull red light appeared to kindle beneath its dark surface.

Sometimes this light was brighter, and then it seemed to grow dull again.

"Do you observe that light?" asked the captain of his friend, in an undertone.

"Yes, distinctly," he replied. "What can it be?"

"I shall begin to think it is a phantom building, inhabited by spectres."

As if to give some colour to such an idea, the light increased in bulk and intensity, and rendered it evident that the illumination proceeded from windows in the mansion, whilst to and fro, reflected by the light within, strange fantastic figures appeared to move about and pass and repass.

As the highwaymen remained with riveted eyes, gazing upon this strange spectacle, the report of a gun startled the silent night, and in an instant the lights disappeared from the windows.

Our heroes lingered for some moments watching whether the illumination would reappear, but it did not.

The weird mansion alone remained as dark, gloomy, and portentous as before.

"'Tis strange!" said Captain Hawk. "But that dark house, with its gloom and its fantastic shadows, has excited an unusual interest in my breast."

"It is certainly most singular, and to say the least, invites inquiry."

"What say you, then, shall we resolve that that mysterious mansion be the first spot to which we direct our steps?"

"I am perfectly willing, for I confess I feel an anxiety to know something of it little less than your own."

"Let us, then, follow the stream, still keeping that old building in sight till we can form some idea of the best way to cut across to reach it."

The highwaymen turned their horses' heads and were about to retrace their steps, when a shrill scream rose upon the night air, followed by another and then another.

"Hark! D'ye hear that, Harcliffe?" cried the captain.

"Hear it, Dick!—it curdled my blood to listen to it!" returned his lordship.

"It came from that direction, I am certain," said the captain, pointing exactly away from the course they had been about to pursue.

Again the scream rang out distinctly, and this time the cries were heard:

"Help!—help!—help!"

"'Tis a woman's voice!" cried the captain, vehemently. "By Heaven, there is either danger or death in that cry. Forward, Harcliffe! To rescue or avenge her!"

A slight touch of the heel sent their steeds flying across the fields and over hedges with lightning speed, but they found the river wound and stopped their progress.

Delay was not to be thought of.

They dashed in, and in a moment were on the opposite bank.

They were still at a loss which way to go, when by the light of the moon they perceived a carriage drawn up in a field.

This was sufficient.

"There is the point for which we must make," cried the captain; and as if to prove the correctness of his opinion, a piercing scream came from a woman who was evidently in some great peril in the road which the hedge of the field concealed from view.

"Forward!" cried the captain, as they dashed on. At the same moment the gate of the field swung open, and two gentlemen—or rather two ruffians in the garb of gentlemen—entered, dragging with them a young and lovely woman, who resisted violently.

But for the sake of the lady they would have ridden forward and crushed the cowardly miscreants under their horses' hoofs.

But they feared to injure at the same time the helpless being who struggled against such cruel odds.

"We must dismount," whispered Captain Hawk.

In an instant they had descended, leaving their horses standing side by side.

In another moment their masks were on and their swords drawn.

They approached rapidly.

So occupied were the captors in securing their fair prize, that they were totally unaware of the aid that was approaching.

But the hapless object of their persecution saw more distinctly, and redoubled her cries and entreaties as the highwaymen drew near.

"Oh, help me!—help me!" she cried, despairingly.

"By Heaven, it is the Countess of Blacklake! and—ah, see those scoundrels! D—n them, the cowardly hounds! On to them! Fasten your teeth in the dogs!"

Like lightning the highwaymen, though on foot, dashed upon the recreant assailants.

Without condescending to use their swords upon such miserable ruffians, Captain Hawk with one blow sent Lord Strathern reeling to the ground, whilst Lord Harcliffe seizing Sir Richard by the collar of his coat, lifted him off his feet and jerked him, as if he had been an infant, a distance of some yards.

The noblemen, thus suddenly foiled and completely scared by the rapid attack were at a loss to comprehend it.

Lord Edward made a vague and scrambling effort to rise, on which Captain Hawk knocked him down again, and drawing his sword, placed its point against the villain's breast, whilst with his other hand he gripped him by the throat until he felt on the verge of suffocation.

Sir Richard staggered from the violent impetus he received from Lord Harcliffe up against a tree and rebounded to the earth, but he, like his companion in this cowardly assault, staggered as he best could on to his feet, and drawing instantly, crossed swords with his unknown adversary, who with his arm encircling the trembling but grateful countess, stood coolly gazing at the ruffian noble from behind his mask.*

The first surprise and shock of the sudden attack having somewhat abated, the noblemen were able to discern the persons of those who had thus snatched their prey from their grasp.

To their horror they recognised in their masked opponents the duellists of the garden in St. James's Square.

A strange, superstitious dread fastened on their guilty hearts.

They remained silent, glaring at our heroes, who with the utmost coolness and the most profound contempt, appeared to be considering what would be the most fitting punishment to inflict on these dastardly noblemen.

"Cowardly—unmanly wretches!" cried Captain Hawk, "who have courage sufficient to assail a defenceless woman, but who tremble when opposed to the strength of a man! I blush to think I belong to the same sex as yourselves! Deliver up the sword you are unworthy to wear!"

These words were especially addressed to Lord Strathern, whose throat the fingers of Captain Hawk still clutched, but whom he released as he would have flung from him a venomous reptile, in order to give him the opportunity of tendering his weapon.

Lord Edward, burning with shame and rage, drew his sword, and imagining Captain Hawk was off his guard, made a desperate and deadly lunge, which, had not the latter avoided by a rapid side movement, would have been a mortal blow.

The captain evinced neither passion nor resentment at this treacherous but impotent attempt.

He simply grasped his adversary's weapon by the hilt, and wresting it from his hand, struck him contemptuously on the breast with the flat of the blade, and then coolly snapped it across his knee.

At the same moment the Black Highwayman, who had disarmed the baronet, performed a similar operation with the sword of his opponent.

"That is the way we treat such poltroons as you are!" said Captain Hawk. "You are a couple of dastardly, craven cowards, unworthy of the name of men, much less gentlemen! Had you been worthy of the weapon of an honourable man, I should have let daylight—or rather moonlight—into your ribs long since! As it is, this fair lady shall pronounce your doom. According to her verdict I will act, and, by Heaven! if she orders us to hang you both by the neck to yonder branch, or to spit you like a couple of frogs on our swords, we shall most infallibly obey her. Speak, madam!"

"I have no wish for revenge, gentlemen," replied the countess, who had now completely recovered her self-possession; "I only regret that I am compelled to call one of those who have so basely and cruelly attacked me, a relative. As regards the other, I have nothing to say: he has disgraced his title of nobility, and lowered himself for ever in my estimation. Let them begone, and cease in future to molest me. I desire no further atonement at their hands: the shame they must both feel at this moment will be a sufficient punishment."

"You hear what her ladyship says respecting you pair of scoundrels, and I can only—if she will pardon my venturing to express an opinion in opposition to that of a lady—affirm that she has treated you with a lenity utterly undeserved, and I further beg to remark in the name of my comrade and myself that I sincerely regret not having been permitted to horsewhip you both soundly. Now you can go, and go quickly. There's the gate—let us see you out of it!"

---

*The reader will find this tableau illustrated in the large coloured engraving of the Black Highwayman and Captain Hawk rescuing the Countess of Blacklake.

The two crestfallen aristocrats, with shame, rage, and fear struggling in their breasts for the mastery, slunk away towards the gate.

"Where are the horses?" muttered Sir Richard.

"Never mind the horses," cried Captain Hawk, who had overheard the baronet's remark. "Fellows like you are unworthy to bestride such noble animals! Thank your stars you're permitted to walk. If you had your deserts, you'd be tied to a cart's tail, and be whipped from here to London. Begone!"

Sir Richard and Lord Edward, burning with a fury they could neither repress nor resent, reached the gate.

Then turning to the highwaymen, Lord Edward said, in a voice hoarse and scarcely articulate from passion:

"You'll hear of this again, villains!—that is, unless you're hung before our vengeance can overtake you!"

A scornful laugh was the only reply; and with muttered execrations on their lips, the baffled conspirators slowly left the spot, weaponless, and on foot.

No sooner were they gone than the fair countess poured forth her grateful heart in the most earnest thanks to the highwaymen for the great service they had rendered her.

"B t for you, my friends," she cried, "I should have been lost beyond redemption."

Our heroes assured her that the joy they felt at having been able to rescue her from the peril that threatened her was the highest reward they desired.

"But still—pardon our curiosity," said Captain Hawk, with respectful hesitation—"we are still at a loss to account for your being here, when only yesterday we left you at Windsor."

"You may well be surprised, my friends," returned the countess; "but not long after you left us a messenger arrived post haste from town with a summons recalling my dear husband to the Court."

"I understand; and you accompanied him?"

"Yes, and was on my way to the house of a relative at King's Langley, where I shall remain until I can accompany Captain Nugent to his seat at Cheshire."

"And these vindictive cowards contrived to get acquainted with your plans?"

"Yes, and waylaid me as I passed. But for you, Heaven only knows what would have been my fate!"

"Think no more of it, dear lady!" cried Captain Hawk. 'They will not dare renew the attempt."

"I pray not!" exclaimed the countess, fervently.

"And do you wish to reach King's Langley to-night?"

"Most earnestly!" she replied.

"Then, with your permission, we will be your escort."

The countess thanked them warmly, at the same time apologising for the labour she was imposing on them.

"I should not rest," said Captain Hawk, "unless I was assured you had reached your destination in safety."

The countess, who was rejoiced at the protection thus cheerfully volunteered, made no further objection.

Having handed her into the carriage and mounted their steeds, the *cortege* passed through the gate into the road, and proceeded rapidly in the direction of King's Langley, the highwaymen riding on each side of the vehicle, close to the window.

They had not proceeded far in this manner, when the road became narrower, and from the trees being thick and the foliage dense, more obscure.

Suddenly the loud reports of two pistols, fired evidently from some ambushed foes from each side of the road, caused the startled horses to rear violently.

Both the windows of the carriage were shattered by the bullets; and the crashing of the glass, the terrified scream of the countess, and the plunging of the animals for a moment caused the utmost confusion and anxiety.

But Providence again interfered to save them: the obscurity of the road had proved their safeguard: no one was hurt.

"I'll stake my life," cried Captain Hawk, as soon as by his own and his comrade's exertions he had succeeded in quieting the horses, "that those shots were fired by the vagabonds we permitted to escape instead of pinning them to the ground with our swords."

At this moment a rustling was heard in the hedge at a short distance from the carriage, which was still stationary.

As quick as thought, the captain and Lord Harcliffe fired in the direction of the sound.

A faint cry was heard as the carriage moved onwards.

"One of the traitors is winged at least!" exclaimed Captain Hawk, as he placed his smoking weapon in the holster of his saddle.

Little did he think how true his aim in the dark had been, for as the morning dawned a form, cold, rigid, and ghastly, with clotted blood saturating the hair and temple, lay almost screened from observation in the field skirting the road on the other side of the hedge.

It was the dead body of Lord Edward Strathern.

Thirsting for revenge, the baffled pair, instead of profiting by the forbearance shown them, and relinquishing a vain pursuit, had crept back under cover of the hedge, and hurried forward till they found a suitable spot for concealment.

When the carriage passed they had fired simultaneously, but without effect.

The retaliation had been more fatal, and one at least who sought another's life had himself fallen a victim, and passed in a moment into Eternity 'with all his imperfections on his head.'

Sir Richard Chandos escaped unhurt.

CHAPTER CCXVI.

OUR HEROES CONTINUE THEIR JOURNEY.—THEY RE-ENTER THE WOOD.—POOR WILLIE THE MANIAC.—THE GUN-SHOT.—THE DEAD FACE ON THE RIVER.

A QUICK drive of an hour and a half brought the countess to her destination, where she found her friends anxiously expecting her arrival.

Warmly thanking our heroes for their chivalrous protection, she bade them a cordial farewell, and entered the hospitable roof, where she was safe at least from the machinations of jealousy or violence.

The highwaymen waited till she was safely housed, and then, with the pleasant consciousness in their breasts that they had been able to serve one so beautiful and amiable, retraced the ground they had traversed.

Their reason for so doing was that they might gain some more certain knowledge as to the locality of the house whose portentous appearance so greatly excited their curiosity.

They soon reached the scene of their late encounter, and leaping the hedge, stood once more on the banks of the Lea.

Across this they urged their horses, who appeared to relish their swim greatly.

The opposite side regained, they retraced their path along the banks of the river.

Again the ominous-looking mansion appeared in sight, dark and gloomy as ever.

No lights glowed from the windows, no fantastic figures appeared to perplex and bewilder the beholder.

All was quiet and still as a mansion of the dead might be supposed to be.

They determined now to investigate that portion of the wood through which they had not yet passed.

Accordingly they entered its shadowy precincts, and were soon lost in its intricacies.

The highwaymen left it to their steeds to find their way through the thickly-planted trees that grew in every direction.

The night was deliciously mild, and the grateful, earthy odour that the moisture of the dew seemed to draw forth spoke of the country, its freshness, its freedom, and its healthfulness.

Every now and then the horses paused to crop a little of the crisp, moist grass, and then went on again.

A sense of weariness was beginning to steal over our heroes, and they began to have some strong ideas of throwing themselves on the dewy grass and indulging in a few hours' sleep beneath the forest trees.

"What think you," asked the captain, "of a saddle for a pillow and the turf for a bed?"

"It is all one to me," returned Lord Harcliffe. "I can sleep as well on such a couch as on a bed of down."

They were about to remove the saddles from their steeds, when a peculiar sound caused them to pause.

It was not a cry, nor a groan, but a kind of terrified muttering, or a series of ejaculations that reached their ears at intervals.

"What can it be?" said Captain Hawk, straining his ear to catch a repetition of the sounds.

[THE HIGHWAYMEN GAZE ON THE DEAD FACE IN THE RIVER.]

At a short distance from the spot where the highwaymen were standing was a kind of open space or clearing in the wood, into which the moonbeams, being unimpeded, fell in a bright flood of silver light. As they gazed in this direction, they observed a pale wan figure, so scantily clad as barely to hide its naked body, advance to the edge of the clearing, and after looking back apprehensively as though fearing pursuit, come forward into the moonlight.

Struck with this strange appearance, the highwaymen advanced under the shadow of the trees almost close to the opening, and watched the attenuated form.

It was evidently that of a youth; but though young, there were deep lines stamped in the features that impressed them with the marks of premature old age.

The features were ghastly pale, and the large eyes

roaming suspiciously from side to side were deeply sunken in their hollow sockets.

There was in their expression also something that spoke of that heaviest of all afflictions—insanity—and yet there appeared some lingering consciousness that was yet alive, as the youth would ever and anon look wistfully back to the dark grove from which he had emerged, as though he anticipated some danger in that direction.

Nothing, however, appeared to scare him, and he seemed to enjoy the bright rays of the moon as they fell upon him.

He stretched forth his wasted, fleshless arms towards the luminary, and smiled, but such a wan, faint, sickly smile, that almost any other expression would have been preferable.

"Ha—ha!" he laughed. "How much pleasanter this is

than the dark, dreary place where I have been kept so long! I like this! Ha, ha! I like this—I like this!"

Crouching down as he spoke, the youth seemed to bask as it were in the moonbeams.

"Who can he be?" whispered Lord Harcliffe.

"From his manner, I should be inclined to think he is some unfortunate lunatic escaped from his keepers."

"I fear so."

"Oh, this is delightful—this is lovely!" cried the poor youth, as he rolled himself in a kind of transport on the dewy grass, and buried his face in it as though he would have cooled his aching brain with its moisture. "If I could lie like this," he continued—"here in the fresh air, with the bright moon shining on me every night, the dreadful pain would soon depart from me, the evil spirit would be exorcised, and I should be well again!"

"Poor wretch!" murmured the captain.

"I wonder whence he has come?" said Lord Harcliffe.

"Shall we speak to him?"

"As you please."

"We must be very gentle, or we shall scare him."

Accordingly the highwaymen advanced into the moonlight, and stood for a moment perfectly motionless.

The poor maniac did not at first observe them, but suddenly, in one of his hasty contortions, his eyes rested full upon them.

He started, and seemed inclined to fly from them like a startled hare.

"Don't go, my poor lad!" said Captain Hawk, gently. "We shall not hurt you. We are your friends."

The poor lad paused at the gentle tones that met his ears, and looked wistfully at the captain.

"Friends—friends?" he repeated, doubtfully. "Poor Willie has no friends. He had once, but he has been kept in the dark so long they are all dead long ago—all dead!"

"No, not all, Willie," said Lord Harcliffe; "we are alive."

"And are you my friends indeed?" inquired the youth, with a strange eagerness.

"Indeed we are," answered his lordship.

"You'll not beat me?"

"Beat you, poor boy! No, no!" exclaimed Captain Hawk, warmly.

"They do sometimes," whispered the hapless youth, as he drew nearer towards the highwaymen, attracted by their kind manner. "See," he continued, as he tore aside his tattered shirt and exposed a cruel, hideous mass of cuts and bruises, "this is what they do!"

"Oh, wretches—wretches!" cried our heroes. "What can be too great a punishment for such barbarity as this!"

With tears almost in his eyes, Captain Hawk inquired:

"Whence come you, and who has done this?"

The lad glanced round apprehensively, and then, drawing nearer, said, in a terrified whisper:

"The old man there—there!"

As he spoke, he pointed vaguely through the wood.

The highwaymen looked intently but saw nothing; though, had it been light, they might have noticed an elderly man, with iron-gray hair and keen, wolfish, blood-shot eyes, grasping a firelock, and glaring like a fiend from out the darkness upon the fair face of the poor maniac.

"Where do you mean?" inquired Captain Hawk of the youth.

"There, there!" continued the lad—"the old house yonder with the gaunt, dark front, that frowns upon the beautiful blue sky—there, where there are cries and shrieks and groans! and where he——"

"The old man?"

"Yes—yes!" assented the poor maniac, with forcible gesticulation—"the old man with cruel hair like iron snakes, and burning eyes that scorch and——Ah! see—see!" he shrieked. "I see him now glaring upon me! Oh, save me—save me!"

And before the highwaymen could detain him, he bounded wildly off with the fleetness of a deer.

A muttered execration and a crackling of branches not far off reached their ears, and a shadowy form flitted by, but it was too obscure for certainty.

"It is useless to pursue the poor fellow, is it not?" asked the captain.

"I fear so."

"My heart bleeds for that poor youth!" continued Captain Hawk. "And the old wretch who so ill-treats him—what is he? Is it possible he belongs to that mysterious mansion?"

Before Lord Harcliffe could reply, the report of a gun at some distance echoed through the wood.

This was followed by a wailing cry of agony, and then all was still.

"Good Heaven!" cried Captain Hawk, "that was a death cry! That shot has consigned some poor wretch to eternity! Could it be that poor boy? Let us try and ascertain."

Urging on their horses as fast as they could through the intricacies of the wood, they went on, looking eagerly to the right and left, but they neither saw nor heard anything.

Thus proceeding, they came once more on to the banks of the river, but still no one appeared in sight.

"Umph!" said Captain Hawk, "this is strange!"

Hardly had the words passed his lips when he caught a glimpse of a man's hat through the bushes at some distance.

"See!" he exclaimed, in a hasty whisper, to his comrade, "there is something living there! If that hat be on the head of the man who fired the gun, he must have doubled us like a hare. Let us dismount, and creep forward quietly; we shall most probably drop upon him."

This suggestion being at once acted upon, the highwaymen hastily cut across the grass—the river winding outwards considerably at that spot—and soon approached the bushes from behind which they had sighted the man.

As they drew near these bushes, they found they skirted a wide ditch, or dyke, that ran through the wood into the Lea.

To continue their course there was only one thing to do, and that was either to overleap it or to wade through it.

The former of these operations being the most agreeable, they were about to make the attempt, when their attention and their actions were arrested by a deep grumbling voice, speaking in a low but audible tone, on the other side of the bushes.

"Hush!" whispered Captain Hawk, "we shall probably hear something that may guide us."

"If my aim hasn't failed me strangely," growled the voice, "I've hit him. I must have hit him! The mad fool will never want a second lesson—he'll never blab any more secrets—he'll be quiet enough if he's tasted my bullet—he'll keep his tongue between his teeth now! Where the h—ll has he slunk away to? I lost sight of him here."

A rustling amongst the bushes caused the man to look up eagerly and clap his hand to the trigger of his gun.

He doubtless expected to see the retreating form of his bleeding victim, and his surprise was evident when, instead, he found himself overlooked by two determined-looking strangers.

The consciousness that they were gazing at a man who had evidently just committed a dastardly and atrocious deed, imparted to the countenances of the highwaymen an expression of stern disgust.

Nor were the features they looked upon calculated to change that expression.

The man was roughly attired in a kind of gamekeeper's costume, and consisted of coat, waistcoat, and breeches of well-worn brown velveteen; gaiters of leather reaching half-way up the thigh, falling at the bottom over a pair of heavy boots. A red cotton handkerchief was loosely knotted round his neck, and a broad slouch hat surmounted his coarse, tangled gray hair.

Our heroes gazed for a moment in silent scrutiny at the forbidding features that were thus presented to their view.

Age, that had not yet imparted any apparent feebleness to the gaunt, wiry frame before them, had nevertheless denuded it of all superfluous flesh, whilst crime and evil passions had impressed their unmistakable lineaments on his face.

A complexion whose pallor was ghastly and unnatural, a vulture-like, hungry expression of feature, and a pair of suspicious, keen eyes, that glittered like a snake's as they glanced from under his knitted brows from their cavernous sockets, beneath which the sharp cheekbones stood prominently forth like the ridge of a precipice, from which hung in wrinkled furrows the dried and yellow skin of his fleshless cheeks, formed a combination of terrors that inspired the beholder equally with loathing and horror.

"What are you looking for?" asked Captain Hawk, in a stern, decided tone of command.

The man appeared inclined to be sulky, but there was something in the glance of the captain's eye, and the manner in which he had put the question, that suggested he was not to be trifled with, so the man answered, glancing furtively from side to side as he did so:

"I was looking for a pheasant I hit; it wasn't a dead shot, and he got away. He fell somewheres hereabouts."

"A poacher, eh?" said Lord Harcliffe.

"I'm no poacher!" returned the man, gruffly.

"A strange hour this, then, for pheasant shooting," remarked the captain; "but it strikes me the object you hit was *not* a pheasant. Pheasants do not usually *blab secrets*. It is *something else* you seek!"

Captain Hawk uttered these words in a very pointed tone of suspicion that roused the ruffian's ire and apprehension.

"What is it to you what I seek?" he growled. "You go your way, and leave me to go mine! If you don't——"

He finished his speech by laying his hand ominously on the trigger of his gun, and glaring up like a wolf at bay into the faces of the highwaymen.

This act was immediately responded to by the latter, who covered the man's face with the muzzles of their pistols.

Had they gone off, the eyes and brains of the man would have been clean wiped out.

The scoundrel seemed to think so, for he paused, keeping his eyes fixed on the deadly weapons, and Captain Hawk continued:

"We heard the report of a gun, and a cry—not the cry of a bird, but of a human being—and we believe some dastardly act has been committed."

"Act—what act?" inquired the man, with a quick, convulsive gasp of his breath.

"Murder!" replied Captain Hawk, impressively; "and we order you to assist us in investigating it!"

"I've got no time to be minding other matters besides my own," answered the man, gruffly. "Go your ways, and let me go mine!"

"Not yet!" said Captain Hawk, firmly. "Lower your gun while I speak to you!"

The man scowled, but did not obey.

"Lower it, I say, this instant!" shouted the captain, in a voice of passionate command.

The man, evidently cowed, lowered his weapon, but sulkily.

"Your appearance here is suspicious," continued Captain Hawk, "and your manner still more than your appearance. You will come with us."

"I sha'n't come with you!" returned the man, doggedly. "What I want is the game I shot!"

"You mean," retorted Captain Hawk, sternly, "what you want is the *poor lad* you shot!"

The villain's countenance grew livid at this startling sentence, which proved how much he was suspected.

His fingers worked convulsively, his eyes rolled up and around in all directions.

What he would have replied to this charge remained a mere matter of conjecture, for at this moment a low wailing cry of agony attracted the attention of all present.

"Hark! Do you hear?" cried Captain Hawk, excitedly.

The words were scarcely uttered when a loud splash in the water caused the highwaymen, by an involuntary impulse, to lower their pistols and look away anxiously across the river.

No sooner had they done so than the man, taking advantage of their diverted attention, bounded from the spot with an agility and desperation hardly conceivable in a gray-haired man, and disappeared amongst the trees before the highwaymen had time to arrest his flight.

"No matter," said Captain Hawk; "though he has escaped us for a time, he will not go far. The eye of Heaven and its avenging arm are on the track of the shedder of innocent blood!"

"He will meet his deserved fate. Let us leave him to it, and endeavour to ascertain whence that cry proceeded," added Lord Harcliffe.

Approaching the sedgy banks of the Lea, our heroes looked up and down the stream, but nothing but the rippling waters met their view, now sparkling like silver in the clear moonlight, and anon shadowed by some overhanging branches, or a bed of rushes that reared itself green and fresh from out its bosom.

It was a spot that would have made a youthful angler's mouth water.

The deep stream, and the sheltering rushes—oh, surely there must be some fine old shy, golden-finned roach in those pellucid depths, had we but a rod and line to try our luck. But we are digressing.

Captain Hawk turned to his comrade, and remarked:

"The cry we heard seemed to be yonder, up the river."

"Yes," returned Lord Harcliffe, "and the sound that followed the cry was exactly as though some one had plunged into the water."

"It was. 'Tis strange, though, there should be no signs of a human being as yet. There has been sufficient time for a body to have floated to us down the stream."

"Perhaps he has swum across the river."

"It may be so. Let us proceed along the bank, and reconnoitre as we go."

"We must first cross this dyke."

"I think we can jump it."

The bank, as the dyke neared the river, was free from bushes; consequently it offered a run.

Of this our heroes took advantage.

Captain Hawk was the first to essay the leap, and performed the feat successfully, with no greater mishap than a little mud on the heels of his boots.

Lord Harcliffe followed, and being lighter than his comrade, cleared it completely.

"Now then, let us see if we can discover the source of that cry of anguish," said the captain.

They continued their course along the bank till suddenly a dark object on the surface of the water caused them to pause, riveted to the spot.

This object was close to a bed of rushes, and from the eddying of the water as it flowed past, these weeds had evidently checked its progress down the stream.

"That appears to be the object of our search," remarked the captain.

"It looks like a human body," returned his comrade; "and if it prove to be so, since it is not far from the bank, we shall be able to reach it."

"Yes; let us come on."

They continued to advance, still keeping their eyes fixed upon the dark object in the water, when suddenly the head of the ruffian they had previously encountered appeared from a clump of foliage that extended almost to the river's brink.

Captain Hawk uttered a suppressed exclamation, and instinctively grasped his pistol, his brows knitted in a frown of deep indignation.

"Hush!" whispered Lord Harcliffe, restraining him; "let us remain silent, and watch the movements of this rascal."

The captain immediately acquiesced, and he and his comrade, keeping close behind the trunk of a tree that interposed, remained watching.

The man, utterly unconscious of the close scrutiny he was undergoing, having first peered cautiously around, approached the bank and fixed his eyes upon the dark object in the water.

"Ah!" said Captain Hawk, "there is no doubt that it is a human body, and that wretch is the murderer!"

As he spoke, the man, who had possessed himself of a long branch of a tree, stepped into the water, and after a few efforts dislodged the body from its position, and drew it towards him.

Our heroes could see the fierce contraction of the haggard features as the wretch fastened his hands upon the tattered garments that clung around the senseless clay.

It forcibly reminded them of a hungry vulture that had just swooped upon its prey.

Captain Hawk could no longer restrain the feeling of revulsion that rushed across him.

He levelled his pistol, and at the moment the man had gathered up his strength for the purpose of lifting the dead form on to the bank, he fired.

With a wild yell, the scared ruffian dropped the body,

and splashing through the water like some river monster, plunged into the brake and disappeared.

The body, thus released, floated calmly onwards towards the highwaymen, who, with breathless interest, watched its gradual approach.

They had not long to wait, and, as the clear stream wafted its silent burden past them, the moonbeams fell gently on the fair but worn features of poor Willie, who lay cradled on the cool bosom of the waters, that supported him more kindly than ever human breast had done, with his dark lashes fringing his pale cheek, and smiling placidly in his death sleep like a slumbering infant in the arms of its mother.

A shudder passed through the stout hearts of the highwaymen, and the tears welled up to their eyes.

"Poor boy!—poor boy!" they cried together; "brutality has done its worst; you are now beyond its reach!"

The body at this juncture again became entangled in the reeds, and this slight resistance caused the blood to ooze from the wound and tinge the bright waters with its murderous hue.

"That blood shall be avenged!" cried the captain, in a voice hoarse with emotion.

"It shall, by Heaven!" echoed the Black Highwayman.

With eyes upturned and hands clenched, our heroes recorded the oath.

CHAPTER CCXVII.

THE HIGHWAYMEN RESCUE THE BODY OF POOR WILLIE FROM THE RIVER, AND CONSIGN HIM TO HIS GRAVE.—OUR HEROES INDULGE IN AN OPEN-AIR SIESTA.—THEY SLEEP SOUNDLY, AND ON AWAKING CONTINUE THEIR JOURNEY.—THEY LEARN SOMETHING OF THE MYSTERIOUS MANSION.

LORD HARCLIFFE, grasping the hand of his comrade and leaning over the stream, drew the body to the bank, and then, with gentle, reverent touch, they lifted it out of the water, and laid it quietly upon its mother earth.

There was something inexpressibly touching in the deep calm of that young face; it seemed, in its still eloquence, to speak a whole romance in a single moment.

The highwaymen gazed down upon the lifeless clay, and, unable to restrain their emotions, they wept in silence.

"I think," said Captain Hawk, after a pause, as he wiped the tears from his eyes, "we are the only living creatures who will shed a tear to this poor lad's memory."

"He must be hard-hearted indeed," added Lord Harcliffe, "who can look unmoved on such a sight as this."

"How has he met his death? I see no wound," said the captain.

"He was flying from his murderous assailant when he received the fatal shot," returned Lord Harcliffe. "The wound will most probably be behind."

Kneeling down, they turned the body slightly. The rigidity of death had not yet stiffened the limbs.

The cause of death was then perceptible, and the dark blood trickled from a yawning cavity at the back of the neck.

It was the fatal shot of a good marksman.

The bullet had entered the spine.

They replaced the body, and composed the limbs.

"That murderous ruffian," said Captain Hawk, "doubtless was watching that poor boy, who must have escaped from some place where, for some iniquitous reason, he had been confined. I believe that what he said to us has cost him his life."

"Ay, his vague description of that mysterious mansion."

"True; and from what he said, wandering and wild as his words were, I feel more eager than ever to know more of that strange building."

"And I. But we must not leave the poor youth's body here."

"No, Heaven forbid! We will place him decently beneath the turf; and though the ground in which he will lie has been unconsecrated by the voice of man, the fresh breeze will blow over it, the bright sun will warm it, and the silver moon shed her evening light upon the lonely resting-place, and there are Heaven's voices that will hallow it."

Having procured a strong hedge-stake, our heroes, bent on their charitable work, proceeded to dig a trench sufficiently large to receive the body.

They both assisted in the task, which was one of considerable labour and fatigue from the absence of proper materials.

One loosened the earth with the hedge-stake, whilst the other removed the mould thus loosened with his hands.

At length the grave was finished.

It was not very deep, but sufficiently so to receive its unconscious tenant.

All being ready, they placed the poor lad in the narrow cell, into whose dark confines the moonbeams strove to penetrate.

"Poor boy!" said Captain Hawk, as he took a last look at the calm face of the dead, "thy life was one of suffering, but your pains are now over! Your obsequies are humble: there are no pompous funeral rites, no waving sable plumes, no crowds of mourners to see you to your last home—two strangers only stand by your graveside to drop a farewell tear upon your cold remains, and offer a prayer to Heaven that, your short and weary existence terminated, here in the humble grave our hands have prepared you may rest in peace!"

"Amen!" said the Black Highwayman, in a low, reverent tone.

The grave was then filled up, and, marking a tree that stood near its head, that they might recognise the spot at any future period, their work was ended.

The highwaymen now began to be sensible of considerable fatigue, but still the idea of seeking for an inn did not occur to them.

The night was mild and lovely, and, in the frame of mind the circumstances of the past hour had induced, they felt more disposed to linger amid nature's beauties, in the quiet retreat of that old wood, bordered by the placid river, than to enter the walls of the snuggest inn in Christendom.

They accordingly selected a spot where the grass and moss grew thickly, and, stretching themselves on this soft carpet, wrapped in their cloaks, which were strapped to their saddles in readiness for such service, they were soon soundly asleep, nor were their slumbers less sweet from the thought that they had paid the last tribute of respect to the lifeless clay of the poor lad who slumbered not far from them.

It was broad daylight when they awoke; the sun was shining brightly, and the birds were singing blithely in the leafy canopy over their heads.

"It strikes me," said Captain Hawk, as he threw off his drowsiness and started on to his feet, "we have slept late."

"Very probably," acquiesced Lord Harcliffe, following his example. "I generally sleep longer in the open air than under a roof. I feel, however, much refreshed, and my appetite strongly suggests that it must be near breakfast-time."

"It is twelve o'clock," said Captain Hawk, who had by this time referred to his watch. "It is no wonder we are hungry."

"I think Pharoah packed away some provisions, and gave them to Charles. If so, we shall find them in the saddle-bags," explained Lord Harcliffe.

A moment's investigation removed all doubts on the subject.

A cold fowl, some sandwiches of deliciously potted meat, ox-tongue, and a bottle of brandy, were successively produced from the saddle-bags, to the great delight of our heroes.

"Bravo, Pharoah! Bravo, Charles!" burst from their lips.

Seating themselves upon the grass, they made a hearty meal, which they diluted with draughts of cold brandy-and-water.

At the conclusion, they were entirely resuscitated, and ready for any enterprise.

It must not be imagined that, because Captain Hawk had been a sharer in the adventures recorded since his departure in search of Blanche Allison, he had forgotten the object of his mission.

On the contrary, she still held the first place in his thoughts and his heart.

It must be remembered, too, that the clue he had to

guide him to her was in the highest degree faint and ambiguous.

If, therefore, adventures came in his way, he followed them out as usual, feeling that in those very adventures he would be most likely to arrive at some intelligence of the fair girl he sought.

If, then, in the carrying out of these, the captain, in spite of his anxiety for Blanche, occasionally finds his spirits mount, our readers must not accuse him of want of feeling, but rather look upon it as the natural consequence of the active excitement of the state in which he lived, and which too often compelled him to throw aside his sorrows for a time, whatever they might be, in order to frustrate the attempts of his enemies, and to preserve his own life.

Being now refreshed by sleep and food, the captain became anxious to be on the road again.

"We must make up for lost time," he remarked to his comrade.

"What is the first step you propose taking?" inquired Lord Harcliffe.

"I think our first effort should be to investigate, if possible, the interior of that mysterious mansion."

"I quite agree with you; and since my stay with you may be limited, I should like to be at your side when you make this attempt."

"Come, then, let that be our point of destination."

This being decided on, they mounted their horses, and once more by a cross-ride made for the high-road.

Once only they paused in order, if possible, to arrive at the bearings of the building they sought.

They stood gazing at it in the bright sunlight and the glare of day, and still, as though some dark curse rested on it, the glorious luminary seemed to shun it.

Though all around it was bright and golden in the sunshine, that strange, solitary building caught not a single ray of the pervading brightness.

It stood forth like a frown on the face of nature—dark, portentous, gloomy, and forbidding.

"I am convinced there is some strange mystery attached to that edifice," said Captain Hawk.

"We must inquire of some one in the neighbourhood if it be as you suspect. There will be no lack of legendary terrors connected with it, you may be sure."

Urging on their horses, they soon came in sight of the highway.

As they approached, they saw a country lad sitting on a gate in all the luxuriance of relaxation, a good appetite, and a large lump of bread and bacon, which he was devouring as rapidly as possible.

The sound of the horses' feet made him turn; and struck with the imposing appearance of two such handsome cavaliers as our heroes, he glided from the gate with great rapidity, thinking them nothing less than a couple of dukes or princes, and stood ready to open the gate for the distinguished horsemen.

There was policy in this, as the young countryman soon discovered; for Captain Hawk threw a crown to the young man for his attention.

The country lad pulled his front hair with profound respect as our heroes rode up.

"You needn't open the gate this moment," said the captain. "I wish to ask you a few questions first."

"Ees, zur."

"Can you tell me what house that is. You can see from the high ground yonder in that direction?" inquired the captain, pointing backwards and before him as he spoke in the respective directions.

"What, zur? Do 'ee mean th' large 'oose as do stand yonder oop on th' hill?" said the rustic, answering Captain Hawk's question with another, and pointing also at the same time.

"I think it must be that—a large, gloomy-looking house on which the sun never seems to shine," the captain continued.

"Eh, I know now th' 'oose your honour do mean," said the lad. "You do mean th' Gray Mansion."

The tone of the young countryman was subdued; he spoke cautiously; and as he looked in the direction of the building in question, there was a kind of superstitious timidity in his manner that was sufficiently significant.

"May I ask your honours why 'ee do want to know aboot th' Gray Mansion?" he added.

"Oh," replied Captain Hawk, carelessly, "we have heard strange stories respecting this house, and being in the neighbourhood, we wished to view it."

"Ah!" ejaculated the rustic, with a deep expiration, "there be many strange stories about that old place. Did you notice how dark and black it looked?"

"We did indeed; it was that gloomy peculiarity that particularly impressed us," answered the captain.

"Do you know what it be that do make it look so dark?"

"No; what is the reason?"

"It be covered all over wi' a sort o' dirty moss, that do give it a dark hue different from that of any other 'oose as was ever seen afore."

"And what stories or legends are attached to the place?" inquired Lord Harcliffe.

"Why," answered the countryman, in a subdued whisper, as though half afraid his words should be heard, "they say in former times it were owned by a desperate bad man as murdered his three wives."

"A regular Bluebeard," remarked his lordship.

"Ay; but not only his wives, but his brothers and sisters, so as he might get possession of their money."

"Bloodthirsty rascal!" exclaimed the captain.

"Eh; but he didn't spill no blood," returned the lad. "It were not with knife or bullet he murdered his victims—he *poisoned* and *starved* 'em!"

"Atrocious!"

"But he were never happy."

"I should think not, with such crimes upon his soul," remarked Lord Harcliffe.

"There are some alive who have seen him often. They say he used to walk about wi' his arms folded on his breast, and his head hanging down, as though he were ashamed to be seen, and when he did look up his feace was loike the feace of a corpse."

"Well, and what became of him?"

"Why, his conscience wouldn't let him rest night nor mornin'. He kept on growing thinner an' thinner, an' paler an' more ghastlier-lookin' every day, an' at last he went to follow his victims."

"He died?"

"Ees, zur. It were curious, too, during his last illness he shut himself oop in one of th' rooms, an' wouldn't allow no one to go a-near him—neither doctor, nor nurse, nor nobody!"

"Strange!"

"Well, gentlemen, one night there was most awful shrieks and cries heard in the room where the dying man lay; and they said the inside was lit up with bright blue light, and that then it changed to a red flame like a furnace, though all the time there were only a small wax taper burning in th' chamber."

"Well?"

"Then, all of a soodden, theer come on a dreadful storm o' thunder an' lightnin', an' the rain poured down in torrents. Well, at the height o' the storm a flash o' lightnin' struck the wing in which the wicked master lay, and shivered one side clean away, an' theer, so they says as saw it, were a dark, gigantic figure, exactly like the pictures of Satan, standing by the bedside and pointing at the bad man."

"The fiend, no doubt, who was waiting for his prey," remarked Captain Hawk.

"He didn't wait long; for, almost directly after, there came upon the wind, that blowed a hurricane, a scream louder than any that had been heard before, and then all was as black as night!"

"And then?"

"It were supposed it were at that moment the soul o' th' unfortunate man flitted, for the dark figure was seen no more."

"And was no search made?" inquired the Black Highman.

"Oh, ees," replied the rustic; "arter a day or two, no tidings bein' heard of the sick man, a party of countrymen went oop to th' house, an' asked aboot him. Lor' love ye, gentlemen! all the servants—an' he didn't keep many—were scared, an' didn't dare go near theer master's room when he'd ordered 'em to keep away, and so they told the men as went to inquire. But this didn't satisfy 'em; so away they took themselves to the chamber o' th' master."

"Did they discover anything?" asked the captain.

"The door were fast locked," continued the narrator;

"but theer curiosity wasn't to be baulked like that, so they bursted it open, an' theer they saw a sight so awful as they never forgot to theer dying day!"

"What?"

"The bed furniture were all scorched an' burnt away, an' the bedstead were charred jest like sticks o' charcoal."

"And the body?"

"That lay on the bed like a black mass o' tinder. It were only from the shape o' the figure they knew it were the master."

"And what did they do?"

"One o' th' men—his name were John Styles—put his hand upon the body, an' at the same minute theer were another loud shriek heard, an' everything—body, bedstead, and bed-coverings—crumbled into dust, and fell at their feet!"

As he wound up his narration with this startling conclusion, the young countryman looked earnestly in the faces of his listeners, as if in expectation of great surprise and terror.

He had been accustomed to relate this harrowing history, and to receive his applause in the expressed horror of his audience, and was somewhat disappointed at the look of quiet incredulity that sat on the features of the highwaymen.

"Don't you think it be a most wonderful story?" he inquired at length.

"If we are to accredit the whole of it, it undoubtedly is," replied the captain; "but with respect to the latter portion, I see nothing unnatural in it at all."

"What!" echoed the rustic, opening his mouth in utter consternation, "nothing wonderful in the bed an' the body fallin' to dust the minnit it were touched? I think that were the most wonderfullest of all."

"The wing of the building had evidently been struck by lightning, and the astounding effect you mention was caused solely by the electric fluid," said Captain Hawk.

"But the dark figure an' the bright lights, an' the shrieks—they weren't caused by the 'lectric fluid, was they?" inquired the astonished countryman.

"No," returned the captain; "they were probably the results of the excited imaginations of the spectators, and the fury of the wind."

"I don't think you believe the story, gentlemen," remarked the lad, in a tone as nearly resembling reproachful indignation as he dared exhibit.

"Well, my lad, although we are sorry to appear to doubt facts, of the truth of which you appear to be so confident, still we cannot pledge ourselves to believe *all* the marvellous things we hear," said the captain.

"Eh, it be true though—true as gospel!" replied the young man, pertinaciously.

"And is this mansion inhabited at the present time?" inquired Lord Harcliffe.

"Lor' love 'ee, no sir! nor it hasn't been for the last twenty year!" the boy answered, in evident surprise at the ignorance of his questioners on a point so well known to himself.

The highwaymen looked at each other.

"We have got hold of a mystery at last," whispered the captain to his comrade.

"I think so," was the reply.

"How is it," continued Lord Harcliffe, "it has remained uninhabited for so long a time?"

"Why," returned the rustic, "in the foorst place, because th' old master left in 's will as no one was to live in it as long as one stone stood upon another; an' then the next reason is because it's haunted!"

"Haunted?" echoed the highwaymen, smiling.

"Ah, gentlemen, yow may smile, but it'd be a braver man than any as lives aboot here as'd stay a night in that old 'oose," remarked the lad, with an involuntary shudder.

Our heroes answered evasively, not particularly wishing to enlighten the bumpkin as to their intentions, which were most decidedly to do that which he considered so tremendous a test of courage.

"I'm rather inclined to believe there is something singularly strange about this mansion," said Captain Hawk, "for when we were gazing at it last night from a distance the windows suddenly became illuminated."

"Ay, that be th' *Phantom Lights*," explained the boy.

"And the figures we saw—or fancied we saw—flitting to and fro, we may presume to be the phantoms?"

"'Ees, they was the *ghostes*, safe enough! They do always coom out after dark. I wouldn't go past the geate o' that old 'oose at night not for a 'oondred poun'!" said the timid lad, apprehensively.

"Quite right to be cautious. If you ventured so near, a ghost or a dark figure might either appear before you and carry you away under his arm, or else pop you in his oven an' make tinder of you," suggested Lord Harcliffe.

"Bean't it orful to think of?" exclaimed the youth. "No one," he continued, "goes past theer at night as knows the story of the pleace; and them as do, always 'ears screechings an' groanings enough to scare 'em out o' their senses."

"And who are these screaming spectres supposed to be?" asked the captain.

"Oh, they be the ghosteses of the poor creeturs as th' old master murdered—so people says," answered the boy. "He had three wives, and they all disappeared strangely, an' it's supposed they haunt theer murderer through the old 'oose from room to room, never allowing him a minit's rest all night long!"

"'Alas, poor ghost!'" quoted Lord Harcliffe.

"Well, I don't think he do deserve much pity," said the countryman. "If a man do murder three wives, I think they ha' got a right to haunt 'im! I knows I would if I was one on 'em!"

"Well, my lad," observed Captain Hawk to his rustic informant, "I have to thank you for your information, and for your graphic and vivid recital of the legends attached to this mansion, and as we are strangers here, and desirous of seeing this old building, you would further oblige us by acting in the capacity of guide."

"What, guide 'ee to that dreadful pleace?"

"Yes; we wish to view it."

"Oh, it bean't worth seein'! It be nothin' to look at!" urged the lad, evidently disliking the task, and trying to dissuade our heroes.

"But we have made up our minds on this point. We are curious to visit it."

"It be nought but an old crumbling ruin."

"We are fond of ruins; besides, it is broad daylight, and ghosts never venture out at such a time. They wait for the moonlight."

"Ees, but——" the lad hesitated.

"We'll pay you well for your trouble," remarked the captain.

The inducement of a reward overpowered his scruples, and he at length consented to conduct the highwaymen.

They accordingly placed themselves under his guidance.

The lad led the way, whilst they followed leisurely, conversing in low tones.

It is almost needless to add that the subject of their discourse was the mysterious mansion they were approaching.

"There is mystery enough surrounding this building," said Captain Hawk to his comrade, "to form the groundwork of half a dozen romances."

Lord Harcliffe smiled.

"Yes," he answered, "half a dozen at least. The wicked proprietor—the midnight shrieks—the thunderstorm—the dark figure—the shattered wing—the mysterious lights—the howling ghosts—are capital subjects!"

"Does any idea suggest itself to you with respect to this strange mansion?"

"Yes, one in particular."

"What is that?"

"That it would be an admirable sanctuary in times of danger."

"Your idea was mine."

"There is no better retreat than a haunted house, depend upon it, for hunted fugitives."

"True; no one would dare to approach its precincts. But do you mean to infer that this mansion is inhabited by such?"

"I think it is by no means improbable that it might be."

"Likelier than not; and the ghosts—the spectres?"

"Would, I imagine, be found upon examination to be far more *corporeal* than *spiritual*, though I'd wager not one would object to a glass of good brandy."

"I daresay not. But see, our guide is getting upon

hunted ground! He pauses—and look! I declare, he's quite pale!"

This was a fact.

The young countryman had struggled with his misgivings—in the hope of reward—manfully; but as he drew nearer to the ghost-haunted spot, his courage failed him, his superstitious terrors overpowered him, and he dared not venture further.

"I've come as far as I dare, gentlemen," he said; "but the road be quite straight now, an' if you do keep oop th' hill through the plantation, you'll soon coom in sight of th' oose."

He touched his hat as he spoke, implying that as he did not intend to go any further they might as well reward him for his services, and release him from further attendance.

Our heroes perfectly understood his feelings, and were by no means sorry, now that they were so near the spot they sought, to get rid of their guide, whom they did not desire to be a spy upon their actions.

Captain Hawk, therefore, threw the young man a guinea, and thanking him for his assistance, availed himself of permission to depart, full of joyful astonishment at the liberality of the gift for so trifling a service.

Being alone, the highwaymen pressed forward, and soon reached the plantation, as described by the countryman.

Here the ground ascended considerably. However, they continued their course through the trees, which, from their present position, formed a complete screen to shut out all that was beyond.

But they were not long in passing through this tangled brake, and as they emerged from it they came in sight of the object they so anxiously sought—the *Gray Mansion!*

CHAPTER CCXVIII.

THE HIGHWAYMEN HAVING RECONNOITRED THE EXTERIOR OF THE GRAY MANSION, PROCEED TO INVESTIGATE THE INTERIOR.—THE ABODE OF DESOLATION.—THE ALARM.—THEY RESOLVE TO PASS THE NIGHT THERE.

If anything had been wanting in the descriptive powers of the countryman to describe this strange old pile, it was completely atoned for by the appearance of the building itself and the spot in which it reared its frowning head.

Though standing on a considerable elevation, it looked, from the circumstance of its being surrounded by trees, as though it stood in some secluded romantic glen.

Behind it, on a steep, almost perpendicular ascent, frowned dark masses of vegetation.

In front, the trees of the plantation, through which our heroes had passed, towered upwards as a barrier, whilst through the valley formed by these woody boundaries a stream ran, that seemed to have cut its way just as it pleased, and poured its crystal torrent splashing and sparkling as if in joyful contrast to the dark pile, whose dark walls threw their shadows athwart its clear bosom.

But who shall describe the gloom, the extreme desolation of that old mansion?

There was not a stone in its walls—not a lichen or a fungus on its broken crumbling cornices—not a weed in its lonely courtyard that did not speak in mournful tones of ruin and decay.

The beholder looking at this weird building was at once seized with a profound oppressive melancholy.

All there was silent—even the birds seemed to forget to sing, and chirped as it were in whispers.

It was *too* silent—it was *un*earthly; the calm was not the gentle silence of rest and repose—it was the mute, echoless, awful hush of death.

The edifice itself was an old castellated mansion, over whose hoar front the storms of some hundreds of winters had swept.

One wing—that in which, according to report, the guilty proprietor had met with a terrible fate—had partially fallen to decay, but the rest of the massive pile seemed to stand defiantly in gloomy spite of time, wind, and weather.

It had one peculiarity—it was entirely covered with a kind of greenish-gray moss, whose ghastly hue added to its spectral appearance, and evoked the title by which the building was known—the *Gray Mansion.*

The highwaymen looked on in silence.

At length Captain Hawk spoke.

"This place," said he, "must have been evidently built to stand a siege."

"Undoubtedly!" assented Lord Harcliffe. "Depend upon it, in years gone by, many a stout skirmish has taken place beneath the sight of these old walls."

They walked round the deserted building.

It was encircled by a fosse, or ditch, from which the water had long since dried up.

The drawbridge was raised, and from the fact of its being covered, like the rest of the castle, with the unvarying gray moss, was barely distinguishable save from its position.

"I can fancy," said Captain Hawk, spurred on by his chivalrous imagination, "the time when busy, active feet, cased in mail, trampled over that bridge, when the fierce contest raged, and the battle cry echoed through the ramparts. That, however, belongs to the past," he added, with a sigh "The massive chains and machinery of that bridge have long since rusted to decay: when next it falls it will be with the ruinous crash of desolation."

The day was fine and clear, but the summer brightness seemed to impart no life or beauty to this lonely spot.

An unaccountable depression stole across the spirits of our heroes.

They, however, roused themselves with an effort.

"It will not do to yield to melancholy," said Captain Hawk, "now that we are at the threshold of the place that has awakened in us so much curiosity."

"Certainly not," returned Lord Harcliffe. "As the old song says, 'away with melancholy.' I confess, however, to feeling an inclination myself in that direction just now; the feeling was but transient, and has passed away. I propose we enter."

Dismounting from their steeds, which they fastened by the reins to a sapling, the highwaymen advanced.

"I see no one to interfere with or dispute such a proposition, so here goes!" said Captain Hawk as he stepped over the low wall that surrounded the fosse and ran down the bank into the bed of the moat, that had been formerly filled with water, but was now overgrown with rank grass and nettles.

He was immediately followed by his comrade.

"I think that will be the point to which we must direct our steps," exclaimed the captain, pointing to the drawbridge that stood resting upright, cutting off the passage across the moat and seeming to utter the inhospitable notice to all comers, "No admittance here."

However, it was easier to say this than to enforce it with two men resolved as our heroes were.

Their object was to clamber up and get on the other side of the drawbridge.

The highwaymen looked up at it thoughtfully for a few moments, as though measuring their means and resources.

"There is only one way to accomplish our end," said Captain Hawk, in a decided tone—"we must clamber up somehow. Here," he continued, drawing his companion close to the wall, "you must oblige me with your shoulder."

"Willingly," answered Lord Harcliffe, placing himself firmly against the wall.

In an instant the captain had mounted, and in a few moments after, climbing like a cat, had managed to scramble up a certain distance and then drop in at the side of the bridge, which did not quite close up the arched opening it masked.

Having thus proved the ascent was practicable, his first thought was to facilitate the journey for his friend, who, having no one's shoulder to give him a start, still remained below.

In the arch were strong oak doors.

He pushed one, which grated and creaked on its hinges, and having opened a few inches with a very bad grace, came to a dead lock, and obstinately refused to move a fraction further.

However, the open space was sufficient for the captain to thrust himself through.

It was a small stone chamber, and had a damp, mouldy odour.

All it contained was a strong, horizontal capstan or windlass, round which was coiled one of the massive chains of the drawbridge, which came through a hole in the masonry.

Captain Hawk grasped the iron handle of the windlass, which, like the walls and the entire machine, was covered with blue mould and rust.

He essayed to move it, but he might as well have tried to dislodge the building from its foundations.

"That will never move again," soliloquised the captain, as he gazed upon the ponderous machine; "besides, even if it were in working order, since there is another windlass exactly resembling this in the opposite side of the arch, for the other chain, it would require two pairs of hands to let down the bridge; that idea, therefore, must be abandoned."

He was roused from his reflections by the voice of his comrade.

"Are you safely inside?" it cried.

"I am, my friend," returned the captain, "and I am seeking for the means to enable you to follow me."

"If I could but get a start," cried Lord Harcliffe, "I would soon be at your side."

At this moment the eyes of Captain Hawk fell upon a round mildewed piece of wood that might at one time have been the handle of a spear or partisan, and which lay, forgotten and unused, beneath a mass of leaves and dust.

"This will do!" exclaimed the captain as he extricated it from its obscurity. "I'm with you, Harcliffe!" he cried, as he hastily passed through the stone arch towards the drawbridge.

Clambering up on the inside, and passing out at the side at which he had entered, he grasped the pole and held it out at arm's-length to his comrade.

Lord Harcliffe grasped it, and using it much as he would have done a rope, he effected his ascent with little difficulty.

Having reached the framework of the bridge, the rest was comparatively easy.

In a few moments the friends once more stood side by side.

The first step was accomplished.

They had gained the courtyard of the Gray Mansion.

They might have saved themselves much time and trouble had they tried the postern gate at the back of the mansion, but of this they were ignorant.

"Now, my friend," cried Captain Hawk, 'forward's' the word!"

The highwaymen accordingly advanced towards the great gate of the mansion, which was of massive wood, surmounted by an arched portico of stone.

To their surprise this gate was partially open.

They pushed against it, but it moved not, and on examination it was found that one of the hinges was broken, and the other fast bound with rust.

They listened a moment, but not the slightest sound reached their ears.

"Let us enter," said the captain.

If the exterior of the building had impressed them, the interior was calculated to deepen those impressions tenfold.

They passed along the vaulted stone passages, their footsteps echoing as they went, and entered in succession every room they came to.

Each one, however, repeated again and again the same story—*desolation, ruin, decay.*

The tapestry in some of these chambers hung in mournful tatters from the walls.

The windows looked sadly from beneath their arched frames, begrimed with yellow dust.

The oak panels were gnawn and scratched by the rats, that could be distinctly heard scrambling off in troops, startled from their gambols by the tread of the strangers.

The lower portion of the mansion was completely destitute of furniture; but on ascending a wide stone staircase, the carpet of which had rotted into tatters, they discovered in the apartments there some old-fashioned relics that bespoke a time when something human had lived in them, and when perhaps joyful voices had echoed, where now all was unbroken silence.

The table and chairs were, however, all of very antique appearance and covered with dust.

They passed through the range of apartments on the first story, and then ascended to the upper floor.

The chambers here were smaller than the rest and empty—save one—and in that was a miscellaneous collection of suspicious implements that attracted our heroes' attention.

"What are these?" said Captain Hawk, as he selected an ugly iron instrument, with a screw and sharp teeth.

"It looks like a steel trap," remarked Lord Harcliffe.

"Or a thumb-screw," added his comrade.

His lordship at this moment picked up a heavy whip with knotted leather thongs, that were dry and stiff, and stained unmistakably with human gore.

A thrill passed through the veins of the highwaymen.

"This has been used at a much more recent date than *twenty years ago*," remarked his lordship, significantly.

"Yes," said Captain Hawk, "it sets my suspicions at work. Who knows what we may be destined to discover here?"

They now came to a room at the top of which were six arched windows.

Rubbing off a little of the dust that obscured the view, the highwaymen were able to form an idea of their position.

"According to my judgment," observed the captain, "I believe this to be the room, and those the windows, from whence the illumination was visible."

"I think so too," replied his lordship; "and yet may we not have been deceived: might it not have been the lambent flame of an *ignis fatuus*?"

"Not at that height," said the captain, in reply. "Depend upon it, there are mysteries here that time will alone unravel."

Having explored the upper portion of the house, they descended once more to a large chamber on the first story.

Here, taking advantage of the old-fashioned dusty furniture, they seated themselves, and for a few moments summed up, as it were, the result of their investigation.

"We have discovered nothing at present," said Captain Hawk; "but it by no means follows on that account that there is nothing to be discovered."

"The place seems to be entirely deserted," remarked Lord Harcliffe.

"Yes, my dear friend," answered the captain, "it certainly seems so, but at the same time it may be teeming with life in some of its recesses."

"Do you allude to the rats that infest it?" inquired the Black Highwayman.

"No, I mean *human* rats — two-legged vermin—far more dangerous and voracious than the small four-legged despoilers for which we set iron traps and which we demolish with poisoned grain."

"Do you think, then, this place really *is* inhabited?"

"I am inclined to think so."

"Why?"

"From the accounts given by that credulous country bumpkin."

"I believe this building is the resort of some who have an interest in keeping it in its present ruinous state, and also in feeding by artful means the popular opinion that it is haunted."

"The idea is certainly ridiculous! Have you any belief in ghosts?"

"Not I; and for a very good reason."

"What is that?"

"That all the ghosts I have ever encountered turned out eventually to be alive. No, no; on one point I am convinced: that when a man is really dead and in his grave, he never returns from his narrow prison house to reveal its secrets."

"I am of your opinion. To believe otherwise is gross superstition. Then I presume you imagine that the inhabitants of this lonely mansion act with the greatest caution, and never show themselves by day?"

"Exactly! They show the light, and work out their ends by '*making night hideous*' with spectres and coloured lights, and harrowing shrieks. They are cunning enough too, to make no effort to barricade their retreat (in which every door is off its hinges), knowing that the superstitious dread that surrounds the spot is their greatest safeguard."

"I think you are right, Dick. Then if we wish to discover anything, we must be here during the night?"

[CAPTAIN HAWK CURES A POLICE OFFICER OF HIS CLIMBING PROPENSITIES.]

"Unquestionably!"

"Then let us remain here this night."

"It is what I was about to propose."

"We are not very well provided for a midnight vigil."

"No; but there is ample time to forage, between now and twelve o'clock."

"True! We should want food, wine, and fuel, for the place is damp, and a good log in that old grate would impart a little life to those gloomy oak walls."

"And help to scare away the spirits."

"Or perhaps attract them—induce them to fraternise," laughed Lord Harcliffe.

"Not unlikely," said the captain. "I have known spirits uncommonly fond of brandy. But, as you say, we shall want a fire. Ugh!" he exclaimed, suddenly. "How cold it is! Do you not feel a draught strong enough to cut you in half?"

"It is strange," answered Lord Harcliffe, "but it seems as though a door had been suddenly—— Ah! see!—see!" he cried, starting up and pointing to the end of the room, where some old tapestry was violently agitated, and from whence a sound of the sharp creaking of a door hinge was distinctly audible.

"We shall arrive at something before night, after all," cried Captain Hawk, drawing his sword and rushing to the end of the room.

Lord Harcliffe, with his sword also drawn, was at his side in a moment.

"This is the spot!" they cried.

In a second, the fluttering tapestry was flung aside, but no vestige of a door appeared; only (and this might have been the excitement of their fancy) the faint echo of a muffled footstep and a mocking laugh seemed to deride their baffled effort.

But this event, far from intimidating, only connrmed

our heroes in their determination to pass the night in the very chamber where they then stood.

It was determined, then, that for the present they should take their departure, and return when the shades of evening had fallen over the earth.

They accordingly descended the staircase, and branching off in a direction different from that by which they had entered, they arrived at a small postern gate, which brought them out at the rear of the building, and which, like all the other doors, was rust-bound in a partially open position.

"If this place were the resort of genuine spirits," remarked Captain Hawk, "the keyhole would be sufficient for ingress and egress. These open doors are very suspicious."

The back of the building was remarkable for the rank and prolific growth of shrubs and weeds.

So thickly was the ground overrun with these, that a rapid progress was impossible.

However, by the assistance of their good swords, the highwaymen carved out a path, till they got clear of the rank herbage.

The moat was soon crossed, and having mounted their steeds, our heroes were soon on the high-road again.

It was then arranged that one of them should return to the "Crane with Three Necks" for the purpose of procuring wine and provisions, whilst the other occupied himself in the interim with collecting fuel and fodder for their steeds.

Lord Harcliffe chose the later office, and Captain Hawk, giving Satan the rein, darted off like the wind, promising to use the utmost expedition.

CHAPTER CCXIX.

CAPTAIN HAWK RETURNS WITH PROVISIONS, AND A TROOP OF POLICE OFFICERS AT HIS HEELS.—THE FLIGHT.—THE TACTICS OF THE OFFICIALS.—OUR HEROES CONCEAL THEMSELVES IN A TREE.—WHAT THEY DO THERE.—A DROP FOR THE POLICE.

AN hour and a half had passed, and Lord Harcliffe had, in that space of time, accumulated a handsome collection of branches of all sorts and sizes.

He had laboured hard—the day was warm, and he was parched with thirst.

He looked wistfully up the road for his comrade, but no signs of him appeared.

"Would he were here!" he murmured. "My throat is as dry as the moat yonder."

Suddenly he thought of the stream, and as it was not far, he returned thither, and drank from its cool clear waters till his burning thirst was quenched.

He was descending the steep path to the road once more, when the sound of a horse's feet fell upon his ear, and the next moment, tearing along at lightning speed, and enveloped in a cloud of dust, his comrade came in sight.

"What's up?" he thought, as he quickened Phantom's walk into a trot. "There is some danger in that speed!"

On came Captain Hawk like an arrow from a bow, and by the time the Black Highwayman had gained the road, the former was at his side, his horse covered with dust and foam.

Breathless with excitement, and the lightning speed with which he had flown along, he could only point behind him, and gasp:

"The officers! curse them!"

As he spoke, a large body of mounted police, quite twenty in number, appeared turning the bend in the road.

They raised a loud shout as they sighted the highwaymen, who returned the war cry of defiance, and who, darting at once over the hedge, urged on their gallant steeds towards the wood.

At the same moment, the officers imitated their example, and followed suit, leaping the hedge and coming on at the top of their speed, divided into two separate parties of ten each, one of which took a wide range, making for the extreme boundary of the wood, whilst the other followed directly in the track of our heroes.

It is needless to say the highwaymen, being ahead, reached the shady retreat first.

They had noticed the division of the police into two parties, and at once divined their motive in taking this step.

Their only chance was to be foremost in the chase, and to get through the wood first.

But in this chase our heroes had the odds against them numerically as well as circumstantially

True, they had been the first to gain the wood, but then their pursuers—in the proportion of ten to one—were very close upon their track.

Satan and Phantom, as the reader knows, were unrivalled in endurance and matchless in speed; but how could they exert that speed in the crowded precincts of a wood where trees and tangled bushes grow thickly in every direction? Of what use were two thorough-bred animals under such circumstances? the commonest hack would have answered the purpose equally well.

Besides, the highwaymen were not accustomed to the *ins* and *outs* of the forest, and this was another great disadvantage.

Altogether the prospect of affairs looked somewhat unpromising, but still not hopeless. They had still their trusty swords, their pistols, and, above all, their gallant dauntless hearts.

Not suffering themselves to be discouraged, they pressed forward as rapidly as possible, receiving as they went many passing remembrances from straggling branches and sharp thorns in the shape of punctures and scratches from which the blood trickled freely.

Having penetrated a considerable distance into the wood, they diverged suddenly on one side at right angles to the course they had been pursuing, hoping by this means to get clear of their enemies.

But as they drew near the confines of the forest, they saw with much chagrin several officers stationed at the very point at which they would have wished to emerge.

They therefore branched off, and pressed forward in a slanting direction; but here again they found a similar body of police awaiting them.

The highwaymen were very cautious in their approach, so that they saw their foes without being seen by them.

Finding, therefore, their retreat cut off, they retraced their steps into the recesses of the wood, and there held a brief consultation.

"It is very evident," said Captain Hawk, "that this forest, which is of limited extent, is surrounded by these myrmidons of the law. They think to hem us in, like hares or rabbits in a net, or perhaps they hope to starve us out."

"We are in a very awkward position, certainly," replied the Black Highwayman; "but still I think I can recall times when we have been placed in circumstances equally critical."

"Undoubtedly! The plank, for instance!"

"What will be the best course to pursue? Would it be safe or feasible to make a bold dash out from the wood and run for it?"

"I think not; they are too many for us, and we have no hiding-place to fly too, even if we could distance our pursuers."

"There is the Gray Mansion!"

"I hardly look upon that as an asylum. It may be, for what we know, a hotbed of danger—a den of thieves," said the captain.

"True!"

"Besides, these thick-headed police have no superstitions: they would ride up post-haste to that old, ruinous, weird mansion, as though a ghost had never taken its silent walk through its deserted galleries, and rush with noisy tramp up its stone staircases to take us, though they were sure of finding us in company with the devil himself."

"You are right. But what, then, do you propose?"

"We must play the fox with these dogs—oppose cunning to cunning, and endeavour to outwit them by superior craft."

"All seems quiet," remarked Lord Harcliffe. "I no longer hear the shouts of pursuit."

"No; that is part of their tactics—they have laid their snares—their men are now all placed in their respective positions—the trap is baited, and they are quietly waiting for us to fall into it."

"I think they'll have to wait some time."

"I'm sure they will."

"Then you propose remaining in our present covert?"

"Yes."

"I almost wish our horses were not with us, but in some snug place of safety," said Lord Harcliffe.

"So do I, most sincerely!" returned Captain Hawk. "Never in my life did I so much wish to part with my old beauty here"—patting the glossy neck of his steed as he spoke. "These curs would be glad to disable or destroy our steeds as a sure means of capturing their riders, and I think it would break my heart to lose Satan."

"Is there no place where we could conceal them?"

"None that I should like to trust to for safety," answered Captain Hawk. "Stay! What is here?" he exclaimed, fastening his eyes scrutinisingly on the ground.

"What is it attracts your attention?" inquired the Black Highwayman, at a loss to understand what it was that had so engrossed his comrade.

"See!" said the captain in reply, pointing to a spot where, almost concealed by a mass of brambles and foliage, the commencement of a deep channel or fissure in the ground was perceptible. "That looks as though it might possibly lead to some subterranean retreat that would be the very place we require at this moment."

"Let us search, Dick."

After listening a moment, and throwing a careful glance on all sides, the highwaymen dismounted, and approached the spot alluded to.

To their great joy, they discovered on dragging aside the bushes, a gradually sloping descent, that appeared to lead completely underground.

It was not wider than sufficient to admit a horse, and had been probably used as a place of concealment in some of the stormy periods of the good old times.

Captain Hawk was rejoiced.

"Could anything be more fortunate?" he cried. "We were just wishing for some retreat where we could bestow our steeds, and here we appear to have lighted on the identical spot."

"It will be as well to examine," suggested Lord Harcliffe.

"That I will do in a moment," said the captain, eagerly. "Stand still, old boy," he whispered to his steed; "there are foes at hand!"

As though he comprehended this information, the noble animal remained perfectly quiescent.

Captain Hawk then cautiously descended the narrow gully, which at a distance of about twelve yards widened considerably, so that he could not touch the sides with his arms extended.

His joy was unbounded.

Taking from his pocket a small bottle of phosphorus and a match, he quickly procured a light, which, though dim, enabled him to discover that he was in a small subterranean cavern.

It was almost circular, and about twelve yards in diameter.

A brief glance was sufficient.

It was everything that could be desired as a place of security for the horses.

He immediately returned to his comrade with the joyful intelligence.

Not wishing to lose time, they at once led their horses down the descent.

Captain Hawk kindled a taper to give his friend a glimpse of the interior.

Lord Harcliffe's satisfaction at the sight fully equalled that of his comrade, and a discovery made by the latter completed their self-congratulations.

This was a spring that bubbled from one side, and fell into a kind of basin.

"Our steeds will want here for nothing," cried the captain.

They led the horses to the spring, and they drank eagerly.

"We must now," said Captain Hawk, "supply them with something to eat. I should not be easy if I thought they needed anything."

The two friends having ascended once more into the upper world, hastily gathered handsful of the long rich grass that grew there abundantly, and pulled down such branches of green leaves as grew within their reach.

These they conveyed into the subterranean stable, and in a short time they had collected a considerable quantity—sufficient, at least, to supply the wants of the animals until they could visit them again.

These necessary arrangements completed, the highwaymen removed the bridles and saddles from their favourites, and giving them an affectionate parting caress, left the cavern, taking care to cover the entrance so thoroughly with brambles, that not the slightest trace of such path was perceptible.

"Now, then," said Captain Hawk, "having secured the safety of our steeds, we shall be able to look to ourselves."

"It has just struck me," remarked Lord Harcliffe, "that the same place of concealment would secure our safety."

"I should hardly be inclined to risk it," said the captain.

"May I ask why?"

"I never like to place the safety either of myself or my comrade on anything like a contingency," replied the captain.

"But surely these police officers know nothing of this retreat?" urged his lordship.

"It is almost a certainty they *do not*," answered the captain; "still, since chance revealed it to us, the same chance might favour them. They might, for instance, in searching for us, find themselves suddenly sinking into that chasm; and if we were hemmed in *there*, our starvation would be easily accomplished, for there would be no escape. No! when our time comes, and we must die, let it be with our swords in our hands, not like rats in our burrows!"

"You are quite right, my dear friend," cried Lord Harcliffe. "And now for our task of escape."

Our heroes advanced a few paces in the wood and listened.

All was perfectly quiet.

Lord Harcliffe looked inquiringly at his comrade.

"They have not given up the chase surely?" he said.

Captain Hawk smiled at the idea.

"The cat never gives up watching the mouse till the mouse is either caught or has escaped," he replied; "they are there safe enough."

"Who are there amongst them?" asked his lordship—"the old lot?"

"Oh yes. There's the gallant Peterson, who takes good care to look after number one, and his crony Nicholas, with a few other veterans, who prefer ordering the attack to executing it. The rest are new men, I fancy; at least, so far as I could judge from the hasty view I had: they seem unknown to me."

"Well, the more the merrier," laughed Lord Harcliffe, gaily. "'Tis strange, though, they keep themselves so confoundedly quiet!"

At this juncture the report of a pistol fired from the side of the wood at which the highwaymen had entered rang through the air, causing the startled birds to flutter and fly in all directions.

"What is the meaning of that?" inquired Lord Harcliffe.

As if in answer, there came from the opposite side of the wood the report of another pistol.

"I think I understand," said Captain Hawk. "We shall soon have our work to do; that was *a signal*. I'll give them one in reply."

As he spoke, he discharged one of his own weapons, and coolly reloaded it.

It will now perhaps be as well to return to the police officers, whom we last encountered in hot pursuit of our heroes.

Let us see whether the ideas formed by the highwaymen as to their plans of procedure are near the truth.

Of course the flight of the highwaymen in full view of the entire body of the police, and their rapid and headlong dash into the wood, left no doubt as to their place of concealment.

They were *in* the wood to a certainty, and the object to be attained was to rout them out of it, and to carry them off prisoners in triumph.

Never in their lives had they had two such formidable opponents—two such slippery customers.

As for Nicholas Twigg—old Nick, as he was called—he had almost given them up in despair. He would often say, with an angry grunt:

"It ain't no good a tryin' to grab *them!* Eels is nothin' to 'em! In the first place we can't catch 'em; an' in the next place, we couldn't hold 'em if we had caught 'em."

Peterson, having given his men hasty directions, had

sent off half his force to the other side of the wood to cut off the retreat of the highwaymen.

This our reader knows had been attended with success, inasmuch as our heroes were still *in* the wood.

His orders to his scouts were to separate at short intervals, and watch unremittingly pistol in hand.

At the first glimpse of their prey, a pistol was to be fired as a signal, which was to be answered by another from the opposite party, and then the entire party was to advance towards the centre of the wood, and thus gradually hem in the objects of their pursuit in a circle that would grow every moment less and less.

Peterson, with his colleague Nicholas, remained with his party at the entrance, or near side of the wood.

The gallant officer was somewhat winded with his rapid ride, and so was his friend, old Nick.

Both puffed and phew'd! and looked very red and inflammatory in the face.

It was not till they had refreshed themselves with a prolonged pull at their pocket flasks that they could manage to address their men.

At length, however, Peterson, having recovered his breath, began to speak, which was about all he ever did do, except eat and drink, in which exercise he was a great proficient.

"Now, my lads," he cried, as they all stood together at the entrance of the wood, "I count upon all the vigilance and courage you possess! You know who we're after; you know where they're a lying concealed; you know the kind of men they are; and you also know the reward that's offered for their apprehension—£300! Think of that, my lads!—think of the three hundred! And when yau lay hold of 'em——"

"*When* you do," added Nicholas Twigg, "by all manner o' means 'old 'em tight!"

A shout answered this harangue, and the courage of the officers burnt up with a fierce flame.

They longed to see their prey before them.

Jessop, the youthful and aspiring, unobserved by the rest, crept into the wood, his heart bounding with the thought that he might perhaps light upon the highwaymen, and compel them to submit.

Of course these ideas were in the highest degree playful and fantastic; but after all, they were perhaps not more visionary and impossible than the ideas of inexperienced youth usually are.

Thus, while Peterson was waiting as patiently as possible, and assisting his maintenance of that necessary frame of mind by occasional sips from his flask, the ardent Jessop was pursuing his path.

He had dismounted and, tying his horse to a branch, was following the track with all the perseverance, without the skill, of a Red Indian.

"I wonder 'ow they're a gettin' on at the other side o' th' wood?" remarked Peterson to Nicholas.

"Oh, they're jest where you sent 'em, o' course," said old Nick, in reply. "They ain't seen anythin' at present, or you'd a heerd on it."

Just as these words came from the mouth of Nicholas Twigg, a somewhat similar question was uttered by Jessop to himself, who was creeping along, like an official snake, in his adventurous pursuit.

"They can't have caught sight of these highwaymen yet," he soliloquised, "or I should have heard the report of the pistol that was to be the signal of advance."

As he spoke, a pistol was fired from the entrance of the wood.

P.O. Peterson was getting rather tired of waiting, and thought it would be as well to expedite matters, as the day was wearing, and get back to town; he therefore gave the signal agreed upon.

"There it is!" said Jessop. "And there's the answer!" he added, as a second report echoed through the wood in reply.

He had scarcely made this remark, when a third report, that seemed almost close to his ear, made him start up from his crouching position like a jack-in-the-box.

"What the devil's that?" he cried, in a startled tone.

Before he had time to reply, he felt himself gripped violently by the throat, and in that position standing face to face with the men he sought.

His first impulse was to cry, "Help!"

But the muzzle of a pistol intruded itself between his teeth the moment he opened his mouth, whilst another weapon of a similar kind pressed against his temple.

"Now," said Captain Hawk, in an impressive undertone, "if you wish to preserve what brains you have, you will be perfectly silent!"

The young policeman saw the necessity of obedience, and remained perfectly still.

Captain Hawk continued:

"What are you prowling here after?" he inquired.

"I'm doing my duty!" said Jessop, sulkily.

"What is that? Condescend to be explicit!" returned the captain.

"I'm looking after Captain Hawk and the Black Highwayman!" answered the man.

"Congratulate yourself, then," said the captain: "you have found them!"

"I can't look upon it in that light," returned Jessop, with the faintest and most melancholy attempt at a smile. "It seems to me you've found me."

"Do you know what we usually do with those whom we find dogging our steps?"

"How should I?"

"The means we employ are very efficacious in checking impertinent curiosity."

"What are they?"

"We blow their brains out."

"Well, it won't be the first murder you've committed," returned Jessop, whose courage was greater than his prudence.

"Are you prepared to meet such a fate?" inquired the captain, sternly.

"If you mean, 'Am I tired of life?' I answer no. Only I'm young in the force, and I must do something, or I shall never get promotion," answered Jessop.

"If you run into the lion's jaws in the manner you do, you'll never live to be promoted. Take my word for it, all those police officers who, like Peterson and Twigg, live to grow old in the service, do it by taking care of the main chance and keeping out of harm's way. You do the same. You are young and green in these matters, therefore I spare your life. Deliver up your pistols and begone!"

The young policeman looked very down in the mouth at the idea of being deprived of his weapons.

"You've no right to deprive me of my pistols," he said:

"I have no *right* to deprive you of life, but I shall most assuredly do so if you are obstinate!" answered Captain Hawk.

Jessop glanced at the captain, and then at the Black Highwayman, and seeing a most inflexible determination written on their features, he gave up the contest, and delivered up his weapons.

"And now begone!" cried Captain Hawk, "and thank your youth and inexperience for saving your life."

But Jessop did not appear to be nearly as grateful as he should have been.

After slowly proceeding a few steps, he paused, and, turning round, said to the highwaymen:

"You despise me now, because I'm young, but that is a fault that will mend. I owe you a grudge for the contempt you show me under the mask of kindness. We may meet again as foes before long, and you may perhaps find Mark Jessop a more dangerous antagonist than he looks."

With these words, and an angry, vindictive scowl on his face, he hastily disappeared.

"That's the gratitude of this world!" said Captain Hawk. "We save that fellow's life, and he turns round and bullies us."

"He'll go back now with a glowing, exaggerated account of a desperate struggle he has had with us," added Lord Harcliffe. "It would have been almost better to have shot him at once."

"Umph! We may perform that service for him yet," said the captain, with a short laugh.

At this moment a peculiar crackling sound was heard in the brushwood, and Lord Harcliffe placed his hand upon his arm.

"We are surrounded," he whispered.

"Are we?" cried the captain. "Then the time for action has arrived!"

"We cannot hope to fight through them."

"I am not going to attempt it."

"How, then, can we hope to escape?"

"By stratagem—*finesse*: we must play the fox. Cunning must outwit numbers."

"Quick, then, for I can see them!"

"That is what I desire," said Captain Hawk. "And I also wish them to see us."

A loud shout from the officers, who now, at some little distance, completely surrounded our heroes, proved that the captain's desire to be visible had been fully gratified.

But they did not fire, since, being in a circle, each one feared in the event of doing so, he might miss the object of his aim, and perhaps destroy a comrade.

Captain Hawk's sagacity detected this in a moment.

"Now, then," he cried to Lord Harcliffe, "it's time to be moving!"

"Where can we go? We are completely hemmed in!" said his lordship.

"Look upwards," exclaimed his comrade.

They stood beneath the spreading boughs of a magnificent elm, and as the Black Highwayman cast his eyes at the massive trunk and the densely-clustering leaves over his head, he began to understand his friend.

"I see," said he: "our path to freedom is above."

"It is; and there is not a moment to be lost. Are you ready?"

"Yes."

"Then let us both spring for the lower branch together, and get out of sight as quickly as possible. You will soon see why. Now!"

As these words were uttered, the highwaymen sprang up, and, grasping the lowest branch, hoisted themselves on to it rapidly.

This was a step utterly unforeseen by the police officers, who had halted at the sight of our heroes.

Another loud yell proclaimed their fury at the idea of their attempting to escape in such an irregular manner.

"Fire!" cried Peterson, hoarsely.

Twenty bullets rattled through the branches, and a loud laugh proclaimed that not one had taken effect.

The police rushed forward and closed round the tree, completely encircling it like a swarm of bees.

"Now, then, boys!" cried Peterson, who stuck as close as wax to the trunk, "you must have 'em now! Look out sharp, and let me have a glorious account to deliver of your valour and——"

Bang! went a pistol overhead, and took off that corner of the speaker's cocked hat that was over his eye, shutting him up suddenly in the midst of his speech.

"D—n it!" he shouted. "What are yer about? A little more and it'd a' been my head as was hit!"

The gallant man made a precipitate retreat to the shelter of an adjacent oak, and sucked his flask to compose his nerves.

After a tolerably long draught, rendered necessary by the sudden shock he had undergone, he beckoned to his comrades.

"You'd better stand here," he said, as they approached. "Keep your eyes upon that tree, but don't stand *under* it: it ain't safe."

It was astonishing how the little incident of the bullet just related awakened in the gallant officer's breast a sudden consideration for the lives of others.

When they were all assembled, Mr. Peterson addressed them, taking particular care to keep the trunk of the oak between him and danger.

It might have been observed that Nicholas Twigg followed his comrade's example closely, and remained a fixture on the far side of the oak.

"Well, gentlemen," commenced Mr. P., who was not always so polite—"gentlemen," he repeated, "we've got now to ask ourselves a very important question—which is, what's to be done with those rascals up in the tree yonder?"

There was a pause.

There seemed to be a stagnation of ideas at that moment; but at length two or three voices exclaimed, with a desperate effort at determination:

"Take 'em alive or dead!"

"That's all very well," returned Peterson; "but you can't get a sight of 'em."

"'Ear, 'ear!" murmured Nicholas.

"Now, before you can collar a man, or before you can shoot a man, you're obligated to see him, o' course," continued Peterson.

"O' course!" echoed Nicholas.

"It'd be a burnin' shame an' a disgrace to the force," went on Mr. P., waxing eloquent as he proceeded, "now that we've got these varmints, as it were, under our thumbs——"

"*Over* our thumbs you mean," suggested Nicholas, who was inclined to be facetious.

"Over our thumbs, then, if you like," said Peterson, accepting the amendment rather irritably; "though," he added, pointedly, to his friend, "I don't see that it's a pertickler good joke either; but," he went on, "I do think as it would be too bad, now we've got 'em up there, not to bring 'em down by hook or by crook!"

A murmur of assent followed this, and Peterson, during the pause, took another sip of rum.

"If I might speak," said Jessop, who had rejoined the party, "I should advise surrounding the tree and firing a volley into it."

"Hear, hear, hear!" exclaimed his companions, who admired this wholesale demonstration as safer and more expeditious.

"Very good!" answered Peterson; "then p'r'aps you'll be kind enough, Mr. Jessop, to walk round the tree first, and make your observations. Try an' see if you can discover where the vagabonds are posted, an' then let us know."

Jessop, who had in reality more courage than any of his comrades, far from being chagrined at this order, assented willingly, and quietly commenced his scrutiny.

During this time our heroes had ascended almost to the top of the giant tree that had afforded them so secure and impervious a hiding-place.

But it had one disadvantage: if it concealed them from their pursuers, it also prevented them from seeing what they were doing, and as the officers spoke in an undertone, they could gain no information as to their plans.

Captain Hawk and his comrade were perched aloft astride the branches of the tree, and had taken especial care so to post themselves that those branches should protect them as much as possible.

Still they could not conceal from themselves their position was one of imminent danger.

A chance bullet might in a moment close their mortal career.

The shot fired by Captain Hawk at Peterson had done them some service in removing their foes to some little distance; but of this they were unaware.

"How the deuce are we to get out of this infernal mesh?" exclaimed Lord Harcliffe, somewhat impatiently.

"I have been thinking for some time," answered his comrade, "and I am of opinion that if we are to get off *scot* free, we shall have to make one of those bold, decisive, desperate hair-breadth efforts, which, like doctors' remedies in some medicinal cases, either *kill* or *cure*, but which with us is almost sure to be successful."

"I am ready to attempt anything," replied Lord Harcliffe, "rather than be hung up here to be made a target of by those curs below."

"Then listen to me," continued Captain Hawk. "We are surrounded on every side by trees, so that there is one great advantage in our favour: our movements are entirely concealed from our enemies beneath."

"Yes; well?"

"Well, then, the tree we are now in being the only one watched by these acute intellects, it must be our task to remove to *another* tree at the earliest possible moment."

"I see! Excellent!"

"The difficulties are these: First, to take our flight unseen, for if they suspect or discover our design, all hope of escape is lost; then it is questionable whether the extremities of the upper branches would be strong enough to support us whilst we swung ourselves from one tree to the other."

"I fear not."

Captain Hawk paused an instant, and then suddenly exclaimed:

"There is only one way."

"What is that?"

"We must jump for our lives!"

"Jump?"

"Yes."

"From one tree to the other?"

"Precisely! We will mount as high as we can consistent with safety, and then walking out as far as we dare upon the strongest branch we can find, plunge from that into the very heart of the adjoining tree!"

"Yes; that will be the only way to ensure success; but still——"

"What?"

"The crash we must inevitably make will betray us, even though we perform the leap in safety."

"We must chance that," replied the captain; "though I should take care to do something just before we made the plunge to distract the attention of our foes."

"A bullet in the head of that old donkey, Peterson, would, I think, be effectual."

"Would I could get a fair shot at the idiot!" exclaimed the captain. "But hark!" he added, suddenly. "Do you not hear something?"

Both held their breath and listened intently.

"They are assembled beneath the tree, I fancy," whispered Lord Harcliffe.

"Then they mean treachery," returned the captain, quickly. "Gather yourself into as small a space as possible."

This advice came not an instant too soon, for the words were scarcely uttered when a tremendous volley from the entire body of the officers who encircled the trunk of the tree came whistling and crashing through the leaves and branches.

It was a terrible moment of suspense for our heroes.

Each clasped the other's hand involuntarily.

"Are you hurt, my friend?" whispered the captain, in a quivering voice.

"No, old fellow!" returned the Black Highwayman.

"Thank Heaven for that!" said Captain Hawk, fervently.

"These clever marksmen will rest now for a time after that last courageous feat."

The police, having fired their volley, remained stationary for a moment, fully expecting to see the bleeding and mangled bodies of the highwaymen come toppling down headlong.

To their great surprise, however, nothing occurred.

They accordingly removed with all convenient expedition to the oak tree adjacent.

Peterson, who had partaken freely of rum, felt inclined to be indignant.

"This is child's play!" he cried. "It's treating the agents of the law as though they was dummies or nobodies."

It was, of course, an enormous piece of impertinence for two individuals to dare to be alive after twenty police officers had condescended to fire at them.

"It's no use going on in this way," continued Peterson. "I'll speak to 'em!"

"'Ear—'ear—'ear!" cried Nicholas.

"Ahem—a-hem!" coughed the officer, clearing his throat as a preliminary step. "Here—heigh!—you, up in the tree," he continued—"you, Captain Hawk, and you, Mr. Black Highwayman! We know you're there; and I feel it my duty to caution you not to resist the law—for your own sakes, don't resist it! In the name of his Gracious Majesty King George, I, Sergeant Peterson, police officer, order you to come down and surrender yourselves prisoners!"

There was a pause, and then a mocking laugh of the most deliberate and profound contempt; and then Captain Hawk's voice was distinctly heard.

"Mr. P. O. Peterson," said the voice, "you will be good enough to present our compliments to the king, and tell him that as we prize our liberties beyond anything else in the world, we decline obeying the orders of his Gracious Majesty, even when issued by so renowned a personage as Sergeant Peterson, backed by his body of Bow Street runners."

At this audacious speech Peterson positively grew pale.

"Did ever anyone hear such infernal impertinence?" he cried, puffing and blowing with passion. "I see," he continued, "there's only one thing to be done: we must dislodge 'em. Mercy, an' that kind o' thing's no use at all. If I wasn't too old, I'd be up in the branches after 'em, that I would!"

"So 'ud I!" echoed Nicholas Twigg.

One of the number, a broad-headed, thick-set fellow stepped forward.

"I'll go up, if you like, sergeant," he said, "if anyone'll go with me."

"I will!" answered the plucky Jessop, who had to rise in his profession and either to *dis*tinguish or extinguish himself.

Peterson gave a sigh, whether of relief at being exempt from such a perilous duty, or regret at being deprived of so excellent an opportunity of proving his courage and skill, we cannot undertake to determine.

He, however, gave the volunteers permission to ascend; and after cautioning them to be very careful, and to look to their pistols, the two gallant fellows—for they were so—commenced their ascent.

The stronger and more bulky of the two, by name Morrison, went first; Jessop followed.

It was precisely at this moment that our heroes had fixed themselves on two branches, ready to spring off at the first favourable opportunity.

The crackling of the branches below first arrested their attention.

"Some one is ascending," whispered Captain Hawk, as he quietly drew forth and cocked one of his deadly pistols.

"There are more than one," said Lord Harcliffe.

"How many?"

"Two, I think, from the sound."

"All the better. Let them come. In a few moments we shall have two enemies the less," remarked the captain, with an ominous smile.

The agitation and crackling amongst the boughs and branches continued, becoming more and more distinct each moment.

The highwaymen, whose ears were strained to catch the slightest sound, could now hear the deep breathings of the daring climbers, who were voluntarily advancing into the very jaws of destruction.

There was something in the very natures of our heroes that compelled them to admire bravery, even in their enemies; and it was a feeling of this kind that induced Captain Hawk to say to his comrade:

"These two poor devils are doubtless the cat's paw of the troop—two raw aspirants, with more courage than discretion, who seek 'the bubble reputation even at the cannon's mouth.'"

"They are labouring hard," said Lord Harcliffe. "Hark to their deep inspirations!"

"Fools that they are!" exclaimed the captain; "I do not seek their destruction; I abhor shedding blood that might be spared! Why should I have their deaths to answer for in addition to my other sins?"

Hardly had he uttered these words, when, with a sudden jerk, the head and shoulders of the stalwart Morrison started upwards into view.

"So," he exclaimed, as well as his breathless state would permit, "I thought I should get at you at last!"

It was evident this adventurous individual totally misunderstood the characters of the men who were looking down upon him.

He was young in the service, and had an idea that the very name, much less the sight, of a police officer was sufficient to strike terror to the heart of the most daring defier of the laws.

Captain Hawk could read this as he gazed upon him; and, in a tone in which pity and contempt were mingled, he said:

"If you will take my advice, my friend, you will at once descend from your present position."

"What!" cried the young man, in a tone of arrogant contempt, "descend, after the trouble I've had to climb to the top?"

"You will find it much easier to go down than to come up," remarked the captain, coolly.

"I know that," answered the officer, in an inflated, self-sufficient manner, "but I don't go down without you two chaps! Dy'e see that?"

"That's right!" called out Jessop, thrusting his head up from the branch beneath that on which his companion rested; "they'll try to bounce you off if they can, as they did me. But don't give in; it's only talk."

"You're a very foolish young man," continued Captain Hawk, addressing himself to the former speaker, but keeping his eye fixed on his companion also, who began to feel a little uncomfortable under its piercing glance.

"If you think," continued the captain, "that I shall allow you to take me, dismiss the idea at once. If your whole troop were seated by your side—if that were possible—I should only have one word to reply: that word is—'Defiance!'"

Before Morrison could frame an answer to this deliberate speech, Jessop interposed, vehemently:

"Here!" he cried, "change places with me: I'll talk to 'em! You don't understand 'em!"

As he spoke, he, by a sudden effort, jerked himself up into his comrade's place, who as quickly dropped on to the branch beneath.

"Now, then," said the impudent Jessop, "you told me not long ago I should never live to grow old in the force if I didn't keep out of harm's way. What dy'e think of this—eh?"

He grinned impertinently in Captain Hawk's face as he spoke, and dangled his legs on the branch.

The captain made no reply, but regarded him sternly.

"You're an idiot!" he remarked at length, quietly.

"Oh no, I'm not!" cried Jessop, with a knowing shake of the head; "I'm a police officer, and I'm here to arrest you two. If you're wise, you'll come; if not——"

Here he thrust his hand into his pocket, and drew forth a heavy pistol.

"If you resist," he continued, "I shall blow you to the devil!"

He cocked the weapon he held as he spoke, but that was the last earthly act he ever accomplished, for, ere he could level it, there was a loud report, and the bullet of Captain Hawk had pierced his skull.

At the same moment a tremendous crash, as though every tree in the vicinity had been breaking into fragments, reached the ears of the expectant party below.

"There's one of 'em gone!" exclaimed Peterson.

"We shall hear th' hother in a minnit!" added Nicholas Twigg.

The words were barely delivered when two bodies fell with tremendous violence to the ground.

"There they are!" cried the officials, as they rushed forward.

Their words were perfectly true.

There they were!

Not the highwaymen, but the aspiring Jessop, stone dead, with a bullet in his brain; and Alec Morrison, who had been dislodged by the weight of the dead body falling upon him, stunned and senseless.

CHAPTER CCXX.

THE OFFICERS SET FIRE TO THE TREE.—SUPPOSED DESTRUCTION OF OUR HEROES.—PETERSON PUTS HIS FOOT IN A WASPS' NEST.—CAPTAIN HAWK AND LORD HARCLIFFE RETURN TO THE HAUNTED MANSION.—THE SPIRIT OF THE STORM.

The revulsion of feeling was so strong at the sight, that the whole body rushed furiously to the giant elm, and seemed inclined to attack the unoffending trunk in their excited fury.

"The cowardly assassins!" "The dastardly murderers!" "The bloodthirsty wretches!" were exclamations breathed rather than spoken on every side.

Mr. Peterson and Nicholas Twigg were a great deal more than considerably astounded.

"I never see anything like it in all my professional experience!" asserted the former.

"In times gone by," said Nicholas, "when a gentleman of the road saw his time was come, he gave in *like* a gentleman, but these varmints—there's no such thing as giving in about 'em!"

"I said before," exclaimed Peterson, "and I say again, these two beings are not men, they're devils!—fiends!"

"We'll be revenged for the death of our comrades!" shouted the indignant men.

"But how are you to get at them?" said Peterson. "We can't all get up to the top of a lofty tree, to be hurled to the bottom like sacks of sawdust."

But the popular feeling was not to be subdued.

Nothing would appease the thirst for vengeance but the destruction of the destroyers.

One of the number was suddenly struck with an idea that promised a swift and terrible retribution.

This was, that the tree should be set on fire, and the highwaymen burnt *out of*, or burnt *in*, their lofty retreat.

The proposal met with unanimous approval, and the necessary materials were rapidly collected.

Dried grass, sticks, branches—everything that would burn that could be found was piled around the fatal tree.

The vengeance of the officers was sharpened to a keener edge by the certainty of the success of their project.

Those reckless defiers of the law might dispute the sovereign pleasure of the king, transgress his laws, and defy and murder the agents appointed to enforce them, but they could not hold out against the devouring flames that would in a few moments encircle them.

And now the pile of combustible materials being prepared, a match was lighted, and the flame applied to different parts.

At first it burnt sluggishly, but gradually the heat becoming greater, the fire got a hold, and the flames mounted rapidly, clinging to, and licking the trunk with their burning tongues, till it hissed and steamed again.

Gradually the devouring element, fanned by the breeze, began to rise, and the lower branches of the elm were caught.

Crackling, sputtering, and smoking, now seeming to die out, and then bursting forth again into life, the conflagration continued.

In the meantime, the officers piled fresh fuel round the trunk, which at length, being thoroughly heated, sent forth huge volumes of flame and smoke.

The work of destruction n w went on more rapidly.

The flames ascended in long, bright streaks, and clung to the branches above, over and betwixt which they darted and leaped like fiery snakes.

The officers cheered triumphantly as they watched the monarch of the forest gradually enveloped in its fiery robe; and when at length the flames, having got a firm hold, darted upwards with a roaring sound like the bellowing of a furnace, shrouding the elm in a burning winding-sheet, a loud burst of exultation from the throats of the gazers rose on the air.

Their vengeance was consummated, and the objects of their indignation must by that time have become blackened and charred masses involved in the general destruction—at least, such was the general impression.

There was only one thing to be desired by the eager spectators, and that was to see the disfigured trunks of their victims fall hissing through the torrents of flame on to the ground before them.

But this pleasure was denied them.

The tree still burnt fiercely; the trees, too, in the immediate vicinity caught fire, and burnt in company, but still no signs of the bodies of the highwaymen.

"How fierce the fire must 'a been!" exclaimed Peterson. "It's burnt them up to ashes!"

"But flames don't burn up the steel of swords, or the barrels of pistols," suggested old Nick, doubtfully.

"You're a ignoramus!" returned Peterson. "If it don't burn 'em, it melts 'em."

"Well, melted or not, I should like to see em," continued Nicholas, suspiciously.

"You ought to be very glad to think that everything belonging to such vagabonds is consumed," replied Peterson.

"So I should be if I *could* think so," retorted Nicholas, "but somehow or other I don't."

"Not?"

"No."

"You mean to say that you believe the scoundrels are not burnt?"

"I do."

"Oh, you're mad!"

"Very likely, but I hold to my opinion for all that!"

"Mad people are usually very obstinate."

"I always like proofs."

Peterson also liked proofs, and though he condemned his comrade for venturing to doubt, he had at the same time some uncomfortable suspicions himself.

A sword-blade, or the lock of a pistol falling to the ground from the burning mass would have been satisfactory; but there was nothing—not the least vestige of anything to confirm a belief of the highwaymen's destruction.

Peterson was very unwillingly obliged to acknowledge to himself that it was possible he might have been mistaken, and that after all the prey had once more escaped the hunters.

The upper portion of the tree was now entirely consumed.

All that remained was the massive trunk, and that, from its solidity, being once kindled, still burnt with great fury.

But even that by degrees began to abate.

Peterson now thought it was time for himself and party to retrace their steps towards town.

He accordingly gave orders that temporary litters should be formed for the conveyance of their dead and wounded comrade, and then directed their return to London.

He took a farewell glance at the smouldering and blackened trunk, and then, having once more applied to his flask for the last time, it being now emptied, he walked with a very unsteady step towards his horse.

As he went along, one of his legs was seen to disappear into the earth very suddenly.

So suddenly that the gallant officer was compelled to fall forward on his hands.

"Confound it!—dash it!—d—n it!" cried Peterson, angrily. "Where have I got to now?"

A sharp and piercing pain at that instant seized upon the calf of his leg.

It was so vividly acute, that he could not forbear a yell of agony.

"Help me out!" he roared; "something's stinging me!"

His comrades assisted him, and then the cause of his pain was at once perceptible.

He had planted his foot in a wasps' nest, and the animals, indignant at the assault, swarmed out in vast quantities.

They seemed—these unpleasant insects—to have a great affection for the faces of the police officers.

Nicholas Twigg attracted several of these winged and venomous tormentors, and was stung on the nose, to his intense horror.

The entire company more or less suffered from the attacks of the wasps.

As for Peterson, his boot was full of these insects, and his punishment from their stings was so severe that he danced and howled with the pain.

Altogether the cavalcade made a most inglorious exit from the wood, inwardly vowing vengeance and murmuring curses, not loud but deep, against those in pursuit of whom they had entered its precincts.

In the meantime Captain Hawk and the Black Highwayman were making their way with much expedition, considering they had been *burnt to ashes*, out of the reach of the police.

Their efforts had been crowned with success.

Their leap into the tree had saved them, having enabled them to get clear of their unsuspicious foes; and they had now made a *detour* to reach their steeds and refresh themselves previous to their return to the Gray Mansion.

The day was beginning to decline, and as they sat outside their forest cave enjoying a brief repast, and resting at the same time from their past fatigues, the hairbreadth escapes they had had came home to them vividly.

Nor were they less impressed when, mounted on their horses, they passed by the scene of their late adventures, and beheld the blackened, smouldering trunk of the noble tree that had so short a time previously sheltered them in its branches.

It was growing dusk as they once more approached the vicinity of the Gray Mansion.

The aspect, too, of Nature's face had changed.

The sky was dark and lowering, and thick driving clouds scudded past driven by the wind that blew in sharp fitful gusts across the plain.

Large drops of rain began to fall, and so far as appearances went there seemed every prospect of a tempestuous night.

"It is fortunate we have decided upon our lodging for to-night," remarked Captain Hawk, "or we might stand a chance of reaching home with wet skins."

"Your words remind me that I had collected a supply of fuel for our night's vigil. We must call and pick it up," said Lord Harcliffe.

This being done, the highwaymen urged on their horses, and in a short time arrived at the Gray Mansion.

They entered by the small postern gate at the back of the building, and, having arrived thus far, their first care was to stable their horses, which they did in one of the deserted rooms, where, having supplied them with some freshly gathered long grass, they left them for the night.

Our heroes had not reached their quarters one moment too early.

Scarcely had they finished their task of gathering provender for their steeds than the storm, which had been for some time brewing, burst forth in its full strength.

The rain poured in torrents, and driven by the wind, battered at and shook the windows of the old mansion in a most threatening manner, whilst ever and anon the vivid lightning flashed with a blue glare through the empty rooms, and the hoarse thunder rolled over its turrets like a peal of ordnance.

Our heroes, laden with fuel and provisions, ascended the stone staircase and established their quarters in the chamber they had previously occupied for a short time on their first visit.

Everything about the place was cold and cheerless.

The heavy rain filled the atmosphere with a damp earthy odour, and the wind as it came streaming along the vaulted passages with its melancholy, wailing music, struck a chill to their hearts.

"The sooner we can kindle a fire, the better, in my opinion," said Captain Hawk.

"There will be little difficulty, I imagine," remarked Lord Harcliffe, as he assisted his comrade in arranging the branches and logs in the old-fashioned grate. "The wood is dry."

"Such a luxury will astonish this gloomy chamber," the captain continued. "It must be some years since a cheerful blaze shed its light over these sombre walls."

"I am anxious to see their effect under such an inspiring influence."

"Here goes, then, to try!" exclaimed his lordship, lighting a match as he spoke, and applying it to the fuel.

In a few moments it began to blaze, but not freely, the chimney being damp; but as the heat became stronger, so the smoke that threatened to render the apartment uninhabitable gradually decreased, and in half an hour a bright light burnt in the old grate.

But though in the immediate vicinity of the fire the bright rays imparted a certain life, still, the extremities of the large chamber were wrapped in obscurity.

This gloom was increased by the oak walls, that reflected no light save when the lightning flashed with lurid glare through the arched windows, and for a moment seemed to stamp the pattern of the lattice-work upon their illuminated surfaces, and then for a brief space all was dark again.

The highwaymen, desirous of throwing as much vitality as possible into this weird abode, spread out upon the table the provisions they possessed, to the greatest advantage.

A delicious pigeon-pie, a ham, and a brace of young pullets, completed the bill of fare, with a loaf of home-made bread.

Two bottles of old sherry flanked these comestibles, and an additional bottle of champagne in which to drink destruction and annihilation to all ghostly intruders.

Nor had Captain Hawk been unmindful of another necessity—light—for he had brought with him a pair of wax tapers, which greatly assisted in cheering up the prospect which, without them, was extremely gloomy and cheerless.

As it was necessary to be economical of such luxuries, one of these only was lit, the other being reserved in case of necessity.

But although the door of the apartment was closed, the wind would intrude itself into the interior, and make its presence known by its shrill whispers and the flickering of the taper.

"How cold it is!" remarked Captain Hawk, with an involuntary shudder "It is enough to make even a spirit complain."

As he spoke, a long, mournful cry, like the wail of the *banshee*, seemed to float upon the air without; then there came a terrific blast of wind that at once extinguished the taper.

These ominous indications were followed by a blinding

[THE GRAY FIGURE ENDEAVOURS TO PROVE HIMSELF INVULNERABLE.]

flash of lightning that seemed to fill the entire chamber with its lurid glare, and a peal of thunder loud enough to wake the dead.

But this was not all; for as our heroes—whose preparations were suddenly interrupted by these events following in quick succession—stood with eyes riveted upon the windows, lit up by the lightning with a brightness exceeding that of the day, they saw floating in the space without a figure robed in white drapery, with long fair hair that streamed behind in the wind.

It was evidently a female, and the expression of its features was that of extreme sadness.

With limbs rigid with a sudden paralysis, and eyes riveted upon this unusual spectacle, our heroes remained as if spellbound watching this spirit of the storm.

This strange visitant approached the windows and floated past each one successively, uttering the same melancholy cry they had previously heard.

But who could describe the deep sadness—the terrible despair that lived in those pallid features?

She seemed to peer wistfully, with her face close to the glass of the windows, as though soliciting admission from the pitiless storm.

Had it been on the ground floor, instead of the first story, the highwaymen would instantly have opened the window and invited the pale wanderer to enter, with the courtesy inherent to their natures; but it was the very singularity of this mysterious appearance at such a distance from *terra firma* that chained their limbs and fettered their tongues.

They could only stand rooted to the spot and gaze in silence.

The figure, after her vain and silent appeal, uttered once more the wailing cry that went to the hearts of the listeners, and floated away.

Her departure broke the spell that held our heroes.

"By Heaven, Harcliffe!" cried Captain Hawk, "if I remain long in this place, I shall begin to share in its superstitions, and believe against my own sense of truth that it is the abode of disembodied spirits!"

"It is indeed strange," replied his lordship, in a dreamy, thoughtful tone. "I confess my own mind seems shaken from its balance."

They approached the window, opened it, and looked out, but no vestige of anything appeared beyond the dark, stormy sky and the waving, agitated trees as they swayed to and fro in the blast.

They closed the window and rekindled the taper.

"Come, my friend," said the captain, "we must make an effort to throw off these timid fancies, or we shall grow cowardly, and be utterly unfit for the duties we have to perform."

"As an antidote, then," said Lord Harcliffe, "I propose we have supper. A good meal and a few glasses of wine will recruit our jaded spirits, and drive the phantoms from our brains, at least."

"I second your proposal with all my heart," returned his comrade.

Having raked the fire together, and replenished it with fresh fuel, our heroes sat down to their repast.

It was soon evident enough that their nerves had been unstrung by previous fatigue and over-excitement—an excitement which the excellent fare of which they were partaking rapidly allayed.

The good old wine, too, from John Tonks's cellar acted as a stimulating cordial; and in less than half an hour the highwaymen felt completely resuscitated.

"I am in a condition now," remarked Captain Hawk, draining his glass, "to defy all the ghosts in England——"

"Ireland and Scotland!" added Lord Harcliffe, quaffing a bumper as he spoke. "There is only one thing I should like as an addition to mine host's excellent wine," he continued.

"What is that?" asked the captain.

"One of mine host's excellent cigars," answered the Black Highwayman.

"Conjure, *hocus-pocus!*" laughed his comrade, holding up a small leathern case. "No sooner said than done. Open *sesame!*"

He pushed the cigar-case across the table to Lord Harcliffe, who selected one of the fragrant weeds, and returned it to his friend, who also abstracted one.

Having lighted their cigars from one of the burning embers, the old chamber was soon redolent with the comfortable aromatic odour that rose in thin blue vapour to the very ceiling.

"Ha, ha!" laughed Captain Hawk, "if there are any invisible agents floating in the upper regions of this chamber, I rather think we shall smoke them out."

"I should imagine so," said Lord Harcliffe; "I am rather inclined to believe that the most strong-minded spirit would have to yield to the antagonistic vapours of our Havannahs. I declare," he continued, laughing, "we have shrouded ourselves in a 'robe of mist.'"

This was perfectly true, for our heroes, in the full enjoyment of their "smokes," had puffed away like a couple of steam engines, and the natural result was a cloud of ambrosial vapour all round them.

But it smelt warm and comfortable, and was in every way preferable to the close, musty odour that had previously prevailed there.

"This is delightful!" exclaimed Lord Harcliffe. "I feel now, seated as I am in this silent, lonely, ghostly old building, as though I were in the land of *romance!*"

"Well," replied his comrade, smiling, and stretching his limbs in the genial warmth of the fire, "I don't exactly agree with your sensations, my friend, for I feel more as though I were in the land of *reality.*"

"Oh," laughed Lord Harcliffe, "we must banish everything so commonplace as reality, or we shall destroy all the *romance* of our position."

"Oh, hang the *romance!*" cried the captain, jovially. "What would this gloomy old, dusty chamber be without fire, wine, food and cigars?"

"A very miserable tenement indeed!" said his lordship.

"Exactly!" responded Captain Hawk; "but yet it is the darkness, the dust, the draughts, and the damp that invest it with the ideal delights of *romance*, while all that is comfortable in it belongs to the solid appliances of reality. I drink its health!"

"I won't dispute the point," said his lordship, as he emptied his glass with great relish.

Our heroes could scarcely remember the time when they had passed a more cosy hour than that which had flown over their heads in that ghostly old room.

Perhaps it was the sudden contrast from dark to light, or that kind of unexpected treat which is almost more delightful than any anticipated banquet.

But whatever it was, it is certain they felt in such excellent spirits that if a troop of white-faced ghosts, or imps of a darker hue had shown their noses at the door, it is more than probable they would have received a hearty invitation to come in and "share and share alike."

But though they each felt a strong tendency to indulgence and conviviality, they did not forget that there was work to be done, and that they were not passing the night under the roof of the Gray Mansion out of mere *bravado*, or for the simple pleasure of smoking and drinking within its precincts.

The object of their visit was, if possible, to bring to light some of the secrets which they believed were hidden there, to clear up the dark mysteries that surrounded the time-worn edifice and shrouded it with vague terrors, and either prove them fables altogether, or if not, discover who it was that really did inhabit there.

"Well, comrade," said Captain Hawk, as he threw the relics of his cigar, smoked down to the smallest stump, into the grate, "what say you to a ghostly ramble through the rooms?"

"I am with you," answered his lordship, rising from his seat, and throwing out his arms with a comfortable yawn. "It's almost time we began to be moving, for I'm inclined to feel drowsy."

"A ramble through the cool galleries of *Grim Gray Hall* will speedily remove all such sensations!" laughed Captain Hawk. "Are you ready?"

"Quite."

"Our cold collation and wine will, I presume, be safe here till we return?"

"Oh, yes! Ghosts have no appetites!"

Had the captain known all at that moment, he might perhaps have altered his opinion.

"Come on!" he cried, taking the wax taper from the table—"lead the way!"

They went out of the apartment on to the stone gallery and descended the staircase, Lord Harcliffe going first and Captain Hawk following, shading the light with his hand.

The large room they had quitted was transformed into its usual ghostliness.

Though the thunder still rolled at intervals, and the lightning flashed ever and anon with great brilliancy, the storm had somewhat abated, and a pallid moon peered forth.

As the electric fluid played in the heavens, it lit up the dark chamber, casting the shadows of its windows and their latticed panes on the oak floor.

The fire being of wood, began to burn out, and gave but a feeble light; but feeble as it was, it was still sufficient to show the outline of a figure that seemed to start suddenly from behind some tattered drapery, and glide towards the door of the apartment.

After listening a moment, the mysterious being uttered a low, chuckling laugh, and returned to the table, where, seating himself in a chair, he began to devour a pullet with great voracity, moistening this operation with prolonged draughts of sherry, which he drank from the bottle.

The manner in which this phantom attacked the provisions was so decidedly *un*ghostlike that in any other place than the Gray Mansion a spectator would have been inclined to lay odds that the spectre inclined more to the *corporeal* than the *spiritual*; but of course, in that ghostly, dreary place, how could anything human exist unless itself a ghost?

The repast being finished, the silent, self-invited guest rose, stretched himself, and departed as he came, taking with him—probably in a fit of absence of mind—the remainder of the sherry.

In the meantime Captain Hawk and the Black Highwayman, little imagining the pillage that was going on above stairs, were exploring the rooms below.

This was a task of some difficulty, since the wind blew in such sudden gusts and came upon them in such unexpected streams and puffs, that it was with the utmost difficulty the taper, although shrouded carefully by the captain's hand, could be induced to keep alight.

And even then its feeble rays in the large rambling rooms did little more than render darkness visible.

Their discoveries, therefore, had been of the most limited kind—an old hunting-whip and a small troop of rats being all they had come across.

They visited Satan and Phantom in their apartment, who not being at all impressed with ghostly terrors, were placidly nibbling the branches before them.

All this silence was in its way very well; but the highwaymen were eager for some adventure—anything that promised a clue to guide them to the solution of the mysteries of the Gray Mansion.

After leaving the chamber in which their steeds were located, they paused in the vaulted passage at a spot where two other turnings branched off.

They were a little undecided which course to pursue.

"This place," remarked Captain Hawk, in a tone of chagrin, "though it certainly promises much from its appearance, seems to me remarkably barren of adventures."

"I think so myself," assented Lord Harcliffe. "As to a ghost, or a goblin, there seems no signs of any such things."

"Oh, d—n the ghosts and goblins!" cried the captain. "Let us have flesh and blood! But this place is so confoundedly quiet that——"

At this moment, as if in flat contradiction to the highwayman's remark, a wild and prolonged scream echoed through the surrounding silence.

It was not, however, close at hand; but it was borne to the ears of the listeners on the night air with remarkable distinctness.

At another time such a harrowing shriek would have curdled their blood, but now it was almost a relief, inasmuch as it suggested something to be attempted or some danger to be encountered.

"It is very perplexing," said Captain Hawk, "that, as we are in this intricate building, we are utterly at a loss which way to proceed."

"Yes," replied Lord Harcliffe, thoughtfully. "That ringing cry evidently came from the lips of a woman!"

"Woman!" repeated Captain Hawk, eagerly, as the word brought Blanche vividly to his mind. "Surely it could not have been she who uttered that piercing shriek?"

He had hardly spoken these words when the cry was repeated, and then died away into a succession of fainter wails.

"Good Heaven!" cried the captain, clenching his hand fiercely. "There is some infernal work going on here that the world without knows nothing of, and we seem to be powerless to render any assistance!"

"Let us take this path," suggested Lord Harcliffe, pointing as he spoke to a vaulted passage on the left.

"Any path that promises to lead us to a human foe!" replied Captain Hawk, excitedly.

They proceeded as rapidly as possible, guided partly by the flickering taper, and partly by the lightning that flashed at intervals, along the narrow corridor indicated, and after following its windings for a considerable distance, they found themselves, without having encountered any adventure, on the spot from which they had started.

The highwaymen stamped their feet in despair.

"Let us try the passage to the right," said the captain, impatiently.

"Forward, then!" exclaimed his comrade.

As they proceeded, screams, such as they had heard before, mingled with groans, again assailed their ears.

They paused.

"It is my opinion," said Captain Hawk, "that there is some portion of this building—a wing probably—detached from the rest, that we have not yet discovered."

"I think it very likely," replied Lord Harcliffe. "The screams, then, that we have heard would proceed from that wing?"

"Yes."

"It will be our plan, then, to discover where it is situated."

"I do not apprehend any great difficulty in that."

"But there may be a great difficulty in effecting an entrance."

"Yes; for depend upon it, whatever secrets are held—whatever dark deeds are perpetrated within these walls—that wing is the spot that can alone disclose them."

"It is something, however, to know in what direction to point our efforts," said the Black Highwayman.

"It is *everything*," returned Captain Hawk. "As we are at present, we are entirely in the dark; but since this new idea has fastened upon us, we will at the earliest dawn of day thoroughly reconnoitre the building, for I swear not to leave this place until I have dragged some of its infernal secrets to light!"

The last word of this speech had scarcely passed from his lips when he felt his comrade's arm upon his wrist, and at the same moment an eddying gust of wind extinguished the wax taper, and they were left in total darkness.

"Hist!" whispered Lord Harcliffe.

"What is it?" inquired his comrade, in an undertone.

"Listen!"

"Well?"

"Do you hear anything?"

"Nothing—that is, only the wind."

"Nothing else? Are you sure?"

"Quite—no—stay!" added the captain, suddenly. "I hear a sound like the suppressed breathing of some one near us."

"That is what I meant. I hear it too."

"I see nothing," continued Captain Hawk, straining his eyes through the darkness; "and yet I experience a sensation as though some one were near us."

"Whoever it may be," remarked the Black Highwayman, "it will be well for him to be careful."

The highwaymen drew their swords.

"Let us keep close together, and keep our swords on the alert in front of us," whispered Captain Hawk; "and as we can do nothing until the day dawns, I propose we return to our quarters until then."

"Agreed!" said his lordship.

Walking side by side, and feeling their way with their swords, they groped their way back to their point of starting.

The storm, which had lulled, seemed to have burst forth again.

They moved forwards, when as they turned the corner of the passage a vivid flash of lightning and a deafening discharge of Nature's ordnance, caused them to pause suddenly.

But it was not the thunder or the lightning that checked them.

It was that, right in their path at the foot of the staircase, the lurid glare of the electric fluid revealed a figure that looked colossal, standing motionless, shrouded from head to food in a robe and cowl of dark gray.

"The phantom at last!" shouted Captain Hawk, as he and his comrade rushed forward.

But the lightning was but for a moment, and all was the next instant dark as before.

Still there came a sensation similar to that they had previously experienced—that the object was near at hand.

They fancied even in the gloom they could trace the tall form gliding noiselessly up the massive staircase; but when the next flash lighted up the scene, the figure was no longer visible.

CHAPTER CCXXI.

CAPTAIN HAWK AND LORD HARCLIFFE MISS THEIR BOTTLE, BUT COMFORT THEMSELVES WITH A FRESH ONE.—THEY MAKE A NOVEL DISCOVERY IN THE CHIMNEY.—CAPTAIN HAWK HAS A LONG CONVERSATION WITH THE GRAY PHANTOM, AND UNMASKS HIM.

"Let us follow on," cried Captain Hawk. "It is only by keeping close to the heels of these phantoms, or prowling figures, or whatever they are, we can hope to unmask them. Forward!"

With these words our heroes rushed up the stairs and entered the apartment they had previously occupied.

The fire had burnt so low that its mere embers alone remained, but they were alight.

The taper Captain Hawk held in his hand had been extinguished, so that, save from the faint reflections from the windows, the chamber was in darkness.

Still, in spite of the obscurity, there was the same unpleasant sensation that there was *another person* in the room besides themselves.

Besides, they distinctly heard the rustling of the tapestry at the extremity of the chamber and the slight creak as of the hinge of a door grating, as they had observed once before.

"We must re-light our taper," said the captain. "It is confoundedly annoying, being dogged at every turn by mysterious visitants, who will neither speak nor show themselves."

"Can you succeed?" asked Lord Harcliffe of the captain, who was fanning the fire with his hat in order to resuscitate it.

"I am trying what perseverance can effect," answered the captain, as he threw on some fresh twigs, which presently began to burn.

"At last!" he exclaimed as he lit the wax taper.

Lord Harcliffe then replenished the fire, and in a few moments there was once more life and light in the old chamber.

Nothing human, however, appeared there save themselves.

"Would it were morning!" cried Captain Hawk. "I am quite anxious to reconnoitre this old ghost-haunted tenement from the exterior."

"I share your anxiety," said Lord Harcliffe. "Ugh!" he continued, with a shudder, "rambling through those cold vault-like passages has chilled my blood! I must restore a proper circulation with a glass of wine."

As he spoke, his lordship stretched forth his hand mechanically, expecting to grasp the bottle.

No such article, however, was to be seen.

"The bottle has disappeared!" he exclaimed, in a tone of surprise.

"So it seems," returned Captain Hawk, with a smile and slight elevation of his eyebrows. "It was, however, on the table when we quitted the room."

"Are you sure you did not remove it?"

"Positive."

"Where can it have gone?"

"Some thirsty spectre has probably walked off with it."

"I thought all ghosts were members of the temperance society?" remarked Lord Harcliffe, smiling, although somewhat disappointed at the loss of the wine.

"Well, I don't know what to say to that!" returned his comrade, following up the joke. "I should rather think *ghosts* would have a natural partiality for *spirits*."

His lordship laughed at this little sally on the part of the captain, who joined him, and then stooping down and passing his hand under the table, produced another full bottle, corked and sealed.

"Here, my friend," he cried, "this will make amends for our loss; therefore, instead of regretting what is gone, let us solace ourselves with what remains."

A beaming smile lit up the features of the Black Highwayman as the captain held up the golden liquor before the light.

"Will you act as waiter and uncork it?" said his lordship.

"With much pleasure, for I'm longing for a glass myself," answered the captain.

This operation was speedily performed, and the fragrant aroma of the generous vintage dispersed itself delightfully under the olfactory organs of our heroes.

"Our worthy host of the Crane with Three Necks keeps excellent wine," remarked Captain Hawk, as he filled the glasses.

"He does indeed," returned Lord Harcliffe, as he emptied his with infinite gusto. "I must have another to drink his health."

The glasses were replenished and raised aloft.

"The health of John Tonks!" they cried, as they drained their glasses.

"And now for a weed," proposed the captain.

"Truly there is much of the comfort of life in a good fire, sherry, and cigars," he added, as he puffed out a thin blue volume of smoke from his lips.

"Unquestionably there is!" acquiesced Lord Harcliffe, leaning back in his chair in luxurious enjoyment.

They smoked some little time in silence.

The vapours of the ambrosial Havannah probably induced meditation.

At length Lord Harcliffe broke the silence.

"I'm thinking about that bottle of wine," he said.

"The one that made so mysterious a disappearance?"

"Yes."

"Strange! So was I."

"It seems to me to prove one fact incontestibly, that if this mansion be haunted by spirits, it is also occupied by the living."

"Undoubtedly; only the living tenants have acquired a remarkable facility in keeping themselves invisible."

"That mysterious figure in the cloak! That was strange! Who could he be?"

"The proprietor, I presume, of the mansion."

"I suppose so. This place being designated *The Gray Mansion*, it is supposed the owner would wear a cloak to match of the same colour."

"I should like to have seen his face."

"Ha, ha—no doubt! My gentleman was too cunning to show that."

"Mystery and secrecy seem to be the presiding genii of this tenement."

"Yes; your lovers of marvels and romance would find a week or two in this place extremely congenial, I should think. Hark! how the wind howls!"

Just at this juncture, the fierce element, as though it had just awoke out of sleep, whirled furiously round the old mansion, till its antique walls quivered again.

The rain, driven by the wind, splashed and rattled against the windows like showers of hailstones, whilst vivid flashings of lightning and hoarse rolling thunder completed the elemental din.

The highwaymen sat listening for a few moments to this strife of nature, which had broken in suddenly upon their conversation.

"Well," said Captain Hawk, "whatever this place may be, I prefer its shelter at the present moment to being exposed to the fury of the storm without."

"Heavens! how the wind howls! as though it would uproot the walls from their foundations. I never remember a more violent tempest," remarked his lordship.

"It seems to have with all its fury a somewhat composing effect upon me," answered the captain, yawning drowsily.

"Either that or the sherry," returned his comrade, catching the infection and yawning, in concert.

"I think it is probably a combination of warmth, sherry, and cigars."

"Yes."

"I vote," continued the captain, "we wrap ourselves in our riding cloaks and compose ourselves for the night in these high-backed arm-chairs."

"I am quite agreeable," answered his comrade, yawning again, "for I candidly confess I am uncommonly sleepy."

Our heroes accordingly spread their cloaks over their seats, and, as was their unfailing practice, examined the primings of their pistols.

"These," said Captain Hawk, are the best ghost detectors."

"Yes," returned the Black Highwayman, as he placed the handsome, but formidable, polished weapons he had been examining by his side on the table, "it must be a genuine ghost without flesh and bones that can stand against these."

"We may now sleep securely," said the captain, sinking back in his chair, and putting his weapons on the table within reach of his hand. "At the least alarm, we have only to grasp our pistols, and woe be to him who endeavours to trifle with us!"

Having uttered these words, Captain Hawk and his comrade pulled their voluminous cloaks around them and composed themselves to slumber, whilst the wind, as if in mockery at the captain's last words, howled its defiance in his ears.

But he heeded not its rude voice.

Ere the blast had died away, our heroes were asleep.

The storm still raged its fury over the Gray Mansion, heedless of the slumberers.

The fire flickered, and the green wood in the grate hissed and sputtered, and at length, having become thoroughly dry, sent a bright, roaring flame up the wide chimney.

The sudden brightness startled Captain Hawk, who awoke and looked around.

"It was the fire—nothing else!" he exclaimed; "but at first I thought——"

He was about to compose himself again to sleep, when a strange noise arrested his attention.

He listened attentively.

It seemed to proceed from the chimney.

Lord Harcliffe slumbered on unconsciously.

"I will not rouse him," thought the captain. "It may be nothing, after all."

Whatever it was, however, the sounds, instead of diminishing, increased.

The captain rose from his seat and approached the grate.

There was no doubt of the direction from which the noise proceeded.

It was from the chimney.

"There must be a chamber above, occupied by several persons," he thought. He listened attentively. "Are they quarrelling?" he exclaimed to himself.

The tumult now became louder than ever.

Captain Hawk's curiosity became roused to an uncontrollable extent.

"I'll bring you down, my friends, whoever you are!" he said to himself.

However, not wishing to injure the parties, but simply to assure himself, he withdrew the bullet from one of his pistols, and having done so, he discharged it up the chimney.

The result of this was a very wild and startled shriek that caused Lord Harcliffe to wake from his slumbers just in time to witness the rapid descent from the upper region of the chimney of——

A nest of young owls!

The unfortunate little birds, that had been first smoked, next scorched, and finally ousted in this unceremonious manner from their lodgings in the chimney-top, made a prodigious fluttering and screaming as Captain Hawk and Lord Harcliffe precipitately snatched them from the flames, which would else have consumed them.

"Poor little wretches!" cried Captain Hawk. "I regret I've disturbed them! However, it's too late to remedy the evil, so we must make the best of it."

"It's unfortunate," said Lord Harcliffe, "that owls do not appreciate sherry and cigars, or we might treat the little rascals all round."

The captain laughed as he collected the fragments of the nest, and endeavoured to establish a temporary asylum for the expatriated birds.

This was, to a certain extent, accomplished, and the young owlets sat huddled together by the side of the fireplace, looking wondrous wise and astonished, winking and blinking at the highwaymen, who took quite a fancy to them.

But the sensation was not yet concluded, for a few moments after there was a tremendous flap heard, and down came the mamma owl to look after her young, with a mouse in her beak.

Without condescending to take the smallest notice of our heroes, she divided the dainty she carried among her brood, and then her duties to her family having been performed, she turned her large round eyes upon the highwaymen, as much as to say, "Who are you?"

But the family circle was not yet completed, for presently a large, venerable-looking old gentleman—who turned out to be the father of the family—came also tumbling down, narrowly escaping pitching head first into the fire.

He also had a mouse in his claws, which, having handed over to the four little beaks that were quite ready to receive it, he joined his consort in staring at our heroes with such imperturbable gravity that they roared again.

Nothing, however, disconcerted, the wise birds, after a time, lulled by the warmth of the fire, closed their eyes and went to sleep.

The highwaymen, whom this little episode had disturbed, addressed themselves once more to sleep.

Lord Harcliffe was soon in blissful unconsciousness.

Not so, however, his companion.

Having been startled from his first sleep, the spell seemed to have been broken, and he found it difficult to place himself again under the dominion of the drowsy god.

He therefore lay back, wrapped in his cloak as before, having first reloaded his pistol, and closed his eyes, to sleep if possible.

But his thoughts prevented him.

The dislodgment of the owls' nest from the chimney suggested an explanation of much that had appeared strange in that place.

Might not the sounds which they had construed into the shrieks of human beings have been, after all, merely the hooting of these solitary birds?

Still there was the *Gray Figure*, and the *White-Robed Apparition*, that floated past the windows.

How were they to be accounted for?

The captain's thoughts then wandered to his beloved Blanche, and seemed to linger there.

His reverie was so profound that, at the same time, he imagined he was wishing he could sleep.

He *was* asleep.

But his slumber was not pleasant.

It was more like a lethargy—a sort of waking trance, in which his senses seemed to be partially active, but his limbs coerced and fettered as with an iron weight.

In this state, as he lay back in his chair, he could distinctly hear the wailing of the melancholy wind, and the hollow rolling of the thunder.

He became wrapt in a strange medley of truth and improbability.

His adventures of the past few days were jumbled together in fantastic distortion.

At one moment he spoke to Blanche, he folded her to his heart; then, as he gazed in her fair face, and drank from the beauty of her lustrous eyes, the glowing features gradually seemed to fade away before him, and their place become supplied by the pale, dead face of poor Willie.

This, in its turn, would gradually become indistinct, like the *phantasmagoria* of a dissolving view, and then, starting up into fresh vividness, stood the dark, motionless Gray Phantom, in its robe and cowl.

And in this manner the creations of his brain came, and disappeared, and came again.

Still the captain stirred not; his lethargy was as profound as the deepest sleep, the repose of his limbs as perfect.

And yet, withal, there was the latent sense of consciousness.

He was sensible of a *dark shadow* passing between his eyes and the light, like a cloud obscuring the face of the sun.

Yet he made no effort to see what the cloud portended.

He did not dream that it was a *man's hand* thus interposed for the purpose of testing whether he slept or not.

He was utterly unconscious that a dark, mysterious figure, whose hand grasped the glittering blade of a keen knife, crouched behind him, like a hidden snake, waiting the moment to strike.

The opportunity was favourable.

With suppressed breath, the dark form drew near.

The gaunt hand, passed backwards and forwards before the sleeper's eyes, elicited neither motion nor response.

It was time to strike.

The shrouded arm was uplifted.

The glittering blade flashed in the light; another moment, and it would have been buried to the hilt in the slumberer's breast.

But at that moment a tremendous peal of thunder rattled like a discharge of a battery of cannon over the mansion's roof.

The captain stirred.

The shrouded figure was gone!

The intended victim lived!

But still so powerful was the drowsy chain that held the faculties of the captain in temporary abeyance, that although the noise of the thunder had caused him to start, he had instantly relapsed into his quiescent state.

In this abnormal condition he lay, and became the subject of a strange delusion.

In the position he occupied his face was turned towards the table.

Suddenly—without any previous sound or warning—a *solitary hand* appeared.

This hand slowly descended and fell lightly on the pistol that lay on the table.

Still the captain stirred not.

All he seemed to have the power to do was to make a strong mental effort to solve the mystery, and in that effort the hand gradually disappeared. Then as the tension of his mind became relaxed, and he had almost ceased to wonder as to the cause of this illusion, the hand was there again, *and on the pistol.*

This was repeated four times.

Then the light gradually faded out, and as it grew more and more indistinct, a dark gigantic figure seemed to rise slowly from the oaken floor, and enlarge itself till it towered above the sleeper's head.

As the last ray expired, another terrific peal of thunder, preceded by a blinding flash of lightning, broke the lethargy that had bound the senses of Captain Hawk.

He awoke, and mechanically seizing his pistol, looked eagerly through the darkness.

His inmost soul seemed to warn him of something dread to be encountered.

Yes! There was no doubt this time. It was no vain dream; for there, only a few yards from the chair in which he sat, stood, in silent and imposing rigidity, the shrouded form of *the Gray Phantom!*

Yes! There it stood like a veiled horror, inspiring more terrible thoughts than had its face been displayed, even had the lineaments been those of a demon. Imagination is always stronger than reality; and as the captain gazed with riveted eyes upon this awful visitant, was it strange if a sensation stole across him something akin to fear?

It would rather have been strange if the reverse had been the case. Anyone who could have looked upon that dark silent figure, at that lonely midnight hour, in that solitary chamber, without a chilling of the heart, or a tremor of the limbs, must have been more than mortal.

But it was not the fear of danger that influenced Captain Hawk—it was an impression forced upon him by the state of his mind at that particular moment.

He had been startled from a trance-like lethargy—that was in itself filled with fantastic, strange apparitions—to gaze upon a veiled spectre—a nameless horror—and his heart yielded to the influence of a superstitious dread the time, place, and circumstances inspired.

He sat with his pistol grasped in his hand, as motionless as the object on which his dilated eyes were fixed.

But his tongue seemed paralysed, and he uttered no sound.

His companion, Lord Harcliffe, slept on soundly, and so occupied was the captain with his mysterious visitor, that he never even thought to arouse him.

A nature like Captain Hawk's, brave, impetuous, and excitable, could not long endure this silent interchange of looks.

Any *known* danger, he had always the courage to look boldly in the face.

Never in his life had he turned his face from peril on account of personal fear.

But there was a mystery about this Gray Phantom—a *quality*—that seemed beyond his reach.

Had he been assured that the strange being were a corporeal shape, he would at once have gripped him with his strong hands.

But the idea of grasping at a spirit—a shadow—*nothing!* seemed to forbid his approach.

He dared not encounter one from the dark regions of the world of spirits!

But in a few moments he felt the blood gradually returning to his heart, and beginning to circulate in his veins.

His vital energies were increasing—the healthy action of his mind returning—and as a natural consequence his fears diminishing.

He began to be ashamed of his terrors—to despise himself. Whatever might be the result, he would speak to the figure.

He acted at once upon this resolve.

"Mysterious being," he exclaimed, "who art thou?"

His voice seemed strangely hollow and startling, even to himself, as he asked this question.

The reply came in tones still deeper:

"*The Wandering Spirit of the Restless Dead!*"

The captain started, and drew in his breath in quick, spasmodic gulps.

This was what he had feared.

He struggled, however, to preserve his self-control.

"Whence have you come?" he demanded.

"*From the Grave!*" replied the spirit, in a voice so awful in its tone, that his listener's blood well-nigh curdled in his veins.

"For what purpose?" he inquired, with enforced calmness.

"To see who it is that dares intrude his mortal presence beneath the roof under which I dwelt while living."

This reply struck the captain as strange.

"How can it affect the dead who occupy their places after they have for ever quitted them?" he thought; and then inquired, aloud:

"Were you the master here?"

"I was; nay, I *am* so still!"

"How can that be since you have done with earthly things?"

"I have never relinquished my title to this mansion. That which I held *living*, I claim when *dead*."

"And you object to my presence here?"

"I do! and command your instant departure!"

"On such a night as this?—in such a storm?"

The thunder rolled heavily as the captain put this question, and the wind howled past the windows with gusty violence.

"What is the storm to me?" said the figure, in a tone of contempt.

"Nothing, I am ready to admit," replied the captain, growing gradually bolder as he spoke; and feeling perhaps some little pride at thus arguing the point with the spectral owner of the mansion, "but it is everything to me; I do not care to be buffeted by the wind or drenched by the rain."

"What is your purpose in coming here?"

"Curiosity. I had heard strange reports of this mansion, and wished to ascertain if there was any truth in them."

"Beware! Seek not to know too much. Depart while yet you are safe!"

Captain Hawk was struck with the idea that the spirit, from his evident desire to impress upon his listener the necessity of departure, admitted a certain fear of him; at the same time, he fancied he had heard his voice before. He therefore replied, boldly:

"I have made up my mind to stop here to-night, and would not alter my determination, though all the ghosts in the churchyard you came from joined in commanding me!"

"My body rests not in *hallowed* ground!" answered the phantom, in a tone of deep despair. "I am a *thing accursed!*"

"I understand," returned the captain, who was somewhat more impressed with the last words of the spectre: "the crimes of your life forbade your burial in consecrated earth, and forbid you to repose."

"That is more than you can say," answered the figure; "but even were it true, am I the only one in all the world who has crime to answer for?"

"No, but such crimes!"

"What crimes?"

"Did you not sell your soul to the Arch Fiend? Did not his dark presence haunt your death-bed on that fearful night when your soul passed from its mortal tenement?"

A deep groan of inexpressible anguish was the reply to this.

"Do not the mouldering skeletons of three wives lie entombed in the dark vaults beneath this time-worn mansion?"

The figure groaned again, whether with real or feigned emotion was known to itself alone.

Captain Hawk, now that he had addressed the spectre, had become gradually suspicious of his right to the title, but he continued;

"I can judge from your words, your groans, that your restless spirit is charged with heavy crimes."

"Yes, yes! I have crimes to answer for!—deep, heavy, burdensome crimes! There, there!" continued the veiled figure, in an agonized voice, pointing as he spoke to a dark spot on the floor. "In that place my hands shed innocent blood! The stain will never wash out!—the curse of that deed will never depart from this roof!"

"So much for the past," returned the captain; "but for crimes of more recent date?" he added.

"Do you call a hundred years recent?" asked the spirit. "It has been beyond my power to commit crime since that date."

"Are you sure of that?" said Captain Hawk.

"Alas! too sure!" was the answer.

"What, then, of Blanche Allison?"

This may seem to our readers a very strange and irrelevant question; but the captain, who had during his conversation with the veiled figure been becoming more and more convinced that his spiritual character was a mere sham, put this query as a random shot to see what effect it would take.

Captain Hawk saw, or fancied he saw, a sudden agitation of the spectre's robe at his inquiry, and he also detected—or imagined so—a slight unsteadiness in its voice as it re-echoed the words:

"Blanche Allison?"

The utterance of this name confirmed the captain in his opinion that, under a different aspect, he and the mysterious figure had met before.

"Yes, Blanche Allison! She has been abducted from her home," he continued. "Spirits, it is supposed, have a knowledge of events that are hidden from mere mortals. Tell we where is she?"

"You speak in riddles. I know not what you mean. This earth and its affairs are nothing now to me," said the figure.

"Why then need you have come from your grave to complain of my presence here?"

This was rather an embarrassing question for the spirit to answer.

He therefore evaded it, and in a voice of apprehension remarked:

"I have o'erstayed my time——"

"Wants to be off," thought the captain.

"I must be gone," the figure continued; "I must return to my prison-house. For yourself, take heed to my warning, and depart at once."

"Not I," replied Captain Hawk, with all his usual boldness and decision; "neither shall you until I am satisfied on one point."

"What mean you?"

"I am one of those matter-of-fact persons," answered the captain, "who fear the *living* far more than the *dead*. To speak plainly, I do not believe in the existence of ghosts! I believe you are an impostor!"

"Rash fool! you know not what you say! Begone!" —once more I warn you—while you are safe!"

With an imperious wave of the hand, the spirit stepped back, as though it would have taken its departure.

But Captain Hawk, who was resolved not to be baulked, cried in a determined voice:

"Stay! Before you depart, let me see your face."

"It is too dark. Be thankful that it is so."

"I demand! I can light the taper."

"The sight of it would strike you dead, or leave you a gibbering idiot!"

"Psha!"

"You would not dare to gaze upon it!"

"I dare anything!"

"You know not what you ask. Those who gaze on the face of the Gray Phantom never live long after. Be wise and depart!"

"That would be a proof not of wisdom, but of cowardice and folly. I have been holding a long conversation with you in semi-darkness: I am now about to light the taper."

As he spoke, the captain rose hastily, and thrust the wax candle between the bars of the grate. It ignited, and a little of the melted wax falling on the hot embers, caused for a few moments a bright light.

Captain Hawk now perceived that the spectre had gradually retreated towards the drapery at the end of the room.

There was no doubt now in his mind that the intention of the ghost was a sudden *bolt*.

"Mark me!" cried the captain; "I know you wish to escape me; but I am determined not to lose sight of you, whatever be the consequence! Therefore remove the cowl that shrouds your features. If not, I swear I will fire!"

As he spoke he cocked his pistol with an ominous click.

"Fire!" echoed the spectre, with a scornful laugh that somewhat disconcerted Captain Hawk. "Do you imagine earthly weapons can injure me? I defy you! Farewell!"

The figure appeared to glide backwards towards the wall.

But ere he had progressed ten yards, Captain Hawk kept his promise, and discharged his pistol.

"Ha, ha, ha!" laughed the spectre, quite unmoved.

At the same moment Lord Harcliffe, roused by the report, started from his slumbers.

The captain grasped his friend's arm excitedly, and pointed to the Gray Figure.

His mind began to be shaken.

If anything would have induced him to believe that the strange visitor was indeed a being from the other world it was his apparent invulnerability.

He began to feel his old supernatural sensations creeping over him.

He had fired at the figure with an aim that was unerring, at a distance of only a few yards, without the slightest effect.

"If he be bullet proof, I shall begin to think he is the Fiend himself!" he murmured.

"I will try!" said his comrade, as without the least hesitation he cocked and discharged his weapon.

Again the only reply was the mocking laugh of the fiend, as he now undoubtedly appeared to be, who deliberately held up a bullet between his thumb and finger.

The tables were now turned, and the big drops of terror bedewed the foreheads of our heroes.

It was, then, a veritable spirit, after all!

The Gray Figure had now reached the drapery at the end of the room, and a very perceptible movement of the drapery pointed out that spot as the locality at which he would depart.

Captain Hawk had given up any further idea of arresting his departure.

The triumph of the *im*material over the corporeal appeared to be complete.

But it was in appearance only.

The panel from whence the spectre had entered had closed, and no effort on his part could open it.

But of this our heroes were unconscious.

A muttered oath from the figure caught their ears.

Suddenly Lord Harcliffe whispered to his comrade:

"The bullets of my pistols have been extracted."

These words formed a clue to the mystery.

"And so must mine have been!" he cried.

"Juggling impostor!" he shouted, to the figure, furious at the trick he felt convinced had been played upon him, "you shall find, in the absence of other weapons, my own arms are strong enough to unveil you!"

As he spoke, he bounded forward; but ere he could reach the figure, the cowl fell from his face, and revealed features so death-like and appalling that the captain recoiled with horror.

The spectre evidently congratulated himself at the effect he had produced.

"Did I not tell you you could not bear to look upon my unveiled face?" he exclaimed.

"You did!" shouted the highwayman. "But you forgot to tell me at the same time that you wore a mask!"

As he spoke, he rushed desperately towards the spectre, and, with a rapid movement, tore away the covering from his face.

A mingled cry of hate and indignation burst from his lips as he recognised in the Gray Figure the person of the abductor of his beloved Blanche—

Ridley Massingham!

Quick as lightning, he bounded on to the villain, who, cowed and trembling, and baffled in his means of escape, could but faintly struggle against his impetuous assailant.

Like a child in his excited grasp, the captain swung him round, when at the same moment the latter found himself grasped by a pair of iron arms and hurled violently to the floor.

When he arose, breathless from the shock, the Gray Figure and his accomplice had disappeared.

CHAPTER CCXXII.

THE POLICE OFFICERS, DRIVEN BY THE STORM, SEEK SHELTER IN THE HAUNTED MANSION.—THEY ENCOUNTER VARIOUS OBJECTS IN THE DARK.—PETERSON SINGS A SONG, AND NICHOLAS TWIGG TELLS A GHOST STORY.—ARRIVAL OF THE SPECTRE, AND RAPID DEPARTURE OF THE POLICE.

THE assault upon the captain had been so sudden and unexpected that he could not possibly have guarded against it, neither could he see the means by which his prey had escaped his grasp.

But his comrade, although from the rapidity with which the manœuvre had been executed, had been unable to assist his friend, still saw distinctly that the place of exit was behind the tattered drapery that hung from a particular portion of the wall.

This he pointed out at once to his friend.

"Quick!" cried Captain Hawk, in a fever of excited rage. "Bring the light this way!"

His lordship advanced hastily with the taper.

Throwing aside the tapestry, they, after a brief scrutiny, discovered a small narrow panel in the wall.

To their great joy it was not closely shut.

In the anxiety of the retreating parties to effect their escape, they had closed the panel too hastily, and it had rebounded without fastening.

Pushing open the door, they entered without hesitation, taking care, however, to keep the door wide open.

It was a small stone chamber, entirely unfurnished, and looked miserably cold and bare.

Neither did it afford them any assistance, since it appeared to lead nowhere.

A shade of disappointment stole over their features.

"There must be some means of egress," said Captain Hawk, "or else those we seek would be here."

"We must search carefully: we shall find it presently," replied the Black Highwayman.

This appeared to be a more difficult discovery to arrive at than they at first imagined.

The walls were of stone, without anything in them approaching a door.

Neither was there any trap in the floor.

"It's strange," remarked the captain.

"Yes; but patience. We shall arrive at it in time."

At length, when both were inclined to give up the search as useless, Captain Hawk noticed a slab of stone in the wall that bore every appearance of being m ovable.

"This is the spot!" he cried; "but we are in as unsatisfactory a plight as ever, since we can never hope to remove the stone."

"We have at least discovered this room, and are therefore so much nearer to the nest where these villains burrow," said Lord Harcliffe.

"We will hunt them out yet!" exclaimed Captain Hawk. "A ray of hope shines in my heart, for I believe I shall ere long gain tidings of my beloved Blanche."

"In the meantime," suggested Lord Harcliffe, "we will secure access to this cell by damaging the lock of the door that leads to it."

This was easily done, and having so battered it as to leave it perfectly useless, they re-entered their old quarters.

Hardly had they established themselves there once more when the sound of footsteps tramping below, and echoing with prodigious clamour through the vaulted passages, reached their ears.

"What new adventure now?" exclaimed Captain Hawk.

"If these are phantoms, they are very noisy ones," answered Lord Harcliffe.

"Let us see."

Opening the door, they walked out on to the gallery at the top of the staircase and listened.

They had little difficulty in recognising the new-comers.

For as Peterson's voice was heard giving directions, Captain Hawk exclaimed, in a low tone:

"The police officers, by Jove! What brings them here?"

"That question is almost superfluous, my dear Dick," answered his comrade. "Whenever the police are within a mile of Captain Hawk and the Black Highwayman, there need never be any doubt *who they want*."

"You imagine, then, they're after us?"

"Is it not the most reasonable supposition?"

"Perhaps so! They have discovered at length that the birds they expected to net have flown from the tree; and are now probably full of irritation and chagrin, scouring the country and searching every hole and corner in search of us."

It may be mentioned here, that after our heroes took the break-neck leap from one tree to the other, they lost no time in still further increasing the distance between themselves and their pursuers by dropping to the ground and creeping carefully away through the brushwood. This was an easy task, since the police were so scared and engrossed at the fate of their comrades who had ventured to essay the task of climbing after the highwaymen, that they had neither eyes nor ears for anything else.

Of the burning of the tree and their supposed destruction in the flames our heroes knew nothing at present.

They stood listening to the scuffling of feet and the exclamations of the officials, who did not appear to be in the most amiable of humours, either with themselves or the weather.

"Come on!" they heard Peterson exclaim, in an authoritative tone. "We're on his Majesty's service, an' whether there's anyone here, or whether there ain't, what's the odds? The 'orses 'll catch their deaths o' cold standin' in the damp!"

"I knows as I shall," said Nicholas Twigg, in a wheezy voice. "I never could stand damp, no more could my father or grandfather. Ugh! ugh! ugh!" he coughed.

"Now then, Nick!" cried Peterson, "when you're quite done coughin' an' spittin', per'aps yer'll bring in yer 'orse!"

"What! inside?"

"Yes, inside, o' course!" returned Peterson. "What's good for christians, is good for 'orses."

Whether he considered this remark held good with respect to rum, we know not, but he took a good swig from his pocket-flask as he made the remark.

Nicholas, coughing and grunting, went out of the passage, and presently there was a tremendous clatter caused by the hoofs of twenty horses that were led in to be stabled there till the morning.

"By Heaven!" exclaimed Captain Hawk, suddenly, "if they go blundering into any of the rooms they'll discover Satan and Phantom, and in that case we're done!"

"No, my friend, we must be on the watch," returned his comrade. "We shall easily hear if they make this important discovery; and if so, there will be still an opportunity between now and daylight to get away. They are sure to be drowsy."

"True," answered the captain; "I forgot that."

The police officers, however, did not appear desirous of investigating the apartments, but simply contented themselves with ranging their horses in the passage.

This done, they assembled at the foot of the stairs and held a consultation.

Our heroes, shrouded in darkness at the top of the staircase, could hear all that was said without being visible.

"It's a cussed noosance this rain a comin' on!" croaked Old Nick. "Ugh! 'ow the blessed wind comes a drivin' up this passage—enough to blow a feller's 'ead off!"

"Well, we must make the best of it," returned Peterson; "though if I'd known as much as I do now, I'd a given orders to stop where we was. The inn was comfortable, an' we could have put up there for the night."

"Wishes as we 'ad!" grumbled Nicholas.

The entire body joined in this wish.

"Well, there's one comfort," continued Peterson, "we've left poor Morrison behind. One'll be looked after; and the other dcn't want any looking to: he's done for."

"An' there's another comfort," said Nicholas, "as them two vagabones was roasted in the tree."

"What does he mean?" whispered Captain Hawk to his comrade.

"We shall hear, most likely, if we listen!" replied his lordship.

"It's the first time I ever burnt a brace of highwaymen," remarked Peterson; "that is, if they are burnt."

"If they are burnt?" echoed Nicholas, indignantly. "I should think there can't be no manner o' doubt about that?"

"Well, I'm not quite sure," answered Peterson, dubiously.

[THE POLICE OFFICERS ENCOUNTER A GHASTLY SPECTRE IN THE HAUNTED MANSION.]

"Not sure? Why, didn't the tree burn like blazes?—didn't we see the flames pitch into it till it was entirely consoomed?" asked Nicholas.

"Yes, we see that," replied Peterson, sententiously.

"Very well, then, what more could yer want to see?" asked Nicholas.

"I should like to see proofs."

"Proofs?"

"Yes. These rascals are as artful as ole Nick 'imself! I don't mean you!"

"Thankee!"

"An' all the time as we're a congraterlatin' ourselves as these 'ighwaymen are dead, 'ow do we know as they ain't escaped, an' got clear off?"

"Ho, ho!" laughed Nicholas, derisively. "That is a good idear! Got clear off! Ho, ho!"

"Well, you may laugh; but how do you know they haven't?"

"'Ow do I know? Why, in the fust place, didn't I see the combusterbles piled round the tree?"

"I saw that much myself."

"Well, then, didn't I see a light applied to them combusterbles?"

"I saw that, too. Well?"

"Well, then, didn't the tree burn up an' blaze like a bonfire?"

"No doubt of it."

"Very good! Then, what I wants to know is—'ow could two men sit up in the top of a tree that was a blazin' like a bonfire, an' not be consoomed, when the tree itself was burnt to ashes, right down to 'is stump?"

Nicholas Trigg wound up in a tone of triumph, and had a good cough to relieve himself after this vehement questioning.

"There's no doubt about it," replied Peterson, "that

these highwaymen were consumed, if they were in the tree, and I thought so myself as I looked at it burning; but it has since occurred to me that they're not exac'ly the sort o' men to sit quietly on a branch an' be roasted when there's the slightest chance o' gettin' away."

Captain Hawk and Lord Harcliffe felt rather tickled by this sage remark of Peterson, but they remained perfectly still.

This was another way of representing the circumstances that for a moment staggered even the confident Nicholas, but he still clung to his opinion.

"They couldn't 'a got away!" he exclaimed. "Besides, 'ow did they know as we was agoin' to roast 'em?"

"Well, but just look ere," Peterson continued: "if flames can burn bodies and clothes to ashes, they can't consume sword hilts, or pistol barrels."

"Well, who said as they could?"

"Very good. Then, if the men we are after were burnt in their hiding-place in the tree, we should have found the remains of their weapons, shouldn't we?"

This was a very awkward question to get over, and one which Nicholas, with all his desire to imagine the troublesome customers annihilated, found it difficult to answer.

"Oh!" said he, petulantly, "they must 'a melted!"

"Oh, no!" replied the obdurate Peterson, "sword blades and pistol barrels don't melt."

"Well, then, d—n it! what does they do?" cried Nicholas, quite out of patience at his comrade's objections.

"They stop where they are, an' remain just as they are—pistols an' sword blades!"

"Well, 'ave it 'ow yer like!" said Nicholas, in a tone of resignation: "of course I'm wrong—I allus am."

"There's no doubt you're wrong, Nick, this time," returned his comrade, "for depend upon it, since they left no relics of any sort behind 'em, they've given us the double again."

"D—n 'em!" growled Nicholas. "Then I s'pose we may look upon 'em as got loose again?"

"I'm afraid so; an' of course our bus'ness will be to find 'em."

At this moment the wind gave a fearful whirl round the gray mansion, accompanied by a howl that suggested an outburst of fiends from *Pandemonium*, and as the fierce element had no respect whatever for police officers, no matter how vigilant or trustworthy, it came rushing in a torrent up the passage where they were congregated.

At the same moment, Captain Hawk drew his comrade gently into the chamber where they had established their quarters.

"So, then, it seems," he said, "we have had a narrow escape of being burnt alive."

"Yes; but it unfortunately happens that our escape is suspected, or it would have been the most advantageous incident that has ever occurred to us."

"From what I can gather from the conversation of these officers, they have evidently come here for the sake of shelter, and not in pursuit of us."

"No. But it is more than probable they will enter this apartment."

"If so, we must be prepared."

"You do not mean to attack them?"

"Certainly not: at least, not with offensive weapons."

"How then?"

"We must scare them away—frighten them to death!"

"If possible!"

"I think we can effect our purpose. This old mansion, invested as it is with superstitious terrors, may be of inestimable service to us from time to time as a place of concealment when hunted by our foes."

"True, in spite of the Gray Phantom."

"It will therefore be our policy so to work upon the fears of the officers as to give them a wholesome dread of ever again coming within miles of this spot."

"What do you intend to do?"

"In the first place, we must remove the remains of our repast, and everything that betokens the recent presence of human beings, into the small cell we have just discovered within yonder panel."

"But suppose our retreat should be cut off?"

"There is little fear; but at all events, we must risk that. Having gone so far, I am prepared to risk anything rather than quit this place until my doubts are satisfied—till I have unmasked some of its dark mysteries."

"Come, then, let us remove our banquet."

In a few moments everything was conveyed into the small chamber through the panel, and the ashes of the fire, which was now extinguished, raked out and scattered.

All looked as cold and forlorn as when our heroes first entered it.

Being now prepared for any emergency, the highwaymen went out once more on to the gallery.

The officials, who had not yet recovered the violent gust of cold air that had assailed them, were blowing their fingers and stamping their feet to warm themselves.

Peterson and Nicholas were mutually comforting their inner regions with the contents of their flasks.

The men who were not, however, so well supplied, but who only caught transient sniffs of the fragrant spirit exhaled from the mouths of their superiors, began to grumble at their position.

"Are we going to stop here all night?" inquired one.

"O' course we are, Tomkisson," replied Nicholas; "'an grateful too we ought to be to be able to put our 'eads anywhere out o' the way of a storm like this."

A loud volley of thunder rolled over the mansion, as though enforcing the speaker's words.

"We might a' been 'xposed to all this," added Nicholas, "if it warn't for this 'ospitable domicile."

"If this is hospitality," returned the ungrateful Tomkisson, "I say d—n it!"

"What's the good o' swearin' about it?" said Nick, reprovingly. "They say as this place is 'aunted; an' if yer goes a usin' bad languidge, yer'll be a' 'avin' a ghost or a 'obgoblin, or summat o' that sort a droppin' on to yer."

"We might just as well a stayed where we was, at the inn," growled the discontented officer: "we were warm there, at least."

"'Ow was we to know the weather was a going to change like this?" asked Nicholas. "It don't send us a special hintimation every time it is a goin' to be uproarious."

Peterson, who was beginning, in spite of his potations—and they were plentiful—to feel chilled and drowsy, interposed.

"I don't see why we should stand here in the passage all night, catching colds and rheumatism!" he said.

"No more do I!" growled several voices in concert.

"There's no reason," continued Peterson, "why we shouldn't establish ourselves in one of the rooms; as there's no one here to interfere with us, we can make a choice."

This was not difficult in a house where all the chambers were equally uncomfortable.

But the prevailing opinion seemed to be in favour of the upper regions.

"Let's go upstairs," cried several of the men.

"It's time for us to be off to our retreat," whispered Captain Hawk to his comrade.

This suggestion was at once acted upon by our heroes, who reached their hiding-place just as the heels of the police officers came clattering with heavy tread into the room.

The highwaymen smiled to themselves as they placed their taper in a snug corner, and drank a glass of wine each to the success of their plans.

On entering the room, Peterson and Nicholas Twigg, with their usual keen sense of comfort, seized at once upon the two arm-chairs.

Perhaps they felt that, being the eldest members of the force, it was a preference due to their greater age and experience.

The rest of the tired members threw themselves on the ground anywhere.

Peterson drew forth his lanthorn and glanced around the room.

The eyes of the company followed the rays of light as they rested on the gloomy walls.

"Not a pertickler lively spot, this 'ere," remarked Peterson.

"Looks like a undertaker's," remarked Tomkisson, whose tendencies, operated upon by hunger and cold, were decidedly morbid.

"There's a grate," said Nicholas, looking wistfully at the empty appearance it presented.

"We can all see that!" growled the morose Tomkisson.

"If I was a young man, do you know what I should do?" he inquired.

"What?" asked several voices.

"Why, there's plenty o' trees outside," he replied, "an' I should jest make it my business to go an' strip off some o' their branches, an' 'ave a bit o' fire in that 'ere grate."

It was not a bad idea by any means, and so most of them thought.

"Come on!" cried several; "let's go and collect some branches."

Four of the number departed, and in a short time returned loaded.

These were piled in the grate, and a light applied.

But the wood was green and damp, and obstinately refused to ignite.

It was a long time before, in spite of fanning and blowing—which operation filled the room with smoke, and set Nicholas coughing furiously—the branches could be induced to catch the flame.

And then they steamed and hissed, until thoroughly heated; after which they gave out a cheerful blaze, much to the comfort of those assembled.

Most of them lit their pipes, and the odour and smoke of tobacco soon had entire possession of the chamber.

"We only want a barrel of ale," said one, "to make us as jolly as sandboys."

But there was not such luxury at hand, and, consequently, the jollity was of a very limited description.

It was very dull work sitting puffing their pipes in that large empty room, that looked as if it was capable of containing a ghost in every corner.

"This 'ere 'ud be very snug if we'd got somethin' to drink," observed one of the party.

"Never give your mind to drinking!" said Nicholas Twigg, impressively. "I never did when I was a young man!"

"No more did I!" added Peterson, although a powerful odour of rum at that moment suggested the idea that both these worthy creatures had been intent upon such an operation at no very recent period.

"Drinkin' 's destructive to young hofficers!" continued Nicholas, proudly: "old ones require it—in moderation o' course—but still they wants a little; but that little must be good."

Here he took a sip from his flask.

"Spirits," he continued, "is bad, inasmuch as they're too stimulatin'—they makes a man wentursome an' fool-'ardy, while e's hunder th' hinfluence on it; an' then arterwards, e's no good, bein' shaky and nervous. Take the advice o' me—a old member o' the force—chew tobaccy, if you likes, but *es*chew spirits as is neat."

The younger members were doubtless very much edified by this advocation of temperance, but they began to feel the want of something to make the hours pass agreeably.

At length one proposed a song.

"Well, there's no objection to that," said Peterson—"a song will help to frighten away the ghosts!"

"Ghosts!" inquired several voices at once—"are there ghosts here?"

"*Are* there ghosts?" echoed Paterson, emphasising the *are* vehemently. "Why the place swarms with 'em."

The listeners looked rather ominously at this intelligence.

"Why," dropped in Nicholas, "they say there's more ghosteses an' spectres in this 'ere ole 'ouse than there is rats."

"I ain't seen any," remarked one.

"'Ow can ye see what's unwisible?" asked Nicholas.

"Ah, ah, I forgot that," said the former speaker.

"Why," resumed Peterson, "don't you know that in former times the proprietor of this place murdered his three wives, and was carried off one night by the devil himself?"

"No," replied his listeners, "it's the first time we ever heard of it."

"It was just such a night as this too—the thunder rolled, and the lightning glared, and the wind howled."

Whoo-oo-oo-oo, oo, oo! piped the wind at that moment.

"Whoo-oo-oo-oo, oo, oo!" piped a voice in reply.

"What's that?" inquired everybody.

Nobody knew.

"It was the wind," suggested Peterson—"it must have been the wind."

"The first '*whoo-hoo!*' was wind," explained the experienced Nicholas, "but the last was—a—summat else, though what that summat was, it's more than I can undertake to pint out."

"*Ha, ha, ha!*" laughed a voice near at hand. "What an old fool!" it cried.

"Eh? what's that?" cried Nicholas. "Old fool! Who said I was an old fool?"

Nobody pleaded guilty to this charge, and Peterson, who rather flattered himself he could sing, in order to set matters right, volunteered a song with a chorus.

The proposal was received with much approbation on all sides.

Peterson, therefore, having cleared his throat and taken a preliminary suck at his rum-bottle, chanted as follows:—

"A long time ago there liv'd a man,
Whose name I'm told was sorrowful Sam;
Such a mournful buffer you never could see,
He was groanin' an' cryin' continival-lee:
Oh dear me! how wretched I am!
Have a good cry with sorrowful Sam!
Sorrowful Sam! sorrowful Sam!
Have a good cry with sorrowful Sam!
Chorus: Sorrowful Sam! sorrowful Sam!
Have a good cry with sorrowful Sam!"

"Have a good cry with sorrowful Sam!" repeated a little quiet voice, that seemed to come from the chimney.

"Eh?" said Peterson, pausing. "Keep together with the chorus, gentlemen, if you please."

He then continued:

To such an extent went his mournin' an' woes,
His eyes were like ferrets, an' red was 'is nose;
Wherever 'e went you was certain to find 'im,
From 'is leavin' a stream of cold water behind 'im.
An' 'e cried, Oh dear! how wretched I am!
Have a good cry with sorrowful Sam!
Chorus: Sorrowful Sam! sorrowful Sam!
'Have a good cry with sorrowful Sam!'

"Have a good cry with sorrowful Sam!" again repeated the peculiar voice as before.

Peterson was indignant at this.

"I wish!" said he, rising, "that the gen'l'man who keeps droppin' in with 'Have a good cry with sorrowful Sam!' after everybody else is finished, 'ud try an' keep proper time."

He seated himself grandly, and continued:

"He caused such a stir as he walked in the street,
All who met him were certain to cry for a week;
An' th' gutters were flooded with tears as they ran
From the eyes that were cryin' with sorrowful Sam.
Sorrowful Sam! sorrowful Sam!
Have a good cry with sorrowful Sam!
Chorus: Have a good cry with sorrowful Sam!
Poor Samuel's friends were in terrible plights,
What to do to poor Sammy to set 'im to rights;
Till one of their number suggested at last,
Sam should swallow a bladder o' strong laughin' gas.
To the chemist at once in a body they ran
For a bladder of gas for sorrowful Sam.
Chorus: A bladder of gas for sorrowful Sam!"

"A bladder of gas for sorrowful Sam!" exclaimed the little peculiar voice once more.

Peterson looked round indignantly as usual, but without remark continued:

"Sam emptied the bladder, and strange to tell,
It was no sooner empty than Sam got well;
If he'd cried before too much by half,
He could now do nothing but giggle and laugh,
Ha, ha, ha! how jolly I am!
Come and have a good laugh with comical Sam!
Chorus: Have a good laugh with comical Sam!

"He laughed so much an' grew so stout,
That Sam was obliged to be carried about;
But he kept on laughing the same as at first,
Until one fine mornin' poor Samuel burst;
But he still kept laughing, How happy I am!
Come and have a good roar with comical Sam!
Chorus: Have a good roar with comical Sam!

"They screw'd him down in a coffin tight,
But Sam kept roarin' with all his might;
They buried him deep 'neath an ivied wall,
But he laugh'd till he shook it down, ivy and all
Ha, ha, ha! how jolly I am!
Come and have a good laugh with comical Sam
Chorus: Have a good laugh with comical Sam!

When you pass the old church, to this very day
You may 'ear old Sam a laughin' away;
An' the more folks tells 'im to 'old 'is riot,
The more he vows 'e'll never be quiet.
He shouts aloud, How jolly I am!
Come an' be buried with comical Sam!
Chorus: Comical Sam! comical Sam!
Come an' be buried with comical Sam!"

Loud applause followed this effusion.

When the murmurs of approbation had subsided, the same peculiar quiet voice distinctly repeated the words:

"Come an' be buried with comical Sam!"

"D—n it all!" cried Peterson, "what's that?"

Everybody looked, but nothing appeared.

Only the voice echoed:

"D—n it all! what's that?"

"Who is it?" exclaimed the irate officer, starting on to his feet and looking round.

Everybody declared it was nobody.

"Nonsense—nobody!" shouted Peterson. "It must be somebody!"

"Must be somebody!" repeated the voice.

"There again!"

"There again!" was echoed.

This was getting so mysterious as to be past a joke.

The officials found themselves gradually drawing as closely as possible to each other.

Nicholas Twigg suddenly caught hold of his comrade by the arm and clung to it.

"P'r'aps," he whispered, "there may be some truth in the reports we 'eard as this ole house is 'aunted——"

"'Aunted!" was repeated.

"Do any of you see anythin'?" inquired Peterson.

"Nothing! Not a sign—or a ghost of—— Ha! see! Look there!" shrieked one of the terrified individuals, pointing distractedly into the darkness.

They all looked, of course, and there, to their dismay, they saw two bright round eyes shining on them like diamonds.

At the same moment, a dark object flopped on the floor, and came hopping forwards.

"The devil—the devil!" cried the officers, as they clung to each other in all the horrors of superstitious terror.

But the *devil*, without taking any notice of the alarm he had inspired, leapt nimbly on the table, and looked down upon them, uttering a loud "Caw!—caw!"

And, after all, what was this frightful apparition?

Merely a poor raven, who was bidding the intruders welcome in the best manner he could.

"Well I'm blest!" cried Nicholas, as he recognised the new guest, "if it ain't a raven as 'as been a jinin' in chorus!"

This was a relief to the agitated nerves of the party.

"We're werry glad to see yer, Master Caw—caw!" said Nicholas; "but you're a interruption to 'armony, so out yer goes!"

Grasping the black, ominous bird, he opened the window, and threw him forth to enliven some other party with his presence.

"The idea," cried Peterson, "of an ugly black imp of a bird startling us all like that!"

Order being restored, Nicholas Twigg was next called upon to contribute to the amusement of the party.

"Well, yer see, gents, I can't sing, seein' as I ain't got a singin' woice, but I can tell yer a story, if yer likes to 'ear it."

"Oh yes, a story—a story!" cried the party.

"An', in order to be quite sootable an' in accordance with the present time an' place as we're in, I'll tell yer a *ghost* story."

"Ay, ay, a ghost story—a ghost story!" burst forth in general assent, as the audience drew closer together with listening eagerness.

"What I'm goin' to tell you was told me by a old brother officer as is dead an' gone long ago. 'E swore as it was true, but you can believe it or not, as yer likes. I shall call it—

"OLD NICK'S GHOST STORY.

"Well, then, you must know as Mat Mullins—that was my comrade's name—was married twice. That warn't anything partickler, cos there's numbers o' people as enters the matermoneral state as often as that.

"But there was somethin' *very* strange about what happened to these 'ere wives of 'is'n, an' what appeared arter their deaths to 'im.

"Well, 'is fust wife's name was Soosan, an' a werry pretty gal she was too. 'E was a young man when 'e married 'er, an' they lived together five years exactly.

"Doorin' the last month of the fifth year Soosan calls Mat to her one day, an' says:

"'Mat, I'm a goin' to tell yer somethin'.'

"'What is it, my dear?' says 'e.

"'I'm goin to 'ave a fit of illness,' she answers; 'I shall be taken ill to-morrow, an' I shall die on the last day of the year.'

"O' course Mat was rayther skeered like at this, an' tried to laugh it off.

"But Soosan wouldn't be laughed off, an' sure enough she were took ill, an' got wuss an' wuss, till, on the last night of the old year—that was the 31st of December—as Mat, who was a very good nuss, was a makin' some gruel at the fire, 'is wife calls 'im to 'er bedside.

"'Come directly, Mat!' she says. 'Never mind the gruel, I sha'n't want it.'

"'E went to 'er, an' saw as 'er face was awful white an' death-like.

"'My gal,' says 'e, with a falterin' voice, for 'e were werry fond on 'er, 'what's the matter?'

"'I'm goin' now, Mat!' she gasped out.

"Mat was so floored he was a goin' to bolt out arter a doctor, but Soosan held his hand fast.

"'Don't leave me!' she cried, 'my time's come, an' no doctor can do me good. I shall die to-night!'

"'She's a goin' to die!—she's a goin' from me! I shall never see 'er no more!' cried Mat, with the tears rollin' down his cheeks.

"'Yes,' said 'is wife, 'you'll see me once more.'

"'I knows that,' sobbed poor Mat, 'when I jines yer in th' hother world.'

"'Long before that,' answered Soosan; 'I shall come to supper with you, Mat.'

"'When?' he inquired, feelin' cold all over at 'er words.

"'On Twelfth Night!'

"'At what time?'

"'Ten o'clock!' she exclaimed, as she fell back on 'er piller—dead!

"Poor Mat cried a good deal about 'er; 'owever, all 'is tears couldn't bring 'er to life agin, so 'e tried to comfort 'imself with the th' idear of 'avin' supper with 'er once more at least.

"One thing, 'owever, puzzled him, an' that was what 'e should get 'er for supper.

"'She won't be able to heat,' 'e kept athinkin' to 'isself, 'the sort o' things she used to when she were alive.'

"Well, 'e puzzled is brains to no purpose, 'an at last 'e give it up.

"'It ain't no good a thinkin',' 'e cried; 'I'll get 'er 'er favourite supper—boiled tripe an' onions; an' if she don't like that, poor dear, she must order what she wants when she comes.'

"Well, Twelfth Day came at last.

"Mat gets the place all tidied an' cleaned up, an' the tripe an' onions all cooked beautiful, by half-past nine.

"He set th' dish on th' 'ob to keep 'ot, and lays the clean white table-cloth, an' puts a plate an' knife an' fork for 'er, an' one for 'isself.

"'E kep' a lookin' at the clock; an' as the time drew on, if 'e didn't get awful nervous, no man never did—'e told me this arterwards.

"'I wonder whether she'll come,' e' said to 'isself. 'Five minutes to ten! I think I'll put the tripe on the table.'

"Mat according dusts the covered dish, an' brings it from the 'ob, an' puts it down in its proper place, an' just as e'd done this the clock begins to strike.

"Is 'eart beat with every stroke of the clock, till the whole ten 'ad struck, and then just as 'e was a going' to exclaim, 'She won't come,' blest if there didn't come—

"*Three distinct raps at the door!*"

The speaker added to the effect of this announcement by performing the act very deliberately with his knuckles on the table.

"Mat's hair stood bolt upright, as you may imagine," continued Nicholas, "as with faltering voice he exclaimed:

"'Come in, Soosan, my love, if it's you!'

"That instant the door flew open of 'isself, an' in walked Soosan, all smilin' an' pleasant, an bloomin' as when she were alive.

"Mat were so delighted, 'e forgot all about what she were, an' threw 'is arms round 'er. But, lor bless yer, 'e didn't grasp nothin' but hair.

"'E were awful disappointed, so 'e were obliged to content hisself wi' looking at 'er.

"Well, they sat down to supper, an' Mat took the cover off the dish.

"'Oh, it does smell beautiful!' she exclaimed. 'What is it?'

"'Tripe and honions,' 'e answered.

"'Oh, that's right,' she said.

"Mat helped 'er an' 'imself, an' when supper was over she drew 'er chair up to the fire, an' pointed to Mat's pipe.

"'Smoke your pipe, dear,' she said.

"Mat smoked an' looked, an' looked an' smoked, till near midnight, for there was somethin' in 'er manner as prevented him talkin' to 'er.

"Well, as time drew on, Soosan looked at the clock.

"'I must be gone at twelve,' she said, sorrowfully.

"'I wishes I could kiss yer afore yer goes!' whimpered Mat.

"'You'll soon have somethin' to kiss,' says she.

"'I'll never kiss no hother woman as long as I lives!' exclaimed Mat, quite indignant like.

"'Mark my words!' says Sooson—'the last I shall ever speak—before six months are over you'll marry Mary Wilcox, as lives round the corner.'

"'Mary Wilcox!' repeated Mat—'Mary Wil——

"Before he could finish the word the clock began to strike twelve.

"'Good-bye, dear!' cried Soosan.

"But 'er woice seemed to come from hever sich a long way hoff, an' as 'e looked at 'er she seemed to get more an' more indistinct, till, by the time as the clock 'ad done striking, she'd faded away into nothink—hair—and the chair were empty!

"She was gone for good!

"Well, to come to the pint, jest five months and ten days arterwards Mat was married, as Soosan perdicted, to Mary Wilcox, an' arter five years *she* died, just as 'his fust wife did, on the last day o' the year.

"Well, the same thing 'appened exac'ly as before

"'Is dead wife come to supper; only, afore she took er departure, she told 'im something as weren't quite so pleasant as 'is fust wife's perdiction.'

"'Mat,' she says, 'I must be off at twelve, but before I goes I feels it my duty to tell yer yer'll see me this night twelvemonth.'

"'What, agin?' asked Mat.

"'Yes,' says she.

"'Shall yer come to supper?' he inquires.

"'No, I shall want no supper,' she answered. 'When I come again, it will be to fetch you.'

"She disappeared in the usual manner, an', arter she were gone, Mat came round to me in a great state o' excitement, an' tells me vot I've told you.

"'Is wife's promise o' comin' 'ad give 'im quite a turn.

"It were no good a raisining with 'im, 'e'd made up 'is mind as 'e were booked, an' blest if 'e didn't dwindle an' dwindle away till, on Christmas Day, 'e couldn't 'old up no longer, an' took to 'is bed.

"I went to see 'im, an' tries to cheer 'im up, but it were no go.

"'It ain't no good a tryin' to raise my sperrits,' 'e said. 'All I asks yer is to sit up with me on Twelfth Night till arter twelve o'clock.'

"O' course I couldn't refuse, bein' a ole pal o' is'n.'

'Well, the night came at last.

"I went, an' poor Mat seemed awful restless an' unsettled at the prospect afore 'im. 'E didn't seem to see 'is way clear about goin' with 'is wife.

"I cheered 'im up as well as I could, an' at last 'e seemed quite quiet an' resigned like.

"Well, 'e lay still, an' by-and-by the clock begins to strike twelve.

"'She'll soon be 'ere now,' says Mat, an' he were right.

"As the last stroke went there comes—

"'*Thump!—thump!—thump!*' at the door.

"'Ere she is!' cried Mat, faintly. 'Come in.'

"Sure enough, as 'e spoke, the door opens, and in walks Mrs. Mullins, all nice, an' clean, an' smilin'.

"She goes straight to the bed, an' says:

"'Ere I am, Mat; I'm come again, you see.'

"'All right!' says the poor chap, 'I'm ready. Good-bye, Nick!'

"The figure disappeared like a puff of wind, an when I went to the bedside, poor Mat were gone sure enough: 'e were a corpse. An' that's all."

This story had riveted the attention of the audience, and worked upon their ghostly apprehensions to such an extent that had a mouse ran across the floor they would have magnified it at that moment into a mountain of horror.

When, therefore, as Nicholas concluded, they were suddenly checked from any expressions of gratification by a hoarse, "To whit! To whoo! To whit! To whoo!" close to them, and when, in addition to this, Messrs. Twigg and Peterson, who were quietly sucking at their rum flasks, roared out suddenly that the devil was diggin' his claws in their heads, and when, to crown all this, two gigantic animals, with outstretched wings, were distinctly seen on the respective localities pointed out, they yelled with dismay.

"Take 'em away! knock 'em down! kill 'em!" roared the terrified superiors.

But the idea of killing the devil was too serious an undertaking to be entertained for an instant.

No one stirred, but everyone shrieked.

If the ghosts in the mansion had been at all nervous, they must have had a fine time of it.

But the horror of the two officers, whom the fiend had honoured with such marked attention, became too great for endurance, and accordingly, human nature having been wound up to its highest possible pitch, the terrified beings pitched into their demoniac assailants, and by a sweep of their hands sent them fluttering and hissing into the very midst of their compeers.

The confusion was tremendous; every one gave himself up for lost.

Everyone struck at everyone else.

As for the poor demons, they came in for their share of mauling, and would probably have been entirely limbed in the scuffle, had not one of the number, who happened to be a countryman, discovered their real characters.

"Why, theer two owls!" he cried.

"Owls!" echoed everybody. "Why the deuce didn't yer say so before?"

"Becas I didn't know it mysen!" answered the countryman, as he seized the frightened birds, who made a strong demonstration, and bundled them neck and crop out of the window after the raven.

They now began to laugh at their former terrors, and began to solicit Nicholas for another ghost story.

Peterson volunteered a song, but they were in a ghostly humour, and the song was put aside, much to the disgust of the obliging vocalist.

Nicholas Twigg, who felt equally flattered at the preference, once more cleared his throat, and commenced:

"The story as I'm a going to tell yer now——"

"Let 'un 'ave three knocks in it Measter Twigg," interrupted the countryman.

"It's got six in it this 'as," returned Nicholas.

"Well, then, about fifty-six year ago, when I were a boy," he commenced, "theer were——"

He paused suddenly, and the colour faded from his rubicund physiognomy.

An awful dread fell, too, upon the hearts of all present,

for at the very outset of the story there came a loud and sonorous knock, from whence they could not tell.

The knock was not single, but accompanied by a deep, hollow voice, that counted the strokes as they fell—

"One—two—three—four—five—six!"

"Six knocks!—the exact number promised by Nicholas in his forthcoming tale.

What did it mean?

The voice was unearthly and hollow, and seemed to come from the recesses of the ground.

The fire burnt dimly.

The light of the lantern was flickering and unsteady.

Everything, in short, seemed entirely different from what it ought to be.

No one spoke, but the eyes of all were fastened upon the ghost-story-teller, Nicholas Twigg.

A lurking suspicion that he was perhaps amusing himself at their expense flashed across them.

"You ain't tryin' to frighten us wi' your stories Mr. Twigg, are yer?" inquired one, at length.

"Me—m—e a try—trying to—to frighten yer?" gasped poor Nick. "Not I! I'm a—a—frightened myself!"

This was a death-blow to the enduring powers of his companions.

If he, the old, experienced veteran, who had grown gray in all kinds of encounters, could confess himself *frightened*, surely they, young, raw, and inexperienced, might justifiably admit a sensation of fear!

But whether they admitted it or not, there it was.

The pallid indicator lived in the faces of the whole body.

"What ever can it be?" faltered Peterson.

"Perhaps it's a—a——"

But before the speaker could express his opinion, the loud knocking and the unearthly, calculating voice again scared them.

"One—two—three—four—five—six!"

"There it is agin!" groaned Nicholas.

"I think the sooner we're out o' this place the better!" murmured Peterson to his colleague.

"So say I," returned Nicholas. "I say, boys," he whispered, "we'd better—— Why, what the dooce is the matter with 'em?" he ejaculated, as he noticed the terrified squad, prostrate on the floor, burying their faces in their hands, lest by looking up they should encounter some fearful sight that should drive them raving mad.

"'Ere's a pootty go!" he said. to Peterson. "They're reg'ler collapsed."

"Well, I tell you what," replied his old chum: "if they don't feel inclined to come, we must leave 'em behind. I'm off!"

But though these words were spoken in a decided undertone, they were distinctly heard by their terrified comrades.

As they, therefore, arose softly in order to steal away unperceived, there was a general rising of the rest.

"You're not a going to leave us in this awful place, are yer?" groaned a dozen voices.

"Not we," replied Peterson—"that is, if you'll get up and come with us like brave fellows."

"We ain't cowards," they replied: "we don't mind how many men you bring us against, but we can't fight against ghosts an' devils!"

"Certainly not!" remarked Nicholas Twigg, who, in proportion as his juniors became more timorous grew himself more confident. "We'll all stick together an' defy 'em! We'll go——"

Bang! went the door, blown to by the wind.

"Good!" cried a hollow voice. "Our victims are trapped."

This was an awful announcement.

The idea of being shut in—locked in—to be torn to pieces by howling demons—was perfectly unendurable.

A shriek of dismay rang through the chamber.

This was quieted by the sound of the mysterious voice.

"Molko!" it cried.

"Yes, master?" answered another voice.

"Who the dooce is Molko?" asked Nicholas, who, in spite of his peculiarities and his indifferent grammar, was perhaps the least frightened of the lot.

No one volunteered a reply to Nick's question. and the same voice continued:

"How many are there of these intruding fools, that come in the dark to startle us from our quiet graves?"

"Eighteen!" was the answer.

"The wery number!" groaned Nicholas.

"Summon our spectre band!" continued the voice of one who appeared to be the captain.

"They are ready, most powerful master, and eager to begin the work of destruction," was the answer.

"Oh lor!—oh dear!" exclaimed eighteen voices, in the direst dismay.

"How shall we destroy them?"

"Burn—roast—rack—rend!" returned the stern voice. "Use any means that promises sure and speedy extermination!"

At this moment there was a violent clattering against the walls of the room.

Everyone present expected at any moment to see the oak-panelling come in with a crash, and a troop of yelling goblins, with flaming swords, burst through the aperture to commence the work of destruction.

Suddenly, however, the noises ceased, and a voice was again heard in inquiry.

Every ear was strained to catch the sound.

"Who shall be the first victim?"

"*Peterson!*"

A groan burst from the lips of the doomed official.

"Who next?"

"Nicholas Twigg!"

"Oh, lor!" ejaculated that gallant member of the force.

"Any others in particular, master?"

The voice answered:

"Yes, Molko—Tomkisson!—don't forget Tomkisson!"

Tomkisson, little imagining he was such an object of interest, doubled up with terror instanter.

A yell of triumph burst from unseen lips.

A loud report of fire-arms followed.

The fiends were evidently upon them.

A bright flash of light, like an explosion of gunpowder, burst from the extreme end of the chamber, revealing a dark object with a white, ghastly face, contemplating their terror with a mocking smile of ironical malignity.

"Your doom is sealed, rash fools!" cried an awful voice, so deep that it seemed to ascend from the very feet of the spectre; "not one shall leave this place alive! Are you ready, Molko?"

"Yes, master!"

"Then charge! kill! destroy!"

Bang! crash! went something.

A shower of bullets flew amongst them.

Fortunately, in the excitement of that awful moment, the door which had slammed to was dragged open.

Out they all rolled, the whole troop of these gallant police officers.

Clinging to each other, and encumbering each other's flight, shrieking, howling, vowing all kinds of promises for the future.

In the darkness, forgetting they were at the head of a staircase, they rushed madly on—found out their mistake when too late, and pitched headlong down in dire confusion, one on the top of the other.

Noses, foreheads, elbows, knees, and every portion of their bodies, that could be assailed, came into contact with something antagonistic, whether the sharp edge of the stone steps, or the strong carved oak pilasters, or the heels of heavy boots.

At length, however, having no further to fall, they discovered they had reached the bottom.

Then there was a frantic rush for their horses, and then a still more desperate rush for the door, which nobody could find.

Till, at length, a few of the number accidentally wandered to the postern, and the news having spread that the way of escape was discovered, the entire body, covered with bruises and contusions, hurried out.

Two-thirds of this distracted troop plunged, without knowing where they were going, into the stream, and when at last they managed to gain the high-road, such a set of mounted scarecrows could scarcely be imagined, much less described.

Nicholas Twigg, with his nose swelled to the size of a handsome potato, and his lip protruding to an uncomfortable extent, shook his fist in the direction of the Haunted Mansion.

"Cuss yer!" he cried, vehemently—"cuss yer! an' if ever I ventures on 'aunted ground agin as long as I live, I 'opes as I may be pounded to death by ghoste's marrow-bones!"

With a confirmatory growl, the officers proceeded on their journey, and in a short time had left the ghostly territory far behind them.

Once more its lonely walls were left to their usual dreary silence.

CHAPTER CCXXIII.

THE HIGHWAYMEN RECONNOITRE THE OLD MANSION BY DAYLIGHT, BUT DISCOVER NOTHING.—UNEXPECTED MESSAGE FROM TOWN.—DEPARTURE OF LORD HARCLIFFE.—THE BEREAVED PARENT.—THE BETRAYER AND HIS VICTIM.

No sooner was the coast clear than Captain Hawk and Lord Harcliffe—who had at first entered upon the plan of scaring away their enemies from motives of security, but who, finding their efforts so pleasantly anticipated by the superstitious terrors of the officers, had subsequently enjoyed the whole affair as an excellent joke—came from their retreat, laughing heartily.

Understanding as well as they did the dire confusion that pervaded their ranks, and knowing from previous experience what the result of that disorder would be, they could triumph in the discomfiture of their foes to their hearts' content.

"They will never venture here again!" cried the captain, exultingly—"never—never!"

The gray light of morning was beginning to steal over the east; but owing to the leaden, stormy sky, the approaching dawn was not so apparent as it was wont to be.

Our heroes, therefore, being weary, and having enjoyed but a troubled and brief slumber, resolved to rest for an hour or two, despite the combined efforts of all the ghosts and gray figures on the establishment.

They accordingly barricaded each door with a chair, so that anyone entering would make sufficient noise to alarm them, and stretching themselves on the floor, wrapped in their cloaks, slept soundly.

When they awoke, to their surprise the sun was shining brightly.

It was astonishing what a difference the dark old panelling wore in the cheerful light of the god of day.

The chamber looked comparatively lively and cheerful.

The small cell adjoining was still silent and deserted.

It was evident no one had entered since the departure by that way of the masked villain, Ridley Massingham.

As Captain Hawk reviewed the events of the past night, his heart bounded as he confidently anticipated discovering the prison-house of his beloved Blanche, and setting her free from her thraldom.

The very presence of her designing guardian seemed to be a sufficient security that she was not far distant.

"Now," cried the captain, "we will first breakfast, and after that commence our observations from the exterior."

The remains of their supper afforded them a most substantial breakfast, and that being finished, they descended, and went out by the postern gate.

The dew and the drenching of the previous night's rain, still left the long grass soaked with moisture; the birds, under the influence of the bright sun, warbled their songs to Heaven.

But still the Gray Mansion looked hopelessly gloomy and accursed.

The highwaymen examined every yard of the walls, throughout their extent, but without discovering any wing that they did not appear to have visited.

"It is very strange," said Captain Hawk, "but it appears to me that we have entered every apartment this old mansion contains."

"Above ground, probably we have," returned his comrade, "but there may be a world below, in its subterranean recesses, that would throw a light—out of its very gloom—upon those secrets we long to discover."

"Yes, yes," replied the captain, eagerly, "you are right, my friend: it is from below we must look for what we seek."

At this juncture the sound of a horse's feet attracted their attention.

It was evidently approaching.

But not anticipating any danger, they did not put on any appearance of hostility, but simply remained perfectly still listening to the sound of the footsteps they had heard, and watching the spot from whence they expected the new-comer would make his appearance.

Nor were they long kept in suspense; for ere a moment had elapsed, to their great astonishment, the well-known figure of Charles, mounted on horseback, allayed every apprehension.

"Good mornin', gentlemen!" he cried. "Glad to see you safe an' well!"

"Why, Charles," exclaimed the captain, as soon as his surprise would permit him to reply, "you surely are not seeking us?"

"I assure yer, captain, I ain't seeking anyone else," he answered.

"But how did you contrive to discover our retreat?"

"Simply by inquiring," Charles replied.

"You have not been putting questions at random?" eagerly demanded Captain Hawk.

"Not I," replied Charles. "I was very cautious in what I said."

"And what brings you here, my friend? May I know?"

"Certainly, captain. I bring a letter for his lordship there."

"For me?" exclaimed Lord Harcliffe.

"Yes: here it is!"

As he spoke, Charles held forth the epistle.

"From Pharoah!" ejaculated his lordship. "He is always faithful and vigilant. Let us see what he says."

Lord Harcliffe broke the seal hastily, and ran his eye over the contents of the letter.

As he did so, a shade of disappointment crossed his features.

"I can read its purport in your face, my friend," said Captain Hawk. "You are summoned to town!"

"Confound the summons!" exclaimed the Black Highwayman; "just at this moment, too, when my presence was so necessary! I've half a mind to——"

"Nay, my friend, do not act rashly!" counselled the captain, "your interview with the prince—I presume it is the prince who summons you?"

"Yes."

"Well, this interview may secure us more advantages than your remaining here could possibly do; and though you know, Harcliffe," the captain continued, extending his hand, which his companion grasped, "I shall miss you, still I think under all circumstances it will be wiser to yield obedience to the summons than to neglect it."

"You are right," returned his lordship—"I will go. Still it is most annoying, after commencing the hunt, not to be in at the death."

"It must be looked upon as part of the fatality that accompanies every human enterprise," said Captain Hawk.

"But you will want a companion in your undertaking?"

"Here is Charles."

Charles pricked up his ears at the mention of his name, and advanced, thinking himself called.

"Here I am, captain, ready an' willin'," he said.

"I know that," answered Captain Hawk, "but you, my friend," he added, addressing himself to Lord Harcliffe—"you will then have to return to town alone."

"I have no fear of being able to accomplish that," replied the Black Highwayman; "and since we must part, the sooner I am gone the better."

"Say rather the sooner you return the better, my dear friend; it is a pleasanter subject for contemplation," said the captain; "but at any rate, we will see you fairly on your road; we can then bid each other farewell, and hasten on our different enterprises—you in the abodes of wealth and luxury, mine among the dark vaults of the Gray Mansion."

"Heaven prosper your efforts!" cried Lord Harcliffe, earnestly.

"And yours, my dearest friend!"

With these words our heroes re-entered the silent domicile for their steeds.

Satan and Phantom were speedily led forth, and the Highwaymen mounting, the trio disappeared down the descent, and were soon once more on the high-road.

After a quick ride of five miles they came upon an old man, who, seated by the roadside, with his face buried in his hands, appeared to be a prey to some intense grief.

So engrossed was he by his sorrow that he did not even notice the approach of the party.

But there was something in the appearance of the old man that involuntarily compelled them to pause upon their journey.

He appeared to be a respectable farmer, verging towards the end of his earthly sojourn, and numbering nearly three score and ten years.

Having checked their steeds, the sound caused the old man to look up.

As he did so, pushing back the long white locks from his face, it struck our heroes that in his youth he must have been a remarkably handsome man.

Now, however, his face was pale and deeply indented with many a furrow, and from his swollen, heavy eyelids, our heroes could see plainly that he had been weeping.

"You seem in trouble, my friend," said Captain Hawk.

"I am indeed, sir!" returned the old man; "trouble which I would rather have died than encountered."

"Of what nature is this trouble?" inquired Lord Harcliffe, kindly.

"It is of a nature that I cannot reveal without disgracing myself. My sorrow is a sorrow of the heart, since it appertains to my only child."

"Have you lost her?" asked the captain, gently.

"Alas, yes!" replied the aged parent.

"Dead, I presume?" said Lord Harcliffe, hazarding the remark.

"No, not dead—only to me," replied the old man. "She has brought disgrace upon a hitherto unblemished name!" he continued, wringing his hands.

"Has she left her home?" he inquired.

"She has," groaned the bereaved father, in a voice of anguish. "My curses—the malediction of a broken-hearted parent cling to him who has seduced, beguiled my child of her good name, and covered her parent's head with infamy!"

"Know you not whither she has fled?" inquired Captain Hawk.

"Alas, no! I never even suspected the wrong that was inflicted on her. Oh, Lucy, Lucy!—how could you desert me thus?"

As the old man uttered these words the tears fell fast down his furrowed cheeks.

"And you have only, then, just learnt this fatal intelligence?" said Lord Harcliffe.

"Not an hour since. My child has been absent now a month. I thought her lost—dead—hearing no tidings of her—till last night this letter came, that explained the fatal truth."

As he spoke, the old man drew a letter from his breast, and, opening it, presented it to Captain Hawk, who read in a neat, delicate, female hand, as follows:—

"*My dearest Father,*—

"*Do not, I beseech you, imagine that, because I have left the best of homes and the kindest of parents, I have ever forgotten you.* I never have, nor can I ever become insensible or forgetful of the long years of kindness you have shown me. Oh no! Forgive, then, your poor Lucy, that her love got the better of her prudence. The gentleman who induced me to quit my father's roof loves me—he tells me so, and offers me to share that love. Could I refuse? But in my altered position I shall not forget my dear parent. It will be my pride and greatest happiness to add to your comforts and to support your declining strength Only let me hear from you that you forgive me!"

"And does she think," cried the incensed old man, 'that I would ever accept the fruits of her dishonour? No! I could have forgiven aught but that but that never—never!"

"Well, my good friend, we must be moving forward. Farewell!—and pray Heaven your poor child may be yet restored to you!"

"I pray Heaven she may, and so restored that I may not blush to look upon her! Were her mother living, it would break her heart, as it has broken mine!"

"Take comfort, friend—and farewell!"

Having uttered this parting salutation, the highwaymen and Charles urged on their steeds, and were in a few moments out of sight.

After journeying a few miles further they came to a halt.

"I will take you no further, Dick," said Lord Harcliffe to his friend. "You have your work to perform, and I should be selfish to retain you. Let us not make a long leave-taking. Farewell, and prosper!"

"Farewell, my dear friend, till we meet again!"

A cordial pressure of their hands, and a kind smile in each other's faces, and the comrades separated—Lord Harcliffe going towards London, Captain Hawk retracing his steps with Charles to the Gray Mansion.

The latter was all excitement and exhilaration, and seemed confident of a successful issue to all their undertakings.

"We may have more difficulty, Charles, than you imagine," said the captain. "But whatever the difficulty—however great the peril—I am determined nothing shall deter, nothing shall daunt me till I unkennel those villains, and bring their infamous deeds to light!"

It was wonderful how the bright sun and fresh morning air dispelled the gloomy impressions of the previous night.

Then all seemed stormy, ghostly, and unnatural—now everything seemed to be restored to its proper equilibrium.

After galloping a short time along the road, Charles said:

"I think, capting, a gallop on the grass 'll do my 'orse's 'oofs good, if yer don't mind me leaving the highway."

"Mind it? Not I!" answered the captain. "I'll join you; I prefer the greensward to the hard road at any time."

As the captain uttered these words, he leaped his horse over the hedge, and the morning being so delightfully cool and pleasant, they directed their course across the country, and many a bright view of hill and dale they had during that exhilarating ride.

On every side the dewdrops sparkled like diamonds, and the sweet-scented honeysuckle and woodbine ever and anon wafted their fragrance in the faces of the horsemen.

At length, after an hour's ride, they pulled up in one of those delightful nooks that seem as if made expressly for a tired and hard-worked town-dweller to rest in, and look forth in ecstasy upon the beauties of Nature, clad in her robes of summer green.

Their ride had inspired both with a good appetite—another of the blessings attendant upon fresh air and exercise.

"By Jupiter!" said Captain Hawk, "it is only breakfast time, and I feel ready for dinner!"

"All right, capting!" murmured Charles, with a smile, as he dismounted, and from a bag at his saddle drew forth a delicious pigeon pie and a bottle of the Prince of Wales's claret.

Captain Hawk's eye sparkled at this welcome sight.

"Charles," he cried, "you're the prince of caterers!"

"I thought as yer'd be hungry in course o' time, capting, so when Mr. Pharoah asked me if I could carry anythin', o' course I said 'decidedly yes!'"

"You were decidedly right!" returned the captain, as he descended from his saddle and gave Satan his liberty for a short time.

Seated on the grass, master and man ate and drank together on terms of perfect equality.

"Charles," said the captain, raising his glass, "your health! Those who serve me faithfully—those whom I can trust—are the men I value and call my friends—you are one of these!"

Charles, overpowered by the compliment, was about to reply, when the sound of voices reached them from a short distance.

There seemed nothing to apprehend; therefore the captain continued his repast, and, having finished, lighted a cigar, and began to smoke.

The voices had approached, and now the tones of a woman were distinctly audible.

There was something in the sounds that had an irresistible attraction for Captain Hawk.

[CAPTAIN HAWK RESCUES THE MILLER'S DAUGHTER FROM THE RIVER.]

He rose from the grass on which he had been reclining, and, approaching the hedge, looked cautiously over it.

He had hardly done so when the speakers approached.

There were a young man—evidently of a superior rank to his companion—and a girl some years younger.

The former was attired in a *negligee* kind of shooting-jacket, and from his careless and unconcerned demeanour, as he walked with his hands in his pockets, was evidently entirely unimpressed by the emotion of his companion.

He was handsome, but the expression of his features was sensual, and this gave a coarseness and unprepossessing effect to his face that all its regularity of outline could not counterbalance.

The girl was beautiful, and, with her bright golden locks and blue eyes, formed one of those pictures of rustic perfection occasionally seen in the rural districts of our kingdom.

"Oh, Edgar!" she exclaimed, earnestly, "after all that has passed between us, you cannot surely—you will not cast me off?"

"What can I do?" he replied, petulantly—"how can I help myself? I have explained to you the precise position in which I am placed. My father has set his heart upon my marrying the Lady Clementina; and, even had he not, how could I wed one in your position? You must consider that."

"I did consider it—I have always considered it! Did I not mention this when you first told me you loved me?" she exclaimed, in an anguished voice. "But I am punished! I was foolish—I was mad to listen to the voice of the tempter—and now I am bitterly punished!"

There was a pause, broken only by the sobs of the poor girl

These outpourings of grief, instead of softening, appeared to irritate her companion.

"What nonsense this is!" he cried. "Of what avail is it for you to sob and cry over what is past, and about that which is inevitable? Does it necessarily follow that, because I marry another to please my father, I should not still love you to please myself?"

This atrocious piece of morality appeared particularly offensive to the young girl, for she flung aside the arm outstretched to encircle her indignantly.

"And do you suppose—humble, worthless as you appear to think me—that I would consent to *share* your love—that I would accept of half a heart?" she cried.

"Half is better than none," was the cool reply.

"It would not satisfy me," said the young girl, in a proud tone. "When I yielded my heart to you, Lord Edgar, I kept none back, I gave it *all*—gave it because I believed your vows, because I thought you sincere. Ah, little did I deem how utterly false they were—little did I dream that perjury lingered beneath the honey of your tongue!"

"Psha!—you talk as though I had committed some atrocious crime."

"And have you not? Is it no crime to deceive the one who trusts you—to break the heart that would have made any sacrifice for you?"

"Nonsense! You will find me just as loving as ever!"

"I do not find you so; I find your love—or rather what you called by that name—grows cooler every hour; your toy has ceased to please you, Edgar—you are tired of me!"

"Well, if I am, these reproaches are not calculated to remove that sensation."

"I cannot help it! Indeed—indeed I cannot!" she cried, despairingly. "I would not say anything to grieve you, but if you knew how dearly I have loved you, or how much my happiness is bound up in you, you could not treat me as you do."

"Well, well, I know your partiality for me, but I really did not imagine your prepossession in my favour was so very great; however, as it is, we must make the best we can of it. I will allow you sufficient to keep you——"

Again the flush of outraged affection crimsoned the features of the young girl, and with heaving bosom she exclaimed, excitedly:

"I do not want your money! I am not a courtesan to be bought at a price, and no sum you can offer me will ever restore my peace of mind, or heal my wounded honour. Your offer of money is an insult—speak of it no more!"

"Umph!" exclaimed the young nobleman, irritably, "there's no satisfying you. What the deuce *do* you want?"

"Nothing now!" she cried, sadly. "I coveted your love as a miser covets his treasure, but since I am deprived of that, I care for nothing else."

"Then for Heaven's sake let us shake hands upon that bargain!" said the unfeeling man. "It will be better for both of us in the end."

"In the end!" cried the young girl, in a tortured voice. "Ay! it will, perhaps. You shall have your will; you shall no more be troubled with my presence; my death will secure that to you, and it will release me from an insupportable burden. Lord Edgar, farewell for ever!"

And with these words, uttered with wild excitement, she darted away from the spot.

The young man stood looking after her irresolutely for a moment.

"Does she contemplate self-destruction?" he soliloquised. "Psha! no. Women are not such fools! They often promise, but rarely perform. But even should she keep her word, it will relieve me of a clog that is becoming an intolerable nuisance."

And with these words, without troubling himself further about the matter, the heartless betrayer of the poor girl turned on his heel and departed.

"Unfeeling miscreant!" muttered Captain Hawk, "I should like to have horsewhipped him. But I am anxious about that poor girl. She rushed from the spot in an excited manner, and who knows to what extent her despair may drive her?"

At this moment a scream and a splash foretold the fatal truth that she had kept her word and sought refuge from her misery in the depths of the river.

"Follow me, Charles," cried the Captain, as he galloped forward to the river's bank.

"Ah! see!" he cried, as the form of the young girl appeared struggling in the waters.

Without a moment's hesitation, he slipped from his saddle, threw off his coat, and plunged into the river.

The current was running strongly.

He struck out boldly, and succeeded in grasping her as she was on the verge of sinking for the last time.

No sooner did she feel the outstretched arm, than the poor girl clung to it with a tenacity which those who have ever attempted to rescue a fellow-creature under such circumstances, will well understand.

So tightly did she cling, that the captain, who was encumbered with his heavy riding-boots, had the utmost difficulty in keeping himself and his charge above water.

He began to feel symptoms of terrible exhaustion, and it was only by the most superhuman exertions he kept afloat.

To add to his peril, he was being rapidly borne along in the strong current of a mill-stream, which roared and foamed as it turned two large wheels, one of which was behind and the other in front of the mill.

The force of the current was an advantage, inasmuch as it assisted him in his progress; but he dreaded lest he should not have sufficient power to clear the formidable piece of mechanism, whose revolutions seemed waiting ready to crush him.

He struck out at an angle, and by dint of the most strenuous efforts succeeded fortunately in clearing the first wheel, that would have sucked him under to certain destruction; and, clinging to the woodwork of the mill, he gradually guided himself round to the other side, where, the gyrations of the second wheel being upwards, he grasped one of the crossbars, and was thus borne by the revolution out of the water to the wooden platform above, where Charles, who had seen the captain's peril, was anxiously waiting to drag him with a strong arm from his perilous position with his senseless burden.

Hardly had they been safely deposited upon this wooden bridge when the miller made his appearance, and Captain Hawk, having recovered his breath, explained the circumstance.

To his great surprise, he recognised the features of the old man whom he had not long before discovered in the road bemoaning his daughter's fate.

As the miller glanced at the senseless body of the young girl, he saw his countenance change, and as, with trembling, agitated hands, the old man raised her head and parted asunder the drenched locks that covered it, a cry of anguish broke from his lips.

"Lucy, my child—my poor child!"

It was indeed her own home to which the tide had borne her, and the fond father clasped his child to his heart, and thanked Heaven fervently that had preserved her from the guilt of self-destruction.

CHAPTER CCXXIV.

LORD HARCLIFFE HAS AN INTERVIEW WITH THE PRINCE OF WALES, WHO CLAIMS THE FULFILMENT OF A PROMISE.—AN INFAMOUS PROPOSAL INDIGNANTLY REJECTED. —AN ATTACK, AND A LEAP FOR LIFE.

WHEN Lord Harcliffe reached town, he went at once to the "Prince's Retreat," where he found Pharoah anxiously awaiting his arrival.

The interview had been fixed for the evening, and at the appointed time the Black Highwayman, dressed with the most scupulous accuracy in a suit of costly black velvet, with a cravet and ruffles of the finest lace, proceeded to Leicester House, and was at once ushered into the presence of the Prince of Wales.

A beholder would have been struck with the difference between the bloated sensual appearence of the prince and the dignified carriage and spiritually pale features of his lordship, heightened by the sable dress he wore

Pharoah having introduced the visitor, retired.

"Be seated," said the prince, condescendingly pointing to a chair, "and before we commence our conference, we will drink together."

"Your Royal Highness will pardon me, but I always

prefer transacting all business matters with a clear head."

"As you please," returned the prince, as he poured out a glass of port and drank it off.

There was a slight pause after this, during which the prince looked at the Black Highwayman scutinisingly from under his brows.

He then commenced:

"You will, of course, remember that in return for a service I once rendered you, you pledged yourself to render me an equivalent, should I ever call upon you to do so."

"Always providing the deed you wished me to accomplish was one which a gentleman might perform without forfeiting his honour."

"The message brought to me was simply that you would be at my service when I chose to command you—the word *honour* was not mentioned."

"Then your messenger delivered my message incorrectly."

"You are very punctilious——"

"I am, your Highness."

"I was about to add—for a highwayman!"

"Highwaymen have their *own* ideas about *honour; princes* have *theirs.* It is possible they may clash," returned Lord Harcliffe, satirically.

"I imagine not," said the prince, with a peculiarly sinister smile. "Whatever your *ideas* of *honour* may be, I presume you will not object to earn rank and fortune without the slightest peril to yourself?"

"It depends entirely on what I have to part with in exchange."

"You will have to part with nothing; but, on the contrary, have everything to gain. I wish you would drink!"

"I am not thirsty, your Highness!"

"*Peste!*" exclaimed the prince, impatiently—"how confoundedly temperate you are!" It was more than he could say for himself, for he poured out another glass of wine and emptied it as before. "And now listen to me, and be prepared to welcome fortune, that does not always come so directly in the way of men as it does in yours."

"I listen, your Highness."

"You are of course aware, that on the death of the present King, I shall ascend the throne of England?"

"Unless your Royal Highness happens to *die first,*" interposed Lord Harcliffe, little imagining his words were prophetic of the prince's fate.

"Well, then, *if* I live I shall be king."

"Yes."

"Reigning monarchs," continued the prince, in a deliberate tone, "seem to live on for ever."

"Not for ever, your highness: look back to the line of departed kings."

"I do not wish to look back—my desire is to look forward. Were you in my position, waiting for a crown—that you could not wear until the death of the reigning monarch"—here the prince sank his voice almost to a whisper—"you would wish him dead even were that monarch *your own father!*"

Lord Harcliffe started back in his seat: there was something so diabolical in the idea that for a moment he could only gaze upon the proposer's features.

But they were calm and impassible.

After a few seconds his lordship replied:

"I am not the heir apparent to a throne, but even were I so, I hope I should never give utterance to such a wish."

"It seems to shock you."

"Not only seems—it does shock me!"

"It did me at first, but by constantly accustoming myself to think of it, it has ceased to affect me," said the prince, coolly. "You will, by familiarity with the idea, become as callous to it as I am myself."

"Never!"

"What, then, do you mean to affirm that you will forego all the brilliant prospects that the friendship of the King of England could open to your acceptance?"

"Certainly if they are to be purchased by the crime of——"

"Hush!" interrupted the prince, in a voice scarcely louder than a whisper. "Content yourself with thinking the crime, not speaking it."

"In plain English, then," said Lord Harcliffe, whose rising indignation at the cool manner in which his tempter uttered his fiendish remarks, imparted a settled sternness to his voice, "what is it your Highness wishes me to perform?"

"I wish to be King of England," whispered the prince, "and not to wait until the course of nature opens the way!"

"Well, your Highness?"

"Well, as that step can never be taken—since the crown can never encircle my brow while my father lives," continued the unnatural son, in the same awful cold-blooded whisper, "I wish him dead! Now do you comprehend me perfectly?"

"Not quite. Am I to understand that you wish me to be the instrument to compass his majesty's death."

"Yes!"

Lord Harcliffe drew himself up in his chair, and fixed his clear piercing eyes full upon his questioner.

Had the Prince of Wales been skilful in translating looks, he might have read in the expression of the Black Highwayman's indignant features the utter failure of his murderous negotiation.

But having his end to gain, he was wilfully blind, and continued:

"If what I have heard be true, you are acquainted with some secret means of access into the palace at Kew?"

This was partly put as an assertion, partly as a question, but Lord Harcliffe did not reply to it.

"It would be an easy task," the prince went on, "to enter at the dead of night and perform the deed that would leave the throne open to me."

"Go on!" said his lordship, with peculiar calmness.

"You can choose your own weapons; though if you would be advised by me, poison would be the safest agent and the best."

"It is well your Highness is the King's son, or, by Heaven! if anyone but yourself had made me such a proposition, I think I should have struck him dead before the words had escaped his lips."

"And I may reply to that, had you been any other than the Black Highwayman, the proposal would never have been made to you."

"You think me then so utterly, so irredeemably bad?"

"I look upon you as a man upon whose head a price is set—a man fond of life, and the luxuries that alone make it valuable, and not so scrupulous as to prefer the hangman's rope at Tyburn to the commission of the simple act I solicit."

"I would rather endure fifty hangmen's ropes than escape one by an act of regicide!" returned Lord Harcliffe, boldly.

"Remember, I could and would advance you to the highest post in the kingdom."

"I do not believe your promise! Once let me criminate myself as you would have me, I should be your slave; but that would not be all; you would naturally, after such a deed, despise me; but, whether or not, I should execrate myself, and therefore I refuse to execute your bloodthirsty commission!"

"Positively?"

"Most absolutely!"

"Then your life is not worth the value of a straw. I shall hand you over to the officers of justice!"

"I do not doubt it. Where was there ever an assassin who was not a traitor?"

The prince rang a small hand-bell that was on the table.

Pharoah entered on the instant.

"Introduce the parties who are waiting," said the prince.

Pharoah disappeared, casting as he retired a significant look at his former master.

The look seemed to say:

"Do not be alarmed."

The next moment there was a shuffling of feet heard without, and the portly forms of Peterson and Nicholas Twigg appeared in the doorway.

They entered in a most servile and humble manner, and so impressed were they by the exalted presence in which they found themselves that they entirely overlooked the important personage who was seated in such close proximity.

They were recalled to themselves by the voice of the prince.

"You know that man?" he said, pointing to the Black

Highwayman, who, in order to afford them every facility for a close investigation, turned suddenly in his chair and looked them full in the face.

The effect this act produced on the two officials was wonderful.

Had the ghosts of their ancestors—going back to the fourth generation—started up before them, it could not have rendered these worthies more utterly aghast.

Their mouths opened spasmodically, and their eyes glared as though some mischievous imp were agitating the optic nerve with all his might, whilst the rubicund tints implanted in their faces by the potent draughts of many years, faded away into an almost ashy pallor.

The prince observed their agitation, and rather enjoyed it; but he repeated the question:

"You know these men?"

"Y-es, yer—yer Roil 'Ighniss," they gasped, "we—a—knows 'im."

"Be ready, then," curtly remarked the prince; "you may be wanted presently. Pharoah!"

A movement of the head to his domestic, and the officers were abruptly backed out of the room.

"You see," said his Highness, "I have only to give the order, and you will be arrested as a felon."

The Black Highwayman smiled—a bold, sarcastic smile that annoyed the prince, who replied:

"I can interpret that smile. You imagine probably you have the power to criminate me; if so, dismiss the absurd idea at once. I am beyond the reach of the tongue of a condemned criminal."

His lordship smiled again; but the prince continued:

"Once for all, what is your determination? Will you undertake the task I offer you?"

"No!"

"Your refusal will cost you your life!"

"So be it! I refuse! Not to save a thousand lives would I be the instrument to perpetrate this diabolical—this unnnatural crime! I tell you so to your face, murderer!"

The prince, foaming with rage, started from his seat, and shouted in a voice hoarse with passion:

"Without there!"

Lord Harcliffe, who fully expected the return of the officers, was much surprised to see enter from an opposite door four gentlemen, whom he at once recognised.

"Ha!" he cried, loudly, as they entered. "I know you all: you, Marquis of Rockleigh; you, Sir Hubert Mansfield, and Sir Slingsby Sleuforth; and you, Ashley Fordyce! A fitting escort for such a master!"

The four gentlemen thus accosted, glared suspiciously at the bold speaker, who continued:

"I despise you all: you, Frederick Prince of Wales, and your gang of myrmidons!"

"What means the fellow?" they shouted.

"Where is Antonio Riccioli?" cried the Black Highwayman—"cowards, where is he? There is not one of your number whose conscience does not tell him at this moment he has innocent blood upon his head!"

"Cut him down!" was the universal cry, as four swords leapt from their scabbards.

The Black Highwayman's trusty blade flashed before their eyes as they rushed forward madly to the attack.

But they knew not the accomplished swordsman they had to encounter. In an instant two of the weapons were sent spinning through the air, and beating down the swords of the remaining couple and inflicting by a sweeping blow a severe gash across their foreheads, Lord Harcliffe, seeing that the conflict was too unequal to be prolonged, made a desperate plunge *a la* harlequin through the window, and amidst the crash of glass and the execrations of the baffled crew, alighted safely on the soft mould of a flower-bed in the garden.

Pausing only to recover his feet, he ran forwards till his progress was stopped by a wall.

He sprang up, and reached the top with the agility of a cat.

Not a moment too soon, for, as he dropped into the next garden, the report of several pistols was heard, the bullets of which struck against the top of the wall he had just surmounted.

Without waiting to hear whether he was pursued or not, he continued his course, and it was not till he had scaled six walls and crossed as many gardens he paused to take breath.

All then was silent.

At the end of the enclosure in which he then stood was a chamber leading by wide stone steps to the exterior, in which a dim light burned.

The sound of voices fell upon his ear from within the apartment.

He advanced cautiously, and, holding his breath, he noiselessly ascended the steps to the window.

This was masked by heavy curtains, but, gently pushing a small portion of the drapery aside, he was enabled to see distinctly into the interior.

CHAPTER CCXXV.

LORD HARCLIFFE OVERHEARS AN INTERESTING CONVERSATION IN A LADY'S BED-CHAMBER.—HE PUTS IN AN APPEARANCE AT THE RIGHT MOMENT.—A MUTUAL CASE OF LOVE AT FIRST SIGHT.—THE OLD MAN'S BRIDE.—THE ESCAPE.

In the room were seated three persons.

One an old man of foreign aspect, and the other a shrewd, sharp-featured individual in spectacles, who was unmistakably a lawyer.

But it was upon the third of the party the eyes of Lord Harcliffe particularly rested.

Never in his life had he gazed on anything so transcendently lovely.

The expression of her features was troubled and stormy, but it only seemed to impart a fresh character to her beauty, not to destroy it.

Her dark, lustrous eyes were tearful, but the drops that swam there added to their brightness.

Her raven tresses fell back in evident disorder over her marble shoulders, which peeped forth from beneath the *negligee* robe she wore; and on glancing for a moment on the surrounding furniture, his lordship perceived that it was a bed-chamber in which this group was congregated.

The eyes of the young girl were fastened upon her guardian, the Signor Brambillo, who sat next to her, as though she would have entreated mercy or release from some terrible sacrifice.

It seemed to require not a human heart, but a heart of stone, to resist that earnest look of supplication.

"Oh, signor!" she cried, "do not, I entreat you, condemn me to this detested union!"

"It is necessary," replied the signor—"positively necessary, Beatrice; and, as your guardian, I feel it my duty to direct your choice."

"Not in this way, or to this extent!" she exclaimed. "It cannot be your duty to urge me to a step at which my heart revolts!"

"Your father, who was my friend, counselled me with his dying breath to watch over you——"

"Yes, to *watch over*, not to drive me to despair! Oh, signor!" she continued, earnestly, "by the memory of that dead parent, do not condemn his child to misery!"

"I act for your best interests," returned the old man. "The Marquis of Gavestone is an English nobleman, rich, titled——"

"With one foot in the grave! Is he a fitting match for me, who have scarcely seen nineteen summers? Is my happiness of no account? Is the will of Count Riccioli's daughter to be thus coerced?"

"It is quite fitting, my child, when you are so wilfully blind to your own interests, that some compulsion should be placed upon your will. The day will come when you will thank me for the firmness I display in thus——"

"I will not consent," interposed the young beauty, forcibly. "It is an outrage against all propriety; an old imbecile——"

"If I might suggest," snuffled Mr. Grill, the sharp-featured lawyer, "the wealth of the marquis will more than atone for his age."

"I do not require wealth," retorted Beatrice, with a look of disgust and contempt. "I have sufficient of my own. Am I not rich?"

"Ah!" ejaculated her guardian, with an ominous sigh.

"Am I not?" she repeated, in reply to this deep aspiration. "The wealth left by my father to me and my brother Antonio——"

"Antonio!" echoed the old man. "Alas! you have now touched upon the very key that produces all this discord. "Antonio Riccioli's desperate love of gambling has entirely dissipated the large fortune left by your father."

This was a falsehood, but the mendacious guardian made the assertion boldly, whilst the unseen listener was struck with astonishment at the words he heard.

"How!" exclaimed Beatrice. "Is our fortune all gone—all?"

"Every sixpence."

"I can't believe it—I'll not believe it!" replied Beatrice, excitedly. "Where is my brother? He will never say this—he could not!"

"You are right, Beatrice," sighed the signor, in a melancholy tone: "he never will—it is beyond his power."

"What mean your words?" she asked, in a tone of alarm.

"Your brother's tongue is for ever silent—he is no more!"

The eyes of the poor girl dilated, and her features assumed an appearance of almost stony rigidity, as she gazed upon her torturer.

"Do you mean to tell me," she asked, in a voice full of anguish, "that my brother is dead?"

The signor bowed his head sorrowfully.

"Your brother Antonio, driven to desperation by his losses, attacked his companions at the gaming-table, and, after slaying one in his mad fury, consummated that deed by self-destruction."

At this fearful announcement Beatrice uttered a loud shriek of consternation.

"My brother Antonio dead!" she cried. "My poor brother—my only friend—my dear companion! Oh, take me to him!" she continued, wildly, starting from her seat. "Let me gaze once more upon his beloved features, now cold in death!"

"Alas!" returned the signor. "It is impossible: he is buried."

"And I to know nothing of this!" wailed the afflicted girl. "My brother—my poor brother!"

Her grief had now reached its height, and a torrent of tears came happily to her relief.

"You now see the reason," continued her guardian, after a pause, "why I act as I do. If you do not marry the Marquis of Gavestone you will be a beggar."

"So let me be! I would rather beg my bread from door to door than be his wife!"

But this arrangement would by no means have suited the mercenary Signor Brambillo, since he had been promised a large sum on the dav the marriage should be consummated.

"Consider," he went on, "the wealth, luxury, position such an alliance would secure you!"

"I only consider the wretchedness — the misery!" groaned the unhappy girl. "My whole soul revolts at this unnatural union."

"You are young, foolish, romantic: you know not what it is to be poor."

"There is a poverty harder to bear than any mere external privations," sobbed Beatrice—"the poverty of the heart."

But Signor Brambillo was in no way affected by the evident grief of his ward. He was obdurate—hard as granite.

"There are times," he said, "when it is necessary to enforce obedience. I act for you as though you were my own child. Against your will I compel you for your own good. I say you must accept the marquis, my word is pledged, therefore prepare to yield obedience!"

The old man rose as he uttered these words and so did Mr. Grill the lawyer.

"When is this sacrifice to be consummated?" she inquired, in a voice unnaturally calm.

"This night!" answered her guardian. "I expect the marquis here shortly with his chaplain. Wishing to spare your feelings in every possible way, the marriage will be strictly private, and can be performed in this room."

"Ee, ee!" sniggered Mr. Grill to himself. "Chapel, altar, and nuptial chamber all in one: beautiful!"

Signor Brambillo turned as he reached the door:

"You will make up your mind to recieve your future husband with a smile, and to yield obedience to that which *must be!*" he said; and with these words he quitted the chamber, locking the door behind him.

To-night—to-night!" murmured the fair girl, after a pause of painful reflection. "No—no! I'd rather die than endure anything so horrible!"

She rose from her seat and paced the room with hurried steps, clasping her white hands, and grasping in her despair the clustering raven tresses that fell in wild disorder down her back.

Lord Harcliffe was strangely impressed.

Apart from the desire he felt to rescue this beautiful creature from the fate that threatened her, there had sprung up in his breast from the first moment he beheld her a sentiment that he felt would endure for ever.

It was one of those instances of "love at first sight" by no means uncommon with ardent and impressible natures.

Then again, the name—Beatrice *Riccioli!*

Surely she must be the sister of Antonio Riccioli—of the young Italian he and his comrade had been instrumental in rescuing from a violent death in the Red Chamber.

This supposition a family likeness seemed to confirm.

"It must be the same," he soliloquised: "how can I venture to address without alarming her, or come suddenly upon her in the privacy of her bed-chamber without causing her to suspect the purity of my intentions?"

His meditations were abruptly terminated by the young girl stopping suddenly in her excited march to and fro.

She was calm in a moment.

"I will not—I cannot bear it—I will be free! There is only one road to freedom—death! By that dark portal I will escape this pollution!"

Lord Harcliffe was aghast at these words, and felt inclined to dart forward, but he paused as he saw her open a small ivory box on her dressing-table.

From this she took a small vial, and then half-filling a glass with water from a decanter, she poured into it the contents of the vial.

She then placed it on the toilet-table, and with a sad expression on her lovely face she fell on her knees in prayer.

"Oh, merciful Protector of the helpless, pardon the deed I am about to perform in pity for my great necessity—pardon those who drive me to it, and receive the poor weak creature who now kneels before thee to thine eternal rest, and let the arms of thy mercy be folded around her!"

She rose from her knees, and taking the glass in her hands, was about to raise it to her lips, but started back with a cry of surprise at finding it empty.

Lord Harcliffe had taken advantage of the opportunity while she was on her knees to throw away the deadly draught.

Beatrice gazed for an instant on the empty glass, and then the sense of her guilt rushing forcibly into her mind, she became impressed with the idea that it was a miraculous interposition of Heaven to keep her from the guilt of self-destruction.

Once more she feel on her knees.

"Oh, merciful Heaven!" she cried, "forgive me, pardon me, for this wicked act; and if it be thy will that I should live, preserve me from the bitter sacrifice that awaits me."

She rose, and seated herself in the arm-chair before her dressing-table.

The expression of her lovely features was calmer and more resigned.

"Oh, Antonio—my dear brother!" she cried, "is it possible that you, from whom I so lately parted, strong in life and health, can be no more?—that you are cold, silent, lifeless, in the grave? If so, whither can I fly for help?—whom can I trust?"

"*Trust me!*" said a gentle voice near at hand. She turned suddenly, and her eye fell on the elegant figure, and pale handsome features of the Black Highwayman, who had sunk on his knee at a few paces distance, and respectfully and calmly awaited her reply.

Her first impulse was to start up and fly from the room, but the voice was so melodious, the manner so winning, and the expression of the eyes that met hers so full of sympathy and tender earnestness, that though the form that knelt before her was that of a stranger, she felt she could *not fear*.

She remained therefore still seated gazing at his lordship, and drinking in unconsciously feelings precisely resembling those that had sprung up already in the breast of him on whom her eyes were fixed.

The manner in which Lord Harcliffe had introduced himself was an act of impulse, but the result proved that he could not have made his appearance at a more opportune moment, or in a more effective manner.

"Who are you, sir?" she exclaimed at length.

"One whom you may trust!" replied the Black Highwayman, chivalrously—"your servant, friend, if you will permit me, to the death!"

"You are a stranger," she said: "how came you here?"

"It was chance conducted me hither. I was in the next garden, I heard voices, and, I fancied, a cry for help. I climbed the wall, and—and am here, signora, to serve you if possible in any way you may please to direct."

This account, if not in all points strictly true, was still sufficient to assure the young Italian.

She gazed wistfully at his lordship, and said, with some hesitation:

"You overheard the conversation then that passed in this room?"

"I did, signora; and I feel indignant at the fate your guardian would assign you. I can readily understand the horror you must feel, urging you even to the act—which I thank Heaven I was enabled to preserve you from—of self-destruction."

"Oh, sir," she cried, a deep blush crimsoning her features, "was it you who—who——" She faltered, and drooped her head.

"Yes," replied Lord Harcliffe, "I was the instrument, in the hands of Providence, of preserving one so young, so beautiful, from such an untimely fate."

Beatrice blushed again, but looked at her preserver gratefully.

"How can I thank you, sir," she said, earnestly, "for this kindness to me, a stranger?"

"You do not appear to be strange to me," replied his lordship.

"But we have never met before?"

"No, signora: it is your resemblance to your brother that makes me familiar with your features."

"Ah, my brother—my poor brother Antonio!" cried Beatrice, excitedly.

This name seemed to be an immediate bond of union between them, for the young girl started up, and impulsively darting forward, eagerly clasped the hand of the Black Highwayman as she inquired, looking up in his face, eagerly:

"You knew my brother?"

"Not only *knew*, I *know* him well," answered his lordship.

"Alas, no—he is dead!" she cried, bitterly.

"You have been told so, but I am happy to be able to contradict you."

"What, is he not dead, then?"

"No, signora—he lives!"

"Lives?"

"Yes, I swear it on the honour of a gentleman! I have seen him, spoken to him, within the last three hours."

"And is he well—unwounded?" she asked, eagerly.

"Perfectly! Reasons, which you shall know hereafter, induce him to seclude himself for a time; but, beyond that, there is nothing the matter with him."

"My brother!—my dear Antonio!" exclaimed Beatrice, joyfully. "Then was not the tale of the gambling-house true?" she inquired.

"Partly, signora; but your brother has not lost his property, but won considerably; neither has he been engaged in any conflict to his own injury or that of any other person, although, but for the intervention of myself and a dear friend of mine, he would assuredly have fallen a victim to a gang of assassins."

"And you preserved him?" exclaimed the fair girl, with grateful earnestness, her beautiful eyes thanking Lord Harcliffe more warmly than her words. "How can I ever thank you—repay you?"

"I am repaid, signora" answered the Black Highwayman, fervently; "one smile from those fair lips, one clasp of this fair hand would more than overpay the highest service I could render you!"

As he spoke, his lordship, who was gazing down into the depths of her dark, eloquent eyes, unable to resist the temptation, encircled her waist with his arm, and gently pressed her unresisting hand to his lips.

The young girl did not appear in the least offended or surprised.

During the short time they had been together, she had learned to trust him; and there was in the manly, dignified bearing of the man on whose arm she rested that which disarmed suspicion and invited confidence.

Would it be saying too much to state that the fair Beatrice had in those few moments given more even than this?

Not a whit!

The young girl had given her heart—she *loved* the Black Highwayman.

"You cannot," she said, after a pause of delightful silence, "approve of this ill-assorted union?"

"No, by Heaven!" exclaimed Lord Harcliffe, warmly, "it is, in my opinion, detestable!"

"You will preserve me from it?" she said, clinging to his grasp with almost frenzied earnestness.

"I will—trust me!" answered his lordship.

"My brother will thank you—bless you!"

"And the sister," asked the Black Highwayman, tenderly, "what will she do?"

"She will be bound to you for ever by the ties of—of gratitude——"

"And love?" whispered his lordship, as he pressed his lips to her fair cheek.

Beatrice hid her glowing face on his breast, and from that moment there was no happier man in the universe than Lord Harcliffe.

"The first thing to be done is to leave this place," he said. "Is there any way of egress by the garden?"

"None; the only mode of exit is by that door," pointing to that by which her guardian had departed, and which was locked.

"They will be here soon, I fear," she continued.

"Fear not, dearest signora," said Lord Harcliffe, assuringly, "I defy them all!"

Any doubts of his being able to effect the retreat of himself and his precious charge never entered his lordship's head. It seemed little more than child's play, and he scouted the idea of opposition or failure.

"Hark!" cried Beatrice, suddenly. "I hear footsteps in the ante-chamber! They are returning!"

"Be calm, love!" whispered the Black Highwayman, hastily. "We must have recourse to stratagem. Listen to me, dearest: retire into the garden quickly, conceal yourself in the shrubs near the window; when your guardian and his party enter the chamber, cry out loudly for help. They will of course hurry into the garden to search for you, whilst you will as quickly return to me here, and the difficulty will be over."

The key was now heard in the lock.

Beatrice hastily disappeared through the window, whilst Lord Harcliffe concealed himself behind the hangings of the bed.

At the same instant the door opened, and there entered the Signor Brambillo, followed by the Marquis of Gavestone and his chaplain.

The Black Highwayman smiled as he peeped out at the three formidable opponents he would at the worst have to encounter.

A puff of breath, it seemed to him, would have blown them clean out of the way.

The earl had been a gay Lothario in his time.

He had been twice married, and now, in his seventy-fifth year, affected the *debonair* and sprightly manner which his trembling limbs and shaky voice positively contradicted.

The antiquated nobleman advanced as jauntily as possible to pay his *devoirs* to his intended bride, but the lady was nowhere to be seen.

"Where has the lovely Beatrice concealed herself?" he inquired, in a tone that seemed to imply a suspicion of some little playful jest on her part. "Come out, my love—come out!" exclaimed the ancient Benedict, strutting in a painfully jerky manner towards the cupboard, and trying to open it with his walking-stick.

Signor Brambillo, who was a little more impatient, and who, from knowing the state of his ward's mind respecting the venerable marquis much better than the marquis himself, began to fancy from her absence that all was not quite right.

He therefore advanced hastily to the cupboard.

"Allow me, marquis," he said, pulling open the door, which, however, did not disclose the object of his search.

Signor Brambillo looked puzzled and perplexed.

Not so, however, the gallant marquis.

He had been twice married, and was well up in all the phases of woman's changeable and fickle temperament.

At least, so he thought.

"Leave it to me, signor—leave it to me! I'll find her," he said, in a confident tone. "She's hiding from me: my dear dead first wife did the same: it's maiden coyness, nothing more. I'll discover her presently, and plead my own cause eloquently. The man that can't overcome a woman's scruples is unworthy of the name."

At this moment a loud shriek arose from the garden.

"Diavolo!" shouted the Signor Brambillo. "That is her voice. Something is the matter!"

"Something the matter with my intended bride?" exclaimed the septegenarian lover.

"The cry came from the garden," said the signor. "Let us search."

"Decidedly—let us search!" groaned the marquis, trying to draw his sword, which had got between his legs.

At this moment the shriek from the garden was repeated, with the additional cry:

"Help—help!"

"Follow me!" cried Signor Brambillo, as he hastily descended the steps leading to the garden.

"I'm with you!" said the jaunty old beau; "but, 'fore gad, I can't get my sword from its scabbard!"

He accordingly relinquished his efforts, and strutted off towards the window; but even in this Fortune seemed against him, for in his progress he caught his gracefully-pointed toe in one of the projecting carved feet of the chairs, and took a sudden dive on to the carpet, to the imminent danger of his venerable nose.

He, however, scrambled up just in time to see the object of his solicitude enter hastily by the window.

"Ah, my love!" he cried, puffing and blowing with his exertions, "I'm so glad—phew—phew!—to see you—phew! I heard you—phew!—cry out, and I was—phew!—just coming——"

He had no time to say any more, for Lord Harcliffe, thinking the sooner they were safely out of the house the better, stepped forward, and catching the little old gentleman up under his arm, walked coolly to the cupboard, and depositing him there, closed the door and turned the key.

Then leading Beatrice out of the apartment, he locked the door on the outside, and in a few moments both he and his charge were hastening along the streets to a place of safety.

The Signor Brambillo and the chaplain having explored the utmost limits of the garden, and hunted every bush unsuccessfully, returned to the room.

"It is most extraordinary!" said the signor. "Where can she be? It is most certain we heard her voice in the garden; but there are no signs of her there!"

"She must be somewhere!" remarked the chaplain, sagely.

"I know where—I **know**!" piped a querulous voice of a muffled quality not far off.

"That's the voice of the marquis undoubtedly," cried the reverend gentleman, noticing for the first time that his patron was not to be seen; "but where is *he?*"

"I'm in the cupboard!" responded the ancient beau.

Both immediately rushed thither, and there sure enough was the little marquis, wrong side upwards on the bottom shelf.

Having been rescued from his unpleasant position, he eagerly explained all he knew of the abduction of his intended bride, viz.:—

"That somebody—he didn't know who—had picked him up and dropped him in the cupboard, and that that somebody had run away with his bride, he didn't know where."

This was the sum and substance of the marquis's information, and as his listeners were no better informed than himself, the disappearance of Beatrice Riccioli remained a profound mystery.

CHAPTER CCXXVI.

CAPTAIN HAWK RETURNS TO THE GRAY MANSION WITH CHARLES, AND CONTINUES HIS EXAMINATION OF THE EDIFICE.—THE DECOY.—THE DISCOVERY OF THE SUBTERRANEAN PATH.—THEY EXPLORE THE CELLARS.—THE CAPTAIN HAS A NARROW ESCAPE OF HIS LIFE.

We will now return to Captain Hawk and Charles, who, having restored the unfortunate Lucy to her father, once more retraced their steps to the old mansion.

It was afternoon when they reached this locality. The weather was lovely; the abundant discharge of the electric fluid during the previous night's tempest had cooled the atmosphere, and everything—plants, trees, grass, and flowers, and the entire face of Nature—seemed to have benefited by the storm, and to have sprung forth with renewed vigour.

On one object alone no change had been effected, and this was the Gray Mansion.

While all around seemed to be smiling in the sun's rays and glistening with diamond dewdrops, this obdurate old building seemed—perhaps from contrast—to wear a darker and sterner look than ever. However unpromising as its aspect was, the circumstances connected with it had invested it with an interest in the eyes of Captain Hawk that he had never felt for any other building.

He walked round it, examining, as it were, every stone with the most scrutinising attention, until his eyeballs ached with the uniform dingy gray moss that met him at every glance.

This inspection was conducted in perfect silence, until at length the captain, having arrived at some conclusion, addressed his companion.

"Charles," he said, "from the survey I have just made of the exterior, I feel certain there is one wing of this mansion I have not yet entered."

"Yes, capting," said Charles, submissively, "but I s'pose yer means to enter it?" he added.

"Undoubtedly; though I have to dig the stones from the walls, or undermine the foundations."

"It'd be hard work that, capting!" remarked Charles.

"It seems to me," the captain continued, pointing out the spot with his finger, "that that is the wing to enter which my efforts must be directed, and that this wing is not connected with the other portion of the building."

"Does yer mean, capting, as it's got a different entrance?" inquired Charles.

"Precisely," returned the captain, "though where that entrance is I am at a loss to discern at present. I am inclined to think it must be subterranean."

"You mean underground?"

"Yes, and I believe that wing contains the secrets of this place."

"No doubt on it," assented Charles, who felt himself bound to agree with the captain in everything.

"Let us come this way," said Captain Hawk.

They advanced some distance until they reached the portion of the edifice which the captain's judgment decided as being the unexplored wing.

It looked very dark and forbidding, but there was not the slightest signs of a door or any other opening that might lead to the interior.

"Now, how is this prison-house to be entered, and its dark secrets brought to light?" he cogitated.

While thus reflecting, a faint shriek reached his ears. He started, and glanced at his companion.

"Eh, captain?" said Charles, who had also heard it, and who looked a little scared. "That wur the cry o' a human bein', warn't it?"

"Yes," replied Captain Hawk, biting his lips excitedly, "there is some d—d work going on within. Oh!" he cried, with sudden vehemence, "would I were there!"

"Hark!" exclaimed Charles, listening.

As he spoke, scream after scream followed in rapid succession, and then died away.

"By Heaven!" cried the captain, with stern resolution, "I'll discover the secrets of this Hell, though I hack the flesh from off my bones, and——"

His further speech was suddenly interrupted by Charles.

"See- -see, capting!" he shouted, as he pointed to some ditsance off.

"What do you see?" asked the captain.

"A man, I'll swear to it!"

At this instant there was a crackling sound heard in the bushes at a distance.

"You are right, Charles, there is some one," said the captain.

Just as he spoke, a man's head appeared cautiously reconnoitring.

"Ah, see! he is there!" shouted Captain Hawk. "Quick—let us give chase!"

They started forward, but when they reached the spot no traces of the man were to be seen.

"He's run for'ards, p'raps," suggested Charles.

The truth of this idea was confirmed by the reappearance of the figure at a considerable distance off.

They now gave chase in earnest; but the retreating form contrived to baffle their attempts at capture, though he still, by appearing and disappearing periodically, induced them to follow.

At length, when they had wandered some distance from the mansion, the captain halted.

"This chase is worse than useless," he observed. "I am convinced that fellow, whoever he is, was nothing more or less than a decoy to lure us away from the wing we were contemplating."

"Like enough," said Charles.

"But I'm not to be thrown off the scent like that. Let us return."

They had had a long run, and, being somewhat winded, they went back at their leisure, but as they came in sight of their former position they distinctly beheld a man—cautiously looking round him to see if he was observed—emerge from the shrubby thicket.

"Quick—conceal yourself!" whispered Captain Hawk; "and under cover of these bushes let us advance and see what this scout is doing!"

They did this with considerable success, and with such rapidity that they were almost within pistol-shot in a few moments.

"I'll bring you down, my friend!" exclaimed Captain Hawk, as he drew a pistol from his belt and cocked it.

But whether in so doing he trod upon some dry branch, or whether the click of the hammer startled the man, he suddenly bounded into the thicket.

The captain fired, and with a loud yell the man disappeared.

"You've hit him!" shouted Charles. "Hooray! For'ards, capting!"

"Yes," said Captain Hawk, "I think that shot told! Forward—quickly!"

In a few moments they reached the spot where the man, as they supposed, had received the captain's bullet and fallen to the ground.

They searched in the bushes on every side, but in vain.

There were no signs that any such event had taken place—no groans—no drop of blood.

"I surely could not have missed him!" cried Captain Hawk.

"It ain't possible!" echoed Charles, "unless 'e wur th——"

Charles paused, and a superstitious shudder passed over him.

"They say," he continued, apprehensively, "that devils and sperrits are bullet-proof!"

The drops of perspiration stood on the poor fellow's brow at the idea.

Captain Hawk noticed his pallor and rightly conceived that he was actuated by some mysterious terror.

Wishing, however, to reassure him, he said:

"My dear fellow, I can divine your thoughts. You are inclined to believe that this place is the abode of evil spirits?"

"Well, capting, it do look mortal like it," answered Charles, with evident trepidation.

"I admit it! But I know you are no coward, and if you will be guided by me——"

"Which I will, capting."

"Then, take my word for it, there is nothing here but flesh and blood."

"But that man disappearing wi' your bullet in his body?" urged Charles.

"Only convinces me more firmly that we are not far from some outlet that leads to the secret retreat I wish to penetrate."

"An' do you think the man made his escape by that outlet?"

"I do."

"An' th' screams we heerd?"

"The cries, I imagine, of victims confined either in the vaults below or the cells of this terrible place."

"Then you don't believe in ghosts?"

"No, not at all! Such things are only fit to scare children. Lord Harcliffe and myself passed a night in this place, and we then saw spectres enough to have driven a believer in such phantasies out of his senses."

"You really did see th' spectres then?" asked Charles, still with some degree of doubt and apprehension.

"We saw their *representative* in the shape of the much-dreaded *Gray Phantom.*"

Charles shuddered.

"He was but an impostor," continued the captain, "And I soon found out that this formidable spectre was a living man—in fact, an infernal villain, who was much more alarmed at our presence than we were at his. I unmasked him, and compelled him to run for his life."

"Did you though?" exclaimed Charles, much relieved.

"I assure you I speak the truth."

"Then now I know there aren't no ghostes, I'll go with you anywheres, an' stick to yer, capting, through thick an' thin!"

"Bravely said, Charles!" returned the captain. "For myself, I am determined at any risk to penetrate within these walls, but I do not wish to drag you into any peril on my account."

"I ain't afeared, capting," expostulated Charles.

"Fear would be destruction in a case like this," continued Captain Hawk. "If, therefore, you have the slightest doubt or misgiving clinging to you, you have my full permission to depart."

"What! leave you, capting, to go alone? Never!" cried Charles, with generous indignation.

"Well, then," said Captain Hawk, "dismiss at once from your mind all ideas of anything supernatural, and be assured that what you have to encounter will be living men—fiends, perhaps, but in human shape, and armed with living weapons, and really far more dangerous than any spirits could possibly be."

"I don't care how many men I tackles, so long as they are men; but as for ghostes, as yer can't get hold on nohow, I can't abide 'em."

"Let us commence our search, then, while the daylight lasts," said the captain.

"It's certain," maintained Charles, who brisked up and recovered all his usual boldness, "that the man disappeared hereabouts."

"It must be our task, then, to discover *where* he disappeared."

They both searched on the spot and the immediate vicinity, but at first without any apparent success.

"This is very strange," the captain soliloquised. "I feel confident I am not far from the spot, if I could but light upon it."

Suddenly Charles, who was searching a few yards from the captain, uttered a cry and disappeared through the bushes—all but his head.

"What is the matter, Charles?" exclaimed Captain Hawk.

"Got my foot in a plug-'ole, capting, or somethink—at all events, I'm in a 'ole o' some sort," answered Charles, struggling to extricate himself, but sinking deeper with each effort.

Captain Hawk hastened to his assistance, and, as he grasped his hand and dragged him out, a cry of joy burst from his lips.

"We have found it at last, I believe!" he exclaimed, eagerly.

"What, captain?"

"The way by which the man escaped—the path which leads to the interior of that wing."

"Let us search, capting."

With almost desperate energy they pulled aside the bushes, and in a few moments their eyes were gratified with the sight of an opening in the ground like the entrance to a rabbit-warren on a large scale.

"Be this it, capting?" asked Charles.

"Yes, this is the mouth of the pit—this the shaft of this infernal mine, or if not, I am very much mistaken,"

[CAPTAIN HAWK DISCOVERS THE SECRETS OF THE PRISON-HOUSE.]

answered Captain Hawk, as he bent down to examine it.

After a few moments' scrutiny, he looked up to Charles and said:

"Dare you follow me?"

"You lead th' way, capting, an' I'll soon show yer," replied Charles, boldly.

"Come on, then!" cried Captain Hawk.

Fortunately Charles was provided with a dark lantern and a flask of oil, from which the captain replenished his own.

He then reloaded the pistol he had recently discharged, and grasping the lantern in one hand, said to Charles:

"Now to learn the truth or perish in the effort!" And then crept forward on his hand and knees, that being the only position the smallness of the aperture permitted.

This narrow passage continued in a winding direction for about thirty yards, gradually widening until by a gradual incline it led into a small cellar, or rather cavern.

Charles followed close upon his leader's heels, and having reached the first halting-place on their critical journey, they were able to stand upright. Here, however, they were brought to a dead stop.

On bringing the lanterns into requisition, the cave being totally dark, they discovered a small door at the extremity, securely fastened.

"We must open this," said the captain, in a decided tone.

He was just about to commence the attempt, when Charles whispered hastily to him:

"We are followed!"

"Are we?" returned the captain, with delicious *sang froid*. "He must be a bold hunter who dares to follow his prey into the bowels of the earth."

He drew a pistol from his belt as he spoke, and crept

back along the narrow path he had just traversed. As he listened he heard a sound at the entrance of the passage, and then suddenly a dull thud, followed by a sudden extinction of the daylight.

This was sufficiently explanatory, and he hastily returned.

"We are trapped," he said to his companion; "some one has rolled a stone over the mouth of the passage."

"What's to be done?" asked Charles.

"Only one thing," replied the captain, determinately. "As going back is impossible, we must go forward."

In an instant he had screwed together his steel crowbar, by the skilful use of which, in less than two minutes, the door so apparently formidable began to show signs of yielding, and in another space of time of no longer duration it swung open on its rusty hinges.

On passing through, they found themselves in a cavern of larger dimensions than the former, with a gap at the end large enough for one person to pass through. This opening led into a narrow passage evidently a part of the mansion, inasmuch as the roof and sides were of stone, with doors in the latter at various intervals, leading to small cells.

These they examined, but they were entirely empty. At length they came to one fastened by a chain and padlock.

One vigorous wrench of the crowbar burst asunder these rusty appendages, and the door opened.

A sickening, foul effluvia, like the exhalations of a charnel-house, rose to their nostrils as they entered.

It was a loathsome and disgusting sight that met their view—the cell being crowded with skeletons in the various positions in which they had lain when life departed from them.

Captain Hawk called to mind the countryman's words, and became impressed with the idea that the wild tales of horror attached to this mansion had their foundation in truth.

"Let us come on," he cried, with a slight shudder of disgust—"our business is with the living, not the dead."

Quitting the cell, they continued their course till they came to a flight of stone steps, at the top of which was a strong iron-plated door.

"Umph!" remarked the captain, as he contemplated its massive structure—"stopped again!"

But he did not waste any time in contemplation. "*Nil desperandum*," was his motto, and he prepared for bursting through this formidable barricade by fixing a strong chisel in a handle.

While thus occupied, Charles, whose ears were on the alert for the slightest sound, laid his hand on the captain's arm and said to him in a whisper:

"There is some one in the passage besides ourselves."

"What makes you think so?"

"I can detect a stealthy footstep, and hear the sound of some one breathing, close to us."

"Mask your lantern, then, and let us retrace our footsteps in order that we may learn who the intruder is."

This operation having been performed, they went as rapidly as possible once more over the ground they had just traversed.

They had returned some distance, when suddenly the sound of the turning of a key in a lock arrested their progress.

They turned on their lanterns instantly, and the sudden light revealed the figure of a man opening the door at the top of the stone steps.

"Forward!" cried the captain.

The person, whoever he was, had evidently passed them in the dark. and intended escaping unnoticed that way.

The rays of the lanterns flashing through the dark passage, scared the man.

"Stop!" shouted Captain Hawk, as he and his companion ran forward—"stop, or I fire!"

"Fire, and be d—d!" cried the figure.

A deafening report was the reply to this, and the loud slamming to of the door proved that the man had made good his retreat.

When they reached the steps, the portal was closed as before.

But only for a moment.

The man, in his excitement and eager haste to escape, had pulled the door violently to, but not effectually, for it had no sooner closed than it swung open again, to the captain's great satisfaction, who bounded through, followed by Charles.

As they emerged from the cellar, the waning light of day streamed through an iron-grated window in the passage, and informed them where they were.

It also revealed the retreating form of the fugitive.

This sight stimulated the captain to pursue him.

Heedless of danger, intent only on overtaking this individual, Captain Hawk rushed onwards like an arrow from a bow.

The man, evidently fearful of being overtaken, put forth all his speed, but the captain had the advantage.

A few yards only intervened between them.

"Stay, scoundrel! Escape is impossible!" shouted the captain, stretching forth his hand as he advanced.

The man darted suddenly round a corner, and thus avoided the grip, and before the captain could recover himself, darted through a narrow swing door in the wall, that closed upon him as he entered.

But even here, the extreme precipitation of the man's action defeated his own ends.

The door did not close perfectly, and the captain, throwing himself forward with all his energy, plunged into the cell almost on the heels of the object of his pursuit, whom he at once grasped by the back of the collar.

The man turned desperately as he felt the hand of his pursuer laid upon him.

There was a violent effort for freedom, and in the struggle they lurched heavily against the door, which this time *did* close with a loud snap, most effectually, just in time to exclude Charles, who, thus separated from the captain, remained in a state of great anxiety in the passage without.

All this was the work merely of a few seconds, and when, by a powerful effort, Captain Hawk succeeded in getting a fair glance at the face of the man he held in his grasp, he at once recognised the features of the murderer of poor Willie.

"So, you murderous scoundrel!" he cried, "I have you at last?"

The words had scarcely passed his lips, when the captain suddenly felt his pistols wrenched from his belt, and his sword violently dragged from its scabbard by a hand behind him.

Both his own hands being occupied in grasping the wiry figure he had caught, he was powerless to resist; but on hastily turning his head, he beheld to his chagrin his trusty weapons in the hand of the Gray Figure, or, as we shall now call him, his rival, Ridley Massingham, who, with a sardonic smile on his features, stood contemplating him at a few yards' distance.

"You have rushed into the very jaws of the tiger, like a rash, hot-headed fool!" he said, in a cold-blooded tone, "and you shall now feel the tiger's claws! You shall learn by experience the penalty of attempting to pry into the secrets of the Haunted Mansion!"

"Scoundrel!" shouted Captain Hawk, with indignant contempt, "you are unworthy the name of tiger! Wolf or fox is your fitting title!"

"Bind him!" cried his enemy to his myrmidon.

But it was all that individual could do to hold his prey.

"You must help me!" he gasped.

This necessity was apparent, and without another word Ridley Massingham darted behind the captain, and throwing the noose of a rope over the captain's neck, and tightening it by a sudden jerk, dragged him back with all his power.

Thus assailed by two strong and desperate men, in this narrow cell, the contest was too unequal.

Captain Hawk began to feel his strength fail.

Charles, who heard the struggle from without, and comprehended the peril to which his leader might be exposed, was in an agony of anxiety.

He heard the heavy gaspings of the captain, and hammered at the door with frantic violence.

"What's up, capting?" he shouted.

Charles's voice reached the ears of the gallant but gradually succumbing captain on the other side.

"Help!" he cried, faintly.

"They're murderin' on him!" groaned Charles. "Yer d—d wagabones!" he shouted, "if yer don't take off yer hands, I'll be the death on yer!"

A scornful laugh was the only answer.

Matters were now growing awfully critical with the captain, who was becoming black in the face, and enduring all the agonies of suffocation.

Ridley Massingham, like a hungry bloodhound, having fastened his fangs in his victim, was resolved to show no mercy.

The captain's powers were rapidly failing him, and a few seconds more would have sealed his fate for ever, when the loud report of a pistol was heard, mingled with the crash of wood, and Charles burst into the cell with the impetuosity of a battering-ram.

As a despairing effort, he had discharged his weapon with the muzzle placed close against the lock.

The plan had been successful.

The lock was blown from its place, the door opened, and the faithful fellow stood by the side of the captain.

One blow from the butt-end of his pistol struck down the man who held Captain Hawk, and a second would have prostrated the cowardly Ridley Massingham, but he was nowhere to be seen.

The report of the pistol had scared him; and in the momentary confusion, and under cover of the smoke from the discharge, he had effected his escape, though by what means did not immediately appear.

Charles was at this juncture too anxious about the captain's welfare to trouble himself on account of the villain's flight.

He unfastened the rope from Captain Hawk's neck with trembling eagerness, as though he feared each instant perilled his life.

The captain fortunately still breathed, and the ligature being removed, after a few violent gasps he staggered to his feet.

"I thought it was all over with me!" he exclaimed, in broken sentences, as he leant against the wall to recover himself.

"So did I too, captain," cried Charles. "Phew! the very thought on it puts me all over in a cold sweat!"

"My faithful fellow, I owe my life to you a second time," said Captain Hawk, grasping his hand warmly.

Charles was delighted and affected simultaneously, for he both admired and loved the captain, and could conceive nothing more terrible than any harm befalling him.

"'Ere, capting," he cried, offering him a flask of brandy, "drink—it'll set yer to rights in no time."

Captain Hawk took a prolonged draught of the reviving spirit, and felt himself completely restored.

"Why, yer looks quite yerself again!" exclaimed Charles, examining his patient with an expression of the most intense satisfaction.

"I shall do now," returned the captain; "the unpleasant sensations I experienced have passed off."

"That's right, capting; I thought as there were no bones broke."

Charles now turned his attention to the man he had struck down, and who was just beginning to recover from the effects of the blow.

"Now then, d—n yer!" he cried, giving the prostrate ruffian a kick to stimulate him—"get up!"

Charles was fierce and indignant, and felt strongly inclined to exterminate him at once.

"What shall I do with this warmint?" he asked the captain. "Shall I batter out his brains on the floor?"

"No," replied the captain, who had been picking up and examining his weapons, which Ridley Massingham, in his hasty exit, had forgotten to take with him; "the scoundrel will be more serviceable to us alive than dead."

"'E don't seem o' much good," said Charles.

"I must use him as the key to unlock the cells of this place, and as a guide to reveal their mysteries."

The man groaned.

"Spare me!" he cried, in a faint voice.

"Spare yer!" echoed Charles, indignantly. "Ye're a pretty article to spare! I should like to rope's-end yer!"

"On one condition only you may hope for mercy," said Captain Hawk.

"What's that?" asked the man, eagerly.

"That you conduct me through those portions of this building that I have not yet visited."

"I will—I will!"

"Don't attempt to deceive or hide anything from me; if you do, I'll blow your brains out without mercy!"

"I won't deceive you!"

"I have made up my mind to bring to light the secrets of this dark abode, therefore deal truly with me, or prepare to abide the consequences!"

"You may depend upon me."

"First, then, what is this dwelling used for?"

"A madhouse."

"A madhouse?" echoed the captain.

"Yes, a private madhouse."

"Who are confined here?"

"Anyone whom the proprietors think proper to send."

"Speak definitely!"

"Well, then, suppose a son has a parent who keeps him from his inheritance by living too long, he is declared to be insane and brought here, till torture and privation finish him. If a girl declines the suit of a rich lover, she is decoyed to this mansion and compelled to submit, and after she has served her turn, left to grow mad in darkness and solitude."

"Horrible!" murmured Captain Hawk—"most horrible! Is it possible that such a den as this can exist in the heart of a civilized country—that the law——"

"The law never troubles itself about us, and as for anyone else, they wouldn't dare come near. This place is supposed to be haunted, that's why it was fixed upon; and the screams of those confined here are thought to be the cries and wailings of lost spirits, or the shrieks of furious demons."

"Who have you here at this moment?" inquired the captain.

"Not many; there's been a great mortality among 'em this year, no fewer than six hundred."

"And where are they buried?"

"In the plantation at the back."

"What are those skeletons in the vaults beneath?"

"Oh, they've been there for many years. They belong to the last generation, they do."

"This place, then, seems to have been the abode of crime from its commencement; no wonder a curse rests upon its blood-stained walls!" the captain remarked; and then added:

"Is Ridley Massingham the proprietor of this hell?"

"This place is not the property of *one*," answered the man; "it has *many proprietors*, and he is one of them."

"He seems to be here almost continually; how is that?"

"He is paid to look after it, but there are some of the first names in the country who make use of the Gray Mansion as a hiding-place of the results of their crimes."

"Is it possible?"

"It's a fact!"

"Mention some of the names you know."

"The Marquis of Rockleigh."

"Go on."

"Sir Slingsby Sleuforth."

Captain Hawk drew in his breath.

"Continue," he said.

"Lord Hubert Mansfield—Ashley Fordyce."

"Enough—enough!" cried the captain, in a tone of disgust.

"There's just one more name you ought to hear, because it's the highest of all," said the man.

"What name is that?"

"The *Prince of Wales*."

"Good Heavens! no!" exclaimed Captain Hawk, recoiling incredulously.

"I swear it's truth! I've seen him here with my own eyes!" affirmed the man, earnestly.

"After all, why not?" thought the captain. "He who would countenance a murder at 'The Prince's Retreat,' would have no scruple in doing so at the Gray Mansion. It is indeed a terrible revelation!"

"The prince came not a month since to see an old Spanish gentleman, whose daughter disappeared mysteriously, and who accused the prince—he being the last person with whom she was seen alive—of her destruction."

"Did that lead to his incarceration here?"

"Yes, that was just what *did* lead to it! There'd like to have been the devil to pay. The old man was furious—mad about his daughter—and would have summoned the prince before a court of justice to inquire into his child's fate, when he was suddenly removed here and chained down in one of the cells, from which it was never intended he should escape alive!"

"Heavens! what atrocity!" exclaimed the captain. "And how long has this old man been here?" he inquired.

"About six months."

"Poor old man! They must have appeared to him six years! But go on: who else have you here?"

"An elderly lady. She's a prisoner of Ridley Massingham's. I think he calls her Miss Allison."

"Ha!" vociferated Captain Hawk, violently, the indignant blood rushing into his face. "I have the clue at last, then! And her niece?" he continued, with impetuous eagerness. "Tell me, is she here?"

The man hesitated.

"Her niece?" he repeated.

"Yes, her niece!" furiously reiterated Captain Hawk—"her niece, Blanche Allison, a young, beautiful girl, scarcely nineteen years of age!"

His eyes were riveted upon the man, and blazed with eager expectation like two live coals.

"Is she here?" he shouted.

"No, she is not here," answered the man, but with some hesitation.

"Then she has been here?" quickly interrogated Captain Hawk. "Don't deceive me on this point, or I swear, though you had fifty lives in your worthless carcass, I'd sacrifice them all!"

"Well, then, she has been here, but she is not here now," the man answered

"How is that?"

"The master had some fears that there might be an exposure of the secrets of this place, and he had her removed."

"When?"

"This morning."

"Where?"

"To an old farm-house some miles distant."

"Then she is there now?"

"Yes."

"You must guide me there."

"I will."

"But how is it Ridley Massingham did not accompany her?"

"He remained behind to watch you."

"Is she alone?"

"No."

"Who is with her?"

"One of the master's men."

"Which—what is his name, do you know?"

"His name is Jacob Mawks."

"That hideous wretch!" exclaimed the captain, apprehensively.

"He ain't a beauty, that's certain!" said the man.

"He's enough to scare away the senses of the poor girl, the brutal monster! But I shall shortly be upon his track! And now, quick, what other prisoners?"

"Only one more. She's quite mad, she is. She belongs to the Marquis of Rockleigh. She's the mother of mad Willie."

"Whom you destroyed yesterday, wretch!"

"I'm very sorry, but what could I do? He wouldn't come back. I was obliged to kill him to save myself."

Captain Hawk motioned him abruptly to be silent.

"You are a murderous rascal," he cried, "but less blameable than those whose education and position should have rendered incapable of such atrocities."

The man looked—or pretended to do so—penitent and ashamed.

"Now," cried the captain, "lead me at once to the cells; and mark me once more—no attempt at treachery, or——" He placed his hand menacingly on the handle of his pistol, and said, in a low, earnest tone: "I'll send you to join the poor lad, you so brutally murdered, in the land of spirits!"

The man shuddered.

"I'll not betray you," he answered. "This is the way."

As he spoke, he pushed open a small door in a recess of the cell, and passed through.

Captain Hawk and Charles followed their conductor up a flight of narrow steps and along a gallery till they came to a door.

Here they paused, whilst a moaning sound came feebly from within.

CHAPTER CCXXVII.

CAPTAIN HAWK VISITS THE CELLS, AND RELEASES THE PRISONERS.—MAKES AN EXTRAORDINARY DISCOVERY AND RESCUES BLANCHE FROM IMMINENT PERIL.—DESTRUCTION OF THE HAUNTED MANSION

Taking a bunch of keys from his pocket, the man speedily opened the door.

They entered a small cell, through the narrow window of which some rays of twilight feebly shone.

They were just able to discern an old, white-haired man huddled up against the wall, to which he was attached by a chain and staple, the other end being fastened to an iron band that encircled his waist.

Captain Hawk and Charles turned on their lanterns, the rays of which illuminated the cell, and showed the fearful ravages grief, privation, and ill-treatment had made in the unhappy victim before them.

He looked wistfully as they entered, shading his eyes with his hand from the sudden and unusual light that dazzled them.

"You're come at last," he cried, in a feeble voice—"come to tell me of my child! I haven't seen her for years: I don't know how many, but it seems an age since I last looked upon my poor Inez! Where is she?"

He looked up at the captain as he spoke, as though he recognised in his features a sympathy to which he had been long unaccustomed.

The expression of the old man's eyes was wild, and there was no doubt insanity was fast creeping over him with its fearful oblivion.

He appeared very weak, and kept his hand closed tightly over something he would ever and anon gaze at with the utmost caution and secrecy.

"What is that the old man grasps so tightly?" inquired Captain Hawk, whose curiosity was excited.

"A kind of locket," answered the guide, "that he can never be induced to part with."

"Never—never!" cried the prisoner, who had overheard the words. "With this locket I shall recover my child! She had one like it round her neck when I lost her."

"May I look at it?" asked the captain.

"Yes, yes!" answered the old man "I will let you, but no one else—no one else! See," he continued, in a whisper, as he unclosed his hand and revealed a golden locket glittering with precious stones.

Captain Hawk bent down to gaze at it, but started back with a cry almost of horror.

"Merciful Heaven!" he ejaculated. "It is the very counterpart of the locket we found on the dead body of that poor girl in the sand-pits at Kew."

This opened such a vast field for suspicion that the captain was fairly bewildered.

He pressed his hand to his throbbing brain, and closed his eyes, as he murmured to himself:

"It was, beyond a doubt, this poor old man's child we saw there? But who was her murderer—who?"

He was aroused from his reverie by the plaintive voice of the old man.

"You will take me away from this place, will you not?" he inquired.

"Most certainly," answered Captain Hawk.

The old man's eye lighted up with a hopeful expression at this assurance.

"And you will restore me my child—my Inez?" he asked, eagerly

The captain had not the heart to mention his suspicions at that moment, but answered:

"We will search for her."

"Heaven bless you!" cried the grateful father—Heaven bless you!"

In a paroxysm of joy, the old man endeavoured to rise to his feet, but was dragged back, and then for the first time Captain Hawk's eye fell on the cruel chain that fettered the unhappy prisoner.

"Inhuman wretches!" he cried, with strong indignation in his tone and manner. "Unfasten that chain at once, and set him free! I blush to call myself a man and stand to witness such barbarity."

The jailer stooped down and with a key unlocked the band that encircled the prisoner's waist.

The iron ligature fell with a crash to the floor, and the old man, thus set at liberty, uttered a wild cry of joy, and essayed to start up and embrace the knees of his liberator, but his strength failed him, and, throwing out his arms feebly to express his gratitude, he fell fainting at the captain's feet.

"Poor old man!" exclaimed Captain Hawk, pityingly. "I fear your days are numbered."

Charles, having raised the poor victim, placed him for the present on his straw pallet, and, having induced him to swallow a few drops of brandy, they left him to visit the other cells.

The next they entered was that in which Miss Hester Allison—Blanche's aunt—was confined.

Captain Hawk had never before seen her, but even if he had he would scarcely have recognised her.

Though she had only been a prisoner in that gloomy abode for two days, her hair had become quite gray, and there was no doubt, had the term of her incarceration been extended, it would in a few days longer have grown perfectly white.

She appeared in a state of utter despondency.

As Captain Hawk entered, she rushed eagerly towards him, sobbing piteously.

Her thoughts—in fact, her entire solicitude—seemed fixed upon her niece.

"Oh, sir," she exclaimed, "you come like a good angel to release my poor Blanche! Oh, hasten to deliver her—to set her free!"

"I am about to do so, my dear lady. Fear nothing! Your niece shall speedily be restored to you," said Captain Hawk, in an assuring tone.

He then proceeded to explain to her who he was, and the relation that subsisted between her niece and himself.

Her spirit seemed quite to revive at his words.

"Oh, go, sir—go!" she cried, eagerly. "Do not think of me—fly to the relief of my poor girl! She loves you—your name was ever on her lips!"

"My beloved Blanche!" murmured the captain, at this assurance.

Then, taking leave of Miss Allison for a few moments, and promising to return very shortly, he left the chamber.

"There is now," said Captain Hawk, "only one more cell to visit."

This was speedily reached, and the door flung open.

In this the captain was prepared to encounter the raving maniac whose screams he had so often heard from the exterior.

"But, alas! all was still, and a sight of horror presented itself more appalling in its silence than had it been accompanied with groans and shrieks.

The poor maniac had hanged herself to the iron bars of her prison window, and the spirit of the distraught mother had fled to join her son in another and a better world.

Captain Hawk turned away with a heavy heart from this sickening sight, and ordered his guide, in a voice husky with emotion, to cut down the body.

As there could nothing further be done at that moment, they left the cell.

"Have you a vehicle here of any description?" the captain inquired of the man.

"There's a horse and cart in the shed," he answered.

"Harness the horse instantly. Charles, go with him, and see that he does so, and then let me know. You will find me in Miss Allison's apartment."

Charles and the jailer went their way, and the captain once more entered the cell where Blanche's aunt, in a mingled tumult of hope and fear, anxiously expected his return.

In about ten minutes Charles returned, leading the jailer by the collar—whether out of affection or to prevent his making a sudden bolt we leave to the decision of our readers—to inform the captain that the cart was ready.

The old man was moved downstairs and placed in this somewhat rude conveyance.

He was too weak to sit up, and it seemed apparent, unless a change for the better took place, that his end was fast approaching.

Miss Allison attended to the poor old man during the journey, until they reached a small roadside inn, the landlady of which—a kind, rosy-faced woman—received them, and made immediate preparations to lodge them for the night.

The ostler was despatched for the doctor, and, having seen them at least comfortably and safely housed, Captain Hawk, accompanied by Charles, and the jailer to act as guide, started for the farm-house where Blanche was confined.

This tenement lay across the country several miles—to reach it, therefore, they were obliged to diverge from the high-road.

It was now quite dusk, and, being totally unacquainted with the locality, they were compelled to depend upon the guidance of the jailer.

However, as he protested he meant nothing but fair dealing, and Captain Hawk promising him most infallibly the contents of his pistol if he attempted anything else, they felt pretty well assured that they would arrive at their destination.

As they passed along, in looking back the captain caught a last glimpse of the Gray Mansion, as its gaunt outline frowned forth darker even than the thickening night.

After a quick ride of about half an hour across fields, and over hedges and ditches, the jailer checked his horse.

The spot where he stopped was the end of a dark lane.

"We are near the place now," he said.

"Very well," replied the captain. "Then you had better lead the way as quietly as possible, and remember I am close behind you, with my pistol pointed at your head."

"So am I," said Charles.

It was certain that this jailer never had the necessity of fair dealing so strongly urged upon him in his life before.

He could hardly have found an opportunity of being treacherous even had he wished it.

In a few moments they reached the end of the lane, and emerged into an open space, in which stood a solitary tenement, the dark outline of whose gable roof and projecting windows proclaimed to be a farm-house.

But there were no signs of anything living—no neighing of horses, lowing of cows, or bleating of sheep—not even a solitary grunt of a pig or bark of a dog to give a transient light to the sombre picture.

Everything tended to describe the character of the place in one word—

"Deserted!"

Dismounting from their horses, which they turned loose to crop the dewy grass, they approached the house.

All was profoundly dark, save one of the rooms in the upper storey, and from the window of this a light streamed forth that looked quite cheerful amid the surrounding darkness.

A kind of wooden gallery surrounded this portion of the building, the ascent to which was by a flight of steps.

Telling his companions to remain below, he ascended to the gallery, and cautiously drew near the window and looked in.

It was a very plain, unpretending apartment, with bare floor and white-washed walls not over clean.

A fire smouldered in the grate, and a candle flickered on the table.

But all these objects sunk into utter insignificance before the one sight that presented itself, and which caused the captain's heart to beat so violently that he could almost fancy he heard the strokes vibrate against his ribs.

There, calmly sleeping upon the bed, lay his beautiful—his adored Blanche.

Her face was turned towards him, and, though pale, was not alarmingly so.

It was, however, enough she was still alive, and that no more than the extent of a few yards separated him from her.

He had hardly recovered from the first emotion of joy caused by the sight of the woman he loved when an object presented itself that produced in his breast sensations of an entirely opposite description.

This object was the shock head and repulsive, ogre-like features of Jacob Mawks.

This obnoxious individual did not make his appearance either at a door or a window, but, like some hideous demon rising from his native depths in the bowels of the earth, through a trap in the floor.

This trap opened silently, and the horrible object crept up stealthily, appearing by degrees and cautiously, as though conscious he was treading on forbidden ground in search of forbidden fruit, until the whole of his ungainly carcass was revealed.

Having cautiously closed the trap, he advanced towards the bed, where he remained, like some hideous satyr fascinated by the charms of a slumbering wood-nymph, gloating over the sleeping beauty of the unconscious Blanche.

As he gazed, the monster smacked his lips and rubbed his huge hands one over the other, as though in anticipation of some luxurious banquet.

As he stood there the expression of his countenance, always repulsive, became positively horrible.

"Measter Massin'am sent Oi to look arter 'er, but 'e didn't know as Oi loikes a pootty gurl as well as 'e do."

He drew a little nearer to the bed, and peered earnestly at the sleeping beauty from under his pent-house brows.

His bloodshot eyes dilated, and it seemed for the moment as though he would dart upon the slumbering victim like a vampire, but he paused and drew back.

"She be a foine wench, that she be!" he soliloquised. "Oi'm thinkin' she worn't loike sooch as Oi; boot thart bean't no matter: she moost loike me, when she carn't 'elp 'ersen!"

This soliloquy was heightened by sudden writhings and contortions of the speaker's body.

"Shall Oi waken 'er, or shall Oi loie doon boy 'er soide?" he continued, talking to himself. "Ee, ee!—worn't she be pleased when she waks oop an' finds 'ersen in moi orms!"

He stretched forth the long, straggling members alluded to, as though he were embracing some aerial form, and then, taking a bottle from his pocket, he took a long draught, after which a very powerful odour of rum pervaded the apartment.

He then quietly drew off his heavy boots, and proceeded to divest himself of his attire with the utmost deliberation.

His limbs, which this operation revealed, were prodigiously muscular—unnaturally so—and covered with red hair, that gave him the appearance of an enormous gorilla.

He appeared to be in an exceedingly good humour, and drank again from his rum-bottle.

During this, Captain Hawk, outside the window, with every nerve in his body trembling to grasp the ugly wretch by the throat, remained silent, with his eyes riveted upon him.

"Ee, ee!" the monster grinned. "Measter worn't be 'ere to-noight—ee, ee! Eef 'e could see Oi noo, Oi woonders whort 'e'd say?"

He little thought that at that moment he was so closely watched.

From the increasing unsteadiness of his gait, it was evident Mr. Jacob Mawks had been drinking considerably; and giving a sudden lurch, he stumbled over his heavy boots, making sufficient noise to arouse Blanche from her sleep.

She started up on the bed, and at the same moment the trap-door was gently raised, and the head of Ridley Massingham appeared.

"Who's there?" cried Blanche, in a tone of alarm.

"It be only Oi—dorn't be froightened!" grunted Jacob.

"You d—d hound!" muttered his master between his teeth.

The poor girl at the sight of the hideous object in that lonely chamber in a state of semi-nudity, filled her with violent terror, and she uttered a startled shriek.

"Wretch!" she cried. "How dare you intrude yourself into this room? Begone this instant!"

Jacob looked upon this command as a good joke, and uttered a coarse laugh accordingly.

"It arn't loikely Oi be goin' to go, when Oi've only joost coom! Oi be coomin' to keep yow coompany. Will yow 'ave a drop o' room?"

"Wretch!" exclaimed Blanche, with a shudder of the highest disgust.

"Oh, dorn't call neames—Oi be as good as moi measter," retorted Jacob.

"You are a pair of villains!" cried Blanche, gathering strength from despair, and springing from the bed.

She had lain down in her clothes, and consequently was not undressed.

She flew to the door.

The inebriated Jacob staggered after her and dragged her back.

"At your peril dare to stop me!" shrieked the desperate girl.

"Ee, ee!—the door be lorked, an' Oi dare onythin'!" growled Jacob, as he wound his long arms around her delicate body, and forced her on to the bed.

In an agony of terror she screamed aloud.

But an unexpected crisis was at hand.

At that instant a crushing, mortal blow from the butt-end of Ridley Massingham's pistol fell on the head of Jacob Mawks, who, with his skull frightfully fractured, bit the dust never to rise again; and at the same moment a sudden crash of splintered wood and broken glass was heard, and Captain Hawk sprang into the room, followed by Charles.

With one arm he encircled the trembling Blanche, who welcomed him with a cry of wild, delirious joy, and with his other hand grasped the throat of her villanous abductor.

This was all done so rapidly that ere the astonished culprit could make an effort to extricate himself, a rope was thrown over his head and arms, and drawn tightly by Charles; and being thus rendered utterly powerless, the *Gray Phantom* was to all intents and purposes *laid* at last.

Charles continued his kind offices, inasmuch as he not only confined the arms, but the legs of the *spectre*, who being now thoroughly shorn of his ghostly terrors, was conveyed to the stable by his attentive friend, assisted by the jailer, whose services were brought into requisition to help to lift his master into the hay-rack, where he was placed to be out of harm's way.

The dead body of the wretched Jacob was left where it fell.

But who can express the transports of our hero as he clasped his beloved Blanche to his breast, or describe the raptures of Blanche herself as she felt her faithful lover's protecting arms clasped around her.

The steeds being summoned, Captain Hawk placed Blanche before him in the saddle, and the party returned to the inn.

On their journey back their attention was attracted by a bright light at a distance.

They paused and looked round.

"Is it lightning?" said Captain Hawk.

It was evident it was not so, for the light was too lasting.

"Seems like a fire," said Charles.

As he spoke, a more vivid glare seemed to illuminate the dark horizon, and the next instant a column of flame darted upwards in the air.

There was no longer any doubt as to what this blaze portended.

"See!" cried the captain.

And as he pointed with his finger across the country the dark lineaments of the Haunted Mansion stood boldly forth wrapped in a sheet of burning flame.

"The Gray Mansion is on fire!" exclaimed Captain Hawk, "and I believe it to be the work of an incendiary. Thank Heaven, however, that there is nothing human within its dreary walls to suffer injury. It has stood too long a blot upon the face of nature, and its destruction will be like the removal of a curse from the land whereon it reared its head."

The fire had now got thoroughly hold; but still, as though the old ghostly tenement had resolutely determined not to part with its distinctive character while one stone remained upon the other, it still stood dark and frowning in the midst of the fiery element in which it was envelped.

"I never see sich a place," said Charles, in a kind of wondering soliloquy; "the stones seem as if they wouldn't burn!"

"There's too much blood in them!" remarked the jailer in a deep tone. "Even the furnace that now surrounds its walls cannot burn it out or dry it up; but when the right moment comes it will crumble into dust and its very memory will be swept away!"

"The sooner the better!" Charles observed. "How it flares!"

The flames darted upwards, and the roar of conflagration could be distinctly heard like the foaming of some mighty cataract.

"Strange it does not fall!" said Captain Hawk, as with his arm fondly thrown around Blanche, whose head rested on his breast, he gazed at the sublime but awful spectacle.

"Its time has not yet come!" returned the jailer. "Like a piece of bad coal in a grate that will prevent the fire in it from burning freely, so there is in that old mansion some unholy relics yet to be consumed before the flames can take their full effect."

Captain Hawk looked at the man in astonishment. He, the inhuman, hard-featured jailer, seemed suddenly to be inspired with the prescience and dignity of a prophet.

The captain, without being superstitious, began to feel impressed with his words.

"Hark!" cried the man, suddenly bending his ear to listen.

Everyone of the party was silent, and in an instant, far above the hollow roar of the furnace, a prolonged succession of awful heart-rending shrieks rose on the night air.

"Hark!—hark!" repeated the man, solemnly, "the fires of retribution have burnt home—*the time is near at hand!*"

As he spoke, there burst forth one wild prolonged wail, like the parting death-cry of some mighty giant; and as it died away, a bright column of sparks shot up in the air.

"The time has come," shouted the jailer, "and the curse of the Gray Mansion is purged away. It will burn now!"

And as he spoke, the hitherto dark mass suddenly became lighter and lighter, till at length every stone in its massive walls appeared red hot, and glowed like a tower of molten brass.

"Behold!" cried the jailer, excitedly. "Were not my words true? See how the old walls glow with the fierce heat! The work goes bravely on! Already the foundations are undermined, and the walls totter on their once solid bases!"

Whether it was fancy or not, the lookers-on could not determine, but the glowing mass seemed to oscillate and quiver as he spoke.

"Its moments are numbered!" shouted the man. "Five more short spaces of time, and it will no longer exist! One—two—three—four—five!"

As he uttered the last word, a report like the discharge of a thousand cannons burst from the blazing pile, and the next moment all was darkness.

The Gray Mansion, with its guilty secrets and its blood-stained walls, existed no longer!

CHAPTER CCXXVIII.

THE PRINCE OF WALES RECEIVES A MYSTERIOUS LETTER.—HE RESOLVES TO VISIT THE RETREAT.—LORD HARCLIFFE MAKES A CONFESSION AND RECEIVES FORGIVENESS.—A STRANGE RESOLVE AND ITS CONSEQUENCES.

THE PRINCE OF WALES and his satellites, although annoyed at the escape of Lord Harcliffe, whom they had calculated upon making an easy victim, were not particularly alarmed at his slipping through their fingers.

The former knew very well that the word of a prince opposed to that of a condemned highwayman would be less than nothing, and that any accusation the latter might make against him would be utterly powerless; whilst the latter felt that with the heir apparent for their president, at the head of their iniquitous assemblies, and their still more iniquitous proceedings, they had a powerful ally, under the shadow of whose royal protection they could transgress the laws with the greatest impunity.

The entire party therefore dismissed the idea of any such thing as apprehension, and went on as usual in their midnight orgies and unbridled dissipations.

Little did it concern them that their youthful victim had descended into the dark depths beneath the Red Chamber, cut off suddenly in the full tide of health and strength, and "sent to his account with all his imperfections on his head."

Nor did any such reflections disturb the dreams of the Prince of Wales.

In fact, little ever did disturb him, save when he had a fit of the gout.

He lived for himself essentially, and nothing else.

Luxury, dissipation and sensuality, blinded the better feelings he might once have possessed, and destroyed them as effectually as they were killing him.

His health had been breaking for some time, and there were, perhaps, times when, intoxication not having shrouded his faculties, remorse would dart its stings into his royal breast, as his mind wandered back over the past.

How many young and once happy victims had his lust consigned to the tomb!

It was on a fine summer afternoon, some days after the escape of Lord Harcliffe, the prince sat alone in his private chamber.

He felt on this particular day more than usually depressed and low-spirited.

He tried to read, but the effort made his head ache.

He would have eaten, but he had no appetite.

He tried to cheer his spirits by looking out of the window at the bright sunshine, but even that was insufficient to lighten the gloom within.

He turned away from the radiant face of nature and sank with a hopeless sigh into a luxuriant arm-chair whose Sybaritic softness brought no rest to his aching limbs.

"*Peste!*" he groaned, "what is the meaning of this? I must rouse myself! I seem to be breaking up altogether!"

He reached forth his hand, and drew towards him a small ebony case richly inlaid with silver and mother-of-pearl, from which he drew forth a small bottle of choice liqueur, the stopper of which inverted formed a glass.

This he filled and refilled several times, and then shutting the case, threw himself back in his chair and closed his eyes.

When he opened them again after a short interval, his eye fell upon a letter that lay on the table within reach of his hand.

With a look of surprise, he took it up, and glanced at the address:—

"*Frederick Prince of Wales,*
President of 'The Prince's Retreat.'"

This struck the royal reader as a singular direction, to say the least, and a frown overspread his features.

The very appearance of the letter, too, was mysterious, inasmuch as it was not there a few moments before, and he felt confident no one had entered the room within that time.

He turned it over several times in his hands, and then opened it and read the contents, which were brief and ominous:—

"*Your secret crimes are known to me! Beware!*"

The colour, never very roseate at any time, save when heightened by intemperance, faded from the prince's cheek, leaving it of a sickly, cadaverous yellow tint. But after a time he recovered himself a little.

"Psha!" he murmured to himself, irritably, "this is some practical joke. Who can have played it? I do not recognise the hand."

He examined it more closely, but without being able to identify it.

"This is written by some stranger to intimidate me, I suppose, or for the purpose of extorting money," he continued; "none of my friends would have dared to write such words as these."

Suddenly he thought of Lord Harcliffe.

"It must be that fellow!" he exclaimed. "Yes, it is just such a letter as he would have written. Perhaps Pharoah may know something of this. I wonder it never struck me so before."

His Royal Highness rang the hand-bell

Pharoah appeared.

"Has anyone entered this room within the last ten minutes?" inquired the prince.

"No, your Highness."

"You are certain?"

"Positive! I have not stirred from my post for the last half-hour."

"This letter," said the prince, holding up the concise

but unpleasant epistle, "has been laid upon the table within the last ten minutes."

"I know nothing of it, your Highness," returned Pharoah.

"'Tis very strange! Perhaps some of the other domestics may be better informed—go and inquire."

Pharoah departed, and during his absence the prince, evidently discomfited, endeavoured to allay his anxiety by imbibing several glasses of brandy.

He had grown a little more composed when Pharoah re-entered.

"Well, what news?" asked the prince.

"I have inquired, your Royal Highness," answered Pharoah, "but without success."

"Psha! I shall begin to think it is the work of the devil himself! You can go!"

Pharoah obeyed.

"I must shake off this nervous timidity, this depression," said the prince to himself. "I can understand an insolant rascal like the Black Highwayman writing me a threatening letter, but how he could have contrived to place it here baffles me, unless"—a new idea seemed suddenly to strike him—"his old servant, Pharoah, is in league with him, and has deceived me. This letter looks like the work of a confederate."

The prince little knew how near he was to the truth, and that Pharoah had quietly deposited the letter written by Lord Harcliffe, on the table, while the prince was looking from the window.

"I shall visit 'The Retreat' to-night," soliloquised the royal debauchee; "I need excitement, company; and the presence of my boon companions will cheer me. Would the night were come!"

Having given utterance to this wish, the prince, whose brains were already muddled with liqueurs and brandy, threw himself back in the chair, and endeavoured to expedite the passage of time by sleeping it away.

While the Prince of Wales, therefore, is thus wrapped in slumber, let us look in at a small upper chamber in "The Prince's Retreat."

Our readers will remember this chamber as the former sanctuary of our heroes when the pursuit was hot after them, and that it was here they found a secure asylum.

Here were seated Lord Harcliffe and the beautiful Beatrice Riccioli, looking more lovely than ever.

"The course of true love" with them had not only "run smoothly," but was at the full.

As the Black Highwayman gazed into the depths of her dark speaking eyes, he felt a sense of rapture he had never before experienced.

But with that rapture came a rush of other thoughts that to a certain extent disturbed him.

He felt that he had secured her entire affections without informing her who he *was* to whom she had so willingly surrendered them.

But he resolved to atone for his fault, though he forfeited by so doing the love that was dearer to him than his life.

Clasping the fair girl by his side to his breast, and looking earnestly in her face, he said, tenderly:

"You love me, Beatrice?"

"Love you!" she echoed, almost in a tone of surprise—"*you*, my preserver! Oh, *carissima mia!* what a question! Can you doubt me?"

She threw her white arms round his lordship as she spoke, and looked up in his face with such a sweet assuring smile, that if ever he had been inclined to cherish doubts, they must have been at once and for ever swept away.

"I believe you love me, Beatrice," continued the Black Highwayman: "it is not your love I doubt, or my love for you; it is whether I am worthy of it."

"You are—I am sure you are!" she exclaimed, warmly—"worthy of a reward far greater than my poor love can ever bestow!"

"My dearest, believe me I can wish for nothing greater—nothing better than your love. To be deprived of that would be to lose every joy in life. Still, I think you should know who it is to whom your have given your heart, and with whom you look forward to pass your life."

Beatrice pressed the hand she clasped, and Lord Harcliffe continued:

"The fate of man, the position he occupies in this world is not to be controlled by himself. He finds himself launched upon the tide of this busy stream, and he must sail with the tide, or be submerged in its rapid current.

"Fortune—the fickle goddess—seemed to favour me from my birth, but in her own particular way. Poverty I always abhorred. My nature, early associations, temperament and tastes, led me to desire pleasure, luxury, and refinement.

"Fate led me in the path, and pointed the way to the possession of these; and she said to me these words:—

"'*Everything is possible to a bold heart and a ready hand. That which you desire to have, make up your mind unflinchingly to possess, and you will infallibly gain it.*'

"This was the advice the *voice of Fate* whispered in my ears. I followed her counsel, and succeeded; the result was all I could desire—luxury, wealth, pleasure; but the penalty—a liability at any moment to ruin, disgrace, death!"

"Oh, Heaven!" murmured Beatrice, with a look of terror.

"I thought—I feared—my words would startle you; but I cannot, I will not disguise the truth, even to screen myself," said Lord Harcliffe. "I almost blush to make so painful a confession," he continued, "but the man to whom you have given the rich treasure of your loving heart and lovely self is at this moment nothing less than a proscribed and guilty felon, with the stern finger of the law over his head, pointing him to his goal, the gibbet!"

Beatrice started to her feet, with a wild cry of alarm.

"Oh no, no! it cannot be! You guilty? You a felon? Surely you mock me!" she exclaimed, in a voice of terror.

"I have spoken the truth," answered her lover, in a low, sad tone; "would it were not so!"

"And are you not a lord, then?"

"I have a right to that title from my father, who was of noble birth; but I have another title that eclipses my nobility, and proclaims me a knight of the road. I am the BLACK HIGHWAYMAN!"

The beautiful Beatrice Riccioli drew back a few paces, and remained for a few moments in silence, but there was neither reproach nor abhorrence in her look.

Lord Harcliffe, with his head bowed down with shame, stood like a culprit before his beautiful judge, waiting to hear his sentence.

At length she spoke.

"It is not the position of a man," she said, "whether it be high or low, that gains for him the love of a true woman; it is the man himself. Before I knew who or what you were, I gave you my heart—I loved you! Now that you tell me your name and character, I love you still—innocent or guilty, I shall always love you till I die, my own! my dearest!"

She rushed forward as she spoke, and throwing her arms passionately round his neck, pressed her glowing cheek to his.

"Angel!" cried the Black Highwayman, rapturously, "you have saved me! let my past life be blotted out! If Heaven permit, I will live for you in the future. Your love shall be the amulet to preserve me; your fair image the guiding star to lead me on in the path of honour and virtue, that when old age creeps on, and my hair is white, and my steps are feeble, I may look back, at least upon the close of life, with a quiet and peaceful conscience, and say I owe all to you."

The trusting love and devotion of the beautiful woman who so confidingly entrusted herself to his honour and protection seemed to change the entire current of the Black Highwayman's feelings.

Circumstances which he had before treated lightly, nay jestingly, now became serious realities.

Life, of which he had a few hours ago been reckless, had now become a precious treasure to be prized and retained if possible.

He knew—and the thought fell upon his heart with a crushing weight—that that life was forfeit to the laws—that a large reward had been placed upon his head, and that the gallows, with all its ghastly terrors, awaited him whenever caught.

It was as he pondered sadly over these true but painful facts, that one of those thoughts that sometimes dart like a bright flash of light over the darkness of our mental horizon, came suddenly across him.

It was a desperate plan, but his case was desperate, and it seemed to him as though Heaven itself had suggested

[CAPTAIN HAWK BRINGS THE BLACK HIGHWAYMAN THE ORDER FOR RELEASE.]

the means by which both he and his comrade might secure indemnity for the past, and a prospect of a calm and happy life for the future.

It was this:—

The Prince of Wales had been cognisant of certain great and atrocious crimes committed under his sanction, and would have been guilty of still greater, could he have found an instrument.

Of some of these he and Captain Hawk had proofs, most convincing and damning.

The captain not having yet returned, Lord Harcliffe was ignorant how vastly the chain of evidence his comrade had collected would tend to secure their safety, but that which he did know he confidently counted on to secure their safety.

The Prince of Wales would in his exalted position hardly dare to risk the terrible charges Lord Harcliffe could bring against him, and the Black Highwayman felt confident in his own mind that with the assistance of Pharoah, he could so work upon the prince's mind as to make the silence of his comrade and himself an equivalent for their own free pardon, which the prince would procure.

This idea once presented to his mind, Lord Harcliffe at once set himself to work to arrange his plan of procedure.

The unexpected arrival of Pharoah assisted him greatly.

The announcement that he came to make, that the prince and his companions would visit "The Retreat" that evening, was the most gratifying that could possibly have been made to him, inasmuch as it gave him the opportunity of putting his plan at once into execution.

He detailed his intention to Phareah fully, and his faithful and devoted friend warmly acquiesced in the idea, and predicted every success to his attempt.

It was therefore arranged between them that Lord

Harcliffe should come upon the guilty parties at a moment when they least expected it.

All therefore that remained—the preliminaries and plan of attack being settled—was to wait patiently till the proper moment for striking the blow should arrive.

Lord Harcliffe did not, like the Prince of Wales, seek to sleep away the interim, but employed his mind in collecting all the evidence possible to strike terror into the hearts of those he sought to terrify.

Nor did the prince sleep long.

His dreams disturbed him, the mysterious letter haunted him, and at length, after turning the matter over in every possible way, he resolved to shut his eyes wilfully to that which his *conscience told him* was the truth, and treat the whole affair as a kind of ugly jest.

He thought also that it might be a good plan to enlist some of the police on his side at the very outset, and the more he contemplated this piece of policy, the more he approved it.

He therefore determined to send a private message to Bow Street to Messrs. Peterson and Nicholas Twigg, requiring their presence at "The Retreat" that evening on private business.

This message was confided to Pharoah, who delivered it with every possible tact and secrecy.

The two worthy members of the police force were immensely inflated at being thus privately summoned to a conference with the heir apparent.

They were positively bursting with self-complacency, and the importance of the mission they were about to fulfil.

It seemed after the message had been delivered to them that their very clothes were too small to contain such extensive personages as themselves.

They assumed a stern, impenetrable air, and could scarcely bring themselves to notice inferior officers who had not been summoned to the prince's retreat on private business.

Nicholas found it necessary to step out very frequently during the afternoon for sundry little drops to allay his curiosity and impatience.

He found himself, as he sipped his rum-and-water at the bar of the public-house round the corner in Drury Lane, winking at the barmaid, and making himself more than usually agreeable and condescending.

But then he was a great man, in the confidence of a prince, and he could afford to stoop from his pedestal and flirt a little with a pretty girl, though she was only a barmaid.

But time rolled on, and in due course brought upon its wings the hour for the appointed interview.

Accordingly Peterson and Nicholas, having just looked in at Bow Street, and given a few parting directions, in a very "rum-and-watery" manner to Inspector Nutkins, for whom they felt a profound commiseration, almost contempt, they departed for Pall Mall and "The Retreat."

The prince and his party were already there.

The prince complaining of feeling rather low, he was only surrounded by his own "particular set," that comprised the parties previously introduced to our readers, and who need not, therefore, be particularly enumerated here.

The wine had circulated briskly, and the nerves of the party had been strung up to a very tolerable state of tension, when the prince introduced the subject of the letter.

It was received with considerable apprehension by the guilty revellers, and had the effect of producing several pallid faces, a few internal spasmodic convulsions, and a more vigorous application to the bottle than before.

Their first emotion having passed, the prince produced the epistle itself and laid it on the table.

It was an object of the closest scrutiny.

Some thought one thing—some another; but whatever their real convictions might be, they all affected to treat it lightly, and to laugh at it—not very heartily, though—as an impertinent practical joke.

It was in the midst of one of these questionable outbursts of hilarity, that Pharoah entered and informed the prince that "two police officers from Bow Street were waiting."

It was quite curious to observe the effect this announcement took upon this exclusive few.

Each member seemed to be possessed with a sudden qualm that drove the flush of intemperance from their features.

Some even were so far influenced as to appear desirous of disappearing under the table.

But the prince, after enjoying the joke for his own private satisfaction, removed their apprehension, by informing them that the officers had been expressly sent for by himself.

"It is always as well," he said, "to have the police on our side."

"Oh yes, yes—decidedly!" was the universal cry.

It was astonishing how quickly their fears were hushed, and how the presence of the police, that at first filled them with terror, became in the way the prince put it to them, a source of perfect security.

When, therefore, the clattering of the boots of Messrs. Peterson and Twigg was heard in the ante-room, there was quite a murmur of expectation; and when at length the two worthies appeared, looking very inflammatory and important, the interest arrived at its height.

It was the policy of the prince, and consequently of the prince's "reflectors," to put the officials perfectly at their ease.

His Royal Highness therefore, in a courteous tone, said:

"Good evening, gentlemen. I am happy to see you! Pray take a seat at our table."

"Yer Rile 'Ighness is werry kind," responded Nicholas Twigg, "an' if it aint a' takin' too great a liberty——"

"Not at all, gentlemen—not at all!" interposed the prince, assuringly. "This is a matter of business on which we wish to ask your advice."

"Well, yer 'Ighness, suttin'ly bis'niss is bis'niss," remarked Nicholas, "an' if me an' my brother hofficer Peterson can give yer hany information on hany pint, has it's most likely as we can, from the many long 'ears o' hexperience as we're 'ad, I can only say as we shall be werry proud an' 'appy to give it."

Having thus delivered himself, the worthy official dropped into a seat, an example his comrade instantly followed.

"Pass the bottle to our friends," cried the prince.

Two decanters, in silver machines with wheels, came rattling up the table towards the officers.

"Port!" ejaculated Nicholas, as he seized one of the bottles and poured out for himself and Peterson. "Port," he repeated, "is a wine as I pertickler admires: it seems to do a man good."

He raised his glass and said:

"Yer Ryle 'Ighnessis good 'ealth—gen'lemen hall!" and emptied it at once.

"Pray don't spare the bottle, gentlemen," urged the prince; "you know wine was made to drink."

"That's a werry senserble remark o' your'n, yer 'Ighness," answered Nicholas, pouring out and emptying two glasses successively; "that's jest what I says. Says I, what's the good o' 'avin' good wine if yer don't drink it?"

"The object for which I sent for you two gentlemen is to ask your opinion of a certain letter that I have received," commenced the prince.

"Ah yes, suttinly, a letter! Does yer 'Ighness 'appen to 'ave it anywhere about yer?"

"It is here," replied the prince, handing over the letter to Nicholas.

The police officer looked at it profoundly, and then, after a significant "Um!" put on his spectacles and looked again.

"It *is* a letter, your 'Ighness—there ain't no manner o' doubt o' that!" said Nicholas, in a strong tone of conviction.

"We had no doubt on that point," observed the prince, drily, "but of its contents——"

"I'm a goin' to inwestigate," answered Nicholas.

After tipping off another glass of port, he read the letter.

"'Your secret crimes are known to me! Beware!'

"Ah! um! yes!" he ejaculated, deliberately.

"What do you think of that?" demanded the prince.

"Why, yer 'Ighness, I knows what I knows," returned the officer, with a peculiarly confidential wink. "It's all right—I'm downy!"

The prince and his companions seemed to be slightly mystified as to Mr. Twigg's meaning.

"Perhaps," remarked the prince, "as you seem to understand the meaning of that letter, you will have the kindness to enlighten us on the subject, who are at present very much in the dark."

"This letter was sent by some 'uns, your 'Ighness—that's my impression!" said Nicholas, confidently. "What's your'n, mate?" he inquired of his companion.

"I'm o' your opinion," replied Peterson.

"But what could be the object of sending such a letter as that to me? 'Secret crimes!' What secret crimes have I committed? It is perfectly absurd!" exclaimed the prince.

"O' course it is. Th' hidear o' the Hair aperient a committin' secret crimes is hout o' hall raisin; hit's ridiklus!" Nicholas laughed at the outrageous supposition.

"Then what does it mean?"

"Hin my erpinion, yer 'Ighness, it's a case o' 'timidation an' 'xtortion," continued Nicholas, in a somewhat indistinct tone.

"I think so too," assented the prince.

"It can't be nothink else," Nicholas resumed; "therefore the chap as writ this 'll be sure to come for 'is answer, an' then when 'e does come 'e must be dropped upon by us."

"I presume you mean he must be taken into custody?" inquired the prince.

"D'cid'ly!" hiccupped Mr. Twigg.

The police officer had been drinking incessant drops of rum since the afternoon, and the port-wine coming on the top of the spirit produced a remarkable confusion in his ideas.

He was rapidly getting drunk, and, in his replies to the prince, had to shut one eye in a very peculiar manner in order to see his Royal Highness, who kept waving to and fro, and appeared suddenly to have six heads.

"I don' see no (hic) other way," murmured Mr. Twigg.

Peterson suddenly remembered the glimpse they had had that afternoon of the Black Highwayman, and he whispered his doubts to his companion.

"No (hic) doubt on it!" exclaimed Nicholas. "It's Black 'Ighw'm'n, sure's my name's (hic) Nick!"

It was therefore suggested, owing to the formidable character of the man, that Peterson should depart for further assistance from Bow Street, and that a body of men should remain constantly on the premises, until the impertinent and anonymous letter-writer should arrive.

This seemed perfectly satisfactory to Mr. Twigg, who expressed himself willing to remain while his mate went for a staff of officers.

Accordingly, that no time should be lost, Peterson departed.

Nicholas once more applied himself to the port, and became so elevated that he was on the verge of calling upon the prince for a song, when three peculiar knocks were heard at the door.

The company looked inquiringly at the prince, who whispered to Nicholas:

"This must be he!"

"Who?" asked the officer, whose eyes rolled in his head with liquor.

"The writer of the letter," said the prince, in a low tone. "Quick! get out of sight, and you can listen to his conversation without being seen yourself."

"Cer'nly!" responded the intoxicated official.

His Royal Highness opened the door of a buffet near at hand.

"Get in here, quickly!" urged the prince.

Nicholas complied, and pitched into the recess head first.

Hardly had the door been closed, when the three knocks were repeated.

"Now, gentlemen!" hastily whispered the prince to his companions, "whatever allegations are made by this person, be bold and deny them!"

Having pledged themselves to this, the prince called out:

"Come in!"

The door opened instantly, and Lord Harcliffe walked forward into the centre of the room; where he stood with a calm but stern expression of countenance contemplating the assembled company.

"Well, sir?" at length demanded the Prince of Wales, "what is your business here?"

"First, you received my letter?"

"Relative to 'certain secret crimes,' of which I know nothing. Yes!"

"I sent that to warn you that I know you and your deeds," said Lord Harcliffe, sternly.

"Well, sir?" said the prince.

"At our last interview," continued the Black Highwayman, "your Highness made me certain proposals, which I rejected with indignation."

"I remember nothing of them," returned the Royal liar, coolly.

"Your memory, then, must be remarkably defective; but these gentlemen will probably recollect drawing their swords upon me at Leicester House when I made my escape by the window?"

As he spoke, Lord Harcliffe glanced round at the assembled company.

"We don't understand you!"

"The fellow speaks in riddles!"

"What does he mean?"

Were the remarks that fell from their lips.

"You all seem to have eaten of the fruit of the lotus, you are so utterly forgetful. But whether these facts have or have not vanished from your memory, they have not from mine; and I am here to inquire into the fate of a friend of mine who came into this place alive and well, and who met his death in the room known as the Red Chamber!"

Once more his lordship glanced round scrutinizingly at the guests, on whom this announcement had, in spite of their determination, taken a visible effect.

"Do you take us for a gang of assassins?" demanded the Prince of Wales, in a lofty tone of assumed indignation.

"That is precisely what I *do* take you for!" answered Lord Harcliffe, in a tone of stern conviction.

"Insolent!"

"Scoundrel!"

"Cut him down!"

Rose on all sides.

The members were about to leave their seats.

"Stay!" cried the Black Highwayman, in a voice of such peremptory command, that they paused and remained quite stationary.

"I call you," he continued, "not only assassins, but cowardly murderers and robbers! You not only doomed to an awful and violent death a young and amiable man—whose years, in comparison with yours, should have been his protection—but you despoiled the dead! You would deny the deed, but you have not the hardihood to do so; your consciences convict you and speak in every lineament of your ashy features! Once more I demand where is my friend, Count Antonio Riccioli?"

Agitation, rage, and conscious guilt prevented the confused listeners replying, till the Prince of Wales, who was the most self-possessed of the assembly, replied, fiercely:

"You are mad, and know not what you say! We understand nothing of what you speak. Your words seem to us the incoherent ravings of a maniac!"

"You would wish to consider them so, prince, but you cannot," said Lord Harcliffe. "You know in your inmost heart every word I have uttered is so true that each one pierces like a dart through all your hearts!"

"Scoundrel! no more!" foamed the prince.

"That death-trap in the Red Chamber," continued the Black Highwayman, coolly, unmoved by the outburst of the prince's fury, "although doubtless highly useful to shroud the atrocities committed in this place from the eyes of the world, would wear a very ugly, ghastly appearance when exposed to the light of day—as ghastly as the victims that it receives!"

"Villain! Your words are slanderous falsehoods!"

"I can prove them!"

"'Tis false!"

"I say 'tis true, or I should never dare to utter such an accusation! Remember 'tis possible to search a well—to descend into its depths for truth's sake, and to bring murder to light! Be wise, therefore! Do not pretend to ignore a crime in which you are all concerned, or you may tempt me to a step that would involve you all in ruin!"

"What step?"

"A public accusation!"

"Psha—fool! You know not what you say! Do you remember who you are that you say this?"

"Perfectly! I am a man whose life is forfeit to the law, a price of £300 being set upon my head!"

"And do you imagine a condemned felon would have power to criminate me, or any of my friends?" asked the prince, furiously.

"I might not, perhaps," retorted Lord Harcliffe; "but I should leave the knowledge I possess in the hands of those who would breathe forth the horrid deed throughout the length and breadth of the land, till a million voices should raise the cry of vengeance on the murderer, even though he were the King of England, instead of the heir apparent!"

"You have gone too far!" cried the prince, whose indignation, united to the wine he had drank, rendered him reckless.

He hastily approached the buffet, and throwing open the door, cried:

"Come forth!"

No sooner said than done.

Nicholas Twigg, dead drunk, "came forth" obediently, or rather rolled out on to the carpet as soon as the door was opened.

"I give this man into custody!" cried the prince, wrathfully, pointing to the Black Highwayman.

"Cer'nly—cus'dy! I'man! Hic—hic!" gasped Nicholas, and then fell asleep.

Lord Harcliffe laughed derisively, and then said:

"If these are the instruments with which you seek to arrest me you will require some of rather keener temper!"

"And here they are!" cried a voice behind him, and in an instant four powerful men were upon him.

So suddenly was this performed, that resistance was impossible.

Utterly borne down by numbers, the Black Highwayman, seeing there was no present means of escape, yielded to circumstances and offered no attempt.

"Away with the scoundrel!" cried the prince; "but first drink, my honest fellows!"

The prisoner, being handcuffed and perfectly secure, no objection could be raised against such a desirable offer.

They accordingly imbibed several bumpers of the delicious wine with infinite gusto.

Having finished, the prince said to Peterson, who headed the expedition, slipping at the same time a cheque for £50 into his hand:

"I deliver into your charge the culprit known as the Black Highwayman. The warrants are already out, so that no fresh charge is needed. Away with him to Newgate!"

As Lord Harcliffe was about to be led away he turned to the prince, and said:

"I leave my charge in the hands of others; and my parting warning to you, Frederick, heir apparent to the throne of England, is this: We are both criminals! Take heed lest we meet on the same ground! Newgate is large enough to contain even the Prince of Wales!"

And with these words he was conducted out.

CHAPTER CCXXIX.

LORD HARCLIFFE BECOMES THE INMATE OF A NEWGATE CELL.—THE FRIENDLY JAILER—CAPTAIN HAWK OBTAINS A FREE PARDON FOR HIMSELF AND THE BLACK HIGHWAYMAN.—THE END.

It was with feelings that can be better imagined than described that the Black Highwayman saw the grim, dark walls of the prison in which he was to be incarcerated, and his heart sank within him as he entered its gloomy portals.

Was this strange? Not at all!

Just as the sense of the degradation of his past life had forced itself upon him—just when he had resolved, Providence helping him, that his future career should be one of undeviating rectitude—he found himself cut off from every opportunity—a felon, in a felon's cell, with a felon's manacles upon his limbs.

His plan of intimidation had failed with the Prince of Wales so far as he was concerned, for what hope could he have that the ministers of justice would listen to an accusation from the lips of a criminal against the second person in the kingdom?

No, his case seemed well-nigh hopeless, and yet at the very moment he pronounced this sorrowful verdict against himself, a voice at his heart bade him not "yield to despair," and the form of Beatrice Riccioli seemed to smile upon him from her angel eyes, and whisper to him "all would yet be well."

"Heaven grant it may!" he cried.

The governor paid him a visit shortly after his arrival and recognised him immediately.

"I think," said he, "your lordship and I have met before, have we not?"

"I am sorry to say you are perfectly correct," answered Lord Harcliffe, moodily.

"You have made some stir in the world since you last honoured us with a visit," continued the governor; "your name and that of your comrade have become quite famous."

"The world must always have a lion," retorted the prisoner, who was rather annoyed at the governor's remarks, "and if it makes lions of us, let it do so, but I may remark, that when the animal you allude to has been recently captured, it is a rash policy on the part of the keeper to approach too near, or seek to aggravate him. There are instances on record where an angry lion has torn an aggravating keeper piecemeal!"

Lord Harcliffe spoke these words in such a peculiarly pointed tone that the governor must have been very obtuse indeed if he had not understood their meaning; but this he did perfectly, and edging away from the prisoner, so as to be beyond the reach of his chain, he said, in a different tone:

"Well, well, I did not mean to offend you. To tell you the truth, I am sorry to see you here; you look fit for something far superior to a prison cell in Newgate."

Lord Harcliffe sighed.

The words of the governor seemed earnest and sincere, and his last remark set the thoughts of the Black Highwayman roaming far away back into the past and forward to the future.

"When you were last an inmate of these walls, your stay was of brief duration: let us hope your present visit may be of no longer continuance—that you may find a friend, as you did before," said the governor.

"It is strange," returned Lord Harcliffe, "that the actual cause of my being here at this moment is my refusal to perform a promise to which I was supposed to have pledged myself as the condition of my release when I was first imprisoned here."

"But why did you refuse?"

"Because it was a deed not only unworthy of a man, but characterised by everything that was terrible and unnatural," answered Lord Harcliffe.

"And you refused to perform it?"

"Of course I did."

"You were right; I cannot blame you, even though that refusal has brought you here."

"I care not who blames me, since for once in my life, at least, I cannot blame myself."

"I fear your case is desperate."

"It may be."

"You will be brought to trial."

"Perhaps so."

"Is there any doubt about it?"

"There is doubt about everything."

"Well, if you are?"

"I know my fate beforehand."

"What?"

"Tyburn Tree! There is *no doubt* about that!"

"From your words and manner, I infer a doubt whether you ever will be brought to trial."

"You seem to be full of suppositions, sir."

"I am, in your case. You interest me," said the governor; "you are not one of the common herd."

"No, I am the son of a nobleman."

"There is a certain romance about you that rarely invests those whom I continually encounter here."

"Then you really would be sorry to see me mount the scaffold?"

"I should indeed!"

"You would rather I should escape?"

"Much rather!"

"Then open my prison doors, and set me free."

The governor smiled apologetically.

"That is more than I dare do."

"I always *dare* to do what I *wish*."

"You are very different from myself."

"You are right, I am."

"Were I to let you escape, they would probably hang me as your substitute."

"But would there not be a great satisfaction in the reflection that you had saved a fellow-creature's life by the exchange?"

"It would hardly be an equivalent."

"Ah! you are not in earnest."

"I am indeed, in wishing you safely out of this place; but not sufficiently so to sacrifice myself in your stead."

"You would hardly believe it, but I would not change places with you at this moment."

"I doubt you—but why?"

"I could not endure your occupation. It would kill me in a month."

"You would grow accustomed to it."

"Not I. Do you know how I should inaugurate my entrance into office?"

"No; how?"

"I should, the moment I arrived, knock off the chains of all the prisoners, unlock the doors and set them free. Within an hour the jail would be empty."

"Ha, ha! you're facetious."

"On the contrary, I never felt more depressed."

"And yet you jest?"

"It is the only weapon I have to ward off your questions."

"I beg you pardon, do I annoy you?"

"Not particularly, but I should prefer being alone."

"You shall have your wish."

"Can I do nothing for you?"

"Nothing!"

"Will you take anything?"

"Yes."

"What shall I send you?"

"A glass of brandy-and-water, and a cigar."

"I will, immediately."

"For the present, then, adieu."

"Good-bye."

The door opened and let out the loquacious but friendly disposed governor, and shortly afterwards one of the jailers entered, bringing with him the luxuries his lordship had ordered.

The man placed the brandy and cigars upon the table and civilly asked Lord Harcliffe if he should procure him a light.

His lordship answered in the affirmative; and having lit his cigar, began to smoke in a meditative manner.

The jailer, who had contemplated his noble prisoner very earnestly, having no reason for remaining, went slowly towards the door, and then turned and looked again.

His lordship noticing that he still lingered, said to him:

"Do you want anything? Oh, stay!" he added, suddenly, tendering the man a half-guinea, "my meditations make me forgetful."

"Oh, I don't want your money, sir!" exclaimed the jailer; "I wasn't waiting for that."

"What, then?"

"Your face seems familiar to me, sir," said the man.

"And yours to me," returned Lord Harcliffe. "Where have I seen you before?"

"I used to be head jailer at Huntingdon Jail."

"What! were you there when my comrade, Captain Hawk, was confined there?"

"I was indeed, sir," answered the jailer, eagerly, his features brightening up at the name. "I waited on him all the time."

"To be sure you were. I remember seeing you there; Captain Hawk has often spoken of you to me."

"Has he, though?" said the man, with an expression of intense gratification displayed on his features. "Is he well, sir?"

"Quite!"

"And out of trouble?"

"If you mean by that, is he at liberty—yes!"

"I'm heartily glad of that!" said the man, warmly. "He was a brave gentleman. I was never so rejoiced at anything in my life as when he cheated the gallows so cleverly."

"And so you have removed to London?"

"Yes, sir. There was no chance of getting on down at Huntingdon."

"And do you do better here?"

"I get more money," the man replied; "not that that in particular caused me to leave the country, but my old mother died, and I felt dull at home when I could no longer see her; so I came here for a change."

"And do you find it an agreeable one? If so, it's more than I do!" said his lordship.

"Well, there's more life and variety here. But I don't know that I don't like the country quite as well."

"I should like to be there at this moment, with a good ten-mile gallop before me," remarked Lord Harcliffe. "I'd give them a run before they caught me!"

"I'm sorry they have caught you," exclaimed the jailer, in a regretful tone; "they're not like country folk here; they're so devilish wide-awake; there's no chance for a fellow."

"Not much, I'm afraid. But I mustn't stay any longer," the man answered, "or the governor 'll think I'm up to something with you: they're as suspicious as old gooseberry in this place."

"Well, pray don't get into trouble on my account. I am somewhat fatigued, and not much in the vein for company; in fact, I have been talking incessantly for the last half-hour for the express purpose of driving away the blue devils. But don't let me keep you from your duty."

"All right, your lordship; only I couldn't help speakin' to you—it seemed quite to bring back old times."

"Well, my dear fellow," said the Black Highwayman, consolingly, "I daresay we shall meet occasionally."

"I'm afraid we shall, your lordship; and though I like your company, I would rather see you on the outside than in."

"I endorse your remark; I would much rather see myself there!" exclaimed Lord Harcliffe.

"P'r'aps you will yet—who knows?" replied the man, as he quitted the cell.

"Ah! who knows?" echoed the prisoner, as he threw himself upon his pallet and puffed his cigar in silence.

"I wonder," he soliloquised, "whether my comrade knows where I am?—or Beatrice?—or Pharoah? Surely they will not leave me to perish without an effort to save me?"

And as though ashamed of giving utterance to such a thought, he exclaimed:

"No, no! there is not one I have named who would not die for me if it were necessary!"

Could Lord Harcliffe at that moment have been able to see and know all that was transpiring at a distance, he would have been quite assured that he was not forgotten; and if for a moment he indulged in a doubt that such might be the case, it was rather the natural depression, caused by the surrounding associations, than from a belief that it was so.

As he lay in that gloomy cell, watching the thin wreaths of smoke as they curled upwards to the roof, he became oppressed with an unconquerable drowsiness.

He was by no means inclined to throw it off; and to court the drowsy god, he emptied the tumbler of brandy and-water, and sinking back on his pallet, dropped the cigar from his lips and almost instantaneously fell asleep to dream of freedom.

* * * * *

The lights still blazed in the saloons of the Prince's Retreat.

The prince and his companions, in much self-congratulation at the determined manner in which they had got rid of their accuser and dispatched him to a dungeon, continued their orgies furiously.

They seemed on this particular night to be imbued with the very spirit of intemperance

They drank more than ever.

Why was this? Was it that, although they had got rid of *one* accuser, there remained *another* that would not be ejected in so summary a manner?

Was it that conscience called them ugly names and would not be silenced?

The prince had succeeded in calming their apprehensions, by assuring them that no accusations levelled at him or themselves would have any weight, and on the strength of that assurance they had worked themselves up, by dint of much perseverance with the bottle, to a state of somewhat over-exuberant hilarity.

"The idea of that fellow calling us a gang of assassins!" said Ashley Fordyce, the banker, who could scarcely see out of his eyes.

"Not only assassins," chimed in Sir Slingsby Sleuforth, "but murderers——"

"Robbers!" added Lord Mansfield.

"I wonder how the devil he came to know anything about the matter?" exclaimed the Marquis of Rockleigh. "I thought the Red Chamber was a secret known only to ourselves."

"I thought so too," joined in the Prince of Wales. "But it seems that girl Clarissa has been allowing her tongue to run wild. Psha! it's always the way where women are taken into confidence; they are sure to turn traitors and betray those who trust them."

It was quite a satire upon himself the Prince was uttering; for it was he himself who had first mentioned to Clarissa that there were means of death of a sudden and violent nature in the walls of "The Retreat."

He little knew how the unhappy woman he was thinking of had been punished for her cupidity; he little dreamt the victims had changed places.

"At all events, they can prove nothing; and as for this fellow whom I have packed off to prison to-night, he will——"

The termination of the sentence was suddenly stopped by three very distinct knocks at the door.

"D—n it!" cried the banker. "He's returned!"

Every eye was fixed upon the door.

"Who's there?" demanded the prince, loudly.

There was no answer but the sudden opening of the door, through which passed a figure enveloped in a cloak, and wearing a black mask, and whom our readers will at once divine was no other than Captain Hawk.

The figure coolly closed the door, and advanced with the most perfect calmness.

"What seek you?" demanded the prince, who, together with his companions, was somewhat disturbed at the sight of this apparition.

"I am here, in the first place," answered the captain, in a stern voice, "to demand my friend Lord Harcliffe whom you have packed off to prison to-night."

"It is too late," returned the prince—"he is now in the hands of the law."

"Betrayed by you!" fiercely exclaimed the captain. "And why? Because he called you by your right names—a gang of murderers—because he knew too much of your vile secrets—because you feared him!"

"Feared?" cried the prince. "Psha!"

"I repeat, because you feared him! But if you dreaded him, dread me still more; because, even though he were dead, still I, Phœnix-like, should rise out of his ashes."

The visitors looked at the dark figure with silent apprehension.

Unfortunately, there were no police there.

They began to feel uncomfortable, and at length, as if by common consent, arose to depart.

"Sit still, each one of you!" cried the captain, coolly drawing a pistol from beneath his cloak and cocking it.

The visitors gradually sank again into their seats.

"Now, then, once more," continued Captain Hawk, "I demand my friend! If you do not deliver him, I shall denounce you as the murderers of the Count Antonio Riccioli!"

"We do not understand you."

"Perhaps, then, you will understand one nearer and dearer to your murdered victim—his sister. Enter, signora!" he cried, opening the door, and leading in the lovely Beatrice Riccioli.

"I am here to know what you have done with my brother Antonio?" she said.

"We know nothing of your brother!" answered the prince, roughly.

"No, nothing—nothing!" echoed the rest.

"I will call him, then, from the grave, to which you consigned him, to answer for himself," said Beatrice, solemnly. "Antonio Riccioli, come forth!" she cried.

This adjuration was received at first with an incredulous sneer; but when, with a slow and measured step, the form of Antonio stalked in at the door, and stood before them, a shriek of horror burst from every lip, and a deadly terror fastened on them.

"I accuse you, Frederick Prince of Wales, and all present, with being accessory to an attempt upon my life, which must have been sacrificed had not Heaven preserved me!"

The murderers looked doubtingly at each other.

The victim who descended through the trap was not me, but Clarissa, who sought to rob me, and paid the penalty while she was searching for my gold."

The guilty accomplices shuddered.

"And now," continued Captain Hawk, "having finished the tragedy of the Red Chamber, let us turn to the blood-stained secrets of the Gray Mansion! with which you are all so well acquainted."

There was a pause, whilst a shock like a stream of electricity passed through the assembly.

"The Gray Mansion!" echoed the prince, with a strong effort to be calm. "Where is that supposed to be situated?"

"In Hertfordshire," replied Captain Hawk.

"I know of no such place!" answered his Highness, with unblushing effrontery.

"Allow me, then, to refresh your memory. Ridley Massingham," he cried, "approach!"

With arms bound with ropes, and led by the jailer, the guilty man entered.

"Now!" exclaimed the captain, to the dismayed party, "if you persist in denying your knowledge of the Gray Mansion, here is one who can confute you!"

No one dared repeat the falsehood.

"Marquis of Rockleigh," said Captain Hawk, "the poor woman whom you have kept there a prisoner for many years, and her son, *and yours*, are no more. The unhappy mother destroyed herself—the youth was cruelly murdered!"

The marquis turned ashy pale at this fearful announcement; but the prince, in a tone of pompous indignation—of course assumed—exclaimed:

"What have I to do with this?"

"More than anyone else!" was the prompt and stern reply. "And to you will the consequences come home with more terrible weight."

"Dare you, villain!——"

"Look upon this!" said the captain, in a low tone, suddenly approaching the prince. "Do you know this locket?" displaying before his eyes the trinket as he spoke.

The prince glared upon it, but still refused to recognise it.

"You do not remember it?—you *will* not!"

"I never saw it before!"

"Do you, then, remember a Spanish gentleman, by name Pedro Mendoza, the father of Inez Mendoza?"

At this name the prince's audacity forsook him. He uttered a loud, terror-stricken cry, and turned ghastly pale.

"Ah, I see you do remember her!" continued Captain Hawk. "I thought you would. You will also remember there are sand-pits in Kew Gardens, well adapted for the commission of a deed of blood, and offering great facilities for concealing a dead body!"

The prince, growing more and more moved, positively foamed at the mouth in his fearful agitation. So greatly was he moved, that the captain feared lest a fit of apoplexy should carry him off before the task he had assigned him should be accomplished.

"I see, you admit your guilt!" he said.

"No!" gasped the prince.

"You must yield to proofs, then: I will call your victim's father—he is in the next room."

"No, no!" almost screamed the royal culprit, in his intense excitement, "you drive me mad! What would you?"

"A free and unconditional pardon for all past offences for Lord Alfred Harcliffe, known as the Black Highwayman, and Captain Richard Hawk."

"It is impossible!" almost groaned the prince. "The former of these is in the hands of the law!"

"He must be released, then; and at once!"

"Released?"

"Ay, released! if not, let all here tremble for the consequences!"

There was so much stern determination—so much terrible earnestness—in the voice and manner of the speaker, that a panic fell on the hearts of all.

They staggered to their feet, and essayed to depart.

"We will go!" they faltered.

"Not one!" cried Captain Hawk, levelling his pistol at each in turn. "Remain here, where you are!"

They seemed to have lost the power of volition, and sank hopelessly down again.

"One alone," exclaimed the captain, "must leave this place: that one is yourself," he added, addressing the Prince of Wales. "Lose no time—depart at once! I give you two hours. If within that time you do not bring me here a full pardon for Captain Hawk and the Black Highwayman, signed by the Secretary of State, I swear by Heaven the charges I have laid against you and your iniquitous assembly, shall, with witnesses to substantiate them, be placed before the king—your father—before the clock strikes three of the morning!"

The prince, now thoroughly cowed and alarmed, exclaimed, with much trembling and agitation:

"The effort shall be made!"

His Highness rang the bell.

Pharoah entered, with an ill-concealed smile of exultation on his features.

"Order a coach instantly!" cried the prince.

Pharoah, too happy to receive the commission, hastened off, and in a few moments arrived with one, in which the prince departed to seek the Secretary of State.

Captain Hawk, in the meantime, with the most triumphant hopes of success in his breast, kept guard, pistol in hand, over the assembly of his guilty companions, from whom all mirth had long since departed.

In the meantime, the coach rumbled along on its journey to the mansion of Horace Walpole, the secretary.

The prince had some misgivings as to what this personage might think at seeing him at his door at such an hour of the night, and for such a purpose.

But there was no escape, and as the prince was desperate, he made up his mind to have the pardon, no matter what falsehoods he might have to tell in order to gain his end.

It was now midnight, and the thought that the secretary might be out, or in bed, or indisposed, was torture to him.

At length the dwelling he sought was reached.

A loud knock at the door brought the night porter, who was roused out of his first sleep, to see who it was at that unseasonable hour.

"Tell the secretary," said the prince, hastily, "that the Prince of Wales wishes to see him instantly."

"He has retired to rest, your Royal Highness," answered the porter, humbly.

"He must be aroused," cried the prince, "and at once! It is a matter of life and death!"

"Yes, your Highness," answered the man, who went to knock up the secretary's valet, who then proceeded at once to his master's bed-room.

"What!" exclaimed the secretary, "the Prince of Wales at this time of night? What can have happened?"

Hastily throwing on his dressing-gown, the official descended to the chamber into which his Highness had been conducted.

"You will pardon my disturbing you, Mr. Walpole, at this late hour, but necessity must plead my excuse."

"Don't speak of it, your Royal Highness; business is with me at any hour of the day or night a pleasure."

"I rejoice to hear it, since I can, then, feel I am not putting you to great inconvenience by this untimely visit."

"Be seated, your Royal Highness—pray be seated," said the complaisant secretary.

He had made it a rule always, and under any circumstances, to be civil, and he adhered to it.

At all hours and at all places the Secretary of State was to be found in the same equable tone of the mental temperature.

"And now," he inquired, "in what way can I serve your Royal Highness?"

"There are at present warrants out for the apprehension of two gentlemen of the road—Captain Hawk and Lord Harcliffe, better known as the Black Highwayman."

"Ah, yes, I believe so," replied Mr. Walpole, trying to recollect and identify the names. "Captain Hawk—Lord Harcliffe," he repeated. "Captain Hawk——"

"There's a reward of £200 offered by Government for their apprehension."

"Your Highness is right. Have you caught them, and are you come to claim the reward?" asked the secretary, smiling.

"Not I," returned the prince. "It is on a piece of business entirely opposed to catching them I am here."

"What, may I ask?"

"I wish them to be set free."

"I believe they *are* free. They seem to take good care to keep so," remarked the secretary, who seemed better informed on those points than he at first appeared.

"One only—Captain Hawk. His comrade, the Black Highwayman, was arrested and sent to Newgate this evening."

"The best place for him."

"Excuse me, Mr. Walpole, I cannot quite agree with you. There are many palliating circumstances connected with their history——"

"What, these highwaymen?"

"Yes—that renders them worthy of the highest commiseration."

"Indeed!"

"I assure you their career furnishes a romance of the most painful, but at the same time, most absorbing interest."

"Is it possible?"

"It is true."

"Strange things occur in this life!"

"Would anyone credit that Captain Hawk and the Black Highwayman were both of noble birth?"

"Indeed!" exclaimed the secretary.

"Yes," the prince went on, excitedly; "stolen by gipsies from their parents in infancy, and recognised by a mark set upon them by their kidnappers."

"Extraordinary!"

"Would it not be terrible that two men in whose veins ran noble blood should perish at Tyburn?"

"Undoubtedly. But it is more terrible to think that these men were not hindered by their noble blood from committing deeds worthy of such a fate," said the straightforward Walpole.

"Ah, yes, true!" replied the prince; "but there must always be a great allowance made for early associations. Now these poor children, stolen from their paternal roof by—by gipsies, could have had no sense of—of right and wrong implanted in their minds, consequently, not having such sense, they went a—wrong, of course, mutually."

"Very sad indeed to contemplate!" remarked the secretary, indulging in a slight shudder and a surreptitious yawn.

"Melancholy in the extreme!" exclaimed the prince, who had told lies till he was out of breath, and worked himself up almost to a fever in endeavouring to excite a strong sympathy in the breast of Mr. Walpole.

"We must use our influence to lift these men out of the false position they have been dragged into, and place them——"

"We should always be very careful in effecting such a change as this—that in removing individuals from a position we imagine false, we do not place them in another still more so," urged the cautious secretary.

"Oh, but in the case of these men it is different!" cried the prince, warmly. "They are noble fellows. In fact, Mr. Walpole, between ourselves, they have rendered me an inestimable service—saved my life, in fact, and not only that, but revealed and frustrated a plot that would else have shed the most illustrious blood in the country!"

"Good Heaven!" ejaculated Mr. Walpole. "Treason!"

"Hush, pray! I cannot bear to mention it! But pray write me an order for the immediate release of Lord Harcliffe from Newgate!"

"Your Highness!"

"This instant, my dear sir!"

"But how can I do anything so irregular?"

"This poor fellow is unfortunate!"

"The law says guilty."

"But from circumstances irresponsible for his acts."

"But I am not."

"Mercy should always be shown."

"Not at the expense of justice."

"It is a god-like attribute."

"True; and were men gods, would do very well instead of the other, but since 'men' are 'men,' we are often obliged to put Mercy, beautiful as she is, on the shelf, and pull out the rod of her sterner ally, Justice."

"Mercy and justice should go together."

"Decidedly they should; but human nature is so corrupt that they are compelled to pull different ways."

"You will oblige me with the order I request, and to-morrow I will see his Majesty myself and explain everything," said the prince, earnestly.

"I'm afraid I should——"

"Fear nothing. I will be responsible for everything, my dear sir. See, here are writing materials, seal and wax. Pray sit down and write me the order for release!" the prince still urged.

"You are an earnest pleader, your Royal Highness!" observed the secretary.

"How can I help it? I am full of sympathy."

"Do not forget this man is a robber!"

"True; but he saved my life. I cannot forget that."

"And you desire his release from Newgate?"

"Oh, yes, I must insist on that! I shall have no rest till he is set free."

"I hardly know what to do. It is a step that——"

"My dear Mr. Walpole, you hesitate—you suspect, but you know not the circumstances—the fearful peculiarity connected with these young men. S'death I must tell you, secretary; but you will excuse me, I know."

"Your Highness!"

"Youthful folly—heated blood. I—I——"

"Heaven, what am I about to hear?"

"That which I ought not to be able to speak; but those two outcast highwaymen—those two condemned crim—criminals——"

"Pray go on!"

"I will endeavour. These unhappy youths for whose life the law is thirsting are—are—— Come nearer, Walpole, my——"

The prince whispered in his ear, and then sank, utterly overpowered, with his head resting on his hands—apparently sobbing violently, but in reality taking a sly pinch of snuff under the table.

Walpole, the little secretary, uttered an exclamation of the most bewildered surprise.

"Great Heaven, is it possible, your Highness—my dear sir! Good Heaven! what a painful position for a par—I beg your pardon—for a man who feels like a parent!"

So excited was the worthy secretary that his wig dropped off, and he put his foot in it with the most perfect unconsciousness.

"You may imagine, my dear Walpole," groaned the anguished prince, "what I must have suffered!"

"I do—I do, my prince!"

"I am sure you will no longer refuse me! The sacred—the delicate nature of the case demands secrecy; but at the same time I could not see my own flesh and blood perish!"

The prince had acted his part excellently, and by dint of an utter sacrifice of truth, had so worked upon the tender sympathies of the secretary that, if he had required the release of all the prisoners in Newgate, it is possible he would have had it."

The secretary seated himself at the table, and, utterly regardless of consequences, wrote an order for the immediate release of Lord Alfred Harcliffe, known as the Black Highwayman, and signed and sealed it with the royal signet.

"Thank you, my dear friend!" exclaimed the grateful prince, grasping his hand warmly—"a thousand thanks! I will see the king to-morrow and explain all this. Good night, and Heaven reward you!"

"Good night, your Highness!"

The Prince of Wales entered the coach that waited, and ordered the man to drive as hard as he could to "The Retreat," whilst the Secretary of State went to bed and dreamt the walls of his chamber were papered with orders of release from Newgate.

Captain Hawk was still mounting guard over his prisoners when the prince returned.

"Have you succeeded?" he asked, as the prince entered.

"I have, and here is the order of release. The pardon I cannot procure till to-morrow."

"That will do. To-morrow, then, I shall expect it."

Without losing a moment, Captain Hawk grasped the precious document and hurried off to Newgate.

He would have been something more than mortal who would have arrested him in his headlong career.

The houses and lamps seemed to flash past him like meteors as he galloped along the streets, and in a space of time that seemed not more than a few moments, he pulled up his foaming steed at the governor's door, and saluted it with a prolonged and thundering succession of knocks.

The quiet night echoed with the sounds.

The prisoners woke from their unquiet dreams and wondered what was the cause of the disturbance.

Lord Harcliffe, amongst the rest, started from his slumber, and the thought rushed across him that this nocturnal summons was in some way connected with him.

He was hardly awake when the voice of his faithful comrade was heard without.

"Where is he?" cried Captain Hawk. "Unbar the door—quick!"

There was a rattling of chains, an unfastening of bolts and bars, and as the ponderous door swung open on its hinges, Captain Hawk darted in.

"Joy—joy, my friend!" he cried, excitedly. "You are free—free!"

Throwing his arm round Lord Harcliffe, he hugged him in a perfect paroxysm of joy, and then led him forth into the cool night air to taste once more the blessings of liberty.

An hour after he was seated by the side of his beloved Beatrice, together with Captain Hawk and his equally adored Blanche.

The Prince of Wales kept his word, because he could not possibly avoid it. The next day he had an interview with the old king, his father, and by dint of a host of falsehoods, made it apparent that our heroes should receive an absolute and unconditional pardon.

The document was drawn up and signed by King George II. and the Secretary of State; and a week after, when our heroes entered St. James's Church, Piccadilly, accompanied by Captain Nugent and his fair bride, they had no fear of being interrupted by their friends the police officers.

Their prospects were now entirely changed, and, being wearied with the reckless and hazardous life they had passed, they retired to a quiet estate in the country, where none in the neighbourhood were more beloved and respected than Captain Hawk and his comrade, the Black Highwayman.

Captain Hawk did not forget the promise he had given his friend Dick Turpin to deliver his last message to Matthew Gale. The latter, however, was never destined to receive it, for on Captain Hawk, as soon as his pardon was substantiated, going in quest of Matthew, he found that he had been dead some time; the message, thus remained in his own keeping.

THE END.

www.ingramcontent.com/pod-product-compliance
Lightning Source LLC
Chambersburg PA
CBHW081353050726
47504CB00015B/1901

* 9 7 8 1 5 3 5 8 0 1 1 2 6 *